The Norton Anthology
of Children's Literature

THE TRADITIONS IN ENGLISH

The Norton Anthology
of Children's Literature

THE TRADITIONS IN ENGLISH

Jack Zipes, *General Editor*

UNIVERSITY OF MINNESOTA

Lissa Paul, *Associate General Editor*

BROCK UNIVERSITY

Lynne Vallone, *Associate General Editor*

TEXAS A&M UNIVERSITY

Peter Hunt

CARDIFF UNIVERSITY

Gillian Avery

W · W · NORTON & COMPANY · New York · London

W. W. Norton & Company has been independent since its founding in 1923, when William Warder Norton and Mary D. Herter first publishe lectures delivered at the People's Institute, the adult education division of New York City's Cocer Union. The Nortons soon expanded their program beyond the Institute, publishing books by debrated academics from America and abroad. By mid-century, the two major pillars of Norton's polishing program—trade books and college texts—were firmly established. In the 1950s, the Nonn family transferred control of the company to its employees, and today—with a staff of four hndred and a comparable number of trade, college, and professional titles published each year—W.V. Norton & Company stands as the largest and oldest publishing house owned wholly by its emplcees.

Editor: Julia Reidhead
Developmental Editor: Alice Falk
Assistant Editor: Erin Granville
Electronic Media Editor: Eileen Connell
Production Manager: Diane O'Connor
Text Design: Antonina Krass
Art Research: Meredith Coeyman
Permissions Management: Nancy Rodwan arl Theresa Buswell
Managing Editor, College: Marian Johnson

Digital art file services by Jay's Publishing Scvices
Composition by Binghamton Valley Compostion
Manufacturing by R. R. Donnelley & Sons

Library of Congress Cataloging-in-Publication Data

The Norton anthology of children's literature the traditions in English / Jack Zipes, general editor . . . [et al.].
    p. cm.
    Summary: A collection of fairy tales, picture books, nursery rhymes, fantasy, alphabets, chapbooks, and comics published in English since 1659, representing 170 authors and illustrators, and including more than ninet/ complete works and excerpts from others.
    Includes bibliographical references and irdex.

ISBN 0-393-97538-X (college)
ISBN 0-393-32776-0 (trade)

1. Children's literature, English. 2. Children's literature, American. [1. Literature—Collections.] I. Zipes, Jack David.
PZ5.N655 2004
820.8'09282—dc22

2004054172

W. W. Norton & Company, Inc., 500 Fifth Avenue, New York, NY 10110
www.wwnorton.com

W. W. Norton & Company Ltd., Castle House,
75 / 76 Wells Street, London W1T 3QT

Contents

CHAPBOOKS

PRIMERS AND READERS

FAIRY TALES

ANIMAL FABLES

CLASSICAL MYTHS

LEGENDS

RELIGION: JUDEO-CHRISTIAN STORIES

FANTASY

SCIENCE FICTION

PICTURE BOOKS

COLOR

The Color section of "Picture Books" follows page 1098.

COMICS

VERSE

ROBERT GRAVES (1895–1985)   1229

PLAYS

BOOKS OF INSTRUCTION

LIFE WRITING

ADVENTURE STORIES

SCHOOL STORIES

DOMESTIC FICTION

Preface

Our first encounters with literature take place in childhood, a time saturated with narratives that range from lullabies and hymns, fairy tales and bedtime stories, alphabets and how-to books, jokes and comic strips, beginning readers and school stories, to novels of fantasy, science fiction, and adventure. As children, we listen to many different stories, become acquainted with their rhythms and movements, learn to read narratives and create our own. As adults, we continue this literary tradition through our customs and methods of nurturing, educating, and entertaining children, and these customs and methods have profoundly influenced social structures and cultural mores throughout the centuries. Indeed, the literature of our childhood establishes the foundations of literacies of many kinds. *The Norton Anthology of Children's Literature: The Traditions in English* is designed to introduce students to the variety and abundance of literary works for children.

The history of children's literature runs as a strong current within English literature, on occasion bubbling up to refresh and even reshape the cultural landscape. Though children's literature as a field of study in higher education did not come into its own until after the 1970s, the constant and forceful interaction between children's literature and the broader stream of English literature has been present from the beginning. To understand these strong mutual influences, and to situate the goals of *The Norton Anthology of Children's Literature*, it is important to recall some historical markers of children's literature.

HISTORICAL BACKGROUNDS

Children's literature begins, as does all literature, in the oral traditions of myth, fable, legend, folktale, and religion. The written tradition in English was initiated in the medieval period, when children's literature was essentially for privileged young males and consisted primarily of books with which to teach manners, morals, and Latin. With the introduction of the printing press in the fifteenth century, books for readers of all ages became more readily available and literacy rates increased. The *Orbis Sensualium Pictus* (1658) by Johann Amos Comenius, a Latin grammar that used pictures to convey "sensual" images of the world to young students, is generally acknowledged as the first children's book. By the seventeenth century, English had replaced Latin as the language of instruction, and the audience for most books for children included boys and girls, though girls were still not given the same educational opportunities. The Puritans, deeply committed to instilling religious doctrine in the young, helped expand the audience of young readers with the publication of two landmark works: *The New-England Primer* (1689), which taught religion and the alphabet with pictures and verse, and John Bunyan's *Pilgrim's Progress* (1678), a dramatic religious adventure that for two hundred years after its publication was often the only book in addition to the Bible considered suitable for Sunday reading. In 1744, with John Newbery's publication of *A Little Pretty Pocket-Book*—the first children's book in which amusement rather than religious indoctrination was a central concern—a new publishing market emerged, and with it new marketing strategies. Newbery promoted the text by including gender-appropriate objects (a ball for boys and a pincushion for girls). This packaging of instruction with amusement-plus-toy has proved successful into the twenty-first century.

In the eighteenth century, the French philosopher and political theoriest Jean-Jacques Rousseau was instrumental in introducing radical ideas about childhood education that had a great impact throughout Europe. While democracy took root and spread by way of the American and French revolutions in 1776 and 1789, Rousseau's influential and controversial *Emile; or, On Education* (1762) brought new attention to child development and to education. Rousseau argues that the naturally good child should be raised apart from, and thus uncorrupted by, society. In this hypothetical account of a boy's education, Rousseau recommends only one book for his "natural" child—Daniel Defoe's *Robinson Crusoe* (1719), the work widely considered the first novel in English. By the end of the eighteenth century, Robinson Crusoes proliferated—in English chapbook editions, in French novels, and in the best-selling adaptation by the important German publisher and educator Joachim Friedrich Campe, *The Young Robinson* (1779–80). In an example of the kind of cross-pollinating common in children's literature, Defoe's novel and Campe's work then led to the important crossover novel *Swiss Family Robinson* (1812–13), one of the most popular novels for children and adults in the nineteenth century, written by Johann David Wyss and translated into English in 1814.

In the late eighteenth and early nineteenth centuries, the establishment of new schools for children of the growing middle class led to higher literacy rates, a broader range of publications, and innovations in teaching methods and materials, including early readers by Anna Laetitia Barbauld and moral tales by Maria Edgeworth. The Romantic movement, embodied in the works of William Wordsworth, Samuel Taylor Coleridge, William Blake, and other poets who championed imagination, individuality, and originality, helped usher in what is considered to be the nineteenth century's "golden age" of children's literature. Central to Romantic ideals was the notion of the child as innocent, and childhood as a sacred time of life; this notion inspired writers for adults, such as Charles Dickens, and writers for children, such as George MacDonald. It also informed Lewis Carroll's *Alice* books, published in 1865 and 1871, in which Carroll mocks some of the conventions of didactic literature for children yet sustains a view of childhood as pure and precious. Perfectly in sync with the cultural sensibilities of the time, the *Alice* books were instant hits.

The late nineteenth and early twentieth century saw the beginnings of universal compulsory schooling, which led to dramatically increased literacy among the working classes, as well as greater cultural and linguistic homogenization. In Victorian England, children's literature became a central tool for the education of children scattered throughout the British Empire, a means by which the young (and old) colonized subjects were taught the colonizer's language and culture. Likewise in the United States, works for children facilitated the "Americanization" of the tide of new immigrants to North America. Advances in printing technologies—the ability to reproduce photographs, the mass production of color images—led to lavishly produced and illustrated books for children and helped make best-selling authors of Robert Louis Stevenson, Rudyard Kipling, Mark Twain, Frances Hodgson Burnett, E. Nesbit, Beatrix Potter, Louisa May Alcott, and A. A. Milne. Many of these best sellers, such as Twain's *The Adventures of Tom Sawyer* (1876), Stevenson's *Treasure Island* (1881), and L. M. Montgomery's *Anne of Green Gables* (1908), appealed to both children and adults and were reviewed by leading literary critics in magazines with wide circulation.

In the twentieth century, the interaction of children's literature with mainstream culture exploded beyond the printed page. Technological advances such as radio, film, television, and the Internet, as well as social transformations such as the women's rights and civil rights movements, changed the form and subject matter of works for children. Film and television have cultivated visual literacy, incalculably influencing media for both adults and children. But the printed book is often still the source of new ideas: animated television shows for children frequently originate from works such as the Arthur books by Marc Brown or the Railway Series by the Reverend W. Awdry (the first book was published in 1945), which was transformed into the *Thomas the Tank Engine* program. Many Disney films are based on fairy tales and novels. *Sesame Street* consistently draws on literature for adults and children, and the provocative animated prime-time sitcom *The Simpsons*, aimed at adults but frequently watched by children, abounds in intertextual references. For younger children growing up in the mid–twentieth century and later, the sophisticated picture book has been the preferred medium of instruction and delight. While working out of a culture steeped in modernism, Freudian theory, and Marxism, Dr. Seuss, Maurice Sendak, Maira Kalman, Anthony Browne, and Chris van Allsburg all speak directly and memorably to children. In the twenty-first century, graphic novels, or comix (crosses between novels, picture books, and traditional comic books), have increasingly become part of the fabric of literary culture. The turning point for the shift from underground to mainstream medium probably came with Art Spiegelman's 1992 Pulitzer Prize for his *Maus* books (1986 and 1991).

Likewise, social changes beginning in the mid–twentieth century and ongoing in the twenty-first have led to changes in the content of Anglo-American children's literature, which, like literature for adults, has moved beyond its white, Christian cast to reflect the diverse origins and experiences of its audience. In the United States, poets, illustrators, and authors of color, including Langston Hughes, Alma Flor Ada, Jerry Pinkney, David Diaz, Lensey Namioka, Lucille Clifton, Lawrence Yep, Mildred Taylor, Virginia Hamilton, Rosa Guy, Gary Soto, Joseph Bruchac, Julius Lester, and Ashley Bryan, have opened up the landscape of children's literature to include the rich and varied traditions, stories, and experiences of nonwhite childhood; in England, Anglo-Caribbean poets such as Grace Nichols, James Berry, John Agard, Jackie Kay, Farrukh Dhondy, Benjamin Zephaniah, and Valerie Bloom have infused English verse with the sounds and words of island languages. Children's literature has also begun to resemble adult literature in subject matter, using frank and provocative language to depict and discuss social problems such as homelessness, drug addiction, abuse, and terrorism and expanding the notion of family to include nontraditional families led by single parents, stepparents, and gay and lesbian parents.

The powerful cultural role of children's literature cannot be denied: its "classics" and best sellers have been absorbed into our bloodstream; they are cherished, revisited, and shared like secret toys and secret loves. Its folk and fairy tales have powerfully influenced our ways of thinking and talking about the human mind and social relations. Its characters, images, and narratives underlie much of what is seen on film and television. Children's literature is life-enhancing, life-changing, and profoundly influential; it provides a new lens with which to see the world. As such, writing for children is everything that literature claims to be. Yet, paradoxically, for all of its importance in Anglo-American culture and literature, the huge subject of children's literature long remained untreated in literary and cultural studies.

Ironically, the ubiquity and popularity of children's literature were reasons why it was largely shunned and undervalued at the university level. This attitude began to change during the 1960s, when school and university reforms fostered new disciplines and inclusiveness in the literary canon. Such fields as film studies, popular culture, children's literature, women's studies, African American studies, and so on were introduced into colleges and universities, creating the need for new anthologies and texts and encouraging more serious scholarly explorations into the history and complexity of children's literature. Children's books new and old, like the expanded canon of adult literature, could be read with the tools provided by fresh critical approaches that moved beyond the New Critical and formalist models, with their attention to the text alone without reference to context, that had dominated literary criticism in the middle of the twentieth century. Discourses such as reader-response theory, poststructuralism, semiotics, feminist theory, and postcolonial theory have proven to be valuable in analyzing children's books. Semiotic theory, for example, with its attention to sign systems, could be used to make sense of picture books. Feminist theory drew attention to the power structures implicit in books that are often designed to foreground a lesson being taught by an adult to a child. Reader-response theories proved very useful by engaging a critical community of readers who attend to the puzzles and patterns inherent in texts and by outlining strategies for identifying the core structures of narrative. In the past thirty years, as literary canons have dramatically expanded, the study of children's literature has gradually established itself as a vital and central field of literary and cultural research.

TEACHING ANTHOLOGIES

Despite the growth and development of children's literature as a field of study in higher education, it has not been easy to create appropriate anthologies for use at the college and university level, nor has it even been possible to agree about what constitutes children's literature. Is it literature written only for the very young? When do children become young adults? What is young adult literature? Do children and young adults read only age-specific literature? What do they read? What is the significance of crossover literature—that is, literature read by both young people and adults, such as the work of J. R. R. Tolkien, Ursula Le Guin, J. K. Rowling, and Philip Pullman? Do writers and illustrators create stories and books for children or for themselves? What has been the importance of anthologies in shaping or representing children's literature?

A history of anthologies of children's literature—still unwritten—would show that since the late eighteenth century there has always been an ample supply and variety of collections of children's literature and that the literature and the anthologies had manifold meanings and uses depending on their readership and their historical and cultural context. For example, in 1796 William Spotswood, a Boston publisher, reprinted *The Children's Miscellany,* a book that first appeared in London and contained tales, poems, essays, and other short works to contribute to the education of upper-class children. During the nineteenth century, numerous other kinds of anthologies appeared—collections of religious works, poetry, representative texts for girls and boys, school readers and primers—all with the main purpose of establishing the "proper" canon of children's literature. Also finding an audience were popular anthologies intended as household references, such as Francis Turner Palgrave's *The Golden Treasury of Songs and Lyrics* (1861). By the beginning of the twentieth century there were even multivolume collections, such as Charles Herbert Sylvester's *Journeys through Bookland* (11 vols., 1909), which boasted in its subtitle that it was "a new and original plan for reading, applied to the world's best literature for children." Specialized anthologies of fairy tales, religious texts, plays, poetry, gender-specific stories, and ethnicity-based writings were published, as well as selected works from important children's magazines and parents and teachers associations. By the 1930s, anthologies for use by college students began appearing. Two of the earliest works were Edna Johnson and Carrie Emma Scott's *Anthology of Children's Literature* (1935) and William Lyon Phelps's *The Children's Anthology* (1941). After World War II, publishers and educators saw an even greater need for anthologies that would appeal to both the trade and the educational markets, and thus such books were printed as Mary Arbuthnot's *Arbuthnot Anthology of Children's Literature* (1953), numerous revised editions of Edna Johnson's *Anthology of Children's Literature*, Mary Anne Nelson's *A Comparative Anthology of Children's Literature* (1972), Virginia Haviland and Margaret Coughlan's *Yankee Doodle's Literary Sampler of Prose, Poetry, and Pictures* (1974), Anne Diven's *The Scribner Anthology for Young People* (1976), and Clifton Fadiman and Leslie Morrill's *The World Treasury of Children's Literature* (1984–85).

The common tendency of anthologies for use in higher education up through the 1970s, such as those cited above, was to include canonical texts that would establish values and standards for judging what was the best in the field. For the most part, the editors favored classic authors and divided the collections according to standard genres of poetry, stories, and novels, arranged in some kind of chronological order. Whether the anthology was intended exclusively for children and use in school or was aimed at a general reading public and college students, the notes about the authors and literature were kept to a minimum. Only in the past twenty-five years have anthologies become more scholarly and been directed primarily at college and university students.

The problematic nature of children's literature is underscored not just by the concerns about defining childhood or children's literature described above but also by the increasing tendency of distinctions between child and adult cultures to dissolve. This has caused a shift in genre analogous to the shift in definitions of the spaces of childhood. In the nineteenth century, for example, the nursery referred not just to a room for babies but to a generous household space devoted to children: it was a world complete with its own food, clothes, customs, daily routines, lessons, and "rulers" (generally nurses, tutors, and governesses). By the mid-twentieth century, that culture had almost completely disappeared. In the twenty-first century, the differentiation between adults and children is blurred as they wear the same clothes (jeans and T-shirts), read the same books (*Harry Potter*), watch the same TV shows and movies (films rated PG-13), play the same video games, and eat the same food (fast). These cultural and social contexts must be taken into account when analyzing children's books and creating an anthology sensitive to social and cultural conditions that affect children.

Profound changes in our production, use, and appreciation of children's literature demand profound changes in anthologies. As Anglo-American literature has become more inclusive of other traditions, books for children have both paralleled and heralded this trend. Both in general literature courses and in children's literature courses, more multicultural texts by writers of color are being taught. In addition, children's books themselves are no longer being branded as simply "for" children. Typically, the term *literature* has excluded children's literature—that is, children's literature has generally been marked as separate from "real literature." When the *for children* marker is dropped from a text, it is welcomed into the category of literature. The most obvious example of this change in category is the success of J. K. Rowling's Harry Potter books. The publishing world has literally never seen anything like it. But other children's books have similarly lost their distinctive marker and become "literature," among them Philip Pullman's *His Dark Materials* trilogy (1995–2000) and Mark Haddon's recent crossover book, *The Curious Incident of the Dog in the Night-Time* (2003). Of course, the divisions and categories established by publishing houses and academia have never determined or even closely mirrored the reading customs and practices of children and adults.

Fortunately, twenty-first-century literature departments and undergraduate students have come to realize the full significance of children's literature, though this realization has not yet been completely reflected in practice. Many survey courses that deal with the introduction to literature have been adapted over the years to reflect changing ideas about the canon and literary history, now routinely presenting women and writers of color. Even the category of literature has itself expanded, and now includes works of popular culture and film. However, in most departments of English, children's literature can be studied only in specialty courses isolated from the literary mainstream. Although these courses tend to be very popular, the forcible separation between literature for the adult and literature for the child tends to obscure the overlapping and rich traditions of each.

It is our firm belief that including children's literature within introduction to literature courses or within courses that deal with the teaching of critical reading methods and literary theory will transform the survey and revolutionize the undergraduate curriculum. Young adults rereading children's books—or reading them for the first time—will be stimulated to read afresh, honing their skills in close reading, in visual literacy, and in contextualizing historical and cross-cultural constructions of childhood and adulthood. Studying children's literature and culture can become an integral part of the general education of students, helping them attain the goals of twenty-first century literacy: competence and pleasure in performing the skills of reading, writing, and thinking.

EDITORIAL GOALS

The Norton Anthology of Children's Literature is intended as an introduction to children's literature for students primarily at colleges and universities. It provides access to the work of 170 writers and illustrators, tracing the historical development of genres and traditions through 350 years of children's literature in English. As such, it is a comprehensive and flexible core anthology for a wide range of courses—historical survey and period courses, theme- or topics-based courses (e.g., on heroes, identity, transformation, gender and genre, or the construction of childhood), and interdisciplinary courses. Along with drawing on an unprecedented sweep of print genres—from alphabets to verse—we have endeavored to represent the central role of images in children's literature by including well over 400 images, 60 of them in full color. These range from facsimile images (many heretofore available only in rare book collections) of seventeenth- and eighteenth-century alphabets, primers, and chapbooks to a visual history of comics to an extensive section on picture books from the nineteenth to the twenty-first centuries.

In shaping the anthology, we have been guided by some general aims. Our first aim has been to construct the history of Anglo-American children's books through a chronological account within each subgenre or category. In so doing we have tried to map the ways in which the history of children's literature fits into the history of Anglo-American literature unmarked as being for children. Each section introduction tells a new story about the contours of that history. Because we have had privileged access to collections of rare children's books, it has been possible to select otherwise inaccessible material for inclusion in the anthology. To give instructors flexible teaching clusters within the chronological flow of the volume, *The Norton Anthology of Children's Literature* is organized by form and genre. Each section provides at least one "core" text (a complete reprint) supported by "satellite" texts—shorter or excerpted works—which can be taught as complements or counterpoints. This structure encourages students to draw connections among forms and genres as they developed over time.

Since we believe that it is important to include complete texts for analysis, we have done so wherever possible—forty longer works are included in their entirety, from *The New-England Primer* to Robert Louis Stevenson's *Child's Garden of Verses* (one of nine complete poetry collections) to Mildred Taylor's prize-winning novel of African American childhood, *Roll of Thunder, Hear My Cry,* to the complete text of the picture-book *BAAA,* by David Macaulay. In addition, forty-three complete shorter works give instructors great choice and flexibility. To fill out course offerings in the novel, the anthology can be ordered with Norton Critical Editions of such children's classics as Alcott's *Little Women* or Carroll's *Alice's Adventures in Wonderland* at a low supplemental cost. See the publisher's Web site (www.wwnorton.com) for titles and ordering information.

We have sought to balance the classic and the emergent. Many of our selections are by much-taught and much-loved authors: Louisa May Alcott, J. M. Barrie, L. Frank Baum, Frances Hodgson Burnett, Eric Carle, Walter de la Mare, Kate Greenaway, the Brothers Grimm, Nathaniel Hawthorne, Edward Lear, Rudyard Kipling, L. M. Montgomery, E. Nesbit, Charles Perrault, Beatrix Potter, Robert Louis Stevenson, and Oscar Wilde, among others. We have also sought to convey the multiethnic and multivoiced variety of the contemporary scene by including authors whose work taps into a wide range of cultural traditions, among them such leading authors and illustrators as Alma Flor Ada, Ashley Bryan, Lucille Clifton, Nikki Grimes, Lensey Namioka, Margaret Mahy, Grace Nichols, Ruth Park, Isaac Bashevis Singer, Jerry Pinkney, Mildred Taylor, Tim Wynne-Jones, and Laurence Yep. This rich mix of teachable texts and images, we believe, can form the core of a range of courses designed to introduce undergraduate students to children's literature. Though our focus is primarily on Anglo-American literature, we have made every attempt to include some literary examples from other countries, especially when certain works have played a pivotal role in the development of a genre. For example, the stories of Charles Perrault, the Brothers Grimm, and Hans Christian Andersen have helped shape the fairy tale in Great Britain and America. The development of children's literature has to be understood within a context that is international, not just national, and in our introductions and headnotes we have included references to important works from other cultures that have influenced the Anglo-American tradition.

The Norton Anthology of Children's Literature is dedicated to filling some of the gaps of previous anthologies; however, we do not pretend to compensate for all past omissions. Rather, we seek to be as innovative as possible, to reflect and address the major changes in the field, and to view children's literature historically within the social and cultural contexts that have led to its current status. In our choice of texts and in our introductions, we have paid close attention to the historical contexts of literary production—to the pivotal roles played by religion, domestic culture, education philosophy and policy, literacy, publishing, and perceptions of race, class, and gender, among other topics, in shaping children's literature and childhood itself. Section introductions, headnotes, a historical timeline, and special "Text and Context" sections reflect recent research in these areas. Our critical perspectives, like those of scholars in other literary fields, have been greatly influenced by the research and criticism rooted in the feminist and multicultural movements.

In all we have done, we are very much aware that the term *children's literature* is problematic and complex, as emphasized above. There are hundreds if not thousands of crossover texts, enjoyed by young and adult readers. Children's literature is, after all, primarily read by adults—parents, librarians, teachers, students, and professors—and much of it is now viewed on movie, television, and computer screens before it is read. Incorporating broadcast media or interactive digital technology into this print anthology is beyond our ability, but we have attempted to reflect the shifts in cultural values, technologies, and visual literacies, as they have been taking shape in the last decade of the twentieth century onward, in the appropriate introductions to the categories and subgenres of children's literature we survey.

Although *The Norton Anthology of Children's Literature* has been organized in neatly titled formal or generic groupings, as we shaped the volume we were fully aware that "neat" categories were impossible. In fact, we often debated where period breaks should occur and what to call various groupings, along with the choice of writers and works to be included and their placement. Constraints of space and restrictions on permissions meant that important writers had to be left out—another topic of intense debate. All five editors participated in these collective decisions and likewise contributed to each other's individual work on selections, introductions, headnotes, footnotes, timeline entries, and bibliographies. It is nonetheless helpful to state the particular responsibilities of each editor: Jack Zipes, General Editor, prepared Fairy Tales, Legends, Plays, and Science Fiction; Lissa Paul, Associate General Editor, prepared Verse, Books of Instruction, Primers and Readers, and Adventure Stories; Lynne Vallone, Associate General Editor, prepared Fantasy, Life Writing, Domestic Fiction, and School Stories; Gillian Avery prepared Religious Stories, Chapbooks, Animal Fables, and Alphabets; and Peter Hunt prepared Myths, Picture Books, and Comics. The death in 2002 of Mitzi Myers, an original member of the editorial team, was a great loss to us and to all who work in the field of children's literature. This anthology is richer for her unfailingly original and scrupulous scholarship.

EDITORIAL PROCEDURES

Following the model of other Norton anthologies, we have written period introductions, headnotes, and explanatory (not interpretive) annotations designed to make the anthology self-contained and accessible to general readers and students new to the study of children's literature. For further reference, we have included as backmatter annotated bibliographies selected for student readers and a timeline placing literary works in cultural context. In preparing the texts, we have modernized most spellings and (very sparingly) the punctuation so that archaic spellings and typography do not pose unnecessary problems. We have used square brackets to indicate titles supplied by the editors for the convenience of readers. Whenever a portion of a text has been omitted, we have indicated that omission with three asterisks. If the omitted portion is important for following the plot or argument, we have provided a brief summary within the text or in a footnote.

The final shape of the anthology offers a contemporary object lesson in the financial power of children's books within the publishing industry. There were many selections for which publishers and agents were reluctant to grant reprint permissions or requested exorbitant fees that would have priced the volume out of the reach of its intended audience. The difficulty in obtaining many of the works we desired to include obliged us to change our table of contents in consultation with others in the field. In general, we have heeded the advice of the numerous colleagues who have served as consultants for our project, and of course our own fruitful internal discussions have led to additions to and alterations in our selections.

The course guide prepared by Michael Joseph to accompany *The Norton Anthology of Children's Literature* includes goals and key questions, suggested course outlines, discussion sections for each of the formal or genre groupings in the anthology, essay topics and exam questions, and a multimedia resource list. A copy may be obtained on request from the publisher. Additional instructor resources, also prepared by Michael Joseph, are available in the Norton Resource Library (*www.wwnorton.com/nrl*). This online library includes the course guide's content for downloading and customizing; annotated links to literary and cultural resources—sample syllabi, scholarly essays, bibliographies, archives of texts or images, and links that explore popular film and television adaptations; and annotated links to professional and practical resources—online materials on teaching children's literature in elementary and secondary schools, on reading to children in literary programs and library and community reading programs, and so on. A separate student Web site is available at *www.norton.com/nacl*. This illustrated site includes a rich bank of annotated Web resources for study and research, a timeline, and self-grading review quizzes. Students using *The Norton Anthology of Children's Literature* can also enjoy access to Norton Literature Online (*www.norton.com/literature*), the richest collection of resources on the Web for students of literature.

The editors are deeply grateful to the dozens of teachers worldwide who have helped us shape *The Norton Anthology of Children's Literature*. A list of the advisors follows in the Acknowledgments, beginning on page xxxv.

Gone are the days of defending the right of children's literature to exist in the academic world. Now we turn to the next challenge, which is to give teachers a practical and, we hope, irresistible argument—this anthology—for exploring new ways to teach existing children's literature courses, for creating new courses, and for including children's literature in introduction-to-literature, writing, and survey courses of various kinds. At once cherished and innovative, children's literature keeps readers alive to the transformative power of learning and delight.

Jack Zipes, *General Editor*
Lissa Paul, *Associate General Editor*
Lynne Vallone, *Associate General Editor*
Gillian Avery
Peter Hunt

September 9, 2004

Acknowledgments

The making of this edition has been a collaborative venture from start to finish. Originally conceived in 1997 at the invitation of Julia Reidhead and with help and encouragement from Jennifer Bartlett, *The Norton Anthology of Children's Literature* has undergone various revisions and transformations. Through the intervening years, we have been guided by Julia, our patient and wise editor—she has been the backbone of the anthology. We have been adroitly assisted by numerous other friends at Norton: Nancy Rodwan and Teresa Buswell performed miracles on the permissions front. Erin Granville has been a resourceful and indefatigable assistant editor. We are deeply grateful to Alice Falk and Marian Johnson for expert developmental and manuscript editing and to Diane O'Connor for overseeing production on a tight schedule. Toni Krass's elegant interior design, Meredith Coeyman's invaluable art research, and Carin Berger's charming and evocative cover art have contributed greatly to the visual richness of the anthology.

For wise counsel on selections and draft editorial materials, we have turned repeatedly to scholars who have been, in effect, an informal advisory group. We want to thank Brian Alderson, Marc Aronson, Bob Barton, Lee Bennett Hopkins, Aidan Chambers, and Nancy Chambers; Susan Bloom, Kelly Hager, and Cathryn Mercier (Simmons College); Gerald Clarke, Linda Eyre, and Jennifer Pazienza (University of New Brunswick); Richard Flynn (Georgia Southern University); Matthew Grenby and Kimberley Reynolds (University of Newcastle-Upon-Tyne); Michael Joseph (Rutgers University); Michael Millgate (University of Toronto); Laureen Tedesco (East Carolina University); Joseph Thomas (California State University, Northridge); and John Wadland (Trent University).

We wish to thank the many consultants who have provided us with important advice: Alma Flor Ada (University of San Francisco), Laura Bates (Indiana State University), Sandra Beckett (Brock University), Ruth Bottigheimer (State University of New York, Stony Brook), Beverly Lyon Clark (Wheaton College), Dan Hade (Penn State University), Betsy Hearne (University of Illinois), Andrea Immel (Cotsen Children's Library, Princeton University), Dianne Johnson (University of South Carolina), Ulrich Knoepflmacher (Princeton University), Margaret Mackey (University of Alberta), Rod McGillis (University of Calgary), Claudia Nelson (Texas A&M University), Judith Saltman (University of British Columbia), Jan Susina (Illinois State University), and Kay Vandergrift (Rutgers University). We truly appreciate their helpful suggestions and thorough and critical analyses of our draft table of contents.

Librarians at special collections, reference, interlibrary loan, and library express have been forthcoming and efficient: Richard Langdon (Fisher Rare Books, University of Toronto), Emma Laws (Victoria and Albert Museum), Library of Congress, Pierpont Morgan, and University of New Brunswick. Special thanks to the librarians at the Osborne Collection of Early Children's Books, Toronto Public Library (Elizabeth Derbecker, Yuka-Kajihara-Nolan, Leslie McGrath, Lori MacLeod, and Martha Scott), who contributed significantly to the making of this book. They generously offered thoughtful suggestions on materials, were patient teachers, and handled arrangements for the copying and photographing of rare materials.

We heartily thank and are indebted to the graduate assistants who helped greatly with demanding research: Zenon Fedory and Irene Green (University of New Brunswick) and Misu Kim (Texas A&M University).

For their readiness to furnish much-needed support, invaluable insight, and help in myriad other ways, we thank Geoff Bubbers, Susan Egenolf, Howard Marchitello, Marco and Rita Portales, and Laureen Tedesco.

Alphabets

Learning to read must always start with knowing the letters, and earlier generations set great store on learning the alphabet by heart. Flora Thompson, remembering her Oxfordshire village school in the early 1880s in her memoir, *Lark Rise* (1939), said that while the schoolmistress attended to the older children the beginners in the baby class were set to recite the alphabet first forward, then backward, then on and on all morning. "Once started, they were like a watch wound up, and went on alone for hours." In the afternoon one of the older girls would come and point to the letters on a wall sheet, the little ones repeating their names after her. Then she would teach them to make pothooks (the curves used in cursive handwriting) on their slates, and after that letters. At the end of the school year those who knew their letters were moved up to the infants' class. Those who did not repeated the year.

In the seventeenth century the procedure seems to have been much the same. A London schoolmaster, Charles Hoole (1610–1667), in *A New Discovery of the Old Art of Teaching School* (1660), wrote of the methods of the day:

> The usual way to begin with a child, when he is first brought to Schoole [Hoole thought that three to four years old was the best time to start] is to teach him to know his letters in the Horn-book, where he is made to run over all the letters in the Alphabet or Christ-cross-row, both forwards and backwards, until he can tel any one of them, which is pointed at[.]

The hornbook alphabet, a relic of pre-Reformation days, was usually preceded by a cross—hence the term "Christ-cross-row," which was used in England but never in New England, where Puritans abhorred the symbol of the cross. But this, Hoole said, only worked with "ripe-witted children." Slower ones "have been learning a whole year together (and though they have been much chid and beaten too for want of head) could scarce tell six of their letters at twelve months end."

The hornbook—a small board with a handle, covered with a thin sheet of horn—was a useful and indestructible substitute for a book. It started the child toward literacy. Then came the primer—the first reading book—which gave instruction in religion as well as spelling. The Massachusetts judge Samuel Sewall recorded in his diary for April 27, 1691: "This morning had Joseph to school to Captain Townsend's Mother's, his cousin Jane accompanying him, carried his Horn-book." Joseph was not yet three; his cousin was fourteen. Hornbooks seem to have come into general use in schools toward the end of the sixteenth century, and to have survived there

1

until the end of the eighteenth. On them would be found the alphabet, the syllabarium, the nine digits, and the Lord's Prayer. From the mid–eighteenth century onward, they were gradually replaced by battledores. Their most usual form was a thin varnished sheet of cardboard folded twice to make a booklet of two pages. As with hornbooks, the alphabet was a prominent feature, but this now might be illustrated with simple woodcuts, as in *The Royal Battledore* published by Benjamin Collins of Salisbury in 1746 in conjunction with John Newbery, the enterprising London bookseller and publisher who was the first to make a profit from children's books. The pages with the alphabet and syllabarium also bore a typical Newbery maxim:

> He that ne'er learns his ABC,
> For ever will a Blockhead be.
> But he that learns these Letters fair
> Shall have a Coach to take the Air.

Despite what Hoole said about stupider pupils being beaten "for want of head," he himself seems to have been a humane man with a enlightened interest in teaching methods, as can be seen from his championship of *Orbis Pictus*—or, as he translated it, *The Visible World*, by Johann Amos Comenius. His instinct that pictures were the way to bring children to an interest in learning to read was shared by other schoolmasters of his time. An unidentified T. H., "Teacher of a Private School," devised a picture alphabet with rhymes for a primer that he called *A Guide for the Childe and Youth*, originally published in London in 1667; it was a popular work, frequently reprinted, particularly in Scotland. This alphabet beginning "In Adams fall / We sinned all" was taken by the London printer Benjamin Harris when he was gathering material for the *New-England Primer* and was to become one of the most famous of rhyming alphabets, though verses were changed to suit the prevailing mood. "T. H." was no Puritan—this is evident from the content of *A Guide*—and his alphabet, though containing biblical references and moral reflections, also had lines such as "The Cat doth play / And after slay" and "The Dog will bite / A thief at night." The 1727 Boston *New-England Primer*, the earliest now extant, followed this, though substituting "Job feels the rod / Yet blesses God" for "Jesus did die / For thee and I," because the latter was accompanied by the forbidden image of the cross. But the alphabet in a Boston *Primer* of 1777 was entirely made up of biblical references.

John Newton (1622–1678), a mathematician, astronomer, and advocate of educational reform, in *School Pastime for Young Children* (1669) also included a picture alphabet, though with no rhymes. At the foot of his title page is printed a quotation from Erasmus, translated "I cannot tell whether anything be better learn'd, than that which is learn'd by play." Writers of schoolbooks were increasingly to act on this maxim, and Newton's alphabet was devised so that it could be cut out and made into spelling cards. A progressive educationalist himself who held that the school curriculum of his time was far too narrow, he probably knew the work of the Moravian bishop Comenius and particularly *Orbis Pictus*, a picture encyclopedia printed in Nuremburg in 1658, which Comenius hoped would teach children both Latin and German and instruct them about the world they lived in.

Instruction Through Play

Comenius's alphabet is a very early example of instruction through play. Here the letters represent the sounds that birds and animals (and two humans) make. There is a small picture by each letter; the child imitates the sounds and is taught to recognize the accompanying letters and the name of the creatures in both German and Latin. Hoole admitted that the alphabet, which had been designed for German-speaking children, had presented problems when he was translating the work into English.

Following Comenius's example, others attempted to make learning fun. In 1694 J. G.—one infers he was a schoolmaster—significantly called his reading primer *A Play-Book for Children*. After word lists in alphabetical order, progressing from single syllables to polysyllabic teasers, he gave three sets of short sentences beginning with each letter of the alphabet. These engagingly describe everyday objects and practical matters that his youngest pupils could understand. The first begins

> Ap-ples are for Chil-dren that know the Let-ters.
> Bel-lows blow the Fire to make it burn bet-ter.
> Combs get the Lice out of Child-ren's heads.
> Drums make a noise, that plea-ses lit-tle Boys.

The rhyming alphabet "A Was an Archer" appeared in another primer, *A Little Book for Little Children*, published during Queen Anne's reign (1702–14); whether this was the invention of its author T. W., probably another schoolmaster, is not known. Books such as these were for the more affluent and did not reach the New England colonies, where life was more serious and learning began with the *New-England Primer*.

Many children learned to read at home with their mothers or older sisters, and there must have been other parallels to the pictorial nursery library made by Jane Johnson (1706–1759), the wife of a Buckinghamshire clergyman, to help her children with their reading. This collection of 438 pieces, now in the Lilly Library of Indiana University, consists of homemade alphabet and word cards and tiny hand-written books, with pictures cut out and mounted from sheets sold by booksellers, for each of which Jane Johnson wrote a descriptive sentence. In other affluent families teaching would be relegated to governesses—women of varying degrees of competence but with no formal training. Poor families with a few pence to spare might send children too young to be wage earners to a nearby dame school. Here an old wife whose own family had left home would act as minder and teach them their letters. In these surroundings there would of course be no books such as the ones described above, nor teaching aids such as Jane Johnson's. There would probably be a Bible, and the children themselves might bring hornbooks or, later, battledores.

But by far the most entertaining way of achieving literacy was through eating. The poet Matthew Prior (1664–1721) in his poem *Alma* describes the gingerbread horn-books sold at fairs:

> To Master John the English maid
> A Horn-book gives of Ginger-bread:
> And that the Child may learn the better,
> As he can name, he eats the Letter:
> Proceeding thus with vast Delight,
> He spells, and gnaws, from left to right.

In 1764 John Newbery used this ploy in a little storybook possibly written by himself: *The Renowned History of Giles Gingerbread, a Little Boy Who Lived upon Learning*. Giles, who initially resists learning but who is eager to put poverty behind him and rise to riches, learns his letters from gingerbread ones, which he is allowed to eat when he has mastered them. There were many American editions, including one by Isaiah Thomas, as there were also of *The History of Little Goody Two-Shoes*, which Newbery published the following year. Here the orphaned little Margery teaches herself to read and becomes a "trotting tutoress," her sole teaching aid being wooden letters which she has carved herself.

Alphabet Picture Books

As juvenile publishing expanded during the eighteenth century, illustrations became more important, and the early nineteenth century saw some attractive picture books from London, New York, and Philadelphia publishers. Alexander Anderson (1775–1870), known as the father of American wood engraving, illustrated many of the juvenile books published by Samuel Wood in New York. Wood's "instructive alphabet" of 1814 provides a Quaker-inspired rule of life for young readers. In London John Harris, successor to the family of Newbery, published many alphabets, including *The History of the Apple Pie* (1808) and, under the title of *The Hobby-Horse, or the High Road to Learning* (1820), the old rhyme of "A Was an Archer." He also began a fashion for alphabetic picture books on different subjects; natural history was a favorite. But his most original alphabet, so flippant that one disgusted reviewer called it "a vile book," was *Peter Piper's Practical Principles of Plain and Perfect Pronunciation* (1813), a series of lunatic tongue twisters beginning

> Andrew Airpump asked his aunt her ailment;
> Did Andrew Airpump ask his aunt her ailment?
> If Andrew Airpump asked his aunt her ailment,
> Where was the ailment of Andrew Airpump's aunt?

The unnamed author even manages Q—"Quixote Quicksight quizzed a queerish quidbox"—but is defeated by the final letters and complains "X Y Z have made my brains to crack-o." It was a popular book, frequently reprinted. The first American edition was published in Lancaster, Massachusetts, in about 1830.

Such books as these were expensive—"One shilling plain, eighteenpence coloured"—when the workingman's wage was ten shillings a week or less. Chapbooks, priced at one penny, or even a halfpenny, met the needs of the poorer family. They could be bought from itinerant traders and at fairs as well as from booksellers in the local town. The standard sixteen-page format could accommodate a page of the letters in capitals and lowercase, alphabet rhymes, a few improving sentences, and a list of other publications. *The Picture Alphabet* printed by Thomas Richardson of Derby, probably in the 1830s (chapbooks are very hard to date), is shown here.

Nineteenth-century illustrators, who were beginning to be named, increasingly saw opportunities in the alphabet book for comedy or as the starting point of a picture book, such as Kate Greenaway's ever-popular *A Apple Pie* (1886). But possibly the most impressive was *An Alphabet* (1897) by William Nicholson (1872–1949), who took many of his subjects from old chapbooks—Lady, Ostler, Pedlar, Quaker. There was a limited edition with hand-colored woodcuts for connoisseurs, and a lithographed edition for children. In the latter Earl replaced E for Executioner, and Trumpeter replaced Toper.

An early example of the comic style came from George Cruikshank (1792–1878), best known as the first illustrator of Charles Dickens, who in 1836 produced *A Comic Alphabet*, designed, etched, and published by himself. This assemblage of street and domestic scenes is probably aimed at adults, but the humor is pitched at a level that children could easily understand: V U Very Unpleasant has a stout man being chased by a bull. Edward Lear's nonsense humor was more original. He composed and illustrated many alphabets for friends; the one included here was made for a child he met at an Italian hotel.

The early-nineteenth-century picture books were hand-colored—John Harris's firm specialized in this work. By the 1860s color printing had become cheap enough for mass production of children's picture books. There were scores of alphabets among the toy books from London firms such as Routledge and Frederick Warne, and McLoughlin in New York. These were designed for the child who could already read, and railways now joined the Bible and the animal kingdom as a popular subject. Walter Crane (1845–1915), who designed some fifty toy books for Routledge and Warne (many of them pirated by McLoughlin), produced several alphabet books in the 1870s. Ruth M. Baldwin in *100 Nineteenth-Century Rhyming Alphabets in English* (1972) reproduced both English and American books from her own collection, which was given to the University of Florida in 1977.

As has been seen, alphabet books long ago extended their horizons. There are of course still books, often printed on board or cloth, for the beginner, with simple outline illustrations of familiar objects. Or there are simple stories like Angela Banner's *Ant and Bee* (1963). Ant and Bee live in a Cup and have a friend who is a Dog and so on in a series of inconsequential encounters illustrated with easily recognized objects, ending with the Zoo where Dog lives. There can be movable books like Robert Crowther's *The Most Amazing Hide-and-Seek Alphabet Book* (1977), where an animal hides behind each letter and emerges when a tab is pulled. But alphabets also attract more sophisticated presentation, as in Ann Jonas's *Aardvarks, Disembark!* (1990). In this retelling of the story of Noah and his ark, Noah, preparing to disembark, finds rare, endangered, even extinct species on board whose names he doesn't know and therefore cannot include in his roll call. For the benefit of the reader (and Noah) there is an appendix giving details about these animals whom he leads down Mount Ararat. Illustrators and writers have long seen the opportunities that lie in comic alphabets. In *On Beyond Zebra* (1955), Theodor Geisel—"Dr. Seuss"—invented a further clutch of "useful" letters: "In the places I go there are things that I see / That I *never* could spell if I stopped with the Z." In *Dr. Seuss's ABC* (1963), he limits himself to the usual twenty-six letters but invents words or even the objects themselves—"fiffer-feffer-feff," "quackeroo," "Zizzer-zazzer-zuzz."

Many alphabet picture books are designed more for the adult eye than the child's, such as *Brian Wildsmith's ABC* (1962), whose riot of color covering the whole page was in startling contrast to the drab austerity that had prevailed during the war years and the 1950s. Alice and Martin Provensen's *A Peaceable Kingdom* (1978) is another alphabet that appeals to the adult eye with its muted colors and evocation of a departed American pastoral scene in the shape of Shaker domestic life in the previous century.

Recent alphabets reflect the increasing desire to extend cultural boundaries. An outstanding example is *Ashanti to Zulu* (1976). This award-winning book, with richly glowing illustrations by Leo and Diane Dillon and text by Margaret Musgrove, portrays the ways of life and traditions of twenty-six African tribes, the author having found an example for every letter of the alphabet.

A sophisticated and attentive eye is required to decipher the teasing and ingenious picture puzzles of *Anno's Alphabet* (1975), designed by the Japanese author and illustrator Mitsumasa Anno. The jacket front of this alphabet without words shows a wooden question mark; on the jacket back is the block into which it would fit. Each verso page shows a wooden letter that, though the shape is right, is an impossible construction; the recto page opposite has the object, often similarly impossible (A a wooden anvil on which a metal bar is being beaten into shape, T a wooden typewriter with T on each of its eleven keys). Each page is surrounded with an elaborately drawn pen-and-ink border in which more objects are subtly hidden.

Even greater attention is required for *Anno's Magical Alphabet* (1981), devised with the help of the author's mathematician son. Described as an anamorphic alphabet, it is in fact two alphabets, each beginning from the outside and meeting in the middle. The distorted letters and images can be identified only when seen reflected in a cylindrical object (sheets of reflecting paper are provided), and the center pages give instructions to the mathematically minded on how to devise one's own anamorphic drawings. It is an instance of how far the alphabet has traveled since the hornbook and the wooden letters used by Little Goody Two-Shoes.

JOHANN AMOS COMENIUS
1592–1670

Comenius's *Visible World*, which might be described as a children's picture encyclopedia, opens with an alphabet, two pages from which are reproduced here. Initial letters relate not to objects but to sounds. Thus "Crow" comes first because his cry sounds *á á*, and "Horse Fly" is last—*ds ds* or *Z z*. The alphabet is introduced by a conversation between master and boy. "What doth this mean, to be wise?" says the pupil. "Who will teach me?" "I will shew thee all," says the master. "Before all things thou oughtest to learn the plain sounds . . . [Here] thou hast a lively and vocal Alphabet."

Comenius's aim was not only to teach beginners to read their own language but to make them familiar with Latin, then a universal school subject in Europe. But, as the 1659 translation of his preface phrases it, he also wanted "to take scarecrows out of wisdom's garden," and to "entice" children, so they may not feel it "a torment to be in the School, but dainty-fare."

The book was originally written in Latin and German and printed in Nuremberg in 1658 under the title *Orbis Sensualium Pictus*. The following year it was published in London, the German translated by Charles Hoole (1610–1667), a schoolmaster, whose title page describes the contents as "a picture and nomenclature of all the chief things that are in the world, and of Mens Employments therein." There are some 150 metal engravings, each with a facing page of description. The volume progresses through objects in the visible world, the solar system, natural history, human anatomy, trades and professions, daily life, and amusements, and concludes with more abstract matters, such as government, justice, ethics, philosophy, and religion.

The life of the Czech theologian and educationalist Comenius, born Jan Komenský, was made tragic by the religious wars of seventeenth-century Europe. As a Protestant bishop in Moravia, then part of the Austrian empire, he became a hunted man and saw his wife and two small children die of privation. He finally left in 1628 with his second wife, and in the company of other of his countrymen fled to Poland. It was there that he began to dream of a new form of education teaching universal God-centered knowledge—pansophy—which became the driving force of his life. Poland too was ravaged by a Catholic army, his second wife died, and he fled through hostile countries to Amsterdam, then a place of refuge from religious persecution. Here he devoted the last fourteen years of his life to "the pansophicall worke" that he saw as the great hope for humanity.

The twelfth London edition (the last) of *Orbis Pictus* was published in 1777, with pictures redrawn and brought up to date, but it opened with an admission that it had "now fallen totally into disuse as a School-book, though no other comparable to it has been substituted in its place." It survived longer in America, where it was popular with the Moravian Brethren who settled in Pennsylvania and the Carolinas. There was a New York edition in 1810 with illustrations by Alexander Anderson.

Orbis Pictus was never widely used in English-speaking schools. Though the educational concept was revolutionary, the information and the illustrations rapidly dated and, as Hoole himself admitted, the alphabet was not easily adapted to English. In addition, it was a complicated book to print, and, with more than 300 pages, it was always expensive. Finally, all-embracing tolerance was not to everyone's taste. Yet in spite of its shortcomings we can still admire its ingenuity, unique in its own time and unusual even now.

(4)

Cornix cornicatur.		*á á* A a
The Crow cryeth.		
Agnus balat.		*bé é é* B b
The Lamb blaiteth.		
Cicáda stridet.		*ci ci* C c
The grashopper chirpeth.		
Upupa dicit.		*du du* D d
The Whooppoo saith.		
Infans éjulat.		*é é é* E e
The Infant cryeth.		
Ventus flat.		*fi fi* F f
The wind bloweth.		
Anser gingrit.		*ga ga* G g
The Goose gaggleth.		
Os halat.		*háh háh* H h
The mouth breaketh out.		
Mus mintrit.		*i i i* I i
The Mouse chirpeth.		
Anas tetrinnit.		*kha kha* K k
The Duck quacketh.		
Lupus ululat.		*lu ulu* L l
The Wolf howleth.		
Ursus múrmurat.		*mum mum* M m
The Bear grumbleth.		

112

(5)

Felis clamat.		*nau nau* N n
The Cat cryeth.		
Auriga clamat.		*ó ó* O o
The Carter cryeth.		
Pullus pipit.		*pi pi* P p
The Chicken peepeth.		
Cúculus cúculat.		*kuk ku* Q q
The Cuckow singeth cuckow.		
Canis ringitur.		*rrr* R r
The Dog grinneth.		
Serpens sibilat.		*si* S s
The Serpent hisseth.		
Graculus clamat.		*tac tac* T t
The Jay cryeth.		
Bubo ululat.		*úú* U u
The Owl hooteth.		
Lepus vagit.		*vá* W w
The Hare squealeth.		
Rana coaxat.		*coax* X x
The Frog croaketh.		
Asinus rudit.		*y y y* Y y
The Asse brayeth.		
Tabanus dicit.		*ds ds* Z z
The Breeze or Horse-fle saith.		B z

113

THE CHILDES GUIDE
1667

Famous through its inclusion in the early *New England Primer*, this alphabet made its original appearance in "The Childes Guide," the first part of *A Guide for the Childe and Youth*, published in London in 1667. It was the work of T. H., "a Teacher of a Private School," who may well have composed the alphabet himself. Only one 1667 copy, the sole survivor from the seventeenth century, is extant, but it was a popular work often reprinted in the eighteenth century.

Benjamin Harris (d. ca. 1718), who used it in the *New-England Primer* (whose two earliest copies known were published in Boston in 1727), was not a schoolmaster but a printer out to find new markets. Driven from England because of his inflammatory political views, he came to Boston in 1686, returning to England permanently in 1695. A Boston almanac advertisement of 1690 gave notice of a "Second Impression of the New England Primer enlarged," but no copies from this period have survived. The *New-England Primer* as we know it from the 1727 printing is made up of material scavenged from other men's works, among them "The Childes Guide" alphabet verses and accompanying woodcuts, and probably these were in seventeenth-century editions also.

Harris made three significant changes to the alphabet. For J and Jesus, with its accompanying cut of Christ on the cross, he substituted "Job feels the Rod / Yet blesses God." Harris was catering to a New England readership who, like himself, held that any representation of the cross was idolatrous. Since he was passionately opposed to Charles II (1630–1685)—here "Charles the Good," who was restored to the throne of Great Britain after Oliver Cromwell's Protectorate, which had ruled since the execution of Charles I in 1649—he avoided naming him under K. The later couplet for O shows the oak tree in which the young Charles hid from pursuers after his Royalist supporters had been defeated by Cromwell's army—the "Rebel slave[s]"—at the battle of Worcester in 1651.

Many of the succeeding couplets have biblical references ("Book" in verses 2 and 8 refer to the Bible). P alludes to St. Peter's denial of Jesus as described in the Gospels (e.g., John 18.25–27). Queen Esther was the Jewish wife of Ahasuerus, King of Persia—the Xerxes (ca. 519–465 B.C.E.; r. 486–465) named at X; her story is told in the Old Testament book of Esther. In R Rachel represents the Jewish mothers weeping over Herod's slaughter of male children in Bethlehem (the Massacre of the Innocents) when Jesus was born (Matthew 2.16–18). Samuel was the last of the judges of Israel (I Samuel). Uriah the Hittite was sent into battle by King David to be killed because the king coveted Uriah's wife, Bathsheba (2 Samuel 11). Zaccheus (Luke 19.2–10) was a tax collector who, being "little of stature," climbed a tree to see Jesus pass.

The reading under Y—"Youths forward slips"—should be noticed. "Youths" had been altered to "Youth" by 1727; it was thought to mean that the young person was slipping downward and Death was waiting to pounce. But possessive *s* without an apostrophe was standard in 1667; "forward slips" then meant precocious growth, which Death, like frost, could so easily "nip" and destroy.

In Adams Fall

In Adams fall
We sinned all.

This Book attend,
Thy life to mend.

The Cat doth play
And after slay.

The Dog will bite
A thief at night.

An Eagles flight
Is out of sight.

The idle Fool
Is whipt at School.

As runs the Glass,
Mans life doth pass.

My Book and Heart
Shall never part.

Jesus did die
For thee and I.

King Charles the Good,
No man of blood.

The Lyon bold,
The Lamb doth hold.

The Moon gives light
In time of Night.

Nightingales sing
In time of Spring.

The Royal Oak
  our King did save,
From fatal streak
  of Rebel slave.

Peter denied
His Lord and cried.

Queen Esther comes
  in Royal state,
To save the Jewes
  from dismal fate.

Rachel doth mourn
For her first born.

Samuel anoints
Whom God appoints.

Time cuts down all,
Both great and small.

Uriah's beauteous wife
Made David seek his life.

Whales in the Sea
Gods voice obey.

Xerxes the Great did die,
And so must you and I.

Youths forward slips,
Death soonest nips.

Zaccheus he
Did climb the tree,
His Lord to see.

1667

A LITTLE BOOK FOR CHILDREN
ca. 1705

The first known version of this rhyming alphabet printed below appeared in *A Little Book for Little Children* by "T. W.," a spelling book whose only known copy is in the British Library. The author and the date are unknown, but since the frontispiece is a crude woodcut of Queen Anne, the book is assumed to have been printed in her reign (1702–14). The alphabet has many later variants and imitations. These seem to reflect the whim of the compiler rather than social change, though the opening with an Archer who shot at a frog stayed fairly constant, occasionally varied by an Angler who caught a fine fish. The Archer appears in *Merry Alphabet*,

a toy book published in 1890 by the New York firm of McLoughlin. Although this alphabet kept several of the traditional avocations—Drunkard, Hunter, Sailor, Tailor—it was brought up to date with Engineer (on a railway), Newsboy, and references to lawn tennis and a ten-dollar bill.

It will be noticed that there are only twenty-four letters here—J and V are missing. Until modern times, these capital letters were treated the same as I and U. Even in the earlier twentieth century, the catalogs in Oxford's Bodleian Library used to follow this rule, with names such as Johnson entered as Iohnson.

A Was an Archer

A was an Archer, and shot at a Frog;
B was a Blind-man, and led by a Dog:
C was a Cutpurse, and liv'd in disgrace;
D was a Drunkard, and had a red Face:
E was an Eater, a Glutton was he;
F was a Fighter, and fought with a Flea:
G was a Gyant, and pul'd down a House;
H was a Hunter, and hunted a Mouse:
I was an ill[1] Man, and hated by all;
K was a Knave, and he rob'd great and small:
L was a Liar, and told many Lies;
M was a Madman, and beat out his Eyes:
N was a Nobleman, nobly born;
O was an Ostler, and stole Horses' Corn:
P was a Pedlar, and sold many Pins;
Q was a Quarreller, and broke both his Shins:
R was a Rogue, and ran about Town;
S was a Sailor, a Man of Renown:
T was a Taylor, and Knavishly bent;
U was a Usurer took Ten *per cent*:
W was a Writer, and Money he earn'd;
X was one *Xenophon*,[2] prudent and learn'd:
Y was a Yeoman, and work'd for his Bread;
Z was one Zeno the Great,[3] but he's dead.

ca. 1705

1. Evil.
2. Greek historian and general (ca. 428 / 7–ca. 354 B.C.E.).
3. One of two Greek philosophers: either Zeno of Elea (b. ca. 490 B.C.E.), who gave his name to the paradox of Zeno's arrow, or Zeno of Citium (335–263 B.C.E.), who founded the Stoic school.

THE PICTURE ALPHABET
ca. 1830

This version of the rhyme "A Was an Archer," with a couplet for each letter as was becoming the practice in the nineteenth century, was used in *The Picture Alphabet,* a chapbook published in Derby by Thomas Richardson (d. 1875). (There were other children's books in the same series offering both information and entertainment, all at one penny, as can be seen in the list reproduced in the introduction to Chapbooks, below.) The rhyme offered the amateur poetaster more opportunities for variation than "A Apple Pie," and appealed to humorists and moralists alike. The Richardson version points a disapproving finger at drinking (bouse = booze), gaming, loose behavior (a "quean" was a disreputable woman), and extravagance. "X was expensive and so became poor" was a favorite way to deal with a difficult letter: earlier alphabets like T. W.'s had used historical figures—Xenophon, or Xantippe, the proverbially shrewish wife of Socrates; the *New England Primer*, taking over an alphabet from an English schoolbook of 1667, showed Xerxes. *Souse*, used in the rhyme for W, indicates a very small coin.

Thomas Richardson's chapbook was a relatively sophisticated production, using illustrations that married with the text, instead of old and inappropriate woodblocks as was common practice. And at the foot of each page runs a line from another alphabet—for example, "A apple-pie."

A Was an Archer

2   THE PICTURE ALPHABET.

Was an Archer,

And shot at a frog,

But missing his mark

Shot into a bog.

A apple-pie.

THE PICTURE ALPHABET.   3

Was a Butcher,

And had a great dog,

Who always went round

The street with a clog.

B bit it.

Was a Captain,

So brave and so grand,

He headed in buff

The stately train band.

C cut it.

Was a Drunkard

And lov'd a full pot,

His face and his belly

Show'd him a great sot.

D dealt it.

Was an Esquire,

Both lofty and proud,

His servant was softly,

Though he was full loud.

E ate it.

Was a Farmer,

And follow'd the plough,

And gathered good

From the sweat of his brow.

F fought for it.

Was a Gamester,

And oft would he play

A poor single ace

Against a bold tray.

G got it.

Hunted the Buck,

And likewise the Doe,

The Hare and the Fox,

And also the Roe.

H had it.

Was an Innkeeper,

Who loved a bouse;

But spending his profits,

He soon lost his house.

I itch'd for it.

Was a Joiner,

And built him a house,

A little time after

There came in a mouse.

J join'd for it.

Was a king,   [rouse,
  Who would drink and ca-
But affrighted was he
  At a cat and a mouse.

K kept it.

Was a lady,
  And flirted a fan,
Which no doubt she oft did,
  To show her white hand.

L long'd for it.

Was a Miser,
  Who hoarded up gold;
But hiding his bags,
  A thief stole them all.

M mourn'd for it.

Was a Noble
  Of birth and high power,
To the poor most gentle,
  To the haughty most sour.

N nodded at it.

With her Oysters,
A delicate cry;
Come buy my sweet Oysters,
Come buy, come buy.

O open'd it.

Was a Parson,
And wore a black gown;
For goodness and virtue
Of high renown.

P peep'd in it.

Was a Quean,
Of the lowest degree,
A state that is worse
Perhaps cannot be.

Q quarter'd it.

Was a Robber,
And hung as you see,
A lot that I hope,
Will ne'er befal me.

R ran for it.

Was a Sailor,

And liv'd in a ship,

He made the Spaniards

And French for to skip

S stole it.

Was Tom Tinker,

And mended a kettle,

While he was hammering

Was deaf as a beetle.

T took it.

Was a Usurer,

A miserly elf,

Who car'd not for others,

But only himself.

U unloos'd it.

Was a Vintner,

That loved his bottle,

Went seldom to bed

Without his fair pottle.

V view'd it.

Was a Watchman,

To guard well the house,

That rogues did not strip it

Of every souse.

W wanted it.

Was expensive

And so became poor,

With his little dog begg'd

From door to door.

X cross'd it.

Was a Youngster,

That lov'd not his school,

But play'd with his hoop

Though out of all rule.

Y yok'd it.

Was a Zany,

That look'd like a fool,

With his long tassel'd cap

He was all the boys' tool.

Z and & wish'd they had a piece in hand.

THE INSTRUCTIVE ALPHABET
1814

This rhyming alphabet formed a preface to a little twenty-four-page book printed in New York by Samuel Wood (1760–1844), a Quaker and former schoolmaster and one of the first publishers to specialize in American material. The emphasis here on "useful business" and improvement was characteristic of much that was directed at American children; there was little room for play, and fiction was treated as lies. But there is a gentler, Quaker spirit in the later precepts, especially in the value placed on quiet and on tolerance. Wood may have composed this alphabet himself, together with the verses accompanied by woodcuts and the moral reflections that follow. The description of the ant concludes, for instance, "Thus all their proceedings are conducted apparently by the utmost prudence and persevering principles of forethought and economy—an instructive lesson to man—especially to youth." The same sober outlook pervaded Wood's other publications for children.

At Early Dawn

A t early dawn of day arise,
B less first the Ruler of the skies;
C omb, wash, and cleanse, and e'vry day
D ress, read, or work, ere thou dost play.
E ach hour in useful business spend,
F or time soon hastens to an end;
G overn thy thoughts by wisdom's rule,
H ate every knave, and shun a fool;
I mprove in each ingenious art;
K nowledge, like beauty, wins the heart;
L ove all thy friends, nor hate thy foes,
M ake *these* thy friends as well as those.
N o bribe should tempt thee to a lie,
O r glittering hate allure thy eye:
P lace not thy heart on sordid pelf;
Q uiet and patient keep thyself;
R ail not at others, for thou may
S ome faults commit as well as they;
T ell not a secret, nor pretend,
U nder disguise to be a friend.
V ain is the pomp of gold or lace,
W here virtue does not stamp a grace.
X erxes[1] over millions weeping cried,

---

1. King of Persia (ca. 519–465 B.C.E.; r. 486–465), who often appears under X. He cried because his invasion of Greece in 480 met with crushing defeat.

Y on mighty host, the grave must hide.
Z comes at last—best place of any,
To fit a zealot or a zany.

THE CHILD'S NEW PLAY-THING
1742

The first appearance in print of this rhyme, a favorite with nineteenth-century illustrators and represented here by pages from Kate Greenaway's picture book, seems to have been in *The Child's New Play-thing*, published in 1742 by Mary Cooper, the widow of Thomas Cooper, a London printer. It was subtitled "A Spelling Book Intended to make Learning to Read a Diversion and not a Task." The rhyme had obviously long been well-known; Iona and Peter Opie point out in *The Oxford Dictionary* of *Nursery Rhymes* (1951) that it was quoted in 1670 by John Eachard, a Cambridge academic, in a satirical pamphlet and must have been old then. Mary Cooper's book also contained a second alphabet, seemingly designed to be cut out and used for spelling, together with Bible stories, fables, songs, and simple retellings of favorite chapbook romances such as *Guy of Warwick*. This alphabet is printed at the foot of Thomas Richardson's chapbook "A Was an Archer," also included here.

A Was an Apple-Pie

A was an apple-pie;
B bit it,
C cut it,
D dealt it,
E eat[1] it,
F fought for it,
G got it,
H had it,
I inspected it,
J jumped for it,
K kept it,
L longed for it,
M mourned for it,

N nodded at it,
O opened it,
P peeped in it,
Q quartered it,
R ran for it,
S stole it,
T took it,
U upset it,
V viewed it,
W wanted it,
X, Y, Z, and ampersand
All wished for a piece in hand.

---

1. I.e., ate—the past tense of *eat*, pronounced "et."

KATE GREENAWAY
1846–1901

Kate Greenaway, Randolph Caldecott, and Walter Crane all had their reputations made by Edmund Evans (1826–1905), the most celebrated Victorian printer of colored picture books. Thanks to improved production methods, which allowed far larger print runs, their work acquired a fame that had not been possible for their predecessors. Of the three illustrators, Greenaway was technically the least accomplished; John Ruskin, who admired her work and was to become a much-valued friend and mentor, in vain tried to teach her perspective and to improve her representations of human anatomy. She preferred to drape her costumes on jointed wooden figures rather than use human models. But in an increasingly industrial age, Greenaway's vision of sunlit gardens and placid parlors where orderly children play sedate games or take tea in pretty dresses won a popularity that has never waned. In 1996 an English grandmother stitched a Kate Greenaway alphabet for her new granddaughter from *Kate Greenaway's Alphabet* (ca. 1885), a tiny square picture book (the illustrations had originally appeared under the initials K. G. in *Mavor's Spelling-Book*). *A Apple Pie* followed in 1886.

The Greenaway family home was in London, but two years that Kate spent as a small child at a Nottinghamshire farm made a lasting impression; it was always pastoral scenes that she preferred. Her father was a draftsman and wood engraver; her mother had her own shop where she sold lace and children's dresses. Kate herself was to design and stitch many of those that she used in her illustrations, creating a "Kate Greenaway style" that was her own invention.

The first pictures she sold were of fairy figures and children for the *People's Magazine* in 1868. For ten years she worked mostly at designs for birthday cards and valentines, later at illustrating toy books (mass-produced colored picture books) and drawing for magazines. But as M. H. Spielmann and G. S. Layard say in their 1905 biography, "she disliked being bound by another person's imagination, and her aversion to 'mere illustration' stayed to the end."

In 1877 she showed Edmund Evans, who had long known her father, a collection of drawings she had made, with accompanying verses. Evans says in his *Reminiscences* (1967), "I bought them at once, for I thought they would make a telling child's book: we settled the title *Under the Window* from the first line of one of the verses." In 1878 the large edition of 20,000 was sold out before he could reprint. Her future was now assured, and her style became so well-known that she had to endure imitations. Her preferred subject was verse. Though she was to illustrate Mother Goose rhymes, her style did not suit the earthy vigor characteristic of so many of them; it worked best with her own verse. *A Apple Pie* shows her at her best, with decorous children dressed in romantic otherworldly style and the delicate "greenery-yallery" coloring that she favored. Her concluding illustration for U, V, W, X, Y, and Z is an admirable solution for those difficult letters.

T TOOK IT

UVWXYZ

ALL HAD A LARGE SLICE
AND WENT OFF TO
BED

EDWARD LEAR
1812–1888

Edward Lear began his professional career with drawings of birds. His *Illustrations of the Family of Psittacidae, or Parrots* was published in a limited edition in 1832. For him nonsense writing was a sideline that took root during 1832 and 1837, during visits to Knowsley Hall, Lancashire, where he drew the animals in the Earl of Derby's menagerie. There he used to devise and illustrate limericks to amuse the children of the household. (The limerick verse form was not his invention; it had already been used in a picture book of 1820, *The History of Sixteen Wonderful Old Women*.) The exuberant style of his nonsense illustrations is very different from the accuracy and detail of his animal and bird drawings and from the many landscape watercolors that he produced in later years, when failing eyesight made close detail difficult and poor health—he suffered from epilepsy and fits of deep depression—drove him to spend much of the year in foreign travel. Though there had been comic illustrated books for children in Lear's own childhood, his *Book of Nonsense* (1846) was the first to use a deliberately naive style, which Basil Blackwood must have had in mind in his drawings for Hilaire Belloc's *The Bad Child's Book of Beasts* (1896).

Lear created more than fifteen alphabets, all written for friends, the earliest known dating from about 1846. In these the melancholy that lurks in much of his verse rarely obtrudes. The one whose text is printed below was made for Daisy Terry, a child he met in Italy in August 1870. Many years later Daisy, by then Mrs. Winthrop Chandler, recalled her first meeting with Lear (*Roman Spring*, 1934):

Something seemed to bubble and sparkle in his talk, and his eyes twinkled benignly behind the shining glasses. I had heard of uncles; mine were in America and I had never seen them. I whispered to my mother that I would like to have that gentleman opposite for an uncle. She smiled and did not keep my secret.

On August 30, 1870, Lear, who had written other nonsense for Daisy, copied the text and illustrations of the alphabet for publication in *More Nonsense*, which appeared in 1872. The Yonghy-Bonghy-Bo with his excessively large head and very small hat makes his first appearance in this alphabet. Daisy recalled that this was what Lear and she said when they kicked the chestnut burrs that lay on the ground outside the hotel. He was later to write one of the saddest of his nonsense poems, "The Courtship of the Yonghy-Bonghy-Bo," around this character.

Below the dedication to Daisy and her brother he drew a comic self-portrait—bearded, bespectacled, paunchy. Lear, ever a sad clown, habitually saw himself as a grotesque figure of fun, the butt of the scornful "They" of the limericks who point mocking fingers at eccentricity.

The Absolutely Abstemious Ass

The Absolutely Abstemious Ass,
who resided in a barrel, and only lived on
Soda Water and Pickled Cucumbers.

The Bountiful Beetle,
who always carried a Green Umbrella when it didn't rain,
and left it at home when it did.

The Comfortable Confidential Cow,
who sate in her Red Morocco Arm Chair and
toasted her own Bread at the parlour Fire.

The Dolomphious Duck,
who caught Spotted Frogs for her dinner
with a Runcible Spoon.

The Enthusiastic Elephant,
who ferried himself across the water with the
Kitchen Poker and a New pair of Ear-rings.

The Fizzgiggious Fish,
who always walked about upon Stilts
because he had no Legs.

The Goodnatured Grey Gull,
who carried the Old Owl, and his Crimson Carpet-bag,
across the river, because he could not swim.

The Hasty Higgeldipiggledy Hen,
who went to market in a Blue Bonnet and Shawl,
and bought a Fish for her Supper.

The Inventive Indian,
who caught a Remarkable Rabbit in a
Stupendous Silver Spoon.

The Judicious Jubilant Jay,
who did up her Back Hair every morning with a Wreath of Roses,
Three Feathers, and a Gold Pin.

The Kicking Kangaroo,
who wore a Pale Pink Muslin Dress
with Blue Spots.

The Lively Learned Lobster,
who mended his own Clothes with
a Needle and Thread.

The Melodious Meritorious Mouse,
who played a Merry Minuet on the
Piano-forte.

The Nutritious Newt,
who purchased a Round Plum-pudding,
for his Grand-daughter.

The Obsequious Ornamental Ostrich,
who wore Boots to keep his
Feet quite dry.

The Perpendicular Purple Polly,
who read the Newspaper and ate Parsnip Pie
with his Spectacles.

The Queer Querulous Quail,
who smoked a Pipe of Tobacco on the top of
a Tin Tea-kettle.

The Rural Runcible Raven,
who wore a White Wig and flew away
with the Carpet Broom.

The Scroobious Snake,
who always wore a Hat on his Head for
fear he should bite anybody.

The Tumultous Tom-tommy Tortoise,
who beat a Drum all day long in the
middle of the Wilderness.

The Umbrageous Umbrella-maker,
whose Face nobody ever saw because it was
always covered by his Umbrella.

The Visibly Vicious Vulture,
who wrote some Verses to a Veal-cutlet in a
Volume bound in Vellum.

The Worrying Whizzing Wasp,
who stood on a Table, and played sweetly on a
Flute with a Morning Cap.

The Excellent Double-extra XX
imbibing King Xerxes,[1] who lived a
long while ago.

The Yonghy-Bonghy-Bo,
whose Head was ever so much bigger than his
Body, and whose Hat was rather small.

---

1. King of Persia (ca. 519–465 B.C.E.; r. 486–465), who often appears under X.

The Zigzag Zealous Zebra,
who carried five Monkeys on his Back all
the way to Jellibolee.

1870   1872

THEODOR SEUSS GEISEL
1904–1991

Theodor Geisel ("Dr. Seuss"), whose specialty was high-spirited anarchy, succeeded in introducing this element even into children's reading primers. Taking his lead from Edward Lear, he invented even more bizarrely named creatures than his master, though his skill as a draftsman was far less and these creatures have a certain sameness on the page. Geisel, who had thought of becoming a teacher, graduated from Dartmouth in 1925. He left the United States for Oxford in 1926, but after a year abandoned academe, returned to his own country, and began working as a freelance cartoonist for American magazines and advertising agencies. Though his drawings for Standard Oil captioned "Quick Henry! The Flit!" achieved national fame, he still hoped for something better.

His first children's book was *And to Think That I Saw It on Mulberry Street* (1937), where Marco weaves a fantastic story about what he saw on the way from school, but knows enough about his prosy father to suppress it when he gets home. But Geisel's real success began with *How the Grinch Stole Christmas* (1957) and in the same year *The Cat in the Hat*, which he said was the book that he was proudest of. The textbook editor at Houghton Mifflin had sent him a list of 300 words and asked him if he could make a primer out of them. In the end he contrived a story that combines pace, suspense,

and wit using only 220. Mother is out of the house and the Cat in the Hat suddenly appears to amuse two astonished children:

> "I know it is wet
> And the sun is not sunny.
> But we can have
> Lots of good fun
> That is funny."

Whereupon he summons his sidekicks Thing One and Thing Two, and between them they create mayhem while the outraged goldfish ("my version of Cotton Mather") vainly gasps out warnings. Houghton Mifflin, said Geisel, had difficulty selling it to schools; "my book was considered too fresh and irreverent." It was passed on to Random House, which marketed it as a Beginner Book "and it just took off in the bookstores."

In *The Cat in the Hat Comes Back* (1958)—relying on 253 words—again the children are appalled by the devastation their amiable visitor can cause, this time with replicas of himself, Little Cats A to Z, who emerge from under his hat. But Little Cat Z saves the day: he produces from *his* hat the ultimate detergent, Voom. Seuss stories always end happily.

Dr. Seuss's ABC (1963) was part of the Beginner series, but was designed for fun rather than lessons. (*On Beyond Zebra*, 1955, was even more surreal, adding extra letters to the alphabet, such as Spazz, indispensable for spelling "Spazzim/A Beast who belongs to the Nazzim of Bazzim.") It has the familiar Seuss elongated fantasy creatures, the same crazy ingenuity: "what begins with C?" accompanies a camel walking upside down on the ceiling. When it comes to X Geisel soars far beyond Xerxes, as can be seen below; and as for Z, she is a lolling Zizzer-Zazzer-Zuzz—a pink-haired odalisque with "slightly batty, oval eyes and a smile you might find on the Mona Lisa after her first martini," as one critic memorably described the Seuss style.

From Dr. Seuss's ABC

O is very useful.
You use it when you say:
"Oscar's only ostrich
oiled
an orange owl today."

35

X is very useful
if your name is
Nixie Knox.
It also
comes in handy
spelling axe
and extra fox.

55

I do.

I am a
Zizzer-Zazzer-Zuzz
as you can
plainly see.

63

29

ALICE PROVENSEN *and* MARTIN PROVENSEN
b. 1918   *1916–1987*

Alice and Martin Provensen's *A Peaceable Kingdom* (1978), the title they gave to their illustrated Shaker Abecedarius, reflects their feeling for the American pastoral scene. Their farm near Staatsburg, New York, where they converted a barn into a studio, forms a background to many of their picture books.

Though often persecuted for their pacifism and beliefs, Shakers, who derived originally from a branch of radical English Quakers known as the Shaking Quakers, were admired for their model farms and well-ordered prosperous communities, as well as for the simple beauty of their craftmanship, which is reflected in the Provensen illustrations.

The asceticism, a central part of the ethos, is not reflected in this alphabet rhyme, which is unexpectedly fanciful in its choice of creatures, and certainly not suitable for those beginning to struggle with the alphabet. Nor, in spite of Shaker seriousness, is there any religious element in the alphabet, as in the *New England Primer*. That has been supplied instead by the illustrators, who have included a meetinghouse in the frontispiece. With its muted coloring and evocation of a vanished age, the alphabet seems designed to please the adult rather than the child's eye, making a beautiful picture book rather than a teaching aid.

From A Peaceable Kingdom

The Shaker Abecedarius

Alligator, Beetle, Porcupine, Whale,
Bobolink, Panther, Dragonfly, Snail,
Crocodile, Monkey, Buffalo, Hare,
Dromedary, Leopard, Mud Turtle, Bear,
Elephant, Badger, Pelican, Ox,
Flying Fish, Reindeer, Anaconda, Fox,
Guinea Pig, Dolphin, Antelope, Goose,
Hummingbird, Weasel, Pickerel, Moose,
Ibex, Rhinoceros, Owl, Kangaroo,
Jackal, Opposum, Toad, Cockatoo,
Kingfisher, Peacock, Anteater, Bat,
Lizard, Ichneumon, Honeybee, Rat,
Mockingbird, Camel, Grasshopper, Mouse,
Nightingale, Spider, Cuttlefish, Grouse,
Ocelot, Pheasant, Wolverine, Auk,
Periwinkle, Ermine, Katydid, Hawk,
Quail, Hippopotamus, Armadillo, Moth,
Rattlesnake, Lion, Woodpecker, Sloth,
Salamander, Goldfinch, Angleworm, Dog,
Tiger, Flamingo, Scorpion, Frog,
Unicorn, Ostrich, Nautilus, Mole,
Viper, Gorilla, Basilisk, Sole,
Whippoorwill, Beaver, Centipede, Fawn,

XANTHOS,[1] Canary, Polliwog, Swan,
YELLOWHAMMER, Eagle, Hyena, Lark,
ZEBRA, Chameleon, Butterfly, Shark.
—*from The Shaker Manifesto, 1882*

1978

WHIPPOORWILL,

Beaver, Centipede, Fawn,

XANTHOS,

Canary, Polliwog, Swan,

1. Horse of the Greek hero Achilles who predicts his master's death (*Iliad* 19.408–17).

Chapbooks

Chapbooks, the cheap literature of the masses sold by peddlers at cottage doors or bought at fairs or at printers' shops in town, played an important part in keeping old tales alive. Medieval romances such as Guy of Warwick and Bevis of Hampton, both stories of British heroes, and romances of foreign origin such as Valentine and Orson, Reynard the Fox, and Fortunatus, had a popularity that lasted over many centuries. Reduced to a fraction of their original length, they were the early reading of many well-known writers, John Bunyan and William Wordsworth among them.

The term "chapbook" is a relatively modern one given to the little sixteen- or twenty-four-page booklets costing as little as a halfpenny that were in circulation in the eighteenth and early nineteenth centuries. But from the middle of the sixteenth century on, cheap publications, often just broadside sheets containing ballads or other ephemeral matter, were being hawked around the British countryside, where they were bought and read by the unsophisticated and semiliterate. The many who could not afford to buy them might find them on the walls of alehouses. Thomas Holcroft, an actor and author (1745–1809), whose own parents had been peddlers and who had taught himself to read from the Bible and chapbooks, saw no print except the ballads he came across pasted up in this way for six or seven years in his adolescence when he was working as a stableboy.

Broadside ballads were printed in columns down the width of the sheet of paper, and the subjects ranged from topical events such as murders and other sensational crimes, to redactions of medieval romances such as those named above, fairy tales such as Tom Thumb and Jack the Giant Killer, and folk heroes—Dick Whittington and Robin Hood being far the most popular. There was also much bawdy humor; *The Friar and the Boy,* for instance, a ballad that first appeared in print in 1512, tells of a boy with a magic pipe that makes everyone dance, and causes his shrewish stepmother to break wind. Many of these ballads remained popular for centuries and were reprinted in eighteenth- and nineteenth-century chapbooks, where, relegated to children, they were reworded and made more decorous.

Protestant moralists and preachers frowned on such reading matter. Undoubtedly much of the old humor was crude and earthy, but there was also deep distrust of "fayned fables, vayne fantasyes, and wanton stories," as one sixteenth-century writer called the sort of fiction enjoyed by young readers (Hugh Rhodes, *The Boke of Nurture,* 1577). The author of *The History of Genesis* (1690) lamented that while Protestant children were blessed with liberty to read the Bible when others were denied it, "yet alas! how often do we see Parents prefer Tom Thumb, Guy of Warwick, Valentine and Orson, or some such Foolish Book, before the Book of Life!" *The Famous Adventures of Tom Thumb . . . Full of Wonder and Merriment*, which first appeared in print in 1621, was a ballad particularly abhorrent to Puritan preachers and frequently denounced. Distrust of works of imagination was strong in New England where fairy tales, being wholly false, were long denounced as pernicious. Indeed they were treated as tantamount to pornography in a Presbyterian Sunday school book of 1876 (Mary D. R. Boyd, *Wat Adams, the Young Machinist*).

The Eighteenth-Century Chapbook

As restrictions on printing in Great Britain eased during the later seventeenth century, the numbers of printers increased and with them the output of cheap books. Chapbook printers did not use original material; they drew on what had been written in the past. For eighteenth-century children, chapbooks were the only source of fairy tales and heroic legends, and as adults many were to recall what these had meant to them. Wordsworth, for instance, in book 5 of *The Prelude* (1805), contrasts the forced diet of grammar and facts that he endured at school with the stories he had loved:

> Oh! give us once again the Wishing-Cap
> Of Fortunatus, and the invisible Coat
> Of Jack the Giant-killer, Robin Hood,
> And Sabra in the forest with St. George!

The eighteenth-century chapbook was usually printed on one side of a sheet of coarse gray paper. This was then folded to make a booklet of twelve or twenty-four pages, roughly 6 × 4 inches in size. There were usually a couple of crude woodcuts, often not particularly relevant since they had been taken from blocks the printer already had in stock. Titles with a special appeal to children included the ancient stories mentioned by Wordsworth. Fortunatus is given a magic purse that never empties and a hat that will carry him anywhere in the world; the story of St. George and the Egyptian princess Sabra is an episode in *The Seven Champions of Christendom*, a long romance by Richard Johnson (published 1596–97), which was also a favorite with John Bunyan. Other popular titles included *The History of the Two Children in the Wood, The History of Sir Richard Whittington, Robinson Crusoe* (very much reduced), *Tom Thumb* and other accounts of juvenile miscreants such as Jack Horner, and Jack, the hero of *The Friar and the Boy*. The old rhyme *The Death and Burial of Cock Robin* also made many appearances in chapbook form.

Cotton Mather in a diary entry for September 27, 1713, deplored "the foolish Songs and Ballads, which the Hawkers and Peddlars carry into all parts of the Countrey." These may have been imported from England, though Isaiah Thomas said of Thomas Fleet, an English printer who arrived in Boston about 1712, that he was publishing "small books for children [probably primers and catechisms] and ballads" (*The History of Printing in America*, 1810). But Harry Weiss in *American Chapbooks* (1938) declares that chapbooks never achieved anything like the popularity that they did in Great Britain; "the population had gotten beyond the elementary tastes and childlike intelligence required for the enjoyment of such works." Newspapers, almanacs, printed sermons, and the American contribution to chapbook literature, Indian captivity stories, took their place as far as adults were concerned. Nevertheless, Caleb

Bingham, a Boston schoolmaster, in *The Columbian Orator* (1797) composed a recitation for "a very small boy" in which the boy, announcing that he is "a monstrous
great student," reels off a list of his favorite stories, all of them old chapbook titles
such as *The Seven Champions of Christendom, Valentine and Orson,* and *Reynard the
Fox.* Although Bingham makes it clear that he thought such reading was puerile, he
must have assumed that his audience would recognize the titles.

Only two of the books named by Bingham's young student were written specifically
for children. Still, there were many American children's chapbooks published in the
late eighteenth and early nineteenth centuries; Dick Whittington, Tom Thumb, and
the Children in the Wood were all popular. But not with the literal-minded Samuel
Goodrich (1793–1860), the original Peter Parley, who was to write many books of
information for the young. Even as a child he looked for facts and despised fiction.
He had led a sheltered life and did not encounter the latter until he was ten, when
his father bought him three chapbooks—the stories of Giles Gingerbread, an ambitious little boy who learned to read from gingerbread letters, and of the worthy little
"trotting tutoress" Goody Two-Shoes, together with some Mother Goose rhymes. He
dismissed them all as ineffably silly nonsense, but his real outrage came when he
later met Red Riding Hood, Puss in Boots, and Jack the Giant Killer, all of which
he said could only reconcile readers to vice and crime.

However, none of these titles could compete in popularity with *The Prodigal
Daughter,* a broadside ballad from England probably of seventeenth-century origin,
first published in Boston ca. 1737–41. A warning story to both parents and children,
it is a great rarity in the country of its origin, where it seems to have been printed
only once in chapbook form. But there are twenty-nine recorded American printings
before 1821, at first from New England but later from New York and Philadelphia
as well. The prodigal daughter, overindulged by wealthy parents and resentful when
at last they try to curb her, is given poison by Satan himself so that she can kill them.
An angel warns them of the plot, saving their lives. The girl seems to die of remorse,
but comes to life as the coffin is about to be laid in the grave, and she is able to edify
the congregation by relating her experiences at the Judgment Seat and her penitence:

> And now she is a christian just and true,
> No more her wicked vices does pursue.

Nineteenth-Century Juvenile Chapbooks

The British market for the old chapbook favorites had declined by the end of the
eighteenth century, and by the nineteenth century mainly catered to children. Many
provincial printers in Britain in such towns as Banbury, Derby, Glasgow, and York
had extensive lists of children's chapbooks. Thomas Richardson of Derby in the
1830s was advertising twenty-five well-designed little books in a wide range of subjects, all at one penny each. These were smaller than chapbooks of the previous
century, some 3¾ × 2½ inches with twelve or sixteen leaves. Chapbooks are noto-
riously difficult to date; the same titles are repeated over many years with illustrations
that usually refer to a past epoch.

What is noticeable in the early nineteenth century is a greater fastidiousness and
a desire to improve young readers. Richardson like most other provincial printers
was providing a modicum of Sunday reading; F. Houlston of Wellington, Shropshire
(fl. 1807–1840), specialized in evangelical stories. And Hannah More (1745–1833)
dexterously used chapbook format and alluring titles (*Black Giles the Poacher* and *The
Gin Shop,* for example) in her Cheap Repository Tracts, all written in a lively style

CHILDREN'S BOOKS,
Printed and Published by
THOMAS RICHARDSON, DERBY,
AT ONE PENNY EACH.

Children in the Wood.
Child's First Book.
Cinderella; or, the Little Glass Slipper.
Death and Burial of Cock Robin.
First Step to Christian Knowledge.
Goody Two-Shoes.
House that Jack Built.
Jack the Giant-Killer.
John Gilpin.
Juvenile Gazetteer.
Little Red Riding-Hood.
Merry-Andrew.
Moral Tales.
Natural History of Beasts and Birds.
Nursery Rhymes.
Old Mother Hubbard and her Dog.
Picture Alphabet.
Picture Exhibition.
Puss in Boots.
Riddle Book; or, Fireside Amusements.
Select Pieces for the Nursery.
Sunday-School Scholar's Reward.
Tommy and Harry.
Tom Thumb.
Whittington and his Cat.

An excellent Assortment of halfpenny
Books and Lotteries.

and aimed at the children and young people of the poor who might otherwise have turned to more lurid reading or to inflammatory political pamphlets. There were many American reprintings, particularly from Philadelphia printers, of More's titles.

The street cries or slogans called out by London sellers to draw attention to their wares, which had been chapbook subjects from the late eighteenth century, now often inspired moral reflections. This is particularly noticeable in America, where their popularity approached that of *The Prodigal Daughter*. Samuel Wood (1760–1844), a former schoolmaster who specialized in children's books, published many books of London cries but seems to have been the first to produce a New York equivalent, *The Cries of New-York* (1808). Here the picture of the muffin man is accompanied by admonitions about the moral dangers that lurk in tea parties. More seriously, he is fired with indignation about those whose political creed is "all men are born free and equal" yet employ slave labor; this comment accompanies the text about the sellers of watermelons. His book was copied in Philadelphia in 1810 with added localized detail, such as a page about a Philadelphia delicacy, Pepper Pot. Mahlon Day, in business in New York from about 1816 on, also published *New-York Cries in Rhyme*, with improving sentiments in Samuel Wood's style. *The Art of Making Money Plenty*, alternatively titled *The Way to Wealth*, always attributed to Benjamin Franklin and certainly drawing on his "Poor Richard" maxims, was another very popular chapbook subject. The Quaker firm of Darton, Harvey, and Darton published it in London. As in Britain in the nineteenth century, there was a plethora of moral and religious booklets for the young published by such organizations as the American Tract Society and the Massachusetts Sabbath School Society.

James Catnach (1792–1841), who was publishing in London between 1813 and 1831, briefly revived the old chapbook tradition, supplying hawkers—who were said to pay him in copper coins—with eye-catching illustrated accounts of murders, trials, and executions. For children there was reading that aimed to entertain rather than to improve: nursery rhymes and fairy tales, as well as stories of criminals—Dick Turpin the highwayman, and Jack Sheppard, heroic because of his repeated escapes from prison—all of them boldly illustrated and ranging in price from one farthing (i.e., a quarter of a penny) to a halfpenny; a large quarto cost one penny. When Catnach retired the business was taken over by William Fortey, who ran it until about 1883. Under him the list became more decorous. There were still colored penny and halfpenny books, even farthing ones, but he also published schoolbooks, hymns, and scripture sheets. By the time Fortey went out of business the day of chapbooks was truly over; penny dreadfuls and dime novels had taken their place. As far as children were concerned, fairy stories, traditional tales, and marvelous adventures were at last considered respectable and were available in a variety of books, ranging from expensive editions to colored toy books costing only a few pence.

TOM THUMB
ca. 1790–1810

Tom Thumb was one of the most popular chapbook heroes. Although the tale is an English one, the idea of a "thumbling," a miniature child born to a hitherto childless couple, has parallels in many other cultures. As a mischievous prankster too Tom Thumb has counterparts—the German Till Eulenspiegel, for instance, though unlike Tom, Till had no magical powers. His more recent equivalents in popular literature are full-sized. Spring-heeled Jack was a favorite character in Victorian penny dreadfuls; Superman, the American comic strip hero, was created in 1938 by Jerry Siegel and Joe Shuster when they were both seventeen years old; Batman was created in 1939 by Bob Kane.

Though Tom Thumb was a well-known figure in English folk legend in the sixteenth century, no story about him exists before 1621. The author of this tale only signed himself R. J., but is supposed to have been Richard Johnson, author of *The Seven Champions of Christendom*. In his preface he speaks of the days when "Batchelors and Maides . . . the old Shepheard and the young Plow boy after their dayes labour" listened to such stories on winter nights. Metrical versions of R. J.'s tale appeared on seventeenth-century broadsides and in chapbooks that came later, becoming more genteel to suit changing taste—so that Tom's mother was made to rescue her child from the cow's mouth rather than from its backside.

Printed here are the first fifteen pages of a twenty-four-page book. In the second half we are told about Tom's exploits as one of King Arthur's knights, how he becomes sick and dies, and how his ghost goes to Fairy Land. But this is not the end of him; we are told that in part 2 we will see him again.

The last few lines in this chapbook version, speculatively dated 1790–1810, advertise part 2 and Tom's return to King Arthur's court:

> Where in the presence of the King
>   He many wonders wrought,
> Recited in the second part,
>   Which now is to be bought
>
> In Irongate, in Derby Town
>   Where are sold fine Histories many,
> And pleasant tales as e'er was told,
>   For purchase of One Penny.

This suggests that the London printers had copied their text from a Derby original.

The First Part of the Life of Tom Thumb

Of the Parentage, Birth & education of *Tom Thumb*, with all the merry Pranks he played in his childhood.

> In Arthur's Court Tom Thumb did live
> A man of mickle might,
> Who was the best of the Table Round,
> And eke a worthy Knight.
>
> In stature but an inch in height,
> Or quarter of a span,
> How think you this courageous Knight
> Was prov'd a valiant man.

His father was a ploughman plain,
   His mother milk'd the cow,
And yet the way to get a Son
   This couple knew not how.

Until the time the good old man
   To learned Merlin goes,
And there to him in deep distress,
   In secret manner shews,

How in his heart he'd wish to have
   A Child in time to come,
To be his heir, tho' it might be,
   No bigger than his thumb.

Of this old Merlin then foretold,
   How he his wish should have;
And so a son of stature small,
   This charmer to him gave.

No blood nor bones in him should be.
   His shape it being such,
That he should hear him speak, but not
   His wandering shadow touch.

But so unseen to overcome,
   Whereat it pleas'd him well,
Begat and born in half an hour,
   For to fit his father's will;

And in four minutes grew so fast,
   That he became so tall,
As was the ploughman's thumb in length
   And so she did him call.

Tom Thumb, the which the Fairy Queen,
   Did give him to his name,
Who with her train of gobblings[1] grim
   Unto the christening came.

When they cloathed him so fine and gay
   In garments rich and fair;
The which did serve him many years
   In seemly sort to wear.

1. Goblins.

His hat made of an oaken leaf,
  His shirt a spider's webb,
Both light and soft for his small limbs,
  Which were so smally bred.

His hose and doublet thistle down,
  Together weav'd full fine;
And stockings of the apple green,
  Made of the outer rhine.[2]

His garters were two little hairs,
  Pluck'd from his mother's eye;
His shoes made of a mouse's skin,
  And tann'd most curiosly.

Thus like a valiant Gallant he
  Does venture forth to go
With other children in the street,
  His pretty pranks to show;

Where for counters, pins, and points,
  And cherry stones did play,
Till he amongst the gamsters young,
  Lost all his stock away.

Yet he could not the same renew,
  When as most nimbly he
Would dive into the cherry bags,
  And there partaker be.

2. Rind, skin.

Unseen or felt by any one,
   Until a scholar shut
The nimble youth into a box
   Wherein his pins were put.

Of whom to be reveng'd he took,
   In mirth and pleasant game,
Black pots and glasses which he hung
   Upon a light sun-beam.

The other boys did do the same,
   In pieces tore them quite,
For which they were severely whipt,
   Which made him laugh outright.

So poor Tom Thumb restrained was,
   From this his sport and play;
And by his mother after that
   Compell'd at home to stay.

Whereas about Christmas time,
   His mother a hog had ki'll'd,
And Tom would see the pudding made,
   For fear it should be spoil'd.

Of Tom's falling into the Pudding Bowl, and his Escape out of the Tinker's Budget.

He sat the candle for to light,
   Upon the pudding bowl,
Of which there is unto this day,
   Some pretty stories told.

For Tom fell in, and could not be
   For some time after found,
For in the blood and batter he
   Was lost and almost drown'd.

But she not knowing of the same,
   Directly after that,
Into the pudding stir'd her son,
   Instead of mincing fat.

Now this pudding of the largest size.
   Into the kettle thrown,
Made all the rest to jump about,
   As with a whirlwind blown.

But so it tumbled up and down,
    Within the liquor there,
As if the devil had been boil'd,
    Such was the mother's fear.

That up she took the pudding strait,
    So gave it at the door
Unto a Tinker, which from thence
    He in his budget[3] bore.

But as the Tinker climb'd a stile,
    He chanc'd to let a crack
How good old man, cry'd Tom Thumb
    Still hanging at his back.

Which made the Tinker for to run,
    And would no longer stay,
But cast both bag and pudding too
    Over the hedge away.

From whence poor Tom got loose at last,
    And home return'd again,
For he from great dangers long
    In safety did remain.

Until such time his mother went
    For to milk her kine;
Where Tom unto a thistle fast,
    She linked with a line.

3. Bag.

Of Tom Thumb being tied to a thistle; of his Mother's Cow eating him up; with his
strange Deliverance out of the Cow's Belly.

> A Thread that held him to the same,
>   For fear the blustering wind
> Would blow him thence, so as she might
>   Her son in safety find.
>
> But mark the hap, a cow came by
>   And up the Thistle eat:[4]
> Poor Tom withal, who as a dock,
>   Was made the red cows meat.
>
> But being mist his mother went
>   Calling him every where;
> Where art thou Tom? where art thou?
>   Quoth he, here mother, here.
>
> In the red Cows Belly here,
>   Your Son is swallow'd up;
> All which within her fearful heart
>   Much woe this cholar[5] put.

4. I.e., ate.
5. May refer to the "caller," Tom, or to the call or shout that Tom makes from within the cow.

Mean time the cow was troubled sore,
   In this her rumbling womb,
And could not rest until that she
   Had backwards cast Tom Thumb,

Now all besmeared as he was,
   His mother took him up,
And home to bear him hence, poor lad,
   She in her apron put.

Tom Thumb is carried away by a Raven, and swallowed up by a Giant; with several
other strange accidents that befel him.

Now after this, in sowing time
   His father would him have
Into the field to drive the plough,
   And therewithal him gave

A whip made of a barley straw,
   For to drive the cattle on;
There in a furrow'd land new sown,
   Poor Tom was lost and gone.

Now by a raven of great strength,
   Poor Tom away was born;
And carried in a carrion's beak,
   Just like a grain of corn.

Unto a giants castle top,
   Whereon he let him fall,
And soon the Giant swallow'd up,
   His body, cloaths and all.

But in his Belly Tom Thumb did
   So great a rumbling make,
That neither night nor day he could
   The smallest quiet take.

Until the giant him had spew'd
   Full three miles in the sea;
There a large Fish soon took him up,
   And bore him hence away,

The lusty Fish was after caught,
   And to King Arthur sent,
Where Tom was kept, being a Dwarf,
   Until his time was spent.

Long time he liv'd in loyalty,
   Beloved of the Court,
And none like Tom was so esteemed
   Amongst the better sort.

Tom Thumb by the Command of King Arthur dances a Galliard upon the Queen's left hand.

Among the deeds of courtship done,
   His Highness did command,
That he should dance a galliard brave
   Upon the Queen's left-hand.

All which he did, and for the same
    Our King his signet[6] gave.
Which Tom about his middle wore
    Long time a girdle brave.

Behold it was a rich reward
    And given by the King,
Which to his Praise and worthiness
    Did lasting honour bring.

For while he lived in the court,
    His pleasant pranks were seen,
And he, according to Report
    Was favoured by the Queen.

1790–1810

6. Ring.

JACK THE GIANT KILLER

ca. 1845–50

Giants play a prominent part in mythology and folk legends. Traditionally brutish and slow-witted, they are easily fooled by heroes such as Odysseus or the Jack of this story, who is of Cornish extraction and a favorite chapbook character. Joseph Jacobs in *English Fairy Tales* (1890) calls the story "a curious jumble," and it does seem to be an amalgam of various giant legends put together in the late seventeenth century. The earliest printed version known

(1711) is now lost; it was transcribed by James Orchard Halliwell (1820–1889), a collector of nursery rhymes and fairy tales. It was a great favorite, particularly with boys, but many in authority disapproved of the tale's violence. W. S. Johnson, the publisher of this version, was in business in St. Martin's Lane from 1845 to 1890. The book probably dates from his earlier years there.

THE HISTORY OF
JACK THE GIANT KILLER.

Printed by W. S. Johnson, 60, St. Martin's Lane,
Charing Cross.

The History of Jack the Giant Killer

In the reign of King Arthur, near to the Land's-end of England, in the county of Cornwall, lived a worthy farmer, who had a son named Jack. He was brisk and of ready wit, and what he could not perform by force, he completed by wit and policy; none could surpass him for the very learned he baffled by his cunning and sharp inventions.

In those days the Mount of Cornwall was kept by a Giant eighteen feet high, and about three yards in circumference, of a fierce countenance, the terror of the neighbouring towns and villages. His habitation was in a cave in the midst of the Mount; he would suffer no living thing to be near him. He fed on other people's cattle, and when he wanted food he waded over to the main land, where he helped himself to anything he could find, the people all running away. He made nothing to carry over on his back half a dozen cows and oxen at once; as for ducks and geese, he would tie them round his waist like a bunch of candles. This he practised for many years, so that a great part of the county of Cornwall was impoverished by him.

Jack undertook to destroy this monster; so furnishing himself with a horn, shovel, and pickaxe, over the mountains he went, in the beginning of a dark winter's evening, fell to work, and in the morning had dug a pit twenty feet deep, and almost as broad; covering it over with long sticks and straws, and strewing a little mould over it, it appeared like plain ground; then putting the horn to his mouth he blew tantivy;[1] which noise awoke the giant, who came roaring towards Jack, crying out, "you incorrigible villain, you shall pay dearly for disturbing me, for I will broil you for my breakfast!" He had scarcely said this when he tumbled into the pit. "Oh! Mr. Giant," says Jack, "where are you now? What do you now think of having for breakfast?" so saying, he struck him such a blow on the crown of his head, that he fell down dead to the bottom of the pit, and Jack shovelled the earth on him as he lay, and there left him.

When the Magistrates heard that Jack had destroyed this enormous Giant they were delighted, and declared that he should henceforth be called Jack the Giant Killer, and presented him with a superb sword and belt, upon which these words were written in letters of gold:—

> Here's the valiant Cornish man,
> Who slew the Giant Cormoran.

The news of Jack's victory soon spread over the western parts, and another Giant, named Blunderbore, who had heard of it, vowed to destroy him should he ever meet with him. This Giant kept an enchanted castle in the midst of a lone wood.

About four months after, as Jack was walking by the borders of a wood, on his journey into Wales, he grew weary, and sitting down by a well, fell asleep. A Giant coming for water, espied Jack, and seeing the gold letters on his belt, soon knew him. Overjoyed at his prize, he put him over his shoulder, to carry him to the castle. As he passed through a thicket, the rustling of the trees woke poor Jack, who was not a little terrified at finding himself in the hands of a monstrous giant, but more so on arriving at the castle, and seeing the mangled heaps of bodies and bones strewed about. The giant took great pleasure in shewing him these things, telling him that

---

1. Sound of a hunting horn.

human hearts were his favourite food, and he had no doubt Jack's would make him a relish for his breakfast. He then locked him in an upper room over the gateway, saying, he would fetch another giant, a friend of his, to breakfast with him off poor Jack.

Jack was almost distracted; he ran to the window, and saw the two giants coming towards the castle; now, quoth he, my death or deliverance is at hand. On looking round the room, he found some strong ropes, and making a running noose at one end, he put the other through a pulley which happened to be just over the window; while the giants were unlocking the gate Jack contrived to throw the noose over both their heads, and instantly pulling the rope, he managed, though he could not pull them off their feet, to choke them both. This was the hardest job he ever did, for the giants kicked and spluttered at a rare rate, but at length he was successful, and rejoiced at his deliverance. He then took the giant's keys, and in searching about the castle, found three ladies tied by the hair of their heads, who told Jack the giant had murdered their husbands. Jack released them, and told them he had killed the giant, so giving them the keys, he departed very well pleased with the termination of this fearful adventure.

Jack having but little money, thought it prudent to travel hard; but losing his way he was benighted, and could find no place of entertainment, until coming to a valley between two hills, he found a very large house in a lonesome place, and being greatly in need of rest and refreshment, he took courage to knock at the gate, when, to his amazement, out came a monstrous giant with three heads; however he did not seem so fierce as the other giants, but it appeared that he hid his wickedness under an appearance of civility, as the sequel will prove. Jack told him his distress, and the giant civilly invited him in, gave him a supper, and then shewed him into a bed-room, where he left him. Jack had scarcely got into bed, when he heard the giant muttering to himself, seemingly very merry:—

> Though here you lodge with me this night,
> You shall not see the morning light,
> My club shall dash your brains out quite.

That's your game, Mr. Giant, says Jack to himself, is it! then I must endeavour to be even with you. So, getting out of bed, he placed a billet of wood (of which there were many in the room) in his place, and then hid himself behind the curtains.

In the middle of the night the giant came with his great club, and, thinking it was Jack, belaboured the billet without mercy. After a while he stopped and left the room, laughing to think how he had taken poor Jack in. Early in the morning Jack put on a bold face, and went to thank the giant for his night's lodging. The giant started when he saw him, and asked him how he had slept, and if any thing had disturbed him in the night? "Oh no, says Jack, nothing worth speaking of; a rat, I believe, gave me two or three slaps with his tail, but I soon went to sleep again."

The giant wondered at this, yet did not answer a word, but got two great bowls of hasty-pudding, and putting one before Jack, began eating the other himself. Jack buttoned his leather provision bag inside his coat, and slyly filled it with the hasty pudding. "Now," says Jack, "I'll do what you can't." So he takes a knife and ripping up the bag, let's out the hasty pudding. "I can do that," says the giant, and instantly ripped up his belly, and killed himself.

Jack now started once more on his travels, and on the third day he entered an extensive forest, and presently heard the cries of some one in distress. Hastening towards the spot, he beheld an enormous giant dragging a lady and gentleman by the hair of their heads. His heart melted at the sight, when, alighting from his horse, he put on an invisible coat, which he had received as a present, and ran up to him, when aiming a blow at his legs he cut them both off at one stroke, and he fell to the ground with such force as made the earth shake. The lady and gentleman not only returned their grateful thanks, but wished him to go to their house. "No," said Jack, "I must haste to relieve a duke's daughter, who is enchanted" he then took his leave. The Enchanter lived with a huge giant in a castle on the top of a mountain guarded by two dragons; but Jack put on his invisible coat and got in unseen. Here he was astonished at the number of birds and animals, who were all enchanted persons, and getting past them, he came up to the enchanter and cut off his head. The charm now ceased—the castle fell to pieces, killed the giant, and the enchanted persons returned to their proper shapes. Jack released the duke's daughter, and many others. He then set off for the court of King Arthur, where he was well received, and in a short time he and the duke's daughter were united.

ca. 1845–50

THE HISTORY OF GOODY TWO-SHOES
ca. 1800

The full title of this story, originally published by John Newbery in 1765, runs *The History of Little Goody-Shoes; Otherwise called, Mrs Margery Two-Shoes. With the Means by which she acquired her Learning and Wisdom, and in consequence thereof her Estate*. Like Newbery, Margery was a meritocrat; her good behavior and industry bring her wealth and position in society, though necessarily through marriage since she is a woman. Though Newbery had never been shoeless like his heroine, he had been largely self-educated and had risen to prosperity through his patent medicines. He had a keen business instinct and in the style of the times advertised himself in his books. In the 1765 text Margery's father dies of a fever because he is in a place "where Dr James's Powder was not to be had." (Dr. James's Fever Powder was one of Newbery's most successful products.)

This early-nineteenth-century version, rewritten and shortened from the diffuse and digressive original, and published by Thomas Richardson of Derby, is still considerably fuller than many of the redactions; the original 156 pages were sometimes summarized in 8. The author is not known; possibly it was Newbery himself. Some have claimed that it was Oliver Goldsmith, who certainly was working for Newbery at the time, but there is no evidence for this. The themes of the story—application, self-help, rags to riches—made it very popular with American readers; Nathaniel Coverly printed it in Boston in 1783, Isaiah Thomas in 1787, and there were several Philadelphia and Hartford editions before 1820.

THE

HISTORY OF

Goody Two-Shoes.

DERBY:

Printed by and for

T. RICHARDSON, FRIAR-GATE.

Price One Halfpenny.

Goody Two-Shoes

It will be readily understood by our young readers, that the real name of the little girl who is the heroine of this story was not Goody Two-Shoes, but Margery Meanwell. Her father, Mr. Meanwell, was for many years a very respectable farmer in the parish of Mouldwell, where Margery was born; but misfortunes, and the cruel persecutions of Sir Timothy Gripe, his landlord, and the rich Farmer Graspall, ruined this worthy man, and was the source of all poor Margery's troubles.

The estate was formerly divided into small farms; but when it came into the possession of the selfish and avaricious Sir Timothy, he accepted the offer of Farmer Graspall, to take the whole farms at an advanced rent; and they had succeeded in getting all the tenants out, except Margery's father. The overbearing Graspall was overseer and churchwarden, and the maintenance of the poor passed through his hands; therefore, besides being anxious to get this farm, he had a great hatred to Mr. Meanwell, who always befriended the poor, when oppressed by him or Sir Timothy. At last, after various schemes of villainy, with the assistance of this wicked baronet, he succeeded in driving the worthy Meanwell out of his farm, and utterly ruining him. Sir Timothy, after selling off all their goods for the rent, turned the whole family out of doors; and they left the village in a state of beggary.

Farmer Meanwell died soon after of a broken heart, and his poor wife, unable to struggle with misfortunes, only survived him a few days, leaving their unfortunate offspring, Margery and Tommy, friendless orphans in an unpitying world.

The loss of their parents seemed to endear these orphans more to each other, and they were continually seen strolling hand in hand about the village, as if they were afraid of being separated. Having no mother to take care of them, they were both in rags, and those of the meanest description. Tommy, indeed, had a pair of shoes, but poor Margery had only one. Their only sustenance was the haws[1] which they pulled off the hedges, or a small morsel received from the poor villagers, and they slept every night in a barn. They had relations, but, as they were rich, they took no notice of these poor children; being ashamed to own such a little ragged girl as Margery, and such a dirty curly-headed boy as Tommy.

Mr. Smith, the clergyman of the parish where Margery and Tommy were born, was a very worthy man, and being at this time visited by a rich and charitable friend, he told him the story of the poor orphans. The gentleman expressed a desire to see them, and Mr. Smith sent a person to bring them to the parsonage. They soon arrived at the house, where their appearance made a favourable impression on the stranger, who gave Mr. Smith money to buy some clothes for Margery, and said that he would make Tommy a little sailor. Tommy was happy to hear this, and next day the gentleman bought him a jacket and trowsers, of which he was very proud. Margery could never give over admiring Tommy in his new dress; but her happiness met with a severe check, for the gentleman was to return to London in a few days, and to take Tommy along with him.

The parting of these children was very affecting; poor Margery's eyes were red with crying, and her cheeks pale with grief; while little Tommy, by way of consolation, said he would never forget his dear sister, and kissed her a hundred times over. As Tommy left his sister, he wiped her eyes with the corner of his jacket, and promised to return, and bring her fine things from abroad.

When Margery found that Tommy did not come back, she cried all day until she went to bed, and next morning she went round to every one in the village, weeping and lamenting that her brother Tommy was gone. Fortunately, while she was in this distress, the shoemaker came with a pair of new shoes, which the gentleman had ordered for her, and it being so long since little Margery wore a pair of shoes, her attention was so engaged as to give a new turn to her thoughts. Nothing but the pleasure of examining her two shoes could have put a stop to the violence of her grief. She immediately put on the shoes, and then went to let Mrs. Smith see them. It was with delight that little Margery exhibited them to her benefactress, saying, "Two shoes, Ma'am! see, two shoes!" She then went through the whole villagers to show her new shoes, addressing them in the same way, until she got the name of "Little Two-Shoes;" but, being a very good child, they usually called her "Little Goody Two-Shoes," and she never entirely lost that name.

Little Margery could have passed her life happily with Mr. and Mrs. Smith, who were very kind to her; but the cruel Farmer Graspall, whose hatred to Mr. Meanwell even descended to his offspring, told Mr. Smith, that he must turn Margery away, or he would reduce his tithes, and also added the commands of Sir Timothy Gripe. The worthy clergyman and his wife were sorry to part with Margery, but being so much in the power of their landlord, they were obliged to send her away.

Poor Margery was again destitute of friends; but, although very young, she had observed the goodness and wisdom of Mr. Smith, and believing that it was owing to his great learning, she became very desirous to know how to read. Therefore she contrived to meet the children as they returned from school, and prevailed on one

1. Berries.

of them to learn her the alphabet. She used to borrow their books, and sit down and read till they came from dinner.[2] It was by these means that she soon acquired more learning than her playmates at school, and in a short time she formed a little plan for instructing children who had not yet learned to read.

She found that there were twenty-six letters in the alphabet, and every word spelled with them; but as these letters might be either large or small, she cut, out of little pieces of wood, ten sets of the alphabet in small letters, and ten of the large, or capitals. With the assistance of an old spelling-book she made her companions arrange the words they wanted to spell out of her wooden alphabets, and then showed them how to make sentences. When they wished to play at this game, she placed the children around her, and gave them a word to spell. If the word was plum-pudding, the first brought the letter *p*, the second *l*, the third *u*, the fourth *m*, and so on, till the whole was completed.

By this method, in a short time Margery gained such great credit among the parents of the children, that they were all happy when she appeared with the basket of letters in her hand, which proved a source of amusement, as well as instruction, and she at last had a regular set of scholars.

Margery usually left home at seven o'clock in the morning, and the first house she called at was Farmer Wilson's. Mrs. Wilson always received her with pleasure, saying, "O Little Goody, I am glad to see you—Billy has learned his lesson." The little boy was equally happy to see her; and after giving him his lesson, she went to Farmer Simpson's. A dog used to bark at her when she first went to that house, but he soon learned to know her. "Come in, Margery," said Mrs. Simpson, "Sally wants you very much, for she has learned her lesson." Little Sally began her lesson, by placing the syllables of two letters, which she did very correctly, and pronounced them as Goody Two-Shoes had taught her.

After giving her a new lesson in words of four letters, Goody took leave, and proceeded to Farmer Cooke's, where a number of poor children were assembled to receive her instructions. The moment she appeared, they all flocked round her, and she made them spell what they had got to dinner. Goody gave them another lesson, and then went to Farmer Thompson's, where she had a great many scholars waiting for her. These children were farther advanced, and not only able to spell words, but some of them put long sentences together, and they all acquitted themselves to the satisfaction of their little instructress.

It was during the time that Goody Two-Shoes went about teaching the children, that the rich Lady Ducklington died, and was buried in the parish church-yard.

The whole county seemed to be assembled on this occasion, and it was late before the funeral was over. In the night-time, when every one was in bed, the bells in the church-steeple were heard to jingle, which frightened the villagers very much, for they thought it must be the ghost of Lady Ducklington amusing itself with the bell-ropes.

The people all flocked to Will Dobbins, the clerk, and begged him to go and see what it was; but Will said he knew it was a ghost, and therefore he would not open the door. However, the rector, Mr. Long, hearing such an uproar, came to the clerk, and inquired why he did not go to the church. "I go to the church, Sir!" said he; "bless me! the ghost would frighten me to death."

"Did you ever see a ghost?" said Mr. Long.

2. I.e., lunch.

"My father once saw one in the shape of a windmill, and it walked round the church in a white sheet, with jack-boots, and a sword by its side."

Mr. Long, who could not help smiling at this ridiculous story, requested the key of the church; and on receiving it, went away, followed by a great number of the villagers, and opened the door, when out came Little Goody Two-Shoes, who, being tired with walking about all the day, had fallen asleep during the funeral service, and been shut up in the church.

Goody begged Mr. Long's pardon for the trouble she had given him; and said, that when she found herself locked into the church, she did not wish to ring the bells; but growing very cold, and hearing Farmer Dawson's man pass by, she thought he would have gone to the clerk for the key. When Mr. Long went away, the people all crowded about little Margery, to learn what she had heard or seen, and she told them as follows:—

"I went to the church with you all to the funeral, and fell asleep in Mr. Jones's pew; the striking of the clock awakened me, and I scarcely knew where I was. It was very dark, and while I was in the pew, something jumped upon me behind, and I thought it placed its hands upon my shoulders; I was afraid, at first, and I knelt down and said my prayers; but something very cold touched my neck, and made me start. I walked down the church aisle, and something followed me, the feet of which went pit pat; something then touched my hand; however, as I was very cold, I felt my way up into the pulpit. I then meant to go to sleep on the mat and cushion, but something pushed against the door, and presently I found that it was Mr. Sanderson's dog, which had come with me to the church. When I heard Farmer Dawson's man, I immediately went to the belfry, and made the noise you heard."

Some days after this, as Little Goody was returning from her pupils rather later than usual, she was overtaken by a violent storm of thunder and lightning; but she took refuge in a farmer's barn, and lay down among some straw at the farther end. She had not remained long, before four robbers also sought shelter from the storm in the same place, and not observing Little Goody, who was at some distance, they began to arrange their future plans of depredation.

Among other schemes of villainy, they formed the resolution of breaking into the houses of Sir William Dove and Sir Timothy Gripe on the night following, and to plunder them of all their money, plate, and jewels.

During their conversation, Little Goody listened with great attention; but the tempest being over, the robbers left the barn, without discovering that they had been overheard. When she thought they were fairly gone, Goody made the best of her way home, and, rising early next morning, went to Sir William Dove, and told him all that she had heard. The knight asked her name, and then giving her some money, desired her to call on him next day.—Goody next proceeded to Sir Timothy Gripe's, and sent in her name by the servant; but, as he refused to see her, she, with some difficulty, got admittance to Lady Gripe, and related what she had heard in the barn. This lady was a very sensible woman, and did not despise the information; but she secretly engaged people to guard the house; and when the robbers came in two parties to attack both houses, they were all taken and sent to gaol.

Sir William Dove, who was grateful for the service Little Goody had done him, said she should no longer sleep in a barn, as he would try to get some proper situation for her; but the wicked Sir Timothy was vexed that his life had been saved by her means, and never rewarded, or even thanked her.

The most respectable school in that neighbourhood was conducted by a Mrs. Williams, a very good lady; but old age induced her to resign the situation, which Sir William Dove getting notice of, sent for her, and recommended Little Goody as a person worthy to succeed her. As Mrs. Williams already knew that Margery had a good heart, she found, upon examination, her head to be equally so; and being every way qualified for the place, Margery was, at the old lady's request, appointed to succeed her.

This event Margery always considered as the happiest of her life, and she made every exertion to be useful to the children who were put under her charge. She was now no longer called *Margery*, or *Little Goody Two-Shoes*, but only known by the name of *Mrs. Margery*.

The school-room was large, and she hung her old wooden letters around it; so that every scholar had to bring a letter in turn, which she considered as conducive to health. As her chief object was not to gain money, but to be of service to the children, she taught all those for nothing whose parents could not afford to pay for their instruction.

Margery had a very feeling heart, and could not endure to see even a dumb animal used with cruelty, without trying to prevent it. As she was one day walking through the village, her attention was drawn to some boys, who were tying a poor raven, which they had caught, to a post, on purpose to amuse themselves with the cruel diversion of shying, or throwing a stick at it. Margery, to get the raven out of their hands, gave them a penny, and brought it home with her. She called the raven Ralph; taught him to speak and spell; and as he was fond of playing with the capital letters, the children called them "Ralph's Alphabet."

Shortly after, when rambling in the fields, she saw two boys torturing a beautiful dove, by allowing it to fly a little way, and then pulling it back again, with a string which was tied to its foot. Margery also rescued this bird for a mere trifle, and carried it away with her. She likewise learned the dove to spell with her letters, besides many other curious things; and being very useful in carry letters, she called him Tom. It is a most curious fact, that Tom showed as great a liking to the small letters as Ralph had for the large, and the scholars used to give them the appellation of "Tom's Alphabet."

Another useful assistant of Mrs. Margery's was a fine skylark, which some of the neighbours made her a present of. As some children are very fond of lying in bed too long in the morning, she sent this pretty bird, which sung sweetly at their window, and taught them when to rise.

A poor little lamb, which had lost its dam, was about to be killed by the butcher, when Margery making a bargain with him for it, took it home, and called it Will. He taught the children when to go to bed, and being very gentle, was a great favourite; but he only carried home the satchel of those who behaved best, and brought it again in the morning. She also got a present of a little dog, called Jumper, who was very sagacious, and might have been termed Porter of the School, for he never allowed any unknown person to enter.

One day, as Mrs. Margery was amusing the children after school-time with some innocent diversion, a man brought the sad news, that Sally Jones's father was thrown from his horse, and in great danger, which affected the poor girl very much. Margery gave Tom, the pigeon, to the messenger, unknown to the children, that he might bring back an account of Mr. Jones's health, and then did every thing she could to sooth Sally. It was not long before the pigeon returned with a letter in his bill, which informed them that he was considered out of danger.

A few days afterwards, little Jumper gave a wonderful proof of his sagacity. The children had just finished their lessons, when the dog ran in, and, seizing Margery's apron, tried to pull her out of the school-room. She allowed the dog to drag her out to the garden, and he returned and brought out one of the children in the same manner; upon which Mrs. Margery called them all into the garden. This saved all their lives, for in less than five minutes after the roof of the house fell in.

This was a great loss to Mrs. Margery, who had now no place to teach in; but Sir William Dove caused another school to be built at his own expense, and she got the use of Farmer Grove's hall till it was ready, which was in the centre of the village. While there, she learned the farmer's servants and neighbours to read and write, and by degrees became so esteemed in the parish, that almost every one consulted her, and many serious disputes were settled by her advice. Mrs. Margery was so frequently employed in making up differences, that she invented what she called, a Charm for the Passions, or a Considering Cap, which had three equal sides. On the first was written, "I may be wrong;" on the second, "It is fifty to one but you are;" and on the third, "I will consider of it:" the other parts were covered with curious hieroglyphics, and in the inside a direction for using it. The possessor was requested to put on the cap whenever he found his passion rising, and not to speak a single word, but with coolness and deliberation.

Most of the grounds farmed by Mr. Grove, and in that neighbourhood, were meadows, and the great dependence of the farmers was on their hay, which for some years had been much injured by the rain. Mrs. Margery, who was always doing good, contrived an instrument to tell when the weather was to continue favourable or unfavourable; by which means she told the farmers when to mow their grass and gather in the hay with safety. Several persons, who suffered in their crops by not consulting Margery, were so angry at their losses, that they accused her of being a witch, and sent Gaffer Goosecap, a silly old meddling fool, to obtain evidence against her.

This old fellow entered the school as Margery was walking about, having the raven on one shoulder, the pigeon on the other, the lark on her hand, and the lamb and dog at her side, and he was so frightened, that he cried, "A witch! a witch!" Margery exclaimed, smiling, "A conjurer! a conjurer!" and he ran off; but soon after a warrant was issued against her, and she was carried before a meeting of the justices, followed by all the neighbours. Although this accusation met with the contempt it deserved, yet one of the magistrates was silly enough to believe the slander, and asked, who could give her a character. Margery inquired if any one there could speak against it; and told them, that she had many friends both able and willing to defend her, but she could not think of troubling them on such a silly business, for if she was a witch, she would show them her charm. She then took out her weather-glass,[3] and placed it upon the table.

This simple defence pleased every one, and Sir William Dove, who was one of the justices, said, "I am surprised that any person can be so foolish as to believe in the existence of witches.

"This puts me in mind of a story of a poor industrious widow, against whom the same silly charge was made. The foolish people had got it into their heads that she was a witch, and requested the parson not to allow her to come to church. He very properly refused their request; but the poor woman, to avoid insult, was forced to sit in some obscure corner. However, some time after this, she was left five thousand pounds by a brother, which changed the public opinion so much, that they all treated her with respect."

Sir Charles Jones, who was present on this occason, was so delighted with her conduct, that he offered her a handsome annuity to superintend his family and the education of his daughter. This she refused at first, but Sir Charles being seized with a severe fit of illness, and again entreating her, she at last consented. In this situation,

3. Barometer.

she conducted herself with so much propriety, and behaved so tenderly to his daughter, that, on his recovery, when she proposed to leave him, he made her an offer of his hand. Margery was neither ambitious of title nor wealth, but she knew the real value of the worthy baronet, and esteemed him as he deserved; therefore, after he had amply provided for his daughter, she consented to become Lady Jones.

When this circumstance was understood in the neighbourhood, it diffused a general joy throughout the village, where Margery was greatly beloved, and brought crowds to witness the marriage. The clergyman was proceeding with the ceremony, when a young gentleman, handsomely dressed, came running into the church, and requested that the ceremony might be stopped until he had a conversation with the bride. The whole assembly were astonished at his request, particularly the bride and bridegroom, who stood motionless without having power to return an answer to the stranger. However, the gentleman coming forward, discovered himself to be Tommy, her brother, and she fainted away in his arms.

Tommy Meanwell had just landed from abroad, where he had made a great fortune, which he intended to share with his dear sister, when he heard of her intended marriage, and posted[4] to be present on the occasion. After mutual congratulations, this happy pair were united, and lived happily together many years, doing all the good in their power.

Sir Timothy Gripe was struck off the list of justices; and one of his relations gained possession of his estates, which he sold to Lady Jones, who divided them again into small farms. In the course of time, both Sir Timothy and Farmer Graspall were so reduced as to be supported by the charity of Lady Jones, who delighted in relieving the indigent, rewarding the industrious, and instructing the children in the neighbourhood.

Having lived to an advanced age in the constant practice of virtue, and having made some liberal bequests in favour of her fellow-creatures, her spirit returned to God who gave it, leaving all who knew her to mourn her departure.

ca. 1800

4. Traveled with speed.

CHILDREN IN THE WOOD
ca. 1800

This ballad, registered in 1595, has always been popular in Britain and America. In 1711 Joseph Addison, writing in *The Spectator*, called it "one of the darling songs of the common people," and d'Alté Welch in his *Bibliography of American Children's Books Printed Prior to 1821* (1972) found thirty different printings. The story, sometimes told in prose, has been a favorite with illustrators, notably Randolph Caldecott (*The Babes in the Wood*, 1879) and Edward Ardizzone (*The Old Ballad of the Babes in the Wood*, 1972). The illustrations in this early-nineteenth-century chapbook were crudely hand-colored. Hand-coloring was a domestic industry in which very young children were used. Each had a different saucer of color and dabbed a patch on the printed sheets laid out on the table. They "colour prints, maps, or children's books from morning till night, and never play or chat about them," said one pitying observer (James Hain Friswell, *Houses with the Fronts Off*, 1854). He thought that if readers knew the misery inflicted on child workers as young as five, they would take no pleasure in the books.

CHILDREN

IN THE

WOOD.

LONDON:

SOLD BY THE BOOKSELLERS.

Children in the Wood

A gentleman of good account,
  In Norfolk dwelt of late,
Who did in honour far surmount,
  Most men of his estate.

Sore sick he was, and like to die,
  No help his life could save;
His wife by him as sick did lie,
  And both possest one grave.

No love between these two was lost,
  Each was to other kind:
In love they lived, in love they died,
  And left two babes behind.

The father left his little son,
  As plainly doth appear,

When he to perfect age should come,
 Three hundred pounds a year.

And to his little daughter Jane,
 Five hundred pounds in gold,
To be paid on her marriage-day,
 Which might not be controll'd.

But if the children chance to die,
 Ere they to age should come,
Their uncle should possess their wealth,
 For so the will did run.

"Now, brother," said the dying man,
 "Look to my children dear;
Be good unto my boy and girl,
 No friends else have they here."

With lips as cold as any stone,
 They kiss'd their children small:
"God bless you both, my children dear;"
 With that the tears did fall.

These speeches then their brother spake,
 To this sick couple there:
"The keeping of your children small,
 Sweet sister, do not fear.

God never prosper me nor mine,
 Nor aught else that I have,
If I do wrong your children dear,
 When you're laid in the grave."

He had not kept these pretty babes
 A twelvemonth and a day,
But, for their wealth, he did devise
 To make them both away.

He bargain'd with two ruffians strong,
 Who were of furious mood,
That they should take these children young,
 And slay them in a wood.

And told his wife and all he had,
 He did the children send
To be brought up in fair London,
 With one that was his friend.

They prate and prattle pleasantly,
 As they rode on their way,
To those who should their butchers be,
 And work their life's decay.

So that the pretty speech they had,
    Made murderer's heart relent,
And they that undertook the deed,
    Full sore did now repent.

Yet one of them more hard of heart,
    Did vow to do his charge,
Because the wretch that hired him,
    Had paid him very large.

The other won't agree thereto;
    So here they fell to strife,
With one another they did fight,
    About the children's life.

And he that was of mildest mood,
    Did slay the other there,
Within an unfrequented wood,
    While babes did quake for fear.

He took the children by the hand,
    Tears standing in their eye,
And bade them straightway follow him,
    And look they did not cry.

And two long miles he led them on,
    While they for bread complain;
"Stay here," quoth he, "I'll bring you some
    When I come back again."

These pretty babes, with hand in hand,
    Went wandering up and down;
But never more could see the man
    Approaching from the town.

Their pretty lips with black-berries,
    Were all besmear'd and dyed,
And when they saw the darksome night,
    They sat them down and cried.

Thus wandered these two little babes,
    Till death did end their grief,
In one another's arms they died,
    As babes wanting relief.

No burial this pretty pair,
    Of any man receives,
Till Robin-redbreast painfully,
    Did cover them with leaves.

ca. 1800

THE HISTORY OF SIR RICHARD WHITTINGTON AND HIS CAT
ca. 1840

The legend of Dick Whittington, the poor boy who rose to become "thrice Lord Mayor of London town," had obvious appeal as a chapbook and later as a Sunday school story. Though nothing is known about his early life, there is no reason to suppose that the real Sir Richard Whittington, who died in 1423, came to London a destitute orphan. He was a mercer, or cloth merchant, already prosperous enough in 1379 to contribute to a city loan. He held many public offices, and was three times Lord Mayor. He lent considerable sums to the king, and after his wife's death devoted his wealth to the public good. The story that this fortune was made through his cat, which was sent on a voyage to a rat-infested country, first appears in a play, now lost, which was licensed in 1605, though the play in turn may have been derived from a ballad. The dates and historical details at the end of this version do not tally with the known facts.

Houlston's juvenile publications (a list is at the end) were in general serious, and included many Sunday stories. The chapbook dates from before the firm's move from Shropshire to London in about 1840.

FRONTISPIECE.

Behold a Cat whose merit wants a name:
'Twas she that rais'd poor Whittington to fame:
E'en so shall Providence provide for those
Who duly honour him, and keep his laws.

THE

HISTORY

OF

Sir Richard Whittington,

AND

HIS CAT.

ADORNED WITH CUTS.

WELLINGTON:

Printed by F. Houlston and Son.

Price One Penny.

The History of Whittington

Dick Whittington was such a little boy, when his parents died, that he never knew them, nor the place where he was born. He wandered about as ragged as a colt, till he met with a waggoner going to London, who gave him leave to walk all the way by the side of his waggon. This much obliged little Whittington, as he was desirous to see London, for he had heard that the streets were paved with gold, and he was willing to get a bushel of it. But the poor boy was disappointed when he saw them covered with dirt instead of gold, and found himself in a strange place without friends, without food, and without money.

Though the waggoner was so charitable as to let him walk by the side of the waggon for nothing, yet he took care not to know him when he came to town. In a little time the poor boy was almost starved to death for want of support. In this distress he asked charity of several people, and one of them bid him go work in the fields. That I will, says Whittington, and with all my heart. I will work for you, if you will permit me. The man immediately sent him to make hay; but when the season was over, he was again in great distress.

In this condition, and fainting for want of food, he laid himself down at the door of one Mr. Fitzwarren, a merchant, where the cook saw him, and being an ill-natured hussey, ordered him to go about his business, or she would scold him. At this time Mr. Fitzwarren came from the Exchange,[1] and began also to scold at the poor boy, bidding him to go to work.

Whittington answered he should be glad to work; but was unable at present, for he had eat nothing for three days, and knew nobody. He then endeavoured to get up, but was so very weak that he fell down again. This excited the merchant's pity, who ordered the servants to take him in, give him some food, and let him help the cook to do any

---

1. The building where merchants transacted business.

drudgery that she had to set him about. People are too apt to reproach those who beg with being idle, but strive not to put them in a way of getting business, or considering whether they are able to do it. I remember a circumstance of this sort which Sir William Thompson told my father, and it is so affecting that I shall never forget it.

When Sir William was in the plantations[2] abroad, one of his friends told him he had an intended servant, whom he had just bought, that was a lusty man, but he is so idle, says he, that I cannot get him to work. Ah! says Sir William, let me see him: accordingly they walked out, and found the man sitting on a heap of stones. Sir William asked why he did not go to work? I am not able, answered the man. Not able! says Sir William; I am sure you look very well, give him a few stripes. Upon this the planter struck him several times, but the poor man still kept his seat. They then left him to look over the plantation, exclaiming against his obstinacy. But how surprised were they, on their return, to find the poor man fallen off the place where he had been sitting, and dead! The cruelty, says Sir William, of my ordering the poor creature to be beaten while in the agonies of death, lies always next my heart. It is what I shall never forget, and will for ever prevent my judging rashly of people who appear in distress.

But we return to Whittington, who would have lived happily in this worthy family, had he not been bumped about by the cross cook, who must always be roasting or basting, and, when the spit was still, she employed her hands upon poor Whittington, till Miss Alice, his master's daughter, was informed of it, who made the servants use him kindly.

Besides the crossness of the cook, Whittington had another difficulty to get over. He had a flock bed placed for him in the garret, where there were such a number of rats and mice that they often ran over the poor boy's nose, and disturbed him in his sleep. After some time, however, a gentleman who came to his master's house gave Whittington a penny for brushing his shoes. This he determined to lay out to the best advantage; and the next day seeing a woman in the street with a cat under her arm, he ran up to her, desiring to know the price of it. The woman asked a great deal of money for it, as the cat was a good mouser; but on Whittington's telling her he had but a penny in the world, and that he wanted a cat sadly, she let him have it, and a fine cat she was.

This cat Whittington concealed in the garret, and here she soon killed or frightened away the rats and mice, so that he could sleep soundly.

Soon after this, the merchant, who had a ship ready to sail, called for all his servants, as his custom was, in order that each of them might venture something to try their luck; and whatever they sent was to pay neither freight nor custom; for he justly thought that God would bless him the more for letting the poor partake of his good fortune.

All the servants appeared but poor Whittington, who having neither money nor goods, could not think of sending any thing to try his luck; but his good friend, Miss Alice, thinking his poverty kept him away, ordered him to be called.

She then offered to lay down something for him; but the merchant told his daughter that would not do, for it must be something of his own. Upon which poor Whittington said he had nothing but a cat, which he had bought for a penny that was given him. Fetch thy cat, boy, says the merchant, and send her. Whittington brought poor puss; and delivered her to the captain with tears in his eyes, for he said he should now be disturbed by the rats and mice as before. All the company laughed at the oddity of the adventure, and Miss Alice, who pitied the poor boy, gave him something to buy him another cat.

2. Sugar plantations in the West Indies.

While puss was beating the billows at sea, poor Whittington was severely beaten at home by his tyrannical mistress the cook, who used him so cruelly, and made such game of him for sending his cat to sea, that at last the poor boy determined to run away from his place; and having packed up a few things he had, he set out very early in the morning on All-hallows-day. He travelled as far as Holloway, and there sat down on a stone, now called Whittington's stone, to consider what course he should take; but whilst he was thus ruminating, Bow bells,[3] of which there were then only six, began to ring; and he thought their sounds addressed him in this manner:

Turn again Whittington,
Lord Mayor of great London.

"Lord Mayor of London!" said he to himself, "what would not one endure to be Lord Mayor of London, and ride in such a fine coach? well, I'll go back again, and bear all the pummelling and ill usage of Cicely, rather than miss the opportunity of being Lord Mayor." So home he went, and happily got into the house, and about his business, before Mrs. Cicely made her appearance. The ship, with the cat on board, was long beating about at sea, and at last, by contrary winds, driven on a part of the coast of Barbary,[4] which was inhabited by Moors unknown to the English. These people received our country men with civility; and therefore the captain, in order to trade with them, showed them patterns of the goods he had on board, and sent some of them to the king of the country, who was so well pleased, that he sent for the captain and the factor to his palace. Here they were placed, according to the custom of the country, on rich carpets flowered with gold and silver; and the king and queen being seated at the upper end of the room, dinner was brought in, which consisted of many dishes; but no sooner were the dishes put down, than an amazing number of rats and mice came from all quarters, and devoured all the meat in an instant. The factor,[5] in

3. The bells of St. Mary-le-Bow, Cheapside, London's most famous church bells. After the Great Fire of London in 1666, the church was rebuilt with eight bells; two more were added in 1762, and the current total of twelve was reached in 1881.
4. The coast of North Africa, including present-day Morocco, Algeria, Tunisia, and western Libya.
5. Mercantile agent.

surprise, turned round to the nobles, and asked if these vermin were not offensive? O yes, said they, very offensive; and the king would give half his treasure to be free of them; for they not only destroy his dinner, as you see, but they assault him in his chamber, and even in his bed, so that he is obliged to be watched while he is sleeping for fear of them.

The factor jumped for joy: he remembered poor Whittington and his cat, and told the king he had a creature on board his ship that would dispatch all these vermin immediately. The king was overjoyed at the news. Bring this creature to me, says he; and if she will perform what you say, I will load your ship with jewels in exchange for her. The factor took this opportunity to set forth the merits of Mrs. Puss, and said that it would be inconvenient for him to part with her, but that, to oblige his majesty, he would fetch her. Run, run, said the queen, for I am impatient to see the dear creature. Away flew the factor, while another dinner was providing, and returned with the cat, just as the rats and mice were devouring that also. He immediately put down Mrs. Puss, who killed great part of them, and the rest ran away.

The king rejoiced greatly to see his old enemies destroyed by so small a creature, and the queen was highly pleased, and desired the cat might be brought near, that she might look at her. Upon which the factor called, Pussey, pussey, pussey, and she came to him; he then presented her to the queen, who started back, and was afraid to touch a creature which had made such havock among the rats and mice; however, when the factor stroked the cat, and cried, Pussey, pussey, pussey, the queen also touched her, and cried, Putty, putty, putty, for she had not learned English. He then put her down on the queen's lap, where she purred, played with her majesty's hand, and then sung herself to sleep.

The king having seen the wonderful exploits of Mrs. Puss, and being informed that she was with young, and would furnish the whole country, bargained with the captain and factor for the whole ship's cargo, and then gave them ten times as much for the cat as all the rest amounted to; with which, after taking leave of their majesties, and other great personages at court, they sailed with a fair wind for England, whither we must now attend them.

> The morn, ensuing from the mountain's height,
> Had scarcely ting'd the skies with rosy light,

when Mr. Fitzwarren stole from the bed of his beloved wife, to count over the cash, and settle the business of the day. He had but just entered the compting-house,[6] and seated himself at the desk, when somebody came tap, tap, tap, at the door. Who's there? says Mr. Fitzwarren. A friend, answered the other. What friend

6. Countinghouse.

can come at this unseasonable time? says Mr. Fitzwarren. A real friend is never unseasonable, answered the other; I come to bring you good news of the ship Unicorn. The merchant instantly got up, opened the door, and who should be seen waiting but the captain and factor with a cabinet of jewels, and a bill of lading, for which the merchant lifted up his eyes, and thanked heaven for sending him such a prosperous voyage. They then told him of the adventures of the cat, and showed him the cabinet of jewels which they had brought for Mr. Whittington. Upon which he cried out with great earnestness,

> Go call him, and tell him of his fame,
> And call him Mr. Whittington by name.

Though we may not prove Mr. Fitzwarren a good poet, yet we shall convince the reader he was a good man; for when some told him that this treasure was too much for such a boy as Whittington, he said, God forbid that I should deprive him of a penny; it is all his own, and he shall have it to a farthing. He then ordered Mr. Whittington in, who was at this time cleaning the kitchen, and would have excused himself from going into the parlour, saying, the room was rubbed, and his shoes were dirty and full of hob-nails. The merchant, however, made him come in, and ordered a chair to be set for him. Upon which, thinking they intended to make sport of him, as had been too often the case in the kitchen, he besought his master not to mock a poor simple fellow, but to let him go about his business. The merchant taking him by the hand, said, Indeed, Mr. Whittington, I am in earnest with you, and sent for you to congratulate you on your great success. Your Cat has produced you more money than I am worth in the world; and may you long enjoy it. Being at length shown the treasure, and convinced by them that all of it belonged to him, he fell upon his knees, and thanked the Almighty for his providential care of such a miserable creature. He then laid all the treasure at his master's feet, who refused to take any part of it, but told him he heartily rejoiced at his prosperity, and hoped the wealth he had acquired would be a comfort to him. He then applied to his mistress and to his good friend, Miss Alice, who likewise refused to take any part of his money, but told him she really rejoiced at his success, and wished him all imaginable felicity. He then gratified the captain, factor, and ship's crew for the care they had taken of his cargo, and distributed presents to all the servants in the house, not forgetting even his old enemy the cook.

After this, Mr. Fitzwarren advised Mr. Whittington to send for the necessary people, and dress himself like a gentleman, and made him the offer of his house to live in till he could provide himself with a better.

When Mr. Whittington's face was washed, his hair curled, his hat cocked, and he was dressed in a rich suit of clothes, then he turned out a very genteel young man indeed, and in a little time dropped that sheepish behaviour, which was principally occasioned by a depression of spirits, and soon became a sprightly and good companion, insomuch that Miss Alice, who had formerly seen him with an eye of compassion, now beheld him differently. This was perhaps occasioned by his readiness to oblige her, and by continually making her presents of such things as he thought might be agreeable. When the father perceived they had this good liking for each other, he proposed a match betwixt them. Both parties cheerfully consented, and the lord mayor, the court of aldermen, the sheriffs, the company of stationers,[7] and a number of eminent merchants, attended the ceremony, and were elegantly treated at an entertainment made for that purpose.

History tells us that they lived happily, and had several children; that he was sheriff of London in the year 1340, and afterwards lord mayor; that in the latter part of his mayoralty he entertained King Henry the Fifth and his Queen, after the conquest of France. Upon this occasion, the king, in consideration of Whittington's merit, said, "Never had prince such a subject." This being told Whittington at table, he replied, "Never had subject such a king."

He constantly fed great numbers of the poor; he built a church and a college to it, with a yearly allowance for poor scholars, and near it erected an hospital.

ca. 1840

BOOKS

Printed and sold by F. Houlston and Son, Wellington, Salop.

TRUE COURAGE; or, Heaven never forsakes the Innocent: adorned with Cuts. Price 1d.

The TRIFLER; or Pretty Plaything: with numerous Cuts. Price 1d.

The HOUSE THAT JACK BUILT: to which is added, the Life of Master and Miss Supine: adorned with Cuts. Price 1d.

The History of LITTLE RED RIDING-HOOD; and Diamonds and Toads: adorned with Cuts. Price 1d.

The CRIES of LONDON: adorned with Cuts. Price 1d.

COCK ROBIN; with the Tragical Death of an Apple-pie: adorned with Cuts. Price 1d.

GLEANINGS from Natural History, with a Cut to each Subject. Price 1d.

WILLIAM AND GEORGE, the rich Boy, and the poor Boy: adorned with Cuts. Price 1d.

7. One of the City of London guilds. Their supposed presence at the funeral must have been a humorous reference to the use made of the Whittington legend.

THE ART OF MAKING MONEY PLENTY
1817

The text of this little work, also known as *The Way to Wealth*, has usually been attributed to Benjamin Franklin, though the editor of the 1836–42 collected edition of Franklin's works questioned that attribution. However, Franklin's name appears on the many early-nineteenth-century American printings, and the maxims are certainly derived from *Poor Richard's Almanack* (1733). For many young Americans, these maxims were their guide to life. William Henry Venable, born in 1836, said that the mandates "were virtuously and strenuously enforced and obeyed as if they were holy Scripture" (*A Buckeye*

Boyhood, 1911). And Samuel Goodrich ("Peter Parley") recommended *Poor Richard* to all his young readers: "He [Richard] instructed me never to eat my breakfast until I had earned it."

The London firm Darton, Harvey, and Darton, Quakers whose philosophy was much the same as Poor Richard's, imitated the idea of a rebus version (where pictures represent syllables or words) of the precepts from one earlier issued in New York by Samuel Wood, but used new illustrations. The elegant copperplate engravings give it an appeal more opulent than that of ordinary chapbooks.

THE ART OF
MAKING MONEY PLENTY,
IN EVERY MAN'S POCKET.

By Dr Franklin.

London, Printed for Darton, Harvey and Darton, Gracechurch Street,
and for Wm Alexander, York.
1817.

2

At this [eye] [w—bird] the complaint

is t[hat] [money] s so s[car]ce,

[eye]t must [bee] an act of kindness

the [money]le[s]s how they

At this time when the general complaint is that money
is so scarce, it must be an act of kindness to inform
the moneyle[s]s how they

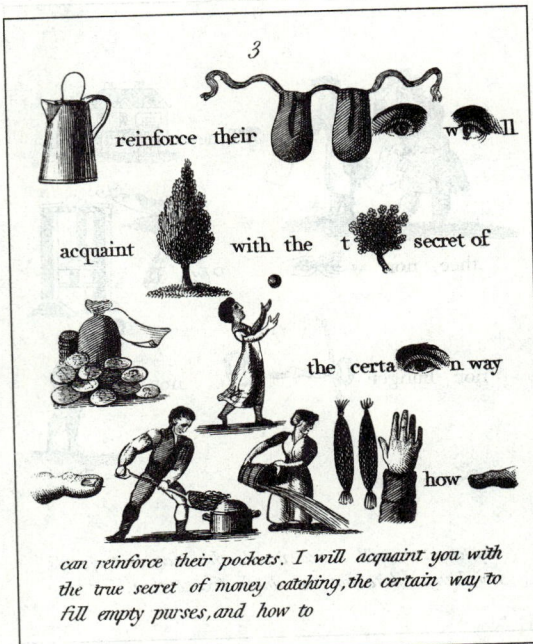

3

reinforce their [pockets] w[ill]

acquaint with the t[rue] secret of

the certa[i]n way

how

can reinforce their pockets. I will acquaint you with
the true secret of money catching, the certain way to
fill empty purses, and how to

4

keep them [al]ways Two simple

d w[ill] do the

bus[i]ne[s]s. 1st Let ho[nest]y

and thy const[ant]

keep them always full. Two simple rules, well obser
ved, will do the busine[s]s. 1st Let honesty and industry
be thy constant

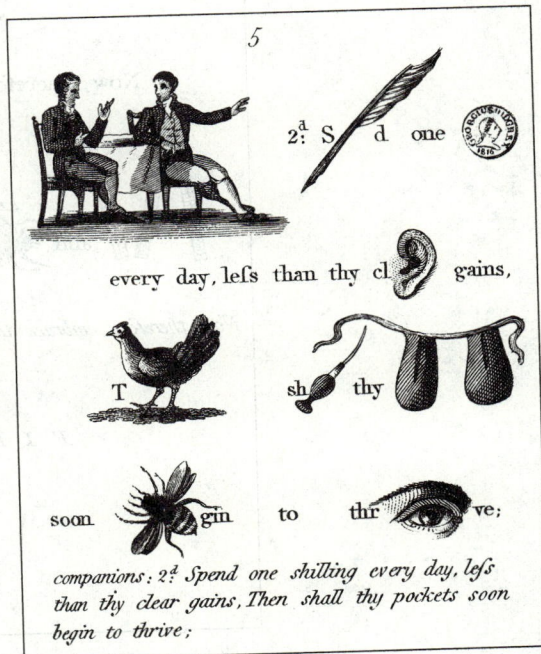

5

2d S[pen]d one

every day, le[s]s than thy cl[ear] gains,

T[hen] sh[all] thy

soon [be]gin to thr[i]ve;

companions: 2d Spend one shilling every day, le[s]s
than thy clear gains, Then shall thy pockets soon
begin to thrive;

6

thy w ll never sult thee, nor w o nor hunger e, nor freeze thee.

thy creditors will never insult thee, nor want oppress,
nor hunger bite, nor nakedness freeze thee.

7

The whole hemi w ll sh ne hter, and leasure s u every er of thy

The whole hemisphere will shine brighter, and plea-
sure spring up in every corner of thy heart.

8

Now; therefore, these and ha y.

Now; therefore, embrace these rules, and be happy.

F I N I S.

THE NEW-YORK CRIES
1826

Street cries, the slogans called out by itinerant traders advertising their wares or skills, were often gathered in books for children in the late eighteenth and early nineteenth centuries, being both an attractive subject to illustrate and a useful one on which to hang gobbets of information or moral maxims. Some of the cries have survived in rhyme and verse. The Mother Goose "Young lambs to sell! Young lambs to sell! / I never would cry young lambs to sell / If I'd as much money as I could tell" (no. 297 in Iona and Peter Opie's *Oxford Dictionary of Nursery Rhymes,* 1951) was once cried by vendors of toy lambs. "Cherry-ripe, ripe, ripe, I cry" was made into a poem by Robert Herrick (1591–1674). Stallhold-

ers in street markets can still be heard crying their wares, and in London, until the first two papers ceased publication, the news vendors' shout of "Star, News, or Standard" used to be a familiar sound in the evening. Books of London street cries were frequently copied by American publishers in the late eighteenth century, but it was some time before American city cries were collected. Samuel Wood published *The Cries of New-York* in 1808, and in 1826 Mahlon Day produced a different compilation, of which this is a later edition. It contains interesting geographical and historical information. There are nineteen cries on twelve leaves.

THE

NEW-YORK CRIES,

IN RHYME.

NEW-YORK:
MAHLON DAY, 374 PEARL-STREET.
1837.

5

MATS! MATS!
Buy a Mat! Buy a Mat!

Here's excellent Mats,
　　Made of oakum all o'er,
So nice and so proper,
　　To keep a clean floor.

One's pity would be raised to see this poor old blind man led along the streets of New-York by his little dutiful son. The manner of their carrying their Mats, adds a good deal to the interest of the scene. They string some on their backs, while others hang before, thus appearing almost covered up with their commodity, and silently but very forcibly appealing to the humane feelings of the citizens to buy their rugs.—No honest business is to be despised by its being humble; nor should any person be shunned or neglected because he is poor. Worth makes the man: and industry leads to plenty. Want looks into a diligent man's door, but dares not enter.

73

NEW MILK.

"Meeleck, Come! Meeleck, Come!

Here's New Milk from the Cow,
Which is so nice and so fine,
That the doctors do say,
It is much better than wine.

● ●

This wholesome beverage is carried all around the city by men in carts, wagons, and very large tin kettles, as we see in the cut. The cows are pastured on the Island of New-York, some along the New-Jersey shore, and large droves on Long-Island. Milk sells from 4 to 6 cents per quart, delivered at our doors every morning in the winter season, and twice a day in summer.

In warm weather, one may see large churns, mounted on a wheelbarrow, pushed along by colored men, mostly from Bergen, on the Jersey shore, crying, BUT-TER MEE-LECK! WHITE WINE!!

SAND O!

"S-A-N-D! Here's your nice white S-A-N-D!"

Sand, O! white Sand, O!
Buy Sand for your floor;
For so cleanly it looks
When strew'd at your door.

● ●

This Sand is brought from the seashore in vessels, principally from Rockaway Beach, Long Island. It is loaded into carts, and carried about the streets of New-York, and so'd for about 12½ cents a bushel. Almost every little girl or boy knows that it is put on newly scrubbed floors, to preserve them clean and pleasant.

But since people have become rich, and swayed by the vain fashions of the world, by carpeting the floors of their houses, there does not appear to be so much use for Sand, as in the days of our worthy ancestors.

Primers and Readers

In *Alice's Adventures in Wonderland* (1865), the Mock Turtle patronizingly explains to Alice that the curriculum in his school consists of "Reeling and Writhing," as well as "different branches of Arithmetic—Ambition, Distraction, Uglification, and Derision." An "Old crab" of a Latin master taught "Laughing and Grief." Lewis Carroll's mock curriculum reads as a telescoped history, and as a cunning critique, of schooling.

"Laughing and Grief" (Latin and Greek) are at the medieval root of Eurocentric ideas about school. Until about the fifteenth century, "reeling" (reading) referred not to any vernacular language but to Latin, which dominated education through the seventeenth century. "Writhing" (writing) was regarded as a specialized vocational skill (until the printing press with movable type was invented around 1440), taught after school hours in the towns and by itinerant writing masters whose visits to country schools were rare. "Ambition, Distraction, Uglification, and Derision" (addition, subtraction, multiplication, and division) cover basic arithmetic.

Schooling was a contentious issue in Carroll's time, hotly debated in Parliament and in the newspapers. Between 1861 and 1895, royal commissions studied and issued critical reports on elementary education, endowed schools, and secondary education; widespread dissatisfaction with the traditional curriculum created pressure to introduce such subjects as the natural sciences, modern languages, and history; traditional methods of teaching were criticized; there were fierce disagreements over the extent to which the state should be involved at all levels and over the role of religion in schools; and agitation regarding women's education was growing.

More broadly, the history of schooling is so closely tied to the history of literacy education that their stories must be told together. The word *literacy* enters the English language in 1883—more than two centuries after *illiteracy* but only thirteen years after the Elementary Education Act of 1870 first made elementary education the responsibility of the state. Local school boards were established and authorized to open schools in areas where they were lacking. In 1880 education to the age of ten became both compulsory and free. This nineteenth-century embrace of compulsory schooling in much of the anglophone world as well as in Europe was an extraordinary and momentous development. For though many had long agreed about the value of education, the widespread view that everybody had the right to be literate and that schools were the responsibility of the state, was something new. Before 1870, elementary education was a patchwork of "voluntary" schools, established and maintained by individuals, religious groups, and other organizations, and an individual's access to it was determined by class, gender, and religion.

Upper-class boys in the nineteenth century were defined, by their classical education in Latin and Greek, as cultured gentlemen suited for any occupation (or none). Upper-class women were educated to be good wives, perhaps (if they were lucky) learning modern languages as well as sewing, music, art, and dancing. It is important to note that school and education were not at all synonymous among the upper classes. Many parents hired private tutors to educate their children at home. Among the lower classes, after the Reformation put new stress on an individual's ability to read the Bible, churches were largely responsible for the spread of literacy; particularly important was the Evangelical Sunday school movement of the eighteenth century. Even more crucial were political changes, as the revolutions in America and France, followed by reform in Great Britain, underscored the need for a literate populace. The right to vote was extended gradually to British men in the nineteenth century (and to women in England, as elsewhere, only in the twentieth). Those arguing for universal suffrage recognized that participatory democracy required an educated electorate. To be literate, to be able to read and write, is to possess a kind of power. The history of literacy education is, in part, the story of democracy.

Learning to Read

In the medieval period in England, being educated meant being able to read and, to a lesser extent, write Latin. Mastery of Latin was a source of real power, held mainly by those associated with the church. The teaching of classical languages was primarily the responsibility of a bishop, who then gave the job of pedagogical overseer to a "chancellor" (a top job category that still exists in some universities, though it has become largely honorary and ceremonial). As the curriculum focused on Latin and Greek grammar instruction, the schools themselves were called "grammar" schools—a designation that still exists in England, though it has come to mean preparation for an intellectual rather than a vocational education.

Schools were directly connected with cathedrals and monasteries, and many though not all of the pupils were preparing to take religious orders. Their curriculum was the trivium—dialectic, rhetoric, and grammar—and the texts were Christian and classical authors in Latin. As students flocked to the best teachers, the medieval universities arose (in Bologna in the eleventh century, Paris in the twelfth century, and in Oxford and Cambridge in the thirteenth), giving impetus to the opening of still more grammar schools (in England, Winchester was founded in 1382 and Eton in 1440). Other schools were founded in connection with chantries, teaching students to sing or chant mass—sometimes with little or no comprehension. Thus the "litel child" in the tale told by Chaucer's Prioress learned his verses "al by rote," but "Noght wiste he what this Latin was to saye" (*Canterbury Tales*, 1386–1400). One of the earliest to urge reform of such rote-based pedagogy was the Czech theologian Johann Amos Comenius, whose *Orbis Sensualium Pictus* (1658; English trans., 1659) was a picture book that attempted to offer beginners a more enticing introduction to their own language and Latin (see the Alphabets section, above).

Reading instruction in English was a haphazard affair. Boys were prepared for grammar school at petty (from the French *petit*, "small") or elementary schools, where the rudiments of reading and spelling were taught by abecedarians. There were also charity schools, run by church parishes, and dame schools—often little more than babysitting services provided by an old woman in her home. Charles

Hoole, the man who brought Comenius's *Orbis* to England, was like Comenius an advocate of universal elementary education in the vernacular. He recognized that reading instruction was too important to be left to untrained people just trying to make some extra money. Hoole produced a kind of handbook for teachers, *A New Discovery of the Old Art of Teaching School* (1660), containing practical pedagogical tips. But with no regulation of who could teach, poor children often were taught by the barely literate.

That a good number of people did manage to learn to read the vernacular is clear from the demand for printed books when they became available, especially chapbooks—cheap books containing fairy tales, romances, ballads, sensational tales, and the like that were sold door-to-door by itinerant peddlers, or chapmen (see the Chapbooks section, above). The printed material being sold was not literature. It was more the type of material that twenty-first-century readers associate with tabloid newspapers and comic books, but it was ideal for those who were teaching themselves to read. And of course Johannes Gutenberg's invention of the printing press was key to spreading literacy much further. William Caxton produced the first book printed in English in 1475, and about 100 more followed (including two editions of Chaucer's *Canterbury Tales*). By 1500 the copying of manuscripts by hand, which had been an important function of church-run scriptoriums, had almost ceased. The introduction of a new technology, as often happens (the Internet is a recent example), led to enormous and relatively swift social changes. The printing press democratized literacy by mass-producing texts and making them widely available across great distances and to men and women of all classes and ages.

Literacy rates in the sixteenth and seventeenth centuries are difficult to ascertain, but it appears that many books were being published and were circulating. In "The Educational Revolution in England, 1560–1640" (1964), the historian Lawrence Stone points to suggestive evidence that by the early seventeenth century, about half the population of England could read at least some of the Bible. He notes that between 1612 and 1614, 95 of the 204 men found guilty of theft and sentenced to death by hanging (47 percent) saved themselves by claiming "benefit of clergy," or their exemption from the judgment of temporal courts. The test of being a cleric was the ability to read Psalm 51.1 (which thereby gained the name "the neck-verse"): "Have mercy upon me, O God, according to Thy loving kindness: according unto the multitude of Thy tender mercies blot out my transgressions." It is however, sobering to remember that in the United States, well into the nineteenth century, African American slaves who learned to read were breaking the law. The 1819 Missouri Literacy Law, for example, forbade both assembling slaves and teaching them to read and write. The 1832 Literacy Laws in Alabama and Virginia ordered whipping and fines for people who taught slaves to read. Flogging was the most common punishment that the slaves themselves received for pursuing literacy, but they could also be branded or mutilated (their tongues slit)—or even have their hands cut off.

The Christian Curriculum and the Beginning of Literacy Education

In anglophone cultures, the links between literacy, power, and a Christian education are very deep. From about the sixteenth century, rich and poor children learned their letters from hornbooks. The size and shape of a Ping-Pong paddle (and often used for batting balls around), a hornbook consisted of a printed alphabet preceded by a cross, from which it also came to be called a *criss-cross row*; a short syllabarium, or list of common syllables; the Lord's Prayer; and the first ten numerals. The name *hornbook* derives from the translucent pieces of animal horn that covered the printed text and provided a tough, durable coating similar to a contemporary clear hard plastic coating. Because this earliest book of instruction was shaped like a bat, the name *battledore* was given to the more elaborate instructional device that superseded it in the late eighteenth century. The first battledores, published around 1750, were made of an oblong piece of heavy card stock, folded into three pages. Each contained a little more text than could be held on a hornbook: an alphabet, a longer syllabarium, a few rhyming couplets, and a new feature—pictures in the form of woodcuts.

Throughout the history of reading instruction, increasingly longer, more complex texts come into use: the single-sheet sixteenth-century hornbook gives way to the eighteenth-century battledore, which is followed by the book-length primer. The name *primer* initially applied only to prayer books used by the laity; but because children learned to read from such books, the term came to mean any elementary book used to teach children to read. In a scene still familiar to elementary school children, the child in Chaucer's "The Prioress's Tale" is depicted as follows: "This litel child, his litel book lernynge, / As he sat in the scole at his prymer." Like the hornbook and the battledore, the primer provided an alphabet (upper- and lower-case) and a syllabarium (consisting of words of one to six syllables); but it also contained a series of brief stories. The most famous example was *The New-England Primer*, first published by Benjamin Harris around 1690 and widely used until well into the nineteenth century. Harris included a long syllabarium (filled with words likely to be encountered in the Bible), hymns by Isaac Watts, prayers (including "Now I lay me down to sleep"), and catechisms (questions and answers about religious doctrine). His major innovation was a picture alphabet with rhyming couplets; they began

> A In Adam's Fall
> We sinned all.
> B Thy Life to Mend
> This Book Attend.

Harris's primer thus distinctly welded the learning of letters to the learning of Christian (specifically, Protestant) doctrine.

Though the first charity schools in England had multiplied under the direction of the Society for Promoting Christian Knowledge, an Anglican society founded in 1698, the most highly organized attempt to teach poor children to read came with the Sunday School movement launched in 1782 by Robert Raikes, an Evangelical. Among those leading the movement in England was the playwright, poet, and essayist Hannah More, who in the 1790s both set up schools herself in Somerset, where she and her sisters had begun to spend their summers, and urged the necessity of the poor learning to read (though not to write). She was shocked at the vice, impiety, and ignorance of the local mine workers, and, as she wrote in a letter to the Bishop of Bath and Wells, her self-proclaimed mission was "to train up the lower classes in habits of industry and piety." Her series of nearly fifty Cheap Repository Tracts (1794–97), addressed to working-class parents, contained stories explicitly designed to illuminate the Christian virtues of obedience and piety. They also brought the condition of the poor to the attention of the middle and upper classes. By 1796 more than two million copies had been sold, indicating the existence of a large literate population.

The idea of school on Sunday was itself an innovation. Though inspired by the necessity of not interfering with the Monday to Saturday work week, the Sunday school movement deserves credit for promoting the growing belief that all children had the right to a free education. The movement also required an increasing supply of instructional material—works such as *The Sunday-Scholar's Manual* (1788) and *The Charity School Spelling Book* (ca. 1798) by Sarah Trimmer, the mother of twelve children and another Sunday school founder and polemicist.

Two other forces were at work in urging a new phase of literacy education in the late eighteenth and early nineteenth centuries. The first was the creation of a children's book publishing industry. For the first time, publishers were soliciting authors to meet a strong demand for books to be used both at home and in schools. The second was a new view of society, sparked in part by the American and French revolutions. Together, they jump-started the push toward universal literacy education.

The Revolutionary Agenda and the Spread of Literacy Education

The starting date for children's literature is generally given as 1744, the year the London printer John Newbery (1713–1767) published *A Little Pretty Pocket-Book* and invented a winning marketing strategy: selling the combination of instruction, delight, and toys to an emerging middle class. But Newbery wasn't alone in selling secular literacy.

The Entertaining History of Little Goody Goosecap (1790), published by John Marshall almost exactly one hundred years after *The New-England Primer*, emphasizes learning to read—rather than learning to read the Bible. The enterprising and long-suffering Goosecap (who bears a certain resemblance to Newbery's Little Goody Two-Shoes; the story is reprinted in the Chapbooks section, above) invents a new alphabet with which to instruct the children in her charge. Its verses are secular, not religious:

A
Was an Angler, who fished in a brook,
B
Was a Blockhead, who ne'er learn'd his book.
C
Was a Captain, a very bold man,
D
Was a Drunkard, say all you can.

Though today's reader of an alphabet book would be surprised by references to the "Drunkard" and the "Blockhead," the stress on learning one's book would seem quite familiar. A letter of 1858 from an American father to his son, preserved in the Johnson Family Papers (archived at the Virginia Military Institute), displays a similar emphasis:

> I received your letter this morning and was glad to hear that you are well and that you have made up your mind to be a good boy and learn to read and write. . . . It would please you very much to see the big brass horse on the Washington monument. But Leake, if you will be a good boy and learn your book and acquire a great deal of information and knowledge, you can come down here yourself some day and see Richmond.

For the son, learning his letters is connected not to learning to be a Christian but to a secular reward: being with his father and seeing the brass horse on the Washington monument.

This uncoupling of literacy from religious instruction has its roots in seventeenth- and eighteenth-century thought. Especially important were the writings of two philosophers, one English and the other French: John Locke, in *Some Thoughts Concerning Education* (1693), and Jean-Jacques Rousseau, in *Emile: or, On Education* (1762).

Locke, an empiricist who argued that the mind is like a "white paper" whose ideas are all furnished by experience, insisted on the importance of environment in education. Ideally, the child should have a sensitive teacher able to adjust the method of instruction to the individual student, who is thereby encouraged to mold himself correctly and learn good physical as well as mental habits. The child should have early practice in reasoning about sense experiences and human situations, and to that end Locke recommended he be given "some easy pleasant book suited to his capacity." Rousseau also emphasized the environment in which learning occurs, but he believed that the child is born naturally good: thus the tutor's role is largely to not interfere with the natural progress of his pupil through childhood's different developmental stages, as he learns by experience, through trial and error—and preferably in the context of the natural world. The student should not read at all until age twelve or so, and then the only suitable book is a story of self-sufficiency in nature: Daniel Defoe's *Robinson Crusoe* (1719). Religious instruction should begin only at about age fifteen.

The massive political and social upheavals of the late eighteenth century were also heavily indebted to the two philosophers: Locke's emphasis in *Two Treatises of Government* (1690) on the natural rights of citizens and on the importance of limiting state responsibility strongly influenced the American revolutionaries, while Rousseau's description in *The Social Contract* (1762) of the government that would enable men to be free helped inspire the French. Amid the heady calls for liberty and equality for men, it is not surprising that some would argue (against Rousseau himself) that the revolutionary spirit should apply to women. Most strikingly, Mary Wollstonecraft followed her defense of the French Revolution, *A Vindication of the Rights of Men* (1790), with *A Vindication of the Rights of Woman* (1792), often called the earliest treatises of modern feminism. In her excoriating attack on the miseducation of women, she explicitly recognizes the key link between education, especially literacy, and the political health of the state: "Public education, of every denomination," she declares, "should be directed to form citizens." Wollstonecraft, who had herself been a teacher, wrote for children *Original Stories from Real Life; with Conversations, Calculated to Regulate the Affections, and Form the Mind to Truth and Goodness* (1788). She sought to win for women full educational and political equality with men.

Though few of her female contemporaries were as radical as Wollstonecraft, a number of them—notably Anna Laetitia Barbauld, Lady Eleanor Fenn (who usually published as Mrs. Lovechild), and Maria Edgeworth—similarly believed in the transformative power of education; all wrote influential books that outlined new maternal pedagogical practices.

Barbauld, the unusually well-educated daughter of a schoolmaster, is credited with developing the first formalized program of reading instruction, designed for children from two to four years old. Moreover, her *Lessons for Children* (1778–79) followed new principles of physical production that she insisted were crucial: the books were small (about 3¼ by 5½ inches square) and printed on good paper with clear and large type. Barbauld's emphasis on the practical, in form and content, owed much to her having grown up at her father's Dissenting schools and having taught at her husband's. Because the members of non-Anglican Protestant denominations were excluded from the dominant grammar schools as well as from Oxford and Cambridge, they set up their own schools. Dissenting academies often embraced a utilitarian curriculum that would enable their students to succeed in the new industrial, scientific world that was coming into being.

Strongly emphasized in Barbauld's *Lessons* is the role of the mother. Lady Eleanor Fenn speaks to the mother as an ideal pedagogue in her introduction to *Cobwebs to Catch Flies; or, Dialogues in Short Sentences: Adapted to Children from the Ages of Three to Eight Years* (ca. 1783):

> The mother who herself watches the dawn of reason in her babe, who teaches him the first rudiments of knowledge, who infuses the first ideas in his mind, will approve my "Cobwebs." She will, if she be desirous of bringing her little darling forward (and where it can be done with ease and satisfaction, who is not?)—she will be aware of the consequence of the first lessons, where nothing meets the eye of the learner but objects with which he is already familiar.

Maternal instruction is seen at work in "Morning," a dialogue that appears early in *Cobwebs to Catch Flies* and that, as text just below the title points out, contains "words of [no more than] three letters":

> BOY: May I go to-day, and buy my top?
> MAMA: Yes, you may.
> BOY: A peg-top? Sam has a peg-top. He let me see his.
> One day he did. I met Tom one day, and he had a top so big!
> I can hop as far as Tom can.
> Tom has a bat too; and Tom is but of my age.
> . . . .
> MAMA: Can you pay for it?
> BOY: Oh, no; but you can pay for all.

Although the sense of the passage is a little tenuous, the significant innovation is that learning to read is now disconnected from religious instruction. Instead, here are stories describing homely scenes and familiar, domestic objects—a middle-class boy's spinning top and a bat, presented with a practical touch of fiscal responsibility ("Can you pay for it?"). And it is the mother who is depicted as the most fitting teacher. Any sophisticated twenty-first-century parent or teacher will recognize the deployment of what is now called "age-appropriate" material: vocabulary and syntax moving in an orderly sequence from the simple to the complex.

Because the pedagogical principle seems so obvious, it likely was not wholly original with Barbauld and Fenn. Though the evidence of earlier maternal teaching is scant, the cache of instructional materials created by one British mother, Jane Johnson (1707–1759), has been preserved. These little card games, mobiles with letters, and little books labeled with the name of his or her young owner are now in the Lilly Library at Indiana University. Johnson may not have been unique: perhaps a whole philosophy of maternal pedagogy was shared by other young mothers of her comfortably middle-class community in the eighteenth century.

By the early nineteenth century, a tradition of maternal teaching had been established. Besides Barbauld and Fenn, the period's most significant figure was probably the novelist Maria Edgeworth, who, as the second of her father's twenty-one children, had a great deal of practical experience. Her father, the Anglo-Irish inventor and educator Richard Lovell Edgeworth, was a proponent of educational reform (though his experiment in applying Rousseau's principles to the upbringing of his oldest son was sadly unsuccessful) and a strong influence on his daughter. Maria Edgeworth's popular works for children included *The Parent's Assistant; or, Stories for Children* (1796), clearly aimed at children's moral development, and *Early Lessons* (1801), aimed at beginning readers. In line with her father's pedagogical beliefs, Maria Edgeworth's stories were designed to build verbal skills step-by-step, and they often portrayed mothers teaching their daughters. Elizabeth Helme outlines a similar maternal agenda in the preface to *Maternal Instruction; or, Family Conversations on Moral and Entertaining Subjects Interspersed with History, Biography and Original Stories Designed for the Perusal of Youth* (1802): "As I regard an informed mother the most proper and attractive of all teachers, I have chosen that character as the principal in the following sheets . . . to excite a desire of reading history, to render industry habitual, and to indicate that piety alone is the real source of happiness, has been my wish."

These and other women of the time represent an intellectual moment that was important in the history of education. Because their works were published and circulated, they entered into the public discourse and became part of the debate over the best pedagogical practices. Publishers began soliciting personal teaching materials from women; an advertisement for one such book, *Introduction to the Elementary Principles of the English Language* (1825), praises it as a "useful manual and assistant to the anxious mother in the most delightful of all employments,—that of communicating to her beloved offspring the first dawnings of useful knowledge." But maternal teaching was labor-intensive, as each loving mother lavished individual attention on her child. Such an approach was not going to address the emerging pedagogical problem created by social changes in England and the United States: mass education, or how to educate large numbers of children quickly, effectively, and cheaply.

Reform Movements and the Rise of Public Education

The late nineteenth century saw both the triumph of mass public education—and the tragedy. The principle of a republican, egalitarian society necessitated a literate population, but the intimate, relaxed, affectionate, and dedicated teaching methods of Mrs. Barbauld and her sister educators proved too expensive. If everyone was to be educated, a cost-effective system had to be put into place quickly. One such system for mass education was devised first in the late 1780s by the Scottish educator Andrew Bell and then implemented in London in 1801 by Joseph Lancaster. To educate large groups of elementary school children cheaply, they used older student assistants, or "monitors." As the rest of society was industrializing, so too was instruction, which had been so long the responsibility of the home and the church. Lancaster also relied on rote memorization of questions and responses, a kind of secular catechism (his curriculum was deliberately undenominational). He observed in *The British System of Education* (1821; 1st ed., 1810):

> The practice of giving short commands aloud, and seeing them instantly obeyed by the whole class, will effectually train the monitor in the habit of giving them with

propriety. Thus, for instance, *"Front"*; *"Right"* or *"Left"*; *"Show Slates,"* or *"Clean Slates"*; . . . without a command, they would be done at random—with it, they are done in an instant.

The militaristic commands of Lancaster's system of reading instruction are a far cry from Fenn's *Cobwebs to Catch Flies*.

The monitorial system immediately won strong support in the early nineteenth century. Bell's National Society for Promoting the Education of the Poor in the Principles of the Established Church (founded 1811), which promoted his method, was warmly defended by, among others, the Romantic poets William Wordsworth and Samuel Taylor Coleridge, who regarded it as an engine for social change. The monitorial system made each student a cog in an endlessly turning wheel. As a child progressed through the curriculum, he or she was given the responsibility of teaching and controlling younger children. Schools thus became factories of learning. The picture of criminals on a treadmill on the cover of one nineteenth-century copybook (reproduced in this section, below) simultaneously warned of the dangers of failing to apply oneself in school and (no doubt unwittingly) established a visual link between manual and intellectual labor.

Although even today rich children and poor children receive different educations in England and America, efforts in the nineteenth century toward free and universal education did much to subvert the tyranny of class. The Elementary Education Act of 1880 made British elementary education compulsory and effectively free, requiring poor children who had worked in factories or lived on the streets to attend school. In the United States, where education is a state and not national responsibility, all states were offering free elementary education by the end of the nineteenth century, and it was compulsory everywhere by 1918. These laws marked the formal beginning of a new social agenda—and the beginning of a huge demand for materials with which to teach all children to be literate.

Toward the Textbook

Once elementary education became mandatory, the need to construct large numbers of new schools, train and license teachers, and provide instructional materials became immediate. The most pressing demand was for texts that could teach all children to read—and so the race to find the best method was on.

In the United States, Truman and Smith, publishers in Cincinnati who had their eye on the market opening up in the new western states and on the frontier, chose a professor at Miami University of Ohio to write a series of elementary readers. William Holmes McGuffey had begun his academic career in 1825 as a professor of ancient languages, was ordained a Presbyterian minister in 1829, and in 1832 began teaching moral philosophy (from 1845 until his death in 1873, he was a professor of moral philosophy at the University of Virginia). *The Eclectic First* and *Second Readers* were published in 1836, and two more in the series and a primer followed in 1837; McGuffey attempted to arrange the selected texts to match children's interests, abilities, and levels of comprehension. By the beginning of the twentieth century, the name "McGuffey" was synonymous with reading instruction. Teachers were assured that when using McGuffey readers, they would be using the most modern, scientific, and up-to-date approaches available. The introductory note to *The New McGuffey First Reader* (1901) boasts that what follows "has been prepared in conformity with the latest and most approved ideas regarding the teaching of reading," and that the "lessons embody and illustrate the best features of the word, the phonic, and the sentence or thought methods." The claim that the methods were scientific, and thus guaranteed to succeed, was important in selling the McGuffey series to schools across the United States and Canada.

In the traditional approach, relied on from the hornbook through the battledore to the primer and Mrs. Barbauld's *Lessons*, the teaching of reading began with recitation: children progressed from the alphabet to syllables to simple texts, with the ultimate aim of reading stories deemed worthy on religious, moral, or literary grounds. The modern method that most closely resembles this reliance on the syllabarium is phonics, discussed below. While other systems were sometimes used, none achieved dominance until the look-say method became standard in the graduated basal readers (called *reading schemes* in anglophone countries outside North America) used in the first half of the twentieth century. Look-say was derived from the research of the psychologist Edmund Huey, who presented his results in *The Psychology and Pedagogy of Reading, with a Review of the History of Reading and Writing and of Methods, Texts, and Hygiene in Reading* (1908). Huey's experiments had demonstrated that university students could read entire words as quickly as single letters, and he believed that children would learn to read most efficiently if they were taught whole words (beginning with the simplest and most common): they should look at a common word, then say it.

A number of factors worked in favor of the swift adoption of the look-say method. It was apparently backed by science (though in fact Huey's interpretation of his research results later came under attack). And it was suitable for use with large groups of children, who could be drilled using inexpensive flash cards, each printed with a word and a picture. It was a series of readers written on look-say principles that finally drove the McGuffey Eclectic Readers—whose primer began with letters and sounds—out of the market.

Scott, Foresman and Company was an educational publisher founded in 1894 by Erastus H. Scott, who held chief editorial power, and Hugh A. Foresman, a master salesman. They were already selling readers of the more traditional type, written by William H. Elson (7 vols., 1909–14), when Elson joined forces with William S. Gray to create a revolutionary new series. Gray, a prominent specialist in reading development and early exponent of the whole word method, was then a senior editor at Scott, Foresman as well as dean of the College of Education at the University of Chicago; in 1955 he helped found the International Reading Association, and was president during its inaugural year. In 1930 the Elson-Gray Basic Readers introduced Dick and Jane to elementary education, and in 1940 the characters gave their names to the series with *Fun with Dick and Jane*. These readers, which relied on the incessant repetition of a limited number of carefully chosen words, dominated literacy education in the United States and Canada well into the 1960s. Other publishers imitated the series—Ginn and Company had Tom and Betty; in England, James Nisbet and Company published Janet and John books, containing such passages as "Janet, Janet. / Come and look. / See the little dog" (*Here We Go*, 1949).

A fervent and highly effective assault on the look-say method was launched in 1955 by Rudolf Flesch, who declared in *Why Johnny Can't Read—and What You Can Do about It* that the look-say method was a disastrous failure whose true justification lay not in scientific studies but in publishers' desire for profits. He argued for a return to learning to read by learning to sound out words: the direct teaching of how written letters combine to make sounds (e.g., that *s* and *h* combine in the *sh* sound). Thus, rather than being restricted to the narrow range of words offered in the basal readers, children will be able to read any word they encounter—whether they understand it or not. Beginning in the late 1950s, many schools turned to explicit phonics instruction; but criticism arose of this method, too. It became clear that many students emerged from these classrooms sounding out words perfectly well, but unable to understand what they were reading. What they'd lost was the idea that words on a page make *narrative* sense.

The corrective of the 1970s and 1980s was the whole language approach, based on the premise that children learn to read in much the same way that they learn to talk. That is, children learn a native language because they are spoken to: words are used in context, and the prose rhythms in the text should be the rhythms of natural speech. The education professor Kenneth S. Goodman, an early advocate, describes the theory clearly in *What's Whole in Whole Language?* (1986).

The adoption of a whole language approach came as anglophone countries were enjoying a new golden age of children's literature. The first golden age began with Charles Kingsley's *Water Babies* (1863) and Lewis Carroll's *Alice's Adventures in Wonderland* (1865) and ended about the time of Kenneth Grahame's *The Wind in the Willows* (1908); the second, which began in the 1960s, was a golden age for beginning readers, with such authors and illustrators as John Burningham, Arnold Lobel, and Maurice Sendak. The upsurge in high-quality publications aided a push to bring real books, genuine works of imaginative literature, into the classroom. Many authors actively employed literary techniques and styles—satire, irony, linguistic play, and so on—in intelligent prose; they focused on the stories they had to tell, not on writing to fit a one-size-fits-all method of reading instruction. Their works thus provided ideal material for those wishing to use the whole language approach. One of the best books on the subject, Liz Waterland's *Read with Me: An Apprenticeship Approach to Reading* (1985), offers practical advice for using children's books in the classroom to induct new readers into a literate community.

But teachers who assumed that whole language meant that children would pick up reading on their own failed to negotiate individual differences, and not surprisingly a back-to-basics backlash ensued. Yet it was of course as silly to assume that phonics instruction was absent from a "good" whole language classroom as it was to assume that literature was absent from a classroom in which there was direct phonics instruction. In pedagogical terms, problems arise when any one methodology is touted as right—to the exclusion of all others. As anyone who works with children knows, all children are different, so that the chances of one methodology being foolproof are slim.

Today, as demands for accountability dominate discussions of education and standardized testing is advocated at every level, the factory models of the early nineteenth century appear to be returning and are threatening to circumscribe our understanding of literacy. Literacy is again being defined narrowly as a skill rather than more complexly as the ability to gain access to a long literary tradition and to engage with a text's interpretive possibilities. Although there is now general consensus about the value of universal literacy, and about the rights of all children, rich and poor, to have access to a good education (even if the educations they receive remain sadly unequal), the problems of defining, achieving, and assessing literacy are far from resolved.

The backlash against standardized testing began growing in the early years of the twenty-first century. In February 2003, a group of almost ninety British children's authors signed a petition against the increased use of standardized testing, declaring their conviction that "children's understanding, empathy, imagination and creativity are developed best by reading whole books, not by doing comprehension exercises on short excerpts and not from ticking boxes or giving one-word answers." As these authors know, the reliance on such tests is driven by the desire for efficiency in a mass system of education. Much as the monitorial system of Bell and Lancaster had done two centuries earlier, it reduces the number of educators required to tightly control large numbers of students.

As long as scholars and educators debate literacy instruction rather than literacy itself, their acrimony will focus only on choosing the best methodology. Yet to date, each approach that has been dominant in turn—look-say, phonics, whole language— has demonstrably failed to produce literacy among all the children all the time. Margaret Meek, a prominent British figure in literacy studies, urges that we stop arguing over methodology and concentrate on "redescribing" reading itself in a way that includes our notions of the uses and functions of literacy, finding a definition that will encompass the "reading" of other forms of expression (including music and art) present in our culture. Reading and writing are about more than decoding and copying. As Carroll suggests in his punning names "Reeling and Writhing," perhaps they are closer to fishing—and being hooked.

THE NEW-ENGLAND PRIMER
ca. 1690

As an Anabaptist London printer, Benjamin Harris published vituperative, seditious attacks on Catholicism that frequently landed him in legal trouble. He fled to Boston (in 1686, after the nominally Anglican Charles II had been succeeded on the throne by his Roman Catholic brother, James II). Though Harris returned to London in 1695, he had a lasting influence on American culture through the enormous success of a book for which he is primarily responsible: *The New-England Primer*. It was adapted from his earlier work, *The Protestant Tutor: instructing children to spel and read English, and grounding them in the true Protestant religion, and discovering the errors and deceits of the Papists* (1679), omitting that text's savage political attacks on Catholicism but retaining a Protestant emphasis that was attractive to New England's Puritan audience. The new primer managed to capture an emerging American sensibility, coupling a strong moral and religious code with a push toward a literate community.

The first edition of *The New-England Primer* was published around 1690 or a bit earlier (an enlarged edition appeared in 1691). It combined religious and reading instruction with woodcuts—thereby drawing on Comenius's idea (demonstrated in his *Orbis Sensualium Pictus*, 1658) that instruction could be engaging. A variety of texts were contained within the book's small (4½-inch by 3-inch) covers. The primer begins with a hymn by Isaac Watts (1674–1748), then proceeds to step-by-step instructions on reading, moving from alphabets, lists of vowels and consonants, and upper- and lowercase letters, to 'syllabaries' containing words of one to six syllables. There follows a famous rhyming picture alphabet ("In Adam's Fall / We sinned All") and catechisms of various kinds. The most explicitly American text is John Cotton's catechism *Milk for Babes* (1646), whose questions and answers include

Q. *Are you then born a sinner?*
A. I was conceived in sin, & born in iniquity.
Q. *What is your birth sin?*
A. Adam's sin imputed to me, and a corrupt nature dwelling in me.
Q. *What is your corrupt nature?*
A. My corrupt nature is empty of grace, bent unto sin, only unto sin, and that continually.

The New-England Primer immediately became a staple of the American schoolroom, and millions of copies were sold in the next two centuries. By 1830, there had been 360 editions. The earliest surviving edition dates from 1727; reprinted below, in facsimile, is a 1777 edition.

THE

NEW-ENGLAND

PRIMER

IMPROVED

For the more easy attaining the true
reading of English.

TO WHICH IS ADDED

The Assembly of Divines, and
Mr. COTTON's *Catechism*.

BOSTON:

Printed by EDWARD DRAPER, *at*
his Printing-Office, in *Newbury-*
Street, and *Sold* by JOHN BOYLE
in *Marlborough-Street.* 1777.

The Honorable JOHN HANCOCK, Esq:
Prefident of the *American* CONGRESS

A Divine Song of Praife to GOD, for a Child,
by the Rev. Dr. WATTS.

HOW glorious is our heavenly King,
Who reigns above the Sky!
How fhall a Child prefume to fing
His dreadful Majefty!

How great his Power is none can tell,
Nor think how large his Grace:
Nor men below, nor Saints that dwell
On high before his Face.

Nor Angels that ftand round the Lord,
Can fearch his fecret will;
But they perform his heav'nly Word,
And fing his Praifes ftill.

Then let me join this holy Train;
And my firft Off 'rings bring;
The eternal GOD will not difdain
To hear an Infant fing.

My Heart refolves, my Tongue obeys,
And Angels fhall rejoice,
To hear their mighty Maker's Praife,
Sound from a feeble Voice.

Hancock: Massachusetts-born politician (1786–1865), active in the American Revolution.

Dr. Watts: Isaac Watts (1674–1748), English theologian and hymn writer. His *Divine Songs* (1715) were recited by children for centuries.

The young INFANT'S or CHILD'S morning Prayer.   *From* Dr. WATTS.

ALMIGHTY God the Maker of every
Thing in Heaven and Earth; the Dark-
nefs goes away, and the Day light comes at thy
Command.   Thou art good and doeſt good con-
tinually.
  I thank thee that thou haſt taken ſuch Care of
me this Night, and that I am alive and well this
Morning.
  Save me, O God, from Evil, all this Day long,
and let me love and ſerve thee forever, for the
Sake of Jeſus Chriſt thy Son.   AMEN.

The INFANT'S or young CHILD'S
Evening Prayer.   *From* Dr. WATTS.

O LORD God who knoweſt all Things, thou
ſeeſt me by Night as well as by Day.
  I pray thee for Chriſt's Sake, forgive me what-
ſoever I have done amiſs this Day, and keep me
all this Night, while I am aſleep.
  I deſire to lie down under thy Care, and
to abide forever under thy Bleſſing, for thou
art a God of all Power and everlaſting Mercy.
AMEN.

---

a b c d e f g h i j k l m
n o p q r ſ s t u v
w x y z &.
Vowels.
a e i o u y.
Conſonants.
b c d f g h j k l m n p q r ſ s t v w x z
Double Letters.
ct ff fi fl ffi ffl ſh ſi ſſi ſl ſſ ſt
Italick Letters.
Aa Bb Cc Dd Ee Ff Gg Hh
Ii Jj Kk Ll Mm Nn Oo Pp Qq
Rr Sſs Tt Uu Vv Ww Xx Yy Zz
Italick Double Letters.
ct ff fi ffi fl ffl ſh ſi ſſ ſſi ſl ſt.

Words of one Syllable.

Eat	ear	eggs	eyes
Face	feet	fifh	foul
Gate	good	grafs	great
Hand	hat	head	heart
Ice	ink	ifle	jobb
Kick	kind	kneel	know
Lamb	lame	land	long
Made	mole	moon	mouth
Name	night	noife	noon
Oak	once	one	ounce
Pain	pair	pence	pound
Quart	queen	quick	quilt
Rain	raife	rofe	run
Saint	fage	falt	faid
Take	talk	time	throat
Vain	vice	vile	view
Way	wait	wafte	would

Words of two Syllables.

Ab-fent	ab-hor	a-pron	au-thor
Ba-bel	be-came	be-guile	bold-ly
Ca-pon	cel-lar	con-ftant	cub-board
Dai-ly	de-pend	di-vers	du-ty
Ea-gle	ea-ger	en-close	e-ven
Fa-ther	fa-mous	fe-male	fu-ture
Ga-ther	gar-den	gra-vy	glo-ry

Words of two Syllables.

Hei-nous	hate-ful	hu-mane	hus-band
In-fant	in-deed	in-cence	i-fland
Ja-cob	jeal-ous	juf-tice	ju-lep
La-bour	la-den	la-dy	la-zy
Ma-ny	ma-ry	mo-tive	mu-fick

Words of three Syllables.

A-bu-fing	a-mend-ing	ar-gu-ment
Bar-ba-rous	be-ne-fit	beg-gar-ly
Cal-cu-late	can-dle-stick	con-foun-ded
Dam-ni-fy	dif-fi-cult	drow-fi-nefs
Ea-ger-ly	em-ploy-ing	evi-dence
Fa-cul-ty	fa-mi-ly	fu-ne-ral
Gar-de-ner	glo-ri-ous	gra-ti-tude
Hap-pi-ness	har-mo-ny	ho-li-nefs

Words of four Syllables.

A-bi-li-ty	ac-com-pa-ny	af-fec-ti-on
Be-ne-fi-ted	be-a-ti-tude	be-ne-vo-lent
Ca-la-mi-ty	ca-pa-ci-ty	ce-re-mo-ny
De-li-ca-cy	di-li-gent-ly	du-ti-ful-ly
E-dy-fy-ing	e-ver-laft-ing	e-vi-dent-ly
Fe-bru-a-ry	fi-de-li-ty	for-mi-da-bly
Ge-ne-ral-ly	glo-ri-fy-ing	gra-ci-ous-ly

Capon: castrated cock.

Words of five Syllables.

A-bo-mi-na-ble	ad-mi-ra-ti-on
Be-ne-dic-ti-on	be-ne-fi-ci-al
Ce-le-bra-ti-on	con-fo-la-ti-on
De-cla-ra-ti-on	de-di-ca-ti-on
E-du-ca-ti-on	ex-hor-ta-ti-on
For-ni-ca-ti-on	fer-men-ta-ti-on
Ge-ne-ra-ti-on	ge-ne-ro-fi-ty

Words of fix Syllables.

A-bo-mi-na-ti-on	Gra-ti-fi-ca-ti-on
Be-ne-fi-ci-al-ly	Hu-mi-li-a-ti-on
Con-ti-nu-a-ti-on	I-ma-gi-na-ti-on
De-ter-mi-na-ti-on	Mor-ti-fi-ca-ti-on
E-di-fi-ca-ti-on	Pu-ri-fi-ca-ti-on
Fa-mi-li-a-ri-ty	Qua-li-fi-ca-ti-on

A Leffon for Children.

Pray to God.	Call no ill names.
Love God.	Ufe no ill words.
Fear God.	Tell no lies.
Serve God.	Hate Lies.
Take not God's Name in vain.	Speak the Truth.
	Spend your Time well.
Do not Swear.	Love your School.
Do not Steal.	Mind your Book.
Cheat not in your play.	Strive to learn.
Play not with bad boys.	Be not a Dunce.

A	In ADAM'S Fall We finned all.
B	Heaven to find; The Bible Mind.
C	Chrift crucify'd For finners dy'd.
D	The Deluge drown'd The Earth around.
E	ELIJAH hid By Ravens fed.
F	The judgment made FELIX afraid.

The Deluge: the Flood (Genesis 7.17–24).
Elijah: the prophet (1 Kings 17.4–7).
The judgment: i.e., the judgment that will come after death.
Felix was the Roman governor before whom Paul was tried
(Acts 24.24, 25).

G As runs the Glass,
   Our Life doth pass.

H My Book and Heart
   Must never part.

I JOB feels the Rod,—
   Yet bleſſes GOD.

K Proud Korah's troop
   Was ſwallowed up

L LOT fled to *Zoar*,
   Saw fiery Shower
   On *Sodom* pour.

M MOSES was he
   Who *Israel's* Hoſt
   Led thro' the Sea

N NOAH did view
   The old world & new.

O Young OBADIAS,
   DAVID, JOSIAS,
   All were pious.

P PETER deny'd
   His Lord and cry'd.

Q Queen ESTHER ſues
   And ſaves the *Jews*.

R Young pious RUTH,
   Left all for Truth.

S Young SAM'L dear,
   The Lord did fear.

Job . . . GOD: the theme of the book of Job.
Proud Korah: Korah and his followers rebelled against Moses during the Israelites' wandering in the desert (Numbers 16.28–35).
Lot . . . pour: Genesis 19.
Moses . . . Sea: i.e., through the Red Sea as they fled from Egypt (Exodus 14).

Noah . . . new: i.e., the world before and after the Flood.
Obadias . . . : King David and some of his descendants (properly, Obadiah; 1 Chronicles 3).
Peter deny'd: e.g., Matthew 26.69–75.
Esther . . . Jews: i.e., the Jews of Persia (the story of the book of Esther).
Ruth: Ruth 1.16, 17.
Young Sam'l: 1 Samuel 2–3.

T Young TIMOTHY
Learnt sin to fly.

U VASTHI for Pride,
Was set aside.

W Whales in the Sea,
GOD's Voice obey.

X XERXES did die,
And so must I.

Y While youth do chear
Death may be near.

Z ZACCHEUS he
Did climb the Tree
Our Lord to see.

WHO was the first man ?   *Adam.*
   Who was the first woman ?   *Eve.*
Who was the first Murderer ?   *Cain.*
Who was the first Martyr ?   *Abel.*
Who was the first Translated ?   *Enoch.*
Who was the oldest Man ?   *Methuselah.*
Who built the Ark ?   *Noah.*
Who was the Patientest Man ?   *Job.*
Who was the Meekest Man ?   *Moses.*
Who led *Israel* into *Canaan* ?   *Joshua.*
Who was the strongest Man ?   *Sampson.*
Who killed *Goliah* ?   *David.*
Who was the wisest Man ?   *Solomon.*
Who was in the Whale's Belly ?   *Jonah.*
Who saves lost Men ?   *Jesus Christ.*
Who is *Jesus Christ* ?   The *Son of God.*
Who was the Mother of *Christ* ?   *Mary.*
Who betrayed his Master ?   *Judas.*
Who denied his Master ?   *Peter.*
Who was the first Christian Martyr ? *Stephen.*
Who was chief Apostle of the *Gentiles* ? *Paul.*

The Infant's Grace before and after Meat.

BLESS me, O Lord, and let my food
strengthen me to serve thee, for Jesus
Christ's sake.   AMEN.

I Desire to thank God who gives me food
to eat every day of my life.   AMEN.

Young Timothy: see 1 Timothy.
Vasthi: the queen and wife of Ahasuerus (Xerxes, king of Persia; r. 486–465 B.C.E.), who refuses to obey his commandments (Esther 1.10–22).
Zaccheus: A rich man of Jericho (Luke 19.1–10).

Translated: carried to heaven without having died (Genesis 5.24).

WHAT's right and good now shew me Lord, and lead me by thy grace and word. Thus shall I be a child of God, and love and fear thy hand and rod.

An Alphabet of Lessons for Youth.

A Wife son maketh a glad father, but a foolish son is the heaviness of his mother.

B Etter is a little with the fear of the Lord, than great treasure & trouble therewith.

C Ome unto Christ all ye that labor and are heavy laden and he will give you rest.

D O not the abominable thing which I hate faith the Lord.

E Xcept a man be born again, he cannot see the kingdom of God.

F Oolishness is bound up in the heart of a child, but the rod of correction shall drive it far from him.

G ODLINESS is profitable unto all things, having the promise of the life that now is, and that which is to come.

H OLINESS becomes G O D ' s house for ever.

I T is good for me to draw near unto G O D.

K EEP thy heart with all diligence, for out of it are the issues of life.

L IARS shall have their part in the lake which burns with fire and brimstone.

M ANY are the afflictions of the right-ous, but the LORD delivereth them out of them all.

N OW is the accepted time, now is the day of salvation.

O UT of the abundance of the heart the mouth speaketh.

P RAY to thy Father which is in secret ; and thy Father which sees in secret shall reward thee openly.

Q UIT you like men, be strong, stand fast in the faith.

R EMEMBER thy Creator in the days of thy youth.

S Eest thou a man wise in his own conceit, there is more hope of a fool than of him.

T RUST in God at all times, ye people, pour out your hearts before him.

U PON the wicked, God shall rain an horrible tempest.

W O to the wicked, it shall be ill with him, for the reward of his hands shall be given him.

EXHORT one another daily while it is called to day, left any of you be hardened thro' the deceitfulnefs of fin.

YOUNG men ye have overcome the wicked one.

ZEal hath confumed me, becaufe thy enemies have forgotten the word of God.

The LORD's Prayer.

OUR Father which art in heaven, hallowed be thy name. Thy kingdom come. Thy will be done on earth as it is heaven. Give us this day our daily bread. And forgive us our debts as we forgive our debtors. And lead us not into temptation. But deliver us from evil. For thine is the kingdom, the power and the glory, forever. AMEN.

The CREED.

I BELIEVE in God the Father Almighty Maker of heaven and earth, and in Jefus Chrift his only Son our Lord, which was conceived by the Holy Ghoft, born of the Virgin Mary, fuffered under Pontius Pilate, was crucified, dead and buried. He defcended into hell. The third day he arofe again from the dead, and afcended into heaven, and fitteth on the right hand of God, the Father, Almighty. From thence he fhall come to judge both the quick and the dead. I believe in the Holy Ghoft, the Holy Catholic Church, the communion of Saints, the forgivenefs of fins, the refurrection of the body, and the life everlafting. AMEN.

Dr. WATTS's Cradle Hymn.

HUSH my dear, lie ftill and flumber,
   holy angels guard thy bed,
Heavenly bleffings without number,
   gently falling on thy head.
Sleep my babe, thy food and raiment
   houfe and home thy friends provide,
All without thy care or payment,
   all thy wants are well fupply'd.
How much better thou'rt attended,
   than the Son of God could be,
When from heaven he defcended,
   and became a child like thee.
Soft and eafy is thy cradle,
   coarfe and hard thy Saviour lay,
When his birth-place was a ftable,
   and his fofteft bed was hay.
Bleffed Babe ! what glorious features
   fpotlefs fair, divinely bright !!
Muft he dwell with brutal creatures,

The Lord's Prayer: Matthew 6.9–13.
The Creed: i.e., the Apostles' Creed, commonly used by Protestants; it took its present form around 650 but has its origins in the second century.

how could angels bear the fight !
Was there nothing but a manger,
  curfed finners could afford,
To receive the heavenly ftranger ;
  did they thus affront their Lord.
Soft my child I did not chide thee,
  tho' my fong may found too hard ;
'Tis thy mother fits befide thee,
  and her arms fhall be thy guard.
Yet to read the fhameful ftory,
  how the Jews abus'd their King,
How they ferv'd the Lord of glory,
  makes me angry while I fing.
See the kinder fhepherds round him,
  telling wonders from the fky ;
There they fought him, there they found him,
  with his Virgin Mother by.
See the lovely Babe a dreffing ;
  lovely Infant how he fmil'd !
When he wept, the Mother's bleffing
  sooth'd and hufh'd the holy child.
Lo ! he flumbers in his manger,
  where the horned oxen fed ;
Peace my darling here's no danger
  here's no Ox a near thy bed.
'Twas to fave thee, child from dying,
  fave my dear from burning flame,

Bitter groans and endlefs crying,
  that thy bleft Redeemer came.
May'ft thou live to know and fear him,
  truft and love him all thy days !
Then go dwell for ever near him,
  fee his face and fing his praife.
I could give thee thoufand kiffes,
  hoping what I moft defire :
Not a mother's fondeft wifhes,
  can to greater joys afpire.

VERSES *for Children.*

THOUGH I am young a little one,
  If I can fpeak and go alone,
Then I muft learn to know the Lord,
And learn to read his holy word.
'Tis time to feek to God and pray
For what I want for every day :
I have a precious foul to fave,
And I a mortal body have,
Tho' I am young yet I may die,
And haften to eternity :
There is a dreadful fiery hell,
Where wicked ones muft always dwell :
There is a heaven full of joy,
Where godly ones muft always ftay :
To one of thefe my foul muft fly,
  As in a moment when I die :

When God that made me, calls me home,
I muſt not ſtay I muſt be gone.
He gave me life, and gives me breath,
And he can ſave my ſoul from death,
By JESUS CHRIST my only Lord,
According to his holy word.
He clothes my back and makes me warm:
He ſaves my fleſh and bones from harm.
He gives me bread and milk and meat
And all I have that's good to eat.
When I am ſick, he if he pleaſe,
Can make me well and give me eaſe:
He gives me ſleep and quiet reſt,
Whereby my body is refreſh'd
The Lord is good and kind to me,
And very thankful I muſt be:
I muſt obey and love and fear him,
By faith in Chriſt I muſt draw near him.
I muſt not ſin as others do,
Leſt I lie down in ſorrow too:
For God is angry every day,
With wicked ones who go aſtray,
All ſinful words I must reſtrain:
I muſt not take God's name in vain.
I muſt not work, I muſt not play,
Upon God's holy ſabbath day.
And if my parents ſpeak the word,

I muſt obey them in the Lord.
Nor ſteal, nor lie, nor ſpend my days,
In idle tales and fooliſh plays,
I muſt obey my Lord's commands,
Do ſomething with my little hands:
Remember my creator now,
In youth while time will it allow.
Young SAMUEL that little child,
He ſerv'd the Lord, liv'd undefil'd;
Him in his ſervice God employ'd,
While ELI's wicked children dy'd:
When wicked children mocking ſaid,
To a good man, *Go up bald head*,
God was diſpleas'd with them and ſent
Two bears which them in pieces rent,
I muſt not like theſe children vile,
Diſpleaſe my God, myſelf defile.
Like young ABIJAH, I muſt ſee,
That good things may be found in me,
Young King JOSIAH, that bleſſed youth,
He ſought the Lord and lov'd the truth;
He like a King did act his part,
And follow'd God with all his heart.
The little children they did ſing,
Hoſannahs to their heavenly King.
That bleſſed child young TIMOTHY,
Did learn God's word moſt heedfully.
2

Young Samuel: 1 Samuel 2.12–18, 4.11.
Eli's wicked children: the children mocked the prophet Eli-sha (2 Kings 2.23–24).
Abijah: second son of Samuel (1 Samuel 8.2).
Young King Josiah: 2 Kings 22–23.

It seem'd to be his recreation,
Which made him wise unto salvation :
By faith in Christ which he had gain'd
With prayers and tears that faith unfeign'd
These good examples were for me ;
Like these good children I must be.
Give me true faith in Christ my Lord,
Obedience to his holy word,
No word is in the world like thine,
There's none so pure, sweet and divine.
From thence let me thy will behold,
And love thy word above fine gold.
Make my heart in thy statutes found,
And make my faith and love abound.
Lord circumcise my heart to love thee :
And nothing in this world above thee :
Let me behold thy pleased face,
And make my soul to grow in grace,
And in the knowledge of my Lord
And Saviour Christ, and of his word.

Another.

A WAKE, arise, behold thou hast,
Thy life a leaf, thy breath a blast ;
At night lay down prepar'd to have
Thy sleep, thy death, thy bed, thy grave.
L ORD if thou lengthen out my days,
Then let my heart so fixed be,

That I may lengthen out thy praise,
And never turn aside from thee.
So in my end I shall rejoice,
In thy salvation joyful be ;
My soul shall say with loud glad voice,
JEHOVAH who is like to thee ?
Who takest the lambs into thy arms,
And gently leadest those with young,
Who savest children from all harms,
Lord, I will praise thee with my song.
And when my days on earth shall end,
And I go hence and be here no more,
Give me eternity to spend,
My G O D to praise forever more.

Another.

Good children must,
Fear God all day,   Love Christ alway,
Parents obey,   In secret pray,
No false thing say,   Mind little play,
By no sin stray,   Make no delay,
In doing good.

Another.

I In the burying place may see,
Graves shorter there than I,
From death's arrest no age is free,
Young children too must die.
My God may such an awful sight,

Awakening be to me!
Oh! that by early grace I might
   For death prepared be.
               Another.

NOW I lay me down to take my *sleep,*
   I pray the Lord my soul to keep,
If I should die before I wake,
I pray the Lord my soul to take.
               Another.

FIrst in the morning when thou dost awake,
   To God for his grace thy petition make,
Some heavenly petition use daily to say,
That the God of heaven may bless thee alway.
      Duty to God and our neighbour.

LOVE God with all your soul & strength,
   With all your heart and mind;
And love your neighbour as yourself,
   Be faithful, just and kind.
Deal with another as you'd have
   Another deal with you:
What you're unwilling to receive,
   Be sure you never do.
         Our Saviour's Golden Rule.

BE you to others kind and true,
   As you'd have others be to you:
And neither do nor say to men,
   Whate'er you would not take again.

The Sum of the ten Commandments.

WITH all thy soul love God above,
   And as thyself thy neighbour love.
      Advice to Youth. Eccle. xii.

NOW in the heat of youthful blood,
   Remember your Creator God;
Behold the months come hast'ning on,
When you shall say, *My joys are gone.*
   Behold the aged sinner goes
Laden with guilt and heavy woes,
Down to the regions of the dead,
With endless curses on his head.
   The dust returns to dust again,
The soul in agonies of pain,
Ascends to God not there to dwell,
But hears her doom and sinks to hell.
Eternal King I fear thy name,
Teach me to know how frail I am,
And when my soul must hence remove,
Give me a mansion in thy love.
Remember thy Creator in the days of thy youth.

CHILDREN your great Creator fear,
   To him your homage pay,
While vain employments fire your blood,
   And lead your thoughts astray.
The due remembrance of his name
   Your first regard requires:

Till your breaſt glows with ſacred love,
  Indulge no meaner ſires.
Secure his favour, and be wiſe,
  Before theſe cheerleſs days,
When age comes on, when mirth's no more,
  And health and ſtrength decays.

Some proper Names of MEN *and* WOMEN,
to teach Children to ſpell their own.

Men's Names.

ADam, Abel, Abraham,
Amos, Aaron,
Abijah, Andrew,
Alexander, Anthony,
Bartholomew,
Benjamin, Barnabas,
Benoni, Barzillai,
Caleb, Cæſar,
Charles, Christopher,
Clement, Cornelius,
David, Daniel,
Ephraim, Edward,
Edmund, Ebenezer,
Elijah, Eliphalet,
Eliſha, Eleazer,
Elihu, Ezekiel,
Elias, Elizur,
Frederick, Francis,
Gilbert, Giles,
George, Gamalial,
Gideon, Gerſhom,
Heman, Henry,
Hezekiah, Hugh,
John, Jonas, Iſaac,
Jacob, Jared, Job,
James, Jonathan,
Iſrael, Joſeph,
Jeremiah, Joſhua,
Joſiah, Jedediah,
Jabez, Joel, Judah,
Lazarus, Luke,
Mathew, Michael,
Moſes, Malachi,
Nathaniel, Nathan,
Nicholas, Noadiah,
Nehemiah, Noah,
Obadiah, Ozias,
Paul, Peter, Philip,
Phineas, Peletiah,
Ralph, Richard,
Samuel, Sampſon,
Stephen, Solomon,
Seth, Simeon, Saul,
Shem, Shubal,
Timothy, Thomas,
Titus, Theophilus,
Uriah, Uzzah,
Walter, William,
Xerxes, Xenophon,
Zachariah, Zebdiel,
Zedekiah, Zadock,
Zebulon, Zebediah,

Women's Names.

ABigail, Anne,
Alice, Anna,
Bethiah, Bridget,
Cloe, Charity,
Deborah, Dorothy,
Dorcas, Dinah,
Damaris,
Elizabeth, Eſther,
Eunice, Eleanor,
Frances, Flora,
Grace, Gillet,
Hannah, Huldah,
Hepzibah,
Henrietta, Hagar.
Joanna, Jane,
Jamima, Iſabel,
Judith, Jennet,
Katharine, Katura,
Kezia, Lydia,
Lucretia, Lucy,
Louis, Lettice,
Mary, Margaret,
Martha, Mehitable,
Marcy, Merial,
Patience, Phylis,
Phebe, Priſcilla,
Rachel, Rebecca,
Ruth, Rhode, Roſe,
Sarah, Suſanna,
Tabitha, Tameſin,
Urſula,
Zipporah, Zibiah

M̲R. J O H N R O G E R S, miniſter of the
goſpel in *London*, was the firſt martyr in Queen M A R Y ' s reign, and was
burnt at *Smithfield, February* 14, 1554.—His
wife with nine small children, and one at
her breaſt following him to the ſtake ; with
which ſorrowful ſight he was not in the
leaſt daunted, but with wonderful patience
died courageouſly for the goſpel of J E S U S
C H R I S T.

*Some few days before his death, he wrote the
following Advice to his Children.*

G̲IVE ear my children to my words
Whom God hath dearly bought,
Lay up his laws within your heart,
and print them in your thoughts.
I leave you here a little book
for you to look upon,
That you may ſee your father's face
when he is dead and gone :
Who ſor the hope of heavenly things,
While he did here remain,
Gave over all his golden years
to priſon and to pain.
Where I, among my iron bands,
incloſed in the dark,
Not many days before my death,
I did compoſe this work :
And for example to your youth,
to whom I wiſh all good,
I ſend you here God's perfect truth,
and ſeal it with my blood.
To you my heirs of earthly things :
which I do leave behind,
That you may read and underſtand
and keep it in your mind.
That as you have been heirs of that
2*

Mr. John Rogers: a Roman Catholic priest (ca. 1500–1555)
who became a Protestant in 1535. He was burned at the stake
following his denunciation of "papist errors" after the accession of Mary I, a Roman Catholic.

that once shall wear away,
You also may possess that part,
  which never shall decay.
Keep always God before your eyes,
  with all your whole intent,
Commit no sin in any wise,
  keep his commandment.
Abhor that arrant whore of ROME,
  and all her blasphemies,
And drink not of her cursed cup,
  obey not her decrees.
Give honor to your mother dear,
  remember well her pain,
And recompence her in her age,
  with the like love again.
Be always ready for her help,
  and let her not decay,
Remember well your father all,
  who would have been your stay.
Give of your portion to the poor,
  as riches do arise,
And from the needy naked soul,
  turn not away your eyes:
For he that doth not hear the cry
  of those that stand in need,
Shall cry himself and not be heard,
  when he does hope to speed.

If GOD hath given you increase,
  and blessed well your store,
Remember you are put in trust,
  and should relieve the poor.
Beware of soul and filthy lust,
  let such things have no place,
Keep clean your vessels in the LORD,
  that he may you embrace.
Ye are the temples of the LORD,
  for you are dearly bought,
And they that do defile the same,
  shall surely come to nought.
Be never proud by any means,
  build not your house too high,
But always have before your eyes,
  that you are born to die.
Defraud not him that hired is,
  your labour to sustain,
But pay him still without delay,
  his wages for his pain.
And as you would that other men
  against you should proceed,
Do you the same to them again,
  when they do stand in need.
Impart your portion to the poor,
  in money and in meat

Whore of Rome: i.e., the pope (adapted from the reference
to the whore of Babylon in Revelation 17.15–18).

And fend the feeble fainting foul,
  of that which you do eat.
Afk counfel always of the wife,
  give ear unto the end,
And ne'er refufe the fweet rebuke
  of him that is thy friend.
Be always thankful to the LORD,
  with prayer and with praife,
Begging of him to blefs your work,
  and to direct your ways.
Seek firft, I fay, the living GOD,
  and always him adore,
And then be fure that he will blefs,
  your bafket and your ftore.
And I befeech Almighty GOD,
  replenifh you with grace,
That I may meet you in the heavens,
  and fee you face to face.
And though the fire my body burns,
  contrary to my kind,
That I cannot enjoy your love
  according to my mind :
Yet I do hope that when the heavens
  fhall vanifh like a fcroll,
I fhall fee you in perfect fhape,
  in body and in foul.
And that I may enjoy your love,

and you enjoy the land,
I do befeech the living LORD,
  to hold you in his hand.
Though here my body be adjudg'd
  in flaming fire to fry,
My foul I truft, will ftraight afcend
  to live with GOD on high.
What though this carcafe fmart awhile
  what though this life decay,
My foul I hope will be with GOD,
  and live with him for aye.
I know I am a finner born,
  from the original,
And that I do deferve to die
  by my fore-father's fall :
But by our SAVIOUR's precious **blood,**
  which on the crofs was fpilt,
Who freely offer'd up his life,
  to fave our fouls from guilt :
I hope redemption I fhall have,
  and all who in him truft,
When I fhall fee him face to face,
  and live among the juft.
Why then fhould I fear death's grim **look**
  fince CHRIST for me did die,
For King and *Cæfar*, rich and poor,
  the force of death muft try.

When I am chained to the stake,
   and fagots girt me round,
Then pray the LORD my soul in heaven
   may be with glory crown'd.
Come welcome death the end of fears,
   I am prepar'd to die :
Those earthly flames will send my soul
   up to the Lord on high.
Farewell my children to the world,
   where you must yet remain ;
The LORD of hosts be your defence,
   'till we do meet again.
Farewell my true and loving wife,
   my children and my friends,
I hope in heaven to see you all,
   when all things have their end.
If you go on to serve the LORD,
   as you have now begun,
You shall walk safely all your days,
   until your life be done.
GOD grant you so to end your days,
   as he shall think it best,
That I may meet you in the heavens,
   where I do hope to rest.

OUR days begin with trouble here,
   our life is but a span,

And cruel death is always near,
   so frail a thing is man.
Then sow the seeds of grace whilst young,
   that when thou com'st to die,
Thou may'st sing forth that triumph song,
   Death where's thy victory.

Choice Sentences.

1. P R A Y I N G will make us leave sinning,
or sinning will make us leave praying.

2. O U R weakness and inabilities break
not the bond of our duties.

3. W H A T we are afraid to speak before
men, we should be afraid to think before
GOD.

Learn these four lines by heart.

HAVE communion with few,
   Be intimate with ONE,
Deal justly with all,
Speak evil of none.

A G U R's Prayer.

REMOVE far from me vanities and
   lies ; give me neither poverty nor
riches ; feed me with food convenient for
me : lest I be full and deny thee, and say,
Who is the Lord ? Or lest I be poor and
steal and take the name of my GOD in vain.

Death where's thy victory: an echo of 1 Corinthians 15.55.
Have communion . . . : Proverbs 30.8–9.

T H E   S H O R T E R
CATECHISM,
Agreed upon by the Reverend Affembly of
DIVINES at *Weftminfter.*

Queft. **W**HAT *is the chief end of man?*
Anf. Man's chief end is to glorify God and enjoy him forever.

Q. 2. *What rule hath God given to direct us how we may glorify and enjoy him?*

A. The word of God which is contained in the fcriptures of the old and new teftament is the only rule to direct us how we may glorify God and enjoy him.

Q.3. *What do the fcriptures principally teach?*

A. The fcriptures principally teach what man is to believe concerning God, and what duty God requireth of man.

Q. 4. *What is God?*

A. God is a fpirit, infinite, eternal, and unchangeable, in his being, wifdom, power, holinefs, juftice, goodnefs and truth.

Q. 5. *Are there more Gods than one?*

A. There is but ONE only, the living and true GOD.

Q. 6. *How many persons are there in the God-head?*

A. There are three perfons in the God-head, the Father, the Son, and the Holy Ghoft, and thefe three are one GOD, the fame in fubftance, equal in power and glory.

Q. 7. *What are the decrees of God?*

A. The decrees of God are his eternal purpofe, according to the counfel of his own will, whereby for his own glory he hath fore-ordained whatfoever comes to pafs.

Q. 8. *How doth God execute his decrees?*

A. God executeth his decrees in the works of creation and providence.

Q. 9. *What is the work of creation?*

A. The work of creation is God's making all things of nothing by the word of his power, in the fpace of fix days, and all very good.

Q. 10. *How did God create man?*

A. God created man male & female after his own image, in knowledge, righteoufnefs and holinefs, with dominion over the creatures

Q. 11. *What are God's works of providence?*

A. God's works of providence are his moft holy, wife and powerful, preferving & govern-

The Shorter Catechism: completed in 1647; it serves as part of the doctrinal standards of many Presbyterian churches.

ing all his creatures and all their actions.

Q. 12. *What special act of providence did God exercise towards man in the estate wherein he was created?*

A. When God had created man, he entered into a covenant of life with him upon condition of perfect obedience, forbidding him to eat of the tree of knowledge of good and evil, upon pain of death.

Q. 13. *Did our first parents continue in the estate wherein they were created?*

A. Our first parents being left to the freedom of their own will, fell from the estate wherein they were created, by sinning against God.

Q. 14. *What is sin?*

A. Sin is any want of conformity unto, or transgression of the law of God.

Q. 15. *What was the sin whereby our first parents fell from the estate wherein they were created?*

A. The sin whereby our first parents fell from the estate wherein they were created, was their eating the forbidden fruit.

Q. 16, *Did all mankind fall in* Adam's *first transgression?*

A. The covenant being made with *Adam*, not only for himself, but for his posterity.

all mankind descending from him by ordinary generation, sinned in him, and fell with him in his first transgression.

Q. 17. *Into what estate did the fall bring mankind?*

A. The fall brought mankind into an estate of sin and misery.

Q. 18. *Wherein consists the sinfulness of that estate whereinto man fell?*

A. The sinfulness of that estate whereinto man fell, consists in the guilt of *Adam's* first sin, the want of original righteousness, & the corruption of his whole nature, which is commonly called original sin, together with all actual transgressions which proceed from it.

Q. 19. *What is the misery of that estate whereinto man fell?*

A. All mankind by the fall lost communion with God, are under his wrath & curse, and so made liable to the miseries in this life, to death itself, & to the pains of hell forever.

Q. 20. *Did God leave all mankind to perish in the state of sin and misery?*

A. God having out of his mere good pleasure from all eternity elected some to everlasting life, did enter into a covenant of grace, to deliver them out of a state of fin and mifery, and to bring them into a ftate of falvation by a Redeemer.

Q. 21. *Who is the Redeemer of God's elect?*

A. The only Redeemer of God's elect, is the Lord Jefus Chrift, who being the eternal Son of God, became man, and fo was, and continues to be God and man, in two diftinct natures, and one perfon forever.

Q. 22. *How did Chrift being the Son of God become man ?*

A. Chrift the Son of God became man by taking to himfelf a true body and a refonable foul, being conceived by the power of the Holy Ghoft, in the womb of the virgin *Mary*, and born of her, and yet without fin.

Q. 23. *What offices doth Chrift execute as our Redeemer ?*

A. Chrift as our Redeemer executes the office of a prophet, of a prieft, & of a king, both in his eftate of humiliation and exaltation.

Q. 24. *How doth Chrift execute the office of a prophet ?*

A. Chrift executeth the office of a prophet in revealing to us by his word and fpirit, the will of God for our falvation.

Q. 25. *How doth Chrift execute the office of a prieft ?*

A. Chrift executeth the office of a prieft in his once offering up himfelf a facrifice to fatisfy divine juftice, and reconcile us to God, and in making continual interceffion for us.

Q. 26. *How doth Chrift execute the office of a king ?*

A. Chrift executeth the office of a king in fubduing us to himfelf, in ruling and defending us, and in reftraining and conquering all his and our enemies.

Q 27 *Wherein did Chrift's humiliation confift?*

A. Chrift's humiliation confifted in his being born and that in a low condition, made under the law, undergoing the miferies of this life, the wrath of God, and the curfed death of the crofs, in being buried and continuing under the power of death for a time.

Q. 28. *Wherein confifts Chrift's exaltation?*

A. Chrift's exaltation confifteth in his rifing again from the dead on the third day, in afcending up into heaven, and fitting at the right hand of God the Father, and in coming to judge the world at the last day.

Q. 29. *How are we made partakers of the redemption purchased by Chrift ?*

A. We are made partakers of the redemption purchafed by Chrift by the effectual application of it to us by his holy Spirit.

Q. 30. *How doth the Spirit apply to us the redemption purchased by Christ?*

A. The Spirit applieth to us the redemption purchased by Christ, by working faith in us, and thereby uniting us to Christ in our effectual calling.

Q. 31. *What is effectual calling?*

A. Effectual calling is the work of God's Spirit, whereby convincing us of our sin and misery, enlightening our minds in the knowledge of Christ, and renewing our wills, he doth persuade and enable us to embrace Jesus Christ, freely offered to us in the gospel.

Q. 32. *What benefits do they that are effectually called partake of in this life?*

A. They that are effectually called do in this life partake of justification, adoption, and sanctification, and the several benefits which in this life do either accompany or flow from them.

Q. 33. *What is justification?*

A. Justification is an act of God's free grace, wherein he pardoneth all our sins, and accepteth us as righteous in his sight only for the righteousness of Christ imputed to us, and received by faith alone.

Q. 34. *What is adoption?*

A. Adoption is an act of God's free grace, whereby we are received into the number, and have a right to all the privileges of the sons of God.

Q. 35. *What is sanctification?*

A. Sanctification is the work of God's free grace, whereby we are renewed in the whole man, after the image of God, and are enabled more and more to die unto sin, and live unto righteousness.

Q. 36. *What are the benefits which in this life do accompany or flow from justification, adoption and sanctification?*

A. The benefits which in this life do accompany or flow from justification, adoption and sanctification, are assurance of God's love, peace of conscience, joy in the holy Ghost, increase of grace, and perseverance therein to the end.

Q. 37. *What benefits do believers receive from Christ at their death?*

A. The souls of believers are at their death made perfect in holiness, and do immediately pass into glory, and their bodies being still united to Christ do rest in their graves 'till the resurrection.

Q. 38. *What benefits do believers receive from Chrift at the resurrection?*

A. At the refurrection believers being raifed up to glory, shall be openly acknowledged and acquitted in the day of judgment, and made perfectly bleffed in the full enjoyment of God to all eternity.

Q. 39. *What is the duty which God requires of man?*

A. The duty which God requires of man, is obedience to his revealed will.

Q. 40. *What did God at firft reveal to man for the rule of his obedience?*

A. The rule which God at firft revealed to man for his obedience was the moral law.

Q. 41. *Where is the moral law fummarily comprehended?*

A. The moral law is fummarily comprehended in the ten commandments.

Q. 42. *What is the fum of the ten commandments?*

A. The fum of the ten commandments is, to love the Lord our God with all our heart, with all our foul, with all our ftrength, and with all our mind, and our neighbour as ourfelves.

Q. 43. *What is the preface to the ten commandments?*

A. The preface to the ten commandments is in thefe words, *I am the Lord thy God which have brought thee out of the land of* Egypt, *and out of the houfe of bondage.*

Q. 44. *What doth the preface to the ten commandments teach us?*

A. The preface to the ten commandments teacheth us, that becaufe God is the Lord, and our God and Redeemer, therefore we are bound to keep all his commandments.

Q. 45. *Which is the first commandment?*

A. The firft commandment is, *Thou fhalt have no other Gods before me.*

Q. 46. *What is required in the firft commandment?*

A. The firft commandment requireth us to know and acknowledge God, to be the only true God, and our God, and to worfhip and glorify him accordingly.

Q. 47. *What is forbidden in the first commandment?*

A. The firft commandment forbiddeth the denying or not worfhipping and glorifying the true God, as God, and our God, and the giving that worfhip and glory to any other which is due to him alone.

3

I am the Lord thy God: Exodus 20.2 (the commandments are given in verses 5–17).

Q. 48. *What are we especially taught by these words* (before me) *in the first commandment?*

A. These words (*before me*) in the first commandment, teach us, that God who seeth all things, taketh notice of and is much displeased with the sin of having any other God.

Q. 49. *Which is the second commandment?*

A. The second commandment is, *Thou shalt not make unto thee any graven image, or the likeness of any thing that is in heaven above, or that is in the earth beneath, or that is in the water under the earth; thou shalt not bow down thyself to them nor serve them, for I the Lord thy God am a jealous God, visiting the iniquities of the fathers upon the children, unto the third and fourth generation of them that hate me and shewing mercy unto thousands of them that love me & keep my commandments.*

Q. 50. *What is required in the second commandment?*

A. The second commandment requireth the receiving, observing, & keeping pure and entire all such religious worship and ordinances, as God hath appointed in his word.

Q. 51. *What is forbidden in the second commandment?*

A. The second commandment forbiddeth the worshipping of God by images or any other way not appointed in his word.

Q. 52. *What are the reasons annexed to the second commandment?*

A. The reasons annexed to the second commandment, are God's sovereignty over us, his propriety in us, and the zeal he hath to his own worship.

Q. 53. *Which is the third commandment?*

A. The third commandment is, *Thou shalt not take the name of the Lord thy God in vain, for the Lord will not hold him guiltless, that taketh his name in vain.*

Q. 54. *What is required in the third commandment?*

A. The third commandment requireth the holy and reverent use of God's names, titles, attributes, ordinances, word and works.

Q. 55. *What is forbidden in the third commandment?*

A. The third commandment forbiddeth all profaning or abusing of any thing whereby God maketh himself known.

Q. 56. *What is the reason annexed to the third commandment?*

A. The reason annexed to the third commandment is, That however the breakers of this commandment may escape punishment from men, yet the Lord our God will not suffer them to escape his righteous judgment.

Q. 57. *Which is the fourth commandment?*

A. The fourth commandment is, *Remember the sabbath day to keep it holy, six days shalt thou labor and do all thy work, but the seventh day is the sabbath of the Lord thy God, in it thou shalt not do any work, thou nor thy son, nor thy daughter, thy man-servant, nor thy maid servant, nor thy cattle, nor the stranger that is within thy gates, for in six days the Lord made heaven and earth, the sea and all that in them is, and rested the seventh day, wherefore the Lord blessed the sabbath day and hallowed it.*

Q. 58. *What is required in the fourth commandment?*

A. The fourth commandment requireth, the keeping holy to God such set times as he hath appointed in his word, expressly one whole day in seven to be an holy Sabbath to himself.

Q. 59. *Which day of the seven hath God appointed to be the weekly sabbath?*

A. From the beginning of the world, to the resurrection of Christ, God appointed the seventh day of the week to be the weekly sabbath, and the first day of the week ever since to continue to the end of the world, which is the Christian Sabbath.

Q. 60. *How is the sabbath to be sanctified?*

A. The sabbath is to be sanctified by an holy resting all that day, even from such worldly employments and recreations as are lawful on other days, and spending the whole time in public and private exercises of God's worship, except so much as is to be taken up in the works of necessity and mercy.

Q. 61. *What is forbidden in the fourth commandment?*

A. The fourth commandment forbiddeth, the omission or careless performance of the duties required, and the profaning the day by idleness, or doing that which is in itself sinful, or by unnecessary thoughts, words or works, about worldly employments or recreations.

Q. 62. *What are the reasons annexed to the fourth commandment?*

A. The reasons annexed to the fourth commandment, are God's allowing us six days of the week for our own employment, his challenging a special propriety in the seventh, his own example, & his blessing the sabbath day.

Q. 63. *Which is the fifth commandment?*

A. The fifth commandment is, *Honor thy father and thy mother, that thy days may be long upon the land which the Lord thy God giveth thee.*

Q. 64. *What is required in the fifth commandment?*

A. The fifth commandment requireth the preserving the honor, and performing the duties belonging to every one in their several places and relations, as superiors, inferiors, or equals.

Q. 65. *What is forbidden in the fifth commandment?*

A. The fifth commandment forbiddeth the neglecting of, or doing any thing against the honour and duty which belongeth to every one in their several places and relations.

Q. 66. *What is the reason annexed to the fifth commandment?*

A. The reason annexed to the fifth commandment is a promise of long life and prosperity, (as far as it shall serve for God's glory and their own good) to all such as keep this commandment.

Q. 67. *Which is the sixth commandment?*

A. The sixth commandment is, *Thou shalt not kill.*

Q. 68. *What is required in the sixth commandment?*

A. The sixth commandment requireth all lawful endeavors to preserve our own life, and the life of others.

Q. 69. *What is forbidden in the sixth commandment?*

A. The sixth commandment forbiddeth the taking away of our own life, or the life of our neighbour unjustly, and whatsoever tendeth thereunto.

Q. 70. *Which is the seventh commandment?*

A. The seventh commandment is, *Thou shalt not commit adultery.*

Q. 71. *What is required in the seventh commandment?*

A. The seventh commandment requireth the preservation of our own and our neighbor's chastity, in heart, speech & behaviour.

Q. 72. *What is forbidden in the seventh commandment?*

A. The seventh commandment forbiddeth all unchaste thoughts, words and actions.

Q. 73. *Which is the eighth commandment?*

A. The eighth commandment is, *Thou*

ſhalt not ſteal.

Q. 74. *What is required in the eighth commandment?*

A. The eighth commandment requireth the lawful procuring & furthering the wealth and outward eſtate of ourſelves and others.

Q. 75. *What is forbidden in the eighth commandment?*

A. The eighth commandment forbiddeth whatſoever doth, or may unjuſtly hinder our own or our neighbour's wealth or outward eſtate.

Q. 76. *Which is the ninth commandment?*

A. The ninth commandment is, *Thou ſhalt not bear falſe witneſs againſt thy neighbour.*

Q. 77. *What is required in the ninth commandment?*

A. The ninth commandment requireth the maintaining and promoting of truth between man & man, & of our own & our neighbor's good name, eſpecially in witneſs bearing.

Q 78. *What is forbidden in the ninth commandment?*

A. The ninth commandment forbiddeth whatſoever is prejudicial to truth, or injurious to our own or our neighbor's good name.

Q. 79. *Which is the tenth commandment?*

A. The tenth commandment is, *Thou ſhalt not covet thy neighbour's houſe, thou ſhalt not covet thy neighbour's wife, nor his man-ſervant, nor his maid-ſervant, nor his ox, nor his aſs, nor any thing that is thy neighbour's.*

Q. 80. *What is required in the tenth commandment?*

A. The tenth commandment requireth full contentment with our own condition, with a right and charitable frame of ſpirit towards our neighbour, and all that is his.

Q. 81. *What is forbidden in the tenth commandment?*

A. The tenth commandment forbiddeth all diſcontentment with our own eſtate, envying or grieving at the good of our neighbour, and all inordinate motions and affections to any thing that is his.

Q. 82. *Is any man able perfectly to keep the commandments of God?*

A. No mere man ſince the fall is able in this life perfectly to keep the commandments of God, but daily doth break them in thought, word and deed.

Q. 83. *Are all tranſgreſſions of the law equally heinous?*

A. Some ſins in themſelves, and by rea-

3*

son of several aggravations, are more heinous in the sight of God than others.

Q. 84. *What doth every sin deserve?*

A. Every sin deserves God's wrath & curse both in this life, and that which is to come.

Q. 85. *What doth God require of us that we may escape his wrath and curse due to us for sin?*

A. To escape the wrath and curse of God due to us for sin, God requireth of us faith in Jesus Christ, repentance unto life, with the diligent use of all outward means whereby Christ communicateth to us the benefits of redemption. Q. 86. *What is faith in Jesus Christ?*

A. Faith in Jesus Christ is a saving grace whereby we receive & rest upon him alone for salvation as he is offered to us in the gospel.

Q. 87. *What is repentance unto life?*

A. Repentance unto life is a saving grace, whereby a sinner out of the true sense of his sin and apprehension of the mercy of God in Christ, doth with grief and hatred of his sin turn from it unto God, with full purpose of and endeavours after new obedience.

Q. 88. *What are the outward and ordinary means whereby Christ communicateth to us the benefits of redemption?*

A. The outward and ordinary means where by Christ communicateth to us the benefits of redemption, are his ordinances, especially the word, sacraments and prayer; all which are made effectual to the elect for salvation.

Q. 89. *How is the word made effectual to salvation?*

A. The spirit of God maketh the reading, but especially the preaching of the word an effectual means of convincing and converting sinners, and of building them up in holiness and comfort, through faith unto salvation.

Q. 90. *How is the word to be read and heard that it may become effectual to salvation?*

A. That the word may become effectual to salvation, we must attend thereunto with diligence, preparation and prayer, receive it with faith and love, lay it up in our hearts, and practice it in our lives.

Q. 91 *How do the sacraments become effectual means of salvation?*

A. The sacraments become effectual means of salvation not from any virtue in them or in him that doth administer them, but only by the blessing of Christ, and the working of the Spirit in them that by faith receive them.

Q. 92. *What is a sacrament?*

A. A sacrament is an holy ordinance inſtituted by Chriſt, wherein by ſenſible ſigns, Chriſt & the benefits of the new covenant are repreſented ſealed and applied to believers.

Q. 93. *What are the ſacraments of the New Teſtament?*

A. The ſacraments of the New Teſtament are baptiſm and the Lord's ſupper.

Q. 94. *What is baptiſm?*

A. Baptiſm is a ſacrament wherein the waſhing of water in the name of the Father and of the Son and of the Holy Ghoſt, doth ſignify and ſeal our ingraſting into Chriſt and partaking of the benefits of the covenant of grace, & our engagements to be the Lord's.

Q. 95. *To whom is baptiſm to be adminiſtered?*

A. Baptiſm is not to be adminiſtered to any that are out of the viſible church, till they profeſs their faith in Chriſt, and obedience to him, but the infants of ſuch as are members of the viſible church are to be baptized.

Q. 96. *What is the Lord's ſupper?*

A. The Lord's ſupper is a ſacrament, wherein by giving and receiving bread and wine according to Chriſt's appointment, his death is ſhewed forth, and the worthy receivers are not after a corporal and carnal manner, but by faith made partakers of his body and blood, with all his benefits, to their ſpiritual nouriſhment and growth in grace.

Q. 97. *What is required in the worthy receiving the Lord's ſupper?*

A. It is required of them that would worthily partake of the Lord's ſupper, that they examine themſelves of their knowledge to diſcern the Lord's body, of their faith to feed upon him, of their repentance, love and new obedience, leſt coming unworthily, they eat and drink judgment to themſelves.

Q. 98. *What is prayer?*

A. Prayer is an offering up of our deſires to God for things agreeable to his will, in the name of Chriſt, with confeſſion of our ſins, & thankful acknowledgment of his mercies.

Q. 99. *What rule hath God given for our direction in prayer?*

A. The whole word of God is of uſe to direct us in prayer but the ſpecial rule of direction is that form of prayer which Chriſt taught his diſciples commonly called, *The Lord's Prayer.*

Q. 100. *What doth the preface of the Lord's prayer teach us?*

A. The preface of the Lord's prayer which is *Our Father which art in heaven,* teacheth us, to draw near to God with all holy reverence and confidence, as children to a father, able and ready to help us, and that we should pray with and for others.

Q.101. *What do we pray for in the first petition?*

A. In the first petition, which is, *Hallowed be thy name,* we pray that God would enable us and others to glorify him in all that whereby he makes himself known, and that he would dispose all things to his own glory.

Q. 102. *What do we pray for in the second petition?*

A. In the second petition, which is, *Thy kingdom come,* we pray that satan's kingdom may be destroyed, the kingdom of grace may be advanced, ourselves and others bro't into it, and kept in it, and that the kingdom of glory may be hastened.

Q. 103. *What do we pray for in the third petition?*

A. In the third petition, which is, *Thy will be done on earth as it is in heaven,* we pray that God by his grace would make us able and willing to know, obey and submit to his will in all things, as the angels do in heaven.

Q. 104. *What do we pray for in the fourth petition?*

A. In the fourth petition, which is, *Give us this day our daily bread,* we pray, that of God's free gift we may receive a competent portion of the good things of this life, and enjoy his blessing with them.

Q. 105. *What do we pray for in the fifth petition?*

A. In the fifth petition, which is, *And forgive us our debts as we forgive our debtors,* we pray that God for Christ's sake, would freely pardon all our sins, which we are the rather encouraged to ask, because by his grace we are enabled from the heart to forgive others.

Q. 106. *What do we pray for in the sixth petition?*

A. In the sixth petition, which is, *And lead us not into temptation, but deliver us from evil,* we pray that God would either keep us from being tempted to sin, or support and deliver us when we are tempted.

Q. 107. *What doth the conclusion of the Lord's prayer teach us?*

A. The conclusion of the Lord's prayer, which is, *For thine is the kingdom, and the power, and the glory, forever,* A M E N, teacheth us, to take our encouragement in prayer from God only, and in our prayers to praise him, ascribing kingdom, power and glory to him, and in testimony of our desire and assurance to be heard, we say, A M E N.

Blessed are they that do his commandments that they may have right to the tree of life, and may enter in through the gates into the city. Rev. xxii. 14.

❊❊❊❊❊❊❊❊❊❊❊❊❊❊❊❊❊❊

S P I R I T U A L   M I L K

F O R

American BABES,

Drawn out of the Breasts of both *Testaments,* for their Souls Nourishment.

By J O H N   C O T T O N.

Q. **W**HAT *hath God done for you ?*   A. God hath made me, he keepeth me, and he can save me.

Q. *What is God ?*

A. God is a Spirit of himself & for himself.

Q. *How many Gods be there ?*

A. There is but one God in three Persons, the Father, and the Son, and the Holy Ghost.

Q. *How did God make you ?*

A. In my first parents holy and righteous.

Q. *Are you then born holy and righteous.*

A. No, my first father sinned and I in him.

Q. *Are you then born a sinner ?*

A. I was conceived in sin, & born in iniquity.

Q. *What is your birth sin ?*

A. Adam's sin imputed to me, and a corrupt nature dwelling in me.

Q. *What is your corrupt nature ?*

A. My corrupt nature is empty of grace, bent unto sin, only unto sin, and that continually.

Q. *What is sin ?*

A. Sin is a transgression of the law.

Q. *How many commandments of the law be there ?*   A. Ten.

Q. *What is the first commandment ?*

A. Thou shalt have no other Gods before me.

Q. *What is the meaning of this commandment ?*

A. That we should worship the only true God, and no other besides him.

Q. *What is the second commandment ?*

A. Thou shalt not make to thyself any graven image, &c.

Q. *What is the meaning of this commandment ?*

A. That we should worship the only true God, with true worship, such as he hath ordained, not such as man hath invented.

Q. *What is the third commandment ?*

John Cotton: English Puritan clergyman (1585–1652); he emigrated to Boston in 1633 and eventually became the head of Congregationalism in America. This catechism was first published in 1646.

A. Thou shalt not take the name of the Lord thy God in vain.

Q. What is meant by the name of God?

A. God himself & the good things of God, whereby he is known as a man by his name, and his attributes, worship, word and works.

Q. What is it not to take his name in vain?

A. To make use of God & the good things of God to his glory, and our own good, not vainly, not irreverently, not unprofitably.

Q. Which is the fourth commandment?

A. Remember that thou keep holy the sabbath day.

Q. What is the meaning of this commandment?

A. That we should rest from labor, and much more from play on the Lord's day, that we may draw nigh to God in holy duties.

Q. What is the fifth commandment?

A. Honor thy father and thy mother, that thy days may be long in the land which the Lord thy God giveth thee.

Q. What are meant by father and mother?

A. All our superiors whether in family, school, church and common wealth.

Q. What is the honor due unto them?

A. Reverence, obedience, and (when I am able) recompence.

Q. What is the sixth commandment?

A. Thou shalt do no murder.

Q. What is the meaning of this commandment?

A. That we should not shorten the life or health of ourselves or others, but preserve both

Q. What is the seventh commandment?

A. Thou shalt not commit adultery.

Q. What is the sin here forbidden?

A. To defile ourselves or others with unclean lusts.

Q. What is the duty here commanded?

A. Chastity to possess our vessels in holiness and honor.

Q. What is the eighth commandment?

A. Thou shalt not steal.

Q. What is the stealth here forbidden?

A. To take away another man's goods without his leave, or to spend our own without benefit to ourselves or others.

Q. What is the duty here commanded?

A. To get our goods honestly, to keep them safely, and spend them thriftily.

Q. What is the ninth commandment?

A. Thou shalt not bear false witness against thy neighbour.

Q. What is the sin here forbidden?

John Cotton, English Puritan clergyman (1585-1652), he emigrated to Boston in 1633 and eventually became the head of Congregationalism in America. His catechism was first published in 1646.

A. To lie falsely, to think or speak untruly of ourselves or others.

Q. *What is the duty here required?*

A. Truth and faithfulness.

Q. *What is the tenth commandment?*

A. Thou shalt not covet, &c.

Q. *What is the coveting here forbidden?*

A. Lust after the things of other men, and want of contentment with our own.

Q. *Whether have you kept all these commandments?*

A. No, I and all men are sinners.

Q. *What are the wages of sin?*

A. Death and damnation.

Q. *How then look you to be saved?*

A. Only by Jesus Christ.

Q. *Who is Jesus Christ?*

*A.*The eternal Son of God, who for our sakes became man, that he might redeem & save us.

Q. *How doth Christ redeem and save us?*

A. By his righteous life, and bitter death, and glorious resurrection to life again.

Q. *How do we come to have a part & fellowship with Christ in his death & resurrection?*

A. By the power of his word and spirit, which brings us to him, and keeps us in him.

Q. *What is the word?*

A. The holy scriptures of the prophets and apostles, the old and new testament, the law and gospel.

Q. *How doth the ministry of the law bring you toward Christ?*

A. By bringing me to know my sin, and the wrath of God, against me for it.

Q. *What are you hereby the nearer to Christ?*

A. So I come to feel my cursed estate and need of a Saviour.

Q. *How doth the ministry of the Gospel help you in this cursed estate?*

A. By humbling me yet more, and then raising me out of this estate.

Q. *How doth the ministry of the Gospel humble you yet more?*

A. By revealing the grace of the Lord Jesus in dying to save sinners, and yet convincing me of my sin in not believing on him, and of my utter insufficiency to come to him, and so I feel myself utterly lost.

Q. *How doth the ministry of the gospel raise you up out of this lost estate to come to Christ?*

A. By teaching me the value and virtue of the death of Christ, and the riches of his grace to lost sinners by revealing the promise of grace to such, and by ministring the Spirit of grace to apply Christ, and his promise of grace unto myself, and to keep me in him.

Q. *How doth the Spirit of grace apply Christ & his promise grace unto you and keep you in him?*

A. By begetting in me faith to receive him, prayer to call upon him, repentance to mourn after him, and new obedience to serve him.

Q. *What is faith ?*

A. Faith is the grace of the Spirit, whereby I deny myself, and believe on Christ for righteousness and salvation.

Q. *What is prayer ?*

A. It is calling upon God in the name of Christ by the help of the Holy Ghost, according to the will of God.

Q. *What is repentance ?*

A. Repentance is a grace of the Spirit, whereby I loath my sins, and myself for them and confess them before the Lord, and mourn after Christ for the pardon of them, and for grace to serve him in newness of life.

Q. *What is the newness of life, or new obedience?*

A. Newness of life is a grace of the Spirit, whereby I forsake my former lust & vain company, and walk before the Lord in the light of his word, and in the communion of saints.

Q. *What is the communion of saints ?*

A. It is the fellowship of the church in the blessings of the covenant of grace, and the seals thereof. Q. *What is the church ?*

A. It is a congregation of saints joined together in the bond of the covenant, to worship the Lord, and to edify one another in all his holy ordinances.

Q, *What is the bond of the covenant by which the church is joined together ?*

A. It is the profession of that covenant which God has made with his faithful people, to be a God unto them, and to their seed.

Q. *What doth the Lord bind his people to in this covenant ?*

A. To give up themselves & their seed first to the Lord to be his people, & then to the elders & brethren of the church to set forward the worship of God & their mutual edification.

Q. *How do they give up themselves and their seed to the Lord ?*

A. By receiving thro' faith the Lord & his covenant to themselves, & to their seed & accordingly walking themselves & training up their children in the ways of the covenant.

Q. *How do they give up themselves and their seed to the elders and brethren of the church ?*

A. By confessing of their sins, and profesfion of their faith, and of their fubjection to the gofpel of Chrift ; and fo they and their feed are received into the fellowfhip of the church and the feals thereof.

Q. *What are the feals of the covenant now in the days of the gofpel?*

A. Baptifm and the Lord's Supper.

Q. *What is done for you in baptifm ?*

A. In baptifm the wafhing with water is a fign and feal of my wafhing in the blood and fpirit of Chrift, and thereby of my in-grafting into Chrift, of the pardon and clean-fing of my fins, of my raifing up out of afflic-tions, and alfo of my refurrection from the dead at the laft day.

Q. *What is done for you in the Lord's fupper?*

A. In the Lord's fupper, the receiving of the bread broken and the wine poured out is a fign and feal of my receiving the communion of the body of Chrift broken for me, and of his blood fhed for me, and thereby of my growth in Chrift, and the pardon and healing of my fins, of the fellowfhip of the Spirit, of my ftrengthening and quickening in grace, and of my fitting together with Chrift on his throne of glory at the laft judgment.

Q. *What was the refurrection from the*

dead, which was fealed up to you in baptifm ?

A. When Chrift fhall come in his laft judgment, all that are in their graves fhall rife again, both the juft and unjuft.

Q. *What is the judgment, which is fealed up to you in the Lord's supper ?*

A. At the laft day we fhall all appear be-fore the judgment feat of Chrift, to give an account of our works, and receive our re-ward according to them.

Q. *What is the reward that fhall then be given?*

A. Tho righteous fhall go into life eter-nal, and the wicked fhall be caft into ever-lafting fire with the Devil and his angels.

A DIALOGUE *between* CHRIST, YOUTH, *and the* Devil.　　　YOUTH

THofe days which God to me doth fend,
　In pleafure I'm refolv'd to fpend ;
Like as the birds in th' lovely spring,
Sit chirping on the bough, and fing ;
Who ftraining forth thofe warbling notes,
Do make fweet mufic in their throats,
So I refolve in this my prime,
In fports and plays to fpend my time.
Sorrow and grief I'll put away,
Such things agree not with my day:

4

From clouds my morning fhall be free ;
And nought on earth fhall trouble me.
I will embrace each fweet delight,
This earth affords me day and night :
Though parents grieve and me correct,
Yet I their counsel will reject.

Devil.

The refolution which you take,
Sweet youth it doth me merry make.
If thou my counsel wilt embrace,
And fhun the ways of truth and grace,
And learn to lie, and curfe and swear,
And be as proud as any are ;
And with thy brothers wilt fall out,
And fifters with vile language flout :
Yea, fight and fcratch, and alfo bite,
Then in thee I will take delight.
If thou wilt but be rul'd by me,
An artift thou fhalt quickly be,
In all my ways which lovely are,
Ther'e few with thee who fhall compare.
Thy parents always difobey ;
Don't mind at all what they do fay :
And alfo pout and fullen be,
And thou fhalt be a child for me.
When others read, be thou at play,
Think not on God, don't sigh nor pray

Nor be thou fuch a filly fool,
To mind thy book or go to fchool ;
But play the truant ; fear not I
Will ftraitway help you to a lie,
Which will excufe thee from the fame,
From being whipp'd and from all blame ;
Come bow to me, uphold my crown,
And I'll thee raife to high renown.

YOUTH.

Thefe motions I will cleave unto,
And let all other counsels go ;
My heart againft my parents now,
Shall harden'd be, and will not bow :
I won't fubmit at all to them,
But all good counsels will condemn,
And what I lift that do will I,
And ftubborn be continually.

CHRIST.

Wilt thou, O youth make fuch a choice,
And thus obey the devil's voice !
Curft finful ways wilt thou embrace,
And hate the ways of truth and grace ?
Wilt thou to me a rebel prove ?
And from thy parents quite remove
Thy heart alfo ? Then fhalt thou fee,
What will e'er long become of thee.
Come, think on God, who did thee make,

And at his prefence dread and quake,
Remember him now in thy youth,
And let thy foul take hold of truth :
The Devil and his ways defy,
Believe him not, he doth but lie :
His ways feem fweet, but youth beware,
He for thy foul hath laid a fnare.
His fweet will into bitter turn,
If in thofe ways thou ftill wilt run,
He will thee into pieces tear,
Like lions which moft hungry are.
Grant me thy heart, thy folly leave,
And from this lion I'll thee fave ;
And thou fhalt have fweet joy from me,
Which fhall laft to eternity.

YOUTH.

My heart fhall chear me in my youth,
I'll have my frolicks in good truth,
What e'er feems lovely in mine eye,
Myfelf I cannot it deny.
In my own ways I ftill will walk,
And take delight among young folk,
Who fpend their days in joy and mirth,
Nothing like that I'm fure on earth :
Thy ways, O Chrift ! are not for me,
They with my age do not agree.
If I unto thy laws fhould cleave,

No more good days then fhould I have.

CHRIST.

Woul'ft thou live long and good days fee
Refrain from all iniquity :
True good alone doth from me flow,
It can't be had in things below.
Are not my ways, O youth ! for thee,
Then thou fhalt never happy be ;
Nor ever fhall thy foul obtain,
True good, whilft thou doft here remain.

YOUTH.

To thee, O Chrift, I'll not adhere,
What thou fpeak'ft of does not appear
Lovely to me I cannot find,
'Tis good to fet or place my mind
On ways whence many forrows fpring,
And to the flefh fuch croffes bring,
Don't trouble me, I muft fulfil,
My flefhly mind, and have my will.

CHRIST.

Unto thyfelf then I'll thee leave,
That Satan may thee wholly have :
Thy heart in fin fhall harden'd be,
And blinded in iniquity.
And then in wrath I'll cut thee down,
Like af the grafs and flowers mown ;
And to thy woe thou fhalt efpy,

4*

Childhood and youth are vanity;
For all fuch things I'll make thee know
To judgment thou fhall come alfo.
In hell at laft thy foul fhall burn,
When thou thy finful race haft run.
Confider this, think on thy end
Left God do thee in pieces rend.

YOUTH.

Amazed, Lord! I now begin,
O help me and I'll leave my fin:
I tremble, and do greatly fear,
To think upon what I do hear.
Lord! I religious now will be,
And I'll from Satan turn to thee.

Devil.

Nay, foolifh youth, don't change thy mind,
Unto fuch thoughts be not inclin'd.
Come, cheer up thy heart, roufe up, be glad;
There is no hell; why art thou fad?
Eat, drink, be merry with thy friend,
For when thou dieft, that's thy laft end.

YOUTH.

Such thoughts as thefe I can't receive,
Becaufe God's word I do believe;
None fhall in this deftroy my faith,
Nor do I mind what Satan faith.

Devil.

Although to thee herein I yield.
Yet e'er long I fhall win the field.
That there's a heaven I can't deny,
Yea, and a hell of mifery:
That heaven is a lovely place
I can't deny; 'tis a clear cafe;
And eafy 'tis for to come there,
Therefore take thou no further care,
All human laws do thou obferve,
And from old cuftoms never fwerve;
Do not oppofe what great men fay,
And thou fhalt never go aftray.
Thou may'ft be drunk, and fwear and curfe,
And finners like thee ne'er the worfe;
At any time thou may'ft repent;
'Twill ferve when all thy days are fpent.

CHRIST.

Take heed or elfe thou art undone;
Thefe thoughts are from the wicked One,
Narrow's the way that leads to life,
Who walk therein do meet with ftrife.
Few fhall be faved, young man know,
Moft do unto deftruction go.
If righteous ones fcarce faved be,
What will at laft become of thee!
Oh! don't reject my precious call,
Left suddenly in hell thou fall;

Unlefs you foon converted be,
God's kingdom thou fhalt never fee.
YOUTH.
Lord, I am now at a great ftand:
If I fhould yield to thy command,
My comrades will me much deride,
And never more will me abide.
Moreover, this I alfo know,
Thou can'ft at laft great mercy fhow.
When I am old, and pleafure gone,
Then what thou fay'ft I'll think upon.
CHRIST.
Nay, hold vain youth, thy time is fhort,
I have thy breath, I'll end thy fport;
Thou fhalt not live till thou art old,
Since thou in fin art grown fo bold.
I in thy youth grim death will fend,
And all thy fports fhall have an end.
YOUTH.
I am too young, alas to die,
Let death fome old grey head efpy.
O fpare me, and I will amend,
And with thy grace my foul befriend,
Or elfe I am undone alas,
For I am in a woful cafe.
CHRIST.
When I did call, you would not hear,

But didft to me turn a deaf ear;
And now in thy calamity,
I will not mind nor hear thy cry;
Thy day is paft, begone from me,
Thou who didft love iniquity,
Above thy foul and Saviour dear;
Who on the crofs great pains did bear,
My mercy thou didft much abufe,
And all good counfel didft refufe,
Juftice will therefore vengeance take,
And thee a fad example make.
YOUTH.
O fpare me, Lord, forbear thy hand,
Don't cut me off who trembling ftand,
Begging for mercy at thy door,
O let me have but one year more.
CHRIST.
If thou fome longer time fhould have,
Thou wouldft again to folly cleave:
Therefore to thee I will not give,
One day on earth longer to live.
Death.
Youth, I am come to fetch thy breath,
And carry thee to th' fhades of death,
No pity on thee can I fhow,
Thou haft thy God offended fo.
Thy foul and body I'll divide,

Thy body in the grave I'll hide,
And thy dear soul in hell muſt lie,
With Devils to eternity.

The concluſion.

Thus end the days of woful youth,
Who won't obey nor mind the truth ;
Nor hearken to what preachers ſay,
But do their parents diſobey.
They in their youth go down to hell,
Under eternal wrath to dwell.
Many don't live out half their days,
For cleaving unto ſinful ways.

*The late Reverend and Venerable Mr. NA-
THANIEL CLAP, of Newport on Rhode
Iſland ; his Advice to children.*

GOOD children ſhould remember daily,
God their Creator, Redeemer, and
Sanctifier ; to believe in, love and ſerve him ;
their parents to obey them in the LORD ;
their bible and catechiſm ; their baptiſm ;
the LORD's day ; the LORD's death and re-
ſurrection ; their own death and reſurrecti-
on ; and the day of judgment, when all that
are not fit for heaven muſt be ſent to hell.
And they ſhould pray to GOD in the name
of CHRIST, for ſaving grace.

Mr. Nathaniel Clap: Clap (1669–1745), who began preaching at Newport in 1695, published "Advice to Children" in
1691.

1777

A LITTLE PRETTY POCKET-BOOK
1744

Traditionally, the history of children's book publishing is dated from 1744, when John Newbery (1713–1767) married the manufacture and sale of books for children (produced in accord with the philosophical and pedagogical ideal of both instructing and delighting) to toys. His *A Little Pretty Pocket-Book* was sold with a ball and pincushion. The book's marketing strategy and emphasis on entertainment guaranteed its status in the history of children's literature. Newbery's winning formula of instruction, delight, and toys is still regularly used in marketing children's books. The gilt cover and woodcuts of *A Little Pretty Pocket-Book* attracted buyers, though the pictures seem to bear little relation to the scraps of stories and rhymes they accompany.

Newbery is best remembered today as the pioneering publisher of children's books and the first children's periodical, the monthly *Lilliputian Magazine* (1751). His name lives on in the Newbery Medal, created in 1922 by the American Library Association and awarded each year to an American author "for the most distinguished contribution to literature for children." But Newbery engaged in a variety of businesses, eventually focusing on publishing and patent medicines (whose sales—particularly of Dr. James's Fever Powder—apparently provided a considerable portion of his income). Like other publishers of his day, he printed and sold books, and he solicited work from the eighteenth century's leading writers, including Oliver Goldsmith and Samuel Johnson.

The extract from *A Little Pretty Pocket-Book* reprinted below is from a 1767 edition.

Delectando monemus
Instruction with Delight

A Little Pretty
POCKET-BOOK,
Intended for the
INSTRUCTION and AMUSEMENT
OF
LITTLE MASTER *TOMMY,*
AND
PRETTY MISS *POLLY.*
With Two Letters from
JACK the GIANT-KILLER;
AS ALSO
A BALL and PINCUSHION;
The Use of which will infallibly make *Tommy*
a good Boy, and *Polly* a good Girl.

To which is added,
A LITTLE SONG-BOOK,
BEING
A *New Attempt* to teach Children the Use of
the *English* Alphabet, by Way of Diversion.

LONDON:
Printed for J. NEWBERY, at the *Bible and Sun*
in St. *Paul's Church-Yard.* 1767.
[Price Six-pence bound.]

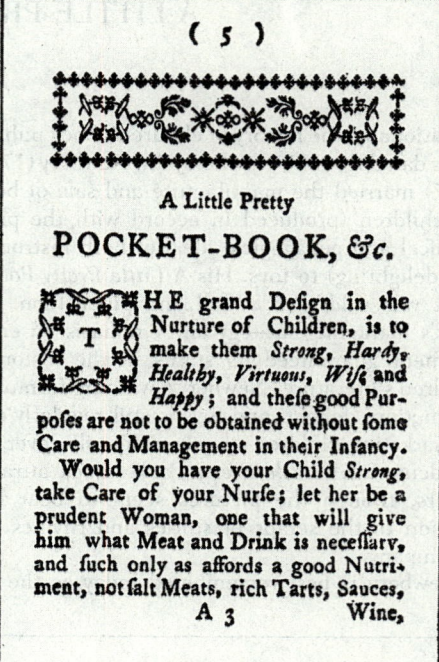

The grand Design in the Nurture of Children, is to make them *Strong, Hardy, Healthy, Virtuous, Wise,* and *Happy*; and these good Purposes are not to be obtained without some Care and Management in their Infancy.

Would you have your Child *Strong*, take Care of your Nurse; let her be a prudent Woman, one that will give him what Meat and Drink is necessary, and such only as affords a good Nutriment, not salt Meats, rich Tarts, Sauces, Wine, &c. a Practice too common amongst some indulgent People. She must also let the child have due Exercise; for 'tis this that gives Life and Spirits, circulates the Blood, strengthens the Sinews, and keeps the whole Machinery in Order.

Would you have a *Hardy* Child, give him common Diet only, cloath him thin, let him have good Exercise, and be as much exposed to Hardships as his natural Constitution will admit. The Face of a Child, when it comes into the World, (says the great Mr. *Locke*)[1] is as tender and susceptible of Injuries as any other Part of the Body; yet, by being always exposed, it becomes Proof against the severest Season and the most inclement Weather; even at a Time when the Body (tho' wrapp'd in Flannels) is pierced with Cold. It is beside my Purpose to give a physical Reason for this; nor indeed will the Brevity of my Design admit of it. 'Tis a Fact sufficiently known, what every Man must be sensible of, and therefore can need no Demonstration.

Would you have a *Healthy* Son, observe the Directions already laid down with Regard to Diet and Exercise, and keep him, as much as possible, from Physic;[2] for

1. John Locke (1632–1704), English philosopher; this observation is found in *Some Thoughts Concerning Education* (1693).
2. Medicine.

Physic is to the Body, as Arms to the State; both are necessary, but neither to be used but in Cases of Emergency and Danger.

Would you have a *Virtuous* Son, instil into him the Principles of Morality early, and encourage him in the Practice of those excellent Rules, by which whole Societies, States, Kingdoms, and Empires are knit together. Take heed what Company you intrust him with, and be always sure to set him a good Example yourself.

Would you have a *Wise* Son, teach him to reason early. Let him read, and make him understand what he reads. No Sentence should be passed over without a strict Examination of the Truth of it; and though this may be thought hard at first, and seem to retard the Boy in his Progress, yet a little Practice will make it familiar, and a Method of Reasoning will be acquired, which will be of Use to him all his Life after. Let him study Mankind; shew him the Springs and Hinges on which they move; teach him to draw Consequences from the Actions of others; and if he should hesitate or mistake, you are to set him right: But then take Care to do it in such a Manner, as to forward his Enquiries, and pave this his grand Pursuit with Pleasure. Was this Method of Reasoning put more in Practice by Tutors, Parents, &c. we should not see so many dismal Objects in the World; for People would learn by the Misfortunes of others to avert their own.

I doubt not but every Parent, every Father and Mother, would gladly contribute what they could towards the Happiness of their Children; and yet it is surprising to see how blind they are, and how wide they mistake the Mark. What the indulgent Parent generally proposes for the Happiness of his Child, is a good Fortune to bear him up under the Calamities of Life; but daily Experience tells us, this is insufficient. Happiness and Misery have their Source from the Passions: If, in the Midst of the greatest Affluence, we are always repining, and think ourselves poor and miserable, we are so; and the Beggar in the Straw, who is content, and thinks he has sufficient, is rich and happy. The whole Matter subsists in the Mind, and the Constitution: Subdue therefore your Childrens Passions; curb their Tempers, and make them subservient to the Rules of Reason. And this is not to be done by chiding, whipping, or severe Treatment, but by Reasoning and mild Discipline. Were I to see my Son too much ruffled and discomposed, I should take him aside, and point out to him the Evils that attend passionate Men; tell him, that my Love for him would make me overlook many Faults, but that this was of so heinous a Nature, that I could not bear the Sight of him while he continued so wicked; that he should not see his Mother, nor any of his Play-mates, till he had sufficiently repented of that Crime: Upon which, I would immediately order him (in a very calm Manner) to be shut up from any Company for five or six Hours, and then, upon his Confession of the Fault, asking Pardon on his Knees, and promising Amendment for the future, I would forgive him. This Method, regularly pursued, would soon break his Passion of Resentment, and subdue it to Reason. The next prudent Step to be taken, is to check his inordinate craving and desiring almost every Thing he sees; and this, I think, might be as easily effected as the other; for, in the first Place, I would lay down this as a Maxim with him, that he should never have any thing he cryed for; and therefore, if he was willing to obtain any Favour, he must come with a reasonable Request, and withdraw without the Appearance of any Uneasiness in case of a Disappointment.

Some over-fond People will think these are harsh Precepts. What, say they, are Children never to be obliged? I answer, Yes, I would have them obliged and pleased, but not humoured and spoiled. They should have what they asked for in a proper Manner; but then they should wait my Time, without seeming over solicitous, or crying after it. I would make them exercise their Patience, that they might know the

Use of it, when the Cares of the World came on. And therefore, I say again, Children should never have any Thing they cryed for; no, not on any Consideration whatsoever.

Children, *like tender* Osiers, *take the Bow, And as they* first are *fashion'd, always grow.*
                                                                      DRYDEN.[3]

'Tis Education *forms the tender* Mind; *Just as the* Twig *is bent, the* Tree's *inclin'd.*[4]
                                                                      POPE.

A LETTER FROM JACK THE GIANT-KILLER, TO LITTLE MASTER TOMMY

My dear TOMMY,

Your Nurse called upon me To-day, and told me that you was a good Boy; that you was dutiful to your Father and Mother, and that, when you had said your Prayers in the Morning and the Evening, you asked their Blessings, and in the Day-time did every Thing they bid you. She says, you are obedient to your Master, loving and kind to your Play-fellows, and obliging to every body; that you rise early in the Morning, keep yourself clean, and learn your Book; that when you have done a Fault you confess it, and are sorry for it. And though you are sometimes naughty, she says you are very honest and good-humoured; that you don't swear, tell Lies, nor say indecent Words, and are always thankful when any body gives you good Advice; that you never quarrel, nor do wicked Things, as some other Boys do.

This Character, my Dear, has made every body love you; and, while you continue so good, you may depend on my obliging you with every thing I can. I have here sent you a *Little Pretty Pocket-Book*, which will teach you to play at all those innocent Games that good Boys and Girls divert themselves with: And, while you behave so well, you shall never want Play I assure you. But then, my dear *Tommy*, in order that you may be as good as possible, I have also sent you a *Ball*, the one Side of which is *Red*, and the other *Black*, and with it ten *Pins*; and I must insist upon making this Bargain, that your Nurse may hang up the *Ball* by the String to it, and for every good Action you do a *Pin* shall be stuck on the *Red Side*, and for every bad Action a *Pin* shall be stuck on the *Black Side*. And when by doing good and pretty Things you have got all the ten *Pins* on the *Red Side*, then I'll send you a *Penny*, and so I will as often as all the *Pins* shall be fairly got on that Side. But if ever the *Pins* be all found on the *Black Side* of the *Ball*, then I'll send a *Rod*, and you shall be whipt as often as they are found there. But this, my Dear, I hope you'll prevent by continuing a good Boy, that every body may still love you, as well as

                                                    Your Friend,
                                                    JACK *the* GIANT-KILLER.

P.S. When you are tired with playing, I have added, for your further Amusement, a Collection of pretty Songs, which your Nurse will take Care to teach you; and I must insist on your getting them perfectly, because the Knowledge of these

3. John Dryden (1631–1700), English poet.
4. Alexander Pope (1688–1744), English poet; slightly misquoted from "Moral Essays, Epistle I: To Richard Temple, Viscount Cobham."

Songs will recommend you to the Favour of all the Gentlemen and Ladies of *England* who sing in that Manner.

A Letter from Jack the Giant-Killer, to Pretty Miss Polly

Dear Miss POLLY,

Your Nurse called upon me To-day, and told me that you was a good Girl; that you was dutiful to your Father and Mother, and that, when you had said your Prayers in the Morning and the Evening, you asked their Blessings, and in the Day-time did every Thing they bid you. She says, you are obedient to your Mistress, loving and kind to your Play-fellows, and obliging to every body; that you rise early in the Morning, keep yourself clean, and learn your Book; that when you have done a Fault you confess it, and are sorry for it. And though you are sometimes naughty, she says you are very honest and good-humoured; that you don't tell Lies, nor say indecent Words, and are always thankful when any body gives you good Advice; that you never quarrel, nor do wicked Things, as some other Girls do.

This Character, my Dear, has made every body love you; and, while you continue so good, you may depend on my obliging you with every thing I can. I have here sent you a *Little Pretty Pocket-Book*, which will teach you to play at all those innocent Games that good Boys and Girls divert themselves with: And, while you behave so well, you shall never want Play I assure you. But then, my dear *Polly*, in order that you may be as good as possible, I have also sent you a *Pincushion*, the one Side of which is *Red*, and the other *Black*, and with it *ten Pins*; and I must insist upon making this Bargain, that your Nurse may hang up the *Pincushion* by the String to it, and for every good Action you do, a *Pin* shall be stuck on the *Red Side*, and for every bad Action a *Pin* shall be stuck on the *Black Side*. And when by doing good and pretty Things you have got all the *ten Pins* on the *Red Side*, then I'll send you a *Penny*, and so I will as often as all the *Pins* shall be fairly got on that Side. But if ever the *Pins* be all found on the *Black Side* of the *Pincushion*, then I'll send a *Rod*, and you shall be whipt as often as they are found there. But this, my Dear, I hope you'll prevent by continuing a good Girl, that every body may still love you, as well as

> *Your Friend,*
> JACK *the* GIANT-KILLER.

P.S. When you are tired with playing, I have added, for your further Amusement, a Collection of pretty Songs, which your Nurse will take Care to teach you; and I must insist on your getting them perfectly, because the Knowledge of these Songs will recommend you to the Favour of all the Gentlemen and Ladies of *England* who sing in this Manner.

Advertisement

A worthy and learned Gentleman, whose Presence I am at this time honoured with, intimates, that it would not be amiss for some Gentlemen to keep a *Ball* contrived in this Manner, and some Ladies a *Pincushion*, by way of Diary, especially if they are often apt to forget themselves.

Chuck—Farthing[5]

As you value your Pence,
  At the *Hole* take your Aim;
Chuck all safely in,
  And you'll win the Game.

Moral

Chuck-Farthing, like Trade,
  Requires great Care;
The more you observe,
  The better you'll fare.

1744   1767

5. A game in which coins are pitched at a mark, then tossed at a hole by the player who comes nearest to the mark (a farthing is a quarter of a penny).

ANNA LAETITIA BARBAULD
1743–1825

When Rochemont Barbauld, Anna's husband of over thirty years, insisted she kill herself in his presence by drinking a bottle of laudanum (opium), she saved herself by jumping out of a nearby window. She used the same escape tactic when he grabbed a knife and chased her around the dinner table. On both occasions, Anna coped with her husband's violent insanity by relying on her courage, agility, and presence of mind, all traits that served her well both as a wife and as an author.

Before she was thirty, Anna Laetitia Barbauld (then Aikin) established herself as an important literary figure with her first published volume, *Poems* (1773), which went through four editions within the year. Her *Miscellaneous Pieces in Prose* (1773), some of whose essays were written by her brother,

John (four years younger than she), was also a popular and critical success. Barbauld was renowned in her time as a political pamphleteer favoring Dissenting causes, an editor, and especially a poet—such leading thinkers and writers as Samuel Taylor Coleridge, William Wordsworth, and Joseph Priestley knew and admired her—but she was most loved and found her lasting influence as a writer of pedagogical material.

Barbauld herself had an exceptional education, as she was raised with her brother and the boys at the Dissenting academy that her father, the Reverend John Aikin, had founded in a small village in Leicestershire. She was highly precocious: according to her mother, before she was three she was reading "as well as most women," and she not only learned modern languages and literatures but also was tutored by her father in Latin and Greek. When she was fifteen, her father became a classical tutor at a prominent Dissenting academy in Warrington, Lancashire, where she found much greater intellectual and social stimulation.

In 1774 she married a former Warrington student, the Reverend Rochemont Barbauld. He was offered a position as minister of a Dissenting congregation in Palgrave, Suffolk, where he opened a boarding school for boys. Its success probably owed something to Anna's literary celebrity, and she taught the youngest students; some of the school's graduates became very prominent men. She carefully corrected students' written work; she also managed school productions of Shakespeare's plays and each week produced a four-page chronicle containing verses, rhymes, games, and puzzles. In 1777 Rochemont and Anna, who had no children of their own, adopted her brother John Aikin's son Charles (the third of five children); he was the "little Charles" addressed in the four volumes of Anna Barbauld's *Lessons for Children* (1778–79), which remained widely read in the century after her death. Even more popular was her *Hymns in Prose for Children* (1881), which by 1850 had gone through more than thirty editions.

After the Barbaulds closed the school in 1785, they traveled for nearly a year on the Continent and returned to Hampstead, where Rochemont became pastor of a Dissenting congregation. There Anna began her work as an editor (including an edition of the poems of Williams Collins with a well-regarded critical essay, 1797) and produced a number of essays and poems dealing with such social themes as the slave trade and discrimination against non-Anglicans. During this time, she also collaborated with her brother on *Evenings at Home; or, The Juvenile Budget Opened* (6 vols., 1792–96), another popular work for children. In 1802 she moved again—to Stoke Newington, near her brother John and his family—perhaps because Rochemont was showing signs of the mental instability that by the end of his life (in 1808) would grow to violent insanity. There Anna concentrated primarily on editing, completing a six-volume edition of Samuel Richardson's letters (1804) and, after her husband's death, a fifty-volume series of British novels (1810). A final work aimed at children was *The Female Speaker; or, Miscellaneous Pieces in Prose and Verse* (1816), intended for the education of girls.

Lessons for Children in many ways initiated revolutionary changes in books for early readers. Perhaps most obvious, but easy for a modern reader to overlook because the innovation is now so familiar, is the size of the letters. Barbauld notes in her introduction to the first volume that earlier children's books had lacked the "*good paper, a clear and large type*, and *large spaces*" suitable for young eyes. As she points out, only those "who have actually taught young children, can be sensible how necessary these assistances are." Moreover, *Lessons* features informal conversation between mother and child, offering the beginning reader a context in which to understand words (compare the abstract, mechanical approach in *The New-England Primer*, reprinted above). Barbauld drew on her own experience to create text appropriate to the child's developmental capacity, which rises through the volumes; and her work with real children inspired other women, including Lady Eleanor Fenn (who wrote under the name Mrs. Lovechild, 1743–1813) and Maria Edgeworth (1767–1849), to venture into the business of publishing materials for the education of children.

Anna Laetitia
Barbauld

From Lessons for Children

ADVERTISEMENT

This little publication was made for a particular child, but the public is welcome to the use of it. It was found that, amidst the multitude of books professedly written for children, there is not one adapted to the comprehension of a child from two to three years old. A grave remark, or a connected story, however simple, is above his capacity; and *nonsense* is always below it; for Folly is worse than Ignorance. Another great defect is the want of *good paper, a clear and large type*, and *large spaces*. They only, who have actually taught young children, can be sensible how necessary these assistances are. The eye of a child and of a learner cannot catch, as ours can, a small, obscure, ill-formed word amidst a number of others all equally unknown to him.—To supply these deficiencies is the object of this book. The task is humble, but not mean; for to lay the first stone of a noble building, and to plant the first idea in a human mind, can be no dishonour to any hand.

BARBAULD'S LESSONS

Part I

Come hither, Charles, come to mamma.
Make haste.
Sit in mamma's lap.
Now read your book.
Where is the pin to point with?
Here is a pin.
Do not tear the book.
Only bad boys tear books.
Charles shall have a pretty new lesson.
Spell that word. Good boy.
Now go and play.
Where is puss?
Puss has got under the table.
You cannot catch puss.
Do not pull her by the tail, you hurt her.
Stroke poor puss. You stroke her the wrong way. This is the right way.
But, puss, why did you kill the rabbit?
You must catch mice: you must not kill rabbits.
Well, what do you say? Did you kill the rabbit?
Why do you not speak, puss?
Puss cannot speak.
Will Charles feed the chickens?
Here is some corn for the pigeons. Pretty pigeons!

The sun shines. Open your eyes, little boy. Get up.
Maid, come and dress Charles.
Go down stairs. Get your breakfast.
Boil some milk for a poor little hungry boy.
Do not spill the milk.
Hold the spoon in the other hand.

Do not throw your bread upon the ground.
Bread is to eat, you must not throw it away.
Corn[1] makes bread.
Corn grows in the fields.
Grass grows in the fields.
Cows eat grass, and sheep eat grass, and horses eat grass.
Little boys do not eat grass; no, they eat bread and milk.

Letters make a syllables.
Syllables make words.
Words make a sentence.
It is a pleasant thing to read well.
When you are older you shall learn to write: but you must know how to read first.
Once papa could not read, nor tell his letters.
If you learn a little every day you will soon know a great deal.
Mamma, shall I ever have learned all that there is to be learned?
No, never, if you were to live longer than the oldest man, but you may learn something
    every day.

Papa, where is Charles?
Ah! where is the little boy?
Papa cannot find him.
Lie still. Do not stir.
Ah! here he is. He is under mamma's apron.
Ride upon papa's cane.
Here is a whip. Whip away.
Make haste, horse.
I want to ride a live horse.
Saddle the horse for the little boy.
The horse prances, he tosses his head, he pricks up his ears, he starts.
Sit fast; take care he does not throw you; he ambles, he trots, he gallops. The horse
    stumbles. Down comes poor Charles in the dirt.—Hark; the huntsman's horn
    sounds.
The hounds come by with their long sweeping ears.
The horses are in a foam.
See how they break down the farmers' fences.
They leap over the ditch.
One, two, three. They are all gone over.
They are running after the hare.
Poor little hare, I believe you must be caught.
In Germany they hunt the tusky boar.

Come and give mamma three kisses. One, two, three.
Little boys must come when mamma calls them.
Blow your nose.
Here is a handkerchief.
Come and let me comb your hair.
Stand still.
Here is the comb case for you to hold.

1. I.e., wheat.

Your frock[2] is untied.
Pray clasp my shoe.
Somebody knocks at the door.
Open the door.
Come in.
Reach a chair.
Sit down.
Come to the fire.
How do you do?
Very well.
Bring some coals.
Make up the fire.
Sweep up the hearth.
Where is the brush?
Stand upon the carpet.
Do not meddle with the ink-horn.
See, you have inked your frock.
Here is a slate for you, and here is a pencil.
Now sit down on the carpet and write.
What is this red stick?
It is sealing-wax.
What is it for?
To seal letters with.
I want papa's watch.
No, you will break the glass.
You broke it once.
You may look at it.
Put it to your ear.
What does it say?
Tick, tick, tick.

Squirrels crack nuts.
Monkeys are very comical.
You are very comical sometimes.
Kittens are playful.
Old cats do not play.
Mice nibble cheese.
An old rat is in the trap.
He has fine whiskers, and a long tail.
He will bite hard, he will bite through wood.
Owls eat mice. Owls live in barns and hollow trees. "Then nightly sings the staring
    owl, To whit, To whoo."[3]
Frogs live in marshes.
Do not kill that toad, it will not hurt you.
See what a fine eye he has.
The snake has a new skin every year.
The snake lays eggs.
The snake will do you no harm.

---

2. A short garment worn by children.
3. William Shakespeare, *Love's Labour's Lost* (1594–95), 5.2. 900–901.

The viper is poisonous.
An old fox is very cunning.
The lamb is gentle.
The ass is patient.
The deer are feeding in the park.

There is a pretty butterfly.
Come, shall we catch it?
Butterfly, where are you going?
It is flown over the hedge.
He will not let us catch him.
There is a bee sucking the flowers.
Will the bee sting Charles?
No, it will not sting you if you let it alone.
Bees make wax and honey.
Honey is very sweet.
Charles shall have some honey and bread for supper.
Caterpillars eat cabbages.
Here is a poor little snail crawling up the wall.

1778–79   1834

NEW CANADIAN READERS
1881–1901

Although the reader featured below is Canadian, it closely follows the pattern of a very famous American model of the late nineteenth and early twentieth centuries: the Eclectic Readers (1836–57) designed by William Holmes McGuffey. These were the first books intended for mass instruction of beginning readers. The selections were ostensibly chosen to match the interest and abilities of children at each reading level, as ascertained by test groups.

The McGuffey readers were hugely successful in the United States through the 1920s. By then, the Elson readers (9 vols., 1909–14) written by William H. Elson for Scott, Foresman and Company were gaining ground. The publisher won market dominance when Elson began collaborating with William S. Gray in 1930 to create the Elson-Gray basal readers (i.e., reading instruction texts that gradually and with rigid control introduce limited vocabulary; outside of North America, these are known as *reading schemes*), the forerunners of the Dick and Jane series (see below).

Throughout the anglophone world, the development of beginning readers proceeded roughly in parallel. The early twentieth century was a heady time, as compulsory public education was firmly established and universal literacy seemed within grasp. It appeared possible to educate the masses into literature and culture. The table of contents of the *New Canadian Readers: 20th Century Edition* speaks to the view of education in a new century, presenting vaguely scientific pieces about nature as well as traditional folktales and fables, a prayer, and little moral stories. As the volume's preface explains, the breadth of material was designed to promote lessons "in which *children* are interested," which would "lead to a love of literature." By the middle of the century, this range had vanished, replaced by a narrow, decontextualized focus on the middle-class world of Dick and Jane. Today's first reading books never mention "love of literature" in their prefaces.

From A First Reader

PREFACE

The lessons contained in this book are a product of experience in the schoolroom. They go forth in the hope of rendering some service to teachers and to children alike.

Throughout the work, the child's point of view has been kept in mind as well as the teacher's; and the aim has been to prepare, first of all, a book which children will like to read. Every lesson centers about something in which *children* are interested. All teachers know that the labor of teaching is lessened when the interest of the pupils is assured.

The name of the Series testifies to another aim of the book,—to lead to a love of literature. Many of the stories and poems herein contained will be found again and again by the children in the world's best books. A taste for good things, developed now, will lead the pupils to demand good things when free to choose.

The value of these lessons will be greatly enhanced if the teacher reads to the children, in connection with the lessons, such selections as are suggested by the text. A good collection of poems should be in every school library to be read to the little ones by the teacher.

It is hoped that many of the poems will be memorized as well as read by the children. Thus the words, as well as the *thought*, become their possession. Nearly every lesson suggests language lessons, which the skillful teacher will readily plan in connection with the reading. For example, a study of the turtle would naturally follow the lesson on "Jack and Joe."

The pictures, as well as the lessons, have been carefully prepared or selected with reference to accepted standards and to the children's tastes. They should be studied until some appreciation of their meaning is gained. Artists' names should become as familiar to the children as are the names of poets.

Many forms of study have been indicated. The word study should demand thought, and result in added power to do independent work. The language lessons, rhyming exercises, and questions will help to form the habit of study. Attention is called to the script lessons, which present beautiful forms, as well as beautiful thoughts, for copying. They thus possess a double advantage for seat work.

Many suggestions for teaching reading will be found in the pages of a "Manual for Teachers," issued by the publishers of these Readers.

CHICKEN LITTLE

Chicken Little was in a gentleman's garden, where she had no right to be, when a rose leaf fell on her tail. Away she ran in great fright until she met Hen Pen. "O Hen Pen!" she cried, "the sky is falling."

"How do you know that?" asked Hen Pen.

"Oh! I saw it with my eyes, and I heard it with my ears, and a part of it fell on my tail."

"Let us run," said Hen Pen.

So they ran to Duck Luck.

"O Duck Luck!" cried Hen Pen, "the sky is falling."

"Pray, how do you know that?" asked Duck Luck.

"Chicken Little told me."

"How do you know that, Chicken Little?"

"Oh!" answered Chicken Little, "I saw it with my eyes, I heard it with my ears, and a part of it fell on my tail."

"Let us run," said Duck Luck.

So they ran until they came to Goose Loose.

"O Goose Loose!" cried Duck Luck, "the sky is falling."

"How do you know that, Duck Luck?"

"Hen Pen told me."

"How do you know that, Hen Pen?"

"Chicken Little told me."

"How do you know that, Chicken Little?"

"Oh! I saw it with my eyes, and I heard it with my ears, and a part of it fell on my tail."

"Let us run," said Goose Loose.

So they ran until they met Turkey Lurkey.

"O Turkey Lurkey!" cried Goose Loose, "the sky is falling."

"How do you know that, Goose Loose?"

"Duck Luck told me."

"How do you know that, Duck Luck?"

"Hen Pen told me."

"How do you know that, Hen Pen?"

"Chicken Little told me."

"How do you know that, Chicken Little?"

"Oh! I saw it with my eyes, I heard it with my ears, and part of it fell on my tail."

"Let us run to tell the Queen," said Turkey Lurkey.

So they ran with all their might, until they met Foxy Loxy.

"O Foxy Loxy!" cried Turkey Lurkey, "the sky is falling."

"How do you know that?" asked Foxy Loxy.

"Goose Loose told me."

"How do you know that, Goose Loose?"

"Duck Luck told me."

"How do you know that, Duck Luck?"

"Hen Pen told me."

"How do you know that Hen Pen?"

"Chicken Little told me."

"How do you know that Chicken Little?"

"Oh! I saw it with my eyes, I heard it with my ears, and a part of it fell on my tail."

"Come with me," said Foxy Loxy. "I will lead you to the Queen."

So Chicken Little, Hen Pen, Duck Luck, Goose Loose, and Turkey Lurkey followed Foxy Loxy, as they had been told to do.

But he led them into his den, and they never came out again.

For Study

Study the pictures in the story of Chicken Little.

What do they tell you?

What do you know about ducks? hens? geese? turkeys? foxes?

Look at the feet of the duck, hen, goose, and turkey, and see the different kinds of feet.

Which have feet alike? Why are not all alike?

1901

FUN WITH DICK AND JANE
1940

Between about 1940 and the late 1960s, most North American schoolchildren were inducted into literacy through Dick and Jane readers. This educational hegemony was made possible by the advent of large-scale curriculum development, the growth of large-scale educational publishing, and the embrace of an industrialized approach to education, premised on a scientific model.

The educational publisher Scott, Foresman and Company already had a successful series of readers by William H. Elson (7 vols., 1909–14) when they introduced the Elson-Gray readers in 1930: Elson was joined by William S. Gray, a leading specialist in reading at the University of Chicago (and later the first president of the International Reading Association, founded in 1956), to create books that would integrate pictures with a basic text—an idea put forth by Zerna Sharp, a reading consultant for the publisher who was responsible for developing the series. *The Elson-Gray Basic Pre-Primer* (1930) was repackaged in 1936 as *Dick and Jane: Elson-Gray Basic Pre-Primer,* and *Fun with Dick and Jane* appeared in 1940.

This enormously popular reading program provided what are called *basal readers* in the United States and *reading schemes* in Great Britain: scientifically designed books that ensured new readers would progress incrementally, in carefully ordered baby steps. Words were introduced in the Dick and Jane readers in a specific order, beginning with those of one syllable; they were repeated often. Texts were short and simple, offering no access to literature. The world of Dick and Jane was the idealized image of white, middle-class America in the mid–twentieth century: father in a business suit, mother in at home in an apron, children at play in an emotionally empty, shallow, repetitious life without reference to the outside world, to history, or to literature. The tight control on vocabulary led to dialogues unlike anything children would hear in real life. Growing criticism of the narrow scope of and obvious stereotyping in the Dick and Jane readers (not silenced by the introduction of African American characters in 1965), coupled with attacks on the look-say whole word methodology that underlies the series, helped lead to its retirement in 1970.

From Fun with Dick and Jane

JANE HELPS

"I can work," said Dick.
"I can help Mother."

Jane said, "I can work, too.
I can help.
Look, Dick.
This is for Father.
Father will eat here."

Jane said, "One, two, three, four.
One is for Father.
One is for Mother.
One is for Dick.
And one is for Baby Sally.
One, two, three, four.
One for Father.
One for Mother.
One for Dick.
And one for Baby Sally."

Jane said, "Look, Dick.
You may eat here."

"Oh, Jane!" said Dick.
"Where will you eat?"

"Oh, my!" said Sally.
"Where will Jane eat?"

Jane said, "One, two, three, four.
I see four in this family.
Father, Mother, Dick, and Sally.
Father is one.
Mother is two.
Dick is three.
Sally is four.
One, two, three, four."

Dick laughed and laughed.
He said, "Oh, Jane!
You are funny.
You are in this family, too.
Where will you eat?
Where is one for you?
Get one for Jane."

"Oh, oh!" laughed Jane.
"Where is one for me?
I will get one for Jane."

1940

ARNOLD LOBEL
1933–1987

According to his wife, Anita (also a children's book author and illustrator), Arnold Lobel was often praised for his gardening skills, his "success with greenery." She credits that success to his abilities not so much as a nurturer but as an editor. Any plant suffering from "vegetal droop" was "removed unceremoniously and replaced by a new and healthy specimen." Only those plants who "behaved themselves" survived in the Lobel household. The same "pleasant omnipotence" that governed Lobel as a gardener also governed his work at the drawing board, where he could be "the stage director, the costume designer and the man who pulls the curtain." If a character was not behaving, she said, he would dismiss him with a "wave" of his eraser.

Such ruthless editing helps explain the elegant grace of all Lobel's work. It was particularly important for the minimalist "I Can Read" books, a series for beginning readers (launched by Harpers in 1957) to which he often contributed. With their limited vocabularies, these books required the tight control more usually associated with verse. In deftly handling the economical and dense form, Lobel imbued his books with humor, basic truths, and much affection for his characters, who are often animals standing in for children.

The most enduring of these characters are Frog and Toad. Lobel's four collections of Frog and Toad tales—*Frog and Toad Are Friends* (1970), *Frog and Toad Together* (1972), *Frog and Toad All Year*

(1976), and *Days with Frog and Toad* (1979)—have been beloved by generations of children being initiated into the print world. They are perfect books of their kind. The spacious design, the breathing space on the page and between the lines, the soothing pastoral greens and browns of Frog and Toad—all are welcoming to new readers. And the humor is gently sophisticated and self-mocking, as it plays on serious, grown-up pastimes: doing housework, making lists, planting a garden, mailing a letter, and the like. Lobel comedically elevates the common to something worthy of literary craft and attention. In a reflective moment, Lobel once commented that if Frog and Toad have "validity and truth" as characters, it is because those qualities came out of the "validity and truth" in himself.

Lobel grew up in upstate New York, and attended the Pratt Institute in Brooklyn. There he met Anita Kempler; they married in 1955, soon after graduation, and settled in Brooklyn, initially sharing a drawing table. Lobel began by doing artwork for advertising agencies, and then illustrating others' books (he would provide the drawings for more than sixty-five in his life). His own first picture book for children soon followed, *A Zoo for Mr. Munster* (1962), and he eventually wrote more than thirty; later in his career, four of them were illustrated by his wife. After their daughter and son were born, they spent many summers in Vermont in a rented house. The children's pursuit of frogs and toads—they found that the toads, though not frogs, made good house pets—helped inspire Lobel's imagination.

The characters of Frog and Toad clearly have literary as well as domestic antecedents. They are in the long tradition of animal fables (Lobel later won the Caldecott Medal for his original collection, *Fables*, 1980). But they also recall the anthropomorphic animals found in late-nineteenth- and early-twentieth-century children's literature. Toad from Kenneth Grahame's *The Wind in the Willows* (1908) is one obvious example. More important are the creations of the two author/illustrators Lobel credits directly: Edward Lear (1812–1888) and Beatrix Potter (1866–1943). Lobel echoes Lear's sense of comic irony in the Frog and Toad books and pays direct homage to the Victorian nonsense poet in *The Book of Pigericks: Pig Limericks* (1983) and *Whiskers and Rhymes* (1985). Lobel's animal characters—like Potter's rabbits and kittens, and her frog, Jeremy Fisher—are not cute or at all cuddly. They display a full range of human emotions and foibles. And their simple adventures, which emphasize the centrality of friendship, make them equally timeless.

Lobel was just fifty-four when he died. Never static, his work evolved throughout his twenty-seven-year career, repeatedly demonstrating his originality and versatility. A fitting epitaph is probably his last limerick in *Pigericks*:

> There was an old pig with a pen
> Who had finished his work once again.
> Then he quietly?
> With his comfortable cat . . .
> While he rested his brushes and pen.

From Frog and Toad Are Friends

THE LETTER

Toad was sitting on his front porch.
Frog came along and said,
"What is the matter, Toad?
You are looking sad."

"Yes," said Toad.
"This is my sad time of day.
It is the time.
when I wait for the mail to come.
It always makes me very unhappy."
"Why is that?" asked Frog.
"Because I never get any mail,"
said Toad.

"Not ever?" asked Frog.

"No, never," said Toad.
"No one has ever sent me a letter.
Every day my mailbox is empty.
That is why waiting for the mail
is a sad time for me."
Frog and Toad sat on the porch,
feeling sad together.

Then Frog said, "I have to go home now, Toad.
There is something that I must do."
Frog hurried home.
He found a pencil
and a piece of paper.
He wrote on the paper.

He put the paper in an envelope.
On the envelope he wrote
"A LETTER FOR TOAD."
Frog ran out of his house.
He saw a snail that he knew.
"Snail," said Frog, "please take
this letter to Toad's house
and put it in his mailbox."
"Sure," said the snail. "Right away."

Then Frog ran back to Toad's house.
Toad was in bed, taking a nap.
"Toad," said Frog,
"I think you should get up
and wait for the mail some more."
"No," said Toad,
"I am tired of waiting for the mail."

Frog looked out of the window
at Toad's mailbox.
The snail was not there yet.
"Toad," said Frog, "you never know
when someone may send you a letter."
"No, no," said Toad. "I do not think
anyone will ever send me a letter."

Frog looked out of the window.
The snail was not there yet.
"But, Toad," said Frog,
"someone may send you a letter today."
"Don't be silly," said Toad.
"No one has ever sent me
a letter before, and no one
will send me a letter today."

Frog looked out of the window.
The snail was still not there.
"Frog, why do you keep looking
out of the window?" asked Toad.
"Because now I am waiting
for the mail," said Frog.
"But there will not be any," said Toad.

"Oh, yes there will," said Frog,
"because I have sent you a letter."
"You have?" said Toad.
"What did you write in the letter?"
Frog said, "I wrote
'Dear Toad, I am glad
that you are my best friend.
Your best friend, Frog.'"

"Oh," said Toad,
"that makes a very good letter."
Then Frog and Toad went out
onto the front porch
to wait for the mail.
They sat there,
feeling happy together.

Frog and Toad waited a long time.
Four days later
the snail got to Toad's house
and gave him the letter from Frog.
Toad was very pleased to have it.

1970

From Frog and Toad Together

A LIST

One morning Toad sat in bed.
"I have many things to do," he said.
"I will write them
all down on a list
so that I can remember them."
Toad wrote on a piece of paper:

A List of things to do today

Then he wrote:

Wake up

"I have done that," said Toad,
and he crossed out:

~~Wake up~~

Then Toad wrote other things
on the paper.

A List
of things to do
today

~~Wake up~~
Eat Breakfast
Get Dressed
Go to Frog's House
Take walk with Frog
Eat lunch
Take nap
Play games with Frog
Eat Supper
Go To Sleep

"There," said Toad.
"Now my day

is all written down."
He got out of bed
and had something to eat.
Then Toad crossed out:

~~Eat Breakfast~~

Toad took his clothes
out of the closet
and put them on.
Then he crossed out:

~~Get Dressed~~

Toad put the list in his pocket.

He opened the door
and walked out into the morning.
Soon Toad was at Frog's front door.
He took the list from his pocket
and crossed out:

~~Go to Frog's House~~

Toad knocked at the door.
"Hello," said Frog.
"Look at my list
of things to do,"
said Toad.
"Oh," said Frog,
"that is very nice."
Toad said, "My list tells me
that we will go
for a walk."
"All right," said Frog.
"I am ready."

Frog and Toad
went on a long walk.
Then Toad took the list
from his pocket again.
He crossed out:

~~Take walk with Frog~~

Just then there was a strong wind.
It blew the list
out of Toad's hand.
The list blew high up
into the air.

"Help!" cried Toad.
"My list is blowing away.
What will I do without my list?"

"Hurry!" said Frog.
"We will run and catch it."
"No!" shouted Toad.
"I cannot do that."
"Why not?" asked Frog.
"Because," wailed Toad,
"running after my list
is not one of the things
that I wrote
on my list of things to do!"

Frog ran after the list.
He ran over hills and swamps,
but the list blew on and on.
At last Frog came back to Toad.
"I am sorry," gasped Frog,
"but I could not catch
your list."
"Blah," said Toad.

"I cannot remember any of the things
that were on my list of things to do.
I will just have to sit here
and do nothing," said Toad.
Toad sat and did nothing.
Frog sat with him.
After a long time Frog said,
"Toad, it is getting dark.
We should be going to sleep now."

"Go to sleep!" shouted Toad.
"That was the last thing on my list!"
Toad wrote on the ground
with a stick:

Go to sleep

Then he crossed out:

~~Go to sleep~~

"There," said Toad.
"Now my day
is all crossed out!"
"I am glad,"
said Frog.
Then Frog and Toad
went right to sleep.

1972

TEXTS AND CONTEXTS

Writing

———————————————

Homesick: My Own Story (1982), an autobiographical novel by Jean Fritz (reprinted in the Life Writing section below), contains a scene in which Fritz describes a penmanship lesson on her first day in the eighth grade of a Pennsylvania school in the late 1920s. She'd returned there with her American missionary parents after her early education at a British school in China. Fritz had been proud of her "straight and even" handwriting, which she saw as "round and neat and happy-looking." But her new teacher demanded that she use the Palmer method, devised by A. N. Palmer (1859–1927). Palmer, a teacher and founder of the magazine *The Western Penman* (1884–1900), observed that clerks who wrote quickly and tirelessly appeared to form their letters with little or no motion of the fingers. He believed this "muscular movement" writing could be taught be accustoming the muscles to the proper habit: he thus developed exercises to teach these techniques (for example, the repeated practice of drawing large loops rather than letters). Fritz was dismayed at the results: the oversized, sober-looking letters, slanting to the right, looked as if when "you pulled one letter out of a word . . . the rest would topple over like a row of dominoes."

By the time Fritz was learning the Palmer method of penmanship in the early twentieth century, the quest for a looser, faster handwriting model had been under way for about a hundred years. The Palmer method was in fact the new and improved replacement for Spencerian penmanship, a sloping, semiangular style devised by Platt R. Spencer (1800–1864), which had dominated much of the second part of the nineteenth century. Spencer was a marketing genius. He had combined his new technique for a faster "hand" for business writing with the promotion of his new business colleges. His system of penmanship dominated American business for much of the nineteenth century.

Though today's schoolchildren are still taught handwriting, in the twenty-first century, accurate and fast keyboarding is clearly more valued than elegant penmanship. Yet historically it is important to remember how critical a skill handwriting was in the history of civilization, not just before the inventions of the typewriter and the computer, but before the invention of the printing press in the mid-fifteenth century.

In the Middle Ages, all books had to be copied out by hand; this labor-intensive, specialized occupation was, for the most part, monopolized by the clergy. Even after the invention of the printing press, the increasing availability of printed books, and the consequent sharp rise in literacy rates, penmanship remained a highly regarded vocational skill, one that was increasingly required by a rising mercantile class engaged in international trade. Professional clerks were needed to keep accounts and manage correspondence. The changes in handwriting styles at least partly reflected changes in the production of paper and writing implements themselves.

Vellum gave way to paper made out of rags and ultimately to the paper we know made primarily out of wood pulp. Feather quills had to be sharpened repeatedly into a tip. Metal nibs had to be dipped frequently into ink. Fountain pens with internal reservoirs required refilling. And ink had to be made. Here is an early nineteenth-century recipe for ink published by Ezra Eastman of Hopkinton, New Hampshire:

Take 1 quart soft water on boil
¼ lb chips logwood in it for half an hour
pour it off while boiling in
¼ pound Nut Galls and ½ oz Pomegranate peels
Stir well the whole with a wooden spatula
Set in summer sun or in a warm place for 3 or 4 days.
Stir the mixture often
Add ¼ pound green vitriol. Let it stand for 4 or 5 days.
Stir it frequently and then add
1 oz. gum Arabic dissolved in
½ pint boiling water.
After a few days strain it off from the dregs and keep well stopped for use. Add pearl
ashes to keep it from moulding and if you please a little spirits wine.*

Because so much technical knowledge was required to produce written text, there
is a long history of the pedagogy of writing instruction. Some schools, like the Writing
School founded in 1694 within Christ's Hospital, London (founded in 1552), specialized in teaching children to become professional scribes. Writing masters taught
children the art of penmanship in several identifiable hands (the term used to
describe a style of handwriting), each used for a specific purpose: so a court hand
was used for official documents, a secretary hand for accounts, and so on. By the
eighteenth century, both in England and in the United States, several books about
commercial handwriting were in circulation. The most famous was probably *The
Universal Penman: Penmanship Made Easy* (1743) by George Bickham. Five typical
styles of handwriting were designated as Round Hand, Italian Hand, the Flourishing
Alphabet, Print Hand, and Gothic Secretary. Other terms for descriptions of handwriting styles included Italic, Ornamental, and Old English, which appears to be
much like script described as Gothic and German. The term "a running hand" was
often used to describe a style in which letters could be joined to each other—as
opposed to something slower in which letters are kept separate from each other, as
in the style of printing still first taught to young children. One running hand was
even touted as being suitable for "business and social needs" as well as being suitable
for "ladies and others of limited capacity."† As recently as the nineteenth century,
large numbers of clerks or scriveners, like the title character of Herman Melville's
"Bartleby the Scrivener" (1853), spent their working lives copying business documents. The samples from the nineteenth-century copybooks that follow offer a
glimpse of the range of styles taught to children and the kinds of proverbial messages
they used as practice. One popular maxim (not represented here) was "Your hand is
your fortune if well you can write."

Besides being a vocational skill, writing was also—in the days before e-mail—an
essential art at all levels of society. Letter writing was a social accomplishment, and
children received direct instruction in how to do it well—as the examples included
by both Newbery and Carroll demonstrate. Carroll himself, incidentally, was a prodigious letter writer and had a careful, complicated filing system for keeping track of
his correspondence.

The publication of the collected letters of famous people, especially authors and
politicians, and the sense that letters could be an art form in themselves, must have

*From Ray Nash, *American Penmanship, 1800–1850* (1969).
†Nash 9.

inspired generations of children. The epistolary novel, which arose in the eighteenth century, developed in a cultural climate that valued letter writing itself as an art form. Samuel Richardson's epistolary novels *Pamela* (1740–41) and *Clarissa* (1747–48) were popular English examples. *Les Liaisons dangereuses* (1782) by Laclos was popular in France and was ultimately made into a stylish period film, in English, in 1988.

In an age of laptop computers in classrooms, e-mail, and text-messaging, the arts of both handwriting and letter writing seem cumbersome and quaint. The style of handwriting still most frequently taught in North American schools (see sample) comes out of the form developed in 1888 by Charles Paxton Zaner (1864–1918), who founded the Zanerian College of Penmanship in Columbus, Ohio, teaching ornamental and business writing. In 1891 he was joined in this venture by another skilled penman, Elmer Ward Bloser (1865–1929), and by 1895 the college had become the Zaner-Bloser Company. In 1904 Zaner-Bloser published *The Zaner Method of Arm Movement* to teach children a simplified style of writing matched to their still developing level of fine motor control. The inane twenty-first-century practice samples (see "Happy Hippos") seem unlikely to provide the impetus necessary to tune children to the elegant possibilities of prose writing that inspired children of earlier generations.

WRITING SHEET
1809

In the same way that girls stitched samplers to demonstrate their accomplished needlework, middle- and upper-class children of both sexes produced equivalent samplers of their handwriting. The writing sheet on the following page, with its border of scenes from Cinderella, was probably, judging from the December 19, 1809, date, given as a Christmas gift by young John Ellyatt to his parents that year. This sheet was printed and sold by Langley & Belch, 173 High Street, Borough, London, and by Champante & Wittrow, Jewry Street, Aldgate.

Writing sheets—large sheets of paper, blank in the center with decorative borders, sometimes colored—had been printed by publishing companies as early as the seventeenth century. Children were supposed to fill the blank spaces with examples of their best handwriting: sometimes they wrote an alphabet, sometimes they copied a prayer or a phrase of proverbial wisdom or, as on this sheet, an admonition to children to obey their parents. Extant examples of completed sheets often, touchingly, display the child's carefully made corrections. Whereas misplaced or botched stitches can be ripped out of a needlework sampler and fully corrected, an inked error is impossible to erase.

Writing sheet, 1809

THE COPYBOOK
nineteenth century

Because accounts and ledgers were handwritten, penmanship was important well into the nineteenth century. In the pages of a copybook excerpted here, an English child named Joseph Crocott practiced various styles of handwriting in 1850. "Happiness is desired by all," for example, is written in both a Running hand and a Gothic script. Children might have learned to write chancery, italic, copperplate, or secretary hands as well. The different kinds of scripts required specific pens, which had to be held in particular ways. The maxims copied typically were timeless aphorisms or received wisdom. On the cover of Crocott's copybook, the publisher placed a reproduction of a treadmill—a punishment for prisoners, described as a "terror to evildoers." Here it seems to warn students of their possible fate should they fail to apply themselves.

What speaks to schoolchildren across the centuries, however, is the caricature at the end of another nineteenth-century copybook: a ghoulish, beak-faced figure reaching greedily for a bag of guineas (gold coins worth 21 shillings each).

Gain stimulates ambition

Gain stimulates ambition

Gain stimulates ambition

Gain stimulates ambi

Gain stimulates ambi

Joseph Groiott 1550.

Put trust in God.

Put trust in God.

Put trust in God.

Put trust in God.

Put trust in God.

Joseph Groiott 1550

Guineas

THE TREAD MILL.

THIS "terror to evil-doers" is now introduced into most of the prisons in the kingdom; the wheel is similar to a common water-wheel; the tread-boards upon its circumference are of considerable length, so as to allow of standing room for a row of from ten to twenty persons; the weight of the culprits forms the first moving power of the machine, and produces the greatest effect when applied upon the circumference of the wheel at or near the level of its axle; to secure therefore this mechanical advantage, a screen of boards is fixed up in an inclined position above the wheel, in order to prevent the prisoners from stepping up higher than the level required: a hand-rail is seen fixed upon this screen, by holding which, they retain their upright position upon the revolving wheel. By means of steps, the gang ascends at one end, and when the requisite number range themselves upon the wheel, it commences its revolution; the effort then to each individual is that of ascending an endless flight of steps: each prisoner gradually advances from the end at which he mounted towards the opposite end of the wheel, from whence the last man, taking his turn, descends for rest for a few minutes, another prisoner immediately mounting, as before, to fill up the number, without stopping the machine. The wheel, five feet diameter, revolves twice in a minute, and the space stepped over by each culprit is 2193 feet per hour. By an excellent contrivance, when the machinery has attained its proper speed, certain balls rise, so as to draw a box out of the reach of a bell-handle, which will then cease to ring a bell, placed in a convenient situation for that purpose; but should the prisoners slacken their speed, the balls descend, and a projecting pin on the box, striking a handle, will continue to ring the bell till they go on again properly; and the taskmaster is apprised, even at a distance, that the full work is not performed: the labour is very fatiguing.

Cover of copybook belonging to Joseph Crocott, Chorlton School (1850).

HAPPY HIPPOS
twenty-first century

This page from *Homework Helpers: Beginning Cursive Writing, Grade* 3, sold in the twenty-first century by Frank Schaffer Publications, features letter forms in the Zaner-Bloser style. The moral phrases characteristic of earlier copy books have been replaced by a string of *h* words connected in a cheerful nonsense sentence lacking any ethical, moral, or religious resonance.

abcdefghijklmnopqrstuvwxyz

H H H H

h h h h

Happy hippos hang in their hammocks.

JOHN NEWBERY
1713–1767

The publisher John Newbery excelled at collecting materials that could be assembled cheaply and attractively to be marketed to prospective buyers of instructional materials for children. Letter writing was an important skill, and members of the growing middle class in the eighteenth and nineteenth centuries were eager for manuals that would help explain its very elaborate, formal codes. Newbery offered *Letters on the Most Common, as Well as* *Important, Occasions in Life: By Cicero, Pliny, Voiture, Balzac, St. Euremont, Locke, Ld. Lansdowne, Temple, Dryden, Garth, Pope, Gay, Swift, Rowe, and other writers of distinguish'd merit . . . with proper directions for addressing persons of rank and eminence for the use of young gentlemen and ladies* (1757). Anne Boleyn's plea to Henry VIII, included here, is a poignant example of an "important" letter.

From Letters on the Most Common, as Well as Most Important, Occasions in Life

TO THE

PARENTS,

GUARDIANS,

AND

GOVERNESSES,

IN

Great Britain and *Ireland,*

THIS

Collection of Letters

Is humbly Inscribed,

BY

Their most obedient Servant,

JOHN NEWBERY.

THE PREFACE

The editor of the following sheets has selected from our most admired English authors, and the best translations we have of the Classics and the French writers, a series of letters, which he apprehends will be not only useful to our youth of both sexes, but also afford some entertainment to those of age and experience: more especially as he has been particularly careful to select those Letters that are esteemed for their natural ease and elegance of style, or that are replete with sentiment, and fraught with the knowledge of mankind. Besides, the young student has here, for his practice and improvement, many examples from great men in view, all of them good, though not equally so, and he may form his style and manner upon the model of that author who pleases him best.

To render this volume of letters the more complete, and that there may be something said suitable to every circumstance in life, the author has added a great number of original letters, mostly his own, and wrote for this purpose, which he hopes will be found useful to the reader.

INSTRUCTIONS FOR EPISTOLARY WRITING

To take up the reader's time in expatiating on the necessity of teaching youth to write letters, would be absurd and ridiculous; its usefulness is allowed on all hands; for *epistolary writing* enters so much into the common concerns of life, that there is no doing without it. Our business, therefore, is to point out to the reader the method by which a proficiency in this art may be best obtained: and that is, by imitating very frequently, and with due attention, the letters of those who have been most celebrated and distinguished for this species of writing. In conformity to this opinion, we have selected, from our most admired writers, this little volume, as so many examples for the young student's practice and improvement: among these, he will also find original letters on various subjects which however inferior to the rest in point of style and sentiment, will be found useful to the youth of both sexes, who may, perhaps, be glad to know how others have handled the subjects about which they have occasion to write.

Besides this book, the young student would do well to read such authors as may tend to form his style, and those especially are to be selected for the purpose, that are remarkable for their purity of language, and elegant easiness of expression. We have had several works of this kind published lately, which justly deserves the reader's consideration, and among the rest, due regard, I think, should be paid to the letters that bear the name of *Fitzosborn*, to those between Mr. *Pope* and his friends that are written on familiar subjects, and to the translations we have lately had of the epistles of *Cicero* and *Pliny*.[1] But above all, let me recommend the *Spectators*[2] to his frequent perusal.

Ease, elegance, perspicuity and correctness are admirably blended in the essays of Mr. *Addison*;[3] and, after reading this little book and those I have mentioned, nothing, perhaps, can be recommended to young persons, that is so likely to polish their style, as his pieces that are scattered through the several volumes of the *Spectators*, and marked at the bottom with some one of these letters—C. L. I. O.[4] There is a happiness in Mr. *Addison's* manner, that is not to be described, but which, perhaps, may be attained, by making him your constant companion.

Those who keep polite company acquire, as it were naturally, an air of politeness. They speak correctly, and with a becoming boldness, ease and freedom: and so it is in writing; those who constantly read polite, correct, and elegant authors, will acquire not only their manner of expression, but, in some measure, their manner of thinking; and notwithstanding the numerous tracts that have been written on *style*, there is in

---

1. Pliny the Younger (ca. 61–ca. 112 C.E.), Roman administrator and author of nine books of literary letters. Fitzosborn: Sir Thomas Fitzosborne, the pseudonym of William Melmoth (ca. 1710–1799), who both published his own letters and translated the letters of a number of Roman writers. Alexander Pope (1688–1744), English poet whose works include a number of verse epistles in imitation of Horace; his own letters began to be published before his death. Marcus Tullius Cicero (106–43 B.C.E.), statesman and rhetorician, generally held to be the greatest Roman orator; more than 900 of

his letters to his friends and brother survive.
2. Issues of a journal, written almost entirely by Joseph Addison and Richard Steele, that appeared daily except Sundays between March 1, 1711, and December 6, 1712 (Addison revived it briefly, June 18–December 29, 1714); *The Spectator* provided the model of the periodical essay.
3. Joseph Addison (1672–1719), English playwright, essayist, and critic. He wrote most of the *Spectator* essays.
4. Each *Spectator* essay ended with an initial; those signed with C, L, I, or O were Addison's.

reality no acquiring a good one, by any rules whatever, nor is it to be obtained in any other manner, than by conversing with polite company, who speak correctly, and by frequently reading the best authors, Read, therefore, Mr. *Addison* again and again; make him your constant companion; and never leave him, till you have obtained a due portion of his elegance and ease. And though some of his essays, those especially on the pleasures of imagination, and the subject of criticism, are wrote in a more elevated style, than the familiarity of an epistle will admit of, yet there are others in abundance, which, though replete with character, and charged with the manners and humours of mankind, are nevertheless as familiar and easy, as if wrote from one friend to another, about any matter of the least concern. The following account of the behaviour of Sir *Roger de Coverly*[5] at church, is, I think, a proof of what I have asserted, and may serve as an example of his manner of writings.

"I am always very well pleased with a country *Sunday*, and think, if keeping holy the seventh day were only a human institution, it would be the best method that could have been thought of for the polishing and civilizing of mankind. It is certain, the country people would soon degenerate into a kind of savages and barbarians, were there not such frequent returns of a stated time, in which the whole village meet together with their best faces and in their cleanliest habits, to converse with one another, upon different subjects, hear their duties explained to them, and join together in adoration of the Supreme Being. *Sunday* clears away the rust of the whole week, not only as it refreshes in their minds the notions of religion, but as it puts both sexes upon appearing in their most agreeable forms, and exerting all such qualities as are apt to give them a figure[6] in the eye of the village. A country fellow distinguishes himself as much in the *church-yard*, as a citizen does upon the *Exchange*,[7] the whole parish-politics being generally discussed in that place, either after sermon, or before the bell rings.

"My friend, Sir ROGER, being a good church-man, has beautified the inside of his church with several texts of his own chusing. He has likewise given an handsome pulpit-cloth, and railed in the communion-table at his own expence. He has often told me, that at his coming to his estate, he found his parishioners very irregular; and that in order to make them kneel and join in the responses, he gave every one of them a hassock[8] and a common-prayer-book; and at the same time employed an itinerant singing-master, who goes about the country for that purpose, to instruct them rightly in the tunes of the Psalms: upon which they now very much value themselves, and indeed out-do most of the country churches that I have ever heard.

"As Sir ROGER is landlord to the whole congregation, he keeps them in very good order, and will suffer no-body to sleep in it besides himself; for if by chance he has been surprized into a short nap at sermon, upon recovering out of it, he stands up, and looks about him, and if he sees any body else nodding, either wakes them himself, or sends his servants to them. Several other of the old knights particularities break out upon these occasions. Sometimes he will be lengthening out a verse in the singing-psalms, half a minute after the rest of the congregation have done with it; sometimes when he is pleased with the matter of his devotion, he pronounces *Amen*, three or four times to the same prayer; and sometimes stands up, when every body else is upon their knees, to count the congregation, or see if any of his tenants are

5. A character invented by Addison to represent the type of the country gentleman; the following essay appeared in *The Spectator*, no. 112 (July 9, 1711).
6. A good appearance.

7. The Royal Exchange, founded as a center of commerce in London in 1565; it was located between Cornhill and Threadneedle Street.
8. A cushion for kneeling.

missing. I was yesterday very much surprized to hear my old friend, in the midst of the service, calling out to one *John Matthews*, to mind what he was about, and not disturb the congregation. This *John Matthews*, it seems, is remarkable for being an idle fellow, and, at that time, was kicking his heels for his diversion. This authority of the knight, though exerted in that odd manner which accompanies him in all circumstances of life, has a very good effect upon the parish, who are not polite[9] enough to see any thing ridiculous in his behaviour; besides that, the general good sense, and worthiness of his character, makes his friends observe these little singularities, as foils that rather set off than blemish his good qualities.

"As soon as the sermon is finished, no body presumes to stir, till Sir ROGER is gone out of the church. The knight walks down from his seat in the chancel, between a double row of his tenants, that stand bowing to him, on each side; and every now and then, enquires after such a one's wife, or mother, or son, or father do, whom he does not see at church; which is understood as a secret reprimand to the person that is absent. The chaplain has often told me, that upon a catechising day, when Sir ROGER has been pleased with a boy that answers well, he has ordered a bible to be given him, next day, for his encouragement; and sometimes accompanies it with a flitch of bacon to his mother. Sir ROGER has likewise added five pounds a year to the clerk's place; and that he may encourage the young fellows to make themselves perfect in the Church-service, has promised upon the death of the present incumbent, who is very old, to bestow it according to merit. The fair understanding between Sir ROGER and his chaplain, and their mutual concurrences in doing good, is the more remarkable, because the very next village is famous for the differences and contentions that arise between the Parson and the 'Squire, who live in a perpetual state of war. The Parson is always preaching at the 'Squire, and the 'Squire, to be revenged on the parson, never comes to church. The 'Squire has made all his tenants Atheists and tithe-stealers:[1] whilst the parson instructs them every Sunday, in the dignity of his order, and insinuates to them, in almost every sermon, that he is a better man than his patron. In short, matters are come to such an extremity, that the 'Squire has not said his prayers either in publick or private, this half year; and that the parson threatens him, if he does not mend his manners, to pray for him in the face of the whole congregation. Feuds of this nature, though too frequent in the country, are very fatal to the ordinary people; who are so used to be dazzled with riches, that they pay as much deference to the understanding of a man of an estate, as of a man of learning; and are very hardly brought to regard any truth, how important soever it may be, that is preached to them, when they know there are several men of five hundred a year,[2] who do not believe it."

Now, though there is character, humour, and a knowledge of mankind displayed in this piece, yet every thing is easy and elegant, gentle and familiar, nor is there a figurative expression in the whole essay, except *clearing away the rust of the week*, and *giving them a figure in the eye of the village*; and those are so aptly applied, and fall in so naturally with the subject, that the sense is as evident, even to an illiterate person, as if it was conveyed in a downright country phrase.

But figures are not wholly to be excluded from epistles any more than from *conversation*. For they are a sort of coin, without which, the commerce of conversation, either literary or verbal, cannot be carried on. The most ignorant people make use

---

9. Refined.
1. Because the tenants do not attend services, they do not pay the tithe (10 percent of their income)

due to the church.
2. I.e., with incomes of £500 a year.

of figures (though unknowingly) in their intercourse with each other, and very often, those of the most dignified kind. Figures are the language of the heart. They are a sort of wings, with which nature has furnished the passions to convey themselves the more forcibly, and are therefore not to be so scrupulously avoided, as the critics have insinuated: for the language of nature can never be unnatural.

The objection they would make, seems to lie here. *Epistolary Writing* should be as much as possible like conversation; for 'tis supposed you are writing those very sentiments to an absent person, cloathed in the same, or nearly the same language, in which you would deliver them if he was present. Whence it will follow, that the style of a letter, if natural, must depend on the disposition of mind the writer is in, and the subject he is upon.

Was I writing to a man in the height of passion, who had done me a great injury, nobody, I suppose, would condemn my letter as unnatural, because it contained some figurative expressions, which nature herself had there imprinted to express the violent agitation of my mind. Nor would a merchant, deeply in love, be condemned, for not writing to his mistress in the same easy, unaffecting strain, as he wrote to his correspondent for a few bales of goods: since, if the mistress and correspondent were both present, they would be addressed in a very different manner, and with a style not altogether similar.

But when we are told that *Epistolary Writing* should be like conversation, we are not to suppose that it is the conversation of the illiterate and vulgar, but, as much as possible, like that of the learned and polite; for it would be inverting the order of things, and debasing human nature, to make the gentleman and scholar speak and write like the plowman.

Some critics, while they are intent on leading others, *mislead* themselves. Instead of setting up nature as a standard, they pervert her order, and change her course. Things with them must have a perpetual sameness, and nature is to buckle to the sturdy precepts of *Aristotle*[3] and his followers. What a clamour have we had about what constitutes a perfect tragedy, and what invectives have been thrown out against the tragi-comedies of *Shakespeare*[4] and others? When, after all, if you consult nature, she will tell you, that, these last are the most perfect pictures of human life; for we very often hear the servants merry, when their masters are sad, and see the parlour in tears, while gambols are going forward in the kitchen. And in a state divided by parties, this will always be the case; for the downfal of one will prove the exaltation of the other. This, however, by way of digression.——We shall now return to our subject, give the young student a few general rules, and conclude.

We have already observed, that letter-writing is but a sort of epistolary conversation, and that you are to write to the person absent, in the manner you would speak to him, if present. The best and only way to do this, and to avoid being unnatural and affected, is, for the writer, after he has duly considered the subject he is upon, and formed the letter in his mind, to sit down and write it immediately, in the words that nature dictates to him, neither hunting after elegant phrases, nor rejecting them, if they naturally occur. They mistake, who suppose that perspicuity depends on expression only; 'tis rather a character of the thought; for he who thinks clearly, will generally write so; but if there be a confusion in the head, perspicuity will never flow from the pen. Accustom yourself, therefore, to think justly, and then let your words

3. Greek philosopher and rhetorician (384–322 B.C.E.); his precepts on poetry and drama, the *Poetics,* greatly influenced eighteenth-century critics.
4. Those who believed in strictly defined genres attacked "mixed" forms such as William Shakespeare's late tragicomedies (e.g., *The Winter's Tale,* 1609).

follow one another from the pen, as they would from your tongue, if you were speaking upon some subject, with which you were perfectly well acquainted, and to a person, whose abilities you thought not superior to your own. This sort of confidence prevents the mind from being disturbed by that diffidence which generally attends men of merit, and which often obscures and envelopes the rich talents they possess; for what is done with pain, is seldom done with grace.

Though you ought to write down your thoughts in the first words that occur, I would not have you neglect a careful revisal of them, when the whole letter is finished. I say, when your letter is finished, because, was you to attempt this sooner, and offer to substitute one word for another, or vary the phrase in the course of your writing, you would probably break in upon your thought, lose the beauty of your sentence, and make that stiff, affected and obscure, that would be otherwise natural, easy, and clear. But when you have thus penned down your thoughts, it would be injustice to yourself, and an affront to the person you address, not to revise the language, and make what alternations are necessary. If your correspondent is a person of understanding, he will not be displeased with an erasement, and if there should be too many (which cannot be the case, if you accustom yourself to this regular manner of deliberately thinking and writing) you may then transcribe your letter, and send a fair copy, which is better than exposing yourself, and affronting your friend, by offering him a bundle of inaccuracies.

But as I have already observed, there is no obtaining a natural, easy style, and a graceful manner, either of writing or speaking, but by practice; custom overcomes many difficulties.—The young student, therefore, should in this, imitate the rules laid down by the most eminent painters, and both read and write something every day, till he has acquired a proficiency in the art. Nor need he ever be afraid of writing too well, if what he writes is natural, and to the purpose. The observation of a certain eminent author, *That letters which pass between familiar friends, if written as they should be, can scarce ever be fit to see the light,* will upon examination be found erroneous; for we daily hear gentlemen speak correctly and elegantly in company, upon almost any subject, without the appearance of affectation; and is it any matter of wonder, that men of great abilities should write in that manner? In short, both speaking and writing, if a man is not over diffident, and has the requisite talents, may be acquired by practice, founded upon a few good rules, to a greater degree of perfection and with more ease than is generally imagined.

With regard to the manner, form, and superscription of letters, the following rules may be observed.

When you write to a person of consequence, let it be on gilt paper, and close it in a cover, and not write the superscription on the letter itself; unless it be to go by the post, in which case, it will be necessary to save expence.[5]

Begin your letter at a good distance from the top of the paper, and if you have compliments to send to any of the family, or to your correspondent's friends, insert them in the body of the letter, and not in the postscript, as is too frequently done; for the placing of them there, betrays an inattention to your friends, and intimates that you had almost forgot them.

It is usual with polite people to sign their names at a considerable distance from the bottom of their letter, which is a needless and useless compliment; and, as it may expose the writer to some difficulties, I would have him avoid it, and sign his name

---

5. Until the nineteenth century, the recipient paid the cost of mailing letters, which depended on the number of sheets as well as the distance sent.

immediately under, and nearly close to the latter part of the letter; for when it is set at so great a distance, if the paper should fall into bad hands, that part may be taken off, and a promissory note wrote over the name, and the person obliged to pay it; for the hand-writing can be proved, which supposes the value received; and who, in this case, can prove a negative? This caution may likewise serve for members of parliament, who frank letters for their friends.[6]

The first letter in any title, as also the personal pronoun, if you are writing to any one of eminence and distinction, should begin with a capital.

You should not be too particular in the superscription of your letters to those who are well known, for it is in some measure an affront, as it supposes the person not to be conspicuous.

These rules I thought proper to fix to the terms of address, as they have not hitherto been taken notice of in any book that I have seen. The following are what are generally inserted in books of this kind, which, therefore, are here placed in their usual form.

How to address persons of distinction, either in writing or discourse.

To the ROYAL FAMILY

To the King's most excellent Majesty, *Sir,* or, *may it please your Majesty.*

To his royal highness George, Prince of Wales,[7] *Sir,* or, *may it please your royal Highness.*

In the same manner to the rest of the royal family; altering the addresses according to the different rank and degrees of dignity.

To the NOBILITY

To his Grace A. Duke of S. *my Lord Duke,* or, *may it please your Grace,* or, *your Grace.*

To the most honourable G. Lord Marquiss of H. *my Lord Marquiss, your Lordship.*

To the right hon. A. Earl of B. *my Lord, your Lordship.*

To the right hon. C. Lord Viscount D. *my Lord, your Lordship.*

To the right hon. E. Lord F. *my Lord, your Lordship.*

The *ladies* are addressed according to the rank of their husbands.

The sons of Dukes, Marquisses, and the eldest sons of Earls, have, by courtesy of *England,* the title of *Lord,* and *right honourable*; and the title of *Lady* and right honourable is given to all their daughters.

But the youngest sons of Earls, are only *honourable* and *Esquires.*

The sons of *Viscounts* and *Barons* are stiled *Esquires,* and *honourable,* and their daughters are directed to, *The honourable Mrs.* A. B. but without any other stile; and they have rank among the first gentry, without title.

The title of *honourable* is likewise conferred on certain persons who have the king's commission, and upon those gentlemen who enjoy places of trust and honour; and every considerable servant to the king, upon the civil or military list, or to any of the royal family, is stiled *Esquire, pro tempore.*

The title of *right honourable* is given to no Commoners, excepting those who are members of his Majesty's most honourable privy-council, and to the three Lord-

---

6. Members of Parliament could send mail free of charge within the country.

7. I.e., the future George III (1738–1820; r. 1760–1820).

mayors, *viz.* of *London, York,* and *Dublin,* and the Lord-provost of *Edinburgh,* during their office.

To the PARLIAMENT

To the right honourable the Lords spiritual and temporal, in parliament of *Great Britain* assembled, *my Lords,* or, *may it please your Lordships.*

To the honourable the Knights, Citizens, and Burgesses in parliament of *Great Britain* assembled, *Gentlemen,* or *may it please your Honours.*

To *the right honourable* C. D. Speaker of the honourable house of Commons, who is generally one of his Majesty's most honourable privy-council, *Sir.*

To the CLERGY

To the most reverend father in God Thomas,[8] Lord Archbishop of Canterbury, *my Lord,* or, *your Grace.*

To the right reverend father in God W. Lord Bishop of S. *my Lord, your Lordship.*

To the right reverend Lord Bishop of G. Lord almoner to his Majesty, *my Lord, your Lordship.*

To the reverend Mr. (or Doctor, if the degree of doctor has been taken) A. B. dean of C. or archdeacon, or chancellor of D. or prebendary, &c. *Mr. Dean, Mr. Archdeacon, reverend Sir,* &c.

All Rectors, Vicars, Curates, Lecturers, and clergymen of all denominations, are stiled *reverend.*

To the Officers of his MAJESTY'S *Houshold*

They are for the most part addressed according to their rank and quality, though sometimes agreeably to the nature of their office, as, *my Lord Steward, my Lord Chamberlain, Mr. Vice Chamberlain,* &c. and in all superscriptions of letters, which relate to gentlemens employments, their stile of office should never be omitted.

To the COMMISSIONERS *and* OFFICERS *on the* CIVIL LISTS

To the right honourable R. Earl of G. Lord privy-seal—Lord president of the council—Lord great chamberlain—Earl marshal of *England*—His majesty's principal secretaries of state, &c. *my Lord, your Lordship.*

To the right honourable the Lords Commissioners—of the admiralty—of treasury—of the trade and plantations, &c. *my Lords, your Lordships.*

N.B. If there be a nobleman, or even a commoner, who is a privy-counsellor, among any set of commissioners, it will be proper to stile them collectively *right honourable*; the usual address then is *your Lordships.*

To the honourable the commissioners of his majesty's customs—Ditto of the revenue of excise—Ditto for the duty on salt—Ditto for his majesty's stamp duties—Ditto for victualing his majesty's navy, &c. &c.

---

8. Thomas Herring (1693–1757; archbishop, 1747–57).

To the Officers of the Army and Navy

In the army, all noblemen are stiled according to their rank, to which is added their employ.

To the honourable A. B. lieutenant-general—Major general—Brigadier-general of his majesty's forces, *Sir, your Honour.*

To the right honourable J. earl of S. captain of his majesty's first troop of horse-guards Band of gentlemen pensioners—Band of yeomen of the guards, &c. *my Lord, your Lordship.*

All colonels are stiled *honourable*; and all inferior officers should have the names of their employments set first; as for example, to Major W. C. to Captain T. H. &c. *Sir.*

In the *navy*, all admirals are stiled *honourable*, and noblemen according to quality and office. The other officers as in the army.

To the Ambassadry

To his excellency Sir A. B. bart. his *Britannic* majesty's envoy extraordinary, and plenipotentiary of the *Ottoman Porte*,[9] *Sir, your Excellency.*

To his excellency C. D. esq; ambassador to his most christian majesty, *Sir, your Excellency.*

To his excellency the baron de E. his *Prussian* majesty's resident at the court of *Great Britain, Sir, your Excellency.*

To seignior F. G. Secretary from the republick of *Venice* at *London, Sir.*

To seignior H. J. Secretary from the great Duke of *Tuscany* at *London, Sir.*

To K. L. esq; his *Britannic* majesty's consul at *Smyrna, Sir.*

To the Judges and Lawyers

All judges, if privy counsellors, are stiled *right honourable*; as for instance:

To the right honourable A. B. lord high chancellor of *Great Britain, my lord, your Lordship.*

To the right honourable P. V. master of the Rolls, *Sir, your Honour.*

To the right honourable Sir G. L. bart. lord chief justice of the king's bench—ditto of the common pleas, *my Lord, your Lordship.*

To the honourable Sir A. B. lord chief baron of the exchequer, *Sir, or may it please you, Sir.*

To the honourable A. D. one of the justices of the court of—or to judge D. *Sir, or, may it please you, Sir.*

To Sir R. D. his majesty's attorney—sollicitor—or advocate-general, *Sir.*

All others in the law, according to the offices and rank they bear, every barrister[1] having the title of *Esquire* given him.

N.B. *Upon the circuits, and when they sit singly, every one of the Judges is addressed and treated with the same respect and ceremony as the chief justices.*

9. The government of the Ottoman empire. "Bart.": baronet.
1. In Great Britain, the duties of lawyers are divided between barristers, who argue cases in the higher courts, and solicitors, who advise clients and argue cases in the lower courts.

Of the LIEUTENANCY *and* MAGISTRACY

To the right honourable S. earl of B. lord lieutenant and *custos rotulorum*[2] of the county of H. *my Lord, your Lordship.*

To P. E. esq; high sheriff for the county of C. *Mr. High Sheriff, Sir.*

To the right honourable A. B. lord mayor of the city of *London; my Lord, your Lordship.*

To the right worshipful C. D. esq; alderman of *Tower-ward, London; Sir, Mr. Alderman.*

To the right worshipful Sir E. F. recorder of the city of *London; Sir, Mr. Recorder.*

To the worshipful G. H. esq; mayor of L. *Mr. Mayor, Sir, your Worship.*

To the worshipful J. K. esq; one of his majesty's justices of the peace for the county of S. *Sir, your Worship.*

To L. M. esq; deputy steward of the city and liberty[3] of W. *Mr. Deputy, Sir.*

To the GOVERNORS *under the* CROWN

To his excellency J. lord C. lord lieutenant of the kingdom of *Ireland; my Lord Lieutenant, your Excellency.*

To their excellencies the lords justices of the kingdom of *Ireland; your Excellencies.*

To the right honourable J. earl of L. governor of *Dover-Castle,* and lord warden of the *Cinque ports;*[4] *my Lord, your Lordship.*

To the right honourable C. lord viscount D. constable of the *Tower.*

To his excellency J. H. esq; captain-general and governor in chief of the *Leward Carribee* islands in *America; Sir, Governor, your Excellency.*

To the honourable F. N. esq; lieutenant-governor of *South Carolina.*

To the honourable Sir J. G. deputy-governor of *Portsmouth.*

To the honourable G. P. esq; governor of *Fort St. George, Madrass,* in *East India.*

To the worshipful the president, and governors of *Christ's Hospital, London.*[5]

The second governors of colonies appointed by the king, are styled lieutenant-governors: those appointed by proprietors, as the East India *company, &c. are called deputy-governors.*

To INCORPORATE BODIES

To the honourable the court of directors of the united company of merchants of *England,* trading to the *East Indies.*

To the honourable the sub-governor, deputy-governor, and directors of the *South-Sea company.*

To the honourable the governor, deputy-governor, and directors of the bank of *England.*

To the master and wardens of the worshipful company of *Drapers.*[6]

To a baronet: To Sir C. D. bart. at *Binfield, Sir.*

To a knight: To Sir W. H. at *Richmond, Sir.*

---

2. Keeper of the rolls (Latin), the title of the chief justice of peace in a county.
3. The district beyond the bounds of a city that is subject to the control of the municipal authority.
4. A confederation of ports in southeast England, dating from at least the twelfth century (originally comprising Hastings, Romney, Hythe, Dover, and Sandwich).
5. A school founded in 1552.
6. I.e., a guild.

To T. Y. esq; at *Wickhman*, *Sir*.
To Dr. W. Jones at *Reading*, *Berks*.
To Mr. John Long, merchant in *London*, or *Bristol*, &c.
To Mr. Swan, *surgeon* at *Bath*.

N.B. The wives of *baronets* and *knights*, are styled *Ladies*.

QUEEN ANN BOLEYN'S LAST LETTER TO KING HENRY VIII[7]

Sir,
Your Grace's displeasure and my imprisonment are things so strange unto me,
as what to write, or what to excuse, I am altogether ignorant: Whereas you send
unto me (willing me to confess a truth, and so obtain your favour) by such a
one, whom you know to be mine ancient professed enemy, I no sooner received
this message by him, than I rightly conceived your meaning; and if, as you say,
confessing a truth indeed may procure my safety, I shall, with all willingness
and duty, perform your command. But let not your Grace ever imagine, that
your poor wife will ever be brought to acknowledge a fault, where not so much
as a thought thereof proceeded! And to speak a truth, never prince had wife
more loyal in all duty, and in all true affection, than you have ever found in *Ann
Boleyn*; with which name and place I could willingly have contented myself, if
God and your grace's pleasure had been so pleased. Neither did I at any time so
far forget myself in my exaltation, or received queenship, but that I always looked
for such an alteration as I now find; for the ground of my preferment being on
no surer foundation than your Grace's fancy, the least alteration I knew was fit
and sufficient to draw that fancy to some other object. You have chosen me,
from a low estate to be your queen and companion, far beyond my desert or
desire. If then you found me worthy of such honour, good your Grace let not
any light fancy, or bad counsel of mine enemies, withdraw your princely favour
from me; neither let that stain, that unworthy stain, of a disloyal heart towards
your good Grace, ever cast so foul a blot on your most dutiful wife, and the
infant princess your daughter.[8] Try me, good King, but let me have a lawful trial,
for my truth shall fear no open shame; then shall you see either mine innocence
cleared, your suspicion and conscience satisfied, the ignominy and slander of
the world stopped, or my guilt openly declared. So that whatsoever God or you
may determine of me, your Grace may be freed from an open censure, and mine
offences being so lawfully proved, your Grace is at liberty, both before God and
man, not only to execute worthy punishment on me as an unlawful wife, but to
follow your affection, already settled on that party,[9] for whose sake I am now as
I am; whose name I could, some good while since, have pointed unto, your Grace
not being ignorant of my suspicion therein.

7. Henry VIII (1491–1547; r. 1509–47) took Anne
Boleyn (ca. 1507–1536) first as his mistress and
then as his second wife (1533). Infatuated with
another woman, and infuriated at Anne's failure to
produce a male heir, Henry charged her with adultery and incest; she was found guilty and beheaded.

8. The future Elizabeth I (1533–1603; r. 1558–
1603).
9. Jane Seymour (ca. 1509–1537), who married
Henry VIII in 1536, less than two weeks after
Anne's execution (she died days after giving birth
to a son, later Edward VI).

But if, you have already determined of me, and that not only my death, but an infamous slander must bring you the enjoying of your desired happiness; then I desire of God, that he will pardon your great sin therein, and likewise mine enemies, the instruments thereof; and that he will not call you to a strict account for your unprincely and cruel usage of me, at his general judgment-seat, where both you and myself must shortly appear, and in whose judgment I doubt not (whatsoever the world may think of me) mine innocence shall be openly known, and sufficiently cleared.

My last and only request shall be, that myself may only bear the burden of your Grace's displeasure, and that it may not touch the innocent souls of those poor gentlemen,[1] who (as I understand) are likewise in straight imprisonment for my sake. If ever I have found favour in your sight, if ever the name of *Ann Boleyn* hath been pleasing in your ears, then let me obtain this request; and I will so leave to trouble your Grace any farther, with mine earnest prayers to the Trinity to have your Grace in his good keeping, and to direct you in all your actions.

From my doleful prison in the *Tower*,[2] this 6th of *May*.

Your loyal and ever faithful wife.
Ann Boleyn.

1757

1. The five men with whom Anne was accused of having sexual relations (including her brother, George). All were sentenced to death.

2. The Tower of London, the ancient fortress used as a jail for illustrious prisoners.

LEWIS CARROLL
1832–1898

Charles Dodgson, the Oxford mathematics don who became famous for the children's books that appeared under the name Lewis Carroll, was a prolific and meticulous letter writer. The modern edition of his correspondence, produced in two thick volumes by Morton N. Cohen and Roger Lancelyn Green (1979), contains only a fraction of the 98,721 items he recorded in what he called his "Register of Letters Sent and Received."

Carroll's pamphlet *Eight or Nine Wise Words about Letter-Writing* (1890), a portion of which is reproduced here, was originally published as part of a package that included a stamp case—a cardboard envelope with little pockets for holding stamps. The "Wonderland" stamp case itself, decorated with illustrations by Sir John Tenniel from *Alice's Adventures in Wonderland* (1865), was a spin-off from the enormously popular book.

From Eight or Nine Wise Words about Letter-Writing

1. ON STAMP-CASES

Some American writer has said "the snakes in this district may be divided into one species—the venomous." The same principle applies here. Postage-Stamp-Cases may be divided into one species, the "Wonderland." Imitations of it will soon appear, no doubt: but they cannot include the two Pictorial Surprises,[1] which are copyright.

You don't see why I call them 'Surprises'? Well, take the Case in your left-hand, and regard it attentively. You see Alice nursing the Duchess's Baby? (An entirely new combination, by the way: it doesn't occur in the book.) Now, with your right thumb and forefinger, lay hold of the little book, and suddenly pull it out. *The Baby has turned into a Pig!* If *that* doesn't surprise you, why, I suppose you wouldn't be surprised if your own Mother-in-law suddenly turned into a Gyroscope!

This Case is *not* intended to carry about in your pocket. Far from it. People seldom want any other Stamps, on an emergency, than Penny-Stamps for Letters, Sixpenny-Stamps for Telegrams, and a bit of Stamp-edging for cut fingers (it makes capital sticking-plaster, and will stand three or four washings, cautiously conducted): and all these are easily carried in a purse or pocket-book. No, *this* is meant to haunt your envelope-case, or wherever you keep your writing-materials. What made me invent it was the constantly wanting Stamps of other values, for foreign Letters, Parcel Post, &c., and finding it very bothersome to get at the kind I wanted in a hurry. Since I have possessed a "Wonderland Stamp-Case", Life has been bright and peaceful, and I have used no other. I believe the Queen's laundress uses no other.

Each of the pockets will hold 6 stamps, comfortably. I would recommend you to arrange the 6, before putting them in, something like a *bouquet*, making them lean to the right and to the left alternately: thus there will always be a free *corner* to get hold off, so as to take them out, quickly and easily, one by one: otherwise you will find them apt to come out two or three at a time.

According to *my* experience, the 5*d*., 9*d*., and 1*s*.[2] Stamps are hardly ever wanted, though I have constantly to replenish all the other pockets. If your experience agrees with mine, you may find it convenient to keep only a couple (say) of each of these 3 kinds, in the 1*s*. pocket, and to fill the other 2 pockets with extra 1*d*. stamps.

2. HOW TO BEGIN A LETTER

If the Letter is to be in answer to another, begin by getting out that other letter and reading it through, in order to refresh your memory, as to what it is you have to answer, and as to your correspondent's *present address* (otherwise you will be sending your letter to his regular address in *London*, though he has been careful in writing to give you his *Torquay*[3] address in full).

Next, Address and Stamp the Envelope. "What! Before writing the *Letter?*" Most certainly. And I'll tell you what will happen if you don't. You will go on writing till the last moment, and, just in the middle of the last sentence, you will become aware

1. Two illustrations by Sir John Tenniel from *Alice's Adventures in Wonderland* (1865); the Duchess's baby turns into a pig in chapter 6.
2. *s.* is the abbreviation for shilling, and *d.* for penny or pence (from the Latin *denarius*, "penny"). There were twelve pence in a shilling.
3. Seaside resort in southwest England.

that 'time's up!' Then comes the hurried wind-up—the wildly-scrawled signature—the hastily-fastened envelope, which comes open in the post—the address, a mere hieroglyphic—the horrible discovery that you've forgotten to replenish your Stamp-Case—the frantic appeal, to every one in the house, to lend you a Stamp—the headlong rush to the Post Office, arriving, hot and gasping, just after the box has closed—and finally, a week afterwards, the return of the Letter, from the Dead-Letter Office, marked "address illegible"!

Next, put your own address, *in full*, at the top of the note-sheet. It is an aggravating thing——I speak from bitter experience——when a friend, staying at some new address, heads his letter "Dover," simply, assuming that you can get the rest of the address from his previous letter, which perhaps you have destroyed.

Next, put the date *in full*. It is another aggravating thing, when you wish, years afterwards, to arrange a series of letters, to find them dated "Feb. 17", "Aug. 2", without any *year* to guide you as to which comes first. And never, never, dear Madam (N.B. this remark is addressed to ladies *only*: no *man* would ever do such a thing), put "Wednesday", simply, as the date!

"That way madness lies."[4]

3. How to Go On with a Letter

Here is a golden Rule to begin with. *Write legibly*. The average temper of the human race would be perceptibly sweetened, if everybody obeyed this Rule! A great deal of the bad writing in the world comes simply from writing *too quickly*. Of course you reply, "I do it to save *time*". A very good object, no doubt: but what right have you to do it at your friend's expense? Isn't *his* time as valuable as yours? Years ago, I used to receive letters from a friend——and very interesting letters too——written in one of the most atrocious hands ever invented. It generally took me about a *week* to read one of his letters! I used to carry it about in my pocket, and take it out at leisure times, to puzzle over the riddles which composed it——holding it in different positions, and at different distances, till at last the meaning of some hopeless scrawl would flash upon me, when I at once wrote down the English under it; and, when several had been thus guessed, the context would help one with the others, till at last the whole series of hieroglyphics was deciphered. If *all* one's friends wrote like that, Life would be entirely spent in reading their letters!

This Rule applies, specially, to names of people or places——and *most* specially to *foreign names*. I got a letter once, containing some Russian names, written in the same hasty scramble in which people often write "yours sincerely". The *context*, of course, didn't help in the least: and one spelling was just as likely as another, so far as *I* knew: it was necessary to write and tell my friend that I couldn't read any of them!

My second Rule is, don't fill *more* than a page and a half with apologies for not having written sooner!

The best subject, to *begin* with, is your friend's last letter. Write with the letter open before you. Answer his questions, and make any remarks his letter suggests. *Then* go on to what you want to say yourself. This arrangement is more courteous, and pleasanter for the reader, than to fill the letter with your own invaluable remarks, and then hastily answer your friend's questions in a postscript. Your friend is much

---

4. William Shakespeare, *King Lear* (ca. 1605), 3.4.

more likely to enjoy your wit, *after* his own anxiety for information has been satisfied.

In referring to anything your friend has said in his letter, it is best to *quote the exact words*, and not to give a summary of them in *your* words. *A*'s impression, of what *B* has said, expressed in *A*'s words, will never convey to *B* the meaning of his own words.

This is specially necessary when some point has arisen as to which the two correspondents do not quite agree. There ought to be no opening for such writing as "You are quite mistaken in thinking I said so-and-so. It was not in the least my meaning, &c., &c.", which tends to make a correspondence last for a life-time.

A few more Rules may fitly be given here, for correspondence that has unfortunately become *controversial*.

One is, *don't repeat yourself.* When once you have said your say, fully and clearly, on a certain point, and have failed to convince your friend, *drop that subject*: to repeat your arguments, all over again, will simply lead to his doing the same; and so you will go on, like a Circulating Decimal.[5] *Did you ever know a Circulating Decimal come to an end?*

Another Rule is, when you have written a letter that you feel may possibly irritate your friend, however necessary you may have felt it to so express yourself, *put it aside till the next day.* Then read it over again, and fancy it addressed to yourself. This will often lead to your writing it all over again, taking out a lot of the vinegar and pepper, and putting in honey instead, and thus making a *much* more palatable dish of it! If, when you have done your best to write inoffensively, you still feel that it will probably lead to further controversy, *keep a copy of it.* There is very little use, months afterwards, in pleading "I am almost sure I never expressed myself as you say: to the best of my recollection I said so-and-so". *Far* better to be able to write "I did *not* express myself so: these are the words I used."

My fifth Rule is, if your friend makes a severe remark, either leave it unnoticed, or make your reply distinctly *less* severe: and if he makes a friendly remark, tending towards 'making up' the little difference that has arisen between you, let your reply be distinctly *more* friendly. If, in picking a quarrel, each party declined to go more than *three-eighths* of the way, and if, in making friends, each was ready to go *five-eighths* of the way—why, there would be more reconciliations than quarrels! Which is like the Irishman's remonstrance to his gad-about daughter—"Shure, you're *always* goin' out! You go out *three* times, for *wanst* that you come in!"

My sixth Rule (and my last remark about controversial correspondence) is, *don't try to have the last word!* How many a controversy would be nipped in the bud, if each was anxious to let the *other* have the last word! Never mind how telling a rejoinder you leave unuttered: never mind your friend's supposing that you are silent from lack of anything to say: let the thing drop, as soon as it is possible without discourtesy: remember 'speech is silvern, but silence is golden'! (N.B.—If you are a gentleman, and your friend a lady, this Rule is superfluous: *you won't get the last word!*)

My seventh Rule is, if it should ever occur to you to write, jestingly, in *dispraise* of your friend, be sure you exaggerate enough to make the jesting *obvious*: a word spoken in *jest*, but taken as *earnest*, may lead to very serious consequences. I have known it to lead to the breaking-off of a friendship. Suppose, for instance, you wish to remind your friend of a sovereign[6] you have lent him, which he has forgotten to repay—you

---

5. A decimal fraction with a digit or a sequence of digits that repeats itself indefinitely.

6. A gold coin worth one pound.

might quite *mean* the words "I mention it, as you seem to have a conveniently bad memory for debts", in jest: yet there would be nothing to wonder at if he took offence at that way of putting it. But, suppose you wrote "Long observation of your career, as a pickpocket and a burglar, has convinced me that my one lingering hope, for recovering that sovereign I lent you, is to say 'Pay up, or I'll summons yer!'" he would indeed be a matter-of-fact friend if he took *that* as seriously meant!

My eighth Rule. When you say, in your letter, "I enclose cheque for £5", or "I enclose John's letter for you to see", leave off writing for a moment—go and get the document referred to—and *put it into the envelope*. Otherwise, you are pretty certain to find it lying about, *after the Post has gone!*

My ninth Rule. When you get to the end of a note-sheet, and find you have more to say, take another piece of paper—a whole sheet, or a scrap, as the case may demand: but, whatever you do, *don't cross!* Remember the old proverb '*Cross-writing*[7] *makes cross reading*'. "The *old* proverb?" you say, enquiringly. "*How* old?" Well, not so *very* ancient, I must confess. In fact, I'm afraid I invented it while writing this paragraph! Still, you know, 'old' is a *comparative* term. I think you would be *quite* justified in addressing a chicken, just out of the shell, as "Old boy!", *when compared* with another chicken, that was only half-out!

4. HOW TO END A LETTER

If doubtful whether to end with 'yours faithfully', or 'yours truly', or 'yours most truly', &c. (there are at least a dozen varieties, before you reach 'yours affectionately'), refer to your correspondent's last letter, and make your winding-up *at least as friendly as his*: In fact, even if a shade *more* friendly, it will do no harm!

A Postscript is a very useful invention: but it is *not* meant (as so many ladies suppose) to contain the real *gist* of the letter: it serves rather to throw into the shade any little matter we do *not* wish to make a fuss about. For example, your friend had promised to execute a commission for you in town, but forgot it, thereby putting you to great inconvenience: and he now writes to apologize for his negligence. It would be cruel, and needlessly crushing, to make it the main subject of your reply. How much more gracefully it comes in thus! "P.S. Don't distress yourself any more about having omitted that little matter in town. I won't deny that it *did* put my plans out a little, at the time: but it's all right now. I often forget things, myself: and 'those, who live in glass-houses, mustn't throw stones', you know!"

When you take your letters to the Post, *carry them in your hand*. If you put them in your pocket you will take a long country-walk (I speak from experience), passing the Post-Office *twice*, going and returning, and, when you get home, will find them *still* in your pocket.

* * *

1890

---

7. A method of conserving paper in writing letters (before the institution of the penny post in 1839, the cost of sending a letter rose with every added sheet): after filling the page with horizonal lines of text, the correspondent turns the sheet 90 degrees and writes across what he or she has just written.

Fairy Tales

The Wonder Tale

Like most genres of children's literature, the fairy tale never was told or written explicitly for children. Nor is its audience limited to children today. The fairy tale distinguished itself as a genre a few centuries ago when storytellers began appropriating different kinds of magical folktales and transforming them and conventionalizing them, for it became necessary in the modern world to adapt the oral tales to the moral, literary, and aesthetic standards of a particular society and to make them acceptable for diffusion in the public sphere.

The fairy tale is only one type of appropriation of a particular oral storytelling tradition—the wonder folktale, often called the *magic tale*, which generally focuses on miraculous transformations that overcome the disadvantages of the protagonists and enable them to succeed in life. Typically, wonder tales recount the adventures of banished heroes and heroines, youngest sons and daughters, impoverished and abused characters, and people who have been cursed. For the most part the tales are secular and incorporate pagan beliefs and superstitions. Some are stories of warning; others are didactic and moral, displaying motifs from Greek and Roman myths as well as from Judeo-Christian sacred writings.

While tales were the common people's mode of entertainment in the fields and at the hearth, storytelling flourished among all social classes: the wonder tales provided wish fulfillment for listeners, reflected their desire to improve their lot, compensated for their misery, and helped preserve and celebrate rituals within their community. Members of the upper class often heard them directly from peasants who worked as servants, wet nurses, maids, and day laborers. The stories were also told by travelers when they relaxed at inns, by soldiers and sailors in their leisure hours, and by troubadors and professional storytellers. Although the tales in their crude form were considered unsuitable for polite society, portions of them began to be used as exempla and parables in sermons to illustrate a moral message. As priests "Christianized" certain folktales, they created new stories—which were, in turn, reappropriated by peasants and retold in altered forms, without their religious elements. Similarly, the performances of professional storytellers and troubadours, designed to startle, delight, and impress the refined listener, were also adapted by peasants and included in their repertoire.

There is no evidence that any of these tales, even those containing warnings about dangerous animals, were intended especially for children. Still, no matter how frank, bawdy, violent, or erotic the story, children were not excluded from the audience. It was through listening to the tales that one gained a sense of values and of one's place within society. The oral tradition was in the hands of the peasantry for hundreds of years, and each peasant community made its mark on tales that circulated beyond its borders.

The Rise of the Literary Fairy Tale

The oral tradition of the wonder tale continued largely unaltered throughout the late Middle Ages. What changes there were in the social function of the tales reflected developments in the communities themselves. For instance, the growth of towns, religious conflicts, and peasant uprisings affected both the subject matter and the use of the tales. Early collections of tales such as Boccaccio's *Decameron* (1348–53) and Chaucer's *Canterbury Tales* (1386–1400) are good examples of how writers responded to the changes, and their works had a great influence on the format of fairy tales, their functions and frames. No development in this period was more important than the introduction of the printing press, which revolutionized the transmission of these wonder tales. As more and more were printed in the fifteenth, sixteenth, and seventeenth centuries, they began to constitute a new genre: the *literary* fairy tale, which gradually took on its own conventions (rooted in its oral antecedents) that appealed to a smaller and more aristocratic reading public. It was first in Giovan Francesco Straparola's *Piacevoli notti* (translated as *The Facetious Nights* and *The Delectable Nights*, 1550–53) and then in Giambattista Basile's *Lo cunto de li cunti* (better known as *The Pentamerone*, 1634–36) and Pompeo Sarnelli's *Posilecheata* (1684) that wonder tales were fully adapted and transcribed to amuse educated readers. Though the stories contained a good deal of social commentary about love, marriage, and power, the social function of representation and entertainment remained dominant in these collections. Essentially, however, the authors altered the motifs and topoi of the oral tradition to mirror upper-class interests. They had wide latitude in content and approach, which could be critical or noncritical so long as they addressed the concerns of the aristocracy and ruling classes in tales that were enjoyable and entertaining.

Because these early authors of fairy tales neither sought to create a new mode of writing nor formed a social network to support its spread, the genre did not take a firm hold in Italy. It thus was France that effectively gave birth to the literary fairy tale. There, by the mid-seventeenth century, aristocratic women had established literary salons and were promoting a type of parlor game that incorporated the use of folk motifs and narrative conventions. The participants were expected to show their wit and expressiveness by inventing wondrous tales (*contes de fées*) that dealt with such subjects as tender love, courtship, proper comportment, and the use of power. As these games grew increasingly popular in Paris, players often wrote down or rehearsed the fairy tales at home so that they might appear *précieux* (unique) or as natural as possible when asked to recite. By 1690, authors such as Marie-Catherine d'Aulnoy and Catherine Bernard began first to incorporate fairy tales into their novels and then to publish entire collections of fairy tales. It is common today to speak of a veritable vogue if not a deluge of fairy tales from 1696 to 1704 in France. Marie-Jeanne Lhéritier, Charlotte-Rose de la Force, Marguerite de Lubert, and Henriette Julie de Murat were among the gifted writers who published remarkable collections of fairy tales. The most famous writer from that era is Charles Perrault, who in 1697 published his collection *Histoires ou contes du temps passé* (*Stories or Tales of Times Past*), often mistakenly referred to as "Tales of Mother Goose."

These aristocratic and bourgeois women and men performed their tales in the salons and published them so that they might demonstrate their individuality, their eloquence, and their wit or *esprit*. The tales were intended not just to amuse the listeners but also to establish the conventions of a discourse on manners and *civilité*, with an implicit code that corresponded to the standards of propriety. The resulting tales differed radically in content and style from their originals, whether those had been heard from nurses, governesses, or servants or had been read in books such as those by Straparola, Basile, and other Italian writers. When transferred from the salon to the page they were adapted even more, for the author could employ even more florid language and invent even more extraordinary events. In addition, the literary fairy tales had a serious undertone. Many, particularly those by women, criticize the policies of Louis XIV, whose wars and conversion to orthodox Catholicism had ended France's dominance as the ruling power in Europe. The utopian projections of magnificent courtly life, where a just ruler guarantees peace and happiness for his subjects, reveal the discontent of the writers and their desire to change French society during the latter days of the Sun King's rule. The authors of early French fairy tales thus give wonder a certain nationalist tinge. Ironically, they thereby echo the project of their king, who sought to have the world admire his court and to make French culture the standard for all cultures. As the fairy-tale realms become magnificent in the tales, the fortunate destinies that are depicted celebrate the wonders of the French or the possibilities that the French have to become wondrous.

All these fairy tales were written explicitly for adults, even those by Perrault—a point worth stressing because many date the origin of the fairy tale for children to this period. Yet there is no evidence that these complex and subtle tales were read to children, or that children read them on their own. To be sure, François de Salignac de la Mothe Fénelon, an important theologian and the archbishop of Cambrai, who was in charge of the education of Louis's grandson during the 1690s, did write several didactic fairy tales—published posthumously as *Recueil des fables composées pour l'éducation de feu Monseigneur le duc de Bourgogne* (*Collection of Fables Written for the Education for the Late Monseigneur the Duke of Burgundy*, 1718)—as an experiment to make the Dauphin's lessons more enjoyable. But the fairy tales to which children were exposed generally were those that had been written for an adult audience.

Of course, the writings for adults did influence the tales that were later developed for children. For instance, soon after their publication, the fairy tales of d'Aulnoy, Perrault, and others were printed in a series of chapbooks called the *Bibliothèque bleue* that were sold by peddlers (*colporteurs*) throughout France, central Europe, and England. In this format the tales were often translated and shortened, and their language simplified. As early as 1729 a complete version of Perrault's tales had been translated into English. Despite the hostility of puritan censors in England, the incorporation of some fairy tales in volumes intended for children gradually became acceptable. The most notable examples are found in *The Governess: or, Little Female Academy* (1749) by Sarah Fielding and in *Magasin des enfans* (translated in 1757 as *The Young Misses' Magazine*) by Jeanne-Marie Leprince de Beaumont. Both Fielding and Leprince de Beaumont use a larger frame tale of schooling to hold stories that illustrate lessons of morals and manners. Often such embedded tales were later published separately. These works, together with memoirs, social histories, biographies, and other publications, indicate that most educated adults in Great Britain had a familiarity with classic French fairy tales, that English folktales in the oral tradition still circulated across the classes, and that the popular literature contained in chapbooks included fairy tales, legends, and fables.

Although the genre had become fully acceptable for adults, fairy tales for children were in a transitional stage in the eighteenth century; a specific children's culture was developing (by the end of the century, some publishers would be specializing in children's literature), but the literary fairy tales to which educated children in Great Britain were exposed were not aimed specifically at them. Indeed, in North America and much of Europe, fairy tales were generally considered to be at best useless for children, at worst dangerous: detractors pointed to their frivolity and accused them of promoting a sense of wonder based in superstitions, magic, and fantasy. Though most poor children—the modern peasantry—continued to hear oral wonder tales, children of the upper and educated classes were urged toward reading material that would encourage them to think and live rationally, in accordance with Christian ideas and proper manners. If fairy tales taught anything, it was to hope, wish, and fantasize. The fairy tales of Fénelon, Sarah Fielding, Mme Leprince de Beaumont, and other traditional writers of the eighteenth century won approval only because they were overly didactic and moralistic and sustained patriarchal notions of power. Though pleasurable to read, the literary fairy tale for children was clearly intended to instruct. Amusement was a secondary goal.

The Influence of Romanticism

At the beginning of the nineteenth century, the function of fairy tales for adults underwent a major shift throughout Europe, thanks to the German Romantic movement. Novalis, Ludwig Tieck, Adelbert von Chamisso, and E. T. A. Hoffmann, among others, made them appropriate venues for sophisticated dialogues about social and political issues. The fairy tale for children remained suspect a while longer, though various collections of fairy tales were published for children in England by John Harris (*Mother Bunch's Fairy Tales*, 1802) and Benjamin Tabart (*Popular Fairy Tales*, 1804–08), along with illustrated chapbooks containing "Little Red Riding Hood," "Cinderella," "Sleeping Beauty," "Jack the Giant Killer," "Beauty and the Beast," and so on. Such collections and tales were popular with children and adults throughout Europe, but they were not viewed as prime reading material for children. Nor were they considered to be healthy for the development of children's minds. Most stories for children were sentimental, realistic, and didactic, intended to demonstrate manners and morals. Even the Brothers Grimm, in particular Wilhelm, began in 1819 to revise their collected tales, *Kinder- und Hausmärchen* (*Children's and Household Tales*, first published in 1812 and 1815), to make them more suitable for children, adding Christian sentiments and removing erotic, cruel, or bawdy passages. Nevertheless, the fantastic and wondrous elements remained; thus the publication in England of Edgar Taylor's translation of the Grimms' tales under the title *German Popular Stories* (1823) signaled a change in attitude toward the fairy tale for children.

Parents began to realize that fantasy literature and amusement would not necessarily destroy or pervert their children's minds. The ideas of progressive educators began to gain broader acceptance. The Swiss-born French philosopher and political theorist Jean-Jacques Rousseau (1712–1778) was among the first to insist that children must be treated as children, not as miniature adults; the Swiss educational reformer Johann Heinrich Pestalozzi (1746–1827) and the German educator Friedrich Froebel (1782–1852), inventor of the "Kinder-Garten," emphasized liberty and play in learning. More generally, the belief took hold that children needed amusement, and the old saying "All work and no play make Jack a dull boy" began to be taken seriously. On this account, children of all classes needed a recreation period— the time and space to re-create themselves without having morals and ethics imposed on them, without being indoctrinated.

Significantly, it was from 1830 to 1900, during the explosive growth of the middle classes fueled by the Industrial Revolution, that the fairy tale for children came into its own. At just this time—from 1835 onward—Hans Christian Andersen began publishing his tales, which won great popular acclaim around the world; almost all were immediately translated and published in England and America. Andersen brilliantly combined humor, Christian sentiments, and fantastic plots to form tales that amused and instructed young and old alike. This was exactly what Fénelon had endeavored to do some 140 years before him, but the social conditions had not been ripe for such tales to spread in Europe, especially because they were so class-specific. By 1830, however, educators and the clergy had come to believe that children needed fantasy in their lives, and the purpose of good literature for children shifted from pure instruction to instruction and amusement.

From the 1820s through the 1850s, the majority of fairy-tale writers for children— including Catherine Sinclair, George Cruikshank, and Alfred Crowquill in England; Comtesse Sophie de Ségur in France; and Ludwig Bechstein in Germany—emphasized lessons to be learned in keeping with the principles of the Protestant ethic. These were industriousness, honesty, cleanliness, diligence, virtuousness—and male supremacy. The fairy tale had a major role to play in the socialization process. But much as the Romantics had subverted the conventional fairy tales for adults, so the second half of the nineteenth century saw a major movement to write parodies of fairy tales for children, to turn them upside down and inside out, to question the traditional value system, and to provide new endings—endings that appeared to contradict the notions of wonder and transformation that had been so dominant in the wonder folktales. William Makepeace Thackeray (*The Rose and the Ring*, 1855), George MacDonald ("The Light Princess," 1863), Lewis Carroll (*Alice's Adventures in Wonderland*, 1865), Jean Ingelow (*Mopsa the Fairy*, 1869), Juliana Ewing (*Old-Fashioned Fairy Tales*, 1822), Andrew Lang (*Princess Nobody*, 1884), Oscar Wilde (*The Happy Prince and Other Tales*, 1888), Kenneth Grahame ("The Reluctant Dragon," 1898), Edith Nesbit ("The Last of the Dragons," 1899), and many other writers began to experiment with the fairy tale in ways that encouraged young readers to question the world around them. Their tales did not offer prescriptions on good housekeeping and clean living. Instead, they suggested that conventional living could fetter the soul and mind, and they offered utopian alternatives.

The British writers had a great impact on contemporary Americans, who were then in the process of developing their culturally specific fairy-tale tradition. The firm of John McLoughlin began publishing numerous fairy-tale toy books at midcentury. Beginning in the 1850s, Nathaniel Hawthorne, James Kirke Paulding, Horace Scudder, Louisa May Alcott, Howard Pyle, and others contributed fairy tales to children's magazines (notably, *St. Nicholas*) or published their own collections. There even appeared a compilation of Native American fairy tales, *The Indian Fairy Book* (1869). The major writer in this genre was Frank Stockton, who published some unusual tales in such books as *Ting-a-ling* (1870) and *The Bee-Man of Orn and Other Fanciful Fairy Tales* (1887). Here, as in other genres, we can discern a movement to establish a genuine *American* literature.

The process of "Americanization" took time, and the most notable and memorable American fairy tale was produced at the very end of the nineteenth century: *The*

Wonderful Wizard of Oz (1900), whose structure is clearly based on the European model. L. Frank Baum depicts Dorothy's great desire and need to escape from the gray bleakness of Kansas. Once her imagination and initiative are awakened, she can ultimately determine her destiny (with the aid of three helpers). Though Dorothy returns to America, she realizes in the sixth Oz book, *The Emerald City of Oz* (1910), that she cannot stay in a country where farmers are driven to ruin by bankers and where exploitation is an accepted fact of life. In his fourteen Oz books, Baum created an American fairy-tale saga; its use of political and cultural commentary profoundly influenced other fairy-tale novels and series, as can be seen in the works of twentieth-century authors such as J. R. R. Tolkien, C. S. Lewis, T. H. White, Lloyd Alexander, and Michael Ende. The Angelo-Indian author Salman Rushdie, who has himself written a fairy-tale novel for children (*Haroun and the Sea of Stories*, 1990), acknowledges a long fascination with *The Wonderful Wizard of Oz*, a work that continues to shape books and films today.

At the same time that Baum was making history in America, J. M. Barrie helped imaginatively radicalize the fairy tale in England with *Peter Pan, or The Boy Who Wouldn't Grow Up* (1904), based on characters who first appeared in his novel *The Little White Bird* (1902). Barrie's drama, later adapted as a novel, *Peter and Wendy* (1911), treats resistance to conformity and convention, a subject that resonates with readers and spectators of all ages. Indeed, during the London premiere of *Peter Pan*, the largely adult audience shouted "Yes!" when Peter Pan asked whether they believed in fairies. It was a "Yes" heard again the following year in New York, and it still echoes wherever and whenever versions appear on stage or screen. Perhaps more than Baum's Dorothy, Peter Pan has captured the imagination of young and old audiences throughout the world.

Twentieth-Century Developments

By the beginning of the twentieth century, in Europe and America the functions of the fairy tale had shifted and expanded. The genre had become fully institutionalized: that is, its production, distribution, and reception gained full acceptance within the public sphere as it played a role in forming and maintaining a given society's cultural heritage. Such institutionalization both preserves the genre and involves it in socializing and acculturating readers. Thus, in every specific time and place the genre is defined by the interaction of writer, publisher, and audience. The aesthetics of each fairy tale will depend on how and why an individual writer chooses to intervene in an ongoing discourse.

In the early twentieth century, three currents in the fairy-tale tradition existed side by side, the classic or conventional fairy tales of Perrault, the Grimms, and Andersen—increasingly sanitized and made more "appropriate" (to fit the modern concept of children and childhood); innovative fairy tales that were often parodic (frequently with a political edge) and that introduced radical aesthetic changes; and orally presented fairy tales of different kinds heard in homes, libraries, schools, and recreation centers and spaces, often through the mass media. The first group of tales were dominant. Through the 1940s they were often republished in collections with illustrations, sometimes by notable artists such as Arthur Rackham, Margaret Tarrant, Edmund Dulac, and W. W. Denslow. They also appeared in individual picture books in a wide range of formats, from tiny four-by-four-inch booklets to gigantic volumes more than a foot square, as well as in comic books and cartoons. Some illustrations brilliantly interpreted the stories, while others were hackwork. Often the writer or the illustrator or both simplified and prettified the stories. Among the better creators of fairy tales between the wars were Walter de la Mare in England and Johnny Gruelle and Wanda Gág in America. De la Mare's work, which includes *Told Again: Traditional Tales* (1927) and *The Lord Fish* (1933), is characterized by gentle irony, careful exploration of characters' motivations, and original plots. Johnny Gruelle's Raggedy Ann and Andy books of the 1920s and 1930s also display unusual plots. His whimsical fairy tales continued Baum's emphasis on nonviolence and the importance for children of imaginative play. Wanda Gág, who made her mark with *Millions of Cats* in 1928, published four volumes of adaptations from the Brothers Grimm between 1936 and 1947. She illustrated the tales with unusual ink drawings, altering them to Americanize their plots and to recapture the authentic tone of a traditional storyteller.

A major change in the use of fairy tales that fully took hold in the twentieth century was their incorporation into children's formal education. By the end of the nineteenth century, the fairy tale had been introduced into the school curriculum in Great Britain and the United States, via primers, and this trend continued and was reinforced in the twentieth century. With the help of teachers and librarians, the fairy tale became a staple of education throughout the West, and naturally a canon for children was established: "Cinderella," "Little Red Riding Hood," "The Frog Prince," "Jack and the Beanstalk," "The Ugly Duckling," "Beauty and the Beast," "Rumpelstiltskin," "Sleeping Beauty," "Bluebeard," "Hansel and Gretel," "Rapunzel," and so on. As fairy tales were carried into schools, libraries, and households not just in print but in plays, radio productions, and (beginning in the 1920s) cinematic animation, theoretical works began to appear; they established the "proper" age (five to ten) for first encountering fairy tales and expounded on their spiritual and psychological value. This development was in stark contrast to the heated controversy about the fairy tale in the early nineteenth century, when educators and clergy tried to prevent it from entering the nursery.

Of course, some still distrusted fairy tales, believing (then as now) that their violence and cruelty affect children too powerfully. For instance, following the end of World War II the Allies' forces briefly banned the publication of the Grimms' tales in Germany because they were thought to encourage the aggressive and amoral fascist mentality. The impulse to sanitize the classic tales, already seen in the Grimms themselves, gained force in the United States after 1945 out of fears that the original versions might give children nightmares or strange ideas. Some religious groups have always objected to stories containing witches and magic and have led campaigns to ban fairy tales (and, into the twenty-first century, the Harry Potter novels by J. K. Rowling) from schools and public libraries. It was largely to oppose the continuing censorship of fairy tales that Bruno Bettelheim wrote his significant study, *The Uses of Enchantment* (1976). Though in many respects wrong-headed, Bettelheim's work stimulated others to explore how all kinds of fairy tales are not simply harmless but actively beneficial. In fact, fairy tales are now widely used in therapy, particularly with disturbed or abused children, because they provide a child with distance from trauma and make it possible to deal with problems on a symbolic level, enabling the therapist to work with the child.

The twentieth century also brought a major shift in how fairy tales were told. Their transmission through animated films, especially those of Walt Disney, has had an enormous impact. During his lifetime, Disney produced several major animated fairy-tale features: *Snow White and the Seven Dwarfs* (1937), *Pinocchio* (1940), *Cinderella* (1950), and *Sleeping Beauty* (1959). After his death, the company he founded continued in this vein with *The Little Mermaid* (1989), *Beauty and the Beast* (1991), *Aladdin* (1992), and so on. Accompanying its films, the Disney Corporation has published thousands of fairy-tale books worldwide, so that today probably most children, if not adults, learn about the classic fairy tale as well as many classics in children's literature through something marketed by Disney. For better or worse—and some have criticized the Disney adaptations as sexist, racist, and imperialist—the dominant notion of what a fairy tale is and should be now corresponds to Disney's conventions. Moreover, these conventions were applied to modern as well as classic works. For example, Disney adapted Lloyd Alexander's highly original and critically acclaimed five-volume Prydain Chronicle (1964–68), which tells the adventures of a young hero (the pig-keeper Taran) destined for greatness, into one undistinguished eighty-minute animated feature, *The Black Cauldron* (1985).

But even as Disney was making fairy tales conventional, some authors were undercutting convention. Among those who published fascinating and original fairy tales following World War II is Joan Aiken. Stories in such collections as *All You've Ever Wanted* (1953), *A Necklace of Raindrops* (1968), *A Harp of Fishbones* (1972), *The Faithless Lollybird, and Other Stories* (1977), and *The Last Slice of Rainbow* (1985) challenge conventional notions of fairy tales, and Aiken consistently parodied and satirized the genre while creating new possibilities for its development. Other British and American authors playing with the genre's rules include Catherine Storr, Nicholas Stuart Gray, and Theodor Geisel (Dr. Seuss). However, the most radical experimentation began in the 1960s and 1970s, when the fairy tale became overtly politicized.

Some used the form to comment on the issues of war (the Vietnam War and the arms race had radicalized many) or of the environment. Ted Hughes addresses both in *The Iron Man* (1968; U.S. title, *The Iron Giant*), which combines elements of science fiction and the fairy tale. But the most significant development in the field has been the emergence of feminist fairy tales for children and adults. Their evolution has been aided by anthologies such as Rosemary Minard's *Womenfolk and Fairy Tales* (1975), Ethel Johnston Phelps's *Tatterhood and Other Tales: Stories of Magic and Adventure* (1978), Alison Lurie's *Clever Gretchen, and Other Forgotten Folktales* (1980), Jack Zipes's *Don't Bet on the Prince: Contemporary Feminist Fairy Tales in North America and England* (1986), and Jane Yolen's *Not One Damsel in Distress: World Folktales for Strong Girls* (2000), as well as by the tales produced by the Merseyside Fairy Tale Collective (Liverpool) in 1978 and by the Feminist Collective of the Attic Press (Dublin) from 1985 to 1992. Well over a hundred writers and illustrators have rearranged familiar motifs and characters and reversed plot lines to provoke readers into rethinking conservative views of gender and power. The aesthetics of these tales are ideological, for their structural changes depend on a non-sexist worldview that advocates dramatically different practices. Particularly significant works produced for young readers include Tanith Lee, *Princess Hynchatti and Some Other Surprises* (1972), Jane Yolen, *The Hundredth Dove and Other Tales* (1978), Jay Williams, *The Practical Princess and Other Liberating Fairy Tales* (1978), Robert Munsch, *The Paper Bag Princess* (1980), Babette Cole, *Princess Smartypants* (1986), Katherine Paterson, *The King's Equal* (1992), Priscilla Galloway, *Truly Grim Tales* (1995), Emma Donoghue, *Kissing the Witch: Old Tales in New Skins* (1997), Francesca Lia Block, *The Rose and the Beast: Fairy Tales Retold* (2000), and Katrin Tchana, *The Serpent Slayer and Other Stories of Strong Women* (2000).

Ethnic and multicultural tales have also become increasingly important. Many of their writers seek to preserve ancestral traditions and to revise misconceptions about ethnic identity and history. Julius Lester helped pioneer this endeavor with the publication of *Black Folktales* in 1969, and other writers—notably Virginia Hamilton (*The People Could Fly: American Black Folktales*, 1985)—and talented illustrators such as Jerry Pinkney have followed. Laurence Yep has been prominent among those focusing on Chinese and Chinese American folktales, both in collections—*The Rainbow People* (1990) and *Tongues of Jade* (1991)—and several picture books (e.g., *The Man Who Tricked a Ghost*, 1993; *The Tiger Woman*, 1996). The Native American tradition has also received attention; for example, Michael Lacapa has written and illustrated such Apache folktales as *Flute Player* (1990) and *Antelope Woman* (1992).

Other experimentation in the genre has been psychological rather than sociopolitical. Thus Donna Jo Napoli has produced a series of intriguing novellas, including *The Prince of the Pond* (1992), *Zel* (1996), and *Beast* (2000), which explore classic tales (here, respectively, "The Frog King," "Rapunzel," and "Beauty and the Beast") with unusual depth. Similarly, Robin McKinley and Gregory Maguire have produced novels that undercut the conventional view of familiar fairy tales. McKinley's *Beauty* (1978) and *Rose Daughter* (1997), for example, are quite different retellings of "Beauty and the Beast" that depict the heroine as a strong, independent young woman; *Spindle's End* (2000) turns "Sleeping Beauty" into a tale of rebellion. Maguire's *Wicked: The Life and Times of the Wicked Witch of the West* (1997), a heretical version of *The Wizard of Oz*, recounts the life of the little green girl who grows up to become the Wicked Witch of the West. His *Confessions of an Ugly Stepsister* (1999) is a masterful retelling of "Cinderella" that focuses on a woman's machinations to ensure her and her daughters' survival in seventeenth-century Holland.

Most revisions of classic fairy tales engage seriously with contemporary mores and values, but others are hugely entertaining parodies. Jon Scieska is probably the best-known parodist; his first book was *The True Story of the Three Little Pigs* (1989), brilliantly and surrealistically illustrated by Lane Smith, who also collaborated with him on *The Stinky Cheese Man and Other Fairly Stupid Tales* (1992) and other books. Perhaps most important for this approach were the "Fractured Fairy Tales" produced for television by Jay Ward for the animated series *Rocky and His Friends* (1959–61) and *The Bullwinkle Show* (1961–64). Highly irreverent, these humorous sketches influenced Jim Henson's Muppet fairy tales and some of the productions in Shelley Duvall's Faerie Tale Theater.

The enormous output of fairy-tale films for the theater and television and the steady growth of multimedia fairy tales on the Internet have not diminished the effect of the genre, which can be regarded as dominating children's literature. If anything, the new media have provided new possibilities for its development—both orally and visually and as literature. Today thousands of parents read fairy tales to their children during the day and as bedtime stories. Thousands of teachers and librarians read fairy tales to children, sometimes as a formal part of a school's curriculum, and encourage them to create their own versions. Children may also be exposed to the performances of storytellers of all types and traditions in schools and libraries, as well as to television and cinematic versions of fairy tales. They may play with and revise these or, relying on the conventions they have assimilated, fashion new stories that enact their own family dramas or struggles to understand existence.

Fairy tales have thus come to provide a way of approaching reality. As noted above, therapists may rely on them to uncover the problems of their patients, both children and adults—in the process devising new methods of listening to as well as of telling tales. More generally, advertisers often rely on their audience's familiarity with fairy-tale plots and motifs to attach a sense of wonder and magic to the products being offered for sale. In addition, the conventions of fairy tales provide a shorthand for professional writers and artists, which they use in all imaginable media to make statements about themselves, society, and the fairy-tale tradition itself.

In short, the fairy tale in our society is part of the public sphere, with its own specific code and forms that we use to communicate about social and psychological phenomena. While children are expected to learn its keywords, icons, and metaphors, the code is not static. As long as the fairy tale continues to awaken the wonderment of the young and offer alternative worlds where yearnings and wishes may be fulfilled, it will serve a meaningful social function, providing not just compensation but revelation.

CHARLES PERRAULT
1628–1703

Though Charles Perrault wrote what became the first classic literary fairy tales for children in the eighteenth century, he never intended them for young readers. In fact, given their subtle themes and ironic style, he would have been surprised by their transformation through chapbooks and picture books into canonical stories for children. Perrault was born in Paris into a highly distinguished bourgeois family; his father was a lawyer and member of parliament, and his four older brothers all won renown in such fields as architecture and law. He himself practiced law for three years before becoming secretary to his brother Pierre, who was the tax receiver of Paris, in 1654; around the same time, he began drawing attention as a poet. In 1663 Perrault was appointed secretary to Jean Baptiste Colbert, controller general of finances and perhaps the most influential minister in Louis XIV's government. For the next twenty years, Perrault used that position to accomplish a great deal in the arts and sciences, and he also established a reputation as a gifted poet and essayist.

In 1671 he was elected to the French Academy and was placed in charge of the royal buildings; he continued to write poetry and to play an important role in the cultural affairs of the court. When Colbert died in 1683, Perrault was dismissed from government service with a pension that enabled him to support his family while concentrating more on literary affairs. In 1687 he helped inaugurate the far-reaching "Quarrel of the Ancients and the Moderns" ("Querelle des anciens et des modernes") by reading his poem "Le siècle de Louis le Grand" ("The Century of Louis the Great"). Perrault defended the moderns, believing that France and Christianity could progress only by incorporating pagan beliefs and folklore and developing a culture of enlightenment. On the other side, the literary critic Nicolas Boileau and the dramatist Jean Racine argued that France had to imitate the great empires of Greece and Rome in the arts and maintain stringent classical rules. This cultural quarrel lasted until 1697, when Louis XIV made it known that he favored

Boileau and Racine. Nevertheless, Perrault kept trying to incorporate his ideas into his poetry and prose, and his fairy tales are closely related to his desire to imbue French popular culture with deeper meaning.

Perrault had always frequented women's literary salons, including those of his niece Marie-Jeanne Lhéritier and of Marie-Catherine d'Aulnoy, and he had been annoyed by Boileau's satirical attacks on women. Thus, he wrote three verse tales—"Griseldis" (1691), "Les souhaits ridicules" ("The Foolish Wishes," 1693), and "Peau d'ane" ("Donkey Skin," 1694)—along with a long poem, "Apologie des femmes" (1694), in women's defense. Today these works might not be considered pro-women, for despite extolling the intelligence and capabilities of women, Perrault maintained that their talents should be put to use in the domestic and social realm (a perspective seen in most of his fairy tales). However, his poems and tales use both a highly sophisticated style and folk motifs to stress the necessity of assuming an enlightened moral attitude toward women.

In 1696 Perrault embarked on an ambitious project: subtly transforming several popular folk stories, with all their superstitious beliefs and magic, into moralistic tales that would demonstrate a modern approach to literature and convey his views on the development of French civility. He, like most writers of fairy tales of the time, was writing for his peers in the literary salons and not (as many critics claim) directly for children; indeed, children's literature per se did not yet exist. Perrault's prose version of "Sleeping Beauty" ("La belle au bois dormant") was printed in the journal *Mercure galant* in 1696, and in 1697 he published *Histoires ou contes du temps passé* (*Stories or Tales of Times Past*), which consisted of a new version of "Sleeping Beauty" together with "Le petit chaperon rouge" ("Little Red Riding Hood"), "Barbe bleue" ("Bluebeard"), "Cendrillon" ("Cinderella"), "Le petit poucet" ("Little Thumbling"), "Riquet à la houppe" ("Riquet with the Tuft"), "Le chat botté" ("Puss in Boots"), and "Les fées" ("The Fairies"). It appeared under the name of Pierre Perrault Darmancour, Perrault's son, but the evidence strongly suggests Perrault was sole author. He was simply masking his own identity so that he would not be blamed for reigniting the Quarrel of the Ancients and the Moderns.

During the eighteenth century, most of Perrault's tales were published as chapbooks or in inexpensive editions, often abridged or adapted for a mass reading public that included children. They were also translated into many different languages. In this way, his tales gradually became part of the literary canon of fairy tales. "Puss in Boots" is one of the most popular tales in the world, and Perrault may have been influenced by the earlier Italian versions of Giovan Francesco Straparola (1553) and Giambattista Basile (1634). In some variants, cats are not the magic helpers: foxes, jackals, fairies, dead people, and trees may aid a common man to rise in society to become a rich nobleman, or a peasant maiden to become a princess. The theme "clothes make the person" is very important, and the helper is sometimes depicted as the main character's alter ego. Perrault was the first writer to depict the cat as male, not female (as in the Italian tales). Indeed, this master cat is clearly the protagonist, using his wits not only to help his master and to survive but also to climb the social ladder. In this regard, Puss takes his place in a long line of ambitious tricksters, found in most cultures throughout the world, who will not stop at killing to succeed in life. Perrault's version profoundly influenced most of the literary and oral versions that have circulated from the eighteenth century up to the present.

The Master Cat; or, Puss in Boots

A miller left his three sons all his worldly possessions, which amounted to nothing more than his mill, his ass, and his cat.[1] The division was made quickly. Neither notary nor attorney was summoned or requested, for they would have charged too much and consumed all of the meager patrimony. The eldest received the mill; the second son, the ass; the youngest got just the cat, and naturally, he was upset at inheriting such a poor portion.

"My brothers can now earn an honest living as partners," he said, "but, as for me, I'll surely die of hunger once I have eaten my cat and made a muff of his skin."

The cat, who had heard these words but pretended not to have been listening, said to him with a sober and serious air, "Don't trouble yourself, master. All you have to do is to give me a pouch and have a pair of boots made for me to go into the bushes. Then you'll see that your share of the inheritance is not as bad as you believe."

Although the cat's master did not place much stock in this assertion, he had seen the cat play such cunning tricks as catching rats and mice by hanging himself upside down by the heels or lying in the flour as if he were dead that he was willing to give the cat a chance to help him.

As soon as the cat had what he had asked for, he boldly pulled on his boots, and after hanging the pouch around his neck, he took the strings in his forepaws and went to a warren where there were a great number of rabbits. He put some bran and lettuce into his pouch and, stretching himself out as if he were dead, he waited for some young rabbit, little versed in the wiles of the world, to come and hunt for something to eat in the pouch. He had hardly laid down when his expectations were met. A young scatterbrain of a rabbit entered the pouch, and master cat instantly pulled the strings, caught it, and killed it without mercy. Proud of his prey, he went

---

1. In his title Perrault applies to the cat the French familiar term *maître* (master), which referred to someone whose social standing was not very high. At the same time, he is punning on its sense as a teacher who instructs a young man and determines his destiny.

to the king's palace and demanded an audience. He was ushered up to the royal apartment, and upon entering, he made a low bow to the king and said, "Sire, here's a rabbit from the warren of my lord, the Marquis de Carabas (such was the name[2] he had dreamed up for his master). He has instructed me to present it to you on his behalf."

"Tell your master," replied the king, "that I thank him and that he's given me great pleasure."

Another time the cat went and hid in a wheatfield, keeping the mouth of the pouch open as he always did, and when two partridges entered it, he pulled the strings and caught them both. Then he went directly to the king and presented them to him just as he had done with the rabbit from the warren. The king was equally pleased by the two partridges and gave the cat a small token for his efforts.

During the next two or three months, the cat continued every now and then to carry presents of game from his master to the king. One day, when he knew the king was going to take a drive on the banks of the river with his daughter, the most beautiful princess in the world, he said to his master, "If you follow my advice, your fortune will be made. Just go and bathe in the river that I'll point out to you, and leave the rest to me."

The Marquis de Carabas did as his cat had advised him, without knowing what good would come of it. While he was bathing, the king passed by, and the cat began to shout with all his might, "Help! Help! My lord, the Marquis de Carabas, is drowning!"

At this cry, the king stuck his head out of the coach window and, recognizing the cat who had often brought game to him, he ordered his guards to rush to the help of the Marquis de Carabas. While they were pulling the poor marquis out of the river, the cat approached the royal coach and told the king that some robbers had come and carried off his master's clothes while he was bathing, even though he had shouted "Thieves!" as loud as he could. But in truth the rascal had hidden his master's clothes himself under a large rock. The king immediately ordered the officers of his wardrobe to go and fetch one of his finest suits for the Marquis de Carabas. The king embraced him a thousand times, and since the fine clothes given to the marquis brought out his good looks (for he was handsome and well-built), the king's daughter found him much to her liking. And no sooner had the Marquis de Carabas cast two or three respectful and rather tender glances at her than she fell in love with him. Then the king invited him to get into the coach and to accompany them on their drive.

Delighted to see that his scheme was succeeding, the cat ran on ahead and soon came upon some peasants who were mowing a field.

"Listen, my good people," he said. "You who are mowing here, if you don't tell the king that the field you are mowing belongs to my lord, the Marquis de Carabas, you'll all be cut into tiny pieces like minced meat!"

Indeed, the king did not fail to ask the mowers whose field it was they were mowing.

"It belongs to our lord, the Marquis de Carabas," they said altogether, for the cat's threat had frightened them.

2. The derivation of the name is not certain. According to legend, a fool in Alexandria was referred to as Carabas by the inhabitants of the city, and they mocked him by treating him as if he were a king. The Turkish word *Carabag* designates a beautiful place in the mountains where sultans and princes would spend the summer months; Perrault might have come on this term in Barthélemy d'Herbelot's *Bibliothèque orientale* (1697).

"You can see, sire," rejoined the marquis, "it's a field that yields an abundant crop every year."

Master cat, who kept ahead of the party, came upon some reapers and said to them, "Listen, my good people, you who are reaping, if you don't say that all this wheat belongs to my lord, the Marquis de Carabas, you'll be cut into tiny pieces like minced meat!"

A moment later the king passed by and wished to know who owned all the wheat-fields that he saw there.

"Our lord, the Marquis de Carabas," responded the reapers, and the king again rejoiced about this with the marquis.

Running ahead of the coach, the cat uttered the same threat to all whom he encountered, and the king was astonished at the great wealth of the Marquis de Carabas. At last master cat arrived at a beautiful castle owned by an ogre, the richest ever known, for all the lands through which the king had driven belonged to the lord of this castle. The cat took care to inquire who the ogre was and what his powers were. Then he requested to speak with him, saying that he could not pass so near his castle without doing himself the honor of paying his respects to him. The ogre received him as civilly as an ogre can and asked him to sit down.

"I've been told," said the cat, "that you possess the power of changing yourself into all sorts of animals. For instance, it has been said that you can transform yourself into a lion or an elephant."

"It's true," said the ogre brusquely, "and to prove it, watch me become a lion."

The cat was so frightened at seeing a lion standing before him that he immediately scampered up into the gutters of the roof, and not without difficulty and danger, for his boots were not made to walk on tiles. Upon noticing that the ogre shortly resumed his previous form, the cat descended and admitted that he had been terribly frightened.

"I've also been told," said the cat, "but I can't believe it, that you've got the power to assume the form of the smallest of animals. For instance, they say that you can change yourself into a rat or mouse. I confess that it seems utterly impossible to me."

"Impossible!" replied the ogre. "Just watch!"

And immediately he changed himself into a mouse which began to run about the floor. No sooner did the cat catch sight of it than he pounced on it and devoured it.

In the meantime, the king saw the ogre's beautiful castle from the road and desired to enter it. The cat heard the noise of the coach rolling over the drawbridge and ran to meet it.

"Your majesty," he said to the king, "welcome to the castle of my lord, the Marquis de Carabas."

"What!" exclaimed the king. "Does this castle also belong to you, Marquis? Nothing could be finer than this courtyard and all these buildings surrounding it. If you please, let us look at the inside of it."

The marquis gave his hand to the young princess, and they followed the king, who led the way upstairs. When they entered a grand hall, they found a magnificent banquet, which the ogre had ordered to be prepared for some friends who were to have visited him that very day. But they did not presume to enter when they found the king was there. The king was now just as much delighted by the accomplishments of the Marquis de Carabas as his daughter, who doted on him, and realizing how wealthy he was, he said to him, after having drunk five or six cups of wine, "The choice is entirely yours, Marquis, whether or not you want to become my son-in-law."

After making several low bows, the marquis accepted the honor the king had offered him, and on that very same day, he married the princess. In turn, the cat became a great lord and never again ran after mice, except for his amusement.

Moral

Although the advantage may be great
When one inherits a grand estate
Passed on from father to son,
Young men often find their industry,
Combined with ingenuity,
Leads to greater prosperity.

Another Moral

Though the miller's son did quickly gain
The heart of a princess whose eyes he tamed,
As he charmed her in a natural way,
It's due to good manners, looks, and dress
That inspired her deepest tenderness
And always help to win the day.

1697

SARAH FIELDING
1710–1768

The British novelist Sarah Fielding was educated at a boarding school in Salisbury as well as privately; that institution may have provided her both with basic knowledge of classical languages (in 1762 she published translations of Greek works by Xenophon) and with the setting of her extremely popular work *The Governess; or, Little Female Academy* (1749), the earliest known long work of fiction for young readers. As she explains in the preface to her first novel, *The Adventures of David Simple* (1744), she wrote out of financial necessity; she relied on a small income and the support of her older brother, the novelist and playwright Henry Fielding. Her sentimental fiction won her success though not great wealth, as she lived in London and finally in Bath.

Fielding had read and loved fairy tales during her youth, and she included two in *The Governess*; yet she felt that she had to apologize for and justify their inclusion. *The Governess* is a frame tale in which Mrs. Teachum, who is in charge of nine young girls, imparts lessons to her wards about proper behavior and etiquette. During their leisure time, Jenny Peace, the oldest of the girls, tells two fairy tales to her companions: "The Story of the Cruel Giant Barbarico, the Good Giant Benefico, and the Little Pretty Dwarf Mignon" and "The Princess Hebe." These stories were apparently influenced by French literary fairy tales, especially those of Marie-Catherine d'Aulnoy. Though Fielding remained very much within the tradition of moralistic storytelling, she used Mrs. Teachum to warn Jenny and her friends about the dangers of fairy tales:

I have no objection, Miss *Jenny*, to your reading any Stories to amuse you, provided you read them with the Disposition of a Mind not to be hurt by them. A very good Moral may indeed be drawn from the Whole. . . . But here let me observe to you (which I would have you communicate to your little Friends) that Giants, Magic, Fairies, and all sorts of supernatural Assistances in a Story, are introduced only to amuse and divert: For a Giant is called so only to express a Man of great power; and the magic Fillet round the Statue was intended only to shew you, that by Patience you will overcome all Difficulties. Therefore by no means let the Notion of Giants or Magic dwell upon your Minds.

For Fielding and other eighteen-century writers like Jeanne-Marie Leprince de Beaumont (who was strongly influenced by Fielding), the fairy tale was suspect for its alleged powers over the imagination of young readers, provoking them to become wild and irresponsible. Fielding endeavored to tame fairy-tale magic by transforming it into a moral allegory. "The Story of the Cruel Giant Barbarico" was regarded so exemplary that it was published separately in chapbook form. However, in the 1824 version of *The Governess* edited by the writer Mary Martha Sherwood (1775–1851), the two fairy tales were eliminated—a cut that reflects the growing influence of the moral guardians of children's literature on the publishing industry. The text reprinted here is from the first edition (1749). The preface and first two chapters of *The Governess* appear in the School Stories section of this anthology, below.

From The Governess; or, Little Female Academy

THE STORY OF THE CRUEL GIANT BARBARICO, THE GOOD GIANT BENEFICO, AND THE LITTLE PRETTY DWARF MIGNON

A Great many hundred Years ago, the Mountains of *Wales* were inhabited by Two Giants; one of whom was the Terror of all his Neighbours, and the Plague of the whole Country. He greatly exceeded the Size of any Giant recorded in History; and his Eyes looked so fierce and terrible, that they frightened all who were so unhappy as to behold them.

The Name of this *enormous Wretch* was *Barbarico*. A Name, which filled all who heard it, with Fear and Astonishment. The whole Delight of this Monster's Life was in Acts of Inhumanity and Mischief; and he was the most miserable as well as the most wicked Creature that ever yet was born. He had no sooner committed one Outrage, but he was in Agonies till he could commit another; never satisfied, unless he could find an Opportunity of either torturing or devouring some innocent Creature. And whenever he happened to be disappointed in any of his malicious Purposes, he would stretch his immense Bulk on the Top of some high Mountain, and groan, and beat the Earth, and bellow with such a hollow Voice, that the whole Country heard and trembled at the Sound.

The other Giant, whose Name was *Benefico*, was not so tall and bulky as the *hideous Barbarico*: He was handsome and well-proportioned, and of a very good-natured Turn of Mind. His Delight was no less in Acts of Goodness and Benevolence than the other's was in Cruelty and Mischief. His constant Care was to endeavour if possible to repair the Injuries committed by this horrid Tyrant: Which he had sometimes an Opportunity of doing; for tho' *Barbarico* was much larger and stronger than *Benefico*, yet his coward Mind was afraid to engage with him, and always shunned a Meeting; leaving the Pursuit of any Prey, if he himself was pursued by *Benefico*: Nor could the good *Benefico* trust farther to this coward Spirit of his base Adversary, than only to make the horrid Creature fly; for he well knew, that a close Engagement might make him desperate; and fatal to himself might be the Consequence of such a brutal Desperation: Therefore he prudently declined any Attempt to destroy this cruel Monster, till he should gain some sure Advantage over him.

It happened on a certain Day, that as the *inhuman Barbarico* was prowling along the Side of a craggy Mountain, o'ergrown with Brambles and briery Thickets, taking most horrid Strides, rolling his ghastly Eyes around in quest of human Blood, and having his Breast tortured with inward Rage and Grief, that he had been so unhappy as to live One whole Day without some Act of Violence, he beheld, in a pleasant Valley at a Distance, a little Rivulet winding its gentle Course thro' Rows of Willows mixt with flowery Shrubs. Hither *the Giant* hasted: And being arrived, he gazed about, to see if in this sweet Retirement any were so unhappy as to fall within his Power: But finding none, the Disappointment set him in a Flame of Rage, which, burning like an inward Furnace, parched his Throat. And now he laid him down upon the Bank, to try if in the cool Stream, that murmured as it flowed, he could asswage or slack the fiery Thirst that burnt within him.

He bent him down to drink: And at the same time casting his baleful Eyes towards the opposite Side, he discovered within a little natural Arbour formed by the Branches of a spreading Tree within the Meadow's flowery Lawn, the Shepherd *Fidus* and his lov'd *Amata*.

The *gloomy Tyrant* no sooner perceived this happy Pair, than his Heart exulted with Joy; and suddenly leaping up on the Ground, he forgot his Thirst, and left the Stream untasted. He stood for a short Space to view them in their sweet Retirement; and was soon convinced, that in the innocent Enjoyment of reciprocal Affection their Happiness was complete. His Eye, inflamed with Envy to behold such Bliss, darted a fearful Glare; and his Breast swelling with Malice and envenom'd Rage, he with gigantic Pace approached their peaceful Seat.

The happy *Fidus* was at that time busy in entertaining his lov'd *Amata* with a Song which he had that very Morning composed in Praise of Constancy; and the *Giant* was now within one Stride of them, when *Amata*, perceiving him, cried out in a trembling Voice, Fly, *Fidus*, fly, or we are lost for ever: We are pursued by the *hateful Barbarico!* She had scarce uttered these Words, when the *savage Tyrant* seized them by the Waste in either Hand, and holding them up to his nearer View, thus said: 'Speak, Miscreants, and, if you would avoid immediate Death, tell me who you are, and whence arises that Tranquility of Mind, which even at a Distance was visible in your Behaviour.'

Poor *Fidus*, with Looks that would have melted the hardest Heart, innocently replied, 'That they were wandering that way, without designing Offence to any Creature on Earth: That they were faithful Lovers; and, with the Content of all their Friends and Relations, were soon to be married; therefore intreated him not to part them.'

The Giant now no sooner perceived, from the last Words of the affrighted Youth, what was most likely to give them the greatest Torment, than with a spiteful Grin, which made his horrible Face yet more horrible, and in a hollow Voice, as loud as Thunder, he tauntingly cried out, 'Ho hoh! You'd not be parted? Would you? For once I'll gratify thy Will, and thou shalt follow this thy whimpering Fondling[1] down my capacious Maw.' So saying, he turned his ghastly Visage on the trembling *Amata*, who being now no longer able to support herself under his cruel Threats, fainted away, and remained in his Hand but as a lifeless Corpse. When lifting up his Eyes towards the Hill on the opposite Side, he beheld *Benefico* coming hastily towards him. This good Giant, having been that Morning informed that *Barbarico* was roam-

---

1. One who is fondly loved; one who is much caressed.

ing in the Mountains after Prey, left his peaceful Castle, in hopes of giving Protection to whatever unfortunate Creature should fall into the Clutches of this so cruel a Monster.

Barbarico, at the Sight of the friendly *Benefico*, started with Fear: For altho' in Bulk and Stature he was, as we have said, the Superior, yet that Cowardice which ever accompanies Wickedness now wrought in him in such a manner, that he could not bear to confront him, well knowing the Courage and Fortitude that always attend the Good and Virtuous; and therefore instantly putting *Fidus* into the Wallet[2] that hung over his Shoulder, he flung the fainting *Amata*, whom he took to be quite expired, into the Stream that ran hard by, and fled to his Cave, not daring once to cast his Eyes behind him.

The good *Benefico* perceiving *the Monster's Flight*, and not doubting but he had been doing some horrid Mischief, immediately hasted to the Brook; where he found the half-expiring *Amata* floating down the Stream; for her Cloaths had yet borne her up on the Surface of the Water. He speedily stepped in, and drew her out; and taking her in his Arms, pressed her to his warm Bosom; and in a short Space perceiving in her Face the visible Marks of returning Life, his Heart swelled with kind Compassion, and he thus bespoke the tender Maid: 'Unhappy Damsel, lift up thy gentle Eyes, and tell me by what hard Fate thou wast fallen into the Power of *that barbarous Monster*, whose savage Nature delights in nothing but Ruin and Desolation. Tremble not thus, but without Fear or Terror behold one who joys in the Thought of having saved thee from Destruction, and will bring thee every Comfort his utmost Power can procure.'

The gentle *Amata* was now just enough recovered to open her Eyes: But finding herself in a Giant's Arms, and still retaining in her Mind the frightful Image of the *horrid Barbarico*, she fetched a deep Sigh, crying out in broken Accents, Fly, *Fidus*, fly; and again sunk down upon the friendly Giant's Breast. On hearing these Words, and plainly seeing by the Anguish of her Mind that some settled Grief was deeply rooted at her Heart, and therefore despairing to bring her to herself immediately, the kind *Benefico* hastened with her to his hospitable Castle; where every imaginable Assistance was administred to her Relief, in order to recover her lost Senses, and reconcile her to her wretched Fate.

The *cruel Barbarico* was no sooner arrived at his gloomy Cave, than he called to him his little Page; who, trembling to hear the *Tyrant* now again returned, quickly drew near to attend his stern Commands: When drawing out of the Wallet the poor *Fidus*, more dead than alive, the *Monster* cried out, 'Here, Caitiff,[3] take in Charge this smooth-faced Miscreant; and, d'ye hear me? See that his Allowance be no more than one small Ounce of mouldy Bread, and half a Pint of standing Water, for each Day's Support, till his now blooming Skin be withered, his Flesh be wasted from his Bones, and he dwindle to a meagre Skeleton.' So saying, he left them, as he hoped, to bewail each other's sad Condition. But the unhappy *Fidus*, bereft of his *Amata*, was not to be appalled by any of the most horrid Threats; for now his only Comfort was, the Hopes of a speedy End to his miserable Life, and to find a Refuge from his Misfortunes in the peaceful Grave. With this Reflection the faithful *Fidus* was endeavouring to calm the inward Troubles of his Mind, when the little Page, with Looks of the most tender Compassion, and in gentle Words, bid him be comforted, and with Patience endure his present Affliction; adding, that he himself had long suffered the most rigorous Fate, yet despaired not but that one Day would give them

---

2. Sack, bag.   3. Captive; a wretched, miserable person.

an Opportunity to free themselves from the *wicked Wretch*, whose sole Delight was in others Torments. As to his inhuman Commands, continued he, I will sooner die than obey them; and in a mutual Friendship perhaps we may find some Consolation, even in this dismal Cave.

This little Page the *cruel Barbarico* had stolen from his Parents at Five Years old; ever since which time, he had tortured and abused him, till he had now attained the Age of One-and-twenty. His Mother had given him the Name of *Mignon*;[4] by which Name the *Monster* always called him, as it gratified his insolence to make use of that fond Appellation whilst he was abusing him: Only when he said *Mignon*, he would in Derision add the Word *Dwarf*; for, to say the Truth, *Mignon* was one of the least Men that was ever seen, tho' at the same time one of the prettiest: His Limbs, tho' small, were exactly proportioned: His Countenance was at once sprightly and soft; and whatever his Head thought, or his Heart felt, his Eyes by their Looks expressed; and his Temper was as sweet as his Person was amiable. Such was the gentle Creature *Barbarico* chose to torment: For wicked Giants, no less than wicked Men and Women, are constantly tormented at the Appearance of those Perfections in another, to which they themselves have no Pretensions.

The Friendship and Affection of *Fidus* and *Mignon* now every Day increased; and the longer they were acquainted, the more Delight they took in each other's Company. The faithful *Fidus* related to his Companion the Story of his loved *Amata*, whilst the tender *Mignon* consoled his Friend's inward Sorrows, and supplied him with Necessaries, notwithstanding the Venture he run[5] of the *cruel Tyrant's* heavy Displeasure. The *Giant* ceased not every Day to view the hapless *Fidus*, to see if the Cruelty of his Intentions had in any Degree wrought its desired Effect: But perceiving in him no Alteration, he now began to be suspicious that the little *Mignon* had not punctually obeyed his savage Command. In order therefore to satisfy his wicked Curiosity, he resolved within himself narrowly to watch every Occasion these poor unhappy Captives had of conversing with each other. *Mignon*, well knowing the implacable and revengeful Disposition of this *barbarous Tyrant*, had taken all the Precautions imaginable to avoid Discovery; and therefore generally sought every Opportunity of being alone with *Fidus*, and carrying him his daily Provisions, at those Hours he knew the *Giant* was most likely to be asleep.

It so befel, that on a certain Day the *wicked Giant* had, as was his usual Custom, been abroad for many Hours, in Search of some unhappy Creature on whom to glut his hateful Inhumanity; when tired with fruitless Roaming, he returned back to his gloomy Cave, beguiled of[6] all his horrid Purposes; for he had not once that Day espied so much as the Track of Man, or other harmless Animal, to give him even Hopes to gratify his Rage or Cruelty: But now raving with inward Torment and Despair, he laid him down upon his Iron Couch, to try if he could close his Eyes and quiet the tumultuous Passions of his Breast. He tossed, and tumbled, and could get no Rest; starting with fearful Dreams, and horrid Visions of tormenting Furies.[7]

Mean while, the gentle *Mignon* had prepared a little delicate Repast, and having seen the *Monster* lay himself at Length, and thinking now that fit Occasion offered in which to comfort and refresh his long-expecting Friend, was hastening with it to the Cell where the faithful *Fidus* was confined. At this fatal Moment the *Giant*,

---

4. I.e., "pretty child" (French).
5. The risk he ran.
6. Disappointed in.
7. In Greek mythology the Furies, or Erinyes, pun-

ished crimes against human society generally (e.g., those committed by host against guest) but especially the murder of blood relatives.

rearing himself up on his Couch, perceived the little *Mignon* just at the Entrance of the Cell: When calling to him in a hollow Voice, that dismally resounded thro' the Cave, he so startled the poor unhappy Page, that he dropped the Cover[8] from his trembling Hand, and stood fixed and motionless as a Statue.

Come hither, *Mignon*, Caitiff, Dwarf, said then the *taunting Homicide*: But the poor little Creature was so thunderstruck, he was quite unable to stir one Foot. Whereat the *Giant* rousing himself from off his Couch; with one huge Stride, reached out his brawny Arm; and seized him by the Waste; and, pointing to the scattered Delicates, cried out, 'Vile Miscreant! is it thus thou hast obeyed my Orders? Is this the mouldy Bread and muddy Water, with which alone it was my Command thou shouldst sustain that puny Mortal? But I'll'—Here raising him aloft, he was about to dash him to the Ground: When suddenly revolving in his wicked Thoughts, that if at once he should destroy his patient Slave, his Cruelty to him must also have an End, he paused—and then recovering his stretched-out Arm, and bringing the little Trembler near his glaring Eyes, he thus subjoins: 'No; I'll not destroy thy wretched Life: But thou shalt waste thy weary Days in a dark Dungeon, as far remote from the least Dawn of Light, as from thy beloved Companion: And I myself will carefully supply you both, so equally, with mouldy Bread and Water, that each by his own Sufferings shall daily know what his dear Friend endures.' So saying, he hastened with him to his deepest Dungeon; and having thrust him in, he doubly barred the Iron Door. And now again retiring to his Couch, this new wrought Mischief, which greatly gratified his raging Mind, soon sunk him down into a sound and heavy Sleep. The Reason this *horrid Monster* had not long ago devoured his little Captive (for he thought him a delicious Morsel) was, that he might never want[9] an Object at hand to gratify his Cruelty: For tho' extremely great was his voracious Hunger, yet greater still was his Desire of Tormenting; and oftentimes when he had teazed, beat, and tortured the poor gentle *Mignon*, so as to force from him Tears, and sometimes a soft Complaint, he would, with a malicious Sneer, scornfully reproach him in the following Words: 'Little does it avail to whine, to blubber, or complain; for, remember, abject Wretch,

> I am a Giant, and I can eat thee:
> Thou art a Dwarf, and canst not eat me.'

When *Mignon* was thus alone, he threw himself on the cold Ground, bemoaning his unhappy Fate. However, he soon recollected, that Patience and Resignation were his only Succour in this distressful Condition; not doubting, but that as Goodness cannot always suffer, he should in time meet with some unforeseen Deliverance from the savage Power of the *inhuman Barbarico*.

Whilst the gentle *Mignon* was endeavouring to comfort himself in his Dungeon with these good Reflections, he suddenly perceived, at a little Distance from him, a small glimmering Light. Immediately he rose from the Ground, and going towards it, found that it shone through a little Door that had been left a-jar, which led him to a spacious Hall, wherein the *Giant* hoarded his immense Treasures. *Mignon* was at first dazzled with the Lustre of so much Gold, and Silver, and sparkling Jewels, as were there heaped together. But casting his Eyes on a Statue that was placed in the

8. Place setting with which a table is covered or laid.
9. Lack.

> Wouldst thou from the Rage be free
> Of the Tyrant's Tyranny,
> Loose the Fillet which is bound
> Thrice three times my Brows around;
> Bolts and Bars shall open fly,
> By a magic Sympathy.
> Take him in his sleeping Hour;
> Bind his Neck, and break his Pow'r.
> PATIENCE bids, make no Delay:
> Haste to bind him, haste away.

Mignon's little Heart now leapt for Joy, that he had found the Means of such a speedy Deliverance; and eagerly climbing up the Statue, he quickly unbound the magic Fillet: Which was no sooner done, but suddenly the Bolts and Bars of the great brazen Gates thro' which the Giant used to pass to this his Treasury were all unloosed, and the Folding-doors of their own accord flew open, grating harsh Thunder on their massy Hinges. At the same Instant, stretched on his Iron Couch in the Room adjoining to the Hall, the Giant gave a deadly Groan. Here again the little *Mignon's* trembling Heart began to fail; for he feared the Monster was awakened by the Noise, and that he should now suffer the cruellest Torments his wicked Malice could invent. Wherefore for a short Space he remained clinging round the Statue, till he perceived that all again was hushed and silent. When getting down, he gently stole into the Giant's Chamber; where he found him still in a profound Sleep.

* * *

Now, thought *Mignon*, is the lucky Moment to fulfil the Instructions of the Oracle: And then cautiously getting up the Side of the Couch, with trembling Hands he put the Fillet round the Monster's Neck, and tied it firmly in a threefold Knot: And again softly creeping down, he retired into a Corner of the Room, to wait the wished Event. In a few Minutes the Giant waked; and opening his enormous Eyes, he glared their horrid Orbs around (but without the least Motion of his Head or Body) and spy'd the little *Mignon* where he lay, close shrinking, to avoid his baleful Sight.

The Giant no sooner perceived his little Page at Liberty, but his Heart sorely smote him, and he began to suspect the worst that could befal: For, recollecting that he had carelessly left open the little Door leading from the Dungeon to the great Hall wherein was placed the fatal magic Statue, he was now intirely convinced that *Mignon* had discovered the secret Charm on which his Power depended; for he already found the magic of the Fillet round his Neck fully to operate, his Sinews all relax, his joints all tremble; and when he would by his own Hand have tried to free himself, his shivering Limbs, he found, refused Obedience to their Office.[1] Thus bereft of all his Strength, and well nigh motionless, in this Extremity of Impotence he cast about within himself, by what sly Fraud (for Fraud and Subtilty were now his only Refuge) he best might work upon the gentle *Mignon* to lend his kind Assistance to unloose him. Wherefore with guileful Words, and seeming Courtesy, yet striving to conceal his curst Condition, he thus bespake his little Captive:

---

1. Function, duty.

'Come hither, *Mignon*; my pretty gentle Boy, come near me. This Fillet thou hast bound around my Neck, to keep me from the Cold, gives me some Pain. I know thy gentle Nature would not let thee see thy tender Master in the least Uneasiness, without affording him thy chearful Aid and kind Relief. Come hither, my dear Child, I say, and loose the Knot which in thy kind Concern (I thank thee for thy Care) thou'st tied so hard, it somewhat frets my Neck.'

These Words the insidious Wretch uttered in such a low trembling Tone of Voice, and with such an Affectation of Tenderness, that the little Page, who had never before experienced from him any such kind of Dialect, and but too well knew his savage Nature to believe that any thing but Guile, or Want of Power, could move him to the least friendly Speech, or kind Affection, began now strongly to be persuaded that all was as he wished, and that the Power of the inhuman Tyrant was at an End. He knew full well, that if the Giant had not lost the Ability of rising from the Couch, he should ere now too sensibly have felt the sad Effects of his malicious Resentment; and therefore boldly adventured to approach him; and coming near the Couch, and finding not the least Effort in the Monster to reach him, and from thence quite satisfied of the Giant's total Incapacity of doing farther Mischief, he flew with Raptures to the Cell where *Fidus* lay confined.

Poor *Fidus* all this time was quite disconsolate: Nor could he guess the Cause why his little Friend so long had kept away: One while he thought the Giant's stern Commands had streighten'd[2] him of all Subsistence; another while his Heart misgave him for his gentle Friend, lest unawares his kind Beneficence towards *him* had caused him to fall a Sacrifice to the Tyrant's cruel Resentment. With these, and many other like Reflections, the unhappy Youth was busied, when *Mignon*, suddenly unbarring the Cell, flew to his Friend, and eagerly embracing him, cried out, 'Come, *Fidus*, haste, my dearest Friend; for thou, and all of us, are from this Moment free. Come and behold the cruel Monster, where he lies, bereft of all his Strength. I cannot stay to tell thee now the Cause; but haste, and thou shalt see the dreaded Tyrant stretched on his Iron Couch, deprived of all his wicked Power: But first let us unbar each Cell, wherein is pent some wretched Captive, that we may share a general Transport for this our glad Deliverance.'

The faithful *Fidus*, whose Heart had known but little Joy since he had lost his lov'd *Amata*, now felt a dawning Hope that he might once more chance to find her, if she had survived their fatal Separation; and, without one Word of Answer, he followed *Mignon* to the several[3] Cells, and soon released all the astonished Captives.

Mignon first carried them to behold their former Terror, now, to Appearance, almost a lifeless Corpse; who, on seeing them all surround his Couch, gave a most hideous Roar, which made them tremble, all but the gentle *Mignon*, who was convinced of the Impotence of his Rage, and begged them to give him their Attendance in the Hall; where they were no sooner assembled, than he shewed them the Statue, read them the Oracle, and told them every Circumstance before related.

They now began to bethink themselves of what Method was to be taken to procure their entire Liberty; for the Influence of the magic Fillet extended only to the Gates of the Hall; and still they remained imprisoned within the dismal Cave: And though they knew from the Oracle, as well as from what appeared, that the Monster's Power was at an End; yet still were they to seek the Means of their Escape from this his horrid Abode. At length *Mignon* again ascended the Couch to find the massy Key; and, spying one End of it peep out from under the Pillow, he called to *Fidus*, who

2. Deprived.   3. Separate.

first stepped up to his Friend's Assistance; the rest by his Example quickly followed: And now, by their united Force, they dragged the ponderous Key from under the Monster's Head; and then descending, they all went to the outer Door of the Cave, where, with some Difficulty, they set wide open the folding Iron Gates.

They now determined to dispatch a Messenger to the good *Benefico*, with the News which they knew would be so welcome to him and all his Guests; and with one Voice agreed, that *Fidus* should bear the joyful Tidings; and then returned to observe the Monster, and to wait the coming of *Benefico*. The nimble *Fidus* soon reached the Giant's Dwelling, where, at a little Distance from the Castle, he met the good *Benefico*, with a Train of happy Friends, enjoying the Pleasures of the Evening, and the instructive and chearful Conversation of their kind Protector. *Fidus* briefly told his Errand; and instantly *Benefico*, with all his Train, joyfully hastened to behold the Wonders he had related; for now many a Heart leapt for Joy, in Hopes of meeting some Friend of whom they had been bereft by the Cruelty of the savage *Barbarico*.

They were not long before they arrived at the horrid Cave, where *Benefico*, proceeding directly to the Monster's Chamber, suddenly appeared to him at the Side of his Couch. *Barbarico*, on seeing him, gave a hideous Yell, and rolled his glaring Eyes in such a manner, as expressed the Height of Rage and envious Bitterness.

Benefico, turning to all the Company present, thus spoke: 'How shall I enough praise and admire the gentle *Mignon*, for having put it in my Power to do Justice on this execrable Wretch, and freeing you all from an insufferable Slavery, and the whole Country from their Terror?' Then reaching the Monster's own Sword, which hung over his Couch, his Hand yet suspended over the impious Tyrant, he thus said: 'Speak, Wretch, if yet the Power of Speech is left thee; and with thy latest[4] Breath declare, what Gain, or what Advantage, hast thou found of all thy wicked Life?'

Barbarico well knew, that too bad had been that Life, to leave the least room for Hope of Mercy; and therefore, instead of an Answer, he gave another hideous Yell, gnashing his horrid Teeth, and again rolling his ghastly Eyes on all around.

Benefico, seeing him thus impenitent and sullen, lifted on high the mighty Sword, and, with one Blow severed his odious Head from his enormous Body.

The whole Assembly gave a Shout for Joy; and *Benefico* holding in his Hand the Monster's yet grinning Head, thus addressed his half-astonished Companions: 'See here, my Friends, the proper Conclusion of a rapacious cruel Life. But let us hasten from this Monster's gloomy Cave; and on the Top of one of our highest Mountains, fixed on a Pole, will I set up this joyful Spectacle, that all the Country round may know themselves at Liberty to pursue their rural Business, or Amusements, without the Dread of any Annoyance from a devouring vile Tormentor: And when his Treasures, which justly all belong to the good patient *Mignon*, are removed, we will shut up the Mouth of this abominable Dwelling; and, casting on the Door a Heap of Earth, we hope, that both the Place and the Remembrance of this cruel Savage may in time be lost.'

The sweet little *Mignon* declared, 'That he should never think of accepting more than a Part of that mighty Wealth; for it was his Opinion, that every Captive who had suffered by the Tyrant's Cruelty, had an equal Right to share in all the Advantages of his Death: But if they thought he had any just Title to those Treasures, he begged they might instantly be removed to *Benefico*'s Castle:' For, continued *Mignon*, He who has already shewn how well he knows the true Use of Power and Riches, by employing them for the Happiness of others; 'tis he alone who has the just and true

4. Last.

Claim to them; and I doubt not but you will all willingly consent to this Proposal.'

Every one readily cried out, 'That to *Benefico*, the good *Benefico*, alone belonged the Tyrant's Treasures; that *Benefico* should ever be, as heretofore, their Governor, their Father, and their kind Protector.'

The beneficent Heart of the *good Giant* was quite melted with this their kind Confidence and Dependence upon him, and assured them, he should ever regard them as his Children: And now, exulting in the general Joy that must attend the Destruction of this savage Monster, when the whole Country should find themselves freed from the Terror of his Rapine and Desolation, he sent before to his Castle, to give Intelligence to all within that happy Place of the grim Monster's Fall, and little *Mignon*'s Triumph; giving in Charge to the Harbinger of these Tidings, that it should be his first and chiefest Care to glad the gentle Bosom of a fair Disconsolate (who kept herself retired and pent up within her own Apartment) with the Knowledge that the inhuman Monster was no more; and that henceforth sweet Peace and rural Innocence might reign in all their Woods and Groves. The Hearts of all within the Castle bounded with Joy, on hearing the Report of the inhuman Monster's Death, and the Deliverance of all his Captives; and with speedy Steps they hastened to meet their kind Protector; nor did the melancholy Fair-one, lest she should seem unthankful for the general Blessing, refuse to join the Train.

It was not long after the Messenger that *Benefico*, and those his joyful Friends, arrived: But the faithful *Fidus* alone, of all this happy Company, was tortured with the inward Pangs of a sad Grief he could not conquer, and his fond Heart remained still captivated to a melting Sorrow: Nor could even the tender Friendship of the gentle *Mignon* quite remove, tho' it alleviated, his Sadness; but the Thoughts of his loved lost *Amata* embitter'd every Joy, and overwhelmed his generous Soul with Sorrow.

When the Company from the Castle joined *Benefico*, he declared to them in what manner their Deliverance was effected; and, as a general Shout of Joy resounded thro' the neighbouring Mountains, *Fidus*, lifting up his Eyes, beheld in the midst of the Multitude, standing in a pensive Posture, the fair Disconsolate. Her tender Heart was at that Instant overflowing in soft Tears, caused by a kind Participation of their present Transport, yet mixed with the deep sad Impression of a Grief her Bosom was full fraught with. Her Face, at first, was almost hid by her white Handkerchief, with which she wiped away the trickling Drops, which falling had bedew'd her beauteous Cheeks: But as she turned her lovely Face to view the joyful Conquerors, and to speak a Welcome to her kind Protector, what Words can speak the Raptures, the Astonishment, that swell'd the Bosom of the faithful Youth, when in this fair Disconsolate he saw his loved, his constant, his long-lost *Amata!* Their delighted Eyes in the same Instant beheld each other; and, breaking on each Side from their astonished Friends, they flew like Lightning into each other's Arms.

After they had given a short Account of what had passed in their Separation, *Fidus* presented to his loved *Amata* the kind, the gentle *Mignon*, with lavish Praises of his generous Friendship, and steady Resolution, in hazarding his Life by disobeying the Injunctions of the cruel Tyrant. No sooner had *Amata* heard the Name of *Mignon*, but she cried out, 'Surely my Happiness is now complete, and all my Sorrows, by this joyful Moment, are more than fully recompensed; for, in the kind Preserver of my *Fidus*, I have found my Brother. My Mother lost her little *Mignon* when he was Five Years old; and pining Grief, after some Years vain Search, ended her wretched Life.'

The generous Hearts of all who were present shared the Raptures of the faithful

Fidus, the lovely *Amata*, and gentle *Mignon*, on this happy Discovery; and in the warmest Congratulations they expressed their Joy.

Benefico now led all the delighted Company into his Castle, where Freedom was publicly proclaimed; and every one was left at Liberty either to remain there with *Benefico*, or, loaded with Wealth sufficient for their Use, to go where their Attachments or Inclinations might invite them.

Fidus, Amata, and the little *Mignon*, hesitated not one Moment to declare their Choice of staying with the generous *Benefico*.

The Nuptials of the faithful *Fidus*, and his loved *Amata*, were solemnized in the Presence of all their Friends.

Benefico passed the Remainder of his Days in pleasing Reflections on his well-spent Life.

The Treasures of the dead Tyrant were turned into Blessings, by the Use they were now made of: Little *Mignon* was loved and cherished by all his Companions. Peace, Harmony, and Love reigned in every Bosom; Dissension, Discord, and Hatred were banished from this friendly Dwelling; and that Happiness, which is the natural Consequence of Goodness, appeared in every chearful Countenance throughout the Castle of the good *Benefico*; and as heretofore Affright and Terror spread itself from the Monster's hateful Cave, so now from this peaceful Castle were diffused Tranquillity and Joy thro' all the happy Country round.

1749

JEANNE-MARIE LEPRINCE DE BEAUMONT
1711–1780

Jeanne-Marie Leprince de Beaumont, active in England and France, was one of the most prolific writers and most progressive educators of the eighteenth century. Although she, like her British contemporary Sarah Fielding, had doubts about the moral nature of fairy tales, she wrote "Beauty and the Beast," which has become one of the most famous fairy tales in the world. Born in the small city of Rouen, she received an excellent education, unlike most girls at that time, and worked as a teacher. In 1745 she married a dissolute libertine named de Beaumont, and the marriage was annulled two years later. Soon thereafter, she departed for England, where she earned her living as a governess; she often returned to France for visits. At one point she married a certain M. Pichon and raised several children in England.

During this time, she began publishing novels and stories with a strong didactic bent, in keeping with current taste. Above all Mme Leprince de Beaumont favored prose fiction that instructed readers about good manners and morals. Her first work was a novel published in France, *Le triomphe de la vérité* (*The Triumph of Truth*, 1748). However, it was in London that she made a name for herself with short stories in magazines and collections of anecdotes, stories, fairy tales, commentaries, and essays directed at specific social groups of particular ages. For instance, she published a series of pedagogical works to improve the manners of young people: *Magasin des enfans* (*The Magazine of Children*, 1757), *Magasin des adolescents* (*The Magazine of Adolescents*, 1760), *Magasin des pauvres* (*The Magazine of the Poor*, 1768), *Le mentor moderne* (*The Modern Mentor*, 1770), *Manuel de la jeunesse* (*The Manual of Youth*, 1773), and *Magasin des dévotes* (*The Magazine of Devotees*, 1779). In 1762 she returned to France, where she continued her voluminous production, and retired to a country estate in Haute-Savoie in 1768. Among her major works of this period were *Mémoires de La Baronne de Batteville* (1776), *Contes moraux* (*Moral Tales*, 1774), and *Oeuvres mêlées* (*Miscellaneous Works*, 1775). By the time of her death, she had written more than seventy books.

Leprince de Beaumont's major fairy tales were all published in *Magasin des enfans*, translated into English in 1761 as *The Young Misses Magazine, Containing Dialogues between a Governess and Several Young Ladies of Quality, Her Scholars*; aside from "La Belle et la Bête" ("Beauty and the Beast"), it includes "Le Prince Chéri," "Le Prince Désir," "Fatal et Fortuné," "Le Prince Charmante," and "Bellotte et Laidronette." Her now-familiar version of "Beauty and the Beast" is based on Gabrielle de Villeneuve's longer narrative in *La jeune Américquaine et les contes marins* (*The Young American and Sea Stories*, 1740). She emphasized the proper upbringing of young girls like Beauty, continually stressing that happiness depends on industriousness, self-sacrifice, modesty, and diligence. Throughout the tale, Leprince de Beaumont celebrates the virtue of self-denial, specifically for young girls, and Beauty exemplifies a social code that was to be identified with her character through Disney's series of *Beauty and the Beast* films in the late 1990s.

Mme Leprince de Beaumont was one of the first French writers to write fairy tales explicitly for children, and one of the first whose work was widely distributed throughout the world. As "Beauty and the Beast" demonstrates, she keeps her language and plot simple to convey more clearly her major moral messages. Though her style is limited by the lesson she wants to teach, she is careful not to destroy the magic in her tales—magic that triumphs despite her preaching.

Beauty and the Beast

Once upon a time, there was an extremely rich merchant who had six children, three boys and three girls. Since he was a sensible man, the merchant spared no expense in educating his children, and he hired all kinds of tutors for their benefit.

His daughters were very pretty, but everyone admired the youngest one in particular. When she was a small child, they simply called her "Little Beauty." As a result, the name stuck and led to a great deal of jealousy on the part of her sisters. Not only was the youngest girl prettier than her sisters, but she was also better. The two elder girls were very arrogant because they were rich. They pretended to be ladies and refused to receive the visits of daughters who belonged to merchant families. They chose only people of quality for their companions. Every day they went to the balls, the theater, and the park, and they made fun of their younger sister, who spent most of her time reading books.

Since these girls were known to be very rich, many important merchants sought their hand in marriage. But the two elder sisters maintained that they would never marry unless they found a duke, or, at the very least, a count. But Beauty—as I have mentioned, this was the name of the youngest daughter—thanked all those who proposed marriage to her and said that she was too young and that she wanted to keep her father company for some years to come.

Suddenly the merchant lost his fortune, and the only property he had left was a small country house quite far from the city. With tears in his eyes, he told his children that they would have to go and live in this house and work like farmers to support themselves. His two elder daughters replied that they did not want to leave the city and that they had many admirers who would be only too happy to marry them, even though they no longer had a fortune. But these fine young ladies were mistaken. Their admirers no longer paid them any attention now that they were poor. Moreover, since they were so arrogant, everyone disliked them and said, "They don't deserve to be pitied. It's quite nice to see their pride take a fall. Now let's see them pretend to be ladies while minding the sheep in the country."

Yet, at the same time, people said, "As for Beauty, we're disturbed about her misfortune. She's such a good girl. She was always kind to poor people. She's such a good girl, so sweet and so forthright!"

There were even several gentlemen who wanted to marry her, despite the fact that she told them that she could not bring herself to abandon her poor father in his distress, and that she was going to follow him to the country to console him and help him in his work. Poor Beauty had been greatly upset by the loss of her fortune, but she said to herself, "My tears will not bring back my fortune. So I must try to be happy without it."

When they arrived at the country house, the merchant and his three daughters began farming the land. Beauty got up at four o'clock in the morning and occupied herself by cleaning the house and preparing breakfast for the family. At first she had a great deal of difficulty because she was not accustomed to working like a servant. But after two months she became stronger, and the hard work improved her health. After finishing her chores, she generally read, played the harpsichord, or sung while spinning. On the other hand, her two sisters were bored to death. They arose at ten o'clock in the morning, took walks the entire day, and entertained themselves bemoaning the loss of their beautiful clothes and the fine company they used to have.

"Look at our little sister," they would say to each other. "Her mind is so dense, and she's so stupid that she's quite content in this miserable situation."

The good merchant did not agree with his daughters. He knew that Beauty was more suited to stand out in company than they were. He admired the virtues of this young girl—especially her patience, for her sisters were not merely content to let her do all the work in the house, but they also insulted her at every chance they got.

After living one year in this secluded spot, the merchant received a letter informing him that one of his ships that contained some of his merchandise had just arrived safely. This news turned the heads of the two elder girls, for they thought that they would finally be able to leave the countryside where they had been leading a life of boredom. When they saw their father getting ready to depart for the city, they begged him to bring them back dresses, furs, caps, and all sorts of finery. Beauty asked for nothing because she thought that all the profit from the merchandise would not be sufficient to buy what her sisters had requested.

"Don't you want me to buy you something?" her father said to her.

"Since you are so kind to think of me," she replied, "please bring me a rose, for there are none here."

Beauty was not really anxious to have a rose, but she did not want to set an example that would disparage her sisters, who would have said that she had requested nothing to show how much better she was than they were.

The good man set out for the city, but when he arrived, he found there was a lawsuit concerning his merchandise, and after a great deal of trouble, he began his return journey much poorer than he had been before. He had only thirty miles to go before he would reach his house, and he was already looking forward to seeing his children again. But he had to pass through a large forest to get to his house, and he got lost. There was a brutal snowstorm, and the wind was so strong that he was knocked from his horse two times. When nightfall arrived, he was convinced that he would die of hunger and cold or be eaten by the wolves that were howling all around him. Suddenly he saw a big light at the end of a long avenue of trees. It appeared to be quite some distance away, and he began walking in that direction. Soon he realized that the light was coming from a huge palace that was totally illuminated. The merchant thanked God for sending this help, and he hurried to the castle, but he was very surprised to find nobody in the courtyards. His horse, which had followed him, saw a large open stable and entered. Upon finding hay and oats, the poor animal, who was dying of hunger, began eating with a rapacious appetite. The merchant tied the horse up in the stable and walked toward the palace without encountering a soul. However, when he entered a large hall, he discovered a good fire and a table covered with food that was set for just one person. Since the rain and snow had soaked him from head to foot, he approached the fire to dry himself. "The master of this house will forgive the liberty I'm taking," he said to himself, "and I'm sure that he'll be here soon."

He waited a considerable time, but when the clock struck eleven, and he still did not see anyone, he could not resist his hunger anymore and took a chicken that he devoured in two mouthfuls while trembling all over. As he became more hardy, he left the hall and went through several large and magnificently furnished apartments. Finally he found a room with a good bed, and since it was past midnight and he was tired, he decided to shut the door and go to bed. It was ten o'clock in the morning when he awoke the next day, and he was greatly surprised to find very clean clothes in place of his own, which had been completely tarnished.

"Surely," he said to himself, "this palace belongs to some good fairy who has taken pity on my predicament."

He looked out the window and no longer saw snow but arbors of flowers that gave rise to an enchanting view. He went back to the large hall where he had dined the night before and saw a small table with a cup of chocolate on it.

"I want to thank you, madame fairy," he said aloud, "for being so kind as to think of my own breakfast."

After drinking his chocolate, the good man went to look for his horse, and as he passed under an arbor of roses, he remembered that Beauty had asked for one, and he plucked a rose from a branch filled with roses. All of a sudden he heard a loud noise and saw a beast coming toward him. It was so horrible-looking that he almost fainted.

"You're very ungrateful," the beast said in a ferocious voice. "I saved your life by offering you hospitality in my castle, and then you steal my roses, which I love more than anything else in the world. You shall have to die for this mistake. I'll give you just a quarter of an hour to ask for God's forgiveness."

The merchant threw himself on his knees and pleaded with his hands clasped. "Pardon me, my lord. I didn't think that I'd offend you by plucking a rose for one of my daughters who had asked me to bring her one."

"I'm not called lord," replied the monster, "but Beast. I don't like compliments and prefer that people speak their minds. So don't think that you can move me by flattery. But you didn't tell me that you had daughters. Now I'll pardon you on the condition that one of your daughters will come here voluntarily to die in your place. Don't try to reason with me. Just go. And if your daughters refuse to die for you, swear to me that you'll return within three months."

The good man did not intend to sacrifice one of his daughters to this hideous monster, but he thought, "At least I'll have the pleasure of embracing them one more time."

So he swore he would return, and the beast told him he could leave whenever he liked. "But," he added, "I don't want you to leave empty-handed. Go back to the room where you slept. There you'll find a large empty chest. You may fill it with whatever you like, and I shall have it carried home for you."

Meanwhile, the Beast withdrew, and the good man said to himself, "If I must die, I shall still have the consolation of leaving my children with something to sustain themselves."

He returned to the room where he had slept, and upon finding a large quantity of gold pieces, he filled the big chest that the Beast had mentioned. After closing it, he went to his horse, which he found in the stable, and he left the palace with a sadness that matched the joy that he had experienced upon entering it. His horse took one of the forest roads on its own, and within a few hours the good man arrived at his small house, where his children gathered around him. But instead of responding to their caresses, the merchant burst into tears at the sight of them. His hand held the branch of roses that he had brought for Beauty, and he gave it to her saying, "Beauty, take these roses. They will cost your poor father dearly."

Immediately thereafter he told his family about the tempestuous adventure that he had experienced. On hearing the tale, the two elder daughters uttered loud cries and berated Beauty, who did not weep.

"See what this measly creature's arrogance has caused!" they said. "Why didn't she settle for the same gifts as ours. But no, our lady had to be different. Now she's going to be the cause of our father's death, and she doesn't even cry."

"That would be quite senseless," replied Beauty. "Why should I lament my father's death when he is not going to perish. Since the monster is willing to accept one of his daughters, I intend to offer myself to placate his fury, and I feel very happy to be in a position to save my father and prove my affection for him."

"No, sister," said her three brothers, "you won't die. We shall go and find this monster, and we'll die under his blows if we can't kill him."

"Don't harbor any such hopes, my children," said the merchant. "The Beast's power is so great that I don't have the slightest hope of having him killed. I'm delighted by the goodness of Beauty's heart, but I won't expose her to death. I'm old, and I don't have much longer to live. Therefore, I'll only lose a few years of my life, which I won't regret losing on account of you, my dear children."

"Rest assured, Father," said Beauty, "you won't go to this palace without me. You can't prevent me from following you. Even though I'm young, I'm not all that strongly tied to life, and I'd rather be devoured by this monster than to die of the grief that your loss would cause me."

Words were in vain. Beauty was completely determined to depart for this beautiful palace. And her sisters were delighted by this because the virtues of their younger sister had filled them with a good deal of jealousy. The merchant was so concerned by the torment of losing his daughter that he forgot all about the chest that he had filled with gold. But as soon as he returned to his room to sleep, he was quite astonished to find it by the side of his bed. He decided not to tell his children that he had become rich because his daughters would have wanted to return to the city, and he was resolved to die in the country. However, he confided his secret to Beauty, who informed him that several gentlemen had come during his absence and that there were two who loved her sisters. She pleaded with her father to let her sisters get married, for she was of such a kind nature that she loved them and forgave the evil they had done her with all her heart.

When Beauty departed with her father, the two nasty sisters rubbed their eyes with onions to weep. But her brothers wept in reality as did the merchant. Beauty was the only one who did not cry because she did not want to increase their distress.

The horse took the road to the palace, and by nightfall, they spotted it totally illuminated as before. The horse was installed in the stable all alone, and the good man entered the large hall with his daughter. There they found a table magnificently set for two people. However, the merchant did not have the heart to eat. On the other hand, Beauty forced herself to appear calm, and she sat down at the table and served him. Then she said to herself, "It's clear that the Beast is providing such a lovely feast to fatten me up before eating me."

After they had finished supper, they heard a loud noise, and the merchant said good-bye to his daughter with tears in his eyes, for he knew it was the Beast. Beauty could only tremble at the sight of this horrible figure, but she summoned her courage. The monster asked her if she had come of her own accord, and she responded yes and continued to shake.

"You are, indeed, quite good," said the Beast, "and I am very much obliged to you. As for you, my good man, you are to depart tomorrow, and never think of returning here. Good-bye, Beauty."

"Good-bye, Beast," she responded.

Suddenly the Beast disappeared.

"Oh, my daughter!" said the merchant embracing Beauty. "I'm half dead with fear. Believe me, it's best if I stay."

"No, my father," Beauty said firmly. "You're to depart tomorrow morning, and you'll leave me to the mercy of heaven. Perhaps heaven will take pity on me."

After they had gone to bed, they thought they would not be able to sleep the entire night. But they were hardly in their beds when their eyes closed shut. During her sleep, Beauty envisioned a lady who said to her, "Your kind heart pleases me, Beauty. The good deed you're performing to save your father's life shall not go unrewarded."

When Beauty awoke the next morning, she told her father about the dream, and though this consoled him somewhat, it did not prevent him from sobbing loudly when he had to separate himself from his dear child. After he departed, Beauty sat down in the great hall and also began to weep. Yet, since she had a great deal of courage, she asked God to protect her and resolved not to grieve any more during the short time she had to live. She firmly believed that the Beast was going to eat her that night, and in the meantime she decided to take a walk and explore this splendid castle. She could not help but admire its beauty, and she was quite surprised when she found a door on which were written the words "Beauty's Room." She opened the door quickly, and she was dazed by the magnificence that radiated throughout the room. But what struck her most of all was a large library, a harpsichord, and numerous books of music. "They don't want me to get bored," she whispered to herself. "If I'm only supposed to spend one day here, they wouldn't have made all these preparations."

This thought renewed her courage. She opened the library, saw a book, and read these letters on it: "Your wish is our command. You are queen and mistress here."

"Alas!" she said with a sigh. "My only wish is to see my poor father again and to know what he's doing at this very moment."

She had said this only to herself, so you can imagine her surprise when she glanced at a large mirror and saw her home, where her father was arriving with an extremely sad face. Her sisters went out to meet him, and despite the grimaces they made to pretend to be distressed, the joy on their faces at the loss of their sister was visible. One moment later, everything in the mirror disappeared, and Beauty could not but think that the Beast had been most compliant and that she had nothing to fear from him.

At noon she found the table set, and during her meal she heard an excellent concert, even though she did not see a soul. That evening, as she was about to sit down at the table, she heard the noise made by the Beast and could not keep herself from trembling.

"Beauty," the monster said to her, "would you mind if I watch you dine?"

"You're the master," replied Beauty trembling.

"No," responded the Beast. "You are the mistress here, and you only have to tell me to go if I bother you. Then I'll leave immediately. Tell me, do you find me very ugly?"

"Yes, I do," said Beauty. "I don't know how to lie. But I believe that you're very good."

"You're right," said the monster. "But aside from my ugliness, I'm not all that intelligent. I know quite well that I'm just a beast."

"A stupid person doesn't realize that he lacks intelligence," Beauty replied. "Fools never know what they're missing."

"Enjoy your meal, Beauty," the monster said to her, "and try to amuse yourself in your house, for everything here is yours. I'd feel upset if you were not happy."

"You're quite kind," Beauty said. "I assure you that I am most pleased with your kind heart. When I think of that, you no longer seem ugly to me."

"Oh, yes," the Beast answered, "I have a kind heart, but I'm still a monster."

"There are many men who are more monstrous than you," Beauty said, "and I prefer you with your looks rather than those who have a human face but conceal false, ungrateful, and corrupt hearts."

"If I had the intelligence," the Beast responded, "I'd make you a fine compliment to thank you. But I'm stupid so that I can only say that I'm greatly obliged to you."

Beauty ate with a good appetite. She was no longer afraid of the Beast, but she nearly died of fright when he said, "Beauty, will you be my wife?"

She did not answer right away, for she was fearful of enraging the monster by refusing him. At last, however, she said, trembling, "No, Beast."

At that moment, the poor monster wanted to sigh, but he made such a frightful whistle that it echoed through the entire palace. Beauty soon regained her courage, for the Beast said to her in a sad voice, "Farewell, then, Beauty."

He left the room, turning to look at her from time to time as he went. When Beauty was alone, she felt a great deal of compassion for the Beast. "It's quite a shame," she said, "that he's so ugly, for he's so good."

Beauty spent three months in the palace in great tranquillity. Every evening the Beast paid her a visit and entertained her at supper in conversation with plain good sense, but not what the world calls wit. Every day Beauty discovered new qualities in the monster. She had become so accustomed to seeing him that she adjusted to his ugliness, and far from dreading the moment of his visit, she often looked at her watch to see if it was already nine o'clock, for the Beast never failed to appear at that hour.

There was only one thing that troubled Beauty. Before she went to bed each night, the Beast would always ask her if she would be his wife, and he seemed deeply wounded when she refused.

"You're making me uncomfortable, Beast," she said one day. "I'd like to be able to marry you, but I'm too frank to allow you to believe that this could ever happen. I'll always be your friend. Try to be content with that."

"I'll have to," responded the Beast. "To be honest with myself, I know I'm quite horrible-looking. But I love you very much. However, I'm happy enough with the knowledge that you want to stay here. Promise me that you'll never leave me."

Beauty blushed at these words, for she had seen in her mirror that her father was sick with grief at having lost her, and she wished to see him again.

"I could very easily promise never to leave you," she said to the Beast. "But I have such a desire to see my father again that I would die of grief if you were to refuse me this request."

"I'd rather die myself than to cause you grief," the monster said. "I'll send you to your father's home. You shall stay with him, and your poor beast will die of grief."

"No," Beauty said to him with tears in her eyes. "I love you too much to want to cause your death. I promise to return in a week's time. You've shown me that my sisters are married and my brothers have left home to join the army. Just let me stay a week with my father since he's all alone."

"You shall be there tomorrow morning," the Beast said. "But remember your promise. You only have to place your ring on the table before going to bed if you want to return. Farewell, Beauty."

As was his custom, the Beast sighed when he said these words, and Beauty went to bed very sad at having disturbed him. When she awoke the next morning, she found herself in her father's house, and when she rang a bell that was at her bedside, it was answered by a servant who uttered a great cry upon seeing her. Her good father came running when he heard the noise and almost died of joy at seeing his dear daughter again. They kept hugging each other for more than a quarter of an hour. After their excitement subsided, Beauty recalled that she did not have any clothes to wear. But the servant told her that he had just found a chest in the next room, and it was full of dresses trimmed with gold and diamonds. Beauty thanked the good Beast for looking after her. She took the least rich of the dresses and told the servant to lock up the others, for she wanted to send them as gifts to her sisters. But no sooner had she spoken those words than the chest disappeared. Her father told Beauty that the Beast probably wanted her to keep them for herself, and within seconds the dresses and the chest came back again.

While Beauty proceeded to get dressed, a message was sent to inform her sisters of her arrival, and they came running with their husbands. Both sisters were exceedingly unhappy. The oldest had married a young gentleman who was remarkably handsome but was so enamored of his own looks that he occupied himself with nothing but his appearance from morning until night, and he despised his wife's beauty. The second sister had married a man who was very intelligent, but he used his wit only to enrage everyone, first and foremost his wife. The sisters almost died of grief when they saw Beauty dressed like a princess and more beautiful than daylight. It was in vain that she hugged them, for nothing could stifle their jealousy, which increased when she told them how happy she was.

The two envious sisters went down into the garden to vent their feelings in tears. "Why is this little snip happier than we are?" they asked each other. "Aren't we just as pleasing as she is?"

"Sister," said the oldest, "I've just had an idea. Let's try to keep her here more than a week. That stupid beast will become enraged when he finds out that she's broken her word, and perhaps he'll devour her."

"Right you are, sister," responded the other. "But we must show her a great deal of affection to succeed."

Having made this decision, they returned to the house and showed Beauty so much attention that Beauty wept with joy. After a week had passed, the two sisters tore their hair and were so distressed by her departure that she promised to remain another week. However, Beauty reproached herself for the grief she was causing her poor Beast, whom she loved with all her heart. In addition, she missed not being able to see him any longer. On the tenth night that she spent in her father's house, she dreamt that she was in the palace garden and saw the Beast lying on the grass nearly dead and reprimanding her for her ingratitude. Beauty awoke with a start and burst into tears.

"Aren't I very wicked for causing grief to a beast who's gone out of his way to please me?" she said. "Is it his fault that he's so ugly and has so little intelligence? He's so kind, and that's worth more than anything else. Why haven't I wanted to marry him? I'm more happy with him than my sisters are with their husbands. It is neither handsome looks nor intelligence that makes a woman happy. It is good character, virtue, and kindness, and the Beast has all these good qualities. It's clear that I don't love him, but I have respect, friendship, and gratitude for him. So there's no reason to make him miserable, and if I'm ungrateful, I'll reproach myself my entire life."

With these words Beauty arose, placed her ring on the table, and lay down again. No sooner was she in her bed than she fell asleep, and when she awoke the next morning, she saw with joy that she was in the Beast's palace. She put on her most magnificent dress to please him and spent a boring day waiting for nine o'clock in the evening to arrive. But the clock struck in vain, for the Beast did not appear.

Now Beauty feared that she had caused his death. She ran throughout the palace sobbing loudly and was terribly despondent. After searching everywhere, she recalled her dream and ran into the garden toward the canal where she had seen him in her sleep. There she found the poor Beast stretched out and unconscious, and she thought he was dead. She threw herself on his body without being horrified by his looks, and she felt his heart still beating. So she fetched some water from the canal and threw it on his face.

Beast opened his eyes and said to Beauty, "You forgot your promise. The grief I felt upon having lost you made me decide to die of hunger. But I shall die content since I have the pleasure of seeing you one more time."

"No, my dear Beast, you shall not die," said Beauty. "You shall live to become my husband. From this moment on, I give you my hand and swear that I belong only to you. Alas! I thought that I only felt friendship for you, but the torment I am feeling makes me realize that I cannot live without you."

Beauty had scarcely uttered these words when the castle radiated with light. Fireworks and music announced a feast. But these attractions could not hold her attention. She returned her gaze toward her dear Beast, whose dangerous condition made her tremble. But how great was her surprise! The Beast had disappeared, and at her feet was a prince more handsome than Eros[1] himself, and he thanked her for having put an end to his enchantment. Although the prince merited her undivided attention, she could not refrain from asking what had happened to the Beast.

"You're looking at him right at your feet," the prince said. "A wicked fairy had condemned me to remain in this form until a beautiful girl would consent to marry me, and she had prohibited me from revealing my intelligence. You were the only person in the world kind enough to allow the goodness of my character to touch you, and in offering you my crown, I'm only discharging the obligations I owe you."

Beauty was most pleasantly surprised and assisted the handsome prince in rising by offering her hand. Together they went to the castle, and Beauty was overwhelmed by joy in finding her father and entire family in the hall, for the beautiful lady who had appeared to her in her dream had transported them to the castle.

1. The Greek god of love, who came to be the patron god of handsome young men.

"Beauty," said this lady, who was a grand fairy, "come and receive the reward for your good choice. You've preferred virtue over beauty and wit, and you deserve to find these qualities combined in one and the same person. You're going to become a great queen, and I hope that the throne will not destroy your virtues. As for you, my young ladies," the fairy said to Beauty's two sisters, "I know your hearts and all the malice they contain. You shall become statues, but you shall retain your ability to think beneath the stone that encompasses you. You shall stand at the portal of your sister's palace, and I can think of no better punishment to impose on you than to witness her happiness. I'll only allow you to return to your original shape when you recognize your faults. But I fear that you'll remain statues forever. Pride, anger, gluttony, and laziness can all be corrected, but some sort of miracle is needed to convert a wicked and envious heart."

All at once the fairy waved her wand and transported everyone in the hall to the prince's realm. His subjects rejoiced upon seeing him again, and he married Beauty, who lived with him a long time in perfect happiness because their relationship was founded on virtue.

1757

JACOB GRIMM *and* WILHELM GRIMM
1785–1863
1786–1859

Although the Brothers Grimm had hoped to collect and publish folktales that would testify to the greatness of ancient German culture, the anthology they produced was more international in scope than they realized. At the same time, their great insight and artistry in editing and refining the material made the tales second only to the Bible in German readership. Indeed, appearing in numerous editions and translated under various titles, they gradually became the greatest exemplary collection of fairy tales in the world—quite an accomplishment by two scholars who were more interested in philology than in magical fairy tales for children.

Jacob and Wilhelm Grimm were born in the village of Hanau. The family's economic security and social status were abruptly lost with the early death of their father in 1796; two years later Jacob and Wilhelm were sent to a well-to-do aunt in Kassel to prepare for college at a famous lyceum. Each one graduated at the head of his class, and each went to the University of Marburg to study law. By 1805, they both decided to dedicate themselves to researching old German literature and customs. The French occupation of Kassel from 1807 to 1813 brought some turmoil, but Jacob and Wilhelm were

able to collect oral and literary tales and other historical materials. The first publication of each appeared in 1811: Jacob's *Über den altdeutschen Meistergesang* (*On the Old German Mastersong*) and Wilhelm's *Altdänische Heldenlieder* (*Danish Heroic Songs*). More important, they together published the first volume of the *Kinder- und Hausmärchen* (*Children's and Household Tales*) with scholarly annotations in 1812.

After the French withdrew from Kassel, Jacob was appointed legation secretary for Hessian diplomats and served in Paris and Vienna. During his absence Wilhelm became secretary to the royal librarian in Kassel and was able to concentrate on bringing out the second volume of *Children's and Household Tales* in 1815. On Jacob's return to Kassel, he became a librarian in the royal library and joined Wilhelm in editing the first volume of *Deutsche Sagen* (*German Legends*, 1816). Over the next thirteen years, the Grimms enjoyed a period of relative calm during which they could devote themselves to scholarly research and publication, producing numerous volumes on folklore and philology. Wilhelm married in 1825 (and would have four children). Both brothers felt undercompensated in

Kassel, and in 1829 they accepted positions at the University of Göttingen; Jacob became professor of old German literature and head librarian, and Wilhelm became a librarian and, eventually, professor in 1835. Jacob's important works during this time include the third volume of *German Grammar* (1831) and *Deutsche Mythologie* (*German Mythology*, 1835); Wilhelm prepared the third edition of *Children's and Household Tales* (1837).

When King Ernst August II succeeded to the throne of Hannover in 1837, he revoked the relatively liberal constitution of 1833, dissolved parliament, and declared that all civil servants had to pledge an oath to serve him personally. The Grimms and five other professors who refused to comply were immediately dismissed; after spending three years in Kassel living with one of their younger brothers, both received offers to become professors at the University of Berlin and members of the Academy of Sciences. In March 1841 the Grimms took up residence in Berlin and were able to continue their labor, begun in Kassel, on the *Deutsches Wörterbuch* (*German Dictionary*)—one of the most ambitious lexicographical undertakings of the nineteenth century. For the rest of their lives, the Grimms devoted most of their energy to completing the monumental dictionary, but they got only as far as the letter F; indeed, the final volume was not published until 1961. Yet the Grimms did complete a remarkable body of work, contributing significantly to scholarship in folklore, history, ethnology, religion, jurisprudence, lexicography, and literary criticism.

During their lifetimes there were seven major editions of *Children's and Household Tales*. The first edition, containing 156 tales, appeared in two volumes (1812, 1815) intended for scholars. Thereafter the tales were always published in one volume, with new tales being added until the seventh edition of 1857 contained 210. Beginning with the second edition in 1819, Wilhelm Grimm was chiefly responsible for revising and expanding the collection, and most of the subsequent additions came from literary rather than oral sources. Also beginning with the second edition, the collection was edited with children and use in households more in mind. In addition, an abbreviated version that included fifty of the more popular tales went through ten editions from 1825 to 1858.

The history of these texts reveals how assiduously the Grimms sought through constant revision to influence our notions of how to socialize and rear children. The case of "Hansel and Gretel" is exemplary. Wilhelm heard the story from Dortchen Wild, daughter of a pharmacist in Kassel, about 1809. The Grimms indicated in their notes that they knew Charles Perrault's "Le petit poucet" ("Little Thumbling," 1697), with which it shares many plot elements, as well as other folk versions. By the time Wilhelm rewrote the story for the second edition of 1819, he was also familiar with Giambattista Basile's "Ninnillo and Nennella" (1634), a similar tale well-known in southern Italy. Wilhelm repeatedly revised "Hansel and Gretel," in each edition making it more Christian in tone and placing greater blame on a stepmother for abandoning the children (the tale as told to Wilhelm featured a biological mother). In essence, his version, like many others, depicts women as threatening figures while it apologizes for the father's behavior.

Popular and important tales similar to the Grimms' version can be found throughout Europe in the oral and literary tradition because the theme of child abandonment and abuse is so powerful. Although we cannot accurately estimate how widespread child abandonment was, the combination of famines, poor living conditions, and lack of contraceptives clearly resulted in the birth of many unwanted children. In the Middle Ages children who could not be fed were sometimes left in front of a church, in a special area of the village square, or in the forest. Sometimes abandonment or abuse followed a parent's remarriage to a man or woman who could not tolerate the children from a previous marriage. In the fairy tales, abandoned children do not always meet a witch—but they do encounter a dangerous character who threatens their lives, and they must use their wits to find their way home. In part because it celebrates the patriarchal home as haven, in the nineteenth century "Hansel and Gretel" became one of the most beloved of the Grimms' tales. Ludwig Bechstein probably based his version in *Deutsches Märchenbuch* (*Book of German Fairy Tales*, 1857) on the Grimms' tale, which similarly inspired Engelbert Humperdinck's famous opera *Hänsel und Gretel* (1893).

Hansel and Gretel

A poor woodcutter lived with his wife and his two children on the edge of a large forest. The boy was called Hansel and the girl Gretel. The woodcutter did not have much food around the house, and when a great famine devastated the entire country, he could no longer provide enough for his family's daily meals. One night, as he was lying in bed and thinking about his worries, he began tossing and turning. Then he sighed and said to his wife, "What's to become of us? How can we feed our poor children when we don't even have enough for ourselves?"

"I'll tell you what," answered his wife. "Early tomorrow morning we'll take the children out into the forest where it's most dense. We'll build a fire and give them each a piece of bread. Then we'll go about our work and leave them alone. They won't find their way back home, and we'll be rid of them."

"No, wife," the man said. "I won't do this. I don't have the heart to leave my children in the forest. The wild beasts would soon come and tear them apart."

"Oh, you fool!" she said. "Then all four of us will have to starve to death. You'd better start planing the boards for our coffins!" She continued to harp on this until he finally agreed to do what she suggested.

"But still, I feel sorry for the poor children," he said.

The two children had not been able to fall asleep that night either. Their hunger kept them awake, and when they heard what their stepmother said to their father, Gretel wept bitter tears and said to Hansel, "Now it's all over for us."

"Be quiet, Gretel," Hansel said. "Don't get upset. I'll soon find a way to help us."

When their parents had fallen asleep, Hansel put on his little jacket, opened the bottom half of the door, and crept outside. The moon was shining very brightly, and the white pebbles glittered in front of the house like pure silver coins. Hansel stooped down to the ground and stuffed his pocket with as many pebbles as he could fit in. Then he went back and said to Gretel, "Don't worry, my dear little sister. Just sleep in peace. God will not forsake us." And he lay down again in his bed.

At dawn, even before the sun began to rise, the woman came and woke the two children.

"Get up, you lazybones!" she said. "We're going into the forest to fetch some wood." Then she gave each one of them a piece of bread and said, "Now you have something for your noonday meal, but don't eat it before then because you're not getting anything else."

Gretel put the bread under her apron because Hansel had the pebbles in his pocket. Then they all set out together toward the forest. After they had walked a while, Hansel stopped and looked back at the house. He did this time and again until his father said, "Hansel, what are you looking at there? Why are you dawdling? Pay attention, and don't forget how to use your legs!"

"Oh, father," said Hansel, "I'm looking at my little white cat that's sitting up on the roof and wants to say good-bye to me."

"You fool," the mother said. "That's not a cat. It's the morning sun shining on the chimney."

But Hansel had not been looking at the cat. Instead, he had been taking the shiny pebbles from his pocket and constantly dropping them on the ground. When they reached the middle of the forest, the father said, "Children, I want you to gather some wood. I'm going to make a fire so you won't get cold."

Hansel and Gretel gathered together some brushwood and built quite a nice little pile. The brushwood was soon kindled, and when the fire was ablaze, the woman said, "Now, children, lie down by the fire, and rest yourselves. We're going into the forest to chop wood. When we're finished, we'll come back and get you."

Hansel and Gretel sat by the fire, and when noon came, they ate their pieces of bread. Since they heard the sounds of the ax, they thought their father was nearby. But it was not the ax. Rather, it was a branch that he had tied to a dead tree, and the wind was banging it back and forth. After they had been sitting there for a long time, they became so weary that their eyes closed, and they fell sound asleep. By the time they finally awoke, it was already pitch-black, and Gretel began to cry and said, "How are we going to get out of the forest?"

But Hansel comforted her by saying, "Just wait a while until the moon has risen. Then we'll find the way."

And when the full moon had risen, Hansel took his little sister by the hand and followed the pebbles that glittered like newly minted silver coins and showed them the way. They walked the whole night long and arrived back at their father's house at break of day. They knocked at the door, and when the woman opened it and saw that it was Hansel and Gretel, she said, "You wicked children, why did you sleep so long in the forest? We thought you'd never come back again."

But the father was delighted because he had been deeply troubled by the way he had abandoned them in the forest.

Not long after that the entire country was once again ravaged by famine, and one night the children heard their mother talking to their father in bed: "Everything's been eaten up again. We only have half a loaf of bread, but after it's gone, that will be the end of our food. The children must leave. This time we'll take them even farther into the forest so they won't find their way back home again. Otherwise, there's no hope for us."

All this saddened the father, and he thought, "It'd be much better to share your last bite to eat with your children." But the woman would not listen to anything he said. She just scolded and reproached him. Indeed, whoever starts something must go on with it, and since he had given in the first time, he also had to yield a second time.

However, the children were still awake and had overheard their conversation. When their parents had fallen asleep, Hansel got up, intending to go out and gather pebbles as he had done before, but the woman had locked the door, and Hansel could not get out. Nevertheless, he comforted his little sister and said, "Don't cry, Gretel. Just sleep in peace. The dear Lord is bound to help us."

Early the next morning the woman came and got the children out of bed. They each received little pieces of bread, but they were smaller than the last time. On the way into the forest Hansel crumbled the bread in his pocket and stopped as often as he could to throw the crumbs on the ground.

"Hansel, why are you always stopping and looking around?" asked the father. "Keep going!"

"I'm looking at my little pigeon that's sitting on the roof and wants to say goodbye to me," Hansel answered.

"Fool!" the woman said. "That's not your little pigeon. It's the morning sun shining on the chimney."

But little by little Hansel managed to scatter all the bread crumbs on the path. The woman led the children even deeper into the forest until they came to a spot they had never in their lives seen before. Once again a large fire was made, and the mother said, "Just keep sitting here, children. If you get tired, you can sleep a little.

We're going into the forest to chop wood, and in the evening, when we're done, we'll come and get you."

When noon came, Gretel shared her bread with Hansel, who had scattered his along the way. Then they fell asleep, and evening passed, but no one came for the poor children. Only when it was pitch-black did they finally wake up, and Hansel comforted his little sister by saying, "Just wait until the moon has risen, Gretel. Then we'll see the little bread crumbs that I scattered. They'll show us the way back home."

When the moon rose, they set out but could not find the crumbs because the many thousands of birds that fly about the forest and fields had devoured them.

"Don't worry, we'll find the way," Hansel said to Gretel, but they could not find it. They walked the entire night and all the next day as well, from morning till night, but they did not get out of the forest. They were now also very hungry, for they had had nothing to eat except some berries that they had found growing on the ground. Eventually they became so tired that their legs would no longer carry them, and they lay down beneath a tree and fell asleep.

It was now the third morning since they had left their father's house. They began walking again, and they kept going deeper and deeper into the forest. If help did not arrive soon, they were bound to perish of hunger and exhaustion. At noon they saw a beautiful bird as white as snow sitting on a branch. It sang with such a lovely voice that the children stood still and listened to it. When the bird finished its song, it flapped its wings and flew ahead of them. They followed it until they came to a little house that was made of bread. Moreover, it had cake for a roof and pure sugar for windows.

"What a blessed meal!" said Hansel. "Let's have a taste. I want to eat a piece of the roof. Gretel, you can have some of the window since it's sweet."

Hansel reached up high and broke off a piece of the roof to see how it tasted, and Gretel leaned against the windowpanes and nibbled on them. Then they heard a shrill voice cry from inside:

> "Nibble, nibble, I hear a mouse.
> Who's that nibbling at my house?"

The children answered:

> "The wind, the wind; it's very mild,
> blowing like the Heavenly Child."

And they did not bother to stop eating or let themselves be distracted. Since the roof tasted so good, Hansel ripped off a large piece and pulled it down, while Gretel pushed out a round piece of the windowpane, sat down, and ate it with great relish. Suddenly the door opened, and a very old woman leaning on a crutch came slinking out of the house. Hansel and Gretel were so tremendously frightened that they dropped what they had in their hands. But the old woman wagged her head and said, "Well now, dear children, who brought you here? Just come inside and stay with me. Nobody's going to harm you."

She took them both by the hand and led them into her house. Then she served them a good meal of milk and pancakes with sugar and apples and nuts. Afterward, she made up two little beds with white sheets, whereupon Hansel and Gretel lay down in them and thought they were in heaven.

The old woman, however, had only pretended to be friendly. She was really a wicked witch on the lookout for children and had built the house made of bread only to lure them to her. As soon as she had any children in her power, she would kill, cook, and eat them. It would be like a feast day for her. Now witches have red eyes and cannot see very far, but they have a keen sense of smell, like animals, and can detect when human beings are near them. Therefore, when Hansel and Gretel had come into her vicinity, she had laughed wickedly and scoffed, "They're mine! They'll never get away from me!"

Early the next morning, before the children were awake, she got up and looked at the two of them sleeping so sweetly with full rosy cheeks. Then she muttered to herself, "They'll certainly make for a tasty meal!"

She seized Hansel with her scrawny hands and carried him into a small pen, where she locked him up behind a grilled door. No matter how much he screamed, it did not help. Then she went back to Gretel, shook her until she woke up, and yelled, "Get up, you lazybones! I want you to fetch some water and cook your brother something nice. He's sitting outside in a pen, and we've got to fatten him up. Then, when he's fat enough, I'm going to eat him."

Gretel began to weep bitter tears, but they were all in vain. She had to do what the wicked witch demanded. So the very best food was cooked for poor Hansel, while Gretel got nothing but crab shells. Every morning the old woman went slinking to the little pen and called out, "Hansel, stick out your finger so I can feel how fat you are."

However, Hansel stuck out a little bone, and since the old woman had poor eyesight, she thought the bone was Hansel's finger. She was puzzled that Hansel did not get any fatter, and when a month had gone by and Hansel still seemed to be thin, she was overcome by her impatience and decided not to wait any longer.

"Hey there, Gretel!" she called to the little girl. "Get a move on and fetch some water! I don't care whether Hansel's fat or thin. He's going to be slaughtered tomorrow, and then I'll cook him."

Oh, how the poor little sister wailed as she was carrying the water, and how the tears streamed down her cheeks!

"Dear God, help us!" she exclaimed. "If only the wild beasts had eaten us in the forest, then we could have at least died together!"

Early the next morning Gretel had to go out, hang up a kettle full of water, and light the fire.

"First we'll bake," the old woman said. "I've already heated the oven and kneaded the dough." She pushed poor Gretel out to the oven, where the flames were leaping from the fire. "Crawl inside," said the witch, "and see if it's properly heated so we can slide the bread in."

The witch intended to close the oven door once Gretel had climbed inside, for the witch wanted to bake her and eat her, too. But Gretel sensed what she had in mind and said, "I don't know how to do it. How do I get in?"

"You stupid goose," the old woman said. "The opening's large enough. Watch, even I can get in!"

She waddled up to the oven and stuck her head through the oven door. Then Gretel gave her a push that sent her flying inside and shut the iron door and bolted it. *Whew!* The witch began to howl dreadfully, but Gretel ran away, and the godless witch was miserably burned to death.

Meanwhile, Gretel ran straight to Hansel, opened the pen, and cried out, "Hansel, we're saved! The old witch is dead!"

Then Hansel jumped out of the pen like a bird that hops out of a cage when the door is opened. My how happy they were! They hugged each other, danced around, and kissed. Since they no longer had anything to fear, they went into the witch's house, and there they found chests filled with pearls and jewels all over the place.

"They're certainly much better than pebbles," said Hansel, and he put whatever he could fit into his pocket, and Gretel said, "I'm going to carry some home, too." And she filled her apron full of jewels and pearls.

"We'd better be on our way now," said Hansel, "so we can get out of the witch's forest."

When they had walked for a few hours, they reached a large river.

"We can't get across," said Hansel. "I don't see a bridge or any way over it."

"There are no boats either," Gretel responded, "but there's a white duck swimming over there. It's bound to help us across if I ask it." Then she cried out:

> "Help us, help us, little duck!
> We're Hansel and Gretel, out of luck.
> We can't get over, try as we may.
> Please take us across right away!"

The little duck came swimming up to them, and Hansel got on top of its back and told his sister to sit down beside him.

"No," Gretel answered. "We'll be too heavy for the little duck. Let it carry us across one at a time."

The kind little duck did just that, and when they were safely across and had walked on for some time, the forest became more and more familiar to them, and finally they caught sight of their father's house from afar. They began to run at once, and soon rushed into the house and threw themselves around their father's neck. The man had not had a single happy hour since he had abandoned his children in the forest, and in the meantime his wife had died. Gretel opened and shook out the apron so that the pearls and jewels bounced about the room, and Hansel added to this by throwing one handful after another from his pocket. Now all their troubles were over, and they lived together in utmost joy.

My tale is done. See the mouse run. Catch it, whoever can, and then you can make a great big cap out of its fur.

1812, rev. 1857

HANS CHRISTIAN ANDERSEN
1805–1875

Although Hans Christian Andersen titled the third version of his autobiography *The Fairy Tale of My Life* (1855), his life was anything but idyllic. Indeed, he wrote his fairy tales to deal with his inner turmoil: a gifted artist, he felt unappreciated and humiliated most of his life. Like the ugly duckling that he created, he desperately sought to prove that he was an authentic noble creature, but he could never feel entirely accepted by the nobility. Born in Odense, Denmark, of an extremely poor family, Andersen left home at an early age and settled in Copenhagen in 1819. A wealthy patron enabled him to receive a formal education at a private school in Slagelse; after his graduation in 1828, he began a career as writer. Extremely ambitious, Andersen sought to establish himself as the most gifted writer in Denmark in the early 1830s. He wrote plays, poems, travel books, and stories, taking numerous trips outside Denmark to seek fresh inspiration for his writing. His first taste of fame did not come until 1835, when he published *Improvisatoren* (*The Improvisatore*), the first Danish experimental novel of social realism. More important, he wrote his first volume of fairy tales, *Eventyr foralte for Born* (*Fairy Tales Told for Children*). With each successive volume, which he generally published annually at Christmas until his death in 1875, Andersen's reputation spread throughout Europe and North America.

Altogether he published 156 tales during his lifetime. The first collection consisted of five: "The Tinder Box," "The Princess and the Pea," "Little Claus and Big Claus," "Little Ida's Flowers," and "Thumbelina." For the most part these were folktales expressly adapted for a young audience. In 1837 Andersen added "The Little Mermaid," "The Naughty Boy," "The Traveling Companion," and "The Emperor's New Clothes," and continued adding tales almost every year. Until 1843 he dedicated the tales to children, but thereafter he changed the title of his anthologies to *Nye Eventyr* (*New Fairy Tales*), a more accurate indication of the direction he was taking: he no longer wrote exclusively for young audiences (if he ever had), and many of his compositions broke away from conventions of the fairy-tale genre.

Andersen published fables, allegories, anecdotes, legends, satires, farces, philosophical commentaries, and didactic stories. His themes vary greatly, but generally—as in "The Swineherd" (1842)—he depicts the difficulties of underdogs trying to prove their merit and gain revenge on their oppressors. He was one of the first writers to introduce modern elements into fairy tales and give them contemporary settings. In so doing, he developed and revitalized the newly popular genre of the *Kunstmärchen*, the literary fairy tale. A number of German Romantics—writers as different as Clemens Brentano, Joseph von Eichendorff, Adelbert von Chamisso, and E. T. A. Hoffmann—reworked folklore and introduced into their tales fantastic events and characters, together with complex ideas expressed in subtle styles. They catered to the tastes and needs of a middle-class reading public, whereas the oral folktales appealed to the lower classes and peasantry. Influenced greatly by these German romantics, Andersen gradually developed his own themes and a refreshing, humorous style, distinguished by lively, colloquial dialogues, that made his tales the most popular in Europe among children and adults alike. Much more than the tales of Charles Perrault and of Jacob and Wilhelm Grimm, Andersen's stories bring out the individual personality of his characters, who are often tragicomic figures left unfulfilled at the end of the tales.

"The Nightingale" can be viewed as a meditation on art, genius, and the role of the artist. It involves a series of transformations in power relations and service. Though Andersen intends to show in this tale how the health of an emperor—that is, the spirit of an empire—is dependent on genuine art, he also makes it clear that the artist wants to be the devoted servant of an autocrat (with no strings attached, of course). Such was Andersen's private resolution of the artist's dilemma: he proclaimed the cult of genius and yet relegated the artist to the humble role of servant because he feared the loss of patronage and social prestige. But this tale is more than just a personal declaration about the artist's function. Andersen's genius lay in his ability to transform his private conflicts into metaphorical tales that address universal social problems. Here, the mechanization of art and the issue of patronage are major themes that continue to be very relevant today.

The Nightingale

In China, you must know, the Emperor is a Chinaman, and all whom he has about him are Chinamen too. It happened a good many years ago, but that's just why it's worth while to hear the story, before it is forgotten. The Emperor's palace was the most splendid in the world; it was made entirely of porcelain, very costly, but so delicate and brittle that one had to take care how one touched it. In the garden were to be seen the most wonderful flowers, and to the costliest of them silver bells were tied, which sounded, so that nobody should pass by without noticing the flowers. Yes, everything in the Emperor's garden was admirably arranged. And it extended so far that the gardener himself did not know where the end was. If a man went on and on, he came into a glorious forest with high trees and deep lakes. The wood extended straight down to the sea, which was blue and deep; great ships could sail to beneath the branches of the trees; and in the trees lived a Nightingale, which sang so splendidly that even the poor fisherman, who had many other things to do, stopped still and listened, when he had gone out at night to throw out his nets, and heard the Nightingale.

"How beautiful that is!" he said; but he was obliged to attend to his property, and thus forgot the bird. But when in the next night the bird sang again, and the fisherman heard it, he exclaimed again, "How beautiful that is!"

From all the countries of the world travellers came to the city of the Emperor, and admired it, and the palace, and the garden, but when they heard the Nightingale, they said, "That is the best of all!"

And the travellers told of it when they came home; and the learned men wrote many books about the town, the palace, and the garden. But they did not forget the Nightingale; that was placed highest of all; and those who were poets wrote most magnificent poems about the Nightingale in the wood by the deep lake.

The books went through all the world, and a few of them once came to the Emperor. He sat in his golden chair, and read, and read: every moment he nodded his head, for it pleased him to peruse the masterly descriptions of the city, the palace, and the garden. "But the Nightingale is the best of all," it stood written there.

"What's that?" exclaimed the Emperor. "I don't know the Nightingale at all! Is there such a bird in my empire, and even in my garden? I've never heard of that. To think that I should have to learn such a thing for the first time from books!"

And hereupon he called his cavalier. This cavalier was so grand that if any one lower in rank then himself dared to speak to him, or to ask him any question, he answered nothing but "P!"—and that meant nothing.

"There is said to be a wonderful bird here called a Nightingale!" said the Emperor. "They say it is the best thing in all my great empire. Why have I never heard anything about it?"

"I have never heard him named," replied the cavalier. "He has never been introduced at Court."

"I command that he shall appear this evening, and sing before me," said the Emperor. "All the world knows what I possess, and I do not know it myself!"

"I have never heard him mentioned," said the cavalier. "I will seek for him. I will find him."

But where was he to be found? The cavalier ran up and down all the staircases, through halls and passages, but no one among all those whom he met had heard talk of the Nightingale. And the cavalier ran back to the Emperor, and said that it must be a fable invented by the writers of books.

"Your Imperial Majesty cannot believe how much is written that is fiction, besides something that they call the black art."

"But the book in which I read this," said the Emperor, "was sent to me by the high and mighty Emperor of Japan, and therefore it cannot be a falsehood. I will hear the Nightingale! It must be here this evening! It has my imperial favour; and if it does not come, all the Court shall be trampled upon after the Court has supped!"

"Tsing-pe!" said the cavalier; and again he ran up and down all the staircases, and through all the halls and corridors; and half the Court ran with him, for the courtiers did not like being trampled upon.

Then there was a great inquiry after the wonderful Nightingale, which all the world knew excepting the people at Court.

At last they met with a poor little girl in the kitchen, who said:

"The Nightingale? I know it well; yes, it can sing gloriously. Every evening I get leave to carry my poor sick mother the scraps from the table. She lives down by the strand, and when I get back and am tired, and rest in the wood, then I hear the Nightingale sing. And then the water comes into my eyes, and it is just as if my mother kissed me!"

"Little kitchen-girl," said the cavalier, "I will get you a place in the kitchen, with permission to see the Emperor dine, if you will lead us to the Nightingale, for it is announced for this evening."

So they all went out into the wood where the Nightingale was accustomed to sing; half the Court went forth. When they were in the midst of their journey a cow began to moo.

"Oh!" cried the Court pages, "now we have it! That shows a wonderful power in so small a creature! I have certainly heard it before."

"No, those are cows mooing!" said the little kitchen-girl. "We are a long way from the place yet."

Now the frogs began to croak in the marsh.

"Glorious!" said the Chinese Court preacher. "Now I hear it—it sounds just like little church bells."

"No, those are frogs!" said the little kitchen-maid. "But now I think we shall soon hear it."

And then the Nightingale began to sing.

"That is it!" exclaimed the little girl. "Listen, listen! And yonder it sits."

And she pointed to a little grey bird up in the boughs.

"Is it possible?" cried the cavalier. "I should never have thought it looked like that! How simple it looks! It must certainly have lost its colour at seeing such grand people around."

"Little Nightingale!" called the little kitchen-maid, quite loudly, "our gracious Emperor wishes you to sing before him."

"With the greatest pleasure!" replied the Nightingale, and began to sing most delightfully.

"It sounds just like glass bells!" said the cavalier. "And look at its little throat, how it's working! It's wonderful that we should never have heard it before. That bird will be a great success at Court."

"Shall I sing once more before the Emperor?" asked the Nightingale, for it thought the Emperor was present.

"My excellent little Nightingale," said the cavalier, "I have great pleasure in inviting you to a Court festival this evening, when you shall charm his Imperial Majesty with your beautiful singing."

"My song sounds best in the green wood!" replied the Nightingale; still it came willingly when it heard what the Emperor wished.

The palace was festively adorned. The walls and the flooring, which were of porcelain, gleamed in the rays of thousands of golden lamps. The most glorious flowers, which could ring clearly, had been placed in the passages. There was a running to and fro, and a thorough draught, and all the bells rang so loudly that one could not hear oneself speak.

In the midst of the great hall, where the Emperor sat, a golden perch had been placed, on which the Nightingale was to sit. The whole Court was there, and the little cook-maid had got leave to stand behind the door, as she had now received the title of a real Court cook. All were in full dress, and all looked at the little grey bird, to which the Emperor nodded.

And the Nightingale sang so gloriously that the tears came into the Emperor's eyes, and the tears ran down over his cheeks; and then the Nightingale sang still more sweetly, that went straight to the heart. The Emperor was so much pleased that he said the Nightingale should have his golden slipper to wear round its neck. But the Nightingale declined this with thanks, saying it had already received a sufficient reward.

"I have seen tears in the Emperor's eyes—that is the real treasure to me. An Emperor's tears have a peculiar power. I am rewarded enough!" And then it sang again with a sweet glorious voice.

"That's the most amiable coquetry I ever saw!" said the ladies who stood round about, and then they took water in their mouths to gurgle when any one spoke to them. They thought they should be nightingales too. And the lackeys and chambermaids reported that they were satisfied too; and that was saying a good deal, for they are the most difficult to please. In short, the Nightingale achieved a real success.

It was now to remain at Court, to have its own cage with liberty to go out twice every day and once at night. Twelve servants were appointed when the Nightingale went out, each of whom had a silken string fastened to the bird's leg, and which they held very tight. There was really no pleasure in an excursion of that kind.

The whole city spoke of the wonderful bird, and when two people met, one said nothing but "Nightin," and the other said "gale;" and then they sighed, and understood one another. Eleven pedlars' children were named after the bird, but not one of them could sing a note.

One day the Emperor received a large parcel, on which was written "The Nightingale."

"There we have a new book about this celebrated bird," said the Emperor.

But it was not a book, but a little work of art contained in a box, an artificial nightingale, which was to sing like a natural one, and was brilliantly ornamented with diamonds, rubies, and sapphires. So soon as the artificial bird was wound up, he could sing one of the pieces that he really sang, and then his tail moved up and down, and shone with silver and gold. Round his neck hung a little ribbon, and on that was written, "The Emperor of China's nightingale is poor compared to that of the Emperor of Japan."

"That is capital!" said they all, and he who had brought the artificial bird immediately received the title, Imperial Head-Nightingale-Bringer.

"Now they must sing together; what a duet that will be!"

And so they had to sing together; but it did not sound very well, for the real Nightingale sang in its own way, and the artificial bird sang waltzes.

"That's not his fault," said the playmaster; "he's quite perfect, and very much in my style."

Now the artificial bird was to sing alone. He had just as much success as the real one, and then it was much handsomer to look at—it shone like bracelets and breast-pins.

Three and thirty times over did it sing the same piece, and yet was not tired. The people would gladly have heard it again, but the Emperor said that the living Nightingale ought to sing something now. But where was it? No one had noticed that it had flown away out of the open window, back to the green wood.

"But what is become of that?" said the Emperor.

And all the courtiers abused the Nightingale, and declared that it was a very ungrateful creature.

"We have the best bird, after all," said they.

And so the artificial bird had to sing again, and that was the thirty-fourth time that they listened to the same piece. For all that they did not know it quite by heart, for it was so very difficult. And the playmaster praised the bird particularly; yes, he declared that it was better than a nightingale, not only with regard to its plumage and the many beautiful diamonds, but inside as well.

"For you see, ladies and gentlemen, and above all, your Imperial Majesty, with a real nightingale one can never calculate what is coming, but in this artificial bird everything is settled. One can explain it; one can open it and make people understand where the waltzes come from, how they go, and how one follows up another."

"Those are quite our own ideas," they all said.

And the speaker received permission to show the bird to the people on the next Sunday. The people were to hear it sing too, the Emperor commanded; and they did hear it, and were as much pleased as if they had all got tipsy upon tea, for that's quite the Chinese fashion; and they all said, "Oh!" and held up their forefingers and nodded. But the poor fisherman, who had heard the real Nightingale, said:

"It sounds pretty enough, and the melodies resemble each other, but there's something wanting, though I know not what!"

The real Nightingale was banished from the country and empire. The artificial bird had its place on a silken cushion close to the Emperor's bed; all the presents it had received, gold and precious stones, were ranged about it; in title it had advanced to be the High Imperial After-Dinner-Singer, and in rank to number one on the left hand; for the Emperor considered that side the most important on which the heart is placed, and even in an Emperor the heart is on the left side; and the playmaster wrote a work of five and twenty volumes about the artificial bird; it was very learned and very long, full of the most difficult Chinese words; but yet all the people declared that they had read it and understood it, for fear of being considered stupid, and having their bodies trampled on.

So a whole year went by. The Emperor, the Court, and all the other Chinese knew every little twitter in the artificial bird's song by heart. But just for that reason it pleased them best—they could sing with it themselves, and they did so. The street boys sang, "Tsi-tsi-tsi-glug-glug!" and the Emperor himself sang it too. Yes, that was certainly famous.

But one evening, when the artificial bird was singing its best, and the Emperor lay in bed listening to it, something inside the bird said, "Whizz!" Something cracked. "Whir-r-r!" All the wheels ran round, and then the music stopped.

The Emperor immediately sprang out of bed, and caused his body physician to be called; but what could *he* do? Then they sent for a watchmaker, and after a good deal of talking and investigation, the bird was put into something like order; but the watchmaker said that the bird must be carefully treated, for the barrels were worn, and it would be impossible to put new ones in in such a manner that the music would go. There was a great lamentation; only once in a year was it permitted to let the bird sing, and that was almost too much. But then the playmaster made a little speech, full of heavy words, and said this was just as good as before—and so of course it was as good as before.

Now five years had gone by, and a real grief came upon the whole nation. The Chinese were really fond of their Emperor and now he was ill, and could not, it was said, live much longer. Already a new Emperor had been chosen, and the people stood out in the street and asked the cavalier how their old Emperor did.

"P!" said he, and shook his head.

Cold and pale lay the Emperor in his great gorgeous bed, the whole Court thought
him dead, and each one ran to pay homage to the new ruler. The chamberlains ran
out to talk it over, and the ladies' maids had a great coffee-party. All about, in all the
halls and passages, cloth had been laid down so that no footstep could be heard, and
therefore it was quiet there, quite quiet. But the Emperor was not dead yet: still and
pale he lay on the gorgeous bed with the long velvet curtains and the heavy gold
tassels; high up, a window stood open, and the moon shone in upon the Emperor
and the artificial bird.

The poor Emperor could scarcely breathe; it was just as if something lay upon his
chest: he opened his eyes, and then he saw that it was Death who sat upon his chest,
and had put on his golden crown, and held in one hand the Emperor's sword, and
in the other his beautiful banner. And all around from among the folds of the splendid
velvet curtains, strange heads peered forth; a few very ugly, the rest quite lovely and
mild. These were all the Emperor's bad and good deeds, they stood before him now
that Death sat upon his heart.

"Do you remember this?" whispered one to the other. "Do you remember that?"
and then they told him so much that the perspiration ran from his forehead.

"I did not know that!" said the Emperor. "Music! music! the great Chinese drum!"
he cried, "so that I need not hear all they say!"

And they continued speaking, and Death nodded like a Chinaman to all they said.

"Music! music!" cried the Emperor. "You little precious golden bird, sing, sing! I
have given you gold and costly presents; I have even hung my golden slipper around
your neck—sing now, sing!"

But the bird stood still; no one was there to wind him up, and he could not sing
without that; but Death continued to stare at the Emperor with his great hollow eyes,
and it was quiet, fearfully quiet.

Then there sounded from the window, suddenly, the most lovely song. It was the
little live Nightingale, that sat outside on a branch. It had heard of the Emperor's
sad plight, and had come to sing to him of comfort and hope. And as it sang the
spectres grew paler and paler; the blood ran quicker and more quickly through the
Emperor's weak limbs; and even Death listened, and said:

"Go on, little Nightingale, go on!"

"But will you give me that splendid golden sword? Will you give me that rich
banner? Will you give me the Emperor's crown?"

And Death gave up each of these treasures for a song. And the Nightingale sang
on and on; and it sang of the quiet churchyard where the white roses grow, where
the elder blossom smells sweet, and where the fresh grass is moistened by the tears
of survivors. Then Death felt a longing to see his garden, and floated out at the
window in the form of a cold white mist.

"Thanks! thanks!" said the Emperor. "You heavenly little bird! I know you well. I
banished you from my country and empire, and yet you have charmed away the evil
faces from my couch, and banished Death from my heart! How can I reward you?"

"You have rewarded me!" replied the Nightingale. "I have drawn tears from your
eyes, when I sang the first time—I shall never forget that. Those are the jewels that
rejoice a singer's heart. But now sleep and grow fresh and strong again. I will sing
you something."

And it sang, and the Emperor fell into a sweet slumber. Ah! how mild and refreshing that sleep was! The sun shone upon him through the windows, when he awoke
refreshed and restored: not one of his servants had yet returned, for they all thought
he was dead; only the Nightingale still sat beside him and sang.

"You must always stay with me," said the Emperor. "You shall sing as you please; and I'll break the artificial bird into a thousand pieces."

"Not so," replied the Nightingale. "It did well as long as it could; keep it as you have done till now. I cannot build my nest in the palace to dwell in it, but let me come when I feel the wish; then I will sit in the evening on the branch yonder by the window, and sing you something, so that you may be glad and thoughtful at once. I will sing of those who are happy and of those who suffer. I will sing of good and of evil that remains hidden round about you. The little singing bird flies far around, to the poor fisherman, to the peasant's roof, to every one who dwells far away from you and from your Court. I love your heart more than your crown, and yet the crown has an air of sanctity about it. I will come and sing to you—but one thing you must promise me."

"Everything!" said the Emperor; and he stood there in his imperial robes, which he had put on himself, and pressed the sword which was heavy with gold to his heart.

"One thing I beg of you: tell no one that you have a little bird who tells you everything. Then it will go all the better."

And the Nightingale flew away.

The servants came in to look to their dead Emperor, and—yes, there he stood, and the Emperor said, "Good morning!"

1843

GEORGE MacDONALD
1824–1905

George MacDonald was a nonconformist at heart, and his fairy tales reflect his skeptical questioning of traditional religious and philosophical thinking. Along with his friend Charles Dodgson (Lewis Carroll), he was one of the first innovators of the fairy tale during the Golden Age of children's literature in England. Born in Aberdeenshire, Scotland, he attended Aberdeen University between 1842 and 1845, completing his studies at a theological seminary in London in 1851. After serving as a minister at a small Congregational church outside London for two years, MacDonald was dismissed because of his heretical views. He had always been drawn to German transcendentalism and mysticism—he admired Novalis and had translated *Hymns to the Night* in 1849—and he was convinced that all earthly creatures, including so-called heathens, could discover the essence of divinity in themselves by perceiving God's truth in nature. Thus salvation could be attained by everyone, a notion that was not acceptable to the Congregational Church. But Mac-

Donald found another way to preach his views: he spent the remainder of his life giving public lectures and sermons and writing poems, novels, fairy tales, and religious essays. MacDonald was an indefatigable writer and brilliant orator, and through his books and lectures he was able to support a family of eleven children. Indeed, he became one of the leading writers of the Victorian period; among his fifty-one works were best sellers such as *David Elginbrod* (1863) and *Malcolm* (1875), novels with conventional plots that stress Christian charity and philanthropy. MacDonald's realistic novels display little original thought. However, his fantasy works such as *Phantastes* (1858) and *Lilith* (1895) are marked by innovative compositional techniques and striking erotic features; so, too, are his three major books for children—*At the Back of the North Wind* (1871), *The Princess and the Goblin* (1872), and *The Princess and Curdie* (1883)—which all emphasize a search for spirituality.

MacDonald's most significant narratives are

undoubtedly his fairy tales, written for both children and adults. He was a pioneer in experimenting with the traditional motifs and themes of well-known tales such as "Sleeping Beauty" and "Rapunzel," successfully mocking them and developing new ideas of sexuality and love. He rebelled against the strict Victorian code by questioning traditional sex roles and creating young protagonists who share their dreams as they pursue love and equal partnership. This approach is most evident in those tales, including "The Light Princess" (1863) and "Little Daylight" (1867), in which mutual recognition forms the basis for the love between the male and female protagonists. "The Light Princess"—which is one of MacDonald's most popular tales, and has often been reprinted as a separate picture book—mixes humor with philosophical reflections about the notion of gravity. Here self-discovery occurs through compassion and social interaction. In most of MacDonald's tales the hero is a composite figure, not a single individual. That is, the triumph of the self is a union of the masculine and feminine elements, an erotic display of the utopian drive that MacDonald expressed primarily in symbolic form.

The Light Princess

I. What! No Children?

Once upon a time, so long ago that I have quite forgotten the date, there lived a king and queen who had no children.

And the king said to himself, "All the queens of my acquaintance have children, some three, some seven, and some as many as twelve; and my queen has not one. I feel ill-used." So he made up his mind to be cross with his wife about it. But she bore it all like a good patient queen as she was. Then the king grew very cross indeed. But the queen pretended to take it all as a joke, and a very good one too.

"Why don't you have any daughters, at least?" said he. "I don't say *sons*; that might be too much to expect."

"I am sure, dear king, I am very sorry," said the queen.

"So you ought to be," retorted the king; "you are not going to make a virtue of *that*, surely."

But he was not an ill-tempered king, and in any matter of less moment would have let the queen have her own way with all his heart. This, however, was an affair of state.

The queen smiled.

"You must have patience with a lady, you know, dear king," said she.

She was, indeed, a very nice queen, and heartily sorry that she could not oblige the king immediately.

The king tried to have patience, but he succeeded very badly. It was more than he deserved, therefore, when, at last, the queen gave him a daughter—as lovely a little princess as ever cried.

II. Won't I, Just?

The day drew near when the infant must be christened. The king wrote all the invitations with his own hand. Of course somebody was forgotten.

Now it does not generally matter if somebody *is* forgotten, only you must mind who. Unfortunately, the king forgot without intending to forget; and so the chance fell upon the Princess Makemnoit, which was awkward. For the princess was the king's own sister; and he ought not to have forgotten her. But she had made herself so disagreeable to the old king, their father, that he had forgotten her in making his will; and so it was no wonder that her brother forgot her in writing his invitations. But poor relations don't do anything to keep you in mind of them. Why don't they? The king could not see into the garret she lived in, could he?

She was a sour, spiteful creature. The wrinkles of contempt crossed the wrinkles of peevishness, and made her face as full of wrinkles as a pat of butter. If ever a king could be justified in forgetting anybody, this king was justified in forgetting his sister, even at a christening. She looked very odd, too. Her forehead was as large as all the rest of her face, and projected over it like a precipice. When she was angry, her little eyes flashed blue. When she hated anybody, they shone yellow and green. What they looked like when she loved anybody, I do not know; for I never heard of her loving anybody but herself, and I do not think she could have managed that if she had not somehow got used to herself. But what made it highly imprudent in the king to forget her was—that she was awfully clever. In fact, she was a witch; and when she bewitched anybody, he very soon had enough of it; for she beat all the wicked fairies in wickedness, and all the clever ones in cleverness. She despised all the modes we read of in history, in which offended fairies and witches have taken their revenges; and therefore, after waiting and waiting in vain for an invitation, she made up her mind at last to go without one, and make the whole family miserable, like a princess as she was.

So she put on her best gown, went to the palace, was kindly received by the happy monarch, who forgot that he had forgotten her, and took her place in the procession to the royal chapel. When they were all gathered about the font, she contrived to get next to it, and throw something into the water; after which she maintained a very respectful demeanour till the water was applied to the child's face. But at that moment she turned round in her place three times, and muttered the following words, loud enough for those beside her to hear:

> "Light of spirit, by my charms,
> Light of body, every part,
> Never weary human arms—
> Only crush thy parents' heart!"

They all thought she had lost her wits, and was repeating some foolish nursery rhyme; but a shudder went through the whole of them notwithstanding. The baby, on the contrary, began to laugh and crow; while the nurse gave a start and a smothered cry, for she thought she was struck with paralysis: she could not feel the baby in her arms. But she clasped it tight and said nothing.

The mischief was done.

III. She Can't Be Ours

Her atrocious aunt had deprived the child of all her gravity. If you ask me how this was effected, I answer, "In the easiest way in the world. She had only to destroy gravitation." For the princess was a philosopher, and knew all the *ins* and *outs* of the laws of gravitation as well as the *ins* and *outs* of her boot-lace. And being a witch as well, she could abrogate those laws in a moment; or at least so clog their wheels and rust their bearings, that they would not work at all. But we have more to do with what followed than with how it was done.

The first awkwardness that resulted from this unhappy privation was, that the moment the nurse began to float the baby up and down, she flew from her arms towards the ceiling. Happily, the resistance of the air brought her ascending career to a close within a foot of it. There she remained, horizontal as when she left her nurse's arms, kicking and laughing amazingly. The nurse in terror flew to the bell, and begged the footman, who answered it, to bring up the house-steps[1] directly. Trembling in every limb, she climbed upon the steps, and had to stand upon the very top, and reach up, before she could catch the floating tail of the baby's long clothes.

When the strange fact came to be known, there was a terrible commotion in the palace. The occasion of its discovery by the king was naturally a repetition of the nurse's experience. Astonished that he felt no weight when the child was laid in his arms, he began to wave her up and—not down; for she slowly ascended to the ceiling as before, and there remained floating in perfect comfort and satisfaction, as was testified by her peals of tiny laughter. The king stood staring up in speechless amazement, and trembled so that his beard shook like grass in the wind. At last, turning to the queen, who was just as horror-struck as himself, he said, gasping, staring, and stammering,—

"She *can't* be ours, queen!"

Now the queen was much cleverer than the king, and had begun already to suspect that "this effect defective came by cause."

"I am sure she is ours," answered she. "But we ought to have taken better care of her at the christening. People who were never invited ought not to have been present."

"Oh, ho!" said the king, tapping his forehead with his forefinger, "I have it all. I've found her out. Don't you see it, queen? Princess Makemnoit has bewitched her."

"That's just what I say," answered the queen.

"I beg your pardon, my love; I did not hear you.—John! bring the steps I get on my throne with."

For he was a little king with a great throne, like many other kings.

The throne-steps were brought, and set upon the dining-table, and John got upon the top of them. But he could not reach the little princess, who lay like a baby-laughter-cloud in the air, exploding continuously.

"Take the tongs, John," said his Majesty; and getting up on the table, he handed them to him.

John could reach the baby now, and the little princess was handed down by the tongs.

IV. WHERE IS SHE?

One fine summer day, a month after these her first adventures, during which time she had been very carefully watched, the princess was lying on the bed in the queen's own chamber, fast asleep. One of the windows was open, for it was noon, and the day was so sultry that the little girl was wrapped in nothing less ethereal than slumber itself. The queen came into the room, and not observing that the baby was on the bed, opened another window. A frolicsome fairy wind, which had been watching for a chance of mischief, rushed in at the one window, and taking its way over the bed where the child was lying, caught her up, and rolling and floating her along like a piece of flue,[2] or a dandelion seed, carried her with it through the opposite window,

1. Stepladder.   2. Down, fluff.

and away. The queen went down-stairs, quite ignorant of the loss she had herself occasioned.

When the nurse returned, she supposed that her Majesty had carried her off, and, dreading a scolding, delayed making inquiry about her. But hearing nothing, she grew uneasy, and went at length to the queen's boudoir, where she found her Majesty.

"Please, your Majesty, shall I take the baby?" said she.

"Where is she?" asked the queen.

"Please forgive me. I know it was wrong."

"What do you mean?" said the queen, looking grave.

"Oh! don't frighten me, your Majesty!" exclaimed the nurse, clasping her hands.

The queen saw that something was amiss, and fell down in a faint. The nurse rushed about the palace, screaming, "My baby! my baby!"

Every one ran to the queen's room. But the queen could give no orders. They soon found out, however, that the princess was missing, and in a moment the palace was like a beehive in a garden; and in one minute more the queen was brought to herself by a great shout and a clapping of hands. They had found the princess fast asleep under a rose-bush, to which the elvish little wind-puff had carried her, finishing its mischief by shaking a shower of red rose-leaves all over the little white sleeper. Startled by the noise the servants made, she woke, and, furious with glee, scattered the rose-leaves in all directions, like a shower of spray in the sunset.

She was watched more carefully after this, no doubt; yet it would be endless to relate all the odd incidents resulting from this peculiarity of the young princess. But there never was a baby in a house, not to say a palace, that kept the household in such constant good humour, at least below-stairs.[3] If it was not easy for her nurses to hold her, at least she made neither their arms nor their hearts ache. And she was so nice to play at ball with! There was positively no danger of letting her fall. They might throw her down, or knock her down, or push her down, but couldn't *let* her down. It is true, they might let her fly into the fire or the coal-hole, or through the window; but none of these accidents had happened as yet. If you heard peals of laughter resounding from some unknown region, you might be sure enough of the cause. Going down into the kitchen, or *the room*, you would find Jane and Thomas, and Robert and Susan, all and sum, playing at ball with the little princess. She was the ball herself, and did not enjoy it the less for that. Away she went, flying from one to another, screeching with laughter. And the servants loved the ball itself better even than the game. But they had to take some care how they threw her, for if she received an upward direction, she would never come down again without being fetched.

V. WHAT IS TO BE DONE?

But above-stairs it was different. One day, for instance, after breakfast, the king went into his counting-house, and counted out his money.

The operation gave him no pleasure.

"To think," said he to himself, "that every one of these gold sovereigns weighs a quarter of an ounce, and my real, live, flesh-and-blood princess weighs nothing at all!"

3. I.e., in the servants' quarters.

And he hated his gold sovereigns, as they lay with a broad smile of self-satisfaction all over their yellow faces.

The queen was in the parlour, eating bread and honey.[4] But at the second mouthful she burst out crying, and could not swallow it. The king heard her sobbing. Glad of anybody, but especially of his queen, to quarrel with, he clashed his gold sovereigns into his money-box, clapped his crown on his head, and rushed into the parlour.

"What is all this about?" exclaimed he. "What are you crying for, queen?"

"I can't eat it," said the queen, looking ruefully at the honey-pot.

"No wonder!" retorted the king. "You've just eaten your breakfast—two turkey eggs, and three anchovies."

"Oh, that's not it!" sobbed her Majesty. "It's my child, my child!"

"Well, what's the matter with your child? She's neither up the chimney nor down the draw-well.[5] Just hear her laughing."

Yet the king could not help a sigh, which he tried to turn into a cough, saying,—

"It is a good thing to be light-hearted, I am sure, whether she be ours or not."

"It is a bad thing to be light-headed," answered the queen, looking with prophetic soul far into the future.

" 'Tis a good thing to be light-handed," said the king.

" 'Tis a bad thing to be light-fingered," answered the queen.

" 'Tis a good thing to be light-footed," said the king.

" 'Tis a bad thing—" began the queen; but the king interrupted her.

"In fact," said he, with the tone of one who concludes an argument in which he has had only imaginary opponents, and in which, therefore, he has come off triumphant—"in fact, it is a good thing altogether to be light-bodied."

"But it is a bad thing altogether to be light-minded," retorted the queen, who was beginning to lose her temper.

This last answer quite discomfited his Majesty, who turned on his heel, and betook himself to his counting-house again. But he was not half-way towards it, when the voice of his queen overtook him.

"And it's a bad thing to be light-haired," screamed she, determined to have more last words, now that her spirit was roused.

The queen's hair was black as night; and the king's had been, and his daughter's was, golden as morning. But it was not this reflection on his hair that arrested him; it was the double use of the word *light*. For the king hated all witticisms, and punning especially. And besides, he could not tell whether the queen meant light-*haired* or light-*heired*; for why might she not aspirate her vowels when she was ex-asperated herself?

He turned upon his other heel, and rejoined her. She looked angry still, because she knew that she was guilty, or, what was much the same, knew that he thought so.

"My dear queen," said he, "duplicity of any sort is exceedingly objectionable between married people of any rank, not to say kings and queens; and the most objectionable form duplicity can assume is that of punning."

"There!" said the queen, "I never made a jest, but I broke it in the making. I am the most unfortunate woman in the world!"

---

4. The second stanza of the nursery rhyme "Sing a Song of Sixpence" begins: "The King was in his counting house, counting out his money, / The Queen was in the parlor, eating bread and honey."
5. A deep well from which water is drawn in a bucket.

She looked so rueful, that the king took her in his arms; and they sat down to consult.

"Can you bear this?" said the king.

"No, I can't," said the queen.

"Well, what's to be done?" said the king.

"I'm sure I don't know," said the queen. "But might you not try an apology?"

"To my old sister, I suppose you mean?" said the king.

"Yes," said the queen.

"Well, I don't mind," said the king.

So he went the next morning to the house of the princess, and, making a very humble apology, begged her to undo the spell. But the princess declared, with a grave face, that she knew nothing at all about it. Her eyes, however, shone pink, which was a sign that she was happy. She advised the king and queen to have patience, and to mend their ways. The king returned disconsolate. The queen tried to comfort him.

"We will wait till she is older. She may then be able to suggest something herself. She will know at least how she feels, and explain things to us."

"But what if she should marry?" exclaimed the king, in sudden consternation at the idea.

"Well, what of that?" rejoined the queen.

"Just think! If she were to have children! In the course of a hundred years the air might be as full of floating children as of gossamers in autumn."

"That is no business of ours," replied the queen. "Besides, by that time they will have learned to take care of themselves."

A sigh was the king's only answer.

He would have consulted the court physicians; but he was afraid they would try experiments upon her.

VI. She Laughs Too Much

Meantime, notwithstanding awkward occurrences, and griefs that she brought upon her parents, the little princess laughed and grew—not fat, but plump and tall. She reached the age of seventeen, without having fallen into any worse scrape than a chimney; by rescuing her from which, a little bird-nesting urchin got fame and a black face. Nor, thoughtless as she was, had she committed anything worse than laughter at everybody and everything that came in her way. When she was told, for the sake of experiment, that General Clanrunfort was cut to pieces with all his troops, she laughed; when she heard that the enemy was on his way to besiege her papa's capital, she laughed hugely; but when she was told that the city would certainly be abandoned to the mercy of the enemy's soldiery—why, then she laughed immoderately. She never could be brought to see the serious side of anything. When her mother cried, she said,—

"What queer faces mamma makes! And she squeezes water out of her cheeks! Funny mamma!"

And when her papa stormed at her, she laughed, and danced round and round him, clapping her hands, and crying—

"Do it again, papa. Do it again! It's such fun! Dear, funny papa!"

And if he tried to catch her, she glided from him in an instant, not in the least afraid of him, but thinking it part of the game not to be caught. With one push of her foot, she would be floating in the air above his head; or she would go dancing backwards and forwards and sideways, like a great butterfly. It happened several times, when her father and mother were holding a consultation about her in private, that they were interrupted by vainly repressed outbursts of laughter over their heads; and looking up with indignation, saw her floating at full length in the air above them, whence she regarded them with the most comical appreciation of the position.

One day an awkward accident happened. The princess had come out upon the lawn with one of her attendants, who held her by the hand. Spying her father at the other side of the lawn, she snatched her hand from the maid's, and sped across to him. Now when she wanted to run alone, her custom was to catch up a stone in each hand, so that she might come down again after a bound. Whatever she wore as part of her attire had no effect in this way: even gold, when it thus became as it were a part of herself, lost all its weight for the time. But whatever she only held in her hands retained its downward tendency. On this occasion she could see nothing to catch up but a huge toad, that was walking across the lawn as if he had a hundred years to do it in. Not knowing what disgust meant, for this was one of her peculiarities, she snatched up the toad and bounded away. She had almost reached her father, and he was holding out his arms to receive her, and take from her lips the kiss which hovered on them like a butterfly on a rosebud, when a puff of wind blew her aside into the arms of a young page, who had just been receiving a message from his Majesty. Now it was no great peculiarity in the princess that, once she was set agoing, it always cost her time and trouble to check herself. On this occasion there was no time. She *must* kiss—and she kissed the page. She did not mind it much; for she had no shyness in her composition; and she knew, besides, that she could not help it. So she only laughed, like a musical box. The poor page fared the worst. For the princess, trying to correct the unfortunate tendency of the kiss, put out her hands to keep her off the page; so that, along with the kiss, he received, on the other cheek, a slap with the huge black toad, which she poked right into his eye. He tried to laugh, too, but the attempt resulted in such an odd contortion of countenance, as showed that there was no danger of his pluming himself on the kiss. As for the king, his dignity was greatly hurt, and he did not speak to the page for a whole month.

I may here remark that it was very amusing to see her run, if her mode of progression could properly be called running. For first she would make a bound; then, having alighted, she would run a few steps, and make another bound. Sometimes she would fancy she had reached the ground before she actually had, and her feet would go backwards and forwards, running upon nothing at all, like those of a chicken on its back. Then she would laugh like the very spirit of fun; only in her laugh there was something missing. What it was, I find myself unable to describe. I think it was a certain tone, depending upon the possibility of sorrow—*morbidezza*,[6] perhaps. She never smiled.

VII. TRY METAPHYSICS

After a long avoidance of the painful subject, the king and queen resolved to hold a council of three upon it; and so they sent for the princess. In she came, sliding and flitting and gliding from one piece of furniture to another, and put herself at last in an arm-chair, in a sitting posture. Whether she could be said to *sit*, seeing she received no support from the seat of the chair, I do not pretend to determine.

6. Softness, tenderness (Italian).

"My dear child," said the king, "you must be aware by this time that you are not exactly like other people."

"Oh, you dear funny papa! I have got a nose, and two eyes, and all the rest. So have you. So has mamma."

"Now be serious, my dear, for once," said the queen.

"No, thank you, mamma; I had rather not."

"Would you not like to be able to walk like other people?" said the king.

"No indeed, I should think not. You only crawl. You are such slow coaches!"

"How do you feel, my child?" he resumed, after a pause of discomfiture.

"Quite well, thank you."

"I mean, what do you feel like?"

"Like nothing at all, that I know of."

"You must feel like something."

"I feel like a princess with such a funny papa, and such a dear pet of a queen-mamma!"

"Now really!" began the queen; but the princess interrupted her.

"Oh yes," she added, "I remember. I have a curious feeling sometimes, as if I were the only person that had any sense in the whole world."

She had been trying to behave herself with dignity; but now she burst into a violent fit of laughter, threw herself backwards over the chair, and went rolling about the floor in an ecstasy of enjoyment. The king picked her up easier than one does a down quilt, and replaced her in her former relation to the chair. The exact preposition expressing this relation I do not happen to know.

"Is there nothing you wish for?" resumed the king, who had learned by this time that it was useless to be angry with her.

"Oh, you dear papa!—yes," answered she.

"What is it, my darling?"

"I have been longing for it—oh, such a time!—ever since last night."

"Tell me what it is."

"Will you promise to let me have it?"

The king was on the point of saying Yes, but the wiser queen checked him with a single motion of her head.

"Tell me what it is first," said he.

"No, no. Promise first."

"I dare not. What is it?"

"Mind, I hold you to your promise.—It is—to be tied to the end of a string—a very long string indeed, and be flown like a kite. Oh, such fun! I would rain rose-water, and hail sugar-plums, and snow whipped-cream, and—and—and—"

A fit of laughing checked her; and she would have been off again over the floor, had not the king started up and caught her just in time. Seeing that nothing but talk could be got out of her, he rang the bell, and sent her away with two of her ladies-in-waiting.

"Now, queen," he said, turning to her Majesty, "what is to be done?"

"There is but one thing left," answered she. "Let us consult the college of Meta-physicians."

"Bravo!" cried the king; "we will."

Now at the head of this college were two very wise Chinese philosophers—by name Hum-Drum, and Kopy-Keck. For them the king sent; and straightway they came. In a long speech he communicated to them what they knew very well already—as who did not?—namely, the peculiar condition of his daughter in relation to the globe on which she dwelt; and requested them to consult together as to what might be the cause and probable cure of her *infirmity*. The king laid stress upon the word, but failed to discover his own pun. The queen laughed; but Hum-Drum and Kopy-Keck heard with humility and retired in silence.

Their consultation consisted chiefly in propounding and supporting, for the thousandth time, each his favourite theories. For the condition of the princess afforded delightful scope for the discussion of every question arising from the division of thought—in fact, of all the Metaphysics of the Chinese Empire. But it is only justice to say that they did not altogether neglect the discussion of the practical question, *what was to be done*.

Hum-Drum was a Materialist, and Kopy-Keck was a Spiritualist. The former was slow and sententious; the latter was quick and flighty: the latter had generally the first word; the former the last.

"I reassert my former assertion," began Kopy-Keck, with a plunge. "There is not a fault in the princess, body or soul; only they are wrong put together. Listen to me now, Hum-Drum, and I will tell you in brief what I think. Don't speak. Don't answer me. I *won't* hear you till I have done.—At that decisive moment, when souls seek their appointed habitations, two eager souls met, struck, rebounded, lost their way, and arrived each at the wrong place. The soul of the princess was one of those, and she went far astray. She does not belong by rights to this world at all, but to some other planet, probably Mercury. Her proclivity to her true sphere destroys all the natural influence which this orb would otherwise possess over her corporeal frame. She cares for nothing here. There is no relation between her and this world.

"She must therefore be taught, by the sternest compulsion, to take an interest in the earth as the earth. She must study every department of its history—its animal history; its vegetable history; its mineral history; its social history; its moral history; its political history; its scientific history; its literary history; its musical history; its artistical history; above all, its metaphysical history. She must begin with the Chinese dynasty and end with Japan. But first of all she must study geology, and especially the history of the extinct races of animals—their natures, their habits, their loves, their hates, their revenges. She must—"

"Hold, h-o-o-old!" roared Hum-Drum. "It is certainly my turn now. My rooted and insubvertible conviction is, that the causes of the anomalies evident in the princess's condition are strictly and solely physical. But that is only tantamount to acknowledging that they exist. Hear my opinion.—From some cause or other, of no importance to our inquiry, the motion of her heart has been reversed. That remarkable combination of the suction and the force-pump works the wrong way—I mean in the case of the unfortunate princess: it draws in where it should force out, and forces out where it should draw in. The offices of the auricles and the ventricles are subverted. The blood is sent forth by the veins, and returns by the arteries. Consequently it is running the wrong way through all her corporeal organism—lungs and all. Is it then at all mysterious, seeing that such is the case, that on the other particular of gravitation as well, she should differ from normal humanity? My proposal for the cure is this:—

"Phlebotomize[7] until she is reduced to the last point of safety. Let it be effected, if necessary, in a warm bath. When she is reduced to a state of perfect asphyxy,[8] apply a ligature to the left ankle, drawing it as tight as the bone will bear. Apply, at

---

7. Bleed her.   8. Stoppage of the pulse.

the same moment, another of equal tension around the right wrist. By means of plates constructed for the purpose, place the other foot and hand under the receivers of two air-pumps. Exhaust the receivers. Exhibit a pint of French brandy, and await the result."

"Which would presently arrive in the form of grim Death," said Kopy-Keck.

"If it should, she would yet die in doing our duty," retorted Hum-Drum.

But their Majesties had too much tenderness for their volatile offspring to subject her to either of the schemes of the equally unscrupulous philosophers. Indeed, the most complete knowledge of the laws of nature would have been unserviceable in her case; for it was impossible to classify her. She was a fifth imponderable body,[9] sharing all the other properties of the ponderable.

VIII. TRY A DROP OF WATER

Perhaps the best thing for the princess would have been to fall in love. But how a princess who had no gravity could fall into anything is a difficulty—perhaps *the* difficulty. As for her own feelings on the subject, she did not even know that there was such a beehive of honey and stings to be fallen into. But now I come to mention another curious fact about her.

The palace was built on the shores of the loveliest lake in the world; and the princess loved this lake more than father or mother. The root of this preference no doubt, although the princess did not recognise it as such, was, that the moment she got into it, she recovered the natural right of which she had been so wickedly deprived—namely, gravity. Whether this was owing to the fact that water had been employed as the means of conveying the injury, I do not know. But it is certain that she could swim and dive like the duck that her old nurse said she was. The manner in which this alleviation of her misfortune was discovered was as follows.

One summer evening, during the carnival of the country, she had been taken upon the lake by the king and queen, in the royal barge. They were accompanied by many of the courtiers in a fleet of little boats. In the middle of the lake she wanted to get into the lord chancellor's barge, for his daughter, who was a great favourite with her, was in it with her father. Now though the old king rarely condescended to make light of his misfortune, yet, happening on this occasion to be in a particularly good humour, as the barges approached each other, he caught up the princess to throw her into the chancellor's barge. He lost his balance, however, and, dropping into the bottom of the barge lost his hold of his daughter; not, however, before imparting to her the downward tendency of his own person, though in a somewhat different direction; for, as the king fell into the boat, she fell into the water. With a burst of delighted laughter she disappeared in the lake. A cry of horror ascended from the boats. They had never seen the Princess go down before. Half the men were under water in a moment; but they had all, one after another come up to the surface again for breath, when—tinkle, tinkle, babble, and gush! came the princess's laugh over the water from far away. There she was, swimming like a swan. Nor would she come out for king or queen, chancellor or daughter. She was perfectly obstinate.

But at the same time she seemed more sedate than usual. Perhaps that was because a great pleasure spoils laughing. At all events, after this, the passion of her life was to get into the water, and she was always the better behaved and the more beautiful

---

9. The four natural classifications are earth, air, fire, and water; because she is weightless, she is literally imponderable (a word derived from the Latin *pondus*, "weight").

the more she had of it. Summer and winter it was quite the same; only she could not stay so long in the water when they had to break the ice to let her in. Any day, from morning till evening in summer, she might be descried—a streak of white in the blue water—lying as still as the shadow of a cloud, or shooting along like a dolphin; disappearing, and coming up again far off, just where one did not expect her. She would have been in the lake of a night too, if she could have had her way; for the balcony of her window overhung a deep pool in it; and through a shallow reedy passage she could have swum out into the wide wet water, and no one would have been any the wiser. Indeed, when she happened to wake in the moonlight she could hardly resist the temptation. But there was the sad difficulty of getting into it. She had as great a dread of the air as some children have of the water. For the slightest gust of wind would blow her away; and a gust might arise in the stillest moment. And if she gave herself a push towards the water and just failed of reaching it, her situation would be dreadfully awkward, irrespective of the wind; for at best there she would have to remain, suspended in her nightgown, till she was seen and angled for by somebody from the window.

"Oh! if I had my gravity," thought she, contemplating the water, "I would flash off this balcony like a long white sea-bird, headlong into the darling wetness. Heigh-ho!"

This was the only consideration that made her wish to be like other people.

Another reason for her being fond of the water was that in it alone she enjoyed any freedom. For she could not walk out without a *cortége*, consisting in part of a troop of light-horse, for fear of the liberties which the wind might take with her. And the king grew more apprehensive with increasing years, till at last he would not allow her to walk abroad at all without some twenty silken cords fastened to as many parts of her dress, and held by twenty noblemen. Of course horseback was out of the question. But she bade good-by to all this ceremony when she got into the water.

And so remarkable were its effects upon her, especially in restoring her for the time to the ordinary human gravity, that Hum-Drum and Kopy-Keck agreed in recommending the king to bury her alive for three years; in the hope that, as the water did her so much good, the earth would do her yet more. But the king had some vulgar prejudices against the experiment, and would not give his consent. Foiled in this, they yet agreed in another recommendation; which, seeing that one imported his opinions from China and the other from Thibet, was very remarkable indeed. They argued that, if water of external origin and application could be so efficacious, water from a deeper source might work a perfect cure; in short, that if the poor afflicted princess could by any means be made to cry, she might recover her lost gravity.

But how was this to be brought about? Therein lay all the difficulty—to meet which the philosophers were not wise enough. To make the princess cry was as impossible as to make her weigh. They sent for a professional beggar; commanded him to prepare his most touching oracle of woe; helped him out of the court charade box, to whatever he wanted for dressing up, and promised great rewards in the event of his success. But it was all in vain. She listened to the mendicant artist's story, and gazed at his marvellous make up, till she could contain herself no longer, and went into the most undignified contortions for relief, shrieking, positively screeching with laughter.

When she had a little recovered herself, she ordered her attendants to drive him away, and not give him a single copper; whereupon his look of mortified discomfiture wrought her punishment and his revenge, for it sent her into violent hysterics, from which she was with difficulty recovered.

But so anxious was the king that the suggestion should have a fair trial, that he put himself in a rage one day, and, rushing up to her room, gave her an awful whipping. Yet not a tear would flow. She looked grave, and her laughing sounded uncommonly like screaming—that was all. The good old tyrant, though he put on his best gold spectacles to look, could not discover the smallest cloud in the serene blue of her eyes.

IX. PUT ME IN AGAIN

It must have been about this time that the son of a king, who lived a thousand miles from Lagobel, set out to look for the daughter of a queen. He travelled far and wide, but as sure as he found a princess, he found some fault in her. Of course he could not marry a mere woman, however beautiful; and there was no princess to be found worthy of him. Whether the prince was so near perfection that he had a right to demand perfection itself, I cannot pretend to say. All I know is, that he was a fine, handsome, brave, generous, well-bred, and well-behaved youth, as all princes are.

In his wanderings he had come across some reports about our princess; but as everybody said she was bewitched, he never dreamed that she could bewitch him. For what indeed could a prince do with a princess that had lost her gravity? Who could tell what she might not lose next? She might lose her visibility, or her tangibility; or, in short, the power of making impressions upon the radical sensorium; so that he should never be able to tell whether she was dead or alive. Of course he made no further inquiries about her.

One day he lost sight of his retinue in a great forest. These forests are very useful in delivering princes from their courtiers, like a sieve that keeps back the bran. Then the princes get away to follow their fortunes. In this they have the advantage of the princesses, who are forced to marry before they have had a bit of fun. I wish our princesses got lost in a forest sometimes.

One lovely evening, after wandering about for many days, he found that he was approaching the outskirts of this forest; for the trees had got so thin that he could see the sunset through them; and he soon came upon a kind of heath. Next he came upon signs of human neighbourhood; but by this time it was getting late, and there was nobody in the fields to direct him.

After travelling for another hour, his horse, quite worn out with long labour and lack of food, fell, and was unable to rise again. So he continued his journey on foot. At length he entered another wood—not a wild forest, but a civilized wood, through which a footpath led him to the side of a lake. Along this path the prince pursued his way through the gathering darkness. Suddenly he paused, and listened. Strange sounds came across the water. It was, in fact, the princess laughing. Now there was something odd in her laugh, as I have already hinted; for the hatching of a real hearty laugh requires the incubation of gravity; and perhaps this was how the prince mistook the laughter for screaming. Looking over the lake, he saw something white in the water; and, in an instant, he had torn off his tunic, kicked off his sandals, and plunged in. He soon reached the white object, and found that it was a woman. There was not light enough to show that she was a princess, but quite enough to show that she was a lady, for it does not want much light to see that.

Now I cannot tell how it came about,—whether she pretended to be drowning, or whether he frightened her, or caught her so as to embarrass her,—but certainly he brought her to shore in a fashion ignominious to a swimmer, and more nearly drowned than she had ever expected to be; for the water had got into her throat as often as she had tried to speak.

At the place to which he bore her, the bank was only a foot or two above the water;

so he gave her a strong lift out of the water, to lay her on the bank. But, her gravitation ceasing the moment she left the water, away she went up into the air, scolding and screaming.

"You naughty, *naughty*, NAUGHTY, NAUGHTY man!" she cried.

No one had ever succeeded in putting her into a passion before.—When the prince saw her ascend, he thought he must have been bewitched, and have mistaken a great swan for a lady. But the princess caught hold of the topmost cone upon a lofty fir. This came off; but she caught at another; and, in fact, stopped herself by gathering cones, dropping them as the stalks gave way. The prince, meantime, stood in the water, staring, and forgetting to get out. But the princess disappearing, he scrambled on shore, and went in the direction of the tree. There he found her climbing down one of the branches towards the stem. But in the darkness of the wood, the prince continued in some bewilderment as to what the phenomenon could be; until, reaching the ground, and seeing him standing there, she caught hold of him, and said,—

"I'll tell papa."

"Oh no, you won't!" returned the prince.

"Yes, I will," she persisted. "What business had you to pull me down out of the water, and throw me to the bottom of the air? I never did you any harm."

"Pardon me. I did not mean to hurt you."

"I don't believe you have any brains; and that is a worse loss than your wretched gravity. I pity you."

The prince now saw that he had come upon the bewitched princess, and had already offended her. But before he could think what to say next, she burst out angrily, giving a stamp with her foot that would have sent her aloft again but for the hold she had of his arm,—

"Put me up directly."

"Put you up where, you beauty?" asked the prince.

He had fallen in love with her almost, already; for her anger made her more charming than any one else had ever beheld her; and, as far as he could see, which certainly was not far, she had not a single fault about her, except, of course, that she had not any gravity. No prince, however, would judge of a princess by weight. The loveliness of her foot he would hardly estimate by the depth of the impression it could make in mud.

"Put you up where, you beauty?" asked the prince.

"In the water, you stupid!" answered the princess.

"Come, then," said the prince.

The condition of her dress, increasing her usual difficulty in walking, compelled her to cling to him; and he could hardly persuade himself that he was not in a delightful dream, notwithstanding the torrent of musical abuse with which she overwhelmed him. The prince being therefore in no hurry, they came upon the lake at quite another part, where the bank was twenty-five feet high at least; and when they had reached the edge, he turned towards the princess, and said,—

"How am I to put you in?"

"That is your business," she answered, quite snappishly. "You took me out—put me in again."

"Very well," said the prince; and, catching her up in his arms, he sprang with her from the rock. The princess had just time to give one delighted shriek of laughter before the water closed over them. When they came to the surface, she found that, for a moment or two, she could not even laugh, for she had gone down with such a rush, that it was with difficulty she recovered her breath. The instant they reached the surface—

"How do you like falling in?" said the prince. After some effort the princess panted out,—

"Is that what you call *falling in?*"

"Yes," answered the prince, "I should think it a very tolerable specimen."

"It seemed to me like going up," rejoined she.

"My feeling was certainly one of elevation too," the prince conceded.

The princess did not appear to understand him, for she retorted his question:—

"How do *you* like falling in?" said the princess.

"Beyond everything," answered he; "for I have fallen in with the only perfect creature I ever saw."

"No more of that: I am tired of it," said the princess.

Perhaps she shared her father's aversion to punning.

"Don't you like falling in, then?" said the prince.

"It is the most delightful fun I ever had in my life," answered she. "I never fell before. I wish I could learn. To think I am the only person in my father's kingdom that can't fall!"

Here the poor princess looked almost sad.

"I shall be most happy to fall in with you any time you like," said the prince, devotedly.

"Thank you. I don't know. Perhaps it would not be proper. But I don't care. At all events, as we have fallen in, let us have a swim together."

"With all my heart," responded the prince.

And away they went, swimming, and diving, and floating, until at last they heard cries along the shore, and saw lights glancing in all directions. It was now quite late, and there was no moon.

"I must go home," said the princess. "I am very sorry, for this is delightful."

"So am I," returned the prince. "But I am glad I haven't a home to go to—at least, I don't exactly know where it is."

"I wish I hadn't one either," rejoined the princess; "it is so stupid! I have a great mind," she continued, "to play them all a trick. Why couldn't they leave me alone? They won't trust me in the lake for a single night!—You see where that green light is burning? That is the window of my room. Now if you would just swim there with me very quietly, and when we are all but under the balcony, give me such a push—*up* you call it—as you did a little while ago, I should be able to catch hold of the balcony, and get in at the window; and then they may look for me till tomorrow morning!"

"With more obedience than pleasure," said the prince, gallantly; and away they swam, very gently.

"Will you be in the lake to-morrow night?" the prince ventured to ask.

"To be sure I will. I don't think so. Perhaps," was the princess's somewhat strange answer.

But the prince was intelligent enough not to press her further; and merely whispered, as he gave her the parting lift, "Don't tell." The only answer the princess returned was a roguish look. She was already a yard above his head. The look seemed to say, "Never fear. It is too good fun to spoil that way."

So perfectly like other people had she been in the water, that even yet the prince could scarcely believe his eyes when he saw her ascend slowly, grasp the balcony, and disappear through the window. He turned, almost expecting to see her still by his side. But he was alone in the water. So he swam away quietly, and watched the lights roving about the shore for hours after the princess was safe in her chamber. As soon as they disappeared, he landed in search of his tunic and sword, and, after some trouble, found them again. Then he made the best of his way round the lake to the other side. There the wood was wilder, and the shore steeper—rising more immediately towards the mountains which surrounded the lake on all sides, and kept sending it messages of silvery streams from morning to night, and all night long. He soon found a spot whence he could see the green light in the princess's room, and where, even in the broad daylight, he would be in no danger of being discovered from the opposite shore. It was a sort of cave in the rock, where he provided himself a bed of withered leaves, and lay down too tired for hunger to keep him awake. All night long he dreamed that he was swimming with the princess.

X. LOOK AT THE MOON

Early the next morning the prince set out to look for something to eat, which he soon found at a forester's hut, where for many following days he was supplied with all that a brave prince could consider necessary. And having plenty to keep him alive for the present, he would not think of wants not yet in existence. Whenever Care intruded, this prince always bowed him out[1] in the most princely manner.

When he returned from his breakfast to his watch-cave, he saw the princess already floating about in the lake, attended by the king and queen—whom he knew by their crowns—and a great company in lovely little boats, with canopies of all the colours of the rainbow, and flags and streamers of a great many more. It was a very bright day, and soon the prince, burned up with the heat, began to long for the cold water and the cool princess. But he had to endure till twilight; for the boats had provisions on board, and it was not till the sun went down that the gay party began to vanish. Boat after boat drew away to the shore, following that of the king and queen, till only one, apparently the princess's own boat, remained. But she did not want to go home even yet, and the prince thought he saw her order the boat to the shore without her. At all events, it rowed away; and now, of all the radiant company, only one white speck remained. Then the prince began to sing.

And this is what he sung:—

"Lady fair,
Swan-white,
Lift thine eyes,
Banish night
By the might
Of thine eyes.

Snowy arms,
Oars of snow,
Oar her hither,
Plashing low.
Soft and slow,
Oar her hither.

1. I.e., ushered him out with a bow.

Stream behind her
O'er the lake,
Radiant whiteness!
In her wake
Following, following for her sake,
Radiant whiteness!

Cling about her,
Waters blue;
Part not from her,
But renew
Cold and true
Kisses round her.

Lap me round,
Waters sad
That have left her
Make me glad,
For ye had
Kissed her ere ye left her."

Before he had finished his song, the princess was just under the place where he sat, and looking up to find him. Her ears had led her truly.

"Would you like a fall, princess?" said the prince, looking down.

"Ah! there you are! Yes, if you please, prince," said the princess, looking up.

"How do you know I am a prince, princess?" said the prince.

"Because you are a very nice young man, prince," said the princess.

"Come up then, princess."

"Fetch me, prince."

The prince took off his scarf, then his sword-belt, then his tunic, and tied them all together, and let them down. But the line was far too short. He unwound his turban, and added it to the rest, when it was all but long enough; and his purse completed it. The princess just managed to lay hold of the knot of money, and was beside him in a moment. This rock was much higher than the other, and the splash and the dive were tremendous. The princess was in ecstasies of delight, and their swim was delicious.

Night after night they met, and swam about in the dark clear lake; where such was the prince's gladness, that (whether the princess's way of looking at things infected him, or he was actually getting light-headed) he often fancied that he was swimming in the sky instead of the lake. But when he talked about being in heaven, the princess laughed at him dreadfully.

When the moon came, she brought them fresh pleasure. Everything looked strange and new in her light, with an old, withered, yet unfading newness. When the moon was nearly full, one of their great delights was, to dive deep in the water, and then, turning round, look up through it at the great blot of light close above them, shimmering and trembling and wavering, spreading and contracting, seeming to melt away, and again grow solid. Then they would shoot up through the blot; and lo! there was the moon, far off, clear and steady and cold, and very lovely, at the bottom of a deeper and bluer lake than theirs, as the princess said.

The prince soon found out that while in the water the princess was very like other people. And besides this, she was not so forward in her questions or pert in her replies at sea as on shore. Neither did she laugh so much; and when she did laugh, it was more gently. She seemed altogether more modest and maidenly in the water than out of it. But when the prince, who had really fallen in love when he fell in the lake, began to talk to her about love, she always turned her head towards him and laughed. After a while she began to look puzzled, as if she were trying to understand what he meant, but could not—revealing a notion that he meant something. But as soon as ever she left the lake, she was so altered, that the prince said to himself, "If I marry her, I see no help for it: we must turn merman and mermaid, and go out to sea at once."

XI. HISS!

The princess's pleasure in the lake had grown to a passion, and she could scarcely bear to be out of it for an hour. Imagine then her consternation, when, diving with the prince one night, a sudden suspicion seized her that the lake was not so deep as it used to be. The prince could not imagine what had happened. She shot to the surface, and, without a word, swam at full speed towards the higher side of the lake. He followed, begging to know if she was ill, or what was the matter. She never turned her head, or took the smallest notice of his question. Arrived at the shore, she coasted the rocks with minute inspection. But she was not able to come to a conclusion, for the moon was very small, and so she could not see well. She turned therefore and swam home, without saying a word to explain her conduct to the prince, of whose presence she seemed no longer conscious. He withdrew to his cave, in great perplexity and distress.

Next day she made many observations, which, alas! strengthened her fears. She saw that the banks were too dry; and that the grass on the shore, and the trailing plants on the rocks, were withering away. She caused marks to be made along the borders, and examined them, day after day, in all directions of the wind; till at last the horrible idea became a certain fact—that the surface of the lake was slowly sinking.

The poor princess nearly went out of the little mind she had. It was awful to her to see the lake, which she loved more than any living thing, lie dying before her eyes. It sank away, slowly vanishing. The tops of rocks that had never been seen till now, began to appear far down in the clear water. Before long they were dry in the sun. It was fearful to think of the mud that would soon lie there baking and festering, full of lovely creatures dying, and ugly creatures coming to life, like the unmaking of a world. And how hot the sun would be without any lake! She could not bear to swim in it any more, and began to pine away. Her life seemed bound up with it; and ever as the lake sank, she pined. People said she would not live an hour after the lake was gone.

But she never cried.

Proclamation was made to all the kingdom, that whosoever should discover the cause of the lake's decrease, would be rewarded after a princely fashion. Hum-Drum and Kopy-Keck applied themselves to their physics and metaphysics; but in vain. Not even they could suggest a cause.

Now the fact was that the old princess was at the root of the mischief. When she heard that her niece found more pleasure in the water than any one else had out of it, she went into a rage, and cursed herself for her want of foresight.

"But," said she, "I will soon set all right. The king and the people shall die of thirst; their brains shall boil and frizzle in their skulls before I will lose my revenge."

And she laughed a ferocious laugh, that made the hairs on the back of her black cat stand erect with terror.

Then she went to an old chest in the room, and opening it, took out what looked like a piece of dried seaweed. This she threw into a tub of water. Then she threw some powder into the water, and stirred it with her bare arm, muttering over it words of hideous sound, and yet more hideous import. Then she set the tub aside, and took from the chest a huge bunch of a hundred rusty keys, that clattered in her shaking hands. Then she sat down and proceeded to oil them all. Before she had finished, out from the tub, the water of which had kept on a slow motion ever since she had ceased stirring it, came the head and half the body of a huge gray snake. But the witch did not look round. It grew out of the tub, waving itself backwards and forwards with a slow horizontal motion, till it reached the princess, when it laid its head upon her shoulder, and gave a low hiss in her ear. She started—but with joy; and seeing the head resting on her shoulder, drew it towards her and kissed it. Then she drew it all out of the tub, and wound it round her body. It was one of those dreadful creatures which few have ever beheld—the White Snakes of Darkness.

Then she took the keys and went down to her cellar; and as she unlocked the door she said to herself,—

"This *is* worth living for!"

Locking the door behind her, she descended a few steps into the cellar, and crossing it, unlocked another door into a dark, narrow passage. She locked this also behind her, and descended a few more steps. If any one had followed the witch-princess, he would have heard her unlock exactly one hundred doors, and descend a few steps after unlocking each. When she had unlocked the last, she entered a vast cave, the roof of which was supported by huge natural pillars of rock. Now this roof was the under side of the bottom of the lake.

She then untwined the snake from her body, and held it by the tail high above her. The hideous creature stretched up its head towards the roof of the cavern, which it was just able to reach. It then began to move its head backwards and forwards, with a slow oscillating motion, as if looking for something. At the same moment the witch began to walk round and round the cavern, coming nearer to the centre every circuit; while the head of the snake described the same path over the roof that she did over the floor, for she kept holding it up. And still it kept slowly oscillating. Round and round the cavern they went, ever lessening the circuit, till at last the snake made a sudden dart, and clung to the roof with its mouth.

"That's right, my beauty!" cried the princess; "drain it dry."

She let it go, left it hanging, and sat down on a great stone, with her black cat, which had followed her all round the cave, by her side. Then she began to knit and mutter awful words. The snake hung like a huge leech, sucking at the stone; the cat stood with his back arched, and his tail like a piece of cable, looking up at the snake; and the old woman sat and knitted and muttered. Seven days and seven nights they remained thus; when suddenly the serpent dropped from the roof as if exhausted, and shrivelled up till it was again like a piece of dried seaweed. The witch started to her feet, picked it up, put it in her pocket, and looked up at the roof. One drop of water was trembling on the spot where the snake had been sucking. As soon as she saw that, she turned and fled, followed by her cat. Shutting the door in a terrible hurry, she locked it, and having muttered some frightful words, sped to the next, which also she locked and muttered over; and so with all the hundred doors, till she arrived in her own cellar. Then she sat down on the floor ready to faint, but listening with malicious delight to the rushing of the water, which she could hear distinctly through all the hundred doors.

But this was not enough. Now that she had tasted revenge, she lost her patience. Without further measures, the lake would be too long in disappearing. So the next night, with the last shred of the dying old moon rising, she took some of the water in which she had revived the snake, put it in a bottle, and set out, accompanied by her cat. Before morning she had made the entire circuit of the lake, muttering fearful words as she crossed every stream, and casting into it some of the water out of her bottle. When she had finished the circuit she muttered yet again, and flung a handful of water towards the moon. Thereupon every spring in the country ceased to throb and bubble, dying away like the pulse of a dying man. The next day there was no sound of falling water to be heard along the borders of the lake. The very courses were dry; and the mountains showed no silvery streaks down their dark sides. And not alone had the fountains of mother Earth ceased to flow; for all the babies throughout the country were crying dreadfully—only without tears.

XII. WHERE IS THE PRINCE?

Never since the night when the princess left him so abruptly had the prince had a single interview with her. He had seen her once or twice in the lake; but as far as he could discover, she had not been in it any more at night. He had sat and sung, and looked in vain for his Nereid;[2] while she, like a true Nereid, was wasting away with her lake, sinking as it sank, withering as it dried. When at length he discovered the change that was taking place in the level of the water, he was in great alarm and perplexity. He could not tell whether the lake was dying because the lady had forsaken it; or whether the lady would not come because the lake had begun to sink. But he resolved to know so much at least.

He disguised himself, and, going to the palace, requested to see the lord chamberlain. His appearance at once gained his request; and the lord chamberlain, being a man of some insight, perceived that there was more in the prince's solicitation than met the ear. He felt likewise that no one could tell whence a solution of the present difficulties might arise. So he granted the prince's prayer to be made shoe-black to the princess. It was rather cunning in the prince to request such an easy post, for the princess could not possibly soil as many shoes as other princesses.

He soon learned all that could be told about the princess. He went nearly distracted; but after roaming about the lake for days, and diving in every depth that remained, all that he could do was to put an extra polish on the dainty pair of boots that was never called for.

For the princess kept her room, with the curtains drawn to shut out the dying lake. But could not shut it out of her mind for a moment. It haunted her imagination so that she felt as if the lake were her soul, drying up within her, first to mud, then to madness and death. She thus brooded over the change, with all its dreadful accompaniments, till she was nearly distracted. As for the prince, she had forgotten him. However much she had enjoyed his company in the water, she did not care for him without it. But she seemed to have forgotten her father and mother too.

The lake went on sinking. Small slimy spots began to appear, which glittered stead-

---

2. In Greek mythology, a sea nymph. Naiads, the nymphs associated with rivers, lakes, and springs, were strongly identified with specific bodies of water.

ily amidst the changeful shine of the water. These grew to broad patches of mud, which widened and spread, with rocks here and there, and floundering fishes and crawling eels swarming. The people went everywhere catching these, and looking for anything that might have dropped from the royal boats.

At length the lake was all but gone, only a few of the deepest pools remaining unexhausted.

It happened one day that a party of youngsters found themselves on the brink of one of these pools in the very centre of the lake. It was a rocky basin of considerable depth. Looking in, they saw at the bottom something that shone yellow in the sun. A little boy jumped in and dived for it. It was a plate of gold covered with writing. They carried it to the king.

On one side of it stood these words:—

> "Death alone from death can save.
> Love is death, and so is brave—
> Love can fill the deepest grave.
> Love loves on beneath the wave."

Now this was enigmatical enough to the king and courtiers. But the reverse of the plate explained it a little. Its writing amounted to this:—

"If the lake should disappear, they must find the hole through which the water ran. But it would be useless to try to stop it by any ordinary means. There was but one effectual mode.—The body of a living man could alone stanch the flow. The man must give himself of his own will; and the lake must take his life as it filled. Otherwise the offering would be of no avail. If the nation could not provide one hero, it was time it should perish."

XIII. HERE I AM

This was a very disheartening revelation to the king—not that he was unwilling to sacrifice a subject, but that he was hopeless of finding a man willing to sacrifice himself. No time was to be lost, however, for the princess was lying motionless on her bed, and taking no nourishment but lake-water, which was now none of the best. Therefore the king caused the contents of the wonderful plate of gold to be published throughout the country.

No one, however, came forward.

The prince, having gone several days' journey into the forest, to consult a hermit whom he had met there on his way to Lagobel, knew nothing of the oracle till his return.

When he had acquainted himself with all the particulars, he sat down and thought,—

"She will die if I don't do it, and life would be nothing to me without her; so I shall lose nothing by doing it. And life will be as pleasant to her as ever, for she will soon forget me. And there will be so much more beauty and happiness in the world!—To be sure, I shall not see it." (Here the poor prince gave a sigh.) "How lovely the lake will be in the moonlight, with that glorious creature sporting in it like a wild goddess!—It is rather hard to be drowned by inches, though. Let me see—that will be seventy inches of me to drown." (Here he tried to laugh, but could not.) "The longer the better, however," he resumed; "for can I not bargain that the princess shall be beside me all the time? So I shall see her once more, kiss her perhaps,—who knows?

and die looking in her eyes. It will be no death. At least, I shall not feel it. And to see the lake filling for the beauty again!—All right! I am ready."

He kissed the princess's boot, laid it down, and hurried to the king's apartment. But feeling, as he went, that anything sentimental would be disagreeable, he resolved to carry off the whole affair with nonchalance. So he knocked at the door of the king's counting-house, where it was all but a capital crime to disturb him.

When the king heard the knock he started up, and opened the door in a rage. Seeing only the shoe-black, he drew his sword. This, I am sorry to say, was his usual mode of asserting his regality when he thought his dignity was in danger. But the prince was not in the least alarmed.

"Please your majesty, I'm your butler," said he.

"My butler! you lying rascal! What do you mean?"

"I mean, I will cork your big bottle."

"Is the fellow mad?" bawled the king, raising the point of his sword.

"I will put a stopper—plug—what you call it, in your leaky lake, grand monarch," said the prince.

The king was in such a rage that before he could speak he had time to cool, and to reflect that it would be great waste to kill the only man who was willing to be useful in the present emergency, seeing that in the end the insolent fellow would be as dead as if he had died by his majesty's own hand.

"Oh!" said he at last, putting up his sword with difficulty, it was so long; "I am obliged to you, you young fool! Take a glass of wine?"

"No, thank you," replied the prince.

"Very well," said the king. "Would you like to run and see your parents before you make your experiment?"

"No, thank you," said the prince.

"Then we will go and look for the hole at once," said his majesty, and proceeded to call some attendants.

"Stop, please your majesty; I have a condition to make," interposed the prince.

"What!" exclaimed the king, "a condition! and with me! How dare you?"

"As you please," returned the prince, coolly. "I wish your majesty a good morning."

"You wretch! I will have you put in a sack, and stuck in the hole."

"Very well, your majesty," replied the prince, becoming a little more respectful, lest the wrath of the king should deprive him of the pleasure of dying for the princess. "But what good will that do your majesty? Please to remember that the oracle says the victim must offer himself."

"Well, you *have* offered yourself," retorted the king.

"Yes, upon one condition."

"Condition again!" roared the king, once more drawing his sword. "Begone! Somebody else will be glad enough to take the honour off your shoulders."

"Your majesty knows it will not be easy to get another to take my place."

"Well, what is your condition?" growled the king, feeling that the prince was right.

"Only this," replied the prince: "that, as I must on no account die before I am fairly drowned, and the waiting will be rather wearisome, the princess, your daughter, shall go with me, feed me with her own hands, and look at me now and then to comfort me; for you must confess it *is* rather hard. As soon as the water is up to my eyes, she may go and be happy, and forget her poor shoe-black."

Here the prince's voice faltered, and he very nearly grew sentimental, in spite of his resolution.

"Why didn't you tell me before what your condition was? Such a fuss about nothing!" exclaimed the king.

"Do you grant it?" persisted the prince.

"Of course I do," replied the king.

"Very well. I am ready."

"Go and have some dinner, then, while I set my people to find the place."

The king ordered out his guards, and gave directions to the officers to find the hole in the lake at once. So the bed of the lake was marked out in divisions and thoroughly examined, and in an hour or so the hole was discovered. It was in the middle of a stone, near the centre of the lake, in the very pool where the golden plate had been found. It was a three-cornered hole of no great size. There was water all round the stone, but very little was flowing through the hole.

XIV. THIS IS VERY KIND OF YOU

The prince went to dress for the occasion, for he was resolved to die like a prince.

When the princess heard that a man had offered to die for her, she was so transported that she jumped off the bed, feeble as she was, and danced about the room for joy. She did not care who the man was; that was nothing to her. The hole wanted stopping; and if only a man would do, why, take one. In an hour or two more everything was ready. Her maid dressed her in haste, and they carried her to the side of the lake. When she saw it she shrieked, and covered her face with her hands. They bore her across to the stone, where they had already placed a little boat for her. The water was not deep enough to float it, but they hoped it would be, before long. They laid her on cushions, placed in the boat wines and fruits and other nice things, and stretched a canopy over all.

In a few minutes the prince appeared. The princess recognized him at once, but did not think it worth while to acknowledge him.

"Here I am," said the prince. "Put me in."

"They told me it was a shoe-black," said the princess.

"So I am," said the prince. "I blacked your little boots three times a day, because they were all I could get of you. Put me in."

The courtiers did not resent his bluntness, except by saying to each other that he was taking it out in impudence.

But how was he to be put in? The golden plate contained no instructions on this point. The prince looked at the hole, and saw but one way. He put both his legs into it, sitting on the stone, and, stooping forward, covered the corner that remained open with his two hands. In this uncomfortable position he resolved to abide his fate, and turning to the people, said,—

"Now you can go."

The king had already gone home to dinner.

"Now you can go," repeated the princess after him, like a parrot.

The people obeyed her and went.

Presently a little wave flowed over the stone, and wetted one of the prince's knees. But he did not mind it much. He began to sing, and the song he sang was this:—

> "As a world that has no well,
> Darkly bright in forest dell;
> As a world without the gleam

Of the downward-going stream;
As a world without the glance
Of the ocean's fair expanse;
As a world where never rain
Glittered on the sunny plain;—
Such, my heart, thy world would be,
If no love did flow in thee.

As a world without the sound
of the rivulets underground;
Or the bubbling of the spring
Out of darkness wandering;
Or the mighty rush and flowing
Of the river's downward going;
Or the music-showers that drop
On the outspread beech's top;
Or the ocean's mighty voice,
When his lifted waves rejoice;—
Such, my soul, thy world would be,
If no love did sing in thee.

Lady, keep thy world's delight;
Keep the waters in thy sight.
Love hath made me strong to go,
For thy sake, to realms below,
Where the water's shine and hum
Through the darkness never come:
Let, I pray, one thought of me
Spring, a little well, in thee;
Lest thy loveless soul be found
Like a dry and thirsty ground."

"Sing again, prince. It makes it less tedious," said the princess.

But the prince was too much overcome to sing any more, and a long pause followed.

"This is very kind of you, prince," said the princess at last, quite coolly, as she lay in the boat with her eyes shut.

"I am sorry I can't return the compliment," thought the prince; "but you are worth dying for, after all."

Again a wavelet, and another, and another flowed over the stone, and wetted both the prince's knees; but he did not speak or move. Two—three—four hours passed in this way, the princess apparently asleep, and the prince very patient. But he was much disappointed in his position, for he had none of the consolation he had hoped for.

At last he could bear it no longer.

"Princess!" said he.

But at the moment up started the princess, crying,—

"I'm afloat! I'm afloat!"

And the little boat bumped against the stone.

"Princess!" repeated the prince, encouraged by seeing her wide awake and looking eagerly at the water.

"Well?" said she, without looking round.

"Your papa promised that you should look at me, and you haven't looked at me once."

"Did he? Then I suppose I must. But I am so sleepy!"

"Sleep then, darling, and don't mind me," said the poor prince.

"Really, you are very good," replied the princess. "I think I will go to sleep again."

"Just give me a glass of wine and a biscuit first," said the prince, very humbly.

"With all my heart," said the princess, and gaped as she said it.

She got the wine and the biscuit, however, and leaning over the side of the boat towards him, was compelled to look at him.

"Why, prince," she said, "you don't look well! Are you sure you don't mind it?"

"Not a bit," answered he, feeling very faint indeed. "Only I shall die before it is of any use to you, unless I have something to eat."

"There, then," said she, holding out the wine to him.

"Ah! you must feed me. I dare not move my hands. The water would run away directly."

"Good gracious!" said the princess; and she began at once to feed him with bits of biscuit and sips of wine.

As she fed him, he contrived to kiss the tips of her fingers now and then. She did not seem to mind it, one way or the other. But the prince felt better.

"Now, for your own sake, princess," said he, "I cannot let you go to sleep. You must sit and look at me, else I shall not be able to keep up."

"Well, I will do anything I can to oblige you," answered she, with condescension;[3] and, sitting down, she did look at him, and kept looking at him with wonderful steadiness, considering all things.

The sun went down, and the moon rose, and, gush after gush, the waters were rising up the prince's body. They were up to his waist now.

"Why can't we go and have a swim?" said the princess. "There seems to be water enough just about here."

"I shall never swim more," said the prince.

"Oh, I forgot," said the princess, and was silent.

So the water grew and grew, and rose up and up on the prince. And the princess sat and looked at him. She fed him now and then. The night wore on. The waters rose and rose. The moon rose likewise higher and higher, and shone full on the face of the dying prince. The water was up to his neck.

"Will you kiss me, princess?" said he, feebly. The nonchalance was all gone now.

"Yes, I will," answered the princess, and kissed him with a long, sweet, cold kiss.

"Now," said he, with a sigh of content, "I die happy."

He did not speak again. The princess gave him some wine for the last time: he was past eating. Then she sat down again, and looked at him. The water rose and rose. It touched his chin. It touched his lower lip. It touched between his lips. He shut them hard to keep it out. The princess began to feel strange. It touched his upper lip. He breathed through his nostrils. The princess looked wild. It covered his nostrils. Her eyes looked scared, and shone strange in the moonlight. His head fell back; the water closed over it, and the bubbles of his last breath bubbled up through the water. The princess gave a shriek, and sprang into the lake.

3. Considerate deference.

She laid hold first of one leg, and then of the other, and pulled and tugged, but she could not move either. She stopped to take breath, and that made her think that he could not get any breath. She was frantic. She got hold of him, and held his head above the water, which was possible now his hands were no longer on the hole. But it was of no use, for he was past breathing.

Love and water brought back all her strength. She got under the water, and pulled and pulled with her whole might, till at last she got one leg out. The other easily followed. How she got him into the boat she never could tell; but when she did, she fainted away. Coming to herself, she seized the oars, kept herself steady as best she could, and rowed and rowed, though she had never rowed before. Round rocks, and over shallows, and through mud she rowed, till she got to the landing-stairs of the palace. By this time her people were on the shore, for they had heard her shriek. She made them carry the prince to her own room, and lay him in her bed, and light a fire, and send for the doctors.

"But the lake, your highness!" said the chamberlain, who, roused by the noise, came in, in his nightcap.

"Go and drown yourself in it!" she said.

This was the last rudeness of which the princess was ever guilty; and one must allow that she had good cause to feel provoked with the lord chamberlain.

Had it been the king himself, he would have fared no better. But both he and the queen were fast asleep. And the chamberlain went back to his bed. Somehow, the doctors never came. So the princess and her old nurse were left with the prince. But the old nurse was a wise woman, and knew what to do.

They tried everything for a long time without success. The princess was nearly distracted between hope and fear, but she tried on and on, one thing after another, and everything over and over again.

At last, when they had all but given it up, just as the sun rose, the prince opened his eyes.

XV. Look at the Rain!

The princess burst into a passion of tears, and *fell* on the floor. There she lay for an hour, and her tears never ceased. All the pent-up crying of her life was spent now. And a rain came on, such as had never been seen in that country. The sun shone all the time, and the great drops, which fell straight to the earth, shone likewise. The palace was in the heart of a rainbow. It was a rain of rubies, and sapphires, and emeralds, and topazes. The torrents poured from the mountains like molten gold; and if it had not been for its subterraneous outlet, the lake would have overflowed and inundated the country. It was full from shore to shore.

But the princess did not heed the lake. She lay on the floor and wept. And this rain within doors was far more wonderful than the rain out of doors. For when it abated a little, and she proceeded to rise, she found, to her astonishment, that she could not. At length, after many efforts, she succeeded in getting upon her feet. But she tumbled down again directly. Hearing her fall, her old nurse uttered a yell of delight, and ran to her, screaming,—

"My darling child! she's found her gravity!"

"Oh, that's it! is it?" said the princess, rubbing her shoulder and her knee alternately. "I consider it very unpleasant. I feel as if I should be crushed to pieces."

"Hurrah!" cried the prince from the bed. "If you've come round, princess, so have I. How's the lake?"

"Brimful," answered the nurse.

"Then we're all happy."

"That we are indeed!" answered the princess, sobbing.

And there was rejoicing all over the country that rainy day. Even the babies forgot their past troubles, and danced and crowed amazingly. And the king told stories, and the queen listened to them. And he divided the money in his box, and she the honey in her pot, among all the children. And there was such jubilation as was never heard of before.

Of course the prince and princess were betrothed at once. But the princess had to learn to walk, before they could be married with any propriety. And this was not so easy at her time of life, for she could walk no more than a baby. She was always falling down and hurting herself.

"Is this the gravity you used to make so much of?" said she one day to the prince, as he raised her from the floor. "For my part, I was a great deal more comfortable without it."

"No, no, that's not it. This is it," replied the prince, as he took her up, and carried her about like a baby, kissing her all the time. "This is gravity."

"That's better," said she. "I don't mind that so much."

And she smiled the sweetest, loveliest smile in the prince's face. And she gave him one little kiss in return for all his; and he thought them overpaid, for he was beside himself with delight. I fear she complained of her gravity more than once after this, notwithstanding.

It was a long time before she got reconciled to walking. But the pain of learning it was quite counterbalanced by two things, either of which would have been sufficient consolation. The first was, that the prince himself was her teacher; and the second, that she could tumble into the lake as often as she pleased. Still, she preferred to have the prince jump in with her; and the splash they made before was nothing to the splash they made now.

The lake never sank again. In process of time, it wore the roof of the cavern quite through, and was twice as deep as before.

The only revenge the princess took upon her aunt was to tread pretty hard on her gouty toe the next time she saw her. But she was sorry for it the very next day, when she heard that the water had undermined her house, and that it had fallen in the night, burying her in its ruins; whence no one ever ventured to dig up her body. There she lies to this day.

So the prince and princess lived and were happy; and had crowns of gold, and clothes of cloth, and shoes of leather, and children of boys and girls, not one of whom was ever known, on the most critical occasion, to lose the smallest atom of his or her due proportion of gravity.

1863

FRANK STOCKTON
1834–1902

Although rarely read today, Frank Stockton was once viewed as a leading American humorist and man of letters; he was also a pioneer in the fairy tale, combining a light comic tone with serious social commentary in original narratives about eccentric characters. Born and raised in Philadelphia, he dreamed of being a writer, but his father insisted that he learn a profession after graduating from high school. Thus from 1852 to 1860 he worked as a wood engraver, even while participating in the Forensic and Literary Circle—a literary society that he, his brother, and other Central High School graduates formed—and submitting stories to publishers. After numerous rejections, his first short story, "The Slight Mistake" (1855), was printed in the *American Courier*, but it was not until a second story, "Kate" (1859), was published by the prestigious *Southern Literary Messenger* that Stockton gained the confidence to actively pursue a literary career. He continued engraving only when necessary to support himself and Mary Ann Tuttle, whom he had married in 1860. In 1870 he published his first collection of fairy tales, *Ting-a-ling*, many of which had appeared in magazines for young readers. After working for the magazine *Hearth and Home*, he served as associate and then chief editor for *St. Nicholas Magazine*, the leading juvenile publication of the 1880s. A series of fairy-tale books intended for both children and adults followed. Among his best works are *The Floating Prince and Other Fairy Tales* (1881), *The Bee-Man of Orn and Other Fanciful Tales* (1887), and *The Queen's Museum* (1887). Stockton also wrote many novels as well as science fiction and utopian stories. In fact, he ranked as one of the most popular American authors of his day; his short story "The Lady, or the Tiger?" (1882) is still considered one of the best in the genre.

Stockton's technique as a writer was to describe all conditions and scenes, no matter how fabulous, as realistically as possible and to turn the world upside down by matter-of-factly introducing extraordinary events and characters. Blending the normal with the abnormal enabled Stockton to create probable situations in which questions about arbitrary actions could be raised. Indeed, Stockton's major concern in his fairy tales was to reveal the absurdity of commands, impositions, and laws that are not developed by people themselves and that display no common sense.

In "The Griffin and the Minor Canon," first published in *St. Nicholas* in 1885, Stockton examines the life of a seemingly insignificant clergyman, depicting what would happen if people were ungrateful for their freedom. Like some of Mark Twain's tales, "The Griffin and the Minor Canon" focuses on social hypocrisy and conformity. Stockton condemns the people in this town for their cowardice and selfishness and leaves his readers with a dark picture of the future. Yet not everything is bleak in this fairy tale, for it also contains something positive—American individualism, as represented by the canon himself. In fact, Stockton's tales were generally optimistic and they prepared the way for the next great American writer of fairy tales and fantasy, L. Frank Baum, who began publishing his Oz books two years before Stockton's death.

The Griffin and the Minor Canon

Over the great door of an old, old church, which stood in a quiet town of a far-away land, there was carved in stone the figure of a large griffin.[1] The old-time sculptor had done his work with great care, but the image he had made was not a pleasant

---

1. In Greek mythology, a legendary animal with the head and the wings of an eagle and the body of a lion, sometimes depicted with the tail of a serpent or scorpion. The Greeks believed that griffins fought Scythians for gold.

one to look at. It had a large head, with enormous open mouth and savage teeth. From its back arose great wings, armed with sharp hooks and prongs. It had stout legs in front, with projecting claws, but there were no legs behind, the body running out into a long and powerful tail, finished off at the end with a barbed point. This tail was coiled up under him, the end sticking up just back of his wings.

The sculptor, or the people who had ordered this stone figure, had evidently been very much pleased with it, for little copies of it, also in stone, had been placed here and there along the sides of the church, not very far from the ground, so that people could easily look at them and ponder on their curious forms. There were a great many other sculptures on the outside of this church—saints, martyrs, grotesque heads of men, beasts, and birds, as well as those of other creatures which cannot be named, because nobody knows exactly what they were. But none were so curious and interesting as the great griffin over the door and the little griffins on the sides of the church.

A long, long distance from the town, in the midst of dreadful wilds scarcely known to man, there dwelt the Griffin whose image had been put up over the church door. In some way or other the old-time sculptor had seen him, and afterwards, to the best of his memory, had copied his figure in stone. The Griffin had never known this until, hundreds of years afterwards, he heard from a bird, from a wild animal, or in some manner which it is not easy to find out, that there was a likeness of him on the old church in the distant town.

Now, this Griffin had no idea whatever how he looked. He had never seen a mirror, and the streams where he lived were so turbulent and violent that a quiet piece of water, which would reflect the image of anything looking into it, could not be found. Being, as far as could be ascertained, the very last of his race, he had never seen another griffin. Therefore it was that, when he heard of this stone image of himself, he became very anxious to know what he looked like, and at last he determined to go to the old church and see for himself what manner of being he was. So he started off from the dreadful wilds, and flew on and on until he came to the countries inhabited by men where his appearance in the air created great consternation. But he alighted nowhere, keeping up a steady flight until he reached the suburbs of the town which had his image on its church. Here, late in the afternoon, he alighted in a green meadow by the side of a brook, and stretched himself on the grass to rest. His great wings were tired, for he had not made such a long flight in a century or more.

The news of his coming spread quickly over the town, and the people, frightened nearly out of their wits by the arrival of so extraordinary a visitor, fled into their houses and shut themselves up. The Griffin called loudly for some one to come to him; but the more he called, the more afraid the people were to show themselves. At length he saw two laborers hurrying to their homes through the fields, and in a terrible voice he commanded them to stop. Not daring to disobey, the men stood, trembling.

"What is the matter with you all?" cried the Griffin. "Is there not a man in your town who is brave enough to speak to me?"

"I think," said one of the laborers, his voice shaking so that his words could hardly be understood, "that—perhaps—the Minor Canon[2]—would come."

"Go, call him!" said the Griffin. "I want to see him."

The Minor Canon, who filled a subordinate position in the old church, had just

---

2. A clergyman who assists in the daily service in a cathedral but is not a full member of the chapter.

finished the afternoon service, and was coming out of a side door, with three aged women who had formed the week-day congregation. He was a young man of a kind disposition, and very anxious to do good to the people of the town. Apart from his duties in the church, where he conducted services every week-day, he visited the sick and the poor; counselled and assisted persons who were in trouble, and taught a school composed entirely of the bad children in the town, with whom nobody else would have anything to do. Whenever the people wanted something difficult done for them, they always went to the Minor Canon. Thus it was that the laborer thought of the young priest when he found that some one must come and speak to the Griffin.

The Minor Canon had not heard of the strange event which was known to the whole town except himself and the three old women, and when he was informed of it, and was told that the Griffin had asked to see him, he was greatly amazed and frightened.

"Me!" he exclaimed. "He has never heard of me! What should he want with *me?*"

"Oh, you must go instantly!" cried the two men. "He is very angry now because he has been kept waiting so long, and nobody knows what may happen if you don't hurry to him."

The poor Minor Canon would rather have had his hand cut off than to go out to meet an angry griffin; but he felt that it was his duty to go, for it would be a woful thing if injury should come to the people of the town because he was not brave enough to obey the summons of the Griffin; so, pale and frightened, he started off.

"Well," said the Griffin, as soon as the young man came near, "I am glad to see that there is some one who has the courage to come to me."

The Minor Canon did not feel very courageous, but he bowed his head.

"Is this the town," said the Griffin, "where there is a church with a likeness of myself over one of the doors?"

The Minor Canon looked at the frightful creature before him, and saw that it was, without doubt, exactly like the stone image on the church. "Yes," he said, "you are right."

"Well, then," said the Griffin, "will you take me to it? I wish very much to see it."

The Minor Canon instantly thought that if the Griffin entered the town without the people knowing what he came for, some of them would probably be frightened to death, and so he sought to gain time to prepare their minds.

"It is growing dark now," he said, very much afraid, as he spoke, that his words might enrage the Griffin, "and objects on the front of the church cannot be seen clearly. It will be better to wait until morning, if you wish to get a good view of the stone image of yourself."

"That will suit me very well," said the Griffin. "I see you are a man of good sense. I am tired, and I will take a nap here on this soft grass, while I cool my tail in the little stream that runs near me. The end of my tail gets red-hot when I am angry or excited, and it is quite warm now. So you may go; but be sure and come early to-morrow morning, and show me the way to the church."

The Minor Canon was glad enough to take his leave, and hurried into the town. In front of the church he found a great many people assembled to hear his report of his interview with the Griffin. When they found that he had not come to spread ruin and devastation, but simply to see his stony likeness on the church, they showed neither relief nor gratification, but began to upbraid the Minor Canon for consenting to conduct the creature into the town.

"What could I do?" cried the young man. "If I should not bring him he would come himself, and perhaps end by setting fire to the town with his red-hot tail."

Still the people were not satisfied, and a great many plans were proposed to prevent the Griffin from coming into the town. Some elderly persons urged that the young men should go out and kill him. But the young men scoffed at such a ridiculous idea. Then some one said that it would be a good thing to destroy the stone image, so that the Griffin would have no excuse for entering the town. This proposal was received with such favor that many of the people ran for hammers, chisels, and crowbars with which to tear down and break up the stone griffin. But the Minor Canon resisted this plan with all the strength of his mind and body. He assured the people that this action would enrage the Griffin beyond measure, for it would be impossible to conceal from him that his image had been destroyed during the night.

But they were so determined to break up the stone griffin that the Minor Canon saw that there was nothing for him to do but to stay there and protect it. All night he walked up and down in front of the church door, keeping away the men who brought ladders by which they might mount to the great stone griffin and knock it to pieces with their hammers and crowbars. After many hours the people were obliged to give up their attempts, and went home to sleep. But the Minor Canon remained at his post till early morning, and then he hurried away to the field where he had left the Griffin.

The monster had just awakened, and rising to his fore legs and shaking himself, he said that he was ready to go into the town. The Minor Canon, therefore, walked back, the Griffin flying slowly through the air at a short distance above the head of his guide. Not a person was to be seen in the streets, and they proceeded directly to the front of the church, where the Minor Canon pointed out the stone griffin.

The real Griffin settled down in the little square before the church and gazed earnestly at his sculptured likeness. For a long time he looked at it. First he put his head on one side, and then he put it on the other. Then he shut his right eye and gazed with his left, after which he shut his left eye and gazed with his right. Then he moved a little to one side and looked at the image, then he moved the other way. After a while he said to the Minor Canon, who had been standing by all this time:

"It is, it must be, an excellent likeness! That breadth between the eyes, that expansive forehead, those massive jaws! I feel that it must resemble me. If there is any fault to find with it, it is that the neck seems a little stiff. But that is nothing. It is an admirable likeness—admirable!"

The Griffin sat looking at his image all the morning and all the afternoon. The Minor Canon had been afraid to go away and leave him, and had hoped all through the day that he would soon be satisfied with his inspection and fly away home. But by evening the poor young man was utterly exhausted, and felt that he must eat and sleep. He frankly admitted this fact to the Griffin, and asked him if he would not like something to eat. He said this because he felt obliged in politeness to do so; but as soon as he had spoken the words, he was seized with dread lest the monster should demand half a dozen babies, or some tempting repast of that kind.

"Oh, no," said the Griffin, "I never eat between the equinoxes. At the vernal and at the autumnal equinox I take a good meal, and that lasts me for half a year. I am extremely regular in my habits, and do not think it healthful to eat at odd times. But if you need food, go and get it, and I will return to the soft grass where I slept last night, and take another nap."

The next day the Griffin came again to the little square before the church, and remained there until evening, steadfastly regarding the stone griffin over the door. The Minor Canon came once or twice to look at him, and the Griffin seemed very glad to see him. But the young clergyman could not stay as he had done before, for he had many duties to perform. Nobody went to the church, but the people came to the Minor Canon's house, and anxiously asked him how long the Griffin was going to stay.

"I do not know," he answered, "but I think he will soon be satisfied with looking at his stone likeness, and then he will go away."

But the Griffin did not go away. Morning after morning he went to the church, but after a time he did not stay there all day. He seemed to have taken a great fancy to the Minor Canon, and followed him about as he pursued his various avocations. He would wait for him at the side door of the church, for the Minor Canon held services every day, morning and evening, though nobody came now. "If any one should come," he said to himself, "I must be found at my post." When the young man came out, the Griffin would accompany him in his visits to the sick and the poor, and would often look into the windows of the school-house where the Minor Canon was teaching his unruly scholars. All the other schools were closed, but the parents of the Minor Canon's scholars forced them to go to school, because they were so bad they could not endure them all day at home—griffin or no griffin. But it must be said they generally behaved very well when that great monster sat up on his tail and looked in at the school-room window.

When it was perceived that the Griffin showed no sign of going away, all the people who were able to do so, left the town. The canons and the higher officers of the church had fled away during the first day of the Griffin's visit, leaving behind only the Minor Canon and some of the men who opened the doors and swept the church. All the citizens who could afford it shut up their houses and travelled to distant parts, and only the working-people and the poor were left behind. After some days these ventured to go about and attend to their business, for if they did not work they would starve. They were getting a little used to seeing the Griffin, and having been told that he did not eat between equinoxes, they did not feel so much afraid of him as before.

Day by day the Griffin became more and more attached to the Minor Canon. He kept near him a great part of the time, and often spent the night in front of the little house where the young clergyman lived alone. This strange companionship was often burdensome to the Minor Canon. But, on the other hand, he could not deny that he derived a great deal of benefit and instruction from it. The Griffin had lived for hundreds of years, and had seen much, and he told the Minor Canon many wonderful things.

"It is like reading an old book," said the young clergyman to himself. "But how many books I would have had to read before I would have found out what the Griffin has told me about the earth, the air, the water, about minerals, and metals, and growing things, and all the wonders of the world!"

Thus the summer went on, and drew towards its close. And now the people of the town began to be very much troubled again.

"It will not be long," they said, "before the autumnal equinox is here, and then that monster will want to eat. He will be dreadfully hungry, for he has taken so much exercise since his last meal. He will devour our children. Without doubt, he will eat them all. What is to be done?"

To this question no one could give an answer, but all agreed that the Griffin must not be allowed to remain until the approaching equinox. After talking over the matter a great deal, a crowd of the people went to the Minor Canon, at a time when the Griffin was not with him.

"It is all your fault," they said, "that that monster is among us. You brought him here, and you ought to see that he goes away. It is only on your account that he stays here at all, for, although he visits his image every day, he is with you the greater part of the time. If you were not here he would not stay. It is your duty to go away, and then he will follow you, and we shall be free from the dreadful danger which hangs over us."

"Go away!" cried the Minor Canon, greatly grieved at being spoken to in such a way. "Where shall I go? If I go to some other town, shall I not take this trouble there? Have I a right to do that?"

"No," said the people, "you must not go to any other town. There is no town far enough away. You must go to the dreadful wilds where the Griffin lives, and then he will follow you and stay there."

They did not say whether or not they expected the Minor Canon to stay there also, and he did not ask them anything about it. He bowed his head, and went into his house to think. The more he thought, the more clear it became to his mind that it was his duty to go away, and thus free the town from the presence of the Griffin.

That evening he packed a leather bag full of bread and meat, and early the next morning he set out on his journey to the dreadful wilds. It was a long, weary, and doleful journey, especially after he had gone beyond the habitations of men; but the Minor Canon kept on bravely, and never faltered. The way was longer than he had expected, and his provisions soon grew so scanty that he was obliged to eat but a little every day; but he kept up his courage, and pressed on, and after many days of toilsome travel he reached the dreadful wilds.

When the Griffin found that the Minor Canon had left the town, he seemed sorry, but showed no disposition to go and look for him. After a few days had passed, he became much annoyed, and asked some of the people where the Minor Canon had gone. But although the citizens had been so anxious that the young clergyman should go to the dreadful wilds, thinking that the Griffin would immediately follow him, they were now afraid to mention the Minor Canon's destination, for the monster seemed angry already, and if he should suspect their trick, he would doubtless become very much enraged. So every one said he did not know, and the Griffin wandered about disconsolate. One morning he looked into the Minor Canon's school-house, which was always empty now, and thought that it was a shame that everything should suffer on account of the young man's absence.

"It does not matter so much about the church," he said, "for nobody went there. But it is a pity about the school. I think I will teach it myself until he returns."

It was the hour for opening the school, and the Griffin went inside and pulled the rope which rang the school bell. Some of the children who heard the bell ran in to see what was the matter, supposing it to be a joke of one of their companions. But when they saw the Griffin they stood astonished and scared.

"Go tell the other scholars," said the monster, "that school is about to open, and that if they are not all here in ten minutes I shall come after them."

In seven minutes every scholar was in place.

Never was seen such an orderly school. Not a boy or girl moved or uttered a whisper. The Griffin climbed into the master's seat, his wide wings spread on each side of him, because he could not lean back in his chair while they stuck out behind, and his great tail coiled around in front of the desk, the barbed end sticking up, ready to tap any boy or girl who might misbehave. The Griffin now addressed the scholars, telling them that he intended to teach them while their master was away. In speaking he endeavored to imitate, as far as possible, the mild and gentle tones of the Minor Canon, but it must be admitted that in this he was not very successful. He had paid a good deal of attention to the studies of the school, and he determined not to attempt to teach them anything new, but to review them in what they had been studying. So he called up the various classes, and questioned them upon their previous lessons. The children racked their brains to remember what they had learned. They were so afraid of the Griffin's displeasure that they recited as they had never recited before. One of the boys, far down in his class, answered so well that the Griffin was astonished.

"I should think you would be at the head," said he. "I am sure you have never been in the habit of reciting so well. Why is this?"

"Because I did not choose to take the trouble," said the boy, trembling in his boots. He felt obliged to speak the truth, for all the children thought that the great eyes of the Griffin could see right through them, and that he would know when they told a falsehood.

"You ought to be ashamed of yourself," said the Griffin. "Go down to the very tail of the class, and if you are not at the head in two days, I shall know the reason why."

The next afternoon this boy was number one.

It was astonishing how much these children now learned of what they had been studying. It was as if they had been educated over again. The Griffin used no severity toward them, but there was a look about him which made them unwilling to go to bed until they were sure they knew their lessons for the next day.

The Griffin now thought that he ought to visit the sick and the poor, and he began to go about the town for this purpose. The effect upon the sick was miraculous. All, except those who were very ill indeed, jumped from their beds when they heard he was coming, and declared themselves quite well. To those who could not get up he gave herbs and roots, which none of them had ever before thought of as medicines, but which the Griffin had seen used in various parts of the world, and most of them recovered. But, for all that, they afterwards said that no matter what happened to them, they hoped that they should never again have such a doctor coming to their bedsides, feeling their pulses and looking at their tongues.

As for the poor, they seemed to have utterly disappeared. All those who had depended upon charity for their daily bread were now at work in some way or other, many of them offering to do odd jobs for their neighbors just for the sake of their meals—a thing which before had been seldom heard of in the town. The Griffin could find no one who needed his assistance.

The summer now passed, and the autumnal equinox was rapidly approaching. The citizens were in a state of great alarm and anxiety. The Griffin showed no signs of going away, but seemed to have settled himself permanently among them. In a short time the day for his semi-annual meal would arrive, and then what would happen? The monster would certainly be very hungry, and would devour all their children.

Now they greatly regretted and lamented that they had sent away the Minor Canon. He was the only one on whom they could have depended in this trouble, for he could talk freely with the Griffin, and so find out what could be done. But it would not do to be inactive. Some step must be taken immediately. A meeting of the citizens was called, and two old men were appointed to go and talk to the Griffin. They were instructed to offer to prepare a splendid dinner for him on equinox day—one which would entirely satisfy his hunger. They would offer him the fattest mutton, the most tender beef, fish and game of various sorts, and anything of the kind he might fancy. If none of these suited, they were to mention that there was an orphan asylum in the next town.

"Anything would be better," said the citizens, "than to have our dear children devoured."

The old men went to the Griffin, but their propositions were not received with favor.

"From what I have seen of the people of this town," said the monster, "I do not think I could relish anything which was prepared by them. They appear to be all cowards, and, therefore, mean and selfish. As for eating one of them, old or young, I could not think of it for a moment. In fact, there was only one creature in the whole place for whom I could have had any appetite, and that is the Minor Canon, who has gone away. He was brave and good and honest, and I think I should have relished him."

"Ah!" said one of the old men, very politely, "in that case I wish we had not sent him to the dreadful wilds!"

"What!" cried the Griffin. "What do you mean? Explain instantly what you are talking about!"

The old man, terribly frightened at what he had said, was obliged to tell how the Minor Canon had been sent away by the people, in the hope that the Griffin might be induced to follow him.

When the monster heard this he became furiously angry. He dashed away from the old men and, spreading his wings, flew backward and forward over the town. He was so much excited that his tail became red-hot, and glowed like a meteor against the evening sky. When at last he settled down in the little field where he usually rested, and thrust his tail into the brook, the steam arose like a cloud, and the water of the stream ran hot through the town. The citizens were greatly frightened, and bitterly blamed the old man for telling about the Minor Canon.

"It is plain," they said, "that the Griffin intended at last to go and look for him, and we should have been saved. Now who can tell what misery you have brought upon us?"

The Griffin did not remain long in the little field. As soon as his tail was cool he flew to the town hall and rang the bell. The citizens knew that they were expected to come there, and although they were afraid to go, they were still more afraid to stay away, and they crowded into the hall. The Griffin was on the platform at one end, flapping his wings and walking up and down, and the end of his tail was still so warm that it slightly scorched the boards as he dragged it after him.

When everybody who was able to come was there, the Griffin stood still and addressed the meeting.

"I have had a contemptible opinion of you," he said, "ever since I discovered what cowards you are, but I had no idea that you were so ungrateful, selfish, and cruel as I now find you to be. Here was your Minor Canon, who labored day and night for your good, and thought of nothing else but how he might benefit you and make you happy; and as soon as you imagine yourselves threatened with a danger,—for well I know you are dreadfully afraid of me,—you send him off, caring not whether he returns or perishes, hoping thereby to save yourselves. Now, I had conceived a great liking for that young man, and had intended, in a day or two, to go and look him up. But I have changed my mind about him. I shall go and find him, but I shall send him back here to live among you, and I intend that he shall enjoy the reward of his labor and his sacrifices. Go, some of you, to the officers of the church, who so cowardly ran away when I first came here, and tell them never to return to this town under penalty of death. And if, when your Minor Canon comes back to you, you do not bow yourselves before him, put him in the highest place among you, and serve and honor him in his life, beware of my terrible vengeance! There were only two good things in this town: the Minor Canon and the stone image of myself over your church door. One of these you have sent away, and the other I shall carry away myself."

With these words he dismissed the meeting; and it was time, for the end of his tail had become so hot that there was danger of its setting fire to the building.

The next morning the Griffin came to the church, and tearing the stone image of himself from its fastenings over the great door, he grasped it with his powerful forelegs and flew up into the air. Then, after hovering over the town for a moment, he gave his tail an angry shake, and took up his flight to the dreadful wilds. When he reached this desolate region, he set the stone griffin upon a ledge of a rock which rose in front of the dismal cave he called his home. There the image occupied a position somewhat similar to that it had had over the church door; and the Griffin, panting with the exertion of carrying such an enormous load to so great a distance, lay down upon the ground, and regarded it with much satisfaction. When he felt somewhat rested he went to look for the Minor Canon. He found the young man, weak and half-starved, lying under the shadow of a rock. After picking him up and carrying him to his cave, the Griffin flew away to a distant marsh, where he procured some roots and herbs which he well knew were strengthening and beneficial to man, though he had never tasted them himself. After eating these the Minor Canon was greatly revived, and sat up and listened while the Griffin told him what had happened in the town.

"Do you know," said the monster, when he had finished, "that I have had, and still have, a great liking for you?"

"I am very glad to hear it," said the Minor Canon, with his usual politeness.

"I am not at all sure that you would be," said the Griffin, "if you thoroughly understood the state of the case, but we will not consider that now. If some things were different, other things would be otherwise. I have been so enraged by discovering the manner in which you have been treated that I have determined that you shall at last enjoy the rewards and honors to which you are entitled. Lie down and have a good sleep, and then I will take you back to the town."

As he heard these words, a look of trouble came over the young man's face.

"You need not give yourself any anxiety," said the Griffin, "about my return to the town. I shall not remain there. Now that I have that admirable likeness of myself in front of my cave, where I can sit at my leisure and gaze upon its noble features and magnificent proportions, I have no wish to see that abode of cowardly and selfish people."

The Minor Canon, relieved from his fears, lay back, and dropped into a doze; and when he was sound asleep, the Griffin took him up and carried him back to the town. He arrived just before daybreak, and putting the young man gently on the grass in the little field where he himself used to rest, the monster, without having been seen by any of the people, flew back to his home.

When the Minor Canon made his appearance in the morning among the citizens, the enthusiasm and cordiality with which he was received were truly wonderful. He was taken to a house which had been occupied by one of the banished high officers of the place, and every one was anxious to do all that could be done for his health and comfort. The people crowded into the church when he held services, so that the three old women who used to be his week-day congregation could not get to the best seats, which they had always been in the habit of taking; and the parents of the bad children determined to reform them at home, in order that he might be spared the trouble of keeping up his former school. The Minor Canon was appointed to the highest office of the old church, and before he died he became a bishop.

During the first years after his return from the dreadful wilds, the people of the town looked up to him as a man to whom they were bound to do honor and reverence. But they often, also, looked up to the sky to see if there were any signs of the Griffin coming back. However, in the course of time they learned to honor and reverence their former Minor Canon without the fear of being punished if they did not do so.

But they need never have been afraid of the Griffin. The autumnal equinox day came round, and the monster ate nothing. If he could not have the Minor Canon, he did not care for anything. So, lying down with his eyes fixed upon the great stone griffin, he gradually declined, and died. It was a good thing for some of the people of the town that they did not know this.

If you should ever visit the old town, you would still see the little griffins on the sides of the church, but the great stone griffin that was over the door is gone.

1885

OSCAR WILDE
1854–1900

In one of his most prophetic statements in *The Soul of Man under Socialism* (1891), Oscar Wilde remarked: "A map of the world that does not include Utopia is not worth even glancing at, for it leaves out the one country at which Humanity is always landing. And when Humanity lands there, it looks out, and seeing a better country, sets sail. Progress is the realisation of Utopia." Unfortunately, the maps of Wilde's time did not include utopia, an omission that may help explain why so much of a utopian spirit pervades his fairy tales. Born in Dublin, Wilde left Ireland in 1874, having won a scholarship to study classics at Oxford. There he came under the influence of John Ruskin and Walter Pater, England's foremost social and aesthetic critics of the day. They stimulated his thinking in different ways: Ruskin drew Wilde's attention to social questions and the significance of incorporating these questions into art, while Pater demonstrated how private experience is essential for grasping the beautiful and profound nature of the external world. Eventually, Wilde synthesized the notions of these two remarkable thinkers to form his own social concept of aesthetics. Although that notion is most familiar to today's readers from Wilde's dramas, critical essays, and novel *The Picture of Dorian Gray*

(1891), it received its first full expression in his fairy tales.

The Happy Prince and Other Tales (1888) appeared at the beginning of his most productive period: it was followed by *The Soul of Man under Socialism* (1891), *The House of Pomegranates* (1891), *Lady Windermere's Fan* (1892), *A Woman of No Importance* (1893), *The Ideal Husband* (1895), and *The Importance of Being Earnest* (1895). This great success came to a calamitous end in 1895, when Wilde brought an unsuccessful libel action against the Marquis of Queensberry—the father of his lover, Lord Alfred Douglas—for publicly labeling him a sodomite. The loss left Wilde bankrupt and in prison, for he was promptly charged with and found guilty of homosexual activity. Released in 1897 after two years' hard labor, he left for France, where he wrote his best-known poem, "The Ballad of Reading Gaol" (1898), about the horrors of prison. Wilde never returned to England; the aftereffects of an ear injury suffered in prison led to his early death in Paris in 1900.

It is fitting that fairy tales for young readers launched his major phase of creativity, for Wilde had always been disturbed by the rigid constraints that society put on young people, who were punished if they did not conform to arbitrary proper rules. Thus his tales, which grew in part from stories he told his two young sons (he had married Constance Lloyd in 1884), are imbued with a Christian socialist humanism that contradicts the English authoritarian approach to "civilizing" children. To achieve the effect he desired, Wilde broke with the apologetics of classical fairy tales and mawkish Victorian stories for children; instead, he portrayed social problems in England with a glimmer of hope—a utopian impulse for change. The symbolic form of the fairy tale seems to have given Wilde needed distance from the material, enabling him to be innovative in how he cast his social criticism. Relying heavily on motifs from Hans Christian Andersen's tales, which he often reversed to criticize Andersen, Wilde developed a poetical style that recalled the rhythm and language of the Bible as he exposed the narrow-mindedness of the church. This critique of both Andersen and organized religion is most noticeable in the tales "The Young King" and "The Fisherman and His Soul," which are included in *The House of Pomegranates*.

"The Happy Prince" is perhaps the best known of all his tales, and the title already indicates the hallmark of Wilde's style as fairy-tale author—irony. The prince, made into a statue after his death, is anything but happy. It is only then, as he sees beyond the court and realizes how irresponsible he was in life, that he chooses to make amends for his past heedlessness. Ironically, the more he sacrifices himself, the more happy and fulfilled he becomes. As a Christlike figure, the prince represents the artist, whose task is to enrich other people's lives without expecting acknowledgement or rewards. On another level, the love between the prince and the swallow creates a spiritual bond that provides a stark contrast to the materialism and petty values of the town councillors. Society, this tale implies, is not yet ready to appreciate the noble role of the artist, who seeks through his gifts to alleviate impoverishment and beautify people's souls.

The Happy Prince

High above the city, on a tall column, stood the stature of the Happy Prince. He was gilded all over with thin leaves of fine gold, for eyes he had two bright sapphires, and a large red ruby glowed on his sword-hilt.

He was very much admired indeed. "He is as beautiful as a weathercock," remarked one of the Town Councillors who wished to gain a reputation for having artistic tastes; "only not quite so useful," he added, fearing lest people should think him unpractical, which he really was not.

"Why can't you be like the Happy Prince?" asked a sensible mother of her little boy who was crying for the moon. "The Happy Prince never dreams of crying for anything."

"I am glad there is some one in the world who is quite happy," muttered a disappointed man as he gazed at the wonderful statue.

"He looks just like an angel," said the Charity Children as they came out of the cathedral in their bright scarlet cloaks and their clean white pinafores.

"How do you know?" said the Mathematical Master, "you have never seen one."

"Ah! but we have, in our dreams," answered the children; and the Mathematical Master frowned and looked very severe, for he did not approve of children dreaming.

One night there flew over the city a little Swallow. His friends had gone away to Egypt six weeks before, but he had stayed behind, for he was in love with the most beautiful Reed. He had met her early in the spring as he was flying down the river after a big yellow moth, and had been so attracted by her slender waist that he had stopped to talk to her.

"Shall I love you?" said the Swallow, who liked to come to the point at once, and the Reed made him a low bow. So he flew round and round her, touching the water with his wings, and making silver ripples. This was his courtship, and it lasted all through the summer.

"It is a ridiculous attachment," twittered the other Swallows; "she has no money, and far too many relations"; and indeed the river was quite full of Reeds. Then, when the autumn came they all flew away.

After they had gone he felt lonely, and began to tire of his lady-love. "She has no conversation," he said, "and I am afraid that she is a coquette, for she is always flirting with the wind." And certainly, whenever the wind blew, the Reed made the most graceful curtseys. "I admit that she is domestic," he continued, "but I love travelling, and my wife, consequently, should love travelling also."

"Will you come away with me?" he said finally to her; but the Reed shook her head, she was so attached to her home.

"You have been trifling with me," he cried. "I am off to the Pyramids. Good-bye!" and he flew away.

All day long he flew, and at night-time he arrived at the city. "Where shall I put up?" he said; "I hope the town has made preparations."

Then he saw the statue on the tall column.

"I will put up there," he cried; "it is a fine position, with plenty of fresh air." So he alighted just between the feet of the Happy Prince.

"I have a golden bedroom," he said softly to himself as he looked round, and he prepared to go to sleep; but just as he was putting his head under his wing a large drop of water fell on him. "What a curious thing!" he cried; "there is not a single cloud in the sky, the stars are quite clear and bright, and yet it is raining. The climate in the north of Europe is really dreadful. The Reed used to like the rain, but that was merely her selfishness."

Then another drop fell.

"What is the use of a statue if it cannot keep the rain off?" he said; "I must look for a good chimney-pot," and he determined to fly away.

But before he had opened his wings, a third drop fell, and he looked up, and saw——Ah! what did he see?

The eyes of the Happy Prince were filled with tears, and tears were running down his golden cheeks. His face was so beautiful in the moonlight that the little Swallow was filled with pity.

"Who are you?" he said.

"I am the Happy Prince."

"Why are you weeping then?" asked the Swallow; "you have quite drenched me."

"When I was alive and had a human heart," answered the statue, "I did not know what tears were, for I lived in the Palace of Sans-Souci,[1] where sorrow is not allowed to enter. In the daytime I played with my companions in the garden, and in the evening I led the dance in the Great Hall. Round the garden ran a very lofty wall, but I never cared to ask what lay beyond it, everything about me was so beautiful. My courtiers called me the Happy Prince, and happy indeed I was, if pleasure be happiness. So I lived, and so I died. And now that I am dead they have set me up here so high that I can see all the ugliness and all the misery of my city, and though my heart is made of lead yet I cannot choose but weep."

"What! is he not solid gold?" said the Swallow to himself. He was too polite to make any personal remarks out loud.

"Far away," continued the statue in a low musical voice, "far away in a little street there is a poor house. One of the windows is open, and through it I can see a woman seated at a table. Her face is thin and worn, and she has coarse, red hands, all pricked

---

1. Literally, "Without Care" (French).

by the needle, for she is a seamstress. She is embroidering passion-flowers on a satin gown for the loveliest of the Queen's maids-of-honour to wear at the next Court-ball. In a bed in the corner of the room her little boy is lying ill. He has a fever, and is asking for oranges. His mother has nothing to give him but river water, so he is crying. Swallow, Swallow, little Swallow, will you not bring her the ruby out of my sword-hilt? My feet are fastened to this pedestal and I cannot move."

"I am waited for in Egypt," said the Swallow. "My friends are flying up and down the Nile, and talking to the large lotus-flowers. Soon they will go to sleep in the tomb of the great King. The King is there himself in his painted coffin. He is wrapped in yellow linen, and embalmed with spices. Round his neck is a chain of pale green jade, and his hands are like withered leaves."

"Swallow, Swallow, little Swallow," said the Prince, "will you not stay with me for one night, and be my messenger? The boy is so thirsty, and the mother so sad."

"I don't think I like boys," answered the Swallow. "Last summer, when I was staying on the river, there were two rude boys, the miller's sons, who were always throwing stones at me. They never hit me, of course; we swallows fly far too well for that, and besides, I come of a family famous for its agility; but still, it was a mark of disrespect."

But the Happy Prince looked so sad that the little Swallow was sorry. "It is very cold here," he said; "but I will stay with you for one night, and be your messenger."

"Thank you, little Swallow," said the Prince.

So the Swallow picked out the great ruby from the Prince's sword, and flew away with it in his beak over the roofs of the town.

He passed by the cathedral tower, where the white marble angels were sculptured. He passed by the palace and heard the sound of dancing. A beautiful girl came out on the balcony with her lover. "How wonderful the stars are," he said to her, "and how wonderful is the power of love!"

"I hope my dress will be ready in time for the State-ball," she answered; "I have ordered passion-flowers to be embroidered on it; but the seamstresses are so lazy."

He passed over the river, and saw the lanterns hanging to the masts of the ships. He passed over the Ghetto,[2] and saw the old Jews bargaining with each other, and weighing out money in copper scales. At last he came to the poor house and looked in. The boy was tossing feverishly on his bed, and the mother had fallen asleep, she was so tired. In he hopped, and laid the great ruby on the table beside the woman's thimble. Then he flew gently round the bed, fanning the boy's forehead with his wings. "How cool I feel," said the boy, "I must be getting better"; and he sank into a delicious slumber.

Then the Swallow flew back to the Happy Prince, and told him what he had done. "It is curious," he remarked, "but I feel quite warm now, although it is so cold."

"That is because you have done a good action," said the Prince. And the little swallow began to think, and then he fell asleep. Thinking always made him sleepy.

When day broke he flew down to the river and had a bath. "What a remarkable phenomenon," said the Professor of Ornithology as he was passing over the bridge. "A swallow in winter!" And he wrote a long letter about it to the local newspaper. Every one quoted it, it was full of so many words that they could not understand.

"To-night I go to Egypt," said the Swallow, and he was in high spirits at the prospect. He visited all the public monuments, and sat a long time on top of the church steeple. Wherever he went the Sparrows chirruped, and said to each other, "What a distinguished stranger!" so he enjoyed himself very much.

2. The quarter of the city in which Jews were required to live.

When the moon rose he flew back to the Happy Prince. "Have you any commissions for Egypt?" he cried; "I am just starting."

"Swallow, Swallow, little Swallow," said the Prince, "will you not stay with me one night longer?"

"I am waited for in Egypt," answered the Swallow. "To-morrow my friends will fly up to the Second Cataract. The river-horse couches there among the bulrushes, and on a great granite throne sits the God Memnon.[3] All night long he watches the stars, and when the morning star shines he utters one cry of joy, and then he is silent. At noon the yellow lions come down to the water's edge to drink. They have eyes like green beryls, and their roar is louder than the roar of the cataract."

"Swallow, Swallow, little Swallow," said the Prince, "far away across the city I see a young man in a garret. He is leaning over a desk covered with papers, and in a tumbler by his side there is a bunch of withered violets. His hair is brown and crisp, and his lips are red as a pomegranate, and he has large and dreamy eyes. He is trying to finish a play for the Director of the Theatre, but he is too cold to write any more. There is no fire in the grate, and hunger has made him faint."

"I will wait with you one night longer," said the Swallow, who really had a good heart. "Shall I take him another ruby?"

"Alas! I have no ruby now," said the Prince; "my eyes are all that I have left. They are made of rare sapphires, which were brought out of India a thousand years ago. Pluck out one of them and take it to him. He will sell it to the jeweller, and buy food and firewood, and finish his play."

"Dear Prince," said the swallow, "I cannot do that"; and he began to weep.

"Swallow, Swallow, little Swallow," said the Prince, "do as I command you."

So the Swallow plucked out the Prince's eye, and flew away to the student's garret. It was easy enough to get in, as there was a hole in the roof. Through this he darted, and came into the room. The young man had his head buried in his hands, so he did not hear the flutter of the bird's wings, and when he looked up he found the beautiful sapphire lying on the withered violets.

"I am beginning to be appreciated," he cried; "this is from some great admirer. Now I can finish my play," and he looked quite happy.

The next day the Swallow flew down to the harbour. He sat on the mast of a large vessel and watched the sailors hauling big chests out of the hold with ropes. "Heave a-hoy!" they shouted as each chest came up. "I am going to Egypt!" cried the Swallow, but nobody minded, and when the moon rose he flew back to the Happy Prince.

"I am come to bid you good-bye," he cried.

"Swallow, Swallow, little Swallow," said the Prince, "will you not stay with me one night longer?"

"It is winter," answered the Swallow, "and the chill snow will soon be here. In Egypt the sun is warm on the green palm-trees, and the crocodiles lie in the mud and look lazily about them. My companions are building a nest in the Temple of Baalbec,[4] and the pink and white doves are watching them, and cooing to each other. Dear Prince, I must leave you, but I will never forget you, and next spring I will bring you back two beautiful jewels in place of those you have given away. The ruby shall be redder than a red rose, and the sapphire shall be as blue as the great sea."

"In the square below," said the Happy Prince, "there stands a little match-girl. She

3. In Greek mythology, the son of Tithonus and Eos (Dawn). The Greeks gave his name to the statue of Amenhotep III at Thebes, which was said to make a musical sound at daybreak as Memnon greeted his mother.

4. The great Temple of the Sun in the town known to the Greeks as Heliopolis, in eastern Lebanon.

has let her matches fall in the gutter, and they are all spoiled. Her father will beat her if she does not bring home some money, and she is crying. She has no shoes or stockings, and her little head is bare. Pluck out my other eye, and give it to her, and her father will not beat her."

"I will stay with you one night longer," said the Swallow, "but I cannot pluck out your eye. You would be quite blind then."

"Swallow, Swallow, little Swallow," said the Prince, "do as I command you."

So he plucked out the Prince's other eye, and darted down with it. He swooped past the match-girl, and slipped the jewel into the palm of her hand. "What a lovely bit of glass," cried the little girl; and she ran home, laughing.

Then the Swallow came back to the Prince. "You are blind now," he said, "so I will stay with you always."

"No, little Swallow," said the poor Prince, "you must go away to Egypt."

"I will stay with you always," said the Swallow, and he slept at the Prince's feet.

All the next day he sat on the Prince's shoulder, and told him stories of what he had seen in strange lands. He told him of the red ibises, who stand in long rows on the banks of the Nile, and catch gold-fish in their beaks; of the Sphinx,[5] who is as old as the world itself, and lives in the desert, and knows everything; of the merchants, who walk slowly by the side of their camels and carry amber beads in their hands; of the King of the Mountains of the Moon, who is as black as ebony, and worships a large crystal; of the great green snake that sleeps in a palm-tree, and has twenty priests to feed it with honey-cakes; and of the pygmies who sail over a big lake on large flat leaves, and are always at war with the butterflies.

"Dear little Swallow," said the Prince, "you tell me of marvellous things, but more marvellous than anything is the suffering of men and of women. There is no Mystery so great as Misery. Fly over my city, little Swallow, and tell me what you see there."

So the Swallow flew over the great city, and saw the rich making merry in their beautiful houses, while the beggars were sitting at the gates. He flew into dark lanes, and saw the white faces of starving children looking out listlessly at the black streets. Under the archway of a bridge two little boys were lying in one another's arms to try and keep themselves warm. "How hungry we are!" they said. "You must not lie here," shouted the Watchman, and they wandered out into the rain.

Then he flew back and told the Prince what he had seen.

"I am covered with fine gold," said the Prince, "you must take it off, leaf by leaf, and give it to my poor; the living always think that gold can make them happy."

Leaf after leaf of the fine gold the Swallow picked off, till the Happy Prince looked quite dull and grey. Leaf after leaf of the fine gold he brought to the poor, and the children's faces grew rosier, and they laughed and played games in the street. "We have bread now!" they cried.

Then the snow came, and after the snow came the frost. The streets looked as if they were made of silver, they were so bright and glistening; long icicles like crystal daggers hung down from the eaves of the houses, everybody went about in furs, and the little boys wore scarlet caps and skated on the ice.

The poor little Swallow grew colder and colder, but he would not leave the Prince, he loved him too well. He picked up crumbs outside the baker's door when the baker was not looking, and tried to keep himself warm by flapping his wings.

But at last he knew that he was going to die. He had just strength to fly up to the

---

5. In Greek mythology, a winged monster with the head of a woman and the body of a lion (in Egypt, it was usually represented wingless and with the head of a man).

Prince's shoulder once more. "Good-bye, dear Prince!" he murmured, "will you let me kiss your hand?"

"I am glad that you are going to Egypt at last, little Swallow," said the Prince, "you have stayed too long here; but you must kiss me on the lips, for I love you."

"It is not to Egypt that I am going," said the Swallow. "I am going to the House of Death. Death is the brother of Sleep, is he not?"

And he kissed the Happy Prince on the lips, and fell down dead at his feet.

At that moment a curious crack sounded inside the statue, as if something had broken. The fact is that the leaden heart had snapped right in two. It certainly was a dreadfully hard frost.

Early the next morning the Mayor was walking in the square below in company with the Town Councillors. As they passed the column he looked up at the statue: "Dear me! how shabby the Happy Prince looks!" he said.

"How shabby indeed!" cried the Town Councillors, who always agreed with the Mayor; and they went up to look at it.

"The ruby has fallen out of his sword, his eyes are gone, and he is golden no longer," said the Mayor; "in fact, he is little better than a beggar!"

"Little better than a beggar," said the Town Councillors.

"And here is actually a dead bird at his feet!" continued the Mayor. "We must really issue a proclamation that birds are not to be allowed to die here." And the Town Clerk made a note of the suggestion.

So they pulled down the statue of the Happy Prince. "As he is no longer beautiful he is no longer useful," said the Art Professor at the University.

Then they melted the statue in a furnace, and the Mayor held a meeting of the Corporation to decide what was to be done with the metal. "We must have another statue, of course," he said, "and it shall be a statue of myself."

"Of myself," said each of the Town Councillors, and they quarrelled. When I last heard of them they were quarrelling still.

"What a strange thing!" said the overseer of the workmen at the foundry. "This broken lead heart will not melt in the furnace. We must throw it away." So they threw it on a dust-heap where the dead Swallow was also lying.

"Bring me the two most precious things in the city," said God to one of His Angels; and the Angel brought Him the leaden heart and the dead bird.

"You have rightly chosen," said God, "for in my garden of Paradise this little bird shall sing for evermore, and in my city of gold the Happy Prince shall praise me."

1888

KENNETH GRAHAME
1859–1932

Kenneth Grahame's writings are all marked by a nostalgic longing for a gentler, more humane past and for jovial male company. Disturbed by the rapid industrialization of English society and its accom-panying radical social and political changes, he turned to fiction to reflect on ephemeral idyllic moments; childhood was often at the center of his thoughts. Grahame was born in Edinburgh, but the family soon moved to western Scotland. After his mother died in 1864, shortly after giving birth to a fourth child, his father—incapacitated by grief and growing alcoholism—sent the children to live with their maternal grandmother in a small English town on the Thames in Berkshire. Cunningham Grahame's attempt in 1866 to reunite his family in Inverary failed, and in 1867 he moved to France; his children never heard from him again. From 1868 to 1876 Grahame enjoyed academic success at St. Edward's School in Oxford. Though he looked forward to continuing his education at the University of Oxford, his uncle John Grahame insisted that he seek employment at the Bank of England. In 1879 he began working as a clerk.

Grahame was a very competent banker and rose swiftly through the ranks, but he aspired to become a writer and spent his leisure time among bohemians and intellectuals in London. After trying his hand at poetry, he had some essays and sketches published in various magazines, which were eventually collected in his first book, Pagan Papers (1893). In 1894 he joined with a few other friends and writers to establish the literary magazine The Yellow Book, which between 1894 and 1897 printed his nostalgic essays and stories based on his childhood. A number of these were reprinted in his second book, The Golden Age (1895). The children featured in that volume reappear in Dream Days (1898), where they are the audience for "The Reluctant Dragon"—a tale that many critics consider Grahame's finest work and that was later republished separately.

The year 1898 also marked his promotion to the post of secretary of the Bank of England, one of the institution's three top positions; a year later he married Elspeth Tomson, and in 1900 their only child, Alastair, was born. Grahame began telling him stories that later, when business separated the two, were continued in a series of letters featuring Mole, Badger, Rat, and Toad, the main characters in his great novel of fantasy for children, The Wind in the Willows (1908). This book—his last major publication—capped his fame as a writer of nostalgia, and many readers in England were drawn to its general mood of longing for bygone days and a carefree life close to nature. Grahame himself seems to have heeded the book's call. Earlier in 1908 he had retired from the bank, and in 1910 the family moved to a farmhouse near Didcot. Indeed, Grahame's focus in his works on a pursuit of childhood and innocent nature suggests that he viewed the trajectory of his own professional life as a mistake. Writing was his way of breaking out and away from the drudgery of banking. Though this escapist and rebellious tendency is strong in his works, it is balanced by a commonsense attitude that always strikes a happy compromise with his imaginative longings.

Dream Days exemplifies this stance. It contains eight episodes in the childhood of five orphaned brothers and sisters: Edward, Harold, Selina, Charlotte, Martha, and the unnamed narrator. The work is a sequel to The Golden Age; all the pieces seek to reformulate childhood's rites of passage from the idealistic viewpoint of the adult who would like to recapture the past, extolling the virtues of youth in contrast to the petty societal demands of the present. Accordingly, the Boy in "The Reluctant Dragon" acts as Grahame's moral arbiter, who confidently satisfies the expectations of his society while protecting the innocent nature of fantasy. But it was not the Boy alone who championed Grahame's views of youth: he employed the fairy-tale form itself in a deft and unusual manner to defend the realm of imagination. Like many great writers of fairy tales, Grahame was concerned about violence and brutality, and in many tales he reversed the traditional notion of "might makes right" to reveal how conflicts can be "miraculously" resolved by kind and humane action.

The Reluctant Dragon

Footprints in the snow have been unfailing provokers of sentiment ever since snow was first a white wonder in this drab-coloured world of ours. In a poetry-book presented to one of us by an aunt, there was a poem by one Wordsworth[1] in which they stood out strongly with a picture all to themselves, too—but we didn't think very

1. The British poet William Wordsworth (1770–1850). In his poem "Lucy Gray" (1800), a mother sees her lost daughter's footprints in the snow.

highly either of the poem or the sentiment. Footprints in the sand, now, were quite another matter, and we grasped Crusoe's attitude of mind[2] much more easily than Wordsworth's. Excitement and mystery, curiosity and suspense—these were the only sentiments that tracks, whether in sand or in snow, were able to arouse in us.

We had awakened early that winter morning, puzzled at first by the added light that filled the room. Then, when the truth at last fully dawned on us and we knew that snow-balling was no longer a wistful dream, but a solid certainty waiting for us, outside, it was a mere brute fight for the necessary clothes, and the lacing of boots seemed a clumsy invention, and the buttoning of coats an unduly tedious form of fastening, with all that snow going to waste at our very door.

When dinner-time came we had to be dragged in by the scruff of our necks. The short armistice over, the combat was resumed; but presently Charlotte and I, a little weary of contests and of missiles that ran shudderingly down inside one's clothes, forsook the trampled battlefield of the lawn and went exploring the blank virgin spaces of the white world that lay beyond. It stretched away unbroken on every side of us, this mysterious soft garment under which our familiar world had so suddenly hidden itself. Faint imprints showed where a casual bird had alighted, but of other traffic there was next to no sign; which made these strange tracks all the more puzzling.

We came across them first at the corner of the shrubbery, and pored over them long, our hands on our knees. Experienced trappers that we knew ourselves to be, it was annoying to be brought up suddenly by a beast we could not at once identify.

"Don't you know?" said Charlotte rather scornfully. "Thought you knew all the beasts that ever was."

This put me on my mettle, and I hastily rattled off a string of animal names embracing both the arctic and the tropic zones, but without much real confidence.

"No," said Charlotte, on consideration; "they won't any of 'em quite do. Seems like something *lizardy*. Did you say a iguanodon? Might be that, p'raps. But that's not British, and we want a real British beast. I think it's a dragon!"

" 'Tisn't half big enough," I objected.

"Well, all dragons must be small to begin with," said Charlotte: "like everything else. P'raps this is a little dragon who's got lost. A little dragon would be rather nice to have. He might scratch and spit, but he couldn't *do* anything really. Let's track him down!"

So we set off into the wide snow-clad world, hand in hand, our hearts big with expectation,—complacently confident that by a few smudgy traces in the snow we were in a fair way to capture a half-grown specimen of a fabulous beast.

We ran the monster across the paddock and along the hedge of the next field, and then he took to the road like any tame civilized tax-payer. Here his tracks became blended with and lost among more ordinary footprints, but imagination and a fixed idea will do a great deal, and we were sure we knew the direction a dragon would naturally take. The traces, too, kept reappearing at intervals—at least Charlotte maintained they did, and as it was *her* dragon I left the following of the slot[3] to her and trotted along peacefully, feeling that it was an expedition anyhow and something was sure to come out of it.

Charlotte took me across another field or two, and through a copse, and into a

---

2. I.e., astonishment. Robinson Crusoe, the eponymous hero of Daniel Defoe's novel (1719), is thunderstruck to find a single footprint in the sand of the island on which he has been living for six years as the sole survivor of a shipwreck.
3. The track or trail of an animal.

fresh road; and I began to feel sure it was only her confounded pride that made her go on pretending to see dragon-tracks instead of owning she was entirely at fault, like a reasonable person. At last she dragged me excitedly through a gap in a hedge of an obviously private character; the waste, open world of field and hedgerow disappeared, and we found ourselves in a garden, well-kept, secluded, most undragon-haunted in appearance. Once inside, I knew where we were. This was the garden of my friend the circus-man, though I had never approached it before by a lawless gap, from this unfamiliar side. And here was the circus-man himself, placidly smoking a pipe as he strolled up and down the walks. I stepped up to him and asked him politely if he had lately seen a Beast.

"May I inquire" he said, with all civility, "what particular sort of a Beast you may happen to be looking for?"

"It's a *lizardy* sort of Beast," I explained. "Charlotte says it's a dragon, but she doesn't really know much about beasts."

The circus-man looked round about him slowly. "I don't *think*," he said, "that I've seen a dragon in these parts recently. But if I come across one I'll know it belongs to you, and I'll have him taken round to you at once."

"Thank you very much," said Charlotte, "but don't *trouble* about it, please, 'cos p'raps it isn't a dragon after all. Only I thought I saw his little footprints in the snow, and we followed 'em up, and they seemed to lead right in here, but maybe it's all a mistake, and thank you all the same."

"Oh, no trouble at all," said the circus-man cheerfully. "I should be only too pleased. But of course, as you say, it *may* be a mistake. And it's getting dark, and he seems to have got away for the present, whatever he is. You'd better come in and have some tea. I'm quite alone, and we'll make a roaring fire, and I've got the biggest Book of Beasts you ever saw. It's got every beast in the world, and all of 'em coloured; and we'll try and find *your* beast in it!"

We were always ready for tea at any time, and especially when combined with beasts. There was marmalade, too, and apricot jam, brought in expressly for us; and afterwards the beast-book was spread out, and, as the man had truly said, it contained every sort of beast that had ever been in the world.

The striking of six o'clock set the more prudent Charlotte nudging me, and we recalled ourselves with an effort from Beast-land, and reluctantly stood up to go.

"Here, I'm coming along with you," said the circus-man. "I want another pipe, and a walk'll do me good. You needn't talk to me unless you like."

Our spirits rose to their wonted level again. The way had seemed so long, the outside world so dark and eerie, after the bright warm room and the highly-coloured beast-book. But a walk with a real Man—why, that was a treat in itself! We set off briskly, the Man in the middle. I looked up at him and wondered whether I should ever live to smoke a big pipe with that careless sort of majesty! But Charlotte, whose young mind was not set on tobacco as a possible goal, made herself heard from the other side.

"Now, then," she said, "tell us a story, please, won't you?"

The Man sighed heavily and looked about him. "I knew it," he groaned. "I *knew* I should have to tell a story. Oh, why did I leave my pleasant fireside? Well, I *will* tell you a story. Only let me think a minute."

So he thought a minute, and then he told us this story:

Long ago—might have been hundreds of years ago—in a cottage half-way between this village and yonder shoulder of the Downs up there, a shepherd lived with his wife and their little son. Now the shepherd spent his days—and at certain times of the year his nights too—up on the wide ocean-bosom of the Downs, with only the sun and the stars and the sheep for company, and the friendly chattering world of men and women far out of sight and hearing. But his little son, when he wasn't helping his father, and often when he was as well, spent much of his time buried in big volumes that he borrowed from the affable gentry and interested parsons of the country round about. And his parents were very fond of him, and rather proud of him too, though they didn't let on in his hearing, so he was left to go his own way and read as much as he liked; and instead of frequently getting a cuff on the side of the head, as might very well have happened to him, he was treated more or less as an equal by his parents, who sensibly thought it a very fair division of labour that they should supply the practical knowledge, and he the book-learning. They knew that book-learning often came in useful at a pinch, in spite of what their neighbours said. What the Boy chiefly dabbled in was natural history and fairy-tales, and he just took them as they came, in a sandwichy sort of way, without making any distinctions; and really his course of reading strikes one as rather sensible.

One evening the shepherd, who for some nights past had been disturbed and preoccupied, and off his usual mental balance, came home all of a tremble, and, sitting down at the table where his wife and son were peacefully employed, she with her seam, he in following out the adventures of the Giant with no Heart in his Body,[4] exclaimed with much agitation:

"It's all up with me, Maria! Never no more can I go up on them there Downs, was it ever so!"

"Now don't you take on like that," said his wife, who was a *very* sensible woman: "but tell us all about it first, whatever it is as has given you this shake-up, and then me and you and the son here, between us, we ought to be able to get to the bottom of it!"

"It began some nights ago," said the shepherd. "You know that cave up there—I never liked it, somehow, and the sheep never liked it neither, and when sheep don't like a thing there's generally some reason for it. Well, for some time past there's been faint noises coming from that cave—noises like heavy sighings, with grunts mixed up in them; and sometimes a snoring, far away down—*real* snoring, yet somehow not *honest* snoring, like you and me o' nights, you know!"

"I know," remarked the Boy quietly.

"Of course I was terrible frightened," the shepherd went on; "yet somehow I couldn't keep away. So this very evening, before I come down, I took a cast round by the cave, quietly. And there—O Lord! there I saw him at last, as plain as I see you!"

"Saw *who*?" said his wife, beginning to share in her husband's nervous terror.

"Why *him*, I'm a-telling you!" said the shepherd. "He was sticking half-way out of the cave, and seemed to be enjoying of the cool of the evening in a poetical sort of way. He was as big as four cart-horses, and all covered with shiny scales—deep-blue scales at the top of him, shading off to a tender sort o' green below. As he breathed, there was a sort of flicker over his nostrils that you see over our chalk roads on a baking windless day in summer. He had his chin on his paws, and I should say he was meditating about things. Oh, yes, a peaceable sort o' beast enough, and not ramping[5] or carrying on or doing anything but what was quite right and proper. I

4. A Norwegian folktale.   5. Menacing with his forelegs.

admit all that. And yet, what am I to do? Scales, you know, and claws, and a tail for certain, though I didn't see that end of him—I ain't *used* to 'em, and I don't *hold* with 'em, and that's a fact!"

The Boy, who had apparently been absorbed in his book during his father's recital, now closed the volume, yawned, clasped his hands behind his head, and said sleepily:

"It's all right, father. Don't you worry. It's only a dragon."

"Only a dragon?" cried his father. "What do you mean, sitting there, you and your dragons? *Only* a dragon indeed! And what do *you* know about it?"

" 'Cos it *is*, and 'cos I *do* know," replied the Boy quietly. "Look here, father, you know we've each of us got our line. *You* know about sheep, and weather, and things; *I* know about dragons. I always said, you know, that that cave up there was a dragon-cave. I always said it must have belonged to a dragon some time, and ought to belong to a dragon now, if rules count for anything. Well, now you tell me it *has* got a dragon, and so *that's* all right. I'm not half as much surprised as when you told me it *hadn't* got a dragon. Rules always come right if you wait quietly. Now, please, just leave this all to me. And I'll stroll up to-morrow morning—no, in the morning I can't, I've got a whole heap of things to do—well, perhaps in the evening, if I'm quite free, I'll go up and have a talk to him, and you'll find it'll be all right. Only please, don't you go worrying round there without me. You don't understand 'em a bit, and they're very sensitive, you know!"

"He's quite right, father," said the sensible mother. "As he says, dragons is his line and not ours. He's wonderful knowing about book-beasts, as every one allows. And to tell the truth, I'm not half happy in my own mind, thinking of that poor animal lying alone up there, without a bit o' hot supper or anyone to change the news with; and maybe we'll be able to do something for him; and if he ain't quite respectable our Boy'll find it out quick enough. He's got a pleasant sort o' way with him that makes everybody tell him everything."

Next day, after he'd had his tea, the Boy strolled up the chalky track that led to the summit of the Downs; and there, sure enough, he found the dragon, stretched lazily on the sward in front of his cave. The view from that point was a magnificent one. To the right and left, the bare and billowy leagues of Downs; in front, the vale, with its clustered homesteads, its threads of white roads running through orchards and well-tilled acreage, and, far away, a hint of grey old cities on the horizon. A cool breeze played over the surface of the grass, and the silver shoulder of a large moon was showing above distant junipers. No wonder the dragon seemed in a peaceful and contented mood; indeed, as the Boy approached he could hear the beast purring with a happy regularity. "Well, we live and learn!" he said to himself. "None of my books ever told me that dragons purred!"

"Hullo, dragon!" said the Boy quietly, when he had got up to him.

The dragon, on hearing the approaching footsteps, made the beginning of a courteous effort to rise. But when he saw it was a Boy, he set his eyebrows severely.

"Now don't you hit me," he said; "or bung stones, or squirt water, or anything. I won't have it, I tell you!"

"Not goin' to hit you," said the Boy wearily, dropping on the grass beside the beast: "and don't, for goodness' sake, keep on saying 'Don't'; I hear so much of it, and it's monotonous, and makes me tired. I've simply looked in to ask you how you were and all that sort of thing; but if I'm in the way I can easily clear out. I've lots of friends, and no one can say I'm in the habit of shoving myself in where I'm not wanted!"

"No, no, don't go off in a huff," said the dragon hastily; "fact is—I'm as happy up here as the day's long; never without an occupation, dear fellow, never without an occupation! And yet, between ourselves, it *is* a trifle dull at times."

The Boy bit off a stalk of grass and chewed it. "Going to make a long stay here?" he asked politely.

"Can't hardly say at present," replied the dragon. "It seems a nice place enough— but I've only been here a short time, and one must look about and reflect and consider before settling down. It's rather a serious thing, settling down. Besides—now I'm going to tell you something! You'd never guess it if you tried ever so!—fact is, I'm such a confoundedly lazy beggar!"

"You surprise me," said the Boy civilly.

"It's the sad truth," the dragon went on, settling down between his paws and evidently delighted to have found a listener at last: "and I fancy that's really how I came to be here. You see all the other fellows were so active and *earnest* and all that sort of thing—always rampaging, and skirmishing, and scouring the desert sands, and pacing the margin of the sea, and chasing knights all over the place, and devouring damsels, and going on generally—whereas I liked to get my meals regular and then to prop my back against a bit of rock and snooze a bit, and wake up and think of things going on and how they kept going on just the same, you know! So when it happened I got fairly caught."

"When *what* happened, please?" asked the Boy.

"That's just what I don't precisely know," said the dragon. "I suppose the earth sneezed, or shook itself, or the bottom dropped out of something. Anyhow there was a shake and a roar and a general stramash,[6] and I found myself miles away underground and wedged in as tight as tight. Well, thank goodness, my wants are few, and at any rate I had peace and quietness and wasn't always being asked to come along and *do* something. And I've got such an active mind—always occupied, I assure you! But time went on, and there was a certain sameness about the life, and at last I began to think it would be fun to work my way upstairs and see what you other fellows were doing. So I scratched and burrowed, and worked this way and that way and at last I came out through this cave here. And I like the country, and the view, and the people—what I've seen of 'em—and on the whole I feel inclined to settle down here."

"What's your mind always occupied about?" asked the Boy. "That's what I want to know."

The dragon coloured slightly and looked away. Presently he said bashfully:

"Did you ever—just for fun—try to make up poetry—verses, you know?"

" 'Course I have," said the Boy. "Heaps of it. And some of it's quite good, I feel sure, only there's no one here cares about it. Mother's very kind and all that, when I read it to her, and so's father for that matter. But somehow they don't seem to——"

"Exactly," cried the dragon; "my own case exactly. They don't seem to, and you can't argue with 'em about it. Now you've got culture, you have, I could tell it on you at once, and I should just like your candid opinion about some little things I threw off lightly, when I was down there. I'm awfully pleased to have met you, and I'm hoping the other neighbours will be equally agreeable. There was a very nice old gentleman up here only last night, but he didn't seem to want to intrude."

"That was my father," said the boy, "and he *is* a nice old gentleman, and I'll introduce you some day if you like."

"Can't you two come up here and dine or something to-morrow?" asked the dragon eagerly. "Only, of course, if you've got nothing better to do," he added politely.

"Thanks awfully," said the Boy, "but we don't go out anywhere without my mother,

6. Crash, smashup.

and, to tell you the truth, I'm afraid she mightn't quite approve of you. You see there's no getting over the hard fact that you're a dragon, is there? And when you talk of settling down, and the neighbours, and so on, I can't help feeling that you don't quite realize your position. You're an enemy of the human race, you see!"

"Haven't got an enemy in the world," said the dragon cheerfully. "Too lazy to make 'em, to begin with. And if I *do* read other fellows my poetry, I'm always ready to listen to theirs!"

"Oh, dear!" cried the boy, "I wish you'd try and grasp the situation properly. When the other people find you out, they'll come after you with spears and swords and all sorts of things. You'll have to be exterminated, according to their way of looking at it! You're a scourge, and a pest, and a baneful monster!"

"Not a word of truth in it," said the dragon, wagging his head solemnly. "Character'll bear the strictest investigation. And now, there's a little sonnet-thing I was working on when you appeared on the scene—"

"Oh, if you *won't* be sensible," cried the Boy, getting up, "I'm going off home. No, I can't stop for sonnets; my mother's sitting up. I'll look you up to-morrow, sometime or other, and do for goodness' sake try and realize that you're a pestilential scourge, or you'll find yourself in a most awful fix. Good night!"

The Boy found it an easy matter to set the mind of his parents at ease about his new friend. They had always left that branch to him, and they took his word without a murmur. The shepherd was formally introduced and many compliments and kind enquiries were exchanged. His wife, however, though expressing her willingness to do anything she could—to mend things, or set the cave to rights, or cook a little something when the dragon had been poring over sonnets and forgotten his meals, as male things *will* do, could not be brought to recognize him formally. The fact that he was a dragon and "they didn't know who he was" seemed to count for everything with her. She made no objection, however, to her little son spending his evenings with the dragon quietly, so long as he was home by nine o'clock: and many a pleasant night they had, sitting on the sward, while the dragon told stories of old, old times, when dragons were quite plentiful and the world was a livelier place than it is now, and life was full of thrills and jumps and surprises.

What the Boy had feared, however, soon came to pass. The most modest and retiring dragon in the world, if he's as big as four cart-horses and covered with blue scales, cannot keep altogether out of the public view. And so in the village tavern of nights the fact that a real live dragon sat brooding in the cave on the Downs was naturally a subject for talk. Though the villagers were extremely frightened, they were rather proud as well. It was a distinction to have a dragon of your own, and it was felt to be a feather in the cap of the village. Still, all were agreed that this sort of thing couldn't be allowed to go on. The dreadful beast must be exterminated, the country-side must be freed from this pest, this terror, this destroying scourge. The fact that not even a hen-roost was the worse for the dragon's arrival wasn't allowed to have anything to do with it. He was a dragon, and he couldn't deny it, and if he didn't choose to behave as such that was his own look-out. But in spite of much valiant talk no hero was found willing to take sword and spear and free the suffering village and win deathless fame; and each night's heated discussion always ended in nothing. Meanwhile the dragon, a happy Bohemian, lolled on the turf, enjoyed the sunsets, told antediluvian anecdotes to the Boy, and polished his old verses while meditating on fresh ones.

One day the Boy, on walking into the village found everything wearing a festal appearance which was not to be accounted for in the calendar. Carpets and gay-coloured stuffs were hung out of the windows, the church-bells clamoured noisily, the little street was flower-strewn, and the whole population jostled each other along either side of it, chattering, shoving, and ordering each other to stand back. The Boy saw a friend of his own age in the crowd and hailed him.

"What's up?" he cried. "Is it the players, or bears, or a circus, or what?"

"It's all right," his friend hailed back. "He's a-coming."

"Who's a-coming?" demanded the Boy, thrusting into the throng.

"Why, St. George,[7] of course," replied his friend. "He's heard tell of our dragon, and he's comin' on purpose to slay the deadly beast, and free us from his horrid yoke. O my! won't there be a jolly fight!"

Here was news indeed! The Boy felt that he ought to make quite sure for himself, and he wriggled himself in between the legs of his good-natured elders, abusing them all the time for their unmannerly habit of shoving. Once in the front rank, he breathlessly awaited the arrival.

Presently from the far-away end of the line came the sound of cheering. Next, the measured tramp of a great war-horse made his heart beat quicker, and then he found himself cheering with the rest, as, amidst welcoming shouts, shrill cries of women, uplifting of babies, and waving of handkerchiefs, St. George paced slowly up the street. The Boy's heart stood still and he breathed with sobs, the beauty and the grace of the hero were so far beyond anything he had yet seen. His fluted armour was inlaid with gold, his plumed helmet hung at his saddle-bow, and his thick fair hair framed a face gracious and gentle beyond expression till you caught the sternness in his eyes. He drew rein in front of the little inn, and the villagers crowded round with greetings and thanks and voluble statements of their wrongs and grievances and oppressions. The Boy heard the grave gentle voice of the Saint, assuring them that all would be well now, and that he would stand by them and see them righted and free them from their foe; then he dismounted and passed through the doorway and the crowd poured in after him. But the Boy made off up the hill as fast as he could lay his legs to the ground.

"It's all up, dragon!" he shouted as soon as he was within sight of the beast. "He's coming! He's here now! You'll have to pull yourself together and *do* something at last!"

The dragon was licking his scales and rubbing them with a bit of house-flannel the Boy's mother had lent him, till he shone like a great turquoise.

"Don't be *violent*, Boy," he said without looking round. "Sit down and get your breath, and try and remember that the noun governs the verb, and then perhaps you'll be good enough to tell me *who's* coming?"

"That's right, take it coolly," said the Boy. "Hope you'll be half as cool when I've got through with my news. It's only St. George who's coming, that's all; he rode into the village half an hour ago. Of course you can lick him—a great big fellow like you! But I thought I'd warn you, 'cos he's sure to be round early, and he's got the longest, wickedest-looking spear you ever did see!" And the Boy got up and began to jump round in sheer delight at the prospect of the battle.

"O deary, deary me," moaned the dragon; "this is too awful. I won't see him, and

7. England's patron saint, whose picture King Arthur is said to have placed on his banner (the historical St. George was martyred in Asia Minor, probably before the 4th c. C.E., and is the ancient patron of soldiers). St. George's slaying of the dragon is interpreted as an allegory of the triumph of the Christian hero over evil.

that's flat. I don't want to know the fellow at all. I'm sure he's not nice. You must tell him to go away at once, please. Say he can write if he likes, but I can't give him an interview. I'm not seeing anybody at present."

"Now, dragon, dragon," said the Boy imploringly, "don't be perverse and wrong-headed. You've *got* to fight him some time or other, you know, 'cos he's St. George and you're the dragon. Better get it over and then we can go on with the sonnets. And you ought to consider other people a little, too. If it's been dull up here for you, think how dull it's been for me!"

"My dear little man," said the dragon solemnly, "just understand, once for all, that I can't fight and I won't fight. I've never fought in my life, and I'm not going to begin now, just to give you a Roman holiday.[8] In old days I always let the other fellows—the *earnest* fellows—do all the fighting, and no doubt that's why I have the pleasure of being here now."

"But if you don't fight he'll cut your head off!" gasped the Boy, miserable at the prospect of losing both his fight and his friend.

"Oh, I think not," said the dragon in his lazy way. "You'll be able to arrange something. I've every confidence in you, you're such a *manager*. Just run down, there's a dear chap, and make it all right. I leave it entirely to you."

The Boy made his way back to the village in a state of great despondency. First of all, there wasn't going to be any fight; next, his dear and honoured friend the dragon hadn't shown up in quite such a heroic light as he would have liked; and lastly, whether the dragon was a hero at heart or not, it made no difference, for St. George would most undoubtedly cut his head off. "Arrange things indeed!" he said bitterly to himself. "The dragon treats the whole affair as if it was an invitation to tea and croquet."

The villagers were straggling homewards as he passed up the street, all of them in the highest spirits, and gleefully discussing the splendid fight that was in store. The Boy pursued his way to the inn, and passed into the principal chamber, where St. George now sat alone, musing over the chances of the fight, and the sad stories of rapine and of wrong that had so lately been poured into his sympathetic ears.

"May I come in, St. George?" said the Boy politely, as he paused at the door. "I want to talk to you about this little matter of the dragon, if you're not tired of it by this time."

"Yes, come in, Boy," said the Saint kindly. "Another tale of misery and wrong, I fear me. Is it a kind parent, then, of whom the tyrant has bereft you? Or some tender sister or brother? Well, it shall soon be avenged."

"Nothing of the sort," said the Boy. "There's a misunderstanding somewhere, and I want to put it right. The fact is, this is a *good* dragon."

"Exactly," said St. George, smiling pleasantly, "I quite understand. A good *dragon*. Believe me, I do not in the least regret that he is an adversary worthy of my steel, and no feeble specimen of his noxious tribe."

"But he's *not* a noxious tribe," cried the Boy distressedly. "Oh dear, oh dear, how *stupid* men are when they get an idea into their heads! I tell you he's a *good* dragon, and a friend of mine, and tells me the most beautiful stories you ever heard, all about old times and when he was little. And he's been so kind to mother, and mother'd do anything for him. And father likes him too, though father doesn't hold with art and poetry much, and always falls asleep when the dragon starts talking about *style*. But

8. A violent public spectacle.

the fact is, nobody can help liking him when once they know him. He's so engaging and so trustful, and as simple as a child!"

"Sit down, and draw your chair up," said St. George. "I like a fellow who sticks up for his friends, and I'm sure the dragon has his good points, if he's got a friend like you. But that's not the question. All this evening I've been listening, with grief and anguish unspeakable, to tales of murder, theft, and wrong; rather too highly coloured, perhaps, not always quite convincing, but forming in the main a most serious roll of crime. History teaches us that the greatest rascals often possess all the domestic virtues; and I fear that your cultivated friend, in spite of the qualities which have won (and rightly) your regard, has got to be speedily exterminated."

"Oh, you've been taking in all the yarns those fellows have been telling you," said the Boy impatiently. "Why, our villagers are the biggest story-tellers in all the country round. It's a known fact. You're a stranger in these parts, or else you'd have heard it already. All they want is a *fight*. They're the most awful beggars for getting up fights—it's meat and drink to them. Dogs, bulls, dragons—anything so long as it's a fight. Why, they've got a poor innocent badger in the stable behind here, at this moment. They were going to have some fun with him to-day, but they're saving him up now till *your* little affair's over. And I've no doubt they've been telling you what a hero you were, and how you were bound to win, in the cause of right and justice, and so on; but let me tell you, I came down the street just now, and they were betting six to four on the dragon freely!"

"Six to four on the dragon!" murmured St. George sadly, resting his cheek on his hand. "This is an evil world, and sometimes I begin to think that all the wickedness in it is not entirely bottled up inside the dragons. And yet—may not this wily beast have misled you as to his real character, in order that your good report of him may serve as a cloak for his evil deeds? Nay, may there not be, at this very moment, some hapless Princess immured within yonder gloomy cavern?"

The moment he had spoken, St. George was sorry for what he had said, the Boy looked so genuinely distressed.

"I assure you, St. George," he said earnestly, "there's nothing of the sort in the cave at all. The dragon's a real gentleman, every inch of him, and I may say that no one would be more shocked and grieved than he would, at hearing you talk in that—that *loose* way about matters on which he has very strong views!"

"Well, perhaps I've been over-credulous," said St. George. "Perhaps I've misjudged the animal. But what are we to do? Here are the dragon and I, almost face to face, each supposed to be thirsting for each other's blood. I don't see any way out of it, exactly. What do you suggest? Can't you arrange things, somehow?"

"That's just what the dragon said," replied the Boy, rather nettled. "Really, the way you two seem to leave everything to me—I suppose you couldn't be persuaded to go away quietly, could you?"

"Impossible, I fear," said the Saint. "Quite against the rules. *You* know that as well as I do."

"Well, then, look here," said the Boy, "it's early yet—would you mind strolling up with me and seeing the dragon and talking it over? It's not far, and any friend of mine will be most welcome."

"Well, it's *irregular*," said St. George, rising, "but really it seems about the most sensible thing to do. You're taking a lot of trouble on your friend's account," he added good-naturedly, as they passed out through the door together. "But cheer up! Perhaps there won't have to be any fight after all."

"Oh, but I hope there will, though!" replied the little fellow wistfully.

"I've brought a friend to see you, dragon," said the Boy rather loud.

The dragon woke up with a start. "I was just—er—thinking about things," he said in his simple way. "Very pleased to make your acquaintance, sir. Charming weather we're having!"

"This is St. George," said the Boy, shortly. "St. George, let me introduce you to the dragon. We've come up to talk things over quietly, dragon, and now for goodness' sake do let us have a little straight common sense, and come to some practical business-like arrangement, for I'm sick of views and theories of life and personal tendencies, and all that sort of thing. I may perhaps add that my mother's sitting up."

"So glad to meet you, St. George," began the dragon rather nervously, "because you've been a great traveller, I hear, and I've always been rather a stay-at-home. But I can show you many antiquities, many interesting features of our countryside, if you're stopping here any time——"

"I think," said St. George in his frank, pleasant way, "that we'd really better take the advice of our young friend here, and try to come to some understanding, on a business footing, about this little affair of ours. Now don't you think that after all the simplest plan would be just to fight it out, according to the rules, and let the best man win? They're betting on you, I may tell you, down in the village, but I don't mind that!"

"Oh, yes, do, dragon," said the Boy delightedly; "it'll save such a lot of bother!"

"My young friend, you shut up," said the dragon severely. "Believe me, St. George," he went on, "there's nobody in the world I'd sooner oblige than you and this young gentleman here. But the whole thing's nonsense, and conventionality, and popular thick-headedness. There's absolutely nothing to fight about, from beginning to end. And anyhow I'm not going to, so that settles it!"

"But supposing I make you?" said St. George, rather nettled.

"You can't," said the dragon triumphantly. "I should only go into my cave and retire for a time down the hole I came up. You'd soon get heartily sick of sitting outside and waiting for me to come out and fight you. And as soon as you'd really gone away, why, I'd come up again gaily, for I tell you frankly, I like this place, and I'm going to stay here!"

St. George gazed for a while on the fair landscape around them. "But this would be a beautiful place for a fight," he began again persuasively. "These great bare rolling Downs for the arena—and me in my golden armour showing up against your big blue scaly coils! Think what a picture it would make!"

"Now you're trying to get at me through my artistic sensibilities," said the dragon. "But it won't work. Not but what it would make a very pretty picture, as you say," he added, wavering a little.

"We seem to be getting rather nearer to business," put in the Boy. "You must see, dragon, that there's got to be a fight of some sort, 'cos you can't want to have to go down that dirty old hole again and stop there till goodness knows when."

"It might be arranged," said St. George thoughtfully. "I must spear you somewhere, of course, but I'm not bound to hurt you very much. There's such a lot of you that there must be a few spare places somewhere. Here, for instance, just behind your foreleg. It couldn't hurt you much, just here!"

"Now you're tickling, George," said the dragon coyly. "No, that place won't do at all. Even if it didn't hurt—and I'm sure it would, awfully—it would make me laugh, and that would spoil everything."

"Let's try somewhere else, then," said St. George patiently. "Under your neck, for instance—all these folds of thick skin,—if I speared you here you'd never even know I'd done it!"

"Yes, but are you sure you can hit off the right place?" asked the dragon anxiously.

"Of course I am," said St. George, with confidence. "You leave that to me!"

"It's just because I've *got* to leave it to you that I'm asking," replied the dragon rather testily. "No doubt you would deeply regret any error you might make in the hurry of the moment; but you wouldn't regret it half as much as I should! However, I suppose we've got to trust somebody, as we go through life, and your plan seems, on the whole, as good a one as any."

"Look here, dragon," interrupted the Boy, a little jealous on behalf of his friend, who seemed to be getting all the worst of the bargain: "I don't quite see where *you* come in! There's to be a fight, apparently, and you're to be licked; and what I want to know is, what are *you* going to get out of it?"

"St. George," said the dragon, "just tell him, please—what will happen after I'm vanquished in the deadly combat?"

"Well, according to the rules I suppose I shall lead you in triumph down to the market-place or whatever answers to it," said St. George.

"Precisely," said the dragon. "And then——?"

"And then there'll be shoutings and speeches and things," continued St. George. "And I shall explain that you're converted, and see the error of your ways, and so on."

"Quite so," said the dragon. "And then——?"

"Oh, and then——" said St. George, "why, and then there will be the usual banquet, I suppose."

"Exactly," said the dragon; "and that's where *I* come in. Look here," he continued, addressing the Boy, "I'm bored to death up here, and no one really appreciates me. I'm going into Society, I am, through the kindly aid of our friend here, who's taking such a lot of trouble on my account; and you'll find I've got all the qualities to endear me to people who entertain! So now that's all settled, and if you don't mind—I'm an old-fashioned fellow—don't want to turn you out, but——"

"Remember, you'll have to do your proper share of the fighting, dragon!" said St. George, as he took the hint and rose to go; "I mean ramping, and breathing fire, and so on!"

"I can *ramp* all right," replied the dragon confidently; "as to breathing fire, it's surprising how easily one gets out of practice; but I'll do the best I can. Good night!"

They had descended the hill and were almost back in the village again, when St. George stopped short. "*Knew* I had forgotten something," he said. "There ought to be a Princess. Terror-stricken and chained to a rock, and all that sort of thing. Boy, can't you arrange a Princess?"

The Boy was in the middle of a tremendous yawn. "I'm tired to death," he wailed, "and I *can't* arrange a Princess, or anything more, at this time of night. And my mother's sitting up, and *do* stop asking me to arrange more things till to-morrow!"

Next morning the people began streaming up to the Downs at quite an early hour, in their Sunday clothes and carrying baskets with bottle-necks sticking out of them, every one intent on securing good places for the combat. This was not exactly a simple matter, for of course it was quite possible that the dragon might win, and in that case even those who had put their money on him felt they could hardly expect him to deal with his backers on a different footing to the rest. Places were chosen, therefore, with circumspection and with a view to a speedy retreat in case of emergency; and the front rank was mostly composed of boys who had escaped from paren-

tal control and now sprawled and rolled about on the grass, regardless of the shrill
threats and warnings discharged at them by their anxious mothers behind.

The Boy had secured a good front place, well up towards the cave, and was feeling
as anxious as a stage-manager on a first night. Could the dragon be depended upon?
He might change his mind and vote the whole performance rot; or else, seeing that
the affair had been so hastily planned without even a rehearsal, he might be too
nervous to show up. The Boy looked narrowly at the cave, but it showed no sign of
life or occupation. Could the dragon have made a moonlight flitting?

The higher portions of the ground were now black with sightseers, and presently
a sound of cheering and a waving of handkerchiefs told that something was visible
to them which the Boy, far up towards the dragon-end of the line as he was, could
not yet see. A minute more and St. George's red plumes topped the hill, as the Saint
rode slowly forth on the great level space which stretched up to the grim mouth of
the cave. Very gallant and beautiful he looked on his tall war-horse, his golden armour
glancing in the sun, his great spear held erect, the little white pennon, crimson-
crossed, fluttering at its point. He drew rein and remained motionless. The lines of
spectators began to give back a little, nervously; and even the boys in front stopped
pulling hair and cuffing each other, and leaned forward expectant.

"Now then, dragon!" muttered the Boy impatiently, fidgeting where he sat. He
need not have distressed himself, had he only known. The dramatic possibilities of
the thing had tickled the dragon immensely, and he had been up from an early hour,
preparing for his first public appearance with as much heartiness as if the years had
run backwards, and he had been again a little dragonlet, playing with his sisters on
the floor of their mother's cave, at the game of saints-and-dragons, in which the
dragon was bound to win.

A low muttering, mingled with snorts, now made itself heard; rising to a bellowing
roar that seemed to fill the plain. Then a cloud of smoke obscured the mouth of the
cave, and out of the midst of it the dragon himself, shining, sea-blue, magnificent,
pranced splendidly forth; and everybody said, "Oo-oo-oo!" as if he had been a mighty
rocket! His scales were glittering, his long spiky tail lashed his sides, his claws tore
up the turf and sent it flying high over his back, and smoke and fire incessantly jetted
from his angry nostrils. "Oh, well done, dragon!" cried the Boy excitedly. "Didn't
think he had it in him!" he added to himself.

St. George lowered his spear, bent his head, dug his heels into his horse's sides,
and came thundering over the turf. The dragon charged with a roar and a squeal,—a
great blue whirling combination of coils and snorts and clashing jaws and spikes and
fire.

"Missed!" yelled the crowd. There was a moment's entanglement of golden
armour and blue-green coils and spiky tail, and then the great horse, tearing at his
bit, carried the Saint, his spear swung high in the air, almost up to the mouth of the
cave.

The dragon sat down and barked viciously, while St. George with difficulty pulled
his horse round into position.

"End of Round One!" thought the Boy. "How well they managed it! But I hope the
Saint won't get excited. I can trust the dragon all right. What a regular play-actor the
fellow is!"

St. George had at last prevailed on his horse to stand steady, and was looking
round him as he wiped his brow. Catching sight of the Boy, he smiled and nodded,
and held up three fingers for an instant.

"It seems to be all planned out," said the Boy to himself. "Round Three is to be the finishing one, evidently. Wish it could have lasted a bit longer. Whatever's that old fool of a dragon up to now?"

The dragon was employing the interval in giving a ramping performance for the benefit of the crowd. Ramping, it should be explained, consists in running round and round in a wide circle, and sending waves and ripples of movement along the whole length of your spine, from your pointed ears right down to the spike at the end of your long tail. When you are covered with blue scales, the effect is particularly pleasing; and the Boy recollected the dragon's recently expressed wish to become a social success.

St. George now gathered up his reins and began to move forward, dropping the point of his spear and settling himself firmly in the saddle.

"Time!" yelled everybody excitedly; and the dragon, leaving off his ramping, sat up on end, and began to leap from one side to the other with huge ungainly bounds, whooping like a Red Indian. This naturally disconcerted the horse, who swerved violently, the Saint only just saving himself by the mane; and as they shot past the dragon delivered a vicious snap at the horse's tail which sent the poor beast careering madly far over the Downs, so that the language of the Saint, who had lost a stirrup, was fortunately inaudible to the general assemblage.

Round Two evoked audible evidence of friendly feeling towards the dragon. The spectators were not slow to appreciate a combatant who could hold his own so well and clearly wanted to show good sport; and many encouraging remarks reached the ears of our friend as he strutted to and fro, his chest thrust out and his tail in the air, hugely enjoying his new popularity.

St. George had dismounted and was tightening his girths, and telling his horse, with quite an Oriental flow of imagery, exactly what he thought of him, and his relations, and his conduct on the present occasion; so the Boy made his way down to the Saint's end of the line, and held his spear for him.

"It's been a jolly fight, St. George!" he said, with a sigh. "Can't you let it last a bit longer?"

"Well, I think I'd better not," replied the Saint. "The fact is, your simple-minded old friend's getting conceited, now they've begun cheering him, and he'll forget all about the arrangement and take to playing the fool, and there's no telling where he would stop. I'll just finish him off this round."

He swung himself into the saddle and took his spear from the Boy. "Now don't you be afraid," he added kindly. "I've marked my spot exactly, and *he's* sure to give me all the assistance in his power, because he knows it's his only chance of being asked to the banquet!"

St. George now shortened his spear, bringing the butt well up under his arm; and, instead of galloping as before, he trotted smartly towards the dragon, who crouched at his approach, flicking his tail till it cracked in the air like a great cart-whip. The Saint wheeled as he neared his opponent and circled warily round him, keeping his eye on the spare place; while the dragon, adopting similar tactics, paced with caution round the same circle, occasionally feinting with his head. So the two sparred for an opening, while the spectators maintained a breathless silence.

Though the round lasted for some minutes, the end was so swift that all the Boy saw was a lightning movement of the Saint's arm, and then a whirl and a confusion of spines, claws, tail, and flying bits of turf. The dust cleared away, the spectators whooped and ran in cheering, and the Boy made out that the dragon was down, pinned to the earth by the spear, while St. George had dismounted, and stood astride of him.

It all seemed so genuine that the Boy ran in breathlessly, hoping the dear old dragon wasn't really hurt. As he approached, the dragon lifted one large eyelid, winked solemnly, and collapsed again. He was held fast to earth by the neck, but the Saint had hit him in the spare place agreed upon, and it didn't even seem to tickle.

"Bain't you goin' to cut 'is 'ed orf, master?" asked one of the applauding crowd. He had backed the dragon, and naturally felt a trifle sore.

"Well, not *to-day*, I think," replied St. George pleasantly. "You see, that can be done at *any* time. There's no hurry at all. I think we'll all go down to the village first, and have some refreshment, and then I'll give him a good talking-to, and you'll find he'll be a very different dragon!"

At that magic word *refreshment* the whole crowd formed up in procession and silently awaited the signal to start. The time for talking and cheering and betting was past, the hour for action had arrived. St. George, hauling on his spear with both hands, released the dragon, who rose and shook himself and ran his eye over his spikes and scales and things, to see that they were all in order. Then the Saint mounted and led off the procession, the dragon following meekly in the company of the Boy, while the thirsty spectators kept at a respectful interval behind.

There were great doings when they got down to the village again, and had formed up in front of the inn. After refreshment St. George made a speech, in which he informed his audience that he had removed their direful scourge, at a great deal of trouble and inconvenience to himself, and now they weren't to go about grumbling and fancying they'd got grievances, because they hadn't. And they shouldn't be so fond of fights, because next time they might have to do the fighting themselves, which would not be the same thing at all. And there was a certain badger in the inn stables which had got to be released at once, and he'd come and see it done himself. Then he told them that the dragon had been thinking over things, and saw that there were two sides to every question, and he wasn't going to do it any more, and if they were good perhaps he'd stay and settle down there. So they must make friends, and not be prejudiced, and go about fancying they knew everything there was to be known, because they didn't, not by a long way. And he warned them against the sin of romancing, and making up stories and fancying other people would believe them just because they were plausible and highly-coloured. Then he sat down, amidst much repentant cheering, and the dragon nudged the Boy in the ribs and whispered that he couldn't have done it better himself. Then every one went off to get ready for the banquet.

Banquets are always pleasant things, consisting mostly, as they do, of eating and drinking; but the specially nice thing about a banquet is, that it comes when something's over, and there's nothing more to worry about, and to-morrow seems a long way off. St. George was happy because there had been a fight and he hadn't had to kill anybody; for he didn't really like killing, though he generally had to do it. The dragon was happy because there had been a fight, and so far from being hurt in it he had won popularity and a sure footing in Society. The Boy was happy because there had been a fight, and in spite of it all his two friends were on the best of terms. And all the others were happy because there had been a fight, and—well, they didn't require any other reasons for their happiness. The dragon exerted himself to say the right thing to everybody, and proved the life and soul of the evening; while the Saint and the Boy, as they looked on, felt that they were only assisting at a feast of which the honour and the glory were entirely the dragon's. But they didn't mind that, being good fellows, and the dragon was not in the least proud or forgetful. On the contrary, every ten minutes or so he leant over towards the Boy and said impressively: "Look here! you *will* see me home afterwards, won't you?" And the Boy always nodded, though he had promised his mother not to be out late.

At last the banquet was over, the guests had dropped away with many good nights and congratulations and invitations, and the dragon, who had seen the last of them off the premises, emerged into the street followed by the Boy, wiped his brow, sighed, sat down in the road and gazed at the stars. "Jolly night it's been!" he murmured. "Jolly stars! Jolly little place this! Think I shall just stop here. Don't feel like climbing up any beastly hill. Boy's promised to see me home. Boy had better do it then! No responsibility on my part. Responsibility all Boy's!" And his chin sank on his broad chest and he slumbered peacefully.

"Oh, *get* up, dragon," cried the Boy piteously. "You *know* my mother's sitting up, and I'm so tired, and you made me promise to see you home, and I never knew what it meant or I wouldn't have done it!" And the Boy sat down in the road by the side of the sleeping dragon, and cried.

The door behind them opened, a stream of light illumined the road, and St. George, who had come out for a stroll in the cool night-air, caught sight of the two figures sitting there—the great motionless dragon and the tearful little Boy.

"What's the matter, Boy?" he inquired kindly, stepping to his side.

"Oh, it's this great lumbering *pig* of a dragon!" sobbed the Boy. "First he makes me promise to see him home, and then he says I'd better do it, and goes to sleep! Might as well try to see a *haystack* home! And I'm so tired, and mother's——" Here he broke down again.

"Now don't take on," said St. George. "I'll stand by you, and we'll *both* see him home. Wake up, dragon!" he said sharply, shaking the beast by the elbow.

The dragon looked up sleepily. "What a night, George!" he murmured; "what a——"

"Now look here, dragon," said the Saint firmly. "Here's this little fellow waiting to see you home, and you *know* he ought to have been in bed these two hours, and what his mother'll say I don't know, and anybody but a selfish pig would have *made* him go to bed long ago——"

"And he *shall* go to bed!" cried the dragon, starting up. "Poor little chap, only fancy his being up at this hour! It's a shame, that's what it is, and I don't think, St. George, you've been very considerate—but come along at once, and don't let us have any more arguing or shilly-shallying. You give me hold of your hand, Boy—thank you, George, an arm up the hill is just what I wanted!"

So they set off up the hill arm-in-arm, the Saint, the Dragon, and the Boy. The lights in the little village began to go out; but there were stars, and a late moon, as they climbed to the Downs together. And, as they turned the last corner and disappeared from view, snatches of an old song were borne back on the night-breeze. I can't be certain which of them was singing, but I *think* it was the Dragon!

"Here we are at your gate," said the man abruptly, laying his hand on it. "Good night. Cut along in sharp, or you'll catch it!"

Could it really be our own gate? Yes, there it was, sure enough, with the familiar marks on its bottom bar made by our feet when we swung on it.

"Oh, but wait a minute!" cried Charlotte. "I want to know a heap of things. Did the dragon really settle down? And did——"

"There isn't any more of that story," said the man, kindly but firmly. "At least, not to-night. Now be off! Good-bye!"

"Wonder if it's all true?" said Charlotte, as we hurried up the path. "Sounded dreadfully like nonsense, in parts!"

"P'raps it's true for all that," I replied encouragingly.

Charlotte bolted in like a rabbit, out of the cold and the dark; but I lingered a moment in the still, frosty air, for a backward glance at the silent white world without, ere I changed it for the land of firelight and cushions and laughter. It was the day for choir-practice, and carol-time was at hand, and a belated member was passing homewards down the road, singing as he went:

> Then St. George: ee made rev'rence: in the stable so dim,
> Oo vanquished the dragon: so fearful and grim.
> So-o grim: and so-o fierce: that now may we say
> All peaceful is our wakin': on Chri-istmas Day!

The singer receded, the carol died away. But I wondered, with my hand on the door-latch, whether that was the song, or something like it, that the dragon sang as he toddled contentedly up the hill.

1898

JOHN B. GRUELLE
1880–1938

Known primarily as the creator of Raggedy Ann and Raggedy Andy, Johnny Gruelle was one of the more versatile and gifted American illustrators of the first half of the twentieth century. Born in Arcalo, Illinois, he spent his childhood largely in Indianapolis, and the Midwest left its mark on his imagination: friendly, open-hearted country characters, idyllic farm scenes, and placid natural settings are found throughout his works. He was also influenced by his father, Richard B. Gruelle, a noted landscape painter, and he developed rapidly as an artist. While still in his teens, Gruelle became a cartoonist for the *Indianapolis Star*, and at twenty he was working for the *Cleveland Press*. He could draw any kind of cartoon or illustration, whether for advertisements or for articles. Indeed, he worked so quickly that he found himself with spare time, which he used to begin writing and illustrating stories for children. Perhaps these grew out of stories he told his young daughter, Marcella, born in 1903; he had married Myrtle Swann in 1900, and they would have two more children.

In 1910 Gruelle won a contest that the *New York Herald* had devised to select the author of a new Sunday comic, and he moved with his family to Silvermine, an artists' colony in Norwalk, Connecticut.

It marked the turning point in his career, as he produced a remarkably varied and abundant range of work for numerous newspapers and magazines, including *Physical Culture, Judge*, and *Life*, while he continued to write and illustrate children's stories for *Good Housekeeping* and *Woman's World*.

During this time he was commissioned by the publishers Cupples and Leon to illustrate Margaret Hunt's translation of the Grimms' tales. The book appeared in 1914, and although the color illustrations are often sentimental, Gruelle's black-and-white ink drawings add a new dimension to the tales: they introduce American motifs and settings that would be familiar to his readers. He also sought to emphasize the humor and optimism in the Grimms' tales, choosing scenes that captured both the mood of each story and a child's perspective. For Gruelle, a fairy-tale illustration always had to make a happy ending seem attainable; thus here, as in his later Raggedy Ann and Raggedy Andy books, the contrasts between the line drawings of good and evil figures create an atmosphere of hope. The first volume of Raggedy Ann stories—based on a favorite doll belonging to Marcella, who died in 1917—appeared in 1918. Before his death in 1938, Gruelle went on to publish twelve more Raggedy Ann and

Raggedy Andy books as well as several original fairy-tale collections. In almost all his stories, the influence of the Grimms' tales can be readily seen. Like his contemporary Wanda Gág, however, Gruelle "Americanized" the European fairy-tale tradition by using American jargon, settings, and recognizable character types.

"The Discontented King" is taken from *Raggedy Ann's Fairy Stories* (1928), a volume filled with characters that have more in common with American than European culture. In this story, Gruelle

employs the traditional motif of the disguised king who learns a lesson from the common people—a story line found in *The Arabian Nights* and elsewhere—and develops it with gentle irony. "The Discontented King" is one of the earliest fairy tales written for children that pokes fun at men with a feminist touch. In this regard, Gruelle closely followed the tradition of the creator of Oz, L. Frank Baum (1856–1919). Gruelle shunned violence and always depicted female protagonists in a positive light.

The Discontented King

Once there was a King who was never satisfied with anything.

He was just like some boys and girls.

He had everything that he could wish for and he worried everyone about the court making them think up new things for him to wish for.

He had so many things already he could think of nothing more, so one day he called to his Wise Men to come into his room.

"I command you to think of something new!" he cried to them, "and unless you can think of something new I will make you leave the country."

The Wise Men knew the King would do just as he said if they did not obey his commands, and they were very uneasy.

And as soon as they had left the King they shook their heads and wiped their glasses. They had tried and tried their best to think of something all morning, for they knew the King would send for them.

"Let's see!" said one, "can't we think of something to eat?"

"That will never do!" another cried, "for the King eats so much that he has tried everything; so I am sure he will turn up his nose at anything to eat!"

"Yes, that is true!" another Wise Man said, "it cannot be food. Can it be clothes?"

"Oh dear no!" all the rest cried. "He has more clothes than he can wear if he spends all his time changing! It must be something else!"

"If he realized what a hard time it is thinking of new things for him he would not ask us," grumbled one Wise Man.

"That is just the trouble!" cried another Wise Man. "The King does not consider that there is anyone else in the world with feelings, for if he could occasionally put himself in another's place, he would realize what a delightful time he is having now!"

"I wish he could be a Wise Man for three or four days and have some old fat fussy King to make him think and think of something new all the time."

"Well, we are getting no closer to the point," one Wise Man finally cried. "We had better pack up our belongings and start to leave the country now! We can think of nothing new."

So the Wise Men went to their homes to pack up their things, and while one of the Wise Men was tying up the last bundle his wife came in from the neighbor's.

"What in the world are you doing, Thadius?" she exclaimed.

281

"All of us Wise Men have to leave the country because we cannot think of anything new for the King to do!"

When the Wise Man's wife heard this she laughed and laughed.

"Of all silly people," she cried, "you Wise Men are the silliest!"

And that is just what all of the rest of the Wise Men's wives said when they came home from the neighbor's and found their husbands getting ready to leave the country.

So one Wise Man's wife said to him, "Why don't you tell the King to let the wives of you Wise Men take your places for a month or two? That will be something new."

"It will never do," replied the Wise Man, "for Wise Men's wives are never wise and you would all make a muddle of it. But I will run and ask the other Wise Men about it."

So he ran and met the rest of the Wise Men just as they were leaving town, and he told them of his wife's foolish suggestion.

"Perhaps it will work!" one said. "At least let us try it for a while, and if it fails we will blame it on our wives."

So they all went back home and unpacked their bags and went to the King and told him of their idea.

"Send for your wives at once!" commanded the King. And when they came before him he frowned and cried, "Now you must think of something quickly or I will throw you into a dungeon!"

"We have a number of things for you to do, Oh! King!" said the leader. "But first we must get your royal promise that you will do everything that we suggest!"

"Will everything you suggest be something that I have never done before?" asked the King, who was beginning to be interested.

"Yes, Oh! King, everything will be something new!"

"Then I promise!" said the King; and he crossed his heart before all the people and swore that he would do all the things the Wise Men's wives could think of.

"Then," said one of the Wise Men's wives, "you will put on the clothes of a Chimney Sweep and go out in search of work!"

The King would have liked to get out of this, but he had given his promise and he knew he could not break it; so he put on the clothes of a Chimney Sweep and went down the street. At the first back door he came to they gave him a job, and the King was covered with soot from head to feet in a short time. And, as he was very fat, he became wedged in the chimney and stuck fast for two hours. He raised so much fuss and noise the man who owned the house climbed to the roof and poured cold water down the chimney upon the King.

This only made the King howl all the louder, and then the man got a stout rope and, with the help of neighbors, he pulled the King from the chimney.

"I will go back to the Castle and have all those Wise Men's wives hung!" he shouted. And at this all the men who had gathered around the Fat Chimney Sweep gathered up barrel staves and drove him from the town. And as the King passed the keeper of the gate, that person gave him a prod with his spear.

So the King wandered about until he came to a Woodchopper's house, and he was so hungry he asked for food.

"If you chop me a cord of wood, I will give you something to eat," said the Woodchopper. And the King was so hungry he had to chop the cord of wood.

He had never swung an ax before and the exertion made his arms ache; and he came back to the Woodchopper's house with blisters upon his hands.

The Woodchopper placed a greasy bowl upon the table and filled it with coarse mush, and placed a piece of dry black bread upon the table.

"Haven't you any tenderloin or venison, or any broiled quail?" asked the King, as he pushed the mush and black bread away from him. "I can't eat this!"

The Woodchopper turned and called to his wife in another room and said: "Ella, come see this creature who turns up his nose at our good, wholesome food. Anyone would think he were a fine Prince instead of a Chimney Sweep, and a lazy one at that!"

And the Woodchopper's wife, who was a large woman, caught the King by the ear and led him squealing from the house. And when she had him outside she gave him a hearty cuff which sent him sprawling.

The King made off as fast as he could and did not stop running until he came to the next town. Here he got another job at which he had to work very hard. And when he had finished working he was given nothing but the coarsest of food to eat, for the poor peasants had nothing but coarse foods to eat. Day after day from one town to another the King wandered, working hard and eating humble fare, until finally, after a month of this, he came to the city in which lived his sister and her husband. They were King and Queen of that province.

Now the King with his sooty clothes and dirty face had quite a time convincing them that he was really their brother, but when he finally did, they asked him what he intended doing, and the King said: "If I can get back upon my throne in my own country I will throw all those foolish wives of the foolish Wise Men into prison, where they will have nothing to eat but mush and dry bread; and I will make them work as hard as I have had to work in the thirty days I have wandered about."

"But, my dear brother!" exclaimed the Queen, "you have lost your fat look and you look stronger and in better health than when I saw you last!"

"That is true," the poor King admitted. "I have had to work so hard it has made my arms and legs strong, to be sure, but I have had to eat nothing but the coarsest of foods."

"Ah, my brother," the Queen laughed, "if you feel better by your coarse food and hard work, doesn't it prove that you were living in too much luxury and laziness before, and that you have experienced just what you needed most to make you better?"

"I am afraid so!" said the King, who hated to admit that he could ever make a mistake. "Perhaps, after all, I should appreciate the joke that the Foolish Men's Wise Wives have played upon me. Arrange then for me to return to my country, and I promise that I will not punish anyone for my experience!"

Then the Queen arranged for him to return. And the people were glad to see that he had improved in appearance and in manners. And when he found that the wives of the Wise Men had ruled the country well in his absence, he knew he must treat everyone right if he wished to remain King long.

So the wives of the Wise Men are still at the Castle, and they make all the laws; for the King spends most of his time working at something useful, and finds it far more pleasant than lying around doing nothing except grumbling and acting discontented.

And the best part of it all is, that the discontented King is never discontented any more. His subjects, who once hated and feared him, now love him and call him "the Good King."

1928

WANDA GÁG
1893–1946

Wanda Gág was one of the first American women to win acclaim as a writer and illustrator of fairy tales, creating extraordinary ink drawings. She was greatly influenced by the tales of the Brothers Grimm, some of which she adapted for American readers, but she is equally renowned for her own unusual tales. Born in New Ulm, Minnesota, the oldest of seven children, Gág grew up in a German-speaking community steeped in Old World customs and the German folktale tradition. She also experienced many torments because her parents were freethinkers and her father, a painter, could barely feed the family; his death, when she was fifteen, plunged them deeper into poverty. Gág won scholarships to art school in St. Paul and Minneapolis, and then, in 1917, to the Art Students League in New York, where she gradually established a reputation as commercial artist, painter, and illustrator.

By then her mother had died, and she continued to help support her younger sisters and brother. Determined to concentrate on expressing her own ideas, she gave up commercial art in the mid-1920s and left the city for rural Connecticut. In 1932 her brother and a sister joined her in a house in New Jersey. She had married Earle Humphreys, a labor organizer and salesman, in 1930; they had no children.

During the 1920s, wishing to refresh her knowledge of German, Gág had returned to reading the Grimms' fairy tales and played with the idea of translating them anew. The great success of her first and most famous children's book, *Millions of Cats* (1928), a unique fairy tale in its own right, gave her considerable leverage with her publisher, Coward-McCann; its children's department was still new, and it wanted to enter the field of fairy tales with its own edition of the Brothers Grimm. Gág was a natural choice, particularly after her 1932 illustration of Hansel and Gretel commissioned by the *New York Herald Tribune* was well received. She thus undertook to translate and adapt sixty tales of her choice—the least gory and most amusing—planning to publish them with her own illustrations. Gág appropriated the Grimms' fairy tales with tremendous earnestness and zeal, "Americanizing" them by using American idiomatic expressions and a conversational style that would appeal to children. With the help of Anne Carroll Moore, a leading specialist in storytelling and children's literature at the New York Public Library; her sister Flavia; her friend Carl Zigrosser, a critic and director of the Weyhe Gallery; and her husband, she worked continuously on the project throughout the 1930s and 1940s. Ultimately she translated and illustrated fifty-one tales in *Tales from Grimm* (1936), *Three Gay Tales from Grimm* (1943), and *More Tales from Grimm* (1947), the last published one year after her death.

Among her most successfully Americanized tales is "The Sorcerer's Apprentice," freely adapted from the Grimms' "The Thief and His Master." It illustrates how Gág, who openly supported the women's movement and progressive political causes, positioned herself through the figure of the child protagonist to defend the rights of the young and introduced a revolutionary spirit to the story. Though she never directly inserted her politics and personal experiences into her works for children, Gág here completely transforms the Grimms' version; the result is a kind of autobiographical fairy tale about a young person who learns from an adult and at the same time struggles against the oppressive adult world for the sake of mastering art. In the process the apprentice kills off the master, as also happens in "The Thief and His Master"; but in Gág's tale, rather than tricking the master out of money with the help of his father, the young man is left alone to do good in the world with his art. Gág's utopian vision transcends the personal: the apprentice becomes an exemplary figure for all young men and women who must negotiate their place in the world, as he seeks to determine his own worth. His triumph is also a declaration of independence in keeping with the radical political currents of the 1920s and 1930s.

The Sorcerer's Apprentice

A man found himself in need of a helper for his workshop, and one day as he was walking along the outskirts of a little hamlet he met a boy with a bundle slung over his shoulder. Stopping him, the man said, "Good morning, my lad. I am looking for an apprentice. Have you a master?"

"No," said the boy, "I have just this morning said good-bye to my mother and am now off to find myself a trade."

"Good," said the man. "You look as though you might be just the lad I need. But wait, do you know anything about reading and writing?"

"Oh yes!" said the boy.

"Too bad!" said the man. "You won't do after all. I have no use for anyone who can read and write."

"Pardon me?" said the boy. "If it was *reading* and *writing* you were talking about, I misunderstood you. I thought you asked if I knew anything about *eating* and *fighting*—those two things I am able to do well, but as to reading and writing that is something I know nothing about."

"Well!" cried the man. "Then you are just the fellow I want. Come with me to my workshop, and I will show you what to do."

The boy, however, had had his wits about him. He could read and write well enough and had only pretended to be a fool. Wondering why a man should prefer to have an unschooled helper, he thought to himself, "I smell a rat. There is something strange about this, and I had better keep my eyes and ears open."

While he was pondering over this, his new master was leading him into the heart of a deep forest. Here in a small clearing stood a house and, as soon as they entered it, the boy could see that this was no ordinary workshop.

At one end of a big room was a huge hearth with a copper cauldron hanging in it; at the other end was a small alcove lined with many big books. A mortar and pestle stood on a bench; bottles and sieves, measuring scales and oddly-shaped glassware were strewn about on the table.

Well! It did not take the clever young apprentice very long to realize that he was working for a magician or sorcerer of some kind and so, although he pretended to be quite stupid, he kept his eyes and ears open, and tried to learn all he could.

"Sorcery—that is a trade I would dearly love to master!" said the boy to himself. "A mouthful of good chants and charms would never come amiss to a poor fellow like me, and with them I might even be able to do some good in the world."

There were many things the boy had to do. Sometimes he was ordered to stir the evil-smelling broths which bubbled in the big copper cauldron; at other times he had to grind up herbs and berries—and other things too gruesome to mention—in the big mortar and pestle. It was also his task to sweep up the workshop, to keep the fire burning in the big hearth, and to gather the strange materials needed by the man for the broths and brews he was always mixing.

This went on day after day, week after week, and month after month, until the boy was almost beside himself with curiosity. He was most curious about the thick heavy books in the alcove. How often he had wondered about them, and how many times had he been tempted to take a peep between their covers! But, remembering that he was not supposed to know how to read or write, he had been wise enough never to show the least interest in them. At last there came a day when he made up his mind to see what was in them, no matter what the risk.

"I'll try it before another day dawns," he thought.

That night he waited until the sorcerer was sound asleep and was snoring loudly in his bedchamber; then, creeping out of his straw couch, the boy took a light into the corner of the alcove and began paging through one of the heavy volumes. What was written in them has never been told, but they were conjuring books, each and every one of them; and from that time on, the boy read in them silently, secretly, for an hour or two, night after night. In this way he learned many magic tricks: chants and charms and countercharms; recipes for philters and potions, for broths and brews and witches' stews; signs mystic and cabalistic, and other helpful spells of many kinds. All these he memorized carefully, and it was not long before he sometimes was able to figure out what kind of charms his master was working, what brand of potion he was mixing, what sort of stews he was brewing. And what kind of charms and potions and stews were they? Alas, they were all wicked ones! Now the boy knew that he was not working for an ordinary magician, but for a cruel, dangerous sorcerer. And because of this, the boy made a plan, a bold one.

He went on with his nightly studies until his head was swarming with magic recipes and incantations. He even had time to work at them in the daytime, for the sorcerer sometimes left the workshop for hours—working harm and havoc on mortals, no doubt. At such times the boy would try out a few bits of his newly-learned wisdom. He began with simple things, such as changing the cat into a bee and back to cat again, making a viper out of the poker, an imp out of the broom, and so on. Sometimes he was successful, often he was not; so he said to himself, "The time is not yet ripe."

One day, after the sorcerer had again gone forth on one of his mysterious trips, the boy hurried through his work, and had just settled himself in the dingy alcove with one of the conjuring books on his knees, when the master returned unexpectedly. The boy, thinking fast, pointed smilingly at one of the pictures, after which he quietly closed the book and went on with his work as though nothing were amiss.

But the sorcerer was not deceived.

"If the wretch can read," he thought, "he may learn how to outwit me. And I can't send him off with a beating and a 'bad speed to you', either—doubtless he knows too much already and will reveal all my fine mean tricks, and then I can't have any more sport working mischief on man and beast."

He acted quickly.

With one leap he rushed at the boy, who in turn made a spring for the door.

"Stop!" cried the sorcerer. "You shall not escape me!"

He was about to grab the boy by the collar when the quick-witted lad mumbled a powerful incantation by which he changed himself into a bird—and—Wootsch!— he had flown into the woods.

The sorcerer, not to be outdone, shouted a charm, thus changing himself into a larger bird—and Whoosh!—he was after the little one.

With a new incantation the boy made himself into a fish—and Whish!—he was swimming across a big pond.

But the master was equal to this, for, with a few words he made himself into a fish too, a big one, and swam after the little one.

At this the boy changed himself into a still bigger fish but the magician, by a master stroke, turned himself into a tiny kernel of grain and rolled into a small crack in a stone where the fish couldn't touch him.

Quickly the boy changed himself into a rooster, and—Peck! Peck! Peck!—with his sharp beak he snapped at the kernel of grain and ate it up.

That was the end of the wicked sorcerer, and the boy became the owner of the magic workshop. And wasn't it fine that all the powers and ingredients which had been used for evil by the sorcerer were now in the hands of a boy who would use them only for the good of man and beast?

1947

LLOYD ALEXANDER
b. 1924

Lloyd Alexander has remarked, "Whether writing realism or fantasy . . . my concerns are the same: how we learn to be genuine human beings. To me, fantasy is one of the many ways to express whatever truths we manage to perceive about our own human condition, not there-and-then but here-and-now." One of the foremost and most prolific writers of fantasy in the second half of the twentieth century, the Philadelphia native early announced his intention to write; to that end, he left school at fifteen to work as a bank messenger to earn money for college. He soon decided that the army would better prepare him for his chosen career, and he enlisted in 1942. He was sent to Wales for training, and then to France as a translator-interpreter. In 1946 he married Janine Denni, a Parisian with a young daughter, and after being discharged from the army he studied at the Sorbonne. When he finally returned to Philadelphia in the late 1940s, he worked at a variety of jobs—as a cartoonist, layout artist, and advertising agent—while writing novels for adults that for the most part were rejected by publishers. During this period, Alexander published several translations of French fiction and poetry (by Jean-Paul Sartre, Paul Eluard, and Paul Vialar).

The success of his first work of fiction for children, *Time Cat* (1963), shifted his creative direction; his next undertaking won him recognition as a major writer of fantasy. The Prydain Chronicle comprises *The Book of Three* (1964; included complete in the Fantasy section, below), *The Black Cauldron* (1965), *The Castle of Llyr* (1966), *Taran Wanderer* (1967), and *The High King* (1968); the final volume

won the 1969 Newbery Medal. The central focus of this series is Taran, a pig-keeper who desires a more heroic life. Like major protagonists of the Arthurian legends and the Welsh traditional folktales in the Mabinogion, Taran has many adventures and long journeys of self-discovery: he eventually becomes High King of Prydain. Alexander's two other important fairy-tale series are the Westmark Trilogy (1981–83) and the Vesper books (1986–90). He has published more than forty books and won many awards; among his best works are *The Marvelous Misadventures of Sebastian* (1970), *The Cat Who Wished to Be a Man* (1973), *Westmark* (1981), *The Illyrian Adventure* (1986), *The Arkadians* (1995), and *The Iron Ring* (1997). Although almost all of his work is connected to fantasy, legend, and the fairy tale, Alexander's books draw parallels with real conditions confronted by today's children, and the conflicts that he depicts are related to social and political problems.

"The Truthful Harp" (1967) features an important character in the Prydain Chronicle, and it is representative of many of the fairy-tale narratives that Alexander has produced throughout his career. King Flewddur Fflam, who rules a tiny land in Prydain, must undergo a quest to discover his genuine talents—which turn out to be other than what he expected. Alexander deftly combines traditional folklore motifs with gentle tongue-in-cheek irony to tell the unusual story of a protagonist whose success lies in learning the truth about himself. Fflam is greater than he thinks, for his deeds are achieved through his humanity, not his artistry.

The Truthful Harp

This is the tale of King Fflewddur Fflam and his truthful harp, as the bards tell it in the Land of Prydain.

And this is the beginning of it.

Fflewddur Fflam ruled a kingdom so small he could almost stride across it between midday and high noon. The fields and pastures grew so near his castle that sheep and cows ambled up to gaze into his bed-chamber; and the cottagers' children played in his Great Hall, knowing he would sooner join their games than order them away.

"My crown's a grievous burden!" Fflewddur cried. "That is, it would be if I ever wore it. But a Fflam is dutiful! My subjects need me to rule this vast kingdom with a firm hand and a watchful eye!"

Nevertheless, one secret wish lay closest to his heart. He yearned to adventure as a wandering bard.

"A Fflam is eager!" he declared. "I'll be as great a bard as I am a king!"

So he puzzled over tomes of ancient lore, striving to gain the wisdom every true bard must have. And he strained and struggled with his harp until his fingers blistered.

"A Fflam is clever!" he exclaimed. "I'll soon have the knack of it, and play my harp as well as I rule my kingdom!"

At last he fancied himself ready to stand before the High Council of Bards and ask to be ranked among their number.

"A Fflam goes forth!" cried Fflewddur. "Gird on my sword! Saddle my charger! But have a care, she's wild and mettlesome."

All his subjects who could spare the time gathered to cheer him on, to wave farewell, and to wish him good speed.

"It saddens them to see me go," Fflewddur sighed. "But a Fflam is faithful! Even as a famous bard, I'll do my kingly duty as carefully as ever."

And so he journeyed to golden-towered Caer[1] Dathyl and eagerly hastened to the Council Chamber.

"A Fflam is quick-witted!" he cried confidently. "Prove me as you please! I've got every morsel of learning on the tip of my tongue, and every harp-tune at my fingers' ends!"

However, when the Council and the Chief Bard questioned him deeply, all that Fflewddur had learned flew out of his head like a flock of sparrows. He gave the right answers to the wrong questions, the wrong answers to the right questions; and worst of all, when he fumbled to strike a tune on his harp it slipped from his grasp and shattered in a thousand splinters on the flagstones. Then Fflewddur bowed his head and stared wretchedly at his boots, knowing he had failed.

"Alas, you are not ready to be one of us," the Chief Bard regretfully told him. But then, with all his poet's wisdom and compassion, the Chief Bard pitied the hapless king, and spoke apart with a servant, desiring him to bring a certain harp which he put in Fflewddur's hands.

"You still have much to learn," said the Chief Bard. "Perhaps this may help you."

Seeing the harp, Fflewddur's dismay vanished in that instant, and his face beamed with delight. The beautiful instrument seemed to play of itself. He needed only touch

---

1. Castle (Welsh).

his fingers to the strings and melodies poured forth in a golden tide.

"Good riddance to my old pot!" Fflewddur cried. "Here's a harp that shows my true skill. A Fflam is grateful!"

The Chief Bard smiled within himself. "May you ever be as grateful as you are now. Come back when it pleases you to tell us how you have fared."

High-hearted, Fflewddur set out from Caer Dathyl. His new harp gladdened him as much as if he were in fact a bard, and he rode along playing merrily and singing at the top of his voice.

Nearing a river he came upon an old man painfully gathering twigs for a fire. Winter had hardly ended, and a chill wind still bit sharply, and the old man's threadbare garments gave no comfort against the cold. He shivered in the gale, his lips were bitter blue, and his fingers were so numb he could scarcely pick up his twigs.

"A good greeting, friend," called Fflewddur. "Brisk weather may be good for the blood, but it seems to me you're ill-garbed for a day like this."

"No warmer clothing do I have," replied the old man. "Would that I did, for I'm frozen to the marrow of my bones."

"Then take my cloak," urged Fflewddur, doffing his garment and wrapping it about the old man's shoulders.

"My thanks to you," said the old man, wistfully fondling the cloak. "But I cannot take what you yourself need."

"Need?" exclaimed Fflewddur. "Not at all," he added, though his own lips had begun turning blue and his nose felt as if it had grown icicles. "Take it and welcome. For the truth of the matter is, I find the day uncomfortably hot!"

No sooner had he spoken these words than the harp shuddered as if it were alive, bent like an overdrawn bow, and a string snapped in two with a loud twang.

"Drat that string!" muttered Fflewddur. "The weather's got into it somehow."

Knotting up the string, he set out on his way again, shivering, shaking, and playing for all he was worth to keep himself warm.

He wandered on, following the swiftly flowing river. Suddenly he heard a child's voice crying in distress and terror. Clapping heels to his horse's flanks he galloped down the riverbank. A small girl had tumbled into the water and the hapless child struggled vainly against the current already sweeping her away.

Fflewddur leaped from his mount and plunged with a great splash into the river, flailing his arms, thrashing his legs, striving with all his might to reach the drowning child.

"This would be an easy task," he gasped, "if only I could swim!"

Nonetheless, he pressed on, choking and sputtering, until he caught up the child. Keeping afloat as best he could, he turned shoreward; at last his long shanks found footing on the river bed, and he bore the girl safely to dry land.

Comforting her all the while, though water streamed from his nose, ears, and mouth, he made his way to the cottage from which she had strayed. There, the husbandman and his wife joyously threw their arms about their daughter and the bedraggled Fflewddur as well.

"Poor folk are we," cried the farm wife. "What reward can we give? All we have is yours, and small payment for saving our greatest treasure."

"Don't give it a thought," Fflewddur exclaimed, his face lighting up as he warmed to his tale. "Why, to begin with, it was in my mind to have a dip in the river. As for the rest—a triffle! A Fflam swims like a fish! With only a few powerful strokes—"

The harp twitched violently and a pair of strings gave way with an ear-splitting crack.

"Drat and blast!" muttered Fflewddur. "What ails these beastly strings? The dampness, I'll be bound."

Taking his leave of the family, for some days he wandered happily to his heart's content, finding himself at last before the stronghold of a noble lord. To the guards at the gate, Fflewddur called out that a bard had come with music and merriment, whereupon they welcomed him and led him to the lord's Great Hall.

No sooner had Fflewddur begun to play than the lord leaped angrily from his throne.

"Have done!" he burst out. "You yelp like a cur with its tail trodden, and your harp rattles worse than a kettle of stones! Away with you!"

Before Fflewddur could collect his wits, the lord snatched up a cudgel, collared the harper, and began drubbing him with all his strength.

"Ai! Ow! Have a care!" cried Fflewddur, struggling vainly to escape the blows and shield his harp at the same time. "A king am I! Of the mightiest realm in Prydain! You'll rue this day when you see my battle host at your gates! A thousand warriors! Spearmen! Bowmen! A Fflam at their head!"

While the harp strings broke right and left, the lord seized Fflewddur by the scruff of the neck and flung him out the gate, where he landed headlong in the mire.

"A Fflam humiliated!" Fflewddur cried, painfully climbing to his feet. "Affronted! Beaten like a knave!" He rubbed his aching shoulders. "Yes, well, it's clear," he sighed. "Some people have no ear for music."

His bones too sore for the saddle, he made the best of his way afoot, with his horse jogging after him. He had trudged a little distance when the selfsame lord and his train of servants galloped by.

"What, are you still in my domain?" shouted the lord. "Begone, you spindle-shanked scarecrow! If once again I see that long nose of yours, you'll have a drubbing better than the first!"

Fflewddur held his tongue as the horsemen rode past, fearing more for his harp than his skin. "Stone-eared clot!" he grumbled under his breath. "A Fflam is forgiving, but this is more than any man can bear." And he consoled himself with delicious dreams of how he would even the score—should he ever have a host of warriors at his command.

Suddenly he realized the clash of arms and noise of battle came not from his imaginings but from a short way down the road. A band of robbers, lying in ambush, had set upon the riders. The servants had fled bawling in terror and the lord himself was hard pressed and sorely in danger of losing his head as well as his purse.

Snatching out his sword and shouting his battle cry, "A Fflam! A Fflam!" Fflewddur rushed into the fray, and laid about him so fiercely and ferociously the robbers turned and fled as if a whole army of long-legged madmen were at their heels.

Shamefaced, the lord knelt humbly before him, saying: "Alas, I gave you a cudgel to your back, but you gave me a bold sword at my side."

"Ah—yes, well, for the matter of that," replied Fflewddur, a little tartly now the danger was past, "the truth is, a Fflam is hotblooded! I'd been itching for a good fight all this day. But had I known it was you," he added, "believe me, I'd have kept on my way—Oh, not again! Drat and blast the wretched things!" He moaned as three harp strings broke one after the other, and the instrument jangled as if it would fall to bits.

More than ever dismayed at the state of his harp strings, Fflewddur left the lord's domain and turned back toward Caer Dathyl, journeying to stand once again before the Chief Bard.

"A Fflam is thankful," he began, "and not one to look a gift horse—in this case, harp—in the mouth. But the strings are weak and worn. As for my wanderings, I was dined and feasted, welcomed and treated royally wherever I went. But the strings—there, you see, they're at it again!" he exclaimed, as several broke in two even as he spoke.

"I've only to take a breath!" Fflewddur lamented. "Why, the wretched things break at every word—" He stopped short and stared at the harp. "It would almost seem—" he murmured, his face turning sickly green. "But it can't be! But it is!" He groaned, looking all the more woebegone.

The Chief Bard was watching him closely and Fflewddur glanced sheepishly at him.

"Ah—the truth of it is," Fflewddur muttered, "I nearly froze to death in the wind, nearly drowned in the river; and my royal welcome was a royal cudgeling.

"Those beastly strings," he sighed. "Yes, they do break whenever I, ah, shall we say, adjust the facts. But facts are so gray and dreary, I can't help adding a little color. Poor things, they need it so badly."

"I have heard more of your wanderings than you might think," said the Chief Bard. "Have you indeed spoken all the truth? What of the old man you warmed with your cloak? The child you saved from the river? The lord at whose side you fought?"

Fflewddur blinked in astonishment. "Ah—yes, well, the truth of it is: it never occurred to me to mention them. They were much too dull and drab for any presentable tale at all."

"Yet those deeds were far more worthy than all your gallant fancies," said the Chief Bard, "for a good truth is purest gold that needs no gilding. You have the modest heart of the truly brave; but your tongue, alas, gallops faster than your head can rein it."

"No longer!" Fflewddur declared. "Never again will I stretch the truth!"

The harp strings tightened as if ready to break all at once.

"That is to say," Fflewddur added hastily, "never beyond what it can bear. A Fflam has learned his lesson. Forever!"

At this, a string snapped loudly. But it was only a small one.

Such is the tale of Fflewddur Fflam, the breaking of the strings, and the harp he carried in all his wanderings from that day forward.

And such is the end of it.

1967

JOAN AIKEN
1924–2004

There have been few writers for children as prolific, versatile, and inventive as Joan Aiken, who created Dickensian characters and plots that nevertheless have a very modern tone. Most of her books—poetry, plays, picture books, mysteries, novels, and fairy tales—reflect her view that adults are the main cause of children's problems, problems with which her young protagonists contend. She was also the author of adult thrillers, gothic novels and stories, and historical romances. The daughter of the American poet Conrad Aiken and the Canadian writer Jessie McDonald, Aiken was born in the village of Rye in Sussex, England. Four years later Aiken went back to the United States, and her mother later married the writer Martin Armstrong. They could not afford to pay for Joan's schooling at the same time as that of her older siblings, so her mother taught her at home. At ten, Joan began making up stories that she told to her younger half-brother; at twelve she was sent to a boarding school near Oxford. Illness in her final term led her to fail her university entrance exams, and in 1941 she found a job—initially as a clerk for the British Broadcasting Corporation. In 1945 she married Ronald George Brown, and they went on to have two children.

Aiken had been writing since she was five, and she began selling stories to the BBC when she was seventeen. She continued writing throughout her marriage, and in 1953 her first collection of fairy-tale fiction appeared, *All You've Ever Wanted and Other Stories*. When she found herself alone in supporting her family after her husband's death in 1955, she sold as many stories as she could while working first as an editor at *Argosy Magazine* and then, for a year, at the J. Walter Thompson Advertising Agency. Her first novel, *The Kingdom and the Cave*, was published in 1960, and in 1961 she began writing full-time. Aiken's final manuscript, *The Witch of Clatteringshaws*, was sent to her publisher days before her death in West Sussex, England.

The Wolves of Willoughby Chase (1962) marks the beginning of her financial and critical success. It was the first in a compelling series of novels of alter-native history: in this nineteenth-century England, the Stuarts remain monarchs (King James III is on the throne) and the Hanoverians scheme to usurp the throne (the pretender is "Bonnie Prince Georgie"). The "Wolves chronicles," which include *Blackhearts at Battersea* (1964), *The Stolen Lake* (1981), and *Is Underground* (1993), span Aiken's entire career. Though fantasies with incredible plots, they are grounded in accurate historical detail; the young protagonists face their adventures with intelligence, determination, and humor. In all, Aiken published more than sixty children's books as well as more than thirty adult novels. Among the best of her highly original fairy-tale collections are *More Than You've Bargained For* (1955), *A Necklace of Raindrops* (1968), *A Harp of Fishbones* (1972), and *Past Eight O'Clock* (1987).

In 1977 Aiken published *The Faithless Lollybird, and Other Stories*; the title story is a brilliant reinterpretation and modernization of Hans Christian Andersen's "The Nightingale" (1843). As often in her fairy-tale collections, Aiken combines traditional motifs and characters with very contemporary characters and settings. Here she echoes Andersen's plea for genuine art while criticizing the pressures placed on artists in the modern world to produce and to meet market demands. The title is ironic, for the bird is more faithful than his faithless master, to whom he teaches the true meaning of art. Aiken plays with the notion of master and slave in original ways with strong alternative figures, putting into question the subservient characters created by Andersen.

The Faithless Lollybird

Far away to the north, in a small hut in the middle of a large forest, there lived a weaver whose name was Luke. All this happened not long ago as the clock ticks, but a long way off as the crow flies.

In his hut, Luke had a loom, taking up most of the floor space. And every day, on his loom, he wove the most beautiful cloth—material for coats and cloaks and carpets, for sheets and shirts and shawls, for towels and tablecloths and tapestries, for babies' blankets and bishops' aprons. Some of the things he made seemed almost too good for everyday wear and tear. They were so beautiful that it seemed wrong to do anything but hang them on the wall and gaze at them. But everything he made was really meant to be used.

And to help him with his weaving, Luke had a bird, a Lollybird. When he had strung up his loom ready to start, with the woollen, or cotton, or silk threads going longways—the warp—Luke would tie another length of wool to a shuttle and hand it to the Lollybird, which up to that moment would have been sitting very still on the chimney-piece, or a corner of the loom, or Luke's shoulder, carefully watching all that he did, without moving a single feather.

However, as soon as he handed the shuttle to it, this Lollybird would begin to fly with the most amazing speed back and forth, in and out, up and down, among the strings on the loom, going so fast that nothing of it could be seen at all except a blur of colour as it shot to and fro. The Lollybird itself was just a little grey creature, but as it worked it would snatch one thread and then another from Luke. Sometimes dropping the shuttle entirely it would wind a scarlet strand round its neck and a green one round its stomach, it would carry a pink thread in its beak and clutch a silver one in its claws, so that if it had ever stopped, if you could have caught a glimpse of it, you would have thought it was a travelling Christmas tree, all sparkling and rainbow-coloured. But it never did stop, until the work was finished, and the last knot made, the last thread pulled tightly into place. Then with a final swoop and a last flash of its wings it would come to rest on Luke's shoulder, or the top of his head, and together they would take a careful look at the piece of cloth they had just woven.

Perhaps it was a coronation robe for a king, all scarlet and gold, with fur round the border and a roaring lion in the middle. Or perhaps it was a carpet for a cathedral with angels and lilies and harps, all in blue and green and silver. Or maybe it was a curtain for some great gallery in a Lord Mayor's house, with a picture of unicorns roaming through a forest and butterflies fluttering among the apples on the branches. Or it might be a tablecloth for a children's school, with cats and dogs, and the sun and moon, and birds and fish, and letters and numbers, to give the children something to look at as they were eating their dinner.

Whatever the piece of cloth was that they had just woven, Luke and his Lollybird would carefully inspect it, making sure there were no rough edges, or lumpy places, or loose threads anywhere. But there never were.

Then Luke would give a sigh of satisfaction, and say,

"Well, I think we did a good bit of work that time, my dear Lollybird," and the Lollybird would cock its head on one side in approval and say,

"Certainly can't see anything wrong with that little job, master," and the two friends would stop work for a short time.

Sometimes, in these spells off between jobs, Luke might play on his flute, while the Lollybird chirped a little song. The Lollybird had no voice to speak of, and its song sounded like somebody scratching a twig down the side of a nutmeg grater. Indeed, the Lollybird was a little embarrassed about its lack of singing ability, but Luke didn't mind. He had a mandolin as well as the flute and sometimes the Lollybird, hopping to and fro on the mandolin's strings, would scratch them with its claws and fetch out a faint thread of tune while Luke softly whistled a few matching notes. Then, if the day was a fine one, they might go for a walk in the forest, the Lollybird sitting on Luke's shoulder or flying ahead of him through the great trunks of the trees.

On these walks they searched for the leaves and flowers and roots which Luke needed to dye the silk and wool that he used in his weaving. There was a plant with golden flowers whose root gave a beautiful yellow, and a purple flower that dyed red, and a kind of toadstool which, pounded to a pulp, produced a fine dark orange, and the bark of a tree which could be ground up to make a deep rose-pink. Wild spinach gave them bright green, and certain nuts and berries were good for browns and crimsons. The only colour they could not get from any plant in the forest was a blue to satisfy them; for that, Luke had to send away many hundreds of miles. A kind of shellfish, only found in southern seas, gave a beautiful clear dark blue, but Luke often grumbled because the loads of shellfish, which had to be brought through the forest by sledge, took a long time on the way, and sometimes, if a pattern they were working on used a lot of blue, they might have to wait for a new supply to arrive.

"I wish we could find a decent blue close at hand," Luke would say.

On their walks through the wood the two friends also found tufts of coloured moss and flower petals, bright leaves, flakes of glossy bark, gay feathers dropped by birds, even small sparkling stones and chips of rock, which they wove into their fabrics, so that often the lengths of material they made were quite dazzling and seemed to shine and ripple the way a brook does when it catches the sun's light.

Because the things he made were so beautiful, Luke's fame began to spread all over the world. More and more people wanted to buy his work. Customers came from farther and farther away, in ships and on camels, by sledge and bicycle and caravan, in lorries and balloons, on horseback and in helicopters. So that presently, after a few years had passed, Luke and his Lollybird had to work harder and harder if they were to keep up with all the orders that poured in.

"I never get a chance to sit in the sun any more," complained the Lollybird. "We haven't had time for any music since the last new moon. We don't even get a breath of fresh air."

Lately Luke had hired two boys to hunt for his dye-plants and mosses. The ones they brought back were not always so good, but there was no time for Luke and his Lollybird to go into the forest. They had to work all the hours of daylight. By the time night came the Lollybird was tired out, and would fall asleep perched on the loom with its head tucked under its wing.

"You should refuse to take any more orders," it said to Luke one morning.

"It would be wrong to disappoint people," said Luke. "Specially when they have come all this way. Why, only today we had the Emperor of Japan, wanting a new dressing-gown, and the Mayor of New York, needing a carpet for his town hall, and the Queen of the Windward Islands,[1] with an order for a screen to keep the wind off, and the manager of the Milan Opera, about a new stage curtain for his opera house, and the President of Finland, ordering new tapestry for the Finnish—"

"Finnish? We never *shall* finish!" wailed the Lollybird, and it snatched up a shuttle and darted angrily between the warp strings of a beautiful white and silver christening shawl which they were making for a little princess in Denmark. "*She* wouldn't know the difference if they wrapped her in an old bath towel," it muttered as it flew back and forth.

"It would be wrong to disappoint people," repeated Luke.

"What about me? *I'm* disappointed if I don't have a bit of music, or get out for my evening stroll," said the indignant Lollybird.

Matters became even worse. For now a railway was built through the forest, with a station right beside Luke's hut, so that more and more people would come to order things, and to watch the weavers at work. The visitors stood around, and picked up the shuttles, and tangled the wool, and were a dreadful nuisance all day long. In the evening they invited Luke out to the café which had been built just down the road, and they talked to him and praised his work and asked him how he planned his patterns. He quite enjoyed all the company and cheerfulness. It made a change from

1. A group of islands in the West Indies, extending south from Martinique.

the long quiet evenings he had spent alone with the Lollybird, after it grew too dark to go on weaving, when he had had nothing to do but play his flute, not very well, while the Lollybird sang its little scratchy song, like a pencil being scraped down a nutmeg grater.

The Lollybird did not enjoy all this extra company at all. It never took part in the conversation, or went out to the café. As soon as the light was gone it would retire to the back of the loom and go to sleep there, hidden among dangling hanks of wool, with its head under its wing. And, even during the day, when the Lollybird was working, very few people noticed it flashing to and fro under the strands of the warp, for it went faster than their eyes could follow. Many people, in fact, did not realise that the Lollybird even existed. If they praised the work and Luke said,

"Oh, it is partly the Lollybird's doing too, you know," they believed that he was joking, and laughed politely.

So by and by he gave up mentioning the Lollybird.

One morning the Lollybird said, "Master, it's spring. The cuckoos have come back to the forest, and the swallows are here, and the storks are building their houses, and the wild geese keep flying past, and I need to go out and stretch my wings."

"Rubbish," said Luke. "You have quite enough healthy exercise flying up and down inside the loom. And we are two days late on the set of flags for the new Mandolian Republic. Hurry up and get to work."

The Lollybird got to work, but it was sulking dreadfully as it flew backwards and forwards with the red, black, and yellow silk threads for the Mandolian flags; indeed it clutched some of the threads so tightly in its little hot angry claws that, although they did not snap immediately, the very first time that the flags were flown in a hurricane (and hurricanes are very common in Mandolia) several of them tore in half.

Now this was the first time that the Lollybird had ever done bad work. At the end of the day it felt guilty and miserable and sulkier than ever.

That evening a group of admirers called in to sit round Luke and look at the work half-finished on the loom, and praise it. They brought a bottle of wine, and presently they all began drinking and singing songs.

"Don't you keep a bird in here?" one of them said presently. "Wouldn't the bird sing us a song?"

"Oh," said Luke carelessly. "It will be asleep by now. And in any case it's only a working-bird, not a songbird. Its song is no better than a frog croaking."

Now the Lollybird had not been asleep. The voices and talk and laughter had kept it awake. And at these words of Luke's its heart swelled inside it with shame.

One of the visitors had left the door open a crack and, under cover of the noise and singing, which had started up again, the Lollybird crept to the end of the loom and then flew swiftly and silently out through the crack of the door, although it was black dark in the forest and none but night creatures were stirring.

The Lollybird had never been out at night. It was not accustomed to flying in the dark, and bumped into several trees. Soon it was lost. Nevertheless it flew on listening to the songs of the nightingales and envying their voices. Presently it reached a wide open space. This was an airstrip, for now Luke had his blue shellfish flown in by plane, and there was the freight-plane sitting in the middle of the space.

"What an enormous bird," thought the Lollybird, which had not had a chance to fly out that way since the plane began coming.

Just then the Lollybird itself nearly came to a sudden end, for a large horned owl, which had noticed it bumping among the trees and followed out of curiosity, swooped down to grab this clumsy stranger and missed it by no more than the flutter of a feather. The Lollybird saw two great golden eyes coming faster than a train and nipped out of the way with a skilful twist learned from years of flying up and down inside the loom.

The owl thumped against the plane's wing, and the terrified Lollybird flew straight through an open hatchway and into the plane itself.

"Hoooo! Ha!" shouted the owl outside. "I can see you, you miserable little beggar! I'm going to eat you up in one mouthful. Come out of there!"

In fact he couldn't see the Lollybird at all, and presently he gave up and flew off in search of other prey. But the Lollybird didn't know he had gone and stayed trembling in its dark corner for a long time.

After a while the pilot arrived, climbed in, slammed the door, and started up the engine. Now the Lollybird was even more frightened, but what could it do? Nothing at all. The plane took off, circled round, climbed higher, flew and flew through the black hours of night, until they were many many thousands of miles from the airstrip, and the forest, and Luke's little hut.

At last morning came, and the sun rose, and the plane landed, and the pilot opened the door and got down and walked away.

Then at last the Lollybird dared to creep stiffly out of its hiding-place and scramble through the hatchway into the noise and light and muddle of a great airport.

There were so many things to see that it saw nothing at all. By pure good luck it escaped being run over by a truck, or squashed flat by a crane, or squeezed in a pair of automatic doors. Avoiding a Boeing 707 and a firewagon, and a limousine, it darted between two taxis and flew straight into the open doorway of a bus, which immediately started up and sped off along the wide straight road that led into the middle of London.

"My goodness!" thought the Lollybird, hanging upside down by one claw from the luggage rack and gazing out with astonishment at all the houses and supermarkets and cats and dogs and people whizzing past. "To think there was all this in the world and I never knew it!"

In Piccadilly Circus the bus came to a stop. By this time dusk was falling, and nobody noticed the Lollybird, which flew out and perched on a windowsill where it looked at the dazzling lights of the advertisements and the many-coloured cars and the people in their gay clothes and the stalls selling apples and pears and strawberries and the brightly lit windows of the restaurants and the police cars and ambulances with their flashing blue beacons and the fire engines all red and gold rushing along ringing their bells.

"My goodness," thought the Lollybird again, "I wish Luke could see this. If we had our loom here, what a picture we could weave."

But then it remembered how angry it was with Luke. "Anyway I can manage without him," it thought. "All I have to do is string a web from those prongs."

The Lollybird began to bustle about, collecting threads and strands, of which there were plenty to be found in the untidy streets. First it drew out a long streamer of the smoke trailing from a car's exhaust pipe and wound it into a spiral, then it snatched a string from a boy's balloon, and twitched a length of raffia from a woman's shopping-basket. Here it tweaked a dangling end of wool from a girl's shawl, there it snatched a spare hair from a man's beard. All these and many other things were threaded with wonderful skill between the TV aerials that sprouted from the roofs.

Now the Lollybird really began to enjoy itself. It picked up coloured ribbons and bits of tissue paper, metal foil, orange-peel, tufts of fur from poodles, silvery rings from Coke cans, and long shining strands from the tails of police horses. Everything was woven into a huge and sparkling canopy which presently dangled all over the top of Piccadilly Circus like a beautiful tent.

"Oh, what a clever Lollybird I am!" cried the Lollybird with great enthusiasm, and it flew off to do the same thing somewhere else.

But meanwhile poor Luke was in a dreadful state without his Lollybird.

He had just managed to finish the job they had been working on when the Lollybird left home, but he found that he was quite unable to start anything else. He had no idea how to set about it. His fingers were too clumsy, he kept dropping the shuttle, his patterns got into a muddle, and in less than two days the inside of his hut was one complete tangle of wool, so that nobody could so much as get through the door.

At first Luke was very angry at the Lollybird's disappearance.

He went stamping through the forest, bawling and shouting.

"Lollybird! Hey, you Lollybird! Where are you? Come back at once!"

But there was no answer.

All night he called and called. "Where are you, you naughty Lollybird? Where are you, you faithless Lollybird?"

But still there was no answer.

Then Luke began to wonder if some owl or eagle had caught the Lollybird, and to worry, and feel sorry. Then he began to remember that he had not always treated the Lollybird very well, that he had made it work when it wanted to fly out into the forest, that sometimes he had given it nothing but dry biscuits to eat for days on end, when he was too busy to stop and cook the millet porridge that the Lollybird liked best. And sometimes, he remembered, he had insisted on finishing a job of work when the Lollybird was tired and stiff, when it was yawning into its wing and having difficulty keeping its eyes open.

"Oh my dear Lollybird! Where are you? Come back, come back and I won't make you work so hard."

But still there was no answer.

By this time most of the people who had come with orders for more work, or to watch and wonder at the weaving, had become impatient and gone back home again. The forest was empty and silent. But somebody, just as they left, reported that somebody else had been told that yet another person thought he had heard tell that someone else had seen the Lollybird climb into a plane and fly off in it.

"In that case the Lollybird may be anywhere in the world," thought Luke. "How shall I ever find it again? But there's no use staying here, that's certain."

So Luke shut up his hut and climbed on to the last shellfish plane and flew to London.

When he reached London, one of the first things he heard was a story of a wonderful bird which had spread a sparkling web all over the top of Piccadilly Circus.

"Oh, that must be my Lollybird!" cried Luke, and he leapt into a taxi and told the driver to go as fast as possible to Piccadilly. Luckily Luke had plenty of money; all these years he had never spent a hundredth part of what he and the Lollybird earned between them. When he reached Piccadilly Circus he looked about for the beautiful canopy. But it was gone. The Westminster City Council Cleaning Department had come with brooms and mops and suction cleaners and had swept it down and tidied it all away.

But now Luke heard stories about a wonderful bird which had spun a cover like a huge egg-cosy, only bigger, all glittering and rainbow-coloured, over the dome of St Peter's church in Rome.

"That must, that must be my wandering Lollybird!" he cried, and he took another plane and flew to Rome. But when he got to St Peter's he found that the Rome City Council had sent helicopters with mops and hoses and had removed the wonderful cover.

"Oh," cried Luke sorrowfully, "where, where shall I find my wayward Lollybird?"

But now he heard tales of a marvellous bird that was weaving a multi-coloured canopy over the elephant house in the Berlin Zoo.

He sent a telegram: "Please, please do not stop the bird," and jumped into another plane and flew to Berlin.

When he reached the Berlin Zoo everybody was watching in admiration as the tiny bird flew darting about, snatching a hank of wool from a llama, catching a plume from the tail of an ostrich, gathering a tuft of black fur from a gorilla, whisking up a dropped peacock's feather, and a bright scale that some fish had cast off, and weaving them all into its beautiful sparkling web, while a whole ring of elephants stood underneath and gazed at it spellbound with uplifted trunks.

"Oh," cried Luke in rapture, "it is, it must be, my faithless Lollybird!"

And the Lollybird heard his voice among all the other voices in the crowd and answered him,

"Yes I am, I am your faithless Lollybird!"

"Come back, come back, you naughty thoughtless Lollybird! I can't manage without you!"

"No," said the Lollybird, "you can't manage without me, but I can manage very well without you. Goodbye, I'm off to London again."

And it flew tauntingly away with a flip of its tail.

"Come back, come back, you disobedient Lollybird!"

"Goodbye, goodbye! You can't manage without me, but I can manage very well without you."

Poor Luke had to follow as best he could. There was no plane just then, so he caught a boat. When it came chugging up the Thames he saw that the naughty Lollybird had woven a glittering web across Tower Bridge, all made of straw wine-bottle-vases, and scraps of polystyrene, and bus tickets, and milk-bottle tops.

But when Luke stepped off the boat, just too late, the vagrant Lollybird flew gaily away, crying,

"You can't manage without me, but I can manage very well without you!"

"Come back! Come back to your proper work, you wicked Lollybird!"

"Not yet! Not yet! Maybe never at all. Not till you have called me a hundred, hundred times, not till you have found a blue dye in the forest, not till I can sing as well as the nightingales, not till you promise never to overwork me ever, ever again!"

"I promise now!" cried the sorrowful Luke.

"Promises cost nothing. You'll have to prove you are telling the truth before I believe you," replied the uncaring Lollybird, and away it flew.

Luke didn't know what to do. He rented a room with a telephone, he rang up the police, he put advertisements in all the papers, saying, "LOST! My faithless Lollybird. Large reward to finder."

Many people had seen the elusive Lollybird, and rang up to say so, but wherever it had been seen, by the time Luke arrived, the bird was always gone. Luke wandered through the streets of London by day and night, calling and crying,

"Where are you, you mocking Lollybird? Where are you, you thankless Lollybird?"

Then Luke began to hear that the bird had been seen at concerts, and at musical instrument shops, and at schools where pupils were taught singing.

One night Luke went to a concert at the Royal Festival Hall. Sure enough, there was the Lollybird, perched on the conductor's rostrum, listening hard to the music. After a while, though, it couldn't resist beginning to flit about and pick things up here and there, a gold thread from a lady's evening cape, a white hair from the conductor's head, a fern frond out of a pot of growing plants, a tie from a flute-player's neck, a length of spaghetti from a plate in the restaurant. Then it began to weave a web across from the bows of the violinists to the boxes on the opposite side of the hall.

The violinists couldn't play with their bows tied down, the music came to a stop, and Luke cried out,

"Lollybird! You are behaving very badly. Come back to your master!"

"Not yet! Not yet! I'm having far too good a time to come home!" replied the teasing Lollybird, and away it flew, through a window and across the Thames, into a great hotel where it tied all the table-napkins into a fluttering string and knotted them round the chandelier.

Then it flew all the way down the river, snatching up strings of streetlights and trailing them in the water behind it.

Luke was tired out and went back to his room to bed.

But by now the provoking Lollybird had learned how to use the telephone. Luke had no sooner gone off to sleep than the phone would ring and when he picked up the receiver he heard a shrill voice calling in his ear,

"Hullo, hullo, hullo, hullo, this is your faithless Lollybird!"

Night after night the Lollybird woke him in this way until Luke grew pale and thin and had great black circles under his eyes from want of sleep.

"Come back! Come back, you heartless Lollybird," he cried into the telephone.

"Not yet! Not for a long time yet!"

The Lollybird was taking singing lessons from a famous opera singer. In exchange for the lessons it was weaving her a beautiful cloak from brown paper and string and bits of tinsel and pine-needles and photographers' flash-bulbs. The Lollybird wove its web, and the singer sang scales, and the Lollybird repeated them; its voice was growing louder and sweeter with every lesson. And at the end of each lesson it would borrow the singer's telephone to ring up Luke and call,

"Hullo, hullo, hullo, hullo! This is your faithless Lollybird."

"Come back home! Come back and do your proper work!"

"Not till you have called me a hundred, hundred times," replied the wayward bird, and it sang like a snatch of music from *The Magic Flute*,[2] and plunked down the receiver.

Now, by chance, Luke heard tell of a famous echo, in a cave in a valley in Derbyshire, an echo that would repeat the same word for half an hour at a time, throwing it from one side of the valley to the other. So he took a train, and a bus, and a taxi, and went to the cave. The Lollybird was piqued and inquisitive at being left behind, and it flew after Luke secretly to see what he was up to, and perched on a bush outside the entrance to the cave.

"Lollybird!" cried Luke inside the tunnel. "Come back, come back, come back to your proper work, you teasing Lollybird!"

A hundred times he called it, and each word was repeated by the echo a hundred times, so that the whole valley was filled with Luke's voice calling Come back, come back, come back!

2. The 1791 opera by Wolfgang Amadeus Mozart.

"Well, well, perhaps I will, some day," said the Lollybird, darting about the valley, listening to all the echoes, and cocking its head on one side to count them. "But not just yet, not just yet, my dear master!"

And away it flew.

Not just yet, not just yet, not just yet, repeated the echoes in the valley, as Luke came out of the cave and saw the Lollybird, a tiny speck, flying farther and farther away over the distant hills.

After this Luke became very discouraged. He began to feel that he might grow into an old man before the runaway Lollybird decided to come back, that he might as well give up hope of trying to persuade it.

So, very sadly, he went back to the airport and took a plane (he had to charter one specially, for no planes flew that way any more, and this took the last of his money) and he returned to his forest.

The hut was dark and cold, half fallen down, and it was still full of a dreadful tangle of knotted wool and yarn and silk and cotton. Luke was too tired to do anything about the tangle that night, and he had no oil for his lamp, so he lay down in the dark in the middle of it all and went to sleep. But next day he slowly and clumsily set about the disagreeable task of unknotting all the knots and unsnarling all the snarls, winding up all the different lengths of wool and silk, and setting the hut to rights.

But when he had finished it was still empty and cold and silent. The people who had once come to see him weave had long ago left; the railway was closed down and grass grew along the track; no planes flew that way any more; winter was coming and the birds were quiet in the forest.

Luke walked slowly through the trees. The silence lay thick as mist. He remembered how the Lollybird used to fly out with him, looking for plants and mosses.

"Oh," he cried sadly, "oh how very much I miss you, my dearest Lollybird."

He remembered how helpful the Lollybird had always been, and how cheerful, how much it enjoyed inventing new patterns and finding new bits of stuff to weave with, how lively it woke in the mornings, how willingly it worked long hours, and how much, when work was done, it had liked to sing its little grating song and pick out a tune on the strings of the mandolin.

"I am sorry I was unkind about its voice," he thought.

Then he remembered the Lollybird's declaration that it would never return till Luke had found a blue dye in the forest.

"But even if I did find one, how would it ever know?" he thought, and as he wandered along the forest track, tears ran down his face and fell among the withered leaves beside the path.

At last it grew too cold to stay outside any longer, and he went back to the hut.

But, to his astonishment, he saw a light shining in the window. And when he went in, there was his Lollybird. It had lit the lamp, and kindled a little fire, and set a saucepan full of millet porridge on the hob. And it was looking at the empty loom, and the stacked-up shuttles and skeins of wool and yarn, very disapprovingly, with its head on one side.

"Am I dreaming?" said Luke. "Are you a dream, or are you really my Lollybird come back at last?"

"No, I'm not a dream," said the Lollybird, giving the porridge a stir.

"Oh, my dear friend, my long-lost Lollybird! How very, very glad I am to see you!"

"It's plain I've come back none too soon," said the Lollybird tartly. "For you don't appear to have done a stroke of work since I left home. We'd best have our supper quickly and go to bed, for we'll need to get started early in the morning."

Luke was too happy to ask any questions that night. But, next morning, when they had started work, and the Lollybird was flashing to and fro across the loom with a strand of rose-pink wool in its beak and another under its wing, he did venture to ask timidly,

"I thought you said that you wouldn't come back till I'd found a blue dye in the forest. Why did you change your mind?"

"Oh well," said the Lollybird looking down its beak with a casual air, "if I'd waited for *that*, I've no doubt I'd have had to wait a mighty long time. And to tell the truth I was getting a little bored flying about the world."

All day they worked, weaving a curtain that was rose-coloured and black and blue and olive-green. When it was done Luke took a thoughtful look at it and said, "I reckon that's the best bit of work we ever did, my dear Lollybird," and the Lollybird, also after a careful scrutiny and tweaking all the strands with its beak to make sure that none were loose, replied, "No, I can't see anything wrong with that little job, master. Who did we make it for?"

"I really forget," said Luke. "But I daresay it'll come in handy for something. Now, how about a bit of music?"

He fetched out his old flute and played a tune. And because of all its lessons the Lollybird was able to sing him arias from all the greatest operas, in a voice that any nightingale might have envied.

Never again did Luke make his Lollybird work too hard or too long. They took no more orders than would keep them busy for a reasonable part of the day; and when work was over they would go off into the forest, looking for feathers and bright stones, shining petals and gaily coloured leaves.

Next spring, to Luke's astonishment, a new flower came up under the trees, a flower that he had never seen before, which, when picked and dried and powdered, gave them a most beautiful blue dye, a blue as dark and clear as the middle of the ocean on a fine winter day.

"I wonder where the seeds can have come from?" Luke said. "Maybe some bird dropped them as it flew over. What a mysterious thing!"

But the Lollybird knew that the flowers had sprung up from Luke's tears, as he wandered sadly along the forest path, crying, "Oh, how very much I miss you, my dearest Lollybird."

1977

TED HUGHES
1930–1998

Ted Hughes's earliest publications established him as a bold new voice in British poetry, and though he was named poet laureate of England in 1984, his work—dealing with elemental themes in powerful language, seemingly obsessed with animals and nature, often dark—remained controversial throughout his life. He is best known for his poetry and plays, for children as well as adults, but he also wrote essays and fiction. His two linked fairy-tale books, *The Iron Man: A Story in Five Nights* (1968) and *The Iron Woman* (1993), display the new direction taken by the fairy tale in the latter part of the twentieth century.

Hughes was born Edward James Hughes in Mytholmoyd, West Yorkshire, and both the distinctive language of the region and the natural beauty of its stark landscape strongly influenced his writing. By fifteen he was writing poetry, and it was apparently in pursuit of his poetic vision—his poems often draw on myth and ritual—that in his final year of study at Cambridge University he changed his field from English to archaeology and anthropology. After earning his degree in 1954 he supported himself with odd jobs (rose gardener, night watchman, and the like) while he continued to write and occasionally publish verse. Early in 1956 he met the American poet Sylvia Plath, and before the end of the year, they married and moved to America. There Plath encouraged him to enter a poetry competition, and his manuscript won the prize and was published by Harpers. *The Hawk in the Rain* (1957) marked the start of an extraordinary literary career that was to encompass dramas, stories, translations, and essays. By 1960, Hughes and Plath had returned to England, and Hughes began writing poetry for children: *Meet My Folks!* (1961) was followed by two other collections (1963, 1964). In the 1960s and 1970s, his works for children included short stories, fables, creation tales, and numerous plays for radio and the stage. The radio plays were collected in *The Coming of the Kings and Other Plays* (1970; an enlarged U.S. edition was published in 1974 as *The Tiger's Bones and Other Plays for Children*).

In 1968 Hughes published his most famous work for children, *The Iron Man*, which appeared in the United States as *The Iron Giant* (also the title of the 1999 animated film version). It consists of five chapters to be read as bedtime stories, presenting in lyrical prose the atypical adventures of its fairy-tale hero. Hogarth, a country boy, resembles many of the small protagonists of folk and fairy tales, who defeat ogres and marry beautiful princesses, but Hughes shifts the setting to the contemporary world and adds science fiction to the mix. Moreover, he clearly makes a statement against war and inhumane technology, while the unusual combination of clever little hero and inscrutable giant saves the day. In *The Iron Woman*, a sequel to *The Iron Man*, a young girl named Lucy joins with Hogarth and the iron man to protect nature from the pollution thoughtlessly created by humankind. In their experimental approach, both these works parallel the endeavors by many contemporary authors to deal with real social issues metaphorically through the form of the fairy tale for young readers.

The Iron Giant: A Story in Five Nights

1. THE COMING OF THE IRON GIANT

The Iron Giant came to the top of the cliff.

How far had he walked? Nobody knows. Where had he come from? Nobody knows. How was he made? Nobody knows.

Taller than a house, the Iron Giant stood at the top of the cliff, on the very brink, in the darkness.

The wind sang through his iron fingers. His great iron head, shaped like a dustbin but as big as a bedroom, slowly turned to the right, slowly turned to the left. His iron ears turned, this way, that way. He was hearing the sea. His eyes, like headlights, glowed white, then red, then infrared, searching the sea. Never before had the Iron Giant seen the sea.

He swayed in the strong wind that pressed against his back. He swayed forward, on the brink of the high cliff.

And his right foot, his enormous iron right foot, lifted—up, out, into space, and the Iron Giant stepped forward, off the cliff, into nothingness.

CRRRAAAASSSSSSSH!

Down the cliff the Iron Giant came toppling, head over heels.

CRASH!

CRASH!

CRASH!

From rock to rock, snag to snag, tumbling slowly. And as he crashed and crashed and crashed

His iron legs fell off.

His iron arms broke off, and the hands broke off his arms.

His great iron ears fell off and his eyes fell out.

His great iron head fell off.

All the separate pieces tumbled, scattered, crashing, bumping, clanging, down onto the rocky beach far below.

A few rocks tumbled with him.

Then

Silence.

Only the sound of the sea, chewing away at the edge of the rocky beach, where the bits and pieces of the Iron Giant lay scattered far and wide, silent and unmoving.

Only one of the iron hands, lying beside an old, sand-logged washed-up seaman's boot, waved its fingers for a minute, like a crab on its back. Then it lay still.

While the stars went on wheeling through the sky and the wind went on tugging at the grass on the cliff top and the sea went on boiling and booming.

Nobody knew the Iron Giant had fallen.

Night passed.

Just before dawn, as the darkness grew blue and the shapes of the rocks separated from each other, two seagulls flew crying over the rocks. They landed on a patch of sand. They had two chicks in a nest on the cliff. Now they were searching for food.

One of the seagulls flew up—Aaaaaark! He had seen something. He glided low over the sharp rocks. He landed and picked something up. Something shiny, round, and hard. It was one of the Iron Giant's eyes. He brought it back to his mate. They both looked at this strange thing. And the eye looked at them. It rolled from side to side looking first at one gull, then at the other. The gulls, peering at it, thought it was a strange kind of clam, peeping at them from under its shell.

Then the other gull flew up, wheeled around, and landed and picked something up. Some awkward, heavy thing. The gull flew low and slowly, dragging the heavy thing. Finally, the gull dropped it beside the eye. This new thing had five legs. It moved. The gulls thought it was a strange kind of crab. They thought they had found a strange crab and a strange clam. They did not know they had found the Iron Giant's eye and the Iron Giant's right hand.

But as soon as the eye and the hand got together the eye looked at the hand. Its light glowed blue. The hand stood up on three fingers and its thumb, and craned its forefinger like a long nose. It felt around. It touched the eye. Gleefully it picked up the eye, and tucked it under its middle finger. The eye peered out, between the forefinger and the thumb. Now the hand could see.

It looked around. Then it darted and jabbed one of the gulls with its stiffly held finger, then darted at the other and jabbed him. The two gulls flew up into the wind with a frightened cry.

Slowly then the hand crept over the stones, searching. It ran forward suddenly, grabbed something, and tugged. But the thing was stuck between two rocks. The thing was one of the Iron Giant's arms. At last the hand left the arm and went scuttling hither and thither among the rocks, till it stopped, and touched something gently. This thing was the other hand. This new hand stood up and hooked a finger round the little finger of the hand with the eye, and let itself be led. Now the two hands, the seeing one leading the blind one, walking on their fingertips, went back together to the arm, and together they tugged it free. The hand with the eye fastened itself onto the wrist of the arm. The arm stood up and walked on its hand. The other hand clung on behind as before, and this strange trio went searching.

An eye! There it was, blinking at them speechlessly beside a black and white pebble. The seeing hand fitted the eye to the blind hand and now both hands could see. They went running among the rocks. Soon they found a leg. They jumped on top of the leg and the leg went hopping over the rocks with the arm swinging from the hand that clung to the top of the leg. The other hand clung on top of that hand. The two hands, with their eyes, guided the leg, twisting it this way and that, as a rider guides a horse.

Soon they found another leg and the other arm. Now each hand, with an eye under its palm and an arm dangling from its wrist, rode on a leg separately about the beach. Hop, hop, hop, they went, peering among the rocks. One found an ear and at the same moment the other found the giant torso. Then the busy hands fitted the legs to the torso, then they fitted the arms, each fitting the other, and the torso stood up with legs and arms but no head. It walked about the beach, holding its eyes up in its hands, searching for its lost head. At last, there was the head—eyeless, earless, nested in a heap of red seaweed. Now in no time the Iron Giant had fitted his head back, and his eyes were in place, and everything in place except for one ear. He strode about the beach searching for his lost ear, as the sun rose over the sea and the day came.

The two gulls sat on their ledge, high on the cliff. They watched the immense man striding to and fro over the rocks below. Between them, on the nesting ledge, lay a great iron ear. The gulls could not eat it. The baby gulls could not eat it. There it lay on the high ledge.

Far below, the Iron Giant searched.

At last he stopped, and looked at the sea. Was he thinking the sea had stolen his ear? Perhaps he was thinking the sea had come up while he lay scattered, and had gone down again with his ear.

He walked toward the sea. He walked into the breakers, and there he stood for a while, the breakers bursting around his knees. Then he walked in deeper, deeper, deeper.

The gulls took off and glided down low over the great iron head that was now moving slowly out through the swell. The eyes blazed red, level with the wavetops, till a big wave covered them and foam spouted over the top of the head. The head still moved out under the water. The eyes and the top of the head appeared for a moment in a hollow of the swell. Now the eyes were green. Then the sea covered them and the head.

The gulls circled low over the line of bubbles that went on moving slowly out into the deep sea.

2. The Return of the Iron Giant

One evening a farmer's son, a boy called Hogarth, was fishing in a stream that ran down to the sea. It was growing too dark to fish, his hook kept getting caught in weeds and bushes. So he stopped fishing and came up from the stream and stood listening to the owls in the wood further up the valley, and to the sea behind him. Hush, said the sea. And again, Hush. Hush. Hush.

Suddenly he felt a strange feeling. He felt he was being watched. He felt afraid. He turned and looked up the steep field to the top of the high cliff. Behind that skyline was the sheer rocky cliff and the sea. And on that skyline, just above the edge of it, in the dusk, were two green lights. What were two green lights doing at the top of the cliff?

Then, as Hogarth watched, a huge dark figure climbed up over the cliff top. The two lights rose into the sky. They were the giant figure's eyes. A giant black figure, taller than a house, black and towering in the twilight, with green headlight eyes. The Iron Giant! There he stood on the cliff top, looking inland. Hogarth began to run. He ran and ran. Home. Home. The Iron Giant had come back.

So he got home at last and, gasping for breath, he told his dad. An Iron Giant! An Iron Man! A giant!

His father frowned. His mother grew pale. His little sister began to cry.

His father took down his double-barreled gun. He believed his son. He went out. He locked the door. He got in his car. He drove to the next farm.

But that farmer laughed. He was a fat, red man, with a fat, red-mouthed laugh. When he stopped laughing, his eyes were red too. An Iron Giant? Nonsense, he said.

So Hogarth's father got back in his car. Now it was dark and it had begun to rain. He drove to the next farm.

That farmer frowned. He believed. Tomorrow, he said, we must see what he is, this iron giant. His feet will have left tracks in the earth.

So Hogarth's father again got back into his car. But as he turned the car in the yard, he saw a strange thing in the headlights. Half a tractor lay there, just half, chopped clean off, the other half missing. He got out of his car and the other farmer came to look too. The tractor had been bitten off—there were big teeth marks in the steel.

No explanation! The two men looked at each other. They were puzzled and afraid. What could have bitten the tractor in two? There, in the yard, in the rain, in the night, while they had been talking inside the house.

The farmer ran in and bolted his door.

Hogarth's father jumped into his car and drove off into the night and the rain as fast as he could, homeward.

The rain poured down. Hogarth's father drove hard. The headlights lit up the road and bushes.

Suddenly—two headlights in a tall treetop at the roadside ahead. Headlights in a treetop? How?

Hogarth's father slowed, peering up to see what the lights might be, up there in the treetop.

As he slowed, a giant iron foot came down in the middle of the road, a foot as big as a single bed. And the headlights came down closer. And a giant hand reached down toward the windshield.

The Iron Giant!

Hogarth's father put on speed, he aimed his car at the foot.

Crash! He knocked the foot out of the way.

He drove on, faster and faster. And behind him, on the road, a clanging clattering boom went up, as if an iron skyscraper had collapsed. The iron man, with his foot knocked from under him, had toppled over.

And so Hogarth's father got home safely.

BUT

Next morning all the farmers were shouting with anger. Where were their tractors? Their earth-diggers? Their plows? Their harrows? From every farm in the region, all the steel and iron farm machinery had gone. Where to? Who had stolen it all?

There was a clue. Here and there lay half a wheel, or half an axle, or half a mud-guard, carved with giant toothmarks where it had been bitten off. How had it been bitten off? *Steel* bitten off?

What had happened?

There was another clue.

From farm to farm, over the soft soil of the fields, went giant footprints, each one the size of a single bed.

The farmers, in a frightened, silent, amazed crowd, followed the footprints. And at every farm the footprints visited, all the metal machinery had disappeared.

Finally, the footprints led back up to the top of the cliff, where the little boy had seen the Iron Giant appear the night before, when he was fishing. The footprints led right to the cliff top.

And all the way down the cliff were torn marks on the rocks, where a huge iron body had slid down. Below, the tide was in. The gray, empty, moving tide. The Iron Giant had gone back into the sea.

SO

The furious farmers began to shout. The Iron Giant had stolen all their machinery. Had he eaten it? Anyway, he had taken it. It had gone. What if he came again? What would he take next time? Cows? Houses? People?

They would have to do something.

They couldn't call in the police or the army, because nobody would believe them about this Iron Monster. They would have to do something for themselves.

So, what did they do?

At the bottom of the hill, below where the Iron Giant had come over the high cliff, they dug a deep, enormous hole. A hole wider than a house, and as deep as three trees one on top of the other. It was a colossal hole. A stupendous hole! And the sides of it were sheer as walls.

They pushed all the earth off to one side. They covered the hole with branches and the branches were covered with straw and the straw with soil, so when they finished, the hole looked like a freshly plowed field.

Now, on the side of the hole opposite the slope up to the top of the cliff, they put an old rusty truck. That was the bait. Now they reckoned the Iron Giant would come over the top of the cliff out of the sea, and he'd see the old truck, which was painted red, and he'd come down to get it to chew it up and eat it. But on his way to the truck he'd be crossing the hole, and the moment he stepped with his great weight onto that soil held up only with straw and branches, he would crash through into the hole and would never get out. They'd find him there in the hole. Then they'd bring the few bulldozers and earth-movers that he hadn't already eaten, and they'd push the pile of earth in on top of him, and bury him forever in the hole. They were certain now that they'd get him.

Next morning, in great excitement, all the farmers gathered together to go along to examine their trap. They came carefully closer, expecting to see hands tearing at the edge of the pit. They came carefully closer.

The red truck stood just as they had left it. The soil lay just as they had left it, undisturbed. Everything was just as they had left it. The Iron Giant had not come.

Nor did he come that day.

Next morning, all the farmers came again. Still, everything lay just as they had left it.

And so it went on, day after day. Still the Iron Giant never came.

Now the farmers began to wonder if he would ever come again. They began to wonder if he had ever come at all. They began to make up explanations of what had happened to their machinery. Nobody likes to believe in an Iron Monster that eats tractors and cars.

Soon, the farmer who owned the red truck they were using as bait decided that he needed it, and he took it away. So there lay the beautiful deep trap, without any bait. Grass began to grow on the loose soil.

The farmers talked of filling the hole in. After all, you can't leave a giant pit like that, somebody might fall in. Some stranger coming along might just walk over it and fall in.

But they didn't want to fill it in. It had been such hard work digging it. Besides, they all had a sneaking fear that the Iron Giant might come again, and the hole was their only weapon against him.

At last they put up a little notice: DANGER: KEEP OFF, to warn people away, and they left it at that.

Now the little boy Hogarth had an idea. He thought he could use that hole to trap a fox. He found a dead hen one day, and threw it out on the loose soil over the trap. Then toward evening, he climbed a tree nearby and waited. A long time he waited. A star came out. He could hear the sea.

Then—there, standing at the edge of the hole, was a fox. A big red fox, looking toward the dead hen. Hogarth stopped breathing. And the fox stood without moving—sniff, sniff, sniff, out toward the hen. But he did not step out onto the trap. Slowly, he walked around the wide patch of raw soil till he got back to where he'd started, sniffing all the time out toward the bird. But he did not step out onto the trap. Was he too smart to walk out there where it was not safe?

But at that moment he stopped sniffing. He turned his head and looked toward the top of the cliff. Hogarth, wondering what the fox had seen, looked toward the top of the cliff.

There, enormous in the blue evening sky, stood the Iron Giant, on the brink of the cliff, gazing inland.

In a moment, the fox had vanished.

Now what?

Hogarth carefully, quietly, hardly breathing, climbed slowly down the tree. He must get home and tell his father. But at the bottom of the tree he stopped. He could no longer see the Iron Giant against the twilight sky. Had he gone back over the cliff into the sea? Or was he coming down the hill, in the darkness under that high skyline, toward Hogarth and the farms?

Then Hogarth understood what was happening. He could hear a strange tearing and creaking sound. The Iron Giant was pulling up the barbed wire fence that led down the hill. And soon Hogarth could see him, as he came nearer, tearing the wire from the fence posts, rolling it up like spaghetti, and eating it. The Iron Giant was eating the barbed fencing wire.

But if he went along the fence, eating as he moved, he wouldn't come anywhere near the trap, which was out in the middle of the field. He could spend the whole night wandering about the countryside along the fences, rolling up the wire and eating it, and never would any fence bring him near the trap.

But Hogarth had an idea. In his pocket, among other things, he had a long nail and a knife. He took these out. Did he dare? His idea frightened him. In the silent dusk, he tapped the nail and the knife blade together.

Clink, Clink, Clink!

At the sound of the metal, the Iron Giant's hands became still. After a few seconds, he slowly turned his head and the headlight eyes shone toward Hogarth.

Again, Clink, Clink, Clink! went the nail on the knife.

Slowly, the Iron Giant took three strides toward Hogarth, and again stopped. It was now quite dark. The headlights shone red. Hogarth pressed close to the tree trunk. Between him and the Iron Giant lay the wide lid of the trap.

Clink, Clink, Clink! Again he tapped the nail on the knife.

And now the Iron Giant was coming. Hogarth could feel the earth shaking under the weight of his footsteps. Was it too late to run? Hogarth stared at the Iron Giant, looming, searching toward him for the taste of the metal that had made that inviting sound.

Clink, Clink, Clink! went the nail on the knife. And

CRASSSHHH!

The Iron Giant vanished.

He was in the pit. The Iron Giant had fallen into the pit. Hogarth went close. The earth was shaking as the Iron Giant struggled underground. Hogarth peered over the torn edge of the great pit. Far below, two deep red headlights glared up at him from the pitch blackness. He could hear the Iron Giant's insides grinding down there and it sounded like a big truck grinding its gears on a steep hill. Hogarth set off. He ran, he ran, home—home with the great news. And as he passed the cottages on the way, and as he turned down the lane toward his father's farm, he was shouting, "The Iron Giant's in the trap!" and "We've caught the Iron Giant."

When the farmers saw the Iron Giant wallowing in their deep pit, they sent up a great cheer. He glared up toward them, his eyes burned from red to purple, from purple to white, from white to fiery whirling black and red, and the cogs inside him ground and screeched, but he could not climb out of the steep-sided pit.

Then, under the beams of car headlights, the farmers brought bulldozers and earthpushers, and they began to push in on top of the struggling Iron Giant all the earth they had dug when they first made the pit and that had been piled off to one side.

The Iron Giant roared again as the earth began to fall on him. But soon he roared no more. Soon the pit was full of earth. Soon the Iron Giant was buried silent, packed down under all the soil, while the farmers piled the earth over him in a mound and in a hill. They went to and fro over the mound on their new tractors, which they'd bought since the Iron Giant ate their old ones, and they packed the earth down hard. Then they all went home talking cheerfully. They were sure they had seen the last of the Iron Giant.

Only Hogarth felt suddenly sorry. He felt guilty. It was he, after all, who had lured the Iron Giant into the pit.

3. What's to Be Done with the Iron Giant?

So the spring came round the following year, leaves unfurled from the buds, daffodils speared up from the soil, and everywhere the grass shook new green points. The round hill over the Iron Giant was covered with new grass. Before the end of the summer, sheep were grazing on the fine grass on the lovely hillock. People who had never heard of the Iron Giant saw the green hill as they drove past on their way to the sea, and they said: "What a lovely hill! What a perfect place for a picnic!"

So people began to picnic on top of the hill. Soon, quite a path was worn up there, by people climbing to eat their sandwiches and take snapshots of each other.

One day, a father, a mother, a little boy, and a little girl stopped their car and climbed the hill for a picnic. They had never heard of the Iron Giant and they thought the hill had been there forever.

They spread a tablecloth on the grass. They set down a plate of sandwiches, a big pie, a roasted chicken, a bottle of milk, a bowl of tomatoes, a bagful of boiled eggs, a dish of butter, and a loaf of bread, with cheese and salt and cups. The father got his stove going to boil some water for tea, and they all lay back on blankets, munching food and waiting for the kettle to boil, under the blue sky.

Suddenly the father said: "That's funny!"

"What is?" asked the mother.

"I felt the ground shake," the father said. "Here, right beneath us."

"Probably an earthquake in Japan," said the mother.

"An earthquake in Japan?" cried the little boy. "How could that be?"

So the father began to explain how an earthquake in a far distant country that shakes down buildings and empties lakes sends a jolt right around the earth. People far away in other countries feel it as nothing more than a slight trembling of the ground. An earthquake that knocks a city flat in South America might do no more than shake a picture off a wall in Poland. But as the father was talking, the mother gave a little gasp, then a yelp.

"The chicken!" she cried. "The cheese! The tomatoes!"

Everybody sat up. The tablecloth was sagging in the middle. As they watched, the sag got deeper and all the food fell into it, dragging the tablecloth right down into the ground. The ground underneath was splitting and the tablecloth, as they watched, slowly folded and disappeared into the crack, and they were left staring at a jagged black crack in the ground. The crack grew, it widened, it lengthened, it ran between them. The mother and the girl were on one side, and the father and the boy were on the other side. The little stove toppled into the growing crack with a clatter and the kettle disappeared.

They could not believe their eyes. They stared at the widening crack. Then, as they watched, an enormous iron hand came up through the crack, groping around in the air, feeling over the grass on either side of the crack. It nearly touched the little boy, and he rolled over backward. The mother screamed. "Run to the car," shouted the father. They all ran. They jumped into the car. They drove. They did not look back.

So they did not see the great iron head, square like a bedroom, with red glaring headlight eyes, and with the tablecloth, still with the chicken and the cheese, draped across the top of it, rising out of the top of the hillock as the Iron Giant freed himself from the pit.

When the farmers realized that the Iron Giant had freed himself, they groaned. What could they do now? They decided to call the army, who could pound him to bits with antitank guns. But Hogarth had another idea. At first, the farmers would not hear of it, least of all his own father. But at last they agreed. Yes, they would give Hogarth's idea a trial. And if it failed, they would call in the army.

After spending a night and a day eating all the barbed wire for miles around, as well as hinges he tore off gates and the tin cans he found in ditches, and three new tractors and two cars and a truck, the Iron Giant was resting in a clump of huge branches, almost hidden by the dense leaves, his eyes glowing a soft blue.

The farmers came near, along a lane, in cars so that they could make a quick getaway if things went wrong. They stopped fifty yards from the clump of elm trees. He really was a monster. This was the first time most of them had had a good look at him. His chest was as big as a cattle truck. His arms were like cranes, and he was getting rust, probably from eating all the old barbed wire.

Now Hogarth walked up toward the Iron Giant.

"Hello!" he shouted, and stopped. "Hello, Mr. Iron Giant."

The Iron Giant made no move. His eyes did not change.

Then Hogarth picked up a rusty old horseshoe, and knocked it against a stone: Clonk, Clonk, Clonk!

At once, the Iron Giant's eyes turned darker blue. Then purple. Then red. And finally white, like car headlights. It was the only sign he gave of having heard.

"Mr. Iron Giant," shouted Hogarth. "We've got all the iron you want, all the food you want, and you can have it for nothing, if only you'll stop eating up the farms."

The Iron Giant stood up straight. Slowly he turned, till he was looking directly at Hogarth.

"We're sorry we trapped you and buried you," shouted the little boy. "We promise we'll not deceive you again. Follow us and you can have all the metal you want. Brass too. Aluminum too. And lots of old chrome. Follow us."

The Iron Giant pushed aside the boughs and came into the lane. Hogarth joined the farmers. Slowly they drove back down the lane, and slowly, with all his cogs humming, the Iron Giant stepped after them.

They led through the villages. Half the people came out to stare, half ran to shut themselves inside bedrooms and kitchens. Nobody could believe their eyes when they saw the Iron Giant marching behind the farmers.

At last they came to the town, and there was a great scrap-metal yard. Everything was there, old cars by the hundred, old trucks, old railway engines, old stoves, old refrigerators, old springs, bedsteads, bicycles, girders, gates, pans—all the scrap iron of the region was piled up there, rusting away.

"There," cried Hogarth. "Eat all you can."

The Iron Giant gazed, and his eyes turned red. He kneeled down in the yard, he stretched out on one elbow. He picked up a greasy black stove and chewed it like a toffee. There were delicious crumbs of chrome on it. He followed that with a double-decker bedstead, and the brass knobs made his eyes crackle with joy. Never before had the Iron Giant eaten such delicacies. As he lay there, a big truck turned into the yard and unloaded a pile of rusty chain. The Iron Giant lifted a handful and let it dangle into his mouth—better than any spaghetti.

So there they left him. It was an Iron Giant's heaven. The farmers went back to their farms. Hogarth visited the Iron Giant every few days. Now the Iron Giant's eyes were constantly a happy blue. He was no longer rusty. His body gleamed blue, like a new gun barrel. And he ate, ate, ate, ate—endlessly.

4. THE SPACE-BEING AND THE IRON GIANT

One day there came strange news. Everybody was talking about it. Round eyes, busy mouths, frightened voices—everybody was talking about it.

One of the stars of the night sky had begun to change. This star had always been a very tiny star, of no importance at all. It had shone up there for billions and trillions and zillions of years in the constellation of Orion, that great shape of the giant hunter that strides across space on autumn and winter nights. In all its time this tiny star had never changed in any way.

Now, suddenly, it began to get bigger.

Astronomers, peering through their telescopes, noticed it first. They watched it with worried frowns.

That tiny star was definitely getting bigger. And not just bigger. But bigger and Bigger and BIGger. Each night it was BIGGER.

Bigger than the Dog Star, the large colored twinkler at the heel of the Hunter Orion.

Bigger than Jupiter, the great blazing planet.

Everybody could see it clearly, night after night, as it grew and Grew and GREW. They stared up with frightened faces.

Till at last it hung there in the sky over the world, blazing down, the size of the moon, a deep, gloomy red. And now there could be only one explanation. That star was getting bigger because it was getting nearer. And nearer and NEARer and NEARER.

It was rushing toward the world.

Faster than a bullet.

Faster than any rocket.

Faster even than a meteorite.

And if it hit the world at that speed, why, the whole world would simply be blasted to bits in the twinkling of an eye. It would be like an express train hitting a bowl of goldfish.

No wonder the people stared up with frightened faces. No wonder the astronomers watched it through their telescopes with worried frowns.

But all of a sudden—a strange thing!

There it hung, a deep and gloomy red, just the size of the moon. It got no smaller. It got no bigger. It wasn't coming any nearer. But it wasn't going away either.

Now everybody tried to explain why and how this was. What had happened? What was happening? What was going to happen?

And now it was that the next strange thing occurred—the astronomers noticed it first.

In the middle of the giant star, a tiny black speck had appeared. On the second night this speck was seen to be wriggling, and much bigger. On the third night, you could see it without a telescope. A struggling black speck in the center of that giant, red, gloomy star.

On the fifth night, the astronomers saw that it seemed to be either a bat, or a black angel, or a flying lizard—a dreadful silhouette, flying out of the center of that giant star, straight toward the earth. What was coming out of the giant star?

Each night, when the astronomers returned to their telescopes to peer up, this black flying horror was bigger. With slow, gigantic wingbeats, with long, slow writhings of its body, it was coming down through space, outlined black against its red star.

Within a few more nights, its shape had completely blotted out the red star. The nameless, immense bat-angel was flying down at the earth, like a great black swan. It was definitely coming straight at the earth.

It took several days to cover the distance.

Then, for one awful night, its wings seemed to be filling most of the sky. The moon peered fearfully from low on the skyline and all the people of earth stayed up, gazing in fear at the huge black movement of wings that filled the night.

Next morning it landed—on Australia.

Barrrump!

The shock of its landing rolled round the earth like an earthquake, spilling teacups in London, jolting pictures off walls in California, cracking statues off their pedestals in Russia.

The thing had actually landed—and it was a terrific dragon.

Terribly black, terribly scaly, terribly knobbly, terribly horned, terribly hairy, terribly clawed, terribly fanged, with vast indescribably terrible eyes, each one as big as Switzerland. There it sat, covering the whole of Australia, its tail trailing away over Tasmania into the sea, its foreclaws on the headlands of the Gulf of Carpentaria. Luckily, the mountains and hills propped its belly up clear of the valleys, and the Australians could still move about in the pitch darkness, under this new sky, this low queer covering, of scales. They crowded toward the light that came in along its sides. Of course, whoever had been on a mountain top when the dragon landed had been squashed flat. Nothing could be done about them. And there the horror sat, glaring out over the countries of the world.

What had it come for? What was going to happen to the world now that this monstrosity had arrived?

Everybody waited. The newspapers spoke about nothing else. Aircraft flew near this space-bat-angel-dragon, taking photographs. It lay over Australia higher than any mountains, higher than the Hindu Kush[1] in Asia, and its head alone was the size of Italy.

For a whole day, while the people of the earth trembled and wept and prayed to God to save them, the space-bat-angel-dragon lay resting, its chin sunk in the Indian Ocean, the sea coming not quite up to its bottom lip.

But the next morning, early, its giant voice came rumbling round the world. The space-bat-angel-dragon was speaking. It wanted to be fed. And what it wanted to eat was . . . living things. People, animals, forests, it didn't care which, so long as the food was alive. But it had better be fed quickly, otherwise it would roll out its tongue longer than the Trans-Siberian railway,[2] and lick huge swaths of life off the surface of the earth—cities, forests, farmlands, whatever there was. It would leave the world looking like a charred pebble—unless it were fed and fed quickly.

Its voice shook and rumbled round the earth for a whole hour as it delivered its message. Finally it ended, and lay waiting.

The peoples of the world got together. If they fed it, how could they ever satisfy it? It would never be full, and every new day it would be as hungry as ever. How can you feed a beast the size of Australia? Australia is a vast land, all the countries of Europe will fit easily into Australia. The monster's stomach alone must be the size of Germany.

No, they would not feed it. The people of the world decided they would not feed this space-bat-angel-dragon or whatever it was—they would fight it. They would declare war on it, and all get together to blast it off the face of the earth. And so it was that all the peoples of earth declared war on the monster, and sent out their armed forces in a grand combined operation.

What a terrific attack!

Rockets, projectiles of all sorts, missiles and bombs, shells and flame throwers—everything was tried. The smoke of the explosions drifted out over the Pacific like a black, crawling continent. The noise of the battle shook the world almost as much as the landing of the dragon had done, and for much longer.

---

1. One of the major mountain ranges in central Asia, with many peaks above 20,000 feet.

2. The railway joining Moscow and Vladivostok, which runs more than 5,500 miles.

Then the noise died down and the smoke cleared. And the peoples of the world cried in dismay. The dragon was actually smiling. Smiling! Aircraft flying daringly near photographed the vast face smiling, and the picture was in all the papers.

It was smiling as if it had been well tickled.

Now the peoples of the world were worried. They were all great fighters. All spent their spare money on preparing for wars, always making bigger and better weapons, and now they had all tried their utmost to blast this thing off the earth, and what was the result?

The dragon merely smiled, and not a scratch could be seen anywhere on its body.

Human weapons had no effect on it.

But that wasn't surprising. This creature had come from the depths of space, out of the heart of a star. Nobody knew what it was made of. Perhaps it could not be destroyed by any means whatsoever.

And now the space-bat-angel-dragon spoke again.

It gave the peoples of the world one week in which to prepare its first meal. They could prepare what they liked, said the dragon. But if the meal was not ready in a week, then he would start on the cities and the towns.

The peoples of the earth, the kings, the presidents and ministers, the farmers and the factory workers and the office workers, began to lament. Now what would happen to them? They would like to say the monster didn't exist, but how could they? There it was, covering Australia, staring out over all the countries of the world.

Now the little boy Hogarth heard all about this. Everybody in the world was talking about it, worrying about it.

He was sure the Iron Giant could do something. Compared to the space-bat-angel-dragon, the Iron Giant wasn't very big, of course. The Iron Giant was only the size of a tall tree. Nevertheless, Hogarth had faith in the Iron Giant.

He visited the Iron Giant in his scrap-yard, and talked to him about this great monster that was threatening the earth.

"Please," he asked, "please can't you think of some way of getting rid of it? If you can't, then it's the end of us all."

The Iron Giant chewed thoughtfully at his favorite tidbit, a juicy, spicy old gas stove. He shook his head slowly.

"Please think of something," cried Hogarth. "If this space-bat-angel-dragon licks all life off the earth, that'll be the end of your scrap iron—there'll be no people left to make it."

The Iron Giant became still. He seemed to be thinking. Suddenly his headlights blazed red, green, blue, and white all at once. And he stood up. In a great grinding voice he gave his commands. Hogarth danced for joy. The Iron Giant had had the most stupendous idea. The Iron Giant would go out, as the champion of the earth, against the monster from space.

5. THE IRON GIANT'S CHALLENGE

There was no time to be wasted. The Iron Giant allowed himself to be taken to pieces, arms, legs, body, head, all separate, so each part could be flown out to Australia on a different airliner. He was too big to be flown out in one piece.

At the same time a ship sailed from China, loaded with great iron girders, and another ship sailed from Japan loaded with fuel oil. The Iron Giant had ordered these. The girders and the oil and a team of engineers were unloaded on the beach of Northern Australia, near the space-bat-angel-dragon's neck. Then the Iron Giant's parts were landed at the same spot, and the engineers fitted him together. He stood up on the beach and shouted his challenge.

"Sit up," he roared. "Sit up and take notice, you great space-lizard."

The space-bat-angel-dragon sat up slowly. He had never noticed the fussing of the boats and airplanes down there on the beach near his neck. Now he gazed in surprise at the Iron Giant, who seemed very tiny to him, though his voice was big enough.

The Iron Giant spoke again.

"I challenge you," he shouted, "to a test of strength."

A test of strength? The space-bat-angel-dragon couldn't believe his ears. A tiny little creature like the Iron Giant challenging him to a test of strength? He simply laughed. Loud and long. Then he peered down again at the Iron Giant, while the echo of his laugh was still rolling round the earth. He peered down out of the sky at this odd little thing on the beach, with the even tinier men scuttling around it.

"And if I can prove myself stronger than you are, then you must promise to become my slave," cried the Iron Giant.

The dragon smiled. Aircraft flew around, watching this amazing conversation between the space-bat-angel-dragon and the Iron Giant. Ships out at sea watched through telescopes.

"And if you don't accept my challenge," shouted the Iron Giant, "then you're a miserable cowardly reptile, not fit to bother with."

The space-bat-angel-dragon was so astounded that he agreed. Why, he thought, when this silly little creature has finished his antics, I'll just lick him up. So the monster agreed, and watched to see what the test of strength was to be. After all, if he wanted, he could flatten the Iron Giant with one eyelash.

The engineers had fastened all the girders together in the shape of a grid, a huge iron bed the size of a house. Under this they had made a steel-lined pit. Now they poured fuel oil into the pit. The space-bat-angel-dragon watched.

Now they lit the fuel oil and the flames roared up fiercely through the bars of the grid.

And now the space-bat-angel-dragon got his first shock. The Iron Giant was stretching himself out on his back, on the grid, among the flames, his ankles crossed, his hands folded behind his head—just as if he were in bed, while the flames raged under and around him.

The monster stared down, and the Iron Giant smiled up out of the midst of the flames.

The flames became fiercer. The grid became red-hot. The Iron Giant's hair and elbows and toes became red-hot. His body became first blue, then black, then began to glow dully. He was getting red-hot. Still he smiled up at the monster, and still the flames grew fiercer.

And now the Iron Giant was entirely red-hot. Pretty soon, he was almost white-hot. And still he smiled, out of white-hot eyes and with white-hot lips. And all the time the space-bat-angel-dragon stared down in astonishment.

But now the fuel oil was all burned away. Suddenly the flames died, flickered, and went out. The white-hot Iron Giant sat up, stood up, got stiffly off his glowing bed, and began to walk to and fro on the sand, cooling. He cooled slowly. He went from white to orange, from orange to red, red to black, as he walked, coolly swinging his arms.

Now at last he spoke to the monster.

"If you can't bear to be made red-hot like me, then you are weaker than I am, and I have won, and you are my slave."

The monster began to laugh.

"All right," he roared. "Build the fire, and I'll lie on it."

He laughed again. He knew the Iron Giant couldn't build a fire the size of Australia. But then his laugh stopped. The Iron Giant was pointing upward, at the sun.

"There is the fire for you," he shouted. "You go and lie there. Go and lie on the sun till you are red-hot."

The monster gazed up at the sun. He felt strangely cold suddenly. But how could he refuse? All right! And he set off.

With slow giant wingbeats, he lifted his immense body off the earth, and flew slowly up toward the sun, while the whole earth watched . . .

Slowly he covered the distance, getting smaller and smaller as he went. At last he landed, a ragged black shape sprawled across the sun. Everybody watched. And now they saw the monster begin to glow. Blue at first, then red, then orange. Finally his shape was invisible, the same blazing white as the sun itself. The monster was white-hot on the sun.

Then they saw him returning, a blazing shape tearing itself off the sun. This shape became red as it flew. It was writhing and growing larger. Slowly once more it became the black bat-winged shape of the dragon flying back to earth, down and down, bigger and bigger, cooling as he came, until

BUMP!!!!

He landed—this time much more heavily than before, on Australia. He landed so heavily that all over the world bells tumbled out of church towers and birds' eggs were jarred out of their nests. The monster stared down at the Iron Giant.

But it was hardly the same monster! His horns drooped, his face was wizened and black, his claws were scorched blunt, his crest flopped over limply, and great ragged holes were burned in his wings. It had been terrible for him on the fires of the sun. But he had done it, and here he was. The fires of the sun are far, far hotter than any fires here on earth can ever be.

"There," he roared. "I've done it."

The Iron Giant nodded. But his answer was to signal to the engineers. Once more they poured oil into the trough under the grid. Once more they lit it. Once more the flames roared up and black smoke billowed up into the clear blue. And once more the Iron Giant stretched himself on the grid of the raging furnace.

The space-bat-angel-dragon watched in horror. He knew what this meant for him. He would have to go once more into the sun's flames.

And now the Iron Giant's hair and toes and elbows were red-hot. He lay back in the flames, smiling up at the dragon. And his whole body was becoming red-hot, then orange, and finally white, like the blazing wire inside an electric bulb.

At this point, the Iron Giant was terribly afraid. For what would happen if the flames went on getting fiercer and fiercer? He would melt. He would melt and drip into the flames like so much treacle and that would be the end of him. So even though he grinned up at the dragon as though he were enjoying the flames, he was not enjoying them at all, and he was very, very frightened.

Even the engineers, who were hiding behind thick asbestos screens over a mile away along the beach, felt the hair singeing on their heads, and they too thought it was the end of the Iron Giant. Perhaps they had poured in just a bit too much fuel oil.

But at that very moment, and the very second that the edge of the Iron Giant's ear started to melt, the fuel was used up and the flames died. The engineers came running down the beach. They saw the red-hot Iron Giant getting off his fearful bed, and they saw him moving to and fro on the sand, cooling off.

At last, the Iron Giant looked up at the dragon. He could hardly speak after his ordeal in the flames. Instead, he simply pointed toward the sun, and jabbed his finger toward the sun, as he gazed up at the monster.

"That's twice," he managed to say. "Now it's your turn."

The monster did not laugh. He set off, up from the earth, beating his colossal wings, writhing his long ponderous body up into the sky toward the sun. Now it was his turn. And he did not laugh. Last time had been too dreadful. But he went. He couldn't let the Iron Giant win. He couldn't let the Iron Giant of the earth beat him in this terrible contest.

And so all the telescopes and cameras of the world watched him flying into the sun. They saw him land among the flames, as before. As before, they saw his great ragged shape like an ink blot sprawled over the center of the sun. And at last they could no longer see him. He and the sun were one blinding whiteness.

He had done it again! But was the sun burning him up? Had he melted in the sun? Where was he?

No, here he was, here he came. Slowly, slowly, down through space. Much more slowly than before. His white-hot flying body cooled slowly to red as he came, and as he grew larger, coming nearer, he finally became once more black. And the great black shape flagged its way down through space until

BUMP!!!!!!

Heavier than ever, he landed on Australia. This time the bump was so heavy, it knocked down certain skyscrapers, sent tidal waves sweeping into harbors, and threw herds of cows onto their backs. All over the world, anybody who happened to be riding a bicycle at that moment instantly fell off. The space-bat-angel-dragon landed so ponderously because he was exhausted. And now he was a very changed monster. The fires of the sun had worked on him in a way that was awful to see. His wings were only rags of what they had been. His skin was crisped. And all his fatness had been changed by the fires of the sun into precious stones—jewels, emeralds, rubies, turquoises, and substances that had never been found on earth. And when he landed, with such a jolt, these loads of precious gems burst through the holes scorched in his skin and scattered down onto the Australian desert beneath.

But the Iron Giant could not allow himself to pity the space-bat-angel-dragon. He signaled to the engineers.

"Round three!" he shouted.

And the engineers began to pour in the oil. But what was this? An enormous whoofing sound. A booming, wheezing, sneezing sound. The space-bat-angel-dragon was weeping. If the Iron Giant got onto his furnace again, it would mean that he, the monster, would have to take another roasting in the sun—and he could not stand another.

"Enough, enough, enough!" he roared.

"No, no," replied the Iron Giant. "I feel like going on. We've only had two each."

"It's enough," cried the dragon. "It's too much. I can't stand another. The fires of the sun are too terrible for me. I submit."

"Then I've won," shouted the Iron Giant. "Because I'm quite ready to roast myself red-hot again. If you daren't, then I've won."

"You've won, yes, you've won, and I am your slave," cried the space-bat-angel-dragon. "I'll do anything you like, but not the sun again."

And he plunged his chin in the Pacific, to cool it.

"Very well," said the Iron Giant. "From now on you are the slave of the earth. What can you do?"

"Alas," said the space-bat-angel-dragon, "I am useless. Utterly useless. All we do in space is fly, or make music."

"Make music?" asked the Iron Giant. "How? What sort of music?"

"Haven't you heard of the music of the spheres?" asked the dragon. "It's the music that space makes to itself. All the spirits inside all the stars are singing. I'm a star spirit. I sing too. The music of the spheres is what makes space so peaceful."

"Then whatever made you want to eat up the earth?" asked the Iron Giant. "If you're all so peaceful up there, how did you get such greedy and cruel ideas?"

The dragon was silent for a long time after this question. And at last he said: "It just came over me. I don't know why. It just came over me, listening to the battling shouts and the war cries of the earth—I got excited, I wanted to join in."

"Well, you can sing for us instead," said the Iron Giant. "It's a long time since anybody here on earth heard the music of the spheres. It might do us all good."

And so it was fixed. The space-bat-angel-dragon was to send his star back into the constellation of Orion, and he was to live inside the moon. And every night he was to fly around the earth, through the heavens, singing.

So his fearful shape, slowly swimming through the night sky, didn't frighten people, because it was dark and he couldn't be seen. But the whole world could hear him, a strange soft music that seemed to fill the whole of space, a deep weird singing, like millions of voices singing together.

Meanwhile, the Iron Giant was the world's hero. He went back to his scrap-yard. But now everybody in the world sent him a present. Some only sent him a nail. Some sent him an old car. One rich man even sent him an ocean liner. He sprawled there in his yard, chewing away, with his one ear slightly drooped where the white heat of that last roasting had slightly melted it. As he chewed, he hummed in harmony to the singing of his tremendous slave in heaven.

And the space-bat-angel's singing had the most unexpected effect. Suddenly the world became wonderfully peaceful. The singing got inside everybody and made them as peaceful as starry space, and blissfully above all their earlier little squabbles. The strange, soft, eerie space-music began to alter all the people of the world. They stopped making weapons. The countries began to think how they could live pleasantly alongside each other, rather than how to get rid of each other. All they wanted to do was to have peace to enjoy this strange, wild, blissful music from the giant singer in space.

1968

JULIUS LESTER
b. 1939

Consistent with his belief that ordinary people are capable of doing great things, Julius Lester has written numerous stories and folktales that depict the extraordinary cunning, humor, and courage of common people who become heroes in their own right.

One of the major writers of African American literature for young adults, he was born in St. Louis, the son of a Methodist minister; he also lived in Kansas City, Kansas, and Nashville during his youth. He noted in an autobiographical sketch that he "absorbed so much of Southern rural black traditions, particularly the music and stories," while growing up, and that he profited from this exposure despite the segregation and discrimination he faced in the South. After graduating from Fisk University in Nashville in 1960, he became involved in the civil rights movement and joined the Student Non-Violent Coordinating Committee (SNCC). Aside from heading SNCC's photo department, he also played the guitar and banjo at demonstrations, and his first publications were a direct outgrowth of these experiences: *The 12-String Guitar as Played by Leadbelly: An Instructional Manual* (1965, coauthored by Pete Seeger) and books on political themes, including *The Angry Children of Malcolm X* (1966) and *Look Out, Whitey! Black Power's Gon' Get Your Mama!* (1968). It was also about this time that an editor at Dial Press suggested that he try his hand at writing for children, and Lester responded with *To Be a Slave* (1969), a collection of six stories based on slaves' oral histories that was a Newbery Honor Book, and *Black Folktales* (1969), a collection of African legends and slave narratives given new life by their retelling in contemporary language. These two books were to mark a turning point in Lester's career, establishing both his main subjects (black history and folklore) and his primary audience. Although he has continued to write for adults, Lester concentrates on children's literature, which he finds more rewarding because he can provide children with books of a kind that were unavailable to him in the segregated South.

Lester has often argued for the importance of an authentic black voice in children's literature. In his own works he has sought to convey African American heritage and experience, thereby encouraging African American children as well as writers and artists to reclaim their history. Lester's contributions to this project of reclamation have often involved the illustrator Jerry Pinkney, in such books as *John Henry* (1994), *Sam and the Tigers: A New Telling of Little Black Sambo* (1996), *Black Cowboy, Wild Horses* (1998), and their four volumes of Uncle Remus stories (published together in *Uncle Remus, Tales from the Briar Patch*, 1999).

"Jack and the Devil's Daughter," from *Black Folktales*, is based on a tale collected by the pathbreaking African American folklorist Zora Neale Hurston in *Mules and Men* (1935). Aside from showing a clear affinity with the familiar "Jack" tales of the British and Continental tradition, which feature a small hero who manages to triumph because he is blessed with luck or who uses his cleverness to outsmart an ogre, witch, or devil, Lester's story draws on African American tall tales that feature the trickster, a rascal who manages to live a charmed life. This figure, found in many traditions, is always an amoral, provocative character who questions how power is used. In the hands of Lester and many other writers of ethnic literature, the trickster is a subversive figure whose antics have their serious side.

Jack and the Devil's Daughter

Once there was a man who had two sons. One day when the sons were almost grown, the old man called them in. "I've decided to give you boys what you got coming to you right now. I don't want y'all hanging around the house waiting for me to die. So here." He gave each of them $1,000, which was their inheritance. "Now I don't want either one of you ever coming to me again for anything in the world. Do with the money what you want to, but if you end up broke, shame on you."

The first son, whose name was John, bought a little grocery store, got married, and settled down.

The other son, whose name was Jack, put the $1,000 in one pocket, a deck of cards in the other, and took off down the road. Jack was a natural-born gambler. Everybody else had to have bad luck, because Jack had all the good luck. There wasn't a card game in the world he couldn't play. And when the money started to hit the table, there wasn't anybody around who could beat Jack.

It was a very good thing that Jack was talented at gambling, because if he had had to work for a living, he would've died. Jack treated work like he treated his mama, and he wouldn't hit his mama a lick. His hands were still baby-soft. But don't let that fool you. If Jack had to, he could shoot out a flea's eye at 100 yards and cut a man so quick, the man would be afraid to bleed if Jack told him not to.

Well, this one day, Jack walked into this place and saw a man sitting by himself at a table. "You look like you might be a card player," Jack said to the man.

The man didn't say a word. He just nodded.

Jack sat down, shuffled the cards, and started dealing. Jack looked at his cards. The man looked at his and laid $100 on the table.

"Aw, man, I thought you wanted to gamble," Jack laughed, laying down $500 plus $100 to cover the man's bet.

The man didn't blink an eye. He laid down another $500 and raised Jack $300 more. Jack threw away two cards and pulled two more from the top of the deck. He laid down $300. "You ain't gon' take no cards?" Jack asked the man.

There was no response.

Jack shrugged. "It's your money you losing." He grinned and laid down three tens. The man spread three queens and a pair of deuces and took the money.

Jack laughed. "Well, you got lucky that time. Let's go 'round again."

They played another hand, and Jack lost all of his money. "Well, mister, you the best I ever run into. I guess the game's over, 'cause you got all my money."

The man spoke for the first time. "I'll bet you all the money on the table against your life."

Jack laughed. "Why not? I'm a gambling man, sure as you're born." Jack wasn't worried. Even if he lost the game, he knew he could out-cut, out-shoot, and out-fight any man around. So if the man did try to kill him, Jack had no doubt that he'd kill him first.

They played another hand and Jack lost. Then the man got up from the table and he stood fourteen feet tall. Jack was as scared as he could be. The man looked down at him and said in a deep voice, "My name is the Devil, and I live across the deep blue sea. I'm not going to kill you right now, because I like your style. If you get to my house by this time tomorrow, I'll spare you. If you don't, you're mine." And he disappeared.

Jack didn't know what he was going to do. He had sat there and played cards with the Devil. Wasn't no way in the world he could've won! The more he thought about it, the worse he felt. And the worse he felt, the more he thought about it.

An old man came in the place and saw Jack sitting there with tears rolling down his face. "What's the matter with you, son?"

"I played cards with the Devil, and he won. He said if I don't get to his house across the ocean by this time tomorrow, he's going to kill me."

The old man said, "You got problems. Ain't no doubt about that. There ain't but one thing that can cross the ocean to where the Devil live at."

"What's that?"

"The bald eagle. There's a bald eagle that comes down to the edge of the ocean every morning, washes in the water, and picks off the dead feathers. When she dips herself in the water the third time, she kinda rocks a little bit, then spreads her wings and takes off again. Now if you could be there with a yearling bull, after she dips in the water the third time, and then rocks, you jump on her back and she'll take you there."

"What's the yearling bull for?"

"She gets hungry going across the ocean, and every time she hollers, you give her some of the yearling bull and you'll be all right. If you don't, she'll eat you."

The next morning, Jack was there bright and early. Sure enough, he hadn't been there long when a bald eagle came flying from the other side of the ocean. Jack watched, and when she dipped herself in the water the third time and rocked a little bit, Jack jumped on her back, the yearling bull under his arm, and the bald eagle started climbing toward the sun.

They'd been flying for a short while when the eagle started twisting her head from side to side, and her blazing eyes lit up the northern sky and then the southern sky, and she hollered:

> One-quarter 'cross the ocean!
> Don't see nothing but blue water!

> One-quarter 'cross the ocean!
> Don't see nothing but blue water!

Jack got scared when he heard the eagle sing like that, and, instead of giving her just a piece of the yearling bull, he gave her all of it. The eagle swallowed it down and kept on flying.

After a while, the eagle twisted her head from side to side, and her blazing eyes lit up the northern sky and the southern sky, and she hollered:

> Halfway 'cross the ocean!
> Don't see nothing but blue water!

> Halfway 'cross the ocean!
> Don't see nothing but blue water!

Jack didn't have any meat left, but he was so scared that he tore off his leg and gave it to her. She swallowed that down and flew on. After a while, she twisted her head to one side, then the other, and her blazing eyes lit up the northern sky and the southern sky, and she hollered:

> Three-quarters 'cross the ocean!
> Don't see nothing but blue water!

> Three-quarters 'cross the ocean!
> Don't see nothing but blue water!

Jack tore off an arm and gave it to her. She swallowed that down and flew on. Pretty soon the eagle landed, and Jack jumped off and started down the road looking for the Devil's house. He didn't know exactly where the Devil lived, so he asked the first person he saw.

"It's the first big white house 'round the curve in the road," Jack was told.

He went on to the house and knocked on the door.

"Who's that?" a voice called out.

"One of the Devil's friends. One without an arm or a leg."

The Devil told his wife, "Reach behind the door and hand that fool an arm and a leg and let him in."

Jack put on the arm and leg and stepped in the house.

"Well," said the Devil, "I see you got here. You just in time for breakfast."

"That's good, 'cause I sure am hungry."

"I'm sure you are. Well, before you eat, I wonder if you'd do a little job for me."

"Be glad to help out," Jack said.

"Glad to hear it. I got a hundred acres of forest out back that I need cut down to keep the fires of Hell burning."

"A hundred acres, you say?"

"That ain't much for a man who played cards with the Devil."

"And you want me to do it before breakfast?"

"If you don't," the Devil said, "I'm going to take your life."

Jack picked up an axe and went out back. When he saw the 100 acres of trees, he knew that it would take 100 men working 100 years to cut all that forest down. It would take him a year just to cut one side of one tree. Jack had never seen trees that were so big and tall. Jack didn't need to take a second look at the trees to know that he was beat. So, instead of sitting down and worrying about it, Jack lay down and went to sleep.

Now the Devil had a daughter named Beulah Mae, and she had been peeping at Jack from the back room and had fallen in love with him. Nobody can tell why somebody falls in love with somebody else. Maybe she fell in love with him because of the green suede shoes he had on. Maybe she liked the pink shirt he was wearing. Maybe she liked the way the sequins on his suit sparkled. Maybe she liked the way his gold tooth sparkled. Whatever it was, she was madly in love with Jack, and when she heard her father give Jack all that work to do, she knew that her father was simply looking for an excuse to kill him. She'd seen it happen before. But she liked Jack, and she didn't want it to happen to him. So she went out back and found Jack sleeping like Daniel in the lion's den.[1]

"Don't you know my father's going to kill you if you don't get this work done?" she asked, waking him up.

"Who're you?" Jack asked, opening one eye.

"I'm Beulah Mae, the Devil's daughter."

Jack opened the other eye. "Well, Beulah Mae, I'm just glad your daddy let me live long enough to rest my eyes on you. Honey, you're prettier than a royal flush.[2] You look as good as Aretha[3] sounds."

Beulah Mae blushed. "Well, I'll help you get this forest cut. You just put your head in my lap and go back to sleep."

Jack didn't need a second invitation, and when he went to sleep, Beulah Mae looked at the axe and sang:

> Axe cut on one side,
> Cut on the other.
> When one tree falls
> All fall together.

And just like that, the whole 100 acres of trees came down.

After a while, Beulah Mae woke Jack up, and he went into the house to get his breakfast.

---

1. According to the Bible, Daniel passed a night unscathed in a den of lions (Daniel 6.16–23).
2. The poker hand of highest value (unless the use

of wild cards makes five of a kind possible).
3. Aretha Franklin (b. 1942), singer widely acclaimed as the Queen of Soul.

"You all through?" the Devil asked.

Jack nodded. "Yeah, and it sho' gave me a good appetite, too."

The Devil went out back, and sure enough, the whole 100 acres was down. "Well, Jack," the Devil said when he came back in, "you're almost as good a man as I am."

Jack grinned. "Almost."

The Devil couldn't figure out how Jack had cut down that 100 acres of trees. No one had ever been able to do it, and he wasn't too sure that Jack had done it. "When you get through breakfast, I got another thing I want you to help me out on."

"What's that?"

"I got a well. It's a hundred feet deep and I want you to dip it dry. And when I say dry, I don't mean muddy. I mean dry! I want that well so dry I want to see dust in the bottom. And then I want you to bring me what's in the bottom of the well."

"Is that all?" Jack asked, without looking up from his breakfast.

"That's all for now."

Jack took his time finishing breakfast, because he knew it was going to be his last meal. Dip a well so dry that there'd be dust in the bottom. The Devil was out of his mind. Jack spent a couple of hours picking his teeth and then went on out to the well and looked it over. Sure enough. It was 100 feet deep, at least. Jack took one look at it, turned his back, and went and stretched out on the grass. The minute he shut his eyes, he was asleep.

In a little while, Beulah Mae came out and woke Jack up. "What did daddy ask you to do this time?"

Jack woke up. "That fool told me to dip that hundred-foot-deep well dry and dip it so dry that there'd be dust in the bottom. Then he said to bring him what was at the bottom. Honey, your daddy is stone crazy!"

"No, he's not. He's the Devil."

"He's the Devil, and he's stone crazy!"

"Well, don't you worry about it. Just put your head in my lap and finish taking your nap. I'll take care of this well." As soon as Jack was asleep, Beulah Mae took a dipper and started singing:

Dipper, dipper,
Dip one drop.
When you dip one drop,
Dip every drop.

And no sooner had she said it than the well was so dry you could see the dust pouring out of it. She called her pet bird to her and told it to fly down to the bottom of the well and bring her what was there.

After a while, she woke Jack up and gave him a ring. "Go give this to daddy. Mama dropped it in the well yesterday."

Jack went in the house and gave the ring to the Devil. "Hey, man. You got to tell your ol' lady to be careful about where she let that ring slip off her finger from now on."

The Devil was really mad now. Not only did Jack get everything done, but he had the nerve to come in bragging about it. But the Devil didn't let on that he was angry. "Jack, you're almost as smart as I am. I tell you what. I been looking for a good number-two man that I could train. I got one more job for you, and, if you do it, I'll make you my number-two man, plus you can marry my daughter, Beulah Mae."

"Well, that's mighty nice of you, Mr. Devil. What'cha want me to do?"

"I got a goose. I want you to go up to the tallest tree and pick all the feathers off the goose, bring me the goose and all the feathers when you get through. If one feather is missing, you're mine."

"Aw, is that all?"

"Don't forget. If one feather is missing, you're mine."

"Don't you worry about it, dude. Ain't gon' be no feathers missing. It oughta be obvious to you by now that I don't mess around."

Jack got the goose, tied him to a bush, and went to sleep on the other side of the bush. He was sure that even Beulah Mae couldn't save him this time. Beulah Mae came to him, and he told her what her father wanted him to do.

"Just put your head in my lap and go back to sleep." After a while, she woke him up and handed him all the feathers tied into a neat little bundle. "That was a hard one, Jack."

"Honey, you ain't told me nothing."

"Here're the feathers and the goose. Take 'em in to daddy."

Jack strutted into the house and gave the feathers and the goose to the Devil. "Now, where's your daughter?"

The Devil was so angry, he wanted to kill Jack on the spot. Instead, he called Beulah Mae. "This is the man I've picked out for you to marry, Beulah Mae. He's going to be my assistant."

"That's nice, daddy."

The Devil noticed how she was looking at him, and how he was looking at her, and he knew who had done all the work. His own daughter, Beulah Mae Devil, had betrayed him.

"Jack, you and Beulah Mae can have that little pink stucco house down the road."

"Thank you, Devil. I sure appreciate all you've done for me."

Jack and Beulah Mae went to their house and had a big supper, and, after they did the dishes, went to bed. 'Way over in the night, Beulah Mae woke Jack up. "Jack! Jack! Wake up! Daddy's on his way here to kill you."

Jack woke up, but he didn't hear anything. "How do you know? I don't hear nothing."

"I'm the Devil's daughter, ain't I? The same powers he got, I got. And I can hear him coming. Now get up and go to the barn. Daddy's got two horses that can jump a thousand miles at a jump. One of them is named Hallowed-Be-Thy-Name. The other one is called Thy-Kingdom-Come. You hitch 'em to the buckboard so we can get out of here."

When the Devil got to the house, he found that Jack and Beulah Mae had gone. He ran to the barn to get his two fast horses, and they were gone. Then he got his bull, which could jump 500 miles at a jump, and he was after 'em.

The Devil was tearing up some road, and every time the bull jumped, the Devil would holler: "Hallowed-Be-Thy-Name! Thy-Kingdom-Come!" And the horses would fall to their knees when they heard his voice, and the Devil would be steady gaining.

"He's going to catch us," Beulah Mae said. "Jack, you get out and draw your feet backwards nine steps, throw some sand over your left shoulder, and let's go."

Jack did what she'd told him, and the horses were off again, 1,000 miles at a jump.

"Hallowed-Be-Thy-Name! Thy-Kingdom-Come!" the Devil hollered.

The horses fell to their knees again, and the Devil was getting closer.

"It's too late," Beulah Mae said. "He's going to catch us."

"Well, what we gon' do?"

"I'll turn into a lake, and I'll turn you into a duck swimming on the lake." She tried to turn Jack into a duck, but he was so tough that he wouldn't turn into nothing.

"Oh, Lord! What we gon' do, Beulah Mae, honey?"

"That's O.K. I'll turn myself into the lake and the horses into ducks, and you be a hunter." She pulled a gun out of the air and handed it to him.

She had scarcely done it when the Devil came by on his bull, and he was steady trucking. He went on by them, five hundred miles a jump. As soon as he was out of sight, Beulah Mae turned back into herself and turned the ducks back into horses, and they started off in another direction at 1,000 miles a jump.

It wasn't long, though, before the Devil realized he'd been tricked, and he came back, got on their trail, and was after them. "Hallowed-Be-Thy-Name! Thy-Kingdom-Come!" And the horses fell to their knees.

Beulah Mae jumped out of the buckboard, pulled a thorn off a rosebush, and stuck it in the ground.

> When I plant one thorn,
> I plant 'em all.
> Grow thorns!
> Three thousand miles high,
> Three thousand miles wide,
> Three thousand miles long.
> Grow thorns!

And no sooner had she said it than the biggest thornbush the world has even seen grew in that place.

When the Devil got to the wall of thorns, there was nothing he could do. By the time he had cast the spell to make the thorns disappear, Jack and Beulah Mae were riding across the ocean on the back of the eagle. Jack took Beulah Mae to Harlem, and they settled down. Jack went into business at the store with his brother, selling numbers.[4] They raised a big family, and, whenever you hear a mother saying to her child, "Boy, you got the Devil in you," more than likely it's one of Jack and Beulah Mae's grandchildren.

1969

4. I.e., running an illegal lottery.

JANE YOLEN
b. 1939

In *Mirror, Mirror: Forty Folktales for Mothers and Daughters to Share* (2000), Jane Yolen remarked to her daughter that folktales do more than simply teach lessons about life: "they can offer us platforms upon which we can play out our inner conflicts." Yolen has deeply explored fairy tales, not only to bring out the genre's implicit psychodramas but also to question its conventional gender relations, re-forming them from a perspective that is clearly but not dogmatically feminist. Poet, playwright, and writer and editor of all manner of children's books as well as fantasy and science fiction for adults,

Yolen is one of today's most prolific and experimental writers of fairy tales. She was born and spent most of her childhood in New York City, and she claims descent from a long line of storytellers—starting with her great-grandfather, "the storyteller in a small village in Finno-Russia." After graduating from Smith College in 1960 and working for different publishing houses, Yolen turned to full-time professional writing in 1965. Her first book was a delightful comical fairy tale for children, *The Witch Who Wasn't* (1964). She has subsequently published well over 250 titles, including such important nonfiction books as *Touch Magic: Fantasy, Faerie, and Folktale in the Literature of Childhood* (1981). She has also produced film scripts and cassettes based on her work.

One of Yolen's main goals has been to recapture the flavor and spirit of the oral tradition in her literary fairy tales. She writes with grace and painstaking care to create tales that evoke the atmosphere of long ago and other worlds, employing metaphors and symbols in unusual combinations that produce new associations. Although she has adapted numerous folktales and classical fairy tales, her best stories are those she herself has created in such books as *The Girl Who Loved the Wind* (1972), *The Girl Who Cried Flowers and Other Tales* (1974), *The Moon Ribbon and Other Tales* (1976), *The Lady and the Merman* (1977), *The Hundredth Dove and Other Tales* (1977), *Dream Weaver and Other Tales* (1979), *Dragonfield and Other Stories* (1985), and *Child of Faerie, Child of Earth* (1997).

Drawing on her comprehensive knowledge of folk and fairy tales throughout the world—she has edited important collections, including *Favorite Folktales from around the World* (1986) and *Not One Damsel in Distress: World Folktales for Strong Girls* (2000)—Yolen often subtly alters popular narratives to undermine readers' expectations and provoke her audience, whether that be adults or children. Such stories as "Moon Ribbon," "Brother Hart," "The Thirteenth Fey," "Happy Dens or A Day in the Old Wolves Home," and "The Undine" use startling metaphors and unusual plots to cast a new light on traditional tales and their meaning. For instance, in "Undine" Yolen emphasizes the notion of male betrayal and female autonomy in an implicit critique of Hans Christian Andersen's "The Little Mermaid" (1837); here the mermaid leaves a charming prince to return to her sisters in the sea. In "The Thirteenth Fey" Yolen evokes the story of "Sleeping Beauty" in the first-person narrative by the youngest daughter of a family of fairies and produces a philosophical critique of decadent monarchy. Though not a writer with a strong ideological bent, Yolen has been influenced by the feminist movement. One of her major achievements has been to subvert the male discourse that has dominated the fairy tale as genre so that the repressed concerns of women are addressed, and the predictable happy ends that signify male hegemony and closure are exploded or put into question. Thus, in "The White Seal Maid" and "The Lady and the Merman" she has her female protagonists seek refuge in their origins, the sea, which represents for Yolen the essence of restlessness, change, tenderness, and humanity.

The Lady and the Merman

Once in a house overlooking the cold northern sea a baby was born. She was so plain, her father, a sea captain, remarked on it.

"She shall be a burden," he said. "She shall be on our hands forever." Then, without another glance at the child, he sailed off on his great ship.

His wife, who had longed to please him, was so hurt by his complaint that she soon died of it. Between one voyage and the next, she was gone.

When the captain came home and found this out, he was so enraged, he never spoke of his wife again. In this way he convinced himself that her loss was nothing.

But the girl lived and grew as if to spite her father. She looked little like her dead mother but instead had the captain's face set round with mouse-brown curls. Yet as plain as her face was, her heart was not. She loved her father, but was not loved in return.

And still the captain remarked on her looks. He said at every meeting, "God must have wanted me cursed to give me such a child. No one will have her. She shall never be wed. She shall be with me forever." So he called her Borne, for she was his burden.

Borne grew into a lady, and only once gave a sign of this hurt.

"Father," she said one day when he was newly returned from the sea, "what can I do to heal this wound between us?"

He looked away from her, for he could not bear to see his own face mocked in hers, and spoke to the cold stone floor. "There is nothing between us, Daughter," he said. "But if there were, I would say *Salt for such wounds*."

"Salt?" Borne asked, surprised for she knew the sting of it.

"A sailor's balm," he said. "The salt of tears or the salt of sweat or the final salt of the sea." Then he turned from her and was gone next day to the furthest port he knew of, and in this way he cleansed his heart.

After this, Borne never spoke again of the hurt. Instead, she carried it silently like a dagger inside. For the salt of tears did not salve her, so she turned instead to work. She baked bread in her ovens for the poor, she nursed the sick, she held the hands of the sea widows. But always, late in the evening, she walked on the shore looking and longing for a sight of her father's sail. Only, less and less often did he return from the sea.

One evening, tired from the work of the day, Borne felt faint as she walked on the strand. Finding a rock half in and half out of the water, she climbed upon it to rest. She spread her skirts about her, and in the dusk they lay like great gray waves.

How long she sat there, still as the rock, she did not know. But a strange, pale moon came up. And as it rose, so too rose the little creatures of the deep. They leaped free for a moment of the pull of the tide. And last of all, up from the depths, came the merman.

He rose out of the crest of the wave, sea-foam crowning his green-black hair. His hands were raised high above him and the webbings of his fingers were as colorless as air. In the moonlight he seemed to stand upon his tail. Then, with a flick of it, he was gone, gone back to the deeps. He thought no one had remarked his dive.

But Borne had. So silent and still, she saw it all, his beauty and his power. She saw him and loved him, though she loved the fish half of him more. It was all she could dare.

She could not tell what she felt to a soul, for she had no one who cared about her feelings. Instead she forsook her work and walked by the sea both morning and night. Yet strange to say, she never once looked for her father's sail.

That is why her father returned one day without her knowing it. He watched her through slotted eyes as she paced the shore, for he would not look straight upon her. At last he went to her and said, "Be done with it. Whatever ails you, give it over." For even he could see *this* wound.

Borne looked up at him, her eyes shimmering with small seas. Grateful even for this attention, she answered, "Yes, Father, you are right. I must be done with it."

The captain turned and left her then, for his food was growing cold. But Borne went directly to the place where the waves were creeping onto the shore. She called out in a low voice, "Come up. Come up and be my love."

There was no answer except the shrieking laughter of the birds as they dove into the sea.

So she took a stick and wrote the same words upon the sand for the merman to see should he ever return. Only, as she watched, the creeping tide erased her words one by one by one. Soon there was nothing left of her cry on that shining strand.

So Borne sat herself down on the rock to weep. And each tear was an ocean.

But the words were not lost. Each syllable washed from the beach was carried below, down, down, down to the deeps of the cool, inviting sea. And there, below on his coral bed, the merman saw her words and came.

He was all day swimming up to her. He was half the night seeking that particular strand. But when he came, cresting the currents, he surfaced with a mighty splash below Borne's rock.

The moon shone down on the two, she a grave shadow perched upon a stone and he all motion and light.

Borne reached down with her white hands and he caught them in his. It was the only touch she could remember. She smiled to see the webs stretched taut between his fingers. He laughed to see hers webless, thin, and small. One great pull between them and he was up by her side. Even in the dark, she could see his eyes on her under the phosphorescence of his hair.

He sat all night by her. And Borne loved the man of him as well as the fish, then, for in the silent night it was all one.

Then, before the sun could rise, she dropped her hands on his chest. "Can you love me?" she dared to ask at last.

But the merman had no tongue to tell her above the waves. He could only speak below the water with his hands, a soft murmuration. So, wordlessly, he stared into her eyes and pointed to the sea.

Then, with the sun just rising beyond the rim of the world, he turned, dove arrow-slim into a wave, and was gone.

Gathering her skirts, now heavy with ocean spray and tears, Borne stood up. She cast but one glance at the shore and her father's house beyond. Then she dove after the merman into the sea.

The sea put bubble jewels in her hair and spread her skirts about her like a scallop shell. Tiny colored fish swam in between her fingers. The water cast her face in silver and all the sea was reflected in her eyes.

She was beautiful for the first time. And for the last.

1977

ROBERT MUNSCH
b. 1945

Many writers for children have first worked as story-tellers in schools, youth centers, and libraries and then gradually begun writing down their tales for publication. The enrichment that results from such live contact and experience with children is clearly evident in the work of Robert Munsch, whose writings often grow out of performances and whose tales have had enormous success in both forms. Born in 1945, Munsch grew up in Pittsburgh in a family with nine children. He studied many years to be a priest, but the pleasure he found in a part-time job at a day care center persuaded him to change his career. While doing his practice teaching at the Eliot Pearson School of Child Studies at Tufts University, where he earned an M.Ed. in 1973, he discovered a certain talent in improvised storytelling. In 1973 Munsch married Ann Beeler, and in 1975 they moved to Guelph, Ontario, where he worked at the Family Studies Laboratory Preschool at the University of Guelph. He remained at the university until 1984, when he began writing full-time.

Encouraged by a librarian to publish the stories he was telling to the children, Munsch began his writing career with *Mud Puddle* (1979), a comic tale in which a young girl named Jule Ann is harassed by a villainous mud puddle wherever she goes. Eventually she defeats the puddle by throwing a smelly orange soap on it. Since its publication Munsch has produced at least one picture book every other year, including *Murmel, Murmel, Murmel* (1982), *Moira's Birthday* (1987), *Stephanie's Ponytail* (1996), and *Makeup Mess* (2001). He has worked with a number of illustrators, especially Michael Martchenko. Munsch's most successful book, *Love You Forever* (1986), is also his most controversial; some view the mother's love for her son as obsessive and infantilizing, while others see it as unconditional. He generally treats ordinary situations involving children and their parents that suddenly become extraordinary and difficult, as he develops imaginative plots and comic characters who do outlandish things. Munsch is very candid in raising problems faced by children but always reassuringly suggests that they can restore order to their world.

Munsch's tales often follow the general framework of a fairy tale, but with the exception of *Giant* (1989) and *The Paper Bag Princess* he has not explicitly worked in this genre. Nevertheless, with well over 3 million copies in print *The Paper Bag Princess* (illustrated by Martchenko) is one of the best-selling feminist fairy tales ever published. Munsch began telling the story in a day care center in 1973, at the height of the second wave of the women's movement, but it was not until 1980 that he published it. His feisty heroine Elizabeth, who refuses to play the stereotypical role of the passive princess, resembles the strong female protagonists in the works of Tanith Lee, Jane Yolen, and other contemporary writers. Though some argue that the end of Munsch's work is anti-boy, the picture book sets a model of nonsexist literature for children.

The Paper Bag Princess

Elizabeth was a beautiful princess.

She lived in a castle and had expensive princess clothes.

She was going to marry a prince named Ronald.

Unfortunately, a dragon smashed her castle, burned all her clothes with his fiery breath, and carried off Prince Ronald.

Elizabeth decided to chase the dragon and get Ronald back.

She looked everywhere for something to wear but the only thing she could find that was not burnt was a paper bag. So she put on the paper bag and followed the dragon.

He was easy to follow because he left a trail of burnt forests and horses' bones.

Finally, Elizabeth came to a cave with a large door that had a huge knocker on it.

She took hold of the knocker and banged on the door.

The dragon stuck his nose out of the door and said, "Well, a princess! I love to eat princesses, but I have already eaten a whole castle today. I am a very busy dragon. Come back tomorrow."

He slammed the door so fast that Elizabeth almost got her nose caught.

Elizabeth grabbed the knocker and banged on the door again.

The dragon stuck his nose out of the door and said, "Go away. I love to eat princesses, but I have already eaten a whole castle today. I am a very busy dragon. Come back tomorrow."

"Wait," shouted Elizabeth. "Is it true that you are the smartest and fiercest dragon in the whole world?"

"Yes," said the dragon.

"Is it true," said Elizabeth, "that you can burn up ten forests with your fiery breath?"

"Oh, yes," said the dragon, and he took a huge, deep breath and breathed out so much fire that he burnt up fifty forests.

"Fantastic," said Elizabeth, and the dragon took another huge breath and breathed out so much fire that he burnt up one hundred forests.

"Magnificent," said Elizabeth, and the dragon took another huge breath, but this time nothing came out.

The dragon didn't even have enough fire left to cook a meat ball.

Elizabeth said, "Dragon, is it true that you can fly around the world in just ten seconds?"

"Why, yes," said the dragon and jumped up and flew all the way around the world in just ten seconds.

He was very tired when he got back, but Elizabeth shouted, "Fantastic, do it again!"

So the dragon jumped up and flew around the whole world in just twenty seconds.

When he got back he was too tired to talk and he lay down and went straight to sleep.

Elizabeth whispered very softly, "Hey, dragon." The dragon didn't move at all.

She lifted up the dragon's ear and put her head right inside. She shouted as loud as she could, "Hey, dragon!"

The dragon was so tired he didn't even move.

Elizabeth walked right over the dragon and opened the door to the cave.

There was Prince Ronald.

He looked at her and said, "Elizabeth, you are a mess! You smell like ashes, your hair is all tangled and you are wearing a dirty old paper bag. Come back when you are dressed like a real princess."

"Ronald," said Elizabeth, "your clothes are really pretty and your hair is very neat. You look like a real prince, but you are a bum."

They didn't get married after all.

1980

LAURENCE YEP

b. 1948

Laurence Yep's first love was science fiction, but he gradually developed an interest in his Chinese ancestry. He has written poignantly about his interest in family history, especially from a child's perspective: "It may be something as simple and yet as indestructible as a weed that links us to our past and binds us to our dreams. Seed, cast into strange soil, may thrive and grow—just like children and just like their history. In fact, a child's history is about growth itself, not only in terms of the body but also in terms of consciousness. Despite all of its limitations, a child's version of history is more useful for writing than adult history." In turning to his own childhood and seeking to understand his ancestors, Yep has become one of the most distinguished writers of Chinese American literature for young people.

Born in 1948, he grew up in San Francisco, where his father, originally from China, and his mother, a Chinese American from West Virginia, owned a grocery shop. The family lived in a predominantly black neighborhood, but Yep attended a bilingual parochial school in San Francisco's Chinatown. His sense of being between two cultures drew him to science fiction, which he saw as being "about adapting." He began to write science fiction stories in high school, and he had his first story accepted when he was a freshman at Marquette University in Milwaukee. He completed his B.A. at the University of California at Santa Cruz in 1970 and, still writing stories and novellas, continued his studies in English, earning a Ph.D. in 1975 from the State University of New York at Buffalo. When he returned to California he taught briefly at San Jose City College, but he decided to concentrate on his writing.

Yep was already enjoying literary success, having published *Sweetwater* (1973), a science fiction novel for young adults. Its thirteen-year-old protagonist, a boy named Tyree, belongs to a minority group of human settlers on a distant planet; he goes against his family wishes to form a friendship through music with an old native named Amadeus, a bond that ultimately protects his family. Yep later realized that he was exploring his own feelings of alienation, and many of the book's themes—racism, family loyalty, personal freedom—would reappear in later works. He addressed his Chinese American heritage directly in his second novel, *Dragonwings* (1975), which has won widespread critical acclaim

and many awards, and which has also been adapted as a play (see the Plays section, below). Yep drew on the life of a historical Chinese American aviator, Fung Joe Guey, and on many years of research in telling this story of the dream of a Chinese immigrant named Windrider, a kite builder who wants to fly a biplane of his own construction over Oakland. Aided by his son, Moon Shadow, who at age eight comes to America to work with him in a San Francisco laundry, and by his white landlady and her young niece, he manages to overcome the prejudices of others and fly his plane. From this point on in his career, Yep began exploring the history of his relatives and of Chinese Americans generally in such works as *Child of the Owl* (1977), *The Sea Glass* (1979), *The Star Fisher* (1991), and *The Thief of Hearts* (1995). Most important are his two collections, *The Rainbow People* (1989) and *Tongues of Jade* (1991), based on tales told by Chinese immigrants in California: some were collected by Jon Lee in Oakland's Chinatown during the 1930s as part of a Works Progress Administration project and others were recorded later from San Francisco's Chinatown by the folklorist Wolfram Eberhard.

"The Phantom Heart" is taken from *Tongues of Jade*, a title that refers to an ancient Chinese practice of setting pieces of jade on the dead to preserve their bodies. Sometimes their tongues were covered with jade, and Yep's tales in this volume enable them to speak again. In this story we find a shopkeeper whose heart is initially closed and a wife whose kindness and devotion have the power to bring him back to life—motifs that are common in fairy tales throughout the world. Here they are closely tied to endeavours by many Chinese American writers to renew young readers' interest in Chinese culture.

The Phantom Heart

A long time ago there was a shopkeeper who hated children. When he and his wife couldn't have any children, he was rather relieved. But his wife talked about adopting someone. "I know you don't like children, but when we pass on, we need someone to send us food and money and all sorts of things."[1]

The shopkeeper agreed, but said that they had plenty of time and kept postponing the moment. "When you're alive, there's no profit in children. They're dirty, noisy,

1. Traditionally, Chinese families honor dead relatives with offerings of food, drink, and paper "money," which is burned so that the dead may use it in the afterlife; paper representations of other goods may be burned as well.

wasteful creatures. And when you're dead, you're lucky if the ungrateful little things remember their duty."

His wife sighed in exasperation. "That's what I get for being married to the most practical man in the world."

"I am what I am," the shopkeeper insisted firmly, "and I don't pretend to be any more."

Then one day when he left their house and went down to open up their shop, a little girl walked by, bearing a huge basket of fruit. As she trudged along, tears fell from her eyes.

"What's wrong?" the shopkeeper asked her.

She whirled like some startled bird, stared at him a moment, and then ran away as fast as she could with her burden of fruit.

The sad little girl made him feel as if there were truly something missing from his life. Finally, he slapped the side of his head and tried to laugh. "You're getting as flighty as a poet," he scolded himself. "Get ahold of yourself."

However, the rest of that day he went about his chores with only half a mind. He could not forget that sad little face. He spent the rest of the day puzzling over the girl. Why was she so sad? What was the poor thing afraid of?

And the shopkeeper, who prided himself upon being so sensible and down-to-earth, lay awake all night pondering the mystery that had stumbled into his life.

When he and his wife got up the next day, she studied him, worried. "You look like something the cat dragged in. Didn't you sleep well?"

"I had a lot on my mind," he mumbled.

She clicked her tongue. "I'll go to the herbalist and get some tea to help you sleep."

He was irritable from lack of sleep. "You think teas can solve everything!" he snapped at his startled wife.

He dressed quickly and ate a breakfast of cold rice and tea and hurried to his shop. Again he saw the little girl, and again she was crying. "What's wrong?" he asked her. "Is it indigestion?"

Fearfully, she looked all around as if she were afraid of being spied upon. Then, still weeping, she scurried away.

The third morning the sorrowful girl appeared at the same time as the other two days. Once more, she looked around with that sad, frightened face and almost stepped inside his shop. But fear made her stop and turn to go.

Just as she was leaving, the shopkeeper ran out of his shop. "Wait," he called. The little girl would have run like some frightened deer, but he caught her hand. "I've watched you for three mornings now. What's troubling you?"

She gazed at the shopkeeper and clasped his hand as if she were drowning. "You have such a kind face, I think you truly want to hear." Tears streamed from her eyes. "My parents were poor farmers. When they could no longer feed me, they sold me to a rich man. They did not want to, but it was either that or watch me starve. They couldn't know the rich man and his wife are cruel people. No matter how hard I try, I never satisfy them, and they beat me every day. I can't stand it anymore."

The shopkeeper was touched. "Perhaps we can find someone to buy your freedom."

"They are so disgusted with me, they say they would sell me for a handful of cash. But I don't even have that." The girl wept even harder, her hot tears falling upon his hand.

"Well, I do," the shopkeeper said. "Where do they live? I'll talk to them."

The girl bowed respectfully. "Lord, if you should go to them, they would ask far too much. However, if I were to break a few things today, they would be ready to kick me out. Then I might pretend the money is my life savings and buy my freedom."

The shopkeeper went inside and came out a moment later with a string of cash. "Take this, and good luck," he said.

Crying, the girl thanked him for his generosity and left. Idly, as he stared at the back of his hand, which was still moist with her tears, he realized what he had done. "Great Heavens. I've just given away money."

Stunned, he returned to his little shop and sat down on a stool. "She's probably some little thief who cheats fools like me. Well, I deserve it. Such nonsense is for shopkeepers as well as for poets. So the lesson is cheap at the price." And he had a good laugh at himself.

However, that very afternoon, the girl walked into his shop and presented herself. "Thank you. Now I'll work off my debt to you."

"But you're free," the shopkeeper protested.

The girl clutched the small basket of her belongings. "Did you ever think of what I was to do once I was free? Do you want me to become a beggar on the roads?"

"Of course not," the shopkeeper said, and scratched his head. "But what do I tell my wife?"

The girl looked around the little shop and then back at the shopkeeper. "She's the wife of a prosperous merchant—an important man in the town. It's time she started living like the wife of a man of substance. She shouldn't be doing the cooking and the washing and the cleaning. She should have a maid."

The shopkeeper was glad that the clever girl had given him an excuse, but his wife was annoyed when he repeated it to her. "We don't have any room," she told him.

"There's a long, narrow closet that I've been using as a storeroom. She can sleep there," the shopkeeper said hastily.

"I'll hire my own maid." His wife sniffed and went down to the store with every intention of firing the girl. However, when she saw how small and young she was, she softened. "She's hardly more than a baby," she whispered to her husband. "Let's see how good a maid she is."

The girl proved as respectful as anyone could ask and did everything promptly and smartly. And she seemed to be exactly what she claimed to be: someone who was grateful to have a kind master and mistress.

The shopkeeper grew quite contented with himself for his good deed. Lately, he found himself sitting more and more. "I must be growing old," he said to himself. "It's good to have young legs around."

Then one day, when he was walking through town on an errand, he heard the fish clapper of a monk. A fish clapper was a kind of wooden knocker in the shape of a fish. Feeling especially virtuous, the shopkeeper stopped and took out some cash.

The monk stood there in an old yellow robe. Though his head was shaved, the elderly man had a wispy gray beard. As the shopkeeper made a show of putting the cash into the monk's begging bowl, the monk dropped his clapper and seized the man's wrist.

"Let me repay your kindness," the monk said. "People's faces are like pages in a book to me, and I can read their futures."

The shopkeeper, who liked to get his money's worth, told the monk to go ahead, but after a moment the monk sighed and shook his head. "You're going to die very soon."

Frightened, the shopkeeper felt his cheeks and jaws. "What's wrong with my face?"

"You're living with a monster," the monk stated calmly. "And the monster will kill you and make your ghost into its slave."

"But I live with my wife and our maid," the shopkeeper protested. "I've been with my wife for years without any trouble."

"Then it must be the maid," the monk said. "How have you been feeling lately?"

"I've been a little tired," the shopkeeper admitted, "but that's because I've been so busy in the shop."

The monk could feel the veins and arteries in the shopkeeper's wrist. "Your pulse is irregular. She's draining you. Beware of her." Releasing the shopkeeper, the monk picked up his clapper and started on.

The shopkeeper stood in a daze as he listened to the knocking of the clapper gradually fade into the distance. He didn't know whether to believe the monk or not, but the monk had been so certain.

I'll ask her who her former master and mistress were, he said to himself. Then I can check up on her story and have a good laugh about that old monk.

Determined to prove his maid innocent, he returned home. As it happened, his wife was also out of the house. When the shopkeeper went to the maid's room, he found the door locked. From inside, there came an odd cackling sound. Puzzled, he sneaked around to the rear of the building.

The windows were of translucent rice paper in a frame of bamboo. Wetting his finger, he rubbed it against the rice paper so it became almost transparent. Then he peeked inside.

Horrified, he saw a monster inside with long white hair flowing like withered old moss down its back to the floor. Wicked-looking fangs thrust out of its lower jaw, and its sunken eyes were as large as saucers and glowed a fiery red. When it raised a hand, he saw nails as long and sharp as daggers. Carefully the creature smoothed out a crisp roll of parchment. But as it unrolled on the floor, the shopkeeper realized it was not parchment at all but a human skin.

Dipping a long nail into a pot of ink, the creature smoothed out the skin and began to scratch out the outline of a human being. Once it had put in all the features, the monster sketched clothing over the human picture. Then it carefully picked up the painted skin, stretched it out, and put it on. Almost at once, the skin fitted itself snugly to the monster like a glove over a hand. And where the monster had once stood was now the young girl.

Horrified, the shopkeeper rounded up some of his neighbors and stormed into his own house, where the maid was calmly preparing lunch.

"You must go," he commanded.

The girl tried to take his hand. "Have I displeased you?"

"I order you out of this house," the shopkeeper insisted.

"I don't want to leave you," the girl insisted.

No matter how the girl protested, the shopkeeper refused to listen. Instead, he and his neighbors forced her out of the house. Packing up her few belongings, he dumped them outside and added a packet of money in the hopes of buying her off.

"Here, you can go anywhere now. Just leave my wife and me alone."

As he watched the little girl leave weeping so piteously, the shopkeeper almost changed his mind, but he reminded himself again of what he had seen. Once she was out of sight, he thanked his neighbors and locked up both his house and shop.

Naturally his strange behavior was the talk of the street, so his wife heard all about it before she actually unlocked their door and stepped inside.

The shopkeeper told her everything about the monster. "I was a fool," he confessed. "Can you ever forgive me for bringing that thing into the house?"

It was the first time she could remember her hard, practical husband ever apologizing. "With all my heart," she said, and stroked his cheek gently.

That night they locked up the house and shop tight, but nothing happened. However, the next night, a storm roared through the town. The wind shook the roofs like a wild animal while the rain clawed at the windows. Listening to the storm howl, he thought of the monk's prophecy that the monster would kill him. Frightened, the shopkeeper rolled over and put his arms around his wife. She asked him what was wrong; but the shopkeeper, who had once been hard-nosed, was now so afraid that he couldn't even utter a squeak. He could only hold on more tightly to his wife.

The storm returned the third night worse than ever. The rain crashed against the house like an ocean wave, and the roaring wind battered at the house like a giant bull. The house itself began to rock on its foundations like a ship in a stormy sea. Again, the shopkeeper clutched at his wife, and she tried to soothe him, though she herself felt afraid.

However, they had slept little the previous night, and so, even as frightened as they were, they eventually fell asleep despite the storm. As they lay now, side by side, the wind rose to a triumphant roar as it rocked the house back and forth.

Under cover of the storm, a little figure slid underneath the locked door. Darting across the floor, it jumped on top of the shopkeeper. With a quick slash of its claws, it laid open his chest and cut out his heart.

The next morning when the wife woke up and saw what had happened to her husband, she rushed out into the street, but before she could wake their neighbors, she saw the old monk.

The old monk scrutinized her face. "The fool is dead," he said. "Just as I predicted." Remembering her husband's story, the woman fell on her knees. "Yes, he is, but I beg you to help him." And she began to weep as she pleaded for her husband.

Touched by her love, the old monk sighed regretfully. "I'm afraid the monster's power is greater than mine." He pointed to a mountain. "But there is a master who lives upon that peak with enough magic to control even that monster." He paused and added, "It is a long journey, though."

"I would walk through fire," the wife insisted.

"And you must do whatever the master asks, no matter what," the monk warned.

"I will do whatever I need to do to save my husband," the wife promised.

Shutting up their house and shop, the woman set out at once. Following the monk's directions, she climbed the steep path, though her lungs and legs both ached. When she reached a waterfall, she turned right and entered into a little clearing. Just before the wet rocks was a dirty, ragged old beggar squatting on a boulder with his head tilted back, sunning himself like an old turtle.

"Is the master in?" she asked politely.

The old beggar did not even open his eyes. "I am the master, and I know why you came." When he scratched himself under his shirt, dirt pattered down in a little shower. "Will you do as I say?"

"Yes," the wife promised.

The old beggar kept scratching himself until he had a ball of dirt in his hands. "Then eat this."

The wife stared at the disgusting lump in his clawlike hand. "I don't know if I can."

"Then you don't want my help," the beggar said, and threw it on the ground.

Gathering up her courage, the woman knelt and picked up the lump gingerly.

"Eat it, eat it, eat it!" the beggar began to chant.

Closing her eyes, she swallowed it in one gulp so as not to taste it.

From the boulder, the old beggar began to laugh crazily, but when she opened her eyes, he had slipped to the ground and was dashing up the rocky slope.

"Come back," she called after him. "You said you would help."

However, the old beggar, still cackling insanely, disappeared from view. The woman rose heavily. "He's no master—just some crazy old man playing a practical joke."

Discouraged, she made the long return journey to town. Plodding wearily into the bedroom, she knelt beside her husband. Instantly, her stomach began to cramp. "I tried to save you, but I couldn't," she apologized to her husband. "And now I'm sick."

She knelt there, weeping as she mourned for her husband, when suddenly the cramps grew more violent. Suddenly a warm object dropped out of her mouth. When she looked at it, she saw it was a heart.

"The old beggar did keep his promise," the wife said. Scooping up the heart, she set it carefully within her husband's chest. Instantly, the corpse began to twitch. Springing to her feet, the woman got her sewing basket. Taking out a needle and thread, she quickly sewed the heart into the chest.

For three days and nights, the shopkeeper lay there in the room, every now and then moving a limb or writhing on his back. On the fourth day, he woke and smiled up gratefully at his wife.

She fed him warm broth and bit by bit nursed him back to health. Even so, the slightest noise would wake him at night. "I keep thinking the monster will come back to fetch my new heart."

One day, the shopkeeper met the monk. After giving him a generous donation, the shopkeeper thanked him for all his advice and then confessed his anxieties.

"The monster will most certainly be back," the monk agreed. "Your wife had better journey to the mountain again and ask the master for his help a second time."

So the wife set out once more. When she met the old beggar by the falls, she begged for his help once more.

This time, he was as calm and reasonable as anybody on the street. From inside his ragged clothes, he pulled out a small black sack. Pasted on the sack was a red sign with magical words written on it. "Open this when you see the monster; and when you've caught it, burn the creature, sack, paper, and charm."

Thanking the beggar, the wife returned to her husband. For three nights, they sat up anxiously, waiting for the monster to come. Then on the fourth, the storm came. The wind rattled the roof tiles, and sheets of water drummed against the windows.

And at the height of the storm, the little figure slipped under the door once again. As it started to race across the floor, the woman held up the little black sack toward the monster. Instantly, a hand shot out of the sack, stretching across the floor on a rubbery arm that never seemed to end.

With a tiny shriek, the monster tried to turn and run, but too late. The hand snatched up the creature and pulled it back inside the sack. Immediately, the shopkeeper and his wife took it down to the kitchen, where they had the stove all prepared. Lighting the fire, they threw the sack into it.

Monster, sack, and hand disappeared in a burst of fire. As the ashes went whirling outside, the storm stopped instantly.

High on his mountaintop, the beggar had stood waiting. Now he cupped his dirty palms together and gathered the ashes, burying them in a special spot he had picked out on the mountain.

Whether it was his new heart or gratitude to his wife, the shopkeeper didn't argue when she said she wanted to adopt a baby. To his shock, he found he rather liked being a father and suggested they adopt another one.

His surprised wife stared at him. "What's gotten into you?"

"I can't give you a practical reason why," he said, and tapped his chest. "It must be this new heart. I don't think it works right."

But, in fact, it was working quite well.

1991

MICHAEL LACAPA
b. 1955

Like Robert Munsch, Michael Lacapa is a gifted storyteller; he has used his talents as an artist to also illustrate traditional tales of Native Americans in the Southwest. Born in Phoenix, he was one year old when his family moved to Whiteriver, Arizona, a town inside the Fort Apache Indian Reservation. He grew up the second of eight children of Hopi, Tewa, and Apache ancestry. As a young boy, he loved to draw, and after studying secondary art education at Arizona State University, he did graduate work in printmaking at Northern Arizona University. He taught for a few years in Phoenix, at the Phoenix Indian and Chaparral high schools, but he left to help the Apache tribe develop multicultural educational curricula for Native children. The project viewed storytelling as a teaching tool, and it was at this time that Lacapa coauthored and illustrated his first book, *Ndee Benagode'i* (*Three Stories of the White Mountain Apache Tribe*, 1981). From 1982 to 1984, he taught at Whiteriver Elementary School, where he continued to hone his skills as a storyteller. He began illustrating and sometimes writing tales—*Mouse Couple: A Hopi Folktale* (1988), retold by Ekkehart Malotki; *Flute Player: An Apache Folktale* (1990); *Magic Hummingbird: A Hopi Folktale* (1996), translated by Ekkehart Malotki, narrated by Michael Lomatuway'ma; *Quest for the Eagle Feather* (1997), by John Dunklee; and others—drawn directly from Native tradition. With his wife, Kathleen, he wrote *Less Than Half, More Than Whole* (1994), which deals with problems of identity faced by children from multicultural backgrounds. Michael Lacapa's teaching of art and his storytelling are no longer limited to the classroom, as he spends a good deal of time participating in programs and conventions around the country.

Antelope Woman: An Apache Folktale (1992), which Lacapa both wrote and illustrated, reflects the great reverence that the Apaches have for all things in nature, big and small. The magical transformation of the young woman is both fortunate and unfortunate, for it leads to a rupture between her people and nature. Lacapa mourns the loss of Native tradition while insisting on the need to recapture spiritual reverence. Like many writers seeking to convey non-European traditions, Lacapa simultaneously returns to the oral folktale and clearly uses motifs taken from literary fairy tales, thereby highlighting the interconnections between the oral and literary traditions.

Antelope Woman: An Apache Folktale

"Listen, my son. As we go to hunt today, let me tell you of the people who lived here long ago and why we honor all things around us, great and small.

"Here in this valley, the people lived, and among the people was a beautiful young woman, a strong worker. She knew how to gather berries early in the morning and how to gather wood for her family. She also knew how to make strong baskets. You see, she was very special.

"Young men from other villages would come to see her and try to get her attention by walking in front of her with their horses, bows and arrows, and colorful shirts and shoes. But they did not interest her.

"One day, a young man who was not like the other young men came to the village. He came to talk to all the people in the village.

"He went to the men, sat down, and began telling them of ways in which to hunt and protect their families. He said, 'When hunting, remember to respect all things great and small.' In the evening, he left.

"The next morning, when the young woman got up to gather wood and berries, she saw the young man helping an elderly man make a bow. He said, 'This is how to make it stronger and, remember, as you hunt with this bow, respect all things great and small.' The older man agreed, and the young woman too. Later that evening, the young man left the village. No one knew when he left or where he had gone.

"The next day, he returned. The young woman saw him helping a woman carry water from the river. As they walked, the young man told the woman, 'We must even honor the water, for it flows down from the mountains to nourish the plants. It nourishes our brothers, the animals. It also nourishes us, the people. We must respect all things great and small.'

"The young woman knew that when the young man left the village that day she would follow him and watch where he went. As he walked from the village at the end of the day, he knew the young woman had been watching him, and he let her follow. Soon, he came to a patch of bushes and trees. There, he disappeared. The young woman ran quickly to see where he had gone.

"Just as she reached the trees, she saw him jump through four hoops, and then something happened.

"Looking back at her, the young man nodded, but she noticed he was not a man anymore. He was an antelope. He motioned for her to follow him, and she did.

"She began to go through the hoops, one after another. As she jumped through the fourth one, she felt herself changed.

"Then the young man told her, 'You must come with me. I will teach you so you too can tell the people to honor all things great and small.'

"The young man and woman walked to a pool of deep water. On the far side of the water were more antelope, who began talking to the young man in a different language. For, you see, they were his people, the antelope. The young woman felt thirsty and began to drink. As she looked into the water, she saw her reflection. She was no longer a woman but an antelope. The young man said, 'You must come with me. I will show you why we must be thankful for all things.'

"Then he called to her, 'Come here quickly. Quickly!' Suddenly all of the antelope were running. They ran until they came to a patch of prickly pear cactus and then they ran through it. The young woman was surprised to find she could somehow step through the prickly pear without hurting her feet. She looked behind her and saw the coyote who had been chasing them. He looked hungry and angry because he could not get to them through the cactus. The young man said to her, 'See, we must be thankful for the sharp prickly pear because it gives us protection from those who wish to have us. It is good to honor all things great and small.'

"After the coyote left, the young woman was happy—and thankful. When the herd began running again, quickly and gracefully, she was thankful that she, too, could run and jump across the plain, through the high grass, and over bushes and small trees. Then she thought of her family. Her family! While learning about things for which to be thankful, she had forgotten her family and her people. She said to the young man, 'We must return to the people and share this knowledge with them.' The young man agreed.

"The next day, they returned through the hoops, were changed back into people, and entered the village. The young man carried with him many gifts—deer hides, jewelry, beads, corn, bows and arrows, and many colorful stones. He brought these gifts for the young woman's family, for he was to marry her.

"The young woman's mother was excited to see her daughter, for, you see, time had passed, and the people had been very worried about her. She told her parents that she and the young man were to be married. The family agreed by accepting his gifts. Soon the young couple married and stayed in the village.

"The people were happy, for the young man showed them many things that would help them through the long, cold winters and the hot, dry summers. He showed them ways to live and ways to learn. During this time, the young woman became pregnant and gave birth. The young man was proud of his children, a boy and a girl.[1] But because they were twins, the people did not accept them.

"The young couple felt sad and began to talk. The young father said, 'Remember when we ran together with my family? It was special. You knew at that time it was important to honor the family. Now you must honor our family by going where we will be accepted. We are not like your people, and they do not accept us. My people will accept us because they have learned how to honor the family and all things great and small.'

"With that, the young mother agreed. She told her parents that she would have to go with her husband to his village. The people watched the young family walk to the place of the four hoops. After the young couple passed through the hoops, they were never seen again.

"Since then, we have learned to honor all things great and small. So today, my son, we honor the antelope by never hunting or killing them. For out there among the antelope are Antelope Woman and her children and they are a part of us. Now as we hunt, my son, we must be thankful to the creator, who gives us all things great and small and who teaches us to honor them all.

"Shí goshk'án dasjaá."

(*The story ends here.*)

1995

1. Antelope usually give birth to two fawns.

TEXTS AND CONTEXTS

Little Red Riding Hood

Most of the classic fairy tales for children in the Western world have a long history connected to an oral tradition of storytelling. The most important ones have evolved through an intricate and complicated interaction of distinct narratives, as themes, plots, and characters have been appropriated and reappropriated. More specifically, each tale has its own discursive history, determined by writers, audience expectations, and its conditions of production and dissemination. What the tales signify is much debated, and those debates have come to greatly affect the socialization of children. By focusing on the case of "Little Red Riding Hood," we can see more clearly how "Cinderella," "Snow White," "Sleeping Beauty," and all the other prominent fairy tales have played a major role in Western civilization.

Anthropologists, folklorists, and historians long maintained that the plot of "Little Red Riding Hood" derived from ancient myths about sunrise and sunset. The protagonist's red garment was associated with the sun, and the wolf was considered to be the personification of darkness. Other scholars viewed the tale as an offshoot of legends about being swallowed alive, which hark back to the story of Jonah and the whale. Still others saw it as a traditional Manichaean myth about the forces of darkness seeking to engulf the purity of Christian goodness. In the past thirty years, however, research has convincingly demonstrated that "Little Red Riding Hood" is of fairly modern vintage. Here *modern* means that the basic elements of the tale were developed in an oral tradition during the late Middle Ages (largely in France, Tirol, and northern Italy), and they gave rise to a widespread group of warning and initiation tales intended for children and adults. These undoubtedly influenced Charles Perrault's literary version of 1697, which for many years had been thought to be an entirely original work. We now know that Perrault did not invent the plot and characters of "Little Red Riding Hood" but borrowed elements from popular folklore, recreating the tale to suit the needs of an upper-class audience whose social and aesthetic standards differed from those of the common folk.

Perrault probably drew on stories about werewolves that were circulating in Touraine when his mother grew up there. Though we cannot be sure precisely what folktale Perrault heard, French folklorists have concluded that it most likely was similar to one collected in 1885 titled "The Story of Grandmother":

> There was a woman who had made some bread. She said to her daughter: "Go carry this hot loaf and bottle of milk to your granny."
>
> So the little girl departed. At the crossway she met *bzou*, the werewolf, who said to her: "Where are you going?"
>
> "I'm taking this hot loaf and a bottle of milk to my granny."
>
> "What path are you taking," said the werewolf, "the path of needles or the path of pins?"
>
> "The path of needles," the little girl said.
>
> "All right, then I'll take the path of pins."
>
> The little girl entertained herself by gathering needles. Meanwhile the werewolf arrived at the grandmother's house, killed her, put some of her flesh in the cupboard and a bottle of her blood on the shelf. The little girl arrived and knocked at the door.
>
> "Push the door,' said the werewolf, "It's barred by a piece of wet straw."
>
> "Good day, Granny. I've brought you a hot loaf of bread and a bottle of milk."
>
> "Put it in the cupboard, my child. Take some of the meat which is inside and the bottle of wine on the shelf."
>
> After she had eaten, there was a little cat which said: "Phooey! . . . A slut is she who eats the flesh and drinks the blood of her granny."
>
> "Undress yourself, my child," the werewolf said, "and come lie down beside me."
>
> "Where should I put my apron?"
>
> "Throw it into the fire, my child, you won't be needing it anymore."
>
> And each time she asked where she should put all her other clothes, the bodice, the dress, the petticoat, and the long stockings, the wolf responded:
>
> "Throw them into the fire, my child, you won't be needing them anymore."
>
> When she laid herself down in the bed, the little girl said: "Oh, Granny, how hairy you are!"
>
> "The better to keep myself warm, my child!"
>
> "Oh, Granny, what big nails you have!"
>
> "The better to scratch me with, my child!"
>
> "Oh, Granny, what big shoulders you have!"
>
> "The better to carry the firewood, my child!"

"Oh, Granny, what big ears you have!"

"The better to hear you with, my child!"

"Oh, Granny, what big nostrils you have!"

"The better to snuff my tobacco with, my child!"

"Oh, Granny, what a big mouth you have!"

"The better to eat you with, my child!"

"Oh, Granny, I've got to go badly. Let me go outside."

"Do it in bed, my child!"

"Oh, no, Granny, I want to go outside."

"All right, but make it quick."

The werewolf attached a woolen rope to her foot and let her go outside.

When the little girl was outside, she tied the end of the rope to a plum tree in the courtyard. The werewolf became impatient and said: "Are you making a load out there? Are you making a load?"

When he realized that nobody was answering him, he jumped out of bed and saw that the little girl had escaped. He followed her but arrived at her house just at the moment she entered.

The direct precursors of Perrault's literary tale were influenced not by sun worship or Christian theology but by the very material conditions of their tellers' existence and by traditional pagan superstitions. Young people were sometimes attacked and killed in the woods and fields by animals as well as by human predators. Hunger drove people to atrocious acts. In the fifteenth and sixteenth centuries, rational explanations of violence were scarce. Peasants instead strongly believed that nature contained uncontrollable magical forces, including werewolves and witches that threatened their lives. Since antiquity, tales had been spread about vicious creatures in France. Consequently, the warning tale became part of a stock oral repertoire of storytellers. No doubt then, as now, the teller often seized a nearby child when pronouncing the climactic line in the well-known dialogue between girl and werewolf / wolf—"The better to eat you with!"—thereby delighting listeners by enabling them to triumph over their momentary terror. Indeed, it seems that in most folktale versions the little girl also triumphs: rather than being killed, she shrewdly outwits the wolf and saves herself with no help from granny, hunter, or father.

Clearly, the folktale does more than convey a warning, for it also celebrates a young girl's coming of age. The pins and needles mentioned in the version quoted above were related to the apprenticeship in needlework undergone by young peasant girls; it began at puberty and marked their initiation into society in specific regions of France where the oral tale was common. The story thus depicts self-assertion through learning and conflict. Unlike in the literary versions, which reduce the grandmother to a meaningless object, her death in the folktale signifies the continuity of custom through her granddaughter, who symbolically replaces her by eating her flesh and drinking her blood.

Perrault's changes were substantive in both style and content. He appealed to sophisticated adult readers by enabling them to understand the tale as a naughty story of seduction, while younger readers could still enjoy its warning aspect and interplay between the wolf and Little Red Riding Hood (with the verse moral a didactic anticlimax). Perrault's great artistic achievement was to appropriate folk motifs, imbue them with a different ideological content, and stylize the elements in ways that made them more acceptable to upper-class audiences. Rather than referring to specific aspects of villagers' lives, Perrault's literary version treated issues of vanity, power, and seduction, and it introduced a new figure: the helpless girl who unconsciously enables her own violation or rape. While the alleged cruelty and coarseness of the oral tale were gone, the literary tale's refinements contributed to an image of Little Red Riding Hood that was to make her life considerably more difficult.

The process initiated by Perrault gave rise to further oral and literary versions within Western cultures. Perrault's version was pivotal. Before it, there was a separate oral tradition, shaped by peasants (most likely women). But once Perrault had appropriated the story and reshaped it to the tastes of a largely female audience of the upper class, it became practically impossible for oral storytellers or for other writers not to take his text into account. Thus storytellers and writers became the conveyors of both the oral and literary tradition of this particular tale.

The crucial point here is that though the debate over Little Red Riding Hood and her destiny has been volatile, the ground rules for this multifaceted discourse were determined by Perrault, who set the direction taken by almost all the hundreds of subsequent writers, storytellers, and illustrators engaging with this tale. Because of its generality, ambiguity, and clever sexual innuendoes, "Little Red Riding Hood"—like many other fairy tales written by Perrault, such as "Cinderella," "Puss in Boots," "Bluebeard," and "Sleeping Beauty"—was reabsorbed by the oral folk tradition. Its enormous success and massive circulation in print in the eighteenth and nineteenth centuries made it highly influential. One result was the creation of the even more popular Grimms' tale, which in its turn also shaped both the oral and literary traditions.

After Perrault's tale was translated into English in 1729, it was constantly reprinted in chapbooks, broadsheets, and collections of children's tales. Eventually it made its way to America, where it became extremely popular. Aside from the Grimms' "Little Red Cap" in *Kinder- und Hausmärchen* (*Children's and Household Tales*, 1812–15), some of the more important versions in the nineteenth century were F. W. N. Bayley's "Little Red Riding Hood" (1846), Richard Henry Stoddard's *The Story of Little Red Riding Hood* (1864), Charles Marelle's "The True History of Little Golden-hood" (1888), Andrew Lang's rendition of Perrault's "Little Red Riding Hood" in *The Blue Fairy Book* (1889), and Sabine Baring-Gould's "Little Red Riding-Hood" (1895). In addition, numerous anonymous collections of tales and picture books featured Little Red Riding Hood. By the end of the nineteenth century such great illustrators as Gustav Doré and Walter Crane had made their mark, and hundreds of other artists imitated them or contributed their own unusual designs.

In the twentieth century the treatments of "Little Red Riding Hood" expanded vastly, both in approach—from parody to tragedy to serious commentary—and in medium. In cartoon, radio play, commercial, and beyond, the encounter of Little Red Riding Hood with the wolf in the woods has been represented and reflected on. Among the more significant text and illustrated versions for children are Walter de la Mare, "Little Red Riding Hood" (1927); James Thurber, "The Girl and the Wolf" (1939); Catherine Storr, "Little Polly Riding Hood" (1955); Merseyside Fairy Story Collective, "Red Riding Hood" (1972); Tomi Ungerer, "Little Red Riding Hood" (1974); Tony Ross, *Little Red Hood: A Classic Story Bent out of Shape* (1979); Michael Emberley, *Ruby* (1990); Lisa Campbell Ernst, *Little Red Riding Hood: A Newfangled Prairie Tale* (1995); Susan Lowell, *Little Red Cowboy Hat* (1997); Lauren Child, *Beware of the Storybook Wolves* (2001); Francesca Lia Block, "Wolf" (2000); and Neal Gilbertsen, *Little Red Snapperhood: A Fishy Fairy Tale* (2003).

Many of the published versions of "Little Red Riding Hood" are hackwork: picture books and stories in fairy-tale collections written and illustrated by mediocre writers and artists, often dumbed down and sanitized in the belief that children are too sensitive to tolerate exposure to more robust adaptations unharmed. The more serious approaches include the diverse perspectives offered by advocates of feminism, Jungian theory, Marxism, animal rights, Freudianism, and multiculturalism. There is no end in sight to our engagement with Little Red Riding Hood, and clearly more surprises about her fate are in store for future generations of adults as well as children.

CHARLES PERRAULT
1628–1703

As the first literary version of "Little Red Riding Hood," Charles Perrault's story engendered a mammoth international debate about the cruel fate of a little girl who foolishly talks to a wolf and strays from a path, and whether she deserves such a horrid punishment. It was originally published in *Histoires ou contes du temps passé* (*Histories or Tales of Times Past* 1697), with the French title "Le petit chaperon rouge" (literally, "Little Red Cap"); Robert Samber translated it into English in 1729 as "Little Red Riding Hood." This name has stuck in English just as the classic story is constantly retold in more or less the same fashion with a poor naive girl always eaten by a wolf. However, the ravaging of the grandmother and girl depicted by Perrault as a warning to "proper" girls may not have been characteristic of the original tale. In many of the oral tales, including the one reprinted in the introduction to this section, a peasant girl goes through the woods to her grandmother's as a test of her maturity. On the way she meets a werewolf, who arrives at her grandmother's house before her. After being given "meat" and "wine" that is in fact her grandmother's flesh and blood, the girl gets into bed naked with the werewolf—whom she tricks into allowing her to escape. She runs home safely, proving that she is clever and courageous and can hold her own with wolves.

Perrault obviously had a different view. His version is addressed to upper-class young women, and he places the blame for the grandmother's and Little Red Riding Hood's violation on the girl, as the moral at the end of his tale makes clear. His was the very first literary text about the conflict between innocent girls and predatory wolves. As such, it began a major debate within the discourse of fairy tales about gender conflict, bestial behavior, and the need to curb violence. Perrault's story, which compresses so much loaded meaning in its terse language and brief action, has become one of the world's best-known fairy tales, interpreted variously as a positive tale of warning, a sexist depiction of stupid girls, an erotic assignation enjoyed by girl and wolf, and more.

Little Red Riding Hood

Once upon a time, there was a little village girl, the prettiest that had ever been seen. Her mother doted on her, and her grandmother even more. This good woman made her a little red hood[1] which suited her so well that she was called Little Red Riding Hood wherever she went.

One day, after her mother had baked some biscuits, she said to Little Red Riding Hood, "Go see how your grandmother's feeling. I've heard that she's sick. You can take her some biscuits and this small pot of butter."

Little Red Riding Hood departed at once to visit her grandmother, who lived in another village. In passing through the forest she met old neighbor wolf, who had a great desire to eat her. But he did not dare because of some woodcutters who were in the forest. He asked her where she was going, and the poor child, who did not know that it is dangerous to stop and listen to a wolf, said to him, "I'm going to see my grandmother, and I'm bringing her some biscuits with a small pot of butter that my mother's sending her."

"Does she live far from here?" the wolf asked.

"Oh, yes!" Little Red Riding Hood said. "You've got to go by the mill, which you can see right over there, and hers is the first house in the village."

"Well, then," said the wolf, "I'll go and see her, too. You take that path there, and I'll take this path here, and we'll see who'll get there first."

The wolf began to run as fast as he could on the path that was shorter, and the little girl took the longer path, and she enjoyed herself by gathering nuts, running after butterflies, and making bouquets of small flowers that she found along the way. It did not take the wolf long to arrive at the grandmother's house, and he knocked:

"Tic, toc."

"Who's there?"

"It's your granddaughter, Little Red Riding Hood," the wolf said, disguising his voice. "I've brought you some biscuits and a little pot of butter that my mother's sent for you."

The good grandmother, who was in her bed because she was not feeling well, cried out to him, "Pull the bobbin, and the latch will fall."

The wolf pulled the bobbin, and the door opened. He pounced on the good woman and devoured her quicker than a wink, for it had been more than three days since he had eaten last. After that he closed the door and lay down in the grandmother's bed to wait for Little Red Riding Hood, who after a while came knocking at the door:

"Toc, toc."

"Who's there?"

When she heard the gruff voice of the wolf, Little Red Riding Hood was scared at

---

1. The French here and in the title is "petit chaperon rouge," which literally means "little red cap"; *chaperon* was misleadingly rendered "riding hood" in the first English translation of 1729, and the phrase has stuck ever since. This little cap was worn by bourgeois women and girls of the period, and Perrault used it to identify the girl with the bourgeoisie (or with aspirations toward that class). Another layer of complexity is added by the idiomatic expression *grand chaperon*, which refers to an older matron who is supposed to escort young women. That Little Red Riding Hood has only a *petit chaperon* suggests that she lacks sufficient protection. The cap's color is obviously highly significant. Red is associated not only with blood, thus signifying menstruation or a girl's sexual coming-of-age, but also with the devil. In the Middle Ages and Reformation, social nonconformists and outcasts were stigmatized by being forced to wear a red hat or some red symbol.

first, but she thought her grandmother had a cold and responded, "It's your grand-daughter, Little Red Riding Hood. I've brought you some biscuits and a little pot of butter that my mother's sent for you."

The wolf softened his voice and cried out to her, "Pull the bobbin, and the latch will fall."

Little Red Riding Hood pulled the bobbin, and the door opened.

Upon seeing her enter, the wolf hid himself under the bedcovers and said to her, "Put the biscuits and the pot of butter on the bin and come lie down beside me."

Little Red Riding Hood undressed and went to get into bed, where she was quite astonished to see the way her grandmother was dressed in her nightgown, and she said to her, "What big arms you have, grandmother!"

"The better to hug you with, my child."

"What big legs you have, grandmother!"

"The better to run with, my child."

"What big ears you have, grandmother!"

"The better to hear you with, my child."

"What big eyes you have, grandmother!"

"The better to see you with, my child."

"What big teeth you have, grandmother!"

"The better to eat you with."

And upon saying these words, the wicked wolf pounced on Little Red Riding Hood and ate her up.

Moral

One sees here that young children,
Especially pretty girls,
Polite, well-taught, and pure as pearls,
Should stay on guard against all sorts of men.
For if one fails to stay alert, it won't be strange
To see one eaten by a wolf enraged.
I say a wolf since not all types are wild,
Or can be said to be the same in kind.
Some are winning and have sharp minds.
Some are loud or smooth or mild.
Others appear just kind and unriled.
They follow young ladies wherever they go,
Right into the halls of their very own homes.
Alas for those who've refused the truth:
Sweetest tongue has the sharpest tooth.

JACOB GRIMM *and* WILHELM GRIMM
1785–1863   *1786–1859*

More sympathetic to Little Red Riding Hood than Charles Perrault and less prone to do her violence, Jacob and Wilhelm Grimm made some very important changes in the literary tradition of the narrative. Yet they preserved the basic tendency of blaming the girl for her violation. Their treatment of "Little Red Riding Hood" is "Rotkäppchen," which exactly translates Perrault's French "little red cap," and there is no doubt that the Grimms knew the French text. However, they were also influenced by Ludwig Tieck's dramatic tragedy, *The Life and Death of Little Red Cap* (*Leben und Tod des kleinen Rotkäppchens*, 1800), and by folktales that were becoming more widely known as they began to circulate in chapbooks. Their version, which is more quaint than Perrault's though perhaps more moralistic, was first published in *Children's and Household Tales* (*Kinder- und Hausmärchen*) in 1812, and they introduced a new character—the *Jäger*, or gamekeeper—who saves Little Red Cap and her grandmother by cutting open the belly of the wolf. They also introduced a new motif: old woman and granddaughter place stones into the wolf's belly to punish the predator and to show that they now have mastery. The Grimms added the anticlimactic story of another temptation to emphasize the importance of learning one's lesson (here, the lesson taught by a male hunter). This tale of "another wolf" is related to such other famous stories as "The Wolf and Seven Kids" and "The Three Little Pigs."

Ever since the Grimms' tale of "Little Red Riding Hood" was published, it and Perrault's story have been reprinted hundreds of thousands of times, in many different formats and variants; they have also been mixed with oral versions. Most of the adaptations have been directed at children, and they often have been somewhat sanitized—the wolf rarely succeeds in touching or gobbling up the grandmother and the naive girl. At the same time, hundreds of notable literary revisions and fractured fairy tales have used the tales framework to question gender stereotypes and the nature of sexuality.

Little Red Cap

Once upon a time there was a sweet little maiden. Whoever laid eyes upon her could not help but love her. But it was her grandmother who loved her most. She could never give the child enough. One time she made her a present, a small, red velvet cap, and since it was so becoming and the maiden insisted on always wearing it, she was called Little Red Cap.

One day her mother said to her, "Come, Little Red Cap, take this piece of cake and bottle of wine and bring them to your grandmother. She's sick and weak, and this will strengthen her. Get an early start, before it becomes hot, and when you're out in the woods, be nice and good and don't stray from the path; otherwise, you'll fall and break the glass, and your grandmother will get nothing. And when you enter her room, don't forget to say good morning, and don't go peeping into all the corners."

"I'll do just as you say," Little Red Cap promised her mother. Well, the grandmother lived out in the forest, half an hour from the village, and as soon as Little Red Cap entered the forest, she encountered the wolf. However, Little Red Cap did not know what a wicked sort of an animal he was and was not afraid of him.

"Good day, Little Cap," he said.

"Thank you kindly, wolf."

"Where are you going so early, Little Red Cap?"

"To grandmother's."

"What are you carrying under your apron?"

"Cake and wine. My grandmother's sick and weak, and yesterday we baked this so it will help her get well."

"Where does your grandmother live, Little Red Cap?"

"About a quarter of an hour from here in the forest. Her house is under the three big oak trees. You can tell it by the hazel bushes," said Little Red Cap.

The wolf thought to himself, "This tender young thing is a juicy morsel. She'll taste even better than the old woman. You've got to be real crafty if you want to catch them both." Then he walked next to Little Red Cap, and after a while he said, "Little Red Cap, just look at the beautiful flowers that are growing all around you! Why don't you look around? I believe you haven't even noticed how lovely the birds are singing. You march along as if you were going straight to school, and yet it's so delightful out here in the woods!"

Little Red Cap looked around and saw how the rays of the sun were dancing through the trees back and forth and how the woods were full of beautiful flowers. So she thought to herself, "If I bring grandmother a bunch of fresh flowers, she'd certainly like that. It's still early, and I'll arrive on time."

So she ran off the path and plunged into the woods to look for flowers. And each time she plucked one, she thought she saw another even prettier flower and ran after it, going deeper and deeper into the forest. But the wolf went straight to the grandmother's house and knocked at the door.

"Who's out there?"

"Little Red Cap. I've brought you some cake and wine. Open up."

"Just lift the latch," the grandmother called. "I'm too weak and can't get up."

The wolf lifted the latch, and the door sprang open. Then he went straight to the grandmother's bed without saying a word and gobbled her up. Next he put on her clothes and her nightcap, lay down in her bed, and drew the curtains.

Meanwhile, Little Red Cap had been running around and looking for flowers, and only when she had as many as she could carry did she remember her grandmother and continue on the way to her house again. She was puzzled when she found the door open, and as she entered the room, it seemed so strange inside that she thought, "Oh, my God, how frightened I feel today, and usually I like to be at grandmother's." She called out, "Good morning!" But she received no answer. Next she went to the bed and drew back the curtains. There lay her grandmother with her cap pulled down over her face giving her a strange appearance.

"Oh, grandmother, what big ears you have!"

"The better to hear you with."

"Oh, grandmother, what big hands you have!"

"The better to grab you with."

"Oh, grandmother, what a terribly big mouth you have!"

"The better to eat you with!"

No sooner did the wolf say that than he jumped out of bed and gobbled up poor Little Red Cap. After the wolf had satisfied his desires, he lay down in bed again, fell asleep, and began to snore very loudly. The huntsman[1] happened to be passing by the house and thought to himself, "The way the old woman's snoring, you'd better

---

1. The German term used by the Grimms is *Jäger*, a gameskeeper hired by the lord of a grand estate to patrol the grounds and forest to prevent poaching or other illegal activity. In other words, he was, among others things, a kind of policeman or security guard.

see if something's wrong." He went into the room, and when he came to the bed, he saw the wolf lying in it.

"So, I've found you at last, you old sinner," said the huntsman. "I've been looking for you a long time."

He took aim with his gun, and then it occurred to him that the wolf could have eaten the grandmother and that she could still be saved. So he did not shoot but took some scissors and started cutting open the sleeping wolf's belly. After he made a couple of cuts, he saw the little red cap shining forth, and after he made a few more cuts, the girl jumped out and exclaimed, "Oh, how frightened I was! It was so dark in the wolf's body."

Soon the grandmother came out. She was alive but could hardly breathe. Little Red Cap quickly fetched some large stones, and they filled the wolf's body with them. When he awoke and tried to run away, the stones were too heavy so he fell down at once and died.

All three were delighted. The huntsman skinned the fur from the wolf and went home with it. The grandmother ate the cake and drank the wine that Little Red Cap had brought, and soon she regained her health. Meanwhile Little Red Cap thought to herself, "Never again will you stray from the path by yourself and go into the forest when your mother has forbidden it."

There is also another tale about how Little Red Cap returned to her grandmother one day to bring some baked goods. Another wolf spoke to her and tried to entice her to leave the path, but this time Little Red Cap was on her guard. She went straight ahead and told her grandmother that she had seen the wolf, that he had wished her good day, but that he had had such a mean look in his eyes that "he would have eaten me if we hadn't been on the open road."

"Come," said the grandmother. "We'll lock the door so he can't get in."

Soon after, the wolf knocked and cried out, "Open up, grandmother. It's Little Red Cap, and I've brought you some baked goods."

But they kept quiet and did not open the door. So Grayhead circled the house several times and finally jumped on the roof. He wanted to wait till evening when Little Red Cap would go home. He intended to sneak after her and eat her up in the darkness. But the grandmother realized what he had in mind. In front of the house was a big stone trough, and she said to the child, "Fetch the bucket, Little Red Cap. I cooked sausages yesterday. Get the water they were boiled in and pour it into the trough."

Little Red Cap kept carrying the water until she had filled the big, big trough. Then the smell of sausages reached the nose of the wolf. He sniffed and looked down. Finally he stretched his neck so far that he could no longer keep his balance on the roof. He began to slip and fell right into the big trough and drowned. Then Little Red Cap went merrily on her way home, and no one harmed her.

1812

CHARLES MARELLE
1827–ca. 1892

By the end of the nineteenth century, numerous versions of "Little Red Riding Hood" were circulating in Europe and America. In France, the country of its written origins, folklorists had discovered versions with tragicomic and tragic endings, but "The True History of Little Golden-hood" belongs more to a comic tradition. Very little is known about Charles Marelle except that he was a French folklorist and writer of miscellaneous works for young readers, including *Le petit monde* (*The Little World*, 1863), *Poésie enfantines* (*Children's Poetry*, 1866), and *Contes et chants populaires français* (*Tales and Popular Songs*, 1876). His major work is *Affenschwanz* (*The Monkey's Tail*, 1880), a collection of folktales; it caught the attention of the Scottish anthropologist Andrew Lang (1844–1912), who was interested in collecting different versions of classic fairy tales and legends. He decided to publish two of Marelle's fairy tales, "The Rat Catcher" and "The True History of Little Golden-hood," in *The Red Fairy Book* (1890). Lang had begun his famous series a year earlier with *The Blue Fairy Book*; the final (twelfth) volume was *The Lilac Fairy Book* (1910). He preferred stories from the oral tradition, but most of the volumes contain literary fairy tales, rewritten and adapted in large part by many female assistants (including his wife). The books were aimed at both young and old readers.

"The True History of Little Golden-hood" shows clear signs of influence by the oral tradition; its selection also reveals Lang's preference for myths. The tale is unusual in its depiction of a resourceful and strong grandmother who serves as Little Golden-hood's protectress. The didactic message— "never talk to strangers"—is stressed, but more important is Little Golden-hood's association with the sun, a symbol of regeneration and also of warning for the readers, especially young ones, who might be foolish enough to talk to wolves.

The True History of Little Golden-hood

You know the tale of poor Little Red Riding-hood, that the Wolf deceived and devoured, with her cake, her little butter can, and her Grandmother; well, the true story happened quite differently, as we know now. And first of all the little girl was called and is still called Little Golden-hood; secondly, it was not she, nor the good grand-dame, but the wicked Wolf who was, in the end, caught and devoured.

Only listen.

The story begins something like the tale.

There was once a little peasant girl, pretty and nice as a star in its season. Her real name was Blanchette, but she was more often called Little Golden-hood, on account of a wonderful little cloak with a hood, gold- and fire-coloured, which she always had on. This little hood was given her by her Grandmother, who was so old that she did not know her age; it ought to bring her luck, for it was made of a ray of sunshine, she said. And as the good old woman was considered something of a witch, everyone thought the little hood rather bewitched too.

And so it was, as you will see.

One day the mother said to the child: "Let us see, my little Golden-hood, if you know how to find your way by yourself. You shall take this good piece of cake to your

Grandmother for a Sunday treat to-morrow. You will ask her how she is, and come back at once, without stopping to chatter on the way with people you don't know. Do you quite understand?"

"I quite understand," replied Blanchette gaily. And off she went with the cake, quite proud of her errand.

But the Grandmother lived in another village, and there was a big wood to cross before getting there. At a turn of the road under the trees, suddenly 'Who goes there?'

"Friend Wolf."

He had seen the child start alone, and the villain was waiting to devour her; when at the same moment he perceived some woodcutters who might observe him, and he changed his mind. Instead of falling upon Blanchette he came frisking up to her like a good dog.

" 'Tis you! my nice Little Golden-hood," said he. So the little girl stops to talk with the Wolf, who, for all that, she did not know in the least.

"You know me, then!" said she; "what is your name?"

"My name is friend Wolf. And where are you going thus, my pretty one, with your little basket on your arm?"

"I am going to my Grandmother, to take her a good piece of cake for her Sunday treat tomorrow."

"And where does she live, your Grandmother?"

"She lives at the other side of the wood, in the first house in the village, near the windmill, you know."

"Ah! yes! I know now," said the Wolf. "Well, that's just where I'm going; I shall get there before you, no doubt, with your little bits of legs, and I'll tell her you're coming to see her; then she'll wait for you."

Thereupon the Wolf cuts across the wood, and in five minutes arrives at the Grandmother's house.

He knocks at the door: *toc, toc.*

No answer.

He knocks louder.

Nobody.

Then he stands up on end, puts his two fore-paws on the latch and the door opens.

Not a soul in the house.

The old woman had risen early to sell herbs in the town, and she had gone off in such haste that she had left her bed unmade, with her great night-cap on the pillow.

"Good!" said the Wolf to himself, "I know what I'll do."

He shuts the door, pulls on the Grandmother's night-cap down to his eyes, then he lies down all his length in the bed and draws the curtains.

In the meantime the good Blanchette went quietly on her way, as little girls do, amusing herself here and there by picking Easter daisies, watching the little birds making their nests, and running after the butterflies which fluttered in the sunshine.

At last she arrives at the door.

Knock, knock.

"Who is there?" says the Wolf, softening his rough voice as best he can.

"It's me, Granny, your little Golden-hood. I'm bringing you a big piece of cake for your Sunday treat to-morrow."

"Press your finger on the latch, then push and the door opens."

"Why, you've got a cold, Granny," said she, coming in.

"Ahem! a little, a little . . ." replies the Wolf, pretending to cough. "Shut the door well, my little lamb. Put your basket on the table, and then take off your frock and come and lie down by me: you shall rest a little."

The good child undresses, but observe this! She kept her little hood upon her head. When she saw what a figure her Granny cut in bed, the poor little thing was much surprised.

"Oh!" cries she, "how like you are to friend Wolf, Grandmother!"

"That's on account of my night-cap, child," replies the Wolf.

"Oh! what hairy arms you've got, Grandmother!"

"All the better to hug you, my child."

"Oh! what a big tongue you've got, Grandmother!"

"All the better for answering, child."

"Oh! what a mouthful of great white teeth you have, Grandmother!"

"That's for crunching little children with!" And the Wolf opened his jaws wide to swallow Blanchette.

But she put down her head crying:

"Mamma! Mamma!" and the Wolf only caught her little hood.

Thereupon, oh dear! oh dear! he draws back, crying and shaking his jaw as if he had swallowed red-hot coals.

It was the little fire-coloured hood that had burnt his tongue right down his throat.

The little hood, you see, was one of those magic caps that they used to have in former times, in the stories, for making oneself invisible or invulnerable.

So there was the Wolf with his throat burnt, jumping off the bed and trying to find the door, howling and howling as if all the dogs in the country were at his heels.

Just at this moment the Grandmother arrives, returning from the town with her long sack empty on her shoulder.

"Ah, brigand!" she cries, "wait a bit!" Quickly she opens her sack wide across the door, and the maddened Wolf springs in head downwards.

It is he now that is caught, swallowed like a letter in the post.

For the brave old dame shuts her sack, so; and she runs and empties it in the well where the vagabond, still howling, tumbles in and is drowned.

"Ah, scoundrel! you thought you would crunch my little grandchild! Well, to-morrow we will make her a muff of your skin, and you yourself shall be crunched, for we will give your carcass to the dogs."

Thereupon the Grandmother hastened to dress poor Blanchette, who was still trembling with fear in the bed.

"Well," she said to her, "without my little hood where would you be now, darling?" And, to restore heart and legs to the child, she made her eat a good piece of her cake, and drink a good draught of wine, after which she took her by the hand and led her back to the house.

And then, who was it who scolded her when she knew all that had happened?

It was the mother.

But Blanchette promised over and over again that she would never more stop to listen to a Wolf, so that at last the mother forgave her.

And Blanchette, the little Golden-hood, kept her word. And in fine weather she may still be seen in the fields with her pretty little hood, the colour of the sun.

But to see her you must rise early.

1888

WALTER DE LA MARE
1873–1956

One of the foremost poets and writers for children in England during the first half of the twentieth century, Walter de la Mare ended his formal education at seventeen, when he graduated from the St. Paul's Cathedral Choir School in London. He then went to work as a bookkeeper at the London office of an international oil company. In the evenings he concentrated on writing poems, novels, and stories for both children and adults. When he turned thirty-five, he had the good fortune to be granted an annual government stipend intended to enable him to devote himself to his literary career. De la Mare was a careful and graceful writer, who sought to capture the consciousness and fancies of childhood in his poems and stories. His best collections of poetry—including *Songs of Childhood* (1902), *Peacock Pie* (1913), and *This Year: Next Year* (1937)—exhibit his predilection for whimsy, mystery, and, at times, ironic humor; *Down-Adown-Derry* (1922) gathers together all his fairy-tale poems. All his works display his familiarity with the major literary fairy tales of the nineteenth and early twentieth centuries, and in his novels (e.g., *Memoirs of a Midget*, 1921) he often uses fairy-tale motifs in innovative ways that open up the classic canon to new interpretations. He also published three important collections of fairy tales and fantasy stories—*Broomsticks, and Other Tales* (1925), *Told Again: Traditional Tales* (1927), and *The Lord Fish* (1933), all reproduced in *Collected Stories for Children* (1947). Some introduce surprising elements into well-known stories, while others are highly original and could be regarded as forerunners to magic realism. An example of the latter is "Broomsticks," in which a very conventional lady gradually learns that her own cat is associated with a witch.

"Little Red Riding-Hood" is one of eighteen classic fairy tales adapted by de la Mare in *Told Again*. De la Mare did not so much alter the familiar plot, based on the Grimms' version, as embellish it with droll humor. However, de la Mare was clearly critical of *vain* Red Riding-Hood, and she is punished for her vanity just as the wolf is punished for his gluttony.

Little Red Riding-Hood

In the old days when countrywomen wore riding-hoods to keep themselves warm and dry as they rode to market, there was a child living in a little village near the Low Forest who was very vain. She was so vain she couldn't even pass a puddle without peeping down into it at her apple cheeks and yellow hair. She could be happy for hours together with nothing but a comb and a glass; and then would sit at the window for people to see her. Nothing pleased her better than fine clothes, and when she was seven, having seen a strange woman riding by on horseback, she suddenly had a violent longing for just such a riding-hood as hers, and that was of a scarlet cloth with strings.

After this, she gave her mother no peace, but begged and pestered her continually, and flew into a passion or sulked when she said, No. When, then, one day a pedlar came to the village, and among the rest of his wares showed her mother a strip of scarlet cloth which he could sell cheap, partly to please the child and partly to get a little quiet, she bought a few yards of this cloth and herself cut out and stitched up a hood of the usual shape and fashion, but of midget size and with ribbons for strings.

When the child saw it she almost choked with delight and peacocked about in it whenever she had the chance. So she grew vainer than ever, and the neighbours became so used to seeing her wearing it in all weathers, her yellow curls dangling on her cheeks and her bright blue eyes looking out from under its hood, that they called her Little Red Riding-Hood.

Now, one fine sunny morning her mother called Little Red Riding-Hood in from her playing and said to her: "Now listen. I've just had news that your poor old Grannie is lying ill in bed and can't stir hand or foot; so as I can't go to see her myself, I want *you* to go instead, and to take her a little present. It's a good long step to Grannie's, mind; but if you don't loiter on the way there'll be plenty of time to be there and back before dark, and to stay a bit with Grannie, too. But *mind*, go straight there and come straight back, and be sure not to speak to anybody whatsoever you meet in the forest. It doesn't look to me like rain, so you can wear your new hood. Poor Grannie will hardly know you!"

Nothing in this long speech pleased Red Riding-Hood so much as the end of it. She ran off at once, and as she combed her hair and put on her hood, she talked to herself in the glass. There was one thing: Red Riding-Hood liked her Grannie pretty well, but she liked the goodies her Grannie gave her even better. So she thought to herself: "If the basket is heavy, I shall take a little rest on the way; and as Grannie's in bed, I shall have plenty to eat when I get there because I can help myself, and I can bring something home in the empty basket. Grannie would like that. Then I can skip along as I please."

Meanwhile, her mother was packing up the basket—a dozen brown hen's eggs, a jar of honey, a pound of butter, a bottle of elderberry wine, and a screw[1] of snuff. After a last look at herself in a polished stewpan, Red Riding-Hood took the basket on her arm and kissed her mother goodbye.

"Now, mind," said her mother yet again, "be sure not to lag or loiter in the Low Forest, picking flowers or chasing the butterflies, and don't speak to any stranger there, not even though he looks as if butter wouldn't melt in his mouth. Do all you can for Grannie, and come straight home."

Red Riding-Hood started off, so pleased with herself and with her head so packed up with greedy thoughts of what she would have to eat at the end of her journey that she forgot to wave back a last goodbye before the path across the buttercup meadow dipped down towards the woods and her mother was out of sight.

On through the sunny lanes among the butterflies she went. The hawthorns, snow-white and crimson, were in fullest flower, and the air was laden with their smell. All the trees of the wood, indeed, were rejoicing in their new green coats, and there was such a medley and concourse of birds singing that their notes sounded like drops of water falling into a fountain.

When Red Riding-Hood heard this shrill sweet warbling she thought to herself: "They are looking at *me* as I go along all by myself with my basket in my bright red hood." And she skipped on more gaily than ever.

But the basket grew heavier and heavier the further she journeyed, and when at last she came to the Low Forest the shade there was so cool and so many strange flowers were blooming in its glens and dingles, that she forgot everything her mother had told her and sat down to rest. Moss, wild thyme and violets grew on that bank, and presently she fell asleep.

In her sleep she dreamed a voice was calling to her from very far away. It was a

1. A small portion (wrapped in a twist of paper).

queer husky voice, and seemed to be coming from some dark dismal place where the speaker was hiding.

At sound of this voice calling and calling her ever more faintly, she suddenly awoke, and there, not more than a few yards away, stood a Wolf, and he was steadily looking at her. At first she was so frightened she could hardly breathe, and could only stare back at him.

But the moment the Wolf saw that she was awake he smiled at her, or rather his jaws opened and he grinned; and then in tones as wheedling and buttery-smooth as his tongue could manage he said: "Good-afternoon, my dear. I hope you are refreshed after your little nap. But what, may I ask, are *you* doing here, all alone in the forest, and in that beautiful, bright red hood, too?" As he uttered these words he went on grinning at her in so friendly a fashion that little Red Riding-Hood could not but smile at him in return.

She told him she was on her way to her Grannie's.

"I see," said the Wolf, not knowing that through his very wiliness he would be stretched out that evening as cold as mutton! "And what might you have in that heavy basket, my dear?"

Little Red Riding-Hood tossed her head so that her curls glinted in a sunbeam that was twinkling through the leaves of the tree beneath which she was sitting, and she said, "My Grannie is very very ill in bed. Perhaps she'll die. So that's why I'm carrying this heavy basket. It's got eggs and butter, and honey and wine, and snuff inside it. And I'm all by myself!"

"My!" said the Wolf. "All by yourself; and a packet of snuff, too! But how, my little dear, will you be able to get in at the door if your Grannie is ill in bed? How will you manage that?"

"Oh," said Red Riding-Hood, "that will be quite easy. I shall just tap seven times and say, 'It's me, Grannie'; then Grannie will know who it is and tell me how to get in."

"But how clever!" said the Wolf. "And where does your poor dear Grannie live? And which way are *you* going?"

Little Red Riding-Hood told him; then he stopped grinning and looked away. "I was just thinking, my dear," he went on softly, "how very lucky it was we met! I know your Grannie's cottage well. Many's the time I've seen her sitting there at her window. But I can tell you a much, *much* shorter way to it. If you go *your* way, I'm afraid you won't be home till long after dark, and that would never do. For sometimes one meets queer people in the Low Forest, not at all what you would care for."

But what this crafty wretch told her was a way which was at least half a mile further round. Red Riding-Hood thanked him, seeing no harm in his sly grinning, and started off by the way he had said. But he himself went louping[2] off by a much shorter cut, and came to her grandmother's cottage long before she did. And there was not a living thing in sight.

Having entered the porch, the Wolf lifted his paw and, keeping his claws well in, rapped seven times on the door.

An old quavering voice called, "Who's there?"

And the Wolf, muffling his tones, said, "It's me, Grannie!"

"Stand on the stone, pull the string, and the door will come open," said the old woman.

2. Leaping.

So the Wolf got up on to his hind legs and with his teeth tugged at the string. The door came open, and in he went; and that (for a while) was the end of Grannie.

But what Master Wolf had planned for his supper that evening was not just Grannie, but Grannie *first* and then—for a titbit—Red Riding-Hood afterwards.

And he knew well there were woodmen in the forest, and that it would be far safer to wait in hiding for her in the cottage than to carry her off openly.

So, having drawn close the curtains at the window, he put on the old woman's clean nightgown which was lying upon a chair, tied her nightcap over his ears, scrambled into her bed, drew up the clothes over him, and laid himself down at all his long length with his head on the pillow. There then he lay, waiting for Red Riding-Hood and thinking he was safe as safe; and an ugly heap he looked.

All this time Red Riding-Hood had been still loitering, picking wild flowers and chasing bright-winged butterflies, and once she had sat down and helped herself to a taste or two of her Grannie's honey.

But at last her footsteps sounded on the cobbles; and there came seven taps at the door.

Then the Wolf, smiling to himself and mimicking the old woman, and trying to say the words as she had said them, called, "Who's there?"

Red Riding-Hood said, "It's me, Grannie!"

And the Wolf said, "Stand on the stone, pull the string, and the door will come open."

Red Riding-Hood stood on her tiptoes, pulled the string, and went in; and one narrow beam of sunshine strayed in after her, for she left the door a little ajar. And there was her Grannie, as she supposed, lying ill in bed. The Wolf peered out at her from under the old woman's nightcap, but the light was so dim in the cottage that at first Red Riding-Hood could not see him at all clearly, only the frilled nightcap and the long, bony hump of him sticking up under the bedclothes.

"Look what *I've* brought you, Grannie," she said. "Some butter, a jar of honey, some eggs, a bottle of wine, and a packet of snuff. And I've come all the way by myself in my new red riding-hood!"

The Wolf said, "Umph!"

Red Riding-Hood peeped about her. "*I expect*, Grannie," she said, "if I was to look in that cupboard over there, there'd be some of those jam-tarts you made for me last time I came, and some cake too, I *expect*, to take home, Grannie; and please may I have a drink of milk *now*?"

The Wolf said, "Umph!"

Then Red Riding-Hood went a little nearer to look at her Grannie in bed. She looked a long, long time, and at last she said, "Oh, Grannie, what very bright eyes you have!"

And the Wolf said, "All the better to *see* with, my dear."

Then Red Riding-Hood said, "And oh, Grannie, what long pointed nails you have!"

And the Wolf said, "All the better to *scratch* with, my dear."

Then Red Riding-Hood said, "And what high hairy sticking-up ears you have, Grannie!"

"All the better to *hear* with, my dear," said the Wolf.

"And, oh, Grannie," cried Red Riding-Hood, "what great huge big teeth you have!"

"All the better to *eat* with!" yelled the Wolf, and with that he leapt out of bed in his long nightgown, and before she could say "Oh!" Little Red Riding-Hood was gobbled up, nose, toes, hood, snuff, butter, honey and all.

Nevertheless, that cunning greedy crafty old Wolf had not been quite cunning enough. He had bolted down such a meal that the old glutton at once went off to sleep on the bed, with his ears sticking out of his nightcap, and his tail lolling out under the quilt. And he had forgotten to shut the door.

Early that evening a woodman, coming home with his axe and a faggot[3] when the first stars were beginning to shine, looked in at the open cottage door, and instead of the old woman saw the Wolf lying there on the bed. He knew the villain at sight.

"Oho! you old ruffian," he cried softly, "is it *you?*"

At this far-away strange sound in his dreams, the Wolf opened—though by scarcely more than a hair's breadth—his dull, drowsy eyes. But at glimpse of the woodman, his wits came instantly back to him, and he knew his danger. Too late! For even, clogged up in Grannie's nightgown, he could gather his legs together to spring out of bed, the woodman with one mighty stroke of his axe had finished him off.

And as the woodman stooped over him to make sure, he fancied he heard muffled voices squeaking in the wolf's inside as if calling for help. He listened, then at once cut him open, and out came Red Riding-Hood, and out at last crept her poor old Grannie. And though the first thing Red Riding-Hood did, when she could get her breath again, was to run off to the looking-glass and comb out her yellow curls and uncrumple her hood, she never afterwards forgot what a wolf looked like, and never afterwards loitered in the Low Forest.

As for her poor old Grannie, though that one hour's warmth and squeezing had worked wonders with her rheumatism, she lived only for twenty years after. But then, it was on the old woman's seventieth birthday that Red Riding-Hood had set out with her basket.

It was a piece of rare good fortune for them both, at any rate, first, that the woodman had looked in at the cottage door in the very nick of time; next, that he had his axe; and last, that this Wolf was such a senseless old glutton that he never really enjoyed a meal, but swallowed everything whole. Else, Red Riding-Hood and her Grannie would certainly not have come out of him alive, and the people in the village would have had to bury the wicked old rascal in the churchyard—where he would have been far from welcome.

1927

3. A bundle of sticks.

CATHERINE STORR
1913–2001

Although there had been some feminist revisions of "Little Red Riding Hood" before World War II, it was not until Catherine Storr began challenging the stereotypical portrayal of little girls that the feminist perspective began to take root. Born in London, Storr studied at Cambridge and later at West London Hospital. She qualified as a physician in 1947 and specialized in psychiatry. In 1948 Storr began working as a psychiatrist in West London Hospital; in 1950 she was appointed the Senior Hospital Medical Officer in the Department of Psychological Medicine at Middlesex Hospital, where she remained until 1962. She also worked as an editor of Penguin Books. In 1951 she created the Clever Polly Series to project a positive image of independent girls in fantasy literature for children; it included *Clever Polly and the Stupid Wolf* (1955) and *Polly, the Giant's Bride* (1956). She published more than thirty-five books for children and adults, and many of her works deal with such social and psychological problems as alienation and the lack of communication between generations. In the novels *Thursday* (1971), *Winter's End* (1978), and *Two's Company* (1984), she sensitively depicts young people who lose their grasp on reality because of conflicts with their parents or traumatic experiences. While her longer works tend to be serious and often explore the inner worlds of children, her fairy tales are more lighthearted and optimistic. Among her best fairy-tale books are *The Chinese Egg* (1975), *The Painter and the Fish* (1975), *The Boy and the*

Swan (1987), *Daljit and the Unqualified Wizard* (1989), and *Last Stories of Polly and the Wolf* (1990).

Her story "Little Polly Riding Hood" is one of the most original revisions of the traditional versions, with clear intertextual references that play with the differences between reality and fiction. By refusing to be victimized, Polly offers a model of behavior that challenges stereotypes and gives young readers new options. At the same time, the story's ending places the narrative form of the fairy tale itself into question and suggests that the classic tale of Little Red Riding Hood does not really help in confronting the reality of predatory behavior.

Little Polly Riding Hood

Once every two weeks Polly went over to the other side of the town to see her grandmother. Sometimes she took a small present, and sometimes she came back with a small present for herself. Sometimes all the rest of the family went too, and sometimes Polly went alone.

One day, when she was going by herself, she had hardly got down the front door steps when she saw the wolf.

"Good afternoon, Polly," said the wolf. "Where are you going to, may I ask?"

"Certainly," said Polly. "I'm going to see my grandma."

"I thought so!" said the wolf, looking very much pleased. "I've been reading about a little girl who went to visit her grandmother and it's a very good story."

"Little Red Riding Hood?" suggested Polly.

"That's it!" cried the wolf. "I read it out loud to myself as a bed-time story. I did enjoy it. The wolf eats up the grandmother, *and* Little Red Riding Hood. It's almost the only story where a wolf really gets anything to eat," he added sadly.

"But in my book he doesn't get Red Riding Hood," said Polly. "Her father comes in just in time to save her."

"Oh, he doesn't in *my* book!" said the wolf. "I expect mine is the true story, and yours is just invented. Anyway, it seems a good idea."

"What is a good idea?" asked Polly.

"To catch little girls on their way to their grandmothers' cottages," said the wolf. "Now where had I got to?"

"I don't know what you mean," said Polly.

"Well, I'd said, 'Where are you going to?'" said the wolf. "Oh, yes. Now I must say 'Where does she live?' Where does your grandmother live, Polly Riding Hood?"

"Over the other side of the town," answered Polly.

The wolf frowned.

"It ought to be 'Through the Wood'," he said. "But perhaps town will do. How do you get there, Polly Riding Hood?"

"First I take a train and then I take a bus," said Polly.

The wolf stamped his foot.

"No, no, no, no!" he shouted. "That's all wrong. You can't say that. You've got to say, 'By that path winding through the trees', or something like that. You can't go by trains and buses and things. It isn't fair."

"Well, I could say that," said Polly, "but it wouldn't be true. I do have to go by bus and train to see my grandma, so what's the good of saying I don't?"

"But then it won't work," said the wolf impatiently. "How can I get there first and gobble her up and get all dressed up to trick you into believing I am her, if we've got a great train journey to do? And anyhow I haven't any money on me, so I can't even take a ticket. You just can't say that."

"All right, I won't say it," said Polly agreeably. "But it's true all the same. Now just excuse me, Wolf, I've got to get down to the station because I am going to visit my grandma even if you aren't."

The wolf slunk along behind Polly, growling to himself. He stood just behind her at the booking-office and heard her ask for her ticket, but he could not go any further. Polly got into a train and was carried away, and the wolf went sadly home.

But just two weeks later the wolf was waiting outside Polly's house again. This time he had plenty of change in his pocket. He even had a book tucked under his front leg to read in the train.

He partly hid himself behind a corner of brick wall and watched to see Polly come out on her way to her grandmother's house.

But Polly did not come out alone, as she had before. This time the whole family appeared, Polly's father and mother too. They got into the car which was waiting in the road, and Polly's father started the engine.

The wolf ran along behind his brick wall as fast as he could, and was just in time to get out into the road ahead of the car, and to stand waving his paws as if he wanted a lift as the car came up.

Polly's father slowed down, and Polly's mother put her head out of the window.

"Where do you want to go?" she asked.

"I want to go to Polly's grandmother's house," the wolf answered. His eyes glistened as he looked at the family of plump little girls in the back of the car.

"That's where we are going," said her mother, surprised. "Do you know her then?"

"Oh no," said the wolf. "But you see, I want to get there very quickly and eat her up and then I can put on her clothes and wait for Polly, and eat her up too."

"Good heavens!" said Polly's father. "What a horrible idea! We certainly shan't give you a lift if that is what you are planning to do."

Polly's mother screwed up the window again and Polly's father drove quickly on. The wolf was left standing miserably in the road.

"Bother!" he said to himself angrily. "It's gone wrong again. I can't think why it can't be the same as the Little Red Riding Hood story. It's all these buses and cars and trains that make it go wrong."

But the wolf was determined to get Polly, and when she was due to visit her grandmother again, a fortnight later, he went down and took a ticket for the station he had heard Polly ask for. When he got out of the train, he climbed on a bus, and soon he was walking down the road where Polly's grandmother lived.

"Aha!" he said to himself, "this time I shall get them both. First the grandma, then Polly."

He unlatched the gate into the garden, and strolled up the path to Polly's grandmother's front door. He rapped sharply with the knocker.

"Who's there?" called a voice from inside the house.

The wolf was very much pleased. This was going just as it had in the story. This time there would be no mistakes.

"Little Polly Riding Hood," he said in a squeaky voice. "Come to see her dear grandmother, with a little present of butter and eggs and—er—cake!"

There was a long pause. Then the voice said doubtfully, "*Who* did you say it was?"

"Little Polly Riding Hood," said the wolf in a great hurry, quite forgetting to disguise his voice this time. "Come to eat up her dear grandmother with butter and eggs!"

There was an even longer pause. Then Polly's grandmother put her head out of a window and looked down at the wolf.

"I beg your pardon?" she said.

"I am Polly," said the wolf firmly.

"Oh," said Polly's grandma. She appeared to be thinking hard. "Good afternoon, Polly. Do you know if anyone else happens to be coming to see me to-day? A wolf, for instance?"

"No. Yes," said the wolf in great confusion. "I met a Polly as I was coming here—I mean, I, Polly, met a wolf on my way here, but she can't have got here yet because I started specially early."

"That's very queer," said the grandma. "Are you quite sure you are Polly?"

"Quite sure," said the wolf.

"Well, then, I don't know who it is who is here already," said Polly's grandma. "She said she was Polly. But if you are Polly then I think this other person must be a wolf."

"No, no, I am Polly," said the wolf. "And, anyhow, you ought not to say that. You ought to say 'Lift the latch and come in'."

"I don't think I'll do that," said Polly's grandma. "Because I don't want my nice little Polly eaten up by a wolf, and if you come in now the wolf who is here already might eat you up."

Another head looked out of another window. It was Polly's.

"Bad luck, Wolf," she said. "You didn't know that I was coming to lunch and tea to-day instead of just tea as I generally do—so I got here first. And as you are Polly, as you've just said, I must be the wolf, and you'd better run away quickly before I gobble you up, hadn't you?"

"Bother, bother, bother and *bother*!" said the wolf. "It hasn't worked out right this time either. And I did just what it said in the book. Why can't I ever get you, Polly, when that other wolf managed to get his little girl?"

"Because this isn't a fairy story," said Polly, "and I'm not Little Red Riding Hood, I am Polly and I can always escape from you, Wolf, however much you try to catch me."

"Clever Polly," said Polly's grandma. And the wolf went growling away.

1955

ROALD DAHL
1916–1990

Though many of Roald Dahl's works have a cynical and even cruel quality, he is viewed as one of the most innovative writers for children in the latter half of the twentieth century. Born in Wales of Norwegian immigrants, he felt a strong attachment to Norwegian folklore as a child. However, much about his childhood, which he describes in the first volume of his autobiography, *Boy: Tales of Childhood* (1984), was unhappy: his father died when he was four, he hated the rigid schools that he attended, and he rebelled against their authority figures. He rejected his mother's offer to pay for a university education and instead took a job with Shell Oil in East Africa. When World War II began, he joined the Royal Air Force. After being seriously injured in a crash, he returned briefly to flying before he was sent to work for the British Embassy in Washington, D.C. (events described in the second volume of his autobiography, *Going Solo*, 1986). It was in Washington that Dahl turned his attention to writing, and he published his first collection of short stories for adults, *Over to You* (1946); *Someone Like You* (1953) and *Kiss, Kiss* (1960) followed.

Dahl married the actress Patricial Neal in 1953, and many of the stories that he told to their five children inspired the extraordinary fantasy books that he began producing for young readers in the 1960s. Yet during this period he also experienced bitter tragedies. His four-month-old son suffered permanent brain damage after being struck by a taxi; his seven-year-old daughter Olivia died of measles

in 1962; and his wife had a series of massive strokes in 1965 that left her incapacitated for two years. It is no wonder that his stories so often involve violence, cruelty, and revenge. For instance, the hero of *James and the Giant Peach* (1961) is a mild young orphan who is abused by his nasty aunts. After James spills some magic seeds, a giant peach grows. Once the peach crushes his aunts, he can have some amusing adventures. In *Charlie and the Chocolate Factory* (1964), an impoverished boy tours a chocolate factory, along with four spoiled, nasty children; they suffer gruesome punishments, and he ultimately inherits the factory. Only the poor and downtrodden children are rewarded. Dahl insisted that children are cruel and have a vulgar sense of humor, and he believed that they respond to forthright portrayals of their lives exaggerated through fantasy. Given that these and his other works, such as *Fantastic Mr. Fox* (1970), *The Enormous Crocodile* (1978), *The BFG* (1982), and *Matilda* (1988), made him one of the most successful writers of children's books of all time, he may have had a point.

"Little Red Riding Hood and the Wolf" appeared in *Roald Dahl's Revolting Rhymes* (1982), illustrated by Quentin Blake. In these poems, like those in *Rhyme Stew* (1989), we clearly see the delight Dahl took in shocking readers. Here he portrays the wolf as grotesquely voracious. In addition, his Little Red Riding Hood recalls the similarly violent heroine of James Thurber's version, "The Little Girl and the Wolf" (1939).

Little Red Riding Hood and the Wolf

As soon as Wolf began to feel
That he would like a decent meal,
He went and knocked on Grandma's door.
When Grandma opened it, she saw
The sharp white teeth, the horrid grin,
And Wolfie said, "May I come in?"
Poor Grandmamma was terrified,
"He's going to eat me up!" she cried.
And she was absolutely right.

He ate her up in one big bite.
But Grandmamma was small and tough,
And Wolfie wailed, "That's not enough!
"I haven't yet begun to feel
"That I have had a decent meal!"
He ran around the kitchen yelping,
"I've *got* to have a second helping!"
Then added with a frightful leer,
"I'm therefore going to wait right here
"Till Little Miss Red Riding Hood
"Comes home from walking in the wood."
He quickly put on Grandma's clothes,
(Of course he hadn't eaten those.)
He dressed himself in coat and hat.
He put on shoes and after that
He even brushed and curled his hair,
Then sat himself in Grandma's chair.
In came the little girl in red.
She stopped. She stared. And then she said,

"What great big ears you have, Grandma."
"All the better to hear you with," the Wolf replied.
"What great big eyes you have, Grandma,"
    said Little Red Riding Hood.
"All the better to see you with," the Wolf replied.

He sat there watching her and smiled
He thought, I'm going to eat this child.
Compared with her old Grandmamma
She's going to taste like caviare.

Then Little Red Riding Hood said, *"But Grandma,*
what a lovely great big furry coat you have on."

"That's wrong!" cried Wolf. "Have you forgot
"To tell me what BIG TEETH I've got?
"Ah well, no matter what you say,
"I'm going to eat you anyway."
The small girl smiles. One eyelid flickers.
She whips a pistol from her knickers.
She aims it at the creature's head
And *bang bang bang*, she shoots him dead.
A few weeks later, in the wood,
I came across Miss Riding Hood.
But what a change! No cloak of red,
No silly hood upon her head.
She said, "Hello, and do please note
"My lovely furry WOLFSKIN COAT."

1982

TOMI UNGERER
b. 1931

Tomi Ungerer is one of the most controversial contemporary illustrators and writers for children and adults. His childhood in Strasbourg, France, was difficult because of the Great Depression and the death of his father, a watchmaker. It was made worse when the Nazis occupied the region and took over the schools, which began teaching only in German. The cruelty and atrocities witnessed by Ungerer during the war profoundly affected his vision of the world. After 1945 he hitchhiked through Europe, studied art in Strasbourg and Paris, and worked as a freelance artist. In 1956 he emigrated to the United States. Soon thereafter he published his first book in English, *The Mellops Go Flying* (1957), which revealed his predilection for irony and the absurd. It tells the story of gentle, middle-class pigs who go off into the world looking for adventures, are nearly destroyed, but use their wits to escape disaster and return home. He returned to his unusual pigs in several other books, including *The Mellops Go Diving for Treasure* (1958) and *The Mellops Go Spelunking* (1963). While these self-illustrated children's books are light and cheerful in tone, most of his other works

deal with violence, hypocrisy, and maliciousness; he also became renowned as a political cartoonist in the 1960s. Evil in Ungerer's stories can be vanquished only by extraordinary beasts or by forthright, courageous children who call things as they see them. In *The Three Robbers* (1962) the thieves are overcome by the charm of a child. In *Zeralda's Ogre* (1967) a young cook uses her culinary art to persuade the ogre to stop eating children. *Allumette* (1974), a disturbing adaptation of Hans Christian Andersen's "The Match Girl" (1845), is much darker, as it depicts the poverty and callousness that children endure in a heartless world.

Ungerer's adaptation of "Little Red Riding Hood" appeared in *A Storybook from Tomi Ungerer* (1974), a collection of stories that challenge the traditional versions of fairy tales. His wry interpretation, which he calls "reruminated," brings out the erotic side of the tale in a surprising manner, and his wolf is one of the few who escapes punishment and maltreatment. Indeed, Ungerer is one of the first writers and illustrators to display a hilarious and courtly wolf and a threatening and unpleasant grandmother.

Little Red Riding Hood

Once upon many times, in the middle of a godforsaken forest there stood a castle. In that castle lived a wolf. The woods were dark and pathless, the castle was sumptuous, and the wolf, like all wolves, was mean, broody, and ferociously ferocious. His reputation was even worse than his deeds. He lived there all alone—for he was feared by everyone—but for a rookery of ravens employed in his service. Wifeless, heirless, with whiskers turning to silver, he spent his days scanning the woods for some juicy fare.

One day, as he was gazing over a multitude of treetops from one of his many ramparts, there flew to him one of his watchcrows.

"Master venerable, lordly Duke and beloved ruler," he cawed, "in a thicket, three miles due northeast, beyond the moor, below the barrens, I sighted a little girl, morsel of a maiden, picking berries off your domain. She is dressed in reds all over like a stop sign. Yes, master, as red as a little beet."

"Well done, trusted lackey," growled the wolf, smacking his flapping chops. "We

"Yes, master, as red as a little beet."

shall settle the matter anon." Anon was right away and off went the wolf.

The little girl in red, her name was—yes, you guessed it—Little Red Riding Hood. Not the one you might already have read about. No. This Little Red Riding Hood was the real, no-nonsense one, and this story is one-hundred-to-a-nickel genuine.

She was as pretty as anything, pink and soft. Her braided blond hair shone like fresh bread, and birds could have flown off into the blue of her eyes. Besides, she had wit and sense. She was dressed in red because it was one of her mother's out-landish notions that her daughter might always easily be spotted that way. Little Red Riding Hood didn't mind. She thought it made her special.

Little Red Riding Hood was on her way to deliver a weekly supply of food to her mean and cranky grandmama, who lived in a run-down shack overlooking a greenish pond. The baskets she was carrying were heavy with three hogs' heads, two pints of rendered lard, two quarts of applejack, and two loaves of wrinkled bread. The old woman was a retired diva whose voice had gone sour. She was filled with superstitions and believed staunchly that she would restore her smithereened voice by eating pigs' heads—eyes, brains, and all. Her place was buzzing with flies who liked pigs' heads, too, in summer especially.

Little Red Riding Hood hated to go there. It was a hot and clammy day and her red Cheviot cape was itching and sticking to her back. The baskets were getting heavier and heavier, her arms longer and longer. Exhausted, she stopped in the cool-ing shade of the forest and started picking fragrant berries.

"I might just as well stop and be late and rest," she reflected. "These baskets are so heavy they feel as if something is growing inside them. All I get for my trouble is blows and insults, anyway. Each time I get there she accuses me of things I haven't done yet—that I guzzled off some of the applejack and nibbled at some pig's snout, and so on and so forth, and so beside the point,[1] the comma, and the asterisk. I still carry on my tender skin the bluish marks of the old woman's beatings. And, here, look at the marks where she bit me in the shoulder last week. Vicious to the core, that's what she is."

"Hullo, there," growled a deep and raucous voice from behind a tree. It was the wolf, who had silently sneaked up on the trespassing child. "Hullo, cute damsel dear, what brings you browsing in my very own berry bushes?"

"Well, ho, you startled me. But yes, good day, Your Excellency," replied the damsel

---

1. One meaning of *point* is a punctuation mark, the period.

dear. "You find me here picking berries for my impatient little belly, and I was on my way to deliver these baskets here, full with food, to my mean and old grandmother who lives by the green fly pond, and besides I have noticed no trespassing signs ever, so how should I know whose bushes I am molesting, noble Prince?"

"Coriander and marjoram, lady young, lady bright. Maybe you are sassy, maybe you are clever, but I fancy your bearings. These baskets seem heavy indeed. Ha! Do you know what? I shall help you carry them. I am strong and efficient and it's a bleeding shame, if you ask me, to burden such a sweet little red maiden with loads like that. I know of your grandmother and all I can say is that her reputation is worse than mine."

"What is a reputation, noble Prince?" queried our heroine.

"Call me Duke," replied the wolf. "A reputation is what people think you are. Reputations come in all sizes. Some are good, some are bad or very bad, like mine. Anyway, here is my plan, and it comes from somebody who has far more experience of life than you. With my strong arms, I shall carry the baskets, not to your granny's bungalow, but to my very own castle. Come along, I live lonely and bored. Come with me and I shall share with you my secrets and more of my secrets. My vaults are plastered with treasures. You will sleep in satins and live in silks. My closets sag with brocade dresses on hangers of solid gold. Your winters will be wrapped in sable furs. My servants shall kiss the very ground you walk upon. I'll make you happy, you'll make me happy, as in a fairy tale."

There was a pensive silence and Little Red Riding Hood took three steps back in distrust.

"I was told wolves feed on little children. I don't quite trust you, Mister Duke. You wouldn't eat me, would you? With a big mouth like that, you could gobble me up in a jiffy and a spiffy, bones, cape, and all."

"Nonsense, child, mere slander, that is. Wolves feed only upon ugly children, and then only on special request," replied the beast with a sugar smile. "Never, ever would I do such a thing. Upon my mother's truffle, never."

"But your jowls are enormous, they look scary, and those huge fangs, why do they twinkle like that?" asked the girl unabashedly.

"Because I brush them every morning with powdered tripoli."[2]

"And your tongue? Why is it so pink?"

"From chewing on rosebuds. Pink and red are my favorite colors," said the wolf.

"And why do—"

"Stop asking foolish questions," interrupted the wolf. "We must get started if we want to reach my palatial abode before dark. Besides, questions are bad for your happiness. Come along," said the wolf as he lifted the baskets. "Come along, there is an exotic library in my castle, and a splash of a swimming pool in my tropical greenhouse."

"But I cannot swim," said Little Red Riding Hood. "And what happens to my parents and my mean grandmother?"

"Read the end of this story, and you'll find out," said the wolf. "We shall send your parents post cards and invite them to the wedding. Your grandmother is old enough to take care of herself, and if you cannot swim all we have to do is empty the swimming pool."

Off they went to live happily ever after. They did get married and they had all sorts of children who all lived happily, too.

---

2. A powder made from a type of lightweight rock containing silica; it is used to polish metal and glass.

And the grandmother? Left without food, she shrank and shrank, until she was just inches high. When last seen, she was scavenging someone's larder in the company of a Norway rat. And, tiny and hungry, she was just as mean as ever.

1974

TONY ROSS
b. 1938

By the time Tony Ross began writing and illustrating fairy tales, numerous cartoons, animated films, and picture books had mocked the traditional characters and themes of "Little Red Riding Hood." However, he has sought to take their comic aspects even further, making burlesques out of the story. Born in London, Ross studied at the Liverpool School of Art; after graduation he worked as a cartoonist and for a number of graphic art studios and advertising companies. He began teaching art at Manchester Polytechnic in 1965, but since 1985 he has been a full-time writer and illustrator.

Ross is best known for his own Towser series and for illustrating Jeannie Willis's Dr. Xargle series. His illustrations reflect his training as an etcher and his experience as a cartoonist, as they reveal his love of line drawings. Ross frequently uses unusual plots and extraordinary characters to challenge readers' expectations. He has often focused on the fairy tale,

turning it inside out with innovative versions in *Goldilocks and the Three Bears* (1976), *Jack and the Beanstalk* (1980), and *Puss in Boots* (1981). In addition, he has created his own original fairy tales, such as *A Fairy Tale* (1991), and has illustrated the stories of others, such as Hiawyn Oram's *The Second Princess* (1994).

"Little Red Hood: A Classic Story Bent Out of Shape" (1978), which is typical of all of Ross's fairy-tale work, resembles the "Fractured Fairy Tales" featured on *The Bullwinkle Show* that began a trend in the 1960s and 1970s of mocking the traditional stories in animation. Ross, who may have also been influenced by the British comic troupe Monty Python, sets his adaptation in the present. Not only does he parody the classic versions of Charles Perrault and the Brothers Grimm, but he also satirizes contemporary mores.

Little Red Hood: A Classic Story Bent Out of Shape

Once upon a time, there was a little kid without a name. Her father was into lumber, but he was a small-timer. Even though he sometimes sat it out with a cool one while the kid did the heavy hitting, Rocky was okay. She loved him and so what if he and her mother had been too busy to give her a name?

Still, she used to whack away at the wood, wondering whatever happened to the child-labor laws and thinking that she might get a couple of organizers and start a union.

Once in a while, she got time off to visit her grandmother, who lived in a forest—or at least someplace in Jersey.

The grandmother, Crazy Carmela, was a batty old biddy who loved to make clothes. She once worked in the garment industry and she still sewed up a storm like the old days in the rag trade, sitting in front of a big blown-up Polaroid of her father, Abe, when he was doorman at the Hilton and controlled the cabs, the numbers,[1] and kept out the riffraff.

"Run me up a pair of jeans," said the little girl one day. But the old lady, who wasn't much in the head, made her a red cape instead.

Okay, so it wasn't Sasson,[2] but the kid dug the cape anyhow and wore it around the neighborhood, showing a lot of leg. Her O.M.[3] chased her, warning about muggers and telling her to get home and slice up some more trees.

"I'm bored with boards," the kid said, and the father knew his daughter had hit puberty and was almost out of sight. She yelled back that she was striking for better working conditions and fringes, one of which was the right to trade in the bike for a Yamaha. He called her a commie and soon the other kids had laid Little Red Hood on her as a name.

That was cool with her, better than no name, and after that Little Red Hood had more time on her hands. One day, the mother, Linda, who had just been to the deli, said: "Take some of these meatballs and pizza and a six-pack over to my mother's. It'll keep her off the streets."

"You been *cooking*?" said Red.

"Nah," said the mother. "Frozen. Linda's liberated."

Then Red and the folks did a big farewell number, just in case there was a photographer around from *People* magazine, and she schlepped along, wondering when she would take delivery of her Honda. (The big Yamaha bikes were back-ordered for five months.) Suddenly, she saw this dog, a great deal of dog, *humongous*, a real Mama Mutt.

She pulled a weed and tickled him, figuring that if this hunk sneezed, he'd clear enough trees to keep her father's lumberyard swinging for a year.

But the big thing was that the big thing was no dog. And no dummy either. The wolf figured fast that if he was going to get some local action, he'd better make nice.

He was just in from Detroit and he was, you know, meaner than a junkyard dog, but he took the tickling, smiled, showing his new caps, and said: "Listen, Farrah, there's lotsa' fine stuff growing around here. Why don't you gather some, we'll sniff a little, and maybe go nuts in May?"

"Hey, animal," the kid said, "nobody uses that stuff anymore. But there are some nice organic greens here." Fine and funky, they agreed. While the kid picked, the

---

1. I.e., an illegal lottery.
2. I.e., designer clothing.

3. Old man.

wolf dropped the smile—Redford was never in any danger—and his eyes went to slits until he could have doubled for Dustin Hoffman.[4] Now this wolf had a bigger nose for news than your average neighborhood wiretap. He knew the scene because he'd planted a bug in the old lady's Luxo lamp. So he figured: First blow away the bag of bones and then the kid.

Using his beak, he hit the buzzer.

"Yeah?" said Grandma Moses. She wasn't too happy about leaving the good-looking dude who was doing the six-o'clock news. Hair spray and all, he could really read a Teleprompter.

The wolf shriveled his sound and said, "It's little Red Hood, Grannie."

"Whatt'ya want?" said the crone.

"I'm your granddaughter, you turkey. You're supposed to love me. Besides, I brought you some diet Bud."

"Fan*tastic*!" said Grams. "Come on in and pull off a couple of caps."

So the stud from Detroit busts in, puts the hit on Miss America 1918, and a minute later is licking his lips. The old bag wasn't all bones at that.

He walked up three steps in the split-level, put on the nightgown he found in the bedroom, and slipped into the sack. Until he caught a profile shot of himself in the mirror. "*Yucch*," he said, got up and flicked off the light. Saves energy, he thought— and maybe this whole bit.

The shades of night were falling fast and so were the wolf's spirits, when he finally heard the kid bop on the door downstairs.

"Come in, dearie," he squeaked, trying to make his voice sound as old as the gag was getting. "I'm topside, flaked out."

"Okay," the kid said. "See you tomorrow."

"NO!" the wolf shouted, losing his cool and what was left of his falsetto.

The kid went in cautiously. "You sure you're okay?" Then she looked closely. "Hey, Gran—you better get your ears cleaned. Or your hair done."

"I heard okay."

"And those *eyes*! You been to the optometrist—or you just giving blood?"

"Contacts," said the wolf and, scrambling to remember his lines, added: "All the better to watch TV with."

The kid touched a paw. "Wow, it's dark as a disco in here," she said, "but I *mean*. You got the only hands I ever felt that need a pedicure *and* a skin graft."

The wolf opened his mouth and she reeled back. "And those teeth! That breath! Try a lung transplant. . . ."

"All the better to eat you with, my dear," he rasped in his own voice, finally trying to get the script straight, and then he zapped her.

"Man, I'm full," said the wolf three minutes later, already desperate for a Fresca.

Meanwhile, the father, pushed by Linda, who was a *noodge*[5] anyhow, was out cruising. Even if the kid had trouble getting a bus, she was overdue. Rocky swore that if she kept on staying out late, he would lock her out of the house.

While he was mentally denying her entree, he didn't know that she had *become* the entree. And his mother-in-law the hors d'oeuvres.

Before long, with the other cats in the region sweating it out—for they liked Little Red, she was a *mensch*, real people—the father found Carmela's house. He broke open the door (which was a little unnecessary since it was unlocked) and saw the

---

4. An American actor (b. 1937) who lacks the classic good looks of Robert Redford (b. 1937), another American actor.

5. I.e., a *nudzh*, a nag (Yiddish, as are *shlep* and *mensch*).

wolf with the fat gut. He fetched him a clout on the snout, followed with a right cross to the basket, and shook him until he gave up his ill-gotten goodies. It was a little overdone, like the front door, but what did Rocky know? He was just muscle.

The wolf split, but not before old Grannie Goose and Little Red had hit him with everything that wasn't nailed down—and a few things that were. He soon had more stuff coming at him than a garage sale.

That night Rocky, Linda, Carmela, Little Red Hood, and some of the crowd went off to the local *cantina* to celebrate, and there wasn't a loose clam or bowl of linguini or jug of Chianti that stood a chance.

Meanwhile, the wolf moved on to other turf, reached an agreement with the regional capo that he'd stay out of the way, went straight, and settled down.

It used to mean when somebody "Bought the farm" that he was dead—but do you want a happy ending or don't you?

1978

MICHAEL EMBERLEY
b. 1960

It seems that Michael Emberley had no choice but to become an illustrator. He grew up in an old colonial house in Ipswich, Massachusetts, and his father Ed, a well-known illustrator, often involved his entire family—his wife Barbara and his daughter Rebecca as well as his son—in the making of his books. In fact, it was while Michael Emberley was working on one of the sections of *Ed Emberley's Big Drawing Book* that his father encouraged him to produce a series of his own books, leading to the start of Michael's independent career: *Dinosaurs! A Drawing Book* (1980). After creating *More Dinosaurs! And Other Prehistoric Beasts: A Drawing Book* (1983), Emberley focused a great deal of his attention on collaborating with Robie H. Harris on an important series of frank, humorous books for young readers about reproduction and their own sexuality: *It's Perfectly Normal: Changing Bodies, Growing Up, Sex, and Sexual Health* (1994), *Happy Birth Day!* (1996), *It's So Amazing! A Book about Eggs, Sperm, Birth, Babies, and Families* (1999), and a new series beginning with *Hello Benny! What It's Like to Be a Baby* (2002). Emberley studied at the Rhode Island School of Design (1979–80) and at the California College of Arts and Crafts (1981–82), but his major schooling was in his father's home. Influenced as well by the cartoon style of William Steig (1907–2003) and Richard Scarry (1919–1994), he has clearly developed his own unique mode of comic illustrating: his images are lively, clever, and droll. He uses fine ink drawings and graphics to emphasize relevant points in the texts and to stress that learning can be fun and can lead to unexpected discoveries. In particular, Emberley has a keen sense for the ironic in life, which is fully expressed in *Ruby* (1990).

The feminist slant in *Ruby* simply reflects Emberley's strong belief that women can master difficult situations by themselves. He also notes that

the folk tale slant came about by chance as I was writing a story that sounded a lot like Little Red Riding Hood, and I ended up just riding that wave to the beach, as they say. Creativity is not always about reinventing the wheel each time. Sometimes the best paths are part of the continuum. After all, the great history of storytelling that propelled much of early civilization involved adapting stories that came from before. I like the notion of being part of an ancient tradition. The story is one of the oldest forms of communication.

Certainly the story of Ruby is steeped in the narrative tradition of the little girl who walks into the woods and is violated, but Emberley's witty illustrations and insightful retelling also demonstrate how major changes in women's lives continue to transform that tradition.

Ruby

Ruby's whiskers twitched. Out in the kitchen, Ruby's mother was just finishing a batch of her famous triple-cheese pies.

"Ruby!" her mother called.

"Yeah?" said Ruby.

"I'd like you to go over to your granny's this afternoon."

"But, Ma . . ." Ruby groaned.

"She's not feeling too well," said her mother.

"But . . ."

"Now I've put in a couple of pies for each of you, plus a few extra in case Granny's neighbor Mrs. Mastiff stops by. You remember Mrs. Mastiff, don't you, Ruby?"

"Sure, Ma," Ruby mumbled.

"Now I want you to go straight there," her mother warned. "No talking to strangers, especially cats. Do you hear me, Ruby? Never, never trust a cat."

"Never, never, never," said Ruby flatly.

"And please don't read as you walk," called her mother. "You'll walk right in front of a bus one of these days."

"OK, Ma," grumbled Ruby.

Ruby got as far as the corner before she forgot her mother's advice and pulled out her book. A few paragraphs later . . . .

KA-PUMPH!

"Hey, kid, what's the rush?"

Ruby looked up. She had run into a grimy-looking reptile whose hot breath smelled very much like dirty gym socks.

"Buzz off, barf breath," Ruby replied, forgetting more of her mother's advice.

"Smart-mouth twerp," grunted the grimy reptile. "What's in the bag?"

"None of your beeswax, creepo," snapped Ruby, trying not to breathe. The creature's odor was so foul, Ruby's whiskers began to wilt.

"You better watch your yap, rodent," hissed the reptile. "Or I might tie your scrawny tail to a brick and take you for a swim."

"Right," snorted Ruby. "And you can't even tie your own shoes."

The grimy reptile turned an alarming shade of purple. Its eyes narrowed to slits.

Its forked tongue flicked in and out. Instinctively, Ruby took a step backward. But suddenly a grimy claw shot out and snatched the cheese pies.

"YOW!" shrieked Ruby.

"Put a cork in it, rodent!" spat the grimy reptile.

Then, as he turned to make his escape, an extremely well-dressed stranger appeared out of nowhere, stopping the thief in his tracks.

"Is there a problem here?" said the stranger casually in a smooth, velvety voice.

Ruby was speechless. The grimy reptile spluttered. "What the . . . ack . . . what is that stuff?"

"Just some warm soapy water," said the stranger. "Now what do you say, my scaly friend? Why don't you find your way back to whatever dark hole you crawled out of?" He paused to show some teeth. "Or perhaps you would enjoy another long overdue bath?"

MICHAEL
EMBERLEY

The grimy reptile glared at them. Then, deciding to stay dry and dirty, he slithered off, muttering foul curses.

"I hope that you are all right, my dear," purred the stranger, turning to Ruby.

"Yes, thank you," said Ruby politely. His breath smelled like cat food mixed with cheap peppermint mouthwash.

"You know," purred the stranger, "a tender, er, pretty thing like you really shouldn't be strolling the streets alone. You never know what nasty creatures may be prowling the dark alleys. I say, I would find it a great pleasure if you would allow me to escort you for the remainder of your journey today."

"Um . . . I don't think so," said Ruby, watching a bead of drool slip down a whisker.

"I beg you to reconsider," persisted the stranger.

"I'm only going to have tea with my granny and a neighbor," said Ruby. "I think I can make it."

"Really? Well, just where do Granny and this, um, neighbor live?" purred the stranger.

Ruby squinted at the stranger a moment. Then she answered slowly, "She has an apartment right at the top of Beacon Hill, number thirty-four."

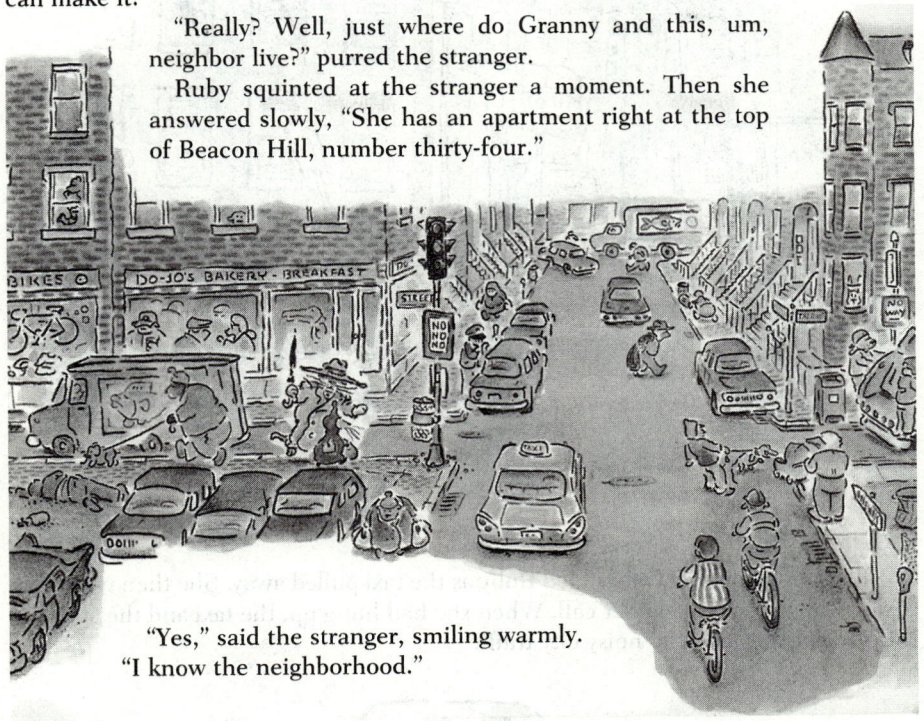

"Yes," said the stranger, smiling warmly. "I know the neighborhood."

"Well," said Ruby, "if you'll excuse me, I should call Granny. She'll be worried if I'm late, so—"

But the stranger was not listening. He waved for a taxi. "Please be careful," he said as he got in. "You won't find a friendly face like mine around every corner. And I certainly wouldn't want anything to happen to you."

"I'll bet you wouldn't," mumbled Ruby as the taxi pulled away. She then went over to a pay phone and made her call. When she had hung up, the taxi and the stranger had disappeared into the noisy city traffic.

"Where to?" grunted the taxi driver.

"Thirty-four Beacon Street," said the cat. "And step on it."

The cat couldn't help chuckling to himself. "What a wonderfully stupid child. Now I'll have *three* mice for lunch instead of one! I'll be there long before that tender little morsel. Plenty of time to nibble on the other two old rodents as appetizers." He giggled. "How clever I am!" He giggled again. "How wonderfully, wickedly clever!"

The cat arrived and rang the bell at number thirty-four. "Who is it?" asked a deep voice on the intercom.

"It's me," squeaked the cat, "little Ruby. I have some goodies for you."

"Ruby?" said the voice. "Just a minute."

"I hope Granny has some tarragon," thought the cat. "Tarragon is just the thing to have with roast mouse."

"You can come in now," sang the voice.

"Yum, yum," said the cat, as he quickly slipped inside.

Before long, Ruby arrived at number thirty-four nearly worn out from carrying all those cheese pies halfway across town and up Beacon Hill. She rang Granny's bell.

"Hello, Ruby dear," said a rough, squeaky voice.

"Granny? How did you know it was me?"

"I was expecting you, dear."

"You sound funny, Granny."

"It's just my cold, dear," said the voice. "Come on up."

MICHAEL
EMBERLEY

Ruby was just reaching for the doorknob when suddenly . . . the door swung open.

"Hi, Mrs. Mastiff," said Ruby.

"Hello, Ruby dear," said Mrs. Mastiff in her deep, cultured voice. "It was wise of you to call me instead of your granny. You were quite correct. That cat did show up here not long after your call. Doing a rather bad imitation of you, I must say."

"So, where's the slimebag now?" said Ruby.

"Oh, he's . . . gone," said Mrs. Mastiff, burping softly. "I imagine that I was not at all what he was expecting." An impish grin curled her mouth, making her look for a moment like a young pup.

Ruby gave Mrs. Mastiff a long look. "New hat?" she said finally.

"Why, yes," said Mrs. Mastiff, posing. "I just got it."

"Mmmm," said Ruby.

"What's all this?" said Granny, wobbling down the stairs.

"Hi, Granny," said Ruby.

"What? Oh, hello there, honey," said Granny.

"I've brought some of Ma's triple-cheese pies for tea," said Ruby.

"Hot dog! Oh! Sorry, Edna," said Granny, eyeing Mrs. Mastiff. "Didn't see you there. Well, let's get upstairs and dig in, I'm starved. Coming, Edna?"

"Thank you, but . . . I've just eaten," said Mrs. Mastiff.

"Suit yourself," said Granny, starting the long trip back up the stairs. "Phew! Does it stink of cat around here or is it just me? Better get upstairs, Ruby. Can't be too careful. Never trust a cat, I always say."

"Never, never, never," said Ruby.

FRANCESCA LIA BLOCK
b. 1962

Known for her "hip" tales that are permeated with the sense of her own Los Angeles environment, Francesca Lia Block has written several works of what she calls pop magic realism that deal with contemporary social problems and California's subcultures. She seeks to depict the desperate lives of children and teenagers as candidly as possible, revealing how they are often victimized by all the institutions established to school and train them—including the family. The worlds she portrays in her works are colored by the edgy and extravagant lifestyles of their inhabitants. Her major fantasies for young adults are the Weetzie Bat books—*Weetzie Bat* (1989), *Witch Baby* (1991), *Cherokee Bat and the Goat Guys* (1992), *Missing Angel Juan* (1993), and *Baby Be-Bop* (1995)—as well as *I Was a Teenage Fairy* (1998) and *The Rose and the Beast: Fairy Tales Retold* (2000). Her works of fiction for adults include *Ecstasia* (1993) and *Nymph* (2000).

Writing for teenagers, Block deals with homosexuality, drugs, child abuse, racism, anti-Semitism, commercial exploitation of the young, and cults. Los Angeles is painted as both nightmare and fairy-tale landscape in which teenagers seek to express their needs and desires through art and love, but are often thwarted by their own families and by outside predators who exploit and abuse their talents. *Weetzie Bat* sets the tone and introduces the characters for the other four linked novels; the central figure is Weetzie, a skinny teenage girl with a bleached-blonde flattop and pink harlequin sunglasses. Reality and fantasy mix as Weetzie and her gay friend Dirk both seek and find love, and in the process they create an extended family (complete with two babies) in a world that includes not just illicit drugs, sexual promiscuity, and commercial exploitation but also an evil witch and a genie offering three wishes. Block explores the problems of children whose biological families, for whatever reasons, have failed them and who must fashion their own community and sense of caring. Though never ignoring the pain in modern society, her works offer solace and hope as they celebrate faithfulness and love.

"Wolf," a story published in *The Rose and the Beast*, connects fairy tales with rape and violence. As in Matthew Bright's important film *Freeway* (1998), which also deals with the problems facing a contemporary Red Riding Hood, Block's story shows how a young girl can take charge of her life, while at the same time exposing the sado-masochistic ties that exist in many dysfunctional families.

Wolf

They don't believe me. They think I'm crazy. But let me tell you something it be a wicked wicked world out there if you didn't already know.

My mom and he were fighting and that was nothing new. And he was drinking, same old thing. But then I heard her mention me, how she knew what he was doing. And no fucking way was she going to sit around and let that happen. She was taking me away and he better not try to stop her. He said, no way, she couldn't leave.

That's when I started getting scared for both of us, my mom and me. How the hell did she know about that? He would think for sure I told her. And then he'd do what he had promised he'd do every night he held me under the crush of his putrid skanky body.

I knew I had to get out of there. I put all my stuff together as quick and quiet as possible—just some clothes, and this one stuffed lamb my mom gave me when I was little and my piggy-bank money that I'd been saving—and I climbed out the window of the condo. It was a hot night and I could smell my own sweat but it was different. I smelled the same old fear I'm used to but it was mixed with the night and the air and the moon and the trees and it was like freedom, that's what I smelled on my skin.

Same old boring boring story America can't stop telling itself. What is this sicko fascination? Every book and movie practically has to have a little, right? But why do you think all those runaways are on the streets tearing up their veins with junk and selling themselves so they can sleep in the gutter? What do you think the alternative was at home?

I booked because I am not a victim by nature. I had been planning on leaving, but I didn't want to lose my mom and I knew the only way I could get her to leave him was if I told her what he did. That was out of the question, not only because of what he might do to me but what it would do to her.

I knew I had to go back and help her, but I have to admit to you that at that moment I was scared shitless and it didn't seem like the time to try any heroics. That's when I knew I had to get to the desert because there was only one person I had in the world besides my mom.

I really love my mom. You know we were like best friends and I didn't even really need any other friend. She was so much fun to hang with. We cut each other's hair and shared clothes. Her taste was kind of youngish and cute, but it worked because she looked pretty young. People thought we were sisters. She knew all the song lyrics and we sang along in the car. We both can't carry a tune. Couldn't? What else about her? It's so hard to think of things sometimes, when you're trying to describe some-body so someone else will know. But that's the thing about it—no one can ever know. Basically you're totally alone and the only person in the world who made me feel not completely that way was her because after all we were made of the same stuff. She used to say to me, Baby, I'll always be with you. No matter what happens to me I'm still here. I believed her until he started coming into my room. Maybe she was still with me but I couldn't be with her those times. It was like if I did then she'd hurt so bad I'd lose her forever.

I figured the only place I could go would be to the desert, so I got together all my money and went to the bus station and bought a ticket. On the ride I started getting the shakes real bad thinking that maybe I shouldn't have left my mom alone like that and maybe I should go back but I was chickenshit, I guess. I leaned my head on the glass and it felt cool and when we got out of the city I started feeling a little better like I could breathe. L.A. isn't really so bad as people think. I guess. I mean there are gangs at my school but they aren't really active or violent except for the isolated incident. I have experienced one big earthquake in my life and it really didn't bother me so much because I'd rather feel out of control at the mercy of nature than other ways, if you know what I mean. I just closed my eyes and let it ride itself out. I kind of wished he'd been on top of me then because it might have scared him and made him feel retribution was at hand, but I seriously doubt that. I don't blame the earth for shaking because she is probably so sick of people fucking with her all the time— building things and poisoning her and that. L.A. is also known for the smog, but my mom said that when she was growing up it was way worse and that they had to have smog alerts all the time where they couldn't do P.E. Now that part I would have liked because P.E. sucks. I'm not very athletic, maybe 'cause I smoke, and I hate getting undressed in front of some of those stupid bitches who like to see what kind of underwear you have on so they can dis you in yet another ingenious way. Anyway, my smoking is way worse for my lungs than the smog, so I don't care about it too much. My mom hated that I smoke and she tried everything—tears and the patch and Nicorette[1] and homeopathic remedies and trips to an acupuncturist, but finally she gave up.

I was wanting a cigarette bad on that bus and thinking about how it would taste, better than the normal taste in my mouth, which I consider tainted by him, and how I can always weirdly breathe a lot better when I have one. My mom read somewhere that smokers smoke as a way to breathe more, so yoga is supposed to help, but that is one thing she couldn't get me to try. My grandmother, I knew she wouldn't mind the smoking—what could she say? My mom called her Barb the chimney. There is something so dry and brittle, so sort of flammable about her, you'd think it'd be dangerous for her to light up like that.

I liked the desert from when I visited there. I liked that it was hot and clean-feeling, and the sand and rocks and cactus didn't make you think too much about love and if you had it or not. They kind of made your mind still, whereas L.A.—even the best parts, maybe especially the best parts, like flowering trees and neon signs and different kinds of ethnic food and music—made you feel agitated and like you were never really getting what you needed. Maybe L.A. had some untapped resources and hidden treasures that would make me feel full and happy and that I didn't know about yet but I wasn't dying to find them just then. If I had a choice I'd probably like to go to Bali or someplace like that where people are more natural and believe in art and dreams and color and love. Does any place like that exist? The main reason L.A. was okay was because that is where my mom was and anywhere she was I had decided to make my home.

On the bus there was this boy with straight brown hair hanging in his pale freckled face. He looked really sad. I wanted to talk to him so much but of course I didn't. I am freaked that if I get close to a boy he will somehow find out what happened to me—like it's a scar he'll see or a smell or something, a red flag—and he'll hate me and go away. This boy kind of looked like maybe something had happened to him, too, but you can't know for sure. Sometimes I'd think I'd see signs of it in people but then I wondered if I was just trying not to feel so alone. That sounds sick, I guess, trying to almost wish what I went through on someone else for company. But I don't mean it that way. I don't wish it on anyone, believe me, but if they've been there I would like to talk to them about it.

The boy was writing furiously in a notebook, like maybe a journal, which I thought was cool. This journal now is the best thing I've ever done in my whole life. It's the only good thing really that they've given me here.

One of our assignments was to write about your perfect dream day. I wonder what this boy's perfect dream day would be. Probably to get to fuck Pamela Lee[2] or something. Unless he was really as cool as I hoped, in which case it would be to wake up in a bed full of cute kitties and puppies and eat a bowl full of chocolate chip cookies in milk and get on a plane and get to go to a warm, clean, safe place (the cats and dogs would arrive there later, not at all stressed from their journey) where you could swim in blue-crystal water all day naked without being afraid and you could lie in the sun and tell your best friend (who was also there) your funniest stories so that you both laughed so hard you thought you'd pop and at night you got to go to a restaurant full of balloons and candles and stuffed bears, like my birthdays when I

---

1. Nicotine gum.
2. Canadian-born American actress and Playboy model (b. 1967).

was little, and eat mounds of ice cream after removing the circuses of tiny plastic animals from on top.

In my case, the best friend would be my mom, of course, and maybe this boy if he turned out to be real cool and not stupid.

I fell asleep for a little while and I had this really bad dream. I can't remember what it was but I woke up feeling like someone had been slugging me. And then I thought about my mom, I waited to feel her there with me, like I did whenever I was scared, but it was like those times when he came into my room—she wasn't anywhere. She was gone then and I think that was when I knew but I wouldn't let myself.

I think when you are born an angel should say to you, hopefully kindly and not in the fake voice of an airline attendant: Here you go on this long, long dream. Don't even try to wake up. Just let it go on until it is over. You will learn many things. Just relax and observe because there just is pain and that's it mostly and you aren't going to be able to escape no matter what. Eventually it will all be over anyway. Good luck.

I had to get off the bus before the boy with the notebook and as I passed him he looked up. I saw in his journal that he hadn't been writing but sketching, and he ripped out a page and handed it to me. I saw it was a picture of a girl's face but that is all that registered because I was thinking about how my stomach had dropped, how I had to keep walking, step by step, and get off the bus and I'd never be able to see him again and somehow it really really mattered.

When I got off the bus and lit up I saw that the picture was me—except way prettier than I think I look, but just as sad as I feel. And then it was too late to do anything because the bus was gone and so was he.

I stopped at the liquor store and bought a bag of pretzels and a Mountain Dew because I hadn't eaten all day and my stomach was talking pretty loud. Everything tasted of bitter smoke. Then after I'd eaten I started walking along the road to my grandma's. She lives off the highway on this dirt road surrounded by cactus and other desert plants. It was pretty dark so you could see the stars really big and bright, and I thought how cold the sky was and not welcoming or magical at all. It just made me feel really lonely. A bat flew past like a sharp shadow and I could hear owls and coyotes. The coyote howls were the sound I would have made if I could have. Deep and sad but scary enough that no one would mess with me, either.

My grandma has a used stuff store so her house is like this crazy warehouse full of junk like those little plaster statuettes from the seventies of these ugly little kids with stupid sayings that are supposed to be funny, and lots of old clothes like army jackets and jeans and ladies' nylon shirts, and cocktail glasses, broken china, old books, trinkets, gadgets, just a lot of stuff that you think no one would want but they do, I guess, because she's been in business a long time. Mostly people come just to talk to her because she is sort of this wise woman of the desert who's been through a lot in her life and then they end up buying something, I think, as a way to pay her back for the free counseling. She's cool, with a desert-lined face and a bandanna over her hair and long skinny legs in jeans. She was always after my mom to drop that guy and move out here with her but my mom wouldn't. My mom still was holding on to her secret dream of being an actress but nothing had panned out yet. She was so pretty, I thought it would, though. Even though she had started to look a little older. But she could have gotten those commercials where they use the women her age to sell household products and aspirin and stuff. She would have been good at that because of her face and her voice, which are kind and honest and you just trust her.

I hadn't told Grandma anything about him, but I think she knew that he was fucked up. She didn't know how much, though, or she wouldn't have let us stay there.

Sometimes I wanted to go and tell her, but I was afraid then Mom would have to know and maybe hate me so much that she'd kick me out.

My mom and I used to get dressed up and put makeup on each other and pretend to do commercials. We had this mother-daughter one that was pretty cool. She said I was a natural, but I wouldn't want to be an actor because I didn't like people looking at me that much. Except that boy on the bus, because his drawing wasn't about the outside of my body, but how I felt inside and you could tell by the way he did it, and the way he smiled, that he understood those feelings so I didn't mind that he saw them. My mom felt that I'd be good anyway, because she said that a lot of actors don't like people looking at them and that is how they create these personas to hide behind so people will see that and the really good ones are created to hide a lot of things. I guess for that reason I might be okay but I still hated the idea of going on auditions and having people tell me I wasn't pretty enough or something. My mom said it was interesting and challenging but I saw it start to wear on her.

Grandma wasn't there when I knocked so I went around the back, where she sat sometimes at night to smoke, and it was quiet there, too. That's when I started feeling sick like at night in my bed trying not to breathe or vomit. Because I saw his Buick sitting there in the sand.

Maybe I have read too many fairy tales. Maybe no one will believe me.

I poked around the house and looked through the windows and after a while I heard their voices and I saw them in this cluttered little storage room piled up with the stuff she sells at the store. Everything looked this glazed brown fluorescent color. When I saw his face I knew something really bad had happened. I remembered the dream I had had and thought about my mom. All of a sudden I was inside that room, I don't really remember how I got there, but I was standing next to my grandma and I saw she had her shotgun in her hand.

He was saying, Barb, calm down, now, okay. Just calm down. When he saw me his eyes narrowed like dark slashes and I heard a coyote out in the night.

My grandmother looked at me and at him and her mouth was this little line stitched up with wrinkles. She kept looking at him but she said to me, Babe, are you okay?

I said I had heard him yelling at mom and I left. She asked him what happened with Nance and he said they had a little argument, that was all, put down the gun, please, Barb.

Then I just lost it, I saw my grandma maybe start to back down a little and I went ballistic. I started screaming how he had raped me for years and I wanted to kill him and if we didn't he'd kill us. Maybe my mom was already dead.

I don't know what else I said, but I do know that he started laughing at me, this hideous tooth laugh, and I remembered him above me in that bed with his clammy hand on my mouth and his ugly ugly weight and me trying to keep hanging on because I wouldn't let him take my mom away, that was the one thing he could never do and now he had. Then I had the gun and I pulled the trigger. My grandma had taught me how once, without my mom knowing, in case I ever needed to defend myself, she said.

My grandma says that she did it. She says that he came at us and she said to him, I've killed a lot prettier, sweeter innocents than you with this shotgun, meaning the animals when she used to go out hunting, which is a pretty good line and everything, but she didn't do it. It was me.

I have no regrets about him. I don't care about much anymore, really. Only one thing.

Maybe one night I'll be asleep and I'll feel a hand like a dove on my cheekbone and feel her breath cool like peppermints and when I open my eyes my mom will be there like an angel, saying in the softest voice, When you are born it is like a long, long dream. Don't try to wake up. Just go along until it is over. Don't be afraid. You may not know it all the time but I am with you. I am with you.

2000

Animal Fables

"The saddest words of pen or tongue are wisdom's wasted on the young." James Thurber appended this moral to "The Daws on the Dial" in *Further Fables for Our Time* (1956), which with its predecessor of 1940 reflects his pessimism about human nature and human behavior. For centuries—indeed, until juvenile publishing became established in the mid–eighteenth century—fables were the only approved secular reading for the young; their elders hoped that such stories would impart important lessons in how to behave, as well as providing a modicum of entertainment. These tales with origins in antiquity are found in cultures all around the world. Replacing humans with animal characters and embodying a coded meaning (appended morals were a later development), animal fables were originally intended not for the young, but for rulers who might benefit from hidden advice, as in the Indian fable of the talkative tortoise; or as political statements; or for the secret amusement of the oppressed, as in the tales of Brer Rabbit. Many indeed represent the protest of the weak; it is significant that both Aesop and Phaedrus, who six centuries later retold Aesopic fables, had been slaves.

Fables were an inescapable experience for schoolboys from the sixth century B.C.E. until at least the eighteenth century. The stories told by Aesop, an illiterate Thracian slave who lived on the island of Samos with his masters and who died about 560 B.C.E., were first circulated by word of mouth. These few facts are virtually all that is known about Aesop; the description of his physical appearance and details of his life set out in the preface to many fable collections are much later fabrications, just as the Aesop "umbrella" has come to shelter many much later fabulists. In 1692 Roger L'Estrange in his preface to *Fables of Aesop, and Other Eminent Mythologists* wrote that it was impossible to say "which of the Fables are Aesop's, and which are not."

Nor was Aesop the originator of the fable form; the stories associated with him have very ancient Greek roots and may have come from much farther than Asia Minor. Joseph Jacobs (1854–1916), a historian and folklorist, in the preface to *Indian Fairy Tales* (1892) gave as his opinion that "a goodly number of the fables that pass under the name of the Samian slave, Aesop, were derived from India, probably from the same source whence the same tales were utilised in the Jatakas, or Birth stories of Buddha." Aesop's stories well may have been considered subversive by his masters, touching as so many do on the weak getting the better of the strong. Nevertheless they were early used to teach grammar and ethics, and were widely circulated. Demetrius of Phalerum (b. ca. 350 B.C.E.) made an assemblage of 200 Aesopic fables that he found in the great library at Alexandria, the center of literature for the Hellenistic world. Now lost, it was probably the earliest Greek collection and the ultimate source of subsequent retellings. The earliest extant collection of the fables in Greek is that of Babrius (ca. 150–200 C.E.), a Hellenized Roman who also wrote in verse, working from Aesopic and Libyan sources. Some two hundred years later Avianus, a young Roman poet, put them into Latin verse, and quotations and paraphrases show that Avianus was much used in medieval schools.

There never has been an Aesop urtext; contents vary and the tales are a patchwork of different authors, most of them working from Phaedrus (ca. 15 B.C.E.–ca. 50 C.E.), a slave in Italy who was freed by the Emperor Augustus. "Our Aesop is Phaedrus with trimmings," Joseph Jacobs writes in his introduction to *The Fables of Aesop as Printed by William Caxton* (1889). Drawing on Aesop, known to him from Demetrius of Phalerum's compilation, Phaedrus composed five books of fables in Latin verse, adding jokes and anecdotes from his own experience. John Henderson in *Telling Tales on Caesar: Roman Stories from Phaedrus* (2001) points out oblique references to Roman power dynamics in Phaedrus's versions. Or sometimes not so oblique. The first Phaedrus fable is of the Wolf and the Lamb, where the Lamb's pitiful reasons as to why he could not have fouled the water that he and the Wolf are both drinking are brushed aside contemptuously before the latter tears him to pieces. "Innocence is no Protection against the arbitrary Cruelty of a tyrannical Power," said Roger L'Estrange in 1692; "The most savagely crushing presentation of the self-confuting dialectic of power supremacy," observes Henderson. The same tilting at power and authority can be found in African stories of the rascally Hare, who outwits all the larger animals including the Lion; only the Tortoise manages to outwit him.

Fables, particularly from Eastern sources, are to be found in the *Gesta Romanorum* (*The Deeds of the Romans*), a hugely popular hodgepodge of stories from classical literature, legends of the saints, romances, and much else, each with its own elaborate and often far-fetched Christian interpretation. It was assembled in England in about 1300 and provided material for sermons in the Middle Ages as well as for many authors from Chaucer to Shakespeare. Also to be found there are traces of stories from the Panchatantra (lit., the Five Books), a collection of Indian stories told by a wise brahmin named Bidpai (also known as Pilpay) to an all-powerful ruler, counseling him in the ways of the world and whom to trust. Bidpai or Pilpay stories reached the West through an Arabic translation; they were not as old as Aesop but may well have been based on even more ancient material. They were published for children in the eighteenth and early nineteenth centuries but never achieved the popularity of Aesop. "The Talkative Tortoise," included here, is a version of "The Tortoise and the Two Ducks," a Bidpai/Pilpay story retold with racy humor by a Victorian editor. The French poet Jean de La Fontaine (1621–1695), who had drawn on Aesop and Phaedrus for his first book of *Fables choisies, mises en vers* (1668), turned to Pilpay in his second volume ten years later and included a versified "Tortoise and the Two Ducks."

Early Use of Fables in Education

By the seventeenth century the adult reading public had lost interest in prose fables, which had become relegated to children, at school and in the home. Nathaniel Crouch (ca. 1632–ca. 1725), a hack writer who raided other men's works to make books of his own, admitted as much in his preface to *Delightful Fables in Prose and Verse* (1691) when he protested that the reader ought not to think fables were invented only to please children. But this was the general attitude. John Locke, the philosopher and physician, in his wise and enlightened *Some Thoughts Concerning Education* (1693) knew of nothing else "fit to engage the liking of children, and tempt them to read." They were short, the subject of many of them was the appealing one of animals, and they were deemed not to be works of imagination like fairy tales, which Locke's contemporaries in particular found dangerous and corrupting.

Fables on the contrary were held to be improving, and many of those who aimed compilations at children hoped that the character of young readers would be molded thereby. The main lesson is worldly wisdom. What fables seem to teach is at best prudence and caution; at worst ruthlessness, rascality, and self-interest. Compassion and charity have no part in them. The fox climbs out of a well on the horns of the goat who has also fallen in. He has undertaken to help rescue the goat, but once safely at the top he merely jeers at his companion. Roger L'Estrange makes him say, " 'If you had but half so much Brain as Beard, you would have better thought your self how to get up again before you went down.' " The moral that L'Estrange appended to this tale, like the lengthy "reflection" that follows, deplores not the behavior of the fox but the lack of foresight on the goat's part: "We cannot therefore keep too strict an Eye upon the Life and Conversation of those we have to do withal."

For more than two thousand years the Aesopic fables were used to teach grammar and syntax. Latin was deemed essential in European schools; indeed, it was the principal part of a boy's education. For centuries it was often taught by the interlineary method—Latin on one line, a translation in the native language on the line below. Aesop came in for this treatment, and schoolbooks are the earliest juvenile Aesops. The first translation into English designed for the common reader generally was *Subtyl Historyes and Fables of Esope* (1484) by William Caxton. He had worked from a German / Latin original, the famous Ulm Aesop (1476–77) in which Heinrich Steinhöwell had collected all the Aesopic fables then known. It was the first printed collection, and through translations from it the fables became known throughout Europe. F. J. Harvey Darton expressed the opinion in *Children's Books in England* (1932) that Caxton's version was still the best for children. It certainly is simple and succinct, as in the tale of the Fox and the Grapes, which Caxton styled "Of the Foxe and of the Raysyns":

> He is not wyse that desyreth to have a thynge which he may not have. As reciteth this fable of a foxe which loked and beheld the raysyns that grewe upon an hyghe vyne: the whiche raysyns he moche desyred for to ete them.
> And whanne he sawe that none he myght gete: he torned his sorowe in to joye: and sayd these raysyns ben sowre: and if I had some I wold not ete them: And therfore this fable sheweth that he is wyse: whiche fayneth not to desyre that thynge the whiche he may not have.

Caxton had commended the wisdom of the fox; some compilers did the same, but others were contemptuous; asserting that it is easy to despise what you cannot get. Fables are often ambiguous; moralists can make of them what they will.

Illustrations for Aesop and Retellings

Caxton's Aesop had illustrations—robust woodcuts with strongly characterized animals. Locke said that as soon as a child "begins to spell, as many pictures of animals should be got him as can be found." When he wrote in 1693, such books were a rarity. Roger L'Estrange's *Fables of Aesop* published the previous year was unillustrated, though he stressed in his preface that he wanted to present them in an attractive form to young readers who were only stumbling through the words in Latin in their schoolbooks. There had been some splendid fifteenth- and sixteenth-century German, Italian, French, and Flemish illustrated Aesops as well as the Caxton, but these were designed for collectors not juveniles, as were Wenzel Hollar's illustrations for John Ogilby's *Aesop* (1665) and Francis Barlow's for a trilingual edition (Latin, French, English) of 1666. An early, more modest Aesop with pictures for children was published anonymously in 1703. (It was later, after his death, attributed to Locke.) The engravings are unimpressive; crude heraldic beasts cluster sixteen on one page, and little distinction is made between "Dog" and "Lyon," "Lamb" and "Asse."

It was surely the illustrations in Samuel Croxall's *Fables of Aesop and Others* (1722) that made the book so popular. Indeed, as the first fully illustrated children's Aesop, it would seem to be the book that Locke was looking for. Elisha Kirkall provided 196 metal engravings—one for each fable—for Croxall's wordy retellings, each followed by lengthier moral musings. Two examples are included here. In an obsequious dedication to a young nobleman who had been five when Croxall first met him, and was seven when the book was published, he also castigates the "pernicious principles" of L'Estrange, denouncing him for having been "Pensioner to a Popish Prince . . . the Tool and Hireling of the Popish Faction." L'Estrange's political views were anathema to Croxall, as were his Catholicism and moral outlook. However, Croxall's precepts were no loftier, being similarly grounded in expediency and the best way to achieve worldly success. L'Estrange was nearer to Locke in his interest in the child reader and his sympathy with schoolboys struggling over fables in Latin: "The Boys break their Teeth upon the Shells, without ever coming near the Kernel." The L'Estrange translations were used in several twentieth-century compilations.

The Newbery firm did well with fables, beginning with *Fables in Verse for the Improvement of the Young and the Old* by "Abraham Aesop" (1757), which went into some ten editions by 1783. Francis Newbery, the nephew of John, published the ninth edition of Croxall, and his widow Elizabeth published the twelfth edition in 1782. And there were Newbery collections for younger readers, including three stages of a reading primer, *Ladder to Learning,* in which fables were told in words of one syllable, then two, then three. Other publishers began competing. One of the most handsomely produced volumes was Robert Dodsley's *Select Fables of Esop and Other Fabulists* (1761), notable for the fine printing and pretty engravings. This was an upscale book, published by the author from London and printed in Birmingham. John Marshall (fl. 1783–1828), catering to less expensive tastes, produced *Tales and Fables Selected by T. Ticklepitcher from the Works of Eminent Writers* (ca. 1785). The poet John Gay (1685–1732) was among these writers. His fables, published in two parts in 1727 and posthumously in 1738, though all were original, owed much in style to La Fontaine. One especially, "The Hare and Many Friends," was often found in collections such as Ticklepitcher's. The Hare whose "care was never to offend / And ev'ry creature was her friend" realizes only when her life is threatened the mistake of being affable to all without ever making a close friend.

Among all these presentations of Aesopic fables, William Godwin's *Fables Ancient and Modern* (1805) stands out. At the time of publication Godwin had three children of his own and two stepchildren, all under ten, and knew from experience the sort of story they liked. The first question they asked when a fable had been read to them was "What became of the poor dog, the fox, or the wolf?" So to remedy the defect he enlarged the text, made it child-oriented, and provided happy but suitably moral endings. In "The Frog and the Ox" Aesop has an old frog boasting to her young that she can make herself the size of an ox; she bursts in the attempt. Godwin substitutes a conceited young frog "who gave a great deal of trouble to his mamma by pretending on all occasions that he could do any thing he had a mind to do." He tells his mother that he can be as big as an ox, but learns his lesson and survives to be a wiser frog.

In contrast Walter Crane's *The Baby's Own Aesop* (1887), despite its title, makes no concession whatever to child readers; the point of some of the five-line verse stories is often hard to grasp and the page designs are overelaborate, even fussy. By this time Aesop editions were often known by the names of their illustrators: Ernest Griset, Harrison Weir, and so on. Harvey Darton had noted, referring to the 1780s:

> Thus, before George III's reign was half over, the Fable had passed, like an embryo, through the literary and social changes of its full growth. It had been something not far from folk-lore long before, had been regimented for schools and decked out for fashion. It had been Everyman's and now was Everychild's. All its supporters and well-wishers were at last ready for it together—the publisher, the author who could make a living out of it, the artist who could embellish it, and the large solid reading public who merely wished to enjoy it. Its later history, once it was a children's book, is but the record of the redecoration of a known model.

Though the Victorian period offered many fine illustrated Aesops, there was little further scope for retelling the fables. There were, however, notable collections of Indian tales, such as *Wide-Awake Stories* (1884) collected by Flora Annie Steel (1847–1929) "direct from the lips of the narrators," as the preface says. "The Jackal and the Crocodile," which according to her notes has a parallel in most Indian collections, bears a marked resemblance to "The Crocodile and the Monkey," retold by W. H. D. Rouse in 1897 and included here. Mrs. Steel also found parallels in *Uncle Remus*.

African American Fables

Interest in African American fables began at much the same time. Joel Chandler Harris's *Uncle Remus, His Songs and His Sayings* appeared in 1880, and English editions followed at once. In his preface Harris cited the work of contemporary anthropologists on Amazonian folk legends and their parallels with the plantation stories. As with all folktales, it is impossible to track origins. In 1892 Joseph Jacobs in *Indian Fairy Tales* claimed that the story in the Panchatantra "The Demon with the Matted Hair," in which the Bodhisattva five times attacks a demon and each time finds himself stuck to a different part of the creature, might well be the source of the Tar Baby story. Virginia Hamilton in her Tar Baby retelling in *The People Could Fly* (1985) refers to some three hundred different versions, from sources that include Africa, Brazil, India, and the Bahamas. And Henri Junod, a Swiss anthropologist, in *Life of a South African Tribe* (1913) collected stories from the Mozambique region about the wily Hare who outwits all the large animals, including the Lion; "But there was one creature that outdid the Hare in cunning, and that was the Tortoise." This would seem to be the origin of the Uncle Remus story of the race between Brer Rabbit and Brer Tarrypin. But there is also the Aesop story "The Hare and the Tortoise," which may be older than either. Possibly the Uncle Remus tales about how animals acquired their physical characteristics—"How Mr. Rabbit Lost His Fine

Bushy Tale," for example—gave Rudyard Kipling the idea for some of the *Just So Stories for Little Children*. These comic fables mingle many traditions, often parodying the style of the oriental Jataka tales, sometimes the *Arabian Nights*, as in "How the Camel Got His Hump," included here, in which a Djinn—a supernatural being in Arabic mythology—punishes the surly camel. Kipling's lighthearted verses about "the Hump we get / From having too little to do" are very different from the lengthy moral reflections of L'Estrange and Croxall, quoted earlier.

Twentieth-century African Americans have retold African fables, eliminating the slave element of Harris's Uncle Remus and the difficult dialect. Julius Lester's *Tales of Uncle Remus*, beginning with *The Adventures of Brer Rabbit* (1987), used Harris to create a simpler version with contemporary speech patterns and a sharpened story line, so that the stories would read easily but could also be told aloud in the traditional style. Virginia Hamilton included animal fables in her three collections of American black folktales. Ashley Bryan, an author, illustrator, and collector of folktales, built on Henri Junod's summary of how the Tortoise tricked the Hare and created his own story, printed here.

Twentieth Century

The fable form has long been used by writers to make political statements—or, as in the case of James Thurber, to give a wry view of human wiles and folly. An outstanding example of the first is George Orwell's *Animal Farm* (1945), a satire on the Russian Revolution, and by extension on all revolution. After Orwell's animals oust the humans, the pigs become the leaders with the slogan "All animals are equal but some animals are more equal than others." They are corrupted by power, and the new tyranny is infinitely more savage than the old.

Ted Hughes's *What Is the Truth? A Farmyard Fable for the Young*, first published in 1984 as a picture book with evocative black-and-white illustrations by R. J. Lloyd, is a collection of poems linked by prose narration. God and his Son visit the sleeping countryside and listen to what its inhabitants have to say in their dreams about the animals in their lives. The attitude of those whose livelihood depends on these is necessarily subjective. The Shepherd can only see the Lamb as "a machine of problems." The Farmer sees his cows as a factory that provides milk and meat, and also slurry that poisons the rivers. He execrates the rooks and pigeons who demolish his crops, but is eloquent about swallows "whetted on air, every move smoother," and mourns the working horses of his childhood, "our last friendly angels," now supplanted by the tractor. The Poacher is freer to admire nature—even the rat. The Farmer's daughter is passionate about a new foal, the Farmer's wife about the maternal nature of the cow. The Vicar and the Schoolteacher both speak of animals and birds they have watched. " 'You see,' said God to his Son, 'these creatures are their toys. Some they keep, some they break.' 'But have we heard the Truth?' asks God's son. 'What is the Truth?'" To which God replies, as the Buddha might have done, that he is all creation—the foal, the cow, the rat, the fly—even the hedgehog's fleas. " 'And each of these things is Me. It is. It is. That is the Truth.'"

Russell Hoban's *The Sea-Thing Child* (1972), the last fable included in this section, is more in the style of an allegory. Here an unidentified fledgling bird washed up on the seashore develops the confidence and resolution to fly away and find his proper element, while his companion the fiddler crab stays on the shore mourning his loneliness and lost opportunities.

For younger children, as William Godwin could see, the traditional Aesopic fable is bleak, unappealing, and far too terse. His solution, already mentioned, was to rewrite a handful, softening their ruthlessness and often introducing child characters. His latest successors have used picture-book format to make the stories even more accessible. *The Very Best of Aesop's Fables* (1990) presents eleven of the tales, retold by Margaret Clark and illustrated by Charlotte Voake. Though the text has been expanded, its thrust has not been changed and it is the gentle pictures that are most at variance with the Aesopic sharpness. *Aesop's Funky Fables* (1997) is another picture book; the text is by Vivian French, with wild cartoon-style illustrations by Korky Paul. Here the retellings, some of them imitating rock or rap rhythms and seemingly designed to be chanted aloud, are far more elaborate; and the little-known "Bat, Bramble, and Cormorant," which occupies only a few lines in L'Estrange, has been reworked into a powerful short story. This book is that unusual thing—a new departure in the presentation of Aesop to the young.

SAMUEL CROXALL

d. 1752

The Reverend Samuel Croxall's *Fables of Aesop and Others* (1722) long remained the most popular children's Aesop through some two hundred editions. It must have been one of the works William Godwin had in mind when in his own compilation he tried to improve the manner in which Aesop was usually presented to children. The handsome copper engravings by Elisha Kirkall are the most appealing element in the book. In the manner of Roger L'Estrange's *Aesop* (1692), the appended reflections vastly exceed the length of each fable. The work was dedicated in slavish terms to "the most lovely and the most engaging child that ever was born"—seven-year-old George, the young son of Croxall's patron, the Earl of Halifax. He was apparently a paragon of learning as well as of amiability, but despite Croxall's confident predictions about his future (molded by "these lectures of morality") George grew up to be a politician notorious for his office seeking, dissipation, and extravagance.

From Fables of Aesop and Others

THE FOX WITHOUT A TAIL

A Fox, being caught in a Steel-Trap by his Tail, was glad to compound for his Escape with the Loss of it; But, upon coming abroad into the World, began to be so sensible of the Disgrace such a Defect would bring upon him, that he almost wish'd he had died, rather than left it behind him. However, to make the best of a bad Matter, he form'd a Project in his Head, to call an Assembly of the rest of the Foxes, and propose it for their Imitation, as a Fashion which would be very agreeable and becoming. He did so: and made a long Harangue upon the Unprofitableness of Tails in general, and endeavour'd chiefly to shew the Aukwardness and Inconvenience of a Fox's Tail in particular; adding, that it would be both more graceful, and more expeditious to be altogether without them; and that, for his Part, what he had only imagin'd and conjectur'd before, he now found by Experience, for that he never enjoy'd himself so well, and found himself so easy, as he had done, since he cut off his Tail. He said no more, but look'd about with a brisk Air to see what Proselytes he had gain'd; when a sly old Thief in the Company, who understood Trap, answer'd him, with a Leer, I believe you may have found a Conveniency in parting with your Tail, and when we are in the same Circumstances, perhaps we may do so too.

The Application

If the World were but generally as prudent as Foxes, they would not suffer so many silly Fashions to obtain, as are daily brought in Vogue: for which scarce any Reason can be assign'd besides the Humour of some conceited vain Creature; unless, which is full as bad, they are intended to palliate some Defect in the Person that introduces them. The Petticoat of a whole Sex is sometimes swell'd to screen an Enormity, of which only one of them has been guilty. Nay so strangely good-natur'd have the Ladies of some Countries been in this respect, that they were contented to expose some hundred Pair of Mill-posts, to countenance the Opportunity of some body's displaying one Pair of handsom Legs. It is no such Wonder that *Alexander* the Great[1] could bring a wry Neck into Fashion in a Nation of Slaves, when we consider what Power, of this nature, some little, insignificant, dapper Fellows have had among a free People.

THE FOX AND THE CROW

A Crow having taken a Piece of Cheese out of a Cottage-Window, flew up into a high Tree with it, in order to eat it. Which a Fox observing, came and sate underneath, and began to compliment the Crow upon the Subject of her Beauty. I protest, says he, I never observ'd it before, but your Feathers are of a more delicate White than any that ever I saw in my Life: Ah! what a fine Shape, and graceful turn of Body is there! And I make no question but you have a tolerable Voice? If it were but as fine as your Complexion, as I hope to live, I don't know a Bird that could pretend to stand in Competition with you. The Crow, tickled with this very civil Language, nestled and riggled[2] about, and hardly knew where she was; but thinking the Fox a little in the dark as to the Particular of her Voice, and having a mind to set him right in that Matter, she begun to sing, for his Information; and, in the same Instant, let the Cheese drop out of her Mouth. This being what the Fox wanted, he chop'd it up in a Moment; and trotted away, laughing in his Sleeve, at the easie Credulity of the Crow.

1. King of Macedonia (356–323 B.C.E.; r. 336–323), generally thought to be the greatest general of antiquity; he brought the eastern Mediterranean under Macedonian rule, creating an empire that stretched to India.
2. Wriggled.

The Application

They that love Flattery (as I have heard several People declare they do) are in a fair way to repent of their Foible at the long Run. And yet I don't believe there is one to be found among the whole race of Mankind, who may be said to be full Proof against its Attacks. The gross Way, by which it is manag'd by some silly[3] Practitioners, is enough to alarm the dullest Apprehension, and make it value itself upon the Quickness of its Insight into the little Plots of this nature. But, let the Ambuscade be dispos'd with due Judgment, and I will warrant it to surprize the most guarded Heart. I have known a Man tickled to the last degree with the Pleasure of Flattery, while he has been applauded for his honest Detestation of those that are liable to it themselves, or play it off upon others. I know no Way to baffle the Force of this Engine, but by every one's examining impartially for himself, the true Estimate of his own Qualities; If he deals sincerely in the Matter, no body can tell so well as himself, what degree of Esteem ought to attend any of his Actions; and therefore he should be entirely easy, as to the Opinion Men are like to have of them in the World. If they attribute more to him than is his Due, they are either designing or mistaken; if they allow him less, they are envious, or, possibly still mistaken; and, in either Case, are to be despis'd, or disregarded. For he that flatters without designing to make Advantage of it, is a Fool: And whoever encourages that Flattery which he has Sense enough to see thro', is what the *English* call a Coxcomb.

1722

_____

3. Unsophisticated.

WILLIAM GODWIN
1756–1836

William Godwin said in his preface to *Fables Ancient and Modern* (1805): "Half the fables which are to be found in the ordinary books end unhappily, or end in an abrupt and unsatisfactory manner. . . . I have accordingly endeavoured to make almost all my narratives end in a happy and forgiving tone." Ironically, though he was an opponent of organized religion, his Aesop might be taken to be Sunday school tales, as in "The Dog in the Manger," where the little boy feeds the surly cur while admonishing him in schoolmasterly tones, and "The Ass in the Lion's Skin," which becomes a lesson on kindness to animals.

Fables was the first publication of the Juvenile Library that Godwin and his second wife set up in London near Oxford Street in 1805. This children's bookshop, which also published works by the two Godwins and their friends, was primarily an attempt to provide means of support for a household of seven. His first wife, Mary Wollstonecraft, had brought a stepdaughter to the marriage, and had died giving birth to a child in 1797. His second wife, Mary Jane Clairmont, already had two children and another was born soon after her marriage to Godwin in 1801. So by 1803, there were five children under eight years old to feed and educate. Godwin's predicament was that since the publication of his *Enquiry Concerning Political Justice* (1793) and his novel of social protest *Things as They Are, or The Adventures of Caleb Williams* (1794), the works for which he is now best remembered, his name had been equated with atheism and dangerous revolu-

tionary principles. Britain had been at war with revolutionary France, except for one brief interval, since 1793, and the government was determined to uphold the values of church and king and to stifle all dissent. Nor did it help that Godwin's first wife, the author of *A Vindication of the Rights of Woman* (1792), had been associated with his anarchical views. The Juvenile Library therefore displayed not his name as proprietor but that of Thomas Hodgkins, who served in the shop. Similarly, Godwin did not publish his children's books under his own name; for *Fables* he used the pseudonym Edward Baldwin.

The Juvenile Library, which after struggling from crisis to crisis eventually collapsed in 1825, was not just a commercial venture, for Godwin had radical views on education. Children should be treated with respect, not commanded; they should be taught to see the reasons that lie behind the accepted codes of conduct, and to read widely in history and literature so as to gain a better understanding of human nature and behavior. To him the Aesop fables were the ideal starting point, as they had been to more orthodox educators for centuries past. Indeed, in the Library's second premises in Skinner Street, he put over the door a statue of Aesop telling stories to children, and he used an engraving of it as a trademark in subsequent books. His own experience of children's reactions made him greatly expand the text, softening the ruthlessness and introducing child characters and conversation. In the process the fables became Godwin rather than Aesop.

From Fables Ancient and Modern

The Dog in the Manger

A naughty dog once went into a stable, and having looked about him, jumped into the manger, thinking that was a nice, snug place for him to lie down and sleep in. Presently a little boy came into the stable, leading his papa's horse, that had been ploughing a whole field, and was very tired, and very hungry. Come out, poor fellow! said the little boy to the dog, papa's horse wants to eat some hay. But the naughty dog never stirred a bit; he only made up an ugly face, and snarled very much. The little boy went close up to him, and endeavoured to take him out; but then the naughty dog barked and growled, and even tried to bite the little boy. The little boy was not big enough to manage such an ill-natured cur; so he turned in the horse, and stood by to see what would happen. The horse looked very hungry, and very tired, and put up his head to the rack to get a mouthful of hay. But the naughty dog snapped at the poor horse's mouth. The horse was very sorry, and would have said, Pray dog, let me eat! if he had been able. But the naughty dog did not care. You silly dog, said the little boy, hay is of no use to you, dogs do not eat hay, though horses do; and if you stay there, you will soon be as hungry as papa's horse. So the dog staid a long while, and by and by he grew hungry, and came to the little boy, and begged for meat. Silly dog, says the little boy, if I were as naughty as you, I should give you nothing to eat, as you prevented papa's horse from eating. There is a plate of meat for you; and remember another time, that only naughty dogs, and naughty boys and girls, keep away from others what they cannot use themselves.

THE ASS IN THE LION'S SKIN

An ass is a very useful and a very patient animal; one would have expected therefore that every body would have thought of him with respect. To be sure he is not half so handsome as a horse, and his coat is apt to be ragged; but, poor fellow! he cannot help that. The only noise he is able to make is called braying, and you never heard a noise more contemptible and disagreeable. But the worst of him is that he is very slow and awkward in his motions; whatever you do, my dear child, take care not to be slow and awkward in going about it.

A poor ass had long been the sport of all the boys in a village; they shouted and hooted after him, and frightened the poor creature very much; they sometimes beat him and threw stones at him; for vulgar and ragged boys are apt to be cruel, they have never been taught any better; then the ass ran and galloped away from them as fast as he could. All this happened in a country where lions live; I suppose in Africa.

One day this poor ass came to a place when he saw a lion's skin lying on the ground. How I wish I were a lion! thought the ass. Then, instead of these naughty boys frightening me, I should be able to frighten them. Sometimes they have thrown an unlucky stone, which has made me lame for several days; but, if I were a lion, I would not hurt them, I would only terrify them soundly.

Thinking thus, the ass turned over the lion's skin: it was a very fine one. It would make a nice, warm coat for me, thought the ass: and with no more ado he began to put it on. He rolled himself up very snug in it, and pulled down the skin of the lion's head over his face. He then looked at himself in the river. I am vastly like a lion, thought the ass: I dare say I can make my tormentors think I am one; they are only silly boys. So away he went to try.

The ass, quite proud of the new appearance he had put on, trotted along toward the village. Presently he came to where some boys were playing at marbles. To be sure the trotting of an ass is not very much like the port[1] of a lion; but the boys were too much frightened to observe that. They thought they should be eaten all up in a moment. They screamed; and, in their hurry to get away tumbled over one another. They then got up and ran; and away trotted the ass after them.

This succeeded wonderfully well the first day, and the ass was delighted to terrify

---

1. Bearing, carriage.

these naughty boys, who had so richly deserved it. The next day he came again; but he thought the boys did not run so fast as they had done before. He knew that the most alarming thing even in a lion is his tremendous roarings, and he determined to roar too. So he opened his mouth as fiercely as he could; but, alas! instead of a roar, there came out nothing but a bray. It was so loud a bray, that all the fields resounded with it. The boys were astonished. One or two of the boldest stopped, and began to look suspiciously at the pursuer. When any body pretends to be what he is not, if you stop to examine him, it is all over. Aha! Mr. Donkey, said they, is it you all this while? A cheat! A cheat! Cheats are always found out.

The boys however somehow came to know, that, if the ass had happened to be a lion in reality, he had determined not to hurt a bone in their skin; and they resolved not to teaze him any more. They sometimes rode upon him, when their father wanted any thing from the market-town; but they did not disturb him when he was feeding. And now, instead of running away the moment they came in sight, he would trot to meet them, would rub his head against them to tell them how much he loved them, and would eat the thistles and the oats out of their hand: was not that pretty?

1805

WALTER CRANE
1845–1915

In a lifetime concerned chiefly with design, Walter Crane is remembered today for his illustrations for children's books, and especially as one of the triumvirate of artists, with Randolph Caldecott and Kate Greenaway, launched by the printer Edmund Evans (1826–1905). Crane had been introduced to Evans in 1863, the year that the first book with his illustrations had been published. "I availed myself of Walter Crane's talent at once: he did all sorts of things for me—he was a genius," said Evans in his *Reminiscences* (1967) "The only subjects I found he could not draw were figure subjects of everyday life. . . . One of the first children's books he drew for me was a *Railroad Alphabet* and a *Farm Yard Alphabet*." These were "toy" books—a term used by publishers to describe small, colored books of six to eight pages. Evans specialized in these, and in all Crane was to design some fifty of them. There were alphabets, Mother Goose rhymes (*One, Two, Buckle My Shoe* was an early title), and fairy tales, with the text mostly supplied by himself or by his sister Lucy. At first the toy books appeared anonymously but from about 1870 on Crane signed his work, often with a drawing of a crane. The books became

larger and double the price—one shilling instead of sixpence—and such was his popularity that he was soon given a series under his own name, Walter Crane's Toy Books. He went on to design more lavish hardback picture books, including *The Baby's Opera* (1877), a collection of Mother Goose rhymes with music; *The Baby's Bouquet* (1879); and *The Baby's Own Aesop* (1887), which were published together as *Triplets* in 1899. He also did black-and-white illustrations for children's books, including a number by Mary Louisa Molesworth, *Carrots* (1876) and *The Cuckoo Clock* (1877) among them.

Crane's illustrations showed his remarkable talent for including beautifully designed background objects, and this he turned to practical use: "To record the various purposes to which he applied it would be to make a list of wellnigh every article of household decoration," declared the *Dictionary of National Biography* a few years after his death. With William Morris he was associated with the foundation of the Art Workers' Guild, formed to bring before the public the work of the Arts and Crafts Movement; he was the first president of the Guild.

In 1891 he exhibited in London a collection of his varied artistic works that he later took to America, Germany, Austria, and Scandinavia.

Crane's style was influenced by the Pre-Raphaelite movement and by Japanese art. In 1867 he had been presented with a collection of Japanese prints and was to introduce Japanese decorative detail into many of his illustrations. He also mixed such details with motifs drawn from a wide range of styles and periods, with results that could be overpowering. But it suited the mood of the 1870s and 1880s, the time of the Aesthetic movement and "art for art's sake," mocked by Sir William Gilbert and Sir Arthur Sullivan in 1881 in their operetta *Patience.*

The verses and complex designs for *The Baby's Own Aesop* (1887) are "more adult than babyish," as Anne Stevenson Hobbs comments in *Fables* (1986). The limerick form that Crane elected to use has reduced the stark fable text even further, often obscuring the point, as in "The Eagle and the Crow." Nor did this flippant verse style marry well with the cruel truth of fables such as "The Blind Doe."

From The Baby's Own Aesop

THE·BLIND·DOE·

A poor half-blind Doe her one eye
kept shoreward, all danger to spy,
As she fed by the sea,
Poor innocent! she
Was shot from a boat passing by.

·WATCH·ON·ALL·SIDES·

THE CROW & THE PITCHER

How the cunning old
Crow got his drink
When 'twas low in the
pitcher, just think!
Don't say that he spilled it!
With pebbles he filled it,
Till the water rose up to
the brink.

· USE · YOUR · WITS ·

THE · EAGLE · AND · THE · CROW ·

THE Eagle flew off with a lamb;
Then the Crow thought to lift an old ram,
In his eaglish conceit,
The wool tangled his feet,
And the shepherd laid hold of the sham.

· BEWARE · OF · OVERATING · YOUR · OWN · POWERS ·

W. H. D. ROUSE
1863–1950

Because of the latent humor in so many of them, Indian and African animal fables can be more successfully reshaped for young readers than the terse Aesop stories. William Henry Denham Rouse published two collections of Indian folktales: *"The Giant Crab" and Other Tales from Old India* (1897), from which the following two tales have been taken, and *The Talking Thrush* (1899). Both are Jatakas, or birth stories of Buddha. Rouse was born in Cal-

cutta, where his parents worked as missionaries, and his early life in India gave him a strong interest in that country's folklore. He read classics at Cambridge, and later as a schoolmaster he taught Latin and Greek with infectious enthusiasm. He wrote widely on classical subjects, taught Sanskrit at Cambridge, collected folklore in Greece and England, and was president of the Folklore Society from 1904 to 1906. He worked from stories collected by Indians themselves, not hesitating to develop the story and add to its humor. In the original Jataka, the tale of the talkative tortoise was intended as an example of the oblique way the faults of the mighty could be corrected—in this case, a dangerously talkative king.

From "The Giant Crab" and Other Tales from Old India

The Crocodile and the Monkey

Once upon a time there was a deep and wide river, and in this river lived a crocodile. I do not know whether you have ever seen a crocodile; but if you did see one, I am sure you would be frightened. They are very long, twice as long as your bed; and they are covered with hard green or yellow scales; and they have a wide flat snout, and a huge jaw with hundreds of sharp teeth, so big that it could hold you all at once inside it. This crocodile used to lie all day in the mud, half under water, basking in the sun, and never moving; but if any little animal came near, he would jump up, and open his big jaws, and snap it up as a dog snaps up a fly. And if you had gone near him, he would have snapped you up too, just as easily.

On the bank of this river lived a monkey. He spent the day climbing about the trees, and eating nuts or wild fruit; but he had been there so long, that there was hardly any fruit left upon the trees.

Now it so happened that the crocodile's wife cast a longing eye on this Monkey. She was very dainty in her eating, was Mrs Crocodile, and she liked the tit-bits. So one morning she began to cry. Crocodile's tears are very big, and as her tears dropped into the water, splash, splash, splash, Mr Crocodile woke up from his snooze, and looked round to see what was the matter.

'Why, wife,' said he, 'what are you crying about?'

'I'm hungry!' whimpered Mrs Crocodile.

'All right,' said he, 'wait a while. I'll soon catch you something.'

'But I want that Monkey's heart!' said Mrs Crocodile. Splash, splash, splash, went her tears again.

'Come, come, cheer up,' said Mr Crocodile. He was very fond of his wife, and he would have wiped away her tears, only he had no pocket-handkerchief. 'Cheer up!' said he; 'I'll see what I can do.'

His wife dried her tears, and Mr Crocodile lay down again on the mud, thinking. He thought for a whole hour. You see, though he was very big, he was very stupid. At last he heaved a sigh of relief, for he thought he had hit upon a clever plan.

He wallowed along the bank to a place just underneath a big tree. Up on the tree our Monkey was swinging by his tail, and chattering to himself.

'Monkey!' he called out, in the softest voice he could manage. It was not very soft, something like a policeman's rattle; but it was the best he could do, with all those sharp teeth.

The Monkey stopped swinging, and looked down. The Crocodile had never spoken to him before, and he felt rather surprised.

'Monkey, dear!' called the Crocodile, again.

'Well, what is it?' asked the Monkey.

'I'm sure you must be hungry,' said Mr Crocodile. 'I see you have eaten all the fruit on these trees; but why don't you try the trees on the other side of the river? Just look, apples, pears, quinces, plums, anything you could wish for! And heaps of them!'

'That is all very well,' said the Monkey. 'But how can I get across a wide river like this?'

'Oh!' said the cunning Crocodile, 'that is easily managed. I like your looks, and I want to do you a good turn. Jump on my back, and I'll swim across; then you can enjoy yourself!'

Never had the Monkey had an offer so tempting. He swung round a branch three times in his joy; his eyes glistened, and without thinking a moment, down he jumped on the Crocodile's back.

The Crocodile began to swim slowly across. The Monkey fixed his eyes on the opposite bank with its glorious fruit trees, and danced for joy. Suddenly he felt the water about his feet! It rose to his legs, it rose to his middle. The Crocodile was sinking!

'Mr Crocodile! Mr Crocodile! take care!' said he. 'You'll drown me!'

'Ha, ha, ha!' laughed the Crocodile, snapping his great jaws. 'So you thought I was taking you across out of pure good nature! You are a green monkey, to be sure. The truth is, my wife has taken a fancy to you, and wants your heart to eat! If you had seen her crying this morning, I am sure you would have pitied her.'

'What a good thing you told me!' said the Monkey. (He was a very clever Monkey, and had his wits about him.) 'Wait a bit, and I'll tell you why. My heart, I think you said? Why, I never carry my heart inside me; that would be too dangerous. If we Monkeys went jumping about the trees with our hearts inside, we should knock them to bits in no time.'

The Crocodile rose up to the surface again. He felt very glad he had not drowned the Monkey, because, as I said, he was a stupid creature, and did not see that the Monkey was playing him a trick.

'Oh,' said he, 'where is your heart, then?'

'Do you see that cluster of round things up in the tree there, on the further bank? Those are out hearts, all in a bunch; and pretty safe too, at that height, I should hope!' It was really a fig-tree, and certainly the figs did look very much like a bunch of hearts. 'Just you take me across,' he went on, 'and I'll climb up and drop my heart down; I can do very well without it.'

'You excellent creature!' said the Crocodile, 'so I will!'

And he swam across the river. The Monkey leapt lightly off the Crocodile's back, and swung himself up the fig-tree. Then he sat down on a branch, and began to eat the figs with great enjoyment.

'Your heart, please!' called out the Crocodile. 'Can't you see I'm waiting?'

'Well, wait as long as you like!' said the Monkey. 'Are you such a fool as to think that any creature keeps its heart in a tree? Your body is big, but your wit is little. No, no; here I am, and here I mean to stay. Many thanks for bringing me over!'

The Crocodile snapped his jaws in disgust, and went back to his wife, feeling very foolish, as he was; and the Monkey had such a feast in the fig-tree as he never had in his life before.

THE TALKATIVE TORTOISE

Once upon a time there was a Tortoise that lived in a pond. He was a most worthy Tortoise, but he had one fault, he would talk in season and out of season; all day long it was chatter, chatter, chatter in that pond, until the fish said that they would rather live on dry land than put up with it any longer.

But the Tortoise had two friends, a pair of young Geese, who used to fly about near the pond in search of food. And when they heard that things were getting hot for the Tortoise in that pond, because he talked so much, they flew up to him and cried eagerly:

'Oh, Tortoise! do come along with us! We have such a beautiful home away in the mountains, where you may talk all day long, and nobody shall worry you there!'

'All very well,' grumbled the Tortoise, 'but how am I to get there? I can't fly!'

'Oh, we'll carry you, if you can only keep your mouth shut for a little while.'

'Yes, I can do that,' says he, 'when I like. Let us be off.'

So the Geese picked up a stout stick, and one Goose took one end in her bill and the other Goose took the other end, and then they told the Tortoise to get hold in the middle; 'only be careful,' said they, 'not to talk.'

The Tortoise set his teeth fast on the stick, and held on like grim death, while the Geese, flapping their strong wings, rose in the air and flew towards their home.

All went well for a time. But it so happened that some boys were looking up in the air, and were highly amused by what they saw.

'Look there!' cried one to the rest, 'two Geese carrying a Tortoise on a stick!'

The Tortoise on hearing this was so angry that he forgot all about his danger, and opened his mouth to cry out: 'What's that to you? Mind your own business!' But he got no farther than the first word; for when his mouth opened he loosed the stick, down he dropped, and fell with a crash on the stones.

The talkative Tortoise lay dead, with his shell cracked in two.

1897

RUDYARD KIPLING
1865–1936

"How the Camel Got His Hump" is the second of Rudyard Kipling's *Just So Stories for Little Children,* his only writing for the very young. These comic tales, interspersed with poems and his own black-and-white drawings with long humorous captions, were published in 1902. They had evolved from the stories he originally told his eldest daughter, Josephine (1892–1899), and later his two younger children, John and Elsie, and their cousins. After Josephine died of pneumonia in New York following an Atlantic crossing in January, her name could never be mentioned to Kipling, who appended a haunting verse memory of his child to the ninth *Just So* story, "How the Alphabet Was Made." Some of the stories were written while Kipling and his wife, Caroline Balestier, were living in Brattleboro, Vermont, the home of Mrs. Kipling's family, and where Josephine was born. In 1935 he contributed a final *Just So* story, "Ham and the Porcupine," to *The Princess Elizabeth Gift Book.* The camel story is told in mock Arabian Nights style with a djinn—a supernatural figure in that mythology—to effect the magic. Though *djinn* is often the usage in English, in Arabic it is the plural and *djinni* is the singular form.

From Just So Stories for Little Children

How the Camel Got His Hump

Now this is the next tale, and it tells how the Camel got his big hump.

In the beginning of years, when the world was so new-and-all, and the Animals were just beginning to work for Man, there was a Camel, and he lived in the middle of a Howling Desert because he did not want to work; and besides, he was a Howler himself. So he ate sticks and thorns and tamarisks and milkweed and prickles, most 'scruciating idle; and when anybody spoke to him he said 'Humph!' Just 'Humph!' and no more.

Presently the Horse came to him on Monday morning, with a saddle on his back and a bit in his mouth, and said, 'Camel, O Camel, come out and trot like the rest of us.'

'Humph!' said the Camel; and the Horse went away and told the Man.

Presently the Dog came to him, with a stick in his mouth, and said, 'Camel, O Camel, come and fetch and carry like the rest of us.'

'Humph!' said the Camel; and the Dog went away and told the Man.

Presently the Ox came to him, with the yoke on his neck, and said, 'Camel, O Camel, come and plough like the rest of us.'

'Humph!' said the Camel; and the Ox went away and told the Man.

At the end of the day the Man called the Horse and the Dog and the Ox together, and said, 'Three, O Three, I'm very sorry for you (with the world so new-and-all); but that Humph-thing in the Desert can't work, or he would have been here by now, so I am going to leave him alone, and you must work double-time to make up for it.'

That made the Three very angry (with the world so new-and-all), and they held a palaver, and an *indaba*, and a *punchayet*,[1] and a pow-wow on the edge of the Desert; and the Camel came chewing milkweed *most* 'scruciating idle, and laughed at them. Then he said 'Humph!' and went away again.

Presently there came along the Djinn in charge of All Deserts, rolling in a cloud of dust (Djinns always travel that way because it is Magic), and he stopped to palaver and pow-wow with the Three.

'Djinn of All Deserts,' said the Horse, '*is* it right for any one to be idle, with the world so new-and-all?'

'Certainly not,' said the Djinn.

'Well,' said the Horse, 'there's a thing in the middle of your Howling Desert (and he's a Howler himself) with a long neck and long legs, and he hasn't done a stroke of work since Monday morning. He won't trot.'

'Whew!' said the Djinn, whistling, 'that's my Camel, for all the gold in Arabia! What does he say about it?'

'He says "Humph!" ' and the Dog; 'and he won't fetch and carry.'

'Does he say anything else?'

'Only "Humph!"; and he won't plough,' said the Ox.

'Very good,' said the Djinn. 'I'll humph him if you will kindly wait a minute.'

The Djinn rolled himself up in his dust-cloak, and took a bearing across the desert, and found the Camel most 'scruciatingly idle, looking at his own reflection in a pool of water.

---

1. Hindustani synonyms for talk.

'My long and bubbling friend,' said the Djinn, 'what's this I hear of your doing no work, with the world so new-and-all?'

'Humph!' said the Camel.

The Djinn sat down, with his chin in his hand, and began to think a Great Magic, while the Camel looked at his own reflection in the pool of water.

'You've given the Three extra work ever since Monday morning, all on account of your 'scruciating idleness,' said the Djinn; and he went on thinking Magics, with his chin in his hand.

'Humph!' said the Camel.

'I shouldn't say that again if I were you,' said the Djinn; 'you might say it once too often. Bubbles, I want you to work.'

And the Camel said 'Humph!' again; but no sooner had he said it than he saw his back, that he was so proud of, puffing up and puffing up into a great big lolloping humph.

'Do you see that?' said the Djinn. 'That's your very own humph that you've brought upon your very own self by not working. To-day is Thursday, and you've done no work since Monday, when the work began. Now you are going to work.'

'How can I,' said the Camel, 'with this humph on my back?'

'That's made a-purpose,' said the Djinn, 'all because you missed those three days. You will be able to work now for three days without eating, because you can live on your humph; and don't you ever say I never did anything for you. Come out of the Desert and go to the Three, and behave. Humph yourself!'

And the Camel humphed himself, humph and all, and went away to join the Three. And from that day to this the Camel always wears a humph (we call it 'hump' now, not to hurt his feelings); but he has never yet caught up with the three days that he missed at the beginning of the world, and he has never yet learned how to behave.

> The Camel's hump is an ugly lump
>   Which well you may see at the Zoo;
> But uglier yet is the hump we get
>   From having too little to do.
>
> Kiddies and grown-ups too-oo-oo,
> If we haven't enough to do-oo-oo,
>   We get the hump—
>   Cameelious hump—
> The hump that is black and blue!
>
> We climb out of bed with a frouzly head
>   And a snarly-yarly voice.
> We shiver and scowl and we grunt and we growl
>   At our bath and our boots and our toys;
>
> And there ought to be a corner for me
> (And I know there is one for you)
>   When we get the hump—
>   Cameelious hump—
> The hump that is black and blue!
>
> The cure for this ill is not to sit still,
>   Or frowst with a book by the fire;

But to take a large hoe and a shovel also,
  And dig till you gently perspire;

And then you will find that the sun and the wind,
And the Djinn of the Garden too,
    Have lifted the hump—
    The horrible hump—
  The hump that is black and blue!

I get it as well as you-oo-oo—
If I haven't enough to do-oo-oo!
    We all get hump—
    Cameelious hump—
  Kiddies and grown-ups too!

Here is the picture of the Djinn in charge of All Deserts guiding the Magic with his magic fan. The Camel is eating a twig of acacia, and he has just finished saying "humph" once too often (the Djinn told him he would), and so the Humph is coming. The long towelly-thing growing out of the thing like an onion is the Magic, and you can see the Humph on its shoulder. The Humph fits on the flat part of the Camel's back. The Camel is too busy looking at his own beautiful self in the pool of water to know what is going to happen to him.

Underneath the truly picture is a picture of the World-so-new-and-all. There are two smoky volcanoes in it, some other mountains and some stones and a lake and a black island and a twisty river and a lot of other things, as well as a Noah's Ark. I couldn't draw all the deserts that the Djinn was in charge of, so I only drew one, but it is a most deserty desert.

1902

JAMES THURBER
1894–1961

James Thurber, wrote David McCord, "slipped into the field of children's literature by the back front gate, like a cat 'walking on velvet'—an expression of his own." His first children's book—there were to be five in all—was *Many Moons* (1943). A light-hearted fairy story with a happy ending, it was a wholly unexpected work for a writer notorious for his wry view of the human lot. Thurber had begun his lifelong connection with the *New Yorker* in 1927, where the short story "The Secret Life of Walter Mitty" appeared in 1939. The leitmotifs of his *New Yorker* stories and drawings were predatory women, henpecked husbands, and the malignancy of fate. In his subsequent children's books this attitude became more obtrusive.

In *Fables for Our Time* (1940) and *Further Fables for Our Time* (1956), the source of the variations on the Aesop fox and crow story included here, Thurber develops the traditional fable theme of victory through quick wits, translating it into a contemporary idiom; sometimes the fox wins, sometimes the crow outsmarts him. Both collections also reflect Thurber's pessimism, and his obsession with the deadly nature of the female species. In "The Tigress and Her Mate," for example, the tigress tells her cubs to go into the parlor and play with their father: " 'He's the tiger rug just in front of the fireplace. I hope you'll like him.'" Moral: "Never be mean to a tiger's wife, especially if you're the tiger."

From Further Fables for Our Time

THE FOX AND THE CROW

A crow, perched in a tree with a piece of cheese in his beak, attracted the eye and nose of a fox. "If you can sing as prettily as you sit," said the fox, "then you are the prettiest singer within my scent and sight." The fox had read somewhere, and somewhere, and somewhere else, that praising the voice of a crow with a cheese in his beak would make him drop the cheese and sing. But this is not what happened to this particular crow in this particular case.

"They say you are sly and they say you are crazy," said the crow, having carefully removed the cheese from his beak with the claws of one foot, "but you must be nearsighted as well. Warblers wear gay hats and colored jackets and bright vests, and they are a dollar a hundred. I wear black and I am unique." He began nibbling the cheese, dropping not a single crumb.

"I am sure you are," said the fox, who was neither crazy nor nearsighted, but sly. "I recognize you, now that I look more closely, as the most famed and talented of all birds, and I fain would hear you tell about yourself, but I am hungry and must go."

"Tarry awhile," said the crow quickly, "and share my lunch with me." Whereupon he tossed the cunning fox the lion's share of the cheese, and began to tell about himself. "A ship that sails without a crow's nest sails to doom," he said. "Bars may come and bars may go, but crow bars last forever. I am the pioneer of flight, I am the map maker. Last, but never least, my flight is known to scientists and engineers, geometrists and scholars, as the shortest distance between two points. Any two points," he concluded arrogantly.

"Oh, every two points, I am sure," said the fox. "And thank you for the lion's share of what I know you could not spare." And with this he trotted away into the woods, his appetite appeased, leaving the hungry crow perched forlornly in the tree.

MORAL: *'Twas true in Aesop's time, and La Fontaine's, and now, no one else can praise thee quite so well as thou.*

VARIATIONS ON THE THEME

I

A fox, attracted by the scent of something, followed his nose to a tree in which sat a crow with a piece of cheese in his beak. "Oh, cheese," said the fox scornfully. "That's for mice."

The crow removed the cheese with his talons and said, "You always hate the thing you cannot have, as, for instance, grapes."[1]

"Grapes are for the birds," said the fox haughtily. "I am an epicure, a gourmet, and a gastronome."

The embarrassed crow, ashamed to be seen eating mouse food by a great specialist in the art of dining, hastily dropped the cheese. The fox caught it deftly, swallowed it with relish, said *"Merci,"* politely, and trotted away.

II

A fox had used all his blandishments in vain, for he could not flatter the crow in the tree and make him drop the cheese he held in his beak. Suddenly, the crow tossed the cheese to the astonished fox. Just then the farmer, from whose kitchen the loot had been stolen, appeared, carrying a rifle, looking for the robber. The fox turned and ran for the woods. "There goes the guilty son of a vixen now!" cried the crow, who, in case you do not happen to know it, can see the glint of sunlight on a gun barrel at a greater distance than anybody.

III

This time the fox, who was determined not to be outfoxed by a crow, stood his ground and did not run when the farmer appeared, carrying a rifle and looking for the robber.

"The teeth marks in this cheese are mine," said the fox, "but the beak marks were made by the true culprit up there in the tree. I submit this cheese in evidence, as Exhibit A, and bid you and the criminal a very good day." Whereupon he lit a cigarette and strolled away.

IV

In the great and ancient tradition, the crow in the tree with the cheese in his beak began singing, and the cheese fell into the fox's lap. "You sing like a shovel," said the fox, with a grin, but the crow pretended not to hear and cried out, "Quick, give me back the cheese! Here comes the farmer with his rifle!"

"Why should I give you back the cheese?" the wily fox demanded.

"Because the farmer has a gun, and I can fly faster than you can run."

So the frightened fox tossed the cheese back to the crow, who ate it, and said, "Dearie me, my eyes are playing tricks on me—or am I playing tricks on you? Which do you think?" But there was no reply, for the fox had slunk away into the woods.

1956

1. An allusion to another of Aesop's fables, "The Fox and the Grapes."

ASHLEY BRYAN
b. 1923

Ashley Bryan, a poet, illustrator, collector of African folktales, musician, and storyteller, majored in philosophy at Columbia, earned degrees from two art schools, and taught art for many years. The first work of his own that he illustrated was *The Ox of the Wonderful Horns and Other African Tales* (1971). His next, *Walk Together Children: Black American Spirituals* (1974), recalled the music of his childhood. It was followed by *Beat the Story-Drum, Pum-Pum* (1980), another collection of folktales. In 1995 he wrote of himself: "I now live on a small island off the coast of Maine. I paint from the landscape, illustrate books, retell African tales, make puppets from things gathered on daily walks along the shore. I use beach glass to make stained glass panels, and I play instruments."

"Tortoise, Hare, and the Sweet Potatoes" was first published in *The Ox of the Wonderful Horns*. Told with characteristic humor, it was created from the bare bones summarized by Henri Junod in *The Life of a South African Tribe* (1913). Junod's two-volume work, which describes the way of life, beliefs, and folklore of the Thonga tribe on the eastern coast of southern Africa, includes four stories about the wily Hare, seemingly the ancestor of Brer Rabbit, who succeeds in tricking all animals except Tortoise. The same rascally character—Wakaima, also a hare—was to be found in African west coast folk legends brought to the American South by people who had told them in their own country.

From "The Ox of the Wonderful Horns" and Other African Tales

TORTOISE, HARE, AND THE SWEET POTATOES

Listen, brothers and sisters, to this story of how Tortoise outwitted Hare.

Hare was a born trickster. He was always dreaming up new riddles and tricks to try on others. He'd spring an impossible riddle, wait a little, then rattle off the answer. Riddles and tricks. Hare never tired of either.

Tortoise on the other hand was much too busy keeping her little pond clean to worry about tricking anyone. Animals came from field and forest, far and near, to drink in the pond where she lived.

Tortoise believed in the proverb, "Give the passing traveller water and you will drink news yourself." So, although she rarely left her pool, her visitors kept her well informed. She knew more than most and was seldom fooled.

It happened one season then that the news Tortoise heard again and again was disgracefully bad. Someone was stealing, stealing food from all the fields around. Now most creatures were willing to give when another was hungry. But stealing was taboo.

Everyone asked, "Who would do what's taboo?" And no one knew. But Tortoise had a few well-founded ideas.

One day Hare came by Tortoise's pond. He drank his fill, then was ready for mischief. "Aha! Now to muddy the pond and have a little fun," he thought. He had never cared for the proverb, "Do not fill up the well after having drunk. Where would you drink tomorrow?"

Tortoise was on her guard, however, and all Hare could do was sit beside her and ask riddles. Tortoise answered every one.

"I know one you can't answer," said Hare. "Tell me the thing that you can beat without leaving a scar?"

"I live by it and I drink it," said Tortoise. "Water."

So Hare gave up trying to catch Tortoise with riddles. But he was not through. After a while he said, "Now old Tortoise, let's go and till a field together."

"Me! Till the land? I can just manage to scratch out my little garden patch. How could I hoe a whole field with my short legs?"

"Short legs? Your legs are beautiful. Just the right length for hoeing."

"Do say! But how could I hold a hoe?"

"No problem at all. I'll tie you to it. I'd love to do that for you."

There was truth in that statement, Tortoise decided. Hare knew how to trick people, all right. But she wasn't taken in. She said aloud, "I don't think I'll try, thanks."

So they sat in silence. And after a while Hare said, "I'm hungry, Sis. Aren't you?"

"A little, but I don't have a leaf left in my garden."

"Well, poor thing, let me help you. I came upon a wide field of good things on my way here. Come on! Let's help ourselves to some of Wild Boar's sweet potatoes."

"Ooo, ooo! What are you saying? You know better than that, Mr. Hare. No pilfering!"

So they sat on in silence, Hare not willing to give up.

And after a while Tortoise became really hungry. Besides she had a few worthwhile ideas.

"Where did you say that field of sweet potatoes was?" she asked.

"It's not far, just past the bush."

"Well now," said Tortoise, seeming to overcome her scruples, "I guess Wild Boar won't miss a few."

Off they went together. And when they came to Wild Boar's field it was no job at all to root out the sweet potatoes. Soon Hare's sack was filled.

Hare with a great show of strength steadied the bag on Tortoise's back, and they headed for the bush to cook the potatoes. When they found a good quiet spot, they gathered dry grass and made a crackling fire in which the sweet potatoes were soon roasted.

"Mmm-yum," said Tortoise as she bit into one.

"Wait a minute," said Hare. "Did you hear that?"

"Mmm-yum," said Tortoise, her mouth full of sweet potato.

"Stop munching and mumbling!" said Hare. "What if we're caught?"

"Mmm-um-yum," said Tortoise, reaching for another sweet potato.

"Wow-wow," said Hare, "do you want to be beaten and bitten by Wild Boar? Put down that potato! We've got to scout around first and make sure that Boar's not after us."

Hare forced Tortoise to stop eating, and they went off in opposite directions to scout the field.

Tortoise who had a good notion of what was afoot and was ready, waddled a few reluctant steps; Hare bounded out of sight. As soon as he was gone, Tortoise turned back, took another sweet potato, and crawled into the empty sack.

"Mmm-yum," she said. She was about to crawl out for another when suddenly a rain of roasted sweet potatoes fell around her. Hare was back, very quietly, very quickly.

"Good," said Tortoise, biting into another sweet potato, "saves me the trouble."

Old trickster Hare filled his sack in a hurry.

"Mistress Tortoise," he shouted then. "Get going! Take off! Run for your life! Wild Boar and his big, fat wife are coming."

He threw the bag over his back. "Save yourself! Fly!" he cried, but inside he thought: "Best trick in ages. Now to put some miles between me and Slowpoke." He took off, running and laughing as hard as he could.

Tortoise made herself comfortable in the sack. She ate one sweet potato after another. "Too bad Hare is missing the feast," she thought. "But maybe he prefers running to eating."

Hare ran as fast and as far as he could. By the time he stopped to rest, Tortoise had eaten all of the finest and fattest sweet potatoes. In fact, there was only one very small sweet potato left.

"Aha good," said Hare as he put his hand into the sack. "Too bad Tortoise is miles away."

"Sweet potatoes," Hare sang, "sweet, sw-eeeet potatoes!" Tortoise put the last sweet potato into Hare's outstretched hand.

When Hare saw the size of it, he cried, "Ha! What a miserable one this is. I didn't run my head off for that!" And he flung it into the bushes.

Hare put his hand back into the sack. This time he felt a big one, a nice firm, juicy one.

"Oho!" he chortled, "here's a beauty. What a prize!"

Imagine Hare's surprise when he saw what he had in his hand.

"Mistress Tortoise!" he cried as he dropped her to the ground.

Hare shook out the sack. Tears of unbelief welled up in his eyes when he saw it was empty. "My potatoes, the sweet ones I rooted up . . . oh no, oh no! You didn't eat mine, too? Sister Tortoise, how could you be so unfair?"

But Mistress Tortoise didn't stand around for the lecture. She took to her toes and scuttled away to her pond as fast as she could go.

Hungry Hare lay on the ground and screeched, "Woe, woe, that wily Mistress Tortoise ate all my sweet potatoes. Wa, Waa. How awful of her. When I think that I carried her all the while, I could cry!"

And that's just what he did.

1971

RUSSELL HOBAN
b. 1925

Russell Hoban's writing for children covers a wide area. It includes factual books of information, verse, benign picture book stories of family life for the youngest readers, and somber fantasies of which *The Mouse and His Child* (1967) is the most famous. He had tried his hand at many occupations before in his own words he "fell into children's book writing," starting with two books about how mechanical implements work. His earliest fiction was a picture book, *Bedtime for Frances* (1960). This and the Frances successors show a small badger experiencing situations that children under six in a well-ordered family would recognize. The warm and loving home here is very different from the hostile, cutthroat world in *The Mouse and His Child*, his first full-length novel and perhaps his finest work. This is a quest story, which can be interpreted as an allegory of the human condition. Two tin clockwork toys, a mouse father and his son, search for a home and safety, and also for the means of being "self-winding"—that is, having a life of their own, so that they are no longer dependent on others to set them in motion. And much in the same way that J. R. .R. Tolkien's despicable Gollum in the final volume of *The Lord of the Rings* (1955) is the means of destroying the Ring of Power, it is Manny Rat, the toys' former enemy, who brings about the longed-for transformation.

The Sea-Thing Child was first published in 1972 with illustrations by Brom Hoban, and reissued in 1999 illustrated by Patrick Benson. The implied moral of this extended literary fable is very different from the worldly wisdom of Aesop and his kind, which stresses prudence, cunning, and self-advancement. Hoban's sea-child, portrayed by Benson as a young puffin, has to develop the confidence to leave the sheltering igloo on the shore where the storm has washed him up and to fly away to find his real element. But the fiddler crab he has met on the beach stays there, forever mourning the fiddle bow that he knows he never will possess.

The Sea-Thing Child

The wind was howling, the sea was wild, and the night was black when the storm flung the sea-thing child up on the beach. In the morning the sky was fresh and clean, the beach was littered with seaweed, and there he lay—a little black heap of scales and feathers, all alone.

All alone he was, and behind him the ocean roared and shook its fist. He lay there, howling not very loud, "Ow, ow, ow! Ai-ee!" while the foam washed over him and went hissing away again. He was too little to swim very well and he hadn't learned to fly yet. He was nothing but a little draggled heap of fright.

After a while he crawled up among the big old seaweed-bearded rocks by a tidepool and he went to sleep there, cheeping softly to himself.

When he woke up he ate some seaweed and some mussels and he felt stronger. He listened to the pebbles clicking in the tide-wash as the tide came in, then he gathered up some round stones and some broken bits of bottles, cups, and saucers that the sea and sand had smoothed to lumps of sea-glass and sea-china.

He built a sea-stone igloo all around himself with no door and no window, then he sat inside it breathing hard and making faces.

After a while he heard a thin and whispery voice yelling, "Oh, if only I had a bow, what music I could play!" The voice sounded as if it came from something smaller than the sea-thing child, so he peeped through a space between the stones of his igloo.

He saw a fiddler crab waving his fiddle and shouting, "Oh, oh, oh! If only I had a bow, what music I could play! Walruses and great green turtles from the trackless deep would gather to the sound of my fiddling, yes."

The sea-thing child pushed some stones off the top of his igloo and stuck his head out. "Why haven't you got a bow?"

"What a brutal question!" said the crab, and he began to cry. The sea-thing child began to cry too. When they had finished crying the sea-thing child said, "But why *don't* you have a bow?"

"If fiddler crabs had bows," said the crab, "the noise of their fiddling would be deafening, and nobody could hear the long, long magic curve of silence arching

413

underneath the day's long sky. As far as I can see, you are a nobody and you come out of nowhere. And you want to change everything."

"But you were the one who was complaining," said the sea-thing child. "I wasn't."

"Oh ho," said the crab. His eye-stalks stood straight up. "I was *not* complaining, and everything was all right until you showed up."

"If you say," said the sea-thing child. He pulled his head back into his sea-stone igloo, put the stones back on top, and sat in the dark and made faces.

After a while the crab said, "Are you there?"

"Yes," said the sea-thing child.

"Do you still think I should have a bow?" said the crab.

"I don't want to make trouble," said the sea-thing child.

"I want you to be frank with me," said the crab.

The sea-thing child stuck his head out of his igloo. "How many fiddler crabs are there around here?" he said.

"I am the only one," said the crab. "This is a one-fiddler-crab beach."

"In that case," said the sea-thing child, "I think the sound of your fiddle would make one hear even better the long, long magic curve of silence."

"Thank you," said the crab. And he began to cry.

"Why are you crying now?" said the sea-thing child.

"I don't want to talk about it," said the crab, sniffling and sobbing. "Let us put this matter over to another time and go strolling in the foam."

The sea-thing child looked out at the white foam, the sparkling surf, the green waves and the deep and dark blue line of ocean where it met the sky. Then he pulled his head in and put the stones back on top of his sea-stone igloo.

"I don't want to go strolling in the foam," he said.

"All right," said the crab. "But will you come out and play?"

"What do you want to play?" said the sea-thing child.

"Stones?" said the crab.

"Yes," said the sea-thing child.

He took off the top of his igloo and came out. He and the crab played stones all afternoon, and while they played they sang:

> *Perfectly round is seldom found,*
> *But egg-shapes are abounding.*

The sea-thing child was restless in the night, and he left his igloo and went for a walk on the beach all alone, not very close to the edge of the water where the white foam gleamed in the dark. He walked to where a river ran down to the sea, and there he heard an eel singing as it came down the river:

> *Fresh to salt,*
> *Salt to deep.*
> *Need must find—*
> *Finding knows*
> *Water goes*
> *Fresh to salt,*
> *Salt to deep,*
> *Deep to finding.*

"Where are you going?" said the sea-thing child.

"Far and deep," said the eel. "Far and deep."

The sea-thing child looked at the ocean that was black in the night. "How will you find your way?" he said.

"Finding knows," said the eel, dark in the starshine on the river. "The finding is in me, and the finding finds the way."

"Aren't you afraid?" said the sea-thing child.

"Of what?" said the eel, slipping through the water, tasting in his mouth the sea-brine and the salt night.

"Of the deepness and the darkness and the farness of the sea," said the sea-thing child.

When the eel answered he was out beyond the foam, and his voice was almost lost in the slap and gurgle of the waves. "*Born* for the sea!" he called, and headed for the deeps.

The next day the sea-thing child fussed with his igloo all morning, and when the fiddler crab came to visit him, he said that he did not want to play stones again.

"Perhaps today is a good day for strolling in the foam?" said the crab.

"Why don't you make a bow for your fiddle," said the sea-thing child, "and then you can play beautiful music while we stroll in the foam. And perhaps the walruses and green turtles will come strolling in the foam with us."

When the crab heard that he scuttled into his hole and cried all afternoon.

That night the sea-thing child took his igloo apart and scattered his sea-stones and sea-glass and sea-china all over the beach. He went down to the edge of the foam that gleamed in the dark and he smelled the salt air and listened to the surf. He waded in and felt the dark water flow past his tail. He went deeper and it wet the scales on his belly. The water was warm but he knew that farther out he would feel the cold coming up from the deeps. A little wave broke over his head and ran past, then the bottom tried to slide away from under his feet and pull him out to deep water with it. "Ai-ee!" said the sea-thing child.

He came out of the water and ran up to the big old seaweed-bearded rocks. He built his igloo all around him again with no door and no window, and he went to sleep, cheeping in the dark.

The fiddler crab and the sea-thing child had very little to say to each other for a while. The sea-thing child kept making igloos and taking them apart, and as time passed he had to make them bigger and bigger because he was growing fast.

One day an albatross landed on the beach, pulled out a little stubby pipe and sat down to have a smoke. The fiddler crab hid among the rocks but the sea-thing child came over to talk to the albatross.

"Ahoy," said the albatross. "Nice beach you've got here. Good landing-strip. Good fishing. Good rocks. Nice place." He puffed big clouds of smoke from his little black pipe and stared out to sea with fearless eyes. "You don't happen to play the fiddle or anything like that, do you? I like a bit of music and fun when I'm ashore."

"No," said the sea-thing child. "But I have a friend who has a fiddle."

"No bow," said the fiddler crab from his hiding place in the rocks.

"Oh, well," said the albatross. "I'll just sit a while and enjoy the view then. Fine day. See for miles. Lovely wind. Good flying. Made a fine passage today. Miles and miles and miles. But of course you know how it is as well as I do, you being a sea-thing."

"Yes," said the sea-thing child. "I'm a sea-thing."

"Fly and swim, just like me," said the albatross. "But you can go *under*, too. You can do the deep swimming. What have you seen down in the deeps?"

"I've never seen anything," said the sea-thing child, "except the big storm that blew me out of my nest and washed me up here."

"Don't tell me you've been on the beach all this time," said the albatross.

"Yes, I have," said the sea-thing child.

"How come?" said the albatross.

"Well, the storm you know," said the sea-thing child, "and the wind and the waves and the dark, and the ocean being so big and me so small."

"Small!" said the albatross. "What *isn't* small compared to the ocean! The blue whale's the biggest thing that swims, and that's small in the *ocean*. If the ocean wasn't big it wouldn't be the ocean. The whale is whale-size, I'm albatross-size, and you're sea-thing-size. What more do you want?" He stood up and brushed the sand off his bottom.

"You're never afraid?" said the sea-thing child. "Not afraid of getting lost in the middle of the ocean? Not afraid of the storms and the dark and the wind howling all around you?"

"There's no such thing as an afraid albatross," said the albatross. "The ocean wouldn't be the ocean without storms, and the ocean is where I live. How can you get lost when you're where you live? I was born on a rock in the middle of the ocean, and Wandering is my name." He knocked the ash from his pipe and turned into the wind. "Clear the runway," he said. "I'm taking off." He started his run, flapped his wings hard, and went up into the air.

The sea-thing child watched the albatross out of sight. Then he went back to the one of the big old seaweed-bearded rocks and sat on it all afternoon, looking out to sea until the sky grew dark.

The sea-thing child stopped building igloos but sometimes he made little heaps of stones and sea-glass and sea-china and drew a circle in the sand around them and sat inside the circle.

"Do you make a break in the circle when you want to come out or do you just step over it?" said the crab.

"I have to make a break in the circle, of course," said the sea-thing child, "but that's much less bother than moving stones and much easier to close up again."

"Yes," said the crab. "That's very sensible. It's a fine day. Perhaps we might take a walk among the rocks?"

"Why don't we stroll in the foam?" said the sea-thing child.

"In the foam," said the crab. "Right in it, you mean, where it's wet?"

"Yes," said the sea-thing child. He rubbed out just enough of the circle so that he could walk through the space. Then he closed it up again and they went strolling in the foam, singing the song the sea sang:

Breathing and sighing, far and deep—
Hissing and foaming, never sleep.

At night the sea-thing child felt more and more restless. He looked at the stars, and when he closed his eyes he went on seeing the stars in his mind. He could not sleep unless he was facing a particular star that burned and flickered over the sea, and when he slept he dreamed of wind rushing past him. He dreamed of the ocean too, black and heaving in the night, sometimes under him, sometimes over him. He would run along the beach in the dark, cheeping to himself, then he would come back to his circle. And every night before he went to sleep he drew a second circle around the first one.

One day when the sea-thing child woke up, the sky was grey, the sea was rough and huge, the air hummed. The sea-thing child stayed inside his double circle all day, staring at the ocean.

After a while the crab came and stood outside the double circle with his eye-stalks turned away from the sea-thing child. "You never want to play stones any more," he said. "You never want to stroll in the foam. You are tired of listening to my lies."

"What lies?" said the sea-thing child.

"My lies about what I could do if I had a bow," said the crab.

"But you don't have a bow," said the sea-thing child.

"With a bit of bone and seaweed I could make one," said the crab, "but what if I have no music in me?"

"Need must find," said the sea-thing child.

"Find what?" said the crab.

"Whatever there is," said the sea-thing child.

"All right," said the crab. "I'll *make* the bow. Will you stay then, and not go away?"

"I never said I was going away," said the sea-thing child.

"At night I hear you running in the dark," said the crab. "Sometimes I see you looking at the stars and I hear something in the wind."

"What do you hear in the wind?" said the sea-thing child.

"Whatever there is," said the crab.

That night the sea-thing child heard the air humming. He looked up at the sky for the star that he always looked at but it was blotted out. He could not see the stars with his eyes, but in the dark of his mind he saw it burning and flickering over the sea. The humming of the air grew louder, and the sea-thing child stepped out of his double circle and faced into the wind. The ocean was high and wild, and the sky and the sea roared together, heaving in the dark.

The sea-thing child spread his wings to keep from falling down and the wind blew him backwards. He moved forward against the wind, then he began to run, faster and faster. The beach slipped away from under him, he laughed and flapped his wings and left the ground behind.

When the crab heard the beating of wings he came out of his hole and looked up. "Whatever there is?" he shouted.

"Whatever there is!" called the sea-thing child. He swooped down through the dark, dived through the wild waves into the blackness below, rose up out of the foam, soared into the night and away into the storm over the ocean he was born in.

1972

Classical Myths

The Problem of Myth

J. R. R. Tolkien suggested that fairy tales became part of children's literature not because they were suitable for children but because they were no longer suitable for, or fashionable with, adults, and the same might be said of many myths. It is especially true of the classical myths from Greece and Rome (dating broadly from the eighth century B.C.E. to the third century C.E.), for these were appropriated in the West by the educational establishment, as a way of teaching Latin and Greek, from the sixteenth century on. These languages were, and are still, residually, the languages of the professions and associated with the upper classes. The myths have been seen as a respectable part of cultural education and have thus come to be regarded as part of children's literature. Whether they are now kept alive in the present postclassical culture only by unreflective adults rather than by really appealing to children is a question open to debate.

The myths of Greece and Rome, as the scholar Kenneth McLeish put it,

> originally related to specific religious, philosophical, cultural and social ideas. In a metaphorical and poetic way, they offered not so much answers to particular questions as ways of beginning to think about answers—and the questions had to do with the nature of the universe, the relationship between human beings and the supernatural, the reasons for certain customs . . . and the self-image of this or that community. They . . . offered a communal viewpoint—they were a binding force.

This "metaphorical" level may now seem to be rather simple-minded, not to say distasteful. A Titan can father gods who control the elements; a hero can confront monsters that represent our deepest psychological fears, and conquer them either by deviousness or by brutality. There is often a primitive preoccupation with raw sexuality and violent atrocities. Motivations may seem to the twenty-first-century reader to be crude: worlds are created or destroyed out of mere spite. And however fascinating the ramifications of the myths may be to the scholar, their thousands of years of oral variations give the world of classical myth the air of a long-running soap opera, as the characters change their personalities to suit new situations, or plots are rewritten retrospectively.

Apologists for classical mythology argue that it is essential for children to be aware of these stories, which have influenced the whole storytelling behavior of Western civilization and which are still potent today. Certainly, the patterns of exploration and conquest, together with the basic character types of tough or clever male heroes, mysterious or passive or malignant females, demented monsters, and so on, seem to be endlessly repeated. J. K. Rowling's Harry Potter series is typical: it contains many of these elements, but we are not sure whether these actually link back to specific stories or are fundamental to the human psyche. Some of the stories from classical myth are still generally known and carry potent resonances—for example, the tale of the doomed flight of Icarus; others, such as the story of Hercules, are sufficiently familiar to be recycled as films or TV dramas. But most have vanished from popular culture. One curious exception can be found in the comic book *Captain Marvel,* which first appeared in February 1940. To turn into Captain Marvel, Billy Batson had only to shout the magic word "Shazam," which stands for the "wisdom of Solomon" and attributes of the Greek gods and heroes: "the strength of *Hercules,* the stamina of *Atlas,* the power of *Zeus, and* the speed of *Mercury.*"

Yet many of the elements of myth might be seen as unfashionable at best, and positively harmful at worst. The myths are given to strong gender stereotyping— females are passive, males are active—and more than one female critic has pointed out that heroes are good for little more than killing other heroes. The protagonists are devoted to a ruthless elimination of the "other" and to a savagery that is scarcely tolerated in children's literature. Torture, mutilation, murder, rape, and incest are common, and more unusual perversions also appear—such as a mad king (who has murdered his father) eating his babies. If we accept the premise of those who argue that these are powerful stories and *therefore* should be given to children, then we might come to the opposite conclusion and hold that child readers, who are by definition susceptible, should *not* be exposed to them.

There is a further difficulty, centered on the relationship between myth and religion. One view is that myth is religion that no one believes in anymore; but if that is so, then what is the relationship between "true" religion and "old" religion, and what is the value of the myth?

Definitions

Though it is very difficult to draw lines between myth, legend, and romance, scholars generally agree that myths are concerned with creation and the ways in which cultures have understood the world in terms of gods and cosmic creatures. Legends and sagas concern heroes who are recognizably human, but often have superhuman abilities and are closely related to the gods. Both myth and legend operate in worlds that resemble our own, with different physical laws. The romance concerns characters who are more human and more complex, even though they may be larger than life and may live (as in Tolkien's *The Lord of the Rings*) in an unusual world.

Myths and legends certainly predate the written word; and their original nature changes once they are set down on the page, as is true of all oral forms (as illustrated more recently by the nineteenth-century publication of folktales known as the Uncle Remus stories). But although myths seem to have a general influence on literature, art, and music and although they confront issues of life and death, they also rely on one-dimensional characters and unsubtle motivations. As a result, myths became marginalized in the nineteenth century, when literature became more preoccupied with "realism" and the portrayal of complex, subtle human characters, and when elements of fantasy were often frowned on by both the practically and religiously minded as useless if not harmful distractions.

Some have argued that myths relate directly to basic human motivations and psychological patterns, and are therefore universal and fundamentally valuable. This theory, which suggests an inevitability in the tales, is undermined by the almost chaotic variety of classical myths. An opposing view is that these are simply stories that have *become* symbolic, and that each generation creates its own myths to satisfy its needs (the "myth" of flying saucers is sometimes cited as a modern example).

The Basic Greco-Roman Myths

It is impossible to produce a definitive narrative for any of the major cycles, as they exhibit many variants and overlaps, with blurring and contradictions in the characters—both between individual stories and between the Greek and the Roman traditions. The Romans adopted and adapted Hellenic tales, blending them with an indigenous mythology and frequently giving the Greek gods and heroes new names (these appear in parentheses below).

In the basic myths, nature, sky, and earth are personified; their offspring become lesser gods—Zeus (Jupiter) of the heavens and thunder, Poseidon (Neptune) of the sea, Demeter (Ceres) of grain, and so on—whose offspring in turn are the heroes.

A brief sketch of some of the creation myths, bearing in mind their great variation, follows. Uranus and Ge or Gaea (Heaven and Earth) had eighteen children, including three Hecatoncheires (literally, "hundred-handed monsters"), three Cyclopes, and six sons and six daughters, called the Titans. Two of these, Cronus and Rhea, encouraged a revolt against Uranus; Cronus castrated his father with a sickle given to him by Rhea. When Uranus's genitals were thrown into the sea, Aphrodite (Venus), the goddess of love, rose from the foam, while giants and the Furies grew from drops of blood. Cronus then became king of the gods and married his sister, Rhea, but ate his children—all except Zeus, for whom Rhea substituted a stone. When Zeus (who later fought his fellow Titans and established the power of the Olympians) grew up, he forced Cronus to vomit up the children, who included Demeter (goddess of grain and harvest), Hera (Juno, goddess of marriage and women), Hades (Pluto, god of the underworld), and Poseidon (god of the sea). The stories of the Titans predate the rise of Greek civilization and can be found in the writings of Hesiod (fl. ca. 700 B.C.E.).

The best-known cycles of hero stories concern the exploits of Jason, Heracles, Odysseus, and Theseus.

The most ancient tells of Jason and the Argonauts; Jason and fifty heroes encounter such dangers as the Harpies, the clashing (or wandering) rocks that guarded the Bosphorus (the channel that links the Black Sea to the Aegean Sea at present-day Istanbul in Turkey). Jason yokes a pair of fire-breathing bulls, sows dragons' teeth that grow into warriors, defeats dragons, takes the Golden Fleece, and marries the sorceress Medea.

The poems attributed to Homer (ca. eighth century B.C.E.), the *Iliad* and the *Odyssey*, deal respectively with the Trojan War and the subsequent adventures of one of the Greek heroes of the war, Odysseus (Ulysses). In the *Odyssey*, a blend of folktale and epic, Odysseus and his men set out for Ithaca after the ten-year siege is over, encountering the Cyclops Polyphemus; Aeolus, who gives Odysseus a bag of winds; Circe the sorceress; the Sirens; and the twin perils of Scylla and Charybdis. These adventures last ten years before Odysseus returns home to his faithful wife, Penelope.

The stories of Theseus were collected by Apollodorus of Athens (b. ca. 180 B.C.E.) and Plutarch (ca. 50–ca. 120 C.E.) and bear some resemblance to those of Heracles (Hercules). Theseus was heir to Aegeus, king of Athens (although the son of Poseidon), and began his adventures by finding a sword and sandals left under a heavy rock by his father. He kills Procrustes, a bandit famous for his bed, which his victims were always made to fit (by being cut or stretched, if necessary). He is nearly poisoned by Medea but volunteers to go to Crete as one of the seven young men and seven young women of Athens sacrificed at regular intervals to the Minotaur. The history of the Minotaur and its many links with other myths give some indication of the complexity of the legends. It was half-bull and half-man, the offspring of a bull sent from the sea by Poseidon and of Pasiphaë, the wife of Minos, king of Crete (she conceived by concealing herself in a wooden cow made by Daedalus). Minos, later one of the judges of hell, commanded the bloody tribute because Aegeus was responsible for the death of Androgeus, Minos's son. The Minotaur lived in a labyrinth created by Daedalus. Theseus killed the monster, with help from Ariadne, one of Minos's daughters. After his escape with Ariadne, whom he abandoned on the island of Naxos, he became king of Athens and part of many other legends. He fought the Amazons and carried off their queen, abducted the daughter of Leda and Zeus (later famous as Helen of Troy), was one of the Argonauts, and gave sanctuary to the blinded and wandering Oedipus. A modern treatment of the stories can be found in Mary Renault's *The King Must Die* (1958) and *The Bull from the Sea* (1962).

Another major work, the *Aeneid* by the Roman poet Virgil (70–19 B.C.E.), follows the adventures of Aeneas, a Trojan who played a small part in the *Iliad* after the fall of Troy. It is important not as folklore but as a consciously literary work that presents the foundation myth of the Roman state.

William Godwin, in one of the earliest English versions of the tales, *The Pantheon* (1806), gave three reasons for children to read his collection. The first, that they should better understand poetic allusion, may no longer apply, but the second and third seem to resonate in an age confronted with the modern myths of Harry Potter:

2: as a collection of the most agreeable fables that ever were invented, it is admirably calculated to awaken the imagination; imagination, which it cannot be too often repeated, is the great engine of morality; 3. It presents us with an instructive lesson on the nature of the human mind, laying before us the manners and prejudices of a nation extremely different from our own, and showing us to what extravagant and fantastic notions of the invisible world the mind, once bewildered in error, may finally be led.

Modern Developments

The Hollywood movie *Troy* (2004) showed that the classical myths of Greece and Rome are still commercially powerful. In addition, people continue to read books by such authors as Mary Renault, Roger Lancelyn Green (*The Tale of Troy* [1958]), and Rosemary Sutcliff (*Black Sails Before Troy* [1993] and *The Wanderings of Odysseus* [1995]). Not surprisingly there have been many new books dealing with classical myths, ranging from beginner readers to adult novels. Retellings such as Claudia Zeff's *Jason and the Golden Fleece* (2003) and Vivian Webb's *Amazing Adventures of Ulysses* (2003) rely on the simplest elements of the myths. Books for teenagers add human dimensions to the characters: Adèle Geras's *Troy* (2001), for example, gives human flaws to Paris, Hector, and other figures, and the events are viewed through the eyes of two sisters and the old women of the kitchens. A children's author who has specialized in myths is Geraldine McCaughrean, with *Greek Gods and Goddesses* (1997; illustrated by Emma Chichester Clark) and *100 World Myths and Legends* (2001). In *Greek Myths* (1994), Marcia Williams powerfully presents the stories of Theseus, Perseus, and others in strip-cartoon form. Alongside these retellings are "factual" books, such as *Women in Ancient Greece* by Fiona Macdonald (1999), that provide links between history and myth. Adult versions of the myths, which may be accessible to older children, include *The Song of Troy* (1999), from Colleen McCullough (author of *The Thorn Birds* [1977]), and *The War at Troy* (2004), by the award-winning British author Lindsay Clarke.

WILLIAM GODWIN
1756–1836

William Godwin was a writer of radical opinions in a radical age; his best-known political novel (*Caleb Williams*, 1794) and political tract (*Enquiry Concerning Political Justice*, 1793), both written during the decade of the French Revolution, challenged traditional thinking in Britain. He married an early feminist, Mary Wollstonecraft (author of *A Vindication of the Rights of Woman*, 1792); their daughter, Mary, married the poet Percy Bysshe Shelley (a man regarded as dangerous by the political establishment) and wrote the classic horror novel *Frankenstein* (1818). Godwin became a publisher, and under the alias of Edward Baldwin Esq. contributed *The Pantheon* to his own Juvenile Library series. The title page of *The Pantheon* claimed that "the purpose of this book is to place the Heathen Mythology in two points of view: first, as it would have struck a Traveller in Greece, who wished to form a just conception of the Religion of the country . . . ; secondly, regarding Mythology as the introduction and hand-maid to the study of poetry."

Curiously, the book was produced—as was perhaps the most famous English-language rendition of the myths, Charles Kingsley's *The Heroes* (1856)—in reaction to an earlier book, Alexander Tooke's *Pantheon* (1694). Godwin described it in his preface as a dull, malicious, and coarse attack on the myths,

whose author "seems continually haunted by the fear that his pupil might prefer the religion of Jupiter to the religion of Christ." Like Kingsley after him, Godwin went to great pains to argue that there was hardly any danger of Christians being seduced by the myths: "We have a religion in which 'life and immortality are brought to light' and which inculcates the sublime lessons of the unity of God. . . . this religion fears no comparison with the mythology of ancient Greece." But despite his efforts, the *Anti-Jacobin* magazine savaged *The Pantheon* as a "eulogy on idolatry."

Godwin does admit that the Greek writers had a certain licentiousness, but he insists that in his version there is nothing "to administer libertinism in the fancy of the stripling, or to sully the whiteness of mind of the purest virgin." In fact, his version of Theseus's destruction of the Minotaur is so bland that it seems unlikely to affect readers at all. Nevertheless, for some of the Romantic poets—and Godwin was a friend or acquaintance of many, including William Wordsworth (1770–1850)—the stories in *The Pantheon* represented an exotic world in which different ways of thinking and behaving were possible. Among the writers deeply influenced by the work was the poet John Keats (1795–1821).

From The Pantheon

THE MINOTAUR

The most famous of all the adventures of Theseus is the destruction of the Minotaur:[1] this monster was described when I gave an account of the family of Minos: he was shut up in the famous labyrinth of Crete: Androgeus, the son of Minos, having

---

1. The Minotaur was the offspring of a bull and Minos's wife, Pasiphaë (Poseidon, god of the sea, made her fall in love with the animal because he was angry at a slight by Minos).

been killed in a riot at Athens, this powerful monarch imposed as a fine upon the Athenians, that they should send every year seven noble youths, and as many virgins, to be devoured by the Minotaur.

This tribute had already been exacted three years, when Theseus arrived at Athens: hungering and thirsting as the gallant champion did for arduous adventures, he intreated his father that, superseding the ordinary course of lot,[2] he might be admitted as one of the seven noble youths: Ægeus unwillingly consented: Theseus took with him two flags, a black and a white one, the first under which to sail in his voyage out, the second to be unfurled, if he returned victorious, as his heart told him he should do, in his voyage home.

Minos had a favourite daughter Ariadne: Theseus, soon after his arrival in Crete, was shut up with his companions in the fatal labyrinth; but not so soon as not to allow time to Ariadne to fall in love with the gallant presence of the youth, and to communicate to him the necessary instructions for destroying the Minotaur, as well as to present him with a clue[3] of thread, by which to find his way out of the labyrinth when he had accomplished the adventure.

The Minotaur being killed, Theseus returned home in triumph to Athens with the youths and virgins his companions: Ægeus his father, who had but just felt the pleasure of having such a son and being delivered from the tyranny of his graceless nephews, watched day and night for the arrival of the vessel in which Theseus had embarked: for this purpose he remained perpetually on the top of a high turret, which overlooked the waves of the sea: he at length discovered the approach of the ship: he watched for the white or black flag, which was to announce his good fortune or disaster: unhappily in the hurry and tumult of their joy, every one on board had forgotten to take down the black flag, and rear the white: Ægeus saw the fatal signal, and threw himself from the top of his turret into the sea, which from him was named the Ægean sea.

1806

2. I.e., that they should ignore the normal lottery   3. Ball.
procedures.

NATHANIEL HAWTHORNE
1804–1864

Nathaniel Hawthorne was born in Salem, Massachusetts, and some of his earliest stories were published in *The Token*, edited by Samuel Griswold Goodrich (alias Peter Parley). He became part of the Concord circle of American writers—which included Louisa May Alcott, Ralph Waldo Emerson, and Henry David Thoreau—and he has been seen as being more psychologically subtle than his contemporaries. After the success of his novels about the decadence of Puritanism, *The Scarlet Letter* (1850) and *The House of the Seven Gables* (1851), Hawthorne produced two volumes of retellings from classical mythology: *A Wonder-Book for Girls and Boys* (1851) and *Tanglewood Tales for Girls and Boys: Being a Second Wonder-Book* (1853). The first book takes the form of classical stories being told to children at Tanglewood Manor in western Massachusetts by a student, Eustace Bright; in the second, the frame is virtually dispensed with as six myths are retold.

The style of the books is more relaxed than that found in earlier versions. Two quotations from the introduction to *Tanglewood Tales* demonstrate Hawthorne's approach to the knotty question of the religious status of the texts:

> These old legends, so brimming over with everything that is most abhorrent to our Christianized moral sense—some of them so hideous, others so melancholy and miserable, amid which the Greek tragedians sought their themes . . . was such material the stuff that children's plaything should be made of? How were they to be purified? How was the blessed sunshine to be thrown into them?
>
> The objectionable characteristics . . . fall away . . . the instant [the storyteller] puts his imagination in sympathy with the innocent little circle, whose wide-open eyes are fixed so eagerly upon him. Thus the stories . . . transform themselves, and re-assume the shapes which they might be supposed to possess in the pure childhood of the world.

Hawthorne's faith in an Arcadian innocence does not prevent the narrator's tone from becoming patronizing rather than informal, while the occasional lapse into modern dialect ("Come on, then, and try it!" says Theseus to the Minotaur) may be distracting. The drawing of morals—"And O, my good little people, you will perhaps see, one of these days, as I do now, that every human being who suffers anything evil to get into his nature, or to remain there, is a kind of Minotaur"—could have been calculated to annoy a writer like Charles Kingsley (1819–1875), who admired the robustness of the original tales. But perhaps Hawthorne's greatest crime in Kingsley's eyes is the treatment of Ariadne in the extract printed below. Hawthorne simply denies that she and Theseus ran away together (as "some low-minded people, who pretend to tell the story . . . , have the face to say"), or that "Theseus (who would have died sooner than wrong the meanest creature in the world) ungratefully deserted Ariadne[.]" Ariadne, instead, expresses "maiden-like" loyalty to her father. As there is not, of course, any definitive text to deviate from, and as traditional stories are rewritten for each generation and each culture, it could be argued that we have no grounds for objecting to such alterations—or are there limits to the changes that adapters may legitimately make?

From Tanglewood Tales

From The Minotaur

One morning, when Prince Theseus awoke, he fancied that he must have had a very sorrowful dream, and that it was still running in his mind, even now that his eyes were open. For it appeared as if the air was full of a melancholy wail; and when he listened more attentively, he could hear sobs and groans, and screams of woe, mingled with deep, quiet sighs, which came from the king's palace, and from the streets, and from the temples, and from every habitation in the city. And all these mournful noises, issuing out of thousands of separate hearts, united themselves into the one great sound of affliction, which had startled Theseus from slumber. He put on his clothes as quickly as he could (not forgetting his sandals and gold-hilted sword), and hastening to the king, inquired what it all meant.

"Alas! my son," quoth King Ægeus, heaving a long sigh, "here is a very lamentable matter in hand! This is the wofullest anniversary in the whole year. It is the day when we annually draw lots to see which of the youths and maidens of Athens shall go to be devoured by the horrible Minotaur!"

"The Minotaur!" exclaimed Prince Theseus; and, like a brave young prince as he was, he put his hand to the hilt of his sword. "What kind of a monster may that be? Is it not possible, at the risk of one's life, to slay him?"

But King Ægeus shook his venerable head, and to convince Theseus that it was quite a hopeless case, he gave him an explanation of the whole affair. It seems that in the island of Crete there lived a certain dreadful monster, called a Minotaur, which was shaped partly like a man and partly like a bull, and was altogether such a hideous sort of a creature that it is really disagreeable to think of him.[1] If he were suffered to exist at all, it should have been on some desert island, or in the duskiness of some deep cavern, where nobody would ever be tormented by his abominable aspect. But King Minos, who reigned over Crete, laid out a vast deal of money in building a habitation for the Minotaur, and took great care of his health and comfort, merely for mischief's sake. A few years before this time, there had been a war between the city of Athens and the island of Crete, in which the Athenians were beaten, and compelled to beg for peace. No peace could they obtain, however, except on condition that they should send seven young men and seven maidens, every year, to be devoured by the pet monster of the cruel King Minos. For three years past, this grievous calamity had been borne. And the sobs, and groans, and shrieks, with which the city was now filled, were caused by the people's woe, because the fatal day had come again, when the fourteen victims were to be chosen by lot; and the old people feared lest their sons or daughters might be taken, and the youths and damsels dreaded lest they themselves might be destined to glut the ravenous maw of that detestable man-brute.

But when Theseus heard the story, he straightened himself up, so that he seemed taller than ever before; and as for his face, it was indignant, despiteful, bold, tender, and compassionate, all in one look.

"Let the people of Athens, this year, draw lots for only six young men, instead of seven," said he. "I will myself be the seventh; and let the Minotaur devour me, if he can!"

"O my dear son," cried King Ægeus, "why should you expose yourself to this horrible fate? You are a royal prince, and have a right to hold yourself above the destinies of common men."

"It is because I am a prince, your son, and the rightful heir of your kingdom, that I freely take upon me the calamity of your subjects," answered Theseus. "And you, my father, being king over this people, and answerable to Heaven for their welfare, are bound to sacrifice what is dearest to you, rather than that the son or daughter of the poorest citizen should come to any harm."

The old king shed tears, and besought Theseus not to leave him desolate in his old age, more especially as he had but just begun to know the happiness of possessing a good and valiant son. Theseus, however, felt that he was in the right, and therefore would not give up his resolution. But he assured his father that he did not intend to be eaten up, unresistingly, like a sheep, and that, if the Minotaur devoured him, it should not be without a battle for his dinner. And finally, since he could not help it, King Ægeus consented to let him go. So a vessel was got ready, and rigged with black sails; and Theseus, with six other young men, and seven tender and beautiful damsels, came down to the harbor to embark. A sorrowful multitude accompanied them to the shore. There was the poor old king, too, leaning on his son's arm, and looking as if his single heart held all the grief of Athens.

Just as Prince Theseus was going on board, his father bethought himself of one last word to say.

"My beloved son," said he, grasping the prince's hand, "you observe that the sails of this vessel are black; as indeed they ought to be, since it goes upon a voyage of

1. See n. 1, p. 423.

sorrow and despair. Now, being weighed down with infirmities, I know not whether I can survive till the vessel shall return. But, as long as I do live, I shall creep daily to the top of yonder cliff, to watch if there be a sail upon the sea. And, dearest Theseus, if by some happy chance you should escape the jaws of the Minotaur, then tear down those dismal sails, and hoist others that shall be bright as the sunshine. Beholding them on the horizon, myself and all the people will know that you are coming back victorious, and will welcome you with such a festal uproar as Athens never heard before."

Theseus promised that he would do so. Then, going on board, the mariners trimmed the vessel's black sails to the wind, which blew faintly off the shore, being pretty much made up of the sighs that everybody kept pouring forth on this melancholy occasion. But by and by, when they had got fairly out to sea, there came a stiff breeze from the northwest, and drove them along as merrily over the white-capped waves as if they had been going on the most delightful errand imaginable. And though it was a sad business enough, I rather question whether fourteen young people, without any old persons to keep them in order, could continue to spend the whole time of the voyage in being miserable. There had been some few dances upon the undulating deck, I suspect, and some hearty bursts of laughter, and other such unseasonable merriment among the victims, before the high, blue mountains of Crete began to show themselves among the far-off clouds. That sight, to be sure, made them all very grave again.

*　*　*

No sooner had they entered the harbor than a party of the guards of King Minos came down to the waterside, and took charge of the fourteen young men and damsels. Surrounded by these armed warriors, Prince Theseus and his companions were led to the king's palace, and ushered into his presence. Now, Minos was a stern and pitiless king. *　*　* He bent his shaggy brows upon the poor Athenian victims. Any other mortal, beholding their fresh and tender beauty, and their innocent looks, would have felt himself sitting on thorns until he had made every soul of them happy, by bidding them go free as the summer wind. But this immitigable Minos cared only to examine whether they were plump enough to satisfy the Minotaur's appetite. For my part, I wish he himself had been the only victim; and the monster would have found him a pretty tough one.

One after another, King Minos called these pale, frightened youths and sobbing maidens to his footstool, gave them each a poke in the ribs with his sceptre (to try whether they were in good flesh or no), and dismissed them with a nod to his guards. But when his eyes rested on Theseus, the king looked at him more attentively, because his face was calm and brave.

"Young man," asked he, with his stern voice, "are you not appalled at the certainty of being devoured by this terrible Minotaur?"

"I have offered my life in a good cause," answered Theseus, "and therefore I give it freely and gladly. But thou, King Minos, art thou not thyself appalled, who, year after year, hast perpetrated this dreadful wrong, by giving seven innocent youths and as many maidens to be devoured by a monster? Dost thou not tremble, wicked king, to turn thine eyes inward on thine own heart? Sitting there on thy golden throne, and in thy robes of majesty, I tell thee to thy face, King Minos, thou art a more hideous monster than the Minotaur himself!"

"Aha! do you think me so?" cried the king, laughing in his cruel way. "To-morrow, at breakfast-time, you shall have an opportunity of judging which is the greater monster, the Minotaur or the king! Take them away, guards; and let this free-spoken youth be the Minotaur's first morsel!"

Near the king's throne (though I had no time to tell you so before) stood his daughter Ariadne. She was a beautiful and tender-hearted maiden, and looked at these poor doomed captives with very different feelings from those of the iron-breasted King Minos. She really wept, indeed, at the idea of how much human happiness would be needlessly thrown away, by giving so many young people, in the first bloom and rose blossom of their lives, to be eaten up by a creature who, no doubt, would have preferred a fat ox, or even a large pig, to the plumpest of them. And when she beheld the brave, spirited figure of Prince Theseus bearing himself so calmly in his terrible peril, she grew a hundred times more pitiful than before. As the guards were taking him away, she flung herself at the king's feet, and besought him to set all the captives free, and especially this one young man.

"Peace, foolish girl!" answered King Minos. "What hast thou to do with an affair like this? It is a matter of state policy, and therefore quite beyond thy weak comprehension. Go water thy flowers, and think no more of these Athenian caitiffs,[2] whom the Minotaur shall as certainly eat up for breakfast as I will eat a partridge for my supper."

So saying, the king looked cruel enough to devour Theseus and all the rest of the captives, himself, had there been no Minotaur to save him the trouble. As he would hear not another word in their favor, the prisoners were now led away, and clapped into a dungeon, where the jailer advised them to go to sleep as soon as possible, because the Minotaur was in the habit of calling for breakfast early. The seven maidens and six of the young men soon sobbed themselves to slumber! But Theseus was not like them. He felt conscious that he was wiser and braver and stronger than his companions, and that therefore he had the responsibility of all their lives upon him, and must consider whether there was no way to save them, even in this last extremity. So he kept himself awake, and paced to and fro across the gloomy dungeon in which they were shut up.

Just before midnight, the door was softly unbarred, and the gentle Ariadne showed herself, with a torch in her hand.

"Are you awake, Prince Theseus?" she whispered.

"Yes," answered Theseus. "With so little time to live, I do not choose to waste any of it in sleep."

"Then follow me," said Ariadne, "and tread softly."

What had become of the jailer and the guards, Theseus never knew. But however that might be, Ariadne opened all the doors, and led him forth from the darksome prison into the pleasant moonlight.

"Theseus," said the maiden, "you can now get on board your vessel, and sail away for Athens."

"No," answered the young man; "I will never leave Crete unless I can first slay the Minotaur, and save my poor companions, and deliver Athens from this cruel tribute."

"I knew that this would be your resolution," said Ariadne. "Come, then, with me, brave Theseus. Here is your own sword, which the guards deprived you of. You will need it; and pray Heaven you may use it well."

Then she led Theseus along by the hand until they came to a dark, shadowy grove, where the moonlight wasted itself on the tops of the trees, without shedding hardly so much as a glimmering beam upon their pathway. After going a good way through

2. Captives.

this obscurity, they reached a high, marble wall, which was overgrown with creeping plants, that made it shaggy with their verdure. The wall seemed to have no door, nor any windows, but rose up, lofty, and massive, and mysterious, and was neither to be clambered over, nor, so far as Theseus could perceive, to be passed through. Nevertheless, Ariadne did but press one of her soft little fingers against a particular block of marble, and, though it looked as solid as any other part of the wall, it yielded to her touch, disclosing an entrance just wide enough to admit them. They crept through, and the marble stone swung back into its place.

"We are now," said Ariadne, "in the famous labyrinth which Dædalus[3] built before he made himself a pair of wings, and flew away from our island like a bird. That Dædalus was a very cunning workman; but of all his artful contrivances, this labyrinth is the most wondrous. Were we to take but a few steps from the doorway, we might wander about all our lifetime, and never find it again. Yet in the very centre of this labyrinth is the Minotaur; and, Theseus, you must go thither to seek him."

"But how shall I ever find him," asked Theseus, "if the labyrinth so bewilders me as you say it will?"

Just as he spoke they heard a rough and very disagreeable roar, which greatly resembled the lowing of a fierce bull, but yet had some sort of sound like the human voice. Theseus even fancied a rude articulation in it, as if the creature that uttered it were trying to shape his hoarse breath into words. It was at some distance, however, and he really could not tell whether it sounded most like a bull's roar or a man's harsh voice.

"That is the Minotaur's noise," whispered Ariadne, closely grasping the hand of Theseus, and pressing one of her own hands to her heart, which was all in a tremble. "You must follow that sound through the windings of the labyrinth, and, by and by, you will find him. Stay! take the end of this silken string; I will hold the other end; and then, if you win the victory, it will lead you again to this spot. Farewell, brave Theseus."

So the young man took the end of the silken string in his left hand, and his gold-hilted sword, ready drawn from its scabbard, in the other, and trod boldly into the inscrutable labyrinth. How this labyrinth was built is more than I can tell you. But so cunningly contrived a mizmaze[4] was never seen in the world, before nor since. There can be nothing else so intricate, unless it were the brain of a man like Dædalus, who planned it, or the heart of any ordinary man; which last, to be sure, is ten times as great a mystery as the labyrinth of Crete. Theseus had not taken five steps before he lost sight of Ariadne; and in five more his head was growing dizzy. But still he went on, now creeping through a low arch, now ascending a flight of steps, now in one crooked passage and now in another with here a door opening before him, and there one banging behind, until it really seemed as if the walls spun round, and whirled him round along with them. And all the while, through these hollow avenues, now nearer, now farther off again, resounded the cry of the Minotaur; and the sound was so fierce, so cruel, so ugly, so like a bull's roar, and withal so like a human voice, and yet like neither of them, that the brave heart of Theseus grew sterner and angrier at every step; for he felt it an insult to the moon and sky, and to our affectionate and simple Mother Earth, that such a monster should have the audacity to exist.

As he passed onward, the clouds gathered over the moon, and the labyrinth grew so dusky that Theseus could no longer discern the bewilderment through which he

3. An Athenian artisan, famed in Greek mythology for his consummate skill. (His son Icarus did not survive their escape from Crete.)
4. Labyrinth, maze.

was passing. He would have felt quite lost, and utterly hopeless of ever again walking in a straight path, if, every little while, he had not been conscious of a gentle twitch at the silken cord. Then he knew that the tender-hearted Ariadne was still holding the other end, and that she was fearing for him, and hoping for him, and giving him just as much of her sympathy as if she were close by his side. Oh, indeed, I can assure you, there was a vast deal of human sympathy running along that slender thread of silk. But still he followed the dreadful roar of the Minotaur, which now grew louder and louder, and finally so very loud that Theseus fully expected to come close upon him, at every new zigzag and wriggle of the path. And at last, in an open space, at the very centre of the labyrinth, he did discern the hideous creature.

Sure enough, what an ugly monster it was! Only his horned head belonged to a bull; and yet, somehow or other, he looked like a bull all over, preposterously waddling on his hind legs; or, if you happened to view him in another way, he seemed wholly a man, and all the more monstrous for being so. And there he was, the wretched thing, with no society, no companion, no kind of a mate, living only to do mischief, and incapable of knowing what affection means. Theseus hated him, and shuddered at him, and yet could not but be sensible of some sort of pity; and all the more, the uglier and more detestable the creature was. For he kept striding to and fro in a solitary frenzy of rage, continually emitting a hoarse roar, which was oddly mixed up with half-shaped words; and, after listening awhile, Theseus understood that the Minotaur was saying to himself how miserable he was, and how hungry, and how he hated everybody, and how he longed to eat up the human race alive.

Ah, the bull-headed villain! And O, my good little people, you will perhaps see, one of these days, as I do now, that every human being who suffers anything evil to get into his nature, or to remain there, is a kind of Minotaur, an enemy of his fellow-creatures, and separated from all good companionship, as this poor monster was.

Was Theseus afraid? By no means, my dear auditors. What! a hero like Theseus afraid! Not had the Minotaur had twenty bull heads instead of one. Bold as he was, however, I rather fancy that it strengthened his valiant heart, just at this crisis, to feel a tremulous twitch at the silken cord, which he was still holding in his left hand. It was as if Ariadne were giving him all her might and courage; and, much as he already had, and little as she had to give, it made his own seem twice as much. And to confess the honest truth, he needed the whole; for now the Minotaur, turning suddenly about, caught sight of Theseus, and instantly lowered his horribly sharp horns, exactly as a mad bull does when he means to rush against an enemy. At the same time, he belched forth a tremendous roar, in which there was something like the words of human language, but all disjointed and shaken to pieces by passing through the gullet of a miserably enraged brute.

Theseus could only guess what the creature intended to say, and that rather by his gestures than his words; for the Minotaur's horns were sharper than his wits, and of a great deal more service to him than his tongue. But probably this was the sense of what he uttered:—

"Ah, wretch of a human being! I'll stick my horns through you, and toss you fifty feet high, and eat you up the moment you come down."

"Come on, then, and try it!" was all that Theseus deigned to reply; for he was far too magnanimous to assault his enemy with insolent language.

Without more words on either side, there ensued the most awful fight between Theseus and the Minotaur that ever happened beneath the sun or moon. I really know not how it might have turned out, if the monster, in his first headlong rush against Theseus had not missed him, by a hair's-breadth, and broken one of his horns short off against the stone wall. On this mishap, he bellowed so intolerably that a part of the labyrinth tumbled down, and all the inhabitants of Crete mistook the noise for an uncommonly heavy thunder-storm. Smarting with the pain, he galloped around the open space in so ridiculous a way that Theseus laughed at it, long afterwards, though not precisely at the moment. After this, the two antagonists stood valiantly up to one another, and fought sword to horn, for a long while. At last, the Minotaur made a run at Theseus, grazed his left side with his horn, and flung him down; and thinking that he had stabbed him to the heart, he cut a great caper in the air, opened his bull mouth from ear to ear, and prepared to snap his head off. But Theseus by this time had leaped up, and caught the monster off his guard. Fetching a sword-stroke at him with all his force, he hit him fair upon the neck, and made his bull head skip six yards from his human body, which fell down flat upon the ground.

So now the battle was ended. Immediately the moon shone out as brightly as if all the troubles of the world, and all the wickedness and the ugliness that infest human life, were past and gone forever. And Theseus, as he leaned on his sword, taking breath, felt another twitch of the silken cord; for all through the terrible encounter he had held it fast in his left hand. Eager to let Ariadne know of his success, he followed the guidance of the thread, and soon found himself at the entrance of the labyrinth.

"Thou hast slain the monster," cried Ariadne, clasping her hands.

"Thanks to thee, dear Ariadne," answered Theseus, "I return victorious."

"Then," said Ariadne, "we must quickly summon thy friends, and get them and thyself on board the vessel before dawn. If morning finds thee here, my father will avenge the Minotaur."

To make my story short, the poor captives were awakened, and, hardly knowing whether it was not a joyful dream, were told of what Theseus had done, and that they must set sail for Athens before daybreak. Hastening down to the vessel, they all clambered on board, except Prince Theseus, who lingered behind them, on the strand, holding Ariadne's hand clasped in his own.

"Dear maiden," said he, "thou wilt surely go with us. Thou art too gentle and sweet a child for such an iron-hearted father as King Minos. He cares no more for thee than a granite rock cares for the little flower that grows in one of its crevices. But my father, King Ægeus, and my dear mother, Æthra, and all the fathers and mothers in Athens, and all the sons and daughters too, will love and honor thee as their benefactress. Come with us, then; for King Minos will be very angry when he knows what thou hast done."

Now, some low-minded people, who pretend to tell the story of Theseus and Ariadne, have the face to say that this royal and honorable maiden did really flee away, under cover of the night, with the young stranger whose life she had preserved. They say, too, that Prince Theseus (who would have died sooner than wrong the meanest creature in the world) ungratefully deserted Ariadne, on a solitary island,[5] where the vessel touched on its voyage to Athens. But, had the noble Theseus heard these falsehoods, he would have served their slanderous authors as he served the Minotaur! Here is what Ariadne answered, when the brave Prince of Athens besought her to accompany him:—

"No, Theseus," the maiden said, pressing his hand, and then drawing back a step or two, "I cannot go with you. My father is old, and has nobody but myself to love

431

TANGLEWOOD
TALES

---

5. Ariadne was rescued and married by Dionysus, the god of wine.

him. Hard as you think his heart is, it would break to lose me. At first King Minos will be angry; but he will soon forgive his only child; [6] and, by and by, he will rejoice, I know, that no more youths and maidens must come from Athens to be devoured by the Minotaur. I have saved you, Theseus, as much for my father's sake as for your own. Farewell! Heaven bless you!"

All this was so true, and so maiden-like, and was spoken with so sweet a dignity, that Theseus would have blushed to urge her any longer. Nothing remained for him, therefore, but to bid Ariadne an affectionate farewell, and go on board the vessel, and set sail.

In a few moments the white foam was boiling up before their prow, as Prince Theseus and his companions sailed out of the harbor with a whistling breeze behind them.

*　*　*

On the homeward voyage, the fourteen youths and damsels were in excellent spirits, as you will easily suppose. They spent most of their time in dancing, unless when the sidelong breeze made the deck slope too much. In due season, they came within sight of the coast of Attica, which was their native country. But here, I am grieved to tell you, happened a sad misfortune.

You will remember (what Theseus unfortunately forgot) that his father, King Ægeus, had enjoined it upon him to hoist sunshine sails, instead of black ones, in case he should overcome the Minotaur, and return victorious. In the joy of their success, however, and amidst the sports, dancing, and other merriment, with which these young folks wore away the time, they never once thought whether their sails were black, white, or rainbow colored, and, indeed, left it entirely to the mariners whether they had any sails at all. Thus the vessel returned, like a raven, with the same sable wings that had wafted her away. But poor King Ægeus, day after day, infirm as he was, had clambered to the summit of a cliff that overhung the sea, and there sat watching for Prince Theseus, homeward bound; and no sooner did he behold the fatal blackness of the sails, than he concluded that his dear son, whom he loved so much, and felt so proud of, had been eaten by the Minotaur. He could not bear the thought of living any longer; so, first flinging his crown and sceptre into the sea, (useless bawbles[7] that they were to him now!) King Ægeus merely stooped forward, and fell headlong over the cliff, and was drowned, poor soul, in the waves that foamed at its base!

This was melancholy news for Prince Theseus, who, when he stepped ashore, found himself king of all the country, whether he would or no; and such a turn of fortune was enough to make any young man feel very much out of spirits. However, he sent for his dear mother to Athens, and, by taking her advice in matters of state, became a very excellent monarch, and was greatly beloved by his people.

1853

6. Traditionally, Ariadne was not Minos's only child.　　7. Baubles.

CHARLES KINGSLEY
1819–1875

The Heroes; or, Greek Fairy Tales for My Children (1856) was written as a direct response to Nathaniel Hawthorne's versions of the Greek myths, which Charles Kingsley thought were "distressingly vulgar": too comfortable and bland, and too ornate and gothic in style. The result was probably the most successful of all British retellings; indeed, the book was eventually translated into Greek.

Kingsley was one of the major figures in British children's literature, and his most famous book, *The Water Babies* (1863), was a landmark text that ushered in the first golden age of children's books in Britain. Kingsley was a man of very wide interests: he was a parish priest, but was also chaplain to Queen Victoria, professor of history at Cambridge University, professor of English at London University, canon of Westminster Abbey in London, and a fellow of the Geological Society. A friend of the naturalist Charles Darwin, he also wrote political novels and poetry.

It is not surprising that Kingsley should be enthusiastic about the classical myths: he saw Greece as the root of language, mathematics, geography, science, philosophy, and politics. *The Heroes* was his first book for children, intended as a Christmas present for his own children—Rose, Maurice, and Mary. In reaction to Hawthorne, he tried to use a "simple ballad tone" (which has been described as "romantic poetic prose"), and he tends to keep more closely to the versions found in classical authors. Though rejecting Hawthorne's romantic idea that the stories became purified in contact with children, or that they represent the innocent childhood of the world, he saw the tales as part of his children's cultural heritage. Kingsley explains in the preface to *The Heroes*, "I love these old Hellens [Greeks] heartily; and I should be very ungrateful to them if I did not, considering all that they have taught me; and

they seem to me like brothers. . . . So as you must learn about them, whether you choose or not, I wish to be the first to introduce you to them."

Since the beginning of the nineteenth century, British children's books had been dominated by Christian evangelical writers, who frowned upon fantasy. By the 1850s, however, fairy tales and folktales were becoming increasingly popular, although it was not until the next decade that fantasy became widely acceptable, and *The Water Babies* and Lewis Carroll's *Alice's Adventures in Wonderland* (1865) appeared. When Kingsley wrote *The Heroes*, therefore, he was careful to try to integrate these tales into a Christian context: "For you must not fancy, children, that because these old Greeks were heathens, therefore God did not care for them, and taught them nothing. . . . The Bible tells us that it was not so, but that God's mercy is over all His works, and that He understands the hearts of all people, and fashions all their works." His argument (characteristically) is rather erratic, and he blurs the sequence of history somewhat, suggesting that the Greeks "believed at first in the One True God" and only later worshipped other gods and spirits; thus Zeus "the Father of gods and men . . . was some dim remembrance of the blessed true God[. . .]"

It is interesting to compare the style and content of Hawthorne and Kingsley, as they represent the growing distinction between American and British approaches to childhood and children's literature. American children's books in the nineteenth century tended to stress independence of thought and action, in both boys and girls, while in Britain there was an emphasis on tradition and codes of behavior. Thus in British children's books, the controlling voice of the adult narrator lingered far longer than it did in the United States.

CHARLES
KINGSLEY

From The Heroes; or, Greek Fairy Tales for My Children

HOW THESEUS SLEW THE MINOTAUR

And at last they came to Crete, and to Cnossus, beneath the peaks of Ida, and to the palace of Minos the great king, to whom Zeus himself taught laws. So he was the wisest of all mortal kings, and conquered all the Ægean isles; and his ships were as many as the sea-gulls, and his palace like a marble hill. And he sat among the pillars of the hall, upon his throne of beaten gold, and around him stood the speaking statues which Daidalos[1] had made by his skill. For Daidalos was the most cunning of all Athenians, and he first invented the plumb-line, and the auger, and glue, and many a tool with which wood is wrought. And he first set up masts in ships, and yards, and his son made sails for them: but Perdix his nephew excelled him; for he first invented the saw and its teeth, copying it from the back-bone of a fish; and invented, too, the chisel, and the compasses, and the potter's wheel which moulds the clay. Therefore Daidalos envied him, and hurled him headlong from the temple of Athené;[2] but the Goddess pitied him (for she loves the wise), and changed him into a partridge, which flits for ever about the hills. And Daidalos fled to Crete, to Minos, and worked for him many a year, till he did a shameful deed,[3] at which the sun hid his face on high.

Then he fled from the anger of Minos, he and Icaros his son having made themselves wings of feathers, and fixed the feathers with wax. So they flew over the sea toward Sicily; but Icaros flew too near the sun; and the wax of his wings was melted, and he fell into the Icarian Sea. But Daidalos came safe to Sicily, and there wrought many a wondrous work; for he made for King Cocalos a reservoir, from which a great river watered all the land, and a castle and a treasury on a mountain, which the giants themselves could not have stormed; and in Selinos he took the steam which comes up from the fires of Ætna, and made of it a warm bath of vapour, to cure the pains of mortal men; and he made a honeycomb of gold, in which the bees came and stored their honey, and in Egypt he made the forecourt of the temple of Hephaistos in Memphis,[4] and a statue of himself within it, and many another wondrous work. And for Minos he made statues which spoke and moved, and the temple of Britomartis,[5] and the dancing-hall of Ariadne, which he carved of fair white stone. And in Sardinia he worked for Iölaos, and in many a land beside, wandering up and down for ever with his cunning, unlovely and accursed by men.

But Theseus stood before Minos, and they looked each other in the face. And Minos bade take them to prison, and cast them to the monster one by one, that the death of Androgeos[6] might be avenged. Then Theseus cried—

'A boon, O Minos! Let me be thrown first to the beast. For I came hither for that very purpose, of my own will, and not by lot.'

'Who art thou, then, brave youth?'

'I am the son of him whom of all men thou hatest most, Ægeus the king of Athens, and I am come here to end this matter.'

---

1. Daedalus.
2. Goddess of war, wisdom, and handicrafts.
3. Daedalus was imprisoned by Minos for constructing the hollow cow that enabled Pasiphaë, Minos's wife, to conceive the Minotaur with a bull. Pasiphaë released Daedalus from prison.
4. The second-largest city in Egypt at that time.

Hephaistos: Hephaestus, god of fire and metalworking.
5. A companion of Artemis (goddess of the hunt), deified after she successfully fled the amorous pursuit of Minos.
6. Minos's son, killed in an ambush plotted by Aegeus.

And Minos pondered awhile, looking steadfastly at him, and he thought, 'The lad means to atone by his own death for his father's sin'; and he answered at last mildly—

'Go back in peace, my son. It is a pity that one so brave should die.'

But Theseus said, 'I have sworn that I will not go back till I have seen the monster face to face.'

And at that Minos frowned, and said, 'Then thou shalt see him; take the madman away.'

And they led Theseus away into the prison, with the other youths and maids.

But Ariadne, Minos' daughter, saw him, as she came out of her white stone hall; and she loved him for his courage and his majesty, and said, 'Shame that such a youth should die!' And by night she went down to the prison, and told him all her heart; and said—

'Flee down to your ship at once, for I have bribed the guards before the door. Flee, you and all your friends, and go back in peace to Greece; and take me, take me with you! for I dare not stay after you are gone; for my father will kill me miserably, if he knows what I have done.'

And Theseus stood silent awhile; for he was astonished and confounded by her beauty: but at last he said, 'I cannot go home in peace, till I have seen and slain this Minotaur, and avenged the deaths of the youths and maidens, and put an end to the terrors of my land.'

'And will you kill the Minotaur? How, then?'

'I know not, nor do I care: but he must be strong if he be too strong for me.'

Then she loved him all the more, and said, 'But when you have killed him, how will you find your way out of the labyrinth?'

'I know not, neither do I care: but it must be a strange road, if I do not find it out before I have eaten up the monster's carcase.'

Then she loved him all the more, and said—

'Fair youth, you are too bold; but I can help you, weak as I am. I will give you a sword, and with that perhaps you may slay the beast; and a clue[7] of thread, and by that, perhaps, you may find your way out again. Only promise me that if you escape safe you will take me home with you to Greece; for my father will surely kill me, if he knows what I have done.'

Then Theseus laughed, and said, 'Am I not safe enough now?' And he hid the sword in his bosom, and rolled up the clue in his hand; and then he swore to Ariadne, and fell down before her, and kissed her hands and her feet; and she wept over him a long while, and then went away; and Theseus lay down and slept sweetly.

And when the evening came, the guards came in and led him away to the labyrinth.

And he went down into that doleful gulf, through winding paths among the rocks, under caverns, and arches, and galleries, and over heaps of fallen stone. And he turned on the left hand, and on the right hand, and went up and down, till his head was dizzy; but all the while he held his clue. For when he went in he had fastened it to a stone, and left it to unroll out of his hand as he went on; and it lasted him till he met the Minotaur, in a narrow chasm between black cliffs.

And when he saw him he stopped awhile, for he had never seen so strange a beast. His body was a man's: but his head was the head of a bull; and his teeth were the teeth of a lion; and with them he tore his prey. And when he saw Theseus he roared, and put his head down, and rushed right at him.

But Theseus stept aside nimbly, and as he passed by, cut him in the knee; and ere

7. Ball.

he could turn in the narrow path, he followed him, and stabbed him again and again from behind, till the monster fled bellowing wildly; for he never before had felt a wound. And Theseus followed him at full speed, holding the clue of thread in his left hand.

Then on, through cavern after cavern, under dark ribs of sounding stone, and up rough glens and torrent-beds, among the sunless roots of Ida, and to the edge of the eternal snow, went they, the hunter and the hunted, while the hills bellowed to the monster's bellow.

And at last Theseus came up with him, where he lay panting on a slab among the snow, and caught him by the horns, and forced his head back, and drove the keen sword through his throat.

Then he turned, and went back limping and weary, feeling his way down by the clue of thread, till he came to the mouth of that doleful place; and saw waiting for him, whom but Ariadne!

And he whispered 'It is done!' and showed her the sword; and she laid her finger on her lips, and led him to the prison, and opened the doors, and set all the prisoners free, while the guards lay sleeping heavily; for she had silenced them with wine.

Then they fled to their ship together, and leapt on board, and hoisted up the sail; and the night lay dark around them, so that they passed through Minos' ships, and escaped all safe to Naxos; and there Ariadne became Theseus' wife.

1856

LEON GARFIELD *and* EDWARD BLISHEN
1921–1996 *1920–1996*

Leon Garfield was a prolific, award-winning writer of novels for children, set in eighteenth- and nineteenth-century England; these include *Devil-in-the-Fog* (1966) and *The Strange Affair of Adelaide Harris* (1971). One of his outstanding characteristics is his style, which is extravagant, ornate, and witty. Edward Blishen was a schoolteacher turned critic and autobiographer, as well as an important campaigner for the wider use of children's books in schools.

In the afterword to *The God beneath the Sea*, Garfield and Blishen discuss their approach to their task. They felt that most retellings of the myths were influenced by "certain conventions of translation from Greek poetry and have little in them of the literary voice of our own time. We wondered if it might be possible to discover some new style of telling these stories—a language freed in some important respects from these conventions." Their book deals with aspects of the classical myths not usually

included in books for children, or thought suitable for them, and its contents are often extreme and violent. *The God beneath the Sea* won the Carnegie Medal for the best British book for children in 1973; it was both praised for its originality (by the poet laureate Ted Hughes) and condemned for its pretentiousness and artificiality (by the award-winning children's writer and folklorist Alan Garner).

The first part of *The God beneath the Sea* deals with the legends of the first rulers of the universe, the Titans—stories that predate Greek civilization. The account of the killing of Uranus, printed here, shows the difficulty that Garfield and Blishen had in retelling the myths. They either ignore overtly sexual material—notably the castration of Uranus, which appears in other accounts—or use euphemisms, such as "embraced," "chief consolation," "could not endure without her," and "Was there a traitor in his bed?" This is a somewhat illogical course to take, as the text would not make much sense to a reader who does not understand what is not being said. The book and its sequel, *The Golden Shadow* (1973), were forcefully and dramatically illustrated by Charles Keeping (1924–1988) in black and white. The story of Cronus, like so many classical tales, once again raises the question of whether the myths can be said to be suitable reading for children.

From The God beneath the Sea

THE SEEDS OF POWER

The king of the seven Titans was Uranus, and in that ancient time he had seized the earth for his garden. He planted it and tended it till the mountains and valleys were all green and gold in an endless spring. Then Uranus lay with Mother Earth and she brought forth a second race of Titans, who were as harsh and savage as the rocks from which they had sprung. Among them were the one-eyed Cyclopes and the hundred-handed giants: craggy monsters who, in the stillness of night, resembled great configurations of land. Violent in their pride, they rebelled against their father. But they lacked his power. Uranus flung them into a deep, fearful hole called Tartarus. For nine nights and days they dropped like struggling black mountains, till at last they were extinguished in echoing shrieks and groans.

Uranus listened and smiled. There was nothing in heaven and earth that could oppose him. His throne was the very rock of the universe. He closed his eyes and the sun and stars went out. He slept and dreamed that Mother Earth was in his arms. He saw her smile; he heard her sigh. His huge hands tightened till he dreamed her breath came sharp and passionate.

He could even hear each separate intake, which seemed to catch at its return with an almost secret air; and he heard the beating of her heart. But he slept on, and a single lamp cast his heaving shadow against the soaring wall of his bedchamber. The lamp flickered, making the sleeping shadow writhe to the rhythm of his dream.

The beating heart, the hissing breath—they were coming nearer. The flame leaped and danced at the wick. The shadow bulked and cowered, for another shadow had joined it. A dreadful, creeping shadow, at first like a bird with one wing upraised. But it was not a bird. It was Cronus, his eldest son, and the wing was a huge stone sickle!

Uranus opened his eyes and the universe blazed up all round him. Then Cronus struck. And it all went out for ever. Not even his dying scream was heard, for it was drowned in Cronus's mighty shout of triumph. The terrible king was dead.

Doors and passages in the great stone castle rang and thundered as the Titans proclaimed his still more terrible son. They tore dead Uranus in pieces and cast them into the sea. They grinned and laughed and joked as they watched the dark sea crack in a hundred places to let the multitude of Uranus in. Then it closed up after, as if he had never been.

But the ocean could not hide what had been done. Three drops of blood from the death wound had fallen unnoticed on the earth, and silently there rose up three terrible creatures. At first they stood still and quiet in the shadow of the castle's southern wall. They might have been dwarfish trees—or bushes, even, with smooth black foliage that hung down like cloaks. But there was movement among what might have been their topmost twigs, as if some breeze was ruffling them. They were nests of snakes, spitting and twisting as they grew out of shadowy heads. Then, of a sudden, they swayed. The black foliage spread into wide, jointed wings. Once, twice, they beat the air; then the three creatures rose up. Round and round the castle they flew, and their shadows seemed to scratch and scar the stones. They would know that place again. Then they vanished into the upper air. They were the Furies—avengers of fathers murdered by their sons.[1]

Cronus slept in his father's bed, with Rhea, his sister-wife. His dreams were easy and seemed to hang in thick curtains across his mind. Suddenly he awoke, as if the curtains had shifted. He stared uneasily into the dark, but saw nothing. He closed his eyes and tried to smile away whatever had disturbed him. But it would not go. There was, or seemed to be, a rustling and a creaking in the air and a smell of snakes. He turned on his back and looked up. Nothing. Yet some drops of moisture fell on his face. They burned like venom, and he cried out in fear and disgust. He did not sleep again that night.

Next night the Furies came again. They looked down on the new king, smiling in his sleep. Then with their curious sharp instruments they made another hole in the curtain of his dreams and whispered through it that he, like his father, would be ruined by his son. With the coming of the dawn, they flew away, but left the marks of their shadows behind. They would be back.

Night after night they came to visit Cronus, till his sleep hung in tatters and through every rent came the hateful words, 'Cronus, you will be ruined by your son! There is no escape!'

A wind blew through the king's head and all the exposed caverns of his mind began to ache and crack. Nothing comforted him—neither his throne nor his queen. All was swept aside by the nightly terror of the Furies and the threat of the unborn son. Despairingly, he embraced Rhea; then, with a cry of dismay, thrust her from him as he remembered that out of this chief consolation would come his chief danger.

Yet he could not endure without her, and at last she bore him a child. Proudly she brought it to him in swaddling clothes. The Furies' words roared a gale through his head. His hands shook and madness finally seized him. He took the infant almost tenderly from the queen and thrust it, living, into his gigantic mouth. Then he laughed till his stone palace rocked on the mountain top. He had cheated the Furies.

That night they came again. But Cronus was ready and went for them with his bare hands. He clawed the air and beat the walls, but it was not till dawn that they flew away. He saw them like black moths dwindling in the sky.

The mad king grinned in triumph. Sooner or later, he would destroy his tormentors even as he had eaten his child. Nothing would shake his throne. So he kept spears in his bedchamber, and knives and arrows. They flew from the casements and scarred the walls as Cronus killed the air.

Then Rhea bore another child. Was there a traitor in his bed? No matter. Cronus was armoured at all points. Again he ate the child.

He would reign for ever.

Some more children after that the wild Titan swallowed. Yet each time he took them from her almost lovingly, so that Rhea's anguish was multiplied by hope.

Then at last she bore such a son as she could not endure to lose. He shone like a star, and her heart ached as he smiled unknowingly.

1. The Furies, or Erinyes, punished crimes against human society generally (e.g., those committed by host against guest), but especially the murder of blood relatives.

'Fetch me the child!' she heard the mad king shout. 'The child! The child!'

With trembling hands, she hid the infant among the bedclothes, then stared round desperately. Beside the door was a stone that wedged it open in the heat of the day. Its size was the size of the child. Hastily she wound it in the swaddling bands over and over. . . .

A shadow darkened the doorway. Rhea looked up. Cronus stood before her. 'Give me the child!' Cronus's eyes flickered over the tumbled bed linen. Frantically Rhea clasped the swaddled stone. He held out his arms. 'My son! My son!' he half whispered, half groaned, and opened wide his mouth. Rhea turned away. Terror seized her. The bedclothes were stirring. Fearfully she looked back at her husband. Had he seen it? His eyes were hooded and remote and his hands hung empty at his sides.

He reached out and stroked her cheek. Then he wiped his mouth and left the room.

When he was gone, Rhea sank to her knees beside the bed. She stared into the careless folds. Then she started. Two golden eyes were gazing out at her, and an infant's lips were curved in a prophetic smile.

1970

PADRAIC COLUM
1881–1972

Padraic Colum (born Patrick Collumb) was a member of the Irish National Theatre Society and one of the founders of the Abbey Theatre in Dublin. He was a friend of major Irish literary figures such as James Joyce (1882–1941) and William Butler Yeats (1865–1939), had some early success as a playwright, and was founder and editor of the *Irish Review*. He emigrated to the United States in 1914, becoming an American citizen in 1945. He taught comparative literature at Columbia University; his publications include a large number of retellings of Celtic, Norse, and classical myths, as well as two volumes titled *Tales and Legends of Hawaii: At the Gateways of the Day* and *The Bright Islands* (1924–25). Colum's original tales, such as *The White Sparrow* (1933), often combine strong political messages with a desire to interpret Irish folk stories to American children.

His straightforward style has just enough formality to suggest the flavor of a different world and society. The excerpt printed here closely follows book 9 of Homer's *Odyssey*. At this stage in Odysseus's journey, he has been shipwrecked on the coast of Scheria (Corfu); he relates his story to Alcinous, the king of the Phaeacians. Although Homer presents him as a noble hero as well as shrewd, most later Greek authors portray Odysseus as unscrupulously clever; his name became a byword not merely for wandering but for deviousness. These elements of his character, together with pride, can be seen in this extract.

From The Adventures of Odysseus and the Tale of Troy

Then Odysseus spoke before the company and said, "O Alcinous, famous King, it is good to listen to a minstrel such as Demodocus is. And as for me, I know of no greater delight than when men feast together with open hearts, when tables are plentifully spread, when wine-bearers pour out good wine into cups, and when a minstrel sings to them noble songs. This seems to me to be happiness indeed. But thou hast asked me to speak of my wanderings and my toils. Ah, where can I begin that tale? For the gods have given me more woes than a man can speak of!

"But first of all I will declare to you my name and my country. I am Odysseus, son of Laertes, and my land is Ithaka, an island around which many islands lie. Ithaka is a rugged isle, but a good nurse of hardy men, and I, for one, have found that there is no place fairer than a man's own land. But now I will tell thee, King, and tell the Princes and Captains and Councillors of the Phæacians, the tale of my wanderings.

"The wind bore my ships from the coast of Troy, and with our white sails hoisted we came to the cape that is called Malea. Now if we had been able to double[1] this cape we should soon have come to our own country, all unhurt. But the north wind came and swept us from our course and drove us wandering past Cythera.

"Then for nine days we were borne onward by terrible winds, and away from all known lands. On the tenth day we came to a strange country. Many of my men landed there. The people of that land were harmless and friendly, but the land itself was most dangerous. For there grew there the honey-sweet fruit of the lotus that makes all men forgetful of their past and neglectful of their future. And those of my men who ate the lotus that the dwellers of that land offered them became forgetful of their country and of the way before them. They wanted to abide forever in the land of the lotus. They wept when they thought of all the toils before them and of all they had endured. I led them back to the ships, and I had to place them beneath the benches and leave them in bonds. And I commanded those who had ate of the lotus to go at once aboard the ships. Then, when I had got all my men upon the ships, we made haste to sail away.

"Later we came to the land of the Cyclôpes, a giant people. There is a waste[2] island outside the harbor of their land, and on it there is a well of bright water that has poplars growing round it. We came to that empty island, and we beached our ships and took down our sails.

"As soon as the dawn came we went through the empty island, starting the wild goats that were there in flocks, and shooting them with our arrows. We killed so many wild goats there that we had nine for each ship. Afterwards we looked across to the land of the Cyclôpes, and we heard the sound of voices and saw the smoke of fires and heard the bleating of flocks of sheep and goats.

"I called my companions together and I said, 'It would be well for some of us to go to that other island. With my own ship and with the company that is on it I shall go there. The rest of you abide here. I will find out what manner of men live there, and whether they will treat us kindly and give us gifts that are due to strangers— gifts of provisions for our voyage.'

"We embarked and we came to the land. There was a cave near the sea, and round the cave there were mighty flocks of sheep and goats. I took twelve men with me and I left the rest to guard the ship. We went into the cave and found no man there.

---

1. Sail around.   2. Uninhabited.

There were baskets filled with cheeses, and vessels of whey, and pails and bowls of milk. My men wanted me to take some of the cheeses and drive off some of the lambs and kids and come away. But this I would not do, for I would rather that he who owned the stores would give us of his own free will the offerings that were due to strangers.

"While we were in the cave, he whose dwelling it was, returned to it. He carried on his shoulder a great pile of wood for his fire. Never in our lives did we see a creature so frightful as this Cyclops was. He was a giant in size, and, what made him terrible to behold, he had but one eye, and that single eye was in his forehead. He cast down on the ground the pile of wood that he carried, making such a din that we fled in terror into the corners and recesses of the cave. Next he drove his flocks into the cave and began to milk his ewes and goats. And when he had the flocks within, he took up a stone that not all our strengths could move and set it as a door to the mouth of the cave.

"The Cyclops kindled his fire, and when it blazed up he saw us in the corners and recesses. He spoke to us. We knew not what he said, but our hearts were shaken with terror at the sound of his deep voice.

"I spoke to him saying that we were Agamemnon's men on our way home from the taking of Priam's City,[3] and I begged him to deal with us kindly, for the sake of Zeus who is ever in the company of strangers and suppliants. But he answered me saying, 'We Cyclôpes pay no heed to Zeus, nor to any of thy gods. In our strength and our power we deem that we are mightier than they. I will not spare thee, neither will I give thee aught for the sake of Zeus, but only as my own spirit bids me. And first I would have thee tell me how you came to our land.'

"I knew it would be better not to let the Cyclops know that my ship and my companions were at the harbor of the island. Therefore I spoke to him guilefully, telling him that my ship had been broken on the rocks, and that I and the men with me were the only ones who had escaped utter doom.

"I begged again that he would deal with us as just men deal with strangers and suppliants, but he, without saying a word, laid hands upon two of my men, and swinging them by the legs, dashed their brains out on the earth. He cut them to pieces and ate them before our very eyes. We wept and we prayed to Zeus as we witnessed a deed so terrible.

"Next the Cyclops stretched himself amongst his sheep and went to sleep beside the fire. Then I debated whether I should take my sharp sword in my hand, and feeling where his heart was, stab him there. But second thoughts held me back from doing this. I might be able to kill him as he slept, but not even with my companions could I roll away the great stone that closed the mouth of the cave.

"Dawn came, and the Cyclops awakened, kindled his fire and milked his flocks. Then he seized two others of my men and made ready for his midday meal. And now he rolled away the great stone and drove his flocks out of the cave.

"I had pondered on a way of escape, and I had thought of something that might be done to baffle the Cyclops. I had with me a great skin of sweet wine, and I thought that if I could make him drunken with wine I and my companions might be able for him. But there were other preparations to be made first. On the floor of the cave there was a great beam of olive wood which the Cyclops had cut to make a club when the wood should be seasoned. It was yet green. I and my companions went and cut off a fathom's length of the wood, and sharpened it to a point and took it to the fire

3. Troy; Priam was its king. Agamemnon, king of Mycenae, led the Greek expedition to Troy.

and hardened it in the glow. Then I hid the beam in a recess of the cave.

"The Cyclops came back in the evening, and opening up the cave drove in his flocks. Then he closed the cave again with the stone and went and milked his ewes and his goats. Again he seized two of my companions. I went to the terrible creature with a bowl of wine in my hands. He took it and drank it and cried out, 'Give me another bowl of this, and tell me thy name that I may give thee gifts for bringing me this honey-tasting drink.'

"Again I spoke to him guilefully and said, 'Noman is my name. Noman my father and my mother call me.'"

" 'Give me more of the drink, Noman,' he shouted. 'And the gift that I shall give to thee is that I shall make thee the last of thy fellows to be eaten.'

"I gave him wine again, and when he had taken the third bowl he sank backwards with his face upturned, and sleep came upon him. Then I, with four companions, took that beam of olive wood, now made into a hard and pointed stake, and thrust it into the ashes of the fire. When the pointed end began to glow we drew it out of the flame. Then I and my companions laid hold on the great stake and, dashing at the Cyclops, thrust it into his eye. He raised a terrible cry that made the rocks ring and we dashed away into the recesses of the cave.

"His cries brought other Cyclôpes to the mouth of the cave, and they, naming him as Polyphemus, called out and asked him what ailed him to cry. 'Noman,' he shrieked out, 'Noman is slaying me by guile.' They answered him saying, 'If no man is slaying thee, there is nothing we can do for thee, Polyphemus. What ails thee has been sent to thee by the gods.' Saying this, they went away from the mouth of the cave without attempting to move away the stone.

"Polyphemus then, groaning with pain, rolled away the stone and sat before the mouth of the cave with his hands outstretched, thinking that he would catch us as we dashed out. I showed my companions how we might pass by him. I laid hands on certain rams of the flock and I lashed three of them together with supple rods. Then on the middle ram I put a man of my company. Thus every three rams carried a man. As soon as the dawn had come the rams hastened out to the pasture, and, as they passed, Polyphemus laid hands on the first and the third of each three that went by. They passed out and Polyphemus did not guess that a ram that he did not touch carried out a man.

"For myself, I took a ram that was the strongest and fleeciest of the whole flock and I placed myself under him, clinging to the wool of his belly. As this ram, the best of all his flock, went by, Polyphemus, laying his hands upon him, said, 'Would that you, the best of my flock, were endowed with speech, so that you might tell me where Noman, who has blinded me, has hidden himself.' The ram went by him, and when he had gone a little way from the cave I loosed myself from him and went and set my companions free.

"We gathered together many of Polyphemus' sheep and we drove them down to our ship. The men we had left behind would have wept when they heard what had happened to six of their companions. But I bade them take on board the sheep we had brought and pull the ship away from that land. Then when we had drawn a certain distance from the shore I could not forbear to shout my taunts into the cave of Polyphemus. 'Cyclops,' I cried, 'you thought that you had the company of a fool and a weakling to eat. But you have been worsted by me, and your evil deeds have been punished.'

"So I shouted, and Polyphemus came to the mouth of the cave with great anger in his heart. He took up rocks and cast them at the ship and they fell before the prow. The men bent to the oars and pulled the ship away or it would have been broken by the rocks he cast. And when we were further away I shouted to him:

" 'Cyclops, if any man should ask who it was set his mark upon you, say that he was Odysseus, the son of Laertes.'

"Then I heard Polyphemus cry out, 'I call upon Poseidon, the god of the sea, whose son I am, to avenge me upon you, Odysseus. I call upon Poseidon to grant that you, Odysseus, may never come to your home, or if the gods have ordained your return, that you come to it after much toil and suffering, in an evil plight and in a stranger's ship, to find sorrow in your home.'

"So Polyphemus prayed, and, to my evil fortune, Poseidon heard his prayer. But we went on in our ship rejoicing at our escape. We came to the waste island where my other ships were. All the company rejoiced to see us, although they had to mourn for their six companions slain by Polyphemus. We divided amongst the ships the sheep we had taken from Polyphemus' flock and we sacrificed to the gods. At the dawn of the next day we raised the sails on each ship and we sailed away."

1918

Legends

Legends belong to a genre strongly rooted in oral tradition and still vibrantly alive today in numerous forms and various media. Though the term is most often applied to stories from the past that contain a core of historical truth under fictional embellishments—stories that form an important part of the cultural history of a nation or people—legends may also arise in connection with contemporary persons, places, or events and may circulate among relatively small groups. Their ability to explain extraordinary or mysterious deeds or occurrences can give them great psychological force, and they can spread quickly, particularly in a time when mass media can aid word of mouth, and are connected to rumor. As what once seemed so "newsworthy" undergoes transformation over time, the legend can easily become confused with history itself. Children have always been crucial to the circulation of these stories, both because legends are an important part of their religious, ethnic, and cultural upbringing and because children tell, alter, and pass on legends.

The original meaning of the word *legend* was the story of a saint: in the Middle Ages, the *legenda* (from the Latin *legere*, meaning "to gather" or "to read," especially "to read aloud") were the martyrologies that had to be read in church. As the common people told and retold these stories among themselves, their elaborations and additions made the oral legends very different from the official accounts. By the sixteenth century, a legend was a story, popularly regarded as historical despite being unverifiable and often improbable, about a real event or person—usually those of importance, such as saints and rulers, heroes and great villains. Though clearly in large part fictitious, the legend was and still is generally believed to contain a germ of truth, a belief that may explain the legend's appeal to listeners and readers who seek an explanation for what is extraordinary in life. Its seemingly real and somewhat truthful elements distinguish the legend from the fairy tale and myth, which are obviously wholly fictitious, even as it employs those genres' motifs, characters, and conventions. More than any other type of short narrative, the legend was and is constantly used to reflect on notable people and events in families, communities, religions, and nations. Because some of the feats and occurrences described may border on the supernatural, the legend is often associated with the fantastic in real life.

From the Middle Ages to the present, legends have spread through word of mouth and print in many subcategories. The stories were told not just about saints but also about miracles and religious holidays. Heroic legends focus on the secular in recounting the deeds of men and women such as Richard the Lion-Hearted and Charlemagne, Buffalo Bill Cody and Betsy Ross. More recently, celebrities of all kinds—in the arts, in business, in sports—have had legends grow up around them; indeed, even sports teams may give rise to legends. Major historical events, from battles to scientific discoveries, often have legends associated with them. Many legends are attempts to explain various phenomena. These may be etiological narratives, or stories about the origins of things, places, peoples, and so on; some are demonological, involving various kind of monsters (often, like witches and vampires, partly human). Others concern animals, sometimes in their relations with people (e.g., recurrent stories of wolves who suckle and raise human infants). Legends bind together groups that range from local communities (we can even speak of family legends) to a nation, commemorating triumphs and tragedies as well as individuals.

Legends in Print

The very first books that incorporated legends were primers intended to teach young readers (mainly boys) proper morals and manners. One early source of tales, with suitable moral reflections attached, was the *Gesta Romanorum* (*Deeds of the Romans*), compiled in the fourteenth century. Its fables, legends, and religious stories were immediately drawn on by Giovanni Boccaccio (1313–1375), Geoffrey Chaucer (ca. 1343–1400), and later writers, and it was soon translated into the European vernacular languages. Also very influential was the book known as the *Legenda Aurea* (*Golden Legend*) of Jacobus de Voragine (1228–1298), an Italian Dominican friar who became archbishop of Genoa. This saints' calendar, a devotional work that includes saints' lives and descriptions of their festivals, circulated in scores of editions by 1500. In 1483 William Caxton published his English translation, which was reprinted numerous times and read at home and in schools.

More important for the spread of legends in print were chapbooks and broadsides. Chapbooks, inexpensive pamphlets sold by itinerant peddlers, were small—only four to thirty-two pages measuring about 5.5 by 4 inches each—and were often illustrated with woodcuts (see the Chapbooks section, above). Broadsides were large sheets with ballads, sensational news, and the like printed on one side; they were hawked on the streets of cities. From the fifteenth century on, millions of both were printed in Europe and later in North America as well. These publications treated a wide range of subjects, in a range of genres no less impressive; especially popular were shortened versions of the romances and historical legends that had already proved of interest to aristocratic readers. Among the earliest books printed in English were *Recuyell of the Historyes of Troye* (1469–71), Sir Thomas Malory's *Morte Darthur* (1485), and *The Four Sons of Aymon* (ca. 1489), published by Caxton, and *Guy of Warwick* (ca. 1500) and *Valentine and Orson* (ca. 1510), published by Caxton's foreman and then successor, Wynkyn de Worde: these stories were soon distributed in the form of chapbooks and broadsides, together with writings on religious subjects, local legends, the adventures of Robin Hood, sensational tales of royalty, stories of the supernatural, and so on.

Though the upper classes and the church scorned and criticized chapbooks as vulgar works that pandered to the lowest tastes, chapbooks appealed to readers of all social classes and ages and thus were extremely effective in disseminating legends of all types. In particular, as Mary Jackson has noted in *Engines of Instruction, Mischief, and Magic: Children's Literature from Its Beginnings to 1839* (1989), by the end of the eighteenth century, chapbooks became an important catalyst in the growth of children's literature. Sometimes they were the chief, if not only sanctuary for stories and poems temporarily out of favor in the "legitimate" press because of pressures from certain interest groups. Always they were a source of healthy competition to that press, particularly with their different illustrations after 1810. By the early nineteenth century, the vast majority of English chapbooks were produced almost entirely for children and ranged in quality from the gorgeous works of W. Belch to the cheap and crude (but highly prized) products of John Pitts and James [Jemmy] Catnach. Tellingly, many respectable publishers of hardcover volumes for the more affluent also issued paper-cover versions of these and other works, offered at prices to compete with and in forms generally indistinguishable from the better sort of chapbook.

It was in the nineteenth century that a variety of types of legends for children flowered in Great Britain, the United States, and Canada, in such profusion that it is difficult to write a history of or even describe the genre. Overabundance of material plagues all research on legends, particularly when the many legends familiar only to tiny groups of people are taken into account, but an analysis that concentrates on children must face an additional complication. As Linda Dégh observes in *Legend and Belief: Dialectics of a Folklore Genre* (2001):

> The available data does not make it clear what folklorists mean by "children's legends." Is it what children invent to tell other children, or is it what they culturally learn from adults and retell, or is it both? And can we regard both as constituents of the entire repertoire of children? Or do we have to view the two sets of legends known to children separately—one as the reflection of the normal or abnormal developmental stages of mentality (in terms of biological givens such as anxieties, dreams, visions, and aggressive impulses) and the other as inherited cultural conventions and/or educational matter of conscious indoctrination? It seems the two are very distinct yet are inseparable and interactive, as both the instinctive and the educational factors are at work from the earliest point of consciousness.

Given these problems, this section focuses on the hero legend, a subcategory that can be usefully analyzed to illustrate how legends in general have evolved and have been used in children's and adult literature. Often related to the tall tale, it tells the story of national, cultural, or local heroes. Every group, whatever its size and however it constitutes itself, celebrates individuals (even if they never existed) who are believed to have made extraordinary contributions to its culture and are viewed as in some way representative of that particular group or nation. Many of these heroes are idealized; yet over time, figures such as Columbus and General Custer in the United States or Richard the Lion-Hearted and the Duke of Wellington in Great Britain have become controversial as views of their deeds have changed. The intersection of history and legend is often messy. Whether intentionally or not, writers and publishers, particularly during the nineteenth century (a period of nation-building and colonialism), sought to produce stories that would lead children to identification with and pride in their nation. Histories have always served as the "true" basis for biographies written for young people; yet, their depictions of great political leaders, rulers, generals, and revolutionaries never can escape a political bias, and by distorting facts and events they contribute to legends that circulate by word of mouth and in print. The line between legend and history can be very subtle.

The Hero Legend: The Example of Arthur

King Arthur is a figure worth treating at length; he is both a national hero in Great Britain and someone who has long commanded interest in the United States. The widespread and lasting appeal of King Arthur and the knights of the Round Table for writers and young readers alike has no single explanation. Certainly, the stories of a magnificent king and the illustrious deeds of his knights evoke readers' admiration and awe. Nostalgia for a time—perhaps an actual period in history—when nobility and chivalry were in the ascendant can powerfully affect readers who believe those virtues to be lost. And because the reasons for their decline appear to be contained in the Arthurian legends, writers keep returning to the stories to better understand the present. Each new version of the tales must thus be interpreted and understood within its own sociohistorical context.

A review of the Arthurian legend reveals a long history of cultural appropriation. To this day, it is uncertain whether there was an Arthur and whether he was a king. Welsh legend suggests that Arthur was a leader of warriors and won many battles (ca. 600 C.E.) against the Saxons who began to occupy Britain after the Romans withdrew in the early fifth century. Arthur the Celtic warrior is mentioned in *Historia Britonum* (*History of the Britons*), a chronicle written around 800 by a Welsh monk named Nennius. Arthurian literature proliferated, but the first coherent "history" of Arthur appeared only in *Historia regum Britanniae* (*History of the Kings of England*, ca. 1135), which drew on Welsh and English chronicles and folklore. In this work Geoffrey of Monmouth, a prelate of Welsh or Breton descent, traces the genealogy of the British kings back to Aeneas, a prince of Troy (and the legendary founder of Rome). He also laid the groundwork for all future legends about King Arthur, whose great missions were to save the Britons from the Saxons and to establish exemplary standards of chivalry. In this account, Arthur was the son of King Uther Pendragon, and he succeeded to the throne when he was fifteen years old. As king, Arthur defeated the Saxons, killing hundreds with his great sword, Caliburn; he went on to conquer Scotland, Ireland, Iceland, Norway, Denmark, Aquitaine, and Gaul and successfully resisted Roman demands for tribute. His court was at Caerleon, on the river Usk in southeast Wales, and he married the beautiful Guinevere. But Arthur's treacherous nephew Mordred rose up against him, and though Arthur defeated Mordred, he was mortally wounded and was carried to the island of Avalon to be cured.

Geoffrey's successors continued to elaborate on the legend, adding many of the details—Arthur's rearing in secret by the magician Merlin, his possession of the magic sword Excalibur as proof of his legitimacy, his establishment of the Round Table at which all sat as equals, his knights' great quests to prove their merit and loyalty, his promise to return from Avalon as king to save Britain in the future—so familiar today.

On the Continent, the exploits of Arthur and his knights of the Round Table were celebrated in the chivalric romances of Chrétien de Troyes, Wolfram von Eschenbach, and others from the twelfth century onward. These romances (particularly those in French), Monmouth's *History*, and oral tradition shaped Malory's *Morte Darthur*, which greatly influenced all subsequent treatments of Arthur's legend. Most of Arthur's adventures, along with those of the knights Lancelot, Gawain, and Percival, were transformed into crudely illustrated short narratives that were published in chapbooks and broadsides up through the nineteenth century. In these formats, children in the United States and Great Britain first read the Arthurian legends. By the nineteenth century, the legends were also being retold by numerous artists in a wide range of genres, including epic poetry (Alfred, Lord Tennyson's *The Idylls of the King*, 1859–88), satirical novel (Mark Twain's *A Connecticut Yankee in King Arthur's Court*, 1889), and opera (notably Richard Wagner's *Tristan und Isolde* and *Parsifal*, 1865, 1882). Among twentieth-century retellings are popular novels (Mary Stewart's Merlin trilogy, 1970–79) and a Broadway musical (*Camelot*, 1960), and a host of contemporary fantasy writers have incorporated this material into their works (e.g., Susan Cooper's Dark Is Rising series, 1965–77).

The first literary version of Malory's Arthurian legends written expressly for children was *The Story of King Arthur and His Knights of the Round Table* (1861) by Sir James Knowles, who sought to stimulate the interest of boys in reading legends. More significant was Sydney Lanier's *The Boys' King Arthur* (1880). Lanier, an American, sanitized the story by omitting all the sexual and adulterous episodes; Henry Frith took a similar approach in *King Arthur and His Knights of the Round Table* (1883). However, Mary Macleod's *The Book of King Arthur and His Noble Knights* (1900) restored some of the love entanglements, while Howard Pyle, the American illustrator and writer, treated the sexual issues very gingerly in his four moralizing books dedicated to Arthur and his court: *The Story of King Arthur and His Knights* (1903), *The Story of the Champions of the Round Table* (1905), *The Story of Sir Launcelot and His Champions* (1907), and *The Story of the Grail and the Passing of Arthur* (1910). For the most part, these versions of the Arthurian legend stressed chivalric ideals, an emphasis that also characterizes Roger Lancelyn Green's *King Arthur and His Knights* (1953) and *Sir Lancelot of the Lake* (1966), as well as Barbara Leonie Picard's *Stories of King Arthur and His Knights* (1955) and Rosemary Sutcliff's trilogy, *The Light Beyond the Forest: Quest for the Holy Grail* (1979), *The Sword and the Circle: King Arthur and the Knights of the Round Table* (1981), and *The Road to Camlann* (1981). Other versions of the legend have been more experimental: for example, T. H. White's wittily inventive *The Sword in the Stone* (1938), and Jane Yolen's trilogy about Merlin's boyhood, *Passager* (1996), *Hobby* (1996), and *Merlin* (1997). In Michael Morpurgo's *Arthur, High King of Britain* (1994), the king himself tells the tales to a twentieth-century boy; similarly, an aged Sir Gawain recounts his exploits in Neil Philip's *The Tale of Sir Gawain* (1987). Notable recent renditions include Marcia William's *King Arthur and the Knights of the Round Table* (1966), a picture book; James Riordan's *King Arthur* (1998), which draws together the tales for middle readers; and Kevin Crossley-Holland's trilogy, *The Seeing Stone* (2000), *At the Crossing Places* (2002), and *King of the Middle March* (2003), which begins in 1199 with a boy (also an Arthur) discovering a connection to the legendary king. And of course, representations in comic books, cartoons, films, and other media burgeoned in the twentieth century.

Each appropriation must be judged individually, but clearly writers use the heroic legend to comment on the meaning of heroism and history. What is particularly appealing about Arthur and his knights is that they are all flawed heroes. They valiantly endeavor to live up to a code of honor and valor, but all—including Arthur—fall short. Though Guinevere plays a major role in many of the tales, the legend usually focuses on the manliness of the heroes, and in this respect it is typical of most heroic legends written for children in the nineteenth and twentieth centuries. Indeed, heroism has been a mainly a male preoccupation. Brave women like Joan of Arc did appear, but until recently they were the exception. The development of the heroic legend up through the 1970s largely favored the exploits of talented male protagonists, whether they were explorers, adventurers, rebels, rulers, inventors, or notable for any other reason. This state of affairs is hardly surprising; history has generally been written by the victors and the elites, who tend to view those like themselves—white males, for the most part—as heroes. But it should provoke a number of questions: Who determines history? What kinds of actions and behavior are necessary to affect or alter the course of history? Which are admirable? Which are to be avoided? What traits are truly heroic? What does the hero represent? Should one identify with the hero?

The Heroic Legend: A Broader View

Though popular and prominent legends have almost exclusively featured white men and boys, tales whose heroes are female or nonwhite have always been part of the oral tradition. They were simply not published, either because they were unknown to those collecting and retelling legends or because they were deemed unworthy of publication. Such judgments often relied on unexamined racist and sexist assumptions about what kinds of legends are appropriate for children and what are "true" or "genuine" folk traditions. As those assumptions came under increasing critical scrutiny in the second half of the twentieth century, both the representativeness of the heroes presented to the children in print and on film and the accuracy and ethics of their characterizations were challenged. For example, Native Americans have long been depicted in U.S. popular culture as barbarous pagans with a primitive culture—at worst, bloodthirsty brutes; at best, noble savages. The message in most stories was that the Indians needed to be "civilized" and acquiesce to the well-intentioned missionary efforts of the white settlers; courageous leaders who resisted, such as the Apache Geronimo (Goyathlay, ca. 1829–1909), were often depicted as treacherous and murderous. But as political activism among Native Americans in the United States grew (signaled by the emergence of the American Indian Movement, or AIM, in 1969), so did the desire that Geronimo, Sitting Bull, Hiawatha, and other heroes be portrayed more positively and realistically. Thus Jean Fritz's *The Double Life of Pocahontas* (1983) emphasizes the young protagonist's independence and intelligence. However, most "revisionist" Native American legends published in the late twentieth century focused less on heroes than on correcting errors in history and reclaiming neglected legends in single-tale picture books or in collections of stories pertaining to a specific culture. The purpose behind these publications is twofold: to instill in Native American readers pride in their traditions and to correct outsiders' misconceptions.

The impulse to redress wrongs and alter views is also visible in legends published about women of all ethnic groups, African Americans, and Asian Americans. Two important multicultural anthologies—Robert D. San Souci's *Cut from the Same Cloth: American Women of Myth, Legend, and Tall Tale* (1993) and Amy L. Cohn's *From Sea to Shining Sea: A Treasury of American Folklore and Folk Songs* (1993)—offer a more balanced and more interesting view of American culture and those who shaped the country's history than do traditional collections. San Souci's fifteen fascinating tales, arranged geographically, present hitherto overlooked legendary female figures such as Annie Christmas (African American), Bess Call (Anglo-American), Sister Fox and Brother Coyote (Mexican American), Drop Star (Seneca), and Hiiaka (Hawaiian). Cohn's book contains a wide variety of tales and songs, illustrated by some of the leading American artists for children (including Anita Lobel, Jerry Pinkney, David Wiesner, and Chris Van Allsburg). The collection draws most heavily on Native American and African American folklore, though other ethnic groups in America (Mexican, Japanese, Irish, etc.) are also represented. While many of the selections feature heroes, from Harriet Tubman to Martin Luther King Jr., the emphasis is on capturing a broad sense of American culture. A great number of writers have similarly focused on legends less concerned with "heroes" than with customs and places of their respective traditions, including African American (e.g., Julius Lester, *Black Folktales*, 1969; Virginia Hamilton, *The People Could Fly: American Black Folktales*, 1985), Chinese American (e.g., Laurence Yep, *The Rainbow People*, 1989), and Native American (e.g., Joseph Bruchac, *Iroquois Stories: Heroes and Heroines, Monsters and Magic*, 1985). In the United Kingdom, too, authors have increasingly begun to publish stories from traditions other than the Anglo-Saxon, including the Caribbean (e.g., Grace Halworth, *Mouth Open, Story Jump Out*, 1984) and the Irish (e.g., Marie Heaney, *Over Nine Waves: A Book of Irish Legends*, 1994).

The role of legendary figures in the socialization and cultural assimilation of children in the United States and United Kingdom is difficult to judge. Both groups are experiencing the same tension, as the vast size and changing demography of the former and the growing multiculturalism of the latter simultaneously encourage the multiplication of different legends and interpretations of history and make the need for unifying national figures more pressing. Hence, certain legends remain part of a national history and culture despite being challenged. In the case of Christopher Columbus, for instance, it is in the very countries that claim him as a kind of national hero—the United States, Spain, and Italy—that his heroic legend is most strongly contested, even as it continues to circulate. Critical scrutiny of Columbus's character and particularly his treatment of indigenous peoples became especially acute before and during the five hundredth anniversary of his "discovery of the New World." According to legend, and indeed many older history books and biographies, he was an intrepid mariner, possessing the religious zeal of a missionary, who sailed west in 1492 to prove to scoffers that the earth is round. Though many of the details of his life remained unclear, his portrayal was generally heroic.

Beginning in the 1980s, a slew of biographies written for children questioned and started to alter the familiar legend. *Where Do You Think You're Going, Christopher Columbus?* (1980), by Jean Fritz; *Christopher Columbus* (1985), by Rae Bains; *The Story of Christopher Columbus: Admiral of the Ocean Sea* (1987), by Mary Pope Osborne; *Christopher Columbus: The Intrepid Mariner* (1989), by Sean Dolan; and *Christopher Columbus: Voyager to the Unknown* (1990), by Nancy Smiler Levinson present a flawed hero who may have brought as much ill to the New World as good. (In his 1996 novel *Pastwatch: The Redemption of Christopher Columbus*, Orson Scott Card offers an accurate account of the explorer's life as he imagines future scientists traveling back in time to undo the damage that Columbus unwittingly caused.) The authors depict Columbus in far more complex terms than does the old legend, revealing that he was interested in fame and money, mistreated the Indians, never reached the North American continent, and was wrong in his view of the earth (the dispute was over its size, not its shape). Some suggest that Columbus was a poor administrator, a racist, and an imperialist. These critical works and many others have helped encourage the writing of new histories. Three very important books for teachers were published before and shortly after the quincentennial commemoration: *1492—Discovery, Invasion, Encounter: Sources and Interpretation* (ed. Marvin Lunenfeld, 1991), *Columbus, His Enterprise: Exploding the Myth* (Hans Koning, 1991), and *Rethinking Columbus: The Next 500 Years* (ed. Bill Bigelow and Bob Peterson, 1998). The Columbus controversy has led to the reexamined facts being used to create new legends, which will engender new debates.

It seems that the least-disputed stories are those concerning heroes about whom few facts are known, such as Robin Hood or Paul Bunyan. Moreover, legends whose source is foreign, such as that of the Pied Piper, least constrain their retellers to remain within any particular cultural code. For the most part, legendary heroes appeal to children because they have great, mysterious, and extraordinary powers that they use to help people in need and to defeat equally potent antiheroes. There is a clear line of descent from the heroes and villains of legends to the superheroes and mutants of twentieth-century comic books and films. Yet in our postmodern age, in which absolute judgments of "good" and "evil" are no longer easily made, the distinction between heroes and villains is often blurred. In addition, the emergence of female superheroes, potent and sexual in their own right, has complicated the traditional legends' emphasis on male prowess.

Linda Dégh has argued in *Legend and Belief* that "children's legends are true mirrors of society. Their actors, actions, language, mannerisms, and paraphernalia originate in everyday living. Children did not invent witches, bogeymen, vampires, werewolves, Bigfoot, or the Hookman; rather they learned about them from the media the same way they learned everything else prescribed by both private and public education. In script and custom, the canon of legendary characters, heroes, and antiheroes is continually rewritten and updated to stay contemporary." The claim that legends "truly" mirror society is perhaps an exaggeration, but the manner in which a particular writer adapts a well-known legend for a young audience reveals a great deal about the author's ideology and how a particular cultural hero is validated at a specific time. Attitudes toward a given legend can shift with remarkable speed. Thus Davy Crockett, who in the mid-1950s was featured in a series of five Walt Disney television specials—for which a new song was written to honor his deeds and which inspired thousands of children to imitate him by wearing coonskin caps—today is regarded by many people as an Indian killer and racist whose boastfulness was boorish, not humorous. As times change, so do our legends about heroes. The paradox of the legend today is that we are demanding more "truth" from a genre that presents its truths through exaggeration and elaboration, even as we often fail to recognize what is false in our own reductive revisions.

ROBERT BROWNING
1812–1889

Regarded as one of the great poets of the Victorian period, Robert Browning rarely wrote for children, and yet his poetic version of the Pied Piper has won world renown. Born in Camberwell, a suburb of London, Browning was schooled mainly at home, with an emphasis on the classics; he learned Latin, Greek, French, and Italian by the time he was fourteen. In 1828 he attended the University of London, but after one semester he returned to his parents' home, and he lived with them until 1846. It was during this period that he wrote his long, obscure poems *Paracelsus* (1835) and *Sordello* (1840). Between 1836 and 1842 he also wrote a number of plays; they had short runs if they were staged at all, but he put the practice in characterization to good use when he began to explore dramatic monologue, a form at which he would prove a master. These first appeared in *Dramatic Lyrics* (1842); it, too, enjoyed little success, though "My Last Duchess," published in that volume, is today among his best-known poems. Early in 1845 Browning wrote an admiring letter to Elizabeth Barrett, who was six years older than he and already a famous poet; and despite the obstacles—an invalid, she rarely left her house, and her father refused to countenance marriage for any of his children—their romance flourished. The two eloped to Italy in 1846, living in Florence from 1847 until Elizabeth Barrett Browning's death in 1861.

While in Italy Browning published *Men and Women* (1855), which contained important monologues, including "Fra Lippo Lippi," but his greatest productivity began after he and his son returned to England following his wife's death. *Dramatis Personae* (1864), whose monologues (including "Caliban upon Setebos") were even more intricate, was his first popular success. The rapturous critical reception of his most ambitious and accomplished work, *The Ring and the Book* (1868–69), a kind of novel in verse based on a Roman murder trial of 1698, established Browning as one of the leading literary figures in England.

Browning received many honors and came to delight in London's social life as he continued to write long narrative and dramatic poems. He traveled a great deal on the Continent and died while visiting Venice in 1889.

Though Browning has been criticized for obscurity (especially in his early works) and for strained language and syntax, his poems—no matter where they are set—acutely portray human psychology and often address issues of concern to his contemporaries. "The Pied Piper of Hamelin" (1842) was written to amuse a friend's ill young son, but Browning managed in his theme and moral to both appeal to and criticize the Victorian mainstream. In the process, he transformed a little-known German legend into one of the most famous stories in the English-speaking world.

The oldest evidence about the mysterious disappearance of the children from the town of Hamelin was a note in Latin prose, written in about 1430. In 1603 a rhyme was inscribed in the wall of the town's Pied Piper House:

It was on the 26th of June in 1284,
John's and Paul's Day,
that a piper, dressed in all kinds of colors,
led astray 130 children born in Hamelin
who were lost at Mount Calvary near Koppen.

Versions of the story by Goethe, the Brothers Grimm, and other German writers followed the medieval tradition of identifying the piper with death; Browning—drawing on Nathaniel Wanley's *Wonders of the Little World* (1678) and Richard Vestegen's *Restitution of Decayed Intelligence in Antiquities*—shifted the focus. His piper is a musician capable of leading the young into a utopian realm. It is not just the greed of the mayor and the Corporation but their hostility to artistic values (their inability to appreciate the piper) that leads to the disappearance of the children, who are no longer worthy of their care.

The Pied Piper of Hamelin

A Child's Story

Hamelin Town's in Brunswick,
　By famous Hanover city;[1]
The river Weser, deep and wide,
Washes its wall on the southern side;
A pleasanter spot you never spied;
　But, when begins my ditty,
Almost five hundred years ago,
To see the townsfolk suffer so
　From vermin, was a pity.

Rats!
They fought the dogs and killed the cats,
　And bit the babies in the cradles,
And ate the cheeses out of the vats,
　And licked the soup from the cooks' own ladles,
Split open the kegs of salted sprats,
Made nests inside men's Sunday hats,
And even spoiled the women's chats
　By drowning their speaking
　With shrieking and squeaking
In fifty different sharps and flats.

At last the people in a body
　To the Town Hall came flocking:
"'Tis clear," cried they, "our Mayor's a noddy;
　And as for our Corporation[2]—shocking
To think we buy gowns lined with ermine
For dolts that can't or won't determine
What's best to rid us of our vermin!
You hope, because you're old and obese,
To find in the furry civic robe ease?
Rouse up, sirs! Give your brains a racking
To find the remedy we're lacking,
Or, sure as fate, we'll send you packing!"
At this the Mayor and Corporation
Quaked with a mighty consternation.

An hour they sat in council,
　At length the Mayor broke silence:
"For a guilder[3] I'd my ermine gown sell,
　I wish I were a mile hence!
It's easy to bid one rack one's brain—

I'm sure my poor head aches again,
I've scratched it so, and all in vain.
Oh for a trap, a trap, a trap!"
Just as he said this, what should hap
At the chamber door but a gentle tap?
"Bless us," cried the Mayor, "what's that?"
(With the Corporation as he sat,
Looking little though wondrous fat;
Nor brighter was his eye, nor moister
Than a too-long-opened oyster,
Save when at noon his paunch grew mutinous
For a plate of turtle green and glutinous)
"Only a scraping of shoes on the mat?
Anything like the sound of a rat
Makes my heart go pit-a-pat!"

"Come in!"—the Mayor cried, looking bigger:
And in did come the strangest figure!
His queer long coat from heel to head
Was half of yellow and half of red,
And he himself was tall and thin,
With sharp blue eyes, each like a pin,
And light loose hair, yet swarthy skin;
No tuft on cheek nor beard on chin,
But lips where smiles went out and in;
There was no guessing his kith and kin:
And nobody could enough admire[4]
The tall man and his quaint attire.
Quoth one: "It's as my great grandsire,
Starting up at the Trump of Doom's tone,[5]
Had walked his way from his painted tombstone!"

He advanced to the council-table:
And, "Please your honours," said he, "I'm able,
By means of a secret charm, to draw
All creatures living beneath the sun,
That creep or swim or fly or run,
After me so as you never saw!
And I chiefly use my charm
On creatures that do people harm,
The mole and toad and newt and viper;
And people call me the Pied Piper."
(And here they noticed round his neck
    A scarf of red and yellow stripe,
To match with his coat of the self-same cheque;
    And at the scarf's end hung a pipe;
    And his fingers, they noticed, were ever straying

4. Wonder at.
5. I.e., the sounding of the trumpet at Judgment Day.

As if impatient to be playing
Upon this pipe, as low it dangled
Over his vesture so old-fangled.)
"Yet," said he, "poor piper as I am,
In Tartary I freed the Cham,[6]
  Last June, from his huge swarms of gnats;
I eased in Asia the Nizam[7]
  Of a monstrous brood of vampyre-bats:
And as for what your brain bewilders,
  If I can rid your town of rats
Will you give me a thousand guilders?"
"One? fifty thousand!"—was the exclamation
Of the astonished Mayor and Corporation.

Into the street the Piper stept,
  Smiling first a little smile,
As if he knew what magic slept
  In his quiet pipe the while;
Then, like a musical adept,
To blow the pipe his lips he wrinkled,
And green and blue his sharp eyes twinkled,
Like a candle-flame where salt is sprinkled;
And ere three shrill notes the pipe uttered,
You heard as if an army muttered;
And the muttering grew to a grumbling;
And the grumbling grew to a mighty rumbling;
And out of the houses the rats came tumbling.
Great rats, small rats, lean rats, brawny rats,
Brown rats, black rats, grey rats, tawny rats,
Grave old plodders, gay young friskers,
  Fathers, mothers, uncles, cousins,
Cocking tails and pricking whiskers,
  Families by tens and dozens,
Brothers, sisters, husbands, wives—
Followed the Piper for their lives.
From street to street he piped advancing,
And step for step they followed dancing,
Until they came to the river Weser,
  Wherein all plunged and perished!
—Save one who, stout as Julius Caesar,[8]
Swam across and lived to carry
  (As he, the manuscript he cherished)
To Rat-land home his commentary:

6. The Khan, the title of the ruler of Tartary, which
stretched from the Dnieper River (in Ukraine) west
to the Sea of Japan.
7. The ruler of Hyderabad, India (a title that came
into use in the eighteenth century).

8. Roman general and statesman (100–44 B.C.E.);
according to legend, when his ship was captured,
he swam to shore holding the manuscript of his
Commentary on the Gallic War. "Stout": brave,
determined.

Which was, "At the first shrill notes of the pipe,
I heard a sound as of scraping tripe,
And putting apples, wondrous ripe,
Into a cider-press's gripe:[9]
And a moving away of pickle-tub-boards,
And a leaving ajar of conserve-cupboards,
And a drawing the corks of train-oil-flasks,[1]
And a breaking the hoops of butter-casks:
And it seemed as if a voice
   (Sweeter far than by harp or by psaltery
Is breathed) called out, 'Oh rats, rejoice!
  The world is grown to one vast drysaltery![2]
So munch on, crunch on, take your nuncheon,[3]
Breakfast, supper, dinner, luncheon!'
And just as a bulky sugar-puncheon,[4]
All ready staved,[5] like a great sun shone
Glorious scarce an inch before me,
Just as methought it said, 'Come, bore me!'
—I found the Weser rolling o'er me."

You should have heard the Hamelin people
Ringing the bells till they rocked the steeple.
"Go," cried the Mayor, "and get long poles,
Poke out the nests and block up the holes!
Consult with carpenters and builders,
And leave in our town not even a trace
Of the rats!"—when suddenly, up the face
Of the Piper perked in the market-place,
With a, "First, if you please, my thousand guilders!"

A thousand guilders! The Mayor looked blue;
So did the Corporation too.
For council dinners made rare havoc
With Claret, Moselle, Vin-de-Grave, Hock;[6]
And half the money would replenish
Their cellar's biggest butt[7] with Rhenish.
To pay this sum to a wandering fellow
With a gypsy coat of red and yellow!
"Beside," quoth the Mayor with a knowing wink,
"Our business was done at the river's brink;
We saw with our eyes the vermin sink,
And what's dead can't come to life, I think.

9. I.e., grip.
1. Whale oil flasks.
2. The store of a drysalter, who deals mainly in chemical products but sometimes also in sauces, canned meats, and the like.
3. Light refreshment in the afternoon or between meals.
4. A large cask.
5. Broken through.
6. All varieties of wine (as is Rhenish).
7. A large wine cask.

So, friend, we're not the folks to shrink
From the duty of giving you something for drink,
And a matter of money to put in your poke;[8]
But as for the guilders, what we spoke
Of them, as you very well know, was in joke.
Besides, our losses have made us thrifty.
A thousand guilders! Come, take fifty!"

The Piper's face fell, and he cried
"No trifling! I can't wait, beside!
I've promised to visit by dinner-time
Bagdat,[9] and accept the prime
Of the Head-Cook's pottage, all he's rich in,
For having left, in the Caliph's kitchen,
Of a nest of scorpions no survivor:
With him I proved no bargain-driver,
With you, don't think I'll bate a stiver![1]
And folks who put me in a passion
May find me pipe after another fashion."

"How?" cried the Mayor, "d'ye think I brook
Being worse treated than a Cook?
Insulted by a lazy ribald
With idle pipe and vesture piebald?
You threaten us, fellow? Do your worst,
Blow your pipe there till you burst!"

One more he stept into the street
   And to his lips again
    Laid his long pipe of smooth straight cane;
And ere he blew three notes (such sweet
Soft notes as yet musician's cunning
   Never gave the enraptured air)
There was a rustling that seemed like a bustling
Of merry crowds justling[2] at pitching and hustling,
Small feet were pattering, wooden shoes clattering,
Little hands clapping and little tongues chattering,
And, like fowls in a farm-yard when barley is scattering,
Out came the children running.
All the little boys and girls,
With rosy cheeks and flaxen curls,
And sparkling eyes and teeth like pearls,
Tripping and skipping, ran merrily after
The wonderful music with shouting and laughter.

---

8. A small bag, a wallet.
9. Baghdad.

1. A Dutch coin of little value. "Bate": subtract.
2. I.e., jostling.

The Mayor was dumb, and the Council stood
As if they were changed into blocks of wood.
Unable to move a step, or cry
To the children merrily skipping by,
—Could only follow with the eye
That joyous crowd at the Piper's back.
But how the Mayor was on the rack,
And the wretched Council's bosoms beat,
As the Piper turned from the High Street[3]
To where the Weser rolled its waters
Right in the way of their sons and daughters!
However he turned from South to West,
And to Koppelberg Hill his steps addressed,
And after him the children pressed;
Great was the joy in every breast.
"He never can cross the mighty top!
He's forced to let that piping drop,
And we shall see our children stop!"
When, lo, as they reached the mountain-side,
A wondrous portal opened wide,
As if a cavern was suddenly hollowed;
And the Piper advanced and the children followed,
And when all were in to the very last,
The door in the mountain-side shut fast.
Did I say, all? No! One was lame,
    And could not dance the whole of the way;
And in after years, if you would blame
    His sadness, he was used to say,—
"It's dull in our town since my playmates left!
I can't forget that I'm bereft
Of all the pleasant sights they see,
Which the Piper also promised me.
For he led us, he said, to a joyous land,
Joining the town and just at hand,
Where waters gushed and fruit-trees grew
And flowers put forth a fairer hue,
And everything was strange and new;
The sparrows were brighter than peacocks here,
And their dogs outran our fallow[4] deer,
And honey-bees had lost their stings,
And horses were born with eagle's wings:
And just as I became assured
My lame foot would be speedily cured,
The music stopped and I stood still,
And found myself outside the hill,
Left alone against my will,

---

3. The town's main street.   4. Pale brown.

To go now limping as before,
And never hear of that country more!"

Alas, alas for Hamelin!
    There came into many a burgher's pate
    A text which says that heaven's gate
    Opes to the rich at as easy rate
As the needle's eye takes a camel in![5]
The Mayor sent East, West, North, and South,
To offer the Piper, by word of mouth,
    Wherever it was men's lot to find him,
Silver and gold to his heart's content,
If he'd only return the way he went,
    And bring the children behind him.
But when they saw 'twas a lost endeavour,
And Piper and dancers were gone for ever,
They made a decree that lawyers never
    Should think their records dated duly
If, after the day of the month and year,
These words did not as well appear,
"And so long after what happened here
    On the Twenty-second of July,
Thirteen hundred and seventy-six":
And the better in memory to fix
The place of the children's last retreat,
They called it, the Pied Piper's Street—
Where any one playing on pipe or tabor[6]
Was sure for the future to lose his labour.
Nor suffered they hostelry or tavern
    To shock with mirth a street so solemn;
But opposite the place of the cavern
    They wrote the story on a column,
And on the great church-window painted
The same, to make the world acquainted
How their children were stolen away;
And there it stands to this very day.
And I must not omit to say
That in Transylvania[7] there's a tribe
Of alien people who ascribe
The outlandish ways and dress
On which their neighbours lay such stress,
To their fathers and mothers having risen
Out of some subterraneous prison
Into which they were trepanned[8]
Long time ago in a mighty band
Out of Hamelin town in Brunswick land,
But how or why, they don't understand.

5. Matthew 19.24.
6. A small drum, played by a piper or fifer.

7. Region in Romania.
8. Lured.

So, Willy,[9] let me and you be wipers
Of scores out with all men—especially pipers!
And, whether they pipe us free from rats or from mice,
If we've promised them aught, let us keep our promise!

1842

9. The young son of the actor and manager William Macready (1793–1873), Browning's chief theatrical patron; confined to bed with an illness, Willy had asked Browning to write something for him to illustrate.

HISTORY OF ROBIN HOOD
ca. 1860

The first written reference to Robin Hood was a casual mention by William Langland in 1377 of the "rymes of Robyn Hood." None of these "rymes" survived, but by 1600 there were numerous ballads, songs, and recollections of Robin Hood. The earliest Robin Hood ballad, generally called "Robin Hood and the Monk," was printed in 1450, and it does not portray the dashing hero that we have come to know in popular culture. He was a yeoman, rough and cruel at times, who lived in Barnsdale Forest, not in Sherwood Forest. Though later versions often picture him as a wronged nobleman, the legend was more than likely based on a robber who kept the money he stole from the rich and occasionally helped the poor. As a devout Catholic, he is described as robbing corrupt monks, bishops, and sheriffs. But he did not fight to defeat Norman tyranny and help King Richard. Nor did he want to set up an ideal society in the forest. He and his men—there were no women in the early ballads, although respect was paid to the Virgin Mary—sought mainly to rectify social injustices and to live well. Little John, who is in all the stories, is almost as important a figure as Robin Hood himself.

Robin Hood became so popular by the seventeenth century that people named places and ships after him, and other outlaws took on his name to make themselves appear "noble." There were even games based on the ballads or plays. By the nineteenth century, the many chapbooks, stories, and songs in circulation had brought about major changes in the Robin Hood legend. His yeoman origins disappeared, and he increasingly became the heroic outlaw of Sherwood Forest who defended the rights of the poor, fell in love with Maid Marian, and helped King Richard the Lion-Hearted reclaim his throne, perhaps best captured in print by Howard Pyle (*The Merry Adventures of Robin Hood*, 1883) and in film by Errol Flynn (*The Adventures of Robin Hood*, 1938).

History of Robin Hood, published by Webb Millington around 1860, is a good example of the chapbooks, read by all social classes and age groups, that disseminated numerous legends and thereby supported their firm hold on the popular imagination.

ROBIN HOOD.

History of Robin Hood

The village of Locksley, in Nottinghamshire, at no great distance from Sherwood Forest,[1] is stated to have been the birthplace of the famous Robin Hood; and his father, who was a forester, is said to have surpassed every competitor in the use of the bow. His mother was sister to Squire Gamewell, of Gamewell Hall, about twenty miles distant from the place where Robin was brought up with his parents.

When Robin was thirteen years of age, his mother, one morning, requested her husband to allow Robin and her to pay a visit to Squire Gamewell, at the Hall. "By all means, my dear," said he; "and let Robin put the best saddle and bridle on the grey horse; but, as the sun is rising, make haste, for tomorrow is Christmas-day."

Next day great preparations were made for the Christmas dinner; and when the company assembled, the squire said, "You are all heartily welcome to dine here, but no man shall taste my ale till he has sung a Christmas carol." After dinner, his guests made the whole hall ring with their songs and shoutings; and the squire sent for one of his retainers,[2] a clever lad, called Little John, who increased their merriment by playing a number of tricks and gambols; but, to the astonishment of every one present, Robin Hood got up after him, and went through all the tricks in a still more masterly style. The squire was so much pleased with Robin's dexterity, that he told him he must not return home, but stay at the Hall, and heir[3] his property. To this Robin consented, on his uncle's giving him Little John to be his servant; for, from a similarity of dispositions, a great intimacy had already taken place between them.

During the absence of Robin who had gone to pay his father a visit, the squire was suddenly taken ill, and he requested that a messenger should be sent to hasten him home; but Robin's mother was confined to bed, and in so dangerous state of health that he could not leave her till a late hour on the following day. In the mean time,

as the squire found himself dying, he ordered his attendant to go for a monk in order that he might make his peace with Heaven.

At that time, as the whole kingdom professed the Roman Catholic religion, the people were entirely under the guidance of the monks and friars, who extracted money and property, by every possible contrivance, from all who applied to them, and granted dispensations for the most enormous crimes. As Gamewell Hall was very near the monastery of Fountain Abbey, the monk soon made his appearance; and he prevailed on the dying man to sign a deed, conveying all he had to the church, as the only means of saving his soul. When Robin arrived at the Hall, his uncle had been dead some hours, and the monks, who were in possession of the house, shut

---

1. A royal forest in central England near Nottingham.

2. Household servants.
3. Be heir to.

the doors against him, and would give him nothing to support himself. This was a sad reverse to poor Robin, who had been brought up as a gentleman without learning any business, and was unable to gain a livelihood. On turning from the Hall, he found Little John waiting, who told him that he knew what had taken place, and was determined to share the fortunes of his master. After some consultation, they resolved, as they were both excellent marksmen, to go to Sherwood Forest, which then abounded with deer, and support themselves by their bows.

The fame of Robin Hood, and the merry life he led, drew a number of young men, in similar circumstances with himself, to join his band, which very soon increased to more than a hundred of the finest-looking and bravest fellows in the kingdom, all clothed in green. To priests, and the niggardly rich, Robin Hood was an enemy; but he held the person and property of every woman sacred, and always took the part of the weak and injured. By the poor he was adored, for he generously supplied their wants from his own private purse.

Robin Hood, who loved a joke as well as a good booty, meeting one day with a jolly-looking butcher on horseback, with panniers on each side, said to him, "Good morrow, my hearty fellow, where are you going so early?" "To Nottingham market," replied he, "to sell my meat." "I never learned any trade," said Robin, "and I would like to be a butcher;—now, what must I give you for the mare, panniers, and meat?" "They are yours at five marks,"[4] returned the butcher. Robin gave him the money, and then made an exchange of clothes, the butcher putting on the fine green uniform which Robin always wore, while he put on the butcher's clothes and apron. Thus accoutred, Robin Hood rode straight to Nottingham market, where he hired a stall, and began to dispose of his meat, giving more for one penny than the butchers could do for five, so that they sold nothing. The butchers, supposing him to be some senseless spendthrift, and that a good bargain might be got of him, asked him to dine with them. To this Robin consented, and after dinner he insisted on paying the bill; which was no sooner observed by the Sheriff, a cunning old miser, who sat at the head of the table, and who was master both of the market and the tavern, than he determined to take advantage of it, and said to him, "Good fellow, hast thou any horned beasts to sell?"—"Yes good master Sheriff," replied Robin, "if you will please to go to see them."

The Sheriff ordered out his horse, and, putting three hundred pounds in gold into a bag, rode off with Robin on the road that leads through Sherwood Forest. On entering the Forest the Sheriff exclaimed, "God preserve us from that man called Robin Hood!" and they had not proceeded far when a number of fat deer were seen skipping about. "How do you like my horned beasts, Master Sheriff," said Robin;

---

4. A mark was a coin worth about ⅔ of a pound sterling.

"these are the cattle I told you of."—"To tell you the truth," replied he, "I don't much like your company, and I wish I were safely in Nottingham again." Robin blew three blasts with his bugle-horn, and Little John, with a number of the merry men, immediately appeared. "Here, comrades," said he, "I have brought the Sheriff of Nottingham to dine with you to-day, and I hope he will pay for his dinner." The Sheriff was forced, much against his inclination, to go and dine with them. After the entertainment, Robin eased him of the three hundred pounds he had in the bag to pay for his intended purchase, and then, placing him on his horse, he led him out of the Forest, and desired to be kindly remembered to his wife.

One morning, as Robin was strolling in the Forest, he saw a genteel-looking young man sitting under a tree, who appeared to be very melancholy and dejected. He inquired the cause of his sadness. The young man, taking a ring from his pocket, said, "I was to have been married yesterday to a young lady whom I have long courted, and I bought this ring for the occasion; but the Bishop of Hereford, her uncle, has rejected me, and means to give her to an old wealthy knight."

When Robin heard the bishop's name who was his great enemy, and the time and place, he told Allan-a-dale (the name of the young man) to put on a cheerful look, and he would ensure him of getting his mistress. Robin seeing there was no time to lose, disguised himself as a harper, and ordered twenty-four of his bowmen and Allan-

a-dale to follow him. He then proceeded to the church alone, where he found the bishop putting on his robes, who asked him what he wanted. Robin told him he was an harper, come to offer his services at the wedding. On the old knight and the bride making their appearance, Robin stepped forward, and said, "I cannot allow this marriage to go on, for the bride must have her own choice."— Then pulling out his horn, he gave three blasts and the bowmen entered the church. "Young lady," said Robin, "as you are now free, see if there is any one here you would choose for your husband." She no sooner saw Allan-a-dale, than she sprang to him, and said, "Here is my choice!" Robin requested the bishop to proceed; but as he refused, he pulled off his robes, and put them on Little John, who took the book, and went through the ceremony very gracefully, Robin giving away the bride. The bishop and the old knight slunk out of the church, and the rest of the party went off to celebrate the wedding at Sherwood Forest.

At one time, when the finances of the merry men were very low, they resolved to plunder the rich convent of St. Mary, and to carry off the image of the holy Virgin, which was of solid silver.

Under the disguise of a poor blind minstrel and his mother, Robin Hood and Little John gained admittance to the convent; and, when the nuns and friars had returned to their cells, opened the gates to their companions.

The alarm soon spread through the convent, and every one flew to the chapel for protection; but the bowmen having already entered the place, were proceeding to spoil it of what was most valuable, and to take down the silver image, when one of the nuns cried out, "Oh, mercy! will they take away the gift of our queen, even while she is within our walls!" On hearing this, Robin said, "My brave comrades desist, and let not disloyalty be ranked among our errors; this house and all within it are rendered sacred by the presence of Queen Eleanor!"[5] The bowmen instantly obeyed their leader; and, as they quitted the convent, Robin told the nuns to bless the queen for preserving their image, which otherwise would have bought wine to the Sherwood venison.

When the queen heard of the behaviour of Robin Hood, and that his respect for her alone had saved the convent from being plundered, she was so much pleased, that she determined to be a friend to him and his men.

Soon after King Richard's return from the wars in Palestine,[6] he ordered a grand shooting match with the bow to be held in the palace grounds, when prizes were to be awarded to the best marksman. Queen Eleanor, his mother, had heard much of the dexterity of the merry men in the use of that weapon, and she thought this a favourable opportunity to execute her design in favour of Robin Hood; therefore she told the king, that she could bring one hundred archers, who would beat the most skilful in his army or guards. The king, who thought it was impossible to find any equal to his own archers, requested her to bring forward her champions to the trial, and if they were victorious, he would not only bestow on them the prizes, but grant her any boon she asked. When the queen heard this, she called her favourite page, and despatched him with a message to Robin Hood. The page soon reached Sherwood Forest, and found out Robin, to whom he said, "Queen Eleanor greets you well, requesting that you will take one hundred of your

5. Eleanor of Aquitaine (ca. 1122–1204), who married Henry Plantagenet in 1152; she became queen of England in 1154, when he became Henry II.

6. Richard I (1157–1199; r. 1189–99), known as Richard the Lion-Hearted, led the Third Crusade (1189–92) to attempt to recover Jerusalem from the Muslims.

bowmen with you, and hasten to London; for a great match at the bow is to take place there, and she has chosen you and your men to be her champions."

Before the bowmen began, Queen Eleanor craved this boon from the king—that he should not be angry with any of her archers; but that they should be free to stay at court during the match, and have forty days to retire to where they pleased. King Richard agreed to this; and then ordered the targets to be placed. The king's archers first drew their bows, and lodged about forty of their arrows in the target; but when Robin and his bowmen shot, to the astonishment of the king and all the court, all their arrows were placed in the mark.

It was while the king's thoughts were turned on Robin Hood and his band, that his mother, Queen Eleanor, entered, to crave the boon he promised to grant if her champions were victorious. "My dear Richard," said she, "the boon I ask is the free pardon of Robin Hood and his men, who will, I am certain, prove themselves worthy of your clemency, and be a valuable acquisition to your crown." "My dear mother," said he, "I can refuse you nothing; but, before I grant your request, I must see Robin Hood again, in order to discover what his sentiments are, and whether these outlaws are inclined to leave off their bad habits, and become faithful subjects; for which purpose I mean to disguise myself immediately, and go to Sherwood Forest."

The queen approved of this, and Richard, accompanied by twelve of his courtiers, all disguised as monks, mounted their horses, and proceeded to the haunts of the outlaws. They had just entered the Forest, when Robin Hood, who had been strolling about, having observed them at a distance, thought it was a whole monastery of friars, and he determined to plunder them. King Richard, who was taller than the rest, rode foremost, and Robin, taking him for the abbot, seized his horse by the bridle, saying, "Abbot, stand, and deliver your money; it was a monk that ruined me, and I have sworn to spare none of your fraternity." "But we are going on the king's message," said Richard. When Robin heard this, he let go the bridle, saying, "God save him! and confound all his enemies!" "Thou art cursing thyself," said the king; "for art a robber, an outlaw, and a traitor." "Were you not his messenger," returned Robin, "I would say you lied; for I never injured the honest and industrious man; I protect women and children, and the poor people around me; it is only from the miserly rich, and those who live upon the labours of others, that I take any thing; however, as you are King Richard's servants, I will not deprive you of a single penny, and also excuse what you have said." Robin asked them to partake of the good cheer of Sherwood Forest before they proceeded on their journey.

After dinner, the pretended monks again mounted their horses, and were preparing to take their leave of the bowmen, when the king said to Robin Hood, "Now, my brave fellow, if I were to procure your pardon and that of your men, would you turn faithful and useful subjects?" This being the first wish of Robin's heart, and for some time past always uppermost in his thoughts, he replied, "Abbot, I am tired of this kind of life; and though some may praise our bold adventures and generous actions, yet I now hate every thing connected with it. Were King Richard, who is a gallant soldier and a generous prince, to pardon our offences, and take us into favour, he would never have to repent his clemency, for he would find us the most loyal and peaceful of his subjects."

"Behold your king!" said Richard, opening a part of the monk's cloak, which discovered the star[7] and other insignia. Robin and his bowmen were instantly on their knees before him. "Rise up, my brave fellows, your leader is now the Earl of Huntingdon, which is his just right, from being next heir to the late earl. I restore you again to society, by freely pardoning all your past offences; and I expect from your future good behaviour, and the services which you are able to

render me by your skill and bravery, if you are inclined, never to have cause to repent of my kindness."

Robin Hood, now Earl of Huntingdon, and his bowmen, immediately swore allegiance to the king, and by their good conduct afterwards, Richard was induced to place them near his own person as a body-guard.

1860

7. Probably an anachronistic reference to the Order of the Garter, which was founded by Edward III in 1348; the star became part of the insignia in the seventeenth century. "Discovered": exposed.

HOWARD PYLE
1853–1911

Howard Pyle, one of America's most famous illustrators and writers of children's books, was born in Wilmington, Delaware. After finishing his schooling, he studied art for three years in Philadelphia. In 1872 he returned home, continuing to draw while he worked in his father's leather business. The acceptance of an illustrated article by *Scribner's Monthly* and a fairy tale by *St. Nicholas* gave him the confidence to move to New York in 1876, where he studied drawing and sold illustrations and short tales. His contacts with major magazines (including

Harper's Weekly) secure, he returned to Wilmington and set up a studio.

There he began to illustrate books by others as well as continuing to work on his own stories; in 1881 he married Anne Poole, and they went on to have seven children. In 1883 he began publishing literary fairy tales and folktales in *Harper's Young People*; these were later reworked and collected in two popular volumes, *Pepper & Salt; or Seasoning for Young Folk* (1885) and *The Wonder Clock* (1888). Also in 1883 he published his first and perhaps best book, *The*

Merry Adventures of Robin Hood of Great Renown, in Nottinghamshire (1883), whose retelling of a classic legend was widely acclaimed in America and England and whose illustrations, modeled on the engravings of Albrecht Dürer (1471–1528), set a new standard for children's books. Pyle returned to medieval subjects in two later works, and he took on an even richer legend when he focused on tales of King Arthur. He devoted four volumes (1903–10) to the project, beginning with *The Story of King Arthur and His Knights*.

Another crucial aspect of Pyle's career was his role as a teacher. By the 1890s he was recognized as one of America's leading illustrators, and in 1894 he was invited to teach illustration at Philadelphia's Drexel Institute of Art, Science, and Technology; he resigned the position in 1900 to start his own small school in Wilmington. In the summer of 1898, he began offering classes in Chadds Ford, Pennsylvania, at a mill on the Brandywine River, providing the impetus for what became known as the Brandywine school of artists. His students included such talented illustrators and painters as Maxfield Parrish, N. C. Wyeth, Frank Schoonover, and Jessie Wilcox Smith, who were all to bring about major changes in the world of illustration. Even while continuing to produce illustrated books for children Pyle became interested in mural painting. In November 1910 he sailed to Europe for the first time, wishing to study the techniques of the Italian Renaissance masters; he died in Florence a year later.

Pyle was both praised and criticized for the highly stylized and archaic language of his retellings of British legends. He depicted the heroes as chaste, moral, and courageous, in keeping with the bourgeois values of the late nineteenth century. Pyle's Robin Hood and Little John are noble characters who respect each other's virtues and talents. Their meeting sets the tone for the rest of the novel, which depicts valorous heroes who allegedly made history but were to gain immortality in ballads and tales. In particular, Robin Hood becomes the epitome of the noble bandit, serving as a model for his followers and setting an example for young readers by righting the wrongs done by the powerful and sharing his wealth with the poor.

Despite its archaic diction, Pyle's novel was hugely popular and influential. Numerous authors who retold the legend in the twentieth century for young readers—including the British authors Geoffrey Trease (*Bows against the Barons*, 1934) and Antonia Fraser (*Robin Hood*, 1971), and the American Robin McKinley (*The Outlaws of Sherwood*, 1988)—follow or cleverly vary the plot he made canonical. Most of the Robin Hood films and television adaptations also draw on his work.

From The Merry Adventures of Robin Hood of Great Renown, of Nottinghamshire

ROBIN HOOD AND LITTLE JOHN

Up rose Robin Hood one merry morn when all the birds were singing blithely among the leaves, and up rose all his merry men, each fellow washing his head and hands in the cold brown brook that leaped laughing from stone to stone. Then said Robin: "For fourteen days have we seen no sport, so now I will go abroad to seek adventures forthwith. But tarry ye, my merry men all, here in the greenwood; only see that ye mind well my call. Three blasts upon the bugle horn I will blow in my hour of need; then come quickly, for I shall want your aid."

So saying, he strode away through the leafy forest glades until he had come to the verge of Sherwood.[1] There he wandered for a long time, through highway and byway, through dingly[2] dell and forest skirts. Now he met a fair buxom lass in a shady lane, and each gave the other a merry word and passed their way; now he saw a fair lady upon an ambling pad,[3] to whom he doffed his cap, and who bowed sedately in return

---

1. Sherwood Forest, a royal forest in central England near Nottingham.
2. With close-set trees.
3. An easy-paced horse.

to the fair youth; now he saw a fat monk on a pannier-laden ass; now a gallant knight, with spear and shield and armor that flashed brightly in the sunlight; now a page clad in crimson; and now a stout burgher from good Nottingham Town, pacing along with serious footsteps; all these sights he saw, but adventure found he none. At last he took a road by the forest skirts; a bypath that dipped toward a broad, pebbly stream spanned by a narrow bridge made of a log of wood. As he drew nigh this bridge, he saw a tall stranger coming from the other side. Thereupon Robin quickened his pace, as did the stranger likewise; each thinking to cross first.

"Now stand thou back," quoth Robin, "and let the better man cross first."

"Nay," answered the stranger, "then stand back thine own self, for the better man, I wot,[4] am I."

"That will we presently see," quoth Robin; "and meanwhile stand thou where thou art, or else, by the bright brow of Saint Ælfrida, I will show thee right good Nottingham play with a clothyard shaft[5] betwixt thy ribs."

"Now," quoth the stranger, "I will tan thy hide till it be as many colors as a beggar's cloak, if thou darest so much as touch a string of that same bow that thou holdest in thy hands."

"Thou pratest like an ass," said Robin, "for I could send this shaft clean through thy proud heart before a curtal friar could say grace over a roast goose at Michaelmastide."[6]

"And thou pratest like a coward," answered the stranger, "for thou standest there with a good yew bow to shoot at my heart, while I have nought in my hand but a plain blackthorn staff wherewith to meet thee."

"Now," quoth Robin, "by the faith of my heart, never have I had a coward's name in all my life before. I will lay by my trusty bow and eke my arrows, and if thou darest abide my coming, I will go and cut a cudgel to test thy manhood withal."[7]

"Ay, marry, that will I abide thy coming, and joyously, too," quoth the stranger; whereupon he leaned sturdily upon his staff to await Robin.

Then Robin Hood stepped quickly to the coverside and cut a good staff of round oak, straight, without flaw, and six feet in length, and came back trimming away the tender stems from it, while the stranger waited for him, leaning upon his staff, and whistling as he gazed roundabout. Robin observed him furtively as he trimmed his staff, measuring him from top to toe from out the corner of his eye, and thought that he had never seen a lustier or a stouter[8] man. Tall was Robin, but taller was the stranger by a head and a neck, for he was seven feet in height. Broad was Robin across the shoulders, but broader was the stranger by twice the breadth of a palm, while he measured at least an ell around the waist.

"Nevertheless," said Robin to himself, "I will baste thy hide right merrily, my good fellow"; then, aloud, "Lo, here is my good staff, lusty and tough. Now wait my coming, an[9] thou darest, and meet me, an thou fearest not; then we will fight until one or the other of us tumble into the stream by dint of blows."

"Marry, that meeteth my whole heart!"[1] cried the stranger, twirling his staff above his head, betwixt his fingers and thumb, until it whistled again.

---

4. Know.
5. A phrase used in ballads of a long bow's arrow (a cloth-yard is 36 inches). Saint Ælfrida (8th c.), a recluse who was the daughter of King Offa of Mercia.
6. The season of St. Michael, whose feast is September 29. "Curtal friar": a friar wearing a short habit.
7. I.e., with. "Eke": also.
8. Stronger, more determined. "Lustier": more vigorous.
9. If.
1. Conforms to or satisfies my wishes.

Never did the Knights of Arthur's Round Table meet in a stouter fight than did these two. In a moment Robin stepped quickly upon the bridge where the stranger stood; first he made a feint, and then delivered a blow at the stranger's head that, had it met its mark, would have tumbled him speedily into the water; but the stranger turned the blow right deftly, and in return gave one as stout, which Robin also turned as the stranger had done. So they stood, each in his place, neither moving a finger's breadth back, for one good hour, and many blows were given and received by each in that time, till here and there were sore bones and bumps, yet neither thought of crying "Enough!" or seemed likely to fall from off the bridge. Now and then they stopped to rest, and each thought that he never had seen in all his life before such a hand at quarterstaff. At last Robin gave the stranger a blow upon the ribs that made his jacket smoke like a damp straw thatch in the sun. So shrewd was the stroke that the stranger came within a hair's breadth of falling off the bridge; but he regained himself right quickly, and, by a dexterous blow, gave Robin a crack on the crown that caused the blood to flow. Then Robin grew mad with anger, and smote with all his might at the other; but the stranger warded the blow, and once again thwacked Robin, and this time so fairly that he fell heels over head into the water, as the queen pin falls in a game of bowls.[2]

"And where art thou now, good lad?" shouted the stranger, roaring with laughter.

"Oh, in the flood and floating adown with the tide," cried Robin; nor could he forbear laughing himself at his sorry plight. Then, gaining his feet, he waded to the bank, the little fish speeding hither and thither, all frightened at his splashing.

"Give me thy hand," cried he, when he had reached the bank. "I must needs own thou art a brave and a sturdy soul, and, withal,[3] a good stout stroke with the cudgels. By this and by that, my head hummeth like to a hive of bees on a hot June day."

Then he clapped his horn to his lips, and winded a blast that went echoing sweetly down the forest paths. "Ay, marry," quoth he again, "thou art a tall lad, and eke a brave one, for ne'er, I trow, is there a man betwixt here and Canterbury Town could do the like to me that thou hast done."

"And thou," quoth the stranger, laughing, "takest thy cudgeling like a brave heart and a stout yeoman."

But now the distant twigs and branches rustled with the coming of men, and suddenly a score or two of good stout yeomen, all clad in Lincoln green,[4] burst from out the covert, with merry Will Stutely at their head.

"Good master," cried Will, "how is this? Truly thou art all wet from head to foot, and that to the very skin."

"Why, marry," answered jolly Robin, "yon stout fellow hath tumbled me neck and crop[5] into the water, and hath given me a drubbing beside."

"Then shall he not go without a ducking and eke a drubbing himself!" cried Will Stutely. "Have at him, lads!"

Then Will and a score of yeomen leaped upon the stranger, but though they sprang quickly they found him ready and felt him strike right and left with his stout staff, so that, though he went down with press of numbers, some of them rubbed cracked crowns before he was overcome.

"Nay, forbear!" cried Robin, laughing until his sore sides ached again; "he is a right

2. A game played with a hard wooden ball—here, ninepins. The front pin is usually called the king-pin.
3. Besides.

4. A bright green material made at Lincoln, a town about 30 miles northeast of Nottingham.
5. Completely, altogether.

good man and true, and no harm shall befall him. Now hark ye, good youth, wilt thou stay with me and be one of my band? Three suits of Lincoln green shalt thou have each year, beside forty marks in fee,[6] and share with us whatsoever good shall befall us. Thou shalt eat sweet venison and quaff the stoutest ale, and mine own good right-hand man shalt thou be, for never did I see such a cudgel-player in all my life before. Speak! wilt thou be one of my good merry men?"

"That know I not," quoth the stranger, surlily, for he was angry at being so tumbled about. "If ye handle yew bow and apple shaft no better than ye do oaken cudgel, I wot ye are not fit to be called yeomen in my country; but if there be any man here that can shoot a better shaft than I, then will I bethink me of joining with you."

"Now, by my faith," said Robin, "thou art a right saucy varlet, sirrah; yet I will stoop[7] to thee as I never stooped to man before. Good Stutely, cut thou a fair white piece of bark four fingers in breadth, and set it forescore[8] yards distant on yonder oak. Now, stranger, hit that fairly with a gray goose shaft and call thyself an archer."

"Ay, marry, that will I," answered he. "Give me a good stout bow and a fair broad arrow, and if I hit it not, strip me and beat me blue with bow-strings."

Then he chose the stoutest bow amongst them all, next to Robin's own, and a straight gray goose shaft, well-feathered and smooth, and stepping to the mark—while all the band, sitting or lying upon the greensward, watched to see him shoot—he drew the arrow to his cheek and loosed the shaft right deftly, sending it so straight down the path that it clove the mark in the very center. "Aha!" cried he, "mend[9] thou that if thou canst"; while even the yeomen clapped their hands at so fair a shot.

"That is a keen shot, indeed," quoth Robin; "mend it I cannot, but mar it I may, perhaps."

Then taking up his own good stout bow and nocking an arrow with care, he shot with his very greatest skill. Straight flew the arrow, and so true that it lit fairly upon the stranger's shaft and split it into splinters. Then all the yeomen leaped to their feet and shouted for joy that their master had shot so well.

"Now, by the lusty yew bow of good Saint Withold,"[1] cried the stranger, "that is a shot indeed, and never saw I the like in all my life before! Now truly will I be thy man henceforth and for aye. Good Adam Bell[2] was a fair shot, but never shot he so!"

"Then have I gained a right good man this day," quoth jolly Robin. "What name goest thou by, good fellow."

"Men call me John Little whence I came," answered the stranger.

Then Will Stutely, who loved a good jest, spoke up. "Nay, fair little stranger," said he, "I like not thy name and fain would I have it otherwise. Little art thou, indeed, and small of bone and sinew; therefore shalt thou be christened Little John, and I will be thy godfather."

Then Robin Hood and all his band laughed aloud until the stranger began to grow angry.

"An thou make a jest of me," quoth he to Will Stutely, "thou wilt have sore bones and little pay, and that in short season."

"Nay, good friend," said Robin Hood, "bottle thine anger, for the name fitteth thee well. Little John shalt thou be called henceforth, and Little John shall it be. So come,

---

6. As wages. A mark was a coin worth about ⅔ of a pound sterling.
7. Humble myself, yield.
8. I.e., four score (eighty).
9. Surpass, better.
1. Like Ælfrida, Withold was a Saxon saint; the

name also appears in Shakespeare's *King Lear* (3.4; ca. 1605) and in Sir Walter Scott's *Ivanhoe* (1819), a novel in which Robin Hood plays a minor role.
2. A northern outlaw whose skill with the bow was legendary; his story is told in an English ballad popular in the sixteenth century.

my merry men, and we will go and prepare a christening feast for this fair infant."

So turning their backs upon the stream, they plunged into the forest once more, through which they traced their steps till they reached the spot where they dwelt in the depths of the woodland. There had they built huts of bark and branches of trees, and made couches of sweet rushes spread over with skins of fallow[3] deer. Here stood a great oak tree with branches spreading broadly around, beneath which was a seat of green moss where Robin Hood was wont to sit at feast and at merry-making with his stout men about him. Here they found the rest of the band, some of whom had come in with a brace of fat does. Then they all built great fires and after a time roasted the does and broached a barrel of humming[4] ale. Then when the feast was ready, they all sat down, but Robin Hood placed Little John at his right hand, for he was henceforth to be the second in the band.

Then, when the feast was done, Will Stutely spoke up. "It is now time, I ween, to christen our bonny babe, is it not so, merry boys?" And "Aye! Aye!" cried all, laughing till the woods echoed with their mirth.

"Then seven sponsors shall we have," quoth Will Stutely; and hunting among all the band he chose the seven stoutest men of them all.

"Now, by Saint Dunstan,"[5] cried Little John, springing to his feet, "more than one of you shall rue it an you lay finger upon me."

But without a word they all ran upon him at once, seizing him by his legs and arms and holding him tightly in spite of his struggles, and they bore him forth while all stood around to see the sport. Then one came forward who had been chosen to play the priest because he had a bald crown, and in his hand he carried a brimming pot of ale. "Now who bringeth this babe?" asked he right soberly.

"That do I," answered Will Stutely.

"And what name callest thou him?"

"Little John call I him."

"Now Little John," quoth the mock priest, "thou hast not lived heretofore, but only got thee along through the world, but henceforth thou wilt live indeed. When thou livedst not, thou wast called John Little, but now that thou dost live indeed, Little John shalt thou be called, so christen I thee." And at these last words he emptied the pot of ale upon Little John's head.

Then all shouted with laughter as they saw the good brown ale stream over Little John's beard and trickle from his nose and chin, while his eyes blinked with the smart of it. At first he was of a mind to be angry, but found he could not because the others were so merry; so he, too, laughed with the rest. Then Robin took this sweet, pretty babe, clothed him all anew from top to toe in Lincoln green, and gave him a good stout bow, and so made him a member of the merry band.

1883

<hr/>

3. Pale brown.
4. Strong.
5. Abbot of Glastonbury and archbishop of Can-terbury (10th c.); he was one of the greatest saints of the Anglo-Saxon church.

ROGER LANCELYN GREEN
1918–1987

Both as a critic and as a reteller of legends, myths, and fairy tales, Roger Lancelyn Green played a major role in children's literature in Great Britain during the twentieth century. During childhood, illnesses often confined him to his home in Norwich, and he spent his time reading works by Rudyard Kipling, Lewis Carroll, Andrew Lang, and J. M. Barrie that had a lasting influence on him. After he earned his degree from Merton College, part of the University of Oxford, in 1940, he held a variety of jobs— including actor, antiquarian bookseller, and deputy librarian at Merton College—before he started to concentrate on writing. Among his earliest publications were short biographies of two of the writers who had been so important to him, *Andrew Lang* (1946) and *The Story of Lewis Carroll* (1949); at the same time he began adapting fairy tales, myths, and legends, some of which appeared in *Beauty and the Beast, and Other Tales* (1948). In 1950 he became the William Noble Research Fellow in English literature at Liverpool University, where he taught and continued to develop a career as a biographer and author of adaptations and original stories for children. His major works include *King Arthur and His Knights of the Round Table* (1953), *The Adventures of Robin Hood* (1956), *Old*

Greek Fairy Tales (1958), *Tales of the Greeks and Trojans* (1964), and *A Book of Myths* (1965).

Green's stated intention in retelling myths and legends for young readers was to select incidents most likely to interest them and to make a work that is new even if all its contents are traditional or borrow from earlier poets and storytellers. "Sir Gawain and the Green Knight" is an excerpt from one his most successful books, *King Arthur and His Knights of the Round Table*, which draws most heavily on Sir Thomas Malory's version of the Arthurian legend, *Morte Darthur* (1485), but also relies on other sources—in this case, the late-fourteenth-century poem "Sir Gawain and the Green Knight." Most of the recorded deeds of Arthur's knights are meant to defend the court and the king and to display the valor of a particular knight. Gawain here must demonstrate loyalty, bravery, and courage, for the Knight of the Green Chapel is no ordinary adversary: he will test not only Gawain's honor but also the chivalry of the court. Though Green, like Howard Pyle and many other writers, used an antiquated style in retelling these legends set long ago, his writing is more crisp and succinct than most, and he captures the grace and charm of courtly manners.

From King Arthur and His Knights of the Round Table

Sir Gawain and the Green Knight

King Arthur's adventures did not end when he had defeated the Saxons and brought peace to Britain: for though he had set up the Realm of Logres[1]—the land of true good and piety, nobleness and right living—the evil was always breaking in to attack the good. It would need many books to tell of every adventure that befell during his reign—that brief period of light set like a star of Heaven in the midst of the Dark Ages: and we cannot, for example, tell here how Arthur himself fought with the Giant of St Michael's Mount who carried off helpless wayfarers to his dark and evil castle;

---

1. The name derives from the Welsh name for England, Lloegr (literally, "the Lost Lands").

nor how he made war against the Emperor Lucius[2] and was received in Rome; nor even of his fight with the dreadful Cat of Losane.

But year by year the fame of his court grew, and spread far and wide, and the bravest and noblest knights in the world came to his court and strove by their deeds of courage and gentleness to win a place at the Round Table.

Many stories are told of these knights also—of Launcelot and Gawain, of Tristram and Gareth, of Percivale, Ywain, Marhaus, Cleges, Agravaine, and many, many others—and more adventures that befell the most famous of these than may possibly be told in one book.

One of the first and bravest of the knights was Sir Gawain—and it was said indeed that only Sir Launcelot, Sir Galahad, and Sir Percivale could surpass him. He had many exciting adventures: but now only one of them can be told.

King Arthur held his Christmas feast at Camelot one year, with all the bravest of his knights about him, and all the fairest ladies of his court—and his chief celebrations fell upon New Year's Day. Queen Guinevere, clad in fair, shining silk, sat beneath an embroidered canopy studded with gems: fair was she to look upon, with her shining eyes of grey, and each knight bent in reverence before her ere he took his place. Beside her sat King Arthur, well pleased to see the noble gathering and the joy that was in the hall: but he would not begin the feast, for such his custom was, until he had been told of some knightly deed, or set before his knights some strange or terrible new quest.

The minstrels had stopped playing and the whole company sat quietly in the great hall, only the roar and crackle of the log fires in the wide hearths breaking the silence—when suddenly there rang out the clash and clang of iron-shod hooves striking upon stone: the great doors flew open, and into the hall rode a strange and terrible figure.

A great man it was, riding upon a huge horse: a strong-limbed, great-handed man, so tall that an earth-giant almost he seemed. Yet he rode as a knight should, though without armour, and his face, though fierce, was fair to see—but the greatest wonder was that he was green all over. A jerkin and cloak of green he wore above green hose gartered in green, with golden spurs; in the green belt round his waist jewels were set, and his green saddle was inlaid richly, as were also his trappings. But his hair, hanging low to his shoulders, was bright green, and his beard also; green was his face and green his hands; and the horse was also green from head to foot, with gold thread wound and knotted in the mane.

He had no weapons nor shield save for a great axe of green steel and gold, and a bough torn from a holly tree held above his head. He flung the branch upon the inlaid floor of the hall and looked proudly on every side; at the knights seated about the Round Table, and the ladies and squires at the boards on either side, and at Arthur where he sat with Guinevere above the rest. Then he cried in a great voice:

'Where is the governor of this gang? With him would I speak and with none other!'

All sat in amazement gazing at the strange knight: some dire enchantment it must be, they thought—for how else could there be such a man sitting there on his horse, as green as the grass—greener than any grass on this earth?

But at length Arthur, courteous ever, greeted the Green Knight, bade him be welcome and sit down to the feast with them.

2. According to Sir Thomas Malory's *Morte Dar-thur* (1485), Lucius was a Roman emperor slain by Arthur in battle; historically, no "Emperor Lucius" existed. (Many accounts describe Arthur's fight with the giant, and his killing of the devil cat of Losane is related in the fifteenth-century *Prose Merlin*.)

'Not so!' cried the stranger in answer. 'I come not to tarry with you: and by the sign of the green bough I come not in war—else had I clothed me in armour and helmet most sure—for such have I richly stored in my castle in the north. But even in that land have I heard of the fame and valour of your court—the bravery of your knights, and their high virtue also.'

'Sir,' replied the king, 'here may you find many to do battle and joust if such be your will.'

'Not so,' cried the Green Knight in his great booming voice. 'Here I see only beardless children whom I could fell with a stroke! Nay, I come rather in this high season of Our Lord's birth to bring Yule-tide sport, a test of valour to your feast. If any man in this hall is so brave and so courageous as to exchange stroke for stroke, I will give him this noble axe—heavy enough truly to handle as he may desire: yes, and I myself will stand here on the floor and receive the first stroke of the axe wherever he may smite me. Only he must swear, and you, lord king, to give me the right to deal him such another blow, if I may, a twelve-month and a day from now.'

More silent still sat the knights; if they had been surprised before now their amazement was greater still. But none dared answer his challenge, so terrible was the man and so fearsome the great axe which he held in his hand.

Then the Green Knight laughed aloud in mockery: 'Is this indeed the court of King Arthur?' he cried, 'and are these the far-famed Knights of the Round Table? Now is their glory laid low for ever, since even to hear tell of blows makes them all grow silent in fear!'

King Arthur sprang up at this. 'Fellow,' he cried, 'this foolishness of yours shall have a fitting answer. If none other will take your challenge, give me the axe and make ready for the blow!'

But at this Sir Gawain rose to his feet and said:

'My lord king and noble uncle, grant me a boon! Let this adventure be mine, for still there is my old shame unhealed: still have I to prove my worth as a Knight of your Round Table, still to fit myself to be a champion of Logres.'

'Right happy I am that the quest shall be yours, dear nephew,' answered Arthur. And the Green Knight smiled grimly as he sprang from his horse and met with Gawain in the middle of the hall.

'I too am overjoyed to find one brave man amongst you all,' he said. 'Tell me your name, Sir knight, ere we make our bargain.'

'I am Gawain, son of King Lot of Orkney,[3] and nephew to royal Arthur,' was the answer. 'And here I swear by my knighthood to strike but one blow, and bravely to endure such another if you may strike it me a twelve-month hence.'

'Sir Gawain,' cried the Green Knight, 'overjoyed am I indeed that your hand shall strike this blow. Come now and deal the stroke: thereafter shall I tell you who I am and where you may find me. Take now the axe and let us see how well you can smite.'

'Gladly will I,' said Gawain, taking the axe in his hands and swinging it while the Green Knight made ready by kneeling on the floor and drawing his long hair on to the crown of his head to lay bare his neck for the stroke. Putting all his strength into the blow, Gawain whirled up the axe and struck so hard that the keen blade cut through flesh and bone and set the sparks flying from the stone paving, while

3. The Orkney Islands, off the northeast coast of Scotland (according to an earlier tradition, Lot was King of Lothian, or southern Scotland). Because Lot married King Arthur's sister or half-sister (depending on the version of the legend), Gawain is Arthur's nephew.

the Green Knight's head leapt from his shoulders and went rolling across the floor.

But the knight neither faltered nor fell: swiftly he sprang forward with hands outstretched, caught up his head, and turning with it held in his hand by the hair mounted upon the waiting horse. Then, riding easily as if nothing had happened, he turned his face towards Gawain and said:

'See to it that you keep your oath and seek me out a year hence. I am the Knight of the Green Chapel, and as such men know me in the north. Through Wales shall you seek me, and in the Forest of Wirral:[4] and you will not fail to find me there if you be not a coward and a breaker of your knightly word.'

With that he wheeled his horse and galloped out of the door, the sparks flying up round his horse's hooves, and away into the distance, his head still held in his hand, swinging easily by the hair.

But all at the feast sat astonished beyond words at this strange adventure, and it was a little while before the hall was filled once more with laughter and the joy of that festal season.

The year went by full swiftly; the trees grew green with spring, the leaves fading through the bright summer days, turned to red and gold in the early autumn; and upon Michaelmas Day King Arthur held a feast at Caerleon[5] with many of his knights, in honour of Sir Gawain who must on the morrow set forth upon his dreadful quest. Ywain and Agravaine and Erec were there; Launcelot and Lionel and Lucan the Good; Sir Bors and Sir Bedivere and Baldwin the lord bishop; Arthur and Guinevere to bless him and wish him God-speed. Gawain donned his armour, curved and shining and inlaid with gold; he girt his sword to his side and took the Green Knight's axe in his hand; then he mounted upon Gringalet his war-horse, and rode into the forests of South Wales, the shield held before him with the device of the Pentangle, the five-pointed Star of Logres, emblazoned in the midst.

So Sir Gawain set out, and rode through the realm of Logres, seeking for no joy but a deadly danger at the end of his quest. After many days he came into the wild lands of North Wales, and fared through lonely valleys and deep forests, forced often to sleep out under the stars by night, and to do battle by day with robbers and wild men.

Grim winter had closed upon him when he came to the northern sea, left the islands of Anglesey upon his left, and came by Clwyd[6] to the Holy Head, near Saint Winifred's Well on the shore of the wide river Dee. Near to the mouth he forded the stream at low tide, and came across the desolate sands into the wild Forest of Wirral.

4. Peninsula in northwest England, adjacent to the Welsh border.
5. Town in southeast Wales. Michaelmas Day: the feast of St. Michael on September 29.
6. River in north Wales.

Here were many more robbers and evil men, lying in wait by forest path and lonely stream, by rocky defile and by green valley—and he must fight with all who stayed him.

Everywhere he went he asked tidings of a Green Knight and of a Chapel also of Green near which was his dwelling: but none in the forest could help him in his quest. Only a brave knight could have passed that way, and Gawain endured all—foes to overcome, and the bitter weather of mid-winter.

On Christmas Eve he rode upon Gringalet through marsh and mire, and prayed that he might find shelter. And on a sudden he came through open parkland to a fine castle set on a little hill above a deep valley where flowed a wide stream. A fair lawn lay in front of it, and many great oak trees on either side; there was a moat before the castle, and a low palisade of wood.

'Now God be thanked,' said Sir Gawain, 'that I have come to this fair dwelling for Christmas, and may He grant me to find an honourable welcome herein . . . Good sir!' he cried to the porter who came to the great gate when he knocked, 'Grant me entrance, I pray you, and tell the lord of this castle that I am a knight of King Arthur's court passing this way upon a quest.'

With a kindly smile the porter opened the gate, and Gawain rode over the drawbridge and into the courtyard. And there were squires and serving-men waiting who helped him to alight, led Gringalet away to the stable, and brought Gawain into a goodly hall where a fire burned brightly and the lord of the castle came forth from his chamber to greet his guest, saying:

'Welcome to my dwelling, Sir knight: all that I have is here at your service, and you shall be my honoured guest for as long as it shall please you to remain in this castle.'

'I thank you, noble sir,' said Gawain. 'May God bless you for your hospitality.' With that they clasped hands as good friends should; and Gawain looked upon the knight who greeted him so warmly, and thought what a fine warrior that castle had as its lord. For he was a tall man and broad of shoulder, with an open, honest face tanned red by the sun, with red hair and beard, a firm hand-clasp, a free stride, and a straightforward speech: just such a man as was born to be a leader of valiant men and a lord over wide estates.

The squires led Gawain next to a fair chamber in the keep, where they helped him to lay aside his armour, and clad him in rich, flowing robes lined softly with fur. Then they led him back to the hall and set him in a chair near to the fire, beside the lord of the castle. They brought in the tables then, set them upon trestles, covered them with fair white cloths, set thereon salt cellars and spoons of silver, then brought in the dishes and the goblets of wine. The lord of the castle drank to Sir Gawain, and rejoiced with all his followers that chance had brought so far-famed a knight to his lonely dwelling.

When the meal was ended the two knights went together to the chapel of the castle, where the chaplain celebrated Evensong and the whole service for Christmas Eve.

Then the knight brought Sir Gawain into a comely closet and sat him in a chair by the fire. And there the lady of the castle came to visit him, accompanied by her handmaidens—a very lovely lady, fairer even than Queen Guinevere. So the evening passed in jest and joy, and they brought Gawain to his room with bright tapers, set a goblet of hot spiced wine at his bedside, and left him there to his rest.

Three days were spent in feasting and in Christmas rejoicings—dancing and carol-singing, and much merriment. And even the lady of the castle sat by Gawain, and sang to him and talked with him, and attended to his comfort.

'Tarry with me longer,' said the lord of the castle on the evening of the fourth day. 'For while I live I shall be held the worthier because so brave and courteous a knight as Sir Gawain has been my guest.'

'I thank you, good sir,' answered Gawain, 'but I must away to-morrow on my high quest. For I must be at the Green Chapel upon the New Year's day, and I would rather keep mine oath than be ruler of all this land. Moreover as yet I have found none who can instruct me as to where the Green Chapel is.'

The lord of the castle laughed happily. 'This is indeed good news!' he cried. 'Here then you may stay until the very day of your quest's ending. For not two hours' ride from this castle you shall find the Green Chapel—a man of mine shall bring you to it upon the first day of the new year.'

Then Gawain was glad, and he too laughed joyously. 'I thank you, sir, for this news—and greatly also for your kindness. Now that my quest is achieved, I will dwell here in all joy and do what you will.'

'Then these three days,' said the lord of the castle, 'I will ride out hunting in the forest. But you, who have travelled far and endured many things, shall abide in my castle and rest at your ease. And my wife shall attend on you, and entertain you with her company when I am out hunting.'

'I thank you indeed,' said Gawain. 'And in no other wise could I pass with greater joy the three days before my meeting with the Green Knight.'

'Well,' said the lord of the castle, 'so let it be. And as this yet is the festive season of game and jest, let us make a merry bargain together, I vowing each day to give you whatever I may win in the wood, and you giving in exchange anything that may come to you here in the castle. Let us swear to make this exchange, for worse or for better, whatever may happen.'

'With all my heart,' laughed Gawain. And so the oath was sworn.

Next morning the lord of the castle hunted the deer through the forests of Wirral and Delamere; and many a hart and hind fell to his keen arrows.

But Gawain slept long in a soft bed hung about with curtains, and dreamt of many things 'twixt waking and sleeping, until the lady of the castle, stepping silently as a sunbeam, came and sat upon his bed and talked with him merrily. Long they spoke together, and many words of love did the lady utter; but Gawain turned them all with jest and courtesy, as a true knight should who speaks with the lady of his host.

'Now God save you, fair sir,' she said at length, 'and reward you for your merry words. But that you are really Sir Gawain I misdoubt me greatly!'

'Wherefore do you doubt?' asked the knight anxiously, fearing that he had failed in some point of courtesy.

'So true a knight as Gawain,' answered the lady, 'and one so gentle and courteous unto damsels would never have tarried so long with a lady and not begged a kiss of her in parting.'

'Faith, fair lady,' said Gawain, 'and[7] you bid me to it, I will indeed ask a kiss of you: but a true knight asks not otherwise, for fear to displease you.'

So the lady kissed him sweetly, and blessed him and departed, and Gawain rose from his bed and called for the chamberlain to clothe him. And thereafter he ate and

7. I.e., an (if).

drank, and passed his day quietly in the castle until the lord of it came home in the grey evening, bearing the spoils of the chase.

'What think you of this game, Sir knight?' he cried. 'I deserve thanks for my skill as a huntsman, do I not—for all of this is yours, according to our bargain!'

'I thank you,' answered Gawain, 'and I take the gift as we agreed. And I will give to you all that I won within these walls.' And with that he put his hands on the lord of the castle's shoulders and kissed him, saying: 'Take here my spoils, for I have won nothing but this: if more had been mine, as freely would I have given it to you.'

'It is good,' said his host, 'and much do I thank you for it. Yet would I like to know whence came your kiss, and how did you win it?'

'Not so,' answered Gawain, 'that was no part of the bargain!' And thereupon they laughed merrily and sat down to a fine dinner.

Next morning the lord of the castle went forth down the hillside and along the deep valley-bottoms to seek out and slay the wild boar in the marshes.

But Gawain abode in his bed, and the lady came once more to sit by him; and ever she strove to wheedle him into speaking to her words of love unseemly for the lady of a knight. But Gawain the courteous turned all into jest, and defended himself so well by his wit that he won no more than two kisses, given by the lady ere she left him laughing.

'And now, Sir Gawain,' said the lord of the castle when he came home that night and laid the boar's head at his feet. 'Here is my spoil of the day which I give you according to our bargain: now what have you won to give me in exchange?'

'I thank you,' said Gawain, 'for your just dealing in this game. As truly will I give you all that I have gained this day.'

Thereat he took the lord of the castle by the shoulders and gave him two kisses, saying: 'Now are we quits—for this and no more have I got me to-day.'

'By St Giles!'[8] laughed the lord of the castle, 'you will be rich in a short time if we drive such bargains!' Then they went to the feast, and sat late over their meat and wine, while the lady strove ever to please Gawain, making fair, secret glances at him which, for his honour, he must not return.

The morrow would be the last day of the year. Gawain was eager to ride forth in quest of the Green Knight; but the lord of the castle stayed him with hospitable words:

'I swear by mine honour as a true knight that upon New Year's Day you shall come to the Green Chapel long ere the hour of noon. So stay in your bed tomorrow and rest in my castle. I will up with morning and ride to hunt the fox: so let us make once again our bargain to exchange all the winnings that may be ours to-morrow. For twice have I tried you and found you true; but the next is the third time, and that shall be the best.'

So once more they swore the oath, and while the lord of the castle went forth with his huntsmen and his pack of music-mouthed hounds,[9] Gawain lay asleep, dreaming of the terrible meeting with the Green Knight so close before him. Presently the lady came in, blithe as a bird; she flung up the window so that the clear, frosty sunshine streamed into the room, roused Gawain from his slumbers and claimed of him a kiss.

She was fairer than the sunshine itself that morning, her hair falling each side of

---

8. The eventual founder of a monastery (d. early 8th c.), who lived alone for many years in a forest near Nimes, in the south of France.

9. *Music* here refers to the cry of hounds when they see the object of their chase.

her lovely face, and her neck whiter than the snow gleaming between the fur of her gown. Sweetly she kissed Gawain and chid him for a sluggard.

'Surely you are a very man of ice that you take but one kiss! Or is it that you have a lady waiting for you in Camelot?'

'Not so,' answered Gawain gravely, 'no lady yet has my love. But it may not be yours, for you have a lord already—a far nobler knight than ever I shall be!'

'But this one day we may love,' she said. 'Surely it may be so? Then all my life-days I may remember that Gawain held me in his arms.'

'Nay, for the sake of mine oath of knighthood and the glory of Logres, I may not do so—for such were shame indeed.'

Then she blamed him and besought him, but ever he turned aside her words

courteously, and ever held true to his honour as a knight of Logres should. At last she sighed sweetly, and kissed him a second time, saying: 'Sir Gawain, you are a true knight, the noblest ever. So give me but a gift whereby to remember you, that by thinking of my knight I may lessen my mourning.'

'Alas,' said Gawain, 'I have nothing to give. For I travel without baggage on this dangerous quest.'

'Then I will give you this green lace from my girdle,' said the lady. 'Wear that for my sake at least.'

'It may not be so,' answered Gawain, 'for I cannot be your knight and wear your favour.'

'It is but a little thing,' she said, 'and you may wear it hidden. Take it, I pray you, for it is a magic lace and while a man wears it he may not be slain, not even by all the magic upon earth. But I charge you to hide it, and tell not my lord.'

This proved too great a temptation for Gawain, and, mindful of his ordeal with the Green Knight next day, he took the lace and promised never to reveal it. Then the lady kissed him for the third time, and went quickly away.

That evening the lord of the castle came home from the hunt bearing with him the skin of one fox. In the bright hall where the fire shone warmly and the tables were all laid richly for dinner, Gawain met him merrily:

'I come with my winnings, and I will be the first giver this night!' he cried gaily; and with that he kissed him solemnly three times.

'By my faith,' cried the lord of the castle, 'you are a good merchant indeed: you give me three such kisses—and I have only a foul fox-skin to give you in return!'

Then with laughter and jests they sat down to the feast, and were merrier that night than on any of the others. But Gawain spoke no word of the green lace which the lady had given him.

The day of the New Year came in with storm: bitterly the winds howled and the sleet lashed against the window pane, and Gawain, who had slept but little, rose at the first light. He clothed himself warmly and buckled on his armour, setting the green lace about his waist in hope that its magic might protect him. Then he went forth into the courtyard, the squires brought out Gringalet, well fed and well groomed, and helped him to mount.

'Farewell,' he said to the lord of the castle. 'I thank you for your hospitality, and pray Heaven to bless you. If I might live a while longer I would reward you for your kindness: but greatly I fear that I shall not see another sun.'

The drawbridge was let down, the gate flung wide, and Gawain rode out of the castle, with a squire to guide him. Through the bitter dawning they rode, beneath trees dripping drearily, and across meadows where the wind moaned as it bit them to the bone, and they came to a great valley with cliffs at one side of it, all filled with mist.

'Sir,' said the squire, 'go no further, I beg of you. Near here dwells the Green Knight, a terrible and a cruel man. There is none so fierce or so strong in this land— and no man may stand against him. Over yonder at the Green Chapel it is ever his custom to stay all who pass by, and fight with them, and kill them—for none can escape him. Flee away now—and I will not tell ever that you fled for fear of the terrible Green Knight.'

'I thank you,' said Gawain, 'but I must go forward. I would be a coward and unworthy of knighthood if I fled away now. Therefore, whether I like it or not I must go forward . . . And God knows well how to save His servants if so He wills.'

'Well then,' said the squire, 'your death be your own doing. Go down this path by the cliff, into the deep valley, and upon the left hand, beyond the water, you will find the Green Chapel. Now farewell, noble Gawain, for I dare not come with you further.'

Down the path rode Gawain, and came to the bottom of the valley. No chapel could he see, but only the rugged cliff above him, and high, desolate banks in the distance. But at length he saw, under the dripping trees, a low green mound beside the rushing stream; and he heard a sound as of a scythe upon a grindstone coming from a deep hollow in that mound.

'Ah,' said Gawain. 'This must be the Green Chapel! A very devil's oratory[1] it is, and green indeed—a chapel of mischance! And within it I hear the knight himself, sharpening a weapon to smite me this day. Alas that I must perish at his hands in this cursed spot . . . Yet will I go on boldly, for my duty is so to do.'

Gawain sprang from his horse and strode down to the streamside:

'Who waits here,' he cried, 'to keep tryst with me? I am Gawain, who have come to the Green Chapel as I vowed.'

'Wait but a little,' came a mighty voice out of the hollow beneath the mound. 'When my weapon is sharp, you shall have that which I promised you!'

Presently the Green Knight came out with a new, shining axe in his hand. He was as terrible as ever, with his green face and his green hair, as he strode down the bank and leapt over the wide stream.

'You are welcome, Gawain!' he cried in his great voice. 'Now will I repay the stroke you dealt me at Camelot—and none shall come between us in this lonely valley. Now off with your helmet, and make ready for the blow!'

Then Gawain did as he was bidden, bending his head forward, with his neck bare to the stroke.

'Make ready to strike,' he said quietly to the Green Knight, 'for here I shall stand and do nought to stay the blow.'

The Green Knight swung his axe round so that it whistled, and aimed a terrible stroke with the sharp blade of it: and try how he might, Gawain flinched at the sound of it.

'Ha!' grunted the Green Knight, lowering his axe and leaning on the handle of it:

1. A place of prayer.

'You are surely not Gawain the brave, thus to fear even the whistle of the blade! When you struck off my head in King Arthur's hall I never flinched from your blow.'

'I shrank once,' said Gawain, 'but I shall not a second time—even when *my* head falls to the ground, which I cannot replace as you have yours! Come now, strike quickly, I will not stay you again.'

'Have at you then!' cried the Green Knight, whirling his axe. He smote once more, and once more stayed his hand ere the sharp blade drew blood. But Gawain stirred not a jot, nor trembled in any limb. 'Now you are filled with courage once more,' he cried, 'and so I may smite bravely a brave man. Hold aside your hood a little further, I am about to strike my hardest.'

'Strike away,' said Gawain. 'Why do you talk so much? Are you perhaps afraid thus to smite a defenceless man?'

'Then here is the blow I promised!' cried the Green Knight, swinging his axe for the third time. And now he struck truly, yet aimed with such care that the blade only parted the skin at the side of his neck.

But when Gawain had felt the wound and the blood over his shoulders, he sprang away in an instant, put on his helmet, drew his sword, set his shield before him and said to the Green Knight:

'Now I have borne the blow, and if you strike again it is beyond our bargain and I may defend myself, striking stroke for stroke!'

The Green Knight stood leaning on his axe. 'Gawain,' he said, all the fierceness gone out of his voice, 'you have indeed borne the blow—and no other will I strike you. I hold you released of all claims now. If I had wished it, I might have struck you a crueller stroke, and smitten your head off as you smote off mine. The first blow and the second that struck you not—these were for promises truly kept, for the one kiss and the two kisses that my wife gave you in the castle, and you truly rendered to me. But the third time you failed, and therefore had the wound of me: you gave me the three kisses, but not the green lace. Oh, well I know all that passed between you—she tempted you by my will. Gawain, I hold you to be the noblest, the most faultless knight in all the wide world. Had you yielded to dishonour and shamed your knighthood—then would your head be lying now at my feet. As for the lace, you hid it but for love of your life—and that is a little sin, and for it I pardon you.'

'I am ashamed,' said Gawain, handing him the green lace. 'For cowardice and covetousness I betrayed my oath of knighthood. Cut off my head, Sir knight, for I am indeed unworthy of the Round Table.'

'Come now!' cried the Green Knight, laughing merrily, so that Gawain knew him indeed to be the lord of the castle. 'You have borne your penance, and are quite absolved and forgiven. Take and keep this green lace in memory of this adventure; and return to my castle and end the festival in joy.'

'I must back to Camelot,' said Gawain, 'I may not bide longer. But tell me, noble sir, how comes this enchantment? Who are you that ride in Green and die not when beheaded? How come you to dwell, a noble knight in a fine castle, and also to strike axe-blows, the Green Knight of the Green Chapel?'

'My name is Sir Bernlak, the Knight of the Lake,' answered he. 'And the enchantment comes from Nimue, the Lady of the Lake, the favoured of Merlin.[2] She sent me to Camelot, to test the truth of the renown that is spread abroad concerning the valour of the Knights of the Round Table, and the worth of Logres.'

Then the two knights embraced one another and parted with blessings. Gawain rode back swiftly through the Forest of Wirral, and after many more adventures he

---

2. The magician who, according to many versions of the legend, raised Arthur.

came to Camelot, where King Arthur welcomed him, marvelled at his tale, and set him with honour in his place at the Round Table. And of all the knights who ever sat there, few indeed were so worthy as Gawain.

1953

JEAN FRITZ
b. 1915

Jean Fritz's honest, realistic, and often humorous biographies and historical novels have won her both numerous awards and many young readers. She has focused particularly on the Revolutionary War period of American history, but she has written about significant figures both before and after that era, as well as about her own childhood (*Homesick: My Own Story*, 1982; see the Life Stories section, below, with further biographical information in the headnote there).

In *The Double Life of Pocahontas* (1983), Fritz turns to one of the founding legends of early America. The story of the Indian girl who saved the life of a captured English colonist, and whose generous gifts of food kept many of his fellow colonists from starvation, was treated as legendary from its first appearance in John Smith's *The General History of Virginia, New England and the Summer Isles* (1624). Writing of himself in the third person, Smith describes being seized in late 1607 and finally brought before "the King" himself, Powhatan:

> a long consultation was held, but the conclusion was, two great stones were brought before Powhatan; then as many as could, laid hands on him, dragged him to them, and thereon laid his head and being ready with their clubs to beat out his brains, Pocahontas, the King's dearest daughter, when no entreaty could prevail, got his head in her arms and laid her own upon his to save him from death[.]

Though Pocahontas (a nickname, meaning "naughty or playful one"; her given name was Matoaka) had appeared in earlier versions of Smith's narrative of his captivity, only here does she become the heroine of the encounter. This surely appears to be the stuff of romance, and those were the terms in which American folklore cast their meeting (and the Disney Corporation presented it, in the 1995 animated film *Pocahontas*). The facts, not surprisingly, are more complex and more interesting. Smith fails to make clear in the above account that Pocahontas is only about twelve, a point he mentions in a 1616 letter praising her to Queen Anne. Moreover, what he perceived as a threat to his life and subsequent rescue may well have been part of a traditional ceremony to adopt outsiders into the tribe.

The later events of Pocahontas's life added to her legend: she was married to a member of the Potomac tribe in 1610, kidnapped in 1612 by a captain in the colony seeking ransom from her father, instructed in Christianity, and married (with her father's permission) to a widowed colonist, John Rolfe, in 1614—an act that did much to reduce tensions between the Native Americans and English. Brought to London in 1616 (along with her husband, their young son, and a number of Algonquians) by a leader of the colony seeking publicity and greater funding for the Virginia Company, Pocahontas—now called Rebecca—was presented at court and to the best of society, and again saw John Smith; she died in England in 1617.

Fritz's portrayal of Pocahontas is one of the few that presents her relationship with John Smith realistically and depicts the political machinations behind the settlement of Jamestown. The key themes of colonization, exploitation, and trust are already present in *The Double Life*'s first chapter, and it is clear that Pocahontas's life will be shaped by how different men try to use her and by her own exceptional, courageous spirit. In this regard, Fritz succeeds in offering a Pocahontas who is more historically "authentic" than most, and thus a new legend that can serve as a corrective to the old.

From The Double Life of Pocahontas

Pocahontas had every reason to be happy. It was the budding time of the year; who would not be happy? The world was new-green, cherry trees were afroth, and strawberries, like sweet red secrets, fattened on the ground. At first birdcall, Pocahontas would run splashing into the river, and along with the others in the village she would wait to greet the Sun as it rose.

Together they would watch the sky turn from gray to pink, to gold. Then suddenly they would shout. There it came! And was it not a wonder that always it returned again and yet again? All the people welcomed it, scattering sacred tobacco into a circle, lifting up their hands and singing to please their god, Okee, in the way their priests had taught them. One must never forget Okee, for it was He who held danger in his hands—lightning, floods, drought, sickness, war.

Indeed, Pocahontas could hardly help but be happy. At eleven, she was the right age for happiness. Still young enough to romp with the children, yet old enough to join the dance of unmarried girls. And how she danced—whirling and stamping and shouting until her breath was whisked into the wind, until she had grown wings like a bird, until she had become sister to the trees, until she was at one with everything that lived and grew. With the world itself, round like a plate under the sky. And in the center of the plate, there was her father, the great Chief Powhatan,[1] seated high, twelve mats under him, raccoon robe around him with tails dangling. And beside him, there was Pocahontas herself, for was she not her father's favorite? Did he not say that Pocahontas was as dear to him as his own life? So of course Pocahontas was happy.

Around the edges of the world plate, Pocahontas knew, were unfriendly tribes. And somewhere on the far, far rim beyond the waters there were strangers from a land she could not picture at all. Sometimes these strangers came to her father's kingdom, coat-wearing men with hair on their faces. The last time, these men had kidnapped a chief's son and killed a chief, but since then the geese had flown north three times and they had not come back. Perhaps they would not come again.

There was no way, of course, for Pocahontas to know that at that very moment three English ships with one hundred and four such coat-wearing men were approaching Chesapeake Bay. No one told these men that the land was taken, that this was Powhatan's kingdom, but even if they had, the English would not have cared. Naked savages, they would have said—they were like herds of deer. How could they legally own land? The world was made for civilized people, for people who wouldn't let the land go to waste, for people who knew the right way to live. In other words, for Christians.

The year, according to the Christian calendar, was 1607, and these Christians were here to stay. They had already named this place Virginia,[2] and they meant to make it theirs. Still mad at themselves for having said No to Christopher Columbus[3] when they might have said Yes and beaten the Spanish to the New World, they were

---

1. Chief of the Powhatan tribe (d. 1618) and leader of the Powhatan Confederacy that encompassed some thirty Algonquian peoples in the Tidewater area of Virginia and on the eastern shore of Chesapeake Bay; his personal name was Wahunsonacock.
2. In honor of "the Virgin Queen," Queen Elizabeth I (1533–1603; r. 1558–1603). The first patent

for colonizing a region that stretched from Florida to Canada was granted by her in 1584; it was later split into two parts, managed by different sets of investors.
3. Italian-born explorer (1451–1506) who sought royal support to sponsor his expedition to sail west to find a route to Asia. After John (or João) II, King of Portugal, rejected his proposal in 1484, he

going to make up for lost time. They had their directions from London. They were to find gold. And a shortcut to the other ocean. They were to be friendly to the natives and turn them into Christians. Finally, they were to provide goods that would make money for England.

They were told to build their houses in straight lines. And when they wrote home, they were to write cheerful letters.

By the time that the English reached Chesapeake Bay (April 26, 1607), however, they had little cheerful to say. After four months of being cooped up on shipboard, the one hundred and four passengers were sick to death of each other. John Smith, a twenty-seven-year-old adventurer, could not abide Master Edward Wingfield (who would be president of the ruling council) with his high and mighty airs. In turn Master Wingfield heartily disliked John Smith, an upstart who acted as if he knew it all. Both men were suspicious of Captain Gabriel Archer, a born troublemaker, and both were impatient with Captain John Ratcliffe, who wanted to go home when the seas became too rough. Poor Robert Hunt, the preacher, tried to keep peace among the passengers, but it was hard, especially since he was seasick so often. John Smith reported that he made "wild vomits into the black night." One of the few men who seemed to command the respect of all was one-armed Captain Christopher Newport, who was in charge of the expedition while at sea. Everyone thought it was lucky that his name was Christopher, like Christopher Columbus.

But once they had landed and started exploring, the spirits of the men rose. What a paradise Virginia was! Raccoons as big as foxes, they reported. Possums like month-old pigs. Vines the size of a man's thigh. Strawberries four times bigger than English strawberries, and oysters thick as stones. Best of all, there were rocks that sparkled. Gold, John Martin said, and since his father was a goldsmith, he should know. And up the river there was a two-mile-long peninsula, a perfect place to settle. They tied their ships up to the trees and called the place Jamestown in honor of their king[4] at home.

There were also natives whom the English called "savages." They encountered them when they first went ashore. After their long trip, the men were so glad to stretch their legs, they stayed until dark, not noticing the five Indians creeping on hands and knees through the tall grass, their bows in their mouths. Then all at once the air was filled with arrows. Captain Archer was shot in both hands; a sailor was wounded.

Then the English fired their guns, and the natives darted back to the woods.

John Smith was the one who seemed to know most about handling the natives. At least he claimed he did. Before joining this expedition, he had fought the Turks in Europe.[5] He'd been captured, made a slave, and had so many narrow escapes that he figured he understood "savages" pretty well. Gentleness was not the way to deal with them, he said. The English should show strength; they should rely on fear, not love, to keep peace. This was only common sense, but John was afraid there wasn't much common sense among these settlers.

The English built a fort on their peninsula, and as they settled down they found there were natives all around them. Many seemed friendly, glad to exchange corn for tiny bells and pretty glass beads. (Pocahontas would love those beads.) When the

---

unsuccessfully turned to King Henry VII of England; it was finally approved by King Ferdinand and Queen Isabella of Castile in 1492.
4. James I (1566–1625; r. 1603–25). Jamestown was located on the James River, not far from present-day Williamsburg, Virginia.
5. Smith (1580–1631) fought in Hungary with the Austrians in their war against the Turks (1593–1606); captured and enslaved in 1601, he escaped in 1604.

English clapped their hands over their hearts in the sign of friendship, the natives would lower their bows, give two shouts of welcome, and offer food and pipes of tobacco. Once a chieftain, wearing a crown of bear's hair, played a flute. They even told the English that, yes, the ocean they were looking for[6] was just ahead. Up the river and beyond the falls.

Yet other Indians were not one bit friendly. Once they killed an English boy and shot an arrow right through President Wingfield's beard. Often they lay in the tall grass outside the English fort, waiting for someone to come through the gate. Not even a dog could run out safely. Once one did and had forty arrows shot into his body.

But all the Indians were curious. Especially Powhatan. What were the strangers doing here? Did they mean to stay? When after two months (on June 22) Captain Newport and two ships sailed back to England for supplies, the Indians were wild with curiosity. Where were the ships going? What did it mean?

Powhatan's brother, Opechancanough, chief of the Pamunkeys, one of Powhatan's most important tribes, sent a messenger to Jamestown.

Where had the ships gone? he wanted to know.

Oh, not far. Just south a little way, the settlers answered.

A few days later Powhatan himself sent messengers. Where were the ships? they asked.

Nearby, they were told.

Perhaps the strangers would leave soon, Powhatan thought. All they had done here was to trade for corn and more corn and still more corn. Perhaps in their country there was no land for growing corn. So when they had enough food, maybe they would go home. In the meantime he might get guns from the strangers. How he marveled at the power of guns! How he loved their thunderclaps! How he longed for guns of his own!

It would be months, however, before either Powhatan or Pocahontas would meet any strangers face to face. In the meantime Pocahontas went about her life as usual in the village of Werowocomoco[7] where she lived, greeting the Sun as it rose, honoring it again as it left the world in the evening.

In Jamestown the settlers held their own ceremonies. Twice a day their preacher, Robert Hunt, read a prayer written especially for the colonists by King James of England. They prayed that the "savages" would be converted to Christianity. How else, they asked themselves, could they get along in the New World?

But as the summer wore on, all the settlers really wanted was to stay alive. The Indians had run out of corn, and, until Captain Newport returned from England with fresh supplies, the settlers had nothing to eat but half a pint of wheat every day and half a pint of wormy barley boiled in water. All they had to drink was water from the river, salty at high tide, slimy at low tide. They quit trying to hunt or fish because whenever they left the fort, arrows came flying out of the tall grass. So it was no wonder that one after another the settlers fell sick and one after another they died.

By the end of the summer fifty men, almost half the colony, had died and the rest were bickering and quarreling with each other. On one thing, however, they agreed: President Wingfield was wicked. They accused him of hoarding food for himself, of liking the Spaniards (England's enemy), of wanting to be a king, and of being an

6. I.e., the Pacific (the search for a navigable river passage to the Pacific continued for another two centuries).

7. Located on the north bank of the York River, about 12 miles northeast of Jamestown.

atheist since, as far as anyone could see, he didn't own a Bible. Moreover, he wouldn't work and he didn't know how to get others to work. In all this time none of their houses had been finished and hardly anything had been planted. So Edward Wingfield was removed as president. Captain Ratcliffe was elected in his place, and John Smith was put in charge of what went on outside the fort.

Meanwhile in Powhatan's kingdom the corn had ripened and the people were celebrating their harvest. There were games—football (only the foot was allowed to touch the ball), a stickball game (like lacrosse), contests of racing, catching, leaping. There was feasting and dancing. Bonfires blazed over the country while men, women, and children danced around the fires, shaking rattles and clapping hands. The men sang songs about the brave things they would do now that their work was done.

One of the first things they decided to do was to trade. Who knew what those hungry settlers might be willing to part with now? Perhaps a copper kettle (a prize indeed). Perhaps a sword or two. Perhaps even a gun. So off to Jamestown they went, loaded down with corn, fruit, pumpkin, squash, turkey—everything a hungry man would dream of. The settlers, of course, gobbled up everything that the Indians brought, and in return they gave the Indians beads and bells, some copper, a hatchet or two. But no guns. John Smith said Indians should never be given a chance even to handle a gun.

Along with the food, one of the Indians gave the settlers a piece of advice. Cut down that long grass outside the fort, he said.

Now that there was corn again, John Smith began to make trading trips up the river and to go on explorations. Maybe he'd find gold, maybe that other ocean. Who knew what he might find in this wonderful land? As young as he was, John was well traveled. Not only had he fought in every war he could find, he had walked, ridden, hitchhiked over much of Europe, but no place had ever moved him as this one did. He could not round the bend of a river without feeling excited at the newness, the wildness, the bigness of this world. What luck it was that he was young and that he was here and that he had his whole life to give to it. Wherever he went, he made maps, carefully drawing in the winding course of rivers that had never been drawn before, giving names to places that had never had English names.

In December he and nine other men were on such an expedition when they were surprised by a hunting party of Pamunkey Indians. At the moment John and an Indian guide were walking inland and didn't know that back on the riverbank two Englishmen had been killed. (The rest got away.) John knew nothing of the danger until all at once arrows were flying from all directions. He grabbed his Indian guide, buckled the Indian's arm to his own with a garter, and, using him as a shield, he held the Indian in front of him with one hand and held his pistol with the other.

Slowly the Indians encircled him—two hundred of them—while John fired his pistol, killing two in short order. The most excited person there, of course, was the Indian guide who stood between the arrows and the bullets. He called frantically to the hunters to put away their arrows. This man was a chief, he said; *he was a chief.* Indians did not kill a chief carelessly. Not right away. Not without more authority. So the hunters agreed to lay down their bows if the English chief would give up his gun.

But John Smith wouldn't. Still holding on to his guide, he brandished his pistol as he began backing toward the river. At least he supposed he was going toward the river. Instead he and his guide suddenly fell into a swamp, such a deep "oozy" swamp there was no way to get out without help. Yet how could John Smith get help and still hold on to his gun? Obviously he couldn't. So, much as he hated to, he threw his pistol on the ground and let the Indians pull him to dry land and make him their captive. After that, for weeks he was marched across the country to be displayed to one village after another, to meet chiefs, to be examined by priests. The natives were all interested in the same questions: What were the English doing here? How long would they stay? When would their big chief, the man with one arm, be back? In the end John Smith was taken to Werowocomoco to see Powhatan, who would decide what was to be done with him.

Long before he arrived the people at Werowocomoco knew about him. Pocahontas would have heard about his magic disc with its arrow that swung around and pointed in one direction no matter how it was turned or shaken.[8] She would have learned that this stranger said the world was round. Not round like a plate but round like a ball. Like an apple. Everyone agreed that he was a man with much magic.

What would happen to him? Pocahontas knew her father could have him killed. Piece by piece, perhaps. Or by burning. Pocahontas had watched both ways. But sometimes a captive was adopted into a tribe. First he would be purified in a ceremony that looked as if the captive would be killed, but instead at the last minute he would seem to be saved by a member of the tribe, a woman usually, to whom he would forever be kin.

Pocahontas was present in her father's great longhouse when John Smith arrived, a short, straight-standing man with a furry beard and bright, fearless eyes. He marched past two hundred of Powhatan's bodyguards, all glaring at him, but John Smith showed no fear. Not even before Powhatan himself who sat high on his matted throne—a large, stately figure, every inch a king.

Of course Pocahontas was impressed by this short stranger. Indians always admired courage, and, according to all reports, this man had not only stood up alone to two hundred warriors, he had struck fear into their hearts. Not just by his gun but by himself. By his very boldness. And here he was striding into an enemy stronghold, into her father's court, without the slightest sign that he felt danger. She watched him wash his hands in the water that was brought to him and dry them on feathers as if this was his daily custom. And when Powhatan questioned him, she marveled that he did not flinch and quail as so many prisoners did. No, he spoke out firmly.

Why had the English come? Powhatan wanted to know.

It was all a mistake, John Smith said. They had been fighting their enemy, the Spanish, and had been blown here by a storm.

Why were they staying?

Oh, they were just waiting for Captain Newport to come back. Then they'd go home.

Perhaps Powhatan had already decided what to do with John Smith; perhaps he decided later. In any case, he had guns on his mind. And if he adopted John Smith into the tribe, John would be required to give him gifts. What better gift than guns? A couple of cannon to start off with, maybe. Then, as his mind ran on, Powhatan may have caught the eye of Pocahontas. She looked so interested, eager—well, why not let her be the man's sponsor?

All John Smith knew, however, was that a fire was being lighted. The priests were wailing and calling on their gods as if they were preparing for a sacrifice. Powhatan was conferring with his chiefs. Then he gave an order and John was dragged forward and forced to lay his head on two huge stones. Tall men stood around him with raised clubs, and at any moment John expected to have his brains bashed out.

8. I.e., a compass.

Suddenly a little girl rushed up to him. She put his head in her arms and begged for his life. Maybe this was prearranged; maybe not. No one can know for sure, but the important thing was: John was saved. The men with the clubs drew back and John was helped to his feet. Of course he was delighted to have his brains intact. And pleased to make the acquaintance of Pocahontas, who had been his savior.

But she was more than that. In her view, she was his sister now. He was her brother, and Powhatan was father to them both. He could live at Werowocomoco, as adopted members of a family often did. He could play games with her, string beads, and make hatchets for her father. They had a special kinship, and if he stayed he would be her countryman.

Did he understand?

Powhatan also wanted to make sure that John Smith understood he'd been adopted into the tribe. To make it seem official, Powhatan and two hundred of his warriors painted themselves black and descended on John Smith one night. Powhatan explained that John Smith was not only Powhatan's adopted son, he was a chief. Like all his chiefs, he would be expected to give Powhatan gifts. What Powhatan wanted right now were two thunder weapons (cannon) and a millstone for grinding corn. Rawhunt (Powhatan's lieutenant) and twelve guards would go to Jamestown with John Smith to bring back the gifts.

John Smith agreed. Pocahontas would not have let him go without saying goodbye, and John would have made a formal farewell to Powhatan, whom he gladly called "father."

Once at the settlement, John showed Rawhunt the millstone. Rawhunt's body was deformed so that he did not expect to move the millstone himself, but none of the twelve guards could move it, either.

Well, there were the cannon, John Smith pointed out. Rawhunt knew how much Powhatan was counting on those cannon, so he urged the guards to try hard, to use every muscle. But it was no use. Each cannon weighed between 3,000 and 4,500 pounds.

It was too bad, John said, that the Indians couldn't take the cannon home. He'd give them other gifts instead. He gathered up some trinkets, bells, baubles of glass and copper.

But Powhatan was expecting thunder.

No thunder, John said.

So the Indians went home, disgruntled, while John Smith, a free man again after six weeks of captivity, walked happily into Jamestown to report to the council on his narrow escape.

He saw at once that Gabriel Archer had taken his place on the council. He also saw that Archer and Ratcliffe, obviously into some mischief or other, were upset to have him back. Indeed, as he soon found out, he was not a free man, after all.

He was under arrest, Archer told him.

Arrest! For what?

Murder.

Whose murder?

The murder of those two men in his party who had been killed by the Indians. He had been responsible for them, hadn't he? He had *let* them get killed. So he was guilty.

Ratcliffe, who always agreed with Archer, chimed in. Captain Smith knew what the Bible said, didn't he? "An eye for an eye." So, as president of the council, Ratcliffe sentenced John Smith to death. He would be executed the next morning.

Put under guard, John Smith fumed. To have escaped the Indians, only to be put to death by his own people! He had always boasted that he was a lucky fellow, but where was his luck now?

Actually, luck was at that very moment gliding toward him up the river. That same evening, just in the nick of time, Captain Newport arrived back from England. He tied his ship up at Jamestown, and as soon as he heard the news he persuaded the council members to set John Smith free and to remove Captain Archer from the council.

Of course the natives had seen Captain Newport arrive. Like the others, Pocahontas would have wondered. Did this mean the strangers would leave now? John Smith too? In a few days they had more news. Captain Newport had brought eighty new settlers with him. It looked as if they meant to stay.

Powhatan would have felt one way about this. Pocahontas might have felt another.

1983

JULIUS LESTER
b. 1939

Because Julius Lester is one of the foremost contemporary writers of fiction, biographies, and folktales that convey a sense of black American history to children (see his "Jack and the Devil's Daughter" in the Fairy Tales section, above, with further biographical information in the headnote there), his decision to retell the story of John Henry seems almost inevitable: it is probably the best known of all African American legends. Almost nothing is known about the historical John Henry, who apparently was one of the vast number of former slaves who could find only dangerous, backbreaking, ill-paid work after the Civil War. He was a steel driver, helping to make tunnels by hammering a steel shaft into stone to form the hole into which explosives were packed, and ballads and work songs ("hammer songs") about his feats of superhuman strength spread quickly across the country as the railroads expanded.

Most historians believe that John Henry's race against the steam-powered drill, if it actually took place, occurred in the early 1870s at Big Bend Mountain in Talcott, West Virginia, where today a statue representing him stands atop the mountain that took three years and hundreds of lives to tunnel through. Some versions of the ballad depict John Henry as a baby on his father's or mother's knee predicting that the C&O (Chesapeake and Ohio) tunnel would be the death of him. The setting is unimportant, however; what matters is his blend of strength, determination, and pride, which heartened first railroad workers and then prisoners as they sang of John Henry. As stanzas were added and altered, the story appeared in almost endless variations, which have now been recorded hundreds of times. One of the earliest printed versions was a broadside published by W. T. Blankenship around 1900. It begins:

John Henry was a railroad man,
He worked from six 'till five,
"Raise 'em up bullies and let 'em drop down,
I'll beat you to the bottom or die."

John Henry said to his captain:
"You are nothing but a common man
Before that steam drill shall beat me down,
I'll die with my hammer in my hand."

And although he strikes the shaft with incredible speed—he explains away a sound like the mountains caving in with "That's my hammer you hear in the wind" —his boast is ultimately an accurate prediction:

John Henry was hammering on the right side,
The big steam drill on the left,
Before that steam drill could beat him down,
He hammered his fool self to death.

In this ballad, as was usually the case, John Henry has a young wife; often the songs about him ended with her display of grief and faithfulness:

> John Henry had a little woman,
> Her name was Pollie Ann,
> He hugged and kissed her just before he died,
> Saying, "Pollie, do the very best you can."

> . . . .

> They carried John Henry to that new burying
>   ground
> His wife all dressed in blue,
> She laid her hand on John Henry's cold face,
> "John Henry I've been true to you."

Countless ballads and stories spread in the twentieth century telling of John Henry's extraordinary birth and growth, his travels throughout the South as a railroad worker, his challenge to the steam-powered drill that set man against machine, and his victory that is also a sacrificial death. Julius Lester borrows both from earlier versions and from traditional folktales in elaborating on his hero's childhood. He focuses on John Henry's generous heart and desire to help people in difficulties, emphasizing how inspirational a figure who lives "well" can be. In their determination to live well and wield a hammer against seemingly impossible odds, Lester links John Henry and Martin Luther King Jr. That connection adds to the poignance of John Henry's burial in Washington (a detail found in some ballads), where the dream symbolized by his rainbow must be kept alive.

John Henry

There are countless historical personages who do not engage us. Yet John Henry continues to move us by his affirmation of something triumphant which we hope is in all of us. After Phyllis Fogelman approached me to write a text based on the John Henry legend that Jerry Pinkney[1] was researching and planning to illustrate, I called Jerry and asked him what he saw in John Henry. Jerry responded by talking about the transcendent quality of John Henry's humanity. As he talked, the image of Martin Luther King Jr.[2] came to me, and it was then I knew I wanted to do the book.

This retelling is the result of the coming together of the creative spirits of Jerry Pinkney, those from whose lives came the song "John Henry," and myself. I'm still not certain what the connection is between John Henry and King. However, I suspect it is the connection all of us feel to both figures—namely, to have the courage to hammer until our hearts break and to leave our mourners smiling in their tears. J.L.

JOHN HENRY

You have probably never heard of John Henry. Or maybe you heard about him but don't know the ins and outs of his comings and goings. Well, that's why I'm going to tell you about him.

When John Henry was born, birds came from everywhere to see him. The bears and panthers and moose and deer and rabbits and squirrels and even a unicorn came out of the woods to see him. And instead of the sun tending to his business and going

---

1. American illustrator (b. 1939), best known for work that pays tribute to his African American heritage. His illustrations of Lester's story are not included here.

2. American minister and activist (1929–1968), the leader most identified with the nonviolent civil rights movement of the 1960s.

to bed, it was peeping out from behind the moon's skirts trying to get a glimpse of the new baby.

Before long the mama and papa come out on the porch to show off their brand-new baby. The birds "oooooohed" and the animals "aaaaaaahed" at how handsome the baby was.

Somewhere in the middle of one of the "ooooooohs," or maybe it was on the backside of one of the "aaaaaaaahs," that baby jumped out of his mama's arms and started growing.

He grew and he grew and he grew. He grew until his head and shoulders busted through the roof which was over the porch. John Henry thought that was the funniest thing in the world. He laughed so loud, the sun got scared. It scurried from behind the moon's skirts and went to bed, which is where it should've been all the while.

The next morning John Henry was up at sunrise. The sun wasn't. He was tired and had decided to sleep in. John Henry wasn't going to have none of that. He hollered up into the sky, "Get up from there! I got things to do and I need light to do 'em by."

The sun yawned, washed its face, flossed and brushed its teeth, and hurried up over the horizon.

That day John Henry helped his papa rebuild the porch he had busted through, added a wing onto the house with an indoor swimming pool and one of them jacutzis.[3] After lunch he chopped down an acre of trees and split them into fireplace logs and still had time for a nap before supper.

The next day John Henry went to town. He met up with the meanest man in the state, Ferret-Faced Freddy, sitting on his big white horse. You know what he was doing? He was thinking of mean things to do. Ferret-Faced Freddy was so mean, he cried if he had a nice thought.

John Henry said, "Freddy, I'll make you a bet. Let's have a race. You on your horse. Me on my legs. If you and your horse win, you can work me as hard as you want for a whole year. If I win, you have to be nice for a year."

Ferret-Faced Freddy laughed an evil laugh. "It's a deal, John Henry." His voice sounded like bat wings on tombstones.

The next morning folks lined up all along the way the race would go. John Henry was ready. Ferret-Faced Freddy and his horse were ready.

BANG! The race was on.

My great-granddaddy's brother's cousin's sister-in-law's uncle's aunt was there that morning. She said everybody saw Ferret-Faced Freddy ride by on his big white horse and they were sho' 'nuf moving. Didn't nobody see John Henry. That's because he was so fast, the wind was out of breath trying to keep up with him. When Ferret-Faced Freddy crossed the finish line, John Henry was already on the other side, sitting in a rocking chair and drinking a soda mom.[4]

After that Ferret-Faced Freddy was so nice, everybody called him Frederick the Friendly.

John Henry decided it was time for him to go on down the big road. He went home and told his mama and daddy good-bye.

His daddy said, "You got to have something to make your way in the world with, Son. These belonged to your granddaddy." And he gave him two twenty-pound sledge-hammers with four-foot handles made of whale bone.

A day or so later, John Henry saw a crew building a road. At least, that's what they were doing until they came on a boulder right smack-dab where the road was sup-

---

3. I.e., Jacuzzis, or whirlpool baths.   4. I.e., a soda pop, or soda.

posed to go. This was no ordinary boulder. It was as hard as anger and so big around, it took half a week for a tall man to walk from one side to the other.

John Henry offered to lend them a hand.

"That's all right. We'll put some dynamite to it."

John Henry smiled to himself. "Whatever you say."

The road crew planted dynamite all around the rock and set it off.

KERBOOM BLAMMITY-
BLAMMITY BOOMBOOM
BANGBOOMBANG!!!

That dynamite made so much racket, the Almighty looked over the parapets of Heaven and hollered, "It's getting too noisy down there." The dynamite kicked up so much dirt and dust, it got dark. The moon thought night had caught her napping and she hurried out so fast, she almost bumped into the sun who was still climbing the steep hill toward noontime.

When all the commotion from the dynamite was over, the road crew was amazed. The boulder was still there. In fact, the dynamite hadn't knocked even a chip off it.

The crew didn't know what to do. Then they heard a rumbling noise. They looked around. It was John Henry, laughing. He said, "If you gentlemen would give me a little room, I got some work to do."

"Don't see how you can do what dynamite couldn't," said the boss of the crew.

John Henry chuckled. "Just watch me." He swung one of his hammers round and round his head. It made such a wind that leaves blew off the trees and birds fell out of the sky.

RINGGGGGG!

The hammer hit the boulder. That boulder shivered like you do on a cold winter morning when it looks like the school bus is never going to come.

RINGGGGGG!

The boulder shivered like the morning when freedom came to the slaves.

John Henry picked up his other hammer. He swung one hammer in a circle over his head. As soon as it hit the rock—RINGGGG!—the hammer in his left hand started to make a circle and—RINGGGG! Soon the RINGGGG! of one hammer followed the RINGGGG! of the other one so closely, it sounded like they were falling at the same time.

RINGGGG!RINGGGG!
RINGGGG!RINGGGG!

Chips and dust were flying from the boulder so fast that John Henry vanished from sight. But you could still hear his hammers—RINGGGG!RINGGGG!

The air seemed to be dancing to the rhythm of his hammers. The boss of the road crew looked up. His mouth dropped open. He pointed into the sky.

There, in the air above the boulder, was a rainbow. John Henry was swinging the hammers so fast, he was making a rainbow around his shoulders. It was shining and shimmering in the dust and grit like hope that never dies. John Henry started singing:

> I got a rainbow
> RINGGGG!RINGGGG!
> Tied round my shoulder
> RINGGGG!RINGGGG!
> It ain't gon' rain,

No, it ain't gon' rain.
RINGGGG!RINGGGG!

John Henry sang and he hammered and the air danced and the rainbow shimmered and the earth shook and rolled from the blows of the hammer. Finally it was quiet. Slowly the dust cleared.

Folks could not believe their eyes. The boulder was gone. In its place was the prettiest and straightest road they had ever seen. Not only had John Henry pulverized the boulder into pebbles, he had finished building the road.

In the distance where the new road connected to the main one, the road crew saw John Henry waving good-bye, a hammer on each shoulder, the rainbow draped around him like love.

John Henry went on his way. He had heard that any man good with a hammer could find work building the Chesapeake and Ohio Railroad through West Virginia. That was where he had been going when he stopped to build the road.

The next day John Henry arrived at the railroad. However, work had stopped. The railroad tracks had to go through a mountain, and such a mountain. Next to it even John Henry felt small.

But a worker told John Henry about a new machine they were going to use to tunnel through the mountain. It was called a steam drill. "It can hammer faster and harder than ten men and it never has to stop and rest."

The next day the boss arrived with the steam drill. John Henry said to him, "Let's have a contest. Your steam drill against me and my hammers."

The man laughed. "I've heard you're the best there ever was, John Henry. But even you can't outhammer a machine."

"Let's find out," John Henry answered.

Boss shrugged. "Don't make me no never mind. You start on the other side of the mountain. I'll start the steam drill over here. Whoever gets to the middle first is the winner."

The next morning all was still. The birds weren't singing and the roosters weren't crowing. When the sun didn't hear the rooster, he wondered if something was wrong. So he rose a couple of minutes early to see.

What he saw was a mountain as big as hurt feelings. On one side was a big machine hooked up to hoses. It was belching smoke and steam. As the machine attacked the mountain, rocks and dirt and underbrush flew into the air. On the other side was John Henry. Next to the mountain he didn't look much bigger than a wish that wasn't going to come true.

He had a twenty-pound hammer in each hand and muscles hard as wisdom in each arm. As he swung them through the air, they shone like silver, and when the hammers hit the rock, they rang like gold. Before long, tongues of fire leaped out with each blow.

On the other side the boss of the steam drill felt the mountain shudder. He got scared and hollered, "I believe this mountain is caving in!"

From the darkness inside the mountain came a deep voice: "It's just my hammers sucking wind. Just my hammers sucking wind." There wasn't enough room inside the tunnel for the rainbow, so it wrapped itself around the mountain on the side where John Henry was.

All through the night John Henry and the steam drill went at it. In the light from the tongues of fire shooting out of the tunnel from John Henry's hammer blows, folks could see the rainbow wrapped around the mountain like a shawl.

The sun came up extra early the next morning to see who was winning. Just as it did, John Henry broke through and met the steam drill. The boss of the steam drill was flabbergasted. John Henry had come a mile and a quarter. The steam drill had only come a quarter.

Folks were cheering and yelling, "John Henry! John Henry!"

John Henry walked out of the tunnel into the sunlight, raised his arms over his head, a hammer in each hand. The rainbow slid off the mountain and around his shoulders.

With a smile John Henry's eyes closed, and slowly he fell to the ground. John Henry was dead. He had hammered so hard and so fast and so long that his big heart had burst.

Everybody was silent for a minute. Then came the sound of soft crying. Some said it came from the moon. Another one said she saw the sun shed a tear.

Then something strange happened. Afterward folks swore the rainbow whispered it. I don't know. But whether it was a whisper or a thought, everyone had the same knowing at the same moment: "Dying ain't important. Everybody does that. What matters is how well you do your living."

First one person started clapping. Then another, and another. Soon everybody was clapping.

The next morning the sun got everybody up early to say good-bye to John Henry. They put him on a flatbed railroad car, and the train made its way slowly out of the mountains. All along the way folks lined both sides of the track, and they were cheering and shouting through their tears:

"John Henry! John Henry!"

John Henry's body was taken to Washington, D.C.

Some say he was buried on the White House lawn late one night while the President and the Mrs. President was asleep.

I don't know about none of that. What I do know is this: If you walk by the White House late at night, stand real still, and listen real closely, folks say you just might hear a deep voice singing:

> I got a rainbow
> RINGGGG!RINGGGG!
> Tied round my shoulder
> RINGGGG!RINGGGG!
> It ain't gon' rain,
> No, it ain't gon' rain.
> RINGGGG!RINGGGG!

1994

MARY POPE OSBORNE
b. 1949

The prolific and multitalented writer Mary Pope Osborne has often been drawn to American folktales and legends, rewritting them in unusual ways for young readers. Born in Fort Sill, Oklahoma, Mary Pope grew up on a series of army posts (including a three-year stay in Austria) until her father retired and the family settled in North Carolina. She enrolled at the University of North Carolina at Chapel Hill two years later. After earning a B.A. in religion in 1971, she traveled throughout the world and held a series of jobs. In 1976 she married John Osborne, an actor, and they eventually settled in New York City.

Osborne's first publication was *Run, Run as Fast as You Can* (1982), a young adult book whose protagonist grapples with both the social hierarchy at school and the terminal illness of her younger brother. Osborne has written several other young adult novels focusing on adolescents' conflicts and problems, but since the late 1980s she has concentrated on younger readers. Her works for beginning readers include picture books, such as *Mo to the Rescue* (1985), featuring the good-hearted sheriff Mo; feminist revisions of fairy tales, such as *Kate and the Beanstalk* (2000); and the extremely popular Magic Tree House series (more than thirty volumes, beginning with *Dinosaurs before Dark*, 1992), in which a brother and sister magically time-travel to various destinations.

Osborne's fascination with history, obvious from the detailed research she undertakes for each Tree House volume, is even clearer in her books for middle readers, which include several biographies, such as *The Many Lives of Benjamin Franklin* (1990), and historical novels, such as her account of Kit Carson's daughter, *Adaline Falling Star* (2000). In addition, she has written several books in Scholastic Books' Dear America and My America series, which depict events of American history through a teenage girl's diary (e.g., *My Secret War: The World War II Diary of Madeline Beck*, 2000).

Because she is also interested in myths (and has published such works as *Favorite Greek Myths*, 1989), it is hardly surprising that Osborne sometimes mixes myth and history to retell legends. Particularly noteworthy is her collection *American Tall Tales* (1991), which contains stories about figures both well-known, such as Paul Bunyan and Johnny Appleseed, and less familiar, such as Stormalong, and Sally Ann Thunder Ann Whirlwind. She explains in her introduction that she sought to create a kind of map of nineteenth-century America, using characters who engaged in the different occupations required in the country's development, and she chose her words carefully:

> I found it disheartening to come across stories that derided African Americans, Native Americans, women, and animals. And considering our environmental problems today, I was less than enthusiastic about the goal of conquering the wilderness at all costs. Therefore, I decided I would attempt to bring out the more vulnerable and compassionate side of the tall-tale characters in my retellings. I sought to revitalize the stories' essential spirit of gargantuan physical courage and absurd humor, de-emphasizing incidents that would seem cruel or insensitive to today's readers.

In "Davy Crockett," of course, Osborne faced a challenge because the real David Crockett (1786–1836) is so controversial and so emblematic of the rough-and-tumble backwoods hero. He rose to fame in Tennessee as a hunter and Indian fighter, and his folksy humor helped him win election to the state legislature and then to Congress. He was regarded as cunning and uncouth, honest and courageous, and his death defending the Alamo won him lasting fame. Osborne adds to the legend, for in her version the good-natured, boasting Crockett rises to become a hero who saves the world.

MARY POPE
OSBORNE

Davy Crockett

NOTES ON THE STORY

The real Davy Crockett was a backwoodsman born in the mountains of Tennessee in 1786. At that time the settlers in the backwoods of Tennessee and Kentucky lived rugged lives devoted to hunting, trapping, clearing the land, and building homesteads. When Davy ran for Congress in 1827, he became famous for satirizing the difficult lives of these frontier men and women. He gained further legendary status after he died at the Alamo in 1836, fighting for Texas in its struggle for independence from Mexico.

Following Davy Crockett's death, a series of small paperbound books were published that contained comically exaggerated tales and woodcuts about his early life. Called the Davy Crockett Almanacks, these books included stories and sayings of the time, and although no one knows who wrote these first American "tall tales," they are still celebrated for their wit and storytelling. Newspapers, songs, plays, television shows, and films have further expanded the Crockett legend, but the following story is derived mostly from these original almanacs.

DAVY CROCKETT

An extraordinary event once occurred in the land of Tennessee. A comet shot out of the sky like a ball of fox fire. But when the comet hit the top of a Tennessee mountain, a baby boy tumbled off and landed upright on his feet. His name was *Davy Crockett.*

That's the same Davy who could carry thunder in his fist and fling lightning from his fingers. That's the same Davy who liked to holler, "I can slide down the slippery ends of rainbows! I'm half horse, half alligator, and a bit of snapping turtle! I can outrun, outlick, and outholler any ring-tailed roarer east of the Mississippi!"

The truth is Davy Crockett did seem to be half varmint—just as every varmint seemed to be half Crockett. Anyone could see that he walked like an ox, ran like a fox, and swam like an eel. And he liked to tell folks, "When I was a baby, my cradle was the shell of a six-hundred-pound turtle! When I was a boy, I ate so much bear meat and drank so much buffalo milk, I could whip my weight in wildcats!" Which was less amazing than you might think, because by the time Davy Crockett was eight years old, he weighed two hundred pounds with his shoes off, his feet clean, and his stomach empty!

Davy Crockett loved to brag about the things he could lick—from wildcats to grizzly bears. Sometimes, though, his bragging got him into big trouble. Take the time he got caught in a thunderstorm in the middle of the forest, carrying nothing but a stick. After hiking some ten miles in the rain, he was so hungry he could have wolfed down a hickory stump, roots and all. He began to search through a black thicket for something good to eat. Just as he parted some trees with his stick, he saw two big eyes staring at him, lit up like a pair of red-hot coals.

Thinking he'd come across a fun fight and a tasty feast combined, Davy neighed like a horse, then hollered like a screech owl. "Hello there! I'm Davy Crockett, and I'm *real* hungry! Which means bad news to any little warm-blooded, four-legged, squinty-eyed, yellow-bellied creature!"

Lightning suddenly lit the woods, and Davy got a good look at his dinner. "By thunder," he breathed. The hair went up on the back of his neck, and his eyes got as big as dogwood blossoms.

Staring back at him was the Big Eater of the Forest—the biggest panther this side of the Mississippi. He was just sitting there with a pile of bones and skulls all around him like pumpkins in a pumpkin patch.

Before Davy could beg the varmint's pardon, the panther spit a sea of froth at him, and his teeth began to grind like a sixty-horsepower sawmill.

"Ohh, I didn't mean what I just said," Davy apologized, backing away slowly.

But the panther shot white fire from his eyes and gave three or four sweeps of his tail as he advanced.

"You think you can forgive me for making a little joke?" Davy begged.

But the panther let out a growl about as loud as five hundred boulders crashing down a mountainside.

"Wanna sing a duet?" Davy asked.

But the panther just growled again and took another step closer.

"Guess I'm going to have to get serious," Davy said, trying to bluff his way out.

The panther stepped forward.

Davy crouched down. "I'm gettin' serious now!" he warned.

But the panther just put his head real low like he was about to leap.

With disaster staring him in the face, Davy suddenly concentrated on grinding his own teeth—until he sounded like a hundred-horsepower sawmill. Then he concentrated on growling his own growl—until he sounded like five thousand boulders tumbling down a mountainside.

As he stepped toward the panther they were both a-grinding and a-growling, until a final growl and a final grate brought the two together. And there in the rainy forest, they began wrestling each other for death or dinner.

Just as the panther was about to make chopped meat out of Davy's head, Davy gave him an upward blow under the jaw. He swung him around like a monkey and throttled him by the neck. And he threw him over one shoulder and twirled him around by his tail.

As Davy was turning the panther into bread dough, the Big Eater *yowled* for mercy.

"Okay, fine, fine," said Davy, panting. "I'm not about to skin such an amazing feller as yourself. But I'm not about to leave you here to collect any more of them bones and skulls, neither. I guess you better come home with me and learn some manners."

So Davy Crockett led the Big Eater of the Forest back to his cabin, and there he taught him all sorts of civilization. Davy taught him how to fold his paws and sing the tenor of a church song and how to rake the leaves with his claws. Best of all, he taught him how to light the hearth fire at night with his burning eyes, then lead Davy to bed in the dark. From then on, you could say that the two were the best of companions.

But Davy's boasting got him into trouble with more than just wild critters. It also nearly ended his political career. It seems that one year he figured the Tennessee Legislature was in sore need of a feller with natural sense instead of book learning. "And that feller is nobody but me!" he bragged as he went about the state, making campaign speeches. "I can sleep under a blanket of snow, outsqueeze a boa constrictor, and outwit the slyest fox in the woods! I'm your man!"

In one of his speeches, Davy got so carried away that he boasted he'd once grinned an old raccoon right out of a tree. "And folks, I can grin *any* dang raccoon out of any dang tree in the whole dang world! If I can't, you can call me a liar and feed me to a bunch of hungry bears in the winter!" he said.

Well, Davy's opponent recognized that this was his big chance to prove once and for all that Davy Crockett was nothing but a blowhard and a boaster. So one moony night in August, the feller got a crowd together, and as they all stood outside Davy's cabin, the varmint hollered, "Crockett, come out here! These folks wanna see your raccoon trick!"

"Sure!" Davy said. "Be glad to show 'em!"

Feeling pretty confident because he believed all his own boasts, Davy led the crowd through the woods, until he spied a raccoon grinning high up in a hickory tree.

"Jimminy crimminy, here I go! Now watch me, folks!" he said, and he set to grinning at the fellow, and he grinned and grinned. And grinned. But after he'd been grinning like a fool for a spell, that raccoon just kept sitting up in the tree, grinning back down at him, not tumbling down or nothing.

After a while folks began to get restless, and Davy began to get mad. His whole reputation was on the line. He didn't relish being fed to a bunch of bears, neither. He got so mad that he finally stomped home and got an ax. Then he returned to the woods and commenced to cutting down the tree.

Well, when the tree fell and Davy grabbed for the critter, he discovered the grinning raccoon was nothing but an old knothole that looked just like a raccoon!

"But look at this!" Davy said, beaming to the crowd. "The fact is, I done grinned the bark right off of this tree!" He was telling the truth—around the knothole, the tree was perfectly smooth.

"Go figure it," grumbled his opponent as the crowd cheered.

Another tale about Davy's bragging concerned one hot day on the banks of the Mississippi River. As old Davy was straggling along, feeling restless because he hadn't had a fight in ten days, he came across a keelboat being pushed upriver. The fellow pushing it had hair as black as a crow's wing and wore a red flannel shirt. There wasn't a man on the river that wouldn't have recognized Mike Fink, king of the Mississippi Boatmen.

"Hello there!" Davy shouted from the shore. "If you don't watch out, that boat's going to run back down the river! I'm about the only ring-tailed roarer in the world who can tame the Mississippi!"

Mike Fink gave Davy a mean look. "Oh, you don't know beans from buckshot, you old cock-a-doodle-doo," he said.

"Oh! Well, I don't care a johnnycake[1] for you, either!" said Davy. "Come ashore and let me whip you! I've been trying to get a fight going all morning!" Then he flapped his hands near his hips and crowed like a rooster.

Mike Fink, feeling chock-full of fight himself, curved his neck and neighed like a horse.

Davy Crockett thumped his chest and roared like a gorilla.

Mike Fink threw back his head and howled like a wolf.

Davy Crockett arched his back and screamed like a panther.

The two of them kept carrying on—flapping, shaking, thumping, howling, screaming—until they both got too tired to carry on. Then Davy waved his hand. "Farewell, stranger. I'm satisfied now."

"Me too," said Mike. "Feelin' much better myself."

In spite of all his boastin' and braggin' and all his screamin' and fightin', Davy Crockett did do some remarkable things for humankind. Take this story he always liked to tell about himself and the sun:

One day it was so cold, the sunlight froze as fast as it rose. When Davy Crockett saw daybreak was so far behind time, he grew concerned. "I better strike a little fire with my fingers," he said, "light my pipe, and travel a few miles to see what's going on."

---

1. A cornmeal griddle cake.

Davy brought his knuckles together like two thunderclouds. But the sparks froze before he could even begin to collect them. He had no choice but to start on his way and try to keep himself from freezing. So off he went, hop, skip, and jump, whistling the tune of his favorite song, "Fire in the Mountains." Even then, his hat froze to his head and twenty icicles formed under his nose.

After he'd hopped, skipped, and jumped ten miles up to the peak of Daybreak Hill, Davy Crockett discovered exactly what was going on: The earth had frozen on her axis and couldn't turn around! The reason was, the sun had gotten jammed between two giant cakes of ice.

"Cre-ation!" said Davy. "Something must be done—or human life is over!"

So he took a can of bear grease and poured about a ton of it over the sun's face. Then he kicked the cakes of ice until he wrenched the sun loose. "Move along, Charlie, keep goin'!" he shouted.

In about fifteen seconds, the sun woke up with such a beautiful smile that it made Davy sneeze. Then he lit his pipe with a blaze of sunlight. And as the earth began to move on her axis, he headed on home with a piece of sunrise in his pocket.

1991

Religion: Judeo-Christian Stories

Until the late nineteenth century, religion played a dominant part in the juvenile book trade. Throughout three centuries of publishing it was the Protestant arm of the church that was most in evidence—first the works of dissenters such as James Janeway, John Bunyan, and Isaac Watts, who had left the Church of England, and then in the nineteenth century the publications of the Religious Tract Society, the American Tract Society, and the American Sunday School Union. Indeed in 1836 John Henry Newman, still a member of the Church of England, recognized this dominance when he flippantly urged a female correspondent to write from a different viewpoint: "I am sure we shall do nothing until we get some ladies to work to poison the rising generation." But there were to be few examples of Anglican or Roman Catholic literature of the sort suggested by Newman, who joined the Roman church in 1845, and none that could match the potent influence of some of the writing discussed below.

The Puritan Ideal

Religious works specifically for child readers began to appear in the 1670s. There had long been religious primers, catechisms, and such versified summaries of the Bible as John Taylor's *Verbum Sempiternum* (1614), but these were mostly intended for any beginners, adult or child. The dominant subject of the new child-oriented books was death, and this was to be true for many generations. The preparation of children for death at a time when only a few of them survived their parents was something that preoccupied seventeenth-century Puritans, to whom the follies of youth seemed far more dangerous than the complacency and worldly concerns of middle age. They looked for intense religious precocity, and only few of them realized that this state might well not last. Benjamin Keach (1640–1704), an English Anabaptist preacher, wrote *War with the Devil: or the Young Mans Conflict with the Powers of Darkness* in 1673, a work very popular in both Englands, old and New. A dramatic double frontispiece shows on one side "The youth in his Natural state": a sixteen-year-old fop in worldly clothes on a path labeled "Broad is ye Way" to hell (indicated by heads engulfed in flames). On the page opposite is "The youth in his Converted state" in sombre Puritan garb, aged only ten. A horned devil aims an arrow at the book he holds, and on the other side of a path inscribed "narrow is ye way that leads to life" are youths with staves trying to trip him up.

The purpose of Keach's verse dialogue was to show "the corruption and vanity of youth, the horrible nature of sin, and deplorable condition of fallen man." There is much prolix conversation between Youth and his old companions, the Devil, Conscience, and Truth, before Christ finally intervenes, forgives Youth, and promises him eternal felicity. The Devil warns that he will return—"I have so much craft and subtilty." But Youth praises God for the strength he has been given to resist. Keach probably also wrote the much shorter dialogue between Christ, Youth, and the Devil that was a well-known feature of many early editions of the *New England Primer*. (He wrote a similar dialogue in another book of instruction.) This is far more pessimistic. Youth will not heed Christ, who urges penitence and reform, but listens instead to the Devil's persuasive arguments that there is still plenty of time. Death carries him off in spite of his anguished pleas, saying "And thy dear soul in hell must lie / With Devils to eternity."

Keach's dialogues did not long outlive him, unlike James Janeway's *A Token for Children*, which attained enormous popularity in both England and America and influenced many writers. This compilation of spiritual biographies of children who had led exemplary lives and died triumphantly, confident of salvation, was published in two parts in 1671 and 1672. Janeway knew none of the thirteen subjects himself, but took their stories from other men's works or else from accounts brought to his notice. These narratives of children who held the stage, surrounded by awestruck adults, enthralled child readers starved of imaginative literature. The comment of William Godwin, an eighteenth-century freethinker who had been brought up in a strict Nonconformist home, would have been echoed by many others: "I felt as if I were willing to die with them, if I could with equal success, engage the admiration of my friends and mankind." And the pattern of triumphant death (now secular) was to be continued in children's fiction by Victorian writers. One half of Juliana Horatia Ewing's *The Story of a Short Life* (1885) is devoted to the fading of her young hero, who wants to die like a soldier.

There were works that could be enjoyed by children long before there were books written *for* them. *The Pilgrim's Progress* (1678) is an outstanding example, recalled by many as a supreme reading experience. A much earlier work, John Foxe's *Actes and Monumentes* (1563), popularly known as the *Book of Martyrs,* was relished for its brisk narrative and horrific woodcuts of the torture and death of Protestant martyrs. His book was to be more influential than he could have dreamed, and could whip up English mobs into "no popery" frenzy for centuries. Almost all known copies of the *New England Primer* carried the famous account of the burning of John Rogers, the first martyr of Queen Mary's reign, with accompanying woodcut. Foxe was still being reprinted in the nineteenth century; and in 1904 we find a children's version, *Stories from Foxe's Book of Martyrs*. Nathaniel Crouch used it in his inflammatory *Martyrs in Flames: or The History of Popery* (1695). Crouch—a publisher, hack writer, and plagiarist, who wrote under the name of Richard Burton or R. B.— was an astute observer of the market. His customers wanted religious books for their families; his motto, openly stated in *Youths Divine Pastime,* was "He certainly doth hit the White / Who mingles Profit with delight," and he hid sensational and salacious material under innocuous titles. Thus *Remarks upon the Lives of Several Excellent Young Persons* (1678) included detailed accounts of the martyrdom of young women that the modern reader would deem pornographic.

From Janeway and from a book recommended by him—Thomas White's *A Little Book for Little Children* (1660)—we learn the Puritan ideals for children. They should be serious, preoccupied with thoughts of death and hell, well-schooled in their catechism, frequent in prayer, and quick to detect frivolity in others and to rebuke not only their brothers and sisters but also their elders. They eschew the company of other children because their peers might lead them into evil ways, and they do not play because precious time would be wasted that could be spent in prayer. All these precepts were to be repeated over and over again by preachers; "early piety" was the great desideratum, and to attain this a child must discard all childish things. Indeed Cotton Mather held up to children the example of his brother Nathanael who had died in 1688 at age nineteen, having so devoured books "that Books devoured him"; he described Nathanael admiringly as "an Old Man without Gray Hairs upon him."

But Isaac Watts in *Divine Songs* (1715), without shedding any of the Puritan doctrine, used it in a far gentler way; love is stressed rather than fear, and the young readers he addresses are recognizably childish. They play and are not reproached, and are coaxed into piety, not threatened:

> 'Twill save us from a Thousand Snares
> To mind Religion young;
> Grace will preserve our following Years
> And make our Vertue strong.

The trouble was that the very popularity of these verses must have killed them for many; there are only twenty-seven Divine Songs, and two Moral—a few more were to be added later. They appeared in reading primers and children's tracts and were learned by heart, recited and sung by every Sunday school. As Harvey Darton said, very few poems can survive that ordeal; and Charles Dodgson (Lewis Carroll), despite being easily offended by irreverence, treated them like popular songs and parodied two in his *Alice's Adventures in Wonderland* (1865).

Though Anna Laetitia Barbauld's *Hymns in Prose* (1781) were as popular in America as in England, they did not have the lasting appeal of Watts, whose style, while not as impressive, is more accessible. Her majestic prose could not be so easily recited, and her religious unorthodoxy offended the more conservative. Barbauld (1743–1825) came from the same dissenting background as Watts, but there is no trace of religious dogma in anything she wrote. Watts's treatment of death, though milder than that of his Puritan predecessors, uses their language and imagery, and "the place / Of everlasting fire and pain" is frequently evoked. Barbauld never suggests this end; death is not to be feared or mourned, and in Hymn 10 she eloquently describes how Nature is perpetually renewing itself. She moves on to human destiny and Hymn 11 concludes

> Mourn not therefore, child of immortality!—for the spoiler, the cruel spoiler that laid waste the works of God, is subdued: Jesus hath conquered death:—child of immortality! mourn no longer.

Of the multitudes who have used the subject of death in their writing for children, there are few who have presented the Christian attitude so positively and so succinctly.

Barbauld's unorthodoxy was shared by her brother, Dr. John Aikin, with whom she collaborated in *Evenings at Home* (1792–96). Here Aikin's story "Difference and Agreement; or Sunday Morning" shows a religious toleration that was unique at the time and for many years to come. A father takes his son to different Sunday services— Church of England, Roman Catholic, Methodist, Baptist, Quaker. All follow their own practices, but when the dispersing congregations see a man in trouble they all react with the same charity.

The Roman Catholic Church in particular was the target of much abusive writing during the nineteenth century. In *Father and Son* (1907), Edmund Gosse described how in his 1850s childhood he and his father (a fanatical fundamentalist Christian) discussed Rome with contemptuous abhorrence, referring to it as the Scarlet Woman and the Whore of Babylon. Many children's books were written in this vein, such as Mary Martha Sherwood's *The Nun* (1833), which tells of the fearful fate of a French nun who apostatizes to Protestantism. A sensational story, it was often allowed in households where otherwise fiction was barred. Sherwood (1775–1851) was a prolific author whose works ranged from tract stories like *Little Henry and His Bearer* (1814) to *The History of the Fairchild Family*, a chronicle written in three parts (1818, 1842, 1848) whose title page declared it "a collection of stories calculated to show the importance and effects of a religious education."

Little Henry was written toward the end of the ten years Sherwood spent in India with her husband. Henry, a five-year-old orphan, is cared for lovingly by his Hindu bearer, Boosy. From a clergyman's daughter, Henry learns a Calvinistic form of the Christian religion and begins to teach it to Boosy before dying. This was one of the earliest examples of what was to become a favorite evangelical theme—the child converting the adult. *The Fairchild Family*, whose first part has always been the best known, was in all Victorian nurseries. Despite its extreme Calvinistic Protestantism, it cut across sects—it was Sunday reading for High Church, Low Church, and Nonconformist families. Most children seem to have read it for the narrative about the three lifelike and, on occasion, engagingly naughty little Fairchilds. As one reader recalled in adult life: "There was plenty about eating and drinking; one could always skip the prayers [and Mr. Fairchild's sermons], and there were three or four very brightly written accounts of funerals in it." The little Fairchilds were taken to deathbeds and to view corpses as well as to funerals; and following a quarrel, they are brought to a gibbet where they are shown the body of a man who had murdered his brother. (This chapter was removed from later editions.)

Sunday School Publications

American Sunday schools were used by all churchgoing families, but in England they initially served only the poorest classes. They came into being in the 1780s in an effort to keep children off the street and to teach them reading skills so that they could spell their way through the Bible and their catechism. In *The Sunday School* (1795), one of her Cheap Repository Tract stories, the religious writer Hannah More (1745–1833) described from her own personal experience the difficulties of setting up such a school in a backward rural area where money had to be coaxed out of reluctant clergy and farmers, and where the poverty-stricken laborers' families were suspicious and unenthusiastic. For the young people among the latter she wrote her tracts, tempting these reluctant readers with sensational titles that suggested chapbook stories, and creating characters in a rural background that they could recognize. There were 114 tracts, published between 1795 and 1798, of which Hannah More herself wrote about 50.

The excellence of these little works brought them to the notice of educated readers, for whom they were issued in volume form. They were very popular in America, particularly *The Shepherd of Salisbury Plain* (1795), a conversation between "a worthy, charitable gentleman" and the shepherd, a poor man with a sick wife and many children who was nevertheless dignified, articulate, and well contented with his lot. The tracts were the first work, said Samuel Goodrich (alias Peter Parley), that he read with real enthusiasm. (He had been brought up in a strict home where fiction was banned and was treated with contempt by himself.) "The Shepherd of Salisbury Plain was to me only inferior to the Bible narrative of Joseph and his brethren." Years later he visited the author in England. "It was in conversation with that amiable and gifted person, that I first formed the conception of the Parley Tales."

Very few of the many thousands of later tract tales approached the quality of Hannah More's. The Religious Tract Society soon found how difficult it was to find suitable material. The society had been founded in London in 1799 by a number of evangelicals who regretted that Hannah More's tracts "did not contain a fuller statement of the great evangelical principles of Christian truth." They were all agreed that it was vitally important to provide reading for Sunday schools, but could think of no suitable works besides Watts's *Divine Songs* and George Burder's *Early Piety* (1776). In 1810 they published *The Dairyman's Daughter,* a narrative by the Reverend Legh Richmond describing the Janeway-style death of a young female parishioner. This work became so famous that crowds of admirers visited the Isle of Wight to see her grave. There were scores of American editions.

It took some time for the society to overcome its scruples about publishing fiction, which to its clerical founders seemed akin to condoning lies. *The Child's Companion,* a little monthly magazine that began in 1824, had examples of children who died having attained early piety, awful instances of catastrophes that had overtaken the impious, and some factual articles. When stories became permissible for Sunday school students they were austerely didactic and full of prohibitions.

But in 1867 the Religious Tract Society achieved a best-seller, Hesba Stretton's *Jessica's First Prayer,* the story of a London street waif who learns about Christianity by surreptitiously lurking at the back of a Methodist chapel and whose innocent faith softens the proud heart of the chapel caretaker. It was not the first book by Stretton (1832–1911), but the first she had written about slum life, of which she—unlike many later imitators—had had firsthand experience. She swiftly followed it up with other stories in the same vein but none was so enthusiastically received, though *Pilgrim Street* (1867), about Manchester slums, was a better book; so too was *Little Meg's Children* (1868), about a ten-year-old struggling by herself to look after her small brother and sister after her mother dies.

Street arab stories, as this genre was styled, became high fashion, and flowed out by the hundreds during the 1870s and 1880s; they were very often the work of writers who had taken their details from popular journalism, or had been affected by the plight of Jo the crossing sweeper in Charles Dickens's *Bleak House* (1852). Eliza Keary, writing in 1882, referred to them disparagingly as "sensational stories of ragged London depravity," and thought that they were far less suitable for Sunday reading than the works of Mrs. Sherwood that she and her sister had been given. Nevertheless readers in both poor and affluent homes sobbed over such works as *Froggy's Little Brother* (by "Brenda") and *A Peep Behind the Scenes* (by Mrs. O. F. Walton), held by their heady emotion. It was ironic that the evangelicals who had so mistrusted works of imagination should produce the best-selling juvenile fiction of the century.

The image of artless children like Hesba Stretton's Jessica bringing a message of love to hard hearts was a popular and long-lasting one. Amy Le Feuvre (d. 1929), one of the most prolific of the Religious Tract Society's authors, made frequent use of the theme. In her most popular book, *Probable Sons* (1895), little Milly, whose mispronunciation of "prodigal sons" is responsible for the title, brings her Uncle Edward back to Christ. As one of her characters remarks in *A Puzzling Pair* (1898), "They live so near to the throne of the Eternal One that they draw those with whom they live to do the same." The popular American Sunday school writer Elizabeth Wetherell—the pen name of Susan Warner (1819–1885), author of *The Wide, Wide World* (1850) and *Queechy* (1852)—had created a similar child evangelist in *Melbourne House* (1864). Nine-year-old Daisy Randolph, unshakably confident that her interpretation of the Scriptures is the only valid one, sets out to be "a soldier of Christ."

Though popular with adolescent girls, this sort of writing in which a vaguely expressed religious message mingles with titillating love interest had many critics. Among them was Charlotte Yonge (1823–1901), who in *What Books to Lend and What to Give* (1887) said shrewdly that novels such as *The Wide, Wide World* would lead girls to see a lover in anyone who was kind to them. She also was wary of street waif stories, and could recommend only two of these. There were multitudes more, she said, "most of them written from fancy. It is possible to have too many of them." Her pamphlet was written primarily to help Sunday schools choose books for their libraries and to give as prizes, but it also included a category she called "drawing-room" literature for the more affluent. She was the type of children's writer Cardinal Newman had had in mind a generation earlier when he wished for a more Catholic approach to stories for the young. But though all her fiction—both the long family chronicles for "drawing-room" readers and the excellent shorter tales for Sunday schools—maintains an implicit background of religious outlook and practice akin to her own, there is no aim to convert and no emotional message as in the evangelical best-sellers. She was fundamentally a reserved writer who would never have been effective at proselytizing.

Fantasy and Allegory

Of all the nineteenth-century writers for children, the Scottish cleric George Mac-Donald (1824–1905) best conveyed the idea of holiness, relying on fantasy stories that never spell out any one meaning; it is left to readers to find their own. *The Princess and the Goblin* (1871) and the short story "The Golden Key" (first published in *Dealings with the Fairies*, 1867) are both spiritual quests. "The Golden Key" begins with a boy listening to his great-aunt's stories:

> She told him that if he could reach the place where the end of the rainbow stands he would find there a golden key.
>
> "And what is the key for?" the boy would ask. "What is the key of? What will it open?"
>
> "That nobody knows," his aunt would reply. "He has to find that out."

And having found the key, the boy, Mossy, with Tangle, a little girl, makes the journey through dreamlike landscapes seeking the country from which the shadows above them are falling. This they reach at the end of their human life.

There have been retellings of Bible stories since the late seventeenth century, and over the years these included pictorial and hieroglyphic Bibles, Bible alphabets, and chapbook versions. In the twentieth century two retellings stand out, Walter de la Mare's *Stories from the Bible* (1929) and Peter Dickinson's *City of Gold* (1980), in which Old Testament stories are related by witnesses who were present as they unfolded. There have also been Bible plays, of which by far the best-known is *Joseph and the Amazing Technicolour Dreamcoat*. With words by Tim Rice and music by Andrew Lloyd Webber, it was first performed by a junior school in London in 1968. It has universal appeal, is regarded as good entertainment for all ages, has been performed in schools of many different religious affiliations, and has been a smash hit on the New York and London professional stage.

Religious themes in mainstream publishing for children became rarer in the twentieth century and were more often found in fantasy. C. S. Lewis (1898–1963), inspired by MacDonald, in the 1950s created the imaginary land of Narnia, the setting of his seven stories that might also be called spiritual quests. Here the moral is never left in doubt. Christ appears as the lion Aslan, and *The Lion, the Witch, and the Wardrobe* (1950) ends with his death and resurrection. A more powerful and imaginative presentation of the Christian resurrection theme can be found in Bob Hartman's *The Easter Angels* (1999). Other twentieth-century fantasy writers, without directly identifying themselves with Christianity, created imaginary worlds where good is victorious over evil. This approach can be controversial. Madeleine L'Engle's *A Wrinkle in Time* (1963), for instance, incurred criticism from those who thought the implied Christian message inappropriate in science fiction, and from Christian fundamentalists who found her books "contrary to biblical teaching."

Philip Pullman in the *His Dark Materials* trilogy—*The Golden Compass* (published in England as *Northern Lights*, 1995), *The Subtle Knife* (1997), and *The Amber Spyglass* (2000)—made a new departure with an antireligious, humanist fantasy. The pace of the narrative and its wealth of invention fascinate adult and child readers alike. There are parallel universes and a knife with which the bearer can get access into them, an "alethiometer" that will show the skilled user the truth, externalized souls (daemons), balloons fighting with zeppelins, witches, armored bears, and a journey to the world of the dead and their emergence from it (perhaps the most impressive episode). The trilogy ends with unanswered questions; there is no statement of triumph over evil as in *The Lord of the Rings* (1954–55), where the Ring of Power is destroyed, inadvertently and ironically by the most abject and treacherous of J. R. R. Tolkien's characters, Gollum. Lyra and Will, the child heroine and hero of *The Amber Spyglass*, go back to their separate universes knowing they can never meet again, but encouraged by the angel Xaphania to benefit humanity "by thinking and feeling and reflecting, by gaining wisdom and passing it on."

As in fantasy fiction, later twentieth-century writers of family stories preferred to avoid direct religious statement; the qualities of truth, kindness, sympathy, and courage are usually upheld but implied, not preached. Kate Montagnon in a 1996 essay on moral and religious writing called it a species of all-purpose religion, to be found in most mainstream books for children. This is true even in the powerful novels of Katherine Paterson, the daughter of missionary parents who is herself a theologian and formerly a missionary in Japan. In *Bridge to Terebithia* (1977) the first reaction of ten-year-old Jess to the accidental death of Leslie is furious anger. This new friend had mattered to him more than anybody else, and she had acted as leader as they created an imaginary kingdom over which they ruled as king and queen. Then as gradually he accepts the tragedy, he finds himself turning to people he had previously excluded. In *Jacob Have I Loved* (1980), there is a closely observed background of a Methodist fishing community on an island in Chesapeake Bay, but the theme of the novel is the passionate antagonism felt by one twin for the other, gifted and beautiful, favored because as a baby she was physically weaker. It is not religion that softens Katherine Paterson's Esau twin, but a new existence as a midwife in a remote Appalachian valley, where she delivers twins and like her parents finds herself more concerned for the weaker of the two.

An exception to this new reluctance to introduce religion into fiction is Isaac Bashevis Singer (1904–1991), whose works, written in Yiddish, consistently returned to the same themes from the 1930s on. He drew on his own Hasidic background in *The Power of Light: Eight Stories for Hanukkah* (1980), stories that all relate to Jewish legends or aspects of Jewish life. In the one included here, "Hanukkah in the Poorhouse," an old Russian Jew tells the history of his life. As a young boy he was captured by the Cossacks and taken far from his home to be reared for the army. "They could force my body to do all kinds of things but they could not make my soul forsake the faith of my fathers." Many years later he escapes from the army and after a perilous journey reaches his old home, where his parents, though they do not at first recognize him, treat him as an honored guest. In this short narrative Singer succeeds in conveying the tenacity with which Jews have cherished their faith and traditions and the warmth of their family life. A further example of this warmth comes in *The Gift* (1995) by the Canadian Joseph Kertes, in which a Jewish family's celebration of Hanukkah is contrasted with the increasing secularization of the Christian Christmas. It also conveys the longing of the immigrant to be assimilated into the life of the new country.

Singer's *The Golem* (1982) is a powerful allegory, a version of an ancient Jewish legend. A rabbi in old Prague is commanded by God to create the clay figure of a monster man—a Golem—so that it can come to the rescue of a Jewish banker attacked by an age-old slander: he has been accused of kidnapping and killing the child of a Christian client for the blood to be used in making the Passover matzohs. The rabbi obeys and brings the creature to life by inscribing a sacred name on its forehead. The Golem, who has a giant's strength but is mindless, does what is required of him, but then refuses to allow the name to be expunged. Instead he rampages through Prague causing terror and devastation. To the rabbi's horror the emperor hears of this and wishes to arm the Golem and use him for war. This time the creator manages to reduce the monster to clay again. Singer leaves it to the readers to find the meaning for themselves. As had been shown by George MacDonald, in skillful hands allegory and fairy tale can have a greater impact than direct moral or religious teaching.

JAMES JANEWAY
ca. 1636–1674

James Janeway's *Token for Children, being an Exact Account of the Conversion, Holy and Exemplary Lives, and Joyful Deaths, of several young Children,* published in two parts in 1671 and 1672, is one of the most influential books in the history of juvenile publishing. Janeway, a Nonconformist preacher with a chapel in Rotherhithe, south of the Thames in London, had no idea of being original; he freely admitted to collecting his material from stories told to him, or from other men's works. The book seems to have been modeled on Thomas White's *A Little Book for Little Children,* which Janeway recommends in his penultimate paragraph. It first appeared as part of White's *The Manual for Parents* (1660). Both writers focus on death—it was an age when parents expected to see many of their children die—the triumphant death of children who inspire all those around them. Unlike Janeway, White also included a long and lurid narrative, taken from the fourth book of Maccabees, of the hideous tortures and martyrdom inflicted upon seven young Jewish brothers.

A Token remained in print in both Britain and America for more than two hundred years. It was published in Boston in 1700 with added New England examples. Cotton Mather commented in his diary that wishing "to charm the Children of New England into the Fear of God with the Examples of some Children . . . in this Countrey, and being furnished with six or seven remarkable Narratives, I putt them into shape, and gave the little book unto the Booksellers." This added part was

given the title *A Token for the Children of New England.* Hannah Hill of Philadelphia may well have been one of the readers; *A Legacy for Children, Being Some of the Last Expressions, and Dying Sayings of Hannah Hill, Junr.* was published in Philadelphia in 1714, at "the ardent desire of the deceased." This young Quaker, aged "eleven years and near three months," seems to have thought out her deathbed in much detail and had left instructions for how her funeral should be conducted. *A Legacy* was only one of the countless imitations of Janeway that lasted until well into the Victorian period with secularized accounts of protracted but still triumphant deaths of child characters.

The title page of *A Token* carries the text from St. Mark's Gospel "Suffer little Children to come unto me, and forbid them not: for of such is the Kingdom of God." This in itself is unusual at a time when preachers rarely spoke of God's love, but far more often, especially where the young were concerned, emphasized his wrath. The preface printed here certainly mentions the hell that awaits those that "play the Truant, and Lye, and speak naughty words, and break the Sabbath." But there is a tender concern that children should not behave thus, and that the examples given should help them to be good. It is an illuminating outline of what constituted good and bad behavior in a Puritan child.

Janeway died of consumption, a disease that had carried off all his brothers, two years after the second part of *A Token* was published.

From A Token for Children

A PREFACE: CONTAINING DIRECTIONS TO CHILDREN

You may now hear (my dear Lambs) what other good Children have done, and remember how they wept and prayed by themselves, how earnestly they cryed out for an interest in the Lord Jesus Christ: May you not read how dutiful they were to their Parents? How diligent at their Books? how ready to learn the Scripture, and their Catechisms? Can you forget what Questions they were wont to ask? How much they feared a lye, how much they abhorred naughty company, how holy they lived, how dearly they were loved, how joyfully they died?

But tell me, my dear Children, and tell me truly, Do you do as these Children did? Did you ever see your miserable state by Nature? Did you ever get by your self and weep for sin, and pray for grace and pardon? Did you ever go to your Father and Mother, or Master, or Mistress, and beg of them to pity you, and pray for you, and to teach you what you shall do to be saved, what you shall do to get Christ, Heaven and Glory? Dost thou love to be taught good things? Come tell me truly, my dear Child, for I would fain do what I can possibly to keep thee from falling into everlasting Fire. I wou'd fain have you one of those little ones, which Christ will take into his Arms and bless: How dost thou spend thy time? is it in play and Idleness, and with wicked Children? Dare you take Gods Name in vain, or swear, or tell a lie? Dare you do any thing which your Parents forbid you, and neglect to do what they command you? Do you dare to run up and down upon the Lords day? or do you keep in to read your book, and to learn what your good Parents command you? What do you say, Child? Which of these two sorts are you of? Let me talk a little with you, and ask you a few questions.

1. Were not these Children sweet Children, which feared God, and were dutiful to their Parents? Did not their Fathers and Mothers, and every body that fears God, love them, and praise them? What do you think is become of them, now they are dead and gone? Why, they are gone to Heaven, and are singing Hallelujahs with the Angels: They see glorious things, and having nothing but joy and pleasure, they shall never sin no more, they shall never be beat any more, they shall never be sick, or in pain any more.

2. And would not you have your Fathers love; your Mothers Commendation, your Masters good word? Would not you have God and Christ love you? And would you not fain go to Heaven when you die? And live with your godly Parents in Glory, and be happy for ever?

3. Whither do you think those Children go, when they dye, that will not do what they are bid, but play the Truant, and Lye, and speak naughty words, and break the Sabbath? Whither do such Children go, do you think? Why, I will tell you, they which Lye, must go to their Father the Devil into everlasting burning; they which never pray, God will pour out his wrath upon them, and when they beg and pray in Hell Fire, God will not forgive them, but there they must lye for ever.

4. And are you willing to go to Hell to be burned with the Devil and his Angels? Would you be in the same condition with naughty Children? O Hell is a terrible place, that's worse a thousand times than whipping; Gods anger is worse than your Fathers anger; and are you willing to anger God? O Child, this is most certainly true, that all that be wicked, and die so, must be turned into Hell; and if any be once there, there is no coming out again.

5. Would you not do any thing in the World rather than be thrown into Hell Fire? would you not do any thing in the World to get Christ, and grace and glory?

6. Well now, what will you do? will you read this book a little, because your good Mother will make you do it, and because it is a little new Book, but as soon as ever you have done, run away to play, and never think of it?

7. How art thou now affected, poor Child, in the Reading of this Book? Have you shed ever a tear since you begun reading? Have you been by your self upon your knees, and begging that God would make you like these blessed Children? or are you as you use to be, as careless, and foolish and disobedient, and wicked as ever?

8. Did you never hear of a little Child that died? and if other Children die, why may not you be sick and die? and what will you do then, Child, if you should have no grace in your heart, and be found like other naughty children?

9. How do you know but that you may be the next Child that may die? and where are you then, if you be not God's Child?

10. Wilt thou tarry any longer, my dear Child, before thou run into thy chamber, and beg of God to give thee a Christ for thy Soul, that thou mayest not be undone for ever? Wilt thou get presently[1] into a corner to weep and pray? Methinks I see that pretty Lamb begin to weep, and thinks of getting by himself, and will as well as he can cry unto the Lord, so make him one of these little ones that go into the Kingdom of Heaven; Methinks there stands a sweet Child, and there another, that are resolved for Christ and for Heaven: Methinks that little Boy looks as if he had a mind to learn good things. Methinks I hear one say, well, I will never tell a lye more, I will never keep any naughty Boy company more, they will teach me to swear, and they will speak naughty words, they do not love God. I'le learn my Catechism, and get my Mother to teach me to pray, and I will go to weep and cry to Christ, and will not be quiet till the Lord hath given me Grace. O that's my brave Child indeed!

11. But will you not quickly forget your promise? are you resolved by the strength of Christ to be a good child? Are you indeed? nay, but are you indeed? Consider: dear child, God calls you to remember your Creator in the days of your Youth, and he takes it kindly when little ones come to him, and he loves them dearly; and godly people, especially Parents, and Masters and Mistresses, they have no greater joy, than to see their Children walking in the way of truth.

Now tell me, my pretty dear Child, What will you do? Shall I make you a Book? Shall I pray for you, and entreat you? Shall your Good Mother weep over you? And will not you make us all glad, by your turning quickly to the Lord? Shall Christ tell you that he will love you? And will not you love him? Will you strive to be like these Children? I am persuaded, that God intends to do good to the Souls of some little Children by these Papers, because he hath laid it so much upon my heart to pray for them, and over these Papers, and thorow mercy I have already experienced, that something of this nature hath not been in vain: I shall give a word of direction, and so leave you.

1. Take heed of what you know is naught; as lying, O that is a grievous fault indeed; and naughty words, and taking the Lords name in vain, and playing upon the Lords Day, and keeping bad company, and playing with ungodly Children: But, if you do go to School with such, tell them that God will not love them, but that the Devil will have them, if they continue to be so naught.

2. Do what your Father and Mother bids you, cheerfully, and take heed of doing any thing that they forbid you.

3. Be diligent in reading the Scripture, and learning your Catechism; and what you do not understand, to be sure ask the meaning of.

4. Think a little sometimes by your self about God and Heaven, and your Soul, and where you shall go when you die, and what Christ came into the world for.

5. And if you have no great mind to do thus, but had rather be at play, then think what is it that makes me that I do not care for good things; is this like one of Gods dear Children? I am afraid I am none of God's Child, I feel I do not love to come to

---

1. Immediately.

Him: O, what shall I do? Either I must be God's Child or the Devils; O, what shall I do? I would not be the Devils Child for any thing in the world.

6. Then go to your Father or Mother, or some good body, and ask them what thou shalt do to be Gods Child; and tell them that thou art afraid, and that thou canst not be contented, till thou hast got the love of God.

7. Get by thyself, into the Chamber or Garret, and fall upon thy knees, and weep and mourn, and tell Christ, thou art afraid that he doth not love thee, but thou would fain have his love: beg of him to give thee his Grace and pardon for thy sins, and that he would make thee his Child: Tell God thou dost not care who don't love thee, if God will but love thee: Say to him, Father, hast thou not a blessing for me, thy poor little Child? Father, hast thou not a blessing for me, even for me? O give a Christ; O give me a Christ; O let me not be undone for ever: thus beg, as for your lives, and be not contented till you have an answer; and do thus every day, with as much earnestness as you can, twice a day at least.

8. Give your self up to Christ: say, dear Jesus, thou didst bid that little Children should be suffered to come unto thee; and Lord, I am come as well as I can, would fain be thy Child: take my heart, and make it humble, and meek, and sensible, and obedient: I give my self to thee, dear Jesus, do what thou wilt with me, So that thou wilt but love me, and give me thy grace and glory.

9. Get acquainted with godly people, and ask them good questions, and endeavour to love their talk.

10. Labour to get a dear love for Christ; read the History of Christ's sufferings, and ask the reason of his sufferings; and never be contented till you see your need of Christ, and the excellency and use of Christ.

11. Hear the most powerful Ministers; and read the most searching Books; and get your Father to buy you *Mr. White's* Book for little Children, and *A Guide to Heaven.*[2]

12. Resolve to continue in well-doing all your dayes; then you shall be one of those sweet little ones that Christ will take into his Arms, and bless, and give a Kingdom, Crown and Glory to. And now dear Children, I have done, I have written to you, I have prayed for you; but what you will do, I can't tell. O Children, if you love me, if you love your Parents, if you love your Souls; if you would scape Hell Fire, and if you would live in Heaven when you dye, do you go and do as these good Children; and that you may be your Parents joy, your Countreys honour, and live in Gods fear, and dye in his love, is the prayer of your dear Friend.   J. Janeway.

1671

---

2. Thomas White's *A Little Book for Little Children* first appeared as part of his *Manual for Parents* (1660). *A Guide to Heaven* is attributed to Samuel Hardy (1636–1691).

JOHN BUNYAN
1628–1688

The Pilgrim's Progress was for some 150 years perhaps the most important imaginative work encountered by children in households where there was no other fiction. Bunyan, the child of a mender of pots and kettles who later followed his father's trade, had spent an unregenerate youth that he was to deplore in *Sighs from Hell: or the Groans of a Damned Soul* (1658). He had heard plenty of good sermons, he said sorrowfully, from which he had received many a warning that he had not heeded. "The Scriptures, thought I, what are they? a dead letter. . . . [G]ive me a Ballad, a News book, George on Horseback, or Bevis of Southampton[.]" In *The Pilgrim's Progress* Bunyan was to take many elements from the story of St. George and his fight with a dragon as it appeared in the broadside ballad version of *The Seven Champions of Christendom,* and from the even older romance of *Sir Bevis of Hampton* who vanquishes both a dragon and a giant.

Bunyan's change of heart came after his marriage in his early twenties. His wife was a serious young woman who had brought with her two devotional books. These had a profound effect on him, and guided by them and by her influence he threw off his old habits. Though outwardly a reformed character, diligent in his attendance at church and in reading the Bible, a full spiritual rebirth was not to come until after three or four years of intense inner conflict, which he described in *Grace Abounding to the Chief of Sinners* (1666). He left the Church of England and became a Nonconformist preacher, attracting huge crowds who were curious to listen to this once-blaspheming tinker. Preaching without a license being then an indictable offense, he received a prison sentence of twelve years and was not released until 1672. The first part of *The Pilgrim's Progress* was published in 1678. The second part, in which Christian's wife Christiana makes the same journey to join her husband, was published in 1684. In 1686 he wrote *A Book for Boys and Girls,* a collection of verses later given the title of *Divine Emblems.* Here little homilies are built around everyday objects such as a snail, a weathercock, and a pair of spectacles. A few of these poems sometimes appear in anthologies.

At first *The Pilgrim's Progress* circulated among the uneducated; it was to be many years before more sophisticated readers recognized its qualities. Since then it has been translated into almost every known language, rewritten, imitated, and set to music. F. J. Harvey Darton in *Children's Books in England* (1932) elaborates on its versions: "It has been 'adapted,' 'edited,' 'shortened,' cut into 'scenes,' made into little moral plays, [and] . . . has even been put, very superfluously, into words of one syllable. In each and every form it is a children's book, however you frame definitions." Darton himself said that he had read it rapturously as an adventure story. Thomas Burt (1837–1922), a trade unionist and politician who was a coal miner from the age of ten, had seen it as "solid literal history. I believed every word of it. Perhaps it was the only book I ever read with entire, unquestioning acceptation."

Many of Burt's contemporaries felt the same. For them as for Burt it was perhaps the only book besides the Bible that the family owned. In households where there were more books, it was one of the very few that could be read on Sundays. Here too children often took it for fact. In *Stories Told to a Child* (1865), Jean Ingelow describes how a little girl of six sees an illustrated version. "There were lions and hobgoblins, and giants, and angels, and martyrs, and there was the river flowing before the golden gates; nothing that could awe the imagination, and take hold on the spirit of a child was wanting." And the small girl escapes to try to make her own way to the city with the golden gates. But to her deep distress she fails even to find the wicket gate through which Christian had started on his journey. Louisa May Alcott's *Little Women* (1868) opens with memories of how Meg, Jo, Beth, and Amy played at being pilgrims when they were younger; in the course of the account of their family life each is given a chapter written around a *Pilgrim's Progress* episode.

In the early-nineteenth-century chapbook version reproduced here, parts 1 and 2 are compressed into twenty-four pages, with text kept to a minimum.

THE
PILGRIM'S PROGRESS,

FROM THIS WORLD TO THAT WHICH IS TO COME.

GLASGOW;

PUBLISHED BY ORR AND SONS, BRUNSWICK ST.

43

The progress of the Pilgrim is here represented by Christian leaving the City of
Destruction, in terror and alarm at its fate. He
is met by Evangelist, who, directed him to fly
from the wrath to come; and keep yonder
shining light in his eye, where it should be
told him what to do.

Christian had not proceeded far, till he fell in
to the slough of Despond, and was relieved by
one called Help, who set him on his way. He
was afterwards beguiled by Worldly-wiseman;
but was again put right way by Evangelist.

Christian at length arrived at the gate, upon which was inscribed "knock and it shall be opened." He knocked and it was opened by one Goodwill, who let him in. Beelzebub as he entered gave him a pull but Christian escaped.

Christian having fairly escaped Beelzebub and his emissaries; was kindly welcomed by Goodwill, and shewed many rare sights by Interpreter: he passed the walls of salvation and came to a cross, where his bundle dropped off.

Christian now being rid of his burden, pushed on more lightly, and took the narrow path up the hill, and struggled hard till he arrived at the arbour, prepared by the Lord of the place for weary pilgrims, where he sat and refreshed himself.

When Christian had got to the top of the hill he met two men running, named Timorous and Mistrust; who said they had been bound for Mount Zion, but meeting with two Lions, they were afraid: Christian passed the Lions, who, being chained, could not hurt him.

JOHN BUNYAN

When Christian lift up his eyes, he beheld the palace of Beautiful; and after a few interrogations, was admitted by a damsel called Discretion, who with her two sisters, Piety and Prudence, he held a long conversation.

After leaving these good damsels, Christian passed on his way; and in the middle of the Valley of Humiliation, he met with Apollion, with whom he had a bloody struggle; Apollion throwing darts as thick as hail: but at last Christian overcame.

Now at the end of this valley was another called the valley of the shadow of death; in the midst of which he perceived the mouth of hell; from which flame and smoke issued out in such abundance, that he was obliged to put up his sword and betake himself to All-prayer.

Shortly after this he came up with Faithful; with whom he held sweet converse till they came to Vanity Fair. A merchant asking what they would buy, they said the truth; which he took amiss, and raised a hubbub; so that they were both taken up and put in a cage, for public view.

Christian and Faithful were brought before Mr. Hategood, to stand their trial. Envy, Superstition, and Hypocrisy, were brought forward as evidences, who did not fail to tell a partial story; which a partial jury confirmed; and Faithful was condemned to die at the stake.

Faithful was then brought out and suffered at the stake: Thus came he to his end, but there stood behind the multitude a chariot, and horses into which he was taken up and carried through the clouds. Christian escaping went on his way.

Christian soon fell in with Hopeful, another pilgrim, with whom he journeyed; and they having slept in the policies[1] of Doubting Castle, were taken prisoners, by Giant Despair, who treated them harshly: a key found in Christians bosom, opened the doors, and they made their escape.

Having escaped from Giant Despair, they soon met with the Shepherds of the Delectable Mountains. Leaving this country, they came to the enchanted ground, where they fell in with some of the shining inhabitants, of the City.

1. Park, grounds.

JOHN BUNYAN

Christian and Hopeful drawing nigh to the Celestial City, beheld the streets were paved with pure gold, but there was a very deep river through which they must pass the Pilgrims were alarmed and begun to sink; but rose again and were welcomed on the other side by two glorious Persons.

Christian's wife and children wept for him, until a heavenly messenger gave her a letter to follow her husband, and live with him for ever. At first she was overcome, but taking the road with all her children they fell in with Mercy, and went toward the wicket gate.

After they had got safely through the Slough of Despond, they arrived at the gate, where they knocked a long time, till at length the keeper called out "Who's there," and opened the gate, and taking Christiana by the hand welcomed them saying "Suffer little children to come unto me."

With some difficulty Mercy was admitted, and they safely arrived at Interpreter's house; supper being ready, and thanks given, they partook of a hearty repast; Interpreter asked how she became a pilgrim, she said, it was by the loss of her husband, and a letter from the King of Zion.

In the morning they were much refreshed. Greatheart was sent along with them to guide them on their way. They passed the place where the load fell from Christian's back; and came to the place where Simple, Sloth, and Presumption were hanging in chains.

They soon arrived at the Hill of Difficulty; Greatheart shewed them the spring where Christian drank; they then begun to ascend the hill, but Christiana began to pant and want rest; but Greatheart encouraged them, telling them they were near the Arbour, where they would find rest.

Being refreshed at the Arbour, and approaching Doubting Castle, Greatheart determined to level it with the ground. He and the giant had a severe fight, but the giant was overcome. They then demolished the Castle, and released many prisoners, where many strange sights were seen.

They still persevered on in their journey by the straight way, and narrow path of pilgrims; occasionally meeting with difficulties and encouragement, till they arrived at the land of Beulah, where the sun shines night and day; and here they betook themselves to rest.

Now while they lay here there was a post came from the Celestial City, with a letter to Christianna: the contents were "Hail good woman! I bring thee good tidings that the master calleth for thee, and expecteth that thou shouldst stand in his presence within these ten days."

Now the day drew on that Christiana must be gone. So the road was full of people to see her take her journey. So she came forth and entered the river with a beckon of farewell to those that follow her to the river side. The last words she was heard to say, were, "I come, Lord, to be with thee, and bless thee."

So her children and friends returned to their place; for those that waited for Christiana had carried her out of their sight. So she went and called and entered in at the gate with all the ceremonies of Joy that Christian had done before her.

FINIS.

ISAAC WATTS
1674–1748

Isaac Watts's *Divine Songs for Children*, first published in 1715, was an inescapable part of Protestant childhood for well over 150 years. Every Sunday school scholar repeated the poems; they were part of the nursery life of children like the Liddell girls, for whom in 1865 Lewis Carroll parodied "How doth the little busy Bee" and "'Tis the voice of a sluggard." Wilbur Macey Stone in *The Divine and Moral Songs of Isaac Watts* (1918) listed 550 British and American editions and in 1929 added 117 more. And this is without taking into account a multitude of appearances in chapbooks and school books.

Watts, a Nonconformist minister, wrote more than 600 hymns as well as many theological and educational works. From 1702 he presided over a London meetinghouse, but from 1712 until his death he lived with Sir Thomas Abney's family in Hertfordshire as their chaplain and as tutor to the three daughters, to whom *Divine Songs for Children* is dedicated. Watts added six more moral songs to subsequent editions and by popular request "A Cradle Hymn," already published. The title *Divine and Moral Songs* was not used until many years after his death.

The precepts are much the same as in James Janeway's *A Token for Children* (1671). It is interesting that in a 1781 Boston edition of *A Token* three Watts songs, "The Advantages of Early Religion," "The Danger of Delay," and "Examples of Early Piety," were also included. Janeway himself had not used the expression "early piety," which was to be the theme of so many sermons and tracts aimed at youth—"Nothing but early piety! early piety! . . . I am tired to death of early piety!" as one American Sunday school student remarked in 1852. Indeed Jacob Abbott, schoolmaster, author, and himself a clergyman, in his book *Early Piety* (1838) told parents that this sort of pressure could well be counterproductive. While undoubtedly Watts warned about the fate awaiting liars, and those who curse, scoff, or take God's name in vain, he did not push children toward precocious religious maturity, and, unlike so many of his Puritan contemporaries, he recognized that play was an essential part of childhood. His method of cajoling into good behavior was something entirely new, as is shown in the song "Against Quarrelling and Fighting." Very different too from his contemporaries was his gentle tolerance and lack of religious dogmatism; Watts wished to have a universal appeal, saying in his preface to *Divine Songs for Children* that nothing would be found "that savours of party: the children of high and low degree, of the church of England dissenters" [he himself of course being one]. Some doctrinaire Sunday school teachers criticized him for this tolerance.

Watts was not a great poet, but he was a memorable one. He had said in his preface, "What is learnt in Verse is longer retain'd in Memory, and sooner recollected[.]" Some of his lines have been passed down the centuries to become proverbs.

The poems printed here all appeared in the first (1715) edition, with the exception of "A Cradle Hymn," which was added in 1727. "The Sluggard" and "Innocent Play" were printed in the second section of the work, subtitled "A Slight Specimen of Moral Songs."

From Divine Songs for Children

AGAINST QUARRELLING AND FIGHTING

Let dogs delight to bark and bite,
    For God hath made them so;
Let bears and lions growl and fight,
    For 'tis their nature too.

But, children, you should never let
    Such angry passions rise;
Your little hands were never made
    To tear each other's eyes.

Let love through all your actions run,
    And all your words be mild;
Live like the blessed Virgin's Son,
    That sweet and lovely child.

His soul was gentle as a lamb;
    And as his stature grew,
He grew in favour both with man,
    And God his Father too.

Now Lord of all he reigns above,
    And from his heavenly throne,
He sees what children dwell in love,
    And marks them for his own.

AGAINST IDLENESS AND MISCHIEF

How doth the little busy bee
    Improve each shining hour,
And gather honey all the day
    From every opening flower.

How skilfully she builds her cell!
    How neat she spreads the wax!
And labours hard to store it well
    With the sweet food she makes.

In works of labour or of skill,
    I would be busy too;
For Satan finds some mischief still
    For idle hands to do.

In books, or works, or healthful play,
    Let my first years be past;
That I may give for every day
    Some good account at last.

An Evening Song

And now another day is gone,
    I'll sing my Maker's praise;
My comforts every hour make known
    His providence and grace.

But how my childhood runs to waste!
    My sins how great their sum!
Lord, give me pardon for the past,
    And strength for days to come.

I lay my body down to sleep;
    Let angels guard my head,
And through the hours of darkness keep
    Their watch around my bed.

With cheerful heart I close my eyes
    Since thou wilt not remove;
And in the morning let me rise
    Rejoicing in thy love.

The Sluggard

'Tis the voice of a sluggard; I hear him complain,
"You have wak'd me too soon, I must slumber again;"
As the door on its hinges, so he on his bed,
Turns his sides and his shoulders, and his heavy head.

"A little more sleep, and a little more slumber;"
Thus he wastes half his days, and his hours without number;
And when he gets up, he sits folding his hands,
Or walks about sauntering, or trifling he stands;

I pass'd by his garden, and saw the wild brier,
The thorn and the thistle grow broader and higher;
The clothes that hang on him are turning to rags;
And his money still wastes, till he starves or he begs.

I made him a visit still hoping to find
He had took better care for improving his mind;
He told me his dreams, talk'd of eating and drinking,
But he scarce reads his Bible, and never loves thinking.

Said I then to my heart, "Here's a lesson for me;
That man's but a picture of what I might be.
But thanks to my friends for their care in my breeding,
Who taught me betimes to love working and reading."

Innocent Play

Abroad in the meadows, to see the young lambs
Run sporting about by the side of their dams,
    With fleeces so clean and so white;
Or a nest of young doves, in a large open cage,
When they play all in love, without anger or rage,
How much we may learn from the sight!

If we had been ducks, we might dabble in mud;
Or dogs, we might play till it ended in blood;
    So foul so fierce are their natures;
But Thomas and William, and such pretty names;
Should be cleanly and harmless as doves or as lambs,
    Those lovely sweet innocent creatures.

Not a thing that we do, nor a word that we say,
Should injure another in jesting or play;
    For he's still in earnest that's hurt;
How rude are the boys that throw pebbles and mire!
There's none but a madman will fling about fire,
    And tell you " 'Tis all but in sport."

A Cradle Hymn

Hush! my dear, lie still and slumber,
    Holy angels guard thy bed!
Heavenly blessings without number
    Gently falling on thy head.

Sleep, my babe, thy food and raiment,
    House and home, thy friends provide;
All without thy care or payment;
    All thy wants are well supplied.

How much better thou'rt attended
    Than the Son of God could be;
When from heaven he descended,
    And became a child like thee!

Soft and easy is thy cradle:
    Coarse and hard thy Saviour lay,
When his birth-place was a stable,
    And his softest bed was hay.

Blessed babe! what glorious features,
    Spotless fair, divinely bright!
Must he dwell with brutal creatures!
    How could angels bear the sight!

Was there nothing but a manger
   Cursed sinners could afford,
To receive the heavenly stranger?
   Did they thus affront their Lord?

Soft, my child! I did not chide thee,
   Tho' my song might sound too hard;
'Tis thy { *mother / nurse that } sits beside thee,
   And her arms shall be thy guard.

Yet to read the shameful story,
   How the Jews abus'd their King;
How they serv'd the Lord of glory,
   Makes me angry while I sing.

See the kinder shepherds round him,
   Telling wonders from the sky:
Where they sought him, there they found him,
   With his virgin-mother by.

See the lovely babe a-dressing,
   Lovely infant, how he smil'd
When he wept, the mother's blessing
   Sooth'd and hush'd the holy child.

Lo! he slumbers in a manger,
   Where the horned oxen fed,
Peace, my darling, here's no danger,
   Here's no ox a-near thy bed.

'Twas to save thee, child, from dying,
   Save my dear from burning flame,
Bitter groans and endless crying,
   That thy blest Redeemer came.

May'st thou live to know and fear him,
   Trust and love him all thy days;
Then go dwell for ever near him,
   See his face and sing his praise!

I could give thee thousand kisses,
   Hoping what I most desire;
Not a mother's fondest wishes
   Can to greater joys aspire.

1715   1727

*Here you may use the words *brother, sister, neighbour, friend,* &c.

HESBA STRETTON
1832–1911

Hesba Stretton was one of the most successful practitioners of the genre known as street arab stories—tales of the destitute waifs who roamed Victorian city streets. "Their carefully chosen details were guaranteed to touch the heart without turning the stomach or offending the enlarged Victorian sense of delicacy," as Nancy Cutts says in *Ministering Angels* (1979).

Interest in these outcasts came from a new awareness of the abysmal poverty and degradation of city life in industrialized Britain. There had been adult fiction with this background, but use of the subject in children's books began only in the 1860s. The purpose of the stories was twofold: to impart a religious message and to evoke pity for the suffering children. Like Oliver Twist, though surrounded with depravity the central characters remain uncorrupted—something that welfare workers such as Dr. Thomas Barnardo considered rare indeed.

Hesba Stretton, whose real name was Sarah Smith, created her pseudonym from All Stretton near her home in Wellington, Shropshire, and the initial letters of her siblings' names. The family was a strict Methodist one; Hesba Stretton, an austere woman, to the end of her life never entered a theater and indeed disapproved of most forms of entertainment. She had firsthand experience of the conditions about which she wrote, and took a prominent part in the founding of the London Society for the Prevention of Cruelty to Children. She was a prolific writer, publishing some fifty volumes between 1866 and 1906—mostly religious and moral tales for the Religious Tract Society.

Jessica's First Prayer, which first appeared in *Sunday at Home* in 1866, was her most famous work. By the time of her death in 1911 two million copies were said to have been printed; it had been translated into most European languages and circulated by missionaries in Africa and Asia. It is the story of how the unwanted beggar child of a drunken, violent mother discovers Christian faith and brings about a change of heart in her first benefactor, Daniel. At his coffee stall he has grudgingly given her coffee dregs and some crusts of bread, but he is appalled when she finds her way to the chapel where he is a caretaker, feeling that his respectability is at risk. However, the minister and his little daughters welcome her, and Daniel, his proud heart melted, finally adopts her. These four chapters from the 12,000-word book describe Jessica's first marveling experience of the chapel, her meeting with the minister, and her first prayer. In the little-known sequel *Jessica's Mother* (1867), the mother returns, conveying—to an adult reader—that she is now a prostitute. Daniel dies, but Jessica has the promise of a new home with the minister and his motherless daughters.

From Jessica's First Prayer

CHAPTER III

An Old Friend in a New Dress

Week after week, through the three last months of the year, Jessica appeared every Wednesday at the coffee-stall, and, after waiting patiently till the close of the breakfasting business, received her pittance from the charity of her new friend. After a while Daniel allowed her to carry some of his load to the coffee-house, but he never suffered her to follow him farther, and he was always particular to watch her out of sight before he turned off through the intricate mazes of the streets in the direction of his own home. Neither did he encourage her to ask him any more questions; and often but very few words passed between them during Jessica's breakfast time.

As to Jessica's home, she made no secret of it, and Daniel might have followed her any time he pleased. It was a single room, which had once been a hayloft over the stable of an old inn, now in use for two or three donkeys, the property of costermongers dwelling in the court about it. The mode of entrance was by a wooden ladder, whose rungs were crazy and broken, and which led up through a trap-door in the floor of the loft. The interior of the home was as desolate and comfortless as that of the stable below, with only a litter of straw for the bedding, and a few bricks and boards for the furniture. Everything that could be pawned had disappeared long ago, and Jessica's mother often lamented that she could not thus dispose of her child. Yet Jessica was hardly a burden to her. It was a long time since she had taken any care to provide her with food or clothing, and the girl had to earn or beg for herself the meat which kept a scanty life within her. Jess was the drudge and errand-girl of the court; and what with being cuffed and beaten by her mother, and over-worked and ill-used by her numerous employers, her life was a hard one. But now there was always Wednesday morning to count upon and look forward to; and by and by a second scene of amazed delight opened upon her.

Jessica had wandered far away from home in the early darkness of a winter's evening, after a violent outbreak of her drunken mother, and she was still sobbing now and then with long-drawn sobs of pain and weariness, when she saw, a little way before her, the tall, well-known figure of her friend Mr. Daniel. He was dressed in a suit of black, with a white neckcloth, and he was pacing with brisk yet measured steps along the lighted streets. Jessica felt afraid of speaking to him, but she followed at a little distance, until presently he stopped before the iron gates of a large building, and, unlocking them, passed on to the arched doorway, and with a heavy key opened the folding-doors and entered in. The child stole after him, but paused for a few minutes, trembling upon the threshold, until the gleam of a light lit up within tempted her to venture a few steps forward, and to push a little way open an inner door, covered with crimson baize, only so far as to enable her to peep through at the inside. Then, growing bolder by degrees, she crept through herself, drawing the door to noiselessly behind her. The place was in partial gloom, but Daniel was kindling every gaslight, and each minute lit it up in more striking grandeur. She stood in a carpeted aisle, with high oaken pews on each side, almost as black as ebony. A gallery of the same dark old oak ran round the walls, resting upon massive pillars, behind one of which she was partly concealed, gazing with eager eyes at Daniel, as he mounted the pulpit steps and kindled the lights there, disclosing to her curious delight the glittering pipes of an organ behind it. Before long the slow and soft-footed chapel-keeper disappeared for a minute or two into a vestry; and Jessica, availing herself of his short absence, stole silently up under the shelter of the dark pews until she reached the steps of the organ loft, with its golden show. But at this moment Mr. Daniel appeared again, arrayed in a long gown of black serge; and as she stood spell-bound gazing at the strange appearance of her patron, his eyes fell upon her, and he also was struck speechless for a minute, with an air of amazement and dismay upon his grave face.

"Come, now," he exclaimed, harshly, as soon as he could recover his presence of mind, "you must take yourself out of this. This isn't any place for such as you. It's for ladies and gentlemen; so you must run away sharp before anybody comes. How ever did you find your way here?"

He had come very close to her, and bent down to whisper in her ear, looking nervously round to the entrance all the time. Jessica's eager tongue was loosened.

"Mother beat me," she said, "and turned me into the streets, and I see you there, so I followed you up. I'll run away this minute, Mr. Daniel; but it's a nice place. What do the ladies and gentlemen do when they come here? Tell me, and I'll be off sharp."

"They come here to pray," whispered Daniel.

"What is pray?" asked Jessica.

"Bless the child!" cried Daniel, in perplexity. "Why, they kneel down in those pews; most of them sit, though; and the minister up in the pulpit tells God what they want."

Jessica gazed into his face with such an air of bewilderment that a faint smile crept over the sedate features of the pew-opener.

"What is a minister and God?" she said; "and do ladies and gentlemen want anything? I thought they'd everything they wanted, Mr. Daniel."

"Oh!" cried Daniel, "you must be off, you know. They'll be coming in a minute, and they'd be shocked to see a ragged little heathen like you. This is the pulpit, where the minister stands and preaches to 'em; and there are the pews, where they sit to listen to him, or to go to sleep, may be; and that's the organ to play music to their singing. There, I've told you everything, and you must never come again, never."

"Mr. Daniel," said Jessica, "I don't know nothing about it. Isn't there a dark little corner somewhere that I could hide in?"

"No, no," interrupted Daniel, impatiently; "we couldn't do with such a little heathen, with no shoes or bonnet on. Come now, it's only a quarter to the time, and somebody will be here in a minute. Run away, do!"

Jessica retraced her steps slowly to the crimson door, casting many a longing look backwards; but Mr. Daniel stood at the end of the aisle, frowning upon her whenever she glanced behind. She gained the lobby at last, but already some one was approaching the chapel door, and beneath the lamp at the gate stood one of her natural enemies, a policeman. Her heart beat fast, but she was quickwitted, and in another instant she spied a place of concealment behind one of the doors, into which she crept for safety until the path should be clear, and the policeman passed on upon his beat.

The congregation began to arrive quickly. She heard the rustling of silk dresses, and she could see the gentlemen and ladies pass by the niche between the door and the post. Once she ventured to stretch out a thin little finger and touch a velvet mantle as the wearer of it swept by, but no one caught her in the act, or suspected her presence behind the door. Mr. Daniel, she could see, was very busy ushering the people to their seats; but there was a startled look lingering upon his face, and every now and then he peered anxiously into the outer gloom and darkness, and even once called to the policeman to ask if he had seen a ragged child hanging about. After a while the organ began to sound, and Jessica, crouching down in her hiding-place, listened entranced to the sweet music. She could not tell what made her cry, but the tears came so rapidly that it was of no use to rub the corners of her eyes with her hard knuckles; so she lay down upon the ground, and buried her face in her hands, and wept without restraint. When the singing was over, she could only catch a confused sound of a voice speaking. The lobby was empty now, and the crimson doors closed. The policeman, also, had walked on. This was the moment to escape. She raised herself from the ground with a feeling of weariness and sorrow; and thinking sadly of the light, and warmth, and music that were within the closed doors, she stepped out into the cold and darkness of the streets, and loitered homewards with a heavy heart.

Chapter IV
Peeps into Fairy-Land

It was not the last time that Jessica concealed herself behind the baize-covered door. She could not overcome the urgent desire to enjoy again and again the secret and perilous pleasure; and Sunday after Sunday she watched in the dark streets for the moment when she could slip in unseen. She soon learned the exact time when Daniel would be occupied in lighting up, before the policeman would take up his station at the entrance, and again, the very minute at which it would be wise and safe to take her departure. Sometimes the child laughed noiselessly to herself, until she shook with suppressed merriment, as she saw Daniel standing unconsciously in the lobby, with his solemn face and grave air, to receive the congregation, much as he faced his customers at the coffee-stall. She learned to know the minister by sight, the tall, thin, pale gentleman, who passed through a side door, with his head bent as if in deep thought, while two little girls, about her own age, followed him with sedate yet pleasant faces. Jessica took a great interest in the minister's children. The younger one was fair, and the elder was about as tall as herself, and had eyes and hair as dark; but oh, how cared for, how plainly waited on by tender hands! Sometimes, when they were gone by, she would close her eyes, and wonder what they would do in one of the high black pews inside, where there was no place for a ragged, bare-footed girl like her; and now and then her wonderings almost ended in a sob, which she was compelled to stifle.

It was an untold relief to Daniel that Jessica did not ply him with questions, as he feared, when she came for breakfast every Wednesday morning; but she was too shrewd and cunning for that. She wished him to forget that she had ever been there, and by and by her wish was accomplished, and Daniel was no longer uneasy, while he was lighting the lamps, with the dread of seeing the child's wild face starting up before him.

But the light evenings of summer-time were drawing near apace, and Jessica foresaw with dismay that her Sunday treats would soon be over. The risk of discovery increased every week, for the sun was later and later in setting, and there would be no chance of creeping in and out unseen in the broad daylight. Already it needed both watchfulness and alertness to dart in at the right moment in the grey twilight; but still she could not give it up; and if it had not been for the fear of offending Mr. Daniel, she would have resolved upon going until she was found out. They could not punish her very much for standing in the lobby of a chapel.

Jessica was found out, however, before the dusky evenings were quite gone. It happened one night that the minister's children, coming early to the chapel, saw a small tattered figure, bareheaded and barefooted, dart swiftly up the steps before them and disappear within the lobby. They paused and looked at one another, and then, hand in hand, their hearts beating quickly, and the colour coming and going on their faces, they followed this strange new member of their father's congregation. The pew-opener was nowhere to be seen, but their quick eyes detected the prints of the wet little feet which had trodden the clean pavement before them, and in an instant they discovered Jessica crouching behind the door.

"Let us call Daniel Standring," said Winny, the younger child, clinging to her sister; but she had spoken aloud, and Jessica overheard her, and before they could stir a step she stood before them with an earnest and imploring face.

"Oh, don't have me drove away," she cried; "I'm a very poor little girl, and it's all the pleasure I've got. I've seen you lots of times, with that tall gentleman as stoops, and I didn't think you'd have me drove away. I don't do any harm behind the door, and if Mr. Daniel finds me out, he won't give me any more coffee."

"Little girl," said the elder child, in a composed and demure voice, "we don't mean to be unkind to you; but what do you come here for, and why do you hide yourself behind the door?"

"I like to hear the music," answered Jessica, "and I want to find out what pray is, and the minister, and God. I know it's only for ladies and gentlemen, and fine children like you; but I'd like to go inside just for once, and see what you do."

"You shall come with us into our pew," cried Winny, in an eager and impulsive tone; but Jane laid her hand upon her outstretched arm, with a glance at Jessica's ragged clothes and matted hair. It was a question difficult enough to perplex them. The little outcast was plainly too dirty and neglected for them to invite her to sit side by side with them in their crimson-lined pew, and no poor people attended the chapel with whom she could have a seat. But Winny, with flushed cheeks and indignant eyes, looked reproachfully at her elder sister.

"Jane," she said, opening her Testament, and turning over the leaves hurriedly, "this was papa's text a little while ago. 'For if there come into your assembly a man with a gold ring, in goodly apparel, and there come in also a poor man in vile raiment; and ye have respect to him that weareth the gay clothing, and say unto him, Sit thou here in a good place; and say to the poor, Stand thou there, or sit here under my footstool; are ye not then partial in yourselves, and are become judges of evil thoughts?'[1] If we don't take this little girl into our pew, we 'have the faith of our Lord Jesus Christ, the Lord of glory, with respect of persons.'"

"I don't know what to do," answered Jane, sighing; "the Bible seems plain; but I'm sure papa would not like it. Let us ask the chapel-keeper."

"Oh, no, no!" cried Jessica, "don't let Mr. Daniel catch me here. I won't come again, indeed; and I'll promise not to try to find out about God and the minister, if you'll only let me go."

"But, little girl," said Jane, in a sweet but grave manner, "we ought to teach you about God, if you don't know him. Our papa is the minister, and if you'll come with us, we'll ask him what we must do."

"Will Mr. Daniel see me?" asked Jessica.

"Nobody but papa is in the vestry," answered Jane, "and he'll tell us all, you and us, what we ought to do. You'll not be afraid of him, will you?"

No," said Jessica, cheerfully, following the minister's children as they led her along the side of the chapel towards the vestry.

"He is not such a terrible personage," said Winny, looking round encouragingly, as Jane tapped softly at the door, and they heard a voice saying "Come in."

CHAPTER V

A New World Opens

The minister was sitting in an easy chair before a comfortable fire, with a hymn-book in his hand, which he closed as the three children appeared in the open doorway. Jessica had seen his pale and thoughtful face many a time from her hiding-place, but she had never met the keen, earnest, searching gaze of his eyes, which seemed to

---

1. James 2.5.2–3. The little sister is trying to say that by not allowing Jessica to sit with them they will be ignoring the apostle James's teaching.

pierce through all her wretchedness and misery, and to read at once the whole history of her desolate life. But before her eyelids could droop, or she could drop a reverential curtsey, the minister's face kindled with such a glow of pitying tenderness and compassion, as fastened her eyes upon him, and gave her new heart and courage. His children ran to him, leaving Jessica upon the mat at the door, and with eager voices and gestures told him the difficulty they were in.

"Come here, little girl," he said, and Jessica walked across the carpeted floor till she stood right before him, with folded hands, and eyes that looked frankly into his.

"What is your name, my child?" he asked.

"Jessica," she answered.

"Jessica," he repeated, with a smile; "that is a strange name."

"Mother used to play 'Jessica' at the theatre, sir," she said, "and I used to be a fairy in the pantomime, till I grew too tall and ugly. If I'm pretty when I grow up, mother says I shall play too; but I've a long time to wait. Are you the minister, sir?"

"Yes," he answered, smiling again.

"What is a minister?" she enquired.

"A servant!" he replied, looking away thoughtfully into the red embers of the fire.

"Papa!" cried Jane and Winny, in tones of astonishment; but Jessica gazed steadily at the minister, who was now looking back again into her bright eyes.

"Please, sir, whose servant are you?" she asked.

"The servant of God and of man," he answered, solemnly. "Jessica, I am your servant."

The child shook her head, and laughed shrilly as she gazed round the room, and at the handsome clothing of the minister's daughters, while she drew her rags closer about her, and shivered a little, as if she felt a sting of the east wind, which was blowing keenly through the streets. The sound of her shrill, childish laugh made the minister's heart ache, and the tears burn under his eyelids.

"Who is God?" asked the child. "When mother's in a good temper, sometimes she says 'God bless me!' Do you know him, please, minister?"

But before there was time to answer, the door into the chapel was opened, and Daniel stood upon the threshold. At first he stared blandly forwards, but then his grave face grew ghastly pale, and he laid his hand upon the door to support himself until he could recover his speech and senses. Jessica also looked about her, scared and irresolute, as if anxious to run away or to hide herself. The minister was the first to speak.

"Jessica," he said, "there is a place close under my pulpit where you shall sit, and where I can see you all the time. Be a good girl and listen, and you will hear something about God. Standring, put this little one in front of the pews by the pulpit steps."

But before she could believe it for very gladness, Jessica found herself inside the chapel, facing the glittering organ, from which a sweet strain of music was sounding. Not far from her Jane and Winny were peeping over the front of their pew, with friendly smiles and glances. It was evident that the minister's elder daughter was anxious about her behaviour, and she made energetic signs to her when to stand up and when to kneel; but Winny was content with smiling at her, whenever her head rose above the top of the pew. Jessica was happy, but not in the least abashed. The ladies and gentlemen were not at all unlike those whom she had often seen when she was a fairy at the theatre; and very soon her attention was engrossed by the minister, whose eyes often fell upon her, as she gazed eagerly, with uplifted face, upon him. She could scarcely understand a word of what he said, but she liked the tones of his voice, and the tender pity of his face as he looked down upon her. Daniel hovered about a good deal, with an air of uneasiness and displeasure, but she was unconscious of his presence. Jessica was intent upon finding out what a minister and God were.

Chapter VI

The First Prayer

When the service was ended, the minister descended the pulpit steps, just as Daniel was about to hurry Jessica away, and taking her by the hand in the face of all the congregation, he led her into the vestry, whither Jane and Winny quickly followed them. He was fatigued with the services of the day, and his pale face was paler than ever, as he placed Jessica before his chair, into which he threw himself with an air of exhaustion; but bowing his head upon his hands, he said in a low but clear tone, "Lord, these are the lambs of thy flock. Help me to feed thy lambs!"

"Children," he said, with a smile upon his weary face, "it is no easy thing to know God. But this one thing we know, that he is our Father—my Father and your Father, Jessica. He loves you, and cares for you more than I do for my little girls here."

He smiled at them and they at him, with an expression which Jessica felt and understood, though it made her sad. She trembled a little, and the minister's ear caught the sound of a faint though bitter sob.

"I never had any father," she said, sorrowfully.

"God is your Father," he answered, very gently; "he knows all about you, because he is present everywhere. We cannot see him, but we have only to speak, and he hears us, and we may ask him for whatever we want."

"Will he let me speak to him, as well as these fine children that are clean, and have got nice clothes?" asked Jessica, glancing anxiously at her muddy feet, and her soiled and tattered frock.

"Yes," said the minister, smiling, yet sighing at the same time; "you may ask him this moment for what you want."

Jessica gazed round the room with large, wide-open eyes, as if she were seeking to see God; but then she shut her eyelids tightly, and bending her head upon her hands, as she had seen the minister do, she said, "O God! I want to know about you. And please pay Mr. Dan'el for all the warm coffee he's give me."

Jane and Winny listened with faces of unutterable amazement; but the tears stood in the minister's eyes, and he added "Amen" to Jessica's first prayer.

1866

ISAAC BASHEVIS SINGER
1904–1991

Isaac Bashevis Singer was born in Leoncin, Poland, the son and grandson of rabbis; he was educated at Polish religious schools and finally at Warsaw's Tachkemoni Rabbinical Seminary, working later in Warsaw as a proofreader and translator. In 1935 he followed his elder brother, Israel Joshua Singer, to America. There he worked as a journalist for the Yiddish newspaper *Vorwärts* (*Jewish Daily Forward*), in which much of his fiction was published. Though he had written in Hebrew earlier in his career, Yiddish soon became his preferred language; as he said, "Yiddish contains vitamins that other languages don't have." He personally supervised translations of his works into English; the first to appear was *The Family Moskat* (1950), which traced the history of a Jewish family in Warsaw in the first half of the twentieth century. Most of his fiction for adults and his children's books concern the life, faith, culture, and folk traditions of Polish Jews. In 1978 he was awarded the Nobel Prize for Literature "for his impassioned narrative art which with roots in Polish-Jewish cultural tradition brings human conditions to life."

His children's books, which began with *Zlateh the Goat* (1966), a collection of short stories illustrated by Maurice Sendak, often contain supernatural elements; they are present in these stories and in *The Golem* (1982; described in the introduction to this section). In *The Power of Light* (1980), subtitled *Eight Stories for Hanukkah,* from which "Hanukkah in the Poorhouse" is taken, there are stories with angels, as in "The Squire," in which a miraculous visitor comes to lavish gifts on a starv-ing peasant family. But there are also domestic tales such as the opening story of the collection, which is probably a reminiscence of how his own family celebrated Hanukkah. The Jewish Festival of Lights commemorates the purification and rededication of the Temple of Jerusalem in 165 B.C.E. after its desecration by the Syrians. On Hanukkah, which typically begins in mid-December and lasts eight days, candles are lit nightly on an eight-branched candlestick (a menorah) and latkes, potato pancakes, are eaten, as in the opening paragraph of the story below. "Hanukkah in the Poorhouse" is a poignant account of oppression in czarist Russia, the tenacity with which a kidnapped Jewish boy clings to his faith, and his reunion many years later with his family at the festival of Purim. Purim celebrates the deliverance of the Jews brought about by Queen Esther, foster daughter of the righteous Mordecai, from the massacre planned by Haman, an official of Ahasuerus (i.e., Xerxes), the King of Persia, who had married Esther not knowing she was a Jew. The story is told in the Old Testament book of Esther, and Singer describes how young Jews traditionally wear carnival hats and masks to reenact it.

Hanukkah in the Poorhouse

Outside there was snow and frost, but in the poorhouse it was warm. Those who were mortally ill or paralyzed lay in beds. The others were sitting around a large Hanukkah lamp with eight burning wicks. Goodhearted citizens had sent pancakes sprinkled with sugar and cinnamon to the inmates. They conversed about olden times, unusual frosts, packs of wolves invading the villages during the icy nights, as well as encounters with demons, imps, and sprites. Among the paupers sat an old man, a stranger who had arrived only two days before. He was tall, straight, and had a milk-white beard. He didn't look older than seventy, but when the warden of the poorhouse asked him his age, he pondered a while, counted on his fingers, and said, "On Passover I will be ninety-two."

"No evil eye should befall you," the others called out in unison.

"When you live, you get older not younger," the old man said.

One could hear from his pronunciation that he was not from Poland but from Russia. For an hour or so he listened to the stories which the other people told, while looking intensely at the Hanukkah lights. The conversation turned to the harsh decrees against the Jews and the old man said, "What do you people in Poland know about harsh decrees? In comparison to Russia, Poland is Paradise."

"Are you from Russia?" someone asked him.

"Yes, from Vitebsk."

"What are you doing here?" another one asked.

"When you wander, you come to all kinds of places," the old man replied.

"You seem to speak in riddles," an old woman said.

"My life was one great riddle."

The warden of the poorhouse, who stood nearby, said, "I can see that this man has a story to tell."

"If you have the patience to listen," the old man said.

"Here we *must* have patience," the warden replied.

"It is a story about Hanukkah," said the old man. "Come closer, because I like to talk, not shout."

They all moved their stools closer and the old man began.

"First let me tell you my name. It is Jacob, but my parents called me Yankele. The Russians turned Yankele into Yasha. I mention the Russians because I am one of those who are called the captured ones. When I was a child Tsar Nicholas I,[1] an enemy of the Jews, decreed that Jewish boys should be captured and brought up to be soldiers. The decree was aimed at Russian Jews, not at Polish ones. It created turmoil. The child catchers would barge into a house or into a cheder,[2] where the boys studied, catch a boy as if he were some animal, and send him away deep into Russia, sometimes as far as Siberia. He was not drafted immediately. First he was given to a peasant in a village where he would grow up, and then, when he was of age, he was taken into the army. He had to learn Russian and forget his Jewishness. Often he was forced to convert to the Greek Orthodox faith. The peasant made him work on the Sabbath and eat pork. Many boys died from the bad treatment and from yearning for their parents.

"Since the law stipulated that no one who was married could be drafted for military service, the Jews often married little boys to little girls to save the youngsters from being captured. The married little boy continued to go to cheder. The little girl put on a matron's bonnet, but she remained a child. It often happened that the young wife went out in the street to play with pebbles or to make mud cakes. Sometimes she would take off her bonnet and put her toys in it.

"What happened to me was of a different nature. The young girl whom I was about to marry was the daughter of a neighbor. Her name was Reizel. When we were children of four or five, we played together. I was supposed to be her husband and she my wife. I made believe that I went to the synagogue and she prepared supper for me, a shard with sand or mud. I loved Reizel and we promised ourselves that when we grew up we really would become husband and wife. She was fair, with red hair and blue eyes. Some years later, when my parents brought me the good tidings that Reizel was to marry me, I became mad with joy. We would have married immediately; however, Reizel's mother insisted on preparing a trousseau for the eight-year-old bride, even though she would grow out of it in no time.

"Three days before our wedding, two Cossacks broke into our house in the middle of the night, tore me from my bed, and forced me to follow them. My mother fainted. My father tried to save me, but they slapped him so hard he lost two teeth. It was on the second night of Hanukkah. The next day the captured boys were led into the synagogue to take an oath that they would serve the Tsar faithfully. Half the towns-people gathered before the synagogue. Men and women were crying, and in the crowd I saw Reizel. In all misery I managed to call out, 'Reizel, I will come back to you.' And she called back, 'Yankele, I will wait for you.'

---

1. Emperor of Russia (1796–1855; r. 1825–55), known as a despotic ruler. A soldier by training, he repeatedly involved his country in war.

2. School for instruction in Jewish or Hebrew education (Yiddish).

"If I wanted to tell you what I went through, I could write a book of a thousand pages. They drove me somewhere deep into Russia. The trip lasted many weeks. They took me to a hamlet and put me in the custody of a peasant by the name of Ivan. Ivan had a wife and six children, and the whole family tried to make a Russian out of me. They all slept in one large bed. In the winter they kept their pigs in their hut. The place was swarming with roaches. I knew only a few Russian words. My fringed garment was taken away and my sidelocks were cut off.[3] I had no choice but to eat unkosher food. In the first days I spat out the pig meat, but how long can a boy fast? For hundreds of miles around there was not a single Jew. They could force my body to do all kinds of things, but they could not make my soul forsake the faith of my fathers. I remembered a few prayers and benedictions by heart and kept on repeating them. I often spoke to myself when nobody was around so as not to forget the Yiddish language. In the summer Ivan sent me to pasture his goats. In later years I took care of his cows and horse. I would sit in the grass and talk to my parents, to my sister Leah, and to my brother Chaim, both younger than I, and also to Reizel. Though I was far away from them, I imagined that they heard me and answered me.

"Since I was captured on Hanukkah I decided to celebrate this feast even if it cost me my life. I had no Jewish calendar,[4] but I recalled that Hanukkah comes about the time of Christmas—a little earlier or later. I would wake up and go outside in the middle of the night. Not far from the granary grew an old oak. Lightning had burned a large hole in its trunk. I crept inside, lit some kindling wood, and made the benediction. If the peasant had caught me, he would have beaten me. But he slept like a bear.

"Years passed and I became a soldier. There was no old oak tree near the barracks, and you would be whipped for leaving the bunk bed and going outside without permission. But on some winter nights they sent me to guard an ammunition warehouse, and I always found an opportunity to light a candle and recite a prayer. Once, a Jewish soldier came to our barracks and brought with him a small prayer book. My joy at seeing the old familiar Hebrew letters cannot be described. I hid somewhere and recited all the prayers, those of the weekdays, the Sabbath, and the holidays. That soldier had already served out his term, and before he went home, he left me the prayer book as a gift. It was the greatest treasure of my life. I still carry it in my sack.

"Twenty-two years had passed since I was captured. The soldiers were supposed to have the right to send letters to their parents once a month, but since I wrote mine in Yiddish, they were never delivered, and I never received anything from them.

"One winter night, when it was my turn to stand watch at the warehouse, I lit two candles, and since there was no wind, I stuck them into the snow. According to my calculation it was Hanukkah. A soldier who stands watch is not allowed to sit down, and certainly not to fall asleep, but it was the middle of the night and nobody was there, so I squatted on the threshold of the warehouse to observe the two little flames burning brightly. I was tired after a difficult day of service and my eyelids closed. Soon I fell asleep. I was committing three sins against the Tsar at once. Suddenly I felt someone shaking my shoulder. I opened my eyes and saw my enemy, a vicious corporal by the name of Kapustin—tall, with broad shoulders, a curled mustache,

---

3. Orthodox Jewish men wear a kind of undershirt with tassels, in accordance with biblical command (Deuteronomy 22.12, Numbers 15.38–40); these tassels or strings are often left outside the outer clothing and held during prayers. The garment is called *tzitzit* or *tallit katan*. Hasidic Jews (a sect of Orthodox Jews) grow long, curled sideburns, also as the Torah orders (Leviticus 19.27). The cutting of the sideburns and the removal of the *tzitzit* signal the removal of the external marks of the Orthodox Jewish male.

4. Because the Jewish calendar is organized on lunar, rather than solar, cycles, the holidays fall on different solar dates from year to year.

and a thick red nose with purple veins from drinking. Usually he slept the whole night, but that night some demon made him come outside. When I saw that rascal by the light of the still-burning Hanukkah candles, I knew that this was my end. I would be court-martialed and sent to Siberia. I jumped up, grabbed my gun, and hit him over the head. He fell down and I started running. I ran until sunrise. I didn't know where my feet were carrying me. I had entered a thick forest and it seemed to have no end.

"For three days I ate nothing, and drank only melted snow. Then I came to a hamlet. In all these years I had saved some fifteen rubles from the few kopeks that a soldier receives as pay. I carried it in a little pouch on my chest. I bought myself a cotton-lined jacket, a pair of pants, and a cap. My soldier's uniform and the gun I threw into a stream. After weeks of wandering on foot, I came to railroad tracks. A freight train carrying logs and moving slowly was heading south. It had almost a hundred cars. I jumped on one of them. When the train approached a station, I jumped off in order not to be seen by the stationmaster. I could tell from signs along the way that we were heading toward St. Petersburg, the capital of Russia. At some stations the train stood for many hours, and I went into the town or village and begged for a slice of bread. The Russians had robbed me of my best years and I had the right to take some food from them. And so I arrived in Petersburg.

"There I found rich Jews, and when I told them of my predicament, they let me rest a few weeks and provided me with warm clothes and the fare to return to my hometown, Vitebsk. I had grown a beard and no one would have recognized me. Still, to come home to my family using my real name was dangerous because I would be arrested as a deserter.

"The train arrived in Vitebsk at dawn. The winter was about to end. The smell of spring was in the air. A few stations before Vitebsk Jewish passengers entered my car, and from their talk I learned that it was Purim. I remembered that on this holiday it was the custom for poor young men to put on masks and to disguise themselves as the silly King Ahasuerus, the righteous Mordecai, the cruel Haman, or his vicious wife, Zeresh. Toward evening they went from house to house singing songs and performing scenes from the book of Esther, and the people gave them a few groschen. I remained at the railroad station until late in the morning, and then I went into town and bought myself a mask of Haman with a high red triangular hat made of paper, as well as a paper sword. I was afraid that I might be recognized by some townspeople after all, and I did not want to shock my old parents with my sudden appearance. Since I was tired, I went to the poorhouse. The poorhouse warden asked me where I came from and I gave him the name of some faraway city. The poor and the sick had gotten chicken soup and challah from wealthy citizens. I ate a delicious meal—even a slice of cake—washed down by a glass of tea.

"After sunset I put on the mask of the wicked Haman, hung my paper sword at my side, and walked toward our old house. I opened the door and saw my parents. My father's beard had turned white over the years. My mother's face was shrunken and wrinkled. My brother Chaim and my sister Leah were not there. They must have gotten married and moved away.

"From my boyhood I remembered a song which the disguised Haman used to sing and I began to chant the words:

> *I am wicked Haman, the hero great,*
> *And Zeresh is my spiteful mate,*
> *On the King's horse ride I will,*
> *And all the Jews shall I kill.*

"I tried to continue, but a lump stuck in my throat and I could not utter another word. I heard my mother say, 'Here is Haman. Why didn't you bring Zeresh the shrew with you?' I made an effort to sing with a hoarse voice, and my father remarked, 'A great voice he has not, but he will get his two groschen anyhow.'

" 'Do you know what, Haman,' my mother said, 'take off your mask, sit down at the table, and eat the Purim repast with us.'

"I glanced at the table. Two thick candles were lit in silver candlesticks as in my young days. Everything looked familiar to me—the embroidered tablecloth, the carafe of wine. I had forgotten in cold Russia that oranges existed. But on the table there were some oranges, as well as mandelbread,[5] a tray of sweet and sour fish, a double-braided challah, and a dish of poppy cakes. After some hesitation I took off my mask and sat down at the table. My mother looked at me and said, 'You must be from another town. Where do you come from?'

"I named a faraway city. 'What are you doing here in Vitebsk?' my father asked. 'Oh, I wander all over the world,' I answered. 'You still look like a young man. What is the purpose of becoming a wanderer at your age?' my father asked me. 'Don't ask him so many questions,' my mother said. 'Let him eat in peace. Go wash your hands.'

"I washed my hands with water from the copper pitcher of olden days and my mother handed me a towel and a knife to cut the challah. The handle was made of mother-of-pearl and embossed with the words 'Holy Sabbath.' Then she brought me a plate of kreplach filled with mincemeat. I asked my parents if they had children and my mother began to talk about my brother Chaim and my sister Leah. Both lived in other towns with their families. My parents didn't mention my name, but I could see my mother's upper lip trembling. Then she burst out crying, and my father reproached her, 'You are crying again? Today is a holiday.' 'I won't cry any more,' my mother apologized. My father handed her his handkerchief, and said to me, 'We had another son and he got lost like a stone in water.'

"In cheder I had studied the book of Genesis and the story of Joseph and his brothers. I wanted to cry out to my parents: 'I am your son.' But I was afraid that the surprise would cause my frail mother to faint. My father also looked exhausted. Gradually he began to tell me what happened on that Hanukkah night when the Cossacks captured his son Yankele. I asked, 'What happened to his bride-to-be?' and my father said, 'For years she refused to marry, hoping that our Yankele would return. Finally her parents persuaded her to get engaged again. She was about to be married when she caught typhoid fever and died.'

" 'She died from yearning for our Yankele,' my mother interjected. 'The day the murderous Cossacks captured him she began to pine away. She died with Yankele's name on her lips.'

"My mother again burst out crying, and my father said, 'Enough. According to the law, we should praise God for our misfortunes as well as for our good fortunes.'

"That night I gradually revealed to my parents who I was. First I told my father, and then he prepared my mother for the good news. After all the sobbing and kissing and embraces were over, we began to speak about my future. I could not stay at home under my real name. The police would have found out about me and arrested me. We decided that I could stay and live in the house only as a relative from some distant place. My parents were to introduce me as a nephew—a widower without children who came to live in their house after the loss of his wife. In a sense it was true. I had always thought of Reizel as my wife. I knew even then that I could never marry another woman. I assumed the name of Leibele instead of Yankele.

---

5. Almond biscuits, virtually identical to Italian biscotti.

"And so it was. When the matchmakers heard that I was without a wife, they became busy with marriage propositions. However, I told them all that I loved my wife too much to exchange her for another woman. My parents were old and weak and they needed my care. For almost six years I remained at home. After four years my father died. My mother lived another two years, and then she also died and was buried beside him. A few times my brother and sister came to visit. Of course they learned who I really was, but they kept it a secret. These were the happiest years of my adult life. Every night when I went to sleep in a bed at home instead of a bunk bed in the barracks and every day when I went to pray in the synagogue, I thanked God for being rescued from the hands of the tyrants.

"After my parents' deaths I had no reason to remain in Vitebsk. I was thinking of learning a trade and settling down somewhere, but it made no sense to stay in one place all by myself. I began to wander from town to town. Wherever I went I stopped at the poorhouse and helped the poor and the sick. All my possessions are in this sack. As I told you, I still carry the prayer book that the soldier gave me some sixty-odd years ago, as well as my parents' Hanukkah lamp. Sometimes when I am on the road and feel especially downhearted, I hide in a forest and light Hanukkah candles, even though it is not Hanukkah.

"At night, the moment I close my eyes, Reizel is with me. She is young and she wears the white silk bridal gown her parents had prepared for her trousseau. She pours oil into a magnificent Hanukkah lamp and I light the candles with a long torch. Sometimes the whole sky turns into an otherworldly Hanukkah lamp, with the stars as its lights. I told my dreams to a rabbi and he said, 'Love comes from the soul and souls radiate light.' I know that when my time comes, Reizel's soul will wait for me in Heaven. Well, it's time to go to sleep. Good night, a happy Hanukkah."

1980

TIM RICE
b. 1944

Joseph and the Amazing Technicolour Dreamcoat must be the most successful retelling ever of an Old Testament story, and has the rare distinction of also being a long-running musical in London and New York. The story has always been a favorite with children, and Rice's swinging lines and contemporary diction make good reading, which again must be rare for a libretto. This "pop oratorio" with music by Sir Andrew Lloyd Webber (b. 1948) was composed for the choir of Colet Court, the junior school of St. Paul's School in London, and first performed there in 1968. It then lasted only twenty-five minutes. After a successful second London performance at Westminster Central Hall the work was expanded. Its first American performance took place in 1970 at the College of the Immaculate Conception in Doug-

lastown, New York, and since then it has been a worldwide favorite with schools, amateur drama groups, and professional companies. "Every schoolchild and exschoolchild that I meet seems to have 'done *Joseph*' during their formative years," Tim Rice said in his foreword to the 1982 printed version. This was illustrated by Quentin Blake (b. 1928), whose witty style is admirably suited to the text. Blake's familiar cartoon technique and deceptively casual approach bring out all the latent humor in the words.

The story is taken from Genesis, beginning in chapter 37, in Canaan, when Joseph, we are told, is seventeen, and his father, Jacob, who loved Joseph "more than all his children . . . made him a coat of many colours." Joseph's eleven brothers are jealous, even more so when he tells them he has dreamed that there will be a time when he shall reign supreme over them. Plotting to get rid of him, they sell him to Ishmaelites who take him to Egypt, where he becomes a slave in the household of Potiphar, one of Pharaoh's senior officers, who sees his abilities and makes him overseer of the household. But Potiphar's wife tries to seduce him and he is thrown into prison. He is unexpectedly released when Pharoah is told of his power to interpret dreams.

After the triumph related in the excerpt included here, the subsequent songs in the musical describe the famine in Canaan, which sends the brothers to Egypt to beg for help from Pharaoh's most powerful minister, who they do not realize until much later is their brother Joseph:

Grovel grovel cringe now stoop fall
Worship worship beg kneel sponge crawl
We're just eleven brothers—good men and true
Though we know we count for nothing when up
   next to you.

Finally, Jacob comes to Egypt:

No longer feeling old
And Joseph went to meet him in his chariot of
   gold.

Tim Rice and Andrew Lloyd Webber have collaborated on other musicals. Their greatest success was the "rock opera" *Jesus Christ Superstar* (staged 1971, filmed 1973).

From Joseph and the Amazing Technicolour Dreamcoat

Pharaoh Story

Pharaoh he was a powerful man
With the ancient world in the palm of his hand
To all intents and purposes he
Was Egypt with a capital E
Whatever he did he was showered with praise
If he cracked a joke then you chortled for days
No-one had rights or a vote but the king
In fact you might say he was fairly right-wing
When Pharaoh's around then you get down on the ground
If you ever find yourself near Rameses
Get down on your knees

But down at the other end of the scale
Joseph was still doing time in jail
For even though he was in with the guards
A lifetime in prison was still on the cards
But though Joseph's prospects were not looking bright
At the end of the tunnel was a glimmer of light
For all of a sudden there were visions and things
Disturbing the sleep of both peasants and kings
Strange as it seems there'd been a run of crazy dreams
And a man who could interpret would go far
Could become a star
Could be famous, could be a big success

Poor, Poor Pharaoh

Guess what? In his bed Pharaoh had an uneasy night
He had had a dream that pinned him to his sheets with fright
No-one knew the meaning of the dream
What to do? Whatever could it mean?
Then some lively lad said
He knew of a bloke in jail
Who was hot on dreams, could explain old Pharaoh's tale
Pharaoh said—

Fetch this Joseph man
I need him to help me if he can

Chained and bound, afraid, alone
Joseph stood before the throne

My service to Pharaoh has begun
Tell me your problems, mighty one

Song of the King (Seven Fat Cows)

I was wandering along the banks of the river when seven fat cows came up out of the Nile
And right behind these fine healthy animals came seven other cows that were skinny and vile
And then the thin cows ate the fat cows which I thought would do them good
But no it didn't make them fatter like such a monster supper should
The thin cows were as thin as they had ever ever been
This dream has got me baffled, hey Joseph what does it mean?
Now you know that kings ain't stupid
But I don't have a clue
So don't be cruel Joseph
Help me now I beg of you . . .

Then I was standing doing nothing in a field out of town when I saw seven beautiful ears of corn
They were ripe, they were golden, but you've guessed it—right behind them there were seven other ears that were tattered and torn
Then the bad corn ate the good corn, they came up from behind, yes they did

But Joseph here's the punchline I think it's going to blow your mind, flip your lid
The bad corn was as bad as it had ever ever been
This dream has got me all shook up, treat me nice and tell me what it means
Hey, hey Joseph won't you tell poor old Pharoah
What does it mean?

Pharoah's Dream Explained

Seven years of bumper crops are on their way
Years of plenty, endless wheat and tons of hay
Your farms will boom, there won't be room
the surplus food you grow

After that the future doesn't look so bright
Egypt's luck will change completely overnight
And famine's hand will stalk the land
With food an all-time low

Noble king there is no doubt
What your dream is all about
All these things you saw in your pyjamas
Are a long-range forecast for your farmers
And I'm sure it's crossed your mind
What it is you have to find
Find a man to lead you through the famine
With a flair for economic planning
But who this man would be I just don't know

Stone the Crows

Pharaoh
Well stone the crows this Joseph is a clever kid
Who'd have thought that fourteen cows could mean the things he says they did?

Joseph, you must help me further, I have got a job for you
You shall lead us through this crisis, you shall be my number two

Pharaoh told his guards to fetch a chisel from the local store
Whereupon he ordered them to cut the chains that Joseph wore
Joseph got a royal pardon and a host of splendid things
A chariot of gold, a cloak, a medal and some signet rings
Seven summers on the trot were perfect just as Joseph said
Joseph saw that food was gathered ready for the years ahead
Seven years of famine followed, Egypt did not mind a bit
The first recorded rationing in history was a hit

Adoring Girls
Joseph how can we ever say
All we want to about you
We're so glad you came our way
We would have perished without you

Pharaoh

Joseph we are the perfect team
Old buddies that's you and me
I was wise to have chosen you
You will be wise to agree
We were in a jam—would have baffled Abraham
But now we're a partnership it's just a piece of cake

Girls

Greatest man since Noah
Only goes to shoah

Joseph

Anyone from anywhere can make it, if they get a lucky break

1968   1982

Fantasy

> Alice laughed. "There's no use trying," she said: "one *ca'n't*
> believe impossible things." "I dare say you haven't had
> much practice," said the Queen. "When I was your age, I
> always did it for half-an-hour a day. Why, sometimes I've
> believed as many as six impossible things before breakfast."
>
> —Lewis Carroll, *Through the Looking-Glass and
> What Alice Found There* (1871)

In his essay "On Fairy-Stories," J. R. R. Tolkien created a useful word for understanding the powerful hold that fantasy literature has on its readers. Tolkien's term *eucatastrophe* (or "good ending") describes the joy and "consolation" of the closed—and often happy—resolution of every successful fantasy. He declared, "It is the mark of a good fairy-story, of the higher or more complete kind, that however wild its events, however fantastic or terrible the adventures, it can give to child or man that hears it, when the 'turn' comes, a catch of the breath, a beat and lifting of the heart, near to (or indeed accompanied by) tears, as keen as that given by any form of literary art, and having a peculiar quality." In *Strategies of Wonder* (1992), Brian Attebery refines Tolkien's phrase and calls the reader's response to this "final turn toward deliverance" *wonder*. As fantasy both stretches the imagination through its possibilities and contains the imagination within its rules, "in return [fantasy] offers the possibility of generating not merely a meaning but an awareness of and a pattern for meaningfulness. This we call wonder." Although many distinguished and well-known examples of children's fantasy have appeared around the world—such as Carlo Collodi's *Pinocchio* (published in Italy in 1883), Astrid Lindgren's Pippi Longstocking series (published in the 1940s in Sweden and translated into English in the 1950s), Michael Ende's *The Neverending Story* (published in German in 1979 and first translated into English in 1983), and Noriko Ogiwara's *Sorairo Magatama* (1989; published as *Dragon Sword and Wind Child* in 1993)—this overview will consider works from the English-speaking tradition.

Narratives of Wonder

Fantasy literature for children encompasses many kinds of works—legends, ballads, romances, myths, literary fairy tales, magic realism, animal fantasies, time-slip fantasies, and science fiction. The wonder tale, or folktale, is one early form of fantasy literature, depicting a world that, as the folklorist Max Lüthi has pointed out, ultimately embodies order, comfort, and clarity. This description can be aptly applied to the generally utopian form of children's fantasy fiction as well. In both folktale and fantasy more generally, social hierarchies, taboos, supernatural creatures, magic, high moral standards, quests, and villains operate in a world in which chaos is ultimately dispelled and virtue rewarded. But although fantasy literature comforts the reader through the orderly structure and ultimate resolution that can be so unlike the untidiness and injustice of real life, it is also much more significantly tied to the "real" world through the attention paid to social and political structures, complicated familial and domestic relationships, and emotional and character development than is the ultra-condensed folktale. Whether it describes a separate world or fantastic interventions in a realistic setting, fantasy literature must conform to rules of internal logic and participate in the generic conventions of its subgroup. Thus, domestic fantasies such as those by E. Nesbit adhere to the conventions of the family story (a group of children who bicker yet whose allegiance to each other is never in question), J. K. Rowling's Harry Potter books are closely aligned with the traditions of the school story, and J. R. R. Tolkien's *The Hobbit* (1937) is also a quest narrative. The escape from the real that fantasy seems to promise is perhaps illusory. Attebery comments in *The Fantasy Tradition in American Literature* (1980), "The best fantasies perform the trick of investing the familiar with enough touches of the unreal—heightened color, heroic action, unexpected transformations, and dislocations in time—to evoke an acute sense of longing in the reader, a nostalgia for the never-was."

Perhaps more than any other literary genre, fantasy appeals to both the nostalgic adult and the imaginative child. Many of the most beloved characters in children's literature populate works of fantasy: the Victorian child, Alice, who falls down a rabbit hole into another world; Pinocchio, the talking puppet-boy; disobedient Peter Rabbit trapped in the garden; Charlotte the literate and literary spider; Harry Potter and the Hogwarts gang. Indeed, fantasy and children's literature combine seamlessly, as childhood is a time of active imagination and fantasy is the literary equivalent of an exciting daydream. While many works of fantasy for children, particularly in the classic or "high" fantasy tradition, confront large themes such as good versus evil, acculturation, social justice, and loyalty, there is also a strong countertradition of nonsense and satire in children's fantasy, starting with the work of Lewis Carroll and continued in the writings of, for example, Roald Dahl. Dahl's rollicking and irreverent fantasies take on and deflate power-hungry, abusive adults such as Aunts Spiker and Sponge in *James and the Giant Peach* (1961) or the diabolical English witches disguised as genteel ladies in *The Witches* (1983).

England: Fantasy's Foes and Friends

By the twentieth century works of fantasy constituted a large portion of the fiction published for children, but fantasy's relationship to children's literature was at first troubled. The late-eighteenth- and early-nineteenth-century gatekeepers of children's literature—figures such as Sarah Trimmer in her periodical *The Guardian of Education* (1802–06) and the popular author Maria Edgeworth—rejected such literature as unwholesome for children. Edgeworth writes in the preface to her book of instructive tales, *The Parent's Assistant* (1796), "But why should the mind be filled with fantastic visions, instead of useful knowledge? Why should so much valuable time be lost? Why should we vitiate their taste, and spoil their appetite, by suffering them to feed upon sweetmeats?"

In an effort to bridge this gap between instructive texts and imaginative works naturally attractive to children, the earliest fantasies for young readers attempted to marry whimsy with moral purpose, a method that persists in some works to the present day (though now executed with a much lighter touch). Such moral fantasies offer children lessons about proper behavior in a circumscribed world, while at the same time making some use of their natural affinity for make-believe. In Dorothy Kilner's *The Life and Perambulations of A Mouse* (1783) as well as in works by her sister-in-law Mary Ann Kilner, *The Adventures of a Pincushion* (ca. 1780) and *Memoirs of a Peg-Top* (ca. 1793), the fantasy is limited to the ability of the animal or inanimate objects to communicate their experiences. Their monologues never stray from what a pincushion, for example, lost underneath the sofa might be expected to see or hear if it were a living being. In *Mouse*, the protagonist is a rodent named Nimble who tells his life story to the narrator. Nimble relates the discussions he has overheard between parents and children on instructive topics such as proper conduct toward animals and the avoidance of vice. The didactic purpose of such literature is never in question.

The deep interest in children and childhood that emerged in the nineteenth century found a new expression in children's books of the Victorian era. Catherine Sinclair's novel *Holiday House* (1839), though indebted to the generic hybridity of Sarah Fielding's *The Governess* (1740), broke with the past and heralded the spirit of experimentation in children's fiction as it mixed together the traditionally separate literary elements of exaggeration, fantasy, domestic fiction, and, ultimately, the moral tale. Its first half presented children's faults and foibles without relating them to heavenly reward and punishment, as was invariably the case in earlier works for children. "Uncle David's Nonsensical Story about Giants and Fairies," from *Holiday House*, represents an early example of satiric fantasy couched in the terms of didacticism—in this case, embedded in the domestic misadventures of a pair of naughty siblings. The extraordinarily badly behaved but good-natured Laura and Harry Graham are told a tale about idleness and industry by their Uncle David. The amusing allegorical tale fails to have the desired effect on the children, however, and they continue to run riot until their older brother's grave illness and pious death convert them to seriousness, self-reflection, and repentance for their giddiness. Lucy Lane Clifford, too, writing more than forty years after Sinclair, similarly extends the parameters of the moral fantasy tale by blending the cautionary tale with folktale and horror fiction in "The New Mother" (1882).

The later nineteenth century is often called "the golden age" of children's literature because it was a time that imaginative works flowered, particularly in the British Isles. The most innovative work of fantasy to emerge from Victorian England was a masterpiece from an unlikely source: a shy yet passionate bachelor, an Oxford mathematics don, Charles Lutwidge Dodgson, who wrote fiction and poetry under the pen name Lewis Carroll (the Latinized and reversed form of "Charles Lutwidge"). Dodgson, whose love for little girls—especially Alice Liddell, a daughter of the dean of Dodgson's college, Christ Church—is legendary, first told the story that would become *Alice's Adventures in Wonderland* to three of the Liddell children as they rowed on the Thames River on July 4, 1862. This fanciful story about seven-year-old Alice's adventure so impressed Alice Liddell (who was ten years old at the time) that she begged for it to be written down. Dodgson complied, though doing so took him two and a half years, and presented the manuscript to her, complete with his own illustrations, as a Christmas gift in 1864. The story refused to take leave of Dodgson, however, and he read it to other children (most notably to the children of George MacDonald; MacDonald would eventually publish his own distinguished children's fantasies) to great, if private, applause. Dodgson ultimately undertook to publish the book, and it appeared, illustrated by the famous *Punch* political cartoonist John Tenniel, in 1865. The book was an immediate success; its sequel, *Through the Looking-Glass and What Alice Found There*, was published in 1871. *Looking-Glass* relates Alice's negotiations of a chess-game world inhabited by nursery rhyme characters such as Humpty Dumpty, a dueling lion and unicorn, and a kind and clumsy White Knight (Carroll himself).

In his use of satire, parody, and nonsense, Carroll self-consciously and gleefully broke with the earlier tradition of children's books promoted by Edgeworth and others that required moral lessons in every tale. Carroll's dreamscape mocked both the stultifying educational system that required mindless memorization of facts (while in Wonderland, Alice's inability to recite well-known didactic poems such as Isaac Watt's "How Doth the Little Busy Bee" and to perform simple arithmetic points to its ineffectiveness) and serious adult concerns such as etiquette, the criminal justice system, and even the monarchy. Wonderland is a world of contradiction, competition, and chaos—a nightmare world, if real. But in her dream Alice's own anger and emotion ultimately control the action as she wakes up once she names and dismisses her antagonists as "nothing but a pack of cards!" Similarly, Alice ends the chess game that constitutes *Looking-Glass* by upsetting the riotous feast table as she cries, "I can't stand this any longer!" Thus the fantasies end, framed by Alice's waking life as a lively, if conventionally well-brought-up, little girl. Dodgson's own fantasies of childhood innocence, and fears of irrelevance to Alice Liddell—the dreams, that is, of his alter ego, Lewis Carroll—can be found in the poems that introduce and conclude each book.

Although Dodgson, a deacon in the Church of England, kept his deeply held religious beliefs out of the *Alice* books, in the fantasy *The Water-Babies* (1863) the "muscular Christian" Charles Kingsley combined the adventures of a chimney sweep turned immortal water creature with religious themes, didacticism, and social commentary. George MacDonald's fantasies for children—such as *The Princess and the Goblin* (1872) and *The Princess and Curdie* (1883)—deliberately confront questions of faith, loyalty, and death. In MacDonald's created world, the struggles against evil mirror spiritual quests in the real world. This tradition of confronting religious issues in fantasy has proved to be enduring. MacDonald's first fantasy, *At the Back of the North Wind* (1871), focuses on the relationship between the powerful figure of the beautiful, maternal, yet terrifying North Wind—God's will on Earth—and the Christ-like human child, Diamond. C. S. Lewis's debt to MacDonald can be seen in his Chronicles of Narnia, beginning with *The Lion, the Witch, and the Wardrobe* (1950), which can be read as Christian allegory. Philip Pullman's fantasy trilogy, "His Dark Materials" (1995–2000), reconsiders Genesis and John Milton's *Paradise Lost* (1667) and combines thrilling adventure with probing analyses and reinterpretations of conventional views of religion, authority, the soul, creation, death, and sexual love.

Fantasy in Early America

The fantasy literature emerging from young America was certainly linked to both the didactic and nonsense strains of fanciful works for children. Distrust of fantasy literature for children was, if anything, stronger in Yankee America than in Britain. The Puritan inheritance, the lack of an ancient American folk tradition (Native American tales were largely invisible in white America), and the focus on the needs of the here-and-now all helped to create educators' and social commentators' preference for realism. Samuel Griswold Goodrich (1793–1860), who wrote information and travel books under the pseudonym Peter Parley, declared: "Some children, no doubt, have a ready appetite for these monstrosities [folktales such as "Little Red Riding Hood" and "Jack the Giant Killer"], but to others they are revolting, until by repetition and familiarity, the taste is sufficiently degraded to relish them."

Nevertheless, fantasy literature found fertile soil in the American imagination. The poet, painter, and Transcendentalist Christopher Pease Cranch, who had participated in the utopian Brook Farm experiment with Nathaniel Hawthorne and Ralph Waldo Emerson, wrote two stories of fantasy—*The Last of the Huggermuggers* (1855) and its sequel, *Kobboltozo* (1856)—about an intrepid Yankee boy who is shipwrecked on an island of giants and dwarves. Hawthorne's forays into children's literature included adaptations of classical myths in *A Wonder-Book for Girls and Boys* (1852). A generation earlier, in "Rip Van Winkle" and "The Legend of Sleepy Hollow" (both published in 1819), Washington Irving had freshened his retellings of German folktales by setting them within the America landscape. It remained for L. Frank Baum at the turn of the twentieth century, however, to advance American children's fantasy writing with *The Wonderful Wizard of Oz* (1900)—though the enterprise at first appeared to have little going for it. Because Baum's publisher was not interested in an American fairy-tale book, Baum and W. W. Denslow (the illustrator) paid for its production. Baum's innovation was in creating a fully realized fantasy world that reflected the American Midwest, American dreams, and American characters.

High Fantasy

High fantasy, or heroic romance, can be compared to the epic: in lengthy prose (as opposed to the verse of the long narrative poem of traditional epics), within an expansive setting, a hero, often with supernatural or magical assistance, struggles and saves a people or a way of life. J. R. R. Tolkien's trilogy *The Lord of the Rings* (1954–55) typifies the genre. The complex worlds of high fantasy are often indebted to Arthurian legend or European mythology for their scope and serious tone. For example, some of the characters and setting of Lloyd Alexander's Prydain Chronicles (1964–68) were inspired by Welsh mythology, although his judicious use of humor (especially in the first book of the series) sets his tone apart from that of other high fantasists such as Susan Cooper, Ursula K. LeGuin, and Alan Garner. Garner's *The Owl Service* (1967) retells some of the legends found in the medieval Welsh prose narrative known as the Mabinogion (or Mabinogi). The novel is set in twentieth-century Wales rather than a wholly separate world, emphasizing the vital connection between traditional stories and contemporary life.

In works of high or epic fantasy written for children, the hero is generally quite young, and the story is often as much about discovering one's identity, hidden talents, and weaknesses as it is about battles between good and evil. In *Worlds Within* (1988), Sheila Egoff comments that "Epic fantasy, like its forebears [myths and legends], is dominated by high purpose. There are worlds to be won or lost, and the protagonists engage in a deeply personal and almost religious battle for the common good." In the past, high fantasy, like the epic tradition, tended toward stories of masculine sacrifice, battle, and derring-do in which the mettle of a seemingly insignificant young man—such as Le Guin's Ged in the Earthsea trilogy or Alexander's Taran—is tested. Through struggles and self-doubts, however, the hero grows up to become a man of superior wisdom, skill, and moral authority. Fantasy novels by contemporary authors such as Anne McCaffrey, Robin McKinley, Tamora Pierce, and Jane Yolen, by contrast, focus on the empowerment and strengths of female characters succeeding in dangerous worlds; they represent a significant development in fantasy literature for children.

Animal fantasies employ humanlike animals of either sex as main characters. *Black Beauty: The Autobiography of a Horse* by Anna Sewell (1877) was an early text that used the conceit of the talking animal within a realistic, brutal world to deliver a message against cruelty to animals. E. B. White's *Charlotte's Web* (1952), like Kenneth Grahame's *The Wind in the Willows* (1908) before it, combines fantastic elements (talking animals) with a comic real world. In White's masterpiece, a clever and loyal spider demonstrates true friendship to the sophisticated barnyard society and shows the importance of the written word to members of the simple farming community that surrounds it. In this way, the humorous, anthropomorphized animals generally consider themselves to be superior to humans (consider Grahame's Mr. Toad and his tormentor, the bargewoman). Richard Adams brought the animal fantasy to epic heights in *Watership Down* (1972). Although not intended solely for a juvenile audience, this novel about a threatened community of rabbits was quickly adopted by young readers.

Stories about animated toys are a popular genre within fantasy literature; they hark back to the didactic stories of the late eighteenth century in which a spinning top recites its autobiography. Some popular doll texts include *The Raggedy Ann Stories* (1918) by Johnny Gruelle and Rumer Godden's *The Dolls' House* (1947). The Mennyms series by Sylvia Waugh (1994–97) reinvents the conventional animated toy narrative, as the "toys" are life-size ragdolls who function in contemporary London society, though their origins remain a secret. By now, the heavy didacticism of the genre's forebears has mostly fallen away to be replaced by humor, suspense, and sophisticated musings about the nature of the real and of humanity.

Time, Magic, and the Everyday

In contrast to high fantasies that tend to engage a mythic past that never was, most time-slip fantasies allow child characters from the present-day to enter a precise historical or future time and place. Through the disruption of the linear order of time, the child protagonist goes on a voyage of self-discovery through experiences in another time and place. The time-slip fantasy for children was introduced by E. Nesbit in *The Story of the Amulet* (1906), in which the children travel to the past and future. Retelling history by way of crossing the thresholds of time and place frees the individual character (and reader) to experience the past as the here and now. In Jane Yolen's first novel about the Holocaust, *The Devil's Arithmetic* (1988), the past is rescued from memory and becomes lived experience for the angry and confused adolescent Hannah Stern, who begins to understand the tragedy and the triumph of surviving the death camps after she is transported back in time to 1942 Poland. In *The Root Cellar* (1981) by the Canadian writer Janet Lunn, the lonely, petulant, orphaned Rose travels more than one hundred years into the past to the same northern Lake Ontario farmhouse in which she lives with relatives in the present. Rose enters the turbulence of the Civil War years, but as she finds warmth and acceptance in that dangerous time she learns to be loved—and loving—in her own time. An Australian writer sets out a similar theme: Abigail Kirk learns patience, forgiveness, and forbearance after she follows a strange-looking child up a street in The Rocks, the remains of Sydney's original settlement, and enters the world of Orkney immigrants in 1873 in Ruth Park's *Playing Beatie Bow* (1980). In a twist on the usual time-slip narrative, in which child characters enter the past, in Virginia Hamilton's *Justice Cycle* (1980–81) Justice Douglass, her twin brothers, and a neighbor boy slip to the future. All four children possess extraordinary extrasensory powers, and when they join together, their unique abilities enable them to travel to the far future and ultimately save it from a malevolent force. Jon Scieszka's Time Warp Trio books (the first, *Knights of the Kitchen Table,* was published in 1991) about a band of three friends who time travel to places such as ancient Rome, King Arthur's Camelot, and the American Old West combine historical facts with zany and juvenile humor.

In real life, time may seem to be linear and inviolable, yet our experience of time, which can seem to fly or stand still, indicates a certain pliability. Exploring the fabulous flexibility of time by manipulating it creates much of the wonder of fantasy literature from traditional tales to contemporary examples. In a time-slip fantasy, time behaves differently once characters have left the present. An extended stay in the fantastic past can take place within the span of a single breath. Although in Lewis's *The Lion, the Witch, and the Wardrobe* the Pevensey children grow to be adults and rulers of Narnia, when they accidentally find their way back to the lamp-post and the wardrobe that had led them from the Professor's house into a different world the Narnian years fall away; and when they reenter the room as children, only a second has passed. Tom Long's delight, in Philippa Pearce's *Tom's Midnight Garden* (1958), at entering the past when the clock strikes thirteen and at playing with a companion within the beautiful garden turns to deep reflection as he ponders Time and how it might be exploited: "Tom thought again: Time no longer—the angel on the grandfather clock had sworn it. But if Time is ever to end, that means that, here and now, Time itself is only a temporary thing. It can be dispensed with perhaps; or, rather, it can be dodged. Tom himself might be able to dodge behind Time's back and have the Past—that is, Hatty's Present and the garden—here, now and for ever." In Natalie Babbitt's *Tuck Everlasting* (1975), the child Winnie falls in love with a family who cannot die, but she learns that the wheel of time, and the death that accompanies it, is a blessing and immortality a curse.

The blend of magic with the quotidian is an aspect of children's fantasy found in works as diverse as *Charlotte's Web* for younger readers and the witch/magician fantasies of the New Zealand author Margaret Mahy written for adolescents. In Mahy's *The Changeover* (1984), Laura, by using her previously untapped supernatural powers, saves her young brother from the "incubus" Carmody Bracque after she teams up with an attractive older schoolmate who is a successful male witch as well as a prefect. In *The Nargun and the Stars* (1973), Patricia Wrightson's contemporary Australian country life is saturated with the Aboriginal spirits of the land. Diana Wynne Jones's ongoing Chrestomanci series (begun in 1977) is set in parallel worlds, some of which resemble regions of Earth at different historical periods, yet magic exists as part of the fabric of everyday life. J. K. Rowling uses this plot device in the Harry Potter books, in which wizards and witches coexist—sometimes uneasily—within the Muggle (or nonmagic) world.

From the mid–twentieth century forward, much of children's fantasy literature and media (in English) has been dominated and homogenized by the Walt Disney Company. But this fact does not tell the whole story of the vital role played by fantasy literature in the lives of contemporary children. Writers, critics, and psychiatrists from Lloyd Alexander and Bruno Bettelheim to Carl Jung, Jane Yolen, and Jack Zipes have argued that fantasy narrative holds impressive and important powers for individual psychological development, communal social development, or both. Lloyd Alexander argues that "children love [fantasy] and thrive on it, and I believe they need the experience of fantasy as an essential part of growing up." Tamora Pierce contends, "Fantasy is a literature of empowerment." And Jane Yolen declares that fantasy is not "Life Actual but it *is* Life in Truth." She continues; "[Life in Truth] tells us of the world *as it should be*. It holds certain values to be important. It makes issues clear. It is, if you will, a fiction based on great opposites, the clashing of opposing forces, question and answer, speech and echo, yin and yang, the great dance of opposites. And so the fantasy tale, the 'I that is not I,' becomes a rehearsal for the reader for life as it *should* be lived." The strong presence of fantasy in contemporary children's culture attests not only to the desire of adults that the young continue to believe impossible things but also to the organic and enduring power of narratives of wonder to delight, challenge, and affect young readers.

CATHERINE SINCLAIR
1800–1864

"In this age of wonderful mechanical inventions, the very mind of youth seems in danger of becoming a machine; and while every effort is used to stuff the memory, like a cricket-ball, with well-known facts and ready-made opinions, no room is left for the vigour of natural feelings, the glow of natural genius, and the ardour of natural enthusiasm," lamented Catherine Sinclair in the preface to her children's novel *Holiday House* (1839). By championing the "natural" in its depiction of childhood—which includes high spirits, naughtiness, and error—*Holiday House*, published at the very beginning of the Victorian era (1837–1901), marks an important milestone in British children's literature, which had, for didactic effect, previously relied on portrayals of children possessing either superlatively good or bad characters. The British children's book author Jan Mark calls *Holiday House* "the first book for and about children to present them as normally naughty rather than as puppets enacting a morality play." The book showcases the exploits of two well-intentioned but ill-behaved upper-class children, Harry and Laura Graham. They live with an affectionate uncle and grandmother under the supervision of a cruel governess, Mrs. Crabtree, while their father wanders about Europe to recover from the shock of his wife's death. Their pious and steady older brother Frank, though mostly off at sea, returns at the end of the novel, once Harry and Laura have matured, to set a good example by patiently suffering a fatal illness and dying a Christian death before them.

Sinclair was an educated Scots aristocrat born and raised in Edinburgh; her father was the politician Sir John Sinclair and her mother was a daughter of Alexander, Lord Macdonald. Herself the fourth daughter, Sinclair worked for many years as her father's secretary, and it was not until his death in 1835 that she began to write novels for adults, now largely forgotten. *Holiday House* began as a series of comic tales she told to her niece and nephew. Frank's last illness and deathbed scene, however, as Sinclair relates in her preface, were based on the true story of her younger brother, a sailor who died at the age of twenty. Besides her novels for adults, Sinclair published *Charlie Seymour: or the Good Aunt and the Bad Aunt* (1832) and a series of writings in pictograms, *Picture Letters* (1861–64), that sold extremely well. She was renowned as well for her philanthropic works, which included funding the first drinking fountain in Edinburgh.

Although *Holiday House* is primarily a realistic portrayal of an upper-class Scottish family embellished with touches of humorous irony and absurdity as well as sentimentality, the embedded story "Uncle David's Nonsensical Story about Giants and Fairies" is a tongue-in-cheek didactic fantasy—an unusual combination, and the essence of Sinclair's innovation in writing literature for youth. The spoiled and lazy boy, Master No-book, after spending some time with the fairies Do-nothing and Teach-all, realizes the good sense inherent in moderation, activity, and right conduct.

From Holiday House

CHAPTER IX. UNCLE DAVID'S NONSENSICAL STORY ABOUT GIANTS AND FAIRIES

"Pie-crust, and pastry-crust, that was the wall;
The windows were made of black-puddings and white,[1]
And slated with pancakes—you ne'er saw the like!"[2]

In the days of yore, children were not all such clever, good, sensible people as they are now! Lessons were then considered rather a plague—sugar-plums were still in demand—holidays continued yet in fashion—and toys were not then made to teach mathematics, nor story-books to give instruction in chemistry and navigation. These were very strange times, and there existed at that period, a very idle, greedy, naughty boy, such as we never hear of in the present day. His papa and mamma were—no matter who, and he lived—no matter where. His name was Master No-book, and he seemed to think his eyes were made for nothing but to stare out of the windows, and his mouth for no other purpose but to eat. This young gentleman hated lessons like mustard, both of which brought tears into his eyes, and during school-hours he sat gazing at his books, pretending to be busy, while his mind wandered away to wish impatiently for dinner, and to consider where he could get the nicest pies, pastry, ices and jellies,[3] while he smacked his lips at the very thoughts of them. I think he must have been first cousin to Peter Grey;[4] but that is not perfectly certain.

Whenever Master No-book spoke, it was always to ask for something, and you might continually hear him say, in a whining tone of voice, "Papa! may I take this piece of cake? Aunt Sarah! will you give me an apple? Mamma! do send me the whole of that plum-pudding!" Indeed, very frequently, when he did not get permission to gormandize, this naughty glutton helped himself without leave. Even his dreams were like his waking hours, for he had often a horrible nightmare about lessons, thinking he was smothered with Greek Lexicons, or pelted out of the school with a shower of English Grammars,[5] while one night he fancied himself sitting down to devour an enormous plum-cake, and all on a sudden it became transformed into a Latin Dictionary!

One afternoon, Master No-book, having played truant all day from school, was lolling on his mamma's best sofa in the drawing-room, with his leather boots tucked up on the satin cushions, and nothing to do but to suck a few oranges, and nothing to think of but how much sugar to put upon them, when suddenly an event took place, which filled him with astonishment.

A sound of soft music stole into the room, becoming louder and louder the longer he listened, till at length, in a few moments afterwards, a large hole burst open in the wall of his room, and there stepped into his presence two magnificent fairies, just arrived from their castles in the air, to pay him a visit. They had travelled all the way on purpose to have some conversation with Master No-book, and immediately introduced themselves in a very ceremonious manner.

1. Sausages made of blood and suet and of oatmeal and suet, respectively.
2. From the Mother Goose rhyme "Little King Boggen," which begins "Little King Boggen, he built a fine hall."
3. Sweet gelatins.
4. A gluttonous, lazy, and ill-mannered schoolboy character in *Holiday House*.
5. Book of the formal features of the English language. "Greek Lexicons": dictionaries.

The fairy Do-nothing was gorgeously dressed with a wreath of flaming gas round her head, a robe of gold tissue, a necklace of rubies, and a bouquet in her hand of glittering diamonds. Her cheeks were rouged to the very eyes, her teeth were set in gold, and her hair was of a most brilliant purple; in short, so fine and fashionable-looking a fairy never was seen in a drawing-room before.

The fairy Teach-all, who followed next, was simply dressed in white muslin, with bunches of natural flowers in her light brown hair, and she carried in her hand a few neat small books, which Master No-book looked at with a shudder of aversion.

The two fairies now informed him, that they very often invited large parties of children to spend some time at their palaces, but as they lived in quite an opposite direction, it was necessary for their young guests to choose which it would be best to visit first; therefore now they had come to inquire of Master No-book whom he thought it would be most agreeable to accompany on the present occasion.

"In my house," said the fairy Teach-all, speaking with a very sweet smile, and a soft, pleasing voice, "you shall be taught to find pleasure in every sort of exertion; for I delight in activity and diligence. My young friends rise at seven every morning, and amuse themselves with working in a beautiful garden of flowers,—rearing whatever fruit they wish to eat,—visiting among the poor,—associating pleasantly together,—studying the arts and sciences,—and learning to know the world in which they live, and to fulfil the purposes for which they have been brought into it. In short, all our amusements tend to some useful object, either for our own improvement or the good of others, and you will grow wiser, better, and happier every day you remain in the palace of Knowledge."

"But in Castle Needless, where I live," interrupted the fairy Do-nothing, rudely pushing her companion aside, with an angry, contemptuous look, "we never think of exerting ourselves for anything. You may put your head in your pocket, and your hands in your sides as long as you choose to stay. No one is ever even asked a question, that he may be spared the trouble of answering. We lead the most fashionable life imaginable, for nobody speaks to anybody! Each of my visitors is quite an exclusive, and sits with his back to as many of the company as possible, in the most comfortable armchair that can be contrived. There, if you are only so good as to take the trouble of wishing for anything, it is yours, without even turning an eye round to look where it comes from. Dresses are provided of the most magnificent kind, which go on themselves, without your having the smallest annoyance with either buttons or strings,—games which you can play without an effort of thought,—and dishes dressed by a French cook, smoking hot under your nose, from morning till night,—while any rain we have is either made of sherry, brandy, lemonade, or lavender water, and in winter it generally snows iced-punch for an hour during the forenoon."

Nobody need be told which fairy Master No-book preferred; and quite charmed at his own good fortune in receiving so agreeable an invitation, he eagerly gave his hand to the splendid new acquaintance who promised him so much pleasure and ease, and gladly proceeded in a carriage lined with velvet, stuffed with downy pillows, and drawn by milk-white swans, to that magnificent residence, Castle Needless, which was lighted by a thousand windows during the day, and by a million of lamps every night.

Here Master No-book enjoyed a constant holiday and a constant feast, while a beautiful lady covered with jewels was ready to tell him stories from morning till night, and servants waited to pick up his playthings if they fell, or to draw out his purse or his pocket-handkerchief when he wished to use them.

Thus Master No-book lay dozing for hours and days on richly embroidered cushions, never stirring from his place, but admiring the view of trees covered with the richest burned-almonds, grottoes of sugar-candy, a *jet d'eau*[6] of champagne, a wide sea which tasted of sugar instead of salt, and a bright clear pond, filled with goldfish, that let themselves be caught whenever he pleased. Nothing could be more complete; and yet, very strange to say, Master No-book did not seem particularly happy! This appears exceedingly unreasonable, when so much trouble was taken to please him, but the truth is, that every day he became more fretful and peevish. No sweetmeats were worth the trouble of eating, nothing was pleasant to play at, and in the end he wished it were possible to sleep all day, as well as all night.

Not a hundred miles from the fairy Do-nothing's palace, there lived a most cruel monster called the giant Snap-'em-up, who looked, when he stood up, like the tall steeple of a great church, raising his head so high that he could peep over the loftiest mountains, and was obliged to climb up a ladder to comb his own hair!

Every morning regularly, this prodigiously great giant walked round the world before breakfast for an appetite, after which he made tea in a large lake, used the sea as a slop-basin, and boiled his kettle on Mount Vesuvius.[7] He lived in great style, and his dinners were most magnificent, consisting very often of an elephant roasted whole, ostrich patties, a tiger smothered in onions, stewed lions, and whale soup; but for a side dish his greatest favourite consisted of little boys, as fat as possible, fried in crumbs of bread, with plenty of pepper and salt.

No children were so well fed, or in such good condition for eating, as those in the fairy Do-nothing's garden, who was a very particular friend of the giant Snap-'em-up's, and who sometimes laughingly said she would give him a licence, and call her own garden his "preserve," because she allowed him to help himself, whenever he pleased, to as many of her visitors as he chose, without taking the trouble even to count them, and in return for such extreme civility, the giant very frequently invited her to dinner.

Snap-'em-up's favourite sport was to see how many brace of little boys he could bag in a morning; so in passing along the streets, he peeped into all the drawing-rooms without having occasion to get upon tiptoe, and picked up every young gentleman who was idly looking out of the windows, and even a few occasionally who were playing truant from school; but busy children seemed always somehow quite out of his reach.

One day, when Master No-book felt even more lazy, more idle, and more miserable than ever, he lay beside a perfect mountain of toys and cakes, wondering what to wish for next, and hating the very sight of everything and everybody. At last he gave so loud a yawn of weariness and disgust, that his jaw very nearly fell out of joint, and then he sighed so deeply, that the giant Snap-'em-up heard the sound as he passed along the road after breakfast, and instantly stepped into the garden, with his glass[8] at his eye, to see what was the matter. Immediately on observing a large, fat, over-grown boy, as round as a dumpling, lying on a bed of roses, he gave a cry of delight, followed by a gigantic peal of laughter, which was heard three miles off, and picking up Master No-book between his finger and thumb, with a pinch that very nearly broke his ribs, he carried him rapidly towards his own castle, while the fairy Do-nothing laughingly shook her head as he passed, saying, "That little man does me great credit! he has only been fed for a week, and is as fat already as a prize ox! What a dainty morsel he will be. When do you dine to-day, in case I should have time to look in upon you?"

6. Fountain (French).   8. Spyglass or small telescope.
7. Active volcano in southeastern Italy.

On reaching home the giant immediately hung up Master No-book, by the hair of his head, on a prodigious hook in the larder, having first taken some large lumps of nasty suet, forcing them down his throat to make him become still fatter, and then stirring the fire, that he might be almost melted with heat, to make his liver grow larger. On a shelf quite near, Master No-book perceived the dead bodies of six other boys, whom he remembered to have seen fattening in the fairy Do-nothing's garden, while he recollected how some of them had rejoiced at the thoughts of leading a long, useless, idle life, with no one to please but themselves.

The enormous cook now seized hold of Master No-book, brandishing her knife, with an aspect of horrible determination, intending to kill him, while he took the trouble of screaming and kicking in the most desperate manner, when the giant turned gravely round and said, that as pigs were considered a much greater dainty when whipped to death than killed in any other way, he meant to see whether children might not be improved by it also; therefore she might leave that great hog of a boy till he had time to try the experiment, especially as his own appetite would be improved by the exercise. This was a dreadful prospect for the unhappy prisoner; but meantime it prolonged his life a few hours, as he was immediately hung up again in the larder, and left to himself. There, in torture of mind and body,—like a fish upon a hook,—the wretched boy began at last to reflect seriously upon his former ways, and to consider what a happy home he might have had, if he could only have been satisfied with business and pleasure succeeding each other, like day and night, while lessons might have come in as a pleasant sauce to his play-hours, and his play-hours as a sauce to his lessons.

In the midst of many reflections, which were all very sensible, though rather too late, Master No-book's attention became attracted by the sound of many voices laughing, talking, and singing, which caused him to turn his eyes in a new direction, when, for the first time, he observed that the fairy Teach-all's garden lay upon a beautiful sloping bank not far off. There a crowd of merry, noisy, rosy-cheeked boys were busily employed, and seemed happier than the day was long; while poor Master No-book watched them during his own miserable hours, envying the enjoyment with which they raked the flower-borders, gathered the fruit, carried baskets of vegetables to the poor, worked with carpenter's tools, drew pictures, shot with bows and arrows, played at cricket, and then sat in the sunny arbours learning their tasks, or talking agreeably together, till at length, a dinner-bell having been rung, the whole party sat merrily down with hearty appetites, and cheerful good humour, to an entertainment of plain roast meat and pudding, where the fairy Teach-all presided herself, and helped her guests moderately, to as much as was good for each.

Large tears rolled down the cheeks of Master No-book while watching this scene; and remembering that if he had known what was best for him, he might have been as happy as the happiest of these excellent boys, instead of suffering *ennui*[9] and weariness, as he had done at the fairy Do-nothing's, ending in a miserable death; but his attention was soon after most alarmingly roused by hearing the giant Snap-'em-up again in conversation with his cook; who said, that if he wished for a good large dish of scalloped[1] children at dinner, it would be necessary to catch a few more, as those he had already provided would scarcely be a mouthful.

As the giant kept very fashionable hours, and always waited dinner for himself till nine o'clock, there was still plenty of time; so, with a loud grumble about the trouble,

9. Feeling of mental weariness and dissatisfaction (French).

1. Dish in which the food is cut up and baked with a sauce, often with crumbs on top.

he seized a large basket in his hand, and set off at a rapid pace towards the fairy Teach-all's garden. It was very seldom that Snap-'em-up ventured to think of foraging in this direction, as he never once succeeded in carrying off a single captive from the enclosure, it was so well fortified and so bravely defended; but on this occasion, being desperately hungry, he felt as bold as a lion, and walked with outstretched hands, straight towards the fairy Teach-all's dinner-table, taking such prodigious strides, that he seemed almost as if he would trample on himself.

A cry of consternation arose the instant this tremendous giant appeared; and as usual on such occasions, when he had made the same attempt before, a dreadful battle took place. Fifty active little boys bravely flew upon the enemy, armed with their dinner knives, and looked like a nest of hornets, stinging him in every direction, till he roared with pain, and would have run away, but the fairy Teach-all, seeing his intention, rushed forward with the carving-knife, and brandishing it high over her head, she most courageously stabbed him to the heart!

If a great mountain had fallen to the earth, it would have seemed like nothing in comparison with the giant Snap-'em-up, who crushed two or three houses to powder beneath him, and upset several fine monuments that were to have made people remembered for ever; but all this would have seemed scarcely worth mentioning, had it not been for a still greater event which occurred on the occasion, no less than the death of the fairy Do-nothing, who had been indolently looking on at this great battle without taking the trouble to interfere, or even to care who was victorious; but being also lazy about running away, when the giant fell, his sword came with so violent a stroke on her head, that she instantly expired.

Thus, luckily for the whole world, the fairy Teach-all got possession of immense property, which she proceeded without delay to make the best use of in her power.

In the first place, however, she lost no time in liberating Master No-book from his hook in the larder, and gave him a lecture on activity, moderation, and good conduct, which he never afterwards forgot; and it was astonishing to see the change that took place immediately in his whole thought and actions. From this very hour, Master No-book became the most diligent, active, happy boy in the fairy Teach-all's garden; and on returning home a month afterwards, he astonished all the masters at school by his extraordinary reformation. The most difficult lessons were a pleasure to him,— he scarcely ever stirred without a book in his hand,—never lay on a sofa again,— would scarcely even sit on a chair with a back to it, but preferred a three-legged stool,—detested holidays,—never thought any exertion a trouble,—preferred climbing over the top of a hill to creeping round the bottom,—always ate the plainest food in very small quantities, joined a Temperance Society![2]—and never tasted a morsel till he had worked very hard and got an appetite.

Not long after this, an old uncle, who had formerly been ashamed of Master No-book's indolence and gluttony, became so pleased at the wonderful change, that, on his death, he left him a magnificent estate, desiring that he should take his name; therefore, instead of being any longer one of the No-book family, he is now called Sir Timothy Bluestocking,[3]—a pattern to the whole country round, for the good he does to every one, and especially for his extraordinary activity, appearing as if he could do twenty things at once. Though generally very good-natured and agreeable, Sir Timothy is occasionally observed in a violent passion, laying about him with his walking-stick in the most terrific manner, and beating little boys within an inch of

2. Organization dedicated to promoting the benefits of abstinence from alcoholic drinks.

3. A learned or literary person (usually a term of derision applied to women).

their lives; but on inquiry, it invariably appears that he has found them out to be lazy, idle, or greedy, for all the industrious boys in the parish are sent to get employment from him, while he assures them that they are far happier breaking stones on the road, than if they were sitting idly in a drawing-room with nothing to do. Sir Timothy cares very little for poetry in general; but the following are his favourite verses, which he has placed over the chimney-piece at a school that he built for the poor, and every scholar is obliged, the very day he begins his education, to learn them:—

> Some people complain they have nothing to do,
>   And time passes slowly away;
> They saunter about, with no object in view,
>   And long for the end of the day.
>
> In vain are the trifles and toys they desire,
>   For nothing they truly enjoy;
> Of trifles, and toys, and amusements they tire,
>   For want of some useful employ.
>
> Although for transgression the ground was accursed,
>   Yet gratefully man must allow,
> 'Twas really a blessing which doomed him, at first,
>   To live by the sweat of his brow.

"Thank you a hundred times over, Uncle David!" said Harry, when the story was finished. "I shall take care not to be found hanging any day on a hook in the larder! Certainly, Frank, you must have spent a month with the good fairy; and I hope she will some day invite me to be made a scholar of too, for Laura and I still belong to the No-book family."

"It is very important, Harry, to choose the best course from the beginning," observed Lady Harriet. "Good or bad habits grow stronger and stronger every minute, as if an additional string were tied on daily, to keep us in the road where we walked the day before; so those who mistake the path of duty at first, find hourly increasing difficulty in turning round."

"But, grandmamma!" said Frank, "you have put up some finger-posts to direct us right; and whenever I see 'No passage this way,' we shall all wheel about directly."

"As Mrs. Crabtree has not tapped at the door yet, I shall describe the progress of a wise and a foolish man, to see which Harry and you would prefer copying," replied Lady Harriet, smiling. "The fool begins when he is young, with hating lessons, lying long in bed, and spending all his money on trash. Any books he will consent to read are never about what is true or important; but he wastes all his time and thoughts on silly stories that never could have happened. Thus he neglects to learn what was done and thought by all the great and good men who really lived in former times; while even his Bible, if he has one, grows dusty on the shelf. After so bad a beginning, he grows up with no useful or interesting knowledge; therefore his whole talk is to describe his own horses, his own dogs, his own guns, and his own exploits; boasting of what a high wall his horse can leap over, the number of little birds he can shoot in a day, and how many bottles of wine he can swallow without tumbling under the table. Thus 'glorying in his shame,' he thinks himself a most wonderful person, not knowing that men are born to do much better things than merely to find selfish pleasure and amusement for themselves. Presently he grows old, gouty, and infirm—no longer able to do such prodigious achievements; therefore now his great delight is to sit with his feet upon the fender, at a club, all day, telling what a famous rider, shooter, and drinker he was long ago: but nobody cares to hear such old stories; therefore he is called a 'proser,' and every person avoids him. It is no wonder a man talks about himself, if he has never read or thought about anyone else. But at length his precious time has all been wasted, and his last hour comes, during which he can have nothing to look back upon but a life of folly and guilt. He sees no one around who loves him, or will weep over his grave; and when he looks forward, it is towards an eternal world, which he has never prepared to enter, and of which he knows nothing."

"What a terrible picture, grandmamma!" said Frank, rather gravely. "I hope there are not many people like that, or it would be very sad to meet with them. Now pray let us have a pleasanter description of the sort of persons you would like Harry and me to become."

"The first foundation of all is, as you already know Frank, to pray that you may be put in the right course, and kept in it; for of ourselves we are so sinful and weak, that we can do no good thing. Then feeling a full trust in the Divine assistance, you must begin and end every day with studying your Bible; not merely reading it, but carefully endeavouring to understand and obey what it contains. Our leisure should be bestowed on reading of wiser and better people than ourselves, which will keep us humble while it instructs our understandings, and thus we shall be fitted to associate with persons whose society is even better than books. Christians who are enlightened and sanctified in the knowledge of all good things will show us an example of carefully using our time, which is the most valuable of all earthly possessions. If we waste our money, we may perhaps get more; if we lose our health, it may be restored; but time squandered on folly must hereafter be answered for, and can never be regained. Whatever be your station in life, waste none of your thoughts upon fancying how much better you might have acted in some other person's place, but see what duties belong to that station in which you live, and do what that requires with activity and diligence. When we are called to give an account of our stewardship, let us not have to confess at the last that we wasted our one talent,[4] because we wished to have been trusted with ten; but let us prepare to render up what was given to us with joy and thankfulness, perfectly satisfied that the best place in life is where God appoints, and where He will guide us to a safe and peaceful end."

"Yes!" added Major Graham, "we have two eyes in our minds as well as in our bodies. With one of these we see all that is good or agreeable in our lot—with the other we see all that is unpleasant or disappointing; and you may generally choose which eye to keep open. Some of my friends always peevishly look at the troubles and vexations they endure, but they might turn them into good, by considering that every circumstance is sent from the same hand, with the same merciful purpose—to make us better now, and happier hereafter."

"Well! my dear children," said Lady Harriet, "it is time now for retiring to Bedfordshire; so good-night."

"If you please, grandmamma! not yet," asked Harry anxiously. "Give us five minutes longer!"

"And then in the morning you will want to remain five minutes more in bed. That is the way people learn to keep such dreadfully late hours at last, Harry! I knew one

4. An allusion to the parable of the talents (Matthew 25.14–30), where *talent* is a unit of money.

very rich gentleman formerly, who always wished to sit up a little later every night, and to get up a little later in the morning, till at length, he ended by hiring a set of servants to rise at nine in the evening, as he did himself, and to remain in bed all day."

"People should regulate their sleep very conscientiously," added Major Graham, "so as to waste as little time as possible; and our good king George III[5] set us the example, for he remarked, that six hours in the night were quite enough for a man, seven hours for a woman, and eight for a fool. Or perhaps, Harry, you might like to live by Sir William Jones'[6] rule:

> 'Six hours to read, to soothing slumber seven,
> Ten to the world allot—and all to Heaven.'"

1839

5. King of England (1730–1820; r. 1760–1820).   6. English linguist and jurist (1746–1794).

LUCY LANE CLIFFORD
1846–1929

Since its publication in the late nineteenth century, Lucy Lane Clifford's fantastical story "The New Mother" has terrified many readers. The tale of two children, given the nicknames of Clifford's own daughters, tormented into behaving badly through their own desires and through the manipulations of a mysterious, shabby girl who tells them that "the pleasure of goodness centres in itself; the pleasures of naughtiness are many and varied" indeed elicits a quickening sense of dread. The resolve of the children to be good in the future fails to keep the "new mother," with her glass eyes and heavy wooden tail, at bay. Although the children escape from the monster, they are doomed to a homeless, sorrowing life of regret. The psychological terror of "The New Mother," the American novelist Alison Lurie notes, prefigures the work of Henry James, Clifford's dear friend, in his famous supernatural tale "The Turn of the Screw" (1898). Neil Gaiman's fantasy for children, *Coraline* (2001), similarly includes a threatening adult figure—the "glittering button-eyed other mother"—who tests the will and wits of a child character initially attracted to her novelty and uncanniness. "The New Mother" was originally published in Clifford's collection for children, *Anyhow Stories, Moral and Otherwise* (1882).

Clifford was the widow of the brilliant mathematician William K. Clifford, a professor at University College, London, who died young and after only four years of marriage. Following her husband's death, Lucy Clifford redoubled her efforts at writing—her earlier attempts had been unsuccessful—in order to support herself and her two children. Although a well-known Victorian novelist, dramatist, children's author, and salon hostess, Clifford has been largely forgotten today. In their sentimentality and praise for childish imagination and innocence, many of Clifford's children's stories are reminiscent of the original folktales of Hans Christian Andersen (1805–1875) and the fantasies of George MacDonald (1824–1905). The vivid and unrelenting "The New Mother," by contrast, remains Clifford's most enduring children's story.

Lucy Lane
Clifford

The New Mother

I

The children were always called Blue-Eyes and the Turkey, and they came by the names in this manner. The elder one was like her dear father who was far away at sea, and when the mother looked up she would often say, "Child, you have taken the pattern of your father's eyes;" for the father had the bluest of blue eyes, and so gradually his little girl came to be called after them. The younger one had once, while she was still almost a baby, cried bitterly because a turkey that lived near to the cottage, and sometimes wandered into the forest, suddenly vanished in the middle of the winter; and to console her she had been called by its name.

Now the mother and Blue-Eyes and the Turkey and the baby all lived in a lonely cottage on the edge of the forest. The forest was so near that the garden at the back seemed a part of it, and the tall fir-trees were so close that their big black arms stretched over the little thatched roof, and when the moon shone upon them their tangled shadows were all over the white-washed walls.

It was a long way to the village, nearly a mile and a half, and the mother had to work hard and had not time to go often herself to see if there was a letter at the post-office from the dear father, and so very often in the afternoon she used to send the two children. They were very proud of being able to go alone, and often ran half the way to the post-office. When they came back tired with the long walk, there would be the mother waiting and watching for them, and the tea would be ready, and the baby crowing with delight; and if by any chance there was a letter from the sea, then they were happy indeed. The cottage room was so cosy: the walls were as white as snow inside as well as out, and against them hung the cake-tin and the baking-dish, and the lid of a large saucepan that had been worn out long before the children could remember, and the fish-slice,[1] all polished and shining as bright as silver. On one side of the fireplace, above the bellows hung the almanac,[2] and on the other the clock that always struck the wrong hour and was always running down too soon, but it was a good clock, with a little picture on its face and sometimes ticked away for nearly a week without stopping. The baby's high chair stood in one corner, and in another there was a cupboard hung up high against the wall, in which the mother kept all manner of little surprises. The children often wondered how the things that came out of that cupboard had got into it, for they seldom saw them put there.

"Dear children," the mother said one afternoon late in the autumn, "it is very chilly for you to go to the village, but you must walk quickly, and who knows but what you may bring back a letter saying that dear father is already on his way to England." Then Blue-Eyes and the Turkey made haste and were soon ready to go. "Don't be long," the mother said, as she always did before they started. "Go the nearest way and don't look at any strangers you meet, and be sure you do not talk with them."

"No, mother," they answered; and then she kissed them and called them dear good children, and they joyfully started on their way.

The village was gayer than usual, for there had been a fair the day before, and the people who had made merry still hung about the street as if reluctant to own that their holiday was over.

---

1. A knife for carving fish.
2. A book of tables containing a calendar with astronomical data and other useful information.

Then she kissed them.

"I wish we had come yesterday," Blue-Eyes said to the Turkey; "then we might have seen something."

"Look there," said the Turkey, and she pointed to a stall covered with gingerbread; but the children had no money. At the end of the street, close to the Blue Lion where the coaches stopped, an old man sat on the ground with his back resting against the wall of a house, and by him, with smart collars round their necks, were two dogs. Evidently they were dancing dogs, the children thought, and longed to see them perform, but they seemed as tired as their master, and sat quite still beside him, looking as if they had not even a single wag left in their tails.

"Oh, I *do* wish we had been here yesterday," Blue-Eyes said again as they went on to the grocer's, which was also the post-office. The post-mistress was very busy weighing out half-pounds of coffee, and when she had time to attend to the children she only just said "No letter for you to-day," and went on with what she was doing. Then Blue-Eyes and the Turkey turned away to go home. They went back slowly down the village street, past the man with the dogs again. One dog had roused himself and sat up rather crookedly with his head a good deal on one side, looking very melancholy and rather ridiculous; but on the children went towards the bridge and the fields that led to the forest.

They had left the village and walked some way, and then, just before they reached the bridge, they noticed, resting against a pile of stones by the wayside, a strange dark figure. At first they thought it was some one asleep, then they thought it was a poor woman ill and hungry, and then they saw that it was a strange wild-looking girl, who seemed very unhappy, and they felt sure that something was the matter. So they went and looked at her, and thought they would ask her if they could do anything to help her, for they were kind children and sorry indeed for any one in distress.

The girl seemed to be tall, and was about fifteen years old. She was dressed in very ragged clothes. Round her shoulders there was an old brown shawl, which was torn at the corner that hung down the middle of her back. She wore no bonnet, and an old yellow handkerchief which she had tied round her head had fallen backwards and was all huddled up round her neck. Her hair was coal black and hung down uncombed and unfastened, just anyhow. It was not very long, but it was very shiny, and it seemed to match her bright black eyes and dark freckled skin. On her feet were coarse gray stockings and thick shabby boots, which she had evidently forgotten to lace up. She had something hidden away under her shawl, but the children did not know what it was. At first they thought it was a baby, but when, on seeing them coming towards her, she carefully put it under her and sat upon it, they thought they must be mistaken. She sat watching the children approach, and did not move or stir till they were within a yard of her; then she wiped her eyes just as if she had been crying bitterly, and looked up.

The children stood still in front of her for a moment, staring at her and wondering what they ought to do.

"Are you crying?" they asked shyly.

To their surprise she said in a most cheerful voice, "Oh dear, no! quite the contrary. Are you?"

They thought it rather rude of her to reply in this way, for any one could see that they were not crying. They felt half in mind to walk away; but the girl looked at them so hard with her big black eyes, they did not like to do so till they had said something else.

"Perhaps you have lost yourself?" they said gently.

But the girl answered promptly, "Certainly not. Why, you have just found me. Besides," she added, "I live in the village."

The children were surprised at this, for they had never seen her before, and yet they thought they knew all the village folk by sight.

"We often go to the village," they said, thinking it might interest her.

"Indeed," she answered. That was all; and again they wondered what to do.

Then the Turkey, who had an inquiring mind, put a good straightforward question. "What are you sitting on?" she asked.

"On a peardrum," the girl answered, still speaking in a most cheerful voice, at which the children wondered, for she looked very cold and uncomfortable.

"What is a peardrum?" they asked.

"I am surprised at your not knowing," the girl answered. "Most people in good society have one." And then she pulled it out and showed it to them. It was a curious instrument, a good deal like a guitar in shape; it had three strings, but only two pegs by which to tune them. The third string was never tuned at all, and thus added to the singular effect produced by the village girl's music. And yet, oddly, the peardrum was not played by touching its strings, but by turning a little handle cunningly hidden on one side.

But the strange thing about the peardrum was not the music it made, or the strings, or the handle, but a little square box attached to one side. The box had a little flat lid that appeared to open by a spring. That was all the children could make out at

"It really is a most beautiful thing, is a peardrum."

first. They were most anxious to see inside the box, or to know what it contained, but they thought it might look curious to say so.

"It really is a most beautiful thing, is a peardrum," the girl said, looking at it, and speaking in a voice that was almost affectionate.

"Where did you get it?" the children asked.

"I bought it," the girl answered.

"Didn't it cost a great deal of money?" they asked.

"Yes," answered the girl slowly, nodding her head, "it cost a great deal of money. I am very rich," she added.

And this the children thought a really remarkable statement, for they had not supposed that rich people dressed in old clothes, or went about without bonnets. She might at least have done her hair, they thought; but they did not like to say so.

"You don't look rich," they said slowly, and in as polite a voice as possible.

"Perhaps not," the girl answered cheerfully.

At this the children gathered courage, and ventured to remark, "You look rather shabby"—they did not like to say ragged.

"Indeed?" said the girl in the voice of one who had heard a pleasant but surprising statement. "A little shabbiness is very respectable," she added in a satisfied voice. "I must really tell them this," she continued. And the children wondered what she meant. She opened the little box by the side of the peardrum, and said, just as if she were speaking to some one who could hear her, "They say I look rather shabby; it is quite lucky, isn't it?"

"Why, you are not speaking to any one!" they said, more surprised than ever.

"Oh dear, yes! I am speaking to them both."

"Both?" they said, wondering.

"Yes. I have here a little man dressed as a peasant, and wearing a wide slouch hat with a large feather, and a little woman to match, dressed in a red petticoat, and a white handkerchief pinned across her bosom. I put them on the lid of the box, and when I play they dance most beautifully. The little man takes off his hat and waves it in the air, and the little woman holds up her petticoat a little bit on one side with one hand, and with the other sends forward a kiss."

"Oh! let us see; do let us see!" the children cried, both at once.

Then the village girl looked at them doubtfully.

"Let you see!" she said slowly. "Well, I am not sure that I can. Tell me, are you good?"

"Yes, yes," they answered eagerly, "we are very good!"

"Then it's quite impossible," she answered, and resolutely closed the lid of the box.

They stared at her in astonishment.

"But we are good," they cried, thinking she must have misunderstood them. "We are very good. Mother always says we are."

"So you remarked before," the girl said, speaking in a tone of decision.

Still the children did not understand.

"Then can't you let us see the little man and woman?" they asked.

"Oh dear, no!" the girl answered. "I only show them to naughty children."

"To naughty children!" they exclaimed.

"Yes, to naughty children," she answered; "and the worse the children the better do the man and woman dance."

She put the peardrum carefully under her ragged cloak, and prepared to go on her way.

"I really could not have believed that you were good," she said, reproachfully, as if they had accused themselves of some great crime. "Well, good day."

"Oh, but do show us the little man and woman," they cried.

"Certainly not. Good day," she said again.

"Oh, but we will be naughty," they said in despair.

"I am afraid you couldn't," she answered, shaking her head. "It requires a great deal of skill, especially to be naughty well. Good day," she said for the third time. "Perhaps I shall see you in the village to-morrow."

And swiftly she walked away, while the children felt their eyes fill with tears, and their hearts ache with disappointment.

"If we had only been naughty," they said, "we should have seen them dance; we should have seen the little woman holding her red petticoat in her hand, and the little man waving his hat. Oh, what shall we do to make her let us see them?"

"Suppose," said the Turkey, "we try to be naughty to-day; perhaps she would let us see them to-morrow."

"But, oh!" said Blue-Eyes, "I don't know how to be naughty; no one ever taught me."

The Turkey thought for a few minutes in silence. "I think I can be naughty if I try," she said. "I'll try to-night."

And then poor Blue-Eyes burst into tears.

"Oh, don't be naughty without me!" she cried. "It would be so unkind of you. You know I want to see the little man and woman just as much as you do. You are very, very unkind." And she sobbed bitterly.

And so, quarrelling and crying, they reached their home.

Now, when their mother saw them, she was greatly astonished, and, fearing they were hurt, ran to meet them.

"Oh, my children, oh, my dear, dear children," she said; "what is the matter?"

But they did not dare tell their mother about the village girl and the little man and woman, so they answered, "Nothing is the matter; nothing at all is the matter," and cried all the more.

"But why are you crying?" she asked in surprise.

"Surely we may cry if we like," they sobbed. "We are very fond of crying."

"Poor children!" the mother said to herself. "They are tired, and perhaps they are hungry; after tea they will be better." And she went back to the cottage, and made the fire blaze, until its reflection danced about on the tin lids upon the wall; and she put the kettle on to boil, and set the tea-things on the table, and opened the window to let in the sweet fresh air, and made all things look bright. Then she went to the little cupboard, hung up high against the wall, and took out some bread and put it on the table, and said in a loving voice, "Dear little children, come and have your tea; it is all quite ready for you. And see, there is the baby waking up from her sleep; we will put her in the high chair, and she will crow at us while we eat."

But the children made no answer to the dear mother; they only stood still by the window and said nothing.

"Come, children," the mother said again. "Come, Blue-Eyes, and come, my Turkey; here is nice sweet bread for tea."

Then Blue-Eyes and the Turkey looked round, and when they saw the tall loaf, baked crisp and brown, and the cups all in a row, and the jug of milk, all waiting for them, they went to the table and sat down and felt a little happier; and the mother did not put the baby in the high chair after all, but took it on her knee, and danced it up and down, and sang little snatches of songs to it, and laughed, and looked content, and thought of the father far away at sea, and wondered what he would say to them all when he came home again. Then suddenly she looked up and saw that the Turkey's eyes were full of tears.

"Turkey!" she exclaimed, "my dear little Turkey! what is the matter? Come to mother, my sweet; come to own mother." And putting the baby down on the rug, she held out her arms, and the Turkey, getting up from her chair, ran swiftly into them.

"Oh, mother," she sobbed, "oh, dear mother! I do so want to be naughty."

"My dear child!" the mother exclaimed.

"Yes, mother," the child sobbed, more and more bitterly. "I do so want to be very, very naughty."

And then Blue-Eyes left her chair also, and, rubbing her face against the mother's shoulder, cried sadly. "And so do I, mother. Oh, I'd give anything to be very, very naughty."

"But, my dear children," said the mother, in astonishment, "why do you want to be naughty?"

"Because we do; oh, what shall we do?" they cried together.

"I should be very angry if you were naughty. But you could not be, for you love me," the mother answered.

"Why couldn't we be naughty because we love you?" they asked.

"Because it would make me very unhappy; and if you love me you couldn't make me unhappy."

"Why couldn't we?" they asked.

Then the mother thought a while before she answered; and when she did so they hardly understood, perhaps because she seemed to be speaking, rather to herself than to them.

"Because if one loves well," she said gently, "one's love is stronger than all bad feelings in one, and conquers them. And this is the test whether love be real or false, unkindness and wickedness have no power over it."

"We don't know what you mean," they cried; "and we do love you; but we want to be naughty."

"Then I should know you did not love me," the mother said.

"And what should you do?" asked Blue-Eyes.

"I cannot tell. I should try to make you better."

"But if you couldn't? If we were very, very, very naughty, and wouldn't be good, what then?"

"Then," said the mother sadly—and while she spoke her eyes filled with tears, and a sob almost choked her—"then," she said, "I should have to go away and leave you, and to send home a new mother, with glass eyes and wooden tail."

"You couldn't," they cried.

"Yes, I could," she answered in a low voice; "but it would make me very unhappy, and I will never do it unless you are very, very, naughty, and I am obliged."

"We won't be naughty," they cried; "we will be good. We should hate a new mother; and she shall never come here." And they clung to their own mother, and kissed her fondly.

But when they went to bed they sobbed bitterly, for they remembered the little man and woman, and longed more than ever to see them; but how could they bear to let their own mother go away, and a new one take her place?

II

"Good-day," said the village girl, when she saw Blue-Eyes and the Turkey approach. She was again sitting by the heap of stones, and under her shawl the peardrum was hidden. She looked just as if she had not moved since the day before. "Good day," she said, in the same cheerful voice in which she had spoken yesterday; "the weather is really charming."

"Are the little man and woman there?" the children asked, taking no notice of her remark.

"Yes; thank you for inquiring after them," the girl answered; "they are both here and quite well. The little man is learning how to rattle the money in his pocket, and the little woman has heard a secret—she tells it while she dances."

"Oh, do let us see," they entreated.

"Quite impossible, I assure you," the girl answered promptly. "You see, you are good."

"Oh!" said Blue Eyes, sadly; "but mother says if we are naughty she will go away and send home a new mother, with glass eyes and a wooden tail."

"Indeed," said the girl, still speaking in the same unconcerned voice, "that is what they all say."

"What do you mean?" asked the Turkey.

"They all threaten that kind of thing. Of course really there are no mothers with glass eyes and wooden tails; they would be much too expensive to make." And the common sense of this remark the children, especially the Turkey, saw at once, but they merely said, half crying—

"We think you might let us see the little man and woman dance."

"The kind of thing you would think," remarked the village girl.

"But will you if we are naughty?" they asked in despair.

"I fear you could not be naughty—that is, really—even if you tried," she said scornfully.

"Oh, but we will try; we will indeed," they cried; "so do show them to us."

"Certainly not beforehand," answered the girl, getting up and preparing to walk away.

"But if we are very naughty to-night, will you let us see them to-morrow?"

"Questions asked to-day are always best answered to-morrow," the girl said, and turned round as if to walk on. "Good day," she said blithely; "I must really go and play a little to myself; good day," she repeated, and then suddenly she began to sing—

> "Oh, sweet and fair's the lady-bird,
>   And so's the bumble-bee,
> But I myself have long preferred
>   The gentle chimpanzee,
>   The gentle chimpanzee-e-e,
>   The gentle chim——"

"I beg your pardon," she said, stopping, and looking over her shoulder; "it's very rude to sing without leave before company. I won't do it again."

"Oh, do go on," the children said.

"I'm going," she said, and walked away.

"No, we meant go on singing," they explained, "and do let us just hear you play," they entreated, remembering that as yet they had not heard a single sound from the peardrum.

"Quite impossible," she called out as she went along. "You are good, as I remarked before. The pleasure of goodness centres in itself; the pleasures of naughtiness are many and varied. Good day," she shouted, for she was almost out of hearing.

For a few minutes the children stood still looking after her, then they broke down and cried.

"She might have let us see them," they sobbed.

The Turkey was the first to wipe away her tears.

"Let us go home and be very naughty," she said; "then perhaps she will let us see them to-morrow."

"But what shall we do?" asked Blue-Eyes, looking up. Then together all the way home they planned how to begin being naughty. And that afternoon the dear mother was sorely distressed, for, instead of sitting at their tea as usual with smiling happy faces, and then helping her to clear away and doing all she told them, they broke their mugs and threw their bread and butter on the floor, and when the mother told them to do one thing they carefully went and did another, and as for helping her to put away, they left her to do it all by herself, and only stamped their feet with rage when she told them to go upstairs until they were good.

"We won't be good," they cried. "We hate being good, and we always mean to be naughty. We like being naughty very much."

"Do you remember what I told you I should do if you were very very naughty?" she asked sadly.

"Yes, we know, but it isn't true," they cried. "There is no mother with a wooden tail and glass eyes, and if there were we should just stick pins into her and send her away; but there is none."

Then the mother became really angry at last, and sent them off to bed, but instead of crying and being sorry at her anger they laughed for joy, and when they were in bed they sat up and sang merry songs at the top of their voices.

The next morning quite early, without asking leave from the mother, the children got up and ran off as fast as they could over the fields towards the bridge to look for the village girl. She was sitting as usual by the heap of stones with the peardrum under her shawl.

"Now please show us the little man and woman," they cried, "and let us hear the peardrum. We were very naughty last night." But the girl kept the peardrum carefully hidden. "We were very naughty," the children cried again.

"Indeed," she said in precisely the same tone in which she had spoken yesterday.

"But we were," they repeated; "we were indeed."

"So you say," she answered. "You were not half naughty enough."

"Why, we were sent to bed!"

"Just so," said the girl, putting the other corner of the shawl over the peardrum. "If you had been really naughty you wouldn't have gone; but you can't help it, you see. As I remarked before, it requires a great deal of skill to be naughty well."

"But we broke our mugs, we threw our bread and butter on the floor, we did everything we could to be tiresome."

"Mere trifles," answered the village girl scornfully. "Did you throw cold water on the fire, did you break the clock, did you pull all the tins down from the walls, and throw them on the floor?"

"No!" exclaimed the children, aghast, "we did not do that."

"I thought not," the girl answered. "So many people mistake a little noise and foolishness for real naughtiness; but, as I remarked before, it wants skill to do the thing properly. Well, good day," and before they could say another word she had vanished.

"We'll be much worse," the children cried, in despair. "We'll go and do all the things she says;" and then they went home and did all these things. They threw water on the fire; they pulled down the baking-dish and the cake-tin, the fish-slice and the lid of the saucepan they had never seen, and banged them on the floor; they broke the clock and danced on the butter; they turned everything upside down; and then they sat still and wondered if they were naughty enough. And when the mother saw all that they had done she did not scold them as she had the day before or send them to bed, but she just broke down and cried, and then she looked at the children and said sadly—

"Unless you are good to-morrow, my poor Blue-Eyes and Turkey, I shall indeed have to go away and come back no more, and the new mother I told you of will come to you."

They did not believe her; yet their hearts ached when they saw how unhappy she looked, and they thought within themselves that when they once had seen the little man and woman dance, they would be good to the dear mother for ever afterwards; but they could not be good now till they had heard the sound of the peardrum, seen the little man and woman dance, and heard the secret told—then they would be satisfied.

The next morning, before the birds were stirring, before the sun had climbed high enough to look in at their bedroom window, or the flowers had wiped their eyes ready for the day, the children got up and crept out of the cottage and ran across the fields. They did not think the village girl would be up so very early, but their hearts had ached so much at the sight of the mother's sad face that they had not been able to sleep, and they longed to know if they had been naughty enough, and if they might just once hear the peardrum and see the little man and woman, and then go home and be good for ever.

To their surprise they found the village girl sitting by the heap of stones, just as if it were her natural home. They ran fast when they saw her, and they noticed that the box containing the little man and woman was open, but she closed it quickly when she saw them, and they heard the clicking of the spring that kept it fast.

"We have been very naughty," they cried. "We have done all the things you told us; now will you show us the little man and woman?" The girl looked at them curiously, then drew the yellow silk handkerchief she sometimes wore round her head out of her pocket, and began to smooth out the creases in it with her hands.

"You really seem quite excited," she said in her usual voice. "You should be calm; calmness gathers in and hides things like a big cloak, or like my shawl does here, for instance;" and she looked down at the ragged covering that hid the peardrum.

"We have done all the things you told us," the children cried again, "and we do so long to hear the secret;" but the girl only went on smoothing out her handkerchief.

"I am so very particular about my dress," she said. They could hardly listen to her in their excitement.

"But do tell if we may see the little man and woman," they entreated again. "We have been so very naughty, and mother says she will go away to-day and send home a new mother if we are not good."

"Indeed," said the girl, beginning to be interested and amused. "The things that people say are most singular and amusing. There is an endless variety in language." But the children did not understand, only entreated once more to see the little man and woman.

"Well, let me see," the girl said at last, just as if she were relenting. "When did your mother say she would go?"

"But if she goes what shall we do?" they cried in despair. "We don't want her to go; we love her very much. Oh! what shall we do if she goes?"

"People go and people come; first they go and then they come. Perhaps she will go before she comes; she couldn't come before she goes. You had better go back and be good," the girl added suddenly; "you are really not clever enough to be anything else; and the little woman's secret is very important; she never tells it for make-believe naughtiness."

"But we did do all the things you told us," the children cried, despairingly.

"You didn't throw the looking-glass out of window, or stand the baby on its head."

"No, we didn't do that," the children gasped.

"I thought not," the girl said triumphantly. "Well, good-day. I shall not be here to-morrow. Good-day."

"Oh, but don't go away," they cried. "We are so unhappy; do let us see them just once."

"Well, I shall go past your cottage at eleven o'clock this morning," the girl said. "Perhaps I shall play the peardrum as I go by."

"And will you show us the man and woman?" they asked.

"Quite impossible, unless you have really deserved it; make-believe naughtiness is only spoilt goodness. Now if you break the looking-glass and do the things that are desired——"

"Oh, we will," they cried. "We will be very naughty till we hear you coming."

"It's waste of time, I fear," the girl said politely; "but of course I should not like to interfere with you. You see the little man and woman, being used to the best society, are very particular. Good-day," she said, just as she always said, and then quickly turned away, but she looked back and called out, "Eleven o'clock, I shall be quite punctual; I am very particular about my engagements."

Then again the children went home, and were naughty, oh, so very very naughty that the dear mother's heart ached, and her eyes filled with tears, and at last she went upstairs and slowly put on her best gown and her new sun-bonnet, and she dressed the baby all in its Sunday clothes, and then she came down and stood before Blue-Eyes and the Turkey, and just as she did so the Turkey threw the looking-glass out of window, and it fell with a loud crash upon the ground.

"Good-bye, my children," the mother said sadly, kissing them. "Good-bye, my Blue-Eyes; good-bye, my Turkey; the new mother will be home presently. Oh, my poor children!" and then weeping bitterly the mother took the baby in her arms and turned to leave the house.

"But, mother," the children cried, "we are——" and then suddenly the broken clock struck half-past ten, and they knew that in half an hour the village girl would come by playing on the peardrum. "But, mother, we will be good at half-past eleven, come back at half-past eleven," they cried, "and we'll both be good, we will indeed; we must be naughty till eleven o'clock." But the mother only picked up the little bundle in which she had tied up her cotton apron and a pair of old shoes, and went slowly out at the door. It seemed as if the children were spellbound, and they could not follow her. They opened the window wide, and called after her—

"Mother! mother! oh, dear mother, come back again! We will be good, we will be good now, we will be good for evermore if you will come back." But the mother only looked round and shook her head, and they could see the tears falling down her cheeks.

"Come back, dear mother!" cried Blue-Eyes; but still the mother went on across the fields.

"Come back, come back!" cried the Turkey; but still the mother went on. Just by the corner of the field she stopped and turned, and waved her handkerchief, all wet with tears, to the children at the window; she made the baby kiss its hand; and in a moment mother and baby had vanished from their sight.

Then the children felt their hearts ache with sorrow, and they cried bitterly just as the mother had done, and yet they could not believe that she had gone. Surely she would come back, they thought; she would not leave them altogether; but, oh, if she did—if she did—if she did. And then the broken clock struck eleven, and suddenly there was a sound—a quick, clanging, jangling sound, with a strange discordant one at intervals; and they looked at each other, while their hearts stood still, for they knew it was the peardrum. They rushed to the open window, and there they saw the village girl coming towards them from the fields, dancing along and playing as she did so. Behind her, walking slowly, and yet ever keeping the same distance from her, was the man with the dogs whom they had seen asleep by the Blue Lion, on the day they first saw the girl with the peardrum. He was playing on a flute that had a strange shrill sound; they could hear it plainly above the jangling of the peardrum. After the man followed the two dogs, slowly waltzing round and round on their hind legs.

"We have done all you told us," the children called, when they had recovered from their astonishment. "Come and see; and now show us the little man and woman."

The girl did not cease her playing or her dancing, but she called out in a voice that was half speaking half singing, and seemed to keep time to the strange music of the peardrum.

"You did it all badly. You threw the water on the wrong side of the fire, the tin things were not quite in the middle of the room, the clock was not broken enough, you did not stand the baby on its head."

Then the children, still standing spellbound by the window, cried out, entreating and wringing their hands, "Oh, but we have done everything you told us, and mother has gone away. Show us the little man and woman now, and let us hear the secret."

As they said this the girl was just in front of the cottage, but she did not stop playing. The sound of the strings seemed to go through their hearts. She did not stop dancing; she was already passing the cottage by. She did not stop singing, and all she said sounded like part of a terrible song. And still the man followed her, always at the same distance, playing shrilly on his flute; and still the two dogs waltzed round and round after him—their tails motionless, their legs straight, their collars clear and white and stiff. On they went, all of them together.

"Oh, stop!" the children cried, "and show us the little man and woman now."

But the girl sang out loud and clear, while the string that was out of tune twanged above her voice.

"The little man and woman are far away. See, their box is empty."

And then for the first time the children saw that the lid of the box was raised and hanging back, and that no little man and woman were in it.

"I am going to my own land," the girl sang, "to the land where I was born." And she went on towards the long straight road that led to the city many many miles away.

"But our mother is gone," the children cried; "our dear mother, will she ever come back?"

"No," sang the girl; "she'll never come back, she'll never come back. I saw her by the bridge: she took a boat upon the river; she is sailing to the sea; she will meet your father once again, and they will go sailing on, sailing on to the countries far away."

And when they heard this, the children cried out, but could say no more, for their hearts seemed to be breaking.

Then the girl, her voice getting fainter and fainter in the distance, called out once more to them. But for the dread that sharpened their ears they would hardly have heard her, so far was she away, and so discordant was the music.

"Your new mother is coming. She is already on her way; but she only walks slowly, for her tail is rather long, and her spectacles are left behind; but she is coming, she is coming—coming—coming."

The last word died away; it was the last one they ever heard the village girl utter. On she went, dancing on; and on followed the man, they could see that he was still playing, but they could no longer hear the sound of his flute; and on went the dogs round and round and round. On they all went, farther and farther away, till they were separate things no more, till they were just a confused mass of faded colour, till they were a dark misty object that nothing could define, till they had vanished altogether,—altogether and for ever.

Then the children turned, and looked at each other and at the little cottage home, that only a week before had been so bright and happy, so cosy and so spotless. The fire was out, and the water was still among the cinders; the baking-dish and cake-tin, the fish-slice and the saucepan lid, which the dear mother used to spend so much time in rubbing, were all pulled down from the nails on which they had hung so long, and were lying on the floor. And there was the clock all broken and spoilt, the little picture upon its face could be seen no more; and though it sometimes struck a stray hour, it was with the tone of a clock whose hours are numbered. And there was the baby's high chair, but no little baby to sit in it; there was the cupboard on the wall, and never a sweet loaf on its shelf; and there were the broken mugs, and the bits of bread tossed about, and the greasy boards which the mother had knelt down to scrub until they were white as snow. In the midst of all stood the children, looking at the wreck they had made, their hearts aching, their eyes blinded with tears, and their poor little hands clasped together in their misery.

"Oh, what shall we do?" cried Blue-Eyes. "I wish we had never seen the village girl and the nasty, nasty peardrum."

"Surely mother will come back," sobbed the Turkey. "I am sure we shall die if she doesn't come back."

"I don't know what we shall do if the new mother comes," cried Blue-Eyes. "I shall never, never like any other mother. I don't know what we shall do if that dreadful mother comes."

"We won't let her in," said the Turkey.

"But perhaps she'll walk in," sobbed Blue-Eyes.

Then Turkey stopped crying for a minute, to think what should be done.

"We will bolt the door," she said, "and shut the window; and we won't take any notice when she knocks."

So they bolted the door, and shut the window, and fastened it. And then, in spite of all they had said, they felt naughty again, and longed after the little man and woman they had never seen, far more than after the mother who had loved them all their lives. But then they did not really believe that their own mother would not come back, or that any new mother would take her place.

When it was dinner-time, they were very hungry, but they could only find some stale bread, and they had to be content with it.

"Oh, I wish we had heard the little woman's secret," cried the Turkey; "I wouldn't have cared then."

All through the afternoon they sat watching and listening for fear of the new mother; but they saw and heard nothing of her, and gradually they became less and less afraid lest she should come. Then they thought that perhaps when it was dark their own dear mother would come home; and perhaps if they asked her to forgive them she would. And then Blue-Eyes thought that if their mother did come she would be very cold, so they crept out at the back door and gathered in some wood, and at last, for the grate was wet, and it was a great deal of trouble to manage it, they made a fire. When they saw the bright fire burning, and the little flames leaping and playing among the wood and coal, they began to be happy again, and to feel certain that their own mother would return; and the sight of the pleasant fire reminded them of all the times she had waited for them to come from the post-office, and of how she had welcomed them, and comforted them, and given them nice warm tea and sweet bread, and talked to them. Oh, how sorry they were they had been naughty, and all for that nasty village girl! They did not care a bit about the little man and woman now, or want to hear the secret.

They fetched a pail of water and washed the floor; they found some rag, and rubbed the tins till they looked bright again, and, putting a footstool on a chair, they got up on it very carefully and hung up the things in their places; and then they picked up the broken mugs and made the room as neat as they could, till it looked more and more as if the dear mother's hands had been busy about it. They felt more and more certain she would return, she and the dear little baby together, and they thought they would set the tea-things for her, just as she had so often set them for her naughty children. They took down the tea-tray, and got out the cups, and put the kettle on the fire to boil, and made everything look as home-like as they could. There was no sweet loaf to put on the table, but perhaps the mother would bring something from the village, they thought. At last all was ready, and Blue-Eyes and the Turkey washed their faces and their hands, and then sat and waited, for of course they did not believe what the village girl had said about their mother sailing away.

Suddenly, while they were sitting by the fire, they heard a sound as of something heavy being dragged along the ground outside, and then there was a loud and terrible knocking at the door. The children felt their hearts stand still. They knew it could not be their own mother, for she would have turned the handle and tried to come in without any knocking at all.

"Oh, Turkey!" whispered Blue-Eyes, "if it should be the new mother, what shall we do?"

"We won't let her in," whispered the Turkey, for she was afraid to speak aloud, and again there came a long and loud and terrible knocking at the door.

"What shall we do? oh, what shall we do?" cried the children, in despair. "Oh, go away!" they called out. "Go away; we won't let you in; we will never be naughty any more; go away, go away!"

But again there came a loud and terrible knocking.

"She'll break the door if she knocks so hard," cried Blue-Eyes.

"Go and put your back to it," whispered the Turkey, "and I'll peep out of the window and try to see if it is really the new mother."

So in fear and trembling Blue-Eyes put her back against the door, and the Turkey went to the window, and, pressing her face against one side of the frame, peeped out. She could just see a black satin poke bonnet[3] with a frill round the edge, and a long bony arm carrying a black leather bag. From beneath the bonnet there flashed a strange bright light, and Turkey's heart sank and her cheeks turned pale, for she knew it was the flashing of two glass eyes. She crept up to Blue-Eyes. "It is—it is—it is!" she whispered, her voice shaking with fear, "it is the new mother! She has come, and brought her luggage in a black leather bag that is hanging on her arm!"

"Oh, what shall we do?" wept Blue-Eyes; and again there was the terrible knocking.

"Come and put your back against the door too, Turkey," cried Blue-Eyes; "I am afraid it will break."

So together they stood with their two little backs against the door. There was a long pause. They thought perhaps the new mother had made up her mind that there was no one at home to let her in, and would go away, but presently the two children heard through the thin wooden door the new mother move a little, and then say to herself—"I must break open the door with my tail."

For one terrible moment all was still, but in it the children could almost hear her lift up her tail, and then, with a fearful blow, the little painted door was cracked and splintered.

With a shriek the children darted from the spot and fled through the cottage, and out at the back door into the forest beyond. All night long they stayed in the darkness and the cold, and all the next day and the next, and all through the cold, dreary days and the long dark nights that followed.

They are there still, my children. All through the long weeks and months have they been there, with only green rushes for their pillows and only the brown dead leaves to cover them, feeding on the wild strawberries in the summer, or on the nuts when they hang green; on the blackberries when they are no longer sour in the autumn, and in the winter on the little red berries that ripen in the snow. They wander about among the tall dark firs or beneath the great trees beyond. Sometimes they stay to

3. A hat tied under the chin, with a wide, projecting front brim.

rest beside the little pool near the copse where the ferns grow thickest, and they long and long, with a longing that is greater than words can say, to see their own dear mother again, just once again, to tell her that they'll be good for evermore—just once again.

And still the new mother stays in the little cottage, but the windows are closed and the doors are shut, and no one knows what the inside looks like. Now and then, when the darkness has fallen and the night is still, hand in hand Blue-Eyes and the Turkey creep up near to the home in which they once were so happy, and with beating hearts they watch and listen; sometimes a blinding flash comes through the window, and they know it is the light from the new mother's glass eyes, or they hear a strange muffled noise, and they know it is the sound of her wooden tail as she drags it along the floor.

1882

L. FRANK BAUM
1856–1919

"The imaginative child," L. Frank Baum wrote to his readers in *The Lost Princess of Oz* (1917), "will become the imaginative man or woman most apt to create, to invent, and therefore to foster civilization." The "civilization" that Baum was most concerned about, contemporary America, inspired his fantasy world, the Land of Oz. With "laconic Yankee terseness," commented Ruth Plumly Thompson—who would herself pen nineteen Oz books after Baum's death—L. Frank Baum "proceeded to create his believable unbelievable country." In the Author's Note to a new edition of *American Fairy Tales* (1908) that rearranged the order of the stories in the 1901 original and added three more, Baum considers the special parameters of American fairy tales. He explains that these are not the stories of deep history, because "our country has no great age to boast of," and concludes, "So I am obliged to offer our wide-awake youngsters modern tales about modern fairies, and while my humble efforts must not be compared with the classic stories of my masters, they at least bear the stamp of our own times and depict the progressive fairies of to-day." Baum's "American" optimism, his belief that dreams come true through hard work, informs these tales as well as *The Wizard of Oz*—the story of a little girl and fanciful characters who live in a marvelous land and cooperate in order to achieve their goals.

L. Frank Baum was born just outside of Syracuse, New York, to a wealthy family. Though a defective heart limited his physical activities, and required that he be educated primarily at home, Baum enjoyed a pleasant childhood exercising his imagination on their considerable property in upstate New York. In 1881 he met Maud Gage (daughter of a famous suffragist, Matilda Joslyn Gage); they were married in 1882. But by 1887, after a string of misfortunes, the Baum family fortune was essentially lost and Baum had to find work. He chose to go out west to the Dakota Territory. After his business ventures failed, Baum moved to Chicago with his family, which would grow to include four sons. Unhappy in his work as a traveling salesman for a china company and looking for less strenuous work that could be done at home, Baum decided to take the advice of his mother-in-law Matilda Gage and try to publish some of the stories he was fond of telling the children.

Baum's first published book for children, *Mother Goose in Prose* (1897), which was also the first book illustrated by the artist Maxfield Parrish (1870–1966), became the best-selling children's book of the year; it launched his career as a writer of children's fantasies. The first in the Oz series, *The Wonderful Wizard of Oz* (1900), was an immediate success. It is on Baum's fourteen full-length Oz books, generally released at Christmas, that his reputation as the author of the first American wonder tales and one of America's most important authors of juvenile fiction is based. Baum often tried to end the series so that he might devote himself to other kinds of fiction, but chronic mismanagement of his income, his own desire to increase that income, and the continual pressure from his readers and publisher always persuaded Baum to return to Oz.

In his last years, Baum and his wife lived comfortably in Hollywood, California, in a home he named Ozcot, surrounded by gardens reminiscent of those he had enjoyed as a boy. Two of his Oz books were published posthumously. Although librarians and professional critics of children's literature consistently spurned the Oz books as bland and silly, they were immensely popular with child readers; the series was continued by other authors until it reached a total of forty volumes. The public's appetite for Oz has been well-fed by the lavish 1939 MGM film version of *The Wizard of Oz*, as well as by more recent stage productions and adaptations such as the Broadway musical *The Wiz* (1975). Fan clubs remain active today.

Baum's *American Fairy Tales* were originally published in various newspapers between March and May 1901. The stories borrowed European folktale plots (such as wealth gained by the intervention of a grateful magical creature and then lost because of pride in "The Wonderful Pump") yet were set in a vaguely present-day America; they depicted the interplay of stereotypical characters such as the New England farmer, Yale professor, senator, and traveling salesman with magical or supernatural characters and objects. In Baum's humorous yarn "The Capture of Father Time," the young Arizona cowboy Jim pays a visit to some eastern cousins. While on his trip, Jim can't contain his wild spirits (somewhat restrained in the urban East); throwing his lasso about wildly, he inadvertently captures the invisible Father Time and stops all movement on Earth. The mischievous Jim, a true inheritor of Tom Sawyer, holds Time as his prisoner and plays all manner of practical jokes on the frozen townspeople.

FAIRY TALES

The CAPTURE *of* FATHER TIME

Jim was the son of a cowboy, and lived on the broad plains of Arizona. His father had trained him to lasso a broncho or a young bull with perfect accuracy, and had Jim possessed the strength to back up his skill he would have been as good a cowboy as any in all Arizona.

When he was twelve years old he made his first visit to the east, where Uncle Charles, his father's brother, lived. Of course Jim took his lasso with him, for he was proud of his skill in casting it, and wanted to show his cousins what a cowboy could do.

At first the city boys and girls were much interested in watching Jim lasso posts and fence pickets, but they soon tired of it, and even Jim decided it was not the right sort of sport for cities.

But one day the butcher asked Jim to ride one of his horses into the coun-

RALPH FLETCHER SEYMOUR

try, to a pasture that had been engaged, and Jim eagerly consented. He had been longing for a horseback ride, and to make it seem like old times he took his lasso with him.

He rode through the streets demurely enough, but on reaching the open country roads his spirits broke forth into wild jubilation, and, urging the butcher's horse to full gallop, he dashed away in true cowboy fashion.

Then he wanted still more liberty, and letting down the bars that led into a big field he began riding over the meadow and throwing his lasso at imaginary cattle, while he yelled and whooped to his heart's content.

Suddenly, on making a long cast with his lasso, the loop caught upon something and rested about three feet from the ground, while the rope drew taut and nearly pulled Jim from his horse.

This was unexpected. More than that, it was wonderful; for the field seemed bare of even a stump. Jim's eyes grew big with amazement, but he knew he had caught something when a voice cried out:

"Here, let go! Let go, I say! Can't you see what you've done?"

No, Jim couldn't see, nor did he intend to let go until he found out what was holding the loop of the lasso. So he resorted to an old trick his father had taught him and, putting the butcher's horse to a run, began riding in a circle around the spot where his lasso had caught.

As he thus drew nearer and nearer his quarry he saw the rope coil up, yet it looked to be coiling over nothing but air. One end of the lasso was made fast to a ring in the saddle, and when the rope was almost wound up and the horse began to pull away and snort with fear, Jim dismounted. Holding the reins of the bridle in one hand, he followed the rope, and an instant later saw an old man caught fast in the coils of the lasso.

His head was bald and uncovered, but long white whiskers grew down to his waist. About his body was thrown a loose robe of fine white linen. In one hand he bore a great scythe, and beneath the other arm he carried an hourglass.

While Jim gazed wonderingly upon him, this venerable old man spoke in an angry voice:

"Now, then—get that rope off as fast as you can! You've brought everything on earth to a standstill by your foolishness! Well—what are you staring at? Don't you know who I am?"

"No," said Jim, stupidly.

"Well, I'm Time—Father Time! Now, make haste and set me free—if you want the world to run properly."

"How did I happen to catch you?" asked Jim, without making a move to release his captive.

"I don't know. I've never been caught before," growled Father Time. "But I suppose it was because you were foolishly throwing your lasso at nothing."

"I didn't see you," said Jim.

"Of course you didn't. I'm invisible to the eyes of human beings unless they get within three feet of me, and I take care to keep more than that distance away from them. That's why I was crossing this field, where I supposed no one would be. And I should have been perfectly safe had it not been for your beastly lasso. Now, then," he added, crossly, "are you going to get that rope off?"

"Why should I?" asked Jim.

"Because everything in the world stopped moving the moment you caught me. I don't suppose you want to make an end of all business and pleasure, and war and

"You've brought everything on earth to a standstill."

love, and misery and ambition and everything else, do you? Not a watch has ticked since you tied me up here like a mummy!"

Jim laughed. It really was funny to see the old man wound round and round with coils of rope from his knees up to his chin.

"It'll do you good to rest," said the boy. "From all I've heard you lead a rather busy life."

"Indeed I do," replied Father Time, with a sigh. "I'm due in Kamchatka[1] this very minute. And to think one small boy is upsetting all my regular habits!"

"Too bad!" said Jim, with a grin. "But since the world has stopped anyhow, it won't matter if it takes a little longer recess. As soon as I let you go Time will fly again. Where are your wings?"

"I haven't any," answered the old man. "That is a story cooked up by some one who never saw me. As a matter of fact, I move rather slowly."

"I see, you take your time," remarked the boy. "What do you use that scythe for?"

"To mow down the people," said the ancient one. "Every time I swing my scythe some one dies."

"Then I ought to win a life-saving medal by keeping you tied up," said Jim. "Some folks will live this much longer."

"But they won't know it," said Father Time, with a sad smile; "so it will do them no good. You may as well untie me at once."

"No," said Jim, with a determined air. "I may never capture you again; so I'll hold you for awhile and see how the world wags without you."

Then he swung the old man, bound as he was, upon the back of the butcher's horse, and, getting into the saddle himself, started back toward town, one hand holding his prisoner and the other guiding the reins.

1. Asian peninsula, in northeast Russia.

When he reached the road his eye fell on a strange tableau. A horse and buggy stood in the middle of the road, the horse in the act of trotting, with his head held high and two legs in the air, but perfectly motionless. In the buggy a man and a woman were seated; but had they been turned into stone they could not have been more still and stiff.

"There's no Time for them!" sighed the old man. "Won't you let me go now?"

"Not yet," replied the boy.

He rode on until he reached the city, where all the people stood in exactly the same positions they were in when Jim lassoed Father Time. Stopping in front of a big dry goods store,[2] the boy hitched his horse and went in. The clerks were measuring out goods and showing patterns to the rows of customers in front of them, but everyone seemed suddenly to have become a statue.

There was something very unpleasant in this scene, and a cold shiver began to run up and down Jim's back; so he hurried out again.

On the edge of the sidewalk sat a poor, crippled beggar, holding out his hat, and beside him stood a prosperous-looking gentleman who was about to drop a penny into the beggar's hat. Jim knew this gentleman to be very rich but rather stingy, so he ventured to run his hand into the man's pocket and take out his purse, in which was a $20 gold piece. This glittering coin he put in the gentleman's fingers instead of the penny and then restored the purse to the rich man's pocket.

"That donation will surprise him when he comes to life," thought the boy.

He mounted the horse again and rode up the street. As he passed the shop of his friend, the butcher, he noticed several pieces of meat hanging outside.

"I'm afraid that meat'll spoil," he remarked.

"It takes Time to spoil meat," answered the old man.

This struck Jim as being queer, but true.

"It seems Time meddles with everything," said he.

"Yes; you've made a prisoner of the most important personage in the world," groaned the old man; "and you haven't enough sense to let him go again."

Jim did not reply, and soon they came to his uncle's house, where he again dismounted. The street was filled with teams and people, but all were motionless. His two little cousins were just coming out the gate on their way to school, with their books and slates underneath their arms; so Jim had to jump over the fence to avoid knocking them down.

In the front room sat his aunt, reading her Bible. She was just turning a page when Time stopped. In the dining-room was his uncle, finishing his luncheon. His mouth was open and his fork poised just before it, while his eyes were fixed upon the newspaper folded beside him. Jim helped himself to his uncle's pie, and while he ate it he walked out to his prisoner.

"There's one thing I don't understand," said he.

"What's that?" asked Father Time.

"Why is it that I'm able to move around while everyone else is—is—froze up?"

"That is because I'm your prisoner," answered the other. "You can do anything you wish with Time now. But unless you are careful you'll do something you will be sorry for."

Jim threw the crust of his pie at a bird that was suspended in the air, where it had been flying when Time stopped.

2. A store that sells fabrics, drapery, clothing, and articles related to making clothing.

"Anyway," he laughed, "I'm living longer than anyone else. No one will ever be able to catch up with me again."

"Each life has its allotted span," said the old man. "When you have lived your proper time my scythe will mow you down."

"I forgot your scythe," said Jim, thoughtfully.

Then a spirit of mischief came into the boy's head, for he happened to think that the present opportunity to have fun would never occur again. He tied Father Time to his uncle's hitching post, that he might not escape, and then crossed the road to the corner grocery.

The grocer had scolded Jim that very morning for stepping into a basket of turnips by accident. So the boy went to the back end of the grocery and turned on the faucet of the molasses barrel.

"That'll make a nice mess when Time starts the molasses running all over the floor," said Jim, with a laugh.

A little further down the street was a barber shop, and sitting in the barber's chair Jim saw the man that all the boys declared was the "meanest man in town." He certainly did not like the boys and the boys knew it. The barber was in the act of shampooing this person when Time was captured. Jim ran to the drug store, and, getting a bottle of mucilage,[3] he returned and poured it over the ruffled hair of the unpopular citizen.

"That'll probably surprise him when he wakes up," thought Jim.

Near by was the schoolhouse. Jim entered it and found that only a few of the pupils were assembled. But the teacher sat at his desk, stern and frowning as usual.

Taking a piece of chalk, Jim marked upon the blackboard in big letters the following words:

> "Every scholar is requested to yell the minute he enters this room.
> He will also please throw his books at the teacher's head.
> Signed, Prof. Sharpe."

"That ought to raise a nice rumpus," murmured the mischiefmaker, as he walked away.

On the corner stood Policeman Mulligan, talking with old Miss Scrapple, the worst gossip in town, who always delighted in saying something disagreeable about her neighbors. Jim thought this opportunity was too good to lose. So he took off the policeman's cap and brass-buttoned coat and put them on Miss Scrapple, while the lady's feathered and ribboned hat he placed jauntily upon the policeman's head.

The effect was so comical that the boy laughed aloud, and as a good many people were standing near the corner Jim decided that Miss Scrapple and Officer Mulligan would create a sensation when Time started upon his travels.

Then the young cowboy remembered his prisoner, and, walking back to the hitching post, he came within three feet of it and saw Father Time still standing patiently within the toils of the lasso. He looked angry and annoyed, however, and growled out:

"Well, when do you intend to release me?"

"I've been thinking about that ugly scythe of yours," said Jim.

"What about it?" asked Father Time.

---

3. Glue.

"Perhaps if I let you go you'll swing it at me the first thing, to be revenged," replied the boy.

Father Time gave him a severe look, but said:

"I've known boys for thousands of years, and of course I know they're mischievous and reckless. But I like boys, because they grow up to be men and people my world. Now, if a man had caught me by accident, as you did, I could have scared him into letting me go instantly; but boys are harder to scare. I don't know as I blame you. I was a boy myself, long ago, when the world was new. But surely you've had enough fun with me by this time, and now I hope you'll show the respect that is due to old age. Let me go, and in return I will promise to forget all about my capture. The incident won't do much harm, anyway, for no one will ever know that Time has halted the last three hours or so."

"All right," said Jim, cheerfully, "since you've promised not to mow me down, I'll let you go." But he had a notion some people in the town would suspect Time had stopped when they returned to life.

He carefully unwound the rope from the old man, who, when he was free, at once shouldered his scythe, rearranged his white robe and nodded farewell.

The next moment he had disappeared, and with a rustle and rumble and roar of activity the world came to life again and jogged along as it always had before.

Jim wound up his lasso, mounted the butcher's horse and rode slowly down the street.

Loud screams came from the corner, where a great crowd of people quickly assembled. From his seat on the horse Jim saw Miss Scrapple, attired in the policeman's uniform, angrily shaking her fists in Mulligan's face, while the officer was furiously stamping upon the lady's hat, which he had torn from his own head amidst the jeers of the crowd.

As he rode past the schoolhouse he heard a tremendous chorus of yells, and knew Prof. Sharpe was having a hard time to quell the riot caused by the sign on the blackboard.

Through the window of the barber shop he saw the "mean man" frantically belaboring the barber with a hair brush, while his hair stood up stiff as bayonets in all directions. And the grocer ran out of his door and yelled "Fire!" while his shoes left a track of molasses wherever he stepped.

Jim's heart was filled with joy. He was fairly reveling in the excitement he had caused when some one caught his leg and pulled him from the horse.

"What're ye doin' here, ye rascal?" cried the butcher, angrily; "didn't ye promise to put that beast inter Plympton's pasture? An' now I find ye ridin' the poor nag around like a gentleman o' leisure!"

"That's a fact," said Jim, with surprise; "I clean forgot about the horse!"

This story should teach us the supreme importance of Time and the folly of trying to stop it. For should you succeed, as Jim did, in bringing Time to a standstill, the world would soon become a dreary place and life decidedly unpleasant.

1901

E. NESBIT
1858–1924

At the height of her popularity, the animated British writer Edith Nesbit, called "Duchess" (in an allusion to Lewis Carroll's commanding character in *Alice's Adventures in Wonderland*, 1865) or "Madam" by her friends and admirers, cut quite an unconventional figure in her flowing dresses, rows of silver bangles, and ever-present cigarette smoldering in a long holder. Nesbit's bohemian nature revealed itself in other ways as well. Along with her husband, the professional reviewer and columnist Hubert Bland, and friends such as the playwright George Bernard Shaw and the social reformers Beatrice and Sidney Webb, Nesbit was an active and long-standing member of the Fabian Society—a London-based socialist organization founded in 1884 that was dedicated to social justice and the progressive improvement of society for the poor, the working classes, and women.

Nesbit's home life was also unlike a typical Edwardian matron's: the philandering Bland took many mistresses over the years, including Edith's friend Alice Hoatson, who ultimately came to live with the Blands and to bear two of Bland's children. These children, adopted by Nesbit as her own, were brought up with Nesbit's three children with Bland. Nesbit, too, took many lovers and enjoyed the attention bestowed on her by her many followers. Well-known as generous hosts, the Blands moved their lively and chaotic household to a number of different locations in south London and on the Kentish coast. The shortages and rationing of the war years (whose advent coincided with Hubert's death in 1914), decades of spending, and a gradual slowing of her literary production all served to constrain Edith's comfortable, if not lavish, lifestyle. Grieving and harried, she resorted to opening her large Georgian home, Well Hall, to P.G.s ("paying guests") and sold produce from its garden in attempts to make ends meet. In 1917 she married a marine engineer—Thomas Terry Tucker, known as "the Skipper"—and lived quietly and simply with him until her death in the spring of 1924.

As a young woman, Nesbit launched her writing career by selling single poems to journals and newspapers. After her marriage, she began to sell stories and poems written jointly with her husband, publishing under the pseudonym Fabian Bland. (The couple would name their third child Fabian.) This collaboration resulted in two novels and a number of pieces for a radical London newspaper, *The Weekly Dispatch*. Nesbit would go on to publish short stories, volumes of poetry, and novels for adults throughout her writing career, yet during her lifetime and today she was and is primarily known as the author of numerous best-selling books for children.

Nesbit's first extended story for children, an episodic novel about a search for treasure to "restore the fallen fortunes of [their] ancient house" conducted by the irrepressible Oswald Bastable (who was based, in part, on Nesbit's beloved older brother) and his siblings, was published in book form as *The Story of the Treasure Seekers* in time for Christmas 1899. Nesbit's use of comic irony, parodies of literary clichés, and a complicated narrative voice (at times switching from third to first person), together with engaging child characters who act mostly without the interference of grownups, caught the attention of the reading public. Virtually overnight, *The Treasure Seekers* established Nesbit's reputation as an innovative voice in children's literature. Nesbit immediately followed with *The Wouldbegoods, Being the Further Adventures of the Treasure Seekers* (1901) and wrote additional children's works in quick succession; until 1912 or so, after which her productivity slowly fell, she often published two or three novels a year.

Nesbit always wrote with speed, working on more than one project at a time. Her welcome popularity placed additional demands on her to produce quickly as her children's novels were often first serialized. Her most successful relationship with a periodical was in writing fantasies for *The Strand Magazine*, which paid well and established the partnership between Nesbit and H. R. Millar, a young line artist who regularly illustrated *The Strand*'s fairy tales and whose drawings became most closely associated with her work.

The Phœnix and the Carpet (1904)—Nesbit's sequel to *Five Children and It* (1902), which was originally published as "The Psammead" in *The Strand Magazine* from April to December 1902—similarly ran first as a twelve-part series in *The Strand Magazine* from July 1903 until June 1904. *The Phœnix and the Carpet* is an example of Nesbit's domestic fantasies in which a group of bickering and believable middle-class children discover magic quite by accident and experience a series of adventures with unforeseen consequences. Nesbit's good friend H. G. Wells (who was later rejected by the Blands once his plan to run away with Rosamund, Hubert Bland's first child with Alice Hoatson, was discovered) wrote an enthusiastic letter to Nesbit after receiving a copy of *The Phœnix and the Carpet*: "The Phœnix is a great creation; he is the best character you ever invented—or anybody ever invented in his line. It's the best larking I ever saw." The American author Edward Eager based his children's fantasies on Nesbit's. In the opening of *Half Magic* (1954), Eager literally invokes the older writer with this bit of flattery: "This summer the children had found some books by a writer named E. Nesbit, surely the most wonderful books in the world."

Although the patronizing attitudes about race and class expressed in her children's fiction mark Nesbit as coming from another era, the sophisticated comic style, strong narrative voice, and imaginative plots of her children's books have made her one of the first "modern" writers for children. She was widely imitated, and her contribution to children's literature should not be underestimated. Marcus Crouch argues in *The Nesbit Tradition* (1972) that in her writings, "the Victorian conscience lost its self-consciousness; their insight became sharper and more richly aware of the incongruities which make for humour; above all, she threw away their strong, sober, essentially literary style and replaced it with the miraculously colloquial, flexible and revealing prose which was her unique contribution to the children's novel."

The Phœnix and the Carpet

To Hubert[1]

Dear Hubert, if I ever found
A wishing-carpet lying round,
I'd stand upon it, and I'd say:
"Take me to Hubert, right away!"
And then we'd travel very far
To where the magic countries are
That you and I will never see,
And choose the loveliest gifts for you, from me.

But oh! alack! and well-a-day!
No wishing-carpets come my way.
I never found a Phœnix[2] yet,
And psammeads[3] are so hard to get!
So I can give you nothing fine—
Only this book, your book and mine,
And hers, whose name by yours is set;
Your book, my book, the book of Margaret![4]

E. Nesbit.
Dymchurch.

1. Hubert Griffith, Nesbit's godson.
2. Mythical Arabian bird; there was only one, and it consumed itself in fire and was reborn from the ashes.

3. Sand fairies of Nesbit's creation; a psammead was a main character in her previous novel, *Five Children and It* (1902).
4. Hubert Griffith's sister.

CHAPTER I. THE EGG

It began with the day when it was almost the Fifth of November,[5] and a doubt arose in some breast—Robert's, I fancy—as to the quality of the fireworks laid in for the Guy Fawkes celebration.

"They were jolly cheap," said whoever it was, and I think it was Robert, "and suppose they didn't go off on the night? Those Prosser kids would have something to snigger about then."

"The ones *I* got are all right," Jane said; "I know they are, because the man at the shop said they were worth thribble the money——"

"I'm sure thribble isn't grammar," Anthea said.

"Of course it isn't," said Cyril; "one word can't be grammar all by itself, so you needn't be so jolly clever."

Anthea was rummaging in the corner-drawers of her mind for a very disagreeable answer, when she remembered what a wet day it was, and how the boys had been disappointed of that ride to London and back on the top of the tram, which their mother had promised them as a reward for not having once forgotten, for six whole days, to wipe their boots on the mat when they came home from school.

So Anthea only said, "Don't be so jolly clever yourself, Squirrel. And the fireworks look all right, and you'll have the eightpence that your tram fares didn't cost to-day, to buy something more with. You ought to get a perfectly lovely Catharine wheel[6] for eightpence."

"I daresay," said Cyril coldly; "but it's not *your* eightpence anyhow——"

"But look here," said Robert, "really now, about the fireworks. We don't want to be disgraced before those kids next door. They think because they wear red plush[7] on Sundays no one else is any good."

"I wouldn't wear plush if it was ever so—unless it was black, to be beheaded in, if I was Mary Queen of Scots,"[8] said Anthea, with scorn.

Robert stuck steadily to his point. One great point about Robert is the steadiness with which he can stick.

"I think we ought to test them," he said.

"You young duffer,"[9] said Cyril, "fireworks are like postage-stamps. You can only use them once."

"What do you suppose it means by 'Carter's tested seeds' in the advertisement?"

There was a blank silence. Then Cyril touched his forehead with his finger and shook his head.

"A little wrong here," he said. "I was always afraid of that with poor Robert. All that cleverness, you know, and being top in algebra so often—it's bound to tell——"

"Dry up," said Robert, fiercely. "Don't you see? You can't *test* seeds if you do them *all*. You just take a few here and there, and if those grow you can feel pretty sure the others will be—what do you call it?—Father told me—'up to sample.' Don't you think we ought to sample the fireworks? Just shut our eyes and each draw one out, and then try them."

---

5. Guy Fawkes Day, named for one of the foiled Catholic conspirators who plotted to blow up Parliament and King James I on November 5, 1605. It is traditionally celebrated in England with fireworks.
6. A firework that rotates in the manner of a wheel while burning (it takes its name from the legend of the martyrdom of St. Catherine of Alexandria).
7. Long-napped velvet used to make fancy clothes.
8. Queen of Scotland (1542–1587; r. 1542–87), beheaded by her cousin Elizabeth I, Queen of England (1533–1603; r. 1558–1603).
9. A dope or dunce.

"But it's raining cats and dogs," said Jane.

"And Queen Anne is dead,"[1] rejoined Robert. No one was in a very good temper. "We needn't go out to do them; we can just move back the table, and let them off on the old tea-tray we play toboggans with. I don't know what *you* think, but *I* think it's time we did something, and that would be really useful; because then we shouldn't just *hope* the fireworks would make those Prossers sit up—we should *know*."

"It *would* be something to do," Cyril owned with languid approval.

So the table was moved back. And then the hole in the carpet, that had been near the window till the carpet was turned round, showed most awfully. But Anthea stole out on tip-toe, and got the tray when cook wasn't looking, and brought it in and put it over the hole.

Then all the fireworks were put on the table, and each of the four children shut his eyes very tight and put out his hand and grasped something. Robert took a cracker, Cyril and Anthea had Roman candles; but Jane's fat paw closed on the gem of the whole collection, the Jack-in-the-box that had cost two shillings, and one at least of the party—I will not say which, because he was sorry afterwards—declared that Jane had done it on purpose. Nobody was pleased. For the worst of it was that these four children, with a very proper dislike of anything even faintly bordering on the sneakish, had a law, unalterable as those of the Medes and Persians,[2] that one had to stand by the results of a toss-up, or a drawing of lots, or any other appeal to chance, however much one might happen to dislike the way things were turning out.

"I didn't mean to," said Jane, near tears. "I don't care, I'll draw another——"

"You know jolly well you can't," said Cyril, bitterly. "It's settled. It's Medium and Persian. You've done it, and you'll have to stand by it—and us too, worse luck. Never mind. *You'll* have your pocket-money before the Fifth. Anyway, we'll have the Jack-in-the-box *last*, and get the most out of it we can."

So the cracker and the Roman candles were lighted, and they were all that could be expected for the money; but when it came to the Jack-in-the-box it simply sat in the tray and laughed at them, as Cyril said. They tried to light it with paper and they tried to light it with matches; they tried to light it with Vesuvian fusees[3] from the pocket of father's second-best overcoat that was hanging in the hall. And then Anthea slipped away to the cupboard under the stairs where the brooms and dustpans were kept, and the rosiny fire-lighters that smell so nice and like the woods where pine-trees grow, and the old newspapers, and the beeswax and turpentine, and the horrid stiff dark rags that are used for cleaning brass and furniture, and the paraffin[4] for the lamps. She came back with a little pot that had once cost sevenpence-halfpenny when it was full of red-currant jelly; but the jelly had been all eaten long ago, and now Anthea had filled the jar with paraffin. She came in, and she threw the paraffin over the tray just at the moment when Cyril was trying with the twenty-third match to light the Jack-in-the-box. The Jack-in-the-box did not catch fire any more than usual, but the paraffin acted quite differently, and in an instant a hot flash of flame leapt up and burnt off Cyril's eyelashes, and scorched the faces of all four before they could spring back. They backed, in four instantaneous bounds, as far as they could, which was to the wall, and the pillar of fire reached from floor to ceiling.

"My hat," said Cyril, with emotion, "you've done it this time, Anthea."

1. A traditional reply made to the teller of stale news. Anne was Queen of England (1665–1714; r. 1702–14).
2. Inhabitants of Media and Persia (modern Iran), whose law "altereth not" (Daniel 6.8).

3. Matches with large heads tipped with brimstone, used especially for lighting cigars or tobacco pipes.
4. Kerosene.

"A hot flash of flame leapt up."

The flame was spreading out under the ceiling like the rose of fire in Mr. Rider Haggard's exciting story about Allan Quatermain.[5] Robert and Cyril saw that no time was to be lost. They turned up the edges of the carpet, and kicked them over the tray. This cut off the column of fire, and it disappeared and there was nothing left but smoke and a dreadful smell of lamps that have been turned too low. All hands now rushed to the rescue, and the paraffin fire was only a bundle of trampled carpet, when suddenly a sharp crack beneath their feet made the amateur firemen start back. Another crack—the carpet moved as if it had had a cat wrapped in it; the Jack-in-the-box had at last allowed itself to be lighted, and it was going off with desperate violence inside the carpet.

Robert, with the air of one doing the only possible thing, rushed to the window and opened it. Anthea screamed, Jane burst into tears, and Cyril turned the table wrong way up on top of the carpet heap. But the firework went on, banging and bursting and spluttering even underneath the table.

Next moment mother rushed in, attracted by the howls of Anthea, and in a few moments the firework desisted and there was a dead silence, and the children stood looking at each other's black faces, and, out of the corners of their eyes, at mother's white one.

The fact that the nursery carpet was ruined occasioned but little surprise, nor was

5. *King Solomon's Mines* (1885) by Rider Haggard (1856–1925), an English novelist popular for romantic adventure stories.

any one really astonished that bed should prove the immediate end of the adventure. It has been said that all roads lead to Rome; this may be true, but at any rate, in early youth I am quite sure that many roads lead to *bed*, and stop there—or *you* do.

The rest of the fireworks were confiscated, and mother was not pleased when father let them off himself in the back garden, though he said, "Well, how else can you get rid of them, my dear?"

You see, father had forgotten that the children were in disgrace, and that their bedroom windows looked out on to the back garden. So that they all saw the fireworks most beautifully, and admired the skill with which father handled them.

Next day all was forgotten and forgiven; only the nursery had to be deeply cleaned (like spring-cleaning), and the ceiling had to be whitewashed.

And mother went out; and just at tea-time next day a man came with a rolled-up carpet, and father paid him, and mother said—

"If the carpet isn't in good condition, you know, I shall expect you to change it." And the man replied—

"There ain't a thread gone in it nowhere, mum. It's a bargain, if ever there was one, and I'm more'n 'arf sorry I let it go at the price; but we can't resist the lydies, can we, sir?" and he winked at father and went away.

Then the carpet was put down in the nursery, and sure enough there wasn't a hole in it anywhere.

As the last fold was unrolled something hard and loud-sounding bumped out of it and trundled along the nursery floor. All the children scrambled for it, and Cyril got it. He took it to the gas. It was shaped like an egg, very yellow and shiny, half-transparent, and it had an odd sort of light in it that changed as you held it in different ways. It was as though it was an egg with a yolk of pale fire that just showed through the stone.

"I *may* keep it, mayn't I, mother?" Cyril asked. And of course mother said no: they must take it back to the man who had brought the carpet, because she had only paid for a carpet, and not for a stone egg with a fiery yolk to it.

So she told them where the shop was, and it was in the Kentish Town Road, not far from the hotel that is called the Bull and Gate. It was a poky little shop, and the man was arranging furniture outside on the pavement very cunningly, so that the more broken parts should show as little as possible. And directly he saw the children he knew them again, and he began at once, without giving them a chance to speak.

"No you don't," he cried loudly; "I ain't a-goin' to take back no carpets, so don't you make no bloomin' errer. A bargain's a bargain, and the carpet's puffik through-out."

"We don't want you to take it back," said Cyril; "but we found something in it."

"It must have got into it up at your place, then," said the man, with indignant promptness, "for there ain't nothing in nothing as I sell. It's all as clean as a whistle."

"I never said it wasn't *clean*," said Cyril, "but—"

"Oh, if it's *moths*," said the man, "that's easy cured with borax. But I expect it was only an odd one. I tell you the carpet's good through and through. It hadn't got no moths when it left my 'ands—not so much as an hegg."

"But that's just it," interrupted Jane; "there *was* so much as an egg."

The man made a sort of rush at the children and stamped his foot.

"Clear out, I say!" he shouted, "or I'll call for the police. A nice thing for customers to 'ear you a-coming 'ere a-charging me with finding things in goods what I sells. 'Ere, be off, afore I sends you off with a flea in your ears. Hi! constable—"

The children fled, and they think, and their father thinks, that they couldn't have done anything else. Mother has her own opinion. But father said they might keep the egg.

"The man certainly didn't know the egg was there when he brought the carpet," said he, "any more than your mother did, and we've as much right to it as he had."

So the egg was put on the mantelpiece, where it quite brightened up the dingy nursery. The nursery was dingy, because it was a basement room, and its windows looked out on a stone area with a rockery made of clinkers[6] facing the windows. Nothing grew in the rockery except London pride[7] and snails.

The room had been described in the house agent's list as a "convenient breakfast-room in basement," and in the daytime it was rather dark. This did not matter so much in the evenings when the gas was alight, but then it was in the evening that the blackbeetles got so sociable, and used to come out of the low cupboards on each side of the fireplace where their homes were, and try to make friends with the children. At least, I suppose that was what they wanted, but the children never would.

On the Fifth of November father and mother went to the theatre, and the children were not happy, because the Prossers next door had lots of fireworks and they had none.

They were not even allowed to have a bonfire in the garden.

"No more playing with fire, thank you," was father's answer, when they asked him.

When the baby had been put to bed the children sat sadly round the fire in the nursery.

"I'm beastly bored," said Robert.

"Let's talk about the Psammead," said Anthea, who generally tried to give the conversation a cheerful turn.

"What's the good of *talking*?" said Cyril. "What I want is for something to happen. It's awfully stuffy for a chap not to be allowed out in the evenings. There's simply nothing to do when you've got through your homers."

Jane finished the last of her home-lessons and shut the book with a bang.

"We've got the pleasure of memory," said she. "Just think of last holidays."

Last holidays, indeed, offered something to think of—for they had been spent in the country at a white house between a sand-pit and a gravel-pit, and things had happened. The children had found a Psammead, or sand-fairy, and it had let them have anything they wished for—just exactly anything, with no bother about its not being really for their good, or anything like that. And if you want to know what kind of things they wished for, and how their wishes turned out you can read it all in a book called *Five Children and It* (*It* was the Psammead). If you've not read it, perhaps I ought to tell you that the fifth child was the baby brother, who was called the Lamb, because the first thing he ever said was "Baa!" and that the other children were not particularly handsome, nor were they extra clever, nor extraordinarily good. But they were not bad sorts on the whole; in fact, they were rather like you.

"I don't want to think about the pleasures of memory," said Cyril; "I want some more things to happen."

"We're very much luckier than any one else, as it is," said Jane. "Why, no one else ever found a Psammead. We ought to be grateful."

"Why shouldn't we *go on* being, though?" Cyril asked—"lucky, I mean; not grateful. Why's it all got to stop?"

"Perhaps something will happen," said Anthea, comfortably. "Do you know, sometimes I think we are the sort of people that things *do* happen to."

---

6. Paving bricks.   7. A hardy flowering plant.

"It's like that in history," said Jane: "some kings are full of interesting things, and others—nothing ever happens to them, except their being born and crowned and buried, and sometimes not that."

"I think Panther's right," said Cyril: "I think we are the sort of people things do happen to. I have a sort of feeling things would happen right enough if we could only give them a shove. It just wants something to start it. That's all."

"I wish they taught magic at school," Jane sighed. "I believe if we could do a little magic it might make something happen."

"I wonder how you begin?" Robert looked round the room, but he got no ideas from the faded green curtains, or the drab Venetian blinds, or the worn brown oil-cloth on the floor. Even the new carpet suggested nothing, though its pattern was a very wonderful one, and always seemed as though it were just going to make you think of something.

"I could begin right enough," said Anthea; "I've read lots about it. But I believe it's wrong in the Bible."

"It's only wrong in the Bible because people wanted to hurt other people. I don't see how things can be wrong unless they hurt somebody, and we don't want to hurt anybody; and what's more we, we jolly well couldn't if we tried. Let's get the *Ingoldsby Legends*.[8] There's a thing about Abracadabra there," said Cyril, yawning. "We may as well play at magic. Let's be Knights Templars.[9] They were awfully gone on magic. They used to work spells or something with a goat and a goose. Father says so."

"Well, that's all right," said Robert, unkindly; "you can play the goat right enough, and Jane knows how to be a goose."

"I'll get *Ingoldsby*," said Anthea, hastily. "You turn up the hearthrug."

So they traced strange figures on the linoleum, where the hearthrug had kept it clean. They traced them with chalk that Robert had nicked from the top of the mathematical master's desk at school. You know, of course, that it is stealing to take a new stick of chalk, but it is not wrong to take a broken piece, so long as you only take one. (I do not know the reason of this rule, nor who made it.) And they chanted all the gloomiest songs they could think of. And, of course, nothing happened. So then Anthea said, "I'm sure a magic fire ought to be made of sweet-smelling wood, and have magic gums and essences and things in it."

"I don't know any sweet-smelling wood, except cedar," said Robert; "but I've got some ends of cedar-wood lead pencil."

So they burned the ends of lead pencil. And still nothing happened.

"Let's burn some of the eucalyptus oil we have for our colds," said Anthea.

And they did. It certainly smelt very strong. And they burned lumps of camphor out of the big chest. It was very bright, and made a horrid black smoke, which looked very magical. But still nothing happened. Then they got some clean tea-cloths from the dresser drawer in the kitchen, and waved them over the magic chalk-tracings, and sang "The Hymn of the Moravian Nuns at Bethlehem,"[1] which is very impressive. And still nothing happened. So they waved more and more wildly, and Robert's tea-cloth caught the golden egg and whisked it off the mantelpiece, and it fell into the fender[2] and rolled under the grate.

8. Collection of humorous stories in prose and light verse (1840) by Thomas Ingoldsby (pseudonym of Rev. Richard H. Barham).
9. Military religious order established during the medieval Crusades.

1. An early work by the American poet Henry Wadsworth Longfellow (1807–1882).
2. A metal guard placed in front of the fire to keep coals from falling into the room.

"The bird rose in its nest of fire."

"Oh, crikey!" said more than one voice.

And every one instantly fell down flat on his front to look under the grate, and there lay the egg, glowing in a nest of hot ashes.

"It's not smashed, anyhow," said Robert, and he put his hand under the grate and picked up the egg. But the egg was much hotter than any one would have believed it could possibly get in such a short time, and Robert had to drop it with a cry of "Bother!" It fell on the top bar of the grate, and bounced right into the glowing red-hot heart of the fire.

"The tongs!" cried Anthea. But, alas, no one could remember where they were. Every one had forgotten that the tongs had last been used to fish up the doll's teapot from the bottom of the water-butt,[3] where the Lamb had dropped it. So the nursery tongs were resting between the water-butt and the dustbin, and cook refused to lend the kitchen ones.

"Never mind," said Robert, "we'll get it out with the poker and the shovel."

"Oh, stop," cried Anthea. "Look at it! Look! look! look! I do believe something *is* going to happen!"

For the egg was now red-hot, and inside it something was moving. Next moment there was a soft cracking sound; the egg burst in two, and out of it came a flame-coloured bird. It rested a moment among the flames, and as it rested there the four children could see it growing bigger and bigger under their eyes.

Every mouth was a-gape, every eye a-goggle.

The bird rose in its nest of fire, stretched its wings, and flew out into the room. It flew round and round, and round again, and where it passed the air was warm. Then

3. A large barrel situated to collect rainwater from the roof.

it perched on the fender. The children looked at each other. Then Cyril put out a hand towards the bird. It put its head on one side and looked up at him, as you may have seen a parrot do when it is just going to speak, so that the children were hardly astonished at all when it said, "Be careful; I am not nearly cool yet."

They were not astonished, but they were very, very much interested.

They looked at the bird, and it was certainly worth looking at. Its feathers were like gold. It was about as large as a bantam, only its beak was not at all bantam-shaped.

"I believe I know what it is," said Robert. "I've seen a picture—"

He hurried away. A hasty dash and scramble among the papers on father's study table yielded, as the sum-books say, "the desired result." But when he came back into the room holding out a paper, and crying, "I say, look here," the others all said "Hush!" and he hushed obediently and instantly, for the bird was speaking.

"Which of you," it was saying, "put the egg into the fire?"

"He did," said three voices, and three fingers pointed at Robert.

The bird bowed; at least it was more like that than anything else.

"I am your grateful debtor," it said with a high-bred air.

The children were all choking with wonder and curiosity—all except Robert. He held the paper in his hand, and he *knew*. He said so. He said—

"I know who you are."

And he opened and displayed a printed paper, at the head of which was a little picture of a bird sitting in a nest of flames.

"You are the Phœnix," said Robert; and the bird was quite pleased.

"My fame has lived then for two thousand years," it said. "Allow me to look at my portrait."

It looked at the page which Robert, kneeling down, spread out in the fender, and said—

"It's not a flattering likeness. . . . And what are these characters?" it asked, pointing to the printed part.

"Oh, that's all dullish; it's not much about *you*, you know," said Cyril, with unconscious politeness; "but you're in lots of books——"

"With portraits?" asked the Phœnix.

"Well, no," said Cyril; "in fact, I don't think I ever saw any portrait of you but that one, but I can read you something about yourself, if you like."

The Phœnix nodded, and Cyril went off and fetched Volume X of the old *Encyclopedia*, and on page 246 he found the following:

"Phœnix—in ornithology, a fabulous bird of antiquity."

"Antiquity is quite correct," said the Phœnix, "but fabulous—well, do I look it?"

Every one shook his head. Cyril went on—

"The ancients speak of this bird as single, or the only one of its kind."

"That's right enough," said the Phœnix.

"They describe it as about the size of an eagle."

"Eagles are of different sizes," said the Phœnix; "it's not at all a good description."

All the children were kneeling on the hearth-rug, to be as near the Phœnix as possible.

"You'll boil your brains," it said. "Look out, I'm nearly cool now;" and with a whirr of golden wings it fluttered from the fender to the table. It was so nearly cool that there was only a very faint smell of burning when it had settled itself on the tablecloth.

"It's only a very little scorched," said the Phœnix, apologetically; "it will come out in the wash. Please go on reading."

The children gathered round the table.

"The size of an eagle," Cyril went on, "its head finely crested with a beautiful plumage, its neck covered with feathers of a gold colour, and the rest of its body purple; only the tail white, and the eyes sparkling like stars. They say that it lives about five hundred years in the wilderness, and when advanced in age it builds itself a pile of sweet wood and aromatic gums, fires it with the wafting of its wings, and thus burns itself; and that from its ashes arises a worm, which in time grows up to be a Phœnix. Hence the Phœnicians[4] gave—"

"Never mind what they gave," said the Phœnix, ruffling its golden feathers. "They never gave much, anyway; they always were people who gave nothing for nothing. That book ought to be destroyed: It's most inaccurate. The rest of my body was *never* purple, and as for my tail—well, I simply ask you, *is* it white?"

It turned round and gravely presented its golden tail to the children.

"No, it's not," said everybody.

"No, and it never was," said the Phœnix. "And that about the worm is just a vulgar insult. The Phœnix has an egg, like all respectable birds. It makes a pile—that part's all right—and it lays its egg, and it burns itself; and it goes to sleep and wakes up in its egg, and comes out and goes on living again, and so on for ever and ever. I can't tell you how weary I got of it—such a restless existence; no repose."

"But how did your egg get *here?*" asked Anthea.

"Ah, that's my life-secret," said the Phœnix. "I couldn't tell it to any one who wasn't really sympathetic. I've always been a misunderstood bird. You can tell that by what they say about the worm. I might tell *you*," it went on, looking at Robert with eyes that were indeed starry. "*You* put me on the fire——"

Robert looked uncomfortable.

"The rest of us made the fire of sweet-scented woods and gums, though," said Cyril.

"And—and it was an accident my putting you on the fire," said Robert, telling the truth with some difficulty, for he did not know how the Phœnix might take it. It took it in the most unexpected manner.

"Your candid avowal," it said, "removes my last scruple. I will tell you my story."

"And you won't vanish, or anything sudden, will you?" asked Anthea, anxiously.

"Why?" it asked, puffing out the golden feathers, "do you wish me to stay here?"

"Oh, *yes*," said every one, with unmistakable sincerity.

"Why?" asked the Phœnix again, looking modestly at the table-cloth.

"Because," said every one at once, and then stopped short; only Jane added after a pause, "you are the most beautiful person we've ever seen."

"You are a sensible child," said the Phœnix, "and I will *not* vanish or anything sudden. And I will tell you my tale. I had resided, as your book says, for many thousand years in the wilderness, which is a large, quiet place with very little really good society, and I was becoming weary of the monotony of my existence. But I acquired the habit of laying my egg and burning myself every five hundred years—and you know how difficult it is to break yourself of a habit."

"Yes," said Cyril; "Jane used to bite her nails."

"But I broke myself of it," urged Jane, rather hurt, "you know I did."

"Not till they put bitter aloes[5] on them," said Cyril.

---

4. Ancient Middle Eastern navigators and traders.
5. A purgative drug made from the juice of the aloe plant.

"I doubt," said the bird, gravely, "whether even bitter aloes (the aloe, by the way, has a bad habit of its own, which it might well cure before seeking to cure others; I allude to its indolent practice of flowering but once a century), I doubt whether even bitter aloes could have cured *me*. But I *was* cured. I awoke one morning from a feverish dream—it was getting near the time for me to lay that tiresome fire and lay that tedious egg upon it—and I saw two people, a man and a woman. They were sitting on a carpet—and when I accosted them civilly they narrated to me their life-story, which, as you have not yet heard it, I will now proceed to relate. They were a prince and princess, and the story of their parents was one which I am sure you will like to hear. In early youth the mother of the princess happened to hear the story of a certain enchanter, and in that story I am sure you will be interested. The enchanter—"

"Oh, please don't," said Anthea. "I can't understand all these beginnings of stories, and you seem to be getting deeper and deeper in them every minute. Do tell us your *own* story. That's what we really want to hear."

"Well," said the Phœnix, seeming on the whole rather flattered, "to cut about seventy long stories short (though I had to listen to them all—but to be sure in the wilderness there is plenty of time), this prince and princess were so fond of each other that they did not want any one else, and the enchanter—don't be alarmed, I won't go into his history—had given them a magic carpet (you've heard of a magic carpet?), and they had just sat on it and told it to take them right away from every one—and it had brought them to the wilderness. And as they meant to stay there they had no further use for the carpet, so they gave it to me. That was indeed the chance of a lifetime!"

"I don't see what you wanted with a carpet," said Jane, "when you've got those lovely wings."

"They *are* nice wings, aren't they?" said the Phœnix, simpering and spreading them out. "Well, I got the prince to lay out the carpet, and I laid my egg on it; then I said to the carpet, 'Now, my excellent carpet, prove your worth. Take that egg somewhere where it can't be hatched for two thousand years, and where, when that time's up, some one will light a fire of sweet wood and aromatic gums, and put the egg in to hatch'; and you see it's all come out exactly as I said. The words were no sooner out of my beak than egg and carpet disappeared. The royal lovers assisted to arrange my pile, and soothed my last moments. I burnt myself up and knew no more till I awoke on yonder altar."

It pointed its claw at the grate.

"But the carpet," said Robert, "the magic carpet that takes you anywhere you wish. What became of that?"

"Oh, *that?*" said the Phœnix, carelessly—"I should say that that is the carpet. I remember the pattern perfectly."

It pointed as it spoke to the floor, where lay the carpet which mother had bought in the Kentish Town Road for twenty-two shillings and ninepence.

At that instant father's latch-key was heard in the door.

"*Oh*," whispered Cyril, "now we shall catch it for not being in bed!"

"Wish yourself there," said the Phœnix, in a hurried whisper, "and then wish the carpet back in its place."

No sooner said than done. It made one a little giddy, certainly, and a little breathless; but when things seemed right way up again, there the children were, in bed, and the lights were out.

They heard the soft voice of the Phœnix through the darkness.

"I shall sleep on the cornice above your curtains," it said. "Please don't mention me to your kinsfolk."

"Not much good," said Robert, "they'd never believe us. I say," he called through the half-open door to the girls; "talk about adventures and things happening. We ought to be able to get some fun out of a magic carpet *and* a Phœnix."

"Rather," said the girls, in bed.

"Children," said father, on the stairs, "go to sleep at once. What do you mean by talking at this time of night?"

No answer was expected to this question, but under the bedclothes Cyril murmured one.

"Mean?" he said. "Don't know what we mean. I don't know what *anything* means——"

"But we've got a magic carpet *and* a Phœnix," said Robert.

"You'll get something else if father comes in and catches you," said Cyril. "Shut up, I tell you."

Robert shut up. But he knew as well as you do that the adventures of that carpet and that Phœnix were only just beginning.

Father and mother had not the least idea of what had happened in their absence. This is often the case, even when there are no magic carpets or Phœnix in the house.

The next morning—but I am sure you would rather wait till the next chapter before you hear about *that*.

Chapter II. The Topless Tower

The children had seen the Phœnix-egg hatched in the flames in their own nursery grate, and had heard from it how the carpet on their own nursery floor was really the wishing carpet, which would take them anywhere they chose. The carpet had transported them to bed just at the right moment, and the Phœnix had gone to roost on the cornice supporting the window-curtains of the boys' room.

"Excuse me," said a gentle voice, and a courteous beak opened, very kindly and delicately, the right eye of Cyril. "I hear the slaves below preparing food. Awaken! A word of explanation and arrangement. . . . I do wish you wouldn't——"

The Phœnix stopped speaking and fluttered away crossly to the cornice-pole; for Cyril had hit out, as boys will do when they are awakened suddenly, and the Phœnix was not used to boys, and his feelings, if not his wings, were hurt.

"Sorry," said Cyril, coming awake all in a minute. "Do come back! What was it you were saying? Something about bacon and rations?"

The Phœnix fluttered back to the brass rail at the foot of the bed.

"I say—you *are* real," said Cyril. "How ripping! And the carpet?"

"The carpet is as real as it ever was," said the Phœnix, rather contemptuously; "but, of course, a carpet's only a carpet, whereas a Phœnix is superlatively a Phœnix."

"Yes, indeed," said Cyril, "I see it is. Oh, what luck! Wake up, Bobs! There's jolly well something to wake up for to-day. And it's Saturday, too."

"I've been reflecting," said the Phœnix, "during the silent watches of the night, and I could not avoid the conclusion that you were quite insufficiently astonished at my appearance yesterday. The ancients were always *very* surprised. Did you, by chance, *expect* my egg to hatch?"

"Not us," Cyril said.

"And if we had," said Anthea, who had come in in her nightie when she heard the silvery voice of the Phœnix, "we could never, never have expected it to hatch anything so splendid as you."

The bird smiled. Perhaps you've never seen a bird smile?

"You see," said Anthea, wrapping herself in the boys' counterpane, for the morning was chill, "we've had things happen to us before"; and she told the story of the Psammead, or sand-fairy.

"Ah, yes," said the Phœnix; "Psammeads were rare, even in my time. I remember I used to be called the Psammead of the Desert. I was always having compliments paid me; I can't think why."

"Can *you* give wishes, then?" asked Jane, who had now come in too.

"Oh, dear me, no," said the Phœnix, contemptuously, "at least—but I hear foot-steps approaching. I hasten to conceal myself." And it did.

I think I said that this day was Saturday. It was also cook's birthday, and mother had allowed her and Eliza to go to the Crystal Palace[6] with a party of friends, so Jane and Anthea of course had to help to make beds and to wash up the breakfast cups, and little things like that. Robert and Cyril intended to spend the morning in conversation with the Phœnix, but the bird had its own ideas about this.

"I must have an hour or two's quiet," it said, "I really must. My nerves will give way unless I can get a little rest. You must remember it's two thousand years since I had any conversation—I'm out of practice, and I must take care of myself. I've often been told that mine is a valuable life." So it nestled down inside an old hat-box of father's, which had been brought down from the box-room some days before, when a helmet was suddenly needed for a game of tournaments, with its golden head under its golden wing, and went to sleep. So then Robert and Cyril moved the table back and were going to sit on the carpet and wish themselves somewhere else. But before they could decide on the place, Cyril said—

"I don't know. Perhaps it's rather sneakish to begin without the girls."

"They'll be all the morning," said Robert, impatiently. And then a thing inside him, which tiresome books sometimes call the "inward monitor," said, "Why don't you help them, then?"

Cyril's "inward monitor" happened to say the same thing at the same moment, so the boys went and helped to wash up the teacups, and to dust the drawing-room. Robert was so interested that he proposed to clean the front doorsteps—a thing he had never been allowed to do. Nor was he allowed to do it on this occasion. One reason was that it had already been done by cook.

When all the housework was finished, the girls dressed the happy, wriggling baby in his blue highwayman coat and three-cornered hat, and kept him amused while mother changed her dress and got ready to take him over to granny's. Mother always went to granny's every Saturday, and generally some of the children went with her; but to-day they were to keep house. And their hearts were full of joyous and delightful feelings every time they remembered that the house they would have to keep had a Phœnix in it, *and* a wishing carpet.

You can always keep the Lamb good and happy for quite a long time if you play the Noah's Ark game with him. It is quite simple. He just sits on your lap and tells you what animal he is, and then you say the little poetry piece about whatever animal he chooses to be. Of course, some of the animals, like the zebra and the tiger, haven't

6. A large hall, innovative in its use of glass and iron, originally erected in Hyde Park, London, to house the Great Exhibition of 1851. After the exhibition closed, it was moved to Sydenham (in south London) and used as a museum until it was destroyed by fire in 1936.

got any poetry, because they are so difficult to rhyme to. The Lamb knows quite well which are the poetry animals.

"I'm a baby bear!" said the Lamb, snugging down; and Anthea began:

> "I love my little baby bear,
> I love his nose and toes and hair;
> I like to hold him in my arm,
> And keep him very safe and warm."

And when she said "very," of course there was a real bear's hug.

Then came the eel, and the Lamb was tickled till he wriggled exactly like a real one:

> "I love my little baby eel,
> He is so squidglety to feel;
> He'll be an eel when he is big—
> But now he's just—a—tiny *snig!*"

Perhaps you didn't know that a snig was a baby eel? It is, though, and the Lamb knew it.

"Hedgehog now!" he said; and Anthea went on:

> "My baby hedgehog, how I like ye,
> Though your back's so prickly-spiky;
> Your front is very soft, I've found,
> So I must love you front ways round!"

And then she loved him front ways round, while he squealed with pleasure.

It is a very baby game, and, of course, the rhymes are only meant for very, very small people—not for people who are old enough to read books, so I won't tell you any more of them.

By the time the Lamb had been a baby lion and a baby weasel, and a baby rabbit and a baby rat, mother was ready; and she and the Lamb, having been kissed by everybody and hugged as thoroughly as it is possible to be when you're dressed for out-of-doors, were seen to the tram by the boys. When the boys came back, every one looked at every one else and said—

"Now!"

They locked the front door and they locked the back door, and they fastened all the windows. They moved the table and chairs off the carpet, and Anthea swept it.

"We must show it a *little* attention," she said kindly. "We'll give it tea-leaves next time. Carpets like tea-leaves."[7]

Then every one put on his out-door things, because, as Cyril said, they didn't know where they might be going, and it makes people stare if you go out of doors in November in pinafores and without hats.

Then Robert gently awoke the Phœnix, who yawned and stretched itself, and allowed Robert to lift it on to the middle of the carpet, where it instantly went to

---

7. One method for cleaning a Persian carpet was to sprinkle nearly dry tea leaves over it and then sweep the tea leaves away.

sleep again with its crested head tucked under its golden wing as before. Then every one sat down on the carpet.

"Where shall we go?" was of course the question, and it was warmly discussed. Anthea wanted to go to Japan. Robert and Cyril voted for America, and Jane wished to go to the seaside.

"Because there are donkeys there," said she.

"Not in November, silly," said Cyril; and the discussion got warmer and warmer, and still nothing was settled.

"I vote we let the Phœnix decide," said Robert, at last. So they stroked it till it woke.

"We want to go somewhere abroad," they said, "and we can't make up our minds where."

"Let the carpet make up *its* mind, if it has one," said the Phœnix. "Just say you wish to go abroad."

So they did; and the next moment the world seemed to spin upside down, and when it was right away up again and they were ungiddy enough to look about them, they were out of doors.

Out of doors—this is a feeble way to express where they were. They were out of—out of the earth, or off it. In fact, they were floating steadily, safely, splendidly, in the crisp clear air, with the pale bright blue of the sky above them, and far down below the pale bright sun-diamonded waves of the sea: The carpet had stiffened itself somehow, so that it was square and firm like a raft, and it steered itself so beautifully and kept on its way so flat and fearless that no one was at all afraid of tumbling off. In front of them lay land.

"The coast of France," said the Phœnix, waking up and pointing with its wing. "Where do you wish to go? I should always keep *one* wish, of course—for emergencies—otherwise you may get into an emergency from which you can't emerge at all."

But the children were far too deeply interested to listen.

"I tell you what," said Cyril: "let's let the thing go on and on, and when we see a place we really want to stop at—why, we'll just stop. Isn't this ripping?"

"It's like trains," said Anthea, as they swept over the low-lying coast-line and held a steady course above orderly fields and straight roads bordered with poplar trees— "like express trains, only in trains you never can see anything because of grown-ups wanting the windows shut; and then they breathe on them, and it's like ground glass, and nobody can see anything, and then they go to sleep."

"It's like tobogganing," said Robert, "so fast and smooth, only there's no door-mat to stop short on—it goes on and on."

"You darling Phœnix," said Jane, "it's all your doing. Oh, look at that ducky little church and the women with flappy cappy things on their heads."

"Don't mention it," said the Phœnix, with sleepy politeness.

"*Oh!*" said Cyril, summing up all the rapture that was in every heart. "Look at it all—look at it—and think of the Kentish Town Road!"

Every one looked and every one thought. And the glorious, gliding, smooth, steady rush went on, and they looked down on strange and beautiful things, and held their breath and let it go in deep sighs, and said "Oh!" and "Ah!" till it was long past dinner-time.

It was Jane who suddenly said, "I wish we'd brought that jam tart and cold mutton with us. It would have been jolly to have a picnic in the air."

The jam tart and cold mutton were, however, far away, sitting quietly in the larder of the house in Camden Town which the children were supposed to be keeping. A mouse was at that moment tasting the outside of the raspberry jam part of the tart (she had nibbled a sort of gulf, or bay, through the pastry edge) to see whether it was the sort of dinner she could ask her little mouse-husband to sit down to. She had had a very good dinner herself. It is an ill wind that blows nobody any good.

"We'll stop as soon as we see a nice place," said Anthea. "I've got threepence, and you boys have the fourpence each that your trams didn't cost the other day, so we can buy things to eat. I expect the Phœnix can speak French."

The carpet was sailing along over rocks and rivers and trees and towns and farms and fields. It reminded everybody of a certain time when all of them had had wings, and had flown up to the top of a church tower, and had had a feast there of chicken and tongue and new bread and soda-water. And this again reminded them how hungry they were. And just as they were all being reminded of this very strongly indeed, they saw ahead of them some ruined walls on a hill, and strong and upright, and really, to look at, as good as new—a great square tower.

"The top of that's just exactly the same size as the carpet," said Jane. "I think it would be good to go to the top of that, because then none of the Abby-whats-its-names—I mean natives—would be able to take the carpet away even if they wanted to. And some of us could go out and get things to eat—buy them honestly, I mean, not take them out of larder windows."

"I think it would be better if we went——" Anthea was beginning; but Jane suddenly clenched her hands.

"I don't see why I should never do anything I want, just because I'm the youngest. I wish the carpet would fit itself in at the top of that tower—so there!"

The carpet made a disconcerting bound, and next moment it was hovering above the square top of the tower. Then slowly and carefully it began to sink under them. It was like a lift going down with you at the Army and Navy Stores.[8]

"I don't think we ought to wish things without all agreeing to them first," said Robert, huffishly. "Hullo! What on earth?"

For unexpectedly and greyly something was coming up all round the four sides of the carpet. It was as if a wall were being built by magic quickness. It was a foot high—it was two feet high—three, four, five. It was shutting out the light—more and more.

Anthea looked up at the sky and the walls that now rose six feet above them.

"We're dropping into the tower," she screamed. *There wasn't any top to it.* So the carpet's going to fit itself in at the bottom."

Robert sprang to his feet.

"We ought to have—— Hullo! an owl's nest." He put his knee on a jutting smooth piece of grey stone, and reached his hand into a deep window slit—broad to the inside of the tower, and narrowing like a funnel to the outside.

"Look sharp!" cried every one, but Robert did not look sharp enough. By the time he had drawn his hand out of the owl's nest—there were no eggs there—the carpet had sunk eight feet below him.

"Jump, you silly cuckoo!" cried Cyril, with brotherly anxiety.

But Robert couldn't turn round all in a minute into a jumping position. He wriggled and twisted and got on to the broad ledge, and by the time he was ready to jump the walls of the tower had risen up thirty feet above the others, who were still sinking with the carpet, and Robert found himself in the embrasure of a window; alone, for

8. One of the largest department stores in Victorian London. "Lift": an elevator.

even the owls were not at home that day. The wall was smoothish; there was no climbing up, and as for climbing down—Robert hid his face in his hands, and squirmed back and back from the giddy verge, until the back part of him was wedged quite tight in the narrowest part of the window slit.

He was safe now, of course, but the outside part of his window was like a frame to a picture of part of the other side of the tower. It was very pretty, with moss growing between the stones and little shiny gems; but between him and it there was the width of the tower, and nothing in it but empty air. The situation was terrible. Robert saw in a flash that the carpet was likely to bring them into just the same sort of tight places that they used to get into with the wishes the Psammead granted them.

And the others—imagine their feelings as the carpet sank slowly and steadily to the very bottom of the tower, leaving Robert clinging to the wall. Robert did not even try to imagine their feelings—he had quite enough to do with his own; but you can.

As soon as the carpet came to a stop on the ground at the bottom of the inside of the tower it suddenly lost that raft-like stiffness which had been such a comfort during the journey from Camden Town to the topless tower, and spread itself limply over the loose stones and little earthy mounds at the bottom of the tower, just exactly like any ordinary carpet. Also it shrank suddenly, so that it seemed to draw away from under their feet, and they stepped quickly off the edges and stood on the firm ground, while the carpet drew itself in till it was its proper size, and no longer fitted exactly into the inside of the tower, but left quite a big space all round it.

Then across the carpet they looked at each other, and then every chin was tilted up and every eye sought vainly to see where poor Robert had got to. Of course, they couldn't see him.

"I wish we hadn't come," said Jane.

"You always do," said Cyril, briefly. "Look here, we can't leave Robert up there. I wish the carpet would fetch him down."

The carpet seemed to awake from a dream and pull itself together. It stiffened itself briskly and floated up between the four walls of the tower. The children below craned their heads back, and nearly broke their necks in doing it. The carpet rose and rose. It hung poised darkly above them for an anxious moment or two; then it dropped down again, threw itself on the uneven floor of the tower, and as it did so it tumbled Robert out on the uneven floor of the tower.

"Oh, glory!" said Robert, "that was a squeak. You don't know how I felt. I say, I've had about enough for a bit. Let's wish ourselves at home again and have a go at that jam tart and mutton. We can go out again afterwards."

"Righto!" said every one, for the adventure had shaken the nerves of all. So they all got on to the carpet again, and said—

"I wish we were at home."

And lo and behold, they were no more at home than before. The carpet never moved. The Phœnix had taken the opportunity to go to sleep. Anthea woke it up gently.

"Look here," she said.

"I'm looking," said the Phœnix.

"We wished to be at home, and we're still here," complained Jane.

"No," said the Phœnix, looking about it at the high dark walls of the tower. "No; I quite see that."

"But we wished to be at home," said Cyril.

"No doubt," said the bird, politely.

"And the carpet hasn't moved an inch," said Robert.

"No," said the Phœnix, "I see it hasn't."

"But I thought it was a wishing carpet?"

"So it is," said the Phœnix.

"Then why——?" asked the children, altogether.

"I did tell you, you know," said the Phœnix, "only you are so fond of listening to the music of your own voices. It is, indeed, the most lovely music to each of us, and, therefore——"

"You did tell us *what?*" interrupted an Exasperated.

"Why, that the carpet only gives you three wishes a day and *you've had them.*"

There was a heartfelt silence.

"Then how are we going to get home," said Cyril, at last.

"I haven't any idea," replied the Phœnix, kindly. "Can I fly out and get you any little thing?"

"How could you carry the money to pay for it?"

"It isn't necessary. Birds always take what they want. It is not regarded as stealing, except in the case of magpies."

The children were glad to find they had been right in supposing this to be the case, on the day when they had had wings, and had enjoyed somebody else's ripe plums.

"Yes; let the Phœnix get us something to eat, anyway," Robert urged ("If it will be so kind you mean," corrected Anthea, in a whisper); "if it will be so kind, and we can be thinking while it's gone."

So the Phœnix fluttered up through the grey space of the tower and vanished at the top, and it was not till it had quite gone that Jane said—

"Suppose it never comes back."

It was not a pleasant thought, and though Anthea at once said, "Of course it will come back; I'm certain it's a bird of its word," a further gloom was cast by the idea. For, curiously enough, there was no door to the tower, and all the windows were far, far too high to be reached by the most adventurous climber. It was cold, too, and Anthea shivered.

"Yes," said Cyril, "it's like being at the bottom of a well."

The children waited in a sad and hungry silence, and got little stiff necks with holding their little heads back to look up the inside of the tall grey tower, to see if the Phœnix were coming.

At last it came. It looked very big as it fluttered down between the walls, and as it neared them the children saw that its bigness was caused by a basket of boiled chestnuts which it carried in one claw. In the other it held a piece of bread. And in its beak was a very large pear. The pear was juicy, and as good as a very small drink. When the meal was over every one felt better, and the question of how to get home was discussed without any disagreeableness. But no one could think of any way out of the difficulty, or even out of the tower; for the Phœnix, though its beak and claws had fortunately been strong enough to carry food for them, was plainly not equal to flying through the air with four well-nourished children.

"We must stay here, I suppose," said Robert at last, "and shout out every now and then, and some one will hear us and bring ropes and ladders, and rescue us like out of mines; and they'll get up a subscription to send us home, like castaways."

"Yes; but we shan't be home before mother is, and then father'll take away the carpet and say it's dangerous or something," said Cyril.

"I *do* wish we hadn't come," said Jane.

And every one else said "Shut up," except Anthea, who suddenly awoke the Phœnix and said—

"Look here, I believe *you* can help us. Oh, I do wish you would!"

"I will help you as far as lies in my power," said the Phœnix, at once. "What is it you want now?"

"Why, we want to get home," said every one.

"Oh," said the Phœnix. "Ah, hum! Yes. Home, you said? Meaning?"

"Where we live—where we slept last night—where the altar is that your egg was hatched on."

"Oh, there!" said the Phœnix. "Well, I'll do my best." It fluttered on to the carpet and walked up and down for a few minutes in deep thought. Then it drew itself up proudly.

"I *can* help you," it said. "I am almost sure I can help you. Unless I am grossly deceived I can help you. You won't mind my leaving you for an hour or two?" And without waiting for a reply it soared up through the dimness of the tower into the brightness above.

"Now," said Cyril, firmly, "it said an hour or two. But I've read about captives and people shut up in dungeons and catacombs and things awaiting release, and I know each moment is an eternity. Those people always do something to pass the desperate moments. It's no use our trying to tame spiders, because we shan't have time."

"I *hope* not," said Jane, doubtfully.

"But we ought to scratch our names on the stones or something."

"I say, talking of stones," said Robert, "you see that heap of stones against the wall over in that corner. Well, I'm certain there's a hole in the wall there—and I believe it's a door. Yes, look here—the stones are round like an arch in the wall; and here's the hole—it's all black inside."

He had walked over to the heap as he spoke and climbed up to it—dislodged the top stone of the heap and uncovered a little dark space.

Next moment every one was helping to pull down the heap of stones, and very soon every one threw off his jacket, for it was warm work.

"It *is* a door," said Cyril, wiping his face, "and not a bad thing either, if——"

He was going to add "if anything happens to the Phœnix," but he didn't for fear of frightening Jane. He was not an unkind boy when he had leisure to think of such things.

The arched hole in the wall grew larger and larger. It was very, very black, even compared with the sort of twilight at the bottom of the tower; it grew larger because the children kept pulling off the stones and throwing them down into another heap. The stones must have been there a very long time, for they were covered with moss, and some of them were stuck together by it. So it was fairly hard work, as Robert pointed out.

When the hole reached to about halfway between the top of the arch and the tower, Robert and Cyril let themselves down cautiously on the inside, and lit matches. How thankful they felt then that they had a sensible father, who did not forbid them to carry matches, as some boys' father do. The father of Robert and Cyril only insisted on the matches being of the kind that strike only on the box.

"It's not a door, it's a sort of tunnel," Robert cried to the girls, after the first match had flared up, flickered, and gone out. "Stand off—we'll push some more stones down!"

They did, amid deep excitement. And now the stone heap was almost gone—and before them the girls saw the dark archway leading to unknown things. All doubts and fears as to getting home were forgotten in this thrilling moment. It was like Monte Cristo[9]—it was like——

"I say," cried Anthea, suddenly, "come out! There's always bad air in places that have been shut up. It makes your torches go out, and then you die. It's called fire-damp, I believe. Come out, I tell you."

The urgency of her tone actually brought the boys out—and then every one took up his jacket and fanned the dark arch with it, so as to make the air fresh inside. When Anthea thought the air inside "must be freshened by now," Cyril led the way into the arch. The girls followed, and Robert came last, because Jane refused to tail the procession lest "something" should come in after her, and catch at her from behind. Cyril advanced cautiously, lighting match after match, and peering before him.

"It's a vaulting roof," he said, "and it's all stone—all right, Panther, don't keep pulling at my jacket! The air must be all right because of the matches, silly, and there are—look out—there are steps down."

"Oh, don't let's go any farther," said Jane, in an agony of reluctance (a very painful thing, by the way, to be in). "I'm sure there are snakes, or dens of lions, or something. Do let's go back, and come some other time, with candles, and bellows for the fire-damp."

"Let me get in front of you, then," said the stern voice of Robert, from behind. "This is exactly the place for buried treasure, and I'm going on, anyway; you can stay behind if you like." And then, of course, Jane consented to go on.

So, very slowly and carefully, the children went down the steps—there were seventeen of them—and at the bottom of the steps were more passages branching four ways, and a sort of low arch on the right-hand side made Cyril wonder what it could be, for it was too low to be the beginning of another passage.

So he knelt down and lit a match, and stooping very low he peeped in.

"There's something," he said, and reached out his hand. It touched something that felt more like a damp bag of marbles than anything else that Cyril had ever touched.

"I believe it *is* a buried treasure," he cried.

And it was; for even as Anthea cried, "Oh, hurry up, Squirrel—fetch it out!" Cyril pulled out a rotting canvas bag—about as big as the paper ones the greengrocer gives you with Barcelona nuts in for sixpence.

"There's more of it, a lot more," he said.

As he pulled the rotten bag gave way, and the gold coins ran and span and jumped and bumped and chinked and clinked on the floor of the dark passage.

I wonder what you would say if you suddenly came upon a buried treasure? What Cyril said was, "Oh, bother—I've burnt my fingers!" and as he spoke he dropped the match. "*And it was the last!*" he added.

There was a moment of desperate silence. Then Jane began to cry.

"Don't," said Anthea, "don't, Pussy—you'll exhaust the air if you cry. We can get out all right."

"Yes," said Jane, through her sobs, "and find the Phœnix has come back and gone away again—because it thought we'd gone home some other way, and—Oh, I *wish* we hadn't come."

9. Island on which a long-lost treasure is found in Alexandre Dumas's novel *The Count of Monte Cristo* (1844–45).

Every one stood quite still—only Anthea cuddled Jane up to her and tried to wipe her eyes in the dark.

"D—don't," said Jane; "that's my *ear*—I'm not crying with my ears."

"Come, let's get on out," said Robert; but that was not so easy, for no one could remember exactly which way they had come. It is very difficult to remember things in the dark, unless you have matches with you, and then of course it is quite different, even if you don't strike one.

Every one had come to agree with Jane's constant wish—and despair was making the darkness blacker than ever, when quite suddenly the floor seemed to tip up—and a strong sensation of being in a whirling lift came upon every one. All eyes were closed—one's eyes always are in the dark, don't you think? When the whirling feeling stopped, Cyril said "Earthquakes!" and they all opened their eyes.

They were in their own dingy breakfast-room at home, and oh, how light and bright and safe and pleasant and altogether delightful it seemed after that dark underground tunnel! The carpet lay on the floor, looking as calm as though it had never been for an excursion in its life. On the mantelpiece stood the Phœnix, waiting with an air of modest yet sterling worth for the thanks of the children.

"But how *did* you do it?" they asked, when every one had thanked the Phœnix again and again.

"Oh, I just went and got a wish from your friend the Psammead."

"But how *did* you know where to find it?"

"I found that out from the carpet; these wishing creatures always know all about each other—they're so clannish: like the Scots, you know—all related."

"But the carpet can't talk, can it?"

"No."

"Then how——"

"How did I get the Psammead's address? I tell you I got it from the carpet."

"*Did* it speak then?"

"No," said the Phœnix, thoughtfully, "it didn't speak, but I gathered my information from something in its manner. I was always a singularly observant bird."

It was not till after the cold mutton and the jam tart, as well as the tea and bread-and-butter, that any one found time to regret the golden treasure which had been left scattered on the floor of the underground passage, and which, indeed, no one had thought of till now, since the moment when Cyril burnt his fingers at the flame of the last match.

"What owls and goats we were!" said Robert. "Look how we've always wanted treasure—and now——"

"Never mind," said Anthea, trying as usual to make the best of it. "We'll go back again and get it all, and then we'll give everybody presents."

More than a quarter of an hour passed most agreeably in arranging what presents should be given to who, and, when the claims of generosity had been satisfied, the talk ran for fifty minutes on what they would buy for themselves.

It was Cyril who broke in on Robert's almost too technical account of the motor-car on which he meant to go to and from school.

"There!" he said. "Dry up. It's no good. We can't ever go back. We don't know where it is."

"Don't *you* know?" Jane asked the Phœnix, wistfully.

"Not in the least," the Phœnix replied, in a tone of amiable regret.

"Then we've lost the treasure," said Cyril.

And they had.

"But we've got the carpet and the Phœnix," said Anthea.

"Excuse me," said the bird, with an air of wounded dignity, "I do so *hate* to seem to interfere, but surely you *must* mean the Phœnix and the carpet?"

Chapter III. The Queen Cook

It was on a Saturday that the children made their first glorious journey on the wishing carpet. Unless you are too young to read at all, you will know that the next day must have been Sunday.

Sunday at 18, Camden Terrace, Camden Town, was always a very pretty day. Father always brought home flowers on Saturday, so that the breakfast-table was extra beautiful. In November, of course, the flowers were chrysanthemums, yellow and coppery coloured. Then there were always sausages on toast for breakfast, and these are rapture, after six days of Kentish Town Road eggs at fourteen a shilling.

On this particular Sunday there were fowls for dinner,[1] a kind of food that is generally kept for birthdays and grand occasions, and there was an angel pudding, when rice and milk and oranges and white icing do their best to make you happy.

After dinner father was very sleepy indeed because he had been working hard all the week; but he did not yield to the voice that said, "Go and have an hour's rest." He nursed the Lamb, who had a horrid cough that cook said was whooping-cough as sure as eggs, and he said—

"Come along, kiddies; I've got a ripping book from the library, called *The Golden Age*,[2] and I'll read it to you."

Mother settled herself on the drawing-room sofa, and said she could listen quite nicely with her eyes shut. The Lamb snugged into the "arm-chair corner" of daddy's arm, and the others got into a happy heap on the hearthrug. At first, of course, there were too many feet and knees and shoulders and elbows, but real comfort was actually settling down on them, and the Phœnix and the carpet were put away on the back top shelf of their minds (beautiful things that could be taken out and played with later), when a surly solid knock came at the drawing-room door. It opened an angry inch, and the cook's voice said, "Please, m', may I speak to you a moment?"

Mother looked at father with a desperate expression. Then she put her pretty sparkly Sunday shoes down from the sofa, and stood up in them and sighed.

"As good fish in the sea,"[3] said father, cheerfully, and it was not till much later that the children understood what he meant.

Mother went out into the passage, which is called "the hall," where the umbrella-stand is, and the picture of the "Monarch of the Glen"[4] in a yellow shining frame, with brown spots on the Monarch from the damp in the house before last, and there was cook, very red and damp in the face, and with a clean apron tied on all crooked over the dirty one that she had dished up those dear delightful chickens in. She stood there and she seemed to get redder and damper, and she twisted the corner of her apron round her fingers, and she said very shortly and fiercely—

"If you please, ma'am, I should wish to leave at my day month."[5]

---

1. I.e., lunch.
2. An 1895 book about Victorian childhood by the British author Kenneth Grahame.
3. Proverbial: "There are as good fish in the sea as ever came out of it" (i.e., there are many good fish

in the sea).
4. An 1851 oil painting of a majestic stag by Sir Edwin Landseer, whose animal paintings were extremely popular in Victorian England.
5. I.e., a month from that day.

Mother leaned against the hatstand. The children could see her looking pale through the crack of the door, because she had been very kind to the cook, and had given her a holiday only the day before, and it seemed so very unkind of the cook to want to go like this, and on a Sunday too.

"Why, what's the matter?" mother said.

"It's them children," the cook replied, and somehow the children all felt that they had known it from the first. They did not remember having done anything extra wrong, but it is so frightfully easy to displease a cook. "It's them children: there's that there new carpet in their room, covered thick with mud, both sides, beastly yellow mud, and sakes alive knows where they got it. And all that muck to clean up on a Sunday! It's not my place, and it's not my intentions, so I don't deceive you, ma'am, and but for them limbs,[6] which they is if ever there was, it's not a bad place, though I says it, and I wouldn't wish to leave, but—"

"I'm very sorry," said mother, gently. "I will speak to the children. And you had better think it over, and if you *really* wish to go, tell me to-morrow."

Next day mother had a quiet talk with cook, and cook said she didn't mind if she stayed on a bit, just to see.

But meantime the question of the muddy carpet had been gone into thoroughly by father and mother. Jane's candid explanation that the mud had come from the bottom of a foreign tower where there was buried treasure was received with such chilling disbelief that the others limited their defence to an expression of sorrow, and of a determination "not to do it again." But father said (and mother agreed with him, because mothers have to agree with fathers, and not because it was her own idea) that children who coated a carpet on both sides with thick mud, and when they were asked for an explanation could only talk silly nonsense—that meant Jane's truthful statement—were not fit to have a carpet at all, and, indeed, *shouldn't* have one for a week!

So the carpet was brushed (with tea-leaves, too, which was the only comfort Anthea could think of) and folded up and put away in the cupboard at the top of the stairs, and daddy put the key in his trousers pocket.

"Till Saturday," said he.

"Never mind," said Anthea, "we've got the Phœnix."

But, as it happened, they hadn't. The Phœnix was nowhere to be found, and everything had suddenly settled down from the rosy wild beauty of magic happenings to the common damp brownness of ordinary November life in Camden Town—and there was the nursery floor all bare boards in the middle and brown oilcloth round the outside, and the bareness and yellowness of the middle floor showed up the blackbeetles with terrible distinctness, when the poor things came out in the evening, as usual, to try to make friends with the children. But the children never would.

The Sunday ended in gloom, which even junket[7] for supper in the blue Dresden bowl could hardly lighten at all. Next day the Lamb's cough was worse. It certainly seemed very whoopy, and the doctor came in his brougham carriage.[8]

Every one tried to bear up under the weight of the sorrow which it was to know that the wishing carpet was locked up and the Phœnix mislaid. A good deal of time was spent in looking for the Phœnix.

"It's a bird of its word," said Anthea. "I'm sure it's not deserted us. But you know it had a most awfully long fly from wherever it was to near Rochester and back, and

6. Young imps or rascals.
7. A dish of thickened and sweetened cream.

8. A one-horse closed carriage.

I expect the poor thing's feeling tired out and wants rest. I am sure we may trust it."

The others tried to feel sure of this, too, but it was hard.

No one could be expected to feel very kindly toward the cook, since it was entirely through her making such a fuss about a little foreign mud that the carpet had been taken away.

"She might have told *us*," said Jane, "and Panther and I would have cleaned it with tea-leaves."

"She's a cantankerous cat," said Robert.

"I shan't say what I think about her," said Anthea primly, "because it would be evil speaking, lying, and slandering."

"It's not lying to say she's a disagreeable pig, and a beastly blue-nosed Bozwoz," said Cyril, who had read *The Eyes of Light*,[9] and intended to talk like Tony as soon as he could teach Robert to talk like Paul.

And all the children, even Anthea, agreed that even if she wasn't a blue-nosed Bozwoz, they wished cook had never been born.

But I ask you to believe that they didn't do all the things on purpose which so annoyed the cook during the following week, though I daresay the things would not have happened if the cook had been a favourite.

This is a mystery. Explain it if you can.

The things that had happened were as follows:—

Sunday.—Discovery of foreign mud on both sides of the carpet.

Monday.—Liquorice put on to boil with aniseed balls in a saucepan. Anthea did this, because she thought it would be good for the Lamb's cough. The whole thing forgotten, and bottom of saucepan burned out. It was the little saucepan lined with white that was kept for the baby's milk.

Tuesday.—A dead mouse found in pantry. Fish-slice[1] taken to dig grave with. By regrettable accident fish-slice broken. Defence: "The cook oughtn' to keep dead mice in pantries."

Wednesday.—Chopped suet[2] left on kitchen table. Robert added chopped soap, but he says he thought the suet was soap too.

Thursday.—Broke the kitchen window by falling against it during a perfectly fair game of bandits in the area.

Friday.—Stopped up grating of kitchen sink with putty and filled sink with water to make a lake to sail paper boats in. Went away and left the tap running. Kitchen hearthrug and cook's shoes ruined.

On Saturday the carpet was restored. There had been plenty of time during the week to decide where it should be asked to go when they did get it back.

Mother had gone over to granny's, and had not taken the Lamb because he had a bad cough, which, cook repeatedly said, was whooping-cough as sure as eggs is eggs.

"But we'll take him out, a ducky darling," said Anthea. "We'll take him somewhere where you can't have the whooping-cough. Don't be so silly, Robert. If he *does* talk about it no one'll take any notice. He's always talking about things he's never seen."

So they dressed the Lamb and themselves in out-of-doors clothes, and the Lamb chuckled and coughed, and laughed and coughed again, poor dear, and all the chairs and tables were moved off the carpet by the boys, while Jane nursed the Lamb, and Anthea rushed through the house in one last wild hunt for the missing Phœnix.

9. Perhaps the 1901 novel by Arthur Moore.
1. Knife used for carving fish.

2. Fatty tissue from beef or mutton, used in cooking.

"It's no use waiting for it," she said, reappearing breathless in the breakfast-room. "But I know it hasn't deserted us. It's a bird of its word."

"Quite so," said the gentle voice of the Phœnix from beneath the table.

Everyone fell on his knees and looked up, and there was the Phœnix perched on a crossbar of wood that ran across under the table, and had once supported a drawer, in the happy days before the drawer had been used as a boat, and its bottom unfortunately trodden out by Raggett's Really Reliable School Boots on the feet of Robert.

"I've been here all the time," said the Phœnix, yawning politely behind its claw. "If you wanted me you should have recited the ode of invocation; it's seven thousand lines long, and written in very pure and beautiful Greek."

"Couldn't you tell it us in English?" asked Anthea.

"It's rather long, isn't it?" said Jane, jumping the Lamb on her knee.

"Couldn't you make a short English version, like Tate and Brady?"[3]

"Oh, come along, do," said Robert, holding out his hand. "Come along, good old Phœnix."

"Good old *beautiful* Phœnix," it corrected shyly.

"Good old *beautiful* Phœnix, then. Come along, come along," said Robert, impatiently, with his hand still held out.

The Phœnix fluttered at once on to his wrist.

"This amiable youth," it said to the others, "has miraculously been able to put the whole meaning of the seven thousand lines of Greek invocation into one English hexameter—a little misplaced some of the words—but——"

"Oh, come along, come along, good old beautiful Phœnix!"

"Not perfect, I admit—but not bad for a boy of his age."

"Well, *now* then," said Robert, stepping back on to the carpet with the golden Phœnix on his wrist.

"You look like the king's falconer," said Jane, sitting down on the carpet with the baby on her lap.

Robert tried to go on looking like it. Cyril and Anthea stood on the carpet.

"We shall have to get back before dinner," said Cyril, "or cook will blow the gaff."[4]

"She hasn't sneaked[5] since Sunday," said Anthea.

"She——" Robert was beginning, when the door burst open and the cook, fierce and furious, came in like a whirlwind and stood on the corner of the carpet, with a broken basin in one hand and a threat in the other, which was clenched.

"Look 'ere!" she cried, "my only basin; and what the powers am I to make the beefsteak and kidney pudding in that your ma ordered for your dinners? You don't deserve no dinners, so yer don't."

"I'm awfully sorry, cook," said Anthea gently; "it was my fault, and I forgot to tell you about it. It got broken when we were telling our fortunes with melted lead, you know, and I meant to tell you."

"Meant to tell me," replied the cook; she was red with anger, and really I don't wonder—"meant to tell! Well, *I* mean to tell, too. I've held my tongue this week through, because the missus she said to me quiet like, 'We mustn't expect old heads on young shoulders,' but now I shan't hold it no longer. There was the soap you put in our pudding, and me and Eliza never so much as breathed it to your ma—though

---

3. The Irish poet and playwright Nahum Tate (1652–1715) and clergyman Nicholas Brady (1659–1726) published *A New Version of the Psalms of David* (1696).
4. Let out the secret.
5. Told tales (school slang).

well we might—and the saucepan, and the fish-slice, and——My gracious cats alive! what 'ave you got that blessed child dressed up in his outdoors for?"

"We aren't going to take him out," said Anthea; "at least——" She stopped short, for though they weren't going to take him out in the Kentish Town Road, they certainly intended to take him elsewhere. But not at all where cook meant when she said "out." This confused the truthful Anthea.

"Out!" said the cook, "that I'll take care you don't"; and she snatched the Lamb from the lap of Jane, while Anthea and Robert caught her by the skirts and apron.

"Look here," said Cyril, in stern desperation, "will you go away, and make your pudding in a pie-dish, or a flower-pot, or a hot-water can, or something?"

"Not me," said the cook, briefly; "and leave this precious poppet for you to give his deathercold to."

"I warn you," said Cyril, solemnly. "Beware, ere yet it be too late."

"Late yourself! the little popsey-wopsey," said the cook, with angry tenderness. "They shan't take it out, no more they shan't. And—— Where did you get that there yellow fowl?"

She pointed to the Phœnix.

Even Anthea saw that unless the cook lost her situation the loss would be theirs.

"I wish," she said suddenly, "we were on a sunny southern shore, where there can't be any whooping-cough."

She said it through the frightened howls of the Lamb, and the sturdy scolding of the cook, and instantly the giddy-go-round-and-falling-lift feeling swept over the whole party, and the cook sat down flat on the carpet, holding the screaming Lamb tight to her stout print-covered self, and calling on St. Bridget[6] to help her. She was an Irishwoman.

The moment the tipsy-topsy-turvy feeling stopped, the cook opened her eyes, gave one sounding screech and shut them again, and Anthea took the opportunity to get the desperately howling Lamb into her own arms.

"It's all right," she said; "own Panther's got you. Look at the trees, and the sand, and the shells, and the great big tortoises. Oh *dear*, how hot it is!"

It certainly was; for the trusty carpet had laid itself out on a southern shore that was sunny and no mistake, as Robert remarked. The greenest of green slopes led up to glorious groves where palm-trees and all the tropical flowers and fruits that you read of in *Westward Ho!* and *Foul Play*[7] were growing in rich profusion. Between the green, green slope and the blue, blue sea lay a stretch of sand that looked like a carpet of jewelled cloth of gold, for it was not greyish as our northern sand is, but yellow and changing—opal-coloured like sunshine and rainbows. And at the very moment when the wild, whirling, blinding, deafening, tumbling upside-downness of the carpet-moving stopped, the children had the happiness of seeing three large live turtles waddle down to the edge of the sea and disappear in the water. And it was hotter than you can possibly imagine, unless you think of ovens on a baking-day.

Every one without an instant's hesitation tore off his London-in-November outdoor clothes, and Anthea took off the Lamb's highwayman blue coat and his three-cornered hat, and then his jersey, and then the Lamb himself suddenly slipped out of his little blue tight breeches and stood up happy and hot in his little white shirt.

---

6. Irish nun (451/452–525), founder of the first women's religious community in Ireland.
7. Sea adventures by the British novelists Charles

Kingsley (1855) and Charles Reade and Dion Boucicault (1868), respectively.

"I'm sure it's much warmer than the seaside in the summer," said Anthea. "Mother always lets us go barefoot then."

So the Lamb's shoes and socks and gaiters came off, and he stood digging his happy naked pink toes into the golden smooth sand.

"I'm a little white duck-dickie," said he—"a little white duck-dickie what swims," and splashed quacking into a sandy pool.

"Let him," said Anthea; "it can't hurt him. Oh, how hot it is!"

The cook suddenly opened her eyes and screamed, shut them, screamed again, opened her eyes once more and said—

"Why, drat my cats alive, what's all this? It's a dream, I expect. Well, it's the best I ever dreamed. I'll look it up in the dream-book to-morrow. Seaside and trees and a carpet to sit on. I never did!"

"Look here," said Cyril, "it isn't a dream; it's real."

"Ho, yes!" said the cook; "they always says that in dreams."

"It's REAL, I tell you," Robert said, stamping his foot. "I'm not going to tell you how it's done, because that's our secret." He winked heavily at each of the others in turn. "But you wouldn't go away and make that pudding, so we had to bring you, and I hope you like it."

"I do that, and no mistake," said the cook unexpectedly; "and it being a dream it don't matter what I say; and I will say, if it's my last word, that of all the aggravating little varmints——"

"Calm yourself, my good woman," said the Phœnix.

"Good woman, indeed," said the cook; "good woman yourself!" Then she saw who it was that had spoken. "Well, if I ever," said she; "this is something like a dream! Yellow fowls a-talking and all! I've heard of such, but never did I think to see the day."

"Well, then," said Cyril, impatiently, "sit here and see the day now. It's a jolly fine day. Here, you others—a council!"

They walked along the shore till they were out of earshot of the cook, who still sat gazing about her with a happy, dreamy, vacant smile.

"Look here," said Cyril, "we must roll the carpet up and hide it, so that we can get at it at any moment. The Lamb can be getting rid of his whooping-cough all the morning, and we can look about; and if the savages on this island are cannibals, we'll hook it, and take her back. And if not, we'll leave her here."

"Is that being kind to servants and animals, like the clergyman said?" asked Jane.

"Nor she isn't kind," retorted Cyril.

"Well—anyway," said Anthea, "the safest thing is to leave the carpet there with her sitting on it. Perhaps it'll be a lesson to her, and anyway, if she thinks it's a dream it won't matter what she says when she gets home."

So the extra coats and hats and mufflers were piled on the carpet. Cyril shouldered the well and happy Lamb, the Phœnix perched on Robert's wrist, and the "party of explorers prepared to enter the interior."

The grassy slope was smooth, but under the trees there were tangled creepers with bright, strange-shaped flowers, and it was not easy to walk.

"We ought to have an explorer's axe," said Robert. "I shall ask father to give me one for Christmas."

There were curtains of creepers with scented blossoms hanging from the trees, and brilliant birds darted about quite close to their faces.

"Now, tell me honestly," said the Phœnix, "are there any birds here handsomer than I am? Don't be afraid of hurting my feelings—I'm a modest bird, I hope."

"Not one of them," said Robert, with conviction, "is a patch upon you!"

"I was never a vain bird," said the Phœnix, "but I own that you confirm my own impression. I will take a flight." It circled in the air for a moment, and returning to Robert's wrist, went on, "There is a path to the left."

And there was. So now the children went on through the wood more quickly and comfortably, the girls picking flowers and the Lamb inviting the "pretty dickies" to observe that he himself was a "little white real-water-wet duck!"

And all this time he hadn't whooping-coughed once.

The path turned and twisted, and, always threading their way amid a tangle of flowers, the children suddenly passed a corner and found themselves in a forest clearing, where there were a lot of pointed huts—the huts, as they knew at once, of *savages*.

The boldest heart beat more quickly. Suppose they *were* cannibals. It was a long way back to the carpet.

"Hadn't we better go back?" said Jane. "Go *now*," she said, and her voice trembled a little. "Suppose they eat us."

"Nonsense, Pussy," said Cyril, firmly. "Look, there's a goat tied up. That shows they don't eat *people*."

"Let's go on and say we're missionaries," Robert suggested.

"I shouldn't advise *that*," said the Phœnix, very earnestly.

"Why not?"

"Well, for one thing, it isn't true," replied the golden bird.

It was while they stood hesitating on the edge of the clearing that a tall man suddenly came out of one of the huts. He had hardly any clothes, and his body all over was a dark and beautiful coppery colour—just like the chrysanthemums father had brought home on Saturday. In his hand he held a spear. The whites of his eyes and the white of his teeth were the only light things about him, except that where the sun shone on his shiny brown body it looked white, too. If you will look carefully at the next shiny savage you meet with next to nothing on, you will see at once—if the sun happens to be shining at the time—that I am right about this.

The savage looked at the children. Concealment was impossible. He uttered a shout that was more like "Oo goggery bag-wag" than anything else the children had ever heard, and at once brown coppery people leapt out of every hut, and swarmed like ants about the clearing. There was no time for discussion, and no one wanted to discuss anything, anyhow. Whether these coppery people were cannibals or not now seemed to matter very little.

Without an instant's hesitation the four children turned and ran back along the forest path; the only pause was Anthea's. She stood back to let Cyril pass, because he was carrying the Lamb, who screamed with delight. (He had not whooping-coughed a single once since the carpet landed him on the island.)

"Gee-up, Squirrel; gee-gee," he shouted, and Cyril did gee-up. The path was a shorter cut to the beach than the creeper-covered way by which they had come, and almost directly they saw through the trees the shining blue-and-gold-and-opal of sand and sea.

"Stick to it," cried Cyril, breathlessly.

They did stick to it; they tore down the sands—they could hear behind them as they ran the patter of feet which they knew, too well, were copper-coloured.

The sands were golden and opal-coloured—*and bare*. There were wreaths of tropic seaweed, there were rich tropic shells of the kind you would not buy in the Kentish

Town Road under at least fifteen pence a pair. There were turtles basking lumpily on the water's edge—but no cook, no clothes, and no carpet.

"On, on! Into the sea!" gasped Cyril. "They must hate water. I've—heard—savages always—dirty."

Their feet were splashing in the warm shallows before his breathless words were ended. The calm baby-waves were easy to go through. It is warm work running for your life in the tropics, and the coolness of the water was delicious. They were up to their arm-pits now, and Jane was up to her chin.

"Look!" said the Phœnix. "What are they pointing at?"

The children turned; and there, a little to the west, was a head—a head they knew, with a crooked cap upon it. It was the head of the cook.

For some reason or other the savages had stopped at the water's edge and were all talking at the top of their voices, and all were pointing copper-coloured fingers, stiff with interest and excitement, at the head of the cook.

The children hurried towards her as quickly as the water would let them.

"What on earth did you come out here for?" Robert shouted; "and where on earth's the carpet?"

"It's not on earth, bless you," replied the cook, happily; "it's *under me*—in the water. I got a bit warm setting there in the sun, and I just says, 'I wish I was in a cold bath'—just like that—and next minute here I was! It's all part of the dream."

Every one at once saw how extremely fortunate it was that the carpet had had the sense to take the cook to the nearest and largest bath—the sea, and how terrible it would have been if the carpet had taken itself and her to the stuffy little bath-room of the house in Camden Town!

"Excuse me," said the Phœnix's soft voice, breaking in on the general sigh of relief, "but I think these brown people want your cook."

"To—to eat?" whispered Jane, as well as she could through the water which the plunging Lamb was dashing in her face with happy fat hands and feet.

"Hardly," rejoined the bird. "Who wants cooks to *eat*? Cooks are *engaged*, not eaten. They wish to engage her."

"How can you understand what they say?" asked Cyril, doubtfully.

"It's as easy as kissing your claw," replied the bird. "I speak and understand *all* languages, even that of your cook, which is difficult and unpleasing. It's quite easy, when you know how it's done. It just comes to you. I should advise you to beach the carpet and land the cargo—the cook, I mean. You can take my word for it, the copper-coloured ones will not harm you now."

It is impossible not to take the word of a Phœnix when it tells you to. So the children at once got hold of the corners of the carpet, and, pulling it from under the cook, towed it slowly in through the shallowing water, and at last spread it on the sand. The cook, who had followed, instantly sat down on it, and at once the copper-coloured natives, now strangely humble, formed a ring round the carpet, and fell on their faces on the rainbow-and-gold sand. The tallest savage spoke in this position, which must have been very awkward for him; and Jane noticed that it took him quite a long time to get the sand out of his mouth afterwards.

"He says," the Phœnix remarked after some time, "that they wish to engage your cook permanently."

"Without a character?"[8] asked Anthea, who had heard her mother speak of such things.

8. A letter of reference.

"They do not wish to engage her as cook, but as *queen*; and queens need not have characters."

There was a breathless pause.

"*Well,*" said Cyril, "of all the choices! But there's no accounting for tastes."

Every one laughed at the idea of the cook's being engaged as queen; they could not help it.

"I do not advise laughter," warned the Phœnix, ruffling out his golden feathers, which were extremely wet. "And it's not their own choice. It seems that there is an ancient prophecy of this copper-coloured tribe that a great queen should some day arise out of the sea with a white crown on her head, and—and—well, you see! There's the crown!"

It pointed its claw at cook's cap; and a very dirty cap it was, because it was the end of the week.

"That's the white crown," it said; "at least, it's nearly white—very white indeed compared to the colour *they* are—and anyway, it's quite white enough."

Cyril addressed the cook. "Look here!" said he, "these brown people want you to be their queen. They're only savages, and they don't know any better. Now would you really like to stay? or, if you'll promise not to be so jolly aggravating at home, and not to tell any one a word about to-day, we'll take you back to Camden Town."

"No, you don't," said the cook, in firm, undoubting tones. "I've always wanted to be the Queen, God bless her! and I always thought what a good one I should make; and now I'm going to. *If* it's only in a dream, it's well worth while. And I don't go back to that nasty underground kitchen, and me blamed for everything; that I don't, not till the dream's finished and I wake up with that nasty bell a rang-tanging in my ears—so I tell you."

"Are you *sure*," Anthea anxiously asked the Phœnix, "that she will be quite safe here?"

"She will find the nest of a queen a very precious and soft thing," said the bird, solemnly.

"There—you hear," said Cyril. "You're in for a precious soft thing, so mind you're a good queen, cook. It's more than you'd any right to expect, but long may you reign."

Some of the cook's copper-coloured subjects now advanced from the forest with long garlands of beautiful flowers, white and sweet-scented, and hung them respectfully round the neck of their new sovereign.

"What! all them lovely bokays for me!" exclaimed the enraptured cook. "Well, this here is something *like* a dream, I must say."

She sat up very straight on the carpet, and the copper-coloured ones, themselves wreathed in garlands of the gayest flowers, madly stuck parrot feathers in their hair and began to dance. It was a dance such as you have never seen; it made the children feel almost sure that the cook was right, and that they were all in a dream. Small, strange-shaped drums were beaten, odd-sounding songs were sung, and the dance got faster and faster and odder and odder, till at last all the dancers fell on the sand tired out.

The new queen, with her white crown-cap all on one side, clapped wildly.

"Brayvo!" she cried, "brayvo! It's better than the Albert Edward Music-hall in the Kentish Town Road. Go it again!"

But the Phœnix would not translate this request into the copper-coloured language; and when the savages had recovered their breath, they implored their queen to leave her white escort and come with them to their huts.

"The finest shall be yours, O queen," said they.

"Well—so long!" said the cook, getting heavily on to her feet, when the Phœnix had translated this request. "No more kitchens and attics for me, thank you. I'm off to my royal palace. I am; and I only wish this here dream would keep on for ever and ever."

She picked up the ends of the garlands that trailed round her feet, and the children had one last glimpse of her striped stockings and worn elastic-side boots before she disappeared into the shadow of the forest, surrounded by her dusky retainers, singing songs of rejoicing as they went.

"Well!" said Cyril, "I suppose she's all right, but they don't seem to count us for much, one way or the other."

"Oh," said the Phœnix, "they think you're merely dreams. The prophecy said that the queen would arise from the waves with a white crown and surrounded by white-dream children. That's about what they think *you* are!"

"And what about dinner?" said Robert, abruptly.

"There won't be any dinner, with no cook and no pudding-basin," Anthea reminded him; "but there's always bread-and-butter."

"Let's get home," said Cyril.

The Lamb was furiously unwishful to be dressed in his warm clothes again, but Anthea and Jane managed it, by force disguised as coaxing, and he never once whooping-coughed.

Then every one put on his own warm things and took his place on the carpet.

A sound of uncouth singing still came from beyond the trees, where the copper-coloured natives were crooning songs of admiration and respect to their white-crowned queen. Then Anthea said "Home," just as duchesses and other people do to their coachmen, and the intelligent carpet in one whirling moment laid itself down in its proper place on the nursery floor. And at that very moment Eliza opened the door and said—

"Cook's gone! I can't find her anywhere, and there's no dinner ready. She hasn't taken her box nor yet her outdoor things. She just ran out to see the time, I shouldn't wonder—the kitchen clock never did give her satisfaction—and she's got run over or fell down in a fit as likely as not. You'll have to put up with cold bacon for your dinners; and what on earth you've got your outdoor things on for I don't know. And then I'll slip out and see if they know anything about her at the police-station."

But nobody ever knew anything about the cook any more, except the children, and, later, one other person.

Mother was so upset at losing the cook, and so anxious about her, that Anthea felt most miserable, as though she had done something very wrong indeed. She woke several times in the night, and at last decided that she would ask the Phœnix to let her tell her mother all about it. But there was no opportunity to do this next day, because the Phœnix, as usual, had gone to sleep in some out-of-the-way spot, after asking, as a special favour, not to be disturbed for twenty-four hours.

The Lamb never whooping-coughed once all that Sunday, and mother and father said what good medicine it was that the doctor had given him. But the children knew that it was the southern shore where you can't have whooping-cough that had cured him. The Lamb babbled of coloured sand and water, but no one took any notice of that. He often talked of things that hadn't happened.

It was on Monday morning, very early indeed, that Anthea woke and suddenly made up her mind. She crept downstairs in her night-gown (it was very chilly), sat down on the carpet, and with a beating heart wished herself on the sunny shore where you can't have whooping-cough, and next moment there she was.

The sand was splendidly warm. She could feel it at once, even through the carpet. She folded the carpet, and put it over her shoulders like a shawl, for she was determined not to be parted from it for a single instant, no matter how hot it might be to wear.

Then, trembling a little, and trying to keep up her courage by saying over and over, "It is my *duty*, it *is* my duty," she went up the forest path.

"Well, here you are again," said the cook, directly she saw Anthea. "This dream does keep on!"

The cook was dressed in a white robe; she had no shoes and stockings and no cap and she was sitting under a screen of palm-leaves, for it was afternoon in the island and blazing hot. She wore a flower wreath on her hair, and copper-coloured boys were fanning her with peacocks' feathers.

"They've got the cap put away," she said. "They seem to think a lot of it. Never saw one before, I expect."

"Are you happy?" asked Anthea, panting; the sight of the cook as queen quite took her breath away.

"I believe you, my dear," said the cook, heartily. "Nothing to do unless you want to. But I'm getting rested now. To-morrow I'm going to start cleaning out my hut, if the dream keeps on, and I shall teach them cooking; they burns everything to a cinder now unless they eats it raw."

"But can you talk to them?"

"Lor' love a duck, yes!" the happy cook-queen replied; "it's quite easy to pick up. I always thought I should be quick at foreign languages. I've taught them to understand 'dinner,' and 'I want a drink,' and 'You leave me be,' already."

"Then you don't want anything?" Anthea asked earnestly and anxiously.

"Not me, miss; except if you'd only go away. I'm afraid of me waking up with that bell a-going if you keep on stopping here a-talking to me. Long as this here dream keeps up I'm as happy as a queen."

"Good-bye, then," said Anthea, gaily, for her conscience was clear now.

She hurried into the wood, threw herself on the ground, and said "Home"—and there she was, rolled in the carpet on the nursery floor.

"*She's* all right, anyhow," said Anthea, and went back to bed. "I'm glad somebody's pleased. But mother will never believe me when I tell her."

The story is indeed a little difficult to believe. Still, you might try.

Chapter IV. Two Bazaars

Mother was really a great dear. She was pretty and she was loving, and most frightfully good when you were ill, and always kind, and almost always just. That is, she was just when she understood things. But of course she did not always understand things. No one understands everything, and mothers are not angels, though a good many of them come pretty near it. The children knew that mother always *wanted* to do what was best for them, even if she was not clever enough to know exactly what was the best. That was why all of them, but much more particularly Anthea, felt rather uncomfortable at keeping the great secret from her of the wishing carpet and the Phœnix. And Anthea, whose inside mind was made so that she was able to be much more uncomfortable than the others, had decided that she *must* tell her mother the truth, however little likely it was that her mother would believe it.

"Then I shall have done what's right," said she to the Phœnix; "and if she doesn't believe me it won't be my fault—will it?"

"Not in the least," said the golden bird. "And she won't, so you're quite safe."

Anthea chose a time when she was doing her home-lessons—they were Algebra and Latin, German, English, and Euclid—and she asked her mother whether she might come and do them in the drawing-room—"so as to be quiet," she said to her mother; and to herself she said, "And that's not the real reason. I hope I shan't grow up a *liar*."

Mother said, "Of course, dearie," and Anthea started swimming through a sea of *x*'s and *y*'s and *z*'s. Mother was sitting at the mahogany bureau writing letters.

"Mother dear," said Anthea.

"Yes, love-a-duck," said mother.

"About cook," said Anthea. "*I* know where she is."

"Do you, dear?" said mother. "Well, I wouldn't take her back after the way she has behaved."

"It's not her fault," said Anthea. "May I tell you about it from the beginning?"

Mother laid down her pen, and her nice face had a resigned expression. As you know, a resigned expression always makes you want not to tell anybody anything.

"It's like this," said Anthea, in a hurry: "that egg, you know, that came in the carpet; we put it in the fire and it hatched into the Phœnix, and the carpet was a wishing carpet—and——"

"A very nice game, darling," said mother, taking up her pen. "Now do be quiet. I've got a lot of letters to write. I'm going to Bournemouth[9] to-morrow with the Lamb—and there's that bazaar."[1]

Anthea went back to *x y z*, and mother's pen scratched busily.

"But, mother," said Anthea, when mother put down the pen to lick an envelope, "the carpet takes us wherever we like—and——"

"I wish it would take you where you could get a few nice Eastern things for my bazaar," said mother. "I promised them, and I've no time to go to Liberty's[2] now."

"It shall," said Anthea, "but, mother . . ."

"Well, dear," said mother, a little impatiently, for she had taken up her pen again.

"The carpet took us to a place where you couldn't have whooping-cough, and the Lamb hasn't whooped since, and we took cook because she was so tiresome, and then she would stay and be queen of the savages. They thought her cap was a crown, and——"

"Darling one," said mother, "you know I love to hear the things you make up—but I am most awfully busy."

"But it's true," said Anthea, desperately.

"You shouldn't say that, my sweet," said mother, gently. And then Anthea knew it was hopeless.

"Are you going away for long?" asked Anthea.

"I've got a cold," said mother, "and daddy's anxious about it, and the Lamb's cough."

"He hasn't coughed since Saturday," the Lamb's eldest sister interrupted.

"I wish I could think so," mother replied. "And daddy's got to go to Scotland. I do hope you'll be good children."

9. Seaside resort in southern England.
1. Charity sale.
2. Fashionable London store specializing in mer-

chandise from the Orient as well as English-made Eastern-style fabrics and objects.

"We will, we will," said Anthea, fervently. "When's the bazaar?"

"On Saturday," said mother, "at the schools. Oh, don't talk any more, there's a treasure! My head's going round, and I've forgotten how to spell whooping-cough."

Mother and the Lamb went away, and father went away, and there was a new cook who looked so like a frightened rabbit that no one had the heart to do anything to frighten her any more than seemed natural to her.

The Phœnix begged to be excused. It said it wanted a week's rest, and asked that it might not be disturbed. And it hid its golden gleaming self, and nobody could find it.

So that when Wednesday afternoon brought an unexpected holiday, and every one decided to go somewhere on the carpet, the journey had to be undertaken without the Phoenix. They were debarred from any carpet excursions in the evening by a sudden promise to mother, exacted in the agitation of parting, that they would not be out after six at night, except on Saturday, when they were to go to the bazaar, and were pledged to put on their best clothes, to wash themselves to the uttermost, and to clean their nails—not with scissors, which are scratchy and bad, but with flat, sharpened ends of wooden matches, which do no harm to any one's nails.

"Let's go and see the Lamb," said Jane.

But every one was agreed that if they appeared suddenly in Bournemouth it would frighten mother out of her wits, if not into a fit. So they sat on the carpet, and thought and thought and thought till they almost began to squint.

"Look here," said Cyril, "I know. Please carpet, take us somewhere where we can see the Lamb and mother and no one can see us."

"Except the Lamb," said Jane, quickly.

And the next moment they found themselves recovering from the upside-down movement—and there they were sitting on the carpet, and the carpet was laid out over another thick soft carpet of brown pine-needles. There were green pine-trees overhead, and a swift clear little stream was running as fast as ever it could between steep banks—and there, sitting on the pine-needle carpet, was mother, without her hat; and the sun was shining brightly, although it was November—and there was the Lamb, as jolly as jolly and not whooping at all.

"The carpet's deceived us," said Robert gloomily; "mother will see us directly she turns her head."

But the faithful carpet had not deceived them.

Mother turned her dear head and looked straight at them, and *did not see them!*

"We're invisible," Cyril whispered: "what awful larks!"

But to the girls it was not larks at all. It was horrible to have mother looking straight at them, and her face keeping the same, just as though they weren't there.

"I don't like it," said Jane. "Mother never looked at us like that before. Just as if she didn't love us—as if we were somebody else's children, and not very nice ones either—as if she didn't care whether she saw us or not."

"It *is* horrid," said Anthea, almost in tears.

But at this moment the Lamb saw them, and plunged towards the carpet, shrieking, "Panty, own Panty—an' Pussy, an' Squiggle—an' Bobs, oh, oh!"

Anthea caught him and kissed him, so did Jane; they could not help it—he looked such a darling, with his blue three-cornered hat all on one side, and his precious face all dirty—quite in the old familiar way.

"I love you, Panty; I love you—and you, and you, and you," cried the Lamb.

It was a delicious moment. Even the boys thumped their baby brother joyously on the back.

Then Anthea glanced at mother—and mother's face was a pale sea-green colour, and she was staring at the Lamb as if she thought he had gone mad. And, indeed, that was exactly what she did think.

"My Lamb, my precious! Come to mother," she cried, and jumped up and ran to the baby.

She was so quick that the invisible children had to leap back, or she would have felt them; and to feel what you can't see is the worst sort of ghost-feeling. Mother picked up the Lamb and hurried away from the pine-wood.

"Let's go home," said Jane, after a miserable silence. "It feels just exactly as if mother didn't love us."

But they couldn't bear to go home till they had seen mother meet another lady, and knew that she was safe. You cannot leave your mother to go green in the face in a distant pine-wood, far from all human aid, and then go home on your wishing carpet as though nothing had happened.

When mother seemed safe the children returned to the carpet, and said "Home"— and home they went.

"I don't care about being invisible myself," said Cyril, "at least, not with my own family. It would be different if you were a prince, or a bandit, or a burglar."

And now the thoughts of all four dwelt fondly on the dear greenish face of mother.

"I wish she hadn't gone away," said Jane; "the house is simply beastly without her."

"I think we ought to do what she said," Anthea put in. "I saw something in a book the other day about the wishes of the departed[3] being sacred."

"That means when they've departed farther off," said Cyril. "India's coral or Greenland's icy, don't you know; not Bournemouth. Besides, we don't know what her wishes are."

"She *said*"—Anthea was very much inclined to cry—"she said, 'Get Indian things for my bazaar'; but I know she thought we couldn't, and it was only play."

"Let's get them all the same," said Robert. "We'll go the first thing on Saturday morning."

And on Saturday morning, the first thing, they went.

There was no finding the Phœnix, so they sat on the beautiful wishing carpet, and said—

"We want Indian things for mother's bazaar. Will you please take us where people will give us heaps of Indian things?"

The docile carpet swirled their senses away, and restored them on the outskirts of a gleaming white Indian town. They knew it was Indian at once, by the shape of the domes and roofs; and besides, a man went by on an elephant, and two English soldiers went along the road, talking like in Mr. Kipling's[4] books—so after that no one could have any doubt as to where they were. They rolled up the carpet and Robert carried it, and they walked bodily into the town. It was very warm, and once more they had to take off their London-in-November coats, and carry them on their arms.

The streets were narrow and strange, and the clothes of the people in the streets were strange, and the talk of the people was strangest of all.

---

3. I.e., the dead.
4. Rudyard Kipling (1865–1936), a British writer

born in India, where he set many of his tales and poems.

"I can't understand a word," said Cyril. "How on earth are we to ask for things for our bazaar?"

"And they're poor people, too," said Jane; "I'm sure they are. What we want is a rajah or something."

Robert was beginning to unroll the carpet, but the others stopped him, imploring him not to waste a wish.

"We asked the carpet to take us where we could get Indian things for bazaars," said Anthea, "and it will."

Her faith was justified.

Just as she finished speaking a very brown gentleman in a turban came up to them and bowed deeply. He spoke, and they thrilled to the sound of English words.

"My ranee,[5] she think you very nice childs. She asks do you lose yourselves, and do you desire to sell carpet? She see you from her palkee.[6] You come see her—yes?"

They followed the stranger, who seemed to have a great many more teeth in his smile than are usual, and he led them through crooked streets to the ranee's palace. I am not going to describe the ranee's palace, because I really have never seen the palace of a ranee, and Mr. Kipling has. So you can read about it in his books. But I know exactly what happened there.

The old ranee sat on a low-cushioned seat, and there were a lot of other ladies with her—all in trousers and veils, and sparkling with tinsel and gold and jewels. And the brown, turbaned gentleman stood behind a sort of carved screen, and interpreted what the children said and what the queen said. And when the queen asked to buy the carpet, the children said "No."

"Why?" asked the ranee.

And Jane briefly said why, and the interpreter interpreted. The queen spoke, and then the interpreter said—

"My mistress says it is a good story, and you tell it all through without thought of time."

And they had to. It made a long story, especially as it had all to be told twice— once by Cyril and once by the interpreter. Cyril rather enjoyed himself. He warmed to his work, and told the tale of the Phoenix and the Carpet, and the Lone Tower, and the Queen-Cook, in language that grew insensibly more and more Arabian Nightsy,[7] and the ranee and her ladies listened to the interpreter, and rolled about on their fat cushions with laughter.

When the story was ended she spoke, and the interpreter explained that she had said, "Little one, thou art a heaven-born teller of tales"; and she threw him a string of turquoises from round her neck.

"*Oh,* how lovely!" cried Jane and Anthea.

Cyril bowed several times, and then cleared his throat and said—

"Thank her very, very much; but I would much rather she gave me some of the cheap things in the bazaar. Tell her I want them to sell again, and give the money to buy clothes to poor people who haven't any."

"Tell him he has my leave to sell my gift and clothe the naked with its price," said the queen, when this was translated.

---

5. Wife of a rajah, or reigning queen or princess.
6. Palanquin: an enclosed conveyance for one person, carried on the shoulders of men by poles.
7. *The Arabian Nights' Entertainment,* or *A Thousand and One Nights,* is a collection of traditional Arabic tales, framed by the storyteller Scheherazade, that eventually took their present form in the fifteenth century; there were several prominent nineteenth-century English translations.

But Cyril said very firmly, "No, thank you. The things have got to be sold to-day at our bazaar, and no one would buy a turquoise necklace at an English bazaar. They'd think it was sham, or else they'd want to know where we got it."

So then the queen sent out for little pretty things, and her servants piled the carpet with them.

"I must needs lend you an elephant to carry them away," she said, laughing.

But Anthea said, "If the queen will lend us a comb and let us wash our hands and faces, she shall see a magic thing. We and the carpet and all these brass trays and pots and carved things and stuffs and things will just vanish away like smoke."

The queen clapped her hands at this idea, and lent the children a sandal-wood comb inlaid with ivory lotus-flowers. And they washed their faces and hands in silver basins.

Then Cyril made a very polite farewell speech, and quite suddenly he ended with the words—

"And I wish we were at the bazaar at our schools."

And of course they were. And the queen and her ladies were left with their mouths open, gazing at the bare space on the inlaid marble floor where the carpet and the children had been.

"That is magic, if ever magic was," said the queen, delighted with the incident; which, indeed, has given the ladies of that court something to talk about on wet days ever since.

Cyril's stories had taken some time, so had the meal of strange sweet foods that they had had while the little pretty things were being bought, and the gas in the schoolroom was already lighted. Outside, the winter dusk was stealing down among the Camden Town houses.

"I'm glad we got washed in India," said Cyril. "We should have been awfully late if we'd had to go home and scrub."

"Besides," Robert said, "it's much warmer washing in India. I shouldn't mind it so much if we lived there."

The thoughtful carpet had dumped the children down in a dusky space behind the point where the corner of two stalls met. The floor was littered with string and brown paper, and baskets and boxes were heaped along the wall.

The children crept out under a stall covered with all sorts of table-covers and mats and things, embroidered beautifully by idle ladies with no real work to do. They got out at the end, displacing a sideboard-cloth adorned with a tasteful pattern of blue geraniums. The girls got out unobserved, so did Cyril; but Robert, as he cautiously emerged, was actually walked on by Mrs. Biddle, who kept the stall. Her large, solid foot stood firmly on the small, solid hand of Robert—and who can blame Robert if he *did* yell a little?

A crowd instantly collected. Yells are very unusual at bazaars, and every one was intensely interested. It was several seconds before the three free children could make Mrs. Biddle understand that what she was walking on was not a schoolroom floor, or even, as she presently supposed, a dropped pin-cushion, but the living hand of a suffering child. When she became aware that she really had hurt him, she grew very angry indeed. When people have hurt other people by accident, the one who does the hurting is always much the angriest. I wonder why.

"I'm very sorry, I'm sure," said Mrs. Biddle; but she spoke more in anger than in sorrow. "Come out! whatever do you mean by creeping about under the stalls, like earwigs?"

"We were looking at the things in the corner."

"Such nasty, prying ways," said Mrs. Biddle, "will never make you successful in life. There's nothing there but packing and dust."

"Oh, isn't there!" said Jane. "That's all you know."

"Little girl, don't be rude," said Mrs. Biddle, flushing violet.

"She doesn't mean to be; but there *are* some nice things there, all the same," said Cyril; who suddenly felt how impossible it was to inform the listening crowd that all the treasures piled on the carpet were mother's contributions to the bazaar. No one would believe it; and if they did, and wrote to thank mother, she would think—well, goodness only knew what she would think. The other three children felt the same.

"I should like to see them," said a very nice lady, whose friends had disappointed her, and who hoped that these might be belated contributions to her poorly furnished stall.

She looked inquiringly at Robert, who said, "With pleasure, don't mention it," and dived back under Mrs. Biddle's stall.

"I wonder you encourage such behavior," said Mrs. Biddle. "I always speak my mind, as you know, Miss Peasmarsh; and, I must say, I am surprised." She turned to the crowd. "There is no entertainment here," she said sternly. "A very naughty little boy has accidentally hurt himself, but only slightly. Will you please disperse? It will only encourage him in naughtiness if he finds himself the centre of attraction."

The crowd slowly dispersed. Anthea, speechless with fury, heard a nice curate say, "Poor little beggar!" and loved the curate at once and for ever.

Then Robert wriggled out from under the stall with some Benares[8] brass and some inlaid sandalwood boxes.

"Liberty!" cried Miss Peasmarsh. "Then Charles has not forgotten, after all."

"Excuse me," said Mrs. Biddle, with fierce politeness, "these objects are deposited behind *my* stall. Some unknown donor who does good by stealth, and would blush if he could hear you claim the things. Of course they are for me."

"My stall touches yours at the corner," said poor Miss Peasmarsh, timidly, "and my cousin did promise——"

The children sidled away from the unequal contest and mingled with the crowd. Their feelings were too deep for words—till at last Robert said—

"That stiff-starched *pig!*"

"And after all our trouble! I'm hoarse with gassing to that trousered lady in India."

"The pig-lady's very, very nasty," said Jane.

It was Anthea who said, in a hurried undertone, "She isn't very nice, and Miss Peasmarsh is pretty and nice too. Who's got a pencil?"

It was a long crawl, under three stalls, but Anthea did it. A large piece of pale blue paper lay among the rubbish in the corner. She folded it to a square and wrote upon it, licking the pencil at every word to make it mark quite blackly: "All these Indian things are for pretty, nice Miss Peasmarsh's stall." She thought of adding, "There is nothing for Mrs. Biddle"; but she saw that this might lead to suspicion, so she wrote hastily: "From an unknown donna," and crept back among the boards and trestles to join the others.

So that when Mrs. Biddle appealed to the bazaar committee, and the corner of the stall was lifted and shifted, so that stout clergymen and heavy ladies could get to the corner without creeping under stalls, the blue paper was discovered, and all the

8. Holy city (now called Varanasi) on the Ganges River, known for its brassware.

splendid, shining Indian things were given over to Miss Peasmarsh, and she sold them all, and got thirty-five pounds for them.

"I don't understand about that blue paper," said Mrs. Biddle. "It looks to me like the work of a lunatic. And saying you were nice and pretty! It's not the work of a sane person."

Anthea and Jane begged Miss Peasmarsh to let them help her to sell the things, because it was their brother who had announced the good news that the things had come. Miss Peasmarsh was very willing, for now her stall, that had been so neglected, was surrounded by people who wanted to buy, and she was glad to be helped. The children noted that Mrs. Biddle had not more to do in the way of selling than she could manage quite well. I hope they were not glad—for you should forgive your enemies, even if they walk on your hands and then say it is all your naughty fault. But I am afraid they were not so sorry as they ought to have been.

It took some time to arrange the things on the stall. The carpet was spread over it, and the dark colours showed up the brass and silver and ivory things. It was a happy and busy afternoon, and when Miss Peasmarsh and the girls had sold every single one of the little pretty things from the Indian bazaar, far, far away, Anthea and Jane went off with the boys to fish in the fishpond, and dive into the bran-pie,[9] and hear the cardboard band, and the phonograph, and the chorus of singing birds that was done behind a screen with glass tubes and glasses of water.

They had a beautiful tea, suddenly presented to them by the nice curate, and Miss Peasmarsh joined them before they had had more than three cakes each. It was a merry party, and the curate was extremely pleasant to every one, "even to Miss Peasmarsh," as Jane said afterwards.

"We ought to get back to the stall," said Anthea, when no one could possibly eat any more, and the curate was talking in a low voice to Miss Peasmarsh about "after Easter."

"There's nothing to go back for," said Miss Peasmarsh gaily; "thanks to you dear children we've sold everything."

"There—there's the carpet," said Cyril.

"Oh," said Miss Peasmarsh, radiantly, "don't bother about the carpet. I've sold even that. Mrs. Biddle gave me ten shillings for it. She said it would do for her servants' bedroom."

"Why," said Jane, "her servants don't *have* carpets. We had cook from her, and she told us so."

"No scandal about Queen Elizabeth, if *you* please," said the curate, cheerfully; and Miss Peasmarsh laughed, and looked at him as though she had never dreamed that any one *could* be so amusing. But the others were struck dumb. How could they say, "The carpet is ours!" For who brings carpets to bazaars?

The children were now thoroughly wretched. But I am glad to say that their wretchedness did not make them forget their manners, as it does sometimes, even with grown-up people, who ought to know ever so much better.

They said, "Thank you very much for the jolly tea," and "Thanks for being so jolly," and "Thanks awfully for giving us such a jolly time"; for the curate had stood[1] fishponds, and bran-pies, and phonographs, and the chorus of singing birds, and had stood them like a man. The girls hugged Miss Peasmarsh, and as they went away they heard the curate say—

---

9. A game in which small articles are hidden in a tub filled with bran to be drawn out at random. "Fishpond": a game in which small objects can be extracted with a fishing rod.

1. I.e., paid for.

"Jolly little kids, yes, but what about—you will let it be directly after Easter. Ah, do say you will——"

And Jane ran back and said, before Anthea could drag her away, "What are you going to do after Easter?"

Miss Peasmarsh smiled and looked very pretty indeed. And the curate said:

"I hope I am going to take a trip to the Fortunate Islands."

"I wish we could take you on the wishing carpet," said Jane.

"Thank you," said the curate, "but I'm afraid I can't wait for that. I must go to the Fortunate Islands before they make me a bishop. I should have no time afterwards."

"I've always thought I should marry a bishop," said Jane: "his aprons would come in so useful. Wouldn't *you* like to marry a bishop, Miss Peasmarsh?"

It was then that they dragged her away.

As it was Robert's hand that Mrs. Biddle had walked on, it was decided that he had better not recall the incident to her mind, and so make her angry again. Anthea and Jane had helped to sell things at the rival stall, so they were not likely to be popular.

A hasty council of four decided that Mrs. Biddle would hate Cyril less than she would hate the others, so the others mingled with the crowd, and it was he who said to her:

"Mrs. Biddle, *we* meant to have that carpet. Would you sell it to us? We would give you——"

"Certainly not," said Mrs. Biddle. "Go away, little boy."

There was that in her tone which showed Cyril, all too plainly, the hopelessness of persuasion. He found the others and said:

"It's no use; she's like a lioness robbed of its puppies. We must watch where it goes—and——Anthea, I don't care what you say. It's our own carpet. It wouldn't be burglary. It would be a sort of forlorn hope rescue party—heroic and daring and dashing, and not wrong at all."

The children still wandered among the gay crowd—but there was no pleasure there for them any more. The chorus of singing birds sounded just like glass tubes being blown through water, and the phonograph simply made a horrid noise, so that you could hardly hear yourself speak. And the people were buying things they couldn't possibly want, and it all seemed very stupid. And Mrs. Biddle had bought the wishing carpet for ten shillings. And the whole of life was sad and grey and dusty, and smelt of slight gas escapes, and hot people, and cake and crumbs, and all the children were very tired indeed.

They found a corner within sight of the carpet, and there they waited miserably, till it was far beyond their proper bedtime. And when it was ten the people who had bought things went away, but the people who had been selling stayed to count up their money.

"And to jaw about it," said Robert. "I'll never go to another bazaar as long as ever I live. My hand is swollen as big as a pudding. I expect the nails in her horrible boots were poisoned."

Just then someone who seemed to have a right to interfere said:

"Everything is over now; you had better go home."

So they went. And then they waited on the pavement under the gas lamp, where ragged children had been standing all the evening to listen to the band, and their feet slipped about in the greasy mud till Mrs. Biddle came out and was driven away in a cab with the many things she hadn't sold, and the few things she had bought—among others the carpet. The other stall-holders left their things at the school till

Monday morning, but Mrs. Biddle was afraid some one would steal some of them, so she took them in a cab.

The children, now too desperate to care for mud or appearances, hung on behind the cab till it reached Mrs. Biddle's house. When she and the carpet had gone in and the door was shut Anthea said:

"Don't let's burgle—I mean do daring and dashing rescue acts, till we've given her a chance. Let's ring and ask to see her."

The others hated to do this, but at last they agreed, on condition that Anthea would not make any silly fuss about the burglary afterwards, if it really had to come to that.

So they knocked and rang, and a scared-looking parlourmaid opened the front door. While they were asking for Mrs. Biddle they saw her. She was in the dining-room, and she had already pushed back the table and spread out the carpet to see how it looked on the floor.

"I knew she didn't want it for her servants' bedroom," Jane muttered.

Anthea walked straight past the uncomfortable parlourmaid, and the others followed her. Mrs. Biddle had her back to them, and was smoothing down the carpet with the same boot that had trampled on the hand of Robert. So that they were all in the room, and Cyril, with great presence of mind, had shut the room door before she saw them.

"Who is it, Jane?" she asked in a sour voice; and then, turning suddenly, she saw who it was. Once more her face grew violet—a deep, dark violet. "You wicked daring little things!" she cried, "how dare you come here? At this time of night, too. Be off, or I'll send for the police."

"Don't be angry," said Anthea, soothingly, "we only wanted to ask you to let us have the carpet. We have quite twelve shillings between us, and——"

"How *dare* you?" cried Mrs. Biddle, and her voice shook with angriness.

"You do look horrid," said Jane suddenly.

Mrs. Biddle actually stamped that booted foot of hers.

"You rude, barefaced[2] child!" she said.

Anthea almost shook Jane; but Jane pushed forward in spite of her.

"It really *is* our nursery carpet," she said, "you ask *any one* if it isn't."

"Let's wish ourselves home," said Cyril in a whisper.

"No go," Robert whispered back, "she'd be there, too, and raving mad as likely as not. Horrid thing, I hate her!"

"I wish Mrs. Biddle was in an angelic good temper," cried Anthea, suddenly. "It's worth trying," she said to herself.

Mrs. Biddle's face grew from purple to violet, and from violet to mauve, and from mauve to pink. Then she smiled quite a jolly smile.

"Why, so I am!" she said, "what a funny idea! Why shouldn't I be in a good temper, my dears."

Once more the carpet had done its work, and not on Mrs. Biddle alone. The children felt suddenly good and happy.

"You're a jolly good sort," said Cyril. "I see that now. I'm sorry we vexed you at the bazaar to-day."

"Not another word," said the changed Mrs. Biddle. "Of course you shall have the carpet, my dears, if you've taken such a fancy to it. No, no; I won't have more than the ten shillings I paid."

"It does seem hard to ask you for it after you bought it at the bazaar," said Anthea;

2. Impudent, shameless.

"but it really *is* our nursery carpet. It got to the bazaar by mistake, with some other things."

"Did it really, now? How vexing!" said Mrs. Biddle, kindly. "Well, my dears, I can very well give the extra ten shillings; so you take your carpet and we'll say no more about it. Have a piece of cake before you go! I'm so sorry I stepped on your hand, my boy. Is it all right now?"

"Yes, thank you," said Robert. "I say, you *are* good."

"Not at all," said Mrs. Biddle, heartily. "I'm delighted to be able to give any little pleasure to you dear children."

And she helped them to roll up the carpet, and the boys carried it away between them.

"You *are* a dear," said Anthea, and she and Mrs. Biddle kissed each other heartily.

"*Well!*" said Cyril as they went along the street.

"Yes," said Robert, "and the odd part is that you feel just as if it was *real*—her being so jolly, I mean—and not only the carpet making her nice."

"Perhaps it *is* real," said Anthea, "only it was covered up with crossness and tiredness and things, and the carpet took them away."

"I hope it'll keep them away," said Jane; "she isn't ugly at all when she laughs."

The carpet has done many wonders in its day; but the case of Mrs. Biddle is, I think, the most wonderful. For from that day she was never anything like so disagreeable as she was before, and she sent a lovely silver tea-pot and a kind letter to Miss Peasmarsh when the pretty lady married the nice curate; just after Easter it was, and they went to Italy for their honeymoon.

Chapter V. The Temple

"I wish we could find the Phœnix," said Jane. "It's much better company than the carpet."

"Beastly ungrateful, little kids are," said Cyril.

"No, I'm not; only the carpet never says anything, and it's so helpless. It doesn't seem able to take care of itself. It gets sold, and taken into the sea, and things like that. You wouldn't catch the Phœnix getting sold."

It was two days after the bazaar. Every one was a little cross—some days are like that, usually Mondays, by the way. And this was a Monday.

"I shouldn't wonder if your precious Phœnix had gone off for good," said Cyril; "and I don't know that I blame it. Look at the weather!"

"It's not worth looking at," said Robert. And indeed it wasn't.

"The Phœnix hasn't gone—I'm sure it hasn't," said Anthea. "I'll have another look for it."

Anthea looked under tables and chairs, and in boxes and baskets, in mother's work-bag and father's portmanteau, but still the Phœnix showed not so much as the tip of one shining feather.

Then suddenly Robert remembered how the whole of the Greek invocation song of seven thousand lines had been condensed by him into one English hexameter, so he stood on the carpet and chanted—

"Oh, come along, come along, you good old beautiful Phœnix,"

and almost at once there was a rustle of wings down the kitchen stairs, and the Phœnix sailed in on wide gold wings.

"Where on earth *have* you been?" asked Anthea. "I've looked everywhere for you."

"Not *everywhere*," replied the bird, "because you did not look in the place where I was. Confess that that hallowed spot was overlooked by you."

"*What* hallowed spot?" asked Cyril, a little impatiently, for time was hastening on, and the wishing carpet still idle.

"The spot," said the Phœnix, "which I hallowed by my golden presence was the Lutron."

"The *what?*"

"The bath—the place of washing."

"I'm sure you weren't," said Jane. "I looked there three times and moved all the towels."

"I was concealed," said the Phœnix, "on the summit of a metal column— enchanted, I should judge, for it felt warm to my golden toes, as though the glorious sun of the desert shone ever upon it."

"Oh, you mean the cylinder," said Cyril: "it *has* rather a comforting feel, this weather. And now where shall we go?"

And then, of course, the usual discussion broke out as to where they should go and what they should do. And naturally, every one wanted to do something that the others did not care about.

"I am the eldest," Cyril remarked, "let's go to the North Pole."

"This weather! Likely!" Robert rejoined. "Let's go to the Equator."

"I think the diamond mines of Golconda[3] would be nice," said Anthea; "don't you agree, Jane?"

"No, I don't," retorted Jane, "I don't agree with you. I don't agree with anybody."

The Phœnix raised a warning claw.

"If you cannot agree among yourselves, I fear I shall have to leave you," it said.

"Well, where shall we go? You decide!" said all.

"If I were you," said the bird, thoughtfully, "I should give the carpet a rest. Besides, you'll lose the use of your legs if you go everywhere by carpet. Can't you take me out and explain your ugly city to me?"

"We will if it clears up," said Robert, without enthusiasm. "Just look at the rain. And why should we give the carpet a rest?"

"Are you greedy and grasping, and heartless and selfish?" asked the bird, sharply.

"*No!*" said Robert, with indignation.

"Well, then!" said the Phœnix. "And as to the rain—well, I am not fond of rain myself. If the sun knew *I* was here—he's very fond of shining on me because I look so bright and golden. He always says I repay a little attention. Haven't you some form of words suitable for use in wet weather?"

"There's 'Rain, rain, go away,'" said Anthea; "but it never *does* go."

"Perhaps you don't say the invocation properly," said the bird.

> " 'Rain, rain, go away,
> Come again another day,
> Little baby wants to play,'"

said Anthea.

"That's quite wrong; and if you say it in that sort of dull way, I can quite understand the rain not taking any notice. You should open the window and shout as loud as you can:

___

3. Ruined town in India (near Hyderabad), famed for its diamonds.

" 'Rain, rain, go away,
        Come again another day;
        Now we want the sun, and so,
        Pretty rain, be kind and go!'"

You should always speak politely to people when you want them to do things, and especially when it's going away that you want them to do. And to-day you might add:

" 'Shine, great sun, the lovely Phœ-
        Nix is here, and wants to be
        Shone on, splendid sun, by thee!'"

"That's poetry!" said Cyril, decidedly.

"It's like it," said the more cautious Robert.

"I was obliged to put in 'lovely,'" said the Phœnix, modestly, "to make the line long enough."

"There are plenty of nasty words just that length," said Jane; but everyone else said "Hush!"

And then they opened the window and shouted the seven lines as loud as they could, and the Phœnix said all the words with them, except "lovely," and when they came to that it looked down and coughed bashfully.

The rain hesitated a moment and then went away.

"There's true politeness," said the Phœnix, and the next moment it was perched on the window-ledge, opening and shutting its radiant wings and flapping out its golden feathers in such a flood of glorious sunshine as you sometimes have at sunset in autumn time. People said afterwards that there had not been such sunshine in December for years and years and years.

"And now," said the bird, "we will go out into the city, and you shall take me to see one of my temples."

"Your temples?"

"I gather from the carpet that I have many temples in this land."

"I don't see how you can find anything out from it," said Jane: "it never speaks."

"All the same, you can pick up things from a carpet," said the bird; "I've seen you do it. And I have picked up several pieces of information in this way. That papyrus on which you showed me my picture—I understand that it bears on it the name of the street of your city in which my finest temple stands, with my image graved in stone and in metal over against its portal."

"You mean the fire insurance office," said Robert. "It's not really a temple, and they don't——"

"Excuse me," said the Phœnix, coldly, "you are wholly misinformed. It is a temple, and they do."

"Don't let's waste the sunshine," said Anthea; "we might argue as we go along, to save time."

So the Phœnix consented to make itself a nest in the breast of Robert's Norfolk jacket,[4] and they all went out into the splendid sunshine. The best way to the temple of the Phœnix seemed to be to take the tram, and on the top of it the children talked, while the Phœnix now and then put a wary beak, cocked a cautious eye, and contradicted what the children were saying.

---

4. Loose-fitting man's or boy's belted jacket.

It was a delicious ride, and the children felt how lucky they were to have had the money to pay for it. They went with the tram as far as it went, and when it did not go any farther they stopped too, and got off. The tram stops at the end of the Gray's Inn Road, and it was Cyril who thought that one might well find a short cut to the Phœnix Office through the little streets and courts that lie tightly packed between Fetter Lane and Ludgate Circus. Of course, he was quite mistaken, as Robert told him at the time, and afterwards Robert did not forbear to remind his brother how he had said so. The streets there were small and stuffy and ugly, and crowded with printers' boys and binders' girls coming out from work; and these stared so hard at the pretty red coats and caps of the sisters that they wished they had gone some other way. And the printers and binders made very personal remarks, advising Jane to get her hair cut, and inquiring where Anthea had bought that hat. Jane and Anthea scorned to reply, and Cyril and Robert found that they were hardly a match for the rough crowd. They could think of nothing nasty enough to say. They turned a corner sharply, and then Anthea pulled Jane into an archway, and then inside a door; Cyril and Robert quickly followed, and the jeering crowd passed by without seeing them.

Anthea drew a long breath.

"How awful!" she said. "I didn't know there were such people, except in books."

"It was a bit thick; but it's partly you girls' fault, coming out in those flashy coats."

"We thought we ought to, when we were going out with the Phœnix," said Jane; and the bird said, "Quite right, too"—and incautiously put out his head to give her a wink of encouragement. And at the same instant a dirty hand reached through the grim balustrade of the staircase beside them and clutched the Phœnix, and a hoarse voice said—

"I say, Urb, blowed if this ain't our Poll parrot what we lost. Thank you very much, lidy, for bringin' 'im home to roost."

The four turned swiftly. Two large and ragged boys were crouched amid the dark shadows of the stairs. They were much larger than Robert and Cyril, and one of them had snatched the Phœnix away and was holding it high above their heads.

"Give me that bird," said Cyril, sternly: "it's ours."

"Good afternoon, and thankin' you," the boy went on, with maddening mockery. "Sorry I can't give yer tuppence for yer trouble—but I've 'ad to spend my fortune advertising for my vallyable bird in all the newspapers. You can call for the reward next year."

"Look out, Ike," said his friend, a little anxiously; "it 'ave a beak on it."

"It's other parties as'll have the Beak[5] on to 'em presently," said Ike, darkly, "if they come a-trying to lay claims on my Poll parrot. You just shut up, Urb. Now then, you four little gells, get out er this."

"Little girls!" cried Robert; "I'll little girl you!" He sprang up three stairs and hit out.

There was a squawk—the most bird-like noise anyone had ever heard from the Phœnix—and a fluttering, and a laugh in the darkness, and Ike said:

"There now, you've been and gone and strook my Poll parrot right in the fevvers— strook 'im something crool, you 'ave."

Robert stamped with fury. Cyril felt himself growing pale with rage, and with the effort of screwing up his brain to make it clever enough to think of some way of being even with those boys. Anthea and Jane were as angry as the boys, but it made them want to cry. Yet it was Anthea who said:

"Do, please, let us have the bird."

---

5. Magistrate or justice of the peace.

"Dew, *please*, get along and leave us an' our bird alone."

"If you don't," said Anthea, "I shall fetch the police."

"You better!" said he who was named Urb. "Say, Ike, you twist the bloomin' pigeon's neck; he ain't worth tuppence."

"Oh, no," cried Jane, "don't hurt it. Oh, don't; it is such a pet."

"I won't hurt it," said Ike; "I'm 'shamed of you, Urb, for to think of such a thing. Arf a shiner, miss, and the bird is yours for life."

"Half a *what?*" asked Anthea.

"Arf a shiner, quid, thick 'un—half a sov,[6] then."

"I haven't got it—and, besides, it's *our* bird," said Anthea.

"Oh, don't talk to him," said Cyril; and then Jane said suddenly:

"Phœnix—dear Phœnix, we can't do anything. *You* must manage it."

"With pleasure," said the Phœnix—and Ike nearly dropped it in his amazement.

"I say, it do talk, suthin' like," said he.

"Youths," said the Phœnix, "sons of misfortune, hear my words."

"My eyes!" said Ike.

"Look out, Ike," said Urb, "you'll throttle the joker—and I see at wunst 'e was wuth 'is weight in flimsies."[7]

"Hearken. O Eikonoclastes, despiser of sacred images—and thou, Urbanus, dweller in the sordid city. Forbear this adventure lest a worse thing befall."

"Luv' us!" said Ike, "ain't it been taught its schoolin', just!"

"Restore me to my young acolytes and escape unscathed. Retain me—and——"

"They must ha' got all this up, case the Polly got pinched," said Ike. "Lor' lumme, the artfulness of them young uns!"

"I say, slosh 'em in the geseech and get clear off with the swag's wot I say," urged Herbert.

"Right O," said Isaac.

"Forbear," repeated the Phœnix, sternly. "Who pinched the click[8] off of the old bloke in Aldermanbury?" it added, in a changed tone. "Who sneaked the nose-rag out of the young gell's 'and in Bell Court? Who——"

"Stow it," said Ike. "You! ugh! yah!—leave go of me. Bash him off, Urb; 'e'll have my bloomin' eyes outer my 'ed."

There were howls, a scuffle, a flutter; Ike and Urb fled up the stairs, and the Phœnix swept out through the doorway. The children followed and the Phœnix settled on Robert, "like a butterfly on a rose," as Anthea said afterwards, and wriggled into the breast of his Norfolk jacket, "like an eel into mud," as Cyril later said.

"Why ever didn't you burn him? You could have, couldn't you?" asked Robert, when the hurried flight through the narrow courts had ended in the safe wideness of Farringdon Street.

"I could have, of course," said the bird, "but I didn't think it would be dignified to allow myself to get warm about a little thing like that. The Fates, after all, have not been illiberal to me. I have a good many friends among the London sparrows, and I have a beak and claws."

These happenings had somewhat shaken the adventurous temper of the children, and the Phœnix had to exert its golden self to hearten them up.

Presently the children came to a great house in Lombard Street, and there, on each side of the door, was the image of the Phœnix carved in stone, and set forth on shining brass were the words—

6. A sovereign: a gold coin worth one pound (or one "quid").

7. Banknotes.

8. Watch.

"One moment," said the bird. "Fire? For altars, I suppose?"

"I don't know," said Robert; he was beginning to feel shy, and that always made him rather cross.

"Oh, yes, you do," Cyril contradicted. "When people's houses are burnt down the Phœnix gives them new houses. Father told me; I asked him."

"The house, then, like the Phœnix, rises from its ashes? Well have my priests dealt with the sons of men!"

"The sons of men pay, you know," said Anthea; "but it's only a little every year."

"That is to maintain my priests," said the bird, "who, in the hour of affliction, heal sorrows and rebuild houses. Lead on; inquire for the High Priest. I will not break upon them too suddenly in all my glory. Noble and honour-deserving are they who make as nought the evil deeds of the lame-footed and unpleasing Hephæstus."[9]

"I don't know what you're talking about, and I wish you wouldn't muddle us with new names. Fire just happens. Nobody does it—not as a deed, you know," Cyril explained. "If they did the Phœnix wouldn't help them, because it's a crime to set fire to things. Arsenic, or something they call it, because it's as bad as poisoning people. The Phœnix wouldn't help *them*—father told me it wouldn't."

"My priests do well," said the Phœnix. "Lead on."

"I don't know what to say," said Cyril; and the others said the same.

"Ask for the High Priest," said the Phœnix. "Say that you have a secret to unfold that concerns my worship, and he will lead you to the innermost sanctuary."

So the children went in, all four of them, though they didn't like it, and stood in a large and beautiful hall adorned with Doulton tiles,[1] like a large and beautiful bath with no water in it, and stately pillars supporting the roof. An unpleasing representation of the Phœnix in brown pottery disfigured one wall. There were counters and desks of mahogany and brass, and clerks bent over the desks and walked behind the counters. There was a great clock over an inner doorway.

"Inquire for the High Priest," whispered the Phœnix.

An attentive clerk in decent black, who controlled his mouth but not his eyebrows, now came towards them. He leaned forward on the counter, and the children thought he was going to say, "What can I have the pleasure of showing you?" like in a draper's; instead of which the young man said—

"And what do *you* want?"

"We want to see the High Priest."

"Get along with you," said the young man.

An elder man, also decent in black coat, advanced.

"Perhaps it's Mr. Blank" (not for worlds would I give the name). "He's a Masonic High Priest,[2] you know."

A porter was sent away to look for Mr. Asterisk (I cannot give his name), and the children were left there to look on and be looked on by all the gentlemen at the mahogany desks. Anthea and Jane thought that they looked kind. The boys thought they stared, and that it was like their cheek.

The porter returned with the news that Mr. Dot Dash Dot (I dare not reveal his name) was out, but that Mr.——

Here a really delightful gentleman appeared. He had a beard and a kind and merry

9. Greek god of fire and metalworking.
1. Ceramic tiles.
2. Of high rank among the Freemasons, a secret, fraternal order founded in England in the early eighteenth century.

eye, and each one of the four knew at once that this was a man who had kiddies of his own and could understand what you were talking about. Yet it was a difficult thing to explain.

"What is it?" he asked. "Mr.——"—he named the name which I will never reveal—"is out. Can I do anything?"

"Inner sanctuary," murmured the Phœnix.

"I beg your pardon," said the nice gentleman, who thought it was Robert who had spoken.

"We have something to tell you," said Cyril, "but"—he glanced at the porter, who was lingering much nearer than he need have done—"this is a very public place."

The nice gentleman laughed.

"Come upstairs then," he said, and led the way up a wide and beautiful staircase. Anthea says the stairs were of white marble, but I am not sure. On the corner-post of the stairs, at the top, was a beautiful image of the Phœnix in dark metal, and on the wall at each side was a flat sort of image of it.

The nice gentleman led them into a room where the chairs, and even the tables, were covered with reddish leather. He looked at the children inquiringly.

"Don't be frightened," he said; "tell me exactly what you want."

"May I shut the door?" asked Cyril.

The gentleman looked surprised, but he shut the door.

"Now," said Cyril, firmly, "I know you'll be awfully surprised, and you'll think it's not true and we are lunatics; but we aren't, and it is. Robert's got something inside his Norfolk—that's Robert, he's my young brother. Now don't be upset and have a fit or anything, sir. Of course, I know when you called your shop the 'Phœnix' you never thought there was one; but there is—and Robert's got it buttoned up against his chest!"

"If it's an old curio in the form of a Phœnix, I dare say the Board——" said the nice gentleman, as Robert began to fumble with his buttons.

"It's old enough," said Anthea, "going by what it says, but——"

"My goodness gracious!" said the gentleman as the Phœnix, with one last wriggle that melted into a flutter, got out of its nest in the breast of Robert and stood up on the leather-covered table.

"What an extraordinarily fine bird!" he went on. "I don't think I ever saw one just like it."

"I should think not," said the Phœnix, with pardonable pride. And the gentleman jumped.

"Oh, it's been taught to speak! Some sort of parrot, perhaps?"

"I am," said the bird, simply, "the Head of your House, and I have come to my temple to receive your homage. I am no parrot"—its beak curved scornfully—"I am the one and only Phœnix, and I demand the homage of my High Priest."

"In the absence of our manager," the gentleman began, exactly as though he were addressing a valued customer—"in the absence of our manager, I might perhaps be able—— What am I saying?" He turned pale, and passed his hand across his brow. "My dears," he said, "the weather is unusually warm for the time of year, and I don't feel quite myself. Do you know, for a moment I really thought that that remarkable bird of yours had spoken and said it was the Phœnix, and, what's more, that I'd believed it."

"So it did, sir," said Cyril, "and so did you."

"It really—— Allow me."

A bell was rung. The porter appeared.

"Mackenzie," said the gentleman, "you see that golden bird?"

"Yes, sir."

The other breathed a sigh of relief.

"It *is* real, then?"

"Yes, sir, of course, sir. You take it in your hand, sir," said the porter, sympathetically, and reached out his hand to the Phœnix, who shrank back on toes curved with agitated indignation.

"Forbear!" it cried; "how dare you seek to lay hands on me?"

The porter saluted.

"Beg pardon, sir," he said, "I thought you was a bird."

"I *am* a bird—*the* bird—the Phœnix."

"Of course you are, sir," said the porter. "I see that the first minute, directly I got my breath, sir."

"That will do," said the gentleman. "Ask Mr. Wilson and Mr. Sterry to step up here for a moment, please."

Mr. Sterry and Mr. Wilson were in their turn overcome by amazement—quickly followed by conviction. To the surprise of the children every one in the office took the Phœnix at its word, and after the first shock of surprise it seemed to be perfectly natural to every one that the Phœnix should be alive, and that, passing through London, it should call at its temple.

"We ought to have some sort of ceremony," said the nicest gentleman, anxiously. "There isn't time to summon the directors and shareholders—we might do that to-morrow, perhaps. Yes, the board-room would be best. I shouldn't like it to feel we hadn't done everything in our power to show our appreciation of its condescension in looking in on us in this friendly way."

The children could hardly believe their ears, for they had never thought that any one but themselves would believe in the Phœnix. And yet every one did; all the men in the office were brought in by twos and threes, and the moment the Phœnix opened its beak it convinced the cleverest of them, as well as those who were not so clever. Cyril wondered how the story would look in the papers next day.

He seemed to see the posters in the streets:

PHŒNIX FIRE OFFICE.

THE PHŒNIX AT ITS TEMPLE.

MEETING TO WELCOME IT.

DELIGHT OF THE MANAGER AND EVERYBODY.

"Excuse our leaving you a moment," said the nice gentleman, and he went away with the others; and through the half-closed door the children could hear the sound of many boots on stairs, the hum of excited voices explaining, suggesting, arguing, the thumpy drag of heavy furniture being moved about.

The Phœnix strutted up and down the leather-covered table, looking over its shoulder at its pretty back.

"You see what a convincing manner I have," it said proudly.

And now a new gentleman came in and said, bowing low—

"Everything is prepared—we have done our best at so short a notice; the meeting—the ceremony—will be in the board-room. Will the Honourable Phœnix walk—it is only a few steps—or would it like to be—would it like some sort of conveyance?"

"My Robert will bear me to the board-room, if that be the unlovely name of my temple's inmost court," replied the bird.

So they all followed the gentleman. There was a big table in the board-room, but it had been pushed right up under the long windows at one side, and chairs were arranged in rows across the room—like those you have at schools when there is a magic lantern[3] on "Our Eastern Empire," or on "The Way We Do in the Navy." The doors were of carved wood, very beautiful, with a carved Phœnix above. Anthea noticed that the chairs in the front rows were of the kind that her mother so loved to ask the price of in old furniture shops, and never could buy, because the price was always nearly twenty pounds each. On the mantelpiece were some heavy bronze candlesticks and a clock, and on the top of the clock was another image of the Phœnix.

"Remove that effigy," said the Phœnix to the gentlemen who were there, and it was hastily taken down. Then the Phœnix fluttered to the middle of the mantelpiece and stood there, looking more golden than ever. Then every one in the house and the office came in—from the cashier to the women who cooked the clerks' dinners in the beautiful kitchen at the top of the house. And every one bowed to the Phœnix and then sat down in a chair.

"Gentlemen," said the nicest gentleman, "we have met here to-day——"

The Phœnix was turning its golden beak from side to side.

"I don't notice any incense," it said, with an injured sniff.

A hurried consultation ended in plates being fetched from the kitchen. Brown sugar, sealing-wax, and tobacco were placed on these, and something from a square bottle was poured over it all. Then a match was applied. It was the only incense that was handy in the Phœnix office, and it certainly burned very briskly and smoked a great deal.

"We have met here to-day," said the gentleman again, "on an occasion unparalleled in the annals of this office. Our respected Phœnix——"

"Head of the House," said the Phœnix, in a hollow voice.

"I was coming to that. Our respected Phœnix, the Head of this ancient House, has at length done us the honour to come among us. I think I may say, gentlemen, that we are not insensible to this honour, and that we welcome with no uncertain voice one whom we have so long desired to see in our midst."

Several of the younger clerks thought of saying "Hear, hear," but they feared it might seem disrespectful to the bird.

"I will not take up your time," the speaker went on, "by recapitulating the advantages to be derived from a proper use of our system of fire insurance. I know, and you know, gentlemen, that our aim has ever been to be worthy of that eminent bird whose name we bear, and who now adorns our mantelpiece with his presence. Three cheers, gentlemen, for the winged Head of the House!"

The cheers rose, deafening. When they had died away the Phœnix was asked to say a few words.

It expressed in graceful phrases the pleasure it felt in finding itself at last in its own temple.

"And," it went on, "you must not think me wanting in appreciation of your very hearty and cordial reception when I ask that an ode may be recited or a choric song sung. It is what I have always been accustomed to."

The four children, dumb witnesses of this wonderful scene, glanced a little nervously across the foam of white faces above the sea of black coats. It seemed to them that the Phœnix was really asking a little too much.

"Time presses," said the Phœnix, "and the original ode of invocation is long, as

3. A slide show using an early form of projector.

well as being Greek; and, besides, it's no use invoking me when here I am; but is
there not a song in your own tongue for a great day such as this?"

Absently the manager began to sing, and one by one the rest joined—

> "Absolute security!
> No liability!
> All kinds of property
> Insured against fire.
> Terms most favourable,
> Expenses reasonable,
> Moderate rates for annual
> Insurance. . . ."

"That one is *not* my favourite," interrupted the Phœnix, "and I think you've forgotten part of it."

The manager hastily began another—

> "O Golden Phœnix, fairest bird,
> The whole great world has often heard
> Of all the splendid things we do,
> Great Phœnix, just to honour you."

"That's better," said the bird.

And every one sang—

> "Class one, for private dwelling-house,
> For household goods and shops allows;
> Provided these are built of brick
> Or stone, and tiled and slated thick."

"Try another verse," said the Phœnix, "further on."

And again arose the voices of all the clerks and employees and managers and
secretaries and cooks—

> "In Scotland our insurance yields
> The price of burnt-up stacks in fields."

"Skip that verse," said the Phœnix.

> "Thatched dwellings and their whole contents
> We deal with—also with their rents;
> Oh, glorious Phœnix, look and see
> That these are dealt with in class three.

> "The glories of your temple throng
> Too thick to go in any song;
> And we attend, O good and wise,
> To 'days of grace' and merchandise.

> "When people's homes are burned away
> They never have a cent to pay

If they have done as all should do,
O Phœnix, and have honoured you.

> "So let us raise our voice and sing
> The praises of the Phœnix King.
> In classes one and two and three,
> Oh, trust to him, for kind is he!"

"I'm sure *you're* very kind," said the Phœnix; "and now we must be going. And thank you very much for a very pleasant time. May you all prosper as you deserve to do, for I am sure a nicer, pleasanter-spoken lot of temple attendants I have never met, and never wish to meet. I wish you all good-day!"

It fluttered to the wrist of Robert and drew the four children from the room. The whole of the office staff followed down the wide stairs and filed into their accustomed places, and the two most important officials stood on the steps bowing till Robert had buttoned the golden bird in his Norfolk bosom, and it and he and the three other children were lost in the crowd.

The two most important gentlemen looked at each other earnestly and strangely for a moment, and then retreated to those sacred inner rooms, where they toil without ceasing for the good of the House.

And the moment they were all in their places—managers, secretaries, clerks, and porters—they all started, and each looked cautiously round to see if any one was looking at him. For each thought that he had fallen asleep for a few minutes, and had dreamed a very odd dream about the Phœnix and the board-room. And, of course, no one mentioned it to any one else, because going to sleep at your office is a thing you simply *must not* do.

The extraordinary confusion of the board-room, with the remains of the incense in the plates, would have shown them at once that the visit of the Phœnix had been no dream, but a radiant reality, but no one went into the board-room again that day; and next day, before the office was opened, it was all cleaned and put nice and tidy by a lady whose business asking questions was not part of. That is why Cyril read the papers in vain on the next day and the day after that; because no sensible person thinks his dreams worth putting in the paper, and no one will ever own that he has been asleep in the daytime.

The Phœnix was very pleased, but it decided to write an ode for itself. It thought the ones it had heard at its temple had been too hastily composed. Its own ode began—

> "For beauty and for modest worth
> The Phœnix has not its equal on earth."

And when the children went to bed that night it was still trying to cut down the last line to the proper length without taking out any of what it wanted to say.

That is what makes poetry so difficult.

Chapter VI. Doing Good

"We shan't be able to go anywhere on the carpet for a whole week, though," said Robert.

"And I'm glad of it," said Jane, unexpectedly.

"Glad?" said Cyril; "*glad?*"

It was breakfast-time, and mother's letter, telling them how they were all going for Christmas to their aunt's at Lyndhurst,[4] and how father and mother would meet them there, having been read by every one, lay on the table, drinking hot bacon-fat with one corner and eating marmalade with the other.

"Yes, glad," said Jane. "I don't want any more things to happen just now. I feel like you do when you've been to three parties in a week—like we did at granny's once—and extras in between, toys and chocs and things like that. I want everything to be just real, and no fancy things happening at all."

"I don't like being obliged to keep things from mother," said Anthea. "I don't know why, but it makes me feel selfish and mean."

"If we could only get the mater[5] to believe it, we might take her to the jolliest places," said Cyril, thoughtfully. "As it is, we've just *got* to be selfish and mean—if it is that—but I don't feel it is."

"I *know* it isn't, but I *feel* it is," said Anthea, "and that's just as bad."

"It's worse," said Robert; "if you knew it and didn't feel it, it wouldn't matter so much."

"That's being a hardened criminal, father says," put in Cyril, and he picked up mother's letter and wiped its corners with his handkerchief, to whose colour a trifle of bacon-fat and marmalade made but little difference.

"We're going to-morrow, anyhow," said Robert. "Don't," he added, with a good-boy expression on his face—"don't let's be ungrateful for our blessings; don't let's waste the day in saying how horrid it is to keep secrets from mothers, when we all know Anthea tried all she knew to give her the secret, and she wouldn't take it. Let's get on the carpet and have a jolly good wish. You'll have time enough to repent of things all next week."

"Yes," said Cyril, "let's. It's not really wrong."

"Well, look here," said Anthea. "You know there's something about Christmas that makes you want to be good—however little you wish it at other times. Couldn't we wish the carpet to take us somewhere where we should have the chance to do some good and kind action? It would be an adventure just the same," she pleaded.

"I don't mind," said Cyril. "We shan't know where we're going, and that'll be exciting. No one know's what'll happen. We'd best put on our outers in case—"

"We might rescue a traveller buried in the snow, like St. Bernard dogs, with barrels round our necks," said Jane, beginning to be interested.

"Or we might arrive just in time to witness a will being signed—more tea, please," said Robert—"and we should see the old man hide it away in the secret cupboard; and then, after long years, when the rightful heir was in despair, we should lead him to the hidden panel and—"

"Yes," interrupted Anthea; "or we might be taken to some freezing garret in a German town, where a poor little pale, sick child—"

"We haven't any German money," interrupted Cyril, "so *that's* no go. What I should like would be getting into the middle of a war and getting hold of secret intelligence and taking it to the general, and he would make me a lieutenant, or a scout, or a hussar."

When breakfast was cleared away, Anthea swept the carpet, and the children sat down on it, together with the Phœnix, who had been especially invited, as a Christmas

---

4. A village near the port of Southampton, south-west of London.

5. Mother (Latin; this use is schoolboy slang).

treat, to come with them and witness the good and kind action they were about to do.

Four children and one bird were ready, and the wish was wished.

Every one closed his eyes, so as to feel the topsy-turvy swirl of the carpet's movement as little as possible.

When the eyes were opened again the children found themselves on the carpet, and the carpet was in its proper place on the floor of their own nursery at Camden Town.

"I say," said Cyril, "here's a go!"

"Do you think it's worn out? The wishing part of it, I mean?" Robert anxiously asked the Phœnix.

"It's not that," said the Phœnix; "but—well—what did you wish—?"

"Oh! I see what it means," said Robert, with deep disgust; "it's like the end of a fairy story in a Sunday magazine. How perfectly beastly!"

"You mean it means we can do kind and good actions where we are? I see. I suppose it wants us to carry coals for the cook or make clothes for the bare heathens. Well, I simply won't. And the last day and everything. Look here!" Cyril spoke loudly and firmly. "We want to go somewhere really interesting, where we have a chance of doing something good and kind; we don't want to do it here, but somewhere else. See? Now, then."

The obedient carpet started instantly, and the four children and one bird fell in a heap together, and as they fell were plunged in perfect darkness.

"Are you all there?" said Anthea, breathlessly, through the black dark. Every one owned that he was there.

"Where are we? Oh! how shivery and wet it is! Ugh!—oh!—I've put my hand in a puddle!"

"Has any one got any matches?" said Anthea, hopelessly. She felt sure that no one would have any.

It was then that Robert, with a radiant smile of triumph that was quite wasted in the darkness, where, of course, no one could see anything, drew out of his pocket a box of matches, struck a match and lighted a candle—two candles. And every one, with his mouth open, blinked at the sudden light.

"Well done, Bobs," said his sisters, and even Cyril's natural brotherly feelings could not check his admiration of Robert's foresight.

"I've always carried them about ever since the lone tower day," said Robert, with modest pride. "I knew we should want them some day. I kept the secret well, didn't I?"

"Oh, yes," said Cyril, with fine scorn. "I found them the Sunday after, when I was feeling in your Norfolks for the knife you borrowed off me. But I thought you'd only sneaked them for Chinese lanterns, or reading in bed by."

"Bobs," said Anthea, suddenly, "do you know where we are? This is *the* underground passage, and look there—there's the money and the money-bags, and everything."

By this time the ten eyes had got used to the light of the candles, and no one could help seeing that Anthea spoke the truth.

"It seems an odd place to do good and kind acts in, though," said Jane. "There's no one to do them to."

"Don't you be too sure," said Cyril; "just round the next turning we might find a prisoner who has languished here for years and years, and we could take him out on our carpet and restore him to his sorrowing friends."

"Of course we could," said Robert, standing up and holding the candle above his head to see further off; "or we might find the bones of a poor prisoner and take them to his friends to be buried properly—that's always a kind action in books, though I never could see what bones matter."

"I wish you wouldn't," said Jane.

"I know exactly where we shall find the bones, too," Robert went on. "You see that dark arch just along the passage? Well, just inside there——"

"If you don't stop going on like that," said Jane, firmly, "I shall scream, and then I'll faint—so now then!"

"And I will, too," said Anthea.

Robert was not pleased at being checked in his flight of fancy.

"You girls will never be great writers," he said bitterly. "They just love to think of things in dungeons, and chains, and knobbly bare human bones, and——"

Jane had opened her mouth to scream, but before she could decide how you began when you wanted to faint, the golden voice of the Phœnix spoke through the gloom.

"Peace!" it said; "there are no bones here except the small but useful sets that you have inside you. And you did not invite me to come out with you to hear you talk about bones, but to see you do some good and kind action."

"We can't do it here," said Robert, sulkily.

"No," rejoined the bird. "The only thing we can do here, it seems, is to try to frighten our little sisters."

"He didn't, really, and I'm not so very little," said Jane, rather ungratefully.

Robert was silent. It was Cyril who suggested that perhaps they had better take the money and go.

"That wouldn't be a kind act, except to ourselves; and it wouldn't be good, whatever way you look at it," said Anthea, "to take money that's not ours."

"We might take it and spend it all on benefits to the poor and aged," said Cyril.

"That wouldn't make it right to steal," said Anthea, stoutly.

"I don't know," said Cyril. They were all standing up now. "Stealing is taking things that belong to some one else, and there's no one else."

"It can't be stealing if——"

"That's right," said Robert, with ironical approval; "stand here all day arguing while the candles burn out. You'll like it awfully when it's all dark again—and bony."

"Let's get out, then," said Anthea. "We can argue as we go." So they rolled up the carpet and went. But when they had crept along to the place where the passage led into the topless tower they found the way blocked by a great stone, which they could not move.

"There!" said Robert. "I hope you're satisfied!"

"Everything has two ends," said the Phœnix, softly; "even a quarrel or a secret passage."

So they turned round and went back, and Robert was made to go first with one of the candles, because he was the one who had begun to talk about bones. And Cyril carried the carpet.

"I wish you hadn't put bones into our heads," said Jane, as they went along.

"I didn't; you always had them. More bones than brains," said Robert.

The passage was long, and there were arches and steps and turnings and dark alcoves that the girls did not much like passing. The passage ended in a flight of steps. Robert went up them.

Suddenly he staggered heavily back on to the following feet of Jane, and everybody screamed, "Oh! what is it?"

"I've only bashed my head in," said Robert, when he had groaned for some time; "that's all. Don't mention it; I like it. The stairs just go right slap into the ceiling, and it's a stone ceiling. You can't do good and kind actions underneath a paving-stone."

"Stairs aren't made to lead just to paving-stones as a general rule," said the Phœnix. "Put your shoulder to the wheel."

"There isn't any wheel," said the injured Robert, still rubbing his head.

But Cyril had pushed passed him to the top stair, and was already shoving his hardest against the stone above. Of course, it did not give in the least.

"If it's a trap-door——" said Cyril. And he stopped shoving and began to feel about with his hands. "Yes, there *is* a bolt. I can't move it."

By a happy chance Cyril had in his pocket the oil-can of his father's bicycle; he put the carpet down at the foot of the stairs, and he lay on his back, with his head on the top step and his feet straggling down among his young relations, and he oiled the bolt till the drops of rust and oil fell down on his face. One even went into his mouth—open, as he panted with the exertion of keeping up this unnatural position. Then he tried again, but still the bolt would not move. So now he tied his handkerchief—the one with the bacon-fat and marmalade on it—to the bolt, and Robert's handkerchief to that, in a reef knot, which cannot come undone however much you pull, and, indeed, gets tighter and tighter the more you pull it. This must not be confused with a granny knot, which comes undone if you look at it. And then he and Robert pulled, and the girls put their arms round their brothers and pulled too, and suddenly the bolt gave way with a rusty scrunch, and they all rolled together to the bottom of the stairs—all but the Phœnix, which had taken to its wings when the pulling began.

Nobody was hurt much, because the rolled-up carpet broke their fall; and now, indeed, the shoulders of the boys were used to some purpose, for the stone allowed them to heave it up. They felt it give; dust fell freely on them.

"Now, then," cried Robert, forgetting his head and his temper, "push all together. One, two, three!"

The stone was heaved up. It swung up on a creaking, unwilling hinge, and showed a growing oblong of dazzling daylight; and it fell back with a bang against something that kept it upright. Every one climbed out, but there was not room for every one to stand comfortably in the little paved house where they found themselves, so when the Phœnix had fluttered up from the darkness they let the stone down, and it closed like a trap-door, as indeed it was.

You can have no idea how dusty and dirty the children were. Fortunately there was no one to see them but each other. The place they were in was a little shrine, built on the side of a road that went winding up through yellow-green fields to the topless tower. Below them were fields and orchards, all bare boughs and brown furrows, and little houses and gardens. The shrine was a kind of tiny chapel with no front wall—just a place for people to stop and rest in and wish to be good. So the Phœnix told them. There was an image that had once been brightly coloured, but the rain and snow had beaten in through the open front of the shrine, and the poor image was dull and weather-stained. Under it was written: "St. Jean de Luz. Priez pour nous."[6] It was a sad little place, very neglected and lonely, and yet it was nice, Anthea thought, that poor travellers should come to this little rest-house in the hurry and worry of their journeyings and be quiet for a few minutes, and think about being good. The thought of St. Jean de Luz—who had, no doubt, in his time, been very

6. Pray for us (French). St. Jean de Luz: a Basque fishing village.

good and kind—made Anthea want more than ever to do something kind and good.

"Tell us," she said to the Phœnix, "what is the good and kind action the carpet brought us here to do?"

"I think it would be kind to find the owners of the treasure and tell them about it," said Cyril.

"And give it them *all*?" said Jane.

"Yes. But whose is it?"

"I should go to the first house and ask the name of the owner of the castle," said the golden bird, and really the idea seemed a good one.

They dusted each other as well as they could and went down the road. A little way on they found a tiny spring, bubbling out of the hillside and falling into a rough stone basin surrounded by draggled hart's-tongue ferns, now hardly green at all. Here the children washed their hands and faces and dried them on their pocket-handkerchiefs, which always, on these occasions, seem unnaturally small. Cyril's and Robert's handkerchiefs, indeed, rather undid the effects of the wash. But in spite of this the party certainly looked cleaner than before.

The first house they came to was a little white house with green shutters and a slate roof. It stood in a prim little garden, and down each side of the neat path were large stone vases for flowers to grow in; but all the flowers were dead now.

Along one side of the house was a sort of wide verandah, built of poles and trellis-work, and a vine crawled all over it. It was wider than our English verandahs, and Anthea thought it must look lovely when the green leaves and the grapes were there; but now there were only dry, reddish-brown stalks and stems, with a few withered leaves caught in them.

The children walked up to the front door. It was green and narrow. A chain with a handle hung beside it, and joined itself quite openly to a rusty bell that hung under the porch. Cyril had pulled the bell and its noisy clang was dying away before the terrible thought came to all. Cyril spoke it.

"My hat!" he breathed. "We don't know any French!"

At this moment the door opened. A very tall, lean lady, with pale ringlets like whitey-brown paper or oak shavings, stood before them. She had an ugly grey dress and a black silk apron. Her eyes were small and grey and not pretty, and the rims were red, as though she had been crying.

She addressed the party in something that sounded like a foreign language, and ended with something which they were sure was a question. Of course, no one could answer it.

"What does she say?" Robert asked, looking down into the hollow of his jacket, where the Phœnix was nestling. But before the Phœnix could answer, the whitey-brown lady's face was lighted up by a most charming smile.

"You—you ar-r-re fr-r-rom the England!" she cried. "I love so much the England. Mais entrez—entrez donc tous! Enter, then—enter all. One essuyes his feet on the carpet."

She pointed to the mat.

"We only wanted to ask——"

"I shall say you all that what you wish," said the lady. "Enter only!"

So they all went in, wiping their feet on a very clean mat, and putting the carpet in a safe corner of the verandah.

"The most beautiful days of my life," said the lady, as she shut the door, "did pass themselves in England. And since long time I have not heard an English voice to repeal me the past."

This warm welcome embarrassed every one, but most the boys, for the floor of the hall was of such very clean red and white tiles, and the floor of the sitting-room so very shiny—like a black looking-glass—that each felt as though he had on far more boots than usual, and far noisier.

There was a wood fire, very small and very bright, on the hearth—neat little logs laid on brass fire-dogs. Some portraits of powdered ladies and gentlemen hung in oval frames on the pale walls. There were silver candlesticks on the mantelpiece, and there were chairs and a table, very slim and polite, with slender legs. The room was extremely bare, but with a bright foreign bareness that was very cheerful, in an odd way of its own.

At the end of the polished table a very un-English little boy sat on a footstool in a high-backed, uncomfortable-looking chair. He wore black velvet, and the kind of collar—all frills and lacey—that Robert would rather have died than wear; but then the little French boy was much younger than Robert.

"Oh, how pretty!" said every one. But no one meant the little French boy, with the velvety short knickerbockers and the velvety short hair.

What every one admired was a little, little Christmas-tree, very green, and standing in a very red little flower-pot, and hung round with very bright little things made of tinsel and coloured paper. There were tiny candles on the tree, but they were not lighted yet.

"But, yes—is it not that it is genteel?" said the lady. "Sit down you then, and let us see."

The children sat down in a row on the stiff chairs against the wall, and the lady lighted a long, slim red taper at the wood flame, and then she drew the curtains and lit the little candles, and when they were all lighted the little French boy suddenly shouted, "Bravo, ma tante! Oh, que c'est gentil,"[7] and the English children shouted "Hooray!"

Then there was a struggle in the breast of Robert, and out fluttered the Phœnix—spread his gold wings, flew to the top of the Christmas-tree, and perched there.

"Ah! catch it, then," cried the lady; "it will itself burn—your genteel parrakeet!"

"It won't," said Robert, "thank you."

And the little French boy clapped his clean and tidy hands; but the lady was so anxious that the Phœnix fluttered down and walked up and down on the shiny walnut-wood table.

"Is it that it talks?" asked the lady.

And the Phœnix replied in excellent French. It said, "Parfaitement,[8] madame!"

"Oh, the pretty parrakeet," said the lady. "Can it say still of other things?"

And the Phœnix replied, this time in English, "Why are you sad so near Christmas-time?"

The children looked at it with one gasp of horror and surprise, for the youngest of them knew that it is far from manners to notice that strangers have been crying, and much worse to ask them the reason of their tears. And, of course, the lady began to cry again, very much indeed, after calling the Phœnix a bird without a heart; and she could not find her handkerchief, so Anthea offered hers, which was still very damp and no use at all. She also hugged the lady, and this seemed to be of more use than the handkerchief, so that presently the lady stopped crying, and found her own handkerchief and dried her eyes, and called Anthea a cherished angel.

---

7. Bravo, Aunt! Oh, that's nice.   8. Perfectly.

"I am sorry we came just when you were so sad," said Anthea, "but we really only wanted to ask you whose that castle is on the hill."

"Oh, my little angel," said the poor lady, sniffing, "to-day and for hundreds of years the castle is to us, to our family. To-morrow it must that I sell it—to some strangers—and my little Henri, who ignores all, he will not have never the lands paternal. But what will you? His father, my brother—Mr. the Marquis—has spent much of money, and it the must, despite the sentiments of familial respect, that I admit that my sainted father he also——"

"How would you feel if you found a lot of money—hundreds and thousands of gold pieces?" asked Cyril.

The lady smiled sadly.

"Ah! one has already recounted to you the legend?" she said. "It is true that one says that it is long time; oh! but long time, one of our ancestors has hid a treasure—of gold, and of gold, and of gold—enough to enrich my little Henri for the life. But all that, my children, it is but the accounts of fays——"

"She means fairy stories," whispered the Phœnix to Robert. "Tell her what you have found."

So Robert told, while Anthea and Jane hugged the lady for fear she should faint for joy, like people in books, and they hugged her with the earnest, joyous hugs of unselfish delight.

"It's no use explaining how we got in," said Robert, when he had told of the finding of the treasure, "because you would find it a little difficult to understand, and much more difficult to believe. But we can show you where the gold is and help you to fetch it away."

The lady looked doubtfully at Robert as she absently returned the hugs of the girls.

"No, he's not making it up," said Anthea; "it's true, *true*, TRUE!—and we *are* so glad."

"You would not be capable to torment an old woman?" she said; "and it is not possible that it be a dream."

"It really *is* true," said Cyril; "and I congratulate you very much."

His tone of studied politeness seemed to convince more than the raptures of the others.

"If I do not dream," she said, "Henri come to Manon—and you—you shall come all with me to Mr. the Curate. Is it not?"

Manon was a wrinkled old woman with a red and yellow handkerchief twisted round her head. She took Henri, who was already sleepy with the excitement of his Christmas-tree and his visitors, and when the lady had put on a stiff black cape and a wonderful black silk bonnet and a pair of black wooden clogs over her black cashmere house-boots, the whole party went down the road to a little white house—very like the one they had left—where an old priest, with a good face, welcomed them with a politeness so great that it hid his astonishment.

The lady, with her French waving hands and her shrugging French shoulders and her trembling French speech, told the story. And now the priest, who knew no English, shrugged *his* shoulders and waved *his* hands and spoke also in French.

"He thinks," whispered the Phœnix, "that her troubles have turned her brain. What a pity you know no French!"

"I do know a lot of French," whispered Robert, indignantly; "but it's all about the pencil of the gardener's son and the penknife of the baker's niece—nothing that any one ever wants to say."

"If *I* speak," the bird whispered, "he'll think *he's* mad, too."

"Tell me what to say."

"Say 'C'est vrai, monsieur. Venez donc voir,'"[9] said the Phœnix; and then Robert earned the undying respect of everybody by suddenly saying, very loudly and distinctly—

"Say vray, mossoo; venny dong vwaw."

The priest was disappointed when he found that Robert's French began and ended with these useful words; but, at any rate, he saw that if the lady was mad she was not the only one, and he put on a big beavery hat, and got a candle and matches and a spade, and they all went up the hill to the wayside shrine of St. John of Luz.

"Now," said Robert, "I will go first and show you where it is."

So they prised the stone up with a corner of the spade, and Robert did go first, and they all followed and found the golden treasure exactly as they had left it. And every one was flushed with the joy of performing such a wonderfully kind action.

Then the lady and the priest clasped hands and wept for joy, as French people do, and knelt down and touched the money, and talked very fast and both together, and the lady embraced all the children three times each, and called them "little garden angels," and then she and the priest shook each other by both hands again, and talked, and talked, and talked, faster and more Frenchy than you would have believed possible. And the children were struck dumb with joy and pleasure.

"Get away *now*," said the Phœnix softly, breaking in on the radiant dream.

So the children crept away, and out through the little shrine, and the lady and the priest were so tearfully, talkatively happy that they never noticed that the guardian angels had gone.

The "garden angels" ran down the hill to the lady's little house, where they had left the carpet in the verandah, and they spread it out and said "Home," and no one saw them disappear, except little Henri, who had flattened his nose into a white button against the window-glass, and when he tried to tell his aunt she thought he had been dreaming. So that was all right.

"It is much the best thing we've done," said Anthea, when they talked it over at tea-time. "In the future we'll only do kind actions with the carpet."

"Ahem!" said the Phœnix.

"I beg your pardon?" said Anthea.

"Oh, nothing," said the bird. "I was only thinking!"

CHAPTER VII. MEWS FROM PERSIA

When you hear that the four children found themselves at Waterloo Station quite un-taken-care-of, and with no one to meet them, it may make you think that their parents were neither kind nor careful. But if you think this you will be wrong. The fact is, mother arranged with Aunt Emma that she was to meet the children at Waterloo,[1] when they went back from their Christmas holiday at Lyndhurst. The train was fixed, but not the day. Then mother wrote to Aunt Emma, giving her careful instructions about the day and the hour, and about luggage and cabs and things, and gave the letter to Robert to post. But the hounds happened to meet near Rufus Stone that morning, and what is more, on the way to the meet they met Robert, and Robert met

9. It's true, sir. See for yourself.
1. One of London's train stations, serving southwest England.

them, and instantly forgot all about posting Aunt Emma's letter and never thought of it again until he and the others had wandered three times up and down the platform at Waterloo—which makes six in all—and had bumped against old gentlemen, and stared in the faces of ladies, and been shoved by people in a hurry, and "by-your-leaved" by porters with trucks, and were quite, quite sure that Aunt Emma was not there.

Then suddenly the true truth of what he had forgotten to do came home to Robert, and he said, "Oh, crikey!" and stood still with his mouth open, and let a porter with a Gladstone bag[2] in each hand and a bundle of umbrellas under one arm blunder heavily into him, and never so much as said, "Where are you shoving to now?" or, "Look out where you're going, can't you?" The heavier bag smote him at the knee, and he staggered, but he said nothing.

When the others understood what was the matter I think they told Robert what they thought of him.

"We must take the train to Croydon,"[3] said Anthea, "and find Aunt Emma."

"Yes," said Cyril, "and precious pleased those Jevonses would be to see us and our traps."

Aunt Emma, indeed, was staying with some Jevonses—very prim people. They were middle-aged and wore very smart blouses, and they were fond of *matinées* and shopping, and they did not care about children.

"I know *mother* would be pleased to see us if we went back," said Jane.

"Yes, she would, but she'd think it was not right to show she was pleased, because it's Bob's fault we're not met. Don't I know the sort of thing?" said Cyril. "Besides, we've no tin.[4] No; we've got enough for a growler[5] among us, but not enough for tickets to the New Forest. We must just go home. They won't be so savage when they find we've really got home all right. You know auntie was only going to take us home in a cab."

"I believe we ought to go to Croydon," Anthea insisted.

"Aunt Emma would be out to a dead cert," said Robert. "Those Jevonses go to the theatre every afternoon, I believe. Besides, there's the Phœnix at home, *and* the carpet. I votes we call a four-wheeled cabman."

A four-wheeled cabman was called—his cab was one of the old-fashioned kind with straw in the bottom—and he was asked by Anthea to drive them very carefully to their address. This he did, and the price he asked for doing so was exactly the value of the gold coin grandpapa had given Cyril for Christmas. This cast a gloom; but Cyril would never have stooped to argue about a cab-fare, for fear the cabman should think he was not accustomed to take cabs whenever he wanted them. For a reason that was something like this he told the cabman to put the luggage on the steps, and waited till the wheels of the growler had grittily retired before he rang the bell.

"You see," he said, with his hand on the handle, "we don't want cook and Eliza asking us before *him* how it is we've come home alone, as if we were babies."

Here he rang the bell; and the moment its answering clang was heard, every one felt that it would be some time before that bell was answered. The sound of a bell is quite different, somehow, when there is any one inside the house who hears it. I can't tell you why that is—but so it is.

2. Light traveling bag.
3. A borough of Greater London.
4. Money.
5. Four-wheeled cab.

"I expect they're changing their dresses," said Jane.

"Too late," said Anthea, "it must be past five. I expect Eliza's gone to post a letter, and cook's gone to see the time."

Cyril rang again. And the bell did its best to inform the listening children that there was really no one human in the house. They rang again and listened intently. The hearts of all sank low. It is a terrible thing to be locked out of your own house, on a dark, muggy January evening.

"There is no gas on anywhere," said Jane, in a broken voice.

"I expect they've left the gas on once too often, and the draught blew it out, and they're suffocated in their beds. Father always said they would some day," said Robert cheerfully.

"Let's go and fetch a policeman," said Anthea, trembling.

"And be taken up for trying to be burglars—no, thank you," said Cyril. "I heard father read out of the paper about a young man who got into his own mother's house, and they got him made a burglar only the other day."

"I only hope the gas hasn't hurt the Phœnix," said Anthea. "It *said* it wanted to stay in the bathroom cupboard, and I thought it would be all right, because the servants *never* clean that out. But if it's gone and got out and been choked by gas—— And besides, directly we open the door we shall be choked, too. I *knew* we ought to have gone to Aunt Emma at Croydon. Oh, Squirrel, I wish we had. Let's go *now*."

"Shut up," said her brother, briefly. "There's some one rattling the latch inside."

Every one listened with all his ears, and every one stood back as far from the door as the steps would allow.

The latch rattled, and clicked. Then the flap of the letter-box lifted itself—every one saw it by the flickering light of the gas-lamp that shone through the leafless lime-tree by the gate—a golden eye seemed to wink at them through the letter-slit, and a cautious beak whispered—

"Are you alone?"

"It's the Phœnix," said every one, in a voice so joyous, and so full of relief, as to be a sort of whispered shout.

"Hush!" said the voice from the letter-box slit. "Your slaves have gone a-merry-making. The latch of this portal is too stiff for my beak. But at the side—the little window above the shelf whereon your bread lies—it is not fastened."

"Righto!" said Cyril.

And Anthea added, "I wish you'd meet us there, dear Phœnix."

The children crept round to the pantry window. It is at the side of the house, and there is a green gate labelled "Tradesmen's Entrance," which is always kept bolted. But if you get one foot on the fence between you and next door, and one on the handle of the gate, you are over before you know where you are. This, at least, was the experience of Cyril and Robert, and even, if the truth must be told, of Anthea and Jane. So in almost no time all four were in the narrow gravelled passage that runs between that house and the next.

Then Robert made a back, and Cyril hoisted himself up and got his knickerbock-ered[6] knee on the concrete window-sill. He dived into the pantry head first, as one dives into water, and his legs waved in the air as he went, just as your legs do when you are first beginning to learn to dive. The soles of his boots—squarish muddy patches—disappeared.

"Give me a leg up," said Robert to his sisters.

6. Covered in loose-fitting trousers gathered at the knee.

"No, you don't," said Jane firmly. "I'm not going to be left outside here with just Anthea, and have something creep up behind us out of the dark. Squirrel can go and open the back door."

A light had sprung awake in the pantry. Cyril always said the Phœnix turned the gas on with its beak, and lighted it with a waft of its wing; but he was excited at the time, and perhaps he really did it himself with matches, and then forgot all about it. He let the others in by the back door. And when it had been bolted again the children went all over the house and lighted every single gas-jet they could find. For they couldn't help feeling that this was just the dark dreary winter's evening when an armed burglar might easily be expected to appear at any moment. There is nothing like light when you are afraid of burglars—or of anything else, for that matter.

And when all the gas-jets were lighted it was quite clear that the Phœnix had made no mistake, and that Eliza and cook were really out, and that there was no one in the house except the four children, and the Phœnix, and the carpet, and the black-beetles who lived in the cupboards on each side of the nursery fireplace. These last were very pleased that the children had come home again, especially when Anthea had lighted the nursery fire. But, as usual, the children treated the loving little black-beetles with coldness and disdain.

I wonder whether you know how to light a fire? I don't mean how to strike a match and set fire to the corners of the paper in a fire some one has laid ready, but how to lay and light a fire all by yourself. I will tell you how Anthea did it, and if ever you have to light one yourself you may remember how it is done. First, she raked out the ashes of the fire that had burned there a week ago—for Eliza had actually never done this, though she had had plenty of time. In doing this Anthea knocked her knuckle and made it bleed. Then she laid the largest and handsomest cinders in the bottom of the grate. Then she took a sheet of old newspaper (you ought never to light a fire with to-day's newspaper—it will not burn well, and there are other reasons against it), and tore it into four quarters, and screwed each of these into a loose ball, and put them on the cinders; then she got a bundle of wood and broke the string, and stuck the sticks in so that their front ends rested on the bars, and the back end on the back of the paper balls. In doing this she cut her finger slightly with the string, and when she broke it, two of the sticks jumped up and hit her on the cheek. Then she put more cinders and some bits of coal—no dust. She put most of that on her hands, but there seemed to be enough left for her face. Then she lighted the edges of the paper balls, and waited till she heard the fizz-crack-crack-fizz of the wood as it began to burn. Then she went and washed her hands and face under the tap in the back kitchen.

Of course, you need not bark your knuckles, or cut your finger, or bruise your cheek with wood, or black yourself all over; but otherwise, this is a very good way to light a fire in London. In the real country fires are lighted in a different and prettier way. But it is always good to wash your hands and face afterwards, wherever you are.

While Anthea was delighting the poor little blackbeetles with the cheerful blaze, Jane had set the table for—I was going to say tea, but the meal of which I am speaking was not exactly tea. Let us call it a tea-ish meal. There was tea, certainly, for Anthea's fire blazed and crackled so kindly that it really seemed to be affectionately inviting the kettle to come and sit upon its lap. So the kettle was brought and tea made. But no milk could be found—so every one had six lumps of sugar to each cup instead. The things to eat, on the other hand, were nicer than usual. The boys looked about very carefully, and found in the pantry some cold tongue, bread, butter, cheese, and part of a cold pudding—very much nicer than cook ever made when they were at home. And in the kitchen cupboard was half a Christmassy cake, a pot of strawberry jam, and about a pound of mixed candied fruit, with soft crumbly slabs of delicious sugar in each cup of lemon, orange, or citron.

It was indeed, as Jane said, "a banquet fit for an Arabian Knight."

The Phœnix perched on Robert's chair, and listened kindly and politely to all they had to tell it about their visit to Lyndhurst, and underneath the table, by just stretching a toe down rather far, the faithful carpet could be felt by all—even by Jane, whose legs were very short.

"Your slaves will not return to-night," said the Phœnix. "They sleep under the roof of the cook's step-mother's aunt, who is, I gather, hostess to a large party to-night in honour of her husband's cousin's sister-in-law's mother's ninetieth birthday."

"I don't think they ought to have gone without leave," said Anthea, "however many relations they have, or however old they are; but I suppose we ought to wash up."

"It's not our business about the leave," said Cyril, firmly, "but I simply won't wash up for them. We got it, and we'll clear it away; and then we'll go somewhere on the carpet. It's not often we get a chance of being out all night. We can go right away to the other side of the equator, to the tropical climes, and see the sun rise over the great Pacific Ocean."

"Right you are," said Robert. "I always did want to see the Southern Cross and the stars as big as gas-lamps."

"*Don't* go," said Anthea, very earnestly, "because I *couldn't*. I'm *sure* mother wouldn't like us to leave the house, and I should hate to be left here alone."

"I'd stay with you," said Jane loyally.

"I know you would," said Anthea gratefully, "but even with you I'd much rather not."

"Well," said Cyril, trying to be kind and amiable, "I don't want you to do anything you think wrong, *but——*"

He was silent; this silence said many things.

"I don't see," Robert was beginning, when Anthea interrupted—

"I'm quite sure. Sometimes you just think a thing's wrong, and sometimes you *know*. And this is a know time."

The Phœnix turned kind golden eyes on her and opened a friendly beak to say—

"When it is, as you say, a 'know time,' there is no more to be said. And your noble brothers would never leave you."

"Of course not," said Cyril rather quickly. And Robert said so too.

"I myself," the Phœnix went on, "am willing to help in any way possible. I will go personally—either by carpet or on the wing—and fetch you anything you can think of to amuse you during the evening. In order to waste no time I could go while you wash up.—Why," it went on in a musing voice, "does one wash up teacups and wash down the stairs?"

"You couldn't wash stairs up, you know," said Anthea, "unless you began at the bottom and went up feet first as you washed. I wish cook would try that way for a change."

"I don't," said Cyril, briefly. "I should hate the look of her elastic-side boots sticking up."

"This is mere trifling," said the Phœnix. "Come, decide what I shall fetch for you. I can get you anything you like."

But of course they couldn't decide. Many things were suggested—a rocking-horse, jewelled chessmen, an elephant, a bicycle, a motor-car, books with pictures, musical instruments, and many other things. But a musical instrument is agreeable only to the player, unless he has learned to play it really well; books are not sociable, bicycles cannot be ridden without going out of doors, and the same is true of motor-cars and elephants. Only two people can play chess at once with one set of chessmen (and anyway it's very much too much like lessons for a game), and only one can ride on a rocking-horse. Suddenly, in the midst of the discussion, the Phœnix spread its wings and fluttered to the floor, and from there it spoke.

"I gather," it said, "from the carpet, that it wants you to let it go to its old home, where it was born and brought up, and it will return within the hour laden with a number of the most beautiful and delightful products of its native land."

"What *is* its native land?"

"I didn't gather. But since you can't agree, and time is passing, and the tea-things are not washed down—I mean washed up——"

"I votes we do," said Robert. "It'll stop all this jaw, anyway. And it's not bad to have surprises. Perhaps it's a Turkey carpet, and it might bring us Turkish delight."[7]

"Or a Turkish patrol," said Robert.

"Or a Turkish bath," said Anthea.

"Or a Turkish towel," said Jane.

"Nonsense," Robert urged, "it said beautiful and delightful, and towels and baths aren't *that*, however good they may be for you. Let it go. I suppose it won't give us the slip," he added, pushing back his chair and standing up.

"Hush!" said the Phœnix; "how can you? Don't trample on its feelings just because it's only a carpet."

"But how can it do it—unless one of us is on it to do the wishing?" asked Robert. He spoke with a rising hope that it *might* be necessary for one to go—and why not Robert? But the Phœnix quickly threw cold water on his new-born dream.

"Why, you just write your wish on a paper, and pin it on the carpet."

So a leaf was torn from Anthea's arithmetic book, and on it Cyril wrote in large round-hand the following:

"We wish you to go to your dear native home, and bring back the most beautiful and delightful productions of it you can—and not to be gone long, please.
(Signed) "CYRIL,
"Robert,
"ANTHEA,
"JANE."

Then the paper was laid on the carpet.

"Writing down, please," said the Phœnix; "the carpet can't read a paper whose back is turned to it, any more than you can."

It was pinned fast, and the table and chairs having been moved, the carpet simply and suddenly vanished, rather like a patch of water on a hearth under a fierce fire. The edges got smaller and smaller, and then it disappeared from sight.

"It may take it some time to collect the beautiful and delightful things," said the Phœnix. "I should wash up—I mean wash down."

So they did. There was plenty of hot water left in the kettle, and everyone helped—even the Phœnix, who took up cups by their handles with its clever claws and dipped them in the hot water, and then stood them on the table ready for Anthea to dry them. But the bird was rather slow, because, as it said, though it was not above any

---

7. Candy made of boiled gelatin and dusted with sugar.

"Everyone helped—even the Phœnix."

sort of honest work, messing about with dish-water was not exactly what it had been brought up to. Everything was nicely washed up, and dried, and put in its proper place, and the dish-cloth washed and hung on the edge of the copper to dry, and the tea-cloth was hung on the line that goes across the scullery.[8] (If you are a duchess's child, or a king's, or a person of high social position's child, you will perhaps not know the difference between a dish-cloth and a tea-cloth; but in that case your nurse has been better instructed than you, and she will tell you all about it.) And just as eight hands and one pair of claws were being dried on the roller-towel behind the scullery door there came a strange sound from the other side of the kitchen wall— the side where the nursery was. It was a very strange sound, indeed—most odd, and unlike any other sounds the children had ever heard. At least, they had heard sounds as much like it as a toy engine's whistle is like a steam siren's.

"The carpet's come back," said Robert; and the others felt that he was right.

"But what has it brought with it?" asked Jane. "It sounds like Leviathan, that great beast——"

"It couldn't have been made in India, and have brought elephants? Even baby ones would be rather awful in that room," said Cyril. "I vote we take it in turns to squint through the keyhole."

They did—in the order of their ages. The Phœnix, being the eldest by some thousands of years, was entitled to the first peep. But—

"Excuse me," it said, ruffling its golden feathers and sneezing softly; "looking through keyholes always gives me a cold in my golden eyes."

So Cyril looked.

"I see something grey moving," said he.

8. Small room attached to the kitchen in which dishes are washed. "Dish-cloth": cloth used to wash dishes. "Tea-cloth": cloth used to dry dishes.

"It's a zoological garden of some sort, I bet," said Robert, when he had taken his turn. And the soft rustling, bustling, ruffling, scuffling, shuffling, fluffling noise went on inside.

"*I* can't see anything," said Anthea, "my eye tickles so."

Then Jane's turn came, and she put her eye to the keyhole.

"It's a giant kitty-cat," she said; "and it's asleep all over the floor."

"Giant cats are tigers—father says so."

"No, he didn't. He said tigers were giant cats. It's not at all the same thing."

"It's no use sending the carpet to fetch precious things for you if you're afraid to look at them when they come," said the Phœnix, sensibly. And Cyril, being the eldest, said:

"Come on," and turned the handle.

The gas had been left full on after tea, and everything in the room could be plainly seen by the ten eyes at the door. At least, not everything, for though the carpet was there it was invisible, because it was completely covered by the hundred and ninety-nine beautiful objects which it had brought from its birthplace.

"My hat!" Cyril remarked. "I never thought about its being a *Persian* carpet."

Yet it was now plain that it was so, for the beautiful objects which it had brought back were cats—Persian cats, grey Persian cats, and there were, as I have said, one hundred and ninety-nine of them, and they were sitting on the carpet as close as they could get to each other. But the moment the children entered the room the cats rose and stretched, and spread and overflowed from the carpet to the floor, and in an instant the floor was a sea of moving, mewing pussishness, and the children with one accord climbed to the table, and gathered up their legs, and the people next door knocked on the wall—and, indeed, no wonder, for the mews were Persian and piercing.

"This is pretty poor sport," said Cyril. "What's the matter with the bounders?"

"I imagine that they are hungry," said the Phœnix. "If you were to feed them——"

"We haven't anything to feed them with," said Anthea in despair, and she stroked the nearest Persian back. "Oh, pussies, do be quiet—we can't hear ourselves think."

She had to shout this entreaty, for the mews were growing deafening, "and it would take pounds and pounds' worth of cat's-meat."

"Let's ask the carpet to take them away," said Robert.

But the girls said "No."

"They are so soft and pussy," said Jane.

"And valuable," said Anthea, hastily. "We can sell them for lots and lots of money."

"Why not send the carpet to get food for them?" suggested the Phœnix, and its golden voice became harsh and cracked with the effort it had to make to be heard above the increasing fierceness of the Persian mews.

So it was written that the carpet should bring food for one hundred and ninety-nine Persian cats, and the paper was pinned to the carpet as before.

The carpet seemed to gather itself together, and the cats dropped off it, as rain-drops do from your mackintosh when you shake it. And the carpet disappeared.

Unless you have had one hundred and ninety-nine well-grown Persian cats in one small room, all hungry, and all saying so in unmistakable mews, you can form but a poor idea of the noise that now deafened the children and the Phœnix. The cats did not seem to have been at all properly brought up. They seemed to have no idea of its being a mistake in manners to ask for meals in a strange house—let alone to howl for them—and they mewed, and they mewed, and they mewed, and they mewed, till the children poked their fingers into their ears and waited in silent agony, wondering why the whole of Camden Town did not come knocking at the door to ask what was the matter, and only hoping that the food for the cats would come before the neighbours did—and before all the secrets of the carpet and the Phœnix had to be given away beyond recall to an indignant neighbourhood.

The cats mewed and mewed and twisted their Persian forms in and out and unfolded their Persian tails, and the children and the Phœnix huddled together on the table.

The Phœnix, Robert noticed suddenly, was trembling.

"So many cats," it said, "and they might not know I was the Phœnix. These accidents happen so quickly. It quite un-mans me."

This was a danger of which the children had not thought.

"Creep in," cried Robert, opening his jacket.

And the Phœnix crept in—only just in time, for green eyes had glared, pink noses had sniffed, white whiskers had twitched, and as Robert buttoned his coat he disappeared to the waist in a wave of eager grey Persian fur. And on the instant the good carpet slapped itself down on the floor. And it was covered with rats—three hundred and ninety-eight of them, I believe, two for each cat.

"How horrible!" cried Anthea. "Oh, take them away!"

"Take yourself away," said the Phœnix, "and me."

"I wish we'd never had a carpet," said Anthea, in tears.

They hustled and crowded out of the door, and shut it, and locked it. Cyril, with great presence of mind, lit a candle and turned off the gas at the main.

"The rats'll have a better chance in the dark," he said.

The mewing had ceased. Every one listened in breathless silence. We all know that cats eat rats—it is one of the first things we read in our little brown reading books; but all those cats eating all those rats—it wouldn't bear thinking of.

Suddenly Robert sniffed, in the silence of the dark kitchen, where the only candle was burning all on one side, because of the draught.

"What a funny scent!" he said.

And as he spoke, a lantern flashed its light through the window of the kitchen, a face peered in, and a voice said:

"What's all this row about? You let me in."

It was the voice of the police!

Robert tip-toed to the window, and spoke through the pane that had been a little cracked since Cyril accidentally knocked it with a walking-stick when he was playing at balancing it on his nose. (It was after they had been to the circus.)

"What do you mean?" he said. "There's no row. You listen; everything's as quiet as quiet."

And indeed it was.

The strange sweet scent grew stronger, and the Phœnix put out its beak.

The policeman hesitated.

"They're *musk*-rats," said the Phœnix. "I suppose some cats eat them—but never Persian ones. What a mistake for a well-informed carpet to make! Oh, what a night we're having!"

"Do go away," said Robert, nervously. "We're just going to bed—that's our bedroom candle; there isn't any row. Everything's as quiet as a mouse."

A wild chorus of mews drowned his words, and with the mews were mingled the shrieks of the musk-rats. What had happened? Had the cats tasted them before deciding that they disliked the flavour?

"I'm a-coming in," said the policeman. "You've got a cat shut up there."

"A cat," said Cyril. "Oh, my only aunt! A cat!"

"Come in, then," said Robert. "It's your own look out. I advise you not. Wait a shake, and I'll undo the side gate."

He undid the side gate, and the policeman, very cautiously, came in.

And there in the kitchen, by the light of one candle, with the mewing and the screaming going on like a dozen steam sirens, twenty waiting motor-cars, and half a hundred squeaking pumps, four agitated voices shouted to the policeman four mixed and wholly different explanations of the very mixed events of the evening.

Did you ever try to explain the simplest thing to a policeman?

CHAPTER VIII. THE CATS, THE COW, AND THE BURGLAR

The nursery was full of Persian cats and musk-rats that had been brought there by the wishing carpet. The cats were mewing and the musk-rats were squeaking so that you could hardly hear yourself speak. In the kitchen were the four children, one candle, a concealed Phœnix, and a very visible policeman.

"Now then, look here," said the policeman, very loudly, and he pointed his lantern at each child in turn, "what's the meaning of this here yelling and caterwauling? I tell you you've got a cat here, and someone's a ill-treating of it. What do you mean by it, eh?"

It was five to one, counting the Phœnix; but the policeman, who was one, was of unusually fine size, and the five, including the Phœnix, were small. The mews and the squeaks grew softer, and in the comparative silence, Cyril said:

"It's true. There are a few cats here. But we've not hurt them. It's quite the opposite. We've just fed them."

"It don't sound like it," said the policeman grimly.

"I daresay they're not real cats," said Jane madly, "perhaps they're only dream-cats."

"I'll dream-cat you, my lady," was the brief response of the force.

"If you understand anything except people who do murders and stealings and naughty things like that, I'd tell you all about it," said Robert; "but I'm certain you don't. You're not meant to shove your oar into people's private cat-keepings. You're only supposed to interfere when people shout 'murder' and 'stop thief' in the street. So there!"

The policeman assured them that he should see about that; and at this point the Phœnix, who had been making itself small on the pot-shelf under the dresser, among the saucepan lids and the fish-kettle, walked on tip-toed claws in a noiseless and modest manner, and left the room unnoticed by any one.

"Oh, don't be so horrid," Anthea was saying, gently and earnestly. "We love cats—dear pussy-soft things. We wouldn't hurt them for worlds. Would we, Pussy?"

And Jane answered that of course they wouldn't. And still the policeman seemed unmoved by their eloquence.

"Now, look here," he said, "I'm a-going to see what's in that room beyond there, and——"

His voice was drowned in a wild burst of mewing and squeaking. And as soon as it died down all four children began to explain at once; and though the squeaking and mewing were not at their very loudest, yet there was quite enough of both to make it very hard for the policeman to understand a single word of any of the four wholly different explanations now poured out to him.

"Stow it," he said at last. "I'm a-goin' into the next room in the execution of my duty. I'm a-goin' to use my eyes—my ears have gone off their chumps, what with you and them cats."

And he pushed Robert aside, and strode through the door.

"Don't say I didn't warn you," said Robert.

"It's tigers, *really*," said Jane. "Father said so. I wouldn't go in, if I were you."

But the policeman was quite stony; nothing any one said seemed to make any difference to him. Some policemen are like this, I believe. He strode down the passage, and in another moment he would have been in the room with all the cats and all the rats (musk), but at that very instant a thin, sharp voice screamed from the street outside—

"Murder-murder! Stop thief!"

The policeman stopped, with one regulation boot heavily poised in the air.

"Eh?" he said.

And again the shrieks sounded shrilly and piercingly from the dark street outside.

"Come on," said Robert. "Come and look after cats while somebody's being killed outside." For Robert had an inside feeling that told him quite plainly *who* it was that was screaming.

"You young rip," said the policeman, "I'll settle up with you bimeby."[9]

And he rushed out, and the children heard his boots going weightily along the pavement, and the screams also going along, rather ahead of the policeman; and both the murder-screams and the policeman's boots faded away in the remote distance.

Then Robert smacked his knickerbocker loudly with his palm, and said:

"Good old Phœnix! I should know its golden voice anywhere."

And then every one understood how cleverly the Phœnix had caught at what Robert had said about the real work of a policeman being to look after murderers and thieves, and not after cats, and all hearts were filled with admiring affection.

"But he'll come back," said Anthea, mournfully, "as soon as he finds the murderer is only a bright vision of a dream, and there isn't one at all really."

"No, he won't," said the soft voice of the clever Phœnix, as it flew in. *"He does not know where your house is.* I heard him own as much to a fellow mercenary. Oh! what a night we are having! Lock the door, and let us rid ourselves of this intolerable smell of the perfume peculiar to the musk-rat and to the house of the trimmers of beards. If you'll excuse me, I will go to bed. I am worn out."

It was Cyril who wrote the paper that told the carpet to take away the rats and bring milk, because there seemed to be no doubt in any breast that, however Persian cats may be, they must like milk.

"Let's hope it won't be musk-milk," said Anthea, in gloom, as she pinned the paper face-downwards on the carpet. "Is there such a thing as a musk-cow?" she added anxiously, as the carpet shrivelled and vanished. "I do hope not. Perhaps really it *would* have been wiser to let the carpet take the cats away. It's getting quite late, and we can't keep them all night."

"Oh, can't we?" was the bitter rejoinder of Robert, who had been fastening the side door. "You might have consulted me," he went on. "I'm not such an idiot as some people."

"Why, whatever—"

"Don't you see? We've jolly well *got* to keep the cats all night—oh, get down, you furry beasts!—because we've had three wishes out of the old carpet now, and we can't get any more till to-morrow."

9. I.e., by and by; shortly. "Rip": worthless fellow.

The liveliness of Persian mews alone prevented the occurrence of a dismal silence. Anthea spoke first.

"Never mind," she said. "Do you know, I really do think they're quieting down a bit. Perhaps they heard us say milk."

"They can't understand English," said Jane. "You forget they're Persian cats, Panther."

"Well," said Anthea, rather sharply, for she was tired and anxious, "who told you 'milk' wasn't Persian for milk. Lots of English words are just the same in French—at least I know 'miaw' is, and 'croquet,' and 'fiancé.' Oh, pussies, do be quiet! Let's stroke them as hard as we can with both hands, and perhaps they'll stop."

So every one stroked grey fur till their hands were tired, and as soon as a cat had been stroked enough to make it stop mewing it was pushed gently away, and another mewing mouser was approached by the hands of the strokers. And the noise was really more than half purr when the carpet suddenly appeared in its proper place, and on it, instead of rows of milk-cans, or even of milk-jugs, there was a *cow*. Not a Persian cow, either, nor, most fortunately, a musk-cow, if there is such a thing, but a smooth, sleek, dun-coloured Jersey cow, who blinked large soft eyes at the gas-light and mooed in an amiable if rather inquiring manner.

Anthea had always been afraid of cows; but now she tried to be brave.

"Anyway, it can't run after me," she said to herself. "There isn't room for it even to begin to run."

The cow was perfectly placid. She behaved like a strayed duchess till some one brought a saucer for the milk, and some one else tried to milk the cow into it. Milking is very difficult. You may think it is easy, but it is not. All the children were by this time strung up to a pitch of heroism that would have been impossible to them in their ordinary condition. Robert and Cyril held the cow by the horns; and Jane, when she was quite sure that their end of the cow was quite secure, consented to stand by, ready to hold the cow by the tail should occasion arise. Anthea, holding the saucer, now advanced towards the cow. She remembered to have heard that cows, when milked by strangers, are susceptible to the soothing influence of the human voice. So, clutching her saucer very tight, she sought for words to whose soothing influence the cow might be susceptible. And her memory, troubled by the events of the night, which seemed to go on and on forever and ever, refused to help her with any form of words suitable to address a Jersey cow in.

"Poor pussy, then. Lie down, then, good dog, lie down!" was all that she could think of to say, and she said it.

And nobody laughed. The situation, full of grey mewing cats, was too serious for that.

Then Anthea, with a beating heart, tried to milk the cow. Next moment the cow had knocked the saucer out of her hand and trampled on it with one foot, while with the other three she had walked on a foot each of Robert, Cyril, and Jane.

Jane burst into tears.

"Oh, how much too horrid everything is!" she cried. "Come away. Let's go to bed and leave the horrid cats with the hateful cow. Perhaps somebody will eat somebody else. And serve them right."

They did not go to bed, but they had a shivering council in the drawing-room, which smelt of soot—and, indeed, a heap of this lay in the fender. There had been no fire in the room since mother went away, and all the chairs and tables were in the wrong places, and the chrysanthemums were dead, and the water in the pot nearly dried up. Anthea wrapped the embroidered woolly soft blanket round Jane and herself, while Robert and Cyril had a struggle, silent and brief, but fierce, for the larger share of the fur hearthrug.

"It is most truly awful," said Anthea, "and I *am* so tired. Let's let the cats loose."

"And the cow, perhaps?" said Cyril. "The police would find us at once. That cow would stand at the gate and mew—I mean moo—to come in. And so would the cats. No; I see quite well what we've got to do. We must put them in baskets and leave them on people's doorsteps, like orphan foundlings."

"We've got three baskets, counting mother's work one," said Jane, brightening.

"And there are nearly two hundred cats," said Anthea, "besides the cow—and it would have to be a different-sized basket for her; and then I don't know how you'd carry it, and you'd never find a doorstep big enough to put it on. Except the church one—and——"

"Oh, well," said Cyril, "if you simply *make* difficulties——"

"I'm with you," said Robert. "Don't fuss about the cow, Panther. It's simply *got* to stay the night, and I'm sure I've read that the cow is a remunerating[1] creature, and that means it will sit still and think for hours. The carpet can take it away in the morning. And as for the baskets, we'll do them up in dusters, or pillow-cases, or bath-towels. Come on, Squirrel. You girls can be out of it if you like."

His tone was full of contempt, but Jane and Anthea were too tired and desperate to care; even being "out of it," which at other times they could not have borne, now seemed quite a comfort. They snugged down in the sofa blanket, and Cyril threw the fur hearthrug over them.

"Ah," he said, "that's all women are fit for—to keep safe and warm, while the men do the work and run dangers and risks and things."

"I'm not," said Anthea, "you know I'm not."

But Cyril was gone.

It was warm under the blankets and the hearthrug, and Jane snugged up close to her sister; and Anthea cuddled Jane closely and kindly, and in a sort of dream they heard the rise of a wave of mewing as Robert opened the door of the nursery. They heard the booted search for baskets in the back kitchen. They heard the side door open and close, and they knew that each brother had gone out with at least one cat. Anthea's last thought was that it would take at least all night to get rid of one hundred and ninety-nine cats by twos. There would be ninety-nine journeys of two cats each, and one cat over.

"I almost think we might keep the one cat over," said Anthea. "I don't seem to care for cats just now, but I daresay I shall again some day." And she fell asleep. Jane also was sleeping.

It was Jane who awoke with a start, to find Anthea still asleep. As, in the act of awakening, she kicked her sister, she wondered idly why they should have gone to bed in their boots; but the next moment she remembered where they were.

There was a sound of muffled, shuffled feet on the stairs. Like the heroine of the classic poem, Jane "thought it was the boys," and as she felt quite wide awake, and not nearly so tired as before, she crept gently from Anthea's side and followed the footsteps. They went down into the basement; the cats, who seemed to have fallen into the sleep of exhaustion, awoke at the sound of the approaching footsteps and mewed piteously. Jane was at the foot of the stairs before she saw it was not her brothers whose coming had roused her and the cats, but a burglar. She knew he was

---

1. This malapropism puns on "ruminate" (of cows, to chew the cud; more generally, to meditate) and "remunerate" (pay money).

a burglar at once, because he wore a fur cap and a red and black charity-check comforter, and he had no business where he was.

If you had been stood in Jane's shoes you would no doubt have run away in them, appealing to the police and neighbours with horrid screams. But Jane knew better. She had read a great many nice stories about burglars, as well as some affecting pieces of poetry, and she knew that no burglar will ever hurt a little girl if he meets her when burgling.[2] Indeed, in all the cases Jane had read of, his burglarishness was almost at once forgotten in the interest he felt in the little girl's artless prattle. So if Jane hesitated for a moment before addressing the burglar, it was only because she could not at once think of any remark sufficiently prattling and artless to make a beginning with. In the stories and the affecting poetry the child could never speak plainly, though it always looked old enough to in the pictures. And Jane could not make up her mind to lisp and "talk baby," even to a burglar. And while she hesitated he softly opened the nursery door and went in.

Jane followed—just in time to see him sit down flat on the floor, scattering cats as a stone thrown into a pool splashes water.

She closed the door softly and stood there, still wondering whether she _could_ bring herself to say, "What's 'oo doing here, Mithter Wobber?" and whether any other kind of talk would do.

Then she heard the burglar draw a long breath, and he spoke.

"It's a judgment," he said, "so help me bob if it ain't. Oh, 'ere's a thing to 'appen to a chap! Makes it come 'ome to you, don't it neither? Cats an' cats an' cats. There couldn't be all them cats. Let alone the cow. If she ain't the moral of the old man's Daisy. She's a dream out of when I was a lad—I don't mind 'er so much. 'Ere, Daisy, Daisy?"

The cow turned and looked at him.

"_She's_ all right," he went on. "Sort of company, too. Though them above knows how she got into this downstairs parlour. But them cats—oh, take 'em away, take 'em away! I'll chuck the 'ole show—oh, take 'em away."

"Burglar," said Jane, close behind him, and he started convulsively, and turned on her a blank face, whose pale lips trembled. "I can't take those cats away."

"Lor-lumme!" exclaimed the man; "if 'ere ain't another on 'em. Are you real, miss, or something I'll wake up from presently?"

"I am quite real," said Jane, relieved to find that a lisp was not needed to make the burglar understand her. "And so," she added, "are the cats."

"Then send for the police, send for the police, and I'll go quiet. If you ain't no realler than them cats, I'm done, spunchuck—out of time. Send for the police. I'll go quiet. One thing, there'd not be room for 'arf them cats in no cell as ever _I_ see."

He ran his fingers through his hair, which was short, and his eyes wandered wildly round the roomful of cats.

"Burglar," said Jane, kindly and softly, "if you didn't like cats, what did you come here for?"

"Send for the police," was the unfortunate criminal's only reply. "I'd rather you would—honest, I'd rather."

"I daren't," said Jane, "and besides, I've no one to send. I hate the police. I wish he'd never been born."

2. A tongue-in-cheek reference to sentimental stories such as "Editha's Burglar" (first published in _St. Nicholas Magazine_, 1880), by the Anglo-American writer Frances Hodgson Burnett.

"You've a feeling 'art, miss," said the burglar; "but them cats is really a little bit too thick."

"Look here," said Jane, "I won't call the police. And I am quite a real little girl, though I talk older than the kind you've met before when you've been doing your burglings. And they *are* real cats—and they want real milk—and—— Didn't you say the cow was like somebody's Daisy that you used to know?"

"Wish I may die if she ain't the very spit of her," replied the man.

"Well, then," said Jane—and a thrill of joyful pride ran through her—"perhaps you know how to milk cows?"

"Perhaps I does," was the burglar's cautious rejoinder.

"Then," said Jane, "if you will *only* milk ours—you don't know how we shall always love you."

The burglar replied that loving was all very well.

"If those cats only had a good long, wet, thirsty drink of milk," Jane went on with eager persuasion, "they'd lie down and go to sleep as likely as not, and then the police won't come back. But if they go on mewing like this he will, and then I don't know what'll become of us, or you either."

This argument seemed to decide the criminal. Jane fetched the wash-bowl from the sink, and he spat on his hands and prepared to milk the cow. At this instant boots were heard on the stairs.

"It's all up," said the man, desperately, "this 'ere's a plant. *'Ere's* the police." He made as if to open the window and leap from it.

"It's all right, I tell you," whispered Jane, in anguish. "I'll say you're a friend of mine, or the good clergyman called in, or my uncle, or *anything*—only do, do, do milk the cow. Oh, *don't* go—oh—oh, thank goodness it's only the boys!"

It was; and their entrance had awakened Anthea, who, with her brothers, now crowded through the doorway. The man looked about him like a rat looks round a trap.

"This is a friend of mine," said Jane; "he's just called in, and he's going to milk the cow for us. *Isn't* it good and kind of him?"

She winked at the others, and though they did not understand they played up loyally.

"How do?" said Cyril. "Very glad to meet you. Don't let us interrupt the milking."

"I shall 'ave a 'ead, and a 'arf in the morning, and no bloomin' error," remarked the burglar; but he began to milk the cow.

Robert was winked at to stay and see that he did not leave off milking or try to escape, and the others went to get things to put the milk in; for it was now spurting and foaming in the wash-bowl, and the cats had ceased from mewing and were crowding round the cow, with expressions of hope and anticipation on their whisk-ered faces.

"We can't get rid of any more cats," said Cyril, as he and his sisters piled a tray high with saucers and soup-plates, and platters and pie-dishes, "the police nearly got us as it was. Not the same one—a much stronger sort. He thought it really was a foundling orphan we'd got. If it hadn't been for me throwing the two bags of cat slap in his eye and hauling Robert over a railing, and lying like mice under a laurel-bush——Well, it's jolly lucky I'm a good shot, that's all. He pranced off when he'd got the cat-bags off his face—thought we'd bolted. And here we are."

The gentle samishness of the milk swishing into the hand-bowl seemed to have soothed the burglar very much. He went on milking in a sort of happy dream, while the children got a cup and ladled the warm milk out into the pie-dishes and plates, and platters and saucers, and set them down to the music of Persian purrs and lappings.

"It makes me think of old-times," said the burglar, smearing his ragged coat-cuff across his eyes—"about the apples in the orchard at home, and the rats at threshing-time, and the rabbits and the ferrets, and how pretty it was seeing the pigs killed."

Finding him in this softened mood, Jane said:

"I wish you'd tell us how you came to choose our house for your burglaring to-night. I am awfully glad you did. You *have* been so kind. I don't know what we should have done without you," she added hastily. "We all love you ever so. Do tell us."

The others added their affectionate entreaties, and at last the burglar said:

"Well, it's my first job, and I didn't expect to be made so welcome, and that's the truth, young gents and ladies. And I don't know but what it won't be my last. For this 'ere cow, she reminds me of my father, and I know 'ow 'e'd 'ave 'ided me if I'd laid 'ands on a 'a'penny[3] as wasn't my own."

"I'm sure he would," Jane agreed kindly; "but what made you come here?"

"Well, miss," said the burglar, "you know best 'ow you come by them cats, and why you don't like the police, so I'll give myself away free, and trust to your noble 'earts. (You'd best bail out a bit, the pan's getting fullish.) I was a-selling oranges off of my barrow—for I ain't a burglar by trade, though you 'ave used the name so free—an' there was a lady bought three 'a'porth[4] off me. An' while she was a-pickin' of them out—very careful indeed, and I'm always glad when them sort gets a few over-ripe ones—there was two other ladies talkin' over the fence. An' one on 'em said to the other on 'em just like this:

" 'I've told both gells to come, and they can doss in with M'ria and Jane, 'cause their boss and his missis is miles away and the kids too. So they can just lock up the 'ouse and leave the gas a-burning, so's no one won't know, and get back bright an' early by 'leven o'clock. And we'll make a night of it, Mrs. Prosser, so we will. I'm just a-goin' to run out to pop the letter in the post.' And then the lady what had chosen the three ha'porth so careful, she said: 'Lor, Mrs. Wigson, I wonder at you, and your hands all over suds. This good gentleman'll slip it into the post for yer, I'll be bound, seeing I'm a customer of his.' So they give me the letter, and of course I read the direction what was written on it afore I shoved it into the post. And then when I'd sold my barrowful, I was a-goin' 'ome with the chink[5] in my pocket, and I'm blowed if some bloomin' thievin' beggar didn't nick the lot whilst I was just a-wettin' of my whistle, for callin' of oranges is dry work. Nicked the bloomin' lot 'e did—and me with not a farden[6] to take 'ome to my brother and his missus."

"How awful!" said Anthea, with much sympathy.

"Horful indeed, miss, I believe yer," the burglar rejoined, with deep feeling. "You don't know her temper when she's roused. An' I'm sure I 'ope you never may, neither. And I'd 'ad all my oranges off of 'em. So it came back to me what was wrote on the ongverlope, and I says to myself, 'Why not, seein' as I've been done myself, and if they keeps two slaveys there must be some pickings?' An' so 'ere I am. But them cats, they've brought me back to the ways of honestness. Never no more."

"Look here," said Cyril, "these cats are very valuable—very indeed. And we will give them all to you, if only you will take them away."

"I see they're a breedy lot," replied the burglar. "But I don't want no bother with the coppers. Did you come by them honest now? Straight?"

---

3. Halfpenny. " 'ided": flogged.
4. Three and a half pennies' worth.
5. Coins.
6. I.e., a farthing (quarter of a penny).

"They are all our very own," said Anthea, "we wanted them, but the confidement——"

"Consignment," whispered Cyril.

"——was larger than we wanted, and they're an awful bother. If you got your barrow, and some sacks or baskets, your brother's missus would be awfully pleased. My father says Persian cats are worth pounds and pounds each."

"Well," said the burglar—and he was certainly moved by her remarks—"I see you're in a hole—and I don't mind lending a helping 'and. I don't ask 'ow you come by them. But I've got a pal—'e's a mark on[7] cats. I'll fetch him along, and if he thinks they'd fetch anything above their skins I don't mind doin' you a kindness."

"You won't go away and never come back," said Jane, "because I don't think I *could* bear that."

The burglar, quite touched by her emotion, swore sentimentally that, alive or dead, he would come back.

Then he went, and Cyril and Robert sent the girls to bed and sat up to wait for his return. It soon seemed absurd to await him in a state of wakefulness, but his stealthy tap on the window awoke them readily enough. For he did return, with the pal and the barrow and the sacks. The pal approved of the cats, now dormant in Persian repletion, and they were bundled into the sacks, and taken away on the barrow—mewing, indeed, but with mews too sleepy to attract public attention.

"I'm a fence—that's what I am," said the burglar gloomily. "I never thought I'd come down to this, and all acause er my kind 'eart."

Cyril knew that a fence is a receiver of stolen goods, and he replied briskly:

"I give you my sacred the cats aren't stolen. What do you make the time?"

"I ain't got the time on me," said the pal—"but it was just about chucking-out time[8] as I come by the 'Bull and Gate.' I shouldn't wonder if it was nigh upon one now."

When the cats had been removed, and the boys and the burglar had parted with warm expressions of friendship, there remained only the cow.

"She must stay all night," said Robert. "Cook'll have a fit when she sees her."

"All night?" said Cyril. "Why—it's to-morrow morning if it's one. We can have another wish!"

So the carpet was urged, in a hastily written note, to remove the cow to wherever she belonged, and to return to its proper place on the nursery floor. But the cow could not be got to move on to the carpet. So Robert got the clothes line out of the back kitchen, and tied one end very firmly to the cow's horns, and the other end to a bunched-up corner of the carpet, and said "Fire away."

And carpet and cow vanished together, and the boys went to bed, tired out and only too thankful that the evening at last was over.

Next morning the carpet lay calmly in its place, but one corner was very badly torn. It was the corner that the cow had been tied on to.

CHAPTER IX. THE BURGLAR'S BRIDE

The morning after the adventure of the Persian cats, the musk-rats, the common cow, and the uncommon burglar, all the children slept till it was ten o'clock; and then it was only Cyril who woke; but he attended to the others, so that by half-past ten every one was ready to help to get breakfast. It was shivery cold, and there was but little in the house that was really worth eating.

---

7. One with an astonishing appetite or desire for.   8. I.e., pub closing time (usually 11 P.M.).

Robert had arranged a thoughtful little surprise for the absent servants. He had made a neat and delightful booby trap over the kitchen door, and as soon as they heard the front door click open and knew the servants had come back, all four children hid in the cupboard under the stairs and listened with delight to the entrance— the tumble, the splash, the scuffle, and the remarks of the servants. They heard the cook say it was a judgment on them for leaving the place to itself; she seemed to think that a booby trap was a kind of plant that was quite likely to grow, all by itself, in a dwelling that was left shut up. But the housemaid, more acute, judged that someone must have been in the house—a view confirmed by the sight of the breakfast things on the nursery table.

The cupboard under the stairs was very tight and paraffiny, however, and a silent struggle for a place on top ended in the door bursting open and discharging Jane, who rolled like a football to the feet of the servants.

"Now," said Cyril, firmly, when the cook's hysterics had become quieter, and the housemaid had time to say what she thought of them, "don't you begin jawing us. We aren't going to stand it. We know too much. You'll please make an extra special treacle roley for dinner, and we'll have a tinned tongue."[9]

"I daresay," said the housemaid, indignant, still in her outdoor things and with her hat very much on one side. "Don't you come a-threatening me, Master Cyril, because I won't stand it, so I tell you. You tell your ma about us being out? Much I care! She'll be sorry for me when she hears about my dear great-aunt by marriage as brought me up from a child and was a mother to me. She sent for me, she did, she wasn't expected to last the night, from the spasms going to her legs—and cook was that kind and careful she couldn't let me go alone, so——"

"Don't," said Anthea, in real distress. "You know where liars go to, Eliza—at least if you don't——"

"Liars indeed!" said Eliza. "I won't demean myself talking to you."

"How's Mrs. Wigson?" said Robert, "and *did* you keep it up last night?"

The mouth of the housemaid fell open.

"Did you doss with Maria or Emily?" asked Cyril.

"How did Mrs. Prosser enjoy herself?" asked Jane.

"Forbear," said Cyril, "they've had enough. Whether we tell or not depends on your later life," he went on, addressing the servants. "If you are decent to us we'll be decent to you. You'd better make that treacle roley—and if I were you, Eliza, I'd do a little housework and cleaning, just for a change."

The servants gave in once and for all.

"There's nothing like firmness," Cyril went on, when the breakfast things were cleared away and the children were alone in the nursery. "People are always talking of difficulties with servants. It's quite simple, when you know the way. We can do what we like now and they won't peach.[1] I think we've broken *their* proud spirit. Let's go somewhere by carpet."

"I wouldn't if I were you," said the Phœnix, yawning, as it swooped down from its roost on the curtain pole. "I've given you one or two hints, but now concealment is at an end, and I see I must speak out."

It perched on the back of a chair and swayed to and fro, like a parrot on a swing.

"What's the matter now?" said Anthea. She was not quite so gentle as usual, because she was still weary from the excitement of last night's cats. "I'm tired of

9. I.e., canned beef tongue. "Treacle roley": a rolled pudding made with molasses-and-sugar syrup.
1. Turn informer.

things happening. I shan't go anywhere on the carpet. I'm going to darn my stockings."

"Darn!" said the Phœnix, "darn! From those young lips these strange expressions——"

"Mend, then," said Anthea, "with a needle and wool."

The Phœnix opened and shut its wings thoughtfully.

"Your stockings," it said, "are much less important than they now appear to you. But the carpet—look at the bare worn patches, look at the great rent at yonder corner. The carpet has been your faithful friend—your willing servant. How have you requited its devoted service?"

"Dear Phœnix," Anthea urged, "don't talk in that horrid lecturing tone. You make me feel as if I'd done something wrong. And really it *is* a wishing carpet, and we haven't done anything else to it—only wishes."

"Only wishes," repeated the Phœnix, ruffling its neck feathers angrily, "and what sort of wishes? Wishing people to be in a good temper, for instance. What carpet did you ever hear of that had such a wish asked of it? But this noble fabric, on which you trample so recklessly" (every one removed his boots from the carpet and stood on the linoleum), "this carpet never flinched. It did what you asked, but the wear and tear must have been awful. And then last night—I don't blame you about the cats and the rats, for those were its own choice but what carpet could stand a heavy cow hanging on to it at one corner?"

"I should think the cats and rats were worse," said Robert, "look at all their claws——"

"Yes," said the bird, "eleven thousand nine hundred and forty of them—I daresay you noticed? I should be surprised if these had not left their mark."

"Good gracious," said Jane, sitting down suddenly on the floor, and patting the edge of the carpet softly; "do you mean its *wearing out?*"

"Its life with you has not been a luxurious one," said the Phœnix. "French mud twice. Sand of sunny shores twice. Soaking in southern seas once. India once. Goodness knows where in Persia once. Musk-rat-land once. And once, wherever the cow came from. Hold your carpet up to the light, and with cautious tenderness, if *you* please."

With cautious tenderness the boys held the carpet up to the light; the girls looked, and a shiver of regret ran through them as they saw how those eleven thousand nine hundred and forty claws had run through the carpet. It was full of little holes: there were some large ones, and more than one thin place. At one corner a strip of it was torn, and hung forlornly.

"We must mend it," said Anthea: "never mind about my stockings. I can sew them up in lumps with sewing cotton if there's no time to do them properly. I know it's awful and no girl would who respected herself, and all that; but the poor dear carpet's more important than my silly stockings. Let's go out now this very minute."

So out they all went, and bought wool to mend the carpet; but there is no shop in Camden Town where you can buy wishing-wool, no, nor in Kentish Town either. However, ordinary Scotch heather-mixture fingering[2] seemed good enough, and this they bought, and all that day Jane and Anthea darned and darned and darned. The boys went out for a walk in the afternoon, and the gentle Phœnix paced up and down

_____

2. A kind of wool or yarn used mainly in knitting stockings.

the table—for exercise, as it said—and talked to the industrious girls about their carpet.

"It is not an ordinary, ignorant, innocent carpet from Kidderminster,[3] it said, "it is a carpet with a past—a Persian past. Do you know that in happier years, when that carpet was the property of caliphs, viziers, kings, and sultans, it never lay on a floor?"

"I thought the floor was the proper home of a carpet," Jane interrupted.

"Not of a *magic* carpet," said the Phœnix; "why, if it had been allowed to lie about on floors there wouldn't be much of it left now. No, indeed! It has lived in chests of cedar-wood, inlaid with pearl and ivory, wrapped in priceless tissues of cloth of gold, embroidered with gems of fabulous value. It has reposed in the sandal-wood caskets of princesses, and in the rose-attar-scented treasure-houses of kings. Never, never, had any one degraded it by walking on it—except in the way of business, when wishes were required, and then they always took their shoes off. And *you*——"

"Oh, *don't!*" said Jane, very near tears. "You know you'd never have been hatched at all if it hadn't been for mother wanting a carpet for us to walk on."

"You needn't have walked so much or so hard!" said the bird, "but come, dry that crystal tear, and I will relate to you the story of the Princess Zulieka, the Prince of Asia, and the magic carpet."

"Relate away," said Anthea—"I mean, please do."

"The Princess Zulieka, fairest of royal ladies," began the bird, "had in her cradle been the subject of several enchantments. Her grandmother had been in her day——"

But what in her day Zulieka's grandmother had been was destined never to be revealed, for Cyril and Robert suddenly burst into the room, and on each brow were the traces of deep emotion. On Cyril's pale brow stood beads of agitation and perspiration, and on the scarlet brow of Robert was a large black smear.

"What ails ye both?" asked the Phœnix, and it added tartly that story-telling was quite impossible if people would come interrupting like that.

"Oh, do shut up, for any sake!" said Cyril, sinking into a chair.

Robert smoothed the ruffled golden feathers, adding kindly—

"Squirrel doesn't mean to be a beast. It's only that the *most awful* thing has happened, and stories don't seem to matter so much. Don't be cross. You won't be when you've heard what's happened."

"Well, what *has* happened?" said the bird, still rather crossly; and Anthea and Jane paused with long needles poised in air, and long needlefuls of Scotch heather-mixture fingering wool drooping from them.

"The most awful thing you can possibly think of," said Cyril. "That nice chap—our own burglar—the police have got him, on suspicion of stolen cats. That's what his brother's missis told me."

"Oh, begin at the beginning!" cried Anthea impatiently.

"Well, then, we went out, and down by where the undertaker's is, with the china flowers in the window—you know. There was a crowd, and of course we went to have a squint. And it was two bobbies and our burglar between them, and he was being dragged along; and he said, 'I tell you them cats was *give* me. I got 'em in exchange for me milking a cow in a basement parlour up Camden Town way.'

"And the people laughed. Beasts! And then one of the policemen said perhaps he

3. Town in Worcestershire that gave its name to a kind of patterned carpet made with two different colored cloths originally manufactured there.

could give the name and address of the cow, and he said, no, he couldn't; but he could take them there if they'd only leave go of his coat collar, and give him a chance to get his breath. And the policeman said he could tell all that to the magistrate in the morning. He didn't see us, and so we came away."

"Oh, Cyril, how *could* you?" said Anthea.

"Don't be a pudding-head," Cyril advised. "A fat lot of good it would have done if we'd let him see us. No one would have believed a word we said. They'd have thought we were kidding. We did better than let him see us. We asked a boy where he lived and he told us, and we went there, and it's a little greengrocer's shop, and we bought some Brazil nuts. Here they are." The girls waved away the Brazil nuts with loathing and contempt.

"Well, we had to buy *something*, and while we were making up our minds what to buy we heard his brother's missis talking. She said when he came home with all them miaoulers she thought there was more in it than met the eye. But he *would* go out this morning with the two likeliest of them, one under each arm. She said he sent her out to buy blue ribbon to put round their beastly necks, and she said if he got three months' hard it was her dying word that he'd got the blue ribbon to thank for it; that, and his own silly thieving ways, taking cats that anybody would know he couldn't have come by in the way of business, instead of things that wouldn't have been missed, which Lord knows there are plenty such, and——"

"Oh, STOP!" cried Jane. And indeed it was time, for Cyril seemed like a clock that had been wound up, and could not help going on. "Where is he now?"

"At the police-station," said Robert, for Cyril was out of breath. "The boy told us they'd put him in the cells, and would bring him up before the Beak in the morning. I thought it was a jolly lark last night—getting him to take the cats—but now——"

"The end of a lark," said the Phœnix, "is the Beak."

"Let's go to him," cried both the girls jumping up. "Let's go and tell the truth. They *must* believe us."

"They *can't*," said Cyril. "Just think! If any one came to you with such a tale, you couldn't believe it, however much you tried. We should only mix things up worse for him."

"There must be something we could do," said Jane, sniffing very much—"my own dear pet burglar! I can't bear it. And he was so nice, the way he talked about his father, and how he was going to be so extra honest. Dear Phœnix, you *must* be able to help us. You're so good and kind and pretty and clever. Do, do tell us what to do."

The Phœnix rubbed its beak thoughtfully with its claw.

"You might rescue him," it said, "and conceal him here, till the law-supporters had forgotten about him."

"That would be ages and ages," said Cyril, "and we couldn't conceal him here. Father might come home at any moment, and if he found the burglar here *he* wouldn't believe the true truth any more than the police would. That's the worst of the truth. Nobody ever believes it. Couldn't we take him somewhere else?"

Jane clapped her hands.

"The sunny southern shore!" she cried, "where the cook is being queen. He and she would be company for each other!"

And really the idea did not seem bad, if only he would consent to go.

So, all talking at once, the children arranged to wait till evening, and then to seek the dear burglar in his lonely cell.

Meantime Jane and Anthea darned away as hard as they could, to make the carpet as strong as possible. For all felt how terrible it would be if the precious burglar, while being carried to the sunny southern shore, were to tumble through a hole in the carpet, and be lost for ever in the sunny southern sea.

The servants were tired after Mrs. Wigson's party, so every one went to bed early, and when the Phœnix reported that both servants were snoring in a heartfelt and candid manner, the children got up—they had never undressed; just putting their nightgowns on over their things had been enough to deceive Eliza when she came to turn out the gas. So they were ready for anything, and they stood on the carpet and said—

"I wish we were in our burglar's lonely cell," and instantly they were.

I think every one had expected the cell to be the "deepest dungeon below the castle moat." I am sure no one had doubted that the burglar, chained by heavy fetters to a ring in the damp stone wall, would be tossing uneasily on a bed of straw, with a pitcher of water and a mouldering crust, untasted, beside him. Robert, remembering the underground passage and the treasure, had brought a candle and matches, but these were not needed.

The cell was a little white-washed room about twelve feet long and six feet wide. On one side of it was a sort of shelf sloping a little towards the wall. On this were two rugs, striped blue and yellow, and a water-proof pillow. Rolled in the rugs, and with his head on the pillow, lay the burglar, fast asleep. (He had had his tea, though this the children did not know—it had come from the coffee-shop round the corner, in very thick crockery.) The scene was plainly revealed by the light of a gas-lamp in the passage outside, which shone into the cell through a pane of thick glass over the door.

"I shall gag him," said Cyril, "and Robert will hold him down. Anthea and Jane and the Phœnix can whisper soft nothings to him while he gradually awakes."

This plan did not have the success it deserved, because the burglar, curiously enough, was much stronger, even in his sleep, than Robert and Cyril, and at the first touch of their hands he leapt up and shouted out something very loud indeed.

Instantly steps were heard outside. Anthea threw her arms round the burglar and whispered—

"It's us—the ones that gave you the cats. We've come to save you, only don't let on we're here. Can't we hide somewhere?"

Heavy boots sounded on the flagged passage outside, and a firm voice shouted—

"Here—you—stop that row, will you?"

"All right, governor," replied the burglar, still with Anthea's arms round him; "I was only a-talking in my sleep. No offence."

It was an awful moment. Would the boots and the voice come in? Yes! No! The voice said—

"Well, stow it, will you?"

And the boots went heavily away, along the passage and up some sounding stone stairs.

"Now then," whispered Anthea.

"How the blue Moses did you get in?" asked the burglar, in a hoarse whisper of amazement.

"On the carpet," said Jane, truly.

"Stow that," said the burglar. "One on you I could 'a' swallowed, but four—and a yellow fowl."

"Look here," said Cyril, sternly, "you wouldn't have believed any one if they'd told you beforehand about your finding a cow and all those cats in our nursery."

"That I wouldn't," said the burglar, with whispered fervour, "so help me Bob, I wouldn't."

"Well, then," Cyril went on, ignoring this appeal to his brother, "just try to believe what we tell you and act accordingly. It can't do you any *harm*, you know," he went on in hoarse whispered earnestness. "You can't be very much worse off than you are now, you know. But if you'll just trust to us we'll get you out of this right enough. No one saw us come in. The question is, where would you like to go?"

"I'd like to go to Boolong,"[4] was the instant reply of the burglar. "I've always wanted to go on that there trip, but I've never 'ad the ready at the right time of year."

"Boolong is a town like London," said Cyril, well meaning, but inaccurate, "how could you get a living there?"

The burglar scratched his head in deep doubt.

"It's 'ard to get a 'onest living anywheres nowadays," he said, and his voice was sad.

"Yes, isn't it?" said Jane, sympathetically; "but how about a sunny southern shore, where there's nothing to do at all unless you want to."

"That's my billet,[5] miss," replied the burglar. "I never did care about work—not like some people, always fussing about."

"Did you never like any sort of work?" asked Anthea, severely.

"Lor', lumme, yes," he answered, "gardening was my 'obby, so it was. But father died afore 'e could bind me to a nurseryman, an'——"

"We'll take you to the sunny southern shore," said Jane; "you've no idea what the flowers are like."

"Our old cook's there," said Anthea. "She's queen——"

"Oh, chuck it," the burglar whispered, clutching at his head with both hands. "I knowed the first minute I see them cats and that cow as it was a judgment on me. I don't know now whether I'm a-standing on my hat or my boots, so help me I don't. If you *can* get me out, get me, and if you can't, get along with you for goodness' sake, and give me a chanst to think about what'll be most likely to go down with the Beak in the morning."

"Come on to the carpet, then," said Anthea, gently shoving. The others quietly pulled, and the moment the feet of the burglar were planted on the carpet Anthea wished: "I wish we were all on the sunny southern shore where cook is." And instantly they were. There were the rainbow sands, the tropic glories of leaf and flower, and there, of course, was the cook, crowned with white flowers, and with all the wrinkles of crossness and tiredness and hard work wiped out of her face.

"Why, cook, you're quite pretty!" Anthea said, as soon as she had got her breath after the tumble-rush-whirl of the carpet. The burglar stood rubbing his eyes in the brilliant tropic sunlight, and gazing wildly round him on the vivid hues of the tropic land.

"Penny plain and tuppence coloured!" he exclaimed pensively, "and well worth any tuppence, however hard-earned."

The cook was seated on a grassy mound with her court of copper-coloured savages around her. The burglar pointed a grimy finger at these.

"Are they tame?" he asked anxiously. "Do they bite or scratch, or do anything to yer with poisoned arrows or oyster shells or that?"

"Don't you be so timid," said the cook. "Look'e 'ere, this 'ere's only a dream what

4. Boulogne, a city in northern France; a major   5. Desired post or job.
port for ferry service across the English Channel.

you've come into, an' as it's only a dream there's no nonsense about what a young lady like me ought to say or not, so I'll say you're the best looking fellow I've seen this many a day. And the dream goes on and on, seemingly, as long as you behaves. The things what you has to eat and drink tastes just as good as real ones, and——"

"Look 'ere," said the burglar, "I've come 'ere straight outer the pleece station. These 'ere kids'll tell you it ain't no blame er mine."

"Well, you *were* a burglar, you know," said the truthful Anthea gently.

"Only because I was druv to it by dishonest blokes, as well you knows, miss," rejoined the criminal. "Blowed if this ain't the 'ottest January as I've known for years."

"Wouldn't you like a bath?" asked the queen, "and some white clothes like me?"

"I should only look a juggins[6] in 'em, miss, thanking you all the same," was the reply; "but a bath I wouldn't resist, and my shirt was only clean on week before last."

Cyril and Robert led him to a rocky pool, where he bathed luxuriously. Then, in shirt and trousers he sat on the sand and spoke.

"That cook, or queen, or whatever you call her—her with the white bokay on her 'ed—she's my sort. Wonder if she'd keep company!"

"I should ask her."

"I was always a quick hitter," the man went on; "it's a word and a blow with me. I will."

In shirt and trousers, and crowned with a scented flowery wreath which Cyril hastily wove as they returned to the court of the queen, the burglar stood before the cook and spoke.

"Look 'ere, miss," he said. "You an' me bein' all forlorn-like, both on us, in this 'ere dream, or whatever you calls it, I'd like to tell you straight as I likes yer looks."

The cook smiled and looked down bashfully.

"I'm a single man—what you might call a batcheldore. I'm mild in my 'abits, which these kids'll tell you the same, and I'd like to 'ave the pleasure of walkin' out with you next Sunday."

"Lor'!" said the queen cook, " 'ow sudden you are, mister."

"Walking out means you're going to be married," said Anthea. "Why not get married and have done with it? I would——"

"I don't mind if I do," said the burglar. But the cook said—

"No, miss. Not me, not even in a dream. I don't say anythink ag'in the young chap's looks, but I always swore I'd be married in church, if at all—and, anyway, I don't believe these here savages would know how to keep a registering office, even if I was to show them. No, mister, thanking you kindly, if you can't bring a clergyman into the dream I'll live and die like what I am."

"Will you marry her if we get a clergyman?" asked the match-making Anthea.

"I'm agreeable, miss, I'm sure," said he, pulling his wreath straight. " 'Ow this 'ere bokay do tiddle a chap's ears to be sure!"

So, very hurriedly, the carpet was spread out, and instructed to fetch a clergyman. The instructions were written on the inside of Cyril's cap with a piece of billiard chalk Robert had got from the marker at the hotel at Lyndhurst. The carpet disappeared, and more quickly than you would have thought possible it came back, bearing on its bosom the Reverend Septimus Blenkinsop.

The Reverend Septimus was rather a nice young man, but very much mazed and muddled, because when he saw a strange carpet laid out at his feet, in his own study, he naturally walked on it to examine it more closely. And he happened to stand on

6. A simpleton.

one of the thin places that Jane and Anthea had darned, so that he was half on wishing carpet and half on plain Scotch heather-mixture fingering, which has no magic properties at all.

The effect of this was that he was only half there—so that the children could just see through him, as though he had been a ghost. And as for him, he saw the sunny southern shore, the cook and the burglar and the children quite plainly; but through them all he saw, quite plainly also, his study at home, with the books and the pictures and the marble clock that had been presented to him when he left his last situation.

He seemed to himself to be in a sort of insane fit, so that it did not matter what he did—and he married the burglar to the cook. The cook said that she would rather have had a solider kind of a clergyman, one that you couldn't see through so plain, but perhaps this was real enough for a dream.

And of course the clergyman, though misty, was really real, and able to marry people, and he did. When the ceremony was over the clergyman wandered about the island collecting botanical specimens, for he was a great botanist, and the ruling passion was strong even in an insane fit.

There was a splendid wedding feast. Can you fancy Jane and Anthea, and Robert and Cyril, dancing merrily in a ring, hand-in-hand with copper-coloured savages, round the happy couple, the queen cook and the burglar consort? There were more flowers gathered and thrown than you have ever even dreamed of, and before the children took carpet for home the now married-and-settled burglar made a speech.

"Ladies and gentlemen," he said, "and savages of both kinds, only I know you can't understand what I'm a saying of, but we'll let that pass. If this is a dream, I'm on. If it ain't, I'm onner than ever. If it's betwixt and between—well, I'm honest, and I can't say more. I don't want no more 'igh London society—I've got some one to put my arm around of; and I've got the whole lot of this 'ere island for my allotment,[7] and if I don't grow some broccoli as'll open the judge's eye at the cottage flower shows, well, strike me pink! All I ask is, as these young gents and ladies'll bring some parsley seed into the dream, and a penn'orth[8] o' radish seed, and three-penn'orth of onion, and I wouldn't mind goin' to fourpence or fippence for mixed kale, only I ain't got a brown,[9] so I don't deceive you. And there's one thing more, you might take away the parson. I don't like things what I can see 'alf through, so here's how!" He drained a cocoanut-shell of palm wine.

It was now past midnight—though it was tea-time on the island.

With all good wishes the children took their leave. They also collected the clergyman and took him back to his study and his presentation clock.[1]

The Phœnix kindly carried the seeds next day to the burglar and his bride, and returned with the most satisfactory news of the happy pair.

"He's made a wooden spade and started on his allotment," it said, "and she is weaving him a shirt and trousers of the most radiant whiteness."

The police never knew how the burglar got away. In Kentish Town Police Station his escape is still spoken of with bated breath as the Persian mystery.

As for the Reverend Septimus Blenkinsop, he felt that he had had a very insane fit indeed, and he was sure it was due to overstudy. So he planned a little dissipation, and took his two maiden aunts to Paris, where they enjoyed a dazzling round of museums and picture galleries, and came back feeling that they had indeed seen life.

---

7. A plot rented in a communal garden, generally used to grow vegetables.
8. A penny's worth.

9. I.e., a copper coin (a penny or halfpenny).
1. Given as a gift in a ceremonial presentation.

He never told his aunts or any one else about the marriage on the island—because no one likes it to be generally known if he has had insane fits, however interesting and unusual.

CHAPTER X. THE HOLE IN THE CARPET

"Hooray! hooray! hooray!
Mother comes home to-day;
Mother comes home to-day,
Hooray! hooray! hooray!"

Jane sang this simple song directly after breakfast, and the Phœnix shed crystal tears of affectionate sympathy.

"How beautiful," it said, "is filial devotion!"

"She won't be home till past bedtime, though," said Robert. "We might have one more carpet-day."

He was glad that mother was coming home—quite glad, very glad; but at the same time that gladness was rudely contradicted by a quite strong feeling of sorrow, because now they could not go out all day on the carpet.

"I do wish we could go and get something nice for mother, only she'd want to know where we got it," said Anthea. "And she'd never, never believe the truth. People never do, somehow, if it's at all interesting."

"I'll tell you what," said Robert. "Suppose we wished the carpet to take us somewhere where we could find a purse with money in it—then we could buy her something."

"Suppose it took us somewhere foreign, and the purse was covered with strange Eastern devices, embroidered in rich silks, and full of money that wasn't money at all here, only foreign curiosities, then we couldn't spend it, and people would bother about where we got it, and we shouldn't know how on earth to get out of it at all." Cyril moved the table off the carpet as he spoke, and its leg caught in one of Anthea's darns and ripped away most of it, as well as a large slit in the carpet.

"Well, now you *have* done it," said Robert.

But Anthea was a really first-class sister. She did not say a word till she had got out the Scotch heather-mixture fingering wool, and the darning-needle and the thimble and the scissors, and by that time she had been able to get the better of her natural wish to be thoroughly disagreeable, and was able to say quite kindly—

"Never mind, Squirrel, I'll soon mend it."

Cyril thumped her on the back. He understood exactly how she had felt, and he was not an ungrateful brother.

"Respecting the purse containing coins," the Phœnix said, scratching its invisible ear thoughtfully with its shining claw, "it might be as well, perhaps, to state clearly the amount which you wish to find, as well as the country where you wish to find it, and the nature of the coins which you prefer. It would be indeed a cold moment when you should find a purse containing but three oboloi."

"How much is an oboloi?"

"An obol is about twopence halfpenny," the Phœnix replied.

"Yes," said Jane, "and if you find a purse I suppose it is only because some one has lost it, and you ought to take it to the policeman."

"The situation," remarked the Phœnix, "does indeed bristle with difficulties."

"What about a buried treasure," said Cyril, "and every one was dead that it belonged to?"

"Mother wouldn't believe *that*," said more than one voice.

"Suppose," said Robert—"suppose we asked to be taken where we could find a purse and give it back to the person it belonged to, and they would give us something for finding it?"

"We aren't allowed to take money from strangers. You know we aren't, Bobs," said Anthea, making a knot at the end of a needleful of Scotch heather-mixture fingering wool (which is very wrong, and you must never do it when you are darning).

"No, *that* wouldn't do," said Cyril. "Let's chuck it and go to the North Pole, or somewhere really interesting."

"No," said the girls together, "there must be *some* way."

"Wait a sec," Anthea added. "I've got an idea coming. Don't speak."

There was a silence as she paused with the darning-needle in the air! Suddenly she spoke:

"I see. Let's tell the carpet to take us somewhere where we can get the money for mother's present, and—and—and get it some way that she'll believe in and not think wrong."

"Well, I must say you are learning the way to get the most out of the carpet," said Cyril. He spoke more heartily and kindly than usual, because he remembered how Anthea had refrained from snarking[2] about tearing the carpet.

"Yes," said the Phœnix, "you certainly are. And you have to remember that if you take a thing out it doesn't stay in."

No one paid any attention to this remark at the time, but afterwards every one thought of it.

"Do hurry up, Panther," said Robert; and that was why Anthea did hurry up, and why the big darn in the middle of the carpet was all open and webby like a fishing net, not tight and close like woven cloth, which is what a good, well-behaved darn should be.

Then every one put on his outdoor things, the Phœnix fluttered on to the mantelpiece and arranged its golden feathers in the glass, and all was ready. Every one got on to the carpet.

"Please go slowly, dear carpet," Anthea began; "we like to see where we're going." And then she added the difficult wish that had been decided on.

Next moment the carpet, stiff and raftlike, was sailing over the roofs of Kentish Town.

"I wish——No, I don't mean that. I mean it's a *pity* we aren't higher up," said Anthea, as the edge of the carpet grazed a chimney-pot.

"That's right. Be careful," said the Phœnix, in warning tones. "If you wish when you're on a wishing carpet, you *do* wish, and there's an end of it."

So for a short time no one spoke, and the carpet sailed on in calm magnificence over St. Pancras and King's Cross stations and over the crowded streets of Clerkenwell.

"We're going out Greenwich way," said Cyril, as they crossed the streak of rough, tumbled water that was the Thames. "We might go and have a look at the Palace."

On and on the carpet swept, still keeping much nearer to the chimney-pots than the children found at all comfortable. And then, just over New Cross, a terrible thing happened.

2. Finding fault with.

Jane and Robert were in the middle of the carpet. Part of them was on the carpet, and part of them—the heaviest part—was on the great central darn.

"It's all very misty," said Jane; "it looks partly like out of doors and partly like in the nursery at home. I feel as if I was going to have measles; everything looked awfully rum then, I remember."

"I feel just exactly the same," Robert said.

"It's the hole," said the Phœnix; "it's not measles, whatever that possession may be."

And at that both Robert and Jane suddenly, and at once, made a bound to try and get on to the safer part of the carpet, and the darn gave way and their boots went up, and the heavy heads and bodies of them went down through the hole, and they landed in a position something between sitting and sprawling on the flat leads[3] on the top of a high, grey, gloomy, respectable house whose address was 705, Amersham Road, New Cross.

The carpet seemed to awaken to new energy as soon as it had got rid of their weight, and it rose high in the air. The others lay down flat and peeped over the edge of the rising carpet.

"Are you hurt?" cried Cyril, and Robert shouted "No," and next moment the carpet had sped away, and Jane and Robert were hidden from the sight of the others by a stack of smoky chimneys.

"Oh, how awful!" said Anthea.

"It might have been worse," said the Phœnix. "What would have been the sentiments of the survivors if that darn had given way when we were crossing the river?"

"Yes, there's that," said Cyril, recovering himself. "They'll be all right. They'll howl till some one gets them down, or drop tiles into the front garden to attract the attention of passers-by. Bobs has got my one-and-fivepence—lucky you forgot to mend that hole in my pocket, Panther, or he wouldn't have had it. They can tram it home."

But Anthea would not be comforted.

"It's all my fault," she said. "I *knew* the proper way to darn, and I didn't do it. It's all my fault. Let's go home and patch the carpet with your Etons[4]—something really strong—and send it to fetch them."

"All right," said Cyril; "but your Sunday jacket is stronger than my Etons. We must just chuck mother's present, that's all. I wish——"

"Stop!" cried the Phœnix; "the carpet is dropping to earth."

And indeed it was.

It sank swiftly, yet steadily, and landed on the pavement of the Deptford Road. It tipped a little as it landed, so that Cyril and Anthea naturally walked off it, and in an instant it had rolled itself up and hidden behind a gate-post. It did this so quickly that not a single person in the Deptford Road noticed it. The Phœnix rustled its way into the breast of Cyril's coat, and almost at the same moment a well-known voice remarked—

"Well, I never! What on earth are you doing here?"

They were face to face with their pet uncle—their Uncle Reginald.

"We *did* think of going to Greenwich Palace and talking about Nelson,"[5] said Cyril, telling as much of the truth as he thought his uncle could believe.

"And where are the others?" asked Uncle Reginald.

---

3. A flat roof (usually made of lead).
4. Short broadcloth jacket of a kind originally worn by younger boys at Eton College, one of the oldest private schools in England.

5. Horatio Nelson (1758–1805), English naval hero. Greenwich Palace: location of former ancient palace of English kings and queens and site of the Royal Naval College (established in 1873).

"I don't exactly know," Cyril replied, this time quite truthfully.

"Well," said Uncle Reginald, "I must fly. I've a case in the County Court. That's the worst of being a beastly solicitor.[6] One can't take the chances of life when one gets them. If only I could come with you to the Painted Hall[7] and give you lunch at the 'Ship' afterwards! But, alas! it may not be."

The uncle felt in his pocket.

"*I* mustn't enjoy myself," he said, "but that's no reason why you shouldn't. Here, divide this by four, and the product ought to give you *some* desired result. Take care of yourselves. Adieu."

And waving a cheery farewell with his neat umbrella, the good and high-hatted uncle passed away, leaving Cyril and Anthea to exchange eloquent glances over the shining golden sovereign that lay in Cyril's hand.

"Well!" said Anthea.

"Well!" said Cyril.

"Well!" said the Phœnix.

"Good old carpet!" said Cyril, joyously.

"It *was* clever of it—so adequate and yet so simple," said the Phœnix, with calm approval.

"Oh, come on home and let's mend the carpet. I am a beast. I'd forgotten the others just for a minute," said the conscience-stricken Anthea.

They unrolled the carpet quickly and slyly—they did not want to attract public attention—and the moment their feet were on the carpet Anthea wished to be at home, and instantly they were.

The kindness of their excellent uncle had made it unnecessary for them to go to such extremes as Cyril's Etons or Anthea's Sunday jacket for the patching of the carpet.

Anthea set to work at once to draw the edges of the broken darn together, and Cyril hastily went out and bought a large piece of the marble-patterned American oil-cloth which careful housewives use to cover dressers and kitchen tables. It was the strongest thing he could think of.

Then they set to work to line the carpet throughout with the oil-cloth. The nursery felt very odd and empty without the others, and Cyril did not feel so sure as he had done about their being able to "tram it" home. So he tried to help Anthea, which was very good of him, but not much use to her.

The Phœnix watched them for a time, but it was plainly growing more and more restless. It fluffed up its splendid feathers, and stood first on one gilded claw and then on the other, and at last it said—

"I can bear it no longer. This suspense! My Robert—who set my egg to hatch—in the bosom of whose Norfolk raiment I have nestled so often and so pleasantly! I think, if you'll excuse me——"

"Yes—do," cried Anthea, "I wish we'd thought of asking you before."

Cyril opened the window. The Phœnix flapped its sunbright wings and vanished.

"So *that's* all right," said Cyril, taking up his needle and instantly pricking his hand in a new place.

Of course I know that what you have really wanted to know about all this time is not what Anthea and Cyril did, but what happened to Jane and Robert after they fell

---

6. Lawyer.
7. The building that houses the National Gallery of Naval Art, at Greenwich.

through the carpet on to the leads of the house which was called number 705, Amersham Road.

But I had to tell you the other first. That is one of the most annoying things about stories, you cannot tell all the different parts of them at the same time.

Robert's first remark when he found himself seated on the damp, cold, sooty leads was—

"Here's a go!"

Jane's first act was tears.

"Dry up, Pussy; don't be a little duffer," said her brother, kindly. "It'll be all right."

And then he looked about, just as Cyril had known he would, for something to throw down, so as to attract the attention of the wayfarers far below in the street. He could not find anything. Curiously enough, there were no stones on the leads, not even a loose tile. The roof was of slate, and every single slate knew its place and kept it. But, as so often happens, in looking for one thing he found another. There was a trap-door leading down into the house.

And that trap-door was not fastened.

"Stop snivelling and come here, Jane," he cried encouragingly. "Lend a hand to heave this up. If we can get into the house, we might sneak down without meeting any one, with luck. Come on."

They heaved up the door till it stood straight up, and, as they bent to look into the hole below, the door fell back with a hollow clang on the leads behind, and with its noise was mingled a blood-curdling scream from underneath.

"Discovered!" hissed Robert. "Oh, my cats alive!"

They were indeed discovered.

They found themselves looking down into an attic, which was also a lumber-room. It had boxes and broken chairs, old fenders and picture-frames, and rag-bags hanging from nails.

In the middle of the floor was a box, open, half full of clothes. Other clothes lay on the floor in neat piles. In the middle of the piles of clothes sat a lady, very flat indeed, with her feet sticking out straight in front of her. And it was she who had screamed, and who, in fact, was still screaming.

"Don't!" cried Jane, "please don't! We won't hurt you."

"Where are the rest of your gang?" asked the lady, stopping short in the middle of a scream.

"The others have gone on, on the wishing carpet," said Jane truthfully.

"The wishing carpet?" said the lady.

"Yes," said Jane, before Robert could say, "You shut up!" "You must have read about it. The Phœnix is with them."

Then the lady got up, and picking her way carefully between the piles of clothes she got to the door and through it. She shut it behind her, and the two children could hear her calling "Septimus! Septimus!" in a loud yet frightened way.

"Now," said Robert quickly; "I'll drop first."

He hung by his hands and dropped through the trap-door.

"Now you. Hang by your hands. I'll catch you. Oh, there's no time for jaw. Drop, I say."

Jane dropped.

Robert tried to catch her, and even before they had finished the breathless roll among the piles of clothes, which was what his catching ended in, he whispered—

"We'll hide—behind those fenders and things; they'll think we've gone along the roofs. Then, when all is calm, we'll creep down the stairs and take our chance."

They hastily hid. A corner of an iron bedstead stuck into Robert's side, and Jane had only standing room for one foot—but they bore it—and when the lady came back, not with Septimus, but with another lady, they held their breath and their hearts beat thickly.

"Gone!" said the first lady; "poor little things—quite mad, my dear—and at large! We must lock this room and send for the police."

"Let me look out," said the second lady, who was, if possible, older and thinner and primmer than the first. So the two ladies dragged a box under the trap-door and put another box on the top of it, and then they both climbed up very carefully and put their two trim, tidy heads out of the trap-door to look for the "mad children."

"Now," whispered Robert, getting the bedstead leg out of his side.

They managed to creep out from their hiding-place and out through the door before the two ladies had done looking out of the trap-door on to the empty leads.

Robert and Jane tiptoed down the stairs—one flight, two flights. Then they looked over the banisters. Horror! a servant was coming up with a loaded scuttle.[8]

The children with one consent crept swiftly through the first open door.

The room was a study, calm and gentlemanly, with rows of books, a writing table, and a pair of embroidered slippers warming themselves in the fender. The children hid behind the window-curtains. As they passed the table they saw on it a missionary-box[9] with its bottom label torn off, open and empty.

"Oh, how awful!" whispered Jane. "We shall never get away alive."

"Hush!" said Robert, not a moment too soon, for there were steps on the stairs, and next instant the two ladies came into the room. They did not see the children, but they saw the empty missionary box.

"I knew it," said one. "Selina, it *was* a gang. I was certain of it from the first. The children were not mad. They were sent to distract our attention while their confederates robbed the house."

"I am afraid you are right," said Selina; "and *where are they now?*"

"Downstairs, no doubt, collecting the silver milk-jug and sugar-basin and the punch-ladle that was Uncle Joe's, and Aunt Jerusha's teaspoons. I shall go down."

"Oh, don't be so rash and heroic," said Selina. "Amelia, we must call the police from the window. Lock the door. I *will*—I will——"

The words ended in a yell as Selina, rushing to the window, came face to face with the hidden children.

"Oh, don't!" said Jane; "how can you be so unkind? *We aren't* burglars, and we haven't any gang, and we didn't open your missionary-box. We opened our own once, but we didn't have to use the money, so our consciences made us put it back and—— *Don't!* Oh, I wish you wouldn't——"

Miss Selina had seized Jane and Miss Amelia captured Robert. The children found themselves held fast by strong, slim hands, pink at the wrists and white at the knuckles.

"We've got *you*, at any rate," said Miss Amelia. "Selina, your captive is smaller than mine. You open the window at once and call 'Murder!' as loud as you can."

Selina obeyed; but when she had opened the window, instead of calling "Murder!" she called "Septimus!" because at that very moment she saw her nephew coming in at the gate.

8. A metal pail for carrying coal.
9. A box into which contributions to missionary society funds are placed.

In another minute he had let himself in with his latch-key and had mounted the stairs. As he came into the room Jane and Robert each uttered a shriek of joy so loud and so sudden that the ladies leaped with surprise, and nearly let them go.

"It's our own clergyman," cried Jane.

"Don't you remember us?" asked Robert. "You married our burglar for us—don't you remember?"

"I *knew* it was a gang," said Amelia. "Septimus, these abandoned children are members of a desperate burgling gang who are robbing the house. They have already forced the missionary-box and purloined its contents."

The Reverend Septimus passed his hand wearily over his brow.

"I feel a little faint," he said, "running upstairs so quickly."

"We never touched the beastly box," said Robert.

"Then your confederates did," said Miss Selina.

"No, no," said the curate, hastily. "*I* opened the box myself. This morning I found I had not enough small change for the Mothers' Independent Unity Measles and Croup Insurance payments. I suppose this is *not* a dream, is it?"

"Dream? No, indeed. Search the house. I insist upon it."

The curate, still pale and trembling, searched the house, which, of course, was blamelessly free of burglars.

When he came back he sank wearily into his chair.

"Aren't you going to let us go?" asked Robert, with furious indignation, for there is something in being held by a strong lady that sets the blood of a boy boiling in his veins with anger and despair. "We've never done anything to you. It's all the carpet. It dropped us on the leads. *We* couldn't help it. You know how it carried you over to the island, and you had to marry the burglar to the cook."

"Oh, my head!" said the curate.

"Never mind your head just now," said Robert; "try to be honest and honourable, and do your duty in that state of life!"

"This is a judgment on me for something, I suppose," said the Reverend Septimus, wearily, "but I really cannot at the moment remember what."

"Send for the police," said Miss Selina.

"Send for a doctor," said the curate.

"Do you think they *are* mad, then?" said Miss Amelia.

"I think I am," said the curate.

Jane had been crying ever since her capture. Now she said—

"You aren't now, but perhaps you will be, if—— And it would serve you jolly well right, too."

"Aunt Selina," said the curate, "and Aunt Amelia, believe me, this is only an insane dream. You will realise it soon. It has happened to me before. But do not let us be unjust, even in a dream. Do not hold the children; they have done no harm. As I said before, it was I who opened the box."

The strong, bony hands unwillingly loosened their grasp. Robert shook himself and stood in sulky resentment. But Jane ran to the curate and embraced him so suddenly that he had not time to defend himself.

"You're a dear," she said. "It *is* like a dream just at first, but you get used to it. Now *do* let us go. There's a good, kind, honourable clergyman."

"I don't know," said the Reverend Septimus; "it's a difficult problem. It is such a very unusual dream. Perhaps it's only a sort of other life—quite real enough for you to be mad in. And if you're mad, there might be a dream-asylum where you'd be kindly treated, and in time restored, cured, to your sorrowing relatives. It is very hard to see your duty plainly, even in ordinary life, and these dream-circumstances are so complicated——"

"If it's a dream," said Robert, "you will wake up directly, and then you'd be sorry if you'd sent us into a dream-asylum, because you might never get into the same dream again and let us out, and so we might stay there for ever, and then what about our sorrowing relatives who aren't in the dreams at all?"

But all the curate could now say was, "Oh, my head!"

And Jane and Robert felt quite ill with helplessness and hopelessness. A really conscientious curate is a very difficult thing to manage.

And then, just as the hopelessness and the helplessness were getting to be almost more than they could bear, the two children suddenly felt that extraordinary shrinking feeling that you always have when you are just going to vanish. And the next moment they had vanished, and the Reverend Septimus was left alone with his aunts.

"I knew it was a dream," he cried, wildly. "I've had something like it before. Did you dream it too, Aunt Selina, and you, Aunt Amelia? I dreamed that you did, you know."

Aunt Selina looked at him and then at Aunt Amelia. Then she said boldly—

"What do you mean? We haven't been dreaming anything. You must have dropped off in your chair."

The curate heaved a sigh of relief.

"Oh, if it's only I," he said; "if we'd all dreamed it I could never have believed it, never!"

Afterwards Aunt Selina said to the other aunt—

"Yes, I know it was an untruth, and I shall doubtless be punished for it in due course. But I could see the poor dear fellow's brain giving way before my very eyes. He couldn't have stood the strain of *three* dreams. It *was* odd, wasn't it? All three of us dreaming the same thing at the same moment. We must never tell dear Seppy. But I shall send an account of it to the Psychical Society, with stars instead of names, you know."

And she did. And you can read all about it in one of the society's fat Blue-books.[1]

Of course, you understand what had happened?

The intelligent Phœnix had simply gone straight off to the Psammead, and had wished Robert and Jane at home. And, of course, they were at home at once. Cyril and Anthea had not half finished mending the carpet.

When the joyful emotions of reunion had calmed down a little, they all went out and spent what was left of Uncle Reginald's sovereign in presents for mother. They bought her a pink silk handkerchief, a pair of blue and white vases, a bottle of scent, a packet of Christmas candles, and a cake of soap shaped and coloured like a tomato, and one that was so like an orange that almost any one you had given it to would have tried to peel it—if they liked oranges, of course. Also they bought a cake with icing on, and the rest of the money they spent in flowers to put in the vases.

When they had arranged all the things on a table, with the candles stuck up on a plate ready to light the moment mother's cab was heard, they washed themselves thoroughly and put on tidier clothes.

Then Robert said, "Good old Psammead," and the others said so too.

1. Official reports.

"But, really, it's just as much good old Phœnix," said Robert. "Suppose it hadn't thought of getting the wish!"

"Ah!" said the Phœnix, "it is perhaps fortunate for you that I am such a competent bird."

"There's mother's cab," cried Anthea, and the Phœnix hid and they lighted the candles, and next moment mother was home again.

She liked her presents very much, and found their story of Uncle Reginald and the sovereign easy and even pleasant to believe.

"Good old carpet," were Cyril's last sleepy words.

"What there is of it," said the Phœnix, from the cornice-pole.

CHAPTER XI. THE BEGINNING OF THE END

"Well, I *must* say," mother said, looking at the wishing carpet as it lay, all darned and mended and backed with shiny American cloth, on the floor of the nursery—"I *must* say I've never in my life bought such a bad bargain as that carpet."

A soft "Oh!" of contradiction sprang to the lips of Cyril, Robert, Jane, and Anthea. Mother looked at them quickly, and said—

"Well, of course, I see you've mended it very nicely, and that was sweet of you, dears."

"The boys helped too," said the dears, honourably.

"But, still—twenty-two and ninepence! It ought to have lasted for years. It's simply dreadful now. Well, never mind, darlings, you've done your best. I think we'll have cocoanut matting next time. A carpet doesn't have an easy life of it in this room, does it?"

"It's not our fault, mother, is it, that our boots are the really reliable kind?" Robert asked the question more in sorrow than in anger.

"No, dear, we can't help our boots," said mother, cheerfully, "but we might change them when we come in, perhaps. It's just an idea of mine. I wouldn't dream of scolding on the very first morning after I've come home. Oh, my Lamb, how could you?"

This conversation was at breakfast, and the Lamb had been beautifully good until every one was looking at the carpet, and then it was for him but the work of a moment to turn a glass dish of syrupy blackberry jam upside down on his young head. It was the work of a good many minutes and several persons to get the jam off him again, and this interesting work took people's minds off the carpet, and nothing more was said just then about its badness as a bargain and about what mother hoped for from cocoanut matting.

When the Lamb was clean again he had to be taken care of while mother rumpled her hair and inked her fingers and made her head ache over the difficult and twisted house-keeping accounts which cook gave her on dirty bits of paper, and which were supposed to explain how it was that cook had only fivepence-halfpenny and a lot of unpaid bills left out of all the money mother had sent her for housekeeping. Mother was very clever, but even she could not quite understand the cook's accounts.

The Lamb was very glad to have his brothers and sisters to play with him. He had not forgotten them a bit, and he made them play all the old exhausting games: "Whirling Worlds," where you swing the baby round and round by his hands; and "Leg and Wing," where you swing him from side to side by one ankle and one wrist. There was also climbing Vesuvius. In this game the baby walks up you, and when he is standing on your shoulders, you shout as loud as you can, which is the rumbling of the burning mountain, and then tumble him gently on to the floor, and roll him there, which is the destruction of Pompeii.[2]

"All the same, I wish we could decide what we'd better say next time mother says anything about the carpet," said Cyril, breathlessly ceasing to be a burning mountain.

"Well, you talk and decide," said Anthea; "here, you lovely ducky Lamb. Come to Panther and play Noah's Ark."

The Lamb came with his pretty hair all tumbled and his face all dusty from the destruction of Pompeii, and instantly became a baby snake, hissing and wriggling and creeping in Anthea's arms, as she said—

> "I love my little baby snake,
> He hisses when he is awake,
> He creeps with such a wriggly creep,
> He wriggles even in his sleep."

"Crocky," said the Lamb, and showed all his little teeth. So Anthea went on—

> "I love my little crocodile,
> I love his truthful, toothful smile;
> It is so wonderful and wide,
> I like to see it—from outside."

"Well, you see," Cyril was saying; "it's just the old bother. Mother can't believe the real true truth about the carpet, and——"

"You speak sooth, O Cyril," remarked the Phœnix, coming out from the cupboard where the black-beetles lived, and the torn books, and the broken slates, and odd pieces of toys that had lost the rest of themselves. "Now hear the wisdom of Phœnix, the son of the Phœnix."

"There is a society called that," said Cyril.

"Where is it? And what is a society?" asked the bird.

"It's a sort of joined-together lot of people—a sort of brotherhood—a kind of—well, something very like your temple, you know, only quite different."

"I take your meaning," said the Phœnix. "I would fain see these calling themselves Sons of the Phœnix."

"But what about your words of wisdom?"

"Wisdom is always welcome," said the Phœnix.

"Pretty Polly!" remarked the Lamb, reaching his hands towards the golden speaker.

The Phœnix modestly retreated behind Robert, and Anthea hastened to distract the attention of the Lamb by murmuring—

> "I love my little baby rabbit;
> But oh! he has a dreadful habit
> Of paddling out among the rocks
> And soaking both his bunny socks."

"I don't think you'd care about the sons of the Phœnix, really," said Robert. "I have heard that they don't do anything fiery. They only drink a great deal. Much more

---

2. A city in Italy destroyed by the volcanic eruption of Mt. Vesuvius in 79 B.C.E.

than other people, because they drink lemonade and fizzy things, and the more you drink of those the more good you get."

"In your mind, perhaps," said Jane; "but it wouldn't be good in your body. You'd get too balloony."

The Phœnix yawned.

"Look here," said Anthea; "I really have an idea. This isn't like a common carpet. It's very magic indeed. Don't you think, if we put Tatcho[3] on it, and then gave it a rest, the magic part of it might grow, like hair is supposed to do?"

"It might," said Robert; "but I should think paraffin would do as well—at any rate as far as the smell goes, and that seems to be the great thing about Tatcho."

But with all its faults Anthea's idea was something to do, and they did it.

It was Cyril who fetched the Tatcho bottle from father's washhand-stand. But the bottle had not much in it.

"We mustn't take it all," Jane said, "in case father's hair began to come off suddenly. If he hadn't anything to put on it, it might all drop off before Eliza had time to get round to the chemist's[4] for another bottle. It would be dreadful to have a bald father, and it would all be our fault."

"And wigs are very expensive, I believe," said Anthea. "Look here, leave enough in the bottle to wet father's head all over with in case any emergency emerges—and let's make up with paraffin. I expect it's the smell that does the good really—and the smell's exactly the same."

So a small teaspoonful of the Tatcho was put on the edges of the worst darn in the carpet and rubbed carefully into the roots of the hairs of it, and all the parts that there was not enough Tatcho for had paraffin rubbed into them with a piece of flannel. Then the flannel was burned. It made a gay flame, which delighted the Phœnix and the Lamb.

"How often," said mother, opening the door—"how often am I to tell you that you are not to play with paraffin? What have you been doing?"

"We have burnt a paraffiny rag," Anthea answered.

It was no use telling mother what they had done to the carpet. She did not know it was a magic carpet, and no one wants to be laughed at for trying to mend an ordinary carpet with lamp-oil.

"Well, don't do it again," said mother. "And now, away with melancholy! Father has sent a telegram. Look!" She held it out, and the children, holding it by its yielding corners, read—

"Box for kiddies at Garrick. Stalls for us, Haymarket. Meet Charing Cross,[5] 6.30."

"That means," said mother, "that you're going to see 'The Water Babies'[6] all by your happy selves, and father and I will take you and fetch you. Give me the Lamb, dear, and you and Jane put clean lace in your red evening frocks, and I shouldn't wonder if you found they wanted ironing. This paraffin smell is ghastly. Run and get out your frocks."

The frocks did want ironing—wanted it rather badly, as it happened; for, being of tomato-coloured Liberty silk, they had been found very useful for *tableau vivants*

---

3. Brand name of a hair restorer.
4. Pharmacist's.
5. London train station near Trafalgar Square. Garrick: London theatre on Charing Cross Road. Haymarket: the Theatre Royal Haymarket, a few blocks from the Garrick Theatre.

6. There have been a number of dramatizations of the children's novel *The Water-Babies* (1863) by Charles Kingsley; the one performed at the Garrick in 1903 was by Rutland Barrington, with music by Frederick Rosse.

when a red dress was required for Cardinal Richelieu.[7] They were very nice *tableaux*, these, and I wish I could tell you about them; but one cannot tell everything in a story. You would have been specially interested in hearing about the *tableau* of the Princes in the Tower,[8] when one of the pillows burst, and the youthful Princes were so covered with feathers that the picture might very well have been called "Michaelmas Eve; or, Plucking the Geese."

Ironing the dresses and sewing the lace in occupied some time, and no one was dull, because there was the theatre to look forward to, and also the possible growth of hairs on the carpet, for which every one kept looking anxiously. By four o'clock Jane was almost sure that several hairs were beginning to grow.

The Phœnix perched on the fender, and its conversation, as usual, was entertaining and instructive—like school prizes are said to be. But it seemed a little absent-minded, and even a little sad.

"Don't you feel well, Phœnix, dear?" asked Anthea, stooping to take an iron off the fire.

"I am not sick," replied the golden bird, with a gloomy shake of the head; "but I am getting old."

"Why, you've hardly been hatched any time at all."

"Time," remarked the Phœnix, "is measured by heart-beats. I'm sure the palpitations I've had since I've known you are enough to blanch the feathers of any bird."

"But I thought you lived five hundred years," said Robert, "and you've hardly begun this set of years. Think of all the time that's before you."

"Time," said the Phœnix, "is, as you are probably aware, merely a convenient fiction. There is no such thing as time. I have lived in these two months at a pace which generously counterbalances five hundred years of life in the desert. I am old, I am weary. I feel as if I ought to lay my egg, and lay me down to my fiery sleep. But unless I'm careful I shall be hatched again instantly, and that is a misfortune which I really do not think I *could* endure. But do not let me intrude these desperate personal reflections on your youthful happiness. What is the show at the theatre to-night? Wrestlers? Gladiators? A combat of camelopards and unicorns?"

"I don't think so," said Cyril; "it's called 'The Water Babies,' and if it's like the book there isn't any gladiating in it. There are chimney-sweeps and professors, and a lobster and an otter and a salmon, and children living in the water."

"It sounds chilly." The Phœnix shivered, and went to sit on the tongs.

"I don't suppose there will be *real* water," said Jane. "And theatres are very warm and pretty, with a lot of gold and lamps. Wouldn't you like to come with us?"

"*I* was just going to say that," said Robert, in injured tones, "only I know how rude it is to interrupt. Do come, Phoenix, old chap; it will cheer you up. It'll make you laugh like anything. Mr. Bourchier[9] always makes ripping plays. You ought to have seen 'Shock-headed Peter'[1] last year."

"Your words are strange," said the Phoenix, "but I will come with you. The revels of this Bourchier, of whom you speak, may help me to forget the weight of my years."

---

7. Armand-Jean du Plessis (1585–1642), French statesman and cardinal who was the chief minister of Louis XIII. *Tableau vivants*: "living pictures" (French); a form of entertainment in which participants dress up and silently pose to re-create well-known paintings, statues, or scenes.
8. The nephews of Richard III (1452–1485; r. 1483–85) who were imprisoned in the Tower of London and murdered, probably by Richard's orders.
9. Arthur Bourchier (1863–1927), a British actor who became manager of the Garrick Theatre in 1901.
1. A dramatization of *Struwwelpeter* (1844), the absurd and macabre cautionary tales by the German physician and poet Heinrich Hoffmann.

So that evening the Phœnix snugged inside the waistcoat of Robert's Etons—a very tight fit it seemed both to Robert and to the Phœnix—and was taken to the play.

Robert had to pretend to be cold at the glittering, many-mirrored restaurant where they all had dinner, with father in evening dress, with a very shiny white shirt-front, and mother looking lovely in her grey evening dress, that changes into pink and green when she moves. Robert pretended that he was too cold to take off his great-coat, and so sat sweltering through what would otherwise have been a most thrilling meal. He felt that he was a blot on the smart beauty of the family, and he hoped the Phœnix knew what he was suffering for its sake. Of course, we are all pleased to suffer for the sake of others, but we like them to know it—unless we are the very best and noblest kind of people, and Robert was just ordinary.

Father was full of jokes and fun, and everyone laughed all the time, even with their mouths full, which is not manners. Robert thought father would not have been quite so funny about his keeping his overcoat on if father had known all the truth. And there Robert was probably right.

When dinner was finished to the last grape and the last paddle in the finger glasses—for it was a really truly grown-up dinner—the children were taken to the theatre, guided to a box close to the stage, and left.

Father's parting words were: "Now, don't you stir out of this box, whatever you do. I shall be back before the end of the play. Be good and you will be happy. Is this zone torrid enough for the abandonment of great-coats, Bobs? No? Well, then, I should say you were sickening for something—mumps or measles or thrush or teething. Good-bye."

He went, and Robert was at last able to remove his coat, mop his perspiring brow, and release the crushed and dishevelled Phœnix. Robert had to arrange his damp hair at the looking-glass at the back of the box, and the Phœnix had to preen its disordered feathers for some time before either of them was fit to be seen.

They were very, very early. When the lights went up fully, the Phœnix, balancing itself on the gilded back of a chair, swayed in ecstasy.

"How fair a scene is this!" it murmured; "how far fairer than my temple! Or have I guessed aright? Have you brought me hither to lift up my heart with emotions of joyous surprise? Tell me, my Robert, is it not that this, *this* is my true temple, and the other was but a humble shrine frequented by outcasts?"

"I don't know about outcasts," said Robert, "but you can call this your temple if you like. Hush! the music is beginning."

I am not going to tell you about the play. As I said before, one can't tell everything, and no doubt you saw "The Water Babies" yourselves. If you did not it was a shame, or, rather, a pity.

What I must tell you is that, though Cyril and Jane and Robert and Anthea enjoyed it as much as any children possibly could, the pleasure of the Phœnix was far, far greater than theirs.

"This is indeed my temple," it said again and again. "What radiant rites! And all to do honour to me!"

The songs in the play it took to be hymns in its honour. The choruses were choric songs in its praise. The electric lights, it said, were magic torches lighted for its sake, and it was so charmed with the footlights that the children could hardly persuade it to sit still. But when the limelight[2] was shown it could contain its approval no longer.

---

2. Spotlight.

It flapped its golden wings, and cried in a voice that could be heard all over the theatre: "Well done, my servants! Ye have my favour and my countenance!"

Little Tom on the stage stopped short in what he was saying. A deep breath was drawn by hundreds of lungs, every eye in the house turned to the box where the luckless children cringed, and most people hissed, or said, "Shish!" or "Turn them out!"

Then the play went on, and an attendant presently came to the box and spoke wrathfully.

"It wasn't us, indeed it wasn't," said Anthea, earnestly; "it was the bird."

The man said well, then, they must keep their bird very quiet.

"Disturbing every one like this," he said.

"It won't do it again," said Robert, glancing imploringly at the golden bird; "I'm sure it won't."

"You have my leave to depart," said the Phœnix gently.

"Well, he is a beauty, and no mistake," said the attendant, "only I'd cover him up during the acts. It upsets the performance."

And he went.

"Don't speak again, there's a dear," said Anthea; "you wouldn't like to interfere with your own temple, would you?"

So now the Phœnix was quiet, but it kept whispering to the children. It wanted to know why there was no altar, no fire, no incense, and became so excited and fretful and tiresome that four at least of the party of five wished deeply that it had been left at home.

What happened next was entirely the fault of the Phœnix. It was not in the least the fault of the theatre people, and no one could ever understand afterwards how it did happen. No one, that is, except the guilty bird itself and the four children. The Phœnix was balancing itself on the gilt back of the chair, swaying backwards and forwards and up and down, as you may see your own domestic parrot do. I mean the grey one with the red tail. All eyes were on the stage, where the lobster was delighting the audience with that gem of a song, "If you can't walk straight, walk sideways!" when the Phœnix murmured warmly:

"No altar, no fire, no incense!" and then, before any of the children could even begin to think of stopping it, it spread its bright wings and swept round the theatre, brushing its gleaming feathers against delicate hangings and gilded woodwork.

It seemed to have made but one circular wingsweep, such as you may see a gull make over grey water on a stormy day. Next moment it was perched again on the chair-back—and all round the theatre, where it had passed, little sparks shone like tinsel seeds, then little smoke wreaths curled up like growing plants—little flames opened like flower-buds.

People whispered—then people shrieked.

"Fire! Fire!" The curtain went down—the lights went up.

"Fire!" cried every one, and made for the doors.

"A magnificent idea!" said the Phœnix, complacently. "An enormous altar—fire supplied free of charge. Doesn't the incense smell delicious?" The only smell was the stifling smell of smoke, of burning silk, or scorching varnish.

The little flames had opened now into great flame-flowers. The people in the theatre were shouting and pressing towards the doors.

"Oh, how *could* you!" cried Jane. "Let's get out."

"Father said stay here," said Anthea, very pale, and trying to speak in her ordinary voice.

"He didn't mean stay and be roasted," said Robert. "No boys on burning decks for me,[3] thank you."

"Not much," said Cyril, and he opened the door of the box.

But a fierce waft of smoke and hot air made him shut it again. It was not possible to get out that way.

They looked over the front of the box. Could they climb down?

It would be possible, certainly; but would they be much better off?

"Look at the people," moaned Anthea; "we couldn't get through." And, indeed, the crowd round the doors looked as thick as flies in the jam-making season.

"I wish we'd never seen the Phœnix," cried Jane.

Even at that awful moment Robert looked round to see if the bird had overheard a speech which, however natural, was hardly polite or grateful.

The Phœnix was gone.

"Look here," said Cyril, "I've read about fires in papers; I'm sure it's all right. Let's wait here, as father said."

"We can't do anything else," said Anthea bitterly.

"Look here," said Robert, "I'm *not* frightened—no, I'm not. The Phœnix has never been a skunk yet, and I'm certain it'll see us through somehow. I believe in the Phœnix!"

"The Phœnix thanks you, O Robert," said a golden voice at its feet, and there was the Phœnix itself, on the Wishing Carpet.

"Quick!" it said. "Stand on those portions of the carpet which are truly antique and authentic—and——"

A sudden jet of flame stopped its words. Alas! the Phœnix had unconsciously warmed to its subject, and in the unintentional heat of the moment had set fire to the paraffin with which that morning the children had anointed the carpet. It burned merrily. The children tried in vain to stamp it out. They had to stand back and let it burn itself out. When the paraffin had burned away it was found that it had taken with it all the darns of Scotch heather-mixture fingering. Only the fabric of the old carpet was left—and that was full of holes.

"Come," said the Phœnix, "I'm cool now."

The four children got on to what was left of the carpet. Very careful they were not to leave a leg or a hand hanging over one of the holes. It was very hot—the theatre was a pit of fire. Every one else had got out.

Jane had to sit on Anthea's lap.

"Home!" said Cyril, and instantly the cool draught from under the nursery door played upon their legs as they sat. They were all on the carpet still, and the carpet was lying in its proper place on the nursery floor, as calm and unmoved as though it had never been to the theatre or taken part in a fire in its life.

Four long breaths of deep relief were instantly breathed. The draught which they had never liked before was for the moment quite pleasant. And they were safe. And every one else was safe. The theatre had been quite empty when they left. Every one was sure of that.

They presently found themselves all talking at once. Somehow none of their adventures had given them so much to talk about. None other had seemed so real.

"Did you notice——?" they said, and "Do you remember——?"

3. An allusion to the much-anthologized poem "Casabianca" (1826) by Felicia Hemans, which celebrates the heroism of a boy who died because he would not leave a doomed ship without the permission of his father, its commander. The poem begins "The boy stood on the burning deck."

When suddenly Anthea's face turned pale under the dirt which it had collected on it during the fire.

"Oh," she cried, "mother and father! Oh, how awful! They'll think we're burned to cinders. Oh, let's go this minute and tell them we aren't."

"We should only miss them," said the sensible Cyril.

"Well—*you* go then," said Anthea, "or I will. Only do wash your face first. Mother will be sure to think you are burnt to a cinder if she sees you as black as that, and she'll faint or be ill or something. Oh, I wish we'd never got to know that Phœnix."

"Hush!" said Robert; "it's no use being rude to the bird. I suppose it can't help its nature. Perhaps we'd better wash too. Now I come to think of it my hands are rather—"

No one had noticed the Phœnix since it had bidden them to step on the carpet. And no one noticed that no one had noticed.

All were partially clean, and Cyril was just plunging into his great-coat to go and look for his parents—he, and not unjustly, called it looking for a needle in a bundle of hay—when the sound of father's latchkey in the front door sent every one bounding up the stairs.

"Are you all safe?" cried mother's voice; "are you all safe?" and the next moment she was kneeling on the linoleum of the hall, trying to kiss four damp children at once, and laughing and crying by turns, while father stood looking on and saying he was blessed or something.

"But how did you guess we'd come home," said Cyril, later, when every one was calm enough for talking.

"Well, it was rather a rum thing. We heard the Garrick was on fire, and of course we went straight there," said father, briskly. "We couldn't find you, of course—and we couldn't get in—but the firemen told us every one was safely out. And then I heard a voice at my ear say, 'Cyril, Anthea, Robert, and Jane'—and something touched me on the shoulder. It was a great yellow pigeon, and it got in the way of my seeing who'd spoken. It fluttered off, and then some one said in the other ear, 'They're safe at home'; and when I turned again, to see who it was speaking, hanged if there wasn't that confounded pigeon on my other shoulder. Dazed by the fire, I suppose. Your mother said it was the voice of——"

"I said it was the bird that spoke," said mother, "and so it was. Or at least I thought so then. It wasn't a pigeon. It was an orange-coloured cockatoo. I don't care who it was that spoke. It was true—and you're safe."

Mother began to cry again, and father said bed was a good place after the pleasures of the stage.

So every one went there.

Robert had a talk to the Phœnix that night.

"Oh, very well," said the bird, when Robert had said what he felt, "didn't you know that I had power over fire? Do not distress yourself. I, like my high priests in Lombard Street, can undo the work of flames. Kindly open the casement."

It flew out.

That was why the papers said next day that the fire at the theatre had done less damage than had been anticipated. As a matter of fact it had done none, for the Phœnix spent the night in putting things straight. How the management accounted for this, and how many of the theatre officials still believe that they were mad on that night will never be known.

Next day mother saw the burnt holes in the carpet.

"It caught where it was paraffiny," said Anthea.

"I must get rid of that carpet at once," said mother.

But what the children said in sad whispers to each other, as they pondered over last night's events, was:

"We must get rid of that Phœnix."

CHAPTER XII. THE END OF THE END

"Egg, toast, tea, milk, tea-cup and saucer, egg-spoon, knife, butter—that's all, I think," remarked Anthea, as she put the last touches to mother's breakfast-tray, and went very carefully up the stairs, feeling for every step with her toes, and holding on to the tray with all her fingers. She crept into mother's room and set the tray on a chair. Then she pulled one of the blinds up very softly.

"Is your head better, mammy dear?" she asked, in the soft little voice that she kept expressly for mother's headaches. "I've brought your brekkie, and I've put the little cloth with clover-leaves on it, the one I made you."

"That's very nice," said mother sleepily.

Anthea knew exactly what to do for mothers with headaches who had breakfast in bed. She fetched warm water and put just enough eau de Cologne in it, and bathed mother's face and hands with the sweet-scented water. Then mother was able to think about breakfast.

"But what's the matter with my girl?" she asked, when her eyes got used to the light.

"Oh, I'm so sorry you're ill," Anthea said. "It's that horrible fire and you being so frightened. Father said so. And we all feel as if it was our faults. I can't explain, but——"

"It wasn't your fault a bit, you darling goosie," mother said. "How could it be?"

"That's just what I can't tell you," said Anthea. "I haven't got a futile brain like you and father, to think of ways of explaining everything."

Mother laughed.

"My futile brain—or did you mean fertile?—anyway, it feels very stiff and sore this morning—but I shall be quite all right by and by. And don't be a silly little pet girl. The fire wasn't your faults. No; I don't want the egg, dear. I'll go to sleep again, I think. Don't you worry. And tell cook not to bother me about meals. You can order what you like for lunch."

Anthea closed the door very mousily, and instantly went downstairs and ordered what she liked for lunch. She ordered a pair of turkeys, a large plum-pudding, cheese-cakes, and almonds and raisins.

Cook told her to go along, do. And she might as well not have ordered anything, for when lunch came in it was just hashed mutton and semolina pudding, and cook had forgotten the sippets[4] for the mutton hash and the semolina pudding was burnt.

When Anthea rejoined the others she found them all plunged in the gloom where she was herself. For every one knew that the days of the carpet were now numbered. Indeed, so worn was it that you could almost have numbered its threads.

So that now, after nearly a month of magic happenings, the time was at hand when life would have to go on in the dull, ordinary way and Jane, Robert, Anthea, and Cyril would be just in the same position as the other children who live in Camden Town, the children whom these four had so often pitied, and perhaps a little despised.

"We shall be just like them," Cyril said.

---

4. Pieces of toasted or fried bread for dipping into gravy.

"Except," said Robert, "that we shall have more things to remember and be sorry we haven't got."

"Mother's going to send away the carpet as soon as she's well enough to see about that cocoanut matting. Fancy *us* with cocoanut matting—us! And we've walked under live cocoanut-trees on the island where you can't have whooping-cough."

"Pretty island," said the Lamb; "paint-box sands and sea all shiny sparkly."

His brothers and sisters had often wondered whether he remembered that island. Now they knew that he did.

"Yes," said Cyril; "no more cheap return trips by carpet for us—that's a dead cert."

They were all talking about the carpet, but what they were all thinking about was the Phœnix.

The golden bird had been so kind, so friendly, so polite, so instructive—and now it had set fire to a theatre and made mother ill.

Nobody blamed the bird. It had acted in a perfectly natural manner. But every one saw that it must not be asked to prolong its visit. Indeed, in plain English it must be asked to go!

The four children felt like base spies and treacherous friends; and each in his mind was saying who ought not to be the one to tell the Phœnix that there could no longer be a place for it in that happy home in Camden Town. Each child was quite sure that one of them ought to speak out in a fair and manly way, but nobody wanted to be the one.

They could not talk the whole thing over as they would have liked to do, because the Phœnix itself was in the cupboard, among the blackbeetles and the odd shoes and the broken chessmen.

But Anthea tried.

"It's very horrid. I do hate thinking things about people, and not being able to say the things you're thinking because of the way they would feel when they thought what things you were thinking, and wondered what they'd done to make you think things like that, and why you were thinking them."

Anthea was so anxious that the Phœnix should not understand what she said that she made a speech completely baffling to all. It was not till she pointed to the cupboard in which all believed the Phœnix to be that even Cyril understood.

"Yes," he said, while Jane and Robert were trying to tell each other how deeply they didn't understand what Anthea was saying; "but after recent eventfulnesses a new leaf has to be turned over, and, after all, mother is more important than the feelings of any of the lower forms of creation, however unnatural."

"How beautifully you do do it," said Anthea, absently beginning to build a card-house for the Lamb—"mixing up what you're saying, I mean. We ought to practise doing it so as to be ready for mysterious occasions. We're talking about *that*," she said to Jane and Robert, frowning, and nodding towards the cupboard where the Phœnix was. Then Robert and Jane understood, and each opened his mouth to speak.

"Wait a minute," said Anthea quickly; "the game is to twist up what you want to say so that no one can understand what you're saying except the people you want to understand it, and sometimes not them."

"The ancient philosophers," said a golden voice, "well understand the art of which you speak."

Of course it was the Phœnix, who had not been in the cupboard at all, but had been cocking a golden eye at them from the cornice during the whole conversation.

"Pretty dickie!" remarked the Lamb. "*Canary* dickie!"

"Poor misguided infant," said the Phœnix.

There was a painful pause; the four could not but think it likely that the Phœnix had understood their very veiled allusions, accompanied as they had been by gestures indicating the cupboard. For the Phœnix was not wanting in intelligence.

"We were just saying——" Cyril began, and I hope he was not going to say anything but the truth. Whatever it was he did not say it, for the Phœnix interrupted him, and all breathed more freely as it spoke.

"I gather," it said, "that you have some tidings of a fatal nature to communicate to our degraded black brothers who run to and fro for ever yonder."

It pointed a claw at the cupboard, where the black-beetles lived.

"Canary *talk*," said the Lamb joyously; "go and show mammy."

He wriggled off Anthea's lap.

"Mammy's asleep," said Jane, hastily. "Come and be wild beasts in a cage under the table."

But the Lamb caught his feet and hands, and even his head, so often and so deeply in the holes of the carpet that the cage, or table, had to be moved on to the linoleum, and the carpet lay bare to sight with all its horrid holes.

"Ah," said the bird, "it isn't long for this world."

"No," said Robert; "everything comes to an end. It's awful."

"Sometimes the end is peace," remarked the Phœnix. "I imagine that unless it comes soon the end of your carpet will be pieces."

"Yes," said Cyril, respectfully kicking what was left of the carpet. The movement of its bright colours caught the eye of the Lamb, who went down on all fours instantly and began to pull at the red and blue threads.

"Aggedydaggedygaggedy," murmured the Lamb; "daggedy ag ag ag!"

And before any one could have winked (even if they had wanted to, and it would not have been of the slightest use) the middle of the floor showed bare, an island of boards surrounded by a sea of linoleum. The magic carpet was gone, *and so was the Lamb!*

There was a horrible silence. The Lamb—the baby, all alone—had been wafted away on that untrustworthy carpet, so full of holes and magic. And no one could know where he was. And no one could follow him because there was now no carpet to follow on.

Jane burst into tears, but Anthea, though pale and frantic, was dry-eyed.

"It *must* be a dream," she said.

"That's what the clergyman said," remarked Robert forlornly; "but it wasn't, and it isn't."

"But the Lamb never wished," said Cyril; "he was only talking Bosh."[5]

"The carpet understands all speech," said the Phœnix, "even Bosh. I know not this Boshland, but be assured that its tongue is not unknown to the carpet."

"Do you mean, then," said Anthea, in white terror, "that when he was saying 'Aggllety dag,' or whatever it was, that he meant something by it?"

"All speech has meaning," said the Phœnix.

"There I think you're wrong," said Cyril; "even people who talk English sometimes say things that don't mean anything in particular."

"Oh, never mind that now," moaned Anthea; "you think 'Aggety dag' meant something to him and the carpet?"

"Beyond doubt it held the same meaning to the carpet as to the luckless infant," the Phœnix said calmly.

"And *what* did it mean? Oh, *what?*"

"Unfortunately," the bird rejoined, "I never studied Bosh."

5. I.e., baby talk or nonsense.

Jane sobbed noisily, but the others were calm with what is sometimes called the calmness of despair. The Lamb was gone—the Lamb, their own precious baby brother—who had never in his happy little life been for a moment out of the sight of eyes that loved him—he was gone. He had gone alone into the great world with no other companion and protector than a carpet with holes in it. The children had never really understood before what an enormously big place the world is. And the Lamb might be anywhere in it!

"And it's no use going to look for him." Cyril, in flat and wretched tones, only said what the others were thinking.

"Do you wish him to return?" the Phœnix asked; it seemed to speak with some surprise.

"Of course we do!" cried everybody.

"Isn't he more trouble than he's worth?" asked the bird doubtfully.

"No, *no*. Oh, we do want him back! We do!"

"Then," said the wearer of gold plumage, "if you'll excuse me, I'll just pop out and see what I can do."

Cyril flung open the window, and the Phœnix popped out.

"Oh, if only mother goes on sleeping! Oh, suppose she wakes up and wants the Lamb! Oh, suppose the servants come! Stop crying, Jane. It's no earthly good. No, I'm not crying myself—at least I wasn't till you said so, and I shouldn't anyway if—if there was any mortal thing we could do. Oh, oh, oh!"

Cyril and Robert were boys, and boys never cry, of course. Still, the position was a terrible one, and I do not wonder that they made faces in their efforts to behave in a really manly way.

And at this awful moment mother's bell rang.

A breathless stillness held the children. Then Anthea dried her eyes. She looked round her and caught up the poker. She held it out to Cyril.

"Hit my hand hard," she said; "I must show mother some reason for my eyes being like they are."

"Harder," she cried as Cyril gently tapped her with the iron handle. And Cyril agitated and trembling, nerved himself to hit harder, and hit very much harder than he intended.

Anthea screamed.

"Oh, Panther, I didn't meant to hurt, really," cried Cyril, clattering the poker back into the fender.

"It's—all—right," said Anthea breathlessly, clasping the hurt hand with the one that wasn't hurt; "it's—getting—red."

It was—a round red and blue bump was rising on the back of it.

"Now, Robert," she said, trying to breathe more evenly, "you go out—oh, I don't know where—on to the dustbin—anywhere—and I shall tell mother you and the Lamb are out."

Anthea was now ready to deceive her mother for as long as ever she could. Deceit is very wrong, we know, but it seemed to Anthea that it was her plain duty to keep her mother from being frightened about the Lamb as long as possible. And the Phœnix *might* help.

"It always has helped," Robert said; "it got us out of the tower, and even when it made the fire in the theatre it got us out all right. I'm certain it will manage somehow."

Mother's bell rang again.

"Oh, Eliza's never answered it," cried Anthea; "she never does. Oh, I must go."

And she went.

Her heart beat bumpingly as she climbed the stairs. Mother would be certain to notice her eyes—well, her hand would account for that. But the Lamb——

"No, I must *not* think of the Lamb," she said to herself, and bit her tongue till her eyes watered again, so as to give herself something else to think of. Her arms and legs and back, and even her tear-reddened face, felt stiff with her resolution not to let mother be worried if she could help it.

She opened the door softly.

"Yes, mother?" she said.

"Dearest," said mother, "the Lamb——"

Anthea tried to be brave. She tried to say that the Lamb and Robert were out. Perhaps she tried too hard. Anyway, when she opened her mouth no words came. So she stood with it open. It seemed easier to keep from crying with one's mouth in that unusual position.

"The Lamb," mother went on; "he was very good at first, but he's pulled the toilet-cover off the dressing-table with all the brushes and pots and things, and now he's so quiet I'm sure he's in some dreadful mischief. And I can't see him from here, and if I'd got out of bed to see I'm sure I should have fainted."

"Do you mean he's *here?*" said Anthea.

"Of course he's here," said mother, a little impatiently. "Where did you think he was?"

Anthea went round the foot of the big mahogany bed. There was a pause.

"He's not here *now,*" she said.

That he had been there was plain, from the toilet-cover on the floor, the scattered pots and bottles, the wandering brushes and combs, all involved in the tangle of ribbons and laces which an open drawer had yielded to the baby's inquisitive fingers.

"He must have crept out, then," said mother; "do keep him with you, there's a darling. If I don't get some sleep I shall be a wreck when father comes home."

Anthea closed the door softly. Then she tore downstairs and burst into the nursery crying:

"He must have wished he was with mother. He's been there all the time, 'Aggety dag'——"

The unusual word was frozen on her lip, as people say in books.

For there, on the floor, lay the carpet, and on the carpet, surrounded by his brothers and by Jane, sat the Lamb. He had covered his face and clothes with vaseline and violet powder, but he was easily recognisable in spite of this disguise.

"You are right," said the Phœnix, who was also present; "it is evident that, as you say, 'Aggety dag' is Bosh for 'I want to be where my mother is,' and so the faithful carpet understood it."

"But how," said Anthea, catching up the Lamb and hugging him—"how did he get back here?"

"Oh," said the Phœnix, "I flew to the Psammead and wished that your infant brother were restored to your midst, and immediately it was so."

"Oh, I am glad, I am glad!" cried Anthea, still hugging the baby. "Oh, you darling! Shut up, Jane! I don't care *how* much he comes off on me! Cyril! You and Robert roll that carpet up and put it in the beetle-cupboard. He might say 'Aggety dag' again, and it might mean something quite different next time. Now, my Lamb, Panther'll clean you a little. Come on."

"I hope the beetles won't go wishing," said Cyril, as they rolled up the carpet.

Two days later mother was well enough to go out, and that evening the cocoanut matting came home. The children had talked and talked, and thought and thought, but they had not found any polite way of telling the Phœnix that they did not want it to stay any longer.

The days had been days spent by the children in embarrassment, and by the Phœnix in sleep.

And, now the matting was laid down, the Phœnix awoke and fluttered down on to it. It shook its crested head.

"I like not this carpet," it said; "it is harsh and unyielding, and it hurts my golden feet."

"We've jolly well got to get used to its hurting *our* golden feet," said Cyril.

"This, then," said the bird, "supersedes the Wishing Carpet."

"Yes," said Robert, "if you mean that it's instead of it."

"And the magic web?" inquired the Phœnix, with sudden eagerness.

"It's the rag-and-bottle man's day to-morrow," said Anthea, in a low voice; "he will take it away."

The Phœnix fluttered up to its favourite perch on the chair-back.

"Hear me!" it cried, "oh, youthful children of men, and restrain your tears of misery and despair, for what must be must be, and I would not remember you, thousands of years hence, as base ingrates and crawling worms compact of low selfishness."

"I should hope not, indeed," said Cyril.

"Weep not," the bird went on; "I really do beg that you won't weep. I will not seek to break the news to you gently. Let the blow fall at once. The time has come when I must leave you."

All four children breathed forth a long sigh of relief.

"We needn't have bothered so about how to break the news to it," whispered Cyril.

"Ah, sigh not so," said the bird, gently. "All meetings end in partings. I must leave you. I have sought to prepare you for this. Ah, do not give way!"

"Must you really go—so soon?" murmured Anthea. It was what she had often heard her mother say to calling ladies in the afternoon.

"I must, really; thank you so much, dear," replied the bird, just as though it had been one of the ladies.

"I am weary," it went on. "I desire to rest—after all the happenings of this last moon I do desire greatly to rest, and I ask of you one last boon."

"Any little thing we can do," said Robert.

Now that it had really come to parting with the Phœnix, whose favourite he had always been, Robert did feel almost as miserable as the Phœnix thought they all did.

"I ask but the relic designed for the rag-and-bottle man. Give me what is left of the carpet and let me go."

"Dare we?" said Anthea. "Would mother mind?"

"I have dared greatly for your sakes," remarked the bird.

"Well, then, we will," said Robert.

The Phœnix fluffed out its feathers joyously.

"Nor shall you regret it, children of golden hearts," it said. "Quick—spread the carpet and leave me alone; but first pile high the fire. Then, while I am immersed in the sacred preliminary rites, do ye prepare sweet-smelling woods and spices for the last act of parting."

The children spread out what was left of the carpet. And, after all, though this was just what they would have wished to have happened, all hearts were sad. Then they put half a scuttle of coal on the fire and went out, closing the door on the Phœnix— left, at last, alone with the carpet.

"One of us must keep watch," said Robert, excitedly, as soon as they were all out of the room, "and the others can go and buy sweet woods and spices. Get the very best that money can buy, and plenty of them. Don't let's stand to a threepence or so. I want it to have a jolly good send-off. It's the only thing that'll make us feel less horrid inside."

It was felt that Robert, as the pet of the Phœnix, ought to have the last melancholy pleasure of choosing the materials for its funeral pyre.

"I'll keep watch if you like," said Cyril. "I don't mind. And, besides, it's raining hard, and my boots let in the wet. You might call and see if my other ones are 'really reliable' again yet."

So they left Cyril, standing like a Roman sentinel outside the door inside which the Phœnix was getting ready for the great change, and they all went out to buy the precious things for the last sad rites.

"Robert is right," Anthea said; "this is no time for being careful about our money. Let's go to the stationer's first, and buy a whole packet of lead-pencils. They're cheaper if you buy them by the packet."

This was a thing that they had always wanted to do, but it needed the great excitement of a funeral pyre and a parting from a beloved Phœnix to screw them up to the extravagance.

The people at the stationer's said that the pencils were real cedar-wood, so I hope they were, for stationers should always speak the truth. At any rate they cost one-and-fourpence.[6] Also they spent seven-pence three-farthings on a little sandal-wood box inlaid with ivory.

"Because," said Anthea, "I know sandal-wood smells sweet, and when it's burned it smells very sweet indeed."

"Ivory doesn't smell at all," said Robert, "but I expect when you burn it it smells most awful vile, like bones."

At the grocer's they bought all the spices they could remember the names of—shell-like mace, cloves like blunt nails, peppercorns, the long and the round kind; ginger, the dry sort, of course; and beautiful bloom-covered shells of fragrant cinnamon. Allspice too, and caraway seeds (caraway seeds that smelt most deadly when the time came for burning them).

Camphor and oil of lavender were bought at the chemist's, and also a little scent satchet labelled "Violettes de Parme."[7]

They took the things home and found Cyril still on guard. When they had knocked and the golden voice of the Phœnix had said "Come in," they went in.

There lay the carpet—or what was left of it—and on it lay an egg, exactly like the one out of which the Phœnix had been hatched.

The Phœnix was walking round and round the egg, clucking with joy and pride.

"I've laid it, you see," it said, "and as fine an egg as ever I laid in all my born days." Every one said yes, it was indeed a beauty.

The things which the children had bought were now taken out of their papers and arranged on the table, and when the Phœnix had been persuaded to leave its egg for a moment and look at the materials for its last fire it was quite overcome.

"Never, never have I had a finer pyre than this will be. You shall not regret it," it said, wiping away a golden tear. "Write quickly: 'Go and tell the Psammead to fulfil the last wish of the Phœnix and return instantly.'"

But Robert wished to be polite and he wrote:

---

6. I.e., one shilling and four pence (there were twelve pence in a shilling).

7. Parma violets (French), used in perfume.

"Please go and ask the Psammead to be so kind as to fulfil the Phœnix's last wish, and come straight back, if you please."

The paper was pinned to the carpet, which vanished and returned in the flash of an eye.

Then another paper was written ordering the carpet to take the egg somewhere where it wouldn't be hatched for another two thousand years. The Phœnix tore itself away from its cherished egg, which it watched with yearning tenderness till, the paper being pinned on, the carpet hastily rolled itself up round the egg, and both vanished forever from the nursery of the house in Camden Town.

"Oh, dear! oh, dear! oh, dear!" said everybody.

"Bear up," said the bird; "do you think *I* don't suffer, being parted from my precious new-laid egg like this? Come, conquer your emotions and build my fire."

"*Oh!*" cried Robert, suddenly, and wholly breaking down, "I can't *bear* you to go!"

The Phœnix perched on his shoulder and rubbed its beak softly against his ear.

"The sorrows of youth soon appear but as dreams," it said. "Farewell, Robert of my heart. I have loved you well."

The fire had burnt to a red glow. One by one the spices and sweet woods were laid on it. Some smelt nice and some—the caraway seeds and the Violettes de Parme sachet among them—smelt worse than you would think possible.

"Farewell, farewell, farewell, farewell!" said the Phœnix, in a far-away voice.

"Oh, *good-bye*," said every one, and now all were in tears.

The bright bird fluttered seven times round the room and settled in the hot heart of the fire. The sweet gums and spices and woods flared and flickered around it, but its golden feathers did not burn. It seemed to grow red-hot to the very inside heart of it—and then before the eight eyes of its friends it fell together, a heap of white ashes, and the flames of the cedar pencils and the sandal-wood box met and joined above it.

"Whatever have you done with the carpet?" asked mother next day.

"We gave it to some one who wanted it very much. The name began with a P," said Jane. The others instantly hushed her.

"Oh, well, it wasn't worth twopence," said mother.

"The person who began with P said we shouldn't lose by it," Jane went on before she could be stopped.

"I daresay!" said mother, laughing.

But that very night a great box came, addressed to the children by all their names. Eliza never could remember the name of the carrier who brought it. It wasn't Carter Paterson[8] or the Parcels Delivery.

It was instantly opened. It was a big wooden box, and it had to be opened with a hammer and the kitchen poker; the long nails came squeaking out, and the boards scrunched as they were wrenched off. Inside the box was soft paper, with beautiful Chinese patterns on it—blue and green and red and violet. And under the paper—well, almost everything lovely that you can think of. Everything of reasonable size, I mean; for, of course, there were no motors or flying machines or thoroughbred chargers. But there really was almost everything else. Everything that the children had always wanted—toys and games and books, and chocolate and candied cherries and paint-boxes and photographic cameras, and all the presents they had always wanted to give to father and mother and the Lamb, only they had never had the money for

8. Prominent London-based shipping company.

them. At the very bottom of the box was a tiny golden feather. No one saw it but Robert, and he picked it up and hid it in the breast of his jacket, which had been so often the nesting-place of the golden bird. When he went to bed the feather was gone. It was the last he ever saw of the Phœnix.

Pinned to the lovely fur cloak that mother had always wanted was a paper, and it said:

"In return for the carpet. With gratitude.—P."

You may guess how father and mother talked it over. They decided at last the person who had had the carpet, and whom, curiously enough, the children were quite unable to describe, must be an insane millionaire who amused himself by playing at being a rag-and-bone man. But the children knew better.

They knew that this was the fulfilment, by the powerful Psammead, of the last wish of the Phœnix, and that this glorious and delightful boxful of treasures was really the very, very, very end of the Phœnix and the Carpet.

1904

RUTH PARK
b. 1923

As a little girl, Ruth Park was captivated by her father's stories and she exercised her imagination with the solitary games she played in the New Zealand rain forest. She knew from her earliest days that she wanted to be a writer. As she explains in her first memoir, Park was as compelled to follow this destiny "as if a voice spoke from a burning bush."

Park worshipped books and words, though her library contained little beyond the fairy tales of the Brothers Grimm and an anthology of modern poetry. Her dedication to the written word was such that she began publishing stories for the children's page of the *New Zealand Herald* when still a child herself. As an adult, she worked as a copyeditor for the *Auckland Star* while writing stories, poems, and radio programs of every description. After leaving New Zealand and settling in Australia, Park married another aspiring author, D'Arcy Niland; together with their growing family they endured in Sydney the economic hardships brought by World War II as they continued to work as freelance writers. For many years, after her husband's early death and her children's departure from home, Park lived on Norfolk Island, a small island in the South Pacific Ocean.

The Muddle-Headed Wombat series of radio scripts and books (1962–81) established Park's reputation in writing for children. She has written works in other genres as well, including information books, historical novels, and screenplays, and has won many awards. In the early 1990s she published two memoirs, *A Fence around the Cuckoo* (1992) and *Fishing in the Styx* (1993). Park's novels for children are praised for their vivid, living characters, emotional truth, and strong sense of place.

Playing Beatie Bow (1980), a time-slip fantasy set in the Victorian slum areas of Sydney that fascinate Park and appear "as the backbone" of many of her books for both adults and younger readers, won the Children's Book Council of Australia Book of the Year for 1981, among other prizes; in 1986 it was made into a film. Park fixated on the 1899 photograph of a girl "with slitted tiger eyes" and somehow knew that her name was "Beatie Bow" and that her story—together with the story of a confused adolescent girl from contemporary Sydney who is thrust into the world of 1873 and the hard life of the New South Wales colonists—must be told.

Playing Beatie Bow

CHAPTER 1

In the first place, Abigail Kirk was not Abigail at all. She had been christened Lynette.

Her mother apologised. 'It must have been the anaesthetic. I felt as tight as a tick[1] for days. And Daddy was so thrilled to have a daughter that he wouldn't have minded if I'd called you Ophelia.'

So for the first ten years of her life she was Lynnie Kirk, and happy as a lark. A hot-headed rag of a child, she vibrated with devotion for many things and people, including her parents. She loved her mother, but her father was a king.

So when he said good-bye to her, before he went off with another lady, she was outraged to the point of speechlessness that he could like someone so much better than herself that he didn't want to live in the same house with her any more.

'I'll come and see you often, Lynnie, I promise I shall,' he had said. And she, who could not bear to see a puppy slapped or a cockroach trodden on, hit him hard on the nose. She had never forgotten his shocked eyes above the blood-stained hand-kerchief. Very blue eyes they were, for he was half Norwegian.

Later she commanded her mother: 'Don't ever call me Lynnie again. Or any of those other names either.'

Kathy Kirk knew that her daughter was referring to the many pet names her father called her, for she was very dear to him.

Because she was a loving woman, she had put her arms round the little girl and said, 'You don't understand, because you're too young yet. Just because Daddy wants to go away from me doesn't mean that he doesn't love you. But of course you may change your name if you wish. What would you like to be called?'

Weeks and months went past, and the person who had once been Lynette Kirk had no name at all. She would not answer to Lynette at home or at school. There were some puzzled notes from her teachers, which fortunately never had to be answered; because soon after the marriage break-up Kathy Kirk sold the family home and moved into a unit her husband had given her.

Her daughter was enraged that Kathy had accepted it. It was the finest in a high-rise tower her father's firm had designed, a glistening spike of steel and glass jammed in the sandstone amongst the tiny meek cottages and old bond stores[2] of that part of Sydney called The Rocks.

'You ought to be prouder!' she yelled in her passion and grief. 'I'd rather live in the Ladies on the Quay than in something he gave me.'

'Be quiet!' said Grandmother in her razor-blade voice.

'You!' shouted that long-ago child. 'You're glad he's gone. *I* know.'

Because she was right, this was what began Abigail's and her grandmother's silent agreement not to like each other.

Yet, strangely, it was through Grandmother that the ex-Lynette at last found her name.

'You'll have to do something about that hysterical little bore, Katherine,' she said. Grandmother had this spooky habit of turning her eyes up and apparently speaking to a careful careless wave that curled down over her forehead. Lynnie always thought of it as Grandmother talking to her perm. Now she was doing it again. 'Just look at

---

1. Drunk.   2. Warehouses.

her, dear. She looks like a little witch with those wild eyes and her hair all in a bush.'

'You leave Lynnie alone, Mother! I've had enough of your sniping!' said Kathy in a voice in which Grandmother heard the fury and Lynette heard the shakiness.

'Well!' said Grandmother protestingly to her perm, for her daughter Kathy was a sunny-natured young woman and almost never lost her temper.

'Don't mind, darling,' said Kathy to ex-Lynette.

But the ex-Lynette was taken by the idea of being a witch.

'Tell me some witches' names, Mum,' she said.

'Well, there's Samantha, and Tabitha,' Kathy began.

'Oh, I don't want soppy TV names,'[3] said her daughter. 'Some real witches' names.'

'They'd have to be old ones,' said Kathy thoughtfully, 'like Hephzibah, or Susannah, or Petronella, or Abigail.'

'That's the one!' cried the girl.

'But it's so plain, so knobbly, so . . . so awful!' wailed Kathy.

Grandmother smiled. Abigail could see quite easily that Grandmother thought she was plain and knobbly and awful, too. So that settled it.

'From now on I'm Abigail Kirk,' she said, 'and as soon as I'm old enough I'll change the Kirk, too.'

So time passed, one way and another. Now she was fourteen and, as with many other girls of her age, her inside did not match her outside at all. The outside was nothing to beat drums about. Somehow she had missed her mother's winning quaintness and her father's ash-blond distinction. She was thin and flat as a board, with a narrow brown face and black coffee eyes so deep-set that she had only to cry for ten minutes and they disappeared altogether. This was one reason why she never cried.

She was known in the family as a clever student, a reserved girl, self-contained.

'More to that one than meets the eye,' said her grandmother with an ice-cream smile. 'Dodgy.'

Instead of tweaking off Grandmother's glasses and cracking them smartly across the edge of the table, as was her impulse, Abigail gave the old woman an ice-cream smile in return. Thereby proving that she was, perhaps, dodgy.

Or a girl who wished to be private.

Outside, she was composed, independent, not very much liked. The girls at school said she was a weirdie, and there was no doubt she was an outsider. She looked like a stick in jeans and a tank top; so she would not wear them. If everyone else was wearing her hair over her face, Abigail scraped hers back. She didn't have a boy friend, and when asked why she either looked enigmatic as though she knew twenty times more about boys than anyone else, or said she'd never met one who was half-way as interesting as her maths textbook. The girls said she was unreal, and she shrugged coolly. The really unreal thing was that she didn't care in the least what they thought of her. She felt a hundred years older and wiser than this love-mad rabble in her class.

Her chief concern was that no one, not even her mother, should know what she was like inside. Because maybe to adults the turmoil of uncertainties, extravagant glooms, and sudden blisses, might present some kind of pattern or map, so that they could say, 'Ah, so that's the real Abigail, is it?'

The thought of such trespass made her stomach turn over. So she cultivated an expressionless face, a long piercing glance under her eyelashes that Grandmother called slippery. She carefully laid false trails until she herself sometimes could not

3. The very popular television series *Bewitched* (ABC, 1964–72) featured a witch, Samantha; her daughter, Tabitha, was also a witch (and had her own series, 1977–78).

find the way into her secret heart. Yet the older she grew the more she longed for someone to laugh at the false trails with, to share the secrets.

What secrets? She didn't yet know what they were herself.

The May holidays always made her feel forlorn and restless. Maybe it was the chill in the air after all the summer softness, the leaves turning yellow, letting go, whirling away. The dark coming earlier, as though the solitude of space were more tightly enclosing the earth, sunless and melancholy.

It was not possible to go for a holiday, unless it were to her grandmother's, which was unthinkable for them both. So, if her mother didn't want her to help at the shop, she spent hours squashed into the corner of the brown armchair, which had once been a kindly bear and now was only a bear-shaped chair near a window which looked out on cranes and mast tops, on the deck of the Harbour Bridge and the pearly cusps of the Opera House[4] rising through the gauzy murk like Aladdin's palace.

Mumping, her mother called it. But she was not doing that, or even thinking. Mostly she was just aware of something missing.

When she was young she thought it was her father, for she had missed him miserably as well as hating him. Then with a new school and home, and new things to think about, she began to forget about him a little, though even now she could sometimes almost cry with pity for that woebegone, puzzled kid who used to go to bed and pray that her father would fall off a scaffold on one of his inspection tours, and the next moment sweat in terror in case he did.

But now she wasn't a kid she knew that it wasn't the absence of her father that caused the empty place inside. It was a part of her and she didn't know what it was or why it was there.

She and her mother, although they were such different characters, had fought and hugged and scrambled their way through to a close friendship. Kathy became a businesswoman of flair and dash.

When the Kirk family lived in a two-car garden suburb, she had been a fearful packrat, a collector of almost everything. Abigail remembered wet days when big cardboard cartons and wooden tea-chests were thrown open to her and her playmates, and they had turned the entire house into a gorgeous mess of twinkles, spangles, seashells, faceless calico cats; old shoes; a real clown suit still stained with red and black grease-paint; Victorian postcards, some rude; and books and books of dried ferns, painted rosebuds, and autographs with silly poems.

After Abigail's father went away, Kathy had given a last decisive sniff, washed her face, which was somewhat like that of a fat-cheeked finch with a finch's shiny dewdrop eyes, raked her hair up on top of her head in a washerwoman's knot, and rented a black hole of Calcutta[5] in a Paddington lane. This she turned into a treasure-house of trendy trivia. She called the shop Magpies, and soon other magpie people flocked around to shriek and snatch and buy.

What with Kathy being a success, and Grandmother getting more interested in Bridge and less of a carper, Abigail and her mother achieved a kind of happiness.

Now she jumped up with a scowl, banged the door on the empty place, and went to visit the Crowns, her neighbours.

That unit was in its customary state of theatrically awful mess. Justine Crown didn't believe in housework. She said the children came first; but she hadn't made a gold-

---

4. A famous Sydney landmark completed in 1973; its tripartite structure in expressionist modern style is highly distinctive.

5. A small, dark place. The original "Black Hole" was a small cell into which soldiers in a garrison of the British East India Company were placed in 1756 after their capture by the governor of Bengal. By morning, most had died.

medal job of them either. Usually Natalie, the four-year-old, was at kindergarten, and Vincent, the high-rise monster, at school. But as it was holidays they were both at home, and Vincent, who was in Abigail's opinion the grimmest kid two agreeable people could be cursed with, was at his usual game of worrying Natalie like a dog with a bone.

Natalie aroused in Abigail a solemnly protective feeling. This rather embarrassed her. The little girl was prone to sudden fevers, nightmares, fears, and had a kind of helpless affection for the frightful Vincent that did not allow her to defend herself against him.

Vincent was a bundle of bones with a puzzling smell, as though he'd wet himself six weeks earlier and not bothered to bathe. He was as sharp as a knife and had his parents sized up to the last millimetre. Abigail did not see that his face was wretched as well as cunning, and she was sincerely flattered that he hated her more than he hated everyone else.

'You've got Dracula teeth,' he greeted her.

Justine shouted from the kitchen, 'Oh, for heaven's sake don't start on Abigail, you little beast.' She came out, bashing around in a basin with a fork. 'He's been dark blue hell all day.'

'Dracula teeth,' said Vincent. 'Big long white choppers. See them, Fat Nat?'

'Don't call your sister that, and if Abigail's teeth are too big it's because her face hasn't grown up to them yet.'

Instantly Abigail imagined herself with this thin nosy face and fangs sticking out over her lower lip.

She was very depressed with her looks as it was, and had given up hope of developing fascinating high cheekbones or eyelashes an inch long. She liked her eyebrows, which were black and straight, and her long brown hair, which glistened satisfactorily. But although her mother assured her that her figure would arrive some day, she often despaired. Most times people took her for twelve, which was humiliating.

However, she was not going to be bugged by any six-year-old dinosaur like Vincent Crown. She glared at him.

'Knock off the wisecracks!' To Justine she said, 'It's freezing outside, but would you like me to take them down to the playground till it starts to get dark?'

Justine was so jubilant at the thought of being free of Natalie's unexplained tears and silences and Vincent's whining that she had the children into their anoraks[6] and woolly caps before Abigail could think, 'Curse it, why am I such a sucker?'

The high-rise tower was called Mitchell, after a famous man who had been born just where it stood many years before. He was the Mitchell who founded the Mitchell Library. High-rise buildings near by were called Dalley, Campbell, and Reiby,[7] after other celebrated people, though Abigail didn't know for what they were celebrated.

Mitchell stood amongst charming landscaping, which included a covered swimming-pool and a children's playground. In spite of her resentment against her father, Abigail could never hate the building, standing up there severe as a sword, slitting each wind into two streams, reflecting fish-scale seas, and cherry-red sunsets, and a city which, when stretched and crinkled by curved windows, grew itself steeples

---

6. Parkas.

7. Mary Reiby (1777–1855), a former convict who became a savvy businesswoman and founding member of the Bank of New South Wales. David Scott Mitchell (1836–1907), a collector and bibliophile who bequeathed to the Australian people his thousands of books, manuscripts, artifacts, paintings, documents, and maps (these formed the core of the library, which opened in 1910). William Bede Dalley (1831–1888), a barrister and attorney general of New South Wales. Elizabeth Campbell (1778–1835), the second wife of the governor of New South Wales sometimes called the "father of Australia," Lachlan Macquarie.

and domes and trees like minarets, and escarpments floating in cloud. On the lobby wall in polished brass were the letters: *Architects: Weyland Kirk, Casper and Domenici, Sydney, San Francisco, Oslo, Siena.* Abigail tried never to look at it, for, try as she might, she couldn't help feeling proud: she knew that this particular high-riser was all the work of Weyland Kirk.

Now Mitchell was haughtily slicing up a barbed westerly, which did not seem to bother the children climbing the monkey bars, brawling thunderously inside the concrete pipes, or fighting like tom-cats inside the space rocket. Thankfully Abigail released Vincent's hard, sticky paw, and he flitted off to torment a group of fat bundles climbing the stone wall about the playground. Let the fat bundles look after themselves, Abigail thought callously. Likely they'd have parents with them, anyway, who would pluck Vincent away from their darlings and, with any luck, half-strangle him in the process.

The noise was shattering. Most of the children came from Mitchell, but others probably lived in the cottages round about. Abigail observed that those racing dementedly back and forth performed their charges in a certain order. They were playing a group game.

'Would you like to play it, too, Natty?'

Natalie shook her head. Her big grey eyes were now full of tears. Abigail sighed. Justine was for ever trailing Natalie off to a doctor who was supposed to be miraculous with highly strung children, but he hadn't brought off any miracles yet.

'Now what's the matter, little dopey?'

'They're playing Beatie Bow and it scares me. But I like to watch. Please let's watch,' pleaded Natalie.

'Never heard of it,' said Abigail. She noticed Vincent rushing to join in and thought how weird it was that in the few years that had passed since she was six or seven the kids had begun to play such different games. She watched this one just in case Vincent murdered anyone. She could already hear him squealing like a mad rat.

Natalie took hold of a fistful of her shawl, and Abigail held her close to keep her out of the wind. The child was shivering. Yet the game didn't look so exciting; just one more goofy kid's game.

First of all the children formed a circle. They had become very quiet. In the middle was a girl who had been chosen by some counting-out rhyme.

'That's Mudda,' explained Natalie.

'What's Mudda?'

'You know, a mummy like my mummy.'

'Oh, Mother!'

'Yes, but she's called Mudda. That's in the game.'

Someone hidden behind the concrete pipes made a scraping sound. The children chorused, 'Oh, Mudda, what's that?'

'Nothing at all,' chanted the girl in the center. 'The dog at the door, the dog at the door.'

Now a bloodcurdling moan was heard from behind the pipes. Abigail felt Natalie press closer to her. She noticed that the dark was coming down fast; soon it would rain. She resolved she would take the children home as soon as she could gather up Vincent.

'Oh, Mudda, what's that, what can it be?'

'The wind in the chimney, that's all, that's all.'

There was a clatter of stones being dropped. Some of the younger children squawked, and were hushed.

'Oh, Mudda, what's that, what's that, can you see?'

'It's the cow in the byre,[8] the horse in the stall.'

Natalie held on tightly and put her hands over her eyes.

'Don't look, Abigail, it's worse than awful things on TV!'

At this point Mudda pointed dramatically beyond the circle of children. A girl covered in a white sheet or tablecloth was creeping towards them, waving her arms and wailing.

'It's Beatie Bow,' shrieked Mudda in a voice of horror, 'risen from the dead!'

At this the circle broke and the children ran shrieking hysterically to fling themselves in a chaotic huddle of arms and legs in the sandpit at the other end.

'What on earth was all that about?' asked Abigail. She felt cold and grumpy and made gestures at Vince to rejoin them.

'The person who is Beatie Bow is a ghost, you see,' explained Natalie, 'and she rises from her grave, and everyone runs and pretends to be afraid. If she catches someone, that one has to be the next Beatie Bow. But mostly the children *are* frightened, because they play it and play it till it's dark. Vincent gets in a state and that's why he's so mean afterwards. But the little furry girl doesn't get scared,' she added inconsequentially. 'I think she'd like to join in, she smiles so much. Look, Abigail, see her watching over there?'

Before the older girl could look, Vincent panted up, scowling.

'We're going to play it again! I want to! I want to!'

'No way,' said Abigail firmly. 'It's getting dark and it's too cold for Natalie already.'

The boy said bitterly, 'I hate you!'

'Big deal,' said Abigail.

Vincent pinched Natalie cruelly. Tears filled her eyes. 'You see? Just like I told you,' she said without rancour.

'What a creep you are, Vincent,' said Abigail scornfully.

Vincent made a rude gesture and ran on before them into the lobby. As they waited for the lift, Abigail saw that his whole body was trembling. She made up her mind to have a word with Justine about the too-exciting game.

'I saw the little furry girl, Vince,' said Natalie. 'She was watching you all again.'

He ignored her, barged past them into the Crown unit, and flung himself down before the TV.

'I'll stay a little while if you like, Justine,' offered Abigail. 'Mum won't be home till nearly seven. She had to go and look at some old furniture at St Mary's near Penrith.'[9]

Justine was delighted at the prospect of concluding dinner preparations without the usual civil war between her young. She suggested that Abigail help Natty make new clothes for her teddy-bear.

Abigail enjoyed sewing, and made some of her own clothes. She did not do a professional job, but she did her best; and somehow she loved her clothes more because of the sleeves that wouldn't quite fit, the seams she had unpicked over and over again. At the moment she was fond of long dresses and shawls and hooded sweaters. Her favourite belt was a piece of old harness strap, polished deep brown and fastened with the original brass buckles. It had a phantom smell of horse which her grandmother said was disgusting.

'You look like a gipsy or a street Arab,'[1] she said.

'The Arabs own all the streets nowadays, Grandmother.' Abigail smiled. 'You're not up with things.'

'Don't be impertinent!' snapped Grandmother. She appealed to her perm. 'Kath-

---

8. Cow barn.
9. City about 35 miles west of Sydney.

1. A homeless child who lives by begging or stealing.

erine, are you going to stand there and permit this child to speak to me like that?'

'You criticised her clothes, Mother,' answered Kathy, flushing. 'She didn't say a word about yours.'

'About mine?' gasped Grandmother, as though it had never occurred to her that she was not wearing the only type of garment in the world. She swept out—she really did sweep in some extraordinary way—and Kathy looked rueful and fidgety, for she hated to be at outs with anyone.

'All right, don't be sarky,'[2] she said to her daughter. 'You can dress any way you like. But please try not to aggravate her deliberately. She's old and . . .'

'Oh, Mum,' said Abigail impatiently, 'she enjoys a little set-to. It improves her circulation or something. That's why she always used to pick on Dad. Don't you remember how her eyes used to sparkle . . .' She stopped dead. Why had she brought Dad into it? She sneaked a sidelong glance at her mother, and saw that Kathy's eyes were full of tears.

'I was pretty dumb in those days,' said Kathy. Then she laughed, and began to peel vegetables for dinner. But she was still flushed.

Now as they rummaged in the ragbag, trying that piece and this against Teddy's stubby form, Abigail told the little girl that she had almost finished making herself a long dress from an Edwardian curtain that her mother had found in a box of old fabrics bought at an auction. The curtain was still unperished, a heavy cotton with strong striped selvages, which Abigail had wangled around to use as borders for sleeves and skirt.

'It's a very funny colour,' she told Natalie. 'A mucky brownish-green, like pea soup.'

'It wouldn't suit Teddy,' observed Natalie.

'And Teddy is not going to get it either,' said Abigail.

They cut out a pair of red shorts, and Abigail tacked them up for Justine to sew. Then they upended the ragbag to find something spotted for a waistcoat. Tangled amongst all the scraps and remnants and outgrown garments was a strangely shaped piece of yellowed crochet. Abigail smoothed it out, trying to distinguish the pattern. It was very fine work, almost like lace.

Justine came in, battled with Vincent about his bath before dinner, and dragged him away. She came back.

'What have you got there? Oh, that old rag! It's been around for ever. Give it to me, Abigail, and I'll use it for a dishcloth or something.'

'If you don't want it,' said the girl, 'I'd really like to have it.'

She spread the crumpled fabric. 'See, it's a yoke for a high-necked dress. Just right for my new greeny one.'

'It's yours,' said Justine cheerfully. 'Probably fall to bits the first time you wash it.'

The children were quiet and, since Mr Crown was due home, Abigail said good-bye and went. She was very taken with Justine's gift. She decided against bleaching the crochet piece, for the chemical might be too harsh for the old thread. Besides, she liked the creamy colour against the murky green of the dress. She carefully washed the yoke and dried it with a hair-dryer, stretching the fabric as she went. The pattern showed itself at last as a recurrent design of a delicate plant with a flower like a buttercup rising out of five heart-shaped leaves.

With a cry of pleasure, Abigail saw that each flower had been over-embroidered with yellowish green tiny knots which seemed to indicate stamens or hairs. But the coloured thread had so faded that it was almost indiscernible.

2. Sarcastic.

About seven, her mother telephoned. She sounded tired, said she had been delayed, and told Abigail to go ahead and eat something. The girl agreed and went back to her work.

The border of the crochet was a curious twist, almost like a rope, done in a coarser thread, and at the edge of each shoulder Abigail saw, between the leaves of a flower, the tiny initials A.T.

As she worked, she found herself singing, 'The cow in the byre, the horse in the stall.' She broke off. 'Now where did those kids hear a funny word like bryre?'

By the time Kathy had tottered in and collapsed in a chair, Abigail already had the crochet tacked to the dress. Weary as she was, her mother exclaimed at it.

'It's a Victorian piece, I think, although the pattern is unfamiliar. What superb work! I could sell it like a shot if you want me to.'

'No,' said Abigail.

'Don't blame you. Heavens, I'm bushed. No, I don't want anything to eat. Had a bite in town. Sorry, love. Have to fall into bed.'

She limped off, yawning like a lion. Abigail stitched the yoke to her dress with the smallest stitches she could achieve: the fineness of her new treasure seemed to demand it. The yoke fitted the bodice as though it had been made for it, and when she tried on the dress it was as if the two pieces of fabric had never been separate. The girl had an extraordinary sense of pleasure. She felt that she would wear this perfect dress until it fell to bits. Even now she knew that this was one of those mysterious garments in which she always felt happy.

Just before she went to sleep she thought, 'I've seen that flower somewhere. Not real though. A picture.'

At the same moment she recalled the old *Herbal* in the bookcase. She squeezed her eyes tight and tried to go to sleep, but it was no use. She had to get out of bed and look. She riffled through the thick fox-marked[3] pages to the wild-flowers, and there it was: not a buttercup at all, but a peat bog plant called Grass of Parnassus.

Parnassus! Was the plant Greek then? She knew that Parnassus was where the Muses lived, the goddesses of poetry and dance and art and whatever the rest of them were. Parnassus was a lovely word, and perhaps the original Parnassus had grass that was not ordinary grass but blossomed with little hairy flowers of green and faded yellow.

Suddenly she felt intensely happy, almost as blissfully happy as she had been before she was ten, knowing nothing of the world but warmth and sunshine, and loving parents and birthdays and Christmas presents.

She floated off to sleep. She did not dream of an enchanted mountain where goddesses danced and sang, but of a smell of burning sugar, and a closed door with an iron fist for a knocker, and tied to the fist a bit of yellow rag.

CHAPTER 2

At breakfast next morning her mother was fully recovered, talkative and bright-cheeked. She admired the new dress, puzzled over the crochet pattern, and voted for Agnes Timms as the owner of the initials A.T. But Abigail said that, since the design seemed to be of a Greek plant, A.T. probably stood for Anastasia Tassiopolis, or something similar.

Kathy chattered on until at last her daughter said teasingly, 'What are you excited

3. Discolored by age.

about, Apple Annie? Did you find something extra special at St Mary's?'

Kathy's eyes twinkled. 'I might as well tell you. I had dinner with your father last night.'

Weyland Kirk and his wife had never been divorced. Their relations were friendly, and two or three times a year they met to discuss business matters or Abigail's future. Abigail was occasionally taken out by her father to some entertainment; and although they both behaved with careful courtesy it was always an awkward and hateful experience for Abigail. Something lay between them, an ineradicable memory of rejection of love, and Abigail could not pretend it was not there.

He asked her polite questions about her friends, even the ones he could remember from her childhood and she had almost forgotten.

'You seem to be a bit of a loner, pet,' he said, almost apologetically.

She answered coolly, 'I really don't care for people much.'

He had the same quickness of uptake as she, and he shot her a blue glance that laid her thoughts bare. Then he said gently, 'Well, you can always trust your mother, anyway.'

She knew how much she had hurt him. She tried to be glad. He deserved it. But she was not glad; she was sorry and ashamed.

Now she looked without concern at her mother and said 'Oh, yes? Did you just run into him?'

'As a matter of fact I've seen him quite a few times lately,' Kathy said. 'Oh, darling, don't be cross. I know it was deceitful of me, but I thought I wouldn't mention it in case it all fell through.'

Abigail felt a sudden chill. 'Whatever are you talking about, Mum?'

'Oh, Abigail, I don't know how to put it without sounding silly. Dad—well, he wants us to become a family again.'

'You're joking,' said Abigail.

Kathy's face was almost pleading. 'No, I'm not.'

Abigail felt much as she had felt that morning her father had said good-bye. A burning wave of dismay, anger and fright swept up from her feet. But before it reached her face and turned it scarlet she managed to say, 'And what about Miss Thingo? Is she going to join the party?'

Kathy said stiffly, 'You know very well Jan went off to Canada a year ago. She has a name. Use it, and don't be vulgar. What do you think I'm talking about, last Saturday's TV movie? This is a serious matter for me and your father, so please don't fool about with it.'

Abigail could hardly believe what she heard. 'You're really considering it! After what he did four years ago?'

Kathy smiled nervously. She used a cool tone, but it did not go well with her restless hands. 'Next thing you'll be saying he tossed me aside like a worn-out glove.'

'He dumped you and me for a scheming little creep on his secretarial staff, that's what he did, after being married twelve years.'

'Hold on,' said Kathy. 'Fair's fair. Jan wasn't like that at all. And besides that, he fell in love with her. You don't even know what that means yet.'

'Oh, Mum, now you're being wet!'[4]

'Oh, I know all you schoolgirls think you know every last word in the book about the relationships between a man and a woman; but love is a thing you have to experience before you know—' she hesitated, and then blurted out—'how powerful it can be.'

---

4. I.e., weak, sentimental.

'Oh, come on!'

'I'm only thirty-six,' said Kathy. 'I've missed being married.'

Abigail leapt up and began to pile the dishes noisily in the sink.

'You've no self-respect!'

'Okay, okay!' cried Kathy. 'It's awful, it's shameful, it isn't liberated in the slightest—but I happen to love Weyland. I always have, and I always wanted him to come back. And now it's happened and I want to go with him.'

Abigail was so outraged, so disgusted that anyone as capable and independent and courageous as her mother could be so . . . so—*female* was the word that sprang to her mind—that for a moment the significance of what she had said did not strike her.

'What do you mean, *go*?' she said, aghast.

'He has to go to Norway for three years of architectural study, and he wants us to go with him and . . . and be together again as we used to.'

Abigail felt as if her mother had risen and hit her with the teapot. 'Norway! Why Norway?'

'Well, he's always had this strong feeling for Scandinavian design, because of his family, I expect. But he wouldn't be in Norway all the time. He has to take some seminars in the University of Oslo, and of course we could often go to Denmark . . . and England sometimes.' Her voice trailed away.

'Mother,' said Abigail, 'don't you realise that he could easily leave you again?'

'Yes,' admitted Kathy. 'I have to take the risk, you see.'

Flushing, she looked at her daughter, and the innocence and frankness of that gaze was such that Abigail thought, amazed, 'She really *is* in love with him; she has been all along.'

Such jealousy fired up in her heart that she felt dizzy.

'Then you can take it by yourself.'

Her mother looked as if she had been slapped. 'You can't mean that, darling.'

'You forget that he dumped me, too,' said Abigail tartly. 'That's not going to happen to me again. I can't stop you doing something idiotic if that's what you want, but you can't make me do it, too.'

'But, Abigail, how can I . . . I can't leave you here at your age!'

The shock of realisation hit Abigail. 'She'd really leave me, if there had to be a choice.'

Pride forced the hurt into the back of her mind. With an effort she composed her face. She even smiled.

'Oh, well, let's be practical, Mum. I can easily change over to boarding-school until I'm ready for university, and then I'll go and flat with someone, or live in college.'

'Oh, no!'

'Don't try to wheedle me out of it, Mum. I'm not going. No way.'

Her exit was spoiled because the door slipped out of her fingers and slammed. She couldn't very well open it again and explain to her mother that she wasn't so childish as to go around slamming doors. She stood in the middle of her bedroom feeling sick with fury and shock and a horrible kind of triumph, because she knew how much she had wounded her mother.

'She's hurt because she knows I'm right. How could she, how could she be like that, with all she's got—me, and the shop, and her friends and . . . ?' Here a burst of anger made her feel sickish. 'And Dad! The nerve of . . .'

Her mother tapped on the door. 'Abigail, I'd like you to come and help me unpack and catalogue some things today. I got so many items from St Mary's.'

'Thanks, but I don't want to,' answered Abigail curtly.

'But,' wailed Kathy, 'if you go to boarding-school where will you spend the holidays? You'd loathe it with Grandmother and we haven't anyone else. Oh, please, darling, I know it's been a surprise. I suppose I told you all the wrong way. But please come with me and let's talk it out down at Magpies.'

Abigail did not reply. After a while her mother gave the door a ferocious kick. The girl could not help grinning; Kathy was such a child.

After her mother had gone she washed up, and put on her green dress, which made her feel better. But not much better.

She had a terrible feeling that her mother would go to Norway, regardless. She could not mistake that look on her face. It was happiness and hope. All these years, then, she had longed and hankered for Weyland Kirk to come back to where she felt he belonged. It was like some late-late-show movie—brave little wife making the best of desertion and loneliness, and then one rainy night, gaunt and pale, in comes Gene Kelly.[5] Oh, Kathy, can you ever forgive me? I made such a mistake. I ruined my life, but oh, how can I forgive myself for ruining yours? It's always been you, Kathy, always.

Bring up the reunited lovers music, and she falls into his arms and a bit later he dances up and down the stairs on his knees.

Abigail could just imagine what the girls at school would say. Some, the sloppy romantic ones, would think it just lovely. Together again! But the others, the tough-ies, would think it disgusting. Love was for the young, everyone knew that. Like having no wrinkles or varicose veins. And besides, they'd say her mother was being grovelly. He whistles and back she goes like a well-trained dog.

The more she thought about it the angrier and more embarrassed she felt. 'There's the shop, too. After all her hard work building it up. She's not thinking straight—early menopause or something. And what about me? Turning my life upside down once more for him? A lot he cared about me when I was little and needed him! I don't owe him anything,' thought Abigail, white with fury. 'Not one kind word.'

But, oh God, there was Grandmother, chic and glittery and poisonous and probably thrilled to her long claw toes to get her hands on a lonely Abigail and teach her what's what and who's who. Grandmother's house, expensive suburbia, with a surly house-man, Uruguayan or something, who lived in separate quarters at the end of the garden, the Bridge ladies, the theatre parties, and Abigail required to hand round the teensy bits of fish goo on decarbohydrated crackers. They were always on diets, the Bridge ladies, though not one of them had a soul in the world to care a spit if she turned into a porker or not.

She went around the unit saying, 'Norway!' She saw it as a kind of iceberg with houses on it. And Lapps, weren't there Lapps, with funny knitted hats with tops like two horns? Penguins? Polar bears, then. Norway, a million kilometres away from Sydney and the life she and Mum had made for themselves without Dad's help.

Alternatively she raged and sulked, and then reassured herself with little bursts of optimism. 'Of course she didn't mean it, that crazy lady. She'll think it over and see it doesn't make sense.'

And then she imagined Dad dancing up and down the stairs instead of Gene Kelly; but instead of laughing she cried, because even though she hated what he had done all those years ago she knew she still loved him and was afraid that if they lived together she'd come to love him still more and so could be hurt worse.

In this way the day went past dreadfully and speedily, and when the Bridge began to bellow with the home-going traffic she stirred herself, washed her face and, taking her shawl, she went next door.

_____

5. American dancer, actor, and director (1912–1996).

'I'm bored, Justine. Like me to take the kids to the playground for a while?'

The young woman, who usually looked like a starved cat, now looked like a sleepless starved cat. She seemed at the end of her tether.

'If you could just take Natty off my hands. Goodness, how super! Vincent has been moaning all day, and I've just pried open his trap to look at his throat, and it's like a beetroot. I was just about to hustle him and Natalie along to the doctor. But if you could look after Nat—' She threw her arms thankfully about the girl. 'You're a pet, Abigail, bless you. Good heavens, is that the family tatting you have on your dress? I can't believe it.'

'Abigail has big Dracula teeth dripping with blood,' croaked Vincent.

'Oh, shut up, you,' she snapped. Justine looked pained and Abigail felt ashamed, for after all the little viper *was* sick. She busied herself putting Natalie into her outdoor gear.

The child whispered excitedly, 'When I was watching through the window I saw the little furry girl.'

Abigail hugged her. 'You and your little furry girl! And how could you see her all the way down there in the playground?'

'I don't know; I just did. I wonder where she comes from?'

'I expect she lives in one of the little terrace houses,' said Abigail as they went down in the lift.

'I'd like to live in a little house,' said Natalie, 'with sunflowers higher than the roof and little hollows in the stairs. And a bedroom with a slopey roof. And a chimney.'

The little girl, freed from the oppressive presence of her brother, skipped blithely along, looking at the children sliding down slippery-dips, hanging on the bars like rows of orangoutangs and climbing over the gaudily painted locomotive that stood near the sandpit. Abigail lifted Natalie up to the driver's seat, but she was frightened at the height; and, besides, most of the children had begun their obsessive game of Beatie Bow, and she wanted to watch.

'Why do you want to watch when the silly game scares you so, Natty?'

'I just want to look at the little furry girl watching, because I like her, you see.'

'You're a funny little sausage.' Abigail sat on a cement mushroom and watched curiously while the children formed themselves into their hushed circle, and 'Mudda' took her place in the middle. Natalie pulled at her shawl.

'There she is, Abigail. Do look.'

Abigail looked. At the edge of the playground, absorbed in the children's activities, yet seemingly too shy to emerge from the half-shadow of the wall, was a diminutive figure in a dark dress and lighter pinafore. Her face was pale, and her hair had been clipped so close it did indeed look like a cat's fur. Eagerly she watched the children, smiling sometimes, or looking suspenseful, as the game went on, and then jumping up and down excitedly as Beatie Bow emerged from her grave and frightened everyone to death.

'I wonder why she doesn't play. Perhaps she's crippled or something,' said Abigail. 'Let's go and talk to her.'

They were close to the child before she noticed them, so engrossed was she. She was about eleven, Abigail thought, but stunted, with a monkey face and wide-apart eyes that added to the monkey look. She wore a long, washed-out print dress, a pinafore of brown cotton, and over both of them a shawl crossed over her chest and tied behind. Her feet were bare, and Abigail was surprised to see that the skin was peeling from them in big flakes.

'Hullo, little girl!' said Natty shyly.

The child whipped around in what seemed consternation. She looked an ugly, lively little creature, but scared to death. With a stifled squawk she fled along the wall and dived up one of the steep stone alleys that still linked the many irregular levels of The Rocks.

'Well, she didn't like *us*,' said Abigail. 'Or perhaps she comes from another country and didn't understand we wanted to be friends.'

Natalie nodded, her eyes full of tears once more.

'Oh, Natty, do stop crying. You're like a leaky jug or something. What's the matter now?'

'I don't know.' But when Abigail had delivered her back at the unit, she gave the elder girl a hug and whispered, 'I cried because the little furry girl has been unhappy.'

'How do you know?' Abigail asked, but the child just shook her head.

Kathy came home early. She had been steeling herself all day to face discussion of the problem of leaving Sydney.

'Now, Abigail, let's be straightforward and honest . . .'

'I am,' said Abigail. 'But before we get on to that, what are you going to do with Magpies?'

'Lucille said she'd buy it.'

'Wouldn't it be more sensible to lease it to her, so that you can get it back afterwards?'

'Afterwards!' gasped Kathy. 'Of all the cynical . . .' She had turned quite pale. 'If you want to know, Dad said he's never stopped caring for me.'

'And now for the violins,' said Abigail. The moment the words were out of her mouth she felt terrible, as if she'd taken up the vegetable knife and stuck it into her mother. As for Kathy, she exploded: 'That's a lousy thing to say. Especially from you. When did you ever feel anything for me when Dad left home? You were so wrapped up in your own troubles anyone might have thought no one else was hurt.'

'Well, you might remember I was only ten,' protested Abigail, aghast at this broadside from her mother who had never attacked her before.

'You've been twelve since then, and thirteen and fourteen, the wideawake kid who knows all about men and women and sex and love; and never, not once, have you ever said or asked anything about what I felt when Dad left. Did you ever think of me as a deserted wife, or just of yourself as a deserted child?' shouted Kathy. 'And now I have a chance to experience happiness again, you're going to throw a spanner in the works, because you know very well I won't leave you here with no one but Grandmother to look to if you get ill or . . . or . . . anything.'

She hurried off to the bathroom and spent so long there that Abigail went unhappily to bed.

The next morning Kathy said, 'If you're going to help at Magpies today we'd better get going. Are you?'

'Why not?' said Abigail, and she was glad to hear a voice that was hard and flip, as she wanted it to be.

And for the rest of the painful day, and all the next, no word passed between them except those of ordinary civility. Abigail was glad they were busy, for crates of stuff arrived from the old farm at St Mary's—oil paintings black with smoke and grease, battered colonial furniture, goldfish bowls and petit-point[6] evening bags, and all the fascinating detritus of some unknown person's expended life.

Kathy looked as if she had been crying in the night, for she had put on eyeshadow, which she rarely did. She looked ridiculous, like a finch that had lost a fight. Abigail

6. Needlework.

was so upset she felt dislocated; her emotions were so turbulent that she felt like some sea creature with horny shell and poisonous spines, and bits of weed and shell attached as camouflage. Except that all the camouflage she had was her cool expressionless face, and her green dress, which she kept stroking and touching, as though it gave her comfort, the way Natalie stroked her teddy-bear. And she went on doing this, unconsciously, until at last Kathy screamed:

'Stop that! You've been doing it all day; you're driving me up the wall. I wish you'd take that wretched dress off; it's too cold for this weather. Why do you get so obsessed with some stupid garment? It just sends me round the bend.'

'Maybe there's s-something else you'd like to find wrong with me while you're at it!' Abigail could not keep her voice from shaking. It was unreal. She and her mother did not go on like this. They were friends.

'Oh, shut up!' yelped Kathy, turning to her work. Abigail grabbed her old patchwork shawl (it, too, had come from some deceased estate) and tore up to the corner of the street and caught a West Circular Quay bus. She sat there and boiled while the bus bumped and halted and jerked onwards, and inside the tears ran down and put out the fire of her anger.

It was true. She did wear things until they almost fell off. But always before her mother had laughed.

'That's Abigail, always rapt in something. And why not?' she had said. Already there was a change in both of them.

'It's true,' she thought, sorrowfully, 'I never did think of what she must have felt. Never once did I put my arms around her and say, "Don't mind, I'm still here." It was always Mum who did that to me.'

A bus seemed an unlikely place to have your heart broken in, but she felt that was happening. She didn't even have dark glasses to hide behind. All she could do was to open her burning eyes to their utmost so that the tears wouldn't fall out, and put on the calm, slightly scornful face she had, thank God, practised for years.

'It's all his fault, trying to creep in, spoiling what we have,' she thought. But it was not her father that her thoughts returned to over and over again, it was Mum. 'If she's loved him all this while, and not thought of anyone else, it must have been hell for her. But she's never complained, and when I made those snide remarks about Jan she even said I was unfair. I don't think I could ever say a good word for someone my husband left me for. But it's true, I would expect my only daughter to stand by me. And I didn't. I just thought of how awful it was for me, the way I'm doing right now.'

She had left the bus almost without noticing it. Great steely skies, blanched with approaching winter, arched overhead, and amidst these floated the half-circle of the Bridge, spangled with crimson patches from the sunset, long gone but still painted on the high clouds. The windows of Mitchell and other tall buildings shone tremulously with this ruby light. A cold dusty wind blew from the south, bringing in gusts the iron voice of the city, the dirty, down-at-heel city around Central Railway, drowning the hoot of the hydrofoils, the swish-swash of ferries drawing in and pulling out at Circular Quay.

There were still children tearing around in the playground, and she halted for a moment to watch them. Mothers and older brothers were calling them in. There were not enough to play Beatie Bow; they were chasing each other, screeching aimlessly.

Her eyes turned instinctively to the corner of the wall where it met the street. There lurked Natalie's little furry girl, looking cold and forlorn.

'She looks the way I feel,' thought Abigail.

But how did she feel? Not quite lost but almost. Baffled. A sense of too many strange ideas crowding around her, a feeling of helplessness and difficulty with which she could not come to terms. She thought, 'Maybe they're right. Maybe there is such a thing as being too young and inexperienced to know your own mind.'

Or perhaps it was something simpler. In Norway, if there was family discord once more, she would have no bolt-holes,[7] no familiar places or friends, probably not even anyone to whom she could speak in English. At the thought of this her sensation of vulnerability grew so strong that she almost cried out aloud.

'Mum's got to listen to me,' she thought. 'Maybe she could cope if something went wrong, but I couldn't, I know I couldn't.'

Distinctly she saw the little furry girl sigh, as though sadly disappointed.

And for an instant she reminded Abigail of Natalie, when tormented beyond endurance by the demonic Vincent.

'Poor little rat,' she thought. 'The things kids have to put up with!'

All at once she had an irresistible desire to speak once more to this child, to find out why she watched, why her clothes were so poor, why Natalie thought she had been unhappy. Most of all she wanted to see her smile. She tiptoed along in the shadow of the wall. The little furry girl, looking hopefully at the children, did not see her.

'Boo!' whispered Abigail.

The child leapt in the air like a trout, gaping at Abigail. Her eyes were a light hazel, and Abigail noticed that her hair was tufted and bristly as though growing out after having been shaved.

'Did I give you a start?' she said. 'It was only a joke.'

The other blurted, 'I wasna doing naething! I were only watching the bairns!'

Her voice was hoarse, her accent so extraordinary that Abigail caught only a word or two. But before she could ask the girl to repeat what she had said, the hazel eyes glistened and she said in a half-sob, half-cough, 'I dunna want it to be true, but then again I do, oh, I do!'

This time Abigail heard clearly. Involuntarily she stretched out a hand to this odd troubled child as she might have done to Natty, but the girl leapt away like a hare up the cobbled lane she had used the previous time.

More for curiosity than anything else, Abigail stretched her long legs and raced up the steep alley.

She could not remember ever walking up it before, though it was directly opposite the playground. It ascended as abruptly as a staircase between tall stone walls of warehouses or shops. She did not have time to look. At the top was a little flight of crooked stone steps, and there she could see the child's shawl fluttering, as she hesitated and peered back at her pursuer. The shawl showed dark bottle-green under a street lamp.

'Don't be a silly little twit. I only want to talk to you,' cried Abigail breathlessly. She bounded up the steps into the light and saw that she was in Harrington Street, a queer old road, not much used now, all different levels, so that sometimes one had to step down from the footpath and other times up. The little girl had flickered out of the light, but Abigail could see her bare feet and the edge of her skirt showing in the shadow of a thickety shrub that had followed its network of snaky roots down the crevices of a crumbling stone embankment.

---

7. Hiding places.

She called out teasingly, 'I can see you hiding there!'

Just then, down in the city, the Town Hall clock began its baritone booming, distorted and half drowned by the traffic. But Abigail distinctly heard the first four notes of the simple tune which denoted the half-hour, and she thought, 'Five thirty. I'd best be getting home, I suppose.'

Something, she did not know what, made her hold out her hand to the hidden child and say, in a doomed, dramatic voice. 'Oh, Mudda, what's that, what can it be?'

There was a muffled squeal of surprise or terror, Abigail could not guess which, from the little girl; but before she could make another move she heard a clinking and creaking and rattling and the unmistakable sound of a horse's hoofs. And out of the gathering dusk at the south end of Harrington Street, its two side-lamps shining dimly, for they held only stumps of candles, came a high old-fashioned cab, glittering black in the wavering light from the street lamp.

Abigail was stunned. She stood in the middle of the street, as though she'd lost all power to move, until she could see the very breath from the horse's nostrils in the cold air, and the panic on the face of the tall-hatted cabbie. His lips were curled back, displaying a black gap in the middle of his teeth. He half rose.

'Get outa the road, wench! D'ye want to be run down?'

At that moment the little girl darted from the shadows, almost under the nose of the horse, and pushed Abigail sprawling out of the way. She crashed on what seemed to be wet cobblestones, while the cabbie leant over her and flicked at them both with the tip of his whip, shouting 'Danged baggages! Are ye cracked, standing there like two dummies?'

The cab creaked and clattered onwards. Abigail lay looking up at the lamp. The pedestal was a thick pillar of grooved iron; at the top was a glass-windowed lantern in which waved and waggled a blue fishtail of flame. She had seen pictures of such lamps before, and she knew the light came not from electricity but coal gas.

'Dreaming!' she thought. 'That's all. I'm dreaming.'

But the cobbles were cold and dank, her knees were stinging where she had fallen, the air was full of strange smells, horse manure and tidal flats, wood smoke, human sweat, and an all-pervading odour of sewage.

She felt the little girl withdraw, heard the patter of her bare feet along the road, and panic swept through her.

'Don't leave me—I don't know where I am!'

She scrambled up and ran after the child. Strange, foreign-looking women in long aprons came out of dimly lighted doorways to stare. Children, more dirty and ragged and evil-looking than she had imagined children could be, looked up from floating paper boats in the gutter. One of them threw something stinking at her; it was a rabbit's head, half decayed.

She did not know where she was; all she knew was that the furry little girl might be able to tell her, so she held her skirts up to her knees and ran after her in both terror and desperation.

CHAPTER 3

When she thought about it, weeks afterwards, Abigail felt that surely, surely she must have believed herself dreaming for longer than she did. Why didn't I think I'd got into some street where the television people were shooting a film or something? But she knew she hadn't. From the first minute, as she lay dazed on the cobbles, she knew that she was real and the place was real, and so were the people in it.

The furry little girl tried to lose her, ducking up dogleg courts where the houses pressed close to the earth like lichen. They had shingled roofs covered with moss, and heaps of foul debris around their walls. Sometimes the child glanced over her shoulder as she jumped black gullies of water, or dodged urchins with hair like stiffened mop-heads. Her face was distorted with panic.

The houses were like wasps' nests, or Tibetan houses as Abigail had seen them in films, piled on top of each other, roosting on narrow sandstone ledges, sometimes with a lighted candle stuck in half a turnip on the doorstep, as if to show the way. The dark was coming down, and in those mazy alleys it came quicker. The lamplight that streamed through broken grimy windows was sickly yellow.

The little girl darted past the tall stone cliff of a warehouse, its huge door studded with nail-heads as if against invaders. There Abigail almost caught up with her, but a beggar with a wooden stump reared up and waved his crutch at her, shouting something out of a black toothless mouth. And she saw that she had almost trampled on something she thought was a deformed child, until it leapt snarling to its master's crooked shoulder. It was a monkey in a hussar's uniform.[8]

And now she had gained on the little girl, who was beginning to falter.

They had turned into what Abigail did not immediately recognise as Argyle Street, though she had walked up that street a hundred times. The enormous stone arch of The Cut, the cutting quarried through the sandstone backbone of The Rocks, was different. It was narrower, she thought, though so many shops and stalls and barrows clustered along Argyle Street it was hard to see. Where the Bradfield Highway had roared across the top of The Cut there were now two rickety wooden bridges. Stone steps ran up one side, and on the other two tottering stairways curled upon themselves, overhung with vines and dishevelled trees, and running amongst and even across the roofs of indescribable shanties like broken-down farm sheds. These dwellings were propped up with tree trunks and railway sleepers;[9] goats grazed on their roofs; and over all was the smell of rotting seaweed, ships, wood smoke, human ordure, and horses and harness.

She wondered afterwards why people had stared at her, and realised that it was not because she looked strange—for with her long dress and shawl she was dressed much as they were—but because she was running.

Once a youth with a silly face and a fanciful soldier's uniform, or so she thought, stood in her path, stroking his side whiskers and smirking, but she shoved past him.

Picking out the fugitive child's figure she ran onwards, almost to the edge of The Cut, where the child dived into a doorway of a corner house or shop, with a lighted window and a smell of burnt sugar that for a moment made her hesitate, for she had smelt it before.

And while she stood there, hesitating, there was a fearful noise within—a feminine protest, the clatter of metal, and a man's angry roar.

Out of the doorway bounded a grotesquely tall figure in a long white apron, brandishing what she thought was a rusty scimitar above his head. He was bellowing something like 'Charge the heathen devils!' as he rushed past her, knocking her down as he went. She hit her head hard on the edge of the doorstep.

The pain was so sharp she was quite blinded. Other people burst from the doorway, there were cries of consternation, and she was lifted to her feet. The pain seemed to move to her ankle, she could see nothing but darkness and lights gone fuzzy and dim.

8. Members of Hungarian cavalry units wore bright colors and ornaments and tall, fur hats.

9. Timber used to keep rails in place.

'I'm awfully sorry,' she whispered. 'I think I'm going to faint.'

When she came to herself, she kept her eyes shut, for she knew very well that she was in neither a hospital nor her own home. The air was warm and stuffy; she thought there was an open fire in the room, and it was burning coal. She knew the smell, for Grandmother had an open fireplace in her house, and burnt coal in winter. Someone was holding her hand. It was a woman's hand, not a child's, though the palm was as hard as a man's. The hand was placed on her forehead for a moment, and a voice, with the accent of the little furry girl's, said softly, 'Aye, she's no' so burning. Change the bandage, Dovey, pet, and we'll see how the dint is.'

Gentle hands touched a tender spot on her head. She managed to keep still, with her eyes shut, partly because she was filled with apprehension at what or whom she might see, and partly because she still felt confused and ill. A distant throb in her ankle grew into a savage pain.

Still she did not believe she was dreaming. She thought, 'I've gone out of my mind in some way; this can't be real, even though it is.'

A girl's voice said, ''Tis clean, Granny, but I'll put a touch of the comfrey paste[1] on it, shall I?'

'Do that, lass, and then you'd best see if your Uncle Samuel is himself again.'

'He's greeting,[2] Beatie said, heartsick at what he did.'

'Poor man, poor man, 'tis an evil I dunna ken the cure for.'

As with the little furry girl, Abigail at first thought these unknown women were speaking some foreign tongue. Then she realised it was an English she had never heard before. She thought, 'Perhaps it's Scots.' After those first bewildered moments, she found that if she listened closely the words began to make sense. She was so desperate to find out where she was, and who these people were, that she concentrated as well as she could on all they said; and after a little, as though she had become accustomed to their speech, their words seemed to turn into understandable English.

The voices, especially that of the girl, were placid and lilting.

'She's a lady, Granny, no doubt.'

'Aye.'

Abigail felt her hand lifted. Fingers ran over her palm.

'Soft as plush, and will you see the nails? Pink and clean as the Queen's own.'

Abigail's astonishment at this was submerged in a sickening wave of pain from her ankle. Out of her burst a puppy-like yelp of which she was immediately ashamed. But the pain was too much and she began to sob, 'My foot, my foot!' She opened her eyes and gazed wildly about.

Bending over her was one of the sweetest faces she had ever seen, a young girl's, with a soft, baby's complexion. A horsetail of dull fair hair hung over one shoulder.

'Poor bairnie, poor bairnie. Take a sup of Granny's posset,[3] 'tis so good for pain. There now, all's well, Dovey's here, and Granny, and we'll no' leave you, I promise.'

Granny's posset tasted like parsley, with a bitter aftertaste; but although Abigail thought she would instantly be sick she was not. She drifted drowsily away, lulled by the warmth of the fire and the warm hand holding her own.

When she awakened she seemed to be alone. Her clothes had been taken off, and she was wearing a long nightdress of thick hairy material. It had a linen collar that

1. A traditional remedy for inflammation, bruising, and sprains.
2. Crying.
3. Drink made of hot milk curdled with ale or wine, often spiced with herbs and used medicinally.

rubbed her neck and chin. She cautiously felt this collar. It had been starched to a papery stiffness. One foot, the painful one, was raised on a pillow. The other was against something hard but comfortingly warm. She felt cautiously around it with her toes.

Then a child's voice said, ''Tis a hot pig you're poking at.'

Abigail snapped open her eyes. Natalie's furry girl sat on a stool beside her, so close that Abigail could see the freckles on her face. Her eyes were excited.

Seeing the child so close was strange but comforting, for she knew this child belonged in her own world; she had seen her and Natalie Crown had seen her. And yet, viewed at close hand, she did not seem like an ordinary little girl at all. There was something headstrong and fierce and resolute in her face. Her little hands were marked with scars and burns.

A wave of intense fright ran over Abigail. The very hairs on her arms prickled. Her breathing became fast. Deep inside her, in her secret place, she began to repeat to herself, 'I mustn't lose hold. I must pretend I haven't noticed anything . . . anything strange.'

Now that her head was no longer whirling, though it was still paining, she was able to collect her thoughts. She didn't like the fact that her clothes had been taken away. She remembered all the stories at school, about girls who were drugged and taken away to South America and Uganda and Algeria to be slaves in terrible places there. Nicole Price absolutely swore on the snippet of Elvis's silk bandanna[4] (which was the most sacred thing in the world to her) that her own cousin had been standing in Castlereagh Street waiting for a bus in broad daylight and was never seen again.

After a while she whispered, 'What's a hot pig?'

'Daftie,' said the girl. ''Tis a stone bottle filled with hot water. Dunna ye ken anything?'

'Why does my foot hurt?' asked Abigail.

'Why wouldn't it? You sprained your ankle terrible bad when you fell.'

Abigail felt a feeble spark of anger. 'I didn't fall. Some great ox knocked me over.' She thought for a while. 'He didn't really . . . really have a sword, did he?'

'Aye, he did. That's me faither. He has spells.'

Abigail thought this over but could make nothing of it. Briefly she thought that if she went to sleep again she might wake up in her own room. But the strong smell of the tallow candle that burnt on the table beside her, the crash of cartwheels and hoofs on the cobbles outside the window, the blast of a ship's whistle from somewhere near, the anxious look of the little girl, denied this.

'What's your name?'

'Beatie Bow.'

Abigail scowled. 'Quit having me on, whoever you are. That's the name of a kids' game.'

'I ken that well enough. But it's my name. Beatrice May Bow, and I'm eleven years of age, though small for it, I know, because of the fever.'

Suddenly she gripped Abigail's arm. 'Dunna tell, I'm asking you. Dunna tell Granny where you come from, or I'm for it. She'll say I've the Gift and I havena, and don't want it, God knows, because I'm afeared of what it does.'

Abigail thought muzzily, 'There's some sense in this somewhere, and sooner or later there'll be a clue and I'll understand it.' Aloud she said, 'What is this place?'

'It's the best bedroom, and it's in faither's house, behind the confectionery shop.'

---

4. I.e., a supposed relic of Elvis Presley (1935–1977), the American music icon.

'I mean, what country is it?'

The other girl looked flabbergasted. 'Have ye lost your wits? It's the colony of New South Wales.'[5]

Abigail turned her head into the pillow, which was lumpy and smelled puzzlingly of chicken-coops, and sobbed weakly. She understood nothing except that she was hurt, and was afraid to her very toes, and wanted her mother or even her father.

Beatie said urgently, 'Promise you won't tell where you come from. From *there*. I shouldna ha' done it; I were wicked, I know. But when I heard the bairns calling my name, my heart gave a jump like a spring lamb. But I didna mean to bring you here, I didna know it could be done, heaven's truth.'

She was talking riddles. Abigail was frozen with terror. Was she amongst mad people? The memory of some of those terrible hag faces that had confronted her while she was running returned to her—the caved-in mouths, the skin puckered with old blue scars—of what? The fearsome beggar and his wooden leg, a thing shaped like a peg, like Long John Silver's in *Treasure Island*.[6] She gave a loud snuffle of terror.

Beatie shook her, so that her head and her ankle shot forth pangs of agony.

'Promise me or I'll punch ye yeller and green!'

'Leave me alone,' cried Abigail. 'I don't know where I come from, I don't know where this place is, I can't understand anything.'

'You've lost your memory then,' said the little girl with satisfaction. 'Aye, that'll do bonny.'

Abigail trembled. 'Have I? But I remember lots of things: my name, and how old I am, and I live in George Street North, and my mother's name is Kathy, and she's angry with me because . . . .' At the thought of her mother, coming home and finding her missing, ringing the police, Dad, being frantic, she lost her head and began to scream. She saw the elder girl limp into the room. Why did she limp? And Beatie Bow looking frightened and defiant.

Then she became aware that a tall old woman stood beside her, holding her hand. She wore a long black dress and white apron, and on her head was a huge pleated white cap with streamers. Afterwards Abigail realised she looked exactly like a fairy godmother, but at the time she thought nothing. She said wonderingly, 'Granny!'

'She's no' your granny, she's ours!' snapped Beatie. Dovey hushed her, smiling.

The old woman put her arms round Abigail, and rocked her against a bosom corseted as hard as a board. Terrified as she was, she was at once aware of the goodness that dwelt in this old woman.

She stole a look upwards, saw the brown skin creased like old silk, a sculptured smile on the sunken mouth. It was a composed, private face, with the lines of hardship and grief written on it.

'There, there, lassie, dinna take on so. Granny's here.'

Abigail pressed her face into the black tucked cloth, and held on tight. Something strong and calm radiated from the old woman.

Never in your whole life could you imagine her addressing snide remarks to her bonnet, or the grey silky hair that showed beneath it. She was a real grandmother.

Above her head she heard the grandmother murmur, 'Fetch Judah, Beatie, pet. I think I heard his step. He's that good with bairns.'

---

5. New South Wales became a British colony in 1846 and was federated as a state of the Commonwealth of Australia in 1901; it was originally settled in 1788 as a penal colony.

6. The 1883 novel of pirates and adventure by the Scottish author Robert Louis Stevenson.

'I want my mother,' moaned Abigail.

'Rest sure, my bonnie, that you'll have your mother as soon as we know where she lives, and what you're called.'

A tall young man entered the room. She had a glimpse of fair hair, cut strangely, a square-cut jacket of black or dark blue, with metal buttons, crumpled white trousers.

'Faither's in a state, fair adrift with fright and sorrow. You'd best sit with him, Dovey, till he comes out of it.'

'I'm frightened, I'm frightened,' Abigail whispered.

The young man sat beside her. She could not see his face because the light was in her eyes. Instead she saw a big brown hand, on the outstretched forefinger of which perched a bird as big as a thimble, its feathers a tinsel green.

'Would you know what that is, Eliza?'

'My name isn't Eliza,' whispered Abigail, 'it's Abigail. And that's a humming-bird. But it isn't alive, it's stuffed.'

The young man stroked the tiny glittering head with one finger.

'She came from the Orinoco. I got her for a florin from a deepwater man.'[7] Did ye ever see aught as fine?'

He turned the finger this way and that, and the little bird shone like an emerald.

'Will you listen to the way she speaks,' murmured the old woman to Beatie. 'I fear your dada will be in desperate trouble if he's injured her, for she's a lady.'

'I'm not a lady,' muttered Abigail. 'I'm just a girl. *You're* a lady.'

'Not me, child,' said the old woman. 'Why, we Talliskers have been fisherfolk since the Earls of Stewart.'[8]

Abigail could make no sense of any of it. She buried her face in the chickeny pillow. Maybe when she opened her eyes again she would be in her own bed, her own bedroom. But clearly she heard the young man blowing up the fire. It was with a bellows. She knew the rhythmic wheeze, for bellows were a popular item at Magpies. There! She remembered Magpies, even where things were put; Mum's crazy sixty-year-old cash register with all the beautiful bronze-work, the green plush tablecloth draped over the delicate rattan whatnot.[9]

She forced her eyes open. The room was now much brighter. The firelight leapt up, reflecting pinkly on a sloping ceiling. On the table was now a tall oil lamp, and Dovey was carefully turning down the wick.

There was a marble wash-stand in the corner, with a blue flowered thick china wash-basin set into a recess. Underneath stood a tall fluted water jug, and a similarly patterned chamber-pot. The fireplace had an iron hob and on it was a jug of what Abigail thought, from the delicious smell, was hot cocoa. The jug was large and white, and in an oval of leaves was imprinted the face of a youngish man with long dark silky whiskers. She had seen him before in Magpies, too.

'That's Prince Albert,[1] isn't it?' she asked.

'Yes, God rest him. He was taken too soon,' replied the old woman.

Judah brought something out of his pocket and proffered it to her on the palm of his brown hand. It was a pink sugar mouse.

'Our faither makes them. Do you fancy a nibble?'

Abigail did not even see it. She sat shakily up in bed. She saw over the mantel a

---

7. I.e., one who sails across the ocean (rather than along the coast). "Florin": a coin used by several nations; here probably a British silver coin valued at two shillings. The Orinoco: river in Venezuela.
8. Noble, and eventually royal, Scottish family originating in the twelfth century.
9. Open stand of shelves used to display various objects and curios.
1. Albert of Saxe-Coburg Gotha (1819–1861), prince consort (husband) of Queen Victoria.

picture of a middle-aged woman in black, with a small coronet over a white lace veil.

How many times had Abigail seen that sulky, solemn face—on china, miniatures, christening mugs?

'Why ever have you a picture of old Victoria[2] on the wall?' she asked.

'You mustn't speak of our gracious Queen in that way, child!' said Granny severely.

'But our queen is Elizabeth!'

They laughed kindly. 'Why, good Queen Bess[3] died hundreds of years ago, lass. You're still wandering a little; but don't fret: tomorrow you'll be as good as gold.'

Abigail said nothing more. She stared at Queen Victoria in her black widow's weeds and her jet jewellery. Once again, deep inside her, she was saying, 'I must be calm. There's some explanation. I mustn't give myself away.'

Out in the darkness she could hear ships baa-ing on the harbour. 'Is it foggy?' she asked.

'Aye, so maybe I won't be leaving in the morn,' said Judah. 'I'm a seaman, you see, lass.'

Quite near by a bell blommed slow and stately. Abigail jumped.

'It's naught but St Philip's ringing for evensong,' said Dovey softly. 'Ah, she's all of a swither[4] with the shock she got when Uncle Samuel ran into her, poor lamb.'

Abigail tried to still her quaking body. She said to the young man, 'I want to see where I am. Would you help me to the window?'

'Sure as your life, hen,'[5] replied the young fellow heartily. Abigail had expected only to lean on his arm, but he gathered her up, bedclothes and all, and took her to the window. He had the same dark-blue eyes as the old woman.

'What are ye girning[6] about, Beatie?' he chided. 'Open the shutters, lass.'

Sulkily and unwillingly, the little girl unlatched the shutters and threw them wide. Abigail looked out on a gas-lit street, fog forming ghostly rainbows about the lamps. A man pushed a barrow on which glowed a brazier. 'Hot chestnuts, all hot, all hot!' His shout came clearly to Abigail. Women hurried past, all with shawls, some with men's caps pulled over their hair, others with large battered hats with tattered feathers.

But Abigail was looking for something else. She was upstairs, she knew, above the confectionery shop, and she had a wide view of smoking chimneys, hundreds, thousands of smoking chimneys, it seemed, each with a faint pink glow above it.

Mitchell should have been standing there, lit like a Christmas tree at this time of night. The city should have glittered like a galaxy of stars. The city was still there—she could see dimmish blotches of light, and vehicles that moved very slowly and bumpily.

'The Bridge has gone, too,' she whispered. No broad lighted deck strode across the little peninsula, no great arch with its winking ruby at the highest point—nothing. The flower-like outline of the Opera House was missing.

She turned her face against Judah's chest and buried it so deeply that she could even hear his heart thumping steadily.

'What is it, Abby? What ails you, child?'

For the first time she looked into his face. It was brown and ruddy, a snubbed, country kind of face.

'What year is this?' she whispered.

He looked dumbfounded. 'Are you codding[7] me?'

'What year is it?' she repeated.

---

2. Queen of England (1819–1901; r. 1837–1901), often portrayed in black because she was a widow for forty years.
3. Elizabeth I (1533–1603; r. 1558–1603).

4. In a state of anxiety or doubt.
5. A term of endearment (mainly Scottish).
6. Snarling, complaining.
7. Hoaxing, fooling.

'Why, it's 1873, and most gone already,' he said.

Abigail said no more. He took her back to the bed, and Dovey gently folded the covers over her.

'It's true then,' she said uneasily to the old grandmother. 'She's lost her memory. Dear God, what will we do, Granny? For 'twas Uncle Samuel that caused it, and in all charity we've the responsibility of her.'

The tall old woman murmured something. Abigail caught the word 'stranger . . .'

Dovey looked dubious. 'It's my belief she's an immigrant lass, sent to one of the fine houses on the High Rocks to be a parlourmaid, perhaps, for she speaks so bonny. Not like folk hereabouts at all! But where's her traps,[8] do you think, Granny? Stolen or lost? Just what she stood up in, and the Dear knows there was little enough of that!'

Thus they talked in low voices beside the door, while Beatie Bow crept a little closer and stared with thrilled yet terrified eyes at Abigail.

'You!' said Abigail in a fierce whisper. 'You did this to me!'

''Tisn't so,' objected Beatie. 'You chased me up alley and down gully, like a fox after a hare. It wunna my fault!'

Abigail was silent. She kept saying to herself, 'Abigail Kirk, that's who I am. I mustn't forget. I might sink down and get lost in this place—this time, or whatever it is—if I don't keep my mind on it.'

Judah and Granny had gone down the stairs. Dovey limped over and put a hand on Abigail's forehead. 'You've no fever, and the ankle will be a wee bit easier tomorrow. You stay here and talk to Abby, Beatie, seeing that you're getting on so grand, and I'll heat up some broth for your supper.'

Beatie stared at Abigail crossly, defiantly, and yet with anxiety.

'It'd be no skin off your nose if you codded you'd lost your memory because of that dint on the head. I dunna want my granny to know.'

'I want to go back to my own place,' said Abigail in a hard voice.

'I dunna ken where your ain place is,' protested Beatie. 'I didna mean to go there myself. It were the bairnies calling my name. I dunna ken how I did it, honest. I never did it afore I had the fever.'

As though to herself, in a puzzled, worried voice she said, 'One minute I was in the lane, and the next there was a wall there, and the bairnies skittering about, and all those places like towers and castles and that . . . that great road that goes over the water, and strange carriages on it with never a horse amongst them, and I was afeared out of my wits, thinking the fever had turned my brain. And then I heard children calling my name, and they were playing a game we play around the streets here, except that we call it Janey Jo. But they couldna see me, because I tried to speak to one or two. Only you and that wee little one with the yellow coat.'

The child's cocky attitude had vanished. Her face was sallow and the big hollow eyes shone. Abigail remembered that Natalie had wept because she believed that this girl had been unhappy. She had mentioned fever. Perhaps that was why Beatie's hair had been cut so short. Abigail remembered that once it had been the custom to shave the heads of fever patients. She was about to ask about this, when Beatie said in an awed voice, 'Is it Elfland, that place where you come from?'

'Of course it isn't, there isn't any Elfland. Are you crazy?'

Beatie said in a hushed voice. 'Green as a leek, you are. Of course there's Elfland.

8. Belongings.

Isn't that where Granny's great-great-granny got the Gift, the time she was lost so long?'

'You're crazy,' said Abigail. 'You're all crazy.'

She closed her eyes. The fire crackled, the room was full of strange smells, but the smell of burnt sugar was strongest of all. A hand timidly touched hers.

'It's bonny.'

'What is?'

'That place you were. Elfland.'

Abigail opened her eyes and glared into the tawny ones. 'I told you it wasn't Elfland.'

'Where is it then?'

'Guess,' said Abigail snappily.

Beatie Bow was silent. Abigail stared at the ceiling. Then Beatie Bow said, 'How did those children know my name?'

'I wouldn't know, and if I did I wouldn't tell you.'

She wanted to scream like a seagull. With a great effort she kept the sounds of lostness and fright down in her chest. Her head was throbbing again and her ankle felt like a bursting football.

'If it wasna Elfland,' said Beatie slowly and thoughtfully, 'it was some place I dunna ken about. Yet the bairns there don't play Janey Jo any more; they play Beatie Bow.'

Abigail didn't answer.

Suddenly the little girl shouted, 'I will make you tell, I will! I want to know about the castles and palaces, and the lights that went so fast, and the queer old things the bairns were playing on, and how they knew my name. I'll punch ye yeller and green, I swear it, if ye dunna tell!'

'Maybe you've got the Gift,' said Abigail cruelly. Beatie turned so white her freckles seemed twice as numerous. Abigail said, 'You get me back there where I met you, or I'll tell your granny where I come from and who brought me.'

Beatie whipped up a hard little fist as though to clout her.

'I dunna want the Gift. I'm feared of it! I wunna have it!'

Abigail thought hazily, 'When I get back home, or wake up, or whatever I'm going to do, I'll be sorry I didn't ask her what this stupid Gift is. But just now I don't care.'

She turned away from Beatie's anxious, angry face, and pretended to be asleep. Within a moment or two she was.

CHAPTER 4

Twice during the night Abigail awakened to hear a child whimpering forlornly somewhere above the ceiling.

'That can't be,' she thought muzzily. Then she remembered that this was an old-fashioned house. There might be attics.

Dovey had left the lamp turned low. The round glass globe had bunches of grapes etched on it. The fire had gone out and there was a smell of cold ashes.

She heard a halting step on stairs somewhere. So there really must be yet another child, and Dovey was coming down from looking after it.

Abigail didn't know whether she liked Dovey or not. She seemed so gentle and good, but Abigail knew from books and TV that an angelic exterior often hid an interior chock-full of black evil. Besides, she didn't want to be comforted by Dovey at two in the morning or whatever it was; so as the girl limped into the room Abigail pretended to be asleep. Dovey wore a baggy red-flannel dressing-gown, and her hair was in a plait tied with a scrap of wool. She looked worn and sleepy.

Granny was with her in an even baggier red-flannel dressing-gown. Her hair was tucked under what Abigail imagined was a nightcap, a little baby bonnet with a frill about the face, and tapes under the chin.

'The hideous clothes the Victorian working class wore,' marvelled Abigail—a long way from the hailstone muslin[9] and exquisite China silks that sometimes ended up at Magpies.

'Did Judah get away, hen?' asked Granny.

'Aye. He'll sleep on board, for the fog's lifting and he thought the skipper'd be away with the morn's tide. I gave Gibbie a draught and he's asleep, but he looks poorly, Granny. Do you have a good or a bad feeling about him, poor bairn?'

Granny sighed. 'I hae no clear feelings any more, Dovey. They're as mixed up as folk in fog.'

'But you've no doubt that this little one here is the Stranger?'

The two women spoke in whispers, but Abigail heard them, for the night was almost silent. There was no sound of traffic except a dray's wheels rolling like distant thunder over the cobbles at the docks. She could hear the waves breaking on the rocks of Dawes Point and Walsh Bay.

'Aye, when I first saw her I had a flash, clear as it was when I was a lass. Poor ill-favoured little yellow herring of a thing. But still, it came to me then, she was the Stranger that would save the Gift for the family.'

Abigail was so indignant at the description of herself that she almost opened her eyes.

'And then there was the gown, forebye. I swear, Granny, I almost fainted when I set eyes on it. The very pattern that we worked out between us!'

'And not a needle lifted to it yet,' said Granny. 'Hush, Dovey, the child is stirring.'

The lamp's reflections on the ceiling shifted, and the room was left in darkness. Abigail had the impression that Dovey came back to sleep in the other bed, but she was unable to keep awake to see.

'I'll bet I've had one of Granny's possets in the cocoa or something. On top of everything else they'll poison me.'

This was her last outraged thought as she sank into sleep. She was still resentful when she awoke. The trundle-bed had been slept in but was unoccupied; the house was full of unfamiliar noises, metal clinking vigorously (the fire downstairs being raked out?), the continuous puling complaint from above (the mysterious Gibbie?), someone yelling in a temper (Beatie, without a doubt), and Granny's soft full tones, making peace amongst them all.

She struggled to a sitting position. Her head felt better, clearer. Her ankle still hurt frightfully. She peeled back the bedclothes to look at it. Hideous! Yellow and purple and swollen to twice its size. But perhaps it wasn't as painful as yesterday.

'Now then,' thought Abigail, inside this new clear head, 'something very weird has happened to me. I'm in the last century. I don't know why, and that doesn't matter. I've got to get back, before Mum goes mad with worry. Dad, too, I suppose. Now, what were those women talking about last night when they thought I was asleep?'

She concentrated. Some of the words came back.

9. Delicately woven cotton fabric also known as dotted swiss.

'I didn't dream them. Granny said I was the Stranger, without doubt. Well, I'm a stranger all right, but what's *the* Stranger? And there was that other bit about saving the Gift for the family. This creepy Gift that Beatie's always sounding off about.

'Then they said something about my dress, my Edwardian dress.'

She was puzzling her head over the half-remembered words when Dovey entered with a metal can full of steaming water.

She poured it in the basin on the wash-stand.

'How do you feel this morning, Abby love?'

'Better,' said Abby. 'I want to get up. I think I can hop around.'

'We'll ask Granny first.' Dovey smiled. 'Can you remember anything more clear-like today?'

Abigail was about to tell her snippily that she had never forgotten anything at all, but caution kept her silent. She said, 'I'm Abigail Kirk, and I'm fourteen.'

'Never!' said Dovey, astonished. 'I'd thought you about our Beatie's age. Why, you've not filled out in the least.'

Abigail thought bitterly of the 'little yellow herring of a thing' but kept her thoughts to herself. She said with false wistfulness, 'It's a pity, but none of my fault.'

'Perhaps you were not well fed as a babby,' said Dovey sympathetically, briskly washing Abigail down to the waist.

'They've no business sending you out to a situation, under-sized as you are. There now, put on your shift, hen, and I'll give your legs a rub.'

'Can't I have my own clothes?' asked Abigail. 'Where's my dress?'

Dovey looked uncomfortable. A rosebud blush crept over her china-like complexion. 'I believe 'twas so stained with blood and dirt Granny burnt it.'

'But it was new and I loved it,' wailed Abigail. Just in time she clamped her mouth shut. Don't talk. Just listen. You have to be sharper than these people, nice as they seem to be, or you'll never get home.

'It was my best,' she said chokily.

'Ne'er mind,' Dovey said soothingly. 'I've a skirt and bodice you can wear and welcome. But first we must let Granny see if you're well enough to come downstairs.'

Granny said no. She said after a dint on the head-bone rest was necessary.

'But I've nothing to do,' complained Abigail. 'Isn't there anything I can read?'

Dovey and Granny exchanged pleased glances. 'So you can read, lass? Can you figure, too?'

In her astonishment Abigail almost laughed, but she lowered her eyes and said, 'Well enough.'

'In our family we have considerable learning,' said Granny with quiet pride, 'for we had the advantage of a grand dominie back home in Orkney.[1] But here in the colony poor Beatie and Gibbie, who's the wean that's still sickly from the fever that carried off his mother and her babe—they've naught but the Ragged School.[2] And that's no' good enough for Talliskers, even though it may be so for Bows.'

'Now, Granny,' objected Dovey mildly. ''Tisn't Uncle Samuel's fault he can sign his name only with a cross. To be sore wounded for his country's sake is more than enough to ask of a sojer.'

1. Island group off the northeast coast of Scotland. "Dominie": schoolmaster.
2. School that taught poor children basic literacy skills, as well as plain sewing for girls and light carpentry for boys. "Wean": child.

But there was nothing for Abigail to read except the family Bible, and to this she shook her head.

'You're never godless?' asked Granny anxiously. After some thought Abigail understood she was asking about religion.

'I don't remember,' she whispered.

'Poor bairnie,' said Granny. 'Dovey, send Beatie to her when she comes from school, to speak to her of Scripture. It may bring the child's memories back to her. Not to remember our Father in Heaven!'

At the thought of her own father, Abigail's eyes filled with genuine tears. Oh, what was he doing? Thinking her kidnapped or murdered, comforting her mother or blaming her for letting her go home alone?

'Be brave, lass,' said Granny. 'You can do no less.'

Abigail looked blurrily at the strong clear-cut features of the old woman. 'All right for you,' she thought; 'you aren't desperate like me.'

While she lay there the sounds of the nineteenth-century Rocks rose up from out of the street, horses slipping and sliding on slimy cobbles, a refrain from a concertina, market cries: 'Tripe, all 'ot and juicy! Cloes prarps! Windsor apples! Rag 'n' bones, bring 'em out! China pears! Lamp oil, cheapest in town!'

From somewhere near the water came the sweetly harsh summons of a bugle. 'That'll be the Dawes Point Battery,'[3] thought Abigail, marvelling. 'Fancy—real live troops there, and muskets and drums! And all I've ever seen in my time are bits of old wall, and the cannons, and grass, and people sitting under the Bridge eating their lunches.'

Disagreeable things happened to her. She had to use the chamber-pot, while Dovey bustled around tossing up her pillows and pulling the coverlet straight. Of course, it had to be done. Abigail realised that the lavatory, if there was one, would be a little shed at the bottom of the yard, with a can and a wooden seat with a hole in it. But even though Dovey was matter-of-fact about it, Abigail hated it.

To keep her mind off her embarrassment she thought how much her mother would enjoy seeing Dovey. She was so like one of the Victorian china dolls that sold for huge prices at Magpies that Abigail wondered if the dolls' faces hadn't been modelled on those of real girls. She had a tiny chin with a dent in it, blue eyes that Abigail thought bulgy, and a little soft neck with circular wrinkles running around it.

Her real name was Dorcas Tallisker, and she limped because when they were young Judah had run over the cliff with her in a trundle-cart[4] and her thigh-bone had been broken. Sometimes it stiffened up, and then she had to walk with a stick; but the warm New South Wales weather had made the pain lessen.

'The Orkney isles are harsh country,' she said, 'for all there is such beauty there— the heather, and the wild birds crying, and the great craigs and the magic stones.'[5]

'Magic stones?' asked Abigail.

'Aye,' said Dovey simply. 'Built by dwarfies, ye ken, and even giants so they say, long before the Northmen came; for Orkney folk is half Scots and half Norwegian, so 'tis said. Ah, I would that I was there now, milking my wee cow Silky.'

Sad of face, she helped Abigail back to bed and went away with the chamber-pot covered with a cloth. Soon she was back with a little brass shovel with a few red hot coals upon it. Abigail watched with interest as Dovey put sprigs of dried

---

3. Fort constructed in 1791 to guard the approach to Sydney.
4. A low cart on small wheels.

5. The Orkneys contain prominent Stone Age henges, or circles of standing stones.

lavender on the coals and waved the resultant thin blue smoke about the room.

'There now! You're all sweet again.'

'Can't I have the window open?' asked Abigail.

Dovey was shocked. 'But the spring air brings so many fluxes and congestions in the chest,' she said. 'And you're still no' yourself, ye ken, Abby.'

So it was spring. But how? For when she had left home it was already lowering with winter. She recalled how Beatie, in her thin dress and shawl, had shuddered with cold.

How could it be? Where had all the time gone?

But she was unable to puzzle further, because footsteps came up the stairs. Dovey, brushing Abigail's hair, hastily pulled the sheet up to her neck, so that she would look proper, and said, ''Tis Uncle Samuel. Try to forgive him for the harm he did you, love, for, as you'll see, he's a pitiful man.'

The tall man who came stooping through the little doorway was stooped and spindly himself. He was the ruin of what had probably been a handsome trooper in his blue and buff uniform and pipe-clayed gaiters. His ashy hair looked as if it had flour in it, and his bright blue eyes were spectacularly crossed.

''Tis the effect of the head wound,' murmured Dovey. She said in a louder voice, 'Come in, Uncle Samuel. Abigail is much better today.'

Mr Bow wore a long white apron. He smelt deliciously of syrup and almonds. He twisted his scarred hands in his apron and said abjectly, 'Oh, dear Miss, there hain't words to tell how broken up I am for doin' yer such damage. It's these spells, you see. I think I'm back at Balaclava[6] and I hain't seein' a thing but Rooshians like bears in their big coats. And I pray from the bottom of me heart, honest to God, that I didn't do yer too much harm.'

Abigail was much taken with Mr Bow. He looked so much like a Siamese cat. She could see Beatie's little face scowling from under his arm.

'It wasn't your fault, Mr Bow. I just didn't get out of the way quickly enough. And all I have are a sprained ankle and a bump on the head, so you've nothing to worry about.'

'You're sartin sure you forgive me?' he asked pleadingly. 'I hain't been myself since my dear 'Melia died, you see, and then when Granny tells me you're the Stranger . . .'

'Hush, Dada!' said Beatie, and the tall man, mopping his eyes, turned, muttering, 'Ah, she was a good wife, my 'Melia, and the babby, such a fine sonsy[7] lad—make two of Gibbie, he would.'

As he went out, Beatie dawdled in and gave Abby a sullen look.

'Did you do well at school today, hen?' asked Dovey.

'Patching,' Beatie said scornfully, 'and how to curtsey when the Lady Visitor[8] came. And I was sore scolded for wearing no shoes. The Lady Visitor said I might as well be a Chinaman.'

'Indeed!' exclaimed Dovey. Bright scarlet stained her cheeks. 'We'll do something about that. Orkney folk are not to be spoken to in such a way, I tell you. But I'll not soil myself with anger at such trash. Beatie, lass, Granny wants you to read the Gospel to Abby, for she's no memory of the Lord's good words, either.'

---

6. Port on the Crimean Peninsula, which extends into the Black Sea. It was British headquarters during the Crimean War, and the scene of a famous and ill-fated British cavalry charge against the Russian artillery in 1854.

7. Healthy, thriving.

8. One who visits to inspect or supervise a school.

From the tall narrow cupboard she took a huge book bound in half-bald green plush, its edges reinforced with well-polished brass.

'The Sermon on the Mount[9] would be a bonny choice,' she said. 'And now I'll see to Gibbie. Granny's been up with him half the night.'

Beatie grimaced at Abigail. 'I'd liefer read the bloody bits, about slaughtering the enemy and blowing down walls and sticking pikes into the Canaanites.'[1]

'Save your breath,' said Abigail briskly. She pulled herself up on her pillows. 'I want to talk to you.'

'If you're about to ask me to take you back where I got you, you can save your ain breath,' snapped Beatie, 'because I don't know how to do it, and that's the truth of it.'

The two girls glared at each other. Then Abigail laughed. The younger child was such a fierce homely creature, the eyes so bright and intelligent, the small thin hands crooked as though they would claw the eyes out of life itself.

'You've got plenty of brains,' said Abigail.

'Aye,' said Beatie suspiciously. 'And what brings you to say that?'

'Because I think you want to do other things besides learn how to feather-stitch and drop curtseys to rude rich old hags at the Ragged School.'

Beatie's tawny eyes glittered. 'True enough. I want to learn Greek and Latin like the boys. And geography. And algebra. And yet I'll never. Gibbie will learn them afore me, and he's next door to a mumblepate!'

'But why?' asked Abigail.

'Why, why?' cried Beatie. 'Because I'm a girl, that's why, and girls canna become scholars. Not unless their fathers are rich, and most of *their* daughters are learnt naught but how to dabble in paints, twiddle on the pianoforte, and make themselves pretty for a good match!'

Suddenly light broke upon Abigail. 'So that's why you wanted to know why the children were playing Beatie Bow, how they got to know about you?'

'That's what I asked before,' answered Beatie resentfully, 'an' ye wunna tell me, damn ye!'

'Well, I don't truly know,' said Abigail, 'but I think I can guess.'

'Tell me!' cried Beatie, bright-eyed.

'We'll trade,' said Abigail.

'I dinna know what you mean,' said Beatie suspiciously.

'You say you can't get me back to where I came from. Maybe that's true. But could you help me to Harrington Street? Because that's where things started to change. And maybe if I got back there . . .'

'I could. But it wunna be easy because Granny thinks you're none other than . . .' Beatie stopped short.

'I know. The Stranger, whatever that is. But will you help me get to Harrington Street, when my ankle's a little better?'

'I dinna like going agin Granny,' muttered Beatie. 'She's got the Gift. It's not what it was when she was a lass, but she's still got powers.'

'Very well, then. Go away,' said Abigail, and she lay down and turned her back on Beatie. She heard the child fidgeting around, going to the door once or twice, then coming back hesitantly to stand beside the bed.

9. The essence of Jesus' teachings (Matthew 5.1–7.27).
1. Inhabitants of the land that God promised to the Israelites (e.g., Genesis 17.8; Exodus 32.49).

The defeat of the Canaanites is described in the book of Joshua, which also contains the account of "blowing down walls" (the fall of Jericho; Joshua 6.4–20).

'Right, I'll help you, and the dear God help me if Granny kens what I'm doing, for she's dead set on your staying. There, I've given my word. Now for your part of the bargain.'

Abigail sat up again. 'I think those children were using your name in their game because you got to be famous.'

Beatie's face flushed. 'Me? You're daft. Famous? In Elfland?'

'It isn't Elfland,' said Abigail, exasperated. 'How many more times? If I tell you where . . . what . . . that place is, do you solemnly swear it will be our secret?'

'I swear,' said Beatie. 'I swear by my mother's grave, and there inna anything in the world more sacred than that.'

So Abigail told her. The little girl burst into wrathful indignation.

'You ought to be ashamed, telling me such lees. You'll go to hell for it, and be toasted on a pitchfork!'

'You saw it for yourself,' said Abigail, taken aback, 'the Bridge and the Opera House, and all the tall buildings. Why, I live in one of them, right at the top!'

'You're a damned leear. Such things inna possible except in Elfland.' But the girl's voice quavered.

'I wouldn't have thought this place, time, or whatever it is, would be possible either,' Abigail said angrily.

'What's the matter with here then?' shouted Beatie in a whisper.

'For one thing, it stinks like a pig-pen, and for another they won't let a girl have a proper education, and for another people can die here of fever, and smallpox, and diphtheria.'

Beatie was silent. Then she said hoarsely, 'Don't folk die of those things in . . . that time?' When Abigail shook her head, Beatie broke into a passion of sobbing. 'Then Mamma would still be alive, and the babby, and Gibbie wouldn't be so sickly.'

Abigail let her sob. Suddenly she felt towards this wounded tough little scrap as she had felt towards Natalie in that other life. But she did not touch her. She knew instinctively that Beatie would throw off any sympathetic hand.

At last Beatie was silent.

'I thought I was over it,' she said in a stifled voice.

'You will be some day.'

'It wunna lees you told me, then?'

'No,' said Abigail. 'But I want to get back as soon as I can walk properly because my mother and father will be anxious to death about me.'

Beatie nodded. 'I know how you feel about your mother. When I cried when Mamma was dying, Dovey said "Dunna let her go to her reward fretting about you, child"—that's what she said. "For Granny and I are here to look after you and Gib. I'll be your mother, hen," she said. "Smile now and let your mamma be at ease." So I did.'

She was quiet for a while, sniffling. Then she said grudgingly, 'You're no' so bad, you.'

'Neither are you,' said Abigail, grinning. 'Is it a bargain then?'

Beatie stuck out her hard, work-harsh little fist and they shook hands.

During the next two days Abigail learnt a great deal about these people amongst whom she had been thrown in such a strange way. She learnt that the Orkneys were a hard and ancient group of islands set amongst dangerous seas north of Scotland. All of the family had been born there except Mr Bow the Englishman, Gibbie, and the baby boy who had died with his mother.

Dorcas Tallisker was the cousin of the Bows. Her mother had died when she was born, and she was reared by her fisherman father Robert Tallisker, and his mother, Granny. Two years before, Dovey's father was drowned in a squall in Hoy Sound, off Stromness,[2] and Granny had decided to emigrate to New South Wales to live with her daughter, Amelia, who had married an English soldier, Samuel Bow. When Dovey and Granny arrived, they found Amelia, the children Beatie and Gilbert, and a six-months-old infant, deathly ill with the fever.

'What kind of fever?' thought Abigail uneasily, remembering that though she had been immunised against most modern infectious diseases, a dockside area of the 1870s very likely had plenty of lethal bugs of its own.

'The typhoid,' said Beatie. ''Tis very common in these parts.'

Abigail decided she'd drink nothing but tea. At least she would know the water had been boiled.

'And now tell me about the Gift,' she said. Beatie gave her a scared look.

'No, I wunna. Granny would ne'er forgive me. It's the family Gift, you see.'

'But I'm connected with it in some way. I'm the Stranger. Even your father said so. I ought to know what it is; it's my right. Tell me or I'll ask Granny.'

'Dunna,' pleaded the child. 'I'm gey[3] scared of it, Abby. I dunna want it. I just want to be a scholar. I dunna want to see things and know things a mortal body shouldna know.'

'Why,' Abigail thought, 'it's the second sight, ESP, or something. And Beatie's afraid that she might have it too, poor brat.'

But she said nothing.

By the third day she was allowed to get dressed and be carried downstairs by Mr Bow. In fact she was dressed by Dovey: for when confronted with the garments the older girl lent her she had not the faintest idea how to put them on. There was a boned bodice of stiff calico fastened with rows of strong hooks and eyes at the back. Abigail eyed it with distaste.

'Where's my own underwear?' she demanded.

'But you had hardly a thing for underclothes,' answered Dovey. 'Just a few queer rags and drawers the size of a baby's. Now, slip your arms through here, and I'll hook you up, and you'll be more comfortable.'

Scowling, Abigail did so. She also obediently drew on the cotton knickers[4] and the long flannel ones that went over them, a waist petticoat that tied with a tape, and a woollen blouse that had long full sleeves and did up to the neck with an endless row of pearl buttons.

'She's such a skinny wee thing she won't need the stays, Granny,' said Dovey. Abigail thanked heaven.

'I'm boiling,' she said. 'I don't wear heavy clothes like this, ever!'

''Tis the kind of clothes worn at this season,' said Granny with her quiet inflexibility, 'and Dovey's best, at that.'

'I do thank you,' said Abigail awkwardly, 'but it's not what I'm used to, you see.'

When she was completely dressed, in a long dark serge skirt over the blouse, a ribbon belt with a pewter buckle, knee-high stockings of hand-knitted wool in circles of brown and yellow, and one of Granny's best buttoned boots (for Dovey had feet as tiny as her hands, and her boots would not fit Abigail by three sizes) on her good leg, she felt like a wooden image, stiff, clumsy, and half choked with the smell of mothballs and lavender that drifted from the fabric. On her other foot she had a

2. Large port on Pomona (Mainland) Island.
3. Very.
4. Underpants.

knitted slipper with a fringed top. She hopped over to the mirror and recoiled.

'I never saw such a scarecrow in my life!'

She looked so hideous she could have cried. But she had finished with crying; and, anyway, she couldn't afford to lose her eyes as well.

'You'll look more yourself when your hair is brushed,' said Dovey in her soothing way. She brushed Abigail's hair flat off her forehead and plaited it tightly from the nape of her neck. The corners of Abigail's eyes were pulled taut, so that she looked like a beaten-up Oriental. A huge greenish-blue bruise extended from her forehead to her cheek. Her nose had become pointy, and her teeth seemed to stick out.

'Dracula teeth,' she said mournfully, then hurriedly covered her slip[5] by murmuring, 'I look so awful!'

'Beauty does not matter. It is all vanity, the Good Book says,' reproved Dovey gently.

'No wonder people in Victorian photographs look so monstrous,' thought Abigail. 'They didn't have a chance, what with no make-up, ugly hair-dos and clothes that would make the skinniest woman look like a haystack.'

Mr Bow carried her downstairs. He seemed silent and absent-minded. There was a peculiar dull sheen in his eyes, and a red patch on each cheek.

Downstairs the odours of sweet-making were strong. Abigail could smell aniseed, treacle,[6] hot butter, and boiling sugar.

She said, 'I'd so like to see the shop, Mr Bow.' But he did not seem to hear.

'I bet he's working up to another spell,' she thought uneasily. Being so close to his head she could see the old wound in his skull, a scarred hole only half covered by the ashy grey hair. It was so big she could have laid the fingers of one hand in it. She shuddered and looked away.

'What did they fight with in that Crimean War?[7] Axes?' she wondered. 'How it must have hurt!'

He carried her into the little front room. A small fire burnt in the basket grate. The furniture, covered with rose-patterned plush and stuffed as hard as bricks with horsehair, was plainly not for sitting on. Abigail was placed in a rocking-chair to one side of the fireplace. ('As if I were one of a pair of china dogs,' she thought later.) On the other side, in a smaller rocking-chair, swathed in shawls, was a small peaky-faced boy.

'I'm Gilbert Samuel Bow,' he announced in an important and yet tremulous voice, 'and I'm in a decline. But if I live to my next birthday I'll be ten.'

Abigail looked at him with distaste. She felt like saying, 'Why bother?' But Dovey was hovering around, so she didn't.

CHAPTER 5

Gibbie peered out of his huddle of shawls like a small wizened monk. His head had been shaved. It was not an agreeable head, being bony, bumpy, and bluish.

'Mercy on us!' piped this monkish person. 'You're as plain as a toad.'

'Thanks very much,' said Abigail, nettled. 'You're not exactly a dazzler yourself.'

The little face assumed an expression of insufferable piety. 'I expect you know I'm not long for this world. I've been given up by the doctors.'

Dovey limped in with two bowls of broth on a tray and a box of dominoes.

---

5. Bram Stoker's novel *Dracula*, about vampires, was not written until 1897.
6. Molasses. "Aniseed": a spice used for its licorice-like flavor.

7. War (1853–56) between an alliance of Great Britain, France, Sardinia, and the Ottoman Empire against Russia for control of the straits between the Black Sea and the Mediterranean Sea.

'Just to pass the time away,' she said coaxingly. Gibbie turned up his eyes and said, 'I mun turn away from the things of this world.'

'Oh, fiddlesticks!' growled Abigail. 'You'd get better faster if you moved yourself out in the sun and fresh air, instead of lying around like an old granny.'

Dovey reproved her. 'Gibbie has been nigh to death, Abby,' she said.

Gibbie put on a holy face. 'And I still am. Maybe by my birthday I shall be with my mamma and the angels in heaven.'

Abigail looked disgusted. It seemed to her that a good spank on the backside would do wonders for this whiney, self-important little monster. She marvelled at Dovey's patience with him. Typical Victorian morbidity about the sick and the dead, she thought, remembering what her mother had said about this mildewed aspect of the Victorian era. Certainly kilos of 'mourning' stuff came into Magpies—jet jewellery; brooches containing wreaths of the dear departed's hair; once an onyx-framed miniature topped with two delightful tiny weeping angels. The miniature was of a white-eyed gentleman with side-whiskers and carnation cheeks. It had gone off, to the accompaniment of shrieks of laughter, as a conversation piece. At the time Abigail had thought the buyer's mirth unbearably vulgar; because, after all, that man had once been real and someone had loved him and missed him when he died.

But now, in the middle of it all, and real as she was, all she could feel was exasperation and grumpiness. It was partly because she wasn't as clean as she was used to being. She loathed this. Her hair was lank and greasy. That morning she had asked Dovey if she could wash it in the bathroom and the elder girl had gazed at her in innocent dismay.

'But there's no such place, Abby love, only in the grand houses!'

Abigail, who was accustomed to dashing under the shower whenever she felt like it, was aghast.

'But however do you keep clean?'

Dovey explained that on Saturday nights Granny and the girls bathed in front of the bedroom fire. Uncle Samuel brought up the wooden tub and the hot water, and emptied it afterwards.

'The menfolk wash in front of the kitchen fire, do you see? But it must be on Saturday, so as to be clean and proper for the Sabbath.'

'But your clothes, how do you wash them?' asked Abigail.

Dovey said, a little indignantly, 'Our linen is boiled in the downstairs copper every Monday, rain or shine, and hung out to bleach in the yard. And our outer clothes are sponged regular every month with vinegar or ivy water, which is a fine cleanser, and better than the ammonia some use. Oh, we keep good and cleanly, have no fear of that!'

'Oh, sugar!' thought Abigail in despair. 'No wonder everyone whiffs like an old dishcloth.'

It had never occurred to her that manufacturers would actually produce a fabric that couldn't be washed or dry-cleaned (though she supposed the vinegar and ivy-water, whatever that was, was a kind of dry-or-damp cleaning). Probably Granny's black linsey-wool dress had never had a wash in its life, though it smelt clean enough—if you liked the smell of camphor and lavender water, that is.

'Well,' she thought, 'I've just got to get used to it—even beastly grubby hair. Just fancy what these people would think of drip-dry clothes!'

'Ye hae'na noticed I haven't touched a sip of ma broth,' complained Gibbie.

Abigail, who had eaten hers enthusiastically, for she felt hungry this last day or two, said, 'Too bad for you. It's good.'

'I been thinking on my funeral,' Gibbie said pleasurably. 'Six black horses I'll have, with plumes, and four men in tall hats with black streamers and a dead cart covered in flowers. But my coffin will be white because I'm just an innocent child.'

Abigail looked at him both amused and revolted. 'You want to get those ideas out of your head, you silly little twit, or you *will* die. And then think how sad Granny and Dovey and Judah and Beatie will be.'

'Aye,' said Gibbie with satisfaction, 'they'll greet and groan for a month.'

Abigail shook her head disbelievingly. She would never have thought there could be a child as repellent as Vincent Crown, but Gibbie had him licked into a cocked hat. However, she thought she'd better try to do what she could for him, so she said cheerfully, 'Bet I can beat you at dominoes.'

'It's evil to gamble,' said Gibbie, shocked.

'Holy snakes!' protested Abigail. 'Who's going to gamble?'

Gibbie shrank back. 'You *blasphemed*,' he gasped.

'Oh, for heaven's sake, I'm sick of you, you little creep,' said Abigail. She went to the window. There was no doubt, her ankle felt stronger.

'If only I could go barefoot,' she thought, for Granny's best boot felt terrible. The heel was the wrong height, the upper nipped cruelly at the instep, and the toe was pointed like a dachshund's nose.

'You must be from a foreign land, as Dovey said,' observed Gibbie. 'You canna speak proper English like the rest of us, poor soul.'

'Who's talking?' asked Abigail. She pulled the dusty brown curtains aside.

Behind them was a little window made of six square glass panes, and beyond it a busy street. But which street? By standing as high as she could, she caught a glimpse of china-blue sea to her right, a dark peninsula of land with something battlemented like a toy fort built on the end. Bennelong Point, could that be it? But the street itself drew her gaze. Dirty, draggletail, it was nevertheless an important street, as she could see from the carriages and the jaunty horse-drawn sulkies that jolted past. The extraordinary thing was that the pedestrians seemed more important than the wheeled traffic.

Abigail, coming from a time where a pedestrian ventured onto the road at his peril, could scarcely believe it. The roadway itself was crowded with people crossing at all angles; filthy scamps of children played with a skipping rope; a man was driving a small herd of goats; there were street barrows laden with fish, old clothes, boots, garbage, and even a water barrel. A man passed at a fast trot. He wore a dozen hats, one on top of the other. A board about his neck proclaimed *Tanner Heach, Hatts All Clane*.

Abigail mumbled this over to herself and at last worked it out. She laughed.

'Do come and look, Gibbie. It's fun!'

But the boy was bawling: 'She's gunna open the window and kill me! Dovey, Granny, Faither, she'll open the window if you dunna take care!'

Abigail had not thought of opening the window. Now she gave it a heave, but the sash was screwed down. She withdrew her head, and became aware that there was uproar in the shop, Dovey and Granny scolding, a strange male voice, of a customer perhaps, raised in a yell of pain and fury. Mr Bow stormed into the parlour. Ignoring Abigail and the cowering Gibbie, he jerked down a rusty sword that hung by a green tasselled cord above the mantel.

'The Rooshians are coming, fousands of 'em! Let's show 'em what we're made of, lads! Hearts of oak, hearts of oak!' he roared as he charged out, and Abigail hopped to the window just in time to see him pelting down the street, the people scattering before him.

'Wow!' cried Abigail. She went into the shop.

Dovey was pale and frightened. 'I dunna ken how he got at the rum, Granny, honest! He must have had it hid. And he's split all the glessie,[8] just as it was about to crackle, and scattered the lemon bonbons everywhere!'

Abigail saw also that Dovey's arm was streaked with a long burn; but the girl said nothing about it, so neither did Abigail. She understood the situation now. Mr Bow was a placid, timid man until he drank, and then his head filled with fancies and he ran wild.

Mrs Tallisker was taking off her apron. Her firm brown face was calm but stern, her lips compressed.

'I'll be awa' after him, lass. You try to make order here.'

She took Dovey's stick, which was leaning against the wall, and marched out. She took no notice whatsoever of the soldier, treacle-plastered from top to toe, swearing without pause for breath.

Abigail limped over to him. 'You!' she commanded. 'Shut up!'

He ceased in mid-expletive, and snarled, 'I'll get ten days in the clink[9] for having me gear in this state. The sergeant will say I'm a slummerkin and very likely sozzled.'[1]

'And so you are,' said Abigail boldly. 'You stink like a barrel of beer. Tell your officer it was an accident.'

'And who are you, ordering one of the Queen's men around, you damned saucy wench? Sure, you're as homely as a cow's behind.'

'That may be,' replied Abigail, 'but there's one thing I'll tell you . . . get out of here before Mr Bow returns or he'll take you for a Russian and slice off your head like the pumpkin it is!'

The soldier backed out, but not before he shouted, 'They'll have Bow in Bedlam[2] if he don't keep off the wet!'

'But he only drinks because of his sorrow, poor man,' said Dovey. 'And when he does he goes awa' out of his head. But it's true . . . sooner or later they'll come and put him away. Oh, if only Judah were home—he can manage him, and keep him from the drink, too!'

Abigail peeped out the door. There was a brief commotion down on the corner. She saw Granny's tall white bonnet bobbing above the crowd.

'Granny's got him,' Abigail called to Dovey, 'and there's two men with him holding his arms.'

'Oh, the Dear help us,' gasped Dovey. 'Not the constables?'

She, too, hurried down the street. Abigail, her ankle beginning to pain savagely, clung to the lintel of the door and looked eagerly and urgently about her. The shop was on a corner. Five stone steps, scooped out like ladles with wear, led to the footpath of slab timber sunk in the earth and interspersed with areas of cobbles and rough gravel. To her right was the Argyle Cut.[3] She was amazed to see above it a rock precipice surmounted by excellent mansions. Late winter roses wavered over their massive stone walls. It seemed incredible that wealthy people lived up there, with all the stenches and rat-ridden poverty of The Rocks washing up to their back fences like a disgusting tide. But she had no time to ponder that now. Through the struts of the wooden bridge that spanned The Cut she saw the low peaked roof of the Garrison Church. *That* had not changed. Abigail's heart jumped with excitement.

---

8. A kind of traditional Scottish toffee.
9. Jail.
1. Drunk. "Slummerkin": a slum dweller.
2. A lunatic asylum.
3. The tunnel road cut through the sandstone

ridge of The Rocks area of Sydney. Started in 1843 by convicts using hammer and chisels, it was finished in 1867 with the help of explosives. The Cut connects Millers Point with Sydney Cove.

Now she knew where she was. The confectionery shop was on the corner of Cambridge and Argyle streets. To the right was Circular Quay, and George Street, and between them and Mr Bow's shop was Harrington Street, where she had first accidentally stumbled into the nineteenth century.

Looking down there now she caught glimpses of the Harbour, and saw Granny's tall form and white cap, and Mr Bow himself, sagging between a mighty blue-aproned butcher in a bowler hat and a floury-faced baker in a stiff white paper crown. All the fire had gone out of Mr Bow.

Abigail trembled with relief and joy. As far as time went she might be a long way from home, but in space she was just five minutes from the alley up which she had come from Mitchell and the children's playground.

'I don't need Beatie's help after all,' she thought. 'The poor kid hated promising to do it, anyway, going against her granny and everything. But I'll have to wait till my ankle is a little better, and this bruise gone from my face. I can't let poor Mum see that—she'll be frantic enough as it is. I'll just have to bide my time, that's all, and climb out a window if necessary.'

Dovey and Granny gently lowered the collapsed form of Mr Bow to a bench in the shop.

The butcher, who had the rusty old sword over his shoulder, said gruffly, 'You ought to throw this old pig-sticker away, Missus. Only brings back memories to the poor silly cove. Better forgotten, I say, wars and all them things. Well, Barney 'n me'll leave you, me old cocksparrer. Back you go to the gobstoppers.'[4]

Dovey hastily closed the door behind them and barred it. The little shop was an indescribable mess: treacle and half-solidified caramel all over the floor; the piles of shining tins cast down; the huge cauldrons that hung over the fire sullenly spitting and glugging.

'I'll help,' said Abigail. 'Give me an apron.'

While Granny stirred the cauldrons and blew up the fire to redness again, Abby got down on the floor with a brush and bucket and scraped up the sugary mess. Mr Bow, as though in a trance, sat yellowish and silent. He smelled strongly of rum.

Gibbie trailed out from the parlour, saying pathetically, 'I'm a very sick laddie, and there's not one of you has been to see if I'm quick or dead.'

'You go up to bed, if you're poorly,' said Dovey soothingly. She passed a hand over the little boy's forehead. 'There, you're no' so hot today. Why, you're a deal better!'

'Nay, nay,' said Gibbie crossly, 'I'm no' fit to climb all those stairs. I'll wait till I'm carried.'

As he trailed back into the parlour Abigail thought, 'Little fake! Making the most of it.'

Scrubbing away, she found opportunity to look closely at the shop. The walls were whitewashed, and the surrounds of the vast open fireplace made crimson with a glossy paste. The grates, the spits and hooks, were bright. Only the outside of the four large cauldrons, dangling from their hooks and chains, were sooted over. On the wall, over an iron hook, hung a solidified cascade of toffee that Dovey had been pulling to make it creamy and malleable.

'It's ruined, I fear,' Dovey said gloomily. 'That's Black Man, Abby. 'Tis cut into six-inch sticks with scissors. What a sad loss of good treacle.'

'Not so, hen,' said Mrs Tallisker. She lifted the huge irregular slab of toffee onto

4. Jawbreakers (i.e., large, round hard candies).

a marble work bench, gave it a whack with a little mallet. It shattered into hundreds of pieces of glassy amber.

'Put it in the big trencher, lass, and into the window with it. We'll sell it at a ha'penny the quarter.'

The windows were not display windows but cottage windows of many-paned glass, with benches behind them where the wares could be shown. When the girls had cleaned the floor and washed themselves, Dovey showed Abigail the many different sweets Mr Bow could concoct. Gundy,[5] flavoured with cinnamon or aniseed; fig and almond cake, which was a lemon-flavoured toffee poured over pounded fruit or nuts and allowed to set; Peggy's Leg;[6] liquorice; and the favourite glessie, a kind of honeycomb. Abigail had never seen any of these sweets before, but did not say so.

At last everything was spotless again. Gibbie appeared from the parlour and gazed reproachfully at them all.

'And what about poor wee Gibbie?' he inquired.

'Oh, Gibbie love,' pleaded Dovey, 'we must wait for Beatie to come from school to help Granny carry you up. Ye ken verra weel I'm no use at all, and Abby can scarce walk.'

'Me faither is offending Providence by touching the speerits,' pronounced Gibbie, stern as a parson. 'He canna even carry his wee dying laddie up to his bed!'

As though on cue, Mr Bow produced a great roaring sob, dropped his head in his hands and wept bitterly. 'My 'Melia, my 'Melia, how will I raise the young 'uns without you? Why did you go for to leave me, wife?'

'Because God called her, Samuel,' said Granny gently. 'Would you go against His holy will?'

Gibbie began to croak and grunt about the soreness of his throat, the feebleness of his legs, and Abigail gave him a sharp nip on the back of the neck. He yelped once and shot up the stairs roaring. Dovey limped after him.

'That was not kind, Abigail,' said Granny, with the nearest thing to severity the girl had yet heard in the old woman's beautiful voice.

'Maybe not,' said Abigail, 'but it worked, didn't it? That youngster will turn into an invalid and get his four black horses and his wee white coffin if he's not pushed out into the fresh air and sunshine. If Beatie can recover from the fever and go back to her lessons, why can't he?'

'Ah,' said the old woman with a sigh. 'Beatie is different. She has a will like iron. The Dear alone knows what will become of her, with all the wild thoughts she has. But there, hen, you should be resting that ankle. I'll just get Mr Bow to bed, and then I'll put a wee poultice on it for you.'

The poultice was of mashed and heated comfrey leaves, which Mrs Tallisker called 'boneset'. A comfrey paste was also applied to the bruise on the girl's face. It must have been effective, for day by day the bruise faded.

Now that she felt confident of making her escape when she was fit enough, Abigail began to observe the Bows and Talliskers more closely than she had previously done.

When she had first come to this time she had been like a plane passenger who had disembarked in the wrong country, without luggage or passport. But now she knew where she was. She knew that she could leave.

She realised there would be many problems. Her parents would be half crazy with

---

5. A Scottish hard candy, made with brown sugar, butter, and molasses.

6. An Irish creamy candy, made in a tan cylinder.

anxiety; they would certainly have alerted the police. She had no idea what she could tell them back in her own time. No one would believe her.

There was also the problem of clothes. Dovey's blouse and skirt, so heavy, so much the wrong shape and the wrong length, the frightful stockings that made even Abigail's slim legs look like striped woollen table legs—how could she explain them? Even in a Sydney where almost everyone dressed casually Dovey's clothes were so uncouth they could not possibly be anyone's choice.

'Well,' thought Abigail, 'I'll meet those hassles when I come to them. First I have to be able to walk properly on this ankle and, if possible, have a face that doesn't look as if it's been caught in a door.'

She began to look attentively at these people amongst who she had come to live. After all, she thought, there aren't many twentieth-century girls who can speak of Victorian times from experience.

The first thing was their kindness. How amazingly widespread it was . . . the butcher and the baker catching and bringing back Mr Bow in his frenzy; even the treacle-smeared soldier, who she was sure would not blame the confectioner for his accident. And then, herself. Suppose some strange girl had been knocked down outside Magpies, what would her own mother have done? Brought her inside, rung the ambulance, sent her flowers in hospital, perhaps worried a little whether Magpies' insurance covered such accidents. And yet Kathy Kirk was the most soft-hearted of women. But here were these people, not as poor as some of the malformed scarecrows that dawdled around the lanes perhaps, but still far from comfortably settled; people, too, who had recently suffered a painful bereavement: And yet they had believed her worse off than they were, a solitary girl with only the clothes she stood up in. They had taken responsibility for her, nursed and clothed her. Someone had given up her bed, probably Beatie; no one had complained when she was snappish and rude about Dovey's best clothes, about the lack of sanitation; no one had condemned her unsympathetic attitude towards Gibbie.

'I'm not kind,' said Abigail with a sickish surprise. 'Look how I went on with Mum when she said she wanted us to get together with Dad again. Look what I did to Dad when I was little, punched him on the nose and made it bleed. Maybe I've never been really kind in my life.'

And she remembered with a pang what Kathy had said, that awful day: that she had never, either as a child or a fourteen-year-old, offered a word of sympathy to her mother.

'Yet here are these people, happy and grateful to be able to read and write, just to be allowed to earn a living; and they've shared everything they can share with me, whom they don't know from Adam.'

These Victorians lived in a dangerous world, where a whole family could be wiped out with typhoid fever or smallpox, where a soldier could get a hole in his head that you could put your fist in, where there were no pensions or free hospitals or penicillin or proper education for girls, or even poor boys, probably. Yet, in a way, it was a more human world than the one Abigail called her own.

'I wish I could stay awhile,' she thought, 'and find out why all these things are. But I can't think about any of this till I get home. Getting home, that's what I have to plan.'

The day Abigail ran away to go home started like any other day. As usual she was wearing clothes borrowed from Dovey, flannel underwear and a brown gingham dress covered by a long white pinafore. She felt draggy[7] and looked it.

She had noted that the ladies in the carriages dashing through to Kent and Cumberland streets—some of them being real ladies and others, according to the cynical Beatie, only 'high-steppers', or women unacceptable to polite society—wore lace jabots,[8] handsome buttons and silk braids, and tight jackets that narrowed to fish tails at the rear.

Working women wore drab, ankle-length dresses with long sleeves and aprons. And whereas the rich ladies and the dashing high-steppers both peacocked in saucer-shaped hats tipped forward to make room for elaborate chignons of plaits and curls, the working women flung shawls over their centre-parted, smoothly brushed, or, more often, disorderly and dusty, hair.

It was hard to tell a high-stepper from a real lady, thought Abigail; but you would never mistake one or the other for a working-class woman. She understood now why Kathy never got any lower-class Victorian clothing at Magpies. It had all been worn out by unceasing labour a hundred years before.

'Mum knows a lot about Victorian and Edwardian days,' ruminated Abigail, 'but she has no idea how hard the women worked!'

'Are the high-steppers prostitutes?' Abigail innocently asked Dovey.

Dovey flushed 'Oh, Abby, never let Granny hear you use such language! It'd fair make her swoon awa'.'

Abby added prostitutes to the list of things she was not to mention: the Deity, legs (in front of menfolk), any natural function (except in whispers), the privy at the end of the yard, which consisted of a can and a scrubbed wooden seat (this was 'the wee hoosie').

'Lot of blanky rubbish,' said the outspoken Beatie when she was alone with Abigail, 'with The Rocks the way it is, full of seamen and soldiers and language to curl your hair. Not to mind some of the worst grog shops and crimp houses in Sydney.'

'What's a crimp house?' asked Abigail.

'A grog shop where they put opium in the seamen's drink, and then shanghai them away to ships that need crews and can't get them, leaky old tubs bound for China and maybe intended to sink so that the owners will get the insurance. So Judah says.'

'But that's cold-blooded murder,' cried Abigail. 'Things like that can't go on in these days!'

'Do they no' go on in yours?' asked Beatie hopefully.

'I don't think so,' said Abigail.

She could not bring herself to tell the eager Beatie about nuclear bombs, chemical warfare, napalm bombing of peasants' villages and fields. The little girl thought of the late twentieth century as a sort of paradise, a place of marvels. In some ways it was a paradise compared with Beatie's own time. Let her go on believing there was no dark side, thought Abigail. She would not live to see it, anyway.

On the day Abigail tried to run away to her own time she was not wearing Mrs Tallisker's best buttoned boots, though now her ankle was its normal size again. Granny had bought her second-hand shoes from the boot barrow.[9] They were heel-

---

7. Dull.
8. Falling ruffles at the neck, worn by women.

9. I.e., someone selling boots from a pushcart.

less slippers of kid, very uncomfortable, and the barrow man had passed cheeky remarks about the size of her feet. That was another thing she hadn't known: that even Victorian working women had tiny feet.

Beatie went off to the Ragged School. She was excited because Judah's ship was in port; he would be home that night.

'And I've learnt how to decline six Latin verbs,' she told Abigail joyfully. 'Judah teaches me.'

'Has Judah studied Latin, then?'

'Oh, aye, has he not!' said Beatie proudly. 'And wasn't he top of the class when he was only thirteen. Mr Taylor gave him a grand book, *Travels in Africa*, with "First Prize for Scholarship" and his name written in copperplate, and he sorely wanted him to go to Fort Street School for Boys; but Judah, he was that set on the sea and he wunna!'

'Who's Mr Taylor?' asked Abigail.

'Oh, he's the headmaster of Trinity Parish School, y'ken, and he took Judah into his special class for promising boys. Aye, promising, that's what he said about our Judah. Smart as a whip he is, and will be master of his own vessel some day.'

Mr Bow had been very morose and silent since his last escapade; he was a wretched man, and Abigail was sorry for him. It must have been a terrible thing to lose his wife and little son all in a day. This child was not the only one he and Amelia Bow had lost. Three daughters had died of the smallpox. They had come between Judah and Beatie. Judah had taken the disease too, but lightly. The pock on his cheek, that looked like a dimple, was the only sign of it.

Abigail had not looked closely at Judah's face: she had been too frightened and confused that night. But she remembered the quaint way he had got her name out of her, and the ease with which he had lifted her to look out the window—to find that her own world had vanished as if by enchantment. She tried to get Mr Bow to talk about his children, but he only gave her a piteous look from those preposterously crossed eyes, and she desisted.

She was making bonbons for Granny. They were small squares of orange and lemon peel threaded on a fine steel knitting-needle. Abigail dipped the needle into a pot of boiling sugar flavoured with grated lemon and a drop of purest whale-oil.

'To keep the syrup from brittling,' explained Granny. These bonbons were then laid carefully on a buttered slab of marble and allowed to get cold and crisp before they were packed in paper cones for sale.

It was interesting, thought Abigail, how she had been so absorbed into The Rocks area without further question. The fiction that she was an immigrant girl of good education and no kin, bound for a situation on the High Rocks, knocked down and injured by Mr Bow in one of his spells, and now without memory or worldly resources, had been accepted by those customers made curious by her occasional presence in the shop. She had now been two weeks with the Bows, and there had been no further reference to that curious conversation between Granny and Dovey about her lost green dress. Nor would Beatie answer any questions about 'the Stranger'. She shut her mouth like a rat-trap and admitted frankly: 'I'm that scared of Granny. She'd murder me if she knew what I've told ye already. She's got the power, I've told ye over and over again!'

'You're dotty!' said Abigail, 'Granny would never hurt you, or anyone else. She's the best soul in the world.'

''Tisn't that she'd hurt me,' explained Beatie reluctantly. 'But she'd look at me. And I dinna want Granny to look at me.'

And that was all she would say.

Yet Beatie was relentless in her questioning of Abigail about the years to come. Abigail told her about jet aircraft, about men landing on the moon and their voices and pictures coming all the way to earth, clear and bright. She told her about new countries that did not exist in Beatie's day.

'But where is the Empire?' Beatie asked, baffled.

Abigail did not know. 'It just seemed to break up and dribble away,' she admitted lamely.

'But who's looking after the black men?'

'They're looking after themselves,' said Abigail. But Beatie could not understand. 'Black men canna look after themselves. Don't be daft!'

Abigail was constantly surprised at what Beatie would believe and what she could not accept for a second. That men could land on the moon, yes. That people bathed naked from public beaches, no. She scoffed at the idea that there were only three or four kings and queens left in the world, but believed without question that many married folk divorced and married others.

'For rich folk do the same right now,' she said in her matter-of-fact way. 'But for a housewifie now, should her man starve or beat her and the bairns, there's naught but running away or rat poison.'

Most of all she wanted to know about people, whether girls could become doctors, teachers, do good and useful things. Abigail was glad to be able to say 'yes'.

Always these conversations ended the same way.

'But how did those bairnies know my name? Dinna ye ha' some more ideas, Abby? I tell ye, I'm ettlin'[1] to find out, come what may!'

The older children at the Ragged School had their lessons after dinner-time whistle, a midday orchestra of hideous noises from steam cranes, factories, and loading ships. It was taken for granted by the Ragged School board that the children worked for a living. Some were boot blacks or newspaper boys in the city; others ran errands for offices, or delivered for merchants; many were 'sparrow-starvers' or sweepers of manure. Each youngster did something, anything, to earn a few pennies, and many of their parents resented their wasting afternoons at the Ragged School.

On this fateful afternoon, Beatie had long gone off, grizzling[2] and fiery-eyed over the 'lassies' rubbish' she would be taught. Granny and Dovey were upstairs with Gibbie; Mr Bow, hoop-backed, speechless and glum, stirred a cauldron, his back to Abigail.

Abigail delicately placed the last skewer of bonbons to dry on the marble slab, and walked without haste out of the shop.

It was late in the afternoon. The ships' masts, bare as trees after a bushfire, stood up in the Harbour, very straight, like a thousand spillikins, criss-crossed and twigged with spars and lesser gear. The westering sun seized upon bright specks of metal on these masts and made them burn like stars. Abigail walked straight down Argyle Street.

Not for a moment did it occur to her that she was not going home, to her mother, her father, the bear chair, Magpies, school. All she had to do was turn up Harrington Street, find the stairway and the lane up which she and Beatie had run, and she would descend towards George Street and Circular Quay, and see Mitchell standing there in its steel and glassy grandeur.

'My father designed it,' she had told Beatie, who looked at her as if she were lying.

---

1. Intending, planning.   2. Sulking.

There were trees in Argyle Street, oaks, she thought, covered with curdy green. Many alleys spindled away, turning into flights of steps as steep as ships' companionways as they went up and over looming sandstone knobs and reefs. Sometimes houses perched on these outcrops like beached Arks; sometimes they were built into them so that the back wall of the house was living sandstone. The lanes were runnels of wet and filth between mouldering shops, factories and cottages. The whole place was cankered with poverty and neglect. The people also—all had something the matter with them: rotting teeth, clubfeet, a cheek puckered by a burn. A little girl, dressed fantastically in a woman's trailing dress and squashed hat, snarled, 'Ooya starin' at?' and raised a dirty fist as if to strike. Abigail saw that the little one's face was despoiled by a hare-lip.

But who could fix these infirmities in Victorian days? wondered Abigail. If you were born crooked, you stayed crooked and made the best of it, as Granny Tallisker made the best of the violent deprivation of her son Robert, her daughter Amelia, the four grandchildren dead before they grew up. It was all God's will.

The gutters, made of two tipped stones, were full of garbage. Abigail saw scaly tails twitching amongst the rotting debris and sprang away.

'Steady on, Missie!' It was an elderly soldier with a roast-beef face. He held his musket horizontally so that she could not pass, and she saw a gang of convicts clanking across the street. Some had yellow jackets with large letters and figures daubed in black and red. Others wore coarse canvas cover-alls, part grey, part brown, like grotesque harlequins.[3] Those who were chained had hitched up their chains to their belts with fragments of rope or rag, so that they could walk. But their walk was a slow, bandy-legged shuffle.

She said, 'I thought transportation[4] stopped years and years ago!'

'These canaries[5] are long-termers, Miss. They bin loading coal down yonder.'

'It's terrible, terrible,' she whispered.

The soldier said with harsh kindness, 'You just out from the Old Country, Miss? Well, New South Wales ain't no place of harps and angels, that's sartin.'

He stiffened to attention. Abigail saw a young officer, very dandified and bored, ride out from under one of the flattened arches that marked the many courts or wynds.[6] He cut carelessly with his crop at the mob of skeleton, matted-hair urchins that milled about his horse, yelping, 'Chuck us down a copper, Guv!' and rode after the convicts.

Now she was outside the Ragged School. She passed it cautiously, for she did not want to meet Beatie unexpectedly. She heard from within the drone of many voices reciting the Lord's Prayer, the sudden whip-like whistle of a willow cane. But even as she sighed for the pauper children within, she heard behind her the hoarse voice of Beatie Bow.

'Eh, it's Abigail! Abby, come back! Where are ye off to?'

Abigail plunged across the street. A stunted child, face black with a lifetime's dirt, ceased sweeping horse manure and whacked at her legs with his broom so that she almost fell. Her first thought was that Beatie had called from one of the school windows, but now she saw her, accompanied by the sturdy figure of Judah, running along from the direction of the wharves.

It had not occurred to her that Beatie would play truant from school to go to meet

3. Comic characters typically dressed in multicolored diamond-patterned tights.
4. The banishment of criminals overseas to a penal
colony. Transportation to New South Wales ended

in 1840.
5. Rogues, jailbirds.
6. Very narrow streets (Scottish).

her brother. But there they were, dodging amongst the crowd, gaining on her every minute.

She could not see the lamp-post that marked the stairs she had ascended on that first night; it was too late to look for the right alley. So she dived into the first opening she noticed. It was so narrow she could have spanned it with her arms. Its uneven cobbles ran sluggishly with thick green slime. Pressed against the wall, she saw Beatie and Judah run past.

Suddenly a hand fastened round her ankle. She looked down and saw a frightful thing grinning gap-toothed at her. It was a legless man, on a little low trolley like a child's push-cart. He had a big bulging forehead and fingers as sinuous as steel.

'Let me go!' panted Abigail. With her free foot she kicked at the man's face, but he dodged her with the nimbleness of a monkey. Laughing, he dragged her closer, and bit her leg just above the ankle. The pain was bad enough, but the horror that seized the girl was unbearable.

She let out a ringing shriek. 'Beatie, Judah, help, help!'

That was all she could utter, for a bag smelling of rotten fish descended over her head and was pulled tight. She was half carried, half dragged she knew not where. Abigail was a strong girl, and her hands were free. She hammered and punched, scratched and tore. Once her fingers fastened in a beard: she could tell by the bristly texture of it. She gave a great yank and a handful came out. The owner slapped her repeatedly over the ears, cursing in an accent and tones such as she had never heard.

'You've caught yourself no tame puss-cat there, Hannah!' a husky voice said with a chuckle. Abigail's hands were deftly snared and tied behind her back, and the sack was whisked off her head. She was in a dark, evil-smelling room, and before her stood a mountainous woman holding a blood-spattered fist to her hairy chin. She must have weighed nearly a hundred kilos; there seemed no end to her in her full skirts and vast blouse of gaudy striped silk. Out of the sleeves poked sausagey hands covered in rings. Ferret eyes gleamed at Abigail; the sausage hands filled themselves with her hair and jerked brutally.

'I'll have yer bald!' she yelled. Abigail shrieked at the full power of her lungs, and kicked violently at everything she could see or reach.

A hand went over her mouth. It was accustomed to holding captives thus, for it pushed her upper lip down over her teeth so that she could not bite.

'Hold on now, Hannah,' said the husky voice. 'We've a pretty little canary bird here; she'll go for a sweet sum, fifteen quid or more. But not if you take off all her hair at the roots.'

Abigail glared over the hand at the bearded woman. She had never seen anything so grotesque in her life. Whether the creature had come from a circus or not, she was terrifying.

Yet, now that the first shock was over, Abigail felt mad fury rather than panic. The panic ran underneath the anger, like a fast-rising tide. She realised clearly that she was in the kind of peril of which she had never dreamed. For the room contained many people, and there was no way, even if she could get her hands free, that she could fight her way out.

The room was, she thought, an underground kitchen. It was like a lair or cavern, pitch black except for a few candle stubs stuck in bottles or their own grease, and the murky gleam of a vast open fireplace. The smell was terrible, even for The Rocks—not only of unwashed and crowded humanity, but decayed meat and rotting wood.

A girl in a draggletail pink wrapper wandered over and looked at her curiously. She seemed half imbecile, with no front teeth and a nose with a flattened bridge. Picking this nose industriously, she lisped, 'She ain't much to look at, Master. Be she right age, you think? Mebbe with her 'air frizzed out and some paint on she'd pass in twilight.'

Abigail felt her skin creep.

'Shut your trap, Effie,' said the husky voice. 'She's fresh as a new-laid egg. What else matters?'

Abigail felt a hand stealing around the hem of her skirt. Twisting sideways, she saw the terrible little cripple sniffing about her ankles like a dog.

'She taste sweet as a newborn mouse, Hannah,' he cajoled. 'Let poor Barker have a nibble.'

'Sho, you cannibal,' shouted the woman. 'Mark her and I'll do fer yer, I swear I will.'

The husky voice now said, almost with kindness, 'Just out from the Old Country, are you, my pet?'

Abigail nodded.

'Hannah will see you right,' went on the voice. 'Heart of gold, Hannah, though it's a long way in, eh, Hannah?'

The fat woman snarled. But it was plain she was afraid of the man with the husky voice. He now said, 'If I take away my hand, will you be quiet, like the dear child you are?'

Abigail nodded, and the hand was removed from her mouth. Instantly she yelled, 'Ju . . .' But she got no further. A kerchief was thrust between her teeth and tied behind her head, and she was given a push that sent her sprawling into a corner. She was now able to see that the owner of the husky voice was a handsome man, a gentleman, as Beatie would have said, in well-fitted breeches, a tailored coat of cocoa colour, and a dashing tall beaver[7] to match.

He held a tiny bouquet of jonquils and fern to his nose, presumably to keep the smells away.

'She's to be kept close,' he instructed the bearded woman, jerking his head at the ceiling. He took out a gold watch, sprang open its lid, and shut it again. He said, 'In the morning, Hannah, and I don't want the goods damaged.' Without another look at Abigail he strolled out.

Now Abigail began to sweat with growing terror. If Judah and Beatie had not seen her duck into the little alley, what chance would she have? The bearded woman came over, a rag still held to her bloody chin, and said venomously, 'Lucky for you the master took a fancy to yer. But don't think I ain't able to hurt you bad where it don't show.'

Abigail swallowed with difficulty. Her mouth was dry. The scarf was salty with dirt and sweat. She retched a little. She thought desperately, 'I can't lose my head, whatever I do.'

She made herself breathe quietly. But something soft and squashy moved beneath her. She realised with horror that it was a woman, a kind of woman, for shortly it wriggled feebly out from underneath her and showed itself in the candlelight to be a hobgoblin with tangled hay-like hair, cheeks bonfire red with either rouge or fever, and a body hung with parti-coloured rags.

She crept over to the table, and began to tear at a mildewed crust of bread. One of the other women, wearing a flounced red petticoat and a black corset and little

7. Top hat made of beaver fur.

else, good-naturedly pushed over to the wreck an anonymous hunk of meat that might have been a rooster's neck.

'Here, Doll,' she said. 'Don't eat that muck you got there. Ruin your gut it will.'

The wreck stuffed it in her mouth, bone and all, but before she did she said in a voice of extreme refinement, 'Thank you, Sarah, I'm much obliged.'

'Oh, God,' thought Abigail, 'that thing has had an education. It might even have been a *lady*.'

Now she was paralysed with terror. She could imagine herself as another Doll in twenty years' time, all spirit beaten out of her, sodden with booze and disease, not even fit for the life of degradation the gentleman with the husky voice evidently intended for her. No matter how fiercely she blinked, tears filled her eyes and fell down on the gag.

One of the other girls strolled over to her. She was fancily dressed, with much flouncing and many ribbons, and a large hat with a purple ostrich feather. Below this hat was a young plump face, pretty and good-natured. Abigail noticed that she, like Dovey, uncannily resembled a Victorian doll.

'It must be their idea of good looks,' thought Abigail hazily. 'No wonder everyone's always telling me how homely I am.'

The girl smiled, showing chalky teeth. 'Don't pipe your eye,[8] duck; 'tisn't such a bad old life. Better than starving on slop work[9] in the factories, any old how. I'm the dress-lodger, and me name's Em'ly, but I call meself Maude 'cos it's more posh. Come on, Doll, the lamps is lit, time we was getting on the road.'

All of this, spoken in a thick south London accent, was scarcely comprehensible to Abigail. But she was to find out that the handsomest girl in the house was called the dress-lodger, sent out in garments belonging to the proprietor, always with an attendant to see that she didn't run off with them.

But Doll began to cough and splutter. Her eyes rolled up; she looked as if she were going to die.

'Gawd, I'm not going off with that death's head trailing behind me,' protested Maude. 'It'd scare off Robinson Crusoe.'[1]

So another famine-wasted object was dragged out of a corner, arrayed respectably, and pushed forward to follow Maude. Maude protested, but finally laughed and set off.

Doll cringed timidly as Hannah stood over her.

'You good-for-nothing, you scarecrow! You're fit for the bone-yard, that's all, breathing pestilence over us all.'

'Chuck her out, Hannah,' advised one of the men who sat smoking a cutty pipe[2] by the fire. They seemed to have nothing to do with the establishment as customers or protectors. Abigail guessed that they were employed by the gentleman proprietor to bully the women's takings from them and keep an eye on Hannah's honesty.

'Ah, well,' said Hannah, putting on a ludicrous face of long-suffering virtue, 'if I ain't charitable towards me own niece I dunno what the rest of you villains can expect. Here, you, Chow, take the new 'un up to the attic, and you come up and keep an eye on her, Doll.'

Chow, an emaciated half-Asian, seized Abigail as though she weighed no more than a cat, carried her up stairs built of rough-hewn baulks of timber, and at last

8. Shed tears (originally nautical slang).
9. The making of cheap garments.
1. The hero of Daniel Defoe's novel of the same name (1719–20); because he lived more than twenty years on a South American island, first alone and then with a young male native, he would presumably be eager for female companionship.
2. Short pipe.

dropped her on a sagging pallet. Doll sidled breathlessly about Hannah, beseeching, 'Just a little gin, Aunt dear. Twopenceworth would be sufficient. Just enough to keep my cough from annoying our guest.'

'Here y'are, then, and don't say I ain't a good aunt to you, bit o' useless rubbish that you are.'

Hannah dug into a depthless pocket and fished up a small bottle. Doll seized it with tearful gratitude. Hannah cautioned her to keep a keen eye on Abigail.

'Them rats are partial to a nice bit o' fresh chicken,' she said. Abigail could hear rats scampering over the ceiling. Hannah saw her look upwards and grinned, satisfied.

'They come out in their fousands.' She chuckled. Placing the candlestick on a box in the corner, she jerked her head at Chow. The door slammed, and Abigail heard a key turn and a bar clank home.

She wanted to cry but she knew that if she did she would choke on the gag. To distract herself she looked around at the attic. Doll, lying on a sack beside the pallet, sucked luxuriously at her bottle.

The attic did not have the proportions or the sloping roof of the usual attic, such as the one Gibbie slept in. The window, too, was almost as large as a door. And then, those stairs . . . they were not stairs anyone would build in a house. Abby tried to think as sensibly as she could.

Was it likely that houses, however derelict, would stand beside such a narrow alley? The walls of the attic seemed to be made of blocks of bare stone. That, too, was uncommon. There was no fireplace and, as she had now learnt from Beatie, almost every room in every house in Sydney, no matter how poor, had a fireplace.

She realised with despair that she was too frightened to make sense of it. Her thoughts began to chase one another round and round.

'Like those rats up there,' she thought. Sometimes her whole body shuddered spasmodically, as if she were lying on an ice floe. She was aware in the direst way of her great danger. It could be that she would never be seen again in 1873, let alone her own time. She had nothing to hope for except that Judah and Beatie had heard the first great yell she had given.

She forced herself to lie quiet. There was no one to help her, no one at all. But she could not give up without a battle. Whatever she could do to escape, she had to try to do.

She had an imaginative flash of her grandmother, addressing her perm in resigned tones: 'She's dodgy, Katherine. Not one of your nice frank open-faced girls. You're too soft and protective. Heaven help her if she ever has to fend for herself.'

'We'll see about that, you old bat,' thought Abigail. But her bravado was false. If her grandmother had come through the door, smiling her bogus smile, Abigail would have welcomed her like an angel.

But Grandmother would never come through the door. Grandmother had not yet been born.

Abigail, with one eye on Doll, began to strain at the fabric that bound her hands. It seemed to be another kerchief. She twisted it patiently, at last got a thumb free and, after half an hour, the fingers of one hand.

Doll drank, sometimes wept, the tears oozing like oil out of the black-socketed eyes. She mumbled and sang, sometimes seemed to speak to her companion, though perhaps it was to herself.

'My name is Dorothea Victoria Brand. I had God-fearing parents. Mother was ill-educated, like Aunt Hannah, and Father married beneath him. He was a clerk in a counting house. He saw that I went to school, a boarding-school on the moors. It was very cold there, but I was happy. I was a bookish child. Clever and industrious, that's what the Board said. Father wanted me to have private tutoring in French and singing, but he could not afford it. He wept, I remember. He loved me dearly, did my father.'

It's a warehouse or bond store, that's what it is, thought Abigail suddenly. A disused one. And that window might be the kind that opens on a platform, with a pulley and rope for hauling up bags of flour and stuff.

She got the other hand out, and with infinite slowness untied the gag at the back of her head. She clamped the gag between her teeth, did not shift her position, and kept her gaze on Doll.

'Father was taken suddenly. His horse rolled on him. And Mother went labouring in a slop-shop, making sailors' smocks. Twenty girls in a room ten by ten—think of it!—stitch, stitch, fourteen hours a day without a breath of fresh air. So Mother took the lung fever. Thirty-two she was when God took her. So the parish Board sent me out to Mother's sister. I had my thirteenth birthday on the ship *Corona*. That was ten long years ago.'

Abigail froze. Could this tottering ruin of a woman be only twenty-three? Doll pushed herself half upright, fell into a fearful paroxysm of coughing, and subsided once more. Her breath rattled in her chest in a frightening way; she seemed in a stupor.

'Aunt Hannah,' she whispered hoarsely, 'she put me to work. I didn't starve, you know.'

Abigail slipped to her feet. There was an iron bar across the two shutters that formed the window. It took her a long time to work it out of its rusted sockets. As she tried to open the shutter, it squawked alarmingly. Doll opened one glazed eye, but seemed not to have the strength to open the other. A trickle of bloodstained dribble came from her mouth.

'A person will do many things rather than starve,' she murmured. 'That's what the parsons don't understand. Empty bellies speak louder than the Ten Commandments.'

She closed her eyes again. In the uncertain light her face was that of a skull.

Abigail was frightened out of her wits. 'Mum!' she thought. 'I want you, Mum!' She wanted to pray but couldn't think of any words, so instead she put forth all her strength and shouted silently, 'Granny! Help me, help me!'

But it was to Granny Tallisker and not her own grandmother that her thoughts had turned. The shutter moved, and opened, and a gush of damp, kerosene-laden air came into the room. A glaring yellow light, broken by dancing shadows, fanned up from the little court below.

She had guessed right. There was a small wooden platform, supported on struts grown rotten and flimsy, in front of the window, and above it projected a rusty pulley and a frayed rope. She closed the shutter behind her, in case the cold air awakened Doll from her drunken slumber, and crouched on the platform. It groaned and dipped under her weight.

Nervously she gazed over the edge. Dark, shapeless things like bears or trolls gyrated about a brazier; coarse braying music from a tin whistle and a paper-covered comb filtered upwards. She could see above the lower roofs the gaslights of George Street, and she heard the chunk-splosh of the Manly[3] ferry's paddlewheels as it left the Quay.

She saw now that the thread-like alleyway into which she had ducked to hide from

3. Suburb of Sydney.

Beatie and Judah led from Harrington Street to George Street. Half-way down this wretched short-cut was a yard upon which opened the back doors of two taverns. It was plain that they catered for the violent and degraded. A ragged thing flung out of a tavern door, to lie unconscious on the cobbles, had a face that might have belonged to a bulldog. The ruffians gyrating drunkenly around the brazier instantly fell upon this victim, and in a few moments it was naked. Abigail watched, paralysed with horror.

The platform creaked and shuddered. She could climb neither down nor up, unless the rope and pulley were usable. Some time towards morning, surely, the revellers below would be either asleep or dead drunk, and she could let herself down into the courtyard?

After a while she thought of testing the dangling rope. Cautiously she rose on tiptoe and seized it. The frayed ends fell almost into dust in her hand. The rope had not been used for years and was completely perished.

Her eyes filled with tears. There was no hope. As she stood there, looking up at the askew, rusted pulley, and the edge of the roof above it, a small patch of the sky suddenly lost its stars.

Someone was lying on the warehouse roof looking down at her.

CHAPTER 7

When Abigail realised that she was being spied upon, her first horrified impulse was to get back into the room with Doll and bar the shutters. Her hand was on the pin when a voice said, very hushed, 'Dunna be feared, lass—it's me, Judah.'

She could see nothing but the shape of a head. She stood very still.

'Aye, that's bonny,' said the voice. 'That contraption ye're standing on might go any moment. Now, d'ye hear me all right?'

'Yes,' she breathed.

'I've some of the lads from the ship wi' me. I'm droppin' you a line with a loop in it. Put your foot in the loop and hold tight wi' all your might.'

A rope tumbled down to her. She seized it, did as she had been told, and whispered, 'I'm ready.'

As her chin rose above the roof slates, sturdy arms reached down and caught her under the armpits. In a few moments she was lying, limp and sweating, on the dewy slates.

There were several boys, two of them as small as Beatie, on the roof. They had bent the line around the stump of a chimney, and were now swiftly untying and coiling the rope. Barefooted and silent, they moved with the monkey-like nimbleness of apprentice seamen.

'How did you know where I was?' she asked.

'It was Granny,' said Judah, matter-of-factly. 'Go ahead, lads, and take care, for the roof's as rotten as them that own it.'

Keeping low, for fear anyone should see them outlined against the sky, Abigail and the boys crawled to the edge of the warehouse roof, and down the steep slippery gable of the terrace house next to it. If Abigail had not been so numbed with her recent experiences she would have been nervous of falling. But she had lost her shoes, and her stockinged toes, though not as deft as those of the boys, gripped fast in the mossy irregularities of the slates.

The boys pushed and pulled her across the roofs of six or seven little houses, sometimes disturbing rats playing in the guttering, or birds nesting in disused chimney-pots. She began to feel more and more unreal. Sometimes she thought she must have gone to sleep in the attic and was dreaming.

At last they came to a high rock lavishly curtained with convolvulus. A meagre lane squeezed between house and rock. Abigail cleared this space with ease.

'Why, she's as good as a lad!' said one of the boys. 'My sister Mabel would just 'a stood there squalling like a stood-on cat.'

Abigail, having slid down into the lane, was about to say that Mabel couldn't have been blamed when a curious thing happened. A wave of heat rippled up from her feet, leaving her legs boneless behind them.

She said feebly, 'I'm awfully sorry . . . my legs are gone somehow . . . and I think I might be sick . . .'

So she was, shivering and ashamed. But Judah merely said heartily, 'Chuck it up, Abby. It's a living wonder you're not in a dead swoon, what you've been through this night.'

She dimly heard the apprentice with the sister say, 'My sister Mabel would be flat on her back a'kicking and screeching in a fit of the flim-flams.'

'Poor old Mabel,' she tried to say, but nothing came out. Judah gathered her up, and she remembered no more until she realised she was being carried through the door of Mr Bow's shop. The other apprentices had vanished. She did not open her eyes again; it was too safe and comfortable against Judah's chest. If only, she felt drowsily, she could rest there for ever. But she had caught a glimpse of Dovey and Beatie, hovering about anxiously, and Gibbie in his long trailing night-shirt, flickering around like a small grey ghost, mad with curiosity.

Judah took her upstairs and laid her on her own bed. He said to Dovey, 'Granny?'

Dovey shook her head. 'Low.'

Abigail tried to speak, tried to ask, 'Is Granny Tallisker ill?' But although her mouth opened, her tongue moved, not a word came out. Terror filled her. What was the matter now? She caught Dovey's eye, pointed to her mouth, struggled to speak.

Dovey said soothingly, 'It's the shock, without doubt. Come the morning your voice will be back, as good as gold. Now then, so I can tell Granny when she's herself again: Did those villains do anything bad to you?'

Abigail longed to say, they kidnapped me and slapped me and a foul little beast with no legs bit me, and then they locked me up with a drunken consumptive who might be dead, as far as I know; but, no, they didn't do what I know you mean. But she could say nothing. She looked helplessly from Dovey to Judah and shook her head.

Judah said, 'I'll go take a keek[4] at my granny, then.' He came over to the bed, smoothed the tangled hair back from her forehead as if she were a child, and said, 'All's over now, Abby. Fret no more. Go to sleep and dream grand dreams, as you deserve.'

Abigail thought he had the most beautiful smile she had ever seen. The ruddy wholesomeness of his face contrasted so vividly with the fearful half-beast countenances of the inhabitants of the thieves' kitchen that she wanted to say, 'Thank you, thank you, Judah, for everything, not just for saving me. Thank you for being here.' But she could do nothing but press his hand.

He laughed, patted her cheek. 'You're a game lass, no doubt about that.'

Abigail still seemed to have no bones left in her body. Once again she was

---

4. A peep.

undressed by Dovey, given a posset, and put under the quilts. Dovey kissed her forehead, and hastened out.

Abigail thought, 'Mabel has the right idea. Lying on my back kicking and having hysterics is just what I'd do if I had any strength left.'

She became aware that Beatie was squatting on the end of the bed, like a malignant gnome. Abigail, already muzzy from the posset, had never seen her look so ferocious.

'What came over you, you blanky rattlebrain, to go down the Suez Canal? Could you not see it was the abode of cut-throats and mongrels? And what were you doing, fleein' away like that, when I'd given my solemn word to help you back to your ain time? Aye, and I wunna go back on it, neither, even though my poor granny is half dead on your account.'

'How, why?' Abigail wanted to ask. She managed a pitiful squawk.

'Never mind yer greeting, yer numbskull! Oh, couldn't I punch yer yeller and green!'

Abigail was only able to give a faint yelp of protest. She buried her face in the chicken-coop smelling pillow, and went unexpectedly to sleep. She awakened early, feeling stiff and sore all over. A faint daylight crept through the windows, early market carts grumbled over the cobbles. Dovey knelt beside her bed, her face in her hands.

'Oh, kind Lord in heaven, let my grandmother come to herself again, let poor Abby be as innocent as she was when she came to our care.'

Abigail managed a faint croak, and Dovey jumped up and came over to her. Abigail's voice still seemed to belong to someone else, but she whispered, 'Granny?'

'She's come back to herself, but she's no' well at all,' said Dovey evasively.

Abigail could not help it. Tears trickled down her cheeks.

'I'm just so tired of not understanding anything,' she said plaintively. 'It wouldn't matter if I weren't mixed up in it, but I am, and no one will tell me anything. It's not fair at all.'

Dovey looked both dubious and conscience-stricken. Across her childish face flitted a variety of expressions.

'Poor dear, poor child. 'Tis Granny herself who should tell you, as she meant to do. 'Twas a terrible effort for her, finding you last night. Aye, she was like a dead woman for two hours.' She sighed. ''Tis sad, for there ne'er was such a spaewife[5] as Granny in her young days; past and present were as clear as water to her eye. And Beatie, and myself—we dunna ha' the power. Except Beatie a little, when she was wandersome with the fever.'

Abigail said, 'I'm the Stranger, aren't I?'

'Aye,' said Dovey. 'Granny is certain of it. The signs are right.'

'Tell me,' begged Abigail. 'It's very frightening, Dovey. To be me, I mean. Not understanding anything at all.'

Out of the corner of her eye she saw Beatie creep in and sit on the rag rug beside Dovey's bed. Her sallow face was both fascinated and repelled. Dovey looked at her warningly.

'I'll not have any jeering, Beatie,' she said, severely for her. 'We all know verra well, for you've told us a thousand times, that you dunna want the Gift and won't have it; but nevertheless you and your children, should you have any, are in the way of it.'

'Babbies!' cried Beatie disgustedly. 'Who'd want the puling, useless things?'

The Gift was not in the Bow family, but in the Tallisker clan. Mrs Tallisker as a girl had borne the same surname. She had married her cousin, for young men were

5. A woman who makes prophecies.

scarce on Orkney where the sea took so many. It had been the ancestress of both these young people who had been whisked away to Elfland for several years, and then reappeared as mysteriously as she had vanished.

'You see, Abby,' explained Dovey, 'Orkney is a queer old place, where dwarfies and painted men, Picts[6] you might call them, lived long ago, and built great forts and rings of stone where a shepherd might wander and ne'er be seen again. And there are trolls, and spells to be said against them, and the children of the sea who dance on the sands on St John's Eve[7] . . . and it was Granny's seventh grandmother, Osla, who was elf-taken while she was watching the sheep and came back from Elfland with a wean about to be born. And with that wean came the Gift.'

This precious legacy was the gift of seeing the future, of healing, of secret wisdom. The Gift could be handed down by the men of the family, but never possessed by them. With the Gift, Osla's child, fathered in Elfland, had brought the Prophecy.

Granny was the greatest spaewife and healer of them all, explained Dovey. But as she grew older the Gift left her, coming only in erratic, puzzling flashes that she could not always understand. She could not, for instance, correctly interpret the Prophecy, although she was sure that Abigail herself was the Stranger.

'It's this way,' explained Beatie gruffly. 'Whenever the Gift looks like breeding right out, a Stranger comes. You can tell the Stranger because he or she always has something belonging to the Talliskers.'

'Well, I haven't,' thought Abigail. 'Granny's barking up the wrong tree this time. It can't be my dress, because Mum said that was an Edwardian curtain I made it from and she's never wrong about fabrics.'

'And the Stranger makes the Gift strong again,' said Beatie. Her turbulent, troubled little face was solemn. 'The blanky thing!'

'Beatie,' reproved Dovey, 'how can you speak that way?'

'Because,' Beatie said crossly, 'even though I dunna want the Gift myself, I know it's true. Oh, aye, I'm dead afeared of it; but I know it's true.'

For an instant Abby thought Beatie was going to confess that several times she had gone unvolitionally into the next century, but instead she muttered, 'You mind when I was sick, Dovey, and I had the dream of Mother's funeral and the yellow fever rag on the door . . .' Here Abigail started, for she, too, had dreamed of a door with a yellow rag tied to the knocker. 'And my three sisters that died of the smallpox came to me, looking as bonny as angels.'

'Well I remember that dream,' said Dovey. 'I feared they had come for you.'

'Those were only dreams,' said Beatie. 'But that night I had a flash, clear as day, and I knew I was no' to die. I didna like to tell you, in case you thought I had the Gift.'

'Whatever did you see, Beatie?' interposed Abigail.

'My own hands,' said Beatie, 'and they were a woman's hands, and there was no ring on them, and they were holding a book, very heavy, with a leather cover. A scholarly book. And I thought then, maybe I winna be an ignorant lass all my life, but get some education like Judah, or even better. I have kept it from you, Dovey; but all must come out now with Granny so low.'

Both Dovey and Beatie seemed to have forgotten Abigail, and she herself was thinking furiously. 'And why shouldn't she? She's brainy, and as determined as a little

---

6. Ancient inhabitants of central and northern Scotland.
7. Midsummer night. The original festival, a pagan feast celebrating the sun and fertility, was later Christianized to honor the birth of John the Baptist.

red devil. This Mr Taylor, who runs the class for promising boys, he must have a feeling for education . . . Perhaps if Beatie went to see him, let him know how much she has learnt, how much she longs to be properly educated . . .'

There was a piercing wail from above.

'I want the chamber-pot, Dovey. Come quick!'

Beatie sprang to her feet. 'I'll go, Dovey, and won't I shove his head in it if he's doing no more than pester us!'

'I'd like to see Granny,' said Abby. 'Please, Dovey.'

The old woman who lay in the small iron four-poster bed was scarcely recognisable. She had a look of ancient and unbearable fatigue, as though all strength had drained out of her. Abigail saw her eyes flickering under the silken brown eyelids.

'Granny,' said Dovey softly, ''tis Abby, come to show you she is safe.'

The eyes opened. Light had drained out of them also. The glistening vitality and intelligence, so like that in Judah's eyes, had gone. The dark blue had faded to a bleached slate-grey. Abigail was shocked and distressed.

'Oh, Granny,' she cried, 'do you feel very bad? Oh, Granny, I'm so sorry, but I just had to try to go home.'

The knobbly old hand wavered out. Abigail took it. The old woman's grip was feeble, and yet firm. She held Abigail's hand lightly but Abigail felt that even if she wanted to take her hand back she would not be able to.

'She hanna the Power, Dovey,' said the dim, rustling voice. 'She isna one of us. But there's something there, something . . . I can feel it strengthening me. Now, Abigail, isna the time for truth come? For you and for us, too, forbye.[8] You dinna come from another country, but from another time?'

Abigail heard Dovey gasp. She told Mrs Tallisker the year of her birth, and Dovey breathed, 'Dear God, is it possible?'

'Hush, Dovey. Tell me true, Abigail, in that far-off time which is yours and not ours, did ye ever hear the name Tallisker, or Bow?'

'No, never,' said Abigail truthfully.

'Your father's name is Kirk? A Scottish name.'

'Yes, but he's half Norwegian. He was born in Narvik, and brought to Aust . . . to New South Wales as a baby.'

'His mother's name?'

'Emma Rasmussen.'

Granny Tallisker asked the same questions about Abigail's mother. But Kathy was fourth generation Australian, and Abigail knew of no blood strain other than English and German amongst her mother's ancestors.

'Yet you are the Stranger,' murmured the old lady. ''Tis very puzzling, Dovey.'

'I'm not, you know,' said Abigail emphatically. 'You've made a mistake. I got here quite accidentally. It was because . . .' she stopped. She had promised Beatie solemnly that she would not ever tell that the younger girl had visited the twentieth century.

'No, no,' said the old woman almost impatiently. 'You are the Stranger; there is nae possibility of mistake.'

Her voice had grown stronger. The hyacinth colour almost perceptibly flowed back into her eyes. Abigail wondered uneasily if she were withdrawing vitality from her own hand, and she tried to take it away, but could not without a sharp, rude jerk.

Suddenly Dovey spoke rapidly in the broad Orkney dialect. Abigail could scarcely

8. Besides.

catch a word except 'aye' and 'Beatie' and 'unwed'. Mrs Tallisker was excited.

'Then she's not to die, my clever wee hen! God be praised for that, anyway.'

'I have just told Granny what Beatie saw,' Dovey explained; 'the woman's hands without a ring, and a book in them. And she says that is the first part of the Prophecy proved.'

Abigail was bewildered. She was not interested in the Prophecy. What she wanted to know was how Granny had known where she was held captive. But it didn't seem the time to ask.

'The Prophecy,' explained Mrs Tallisker, 'is for each fifth generation, when it is so ordered that the Gift is at risk. This is the fifth generation from my grandfather's time, when there wunna a Tallisker left but himself, after the Stuart wars in Scotland.[9] Tell Abby the words, Dovey, the while I catch my breath.'

Dovey said in a low reluctant voice, 'It is in our Orkney speech, but it means, "One to be barren and one to die."'

'Well, goodness,' said Abigail, 'I can't see that that's so bad.'

'See, Abigail,' explained Dovey, 'I am the sole child of Granny's son Robert Tallisker who drowned, God rest his soul. And of the bairns of my Aunt Amelia, four died young. Of those who can hand on the Gift to the future, there are now no more than four.'

'You, Judah, Beatie and Gibbie,' said Abigail thoughtfully.

'And of those Beatie is to be barren and will not hand on the Gift,' said Mrs Tallisker.

'But you don't know that!' protested Abigail.

'The ringless hand,' reminded Dovey. 'She saw it herself. She will not wed, and will be childless.'

'I think it's absolutely repulsive,' cried Abigail, 'talking about people as if they were part of some superstitious pattern. It's all right for Beatie not to marry if she doesn't want to, don't you see? But that means one of the rest of you will die.'

'And die young,' said Dovey.

'Don't you care?' cried Abigail. 'Why, it might be you! It might be Judah!' Then realisation struck her. 'Gibbie! You believe Gibbie's going to die, don't you?'

'It might well be the poor little one,' said Dovey gently. 'He hasna made headway since the fever, and it is now seven months since he sickened. His little bones are like sticks, and he hasna put on an ounce, feed him up as we may. But on the other hand, Abigail, it may be myself, as you say. It is your coming that will decide.'

'I've nothing to do with it!' cried Abigail. 'I came here without wanting to and I want to go home. I've a life of my own, and I want to live it. My mother, I miss her, don't you understand?' she said chokily. She thought fiercely, 'I won't cry, I won't.' She waited for a moment, and then said quietly, 'I'm not your mysterious Stranger. I'm just someone who came into your life here in some way that's a riddle to me. But I have to go home, I don't belong here. You must see that.'

'We canna let you go,' said Mrs Tallisker. She had relinquished Abigail's hand and was sitting up against her pillows. Except for her sunken eyes she looked almost like her own dignified strong self again.

Abigail glowered. 'I'll run away again and again till I find the place where I came into this horrible century; and I'll go, I swear I will.'

'But we canna let you go until you have done whatever it is the Stranger must do

9. The struggle for power (1479–84) between James III, King of Scotland (1452–1488; r. 1460–88), and his brother, Alexander Stuart (Duke of Albany, ca. 1454–1485).

to preserve the Gift.' Dovey was distressed. 'Oh, dear Abby, it may only be for a little while and then we will help you go to your own place. We do understand what you feel, that you long for your ain folk, but we canna let you go . . . you are our only hope, you see.'

Abigail said unbelievingly, 'This thing . . . is it so precious to you that you'd do this to me? It . . . isn't Christian.'

'The Gift is not Christian,' said Mrs Tallisker. 'But aye, you have it right, girl. It is so precious to us that we would keep you here for ever if this were ordained to be so.'

'Judah wouldn't let you!' burst out Abigail. 'He's got some gumption, he's a seaman, a grown man . . .' But she could see from their pitying faces that Judah believed in the Gift as strongly as they did.

'Either they're all dotty, or I'm dreaming,' thought Abigail. Her knees wobbled. 'But I'm not dreaming. I'm here, in a little Victorian cottage full of oil lamps and iron pots and funny clothes and paintings of people who lived before Queen Victoria was born. It's real, more real than Magpies, or anything.'

At the thought that she was trapped as efficiently as she had been in that gloomy cavern of the Suez Canal, she sniffed dolorously.

'I can't go my whole life without seeing my mother and father again,' she whispered. 'And truly you are mistaken. I'm not this Stranger of whom you talk. I didn't have anything belonging to the family. I wasn't even wearing anything unusual: just my green dress.'

'Aye,' said Mrs Tallisker, and her voice was so tender, so loving, that chills ran up and down Abby's spine.

'My dress? That had something to do with . . . ?'

All at once she remembered the dream-like conversation she had heard that first terrible, confused, and painful night. Dovey and Granny. Whispers. No mistake. Pattern. Not a needle set to it yet.

She cried, 'Not the dress, the crochet! *The crochet!*'

She saw by glancing from one to the other that she was right.

'The pattern . . . the grass of Parnassus . . .'

'It is a common bog plant in Orkney,' said Dovey.

'The initials,' breathed Abigail. 'A.T. Not Anastasia Tassiopolis but Alice Tallisker . . . I don't know what to say. That crochet—you designed it, you made it . . . but not yet.'

Mrs Tallisker nodded. She had wearied again. The small vitality she had absorbed from Abigail seemed to have leaked away now that Abigail herself was trembling and shocked.

'The crochet brought me here in some way; it was a sort of link between me and Beatie . . . and you've burnt the dress, so now I can never get back, never.'

She felt very much older than fourteen. She felt like an old woman.

It was like the terrible lostness and helplessness she had felt when her father went away. The empty place inside her had swallowed her up. She got up to leave the room. Dovey tried to stop her, but Abigail's stony, hating face made her recoil. She went downstairs, with Dovey limping after her.

Mr Bow looked up with surprise from the marble slab where he was moulding liquorice babies.

'What in the name of fortune are you doing, girl? You're still in your night-rail!'

Abigail looked down without interest at her stiff calico nightdress. It struck her then that this was the kind of clothing she would always wear until she was an old woman and graduated to a flannel gown and a baby's bonnet nightcap like Mrs Tallisker. That was if she survived scarlet fever, cholera, plague, and all the things she had not had shots for.

'Fortunately I have had my polio injections and my smallpox inoculations,' she remarked politely to Mr Bow. The man looked flabbergasted. He wiped his hands on his apron and led her gently away from the door. He put his sticky hand on her forehead, and said anxiously to Dovey, 'Would she be sickening for something, walking about this way in her shift?'

Dovey tried to put her arms around Abigail, but she pushed them away. 'You pretend to be kind, but you're cruel. Your father died and your mother died, and you know how hard it is. But you will keep me away from my home and my friends and my mother and I'll never see her again.'

She felt that somewhere inside her she was sobbing broken-heartedly, but outwardly she was calm.

'I can't trust any of you, except Judah.'

She thought then of Judah as a rock in the wilderness. His strength, his frankness and plainness of speech, his understanding of Beatie's longing for education—why else should he be teaching her Latin, and geometry, too, for all Abigail knew?

'Abby, Granny wants to see you. Please come.'

'I don't want to.'

'It's about your dress.' Dovey faltered. 'I told you an untruth, Abby, and verra ashamed I was. But Granny thought it best. Your dress was not burnt, 'tis hid away, safe as houses.'

Abigail leapt up the stairs two at a time. She burst into Granny's room. Beatie was helping the old woman into a clean wrapper. Abigail's rage was beyond bounds. She opened her mouth to yell at Mrs Tallisker, but the old woman looked at her steadfastly. It was if she were being engulfed by those blue eyes. Her anger melted, and she said, gently and politely, 'Is it true that my dress was not destroyed?'

'True indeed,' replied the old woman tranquilly. 'And when you've done what you were sent here to do I shall give it back to you, and you can return home.'

'But I don't know what I have to do,' said Abigail desperately.

'It will show itself in time,' said Granny.

Abigail begged and pleaded, but Mrs Tallisker was adamant.

'The Gift is more precious than you, or any of us here. It munna be more than a couple of days before we know what you must do.'

'Tell me what it is and I'll do it!' pleaded Abigail.

But Granny shook her head. 'That we dinna know, child. But it will reveal itself.'

'Why don't you know, if you have the Gift?' cried Abigail.

'Because I'm old and the Gift is leaving me—' replied Granny with dignity, 'as is the power of my sight and the strength of my hands. If I could still heal would I not make poor Gibbie as strong as his brother?'

'All very well,' thought Abigail contemptuously, 'but how did you know I was in that warehouse, tied up and helpless?'

'Because you called me, child,' answered the old woman readily, 'and I sent out my mind to search for you.'

Distantly the voice of Gibbie could be heard, cheeping wretchedly.

'I'll see to him,' said Abigail to Beatie. She was half-way up to the attic before she realised that Mrs Tallisker had answered a question she had not asked aloud. She shuddered. Did Judah believe all this stuff? Did Mr Bow?

Gibbie was lying back on his little bed, looking holy. Abigail looked at him critically.

No doubt of it, he was a miserable whitebait[1] of a kid, as flimsy within as without, she had no doubt. He opened one eye a slit and peered at her through his eyelashes, and began to wheeze dramatically.

'Don't waste your theatrics on me,' said Abigail.

'Going to the theatre is the devil's work,' said Gibbie in his parson's tone. 'You fall straight into hell fire ten miles down.'

'Sounds fun,' said Abigail. Gibbie blanched.

It was no wonder, thought the girl, that Granny and Dovey thought he would be the one to die. And this conclusion, she knew, would not lie easy on their minds. She recalled Dovey's devotion to the child, her sleepless nights and endless patience with a youngster Abigail felt was as unlovable and obnoxious as a child could get.

The attic had a sloping roof covered with flowered wallpaper. There were framed texts on the walls. In the sharp angle of the ceiling and floor was a small casement window.

'Dunna you open it,' said Gibbie in a fright. ''Twould mean my death of cold, immediate!'

'I'm just looking,' said Abigail. The attic window looked over the back of the house, over midget back yards; 'wee hoosies'; and incredible masses of rubbish: old iron bedsteads, broken hen-coops, rusty corrugated iron. The skillion[2] roof of the Bows' kitchen ran below the window, to extend half over the next yard, where someone had strung a line of deep-grey tattered washing. A small pig was tethered on the roof, rooting listlessly at a heap of rotting cabbage leaves. In the next yard two Chinese with pigtails worked industriously over a steaming copper. *Their* laundry was dazzling white. Baffled by this, Abigail returned to the bed, where Gibbie was watching her with big eyes.

'Why do you look so different from us?'

'You've got me there,' said Abby. 'Haven't you anything to do besides pick your nose? Haven't you anything to read?'

'I dinna read very well, but sometimes Granny tells me stories of the fishermen, and the big storms and such things; and when Judah is home from a voyage he tells me of shipwrecks and rafts, and the forest where the cedar is cut, and how he's going to be master of his own ship, and sail to the Solomons[3] and see the savages.'

'That must be interesting,' said Abigail. The little boy's face had momentarily lost its pinched, old-monkish look, and become vivacious and excited. Then he said in his dreariest tone, 'But I'm going to heaven instead to be with Mamma and the angels, and I daresay that is twice as worthwhile as the Solomon Islands.'

'Poor little rat,' thought Abigail. Then she caught herself: 'I'm going on as if I believe he's going to die, just like the rest of them.' Aloud she said, 'Do you know the story of *Treasure Island?*'

Gibbie's eyes glistened. 'I do not. Can you tell it to me?'

Abby began: 'Once upon a time there was a pirate called Long John Silver . . .'

'But if *he* doesn't die,' she thought, 'there's only Dovey and Judah.' The room seemed to fill with Judah's warmth and liveliness, his boy's joviality and his man's sense of responsibility towards his family. She could almost hear him telling this sick child of tropical forests and coral reefs, never mentioning all the hardships and perils of an apprentice seaman on a coastal brig.

---

1. Small, young fish (especially herring).
2. A lean-to built against the house.

3. South Pacific islands.

'Won't ye be goin' on?' pleaded Gibbie. 'For I'm fair mad to hear about this pirate.'

'He had a wooden leg,' said Abby absently.

'Oh,' she thought, 'don't let it be Judah; it mustn't be Judah!'

CHAPTER 8

In a way, she felt as she had felt when her father went away and left her. Fright, anger and helplessness, the sense of being nobody who could make things happen. But then she had been only ten. Four years of schooling her face to be expressionless, her thoughts to be her private property, had not gone to waste.

After her first despair, she thought, 'I won't let them beat me. If that dress is hidden around the house I'll find it. Or I'll bribe Beatie, or coax Judah, into telling me where it is.'

She had learnt a lot about herself in this new rough world. Her own thoughts and conclusions of just a month before filled her with embarrassed astonishment when she reviewed them.

'What a dummo I was! I knew as much about real life as poor little Natty.'

She stopped being silent and distraught and asked Granny if she could help in the house and the shop until whatever it was that she was fated to do as the Stranger was revealed.

Granny put her arms about her. Orkney folk were an undemonstrative people, as she had realised, and Granny's action touched her. 'My heart aches for you, Abby, but 'twill be worth it, for you as well as the rest of us. It is my duty to see the Gift handed on. I can do no other.'

Abigail nodded gravely. Granny's eyes twinkled. 'And if you are planning on finding your gown, hen, it's nae guid. It's where you'll n'er look for it.'

'Oh, damn you all!' Abigail was furious.

'Fair enough,' said Granny, her eyes still twinkling.

Still, rather than maunder around with nothing to do, Abigail fitted herself into the household routine. She learnt to rake out the shop fire and carry the ash in pails to the ash-pit in the yard. Some of this ash was saved and sifted and used to make soap. Though many of the inhabitants of The Rocks washed themselves, during their rare personal ablutions, with the harsh lye soap, the Talliskers and Bows used it for laundry soap and never applied it to their skins.

'You'd be as chapped as a frost-bitten potato in a week, lass,' explained Granny. They all, even the men, used oatmeal in muslin bags with which to scrub themselves, and as the days went by Abigail noticed her own brown skin taking on the fineness that was characteristic of all the family's complexions.

She scrubbed and dusted, washed and polished the lamp chimneys, and learnt how to set a wick so that the paraffin (which she called kerosene) burnt clear and without odour.

She did approach Beatie about the dress, but the girl said downrightly she had no idea where it was, and would not tell if she did.

'But Beatie, if I could escape to my own time, maybe you could come with me, and go to school, and learn all you want, with no one to discourage you.'

A look of intense yearning passed over the younger girl's face.

'I'd sell my ten toes for it, as ye weel know,' she said, 'but how could I leave Dovey? For she's all in all to me now my mother's gone. Aye, I'd do without anything in life rather than leave Dovey.'

Abigail best liked working in the shop. Very quiet and mild since his last frenzy, Mr Bow was a pleasant companion, though given to bursts of tears, turning away unexpectedly and wiping his eyes on the corner of his apron.

'I'm as right-minded as any man when I don't touch the spirits,' he explained. 'But the pain in my head gets that bad, and hain't it a temptation then to have a halfer and relieve it a little? But I didn't hurt you bad, wench, eh, did I?'

'Only a little, Mr Bow,' Abigail assured him. She said frankly, 'I expect you know that Mrs Tallisker thinks I'm the mysterious Stranger?'

'Don't I just,' he replied, 'and it must be a heart scald for you, kept here amongst folk not your own. But I ain't saying nothing about it, Miss, because I'm skeered to do so, if you must know the truth of it. For 'tis true, you know, the Gift and that.'

'But, Mr Bow,' protested Abigail, 'you're English. You can't believe this Orkney fairy-tale.'

He looked at her sadly. 'I do, dear Miss, and that's a fact. Didn't my pretty 'Melia, when I was a-courting her, tell me that she'd die afore me and leave me with enough sorrow to break my back? I laughed me head off, for you know I was near twenty years older than 'Melia, and in the course of nature it was to be expected that I would be taken afore her. But I said two years of your company, my pretty dear, is worth a lifetime of tears. And I did better than that. Nigh nineteen years we was wed, and never a frown.'

Here he turned away quickly.

'Did you ever see Florence Nightingale?'[4] interposed Abigail hurriedly.

He wiped his eyes, turned once more to his patient pulling and slapping of the rapidly congealing toffee over the great hook. 'Nay,' he said 'not to remember like. I mind only filth and the stink of wounds and green water. And then the ship and England. And after a long time I rejoined my regiment and, unfit for active duty as I was, we was posted to New South Wales to the garrison. And there I served out my term, four years agone now. And what I'd do without Granny and Dovey I can't bear to think, for there's Beatrice needs a mother, and Gibbie a-fading away, and myself that mazy[5] sometimes I dunno if I'm on head or heels.'

Abigail realised dolefully that Mr Bow would never cross Granny in order to help her.

But this did not mean that she did not stealthily investigate every available place where her dress might have been hidden. In such a tiny cottage she was rarely alone, and she was abashed and angry when caught scrabbling behind the sacks of sugar in the cellar under the shop.

'It inna worthy of you, pet,' said Granny quietly. Abigail was crimson.

'It's all your fault,' she retorted. 'You took my dress and hid it. I've never before snooped amongst other people's things in my life!'

'And you'll not have to again,' said Mrs Tallisker, mildly, 'for I'll tell ye where the gown is laid away. In Dovey's bride chest, which is locked.'

Abigail groaned. 'You know very well I'd never as much as lift the lid of Dovey's bride chest, let alone break the lock. You're as crafty as a fox; you ought to be ashamed!'

'Aye,' agreed Granny tranquilly, 'but 'tis all in a good cause.'

4. English nurse (1820–1910) whose reforms in a military hospital during the Crimean War won her fame; she later founded the first institution to train nurses.
5. Dizzy, confused in the head.

'I just want to go home, you know,' whispered Abigail.

'You're as restless as a robin, child,' said Mrs Tallisker. 'But 'twill not be long now.'

There was a great difference in Mrs Tallisker. She had, all at once, become older and smaller. Only a few weeks before she had towered, or so it seemed, over Abigail. Now Abigail was almost as tall. Her skin had crumpled more deeply, more extensively, like a slowly withering flower. She could not work as hard as before, but sat more often in the parlour with Gibbie, knitting thick grey socks for Judah.

'Aye,' she said with her sweet smile, as Abigail secretly stared at her, "'tis a fearful effort to give out the Power when it has decided to leave. If I could do what I did for you, child, you can give me a little of your time, inna that fair enough?'

'Yes, of course,' said Abigail, but in her heart she was grudging.

Sometimes she sat, pondering, in front of Dovey's bride chest. It was a small, green-painted tin box with an arched lid decorated with faded tulips and rosettes. In there was her key to home, but her sense of honour prevented her from taking a knife and forcing the lid.

'It's ridiculous,' she thought, 'but it's true. I can't touch it. Oh, that Granny! She knows me better than I do myself.'

She had no curiosity about the contents of Dovey's bride chest, knowing that from the age of seven every Orkney girl began to prepare household linen against the day when her hand would be asked in marriage. She thought it would be full of towels and sheets and little muslin bags to hold oatmeal.

The Rocks was an uncomfortable place to be at that time of the year. As often in Sydney, it was a time of spectacular electrical storms and erratic summer rain. Wild winds snored and spiralled off the Pacific archipelagoes, their fringes sweeping the Australian coast like the edges of cloudy shawls. Judah's ship, *The Brothers*, had been driven onto the mud at Walsh Bay, and needed repairs. Though he was working on her all day, he was permitted to spend the nights at home, and so she saw far more of him than hitherto.

Now that she was familiar with the household routine, Abigail saw that it turned upon Judah's comings and goings as if he were a pivot. He blew into the house like a bracing nor' easterly, and everyone, from the mourning father to Gibbie languishing before the fire in the suffocatingly hot parlour, seemed to absorb vitality from him. He was unlike any boy Abigail had known in her own world. He was just a well-knit, sturdy person of middle height, yet his muscles were of oak, his mind far-reaching and vigorous.

At first Abigail observed him with friendly curiosity. The difference between him and boys of eighteen in her time was that Judah was a man. She thought of the likeable, aimless brothers of many of her friends, without discipline or ambition, and wondered uneasily how it had come to be that they were so different from this son of a poor family, who had done a man's job, and thought it a right rather than a burden, from his fourteenth year.

He was artless and straightforward, with not the slightest interest in the world from which Abigail had so strangely come.

At first she thought he did not believe her when she told him of ships driven by atomic fission—some under the water—and told him that even ferries no longer used steam, but were oil powered.

'Oh, aye,' he said, unconcerned. 'I believe you. Hanna I seen the Gift at work so often since I was in arms? My mother knew the very day I would return to dock, fair weather or foul, and would have a plum duff in the pot, for as a lad I was fair crazy for a slice of Spotted Dick.[6] But what you tell me, Abby love, well, 'tis like all the fingle-fangles the Government men prate about—Henry Parkes[7] and all that lot—Federation and free trade, and republicanism. I know 'tis true, but it hanna importance for me. 'Tis here I live, do you see, in 1873, and my labour is here, and my own folk, and I'm thankful to God for both. So that's enough for me.'

'But men landing on the moon!' cried Abigail. 'Don't you think *that's* fantastic?'

'Damned foolishness, I call it,' he said, and flushed. 'Your pardon, Abby, for a word Granny would thicken my ear for, but 'tis no more and no less. What good to man or beast is that bare lump of rock?'

'At least it makes the tides,' snapped Abigail, 'and where would you be without them?'

He laughed. 'True for you, but no man has to go there to press a lever or turn a wheel for that!'

Having failed to interest him in the future, she turned to the past, and asked him was he ever homesick for Orkney, as she knew Dovey was.

'Not I,' he said. 'Why, 'tis the past, and dead and gone. I'm a New South Welshman now, and glad about it, aye, gey glad!' His eyes danced. 'Ah, I'm glad to be alive, and at this minute, I tell ye! There's few enough with my good fortune—for in a month or so I'll be an AB,[8] with a decent wage and prospects. Oh, aye,' he added hastily, in case she felt slighted, 'I'm sure the time you came from is a very grand place to be, but it's no' for me, not for all the tea in China.'

The cottage was always noisy when Judah was at home. Either he was doing a sailor's jig with Beatie, twirling Granny in what she called a 'poker', playing tunes on a tin whistle, or giving Gibbie hair-raising pick-a-back rides up and down the twisted stairs. She began to listen for his laugh, his 'Ahoy, who's at home at Bows'?' as he came in, for he had the soft full voice of Dovey and his grandmother, very pleasant to the ear. Other times she would find him, late at night, his bright fair head bent in the circle of light from the paraffin lamp as he corrected Beatie's Latin exercises, or studied his books on navigation.

'For I've a mind to have my own ship one day,' he said cheerfully. 'If Captain Cook[9] could do it, so can I, and sail to the cannibal islands and bring back a cargo of sandalwood.'

'And what will you do when you're rich?' asked Abby laughing.

He gave her his candid blue look. 'I'll take my faither to a fine surgeon and have his trouble fixed, so that he can be happy, and I'll pay a clever tutor to give Beatie all the learning she wants, and I'll buy Dovey a fine silk dress like a princess, and I might give you a white mouse for a pet.'

'Nothing larger or finer?' she asked teasingly.

'Ah, so you'd like a rat? Then I'll catch you one this very night. We have them by the thousand on board *The Brothers*, and the ship's cats are all worn down as small as this with hard work.'

He showed her with finger and thumb.

'Oh, Judah,' she laughed, 'you're a clown. I'll miss you when I go home.'

And all at once it hit her. It was like a physical blow, so that she lost her breath,

6. A pudding made with suet and currants or raisins. "Plum duff": a steamed pudding, usually made with prunes, raisins, or other fruit.
7. Australian politician (1815–1896), best-known for his support of the movement to unite the different Australian states ("Federation").
8. An able-bodied seaman (i.e., qualified to per-

form all routine duties at sea).
9. James Cook (1728–1779), the British mariner and explorer whose achievements included charting the coasts of New Zealand, Australia, and New Guinea. He (like Judah) began his career as a merchant seaman.

and could scarcely gasp a 'Good night' before she fled for the stairs.

Dovey was already in bed and asleep. Abigail undressed hurriedly in the dark, flung herself into bed and buried her face in the feather pillow. It was not possible. Love could not pierce one with a dart, envelop one with an unquenchable fire, all those things that old songs said, that the girls at school said. 'I saw him getting off the bus and my knees went. I didn't know what I was doing. I went down the wrong street and left my school-case at the bus stop.' Or, 'I just sort of burnt all over; it was unreal. I couldn't have answered if he'd spoken to me, I was paralytic.'

Mum, talking about meeting Dad. 'We were both swimming. He was thrashing along and ran into me. Boom! Knocked all the wind out of me. He hauled me out of the water like a wet sack. None of your romantic picking me up and carrying me out. And I lay on the sand whooping. Oh, it was squalid, I can tell you. He said "Why weren't you watching where I was going, you knucklehead?" Typical. My fault, mind you. His hair was all plastered down, like yellow seaweed, yuk! I just lay there making noises like an up-chucking cat and looking at his blue, blue eyes, and thinking, "I've met him at last, my own man. Wonder what his name is?"'

My own man! When her mother had said that, so spontaneously and gaily, Abigail had been so embarrassed she marvelled that she had not come out in hives all over. The idea of one's mother coming out with a golden oldie phrase!

But now she saw it was the only phrase there was.

She could scarcely admit it to herself. The most exquisitely delicate sensation touched her, body and mind. The empty place in her heart opened like a flower and was filled.

'I love him,' she thought. 'I love Judah. I've loved him all along, ever since he carried me to the window that first night. And I didn't know.'

She lay awake for hours, in a daze of happiness.

It was like going to another country, seeing landscapes that were not of this world. Yet she had known those landscapes were there: that was why she had always felt empty, incomplete, because she knew they were there and she belonged in them, but she did not know where to look to find them.

The dark room seemed full of diamonds and spangles, as though the light within her was so exuberant it streamed from her eyes and fingers and toes.

The ships moored at the wharves creaked and groaned, hasty footsteps sounded on the cobbles of a nearby lane. In the Chinamen's laundry the mangle[1] thumped. These sounds were drowned by the bim-bam of thunder, and the dark was suddenly wiped over by lightning. She heard Gibbie shriek above, and Dovey instantly stir.

'I'm awake, Dovey,' she said. 'I'll go up to him.'

'Take the cannle, pet,' said Dovey drowsily and thankfully, 'and my red gown.'

Abby stumbled up the stairs. The baggy red-flannel dressing-gown smelt of perspiration and the vinegar Dovey had used to sponge the collar and cuffs. Normally Abby would have been sickened by it. But now she was different. These small things did not seem to matter any more.

'I dunna want you,' snivelled Gibbie, sitting up in bed like a pale owl, his hair a meagre fuzz. 'I want my Dovey.'

'Dovey's so tired,' said Abigail. 'You'll be a good lad and let her have her sleep, won't you?'

'I'm that skeered of lightning,' he sobbed. ''Twill come and get me and grill me like a kipper!'[2]

---

1. Machine for ironing laundry by pressing it through rollers.   2. Herring.

'It won't if I'm here,' said Abigail confidently. She sat beside him. He smelled sickly and looked like a little death's-head in the candlelight. And Abigail found herself thinking, 'It's a good thing, though. Now Dovey and Judah are safe.'

For an instant she remembered her mother's dark dewdrop eyes, as she said, 'You don't know how powerful love can be', and she thought how strange it was that love had made her both callous and tender. She did not care if this child died. Though she had never liked him, she had not wanted to deprive him of his life. But now, if his death meant that Judah lived, then she did not care a jot if he died.

At the same time she did what would have made her skin creep a day or so before: she put her arms around his shivering, bony little body and held him comfortingly.

She thought, 'I think I could even do the same for foul Vincent, the way I feel now.'

'Want to do Number One,' said Gibbie. She brought him the chamber-pot; put it away on the wash-stand again.

'Lie down now and go to sleep. I'll keep the lightning from hurting you,' she said.

'Are you a witch?' asked Gibbie, big-eyed. 'Beatie said you wunna.'

Abigail considered. 'No, I'm not. But I'm very good with thunder and lightning. Shall I tell you some more about Long John Silver and the other pirates?'

But the little boy was asleep in a few moments. The storm had boiled out to sea; she saw its last rip of light across the dark clouds on the horizon. The rain-glass[3] was falling, Judah had said that evening. Would rain keep his ship from sailing? She wished that a hurricane would blow and keep him at home for a week. She stood for a while outside the room where Judah and his father slept. She did not wish to be with him; it was enough to know that he was there.

The rain was very heavy. It crashed down the slopes of Flagstaff Hill and some feared that the new Observatory itself would come sliding down and perch itself like Noah's Ark on the edge of the cliff. It poured off the High Rocks in torrents and drenched the rat-ridden houses that overhung the alleys. The alleys themselves ran like storm channels. Then the sun would blaze out for a day or two; the air would be full of steams and stinks; people would get out with brooms made of twigs or thick splinters bound in a bush, and sweep away the muck.

Another time Abigail would have been outraged that a city already large and prosperous could tolerate such wretchedness on its front step. But now all the rain meant was that Judah was often at home. She spoke to him little. She helped Dovey wash his wet clothes that reeked of tar and seaweed, turning them constantly as they dried before the kitchen fire.

''Twas at a time like this that Aunt 'Melia and the others took the fever,' said Dovey. 'For the water gets tainted, and even the gentility die.'

But death seemed a long way from Abigail. Her days seemed filled with richness. She did not ask questions of herself, why she felt this enchanted calm, why she no longer fretted about her mother, her home in that other place. She scarcely thought. She just felt, and lived from day to day.

The coming of love was one thing. Yes, it had hit her like a thunderbolt, as other girls and her own mother had described. But what she felt of love itself seemed different from what she had heard and read. She did not long to touch him or be touched by him. Perhaps, she thought, that comes later.

Now, her whole body and mind and emotions had become exquisitely sensitive and delicate. The simple fact of his physical reality was enough to make her world different. To listen to him, to look at him, occasionally to brush past in the narrow

3. Barometer.

passageways of the cottage, this was enough. More would be unbearable. She looked with intense and uncomplicated joy at the golden glint along his jawbone, his close-set ears, the capable width between thumb and forefinger. These seemed marvellous to her.

She was content with loving. She had not thought about being loved in return, though she believed that surely it must be a law of nature that sooner or later he would look up and see her as she saw him, the only one, the precious one.

There seemed no reason to talk to the others, so she did not speak, unless it was necessary. Perhaps they would believe she was just sulking about being kept a virtual prisoner.

Dovey's shattered thigh pained severely in the wet weather. Granny had taken her into her own room, to rub the girl's leg when the pain was worst.

'For I still have a little of the healing touch,' she explained.

Beatie had gone back to her own bed. She was supposed to help Abigail attend to Gibbie, if he needed someone in the night; but the little girl slept like one dead. So the days went past, and on many nights Abby climbed the attic stairs to the sick child and tried to be kind and tolerant with him. She could not help feeling that his insatiable desire for sympathy and attention was not related to his illness, but to his loss of his mother and his constant brooding on death. And how was she to explain these things to people who had never heard of psychology?

She and Beatie had been down to the market to buy vegetables and meat. It was a fine day; the people were out in crowds. She had enjoyed the outing, seeing the old-clo' shops with the wheeled racks of tattered garments outside, the cobbler with a tall Wellington boot hung as a sign above his door, the itinerant cooks with their charcoal braziers—cooking and selling sausages, scallops, baked potatoes, haddocks, chitterlings[4]—positioned every few yards along Argyle and Windmill streets.

Then, almost out of a blue sky, down had come another summer downpour. The girls had run like hares, but they were soaked, both having dragged off their shawls to cover the goods in case of damage.

They were in their bedroom, changing their clothes, when Beatie all at once said, 'I have to talk to you, Abigail.'

'Talk away,' said Abigail cheerfully. She had been aware that Beatie had been more difficult during the last few days, flying into tantrums, bitter about school, churlish even with Dovey.

Judah had threatened to flatten her ears for her, though he had said it with his usual sunny smile.

'What you need, my lass, is an outing. I'll tell ye, I hae the very thing, and we'll take Dovey and Gibbie too, if the lad's fit enough. We'll go cockling[5] next Sabbath . . . I'll get a lend of a dory, and we'll go maybe right across to Billy Blue's Point!'

But Granny was downright about Gibbie's unfitness to go into the open air, and the sea wind at that, and Dovey murmured that she'd never get down Jacob's Ladder at Walsh Bay with her leg as stiff as it was.

'But 'tis a grand idea, Judah, and Abby will enjoy it, isn't that true, hen? And Beatie will be clean out of her mind, she loves an outing so.'

But now, in the bedroom, Beatie said gruffly, 'You! You're stuck on him, inna that right?'

Abigail had been humming happily. Now she felt as though her blood flowed back-

---

4. The small intestine of a pig, usually served fried or in a sauce.　　5. Digging for cockles, an edible mollusk.

wards, so fearful was the sense of privacy breached, of dignity defiled. She stammered, 'I don't know what you mean.'

'Dinna try to hide it from me,' said Beatie. 'I seen it in your face. Look at you now, red as a radish. You're stuck on him, my brother Judah.'

'You mind your own business!' cried Abigail.

'Blind me if it inna my business!' retorted Beatie.

Abigail pulled her shift over her head. In its depths she managed to compose her face, force her outrage to subside.

She pulled down the shift and fastened the tapes of her drawers.

'And suppose you're right, what's the matter with that? Not that I'm saying you're right!'

'Because Judah thinks you're just a child, like me. That's one thing. And the other thing is he's promised.'

'Promised,' whispered Abigail. 'What is promised?'

'Are you daft? He's betrothed to Dovey. He's always been promised to her.'

It was as if the light had diminished. Abigail finished dressing, brushed her damp hair and tied it back. She did all these things automatically, her eyes fixed on Beatie's face.

'Stop girning at me!' ordered Beatie testily. 'What else did you expect? Dinna Judah lame her, when she was but a wean, flitter-brained scamp that he was? Not every man wants a lame wife, so he owes her something. But no matter about that. How could he help loving Dovey, beautiful and good as she is?'

'In my time she wouldn't be thought beautiful,' said Abigail, and was immediately ashamed.

'And in this one you're no oil painting,' snapped back Beatie, 'and neither am I, come to that. But I'm telling you now—Judah belongs to Dovey, and they'll marry as soon as he's out of his time.'[6]

'But I've never seen him kiss her or anything,' said Abigail half to herself. 'How could anyone guess they are promised?'

'Kissing! That's no' for Orkney folk,' cried Beatie haughtily. 'We keep our feelings to ourselves.'

'Not you, I notice!' flashed Abigail.

'And anyway,' continued Beatie, 'such things are for after the betrothal, when Judah is out of his time, and is old enough to wed, and gives her a ring. She's to have a garnet in a band of gold—real gold.'

'Groovy,' said Abigail numbly.

'I dinna ken what that means,' said Beatie gruffly, 'but I can tell by your mug it's no compliment. I'm telling you straight, I'll not have you come between them. I'll break your head first.'

'Be quiet!' said Abigail, in so cold a voice that Beatie faltered. Her fiery gaze dropped, and she muttered, 'I hanna any right to speak like that. I ken no other way but to bluster, you see, Abby, because it's the way of folks about here.'

Abigail was silent.

'Nobody's going to make Dovey unhappy,' said Beatie sullenly. 'Nobody. Not while I'm around. Granny'd let her lose Judah if it meant saving the Gift. The Gift comes first with Granny, but it dinna with me! And Dovey's sae gentle—she'd never stand up for her rights, even if her heart broke.'

'Has Dovey noticed too, then?' asked Abigail. Beatie shook her head. 'She hanna

6. Finished his apprenticeship.

mentioned anything. Well, then,' she said, with a return to her previous aggressive manner, 'what will you do about it?'

'This,' said Abigail. She seized Beatie by the shoulders and shook her with such violence that when she let her go, the little girl fell on the floor.

She gaped at Abigail, not knowing whether to screech maledictions, or leap at the older girl like an infuriated monkey.

'You're a stirrer, that's what you are,' said Abigail. 'Don't you breathe a word of this to Dovey or I'll break *your* head. You don't know that what you said has a word of truth in it.'

'Granny will know,' said Beatie, half tearful, half triumphant.

'Yes, and I'm going to see her, right now,' said Abigail.

Chapter 9

The old lady removed her brass-rimmed spectacles and put aside her knitting.

'Ah, there you are, pet,' she said. 'I've been expecting you this last day or two.'

Abigail sat down beside Mrs Tallisker's chair and leant her head on her knee. The touch of the work-hardened hand on her hair was dear and familiar to her.

'You feel that something verra frail and precious, maybe like a china cup, has been chipped and cracked, is that so, Abby?'

Abigail thought about that.

'No,' she said at last, 'it hasn't been spoiled or changed. I just didn't want her—Beatie—or anyone, to look at it because it was private.'

The hand went on stroking.

'I suppose I'm too young to know anything about—about falling in love,' said Abigail humbly. She knew she could never have spoken like this to her mother. She would have died in torment rather than say such a thing to any of the girls at school. It seemed to her now that they were just a bold-mouthed, sniggering rabble of children, too old to be innocent, too young to be fastidious.

'But I suppose that's not fair, either,' she thought. 'How do I know what they feel in their hearts? They talk like that because other kids think they're freaks if they don't.'

'It wouldna be for me to say that you're too young to know true love, Abby,' said Granny tranquilly, 'for I was wed at fifteen myself.'

'And you've not forgotten what it's like?' asked Abigail, amazed.

'Look into my eyes,' said Granny. She took Abigail's chin in her hand and made the girl look steadfastly at her. The cloudy blue of the old woman's eyes cleared, widened, became a sky with clouds running over it like lizards over a wall, a sea far below, leaping, boiling, a marvellous blue-green.

'Like a mallard drake's neckband.' She heard Granny's voice far, far away, hardly distinguishable from the squealing of the birds, white and dark birds whirling in to and out from precipices that stood like walls and battlements.

'Guillemots, sea-shag and terns,'[7] said Granny. 'Look at yourself, lass.'

Abigail was no longer herself. She was someone else. A dark-brown braid streaked with blond fell over her left shoulder almost to her waist. Her hands were red and chapped. She wore a coarse ankle-length black skirt and a white apron. The very eyes through which she looked were different—clearer, further-seeing, and, she instinctively knew, desperate and wild.

'My own e'en,' said Granny, 'when I was eighteen, new-widowed.'

---

7. All seabirds.

Down that giddy steep Abigail gazed, her whole body thirsting to thrust itself out on that wild wind that whirled the birds down to the sea and up again in tatters and ribbons and shoals of small living bodies; to fall like a stone amongst the black shining reefs and the ever-tossing serpentine arms of the kelp.

'I can't, I can't!' cried Abigail, and her voice was different, her words in a dialect she did not know yet understood. 'There are the bairnies, there are my old parents and yours, Bartle. I cannot come and leave them without a care, I must live on, in spite of pain.'

'I can't bear it,' whispered Abigail. 'I can't bear it!'

In a second she was back in the parlour. Mrs Tallisker, her eyes very bright, was gripping her hands.

'Are you all right, Granny?' panted Abigail. The intensity of her feeling had not left her; she felt she had been through a lifetime of happiness and woe.

'Yes,' said the old woman. She seemed revivified, her bent back straightened, her faded eyes glistening with triumph and excitement.

'Aye, that was a good flash, like a sky full of lightning! Like the old days when past and future were spread out before me like a field of flowers.'

'Was I you?' breathed Abigail. 'Yes, I was you! And Bartle was your husband.'

'Drowned off the Noup[8] like his son Robert. Near nineteen, he was, like his grandson Judah Bow. Aye, the young can experience true love, and true sorrow, and true selflessness too.'

'I don't think I could,' faltered Abigail, 'be unselfish, I mean.'

Mrs Tallisker looked at her with something like scorn.

'If you love truly, you will also know how to live without the beloved, no matter whether you lose him to death or some other.'

Abigail felt helpless and anxious. 'But I don't think I'm good enough to be like that. Maybe when I'm older . . .'

'Age has naught to do with it, Abby,' returned Mrs Tallisker.

'But,' faltered Abby, 'already I feel jealous of Dovey.' She was ashamed. 'When I was shaking Beatie . . .'

The old woman laughed heartily. 'You shook Beatie? 'Twill do that one a world of good.'

'Yes,' confessed Abigail, 'I shook her till her tonsils rattled. But all the time I was wishing it was Dovey. It was horrible, like a kind of black oil smeared over everything. I'm afraid, Granny—that I'll be nasty to Dovey, say something cruel. And I don't want to.'

'And why, Abby? Because you like poor Dovey so much, and she hasna done you anything but kindness?'

'Yes, that,' said Abigail, 'but mostly because I don't want to make Judah unhappy, ever, and he would be if anyone hurt Dovey.'

Mrs Tallisker leant over and kissed Abigail's cheek lightly.

'You'll do, my honey.'

She would say no more, but asked Abigail to fetch the lamp and light it.

'And send Beatie to me, hen.'

Beatie went in glowering and came out snivelling. She joined Abigail at the kitchen table where the girl was scrubbing potatoes in a dish of water.

'Granny said I was to be civil to you, and I will; but 'tis not for your sake! So if I smile at you, 'tis from the teeth outwards!'

Abigail sighed. 'I hope it rains on Sunday, so we can't go cockling. Because it will

8. Noup Head, a promontory on the northwest coast of Westray Island (one of the Orkney Islands).

be hell with you glaring at me with steam coming out of your ears.'

'It inna fair!' said Beatie, crimson with wrath and tears. 'Granny said if I didna behave sweet and kind to you she'd give me a look. And if it inna any better than the one I got ten minutes agone, I dunna want to live to see it. And she said I wasna to give as much as a hint to Dovey that you're mooning over my brother Judah.'

'If you'd hurt Dovey that way, then you don't love Dovey as you say you do,' said Abigail sharply. 'You just watch your tongue, because I for one am sick of it.'

Beatie turned to her forlornly. 'Well, I ken it is sharpened both ends, but your ain inna much better, Abby, all said and done.'

'What did Granny say to you,' asked Abby, 'to upset you so?'

'She said,' confessed Beatie forlornly, 'that on Sunday Judah would know for true whom he loves, and oh, Abigail, I'm afeared it might be you.'

For one moment Abigail's heart filled with bliss. It blazed up and it was gone, she did not know why. All she felt then was a premonitory sadness, not a child's disappointed sadness, but something sterner and more adult. But this was not a thing about which she could speak to Beatie. It was as private as love. She knew now why her mother had been silent all those years about her hurt and loneliness.

'Well, then,' she said composedly to Beatie, 'at least we know that Sunday will be a fine day and we'll go cockling.'

'Will you promise me, solemn, that you won't let Dovey get hurt?' pleaded Beatie.

Abigail thought about that. 'I can't promise it any more than Granny can promise it. But I don't *want* Dovey to get hurt in any way, and that's for true.'

Beatie considered this. 'Verra well,' she said grudgingly. 'But I'll keep my eye on you. Sharp!'

Dovey prepared them a picnic basket. Her excitement over the beauty of the day, the pleasures in store for them, the feast of cockles they would have that night and on the morrow, seemed almost as if, lame as she was, she frolicked with honest joy at the thought of someone else's good fortune. Inside her Abigail felt a bitter humiliation. If Judah thought of her as a child, as Beatie had once said, Dovey thought of her as even more of one. Even if Dovey had guessed her love for Judah, she had no jealousy towards her. But perhaps she didn't know. Gentle and good as she was, she was not as sharp-witted as Beatie or Gibbie.

Abigail gave Dovey's bride chest a spiteful kick. But that made her feel she *was* a child after all. Heavy at heart, she went down the crooked stairs and through the shop. Mr Bow had banked the great open fire, as he always did at night. A downy blanket of grey ash lay over the winking, slow-breathing fire that drowsed in the depths of the immense log at the back of the chimney. Once a month a log was hauled with chains through a little trapdoor specially built in the side of the house next to the fireplace.

Mr Bow sat on the bench beside this sleeping fire, his hands dangling between his legs. Abigail bade him good-bye but he did not answer.

'I'm not gey happy about him,' confessed Judah as they went through The Cut and over The Green. 'His spells are more frequent, there's no denying. But there's no drink in the house, and he's amenable to Granny. Come now, Beatie, you've a lip like a jug. Cheer up, lass, all will be well!'

But Beatie was fidgety and capricious, running ahead of them through the empty Sunday streets, short with Abigail, impudent to Judah, sometimes sullen, sometimes curvetting and prancing like an urchin, vanishing down side lanes and bobbing out at them again, until Judah caught her by the tails of her pinafore and said, 'Will ye take hold of yourself, hen? I'm weary already of ye jumping about like a nag with a chestnut under its tail. Now, quieten down, for once we get in the boat you'll have to turn into a mouse, and you might as well start practising now.'

Beatie meekly took his hand. They walked ahead of Abigail towards what she knew as Darling Harbour, but which The Rocks people still called Cockle Cove.

Occasionally Beatie turned round and glared at Abigail, as though warningly. And, when Judah was not looking, Abigail glared back, knowing what Beatie meant to convey to her.

'Monkey-face,' thought Abigail. 'Blankly little watchdog!'

Several ladder-like wooden stairways ran down to the beaches and slipways below Miller's Point. The beaches were littered with the refuse of ships—broken gear, rotted rope, rusty iron things half-sunken in the sand and gravel. There was a fearful smell of rotted fish and vegetables from a mountain of muck where the Pittwater boats that brought the northern farmers' produce to the markets dumped their unsold cargoes. Children and old women rooted amongst this garbage for anything edible.

The little boat rocked in a foot or so of water. The girls took off their shoes and stockings and waded out. Judah was already barefooted.

'Get in and be smart about it!' he ordered.

Abigail and Beatie climbed in, and Judah pushed the dory off the sand-flat, running alongside till she was well afloat, and then jumping in and taking the oars. With a couple of strong pulls he had them out in deeper water. Cockle Bay stretched to the south, and beyond their bow were the headlands of the North Shore, bronze green and forested, with faint chalk smudges of domestic smoke drifting up from what looked to Abigail like isolated settlements. Only North Sydney seemed fully built upon, though it was eerie to see it without the Bridge's mighty forefoot coming down upon Milson's Point.

What took Abigail's eye was not the majestic half-wilderness of the North Shore, which she had known as a twin city as tall-towered as Sydney, but the Harbour itself.

'The ships, the ships!' she shouted. 'Hundreds . . . thousands of ships!'

For the Harbour was an inhabited place. Barges with rust-brown sails, busy little river ferries with smoke whuffing from tall stacks, fishing-boats and pleasure boats with finned paddle-wheels, sixty-milers, colliers, towering-masted barquentines[9] with sails tied in neat parcels along what Abigail thought of as their branches—every type of vessel imaginable: huddled in coves, lying askew on slipways and beaches, skipping before them over the water, rocking gaily, or slowly and grandly, at buoy or wharf berth.

'What did ye expect, then?' snapped Beatie. 'Cows?'

Abigail, entranced at the magnificent sight, scarcely heard her; but Judah frowned at his sister.

'Whoa, now, lass, what's wi' ye? Is that any way to talk to a guest, and our own Abby at that? Mind your manners, I'm telling you!'

Beatie turned her face away, lip poked out, eyes full of angry tears, which Judah ignored. Abigail rose to her knees, crying, 'It's marvellous! I never dreamt it could be like this!'

'Sit down!' ordered Judah, 'or you'll have us all in the salt. Look overboard and see yon fellow.'

Abigail gingerly sat down, and looked where he pointed. She saw a large shark, with an eye like a willow leaf, cruising three metres below them. A cloud of sprats fled before it. But the green eye was fixed on the boat.

---

9. Large sailing vessel with three or more masts. "Sixty-milers": small cargo vessels used to transport coal from Newcastle (in Australia, some 75 miles up the coast) to Sydney. "Colliers": ships used to carry coal.

Beatie looked at the shark with a shudder and yet a certain satisfaction.

'No doubt,' reflected Abigail, 'she's imagining me falling overboard.'

'There's *The Brothers*,' said Judah, jerking his head towards a sturdy two-masted brig, very shabby. 'She's square-rigged on both masts. Handy for the coastal trade.'

Abigail asked what these hosts of coastal vessels carried.

'Coal from Newcastle,' said Beatie instantly, 'cedar from the northern rivers, whale oil from the whale station at Eden, and wool from up and down the coasts for the clipper ships to take to England.'

She looked triumphantly at Abigail. 'And what do they carry in your time, then?'

'I don't think there *are* many ships,' said Abigail. 'Things like wool come in trains.'

'We've got steam trains,' said Beatie proudly.

'These would be electric or oil-driven, I think,' said Abigail, 'and then a lot of goods come overland in huge semi-trailers . . . that's a kind of horseless carriage,' she added hastily.

Judah listened politely. 'Seems a sad waste of good money when the sea and the wind are free for all,' he remarked.

Judah's complete lack of interest in the marvels of the future cheered Beatie instantly, and Abigail, no longer irked by the sullen ill-temper of her young companion, gave herself up to the joy of the day.

They drifted past innumerable coves, some a rich green with mangrove swamps, empty of all but a tall white heron picking around in the mud, others already claimed by a little ship-yard, a spindly jetty, a half-ribbed whaleboat skeleton on the slips.

Though Abigail had learnt to know the Harbour and its endless bays from her crow's nest at the top of Mitchell, she had long since lost her sense of direction as the dory nosed around the rock inlets, the warm airs sometimes bringing a Wanderer butterfly, or once a Black Prince cicada, a tinselly creature that clung to the bow with hooked feet, creaked once or twice, and flicked away towards land.

Under cliffs dribbling water, Judah pulled in towards a crescent of beach, dragged up the boat a little way, and jabbed the anchor into the mud.

'I'm hungry, I'm hungry!' cried Beatie, hopping out.

'No, cockles first, while the tide's low,' commanded Judah. He took three wooden pails from the dory. 'Tuck your skirts up. The Dear knows I dunna want you both dripping all over me on the trip home.'

He showed Abigail how to find the breathing hole, and sometimes the track of the cockle, and dig for the shellfish with a stick. Beatie stayed close to her brother, and for much of the time Abigail wandered around alone on the cool, faintly sucking sand. A kind of certainty had fallen over her that this day was to be her last in 1873. She could no longer doubt the Gift, and Granny had told Beatie that this day Judah would know whom he loved. She did not know how this would come about, but she knew that it would.

'And it won't be me,' she thought. Her pail full now, she put it in the shade of a tree, and wandered by herself amongst the rocks, shoaly falls from the cliffs, their crevices filled with driftwood, empty crab-shells, dead and dry starfish and sea-eggs.

In the heat there was uncanny silence, as though the sea itself was too exhausted to sigh or murmur. And in this silence she heard the sounds of farewell.

She sat amongst the fallen cities of the rocks and watched Judah and Beatie, high on the beach, lighting a campfire. Beatie filled a billycan[1] at the spring seepage on the cliff, and once or twice Judah went out and towed the now-afloat dory nearer the

---

1. A tin or enamelware-covered can used to make tea or to transport food or liquid.

shore. The tide was rising fast, with a long whispering *hahhhhh*.

The billy must have boiled, for Beatie came running to get her. The little girl's face, though she wore a cabbage-tree hat,[2] as did Abigail and Judah, was scorched with sunburn.

'You've been doing it again!' she accused.

'Doing what?'

'Staring at him. I seen you, sitting on the rocks like a mermaid, staring and gawking.'

Abigail said nothing, but scowled at her and stalked ahead along the beach. A big old redgum, almost one with the sandstone rocks, sheltered them as they ate, hats pulled over their eyes to keep out the sea-dazzle. Judah talked idly of his work: 'Ten bob a month and found,[3] but 'twill be grand pay when I'm an AB.'

Abigail translated this into dollars, couldn't believe the answer, and then remembered that loaves were a penny each, and that Granny often bought a whole fresh fish for twopence. She remarked that being 'a boy' on a coaster seemed to equate with being a man for a boy's pay and status. Judah laughed.

'Well, a boy's a boy, no doubt of that, and he's kept in his place. Me, now, when I started nigh four years ago I brought the food along from the galley and, by jings, I waited till the men had taken their share before I ventured to help myself. Swept the fo'c'sle,[4] took the dishes back to the galley, learnt to know my place right smart after a thick ear or two from one of the crew.'

It seemed to Abigail it would be a hard life, even for a hefty fourteen-year-old as Judah must have been. A boy worked cargo like the rest of the crew, always went aloft to furl the highest sail, and never ventured to offer an opinion during fo'c'sle talk. On the other hand, he was expected to smoke a pipe or chew tobacco.

'Yuk!' said Abigail.

'And sink your quota of rum when you're ashore with the men,' added Judah. 'But Granny—wouldna she skin me alive if she caught me at it and, any old road, I've no taste for either. And I promised Mother besides, so that clinches it.'

He yawned. 'Come on, lassies, let's awa'. I'll show you a pretty place or two, Abby, if you fancy.'

But Beatie wanted to climb the rocks and scramble out onto a little peninsula of grass and pink pigface to be king of the castle, as she said.

'You'll do as I say. Time to move,' he said, stamping out the fire, and gathering up their belongings to put in the basket.

'I want to stay here and paddle,' said Beatie. 'And I'm sick of the boat, up and down, up and down, and nothing to see but water and places with no people in them. I want to play Robinson Crusoe!'

'I don't mind staying a while longer—' began Abigail, but Beatie turned on her roughly. 'Your opinion inna asked! On this voyage you're only the boy!'

Abigail laughed, but Judah took hold of Beatie, gave her a little shake and said sternly, 'What's up with ye today, ye wee smatchit?[5] You've been girning and groaning pretty near since we left home. Are you ailing?'

'I just want to play Robinson Crusoe,' muttered Beatie. Suddenly she aimed a kick at Judah's bare shin.

'Right, that does it,' said her brother. 'You've a temper like a ferret today and I'll

---

2. A hat made out of palm tree leaves.
3. Supplies. "Bob": a shilling ("ten bob" was half a pound).

4. I.e., the forecastle: in a merchant ship, the crew's quarters, in the ship's bow.
5. Chit, nasty child.

stand nae more of it. Stay here and play Robinson Crusoe, while I take Abby for a little row. Get in the dory, Abby.'

He put a wet sack over the cockles and cautioned Beatie: 'Now, see the sun dunna get on them, or they'll all die afore we get them home to Granny. Or do you wish to change your mind and come with us?'

Beatie glowered at him, and he said, 'Stay here then, ye self-willed brat. Dovey's too soft wi' you and Gibbie both. We're off—how do you like that?'

'I dunna care a blanky damn!' screamed Beatie, wading out a little way into the water and shaking her fist at them. 'I hope the boat sinks.'

'No, you don't,' yelled back Judah, laughing. 'You play Robinson Crusoe there for a while, while I show Abby the Harbour. We'll be back before Man Friday[6] comes to eat you up!'

Beatie sat down at the water's edge, her arms around her knees, scowling.

'If she could hurl thunder and lightning she would,' Judah laughed. 'Rest easy, Abby. She'll be as sweet as pie when we come back to get her.'

The dory skidded softly over the water that was coloured like a glass marble, here a clear streak and a sun-speckled sand-bar plain to be seen, there dark blue like polished stone.

'Perhaps we shouldn't have left her . . .' began Abigail, but Judah shushed her. He pulled out into the stream and around the edge of the little peninsula that Beatie had wanted to climb. Waterbirds of all kinds flew up from the brown pocked terraces sluiced with translucent water. A glistening native bee landed on Judah's hand, and Abigail leant forward to brush it off.

'No, no, she'll go in the water. She hasna sting, so don't fret.'

He went on rowing, and in a moment the bee arrowed back to the shore.

'I ha'e a great liking for this land,' he said. 'Man hasna spoiled it yet, not even with steam factories and all the dirt the rich make around them.'

He shipped the oars and sat looking about. Abigail peeped from under the brim of her hat at his brown face shining with sweat, his strong calves and calloused feet. As she peeped, thinking herself unobserved in the shadow of the hat, he reached out and playfully caught her foot with his prehensile toes.

She jumped and blushed.

'What's the matter, Abby? For you seem sad today.'

'I think—I think—' She swallowed. Surely she wasn't going to cry? She looked away. 'I think this is my last day.'

'Did Granny say so?'

'No.'

'Well, then?'

Abigail managed a smile. 'I have gifts of my own, you know.'

'Ah, Abby love, don't go! Not to that grievous world you've described. Stay here with us.'

His arms were around her. Her hat fell off into the water and floated away. His cheek rubbed against hers, and she put up her hand and stroked his face.

'Why, Abby, dinna weep, you must not, what's there to weep about on this bright day?'

But she couldn't stop. A huge shameful gulping hiccup came out of her. Judah grinned.

'Don't laugh at me, damn you!' cried Abigail.

---

6. Crusoe's young native companion, originally a cannibal, whom he made his servant (his "Man") and called "Friday" because on that day Crusoe saved his life.

'Why, Abby—' he said, as though astonished. 'My little one, my Abby.'

Now, although Abigail had no regular boy friend, she had had her share of kisses, everything from the sudden whack on the lips with what appeared to be a hot muffin, to the lingering pressure of a hairy sardine. She had been half-devoured by someone who had been watching too many Italian films, but when her nose got into the act as well, she had stamped on the kisser's foot and alienated him for ever. She had had ear-biters and eyebrow-lickers, and she cared for none of them.

But this was quite different. Her body went off on its own, yielded and clung and moulded itself to Judah's, her head whirled, and so exquisite a melting sensation arose in her middle she thought she was going to die. She could have stayed there under his kiss for ever, but it was he who drew away, breathing quickly. His face was red, his eyes downcast; he seemed not to want to look at her.

'Oh, Abby,' he said hoarsely, 'it were wrong for me to kiss you in such a way.' He stopped and said with difficulty, 'For a little while I felt—I didna know what I felt. Here you're but a bairn, yet I thought for a moment you were a woman grown. And you *were* a woman grown.'

He gazed at her helplessly. 'It were wrong of me, and yet I canna feel regret.'

She whispered, 'I love you, Judah.'

He gazed at her, silent and perturbed, and she saw in his candid eyes that he had no answer.

She remembered then what Mrs Tallisker had said that if one loved truly, one could exist without the loved one. Her whole body cried out for the few frail blisses she had known—to be able to look at him, listen to him, be kissed as if she were a woman and not a child.

And she thought in anguish, 'If I were older I'd know what to say. But I don't.'

She could only say what was in her heart. 'Don't worry, Judah; I know about Dovey. What I feel about you, well . . . that's my worry, not yours.'

He took her hand and held it between his two large ones. 'But it is my worry, Abby, because now I'm in a swither, I dunno what I feel . . .'

From the little peninsula off which the dory was drifting and circling came a sound like an enraged sea-hawk. Abigail jumped, frightened and dislocated.

''Tis Beatie. She's seen.'

Beatie was up on the tumbled rocks. Her small figure seemed to be doing a war-dance. She picked up a stone and threw it with all her might. It fell far short of the boat, but Judah looked disturbed. He took up the oars.

'She wouldna tell poor Dovey, surely,' he muttered. 'The Dear knows I don't want to distress poor little Dovey.'

They were silent until they pulled in to the beach. The tide was now half full, clear green water sliding in to the foot of the redgum, where Beatie stood waiting with the three pails of cockles. Judah threw out the anchor and jumped ashore.

'You!' said Beatie in a voice shrill with rage. 'I saw!'

'Keep it to yourself then,' he said shortly. 'For I dunna want Dovey upset. Take one of the pails to the boat, there's a good lass.'

'Take it yourself!' spat Beatie.

'Right, I will,' he said. He took all three pails, heaved them into the boat, and said to Abigail, 'Move up while I get this wildcat aboard.'

He held out his hand to help Beatie. She flew at him, punched him in the chest, hammered on the arm with which he held her off. Half angry, half laughing, he said, 'Will ye stop it, ye wee devil? Stop it!'

'I'll punch ye yeller and green!' screeched Beatie. 'To do such a thing to Dovey, who trusts you like she trusts God himself!'

He picked her up by the back of the dress, held her kicking and flailing like a maddened cat, and said, 'You've got it wrong, Beatie. There's naught between Abby and me, and Abby will tell you so.'

He put her into the boat. The child subsided into wild sobs.

Abby ventured to put a hand on her shoulder, but Beatie flung it off.

'You're a bad girl! We should have left you in the Suez Canal; it would have suited you grand.'

Judah shipped the oars, leant forward and shook Beatie violently.

'Dunna you speak that way of Abby, when you know nothing of what passed between us. For you're wrong. I'm telling you true, hen!'

Beatie was pale. 'That you could be such a Judas, my own brother! Dovey, expecting to be wed by January; with her bride chest full and her ring chosen, and the down payment made! Don't speak to me, either of you. I'm fair sick to the belly with disgust.'

CHAPTER 10

It was a long, wretched trip home against the tide. Beatie sat huddled, her hands over her ears, and would not listen to a word.

''Tis not new,' said Judah ruefully. 'She's as cross-grained a bairn as ever drew breath. And she's been worse since the fever, and Mother's death. Fanciful, and as obstinate as a mule when she gets a maggot[7] in the head about anything.'

'And Dovey,' he sighed, 'she's trusting and innocent as a bairn. I wouldna like that tender heart to be bruised by me, when already I have gi'en her so much suffering, hare-brained young rip[8] as I was.'

Beatie, who had been listening through her fingers, growled, 'Dovey wunna want you now; you're not true to her!'

'All this fuss over a kiss!' said Abigail, vexed.

'A kiss may not mean over much in your time, for the Dear alone knows what you think good or honourable,' cried Beatie. 'But 'tis different for us. And dunna tell me it was a brother's kiss, for I were watching!'

She covered her ears again.

'She won't say anything,' said Abigail. 'She adores Dovey. She wouldn't say anything to hurt her. You'll see.'

'In this mood,' said Judah, 'she'd do anything. She'd jump out the window if she'd a mind to spite someone by it.'

So they returned to the landing-place below Miller's Point. As soon as the bow touched sand, Beatie jumped out, still looking sullen and resolute.

'I have to tell my mate the dory's safe back,' said Judah, 'and he and I will bring up the cockles to the house directly. Hearken now, Beatie, you stay with Abigail, and none of your nonsense. Go on now, off with the pair of you.'

Beatie turned without a word. The two girls climbed up the precipitous Jacob's Ladder.

Abigail thought, 'I'll speak to her on the way home. Tell her the truth, that he may not know he loves Dovey, but he certainly doesn't love me.'

The moment they reached the top of the cliff, Beatie took off like a rocket.

The little girl was fleet-footed, and she had gained strength since Abigail had first known her. She slung her boots around her neck on their laces, and fled down a narrow crevice between two towering warehouses, over a fence and down a series of

---

7. A whimsical or perverse idea.   8. Worthless fellow.

dog-legged steps. Abigail, surmising that she was taking short-cuts, followed her, her longer steps quickly gaining on Beatie's.

'Beatie!' she yelled. 'You're not to tell Dovey. You don't understand!'

'Shut your face, Judas!' drifted back to Abigail.

Near The Green, she almost caught up with Beatie. Several entertainers were working on The Green: the old beggar with the monkey in the hussar's uniform, playing a tin whistle to which the monkey hopped; a blind singer; and a man playing the bagpipes. The Argyle Cut, just beyond, was crowded with carriages and pedestrians in their Sunday best.

All at once there was a commotion amongst them. Horses reared, men bellowed, a cabbie drove up on the footpath beside the church, sending several ladies with parasols into spasms and screeches.

'Oh, dear God, it's me faither!' gasped Beatie, just as Abby caught up with her. Out of The Cut charged Mr Bow, yelling unintelligibly, sword cutting shining arcs above his head. He made a swipe at the bagpipes; the drones of the pipe, completely severed, flew into the air like so many sticks, and the bag let go its air with a fiendish squeal. The piper, realising that it might have been his bonneted head that had flown in the air, subsided on the grass, uttering hysterical squawks.

A constable waving his staff pursued Mr Bow. As he passed Beatie, he panted, 'He's set the shop afire, wench! Get the Brigade!'

Beatie hovered indecisively, her face yellow with fright. But Abigail picked up her skirts and fled for the shop, and after a moment Beatie followed her. The shop was full of smoke, and Granny was beating at the blazing bench and tables with a wet sack.

A group of urchins, hopping with excitement, clustered about the door.

'Run for the Brigade!' shouted Beatie, 'and it's worth a tanner[9] to you!'

The boys scattered as if by magic, and Abigail and Beatie joined Granny in an effort to smother the flames.

The old woman was exhausted. 'He had drink hid somewhere. He was at it all morning, and then all of a sudden he said, "Here's an end to it!" and tossed the rum bottle into the fireplace. Heaven help me, I thought a cannon had exploded down at the Battery!'

Abigail saw at once that there was no chance of their putting out the fire. A long thread of flame, probably where the rum had splashed, already crawled into the parlour. She said to Granny, 'Where's Dovey?'

'Ran upstairs to throw down her bride chest.'

'For the love of Mike!' cried Abigail. 'At a moment like this? Here, Beatie, help Granny out and safely across the street, and I'll go after Dovey.'

'Your gown is in the bride chest, child,' wheezed the old woman. 'That's why Dovey went up yonder.'

Abigail hurdled the first two stairs, which were smouldering, shooting out small bluish tongues of flame. She found Dovey, a handkerchief tied over her nose and mouth against the smoke, trying to drag the chest towards the door.

'Too late,' said Abigail briefly. 'Anything breakable in here?'

Dovey shook her head.

'Out the window with it then. Here, take the other handle!'

They got the chest to the window. Abigail threw the casements wide, and they hoisted the chest out. It slid down the skillion roof and stuck against the chimney-pot. Dovey cried out in horror.

9. Sixpence.

'If it burns, Abby, you'll not get home again, ever!'

'Don't talk,' said Abby. She dipped a towel in the jug on the wash-stand. 'Put this over your head. The stairs have caught.'

Dovey was trembling, but she limped as fast as she could to the door. Now they could hear the crackle of the old dry wood. Abigail snatched the quilt from the bed, tipped the rest of the water over it, and wrapped it about head and shoulders. Dovey stood on the landing.

'I canna do it, Abby, I'm faintish . . . oh, sweet Saviour, where's Granny?'

'She's out and safe. Down you go, Dovey, or I'll push you, I will!' threatened Abigail.

But the girl clung, weeping and coughing, to the bannisters.

'If we go now, we can get clear down the stairs and out of the door,' begged Abigail. 'You must, Dovey, you must, for Judah's sake!'

The stairs were not yet ablaze, but the bannister was warm. Abigail saw that a patch of fire obstructed the bottom of the stairs where the fire had run across into the parlour. It was a rag mat, well alight.

'Here, wrap this round you, and I'll go first!'

She flung the wet quilt over Dovey's head, and taking her hand, got in front of her. Slowly, the lame girl slipping and stumbling, they got around the awkward corner of the stairs.

Now, in full view of the blazing shop, Dovey froze with terror. Abigail grabbed her, hauled her across the smouldering bottom stairs, and kicked the flaming mat aside. She shouted 'Through the kitchen, quick, Dovey!'

'I canna, I canna!'

'You can!' shrieked Abigail, and she pushed the girl through the smoke, down the passage into the kitchen. The little room under the skillion roof was untouched by flame.

Dovey seemed on the verge of collapse, but Abigail shoved her through the back door. 'Get out of the yard, Dovey, in case the roof falls in . . . for God's sake, what are you doing?'

For Dovey, her eyes wild with terror, was struggling to get past her into the hall.

'Gibbie! We forgot Gibbie!'

Abigail had completely forgotten the boy's existence. With blanched faces the two girls stared at each other, then Abigail snatched the quilt from Dovey, and wound the wet towel around her head.

'I'll get him.'

'But Abby . . .'

'Go. Go!' screamed Abigail, 'And right out of the yard, do you hear me? Find Granny and Beatie, so that they know you're safe!'

She thrust Dovey out the back door and closed it so that there would be no added draught. She shut the kitchen door behind her.

The stairs were now alight. Flames curled around the bannisters. The two bottom stairs were a black gaping hole rimmed with jagged rubies. Abigail took a flying leap across them. She sensed the third step give way under her foot, fell forward entangled in the quilt, and felt the tread above her as hot as iron. The smoke was suffocating. She draped the towel over her face and ran blindly the rest of the way. The door to the attic was closed.

'Thank heavens,' she thought. 'It won't be filled with smoke.'

Now she could hear Gibbie screaming. She burst through the door, slammed it behind her, and said tersely, 'No talk, Gibbie. The place is on fire. We'll have to go through the window.'

The little boy had got out of bed and put on his flannel dressing-gown. He was holding his mother's picture in one hand and the framed text 'Thou, God, Seest Me' in the other.

'I wanna go down the stairs like ordinary,' he wailed.

'You do, and you'll be a cinder. *Come on!*'

She tried to open the window, but it had been nailed shut. She picked up the three-legged stool by the bed and knocked out the glass.

Gibbie said, horrified, 'Look what you done!'

She banged out the remaining splinters of glass, looked to see if the child was wearing slippers, and ordered him:

'Come and see for yourself. It's only a little way down to the roof and we're going to get out and scramble down.'

Gibbie approached and looked down with a ghastly face, as though the drop were twenty metres instead of one. He recoiled.

'I'll break my arms and legs and I dinna want that. And I want to do Number One, forbye.'

'Who doesn't?' yelled Abigail. 'The house is burning down, stupid. Do you want to burn, too?'

But he wouldn't move. At last she snatched the picture of his mother from him, dropped it out on the roof, and tearing the text from his grasp, sent it sailing across the room. Then she clouted him once on each side of the head, and while he was opening his mouth to bawl, she grabbed him round the middle, pushed him feet first through the window and onto the roof. Then she squeezed out after him.

'Dinna you think I won't tell Granny, you wicked girl. You'll go to hell, you just see!'

Now that she was outside, Abigail could see that the entire front of the cottage was blazing. A large crowd had gathered, and two leather-hatted constables wielding long staves drove them back towards the shelter of The Cut.

'Listen, Gibbie, the Fire Brigade is coming! Do you hear the horses? And the bell clanging?'

Up from George Street came the fire engine, the horses galloping, men clinging to the sides of the vehicle. A tanker followed behind. Gibbie showed some faint interest, but there was no time for dawdling and staring. Abigail pushed and pulled him down to the edge of the roof. Dovey was nowhere in sight. While Gibbie hesitated and complained and palpitated at the height, Abigail took the opportunity to push the bride chest from behind the chimney-pot and into the next yard. It fell with a clang. There was an outcry of startled Cantonese from the laundry and angry squealing from the tethered pig. She threw the photograph of Amelia Bow into a basket of unwashed shirts.

Abigail tried her best to wheedle the boy to take her hands as she lay on the roof, and swing down to drop into the yard, but he cowered pitiably.

'Gibbie, there isn't time to argue. You just have to climb down. It's hardly any distance to fall, if I hold you.'

'I want to do Number One.'

A Chinese with a pigtail appeared. He chattered helpfully at Abigail, then ran for a large packing crate and put it below the roof.

'I inna going to be caught by any heathen Chinee,' bawled Gibbie. Abigail, with a nod to the laundryman, seized the boy by the armpits and pushed him off the roof. The little man caught him deftly, cooed comfortingly, and lowered him to the ground.

Then Abby swung herself over to dangle from the roof and be helped to the ground by the Chinaman.

Gibbie sobbed, 'I've lost my picture of Mamma, too.'

Abigail retrieved it from the basket and gave it to him. The Chinese, now joined by another, bowed repeatedly. She could think of nothing else to do, so she bowed back, and on this note of courtesy she left by the lane gate and shepherded Gibbie round to Argyle Street.

The firemen, now augmented by several youthful soldiers from Dawes Battery, directed a stream of water onto the fire.

It was not long before they had it under control.

'It's nobbut[1] what you'd call an *enjoyable* blaze,' remarked a voice near by, deprived of a treat on a dull Sabbath.

Still, the shop was gone. Only smoking, malodorous black timbers showed where it had been. The excitement over, the crowd lingered, coughing melodramatically in the bitter smoke, chatting loudly. Mr Bow wasn't to be blamed for the fire, by no manner of means, the way he suffered with the terrible wound he'd had in the battle at Balaclava. Some said he was a hero; he'd been in the charge of the Light Brigade[2] and the Queen herself had sent him a little box of chocolates. They gave three cheers for Trooper Bow as well as the firemen before they dispersed. Fires were common in The Rocks, but it was still a free and exciting spectacle.

Now that it was all over, Abigail's legs wobbled. She felt she had run twenty miles. Her hands were black with smoke and she knew her face was, too. When she spoke, her voice came out as a squeak.

'Look, Gibbie, by the bond store—Granny and Dovey and Beatie. Run to them now and let them see you're safe.'

'Aye, they'll be worried sick!' said Gibbie gladly. He turned to Abigail and said with dignity, 'You hit me, and broke my window and threw away my text and gave me to a Chinaman, and I willna forget to tell my Granny. Aye, and you look out for yourself!'

'Okay. You do that,' said Abigail. She leant against the castle-like wall of the warehouse, feeling that if she took a step her knees would give way.

She saw Judah bound out of The Cut. He ran straight to Dovey and enfolded her in his arms, lifting her off her feet, rubbing his cheek against her smoke-stained one. Abigail could not take her gaze away. His tenderness and anxiety were beyond question. Ah, Abigail knew the melting sweetness in his heart, for it was in her own for him.

He held Dovey close to him, her dishevelled hair under his chin, while he questioned Granny and Beatie. His free arm went out to hold Gibbie, who had hobbled beside him and plainly was indignantly describing his experiences.

It was several minutes before Judah looked around for Abigail.

Abigail turned her face against the sun-warmed stone of the wall.

'Good-bye, Judah, good-bye,' she said.

CHAPTER 11

The mighty butcher and his thin, goitrous[3] wife took them in. Abigail was washed, fussed over, acclaimed. The constables brought back Mr Bow, who had relapsed into his melancholy trance-like state.

'I'll not put it down in my notebook this time, Ma'am,' said the senior ponderously

---

1. *Nobbut* usually means "only, merely"; here, it must mean "not."
2. The charge of 600 British cavalrymen against entrenched Russian guns at Balaclava in 1854, during the Crimean War, that left three-quarters

of them dead; immortalized by Alfred, Lord Tennyson, in "The Charge of the Light Brigade" (1854).
3. I.e., suffering from goiter (an enlarged thyroid gland, visible as swelling on the neck).

to Mrs Tallisker, 'for the sake of the childer, like. But it's got to stop, oh, yes, or there'll be no way of keeping him out of the madhouse. Why, he could have had some poor creature's napper[4] off, snip-snap!'

The butcher retrieved Dovey's bride chest from the Chinese laundry, and brought it to them. He dropped a vast hand on Mr Bow's shoulder as he crouched in the thin wife's tidy parlour.

'Don't fret, Sam, me old cocksparrer,' he assured him. 'I've already put two of me stoutest apprentices in to see none of the villains about here get into what's left of the cottage during the night, and nab your bits and pieces. And as for rebuilding, why, we'll get some of the lads together and have you back in business afore you can say Walker!'[5]

Granny, very wan and shrunken, but somehow tranquil and content, was with Abigail. 'Well, lass, you did what you were sent for. You saved Dovey for Judah, and now the Gift will hae a double chance of survival.'

'I think it's immortal after all,' said Abigail. She managed to smile. 'I'd like that. I'm tired,' she added inconsequentially. Her eyes closed in spite of themselves. She knew the mighty butcher gathered her up—for she could smell lamb chops and suet—put her into some bed, but she did not stay awake to find out where she was.

'Stay awhile with us,' begged Dovey the next day, 'for you're one of the family, Abby, true!'

'No,' said Abigail. 'I have to go home; you know that.'

Her green dress looked strange to her; it had been so long since she had seen it. She saw it was not very well made; it was not worthy of the lace-like crochet.

Abigail put on the dress. It fitted more tightly across the chest. My figure's coming at last, she thought. Inside she was cold and without feeling, like a volcano covered with ice.

Granny examined the crochet again.

'Well,' she said gaily, 'I'll hae to live long enough to make it! So maybe I'll be with you all awhile yet!'

Granny agreed that it must be Beatie alone who took Abigail to the corner of the lane in Harrington Street where she had so unexpectedly stepped through the door in the century.

'And with the dark coming down, as it was in your time,' she said.

Abigail began to get anxious that the time would not go fast enough, that whatever numbed her heart would vanish and let the pain free. Especially when she had to say good-bye. Dovey wept as she kissed her.

Abigail thought, 'I ought to be feeling that I could kill her, but I don't.' She said, 'I wish you happiness, Dovey. You deserve it.'

Judah. Could she say good-bye to Judah?

He kissed her cheek, a swift, brotherly dab.

'Good-bye,' said Abigail in a low voice. He looked for a moment into her eyes. Did he shake his head, ever so slightly, before he let go her shoulders and hastened away to rejoin his ship? She did not look after him.

'What are ye dilly-dallying for?' cried Beatie tetchily from the door. 'Do you think I want to come home in the pitch dark?'

Gibbie was asleep in bed and Mr Bow did not look up as she said good-bye, but Granny held her close to her corseted bosom.

'Ye think ye've been badly treated, hen,' she said. 'Not so. I told you once and I

4. Head.
5. I.e., express surprise (the interjection "Walker!" expresses incredulity or doubt).

tell ye again, the link between you and us Talliskers and Bows is nae stronger than the link between us and you.'

'Oh, Granny!' cried Abigail. She gave the old woman a hug. 'I wish you were my Granny in truth!'

'For the love of blanky heaven and all eternity will ye come!' yelled Beatie. The little girl hopped from one bare foot to another. Her face was like a thundercloud.

So Abigail went, hastening down Argyle Street with Beatie, not looking back, for she was afraid to do so.

'There's no reason to be still angry,' said Abigail.

'You shunna kissed him when he was Dovey's,' snapped Beatie. She snorted. 'Any road, how do I ken you won't be back, worming your way 'twixt Judah and Dovey? Because I saw the manner he looked at you when he said good-bye, oh, aye, I saw!'

Abigail suddenly felt weary, tired of Beatie's tantrums, and angry with her, too. She was glad to feel angry, because the anger drove down the sadness.

'I won't be back because as soon as I get home I'll burn the crochet, that's why!'

Beatie slid her a look. 'Honour bright?'

'Take it or leave it!' said Abigail cantankerously.

They marched in grumpy silence down the street. It was as crowded as a fair-ground, for Monday was market day. Outside the Penny Dance Hall hung ornate gas lamps on curly brackets. Though the dark had not come they were lit, their long blue and yellow tongues lolling in the salty breeze.

Abigail saw Maude the dress-lodger outside, surrounded by disarrayed redcoats, already half drunk. The girl was in the most vivid of grass-green dresses; a pork-pie hat full of velvet pansies crowned her fantastic coiffure. The sweet smell of hot gin filled the air.

'Look,' said Abby, pulling at Beatie, 'there's one of the girls from the house in the Suez Canal.'

Beatie pulled her arm away haughtily.

The street was full of stalls and barrows and roped-off enclosures where there were dancing dogs, an Indian juggler, and something mysterious called The Infant Phenomenon.[6]

They turned the corner of Harrington Street, past the Ragged School, where the infants of vanished parents, gutter children who lived in cracks in the rocks and under counters and old doors, were taught the rudiments of civilisation side by side with the children of the respectable poor such as Beatie Bow.

'Beatie,' said Abigail. After a moment she shouted, 'Take that blanky look off your obstinate little mug, will you?'

Beatie unwillingly snorted a laugh, quickly retrieved it, and growled, 'Well, what d'ye want? Spit it out!'

'I want to say that you can hate me or whatever you like, but please go to Mr Taylor and tell him what you already have learnt, tell him that you wish to be educated, girl or not. Ask him if he'll tutor you privately.'

Beatie was startled out of her sulks. ''Twould be improper to approach a gentleman. Faither wouldna permit me!'

'Oh, damn Faither!' cried Abigail. 'You have to look out for yourself, you dummy! How will you ever get anything if you don't march in and bullyrag people into giving it to you? Or maybe you're too chicken-hearted?'

---

6. I.e., a supposed child prodigy; in Charles Dickens's *Nicholas Nickleby* (1838–39), the "Infant Phenomenon" was an adult who admitted only to being ten.

Beatie turned scarlet. She clouted Abigail on the arm with her hard little fist. 'I'll punch ye yeller and green, drat ye!'

Abigail saw ahead of her the lamp that lit the steep stairs to the alley which ran down to the playground. Beatie kicked angrily at the kerbstone. Her face was undecided, back to its crabbed urchin look.

'I know you hate me because I fell in love with your brother. Well, he doesn't love me, never did and never will. And I did save Dovey for him.'

''Twas no more than what you were sent for,' said Beatie churlishly.

Abigail lost her temper. 'Oh, you know everything, don't you? Let me tell you, you sulky little pig, you know nothing about love, that's one thing. You have to experience it to know how powerful it is.'

Here she stopped, dumbstruck, remembering who had said the same words to her.

'Anyway,' she said, 'I lost, didn't I? So good-bye and good luck.'

But Beatie said nothing. She did not even look at Abigail. Abigail left her and went down the stairs. Halfway down the lane she saw the brightly painted loco engine, the space rocket, and the monkey bars, waver out of the twilight, like a superimposed photograph.

She looked back, quickly, saw Beatie growing transparent. The bottle-green shawl turned into a cobweb, the pale little oval of her face shone for a moment and was gone. Did she see an uplifted hand waving her good-bye?

'Beatie!' she cried.

But there was nothing at the alley's top but the worn stairs. The blank walls of tall warehouses made walls for that steep crevice, brightly lit by shadowless electric light from some unseen globe.

Abigail turned away. Her eyes blurred. She saw Mitchell spring into sight, incredibly tall to one now accustomed to little houses scarcely higher than sunflowers. It was a fantastic obelisk, its curved windows reflecting a phantom city of another age.

She gazed at this sight as amazed as Beatie herself might have been—and as she did the last note of the half-hour sounded from the Town Hall clock.

Was it possible? That no time had passed at all? That all the weeks, months, she had lived in another world, the kind of growing-up she could never have experienced in this one, had occurred between one sonorous clang and another?

The thought was so eerie she began to tremble. Time . . . who knew anything about it? Because it passed at the common rate in 1873 was no reason at all to believe that time had also passed in the next century. But it was still winter, as it had been when she left her own time. In the light cotton dress she was chilled to the bone. The brown leaves of the plane-trees, desiccated and fragile as brown paper, skidded past her.

'But which winter?'

Nervously she approached the playground. The children seemed to be wearing anoraks and woolly caps that had not changed. Overhead a jetliner arrowed. In its design she could see no change from those she knew.

The lobby of Mitchell beamed with light, but she was afraid to approach it.

'Even if it's next year,' she thought, 'and Mum has gone, what will I do, what will I say?'

But she could not stand there in the freezing wind for ever. Resolutely she approached Mitchell. Something about her feet felt strange. She raised the hem of her skirt and saw that she was still wearing Dovey's circularly striped wool stockings, and Granny Tallisker's best shoes.

'I'll never be able to get them back to her now,' she thought. 'Oh, what will she think of me?'

She ran then into the handsome lobby, into the lift, and upstairs. Suddenly she thought, 'The key of the unit, where is it?' But it was still safety-pinned inside the deep pocket of her dress.

As she unlocked the door she heard what was music to her—Vincent having one of his howling, kicking tantrums next door, and Justine bellowing at him as if she were about to go out of her mind.

'Thank God, thank God,' said Abigail. She switched on the lamps. The clock said twenty to six. A morning paper was tossed on the kitchen bench. Abigail seized it greedily. The date was still the 10th of May. It was incredible. So much had passed, terrors and friendships and shocks, the painful blisses and tender hurts of first love: and it had all happened between one bong from the Town Hall clock and another.

She wanted to fall into the bear chair and cry for days. A burn on her arm stung, her bones ached, the back of her neck was still sunburnt from the cockling expedition. Her heart was beginning to hurt. She would never see Judah again, never in this life or any other.

'I can't think about that,' thought Abigail frantically.

But she knew that after the scene at the shop that day (so far away now she could hardly remember what had been said) her mother would come home early. She ran into her bedroom in panic, ripped off the shoes and stockings and threw them behind the drawer of her divan bed, where all her chief treasures had always been hidden, old diaries and broken beloved toys, and the dress-up clothes of her childhood. A piece of paper fluttered out. On it was written in a childish hand, 'I hope Jann gets pimpels and if I knew a which she would, too.'

Abigail threw it back in amongst the treasures and the dust. How little she had understood anything!

She would think about burning the dress tomorrow. She ripped it off and pulled on sweater and pants. Her face, had it changed? In some indescribable way it had: the skin was paler and finer, and her eyes seemed darker. Or had her eyelashes grown?

'Oh, sugar! My hair!' It had grown nearly to her waist. She shook it out of its plait, still tied with a piece of red ribbon from Dovey's bridal chest, took the scissors and whacked it off to shoulder length. It was crimped horizontally from months of plaiting; her mother would be sure to notice. She knelt down and put her head under the bath faucet, scrubbed her scalp hard.

The front door opened. 'Are you there, Abigail?'

'Sure thing, Mum!'

Quickly she whisked a towel around her wet hair, hid the slashed off hair under her mattress, and went out to the living-room. Kathy was all fluffed-up like an angry bird. Abigail couldn't help smiling like an idiot at her, for she was so pleased to see her, not a day older, not a bit different just Mum, volatile, loving and her very own.

'What are you grinning at, you little wretch? How could you do such a thing, running away like that without a word?'

'I'm sorry, Mum. It was a childish thing to do. But I was upset and mad with you.'

'Well, that's understandable.' Kathy stopped dead and stared at her daughter. 'Funny, for a moment I thought you looked quite different. Older or something.'

'It's my sheikh of Araby get-up,' said Abigail, pushing the towel turban rakishly over one eye. But Kathy took her by the shoulders and turned her to the light.

'It's amazing . . . you do look different . . . I suppose I just haven't looked at you properly lately.' She flung her hand-bag in a chair. 'Oh, I've been in a flurry, not thinking straight. You know how I get. No brains to speak of, just fluff.' She stared at Abigail again. 'Just for a moment there I could see what you'd look like in a few years' time. It was sort of—eerie. I forget you're growing up, you see.'

'So do I,' said Abigail. She threw her arms about her mother and almost lifted her off her feet. 'If only you knew how glad I am to see you.'

'Gosh, it was so awful today,' murmured Kathy. 'Imagine us fighting!'

'I did a lot of thinking on the way home,' began Abigail, but Kathy put a finger to her lip. 'Not a word about it. Not tonight, anyway.'

Abigail nodded.

In bed that night Abigail wondered if Beatie had got back home safely.

'But she didn't come into my time. I think Granny was right. Beatie had the Gift just for a little while, during and after the fever. Well, that will please her, little stirrer.'

But most of her thoughts were for Judah. She could not drive him out of her mind. The look in his eyes when he embraced Dovey, all his northern restraint gone, his gratitude and relief.

'Love, you fool, not relief,' said Abigail cruelly to herself. 'He loves her, and why not? She is much nicer than you in every way. But if he could have looked at me that way, just once . . .'

She tried to turn her thoughts in another direction. Tomorrow she would wait till her mother had gone to Magpies, and she would burn the crochet in the downstairs incinerator. Then the door in the century would be closed for ever.

But Judah was so alive, so vivid to her. He filled her mind as he filled her heart.

'I miss him, that's all,' she said.

She knew girls felt like that when they were fourteen or so. She remembered Samantha Peel crying for a solid week when some pop star or other was discovered dead. 'I would have looked after him and made him happy,' Samantha had sobbed, 'even if he was a druggie.' She remembered girls falling crazily in love with teachers and older girls, making pests of themselves with constant ringings-up, and notes, and gifts, and waylayings.

'I'll get over it,' she thought. But she felt she was different from the others.

She'd never had the frequent infatuations of other girls. She'd never been rapt in anyone before. And also there was that knowledge she'd had, that after she fell in love with Judah the empty place inside her was no longer empty. It still wasn't empty, though very soon it would become so.

But now she had to put him out of her head, go to sleep, lead the ordinary life of that ordinary schoolgirl, Abigail Kirk. She jumped out of bed, slid aside the window and leant out into the icy, whipping sea-wind.

'The winds go through you like a bodkin,[7] taking a stitch or two on the way.' She could hear Granny's voice talking about Orkney.

'I have to forget Granny too, and 1873, and Beatie, and Dovey's little ring with the garnet!'

She stared blindly down upon the scintillant city, up at the gemmy Bridge, across at the Opera House, faintly luminous like a marvellous butterfly poised on the sea.

'Whatever did Beatie think of that? A giant's magic palace? I never did have a chance to explain to her.' She gave a sob that was half a snort because of the wind blowing into her mouth. 'That beastly place is more real than this one! And it isn't, it isn't. There probably isn't any shop any more on the corner of Cambridge and Argyle streets. I mustn't cry. My eyes will swell up, and Mum will notice tomorrow morning. I've got to go to sleep!'

She folded up her green dress and took it to bed with her. She stroked it softly, and after a little while she slept.

_____

7. Sharp instrument for making holes in cloth.

But her sleep was full of dreams.

They were strange dreams. She saw Trooper Bow, his legs and arms chained together, and the chain threaded through an iron ring on the wall. His eyes wandered wildly, and tears ran down his cheeks in a ceaseless stream. She knew they had put him in the lunatic asylum and his family could not rescue him. She struggled desperately to tell the attendants: 'He's not mad. It's just his wound. He's the kindest of fathers. Don't take him away from the children!'

She saw Beatie in someone's study, for the walls were lined with bookshelves. Beatie sat at a leather-topped table, her head bent over a book. Small and upright, she was not a child any longer, but a young woman. Her hair was plastered smooth and parted with mathematical precision in the centre. The rest was caught up in a black knitted snood or net.

'Oh, Beatie,' cried Abigail gladly, 'what are you reading? Is it Latin? Is Mr Taylor tutoring you after all?'

But Beatie did not hear. Her face was severe and resolute. It was then that Abigail noticed that not only the snood was black; the girl was in mourning.

'But for whom? Not dear Granny? Oh, did Gibbie die after all?'

In a flash the study vanished and Abigail was on a ship. The waves ran along the side, leaping and hissing. They were as grey as marble. The ship rolled and creaked. There was a drumming from up in the air, where the wet sails flickered out showers of salty drops. But she felt no movement. Muffled in his pea-jacket, a woollen cap on his bright head, Judah sat on a roll of canvas, mending some ship's gear, or so she thought. He had not got older as Beatie had.

'Judah!' she cried joyfully, but he did not look up. The pulley and rope in his fingers changed to a knife and a little wooden figure he was whittling. Somehow she knew it was herself. With an exclamation she could not hear, he tossed it overboard, where it turned into Abby herself, clad in Dovey's blouse and serge skirt, rising stiffly up and down in the waves like a statue or a ship's figurehead.

'Oh, Judah,' sobbed Abigail, 'how could you?'

She awoke, confused and frightened, to find her mother shaking her. 'You were having such a nightmare, yelling and crying.' She sat down beside her daughter who was blinking dazedly into the light. 'Are you sure you're all right?'

'He threw me away,' sobbed Abigail. 'But I saved Dovey for him, didn't I?'

'There, there, poor pet,' soothed her mother. 'It's just a nightmare. My goodness, what a dramatic one!'

'Oh, Mum,' sobbed Abigail, 'why is life so awful? Why do people have to put up with so many terrible things? Why is it when you love someone they don't love you?'

'Hush, now,' said Kathy. 'You've been dreaming. It's all right now. You'll have forgotten in the morning.'

Next day Abigail did not speak of her dreams, and her mother concluded she had forgotten them. But she took her daughter by the shoulders and looked at her searchingly.

'You *are* different!'

'How could I be, Mum?' asked Abigail with a smile. Kathy shook her head.

'Of course you can't be.'

'The main thing is that you're just the same,' said Abigail.

She walked into Magpies with the sensation that she was returning after a long absence.

It was so different from Samuel Bow, Confectioner, so cunningly arranged, so full of vivid or comical treasures. Against the walls stood painted flats from ballet companies which had visited Sydney in Kathy's childhood: Scheherazade's gold-latticed windows and Ali Baba jars; and mysterious avenues of trees from Les Sylphides' enchanted grove.[8] There was an embroidered stool and an autoharp painted with yellow roses, and miniatures of little boys with sailor suits and tomato cheeks.

Kathy was busy cleaning the family pictures she had brought from the sale at St Mary's. Some of the portraits had been hand-tinted.

'Amazing colours the Victorians wore,' she commented. 'Look at this—blue crinoline skirt, magenta jacket, and a yellow feather on the bonnet.'

'The poor people didn't,' corrected Abigail. 'They wore brown holland, and a grey woollen stuff, and a white pinafore. And funny stockings with stripes going round and round like Glasgow Rock.'[9]

'What on earth do you know about Glasgow Rock?' asked her mother.

'Saw it in an old sweet shop window,' replied her daughter truthfully.

She felt defeated and restless, and as Kathy had come almost to the end of her cataloguing and pricing, she asked if she could go home.

Kathy gave her a keen look. 'Feel all right, do you, pet?'

'Bored with holidays, that's all.' Abigail shrugged. 'But I'm not going home to sit in the bear chair and mump. I thought I'd take a walk around The Rocks and look at things. It's such a funny old place.'

Before she went she hugged her mother and said, 'It's all right about Norway, you know.'

'Well, I'm blowed!' said Kathy. She stammered 'But . . . what . . . how . . .'

'I don't know why I made such a fuss,' said Abigail. 'I just don't know. I suppose it was a shock or something. But it's all right. If Dad still wants me to come, too, then I will.'

Kathy's eyes shone. She gave a little jump of excitement.

'Sssssh!' cautioned Abigail. 'A customer. See you tonight, Mum.'

As she hurried up Argyle Street it was almost as if she were going home. She could almost smell the sugary odour of the sweet shop; she looked around to see if Beatie were stamping up the street, frowning and discontented.

But Argyle Street was sunny and deserted. It was not the right time for tourists, or perhaps they were all in the Argyle Art Centre. She went past the Art Centre, and stood under a bare tree and looked at the wall on the corner of Cambridge Street. A brick wall. She didn't know what was behind it, and didn't care either. Across Cambridge Street fluttered strings of laundry just as they had in Granny's time. The traffic bellowed overhead on the highway.

In this sunny, empty world she wandered about; it was clean, and seemingly uninhabited. Was it only last night she saw this street teeming with ragged, grubby, and vital citizens, selling, buying, yelling, exhibiting fighting dogs, piglets, the Infant Phenomenon? The Garrison Church didn't look any different, except that now it had a symbol of the Trinity on its east end. Broken steps that ran nowhere, a tangle of blue periwinkle and brambles, climbed up behind the church to the ridge where the residence of the schoolmaster had stood in what was then Princes Street. Had Beatie ever run joyfully up those steps to Mr Taylor's study, there to achieve the education for which she had been so famished?

It was amazing, terrifying, that all signs of the family's life could have so completely

8. The ballets referred to are *Schéhérazade* (premiere, 1910; choreographed by Michel Fokine to the music of Nicolas Rimsky-Korsakov) and *Les Sylphides* (premiere, 1909; choreographed by Michel Fokine to the music of Frederic Chopin). 9. A hard candy.

vanished, as if they had never been. It was as if time were a vast black hole which swallowed up all trace of human woes and joys and small hopes and tendernesses. And the same thing would happen to her and her parents.

Abigail turned away, walked through a maze of lanes still familiar. Where the incline became too severe, the alleyway turned into a flight of steps; cottages still clung and perched, or were built into the living rock. The cliffs were water-stained under the winter-flowering vines. Fig-roots snaked down as they had always done. There were still privies at the end of shoebox yards. Only the people had gone, the beggars, the urchins with dirt-stiff hair, the dogs with mange, the hatter with twelve hats, 'all clane'. Queer how independent and jaunty they had been. Poor as dirt, but full of vitality.

She did not dare to go to the top of the cliff above Walsh Bay, where she and Beatie and Judah had climbed down the Jacob's Ladder to the seashore and the dory. It would be all docks, all different.

It was like a dream, and one that hurt as if a knitting needle had been stuck in her chest. The empty place inside her had become so empty she could not bear it any longer and turned towards home. She took her cut-off hair and green dress and went down the back elevator to the big incinerator that belonged to the tower block.

It was easy to rip the Edwardian fabric to pieces. It was perished,[1] anyway, after all. She threw it into the incinerator and poked it down with the iron rake. The crochet yoke remained in one piece. She held it a moment, inhaling those old odours of Dovey's bridal chest, mothballs and lavender and a faint sweetness that came, so Beatie had told her, from the tail of a muskrat, sewn up in muslin.

She threw it in on top of the smouldering rags of her dress. The flames blazed up briefly. She saw a line of crimson run around the outline of a flower, turn black and charred.

'No, I can't!' said Abigail, and she put in her hand and snatched it out. She stamped out the small flames that wagged here and there, shook away the blackened pieces, and folded it up small.

'I didn't say "honour bright" to Beatie,' she remembered.

She put it away with Dovey's stockings and Mrs Tallisker's shoes.

CHAPTER 12

A few days later Kathy brought Abigail's father home for dinner. What a good-looking man he is! thought Abigail. As with many people of Scandinavian descent his hair had faded rather than gone grey. From an ashy gold it had turned to ashy silver.

'Oh, Lynnie,' he said, opening his arms.

Her face pressed against his suede coat, Abigail thought of that other time when her nose was tickled by Judah's coarse woollen shirt. Her longing was unbearable. Her father, seeing the tears in her eyes said, 'I feel rather like that myself. And you didn't object to my calling you Lynnie, either.'

Abigail blinked away the tears. What was the use of crying? She was about to enter upon a new life with new people. She wouldn't even have Mitchell or Natalie any more. The world of Beatie Bow would be a whole earth-distance from her in space as well as time.

And surely space would make things better. It was not like time, that could stretch and twist all in a second and turn into some other aspect of itself.

1. Spoiled.

'What a little dope I was, Daddy,' she said. 'But still, I do feel more like Abigail now.'

Kathy Kirk, watching, crept silently away to the kitchen. She thought she'd let them get on with catching up.

Weyland Kirk told her of his plans, how they would go sailing and ski-ing, how marvellous the Norwegian boys were.

'You ought to see them in their blue velvet evening gear,' he said. 'Breath-taking.'

'I can't wait.' She smiled.

'But you're too young for anything serious,' he said.

'I'll be fifteen soon,' she said. He sighed.

'Yes, not so young, I suppose. Old enough for me to explain about Jan? Because I think we ought to have everything clear before we form a family again. Your mother understands but perhaps . . .'

He looked so anxious, so embarrassed, that Abigail smiled.

'You don't have to talk about it, Dad. I know how it was. You thought she was just a kid, and then you found out she was in love with you, and things got complicated.'

'How did you guess—?' He stopped and said painfully, 'Oh, Lynnie—Abigail—I'm so sorry, for everything.'

So it was decided that Abigail would go back to school for a term. It was, anyway, the long summer vacation in Europe during that time, and they would leave for Oslo in August. That would give Kathy time to tie up the ends at Magpies, find a tenant for the unit at Mitchell, and for them all to prepare themselves for a long Norwegian winter.

It was a time when Abigail's long practice at keeping her feelings to herself was useful. She was sure that neither her father nor her mother realised what was going on inside her. And all she knew herself was that the empty place inside her was so desolate that she fancied she could hear winds blowing within it, round and round, looking for some place to rest.

She took Natalie and Vincent to the playground occasionally. The children there had given up Beatie Bow as a game; they were now crazy about something else. Natalie said wistfully, 'It's queer, Abigail, but I never see the little furry girl any more. I wonder where she is?'

'She's probably at home,' said Abigail, 'brushing her hair and hoping it will grow long enough for her to be bridesmaid at a wedding.'

'Who's getting married?'

'Her brother and her cousin.'

Natalie broke into delighted laughter. 'Oh, you're making up a story about her! And did her hair grow long enough?'

'I don't know, Natalie. I'm not really making up a story. And we have to go home, it's getting so dark.'

'All right,' said the little girl docilely. 'But if you think of some more of the story, Abigail, you'll be sure to tell me, won't you? Will she have a new dress for the wedding?'

'I told you I don't know,' said Abigail, so curtly that she was ashamed of herself. For she longed to sit down somewhere with Natalie—some place Vincent would not find them, or any adult—and begin a story: 'Once upon a time, over a hundred years ago, there was a little girl called Beatrice May Bow who had the fever. Her mother died, and her baby brother died, and they cut off all her hair, because that was what they did in those days . . .'

She realised now that not only did she long for Judah, but she was homesick for all the Bows. She wanted to see Dovey kneeling beside her bed, her lame leg stuck out a little askew from that abominable red-flannel dressing-gown, saying her prayers with such simple faith. She wanted to help Granny make skirl i' the pan, which was fried onions thickened with oatmeal and browned, and rather tasty in a disgusting way; or hotch-potch which was just mutton stew; or oatmeal scones to be baked on the heated round of metal called the girdle. She hadn't even finished telling Gibbie the story of *Treasure Island*. She wondered whether anyone ever would, or would he go to his grave without learning the fate of Long John and the parrot.

She had to know what had become of all those people. She had to find out before she left Australia, so that she could still think about them in Norway.

She knew she was doing a stupid thing—like biting on an aching tooth and rubbing salt into wounds, and all the dusty old sayings; but she went to the Public Library newspaper room and asked for the files of the *Sydney Morning Herald* for December 1873, and January and February of 1874. She had to fill in a form stating why she wished to see the papers, and wrote 'Historical Project', which, she supposed, was correct. The enormous bound files were brought and placed on the sloping reading tables. She was amazed to discover that each newspaper had ten or twelve pages of advertisements before the reader came to what she thought must be the major news pages, though there were no banner headlines.

What was she looking for? She knew Judah and Dovey would never dream of putting a notice of their wedding in the newspaper; that was for the grand people of the High Rocks. Just the same, she read down the births, deaths and marriages column. No Talliskers, no Bows.

On the cable page she saw an occasional reference to a name she knew, Mr Gladstone, the Prime Minister of Great Britain, Disraeli,[2] the Duke of Edinburgh marrying a Russian princess. She hadn't known there was another Duke of Edinburgh.[3]

She looked up to see an old man across the table giving her a poisonous look and realised she was turning the stiff old pages with too much of a rustle. Cautiously she turned to the advertisements. Ah, now she was home—ironmongery departments selling girdles, kerosene lamps, cooking ranges, camp ovens; Mark Foy's corsetry department; David Jones's new shipment of finest velvets, ribbons, osprey and ostrich plumes, ex ship *Oriel*. She was excited, for now she felt that at least the 1870s had really existed, that high-steppers and fashionable ladies bought their hats at David Jones, and when Granny Tallisker's corset wore out she might get a new one at Mark Foy's. Though more likely she'd get a second-hand one from a barrow, she mused, gently turning the pages, the days, the weeks flitting past, throwing up a name here, a headline there, columns of shipping news, random paragraphs, accidental death from bolting horse in Pitt Street, ship *The Brothers* sinks with all hands.

She felt that her heart had stopped. After a little while she realised that her unseeing eyes were fixed on the old man opposite, and he was snarling even more poisonously at her. She returned her gaze to the paragraph. Heavily laden with timber, *The Brothers* had turned turtle in a gale and sunk off the coast a hundred miles north of Sydney. Some of the valuable cargo had drifted ashore and been salvaged. The date was 4 February 1874.

She did not recall walking home along the Quay. As she went into Mitchell's lift,

2. Benjamin Disraeli (1804–1881), Tory statesman, author, and prime minister of Great Britain (1874–80). William Gladstone (1809–1898), Liberal statesman and four-time prime minister of Great Britain (1868–74, 1880–85, 1886, 1892–94).
3. I.e., besides Prince Philip Mountbattan (b. 1921), consort of Queen Elizabeth II. The earlier Duke of Edinburgh is Prince Alfred (1844–1900), the fourth child (and second son) of Queen Victoria; he married the Grand Duchess Marie Alexandrovna, the only daughter of Czar Alexander II of Russia, in January 1874.

Justine and the two children tumbled out. Justine said cheerfully, 'Bet you're in a fluster, getting ready for Norway. Lucky you.'

'Lucky me,' said Abigail with equal cheerfulness.

It was queer how her legs walked, her arms moved, her hand turned the key in the door. It was just as if her body went on knowing what to do, though her mind was numb with shock. She pulled out the drawer of her divan, took out the crochet, and sat in the bear chair.

'Granny,' she said to the empty room, 'I have to warn him; you know that.'

The crochet was more damaged than she had thought. The heat of the incinerator had made some of the old threads disintegrate. It fell into rags in her hands. She gathered up these rags, held them to her chest, and turned her thoughts with all her might to Granny, Beatie at her bench in the Ragged School—anyone at all who might hear her, help her to get back to some time before Judah embarked on *The Brothers* and drowned.

She felt the force of her love and desperation tighten her whole body.

'Granny!' It was a silent yell, as had been the one she had given in her peril at the top of the old warehouse. 'Granny!'

The living-room began to waver as though it were behind a sheet of gauze that a wind gently rippled. The window that showed sea and sky and the Bridge darkened and was no longer there.

She was somewhere, neither in Mitchell nor back in The Rocks. She was suspended as though in a dream, not hearing or feeling, doing nothing but see. And what she saw was a hackney cab, a knot of white ribbons tied to its door, waiting outside the church, Holy Trinity, the Garrison Church. The lean old horse had a rosette of white on his headband, and the cabby himself had stuck a white rose in the ribbon of his hat.

Abigail gazed at this as though at a picture. She could do nothing, she could only wait. Then Beatie ran out of the church. She was in gala dress, a wreath of yellow and purple pansies on her still-short hair, a white dress with a pleated ruffle. The dress showed white stockings and elastic-sided boots.

Then came Mrs Tallisker on the arm of Mr Bow, both still in their mourning clothes, though Mrs Tallisker carried a small basket of lavender stalks.

'Granny! *Granny!*' shouted Abigail, silently within the silence. The old woman looked uneasily around, then her attention was drawn to the church door, where a crowd of sightseers parted, smiling and clapping.

Judah and Dovey appeared, tall Judah towering above the small lame girl. She wore a plain grey print dress, and a modest bonnet with white ribbons tied under her chin.

'Judah! Don't go on *The Brothers*. She will be lost. Don't, don't!'

But Judah was admonishing a crowd of what were probably his shipmates, skylarking and pushing each other as they came out of the church. Beatie began to throw rice, and immediately the sparrows flew down from the trees on the green and snatched the grains almost under the sightseers' feet.

'Get away, you blanky things!' Abigail could see the words form themselves on the child's lips. Granny smiled and drew the little girl close, saying a word or two to her.

'Beatie, can't you hear me?' sobbed Abigail. 'Oh, Beatie, listen to me, I only want him to live and be happy with Dovey. Don't let him go on that ship!'

But Beatie did not hear. She danced about the bridal pair, kicked at the sparrows, half out of her head with delight.

Abigail was able to look into Judah's face as if she were only a few inches away. She saw his clear ruddy skin, his dark blue eyes, his white teeth as he smiled down at Dovey. He looked through Abigail as though she were made of air.

Some of the bedraggled women in the crowd darted forward to touch Dovey's wedding-ring, as though for luck. Solemnly she held out her hand to them, and Abigail saw the tiny red flash of the garnet in her betrothal ring, beside the thin glint of gold.

Then she and Judah kissed Beatie and Granny and Mr Bow, and Judah lifted Dovey into the hackney. Granny threw the lavender in after them, and stood back, smiling.

'Granny, Granny!' sobbed Abigail. She could see the scene losing its colour, fading like an old painting. Granny looked about searchingly for a moment, as though she had heard something as faint as the cheep of a bird, then turned away and waved her handkerchief after the cab as it slowly rattled away, a crowd of urchins following it and pelting it with old boots.

Abigail felt that her hands were full of dust. She looked down, saw them on her lap. The crochet was nothing any more but two handfuls of crumbled threads. Nothing was left, not a leaf of the grass of Parnassus, not a twist of the rope border. It fell over the bear chair like yellowed frost.

The living-room was very cold. She turned on the electric fire and crouched before it, shuddering uncontrollably.

Somewhere inside her a little thought arose: 'He may not have shipped on *The Brothers*.'

But she did not believe it.

'Good-bye, Judah, good-bye,' she said.

CHAPTER 13

When Abigail was almost eighteen, the Kirk family returned to Sydney. They had lived in several countries, and the girl felt an immense gap in both time and space since she had last stepped into the unit on the twentieth floor of Mitchell.

'Quick, look out the window!' squealed Kathy. 'All the new buildings.'

But Abigail was gazing wistfully about her old home.

'Peculiar,' she said to her mother. 'It looks both smaller and larger.'

'And grubbier,' Kathy grumbled, looking at the marks on the walls, the many dents and scratches that were traces of unknown tenants' lives.

'Well,' said Weyland, 'if we can't turn it into something that feels more like home, we'll sell it and find another place.'

'Art deco wallpaper,' mused Kathy, 'fringed lamp-shades.'

'Red plush toot seats?' said her husband. 'I'll shoot myself.'

Abigail went into the bathroom. It was still the prettiest bathroom she had ever seen, but her face seemed to be at a different level in the vanity mirror.

'Can I have grown,' she wondered, 'as well as all the other changes?'

The face that looked back was not very different from that of the fourteen-year-old who had so often looked into the glass and cursed that she would never be a beauty. But time had thinned the cheeks, taken off a sliver here and put one on there, given the narrow dark eyes long fair lashes that looked engaging against the tanned skin. Norway had lightened her hair, too. It was now a streaky sandstone colour.

'A bit like Beatie's,' she thought. It was queer she could recall Beatie's face better than she could remember her own of four years ago.

It had been a curious four years. They had made those months or weeks or minutes in that other century recede a little, like a dream. For the first year, her memories of her life with the Bow family had seemed bitterly real; she had been torn apart with grief for Judah, a true unselfish mourning that he had not lived to be happy with

Dovey, had children, grown old. It had been a long time before she made herself realise that even if he had not drowned, he would have died many years before she herself was born.

'I might have been only a kid, but I did truly love him,' she said, 'and I wanted him to have his life, even though I could never share it.'

Occasionally during those first dislocated miserable months in Bergen[4] she had comforted herself by thinking that she had dreamed the whole story, or created the fantasy because she had been so upset about her parents coming together again. But she knew that was not so.

'And how wrong I was about Mum and Dad, too,' she thought. 'What a silly kid to get so harrowed. And what a sillier one not to realise that adults have as much right to happiness as the young do.'

Her mother peeped into the bathroom.

'What are you mooning about?'

'Just thinking about growing older, looking different,' said Abigail with a smile.

'You look beautiful, I know that,' said Kathy, hugging her.

'You, too,' said Abigail. 'Do you know what, Mother? I think I'll go and see if the Crowns still live next door. Remember little Natalie, and hellish Vincent?'

As she approached the front door of the Crown unit, she almost expected to hear the fearful sounds of domestic battle coming from beyond. But all she heard was a piano. Her heart sank a little. The Crowns had moved, after all. She pressed the bell, and after a little the music ceased and the door was opened by a tall, good-looking boy of ten or eleven. Peering at him, Abigail gasped, 'You can't be Vincent!'

'That's me, all right,' he answered pleasantly. 'But who are you?'

'Abigail Kirk. I used to live next door. I used to take you and Natalie to the playground, remember?'

'Hey, Abigail!' He grinned with genuine pleasure. 'You went away overseas didn't you—Holland or some place?' He turned and called, 'Mum, come here, you'll never guess!'

Justine was overjoyed to see Abigail. The unit had been redecorated and was reasonably tidy. Justine herself looked plump and contented.

'But Natalie, where's she?'

'Oh, she'll be here in a moment, she's out shopping with Robert. It's her eighth birthday, you know. She'll be so thrilled!'

'She won't even recognise me.' Abigail laughed. 'She was so little when I left.'

'I'll get back to my practice, Mum,' said Vincent and, excusing himself, he went off into the next room. The piano started again.

Justine said excitedly, 'He's so promising, his teacher says—something quite out of the ordinary. Remember what a fiend he was? Well, the moment he started music lessons it acted like magic. He just suddenly became an ordinary, decent kid. Bill and I couldn't believe it. We say prayers of gratitude every night.'

'Bill? Isn't your husband called Robert?'

'No, no; Robert's my younger brother. He's Nat's favourite uncle, being so young. He's only twenty. Should be here soon. Now then, start from the very beginning and tell me about everything. Did you go to Oslo University? Did you have any romances with glamorous Norwegians?'

'Oh, three or four.' Abigail smiled. 'They're irresistible people. Not serious though.'

'You'll die being back in this old mundane place,' said Justine.

'No, not at all. Oh, it seems a bit hot and bright after those northern countries,

---

4. Seaport city in southwest Norway.

but I'm going to finish my degree at Sydney University. I'll soon get used to it, and everything that happened in the last four years will seem like a fairy-tale.'

The doorbell rang, and Justine jumped up. An older, bigger Natalie rushed in, her arms laden with parcels.

'And Robert's downstairs with all the big ones,' she cried. Her gaze alighted on the visitor. For a split second she looked dumbfounded; then, yelling 'Abigail!', she dropped all her packages and hurled herself into the older girl's arms. 'Oh, you've turned into a grown-up, but I'd know you anywhere, anywhere!'

As Abigail's arms closed around the wiry strong little body she had an instant pang of regret for the troubled and tearful child Natalie once had been. It was almost as if she were jealous that Natalie had found a braver, surer self without her help. The child's big grey eyes were frank and lively, the mournful little face was gay.

She thought, 'I suppose she's forgotten everything'; but even as the thought entered her mind, Natalie put her lips close to Abigail's and whispered, 'Do you remember the furry little girl?'

Abigail nodded.

'She's always been our secret, hasn't she? Because no one else saw her, you know.'

A key fumbled at the front door, and Natalie shrieked, 'Oh, there's Robert! Wait till you see the super things he's bought for my birthday!'

'How he spoils you monkeys!' scolded Justine as she went to open the door. A tall young man entered, grinning over an armful of large packages. 'Don't jump on me, Natty, or I'll collapse. Where's Vince? There's an un-birthday something here for him.'

Abigail was half-hidden by the arm of a wingchair. She felt as if she were going to faint, as though the blood were draining down to her toenails.

That voice—she felt again the old agony of longing, the tenderness, the unbearable sweetness of being fourteen and drowning in love for someone who thought her a child.

'It's all going to start again,' she thought in panic. 'But it can't; I burnt the crochet. If it does I won't know how to manage it now that I'm older.'

She cringed back into the chair, trying to hide herself until she could collect her thoughts.

'Put all those down and come and meet one of my oldest friends,' she heard Justine say. 'Vincent, stop that racket. Robert's got a surprise for you. Hurry up, Robert.'

She felt him standing there. For a moment she could not look up, she was too afraid.

Justine was chattering. 'Abigail, you must meet my favourite brother, Robert. Robert Bow, Abigail Kirk.'

Abigail raised her eyes.

'It was the most weird thing,' Justine told her long afterwards. 'All you did was to give him the sweetest smile I ever saw. I always thought you a bit of a sobersides, you know—but this! I practically melted. And then Robert said what he said . . . wow, it was really odd!'

'Abby!' the young man exclaimed. Then he turned scarlet and said, 'Oh, I'm sorry. For a moment I thought I knew you. I don't know why I said that; I don't know that people call you Abby for short at all.'

His eyes were deep blue, his hair was fair. He was taller than Judah. His hands were not hard and brown.

'But then, he's lived to be older than Judah ever did,' thought Abigail, 'and he's never worked as hard as Judah.'

The children were making such a commotion over the presents that Justine rocketed away to supervise.

Robert sat down on the floor beside the chair. He shook his head in bewilderment. 'We've never met, have we? You must think me a nut, bursting out that way. Can't think what made me do it.'

All the confused, half-frightened, half-rapturous feelings that had churned in Abigail's interior a few moments previously had gone. Judah had not shipped on *The Brothers*. He had lived, he had lived! The empty place in her heart filled with peaceful benign happiness. She knew that it was settling over her face, that if she looked into a mirror she would see the ghost of a middle-aged woman, still married, still in love, rich with contentment. She almost put out her hand to stroke Robert's cheek as she had dared to do to Judah in that long ago year. But she did not. It was not yet time. He did not know what she knew.

'Tell me,' she said, 'how does your name happen to be Bow when Justine's surname is . . .' she broke off. 'But of course, that's her married name. You must excuse me. I was quite young when I lived in the unit next door.'

'Oh, yes, I know,' said Robert. 'Natalie's often mentioned you. You used to take her to the playground.'

What else, she wondered, had Natalie told him?

'I knew some other Bows once,' she said. 'I had a friend, he was called Judah.'

Robert looked dumbfounded. 'But that's my name too! Robert Judah Bow! Where did you know them? They must be cousins or something. I must ask Justine.'

'No, no,' said Abigail tranquilly. 'She didn't know them. We'll talk about them another time. Just let's sit.'

She wasn't sure afterwards what they talked about. It was too natural and ordinary to remember. She told Robert about Norway, and he told her about the marine engineering course he was doing.

'I've got this feeling about the sea, you see.'

'Yes, of course.'

'I think my ancestors came from Shetland or somewhere, so I suppose the sea is in my genes.'

'Orkney,' said Abigail half to herself. He looked at her half puzzled, half fascinated.

'May I come and see you?'

'Yes, of course. I'm right next door.'

They smiled at each other like old friends.

As she went out, Justine whispered, 'Isn't he a doll?'

Abigail smiled. As she bent to kiss Natalie, the little girl whispered in her old way. 'You won't go away, will you, Abigail? Everything's going to come out all right now, isn't it?'

'Yes,' said Abigail.

When she returned to her parents' unit Kathy said, 'We've decided art deco is too frightful. Maybe Norwegian, with the doors painted with garlands and bouquets in dim colours.'

'You'll start a trend,' said Abigail absently. She did not feel she would be living in that unit very long, so she was not very interested in how it would look. Kathy asked her about the Crowns, nodded with pleasure over the miraculous change in Vincent.

'He was jealous of Natalie, you know,' she said.

'Maybe you're right,' said Abigail. 'Kids . . . whoever knows what they're thinking?'

'And who else was there with Justine, that made you look the way you're looking?' asked Kathy, slyly.

'A university student called Robert Bow,' answered Abigail.

'And?'

'He's dropping in Saturday afternoon. You'll like him.'

Kathy was about to say something teasing when Abigail added, 'He's bringing the family Bible.'

Kathy looked bewildered.

'We just want to look up a family tree,' explained Abigail.

At the week-end Robert arrived. He towered even over Weyland Kirk. Abigail saw now that, aside from his height, there were small differences from Judah's in his face. The eyes and hair and features were the same, but the teeth more regular. The smallpox scar that had dimpled Judah's cheek was missing; the hair was cut altogether differently.

'He's had an easier life than Judah, just as I've had an easier life than Dovey or poor little Beatie, probably. I wonder what happened to her?'

The Bible was a mighty volume. The green plush had hardly any pile left at all; the brass edges were black and bent. They had not been polished for many years.

'Justine had it at the top of the linen cupboard. It belonged to some old great-great aunt or such. She used to be headmistress at Fort Street School, you know the old building up near the Observatory that the National Trust has now?'

'So she made it, the little stirrer!' crowed Abigail. She beamed at Robert, who gaped at her.

'She wasn't any little stirrer; she was a perfect old tartar. Mother remembered her quite well; she was in an old ladies' home or something. Mother was petrified with terror of her, she said.'

'Old Miss Bow?' Abigail laughed marvelling. 'Who would have guessed it? I guess that's how that kids' game sprang up . . . terror lest Miss Beatie Bow would rise from the grave and give them all whatfor!' She laughed. 'Sorry, Robert. I must sound like a witch. But after we've looked at your family tree I'll explain a bit.' Her eyes twinkled as she smiled at him. 'The rest I won't tell you until we know each other lots better.'

'That won't be long if I've anything to say about it.'

'Let's go into the kitchen,' she said. 'Those two are fighting over re-decorating the unit. We've been through the red-plush loo seat phase, and I don't want to be present as they pass into the birchwood and Scandinavian, with Lappish rugs. Besides, in there we can put this monster out flat on the table.'

Robert opened the enormous book and turned to one of the thick mended pages. Hand-painted violets and faded ribbons of lilac enclosed the family tree. Each name was in a little painted oval touched with gold paint. Some of it was in a fanciful Victorian hand with long looping tails, the ink bleached to a light brown. Some names were in a round, childish script, and at the bottom the names of Vincent and Natalie Crown were written in Justine's favourite green biro.[5]

Abigail fell upon it eagerly. 'Your great-grandfather, Judah, where's he?'

'Hold on!' said Robert. 'I didn't have a great-grandfather Judah. That's just a family name. My great-grandfather was Samuel, I think.'

'It couldn't be,' protested Abigail. 'That was Trooper Bow's name, their father, Beatie and Gibbie and Judah's father.'

'How on earth—? Never mind now—Gibbie! That was it. Gilbert. Look, here it is.'

His brown forefinger slid down the painted branches of the tree till it landed on *Gilbert Samuel*, b. 1863, d. 1933.

5. Ballpoint pen.

'That's not possible,' cried Abigail. 'He wasn't supposed to live; he wasn't long for this world. What's Gibbie doing hanging around until he was—what is it?—seventy, mind you!'

Robert gazed at her, flabbergasted.

'Then Judah must have drowned after all,' she said slowly. 'Where is he, Robert?'

Her finger went back to the curly Victorian writing. She found *Judah Bow*, b. 1855, d. 1874.

'Oh, Robert, he was on the ship after all. He died at nineteen. It isn't fair!'

'Oh, Judah, oh, Judah,' she sobbed. In a moment Robert had his arms around her. He tried to make sense of her choked mumbles, but all he could get was: 'And when I saw you I was sure he had lived, and Dovey had had a baby, and you were descended from him. How do you look exactly like him then? Beastly little Gibbie! You've no idea how awful he was, always panting to join his mamma amongst the angels. He even had his funeral worked out.' She raised her head and sniffed angrily. 'It's just him to put it all over everyone and live till seventy, little sneak.'

'But if he hadn't lived,' Robert pointed out softly, 'I wouldn't have had him for a great-grandfather, and I wouldn't be here listening to you.'

'I loved him so much,' wept Abigail. 'Not horrible Gibbie, but Judah; and I knew he would be drowned and tried to warn him but I couldn't get back . . . Oh, Robert, he died when he was nineteen, he never had a real life at all.'

'Now then,' said Robert, and there was in his voice the firmness of Judah Bow, who had been a man, with a man's work and authority, at eighteen. 'You're going to calm down and tell me all about this: how you know things about my family I don't know, why you're crying about someone who died more than a century ago. You know you're going to tell me sooner or later, don't you? So why not sooner?'

He kissed away her tears. It seemed a very natural and accustomed thing to do. So, very simply and without embarrassment, Abigail told him what had happened four years before. He listened seriously.

'Natalie has something to do with this, hasn't she?' he pondered. 'Because, after all, she's a Bow, and perhaps she has the Gift. And the crochet, because it came from the fingers of that Great-great-great-grandmother Alice from the Orkneys, was just enough to tip you over into the last century. She was right, you know: you were the Stranger of the Prophecy.'

'But the rest of the Prophecy—' cried Abigail. 'I mean, it was Granny Tallisker herself who believed that one for death and one for barrenness meant Gibbie for death, because he was so frail, and one for barrenness meant Beatie, because she always said she wouldn't get married no matter what. And instead it was Judah for death, and Dovey for barrenness. The Prophecy was right, but Granny had the wrong people.'

'Dovey wasn't barren,' said Robert gently. 'She's the one called Dorcas, I presume? Look at the family tree again. She had a child, Judith, and it died with her, the same year as she and Granny died.'

'That was the smallpox year,' said Abigail. 'Oh, poor little Dovey, poor little baby. And Granny . . . she was the most wonderful woman. Isn't it strange, Robert, even Granny thought that my importance, as the Stranger I mean, was to go back that day of the fire and save Dovey for Judah, so that their children would have two chances of perpetuating the Gift. But it was getting that little monster Gilbert out of the house as well that mattered. Yes, that was what the whole thing was about. I had to save Gibbie, so that he could continue the Bow family and the Gift.'

She pored over the Bible. 'I suppose there were other children, daughters, perhaps, and some of them had the Gift, too. But whoever has kept the record just hasn't bothered to put them down.'

'I guess old lady Beatie just didn't have time. She was a famous classics scholar and a perfect martinet[6] as headmistress, so Justine says.'

'The interesting thing is,' said Abigail, 'that you believe all I say.'

'Yes,' he said. 'First of all because it's you telling me, and secondly because it wouldn't occur to me not to. I mean, I had this sensation the moment I met you, that you were so familiar I knew all about you except that it had slipped my mind for a moment. I spent that whole night trying to remember what it was.'

'I stayed awake, too,' confessed Abigail. But when he asked her why she would not tell him.

He turned over the page. 'There's lots more room for the family to go on,' he said, 'and already painted. Funny, these flowers are wattle and Christmas bells.[7] They must have been done after the Bows and Talliskers arrived here as immigrants.'

Abigail thought that perhaps Dovey had painted those flowers because entwined amongst them were sprigs of lavender, bog cotton and grass of Parnassus. Poor home-sick Dovey, a wife for such a short while, a widow for only two years.

'You would have liked Granny Tallisker,' said Abigail. She sighed. 'You won't care for mine; she's even worse than she used to be.'

She was silent, thinking of that old woman, Alice Tallisker, her infinite goodness and strength, and how she had said that the link between Abigail and the Talliskers and Bows was no stronger than the link between that family and Abigail. The theory she had had when wandering The Rocks four years before—that time was a great black vortex down which everything disappeared—no longer made sense to her. She saw now that it was a great river, always moving, always changing, but with the same water flowing between its banks from source to sea.

How on earth had ugly, tempestuous little Beatie managed to get as far as being headmistress of Fort Street High, the foremost school of its time?

'I'll find out how, some day,' thought Abigail. 'Maybe I helped a little, but I'll tell Robert about that some other day.'

Her mother came into the kitchen. 'What on earth are you kids doing?'

'Just fooling around,' said Robert. He was still shy with Kathy and Weyland. 'Nothing much.'

'Just playing Beatie Bow,' said Abigail. She knew her mother did not understand, but that didn't matter. Robert did.

1980

---

6. A strict disciplinarian.
7. I.e., flowering plants native to Australia and not Great Britain.

LLOYD ALEXANDER
b. 1924

To the astonishment of his parents and relatives, Lloyd Alexander learned to read fluently at about age three, and from that time forward he read avidly and voraciously. He implored his family to give him books as gifts—in particular, Greek and Celtic mythology, and Welsh legends, and the works of Dickens—to feed his hunger for literature. Alexander "fed" on literature in another way, too: he yearned to eat the meals mentioned in the books he was reading. His patient mother attempted to fulfill young Lloyd's desires as best she could, though she often had to make substitutions for foodstuffs not readily available in Philadelphia, such as the nut-brown ale and venison steaks described in Robin Hood tales.

After graduation from high school, Alexander's ambition to become a writer seemed to be stymied by a number of unfulfilling jobs and false starts in postsecondary education. Alexander decided in 1942 that war adventure would help him to develop as a writer, and he enlisted in the army and was assigned to military intelligence as a translator. During the short time Alexander was stationed in Wales for combat training, he fell in love with the language and the landscape of the country whose legends and tales had inspired his imagination from early youth. For further biographical information about Alexander, see the headnote to "The Truthful Harp," in the Fairy Tales section, above.

When researching different historical periods for his first book for children, *Time Cat: The Remarkable Journeys of Jason and Gareth* (1963), Alexander was reminded of his boyhood love for the tales of Arthur and the traditional Welsh legends found in the *Mabinogion*. He replaced the Welsh episode in *Time Cat* with an Irish one and decided to write an entire book about Wales. That book, *The Book of Three* (1964), would become the first installment in the award-winning five-volume Prydain Chronicles. Alexander also published short fiction for younger readers that featured some of the characters in the Prydain Chronicles, such as the bard, Fflewddur Fflam, the protagonist of "The Truthful Harp" (1967).

As Alexander makes clear in the Author's Note to *The Book of Three,* although elements of Welsh tales and legends inform his stories, Prydain is not Wales and Taran's story is not a retelling of the *Mabinogion.* In writing this first book Alexander realized that he did not want to be beholden to another's mythology, but needed to create his own to reflect his personality and values, and contemporary realism. Thus, while the Prydain Chronicles are firmly within the tradition of high fantasy practiced by children's writers such as Ursula K. Le Guin and Robin McKinley—serious quest narratives set in a secondary world—Alexander's cycle is leavened by humor and inflected by his own search for self-knowledge. At first, Taran, an adolescent Assistant Pig-Keeper, is both headstrong and brave, earnest and easy to anger. Through his adventures with a band of faithful companions and successes and failures in battling evil, Taran develops over the course of the series into a humble, compassionate, and decisive leader who retains his integrity and human qualities. Although Taran's quest is set within a fantastic world of magic and sharply defined good and evil, his search to define himself and his desire to return home a contented, yet changed, young man are as universal as adolescence itself.

In 1985, *The Book of Three* and its sequel, *The Black Cauldron,* were adapted by Disney into an animated film.

The Book of Three

AUTHOR'S NOTE

This chronicle of the Land of Prydain[1] is not a retelling or retranslation of Welsh mythology. Prydain is not Wales—not entirely, at least. The inspiration for it comes from that magnificent land and its legends; but, essentially, Prydain is a country existing only in the imagination.

A few of its inhabitants are drawn from the ancient tales. Gwydion, for example, is a "real" legendary figure. Arawn, the dread Lord of Annuvin, comes from the *Mabinogion*,[2] the classic collection of Welsh legends, though in Prydain he is considerably more villainous. And there is an authentic mythological basis for Arawn's cauldron, Hen Wen the oracular pig, the old enchanter Dallben, and others. However, Taran the Assistant Pig-Keeper, like Eilonwy of the red-gold hair, was born in my own Prydain.

The geography of Prydain is peculiar to itself. Any resemblance between it and Wales is perhaps not coincidental—but not to be used as a guide for tourists. It is a small land, yet it has room enough for gallantry and humor; and even an Assistant Pig-Keeper there may cherish certain dreams.

The chronicle of Prydain is a fantasy. Such things never happen in real life. Or do they? Most of us are called on to perform tasks far beyond what we can do. Our capabilities seldom match our aspirations, and we are often woefully unprepared. To this extent, we are all Assistant Pig-Keepers at heart.

CHAPTER I

The Assistant Pig-Keeper

Taran wanted to make a sword; but Coll,[3] charged with the practical side of his education, decided on horseshoes. And so it had been horseshoes all morning long. Taran's arms ached, soot blackened his face. At last he dropped the hammer and turned to Coll, who was watching him critically.

"Why?" Taran cried. "Why must it be horseshoes? As if we had any horses!"

Coll was stout and round and his great bald head glowed bright pink. "Lucky for the horses," was all he said, glancing at Taran's handiwork.

"I could do better at making a sword," Taran protested. "I know I could." And before Coll could answer, he snatched the tongs, flung a strip of red-hot iron to the anvil, and began hammering away as fast as he could.

"Wait, wait!" cried Coll, "that is not the way to go after it!"

Heedless of Coll, unable even to hear him above the din, Taran pounded harder than ever. Sparks sprayed the air. But the more he pounded, the more the metal

---

1. Welsh word from which "Britain" is derived. See the "Prydain Pronunciation Guide" on pp. 874–75, below.
2. Four native Welsh legends preserved in two manuscripts: the White Book of Rhydderch (1300–1325) and the Red Book of Hergyst (1375–1425). The tales have been known as "The Mabinogion" (or "Mabinogi") since 1838–49, when Lady Charlotte Guest translated the legends into English.

The common element of the four "branches" of the *Mabinogion* is the hero Pryderi.
3. The characters, together with Hen Wen the oracular pig and the enchanter Dallben, are all drawn from Lady Charlotte Guest's notes on the Welsh legends. Although Taran is Alexander's creation, the name appears in the earliest Arthurian tale in the *Mabinogion*.

twisted and buckled, until, finally, the iron sprang from the tongs and fell to the ground. Taran stared in dismay. With the tongs, he picked up the bent iron and examined it.

"Not quite the blade for a hero," Coll remarked.

"It's ruined," Taran glumly agreed. "It looks like a sick snake," he added ruefully.

"As I tried telling you," said Coll, "you had it all wrong. You must hold the tongs—so. When you strike, the strength must flow from your shoulder and your wrist be loose. You can hear it when you do it right. There is a kind of music in it. Besides," he added, "this is not the metal for weapons."

Coll returned the crooked, half-formed blade to the furnace, where it lost its shape entirely.

"I wish I might have my own sword," Taran sighed, "and you would teach me sword-fighting."

"Wisht!" cried Coll. "Why should you want to know that? We have no battles at Caer[4] Dallben."

"We have no horses, either," objected Taran, "but we're making horseshoes."

"Get on with you," said Coll, unmoved. "That is for practice."

"And so would this be," Taran urged. "Come, teach me the sword-fighting. You must know the art."

Coll's shining head glowed even brighter. A trace of a smile appeared on his face, as though he were savoring something pleasant. "True," he said quietly, "I have held a sword once or twice in my day."

"Teach me now," pleaded Taran. He seized a poker and brandished it, slashing at the air and dancing back and forth over the hard-packed earthen floor. "See," he called, "I know most of it already."

"Hold your hand," chuckled Coll. "If you were to come against me like that, with all your posing and bouncing, I should have you chopped into bits by this time." He hesitated a moment. "Look you," he said quickly, "at least you should know there is a right way and a wrong way to go about it."

He picked up another poker. "Here now," he ordered, with a sooty wink, "stand like a man."

Taran brought up his poker. While Coll shouted instructions, they set to parrying and thrusting, with much banging, clanking, and commotion. For a moment Taran was sure he had the better of Coll, but the old man spun away with amazing lightness of foot. Now it was Taran who strove desperately to ward off Coll's blows.

Abruptly, Coll stopped. So did Taran, his poker poised in mid-air. In the doorway of the forge stood the tall, bent figure of Dallben.

Dallben, master of Caer Dallben, was three hundred and seventy-nine years old. His beard covered so much of his face he seemed always to be peering over a gray cloud. On the little farm, while Taran and Coll saw to the plowing, sowing, weeding, reaping, and all the other tasks of husbandry, Dallben undertook the meditating, an occupation so exhausting he could accomplish it only by lying down and closing his eyes. He meditated an hour and a half following breakfast and again later in the day. The clatter from the forge had roused him from his morning meditation; his robe hung askew over his bony knees.

"Stop that nonsense directly," said Dallben. "I am surprised at you," he added, frowning at Coll. "There is serious work to be done."

4. Castle or fortress.

"It wasn't Coll," Taran interrupted. "It was I who asked to learn swordplay."

"I did not say I was surprised at *you*," remarked Dallben. "But perhaps I am, after all. I think you had best come with me."

Taran followed the ancient man out of the forge, across the chicken run, and into the white, thatched cottage. There, in Dallben's chamber, moldering tomes overflowed the sagging shelves and spilled onto the floor amid heaps of iron cook-pots, studded belts, harps with or without strings, and other oddments.

Taran took his place on the wooden bench, as he always did when Dallben was in a mood for giving lessons or reprimands.

"I fully understand," said Dallben, settling himself behind his table, "in the use of weapons, as in everything else, there is a certain skill. But wiser heads than yours will determine when you should learn it."

"I'm sorry," Taran began, "I should not have . . ."

"I am not angry," Dallben said, raising a hand. "Only a little sad. Time flies quickly; things always happen sooner than one expects. And yet," he murmured, almost to himself, "it troubles me. I fear the Horned King may have some part in this."

"The Horned King?" asked Taran.

"We shall speak of him later," said Dallben. He drew a ponderous, leather-bound volume toward him, *The Book of Three,* from which he occasionally read to Taran and which, the boy believed, held in its pages everything anyone could possibly want to know.

"As I have explained to you before," Dallben went on, "—and you have very likely forgotten—Prydain is a land of many cantrevs—of small kingdoms—and many kings. And, of course, their war-leaders who command the warriors."

"But there is the High King above them all," said Taran, "Math Son of Mathonwy. His war-leader is the mightiest hero in Prydain. You told me of him. Prince Gwydion! Yes," Taran went on eagerly, "I know . . ."

"There are other things you do *not* know," Dallben said, "for the obvious reason that I have not told you. For the moment I am less concerned with the realms of the living than with the Land of the Dead, with Annuvin."

Taran shuddered at the word. Even Dallben had spoken it in a whisper.

"And with King Arawn,[5] Lord of Annuvin," Dallben said. "Know this," he continued quickly, "Annuvin is more than a land of death. It is a treasure-house, not only of gold and jewels but of all things of advantage to men. Long ago, the race of men owned these treasures. By craft and deceit, Arawn stole them, one by one, for his own evil uses. Some few of the treasures have been wrested from him though most lie hidden deep in Annuvin, where Arawn guards them jealously."

"But Arawn did not become ruler of Prydain," Taran said.

"You may be thankful he did not," said Dallben. "He would have ruled had it not been for the Children of Don, the sons of the Lady Don and her consort Belin, King of the Sun. Long ago they voyaged to Prydain from the Summer Country and found the land rich and fair, though the race of men had little for themselves. The Sons of Don built their stronghold at Caer Dathyl,[6] far north in the Eagle Mountains. From there, they helped regain at least a portion of what Arawn had stolen, and stood as guardians against the lurking threat of Annuvin."

5. King of the underworld, from the *Mabinogion.* Like the original, Alexander's character has shape-changing abilities.

6. The seat of the High King, borrowed from the *Mabinogion.*

"I hate to think what would have happened if the Sons of Don hadn't come," Taran said. "It was a good destiny that brought them."

"I am not always sure," said Dallben, with a wry smile. "The men of Prydain came to rely on the strength of the House of Don as a child clings to its mother. They do so even today. Math, the High King, is descended from the House of Don. So is Prince Gwydion.[7] But that is all by the way. Prydain has been at peace—as much as men can be peaceful—until now.

"What you do not know," Dallben said, "is this: it has reached my ears that a new and mighty war lord has risen, as powerful as Gwydion; some say more powerful. But he is a man of evil for whom death is a black joy. He sports with death as you might sport with a dog."

"Who is he?" cried Taran.

Dallben shook his head. "No man knows his name, nor has any man seen his face. He wears an antlered mask, and for this reason he is called the Horned King. His purposes I do not know. I suspect the hand of Arawn, but in what manner I cannot tell. I tell you now for your own protection," Dallben added. "From what I saw this morning, your head is full of nonsense about feats of arms. Whatever notions you may have, I advise you to forget them immediately. There is unknown danger abroad. You are barely on the threshold of manhood, and I have a certain responsibility to see that you reach it, preferably with a whole skin. So, you are not to leave Caer Dallben under any circumstances, not even past the orchard, and certainly not into the forest—not for the time being."

"For the time being!" Taran burst out. "I think it will always be for the time being, and it will be vegetables and horseshoes all my life!"

"Tut," said Dallben, "there are worse things. Do you set yourself to be a glorious hero? Do you believe it is all flashing swords and galloping about on horses? As for being glorious . . ."

"What of Prince Gwydion?" cried Taran. "Yes! I wish I might be like him!"

"I fear," Dallben said, "that is entirely out of the question."

"But why?" Taran sprang to his feet. "I know if I had the chance . . ."

"Why?" Dallben interrupted. "In some cases," he said, "we learn more by looking for the answer to a question and not finding it than we do from learning the answer itself. This is one of those cases. I could tell you why, but at the moment it would only be more confusing. If you grow up with any kind of sense—which you sometimes make me doubt—you will very likely reach your own conclusions.

"They will probably be wrong," he added. "However, since they will be yours, you will feel a little more satisfied with them."

Taran sank back and sat, gloomy and silent, on the bench. Dallben had already begun meditating again. His chin gradually came to rest on his collarbone; his beard floated around his ears like a fog bank; and he began snoring peacefully.

The spring scent of apple blossom drifted through the open window. Beyond Dallben's chamber, Taran glimpsed the pale green fringe of forest. The fields, ready to cultivate, would soon turn golden with summer. *The Book of Three* lay closed on the table. Taran had never been allowed to read the volume for himself; now he was sure it held more than Dallben chose to tell him. In the sun-filled room, with Dallben still meditating and showing no sign of stopping, Taran rose and moved through the shimmering beams. From the forest came the monotonous tick of a beetle.

7. A character who appears in the *Mabinogion*.

His hands reached for the cover. Taran gasped in pain and snatched them away. They smarted as if each of his fingers had been stung by hornets. He jumped back, stumbled against the bench, and dropped to the floor, where he put his fingers woefully into his mouth.

Dallben's eyes blinked open. He peered at Taran and yawned slowly. "You had better see Coll about a lotion for those hands," he advised. "Otherwise, I shouldn't be surprised if they blistered."

Fingers smarting, the shamefaced Taran hurried from the cottage and found Coll near the vegetable garden.

"You have been at *The Book of Three*," Coll said. "That is not hard to guess. Now you know better. Well, that is one of the three foundations of learning: see much, study much, suffer much." He led Taran to the stable where medicines for the livestock were kept, and poured a concoction over Taran's fingers.

"What is the use of studying much when I'm to see nothing at all?" Taran retorted. "I think there is a destiny laid on me that I am not to know anything interesting, or do anything interesting. I'm certainly not to *be* anything. I'm not anything even at Caer Dallben!"

"Very well," said Coll, "if that is all that troubles you, I shall make you something. From this moment, you are Taran, Assistant Pig-Keeper. You shall help me take care of Hen Wen: see her trough is full, carry her water, and give her a good scrubbing every other day."

"That's what I do now," Taran said bitterly.

"All the better," said Coll, "for it makes things that much easier. If you want to be something with a name attached to it, I can't think of anything closer to hand. And it is not every lad who can be assistant keeper to an oracular pig. Indeed, she is the only oracular pig in Prydain, and the most valuable."

"Valuable to Dallben," Taran said. "She never tells *me* anything."

"Did you think she would?" replied Coll. "With Hen Wen, you must know how to ask—here, what was that?" Coll shaded his eyes with his hand. A black, buzzing cloud streaked from the orchard, and bore on so rapidly and passed so close to Coll's head that he had to leap out of the way.

"The bees!" Taran shouted. "They're swarming."

"It is not their time," cried Coll. "There is something amiss."

The cloud rose high toward the sun. An instant later Taran heard a loud clucking and squawking from the chicken run. He turned to see the five hens and the rooster beating their wings. Before it occurred to him they were attempting to fly, they, too, were aloft.

Taran and Coll raced to the chicken run, too late to catch the fowls. With the rooster leading, the chickens flapped awkwardly through the air and disappeared over the brow of a hill.

From the stable the pair of oxen bellowed and rolled their eyes in terror.

Dallben's head poked out of the window. He looked irritated. "It has become absolutely impossible for any kind of meditation whatsoever," he said, with a severe glance at Taran. "I have warned you once . . . ."

"Something frightened the animals," Taran protested. "First the bees, then the chickens flew off . . . ."

Dallben's face turned grave. "I have been given no knowledge of this," he said to Coll. "We must ask Hen Wen about it immediately, and we shall need the letter sticks. Quickly, help me find them."

Coll moved hastily to the cottage door. "Watch Hen Wen closely," he ordered Taran. "Do not let her out of your sight."

Coll disappeared inside the cottage to search for Hen Wen's letter sticks, the long rods of ash wood carved with spells. Taran was both frightened and excited. Dallben, he knew, would consult Hen Wen only on a matter of greatest urgency. Within Taran's memory, it had never happened before. He hurried to the pen.

Hen Wen usually slept until noon. Then, trotting daintily, despite her size, she would move to a shady corner of her enclosure and settle comfortably for the rest of the day. The white pig was continually grunting and chuckling to herself, and whenever she saw Taran, she would raise her wide, cheeky face so that he could scratch under her chin. But this time, she paid no attention to him. Wheezing and whistling, Hen Wen was digging furiously in the soft earth at the far side of the pen, burrowing so rapidly she would soon be out.

Taran shouted at her, but the clods continued flying at a great rate. He swung himself over the fence. The oracular pig stopped and glanced around. As Taran approached the hole, already sizable, Hen Wen hurried to the opposite side of the pen and started a new excavation.

Taran was strong and long-legged, but, to his dismay, he saw that Hen Wen moved faster than he. As soon as he chased her from the second hole, she turned quickly on her short legs and made for the first. Both, by now, were big enough for her head and shoulders.

Taran frantically began scraping earth back into the burrow. Hen Wen dug faster than a badger, her hind legs planted firmly, her front legs plowing ahead. Taran despaired of stopping her. He scrambled back over the rails and jumped to the spot where Hen Wen was about to emerge, planning to seize her and hang on until Dallben and Coll arrived. He underestimated Hen Wen's speed and strength.

In an explosion of dirt and pebbles, the pig burst from under the fence, heaving Taran into the air. He landed with the wind knocked out of him. Hen Wen raced across the field and into the woods.

Taran followed. Ahead, the forest rose up dark and threatening. He took a breath and plunged after her.

CHAPTER II

The Mask of the King

Hen Wen had vanished. Ahead, Taran heard a thrashing among the leaves. The pig, he was sure, was keeping out of sight in the bushes. Following the sound, he ran forward. After a time the ground rose sharply, forcing him to clamber on hands and knees up a wooded slope. At the crest the forest broke off before a meadow. Taran caught a glimpse of Hen Wen dashing into the waving grass. Once across the meadow, she disappeared beyond a stand of trees.

Taran hurried after her. This was farther than he had ever dared venture, but he struggled on through the heavy undergrowth. Soon, a fairly wide trail opened, allowing him to quicken his pace. Hen Wen had either stopped running or had outdistanced him. He heard nothing but his own footsteps.

He followed the trail for some while, intending to use it as a landmark on the way back, although it twisted and branched off so frequently he was not at all certain in which direction Caer Dallben lay.

In the meadow Taran had been flushed and perspiring. Now he shivered in the silence of oaks and elms. The woods here were not thick, but shadows drenched the high tree trunks and the sun broke through only in jagged streaks. A damp green scent filled the air. No bird called; no squirrel chattered. The forest seemed to be holding its breath.

Yet there was, beneath the silence, a groaning restlessness and a trembling among the leaves. The branches twisted and grated against each other like broken teeth. The path wavered under Taran's feet, and he felt desperately cold. He flung his arms around himself and moved more quickly to shake off the chill. He was, he realized, running aimlessly; he could not keep his mind on the forks and turns of the path.

He halted suddenly. Hoofbeats thudded in front of him. The forest shook as they grew louder. In another moment a black horse burst into view.

Taran fell back, terrified. Astride the foam-spattered animal rode a monstrous figure. A crimson cloak flamed from his naked shoulders. Crimson stained his gigantic arms. Horror-stricken, Taran saw not the head of a man but the antlered head of a stag.

The Horned King! Taran flung himself against an oak to escape the flying hoofs and the heaving, glistening flanks. Horse and rider swept by. The mask was a human skull; from it, the great antlers rose in cruel curves. The Horned King's eyes blazed behind the gaping sockets of whitened bone.

Many horsemen galloped in his train. The Horned King uttered the long cry of a wild beast, and his riders took it up as they streamed after him. One of them, an ugly, grinning warrior, caught sight of Taran. He turned his mount and drew a sword. Taran sprang from the tree and plunged into the underbrush. The blade followed, hissing like an adder. Taran felt it sting across his back.

He ran blindly, while saplings whipped his face and hidden rocks jutted out to pitch him forward and stab at his knees. Where the woods thinned, Taran clattered along a dry stream bed until, exhausted, he stumbled and held out his hands against the whirling ground.

The sun had already dipped westward when Taran opened his eyes. He was lying on a stretch of turf with a cloak thrown over him. One shoulder smarted painfully. A man knelt beside him. Nearby, a white horse cropped the grass. Still dazed, fearful the riders had overtaken him, Taran started up. The man held out a flask.

"Drink," he said. "Your strength will return in a moment."

The stranger had the shaggy, gray-streaked hair of a wolf. His eyes were deep-set, flecked with green. Sun and wind had leathered his broad face, burnt it dark and grained it with fine lines. His cloak was coarse and travel-stained. A wide belt with an intricately wrought buckle circled his waist.

"Drink," the stranger said again, while Taran took the flask dubiously. "You look as though I were trying to poison you." He smiled. "It is not thus that Gwydion Son of Don deals with a wounded . . ."

"Gwydion!" Taran choked on the liquid and stumbled to his feet. "You are not Gwydion!" he cried. "I know of him. He is a great war leader, a hero! He is not . . ." His eyes fell on the long sword at the stranger's belt. The golden pommel was smooth and rounded, its color deliberately muted; ash leaves of pale gold entwined at the hilt, and a pattern of leaves covered the scabbard. It was truly the weapon of a prince.

Taran dropped to one knee and bowed his head. "Lord Gwydion," he said, "I did not intend insolence." As Gwydion helped him rise, Taran still stared in disbelief at the simple attire and the worn, lined face. From all Dallben had told him of this glorious hero, from all he had pictured to himself—Taran bit his lips.

Gwydion caught Taran's look of disappointment. "It is not the trappings that make the prince," he said gently, "nor, indeed, the sword that makes the warrior. Come," he ordered, "tell me your name and what happened to you. And do not ask me to believe you got a sword wound picking gooseberries or poaching hares."

"I saw the Horned King!" Taran burst out. "His men ride the forest; one of them tried to kill me. I saw the Horned King himself! It was horrible, worse than Dallben told me!"

Gwydion's eyes narrowed. "Who are you?" he demanded. "Who are you to speak of Dallben?"

"I am Taran of Caer Dallben," Taran answered, trying to appear bold but succeeding only in turning paler than a mushroom.

"Of Caer Dallben?" Gwydion paused an instant and gave Taran a strange glance. "What are you doing so far from there? Does Dallben know you are in the forest? Is Coll with you?"

Taran's jaw dropped and he looked so thunderstruck that Gwydion threw back his head and burst into laughter.

"You need not be so surprised," Gwydion said. "I know Coll and Dallben well. And they are too wise to let you wander here alone. Have you run off, then? I warn you; Dallben is not one to be disobeyed."

"It was Hen Wen," Taran protested. "I should have known I couldn't hold on to her. Now she's gone, and it's my fault. I'm Assistant Pig-Keeper . . ."

"Gone?" Gwydion's face tightened. "Where? What has happened to her?"

"I don't know," Taran cried. "She's somewhere in the forest." As he poured out an account of the morning's events, Gwydion listened intently.

"I had not foreseen this," Gwydion murmured, when Taran had finished. "My mission fails if she is not found quickly." He turned abruptly to Taran. "Yes," he said, "I, too, seek Hen Wen."

"You?" cried Taran. "You came this far . . ."

"I need information she alone possesses," Gwydion said quickly. "I have journeyed a month from Caer Dathyl to get it. I have been followed, spied on, hunted. And now," he added with a bitter laugh, "she has run off. Very well. She will be found. I must discover all she knows of the Horned King." Gwydion hesitated. "I fear he himself searches for her even now.

"It must be so," he continued. "Hen Wen sensed him near Caer Dallben and fled in terror . . ."

"Then we should stop him," Taran declared. "Attack him, strike him down! Give me a sword and I will stand with you!"

"Gently, gently," chided Gwydion. "I do not say my life is worth more than another man's, but I prize it highly. Do you think a lone warrior and one Assistant Pig-Keeper dare attack the Horned King and his war band?"

Taran drew himself up. "I would not fear him."

"No?" said Gwydion. "Then you are a fool. He is the man most to be dreaded in all Prydain. Will you hear something I learned during my journey, something even Dallben may not yet realize?"

Gwydion knelt on the turf. "Do you know the craft of weaving? Thread by thread, the pattern forms." As he spoke, he plucked at the long blades of grass, knotting them to form a mesh.

"That is cleverly done," said Taran, watching Gwydion's rapidly moving fingers. "May I look at it?"

"There is a more serious weaving," said Gwydion, slipping the net into his own jacket. "You have seen one thread of a pattern loomed in Annuvin.

"Arawn does not long abandon Annuvin," Gwydion continued, "but his hand reaches everywhere. There are chieftains whose lust for power goads them like a sword point. To certain of them, Arawn promises wealth and dominion, playing on their greed as a bard plays on a harp. Arawn's corruption burns every human feeling from their hearts and they become his liege men, serving him beyond the borders of Annuvin and bound to him forever."

"And the Horned King . . . ?"

Gwydion nodded. "Yes. I know beyond question that he has sworn his allegiance to Arawn. He is Arawn's avowed champion. Once again, the power of Annuvin threatens Prydain."

Taran could only stare, speechless.

Gwydion turned to him. "When the time is ripe, the Horned King and I will meet. And one of us will die. That is my oath. But his purpose is dark and unknown, and I must learn it from Hen Wen."

"She can't be far," Taran cried. "I'll show you where she disappeared. I think I can find the place. It was just before the Horned King . . ."

Gwydion gave him a hard smile. "Do you have the eyes of an owl, to find a trail at nightfall? We sleep here and I shall be off at first light. With good luck, I may have her back before . . ."

"What of me?" Taran interrupted. "Hen Wen is in my charge. I let her escape and it is I who must find her."

"The task counts more than the one who does it," said Gwydion. "I will not be hindered by an Assistant Pig-Keeper, who seems eager to bring himself to grief." He stopped short and looked wryly at Taran. "On second thought, it appears I will. If the Horned King rides toward Caer Dallben, I cannot send you back alone and I dare not go with you and lose a day's tracking. You cannot stay in this forest by yourself. Unless I find some way . . ."

"I swear I will not hinder you," cried Taran. "Let me go with you. Dallben and Coll will see I can do what I set out to do!"

"Have I another choice?" asked Gwydion. "It would seem, Taran of Caer Dallben, we follow the same path. For a little while at least."

The white horse trotted up and nuzzled Gwydion's hand. "Melyngar reminds me it is time for food," Gwydion said. He unpacked provisions from the saddlebags. "Make no fire tonight," he warned. "The Horned King's outriders may be close at hand."

Taran swallowed a hurried meal. Excitement robbed him of appetite and he was impatient for dawn. His wound had stiffened so that he could not settle himself on the roots and pebbles. It had never occurred to him until now that a hero would sleep on the ground.

Gwydion, watchful, sat with his knees drawn up, his back against an enormous elm. In the lowering dusk Taran could barely distinguish the man from the tree; and could have walked within a pace of him before realizing he was any more than a splotch of shadow. Gwydion had sunk into the forest itself; only his green-flecked eyes shone in the reflection of the newly risen moon.

Gwydion was silent and thoughtful for a long while. "So you are Taran of Caer Dallben," he said at last. His voice from the shadows was quiet but urgent. "How long have you been with Dallben? Who are your kinsmen?"

Taran, hunched against a tree root, pulled his cloak closer about his shoulders. "I have always lived at Caer Dallben," he said. "I don't think I have any kinsmen. I don't know who my parents were. Dallben has never told me. I suppose," he added, turning his face away, "I don't even know who *I* am."

"In a way," answered Gwydion, "that is something we must all discover for ourselves. Our meeting was fortunate," he went on. "Thanks to you, I know a little more than I did, and you have spared me a wasted journey to Caer Dallben. It makes me wonder," Gwydion went on, with a laugh that was not unkind, "is there a destiny laid on me that an Assistant Pig-Keeper should help me in my quest?" He hesitated. "Or," he mused, "is it perhaps the other way around?"

"What do you mean?" Taran asked.

"I am not sure," said Gwydion. "It makes no difference. Sleep now, for we rise early tomorrow."

Chapter III

Gurgi

By the time Taran woke, Gwydion had already saddled Melyngar. The cloak Taran had slept in was damp with dew. Every joint ached from his night on the hard ground. With Gwydion's urging, Taran stumbled toward the horse, a white blur in the gray-pink dawn. Gwydion hauled Taran into the saddle behind him, spoke a quiet command, and the white steed moved quickly into the rising mist.

Gwydion was seeking the spot where Taran had last seen Hen Wen. But long before they had reached it, he reined up Melyngar and dismounted. As Taran watched, Gwydion knelt and sighted along the turf.

"Luck is with us," he said. "I think we have struck her trail." Gwydion pointed to a faint circle of trampled grass. "Here she slept, and not too long ago." He strode a few paces forward, scanning every broken twig and blade of grass.

Despite Taran's disappointment at finding the Lord Gwydion dressed in a coarse jacket and mud-spattered boots, he followed the man with growing admiration. Nothing, Taran saw, escaped Gwydion's eyes. Like a lean, gray wolf, he moved silently and easily. A little way on, Gwydion stopped, raised his shaggy head, and narrowed his eyes toward a distant ridge.

"The trail is not clear," he said, frowning. "I can only guess she might have gone down the slope."

"With all the forest to run in," Taran queried, "how can we begin to search? She might have gone anywhere in Prydain."

"Not quite," answered Gwydion. "I may not know where she went, but I can be sure where she did *not* go." He pulled a hunting knife from his belt. "Here, I will show you."

Gwydion knelt and quickly traced lines in the earth. "These are the Eagle Mountains," he said, with a touch of longing in his voice, "in my own land of the north. Here, Great Avren flows. See how it turns west before it reaches the sea. We may have to cross it before our search ends. And this is the River Ystrad. Its valley leads north to Caer Dathyl.

"But see here," Gwydion went on, pointing to the left of the line he had drawn for the River Ystrad, "here is Mount Dragon and the domain of Arawn. Hen Wen would shun this above all. She was too long a captive in Annuvin; she would never venture near it."

"Was Hen in Annuvin?" Taran asked with surprise. "But how . . ."

"Long ago," Gwydion said, "Hen Wen lived among the race of men. She belonged to a farmer who had no idea at all of her powers. And so she might have spent her days as any ordinary pig. But Arawn knew her to be far from ordinary, and of such value that he himself rode out of Annuvin and seized her. What dire things happened while she was prisoner of Arawn—it is better not to speak of them."

"Poor Hen," Taran said, "it must have been terrible for her. But how did she escape?"

"She did not escape," said Gwydion. "She was rescued. A warrior went alone into the depths of Annuvin and brought her back safely."

"That was a brave deed!" Taran cried. "I wish that I . . ."

"The bards of the north still sing of it," Gwydion said. "His name shall never be forgotten."

"Who was it?" Taran demanded.

Gwydion looked closely at him. "Do you not know?" he asked. "Dallben has neglected your education. It was Coll," he said. "Coll Son of Collfrewr."

"Coll!" Taran cried. "Not the same . . ."

"The same," said Gwydion.

"But . . . but . . . ," Taran stammered. "Coll? A hero? But . . . he's so bald!"

Gwydion laughed and shook his head. "Assistant Pig-Keeper," he said, "you have curious notions about heroes. I have never known courage to be judged by the length of a man's hair. Or, for the matter of that, whether he has any hair at all."

Crestfallen, Taran peered at Gwydion's map and said no more.

"Here," continued Gwydion, "not far from Annuvin, lies Spiral Castle. This, too, Hen Wen would avoid at all cost. It is the abode of Queen Achren. She is as dangerous as Arawn himself; as evil as she is beautiful. But there are secrets concerning Achren which are better left untold.

"I am sure," Gwydion went on, "Hen Wen will not go toward Annuvin or Spiral Castle. From what little I can see, she has run straight ahead. Quickly now, we shall try to pick up her trail."

Gwydion turned Melyngar toward the ridge. As they reached the bottom of the slope, Taran heard the waters of Great Avren rushing like wind in a summer storm.

"We must go again on foot," Gwydion said. "Her tracks may show somewhere along here, so we had best move slowly and carefully. Stay close behind me," he ordered. "If you start dashing ahead—and you seem to have that tendency—you will trample out any signs she might have left."

Taran obediently walked a few paces behind. Gwydion made no more sound than the shadow of a bird. Melyngar herself stepped quietly; hardly a twig snapped under her hoofs. Try as he would, Taran could not go as silently. The more careful he attempted to be, the louder the leaves rattled and crackled. Wherever he put his foot, there seemed to be a hole or spiteful branch to trip him up. Even Melyngar turned and gave him a reproachful look.

Taran grew so absorbed in not making noise that he soon lagged far behind Gwydion. On the slope, Taran believed he could make out something round and white. He yearned to be the first to find Hen Wen and he turned aside, clambered through the weeds—to discover nothing more than a boulder.

Disappointed, Taran hastened to catch up with Gwydion. Overhead, the branches rustled. As he stopped and looked up, something fell heavily to the ground behind him. Two hairy and powerful hands locked around his throat.

Whatever had seized him made barking and snorting noises. Taran forced out a cry for help. He struggled with his unseen opponent, twisting, flailing his legs, and throwing himself from one side to the other.

Suddenly he could breathe again. A shape sailed over his head and crashed against a tree trunk. Taran dropped to the ground and began rubbing his neck. Gwydion stood beside him. Sprawled under the tree was the strangest creature Taran had ever seen. He could not be sure whether it was animal or human. He decided it was both. Its hair was so matted and covered with leaves that it looked like an owl's nest in need of housecleaning. It had long, skinny, woolly arms, and a pair of feet as flexible and grimy as its hands.

Gwydion was watching the creature with a look of severity and annoyance. "So it is you," he said. "I ordered you not to hinder me or anyone under my protection."

At this, the creature set up a loud and piteous whining, rolled his eyes, and beat the ground with his palms.

"It is only Gurgi," Gwydion said. "He is always lurking about one place or another. He is not half as ferocious as he looks, nor a quarter as fierce as he should like to be, and more a nuisance than anything else. Somehow, he manages to see most of what happens, and he might be able to help us."

Taran had just begun to catch his breath. He was covered with Gurgi's shedding hair, in addition to the distressing odor of a wet wolfhound.

"O mighty prince," the creature wailed, "Gurgi is sorry; and now he will be smacked on his poor, tender head by the strong hands of this great lord, with fearsome smackings. Yes, yes, that is always the way of it with poor Gurgi. But what honor to be smacked by the greatest of warriors!"

"I have no intention of smacking your poor, tender head," said Gwydion. "But I may change my mind if you do not leave off that whining and sniveling."

"Yes, powerful lord!" Gurgi cried. "See how he obeys rapidly and instantly!" He began crawling about on hands and knees with great agility. Had Gurgi owned a tail, Taran was sure he would have wagged it frantically.

"Then," Gurgi pleaded, "the two strengthful heroes will give Gurgi something to eat? Oh, joyous crunchings and munchings!"

"Afterward," said Gwydion. "When you have answered our questions."

"Oh, afterward!" cried Gurgi. "Poor Gurgi can wait, long, long for his crunchings and munchings. Many years from now, when the great princes revel in their halls— what feastings—they will remember hungry, wretched Gurgi waiting for them."

"How long you wait for your crunchings and munchings," Gwydion said, "depends on how quickly you tell us what we want to know. Have you seen a white pig this morning?"

A crafty look gleamed in Gurgi's close-set little eyes. "For the seeking of a piggy, there are many great lords in the forest, riding with frightening shouts. *They* would not be cruel to starving Gurgi—oh, no—they would feed him . . ."

"They would have your head off your shoulders before you could think twice about it," Gwydion said. "Did one of them wear an antlered mask?"

"Yes, yes!" Gurgi cried. "The great horns! You will save miserable Gurgi from hurtful choppings!" He set up a long and dreadful howling.

"I am losing patience with you," warned Gwydion. "Where is the pig?"

"Gurgi hears these mighty riders," the creature went on. "Oh, yes, with careful listenings from the trees. Gurgi is so quiet and clever, and no one cares about him. But he listens! These great warriors say they have gone to a certain place, but great fire turns them away. They are not pleased, and they still seek a piggy with outcries and horses."

"Gurgi," said Gwydion firmly, "where is the pig?"

"The piggy? Oh, terrible hunger pinches! Gurgi cannot remember. Was there a piggy? Gurgi is fainting and falling into the bushes, his poor, tender head is full of air from his empty belly."

Taran could no longer control his impatience. "Where is Hen Wen, you silly, hairy thing?" he burst out. "Tell us straight off! After the way you jumped on me, you deserve to have your head smacked."

With a moan, Gurgi rolled over on his back and covered his face with his arms.

Gwydion turned severely to Taran. "Had you followed my orders, you would not have been jumped on. Leave him to me. Do not make him any more frightened than he is." Gwydion looked down at Gurgi. "Very well," he asked calmly, "where is she?"

"Oh, fearful wrath!" Gurgi snuffled, "a piggy has gone across the water with swimmings and splashings." He sat upright and waved a woolly arm toward Great Avren.

"If you are lying to me," said Gwydion, "I shall soon find out. Then I will surely come back with wrath."

"Crunchings and munchings now, mighty prince?" asked Gurgi in a high, tiny whimper.

"As I promised you," said Gwydion.

"Gurgi wants the smaller one for munchings," said the creature, with a beady glance at Taran.

"No, you do not," Gwydion said. "He is an Assistant Pig-Keeper and he would disagree with you violently." He unbuckled a saddle-bag and pulled out a few strips of dried meat, which he tossed to Gurgi. "Be off now. Remember, I want no mischief from you."

Gurgi snatched the food, thrust it between his teeth, and scuttled up a tree trunk, leaping from tree to tree until he was out of sight.

"What a disgusting beast," said Taran. "What a nasty, vicious . . . ."

"Oh, he is not bad at heart," Gwydion answered. "He would love to be wicked and terrifying, though he cannot quite manage it. He feels so sorry for himself that it is hard not to be angry with him. But there is no use in doing so."

"Was he telling the truth about Hen Wen?" asked Taran.

"I think he was," Gwydion said. "It is as I feared. The Horned King has ridden to Caer Dallben."

"He burned it!" Taran cried. Until now, he had paid little mind to his home. The thought of the white cottage in flames, his memory of Dallben's beard, and the heroic Coll's bald head touched him all at once. "Dallben and Coll are in peril!"

"Surely not," said Gwydion. "Dallben is an old fox. A beetle could not creep into Caer Dallben without his knowledge. No, I am certain the fire was something Dallben arranged for unexpected visitors.

"Hen Wen is the one in greatest peril. Our quest grows ever more urgent," Gwydion hastily continued. "The Horned King knows she is missing. He will pursue her."

"Then," Taran cried, "we must find her before he does!"

"Assistant Pig-Keeper," said Gwydion, "that has been, so far, your only sensible suggestion."

CHAPTER IV

The Gwythaints

Melyngar bore them swiftly through the fringe of trees lining Great Avren's sloping banks. They dismounted and hurried on foot in the direction Gurgi had indicated. Near a jagged rock, Gwydion halted and gave a cry of triumph. In a patch of clay, Hen Wen's tracks showed as plainly as if they had been carved.

"Good for Gurgi!" exclaimed Gwydion. "I hope he enjoys his crunchings and munchings! Had I known he would guide us so well, I would have given him an extra share.

"Yes, she crossed here," he went on, "and we shall do the same."

Gwydion led Melyngar forward. The air had suddenly grown cold and heavy. The restless Avren ran gray, slashed with white streaks. Clutching Melyngar's saddle horn, Taran stepped gingerly from the bank.

Gwydion strode directly into the water. Taran, thinking it easier to get wet a little at a time, hung back as much as he could—until Melyngar lunged ahead, carrying him with her. His feet sought the river bottom, he stumbled and splashed, while icy waves swirled up to his neck. The current grew stronger, coiling like a gray serpent about Taran's legs. The bottom dropped away sharply; Taran lost his footing and found himself wildly dancing over nothing, as the river seized him greedily.

Melyngar began to swim, her strong legs keeping her afloat and in motion, but the current swung her around; she collided with Taran and forced him under the water.

"Let go the saddle!" Gwydion shouted above the torrent. "Swim clear of her!"

Water flooded Taran's ears and nostrils. With every gasp, the river poured into his lungs. Gwydion struck out after him, soon overtook him, seized him by the hair, and drew him toward the shallows. He heaved the dripping, coughing Taran onto the bank. Melyngar, reaching shore a little farther upstream, trotted down to join them.

Gwydion looked sharply at Taran. "I told you to swim clear. Are all Assistant Pig-Keepers deaf as well as stubborn?"

"I don't know how to swim!" Taran cried, his teeth chattering violently.

"Then why did you not say so before we started across?" Gwydion asked angrily.

"I was sure I could learn," Taran protested, "as soon as I came to do it. If Melyngar hadn't sat on me . . ."

"You must learn to answer for your own folly," said Gwydion. "As for Melyngar, she is wiser now than you can ever hope to become, even should you live to be a man—which seems more and more unlikely."

Gwydion swung into the saddle and pulled up the soaked, bedraggled Taran. Melyngar's hoofs clicked over the stones. Taran, snuffling and shivering, looked toward the waiting hills. High against the blue, three winged shapes wheeled and glided.

Gwydion, whose eyes were everywhere at once, caught sight of them instantly.

"Gwythaints!" he cried, and turned Melyngar sharply to the right. The abrupt change of direction and Melyngar's heaving burst of speed threw Taran off balance. His legs flew up and he landed flat on the pebble-strewn bank.

Gwydion reined in Melyngar immediately. While Taran struggled to his feet, Gwydion seized him like a sack of meal and hauled him to Melyngar's back. The gwythaints, which, at a distance, had seemed no more than dry leaves in the wind, grew larger and larger, as they plunged toward horse and riders. Downward they swooped, their great black wings driving them ever faster. Melyngar clattered up the riverbank. The gwythaints screamed above. At the line of trees, Gwydion thrust Taran from the saddle and leaped down. Dragging him along, Gwydion dropped to the earth under an oak tree's spreading branches.

The glittering wings beat against the foliage. Taran glimpsed curving beaks and talons merciless as daggers. He cried out in terror and hid his face, as the gwythaints veered off and swooped again. The leaves rattled in their wake. The creatures swung upward, hung poised against the sky for an instant, then climbed swiftly and sped westward.

White-faced and trembling, Taran ventured to raise his head. Gwydion strode to the riverbank and stood watching the gwythaints' flight. Taran made his way to his companion's side.

"I had hoped this would not happen," Gwydion said. His face was dark and grave. "Thus far, I have been able to avoid them."

Taran said nothing. He had clumsily fallen off Melyngar at the moment when speed counted most; at the oak, he had behaved like a child. He waited for Gwydion's reprimand, but the warrior's green eyes followed the dark specks.

"Sooner or later they would have found us," Gwydion said. "They are Arawn's spies and messengers, the Eyes of Annuvin, they are called. No one stays long hidden from them. We are lucky they were only scouting and not on a blood hunt." He turned away as the gwythaints at last disappeared. "Now they fly to their iron cages in Annuvin," he said. "Arawn himself will have news of us before this day ends. He will not be idle."

"If only they hadn't seen us," Taran moaned.

"There is no use regretting what has happened," said Gwydion, as they set out again. "One way or another, Arawn would have learned of us. I have no doubt he knew the moment I rode from Caer Dathyl. The gwythaints are not his only servants."

"I think they must be the worst," said Taran, quickening his pace to keep up with Gwydion.

"Far from it," Gwydion said. "The errand of the gwythaints is less to kill than to bring information. For generations they have been trained in this. Arawn understands their language and they are in his power from the moment they leave the egg. Nevertheless, they are creatures of flesh and blood and a sword can answer them.

"There are others to whom a sword means nothing," Gwydion said. "Among them, the Cauldron-Born, who serve Arawn as warriors."

"Are they not men?" Taran asked.

"They were, once," replied Gwydion. "They are the dead whose bodies Arawn steals from their resting places in the long barrows.[8] It is said he steeps them in a cauldron to give them life again—if it can be called life. Like death, they are forever silent; and their only thought is to bring others to the same bondage.

"Arawn keeps them as his guards in Annuvin, for their power wanes the longer and farther they be from their master. Yet from time to time Arawn sends certain of them outside Annuvin to perform his most ruthless tasks.

"These Cauldron-Born are utterly without mercy or pity," Gwydion continued, "for Arawn has worked still greater evil upon them. He has destroyed their remembrance of themselves as living men. They have no memory of tears or laughter, of sorrow or loving kindness. Among all Arawn's deeds, this is one of the cruelest."

After much searching, Gwydion discovered Hen Wen's tracks once more. They led over a barren field, then to a shallow ravine.

"Here they stop," he said, frowning. "Even on stony ground there should be some trace, but I can see nothing."

Slowly and painstakingly he quartered the land on either side of the ravine. The weary and discouraged Taran could barely force himself to put one foot in front of the other, and was glad the dusk obliged Gwydion to halt.

Gwydion tethered Melyngar in a thicket. Taran sank to the ground and rested his head in his hands.

"She has disappeared too completely," said Gwydion, bringing provisions from the saddlebags. "Many things could have happened. Time is too short to ponder each one."

"What can we do, then?" Taran asked fearfully. "Is there no way to find her?"

8. Mounds of earth or stones erected over graves.

"The surest search is not always the shortest," said Gwydion, "and we may need the help of other hands before it is done. There is an ancient dweller in the foothills of Eagle Mountains. His name is Medwyn, and it is said he understands the hearts and ways of every creature in Prydain. He, if anyone, should know where Hen Wen may be hiding."

"If we could find him," Taran began.

"You are right in saying 'if,'" Gwydion answered. "I have never seen him. Others have sought him and failed. We should have only faint hope. But that is better than none at all."

A wind had risen, whispering among the black clusters of trees. From a distance came the lonely baying of hounds. Gwydion sat upright, tense as a bowstring.

"Is it the Horned King?" cried Taran. "Has he followed us this closely?"

Gwydion shook his head. "No hounds bell like those, save the pack of Gwyn the Hunter. And so," he mused, "Gwyn, too, rides abroad."

"Another of Arawn's servants?" asked Taran, his voice betraying his anxiety.

"Gwyn owes allegiance to a lord unknown even to me," Gwydion answered, "and one perhaps greater than Arawn. Gwyn the Hunter rides alone with his dogs, and where he rides, slaughter follows. He has foreknowledge of death and battle, and watches from afar, marking the fall of warriors."

Above the cry of the pack rose the long, clear notes of a hunting horn. Flung across the sky, the sound pierced Taran's breast like a cold blade of terror. Yet, unlike the music itself, the echoes from the hills sang less of fear than of grief. Fading, they sighed that sunlight and birds, bright mornings, warm fires, food and drink, friendship, and all good things had been lost beyond recovery. Gwydion laid a firm hand on Taran's brow.

"Gwyn's music is a warning," Gwydion said. "Take it as a warning, for whatever profit that knowledge may be. But do not listen overmuch to the echoes. Others have done so, and have wandered hopeless ever since."

A whinny from Melyngar broke Taran's sleep. As Gwydion rose and went to her, Taran glimpsed a shadow dart behind a bush. He sat up quickly. Gwydion's back was turned. In the bright moonlight the shadow moved again. Choking back his fear, Taran leaped to his feet and plunged into the undergrowth. Thorns tore at him. He landed on something that grappled frantically. He lashed out, seized what felt like someone's head, and an unmistakable odor of wet wolfhound assailed his nose.

"Gurgi!" Taran cried furiously. "You sneaking . . ." The creature curled into an awkward ball as Taran began shaking him.

"Enough, enough!" Gwydion called. "Do not frighten the wits out of the poor thing!"

"Save your own life next time!" Taran retorted angrily to Gwydion, while Gurgi began howling at the top of his voice. "I should have known a great war-leader needs no help from an Assistant Pig-Keeper!"

"Unlike Assistant Pig-Keepers," Gwydion said gently, "I scorn the help of no man. And you should know better than to jump into thornbushes without first making sure what you will find. Save your anger for a better purpose. . . ." He hesitated and looked carefully at Taran. "Why, I believe you did think my life was in danger."

"If I had known it was only that stupid, silly Gurgi . . ."

"The fact is, you did not," Gwydion said. "So I shall take the intention for the deed. You may be many other things, Taran of Caer Dallben, but I see you are no coward. I offer you my thanks," he added, bowing deeply.

"And what of poor Gurgi?" howled the creature. "No thanks for him—oh, no—

only smackings by great lords! Not even a small munching for helping find a piggy!"

"We didn't find any piggy," Taran replied angrily. "And if you ask me, you know too much about the Horned King. I wouldn't be surprised if you'd gone and told him . . ."

"No, no! The lord of the great horns pursues wise, miserable Gurgi with leaping and galloping. Gurgi fears terrible smackings and whackings. He follows kindly and mighty protectors. Faithful Gurgi will not leave them, never!"

"And what of the Horned King?" Gwydion asked quickly.

"Oh, very angry," whined Gurgi. "Wicked lords ride with mumblings and grumblings because they cannot find a piggy."

"Where are they now?" asked Gwydion.

"Not far. They cross water, but only clever, unthanked Gurgi knows where. And they light fires with fearsome blazings."

"Can you lead us to them?" Gwydion asked. "I would learn their plans."

Gurgi whimpered questioningly. "Crunchings and munchings?"

"I knew he would get around to that," said Taran.

Gwydion saddled Melyngar and, clinging to the shadows, they set out across the moonlit hills. Gurgi led the way, loping ahead, bent forward, his long arms dangling. They crossed one deep valley, then another, before Gurgi halted on a ridge. Below, the wide plain blazed with torches and Taran saw a great ring of flames.

"Crunchings and munchings now?" Gurgi suggested.

Disregarding him, Gwydion motioned for them all to descend the slope. There was little need for silence. A deep, hollow drumming throbbed over the crowded plain. Horses whickered; there came the shouts of men and the clank of weapons. Gwydion crouched in the bracken, watching intently. Around the fiery circle, warriors on high stilts beat upraised swords against their shields.

"What are those men?" Taran whispered. "And the wicker baskets hanging from the posts?"

"They are the Proud Walkers," Gwydion answered, "in a dance of battle, an ancient rite of war from the days when men were no more than savages. The baskets— another ancient custom best forgotten.

"But look there!" Gwydion cried suddenly. "The Horned King! And there," he exclaimed, pointing to the columns of horsemen, "I see the banners of the Cantrev Rheged! The banners of Dau Gleddyn and of Mawr! All the cantrevs of the south! Yes, now I understand!"

Before Gwydion could speak again, the Horned King, bearing a torch, rode to the wicker baskets and thrust the fire into them. Flames seized the osier[9] cages; billows of foul smoke rose skyward. The warriors clashed their shields and shouted together with one voice. From the baskets rose the agonized screams of men. Taran gasped and turned away.

"We have seen enough," Gwydion ordered. "Hurry, let us be gone from here."

Dawn had broken when Gwydion halted at the edge of a barren field. Until now, he had not spoken. Even Gurgi had been silent, his eyes round with terror.

"This is a part of what I have journeyed so far to learn," Gwydion said. His face was grim and pale. "Arawn now dares try force of arms, with the Horned King as his war-leader. The Horned King has raised a mighty host, and they will march against

_____

9. Willow branches used in basketwork.

us. The Sons of Don are ill prepared for so powerful an enemy. They must be warned. I must return to Caer Dathyl immediately."

From a corner of woodland, five mounted warriors cantered into the field. Taran sprang up. The first horseman spurred his mount to a gallop. Melyngar whinnied shrilly. The warriors drew their swords.

Chapter V

The Broken Sword

Gurgi ran off, yelping in terror. Gwydion was at Taran's side as the first rider bore down on them. With a quick gesture, Gwydion thrust a hand into his jacket and pulled out the net of grass. Suddenly the withered wisps grew larger, longer, shimmering and crackling, nearly blinding Taran with streaks of liquid flame. The rider raised his sword. With a shout, Gwydion hurled the dazzling mesh into the warrior's face. Shrieking, the rider dropped his sword and grappled the air. He tumbled from his saddle while the mesh spread over his body and clung to him like an enormous spiderweb.

Gwydion dragged the stupefied Taran to an ash tree and from his belt drew the hunting knife which he thrust in Taran's hand. "This is the only weapon I can spare," he cried. "Use it as well as you can."

His back to the tree, Gwydion faced the four remaining warriors. The great sword swung a glittering arc, the flashing blade sang above Gwydion's head. The attackers drove against them. One horse reared. For Taran there was only a vision of hoofs plunging at his face. The rider chopped viciously at Taran's head, swung around, and struck again. Blindly, Taran lashed out with the knife. Shouting in rage and pain, the rider clutched his leg and wheeled his horse away.

There was no sign of Gurgi, but a white streak sped across the field. Melyngar now had entered the fray. Her golden mane tossing, the white mare whinnied fearsomely and flung herself among the riders. Her mighty flanks dashed against them, crowding, pressing, while the steeds of the war party rolled their eyes in panic. One warrior jerked frantically at his reins to turn his mount away. The animal sank to its haunches. Melyngar reared to her full height; her forelegs churned the air, and her sharp hoofs slashed at the rider, who fell heavily to earth. Melyngar spun about, trampling the cowering horseman.

The three mounted warriors forced their way past the frenzied mare. At the ash tree, Gwydion's blade rang and clashed among the leaves. His legs were as though planted in the earth; the shock of the galloping riders could not dislodge him. His eyes shone with a terrible light.

"Hold your ground but a little while," he called to Taran. The sword whistled, one rider gave a choking cry. The other two did not press the attack, but hung back for a moment.

Hoofbeats pounded over the meadow. Even as the attackers had begun to withdraw, two more riders galloped forward. They reined their horses sharply, dismounted without hesitation, and ran swiftly toward Gwydion. Their faces were pallid; their eyes like stones. Heavy bands of bronze circled their waists, and from these belts hung the black thongs of whips. Knobs of bronze studded their breastplates. They did not bear shield or helmet. Their mouths were frozen in the hideous grin of death.

Gwydion's sword flashed up once more. "Fly!" he cried to Taran. "These are the Cauldron-Born! Take Melyngar and ride from here!"

Taran set himself more firmly against the ash tree and raised his knife. In another instant, the Cauldron-Born were upon them.

For Taran, the horror beating in him like black wings came not from the livid features of the Cauldron warriors or their lightless eyes but from their ghostly silence. The mute men swung their swords, metal grated against metal. The relentless warriors struck and struck again. Gwydion's blade leaped past one opponent's guard and drove deep into his heart. The pale warrior made no outcry. No blood followed as Gwydion ripped the weapon free; the Cauldron-Born shook himself once, without a grimace, and moved again to the attack.

Gwydion stood as a wolf at bay, his green eyes glittering, his teeth bared. The swords of the Cauldron-Born beat against his guard. Taran thrust at one of the livid warriors; a sword point ripped his arm and sent the small knife hurtling into the bracken.

Blood streaked Gwydion's face where an unlucky blow had slashed his cheekbone and forehead. Once, his blade faltered and a Cauldron-Born thrust at his breast. Gwydion turned, taking the sword point in his side. The pale warriors doubled their assault.

The great shaggy head bowed wearily as Gwydion stumbled forward. With a mighty cry, he lunged, then dropped to one knee. With his flagging strength, he fought to raise the blade again. The Cauldron-Born flung aside their weapons, seized him, threw him to the ground, and quickly bound him.

Now the other two warriors approached. One grasped Taran by the throat, the other tied his hands behind him. Taran was dragged to Melyngar and thrown across her back, where he lay side by side with Gwydion.

"Are you badly hurt?" asked Gwydion, striving to raise his head.

"No," Taran said, "but your own wound is grave."

"It is not the wound that pains me," said Gwydion with a bitter smile. "I have taken worse and lived. Why did you not flee, as I ordered? I knew I was powerless against the Cauldron-Born, but I could have held the ground for you. Yet, you fought well enough, Taran of Caer Dallben."

"You are more than a war-leader," Taran whispered. "Why do you keep the truth from me? I remember the net of grass you wove before we crossed Avren. But in your hands today it was no grass I have ever seen."

"I am what I told you. The wisp of grass—yes, it is a little more than that. Dallben himself taught me the use of it."

"You, too, are an enchanter!"

"I have certain skills. Alas, they are not great enough to defend myself against the powers of Arawn. Today," he added, "they were not enough to protect a brave companion."

One of the Cauldron-Born spurred his horse alongside Melyngar. Snatching the whip from his belt, he lashed brutally at the captives.

"Say no more," Gwydion whispered. "You will only bring yourself pain. If we should not meet again, farewell."

The party rode long without a halt. Fording the shallow River Ystrad, the Cauldron-Born pressed tightly on either side of the captives. Taran dared once again to speak to Gwydion, but the lash cut his words short. Taran's throat was parched, waves of dizziness threatened to drown him. He could not be sure how long they had ridden, for he lapsed often into feverish dreams. The sun was still high and he was dimly aware of a hill with a tall, gray fortress looming at its crest. Melyngar's hoofs rang on stones as a courtyard opened before him. Rough hands pulled him from Melyngar's back and drove him, stumbling, down an arching corridor. Gwydion was half-dragged, half-carried before him. Taran tried to catch up with his companion, but the lash of the Cauldron-Born beat him to his knees. A guard hauled him upright again and kicked him forward.

At length, the captives were led into a spacious council chamber. Torches flickered from walls hung with scarlet tapestries. Outside, it had been full daylight; here in the great, windowless hall, the chill and dampness of night rose from the cold flagstones like mist. At the far end of the hall, on a throne carved of black wood, sat a woman. Her long hair glittered silver in the torchlight. Her face was young and beautiful; her pale skin seemed paler still above her crimson robe. Jeweled necklaces hung at her throat, gem-studded bracelets circled her wrists, and heavy rings threw back the flickering torches. Gwydion's sword lay at her feet.

The woman rose quickly. "What shame to my household is this?" she cried at the warriors. "The wounds of these men are fresh and untended. Someone shall answer for this neglect!" She stopped in front of Taran. "And this lad can barely keep his feet." She clapped her hands. "Bring food and wine and medicine for their injuries."

She turned again to Taran. "Poor boy," she said, with a pitying smile, "there has been grievous mischief done today." She touched his wound with a soft, pale hand. At the pressure of her fingers, a comforting warmth filled Taran's aching body. Instead of pain, a delicious sensation of repose came over him, repose as he remembered it from days long forgotten in Caer Dallben, the warm bed of his childhood, drowsy summer afternoons. "How do you come here?" she asked quietly.

"We crossed Great Avren," Taran began. "You see, what had happened . . ."

"Silence!" Gwydion's voice rang out. "She is Achren! She sets a trap for you!"

Taran gasped. For an instant he could not believe such beauty concealed the evil of which he had been warned. Had Gwydion mistaken her? Nevertheless, he shut his lips tightly.

The woman, in surprise, turned to Gwydion. "This is not courtesy to accuse me thus. Your wound excuses your conduct, but there is no need for anger. Who are you? Why do you . . ."

Gwydion's eyes flashed. "You know me as well as I know you, Achren!" He spat the name through his bleeding lips.

"I have heard Lord Gwydion was traveling in my realm. Beyond that . . ."

"Arawn sent his warriors to slay us," cried Gwydion, "and here they stand in your council hall. Do you say that you know nothing more?"

"Arawn sent warriors to find, not slay you," answered Achren, "or you would not be alive at this moment. Now that I see you face to face," she said, her eyes on Gwydion, "I am glad such a man is not bleeding out his life in a ditch. For there is much we have to discuss, and much that you can profit from."

"If you would treat[1] with me," said Gwydion, "unbind me and return my sword."

"You make demands?" Achren asked gently. "Perhaps you do not understand. I offer you something you cannot have even if I loosened your hands and gave back your weapon. By that, Lord Gwydion, I mean—your life."

"In exchange for what?"

"I had thought to bargain with another life," said Achren, glancing at Taran. "But

---

1. Negotiate.

I see he is of no consequence, alive or dead. No," she said, "there are other, pleasanter ways to bargain. You do not know me as well as you think, Gwydion. There is no future for you beyond these gates. Here, I can promise . . ."

"Your promises reek of Annuvin!" cried Gwydion. "I scorn them. It is no secret what you are!"

Achren's face turned livid. Hissing, she struck at Gwydion and her blood-red nails raked his cheek. Achren unsheathed Gwydion's sword; holding it in both hands she drove the point toward his throat, stopping only a hairbreadth from it. Gwydion stood proudly, his eyes blazing.

"No," cried Achren, "I will not slay you; you shall come to wish I had, and beg the mercy of a sword! You scorn my promises! This promise will be well kept!"

Achren raised the sword above her head and smote with all her force against a stone pillar. Sparks flashed, the blade rang unbroken. With a scream of rage, she dashed the weapon to the ground.

The sword shone, still undamaged. Achren seized it again, gripping the sharp blade itself until her hands ran scarlet. Her eyes rolled back into her head, her lips moved and twisted. A thunderclap filled the hall, a light burst like a crimson sun, and the broken weapon fell in pieces to the ground.

"So shall I break you!" Achren shrieked. She raised her hand to the Cauldron-Born and called out in a strange, harsh language.

The pale warriors strode forward and dragged Taran and Gwydion from the hall. In a dark passageway of stone, Taran struggled with his captors, fighting to reach Gwydion's side. One of the Cauldron-Born brought a whip handle down on Taran's head.

CHAPTER VI

Eilonwy

Taran came to his senses on a pile of dirty straw, which smelled as though Gurgi and all his ancestors had slept on it. A few feet above him, pale yellow sunlight shone through a grating; the feeble beam ended abruptly on a wall of rough, damp stone. The shadows of bars lay across the tiny patch of light; instead of brightening the cell, the wan rays made it appear only more grim and closed in. As Taran's eyes grew accustomed to this yellow twilight, he made out a heavy, studded portal with a slot at the base. The cell itself was not more than three paces square.

His head ached; since his hands were still bound behind him, he could do no more than guess at the large and throbbing lump. What had happened to Gwydion he dared not imagine. After the Cauldron warrior had struck him, Taran had regained consciousness only a few moments before slipping once again into whirling darkness. In that brief time, he vaguely remembered opening his eyes and finding himself slung over a guard's back. His confused recollection included a dim corridor with doors on either side. Gwydion had called out to him once—or so Taran believed—he could not recall his friend's words, perhaps even that had been part of the nightmare. He supposed Gwydion had been cast in another dungeon; Taran fervently hoped so. He could not shake off the memory of Achren's livid face and horrible screaming, and he feared she might have ordered Gwydion slain.

Still, there was good reason to hope his companion lived. Achren could easily have cut his throat as he braved her in the council hall, yet she had held back. Thus, she intended to keep Gwydion alive; perhaps, Taran thought wretchedly, Gwydion would be better off dead. The idea of the proud figure lying a broken corpse filled Taran with grief that quickly turned to rage. He staggered to his feet, lurched to the door, kicking it, battering himself against it with what little strength remained to him. In despair, he sank to the damp ground, his head pressed against the unyielding oaken planks. He rose again after a few moments and kicked at the walls. If Gwydion were, by chance, in an adjoining cell, Taran hoped he would hear this signal. But he judged, from the dull and muffled sound, that the walls were too thick for his feeble tapping to penetrate.

As he turned away, a flashing object fell through the grating and dropped to the stone floor. Taran stooped. It was a ball of what seemed to be gold. Perplexed, he looked upward. From the grating, a pair of intensely blue eyes looked back at him.

"Please," said a girl's voice, light and musical, "my name is Eilonwy and if you don't mind, would you throw my bauble[2] to me? I don't want you to think I'm a baby, playing with a silly bauble, because I'm not; but sometimes there's absolutely nothing else to do around here and it slipped out of my hands when I was tossing it . . ."

"Little girl," Taran interrupted, "I don't . . ."

"But I am not a little girl," Eilonwy protested. "Haven't I just been and finished telling you? Are you slow-witted? I'm so sorry for you. It's terrible to be dull and stupid. What's your name?" she went on. "It makes me feel funny not knowing someone's name. Wrongfooted, you know, or as if I had three thumbs on one hand, if you see what I mean. It's clumsy . . ."

"I am Taran of Caer Dallben," Taran said, then wished he had not. This, he realized, could be another trap.

"That's lovely," Eilonwy said gaily. "I'm very glad to meet you. I suppose you're a lord, or a warrior, or a war-leader, or a bard, or a monster. Though we haven't had any monsters for a long time."

"I am none of those," said Taran, feeling quite flattered that Eilonwy should have taken him for any one of them.

"What else is there?"

"I am an Assistant Pig-Keeper," Taran said. He bit his lip as soon as the words were out; then, to excuse his loose tongue, told himself it could do no harm for the girl to know that much.

"How fascinating," Eilonwy said. "You're the first we've ever had—unless that poor fellow in the other dungeon is one, too."

"Tell me of him," Taran said quickly. "Is he alive?"

"I don't know," said Eilonwy. "I peeked through the grating, but I couldn't tell. He doesn't move at all, but I should imagine he is alive; otherwise, Achren would have fed him to the ravens. Now, please, if you don't mind, it's right at your feet."

"I can't pick up your bauble," Taran said, "because my hands are tied."

The blue eyes looked surprised. "Oh? Well, that would account for it. Then I suppose I shall have to come in and get it."

"You can't come in and get it," said Taran wearily. "Don't you see I'm locked up here?"

"Of course I do," said Eilonwy. "What would be the point of having someone in a dungeon if they weren't locked up? Really, Taran of Caer Dallben, you surprise me with some of your remarks. I don't mean to hurt your feelings by asking, but is Assistant Pig-Keeper the kind of work that calls for a great deal of intelligence?"

Something beyond the grating and out of Taran's vision swooped down and the

2. Child's spherical toy; also a jester's staff.

blue eyes disappeared suddenly. Taran heard what he took to be a scuffle, then a high-pitched little shriek, followed by a larger shriek and a moment or two of loud smacking.

The blue eyes did not reappear. Taran flung himself back on the straw. After a time, in the dreadful silence and loneliness of the tiny cell, he began suddenly to wish Eilonwy would come back. She was the most confusing person he had ever met, and surely as wicked as everyone else in the castle—although he could not quite bring himself to believe it completely. Nevertheless, he longed for the sound of another voice, even Eilonwy's prattling.

The grating above his head darkened. Night poured into the cell in a black, chilly wave. The slot in the heavy portal rattled open. Taran heard something being slid into the cell and crawled toward it. It was a shallow bowl. He sniffed carefully and finally ventured to touch his tongue to it, fearing all the while that it might be poisoned food. It was not food at all, but only a little water, warm and musty. His throat was so parched that Taran disregarded the taste, thrust his face into the bowl, and drank it dry.

He curled up and tried to sleep away his pain; the tight thongs pinched, but his swollen hands were mercifully numb. Sleep brought only nightmares and he roused to find himself shouting aloud. He settled down once more. Now there was a rasping sound under the straw.

Taran stumbled to his feet. The rasping grew louder.

"Move away!" cried a faint voice.

Taran looked around him, dumbfounded.

"Get off the stone!"

He stepped backward. The voice was coming from the straw.

"Well, I can't lift it with you standing on it, you silly Assistant Pig-Keeper!" the muffled voice complained.

Frightened and puzzled, Taran jumped to the wall. The pallet began rising upward. A loose flagstone was lifted, pushed aside, and a slender shadow emerged as if from the ground itself.

"Who are you?" Taran shouted.

"Who did you expect?" said the voice of Eilonwy. "And please don't make such a racket. I told you I was coming back. Oh, there's my bauble . . ." The shadow bent and picked up the luminous ball.

"Where are you?" cried Taran. "I can see nothing . . ."

"Is that what's bothering you?" Eilonwy asked. "Why didn't you say so in the first place?" Instantly, a bright light filled the cell. It came from the golden sphere in the girl's hand.

Taran blinked with amazement. "What's that?" he cried.

"It's my bauble," said Eilonwy. "How many times do I have to tell you?"

"But—but it lights up!"

"What did you think it would do? Turn into a bird and fly away?"

Eilonwy, as the bewildered Taran saw her for the first time, had, in addition to blue eyes, long hair of reddish gold reaching to her waist. Her face, though smudged, was delicate, elfin, with high cheekbones. Her short, white robe, mud-stained, was girdled with silver links. A crescent moon of silver hung from a fine chain around her neck. She was one or two years younger than he, but fully as tall. Eilonwy put the glowing sphere on the floor, went quickly to Taran, and unknotted the thongs that bound him.

"I meant to come back sooner," Eilonwy said. "But Achren caught me talking to you. She started to give me a whipping. I bit her.

"Then she locked me in one of the chambers, deep underground," Eilonwy went on, pointing to the flagstones. "There are hundreds of them under Spiral Castle, and all kinds of galleries and little passages, like a honeycomb. Achren didn't build them; this castle, they say, once belonged to a great king. She thinks she knows all the passageways. But she doesn't. She hasn't been in half of them. Can you imagine Achren going through a tunnel? She's older than she looks, you know." Eilonwy giggled. "But I know every one, and most of them connect with each other. It took me longer in the dark, though, because I didn't have my bauble."

"You mean you live in this terrible place?" Taran asked.

"Naturally," Eilonwy said. "You don't imagine I'd want to visit here, do you?"

"Is—is Achren your mother?" Taran gasped and drew back fearfully.

"Certainly not!" cried the girl. "I am Eilonwy Daughter of Angharad, Daughter of Regat Daughter of—oh, it's such a bother going through all that. My ancestors," she said proudly, "are the Sea People. I am of the blood of Llyr Half-Speech, the Sea King. Achren is my aunt, though sometimes I don't think she's really my aunt at all."

"Then what are you doing here?"

"I said I live here," Eilonwy answered. "It must take a lot of explaining before you understand anything. My parents died and my kinsmen sent me here so Achren could teach me to be an enchantress. It's a family tradition, don't you see? The boys are war-leaders, and the girls are enchantresses."

"Achren is leagued with Arawn of Annuvin," cried Taran. "She is an evil, loathsome creature!"

"Oh, everybody knows that," said Eilonwy. "Sometimes I wish my kinsmen had sent me to someone else. But I think they must have forgotten about me by now."

She noticed a deep slash on his arm. "Where did you get that?" she asked. "I don't think you know much about fighting if you let yourself get knocked about and cut up so badly. But I don't imagine Assistant Pig-Keepers are often called on to do that sort of thing." The girl tore a strip from the hem of her robe and began binding Taran's wound.

"I didn't *let* myself be cut up," Taran said angrily. "That's Arawn's doing, or your aunt's—I don't know which and I don't care. One is no better than the other."

"I hate Achren!" Eilonwy burst out. "She is a mean, spiteful person. Of all the people who come here, you're the only one who's the least bit agreeable to talk to— and she had you damaged!"

"That's not the end of it," Taran said. "She means to kill my friend."

"If she does that," said Eilonwy, "I'm sure she'll include you. Achren doesn't do things by halves. It would be a shame if you were killed. I should be very sorry. I know I wouldn't like it to happen to me . . ."

"Eilonwy, listen," Taran interrupted, "if there are tunnels and passages under the castle—can you get to the other cells? Is there a way outside?"

"Of course there is," Eilonwy said. "If there's a way in, there has to be a way out, doesn't there?"

"Will you help us?" Taran asked. "It is important for us to be free of this place. Will you show us the passage?"

"Let you escape?" Eilonwy giggled. "Wouldn't Achren be furious at that!" She tossed her head. "It would serve her right for whipping me and trying to lock me up. Yes, yes," she went on, her eyes dancing, "that's a wonderful idea. I would love to see her face when she comes down to find you. Yes, that would be more fun than anything I could think of. Can you imagine . . ."

"Listen carefully," Taran said, "is there a way you can take me to my companion?"

Eilonwy shook her head. "That would be very hard to do. You see, some of the galleries connect with the ones leading to the cells, but when you try to go across, what happens is that you start to run into passages that . . ."

"Never mind, then," Taran said. "Can I join him in one of the passageways?"

"I don't see why you want to do that," said the girl. "It would be so much simpler if I just go and let him out and have him wait for you beyond the castle. I don't understand why you want to complicate things; it's bad enough for two people crawling about, but with three, you can imagine what that would be. And you can't possibly find your way by yourself."

"Very well," Taran said impatiently. "Free my companion first. I only hope he is well enough to move. If he isn't, then you must come and tell me right away and I'll think of some means of carrying him.

"And there is a white horse, Melyngar," Taran went on. "I don't know what's been done with her."

"She would be in the stable," Eilonwy said. "Isn't that where you'd usually find a horse?"

"Please," Taran said, "you must get her, too. And weapons for us. Will you do that?"

Eilonwy nodded quickly. "Yes, that should be very exciting." She giggled again. She picked up the glowing ball, cupped it in her hands, and once again the cell was dark. The stone grated shut and only Eilonwy's silvery laugh lingered behind.

Taran paced back and forth. For the first time, he felt some hope; though he wondered how much he could count on this scatterbrained girl. She was likely to forget what she started out to do. Worse, she might betray him to Achren. It might be another trap, a new torment that promised him freedom only to snatch it away, but even so, Taran decided, they could be no worse off.

To save his energy, he lay down on the straw and tried to relax. His bandaged arm no longer pained him, and while he was still hungry and thirsty, the water he had drunk had taken some of the edge from his discomfort.

He had no idea how long it would take to travel through the underground galleries. But as time passed, he grew more anxious. He worked at the flagstone the girl had used. It would not move, though Taran's efforts bloodied his fingers. He sank again into dark, endless waiting. Eilonwy did not return.

CHAPTER VII

The Trap

From the corridor, a faint sound grew louder. Taran hastened to press his ear against the slot in the portal. He heard the heavy tread of marching feet, the rattle of weapons. He straightened and stood with his back to the wall. The girl had betrayed him. He cast about for some means to defend himself, for he had determined they would not take him easily. For the sake of having something in his hands, Taran picked up the dirty straw and held it ready to fling; it was a pitiable defense, and he wished desperately for Gwydion's power to set it ablaze.

The footsteps continued. He feared, then, they would enter the other cell. He breathed a sigh of relief when they did not stop but faded away toward what he imagined to be the far end of the corridor. Perhaps the guard was being changed.

He turned away, certain Eilonwy would not be back, and furious with her and her false promises. She was a rattlebrained fool who would undoubtedly giggle and take it as a great joke when the Cauldron-Born came for him. He buried his face in his hands. He could hear her chatter even now. Taran started up again. The voice he heard was real.

"*Must* you always sit on the wrong stone?" it said. "You're too heavy to lift."

Taran jumped up and hurriedly cleared the straw away. The flagstone was raised. The light from the golden ball was dim now, but enough for him to see that Eilonwy looked pleased with herself.

"Your companion is free," she whispered. "And I took Melyngar from the stable. They are hidden in the woods outside the castle. It's all done now," Eilonwy said gleefully. "They're waiting for you. So if you get a move on and stop looking as if you'd forgotten your own name, we can go and meet them."

"Did you find weapons?" Taran asked.

"Well, no. I didn't have a chance to look," Eilonwy said. "Really," she added, "you can't expect me to do everything, can you?"

Eilonwy held the glowing sphere close to the stone floor. "Go first," she said. "Then I'll come down after, so I can put the stone back in place. Then, when Achren sends to have you killed, there won't be any trace at all. She'll think you disappeared into thin air—and that will make it all the more vexing. I know it isn't nice to vex people on purpose—it's like handing them a toad—but this is much too good to miss and I may never have another chance at it."

"Achren will know you let us escape," Taran said.

"No, she won't," said Eilonwy, "because she'll think I'm still locked up. And if she doesn't know I can get out, she can't know I was here. But it's very thoughtful of you to say that. It shows a kind heart, and I think that's so much more important than being clever."

While Eilonwy continued to chatter away, Taran lowered himself into the narrow opening. The passage was low, he discovered, and he was obliged to crouch almost on hands and knees.

Eilonwy moved the stone into place and then began to lead the way. The glow from the sphere showed walls of hard-packed earth. As Taran hunched along, other galleries opened up on either side.

"Be sure you follow me," Eilonwy called. "Don't go into any of those. Some of them branch off and some of them don't go anywhere at all. You'd get lost, and that would be a useless thing to do if you're trying to escape."

The girl moved so quickly Taran had difficulty keeping up with her. Twice he stumbled over loose stones in the passage, clutched at the ground, and pitched forward. The little light bobbed ahead, while behind him long fingers of darkness grasped his heels. He could understand why Achren's fortress was called Spiral Castle. The narrow, stifling galleries turned endlessly; he could not be sure whether they were making real progress or whether the tunnel was merely doubling back on itself.

The earthen ceiling trembled with racing footsteps.

"We're just below the guardroom," Eilonwy whispered. "Something's happening up there. Achren doesn't usually turn out the guard in the middle of the night."

"They must have gone to the cells," Taran said. "There was a lot of commotion just before you came. They surely know we're gone."

"You must be a very important Assistant Pig-Keeper," said Eilonwy with a small laugh. "Achren wouldn't go to all that trouble unless . . ."

"Hurry," Taran urged. "If she puts a guard around the castle we'll never get out."

"I wish you'd stop worrying," Eilonwy said. "You sound as if you were having your toes twisted. Achren can set out all the guards she wants. She doesn't know where the mouth of the tunnel is. And it's hidden so well an owl couldn't see it. After all, you don't think I'd march you out the front gate, do you?"

Despite her chattering, Eilonwy kept a rapid pace. Taran bent close to the ground, moving half by touch, keeping his eyes on the faint glow; he skidded past sharp turns, fetched up against rough walls, skinned his knees, then had to move twice as fast to regain the ground he had lost. At another bend in the passageway, Eilonwy's light wavered and dropped out of sight. In the moment of darkness, Taran lost his footing as the ground rose steeply on one side. He fell and rolled. Before he could recover his balance, he was sliding rapidly downward in a shower of loose stones and earth. He collided with an outcropping of rock, rolled again, and dropped suddenly into the darkness.

He landed heavily on flat stones, legs twisted under him. Taran climbed painfully to his feet and shook his head to clear it. Suddenly he realized he was standing upright. Eilonwy and her light could not be seen. He called as loudly as he dared.

After a few moments he heard a scraping above him and saw the faint reflection of the golden ball. "Where are you?" called the girl. Her voice seemed quite distant. "Oh—I see. Part of the tunnel's given way. You must have slipped into a crevice."

"It's not a crevice," Taran called. "I've fallen all the way down into something and it's deep. Can't you put the light into it? I've got to get up again."

There were more scraping noises. "Yes," Eilonwy said, "you have got yourself into a mess. The ground's all broken through here, and below there's a big stone, like a shelf over your head. How *did* you ever manage to do that?"

"I don't know how," replied Taran, "but I certainly didn't do it on purpose."

"It's strange," Eilonwy said. "This wasn't here when I came through the first time. All that tramping must have jarred something loose; it's hard to say. I don't think these tunnels are half as solid as they look, and neither is the castle, for the matter of that; Achren's always complaining about things leaking and doors not closing right . . ."

"Do stop that prattling," cried Taran, clasping his head. "I don't want to hear about leaks and doors. Show a light so I can climb out of here."

"That's the trouble," the girl said. "I'm not quite sure you can. You see, that shelf of stone juts out so far and goes down so steeply. Can you manage to reach it?"

Taran raised his arms and jumped as high as he could. He could find no handhold. From Eilonwy's description, and from the massive shadow above, he feared the girl was right. He could not reach the stone and, even if he could have, its sharp downward pitch would have made it impossible to climb. Taran groaned with despair.

"Go on without me," he said. "Warn my companion the castle is alerted . . ."

"And what do you intend doing? You can't just sit there like a fly in a jug. That isn't going to help matters at all."

"It doesn't make any difference about me," Taran said. "You can find a rope and come back when things are safe . . ."

"Who knows when that will be? If Achren sees me, there's no telling what might happen. And suppose I couldn't get back? You'd turn into a skeleton while you're waiting—I don't know how long it takes for people to turn into skeletons, though I imagine it would need some time—and you'd be worse off than before."

"What else am I to do?" cried Taran.

Eilonwy's talk of skeletons made his blood run cold. He recalled, then, the sound of Gwyn the Hunter's horn and the memory of it filled him with grief and fear. He bowed his head and turned his face to the rough wall.

"That's very noble of you," said Eilonwy, "but I don't think it's really necessary, not yet, at any rate. If Achren's warriors come out and start beating the woods, I hardly think your friend would stay around waiting. He'd go and hide and find you later, or so I should imagine. That would be the sensible thing to do. Of course, if he's an Assistant Pig-Keeper, too, it's hard to guess how his mind would work."

"He's not an Assistant Pig-Keeper," Taran said. "He's . . . well, it's none of your business what he is."

"That's not a very polite thing to say. Well, nevertheless . . . ," Eilonwy's voice dismissed the matter. "The main thing is to get you out."

"There's nothing we can do," Taran said. "I'm caught here, and locked up better than Achren ever planned."

"Don't say that. I could tear up my robe and plait it into a cord—though I'll tell you right away I wouldn't enjoy crawling around tunnels without any clothes on. But I don't think it would be long enough or strong enough. I suppose I could cut off my hair, if I had a pair of shears, and add it in—no, that still wouldn't do. Won't you please be quiet for a while and let me think? Wait, I'm going to drop my bauble down to you. Here, catch!"

The golden sphere came hurtling over the ledge. Taran caught it in mid-air.

"Now then," Eilonwy called, "what's down there? Is it just a pit of some kind?"

Taran raised the ball above his head. "Why, it's not a hole at all!" he cried. "It's a kind of chamber. There's a tunnel here, too." He took a few paces. "I can't see where it ends. It's big . . ."

Stones rattled behind him; an instant later, Eilonwy dropped to the ground. Taran stared at her in disbelief.

"You fool!" he shouted. "You addlepated . . . What have you done? Now both of us are trapped! And you talk about sense! You haven't . . ."

Eilonwy smiled at him and waited until he ran out of breath. "Now," she said, "if you've quite finished, let me explain something very simple to you. If there's a tunnel, it has to go someplace. And wherever it goes, there's a very good chance it will be better than where we are now."

"I didn't mean to call you names," Taran said, "but," he added sorrowfully, "there was no reason for you to put yourself in danger."

"There you go again," Eilonwy said. "I promised to help you escape and that's what I'm doing. I understand about tunnels and I shouldn't be surprised if this one followed the same direction as the one above. It doesn't have half as many galleries coming off it. And besides, it's a lot more comfortable."

Eilonwy took the glowing sphere from Taran's hand and stepped forward into the new passageway. Still doubtful, Taran followed.

CHAPTER VIII

The Barrow

As Eilonwy had said, the passageway was more comfortable, for they could walk side by side without crouching and scuttling like rabbits in a warren. Unlike those of the upper galleries, the walls were lined with huge, flat stones; the ceiling was formed of even larger stones, whose weight was supported by upright slabs set at intervals along the square corridor. The air, too, smelled slightly better; musty, as if it had lain unstirred for ages, but without the choking closeness of the tunnels.

None of this comforted Taran greatly. Eilonwy herself admitted she had never explored the passage; her blithe confidence did not convince him she had the slightest notion of where she was going. Nevertheless, the girl hurried along, her sandals tapping and echoing, the golden light of the bauble casting its rays through shadows that hung like cobwebs.

They passed a few side galleries which Eilonwy ignored. "We'll go straight to the end of this one," she announced. "There's bound to be something there."

Taran had begun wishing himself back in the chamber. "We shouldn't have come this far," he said, with a frown. "We should have stayed and found some way to climb out; now you don't even know how long it will be before this passage stops. We might go on tramping for days."

Something else troubled him. After all their progress, it seemed the passageway should now follow an upward direction.

"The tunnel's supposed to bring us out above ground," Taran said. "But we haven't stopped going down. We aren't coming out at all; we're only going deeper and deeper."

Eilonwy paid no attention to his remarks.

But she was soon obliged to. Within another few paces, the corridor stopped abruptly, sealed by a wall of boulders.

"This is what I feared," cried Taran, dismayed. "We have gone to the end of your tunnel, that you know so much about, and this is what we find. Now we can only go back; we've lost all our time and we're no better off than when we started." He turned away while the girl stood looking curiously at the barrier.

"I can't understand," said Eilonwy, "why anyone would go to the trouble of building a tunnel and not have it go anyplace. It must have been a terrible amount of work for whoever it was to dig it all and set in the rocks. Why do you suppose . . . ?"

"I don't know! And I wish you'd stop wondering about things that can't make any difference to us. I'm going back," Taran said. "I don't know how I'm going to climb onto that shelf, but I can certainly do it a lot more easily than digging through a wall."

"Well," said Eilonwy, "it is very strange and all. I'm sure I don't know where we are."

"I knew we'd end up being lost. I could have told you that."

"I didn't say I was lost," the girl protested. "I only said I didn't know where I was. There's a big difference. When you're lost, you really don't know where you are. When you just don't happen to know where you are at the moment, that's something else. I know I'm underneath Spiral Castle, and that's quite good for a start."

"You're splitting hairs," Taran said. "Lost is lost. You're worse than Dallben."

"Who is Dallben?"

"Dallben is my—oh, never mind!" His face grim, Taran began retracing his steps.

Eilonwy hurried to join him. "We could have a look into one of the side passageways," she called.

Taran disregarded the suggestion. Nevertheless, approaching the next branching gallery, he slowed his steps and peered briefly into the gloom.

"Go ahead," Eilonwy urged. "Let's try this one. It seems as good as any."

"Hush!" Taran bent his head and listened intently. From a distance came a faint whispering and rustling. "There's something . . ."

"Well, by all means let's find out what," said Eilonwy, prodding Taran in the back. "Go ahead, will you?"

Taran took a few cautious steps. The passage here was lower and seemed to slope still farther down. With Eilonwy beside him, he continued gingerly, setting each foot carefully, remembering the sudden, sickening fall that had brought him there in the first place. The whispering became a high keening, a wail of torment. It was as though voices had been spun out like threads, twisted taut, ready to snap. An icy current wove through the air, carrying along with it hollow sighs and a swell of dull mutterings. There were other sounds, too; raspings and shriekings, like sword points dragged over stones. Taran felt his hands tremble; he hesitated a moment and gestured for Eilonwy to stay behind him.

"Give me the light," he whispered, "and wait for me here."

"Do you think it's ghosts?" Eilonwy asked. "I don't have any beans to spit at them, and that's about the only thing that will really do for a ghost. But you know I don't think it's ghosts at all. I've never heard one, though I suppose they could sound like that if they wanted to, but I don't see why they should bother. No, I think it's wind making all those noises."

"Wind? How could there be . . . Wait," Taran said. "You may be right, at that. There might be an opening." Closing his ears to the horrifying sounds and preferring to think of them as draughts of air rather than spectral voices, Taran quickened his pace. Eilonwy, paying no attention to his order to wait, strode along with him.

They soon arrived at the end of the passage. Once more, fallen stones blocked their way, but this time there was a narrow, jagged gap. From it, the wailing grew louder, and Taran felt a cold ribbon of air on his face. He thrust the light into the opening, but even the golden rays could not pierce the curtain of shadows. Taran slid cautiously past the barrier; Eilonwy followed.

They entered a low-ceilinged chamber, and as they did, the light flickered under the weight of the darkness. At first, Taran could make out only indistinct shapes, touched with a feeble green glow. The voices screamed in trembling rage. Despite the chill wind, Taran's forehead was clammy. He raised the light and took another step forward. The shapes grew clearer. Now he distinguished outlines of shields hanging from the walls and piles of swords and spears. His foot struck something. He bent to look and sprang back again, stifling a cry. It was the withered corpse of a man—a warrior fully armed. Another lay beside him, and another, in a circle of ancient dead guarding a high stone slab on which a shadowy figure lay at full length.

Eilonwy paid scant attention to the warriors, having found something more interesting to her. "I'm sure Achren hasn't any idea all this is here," she whispered, pointing to heaps of otter-skin robes and great earthen jars overflowing with jewels. Weapons glistened amid stacks of helmets; woven baskets held brooches, collarpieces, and chains.

"She'd have hauled it out long ago; she loves jewelry, you know, though it doesn't become her one bit."

"Surely it is the barrow of the king who built this castle," Taran said in a hushed voice. He stepped past the warriors and drew near the figure on the slab. Rich raiment clothed the body; polished stones glowed in his broad belt. The clawed hands still grasped the jeweled hilt of a sword, as if ready to unsheathe it. Taran recoiled in fear and horror. The skull seemed to grimace in defiance, daring a stranger to despoil the royal treasures.

As Taran turned, a gust of wind caught at his face. "I think there is a passage," he called, "there, in the far wall." He ran in the direction of the ghostly cries.

Close to the ground, a tunnel opened; he could smell fresh air, and his lungs drank deeply. "Hurry," he urged.

Taran snatched a sword from a warrior's bony hand and scrambled into the tunnel.

The tunnel was the narrowest they had encountered. Flat on his belly, Taran squeezed and fought his way over the loose stones. Behind him, he heard Eilonwy gasping and struggling. Then a new sound began, a distant booming and throbbing. The earth shuddered as the pounding increased. Suddenly the passageway convulsed, the hidden roots of trees sprang up, the ground split beneath Taran, heaving and crumbling. In another instant, he was flung out at the bottom of a rocky slope.

A great crash resounded deep within the hill. Spiral Castle, high above him, was bathed in blue fire. A sudden gale nearly battered Taran to the ground. A tree of lightning crackled in the sky. Behind him, Eilonwy called for help.

She was half in, half out of the narrow passage. As Taran wrestled with the fallen stones, the walls of Spiral Castle shook like gray rags. The towers lurched madly. Taran clawed away clumps of earth and roots.

"I'm all tangled up with the sword," Eilonwy panted. "The scabbard's caught on something."

Taran heaved at the last rock. "What sword?" he said through gritted teeth. He seized Eilonwy under the arms and pulled her free.

"Oof!" she gasped. "I feel as if I had all my bones taken apart and put together wrong. The sword? You said you needed weapons, didn't you? And you took one, so I thought I might as well, too."

In a violent explosion that seemed ripped from the very center of the earth, Spiral Castle crumbled in on itself. The mighty stones of its walls split like twigs, their jagged ends thrusting at the sky. Then a deep silence fell. The wind was still; the air oppressive.

"Thank you for saving my life," said Eilonwy. "For an Assistant Pig-Keeper, I must say you are quite courageous. It's wonderful when people surprise you that way.

"I wonder what happened to Achren," she went on. "She'll really be furious," she added with a delighted laugh, "and probably blame everything on me, for she's always punishing me for things I haven't even thought of yet."

"If Achren is under those stones, she'll never punish anyone again," Taran said. "But I don't think we'd better stay to find out." He buckled on his sword.

The blade Eilonwy had taken from the barrow was too long for the girl to wear comfortably at her waist, so she had slung it from her shoulder.

Taran looked at the weapon with surprise. "Why—that's the sword the king was holding."

"Naturally," said Eilonwy. "It should be the best one, shouldn't it?" She picked up the glowing sphere. "We're at the far side of the castle, what used to be the castle. Your friend is down there, among those trees—assuming he waited for you. I'd be surprised if he did, with all this going on . . ."

They ran toward the grove. Ahead, Taran saw the shadowy forms of a cloaked figure and a white horse. "There they are!" he cried.

"Gwydion!" he called. "Gwydion!"

The moon swung from behind the clouds. The figure turned. Taran stopped short in the sudden brightness and his jaw dropped. He had never seen this man before.

CHAPTER IX

Fflewddur Fflam

Taran's sword leaped out. The man in the cloak hurriedly dropped Melyngar's bridle and darted behind a tree. Taran swung the blade. Pieces of bark sprayed the air.

While the stranger ducked back and forth, Taran slashed and thrust, hacking wildly at bushes and branches.

"You're not Gwydion!" he shouted.

"Never claimed I was," the stranger shouted back. "If you think I'm Gwydion, you're dreadfully mistaken."

"Come out of there," Taran ordered, thrusting again.

"Certainly not while you're swinging that enormous—here now, watch that! Great Belin, I was safer in Achren's dungeon!"

"Come out now or you won't be able to," Taran shouted. He redoubled his attack, ripping furiously through the underbrush.

"Truce! Truce!" called the stranger. "You can't smite an unarmed man!"

Eilonwy, who had been a few paces behind Taran, ran up and seized his arm. "Stop it!" she cried. "That's no way to treat your friend, after I went to all the bother of rescuing him."

Taran shook off Eilonwy. "What treachery is this!" he shouted. "You left my companion to die! You've been with Achren all along. I should have known it. You're no better than she is!" With a cry of anguish, he raised his sword.

Eilonwy ran sobbing into the woods. Taran dropped the blade and stood with bowed head.

The stranger ventured from behind the tree. "Truce?" he inquired again. "Believe me, if I'd known it was going to cause all this trouble I wouldn't have listened to that redheaded girl."

Taran did not raise his head.

The stranger took a few more cautious steps. "Humblest apologies for disappointing you," he said. "I'm awfully flattered you mistook me for Prince Gwydion. There's hardly any resemblance, except possibly a certain air of . . ."

"I do not know who you are," Taran said bitterly. "I do know that a brave man has bought your life for you."

"I am Flewddur Fflam[3] Son of Godo," the stranger said, bowing deeply, "a bard of the harp at your service."

"I have no need of bards," Taran said. "A harp will not bring my companion to life."

"Lord Gwydion is dead?" Fflewddur Fflam asked. "Those are sorrowful tidings. He is a kinsman and I owe allegiance to the House of Don. But why do you blame his death on me? If Gwydion has bought my life, at least tell me how, and I shall mourn with you."

"Go your way," said Taran. "It is no fault of yours. I trusted Gwydion's life to a traitor and liar. My own life should be forfeit."

"Those are hard words to apply to a winsome lass," said the bard. "Especially one who isn't here to defend herself."

"I want no explanation from her," he said. "There is nothing she can tell me. She can lose herself in the forest, for all I care."

"If she's as much of a traitor and a liar as you say," Fflewddur remarked, "then you're letting her off easily. You may not want her explanation, but I'm quite sure Gwydion would. Allow me to suggest you go and find her before she strays too far."

Taran nodded. "Yes," he said coldly, "Gwydion shall have justice."

He turned on his heel and walked toward the trees. Eilonwy had gone no great

---

3. In the *Mabinogion*, Fflewddur Fflam is one of three kings who choose to remain with King Arthur as knights of the Round Table rather than return to their kingdoms.

distance; he could see the glow of the sphere a few paces ahead, where the girl sat on a boulder in a clearing. She looked small and thin; her head was pressed into her hands, and her shoulders shook.

"Now you've made me cry!" she burst out, as Taran approached. "I hate crying; it makes my nose feel like a melted icicle. You've hurt my feelings, you stupid Assistant Pig-Keeper, and all for something that's your own fault to begin with."

Taran was so taken aback that he began to stammer.

"Yes," cried Eilonwy, "it's every bit your fault! You were so close-mouthed about the man you wanted me to rescue, and you kept talking about your friend in the other cell. Very well, I rescued whoever it was in the other cell."

"You didn't tell me there was anyone else in the dungeon."

"There wasn't," Eilonwy insisted. "Fflewddur Fflam or whatever he calls himself was the only one."

"Then where is my companion?" Taran demanded. "Where is Gwydion?"

"I don't know," Eilonwy said. "He wasn't in Achren's dungeon, that's sure. What's more, he never was."

Taran realized the girl was speaking the truth. As his memory returned, he recalled that Gwydion had been with him only briefly; he had not seen the guards put him in a cell; Taran had only guessed at that.

"What could she have done with him?"

"I haven't any idea in the world," Eilonwy said and sniffed. "She could have brought him to her chambers, or locked him in the tower—there's a dozen places she could have hidden him. All you needed to say was, 'Go and rescue a man named Gwydion,' and I would have found him. But no, you had to be so clever about it and keep everything to yourself . . ."

Taran's heart sank. "I must go back to the castle and find him. Will you show me where Achren might have imprisoned him?"

"There's nothing left of the castle," said Eilonwy. "Besides, I'm not sure I'm going to help you any more at all, after the way you've behaved; and calling me those horrid names, that's like putting caterpillars in somebody's hair." She tossed her head, put her chin in the air, and refused to look at him.

"I accused you falsely," Taran said. "My shame is as deep as my sorrow."

Eilonwy, without lowering her chin, gave him a sidelong glance. "I should think it would be."

"I shall seek him alone," said Taran. "You are right in refusing to help. It is no concern of yours." He turned and started out of the clearing.

"Well, you don't have to agree with me so quickly," Eilonwy cried. She slid off the boulder and hastened after him.

Fflewddur Fflam was still waiting when they returned. In the light of Eilonwy's sphere, Taran had a better view of this unexpected arrival. The bard was tall and lanky, with a long, pointed nose. His great shock of bright yellow hair burst out in all directions, like a ragged sun. His jacket and leggings were patched at knees and elbows, and sewn with large, clumsy stitches—the work, Taran was certain, of the bard himself. A harp with a beautiful, sweeping curve was slung from his shoulder, but otherwise he looked nothing at all like the bards Taran had learned about from *The Book of Three*.

"So it seems that I've been rescued by mistake," Fflewddur said, after Taran explained what had happened. "I should have known it would turn out to be something like that. I kept asking myself, crawling along those beastly tunnels, who could possibly be interested whether I was languishing in a dungeon or not?"

"I am going back to the castle," Taran said. "There may be hope that Gwydion still lives."

"By all means," cried the bard, his eyes lighting up. "A Fflam to the rescue! Storm the castle! Carry it by assault! Batter down the gates!"

"There's not much of it left to storm," said Eilonwy.

"Oh?" said Fflewddur, with disappointment. "Very well, we shall do the best we can."

At the summit of the hill, the mighty blocks of stone lay as if crushed by a giant fist. Only the square arch of the gate remained upright, gaunt as a bone. In the moonlight, the ruins seemed already ancient. Shreds of mist hung over the shattered tower. Achren had learned of his escape, Taran guessed, for at the moment of the castle's destruction, she had sent out a company of guards. Amid the rubble, their bodies sprawled motionless as the stones.

With growing despair, Taran climbed over the ruins. The foundations of the castle had collapsed. The walls had fallen inward. The bard and Eilonwy helped Taran try to shift one or two of the broken rocks, but the work was beyond their strength.

At last, the exhausted Taran shook his head. "We can do no more," he murmured. "This shall stand as Gwydion's burial mound." He stood a moment, looking silently over the desolation, then turned away.

Fflewddur suggested taking weapons from the bodies of the guards. He equipped himself with a dagger, sword, and spear; in addition to the blade she had taken from the barrow, Eilonwy carried a slim dagger at her waist. Taran collected as many bows and quivers of arrows as he could carry. The group was now lightly but effectively armed.

With heavy hearts, the little band made their way down the slope. Melyngar followed docilely, her head bowed, as if she understood that she would not see her master again.

"I must leave this evil place," Taran cried. "I am impatient to be gone from here. Spiral Castle has brought me only grief; I have no wish to see it again."

"What has it brought the rest of us?" Eilonwy asked. "You make it sound as though we were just sitting around having a splendid time while you moan and take on."

Taran stopped abruptly. "I—I'm sorry," he said. "I didn't mean it that way."

"Furthermore," said Eilonwy, "you're mistaken if you think I'm going to go marching through the woods in the middle of the night."

"And I," put in Fflewddur, "I don't mind telling you I'm so tired I could sleep on Achren's doorstep."

"We all need rest," Taran said. "But I don't trust Achren, alive or dead, and we still know nothing of the Cauldron-Born. If they escaped, they may be looking for us right now. No matter how tired we are, it would be foolhardy to stay this close."

Eilonwy and Fflewddur agreed to continue on for a little distance. After a time, they found a spot well protected by trees, and flung themselves wearily to the turf. Taran unsaddled Melyngar, thankful the girl had thought to bring along Gwydion's gear. He found a cloak in a saddlebag and handed it to Eilonwy. The bard wrapped himself in his own tattered garment and set his harp carefully on a gnarled root.

Taran stood the first watch. Thoughts of the livid warriors still haunted him, and he saw their faces in every shadow. As the night wore on, the passage of a forest creature or the restless sighing of wind in the leaves made him start. The bushes rustled. This time it was not the wind. He heard a faint scratching, and his hand flew to his sword.

A figure bounded into the moonlight and rolled up to Taran.

"Crunchings and munchings?" whimpered a voice.

"Who is your peculiar friend?" asked the bard, sitting up and looking curiously at this new arrival.

"For an Assistant Pig-Keeper," remarked Eilonwy, "you do keep strange company. Where did you find it? And what is it? I've never seen anything like that in my life."

"He is no friend of mine," cried Taran. "He is a miserable, sneaking wretch who deserted us as soon as we were attacked."

"No, no!" Gurgi protested, whimpering and bobbing his matted head. "Poor humble Gurgi is always faithful to mighty lords—what joy to serve them, even with shakings and breakings."

"Tell the truth," said Taran. "You ran off when we needed you most."

"Slashings and gashings are for noble lords, not for poor, weak Gurgi. Oh, fearsome whistlings of blades! Gurgi ran to look for help, mighty lord."

"You didn't succeed in finding any," Taran said angrily.

"Oh, sadness!" Gurgi moaned. "There was no help for brave warriors. Gurgi went far, far, with great squeakings and shriekings."

"I'm sure you did," Taran said.

"What else can unhappy Gurgi do? He is sorry to see great warriors in distress, oh, tears of misery! But in battle, what would there be for poor Gurgi except hurtful guttings and cuttings of his throat?"

"It wasn't very brave," said Eilonwy, "but it wasn't altogether stupid, either. I don't see what advantage there was for him to be chopped up, especially if he wasn't any help to you in the first place."

"Oh, wisdom of a noble lady!" Gurgi cried, throwing himself at Eilonwy's feet. "If Gurgi had not gone seeking help, he would not be here to serve you now. But he is here! Yes, yes, faithful Gurgi returns to beatings and bruisings from the terrifying warrior!"

"Just keep out of my sight," Taran said, "or you really will have something to complain about."

Gurgi snuffled. "Gurgi hastens to obey, mighty lord. He will say no more, not even whisperings of what he saw. No, he will not disturb the sleepings of powerful heroes. See how he leaves, with tearful farewells."

"Come back here immediately," Taran called.

Gurgi brightened. "Crunchings?"

"Listen to me," Taran said, "there's hardly enough to go round, but I'll give you a fair share of what we have. After that, you'll have to find your own munchings."

Gurgi nodded. "Many more hosts march in the valley with sharp spears—oh, many more. Gurgi watches so quietly and cleverly, he does not ask *them* for help. No, they would only give harmful hurtings."

"What's this, what's this?" cried Fflewddur. "A great host? I should love to see them. I always enjoy processions and that sort of thing."

"The enemies of the House of Don are gathering," Taran hurriedly told the bard. "Gwydion and I saw them before we were captured. Now, if Gurgi speaks the truth, they have gathered reinforcements."

The bard sprang to his feet. "A Fflam never shrinks from danger! The mightier the foe, the greater the glory! We shall seek them out, set upon them! The bards shall sing our praises forever!"

Carried away by Fflewddur's enthusiasm, Taran seized his sword. Then he shook his head, remembering Gwydion's words in the forest near Caer Dallben. "No—no," he said slowly, "it would be folly to think of attacking them." He smiled quickly at Fflewddur. "The bards would sing of us," he admitted, "but we'd be in no position to appreciate it."

Fflewddur sat down again, disappointed.

"You can talk about the bards singing your praises all you want," said Eilonwy. "I'm in no mood to do battle. I'm going to sleep." With that, she curled up on the ground and pulled the cloak over her head.

Still unconvinced, Fflewddur settled himself against a tree root for his turn at guard. Gurgi curled up at Eilonwy's feet. Exhausted though he was, Taran lay awake. In his mind, he saw again the Horned King and heard the screams from the flaming cages.

He sat up quickly. Grieving for his companion, he had forgotten what had brought him here. His own quest had been for Hen Wen; Gwydion's, to warn the Sons of Don. Taran's head spun. With his companion surely dead, should he now try to make his way to Caer Dathyl? What, then, would become of Hen Wen? Everything had ceased to be simple. He yearned for the peacefulness of Caer Dallben, yearned even to weed the vegetable gardens and make horseshoes. He turned restlessly, finding no answer. At last, his weariness overcame him and he slept, plunged in nightmares.

CHAPTER X

The Sword Dyrnwyn

It was full daylight when Taran opened his eyes. Gurgi was already sniffing hungrily at the saddlebags. Taran rose quickly and shared out as much of the remaining provisions as he dared, keeping a small amount in reserve, since he had no idea how difficult it would be to find food during the coming journey. In the course of the restless night, he had reached his decision, though at present he refrained from speaking of it, still unsure he had chosen wisely. For the moment he concentrated on a meager breakfast.

Gurgi, sitting cross-legged, devoured his food with so many outcries of pleasure and loud smackings of his lips that he seemed to be eating twice as much as he really did. Fflewddur bolted his scant portion as though he had not enjoyed a meal for at least five days. Eilonwy was more interested in the sword she had taken from the barrow. It lay across her knees and, with a perplexed frown, the tip of her tongue between her lips, the girl was studying the weapon curiously.

As Taran grew near, Eilonwy snatched the sword away. "Well," said Taran, with a laugh, "you needn't act as if I were going to steal it from you." Although jewels studded the hilt and pommel, the scabbard was battered, discolored, nearly black with age. For all that, it had an air of ancient lineage, and Taran was eager to hold it. "Come," he said, "let me see the blade."

"I dare not," cried Eilonwy, to Taran's great surprise. He saw that her face was solemn and almost fearful.

"There is a symbol of power on the scabbard," Eilonwy continued. "I've seen this mark before, on some of Achren's things. It always means something forbidden. Of course, all Achren's things are like that, but some are more forbidden than others.

"There's another inscription, too," said Eilonwy, frowning again. "But it's in the Old Writing." She stamped her foot. "Oh, I do wish Achren had finished teaching it to me. I can almost make it out, but not quite, and there's nothing more irritating. It's like not finishing what you started out to say."

Fflewddur came up just then and he, too, peered at the strange weapon. "Comes from a barrow, eh?" The bard shook his spiky, yellow head and whistled. "I suggest getting rid of it immediately. Never had much confidence in things you find in barrows. It's a bad business having anything to do with them. You can't be sure where else they've been and who all's had them."

"If it's an enchanted weapon," Taran began, more interested than ever in getting his hands on the sword, "shouldn't we keep it . . ."

"Oh, do be quiet," Eilonwy cried. "I can't hear myself think. I don't see what you're both talking about, getting rid of it or not getting rid of it. After all, it's mine, isn't it? I found it and carried it out, and almost got stuck in a dirty old tunnel because of it."

"Bards are supposed to understand these things," Taran said.

"Naturally," Fflewddur answered, smiling confidently and putting his long nose closer to the scabbard. "These inscriptions are all pretty much the same. I see this one's on the scabbard rather than the blade. It says, oh, something like 'Beware My Wrath'—the usual sentiments."

At that moment there was a loud twang. Fflewddur blinked. One of his harp strings had snapped. "Excuse me," he said, and went to see about his instrument.

"It doesn't say anything at all like that," Eilonwy declared. "I can read some of it now. Here, it starts near the hilt and goes winding around like ivy. I was looking at it the wrong way. It says *Dyrnwyn*, first. I don't know whether that's the name of the sword or the name of the king. Oh, yes, that's the name of the sword; here it is again:

DRAW DYRNWYN, ONLY THOU OF ROYAL BLOOD,
TO RULE, TO STRIKE THE . . .

"Something or other," Eilonwy went on. "It's very faint; I can't see it. The letters are worn too smooth. No, that's odd. They aren't worn; they've been scratched out. They must have been cut deeply, because there's still a trace. But I can't read the rest. This word looks as if it might be death . . ." She shuddered. "That's not very cheerful."

"Let me unsheathe it," Taran urged again. "There might be more on the blade."

"Certainly not," said Eilonwy. "I told you it had a symbol of power and I'm bound by it—that's elementary."

"Achren cannot bind you any longer."

"It isn't Achren," Eilonwy answered. "I only said she had things with the same mark. This is a stronger enchantment than any she could make, I'm quite sure. I wouldn't dare to draw it, and I don't intend letting you, either. Besides, it says *only royal blood* and doesn't mention a word about Assistant Pig-Keepers."

"How can you tell I haven't royal blood?" Taran asked, bristling. "I wasn't *born* an Assistant Pig-Keeper. For all you know, my father might have been a king. It happens all the time in *The Book of Three*."

"I never heard of *The Book of Three*," said Eilonwy. "But in the first place, I don't think it's good enough to be a king's son or even a king himself. Royal blood is just a way of translating; in the Old Writing, it didn't mean only having royal relatives— anybody can have those. It meant—oh, I don't know what you'd call it. Something very special. And it seems to me that if you have it, you don't need to wonder whether you have it."

"So, of course," said Taran, nettled by the girl's remarks, "you've made up your mind that I'm not—whatever it is."

"I didn't mean to offend you," Eilonwy said quickly. "For an Assistant Pig-Keeper,

I think you're quite remarkable. I even think you're the nicest person I've ever met in my life. It's just that I'm forbidden to let you have the sword and that's that."

"What will you do with it, then?"

"Keep it, naturally. I'm not going to drop it down a well, am I?"

Taran snorted. "You'll make a fine sight—a little girl carrying a sword."

"I am not a little girl," said Eilonwy, tossing her hair in exasperation. "Among my people in the olden days, the Sword-Maidens did battle beside the men."

"It's not the olden days now," Taran said. "Instead of a sword, you should be carrying a doll."

Eilonwy, with a squeal of vexation, raised a hand to slap at Taran, when Fflewddur Fflam returned.

"Here now," said the bard, "no squabbling; there's not a bit of use to it." With a large key he tightened the wooden peg holding the newly repaired harp string.

Eilonwy turned her irritation on Fflewddur. "That inscription was a very important one. It didn't say anything about bewaring anyone's wrath. You didn't read it right at all. You're a fine bard, if you can't make out the writing on an enchanted sword."

"Well, you see, the truth of the matter," said Fflewddur, clearing his throat and speaking with much hesitation, "is this way. I'm not officially a bard."

"I didn't know there were *un*official bards," Eilonwy remarked.

"Oh, yes indeed," said Fflewddur. "At least in my case. I'm also a king."

"A king?" Taran said. "Sire . . ." He dropped to one knee.

"None of that, none of that," said Fflewddur. "I don't bother with it any more."

"Where is your kingdom?" Eilonwy asked.

"Several days' journey east of Caer Dathyl," said Fflewddur. "It is a vast realm . . ."

At this, Taran heard another jangling.

"Drat the thing," said the bard. "There go two more strings. As I was saying. Yes, well, it is actually a rather *small* kingdom in the north, very dull and dreary. So I gave it up. I'd always loved barding and wandering—and that's what I decided to do."

"I thought bards had to study a great deal," Eilonwy said. "A person can't just go and decide . . ."

"Yes, that was one of the problems," said the former king. "I studied; I did quite well in the examinations . . ." A small string at the upper end of the harp broke with a high-pitched tinkle and curled up like an ivy tendril. "I did quite *poorly*," he went on, "and the Council of Bards wouldn't admit me. Really, they want you to know so much these days. Volumes and volumes of poetry, and chants and music and calculating the seasons, and history; and all kinds of alphabets you spell out on your fingers, and secret signs—a man couldn't hope to cram it all into his skull.

"The Council were very nice to me," continued Fflewddur. "Taliesin,[4] the Chief Bard himself, presented me with this harp. He said it was exactly what I needed. I sometimes wonder if he was really doing me a favor. It's a very nice harp, but I have such trouble with the strings. I'd throw it away and get another, but it has a beautiful tone; I should never find one as good. If only the beastly strings . . ."

"They do seem to break frequently," Eilonwy began.

"Yes, that's so," Fflewddur admitted, a little sheepishly. "I've noticed it usually happens when—well, I'm an emotional sort of fellow, and I do get carried away. I might, ah, readjust the facts slightly; purely for dramatic effect, you understand."

"If you'd stop readjusting the facts quite as much," Eilonwy said, "perhaps you wouldn't have that trouble with the harp."

"Yes, I suppose," said the bard with a sigh. "I try, but it's hard, very hard. As a king,

---

4. The greatest bard in Wales, borrowed from the *Mabinogion*.

you get into the habit. Sometimes I think I pass more time fixing strings than playing. But, there it is. You can't have everything."

"Where were you journeying when Achren captured you?" Taran asked.

"No place in particular," said Fflewddur. "That's one advantage. You don't have to hurry to get somewhere. You keep moving, and next thing you know, there you are. Unfortunately, in this case, it was Achren's dungeon. She didn't care for my playing. That woman has no ear for music," he added, shuddering.

"Sire," Taran said, "I ask a boon."

"Please," said the former king, "Fflewddur will do very well. A boon? Delighted! I haven't done any boon-granting since I gave up the throne."

Fflewddur Fflam and Eilonwy seated themselves on the turf, while Taran recounted his search for Hen Wen and what Gwydion had told him of the Horned King and the rising of the cantrevs. Gurgi, having finished his meal, sidled over and squatted on a hillock to listen.

"There is no doubt in my mind," Taran went on, "the Sons of Don must have news of the uprising before the Horned King strikes. If he triumphs, Arawn will have Prydain by the throat. I have seen with my own eyes what that means." He felt ill at ease, speaking as if he himself were a war-leader in a council hall, but soon the words began to come easier. Perhaps, he thought, because he was speaking for Gwydion.

"I see your plan," Fflewddur interrupted. "You shall keep on looking for your pig, and you want me to warn the warriors of Don. Splendid! I shall start off immediately. And if the hosts of the Horned King overtake me . . ." The bard slashed and thrust at the air. "They shall know the valor of a Fflam!"

Taran shook his head. "No, I shall journey to Caer Dathyl myself. I do not question your valor," he said to the bard, "but the danger is too great. I ask no one else to face it in my stead."

"When do you intend to seek your pig?" asked Fflewddur.

"My own quest," said Taran, looking at the bard, "must be given up. If it is possible, after the first task is done, I mean to return to it. Until then, I serve only Gwydion. It was I who cost him his life, and it is justice for me to do what I believe he would have done."

"As I grasp the situation," said the bard, "I think you're taking too much blame on yourself. You had no way of knowing Gwydion wasn't in the dungeon."

"It changes nothing," Taran answered. "I have made my decision."

Fflewddur was about to protest, but the firmness of Taran's words silenced the bard. After a moment, he asked, "What is your boon, then?"

"It is twofold," said Taran. "First, tell me how I may reach Caer Dathyl as quickly as possible. Second, I beg you to conduct this girl safely to her own people."

Before Fflewddur could open his mouth, Eilonwy gave an indignant cry and leaped to her feet. "Conducted? I shall be conducted where I please! I'm not going to be sent back, just so I can be sent somewhere else; and it will be another dreary place, you can be sure. No, I shall go to Caer Dathyl, too!"

"There is risk enough," Taran declared, "without having to worry about a girl."

Eilonwy put her hands on her hips. Her eyes flashed. "I don't like being called 'a girl' and 'this girl' as if I didn't have a name at all. It's like having your head put in a sack. If you've made your decision, I've made my own. I don't see how you're going to stop me. If you," she hurried on, pointing at the bard, "try to conduct me to my mean, stupid kinsmen—and they're hardly related to me in the first place—that harp will be in pieces around your ears!"

Fflewddur blinked and clutched his harp protectively, while Eilonwy went on.

"And if a certain Assistant Pig-Keeper—I won't even mention *his* name—thinks otherwise, he'll be even more mistaken!"

Everyone started talking at once. "Stop it!" cried Taran at the top of his voice. "Very well," he said, after the others grew quiet. "You," he said to Eilonwy, "could be tied up and set on Melyngar. But," he added, raising his hand before the girl could interrupt, "that will not be done. *Not* because of all the commotion you raised, but because I realize now it is best."

The bard looked surprised.

Taran continued. "There is greater safety in greater numbers. Whatever happens, there will be more chance for one of us to reach Caer Dathyl. I believe we should all stay together."

"And faithful Gurgi, too!" shouted Gurgi. "He will follow! Too many wicked enemies are smirking and lurking to jab him with pointy spears!"

"If he agrees," Taran said, "Fflewddur shall act as guide. But I warn you," he added, glancing at Gurgi and Eilonwy, "nothing must hinder our task."

"Ordinarily," said Fflewddur, "I prefer to be in charge of this type of expedition myself. But," he went on, as Taran was about to protest, "since you are acting for Lord Gwydion, I accept your authority as I would accept his." He bowed low. "A Fflam is yours to command."

"Forward, then!" the bard cried. "And if we must give battle, so be it! Why, I've carved my way through walls of spearmen . . ."

Six harp strings broke at once, and the others strained so tautly they looked on the verge of snapping. While Taran saddled Melyngar, the bard set ruefully to work repairing his harp.

CHAPTER XI

Flight Through the Hills

At first, Taran offered to let Eilonwy ride Melyngar, but the girl refused.

"I can walk as well as any of you," she cried, so angrily that Taran made no more of it; he had learned to be wary of the girl's sharp tongue. It was agreed that the white mare would carry the weapons taken from Spiral Castle—except the sword Dyrnwyn, of which Eilonwy had appointed herself guardian.

Scratching in the dirt with his dagger point, Fflewddur Fflam showed Taran the path he intended to follow. "The hosts of the Horned King will surely stay in the Valley of Ystrad. It's the easiest way for an army on the march. Spiral Castle was here," he added, with an angry jab to mark the spot, "west of the River Ystrad. Now, the shortest road would be straight north over these hills."

"That is the one we must take," said Taran, trying hard to make sense of Fflewddur's crisscrossing lines.

"Wouldn't recommend it, my friend. We should be passing a little too near Annuvin. Arawn's strongholds are close to Spiral Castle; and I suggest we keep clear of them. No, what I believe we should do is this: stay on the high ground of the western bank of the Ystrad; we can go quite directly, since we needn't follow the valley itself. That way, we can avoid both Annuvin and the Horned King. The four of us can move faster than heavily armed warriors. We shall come out well ahead of them, not too far from Caer Dathyl. From there, we make a dash for it—and our task is done." Fflewddur straightened up, beaming with satisfaction. "There you have it," he said, wiping the dirt from his dagger. "A brilliant strategy. My own war-leader couldn't have arranged it better."

"Yes," said Taran, his head still muddled with the bard's talk of high ground and western banks, "that sounds very reasonable."

They descended to a broad, sun-swept meadow. The morning had turned bright and warm; dew still clung to bending blades of grass. At the head of the travelers strode Fflewddur, stepping out briskly on his long, spindly shanks. The harp jogged on his back; his shabby cloak was rolled over his shoulder. Eilonwy, hair disheveled by the breeze, the great black sword slung behind her, followed next, with Gurgi immediately after. So many new leaves and twigs had stuck in Gurgi's hair that he had begun to look like a walking beaver dam; he loped along, swinging his arms, shaking his head from side to side, moaning and muttering.

Holding Melyngar's bridle, Taran marched last in line. Except for the weapons lashed to the horse's saddle, these travelers might have been on a spring ramble. Eilonwy chattered gaily; now and then Fflewddur burst into a snatch of song. Taran alone was uneasy. To him, the bright morning felt deceptively gentle; the golden trees seemed to cover dark shadows. He shuddered even in the warmth. His heart was troubled, too, as he watched his companions. In Caer Dallben, he had dreamed of being a hero. But dreaming, he had come to learn, was easy; and at Caer Dallben no lives depended on his judgment. He longed for Gwydion's strength and guidance. His own strength, he feared, was not equal to his task. He turned once for a last look in the direction of Spiral Castle, Gwydion's burial mound. Over the hill crest, stark against the clouds, rose two figures on horseback.

Taran shouted and gestured for his companions to take cover in the woods. Melyngar galloped forward. In another moment, they were all crouching in a thicket. The horsemen followed along the crest, too far away for Taran to see their faces clearly; but from their rigid postures he could guess at the livid features and dull eyes of the Cauldron-Born.

"How long have they been behind us?" asked Fflewddur. "Have they seen us?"

Taran looked cautiously through the screen of leaves. He pointed toward the slope. "There is your answer," he said.

From the crest the pale Cauldron warriors had turned their horses toward the meadow and were steadily picking their way down the hill. "Hurry," ordered Taran. "We must outrun them."

The group did not return to the meadow, but struck out across the woods. The appearance of the Cauldron-Born now forced them to abandon the path Fflewddur had chosen, but the bard hoped they might throw the warriors off the track and circle back again to higher ground.

Staying close to one another, they moved at a dog trot, not daring to stop even for water. The forest offered a measure of protection from the sun, but after a time the pace began to tell on them. Only Gurgi did not seem fatigued or uncomfortable. He loped steadily along, and the swarms of midges and stinging insects could not penetrate his matted hair. Eilonwy, who proudly insisted she enjoyed running, clung to Melyngar's stirrup.

Taran could not be sure how close the warriors were; he knew the Cauldron-Born could hardly fail to track them, by sound if nothing else, for they no longer attempted to move silently. Speed was their only hope, and long after nightfall they pressed on.

It had become a blind race into darkness, under a moon drowned in heavy clouds. Invisible branches grasped at them or slashed their faces. Eilonwy stumbled once, and Taran pulled her to her feet. The girl faltered again; her head drooped. Taran unstrapped the weapons on Melyngar's saddle, shared out the burden with Fflewddur and Gurgi, and hoisted the protesting Eilonwy to Melyngar's back. She slumped forward, her cheek pressed against the horse's golden mane.

All night they struggled through the forest, which grew denser the closer they approached the Ystrad valley. By the time the first hesitating light of day appeared, even Gurgi had begun to stumble with fatigue and could barely put one hairy foot in front of the other. Eilonwy had fallen into a slumber so deep that Taran feared she was ill. Her hair lay bedraggled and damp upon her forehead; her face was pallid. With the bard's help, Taran lifted her from the saddle and propped her against a mossy bank. When he ventured to unbuckle the cumbersome sword, Eilonwy opened one eye, made an irritated face, and pulled the blade away from him—with more determination than he had expected.

"You never understand things the first time," Eilonwy murmured, her grip firm on the weapon. "But I imagine Assistant Pig-Keepers are all alike. I told you before you're not to have it, and now I'll tell you for the second time—or is it the third, or fourth? I must have lost count." So saying, she wrapped her arms around the scabbard and dropped back to sleep.

"We must rest here," Taran said to the bard, "if only a little while."

"At the moment," groaned Fflewddur, who had stretched out full length with his toes and nose pointing straight into the air, "I don't care who catches me. I'd welcome Arawn himself, and ask whether he had any breakfast with him."

"The Cauldron-Born might have lost track of us during the night," Taran said hopefully, but without great conviction. "I wish I knew how far we've left them behind—if we've left them behind at all."

Gurgi brightened a little. "Clever Gurgi will know," he cried, "with seekings and peekings."

In another moment, Gurgi was halfway up a tall pine. He clambered easily to the top and perched there like an enormous crow, scanning the land in the direction they had traveled.

Taran, meanwhile, opened the saddlebags. So little food remained that it was hardly worth dividing. He and Fflewddur agreed to give Eilonwy the last of the provisions.

Gurgi had scented food even at the top of the pine tree, and he came scuttling down, snuffling eagerly at the prospect of his crunchings and munchings.

"Stop thinking about eating for a moment," Taran cried. "What did you see?"

"Two warriors are far, but Gurgi sees them—yes, yes, they are riding full of wickedness and fierceness. But there is time for a small crunching," Gurgi pleaded. "Oh, very small for clever, valiant Gurgi."

"There are no more crunchings," said Taran. "If the Cauldron-Born are still on our heels, you had better worry less about food and more about your own skin."

"But Gurgi will find munchings! Very quickly—oh, yes—he is so wise to get them, to comfort the bellies of great noble lords. But they will forget poor Gurgi, and not even give him snips and snaps for his eatings."

After a hurried discussion with Fflewddur, who looked as ravenous as Gurgi, Taran agreed they might take a little time to search for berries and edible roots.

"Quite right," said the bard. "Better eat what we can get now, while the Cauldron-Born give us a chance to do it. I shall help you. I know all about foraging in the woods, do it constantly . . ." The harp tensed and one string showed signs of giving way. "No," he added quickly, "I had better stay with Eilonwy. The truth is, I can't tell a mushroom from a toadstool. I wish I could; it would make the life of a wandering bard considerably more filling."

With cloaks in which to carry back whatever they might find, Taran and Gurgi set off. At a small stream Taran halted to fill Gwydion's leather water flask. Gurgi, sniffing hungrily, ran ahead and disappeared into a stand of rowans. Near the bank of the stream Taran discovered mushrooms, and gathered them hurriedly. Bent on his own search, he paid little heed to Gurgi, until he suddenly heard anguished yelps from behind the trees. Clutching his precious mushrooms, Taran hastened to see what had happened, and came upon Gurgi lying in the middle of the grove, writhing and whimpering, a honeycomb beside him.

At first, Taran thought Gurgi had got himself stung by bees. Then, he saw the creature was in more serious trouble. While Gurgi had climbed for the honey, a dead branch had snapped under his weight. His twisted leg was pinned to the ground with the heavy wood on top of it. Taran heaved the branch away.

The panting Gurgi shook his head. "Poor Gurgi's leg is broken," he moaned. "There will be no more amblings and ramblings for him now!"

Taran bent and examined the injury. The leg was not broken, though badly torn, and swelling rapidly.

"Now Gurgi's head must be chopped off," the creature moaned. "Do it, great lord, do it quickly. Gurgi will squeeze up his eyes so as not to see hurtful slashings."

Taran looked closely at Gurgi. The creature was in earnest. His eyes pleaded with Taran. "Yes, yes," cried Gurgi. "Now, before silent warriors arrive. Gurgi is better dead at your sword than in their hands. Gurgi cannot walk! All will be killed with fearful smitings and bitings. It is better . . ."

"No," said Taran. "You won't be left in the woods, and you won't have your head chopped off—by me or anyone else." For a moment Taran almost regretted his words. The poor creature was right, he knew. The injury would slow their pace. And Gurgi, like all of them, would be better off dead than in Arawn's grasp. Still, Taran could not bring himself to draw his sword.

"You and Eilonwy can ride Melyngar," Taran said, lifting Gurgi to his feet and putting one of the creature's hairy arms about his shoulder. "Come on, now. One step at a time . . ."

Taran was exhausted when they reached Eilonwy and the bard. The girl had recovered noticeably and was chattering even faster than before. While Gurgi lay silently on the grass, Taran divided the honeycomb. The portions were pitifully small.

Fflewddur called Taran aside. "Your hairy friend is going to make things difficult," he said quietly. "If Melyngar carries two riders, I don't know how much longer she can keep up."

"That is true," said Taran. "Yet I see nothing else we can do. Would you abandon him? Would *you* have cut off his head?"

"Absolutely," cried the bard, "in a flash! A Fflam never hesitates. Fortunes of war and all that. Oh, drat and blast! There goes another string. A thick one, too."

When Taran went back to rearrange the weapons they would now be obliged to bear, he was surprised to find a large oak leaf on the ground before his cloak. On the leaf lay Gurgi's tiny portion of honeycomb.

"For great lord," murmured Gurgi. "Gurgi is not hungry for crunchings and munchings today."

Taran looked at the eager face of Gurgi. For the first time they smiled at one another.

"Your gift is generous," Taran said softly, "but you travel as one of us and you will need all your strength. Keep your share; it is yours by right; and you have more than earned it."

He put his hand gently on Gurgi's shoulder. The wet wolfhound odor did not seem as objectionable as before.

CHAPTER XII

The Wolves

For a time, during the day, Taran believed they had at last outdistanced the Cauldron-Born. But, late that afternoon, the warriors reappeared from behind a distant fringe of trees. Against the westering sun, the long shadows of the horsemen reached across the hill slope toward the flatlands where the small troop struggled onward.

"We must stand against them sooner or later," Taran said, wiping his forehead. "Let it be now. There can be no victory over the Cauldron-Born, but with luck, we can hold them off a little while. If Eilonwy and Gurgi can escape, there is still a chance."

Gurgi, draped over Melyngar's saddle, immediately set up a great outcry. "No, no! Faithful Gurgi stays with mighty lord who spared his poor tender head! Happy, grateful Gurgi will fight, too, with slashings and gashings . . ."

"We appreciate your sentiments," said Fflewddur, "but with that leg of yours, you're hardly up to slashing or gashing or anything at all."

"I'm not going to run, either," Eilonwy put in. "I'm tired of running and having my face scratched and my robe torn, all on account of those stupid warriors." She jumped lightly from the saddle and snatched a bow and a handful of arrows from Taran's pack.

"Eilonwy! Stop!" Taran cried. "These are deathless men! They cannot be killed!"

Although encumbered by the long sword hanging from her shoulder, Eilonwy ran faster than Taran. By the time he caught up with her, she had climbed a hillock and was stringing the bow. The Cauldron-Born galloped across the plain. The sun glinted on their drawn swords.

Taran seized the girl by the waist and tried to pull her away. He received a sharp kick in the shins.

"Must you always interfere with everything?" Eilonwy asked indignantly.

Before Taran could reach for her again, she held an arrow toward the sun and murmured a strange phrase. She nocked the arrow and loosed it in the direction of the Cauldron-Born. The shaft arched upward and almost disappeared against the bright rays.

Open-mouthed, Taran watched while the shaft began its descent: as the arrow plummeted to earth, long, silvery streamers sprang from its feathers. In an instant, a huge spiderweb glittered in the air and drifted slowly toward the horsemen.

Fflewddur, who had run up just then, stopped in amazement. "Great Belin!" he exclaimed. "What's that? It looks like decorations for a feast!"

The web slowly settled over the Cauldron-Born, but the pallid warriors paid it no heed. They spurred their mounts onward; the strands of the web broke and melted away.

Eilonwy clapped a hand to her mouth. "It didn't work!" she cried, almost in tears. "The way Achren does it, she makes it into a big sticky rope. Oh, it's all gone wrong. I tried to listen behind the door when she was practicing, but I've missed something important." She stamped her foot and turned away.

"Take her from here!" Taran called to the bard. He unsheathed his sword and faced the Cauldron-Born. Within moments they would be upon him. But, even as he braced for their onslaught, he saw the horsemen falter. The Cauldron-Born reined up suddenly; then, without a gesture, turned their horses and rode silently back toward the hills.

"It worked! It worked after all!" cried the astonished Fflewddur.

Eilonwy shook her head. "No," she said with discouragement, "something turned them away, but I'm afraid it wasn't my spell." She unstrung the bow and picked up the arrows she had dropped.

"I think I know what it was," Taran said. "They are returning to Arawn. Gwydion told me they could not stay long from Annuvin. Their power must have been waning ever since we left Spiral Castle, and they reached the limit of their strength right here."

"I hope they don't have enough to get back to Annuvin," Eilonwy said. "I hope they fall into pieces or shrivel up like bats."

"I doubt that they will," Taran said, watching the horsemen slowly disappear over the ridge. "They must know how long they can stay and how far they can go, and still return to their master." He gave Eilonwy an admiring glance. "It doesn't matter. They're gone. And that was one of the most amazing things I've ever seen. Gwydion had a mesh of grass that burst into flame; but I've never met anyone else who could make a web like that."

Eilonwy looked at him in surprise. Her cheeks blushed brighter than the sunset. "Why, Taran of Caer Dallben," she said, "I think that's the first polite thing you've said to me." Then, suddenly, Eilonwy tossed her head and sniffed. "Of course, I should have known; it was the spiderweb. You were more interested in that; you didn't care whether I was in danger." She strode haughtily back to Gurgi and Melyngar.

"But that's not true," Taran called. "I—I was . . ." By then, Eilonwy was out of earshot. Crestfallen, Taran followed her. "I can't make sense out of that girl," he said to the bard. "Can you?"

"Never mind," Fflewddur said. "We aren't really expected to."

That night, they continued to take turns at standing guard, though much of their fear had lifted since the Cauldron-Born had vanished. Taran's was the last watch before dawn, and he was awake well before Eilonwy's had ended.

"You had better sleep," Taran told her. "I'll finish the watch for you."

"I'm perfectly able to do my share," said Eilonwy, who had not stopped being irritated at him since the afternoon.

Taran knew better than to insist. He picked up his bow and quiver arrows, stood near the dark trunk of an oak, and looked out across the moon-silvered meadow. Nearby, Fflewddur snored heartily. Gurgi, whose leg had shown no improvement, stirred restlessly and whimpered in his sleep.

"You know," Taran began, with embarrassed hesitation, "that spiderweb . . ."

"I don't want to hear any more about it," retorted Eilonwy.

"No—what I meant was: I really was worried about you. But the web surprised me so much I forgot to mention it. It was courageous of you to stand up against the Cauldron warriors. I just wanted to tell you that."

"You took long enough getting around to it," said Eilonwy, a tone of satisfaction in her voice. "But I imagine Assistant Pig-Keepers tend to be slower than what you might expect. It probably comes from the kind of work they do. Don't misunderstand, I think it's awfully important. Only it's the sort of thing you don't often need to be quick about."

"At first," Taran went on, "I thought I would be able to reach Caer Dathyl by myself. I see now that I wouldn't have got even this far without help. It is a good destiny that brings me such brave companions."

"There, you've done it again," Eilonwy cried, so heatedly that Fflewddur choked on one of his snores. "That's all you care about! Someone to help you carry spears and swords and what-all. It could be *anybody* and you'd be just as pleased. Taran of Caer Dallben, I'm not speaking to you any more."

"At home," Taran said—to himself, Eilonwy had already pulled a cloak over her head and was feigning sleep—"nothing ever happened. Now, everything happens. But somehow I can never seem to make it come out right." With a sigh, he held his bow ready and began his turn at guard. Daylight was long in coming.

In the morning, Taran saw Gurgi's leg was much worse, and he left the campsite to search the woods for healing plants, glad that Coll had taught him the properties of herbs. He made a poultice and set it on Gurgi's wound.

Fflewddur, meanwhile, had begun drawing new maps with his dagger. The Cauldron warriors, explained the bard, had forced the companions too deeply into the Ystrad valley. Returning to their original path would cost them at least two days of hard travel. "Since we're this far," Fflewddur went on, "we might just as well cross Ystrad and follow along the hills, staying out of sight of the Horned King. We'll be only a few days from Caer Dathyl, and if we keep a good pace, we should reach it just in time."

Taran agreed to the new plan. It would, he realized, be more difficult; but he judged Melyngar could still carry the unfortunate Gurgi, as long as the companions shared the burden of the weapons. Eilonwy, having forgotten she was not speaking to Taran, again insisted on walking.

A day's march brought them to the banks of the Ystrad.

Taran stole cautiously ahead. Looking down the broad valley, he saw a moving dust cloud. When he hurried back and reported this to Fflewddur, the bard clapped him on the shoulder.

"We're ahead of them," he said. "That is excellent news. I was afraid they'd be much closer to us and we'd have to wait for nightfall to cross Ystrad. We've saved half a day! Hurry now and we'll be into the foothills of Eagle Mountains before sundown!"

With his precious harp held above his head, Fflewddur plunged into the river, and the others followed. Here, the Ystrad ran shallow, scarcely above Eilonwy's waist, and the companions forded it with little difficulty. Nevertheless, they emerged cold and dripping, and the setting sun neither dried nor warmed them.

Leaving the Ystrad behind, the companions climbed slopes steeper and rockier than any they had traveled before. Perhaps it was only his imagination, but the air of the land around Spiral Castle had seemed, to Taran, heavy and oppressive. Approaching the Eagle Mountains, Taran felt his burden lighten, as he inhaled the dry, spicy scent of pine.

He had planned to continue the march throughout most of the night; but Gurgi's condition had worsened, obliging Taran to call a halt. Despite the herbs, Gurgi's leg was badly inflamed, and he shivered with fever. He looked thin and sad; the suggestion of crunchings and munchings could not rouse him. Even Melyngar showed concern. As Gurgi lay with his eyes half-closed, his parched lips tight against his teeth, the white mare nuzzled him delicately, whinnying and blowing out her breath anxiously, as if attempting to comfort him as best she could.

Taran risked lighting a small fire. He and Fflewddur stretched Gurgi out beside it.

While Eilonwy held up the suffering creature's head and gave him a drink from the leather flask, Taran and the bard moved a little away and spoke quietly between themselves.

"I have done all I know," Taran said. "If there is anything else, it lies beyond my skill." He shook his head sorrowfully. "He has failed badly today, and there is so little of him left I believe I could pick him up with one hand."

"Caer Dathyl is not far away," said Fflewddur, "but our friend, I fear, may not live to see it."

That night, wolves howled in the darkness beyond the fire.

All next day, the wolves followed them; sometimes silently, sometimes barking as if in signal to one another. They remained always out of bow shot, but Taran caught sight of the lean, gray shapes flickering in and out of the scrubby trees.

"As long as they don't come any closer," he said to the bard, "we needn't worry about them."

"Oh, they won't attack us," Fflewddur answered. "Not now, at any rate. They can be infuriatingly patient if they know someone's wounded." He turned an anxious glance toward Gurgi. "For them, it's just a matter of waiting."

"Well, I must say you're a cheerful one," remarked Eilonwy. "You sound as if all we had to look forward to was being gobbled up."

"If they attack, we shall stand them off," Taran said quietly. "Gurgi was willing to give up his life for us; I can do no less for him. Above all, we must not lose heart so close to the end of our journey."

"A Fflam never loses heart!" cried the bard. "Come wolves or what have you!"

Nevertheless, uneasiness settled over the companions as the gray shapes continued trailing them; and Melyngar, docile and obedient until now, turned skittish. The golden-maned horse tossed her head and rolled her eyes at every attempt to lead her.

To make matters worse, Fflewddur declared their progress through the hills was too slow.

"If we go any farther east," said the bard, "we'll run into some really high mountains. The condition we're in, we couldn't possibly climb them. But here, we're practically walled in. Every path has led us roundabout. The cliffs there," he went on, pointing toward the towering mass of rock to his left, "are too rugged to get over. I had thought we'd find a pass before now. Well, that's the way of it. We can only keep on bearing north as much as possible."

"The wolves didn't seem to have any trouble finding their way," said Eilonwy.

"My dear girl," answered the bard, with some indignation, "if I were able to run on four legs and sniff my dinner a mile away, I doubt I'd have any difficulties either." Eilonwy giggled. "I'd love to see you try," she said.

"We do have someone who can run on four legs," Taran said suddenly. "Melyngar! If anyone can find their way to Caer Dathyl, she can."

The bard snapped his fingers. "That's it!" he cried. "Every horse knows its way home! It's worth trying—and we can't be worse off than we are now."

"For an Assistant Pig-Keeper," said Eilonwy to Taran, "you do come up with some interesting ideas now and then."

When the companions started off again, Taran dropped the bridle and gave Melyngar her head. With the half-conscious Gurgi bound to her saddle, the white horse trotted swiftly ahead at a determined gait.

By mid-afternoon, Melyngar discovered one pass which, Fflewddur admitted, he himself would have overlooked. As the day wore on, Melyngar led them swiftly through rocky defiles to high ridges. It was all the companions could do to keep up with her. When she cantered into a long ravine, Taran lost sight of her for a moment and hurried forward in time to glimpse the mare as she turned sharply around an outcropping of white stone.

Calling the bard and Eilonwy to follow quickly, Taran ran ahead. He stopped suddenly. To his left, on a high shelf of rock, crouched an enormous wolf with golden eyes and lolling red tongue. Before Taran could draw his sword, the lean animal sprang.

Chapter XIII

The Hidden Valley

The impact of the heavy, furry body caught Taran full in the chest, and sent him tumbling. As he fell, he caught a glimpse of Fflewddur. The bard, too, had been borne to earth under the paws of another wolf. Eilonwy still stood, though a third animal crouched in front of her.

Taran's hand flew to his sword. The gray wolf seized his arm. The animal's teeth, however, did not sink into his flesh, but held him in an unshakable grip.

At the end of the ravine a huge, robed figure suddenly appeared. Melyngar stood behind him. The man raised his arm and spoke a command. Immediately, the wolf holding Taran relaxed his jaws and drew away, as obediently as a dog. The man strode toward Taran, who scrambled to his feet.

"You saved our lives," Taran began. "We are grateful."

The man spoke again to the wolves and the animals crowded around him, whining and wagging their tails. He was a strange-looking figure, broad and muscular, with the vigor of an ancient but sturdy tree. His white hair reached below his shoulders and his beard hung to his waist. Around his forehead he wore a narrow band of gold, set with a single blue jewel.

"From these creatures," he said, in a deep voice that was stern but not unkind, "your lives were never in danger. But you must leave this place. It is not an abode for the race of men."

"We were lost," Taran said. "We had been following our horse . . ."

"Melyngar?" The man turned a pair of keen gray eyes on Taran. Under his deep brow they sparkled like frost in a valley. "Melyngar brought me four of you? I understood young Gurgi was alone. By all means, then, if you are friends of Melyngar. It is Melyngar, isn't it? She looks so much like her mother; and there are so many I cannot always keep track of the names."

"I know who you are," cried Taran. "You are Medwyn!"

"Am I now?" the man answered with a smile that furrowed his face. "Yes, I have been called Medwyn. But how should you know that?"

"I am Taran of Caer Dallben. Gwydion, Prince of Don, was my companion, and he spoke of you before—before his death. He was journeying to Caer Dathyl, as we are now. I never hoped to find you."

"You were quite right," Medwyn answered. "You could not have found me. Only the animals know my valley. Melyngar led you here. Taran, you say? Of Caer Dallben?" He put an enormous hand to his forehead. "Let me see. Yes, there are visitors from Caer Dallben, I am sure."

Taran's heart leaped. "Hen Wen!" he cried.

Medwyn gave him a puzzled glance. "Were you seeking her? Now, that is curious. No, she is not here."

"But I had thought . . ."

"We will speak of Hen Wen later," said Medwyn. "Your friend is badly injured, you know. Come, I shall do what I can for him." He motioned for them to follow.

The wolves padded silently behind Taran, Eilonwy, and the bard. Where Melyngar waited at the end of the ravine, Medwyn lifted Gurgi from the saddle, as if the creature weighed no more than a squirrel. Gurgi lay quietly in Medwyn's arms.

The group descended a narrow footpath. Medwyn strode ahead, as slowly and powerfully as if a tree were walking. The old man's feet were bare, but the sharp stones and pebbles did not trouble him. The path turned abruptly, then turned again. Medwyn passed through a cut in a bare shoulder of the cliff, and the next thing Taran knew, they suddenly emerged into a green, sunlit valley. Mountains, seemingly impassable, rose on all sides. Here the air was gentler, without the tooth of the wind; the grass spread rich and tender before him. Set among tall hemlocks were low, white cottages, not unlike those of Caer Dallben. At the sight of them, Taran felt a pang of homesickness. Against the face of the slope behind the cottages, he saw what appeared at first to be rows of moss-covered tree trunks; as he looked, to his surprise, they seemed more like the weather-worn ribs and timbers of a long ship. The earth covered them almost entirely; grass and meadow flowers had sprung up to obliterate them further and make them part of the mountain itself.

"I must say the old fellow's well tucked away here," whispered Fflewddur. "I could never have found the path in, and I doubt I could find the path out."

Taran nodded. The valley was the most beautiful he had ever seen. Cattle grazed peacefully in the meadow. Near the hemlocks, a small lake caught the sky and sparkled blue and white. The bright plumage of birds flashed among the trees. Even as he stepped across the lush green of the turf, Taran felt exhaustion drain from his aching body.

"There's a fawn!" Eilonwy cried with delight.

From behind the cottages, a speckled, long-legged fawn appeared, sniffed the air, then trotted quickly toward Medwyn. The graceful creature paid no attention to the wolves, but frisked gaily at the old man's side. The animal drew shyly away from the strangers; but her curiosity got the better of her, and soon she was nuzzling Eilonwy's hand.

"I've never seen a fawn this close," said the girl. "Achren never had any pets—none that would stay with her, at any rate. I can't blame them at all. This one is lovely; it makes you feel all tingly, as if you were touching the wind."

Medwyn, motioning for them to wait, carried Gurgi into the largest of the cottages. The wolves sat on their haunches and watched the travelers through slanted eyes. Taran unsaddled Melyngar, who began cropping the tender grass. Half-a-dozen chickens clucked and pecked around a neat white henhouse. The rooster raised his head to show a notched comb.

"Those are Dallben's chickens!" cried Taran. "They must be! There's the brown hen, the white—I'd know that comb anywhere." He hurried over and clucked at them.

The chickens, more interested in eating, paid little attention.

Medwyn reappeared in the doorway. He carried an enormous wicker basket laden with jugs of milk, with cheese, honeycombs, and fruits that, in the lowlands, would not be in season for another month. "I shall look after your friend directly," he said. "Meantime, I thought you might enjoy—oh, yes, so you've found them, have you?" he said, noticing Taran with the chickens. "Those are my visitors from Caer Dallben. There should be a swarm of bees, too, somewhere about."

"They flew away," Taran said, "the same day Hen Wen ran off."

"Then I imagine they came straight here," Medwyn said. "The chickens were petrified with fright; I could make no sense at all out of them. Oh, they settled down quickly enough, but of course by that time they had forgotten why they flew off in the first place. You know how chickens are, imagining the world coming to an end one moment, then pecking corn the next. They shall all fly back when they're ready, have no fear. Though it's unfortunate Dallben and Coll should be put out in the matter of eggs."

"I would ask you inside," Medwyn continued, "but the disorder at the moment—there were bears at breakfast, and you can imagine the state of things. So I must ask you to attend to yourselves. If you would rest, there is straw in the byre; it should not be too uncomfortable for you."

The travelers lost no time in helping themselves to Medwyn's provisions, or in finding the byre. The sweet scent of hay filled the low-ceilinged building. They scooped out nests in the straw, uncovering one of Medwyn's breakfast guests curled up and fast asleep. Fflewddur, at first uneasy, was finally convinced the bear had no appetite for bards, and soon began snoring. Eilonwy dropped off to sleep in the middle of one of her sentences.

Taran had no desire to rest. Medwyn's valley had refreshed him more than a night's slumber. He left the byre and strolled across the meadow. At the far side of the lake, otters built a slide and were amusing themselves by tumbling down it. At Taran's approach, they stopped for a moment, raised their heads to look at him as though sorry he was unable to join them, and returned to their game. A fish broke water in a twinkle of silver scales; the ripples widened until the last of them lapped gently at the shore.

Medwyn, Taran saw, had gardens of both flowers and vegetables behind the cottage. To his surprise, Taran found himself yearning to work with Coll in his own vegetable plot. The weeding and hoeing he had so despised at Caer Dallben now seemed, as he thought of his past journey and the journey yet to come, infinitely pleasant.

He sat down by the rim of the lake and looked across the hills. With the sun resting above the peaks, the wooden skeleton of the great ship stood out sharply against the mound which nearly enveloped it. He had little chance to study it, for Medwyn appeared, walking deliberately across the field; the fawn trotted beside him, the three wolves followed. With his brown robe and white hair, Medwyn looked as broad and solid as a snow-capped mountain.

"Gurgi is more comfortable than he was," the ancient man said in his deep voice. The fawn danced at the lake shore while Medwyn ponderously sat down and leaned his huge head toward Taran. "He will recover well; there is no longer any danger. Not, at least, while he is here."

"I have thought long of Gurgi," Taran said, looking frankly into the old man's gray eyes. He explained, then, the reason for his journey and the events leading to Gurgi's accident. Medwyn listened carefully, head cocked to one side, thoughtful, while Taran recounted Gurgi's willingness to sacrifice his own life rather than endanger the others. "At first, I wasn't too fond of him," Taran admitted. "Now I've begun to like him in spite of all his whining and complaining."

"Every living thing deserves our respect," said Medwyn, knitting his shaggy brows, "be it humble or proud, ugly or beautiful."

"I wouldn't want to say that about the gwythaints," Taran answered.

"I feel only sorrow for those unhappy creatures," Medwyn said. "Once, long ago, they were as free as other birds, gentle and trusting. In his cunning, Arawn lured them to him and brought them under his power. He built the iron cages which are now their prison house in Annuvin. The tortures he inflicted on the gwythaints were shameful and unspeakable. Now they serve him out of terror.

"Thus would he strive to corrupt every animal in Prydain, no less than the race of men. That is one of the reasons I remain in the valley. Here, Arawn cannot harm them. Even so, were he to become ruler of this land, I doubt I could help them all. Those who fell into his clutches would be counted fortunate if they perished quickly."

Taran nodded. "I understand more and more why I must warn the Sons of Don. As for Gurgi, I wonder if it wouldn't be safer for him to stay here."

"Safer?" asked Medwyn. "Yes, certainly. But you would hurt him grievously were you to turn him away now. Gurgi's misfortune is that he is neither one thing nor the other, at the moment. He has lost the wisdom of animals and has not gained the learning of men. Therefore, both shun him. Were he to do something purposeful, it would mean much to him.

"I doubt he will delay your journey, for he will be able to walk as well as you—by tomorrow, easily. I urge you to take him. He may even find his own way of serving you. Neither refuse to give help when it is needed," Medwyn continued, "nor refuse to accept it when it is offered. Gwythyr Son of Greidawl learned that from a lame ant, you know."

"A lame ant?" Taran shook his head. "Dallben has taught me much about ants, but nothing of a lame one."

"It is a long history," Medwyn said, "perhaps you will hear all of it another time. For the moment, you need only know that when Kilhuch—or was it his father? No, it was young Kilhuch. Very well. When young Kilhuch sought the hand of the fair Olwen, he was given a number of tasks by her father, Yspadadden; he was Chief Giant at the time. What the tasks were does not concern us now, except that they were very nigh impossible, and Kilhuch could not have accomplished them without the aid of his companions.

"One of the tasks was to gather nine bushels of flax seed, though there was scarcely that much in all the land. For the sake of his friend, Gwythyr Son of Greidawl undertook to do this. While he was walking over the hills, wondering how he might accomplish it, he heard a grievous wailing from an anthill; a fire had started around it and the ants were in danger of their lives. Gwythyr—yes, I'm quite sure it was Gwythyr—drew his sword and beat out the fire.

"In gratitude, the ants combed every field until they had collected the nine bushels. Yet the Chief Giant, a picky and disagreeable sort, claimed the measure was not complete. One flax seed was missing, and must be delivered before nightfall.

"Gwythyr had no idea where he could find another flax seed, but at last, just as the sun had begun to set, up hobbled a lame ant carrying a heavy burden. It was the single flax seed, and so the last measure was filled.

"I have studied the race of men," Medwyn continued. "I have seen that alone you stand as weak reeds by a lake. You must learn to help yourselves, that is true; but you must also learn to help one another. Are you not, all of you, lame ants?"

Taran was silent. Medwyn put his hand into the lake and stirred the water. After a moment, a venerable salmon rippled up; Medwyn stroked the jaws of the huge fish.

"What place is this?" Taran finally asked, in a hushed voice. "Are you indeed Medwyn? You speak of the race of men as if you were not one of them."

"This is a place of peace," Medwyn said, "and therefore not suitable for men, at least, not yet. Until it is, I hold this valley for creatures of the forests and the waters. In their mortal danger they come to me, if they have the strength to do so—and in their pain and grief. Do you not believe that animals know grief and fear and pain? The world of men is not an easy one for them."

"Dallben," said Taran, "taught me that when the black waters flooded Prydain, ages ago, Nevvid Nav Neivion built a ship and carried with him two of every living creature. The waters drained away, the ship came to rest—no man knows where. But the animals who came safe again into the world remembered, and their young have never forgotten. And here," Taran said, pointing toward the hillside, "I see a ship, far from water. Gwydion called you Medwyn, but I ask . . ."

"I am Medwyn," answered the white-bearded man, "for all that my name may concern you. That is not important now. My own concern is for Hen Wen."

"You have seen nothing of her, then?"

Medwyn shook his head. "What Lord Gwydion said is true: of all places in Prydain, she would have come here first, especially if she sensed her life in danger. But there has been no sign, no rumor. Yet she would find her way, sooner or later, unless . . ."

Taran felt a chill ripple at his heart. "Unless she has been killed," he murmured. "Do you think that has happened?"

"I do not know," Medwyn answered, "though I fear it may be so."

CHAPTER XIV

The Black Lake

That night Medwyn prepared a feast for the travelers. The disorder left by the breakfasting bears had been cleared away. The cottage was snug and neat, though even smaller than Caer Dallben. Taran could see that Medwyn was indeed unused to entertaining human visitors, for his table was barely long enough to seat them all; and for chairs he had been obliged to make do with benches and milking stools.

Medwyn sat at the head of the table. The fawn had gone to sleep, but the wolves crouched at his feet and grinned happily. On the back of his chair perched a gigantic, golden-plumed eagle, watching every movement with sharp, unblinking eyes. Fflewddur, though still apprehensive, did not allow his fear to affect his appetite. He ate enough for three, without showing the least sign of becoming full. But when he asked for another portion of venison, Medwyn gave a long chuckle and explained to the amazed Fflewddur it was not meat at all but vegetables prepared according to his own recipe.

"Of course it is," Eilonwy told the bard. "You wouldn't expect him to cook his guests, would you? That would be like asking someone to dinner and then roasting him. Really, I think bards are as muddled as Assistant Pig-Keepers; neither one of you seems to think very clearly."

As much as he welcomed food and the chance to rest, Taran was silent throughout the meal, and continued so when he retired to his nest of straw. Until now, he had never imagined Hen Wen might not be alive. He had spoken again with Medwyn, but the old man could give him no assurance.

Wakeful, Taran left the byre and stood outside, looking at the sky. In the clear air, the stars were blue-white, closer than he had ever seen them. He tried to turn his thoughts from Hen Wen; reaching Caer Dathyl was the task he had undertaken and that in itself would be difficult enough. An owl passed overhead, silent as ashes. The shadow appearing noiselessly beside him was Medwyn.

"Not asleep?" Medwyn asked. "A restless night is no way to begin a journey."

"It is a journey I am eager to end," Taran said. "There are times when I fear I shall not see Caer Dallben again."

"It is not given to men to know the ends of their journeys," Medwyn answered. "It may be that you will never return to the places dearest to you. But how can that matter, if what you must do is here and now?"

"I think," said Taran longingly, "that if I knew I were not to see my own home again, I would be happy to stay in this valley."

"Your heart is young and unformed," Medwyn said. "Yet, if I read it well, you are of the few I would welcome here. Indeed, you may stay if you choose. Surely you can entrust your task to your friends."

"No," said Taran, after a long pause, "I have taken it on myself through my own choice."

"If that is so," answered Medwyn, "then you can give it up through your own choice."

From all over the valley it seemed to Taran there came voices urging him to remain. The hemlocks whispered of rest and peace; the lake spoke of sunlight lingering in its depths, the joy of otters at their games. He turned away.

"No," he said quickly, "my decision was made long before this."

"Then," Medwyn answered gently, "so be it." He put a hand on Taran's brow. "I grant you all that you will allow me to grant: a night's rest. Sleep well."

Taran remembered nothing of returning to the byre or falling asleep, but he rose in the morning sunlight refreshed and strengthened. Eilonwy and the bard had already finished their breakfast, and Taran was delighted to see that Gurgi had joined them. As Taran approached, Gurgi gave a yelp of joy and turned gleeful somersaults.

"Oh, joy!" he cried. "Gurgi is ready for new walkings and stalkings, oh, yes! And new seekings and peekings! Great lords have been kind to happy, jolly Gurgi!"

Taran noticed Medwyn had not only healed the creature's leg, he had also given him a bath and a good combing. Gurgi looked only half as twiggy and leafy as usual. In addition, as he saddled Melyngar, Taran found that Medwyn had packed the saddlebags with food, and had included warm cloaks for all of them.

The old man called the travelers around him and seated himself on the ground. "The armies of the Horned King are by now a day's march ahead of you," he said, "but if you follow the paths I shall reveal, and move quickly, you may regain the time you have lost. It is even possible for you to reach Caer Dathyl a day, perhaps two, before them. However, I warn you, the mountain ways are not easy. If you prefer, I shall set you on a path toward the Valley of Ystrad once again."

"Then we would be following the Horned King," Taran said. "There would be less chance of overtaking him, and much danger, too."

"Do not think the mountains are not dangerous," Medwyn said. "Though it is a danger of a different sort."

"A Fflam thrives on danger!" cried the bard. "Let it be the mountains or the Horned King's hosts, I fear neither—not to any great extent," he added quickly.

"We shall risk the mountains," Taran said.

"For once," Eilonwy interrupted, "you've decided the right thing. The mountains certainly aren't going to throw spears at us, no matter how dangerous they are. I really think you're improving."

"Listen carefully, then," Medwyn ordered. As he spoke, his hands moved deftly in the soft earth before him, molding a tiny model of hills, which Taran found easier to follow than Fflewddur's map scratchings. When he finished, and the travelers' gear and weapons were secured on Melyngar's back, Medwyn led the group from the valley. As closely as Taran observed each step of the way, he knew the path to Medwyn's valley would be lost to him as soon as the ancient man left.

In a little while Medwyn stopped. "Your path now lies to the north," he said, "and here we shall part. And you, Taran of Caer Dallben—whether you have chosen wisely, you will learn from your own heart. Perhaps we shall meet again, and you will tell me. Until then, farewell."

Before Taran could turn and thank Medwyn, the white-bearded man disappeared, as if the hills had swallowed him up; and the travelers stood by themselves on a rocky, windswept plateau.

"Well," said Fflewddur, hitching up the harp behind him, "I somehow feel that if we meet any more wolves, they'll know we're friends of Medwyn."

The first day's march was less difficult than Taran had feared. This time he led the way, for the bard admitted—after a number of harp strings had snapped—that he had not been able to keep all Medwyn's directions in his head.

They climbed steadily until long after the sun had turned westward; and, though the ground was rough and broken, the path Medwyn had indicated lay clearly before them. Mountain streams, whose water ran cold and clear, made winding lines of sparkling silver as they danced down the slopes into the distant valley lands. The air was bracing, yet with a cold edge which made the travelers grateful for the cloaks Medwyn had given them.

At a long cleft protected from the wind, Taran signaled a halt. They had made excellent progress during the day, far more than he had expected, and he saw no reason to exhaust themselves by forcing a march during the night. Tethering Melyngar to one of the stunted trees that grew in the heights, the travelers made camp. Since there was no further danger from the Cauldron-Born, and the hosts of the Horned King moved far below and to the west of the group, Taran deemed it safe to build a fire. Medwyn's provisions needed no cooking, but the blaze warmed and cheered them. As the night shadows drifted from the peaks, Eilonwy lit her golden sphere and set it in the crevice of a faulted rock.

Gurgi, who had not uttered a single moan or groan during this part of the journey, perched on a boulder and began scratching himself luxuriously; although, after Medwyn's washing and combing, it was more through habit than anything else. The bard, as lean as ever, despite the huge amount he had eaten, repaired his harp strings.

"You've been carrying that harp ever since I met you," Eilonwy said, "and you've never once played it. That's like telling somebody you want to talk to them, and when they get ready to listen, you don't say anything."

"You'd hardly expect me to go strumming out airs while those Cauldron warriors were following us," Fflewddur said. "Somehow I didn't think it would be appropriate. But—a Fflam is always obliging, so if you really care to hear me play . . . ," he added, looking both delighted and embarrassed. He cradled the instrument in one arm and, almost before his fingers touched the strings, a gentle melody, as beautiful as the curve of the harp itself, lifted like a voice singing without words.

To Taran's ear, the melody had its own words, weaving a supple thread among the rising notes. Home, home, they sang; and beyond the words themselves, so fleeting he could not be quite sure of them, were the fields and orchards of Caer Dallben, the gold afternoons of autumn and the crisp winter mornings with pink sunlight on the snow.

Then the harp fell silent. Fflewddur sat with his head bent close to the strings, a curious expression on his long face. "Well, that was a surprise," said the bard at last. "I had planned something a little more lively, the sort of thing my war-leader always enjoys—to put us in a bold frame of mind, you understand. The truth of the matter is," he admitted with a slight tone of discouragement, "I don't really know what's going to come out of it next. My fingers go along, but sometimes I think this harp plays of itself.

"Perhaps," Fflewddur continued, "that's why Taliesin thought he was doing me a favor when he gave it to me. Because when I went up to the Council of Bards for my examination, I had an old pot one of the minstrels had left behind and I couldn't do more than plunk out a few chants. However, a Fflam never looks a gift horse in the mouth, or, in this case, I should say harp."

"It was a sad tune," Eilonwy said. "But the odd thing about it is, you don't mind the sadness. It's like feeling better after you've had a good cry. It made me think of the sea again, though I haven't been there since I was a little girl." At this, Taran snorted, but Eilonwy paid no attention to him. "The waves break against the cliffs and churn into foam, and farther out, as far as you can see, there are the white crests, the White Horses of Llyr, they call them; but they're really only waves waiting their turn to roll in."

"Strange," said the bard, "personally, I was thinking of my own castle. It's small and drafty, but I would like to see it again; a person can have enough wandering, you know. It made me think I might even settle down again and try to be a respectable sort of king."

"Caer Dallben is closer to my heart," Taran said. "When I left, I never gave it too much thought. Now I think of it a great deal."

Gurgi, who had been listening silently, set up a long howl. "Yes, yes, soon great warriors will all be back in their halls, telling their tales with laughings and chaffings. Then it will be the fearful forest again for poor Gurgi, to put down his tender head in snoozings and snorings."

"Gurgi," Taran said, "I promise to bring you to Caer Dallben, if I ever get there myself. And if you like it, and Dallben agrees, you can stay there as long as you want."

"What joy!" Gurgi cried. "Honest, toiling Gurgi extends thanks and best wishes. Oh, yes, fond, obedient Gurgi will work hard . . ."

"For now, obedient Gurgi had better sleep," Taran advised, "and so should we all. Medwyn has put us well on our way, and it can't take much longer. We'll start again at daybreak."

During the night, however, a gale rose, and by morning a drenching rain beat into the cleft. Instead of slackening, the wind gained in force and screamed over the rocks. It beat like a fist against the travelers' shelter, then pried with searching fingers, as if to seize and dash them into the valley.

They set out nevertheless, holding their cloaks before their faces. To make matters worse, the path broke off entirely and sheer cliffs loomed ahead of them. The rain stopped, after the travelers had all been soaked to the skin, but now the rocks were slippery and treacherous. Even the surefooted Melyngar stumbled once, and for a breathless moment Taran feared she would be lost.

The mountains swung a half-circle around a lake black and sullen below threatening clouds. Taran halted on an outcropping of stone and pointed toward the hills at the far side of the lake. "According to what Medwyn told us," he said to the bard, "we should make for that notch, all the way over there. But I see no purpose in following the mountains when we can cut almost straight across. The lake shore is flat, at least, while here it's getting practically impossible to climb."

Fflewddur rubbed his pointed nose. "Even counting the time it would take us to go down and come up again, I think we should save several hours. Yes, I definitely believe it's worth trying."

"Medwyn didn't say a word about crossing valleys," Eilonwy put in.

"He didn't say anything about cliffs like these," answered Taran. "They seem nothing to him; he's lived here a long time. For us, it's something else again."

"If you don't listen to what somebody tells you," Eilonwy remarked, "it's like putting your fingers in your ears and jumping down a well. For an Assistant Pig-Keeper who's done very little traveling, you suddenly know all about it."

"Who found the way out of the barrow?" Taran retorted. "It's decided. We cross the valley."

The descent was laborious, but once they had reached ground level, Taran felt all the more convinced they would save time. Holding Melyngar's bridle, he led the group along the narrow shore. The lake reached closely to the base of the hills, obliging Taran to splash through the shallows. The lake, he realized, was not black in reflection of the sky; the water itself was dark, flat, and as grim and heavy as iron. The bottom, too, was as treacherous as the rocks above. Despite his care, Taran lurched and nearly got a ducking. When he turned to warn the others, to his surprise he saw Gurgi in water up to his waist and heading toward the center of the lake. Fflewddur and Eilonwy were also splashing farther and farther from land.

"Don't go through the water," Taran called. "Keep to the shore!"

"Wish we could," the bard shouted back. "But we're stuck somehow. There's a terribly strong pull . . ."

A moment later, Taran understood what the bard meant. An unexpected swell knocked him off his feet and even as he put our his hands to break his fall the black lake sucked him down. Beside him, Melyngar thrashed her legs and whinnied. The sky spun overhead. He was pulled along like a twig in a torrent. Eilonwy shot past him. He tried to regain his footing and catch her. It was too late. He skimmed and bobbed over the surface. The far shore would stop them, Taran thought, struggling to keep his head above the waves. A roar filled his ears. The middle of the lake was a whirlpool clutching and flinging him to the depths. Black water closed over him, and he knew he was drowning.

CHAPTER XV

King Eiddileg

Down he spun, battling for air, in a flood that broke upon him like a crumbling mountain. Faster and faster the waters bore him along, tossing him right and left. Taran collided with something—what it was, he could not tell—but he clung to it even as his strength failed him. There was a crash, as though the earth had split asunder; the water turned to foam, and Taran felt himself dashed against an unyielding wall. He remembered nothing more.

When he opened his eyes he was lying on a hard, smooth surface, his hand tightly gripping Fflewddur's harp. He heard the rush of water close by. Cautiously, he felt around him; his fingers touched only wet, flat stone, an embankment of some kind. A pale blue light shone high above him. Taran decided he had come to rest in a cave or grotto. He raised himself and his movement set the harp to jangling.

"Hello! Who's that?" A voice echoed down the embankment. Faint though it was,

Taran recognized it as belonging to the bard. He scrambled to his feet and crept in the direction of the sound. On the way he tripped over a form, which became suddenly vocal and indignant.

"You've done very well, Taran of Caer Dallben, with all your shortcuts. What's left of me is soaked to the skin, and I can't find my bauble—oh, here it is, all wet, of course. And who knows what's happened to the rest of us?"

The golden light flared dimly to reveal the dripping face of Eilonwy, her blue eyes flashing with vexation.

Gurgi's hairy, sputtering shadow rolled toward them. "Oh, poor tender head is filled with sloshings and washings!"

In another moment Fflewddur had found them. Melyngar whinnied behind him. "I thought I heard my harp down here," he said. "I couldn't believe it at first. Never expected to see it again. But—a Fflam never despairs! Quite a stroke of luck, though."

"I never thought I'd see anything again," Taran said, handing the instrument to Fflewddur. "We've been washed into a cave of some kind; but it's not a natural one. Look at these flagstones."

"If you'd look at Melyngar," Eilonwy called, "you'd see all our provisions are gone. All our weapons, too, thanks to your precious short cut!"

It was true. The straps had broken loose and the saddle had torn away in the whirlpool. Luckily, the companions still had their swords.

"I'm sorry," Taran said. "I admit we are here through my fault. I should not have followed this path, but what's done is done. I led us here, and I'll find a way out."

He glanced around. The roar of water came from a wide, swift-running canal. The embankment itself was much broader than he had realized. Lights of various colors glowed in the high arches. He turned to his companions again. "This is very curious. We seem to be deep underground, but it isn't the lake bottom—"

Before he could utter another word, he was seized from behind, and a bag smelling strongly of onions was jammed over his head. Eilonwy screamed, then her voice grew muffled. Taran was being half-pushed, half-pulled in two directions at once. Gurgi began yelping furiously.

"Here! Get that one!" a gruff voice shouted.

"Get him yourself! Can't you see I've got my hands full?"

Taran struck out. A solid, round ball that must have been someone's head butted him in the stomach. There were slapping noises filtering through the oniony darkness around him. Those would be from Eilonwy. Now he was pushed from behind, propelled at top speed, while angry voices shouted at him—and at each other. "Hustle along there!"

"You fool, you didn't take their swords!"—At this, came another shriek from Eilonwy, the sound of what might have been a kick, then a moment of silence—"All right, let them keep their swords. You'll have the blame of it, letting them approach King Eiddileg with weapons!"

At a blind trot, Taran was shoved through what seemed a large crowd of people. Everyone was talking at once; the noise was deafening. After a number of turns, he was thrust forward again. A heavy door snapped behind him; the onion bag was snatched from his head.

Taran blinked. With Fflewddur and Eilonwy he stood in the center of a high-vaulted chamber, glittering with lights. Gurgi was nowhere in sight. Their captors were half-a-dozen squat, round, stubby-legged warriors. Axes hung from their belts and each man had a bow and quiver of arrows on his shoulder. The left eye of the short, burly fellow who stood beside Eilonwy was turning greenish-black.

Before them, at a long stone table, a dwarfish figure with a bristling yellow beard glared at the warriors. He wore a robe of garish red and green. Rings sparkled on his plump fingers. "What's this?" he shouted. "Who are these people? Didn't I give orders I wasn't to be disturbed?"

"But Majesty," began one of the warriors, shifting uneasily, "we caught them . . ."

"*Must* you bother me with details?" King Eiddileg cried, clasping his forehead. "You'll ruin me! You'll be the death of me! Out! Out! No, not the *prisoners,* you idiots!" Shaking his head, sighing and sputtering, the King collapsed onto a throne carved from rock. The guards scurried away. King Eiddileg shot a furious glance at Taran and his companions. "Now, then, out with it. What do you want? You might as well know ahead of time, you shan't have it."

"Sire," Taran began, "we ask no more than safe passage through your realm. The four of us . . ."

"There's only three of you," King Eiddileg snapped. "Can't you count?"

"One of my companions is missing," Taran said regretfully. He had hoped Gurgi would have overcome his fear, but he could not blame the creature for running off after his ordeal in the whirlpool. "I beg your servants to help us find him. Then, too, our provisions and weapons have been lost . . ."

"That's clotted nonsense!" shouted the King. "Don't lie to me, I can't stand it." He pulled an orange kerchief from his sleeve and mopped his forehead. "Why did you come here?"

"Because an Assistant Pig-Keeper led us on a wild-goose chase," Eilonwy interrupted. "We don't even know *where* we are, let alone why. It's worse than rolling downhill in the dark."

"Naturally," said Eiddileg, his voice dripping with sarcasm. "You have no idea you're in the very heart of the Kingdom of Tylwyth Teg, the Fair Folk, the Happy Family, the Little People, or whatever other insipid, irritating names you've put on us. Oh, no, of course not. You just happened to be passing by."

"We were caught in the lake," Taran protested. "It pulled us down."

"Good, eh?" King Eiddileg answered, with a quick smile of pride. "I've added some improvements of my own, of course."

"If you're so anxious to keep visitors away," Eilonwy said, "you should have something better—to make people stay *out.*"

"When people get this close," Eiddileg answered, "they're already *too* close. At that point, I don't want them out. I want them *in.*"

Fflewddur shook his head. "I always understood the Fair Folk were all over Prydain, not just here."

"Of course, not just here," said Eiddileg with impatience. "This is the royal seat. Why, we have tunnels and mines every place you can imagine. But the real work— the real labor of organization—is here, right here, in this very spot—in this very throne room. On my shoulders! It's too much, I tell you, too much. But who else can you trust? If you want something done right . . ." The King stopped suddenly and drummed his glittering fingers on the stone table. "That's not your affair," he said. "You're in trouble enough as it is. It can't be overlooked."

"*I* don't see any work being done," said Eilonwy.

Before Taran could warn Eilonwy not to be imprudent, the door of the throne room burst open and a crowd of folk pressed in. Looking closer, Taran saw not all were dwarfs; some were tall, slender, with white robes; others were covered with glistening scales like fish; still others fluttered large, delicate wings. For some moments Taran heard nothing but a confusion of voices, angry outcries and bick-ering, with Eiddileg trying to shout above them. Finally, the King managed to push them all out again. "No work being done?" he cried. "You don't appreciate everything that goes into it. The Children of Evening—that's another ridiculous name you humans have thought up—are to sing in the forest of Cantrev Mawr tonight. They haven't even practiced. Two are sick and one can't be found.

"The Lake Sprites have been quarreling all day; now they're sulking. Their hair's a mess. And who does that reflect on? Who has to jolly them along, coax them, plead with them? The answer is obvious.

"What thanks do I get for it?" King Eiddileg ranted on. "None at all! Has any of you long-legged gawks ever taken the trouble—even once, mind you—to offer the simplest expression of gratitude, such as, 'Thank you, King Eiddileg, for the tremen-dous effort and inconvenience you've gone to, so that we can enjoy a little charm and beauty in the world above, which would be so unspeakably grim without you and your Fair Folk'? Just a few words of honest appreciation?

"By no means! Just the opposite! If any of you thick-skulled oafs come on one of the Fair Folk above ground, what happens? You seize him! You grab him with your great hammy hands and try to make him lead you to buried treasure. Or you squeeze him until you get three wishes out of him—not satisfied with one, oh, no, but *three*!

"Well, I don't mind telling you this," Eiddileg went on, his face turning redder by the moment, "I've put an end to all this wish-granting and treasure-scavenging. No more! Absolutely not! I'm surprised you didn't ruin us long ago!"

Just then a chorus of voices rose from behind the door of Eiddileg's throne room. The harmonies penetrated even the walls of heavy stone. Taran had never in his life heard such beautiful singing. He listened, enchanted, forgetting, for the moment, all but the soaring melody. Eiddileg himself stopped shouting and puffing until the voices died away.

"That's something to be thankful for," the King said at last. "The Children of Evening have evidently got together again. Not as good as you might want, but they'll manage somehow."

"I have not heard the songs of the Fair Folk until now," Taran said. "I had never realized how lovely they were."

"Don't try to flatter me," Eiddileg cried, trying to look furious, yet beaming at the same time.

"What surprises me," Eilonwy said, while the bard plucked meditatively at his harp, trying to recapture the notes of the song, "is why you go to so much trouble. If you Fair Folk dislike all of us above ground, why do you bother?"

"Professional pride, my dear girl," said the Dwarf King, putting a chubby hand to his heart and bowing slightly. "When we Fair Folk do something, we do it right. Oh, yes," he sighed, "never mind the sacrifices we make. It's a task that needs doing, and so we do it. Never mind the cost. For myself," he added, with a wave of his hand, "it doesn't matter. I've lost sleep, I've lost weight, but that's not important . . ."

If King Eiddileg had lost weight, Taran thought to himself, what must he have been like beforehand? He decided against asking this question.

"Well, *I* appreciate it," Eilonwy said. "I think it's amazing what you've been able to do. You must be extremely clever, and any Assistant Pig-Keepers who happen to be in this throne room might do well to pay attention."

"Thank you, dear girl," said King Eiddileg, bowing lower. "I see you're the sort of person one can talk to intelligently. It's unheard of for one of you big shambling louts to have any kind of insight into these matters. But you at least seem to understand the problems we face."

"Sire," interrupted Taran, "we understand your time is precious. Let us disturb you no more. Give us safe conduct to Caer Dathyl."

"What?" shouted Eiddileg. "Leave here? Impossible! Unheard of! Once you're with the Fair Folk, my good lad, you *stay*, and no mistake about it. Oh, I suppose I could stretch a point, for the sake of the young lady, and let you off easily. Only put you to sleep for fifty years, or turn you all into bats; but that would be a pure favor, mind you."

"Our task is urgent," Taran cried. "Even now we have delayed too long."

"That's your concern, not mine." Eiddileg shrugged.

"Then we shall make our own way," Taran shouted, drawing his sword. Fflewddur's blade leaped out and the bard stood with Taran, ready to fight.

"More clotted nonsense," King Eiddileg said, looking contemptuously at the swords pointed toward him. He shook his fingers at them. "There! And there! Now you might try to move your arms."

Taran strained every muscle. His body felt turned to stone.

"Put your swords away and let's talk this over calmly," said the Dwarf King, gesturing again. "If you give me any decent reason why I should let you go, I might think it over and answer you promptly, say in a year or two."

There could be no use, Taran saw, in concealing the reasons for his journey; he explained to Eiddileg what had befallen them. The Dwarf King ceased his blustering at the mention of Arawn, but when Taran had finished, King Eiddileg shook his head.

"This is a conflict you great gawks must attend to yourselves. The Fair Folk owe you no allegiance," he said angrily. "Prydain belonged to us before the race of men came. *You* drove us underground. You plundered our mines, you blundering clod-poles! You stole our treasures, and you keep on stealing them, you clumsy oafs . . ."

"Sire," Taran answered, "I can speak for no man but myself. I have never robbed you and I have no wish to. My task means more to me than your treasures. If there is ill will between the Fair Folk and the race of men, then it is a matter to be settled between them. But if the Horned King triumphs, if the shadow of Annuvin falls on the land above you, Arawn's hand will reach your deepest caverns."

"For an Assistant Pig-Keeper," said Eiddileg, "you're reasonably eloquent. But the Fair Folk will worry about Arawn when the time comes."

"The time has come," Taran said. "I only hope it has not passed."

"I don't think you really know what's going on above ground," Eilonwy suddenly exclaimed. "You talk about charm and beauty and sacrificing yourself to make things pleasant for people. I don't believe you care a bit for that. You're too conceited and stubborn and selfish . . ."

"Conceited!" shouted Eiddileg, his eyes popping. "Selfish! You won't find anyone more open-hearted and generous. How dare you say that? What do you want, my life's blood?" With that, he tore off his cloak and threw it in the air, pulled the rings from his fingers and tossed them in every direction. "Go ahead! Take it all! Leave me ruined! What else do you want—my whole kingdom? Do you want to leave? Go, by all means. The sooner the better! Stubborn? I'm too soft! It will be the death of me! But little you care!"

At that moment the door of the throne room burst open again. Two dwarf warriors clung frantically to Gurgi, who swung them about as if they were rabbits.

"Joyous greetings! Faithful Gurgi is back with mighty heroes! This time valiant

Gurgi did not run! Oh, no, no! Brave Gurgi fought with great whackings and smackings. He triumphed! But then, mighty lords are carried away. Clever Gurgi goes seeking and peeking to save them, yes! And he finds them!

"But that is not all. Oh, faithful, honest, fearless Gurgi finds more. Surprises and delights, oh, joy!" Gurgi was so excited that he began dancing on one foot, spinning around and clapping his hands.

"Mighty warriors go to seek a piggy! It is clever, wise Gurgi who finds her!"

"Hen Wen?" cried Taran. "Where is she?"

"Here, mighty lord," Gurgi shouted, "the piggy is here!"

CHAPTER XVI

Doli

Taran turned accusingly to King Eiddileg. "You said nothing of Hen Wen."

"You didn't ask me," said Eiddileg.

"That's sharp practice," Fflewddur muttered, "even for a king."

"It's worse than a lie," Taran said angrily. "You'd have let us go our way, and we'd never have known what happened to her."

"You should be ashamed of yourself," Eilonwy put in, shaking her finger at the King, who appeared most embarrassed at being found out. "It's like looking the other way when someone's about to walk into a hole."

"Finders keepers," the Dwarf King snapped. "A troop of the Fair Folk came on her near the Avren banks. She was running through a ravine. And I'll tell you something you don't know. Half-a-dozen warriors were after her, the henchmen of the Horned King. The troop took care of those warriors—we have our own ways of dealing with you clumsy lummoxes—and they brought your pig here, underground most of the way."

"No wonder Gwydion could find no tracks," Taran murmured to himself.

"The Fair Folk rescued her," Eiddileg angrily continued, turning bright red, "and there's another fine example. Do I get a word of thanks? Naturally not. But I do get called disagreeable names and have nasty thoughts thrown at me. Oh, I can see it in your faces. Eiddileg is a thief and a wretch—that's what you're saying to yourselves. Well, just for that you shan't have her back. And you'll stay here, all of you, until I feel like letting you go."

Eilonwy gasped with indignation. "If you do that," she cried, "you *are* a thief and a wretch! You gave me your word. The Fair Folk don't go back on their word."

"There was no mention of a pig, no mention at all." Eiddileg clapped his hands over his paunch and snapped his mouth shut.

"No," Taran said, "there was not. But there is a question of honesty and honor."

Eiddileg blinked and looked sideways. He took out his orange kerchief and mopped his brow again. "Honor," he muttered, "yes, I was afraid you'd come to that. True, the Fair Folk never break their word. Well," he sighed, "that's the price for being openhearted and generous. So be it. You shall have your pig."

"We shall need weapons to replace those we lost," Taran said.

"What?" screamed Eiddileg. "Are you trying to ruin me?"

"And crunchings and munchings!" piped up Gurgi.

Taran nodded. "Provisions, as well."

"This is going too far," Eiddileg shouted. "You're bleeding me to death! Weapons! Food! Pigs!"

"And we beg for a guide who will show us the way to Caer Dathyl."

At this, Eiddileg nearly exploded. When finally he calmed himself, he nodded reluctantly. "I shall lend you Doli," he said. "He is the only one I can spare." He clapped his hands and gave orders to the armed dwarfs, then turned to the companions.

"Off with you now, before I change my mind."

Eilonwy stepped quickly to the throne, bent and kissed Eiddileg on the top of his head. "Thank you," she whispered, "you're a perfectly lovely king."

"Out! Out!" the dwarf cried. As the stone door closed behind him, Taran saw King Eiddileg fondling his head and beaming happily.

The troop of Fair Folk led the company down the vaulted corridors. Taran had at first imagined Eiddileg's realm to be no more than a maze of underground galleries. To his astonishment, the corridors soon broadened into wide avenues. In the great domes far overhead, gems glittered as bright as sunshine. There was no grass, but deep carpets of green lichen stretched out like meadows. There were blue lakes, glistening as much as the jewels above; and cottages, and small farmhouses. It was difficult for Taran and his companions to realize they were underground.

"I've been thinking," whispered Fflewddur, "that it might be wiser to leave Hen Wen here, until we can return for her."

"I thought of that, too," answered Taran. "It's not that I don't trust Eiddileg to keep his word—most of the time. But I'm not sure we should take another chance in that lake, and I doubt we could find another way into his kingdom. He certainly won't make it easy for us to come back, I'm afraid. No, we must take Hen Wen while we have the chance. Once she's with me again, I won't let her out of my sight."

Suddenly the Fair Folk halted at one of the cottages, and from a neatly carpentered pen Taran heard a loud "Hwoinch!"

He raced to the sty. Hen Wen was standing with her front feet on the rails, grunting at the top of her voice.

One of the Fair Folk opened the gate and the white pig burst out, wriggling and squealing.

Taran threw his arms around Hen Wen's neck. "Oh, Hen!" he cried. "Even Medwyn thought you were dead!"

"Hwch! Hwaaw!" Hen Wen chuckled joyfully. Her beady eyes sparkled. With her great pink snout she rooted affectionately under Taran's chin and came close to knocking him down.

"She looks like a wonderful pig," Eilonwy said, scratching Hen Wen behind the ears. "It's always nice to see two friends meet again. It's like waking up with the sun shining."

"She's certainly a great deal of pig," agreed the bard, "though very handsome, I must say."

"And clever, noble, brave, wise Gurgi found her."

"Have no fear," Taran said with a smile to Gurgi, "there's no chance we'll forget it."

Rolling and waddling on short legs, Hen Wen followed Taran happily, while the Fair Folk proceeded across the fields to where a stocky figure waited. The captain of the troop announced that this was Doli, the guide Eiddileg had promised. Doli, short and stumpy, almost as broad as he was tall, wore a rust-colored leather jacket and stout, knee-high boots. A round cap covered his head, but not enough to conceal a fringe of flaming red hair. An axe and short sword hung from his belt; and over his shoulder, he wore the stubby bow of the Fair Folk warrior.

Taran bowed politely. The dwarf stared at him with a pair of bright red eyes and snorted. Then, to Taran's surprise, Doli took a deep breath and held it until his face turned scarlet and he looked about to burst. After a few moments, the dwarf puffed out his cheeks and snorted again.

"What's the trouble?" asked Taran.

"You can still see me, can't you?" Doli burst out angrily.

"Of course, I can still see you." Taran frowned. "Why shouldn't I?"

Doli gave him a scornful look and did not answer.

Two of the Fair Folk led up Melyngar. King Eiddileg, Taran saw with relief, was as good as his word. The saddlebags bulged with provisions, and the white mare also carried a number of spears, bows, and arrows—short and heavy, as were all the weapons of the Fair Folk, but carefully and sturdily crafted.

Without another word, Doli beckoned them to follow him across the meadow. Grumbling and muttering to himself, the dwarf led them to what seemed to be the sheer face of a cliff. Only after he had reached it did Taran see long flights of steps carved into the living rock. Doli jerked his head toward the stairway and they began to climb.

This passageway of the Fair Folk was steeper than any of the mountains they had crossed. Melyngar strained forward. Wheezing and gasping, Hen Wen pulled herself up each step. The stairway turned and twisted; at one point, the darkness was such that the companions lost sight of each other. After a time, the steps broke off and the group trod a narrow pathway of hard-packed stones. Sheets of white light rippled ahead and the travelers found themselves behind a high waterfall. One after the other, they leaped the glistening rocks, splashed through a foaming stream, and at last emerged into the cool air of the hills.

Doli squinted up at the sun. "Not much daylight left," he muttered, more gruffly than King Eiddileg himself. "Don't think I'm going to walk my legs off all night, either. Didn't ask for this work, you know. Got picked for it. Guiding a crew of—of what! An Assistant Pig-Keeper. A yellow-headed idiot with a harp. A girl with a sword. A shaggy what-is-it. Not to mention the livestock. All you can hope for is you don't run into a real war band. They'd do for you, they would. There's not one of you looks as if he could handle a blade. Humph!"

This was the most Doli had spoken since they had left Eiddileg's realm and, despite the dwarf's uncomplimentary opinions, Taran hoped he would finally come around to being civil. Doli, however, had said all he intended to say for a while; later, when Taran ventured to speak to him, the dwarf turned angrily away and started holding his breath again.

"For goodness sake," Eilonwy cried, "I wish you'd stop that. It makes me feel as if I'd drunk too much water, just watching you."

"It still doesn't work," Doli growled.

"Whatever are you trying to do?" Taran asked.

Even Hen Wen stared curiously at the dwarf.

"What does it look like?" Doli answered. "I'm trying to make myself invisible."

"That's an odd thing to attempt," remarked Fflewddur.

"I'm *supposed* to be invisible," snapped Doli. "My whole family can do it. Just like that! Like blowing out a candle. But not me. No wonder they all laugh at me. No wonder Eiddileg sends me out with a pack of fools. If there's anything nasty or dis-agreeable to be done, it's always 'find good old Doli.' If there's gems to be cut or blades to be decorated or arrows to be footed—that's the job for good old Doli!"

The dwarf held his breath again, this time so long that his face turned blue and his ears trembled.

"I think you're getting it now," said the bard, with an encouraging smile. "I can't see you at all." No sooner had this remark passed his lips than a harp string snapped in two. Fflewddur looked sorrowfully at the instrument. "Blast the thing," he muttered, "I knew I was exaggerating somewhat; I only did it to make him feel better. He actually did seem to be fading a bit around the edges."

"If I could carve gems and do all those other things," Taran remarked sympathetically to Doli, "I wouldn't mind not being invisible. All I know is vegetables and horseshoes, and not too much about either."

"It's silly," Eilonwy added, "to worry because you can't do something you simply can't do. That's worse than trying to make yourself taller by standing on your head."

None of these well-intentioned remarks cheered the dwarf, who strode angrily ahead, swinging his axe from side to side. Despite his bad temper, Doli was an excellent guide, Taran realized. Most of the time, the dwarf said little beyond his usual grunts and snorts, making no attempt to explain the path he followed or to suggest how long it would take the companions to reach Caer Dathyl. Taran, nevertheless, had learned a great deal of woodcraft and tracking during his journey, and he was aware the companions had begun turning westward to descend the hills. They had, during the afternoon, covered more ground than Taran thought possible, and he knew it was thanks to Doli's expert guidance. When he congratulated the dwarf, Doli answered only, "Humph!"—and held his breath.

They camped that night on the sheltered slope of the last barrier of mountains. Gurgi, whom Taran had taught to build a fire, was delighted to be useful; he cheerfully gathered twigs, dug a cooking pit, and, to the surprise of all, distributed the provisions equally without saving out a private share for his own crunchings and munchings later on.

Doli refused to do anything whatsoever. He took his own food from a large leather wallet hanging at his side, and sat on a rock, chewing glumly; he snorted with annoyance between every mouthful, and occasionally held his breath.

"Keep at it, old boy!" called Fflewddur. "Another try might do it! Your outline looks definitely blurred."

"Oh, hush!" Eilonwy told the bard. "Don't encourage him or he'll decide to hold his breath forever."

"Just lending support," explained the crestfallen bard. "A Fflam never gives up, and I don't see why a dwarf should."

Hen Wen had not left Taran's side all day. Now, as he spread his cloak on the ground, the white pig grunted with pleasure, waddled over, and hunkered down beside him. Her crinkled ears relaxed; she thrust her snout comfortably against Taran's shoulder and chuckled contentedly, a blissful smile on her face. Soon the whole weight of her head pressed on him, making it impossible for Taran to roll onto his side. Hen Wen snored luxuriously and Taran resigned himself to sleeping, despite the assortment of whistles and groans directly below his ear. "I'm glad to see you, Hen," he said, "and I'm glad you're glad to see me. But I wish you wouldn't be so loud about it."

Next morning they turned their backs on the Eagle Mountains and began heading for what Taran hoped would be Caer Dathyl. As the trees rose more densely around them, Taran turned for a last glimpse of the Eagle itself, tall and serene in the distance. He was grateful their path had not led them over it, but in his heart he hoped one day to return and climb its towers of sun-flecked ice and black stone. Until this journey, he had never seen mountains, but now he understood why Gwydion had spoken longingly of Caer Dathyl.

His thought led Taran to wonder again what else Gwydion had expected to learn from Hen Wen. When they halted, he spoke to Fflewddur about it.

"There may be someone in Caer Dathyl who can understand her," Taran said. "But if we could only get her to prophesy now, she might tell us something important."

The bard agreed; however, as Taran had pointed out, they had no letter sticks.

"I could try a new spell," offered Eilonwy. "Achren taught me some others, but I don't know if they'd be any use. They haven't anything to do with oracular pigs. I do know a wonderful one for summoning toads. Achren was about to teach me the spell for opening locks, but I don't suppose I'll ever learn it now. Even so, locks haven't much to do with pigs, either."

Eilonwy knelt beside Hen Wen and whispered rapidly. Hen Wen seemed to listen politely for a while, grinning broadly, wheezing, and snuffling. She gave no sign of understanding a word of what the girl was saying; and at last, with a joyful "Hwoinch!" she broke away and ran to Taran, wriggling gleefully.

"It's no use," Taran said, "and there's no sense in losing time. I hope they have letter sticks in Caer Dathyl. Though I doubt it. Whatever Dallben has, it seems to be the only one of its kind in all Prydain."

They resumed their march. Gurgi, now official cook and firemaker, strode boldly behind the dwarf. Doli led the companions through a clearing and past a line of alders. A few moments later the dwarf halted and cocked his head.

Taran heard the sound, too: a faint, high-pitched screaming. It seemed to come from a twisted thornbush. Drawing his sword, Taran hurried past the dwarf. At first he could see nothing in the dark tangle. He drew closer, then stopped abruptly.

It was a gwythaint.

CHAPTER XVII

The Fledgling

The gwythaint hung like a crumpled black rag, one wing upraised, the other folded awkwardly on its breast. No larger than a raven, it was young and barely out of its first moult; the head seemed a little too big for its body, the feathers thin and quilly. As Taran cautiously approached, the gwythaint fluttered vainly, unable to free itself. The bird opened its curved beak and hissed warningly; but its eyes were dull and half-closed.

The companions had followed Taran. As soon as Gurgi saw what it was, he hunched up his shoulders, and with many fearful glances behind him, turned and crept off to a safe distance. Melyngar whinnied nervously. The white pig, undisturbed, sat on her haunches and looked cheerful.

Fflewddur, on seeing the bird, gave a low whistle. "It's a stroke of luck the parents aren't about," he said. "Those creatures will tear a man to shreds if their young are in danger."

"It reminds me of Achren," Eilonwy said, "especially around the eyes, on days when she was in a bad temper."

Doli pulled his axe from his belt.

"What are you going to do?" Taran asked.

The dwarf looked at him with surprise. "Going to do? Do you have any other stupid questions? You can't imagine I'd let it sit there, can you? I'm going to chop off its head, to begin with."

"No!" cried Taran, seizing the dwarf's arm. "It's badly hurt."

"Be glad of that," snapped Doli. "If it weren't, neither you nor I nor any of us would be standing here."

"I will not have it killed," Taran declared. "It's in pain and it needs help."

"That's true," Eilonwy said, "it doesn't look comfortable at all. For the matter of that, it looks even worse than Achren."

The dwarf threw his axe to the ground and put his hands on his hips. "I can't make myself invisible," he snorted, "but at least I'm no fool. Go ahead. Pick up the vicious little thing. Give it a drink. Pat its head. Then you'll see what happens. As soon as it's got strength enough, the first thing it'll do is slice you to bits. And next thing, fly straight to Arawn. Then we'll be in a fine stew."

"What Doli says is true," Fflewddur added. "I myself don't enjoy chopping things up—the bird is interesting, in a disagreeable sort of way. But we've been lucky so far, with no trouble from gwythaints, at least. I don't see the use of bringing one of Arawn's spies right into our bosom, as you might say. A Fflam is always kindhearted, but it seems to me this is overdoing it."

"Medwyn would not say so," Taran answered. "In the hills, he spoke of kindness for all creatures; and he told me much about the gwythaints. I think it's important to bring this one to Caer Dathyl. No one has ever captured a live gwythaint, as far as I know. Who can tell what value it may have?"

The bard scratched his head. "Well, yes, I suppose if it had any use at all, it would be better alive than dead. But the proposition is risky, no matter what."

Taran gestured for the others to stand away from the bush. He saw the gwythaint was wounded by more than thorns; perhaps an eagle had challenged it, for blood flecked its back and a number of feathers had been torn out. He reached in carefully. The gwythaint hissed again, and a long, rasping rattle sounded in its throat. Taran feared the bird might be dying even then. He put a hand under its feverish body. The gwythaint struck with beak and talons, but its strength had gone. Taran lifted it free of the thornbush.

"If I can find the right herbs, I'll make a poultice," Taran told Eilonwy. "But I'll need hot water to steep them." While the girl prepared a nest of grass and leaves, Taran asked Gurgi to build a fire and heat some stones, which could be dropped into a cup of water. Then, with Hen Wen at his heels, he quickly set out to search for the plants.

"How long are we going to stay here?" Doli shouted after him. "Not that I care. You're the ones in a hurry, not I. Humph!" He thrust his axe into his belt, jammed his cap tight on his head, and furiously held his breath.

Taran was again grateful for what Coll had taught him of herbs. He found most of what he needed growing nearby. Hen Wen joined the hunt with enthusiasm, grunting happily, rooting under leaves and stones. Indeed, the white pig was the first to discover an important variety Taran had overlooked.

The gwythaint did not struggle when Taran applied the poultice; soaking a piece of cloth torn from his jacket in another healing brew, he squeezed the liquid drop by drop into the bird's beak.

"That's all very well," said Doli, whose curiosity had got the better of him, and who had come to observe the operation. "How do you imagine you'll carry the nasty thing—perched on your shoulder?"

"I don't know," Taran said. "I thought I could wrap it in my cloak."

Doli snorted. "That's the trouble with you great clodhoppers. You don't see beyond your noses. But if you expect me to build a cage for you, you're mistaken."

"A cage would be just the thing," Taran agreed. "No, I wouldn't want to bother you with that. I'll try to make one myself."

The dwarf watched contemptuously while Taran gathered saplings and attempted to weave them together.

"Oh, stop it!" Doli finally burst out. "I can't stand looking at botched work. Here, get out of the way." He shouldered Taran aside, squatted on the ground, and picked up the saplings. He trimmed them expertly with his knife, lashed them with braided vines, and in no time at all the dwarf held up a serviceable cage.

"That's certainly more practical than making yourself invisible," Eilonwy said. The dwarf made no answer and only looked at her angrily.

Taran lined the bottom of the cage with leaves, gently put the gwythaint inside, and they resumed their march. Doli now led them at a faster pace, to make up for the time they had lost. He tramped steadily down the hill slopes without even turning to see whether Taran and the others were able to keep up with him. The speed of their pace, Taran realized, served little purpose, since they were obliged to halt more frequently. But he did not deem it wise to mention this to the dwarf.

Throughout the day the gwythaint steadily improved. At each halt, Taran fed the bird and applied the medicines. Gurgi was still too terrified to come near; Taran alone dared handle the creature. When Fflewddur, endeavoring to make friends, put his finger into the cage, the gwythaint roused and slashed at him with its beak.

"I warn you," snapped Doli, "no good will come of this. But don't pay any attention to what I say. Go right ahead. Cut your own throats. Then come running and complaining afterward. I'm just a guide; I do what I'm ordered to, and that's all."

At nightfall they made camp and discussed plans for the morrow. The gwythaint had entirely recovered, and had also developed an enormous appetite. It squawked furiously when Taran did not bring its food quickly enough, and rattled its beak against the cage. It gobbled up the morsels Taran gave it, then looked around for more. After eating, the gwythaint crouched at the bottom of the cage, its head cocked and listening, its eyes following every movement. Taran finally ventured to put a finger past the bars and scratch the gwythaint's head. The creature no longer hissed, and it made no attempt to bite him. The gwythaint even allowed Eilonwy to feed it, but the bard's attempts to make friends failed.

"It knows perfectly well you'd have agreed to chop off its head," Eilonwy told Fflewddur, "so you can't blame the poor thing for being annoyed at you. If somebody wanted to chop off *my* head, then came around afterward and wanted to be sociable, I'd peck at him too."

"Gwydion told me the birds are trained when young," Taran said. "I wish he were here. He would know best how to handle the creature. Perhaps it could be taught differently. But there's bound to be a good falconer at Caer Dathyl, and we'll see what he can do."

But next morning, the cage was empty.

Doli, who had risen long before the others, was the first to discover it. The furious dwarf thrust the cage under Taran's nose. The sapling bars had been slashed to pieces by the gwythaint's beak.

"And there you have it!" cried Doli. "I told you so! Don't say I didn't warn you. The treacherous creature's halfway to Annuvin by now, after listening to every word we said. If Arawn didn't know where we are, he'll know soon enough. You've done well; oh, very well," Doli snorted. "Spare me from fools and Assistant Pig-Keepers!"

Taran could not hide his disappointment or fear.

Fflewddur said nothing, but the bard's face was grim.

"I've done the wrong thing again, as usual," Taran said angrily. "Doli is right. There's no difference between a fool and an Assistant Pig-Keeper."

"That's probably true," agreed Eilonwy, whose remark did nothing to cheer Taran.

"But," she went on, "I can't stand people who say 'I told you so.' That's worse than somebody coming up and eating your dinner before you have a chance to sit down.

"Even so," she added, "Doli means well. He's not half as disagreeable as he pretends to be, and I'm sure he's worried about us. He's like a porcupine, all prickly on the outside, but very ticklish once you turn him over. If he'd only stop trying to make himself invisible, I think it should do a lot to improve his disposition."

There was no time for further regrets. Doli set them an even swifter pace. They still followed the hills along the Ystrad valley, but at midday the dwarf turned west and once more began to descend toward the plains. The sky had grown as thick and gray as lead. Violent gusts of wind whipped at their faces. The pale sun gave no warmth. Melyngar neighed uneasily; Hen Wen, placid and agreeable until now, began to roll her eyes and mutter to herself.

While the companions rested briefly, Doli went ahead to scout the land. In a short time he was back again. He led them to the crest of a hill, motioned them to stay close to the ground, and pointed toward the Ystrad below.

The plain was covered with warriors, on foot and on horseback. Black banners snapped in the wind. Even at this distance, Taran could hear the clank of weapons, the steady, heavy drumming of marching feet. At the head of the winding columns rode the Horned King.

The giant figure towered above the men-at-arms, who galloped behind him. The curving antlers rose like eager claws. As Taran watched, terrified but unable to turn away, the Horned King's head swung slowly in the direction of the heights. Taran pressed flat, against the earth. Arawn's champion, he was sure, could not see him; it was only a trick of his mind, a mirror of his own fear, but it seemed the Horned King's eyes sought him out and thrust like daggers at his heart.

"They have overtaken us," Taran said in a flat voice.

"Hurry," snapped the dwarf. "Get hustling, instead of dawdling and moaning. We're no more than a day away from Caer Dathyl and so are they. We can still move faster. If you hadn't stopped for that ungrateful spy of Annuvin, we'd be well ahead of them by now. Don't say I didn't warn you."

"We should arm ourselves a little better," the bard said. "The Horned King will have outriders on both sides of the valley."

Taran unstrapped the weapons on Melyngar's back and handed a bow and quiver of arrows to his companions, as well as a short spear for each. King Eiddileg had given them round bronze bucklers; they were dwarf-size and, after his view of the marching hosts, Taran found them pitifully small. Gurgi buckled a short sword around his waist. Of all the band, he was the most excited.

"Yes, yes!" he cried. "Now bold, valiant Gurgi is a mighty warrior, too! He has a grinding gasher and a pointed piercer! He is ready for great fightings and smitings!"

"And so am I!" Fflewddur declared. "Nothing withstands the onslaught of an angry Fflam!"

The dwarf clapped his hands to his head and gnashed his teeth. "Stop jabbering and move!" he sputtered. This time he was too furious to hold his breath.

Taran slung the buckler over his shoulder. Hen Wen hung back and grunted fearfully. "I know you're afraid," Taran whispered coaxingly, "but you'll be safe in Caer Dathyl."

The pig followed reluctantly; but as Doli set off once again, she lagged behind, and it was all Taran could do to urge her forward. Her pink snout trembled; her eyes darted from one side of the path to the other.

At the next halt Doli summoned Taran. "Keep on like this," he cried, "and you'll have no chance at all. First a gwythaint delays us, now a pig!"

"She's frightened," Taran tried to explain to the angry dwarf. "She knows the Horned King is near."

"Then tie her up," Doli said. "Put her on the horse."

Taran nodded. "Yes. She won't like it, but there's nothing else we can do."

A few moments before, the pig had been crouched at the roots of a tree. Now there was no sign of her.

"Hen?" Taran called. He turned to the bard. "Where did she go?" he asked in alarm.

The bard shook his head. Neither he nor Eilonwy had seen her move; Gurgi had been watering Melyngar and had not noticed the pig at all.

"She can't have run off again," Taran cried. He raced back into the woods. When he returned, his face was pale.

"She's gone," he gasped. "She's hiding somewhere, I know it."

He sank to the ground and put his head in his hands. "I shouldn't have let her out of my sight, not even for a moment," he said bitterly. "I have failed twice."

"Let the others go on," Eilonwy said. "We'll find her and catch up with them."

Before Taran could answer, he heard a sound that chilled his blood. From the hills came the voices of a hunting pack in full cry and the long notes of a horn.

The companions stood frozen with dread. With the ice of terror in his throat, Taran looked at the silent faces around him. The dire music trembled in the air; a shadow flickered across the lowering sky.

"Where Gwyn the Hunter rides," murmured Fflewddur, "death rides close behind."

CHAPTER XVIII
The Flame of Dyrnwyn

No sooner had the notes of Gwyn's horn sunk into the hills than Taran started, as though waking from a fearful dream. Hoofbeats drummed across the meadow.

"The Horned King's scouts!" cried Fflewddur, pointing to the mounted warriors galloping toward them. "They've seen us!"

Up from the plains the riders sped, bent over their saddles, urging on their steeds. They drew closer, lances leveled as if each gleaming point sought its own target.

"I could try to make another web," Eilonwy suggested, then added, "but I'm afraid the last one wasn't too useful."

Taran's sword flashed out. "There are only four of them," he said. "We match them in numbers at least."

"Put up your blade," Fflewddur said. "Arrows first. We'll have work enough for swords later."

They unslung their bows. Under Fflewddur's orders, they formed a line and knelt shoulder to shoulder. The bard's spiky yellow hair blew in the wind; his face shone with excitement. "I haven't had a good fight in years," he said. "That's one of the things I miss, being a bard. They'll see what it means to attack a Fflam!"

Taran nocked an arrow to the string. At a word from the bard, the companions drew their bows and took aim.

"Loose!" shouted Fflewddur.

Taran saw his own shaft fly wide of the leading horseman. With a cry of anger, he seized another arrow from the quiver. Beside him, he heard Gurgi shout triumphantly. Of the volley, only Gurgi's bolt had found its mark. A warrior toppled from his horse, the shaft deep in his throat.

"They know we can sting!" Fflewddur cried. "Loose again!"

The horsemen veered. More cautious now, the warriors raised their bucklers. Of the three, two drove directly for the companions; the third turned his mount's head and galloped to the flank of the defenders.

"Now, friends," shouted the bard, "back to back!"

Taran heard Doli grunt as the dwarf loosed an arrow at the nearest warrior. Gurgi's shot had been lucky; now the shafts hissed through the air only to glance off the attackers' light shields. Behind Taran, Melyngar whinnied and pawed the ground frantically. Taran remembered how valiantly she had fought for Gwydion, but she was tethered now and he dared not break away from the defenders to untie her.

The horsemen circled. One turned his exposed side to the companions. Doli's arrow leaped from the bowstring and buried itself in the warrior's neck. The other horsemen spun their mounts and galloped across the meadow.

"We've beaten them!" cried Eilonwy. "That's like bees driving away eagles!"

The panting Fflewddur shook his head. "They'll spend no more men on us. When they come back, they'll come back with a war band. That's highly complimentary to our bravery, but I don't think we should wait for them. A Fflam knows when to fight and when to run. At this point, we had better run."

"I won't leave Hen Wen," cried Taran.

"Go look for her," growled Doli. "You'll lose your head as well as your pig."

"Crafty Gurgi will go," suggested Gurgi, "with bold seekings and peekings."

"In all likelihood," said the bard, "they'll attack us again. We can't afford to lose what little strength we have. A Fflam never worries about being outnumbered, but one sword less could be fatal. I'm sure your pig is able to look out for herself; wherever she may be, she is in less danger than we are."

Taran nodded. "It is true. But it grieves me to lose her for the second time. I had chosen to abandon my search and go to Caer Dathyl; then, after Gurgi found Hen Wen, I had hoped to accomplish both tasks. But I fear it must be one or the other."

"The question is," said Fflewddur, "is there any chance at all of warning the Sons of Don before the Horned King attacks? Doli is the only one who can answer that."

The dwarf scowled and thought for a few moments. "Possible," he said, "but we'll have to go into the valley. We'll be in the middle of the Horned King's vanguard if we do."

"Can we get through?" asked Taran.

"Won't know until you've tried," grunted Doli.

"The decision is yours," said the bard, glancing at Taran.

"We shall try," Taran answered.

For the rest of that day they traveled without a halt. At nightfall, Taran would have been glad to rest, but the dwarf warned against it. The companions pressed on in weary silence. They had escaped the attack Fflewddur expected, but a column of horsemen bearing torches passed within bowshot of them. The companions crouched in the fringe of trees until the streaks of flame wound behind a hill and vanished. In a short time, Doli led the little band into the valley, where they found concealment in the wooded groves.

But the dawn revealed a sight that filled Taran with despair. The valley roiled with warriors wherever he turned his eyes. Black banners whipped against the sky. The host of the Horned King was like the body of an armed giant restlessly stirring.

For a moment, Taran stared in disbelief. He turned his face away. "Too late," he murmured. "Too late. We have failed."

While the dwarf surveyed the marching columns, Fflewddur strode forward. "There is one thing we can do," he cried. "Caer Dathyl lies straight ahead. Let us go on, and make our last stand there."

Taran nodded. "Yes. My place is at the side of Gwydion's people. Doli shall lead Gurgi and Eilonwy to safety." He took a deep breath and buckled his sword belt more tightly. "You have guided us well," he said quietly to the dwarf. "Return to your king with our gratitude. Your work is done."

The dwarf looked at him furiously. "Done!" he snorted. "Idiots and numbskulls! It's not that I care what happens to you, but don't think I'm going to watch you get hacked to pieces. I can't stand a botched job. Like it or not, I'm going with you."

Before the words were out of his mouth, an arrow sang past Doli's head. Melyngar reared up. A party of foot soldiers sprang from the woods behind the companions. "Begone!" the bard shouted to Taran. "Ride as fast as you can, or it will be death for all of us!"

When Taran hesitated, the bard seized him by the shoulders, pitched him toward the horse, and thrust Eilonwy after him. Fflewddur drew his sword. "Do as I say!" shouted the bard, his eyes blazing.

Taran leaped to Melyngar's saddle and pulled Eilonwy up behind him. The white horse shot forward. Eilonwy clung to Taran's waist as the steed galloped straight across the bracken, toward the vanguard of the Horned King. Taran made no attempt to guide her; the horse had chosen her own path. Suddenly he was in the midst of the warriors. Melyngar reared and plunged. Taran's sword was out and he struck right and left. A hand clutched at the stirrups, then was ripped away. Taran saw the warrior stumble back and drown in the press of struggling men. The white horse broke free and streaked for the brow of the hill. One mounted figure galloped behind them now. In a terrified glance, Taran saw the sweeping antlers of the Horned King.

The black steed gained on them. Melyngar turned sharply and drove toward the forest. The Horned King turned with her, and as they crashed through the underbrush and past the first rows of trees, the antlered giant drew closer until both steeds galloped side by side. In a final burst of speed, the horse of the Horned King plunged ahead; the animal's flanks bore against Melyngar, who reared furiously and struck out with her hoofs. Taran and Eilonwy were flung from the saddle. The Horned King turned his mount, seeking to trample them.

Taran scrambled to his feet and struck blindly with his sword. Then, gripping Eilonwy's arm, he pulled her deeper into the protection of the trees. The Horned King sprang heavily to the ground and was upon them in a few long strides.

Eilonwy screamed. Taran swung about to face the antlered man. Dark fears clutched Taran, as though the Lord of Annuvin himself had opened an abyss at his feet and he was hurtling downward. He gasped with pain, as though his old wound had opened once again. All the despair he had known as Achren's captive returned to sap his strength.

Behind the bleached skull, the eyes of the Horned King flamed, as he raised a crimson-stained arm.

Blindly, Taran brought up his sword. It trembled in his hand. The Horned King's blade lashed against the weapon and shattered it with a single blow.

Taran dropped the useless shards. The Horned King paused, a growl of savage joy rose in his throat, and he took a firmer grasp on his weapon.

Mortal terror goaded Taran into action. He leaped back and spun toward Eilonwy. "Dyrnwyn!" he cried. "Give me the sword!"

Before she could move, he tore belt and weapon from her shoulder. The Horned King saw the black scabbard and hesitated a moment, as if in fear.

Taran grasped the hilt. The blade would not come free. He pulled with all his strength. The sword moved only a little from its sheath. The Horned King raised his own weapon. As Taran gave a final wrench, the scabbard turned in his hand. A blinding flash split the air in front of him. Lightning seared his arm and he was thrown violently to the ground.

The sword Dyrnwyn, blazing white with flame, leaped from his hand, and fell beyond his reach. The Horned King stood over him. With a cry, Eilonwy sprang at the antlered man. Snarling, the giant tossed her aside.

A voice rang out behind the Horned King. Through eyes blurred with pain, Taran glimpsed a tall figure against the trees, and heard a shouted word he could not distinguish.

The Horned King stood motionless, his arm upraised. Lightning played about his sword. The giant flamed like a burning tree. The stag horns turned to crimson streaks, the skull mask ran like molten iron. A roar of pain and rage rose from the Antlered King's throat.

With a cry, Taran flung an arm across his face. The ground rumbled and seemed to open beneath him. Then there was nothing.

CHAPTER XIX

The Secret

Sunlight streamed through the high window of a chamber pleasantly cool and fragrant. Taran blinked and tried to lift himself from the low, narrow couch. His head spun; his arm, swathed in white linen, throbbed painfully. Dry rushes covered the floor; the bright rays turned them yellow as wheat. Beside the couch, a white, sundappled shape stirred and rose up.

"Hwoinch!"

Hen Wen, wheezing and chuckling, grinned all over her round face. With a joyful grunt, she began nuzzling Taran's cheek. His mouth opened, but he could not speak. A silvery laugh rang from a corner of the chamber.

"You should really see your expression. You look like a fish that's climbed into a bird's nest by mistake."

Eilonwy rose from the osier stool. "I was hoping you'd wake up soon. You can't imagine how boring it is to sit and watch somebody sleep. It's like counting stones in a wall."

"Where have they taken us? Is this Annuvin?"

Eilonwy laughed again and shook her head. "That's exactly the sort of question you might expect from an Assistant Pig-Keeper. Annuvin? Ugh! I wouldn't want to be there at all. Why must you always think of unpleasant things? I suppose it's because your wound probably did something to your head. You're looking a lot better now than you did, though you still have that greenish-white color, like a boiled leek."

"Stop chattering and tell me where we are!" Taran tried to roll from the couch, then sank back weakly and put a hand to his head.

"You aren't supposed to get up yet," Eilonwy cautioned, "but I imagine you've just discovered that for yourself."

Wriggling and grunting loudly, the delighted Hen Wen had begun to climb onto the couch. Eilonwy snapped her fingers. "Stop that, Hen," she ordered, "you know he isn't to be disturbed or upset and especially not sat on." The girl turned again to Taran. "We're in Caer Dathyl," she said. "It's a lovely place. Much nicer than Spiral Castle."

Taran started up once more as memories flooded over him. "The Horned King!" he cried. "What happened? Where is he?"

"In a barrow, most likely, I should think."

"Is he dead?"

"Naturally," answered the girl. "You don't think he'd stand being put in a barrow if he weren't, do you? There wasn't a great deal left of him, but what there was got buried." Eilonwy shuddered. "I think he was the most terrifying person I've ever met, and that includes Achren. He gave me a dreadful tossing about—just before he was going to smite you." She rubbed her head. "For the matter of that, you pulled away my sword rather roughly. I told you and told you not to draw it. But you wouldn't listen. That's what burned your arm."

Taran noticed the black scabbard of Dyrnwyn no longer hung from Eilonwy's shoulder. "But then what . . ."

"It's lucky you went unconscious," Eilonwy continued. "You missed the worst of it. There was the earthquake, and the Horned King burning until he just, well, broke apart. It wasn't pleasant. The truth of the matter is, I'd rather not talk about it. It still gives me bad dreams, even when I'm not asleep."

Taran gritted his teeth. "Eilonwy," he said at last, "I want you to tell me very slowly and carefully what happened. If you don't, *I'm* going to be angry and *you're* going to be sorry."

"How—can—I—tell—you—anything," Eilonwy said, deliberately pronouncing every word and making extravagant grimaces as she did so, "if—you—don't—want—me—to—talk?" She shrugged. "Well, in any case," she resumed, at her usual breathless rate, "as soon as the armies saw the Horned King was dead, they practically fell apart, too. Not the same way, naturally. With them, it was more sort of running away, like a herd of rabbits—no, that isn't right, is it? But it was pitiful to see grown men so frightened. Of course, by that time the Sons of Don had their chance to attack. You should have seen the golden banners. And such handsome warriors." Eilonwy sighed. "It was—it was like—I don't even know what it was like."

"And Hen Wen . . ."

"She hasn't stirred from this chamber ever since they brought you here," said Eilonwy. "Neither have I," she added, with a glance at Taran. "She's a very intelligent pig," Eilonwy went on. "Oh, she does get frightened and loses her head once in a while, I suppose. And she can be very stubborn when she wants, which sometimes makes me wonder how much difference there is between pigs and the people who keep them. I'm not mentioning anyone in particular, you understand."

The door opposite Taran's couch opened part way. Around it appeared the spiky yellow head and pointed nose of Fflewddur Fflam.

"So you're back with us," cried the bard. "Or, as you might say, we're back with you!"

Gurgi and the dwarf, who had been standing behind the bard, now rushed in; despite Eilonwy's protests, they crowded around Taran. Fflewddur and Doli showed no sign of injury, but Gurgi's head was bound up and he moved with a limp.

"Yes! Yes!" he cried. "Gurgi fought for his friend with slashings and gashings! What smitings! Fierce warriors strike him about his poor tender head, but valiant Gurgi does not flee, oh, no!"

Taran smiled at him, deeply touched. "I'm sorry about your poor tender head," he said, putting a hand on Gurgi's shoulder, "and that a friend should be wounded for my sake."

"What joy! What clashings and smashings! Ferocious Gurgi fills wicked warriors with awful terror and outcries."

"It's true," said the bard. "He was the bravest of us all. Though my stumpy friend here can do surprising things with an axe."

Doli, for the first time, grinned. "Never thought any of you had any mettle to show," he said, attempting to be gruff. "Took you all for milksops at first. Deepest apologies," he added, with a bow.

"We held off the war band," Fflewddur said, "until we were sure you were well away. Some of them should have occasion to think unkindly of us for a while to come." The bard's face lit up. "There we were," he cried, "fighting like madmen, hopelessly outnumbered. But a Fflam never surrenders! I took on three at once. Slash! Thrust! Another seized me from behind, the wretched coward. But I flung him off. We disengaged them and made for Caer Dathyl, chopping and hacking all the way, beset on all sides . . ."

Taran expected Fflewddur's harp strings to sunder at any moment. To his surprise, they held firm.

"And so," Fflewddur concluded with a carefree shrug, "that was our part. Rather easy, when you come down to it; I had no fear of things going badly, not for an instant."

A string broke with a deep twang.

Fflewddur bent down to Taran. "Terrified," he whispered. "Absolutely green."

Eilonwy seized the bard and thrust him toward the door. "Begone!" she cried, "all of you! You'll wear him out with your chatter." The girl shoved Gurgi and the dwarf after Fflewddur. "And stay out! No one's to come in until I say they can."

"Not even I?"

Taran started up at the familiar voice.

Gwydion stood in the doorway.

For a moment Taran did not recognize him. Instead of the stained cloak and coarse jacket, Gwydion wore the shining raiment of a prince. His rich mantle hung in deep folds. On a chain at his throat gleamed a sun-shaped disk of gold. His green eyes shone with new depth and power. Taran saw him now as he had always imagined him.

Heedless of his wounded arm, Taran sprang from the couch. The tall figure strode toward him. The authority of the warrior's bearing made Taran drop to one knee. "Lord Gwydion," he murmured.

"That is no greeting from a friend to a friend," said Gwydion, gently raising Taran to his feet. "It gives me more pleasure to remember an Assistant Pig-Keeper who feared I would poison him in the forest near Caer Dallben."

"After Spiral Castle," Taran stammered, "I never thought to see you alive." He clasped Gwydion's hand and wept unashamedly.

"A little more alive than you are." Gwydion smiled. He helped Taran seat himself on the couch.

"But how did . . ." Taran began, as he noticed a black and battered weapon at Gwydion's side.

Gwydion saw the question on Taran's face. "A gift," he said, "a royal gift from a young lady."

"I girded it on him myself," Eilonwy interrupted. She turned to Gwydion. "I told him not to draw it, but he's impossibly stubborn."

"Fortunately you did not unsheathe it entirely," Gwydion said to Taran. "I fear the flame of Dyrnwyn would have been too great even for an Assistant Pig-Keeper."

"It is a weapon of power, as Eilonwy recognized," Gwydion added. "So ancient that I believed it no more than a legend. There are still deep secrets concerning Dyrnwyn, unknown even to the wisest. Its loss destroyed Spiral Castle and was a severe blow to Arawn."

With a single, firm gesture, Gwydion drew the blade and held it aloft. The weapon glittered blindingly. In fear and wonder, Taran shrank back, his wound throbbing anew. Gwydion quickly returned the blade to its scabbard.

"As soon as I saw Lord Gwydion," Eilonwy put in, with an admiring glance at him, "I knew he was the one who should keep the sword. I must say I'm glad to have done with the clumsy thing."

"Do stop interrupting," Taran cried. "Let me find out what happened to my friend before you start babbling."

"I shall not weary you with a long tale," Gwydion said. "You already know Arawn's threat has been turned aside. He may strike again, how or when no man can guess. But for the moment there is little fear."

"What of Achren?" Taran asked. "And Spiral Castle . . ."

"I was not in Spiral Castle when it crumbled," Gwydion said. "Achren took me from my cell and bound me to a horse. With the Cauldron-Born, we rode to the castle of Oeth-Anoeth."

"Oeth-Anoeth?" questioned Taran.

"It is a stronghold of Annuvin," Gwydion said, "not far from Spiral Castle, raised when Arawn held wider sway over Prydain. A place of death, its walls are filled with human bones. I could foresee the torments Achren had planned for me.

"Yet, before she thrust me into its dungeons, she gripped my arm. 'Why do you choose death, Lord Gwydion?' she cried, 'when I can offer you eternal life and power beyond the grasp of mortal minds?'

" 'I ruled Prydain long before Arawn,' Achren told me, 'and it was I who made him king over Annuvin. It was I who gave him power—though he used it to betray me. But now, if you desire it, you shall take your place on the high throne of Arawn himself and rule in his stead.'

" 'Gladly will I overthrow Arawn,' I answered. 'And I will use those powers to destroy you along with him.'

"Raging, she cast me into the lowest dungeon," Gwydion said. "I have never been closer to my death than in Oeth-Anoeth.

"How long I lay there, I cannot be sure," Gwydion continued. "In Oeth-Anoeth, time is not as you know it here. It is better that I do not speak of the torments Achren had devised. The worst were not of the body but of the spirit, and of these the most painful was despair. Yet, even in my deepest anguish, I clung to hope. For there is this about Oeth-Anoeth: if a man withstand it, even death will give up its secrets to him.

"I withstood it," Gwydion said quietly, "and at the end much was revealed to me which before had been clouded. Of this, too, I shall not speak. It is enough for you to know that I understood the workings of life and death, of laughter and tears, endings and beginnings. I saw the truth of the world, and knew no chains could hold me. My bonds were light as dreams. At that moment, the walls of my prison melted."

"What became of Achren?" Eilonwy asked.

"I do not know," Gwydion said. "I did not see her thereafter. For some days I lay concealed in the forest, to heal the injuries of my body. Spiral Castle was in ruins when I returned to seek you; and there I mourned your death."

"As we mourned yours," Taran said.

"I set out for Caer Dathyl again," Gwydion continued. "For a time I followed the same path Fflewddur chose for you, though I did not cross the valley until much later. By then, I had outdistanced you a little.

"That day, a gwythaint plunged from the sky and flew directly toward me. To my surprise, it neither attacked nor sped away after it had seen me, but fluttered before me, crying strangely. The gwythaint's language is no longer secret to me—nor is the speech of any living creature—and I understood a band of travelers was journeying from the hills nearby and a white pig accompanied them.

"I hastened to retrace my steps. By then, Hen Wen sensed I was close at hand. When she ran from you," Gwydion said to Taran, "she ran not in terror but to find me. What I learned from her was more important than I suspected, and I understood why Arawn's champion sought her desperately. He, too, realized she knew the one thing that could destroy him."

"What was that?" Taran asked urgently.

"She knew the Horned King's secret name."

"His name?" Taran cried in astonishment. "I never realized a name could be so powerful."

"Yes," Gwydion answered. "Once you have courage to look upon evil, seeing it for what it is and naming it by its true name, it is powerless against you, and you can destroy it. Yet, with all my understanding," he said, reaching down and scratching the white pig's ear, "I could not have discovered the Horned King's name without Hen Wen.

"Hen Wen told me this secret in the forest. I had no need of letter sticks or tomes of enchantment, for we could speak as one heart and mind to each other. The gwythaint, circling overhead, led me to the Horned King. The rest you know."

"Where is the gwythaint now?" asked Taran.

Gwydion shook his head. "I do not know. But I doubt she will ever return to Annuvin, for Arawn would rend her to pieces once he learned what she had done. I only know she has repaid your kindness in the fullest measure.

"Rest now," Gwydion said. "Later, we shall speak of happier things."

"Lord Gwydion," Eilonwy called, as he rose to leave, "what was the Horned King's secret name?"

Gwydion's lined face broke into a smile. "It must remain a secret," he said, then patted the girl gently on the cheek. "But I assure you, it was not half as pretty as your own."

A few days afterward, when Taran had regained strength enough to walk unaided, Gwydion accompanied him through Caer Dathyl. Standing high on a hill, the fortress alone was big enough to hold several Caer Dallbens. Taran saw armorers' shops, stables for the steeds of warriors, breweries, weaving rooms. Cottages clustered in the valleys below, and clear streams ran golden in the sunlight. Later, Gwydion summoned all the companions to the Great Hall of Caer Dathyl, and there, amid banners and hedges of spears, they received the gratitude of King Math Son of Mathonwy, ruler of the House of Don. The white-bearded monarch, who looked as old as Dallben and as testy, was even more talkative than Eilonwy. But when at last he had finished one of the longest speeches Taran had ever heard, the companions bowed, and a guard of honor bore King Math from the Hall on a litter draped with cloth of gold. As Taran and his friends were about to take their leave, Gwydion called to them.

"These are small gifts for great valor," he said. "But it is in my power to bestow them, which I do with a glad heart, and with hope that you will treasure them not so much for their value as for the sake of remembrance.

"To Fflewddur Fflam shall be given one harp string. Though all his others break, this shall forever hold, regardless of how many gallant extravagances he may put on it. And its tone shall be the truest and most beautiful.

"To Doli of the Fair Folk shall be granted the power of invisibility, so long as he chooses to retain it.

"To faithful and valiant Gurgi shall be given a wallet of food[5] which shall be always full. Guard it well; it is one of the treasures of Prydain.

"To Eilonwy of the House of Llyr shall be given a ring of gold set with a gem carved by the ancient craftsmen of the Fair Folk. It is precious; but to me, her friendship is even more precious.

"And to Taran of Caer Dallben . . ." Here, Gwydion paused. "The choice of his reward has been the most difficult of all."

"I ask no reward," Taran said. "I want no friend to repay me for what I did willingly, out of friendship and for my own honor."

Gwydion smiled. "Taran of Caer Dallben," he said, "you are still as touchy and headstrong as ever. Believe that I know what you yearn for in your heart. The dreams of heroism, of worth, and of achievement are noble ones; but you, not I, must make them come true. Ask me whatever else, and I shall grant it."

Taran bowed his head. "In spite of all that has befallen me, I have come to love the valleys and mountains of your northern lands. But my thoughts have turned more and more to Caer Dallben. I long to be home."

Gwydion nodded. "So it shall be."

CHAPTER XX

Welcomes

The journey to Caer Dallben was swift and unhindered, for the lords of the southern cantrevs,[6] their power broken, had slunk back each to his own tribe throne. Taran and his companions, with Gwydion himself leading, rode south through the Valley of Ystrad. Eilonwy, who had heard so much of Taran's talk of Coll and Dallben, would not be denied a visit, and she, too, rode with them. Gwydion had given each of the companions a handsome steed; to Taran he had given the finest: the gray, silver-maned stallion, Melynlas, of the lineage of Melyngar and as swift. Hen Wen rode triumphantly on a horse-litter, looking intensely pleased with herself.

Caer Dallben had never seen so joyous a welcome—though by this time Taran was not positive about what Dallben had or had not seen—with such feasting that even Gurgi had his fill for once. Coll embraced Taran, who was amazed that such a hero

5. Motif drawn from the first branch of the *Mabinogion.*   6. Territories.

would deign to remember an Assistant Pig-Keeper, as well as Eilonwy, Hen Wen, and anyone else he could get his hands on; his face beamed like a winter fire and his bald crown glowed with delight.

Dallben interrupted his meditations to be present at the feast; though soon after the festivities, he withdrew to his chamber and was not seen for some time. Later, he and Gwydion spent several hours alone, for there were important matters Gwydion would reveal only to the old enchanter.

Gurgi, making himself completely at home, snored under a pile of hay in the barn. While Fflewddur and Doli went off exploring, Taran showed Eilonwy Hen Wen's enclosure, where the pig chuckled and grunted as happily as before.

"So this is where it all began," Eilonwy said. "I don't want to sound critical, but I don't think you should have had all that trouble keeping her in. Caer Dallben is as lovely as you said, and you should be glad to be home," she went on. "It's like suddenly remembering where you put something you've been looking for."

"Yes, I suppose it is," Taran said, leaning on the railing and examining it closely.

"What will you do now?" asked Eilonwy. "I expect you'll go back to Assistant Pig-Keeping."

Without looking up, Taran nodded. "Eilonwy," he said, with hesitation, "I was hoping—I mean, I was wondering . . ."

Before he could finish, Coll came hurrying up and whispered that Dallben would like to see him privately.

"Eilonwy—" Taran began again, then stopped abruptly and strode off to the cottage.

When he entered the chamber, Dallben was writing with a great quill in *The Book of Three*. As soon as he saw Taran, he shut the volume quickly and put it aside.

"Well, now," Dallben said, "I should like the two of us to speak quietly to each other. First, I am interested to learn what you think of being a hero. I daresay you feel rather proud of yourself. Although," he added, "I do not gain that impression from your face."

"I have no just cause for pride," Taran said, taking his usual place on the familiar bench. "It was Gwydion who destroyed the Horned King, and Hen Wen helped him do it. But Gurgi, not I, found her. Doli and Fflewddur fought gloriously while I was wounded by a sword I had no right to draw. And Eilonwy was the one who took the sword from the barrow in the first place. As for me, what I mostly did was make mistakes."

"My, my," said Dallben, "those are complaints enough to dampen the merriest feast. Though what you say may be true, you have cause for a certain pride nevertheless. It was you who held the companions together and led them. You did what you set out to do, and Hen Wen is safely back with us. If you made mistakes, you recognize them. As I told you, there are times when the seeking counts more than the finding.

"Does it truly matter," Dallben went on, "which of you did what, since all shared the same goal and the same danger? Nothing we do is ever done entirely alone. There is a part of us in everyone else—you, of all people, should know that. From what I hear, you have been as impetuous as your friend Fflewddur; I have been told, among other things, of a night when you dove head first into a thornbush. And you have certainly felt as sorry for yourself as Gurgi; and, like Doli, striven for the impossible."

"Yes," admitted Taran, "but that is not all that troubles me. I have dreamed often of Caer Dallben and I love it—and you and Coll—more than ever. I asked for nothing better than to be at home, and my heart rejoices. Yet it is a curious feeling. I have returned to the chamber I slept in and found it smaller than I remember. The fields are beautiful, yet not quite as I recalled them. And I am troubled, for I wonder now if I am to be a stranger in my own home."

Dallben shook his head. "No, that you shall never be. But it is not Caer Dallben which has grown smaller. You have grown bigger. That is the way of it."

"And there is Eilonwy," Taran said. "What will become of her? Is it—is it possible you would let her stay with us?"

Dallben pursed his lips and toyed with the pages of *The Book of Three*. "By all rights," he said, "the Princess Eilonwy should be returned to her kinsmen—yes, she is a princess. Did she not tell you? But there is no hurry about that. She might consent to stay. Perhaps if you spoke to her."

Taran sprang to his feet. "I shall!"

He hurried from the chamber and ran to Hen Wen's enclosure. Eilonwy was still there, watching the oracular pig with interest.

"You're to stay!" Taran cried. "I've asked Dallben!"

Eilonwy tossed her head. "I suppose," she said, "it never occurred to you to ask *me*."

"Yes—but I mean . . ." he stammered, "I didn't think . . ."

"You usually don't," Eilonwy sighed. "No matter. Coll is straightening up a place for me."

"Already?" cried Taran. "How did *he* know? How did *you* know?"

"Humph!" said Eilonwy.

"Hwoinch!" said Hen Wen.

PRYDAIN PRONUNCIATION GUIDE

Achren AHK-*ren*
Adaon *ah*-DAY-*on*
Aeddan EE-*dan*
Angharad *an*-GAR-*ad*
Annuvin *ah*-NOO-*vin*
Arawn *ah*-RAWN
Arianllyn *ahree*-AHN-*lin*

Briavael *bree*-AH-*vel*
Brynach BRIHN-*ak*

Caer Cadarn *kare* KAH-*darn*
Caer Colur *kare* KOH-*loor*
Caer Dathyl *kare* DA-*thil*
Coll *kahl*

Dallben DAHL-*ben*
Doli DOH-*lee*
Don *dahn*
Dwyvach DWIH-*vak*
Dyrnwyn DUHRN-*win*

Edyrnion *eh*-DIR-*nyon*
Eiddileg *eye*-DILL-*eg*

Eilonwy *eye*-LAHN-*wee*
Ellidyr ELLI-*deer*

Fflewddur Fflam FLEW-*der flam*

Geraint GHER-*aint*
Goewin GOH-*win*
Govannion *go*-VAH-*nyon*
Gurgi GHER-*ghee*
Gwydion GWIH-*dyon*
Gwythaint GWIH-*thaint*

Islimach *iss*-LIM-*ahk*

Llawgadarn *law*-GAD-*arn*
Lluagor *lew*-AH-*gore*
Llunet LOO-*net*
Llyan *lee*-AHN
Llyr *leer*

Melyngar MELLIN-*gar*
Melynlas MELLIN-*lass*

Oeth-Anoeth *eth-AHN-eth*	**Rhuddlum** ROOD-*lum*
Orddu OR-*doo*	**Rhun** *roon*
Orgoch OR-*gahk*	
Orwen OR-*wen*	**Smoit** *smoyt*
Prydain *prih-DANE*	**Taliesin** *tally-ESS-in*
Pryderi *prih-DAY-ree*	**Taran** TAH-*ran*
	Teleria *tell-EHR-ya*

1964

JON SCIESZKA
b. 1954

When Jon Scieszka was in kindergarten, just learning to write, and was asked to put his name on the top of his papers, he wrote "Jon S." Many years later, a successful author of picture books and early chapter books whose name had nevertheless remained a challenge for others, Scieszka wrote a humorous piece for the children's literature journal *Horn Book Magazine* about how to pronounce the tricky names of children's authors and illustrators. Scieszka always responds to a challenge by using his own brand of wacky humor, whether his object is teaching the world how to pronounce his name (it's SHEH-ska), enticing reluctant readers to pick up a book, engaging the interest of boys who sit in the back of the room, or encouraging teachers and parents who might disparage a funny story to laugh and to appreciate the importance of silliness in writing for children. Scieszka has commented, "Good humor is important and educational in an essential way. The best humor is always built from the truth of experience."

Scieszka's off-beat picture books re-create the known in a delightful chaos of reversals, inversions, and interventions; thus in *The Story of the Three Little Pigs* (1989), the conventional tale of victimized pigs and predator wolf is told from a different perspective. In *Math Curse* (1995), everything in the narrator's daily life can be understood as a math problem. The absurd situations are not only entertaining but educational, and they make fun of math as well. In the humorous Time Warp Trio series of short chapter books, three friends travel through time and space by means of a green mist that emanates from a magical book given to one of them as a birthday gift. Wherever and whenever they find themselves—in ancient Egypt, the Stone Age, or the future—the wisecracking boys must find *The Book* in order to return home. Many of Scieszka's books are illustrated by Lane Smith, whose zany and unconventional paintings perfectly capture Scieszka's goofy and ironic worlds and add another dimension to the humor and bad jokes in which children delight.

Because he draws attention to the "bookness" of his books (for example, the ISBN number, the role of the narrator, and the copyright information are all played with in *The Stinky Cheese Man and Other Fairly Stupid Tales*, 1992), invokes intertextual references to other works of children's literature (the running joke of *Summer Reading Is Killing Me!*), and explodes the myth of the "real" version of any text or legend from history, critics have called Scieszka's work "postmodern." Children call it funny.

JON SCIESZKA

Summer Reading Is Killing Me!

The characters and events in this book are fictitious. Any similarity to real characters or real events is very interesting. Does this happen to you often?

A special thanks to Lloyd Alexander, Daniel Pinkwater, and the E. B. White estate for allowing their characters to appear in this book. May millions of kids meet the Horned King, Henrietta, and Charlotte, and go find them in their original books.

Dedicated to all of those authors who saved me
from getting killed by summer reading:

Aesop, Lloyd Alexander, Natalie Babbitt, Ludwig Bemelmans, Raymond Briggs, Jeff Brown, Eric Carle, Lewis Carroll, John Christopher, Beverly Cleary, Roald Dahl, Daniel Defoe, Marjorie Flack, Esther Forbes, Jean Craighead George, William Golding, Kenneth Grahame, Florence Parry Heide, James Howe, Washington Irving, Crockett Johnson, Ruth Krauss, C. S. Lewis, Astrid Lindgren, Arnold Lobel, Patricia MacLachlan, James Marshall, Robert McCloskey, Herman Melville, A. A. Milne, Peggy Parish, Katherine Paterson, Gary Paulsen, Daniel Marius Pinkwater, Beatrix Potter, H. A. Rey, W. H. D. Rouse, Louis Sachar, Dr. Seuss, Marjorie W. Sharmat, Mary Shelley, Donald J. Sobol, William Steig, Robert Louis Stevenson, Bram Stoker, Rosemary Sutcliff, J. R. R. Tolkien, P. L. Travers, Mark Twain, Jules Verne, E. B. White and Laura Ingalls Wilder.[1]

1

"Cluck, cluck," the thing rumbled in a deep voice.

"Is that thing talking to us?" said Fred.

I looked around the small playground. Fred, Sam, and I stood at one end against a chain-link fence. A very large, white, feathered thing stood next to the swing set at the other end. It had yellow, scaly legs as big as baseball bats, little red eyes, and a dog collar.

"I think it's a giant chicken," I said.

Sam cleaned his glasses on his T-shirt and took another look at the other side of the playground. "Yes, that is a two-hundred-fifty-pound chicken standing there."

The sun glittered in its hungry little eyes.

"And yes, he looks like he's planning to hurt us," added Sam.

"Hey, it's not my fault," said Fred. "I didn't touch *The Book*."[2]

"You did too," I said.

"Did not," said Fred.

"Did too."

"Did not."

"Did too."

"Excuse me, guys," said Sam. "Did you ever get the feeling that all of this has happened before, exactly like this?"

---

1. The success of Scieszka's humorous fantasy relies, in part, on the reader's knowledge of the classic and contemporary children's books alluded to in the text. This dedication and the Summer Reading List appendix supply a list of the authors, books, and literary characters that appear in *Summer Reading Is Killing Me!*

2. In Scieszka's Time Warp Trio series, a magical book transports the three boys to far-off lands in the deep past or distant future.

The super-size chicken eyed us. He gave another gut-rumbling "CLUCK."

"Well, except with maybe a black knight instead of a giant chicken, of course."

Fred pushed back his Red Wings hat and scratched his head. "Hey yeah. It's like 'a la mode' or something."

The chicken pecked the ground hungrily with jackhammer blows of its beak.

"You mean 'déjà vu,'" said Sam, backing up against the fence. "And Joe, isn't this right about when you should do some magic trick and get us out of here?"

I stood there stunned, looking at a giant white chicken on a city playground. The swing set, the slide, the gravel, even the impossible chicken . . . Sam was right. Everything did look familiar, but not really familiar. I couldn't put my finger on it.

"Uh, Joe. *Joe?*" said Sam, elbowing me in the ribs while keeping his eye on the hungry chicken. "The magic trick?"

"It's like I've been here before, but I haven't really been here before," I said.

The monster bird twisted its head. It looked us over with one eye, then the other.

"Well, thank you for sharing your feelings," said Sam. "And you know we would just love to hear more . . . later. Right now it looks like that bird is thinking about his own idea of chicken dinner—us. So how about that magic trick?"

The killer fowl started bobbing and walking toward us.

Fred bounced his fist off the top of my head. "Yeah, come, on, Joe. You are the worst magician I've ever known. Your *Book* got us into this. Do a real magic trick for once and get us out of here."

The chicken started trotting.

I racked my brain. There was no way I was going to try the classic "abracadabra" or "hocus pocus" magic words to stop a charging chicken. And don't even remind me of that "please" and "thank you" mistake I made earlier in my career.[3] But I had a flash of an idea. I thought it could work. It just might work. So I gave it a try.

---

3. An allusion to the first Time Warp Trio book, *Knights of the Kitchen Table* (1991).

"Why did the chicken cross the road?" I yelled.

The chicken only flapped its wings and ran faster.

I cupped my hands like a megaphone and yelled punch lines: "To get to the other side. To buy the newspaper. To get away from Colonel Sanders."[4]

Nothing worked. The monster chicken just looked madder and ran at us faster.

"I don't want to end up as chicken feed," wailed Sam, plastered against the fence.

At that moment, I saw a sign out of the corner of my eye. And I knew where we were.

The chicken thundered toward us, its deadly sharp beak pointed directly at us.

I stepped in front of Sam and Fred with my chest out.

"Hoboken," I said.

"Chicken," said Fred.

"Emergency!" screamed Sam.

"Exactly."

2

This is going to be impossible to explain. But give me a chance and just let me try. I think I know what happened.

To go back to the very beginning—my life has not been the same since my uncle Joe gave me *The Book* for my birthday. This book is a small book. A dark blue book with strange silver writing on it. A book like no book I've ever read before or since. It's a time-warping book.

I know. I know. I can hear you laughing right now. You're saying to yourself, "What's with this guy? He probably still believes in the Easter Bunny and the Tooth Fairy. Everybody knows you can't travel through time with a book."

I don't blame you for not believing. I didn't really believe it myself, either. Then we opened *The Book* and started going places.

Since then, my friends Sam and Fred and I have gotten into trouble in just about every time from the Stone Age to the future. We've run into pirates, robots, cavemen, you name it. We've been chased by a woolly mammoth, stampeded by cattle, turned into mummies, and nearly suffocated by one very nasty-smelling giant.

And we still have absolutely no idea how to work *The Book*.

The only thing that seems to stay the same is the green mist that takes us places. And that once we go to another time, the only way to get back home to our time is to find *The Book* in that time.

So anyway, there we were—sitting in my room the very first day of summer vacation. We were trying to be careful. We really were.

Fred was sitting on my bed, putting new wheels on his skates, showing off his new Detroit Red Wings Stanley Cup Champions hat. Sam and I were at my desk.

"No more classes, no more books. No more teachers' dirty looks," chanted Fred.

Sam raised one eyebrow. "What a poet. You wouldn't know it. But your feet show it. They're Longfellows."[5]

Fred looked up from his skates. "Hey, what's that supposed to mean . . . ?"

I stepped in between them before they started anything. "Okay guys. Forget the poetry. We are gathered here today to decide one great question: How do we spend our summer vacation?"

---

4. Harland Sanders (1890–1980), founder of Kentucky Fried Chicken (KFC).

5. A pun on the name of the American poet Henry Wadsworth Longfellow (1807–1882).

Sam raised his hand. "May I first suggest how we *don't* spend our summer vacation?" He pointed to a thin blue book with silver designs on my bookshelf. "Can we please promise not to open *The Book* and get sucked into some time-travel trouble like we always do when we get together?"

I started, "But—"

"No buts," said Sam. "Every time you figure out some new way to keep track of *The Book*, we just get in more trouble. Let's stay right here, right now."

"I'm with you," said Fred, spinning his wheels. "I say we do nothing but skate, skate, skate, and skate. We don't have to open any books."

"Well, now that you mention books," said Sam, "I was thinking we might get an early start on this list. Then we can do whatever we want for the rest of the summer."

Fred grabbed the piece of paper from Sam's hand and read the heading. "Summer reading list? Are you crazy? This is vacation. We don't have to read anything. That's why they call it vacation."

Sam took his list back. He read aloud, "Each student must read four books during the summer and fill out the attached study guide for two of them."

"How can you be thinking about books?" said Fred. "We've got skating moves to practice."

"Hmmm," said Sam. "The list has *Hatchet, The Phantom Tollbooth,*[6] *The Hoboken Chicken Emergency* . . ."

Fred used the edge of my bed to practice his street skating moves. "We've got to perfect the unity, the mute grab, the backside royale . . ."[7]

". . . *Matilda, Flat Stanley* . . ."

". . . gumby, stale Japan . . ."

Fred and Sam traded skate moves and book titles one-on-one.

". . . or here's *Tuck Everlasting* . . ."

". . . rocket three-sixty . . ."

". . . *Bunnicula* . . ."

". . . fishbrain . . ."

Without looking up from the list, Sam grabbed Fred's hat and tossed it on the floor.

"*Encyclopedia Brown.*"

Fred did a half-twist flip off the bed and took Sam's list. He stuck it in a book from my shelf, shoved the book back on the shelf, and jumped back onto the bed.

"*Mistyflip.*"

"*George and Martha.*"

"One-eighty monkey plant."

"Guys—"

"*Frog and Toad.*"

"Alley-oop soul."

"*Forget it, you guys!*" I yelled. "You don't have to decide."

Fred and Sam both stopped and looked at me.

"What do you mean we don't have to decide?"

I pointed to my bookshelf.

"The way I figure it, we have about three seconds before this green mist leaking off my bookshelf decides for us."

6. A humorous fantasy (1961) by the American architect and children's author Norton Juster. Most of the titles mentioned in the text are listed in Scieszka's appendix (those listed there are not glossed in these notes).
7. The first of many skateboarding moves named in the text.

All three of us stared at the wisps of green mist swirling out of the thin blue book with silver designs.

"Aww no," said Fred. "How did that happen? I didn't do nothing."

"Anything," said Sam. "You didn't do anything . . . except put our summer reading list inside *The Book*."

"So, what will that do?" asked Fred.

"We'll find out soon enough," I said.

Then the familiar green mist washed over us. And we were flung through time and space to who knows when or where.

3

The chicken thundered toward us.

"Don't worry," I said, standing in front of Fred and Sam. "I know exactly what's going to happen next."

Sam crouched down and covered his head. "Yeah, death by chicken."

The galloping chicken was ten feet away and closing fast.

"Are you sure you know what's going to happen?" said Fred.

"*Yerrbbfff,*" said Sam's muffled voice.

The enormous chicken hopped, flapped, and launched itself right at us.

I thought I knew what was going to happen. I hoped I knew.

The feathered monster rose up . . . up . . . and . . . just over us. It cleared the fence behind us with a foot to spare, and landed with a groundshaking *thud*. The big bird gave one more "CLUCK" and then disappeared down the street.

Sam froze in his crouch. "I can't bear to look. Are we dead yet?"

"Yes," said Fred. "And I'm the ghost of Fred." Fred nudged Sam with one knee. Sam fell over, still curled in a ball. He carefully opened one eye.

"Fred, Joe—you're alive!" said Sam. "You're sideways, but you're alive!"

Fred rolled Sam back upright.

"Like magic," said Sam. "Now you're perfect." Sam got on his knees and bowed to me. "Joe the Magnificent, I take back all of the bad things I ever said about you. You are a genius. You did know what was going to happen."

"Well—" I began.

Sam wrapped his arms around my knees. "So you must know where *The Book* is and how we can get it and go back home and not stick around to fight giant chickens or slay dragons or wrestle pirates or—"

"Not exactly—" I began.

Fred hopped a handrail, practicing a backside royale. "What do you mean 'not exactly'? And how did you know that chicken was going to jump?"

"That's what I've been trying to tell you," I said. "I saw that sign that says HOBOKEN DELI and I knew exactly where we were."

"Hoboken?" said Fred.

"Brilliant," said Sam.

"Well not exactly Hoboken," I said. "I saw Hoboken, then the chicken, and then Sam said 'emergency.'"

A look of understanding came across Sam's face. "No. This is not possible."

"It's exactly like this book I read," I went on. "*The Hoboken Chicken Emergency*. This kid lives in Hoboken. He gets a two-hundred-sixty-six-pound chicken for Thanksgiving. He takes it to a playground. Then it runs away and jumps over the fence."

Fred and Sam stared at me with their mouths hanging open.

"Are you telling me we are inside the book *The Hoboken Chicken Emergency* by D. Manus Pinkwater?" said Sam.

"It all fits," I said. "The playground. Hoboken. The two-hundred-sixty-six-pound chicken."

"We can't be in a book," said Fred. "That only happens in those geeky movies. Besides, there is no way I am going to spend my summer vacation in a book."

Sam slowly shook his head. "This is very weird, but quite possibly true. What if story characters are real in some way? What if they have a life we just don't know about?"

"That would explain everything," I said.

"Almost everything," said Fred, tugging nervously on his hat. "Everything except that frog in a suit coat and pants over there."

I looked around. "There's no frog in a suit in *The Hoboken Chicken Emergency*. Where?"

"Right there," pointed Fred. "Next to the toad in the plaid jacket."

"Frog?" I said.

"Toad?" Sam said.

We looked at each other in horror.

"Frog and Toad?" we said.

And we knew then and there that something had gone terribly, mixed-uply, summer-reading-listly wrong.

4

Fred, Sam, and I hung on the playground fence. We watched the human-size frog in a green suit coat and striped pants and the toad in a plaid coat turn the corner and run down the street.

"I saw it, but I don't believe it," I said.

"How did they get here?" asked Fred.

"The summer reading list was for the whole school," answered Sam. "First grade through eighth grade. *Green Eggs and Ham* through *20,000 Leagues Under the Sea.*"

I shook my head. "But you don't really think all of those books . . . ? I mean did we . . . ? Are they . . . ?"

Black clouds swept over the sun. A bolt of lightning flashed. Thunder cracked.

A rabbit in a blue coat with brass buttons, a curious-looking monkey, and a boy pushing a wheelbarrow filled with one very large orange carrot ran toward us down the street.

Sam's eyes widened. "Quick, hide!" He pushed us under a bench behind a bush.

"Why are we hiding from Peter Rabbit?" whispered Fred.

Another flash of lightning split the dark Hoboken sky. The crack of thunder shook the ground under us. A giant figure with a bleached skull head and antlers galloped his black horse behind Peter.

I peeked through the slats of the bench and the leaves of the bushes. The antlered giant swung his sword overhead, then reined his horse to a stop. He turned his flaming eyes our way. I could have sworn he was staring right at us. My heart stopped. Just then, the monkey let out a shriek. The antler guy turned his head, then spurred his horse and rode off.

The black cloud passed. It took us a few minutes to get slowly to our feet and brush the dirt off our knees.

"Does that answer your question?" asked Sam.

Even Fred, who has stood up to Blackbeard the pirate, crocodiles on the Nile, and a twelve-foot vert wall half pipe, seemed shaken.

"Who . . . ? What . . . ?"

"That was the Horned King," said Sam. "One very nasty character from Lloyd Alexander's *The Book of Three*."

"Oh no," I said. "We are in huge trouble. If this means what I think it means, all of the characters from every book on the summer reading list are mixed up here in Hoboken. And none of them are in their books where they're supposed to be. The librarian is going to kill us."

Fred slapped me with his hat. "And I'm going to kill you if you blow my whole skating summer chasing Nancy Drew[8] and Pippi Longstocking."

"I don't believe Nancy was on the list," said Sam.

Fred punched Sam. "You know what I mean."

"Knock it off, you guys," I said. "We've got to take care of this before things really go wrong. Like what if the Horned King makes Peter Rabbit stew?"

"What if the Red Queen[9] says, 'Off with Ramona's head!'?" said Sam.

"What if the Twits mess up Wayside School?" I said.

"What if the Tripods[1] take over the Little House on the Prairie?" said Sam.

"Now that might be a good thing," said Fred.

We both gave Fred a look.

"Aw, come on," said Fred. "You've got to admit it would make that book a lot more exciting."

"We've got to get everyone back in the right book," said Sam. "Otherwise it will just . . . just . . . be wrong."

I jumped up on the bench. "I know just what we have to do."

"Now you're even acting like somebody in one of those lame books," said Fred.

I pretended I didn't hear him and went on. "We have to get back *The Book* and take the summer reading list out of it before anything permanent happens."

Sam sat on the bench. "Oh good. We have to find *The Book* to fix everything. That's original."

Fred slumped next to Sam. "We need Sherlock Holmes or somebody. Where are we going to find *The Book*?"

I looked up, trying to figure out where we should look . . . and I saw the answer. "There," I said, pointing to a spiderweb in the corner of the fence. "The answer is right there over your head."

5

Fred and Sam turned to look where I was pointing. We all stared in amazement at the spiderweb. Because there in the center of the web, neatly woven in block letters, was a message. It said:

THE
LIBRARY

8. Title character of series (begun in 1930) by a number of different authors writing under the pseudonym Carolyn Keene.
9. Character in Lewis Carroll's *Through the Looking-Glass* (1872; it is actually the Queen of

Hearts, in *Alice's Adventures in Wonderland*, who repeatedly cries "Off with their heads!").
1. Giant machines who control the human race in *The White Mountains* (1967) and the other volumes of John Christopher's Tripod Trilogy.

We all went weak in the knees. Things were getting stranger by the minute.

"It's Charlotte," whispered Sam.

"The librarian?" said Fred.

"No, you doofus," said Sam. "The spider. Didn't you ever read *Charlotte's Web?*"

"Uh . . . yeah. Sure I did," said Fred. "I must have just missed that Charlotte part."

"She's in the whole book," said Sam. "She spins messages in her web to save the pig."

"Right," said Fred. "I knew that."

"Of course," I said. "Where else would *The Book* be? The library."

"So what are we waiting for?" said Fred. "Let's get to the library, check out *The Book*, and get home to skate."

"There is just one small problem," said Sam, adjusting his glasses like he always does when he knows something we don't know. "We have absolutely no idea where the Hoboken Library is."

The three of us sat back down on the bench. We could waste the whole day looking for the library. By then it might be too late to save Frog and Toad and Peter Rabbit and who knows who else. I glanced up at Charlotte's web again.

"Oh yes we do," I said. Because there in the center of the web, neatly woven in block letters was a message. It said:

500 PARK AVE.

6 BLOCKS WEST ON 5TH STREET

ACROSS FROM

CHURCH SQUARE PARK

M, T, TH: 9-8

W, F: 9-5

SAT: 11-2

CLOSED SUNDAY

We took off west on Fifth Street. We passed old houses, an alley, a street lined with delis, bars, and shops. In just a few minutes we were at the corner of the park.

I looked around the deserted streets. "Does something seem weird to you?"

"Oh no," said Sam. "I get sucked into a book and walk around inside it every day. Of course this seems weird."

"No, I mean how come there are no people walking around?"

"Hey, yeah," said Fred. "It's like that *Twilight Zone*[2] episode where the guy can stop and start time with a watch. But he breaks the watch while everyone is frozen and he's the only one left and he goes crazy and starts screaming and crying and—"

"Thanks for that cheerful little story," said Sam. "But I think we're not in the real Hoboken. We're in the Hoboken from the book. Only characters from the book are here. So—"

Just then we heard a wild yelling and the sound of stomping footsteps behind us. Fred, Sam, and I ran into the park and dove behind a statue with a big base.

Two large gray hippos ran down the street on their hind legs. One wore a red striped dress and a flower behind her ear. The other had one gold tooth.

"Hold the course or I'll keelhaul the both of ye," growled a strangely dressed guy. He hopped along on one leg and a crutch. A parrot perched on his shoulder. He fired a shot from a huge pistol over the hippos' heads.

---

2. American television series (CBS, 1959–64) that featured separate fantasy and science fiction stories. The episode alluded to, "A Kind of Stop Watch," was written by Rod Serling.

"Pieces of eight, pieces of eight," squawked the parrot.

The one-legged pirate chased the hippos up the steps and between the two big columns of an old brick building. Then everything went quiet again.

We sat down behind the statue and looked at each other. We've seen some strange things in our time-warp travels together, but nothing as strange as this.

Sam wiped his glasses with his shirt. "George and Martha?"

"Chased by Long John Silver?"[3] said Fred.

I peeked around the statue to take another look and saw a stranger sight times ten. I saw Homer Price being carried by the Headless Horseman.[4] Dracula was dragging Winnie-the-Pooh in a headlock. Mr. Twit was breaking Harold's purple crayon. I saw twenty different bad guys from twenty different books chasing, hauling, and pushing all kinds of characters up the steps of the big old brick building. And just when I thought things couldn't get any stranger, I saw a sight that froze my blood.

I sat back down behind the statue. I didn't have the heart to tell Sam and Fred.

"What was it?" said Sam. "You look like you've seen a ghost. Is it Frankenstein? Moby Dick? How bad could it be? The Babysitters' Club?"[5]

I could only motion weakly and point to the big brick building.

Sam looked around the statue and collapsed next to me. "No . . ."

Fred looked at the two of us. "What? What is it?"

Sam and I pointed. Fred looked out and read the sign on the big brick building. The building every bad character from the summer reading list was heading into.

Fred read the sign out loud: "Hoboken Public Library." Then he collapsed next to us.

6

"That's it. We're cooked," said Sam.

I tried to think of a plan or even a magic trick to use. But I couldn't.

"Things could be worse," I said.

"Things could be worse?" squeaked Sam. "Things could be worse?" He was starting to look a little hysterical. "The one building in Hoboken that we need to get into is filled with monsters, criminals, and killers. It's packed with every bad guy from every book ever written. We have to sneak in and find one small book in the middle of thousands of library books. And all you can say is, 'Things could be worse'?"

Sam's hair sprouted out in every direction. His glasses hung crookedly. Now he was definitely hysterical.

"Well," said Fred calmly, "we could be captured and getting dragged in there like everybody else. That would be worse."

Sam stared at Fred like he was going to strangle him.

I stared at Fred like I was going to hug him.

"Fred," I said. "You are a genius. That's exactly how we'll get in there. We don't even need a magic trick. You pretend to be a bad guy character from a book who captures us. You chase us into the library."

"I what?" said Fred. "I am? Okay."

Sam wasn't too thrilled with the plan. But even he had to admit we didn't have much choice. We had to get into the library as soon as we could and get our hands on *The Book*.

---

3. Character in Robert Louis Stevenson's *Treasure Island* (1883).
4. Character in Washington Irving's "The Legend of Sleepy Hollow" (1820).
5. Series (1986–2000) by Ann M. Martin.

Fred turned his Red Wings hat backward and rolled his sleeves up over his shoulders to look as nasty as possible. Sam and I combed our hair down to look as nerdy as possible.

Fred, Sam, and I checked each other out. Fred pulled his belt out of his pants.

"Ready?" I asked.

"Ready," said Sam and Fred.

"Then let's go."

Sam and I jumped out from behind the statue and headed for the library. Fred ran behind us, yelling and whipping his belt around. "That's it. Keep moving, you chuckleheads." He landed a solid belt whip on Sam's leg.

"Hey!" said Sam. "That hurts."

"And there's more where that came from," yelled Fred, chasing us up the library steps. "So don't give me any grief, four eyes."

We pushed through the front doors and right into one incredibly ugly troll and a gangster guarding the next doors. The troll had a crazy look in his eye. The gangster had a machine gun.

"Who's that crossing my bridge?" said the troll.[6]

"Yeah. Who are you mugs? And what patty-cake book did you fall out of?" said the gangster, chewing his cigar.

I smoothed my hair and straightened my collar. "We are the Time Warp Trio," I said in my best nerd voice. "Sam and I do good deeds and help people wherever we go. But Fred is the mean kid next door. He always wrecks our plans."

"Time Warp Trio?" said the gangster. "I didn't never hear of no books called the Time Warp Trio. Whaddayou, some kinda science fiction or somethin'?"

The troll hiccupped and drooled a pool of yellowish saliva on his green hairy foot.

"Nah, we're like action adventure fiction," said Fred. "These jerks try to make them educational adventures. I make sure to mess 'em up and keep things moving so the readers don't fall asleep." Fred gave Sam and me a smack on the back of our heads.

The gangster pointed his machine gun at us and gave us a cold stare. Sam and I thought we were goners. He chewed his cigar, then broke into a laugh.

"Hey, dat's funny. You sound like my kinda guy. Reminds me of stories I was in when I was a kid."

Fred smiled and gave us an extra couple of slaps Sam and I didn't think were really necessary.

"Take 'em inside." The gangster motioned with his machine gun. "The Boss has plans for characters like them."

The troll's stomach rumbled. He urped, and another string of drool spilled down his chin.

Fred grabbed Sam and me by the backs of the necks and pushed us quickly through the doors before the gangster changed his mind. The three of us stumbled into the library and stopped dead.

You know how when you read a book you kind of "see" the characters even if they don't show a picture of them? Well, that's what this was like. But instead of seeing book characters in our minds, we saw them for real, wandering all over the Hoboken Public Library, characters from every book on our summer reading list.

"I see it, but I don't believe it," whispered Sam. "That's Mrs. Twit tying up Mary Poppins and Encyclopedia Brown."

"That's Frankenstein holding Pippi Longstocking," I breathed.

6. A character in the Scandinavian folktale "Three Billy Goats Gruff."

"They even got Mother Goose," said Fred.

I could just see Peter Rabbit, Henrietta the 266-pound Hoboken chicken, George and Martha, and ten or twenty other characters already trapped in a kind of cage made out of library shelves behind the main desk. Huge stacks of books towered over them.

"There's that girl with the yellow hat who has her appendix taken out," I said.

"Madeline," said Sam.

"And that vampire rabbit we read about last year," said Fred.

"Bunnicula," said Sam. "And Flat Stanley, Treehorn, Alice in Wonderland, Nate the Great, Amelia Bedelia . . . they're all here," said Sam in amazement.

We couldn't see who "the Boss" was. He was running things from the main check-out desk, completely surrounded by some very bad-looking characters.

"Keelhaul the lot of them," boomed Long John Silver.

"Off with their heads," commanded the Red Queen.

"Kill the pig! Cut his throat! Bash him in!" chanted a scrawny kid dressed in ripped clothes with streaks of mud, pounding his pointed stick spear on a library table.[7]

"I don't know what's going on here, but it doesn't look good," I said. "Let's sneak up those stairs and start looking for *The Book*—quick."

And it probably would have been a good plan. But we were only halfway up the stairs when we heard a voice that could only be talking to us.

"You three boys. What book are you from? Come down here now."

I turned to see who had spotted us. I had to blink to make sure I wasn't seeing things. Because standing between the White Witch from Narnia[8] and The Trunch-bull from *Matilda* was a little red man pointing his finger directly at us.

"This does not look good," I said.

"This looks positively evil," said Sam.

"Is that who I think it is?" said Fred.

I thought about it for a second. "Do you know any other red guy with two horns and a pointed tail?"

7

The Devil motioned us back down to the main desk.

We had no choice but to go.

We walked down the steps and across the floor covered with the books that had been thrown everywhere. Characters from all kinds of stories milled around.

We stepped over a very hungry caterpillar eating his way through a dictionary. We pushed past a mother duck and her line of ducklings. We made our way through a crowd made up of Robinson Crusoe, a blue moose, Julie with some wolves, a snowman, a plain and tall lady named Sarah, a kid with a hatchet,[9] and a very confused-looking Robin Hood helping Eeyore reattach his tail.

We stood in front of the horned guy, speechless. So this was "the Boss" behind this terrible scene.

The Devil sat in the librarian's chair surrounded by outlaws, Wild Things,[1] and a lot of generally bad-looking characters. He looked us over, twirling the little beard on his chin. He checked a list on his clipboard.

---

7. A character from the British author William Golding's *Lord of the Flies* (1954).
8. From C. S. Lewis's *The Lion, the Witch, and the Wardrobe* (1950).

9. Brian Robeson, the main character in Gary Paulsen's *Hatchet* (1988).
1. Characters in *Where the Wild Things Are* (1963), by Maurice Sendak.

"And you are——?"

"Uh . . . Joe, Sam, and Fred," I said.

"And from which book might that be?"

I panicked. I knew the Devil probably wouldn't believe the same weak story we told those not-too-bright guards at the front door. So I decided to just pretend our real lives were a story. They were definitely weird enough to sound like fiction.

"We're the Time Warp Trio," I said. "We travel around in time and have adventures and stuff."

The Devil pulled at his beard while he checked his alphabetical list. "I have a *Time Cat*, a *Time of Wonder*, and then *A Toad for Tuesday*.[2] But no *Time Warp Trio*."

"Off with their heads!" yelled the Red Queen.

The Devil looked up and looked right through me. "Do you know your author?"

That threw me for a loop. "Um . . . sure . . . I mean no . . . I mean I'm not sure . . . I think it starts with an *s* . . . maybe . . . ?" I started making up any answer I could think of.

Sam saw I was in trouble and jumped in to help. "We go a lot of different places. So each adventure has a different title. We're probably not under 'Time Warp Trio' because we're actually a series."

Frankenstein gave a mad groan: "Series—bad!" and made a move to wring our necks. The Devil held him back.

"No, no. Settle down your goose bumps,[3] Frank. They're not from one of those horror series. They look more like kids who would travel around on a magic school bus[4] or something."

"Hey, no way," said Fred, stepping up to the desk and getting into it. "Joe does some unreal magic tricks. Sam is *the* joke-and-riddle brainiac. And I usually save the day with my mad skills."

The Devil looked completely confused.

"Mad skills!" squawked the parrot. "Mad skills!"

"Shiver my timbers," boomed Long John Silver. "He's not even speaking the King's English. Clap him in irons with the rest of them!"

The Devil tapped his pencil on his list. "I'm not quite sure what you said, young man. But maybe you can make this easier on all of us. What we are doing here is separating the good characters from the bad characters. The bad characters stay here and take over any story they like. . . ."

He motioned to the bogeymen, goblins, and people who cut in front of you in the lunch line.

"And the good characters go there . . ."

He motioned to the characters behind him.

". . . to be crushed by those huge stacks of books and wiped out of stories forever."

The bad characters cheered and hooted and howled. The Devil smiled.

"So—are you good characters . . . or bad characters?"

Now I know it's wrong to lie. But I was still trying to figure out if it would be all that wrong to lie to the Devil . . . when Fred solved the problem.

"Oh, we're definitely bad," said Fred. "Watch this." He jumped on top of a library table, spun 570 degrees through the air to land backward on the stair's handrail,

---

2. Books by, respectively, Lloyd Alexander (1963), Robert McCloskey (1957), and Russell E. Erickson (1974).

3. A reference to the popular Goosebumps series (1990s) by the American author R. L. Stine.

4. An American series (begun in 1986), written by Joanna Cole and illustrated by Bruce Degen, that is designed to teach children about science (and is the basis of the PBS animated television program, 1994–98).

then slid down the whole rail fakie stale Japan on his shoes. "Now *that's* bad."

The Horned King nodded his big antlered head.

"And see this book?" I lifted a telephone-book-size volume called *Best Children's Books*. I grabbed a piece of string off the desk. I put the string through the middle of the book, closed it, and tied a knot at the back of the spine. I held the two ends of the string out. "I bet your baddest, strongest character can't pull the string so it's straight horizontally."

Jack's giant stepped up and grabbed the string. He pulled. The string stayed bowed. Frankenstein pulled. The string stayed bowed. The Cyclops[5] pulled and pulled and nearly popped his one eye out of his head. The string stayed bowed.

"That's bad," said a wolf in sheep's clothing.

"What building has the most stories?" said Sam.

"The Empire State Building?" guessed the Sheriff of Nottingham.

"No, the library," said Sam. "Where does Thursday come before Wednesday?"

From the captured good guys came a voice. "On a deserted island?" guessed Robinson Crusoe's Friday.

"No, the dictionary," said Sam. "What would happen if you threw this yellow book into the Red Sea?"

"It would turn pink?" guessed one of the evil stepmothers.

"It would get wet," said Sam.

Everyone groaned.

"Stop, stop," said the Devil. "That is really bad."

All of the bad characters laughed and gathered around us. Fred showed the Horned King a half cab topside grind. Dracula and Sam traded vampire riddles. I was explaining some more impossible tricks to an evil scientist.

We were in. All we had to do was get our hands on *The Book*, and everything and everyone would be back where they belonged. Fred, Sam, and I smiled at each other.

Then the door with LIBRARIAN written on the glass slammed open with a bang.

"What is going on out here?!"

Injun Joe and Captain Ahab[6] tried to hide behind a shelf. Everyone else became instantly quiet. All the nasty, murdering, cutthroat, bad characters in the place were standing looking nervously at their feet.

"Nothing, Boss," said the Devil.

We looked from the Devil to the fuzzy brown figure he was talking to. Then we knew we were in even weirder and bigger trouble.

"The Boss?" said Fred.

"A . . . a . . . teddy bear?" said Sam.

8

"That's *Mr.* Bear to you, kid," growled the soft fuzzy teddy bear with a red ribbon around his neck.

We must have looked more than a little shocked. We didn't say anything else. But the teddy bear went crazy on us.

"This is exactly what I'm talking about. Just because I'm a teddy bear, I get no respect. Everyone thinks I'm soft and huggable and *stupid!*"

---

5. In Greek mythology, a one-eyed giant.
6. The monomaniacal pursuer of the whale in Herman Melville's *Moby-Dick* (1851). Injun Joe:
the villain of Mark Twain's *The Adventures of Tom Sawyer* (1876).

"Hey, we didn't say anything like that," said Fred.

Teddy Bear hopped up on the desk. "No, but I know what you're thinking. And that's all going to change."

Teddy Bear turned around and faced the Devil. "And what exactly is the holdup here? Why isn't everyone being crushed?"

The Devil shuffled his papers and pointed to us. "We were . . . uh . . . I was just . . . checking in these three characters."

Teddy Bear jumped off the desk and touched the ground. "Characters? Hah! That's a good one. They aren't characters from a book. These are three kids. Any moron can see that!"

"Any moron can see that!" screeched Long John's parrot.

Teddy Bear was really fuming now. "In fact, they are just the kind of readers I get no respect from—wise-guy boys." He shook his cute pudgy little paw at us. "Don't think I don't know your type. Nothing but action books, sports books, and nonfiction. Well, I'll give you some action. Throw them in the crusher *now!*"

A giant octopus wrapped its monster tentacles around us, tightly.

"Where the heck did that come from?" gasped Fred.

"*20,000 Leagues Under the Sea* would be my guess," wheezed Sam. "Probably eighth-grade list."

Getting yelled at by a teddy bear was bad enough. But being crushed by books and attacked by a character that wasn't even on our grade's reading list was just too much for me. I snapped.

"Now just one minute!" I screamed. I surprised even myself with how loud I yelled. Everyone stared. The octopus loosened its grip. I saw this was my one chance to save us from the horrible fate of getting flattened by hundreds of books. I decided to try reasoning with the teddy bear.

"Now look, Mr. Teddy—I mean Mr. Bear," I said. "It is probably true that we are not the biggest fans of teddy bear books."

"See! See! I told you. I told you," squealed Teddy Bear, spinning around.

"But crushing all of the good characters from every other book is not going to solve anything," I went on. (I tried my best to sound like my mom and dad when they're telling me what to do, but want me to think I have a choice.) "Just look how dumb these books sound without their main characters."

I bent over the tentacle around my waist and picked a book off the floor. "Look at this. Now *The Hoboken Chicken Emergency* is just *The Emergency*."

Fred picked up another book. "*Sylvester and the Magic Pebble* is *And the Magic Pebble*."

Sam picked up *The Gingerbread Man*.[7] "There are giant holes in every story." He read:

> "'Run run run,
> as fast as you can.
> You can't catch me,
> I'm the blankety blank'?"

Teddy Bear looked at us with his big shining eyes. "Aww, that is so sweet. You are worried about all of the poor little books. Well, don't worry. Because the new titles

---

7. A children's folktale.

of those books will be *The Teddy Bear Emergency, Teddy Bear and the Magic Pebble,* and *The Teddy Bear Man!"*

He raised both fuzzy brown arms in the air and laughed a crazy hyper laugh at the ceiling. He kept laughing and babbling. "And then there will be *Encyclopedia Teddy Bear, Curious Mr. Twit, Bridge to Long John Silver . . ."*

His voice got higher and louder.

"Frankenstein in Wonderland . . ."

The bad characters cheered each new title.

"The Devil in the Willows, Green Eggs and Dracula . . ."

He was totally loony.

"Headless-Horseman-the-Pooh, Teddy Bear Everlasting! We're taking over!"

The bad characters gave a huge cheer. "Ted-dy! Ted-dy! Ted-dy!"

Teddy Bear ran around in little circles with his fuzzy arms raised.

The octopus tossed us into the cage with the good characters and slammed the metal bar door behind us. Fred, Sam, and I bounced off George, Martha, and Ramona. We lay on our backs looking up at the hundreds of books that were about to come crashing down on us.

This is it, I thought. The minute that twisted little bear gives the word, we will be flattened proof of what some kids have always suspected—reading can kill you.

I heard a voice. The books teetered. I closed my eyes.

It was too late to even scream.

9

I heard the voice again. It didn't sound like Teddy Bear's voice.

I opened my eyes to see if we were still alive. Sam sat squeezed between George and Martha. Fred held Peter Rabbit in one arm and Ping in the other. I let out one long sigh of relief and looked at the front desk.

A girl about our age stood in front of Teddy Bear and his bad character pals.

"What the boys said makes sense."

Teddy Bear stared at the girl in amazement.

Long John Silver stared at her like she was a piece of steak about to be thrown to a hungry lion.

"If we're not in our books, who will tell all of the stories? Of how we crossed the river. How we cleared the land. How we cut the trees. Making the logs. Cutting a notch in the—"

"Okay already," said Teddy Bear. "Could you speed it up? I'm just about to knock over these books and crush these characters out of existence."

"Who the heck is she?" whispered Fred.

"I think it's that girl who lived on the prairie," said Sam.

We all shivered, remembering that required-reading book.

"Then there was the time I accidentally poured the currant wine at tea," said the girl. "I was only looking for raspberry cordial and I had so wanted to use the rosebud tea set but of course that was never used except for the minister . . ."

"Or maybe she's Anne of Green Gables,"[8] whispered Sam.

"I see—" began Teddy Bear. But the girl kept going.

"And then that Christmas without Father was so lonely yet so splendid because

8. Title character of a book (1908) and then series by the Canadian novelist Lucy Maud Montgomery.

Father was away as a chaplain and Meg and Jo and Amy and Marmee . . ."

"Yes—" began Teddy Bear. But the girl kept going.

"One of the Little Women?"[9] I guessed.

"Or the time I took trick riding because who knew when it might come in handy when I had a mystery to solve, and sure enough, later that week . . ."

Teddy Bear sat down and started listening.

"Nancy Drew?" guessed Fred. The girl kept going.

". . . after that summer, babysitting was never the same. The club met over at my house . . ."

The Devil propped his chin in his hand to keep his head up.

"Babysitters' Club?" I guessed.

". . . and I knew Annie had beauty, talent, and the drive to be a cheerleader. But I was not about to let her ruin the reputation of our squad . . ."

"Definitely Sweet Valley High,"[1] I said.

Somebody yawned. Sam nudged me in the ribs and pointed to Frankenstein. He was struggling mightily to keep his eyelids open. First one eye would close. Then the other. Both eyes popped open. They closed.

". . . we passed notes in school by curling up the piece of paper, slipping it in the iron scroll of the desk . . ."

The Headless Horseman and the Horned King sat propped up against each other. No one could see their eyes. But neither one of them was moving anymore. Long John Silver let out a soft little snore.

"Betty?" guessed Fred. "Veronica?"[2]

"American Girls?"[3] I guessed.

"That's it," whispered Sam.

"Who's it?"

"She's all of those girls," said Sam. "We never read any of those books. So we couldn't tell one character from another if we had to. She's all of those girl characters rolled into one!"

"Now *that's* scary," said Fred.

Teddy Bear leaned forward, looking at the Girl through half-closed eyes. The Red Queen had long since laid her head on the table. Dracula was wrapped in sweet dreams in his cape. Teddy Bear was the last bad character still awake.

". . . Pa didn't have no nails. But he said a man don't need no nails to make a door. This is how he did it. . . ."

Teddy Bear closed one eye and leaned against the sleeping Devil.

". . . and when you are filled with sadness and in the depths of despair, doesn't it just feel like a lump of caramel in your throat . . ."

Teddy Bear's last open eye winked . . . half closed . . . and then dropped shut. His chin fell forward on his chest. And he snored the biggest growling snore of any of the fast-asleep bad guys.

I put my finger to my lips. Fred slowly and carefully swung open the metal door. Sam led everyone out from under the stack of books teetering above us. Martha carried Piglet. Pooh cradled Peter Rabbit.

". . . 'It takes time to develop a good relationship,' I told Annie . . ."

9. Title of the perennially popular novel (1868) by Louisa May Alcott.
1. Series (begun in 1984) originally written and then plotted by Francine Pascal.

2. Characters in the *Archie* comic; they (and Archie) first appeared in a story in 1941 (by writer Vic Bloom and artist Bob Montana).
3. Series (begun in 1986) by Valerie Tripp.

The Hoboken Chicken tiptoed carefully through the sleeping octopus's tentacles. Madeline stepped over Mr. McGregor's[4] hoe. Fred slipped Flat Stanley between the doors so he could unlock them. Harold, Nate, Pippi, and all the others snuck outside into the sunshine and freedom.

Robin Hood led the last of the kids from Wayside School between the sleeping gangster and the still-drooling troll.

Fred and I stood in the doorway and looked back.

". . . a suspicious character threw a rock. My horse reared almost straight up . . ."

Fred and I looked at each other. We looked back at the Girl who had saved us and all of the characters.

". . . for Christmas in Sweden, one girl in each family would get to dress in a long white dress and red sash with a crown of green leaves and lighted candles . . ."

Fred headed outside. I grabbed him by the arm and dragged him back. We picked the Girl up by each elbow and carried her, still talking, carefully toward the library door.

". . . and what a secret it was! Just three words I whispered in his ear . . ."

We were just at the foot of the stairs when I saw, out of the corner of my eye, a flutter of motion near Long John Silver.

". . . next Pa cut a wide deep notch near the edge—"

"Bbbwwwaaauuukk!" squawked Long John's parrot. "Near the edge! Near the edge!"

Teddy Bear's eyes popped open. The eyes of every bad character in the library popped open. Teddy Bear saw the now-empty room. Teddy Bear saw Fred and me carrying the Girl.

He screamed in a not-very-cuddly voice, "Crush those boys *now!*"

10

Mr. McGregor swung his hoe. The Horned King drew his sword.

"We'll never make it to the door," said Fred. "Quick. Up these stairs."

We charged up the steps two at a time with the Girl leading the way. Captain Ahab and a snake-haired woman[5] climbed after us. The Devil and a red-golden dragon scrambled right behind them.

We reached the top landing, blocked by the stack of books that had been meant to crush us. I had a brainstorm. "Get back here and push!"

The Girl and Fred climbed around behind the books with me. We pushed and pushed and toppled an avalanche of dusty old books down the stairs. I saw the Red Queen disappear under a full set of Funk and Wagnall's encyclopedias. Mrs. Twit took a four-volume *History of the Civil War* right on her chin. Her glass eye popped out, and she flipped over the handrail. A beautiful blue *Historical Atlas of the World* flattened the Headless Horseman.

But a whole new wave of bad characters swarmed over the fallen books.

This time it was the Girl who came up with the brainstorm.

"Come on, boys. Use our only weapon," she called. And she machine-gunned a whole row of Hardy Boys[6] books off one end of a shelf onto the Cyclops' head.

---

4. The villain of Beatrix Potter's *The Tale of Peter Rabbit* (1902).
5. Medusa, a monster from Greek mythology; those who looked at her were turned to stone.

6. Protagonists of series (begun in 1927) by a number of different authors writing under the pseudonym Franklin W. Dixon.

"Nice shot," said Fred. He knocked out a goblin with a rapid-fire set of American Girls. "Don't you love a good series?"

Then we hit them with the heavy artillery. I tossed *The Complete Illustrated Book of All Animals*. Fred chucked *Big Paintings by Everyone Who Ever Did One*. The Girl unloaded *The Big Big Big Dictionary of Names*.

Teddy Bear screamed, "You are making me angry!" and shook his soft fuzzy paw at us.

I knew he was right. And I knew we couldn't hold out for much longer. I looked around for a way to escape. Stairs blocked. Windows too high to reach. Books piled on the other side. That's when I saw our salvation.

Because there, across the lobby, in the piles of books stacked over the desk, in between *Hot Men of Science* and *You and Your Koala Bear*, sat a thin blue book covered with silver stars and moons along the back. A folded list stuck out of the middle of it.

"*The Book!*" I yelled.

"Where?" said Fred.

Surrounded by books, the Girl looked at us like we were crazy.

As I pointed across the room at *The Book*, I suddenly and sadly realized we were no better off than we had been before. There was no way to get to *The Book* without going down the stairs, through a pack of very mad characters we had just conked with some very heavy books, and back up over the desk where Teddy Bear was at this moment throwing a screaming tantrum.

"I will squash you! I will flatten you like the bugs you are!" yelled Teddy Bear. "No one ruins my plans. I will be the most famous character in every story!"

"Why do you need that book?" asked the Girl.

"It's magic enough to get everyone out of here and back into their own books," I said. "But forget it. There is no way we can get there from here."

I figured we were doomed to meet a messy and bookish end at the hands of a crazed teddy bear. I looked over at Fred. And when I saw that look in his eye, and saw him measuring lines and distances, I knew he figured differently.

"Give me some cover," said Fred. "I think a one-eighty monkey plant to an alley-oop fishbrain into a mistyflip rocket air should get me just high enough for a one-handed book grab."

I looked down at the swarming bad guys, then looked back at Fred. "Are you crazy? This isn't a kung-fu skate movie. As soon as those guys see what you're up to, they'll be all over you."

"That's why I need you to keep pelting them with books," said Fred.

"Do you think you can make it?" asked the Girl.

Fred looked over his route once more. He pulled his Red Wings cap low, then nodded.

"So what are you waiting for?" She let out a wild whoop and started firing every book she could get her hands on at the nasty gang below. I gave a yell and started winging books, too.

Fred jumped the handrail and slid halfway down before anyone figured out what was happening. Long John Silver stood up to swing his crutch, but I took him out with volume 7 of *Junior Classics: Legends of Long Ago*. Fred hit the end of the rail, launched a perfect mistyflip over the Devil's horns, and rocketed up toward *The Book*.

"Stop that boy!" screamed Teddy Bear.

Now I don't know if everything really slowed down like it always does in those kung-fu action movies. But it sure looked like it to me.

Fred's hand rose to *The Book*. So did Long John's parrot. Fred's hand. The parrot's beak. Both closed on *The Book* at the same instant. Fred pulled. The parrot pulled. Fred, *The Book*, the parrot . . .

And that's when the Girl tomahawked volume 2 of *Junior Classics: Once upon a Time* through the air. It smacked the parrot and popped it off *The Book* with a loud squawk and a puff of green feathers.

Fred bobbled *The Book*, pulled the summer reading list out, and then fell into the pileup of Teddy Bear, Devil, Red Queen, White Witch, and Horned King below.

The Girl and I looked at each other for one horrified second. We thought Fred was history.

Then I saw the wisp of pale green smoke rising from the pile of characters. The wisp turned into a stream. The stream turned into a twisting river. And the river turned into a whirling tornado of pale green mist that sucked up every character and book inside and outside the Hoboken Public Library.

I had just enough time to give the Girl a wave of thanks . . . and we were gone.

11

Fred landed on top of my desk, surrounded by the pileup of books that had been blown off my shelves. In one hand he held *The Book*. In the other hand he held the summer reading list.

I lay on my bed, still feeling a little time-warp queasy.

Sam was nowhere to be seen.

"Oh no," I said. "Sam was outside with the other characters when the mist scooped us up."

"He must still be in Hoboken," said Fred, jumping down off the desk.

I looked at the pile of books and had a terrible thought. "Or sucked into some other book," I said.

Fred and I attacked the books, flipping through all of them, looking for Sam.

"Here's the Hoboken Chicken," I said. "She made it back into her book."

"The Twits are both here," said Fred.

"Mary Poppins, Charlotte, Frog and Toad—everybody's back. Sam!" I yelled at the pile of books. "Where are you?"

We heard a very faint noise. It sounded like Sam's voice.

"Are you in *The White Mountains*?" called Fred, flipping it open.

"Are you in *Treasure Island*?" I called, leafing through it.

"Help!" came a muffled cry. It was definitely Sam's voice.

"Hang on, Sam," said Fred. "We'll get you out."

We flipped through *Winnie-the-Pooh*, *The BFG*, *Fat Men from Space*, and *Treehorn Times Three*. Still no Sam.

That's when Fred and I both spotted the scariest book on the desk. We saw it, but couldn't bring ourselves to pick it up. It was *Little House on the Prairie*.

"Help! Help! Help!" yelled Sam's muffled voice.

"Oh no," said Fred. "What if we can't get him out? What if he's stuck in there forever?" Fred carefully picked up *Little House on the Prairie* between one finger and thumb.

I took it carefully, breathed a deep breath . . . and opened it.

Sam came tumbling out of my closet, fighting my shirts, pants, and hangers wrapped around him.

Fred and I took one look and fell back laughing. Sam finally pulled my basketball shorts off his head. He stood there still covered in clothes and hangers. We started laughing all over again.

"Ahem."

We froze.

"Ahem."

It was my little sister Anna, standing in the doorway.

"I don't really want to know what you are doing," said Anna. "I just wanted to ask you, Joe, if you have any ribbon I can use for my—"

Anna held out her stuffed toy. And before the words "teddy bear" were even out of her mouth, the three of us dove into my closet screaming, "Nooooooo!"

Anna backed slowly out of my room. She held her teddy bear behind her. We peeked out of the closet.

"You guys are so weird," said Anna. "So weird."

SUMMER READING LIST

Each student must read four books during the summer and fill out the attached study guide for two of them.

Early Readers

Amelia Bedelia (series), by Peggy Parish

The *Carrot Seed*, by Ruth Krauss

The *Cat in the Hat*, by Dr. Seuss

Curious George (series), by H. A. Rey

Frog and Toad (series), by Arnold Lobel

George and Martha (series), by James Marshall

Green Eggs and Ham, by Dr. Seuss

Grimms Fairy Tales

Harold and the Purple Crayon, by Crockett Johnson

The House at Pooh Corner, by A. A. Milne

Madeline (series), by Ludwig Bemelmans

Make Way for Ducklings, by Robert McCloskey

Mother Goose

Nate the Great (series), by Marjorie W. Sharmat

The Snowman, by Raymond Briggs

The Story About Ping, by Marjorie Flack

Sylvester and the Magic Pebble, by William Steig

The Tale of Peter Rabbit, by Beatrix Potter

The Three Billy Goats Gruff, folk tale

The Very Hungry Caterpillar, by Eric Carle

Middle Readers

Blue Moose, Fat Men from Space, The Hoboken Chicken Emergency, and pretty much anything written by Daniel Manus Pinkwater

Bunnicula, by James Howe

Charlotte's Web, by E. B. White

The Devil's Storybook, by Natalie Babbitt

Encyclopedia Brown (series), by Donald J. Sobol

Flat Stanley, by Jeff Brown

Hatchet, by Gary Paulsen

Homer Price, by Robert McCloskey

I Was a Teenage Gangster, by A Badguy
The Lion, the Witch, and the Wardrobe, by C. S. Lewis
Little House on the Prairie, by Laura Ingalls Wilder
Mary Poppins, by P. L. Travers
Pippi Longstocking, by Astrid Lindgren
Ramona (series), by Beverly Cleary
Robin Hood, retold by Rosemary Sutcliff
Sarah, Plain and Tall, by Patricia MacLachlan
Treehorn Times Three, by Florence Parry Heide
The Twits, Matilda, The BFG, and a lot of things by Roald Dahl
Wayside School Is Falling Down, by Louis Sachar
The White Mountains, by John Christopher
The Wind in the Willows, by Kenneth Grahame

Older Readers

Adventures of Tom Sawyer, by Mark Twain
Aesop's Fables, by Aesop
Alice in Wonderland, by Lewis Carroll
The Book of Three, and everything written by Lloyd Alexander
Bridge to Terabithia, by Katherine Paterson
Dracula, by Bram Stoker
Frankenstein, by Mary Shelley
Gods, Heroes and Men of Ancient Greece, by W. H. D. Rouse
The Hobbit, by J. R. R. Tolkien
Julie of the Wolves, by Jean Craighead George
The Legend of Sleepy Hollow, by Washington Irving
Lord of the Flies, by William Golding
Moby Dick, by Herman Melville
Robinson Crusoe, by Daniel Defoe
Treasure Island, by Robert Louis Stevenson
Tuck Everlasting, by Natalie Babbitt
Johnny Tremain, by Esther Forbes
20,000 Leagues Under the Sea, by Jules Verne

Be-Extremely-Careful-When-You-Readers

Anything with Teddy Bears in It, by Anyone

Perfect-for-Knocking-Out-Parrots-and-Saving-the-Day-Readers

Junior Classics, Volume Two: Once upon a Time

Study Guide

• Write the title and author of the book.
• Identify two major characters of the book.
• Imagine who you would have play the major characters in the movie version of
the book.
• Tap your pencil on the paper.
• Stare out the window and daydream.
• Put the study guide away and don't look at it again until the night before the
first day of school.

1998

Science Fiction

The popularity and significance of science fiction for young and old in the twenty-first century cannot be overstated. As the gifted British science fiction writer Brian Aldiss has noted in his book *Trillion Year Spree* (1986), "Films, TV series, computer games, toys, media advertising, music—the science fiction mode is more diverse in its forms than ever before. We live in an SF environment where our children's toys are robots and spacecraft, their cartoon adventures set in the 31st Century or on another planet. We see computer technology proliferating unchecked. We also see our oldest SF dreams being made into believable visual images on the wide screen." More than any genre of literature, science fiction has anticipated how technology can change and still is changing the very essence of human relations. It relies on serious speculation about the use of technology, and it attracts readers not because it predicts what might happen to them in the future but because it actually touches their lives in the present.

Although science fiction has become one of the most popular genres for children and teenagers, especially when presented in comic books, films, and television series, there is very little agreement among critics about its origins and definition. Some scholars cite Mary Shelley's *Frankenstein; or, The Modern Prometheus* (1818) as the first science fiction novel; others point to the works of Jules Verne and H. G. Wells in the latter part of the nineteenth century as the first classics of the genre. The term *science fiction* itself was first coined by William Wilson in an obscure work, *A Little Earnest Book upon a Great Old Subject* (1851)—but few stories and books then being written fit the term, which was soon forgotten. In 1926 Hugo Gernsback founded the magazine *Amazing Stories* and began promoting what he first called stories of "scientifiction" and in 1929 labeled "science fiction." His magazine began publishing fiction in the tradition of Edgar Allan Poe, Verne, and Wells, writers who were among the first to ponder the momentous effects that modern scientific experimentation might have on civilization. Once Gernsback had demonstrated how viable science fiction was for the mass market, existing pulp fiction magazines began including such stories, and new magazines were founded. Yet the mass publication of these stories did not lead to a precise definition of the genre. Nor was it clear whether the intended audience of science fiction was primarily adult or young readers.

Historically, science fiction can be regarded as a crossover genre, read by both adults and children almost from its beginning, and young readers have always consumed so-called adult works as well as the "juveniles" specifically meant for them. It is a branch of literature concerned with technology and science, often (but not only) exploring their effects on the future of humankind. In its speculations, science fiction does not focus solely on the earth's future, but also employs settings in other times and other places, whether in space or on distant planets. Much of science fiction is also inner or psychological exploration of how scientific change affects the human mind and body. Though it carries an implicit hope that humans can be improved by science and that improved human beings will improve society, this hope is not always fulfilled. Science fiction cannot be understood without grasping technology's utopian and dystopian ramifications for the future of civilization. Typical plots and themes include the creation of ideal societies on earth or on another planet, the exploration of space, alien invasion, time travel, genetic experimentation, nuclear apocalypse, postholocaust societies, robots, mind control, totalitarianism, cybernetics, and a computer-controlled universe.

Though the distinction between adult and juvenile science fiction is difficult to make, certain identifiable phases in the genre's development in the United Kingdom and United States must be grasped to understand science fiction's impact on children as well as the meaning of the genre as a whole. While particular authors and their works may be better known or more popular in one or the other country, there is a shared tradition of science fiction appreciation, especially among boys and men, that can be briefly sketched to provide the background for more detailed studies of specific works and authors.

The First Phase

Early science fiction (1863–1919) can be linked to industrialization, colonialism, imperialism, and (in the United States) the exploration and closing of the frontier. The first significant writer of "scientific romances," the term used at that time, was the Frenchman Jules Verne. His extraordinarily successful novels, rapidly translated into English, marked the future of the genre; they include *Five Weeks in a Balloon* (1863), *Journey to the Center of the Earth* (1864), *From the Earth to the Moon* (1865), *Around the Moon* (1870), *Twenty Thousand Leagues under the Sea* (1870), *Round the World in Eighty Days* (1873), and *The Mysterious Island* (1874–75). In all, sixty-four novels in his series *Les voyages extraordinaires* appeared between 1863 and 1910 (publication from manuscripts continued after his death in 1905). Though other writers in France and England were writing about interplanetary travel, Verne was the most inventive and prolific. He sought to base his novels on scientific fact—for instance, the *Nautilus* in *Twenty Thousand Leagues under the Sea* was inspired by the steam-driven submarine developed by his friend Jacques-François Conseil—and he had a comprehensive understanding of science's potential and its effects. There was hardly a realm or an invention that Verne did not explore in his works as he sent his protagonists into space, to other planets, down into the ocean, and around the world in different vehicles to assess how science might shape humankind's destiny.

H. G. Wells was no less far-reaching in his speculations, but he was much more political and philosophical than Verne. His best-known science fiction works, published around the turn of the century, include *The Time Machine: An Invention* (1895), *The Island of Doctor Moreau: A Possibility* (1896), *The Invisible Man: A Grotesque Romance* (1897), *The War of the Worlds* (1897), *Tales of Space and Time* (1899), and *The First Men in the Moon* (1900–01). Rather than stressing the wonder of scientific inventions and technological transformations, Wells was usually more concerned with their implications for society. He sought to use science artfully to open up various perspectives for readers, encouraging them to reflect on human evolution and social conflict.

Verne and Wells greatly influenced the many writers of novels and stories that could be regarded as the first wave of science fiction for young readers at the turn of the century. Some of the more important works of this period were Edward Bellamy's *Looking Backward, 2000–1887* (1888); Mark Twain's *A Connecticut Yankee in King Arthur's Court* (1889); L. Frank Baum's *The Master Key: An Electrical Fairy Tale* (1901); E. Nesbit's time travel novels, *The Story of the Amulet* (1906) and *Harding's Luck* (1909); Jack London's *The Iron Heel* (1908); Sir Arthur Conan Doyle's *The Lost World* (1912); and Edgar Rice Burroughs's *A Princess of Mars* (1917). At the same time, British and American mass magazines such as *The Strand, McClure's Magazine,* and *Argosy* published science fiction stories from the 1890s through the 1920s. Particularly important were the Harmsworth boys' weeklies, which contained a variety of fiction and nonfiction articles that dealt with science. Other crucial forerunners of science fiction were the dime novels and penny dreadfuls that focused on adventures of (always male) young inventors and scientists. As early as 1868 Edward Sylvester Ellis published *The Steam Man of the Prairies,* in which a young inventor takes a steam engine in the shape of a huge man to the western frontier, where it helps three gold miners by scaring away Indians. In 1876 the publisher Frank Tousey commissioned Harry Enton to copy Ellis's work for his paper, *The Boys of New York,* and Enton created a new young inventor for *Frank Reade and His Steam Man of the Plains* (1876). It was followed by *Frank Reade and His Steam Horse* (1876), *Frank Reade and His Steam Team* (1880), and *Frank Reade and His Steam Tally-Ho* (1881), all of which followed the same formula: weapons and steam engines were used to terrorize Indians and settle the frontier. Their success led to other dime novel series whose inventor-heroes, such as Frank Reade Jr., Jack Wright, and even Thomas Edison, were shown leading the way in American progress.

By the beginning of the twentieth century, Edward Stratemeyer, an enterprising publisher of series books for boys and girls, decided to produce new lines of adventure books that revolved around new technologies. The Great Marvel series, written for the most part by Howard Garis under the name Roy Rockwood—*Through the Air to the North Pole* (1906), *Under the Ocean to the South Pole* (1907), and seven more—was very successful. Much more popular still were the Tom Swift novels published between 1910 and 1941, whose title character Stratemeyer modeled on Glenn Curtiss, an inventor and aviation innovator. These, too, were written almost entirely by Garis (in this series working under the name Victor Appleton); he produced five Tom Swift books in 1910 alone. The first, *Tom Swift and His Motor-Cycle,* introduced Tom, his inventor father, and Eradicate Sampson, who becomes their loyal black servant, as Tom's ingenuity keeps his father's latest invention out of the hands of unscrupulous competitors. This series, which ultimately contained forty novels, combined science, information about engineering, and action to form a cultural myth about boy inventors. It also provided a template for science fiction aimed primarily at boys in the first half of the twentieth century.

The Second Phase

Science fiction for young readers between 1919 and 1945 is generally associated with the rise of the pulp magazine and the work of Hugo Gernsback. He left Luxembourg in 1904 for America, hoping to sell a new battery he had invented, and he settled in New York. Various ventures in electronics included the first home radio and the founding of a company that sold radio-building equipment by mail (its catalogue turned into a magazine, *Modern Electrics*, in 1908). After serializations of his own fiction proved to be a popular feature, Gernsback began publishing a story of fictionalized scientific speculation in every issue. By 1920 the magazine (now called *Science and Invention*) was publishing two stories every month, and another was appearing in a second magazine he had started, *Radio News*. These stories both reflected and fed the interest in science fiction, which led to Gernsback's most significant contribution to the genre: the founding of *Amazing Stories*. In its pages, his idealistic and highly influential vision of science fiction took shape. He declared in a June 1927 editorial: "Not only is science fiction an idea of tremendous import, but it is to be an important factor in making the world a better place to live in, through educating the public to the possibilities of science and the influence of science on life which, even today, are not appreciated by the man on the street."

Like Wells, Gernsback strongly believed in the philosophical and pedagogical mission of science fiction. As part of his project, he published and encouraged the leading writers of science fiction in the 1920s and 1930s, such as E. E. "Doc" Smith, Jack Williamson, and John W. Campbell. He also helped form science fiction fan clubs and promoted reviews of science fiction in the popular press. Moreover, by stressing that the stories must be based on science that is real or possible, he literally established the credibility of the genre.

The second important figure of this period was John W. Campbell. Though in the 1930s he was a leading writer of space epics, it was as editor of *Astounding Space-Fiction* (originally titled *Astounding Stories*, and renamed *Analog* in 1960)—a position he assumed in 1937 and kept until his death in 1971—that Campbell changed the genre. He demanded high literary standards in the stories published in his magazine, and as the first truly professional editor of science fiction, he devoted himself to helping authors achieve it. Campbell nurtured the careers of some of the best writers of science fiction, including Robert Heinlein, L. Sprague de Camp, Isaac Asimov, Clifford D. Simak, Theodore Sturgeon, and Lester del Rey. He insisted that authors aim at psychological as well as scientific realism, putting a new stress on characterization and on sociological themes.

Most early science fiction narratives were short, and many other popular magazines in America (e.g., *Thrilling Wonder Stories* and *Planet Stories*) and in England (*Union Jack, Wizard, Champion,* and *Modern Boy*) played a role in disseminating innovative stories that broadened the genre's appeal. To the existing stock characters of science fiction—Frankenstein's monster, the mad scientist, the struggling young inventor, the older inventor's beautiful daughter, and so on—were added more modern figures, such as the dedicated engineer and explorer, the spaceship crew, highly advanced robots, and even typical members of a family or community, such as hardworking mothers and fathers. It was also during this time that comic book superheroes (notably, Superman and Captain Marvel), who were to have a profound influence on the development of science fiction for the young, first appeared.

The Third Phase

After 1945 science fiction flowered and has continued to flourish to the present, as the genre has become much more artistic, experimental, complex, and innovative both in form and in content. In addition, the utopianism of earlier writings was seriously questioned and challenged, often to be replaced by dystopian plots and themes dealing with nuclear holocausts and apocalypses of various kinds. Even as important new science fiction magazines were founded, such as *The Magazine of*

Fantasy and Science Fiction (1949) and *Galaxy Science Fiction* (1950), helping to move the genre further away from simple adventure fiction, the focus of publishing began to shift away from short stories to books. More women started to write science fiction—among the first were C. L. Moore, Leigh Brackett, Judith Merril, and Andre Norton. As they began to include a growing number of female protagonists in their works, science fiction's female audience began to expand. Finally, major writers of science fiction began to create stories and novels deliberately aimed at young readers.

Undoubtedly, the most influential post–World War II science fiction writer for the young was Robert Heinlein, who began his notable career in the late 1930s and won widespread acclaim with a series of juveniles published from 1947 to 1963, including *Rocket Ship Galileo* (1947), *Red Planet* (1949), *Citizen of the Galaxy* (1957), *Have Space Suit—Will Travel* (1958), and *Podkayne of Mars: Her Life and Times* (1963). Most of his juveniles are initiation stories: young protagonists are placed in extraordinary situations that test their valor and talents, and they must learn to cope with changing technological and social conditions. For example, in *Tunnel in the Sky* (1955) students taking their final exam in "advanced survival" are left on an unknown planet for two to ten days, to survive alone or in teams with only whatever equipment they can carry. After they are accidentally stranded and the main characters realize their predicament, they seek out the others in order to form a group large enough for long-term self-sufficiency. More than twenty create a small town, with marriages and births, as they reinvent both basic government and basic technology. After two years, the adults arrive and ironically dismiss the survivors as "kids," ignoring their experiences and knowledge. Heinlein focused critically on the inability of most adults to comprehend or appreciate adolescents. He always stayed close to the facts and extrapolated from sound scientific premises, yet the center of his interest was not science itself but the human reaction to science—its social and political implications. The rites of passage through which his young protagonists passed provided the framework for exploring those implications.

Although Heinlein was often charged with stereotyping women, he was one of the first science fiction writers to depict female characters who are just as skilled and ready for action as their male peers. In doing so, he helped prepare the way for the women who took science fiction in directions, many of them feminist, beyond his imagination. One of the first and most prolific women in the field was Andre Norton (Alice Mary Norton), who, like Heinlein, often wrote adventure stories of adolescents undergoing rites of passage on worlds very different from ours. *Star Man's Son, 2250 A.D.* (1952; later republished as *Daybreak 2250 A.D.*), *Moon of Three Rings* (1966), *The Zero Stone* (1968), and other works affirm the newly tapped talents of their young protagonists, male and female. Other women who began writing science fiction for young readers include Eleanor Cameron, who wrote *The Wonderful Flight to the Mushroom Planet* (1954) and four sequels, three of which feature an Earth-dwelling extraterrestrial scientist named Mr. Bass; Madeline L'Engle, whose interests in time travel, science, and theology were at the center of her important trilogy, *A Wrinkle in Time* (1962), *A Wind in the Door* (1973), and *A Swiftly Tilting Planet* (1978); and Sylvia Engdahl, who wrote a conventional outer-space romance with *Journey Between Worlds* (1970), while *Enchantress from the Stars* (1970) is a much more philosophical depiction of the conflict between a technologically advanced society and another planet's feudal culture. Perhaps the most important female writer of science fiction has been Ursula Le Guin, who is also the author of realist fiction, poetry, fantasy, and essays and is famous for her Earthsea fantasy trilogy for young adults (1968–72). This trilogy, which was expanded by two more novels and several stories of Earthsea by 2001, and her two award-winning novels, *The Left Hand of Darkness*

(1969) and *The Dispossessed* (1975), gained her critical and popular renown. She creates fully imagined and keenly observed societies, with an emphasis on ecology and the environment that reflects a Taoist sense of balance, and her writings have become more overtly feminist over time. In Le Guin's recent novel *The Telling* (2000), she depicts a planet called Aka, which has been completely transformed by a repressive government and by technology, leading to the elimination of old customs and beliefs. The female protagonist Sutty travels to Aka as a neutral observer to discover why Aka's culture has been devastated, and she recovers the art of story-telling as a means of recapturing the essence of humanity in a totally administered world.

Many other women writing juvenile science fiction have been equally critical of how technology has been used to limit the potential of human beings, as they helped reshape the genre's form and interests in the latter half of the twentieth century. In particular, these authors have made female characters more multidimensional, giving them more active roles to play—often within societies in which they had more leeway to counteract stereotypically male tendencies, such as militarism and aggression. Among the more notable American and British authors of science fiction for young readers, and some of their works, are Monica Hughes (the Isis trilogy, 1980–82), Anne McCaffrey (the Pern series, which began in 1968), Virginia Hamilton (the Justice trilogy, 1980–81), Jean Ure (the Plague trilogy, 1989–94), and Diana Wynne Jones (*The Homeward Bounders*, 1981). All have been affected, in varying degrees, by the women's movement, but some writers are particularly feminist in their subjects and concerns. Along with Ursula Le Guin, these include Joanna Russ, whose stories and novel about Alyx (*Alyx*, 1976)—a tough, smart thief from ancient Greece turned agent of the Trans-Temporal Authority—were almost shocking in their subversion of gender expectations, and Vonda McIntyre. In *Dreamsnake* (1978), the Starfarers series (1989–94), and other novels, McIntyre depicts women engaging in a full range of human endeavor (healer, starship captain, scientist, tribal leader) and sometimes in nontraditional sexual partnerships (e.g., three-person marriage).

Certainly, the rise of the feminist movement in the late 1960s and the contributions of female writers had a great impact on the development of science fiction, but there were also other factors that led to greater social reflection, innovation, and experimentation within the genre, such as the Cold War, the Vietnam War, nuclear accidents, the proliferation of computers and the rise of the Internet, experimentation in genetics and nanotechnology, and the development of increasingly deadly weapons of mass destruction—these became the concerns of *all* writers of science fiction, male and female, whose own preferences and ideologies varied widely (and not necessarily along lines of gender or sex). Because science fiction writers often seek to map out alternative societies to highlight the weaknesses and dangers of their own and are at the same time concerned with the future of civilization in general, their interests are often very broad. For instance, Ray Bradbury, one of the most popular of all writers of science fiction, takes on serious sociopolitical topics in such works as *The Martian Chronicles* (1950), whose stories criticize imperialism, racism, and the nuclear arms race, and *Fahrenheit 451* (1953), which attacks censorship and totalitarian mass culture. Arthur C. Clarke's *Childhood End* (1953) and Lester del Rey's *Step to the Stars* (1954) also explore issues of conformity and authoritarianism in mass society. One of the most profound critiques of autocratic and technocratic societies can be found in the British writer John Christopher's Tripods trilogy (1967–68) and its "prequel," *When the Tripods Came* (1988). Christopher shows that ending totalitarianism does not in itself guarantee peace and freedom.

Though a small band of determined fighters manages to destroy the aliens who had for more than a century used sophisticated "caps" to control the very thoughts of almost all adults on earth, the final chapter of the prequel makes clear that the struggle to form a democratic community of nations will be at least as difficult.

The fears most often expressed after World War II by the best of the science fiction writers for young readers are that the reckless use of technology to acquire power and dominate the world will devastate it or that a totally administered society, such as those described by Aldous Huxley in *Brave New World* (1932) or George Orwell in *1984* (1949), will deny its members civil liberties and turn them into virtual automatons. Andre Norton was among the first to write about these fears in *Star Man's Son*, in which a teenage outcast survives his travels through a postholocaust landscape because he is a mutant; she thus celebrates the significance of difference. Robert C. O'Brien's chilling *Z for Zachariah* (1974) is narrated by a sixteen-year-old girl who is the only person alive in a protected valley after a devastating nuclear and chemical war—and who must defend herself against the man who finds her sanctuary.

Though it began for the most part in optimism, science fiction has increasingly taken a more dystopian view of the future, even in the absence of any cataclysmic act of destruction. Robert Westall's *Futuretrack 5* (1983) imagines a twenty-first-century Britain rigidly stratified by class. Birth and examinations are still important in establishing one's place in society, but now "Paramils" in helicopters use psycho-radar to search for the malcontents—and those who are too unhappy or enraged are sent to "lobo-farms" for lobotomies. Almost all productive work is done by robots, and life (even the weather) is controlled by a single national computer, which is itself programmed by an elite group of "Techs." The best hope for a more humane world is to add information about ethics into the computer's memory.

Similar themes are raised in two outstanding recent books for young adults, both of which powerfully imagine "perfect" societies that are disturbingly dehumanizing. Jonas, the protagonist of Lois Lowry's *The Giver* (1993), lives in a world without hunger, prejudice, or insecurity: every individual has a place in the community, assigned at a solemn ceremony when he or she is twelve. When Jonas is selected to be trained for a position he hadn't even known existed, he learns that one person must hold all the community's memories of pain and pleasure. From the current Receiver of Memory, he learns that knowledge without memories is meaningless; he realizes that the comfortable, choiceless life of those around him is also loveless and literally colorless, lacking joy as well as sorrow. Jonas flees, so that they must bear the memories themselves and he may find a more genuine form of community. Titus, the teenage narrator of M. T. Anderson's *Feed* (2002), lives in a near-future in which the Internet has been supplanted by the feed: a neural implant, installed in most Americans shortly after birth, that both enables people to communicate instantly with each other and admits a never-ending string of advertisements, tailored to each individual, from the corporations that have taken over most state functions. With unlimited, instant access to facts, they never have to think for themselves. It never occurs to Titus that this society lacks meaning until he meets an unusual girl named Violet, whose assimilation into the consumer culture is less complete, and whose implant, unable to function properly after they temporarily lose their connection to the feed, ultimately shuts her down.

The rise of science fiction critical of government control, consumerism, globalization, and the loss of cultural diversity began during the 1970s. For instance, George R. R. Martin, like Anderson, foresees advances in computers that benefit corporations and undermine the authenticity of life, focusing in "The Last Super Bowl Game" (1975) on the realm of sports. Craig Strete, the first Native American to write science fiction for young readers, offers a parable of the dominant culture's instrumental approach to what it does not understand in "The Bleeding Man" (1974). A technocratic society that values obedience, conformity, and eagerness to consume and even equates these qualities with patriotism, Strete, Martin, William Sleator, and other authors suggest, has no place for the uniqueness of the individual. They thus paint a grim picture of the future.

In recent decades, works in science fiction's various media—comics and film as well as fiction—have increasingly raised similar concerns about totalitarianism and the elimination of marginalized people, often represented by racial minorities or mutants. Such movies as *The Matrix* (1999), *The X-Men* (2000), and *Spiderman* (2002) and their sequels, as well as the television shows, books, and comics that they have been spun off into or are derived from, have consistently pleaded and argued for more tolerance toward aliens and the other. Many science fiction classics of the big and small screen, including the original *Star Wars* trilogy (1977–83), *E.T. the Extra-Terrestrial* (1982), and various generations of the Star Trek franchise (beginning with the 1966–69 television series), have the same message. Though science fiction has always contained both optimistic and pessimistic strains, there has clearly been a "dystopian turn" in the latter part of the twentieth century, indicating a crisis for the genre. Whereas Verne and Wells were hopeful that science and technology would benefit humankind because they believed that humans were basically good, the more contemporary writers are less optimistic about the goodness of human beings. A growing number of today's science fiction narratives warn that science and technology are being used not to bring liberation but to consolidate power and control—and indeed that science and technology may eventually overpower and enslave the humans they once served.

H. G. WELLS
1866–1946

Along with the French writer Jules Verne (1828–1905), Herbert George Wells is considered to be the founder of science fiction. He was an extraordinarily prolific and versatile author, writing primarily for adults; today, however, his readers are mainly teenagers and college students who concentrate on what he called his "scientific romances," written between 1895 and 1901. Born into a lower-middle-class family in Bromley, Kent, near London, Wells was apprenticed at thirteen to a draper. But no trade interested him, and he persuaded his parents to allow him to return to school in 1883 when he was offered a student assistantship at the Midhurst Grammar School. Two years later he won a scholarship to the Normal School (now Imperial College) of Science in London, where he came under the influence of T. H. Huxley, the famous biologist and champion of Darwin's theory of evolution. He also edited and wrote for the *Science Schools Journal*. Leaving college without a degree, he taught briefly until poor health forced him to resign. He passed the examinations for his B.Sc. and began teaching for the University Correspondence College, publishing two biology textbooks under its auspices.

By 1893 Wells was writing full-time, producing journalistic sketches, book reviews, and speculative articles on science, such as "The Man of the Year Million" (1893), which foresaw human beings evolving through natural selection into huge-brained and nearly immobile creatures. His first scientific short story, "The Stolen Bacillus" (1894), used the frame of science to set up its joke; others, like "The Flowering of the Strange Orchid" (1894), were more concerned with exotic and uncanny plants and animals. Wells published more than thirty stories in 1894 and 1895, but it was his first novel—*The Time Machine: An Invention*, serialized in 1895—that won him fame; many still believe it to be his best work. The Time Traveller, an inventor, tells his disbelieving guests of his journey forward in time, mainly to 802,701. In that year he finds the beautiful but frail and childish people the Eloi as well as the small and apelike Morlocks, who live underground and, he realizes to his horror, feed on the Eloi. Both are descendants of the human race, the logical outcome of the social class disparities of Wells's time.

This bleak view of humanity's future—underscoring that biological evolution did not guarantee continual improvement—was characteristic of Wells's other turn-of-the-century writings, such as *The Island of Dr. Moreau* (1896) and *The War of the Worlds* (1898). But Wells also believed that once science had replaced the falsehoods of theology, the state would evolve toward world socialism. He began writing nonfiction speculations on the future, beginning with *Anticipations of the Reaction of Mechanical and Scientific Progress upon Human Life and Thought* (1901), and became more active politically, joining the socialist Fabian Society in 1903. Though he left the society in 1908 after George Bernard Shaw and others resisted his attempts to dominate it, he continued in his fiction and nonfiction to criticize Edwardian society and to posit alternatives to the present world. Sometimes these took the form of scientific fantasies, such as *In the Days of the Comet* (1905), but more often his fiction took the form of social comedy and realism, such as *Kipps: The Story of a Simple Soul* (1905) and *Tono-Bungay* (1908). His outspoken advocacy of sexual liberation also found its way into his fiction, and his portrayal of an emancipated woman in *Ann Veronica: A Modern Love Story* (1909) was considered scandalous.

Increasingly, Wells was a social crusader concentrating on nonfiction, as he fought against what he saw as the sad likelihood of human degeneration and extinction. Believing that education was needed to avert catastrophe, he published *The Outline of History, Being a Plain History of Life and Mankind* (1919–20), a best-seller that endeavored to discourage militant nationalism (and thus war) by demonstrating the commonalities of peoples throughout the world. In a similar vein were *The Work, Wealth and Happiness of Mankind* (1931) and his "history" of the future, *The Shape of Things to Come* (1935). He became an international public figure, interviewing Lenin—and later Stalin and Franklin Roosevelt—and continuing to promote his socialist ideals. World War II seemed to confirm his pessimism about humanity's chances, and his last work, *Mind at the End of Its Tether* (1945), foretold the destruction of civilization. Yet his work on the Sankey Commission (which led to *The Rights of Man; or, What Are We Fighting For?*, 1940) directly influenced the language of the Declaration of Human Rights in the United Nations charter adopted in 1948.

"The Stolen Body" is representative of Wells's important early short stories that imaginatively blend the supernatural and science. Nevertheless, it is clear in this story that Wells is interested in using science to explain an extraordinary event. The experiments in astral travel and the spiritual possession of a body are motifs that Wells was to develop in his novels. Important, too, is the notion of the misguided experiment that can wreak havoc on the experimenter and cause his own destruction.

The Stolen Body

Mr. Bessel was the senior partner in the firm of Bessel, Hart, and Brown, of St. Paul's Churchyard,[1] and for many years he was well known among those interested in psychical research as a liberal-minded and conscientious investigator. He was an unmarried man, and instead of living in the suburbs, after the fashion of his class, he occupied rooms in the Albany, near Piccadilly. He was particularly interested in the questions of thought transference and of apparitions of the living, and in November, 1896, he commenced a series of experiments in conjunction with Mr. Vincey, of Staple Inn,[2] in order to test the alleged possibility of projecting an apparition of oneself by force of will through space.

Their experiments were conducted in the following manner: At a pre-arranged hour Mr. Bessel shut himself in one of his rooms in the Albany and Mr. Vincey in his sitting-room in Staple Inn, and each then fixed his mind as resolutely as possible on the other. Mr. Bessel had acquired the art of self-hypnotism, and, so far as he could, he attempted first to hypnotise himself and then to project himself as a 'phantom of the living' across the intervening space of nearly two miles into Mr. Vincey's apartment. On several evenings this was tried without any satisfactory result, but on the fifth or sixth occasion Mr. Vincey did actually see or imagine he saw an apparition of Mr. Bessel standing in his room. He states that the appearance, although brief, was very vivid and real. He noticed that Mr. Bessel's face was white and his expression anxious, and, moreover, that his hair was disordered. For a moment Mr. Vincey, in spite of his state of expectation, was too surprised to speak or move, and in that moment it seemed to him as though the figure glanced over its shoulder and incontinently vanished.

It had been arranged that an attempt should be made to photograph any phantasm seen, but Mr. Vincey had not the instant presence of mind to snap the camera that lay ready on the table beside him, and when he did so he was too late. Greatly elated, however, even by this partial success, he made a note of the exact time, and at once took a cab to the Albany to inform Mr. Bessel of this result.

He was surprised to find Mr. Bessel's outer door standing open to the night, and the inner apartments lit and in an extraordinary disorder. An empty champagne magnum lay smashed upon the floor; its neck had been broken off against the inkpot on

1. Street in the City of London.
2. A group of buildings in central London, once one of the Inns of Chancery, where rooms are rented by lawyers.

the bureau and lay beside it. An octagonal occasional table, which carried a bronze statuette and a number of choice books, had been rudely overturned, and down the primrose paper of the wall inky fingers had been drawn, as it seemed for the mere pleasure of defilement. One of the delicate chintz curtains had been violently torn from its rings and thrust upon the fire, so that the smell of its smouldering filled the room. Indeed the whole place was disarranged in the strangest fashion. For a few minutes Mr. Vincey, who had entered sure of finding Mr. Bessel in his easy chair awaiting him, could scarcely believe his eyes, and stood staring helplessly at these unanticipated things.

Then, full of a vague sense of calamity, he sought the porter at the entrance lodge.[3] 'Where is Mr Bessel?' he asked. 'Do you know that all the furniture is broken in Mr. Bessel's room?' The porter said nothing, but, obeying his gestures, came at once to Mr. Bessel's apartment to see the state of affairs. 'This settles it,' he said, surveying the lunatic confusion. 'I didn't know of this. Mr. Bessel's gone off. He's mad!'

He then proceeded to tell Mr. Vincey that about half an hour previously, that is to say, at about the time of Mr. Bessel's apparition in Mr. Vincey's rooms, the missing gentleman had rushed out of the gates of the Albany into Vigo Street, hatless and with disordered hair, and had vanished into the direction of Bond Street. 'And as he went past me,' said the porter, 'he laughed—a sort of gasping laugh, with his mouth open and his eyes glaring—I tell you, sir, he fair scared me!—like this.'

According to his imitation it was anything but a pleasant laugh. 'He waved his hand, with all his fingers crooked and clawing—like that. And he said, in a sort of fierce whisper, *"Life!"* Just that one word, *"Life!"*'

'Dear me,' said Mr. Vincey. 'Tut, tut,' and 'Dear me!' He could think of nothing else to say. He was naturally very much surprised. He turned from the room to the porter and from the porter to the room in the gravest perplexity. Beyond his suggestion that probably Mr. Bessel would come back presently and explain what had happened, their conversation was unable to proceed. 'It might be a sudden tooth-ache,' said the porter, 'a very sudden and violent tooth-ache, jumping on him suddenly-like and driving him wild. I've broken things myself before now in such a case . . .' He thought. 'If it was, why should he say *"life"* to me as he went past?'

Mr. Vincey did not know. Mr. Bessel did not return, and at last Mr. Vincey, having done some more helpless staring, and having addressed a note of brief inquiry and left it in a conspicuous position on the bureau, returned in a very perplexed frame of mind to his own premises in Staple Inn. This affair had given him a shock. He was at a loss to account for Mr. Bessel's conduct on any sane hypothesis. He tried to read, but he could not do so; he went for a short walk, and was so pre-occupied that he narrowly escaped a cab at the top of Chancery Lane; and at last—a full hour before his usual time—he went to bed. For a considerable time he could not sleep because of his memory of the silent confusion of Mr. Bessel's apartment, and when at length he did attain an uneasy slumber it was at once disturbed by a very vivid and distressing dream of Mr. Bessel.

He saw Mr. Bessel gesticulating wildly, and with his face white and contorted. And, inexplicably mingled with his appearance, suggested perhaps by his gestures, was an intense fear, an urgency to act. He even believed that he heard the voice of his fellow experimenter calling distressfully to him, though at the time he considered this to be an illusion. The vivid impression remained though Mr. Vincey awoke. For a space he lay awake and trembling in the darkness, possessed with that vague, unaccountable terror of unknown possibilities that comes out of dreams upon even

3. I.e., the doorkeeper's room.

the bravest men. But at last he roused himself, and turned over and went to sleep again, only for the dream to return with enhanced vividness.

He awoke with such a strong conviction that Mr. Bessel was in overwhelming distress and need of help that sleep was no longer possible. He was persuaded that his friend had rushed out to some dire calamity. For a time he lay reasoning vainly against this belief, but at last he gave way to it. He arose, against all reason, lit his gas and dressed, and set out through the deserted streets—deserted, save for a noiseless policeman or so and the early news carts—towards Vigo Street to inquire if Mr. Bessel had returned.

But he never got there. As he was going down Long Acre some unaccountable impulse turned him aside out of that street towards Covent Garden, which was just waking to its nocturnal activities. He saw the market in front of him—a queer effect of glowing yellow lights and busy black figures. He became aware of a shouting, and perceived a figure turn the corner by the hotel and run swiftly towards him. He knew at once that it was Mr. Bessel. But it was Mr. Bessel transfigured. He was hatless and dishevelled, his collar was torn open, he grasped a bone-handled walking-cane near the ferrule end,[4] and his mouth was pulled awry. And he ran, with agile strides, very rapidly. Their encounter was the affair of an instant. 'Bessel!' cried Vincey.

The running man gave no sign of recognition either of Mr. Vincey or of his own name. Instead, he cut at his friend savagely with the stick, hitting him in the face within an inch of the eye. Mr. Vincey, stunned and astonished, staggered back, lost his footing, and fell heavily on the pavement. It seemed to him that Mr. Bessel leapt over him as he fell. When he looked again Mr. Bessel had vanished, and a policeman and a number of garden porters and salesmen were rushing past towards Long Acre in hot pursuit.

With the assistance of several passers-by—for the whole street was speedily alive with running people—Mr. Vincey struggled to his feet. He at once became the centre of a crowd greedy to see his injury. A multitude of voices competed to reassure him of his safety, and then to tell him of the behaviour of the madman, as they regarded Mr. Bessel. He had suddenly appeared in the middle of the market screaming 'Life! Life!' striking left and right with a blood-stained walking-stick, and dancing and shouting with laughter at each successful blow. A lad and two women had broken heads, and he had smashed a man's wrist; a little child had been knocked insensible, and for a time he had driven every one before him, so furious and resolute had his behaviour been. Then he made a raid upon a coffee stall, hurled its paraffin[5] flare through the window of the post office, and fled laughing, after stunning the foremost of the two policemen who had the pluck to charge him.

Mr. Vincey's first impulse was naturally to join in the pursuit of his friend, in order if possible to save him from the violence of the indignant people. But his action was slow, the blow had half stunned him, and while this was still no more than a resolution came the news, shouted through the crowd, that Mr. Bessel had eluded his pursuers. At first Mr. Vincey could scarcely credit this, but the universality of the report, and presently the dignified return of two futile policemen, convinced him. After some aimless inquiries he returned towards Staple Inn, padding a handkerchief to a now very painful nose.

He was angry and astonished and perplexed. It appeared to him indisputable that Mr. Bessel must have gone violently mad in the midst of his experiment in thought

---

4. I.e., the bottom (a *ferrule* is a protective metal cap or band).
5. Kerosene.

transference, but why that should make him appear with a sad white face in Mr. Vincey's dreams seemed a problem beyond solution. He racked his brains in vain to explain this. It seemed to him at last that not simply Mr. Bessel, but the order of things must be insane. But he could think of nothing to do. He shut himself carefully into his room, lit his fire—it was a gas fire with asbestos bricks—and, fearing fresh dreams if he went to bed, remained bathing his injured face, or holding up books in a vain attempt to read, until dawn. Throughout that vigil he had a curious persuasion that Mr. Bessel was endeavouring to speak to him, but he would not let himself attend to any such belief.

About dawn, his physical fatigue asserted itself, and he went to bed and slept at last in spite of dreaming. He rose late, unrested and anxious and in considerable facial pain. The morning papers had no news of Mr. Bessel's aberration—it had come too late for them. Mr. Vincey's perplexities, to which the fever of his bruise added fresh irritation, became at last intolerable, and, after a fruitless visit to the Albany, he went down to St. Paul's Churchyard to Mr. Hart, Mr. Bessel's partner, and so far as Mr. Vincey knew, his nearest friend.

He was surprised to learn that Mr. Hart, although he knew nothing of the outbreak, had also been disturbed by a vision, the very vision that Mr. Vincey had seen—Mr. Bessel, white and dishevelled, pleading earnestly by his gestures for help. That was his impression of the import of his signs. 'I was just going to look him up in the Albany when you arrived,' said Mr. Hart. 'I was so sure of something being wrong with him.'

As the outcome of their consultation the two gentlemen decided to inquire at Scotland Yard for news of their missing friend. 'He is bound to be laid by the heels,'[6] said Mr. Hart. 'He can't go on at that pace for long.' But the police authorities had not laid Mr. Bessel by the heels. They confirmed Mr. Vincey's overnight experiences and added fresh circumstances, some of an even graver character than those he knew—a list of smashed glass along the upper half of Tottenham Court Road, an attack upon a policeman in Hampstead Road, and an atrocious assault upon a woman. All these outrages were committed between half-past twelve and a quarter to two in the morning, and between those hours—and, indeed, from the very moment of Mr. Bessel's first rush from his rooms at half-past nine in the evening—they could trace the deepening violence of his fantastic career. For the last hour, at least from before one, that is, until a quarter to two, he had run amuck through London, eluding with amazing agility every effort to stop or capture him.

But after a quarter to two he had vanished. Up to that hour witnesses were multitudinous. Dozens of people had seen him, fled from him or pursued him, and then things suddenly came to an end. At a quarter to two he had been seen running down the Euston Road towards Baker Street, flourishing a can of burning colza oil[7] and jerking splashes of flame therefrom at the windows of the houses he passed. But none of the policemen on Euston Road beyond the Waxwork Exhibition, nor any of those in the side streets down which he must have passed had he left the Euston Road, had seen anything of him. Abruptly he disappeared. Nothing of his subsequent doings came to light in spite of the keenest inquiry.

Here was a fresh astonishment for Mr. Vincey. He had found considerable comfort in Mr. Hart's conviction: 'He is bound to be laid by the heels before long,' and in that assurance he had been able to suspend his mental perplexities. But any fresh

6. Put in irons; arrested.
7. Coleseed (i.e., rapeseed) oil, often used in lamps.

development seemed destined to add new impossibilities to a pile already heaped beyond the powers of his acceptance. He found himself doubting whether his memory might not have played him some grotesque trick, debating whether any of these things could possibly have happened; and in the afternoon he hunted up Mr. Hart again to share the intolerable weight on his mind. He found Mr. Hart engaged with a well-known private detective, but as that gentleman accomplished nothing in this case, we need not enlarge upon his proceedings.

All that day Mr. Bessel's whereabouts eluded an unceasingly active inquiry, and all that night. And all that day there was a persuasion in the back of Mr. Vincey's mind that Mr. Bessel sought his attention, and all through the night Mr. Bessel with a tear-stained face of anguish pursued him through his dreams. And whenever he saw Mr. Bessel in his dreams he also saw a number of other faces, vague but malignant, that seemed to be pursuing Mr. Bessel.

It was on the following day, Sunday, that Mr. Vincey recalled certain remarkable stories of Mrs. Bullock, the medium, who was then attracting attention for the first time in London. He determined to consult her. She was staying at the house of that well-known inquirer, Dr. Wilson Paget, and Mr. Vincey, although he had never met that gentleman before, repaired to him forthwith with the intention of invoking her help. But scarcely had he mentioned the name of Bessel when Doctor Paget interrupted him. 'Last night—just at the end,' he said, 'we had a communication.'

He left the room, and returned with a slate on which were certain words written in a handwriting, shaky indeed, but indisputably the handwriting of Mr. Bessel!

'How did you get this?' said Mr. Vincey. 'Do you mean?'——

'We got it last night,' said Doctor Paget. With numerous interruptions from Mr. Vincey, he proceeded to explain how the writing had been obtained. It appears that in her *séances*, Mrs. Bullock passes into a condition of trance, her eyes rolling up in a strange way under her eyelids, and her body becoming rigid. She then begins to talk very rapidly, usually in voices other than her own. At the same time one or both of her hands may become active, and if slates and pencils are provided they will then write messages simultaneously with and quite independently of the flow of words from her mouth. By many she is considered an even more remarkable medium than the celebrated Mrs. Piper. It was one of these messages, the one written by her left hand, that Mr. Vincey now had before him. It consisted of eight words written disconnectedly 'George Bessel . . . trial excav^n . . . Baker Street . . . help . . . starvation.' Curiously enough, neither Doctor Paget nor the two other inquirers who were present had heard of the disappearance of Mr. Bessel—the news of it appeared only in the evening papers of Saturday—and they had put the message aside with many others of a vague and enigmatical sort that Mrs. Bullock has from time to time delivered.

When Doctor Paget heard Mr. Vincey's story, he gave himself at once with great energy to the pursuit of this clue to the discovery of Mr. Bessel. It would serve no useful purpose here to describe the inquiries of Mr. Vincey and himself; suffice it that the clue was a genuine one, and that Mr. Bessel was actually discovered by its aid.

He was found at the bottom of a detached shaft which had been sunk and abandoned at the commencement of the work for the new electric railway near Baker Street Station. His arm and leg and two ribs were broken. The shaft is protected by a hoarding nearly 20 ft. high, and over this, incredible as it seems, Mr. Bessel, a stout, middle-aged gentleman, must have scrambled in order to fall down the shaft. He was saturated in colza oil, and the smashed tin lay beside him, but luckily the flame had been extinguished by his fall. And his madness had passed from him altogether. But he was, of course, terribly enfeebled, and at the sight of his rescuers he gave way to hysterical weeping.

In view of the deplorable state of his flat, he was taken to the house of Dr. Hatton in Upper Baker Street. Here he was subjected to a sedative treatment, and anything that might recall the violent crisis through which he had passed was carefully avoided. But on the second day he volunteered a statement.

Since that occasion Mr. Bessel has several times repeated this statement—to myself among other people—varying the details as the narrator of real experiences always does, but never by any chance contradicting himself in any particular. And the statement he makes is in substance as follows.

In order to understand it clearly it is necessary to go back to his experiments with Mr. Vincey before his remarkable attack. Mr. Bessel's first attempts at self-projection, in his experiments with Mr. Vincey, were, as the reader will remember, unsuccessful. But through all of them he was concentrating all his power and will upon getting out of the body—'willing it with all my might,' he says. At last, almost against expectation, came success. And Mr. Bessel asserts that he, being alive, did actually, by an effort of will, leave his body and pass into some place or state outside this world.

The release was, he asserts, instantaneous. 'At one moment I was seated in my chair, with my eyes tightly shut, my hands gripping the arms of the chair, doing all I could to concentrate my mind on Vincey, and then I perceived myself outside my body—saw my body near me, but certainly not containing me, with the hands relaxing and the head drooping forward on the breast.'

Nothing shakes him in his assurance of that release. He describes in a quiet, matter-of-fact way the new sensation he experienced. He felt he had become impalpable—so much he had expected, but he had not expected to find himself enormously large. So, however, it would seem he became. 'I was a great cloud—if I may express it that way—anchored to my body. It appeared to me, at first, as if I had discovered a greater self of which the conscious being in my brain was only a little part. I saw the Albany and Piccadilly and Regent Street and all the rooms and places in the houses, very minute and very bright and distinct, spread out below me like a little city seen from a balloon. Every now and then vague shapes like drifting wreaths of smoke made the vision a little indistinct, but at first I paid little heed to them. The thing that astonished me most, and which astonishes me still, is that I saw quite distinctly the insides of the houses as well as the streets, saw little people dining and talking in the private houses, men and women dining, playing billiards, and drinking in restaurants and hotels, and several places of entertainment crammed with people. It was like watching the affairs of a glass hive.'

Such were Mr. Bessel's exact words as I took them down when he told me the story. Quite forgetful of Mr. Vincey, he remained for a space observing these things. Impelled by curiosity, he says, he stooped down, and with the shadowy arm he found himself possessed of attempted to touch a man walking along Vigo Street. But he could not do so, though his finger seemed to pass through the man. Something prevented his doing this, but what it was he finds it hard to describe. He compares the obstacle to a sheet of glass.

'I felt as a kitten may feel,' he said, 'when it goes for the first time to pat its reflection in a mirror.' Again and again, on the occasion when I heard him tell this story, Mr. Bessel returned to that comparison of the sheet of glass. Yet it was not altogether a precise comparison, because, as the reader will speedily see, there were interruptions of this generally impermeable resistance, means of getting through the barrier to the material world again. But, naturally, there is a very great difficulty in expressing these unprecedented impressions in the language of everyday experience.

A thing that impressed him instantly, and which weighed upon him throughout all this experience, was the stillness of this place—he was in a world without sound.

At first Mr. Bessel's mental state was an unemotional wonder. His thought chiefly concerned itself with where he might be. He was out of the body—out of his material body, at any rate—but that was not all. He believes, and I for one believe also, that he was somewhere out of space, as we understand it, altogether. By a strenuous effort of will he had passed out of his body into a world beyond this world, a world undreamt of, yet lying so close to it and so strangely situated with regard to it that all things on this earth are clearly visible both from without and from within in this other world about us. For a long time, as it seemed to him, this realisation occupied his mind to the exclusion of all other matters, and then he recalled the engagement with Mr. Vincey, to which this astonishing experience was, after all, but a prelude.

He turned his mind to locomotion in this new body in which he found himself. For a time he was unable to shift himself from his attachment to his earthly carcass. For a time this new strange cloud body of his simply swayed, contracted, expanded, coiled, and writhed with his efforts to free himself, and then quite suddenly the link that bound him snapped. For a moment everything was hidden by what appeared to be whirling spheres of dark vapour, and then through a momentary gap he saw his drooping body collapse limply, saw his lifeless head drop sideways, and found he was driving along like a huge cloud in a strange place of shadowy clouds that had the luminous intricacy of London spread like a model below.

But now he was aware that the fluctuating vapour about him was something more than vapour, and the temerarious excitement of his first essay was shot with fear. For he perceived, at first indistinctly, and then suddenly very clearly, that he was surrounded by *faces!* that each roll and coil of the seeming cloud-stuff was a face. And such faces! Faces of thin shadow, faces of gaseous tenuity. Faces like those faces that glare with intolerable strangeness upon the sleeper in the evil hours of his dreams. Evil, greedy eyes that were full of a covetous curiosity, faces with knit brows and snarling, smiling lips; their vague hands clutched at Mr. Bessel as he passed, and the rest of their bodies was but an elusive streak of trailing darkness. Never a word they said, never a sound from the mouths that seemed to gibber. All about him they pressed in that dreamy silence, passing freely through the dim mistiness that was his body, gathering ever more numerously about him. And the shadowy Mr. Bessel, now suddenly fear-stricken, drove through the silent, active multitude of eyes and clutching hands.

So inhuman were these faces, so malignant their staring eyes, and shadowy, clawing gestures, that it did not occur to Mr. Bessel to attempt intercourse with these drifting creatures. Idiot phantoms, they seemed, children of vain desire, beings unborn and forbidden the boon of being, whose only expressions and gestures told of the envy and craving for life that was their one link with existence.

It says much for his resolution that, amidst the swarming cloud of these noiseless spirits of evil, he could still think of Mr. Vincey. He made a violent effort of will and found himself, he knew not how, stooping towards Staple Inn, saw Vincey sitting attentive and alert in his arm-chair by the fire.

And clustering also about him, as they clustered ever about all that lives and breathes, was another multitude of these vain voiceless shadows, longing, desiring, seeking some loophole into life.

For a space Mr. Bessel sought ineffectually to attract his friend's attention. He tried to get in front of his eyes, to move the objects in his room, to touch him. But

Mr. Vincey remained unaffected, ignorant of the being that was so close to his own. The strange something that Mr. Bessel has compared to a sheet of glass separated them impermeably.

And at last Mr. Bessel did a desperate thing. I have told how that in some strange way he could see not only the outside of a man as we see him, but within. He extended his shadowy hand and thrust his vague black fingers, as it seemed, through the heedless brain.

Then, suddenly, Mr. Vincey started like a man who recalls his attention from wandering thoughts, and it seemed to Mr. Bessel that a little dark-red body situated in the middle of Mr. Vincey's brain swelled and glowed as he did so. Since that experience he has been shown anatomical figures of the brain, and he knows now that this is that useless structure, as doctors call it, the pineal eye. For, strange as it will seem to many, we have, deep in our brains—where it cannot possibly see any earthly light—an eye! At the time this, with the rest of the internal anatomy of the brain, was quite new to him. At the sight of its changed appearance, however, he thrust forth his finger, and, rather fearful still of the consequences, touched this little spot. And instantly Mr. Vincey started, and Mr. Bessel knew that he was seen.

And at that instant it came to Mr. Bessel that evil had happened to his body, and behold! a great wind blew through all that world of shadows and tore him away. So strong was this persuasion that he thought no more of Mr. Vincey, but turned about forthwith, and all the countless faces drove back with him like leaves before a gale. But he returned too late. In an instant he saw the body that he had left inert and collapsed—lying, indeed, like the body of a man just dead—had arisen, had arisen by virtue of some strength and will beyond his own. It stood with staring eyes, stretching its limbs in dubious fashion.

For a moment he watched it in wild dismay, and then he stooped towards it. But the pane of glass had closed against him again, and he was foiled. He beat himself passionately against this, and all about him the spirits of evil grinned and pointed and mocked. He gave way to furious anger. He compares himself to a bird that has fluttered heedlessly into a room and is beating at the window-pane that holds it back from freedom.

And behold! the little body that had once been his was now dancing with delight. He saw it shouting, though he could not hear its shouts; he saw the violence of its movements grow. He watched it fling his cherished furniture about in the mad delight of existence, rend his books apart, smash bottles, drink heedlessly from the jagged fragments, leap and smite in a passionate acceptance of living. He watched these actions in paralyzed astonishment. Then once more he hurled himself against the impassable barrier, and then, with all that crew of mocking ghosts about him, hurried back in dire confusion to Vincey to tell him of the outrage that had come upon him.

But the brain of Vincey was now closed against apparitions, and the disembodied Mr. Bessel pursued him in vain as he hurried out into Holborn to call a cab. Foiled and terror-stricken, Mr. Bessel swept back again, to find his desecrated body whooping in a glorious frenzy down the Burlington Arcade. . . .

And now the attentive reader begins to understand Mr. Bessel's interpretation of the first part of this strange story. The being whose frantic rush through London had inflicted so much injury and disaster had indeed Mr. Bessel's body, but it was not Mr. Bessel. It was an evil spirit out of that strange world beyond existence, into which Mr. Bessel had so rashly ventured. For twenty hours it held possession of him, and for all those twenty hours the dispossessed spirit-body of Mr. Bessel was going to and fro in that unheard-of middle world of shadows seeking help in vain.

He spent many hours beating at the minds of Mr. Vincey and of his friend Mr. Hart. Each, as we know, he roused by his efforts. But the language that might convey his situation to these helpers across the gulf he did not know; his feeble fingers groped vainly and powerlessly in their brains. Once, indeed, as we have already told, he was able to turn Mr. Vincey aside from his path so that he encountered the stolen body in its career, but he could not make him understand the thing that had happened: he was unable to draw any help from that encounter. . . .

All through those hours the persuasion was overwhelming in Mr. Bessel's mind that presently his body would be killed by its furious tenant, and he would have to remain in this shadow-land for evermore. So that those long hours were a growing agony of fear. And ever as he hurried to and fro in his ineffectual excitement innumerable spirits of that world about him mobbed him and confused his mind. And ever an envious applauding multitude poured after their successful fellow as he went upon his glorious career.

For that, it would seem, must be the life of these bodiless things of this world that is the shadow of our world. Ever they watch, coveting a way into a mortal body, in order that they may descend, as furies and frenzies, as violent lusts and mad, strange impulses, rejoicing in the body they have won. For Mr. Bessel was not the only human soul in that place. Witness the fact that he met first one, and afterwards several shadows of men, men like himself, it seemed, who had lost their bodies even it may be as he had lost his, and wandered, despairingly, in that lost world that is neither life nor death. They could not speak because that world is silent, yet he knew them for men because of their dim human bodies, and because of the sadness of their faces.

But how they had come into that world he could not tell, nor where the bodies they had lost might be, whether they still raved about the earth, or whether they were closed for ever in death against return. That they were the spirits of the dead neither he nor I believe. But Doctor Wilson Paget thinks they are the rational souls of men who are lost in madness on the earth.

At last Mr. Bessel chanced upon a place where a little crowd of such disembodied silent creatures was gathered, and thrusting through them he saw below a brightly-lit room, and four or five quiet gentlemen and a woman, a stoutish woman dressed in black bombazine and sitting awkwardly in a chair with her head thrown back. He knew her from her portraits to be Mrs. Bullock, the medium. And he perceived that tracts and structures in her brain glowed and stirred as he had seen the pineal eye in the brain of Mr. Vincey glow. The light was very fitful; sometimes it was a broad illumination, and sometimes merely a faint twilight spot, and it shifted slowly about her brain. She kept on talking and writing with one hand. And Mr. Bessel saw that the crowding shadows of men about him, and a great multitude of the shadow spirits of that shadow land, were all striving and thrusting to touch the lighted regions of her brain. As one gained her brain or another was thrust away, her voice and the writing of her hand changed. So that what she said was disorderly and confused for the most part; now a fragment of one soul's message, and now a fragment of another's, and now she babbled the insane fancies of the spirits of vain desire. Then Mr. Bessel understood that she spoke for the spirit that had touch of her, and he began to struggle very furiously towards her. But he was on the outside of the crowd and at that time he could not reach her, and at last, growing anxious, he went away to find what had happened meanwhile to his body.

For a long time he went to and fro seeking it in vain and fearing that it must have been killed, and then he found it at the bottom of the shaft in Baker Street, writhing furiously and cursing with pain. Its leg and an arm and two ribs had been broken by its fall. Moreover, the evil spirit was angry because his time had been so short and because of the pain—making violent movements and casting his body about.

And at that Mr. Bessel returned with redoubled earnestness to the room where the *séance* was going on, and so soon as he had thrust himself within sight of the place he saw one of the men who stood about the medium looking at his watch as if he meant that the *séance* should presently end. At that a great number of the shadows who had been striving turned away with gestures of despair. But the thought that the *séance* was almost over only made Mr. Bessel the more earnest, and he struggled so stoutly with his will against the others that presently he gained the woman's brain. It chanced that just at that moment it glowed very brightly, and in that instant she wrote the message that Doctor Wilson Paget preserved. And then the other shadows and the cloud of evil spirits about him had thrust Mr. Bessel away from her, and for all the rest of the *séance* he could regain her no more.

So he went back and watched through the long hours at the bottom of the shaft where the evil spirit lay in the stolen body it had maimed, writhing and cursing, and weeping and groaning, and learning the lesson of pain. And towards dawn the thing he had waited for happened, the brain glowed brightly and the evil spirit came out, and Mr. Bessel entered the body he had feared he should never enter again. As he did so, the silence—the brooding silence—ended; he heard the tumult of traffic and the voices of people overhead, and that strange world that is the shadow of our world—the dark and silent shadows of ineffectual desire and the shadows of lost men—vanished clean away.

He lay there for the space of about three hours before he was found. And in spite of the pain and suffering of his wounds, and of the dim damp place in which he lay; in spite of the tears—wrung from him by his physical distress—his heart was full of gladness to know that he was nevertheless back once more in the kindly world of men.

1898

ROBERT A. HEINLEIN
1907–1988

Considered by many critics to be the most influential writer of science fiction in the United States, Robert Heinlein was born in the town of Butler, Missouri, but grew up in Kansas City. He took an early interest in science fiction and read Jules Verne, H. G. Wells, and Edgar Rice Burroughs as well as the stories in science fiction magazines such as *Argos*. He attended the University of Missouri for one year before transferring to the Naval Academy in Annapolis, graduating in 1929. His naval career was cut short when he developed tuberculosis and was forced to retire on medical disability in 1934.

After briefly attending the University of California at Los Angeles, where he studied mathematics and physics, Heinlein tried his hand at several jobs, including silver mining and real estate; he also unsuccessfully ran in a Democratic primary for state assembly. To pay off his mortgage, he later explained, he wrote a story for a competition run by the magazine *Thrilling Wonder Stories*. However, he decided to try selling "Life-Line," whose main character invents a machine that can predict the exact time of a person's death, for more money than the prize offered; the mainstream magazine *Collier's* rejected it, but the best-paying science fiction pulp—*Astounding Science-Fiction*, edited by John W. Campbell Jr.—published it in 1939.

By 1942 Heinlein had published thirty stories (mainly in *Astounding*, sometimes under pseudonyms) and two novels. He spent World War II working as an aviation engineer in Philadelphia. When he returned to science fiction after the war, he turned away from the pulps, instead placing most of his stories in mainstream magazines; he also devoted much of his attention to juvenile novels, which he produced annually for Scribner from 1947 to 1958 (he also wrote several adult novels during this period). Much of Heinlein's work is in fact crossover fiction, enjoyed by both young and old. Though many of his great range of themes were already familiar to his readers, he had unparalleled skill in building on real scientific discoveries to make the future seem believable. His works not only predict technological inventions but also imagine their possible consequences for humanity's social development. His first novel for young readers, *Rocket Ship Galileo* (1947), buttressed its rather implausible plot—teenagers help a scientist build an atomic power rocket—with painstakingly realistic details of their flight to the Moon, including an on-board computer and a disquisition on the distinction between gunnery and rocketry. In later books, such as *Farmer in the Sky* (1950), *Starman Jones* (1953), and *Tunnel in the Sky* (1955), a young hero passes from childhood into adulthood against the backdrop of the social structures needed to explore, colonize, or patrol space, whether within our solar system or across the galaxy. In the maturity and complexity of their concerns, these *Bildungsromane*, or novels of education, set new standards for science fiction intended for young readers.

In 1959 Heinlein wrote another novel intended for young readers, *Starship Troopers*, which was to bring him great notoriety because of its seeming glorification of violence and militarism, and it remains highly controversial. The novel depicts an earth where only those who volunteer to serve in "the Federal Service of the Terran Federation" are allowed to vote; the hero, who has joined against the wishes of his parents, becomes an infantryman in a fierce war with spiderlike aliens who possess a hive mind. Critics have attacked the work as right-wing and even fascist, but a more accurate label of Heinlein's politics throughout his works is "libertarian": he was a passionate defender of individual freedom and an elitist who could be fiercely critical of the government, organized religion, and big business. He demonstrated his iconoclasm in his next novel, *Stranger*

in a Strange Land (1961), his most famous work, which became the first science fiction novel to make the best-seller list and to become a cult classic.

Heinlein uses an innocent with psi powers—Valentine Michael Smith, a man in his twenties who was raised from infancy by Martians, beings whose mental development and culture are far in advance of those of humans—to question assumptions about politics, law, religion, sex, and religion. Smith, who becomes a charismatic founder of a new religion, the "Church of All Worlds," based on a Martian worldview, is willingly martyred. In emphasizing communal life (including group sex); introducing of the idea of "grokking," or understanding the essence of something so thoroughly as to become one with it; and describing a mystic power that could shatter the status quo, the book appealed to many readers in the 1960s. Heinlein's later novels, including *The Moon Is a Harsh Mistress* (1966), *Time Enough for Love: The Lives of Lazarus Long* (1973), and *Friday* (1982), continued to speculate in sometimes controversial ways about sexual mores and social changes of the future. Some of them also reflect the unfortunate tendency, already present in *Stranger*, to replace novelistic development through action with didactic expression of ideas through lecture and dialogue. Moreover, they reflect a cynicism that contradicts the utopianism of his early works.

Podkayne of Mars: Her Life and Times (1963) is one of the earliest science fiction works with an active and intelligent female protagonist. In this *Bildungsroman*, we clearly see Poddy's growing awareness that as a woman she is unlikely to become a "famous explorer captain" and that politics matters. Indeed, Heinlein had meant the lesson to be fatal. But he was persuaded to change that ending. In a 1962 letter to his agent, Lurton Blassingame, Heinlein defended his original version:

> I know that the ending of *Poddy* comes as rather a shock. However, that is the ending that seemed to fit—to me. The story follows a definite progression: a girl child with no worries at all and a preposterous ambition . . . then, step by step, she grows up and discovers that the real world is more complex and not nearly as sweet as she had thought . . . and that the only basic standard for an adult is the welfare of the young.

A 1995 reprint of the novel contains both endings, together with spirited responses by Heinlein fans to the question "Shall Poddy live or die?" Whatever the answer, it is clear that the future Heinlein imagines for any girl like Poddy is difficult. As in all his novels for young readers, the ending is incidental to the development of his protagonists. Heinlein's emphasis is on learning as a process of self-discovery, and in this regard, Poddy's struggles lead to the new self-awareness that Heinlein sought to convey to readers in all his works of juvenile science fiction.

Podkayne of Mars: Her Life and Times

I

All my life I've wanted to go to Earth. Not to live, of course—just to see it. As everybody knows, Terra is a wonderful place to visit but not to live. Not truly suited to human habitation.

Personally, I'm not convinced that the human race originated on Earth. I mean to say, how much reliance should you place on the evidence of a few pounds of old bones plus the opinions of anthropologists who usually contradict each other anyhow when what you are being asked to swallow so obviously flies in the face of all common sense?

Think it through— The surface acceleration of Terra is clearly too great for the human structure; it is known to result in flat feet and hernias and heart trouble. The incident solar radiation on Terra will knock down dead an unprotected human in an amazingly short time—and do you know of any other organism which has to be artificially protected from what is alleged to be its own natural environment in order to stay alive? As to Terran ecology—

Never mind. We humans just *couldn't* have originated on Earth. Nor (I admit) on Mars, for that matter—although Mars is certainly as near ideal as you can find in this planetary system today. Possibly the Missing Planet was our first home—even though I think of Mars as "home" and will always want to return to it no matter how far I travel in later years . . . and I intend to travel a long, *long* way.

But I do want to visit Earth as a starter, not only to see how in the world eight billion people manage to live almost sitting in each other's laps (less than half of the land area of Terra is even marginally habitable) but mostly to see oceans . . . from a safe distance. Oceans are not only fantastically unlikely but to me the very thought of them is terrifying. All that unimaginable amount of water, unconfined. And so deep that if you fell into it, it would be over your head. Incredible!

But now we are going there!

Perhaps I should introduce us. The Fries Family, I mean. Myself: Podkayne Fries— "Poddy" to my friends and we might as well start off being friendly. Adolescent female: I'm eight plus a few months, at a point in my development described by my Uncle Tom as "frying size and just short of husband high"—a fair-enough description since a female citizen of Mars may contract plenary marriage without guardian's waiver on her ninth birthday, and I stand 157 centimeters tall in my bare feet and mass 49 kilograms. "Five feet two and eyes of blue"[1] my daddy calls me, but he is a historian and romantic. But I am not romantic and would not consider even a limited marriage on my ninth birthday; I have other plans.

Not that I am opposed to marriage in due time, nor do I expect to have any trouble snagging the male of my choice. In these memoirs I shall be frank rather than modest because they will not be published until I am old and famous, and I will certainly

---

1. An inexact quotation of the first line of the song "Has Anybody Seen My Gal?" (1914; music by Percy Wenrich and lyrics by Jack Mahoney).

revise them before then. In the meantime I am taking the precaution of writing English in Martian Oldscript—a combination which I'm sure Daddy could puzzle out, only he wouldn't do such a thing unless I invited him to. Daddy is a dear and does not snoopervise me. My brother Clark would pry, but he regards English as a dead language and would never bother his head with Oldscript anyhow.

Perhaps you have seen a book titled: *Eleven Years Old: The Pre-Adolescent Adjustment Crisis in the Male.* I read it, hoping that it would help me to cope with my brother. Clark is just six, but the "Eleven Years" referred to in that title are Terran years because it was written on Earth. If you will apply the conversion factor of 1.8808 to attain real years, you will see that my brother is exactly eleven of those undersized Earth years old.

That book did not help me much. It talks about "cushioning the transition into the social group"—but there is no present indication that Clark ever intends to join the human race. He is more likely to devise a way to blow up the universe just to hear the bang. Since I am responsible for him much of the time and since he has an I.Q. of 160 while mine is only 145, you can readily see that I need all the advantage that greater age and maturity can give me. At present my standing rule with him is: Keep your guard up and *never* offer hostages.

Back to me—I'm colonial mongrel in ancestry, but the Swedish part is dominant in my looks, with Polynesian and Asiatic fractions adding no more than a not-unpleasing exotic flavor. My legs are long for my height, my waist is 48 centimeters and my chest is 90—not all of which is rib cage, I assure you, even though we old colonial families all run to hypertrophied lung development; some of it is burgeoning secondary sex characteristic. Besides that, my hair is pale blond and wavy and I'm pretty. Not beautiful—Praxiteles[2] would not have given me a second look—but real beauty is likely to scare a man off, or else make him quite unmanageable, whereas prettiness, properly handled, is an asset.

Up till a couple of years ago I used to regret not being male (in view of my ambitions), but I at last realized how silly I was being; one might as well wish for wings. As Mother says: "One works with available materials" . . . and I found that the materials available were adequate. In fact I found that I *like* being female; my hormone balance is okay and I'm quite well adjusted to the world and vice versa. I'm smart enough not unnecessarily to show that I am smart; I've got a long upper lip and a short nose, and when I wrinkle my nose and look baffled, a man is usually only too glad to help me, especially if he is about twice my age. There are more ways of computing a ballistic than by counting it on your fingers.

That's me: Poddy Fries, free citizen of Mars, female. Future pilot and someday commander of deep-space exploration parties. Watch for me in the news.

Mother is twice as good-looking as I am and much taller than I ever will be; she looks like a Valkyrie[3] about to gallop off into the sky. She holds a system-wide license as a Master Engineer, Heavy Construction, Surface or Free Fall, and is entitled to wear both the Hoover Medal with cluster and the Christiana Order, Knight Commander, for bossing the rebuilding of Deimos and Phobos.[4] But she's more than just the traditional hairy engineer; she has a social presence which she can switch from warmly charming to frostily intimidating at will, she holds honorary degrees galore, and she publishes popular little gems such as "Design Criteria with Respect to the Effects of Radiation on the Bonding of Pressure-Loaded Sandwich Structures."

---

2. A great Athenian sculptor (fl. ca. 370–330 B.C.E.).
3. One of the warrior maidens of Old Norse mythology, usually represented as riding through the air on horseback.
4. The two moons of Mars.

It is because Mother is often away from home for professional reasons that I am, from time to time, the reluctant custodian of my younger brother. Still, I suppose it is good practice, for how can I ever expect to command my own ship if I can't tame a six-year-old savage? Mother says that a boss who is forced to part a man's hair with a wrench has failed at some point, so I try to control our junior nihilist without resorting to force. Besides, using force on Clark is very chancy; he masses as much as I do and he fights dirty.

It was the job Mother did on Deimos that accounts for Clark and myself. Mother was determined to meet her construction dates; and Daddy, on leave from Ares[5] U. with a Guggenheim grant, was even more frantically determined to save every scrap of the ancient Martian artifacts no matter how much it delayed construction; this threw them into such intimate and bitter conflict that they got married and for a while Mother had babies.

Daddy and Mother are Jack Spratt and his wife;[6] he is interested in everything that has already happened, she is interested only in what is going to happen, especially if she herself is making it happen. Daddy's title is Van Loon Professor of Terrestrial History but his real love is Martian history, especially if it happened fifty million years ago. But do not think that Daddy is a cloistered don given only to contemplation and study. When he was even younger than I am now, he lost an arm one chilly night in the attack on the Company Offices during the Revolution—and he can still shoot straight and fast with the hand he has left.

The rest of our family is Great-Uncle Tom, Daddy's father's brother. Uncle Tom is a parasite. So he says. It is true that you don't see him work much, but he was an old man before I was born. He is a Revolutionary veteran, same as Daddy, and is a Past Grand Commander of the Martian Legion and a Senator-at-Large of the Republic, but he doesn't seem to spend much time on either sort of politics, Legion or public; instead he hangs out at the Elks Club and plays pinochle with other relics of the past. Uncle Tom is really my closest relative, for he isn't as intense as my parents, nor as busy, and will always take time to talk with me. Furthermore he has a streak of Original Sin which makes him sympathetic to my problems. He says that I have such a streak, too, much wider than his. Concerning this, I reserve my opinion.

That's our family and we are all going to Earth. Wups! I left out three—the infants. But they hardly count now and it is easy to forget them. When Daddy and Mother got married, the PEG Board—Population, Ecology, & Genetics—pegged them at five and would have allowed them seven had they requested it, for, as you may have gathered, my parents are rather high-grade citizens even among planetary colonials all of whom are descended from, or are themselves, highly selected and drastically screened stock.

But Mother told the Board that five was all that she had time for and then had us as fast as possible, while fidgeting at a desk job in the Bureau of Planetary Engineering. Then she popped her babies into deep-freeze as fast as she had them, all but me, since I was the first. Clark spent two years at constant entropy, else he would be almost as old as I am—deep-freeze time doesn't count, of course, and his official birthday is the day he was decanted. I remember how jealous I was—Mother was just back from conditioning Juno[7] and it didn't seem fair to me that she would immediately start raising a baby.

5. I.e., Mars (Mars was the Roman god of war, Ares the Greek).
6. I.e., opposites; from the nursery rhyme that begins "Jack Spratt could eat no fat / His wife could eat no lean."
7. An asteroid ca. 120 miles in diameter; its orbit lies between those of Mars and Jupiter.

Uncle Tom talked me out of that, with a lot of lap sitting, and I am no longer jealous of Clark—merely wary.

So we've got Gamma, Delta, and Epsilon in the subbasement of the crèche at Marsopolis, and we'll uncork and name at least one of them as soon as we get back from Earth. Mother is thinking of revivifying Gamma and Epsilon together and raising them as twins (they're girls) and then launching Delta, who is a boy, as soon as the girls are housebroken. Daddy says that is not fair, because Delta is entitled to be older than Epsilon by natural priority of birth date. Mother says that is mere worship of precedent and that she does wish Daddy would learn to leave his reverence for the past on the campus when he comes home in the evening.

Daddy says that Mother has no sentimental feelings—and Mother says she certainly hopes not, at least with any problem requiring rational analysis—and Daddy says let's be rational, then . . . twin older sisters would either break a boy's spirit or else spoil him rotten.

Mother says that is unscientific and unfounded. Daddy says that Mother merely wants to get two chores out of the way at once—whereupon Mother heartily agrees and demands to know why proved production engineering principles should not be applied to domestic economy?

Daddy doesn't answer this. Instead he remarks thoughtfully that he must admit that two little girls dressed just alike would be kind of cute . . . name them "Margaret" and "Marguerite" and call them "Peg" and "Meg"—

Clark muttered to me, "Why uncork them at all? Why not just sneak down some night and open the valves and call it an accident?"

I told him to go wash out his mouth with prussic acid and not let Daddy hear him talk that way. Daddy would have walloped him properly. Daddy, although a historian, is devoted to the latest, most progressive theories of child psychology and applies them by canalizing the cortex through pain association whenever he really wants to ensure that a lesson will not be forgotten. As he puts it so neatly: "Spare the rod and spoil the child."

I canalize most readily and learned very early indeed how to predict and avoid incidents which would result in Daddy's applying his theories and his hand. But in Clark's case it is almost necessary to use a club simply to gain his divided attention.

So it is now clearly evident that we are going to have twin baby sisters. But it is no headache of mine, I am happy to say, for Clark is quite enough maturing trauma for one girl's adolescence. By the time the twins are a current problem I expect to be long gone and far away.

Interlude

Hi, Pod.

So you think I can't read your worm tracks.

A lot you know about me! Poddy—oh, excuse me, "Captain" Podkayne Fries, I mean, the famous Space Explorer and Master of Men—Captain Poddy dear, you probably will never read this because it wouldn't occur to you that I not only would break your "code" but also write comments in the big, wide margins you leave.

Just for the record, Sister dear, I read Old Anglish just as readily as I do System Ortho. Anglish isn't all that hard and I learned it as soon as I found out that a lot of books I wanted to read had never been translated. But it doesn't pay to tell everything you know, or somebody comes along and tells you to stop doing whatever it is you are doing. Probably your older sister.

But imagine calling a straight substitution a "code"! Poddy, if you had actually been able to write Old Martian, it would have taken me quite a lot longer. But you can't. Shucks, even Dad can't write it without stewing over it and he probably knows more about Old Martian than anyone else in the System.

But you won't crack my code—because I haven't any.

Try looking at this page under ultraviolet light—a sun lamp, for example.

II

Oh, *Unspeakables!*

Dirty ears! Hangnails! Snel-frockey! *Spit!* WE AREN'T *GOING!*

At first I thought that my brother Clark had managed one of his more charlatanous machinations of malevolent legerdemain. But fortunately (the only fortunate thing about the whole miserable mess) I soon perceived that it was impossible for him to be in fact guilty no matter what devious subversions roil his id. Unless he has managed to invent and build in secret a time machine, which I misdoubt he *would* do if he could . . . nor am I prepared to offer odds that he can't. Not since the time he rewired the delivery robot so that it would serve him midnight snacks and charge them to my code number without (so far as anyone could ever prove) disturbing the company's seal on the control box.

We'll never know how he did that one, because, despite the fact that the company offered to Forgive All and pay a cash bonus to boot if only he would *please* tell them how he managed to beat their unbeatable seal—despite this, Clark looked blank and would not talk. That left only circumstantial evidence, i.e., it was clearly evident to anyone who knew us both (Daddy and Mother, namely) that *I* would never order candy-stripe ice cream smothered in hollandaise sauce, or—no, I can't go on; I feel ill. Whereas Clark is widely known to eat anything which does not eat him first.

Even this clinching psychological evidence would never have convinced the company's adjuster had not their own records proved that two of these obscene feasts had taken place while I was a house guest of friends in Syrtis Major,[8] a thousand kilometers away. Never mind, I simply want to warn all girls not to have a Mad Genius for a baby brother. Pick instead a stupid, stolid, slightly subnormal one who will sit quietly in front of the solly box, mouth agape at cowboy classics, and never wonder what makes the pretty images.

But I have wandered far from my tragic tale.

We aren't going to have twins.

We already have triplets.

Gamma, Delta, and Epsilon, throughout all my former life mere topics of conversation, are now Grace, Duncan, and Elspeth in all too solid flesh—unless Daddy again changes his mind before final registration; they've had three sets of names already. But what's in a name?—they are here, already in our home with a nursery room sealed on to shelter them . . . three helpless unfinished humans about canal-worm pink in color and no features worthy of the name. Their limbs squirm aimlessly, their eyes don't track, and a faint, queasy odor of sour milk permeates every room even when they are freshly bathed. Appalling sounds come from one end of each— in which they heterodyne each other[9]—and even more appalling conditions prevail at the other ends. (I've yet to find all three of them dry at the same time.)

And yet there is something decidedly engaging about the little things; were it not

8. The name given to a region of Mars that, viewed from Earth, has distinctive black markings.

9. I.e., make noise at different frequencies.

that they are the proximate cause of my tragedy I could easily grow quite fond of them. I'm sure Duncan is beginning to recognize me already.

But, if I am beginning to be reconciled to their presence, Mother's state can only be described as atavistically maternal. Her professional journals pile up unread, she has that soft Madonna look in her eyes, and she seems somehow both shorter and wider than she did a week ago.

First consequence: she won't even discuss going to Earth, with or without the triplets.

Second consequence: Daddy won't go if she won't go—he spoke quite sharply to Clark for even suggesting it.

Third consequence: since they won't go, we *can't* go. Clark and me, I mean. It is conceivably possible that I might have been permitted to travel alone (since Daddy agrees that I am now a "young adult" in maturity and judgment even though my ninth birthday lies still some months in the future), but the question is formal and without content since I am not considered quite old enough to accept full responsible control of my brother with both my parents some millions of kilometers away (nor am I sure that I would wish to, unless armed with something at least as convincing as a morning star[1]) and Daddy is so dismayingly fair with that he would not even discuss permitting one of us to go and not the other when both of us had been promised the trip.

Fairness is a priceless virtue in a parent—but just at the moment I could stand being spoiled and favored instead.

But the above is why I am sure that Clark does not have a time machine concealed in his wardrobe. This incredible contretemps, this idiot's dream of interlocking mishaps, is as much to his disadvantage as it is to mine.

How did it happen? Gather ye round— Little did we dream that, when the question of a family trip to Earth was being planned in our household more than a month ago, this disaster was already complete and simply waiting the most hideous moment to unveil itself. The facts are these: the crèche at Marsopolis has thousands of newborn babies marbleized at just short of absolute zero, waiting in perfect safety until their respective parents are ready for them. It is said, and I believe it, that a direct hit with a nuclear bomb would not hurt the consigned infants; a thousand years later a rescue squad could burrow down and find that automatic, self-maintaining machinery had not permitted the tank temperatures to vary a hundredth of a degree.

In consequence, we Marsmen (not "Martians," please!—Martians are a non-human race, now almost extinct)—Marsmen tend to marry early, have a full quota of babies quickly, then rear them later, as money and time permit. It reconciles that discrepancy, so increasingly and glaringly evident ever since the Terran Industrial Revolution, between the best biological age for having children and the best social age for supporting and rearing them.

A couple named Breeze did just that, some ten years ago—married on her ninth birthday and just past his tenth, while he was still a pilot cadet and she was attending Ares U. They applied for three babies, were pegged accordingly, and got them all out of the way while they were both finishing school. Very sensible.

The years roll past, he as a pilot and later as master, she as a finance clerk in his ship and later as purser—a happy life. The spacelines like such an arrangement; married couples spacing together mean a taut, happy ship.

Captain and Mrs. Breeze serve their ten-and-a-half (twenty Terran) years and put in for half-pay retirement, have it confirmed—and immediately radio the crèche to uncork their babies, all three of them.

---

1. A spiked metal ball attached to a pole by a chain (a medieval weapon).

The radio order is received, relayed back for confirmation; the crèche accepts it. Five weeks later the happy couple pick up three babies, sign for them, and start the second half of a perfect life.

So they thought—

But what they had deposited was two boys and a girl; what they got was two girls and a boy. Ours.

Believe this you must—it took them the better part of a week to notice it. I will readily concede that the difference between a brand-new boy baby and a brand-new girl baby is, at the time, almost irrelevant. Nevertheless there is a slight difference. Apparently it was a case of too much help—between a mother, a mother-in-law, a temporary nurse, and a helpful neighbor, and much running in and out, it seems unlikely that any one person bathed all three babies as one continuous operation that first week. Certainly Mrs. Breeze had not done so—until the day she did . . . and noticed . . . and fainted—and dropped one of our babies in the bath water, where it would have drowned had not her scream fetched both her husband and the neighbor lady.

So we suddenly had month-old triplets.

The lawyer man from the crèche was very vague about how it happened; he obviously did not want to discuss how their "foolproof" identification system could result in such a mixup. So I don't know myself—but it seems logically certain that, for all their serial numbers, babies' footprints, record machines, et cetera, there is some point in the system where one clerk read aloud "Breeze" from the radioed order and another clerk checked a file, then punched "Fries" into a machine that did the rest.

But the fixer man did not say. He was simply achingly anxious to get Mother and Daddy to settle out of court—accept a check and sign a release under which they agreed not to publicize the error.

They settled for three years of Mother's established professional earning power while the little fixer man gulped and looked relieved.

But nobody offered to pay me for the mayhem that had been committed on my life, my hopes, and my ambitions.

Clark did offer a suggestion that was almost a sensible one, for him. He proposed that we swap even with the Breezes, let them keep the warm ones, we could keep the cold ones. Everybody happy—and we all go to Earth.

My brother is far too self-centered to realize it, but the Angel of Death brushed him with its wings at that point. Daddy is a truly noble soul . . . but he had had almost more than he could stand.

And so have I. I had expected today to be actually on my way to Earth, my first space trip farther than Phobos—which was merely a school field trip, our "Class Honeymoon." A nothing thing.

Instead, guess what I'm doing.

Do you have any idea how many times a day *three* babies have to be changed?

III

Hold it! Stop the machines! Wipe the tapes! Cancel all bulletins—
WE ARE GOING TO EARTH *AFTER ALL!!!!*

Well, not *all* of us. Daddy and Mother aren't going, and of course, the triplets are not. But—Never mind; I had better tell it in order.

Yesterday things just got to be Too Much. I had changed them in rotation, only to find as I got the third one dry and fresh that number one again needed service. I had been thinking sadly that just about that moment I should have been entering the dining saloon of S.S. *Wanderlust* to the strains of soft music. Perhaps on the arm of one of the officers . . . perhaps even on the arm of the Captain himself had I the chance to arrange an accidental Happy Encounter, then make judicious use of my "puzzled kitten" expression.

And, as I reached that point in my melancholy daydream, it was then that I discovered that my chores had started all over again. I thought of the Augean Stables[2] and suddenly it was just Too Much and my eyes got blurry with tears.

Mother came in at that point and I asked if I could *please* have a couple of hours of recess?

She answered, "Why, certainly dear," and didn't even glance at me. I'm sure that she didn't notice that I was crying; she was already doing over, quite unnecessarily, the one that I had just done. She had been tied up on the phone, telling someone firmly that, while it was true as reported that she was not leaving Mars, nevertheless she would not now accept another commission even as a consultant—and no doubt being away from the infants for all of ten minutes had made her uneasy, so she just had to get her hands on one of them.

Mother's behavior had been utterly unbelievable. Her cortex had tripped out of circuit and her primitive instincts are in full charge. She reminds me of a cat we had when I was a little girl—Miss Polka Dot Ma'am and her first litter of kittens. Miss Pokie loved and trusted all of us—except about kittens. If we touched one of them, she was uneasy about it. If a kitten was taken out of her box and placed on the floor to be admired, she herself would hop out, grab the kitten in her teeth and immediately return it to the box, with an indignant waggle to her seat that showed all too plainly what she thought of irresponsible people who didn't know how to handle babies.

Mother is just like that now. She accepts my help simply because there is too much for her to do alone. But she doesn't really believe that I can even pick up a baby without close supervision.

So I left and followed my own blind instincts, which told me to go look up Uncle Tom.

I found him at the Elks Club, which was reasonably certain at that time of day, but I had to wait in the ladies' lounge until he came out of the card room. Which he did in about ten minutes, counting a wad of money as he came. "Sorry to make you wait," he said, "but I was teaching a fellow citizen about the uncertainties in the laws of chance and I had to stay long enough to collect the tuition. How marches it, Podkayne mavourneen?"

I tried to tell him and got all choked up, so he walked me to the park under the city hall and sat me on a bench and bought us both packages of Choklatpops and I ate mine and most of his and watched the stars on the ceiling and told him all about it and felt better.

He patted my hand. "Cheer up, Flicka. Always remember that, when things seem darkest, they usually get considerably worse." He took his phone out of a pocket and made a call. Presently he said, "Never mind the protocol routine, miss. This is Senator Fries. I want the Director." Then he added in a moment, "Hymie? Tom Fries here. How's Judith? Good, good . . . Hymie, I just called to tell you that I'm coming over to stuff you into one of your own liquid helium tanks. Oh, say about fourteen or a few minutes after. That'll give you time to get out of town. Clearing." He pocketed

---

2. One of the twelve labors that the legendary Greek hero Heracles had to perform was to clean the dung from the vast stables of King Augeas of Elis in a single day.

his phone. "Let's get some lunch. Never commit suicide on an empty stomach, my dear; it's bad for the digestion."

Uncle Tom took me to the Pioneers Club where I have been only once before and which is even more impressive than I had recalled—It has *real waiters . . .* men so old that they might have been pioneers themselves, unless they met the first ship. Everybody fussed over Uncle Tom and he called them all by their first names and they all called him "Tom" but made it sound like "Your Majesty" and the master of the hostel came over and prepared my sweet himself with about six other people standing around to hand him things, like a famous surgeon operating against the swift onrush of death.

Presently Uncle Tom belched behind his napkin and I thanked everybody as we left while wishing that I had had the forethought to wear my unsuitable gown that Mother won't let me wear until I'm nine and almost made me take back—one doesn't get to the Pioneers Club every day.

We took the James Joyce Fogarty Express Tunnel and Uncle Tom sat down the whole way, so I had to sit, too, although it makes me restless; I prefer to walk in the direction a tunnel is moving and get there a bit sooner. But Uncle Tom says that he gets plenty of exercise watching other people work themselves to death.

I didn't really realize that we were going to the Marsopolis Crèche until we were there, so bemused had I been earlier with my own tumultuous emotions. But when we were there and facing a sign reading: OFFICE OF THE DIRECTOR—PLEASE USE OTHER DOOR, Uncle Tom said, "Hang around somewhere; I'll need you later," and went on in.

The waiting room was crowded and the only magazines not in use were *Kiddie Kapers* and *Modern Homemaker*, so I wandered around a bit and presently found a corridor that led to the Nursery.

The sign on the door said that visiting hours were from 16 to 18.30. Furthermore, it was locked, so I moved on and found another door which seemed much more promising. It was marked: POSITIVELY NO ADMITTANCE—but it didn't say "This Means You" and it wasn't locked, so I went in.

You never saw so many babies in your whole life!

Row upon row upon row, each in its own little transparent cubicle. I could really see only the row nearest me, all of which seemed to be about the same age—and much more finished than the three we had at home. Little brown dumplings they were, cute as puppies. Most of them were asleep, some were awake and kicking and cooing and grabbing at dangle toys that were just in reach. If there had not been a sheet of glass between me and them I would have grabbed me a double armful of babies.

There were a lot of girls in the room, too—well, young women, really. Each of them seemed to be busy with a baby and they didn't notice me. But shortly one of the babies nearest me started to cry whereupon a light came on over its cubicle, and one of the nurse girls hurried over, slid back the cover, picked it up and started patting its bottom. It stopped crying.

"Wet?" I inquired.

She looked up, saw me. "Oh, no, the machines take care of that. Just lonely, so I'm loving it." Her voice came through clearly in spite of the glass—a hear and speak circuit, no doubt, although the pickups were not in evidence. She made soft noises to the baby, then added, "Are you a new employee? You seem to be lost."

"Oh, no," I said hastily, "I'm not an employee. I just—"

"Then you don't belong here, not at this hour. Unless"—she looked at me rather skeptically—"just possibly you are looking for the instruction class for young mothers?"

"Oh, no, no!" I said hastily. "Not yet." Then I added still more hastily, "I'm a guest of the Director."

Well, it wasn't a fib. Not quite. I was a guest of a guest of the Director, one who was with him by appointment. The relationship was certainly concatenative, if not equivalent.

It seemed to reassure her. She asked, "Just what did you want? Can I help you?"

"Uh, just information. I'm making a sort of a survey. What goes on in this room?"

"These are age six-month withdrawal contracts," she told me. "All these babies will be going home in a few days." She put the baby, quiet now, back into its private room, adjusted a nursing nipple for it, made some other sort of adjustments on the outside of the cubicle so that the padding inside sort of humped up and held the baby steady against the milk supply, then closed the top, moved on a few meters and picked up another baby. "Personally," she added, "I think the age six-month contract is the best one. A child twelve months old is old enough to notice the transition. But these aren't. They don't care who comes along and pets them when they cry . . . but nevertheless six months is long enough to get a baby well started and take the worst of the load off the mother. We know how, we're used to it, we stand our watches in rotation so that we are never exhausted from being 'up with the baby all night' . . . and in consequence we aren't short-tempered and we never yell at them—and don't think for a minute that a baby doesn't understand a cross tone of voice simply because he can't talk yet. He knows! And it can start him off so twisted that he may take it out on somebody else, years and years later. There, there, honey," she went on but not to me, "feel better now? Feeling sleepy, huh? Now you just hold still and Martha will keep her hand on you until you are fast asleep."

She watched the baby for a moment longer, then withdrew her hand, closed the box and hurried on to where another light was burning. "A baby has no sense of time," she added as she removed a squalling lump of fury from its crib. "When it needs love, it needs it right now. It can't know that—" An older woman had come up behind her. "Yes, Nurse?"

"Who is this you're chatting with? You know the rules."

"But . . . she's a guest of the Director."

The older woman looked at me with a stern no-nonsense look. "The Director sent you in here?"

I was making a split-second choice among three nonresponsive answers when I was saved by Fate. A soft voice coming from everywhere at once announced: "Miss Podkayne Fries is requested to come to the office of the Director. Miss Podkayne Fries, please come to the office of the Director."

I tilted my nose in the air and said with dignity, "That is I. Nurse, will you be so kind as to phone the Director and tell him that Miss Fries is on her way?" I exited with deliberate haste.

The Director's office was four times as big and sixteen times as impressive as the principal's office at school. The Director was short and had a dark brown skin and a gray goatee and a harried expression. In addition to him and to Uncle Tom, of course, there was present the little lawyer man who had had a bad time with Daddy a week earlier—and my brother Clark. I couldn't figure out how he got there . . . except that Clark has an infallible homing instinct for trouble.

Clark looked at me with no expression; I nodded. The Director and his legal beagle stood up. Uncle Tom didn't but he said, "Dr. Hyman Schoenstein, Mr. Poon Kwai Yau—my niece Podkayne Fries. Sit down, honey; nobody is going to bite you. The Director has a proposition to offer you."

The lawyer man interrupted. "I don't think—"

"Correct," agreed Uncle Tom. "You don't think. Or it would have occurred to you that ripples spread out from a splash."

"But— Dr. Schoenstein, the release I obtained from Professor Fries explicitly binds him to silence, for separate good and sufficient consideration, over and above damages conceded by us and made good. This is tantamount to blackmail. I—"

Then Uncle Tom did stand up. He seemed twice as tall as usual and was grinning like a fright mask. "What was that last word you used?"

"I?" The lawyer looked startled. "Perhaps I spoke hastily. I simply meant—"

"I heard you," Uncle Tom growled. "And so did three witnesses. Happens to be one of the words a man can be challenged for on this still free planet. But, since I'm getting old and fat, I may just sue you for your shirt instead. Come along, kids."

The Director spoke quickly. "Tom . . . sit down, please. Mr. Poon . . . please keep quiet unless I ask for your advice. Now, Tom, you know quite well that you can't challenge nor sue over a privileged communication, counsel to client."

"I can do both or either. Question is: will a court sustain me? But I can always find out."

"And thereby drag out into the open the very point you know quite well I can't afford to have dragged out. Simply because my lawyer spoke in an excess of zeal. Mr. Poon?"

"I tried to withdraw it. I do withdraw it."

"Senator?"

Uncle Tom bowed stiffly to Mr. Poon, who returned it. "Accepted, sir. No offense meant and none taken." Then Uncle Tom grinned merrily, let his potbelly slide back down out of his chest, and said in his normal voice, "Okay, Hymie, let's get on with the crime. Your move."

Dr. Schoenstein said carefully, "Young lady, I have just learned that the recent disruption of family planning in your home—which we all deeply regret—caused an additional sharp disappointment to you and your brother."

"It certainly did!" I answered, rather shrilly I'm afraid.

"Yes. As your uncle put it, the ripples spread out. Another of those ripples could wreck this establishment, make it insolvent as a private business. This is an odd sort of business we are in here, Miss Fries. Superficially we perform a routine engineering function, plus some not unusual boarding nursery services. But in fact what we do touches the most primitive of human emotions. If confidence in our integrity, or in the perfection with which we carry out the service entrusted to us, were to be shaken—" He spread his hands helplessly. "We couldn't last out the year. Now I can show you exactly how the mishap occurred which affected your family, show you how wildly unlikely it was to have it happen even under the methods we did use . . . prove to you how utterly impossible it now is and always will be in the future for such a mistake to take place again, under our new procedures. Nevertheless"—he looked helpless again—"if you were to talk, merely tell the simple truth about what did indeed happen once . . . you could ruin us."

I felt so sorry for him that I was about to blurt out that I wouldn't even *dream* of talking!—even though they had ruined my life—when Clark cut in. "Watch it, Pod! It's loaded."

So I just gave the Director my Sphinx[3] expression and said nothing. Clark's instinctive self-interest is absolutely reliable.

Dr. Schoenstein motioned Mr. Poon to keep quiet. "But, my dear lady, I am not asking you not to talk. As your uncle the Senator says, you are not here to blackmail and I have nothing with which to bargain. The Marsopolis Crèche Foundation, Limited, always carries out its obligations even when they do not result from formal contract. I asked you to come in here in order to suggest a measure of relief for the damage we have unquestionably—though unwittingly—done you and your brother. Your uncle tells me that he had intended to travel with you and your family . . . but that now he intends to go via the next Triangle Line departure. The *Tricorn*, I believe it is, about ten days from now. Would you feel less mistreated if we were to pay first-class fares for your brother and you—round trip, of course—in the Triangle Line?"

Would I! The *Wanderlust* has, as her sole virtue, the fact that she is indeed a spaceship and she was shaping for Earth. But she is an old, slow freighter. Whereas the Triangle Liners, as everyone knows, are utter palaces! I could but nod.

"Good. It is our privilege and we hope you have a wonderful trip. But, uh, young lady . . . do you think it possible that you could give us some assurance, for no consideration and simply out of kindness, that you wouldn't talk about a certain regrettable mishap?"

"Oh? I thought that was part of the deal?"

"There is no deal. As your uncle pointed out to me, we owe you this trip, no matter what."

"Why—why, Doctor, I'm going to be so busy, so utterly rushed, just to get ready in time, that I won't have *time* to talk to anyone about any mishaps that probably weren't your fault anyhow!"

"Thank you." He turned to Clark. "And you, son?"

Clark doesn't like to be called "son" at best. But don't think it affected his answer. He ignored the vocative and said coldly, "What about our expenses?"

Dr. Schoenstein flinched. Uncle Tom guffawed and said, "That's my boy! Doc, I told you he had the simple rapacity of a sand gator. He'll go far—if somebody doesn't poison him."

"Any suggestions?"

"No trouble. Clark. Look me in the eye. Either you stay behind and we weld you into a barrel and feed you through the bunghole so that you *can't* talk—while your sister goes anyhow—or you accept these terms. Say a thousand each—no, fifteen hundred—for travel expenses, and you keep your snapper shut forever about the baby mix-up . . . or I personally, with the aid of four stout, blackhearted accomplices, will cut your tongue out and feed it to the cat. A deal?"

"I ought to get ten percent commission on Sis's fifteen hundred. She didn't have sense enough to ask for it."

"No cumshaw.[4] I ought to be charging *you* commission on the whole transaction. A deal?"

"A deal," Clark agreed.

Uncle Tom stood up. "That does it, Doc. In his own unappetizing way he is as utterly reliable as she is. So relax. You, too, Kwai Yau, you can breathe again. Doc, you can send a check around to me in the morning. Come on, kids."

"Thanks, Tom. If that is the word. I'll have the check over before you get there. Uh . . . just one thing . . ."

3. Enigmatic, like the riddling monster of Greek mythology.
4. Payoff.

"What, Doc?"

"Senator, you were here long before I was born, so I don't know too much about your early life. Just the traditional stories and what it says about you in *Who's Who on Mars*. Just what were you transported for? You *were* transported? Weren't you?"

Mr. Poon looked horror-stricken, and I was. But Uncle Tom didn't seem offended. He laughed heartily and answered, "I was accused of freezing babies for profit. But it was a frameup—I never did no such thing nohow. Come on, kids. Let's get out of this ghouls' nest before they smuggle us down into the sub-basement."

Later that night in bed I was dreamily thinking over the trip. There hadn't even been the least argument with Mother and Daddy; Uncle Tom had settled it all by phone before we got home. I heard a sound from the nursery, got up and paddled in. It was Duncan, the little darling, not even wet but lonely. So I picked him up and cuddled him and he cooed and then he was wet, so I changed him.

I decided that he was just as pretty or prettier than all those other babies, even though he was five months younger and his eyes didn't track. When I put him down again, he was sound asleep; I started back to bed.

And stopped— The Triangle Line gets its name from serving the three leading planets, of course, but which direction a ship makes the Mars-Venus-Earth route depends on just where we all are in our orbits.

But just where were we?

I hurried into the living room and searched for the *Daily War Whoop*—found it, thank goodness, and fed it into the viewer, flipped to the shipping news, found the predicted arrivals and departures.

Yes, yes, *yes!* I am going not only to Earth—but to Venus as well!

Venus! Do you suppose Mother would let me—No, best just say nothing now. Uncle Tom will be more tractable, after we get there.

I'm going to miss Duncan—he's such a little doll.

IV

I haven't had time to write in this journal for *days*. Just getting ready to leave was almost impossible—and would have been truly impossible had it not been that most preparations—all the special Terran inoculations and photographs and passports and such—were mostly done before Everything Came Unstuck. But Mother came out of her atavistic daze and was very helpful. She would even let one of the triplets cry for a few moments rather than leave me half pinned up.

I don't know how Clark got ready or whether he had any preparations to make. He continued to creep around silently, answering in grunts if he answered at all. Nor did Uncle Tom seem to find it difficult. I saw him only twice during those frantic ten days (once to borrow baggage mass from his allowance, which he let me have, the dear!) and both times I had to dig him out of the card room at the Elks Club. I asked him how he managed to get ready for so important a trip and still have time to play cards?

"Nothing to it," he answered. "I bought a new toothbrush. Is there something else I should have done?"

So I hugged him and told him he was an utterly utter beast and he chuckled and mussed my hair. Query: Will I ever become that blasé about space travel? I suppose I must if I am to be an astronaut. But Daddy says that getting ready for a trip is half the fun . . . so perhaps I don't want to become that sophisticated.

Somehow Mother delivered me, complete with baggage and all the myriad pieces of paper—tickets and medical records and passport and universal identification complex and guardians' assignment-and-guarantee and three kinds of money and travelers' cheques and birth record and police certification and security clearance and I don't remember—all checked off, to the city shuttle port. I was juggling one package of things that simply *wouldn't* go into my luggage, and I had one hat on my head and one in my hand; otherwise everything came out even.

(I don't know where that second hat went. Somehow it never got aboard with me. But I haven't missed it.)

Good-bye at the shuttle port was most teary and exciting. Not just with Mother and Daddy, which was to be expected (when Daddy put his arm around me tight, I threw both mine around him and for a dreadful second I didn't want to leave at all), but also because about thirty of my classmates showed up (which I hadn't in the least expected), complete with a banner that two of them were carrying reading:

BON VOYAGE—PODKAYNE

I got kissed enough times to start a fair-sized epidemic if any one of them had had anything, which apparently they didn't. I got kissed by boys who had never even *tried* to, in the past—and I assure you that it is not utterly impossible to kiss me, if the project is approached with confidence and finesse, as I believe that one's instincts should be allowed to develop as well as one's overt cortical behavior.

The corsage Daddy had given me for going away got crushed and I didn't even notice it until we were aboard the shuttle. I suppose it was somewhere about then that I lost that hat, but I'll never know—I would have lost the last-minute package, too, if Uncle Tom had not rescued it. There were photographers, too, but not for me—for Uncle Tom. Then suddenly we had to scoot aboard the shuttle *right now* because a shuttle can't wait; it has to boost on the split second even though Deimos moves so much more slowly than Phobos. A reporter from the *War Whoop* was still trying to get a statement out of Uncle Tom about the forthcoming Three-Planets conference but he just pointed at his throat and whispered, "Laryngitis"—then we were aboard just before they sealed the airlock.

It must have been the shortest case of laryngitis on record; Uncle Tom's voice had been all right until we got to the shuttle port and it was okay again once we were in the shuttle.

One shuttle trip is exactly like another, whether to Phobos or Deimos. Still, that first tremendous *whoosh!* of acceleration is exciting as it pins you down into your couch with so much weight that you can't breathe, much less move—and free fall is always strange and eerie and rather stomach fluttering even if one doesn't tend to be nauseated by it, which, thank you, I don't.

Being on Deimos is just like being in free fall, since neither Deimos nor Phobos has enough surface gravitation for one to feel it. They put suction sandals on us before they unstrapped us so that we could walk, just as they do on Phobos. Nevertheless Deimos is different from Phobos for reasons having nothing to do with natural phenomena. Phobos is, of course, legally a part of Mars; there are no formalities of any sort about visiting it. All that is required is the fare, a free day, and a yen for a picnic in space.

But Deimos is a free port, leased in perpetuity to Three-Planets Treaty Authority. A known criminal, with a price on his head in Marsopolis, could change ships there right under the eyes of our own police—and we couldn't touch him. Instead, we would have to start most complicated legal doings at the Interplanetary High Court on Luna,[5] practically win the case ahead of time and, besides that, prove that the crime was a crime under Three-Planet rules and not just under our own laws . . . and then all that we could do would be to ask the Authority's proctors to arrest the man if he was still around—which doesn't seem likely.

I knew about this, theoretically, because there had been about a half page on it in our school course *Essentials of Martian Government* in the section on "Extraterritoriality." But now I had plenty of time to think about it because, as soon as we left the shuttle, we found ourselves locked up in a room misleadingly called the "Hospitality Room" while we waited until they were ready to "process" us. One wall of the room was glass and I could see lots and lots of people hurrying around in the concourse beyond, doing all manner of interesting and mysterious things. But all we had to do was to wait beside our baggage and grow bored.

I found that I was growing furious by the minute, not at all like my normally sweet and lovable nature. Why, this place had been built by my own mother!—and here I was, caged up in it like white mice in a bio lab.

(Well, I admit that Mother didn't exactly build Deimos; the Martians did that, starting with a spare asteroid that they happened to have handy. But some millions of years back they grew tired of space travel and devoted all their time to the whichness of what and how to unscrew the inscrutable—so when Mother took over the job, Deimos was pretty run down; she had to start in from the ground up and rebuild it completely.)

In any case, it was certain that everything that I could see through that transparent wall was a product of Mother's creative, imaginative and hardheaded engineering ability. I began to fume. Clark was off in a corner, talking privately to some stranger— "stranger" to me, at least; Clark, for all his antisocial disposition, always seems to know somebody, or to know somebody who knows somebody, anywhere we go. I sometimes wonder if he is a member of some vast underground secret society; he has such unsavory acquaintances and never brings any of them home.

Clark is, however, a very satisfactory person to fume with, because, if he isn't busy, he is always willing to help a person hate anything that needs hating; he can even dig up reasons why a situation is even more vilely unfair than you thought it was. But he was busy, so that left Uncle Tom. So I explained to him bitterly how outrageous I thought it was that we should be penned up like animals—free Mars citizens on one of Mars' own moons!—simply because a sign read: *Passengers must wait until called—by order of Three-Planets Treaty Authority.*

"*Politics!*" I said bitterly. "I could run it better myself."

"I'm sure you could," he agreed gravely, "but, Flicka, you don't understand."

"I understand all too well!"

"No, honey bun. You understand that there is no good reason why you should not walk straight through that door and enjoy yourself by shopping until it is time to go inboard the *Tricorn*. And you are right about that, for there is no need at all for you to be locked up in here when you could be out there making some freeport shopkeeper happy by paying him a high price which seems to you a low price. So you say 'Politics!' as if it were a nasty word—and you think that settles it."

He sighed. "But you *don't* understand. Politics is not evil; politics is the human race's most magnificent achievement. When politics is good, it's wonderful . . . and when politics is bad—well, it's still pretty good."

"I guess I don't understand," I said slowly.

5. The Moon.

"Think about it. Politics is just a name for the way we get things done . . . without fighting. We dicker and compromise and everybody thinks he has received a raw deal, but somehow after a tedious amount of talk we come up with some jury-rigged way to do it without getting anybody's head bashed in. That's politics. The only other way to settle a dispute is by bashing a few heads in . . . and that is what happens when one or both sides is no longer willing to dicker. That's why I say politics is good even when it is bad . . . because the only alternative is force—and somebody gets hurt."

"Uh . . . it seems to me that's a funny way for a revolutionary veteran to talk. From what I've heard, Uncle Tom, you were one of the bloodthirsty ones who started the shooting. Or so Daddy says."

He grinned. "Mostly I ducked. If dickering won't work, then you have to fight. But I think maybe it takes a man who has been shot at to appreciate how much better it is to fumble your way through a political compromise rather than have the top of your head blown off." He frowned and suddenly looked very old. "When to talk and when to fight— That is the most difficult decision to make wisely of all the decisions in life." Then suddenly he smiled and the years dropped away. "Mankind didn't invent fighting; it was here long before we were. But we invented politics. Just think of it, hon— Homo sapiens is the most cruel, the most vicious, the most predatory, and certainly the most deadly of all the animals in this solar system. Yet he invented politics! He figured out a way to let most of us, most of the time, get along well enough so that we usually don't kill each other. So don't let me hear you using 'politics' as a swear word again."

"I'm sorry, Uncle Tom," I said humbly.

"Like fun you are. But if you let that idea soak for twenty or thirty years, you may— Oh, oh! There's your villain, baby girl—the politically appointed bureaucrat who has most unjustly held you in durance vile. So scratch his eyes out. Show him how little you think of his silly rules."

I answered this with dignified silence. It is hard to tell when Uncle Tom is serious because he loves to pull my leg, always hoping that it will come off in his hand. The Three-Planets proctor of whom he was speaking had opened the door to our bullpen and was looking around exactly like a zookeeper inspecting a cage for cleanliness. "Passports!" he called out. "Diplomatic passports first." He looked us over, spotted Uncle Tom. "Senator?"

Uncle Tom shook his head. "I'm a tourist, thanks."

"As you say, sir. Line up, please—reverse alphabetical order"—which put us near the tail of the line instead of near the head. There followed maddening delays for fully two hours—passports, health clearance, outgoing baggage inspection—Mars Republic does not levy duties on exports but just the same is a whole long list of things you can't export without a license, such as ancient Martian artifacts (the first explorers did their best to gut the place and some of the most priceless are in the British Museum or the Kremlin; I've heard Daddy fume about it), some things you can't export under *any* circumstances, such as certain narcotics, and some things you can take aboard ship only by surrendering them for safekeeping by the purser, such as guns and other weapons.

Clark picked outgoing inspection for some typical abnormal behavior. They had passed down the line copies of a long list of things we must not have in our baggage— a fascinating list; I hadn't known that there were so many things either illegal, immoral, or deadly. When the Fries contingent wearily reached the inspection counter, the inspector said, all in one word: " 'Nything-t'-d'clare?" He was a Marsman and as he looked up he recognized Uncle Tom. "Oh. Howdy, Senator. Honored to have you with us. Well, I guess we needn't waste time on your baggage. These two young people with you?"

"Better search my kit," Uncle Tom advised. "I'm smuggling guns to an out-planet branch of the Legion. As for the kids, they're my niece and nephew. But I don't vouch for them; they're both subversive characters. Especially the girl. She was soap-boxing revolution just now while we waited."

The inspector smiled and said, "I guess we can allow you a few guns, Senator— you know how to use them. Well, how about it, kids? Anything to declare?"

I said, "Nothing to declare," with icy dignity—when suddenly Clark spoke up.

"Sure!" he piped, his voice cracking. "Two kilos of happy dust! And whose business is it? I paid for it. I'm not going to let it be stolen by a bunch of clerks." His voice was surly as only he can manage and the expression on his face simply ached for a slap.

That did it. The inspector had been just about to glance into one of my bags, a purely formal inspection, I think—when my brattish brother deliberately stirred things up. At the very word "happy dust" four other inspectors closed in. Two were Venusmen, to judge by their accents, and the other two might have been from Earth.

Of course, happy dust doesn't matter to us Marsmen. The Martians use it, have always used it, and it is about as important to them as tobacco is to humans, but apparently without any ill effects. What they get out of it I don't know. Some of the old sand rats among us have picked up the habit from the Martians—but my entire botany class experimented with it under our teacher's supervision and nobody got any thrill out of it and all I got was blocked sinuses that wore off before the day was out. Strictly zero squared.

But with the native Venerians it is another matter—when they can get it. It turns them into murderous maniacs and they'll do anything to get it. The (black market) price on it there is very high indeed . . . and possession of it by a human on Venus is at least an automatic life sentence to Saturn's moons.

They buzzed around Clark like angry jetta wasps.

But they did not find what they were looking for. Shortly Uncle Tom spoke up and said, "Inspector? May I make a suggestion?"

"Eh? Certainly, Senator."

"My nephew, I am sorry to say, has caused a disturbance. Why don't you put him aside—chain him up, I would—and let all these other good people go through?"

The inspector blinked. "I think that is an excellent idea."

"And I would appreciate it if you would inspect myself and my niece now. Then we won't hold up the others."

"Oh, that's not necessary." The inspector slapped seals on all of Uncle's bags, closed the one of mine he had started to open, and said, "I don't need to paw through the young lady's pretties. But I think we'll take this smart boy and search him to the skin and X-ray him."

"Do that."

So Uncle and I went on and checked at four or five other desks—fiscal control and migration and reservations and other nonsense—and finally wound up with our baggage at the centrifuge for weighing in. I never did get a chance to shop.

To my chagrin, when I stepped off the merry-go-round the record showed that my baggage and myself were nearly three kilos over my allowance, which didn't seem possible. I hadn't eaten more breakfast than usual—less actually—and I hadn't drunk any water because, while I do not become ill in free fall, drinking in free fall is very tricky; you are likely to get water up your nose or something and set off an embarrassing chain reaction.

So I was about to protest bitterly that the weightmaster had spun the centrifuge too fast and produced a false mass reading. But it occurred to me that I did not know for surely certain that the scales Mother and I had used were perfectly accurate. So I kept quiet.

Uncle Tom just reached for his purse and said, "How much?"

The weightmaster said, "Mmm . . . let's spin you first, Senator."

Uncle Tom was almost two kilos under his allowance. The weightmaster shrugged and said, "Forget it, Senator. I'm minus on a couple of other things; I think I can swallow it. If not, I'll leave a memo with the purser. But I'm fairly sure I can."

"Thank you. What did you say your name was?"

"Milo. Miles M. Milo—Aasvogel Lodge number seventy-four. Maybe you saw our crack drill team at the Legion convention two years ago—I was left pivot."

"I certainly did, I certainly did!" They exchanged that secret grip that they think other people don't know and Uncle Tom said, "Well, thanks, Miles. Be seeing you."

"Not at all—Tom. No, don't bother with your baggage." Mr. Milo touched a button and called out, "In the *Tricorn!* Get somebody out here fast for the Senator's baggage."

It occurred to me, as we stopped at the passenger tube sealed to the transfer station to swap our suction sandals for little magnet pads that clipped to our shoes, that we need not have waited for anything at anytime—if only Uncle Tom had been willing to use the special favors he so plainly could demand.

But, even so, it pays to travel with an important person—even though it's just your Uncle Tom whose stomach you used to jump up and down on when you were small enough for such things. Our tickets simply read FIRST CLASS—I'm sure, for I saw all three of them—but where we were placed was in what they call the "Owner's Cabin," which is actually a suite with three bedrooms and a living room. I was dazzled!

But I didn't have time to admire it just then. First they strapped our baggage down, then they strapped us down—to seat couches which were against one wall of the living room. That wall plainly should have been the floor, but it slanted up almost vertically with respect to the tiny, not-quite-nothing weight that we had. The warning sirens were already sounding when someone dragged Clark in and strapped him to one of the couches. He was looking mussed up but cocky.

"Hi, smuggler," Uncle Tom greeted him amiably. "They find it on you?"

"Nothing to find."

"That's what I thought. I trust they gave you a rough time."

"Naah!"

I wasn't sure I believed Clark's answer; I've heard that a skin and person search can be made quite annoying indeed, without doing anything the least bit illegal, if the proctors are feeling unfriendly. A "rough time" would be good for Clark's soul, I am sure—but he certainly did not act as if the experience had caused him any discomfort. I said, "Clark, that was a very foolish remark you made to the inspector. And it was a lie, as well—a silly, useless lie."

"Sign off," he said curtly. "If I'm smuggling anything, it's up to them to find it; that's what they're paid for. 'Any-thing-t'd'clare?'" he added in a mimicking voice. "What nonsense! As if anybody would declare something he was trying to smuggle."

"Just the same," I went on, "if Daddy had heard you say—"

"Podkayne."

"Yes, Uncle Tom?"

"Table it. We're about to start. Let's enjoy it."

"But— Yes, Uncle."

There was a slight drop in pressure, then a sudden surge that would have slid us out of our couches if we had not been strapped—but not a strong one, not at all like that giant *whoosh!* with which we had left the surface. It did not last long, then we were truly in free fall for a few moments . . . then there started a soft, gentle push in the same direction, which kept up.

Then the room started very slowly to turn around . . . almost unnoticeable except for a slight dizziness it gave one.

Gradually, gradually (it took almost twenty minutes) our weight increased, until at last we were back to our proper weight . . . at which time the floor, which had been all wrong when we came in, was where it belonged, under us, and almost level. But not quite—

Here is what had happened. The first short boost was made by the rocket tugs of Deimos Port picking up the *Tricorn* and hurling her out into a free orbit of her own. This doesn't take much, because the attraction between even a big ship like the *Tricorn* and a tiny, tiny satellite such as Deimos isn't enough to matter; all that matters is getting the very considerable mass of the ship shoved free.

The second gentle shove, the one that kept up and never went away, was the ship's own main drive—one-tenth of a standard gee.[6] The *Tricorn* is a constant-boost ship; she doesn't dillydally around with economical orbits and weeks and months in free fall. She goes very fast indeed . . . because even 0.1 gee adds up awfully fast.

But one-tenth gee is not enough to make comfortable passengers who have been used to more. As soon as the Captain had set her on her course, he started to spin her and kept it up until the centrifugal force and the boost added up (in vector addition, of course) to exactly the surface gravitation of Mars (or 37 percent of a standard gee) at the locus of the first-class staterooms.

But the floors will not be quite level until we approach Earth, because the inside of the ship had been constructed so that the floors would feel perfectly level when the spin and the boost added up to exactly one standard gravity—or Earth-Normal.

Maybe this isn't too clear. Well, it wasn't too clear to me, in school; I didn't see exactly how it worked out until (later) I had a chance to see the controls used to put spin on the ship and how the centrifugal force was calculated. Just remember that the *Tricorn*—and her sisters, the *Trice* and the *Triad* and the *Triangulum* and the *Tricolor* are enormous cylinders. The thrust is straight along the main axis; it has to be. Centrifugal force pushes away from the main axis—how else? The two forces add up to make the ship's "artificial gravity" in passenger country—but, since one force (the boost) is kept constant and the other (the spin) can be varied, there can be only one rate of spin which will add in with the boost to make those floors perfectly level.

For the *Tricorn* the spin that will produce level floors and exactly one Earth gravity in passenger country is 5.42 revolutions per minute—I know because the Captain told me so . . . and I checked his arithmetic and he was right. The floor of our cabin is just over thirty meters from the main axis of the ship, so it all comes out even.

As soon as they had the floor back under us and had announced the "all clear" I unstrapped me and hurried out. I wanted a quick look at the ship; I didn't even wait to unpack.

---

6. The amount of force that gravity on earth exerts on a body at rest.

There's a fortune awaiting the man who invents a really good deodorizer for a spaceship. That's the one thing you can't fail to notice.

Oh, they try, I grant them that. The air goes through precipitators each time it is cycled; it is washed, it is perfumed, a precise fraction of ozone is added, and the new oxygen that is put in after the carbon dioxide is distilled out is as pure as a baby's mind; it has to be, for it is newly released as a by-product of the photosynthesis of living plants. That air is so pure that it really ought to be voted a medal by the Society for the Suppression of Evil Thoughts.

Besides that, a simply amazing amount of the crew's time is put into cleaning, polishing, washing, sterilizing—oh, they *try!*

But nevertheless, even a new, extra-fare luxury liner like the *Tricorn* simply reeks of human sweat and ancient sin, with undefinable overtones of organic decay and unfortunate accidents and matters best forgotten. Once I was with Daddy when a Martian tomb was being unsealed—and I found out why xenoarchaeologists[7] always have gas masks handy. But a spaceship smells even worse than that tomb.

It does no good to complain to the purser. He'll listen with professional sympathy and send a crewman around to spray your stateroom with something which (I suspect) merely deadens your nose for a while. But his sympathy is not real, because the poor man simply cannot smell anything wrong himself. He has lived in ships for years; it is literally impossible for him to smell the unmistakable reek of a ship that has been lived in—and, besides, he *knows* that the air is pure; the ship's instruments show it. None of the professional spacers can smell it.

But the purser and all of them are quite used to having passengers complain about the "unbearable stench"—so they pretend sympathy and go through the motions of correcting the matter.

Not that I complained. I was looking forward to having this ship eating out of my hand, and you don't accomplish that sort of coup by becoming known first thing as a complainer. But other first-timers did, and I certainly understood why—in fact I began to have a glimmer of a doubt about my ambitions to become skipper of an explorer ship.

But—Well, in about two days it seemed to me that they had managed to clean up the ship quite a bit, and shortly thereafter I stopped thinking about it. I began to understand why the ship's crew can't smell the things the passengers complain about. Their nervous systems simply cancel out the old familiar stinks—like a cybernetic skywatch canceling out and ignoring any object whose predicted orbit has previously been programmed into the machine.

But the odor is still there. I suspect that it sinks right into polished metal and can never be removed, short of scrapping the ship and melting it down. Thank goodness the human nervous system is endlessly adaptable.

But my own nervous system didn't seem too adaptable during that first hasty tour of the *Tricorn*; it is a good thing that I had not eaten much breakfast and had refrained from drinking anything. My stomach did give me a couple of bad moments, but I told it sternly that I was busy—I was very anxious to look over the ship; I simply didn't have time to cater to the weaknesses to which flesh is heir.

Well, the *Tricorn* is lovely all right—every bit as nice as the travel folders say that she is . . . except for that dreadful ship's odor. Her ballroom is gorgeous and so big

7. Archaeologists who study the material remains of aliens.

that you can see that the floor curves to match the ship . . . only it is not curved when you walk across it. It is level, too—it is the only room in the ship where they jack up the floor to match perfectly with whatever spin is on the ship. There is a lounge with a simulated sky of outer space, or it can be switched to blue sky and fleecy clouds. Some old biddies were already in there, gabbling.

The dining saloon is every bit as fancy, but it seemed hardly big enough—which reminded me of the warning in the travel brochure about first and second tables, so I rushed back to our cabin to urge Uncle Tom to make reservations for us quickly before all the best tables were filled.

He wasn't there. I took a quick look in all the rooms and didn't find him—but I found Clark in *my* room, just closing one of my bags!

"What are you doing?" I demanded.

He jumped and then looked perfectly blank. "I was just looking to see if you had any nausea pills," he said woodenly.

"Well, don't dig into my things! You know better." I came up and felt his cheek; he wasn't feverish. "I don't have any. But I noticed where the surgeon's office is. If you are feeling ill, I'll take you straight there and let him dose you."

He pulled away. "Aw, I'm all right—now."

"Clark Fries, you listen to me. If you—" But he wasn't listening; he slid past me, ducked into his own room and closed the door; I heard the lock click.

I closed the bag he had opened—and noticed something. It was the bag the inspector had been just about to search when Clark had pulled that silly stunt about "happy dust."

My younger brother never does anything without a reason. Never.

His reasons may be, and often are, inscrutable to others. But if you just dig deeply enough, you will always find that his mind is never a random-choice machine, doing things pointlessly. It is as logical as a calculator—and about as cold.

I now knew why he had made what seemed to be entirely unnecessary trouble for himself at outgoing inspection.

I knew why I had been unexpectedly three kilos over my allowance on the centrifuge.

The only thing I didn't know was: *What* had he smuggled aboard in my baggage? And *why?*

Interlude

Well, Pod, I am glad to see that you've resumed keeping your diary. Not only do I find your girlish viewpoints entertaining but also you sometimes (not often) provide me with useful bits of information.

If I can do anything for you in return, do let me know. Perhaps you would like help in straightening out your grammar? Those incomplete sentences you are so fond of indicate incomplete thinking. You know that, don't you?

For example, let us consider a purely hypothetical case: a delivery robot with an unbeatable seal. Since the seal is in fact unbeatable, thinking about the seal simply leads to frustration. But a complete analysis of the situation leads one to the obvious fact that any cubical or quasi-cubical object has six sides, and that the seal applies to only one of these six sides.

Pursuing this line of thought one may note that, while the quasi cube may not be moved without cutting its connections, the floor under it may be lowered as much as forty-eight centimeters—if one has all afternoon in which to work.

Were this not a hypothetical case I would now suggest the use of a mirror and light on an extension handle and some around-the-corner tools, plus plenty of patience.

That's what you lack, Pod—patience.

I hope this may shed some light on the matter of the hypothetical happy dust— and do feel free to come to me with your little problems.

V

Clark kept his stateroom door locked all the time the first three days we were in the *Tricorn*—I know, because I tried it every time he left the suite.

Then on the fourth day he failed to lock it at a time when it was predictable that he would be gone at least an hour, as he had signed up for a tour of the ship—the parts passengers ordinarily are not allowed in, I mean. I didn't mind missing it myself, for by then I had worked out my own private "Poddy special" escort service. Nor did I have to worry about Uncle Tom; he wasn't making the tour, it would have violated his no-exercise rule, but he had acquired new pinochle cronies and he was safely in the smoking room.

Those stateroom door locks are not impossible to pick—not for a girl equipped with a nail file, some bits of this and that, and *free* run of the purser's office—me, I mean.

But I found I did not have to pick the lock; the catch had not quite caught. I breathed the conventional sigh of relief, as I figured that the happy accident put me at least twenty minutes ahead of schedule.

I shan't detail the search, but I flatter myself that the Criminal Investigation Bureau could not have done it more logically nor more quickly if limited, as I was, to bare hands and no equipment. It had to be something forbidden by that list they had given us on Deimos—and I had carefully kept and studied my copy. It had to mass slightly over three kilos. It had to bulk so large and be sufficiently fixed in its shape and dimensions that Clark was forced to hide it in baggage—otherwise I am sure he would have concealed it on his person and coldly depended on his youth and "innocence," plus the chaperonage of Uncle Tom, to breeze him through the outgoing inspection. Otherwise he would never have taken the calculated risk of hiding it in my baggage, since he couldn't be sure of recovering it without my knowing.

Could he have predicted that I would at once go sight-seeing without waiting to unpack? Well, perhaps he could, even though I had done so on the spur of the moment. I must reluctantly admit that Clark can outguess me with maddening regularity. As an opponent, he is never to be underrated. But still it was for him a "calculated risk," albeit a small one.

Very well. Largish, rather massy, forbidden—but I didn't know what it looked like and I had to assume that *anything* which met the first two requirements might be disguised to appear innocent.

Ten minutes later I knew that it had to be in one of his three bags, which I had left to the last on purpose as the least likely spots. A stateroom aboard ship has many cover plates, access holes, removable fixtures, and the like, but I had done a careful practice run in my own room; I knew which ones were worth opening, which ones could not be opened without power tools, which ones could not be opened without leaving unmistakable signs of tampering. I checked these all in great haste, then congratulated Clark on having the good sense not to use such obvious hiding places.

Then I checked everything readily accessible—out in the open, in his wardrobe, etc.—using the classic "Purloined Letter" technique, i.e., I never assumed that a book was a book simply because it looked like a book, nor that a jacket on a hanger was simply that and nothing more.

Null, negative, nothing— Reluctantly, I tackled his three pieces of luggage, first noting carefully exactly how they were stacked and in what order.

The first was empty. Oh, the linings could have been tampered with, but the bag was no heavier than it should have been and any false pocket in the linings could not have held anything large enough to meet the specifications.

The second bag was the same—and the bag on the bottom seemed to be the same . . . until I found an envelope in a pocket of it. Oh, nothing nearly mass enough, nor gross enough; just an ordinary envelope for a letter—but nevertheless I glanced at it.

And was immediately indignant!

It had printed on it:

MISS PODKAYNE FRIES
PASSENGER, S.S. *Tricorn*
For delivery in ship

Why, the little wretch! He had been intercepting my mail! With fingers trembling with rage so badly that I could hardly do so I opened it—and discovered that it had already been opened and was angrier than ever. But, at least, the note was still inside. Shaking, I pulled it out and read it.

Just six words—

Hi, Pod. Snooping again, I see.

—in Clark's handwriting.

I stood there, frozen, for a long moment, while I blushed scarlet and chewed the bitter realization that I had been hoaxed to perfection—*again*.

There are only three people in the world who can make me feel stupid—and Clark is two of them.

I heard a throat-clearing sound behind me and whirled around. Lounging in the open doorway (I had left it closed) was my brother. He smiled at me and said, "Hello, Sis. Looking for something? Need any help?"

I didn't waste time pretending that I didn't have jam all over my face; I simply said, "Clark Fries, what did you smuggle into this ship in my baggage?"

He looked blank—a look of malignant idiocy which has been known to drive well-balanced teachers to their therapists. "What in the world are you talking about, Pod?"

"You know what I'm talking about! Smuggling!"

"Oh!" His face lit up in a sunny smile. "You mean those two kilograms of happy dust. Goodness, Sis, is that still worrying you? There never were any two kilos of happy dust; I was just having my little joke with that stuffy inspector. I thought you knew that."

"I do not mean any 'two kilos of happy dust'! I am talking about at least three kilos of something else that you hid in my baggage!"

He looked worried. "Pod, do you feel well?"

"Ooooooh!—*dandruff!* Clark Fries, you stop that! You know what I mean! When I was centrifuged, my bags and I weighed three kilos over my allowance. Well?"

He looked at me thoughtfully, sympathetically. "It *has* seemed to me that you were getting a bit fat—but I didn't want to mention it. I thought it was all this rich food you've been tucking away here in the ship. You really ought to watch that sort of thing, Pod. After all, if a girl lets her figure go to pieces— Well, she doesn't have much else. So I hear."

Had that envelope been a blunt instrument I would have blunted him. I heard a low growling sound, and realized that I was making it. So I stopped. "Where's the letter that was in this envelope?"

Clark looked surprised. "Why, it's right there, in your other hand."

"This? This is all there was? No letter from somebody else?"

"Why, just that note from me, Sis. Didn't you like it? I thought that it just suited the occasion . . . I knew you would find it your very first chance." He smiled. "Next time you want to paw through my things, let me know and I'll help. Sometimes I have experiments running—and you might get hurt. That can happen to people who aren't very bright and don't look before they leap. I wouldn't want that to happen to *you*, Sis."

I didn't bandy any more words; I brushed past him and went to my own room and locked the door and bawled.

Then I got up and did very careful things to my face. I know when I'm licked; I don't have to have a full set of working drawings. I resolved never to mention the matter to Clark again.

But what was I to do? Go to the Captain? I already knew the Captain pretty well; his imagination extended as far as the next ballistic prediction and no further. Tell him that my brother had been smuggling something, I didn't know what—and that he had better search the entire ship most carefully, because, whatever it was, it was not in my brother's room? Don't be triple silly, Poddy. In the first place, he would laugh at you; in the second place, you don't *want* Clark to be caught—Mother and Daddy wouldn't like it.

Tell Uncle Tom about it? He might be just as unbelieving . . . or, if he did believe me, he might go to the Captain himself—with just as disastrous results.

I decided not to go to Uncle Tom—at least not yet. Instead I would keep my eyes and ears open and try to find an answer myself.

In any case I did not waste much time on Clark's sins (if any, I had to admit in bare honesty); I was in my first real spaceship—halfway to my ambition thereby—and there was much to learn and do.

Those travel brochures are honest enough, I guess—but they do not give you the full picture.

For example, take this phrase right out of the text of the Triangle Line's fancy folder: . . . *romantic days in ancient Marsopolis, the city older than time; exotic nights under the hurtling moons of Mars* . . .

Let's rephrase it into everyday language, shall we? Marsopolis is my hometown and I love it—but it is as romantic as bread and butter with no jam. The parts people live in are new and were designed for function, not romance. As for the ruins outside town (which the Martians *never* called "Marsopolis"), a lot of high foreheads including Daddy have seen to it that the best parts are locked off so that tourists will not carve their initials in something that was old when stone axes were the latest thing in super-weapons. Furthermore, Martian ruins are neither beautiful, nor picturesque, nor impressive, to human eyes. The way to appreciate them is to read a really good book with illustrations, diagrams, and simple explanations—such as Daddy's *Other Paths Than Ours*. (Adv.)

As for those exotic nights, anybody who is outdoors after sundown on Mars other than through sheer necessity needs to have his head examined. It's *chilly* out there.

I've seen Deimos and Phobos at night exactly twice, each time through no fault of my own—and I was so busy keeping from freezing to death that I wasted no thought on "hurtling moons."

This advertising brochure is just as meticulously accurate and just as deceptive in effect—concerning the ships themselves. Oh, the *Tricorn* is a palace; I'll vouch for that. It really is a miracle of engineering that anything so huge, so luxurious, so fantastically adapted to the health and comfort of human beings, should be able to "hurtle" (pardon the word) through space.

But take those pictures—

You know the ones I mean: full color and depth, showing groups of handsome young people of both sexes chatting or playing games in the lounge, dancing gaily in the ballroom—or views of a "typical stateroom."

That "typical stateroom" is not a fake. No, it has simply been photographed from an angle and with a lens that makes it look at least twice as big as it is. As for those handsome, gay, young people—well, they aren't along on the trip I'm making. It's my guess that they are professional models.

In the *Tricorn* this trip the young and handsome passengers like those in the pictures can be counted on the thumbs of one hand. The typical passenger we have with us is a great-grandmother, Terran citizenship, widowed, wealthy, making her first trip into space—and probably her last, for she is not sure she likes it.

Honest, I'm not exaggerating; our passengers look like refugees from a geriatrics clinic. I am not scoffing at old age. I understand that it is a condition I will one day attain myself, if I go on breathing in and out enough times—say about 900,000,000 more times, not counting heavy exercise. Old age can be a charming condition, as witness Uncle Tom. But old age is not an accomplishment; it is just something that happens to you despite yourself, like falling downstairs.

And I must say that I am getting a wee bit tired of having youth treated as a punishable offense.

Our typical male passenger is the same sort, only not nearly so numerous. He differs from his wife primarily in that, instead of looking down his nose at me, he is sometimes inclined to pat me in a "fatherly" way that I do not find fatherly, don't like, avoid if humanly possible—and which nevertheless gets me talked about.

I suppose I should not have been surprised to find the *Tricorn* a super-deluxe old folks' home, but (I may as well admit it) my experience is still limited and I was not aware of some of the economic facts of life.

The *Tricorn* is expensive. It is *very* expensive. Clark and I would not be in it at all if Uncle Tom had not twisted Dr. Schoenstein's arm in our behalf. Oh, I suppose Uncle Tom can afford it, but, by age group though not by temperament, he fits the defined category. But Daddy and Mother had intended to take us in the *Wanderlust*, a low-fare, economy-orbit freighter. Daddy and Mother are not poor, but they are not rich—and after they finish raising and educating five children it is unlikely that they will ever be rich.

Who can afford to travel in luxury liners? Ans.: Rich old widows, wealthy retired couples, high-priced executives whose time is so valuable that their corporations gladly send them by the fastest ships—and an occasional rare exception of some other sort.

Clark and I are such exceptions. We have one other exception in the ship, Miss— well, I'll call her Miss Girdle Fitz-Snugglie, because if I used her right name and perchance anybody ever sees this, it would be all too easily recognizable. I think Girdie is a good sort. I don't care what the gossips in this ship say. She doesn't act jealous of me even though it appears that the younger officers in the ship were all her personal property until I boarded—all the trip out from Earth, I mean. I've cut into her monopoly quite a bit, but she isn't catty to me; she treats me warmly woman-to-woman, and I've learned quite a lot about Life and Men from her . . . more than Mother ever taught me.

(It is just possible that Mother is slightly naïve on subjects that Girdie knows best. A woman who tackles engineering and undertakes to beat men at their own game might have had a fairly limited social life, wouldn't you think? I must study this seriously . . . because it seems possible that much the same might happen to a female space pilot and it is no part of my Master Plan to become a soured old maid.)

Girdie is about twice my age, which makes her awfully young in this company; nevertheless it may be that I cause her to look just a bit wrinkled around the eyes. Contrariwise, my somewhat unfinished look may make her more mature contours appear even more Helen-of-Troyish.[8] As may be, it is certain that my presence has relieved the pressure on her by giving the gossips two targets instead of one.

And gossip they do. I heard one of them say about her: "She's been in more laps than a napkin!"

If so, I hope she had fun.

Those gay ship's dances in the mammoth ballroom! Like this: they happen every Tuesday and Saturday night, when the ship is spacing. The music starts at 20.30 and the Ladies' Society for Moral Rectitude is seated around the edge of the floor, as if for a wake. Uncle Tom is there, as a concession to me, and very proudsome and distinguished he looks in evening formal. I am there in a party dress which is not quite as girlish as it was when Mother helped me pick it out, in consequence of some *very* careful retailoring I have done with my door locked. Even Clark attends because there is nothing else going on and he's afraid he might miss something—and looking so nice I'm proud of him, because he has to climb into his own monkey suit or he can't come to the ball.

Over by the punch bowl are half a dozen of the ship's junior officers, dressed in mess jacket uniforms[9] and looking faintly uncomfortable.

The Captain, by some process known only to him, selects one of the widows and asks her to dance. Two husbands dance with their wives. Uncle Tom offers me his arm and leads me to the floor. Two or three of the junior officers follow the Captain's example. Clark takes advantage of the breathless excitement to raid the punch bowl.

But *nobody* asks Girdie to dance.

This is no accident. The Captain has given the Word (I have this intelligence with utter certainty through My Spies) that no ship's officer shall dance with Miss Fitz-Snugglie until he has danced at least two dances with other partners—and I am not an "other partner," because the proscription, since leaving Mars, has been extended to me.

This should be proof to anyone that a captain of a ship is, in sober fact, the Last of the Absolute Monarchs.

There are now six or seven couples on the floor and the fun is at its riotous height. The floor will never again be so crowded. Nevertheless nine-tenths of the chairs are still occupied and you could ride a bicycle around the floor without endangering the dancers. The spectators look as if they were knitting at the tumbrels.[1] The proper

---

8. The legendary Helen, whose abduction from Greece was the cause of the Trojan War, was considered the most beautiful woman in the world.
9. I.e., dress uniforms.
1. I.e., as if they were women supporters of the French Revolution who knitted while they watched political prisoners taken in carts to the guillotine and beheaded (as described in Thomas Carlyle's *The French Revolution*, 1837).

finishing touch would be a guillotine in the empty space in the middle of the floor.

The music stops; Uncle Tom takes me back to my chair, then asks Girdie to dance—since he is a Cash Customer, the Captain has not attempted to make him toe the mark. But I am still out of bounds, so I walk over to the punch bowl, take a cup out of Clark's hands, finish it, and say, "Come on, Clark. I'll let you practice on me."

"Aw, it's a waltz!" (Or a "flea hop," or a "chassé," or "five step"—but whatever it is, it is just too utterly impossible.)

"Do it—or I'll tell Madame Grew that you want to dance with her, only you're too shy to ask her."

"You do and I'll trip her! I'll stumble and trip her."

However, Clark is weakening, so I move in fast. "Look, Bub, you either take me out there and walk on my feet for a while—or I'll see to it that Girdie doesn't dance with you at all."

That does it. Clark is in the throes of his first case of puppy love, and Girdie is such a gent that she treats him as an equal and accepts his attentions with warm courtesy. So Clark dances with me. Actually he is quite a good dancer and I have to lead him only a tiny bit. He likes to dance—but he wouldn't want anyone, especially me, to think that he likes to dance with his sister. We don't look too badly matched, since I am short. In the meantime Girdie is looking very good indeed with Uncle Tom, which is quite an accomplishment, as Uncle Tom dances with great enthusiasm and no rhythm. But Girdie can follow anyone—if her partner broke his leg, she would follow, fracturing her own at the same spot. But the crowd is thinning out now; husbands that danced the first dance are too tired for the second and no one has replaced them.

Oh, we have gay times in the luxury liner *Tricorn!*

Truthfully we *do* have gay times. Starting with the third dance Girdie and I have our pick of the ship's officers, most of whom are good dancers, or at least have had plenty of practice. About twenty-two o'clock the Captain goes to bed and shortly after that the chaperones start putting away their whetstones and fading, one by one. By midnight there is just Girdie and myself and half a dozen of the younger officers— and the Purser, who has dutifully danced with every woman and now feels that he owes himself the rest of the night. He is quite a good dancer, for an old man.

Oh, and there is usually Mrs. Grew, too—but she isn't one of the chaperones and she is always nice to Girdie. She is a fat old woman, full of sin and chuckles. She doesn't expect anyone to dance with her but she likes to watch—and the officers who aren't dancing at the moment like to sit with her; she's fun.

About one o'clock Uncle Tom sends Clark to tell me to come to bed or he'll lock me out. He wouldn't but I do—my feet are tired.

Good old *Tricorn!*

VI

The Captain is slowly increasing the spin of the ship to make the fake gravity match the surface gravitation of Venus, which is 84 percent of one standard gravity or more than twice as much as I have been used to all my life. So, when I am not busy studying astrogation or ship handling, I spend much of my time in the ship's gymnasium, hardening myself for what is coming, for I have no intention of being at a disadvantage on Venus in either strength or agility.

If I can adjust to an acceleration of 0.84 gee, the later transition to the full Earth-normal of one gee should be sugar pie with chocolate frosting. So I think.

I usually have the gymnasium all to myself. Most of the passengers are Earthmen or Venusmen who feel no need to prepare for the heavy gravitation of Venus. Of the dozen-odd Marsmen I am the only one who seems to take seriously the coming burden—and the handful of aliens in the ship we never see; each remains in his specially conditioned stateroom. The ship's officers do use the gym; some of them are quite fanatic about keeping fit. But they use it mostly at hours when passengers are not likely to use it.

So, on this day (Ceres thirteenth actually but the *Tricorn* uses Earth dates and time, which made it March ninth—I don't mind the strange dates but the short Earth day is costing me a half-hour's sleep each night)—on Ceres thirteenth I went charging into the gym, so angry I could spit venom and intending to derive a double benefit by working off my mad (at least to the point where I would not be clapped in irons for assault), and by strengthening my muscles, too.

And found Clark inside, dressed in shorts and with a massy barbell.

I stopped short and blurted out, "What are *you* doing here?"

He grunted, "Weakening my mind."

Well, I had asked for it; there is no ship's regulation forbidding Clark to use the gym. His answer made sense to one schooled in his devious logic, which I certainly should be. I changed the subject, tossed aside my robe, and started limbering exercises to warm up. "How massy?" I asked.

"Sixty kilos."

I glanced at a weight meter on the wall, a loaded spring scale marked to read in fractions of standard gee; it read 52%. I did a fast rough in my mind—fifty-two thirty-sevenths of sixty—or unit sum, plus nine hundred over thirty-seven, so add about a ninth, top and bottom for a thousand over forty, to yield twenty-five—or call it the same as lifting eighty-five kilos back home on Mars. "Then why are you sweating?"

"I am not sweating!" He put the barbell down. "Let's see *you* lift it."

"All right." As he moved I squatted down to raise the barbell—and changed my mind.

Now, believe me, I work out regularly with ninety kilos at home and I had been checking that weight meter on the wall each day and loading that same barbell to match the weight I use at home, plus a bit extra each day. My objective (hopeless, it is beginning to seem) is eventually to lift as much mass under Venus conditions as I had been accustomed to lifting at home.

So I was certain I could lift sixty kilos at 52 percent of standard gee.

But it is a mistake for a girl to beat a male at any test of physical strength . . . even when it's your brother. Most especially when it's your brother and he has a fiendish disposition and you've suddenly had a glimmering of a way to put his fiendish proclivities to work. As I have said, if you're in a mood to hate something or somebody, Clark is the perfect partner.

So I grunted and strained, making a good show, got it up to my chest, started it on up—and squeaked "Help me!"

Clark gave a one-handed push at the center of the bar and we got it all the way up. Then I said, "Catch for me," through clenched teeth, and he eased it down. I sighed. "Gee, Clark, you must be getting awful strong."

"Doing all right."

It works; Clark was now as mellow as his nature permits. I suggested companion tumbling—if he didn't mind being the bottom half of the team?—because I wasn't sure I could hold him, not at point-five-two gee . . . did he mind?

He didn't mind at all; it gave him another chance to be muscular and masculine—and I was certain he could lift me; I massed eleven kilos less than the barbell he had just been lifting. When he was smaller, we used to do quite a bit of it, with me lifting him—it was a way to keep him quiet when I was in charge of him. Now that he is as big as I am (and stronger, I fear), we still tumble a little, but taking turns at the ground-and-air parts—back home, I mean.

But with my weight almost half again what it ought to be I didn't risk any fancy capers. Presently, when he had me in a simple handstand over his head, I broached the subject on my mind. "Clark, is Mrs. Royer any special friend of yours?"

"Her?" He snorted and added a rude noise. "Why?"

"I just wondered. She—Mmm, perhaps I shouldn't repeat it."

He said, "Look, Pod, you want me to leave you standing on the ceiling?"

"Don't you dare!"

"Then don't start to say something and not finish it."

"All right. But steady while I swing my feet down to your shoulders." He let me do so, then I hopped down to the floor. The worst part about high acceleration is not how much you weigh, though that is bad enough, but how *fast* you fall—and I suspected that Clark was quite capable of leaving me head downwards high in the air if I annoyed him.

"What's this about Mrs. Royer?" he asked.

"Oh, nothing much. She thinks Marsmen are trash, that's all."

"She does, huh? That makes it mutual."

"Yes. She thinks it's disgraceful that the Line allows us to travel first class—and the Captain certainly ought not to allow us to eat in the same mess with decent people."

"Tell me more."

"Nothing to tell. We're riffraff, that's all. Convicts. You know."

"Interesting. Very, very interesting."

"And her friend Mrs. Garcia agrees with her. But I suppose I shouldn't have repeated it. After all, they are entitled to their own opinions. Aren't they?"

Clark didn't answer, which is a very bad sign. Shortly thereafter he left without a word. In a sudden panic that I might have started more than I intended to, I called after him but he just kept going. Clark is not hard of hearing but he can be very hard of listening.

Well, it was too late now. So I put on a weight harness, then loaded myself down all over until I weighed as much as I would on Venus and started trotting on the treadmill until I was covered with sweat and ready for a bath and a change.

Actually I did not really care what bad luck overtook those two harpies; I simply hoped that Clark's sleight-of-hand would be up to its usual high standards so that it could not possibly be traced back to him. Nor even guessed at. For I had not told Clark half of what was said.

Believe you me, I had never guessed, until we were in the *Tricorn*, that anyone could despise other persons simply over their ancestry or where they lived. Oh, I had encountered tourists from Earth whose manners left something to be desired—but Daddy had told me that all tourists, everywhere, seem obnoxious simply because tourists are strangers who do not know local customs . . . and I believed it, because Daddy is never wrong. Certainly the occasional visiting professor that Daddy brought home for dinner was always charming, which proves that Earthmen do not have to have bad manners.

I had noticed that the passengers in the *Tricorn* seemed a little bit stand-offish when we first boarded, but I did not think anything of it. After all, strangers do not run up and kiss you, even on Mars—and we Marsmen are fairly informal, I suppose; we're still a frontier society. Besides that, most passengers had been in the ship at least from Earth; they had already formed their friendships and cliques. We were like new kids in a strange school.

But I said "Good morning!" to anyone I met in the passageway and if I was not answered I just checked it off to hard-of-hearing—so many of them obviously *could* be hard of hearing. Anyhow, I wasn't terribly interested in getting chummy with passengers; I wanted to get acquainted with the ship's officers, pilot officers especially, so that I could get some practical experience to chink in what I already knew from reading. It's not easy for a girl to get accepted for pilot training; she has to be about four times as good as a male candidate—and every little bit helps.

I got a wonderful break right away. We were seated at the Captain's table!

Uncle Tom, of course. I am not conceited enough to think that "Miss Podkayne Fries, Marsopolis" means anything on a ship's passenger list (but wait ten years!)—whereas Uncle Tom, even though he is just my pinochle-playing, easygoing oldest relative, is nevertheless senior Senator-at-Large of the Republic, and it is certain that the Marsopolis General Agent for the Triangle Line knows this and no doubt the agent would see to it that the Purser of the *Tricorn* would know it if he didn't already.

As may be—I am not one to scorn gifts from heaven, no matter how they arrive. At our very first meal I started working on Captain Darling. That really is his name, Barrington Babcock Darling—and does his wife call him "Baby Darling"?

But of course a captain does not have a name aboard ship; he is "the Captain," "the Master," "the Skipper," or even "the Old Man" if it is a member of the ship's company speaking not in his august presence. But never a name—simply a majestic figure of impersonal authority.

(I wonder if I will someday be called "the Old Woman" when I am not in earshot? Somehow it doesn't sound quite the same.)

But Captain Darling is not too majestic or impersonal with *me*. I set out to impress him with the idea that I was awfully sweet, even younger than I am, terribly impressed by him and overawed . . . and not too bright. It does not do to let a male of any age know that one has brains, not on first acquaintance; intelligence in a woman is likely to make a man suspicious and uneasy, much like Caesar's fear of Cassius' "lean and hungry look."[2] Get a man solidly on your side first; after that it is fairly safe to let him become gradually aware of your intellect. He may even feel unconsciously that it rubbed off from his own.

So I set out to make him feel that it was a shame that I was not his daughter. (Fortunately he only has sons.) Before that first meal was over I confided in him my great yearning to take pilot training . . . suppressing, of course, any higher ambition.

Both Uncle Tom and Clark could see what I was up to. But Uncle Tom would never give me away and Clark just looked bored and contemptuous and said nothing, because Clark would not bother to interfere with Armageddon unless there was ten percent in it for him.

But I do not mind what my relatives think of my tactics; they work. Captain Darling was obviously amused at my grandiose and "impossible" ambition . . . but he offered to show me the control room.

Round one to Poddy, on points.

---

2. From William Shakespeare, *Julius Caesar* 1.2.

I am now the unofficial ship's mascot, with free run of the control room—and I am almost as privileged in the engineering department. Of course the Captain does not really want to spend hours teaching me the practical side of astrogation. He did show me through the control room and gave me a kindergarten explanation of the work—which I followed with wide-eyed awe—but his interest in me is purely social. He wants to not-quite hold me in his lap (he is much too practical and too discreet to do anything of the sort!), so I not-quite let him and make it a point to keep up my social relations with him, listening with my best astonished-kitten look to his anecdotes while he feeds me liters of tea. I really am a good listener because you never can tell when you will pick up something useful—and all in the world any woman has to do to be considered "charming" by men is to listen while they talk.

But Captain Darling is not the only astrogator in the ship.

He gave me the run of the control room; I did the rest. The second officer, Mr. Savvonavong, thinks it is simply amazing how fast I pick up mathematics. You see, he thinks he taught me differential equations. Well, he did, when it comes to those awfully complicated ones used in correcting the vector of a constant-boost ship, but if I hadn't worked hard in the supplementary course I was allowed to take last semester, I wouldn't know what he was talking about. Now he is showing me how to program a ballistic computer.

The junior third, Mr. Clancy, is still studying for his unlimited license, so he has all the study tapes and reference books I need and is just as helpful. He is near enough my age to develop groping hands . . . but only a very stupid male will make even an indirect pass unless a girl manages to let him know that it won't be resented, and Mr. Clancy is not stupid and I am very careful to offer neither invitation nor opportunity.

I may kiss him—two minutes before I leave the ship for the last time. Not sooner.

They are all very helpful and they think it is cute of me to be so dead serious about it. But, in truth, practical astrogation is *much* harder than I had ever dreamed.

I had guessed that part of the resentment I sensed—resentment that I could not fail to notice despite my cheery "Good mornings!"—lay in the fact that we were at the Captain's table. To be sure, the *Welcome in the Tricorn!* booklet in each stateroom states plainly that new seating arrangements are made at each port and that it is the ship's custom to change the guests at the Captain's table each time, making the selections from the new passengers.

But I don't suppose that warning makes it any pleasanter to be bumped, because I don't expect to like it when I'm bumped off the Captain's table at Venus.

But that is only part—

Only three of the passengers were really friendly to me: Mrs. Grew, Girdie, and Mrs. Royer. Mrs. Royer I met first and at first I thought that I was going to like her, in a bored sort of way, as she was awfully friendly and I have great capacity for enduring boredom if it suits my purpose. I met her in the lounge the first day and she immediately caught my eye, smiled, invited me to sit by her, and quizzed me about myself.

I answered her questions, mostly. I told her that Daddy was a teacher and that Mother was raising babies and that my brother and I were traveling with our uncle. I didn't boast about our family; boasting is not polite and it often is not believed—far better to let people find out nice things on their own and hope they won't notice any unnice things. Not that there is anything unnice about Daddy and Mother.

I told her that my name was Poddy Fries.

" 'Poddy'?" she said. "I thought I saw something else on the passenger list."

"Oh. It's really 'Podkayne,'" I explained. "For the Martian saint, you know."

But she didn't know. She answered, "It seems very odd to give a girl a man's name."

Well, my name *is* odd, even among Marsmen. But not for that reason. "Possibly," I agreed. "But with Martians gender is rather a matter of opinion, wouldn't you say?"

She blinked, "You're jesting."

I started to explain—how a Martian doesn't select which of three sexes to be until just before it matures . . . and how, even so, the decision is operative only during a relatively short period of its life.

But I gave up, as I could see that I was talking to a blank wall. Mrs. Royer simply could not imagine any pattern other than her own. So I shifted quickly. "Saint Podkayne lived a very *long* time ago. Nobody actually knows whether the saint was male or female. There are just traditions."

Of course the traditions are pretty explicit and many living Martians claim descent from Saint Podkayne. Daddy says that we know Martian history of millions of years ago much more accurately than we know human history a mere two thousand years ago. In any case, most Martians include "Podkayne" in their long lists of names (practically genealogies in synopsis) because of the tradition that anyone named for Saint Podkayne can call on him (or "her"—or "it") in time of trouble.

As I have said, Daddy is romantic and he thought it would be nice to give a baby the luck, if any, that is attached to the saint's name. I am neither romantic nor superstitious, but it suits me just fine to have a name that belongs to me and to no other human. I like being Podkayne "Poddy" Fries— It's better than being one of a multitude of Elizabeths, or Dorothys, or such.

But I could see that it simply puzzled Mrs. Royer, so we passed to other matters, speaking from her seniority as an "old space hand," based on her one just-completed trip out from Earth, she told me a great many things about ships and space travel, most of which weren't so, but I indulged her. She introduced me to a number of people and handed me a large quantity of gossip about passengers, ship's officers, et cetera. Between times she filled me in on her aches, pains, and symptoms, what an important executive her son was, what a very important person her late husband had been, and how, when I reached Earth, she really must see to it that I met the Right People. "Perhaps such things don't matter in an outpost like Mars, my dear child, but it is Terribly Important to get Started Right in New York."

I tabbed her as garrulous, stupid, and well intentioned.

But I soon found that I couldn't get rid of her. If I passed through the lounge— which I had to do in order to reach the control room—she would snag me and I couldn't get away short of abrupt rudeness or flat lies.

She quickly started using me for chores. "Podkayne darling, would you mind just slipping around to my stateroom and fetching my mauve wrap? I feel a tiny chill. It's on the bed, I think—or perhaps in the wardrobe—that's a dear." Or, "Poddy child, I've rung and I've rung and the stewardess simply *won't* answer. Would you get my book and my knitting? Oh, and while you're at it, you might bring me a nice cup of tea from the pantry."

Those things aren't too bad; she is probably creaky in the knees and I'm not. But it went on endlessly . . . and shortly, in addition to being her personal stewardess, I was her private nurse. First she asked me to read her to sleep. "Such a blinding headache and your voice is so soothing, my sweet."

I read to her for an hour and then found myself rubbing her head and temples for almost as long. Oh well, a person ought to manage a little kindness now and then, just for practice—and Mother sometimes has dreadful headaches when she has been working too hard; I know that a rub does help.

That time she tried to tip me. I refused it. She insisted. "Now, now, child, don't argue with your Aunt Flossie."

I said, "No, really, Mrs. Royer. If you want to give it to the fund for disabled spacemen as a thank-you, that's all right. But I can't take it."

She said pish and tosh and tried to shove it into my pocket. So I slid out and went to bed.

I didn't see her at breakfast; she always has a tray in her room. But about midmorning a stewardess told me that Mrs. Royer wanted to see me in her room. I was hardly gruntled at the summons, as Mr. Savvonavong had told me that if I showed up just before ten during his watch, I could watch the whole process of a ballistic correction and he would explain the steps to me. If she wasted more than five minutes of my time, I would be late.

But I called on her. She was as cheery as ever. "Oh, there you are darling! I've been waiting ever so long! That stupid stewardess— Poddy dear, you did such wonders for my head last night . . . and this morning I find that I'm positively *crippled* with my back. You can't imagine, dear; it's *ghastly!* Now if you'll just be an angel and give me a few minutes massage—oh, say a half hour—I'm sure it'll do wonders for me. You'll find the cream for it over there on the dressing table, I think . . . And now, if you'll just help me slid out of this robe . . ."

"Mrs. Royer—"

"Yes, dear? The cream is in that big pink tube. Use just—"

"Mrs. Royer, I can't do it. I have an appointment."

"What dear? Oh, tosh, let them wait. No one is ever on time aboard ship. Perhaps you had better warm your hands before—"

"Mrs. Royer, I am not going to do it. If something is wrong with your back, I shouldn't touch it; I might injure you. But I'll take a message to the Surgeon if you like and ask him to come see you."

Suddenly she wasn't at all cheery. "You mean you *won't* do it!"

"Have it your way. Shall I tell the Surgeon?"

"Why, you impertinent— *Get out of here!*"

I got.

I met her in a passageway on my way to lunch. She stared straight through me, so I didn't speak either. She was walking as nimbly as I was; I guess her back had taken a turn for the better. I saw her twice more that day and twice more she simply couldn't see me.

The following morning I was using the viewer in the lounge to scan one of Mr. Clancy's study tapes, one on radar approach and contact. The viewer is off in a corner, behind a screen of fake potted palms, and perhaps they didn't notice me. Or perhaps they didn't care.

I stopped the scan to give my eyes and ears a rest, and heard Mrs. Garcia talking to Mrs. Royer.

". . . that I simply can't stand about Mars is that it is so *commercialized.* Why couldn't they have left it primitive and beautiful?"

MRS. ROYER: "What can you expect? Those *dreadful* people!"

The ship's official language is Ortho but many passengers talk English among themselves—and often act as if no one else could possibly understand it. These two weren't keeping their voices down. I went on listening.

MRS. GARCIA: "Just what I was saying to Mrs. Rimski. After all, they're all *criminals*."

MRS. ROYER: "Or worse. Have you noticed that little Martian girl? The niece— or so they claim—of that big black savage?"

I counted ten backwards in Old Martian and reminded myself of the penalty for murder. I didn't mind being called a "Martian." They didn't know any better, and anyhow, it's no insult; the Martians were civilized before humans learned to walk. But "big black savage"!— Uncle Tom is as dark as I am blond; his Maori blood and desert tan make him the color of beautiful old leather . . . and I love the way he looks. As for the rest—he is learned and civilized and gentle . . . and highly honored wherever he goes.

MRS. GARCIA: "I've seen her. Common, I would say. Flashy but cheap. A type that attracts a certain sort of man."

MRS. ROYER: "My dear, you don't know the half of it. I've tried to help her—I really felt sorry for her, and I always believe in being gracious, especially to one's social inferiors."

MRS. GARCIA: "Of course, dear."

MRS. ROYER: "I tried to give her a few hints as to proper conduct among gentle people. Why, I was even *paying* her for little trifles, so that she wouldn't be uneasy among her betters. But she's an utterly ungrateful little snip—she thought she could squeeze more money out of me. She was rude about it, rude that I feared for my safety. I had to order her out of my room, actually."

MRS. GARCIA: "You were wise to drop her. Blood will tell—bad blood or good blood—blood will always tell. And mixed blood is the Very Worst Sort. Criminals to start with . . . and then that Shameless Mixing of Races. You can see it right in that family. The boy doesn't look a bit like his sister, and as for the uncle—*hmmm*— My dear, you halfway hinted at something. Do you suppose that she is *not* his niece but something, shall we say, a bit *closer*?"

MRS. ROYER: "I wouldn't put it past either one of them!"

MRS. GARCIA: "Oh, come, 'fess up, Flossie. Tell me what you found out."

MRS. ROYER: "I didn't say a word. But I have eyes—and so have you."

MRS. GARCIA: "Right in front of everyone!"

MRS. ROYER: "What I *can't* understand is why the Line permits *them* to mix with *us*. Perhaps they have to sell them passage—treaties or some such nonsense—but we shouldn't be forced to associate with them . . . and certainly not to *eat* with them!"

MRS. GARCIA: "I know. I'm going to write a very strong letter about it as soon as I get home. There are limits. You know, I had thought that Captain Darling was a gentleman . . . but when I saw those *creatures* actually seated at the Captain's table . . . well, I didn't believe my eyes. I thought I would faint."

MRS. ROYER: "I know. But after all, the Captain does come from Venus."

MRS. GARCIA: "Yes, but Venus was never a *prison* colony. That boy . . . he sits in the very chair I used to sit in, right across from the Captain."

(I made a mental note to ask the Chief Steward for a different chair for Clark; I didn't want him contaminated.)

After that they dropped us "Martians" and started dissecting Girdie and complaining about the food and the service, and even stuck pins in some of their shipboard coven who weren't present. But I didn't listen: I simply kept quiet and prayed for strength to go on doing so, because if I had made my presence known I feel sure that I would have stabbed them both with their own knitting needles.

Eventually they left—to rest a while to fortify themselves for lunch—and I rushed out and changed into my gym suit and hurried to the gymnasium to work up a good sweat instead of engaging in violent crime.

It was there that I found Clark and told him just enough—or maybe too much.

VII

Mr. Savvonavong tells me that we are likely to have a radiation storm almost any time now and that we'll have an emergency drill today to practice for it. The solar weather station on Mercury reports that "flare" weather is shaping up and has warned all ships in space and all manned satellites to be ready for it. The flares are expected to continue for about—

Wups! The emergency alarm caught me in the middle of a sentence. We've had our drill and I think the Captain has all the passengers properly scared now. Some ignored the alarm, or tried to, whereupon crewmen in heavy armor fetched them. Clark got fetched. He was the very last they tracked down, and Captain Darling gave him a public scolding that was a work of art and finished by warning Clark that if he failed to be the first passenger to reach shelter the next time the alarm sounded, Clark could expect to spend the rest of the trip *in* the shelter, twenty-four hours of the day, instead of having free run of passenger country.

Clark took it with his usual wooden face, but I think it hit home, especially the threat to confine him. I'm sure the speech impressed the other passengers; it was the sort that raises blisters at twenty paces. Perhaps the Captain intended it mostly for their benefit.

Then the Captain changed his tone to that of a patient teacher and explained in simple words what we could expect, why it was necessary to reach shelter *at once* even if one were taking a bath, why we would be perfectly safe if we did.

The solar flares trigger radiation, he told us, quite ordinary radiation, much like X-rays ("and other sorts," I mentally added), the sort of radiation which is found in space at all times. But the intensity reaches levels from a thousand to ten thousand times as high as "normal" space radiation—and, since we are already inside the orbit of Earth, this is bad medicine indeed; it would kill an unprotected man about as quickly as shooting him through the head.

Then he explained why we would not require a thousand to ten thousand times as much shielding in order to be safe. It's the cascade principle. The outer hull stops over 90 percent of any radiation; then comes the "cofferdam" (cargo holds and water tanks) which absorbs some more; then comes the inner hull which is actually the floor of the cylinder which is first-class passenger country.

This much shielding is plenty for all normal conditions; the radiation level in our staterooms is lower than it is at home, quite a lot lower than it is most places on Earth, especially in the mountains. (I'm looking forward to seeing real mountains. Scary!)

Then one day comes a really *bad* storm on the Sun and the radiation level jumps suddenly to 10,000 times normal—and you could get a killing dose right in your own bed and wake up dying.

No trouble. The emergency shelter is at the center of the ship, four shells farther in, each of which stops more than 90 percent of what hits it. Like this:

10,000
  1,000 (after the first inner shell, the ceiling of passenger country)
    100 (after the second inner shell)

10 (third)

1 (fourth—and you're inside the shelter)

But actually the shielding is better than that and it is safer to be in the ship's shelter during a bad solar storm than it is to be in Marsopolis.

The only trouble is—and no small matter—the shelter space is the geometrical core of the ship, just abaft the control room and not a whole lot bigger; passengers and crew are stacked into it about as intimately as puppies in a basket. My billet is a shelf space half a meter wide, half a meter deep, and just a trifle longer than I am—with other females brushing my elbows on each side of me. I am not a claustrophobe, but a coffin would be roomier.

Rations are canned ones, kept there against emergencies; sanitary facilities can only be described as "dreadful." I hope this storm is only a solar squall and is followed by good weather on the Sun. To finish the trip to Venus in the shelter would turn a wonderful experience into a nightmare.

The captain finished by saying, "We will probably have five to ten minutes' warning from Hermes Station. But don't take five minutes getting here. The instant the alarm sounds *head for the shelter at once* as fast as possible. If you are not dressed, be sure you have clothes ready to grab—and dress when you get here. If you stop to worry about *anything*, it may kill you.

"Crewmen will search all passenger spaces the moment the alarm sounds—and each one is *ordered* to use force to send to shelter any passenger who fails to move fast. He won't argue with you—he'll hit you, kick you, drag you—and I'll back him up.

"One last word. Some of you have not been wearing your personal radiation meters. The law permits me to levy a stiff fine for such failure. Ordinarily I overlook such technical offenses—it's your health, not mine. But during this emergency, this regulation will be enforced. Fresh personal meters are now being passed out to each of you; old ones will be turned over to the Surgeon, examined, and exposures entered in your records for future guidance."

He gave the "all clear" order then and we all went back down to passenger country, sweaty and mussed—at least I was. I was just washing my face when the alarm sounded *again*, and I swarmed up those four decks like a frightened cat.

But I was only a close second. Clark passed me on the way.

It was just another drill. This time all passengers were in the shelter within four minutes. The Captain seemed pleased.

I've been sleeping raw but I'm going to wear pajamas tonight and all nights until this is over, and leave a robe where I can grab it. Captain Darling is a darling but I think he means exactly what he says—and I won't play Lady Godiva;[3] there isn't a horse in the whole ship.

Neither Mrs. Royer nor Mrs. Garcia were at dinner this evening, although they were both amazingly agile both times the alarm sounded. They weren't in the lounge after dinner; their doors are closed, and I saw the Surgeon coming out of Mrs. Garcia's room.

I wonder. Surely Clark wouldn't poison them? Or would he? I don't dare ask him because of the remote possibility that he might tell me.

---

3. An English noblewoman who, according to tradition, around 1040 won tax relief for the people of Coventry by riding naked through the marketplace at midday.

I don't want to ask the Surgeon, either, because it might attract attention to the Fries family. But I surely would like to have ESP sight (if there truly is such a thing) long enough to find out what is behind those two closed doors.

I hope Clark hasn't let his talents run away with him. Oh, I'm as angry at those two as ever . . . because there is just enough truth in the nasty things they said to make it hurt. I *am* of mixed races and I know that some people think that is bad, even though there is no bias against it on Mars. I *do* have "convicts" among my ancestors—but I've never been ashamed of it. Or not much, although I suppose I'm inclined to dwell more on the highly selected ones. But a "convict" is not always criminal. Admittedly there was that period in the early history of Mars when the commissars were running things on Earth, and Mars was used as a penal colony; everybody knows that and we don't try to hide it.

But the vast majority of the transportees were political prisoners—"counterrevolutionists," "enemies of the people." Is this bad?

In any case there was the much longer period, involving fifty times as many colonists, when every new Marsman was selected as carefully as a bride selects her wedding gown—and much more scientifically. And finally, there is the current period, since our Revolution and Independence, when we dropped all bars to immigration and welcome anyone who is healthy and has normal intelligence.

No, I'm not ashamed of my ancestors or my people, whatever their skin shades or backgrounds; I'm proud of them. It makes me boiling mad to hear anyone sneer at them. Why, I'll bet those two couldn't qualify for permanent visa even under our present "open door" policy! Feeble-minded—

But I do hope Clark hasn't done anything too drastic. I wouldn't want Clark to have to spend the rest of his life on Titan;[4] I love the little wretch.

Sort of.

VIII

We've had that radiation storm. I prefer hives. I don't mean the storm itself; it wasn't too bad. Radiation jumped to about 1500 times normal for where we are now—about eight-tenths of an astronomical unit[5] from the Sun, say 120,000,000 kilometers in units you can get your teeth in. Mr. Savvonavong says that we would have been all right if the first-class passengers had simply gone up one deck to second-class passenger country—which certainly would have been more comfortable than stuffing all the passengers and crew into that maximum-safety mausoleum at the center of the ship. Second-class accommodations are cramped and cheerless, and as for third class, I would rather be shipped as freight. But either one would be a picnic compared with spending eighteen hours in the radiation shelter.

For the first time I envied the half-dozen aliens aboard. They don't take shelter; they simply remain locked in their specially conditioned staterooms as usual. No, they aren't allowed to fry; those X-numbered rooms are almost at the center of the ship anyhow, in officers' and crew's country, and they have their own extra layer of shielding, because you can't expect a Martian, for example, to leave the pressure and humidity he requires and join us humans in the shelter; it would be equivalent to dunking him in a bathtub and holding his head under. If he had a head, I mean.

Still, I suppose eighteen hours of discomfort is better than being sealed into one

4. The largest moon of Saturn.
5. One astronomical unit is the distance from the

Sun to Earth (about 93 million miles, or 149.5 million kilometers).

small room for the whole trip. A Martian can simply contemplate the subtle difference between zero and nothing for that long or longer and a Venerian just estivates. But not me. I need unrest oftener than I need rest—or my circuits get tangled and smoke pours out of my ears.

But Captain Darling couldn't know ahead of time that the storm would be short and relatively mild; he had to assume the worst and protect his passengers and crew. Eleven minutes would have been long enough for us to be in the shelter, as shown later by instrument records. But that is hindsight . . . and a captain doesn't save his ship and the lives depending on him by hindsight.

I am beginning to realize that being a captain isn't all glorious adventure and being saluted and wearing four gold stripes on your shoulders. Captain Darling is younger than Daddy and yet he has worry lines that make him look years older.

QUERY: Poddy, are you *sure* you have what it takes to captain an explorer ship?
ANSWERS: What did Columbus[6] have that you don't? Aside from Isabella, I mean. *Semper toujours,*[7] girl!

I spent a lot of time before the storm in the control room. Hermes[8] Solar Weather Station doesn't actually warn us when the storm is coming; what they do is *fail* to warn us that the storm is *not* coming. That sounds silly but here is how it works:

The weathermen at Hermes are perfectly safe, as they are underground on the dark side of Mercury. Their instruments peek cautiously over the horizon in the twilight zone, gather data about Solar weather including running telephotos at several wave lengths.

But the Sun takes about twenty-five days to turn around, so Hermes Station can't watch all of it all the time. Worse yet. Mercury is going around the Sun in the same direction that the Sun rotates, taking eighty-eight days for one lap, so when the Sun again faces where Mercury was, Mercury has moved on. What this adds up to is that Hermes Station faces exactly the same face of the Sun about every seven weeks.

Which is obviously not good enough for weather-predicting storms that can gather in a day or two, peak in a few minutes, and kill you dead in seconds or less.

So the Solar weather is watched from Earth's Luna and from Venus' satellite station as well, plus some help from Deimos. But there is speed-of-light lag in getting information from these more distant stations back to the main station on Mercury. Maybe fifteen minutes for Luna and as high as a thousand seconds for Deimos . . . not good when seconds count.

But the season of bad storms is only a small part of the Sun's cycle as a variable star—say about a year out of each six. (Real years, I mean—Martian years. The Sun's cycle is about eleven of those Earth years that astronomers still insist on using.)

That makes things a lot easier; five years out of six a ship stands very little chance of being hit by a radiation storm.

But during the stormy season a careful skipper (the only sort who lives to draw a pension) will plan his orbit so that he is in the worst danger zone, say inside the orbit of Earth, only during such time as Mercury lies between him and the Sun, so that Hermes Station can always warn him of coming trouble. That is exactly what Captain

---

6. Christopher Columbus (1451–1506), Italian-born explorer who persuaded Isabella, Queen of Castille (1451–1505; r. 1474–1504), to fund his voyages to the Americas.
7. "Always always" (in Latin and French). In this context, Heinlein may be implying "semper fidelus toujours pret" or "always be loyal and ready." Or he might be indicating "always be yourself."
8. The Greek messenger god (the equivalent of the Roman Mercury).

Darling had done; the *Tricorn* waited at Deimos nearly three weeks longer than the guaranteed sightseeing time on Mars called for by the Triangle Line's advertising, in order to place his approach to Venus so that Hermes Station could observe and warn—because we are right in the middle of the stormy season.

I suppose the Line's business office hates these expensive delays. Maybe they lose money during the stormy season. But three weeks' delay is better than losing a whole shipload of passengers.

But when the storm does start, radio communication goes all to pieces at once— Hermes Station can't warn the ships in the sky.

Stalemate? Not quite. Hermes Station can see a storm shaping up; they can spot the conditions on the Sun which are almost certainly going to produce a radiation storm very shortly. So they send out a storm warning—and the *Tricorn* and other ships hold radiation-shelter drills. Then we wait. One day, two days, or a whole week, and the storm either fails to develop, or it builds up and starts shooting nasty stuff in great quantities.

All during this time the space guard radio station on the dark side of Mercury sends a continuous storm warning, never an instant's break, giving a running account of how the weather looks on the Sun.

. . . and suddenly it stops.

Maybe it's a power failure and the stand-by transmitter will cut in. Maybe it's just a "fade" and the storm hasn't broken yet and transmission will resume with reassuring words.

But it may be that the first blast of the storm has hit Mercury with the speed of light, no last-minute warning at all, and the station's eyes are knocked out and its voice is swallowed up in enormously more powerful radiation.

The officer-of-the-watch in the control room can't be sure and he dare not take a chance. The instant he loses Hermes Station he slaps a switch that starts a big clock with just a second hand. When that clock has ticked off a certain number of seconds—and Hermes Station is *still* silent—the general alarm sounds. The exact number of seconds depends on where the ship is, how far from the Sun, how much longer it will take the first blast to reach the ship after it has already hit Hermes Station.

Now here is where a captain bites his nails and gets gray hair and earns his high pay . . . because *he* has to decide how many seconds to set that clock for. Actually, if the first and worst blast is at the speed of light, he hasn't any warning time at *all* because the break in the radio signal from Hermes and that first wave front from the Sun will reach him at the same instant. Or, if the angle is unfavorable, perhaps it is his own radio reception that has been clobbered, and Hermes Station is still trying to reach him with a last-moment warning. He doesn't know.

But he does know that if he sounds the alarm and chases everybody to shelter every time the radio fades for a few seconds, he will get people so worn out and disgusted from his crying "Wolf!" that when the trouble really comes they may not move fast enough.

He knows, too, that the outer hull of his ship will stop almost anything in the electromagnetic spectrum. Among photons (and nothing else travels at speed-of-light) only the hardest X-radiation will get through to passenger country and not much of that. But traveling along behind, falling just a little behind each second, is the really dangerous stuff—big particles, little particles, middle-sized particles, all the debris of nuclear explosion. This stuff is moving very fast but not quite at speed-of-light. He has to get his people safe before it hits.

Captain Darling picked a delay of twenty-five seconds, for where we were and what he expected from the weather reports. I asked him how he picked it and he just grinned without looking happy and said, "I asked my grandfather's ghost."

Five times while I was in the control room the officer of the watch started that clock . . . and five times contact with Hermes Station was picked up again before time ran out and the switch was opened.

The sixth time the seconds trickled away while all of us held our breaths . . . and contact with Hermes wasn't picked up again and the alarm sounded like the wakeful trump of doom.[9]

The Captain looked stony-faced and turned to duck down the hatch into the radiation shelter. I didn't move, because I expected to be allowed to remain in the control room. Strictly speaking, the control room is part of the radiation shelter, since it is just above it and is enclosed by the same layers of cascade shielding.

(It's amazing how many people think that a captain controls his ship by peering out a port as if he were driving a sand wagon. But he doesn't, of course. The control room is inside, where he can watch things much more accurately and conveniently by displays and instruments. The only viewport in the *Tricorn* is one at the top end of the main axis, to allow passengers to look out at the stars. But we have never been headed so that the mass of the ship would protect that sightseeing room from solar radiation, so it has been locked off this whole trip.)

I knew I was safe where I was, so I hung back, intending to take advantage of being "teacher's pet"—for I certainly didn't want to spend hours or days stretched out on a shelf with gabbling and maybe hysterical women crowding me on both sides.

I should have known. The Captain hesitated a split second as he started down the hatch and snapped, "Come along, Miss Fries."

I came. He *always* calls me "Poddy"—and his voice had spank in it.

Third-class passengers were already pouring in, since they have the shortest distance to go, and crew members were mustering them into their billets. The crew has been on emergency routine ever since we first were warned by Hermes Station, with their usual one watch in three replaced by four hours on and four hours off. Part of the crew had been staying dressed in radiation armor (which must be *very* uncomfortable) and simply hanging around passenger country. They can't take that heavy armor off for any reason at all until their reliefs show up, dressed also in armor. These crewmen are the "chasers" who bet their lives that they can check every passenger space, root out stragglers, and still reach the shelter fast enough not to accumulate radiation poisoning. They are all volunteers and the chasers on duty when the alarm sounds get a big bonus and the other half of them who were lucky enough not to be on duty get a little bonus.

The Chief Officer is in charge of the first section of chasers and the Purser is in charge of the second—but they don't get any bonus even though the one on duty when the alarm sounds is by tradition and law the last man to enter the safety of the shelter. This hardly seems fair . . . but it is considered their honor as well as their duty.

Other crewmen take turns in the radiation shelter and are equipped with mustering lists and billeting diagrams.

Naturally, service has been pretty skimpy of late, with so many of the crew pulled off their regular duties in order to do just one thing and do it *fast* at the first jangle of the alarm. Most of these emergency-duty assignments have to be made from the

9. I.e., the sounding of the trumpet at Judgment Day.

stewards and clerks; engineers and communicators and such usually can't be spared. So staterooms may not be made up until late afternoon—unless you make your own bed and tidy your room yourself, as I had been doing—and serving meals takes about twice as long as usual, and lounge service is almost non-existent.

But of course the passengers realize the necessity for this temporary mild austerity and are grateful because it is all done for safety.

You think so? My dear, if you believe that, you will believe anything. You haven't Seen Life until you've seen a rich, elderly Earthman deprived of something he feels is his rightful due, because he figures he paid for it in the price of his ticket. I saw one man, perhaps as old as Uncle Tom and certainly old enough to know better, almost have a stroke. He turned purple, really purple and gibbered—all because the bar steward didn't show up on the bounce to fetch him a new deck of playing cards.

The bar steward was in armor at the time and couldn't leave his assigned area, and the lounge steward was trying to be three places at once and answer stateroom rings as well. This didn't mean anything to our jolly shipmate; he was threatening to sue the Line and all its directors, when his speech became incoherent.

Not everybody is that way, of course. Mrs. Grew, fat as she is, has been making her own bed and she is never impatient. Some others who are ordinarily inclined to demand lots of service have lately been making a cheerful best of things.

But some of them act like children with tantrums—which isn't pretty in children and is even uglier in grandparents.

The instant I followed the Captain into the radiation shelter I discovered just how efficient *Tricorn* service can be when it really matters. I was snatched—snatched like a ball, right out of the air—and passed from hand to hand. Of course I don't weigh much at one-tenth gravity, all there is at the main axis; but it is rather breath-taking. Some more hands shoved me into my billet, already stretched out, as casually and impersonally as a housewife stows clean laundry, and a voice called out, "Fries, Podkayne!" and another voice answered, "Check."

The spaces around me, and above and below and across from me, filled up awfully fast, with the crewmen working with the unhurried efficiency of automatic machinery sorting mail capsules. Somewhere a baby was crying and through it I heard the Captain saying, "Is that the last?"

"Last one, Captain," I heard the Purser answer. "How's the time?"

"Two minutes thirty-seven seconds—and your boys can start figuring their payoff, because this one is no drill."

"I didn't think it was, Skipper—and I've won a small bet from the Mate myself." Then the Purser walked past my billet carrying someone, and I tried to sit up and bumped my head and my eyes bugged out.

The passenger he was carrying had fainted; her head lolled loosely over the crook of his arm. At first I couldn't tell who it was, as the face was a bright, bright red. And then I recognized her and *I* almost fainted. Mrs. Royer—

Of course the first symptom of any bad radiation exposure is erythema. Even with a sunburn, or just carelessness with an ultraviolet lamp, the first thing you see is the skin turning pink or bright red.

But was it possible that Mrs. Royer had been hit with such extremely sharp radiation in so very little time that her skin had *already* turned red in the worst "sunburn" imaginable? Just from being last man in?

In that case she hadn't fainted; she was dead.

And if that was true, then it was equally true that the passengers who were last to reach the shelter must all have received several times the lethal dosage. They might not feel ill for hours yet; they might not die for days. But they were just as dead as if they were already stretched out stiff and cold.

How many? I had no way of guessing. Possibly—*probably* I corrected myself—all the first-class-passengers; they had the farthest to go and were most exposed to start with.

Uncle Tom and Clark—

I felt sudden sick sorrow and wished that I had not been in the control room. If my brother and Uncle Tom were dying, I didn't want to be alive myself.

I don't think I wasted any sympathy on Mrs. Royer. I did feel a shock of horror when I saw that flaming red face, but truthfully, I didn't like her, I thought she was a parasite with contemptible opinions, and if she had died of heart failure instead, I can't honestly say that it would have affected my appetite. None of us goes around sobbing over the millions and billions of people who have died in the past . . . nor over those still living and yet to be born whose single certain heritage is death (including Podkayne Fries herself). So why should you cry foolish tears simply because you happen to be in the neighborhood when someone you don't like—despise, in fact—comes to the end of her string?

In any case, I did not have time to feel sorrow for Mrs. Royer; my heart was filled with grief over my brother and my uncle. I was sorry that I hadn't been sweeter to Uncle Tom, instead of imposing on him and expecting him always to drop whatever he was doing to help me with my silly problems. I regretted all the many times I had fought with my brother. After all, he was a child and I am a woman; I should have made allowances.

Tears were welling out of my eyes and I almost missed the Captain's first words:

"Shipmates," he said, in a voice firm and very soothing, "my crew and our guests aboard . . . this is not a drill; this is indeed a radiation storm.

"Do not be alarmed; we are all, each and every one of us, perfectly safe. The Surgeon has examined the personal radiation exposure meter of the very last one to reach the shelter. It is well within safe limits. Even if it were added to the accumulated exposure of the most exposed person aboard—who is not a passenger, by the way, but one of the ship's company—the total would still be inside the conservative maximum for personal health and genetic hygiene.

"Let me say it again. No one has been hurt, no one is going to be hurt. We are simply going to suffer a mild inconvenience. I wish I could tell you how long we will have to remain here in the safety of the shelter. But I do not know. It might be a few hours, it might be several days. The longest radiation storm of record lasted less than a week. We hope that Old Sol is not that bad-tempered this time. But until we receive word from Hermes Station that the storm is over, we will all have to stay inside here. Once we know a storm is over it usually does not take too long to check the ship and make sure that your usual comfortable quarters are safe. Until then, be patient and be patient with each other."

I started to feel better as soon as the Captain started to talk. His voice was almost hypnotic; it had the soothing all-better-now effect of a mother reassuring a child. I relaxed and was simply weak with the aftereffects of my fears.

But presently I began to wonder. Would Captain Darling tell us that everything was all right when really everything was All Wrong simply because it was too late and nothing could be done about it?

I thought over everything I had ever learned about radiation poisoning, from the simple hygiene they teach in kindergarten to a tape belonging to Mr. Clancy that I had scanned only that week.

And I decided that the Captain had been telling the truth.

Why? Because, even if my very worst fears had been correct, and we had been hit as hard and unexpectedly as if a nuclear weapon had exploded by us, nevertheless something can *always* be done about it. There would be three groups of us—those who hadn't been hurt at all and were not going to die (certainly everybody who was in the control room or in the shelter when it happened, plus all or almost all the third-class passengers if they had moved fast), a second group so terribly exposed that they were certain to die, no matter what (let's say everybody in first class country), and a third group, no telling how large, which had been dangerously exposed but could be saved by quick and drastic treatment.

In which case that quick and drastic action would be going on.

They would be checking our exposure meters and reshuffling us—sorting out the ones in danger who required rapid treatment, giving morphine shots to the ones who were going to die anyhow and moving them off by themselves, stacking those of us who were safe by ourselves to keep us from getting in the way, or drafting us to help nurse the ones who could be helped.

That was certain. But there was nothing going on, nothing at all—just some babies crying and a murmur of voices. Why, they hadn't even looked at the exposure meters of most of us; it seemed likely that the Surgeon had checked only the last few stragglers to reach the shelter.

Therefore the Captain had told us the simple, heart-warming truth.

I felt so good that I forgot to wonder why Mrs. Royer had looked like a ripe tomato. I relaxed and soaked in the warm and happy fact that darling Uncle Tom wasn't going to die and that my kid brother would live to cause me lots more homey grief. I almost went to sleep . . .

. . . and was yanked out of it by the woman on my right starting to scream: "Let me out of here! *Let me out of here!*"

Then I did see some fast and drastic emergency action.

Two crewmen swarmed up to our shelf and grabbed her; a stewardess was right behind them. She slapped a gag over the woman's mouth and gave her a shot in the arm, all in one motion. Then they held her until she stopped struggling. When she was quiet, one of the crewmen picked her up and took her somewhere.

Shortly thereafter a stewardess showed up who was collecting exposure meters and passing out sleeping pills. Most people took them but I resisted—I don't like pills at best and I certainly won't take one to knock me out so that I won't know what is going on. The stewardess was insistent but I can be awfully stubborn, so she shrugged and went away. After that there were three or four more cases of galloping claustrophobia or maybe just plain screaming funk; I wouldn't know. Each was taken care of promptly with no fuss and shortly the shelter was quiet except for snores, a few voices, and fairly continuous sounds of babies crying.

There aren't any babies in first class and not many children of any age. Second class has quite a few kids, but third class is swarming with them and every family seems to have at least one young baby. It's why they are there, of course; almost all of third class are Earth people emigrating to Venus. With Earth so crowded, a man with a big family can easily reach the point where emigration to Venus looks like the best way out of an impossible situation, so he signs a labor contract and Venus Corporation pays for their tickets as an advance against his wages.

I suppose it's all right. They need to get away and Venus needs all the people they can get. But I'm glad Mars Republic doesn't subsidize immigration, or we would be swamped. We take immigrants but they have to pay their own way and have to deposit return tickets with the PEG board, tickets they can't cash in for two of our years.

A good thing, too. At least a third of the immigrants who come to Mars just can't adjust. They get homesick and despondent and use those return tickets to go back to Earth. I can't understand anyone's not *liking* Mars, but if they don't then it's better if they don't stay.

I lay there, thinking about such things, a little bit excited and a little bit bored, and mostly wondering why somebody didn't do something about those poor babies.

The lights had been dimmed and when somebody came up to my shelf I didn't see who it was at first. "Poddy?" came Girdie's voice, softly but clearly. "Are you in there?"

"I think so. What's up, Girdie?" I tried to keep my voice down too.

"Do you know how to change a baby?"

"I certainly do!" Suddenly I wondered how Duncan was doing . . . and realized that I hadn't really thought about him in *days*. Had he forgotten me? Would he know Grandmaw Poddy the next time he saw her?

"Then come along, chum. There's work to be done."

There certainly was! The lowest part of the shelter, four catwalks below my billet and just over the engineering spaces, was cut like a pie into four quarters—sanitary units, two sick bays, for men and for women and both crowded—and jammed into a little corner between the infirmaries was a sorry pretense for a nursery, not more than two meters in any dimension. On three walls of it babies were stacked high in canvas crib baskets snap-hooked to the walls, and more overflowed into the women's sick bay. A sweeping majority of those babies were crying.

In the crowded middle of this pandemonium two harassed stewardesses were changing babies, working on a barely big enough shelf let down out of one wall. Girdie tapped one of them on the shoulder. "All right, girls, reinforcements have landed. So get some rest and a bite to eat."

The older one protested feebly, but they were awfully glad to take a break; they backed out and Girdie and I moved in and took over. I don't know how long we worked, as we never had time to think about it—there was always more than we could do and we never quite got caught up. But it was better than lying on a shelf and staring at another shelf just centimeters above your nose. The worst of it was that there simply wasn't enough room. I worked with both elbows held in close, to keep from bumping Girdie on one side and a basket crib that was nudging me on the other side.

But I'm not complaining about that. The engineer who designed that shelter into the *Tricorn* had been forced to plan as many people as possible into the smallest possible space; there wasn't any other way to do it and still give us all enough levels of shielding during a storm. I doubt if he worried much about getting babies changed and dry; he had enough to do just worrying about how to keep them alive.

But you can't tell that to a baby.

Girdie worked with an easy, no-lost-motions efficiency that surprised me; I would never have guessed that she had ever had her hands on a baby. But she knew what she was doing and was faster than I was. "Where are their mothers?" I asked, meaning: "Why aren't those lazy slobs down here helping instead of leaving it to the stewardesses and some volunteers?"

Girdie understood me. "Most of them—all of them, maybe—have other small children to keep quiet; they have their hands full. A couple of them went to pieces themselves; they're in there sleeping it off." She jerked her head toward the sick bay.

I shut up, as it made sense. You couldn't possibly take care of an infant properly in one of those shallow niches the passengers were stacked in, and if each mother tried to bring her own baby down here each time, the traffic jam would be indescribable. No, this assembly-line system was necessary. I said, "We're running out of Disposies."

"Stacked in a cupboard behind you. Did you see what happened to Mrs. Garcia's face?"

"Huh?" I squatted and got out more supplies. "You mean Mrs. Royer, don't you?"

"I mean both of them. But I saw milady Garcia first and got a better look at her, while they were quieting her down. You didn't see her?"

"No."

"Sneak a look into the women's ward first chance you get. Her face is the brightest, most amazing chrome yellow I've ever seen in a paint pot, much less on a human face."

I gasped. "Gracious! I did see Mrs. Royer—bright red instead of yellow. Girdie— what in the world happened to them?"

"I'm fairly sure I know what happened," Girdie answered slowly, "but no one can figure out *how* it happened."

"I don't follow you."

"The colors tell the story. Those are the exact shades of two of the water-activated dyes used in photography. Know anything about photography, hon?"

"Not much," I answered. I wasn't going to admit what little I did know, because Clark is a very accomplished amateur photographer. And I wasn't going to mention *that*, either!

"Well, surely you've seen someone taking snapshots. You pull out the tab and there is your picture—only there's no picture as yet. Clear as glass. So you dip it in water and slosh it around for about thirty seconds. Still no picture. Then you lay it anywhere in the light and the picture starts to show . . . and when the colors are bright enough to suit you, you cover it up and let it finish drying in darkness, so that the colors won't get too garish." Girdie suppressed a chuckle. "From the results, I would say that they didn't cover their faces in time to stop the process. They probably tried to scrub it off and made it worse."

I said, in a puzzled tone—and I *was* puzzled, about part of it—"I still don't see how it could happen."

"Neither does anybody else. But the Surgeon has a theory. Somebody booby-trapped their washcloths."

"Huh?"

"Somebody in the ship must have a supply of the pure dyes. That somebody soaked two washcloths in the inactive dyes—colorless, I mean—and dried them carefully, all in total darkness. Then that same somebody sneaked those two prepared washcloths into those two staterooms and substituted them for washcloths they found there on the stateroom wash trays. That last part wouldn't be hard for anyone with cool nerves—service in the staterooms has been pretty haphazard the last day or two, what with this flap over the radiation storm. Maybe a fresh washcloth appears in your room, maybe it doesn't—and all the ship's washcloths and towels are the same pattern. You just wouldn't know."

I certainly hope not! I said to myself—and added aloud, "I suppose not."

"Certainly not. It could be one of the stewardesses—or any of the passengers. But the real mystery is: where did the dyes come from? The ship's shop doesn't carry them . . . just the rolls of prepared film . . . and the Surgeon says that he knows enough about chemistry to be willing to stake his life that no one but a master chemist, using a special laboratory, could possibly separate out pure dyes from a roll of film. He thinks, too, that since the dyes aren't even manufactured on Mars, this somebody must be somebody who came aboard at Earth." Girdie glanced at me and smiled. "So you're not a suspect, Poddy. But I am."

"Why are you a suspect?" (And if I'm not a suspect, then my brother isn't a suspect!) "Why, that's silly!"

"Yes, it is . . . because I wouldn't have known how even if I'd had the dyes. But it isn't, inasmuch as I could have bought them before I left Earth, and I don't have reason to like either of those women."

"I've never heard you say a word against them."

"No, but they've said a few thousand words about me—and other people have ears. So I'm a hot suspect, Poddy. But don't fret about it. I didn't do it, so there is no possible way to show that I did." She chuckled. "And I hope they never catch the somebody who did!"

I didn't even answer, "Me, too!" I could think of one person who might figure out a way to get pure dyes out of a roll of film without a complete chemistry laboratory, and I was checking quickly through my mind every item I had seen when I searched Clark's room.

There hadn't been *anything* in Clark's room which could have been photographic dyes. No, not even film.

Which proves precisely nothing where Clark is concerned. I just hope that he was careful about fingerprints.

Two other stewardesses came in presently and we fed all the babies, and then Girdie and I managed a sort of a washup and had a snack standing up, and then I went back up to my assigned shelf and surprised myself by falling asleep.

I must have slept three or four hours, because I missed the happenings when Mrs. Dirkson had her baby. She is one of the Terran emigrants to Venus and she shouldn't have had her baby until long after we reach Venus—I suppose the excitement stirred things up. Anyhow, when she started to groan they carried her down to that dinky infirmary, and Dr. Torland took one look at her and ordered her carried up into the control room because the control room was the only place inside the radiation-safe space roomy enough to let him do what needed to be done.

So that's where the baby was born, on the deck of the control room, right between the chart tank and the computer. Dr. Torland and Captain Darling are godfathers and the senior stewardess is godmother and the baby's name is "Radiant," which is a poor pun but rather pretty.

They jury-rigged an incubator for Radiant right there in the control room before they moved Mrs. Dirkson back to the infirmary and gave her something to make her sleep. The baby was still there when I woke up and heard about it.

I decided to take a chance that the Captain was feeling more mellow now, and sneaked up to the control room and stuck my head in. "Could I please see the baby?"

The Captain looked annoyed, then he barely smiled and said, "All right, Poddy. Take a quick look and get out."

So I did. Radiant masses about a kilo and, frankly, she looks like cat meat, not worth saving. But Dr. Torland says that she is doing well and that she will grow up to be a fine, healthy girl—prettier than I am. I suppose he knows what he is talking about, but if she is ever going to be prettier than I am, she has lots of kilometers to go. She is almost the color of Mrs. Royer and she's mostly wrinkles.

But no doubt she'll outgrow it, because she looks like one of the pictures toward the end of the series in a rather goody-goody schoolbook called *The Miracle of Life*— and the earlier pictures in that series were even less appetizing. It is probably just as well that we can't possibly see babies until they are ready to make their debut, or the human race would lose interest and die out.

It would probably be still better to lay eggs. Human engineering isn't all that it might be, especially for us female types.

I went back down where the more mature babies were to see if they needed me. They didn't, not right then, as the babies had been fed again and a stewardess and a young woman I had never met were on duty and claimed that they had been working only a few minutes. I hung around anyhow, rather than go back up to my shelf. Soon I was pretending to be useful by reaching past the two who really were working and checking the babies, then handing down the ones who needed servicing as quickly as shelf space was cleared.

It speeded things up a little. Presently I pulled a little wiggler out of his basket and was cuddling him; the stewardess looked up and said, "I'm ready for him."

"Oh, he's not wet," I answered. "Or 'she' as the case may be. Just lonely and needs loving."

"We haven't time for that."

"I wonder." The worst thing about the midget nursery was the high noise level. The babies woke each other and egged each other on and the decibels were something fierce. No doubt they were all lonely and probably frightened—I'm sure I would be. "Most of these babies need loving more than they need anything else."

"They've all had their bottles."

"A bottle can't cuddle."

She didn't answer, just started checking the other infants. But I didn't think what I had said was silly. A baby can't understand your words and he doesn't know where he is if you put him in a strange place, nor what has happened. So he cries. Then he needs to be soothed.

Girdie showed up just then. "Can I help?"

"You certainly can. Here . . . hold this one."

In a few minutes I rounded up three girls about my age and I ran across Clark prowling around the catwalks instead of staying quietly in his assigned billet so I drafted him, too. He wasn't exactly eager to volunteer, but doing anything was slightly better than doing nothing; he came along.

I couldn't use any more help as standing room was almost nonexistent. We worked it only by having two baby-cuddlers sort of back into each of the infirmaries with the mistress of ceremonies (me) standing in the little space at the bottom of the ladder, ready to scrunch in any direction to let people get in and out of the washrooms and up and down the ladder—and with Girdie, because she was tallest, standing back of the two at the changing shelf and dealing out babies, the loudest back to me for further assignment and the wet ones down for service—and vice versa: dry ones back to their baskets unless they started to yell; ones that had fallen asleep from being held and cuddled.

At least seven babies could receive personal attention at once, and sometimes as high as ten or eleven, because at one-tenth gee your feet never get tired and a baby doesn't weigh anything at all worth mentioning; it was possible to hold one in each arm and sometimes we did.

In ten minutes we had that racket quieted down to an occasional whimper, quickly soothed. I didn't think Clark would stick it out, but he did—probably because Girdie was part of the team. With a look of grim nobility on his face, the like of which I have never before seen there, he cuddled babies and presently was saying "Kitchy-koo kitchy-koo!" and "There, there, honey bun," as if he had been doing it all his life. Furthermore, the babies seemed to like him; he could soothe one down and put it to sleep quickest of any of us. Hypnotism, maybe?

This went on for several hours, with volunteers moving in and tired ones moving out and positions rotating. I was relieved once and had another snatched meal and then stretched out on my shelf for about an hour before going back on duty.

I was back at the changing shelf when the Captain called us all by speaker: "Attention, please. In five minutes power will be cut and the ship will be in free fall while a repair is made outside the ship. All passengers strap down. All crew members observe precautions for free fall."

I went right on changing the baby under my hands; you can't walk off on a baby. In the meantime, babies that had been being cuddled were handed back and stowed, and the cuddling team was chased back to their shelves to strap down—and spin was being taken off the ship. One rotation every twelve seconds you simply don't notice at the center of the ship, but you do notice when the *un*spinning starts. The stewardess with me on the changing bench said, "Poddy, go up and strap down. Hurry."

I said, "Don't be silly, Bergitta, there's work to be done," and popped the baby I had just dried into its basket and fastened the zipper.

"You're a passenger. That's an order—*please!*"

"Who's going to check all these babies? You? And how about those four in on the floor of the women's sick bay?"

Bergitta looked startled and hurried to fetch them. All the other stewardesses were busy checking on strap-down; she didn't bother me any more with That's-an-order; she was too busy hooking up the changing shelf and fastening baby baskets to the space. I was checking all the others and almost all of them had been left unzipped—logical enough while we were working with them, but zipping the cover on a baby basket is the same as strapping down for a grown-up. It holds them firmly but comfortably with just their heads free.

I still hadn't finished when the siren sounded and the Captain cut the power.

Oh, brother! Pandemonium. The siren woke the babies who were asleep and scared any who were awake, and every single one of those squirmy little worms started to cry at the top of its lungs—and one I hadn't zipped yet popped right out of its basket and floated out into the middle of the space and I snagged it by one leg and was loose myself, and the baby and I bumped gently against the baskets on one wall—only it wasn't a wall any longer, it was just an obstacle to further progress. Free fall can be very confusing when you are not used to it, which I admit I am not. Or wasn't.

The stewardess grabbed us both and shoved the elusive little darling back into her straitjacket and zipped it while I hung onto a handhold. And by then two more were loose.

I did better this time—snagged one without letting go and just kept it captive while Bergitta took care of the other one. Bergitta really knew how to handle herself in zero gravity, with unabrupt graceful movements like a dancer in a slow-motion solly. I made a mental note that this was a skill I must acquire.

I thought the emergency was over; I was wrong. Babies don't like free fall; it frightens them. It also makes their sphincters most erratic. Most of the latter we could ignore—but Disposies don't catch everything; regrettably some six or seven of them had been fed in the last hour.

I know now why stewardesses are all graduate nurses; we kept five babies from choking to death in the next few minutes. That is, Bergitta cleared the throat of the first one that upchucked its milk and, seeing what she had done, I worked on the second one in trouble while she grabbed the third. And so on.

Then we were very busy trying to clear the air with clean Disposies because— Listen, dear, if you think you've had it tough because your baby brother threw up all over your new party dress, then you should try somewhat-used baby formula in free fall, where it doesn't settle anywhere in particular but just floats around like smoke until you either get it or it gets you.

From six babies. In a small compartment.

By the time we had that mess cleaned up, or 95 percent so anyway, we were both mostly sour milk from hair part to ankle and the Captain was warning us to stand by for acceleration, which came almost at once to my great relief. The Chief Stewardess showed up and was horrified that I had not strapped down and I told her in a ladylike way to go to hell, using a more polite idiom suitable to my age and sex—and asked her what Captain Darling would think about a baby passenger choking to death simply because I had strapped down all regulation-like and according to orders? And Bergitta backed me up and told her that I had cleared choke from at least two and maybe more—she had been too busy to count.

Mrs. Peal, the C.S., changed her tune in a hurry and was sorry and thanked me, and sighed and wiped her forehead and trembled and you could see that she was dead on her feet. But nevertheless, she checked all the babies herself and hurried out. Pretty quickly we were relieved and Bergitta and I crowded into the women's washroom and tried to clean up some. Not much good, as we didn't have any clean clothes to change into.

The "All Clear" felt like a reprieve from purgatory, and a hot bath was heaven itself with the Angels singing. "A" deck had already been checked for radiation level and pronounced safe while the repair outside the ship was being made. The repair itself, I learned, was routine. Some of the antennas and receptors and things outside the ship can't take a flare storm; they burn out—so immediately after a storm, men go outside in armored space suits and replace them. This is normal and unavoidable, like replacing lighting tubes at home. But the men who do it get the same radiation bonus that the passenger chasers get, because old Sol could burn them down with one tiny little afterthought.

I soaked in warm, clean water and thought how miserable an eighteen hours it had been. Then I decided that it hadn't been so bad after all.

It's lots better to be miserable than to be bored.

IX

I am now twenty-seven years old.

Venus years, of course, but it sounds so much better. All is relative.

Not that I would stay here on Venus even if guaranteed the Perfect Age for a thousand years. Venusberg is sort of an organized nervous breakdown and the country outside the city is even worse. What little I've seen of it. And I don't want to see much of it. Why they ever named this dreary, smog-ridden place for the Goddess of Love and Beauty[1] I'll never know. This planet appears to have been put together from the scrap left over after the rest of the Solar System was finished.

I don't think I would go outside Venusberg at all except that I've just got to see

---

1. I.e., Venus, in Roman mythology.

fairies in flight. The only one I've seen so far is in the lobby of the hilton we are staying in and is stuffed.

Actually I'm just marking time until we shape for Earth, because Venus is a Grave Disappointment—and now I'm keeping my fingers crossed that Earth will not be a G.D., too. But I don't see how it can be; there is something deliciously *primitive* about the very thought of a planet where one can go outdoors without any special preparations. Why, Uncle Tom tells me that there are places along the Mediterranean (that's an ocean in La Belle France) where the natives bathe in the ocean itself without any clothing of any sort, much less insulasuits or masks.

I wouldn't like that. Not that I'm body proud; I enjoy a good sauna sweat-out as well as the next Marsman. But it would scare me cross-eyed to bathe in an ocean; I don't ever intend to get wet all over in anything larger than a bathtub. I saw a man fished out of the Grand Canal once, in early spring. They had to thaw him before they could cremate him.

But it is alleged that, along the Mediterranean shore, the air in the summertime is often blood temperature and the water not much cooler. As may be. Podkayne is not going to take any silly chances.

Nevertheless I am terribly eager to see Earth, in all its fantastic unlikeliness. It occurs to me that my most vivid conceptions of Earth come from the Oz stories[2]—and when you come right down to it, I suppose that isn't too reliable a source. I mean, Dorothy's conversations with the Wizard are instructive—but about *what*? When I was a child I believed every word of my Oz tapes; but now I am no longer a child and I do not truly suppose that a whirlwind is a reliable means of transportation, nor that one is likely to encounter a Tin Woodman on a road of yellow brick.

Tik-Tok, yes—because we have Tik-Toks in Marsopolis for the simpler and more tedious work. Not precisely like Tik-Tok of Oz, of course, and not called "Tik-Toks" by anyone but children, but near enough, near enough, quite sufficient to show that the Oz stories are founded on fact if *not* precisely historical.

And I believe in the Hungry Tiger, too, in the most practical way possible, because there was one in the municipal zoo when I was a child, a gift from the Calcutta Kiwanis Klub to Marsopolis Kiwanians. It always looked at me as if it were sizing me up as an appetizer. It died when I was about five and I didn't know whether to be sorry or glad. It was beautiful . . . and so *very* Hungry.

But Earth is still many weeks away and, in the meantime, Venus does have some points of interest for the newcomer, such as I.

In traveling I strongly recommend traveling with my Uncle Tom. On arriving here, there were no silly waits in "Hospitality" (!) rooms; we were given the "courtesy of the port" at once—to the *extreme* chagrin of Mrs. Royer. "Courtesy of the port" means that your baggage isn't examined and that nobody bothers to look at that bulky mass of documents—passport and health record and security clearance and solvency proof and birth certificate and I.D.s, and nineteen other silly forms. Instead we were whisked from satellite station to spaceport in the private yacht of the Chairman of the Board and were met there by the Chairman himself!—and popped into his Rolls and wafted royally to Hilton Tannhäuser.[3]

2. The books by the American writer L. Frank Baum, which begin with *The Wonderful Wizard of Oz* (1900), in which Dorothy first arrives in the land of Oz, meets (among others) the Tin Woodman, and walks down the yellow-brick road; Tik-Tok, a mechanical man, is the title character of *Tik-Tok of Oz* (1914), and the Hungry Tiger is introduced in *Ozma of Oz* (1907).

3. Tannhäuser, a legendary German knight, became the lover of Venus in her enchanted mountain, Venusberg.

We were invited to stay at his official residence (his "cottage," that being the Venus word for a palace) but I don't think he really expected us to accept, because Uncle Tom just cocked his left or satirical eyebrow and, "Mr. Chairman, I don't think you would want me to appear to be bribed even if you manage it."

And the Chairman didn't seem offended at all; he just chuckled till his belly shook like Saint Nicholas' (whom he strongly resembles even to the beard and the red cheeks, although his eyes are cold even when he laughs, which is frequently).

"Senator," he said, "you know me better than that. My attempt to bribe you will be much more subtle. Perhaps through this young lady. Miss Podkayne, are you fond of jewelry?"

I told him honestly that I wasn't, very, because I always lose it. So he blinked and said to Clark, "How about you, son?"

Clark said, "I prefer cash."

The Chairman blinked again and said nothing.

Nor had he said anything to his driver when Uncle Tom declined the offer of his roof; nevertheless we flew straight to our hilton—which is why I don't think he ever expected us to stay with him.

But I am beginning to realize that this is not entirely a pleasure trip for Uncle Tom . . . and to grasp emotionally a fact known only intellectually in the past, i.e., Uncle Tom is not merely the best pinochle player in Marsopolis, he sometimes plays other games for higher stakes. I must confess that the what or why lies outside my admittedly youthful horizon—save that everyone knows that the Three-Planets conference is coming up.

Query: Could U.T. conceivably be involved in this? As a consultant or something? I hope not, as it might keep him tied up for weeks on Luna and I have no wish to waste time on a dreary ball of slag while the Wonders of Terra await me—and Uncle Tom just *might* be difficult about letting me go down to Earth without him.

But I wish still more strongly that Clark had not answered the Chairman truthfully.

Still, Clark would not sell out his own uncle for mere money.

On the other hand, Clark does not regard money as "mere." I must think about this—

But it is some comfort to realize that anyone who handed Clark a bribe would find that Clark had not only taken the bribe but the hand as well.

Possibly our suite at the Tannhäuser is intended as a bribe, too. Are we paying for it? I'm almost afraid to ask Uncle Tom, but I do know this: the servants that come with it won't accept tips. Not any. Although I very carefully studied up on the subject of tipping, both for Venus and Earth, so that I would know what to do when the time came—and it had been my understanding that *anyone* on Venus *always* accepts tips, even ushers in churches and bank tellers.

But not the servants assigned to us. I have two tiny little amber dolls, identical twins, who shadow me and would bathe me if I let them. They speak Portuguese but not Ortho—and at present my Portuguese is limited to "gobble-gobble" (which means "Thank you") and I have trouble explaining to them that I can dress and undress myself and I'm not too sure about their names—they both answer to "Maria."

Or at least I don't *think* they speak Ortho. I must think about this, too.

Venus is officially bilingual, Ortho and Portuguese, but I'll bet I heard at least twenty other languages the first hour we were down. German sounds like a man being choked to death, French sounds like a cat fight, while Spanish sounds like molasses gurgling gently out of a jug. Cantonese— Well, think of a man trying to vocalize Bach[4] who doesn't like Bach very much to start with.

Fortunately almost everybody understands Ortho as well. Except Maria and Maria. If true.

I could live a long time without the luxury of personal maids but I must admit that this hilton suite is quite a treat to a plain-living, wholesome Mars girl, namely me. Especially as I am in it quite a lot of the time and will be for a while yet. The ship's Surgeon, Dr. Torland, gave me many of the special inoculations needed for Venus on the trip here—an unpleasant subject I chose not to mention—but there still remain many more before it will be safe for me to go outside the city, or even very much into the city. As soon as we reached our suite a physician appeared and played chess on my back with scratches, red to move and mate in five moves—and three hours later I had several tens of welts, with something horrid that must be done about each of them.

Clark ducked out and didn't get his scratch tests until the next morning and I misdoubt he will die of Purple Itch or some such, were it not that his karma is so clearly reserving him for hanging. Uncle Tom refused the tests. He was through all this routine more than twenty years ago, and anyhow he claims that the too, too mortal flesh is merely a figment of the imagination.

So I am more or less limited for a few days to lavish living here in the Tannhäuser. If I go out, I must wear gloves and a mask even in the city. But one whole wall of the suite's salon becomes a stereo stage simply by voice request, either taped or piped live from any theater or club in Venusberg—and some of the "entertainment" has widened my sophistication unbelievably, especially when Uncle Tom is not around. I am beginning to realize that Mars is an essentially puritanical culture. Of course Venus doesn't actually have laws, just company regulations, none of which seems to be concerned with personal conduct. But I had been brought up to believe that Mars Republic is a free society—and I suppose it is. However, there is "freedom" and "freedom."

Here the Venus Corporation owns everything worth owning and runs everything that shows a profit, all in a fashion that would make Marsmen swoon. But I guess Venusmen would swoon at how straitlaced *we* are. I know this Mars girl blushed for the first time in I don't know when and switched off a show that I didn't really believe.

But the solly screen is far from being the only astonishing feature of this suite. It is so big that one should carry food and water when exploring it, and the salon is so huge that local storms appear distinctly possible. My private bath is a suite in itself, with so many gadgets in it that I ought to have an advanced degree in engineering before risking washing my hands. But I've learned how to use them all and purely love them! I had never dreamed that I had been limping along all my life without Utter Necessities.

Up to now my top ambition along these lines has been not to have to share a washstand with Clark, because it has never been safe to reach for my own Christmas-present cologne without checking to see that it is not nitric acid or worse! Clark regards a bathroom as an auxiliary chemistry lab; he's not much interested in staying clean.

But the most astonishing thing in our suite is the piano. No, no, dear, I don't mean a keyboard hooked into the sound system; I mean a *real* piano. Three legs. Made out

4. Of the several musicians in the Bach family, the most important was Johann Sebastian Bach (1685–1750).

of wood. Enormous. That odd awkward-graceful curved shape that doesn't fit any-thing else and can't be put in a corner. A top that opens up and lets you see that it really does have a harp inside and very complex machinery for making it work.

I think that there are just four real pianos on all of Mars, the one in the Museum that nobody plays and probably doesn't work, the one in Lowell Academy that no longer has a harp inside it, just wiring connections that make it really the same as any other piano, the one in the Rose House (as if any President ever had time to play a piano!), and the one in the Beaux Arts Hall that actually is played sometimes by visiting artists although I've never heard it. I don't think there can be another one, or it would have been banner-lined in the news, wouldn't you think?

This one was made by a man named Steinway[5] and it must have taken him a lifetime. I played Chopsticks on it (that being the best opus in my limited repertoire) until Uncle asked me to stop. Then I closed it up, keyboard and top, because I had seen Clark eying the machinery inside, and warned him sweetly but firmly that if he touched one finger to it I would break all his fingers while he was asleep. He wasn't listening but he knows I mean it. That piano is Sacred to the Muses and is not to be taken apart by our Young Archimedes.[6]

I don't care what the electronics engineers say; there is a vast difference between a "piano" and a *real* piano. No matter if their silly oscilloscopes "prove" that the sound is identical. It is like the difference between being warmly clothed—or climbing up in your Daddy's lap and getting *really* warm.

I haven't been under house arrest all the time; I've been to the casinos, with Girdie and with Dexter Cunha, Dexter being the son of Mr. Chairman of the Board Kurt Cunha. Girdie is leaving us here, going to stay on Venus, and it makes me sad.

I asked her, "Why?"

We were sitting alone in our palatial salon. Girdie is staying in this same hilton, in a room not very different nor much larger than her cabin in the *Tricorn*, and I guess I'm just mean enough that I wanted her to see the swank we were enjoying. But my excuse was to have her help me dress. For now I am wearing (Shudder!) *support* garments. Arch supports in my shoes and tight things here and there intended to keep me from spreading out like an amoeba—and I won't say what Clark calls them because Clark is rude, crude, unrefined, and barbaric.

I hate them. But at 84 percent of one standard gee, I need them despite all that exercise I took aboard ship. This alone is reason enough not to live on Venus, or on Earth, even if they were as delightful as Mars.

Girdie did help me—she had bought them for me in the first place—but she also made me change my makeup, one which I had most carefully copied out of the latest issue of *Aphrodite*.[7] She looked at me and said, "Go wash your face, Poddy. Then we'll start over."

I pouted out my lip and said, "Won't!" The one thing I had noticed most and quickest was that *every* female on Venus wears paint like a Red Indian shooting at the Good Guys in the sollies—even Maria and Maria wear three times as much makeup just to work in as Mother wears to a formal reception—and Mother doesn't wear any when working.

"Poddy, Poddy! Be a good girl."

---

5. I.e., the American piano manufacturer Stein-way (founded 1853), probably the best known in the world.
6. Greek mathematician and inventor (ca. 287–212 B.C.E.). The Muses: in Greek mythology, nine daughters of Memory who preside over the arts and all intellectual pursuits.
7. The Greek goddess equivalent to the Roman Venus.

"I *am* being a good girl. It's polite to do things the way the local people do them, I learned that when I was just a child. And look at yourself in the mirror!" Girdie was wearing as high-styled a Venusberg face-do as any in that magazine.

"I know what I look like. But I am more than twice your age and no one even suspects me of being young and sweet and innocent. Always be what you are, Poddy. Never pretend. Look at Mrs. Grew. She's a comfortable fat old woman. She isn't kittenish, she's just nice to be around."

"You want me to look like a hick tourist!"

"I want you to look like Poddy. Come, dear, we'll find a happy medium. I grant you that even the girls your age here wear more makeup than grown-up women do on Mars—so we'll compromise. Instead of painting you like a Venusberg trollop, we'll make you a young lady of good family and gentle breeding, one who is widely traveled and used to all sorts of customs and manners, and so calmly sure of herself that she knows what is best for her—totally uninfluenced by local fads."

Girdie is an artist, I must admit. She started with a blank canvas and worked on me for more than an hour—and when she got through, you couldn't see that I was wearing any makeup at all.

But here is what you could see: I was at least two years older (real years, Mars years, or about six Venus years); my face was thinner and my nose not pug at all and I looked ever so slightly world-weary in a sweet and tolerant way. My eyes were enormous.

"Satisfied?" she asked.

"I'm *beautiful!*"

"Yes, you are. Because you are still Poddy. All I've done is make a picture of Poddy the way she is going to be. Before long."

My eyes filled with tears and we had to blot them up very hastily and she repaired the damage. "Now," she said briskly, "all we need is a club. And your mask."

"What's the club for? And I won't wear a mask, not on top of this."

"The club is to beat off wealthy stockholders who will throw themselves at your feet. And you will wear your mask, or else we won't go."

We compromised. I wore the mask until we got there and Girdie promised to repair any damage to my face—and promised that she would coach me as many times as necessary until I could put on that lovely, lying face myself. The casinos are safe, or supposed to be—the air not merely filtered and conditioned but freshly regenerated, free of any trace of pollen, virus, colloidal suspension or whatever. This is because lots of tourists don't like to take all the long list of immunizations necessary actually to *live* on Venus; but the Corporation wouldn't think of letting a tourist get away unbled. So the hiltons are safe and the casinos are safe and a tourist can buy a health insurance policy from the Corporation for a very modest premium. Then he finds that he can cash his policy back in for gambling chips any time he wants to. I understand that the Corporation hasn't had to pay off on one of these policies very often.

Venusberg assaults the eye and ear even from inside a taxi. I believe in free enterprise; all Marsmen do, it's an article of faith and the main reason we *won't* federate with Earth (and be outvoted five hundred to one). But free enterprise is not enough excuse to blare in your ears and glare in your eyes every time you leave your own roof. The shops never close (I don't think anything ever closes in Venusberg) and full color and stereo ads climb right inside your taxi and sit in your lap and shout in your ear.

Don't ask me how this horrid illusion is produced. The engineer who invented it probably flew off on his own broom. This red devil about a meter high appeared between us and the partition separating us from the driver (there wasn't a sign of a solly receiver) and started jabbing at us with a pitchfork. "Get the Hi-Ho Habit!" it shrieked. "Everybody drinks Hi-Ho! Soothing, Habit-Forming. Dee-*lishus!* Get High with Hi-Ho!"

I shrank back against the cushions.

Girdie phoned the driver. "Please shut that thing off."

It faded down to just a pink ghost and the commercial dropped to a whisper while the driver answered, "Can't, madam. They rent the concession." Devil and noise came back on full blast.

And I learned something about tipping. Girdie took money from her purse, displayed one note. Nothing happened and she added a second; noise and image faded down again. She passed them through a slot to the driver and we weren't bothered any more. Oh, the transparent ghost of the red devil remained and a nagging whisper of his voice, until both were replaced by another ad just as faint—but we could talk. The giant ads in the street outside were noisier and more dazzling; I didn't see how the driver could see or hear to drive, especially as traffic was unbelievably thick and heart-stoppingly fast and frantic and he kept cutting in and out of lanes and up and down in levels as if he were trying utmostly to beat Death to a hospital.

By the time we slammed to a stop on the roof of Dom Pedro Casino I figure Death wasn't more than half a lap behind.

I learned later why they drive like that. The hackie is an employee of the Corporation, like most everybody—but he is an "enterprise-employee," not on wages. Each day he has to take in a certain amount in fares to "make his nut"—the Corporation gets all of this. After he has rolled up that fixed number of paid kilometers, he splits the take with the Corporation on all other fares the rest of the day. So he drives like mad to pay off the nut as fast as possible and start making some money himself—then keeps on driving fast because he's got to get his while the getting is good.

Uncle Tom says that most people on Earth have much the same deal, except it's done by the year and they call it income tax.

> In Xanadu did Kubla Khan
> A stately pleasure dome decree[8]—

Dom Pedro Casino is like that. Lavish. Beautiful. Exotic. The arch over the entrance proclaims EVERY DIVERSION IN THE KNOWN UNIVERSE, and from what I hear this may well be true. However, all Girdie and I visited were the gaming rooms.

I never saw so much money in my whole life!

A sign outside the gambling sector read:

> **HELLO, SUCKER!**
> **All Games Are Honest**
> **All Games Have a House Percentage**
> **YOU CAN'T WIN!**
> **So Come On In and Have Fun—**
> **(While We Prove It)**
> *Checks Accepted. All Credit*
> *Cards Honored. Free Breakfast*
> *and a Ride to Your Hilton When*
> *You Go Broke. Your Host,*
> **DOM PEDRO**

---

8. From "Kubla Khan" (1816), by Samuel Taylor Coleridge.

I said, "Girdie, there really is somebody named Dom Pedro?"

She shrugged. "He's an employee and that's not his real name. But he does look like an emperor. I'll point him out. You can meet him if you like and he'll kiss your hand. If you like that sort of thing. Come on."

She headed for the roulette tables while I tried to see everything at once. It was like being on the inside of a kaleidoscope. People beautifully dressed (employees mostly), people dressed every sort of way, from formal evening wear to sports shorts (tourists mostly), bright lights, staccato music, click and tinkle and shuffle and snap, rich hangings, armed guards in comic-opera uniforms, trays of drinks and food, nervous excitement, and money everywhere—

I stopped suddenly, so Girdie stopped. My brother Clark. Seated at a crescent-shaped table at which a beautiful lady was dealing cards. In front of him several tall stacks of chips and an imposing pile of paper money.

I should not have been startled. If you think that a six-year-old boy (or eighteen-year-old boy if you use their years) wouldn't be allowed to gamble in Venusberg, then you haven't been to Venus. Never mind what we do in Marsopolis, here there are just two requirements to gamble: a) you have to be alive; b) you have to have money. You don't have to be able to talk Portuguese or Ortho, nor any known language; as long as you can nod, wink, grunt, or flip a tendril, they'll take your bet. And your shirt.

No, I shouldn't have been surprised. Clark heads straight for money the way ions head for an electrode. Now I knew where he had ducked out to the first night and where he had been most of the time since.

I went up and tapped him on the shoulder. He didn't look around at once but a man popped up out of the rug like a genie from a lamp and had me by the arm. Clark said to the dealer, "Hit me," and looked around. "Hi, Sis. It's all right, Joe, she's my sister."

"Okay?" the man said doubtfully, still holding my arm.

"Sure, sure. She's harmless. Sis, this is Josie Mendoza, company cop, on lease to me for tonight. Hi, Girdie!" Clark's voice was suddenly enthusiastic. But he remembered to say, "Joe, slip into my seat and watch the stuff. Girdie, this is swell! You gonna play black jack? You can have my seat."

(It must be love, dears. Or a high fever.)

She explained that she was about to play roulette. "Want me to come help?" he said eagerly. "I'm pretty good on the wheel, too."

She explained to him gently that she did not want help because she was working on a system, and promised to see him later in the evening. Girdie is unbelievably patient with Clark. I would have—

Come to think of it, she's unbelievably patient with me.

If Girdie has a system for roulette, it didn't show. We found two stools together and she tried to give me a few chips. I didn't want to gamble and told her so, and she explained that I would have to stand up if I didn't. Considering what 84 percent gee does to my poor feet I bought a few chips of my own and did just what she did, which was to place minimum bets on the colors, or on odd or even. This way you don't win, you don't lose—except that once in a long while the little ball lands on zero and you lose a chip permanently (that "house percentage" the sign warned against).

The croupier could see what we were doing but we actually were gambling and inside the rules; he didn't object. I discovered almost at once that the trays of food circulating and the drinks were absolutely free—to anyone who was gambling. Girdie had a glass of wine. I don't touch alcoholic drinks even on birthdays—and I certainly wasn't going to drink Hi-Ho, after that obnoxious ad!—but I ate two or three sandwiches and asked for, and got—they had to go get it—a glass of milk. I tipped the amount I saw Girdie tip.

We had been there over an hour and I was maybe three or four chips ahead when I happened to sit up straight—and knocked a glass out of the hand of a man standing behind me, all over him, some over me.

"Oh, dear!" I said, jumping down from my stool and trying to dab off the wet spots on him with my kerchief. "I'm terribly sorry!"

He bowed. "No harm done to me. Merely soda water. But I fear my clumsiness has ruined milady's gown."

Out of one corner of her mouth Girdie said, "Watch it, kid!" but I answered, "This dress? Huh uh! If that was just water, there won't be a wrinkle or a spot in ten minutes. Travel clothes."

"You are a visitor to our city? Then permit me to introduce myself less informally than by soaking you to the skin." He whipped out a card. Girdie was looking grim but I rather liked his looks. Actually not impossibly older than I am (I guessed at twelve Mars years, or say thirty-six of his own—and it turned out he was only thirty-two). He was dressed in the very elegant Venus evening wear, with cape and stick and formal ruff . . . and the cutest little waxed mustaches.

The card read:

DEXTER KURT CUNHA, STK.

I read it, then reread it, then said, "Dexter *Kurt* Cunha— Are you any relation to—"
"My father."
"Why, I know your father!"—and put out my hand.

Ever had your hand kissed? It makes chill bumps that race up your arm, across your shoulders, and down the other arm—and of course nobody would ever do it on Mars. This is a distinct shortcoming in our planet and one I intend to correct, even if I have to bribe Clark to institute the custom.

By the time we had names straight, Dexter was urging us to share a bite of supper and some dancing with him in the roof garden. But Girdie was balky. "Mr. Cunha," she said, "that is a very handsome calling card. But I am responsible for Podkayne to her uncle—and I would rather see your I.D."

For a split second he looked chilly. Then he smiled warmly at her and said, "I can do better," and held up one hand.

The most imposing old gentleman I have ever seen hurried over. From the medals on his chest I would say that he had won every spelling contest from first grade on. His bearing was kingly and his costume unbelievable. "Yes, Stockholder?"

"Dom Pedro, will you please identify me to these ladies?"

"With pleasure, sir." So Dexter was really Dexter and I got my hand kissed again. Dom Pedro does it with great flourish but it didn't have quite the same effect—I don't think he puts his heart into it the way Dexter does.

Girdie insisted on stopping to collect Clark—and Clark suffered an awful moment of spontaneous schizophrenia, for he was still winning. But love won out and Girdie went up on Clark's arm, with Josie trailing us with the loot. I must say I admire my brother in some ways; spending cash money to protect his winnings must have caused even deeper conflict in his soul, if any, than leaving the game while he was winning.

The roof garden is the Brasilia Room and is even more magnificent than the casino proper, with a night-sky roof to match its name, stars and the Milky Way and the

Southern Cross such as nobody ever in history actually saw from anywhere on Venus. Tourists were lined up behind a velvet rope waiting to get in—but not us. It was, "This way, if you please, Stockholder," to an elevated table right by the floor and across from the orchestra and a perfect view of the floor show.

We danced and we ate foods I've never heard of and I let a glass of champagne be poured for me but didn't try to drink it because the bubbles go up my nose—and wished for a glass of milk or at least a glass of water because some of the food was quite spicy, but didn't ask for it.

But Dexter leaned over me and said, "Poddy, my spies tell me that you like milk."

"I do!"

"So do I. But I'm too shy to order it unless I have somebody to back me up." He raised a finger and two glasses of milk appeared instantly.

But I noticed that he hardly touched his.

However, I did not realize I had been hoaxed until later. A singer, part of the floor show, a tall handsome dark girl dressed as a gypsy—if gypsies did ever dress that way, which I doubt, but she was billed as "Romany Rose"—toured the ringside tables singing topical verses to a popular song.

She stopped in front of us, looked right at me and smiled, struck a couple of chords and sang:

> "Poddy Fries-uh came to town,
> Pretty, winsome Poddy—
> Silver shoes and sky blue gown,
> Lovely darling Podkayne—
>
> "She has sailed the starry sea,
> Pour another toddy!
> Lucky Dexter, lucky we!
> Drink a toast to Poddy!"

And everybody clapped and Clark pounded on the table and Romany Rose curtsied to me and I started to cry and covered my face with my hands and suddenly remembered that I mustn't cry because of my makeup and dabbed at my eyes with my napkin and hoped I hadn't ruined it, and suddenly silver buckets with champagne appeared all over that big room and everybody *did* drink a toast to me, standing up when Dexter stood up in a sudden silence brought on by a roll of drums and a crashing chord from the orchestra.

I was speechless and just barely knew enough to stay seated myself and nod and try to smile when he looked at me—

—and he broke his glass, just like story tapes, and everybody imitated him and for a while there was crash and tinkle all over the room, and I felt like Ozma just after she stops being Tip and is Ozma again[9] and I had to remember my makeup very hard indeed!

Later on, after I had gulped my stomach back into place and could stand up without trembling, I danced with Dexter again. He is a dreamy dancer—a firm, sure lead

---

9. At the end *The Marvelous Land of Oz* (1904), Baum's second Oz book, the main character, Tip, is revealed to be Ozma, the rightful ruler of Oz, who had been magically transformed into a boy as an infant; when restored to her proper form, she is an exquisitely beautiful girl.

without ever turning it into a wrestling match. During a slow waltz I said, "Dexter? *You* spilled that glass of soda water. On purpose."

"Yes. How did you know?"

"Because it *is* a sky-blue dress—or the color that is called 'sky-blue,' for Earth, although I've never seen a sky this color. And my shoes *are* silvered. So it couldn't have been an accident. Any of it."

He just grinned, not a bit ashamed. "Only a little of it. I went first to your hilton— and it took almost half an hour to find out who had taken you where and I was furious, because Papa would have been most vexed. But I found you."

I chewed that over and didn't like the taste. "Then you did it because your daddy told you to. Told you to entertain me because I'm Uncle Tom's niece."

"No, Poddy."

"Huh? Better check through the circuits again. That's how the numbers read."

"No, Poddy. Papa would never order me to entertain a lady—other than formally, at our cottage—lady on my arm at dinner, that sort of thing. What he did do was show me a picture of you and ask me if I wanted to. And I decided I did want to. But it wasn't a very good picture of you, didn't do you justice—just one snapped by one of the servants of the Tannhäuser when you didn't know it."

(I decided I had to find some way to get rid of Maria and Maria, a girl needs privacy. Although this hadn't turned out too dry.)

But he was still talking. ". . . and when I did find you I almost didn't recognize you, you were so much more dazzling than the photograph. I almost shied off from introducing myself. Then I got the wonderful idea of turning it into an accident. I stood behind you with that glass of soda water almost against your elbow for so long the bubbles all went out of it—and when you did move, you bumped me so gently I had to slop it over myself to make it enough of an accident to let me be properly apologetic." He grinned most disarmingly.

"I see," I said. "But look, Dexter, the photograph was probably a very good one. This isn't my own face." I explained what Girdie had done.

He shrugged. "Then someday wash it for me and let me look at the real Poddy. I'll bet I'll recognize her. Look, dear, the accident was only half fake, too. We're even."

"What do you mean?"

"They named me 'Dexter' for my maternal grandfather, before they found out I was left-handed. Then it was a case of either renaming me 'Sinister,'[1] which doesn't sound too well—or changing me over to right-handed. But that didn't work out either; it just made me the clumsiest man on three planets." (This while twirling me through a figure eight!)

"I'm always spilling things, knocking things over. You can follow me by the sound of fractured frangibles. The problem was not to cause an accident, but to keep from spilling that water until the right instant." He grinned that impish grin. "I feel very triumphant about it. But forcing me out of left-handedness did something else to me too. It's made me a rebel—and I think you are one, too."

"Uh . . . maybe."

"I certainly am. I am expected to be Chairman of the Board someday, like my papa and my grandpapa. But I shan't. I'm going to space!"

"Oh! So am I!" We stopped dancing and chattered about spacing. Dexter intends to be an explorer captain, just like me—only I didn't quite admit that my plans for

---

1. *Sinister*, in Latin, means "left"; *dexter* means "right."

spacing included pilot and master; it is never well in dealing with a male to let him know that you think *you* can do whatever it is he can do best or wants to do most. But Dexter intends to go to Cambridge and study paramagnetics and Davis mechanics and be ready when the first true starships are ready. Goodness!

"Poddy, maybe we'll even do it together. Lots of billets for women in starships."

I agreed that that was so.

"But let's talk about you. Poddy, it wasn't that you looked so much better than your picture."

"No?" (I felt vaguely disappointed.)

"No. Look. I know your background, I know you've lived all your life in Marsopolis. Me, I've been everywhere. Sent to Earth for school, took the Grand Tour while I was there, been to Luna, of course, and all over Venus—and to Mars. When you were a little girl and I wish I had met you then."

"Thank you." (I was beginning to feel like a poor relation.)

"So I know exactly what a honky-tonk town Venusberg is . . . and what a shock it is to people the first time. Especially anyone reared in a gentle and civilized place like Marsopolis. Oh, I love my hometown but I know what it is— I've been other places. Poddy? Look at me, Poddy. The thing that impressed me about you was your aplomb."

"Me?"

"Your amazing and perfect savoir-faire . . . under conditions I *knew* were strange to you. Your uncle has been everywhere—and Girdie, I take it, has been, too. But lots of strangers here, older women, become quite giddy when first exposed to the fleshpots of Venusberg and behave frightfully. But you carry yourself like a queen. Savoir-faire."

(This man I liked! Definitely. After years and years of "Beat it, runt!" it does something to a woman to be told she has savoir-faire. I didn't even stop to wonder if he told all the girls that—I didn't want to!)

We didn't stay much longer; Girdie made it plain that I had to get my "beauty sleep." So Clark went back to his game (Josie appeared out of nowhere at the right time—and I thought of telling Clark he had better git fer home too, but I decided that wasn't "savoir-faire" and anyhow he wouldn't have listened) and Dexter took us to the Tannhäuser in his papa's Rolls (or maybe his own, I don't know) and bowed over our hands and kissed them as he left us.

I was wondering if he would try to kiss me good night and had made up my mind to be cooperative about it. But he didn't try. Maybe it's not a Venusberg custom, I don't know.

Girdie went up with me because I wanted to chatter. I bounced myself on a couch and said, "Oh, Girdie, it's been the most wonderful night of my life!"

"It hasn't been a bad night for me," she said quietly. "It certainly can't hurt me to have met the son of the Chairman of the Board." It was then that she told me that she was staying on Venus.

"But, Girdie—*why*?"

"Because I'm broke, dear. I need a job."

"You? But you're *rich*. Everybody knows that."

She smiled. "I *was* rich, dear. But my last husband went through it all. He was an optimistic man and excellent company. But not nearly the businessman he thought he was. So now Girdie must gird her loins and get to work. Venusberg is better than Earth for that. Back home I could either be a parasite on my old friends until they got sick of me—the chronic house guest—or get one of them to give me a job that would really be charity, since I don't know anything. Or disappear into the lower depths and change my name. Here, nobody cares and there is always work for anyone who wants to work. I don't drink and I don't gamble—Venusberg is made to order for me."

"But what will you *do?*" It was hard to imagine her as anything but the rich society girl whose parties and pranks were known even on Mars.

"Croupier, I hope. They make the highest wages . . . and I've been studying it. But I've been practicing dealing, too—for black jack, or faro, or chemin de fer. But I'll probably have to start as a change girl."

"*Change girl?* Girdie—would you dress that way?"

She shrugged. "My figure is still good . . . and I'm quite quick at counting money. It's honest work, Poddy—it has to be. Those change girls often have as much as ten thousand on their trays."

I decided I had fubbed and shut up. I guess you can take the girl out of Marsopolis but you can't quite take Marsopolis out of the girl. Those change girls practically don't wear anything but the trays they carry money on—but it certainly was honest work and Girdie has a figure that had all the junior officers in the *Tricorn* running in circles and dropping one wing. I'm sure she could have married any of the bachelors and insured her old age thereby with no effort.

Isn't it more honest to work? And, if so, why shouldn't she capitalize her assets?

She kissed me good night soon after and ordered me to go right to bed and to sleep. Which I did—all but the sleep. Well, she wouldn't be a change girl long; she'd be a croupier in a beautiful evening gown . . . and saving her wages and her tips . . . and someday she would be a stockholder, one share anyway, which is all anybody needs for old age in the Venus Corporation. And I would come back and visit her when I was famous.

I wondered if I could ask Dexter to put in a word for her to Dom Pedro?

Then I thought about Dexter—

I know that can't be love; I was in love once and it feels entirely different. It hurts. This just feels grand.

X

I hear that Clark has been negotiating to sell me (black market, of course) to one of the concessionaires who ship wives out to contract colonists in the bush. Or so they say. I do not know the truth. But There Are Rumors.

What infuriates me is that he is said to be offering me at a ridiculously low price!

But in truth it is this very fact that convinces me that it is just a rumor, carefully planted by Clark himself, to annoy me—because, while I would not put it past Clark to sell me into what is tantamount to chattel slavery and a Life of Shame if he could get away with it, nevertheless he would wring out of the sordid transaction every penny the traffic would bear. This is certain.

It is much more likely that he is suffering a severe emotional reaction from having opened up and become almost human with me the other night—and therefore found it necessary to counteract it with this rumor in order to restore our relations to their normal, healthy, cold-war status.

Actually I don't think he could get away with it, even on the black market, because I don't have any contract with the Corporation and even if he forged one, I could always manage to get a message to Dexter, and Clark knows this. Girdie tells me that the black market in wives lies mostly in change girls or clerks or hilton chambermaids who haven't managed to snag husbands in Venusberg (where men are in short supply) and are willing to cooperate in being sold out back (where women are scarce) in order to jump their contracts. They don't squawk and the Corporation overlooks the matter.

Most of the bartered brides, of course, are single women among the immigrants, right off a ship. The concessionaires pay their fare and squeeze whatever cumshaw they can out of the women themselves and the miners or ranchers to whom their contracts are assigned. All Kosher.

Not that I understand it—I don't understand *anything* about how this planet really works. No laws, just Corporate regulations. Want to get married? Find somebody who claims to be a priest or a preacher and have any ceremony you like—but it hasn't any legal standing because it is not a contract with the Corporation. Want a divorce? Pack your clothes and get out, leaving a note or not as you see fit. Illegitimacy? They've never heard of it. A baby is a baby and the Corporation won't let one want, because that baby will grow up and be an employee and Venus has a chronic labor shortage. Polygamy? Polyandry? Who cares? The Corporation doesn't.

Bodily assault? Don't try it in Venusberg; it is the most thoroughly policed city in the system—violent crime is bad for business. I don't wander around alone in some parts of Marsopolis, couth as my hometown is, because some of the old sand rats are a bit sunstruck and not really responsible. But I'm perfectly safe alone anywhere in Venusberg; the only assault I risk is from super salesmanship.

(The bush is another matter. Not the people so much, but Venus itself is lethal— and there is always a chance of encountering a Venerian who has gotten hold of a grain of happy dust. Even the little wingety fairies are bloodthirsty if they sniff happy dust.)

Murder? This is a *very* serious violation of regulations. You'll have your pay checked for years and years and years to offset both that employee's earning power for what would have been his working life . . . and his putative value to the Corporation, all calculated by the company's actuaries who are widely known to have no hearts at all, just liquid helium pumps.

So if you are thinking of killing anybody on Venus, *don't do it!* Lure him to a planet where murder is a social matter and all they do is hang you or something. No future in it on Venus.

There are three classes of people on Venus: stockholders, employees, and a large middle ground. Stockholder-employees (Girdie's ambition), enterprise employees (taxi drivers, ranchers, prospectors, some retailers, etc.), and of course future employees, children still being educated. And there are tourists but tourists aren't people; they have more the status of steers in a cattle pen—valuable assets to be treated with great consideration but no pity.

A person from out-planet can be a tourist for an hour or a lifetime—just as long as his money holds out. No visa, no rules of any sort, everybody welcome. But you must have a return ticket and you can't cash it in until *after* you sign a contract with the Corporation. If you do. I wouldn't.

I still don't understand how the system works even though Uncle Tom has been very patient in explaining. But he says he doesn't understand it either. He calls it "corporate fascism"—which explains nothing—and says that he can't make up his mind whether it is the grimmest tyranny the human race has ever known . . . or the most perfect democracy in history.

He says that nothing here is as bad in many ways as the conditions over 90 percent of the people on Earth endure, and that it isn't even as bad in creature comforts and standard of living as lots of people on Mars, especially the sand rats, even though we never knowingly let anyone starve or lack medical attention.

I Just Don't Know. I can see now that all my life I have simply taken for granted the way we do things on Mars. Oh, sure, I learned about other systems in school—but it didn't soak in. Now I am beginning to grasp emotionally that There Are Other Ways Than Ours . . . and that people can be happy under them. Take Girdie. I can see why she didn't want to stay on Earth, not the way things had changed for her. But she could have stayed on Mars; she's just the sort of high-class immigrant we want. But Mars didn't tempt her at all.

This bothered me because (as you may have gathered) I think Mars is just about perfect. And I think Girdie is just about perfect.

Yet a horrible place like Venusberg is what she picked. She says it is a Challenge.

Furthermore Uncle Tom says that she is Dead Right; Girdie will have Venusberg eating out of her hand in two shakes and be a stockholder before you can say Extra Dividend.

I guess he's right. I felt awfully sorry for Girdie when I found out she was broke. "I wept that I had no shoes—till I met a man who had no feet."[2] Like that, I mean. I've never been broke, never missed any meals, never worried about the future—yet I used to feel sorry for Poddy when money was a little tight around home and I couldn't have a new party dress. Then I found out that the rich and glamorous Miss FitzSnugglie (I still won't use her right name, it wouldn't be fair) had only her ticket back to Earth and had borrowed the money for that. I was so sorry I hurt.

But now I'm beginning to realize that Girdie has "feet" no matter what—and will always land on them.

She has indeed been a change girl, for two whole nights—and asked me please to see to it that Clark did not go to Dom Pedro Casino those nights. I don't think she cared at all whether or not I saw her . . . but she knows what a horrible case of puppy love Clark has on her and she's just so sweet and good all through that she did not want to risk making it worse and/or shocking him.

But she's a dealer now and taking lessons for croupier—and Clark goes there every night. But she won't let him play at her table. She told him point-blank that he could know her socially or professionally, but not both—and Clark never argues with the inevitable; he plays at some other table and tags her around whenever possible.

Do you suppose that my kid brother actually does possess psionic powers? I know he's not a telepath, else he would have cut my throat long since. But he is still winning.

Dexter assures me that a) the games are absolutely honest, and b) no one can possibly beat them, not in the long run, because the house collects its percentage no matter what. "Certainly you can win, Poddy," he assured me. "One tourist came here last year and took home over half a million. We paid it happily—and advertised it all over Earth—and still made money the very week he struck it rich. Don't you even suspect that we are giving your brother a break. If he keeps it up long enough, we will not only win it all back but take every buck he started with. If he's as smart as you say he is, he'll quit while he's ahead. But most people aren't that smart—and Venus Corporation never gambles on anything but a sure thing."

Again, I don't know. But it was both Girdie and winning that caused Clark to become almost human with me. For a while.

It was last week, the night I met Dexter—and Girdie told me to go to bed and I did but I couldn't sleep and I left my door open so that I could hear Clark come in—or if I didn't, phone somebody and have him chased home because, while Uncle Tom

2. Often described as an Arabian proverb, this saying appears in a slightly different form in Sa'di's *The Gulistān, or Rose Garden* (1258), story 19.

is responsible for both of us, I'm responsible for Clark and always have been. I wanted Clark to be home and in bed before Uncle Tom got up. Habit, I guess.

He did come sneaking in about two hours after I did and I *psst'd* to him and he came into my room.

You never saw a six-year-old boy with so much money!

Josie had seen him to our door, so he said. Don't ask me why he didn't put it in the Tannhäuser's vault—or do ask me: I think he wanted to fondle it.

He certainly wanted to boast. He laid it out in stacks on my bed, counting it and making sure that I knew how much it was. He even shoved a pile toward me. "Need some, Poddy? I won't even charge you interest—plenty more where this came from."

I was breathless. Not the money, I didn't need any money. But the offer. There have been times in the past when Clark has lent me money against my allowance—and charged me exactly 100 percent interest come allowance day. Till Daddy caught on and spanked us both.

So I thanked him most sincerely and hugged him. Then he said, "Sis, how old would you say Girdie is?"

I began to understand his off-the-curve behavior. "I really couldn't guess," I answered carefully. (Didn't need to guess, I knew.) "Why don't you ask her?"

"I did. She just smiled at me and said that women don't have birthdays."

"Probably an Earth custom," I told him and let it go at that. "Clark, how in the world did you win so much money?"

"Nothing to it," he said. "All those games, somebody wins, somebody loses. I just make sure I'm one who wins."

"But how?"

He just grinned his worst grin.

"How much money did you start with?"

He suddenly looked guarded. But he was still amazingly mellow, for Clark, so I pushed ahead. I said, "Look, if I know you, you can't get all your fun out of it unless *somebody* knows, and you're safer telling me than anyone else. Because I've never told on you yet. Now have I?"

He admitted that this was true by not answering—and it is true. When he was small enough, I used to clip him one occasionally. But I never tattled on him. Lately clipping him has become entirely too dangerous; he can give me a fat lip quicker than I can give him one. But I've never tattled on him. "Loosen up," I urged him. "I'm the only one you dare boast to. How much were you paid to sneak those three kilos into the *Tricorn* in my baggage?"

He looked very smug. "Enough."

"Okay. I won't pry any further about that. But what was it you smuggled? You've had me utterly baffled."

"You would have found it if you hadn't been so silly anxious to explore the ship. Poddy, you're stupid. You know that, don't you? You're as predictable as the law of gravity. I can *always* outguess you."

I didn't get mad. If Clark gets you sore, he's got you.

"Guess maybe," I admitted. "Are you going to tell me what it was? Not happy dust, I hope?"

"Oh, no!" he said and looked shocked. "You know what they do to you for happy dust around here? They turn you over to natives who are hopped up with it, that's what they do—and then they don't even have to bother to cremate you."

I shuddered and returned to the subject. "Going to tell me?"

"*Mmm . . .*"

"I swear by Saint Podkayne Not to Tell." This is my own private oath, nobody else would or could use it.

"By Saint Podkayne!" (And I should have kept my lip zipped.)

"Okay," he said. "But you swore it. A bomb."

"A *what?*"

"Oh, not much of a bomb. Just a little squeezer job. Total destruction not more than a kilometer. Nothing much."

I reswallowed my heart. "Why a bomb? And what did you do with it?"

He shrugged. "They were stupid. They paid me this silly amount, see? Just to sneak this little package aboard. Gave me a lot of north wind about how it was meant to be a surprise for the Captain—and that I should give it to him at the Captain's party, last night out. Gift wrapped and everything. 'Sonny,' this silly zero says to me, 'just keep it out of sight and let him be surprised—because last night out is not only the Captain's party, it's his birthday.'

"Now, Sis, you know I wouldn't swallow anything like that. If it had really been a birthday present they would just have given it to the Purser to hold—no need to bribe me. So I just played stupid and kept jacking up the price. And the idiots paid me. They got real jumpy when time came to shove us through passport clearance and paid all I asked. So I shoved it into your bag while you were yakking to Uncle Tom— then saw to it you didn't get inspected.

"Then the minute we were aboard I went to get it—and got held up by a stewardess spraying your cabin and had to do a fast job and go back to relock your bag because Uncle Tom came back in looking for his pipe. That first night I opened the thing in the dark—and opened it from the bottom; I already had a hunch what it might be."

"Why?"

"Sis, use your brain. Don't just sit there and let it rust out. First they offer me what they probably figured was big money to a kid. When I turn it down, they start to sweat and up the ante. I kept crowding it and the money got important. And more important. They don't even give me a tale about how a man with a flower in his lapel will come aboard at Venus and give me a password. It *has* to be that they don't care what happens to it as long as it gets into the ship. What does that add up to? Logic."

He added, "So I opened it and took it apart. Time bomb. Set for three days after we space. *Blooey!*"

I shivered, thinking about it.

"What a horrible thing to do!"

"It could have turned out pretty dry," he admitted, "if I had been as stupid as they thought I was."

"But why would anybody want to do such a thing?"

"Didn't want the ship to get to Venus."

"But *why?*"

"You figure it out. I have."

"Uh . . . what did you do with it?"

"Oh, I saved it. The essential pieces. Never know when you might need a bomb."

And that's all I got out of him—and here I am stuck with a Saint Podkayne oath. And nineteen questions left unanswered. Was there *really* a bomb? Or was I swindled by my brother's talent for improvising explanations that throw one off the obvious track? If there was, *where is it?* Still in the *Tricorn?* Right here in this suite? In an innocent-looking package in the safe of the Tannhäuser? Or parked with his private bodyguard, Josie? Or a thousand other places in this big city? Or is it still more likely that I simply made a mistake of three kilograms in my excitement and that Clark was snooping just to be snooping? (Which he will always do if not busy otherwise.)

No way to tell. So I decided to squeeze what else I could from this Moment of Truth—if it was one. "I'm awful glad you found it," I said. "But the slickest thing you ever did was that dye job on Mrs. Garcia and Mrs. Royer. Girdie admires it, too."

"She does?" he said eagerly.

"She certainly does. But I never let on you did it. So you can still tell her yourself, if you want to."

"Mmm . . ." He looked quite happy. "I gave Old Lady Royer a little extra, just for luck. Put a mouse in her bed."

"Clark! Oh, wonderful! But where did you get a mouse?"

"Made a deal with the ship's cat."

I wish I had a nice, normal, slightly stupid family. It would be a lot more comfortable. Still, Clark has his points.

But I haven't had too much time to worry about my brother's High Crimes and Misdemeanors; Venusberg offers too much to divert the adolescent female with a hitherto unsuspected taste for high living. Especially Dexter—

I am no longer a leper; I can now go anywhere, even outside the city, without wearing a filter snout that makes me look like a blue-eyed pig—and dashing, darling Dexter has been most flatteringly eager to escort me everywhere. Even shopping. Using both hands a girl could spend a national debt there on clothes alone. But I am being (almost) sensible and spending only that portion of my cash assets earmarked for Venus. If I were not firm with him, Dexter would buy me anything I admire, just by lifting his finger. (He never carries any money, not even a credit card, and even his tipping is done by some unobvious credit system.) But I haven't let him buy me anything more important than a fancy ice cream sundae; I have no intention of jeopardizing my amateur status for some pretty clothes. But I don't feel too compromised over ice cream and fortunately I do not as yet have to worry about my waistline—I'm hollow clear to my ankles.

So, after a hard day of sweating over the latest Rio styles Dexter takes me to an ice cream parlor—one that bears the same relation to our Plaza Sweet Shoppe that the *Tricorn* does to a sand car—and he sits and toys with café au lait and watches in amazement while I eat. First some little trifle like an everlasting strawberry soda, then more serious work on a sundae composed by a master architect from creams and syrups and imported fruits and nuts of course, and perhaps a couple of tens of scoops of ice cream in various flavors and named "The Taj Mahal" or "The Big Rock Candy Mountain" or such.

(Poor Girdie! She diets like a Stylite[3] every day of the year. Query: Will I ever make that sacrifice to remain svelte and glamorous? Or will I get comfortably fat like Mrs. Grew? Echo Answereth Not and I'm not afraid to listen.)

I've had to be firm with him in other ways, too, but much less obviously. Dexter turns out to be a master of seductive logic and is ever anxious to tell me a bedtime story. But I have no intention of being a Maid Betrayed, not at my age. The tragedy about Romeo and Juliet[4] is not that they died so young but that the boy-meets-girl reflex should be so overpowering as to defeat all common sense.

My own reflexes are fine, thank you, and my hormonal balance is just dandy. Dexter's fruitless overtures give me a nice warm feeling at the pit of my stomach and hike up my metabolism. Perhaps I should feel insulted at his dastardly intentions

---

3. One of the Christian ascetics who lived in isolation on top of a pillar and mortified their flesh; the practice was begun by Simeon Stylites the Elder in 423.

4. In Shakespeare's play *Romeo and Juliet* (1595).

toward me—and possibly I would, at home, but this is Venusberg, where the distinction between a shameful proposition and a formal proposal of honorable marriage lies only in the mind and would strain a semantician to define. For all I know, Dexter already has seven wives at home, numbered for the days of the week. I haven't asked him, as I have no intention of becoming number eight, on any basis.

I talked this over with Girdie and asked why I didn't feel "insulted." Had they left the moral circuits out of my cybernet, as they so obviously did with my brother Clark?

Girdie smiled her sweet and secret smile that always means she is thinking about something she doesn't intend to be fully frank about. Then she said, "Poddy, girls are taught to be 'insulted' at such offers for their own protection—and it is a good idea, quite as good an idea as keeping a fire extinguisher handy even though you don't expect a fire. But you are right; it is not an insult, it is never an insult—it is the one utterly honest tribute to a woman's charm and femininity that a man can offer her. The rest of what they tell us is mostly polite lies . . . but on this one subject a man is nakedly honest. I don't see any reason ever to be insulted if a man is polite and gallant about it."

I thought about it. "Maybe you're right, Girdie. I guess it is a compliment, in a way. But why is it that that is all a boy is ever after? Nine times out of ten anyhow."

"You've got it just backwards, Poddy. Why should he *ever* be after anything else? Millions of years of evolution is the logic behind every proposition. Just be glad that the dears have learned to approach the matter with handkissing instead of a club. Some of them, anyhow. It gives us more choice in the matter than we've ever had before in all history. It's a woman's world today, dear—enjoy it and be grateful."

I had never thought of it that way. When I've thought of it at all, I've mostly been groused because it is so hard for a girl to break into a "male" profession, such as piloting.

I've been doing some hard thinking about piloting—and have concluded that there are more ways of skinning a cat than buttering it with parsnips. Do I *really* want to be a "famous explorer captain"? Or would I be just as happy to be some member of his crew?

Oh, I want to space, let there be no doubt about that! My one little trip from Mars to Venus makes me certain that travel is for me. I'd rather be a junior stewardess in the *Tricorn* than President of the Republic. Shipboard life is fun; you take your home and your friends along with you while you go romantic new places—and with Davis-drive starships being built those places are going to be newer and more romantic every year. And Poddy is going to go, somehow. I was born to roam—

But let's not kid ourselves, shall we? Is anybody going to let Poddy captain one of those multimegabuck ships?

Dexter's chances are a hundred times as good as mine. He's as smart as I am, or almost; he'll have the best education for it that money can buy (while I'm loyal to Ares U., I know it is a hick college compared with where he plans to go); and also it is quite possible that his daddy could *buy* him a Star Rover ship. But the clincher is that Dexter is twice as big as I am and male. Even if you leave his father's wealth out of the equation, which one of us gets picked?

But all is not lost. Consider Theodora, consider Catherine the Great.[5] Let a man

5. Empress of Russia (1729–1796; r. 1762–96). Theodora (ca. 500–548), a beautiful actress who as wife of Justinian I (m. 525), emperor of the Eastern Roman Empire, exerted great political influence. A later Theodora (980–1056) became joint ruler (in 1042) and then sole ruler (in 1055) of the Eastern Roman Empire.

boss the job . . . then boss that man. I am not opposed to marriage. (But if Dexter wants to marry me—or anything—he'll have to follow me to Marsopolis where we are pretty old-fashioned about such things. None of this lighthearted Venusberg stuff.) Marriage should be every woman's end—but not her finish. I do not regard marriage as a sort of death.

Girdie says always to "be what you are." All right, let's look at ourselves in a mirror, dear, and forget "Captain Podkayne Fries, the famous Explorer" for the nonce. What do we see?

Getting just a touch broad-shouldered in the hips, aren't we, dear? No longer any chance of being mistaken for a boy in a dim light. One might say that we were designed for having babies. And that doesn't seem too bad an idea, now does it? Especially if we could have one as nice as Duncan. Fact is, all babies are pretty nice even when they're not.

Those eighteen miserable hours during the storm in the *Tricorn*—weren't they just about the most fun you ever had in your life? A baby is lots more fun than differential equations.

Every starship has a crèche. So which is better? To study crèche engineering and pediatrics—and be a department head in a starship? Or buck for pilot training and make it . . . and wind up as a female pilot nobody wants to hire?

Well, we don't have to decide now—

I'm getting pretty anxious for us to shape for Earth. Truth is, Venusberg's fleshpots can grow monotonous to one of my wholesome (or should I say "limited") tastes. I haven't any more money for shopping, not if I am to have any to shop in Paris; I don't think I could ever get addicted to gambling (and don't want to; I'm one of those who lose and thereby offset in part Clark's winning); and the incessant noise and lights are going to put wrinkles where I now have dimples. And I think Dexter is beginning to be just a bit bored with my naïve inability to understand what he is driving at.

If there is any one thing I have learned about males in my eight and a half years, it is that one should sign off before he gets bored. I look forward to just one last encounter with Dexter now: a tearful farewell just before I *must* enter the *Tricorn's* loading tube, with a kiss so grown-up, so utterly passionate and all-out giving, that he will believe the rest of his life that Things Could Have Been Different if Only He Had Played His Cards Right.

I've been outside the city just once, in a sealed tourist bus. Once is more than enough; this ball of smog and swamp should be given back to the natives, only they wouldn't take it. Once a fairy in flight was pointed out, so they said, but I didn't see anything. Just smog.

I'll settle now for just one fairy, in flight or even perched. Dexter says that he knows of a whole colony, a thousand or more, less than two hundred kilometers away, and wants to show it to me in his Rolls. But I'm not warm to that idea; he intends to drive it himself—and that dratted thing has automatic controls. If I can sneak Girdie, or even Clark, into the picnic—well, maybe.

But I have learned a lot on Venus and would not have missed it for anything. The Art of Tipping, especially, and now I feel like an Experienced Traveler. Tipping can be a nuisance but it is not quite the vice Marsmen think it is; it is a necessary lubricant for perfect service.

Let's admit it; service in Marsopolis varies from indifferent to terrible—and I simply had not realized it. A clerk waits on you when he feels like it and goes on gossiping with another clerk, not even able to see you until he does feel like it.

Not like that in Venusberg! However, it is not just the money—and here follows the Great Secret of Happy Travel. I haven't soaked up much Portuguese and not everybody speaks Ortho. But it isn't necessary to be a linguist if you will learn just one word—in as many languages as possible. Just "thank you."

I caught onto this first with Maria and Maria—I say "gobble-gobble" to them a hundred times a day, only the word is actually "obrigado" which sounds like "gobble-gobble" if you say it quickly. A *small* tip is much more savoir-fairish—and gets better, more willing service—when accompanied by "thank you" than a big tip while saying nothing.

So I've learned to say "thank you" in as many languages as possible and I always try to say it in the home language of the person I'm dealing with, if I can guess it, which I usually can. Doesn't matter much if you miss, though; porters and clerks and taxi drivers and such usually know that one word in several languages and can spot it even if you can't talk with them at all in any other way. I've written a lot of them down and memorized them:

> Obrigado
> Donkey shane
> Mare-see
> Key toss
> M'goy
> Graht-see-eh
> Arigato
> Spawseebaw
> Gathee-oss
> Tock[6]

Or "money tock" and Clark says this one means "money talks." But Clark is wrong; he has to tip too high because he won't bother to say "thank you." Oh, yes, Clark tips. It hurts him, but he soon discovered that he couldn't get a taxi and that even automatic vending machines were rude to him if he tried to buck the local system. But it infuriates him so much that he won't be pleasant about it and that costs him.

If you say "tock" instead of "key toss" to a Finn, he still understands it. If you mistake a Japanese for a Cantonese and say "m'goy" instead of "arigato"—well, that is the one word of Cantonese he knows. And "obrigado" everybody understands.

However, if you do guess right and pick their home language, they roll out the red carpet and genuflect, all smiles. I've even had tips refused—and this in a city where Clark's greediness about money is considered only natural.

All those other long, long lists of hints on How to Get Along While Traveling that I studied so carefully before I left turn out not to be necessary; this one rule does it all.

Uncle Tom is dreadfully worried about something. He's absent-minded and, while he will smile at me if I manage to get his attention (not easy), the smile soon fades

---

6. The phonetic spelling of "thanks" in, respectively, Portuguese, German, French, Finnish, Cantonese, Italian, Japanese, Russian, Spanish, and Danish.

XI

Things are really grim. Clark hasn't been home for two nights, and Uncle Tom is almost out of his mind. Besides that, I've had a quarrel with Dexter—which isn't important compared with Brother being missing but I could surely use a shoulder to cry on.

And Uncle Tom has had a real quarrel with Mr. Chairman—which was what led to my quarrel with Dexter because I was on Uncle Tom's side even though I didn't know what was going on and I discovered that Dexter was just as blind in his loyalty to his father as I am to Uncle Tom. I saw only a bit of the quarrel with Mr. Chairman and it was one of those frightening, cold, bitter, formally polite, grown-men quarrels of the sort that used to lead inevitably to pistols at dawn.

I think it almost did. Mr. Chairman arrived at our suite, looking not at all like Santa Claus, and I heard Uncle say coldly, "I would rather your friends had called on me, sir."

But Mr. Chairman ignored that and about then Uncle noticed that I was there— back of the piano, keeping quiet and trying to look small—and he told me to go to my room. Which I did.

But I know what part of it is. I had thought that both Clark and I had been allowed to run around loose in Venusberg—although I have usually had either Girdie or Dexter with me. Not so. Both of us have been guarded night and day, every instant we have been out of the Tannhäuser, by Corporation police. I never suspected this and I'm sure Clark didn't or he would never have hired Josie to watch his boodle.[7] But Uncle did know it and had accepted it as a courtesy from Mr. Chairman, one that left him free to do whatever these things are that have kept him so busy here, without riding herd on two kids, one of them nutty as Christmas cake. (And I don't mean me.)

As near as I can reconstruct it Uncle blames Mr. Chairman for Clark's absence— although this is hardly fair as Clark, if he knew he was being watched, could evade eighteen private eyes, the entire Space Corps, and a pack of slavering bloodhounds. Or is it "wolfhounds"?

But, on top of this, Dexter says that they disagree completely on how to locate Clark. Myself, I think that Clark is missing because Clark wants to be missing because he intends to miss the ship and stay here on Venus where a) Girdie is, and b) where all that lovely money is. Although perhaps I have put them in the wrong order.

I keep telling myself this, but Mr. Chairman says that it is a kidnapping, that it has to be a kidnapping, and that there is only one way to handle a kidnapping on Venus if one ever expects to see the kidnappee alive again.

On Venus, kidnapping is just about the only thing a stockholder is afraid of. In fact they are so afraid of it that they have brought the thing down almost to a ritual. If the kidnapper plays by the rules and doesn't hurt his victim, he not only won't be punished but he has the Corporation's assurance that he can keep any ransom agreed on.

---

7. A large amount of money.

But if he doesn't play by the rules and they do catch him, well, it's pretty grisly. Some of the things Dexter just hinted at. But I understand that the mildest punishment is something called a "four-hour death." He wouldn't give me any details on this, either—except that there is some drug that is just the opposite of anesthesia; it makes pain hurt worse.

Dexter says that Clark is absolutely safe as long as Uncle Tom doesn't insist on meddling with things he doesn't understand. "Old fool" is one term that he used and that was when I slapped him.

Long sigh and a wish for my happy girlhood in Marsopolis, where I understood how things worked. I don't here. All I really know is that I can no longer leave the suite save with Uncle Tom—and must leave it and stay with him when he does and wherever he goes.

Which is how I at last saw the Cunha "cottage"—and would have been much interested if Clark hadn't been missing. A modest little place only slightly smaller than the Tannhäuser but much more lavish. Our President's Rose House would fit into its ballroom. That is where I quarreled with Dexter while Uncle and Mr. Chairman were continuing their worse quarrel elsewhere in that "cottage."

Presently Uncle Tom took me back to the Tannhäuser and I've never seen him look so old—fifty at least, or call it a hundred and fifty of the years they use here. We had dinner in the suite and neither of us ate anything and after dinner I went over and sat by the living window. The view was from Earth, I guess. The Grand Canyon of El Dorado, or El Colorado, or whatever it is. Grand, certainly. But all I got was acrophobia and tears.

Uncle was just sitting, looking like Prometheus enduring the eagles.[8] I put my hand in his and said, "Uncle Tom? I wish you would spank me."

"Eh?" He shook his head and seemed to see me. "Flicka! Why?"

"Because it's my fault."

"What do you mean, dear?"

"Because I'm responsibu—bul for Clark. I always have been. He hasn't any sense. Why, when he was a baby I must have kept him from falling in the Canal at least a thousand times."

He shook his head, negatively this time. "No, Poddy. It is my responsibility and not yours at all. I am in loco parentis to both of you—which means that your parents were loco ever to trust me with it."

"But I *feel* responsible. He's my Chinese obligation."[9]

He shook his head still again. "No. In sober truth no person can ever be truly responsible for another human being. Each one of us faces up to the universe alone, and the universe is what it is and it doesn't soften the rules for any of us—and eventually, in the long run, the universe always wins and takes all. But that doesn't make it any easier when we *try* to be responsible for another—as you have, as I have— and then look back and see how we could have done it better." He sighed. "I should not have blamed Mr. Cunha. He tried to take care of Clark, too. Of both of you. I knew it."

He paused and added, "It was just that I had a foul suspicion, an unworthy one,

8. According to Greek mythology, the Titan Prometheus stole fire from the gods and gave it to humans; as punishment, he was chained to a rock where an eagle came every day to eat his liver (which grew back every night).
9. I.e., because Podkayne had saved her brother's life, she is forever responsible for him.

that he was using Clark to bring pressure on me. I was wrong. In his way and by his rules, Mr. Cunha is an honorable man—and his rules do not include using a boy for political purposes."

"Political purposes?"

Uncle looked around at me, as if surprised that I was still in the room. "Poddy, I should have told you more than I have. I keep forgetting that you are now a woman. I always think of you as the baby who used to climb on my knee and ask me to tell her 'The Poddy Story.'" He took a deep breath. "I still won't burden you with all of it. But I owe Mr. Cunha an abject apology—because *I* was using Clark for political purposes. And you, too."

"Huh?"

"As a cover-up, dear. Doddering great-uncle escorts beloved niece and nephew on pleasure tour. I'm sorry, Poddy, but it isn't that way at all. The truth is I am Ambassador Extraordinary and Minister Plenipotentiary for the Republic. To the Three Planets Summit. But it seemed desirable to keep it a secret until I present my credentials."

I didn't answer because I was having a little trouble soaking this in. I mean, I *know* Uncle Tom is pretty special and has done some important things, but all my life he has been somebody who always had time to hold a skein of yarn for me while I wound it and would take serious interest in helping me name paper dolls.

But he was talking. "So I used you, Flicka. You and your brother. Because— Poddy, do you really want to know all the ins and outs and snarls of the politics behind this?"

I did, very much. But I tried to be grown up. "Just whatever you think best to tell me, Uncle Tom."

"All right. Because some of it is sordid and all of it is complex and would take hours to explain—and some of it really isn't mine to tell; some of it involves commitments Bozo—sorry, the President— Some of it has to do with promises he made. Do you know who our Ambassador is now, at Luna City?"

I tried to remember. "Mr. Suslov?"

"No, that was last administration. Artie Finnegan. Artie isn't too bad a boy . . . but he thinks he should have been President and he's certain he knows more about interplanetary affairs and what is good for Mars than the President does. Means well, no doubt."

I didn't comment because the name "Arthur Finnegan" I recognized at once— I had once heard Uncle Tom sound off about him to Daddy when I was supposed to be in bed and asleep. Some of the milder expressions were "a head like a sack of mud," "larceny in his heart," and a "size twelve ego in a size nine soul."

"But even though he means well," Uncle Tom went on, "he doesn't see eye to eye with the President—and myself—on matters that will come before this conference. But unless the President sends a special envoy—me, in this case—the Ambassador in residence automatically speaks for Mars. Poddy, what do you know about Switzerland?"

"Huh? William Tell.[1] The apple."

"That's enough, I guess, although there probably never was an apple. Poddy, Mars is the Switzerland of the solar System—or it isn't anything at all. So the President

---

1. The legendary national hero of Switzerland (14th c.), who is said to have been forced by the Austrian governor of his canton to shoot an apple from the head of his son with his crossbow; he later shot the governor, setting off the rebellion that led to Swiss freedom from Austrian domination.

thinks, and so I think. A small man (and a small country, like Mars or Switzerland) can stand up to bigger, powerful neighbors only by being willing to fight.[2] We've never had a war and I pray we never do, because we would probably lose it. But if we are willing enough, we may never have to fight."

He sighed. "That's the way I see it. But Mr. Finnegan thinks that, because Mars is small and weak, Mars should join up with the Terran Federation. Perhaps he's right and this really is the wave of the future. But I don't think so; I think it would be the end of Mars as an independent country and a free society. Furthermore, I think it is logical that if Mars gives up its independence, it is only a matter of time until Venus goes the same way. I've been spending the time since we got here trying to convince Mr. Cunha of this, cause him to have his Resident Commissioner make a common cause with us against Terra. This could persuade Luna to come in with us too, since both Venus and Mars can sell to Luna cheaper than Terra can. But it wasn't at all easy; the Corporation has such a long-standing policy of never meddling in politics at all. 'Put not your faith in princes'[3]—which means to them that they buy and they sell and they ask no questions.

"But I have been trying to make Mr. Cunha see that if Luna and Mars and Terra (the Jovian moons hardly count), if those three were all under the same rules, in short order Venus Corporation would be no more free than is General Motors or I.G. Farbenindustrie. He got the picture too, I'm sure—until I jumped to conclusions about Clark's disappearance and blew my top at him." He shook his head. "Poddy, I'm a poor excuse for a diplomat."

"You aren't the only one who got sore," I said, and told him about slapping Dexter.

He smiled for the first time. "Oh, Poddy, Poddy, we'll never make a lady out of you. You're as bad as I am."

So I grinned back at him and started picking my teeth with a fingernail. This is an even ruder gesture than you might think—and utterly private between Uncle Tom and myself. We Maori have a very bloodthirsty history and I won't even hint at what it is we are supposed to be picking out of our teeth. Uncle Tom used to use this vulgar pantomime on me when I was a little girl, to tell me I wasn't being lady-like.

Whereupon he really smiled and mussed my hair. "You're the blondest blue-eyed savage I ever saw. But you're a savage, all right. And me, too. Better tell him you're sorry, hon, because, much as I appreciate your gallant defense of me, Dexter was perfectly right. I was an 'old fool.' I'll apologize to his father, doing the last hundred meters on my belly if he wants it that way; a man should admit it in full when he's wrong, and make amends. And you kiss and make up with Dexter—Dexter is a fine boy."

"I'll say I'm sorry and make up—but I don't think I'll kiss him. I haven't yet."

He looked surprised. "So? Don't you like him? Or have we brought too much Norse blood into the family?"

"I like Dexter just fine and you're crazy with the smog if you think Svenska blood is any colder than Polynesian. I could go for Dexter in a big way—and that's why I haven't kissed him."

He considered this. "I think you're wise, hon. Better do your practice kisses on boys who don't tend to cause your gauges to swing over into the red. Anyhow, although he's a good lad, he's not nearly good enough for my savage niece."

2. Though Switzerland has a long tradition of neutrality, all men between 20 and 42 serve in its militia.

3. Psalms 146.3.

"Maybe so, maybe not. Uncle . . . what *are* you going to do about Clark?"

His halfway happy mood vanished. "Nothing. Nothing at all."

"But we've got to do something!"

"But what, Podkayne?"

There he had me. I had already chased it through all the upper and lower segments of my brain. Tell the police? Mr. Chairman *is* the police—they all work for him. Hire a private detective? If Venus has any (I don't know), then they all are under contract to Mr. Cunha, or rather, the Venus Corporation.

Run ads in newspapers? Question all the taxi drivers? Put Clark's picture in the sollies and offer rewards? It didn't matter what you thought of, *everything* on Venus belongs to Mr. Chairman. Or, rather, to the corporation he heads. Same thing, really, although Uncle Tom tells me that the Cunhas' actually own only a fraction of the stock.

"Poddy, I've been over everything I could think of with Mr. Cunha—and he is either already doing it, or he has convinced me that here, under conditions he knows much better than I do, it should not be done."

"Then what do we *do*?"

"We wait. But if you think of anything—*anything*—that you think might help, tell me and if it isn't already being done, we'll call Mr. Cunha and find out if it should be done. If I'm asleep, wake me."

"I will." I doubted if he would be asleep. Or me. But something else had been bothering me. "If time comes for the *Tricorn* to shape for Earth—and Clark isn't back—what do you do then?"

He didn't answer; the lines in his face just got deeper. I knew what the Awful Decision was—and I knew how he had decided it.

But I had a little Awful Decision of my own to make . . . and I had talked to Saint Podkayne about it for quite a while and had decided that Poddy had to break a Saint-Podkayne oath. Maybe this sounds silly but it isn't silly to me. Never in my life had I broken one . . . and never in my life will I be utterly sure about Poddy again.

So I told Uncle all about the smuggled bomb.

Somewhat to my surprise he took it seriously—when I had about persuaded myself that Clark had been pulling my leg just for exercise. Smuggling—oh, sure, I understand that every ship in space has smuggling. But not a bomb. Just something valuable enough that it was worthwhile to bribe a boy to get it aboard . . . and probably Clark had been paid off again when he passed it along to a steward, or a cargo hand, or somebody. If I know Clark—

But Uncle wanted me to describe exactly the person I had seen talking to Clark at Deimos Station.

"Uncle, I can't! I barely glanced at him. A man. Not short, not tall, not especially fat or skinny, not dressed in any way that made me remember—and I'm not sure I looked at his face at all. Uh, yes, I did but I can't call up any picture of it."

"Could it have been one of the passengers?"

I thought hard about that. "No. Or I would have noticed his face later when it was still fresh in my mind. *Mmm* . . . I'm almost certain he didn't queue up with us. I think he headed for the exit, the one that takes you back to the shuttle ship."

"That is likely," he agreed. "Certain—*if* it was a bomb. And not just a product of Clark's remarkable imagination."

"But, Uncle Tom, *why* would it be a bomb?"

And he didn't answer and I already knew why. Why would anybody blow up the *Tricorn* and kill everybody in her, babies and all? Not for insurance like you sometimes find in adventure stories; Lloyd's[4] won't insure a ship for enough to show a profit on that sort of crazy stunt—or at least that's the way it was explained to me in my high school economics class.

Why, then?

To keep the ship from getting to Venus.

But the *Tricorn* had been to Venus tens and tens of times—

To keep somebody in the ship from getting to Venus (or perhaps to Luna) *that trip*.

Who? Not Podkayne Fries. I wasn't important to anybody but me.

For the next couple of hours Uncle Tom and I searched that hilton suite. We didn't find anything, nor did I expect us to. If there was a bomb (which I still didn't fully believe) and if Clark had indeed brought it off the ship and hidden it there (which seemed unlikely with all of the *Tricorn* at one end and all of the city at the other end to choose from), nevertheless he had had days and days in which to make it look like anything from a vase of flowers to a—a *anything*.

We searched Clark's room last on the theory that it was the least likely place. Or rather, we started to search it together and Uncle had to finish it. Pawing through Clark's things got to be too much for me and Uncle sent me back into the salon to lie down.

I was all cried out by the time he gave up; I even had a suggestion to make. "Maybe if we sent for a Geiger counter?"

Uncle shook his head and sat down. "We aren't looking for a bomb, honey."

"We aren't?"

"No. If we found it, it would simply confirm that Clark had told you the truth, and I'm already using that as least hypothesis. Because . . . well, because I know more about this than the short outline I gave to you . . . and I know just how deadly serious this is to some people, how far they might go. Politics is neither a game nor a bad joke the way some people think it is. War itself is merely an extension of politics . . . so I don't find anything surprising about a bomb in politics; bombs have been used in politics hundreds and even thousands of times in the past. No, we aren't looking for a bomb, we are looking for a man—a man you saw for a few seconds once. And probably not even for that man but for somebody that man might lead us back to. Probably somebody inside the President's office, somebody he trusts."

"Oh, gosh, I wish I had really looked at him!"

"Don't fret about it, hon. You didn't know and there was no reason to look. But you can bet that Clark knows what he looks like. If Clark—I mean, *when* Clark comes back, in time we will have him search the I.D. files at Marsopolis. And all the visa photographs for the past ten years, if necessary. The man will be found. And through him the person the President has been trusting who should not be trusted." Uncle Tom suddenly looked all Maori and very savage. "And when we do, I may take care of the matter personally. We'll see."

Then he smiled and added, "But right now Poddy is going to bed. You're up way past your bedtime, even with all the dancing and late-sleeping you've been doing lately."

"Uh . . . what time is it in Marsopolis?"

He looked at his other watch. "Twenty-seventeen. You weren't thinking of phoning your parents? I hope not."

"Oh, no! I won't say a word to them unless—until Clark is back. And maybe not

4. The London association of insurance syndicates, long associated with insuring ships.

then. But if it's only twenty-seventeen, it's not late at all, real time, and I don't want to go to bed. Not until you do."

"I may not go to bed."

"I don't care. I want to sit with you."

He blinked at me, then said very gently, "All right, Poddy. Nobody ever grows up without spending at least one night of years."

We just sat then for quite a while, with nothing to say that had not already been said and would just hurt to say over again.

At last I said, "Unka Tom? Tell me the Poddy story—"

"At your age?"

"Please." I crawled up on his knees. "I want to sit in your lap once more and hear it. I need to."

"All right," he said, and put his arm around me. "Once upon a time, long, long ago when the world was young, in a specially favored city there lived a little girl named Poddy. All day long she was busy like a ticking clock. *Tick tick tick* went her heels, *tick tick tick* went her knitting needles, and, most especially, *tick tick tick* went her busy little mind. Her hair was the color of butter blossoms in the spring when the ice leaves canals, her eyes were the changing blue of sunshine playing down through the spring floods, her nose had not yet made up its mind what it would be, and her mouth was shaped like a question mark. She greeted the world as an unopened present and there was no badness in her anywhere.

"One day Poddy—"

I stopped him. "But I'm *not* young any longer . . . and I don't think the world was ever young!"

"Here's my hanky," he said. "Blow your nose. I never did tell you the end of it, Poddy; you always fell asleep. It ends with a miracle."

"A truly miracle?"

"Yes. This is the end. Poddy grew up and had another Poddy. And then the world was young again."

"Is that all?"

"That's all there ever is. But it's enough."

XII

I guess Uncle Tom put me to bed, for I woke up with just my shoes off and very rumpled. He was gone but he had left a note saying that I could reach him, if I needed to, on Mr. Chairman's private code. I didn't have any excuse to bother him and didn't want to face anyone, so I chased Maria and Maria out and ate breakfast in bed. Ate quite a lot, too, I must admit—the body goes on ticking anyhow.

Then I dug out my journal for the first time since landing. I don't mean I haven't been keeping it; I mean I've been talking it instead of writing it. The library in our suite has a recorder built into its desk and I discovered how easy it was to keep a diary that way. Well, I had really found out before that, because Mr. Clancy let me use the recorder they use to keep the log on.

The only shortcoming of the recorder in the library was that Clark might drop in most any time. But the first day I went shopping I found the most darling little minirecorder at Venus Macy—only ten-fifty and it just fits in the palm of your hand and you can talk into it without even being noticed if you want to and I just couldn't resist it. I've been carrying it in my purse ever since.

But now I wanted to look way back in my journal, the early written part, and see if I had said *anything* that might remind me of what That Man had looked like or anything about him.

I hadn't. No clues. But I FOUND A NOTE FROM CLARK.

It read:

POD,

If you find this at all, it's time you read it. Because I'm using 24-hr. ink and I expect to lift this out of here and you'll never see it.

Girdie is in trouble and I'm going to rescue her. I haven't told anybody because this is one job that is all mine and I don't want you or anybody horning in on it.

However, a smart gambler hedges his bets, if he can. If I'm gone long enough for you to read this, it's time to get hold of Uncle Tom and have him get hold of Chairman Cunha. All I can tell you is that there is a newsstand right at South Gate. You buy a copy of the *Daily Merchandiser* and ask if they carry Everlites. Then say, "Better give me two—it's quite dark where I'm going."

But don't *you* do this, I don't want it muffed up.

If this turns out dry, you can have my rock collection.

Count your change. Better use your
fingers.
CLARK

I got all blurry. That last line—I know a holographic last will and testament when I see one, even though I had never seen one before. Then I straightened up and counted ten seconds backwards including the rude word at the end that discharges nervous tension, for I knew this was no time to be blurry and weak; there was work to be done.

So I called Uncle Tom right away, as I agreed perfectly with Clark on one point: I wasn't going to try to emulate Space Ranger Stalwart, Man of Steel, the way Clark evidently had; I was going to get all the help I could get! With both Clark and Girdie in some sort of pinch I would have welcomed two regiments of Patrol Marines and the entire Martian Legion.

So I called Mr. Chairman's private code—and it didn't answer; it simply referred me to another code. This one answered all right . . . but with a recording. Uncle Tom. And this time all he said was to repeat something he had said in the note, that he expected to be busy all day and that I was not to leave the suite under any circumstances whatever until he got back—only this time he added that I was not to let anyone into the suite, either, not even a repairman, not even a servant except those who were already there, like Maria and Maria.

When the recording started to play back for the third time, I switched off. Then I called Mr. Chairman the public way, through the Corporation offices. A dry deal that was! By pointing out that I was Miss Fries, niece of Senator Fries, Mars Republic, I did get as far as his secretary, or maybe his secretary's secretary.

"Mr. Cunha cannot be reached. I am veree sorree, Miss Fries."

So I demanded that she locate Uncle Tom. "I do not have that information. I am veree sorree, Miss Fries."

Then I demanded to be patched in to Dexter. "Mr. Dexter is on an inspection trip for Mr. Cunha. I am veree sorree."

She either couldn't, or wouldn't, tell me when Dexter was expected back—and wouldn't, or couldn't, find some way for me to call him. Which I just plain didn't believe, because if I owned a planetwide corporation there would be some way to phone every mine, every ranch, every factory, every air boat the company owned. All the time. And I don't even suspect that Mr. Chairman is less smart about how to run such a lash-up[5] than I am.

I told her so, using the colorful rhetoric of sand rats and canal men. I mean I really got mad and used idioms I hadn't known I even remembered. I guess Uncle is right; scratch my Nordic skin and a savage is just underneath. I wanted to pick my teeth at her, only she wouldn't have understood it.

But would you believe it? I might as well have been cussing out a sand gator; it had no effect on her at all. She just repeated, "I'm-veree-sorree-Miss-Fries," and I growled and switched off.

Do you suppose Mr. Chairman uses an androidal Tik-Tok as his phone monitor? I wouldn't put it past him—and any live woman should have shown *some* reaction at some of the implausibilities I showered on her, even if she didn't understand most of the words (Well, I don't understand some of them myself. But they are not compliments.)

I thought about phoning Daddy; I knew he would accept the charges, even if he had to mortgage his salary. But Mars was eleven minutes away; it said so, right on a dial of the phone. And the relays via Hermes Station and Luna City were even worse. With twenty-two minutes between each remark it would take me most of the day just to tell him what was wrong, even though they don't charge you for the waiting time.

But I still might have called except—well, what could Daddy *do*, three hundred million kilometers away? All it would do would be to turn his last six hairs white.

It wasn't until then that I steadied down enough to realize that there had been something else amiss about that note written into my journal—besides Clark's childish swashbuckling. Girdie—

It was true that I had not seen Girdie for a couple of days; she was on a shift that caused her to zig while I zagged, newly hired dealers don't get the best shifts. But I had indeed talked to her at a time when Clark was probably already gone even though at the time I had simply assumed that he had gotten up early for some inscrutable reason of his own, rather than not coming home at all that night.

But Uncle Tom had talked to her just before we had gone to the Cunha cottage the day before, asked her specifically if she had seen Clark—and she hadn't. Not as recently as we had.

I didn't have any trouble reaching Dom Pedro—not the Dom Pedro I met the night I met Dexter but the Dom Pedro of that shift. However, by now all the Dom Pedros know who Poddy Fries is; she's the girl that is seen with Mr. Dexter. He told me at once that Girdie had gone off shift half an hour earlier and I should try her hilton. Unless—he stopped and made some inquiries; somebody seemed to think that Girdie had gone shopping.

As may be. I already knew that she was not at the little hilton she had moved to from the stylish (and expensive) Tannhäuser; a message I had already recorded there was guaranteed to fetch a call back in seconds, if and when.

That ended it. There was no one left for me to turn to, nothing at all left for me to do, save wait in the suite until Uncle returned, as he had ordered me to do.

So I grabbed my purse and a coat and left.

And got all of three meters outside the door of the suite. A tall, wide, muscular character got in my way. When I tried to duck around him, he said, "Now, now, Miss Fries. Your uncle left orders."

5. An outfit.

I scurried the other way and found that he was awfully quick on his feet, for such a big man. So there I was, arrested! Shoved back into our own suite and held in durance vile. You know, I don't think Uncle entirely trusts me.

I went back to my room and closed the door and thought about it. The room was still not made up and still cluttered with dirty dishes because, despite the language barrier, I have made clear to Maria and Maria that Miss Fries becomes quite vexed if *anybody* disturbs my room until I signal that I no longer want privacy by leaving the door open.

The clumsy, two-decker, roll-around table that had fetched my breakfast was still by my bed, looking like a plundered city.

I took everything off the lower shelf, stowed it here and there in my bath, covered the stuff on top of the table with the extra cloth used to shield the tender eyes of cash customers from the sight of dirty dishes.

Then I grabbed the house phone and told them I wanted my breakfast dishes cleared away immediately.

I'm not very big. I mean you can fit forty-nine mass kilos only one hundred fifty-seven centimeters long into a fairly small space if you scrunch a little. That lower shelf was hard but not too cramped. It had some ketchup on it I hadn't noticed.

Uncle's orders (or perhaps Mr. Cunha's) were being followed meticulously, however. Ordinarily a pantry boy comes to remove the food wagon; this time the two Marias took it out the service entrance and as far as the service lift—and in the course of it I learned something interesting but not really surprising. Maria said something in Portuguese; the other Maria answered her in Ortho as glib as mine: "She's probably soaking in the tub, the lazy brat."

I made a note not to remember her on birthdays and at Christmas.

Somebody wheeled me off the lift many levels down and shoved me into a corner. I waited a few moments, then crawled out. A man in a well-spotted apron was looking astonished. I said, "Obrigado!" handed him a deuce note and walked out the service entrance with my nose in the air. Two minutes later I was in a taxi.

I've been catching up on this account while the taxi scoots to South Gate in order not to chew my nails back to the elbows. I must admit that I feel good even though nervous. Action is better than waiting. No amount of bad can stonker me, but not knowing drives me nuts.

The spool is almost finished, so I think I'll change spools and mail this one back to Uncle at South Gate. I should have left a note, I know—but this is better than a note. I hope.

XIII

Well, I can't complain about not having seen fairies. They are every bit as cute as they are supposed to be—but I don't care greatly if I never see another one.

Throwing myself bravely into the fray against fearful odds, by sheer audacity I overcame—

It wasn't that way at all. I fubbed. Completely. So here I am, some nowhere place out in the bush, in a room with no windows, and only one door. That door isn't much use to me as there is a fairy perched over it. She's a cute little thing and the green part of her fur looks exactly like a ballet tutu. She doesn't look quite like a miniature human with wings—but they do say that the longer you stay here the more human they look. Her eyes slant up, like a cat's, and she has a very pretty built-in smile.

I call her "Titania" because I can't pronounce her real name. She speaks a few words of Ortho, not much because those little skulls are only about twice the brain capacity of a cat's skull—actually, she's an idiot studying to be a moron and not studying very hard.

Most of the time she just stays perched and nurses her baby—the size of a kitten and twice as cute. I call it "Ariel" although I'm not sure of its sex. I'm not dead sure of Titania's sex; they say that both males and females do this nursing thing, which is not quite nursing but serves the same purpose; they are not mammalians. Ariel hasn't learned to fly yet, but Titania is teaching it—tosses it into the air and it sort of flops and glides to the floor and then stays there, mewing piteously until she comes to get it and flies back to her perch.

I'm spending most of my time a) thinking, b) bringing this journal up to date, c) trying to persuade Titania to let me hold Ariel (making some progress; she now lets me pick it up and hand it to her—the baby isn't a bit afraid of me), and d) thinking, which seems to be a futile occupation.

Because I can go anywhere in the room and do anything as long as I stay a couple of meters away from that door. Guess why? Give up? Because fairies have very sharp teeth and claws; they're carnivorous. I have a nasty bite and two deep scratches on my left arm to prove it—red and tender and don't seem to want to heal. If I get close to that door, she dives on me.

Completely friendly otherwise— Nor do I have anything physically to complain about. Often enough a native comes in with a tray of really quite good food. But I never watch him come in and I never watch him take it away—because Venerians look entirely too human to start with and the more you look at them the worse it is for your stomach. No doubt you have seen pictures but pictures don't give you the smell and that drooling loose mouth, nor the impression that this *thing* has been dead a long time and is now animated by obscene arts.

I call him "Pinhead" and to him that is a compliment. No doubt as to its being a "him" either. It's enough to make a girl enter a nunnery.

I eat the food because I feel sure Pinhead didn't cook it. I think I know who does. She would be a good cook.

Let me back up a little. I told the news vendor: "Better give me two—it's quite dark where I'm going." He hesitated and looked at me and I repeated it.

So pretty soon I am in another air car and headed out over the bush. Ever make a wide, sweeping turn in smog? That did it. I haven't the slightest idea where I am, save that it is somewhere within two hours' flight of Venusberg and that there is a small colony of fairies nearby. I saw them flying shortly before we landed and was so terribly interested that I didn't really get a good look at the spot before the car stopped and the door opened. Not that it would have done any good—

I got out and the car lifted at once, mussing me up with its fans . . . and here was an open door to a house and a familiar voice was saying, "Poddy! Come in, dear, come in!"

And I was suddenly so relieved that I threw myself into her arms and hugged her and she hugged me back. It was Mrs. Grew, fat and friendly as ever.

And looked around and here was Clark, just sitting—and he looked at me and said, "Stupid," and looked away. And then I saw Uncle—sitting in another chair and was about to throw myself at him with wild shouts of glee—when Mrs. Grew's arms were suddenly awfully strong and she said soothingly, "No, no, dear, not quite so fast" and held me until somebody (Pinhead, it was) did something to the back of my neck.

Then I had a big comfortable chair all to myself and didn't want it because I couldn't move from my neck down. I felt all right, aside from some odd tingles, but I couldn't stir.

Uncle looked like Mr. Lincoln grieving over the deaths at Waterloo.[6] He didn't say anything.

Mrs. Grew said cheerfully, "Well, now we've got the whole family together. Feel a bit more like discussing things rationally, Senator?"

Uncle shook his head half a centimer.

She said, "Oh, come now! We do want you to attend the conference. We simply want you to attend it in the right frame of mind. If we can't agree—well, it's hardly possible to let any of you be found again. Isn't that obvious? And that would be such a shame . . . especially for the children."

Uncle said, "Pass the hemlock."[7]

"Oh, I'm sure you don't mean that."

"He certainly does mean it!" Clark said shrilly. "You illegal obscenity! I delete all over your censored!" And I knew he was really worked up, because Clark is contemptuous of vulgar idioms; he says they denote an inferior mind.

Mrs. Grew looked at Clark placidly, even tenderly. Then she called in Pinhead again. "Take him out and keep him awake till he dies." Pinhead picked Clark up and carried him out. But Clark had the last word. "And besides that," he yelled, *"you cheat at solitaire!* I've watched you!"

For a split moment Mrs. Grew looked really annoyed. Then she put her face back into its usual kindly expression and said to Uncle, "Now that I have both of the kids I think I can afford to expend one of them. Especially as you are quite fond of Poddy. Too fond of her, some people would say. Psychiatrists, I mean."

I mulled that over . . . and decided that if I ever got out of this mess, I would make a rug out of her hide and give it to Uncle.

Uncle ignored it. Presently there was a most dreadful racket, metal on resounding metal. Mrs. Grew smiled. "It's crude but it works. It is what used to be a water heater when this was a ranch. Unfortunately it isn't quite big enough either to sit down or stand up in—but a boy that rude really shouldn't expect comfort. The noise comes from pounding on the outside of it with a piece of pipe." She blinked and looked thoughtful. "I don't see how we can talk things over with such a racket going on. I think I should have the tank moved farther away—or perhaps our talk would march even more quickly if I had it brought nearer, so that you could hear the sounds he makes inside the tank, too. What do you think, Senator?"

I cut in. "Mrs. Grew!"

"Yes, dear? Poddy, I'm sorry but I'm really quite busy. Later we'll have a nice cup of tea together. Now, Senator—"

"Mrs. Grew, you don't understand my Uncle Tom at all! You'll never get anything out of him this way."

She considered it. "I think you exaggerate, dear. Wishful thinking."

"No, no, no! There isn't *any* way you could possibly get my Uncle Tom to do anything against Mars. But if you hurt Clark—or me—you'll just make him more adamant. Oh, he loves me and he loves Clark, too. But if you try to budge him by hurting either one of us, you're just wasting your time!" I was talking rapidly and just as sincerely as I know how. I seemed to hear Clark's screams. Not likely, I guess, not

6. The decisive and very bloody 1815 battle in the Napoleonic Wars; Abraham Lincoln (1809–1865; U.S. president, 1861–65), however, was likely grieving over the battle of Gettysburg (1863), where casualities totaled about 45,000.
7. A poison.

over that infernal clanging. But once when he was a baby he fell into a wastebasket . . . and screamed something dreadful before I rescued him. I guess I was hearing that in my mind.

Mrs. Grew smiled pleasantly. "Poddy dear, you are only a girl and your head has been filled with nonsense. The Senator is going to do just what I want him to do."

"Not if you kill Clark, he won't!"

"You keep quiet, dear. Do keep quiet and let me explain—or I shall have to slap you a few times to keep you quiet. Poddy, I am not going to kill your brother—"

"But you said—"

"*Quiet!* That native who took your brother away didn't understand what I said; he knows only trade Ortho, a few words, never a full sentence. I said what I did for the benefit of your brother . . . so that, when I *do* have him fetched back in, he'll be groveling, begging your uncle to do anything I want him to do."

She smiled warmly. "One piece of nonsense you've apparently been taught is that patriotism, or something silly like that, will overpower a man's own self-interest. Believe me, I have no slightest fear that an old political hack like your uncle will give any real weight to such a silly abstraction. What *does* worry him is his own political ruin if he does what I want him to do. What he is going to do. Eh, Senator?"

"Madam," Uncle Tom answered tightly, "I see no point in bandying words with you."

"Nor do I. Nor shall we. But you can listen while I explain it to Poddy. Dear, your uncle is a stubborn man and he won't accomplish his own political downfall lightly. I need a string to make him dance—and in *you* I have that string, I'm sure."

"I'm not!"

"Want a slap? Or would you rather be gagged? I like you, dear; don't force me to be forceful. In *you*, I said. Not your brother. Oh, no doubt your uncle goes through the solemn farce of treating his niece and his nephew just alike—Christmas presents and birthday presents and such like pretenses. But it is obvious that no one could love your brother . . . not even his own mother, I venture to say. But the Senator *does* love you—rather more than he wants anyone to suspect. So now I am hurting your brother a little—oh, just a smidgen, at worst he'll be deaf—to let your uncle see what will happen to *you*. Unless he is a good boy and speaks his piece just the way I tell him to."

She looked thoughtfully at Uncle. "Senator, I can't decide which of two methods might work the better on you. You see, I want to keep you reminded—after you agree to cooperate—that you *did* agree. Sometimes a politician doesn't stay bought. After I turn you loose, would it be better for me to send your nephew along with you, to keep you reminded? Or would it be better to keep him here and work on him just a little each day—with his sister watching? So that she would have a clear idea of what happens to her . . . if you try any tricks at Luna City. What's your opinion, sir?"

"Madam, the question does not arise."

"Really, Senator?"

"Because I will not be at Luna City unless both children are with me. Unhurt."

Mrs. Grew chuckled. "Campaign promises, Senator. I'll reason with you later. But now"—she glanced at an antique watch pinned to her gross bosom—"I think I had better put a stop to that dreadful racket, it's giving me a headache. And I doubt if your nephew can hear it any longer, save possibly through his bones." She got up and left, moving with surprising agility and grace for a woman her age and mass.

Suddenly the noise stopped.

It was such a surprise that I would have jumped if anything below my neck could jump. Which it couldn't.

Uncle was looking at me. "Poddy, Poddy—" he said softly.

I said, "Uncle, don't you give in a millimeter to that dreadful woman!"

He said, "Poddy, I *can't* give in to her. Not at all. You understand that? Don't you?"

"I certainly do! But look—you could fake it. Tell her anything. Get loose yourself and take Clark along, as she suggested. Then you can rescue me. I'll hold out. You'll see!"

He looked terribly old. "Poddy . . . Poddy darling . . . I'm very much afraid . . . that this is the end. Be brave, dear."

"Uh, I haven't had very much practice at that. But I'll try to be." I pinched myself, mentally, to see if I was scared—and I wasn't, not really. Somehow I couldn't be scared with Uncle there, even though he was helpless just then. "Uncle, what is it she wants? Is she some kind of a fanatic?"

He didn't answer because we both heard Mrs. Grew's jolly, belly-deep laugh. " 'Fanatic'!" she repeated, came over and tweaked my cheek. "Poddy dear, I'm not any sort of fanatic and I don't really care any more about politics than your uncle does. But I learned many years ago when I was just a girl—and quite attractive, too, dear, much more so than you will ever be—that a girl's best friend is cash. No, dear, I'm a paid professional and a good one."

She went on briskly, "Senator, I think the boy is deaf but I can't be sure; he's passed out now. We'll discuss it later, it's time for my nap. Perhaps we had all better rest a little."

And she called in Pinhead and I was carried into the room I am in now. When he picked me up, I really was truly aghast!—and found that I could move my arms and legs just a little bit—pins and needles you wouldn't believe!—and I struggled feebly. Did me no good, I was dumped in here anyhow.

After a while the drug wore off and I felt almost normal, though shaky. Shortly thereafter I discovered that Titania is a very good watchdog indeed and I haven't tried to reach that door since; my arm and shoulder are quite sore and getting stiff.

Instead I inspected the room. Not much in it. A bed with a mattress but no bed-clothes, not that you need any in this climate. A sort of a table suspended from one wall and a chair fastened to the floor by it. Glow tubes around the upper corners of the room. I checked all these things at once after learning the hard way that Titania was not just a cutie with gauzy wings. It was quite clear that Mrs. Grew, or whoever had outfitted that room, had no intention of leaving anything in it that could be used as a weapon, against Titania or anybody. And I no longer had even my coat and purse.

I particularly regretted losing my purse, because I always carry a number of useful things in it. A nail file for example—if I had had even my nail file I might have considered taking on that bloodthirsty little fairy. But I didn't waste time thinking about it; my purse was where I had dropped it when I was drugged.

I did find one thing very interesting: this room had been used to prison Clark before I landed in it. One of his two bags was there—and I suppose I should have missed it from his room the night before, only I got upset and left Uncle to finish the search. The bag held a very odd collection for a knight errant venturing forth to rescue a damsel in distress; some clothing—three T-shirts and two pairs of shorts, a spare pair of shoes—a slide rule,[8] and three comic books.

---

8. A mechanical device that relies on logarithmic scales to enable its user to make rapid calculations.

If I had found a flame gun or supplies of mysterious chemicals, I would not have been surprised—more Clarkish. I suppose, when you get right down to it, for all his brilliance Clark is just a little boy.

I worried a bit then about the possibility—or probability—that he was deaf. Then I quit thinking about it. If true, I couldn't help it—and he would miss his ears less than anything, since he hardly ever listens anyhow.

So I lay down on the bed and read his comic books. I am not a comic-book addict but these were quite entertaining, especially as the heroes were always getting out of predicaments much worse than the one I was in.

After a while I fell asleep and had heroic dreams.

I was awakened by "breakfast" (more like dinner but quite good). Pinhead took the tray away, and light plastic dishes and a plastic spoon offered little in the way of lethal weapons. However, I was delighted to find that he had fetched my purse!

Delighted for all of ten seconds, that is— No nail file. No penknife. Not a darn thing in it more deadly than lipstick and hanky. Mrs. Grew hadn't disturbed any money or my tiny minirecorder but she had taken everything that could conceivably do any good (harm). So I gritted my teeth and ate and then brought this useless journal up to date. That's about all I've done since—just sleep and eat and make friends with Ariel. It reminds me of Duncan. Oh, not alike really—but all babies are sort of alike, don't you think?

I had dozed off from lack of anything better to do when I was awakened. "Poddy, dear—"

"Oh! Hello, Mrs. Grew."

"Now, now, no quick moves," she said chidingly. I wasn't about to make any quick moves; she had a gun pointed at my belly button. I'm very fond of it, it's the only one I have.

"Now be a good girl and turn over and cross your wrists behind you." I did so and in a moment she had them tied, quite firmly. Then she looped the line around my neck and had me on a leash—and if I struggled, all I accomplished was choking myself. So I didn't struggle.

Oh, I'm sure there was at least a moment when she didn't have that gun pointed at me and my wrists were not yet tied. One of those comic-book heroes would have snatched that golden instant, rendered her helpless, tied her with her own rope.

Regrettably, none of those heroes was named "Poddy Fries." My education has encompassed cooking, sewing, quite a lot of math and history and science, and such useful tidbits as freehand drawing and how to dip candles and make soap. But hand-to-hand combat I have learned sketchily if at all from occasional border clashes with Clark. I know that Mother feels that this is a lack (she is skilled in both karate and kill-quick, and can shoot as well as Daddy does) but Daddy has put off sending me to classes—I've gathered the impression that he doesn't really want his "baby girl" to know such things.

I vote with Mother, it's a lack. There must have been a split second when I could have lashed out with a heel, caught Mrs. Grew in her solar plexus, then broken her neck while she was still helpless—and run down the Jolly Roger and run up the Union Jack, just like in *Treasure Island*.[9]

Oppernockity tunes but once—and I wasn't in tune with it.

9. The 1883 adventure novel by Robert Louis Stevenson. When the young hero retrieves his ship from the pirates, he strikes the pirate flag.

Instead I was led away like a puppy on a string. Titania eyed us as we went through the door but Mrs. Grew clucked at her and she settled back on her perch and cuddled Ariel to her.

She had me walk in front of her down a hallway, through that living room where I had last seen Uncle Tom and Clark, out another door and a passage and into a large room—

—and I gasped and suppressed a scream!

Mrs. Grew said cheerfully, "Take a good look, dear. He's your new roommate."

Half the room was closed off with heavy steel bars, like a cage in a zoo. Inside was—well, it was Pinhead, that's what it was, though it took me a long moment of fright to realize it. You may have gathered that I do not consider Pinhead handsome. Well, dear, he was Apollo Belvedere[1] before compared with the red-eyed maniacal horror he had become.

Then I was lying on the floor and Mrs. Grew was giving me smelling salts. Yes, sir, Captain Podkayne Fries the Famous Explorer had keeled over like a silly girl. All right, go ahead and laugh; I don't mind. *You* haven't ever been shoved into a room with a thing like that and had it introduced to you as "your new roommate."

Mrs. Grew was chuckling. "Feel better, dear?"

"You're not going to put me in there with him!"

"What? Oh, no, no, that was just my little joke. I'm sure your uncle will never make it necessary actually to do it." She looked at Pinhead thoughtfully—and he was straining one arm through the bars, trying again and again to reach us. "He's had only five milligrams, and for a long-time happy dust addict that's barely enough to make him tempery. If I ever do have to put you—or your brother—in with him, I've promised him at least fifteen. I need your advice, dear. You see, I'm about to send your uncle back to Venusberg so that he can catch his ship. Now which do you think would work best with your uncle? To put your brother in there right now, while your uncle watches? He's watching this, you know; he saw you faint—and that couldn't have been better if you had practiced. Or to wait and—"

"My uncle is watching us?"

"Yes, of course. Or to—"

"*Uncle Tom!*"

"Oh, do keep quiet, Poddy. He can see you but he can't hear you and he can't possibly help you. *Hmm*— You're such a silly billy that I don't think I want your advice. On your feet, now!"

She walked me back to my cell.

That was only hours ago; it merely seems like years.

But it is long enough. Long enough for Poddy to lose her nerve. Look, I don't have to tell this, nobody knows but me. But I've been truthful all through these memoirs and I'll be truthful now: I have made up my mind that as soon as I get a chance to talk with Uncle I will beg him, plead with him, to do *anything* to keep me from being locked up with a happy-dusted native.

I'm not proud of it. I'm not sure I'll ever be proud of Poddy again. But there it is and you can rub my nose in it. I've come up against something that frightens me so much I've cracked.

---

1. The most celebrated classical statue of Apollo (Greek god of the sun), which is displayed in the Belvedere court of the Vatican; it is thought to be the Roman copy of a Greek original (ca. 4th c. B.C.E.).

I feel a little better about it to have admitted it baldly. I sort of hope that, when the time comes, I won't whimper and I won't plead. But I . . . just . . . don't . . . know.

And then somebody was shoved in with me and it was Clark!

I jumped up off the bed and threw my arms around him and lifted him right off his feet and was blubbering over him. "Oh, Clarkie! Brother, brother, are you hurt? What did they do to you? Speak to me! Are you deaf?"

Right in my ear he said, "Cut out the sloppy stuff, Pod."

So I knew he wasn't too badly hurt, he sounded just like Clark. I repeated, more quietly, "Are you deaf?"

He barely whispered in my ear, "No, but she thinks I am, so we'll go on letting her think so." He untangled himself from me, took a quick look in his bag, then rapidly and very thoroughly went over every bit of the room—giving Titania just wide enough berth to keep her from diving on him.

Then he came back, shoved his face close to mine and said, "Poddy, can you read lips?"

"No. Why?"

"The hell you can't, you just did."

Well, it wasn't quite true; Clark had barely whispered—and I did find that I was "hearing" him as much from watching his mouth as I was from truly hearing him. This is a very funny thing but Clark says that almost everybody reads lips more than they think they do, and he had noticed it and practiced it and can really read lips— only he never told anybody because sometimes it is most useful.

He had me talk so low that I couldn't hear it myself and he didn't talk much louder. He told me, "Look, Pod, I don't know that Old Lady Grew"—he didn't say "Lady"— "has this room wired. I can't find any changes in it since she had me in it before. But there are at least four places and maybe more where a mike could be. So we keep quiet—because it stands to reason she put us together to hear what we have to say to each other. So talk out loud all you want to . . . but just static. How scared you are and how dreadful it is that I can't hear anything and such-like noise."

So we did and I moaned and groaned and wept over my poor baby brother and he complained that he couldn't hear a word I was saying and kept asking me to find a pencil and write what I was saying—and in between we really did talk, important talk that Clark didn't want her to hear.

I wanted to know why he wasn't deaf—had he actually been in that tank? "Oh, sure," he told me, "but I wasn't nearly as limp by then as she thought I was, either. I had some paper in my pocket and I chewed it up into pulp and corked my ears." He looked pained. "A twenty-spot note. Most expensive earplugs anybody ever had, I'll bet. Then I wrapped my shirt around my head and ignored it. But stow that and listen."

He was even more vague about how he had managed to get himself trapped. "Okay, okay, so I got hoaxed. You and Uncle don't look so smart, either—and anyhow, you're responsible."

"I am not either responsible!" I whispered indignantly.

"If you're not responsible, then you're irresponsible, which is worse. Logic. But forget it, we've got important things to do now. Look, Pod, we're going to crush out of here."

"How?" I glanced up at Titania. She was nursing Ariel but she never took her eyes off us.

Clark followed my glance. "I'll take care of that insect when the time comes, forget it. It has to be soon and it has to be at night."

"Why at night?" I was thinking that this smoggy paradise was bad enough when you could see a little, but in pitch-darkness—

"Pod, let that cut in your face heal; you're making a draft. It's got to be while Jojo is locked up."

"Jojo?"

"That set of muscles she has working for her. The native."

"Oh, you mean Pinhead."

"Pinhead, Jojo, Albert Einstein.[2] The happy-duster. He serves supper, then he washes the dishes, then she locks him up and gives him his night's ration of dust. Then he stays locked up until he sleeps it off, because she's as scared of him when he's high as anybody else is. So we make our try for it while he is caged—and maybe she'll be asleep, too. With luck the bloke who drives her sky wagon will be away, too; he doesn't always sleep here. But we can't count on it and it has got to be before the *Tricorn* shapes for Luna. When is that?"

"Twelve-seventeen on the eighth, ship Greenwich."

"Which is?"

"Local? Nine-sixteen Venusberg, Wednesday the twentieth."

"Check," he answered. "On both."

"But why?"

"Shut up." He had taken his slide rule from his bag and was setting it. For the conversation, I assumed, so I asked, "Do you want to know the Venus second for this Terran year?" I was rather proud to have it on the tip of my tongue, like a proper pilot; Mr. Clancy's time hadn't been entirely wasted even though I had never let him get cuddly.

"Nope. I know it." Clark reset the rule, read it and announced, "We both remember both figures the same way and the conversion checks. So check timepieces." We both looked at our wrists. "Mark!"

We agreed, within a few seconds, but that wasn't what I noticed; I was looking at the date hand. "Clark! Today's the nineteenth!"

"Maybe you thought it was Christmas," he said sourly. "And don't yip like that again. I can read you if you don't make a sound."

"But that's tomorrow!" (I did make it soundless.)

"Worse. It's less than seventeen hours from now . . . and we can't make a move until that brute is locked up. We get just once chance, no more."

"Our Uncle Tom doesn't get to the conference."

Clark shrugged. "Maybe so, maybe not. Whether he decides to go—or sticks around and tries to find us—I couldn't care less."

Clark was being very talkative, for Clark. But at best he grudges words and I didn't understand him. "What do you mean—*if he sticks around?*"

Apparently Clark thought he had told me, or that I already knew—but he hadn't and I didn't. Uncle Tom was already gone. I felt suddenly lost and forlorn. "Clark, are you sure?"

"Sure, I'm sure. She darn well saw to it that I saw him go. Jojo loaded him in like a sack of meal and I saw the wagon take off into the smog. Uncle Tom is in Venusberg by now."

2. The brilliant German-born American theoretical physicist (1879–1955).

I suddenly felt much better. "Then he'll rescue us!"

Clark looked bored. "Pod, don't be stupid squared."

"But he will! Uncle Tom . . . and Mr. Chairman . . . and Dexter—"

He cut me off. "Oh, for Pete's sake, Poddy! Analyze it. You're Uncle Tom, you're in Venusberg, you've got all the help possible. *How do you find this place?*"

"Uh . . ." I stopped. "Uh . . ." I said again. Then I closed my mouth and left it closed.

"*Uh,*" he agreed. "Exactly *Uh.* You don't find it. Oh, in eight or ten years with a few thousand people doing nothing but searching, you could find it by elimination. Fat lot of good that would do. Get this through your little head, Sis: nobody is going to rescue us, nobody can possibly help us. We either break out of here tonight—or we've had it."

"Why tonight? Oh, tonight's all right with me. But if we don't get a chance tonight—"

"Then at nine-sixteen tomorrow," he interrupted, "we're dead."

"Huh? Why?"

"Figure it out yourself, Pod. Put yourself in old Gruesome's place. Tomorrow the *Tricorn* leaves. Figure it both ways: Uncle Tom leaves in it, or Uncle Tom won't leave. Okay, you've got his niece and nephew. What do you do with them? Be logical about it. *Her* sort of logic."

I tried, I really tried. But maybe I've been brought up wrong for that sort of logic; I can't seem to visualize killing somebody just because he or she had become a nuisance to me.

But I could see that Clark was right that far: after ship's departure tomorrow we will simply be nuisances to Mrs. Grew. If Uncle Tom *doesn't* leave, we are most special nuisances—and if he *does* leave and she is counting on his worry about us to keep him in line at Luna City (it wouldn't, of course, but that is what she is counting on anyway), in that case every day she risks the possibility that we might escape and get word to Uncle.

All right, maybe I can't imagine just plain murder; it's outside my experience. But suppose both Clark and I came down with green pox and died— That would certainly be convenient for Mrs. Grew—now, wouldn't it?

"I scan it," I agreed.

"Good," he said. "I'll teach you a thing or four yet, Pod. Either we make it tonight . . . or just past nine tomorrow she chills us both . . . and she chills Jojo, too, and sets fire to the place."

"Why Jojo? I mean Pinhead."

"That's the real tipoff, Pod. The happy-duster. This is Venus . . . and yet she let us see that she was supplying dust to a duster. She won't leave any witnesses."

"Uncle Tom is a witness, too."

"What if he is? She's counting on his keeping his lip zipped until the conference is over . . . and by then she's back on Earth and has lost herself among eight billion people. Hang around here and risk being caught? Pod, she's going to wait here only long enough to find out whether or not Uncle Tom catches the *Tricorn.* Then she'll carry out either Plan A, or Plan B—but both plans cancel us out. Get that through your fuzzy head."

I shivered. "All right. I've got it."

He grinned. "But *we* don't wait. We execute our own plan—my plan—first." He looked unbearably smug and added, "You fubbed utterly and came out here without doing any of the things I told you to . . . and Uncle Tom fubbed just about as badly, thinking he could make a straight payoff . . . but I came out here prepared!"

"You did? With what? Your slide rule? Or maybe those comic books?"

Clark said, "Pod, you know I never read comic books; they were just protective coloration."

(And this is true, so far as I know—I thought I had uncovered his Secret Vice.)

"Then what?" I demanded.

"Just compose your soul in patience, Sister dear. All in good time." He moved his bag back of the bed, then added, "Move around here where you can watch down the hallway. If Lady Macbeth[3] shows up, I'm reading comic books."

I did as he told me to but asked him one more question—on another subject, as quizzing Clark when he doesn't want to answer is as futile as slicing water. "Clark? You figure Mrs. Grew is part of the gang that smuggled the bomb?"

He blinked and looked stupid. "What bomb?"

"The one they paid you to sneak aboard the *Tricorn*, of course! *What bomb* indeed!"

"Oh, that. Golly, Poddy, you believe everything you're told. When you get to Terra, don't let anybody sell you the Pyramids—they're not for sale." He went on working and I smothered my annoyance.

Presently he said, "She couldn't possibly know anything about any bombs in the *Tricorn*, or she wouldn't have been a passenger in it herself."

Clark can always make me feel stupid. This was so obvious (after he pointed it out) that I refrained from comment. "How do you figure it, then?"

"Well, she could have been hired by the same people and not have known that they were just using her as a reserve."

My mind raced and another answer came up. "In which case there could be still a third plot to get Uncle Tom between here and Luna!"

"Could be. Certainly a lot of people are taking an interest in him. But I figure it for two groups. One group—almost certainly from Mars—doesn't want Uncle Tom to be there at all. Another group—from Earth probably, at least old Gruesome actually did come from Earth—wants him to be there but wants him to sing their song. Otherwise when she had Uncle Tom, she would never have turned him loose; she would just have had Jojo shove him into a soft spot and wait for the bubbles to stop coming up." Clark dug out something and looked at it. "Pod, repeat this back and don't make a sound. You are exactly twenty-three kilometers from South Gate and almost due south of it—south seven degrees west."

I repeated it. "How do you know?"

He held up a small black object about as big as two packs of cigarettes. "Inertial tracker, infantry model. You can buy them anywhere here, anybody who ever goes out into the bush carries one." He handed it to me.

I looked at it with interest; I had never seen one that small. Sand rats use them, of course, but they use bigger, more accurate ones mounted in their sand buggies— and anyhow, on Mars you can always see either the stars or the Sun. Not like this gloomy place! I even knew how it worked, more or less, because inertial astrogation is a commonplace for spaceships and guided missiles—vector integration of accelerations and times. But whereas the *Tricorn*'s inertial tracker is supposed to be good for one part in a million, this little gadget probably couldn't be read closer than one in a thousand.

But it improved our chances at least a thousand to one!

"Clark! Did Uncle Tom have one of these? 'Cause if he did—"

3. The cold, ambitious, and murderous wife of the title character of Shakespeare's *Macbeth* (1606).

He shook his head. "If he did, he never got a chance to read it. I figure they gassed him at once; he was limp when they lifted him out of the air wagon. And I never had a chance to tell him where this dump is because this has been my first chance to look at mine. Now put it in your purse; you're going to use it to get back to Venusberg."

"Uh . . . it'll be bulky in my purse, it'll show. You better hide it wherever you had it. You won't lose me, I'm going to hang onto your hand every step of the way."

"No."

"Why not?"

"In the first place I'm not going to drag this bag with me and that's where it was hidden, I built a false bottom into it. In the second place we aren't going back together—"

"What? Why not? We certainly are! Clark, I'm responsible for you."

"That's a matter of opinion. Your opinion. Look, Poddy, I'm going to get you out of this silly mess. But don't try to use your head, it leaks. Just your memory. Listen to what I say and then do it exactly the way I tell you to—and you'll be all right."

"But—"

"Do you have a plan to get us out?"

"No."

"Then shut up. You start pulling your Big Sister act now and you'll get us both killed."

I shut up. And I must confess that his plan made considerable sense. According to Clark there is nobody in this house but us, Mrs. Grew, Titania and Ariel, Pinhead—and sometimes her driver. I certainly haven't seen or heard any evidences of anybody else and I suppose that Mrs. Grew has been doing it with an absolute minimum of witnesses—I know I would if I were (God forbid!) ever engaged in anything so outrageously criminal.

I've never seen the driver's face and neither has Clark—on purpose, I'm sure. But Clark says that the driver sometimes stays overnight, so we must be prepared to cope with him.

Okay, assume that we cope. As soon as we are out of the house we split up; I go east, he goes west, for a couple of kilometers, in straight lines as near as bogs and swamps permit, which may be not very.

Then we both turn north—and Clark says that the ring road around the city is just three kilometers north of us; he drew me a sketch from memory of a map he had studied before he set out to "rescue Girdie."

At the ring road I go right, he goes left—and we each make use of the first hitchhike transportation, ranch house phone, or whatever, to reach Uncle Tom and / or Chairman Cunha and get lots of reinforcements in a hurry!

The idea of splitting up is the most elementary of tactics, to make sure that at least one of us gets through and gets help. Mrs. Grew is so fat she couldn't chase anybody on a race track, much less a swamp. We plan to do it when she doesn't dare unlock Pinhead for fear of her own life. If we are chased, it will probably be the driver—and he can't chase two directions at once. Maybe there are other natives she can call on for help, but even so, splitting up doubles our chances.

So I get the inertial tracker because Clark doesn't think I can maneuver in the bush without one, even if I wait for it to get light. He's probably right. But he claims that he can steer well enough to find that road using just his watch, a wet finger for the breeze, and polarized spectacles—which, so help me, he has with him.

I shouldn't have sneered at his comic books; he actually did come prepared, quite a lot of ways. If they hadn't gassed him while he was still locked in the passenger compartment of Mrs. Grew's air buggy, I think he could have given them a very busy, bad time. A flame gun in his bag, a Remington pistol hidden on his person, knives, stun bombs—even a *second* inertial tracker, openly in the bag along with his clothes and comic books and slide rule.

I asked him why, and he put on his best superior look. "If anything went wrong and they grabbed me, they would expect me to have one. So I had one—and it hadn't even been started . . . poor little tenderfoot who doesn't even know enough to switch the thing on when he leaves his base position. Old Gruesome got a fine chuckle out of that." He sneered. "She thinks I'm half-witted and I've done my best to help the idea along."

So they did the same thing with his bag that they did with my purse—cleaned everything out of it that looked even faintly useful for mayhem and murder, let him keep what was left.

And most of what was left was concealed by a false bottom so beautifully faked that the manufacturer wouldn't have noticed it.

Except, possibly, for the weight—I asked Clark about that. He shrugged. "Calculated risk," he said. "If you don't bet, you can't win. Jojo carried it in here still packed and she searched it in here—and didn't pick it up afterwards; she had both arms full of junk I didn't mind her confiscating."

(And suppose she had picked it up and noticed? Well, Brother would still have had his brain and his hands—and I think he could take a sewing machine apart and put it back together as a piece of artillery. Clark is a trial to me—but I have great confidence in him.)

I'm going to get some sleep now—or try to—as Pinhead has just fetched in our supper and we have a busy time ahead of us, later. But first I'm going to backtrack this tape and copy it; I have one fresh spool left in my purse. I'm going to give the copy to Clark to give to Uncle, just in case. Just in case Poddy turns out to be bubbles in a swamp, I mean. But I'm not worried about that; it's a much nicer prospect than being Pinhead's roommate. In fact I'm not worried about anything; Clark has the situation well in hand.

But he warned me very strongly about one thing; "Tell them to get here well before nine-sixteen . . . or don't bother to come at all."

"Why?" I wanted to know.

"Just do it."

"Clark, you know perfectly well that two grown men won't pay any attention unless I can give them a sound reason for it."

He blinked. "All right. There is a very sound reason. A half-a-kiloton bomb isn't very much . . . but it still isn't healthy to be around when it goes off. Unless they can get in here and disarm it before that time—up she goes!"

He has it. I've *seen* it. Snugly fitted into that false bottom. That same three kilograms of excess mass I couldn't account for at Deimos. Clark showed me the timing mechanism and how the shaped charges were nestled around it to produce the implosion squeeze.

But he did not show me how to disarm it. I ran into his blankest, most stubborn wall. He expects to escape, yes—and he expects to come back here with plenty of help and in plenty of time and disarm the thing. But he is utterly convinced that Mrs. Grew intends to kill us, and if anything goes wrong and we don't break out of here, or die trying, or anything . . . well, he intends to take her with us.

I told him it was wrong, I said that he mustn't take the law in his own hands.

"What law?" he said. "There isn't any law here. And you aren't being logical, Pod. Anything that is right for a group to do is right for one person to do."

That one was too slippery for me to answer so I tried simply pleading with him and he got sore. "Maybe you would rather be in the cage with Jojo?"

"Well . . . no."

"Then shut up about it. Look, Pod, I planned all this out when she had me in that tank, trying to beat my ears in, make me deaf. I kept my sanity by ignoring what was being done to me and concentrating on when and how I would blow her to bits."

I wondered if he had indeed kept his sanity but I kept my doubts to myself and shut up. Besides I'm not sure that he's wrong; it may be that I'm just squeamish about bloodshed. "Anything that is moral for a group to do is moral for one person to do." There must be a flaw in that, since I've always been taught that it is wrong to take the law in your own hands. But I can't find the flaw and it sounds axiomatic, self-evident. Switch it around. If something is wrong for one person to do, can it possibly be made *right* by having a lot of people (a government) agree to do it together? Even unanimously?

If a thing is wrong, it is wrong—and vox populi can't change it.

Just the same, I'm not sure I can nap with an atom bomb under my bed.

POSTLUDE

I guess I had better finish this.

My sister got right to sleep after I rehearsed her in what we were going to do. I stretched out on the floor but didn't go right to sleep. I'm a worrier, she isn't. I reviewed my plans, trying to make them tighter. Then I slept.

I've got one of those built-in alarm clocks and I woke just when I planned to, an hour before dawn. Any later and there would be too much chance that Jojo might be loose, any earlier and there would be too much time in the dark. The Venus bush is chancy even when you see well; I didn't want Poddy to step into something sticky, or step on something that would turn and bite her leg off. Nor me, either.

But we had to risk the bush, or stay and let old Gruesome kill us at her convenience. The first was a sporting chance; the latter was a dead certainty, even though I had a terrible time convincing Poddy that Mrs. Grew would kill us. Poddy's greatest weakness—the really soft place in her head, she's not too stupid otherwise—is her almost total inability to grasp that some people are as bad as they are. Evil. Poddy never has understood evil. Naughtiness is about as far as her imagination reaches.

But I understand evil, I can get right inside the skull of a person like Mrs. Grew and understand how she thinks.

Perhaps you infer from this that I am evil, or partly so. All right, want to make something of it? Whatever *I* am, I knew Mrs. Grew was evil before we ever left the *Tricorn* . . . when Poddy (and even Girdie!) thought the slob was just too darling for words.

I don't trust a person who laughs when there is nothing to laugh about. Or is good-natured no matter what happens. If it's that perfect, it's an act, a phony. So I watched her . . . and cheating at solitaire wasn't the only giveaway.

So between the bush and Mrs. Grew, I chose the bush, both for me and my sister.

Unless the air car was there and we could swipe it. This would be a mixed blessing, as it would mean two of them to cope with, them armed and us not. (I don't count a bomb as an arm, you can't point it at a person's head.)

Before I woke Poddy I took care of that alate pseudo-simian, that "fairy." Vicious little beast. I didn't have a gun. But I didn't really want one at that point; they understand about guns and are hard to hit, they'll dive on you at once.

Instead I had shoe trees in my spare shoes, elastic bands around my spare clothes, and more elastic bands in my pockets, and several two-centimeter steel ball bearings.

Shift two wing nuts, and the long parts of the shoe trees become a steel fork. Add elastic bands and you have a slingshot. And don't laugh at a slingshot; many a sand rat has kept himself fed with only a slingshot. They are silent and you usually get your ammo back.

I aimed almost three times as high as I would at home, to allow for the local gravity, and got it right on the sternum, knocked it off its perch—crushed the skull with my heel and gave it an extra twist for the nasty bite on Poddy's arm. The young one started to whine, so I pushed the carcass over in the corner, somewhat out of sight, and put the cub on it. It shut up. I took care of all this before I woke Poddy because I knew she had sentimental fancies about these "fairies" and I didn't want her jittering and maybe grabbing my elbow. As it was—clean and fast.

She was still snoring, so I slipped off my shoes and made a fast reconnoiter.

Not so good— Our local witch was already up and reaching for her broom; in a few minutes she would be unlocking Jojo if she hadn't already. I didn't have a chance to see if the sky car was outside; I did well not to get caught. I hurried back and woke Poddy.

"Pod!" I whispered. "You awake?"

"Yes."

"Wide awake? You've got to do your act, right now. Make it loud and make it good."

"Check."

"Help me up on the perch. Can your sore arm take it?"

She nodded, slid quickly off the bed and took position at the door, hands ready. I grabbed her hands, bounced to her shoulders, steadied, and she grabbed my calves as I let go her hands—and then I was up on the perch, over the door. I waved her on.

Poddy went running out the door, screaming, "Mrs. Grew! Mrs. Grew! Help, help! My brother!" She did make it good.

And came running back in almost at once with Mrs. Grew puffing after her.

I landed on Gruesome's shoulders, knocking her to the floor and knocking her gun out of her hand. I twisted and snapped her neck before she could catch her breath.

Pod was right on the ball, I have to give her credit. She had that gun before it stopped sliding. Then she held it, looking dazed.

I took it carefully from her. "Grab your purse. We go right now! Stick close behind me."

Jojo *was* loose, I had cut it too fine. He was in the living room, looking, I guess, to see what the noise was about. I shot him.

Then I looked for the air car while keeping the gun ready for the driver. No sign of either one—and I didn't know whether to groan or cheer. I was all keyed up to shoot him but maybe he would have shot me first. But a car would have been mighty welcome compared with heading into the bush.

I almost changed my plan at that point and maybe I should have. Kept together, I mean, and headed straight north for the ring road.

It was the gun that decided me. Poddy could protect herself with it—and I would just be darn careful what I stepped on or in. I handed it to her and told her to move slowly and carefully until there was more light—but get going!

She was wobbling the gun around. "But, Brother, I've never shot anybody!"

"Well, you can if you have to."

"I guess so."

"Nothing to it. Just point it at 'em and press the button. Better use both hands. And don't shoot unless you really need to."

"All right."

I smacked her behind. "Now get going. See you later."

And I got going. I looked behind once, but she was already vanished in the smog. I put a little distance between me and the house, just in case, then concentrated on approximating course west.

And I got lost. That's all. I needed that tracker but I had figured I could get along without it and Pod had to have it. I got hopelessly lost. There wasn't breeze enough for me to tell anything by wetting my finger and that polarized light trick for finding the Sun is harder than you would think. Hours after I should have reached the ring road I was still skirting boggy places and open water and trying to keep from being somebody's lunch.

And suddenly there was the most dazzling light possible and I went down flat and stayed there with my eyes buried in my arm and started to count.

I wasn't hurt at all. The blast wave covered me with mud and the noise was pretty rough, but I was well outside the real trouble. Maybe half an hour later I was picked up by a cop car.

Certainly, I should have disarmed that bomb. I had intended to, if everything went well; it was just meant to be a "Samson in the Temple"[4] stunt if things turned out dry. A last resort.

Maybe I should have stopped to disarm it as soon as I broke old gruesome's neck— and maybe Jojo would have caught both of us if I had and him still with a happy-dust hangover. Anyhow I didn't and then I was very busy deciding what to do and telling Poddy how to use that gun and getting her started. I didn't think about the bomb until I was several hundred meters from the house—and I certainly didn't want to go back then, even if I could have found it again in the smog, which is doubtful.

But apparently Poddy did just that. Went back to the house, I mean. She was found later that day, about a kilometer from the house, outside the circle of total destruction—but caught by the blast.

With a live baby fairy in her arms—her body had protected it; it doesn't appear to have been hurt at all.

That's why I think she went back to the house. I don't *know* that this baby fairy is the one she called "Ariel." It could have been one that she picked up in the bush. But that doesn't seem at all likely; a wild one would have clawed her and its parents would have torn her to pieces.

I think she intended to save that baby fairy all along and decided not to mention it to me. It is just the kind of sentimental stunt that Poddy would pull. She knew I was going to have to kill the adult—and she never said a word against that; Pod could always be sensible when absolutely necessary.

Then in the excitement of breaking out she forgot to grab it, just as I forgot to disarm the bomb after we no longer needed it. So she went back for it.

And lost the inertial tracker, somehow. At least it wasn't found on her or near her. Between the gun and her purse and the baby fairy and the tracker she must have dropped it in the bog. Must be, because she had plenty of time to go back and still

4. After being captured by the Philistines, Samson pulled down the pillars that supported their temple, killing them and himself (Judges 16).

get far away from the house. She should have been ten kilometers away by then, so she must have lost the tracker fairly soon and walked in a circle.

I told Uncle Tom all about it and was ready to tell the Corporation people, Mr. Cunha and so forth, and take my medicine. But Uncle told me to keep my mouth shut. He agreed that I had fubbed it, mighty dry indeed—but so had he—and so had everybody. He was gentle with me. I wish he had hit me.

I'm sorry about Poddy. She gave me some trouble from time to time, with her bossy ways and her illogical ideas—but just the same, I'm sorry.

I wish I knew how to cry.

Her little recorder was still in her purse and part of the tape could be read. Doesn't mean much, though; she doesn't tell what she did, she was babbling, sort of:

". . . very dark where I'm going. No man is an island complete in himself.[5] Remember that, Clarkie. Oh, I'm sorry I fubbed it but remember that; it's important. They all have to be cuddled sometimes. My shoulder—Saint Podkayne! Saint Podkayne, are you listening? UnkaTom, Mother, Daddy—is anybody listening? Do listen, please, because this is important. I love—"

It cuts off there. So we don't know whom she loved.

Everybody, maybe.

I'm alone here, now. Mr. Cunha made them hold the *Tricorn* until it was certain whether Poddy would die or get well, then Uncle Tom left and left me behind—alone, that is, except for doctors, and nurses, and Dexter Cunha hanging around all the time, and a whole platoon of guards. I can't go anywhere without one. I can't go to the casinos at all any more—not that I want to, much.

I heard part of what Uncle Tom told Dad about it. Not all of it, as a phone conversation with a bounce time of over twenty minutes is episodic. I heard none of what Dad said and only one monologue of Uncle's:

"Nonsense, sir! I am not dodging my own load of guilt; it will be with me always. Nor can I wait here until you arrive and you know it and you know why—and both children will be safer in Mr. Cunha's hands and *not* close to me . . . and you know *that*, too! But I have a message for you, sir, one that you should pass on to your wife. Just this: people who will not take the trouble to raise children should not have them. You with your nose always in a book, your wife gallivanting off God knows where—between you, your daughter was almost killed. No credit to either of you that she wasn't. Just blind luck. You should tell your wife, sir, that building bridges and space stations and such gadgets is all very well . . . but that a woman has more important work to do. I tried to suggest this to you years ago . . . and was told to mind my own business. Now I am saying it. Your daughter will get well, no thanks to either of you. But I have my doubts about Clark. With him it may be too late. God may give you a second chance if you hurry. Ending transmission!"

I faded into the woodwork then and didn't get caught. But what did Uncle Tom mean by that—trying to scare Dad about *me*? I wasn't hurt at all and he knows it. I just got a load of mud on me, not even a burn . . . whereas Poddy still looks like a corpse and they've got her piped and wired like a crèche.

I don't see what he was driving at.

I'm taking care of that baby fairy because Poddy will want to see it when she gets

---

5. A paraphrase of "No man is an island, entire of itself," from John Donne's *Devotions upon Emergent Occasions* (1624).

well enough to notice things again; she's always been a sentimentalist. It needs a lot of attention because it gets lonely and has to be held and cuddled, or it cries.

So I'm up a lot in the night—I guess it thinks I'm its mother. I don't mind, I don't have much else to do.

It seems to like me.

1963

GEORGE R. R. MARTIN
b. 1948

George Raymond Richard Martin, a multifaceted writer of science fiction, fantasy, and television scripts, grew up in a working-class family in Bayonne, New Jersey. Preferring dream worlds to his real surroundings, he escaped in his imagination, relying in particular on reading works of fantasy, horror, and science fiction by such authors as Robert Heinlein, Andre Norton, H. P. Lovecraft, and J. R. R. Tolkien. He studied journalism at Northwestern University, where he received his B.S. in 1970 and M.S. in 1971, and was already writing fiction. His first published short story, "The Hero," appeared in *Galaxy* magazine in 1971. After graduation he worked for VISTA—a domestic service program that later became part of AmeriCorps—from 1972 to 1974 as communications coordinator for Cook County Legal Assistance Foundation in Chicago, thereby fulfilling his alternative to military service because he was a conscientious objector.

During this time he continued to submit science fiction stories to various magazines and journals. From 1976 to 1978 he taught journalism at Clarke College in Dubuque, Iowa, becoming writer-in-residence in 1978. In 1979 he decided to devote himself full-time to his writing. By then he had already written *Dying of the Light* (1978), a novel whose action takes place on a dying planet, and two well-received short story collections, *A Song for Lya* (1976) and *Song of Stars and Shadows* (1977). In 1981 he published both another novel set on a richly imagined distant planet, *Windhaven* (written with Lisa Tuttle), and another collection of stories, *The Sandkings*.

In the 1980s Martin published two horror novels—*Fevre Dream* (1982), a vampire novel set on the antebellum Mississippi, and *The Armageddon Rag* (1983), in which a writer investigating the ritual murder of a rock promoter is drawn into the supernatural—and four more short story collections, but by the middle of the decade he had moved to Hollywood and shifted his emphasis to writing screenplays, teleplays, and pilots. He wrote episodes for the new version of *The Twilight Zone* (1986) and for the series *Beauty and the Beast* (1987–90). Throughout this time he continued to edit the long-running *Wild Cards* shared-universe anthology series, and in the mid-1990s he returned to writing novels. He is currently halfway through the projected six volumes of an epic fantasy series, "A Song of Ice and Fire," that began in 1996 with *The Game of Thrones* (1996). The novels are historical fantasies, loosely based on England's War of the Roses but set in the mythical Seven Kingdoms where winter and summer may last for decades. Clearly influenced by Tolkien and medieval culture, Martin seeks to explore the meaning of the heroic journey and the extremes of nobility and betrayal in these works.

"The Last Super Bowl Game" (1975) mixes the typical sports story for young readers with science fiction. Unlike writers of traditional sports stories, Martin does not celebrate the "game" or the heroic aspects of American sports culture. Instead, he reveals the dangers of commercialization and shows how technology has been used to alter our sense of what is valuable in games and play.

The Last Super Bowl Game

The last Super Bowl was played in January, 2016, on a muddy field in Hoboken, New Jersey.

It was attended by 832 aging fans, 12 sportswriters, a Boy Scout troop, and the commissioner of the National Football League. The commissioner brought the Boy Scouts. He was also a scoutmaster.

The Packers were the favorites, and that was as it should be. It was somehow right, and appropriate, and just that the Packers should be in the final game.

They were still the Green Bay Packers, after all, the same now, at the end, as in the dim beginnings so many years ago. The teams of the great cities had come and gone, but the Packers stayed on, eternal and unchanging.

They had a perfect record going into the championship, and a defense the likes of which football had never seen. Or at least so the sportswriters wrote. But claims like that had to be taken with several grains of salt. Sportswriters were a dying breed, and they exaggerated a lot to stave off extinction.

The underdogs in the last, lonely showdown were the Hoboken Jets. Formerly the Jersey City Jets. Formerly the Newark Jets. Formerly the New York Jets. The sportswriters, in their fading wisdom, had decreed that the Jets would lose by two touchdowns.

Not that Hoboken had a bad team. They were pretty good, actually. They'd won their conference going away. But then, it was a weak conference, and the Jet defense was a little sloppy. They didn't have a great offense either.

What they did have was Keith Lancer. Lancer, so said the sportswriters, was the greatest quarterback ever to throw a football. Better than Namath, Unitas, Graham, Baugh,[1] any of them. A golden arm; great range, fantastic accuracy. He was a scrambler too. And a brilliant field general.

But he was only one man, and he had never faced a team like the Packers. The Packer front four were creatures out of nightmare. Their rush had been known to drive brilliant quarterbacks into blithering, terrified idiocy.

The sportswriters claimed the Packer defense would grind Lancer into little bits and scatter him all over the field. But that was just what the sportswriters claimed. And nobody listened to sportswriters anymore.

It was a classic confrontation. Offense against defense. One brilliant man against a smoothly oiled machine. A lone hero against a horde of monsters.

The last page of football history. But a great page, a great moment, a great game. And it was played before 832 fans, 12 sportswriters, a Boy Scout troop, and the commissioner of the National Football League.

It had begun, long ago, when someone decided to settle an old argument.

Arguments are the stuff of which sports are made. They go on and on, forever, and no one has ever stopped to figure out how many bars they keep in business. The

---

1. All are Hall of Fame quarterbacks. Joe Namath (b. 1943; player, 1965–78) led the underdog New York Jets to victory in Super Bowl III in 1969; Johnny Unitas (1933–2002; player, 1956–73), who played all but the final five games of his career with the Baltimore Colts, was twice voted the greatest quarterback in football history; Otto Graham (1921–2003; player, 1946–55) led the Cleveland Browns to ten consecutive championship games; and Sammy Baugh (b. 1914; player, 1937–52), who played for the Washington Redskins, has been called the NFL's first great quarterback.

arguments were all different, but all the same. Who's the greatest heavyweight champion of all time? Who should play center field on the all-time All Star team? Name the best football team ever.

Ask a man those questions and listen to his answers. Then you'll know when he was growing up, and where he once lived, and what kind of a man he was.

Eternal questions, never-ending arguments, the raucous music of the locker room and the tavern. Not questions that could be answered. Nor questions that should be answered. There are some things man was not meant to know.

But one day someone tried to answer them. He used a computer.

Computers were still in diapers back then. But still they were treated with deference. They didn't make mistakes. When a computer said something, the man in the street generally listened. And believed.

So they decided to ask a computer to pick the greatest heavyweight champion of all time.

But they didn't merely ask a question. They had more imagination than that. They arranged a tournament, a great tournament between all the heavyweight champions of history, each fighting in his prime. They fed each man's style into the machine, and told it about his strengths and weaknesses and habits and quirks.

And the machine digested all the glass chins[2] and snappy left jabs and dazzling footwork, and set to work producing simulated fights. One by one the heavyweight champions eliminated each other in computerized bouts that were jazzed up and dramatized and broadcast over the radio.

Rocky Marciano[3] won the thing.

It began to rain shortly after the two teams had come onto the field. Not a heavy rain, at first. Just a thin, cold, soggy-wet drizzle that came down and down and wouldn't stop.

Green Bay won the toss and elected to receive. Hoboken decided to defend the south goal.

The kickoff was shallow and wobbly, probably because of the rain and the muddy condition of the field. Mike Strawn, the Packers' speed merchant, fielded the kick and ran it back fifteen yards before being pulled down at the thirty.

The Packer offense took the field. They were a coldly determined bunch that afternoon. They had something to prove. They were tired of hearing, over and over again, about how defense made the Packers great. And Dave Sandretti, the Packers' scrappy young quarterback, was especially tired of hearing about Keith Lancer.

Sandretti went to the air immediately, hitting on a short, flat pass to the sideline for a quick first down. On the next play he handed off, and Mule Mitchell smashed through the center of the Jet line for a four-yard gain. Then Strawn went around end for another first down.

The Packers drove.

Their offense was nothing fancy. The Packer coach believed in basic football. But it was effective. Alternating skillfully between his short passes and his potent running game, Sandretti moved the Packers across the fifty and into enemy territory before the drive finally bogged down near the thirty-five.

The field-goal attempt was wide. The Jets took over on their own twenty.

2. I.e., vulnerabilities to knockout punches.
3. American heavyweight boxer (born Rocco Marchegiano, 1923–1969), champion 1952–56.

Inevitably, other tournaments followed in the wake of the first one. They settled the argument about the greatest middleweight champion of all time, and the best college football team, and the finest baseball squad ever assembled.

And each simulated fight and computerized game seemed to draw larger radio audiences than the one before it. People liked the idea. They didn't always agree with the computer's verdict, but that was okay. It gave them something new to argue about.

It wasn't long before the sponsors of the computerized tournaments realized they had a gold mine on their hands. And, once they did realize it, it took them no time at all to abandon their original purposes. Settling the old arguments, after all, was dangerous. It might lead to loss of interest in forthcoming computerized bouts.

So they announced that the computer's verdicts were far from final. Different tournament pairings might give different results, they claimed. And so it was when they ran the heavyweight elimination over again.

The lords of sport looked on tolerantly. Computerized sports were an interesting sideshow, they thought, but hardly anything to worry about. After all, a phony football game broadcast over the radio could never match the violent color and excitement of the real thing on television.

They even went so far as to feature computer simulations in their pre-game shows, to add a little spice to the presentation. The computer predictions were almost always wrong, and the computer games were drab compared to the spectacle that invariably followed.

The lords of sport were absolutely certain that computer simulations would never be anything more than minor sideshows. Absolutely certain.

At first, Lancer set out to establish his running game.

He abandoned that idea two plays later, after the Packer defense had twice snagged Jet runners short of the line of scrimmage. On third and fifteen, Lancer took to the air for the first time. The pass was complete for a first down.

On first and ten, he went for a long bomb. It fell incomplete when his receiver slipped on the muddy field. But the Jets got a first down anyway. The Packer rush put a bit too much pressure on Lancer, and got assessed fifteen yards for roughing the passer. Lancer had been hit solidly by two defensemen after getting the pass away.

He got up covered with mud, a little shaken, and very mad. When Lancer was mad, the Jets were mad. The team began to move.

If the Packer offense was the soul of simplicity, the Jet offense was a study in devious complexity. Lancer used a whole array of different formations, kept his backfield in constant motion with shift after shift, and had a mind-boggling number of plays to choose from.

The Packers knew all that, of course. They had studied game films. But watching films was not quite the same thing as facing an angry Keith Lancer.

Lancer let the Packers have both barrels now. He started to razzle-dazzle with a vengeance. The Packer rush dumped him a few more times. But in between, the Jets were registering long gains.

It took Lancer nine plays to put Hoboken into the end zone. The Jets went ahead, 7–0.

The sportswriters started muttering.

The problem with the early computer simulations was their lack of depth. Computer games were presented either as flat, colorless predictions, or as overdramatized radio shows. Which was all right. But not to be compared to actually watching a real game.

Then someone got a bright idea. They made a movie.

Rocky Marciano had been retired for years, but he was still around. Muhammad Ali[4] was still one of the premier heavyweights of the era. So they paired them in a computer fight, got Marciano back into reasonable shape, and had the two men act out the computer's prediction of what would have happened if they had met when each was in his prime. Marciano won by a knockout.

The film got wide publicity, and was shown in theaters from coast to coast. It outdrew the crowds that real bouts got in the same theaters when they appeared via closed-circuit television.

The newspapers seemed confused over how to cover it. Some sent movie critics. But many sent sportswriters. And while most of those sportswriters treated it as a joke, a minor and inconsequential diversion, others wrote up the fight quite seriously.

The handwriting was on the wall. But the lords of sport didn't read it. After all, the circumstances that allowed a film like this to be made were pretty unique, they reasoned. The computer people could hardly dig up John L. Sullivan or the Four Horsemen or Babe Ruth[5] for future films. And the public would never accept actors.

So there was nothing to worry about. Nothing at all.

Through the mud and the steadily building rain, the Packers came driving back. They relied mostly on their running game, on Mule Mitchell's tanklike rushes and Mike Strawn's darting zigzags and quick end runs. But Sandretti's passing played a role, too. He didn't have Lancer's arm, by any means. But he was good, and he was accurate, and when the chips were down he seldom missed.

Back upfield they moved, back into Jet territory. The first quarter ended with them on the Jet thirty.

The drive continued in the second period, but once again the Packers seemed to run out of gas when they got within the shadow of the goalposts. They had to settle for a field goal.

More movies followed the success of the first. But the lords of sport had been correct. The idea had built-in limitations. A lavish production that used actors to pit Jack Dempsey against Joe Louis[6] underlined that point. It was a total bust. The fans wanted the real thing. Or close to it, anyway.

But some films could be made, and they were made, and they made money. It became a respectable movie subgenre. One studio, Versus Productions, specialized in film versions of computer sports, and made modest profits.

But real sports continued to do better than ever. The public had more and more leisure, and a voracious hunger for vicarious violence. The lords of sport feasted on huge television contracts, and grew fat and rich. And blind.

4. American heavyweight boxer (born Cassius Clay, 1942), champion 1964–67, 1975–78, and 1978–79.

5. American baseball player (1895–1948; player, 1914–35), who became the game's first superstar with the New York Yankees. Sullivan (1858–1918), American bare-knuckles prizefighter and heavyweight boxing champion (1882–92). The Four Horsemen: a name, alluding to the Four Horsemen of the Apocalypse (famine, pestilence, destruction, and death; Revelation 6.1–8), that was given in

1924 to four devastatingly effective players on Notre Dame's college football team—quarterback Harry Stuhldreher (1901–1965), left halfback Jim Crowley (1902–1986), right halfback Don Miller (1902–1979), and fullback Elmer Layden (1903–1973).

6. American heavyweight boxer (born Joseph Louis Barrow, 1914–1981), champion 1937–49. Dempsey (1895–1983), American heavyweight boxer, champion 1919–26.

They hardly even noticed when some of the old computer films began to turn up on late shows here and there.

They should have.

Lancer got the Jets driving again. But this time their momentum ebbed quickly. The Packer defense wasn't about to get pushed around all day. They were quick to adapt, and now they were beginning to get used to Lancer's bag of tricks.

The Hoboken drive sputtered to a halt on the Green Bay forty, when Lancer was dumped twice in a row by the Packer rush. The field-goal attempt was a valiant but misguided effort to buck the wind and the rain. It fell absurdly short.

The Packers took over. At once they began to move. Sandretti clicked on a series of passes, and Mitchell punched through the Hoboken line again and again.

When the Packers crossed the fifty, the Jets decided to surprise Sandretti with a blitz. They did surprise him. Once.

The next time they tried it, Sandretti flipped a screen pass to Strawn in the flat. He shook off one tackler, sidestepped two more, and outran everybody else on the field.

That made it 10–7 Packers. The sportswriters began to breathe a little easier.

It was such a simple idea.

The name of the man who first thought of it is lost. But there is a legend. The legend says it was an electronics engineer employed by one of the networks, and that the idea came to him when he was watching a television rerun of a computer fight movie.

It wasn't a very good movie, and his attention began to wander, says the legend. He began to think about why filmed computer simulations had never really made it big. The problem, he decided, was actors.

Computer simulations had more veracity and realism than fictional fight movies. But they lost it when they used actors. The public wouldn't buy actors. But, without actors, the possible number of productions was severely limited.

What was needed was another way to make the simulations.

He looked at the television wall, the legend says. And the idea came.

He wasn't watching a picture. Not really. He knew that. He was watching a pattern of multicolored dots. A complex pattern that deluded the human eye into thinking it was a picture. But it wasn't. There was nothing there but a bunch of electronic impulses.

If you got those impulses to join together and form an image of some actor playing Joe Louis, then there was no damn reason in the world that you couldn't get them to join together to form an image of Joe Louis himself.

It was easier if there was a pattern to be broken down and reassembled, of course. But that didn't mean it was impossible to build patterns out of whole cloth. And it wouldn't matter if those patterns had ever really existed anywhere but on the television screen. The images could be made just as real.

Yes. It could work. If you had an instrument fast enough to assemble such complex patterns and change them smoothly enough to simulate motion and action. If you had a computer, a big one. Yes.

The next day, the legend says, the nameless electronics engineer went to speak to the president of his network.

On the second play after the kickoff, the Packers blitzed. Their normal rush was fierce enough. Their blitz was devastating. The Hoboken line shattered under the impact, and the Packers stormed through, hungry for quarterback blood.

Lancer, back to pass, searched desperately for a receiver. He found none. He danced out of the way of the first Packer to reach him, tucked the ball under his arm, and tried to scramble. He got about five yards back toward the line of scrimmage before the Green Bay meat grinder closed in around him.

Afterward, he couldn't get up. They carried him off the field, limping.

There was a stunned silence, then a slowly building cheer as Lancer was carried to the sidelines.

Or as much of a cheer as could be produced by 832 fans, 12 sportswriters, a Boy Scout troop, and the commissioner of the National Football League.

Sports were very big business, and all three networks fought tooth and nail in the bloody bidding wars for the right to telecast the major events. And of all the wars, the football wars were the most gory.

One network won the NFL that year. Another won the NCAA.[7] The third, according to tradition, was in for a bad time. It was going to get badly bludgeoned in the ratings until those contracts ran out.

But that year, the third network refused to lie down meekly and accept its fate. It broke with tradition. It scheduled something new. A show called "Unplayed Football Classics."

The show featured televised computer simulations of great games between the top football teams, both pro and college, in the history of the game. It did not use actors. A gigantic network computer, specially designed and built for the purpose, produced the simulations from scratch.

The show was a bombshell. A glorious, shouting, screaming, disgustingly successful smash hit.

With Lancer out, the Jets went nowhere. They bogged down in the mud and were forced to punt.

Sandretti, sensing that the Hoboken team was badly shaken by the loss of its star quarterback, pressed his advantage ruthlessly. He went for the bomb on the first play from scrimmage.

Strawn, sent out wide on the play, snagged the long throw neatly and took it all the way in for another Packer touchdown. The extra point made it 17–7.

All of a sudden, it seemed to be raining a little harder on the Hoboken side of the field. A few of the 832 fans, those of the least faith,[8] began to drift from the stadium.

"Unplayed Football Classics" was followed by "Matchup," a boxing show that telecast the imaginary bouts most requested by the viewers. Other spin-offs followed in good time when "Matchup," too, made it big.

After the third year of smash ratings, "Unplayed Football Classics" was sent into the front lines. Its time slot was moved so it conflicted, directly, with the NFL Game-of-the-Week.

The resulting holocaust was a ratings draw. But even that was enough to wake the lords of sport from their slumber and set them to yelping. For the very first time,

7. The National Collegiate Athletic Association, which oversees intercollegiate sports.
8. An allusion to a phrase attributed to Jesus in the New Testament, "O ye of little faith" (Matthew 6.30, 8.24, 16.8; Luke 12.28).

computer simulations had demonstrated that they could compete successfully with the real product.

The lords of sport fought back, at first, with an advertising campaign. They set out to convince the public that the computer games were cheap imitations that no *real* sports fan would accept for a moment as a substitute for the real thing.

They failed. The fans were too far removed from the stadium to grasp the point. They were a generation of sports fans that had never seen a football game, except over television. And, over television, the computer games were just as dramatic and unpredictable and exciting as anything the NFL could offer.

So, the games weren't real. So what. They *looked* real. It wasn't like they used actors, or anything.

The lords of sport reeled from their failure, grasped for another weapon. The lawsuits began.

You can't call your simulated team the Green Bay Packers, the lawyers for the lords told the computer people. That name is our property. You can't use it. Or the names of all those players. You'll have to make up your own.

They went to court to prove their point.

They lost.

After all, the judges ruled, they weren't using real games. Besides, they asked the lords of sport, why didn't you object to all those people who did the same thing on radio? No, it's too late. You've set your precedents already.

Meanwhile, the third network was building a bigger computer. It was called Sportsmaster.

Hoboken held onto the ball for the rest of the second quarter, but only to run out the clock. There wasn't enough time left to do anything before the half, anyway.

The halftime show was a dreary affair. The NFL had long passed the point when it could stage big productions. But, given its budget, it still tried. There were a few high school bands on hand, and a holoshow[9] that was an utter disaster thanks to the rain.

It didn't matter. Nobody was watching, anyway. The fans had all gone for hot dogs, and the sportswriters were down in the locker room trying to find out how Keith Lancer was.

The Boy Scouts, meanwhile, went to the Packer locker room, to get autographs— on orders from the scoutmaster, who was also commissioner of the National Football League.

Sportsmaster was the largest civilian computer ever built, and there were some that said it was even bigger than the Pentagon computer that controlled the nation's defenses. Its master memory banks contained all the data on sports and sports figures that anyone anywhere had ever bothered to put down on paper or film or tape. It was designed to prepare detailed, full-color, whole-cloth simulations, for both standard television wall-screens and the new holovision sets.

Its method of operation was an innovation, too. Instead of isolated games, Sportsmaster featured league competition, complete with seasons and schedules. But in the Sportsmaster Baseball League, every team was a pennant winner. In the Sportsmaster Boxing Tournament, every fighter was a champion. In the Sportsmaster Foot-

---

9. A projection of three-dimensional images.

ball League, every competitor had at least a divisional crown to its credit.

Sportsmaster games would not be presented as mere television shows. They would be presented as events, as news, it was decreed. The network sponsoring Sportsmaster immediately began to give the same buildup to future computer simulations as to real sports events. The newspapers, at first, refused to go along. Most insisted on covering Sportsmaster broadcasts in the entertainment section instead of the sports pages.

For a while they insisted, that is. Then, one by one, they began to come around. The fans, it seemed, wanted sports coverage of Sportsmaster presentations.

And the lords of sport suddenly faced war.

Hoboken took the kickoff at the opening of the second half. But Keith Lancer still sat on the sidelines, and without him the Jets seemed vaguely unsure of what they were supposed to do with the ball. They made one first down, then stalled and were forced to punt.

The Packer offense came back onto the field, and they radiated a cold confidence. With methodical precision, Sandretti led his team down the field. He was taking no chances now, so he kept the ball out of the air and relied on his running backs. Again and again Mitchell slammed into the line, and Strawn danced through it, to pick up a yard or two or four. Slowly but inexorably the Packer steamroller ground ahead.

The drive was set back by a few penalties, and slowed here and there when the Jet defense toughened momentarily. But it was never stopped. It was late in the third quarter before Mitchell finally plunged over tackle into the end zone for another Packer touchdown.

Then came the extra point, and it was 24–7 Packers, and a lot of the fans seemed to be leaving.

For a decade the war raged, fierce and bloody. At first, Sportsmaster was the underdog, fighting for acceptance, fighting to be taken seriously. The NFL and the NHL and the NBA won all the early battles.

And then the gap began to close. The viewers and the fans got used to Sportsmaster, and the distinction began to blur. After all, the games all looked the same over television. Except that the Sportsmaster leagues seemed to have better teams, and their games seemed to be a little more exciting.

That was deliberate. The Sportsmaster people had programmed in a drama factor. They were careful about it, however. They knew that nothing can kill a sport faster than obvious staging of games for effect. The predictable, standard scripts of wrestling and roller derby were strictly avoided. Sportsmaster games remained always as unpredictable as the real thing.

Only, they were slightly more exciting, on the average. There were dull games in the Sportsmaster leagues, of course. But never quite as many as in the real leagues.

The turning point in the war was the Battle of the Super Bowl in January, 1994.

In the NFL Super Bowl, the New York Giants were facing the Denver Broncos. The Broncos were one of the most exciting teams in decades; blinding speed, a colorful quarterback, and the highest-scoring offense in football history. The Giants were the mediocre champions of a weak division, who had gotten lucky in the playoffs.

In the Sportsmaster Super Bowl, the 1993 Denver Broncos were facing the Green Bay Packers of the Vince Lombardi era.[1]

In the NFL Super Bowl, the Broncos beat the Giants 34–9 in an utterly undistinguished game. The outcome of the contest was never in doubt for a second.

In the Sportsmaster Super Bowl, the Broncos beat the Packers 21–17, on a long bomb thrown with seconds remaining on the clock.

The two Super Bowls got almost identical ratings. But those who watched the NFL game found that they had missed a classic to watch a dud. It was the last time that would happen, they vowed.

Sportsmaster began to pull ahead.

It was the moment of truth for Hoboken.

The Jets took the Packer kickoff, and started upfield with determination. Yard by yard they fought their way through the mud and the rain, back into the game. And the Packer defense made them pay for every inch with blood.

The Jets drove to the fifty, then past it. They moved into Packer territory. When the quarter ended, they were on the Packer thirty-three-yard line.

Two plays into the fourth quarter, the second-string quarterback fumbled on a handoff. The Packers recovered.

Sandretti took over, and the Packers moved the ball back toward midfield. They picked up one first down. But then, suddenly, the Jet defense got tough.

They stopped the Packers on the forty-five. Green Bay was forced to punt. The punt, against the wind, was a bad one. The Jets called for a fair catch and took the ball on their own thirty.

First and ten. The Jets tried an end sweep. No gain.

Second and ten. A reverse. A three-yard loss.

Third and thirteen. The Jets called time out.

And Keith Lancer came back in.

He wasn't limping now. But he still looked unsteady, wobbly on his feet. This was it for the Jets, the fans told themselves. This was the do-or-die play. A pass, of course. It had to be a pass.

The Packers were thinking the same thing. When the ball was snapped and Lancer faded back, their front four came roaring in like demons out of hell.

Lancer lateraled to one of his halfbacks on the sideline. The rushers changed direction in midstride, and streaked past him.

Lancer, suddenly ignored, ran slowly upfield and caught the pass for a first down. He was tackled with a vengeance. But all that got the Packers was a fifteen-yard penalty.

Lancer stayed in, and started passing. In seven plays, he put Hoboken on the scoreboard again to cut the Packer margin to 24–14.

The long twilight of spectator sports had begun.

Sportsmaster II was unveiled in 1995, a computer bigger and more sophisticated than the original. Sportsmaster, Inc., was sliced from the network that had founded it by government decree, since the combined empire was growing too large.

By the late 1990s, television confrontations between Sportsmaster shows and real

1. I.e., 1959–68, when Lombardi (1913–1970) was the Packers' head coach and the team won five championships.

sports events were confrontations in name only. Sportsmaster ran away with the ratings with monotonous regularity.

In 1996, the network that had been broadcasting NFL games refused to pick up the contract unless the price was slashed almost in half. The league was forced to agree.

In 1998, the NBA television contract was worth only a fourth of what it had gone for five years earlier.

In 1999, no one bid for the right to telecast NHL hockey.

Still, the sports promoters hung on. They still had some television audiences. And the games themselves were still packed.

But the Sportsmaster men were ruthless. They analyzed the reasons why real sports still attracted people. And came up with some innovations.

People who still went to games did so because they preferred to view sports outdoors, or as part of a crowd, they decided. Fine. So they built Sportsmaster Theaters, where fans could eat hot dogs and watch the games as part of a crowd. And they erected a giant Sportsmaster Stadium, where the simulations were staged outdoors as full-color, three-dimensional holoshows.

In 2003, the Super Bowl was not a sellout. The World Series had already failed to sell out for several years running. The live crowds started to shrink.

And didn't stop.

Despite the Jet touchdown, the Packers were still comfortably out in front. The game was theirs, if they could only run out the clock.

Sandretti kept his team on the ground, handing off to Mitchell and Strawn, chalking up one first down after another the hard way by churning through the mud. The Jets began to use their time-outs. The minutes flew by.

The Packers finally were held just past the midfield stripe. But Sandretti had wreaked his damage. There was time left for maybe one Jet drive, but hardly for two.

But Hoboken did not give up. Their time-outs were gone, and the clock was against them. But Lancer was in the game again. And that made anything possible.

The Packers went into a prevent defense to guard against the bomb. They were willing to give up the short gain, the first down. That was all right. Lancer could drive for a touchdown if he wanted to, so long as it wasn't a quick score.

The Jet quarterback tried one bomb, but it fizzled, incomplete, in the rain. Packer defenders were all over the Hoboken deep men. The Jets had no recourse but to drive for the score, eat up the clock, and pray for a break.

They drove. Lancer, no longer wobbly, hit on one short pass after another. Hoboken moved upfield. Hoboken scored. The extra point was dead on target. The score stood at 24–21.

But there was less than a minute left to play.

In 2005, they introduced Sportsmaster III, and the Home Matchmaker. It was a fatal blow.

Sportsmaster III was ten times the size of Sportsmaster II, and had more than a hundred times the capacity. It was built underground in Kansas, and was larger than most cities. Regional extensions were scattered over the nation.

The Home Matchmakers were expensive devices that linked up directly with the Sportsmaster extensions, and through them, with Sportsmaster III. They were programming devices. They allowed each Sportsmaster subscriber to select his own games for home viewing.

Sportsmaster III could accommodate any request, could set up any match, could arrange any conditions. If a subscriber wanted to see the 1962 Los Angeles Rams play the 1980 Notre Dame junior varsity in the Astrodome, Sportsmaster III would digest that request, search its awesome memory banks, and beam up simulation to the subscriber's holovision.

The variations were infinite. The subscriber could punch in weather, injuries, and location. The subscriber could select his own team of All Stars, and pit them against someone else's team, or against a real team of any era. With Sportsmaster III and the Home Matchmaker, the sports fan could sit at home and watch any sort of contest he could dream up.

At first, the Home Matchmakers were very costly. Only the very rich could afford them. Others were forced to pool their resources, form Sportsmaster clubs, and vote on the games they wanted to see.

But soon the price began to come down.

And when it got low enough, spectator sports died.

Boxing went first. It had always been the weak sister. The champions continued to defend their crowns, but there were fewer and fewer challengers, since the game was far from lucrative. The intervals between fights grew steadily longer. And after a while, there were no more fights.

The other sports followed. People continued to play tennis and golf, but they were no longer willing to pay to watch others play. Not when they could watch much better matches, of their own selection, on Sportsmaster hookups. Tournament after tournament was canceled. Until there were no more left to cancel.

The NHL and the NBA both disbanded in 2010. They had been suffering billion-dollar losses for several years before they closed up shop.

Baseball, hoary with age, held on four years longer. It moved its teams to progressively smaller cities, where the novelty always brought out crowds for a while. It slashed costs desperately. It sold stadiums, cut salaries to the bone, skimped on field and equipment maintenance. It went before Congress, and argued that the national pastime should be preserved with a subsidy.

And, in 2014, it folded.

Football was the last to go. Since the 1970s, it had been the biggest, and the richest, and the most arrogant sport of all. It had fought the most bitterly in the days of ads and lawsuits, and it had carried the brunt of the battle throughout the long television war.

And now it refused to die. It used every trick the baseball leagues had tried, and then some. It cut teams, added teams, moved teams, changed the rules, began sideshows. But nothing worked. No one came. No one was interested.

And so it was that the last Super Bowl was played in January, 2016, on a muddy field in Hoboken, New Jersey.

It was going to be an on-sides kick. The Jets knew that. The Packers knew that. Every fan in the stadium knew that. They were all waiting.

But even as they lined up for the kickoff, the rains came.

They came in earnest, a torrent, a sudden downpour. The sky darkened, and the wind howled, and the water came rushing down and down and down. It was a blinding rain, lashing at the mud, sending the remaining fans scrambling for shelter.

In that rain came the kickoff.

It was an on-sides kick, of course. Neither team could see the ball very well. Both converged on it. A Packer reached it first. He threw himself on top of it.

And the mud-covered ball squirted out from under him. Squirted toward Hoboken.

The Jets had the break they needed. It was first and ten near the fifty, and it was their ball. But the clock was ticking, and the rain was a shrieking wall of water that refused to let up.

Lancer and the Jet offense came running back onto the field, and lined up quickly. They didn't bother with a huddle. They had their plays down already.

The Packer defensemen walked out slowly, dragging their heels through the mud, dawdling, eating up the clock. Finally they got lined up, and the ball was snapped.

It was impossible to pass in that rain. Impossible. You couldn't throw through that much water. You couldn't run through mud like that, and puddles that looked like oceans. You couldn't even see the ball in that kind of rain.

It was impossible to pass in that rain. But the Jets had to pass. Their time was running out.

So Lancer passed. Somehow, somehow, he passed.

His first throw was a bullet to the sidelines, good for twenty yards. The receiver didn't see the ball coming. But he caught it anyway, because Lancer laid it right into his hands. Then he stepped out of bounds, and stopped the clock.

There were eighteen seconds left to play.

Lancer passed again. Somehow, through that blinding rain, in that sea of mud, somehow, he passed again. It was complete.

It was complete to the other sideline, to the five. The receiver clutched at the ball, and bobbled it for a second, then grasped it tightly, and took a step toward the goal line.

And the Packer defender roared into him like a Mack truck and knocked him out of bounds. The clock stopped again. With about six seconds left.

It was the last touchdown drive. The very, very last. And now was its climax.

They lined up at the three, with seconds left. Both teams looked the same by now; spattered, soaking, hulking figures in uniforms that had all turned an identical mud-brown.

It was the last confrontation. The Packer defense, in its ultimate test: a wall, an iron-hard, determined, teeth-clenched, mud-brown human wall. Lancer, the last great quarterback: wet and muddy and injured and angry and brilliant.

And the rain, the pounding rain around them both.

The ball was snapped.

Lancer took it. The Jet line surged forward, smashing at the Packers, fighting to clear a hole, clearing one. Lancer moved to it, through it, toward the goal line, the goal line only feet away.

And something rose up from the ground and hit him. Hard and low.

It was the last touchdown drive, the last ever. And it was brilliant and it was poetic and they should have scored. They should have scored.

But they didn't.

And the gun sounded, and the game was over, and the Packers had won. The players began to drift away to the locker room.

And Keith Lancer, who drove for the final touchdown, and didn't make it, picked himself up from the mud, and sighed, and helped up the man who had tackled him.

They shook hands in the rain, and Lancer smiled to hide the tears. And so, strangely, did the Packer. They walked together from the field.

Neither one bothered to look up at the stands.

The empty stands.

VONDA N. McINTYRE
b. 1948

Vonda McIntyre is a leading feminist science fiction writer. Born in Louisville and raised in Seattle, she earned a B.S. in biology from the University of Washington in 1970. That summer, having already published several short stories, she attended the Clarion Writers Workshop in Clarion, Pennsylvania. Though she returned to the university for graduate studies in genetics, she stayed for only a year before deciding to write full-time, and her career has been remarkably successful from the beginning. One early story, "Of Mist, and Grass, and Sand" (1973), won a Nebula award for the best novelette; *Dreamsnake* (1978), which continued the story, won another Nebula and a Hugo for best science fiction novel.

These works, like McIntyre's first novel, *The Exile Waiting* (1975), were set on an earth badly damaged by a nuclear holocaust. In *Exile* the female protagonist is a daring young empath who uses her telepathetic powers to escape to the stars. After publishing *Fireflood and Other Stories* (1979), a collection largely concerned with humans biologically altered (whether through mechanical or genetic means), McIntyre began writing Star Trek novels, including an original story (*The Entropy Effect*, 1981) and best-selling novelizations of three of the Star Trek movies. She also produced her own Starfarers series: four novels (1989–94), beginning with *Starfarers*, that chronicle the first interstellar expedition searching for intelligent alien life. Other publications include a collection of humanist science fiction stories co-edited with Janice Anderson, *Aurora: Beyond Equality* (1976), and her only book written specifically for children, *Barbary* (1986), whose twelve-year-old heroine smuggles her pet cat past adults preoccupied by their preparations for their first contact with aliens. McIntyre's most recent novel, *The Moon and the Sun* (1997), is an alternate history set in France in 1693; it won her another Nebula.

McIntyre is an active outdoorswoman, and her strong interests in feminism, animal rights, and the environment are reflected in all her science fiction. In "Of Mist, and Grass, and Sand," McIntyre voices her concern about the future of the earth and humankind. She purposely sets her story in a post-holocaust world. Technology no longer functions, and nomadic tribes live in primitive conditions and are distrustful and fearful. If there is a sickness or a plague, they need the help of natural healers, mainly women. However, because of their fears and ignorance, the members of the tribe endanger the very person they need, Snake, a young woman with great integrity and strength. Snake's courage and dedication to healing, McIntyre implies, are exemplary, and are crucial if the world is to recuperate after mass devastation.

Of Mist, and Grass, and Sand

The little boy was frightened. Gently, Snake touched his hot forehead. Behind her, three adults stood close together, watching, suspicious, afraid to show their concern with more than narrow lines around their eyes. They feared Snake as much as they feared their only child's death. In the dimness of the tent, the flickering lamplights gave no reassurance.

The child watched with eyes so dark the pupils were not visible, so dull that Snake herself feared for his life. She stroked his hair. It was long and very pale, a striking color against his dark skin, dry and irregular for several inches near the scalp. Had Snake been with these people months ago, she would have known the child was growing ill.

"Bring my case, please," Snake said.

The child's parents started at her soft voice. Perhaps they had expected the screech of a bright jay, or the hissing of a shining serpent. This was the first time Snake had spoken in their presence. She had only watched when the three of them had come to observe her from a distance and whisper about her occupation and her youth; she had only listened, and then nodded, when finally they came to ask her help. Perhaps they had thought she was mute.

The fair-haired young man lifted her leather case. He held the satchel away from his body, leaning to hand it to her, breathing shallowly with nostrils flared against the faint smell of musk in the dry desert air. Snake had almost accustomed herself to the kind of uneasiness he showed; she had already seen it often.

When Snake reached out, the young man jerked back and dropped the case. Snake lunged and barely caught it, gently set it on the felt floor, and glanced at him with reproach. His husband and his wife came forward and touched him to ease his fear. "He was bitten once," the dark and handsome woman said. "He almost died." Her tone was not of apology, but of justification.

"I'm sorry," the younger man said. "It's—" He gestured toward her; he was trembling, and trying visibly to control the reactions of his fear. Snake glanced down at her shoulder, where she had been unconsciously aware of the slight weight and movement. A tiny serpent, thin as the finger of a baby, slid himself around her neck to show his narrow head below her short black curls. He probed the air with his trident tongue in a leisurely manner, out, up and down, in, to savor the taste of the smells. "It's only Grass," Snake said. "He cannot harm you." If he were bigger, he might frighten; his color was pale-green, but the scales around his mouth were red, as if he had just feasted as a mammal eats, by tearing. He was, in fact, much neater.

The child whimpered. He cut off the sound of pain; perhaps he had been told that Snake too would be offended by crying. She only felt sorry that his people refused themselves such a simple way of easing fear. She turned from the adults, regretting their terror of her, but unwilling to spend the time it would take to convince them their reactions were unjustified. "It's all right," she said to the little boy. "Grass is smooth, and dry, and soft, and if I left him to guard you, even death could not reach your bedside." Grass poured himself into her narrow, dirty hand, and she extended him toward the child. "Gently." He reached out and touched the sleek scales with one fingertip. Snake could sense the effort of even such a simple motion, yet the boy almost smiled.

"What are you called?"

He looked quickly toward his parents, and finally they nodded. "Stavin," he whispered. He had no strength or breath for speaking.

"I am Snake, Stavin, and in a little while, in the morning, I must hurt you. You may feel a quick pain, and your body will ache for several days, but you will be better afterward."

He stared at her solemnly. Snake saw that though he understood and feared what she might do, he was less afraid than if she had lied to him. The pain must have increased greatly, as his illness became more apparent, but it seemed that others had only reassured him, and hoped the disease would disappear or kill him quickly.

Snake put Grass on the boy's pillow and pulled her case nearer. The lock opened at her touch. The adults still could only fear her; they had had neither time nor reason to discover any trust. The wife was old enough that they might never have another child, and Snake could tell by their eyes, their covert touching, their concern, that they loved this one very much. They must, to come to Snake in this country.

It was night, and cooling. Sluggish, Sand slid out of the case, moving his head, moving his tongue, smelling, tasting, detecting the warmth of bodies.

"Is that—?" The older husband's voice was low, and wise, but terrified, and Sand sensed the fear. He drew back into striking position and sounded his rattle softly.

Snake spoke, moving her hand, and extended her arm. The pit viper relaxed and flowed around and around her slender wrist to form black and tan bracelets. "No," she said. "Your child is too ill for Sand to help. I know it is hard, but please try to be calm. This is a fearful thing for you, but it is all I can do."

She had to annoy Mist to make her come out. Snake rapped on the bag and finally poked her twice. Snake felt the vibration of sliding scales, and suddenly the albino cobra flung herself into the tent. She moved quickly, yet there seemed to be no end to her. She reared back and up. Her breath rushed out in a hiss. Her head rose well over a meter above the floor. She flared her wide hood. Behind her, the adults gasped, as if physically assaulted by the gaze of the tan spectacle design on the back of Mist's hood. Snake ignored the people and spoke to the great cobra, focusing her attention by her words. "Ah, thou. Furious creature. Lie down; 'tis time for thee to earn thy dinner. Speak to this child, and touch him. He is called Stavin." Slowly, Mist relaxed her hood, and allowed Snake to touch her. Snake grasped her firmly behind the head and held her so she looked at Stavin. The cobra's silver eyes picked up the yellow of the lamplight. "Stavin," Snake said, "Mist will only meet you now. I promise that this time she will touch you gently."

Still, Stavin shivered when Mist touched his thin chest. Snake did not release the serpent's head, but allowed her body to slide against the boy's. The cobra was four times longer than Stavin was tall. She curved herself in stark white loops across his swollen abdomen, extending herself, forcing her head toward the boy's face, straining against Snake's hands. Mist met Stavin's frightened stare with the gaze of lidless eyes. Snake allowed her a little closer.

Mist flicked out her tongue to taste the child.

The younger husband made a small, cut-off, frightened sound. Stavin flinched at it, and Mist drew back, opening her mouth, exposing her fangs, audibly thrusting her breath through her throat. Snake sat back on her heels, letting out her own breath. Sometimes, in other places, the kinfolk could stay while she worked. "You must leave," she said gently. "It's dangerous to frighten Mist."

"I won't—"

"I'm sorry. You must wait outside."

Perhaps the younger husband, perhaps even the wife, would have made the indefensible objections and asked the answerable questions, but the older man turned them and took their hands and led them away.

"I need a small animal," Snake said as he lifted the tent-flap. "It must have fur, and it must be alive."

"One will be found," he said, and the three parents went into the glowing night. Snake could hear their footsteps in the sand outside.

Snake supported Mist in her lap and soothed her. The cobra wrapped herself around Snake's narrow waist, taking in her warmth. Hunger made the cobra even more nervous than usual, and she was hungry, as was Snake. Coming across the black sand desert, they had found sufficient water, but Snake's traps were unsuccessful. The season was summer, the weather was hot, and many of the furry tidbits Sand and Mist preferred were estivating. When the serpents missed their regular meal, Snake began a fast as well.

She saw with regret that Stavin was more frightened now. "I am sorry to send your parents away," she said. "They can come back soon."

His eyes glistened, but he held back the tears. "They said to do what you told me."

"I would have you cry, if you are able," Snake said. "It isn't such a terrible thing." But Stavin seemed not to understand, and Snake did not press him; she knew that his people taught themselves to resist a difficult land by refusing to cry, refusing to mourn, refusing to laugh. They denied themselves grief, and allowed themselves little joy, but they survived.

Mist had calmed to sullenness. Snake unwrapped her from her waist and placed her on the pallet next to Stavin. As the cobra moved, Snake guided her head, feeling the tension of the striking muscles. "She will touch you with her tongue," she told Stavin. "It might tickle, but it will not hurt. She smells with it, as you do with your nose."

"With her tongue?"

Snake nodded, smiling, and Mist flicked out her tongue to caress Stavin's cheek. Stavin did not flinch; he watched, his child's delight in knowledge briefly overcoming pain. He lay perfectly still as Mist's long tongue brushed his cheeks, his eyes, his mouth. "She tastes the sickness," Snake said. Mist stopped fighting the restraint of her grasp, and drew back her head. Snake sat on her heels and released the cobra, who spiraled up her arm and laid herself across her shoulders.

"Go to sleep, Stavin," Snake said. "Try to trust me, and try not to fear the morning."

Stavin gazed at her for a few seconds, searching for truth in Snake's pale eyes. "Will Grass watch?"

She was startled by the question, or rather, by the acceptance behind the question. She brushed his hair from his forehead and smiled a smile that was tears just beneath the surface. "Of course." She picked Grass up. "Thou wilt watch this child, and guard him." The snake lay quiet in her hand, and his eyes glittered black. She laid him gently on Stavin's pillow.

"Now sleep."

Stavin closed his eyes, and the life seemed to flow out of him. The alteration was so great that Snake reached out to touch him, then saw that he was breathing, slowly, shallowly. She tucked a blanket around him and stood up. The abrupt change in position dizzied her; she staggered and caught herself. Across her shoulders, Mist tensed.

Snake's eyes stung and her vision was oversharp, fever-clear. The sound she imagined she heard swooped in closer. She steadied herself against hunger and exhaustion, bent slowly and picked up the leather case. Mist touched her cheek with the tip of her tongue.

She pushed aside the tent-flap and felt relief that it was still night. She could stand the heat, but the brightness of the sun curled through her, burning. The moon must be full; though the clouds obscured everything, they diffused the light so the sky appeared gray from horizon to horizon. Beyond the tents, groups of formless shadows projected from the ground. Here, near the edge of the desert, enough water existed so clumps and patches of bush grew, providing shelter and sustenance for all manner of creatures. The black sand, which sparkled and blinded in the sunlight, at night was like a layer of soft soot. Snake stepped out of the tent, and the illusion of softness disappeared; her boots slid crunching into the sharp hard grains.

Stavin's family waited, sitting close together between the dark tents that clustered in a patch of sand from which the bushes had been ripped and burned. They looked at her silently, hoping with their eyes, showing no expression in their faces. A woman somewhat younger than Stavin's mother sat with them. She was dressed, as they were, in a long loose robe, but she wore the only adornment Snake had seen among these people: a leader's circle, hanging around her neck on a leather thong. She and the older husband were marked close kin by their similarities: sharp-cut planes of face, high cheekbones, his hair white and hers graying early from deep-black, their eyes the dark-brown best suited for survival in the sun. On the ground by their feet a small black animal jerked sporadically against a net, and infrequently gave a shrill weak cry.

"Stavin is asleep," Snake said. "Do not disturb him, but go to him if he wakes."

The wife and young husband rose and went inside, but the older man stopped before her. "Can you help him?"

"I hope we may. The tumor is advanced, but it seems solid." Her own voice sounded removed, slightly hollow, as if she were lying. "Mist will be ready in the morning." She still felt the need to give him reassurance, but she could think of none.

"My sister wished to speak with you," he said, and left them alone without introduction, without elevating himself by saying that the tall woman was the leader of this group. Snake glanced back, but the tent-flap fell shut. She was feeling her exhaustion more deeply, and across her shoulders Mist was, for the first time, a weight she thought heavy.

"Are you all right?"

Snake turned. The woman moved toward her with a natural elegance made slightly awkward by advanced pregnancy. Snake had to look up to meet her gaze. She had small fine lines at the corners of her eyes, as if she laughed, sometimes, in secret. She smiled, but with concern. "You seem very tired. Shall I have someone make you a bed?"

"Not now," Snake said, "not yet. I won't sleep until afterward."

The leader searched her face, and Snake felt a kinship with her in their shared responsibility.

"I understand, I think. Is there anything we can give you? Do you need aid with your preparations?"

Snake found herself having to deal with the questions as if they were complex problems. She turned them in her tired mind, examined them, dissected them, and finally grasped their meanings. "My pony needs food and water—"

"It is taken care of."

"And I need someone to help me with Mist. Someone strong. But it's more important that they aren't afraid."

The leader nodded. "I would help you," she said, and smiled again, a little. "But I am a bit clumsy of late. I will find someone."

"Thank you."

Somber again, the older woman inclined her head and moved slowly toward a small group of tents. Snake watched her go, admiring her grace. She felt small and young and grubby in comparison.

Sand began to unwrap himself from her wrist. Feeling the anticipatory slide of scales on her skin. She caught him before he could drop to the ground. Sand lifted the upper half of his body from her hands. He flicked out his tongue, peering toward the little animal, feeling its body heat, smelling its fear. "I know thou art hungry," Snake said, "but that creature is not for thee." She put Sand in the case, lifted Mist from her shoulder, and let her coil herself in her dark compartment.

The small animal shrieked and struggled again when Snake's diffuse shadow passed over it. She bent and picked it up. The rapid series of terrified cries slowed and diminished and finally stopped as she stroked it. Finally it lay still, breathing hard, exhausted, staring up at her with yellow eyes. It had long hind legs and wide pointed ears, and its nose twitched at the serpent smell. Its soft black fur was marked off in skewed squares by the cords of the net.

"I am sorry to take your life," Snake told it. "But there will be no more fear, and I will not hurt you." She closed her hand gently around it, and stroking it, grasped its spine at the base of its skull. She pulled once, quickly. It seemed to struggle briefly, but it was already dead. It convulsed; its legs drew up against its body, and its toes curled and quivered. It seemed to stare up at her, even now. She freed its body from the net.

Snake chose a small vial from her belt pouch, pried open the animal's clenched jaws, and let a single drop of the vial's cloudy preparation fall into its mouth. Quickly she opened the satchel again and called Mist out. The cobra came slowly, slipping over the edge, hood closed, sliding in the sharp-grained sand. Her milky scales caught the thin light. She smelled the animal, flowed to it, touched it with her tongue. For a moment Snake was afraid she would refuse dead meat, but the body was still warm, still twitching reflexively, and she was very hungry. "A tidbit for thee." Snake spoke to the cobra, a habit of solitude. "To whet thy appetite." Mist nosed the beast, reared back and struck, sinking her short fixed fangs into the tiny body, biting again, pumping out her store of poison. She released it, took a better grip, and began to work her jaws around it; it would hardly distend her throat. When Mist lay quiet, digesting the small meal, Snake sat beside her and held her, waiting.

She heard footsteps in the coarse sand.

"I'm sent to help you."

He was a young man, despite a scatter of white in his black hair. He was taller than Snake and not unattractive. His eyes were dark, and the sharp planes of his face were further hardened because his hair was pulled straight back and tied. His expression was neutral.

"Are you afraid?"

"I will do as you tell me."

Though his form was obscured by his robe, his long fine hands showed strength.

"Then hold her body, and don't let her surprise you." Mist was beginning to twitch from the effects of the drugs Snake had put in the small animal. The cobra's eyes stared, unseeing.

"If it bites—"

"Hold, quickly!"

The young man reached, but he had hesitated too long. Mist writhed, lashing out, striking him in the face with her tail. He staggered back, at least as surprised as hurt. Snake kept a close grip behind Mist's jaws and struggled to catch the rest of her as well. Mist was no constrictor, but she was smooth and strong and fast. Thrashing, she forced out her breath in a long hiss. She would have bitten anything she could reach. As Snake fought with her, she managed to squeeze the poison glands and force out the last drops of venom. They hung from Mist's fangs for a moment, catching light as jewels would; the force of the serpent's convulsions flung them away into the darkness. Snake struggled with the cobra, aided for once by the sand, on which Mist could get no purchase. Snake felt the young man behind her grabbing for Mist's body and tail. The seizure stopped abruptly, and Mist lay limp in their hands.

"I am sorry—"

"Hold her," Snake said. "We have the night to go."

During Mist's second convulsion, the young man held her firmly and was of some real help. Afterward, Snake answered his interrupted question. "If she were making poison and she bit you, you would probably die. Even now her bite would make you ill. But unless you do something foolish, if she manages to bite, she will bite me."

"You would benefit my cousin little, if you were dead or dying."

"You misunderstand. Mist cannot kill me." She held out her hand so he could see the white scars of slashes and punctures. He stared at them, and looked into her eyes for a long moment, then looked away.

The bright spot in the clouds from which the light radiated moved westward in the sky; they held the cobra like a child. Snake found herself half dozing, but Mist moved her head, dully attempting to evade restraint, and Snake woke herself abruptly. "I must not sleep," she said to the young man. "Talk to me. What are you called?"

As Stavin had, the young man hesitated. He seemed afraid of her, or of something. "My people," he said, "think it unwise to speak our names to strangers."

"If you consider me a witch, you should not have asked my aid. I know no magic, and I claim none."

"It's not a superstition," he said. "Not as you might think. We're not afraid of being bewitched."

"I can't learn all the customs of all the people on this earth, so I keep my own. My custom is to address those I work with by name." Watching him, Snake tried to decipher his expression in the dim light.

"Our families know our names, and we exchange names with those we would marry."

Snake considered that custom, and thought it would fit badly on her. "No one else? Ever?"

"Well . . . a friend might know one's name."

"Ah," Snake said. "I see. I am still a stranger, and perhaps an enemy."

"A *friend* would know my name," the young man said again. "I would not offend you, but now you misunderstand. An acquaintance is not a friend. We value friendship highly."

"In this land one should be able to tell quickly if a person is worth calling 'friend.'"

"We take friends seldom. Friendship is a great commitment."

"It sounds like something to be feared."

He considered that possibility. "Perhaps it's the betrayal of friendship we fear. That is a very painful thing."

"Has anyone ever betrayed you?"

He glanced at her sharply, as if she had exceeded the limits of propriety. "No," he said, and his voice was as hard as his face. "No friend. I have no one I call friend."

His reaction startled Snake. "That's very sad," she said, and grew silent, trying to comprehend the deep stresses that could close people off so far, comparing her loneliness of necessity and theirs of choice. "Call me Snake," she said finally, "if you can bring yourself to pronounce it. Saying my name binds you to nothing."

The young man seemed about to speak; perhaps he thought again that he had offended her, perhaps he felt he should further defend his customs. But Mist began to twist in their hands, and they had to hold her to keep her from injuring herself. The cobra was slender for her length, but powerful, and the convulsions she went through were more severe than any she had ever had before. She thrashed in Snake's grasp and almost pulled away. She tried to spread her hood, but Snake held her too tightly. She opened her mouth and hissed, but no poison dripped from her fangs.

She wrapped her tail around the young man's waist. He began to pull her and turn, to extricate himself from her coils.

"She's not a constrictor," Snake said. "She won't hurt you. Leave her—"

But it was too late, Mist relaxed suddenly and the young man lost his balance. Mist whipped herself away and lashed figures in the sand. Snake wrestled with her alone while the young man tried to hold her, but she curled herself around Snake and used the grip for leverage. She started to pull herself from Snake's hands. Snake threw them both backward into the sand; Mist rose above her, open-mouthed, furious, hissing. The young man lunged and grabbed her just beneath her hood. Mist struck at him, but Snake, somehow held her back. Together they deprived Mist of her hold and regained control of her. Snake struggled up, but Mist suddenly went quite still and lay almost rigid between them. They were both sweating; the young man was pale under his tan, and even Snake was trembling.

"We have a little while to rest," Snake said. She glanced at him and noticed the dark line on his cheek where, earlier, Mist's tail had slashed him. She reached up and touched it. "You'll have a bruise," she said. "But it will not scar."

"If it were true that serpents sting with their tails, you would be restraining both the fangs and the stinger, and I'd be of little use."

"Tonight I'd need someone to keep me awake, whether or not they helped me with Mist." Fighting the cobra produced adrenalin, but now it ebbed, and her exhaustion and hunger were returning, stronger.

"Snake . . ."

"Yes?"

He smiled quickly, half-embarrassed, "I was trying the pronunciation."

"Good enough."

"How long did it take you to cross the desert?"

"Not very long. Too long. Six days."

"How did you live?"

"There is water. We traveled at night, except yesterday, when I could find no shade."

"You carried all your food?"

She shrugged. "A little." And wished he would not speak of food.

"What's on the other side?"

"More sand, more bush, a little more water. A few groups of people, traders, the station I grew up and took my training in. And farther on, a mountain with a city inside."

"I would like to see a city. Someday."

"The desert can be crossed."

He said nothing, but Snake's memories of leaving home were recent enough that she could imagine his thoughts.

The next set of convulsions came, much sooner than Snake had expected. By their severity, she gauged something of the stage of Stavin's illness, and wished it were morning. If she were to lose him, she would have it done, and grieve, and try to forget. The cobra would have battered herself to death against the sand if Snake and the young man had not been holding her. She suddenly went completely rigid, with her mouth clamped shut and her forked tongue dangling.

She stopped breathing.

"Hold her," Snake said. "Hold her head. Quickly, take her, and if she gets away, run. Take her! She won't strike at you now, she could only slash you by accident."

He hesitated only a moment, then grasped Mist behind the head. Snake ran, slipping in the deep sand, from the edge of the circle of tents to a place where bushes still grew. She broke off dry thorny branches that tore her scarred hands. Peripherally she noticed a mass of horned vipers, so ugly they seemed deformed, nesting beneath the clump of desiccated vegetation; they hissed at her: she ignored them. She found a narrow hollow stem and carried it back. Her hands bled from deep scratches.

Kneeling by Mist's head, she forced open the cobra's mouth and pushed the tube deep into her throat, through the air passage at the base of Mist's tongue. She bent close, took the tube in her mouth, and breathed gently into Mist's lungs.

She noticed: the young man's hands, holding the cobra as she had asked; his breathing, first a sharp gasp of surprise, then ragged; the sand scrapping her elbows where she leaned; the cloying smell of the fluid seeping from Mist's fangs; her own dizziness, she thought from exhaustion, which she forced away by necessity and will.

Snake breathed, and breathed again, paused, and repeated, until Mist caught the rhythm and continued it unaided.

Snake sat back on her heels. "I think she'll be all right," she said. "I hope she will." She brushed the back of her hand across her forehead. The touch sparked pain: she jerked her hand down and agony slid along her bones, up her arm, across her shoulder, through her chest, enveloping her heart. Her balance turned on its edge. She fell, tried to catch herself but moved too slowly, fought nausea and vertigo and almost succeeded, until the pull of the earth seemed to slip away in pain and she was lost in darkness with nothing to take a bearing by.

She felt sand where it had scraped her cheek and her palms, but it was soft. "Snake, can I let go?" She thought the question must be for someone else, while at the same time she knew there was no one else to answer it, no one else to reply to her name. She felt hands on her, and they were gentle; she wanted to respond to them, but she was too tired. She needed sleep more, so she pushed them away. But they held her head and put dry leather to her lips and poured water into the throat. She coughed and choked and spat it out.

She pushed herself up on one elbow. As her sight cleared, she realized she was shaking. She felt as she had the first time she was snake-bit, before her immunities had completely developed. The young man knelt over her, his water flask in his hand. Mist beyond him, crawled toward the darkness. Snake forgot the throbbing pain. "Mist!" She slapped the ground.

The young man flinched and turned, frightened; the serpent reared up, her head nearly at Snake's standing eye level, her hood spread, swaying, watching, angry, ready to strike. She formed a wavering white line against black. Snake forced herself to rise, feeling as though she were fumbling with the control of some unfamiliar body. She almost fell again, but held herself steady. "Thou must not go to hunt now," she said. "There is work for thee to do." She held out her right hand to the side, a decoy to draw Mist if she struck. Her hand was heavy with pain. Snake feared, not being bitten, but the loss of the contents of Mist's poison sacs. "Come here," she said. "Come here, and stay thy anger." She noticed blood flowing down between her fingers, and the fear she felt for Stavin was intensified. "Didst thou bite me, creature?" But the pain was wrong: poison would numb her, and the new serum only sting . . .

"No," the young man whispered from behind her.

Mist struck. The reflexes of long training took over. Snake's right hand jerked away, her left grabbed Mist as she brought her head back. The cobra writhed a moment, and relaxed. "Devious beast," Snake said. "For shame." She turned and let Mist crawl up her arm and over her shoulder, where she lay like the outline of an invisible cape and dragged her tail like the edge of a train.

"She did not bite me?"

"No," the young man said. His contained voice was touched with awe. "You should be dying. You should be curled around the agony, and your arm swollen purple. When you came back—" He gestured toward her hand. "It must have been a bush viper."

Snake remembered the coil of reptiles beneath the branches and touched the blood on her hand. She wiped it away, revealing the double puncture of a snakebite among the scratches of the thorns. The wound was slightly swollen. "It needs cleaning," she said. "I shame myself by falling to it," The pain of it washed in gentle waves up her arm, burning no longer. She stood looking at the young man, looking around her, watching the landscape shift and change as her tired eyes tried to cope with the low light of setting moon and false dawn. "You held Mist well, and bravely," she said to the young man. "I thank you."

He lowered his gaze, almost bowing to her. He rose and approached her. Snake put her hand gently on Mist's neck so she would not be alarmed.

"I would be honored," the young man said, "if you would call me Arevin."

"I would be pleased to."

Snake knelt down and held the winding white loops as Mist crawled slowly into her compartment. In a little while, when Mist had stabilized, by dawn, they could go to Stavin.

The tip of Mist's white tail slid out of sight. Snake closed the case and would have risen, but she could not stand. She had not quite shaken off the effects of the new venom. The flesh around the wound was red and tender, but the hemorrhaging would not spread. She stayed where she was, slumped, staring at her hand, creeping slowly in her mind toward what she needed to do, this time for herself.

"Let me help you. Please."

He touched her shoulder and helped her stand. "I'm sorry," she said. "I'm so in need of rest . . ."

"Let me wash your hand," Arevin said. "And then you can sleep. Tell me when to awaken you—"

"I can't sleep yet." She collected herself, straightened, tossed the damp curls of her short hair off her forehead. "I'm all right now. Have you any water?"

Arevin loosened his outer robe. Beneath it he wore a loincloth and a leather belt that carried several leather flasks and pouches. His body was lean and well-built, his legs long and muscular. The color of his skin was slightly lighter than the sun-darkened brown of his face. He brought out his water flask and reached for Snake's hand.

"No, Arevin. If the poison gets in any small scratch you might have, it could infect."

She sat down and sluiced lukewarm water over her hand. The water dripped pink to the ground and disappeared, leaving not even a damp spot visible. The wound bled a little more, but now it only ached. The poison was almost inactivated.

"I don't understand," Arevin said, "how it is that you're unhurt. My younger sister was bitten by a bush viper." He could not speak as uncaringly as he might have wished. "We could do nothing to save her—nothing we have would even lessen her pain."

Snake gave him his flask and rubbed salve from a vial in her belt pouch across the closing punctures. "It's a part of our preparation," she said. "We work with many kinds of serpents, so we must be immune to as many as possible." She shrugged. "The process is tedious and somewhat painful." She clenched her fist; the film held, and she was steady. She leaned toward Arevin and touched his abraded cheek again. "Yes . . ." She spread a thin layer of the salve across it. "That will help it heal."

"If you cannot sleep," Arevin said, "can you at least rest?"

"Yes," she said. "For a little while."

Snake sat next to Arevin, leaning against him, and they watched the sun turn the clouds to gold and flame and amber. The simple physical contact with another human being gave Snake pleasure, though she found it unsatisfying. Another time, another place, she might do something more, but not here, not now.

When the lower edge of the sun's bright smear rose above the horizon, Snake rose and teased Mist out of the case. She came slowly, weakly, and crawled across Snake's shoulders. Snake picked up the satchel, and she and Arevin walked together back to the small group of tents.

Stavin's parents waited, watching for her, just outside the entrance of their tent. They stood in a tight, defensive, silent group. For a moment Snake thought they had decided to send her away. Then, with regret and fear like hot iron in her mouth, she asked if Stavin had died. They shook their heads and allowed her to enter.

Stavin lay as she had left him, still asleep. The adults followed her with their stares, and she could smell fear. Mist flicked out her tongue, growing nervous from the implied danger.

"I know you would stay," Snake said. "I know you would help, if you could, but there is nothing to be done by any person but me. Please go back outside."

They glanced at each other, and at Arevin, and she thought for a moment that they would refuse. Snake wanted to fall into the silence and sleep. "Come, cousins," Arevin said. "We are in her hands." He opened the tent-flap and motioned them out. Snake thanked him with nothing more than a glance, and he might almost have smiled. She turned toward Stavin, and knelt beside him. "Stavin—" She touched his forehead; it was very hot. She noticed that her hand was less steady than before. The slight touch awakened the child. "It's time," Snake said.

He blinked, coming out of some child's dream, seeing her, slowly recognizing her. He did not look frightened. For that Snake was glad; for some other reason she could not identify, she was uneasy.

"Will it hurt?"

"Does it hurt now?"

He hesitated, looked away, looked back. "Yes."

"It might hurt a little more. I hope not. Are you ready?"

"Can Grass stay?"

"Of course," she said.

And realized what was wrong.

"I'll come back in a moment." Her voice changed so much, she had pulled it so tight, that she could not help but frighten him. She left the tent, walking slowly, calmly, restraining herself. Outside, the parents told her by their faces what they feared.

"Where is Grass?" Arevin, his back to her, started at her tone. The younger husband made a small grieving sound and could look at her no longer.

"We were afraid," the older husband said. "We thought it would bite the child."

"I thought it would. It was I. It crawled over his face, I could see its fangs—" The wife put her hands on the younger husband's shoulders, and he said no more.

"Where is he?" She wanted to scream; she did not.

They brought her a small open box. Snake took it and looked inside.

Grass lay cut almost in two, his entrails oozing from his body, half turned over, and as she watched, shaking, he writhed once, and flicked his tongue out once, and in. Snake made some sound too low in her throat to be a cry. She hoped his motions were only reflex, but she picked him up as gently as she could. She leaned down and touched her lips to the smooth green scales behind his head. She bit him quickly, sharply, at the base of the skull. His blood flowed cool and salty in her mouth. If he was not dead, she had killed him instantly.

She looked at the parents, and at Arevin; they were all pale, but she had no sympathy for their fear, and cared nothing for shared grief. "Such a small creature," she said. "Such a small creature, who could only give pleasure and dreams." She watched them for a moment more, then turned toward the tent again.

"Wait—" She heard the older husband move up close behind her. He touched her shoulder; she shrugged away his hand. "We will give you anything you want," he said, "but leave the child alone."

She spun on him in a fury. "Should I kill Stavin for your stupidity?" He seemed about to try to hold her back. She jammed her shoulder hard into his stomach and flung herself past the tent-flap. Inside, she kicked over the satchel. Abruptly awakened, and angry, Sand crawled out and coiled himself. When the younger husband and the wife tried to enter, Sand hissed and rattled with a violence Snake had never heard him use before. She did not even bother to look behind her. She ducked her head and wiped her tears on her sleeve before Stavin could see them. She knelt beside him.

"What's the matter?" He could not help but hear the voices outside the tent, and the running.

"Nothing, Stavin," Snake said. "Did you know we came across the desert?"

"No," he said, with wonder.

"It was very hot, and none of us had anything to eat. Grass is hunting now. He was very hungry. Will you forgive him and let me begin? I will be here all the time."

He seemed so tired; he was disappointed, but he had no strength for arguing. "All right." His voice rustled like sand slipping through the fingers.

Snake lifted Mist from her shoulders and pulled the blanket from Stavin's small body. The tumor pressed up beneath his rib cage, distorting his form, squeezing his vital organs, sucking nourishment from him for its own growth, poisoning him with its wastes. Holding Mist's head, Snake let her flow across him, touching and tasting him. She had to restrain the cobra to keep her from striking; the excitement had agitated her. When Sand used his rattle, the vibrations made her flinch. Snake stroked her, soothing her; trained and bred-in responses began to return, overcoming the natural instincts. Mist paused when her tongue flicked the skin above the tumor, and Snake released her.

The cobra reared, and struck, and bit as cobras bite, sinking her fangs their short length once, releasing, instantly biting again for a better purchase, holding on, chewing at her prey. Stavin cried out, but he did not move against Snake's restraining hands.

Mist expended the contents of her venom sacs into the child and released him. She reared up, peered around, folded her hood, and slid across the mats in a perfectly straight line toward her dark close compartment.

"It's done, Stavin."

"Will I die now?"

"No," Snake said. "Not now. Not for many years, I hope." She took a vial of powder from her belt pouch. "Open your mouth." He complied, and she sprinkled the powder across his tongue. "That will help the ache." She spread a pad of cloth across the series of shallow puncture wounds without wiping off the blood.

She turned from him.

"Snake? Are you going away?"

"I will not leave without saying goodbye. I promise."

The child lay back, closed his eyes, and let the drug take him.

Sand coiled quiescently on the dark matting. Snake patted the floor to call him.

He moved toward her and suffered himself to be replaced in the satchel. Snake closed it and lifted it, and it still felt empty. She heard noises outside the tent. Stavin's parents and the people who had come to help them pulled open the tent-flap and peered inside, thrusting sticks in even before they looked.

Snake set down her leather case. "It's done."

They entered. Arevin was with them too; only he was empty-handed. "Snake—" He spoke through grief, pity, confusion, and Snake could not tell what he believed. He looked back. Stavin's mother was just behind him. He took her by the shoulder. "He would have died without her. Whatever happens now, he would have died."

She shook his hand away. "He might have lived. It might have gone away. We—" She could speak no more for hiding tears.

Snake felt the people moving, surrounding her. Arevin took one step toward her and stopped, and she could see he wanted her to defend herself. "Can any of you cry?" she said. "Can any of you cry for me and my despair, or for them and their guilt, or for small things and their pain?" She felt tears slip down her cheeks.

They did not understand her; they were offended by her crying. They stood back, still afraid of her, but gathering themselves. She no longer needed the pose of calmness she had used to deceive the child. "Ah, you fools." Her voice sounded brittle, "Stavin—"

Light from the entrance struck them. "Let me pass." The people in front of Snake moved aside for their leader. She stopped in front of Snake, ignoring the satchel her foot almost touched. "Will Stavin live?" Her voice was quiet, calm, gentle.

"I cannot be certain," Snake said, "but I feel that he will."

"Leave us." The people understood Snake's words before they did their leader's; they looked around and lowered their weapons, and finally, one by one, they moved out of the tent. Arevin remained. Snake felt the strength that came from danger seeping from her. Her knees collapsed. She bent over the satchel with her face in her hands. The older woman knelt in front of her before Snake could notice or prevent her. "Thank you," she said. "Thank you. I am so sorry . . ." She put her arms around Snake and drew her toward her, and Arevin knelt beside them, and he embraced Snake too. Snake began to tremble again, and they held her while she cried.

Later she slept, exhausted, alone in the tent with Stavin, holding his hand. The people had caught small animals for Sand and Mist. They had given her food and supplies and sufficient water for her to bathe, though the last must have strained their resources.

When she awakened, Arevin lay sleeping nearby, his robe open in the heat, a sheen of sweat across his chest and stomach. The sternness in his expression vanished when he slept; he looked exhausted and vulnerable. Snake almost woke him, but stopped, shook her head, and turned to Stavin.

She felt the tumor and found that it had begun to dissolve and shrivel, dying, as Mist's changed poison affected it. Through her grief Snake felt a little joy. She smoothed Stavin's pale hair back from his face. "I would not lie to you again, little one," she whispered, "but I must leave soon. I cannot stay here." She wanted another three days' sleep to finish fighting off the effects of the bush viper's poison, but she would sleep somewhere else. "Stavin?"

He half woke, slowly. "It doesn't hurt any more," he said.

"I am glad."

"Thank you . . ."

"Goodbye, Stavin. Will you remember later on that you woke up, and that I did stay to say goodbye?"

"Goodbye," he said, drifting off again. "Goodbye, Snake. Goodbye, Grass." He closed his eyes.

Snake picked up the satchel and stood gazing down at Arevin. He did not stir. Half-grateful, half-regretful, she left the tent.

Dusk approached with long, indistinct shadows; the camp was hot and quiet. She found her tiger-striped pony tethered with food and water. New, full waterskins bulged on the ground next to the saddle, and desert robes lay across the pommel, though Snake had refused any payment. The tiger-pony whickered at her. She scratched his striped ears, saddled him, and strapped her gear on his back. Leading him, she started west, the way she had come.

"Snake—"

She took a breath and turned back to Arevin. He was facing the sun; it turned his skin ruddy and his robe scarlet. His streaked hair flowed loose to his shoulders, gentling his face. "You must leave?"

"Yes."

"I hoped you would not leave before . . . I hoped you would stay, for a time . . ."

"If things were different, I might have stayed."

"They were frightened—"

"I told them Grass couldn't hurt them, but they saw his fangs and they didn't know he could only give dreams and ease dying."

"But can't you forgive them?"

"I can't face their guilt. What they did was my fault, Arevin. I didn't understand them until too late."

"You said it yourself, you can't know all the customs and all the fears."

"I'm crippled," she said. "Without Grass, if I can't heal a person, I cannot help at all. I must go home and face my teachers, and hope they'll forgive my stupidity. They seldom give the name I bear, but they gave it to me—and they'll be disappointed."

"Let me come with you."

She wanted to; she hesitated, and cursed herself for that weakness. "They may take Mist and Sand and cast me out, and you would be cast out too. Stay here, Arevin."

"It wouldn't matter."

"It would. After a while, we would hate each other. I don't know you, and you don't know me. We need calmness, and quiet, and time to understand each other well."

He came toward her and put his arms around her, and they stood embracing for a moment. When he raised his head, there were tears on his cheeks. "Please come back," he said. "Whatever happens, please come back."

"I will try," Snake said. "Next spring, when the winds stop, look for me. The spring after that, if I do not come, forget me. Wherever I am, if I live, I will forget you."

"I will look for you," Arevin said, and he would promise no more.

Snake picked up her pony's lead and started across the desert.

1973

CRAIG KEE STRETE
b. 1950

Born in Fort Wayne, Indiana, of a Cherokee father and a white mother, Craig Strete often explores the problems of Native Americans forced to live between two cultures, writing for children and adults in a wide range of genres—plays; scripts for radio, television, and film; and short stories, picture books, novels, and poems. He received his B.A. in theater arts from Wright State University in 1974 and earned an M.F.A. at the University of California, Irvine, in 1978. He has worked and published in the Netherlands and the United States.

In his novels and picture books for children, Strete has focused on different aspects of Native American culture. In his early novels, *Paint Your Face on a Drowning in the River* (1978) and *When Grandfather Journeys into Winter* (1979), he depicts the alienation and displacement felt by Native American youth, who abandon traditional ways of living as they try to assimilate into a society hostile to their customs and beliefs. In the picture book *Big Thunder Magic* (1990), illustrated by Craig Brown, a sheep who strays from his home is locked up in a zoo. Only with the magical help of the ghost Thunderspirit is he liberated and able to return to the reservation. The theme of displacement, in the form of coercive relocation policies, is also at the center of *How the Indians Bought the Farm* (1996, written with Michelle Netten Chacon, illustrated by Francisco X. Mora). In this trickster tale, an Indian couple outwits government officials to lay claim to their own farm where they can raise their own animals.

Strete has been particularly successful in blending Native American folklore with themes and motifs from science fiction to make political statements and to develop critiques about the position of Native Americans as marginalized other. In "The Bleeding Man" (1974), his first science fiction story, Strete's critical views take tragicomic form. The mysterious young man of twenty-three is a symbol that whites cannot understand. No matter what scientific experiments are performed or questions asked, the bleeding man does not stop bleeding; nor can he (or his spirit) be killed. Miss Down, the government official, clearly represents the American bureaucracy that has bled the Native Americans but refuses to assume responsibility or attempt to understand the culture it has destroyed, whereas Dr. Santell takes the role of the humane scientist who sacrifices his life so that the Native American spirit can continue to live.

The Bleeding Man

The medicine shaker, the bone breaker. I have seen and been all these. It is nothing but trouble.

I have sat on the good side of the fire. I have cried over young women. It is nothing but trouble.

Miss Dow leaned against the observation window. Her stomach revolted and she backed away. Unable to quell the nausea rising within her, she clamped a hand to her mouth.

Dr. Santell gently took her arm, led her away from the window and helped her to a couch facing away from the observation window.

Nausea passed; Miss Dow smiled weakly. "You did warn me," she said.

Dr. Santell did not return the smile. "It takes getting used to. I'm a doctor, and immune to gore, but still I find it unsettling. He's a biological impossibility."

"Not even human," Miss Dow suggested.

"That's what the government sent you here to decide," said Dr. Santell. "Frankly, I'm glad he's no longer my responsibility."

"I want to look at him again."

Santell shrugged, lit a syntho. Together they walked back to the observation window. He seemed amused at her discomfort.

Again, Miss Dow peered through the window. This time it was easier.

A young man, tall and well-muscled, stood in the middle of the room. He was naked. His uncut black hair fell to the small of his back.

His chest was slit with a gaping wound that bled profusely; his legs and stomach were soaked with blood.

"Why is he smiling? What is he staring at?" she asked, unable to take her eyes off the figure before her.

"I don't know," said Dr. Santell. "Why don't you ask him?"

"Your sense of humor escapes me," said Miss Dow through tightly closed lips.

Dr. Santell grinned and shrugged. His synthetic cigarette reached the cut-off mark and winked out. The butt flashed briefly as he tossed it into the wall disposal.

"Doesn't everything?" suggested Dr. Santell, trying not to laugh at his little joke.

Miss Dow turned away from the window. Her look was sharp, withering. "Tell me about him," she snapped, each word like ice. "How did he get—that way?"

His amusement faded. He licked his lips nervously, nodded. "He has no name, at least no official name. We call him Joe. Sort of a nickname. We gave him that name about—"

"Fascinating," interrupted Miss Dow, "but I didn't come here to be entertained by some droll little tale about his nickname."

"Friendly, aren't you?" asked Santell dryly. A pity, he thought. If she knew how to smile she might have seemed attractive.

"The government doesn't pay me to be friendly. It pays me to do a job." Her voice was cold, dispassionate. But she turned to face Dr. Santell in such a way that she would not see the bleeding man. "How long has he been like this?"

"It's all in my report. If you'd like to read it I could—"

"I'd prefer a verbal outline first. I'll read your report later; I trust that it is a thorough one." She eyed him sharply.

"Yes, quite thorough," Dr. Santell replied, the polite edge in his voice wearing thin.

He turned away from Miss Dow, gazed in at the bleeding man. His words were clipped, impartial. "He is approximately twenty-three years old and has been as he is now since birth."

"Incredible!" said Miss Dow, fascinated in spite of herself. "All this is documented?"

"Completely. There is no possibility of fakery. Nor point either, for that matter."

"Just as you say," echoed Miss Dow. "What have you done to try to cure it? Is it some form of stigmata?"

Dr. Santell shook his head. "If this is stigmata, it is the most extreme case this world will ever see. Besides, it is inconceivable that a psychosomatic illness could cause such a drastic biological malfunction."

"But surely some sort of surgery—?" began Miss Dow. "Some sort of chemical therapy would—"

Dr. Santell shook his head emphatically. "We've tried them all in the seven years he's been here. Psycho-chemistry, primal reconditioning, biofeedback—tried singly and together; none have had any effect. He's a biological impossibility."

"What is his rate of bleeding?" she asked.

"It varies," said Dr. Santell. "Somewhere between two and three pints an hour."

"But it's not possible!" exclaimed Miss Dow. "No one can—"

"He can and does," interrupted Dr. Santell. "He doesn't do anything normally. I can give you ten reasons why he should be dead. Don't ask me why he isn't."

Miss Dow turned her head around and stared at the silent figure standing in the center of the room. The bleeding man had not moved. The blood flowed evenly from the chest wound, gathering in a coagulating pool at his feet.

"I've had enough." She turned away from the window. "Show me to my office. I'm ready to read that report now."

Two hours later, the last page of Dr. Santell's report slipped from nerveless fingers. The bleeding man lay outside the parameters of human biology. By all rights he should have been dead; indeed, could never have lived. Her hands were a little unsteady as she punched in Dr. Santell's office on the videophone. His face appeared on the screen—and it was flushed.

"Report to me immediately," Miss Dow snapped.

"I doubt it, sweetheart," said Dr. Santell, grinning. "I'm off the case, remember?" He drank something out of a dark tumbler.

"You're drinking!" snapped Miss Dow.

"Now that you mention it," admitted Dr. Santell agreeably. He gave her a lopsided grin. "Perhaps you would care to join me?"

"You are a disgusting, undisciplined lout. And I should like to remind you that you are still responsible to me. You may be discharged from this case in your professional capacity, but your standing orders are to cooperate with me in any way possible."

"So I'm cooperating," muttered Dr. Santell. "I'll stay out of your way, you stay out of mine."

"I won't tolerate this!" she raged. "Do you realize to whom you are talking?"

Dr. Santell thought that over slowly. His face tightened. He did realize who she was. It sobered him a little. He took another drink from the tumbler to compensate.

"Are you sober enough to answer a few questions?"

He thought that over for a while too. "I'm drunk enough to answer any questions you have. I don't think I could answer them sober," he said.

"I am trying to be understanding," said Miss Dow, a note of conciliation in her voice. "I realize it is quite natural for you to resent me. After all, I am responsible for your termination at this installation."

Dr. Santell shrugged it off. He took another drink from the tumbler.

"We're both professionals, Dr. Santell," reasoned Miss Dow. "We can't let emotional considerations enter into this. There is no place for emotion here. Our goals must be—"

"Hell! That's easy for you to say!" growled Dr. Santell. "You don't have any!"

"That's quite enough, thank you," said Miss Dow, pressing her lips together in a tight, angry line.

"No, it's not enough—" started Dr. Santell. "You can't—"

"The subject is closed!" she shouted.

There was an uneasy silence.

Miss Dow broke it by changing the subject. "What about his parents?" she asked.

"Didn't you read my report?"

"It said they committed suicide. It did not specify or go into any details. I have to know more than that. Your report was supposed to be thorough. You didn't list your sources of information on his early life, for one thing. I need to know—"

"Ask Nahtari. He can tell you everything," he said. He shrugged as if to say it was out of his hands.

"Who?"

"Nahtari. His uncle. He comes every week to visit his nephew. Nahtari used to exhibit him at the carnival until we discovered him and brought him here. If you'll turn to the financial report near the back, you will see that we pay him a small gratuity for the privilege of studying his nephew. We pay him by the week and he stops in to pick up his check and talk to his relative."

"Did you say he talks to his relative?"

"Yeah. It's pretty strange. Nahtari talks to Joe every week for an hour. I don't know if Joe understands anything that is said to him or even if Nahtari cares if he understands. I've never heard Joe respond in any way, not in the seven years I've been here."

"When does this Nahtari make his weekly visit?"

"He's here now in my office. He brings me a pint of whiskey every week. Makes it himself. You'd never believe how good—"

Miss Dow hit the dial-out button viciously, cutting him off in mid-sentence.

She pushed open the door to Dr. Santell's office. She hadn't bothered to knock Dr. Santell had his feet propped up on the edge of his desk. He held a drink in one hand and a deck of cards in the other. Across the desk from him sat a gray-headed Indian dressed in faded blue jeans, cracked leather boots and a tattered flannel shirt.

"I'll see your dime and raise you a dime," said Dr. Santell, slamming a dime onto the pile of change on the desk between them.

"Are you Nahtari?" demanded Miss Dow, coming into the room. The two studiously ignored her.

"It depends," said the old Indian, not looking up from his cards. "I'll meet your dime and raise you a quarter."

Dr. Santell bit his lip. "You're bluffing! I know you don't have that other ace!"

Miss Dow marched up to the desk, snatched the cards out of Dr. Santell's hands.

Dr. Santell pounded his desk in anger. "Stupid bitch! I had him beat!" He tried to collect the torn cards in his lap.

"Is she some kind of nut?" asked Nahtari, holding his cards out of harm's way.

Dr. Santell dumped the torn pieces of cards on the top of the desk and sighed. "Yeah. A government nut. She's in charge of Joe now."

Nahtari scowled and laid his cards face up on the desk. "And that means she wants to ask me about my relative."

"It certainly does," said Miss Dow. "Would you like to come to my office?"

Nahtari shrugged. There seemed to be no way to avoid it.

"You are owing me twelve dollars," he said to Dr. Santell as he rose to leave the room.

"Don't I always," growled Dr. Santell, staring at the ace that Nahtari had had after all.

"Sit down, Nahtari. This may take a while. I have a great many questions I want to ask you." She put a new cartridge in her tape machine and turned it on.

"If Dr. Santell had taken down all facts from before when I tell him I would not having to be saying again," said Nahtari. "I get tired of telling the story and having no one taking down so I don't have to do all over again."

Miss Dow patted the tape machine. "Don't worry about it," she assured him. "This recorder will make a permanent record of everything you say. I guarantee you won't have to tell it again."

"You going to listen and take down no matter what?"

"Every word," she replied.

She started to ask a question but Nahtari held up his hand. "Let me tell whole story," said Nahtari. "It will be a saving of time and you can ask questions after if you have any. I want to get this over before too long. Got to catch Dr. Santell before he leave with my twelve dollars."

Nahtari scratched his chest over his right shirt pocket.

"That sounds all right to me," agreed Miss Dow. "Could you start with his parents? I'd like to know—"

"He killed them."

"What?" Miss Dow was stunned.

"He killed them," repeated Nahtari matter-of-factly. "I was there the day he was born. His father and mother died within an hour of his birthing. He killed them."

Miss Dow was confused. "But how did it happen? How could—"

"You was not going to ask questions until I finished," accused Nahtari, dragging the back of his hand insolently across his nose.

Miss Dow settled back into her seat with a tight-lipped smile. She motioned for him to continue.

"His parents were medicine people. They were people of great power. My brother was one of the strong ones. They had this child stronger than them."

Miss Dow made a face. "You don't expect me to believe in primitive super—"

"I am expecting of you to keep your stupid mouth shut so this telling can be done and over with. I want to tell this so you will no longer pester me when I come to see my relative. I know all of your kind of government people. You harass a person—"

"Tell the story!" rasped Miss Dow. "For Christ sakes, just tell the story!" She drummed her fingers impatiently on the desk.

"My brother and his woman were filled with the sickness of the world. I knew that my brother did not want to live. His wife knew this and was content to go with him. Then when they had decided the road, she became heavy with child. They had no expecting of this. They became uncertain and did not know the way. But they could not change their decision for the living of the child. They went into the mountains, looking for their road. It was in the fifth month of the child in her belly."

Miss Dow sighed impatiently and settled back in her chair. It looked to be a long story, unrestricted by the inclusion of anything factual. Already she regretted asking him for information.

"They were high in the mountains. They laid down for dying but something strange happened. The child began speaking to them. The child was angry. They ran to the high places, to throw themselves off before the power of the child got too strong for them. But the child stopped them at the edge of the cliff and turned them around. The child forced them back down the mountain. And for four months, they were prisoners of the child."

"Are you seriously telling me that—" began Miss Dow with disgust.

Nahtari snorted contemptuously and passed his hands in front of his eyes. His eyes seemed to be focused on some far horizon. His voice mocked hers. "I just had a vision. I saw you and Dr. Santell embraced upon the ground and then suddenly crushed by a falling outhouse."

"I'm not laughing," said Miss Dow. She wasn't laughing.

"Somebody is," said Nahtari with a straight face. "I knew you was going to not let me finish the story and take it all down so I don't have to tell it again. Nobody ever lets me finish my story," complained Nahtari.

"Christ! I don't blame them!" said Miss Dow. "I've never heard such an outrageous piece of trash." She turned the tape machine off. "You may have all the time in the world, but I haven't got time to listen to this idiocy!" She stood up and marched around the desk. "When you leave, shut the door."

Nahtari came around the desk and sat down in her chair. He tilted the chair back and rested his bootheels on the desk. He turned the tape-recorder microphone around so that it pointed at him. He pushed the recording button and began talking into the machine.

"You bet this time, record is made of all the facts," he said, and went on with the story. "For four months, they were prisoners of the child. Five days before he was born, the child began to fear leaving the belly. The fear did not last long, but it lasted long enough for his father to put poison in their food without the child's knowing. They ate this poison, the mother, the father and the child.

"The child felt the poison and changed it into water in his belly. He felt great sadness in his heart and an anger because they did not want him to live. They did not want him born into a world they had grown sick of. It was not their right to choose for him because his power was greater than theirs. He did not change the poison flowing through them to water. His hatred was at them for they had let the world beat them. They began the agony of poison dying, but they could not die.

"I sat with them through this time. I sat with my brother and my sister by law and they told me these things through their agony. They screamed to die but the child was punishing them for letting the world beat them. I, Nahtari, did not want to see the child born into this world. I feared his coming. There was nothing I could do. He came to birth.

"It was not a child like expected. He bled. His chest was bleeding. I had expected hot roaring fires. I had expected a child of frightful appearance. It was but a small baby that bled and could not talk.

"The father pulled the baby up and beat him into breathing. He laid the baby on the bed and went outside the house. After a little while, my sister by law got to her feet, swaying on dizzy legs, and she staggered out after him. I tried to stop the bleeding of the baby chest but I was too scared about my brother and sister by law. I ran outside. They laid side by side in the black dirt of the garden. They were dead and five days decayed.

"I took the little one into my home, but the bleeding sickened my old woman and she died. So I took the bleeding one to the traveling show. The white people there did not sicken and die at the sight of his bleeding.

"In lines all around the tent they would stand to pay good money to see the bleeding one. They all wanted to see him bleeding and they were not sickened by it and they did not die. But the government people came and took the bleeding man from me and made me sign little pieces of paper and gave me money so they could do what they do. I turned him over to the government ones and that is all there is to the story and it is the truth.

"Now I come every week to talk to him. I know he is too powerful to have a name. I am waiting for him. I am telling so I will not have to tell it again and so that this warning is given to all who would have dealings with him. He is not ready to do what he will one day do. Do not walk in his shadow. Leave him alone, for he is not you. For twenty-three years he has been gathering power. That is all I have to say."

He switched off the tape machine, smiling to himself because there was no one to hear it. He closed the door carefully behind him and went looking for Dr. Santell and his twelve dollars.

Miss Dow pushed open the door cautiously. She was not sure if she had the stomach for what she was doing. But making up her mind, she stepped into the room. She kept telling herself that he was perfectly harmless.

The drain in the center of the floor was stopped up with clotted blood. He stood in a shallow pool of his own blood. His body was motionless, his breathing just barely perceptible by a slight rising and falling of his chest. The blood flowed steadily to the floor.

"Can you hear me?" she asked nervously. She shut the door behind her. She kept her eyes on his face. He stared at her but gave no sign that he had heard her. He seemed to be in no pain, despite the stream of blood flowing down his chest.

"I'm not going to hurt you." She approached him slowly with a small glass lab beaker. Averting her eyes slightly, she placed the glass container below the wound. She felt a little foolish for having spoken to him. It was obvious to her now that he was little better than a cretin and that he could not understand a word she said.

She stood there awkwardly, the glass beaker filling with his blood. The naked man seemed unaware of her presence, yet still she felt an unreasonable fear. There was something frightening about the still figure. Something threatening, otherworldly in the steady flow of blood down his chest. He did not seem vulnerable. Rather it was as if the world were too insignificant for him to notice it.

She backed away with a full glass of his blood. She felt better with each step she took. He stared at her, no expression on his face, his eyes unusually bright. She had felt very uncomfortable under his stare.

Miss Dow had turned and started out the door, watching him all the while. Suddenly he moved. She turned quickly. Fear rose in her like a tide. The bleeding man cupped a hand beneath the wound in his chest.

Slowly, he brought his hands to his lips and drank. Miss Dow fainted.

Dr. Santell found her in the doorway. A tiny red pool of fresh blood was beginning to blacken on the floor beside her head. The glass beaker she had brought into the room was gone. "What happened?" asked Dr. Santell, bending over the couch, his voice oddly gentle despite its gruffness. "Here—take a sip of this," he said, offering her a small glass of whiskey. "It'll steady your nerves."

She was too weak to refuse. The whiskey burned her throat and made her cough. He made her take another sip. It almost made her gag, but seemed to help. A touch of color reappeared in her face.

"He—he—he drank his own blood!" she whispered, tottering on the edge of hysteria.

Dr. Santell leaned forward eagerly. His features sharpened, his manner became intent and forceful. "Are you sure?" he demanded.

"Yes, I'm sure," she said with a trace of her normal sharpness.

"Are you sure—absolutely sure—he drank his own blood?" he asked again, impatiently. The answer seemed unusually important to him.

"Of course, I'm sure, damn it! It was absolutely disgusting!" She wrinkled up her nose. "That revolting animal did it on purpose! Just because I collected a beaker of—"

Dr. Santell suddenly became greatly agitated. "You collected a glass of blood?" he asked.

She nodded, bewildered by his strange behavior.

"God! It's happened again," he muttered. "It's happened again!" A look of dread passed over his face.

"What the devil are you talking about?" demanded Miss Dow.

"When I heard you scream, I started running. I was the first one to reach you. You were sprawled in the doorway. There was a big bloodstain beside your head on the floor. There was no glass on the floor of the room and it wasn't in the hallway."

"Don't be ridiculous! I had it with me. Isn't this an awfully big fuss to be making over a—"

Dr. Santell turned his back on her and dialed security.

"Hobeman? This is Santell. Have room 473 searched for a glass beaker. Delay his feeding time if you have to, but find that beaker!" He shut off the view screen.

He looked at Miss Dow. Her face was blank with bewilderment. Before she could ask a question he began. "Something strange has developed in the last few weeks. Our monitors have been picking up unusual activity levels. They aren't sophisticated enough to tell us exactly what's happening but his heartbeat and galvanic skin responses have been fluctuating wildly."

"But what does that have to do with the glass?" asked Miss Dow.

"I'm coming to that. A week ago, during one of his strange activity levels, the observation port on the wall of his room disappeared."

Miss Dow's face registered shock. "Disappeared? How is that possible?"

Dr. Santell was grim. "I have no idea. We found traces of melted glass on the floor of the room. But what disturbs me the most is that we could detect no coronary activity. For two hours his blood was circulating, but his heart wasn't functioning."

"He's not human, is he?" said Miss Dow.

"I don't know," said Dr. Santell, staring off into space. "I just don't know."

He pushed the carts through the door. The bleeding man stared at him as he had stared for the seven years he had been there.

"Soup's on, Joe," said the man with the feeding carts.

Two men hidden from view by the door were examining two streaks of melted glass on the floor.

"Hey, hold up there," said one of the men. "He's not to be fed until we've finished our search."

"I won't get in the way. What's disappeared this time?"

"Nothing important," grumbled one of the men. "Just a glass jar from the lab."

"Shame on you, Joe," said the cartman, waving a finger at the motionless figure in the center of the room. "You oughtn't to be stealing stuff like that." He opened the top of his cart and took out a pair of gloves.

"It won't hurt if I feed him, will it? I don't have to hose him down until you guys have finished," he said, pulling the gloves over his hands.

"Go ahead. We aren't going to find anything anyway."

The cartman opened a panel on the side of the cart and brought out a bowl of raw meat. He sat it on the floor in front of the bleeding man. From the other cart he got a large bowl of uncooked vegetables and a large wooden ladle.

He detached a water hose from the wall and started backing toward the bleeding man, uncoiling the hose as he walked. When he got to the end of the hose, he turned around.

The bleeding man had overturned the feeding bowls with his feet. He was drinking his own blood from cupped hands.

"This is what you are looking for," said Dr. Santell, handing Miss Dow a clipboard. "His blood type is O lateral. We've run hundreds of tests on it and it seems to be perfectly normal blood, a little more resistant to some diseases than ordinary blood but otherwise normal. It's too bad the government won't let us use his blood. He's a universal donor and at the rate he produces blood, I'll bet he could supply Intercity all by himself."

"But that's just the point. We *are* going to use his blood," said Miss Dow. "We are going to use a lot more besides. That's why I was sent here."

"The government's changed its policy then?" asked Dr. Santell. "Why?"

"We've given transfusions of his blood to prisoners and it seems to have no bad effects. Tell me, you've studied him for seven years. Do you have any idea how something like him is possible?"

Dr. Santell lit a synthetic cigarette slowly. He gave her a curious look.

"Did you listen to Nahtari's explanation?"

"That lunacy," sniffed Miss Dow. "I think we should pay a little more attention to a chromosomal mutation theory than some wild story from some primitive like Nahtari."

Dr. Santell shrugged. "It doesn't really matter what caused it. I couldn't even make an educated guess. His version is the only evidence we have."

"Confine yourself to specifics, please," said Miss Dow. "What biological evidence do we have?"

"There is biological evidence pointing to chromosomal differentiation. He has sixty-four paired chromosomes.[1] I have been unable so far to determine their exact structure. He seems to have all the normal ones. Technically, that makes him a member of our species, I suppose. But it's those extra chromosomes that are so unusual. They seem to be entirely new structures, unlike anything we are familiar with. It must be something outside our experience. I think I pointed this out in more detail in my report."

"But technically, he is human?" asked Miss Dow.

"I would say he is," said Dr. Santell.

"Very well. Then I am going to give the final go-ahead on this project," said Miss Dow.

"And what project is that?"

"We're going to transfer him to the military dome at Intercity where he will be dissected for tissue regeneration. Hopefully, his cellular matrix will produce like functioning biological constructs."

"What!" Dr. Santell jumped to his feet. "You're not serious! That would be murder! Matrix reconstruction from tissue cultures has never advanced beyond the experimental stage! We don't have the technology to stimulate the reproduction of brain and nerve tissue! Good lord, woman, you can't seriously—"

"I am quite aware of our shortcomings in the field of tissue regeneration," said Miss Dow coldly. "For years, our work in this area has been little better than a waste of time and materials. We have yet to produce a successful unit with a well-developed nervous system. Nor have we been able to successfully clone an individual. These matters, however, are not relevant to this case."

"Not relevant! You'll kill him! And to what purpose? A line of research that you yourself admitted has been a waste of time!" stormed Dr. Santell, his face flushed with anger.

---

1. Humans normally have forty-six paired chromosomes.

"Be careful, Dr. Santell," she cautioned him. "I don't think I am happy with your choice of words. We are not going to kill him. Many of our first tissue-regeneration experiments are still alive—alive after a fashion, that is. Their bodies still function, their cells still grow, it is only their minds that are dead." She smiled.

"It's still murder! You have no right!" Dr. Santell looked away from Miss Dow. He had suddenly realized that the things he was saying could be considered treason.

"When's the last time you had an attitude check, Dr. Santell?" asked Miss Dow. "I almost thought I heard you say something that was opposed to the wishes of our government. You did agree that my patient can be made ready for transport tomorrow morning, didn't you?"

"Of course," said Dr. Santell. "He will be ready."

"And did I hear you use the word *murder*, Dr. Santell? I *did* hear you use the word! I'm sure General Talbot will be most interested in your attitude."

Dr. Santell turned and began walking out of the room. He knew that he was in trouble and nothing he could say would make it any better.

"Dr. Santell!"

He turned to look at her.

"I'm really not hard to get along with," said Miss Dow. "You have the reputation of being a brilliant scientist. I've handled your type before. I am willing to overlook a small measure of eccentricity. But I draw the line at treason."

His expression remained blank.

"It's only natural that you're defensive about your patient after seven years," she soothed. "You have personalized him, lost your objectivity. But you must know as well as I do that the bleeding man is a brainless vegetable, hopelessly retarded since birth. You can see that, surely?"

Dr. Santell stared wordlessly.

"It would be a lot easier for me," she continued, "if I had your cooperation on this thing. You've had seven years' experience on this project and you could help us smooth over any rough spots we might encounter. This isn't exactly a normal case. It will require special procedures. Procedures that your cooperation will make possible." She smiled at him. "My report could be a very positive one. It depends on you."

Dr. Santell forced himself to smile. "Believe me," he said, "I shall cooperate in any way I can. I apologize for my behavior."

Miss Dow nodded. "Good. Now, how much blood could, let's say, ten of his regenerations produce in a forty-eight-hour period?"

Dr. Santell began punching up figures on his desk calculator.

The bleeding man continued to drink. The men studying the glass streaks on the floor had fled.

A security guard unlocked the door and looked into the room. The bleeding man did not seem aware of the other's presence. A call went out for Dr. Santell.

Dr. Santell, followed by Miss Dow, arrived just in time to see the heavy door buckling outward.

"He's gone berserk!" screamed Miss Dow as the door was battered off its hinges. The bleeding man walked through the wreckage of the door. He advanced upon them, a crimson trail of blood behind him on the floor. Miss Dow fled, screaming. Dr. Santell stood his ground. The bleeding man brushed him lightly as he walked past. He looked neither to left nor right. He strode down the corridor, moving quickly, relentlessly.

Dr. Santell ran in front of him and tried to push him to a halt. His hands slipped, coming away blood-soaked. His efforts to stop him were futile. Through the plasti-glass corridor walls he could see the security guards gathering around Miss Dow at the corridor exit. Dr. Santell took hold of the bleeding man's arm and tried to drag him to a stop, but found himself being dragged instead. The bleeding man did not even break stride.

Miss Dow stood within a cordon of security men. Dr. Santell knew what she would order them to do even before the bleeding man smashed through the exit door.

"Aim for his head!" she shouted.

A burst of stunner fire took the bleeding man full in the face. He walked several steps, then toppled.

Dr. Santell rushed to his side and put a hand on his chest. "He's still alive," he muttered to himself.

"Good shooting, men," congratulated Miss Dow. "A couple of you carry the body down to the lab."

"Is there very much damage to his head?" she asked. "Is he still alive? Not that it matters. We can't risk another episode like this. We might as well do the dissection here. It'll make him easier to handle. We'd have to ship him frozen anyway, now that we know more about his capabilities."

The security men carried the body away.

"He's still alive," Dr. Santell said, pronouncing each word slowly and distinctly. "He's very much alive."

Miss Dow had a surgical gown on and a mask. "Are you sure you can handle the dissection all by yourself, Dr. Santell? I could fly someone in to assist."

"Quite sure," said Dr. Santell, bending over the still form on the surgery table. "I'll begin soon. You'd better leave now."

"I'll be waiting at the military base in Intercity for the body," said Miss Dow. She came over to the table and stood beside him. Her voice was cold and emotionless, as usual. "You realize I still must report your treasonable remarks to General Talbot."

Dr. Santell nodded, not looking in her direction.

"However, your behavior has shown marked improvement. That too will be noted in my report. Trying to stop this creature single-handedly in the corridor like you did was a very brave if somewhat foolish thing to do. You realize, of course, that the matter is out of my hands. General Talbot will be the one deciding, not I. Perhaps, after a short period of retaining, you may even be reassigned. A man of your reputation, I'm sure, will find it very easy to rejoin the fold. Only a fool—or a traitor—bucks the system."

Dr. Santell seemed not to be listening. He stuck a needle into the arm of the body on the dissection table.

"What a shame a body like that should have no mind," mused Miss Dow. "Just think of the power he must have in order to smash through those doors like he did."

"Yes," Dr. Santell replied tonelessly.

Miss Dow pulled her mask off and turned to leave.

"Wait," said Dr. Santell. "Before you go, could you hand me that box of clamps under the table here?"

She bent over and looked under the table. "I don't see any—"

His scalpel sliced through her right carotid artery. Her body jerked convulsively and she crashed heavily to the floor.

"Yes," said Dr. Santell with a strange look on his face. "It is always a shame to find a good body with a defective mind."

It took him a little over two hours to dissect her. By the time he finished, the stimulant he had injected into him had brought the bleeding man back to consciousness.

As he was putting her dismembered body into the liquid nitrogen packs for shipping, he kept his eyes on the body of the bleeding man. The body sat up slowly and opened its eyes. The head swiveled and the eyes regarded him. The eyes were alive with raw intelligence. The body slid off the table gracefully and stood up, the wound on his chest completely healed.

"I knew," said Dr. Santell. "I knew."

> The medicine shaker, the bone breaker. I have seen and been all these. It is nothing but trouble.
>
> I have sat on the good side of the fire. I have cried over young women. It is nothing but trouble.
>
> These are the words I heard written in his skin. He made me kill her. I had to do it. I am not sorry. I knew. That is enough, knowing.
>
> —Paul Santell

(*This suicide note was found near the charred body of Dr. Santell, who, Intercity Police say, apparently soaked himself with an inflammable liquid and then set himself afire. Dr. Paul Santell, twice recipient of the Nobel Prize in psycho-chemistry, had been experiencing. . . . —excerpt from* Intercity Demographic Area Telepaper.)

The bleeding man, cured of bleeding, walked without haste toward the door leading outside. He remembered the taste of blood, he who no longer had need of it. He pushed the door open and stepped outside. The sky pulled at him, but he resisted for that last little moment. His feet touched the ground. His lungs filled with air. His eyes danced on the horizons of the world. Raising his hands into the air, he let the sky pull him away from the earth. He took the air in his lungs and thrust it out with a shout. Silently his lips formed words.

And then he had no more need of air and words. His fingers curled into the hands of the sky. He disappeared in a cloud.

He Who No Longer Bleeds is gone. He will return. To bleed again.

1974

Picture Books

Picture books are probably the most innovative, experimental, and exciting area of children's literature—but also one of the most difficult to understand. We can define them as books in which pictures dominate the verbal text, or which have no verbal text, or which interact with verbal text in a fundamental way. In contrast, in illustrated stories, such as the original editions of Lewis Carroll's *Alice's Adventures in Wonderland* (1865) or A. A. Milne's *Winnie-the-Pooh* (1926), the pictures are important but the words carry the main message.

Picture books are the form of literature that more than any other is designed specifically for children. The basic idea is that understanding pictures comes before understanding words, and so—obviously—children can handle picture books more easily than word books. Comenius, the author of perhaps the earliest picture book in the Western tradition (the *Orbis Sensualium Pictus,* 1658), wrote that "pictures are the most intelligible books that children can look upon."

Many people therefore assume that picture books must be simple, but in fact they are highly complex—partly because pictures *must* interact with words: to "simply" draw a picture of what the words "say" is impossible. The picture has to have a style, take a viewpoint, and reflect decisions about details (a picture of a cat, for example, necessarily embodies choices about shape, size, color, age, breed, activity, angle of viewing, and so on), and all of these inevitably have social, cultural, and political implications.

Except in wordless books, pictures coexist with words in many creative ways. They can add information or atmosphere, contradict or provide a comment on the words, explain and clarify—or even confuse (and, of course, words can do the same for pictures). They can follow fashions in artistic style, imitate or echo other artists, or develop new techniques.

Therefore, picture books are somewhat paradoxical. They seem to be immediately accessible to—and suitable for—young, inexperienced, and preliterate readers, yet understanding a picture requires a very extensive set of decoding and interpretive skills. Pictures have a "visual vocabulary" and a grammar every bit as complex as that governing the use of words, and we have to learn the implications of space, perspective, size, positioning, relationships, and lighting, as well as conventions of action lines, speech bubbles, and so on. Equally, although picture books have a huge imaginative range and are continually pushing back the boundaries of art and narrative, they also *limit* the imagination of the reader. Rather than having to produce an image for themselves, readers are *given* images, which they may or may not understand, or which may or (more probably) may not match the images in their heads.

Indeed, the apparently "simplest" books, which use few lines and shapes (such as Roger Hargreaves's Mister Men books), in fact make more demands on their readers than those containing images that "look like" what they represent. Books that use only shapes and colors, such as the American classic *Little Blue and Little Yellow* (1959) by Leo Lionni, require considerable interpretive skills from their audience.

Reading Picture Books

Picture books, then, are a greatly underestimated form: in modern critical terms, they are the place where many voices meet (they are multivocal and polyphonic), and a whole new visual-critical vocabulary is needed to discuss them.

It might seem obvious that you open a book, see the picture, and understand it. But looking at a picture is not the same as reading a line of text: when you read words, you set off along the line, from left to right (in the West), and you are equipped only with your unconscious knowledge of the codes of language—what words mean (semantic codes), which order they have to be in to make sense (grammatical codes), and what signals show how words and word groups are related (punctuation codes). We understand a book only because we are in broad agreement about all these things (although we all have personal reactions to words, and it is a myth that everyone will understand the same thing from the same words). Also, reading words is a sequential, not a selective process: you could skip along a line and miss words, or start reading in midsentence at a word that appeals to you, or even read in a random order, but the result is unlikely to make much sense. The order in which you receive information makes a difference to how you understand it—to the meaning that you make.

Reading pictures, in contrast, may or may not be sequential: Do you interpret the whole, or the whole and then the parts, or the parts and then the whole? And if the process is sequential, what determines the sequence? Consider any of the pictures in this book: Where do you look first? What do you see first? How did you construct your own meaning of that picture? There is no prescribed order in which you see things; it depends on what you are expecting to see: in Marjorie Flack's *Angus and the Ducks,* the book is "about" Angus, and so you may well, on each opening, look for him, or you may look for what interests you (ducks? something new?); in John Burningham's *Come Away from the Water, Shirley,* some readers may be interested in what happens to Shirley, others in what happens to her parents. Or perhaps you read the words first and then go to the picture—and if you do that, what difference do the words make to the pictures, or the pictures to the words? That last sequence of events depends largely on how "word oriented" you are, but it might also depend on features of the text—how much it attempts to control your responses and how much you are in control.

There are many theories about what happens when we read a picture and many ways in which we can talk about our responses. Some of these theories are highly sophisticated and may suggest practical ways of understanding what we are doing. Gunter Kress and Theo van Leeuwen, for example, in their *Reading Images: The Grammar of Visual Design* (1996), have developed a system of describing pictures that parallels a word grammar: verbs become vectors, nouns become images of actors, prepositions become colors. There is also a distinction to be made between our responses to "natural" shapes (which tend to be curves) and artificial shapes (which tend to be angular or regular): consider the contrasts between city and nature in Ezra Jack Keats's *The Snowy Day,* or the rural peacefulness that surrounds the curving shapes of Arnold Lobel's Frog and Toad, or even the way that distorted and exaggerated images in Dr. Seuss's work imply how close we are to the edges of "the normal."

Jane Doonan, in *Looking at Pictures in Picture Books* (1993), suggests that pictures consist of "several kinds of interwoven arrangement: a scheme of color, a scheme of light and dark, a system of scale and intervals, an arrangement of shapes, an order of small- and large-scale patterning, [and] a network of linear rhythms." The effectiveness of, for example, schemes of light and dark can be seen in Edward Ardizzone's *Little Tim and the Brave Sea Captain* and in Charles Keeping's *The Highwayman*; the network of linear rhythms and the small- and large-scale patterning in Wanda Gág's *Millions of Cats*. Doonan also points out that pictures have "two basic modes of referring to things outside themselves." The first is denotation, where there is a culturally agreed-on relationship between a symbolic and a real object— Rosie the Hen in Pat Hutchins's *Rosie's Walk* does not look much like any real hen, but readers can understand the codes and interpret those shapes as meaning "hen." The second is exemplification, where we are left to deduce actions or moods or ideas from the pictures: in Gabrielle Vincent's *Merry Christmas, Ernest and Celestine*, the facial expressions and body language of the characters say a great deal more than the words.

William Moebius also sees pictures in terms of codes derived from our general understanding of the world, as set out in his 1986 article "Introduction to Picture-Book Codes." His "Codes of Position, Size and Diminishing Returns" suggest importance, power, safety, and so on. Where a subject is on the page matters: "a character on the left page is likely to be more secure"—as, for example, in *Angus and the Ducks*, or Robert McCloskey's *Make Way for Ducklings*. Moebius's "Codes of Perspective" suggest that the presence or absence of "depth" is significant. Thus the journey of Barbara Cooney's Ox-Cart Man is made safe by its limited perspectives, whereas Edward Gorey's Treehorn is always presented as the same size, from the same angle, which says a great deal about his phlegmatic attitude to life. Equally, the shift in perspective in *Where the Wild Things Are* reflects the frustrations of the character, Max. Maurice Sendak's book is used by Moebius as an example of his "Codes of the Frame"—as Max becomes more liberated, the frame of the page disappears and the images bleed off and across pages. There is a similar contrast in *Come Away from the Water, Shirley*, and in the page design of Blanche Fisher Wright's *Mother Goose* rhymes, or David Macaulay's *Black and White*; the conventionality of the frame of David McKee's *I Hate My Teddy Bear* contains the anarchy of the pictures and, with the words, gives a semblance of order and coherence. And the concept of *frame* can apply to the whole book, as in Jon Scieszka and Lane Smith's *The Stinky Cheese Man*, where the characters stray onto the back cover (the little red hen objects to the bar code and the ISBN as being ugly). There are also, Moebius maintains, "Codes of Line": compare the coziness of *Make Way for Ducklings*, which has soft, blurred drawings, with the remote, retreatist delicacy of Robert Lawson's fine-line drawings in *The Story of Ferdinand*. Moebius's final code, of color, is perhaps the most complex of all: it can act to establish mood (Randolph Caldecott, *Sing a Song for Sixpence*) or contrast (*Come Away from the Water, Shirley*), to focus attention (William Nicholson, *Clever Bill*), to connect characters (*Angus*), or to act as part of "action" codes (Julie Vivas, *Possum Magic*). In different cultures, colors have different symbolic meanings—emotional, religious, social, and political.

Perry Nodelman, a pioneer in this field, has pointed out that reading pictures depends on complex learned behaviors: we "know" that a small figure behind a large figure in a two-dimensional picture indicates perspective, rather than relative size; we have to learn about what he calls "pictorial dynamics"—the way in which objects relate to each other and coexist in a two-dimensional representation of three-dimensional space. Similarly, we are not born with knowledge of action lines, or of other movement indicators: for example, we have to learn that conventionally the progressive movement of characters is from left to right; action the other way suggests difficulty (Florence Upton, *The Adventures of Two Dutch Dolls and a Golliwogg*), opposition (*Where the Wild Things Are*), or completion (Lynley Dodd, *Hairy Maclary's Caterwaul Caper*).

And there are matters of reading specific to the picture-book-as-object: we tend to read picture books in terms of two-page "openings," and so the relationship between those two pages—which sometimes makes use of the gutter (the strip where the two pages meet)—is important. It can be progressive in time (Jean de Brunhoff, *The Story of Babar*) or in space (Roger Duvoisin, *The Happy Lion*) or both (Eric Carle, *The Very Hungry Caterpillar*), or it can be continuous (*The Ox-Cart Man*) or contrastive (*Come Away from the Water, Shirley*), or it can separate words and pictures (Janet and Allan Ahlberg, *Each Peach Pear Plum*)—among other possibilities.

All this is quite apart from the knowledge that we bring to the pictures, knowledge that lets us recognize and react to the artistic traditions that they reflect (such as the differing styles of "primitive" art in Pat Hutchins's *Rosie's Walk* [British] and Barbara Cooney's illustrations for *The Ox-Cart Man* [American]).

Therefore, in talking about pictures in picture books, we need to address the question: What is the *purpose* of each picture? Is it primarily narrative, referential, symbolic, or atmospheric? Remember that pictures are difficult to analyze, because we are analyzing a *process* and not a set of fixed relationships, which a written text more nearly approaches. To come to a single, agreed-on answer about what a picture book says, or what is *in* a picture, or what a picture is *about* is even more difficult than coming to comparable agreements about verbal texts. Everything in and around the picture book is necessarily complex.

The Development of Printing Techniques

Children's books have been illustrated from their beginnings in the seventeenth century, but the true picture book as we know it today did not evolve until the end of the nineteenth century, when printers were able to mass-produce books in color and artists and writers could express themselves freely.

The earliest books for children were generally illustrated by woodcuts—the *Orbis Sensualium Pictus* had more than 150. In woodcuts of the earliest kind, from the sixteenth century, the wood was cut away to leave the design standing out, ink was applied, and the paper took the picture in reverse from the raised surface (relief printing). More expensive books used copper engraving, which employed the opposite technique of filling the cutaway lines with ink and pressing the paper firmly to pick up the picture (intaglio printing). This technique enabled finer detail, and the copperplates lasted longer than the woodcuts; but intaglio images could not be printed at the same time as typeset words, because printing from type is a relief process. The need for large numbers of copies at a low price in the early nineteenth century was met by etched copperplates, steel engraving (which produced cruder results), or the method invented by the British printer Thomas Bewick (1753–1828) of engraving on hard wood in which, as with woodcuts, the image was taken from the relief. Many color-printed books for children were produced by George Baxter's

(1804–1867) process of printing a basic image using a metal plate and then over-printing colors from woodblocks.

The root of modern printing techniques was the lithographic process invented in the 1780s by Alois Senefelder: here ink adheres to greasy areas on a "stone," or metal plate, and is then transferred to the paper. The process of chromolithography—building up a color picture by making several separately colored versions and pressing the paper onto them in sequence—was patented in Britain in 1837. Although chromolithography, in conjunction with the rotary press, later came to dominate printing, it was initially crude and expensive in comparison with wood engraving. An early example of a book that used the technique, Heinrich Hoffmann's *Struwwelpeter* (1845) was transferred to wood engravings in 1858 for cheap mass-printing. There are, however, many examples of the subtle use of the technique, as displayed in the carefully controlled colors of Florence Upton's *Two Dutch Dolls and a Golliwogg* (1895).

Throughout the nineteenth century, much coloring was still done by hand, and colored books were consequently very expensive. Only in the 1860s, when photographic methods of producing printing plates were developed, did color printing become commercially viable. It was refined from the 1890s with the invention of 'halftone' color printing (breaking areas of color into tiny dots, so that shades of color could be reproduced). Despite the development of these techniques, it was not until the 1920s and 1930s that the technique of offset lithography (where there is an intermediary transfer roller between the inked image and the paper) began to be used effectively, and even then it was customary—as in Edward Ardizzone's *Little Tim and the Brave Sea Captain* (1936)—to print in color on one side of the sheet only, leaving the other side either blank or in monochrome.

After World War II, color printing techniques, especially in the United States, allowed top-quality reproduction of any image; recent computerized and digital techniques allow any image to be reproduced accurately, and even to be improved in the printing process.

There were many heavily illustrated "toy books" in the nineteenth century: these were color-printed (sometimes hand-painted) on one side of a sheet of paper, and then folded to make a small book with six or eight pages, with attractive covers in thicker paper. The color printing was of variable quality, but some printers could produce excellent and subtle effects. The modern picture book began with the work of the British printer Edmund Evans (1826–1905), who worked with highly innovative artists to produce the best possible results for publishers such as George Routledge. Artists associated with Evans include Randolph Caldecott, Kate Greenaway, and Walter Crane. Crane used characteristics of Japanese prints—sharp black outlines and flat block coloring; a similar style can be seen in the mid-twentieth-century work of the Belgian comics illustrator Hergé, with his Tintin books. Kate Greenaway reflected British society's nostalgic dreams of innocent, rural childhood, and, as many picture books have done since, her work set fashions in children's clothing (even though her drawings were not always anatomically accurate). Caldecott—often using very old nursery rhymes and folktales—similarly shared a nostalgia for what was seen as the golden age of the eighteenth century. The books that he produced at Christmas from 1878 to 1885 began with *John Gilpin* (1878), based on the poem by William Cowper (1731–1800), and *The House That Jack Built* (1878), and had very large sales over many years.

Another notable British artist of the period was Arthur Rackham (1867–1939), whose work was characterized by a convoluted, grotesque style: his evil characters have ugly, wart-covered faces; bodies are distorted, and backgrounds are dark and threatening. Rackham had a successful career that extended into the 1930s, when he provided the nightmarish woodland background for Walt Disney's first animated feature, *Snow White and the Seven Dwarfs* (1937).

In the United States there were outstanding illustrators, such as N. C. Wyeth (1882–1945), famous for highly dramatic illustrations of books such as *Treasure Island,* by Robert Louis Stevenson; Howard Pyle (1853–1911), whose ornate "medievalism" was highly influential; Maxfield Parrish (1870–1966), who experimented with a pseudo-photo-realism; and W. W. Denslow (1856–1915), who illustrated the first edition of *The Wizard of Oz.* Their work, however, was primarily confined to the illustrated book rather than the picture book.

The Twentieth Century

The picture-book writer who has had the most lasting influence from the beginning of the twentieth century is Beatrix Potter, whose publication history in the late twentieth century demonstrates some of the ways in which tastes in pictures change. When her "little" books about Peter Rabbit and other animals, set in the English Lake District, were first published early in the century, Potter ensured that her skillful and delicate watercolors were printed in the three-color process rather than with the woodblocks still used by her publisher, Frederick Warne. In 1987, new editions were prepared by Ladybird Books (a division of Penguin Books, which by then owned Warne), in order to widen the appeal of the books to new generations of readers. In these editions, the world-famous illustrations were replaced by photographs of stuffed animals, on the grounds that they would be more "accessible." There was an immediate controversy in British newspapers and other media over the "class implications" of the different pictures, and the books became a cause célèbre. On one side it was argued that the new pictures would introduce the stories to a new generation of readers who understood photographs, but who would feel excluded by watercolors that were unfashionable, unfamiliar, and essentially middle-class. On the other side, "traditionalists" felt that the photographs both degraded Potter's art and ghettoized and patronized the "working classes," who would be persuaded to buy the books because they were cheap and familiar. The Ladybird series was short-lived, but it raised a great many issues about who owns children's books, how far texts should be held sacrosanct, and how far they should be changed to suit the sensitivities of a different period. In the United States, where Potter's copyright to *Peter Rabbit* was not secured, several unauthorized editions have appeared with new illustrations. When the books were made into an animated film in 1992 in the United Kingdom, the style imitated Beatrix Potter's artwork, and it was suggested that this approach immediately limited the film's appeal. It is interesting to compare the case of Beatrix Potter with that of A. A. Milne. The Walt Disney Company designed new images of Winnie-the-Pooh, which bore little resemblance to the originals by Ernest H. Shepard (1879–1976), and these new images continue to be successful despite arousing some controversy in Britain.

In broad terms, the 1920s and 1930s represented a period of experimentation. William Nicholson, with *Clever Bill,* and Edward Ardizzone, with *Little Tim and the Brave Sea Captain,* explored the possibilities of offset lithography, a technique then being extensively used in Russian children's books. *Little Tim* was printed in New York in 1935—and a curiosity is that this edition could be printed only on one side of the paper because of the difficulty of drying the ink in the humid weather. Outstanding examples of the technique include two large-format books that became series—one British, featuring Orlando the Marmalade Cat (Kathleen Hale, from 1938), and the other French, with Babar the Elephant (Jean de Brunhoff, from 1931), which proved internationally successful.

Some of the most innovative and stylish work from this period was done in the United States, and in the best American tradition the artists drew eclectically on European roots and styles, whether or not they were recent immigrants. Famous examples include the Russian refugee Boris Artzybasheff's designs for *Gay-Neck* (1927), the Austrian Ludwig Bemelman's *Madeline* (1939), and, from 1933, the Story Book series by Miska Petersham (who had emigrated from Hungary in 1912) and his American wife, Maud. Highly stylized, and often using very bright, flat, lithographed colors, this work stands beside that of Marjorie Flack and Wanda Gág, Virginia Lee Burton's *Mike Mulligan and His Steam Shovel* (1939) and *The Little House* (1942), Kurt Wiese's illustrations for Marjorie Flack's *The Story about Ping* (1933), and Lois Lenski's illustrations for Watty Piper's *The Little Engine That Could* (1945). In contrast to these busy and colorful works, Robert Lawson's illustrations for Munro Leaf's *The Story of Ferdinand* were highly original in their lightness and economy of line, as well as their skillful use of white space. Much distinguished work was produced that explored new directions, from the aerial cityscapes of Robert McCloskey's *Make Way for Ducklings* to the whimsy of Roger Duvoison, the anarchy of Dr. Seuss, and the sophisticated experiments of Maurice Sendak.

From the 1950s on, the history of the picture book becomes the history of major talents, standing out against what is often seen as massive overproduction; the overall quality of illustrations has been unmatched, but at the price of distinctiveness and originality. In the United States, artists such as Ezra Jack Keats, Sendak, and Dr. Seuss went from strength to strength and were followed by a new generation of innovators. Chris Van Allsburg's experiments with surrealism, David Macaulay's complex simultaneous storytelling in *Black and White,* and Lane Smith and Jon Scieszka's anarchic intertextuality demonstrated the range of the picture book.

In the United Kingdom, the lavish color work of Brian Wildsmith in the 1950s led to an unparalleled richness of output and range of styles. The surreal experiments of Anthony Browne and David McKee, the often somber urban visions of Charles Keeping, the quirky individualism of Quentin Blake and Babette Cole, the nostalgia of Janet Ahlberg, and the exploration of adult–child relationships through symbolic color and layout by John Burningham took the picture book to new heights of skill and subtlety.

Across the world, picture books have followed fashions in art and culture, most notably postmodernism, with its blurring of fantasy and reality (as in the picture books of Chris Van Allsburg and David Wiesner), its fragmentation of conventional narratives (as in *I Hate My Teddy Bear* by David McKee), its emphasis on performance and participation (as in the Ahlbergs' *Each Peach Pear Plum*), and its tendency toward "hybridization"—the mixing of conventional genres (seen, along with other such features, in Macaulay's *Black and White*). Although there is a huge output of relatively "conventional" picture books, a good many push self-consciously at the boundaries of form and content.

Content and Culture

The subject matter of picture books continues to cause debate, partly, perhaps, because images are supposed to have an immediate effect, partly because of the unthinking assumption that children's books are innocent or should preserve some kind of innocence (usually by their omissions), and partly on the grounds of good taste. Recent books that have aroused controversy have been Toshi Maruki's unflinching depiction of the bombing of Hiroshima and its tragic effects on one family in *Hiroshima no Pika* (United States, 1980); Babette Cole's cheerful explanation of sexual reproduction, *Mummy Laid an Egg!* (United Kingdom, 1993), which has sperm swimming across the endpapers; *Hello Baby* by Jenni Overend and Julie Vivas (Australia, 1999), with its explicit depiction of natural childbirth; and Werner Holzwarth and Wolf Erlbruch's *The Story of the Little Mole Who Went in Search of Whodunit* (Germany, 1989), in which the mole spends the book trying to discover which animal (to put it delicately) deposited its excrement on his head. In each of these cases, it is interesting to reflect on other images to which children are routinely subjected without comment (such as TV and film violence, or the sexuality in advertising). But it is not new books alone that raise questions, as two books from the end of the nineteenth century illustrate. To the contemporary reader, Florence Upton's Golliwogg or Helen Bannerman's Little Black Sambo may seem undeniably racist, reflecting the endemic prejudices of their day. But the Golliwogg was no more stylized than his playmates, the Dutch dolls; and Sambo is of Indian, not African, origin. Is it any defense to suggest that in both cases the authors were liberals with no intention to patronize, or that the books were for many years seen as charming tales, with heroic central characters?

For the picture-book artist, one traditional way of avoiding irrelevant complexity (such as race) has been to use anthropomorphized animals. Arnold Lobel, for example, has said that by using Frog and Toad, rather than two human bachelors, he avoided the need to provide any backgrounds or jobs for them (nor, curiously, does family or age need to be accounted for). The results of anthropomorphism can be very subtle, as when Gabrielle Vincent makes all her children mice, and all her adults bears: whose view of children and adults is represented there? Sometimes, as in many of Beatrix Potter's books, the animals are only a disguise for humans—mother and children in *The Tale of Peter Rabbit*, or gossipy old women in *The Pie and the Patty-Pan*—while in James Marshall's *Dinner at Alberta's,* a very trying phase of life can be described perhaps a little less painfully. But even displacing human behavior into animal form can be dangerous, as when the marriage of a black rabbit to a white rabbit in Garth Williams's *The Rabbit's Wedding* (1958) caused the book to be banned in some southern states of the United States—and it is becoming progressively less acceptable to use animal stereotypes (for fear of being "foxist," for example).

Picture books have strongly influenced our cultural behavior (from Kate Greenaway's clothes to *Rudolph the Red-Nosed Reindeer*'s contribution to the modern mythology of Christmas), mirrored our attitudes and prejudices, and given young readers the opportunity to expand their experiences in remarkable directions. But they are also at the forefront of the development of children's books. At their very beginning, they were mind-expanding—a revolutionary move into multimedia; in the twenty-first century, it is only natural that they should meld into electronic forms, computer graphics, and the rest; that they should be a natural part of the postmodern world; and that their form and content should shift and expand.

The picture book flourishes around the globe, with a particularly important contribution being made by Australian artists such as Ron Brooks and Julie Vivas. In this context, it is ironic that the greatest danger to the original picture book is blandness: in Europe, economic forces have led to international co-productions that attempt to smooth away national characteristics. Because the markets in each country are relatively small, and large print runs are needed to make large profits, books are designed so that the pictures can be overprinted with different languages—or language is avoided altogether. Consequently, the details of landscapes and artifacts that distinguish countries from each other are lost: Beatrix Potter's idiosyncratic English Lake District characters, or Winnie-the-Pooh and his friends in their middle-class Sussex forest, all living in areas of unique natural and built beauty (and talking in complex and ironic dialects), become generic, timeless, and placeless. In the United States and its sphere of influence, the pressures of commercial spin-offs of movies and computer games threaten to overwhelm original artists.

Finally, it is interesting to consider whether the major awards for picture books have acknowledged the revolutionary potential of their subjects (for example, in the United States, the Caldecott Medal, the Boston Globe–Horn Book Award, and the Coretta Scott King Award; in the United Kingdom, the Kate Greenaway Medal and the Kurt Maschler Award; and in Australia, the Children's Book Council of Australia Book of the Year Award).

Wanda Gág (1893–1946)
From *Millions of Cats* (United States, 1928)

Wanda Gág had a background as an etcher, wood engraver, and lithographer, and her skills are demonstrated in the flowing design of her first book. Both in style and in content, it reflects mid-European influences. Gág was a first-generation American.

He liked to sit just quietly and smell the flowers.

Munro Leaf (1905–1976), with illustrator Robert Lawson (1892–1957)
From *The Story of Ferdinand* (United States, 1936)

Possibly the most famous example of the picture book as political text, *Ferdinand* was written during the Spanish Civil War. It makes its point with great lightness of touch, both in the verbal text and in the illustrations. Ferdinand, the pacifist, refuses to fight in the bullring and is sent back to his field to live happily ever after. Robert Lawson was also remarkable for winning both the Newbery Medal with *Rabbit Hill* (1944) and the Caldecott Medal with *They Were Strong and Good* (1940).

He planted himself in the center of the road, raised one hand to stop the traffic, and then beckoned with the other, the way policemen do, for Mrs. Mallard to cross over.

Robert McCloskey (1914–2003)

From *Make Way for Ducklings* (United States, 1941)

Perhaps the most famous of literary ducks, Robert McCloskey's duck family are commemorated in bronze in their park in Boston. McCloskey's gently nostalgic attitude, emphasized by the softness of line, can also be seen in his Caldecott Medal–winning novel, *Homer Price* (1943).

— they had quite forgotten Tim. He was so small and frightened that nobody had noticed him.

Tim crept on to the bridge where he found the captain, who had refused to leave his ship.

'Hullo, my lad,' said the captain. 'Come, stop crying and be a brave boy. We are bound for Davey Jones's locker and tears won't help us now.'

So Tim dried his eyes and tried not to be too frightened. He felt he would not mind

going anywhere with the captain, even to Davey Jones's locker.

They stood hand in hand and waited for the end.

Edward Ardizzone (1900–1979)

From *Little Tim and the Brave Sea Captain* (United Kingdom, 1955)

Edward Ardizzone was one of the great innovators of the British picture book, and he pioneered the intermingling of text and pictures. His Little Tim series sends a small boy out to sea in adventures that, on principle, do not underestimate the dangers involved. *Little Tim and the Brave Sea Captain* first appeared, with hand-lettered text, in 1936; its spreads were alternately color lithography and monochrome. These illustrations, from the revised and redrawn edition of 1955, demonstrate Ardizzone's sophisticated use of lighting effects.

After recess, Treehorn was thirsty, so he went down the hall to the water bubbler. He couldn't reach it, and he tried to jump up high enough. He still couldn't get a drink, but he kept jumping up and down, trying.

His teacher walked by. "Why, Treehorn," she said. "That isn't like you, jumping up and down in the hall. Just because you're shrinking, it does not mean you have special privileges. What if all the children in the *school* started jumping up and down in the halls? I'm afraid you'll have to go to the Principal's office, Treehorn."

So Treehorn went to the Principal's office.

Florence Parry Heide (b. 1919), with illustrator Edward Gorey (1925–2000)
From *The Shrinking of Treehorn* (United States, 1971)

The wry text of this most famous of books depicting parental neglect and the independent world created by the neglected child, in which everything that Treehorn says is ignored, is matched by Gorey's eccentric and unique illustrations that verge on the macabre. Gorey's use of an unwavering single scale and point of view matches exactly the deadpan insouciance of the hero.

"Look," said Emma,
"now he is feeling the saltshaker."

"Don't feel the saltshaker, Arthur,"
said Father. "Either take some salt
or leave it alone."

"My goodness," said Arthur,
"dinner around here is no fun
if everybody is going to pick on me,"
and he began to diddle with his spoon.

"Arthur is diddling with his spoon,"
said Emma.

"Emma," said Father, "you do not
have to report everything to me.
I am sitting right here
and I can see perfectly well."

"Arthur has no manners," said Emma.

Russell Hoban (b. 1925), with illustrator James Marshall (1942–1992)
From *Dinner at Alberta's* (United States, 1975)

Russell Hoban collaborated with several illustrators, and in James Marshall (who, as Edward Marshall, wrote the Fox series) he found one who could provide the ideal deadpan images to match his wry text. *Dinner at Alberta's* is an understated view of the behavior of teenage boys, as seen by their families. The embarrassment is distanced by the anthropomorphism.

But they gagged his daughter, and bound her, to the foot of her
narrow bed.
Two of them knelt at her casement, with muskets at their side!

Alfred Noyes (1880–1958), with illustrator Charles Keeping (1924–1988)
From *The Highwayman* (United Kingdom, 1981)

Charles Keeping was an award-winning British illustrator whose highly indi-
vidualistic technique is seen at its best in this monochrome text. Alfred
Noyes's 1906 poem has been a staple of children's poetry collections for a
century, and until recently it was widely read in U.K. schools, where the barbarity of what was actually happening was rarely realized by its readers. It took
Keeping, with his mastery of dramatic contrasts of black and white, to portray
the scene as brutal rather than romantic.

Patricia C. McKissack (b. 1944), with illustrator Brian Pinkney (b. 1961)
From *The Dark-Thirty: Southern Tales of the Supernatural* (1992)

Pinkney, who is African American, instantly alerts viewers to inversions of familiar black-on-white, typical in printed texts, by using scratchboard illustrations. This technique begins with a white board covered in black ink. The ink is then scratched off with sharp tools, revealing the white underneath. The African American experience is thereby signaled immediately as different.

THE THIRD-FLOOR BEDROOM

*It all began when someone left
the window open.*

Chris Van Allsburg (b. 1949)

From *The Mysteries of Harris Burdick* (United States, 1984)

Chris Van Allsburg has been one of the great originals of contemporary American picture books; his softly muted monochrome technique contributes an air of otherworldliness to his uneasy texts. *The Polar Express* (1985) and *Jumanji* (1981) each won the Caldecott Medal. All of his books blur the line between fantasy and reality in a clearly postmodernist manner.

DAVID MACAULAY
b. 1946

David Macaulay's *BAAA* may surprise anyone who clings to the idea of the innocence of childhood, or the innocence of children's books. This grim satire takes an apocalyptic view of civilization, politics, and consumer society, using a cannibalistic premise similar to that in Richard Fleischer's 1973 film *Soylent Green*. What is it doing in an anthology of children's literature?

BAAA is in the tradition of the animal fable, which allows writers to comment on human foibles while avoiding specific accusations toward any individual or group. The animal fable allows satire to be, in the words of Jonathan Swift, author of *Gulliver's Travels* (in part an animal fable), "a sort of glass, wherein beholders do generally discover everybody's face but their own." The tradition stretches back to the earliest folktales: Aesop's moral but common-sense fables date from the sixth century B.C.E.; the political satire *Reynard the Fox* (1481) was one of the first English printed books; eighteenth- and nineteenth-century evangelical writers made good use of it—for example, Sarah Trimmer with *Fabulous Histories* (later *The History of the Robins*) (1786). Human cruelty toward animals (and toward other humans) was pilloried in books with animal narrators, such as Anna Sewell's *Black Beauty* (1877) and Marshall Saunders's *Beautiful Jo* (1894). *Winnie-the-Pooh, Paddington Bear*, and the talking animals of C. S. Lewis and Philip Pullman have continued the tradition.

But *BAAA* is also the product of the revolution in children's books that dates from the 1970s, when writers like Robert Cormier and Judy Blume pushed back the boundaries of what children's books could be about. In the wake of this revolution, writers for the young can deal with sex, violence, disease, and death—in particular because many believe that the innocence of childhood has been destroyed by the media and the commodification of childhood.

David Macaulay was born in England in 1946, came to the United States as a boy, and has made his reputation with books of intricate drawings that explain how things, notably buildings, work. Among these are *Cathedral* (1973), *Castle* (1978), and *Mosque* (2003), all drawing on considerable architectural and technical skills. His major reference book, *The Way Things Work* (1989), has been issued on DVD. Macaulay lives in Rhode Island and teaches at the Rhode Island School of Design; he has said that he is "explainer first and foremost and an entertainer second."

Macaulay's remarkable skills as a draughtsman are used only incidentally in *BAAA* but provide a matter-of-fact background of the kind that underpins the best satire, even when that satire might seem a little heavy-handed—perhaps because it is so heartfelt.

BAAA

There is no record of when the last person disappeared. The only person who could have recorded when the last person disappeared was the last person to disappear.

But no matter who left last, the place was deserted.

One day a flock of sheep in a remote pasture ran out of food. Their search for nourishment took them to an abandoned town, where they ate the lawns, flower beds, and potted plants.

9

For the next few days, the sheep did nothing but eat, drink, and sleep. When they ran out of food in one house, they shuffled into another.

Tired of traveling yet still hungry, they wandered into a house where a refrigerator hummed. Its food was cold and hard, but the sheep found it quite tasty.

It was also filled with terrible music, so the sheep took their favorite items back to the houses.

After eating, drinking, and sleeping their way through seventeen houses, they stumbled into a supermarket. They couldn't believe their eyes. It was filled with food.

After three days, some of the sheep became bored. They went outside and frolicked in the fresh air. But that became boring too, so they went back inside to watch more glow.

One day, while gamboling across a family room, a young lamb accidentally turned on a television. When it began to glow, everyone stared and stared.

By watching movies over and over again, the sheep learned to speak and eventually to read.

Then, machines were discovered that made pictures and sounds inside televisions.

They started wearing clothes and discovered that many are made of wool (so that's where it went!).

19

The more they learned about people, the more they wanted to be like them.

18

1075

Careers were pursued. Bank accounts opened.

Schools were established. Thoughts were had.

It was a time of great prosperity. Everything was plentiful. Gas was cheap. The population grew.

Television stations went back on the air. Some sheep became quite famous. Even weather sheep.

Some went on business trips.

Soon sheep were traveling.

Others sought their roots.

At breakfast time, leaders and other interesting sheep appeared on television and discussed timely topics.

Around this time, leaders arose from the sheep population. Some had charisma, others connections.

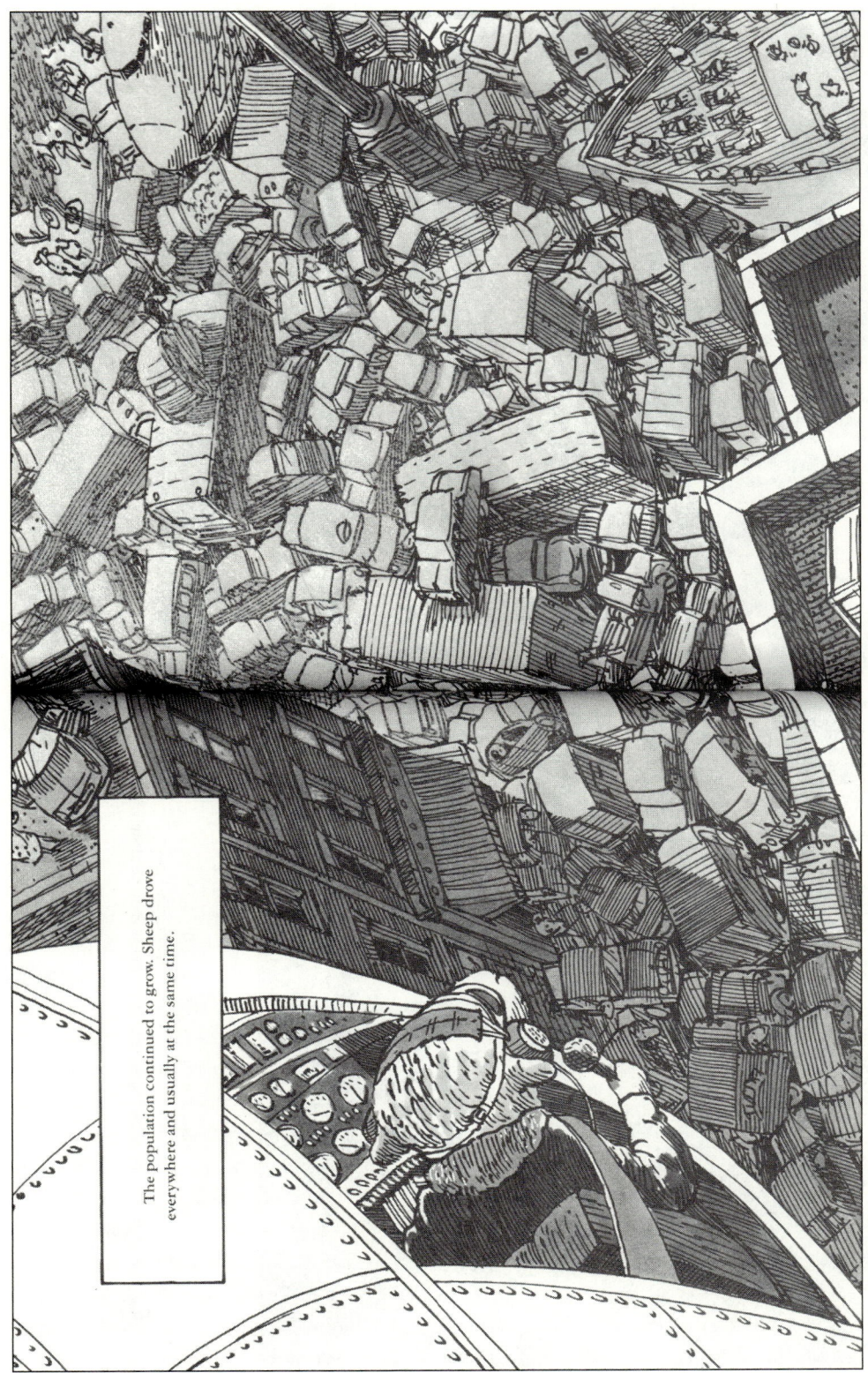

The population continued to grow. Sheep drove everywhere and usually at the same time.

1081

Popular items were often gone from the shelves by ten o'clock in the morning, and for the first time since they left the pasture, some sheep were going to bed hungry.

As the good life continued, it naturally became a little more complicated. Lines at markets and gas stations were growing longer and moving more slowly.

However, when even the leaders couldn't get everything they wanted, rationing was imposed. After this, there was almost enough to go around.

One evening, between commercials, a news sheep announced that things were being used up too fast. But nobody paid much attention.

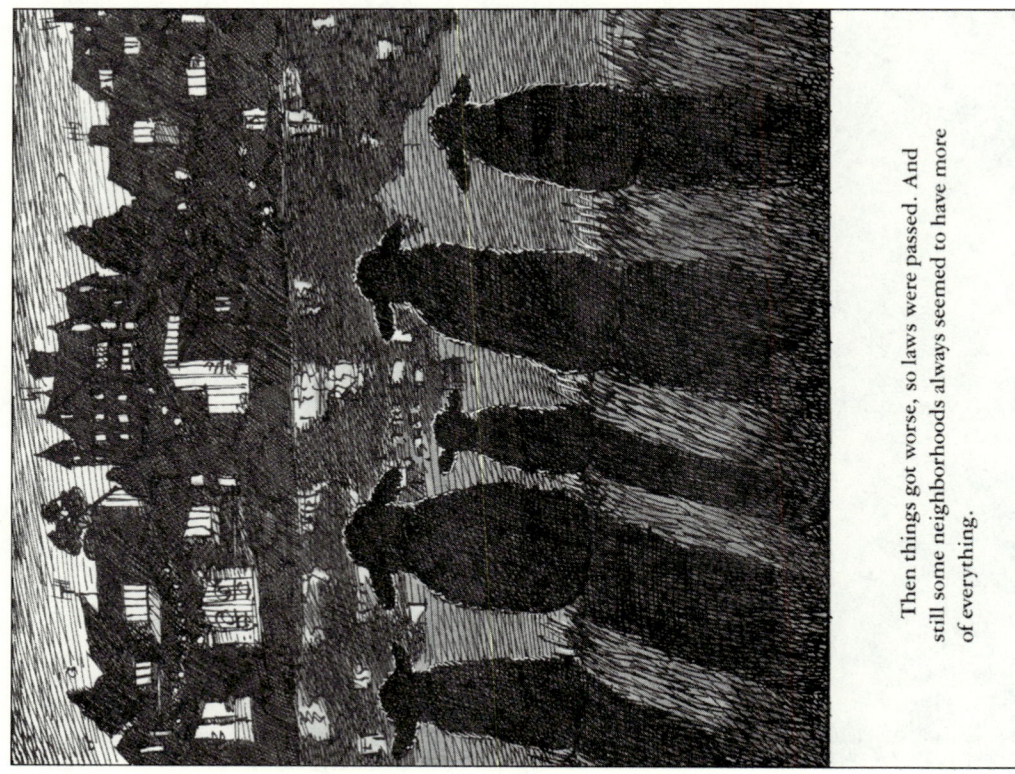

Hungry sheep turned to crime.

Then things got worse, so laws were passed. And still some neighborhoods always seemed to have more of everything.

Riots broke out and injuries were sustained. More comedies were shown on television.

As more and more goods went to fewer and fewer sheep, the number of unhappy sheep grew.

1085

But not everyone heard the good news.

The leaders presented charts and graphs that proved there was no hunger.

Desperate and angry, a number of sheep marched into town to see their leaders. Unfortunately, the leaders were tied up in meetings and could not be disturbed.

Tempers flared. Terrible words were shouted. Things were thrown. Troops arrived to keep the peace.

42

43

1087

The following day, an end to the food shortage was announced. A new product called *Baaa* had been invented. It would be cheap, plentiful, and nutritious.

Everyone tried it and everyone liked it. Peace returned. But then everyone liked it too much, and soon the *Baaa* was all gone. Again, sheep were hungry. Again, they threw things.

While the population steadily declined, the demand for *Baaa* grew.

Once more troops restored the peace, and shortly thereafter *Baaa* shops reopened with fresh supplies. For months this process repeated itself.

By the time the throwing had stopped completely,
Baaa was enormously popular.

The trouble persisted and peace had to be restored
a few more times.

Once again, life was comfortable. There wasn't a single unhappy sheep to be found anywhere.

Baaa vans were familiar to everyone. They passed through some neighborhoods several times a day.

Each evening, more and more houses were vacant, more televisions cold.

As the population grew smaller, fewer leaders were required.

Entire neighborhoods became completely abandoned.

With hardly anyone left to lead, the remaining leaders were unnecessary. They, too, disappeared.

The silence spread. Pools went unfiltered.

And one day they met for lunch.

Eventually, there were only two sheep left.

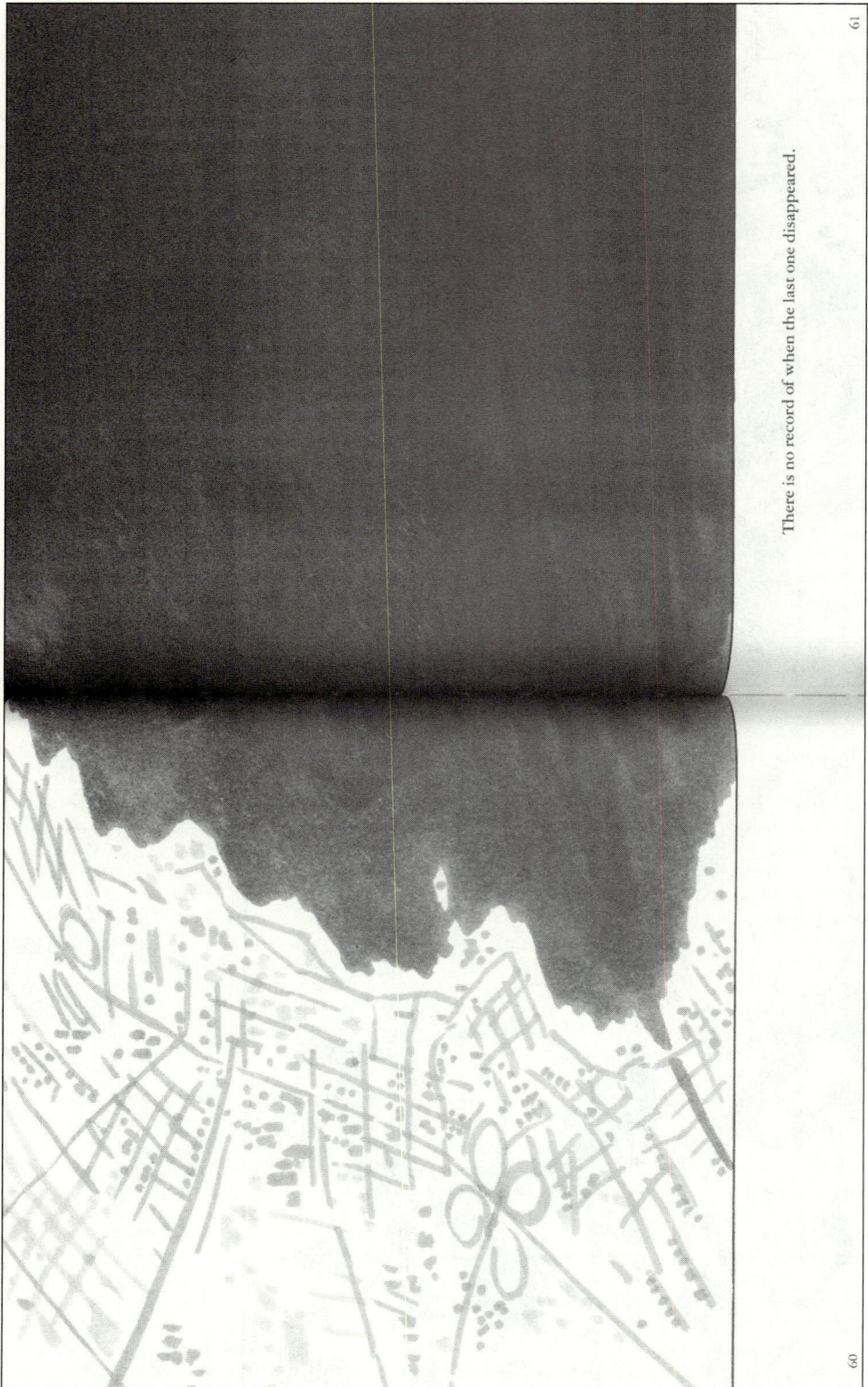

There is no record of when the last one disappeared.

Much later, a fish cautiously swam toward the beach. It stared at the land for a long time and then turned and swam in the opposite direction. The next day, it came back and this time swam a little closer to the beach before turning around. It came back several times that week. On the eighth day, it swam almost to the very edge of the water, intending to crawl onto the dry land. But, at the last moment, it turned again and disappeared into the depths of the ocean.

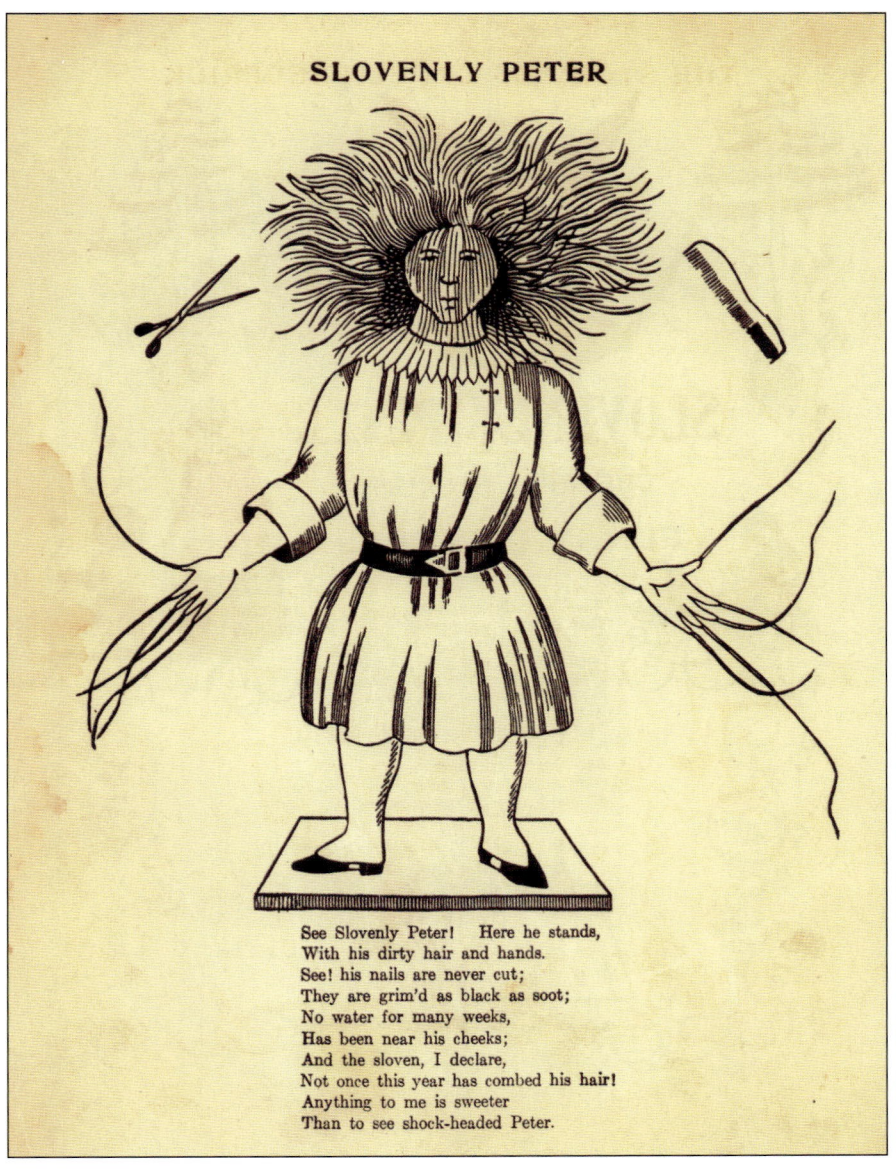

SLOVENLY PETER

See Slovenly Peter! Here he stands,
With his dirty hair and hands.
See! his nails are never cut;
They are grim'd as black as soot;
No water for many weeks,
Has been near his cheeks;
And the sloven, I declare,
Not once this year has combed his **hair**!
Anything to me is sweeter
Than to see shock-headed Peter.

Heinrich Hoffmann (1809–1894)
From *Struwwelpeter* (Germany, 1845)

Struwwelpeter is the classic parody of the cautionary tale that dominated children's books in the first half of the nineteenth century; it has appeared in many hundreds of editions and has had many imitators. Although intended to amuse by exaggerating and ridiculing the extreme punishments threatened by the religious writers of the day, it demonstrates the power of the picture book to frighten, and many of the retributive figures, such as the scissor-man who cuts off sucked thumbs, became features of nightmare. Together with Edward Lear's *A Book of Nonsense* (1846), *Struwwelpeter* set a fashion for crude, humorous drawings. Hoffmann's illustrations were often re-drawn; this English version is typical of many.

You see, merry Phillis, that dear little maid,
   Has invited Belinda to tea ;
Her nice little garden is shaded by trees,—
   What pleasanter place could there be ?

There's a cake full of plums, there are strawberries too,
   And the table is set on the green ;
I 'm fond of a carpet all daisies and grass,—
   Could a prettier picture be seen ?

A blackbird (yes, blackbirds delight in warm weather,)
   Is flitting from yonder high spray ;
He sees the two little ones talking together,—
   No wonder the blackbird is gay !

Kate Greenaway (1846–1901)
From *Under the Window* (United Kingdom, 1879)

Engraved on four or five color woodblocks by Edmund Evans, *Under the Window* was a huge success for Christmas 1879 despite its high price, selling 20,000 copies. It is an example of how children's books can set fashions in clothing; Greenaway persisted in producing an image of a sunlit and idyllic childhood, and contributed to the cult of the "beautiful child" that lasted until the 1920s (A. A. Milne's Christopher Robin is one of the last examples).

Randolph Caldecott (1846–1886)
From *Sing a Song for Sixpence* (United Kingdom, 1880)

Caldecott's books were among the first to truly interrelate words and pictures. He is distinguished by his revolutionary fluidity of line, and, as in this illustration of children catching blackbirds for the king's pie, by the richness of his color work and the subtlety of his compositions. His work influenced Beatrix Potter and is admired by Maurice Sendak, who said: "Caldecott's work heralds the beginning of the modern picture book. He devised an ingenious juxtaposition of picture and word, a counterpoint that never happened before."

Blanche Fisher Wright
From *The Real Mother Goose* (United States, 1916)

The first American edition of *Mother Goose's Melodies* dates from ca. 1785. Here, Blanche Fisher Wright, an American artist, is working in the style of Walter Crane and Kate Greenaway, with simplified line and single block colors demonstrating the same nostalgia for a golden world. The three rhymes are a Scottish popular song collected ca. 1775, a London street vendor's cry from 1733, and an Irish political election jingle from 1761.

RACE

These three treatments of race, in widely differing styles, show how picture books are of their time and need to be understood in their context.

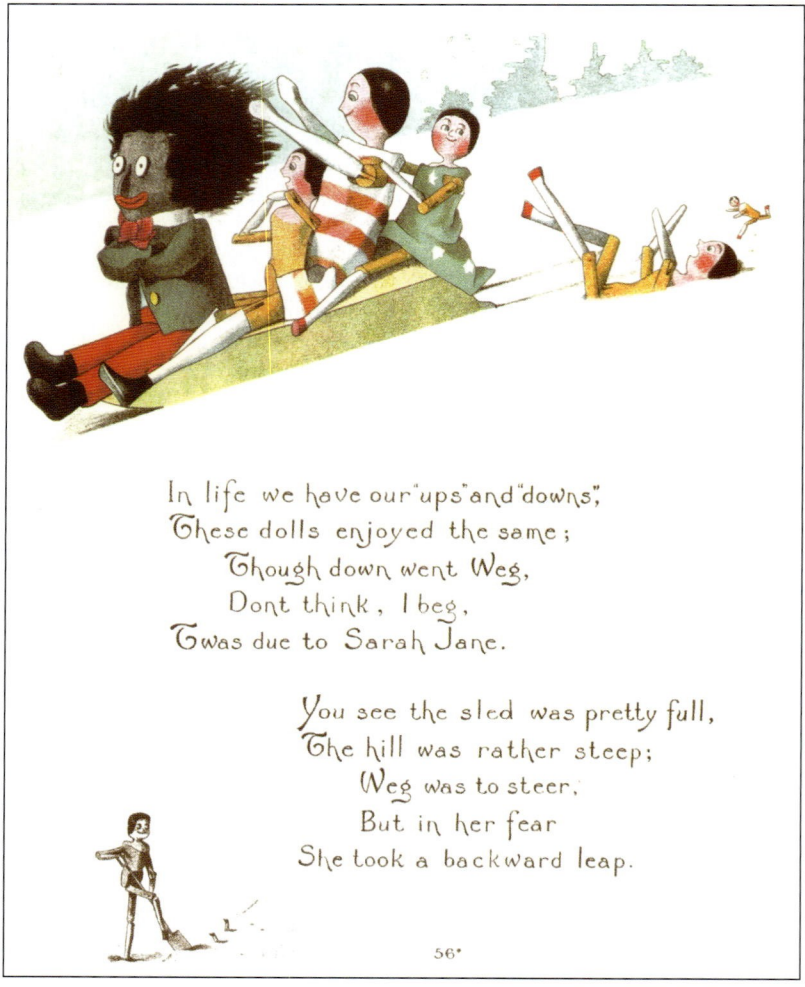

In life we have our "ups" and "downs",
These dolls enjoyed the same;
Though down went Weg,
Dont think, I beg,
Twas due to Sarah Jane.

You see the sled was pretty full,
The hill was rather steep;
Weg was to steer,
But in her fear
She took a backward leap.

56'

Bertha Upton (1849–1912), with illustrator Florence Upton (1873–1922)
From *The Adventures of Two Dutch Dolls and a Golliwogg* (United Kingdom/United States, 1895)

The Golliwogg was the invention of the daughter–mother team of Florence and Bertha Upton, and he became internationally popular as a doll and other merchandise. No more stylized than the white-and-pink "Dutch dolls," he was a friendly, heroic figure, and only in later years became a symbol of racism. In the United Kingdom, the name became associated with the word *wog*—a general opprobrious epithet for non-British people—and in the 1970s references to golliwogs were considered insulting to blacks. As a result, golliwog dolls and other products were withdrawn from sale.

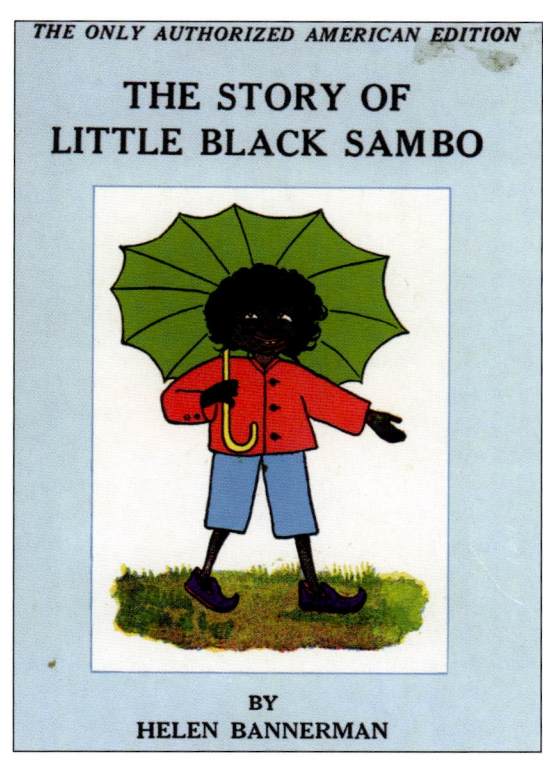

THE ONLY AUTHORIZED AMERICAN EDITION

THE STORY OF
LITTLE BLACK SAMBO

BY
HELEN BANNERMAN

Helen Bannerman (1862–1946)
Cover of *The Story of Little Black Sambo* (first published in the United Kingdom, 1899)

The vigorous, deliberately crude lithographs of *Little Black Sambo* produced perhaps the most notorious of "racist" picture books. It has been widely banned, despite its innocent intentions, possibly mystic interpretations, and Indian rather than African characters. Bannerman wrote several other books of the same kind, including a sequel, *Sambo and the Twins*, commissioned by her American publisher in 1936. She sold the copyright of the original book for $8.00.

Julius Lester (b. 1939), with illustrator Jerry Pinkney (b. 1939)

From *Sam and the Tigers* (United States, 1996)
An attempt to redress the racist imbalance, this adaptation of *Little Black Sambo* is a collaboration between one of the most distinguished American illustrators and one of the most accomplished antiracist activists in children's literature.

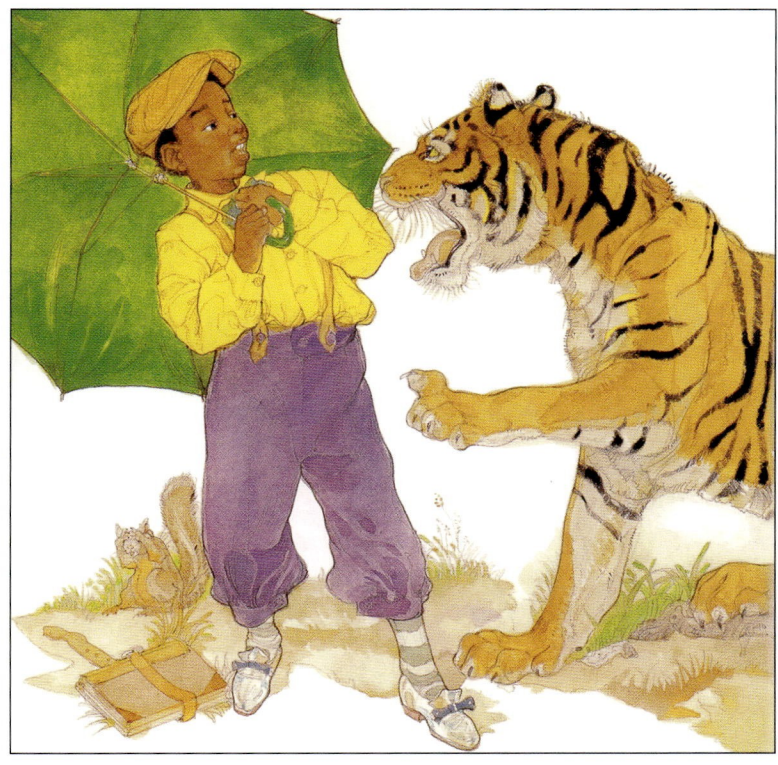

THE TALE OF PETER RABBIT

Beatrix Potter (1866–1943) first sketched Peter Rabbit in a letter to a child (a) and went on to tell the story of his adventure in Mr. McGregor's garden in *The Tale of Peter Rabbit* (1902), published by Frederick Warne & Company. Potter's delicate watercolors (b) and charming characters helped her books "for small hands" become some of the most important picture books of the twentieth century. But despite *Peter Rabbit's* iconic status, an unauthorized edition was published in the United States in 1982, with new, distinctly American illustrations (c). In 1987, Ladybird Books published a new British edition (d), hoping to broaden the audience by using photographs of stuffed toys and softening the text, on the assumption that children could no longer relate to watercolors and would be upset by Potter's attitudes toward punishment and death. Reactions to the Ladybird Book were mixed, and it did not remain long on the market. Several years later (1992), an animated film of the story was released in England, with images closely based on Potter's. Though Warne did produce a book using the stills (e), many felt that the return to a look closer to that of the original limited the film's and book's appeal. Clearly, Peter Rabbit, though he escaped Mrs. McGregor's pie, is not safe from publishers wanting to make him over to suit what they think are contemporary tastes in children's literature.

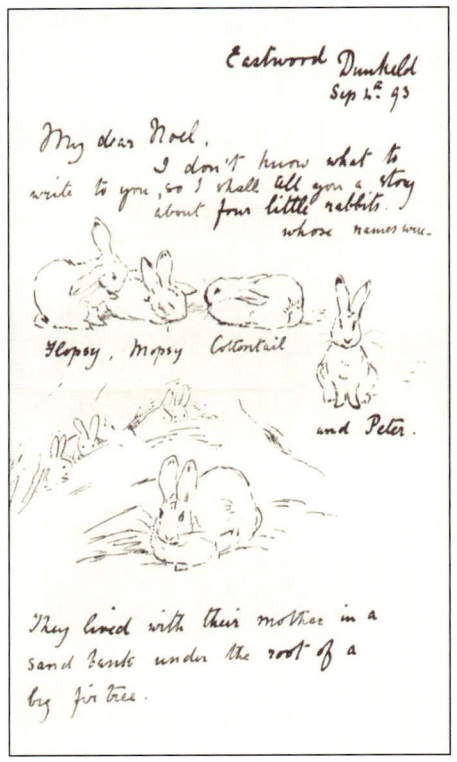

(a) From a letter to Noël Moore (1893)

"NOW, my dears," said old Mrs. Rabbit one morning, "you may go into the fields or down the lane, but don't go into Mr. McGregor's garden: your Father had an accident there; he was put in a pie by Mrs. McGregor."

(b) From *The Tale of Peter Rabbit* (United Kingdom, 1902)

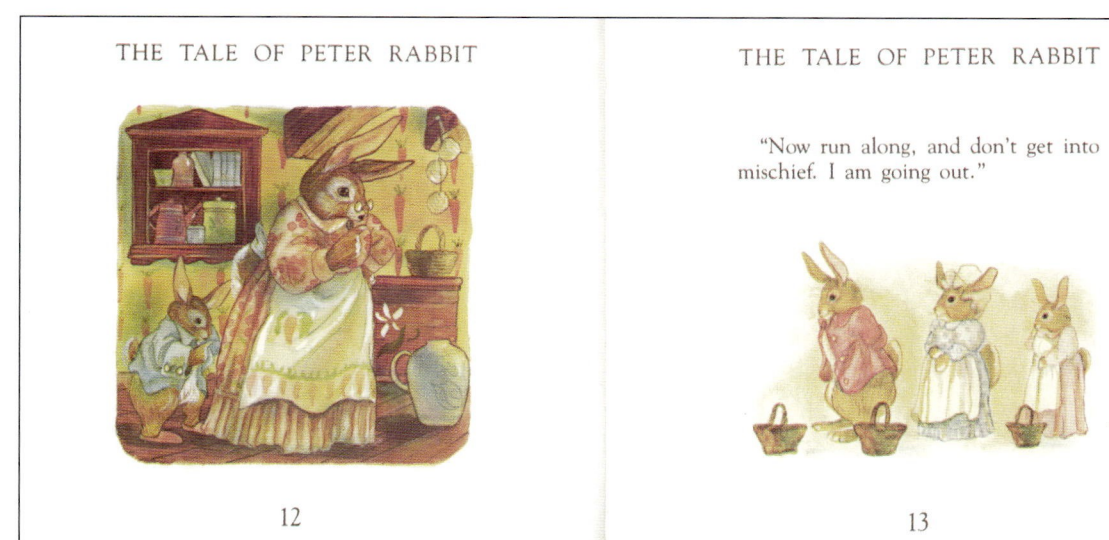

"Now run along, and don't get into mischief. I am going out."

12

13

(c) From an unauthorized edition of *The Tale of Peter Rabbit*, illustrated by Allen Atkinson (United States, 1982)

One day they were allowed to play outside. "Stay near home," said their mother. "Please don't go to Mr McGregor's garden."

"Why not?" asked Peter.

"Because he doesn't like rabbits," answered Mrs Rabbit. "He will try to catch you."

(d) From the Ladybird Books (Penguin) edition of *The Tale of Peter Rabbit,* photographs of stuffed toys (text adapted by David Hately) (United Kingdom, 1987)

They lived with their mother in a sandbank, underneath the root of a very big fir-tree.

'Now, my dears,' said Mrs Rabbit one morning, 'you may go into the fields, or down the lane but *don't* go into Mr McGregor's garden.

(e) From *The Tale of Peter Rabbit and Benjamin Bunny*, the "book of the film" version (United Kingdom, 1992)

Three examples of the bold use of color lithography.

"Clever Bill"

Sir William Nicholson (1872–1949)
From *Clever Bill* (United Kingdom, 1926)

A British classic by a distinguished portrait painter, using the simple lines and colors of the lithographic printing technique and integrating the text and the pictures closely.

But Angus was most curious of all
about a NOISE
which came
from
the OTHER SIDE of
the large green hedge
at the end of
the garden.

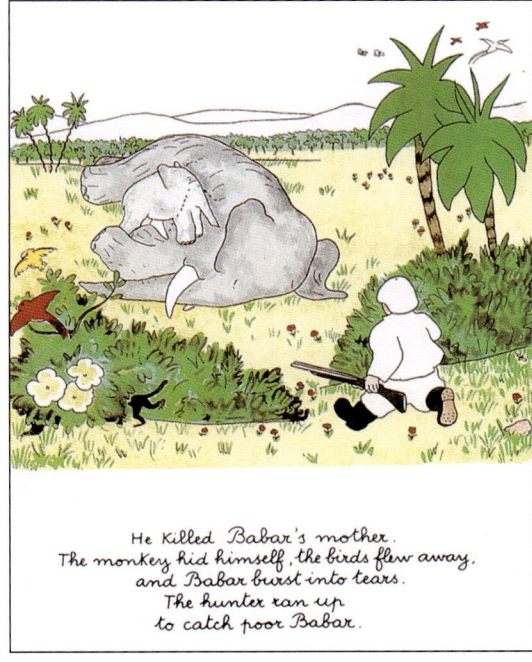

One day Babar was having a lovely ride
on his mother's back,
when a cruel hunter,
hiding behind a bush,
shot at them.

He killed Babar's mother.
The monkey hid himself, the birds flew away,
and Babar burst into tears.
The hunter ran up
to catch poor Babar.

Jean de Brunhoff (1899–1937)
From *The Story of Babar the Little Elephant* (France, 1931; translated 1933)

An example of large-format lithography, this French classic was revolutionary in its size, style, and content. It has been much discussed in terms of imperialism—the way in which Babar adopts the dress and customs of the West and imposes them on Africa—and, as here, for its use of death in a book for young children. Later books in the series, by Jean's son, Laurent de Brunhoff, were simpler and more conventional.

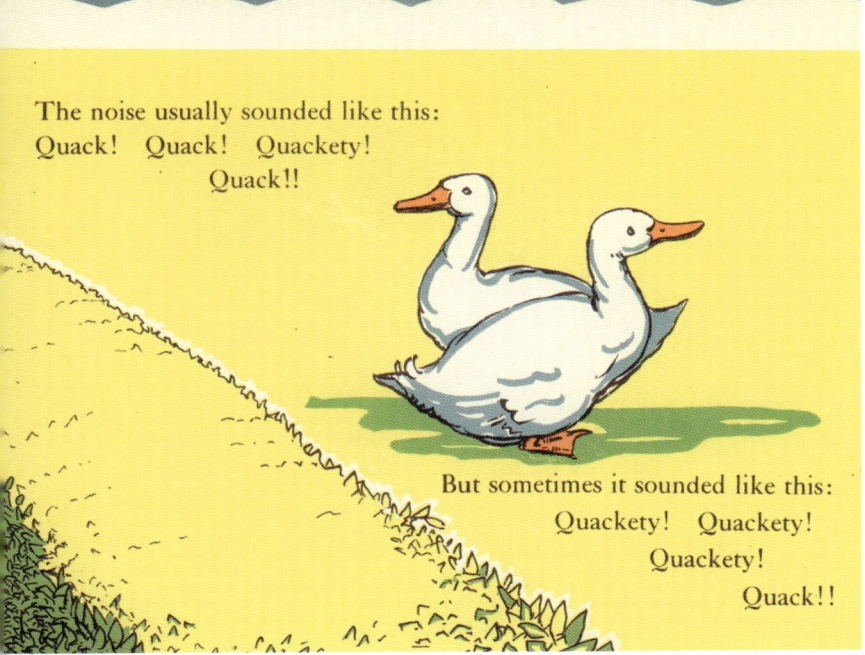

The noise usually sounded like this:
Quack! Quack! Quackety!
    Quack!!

But sometimes it sounded like this:
    Quackety! Quackety!
        Quackety!
            Quack!!

Marjorie Flack (1897–1958)
From *Angus and the Ducks*
(United States, 1930)

Marjorie Flack's Angus books are remarkable for their sweeping, impressionist designs that flow from page to page, as well as for the skillful placement of characters to suggest movement, adventure, and retreat. Color spreads alternate with black-and-white spreads.

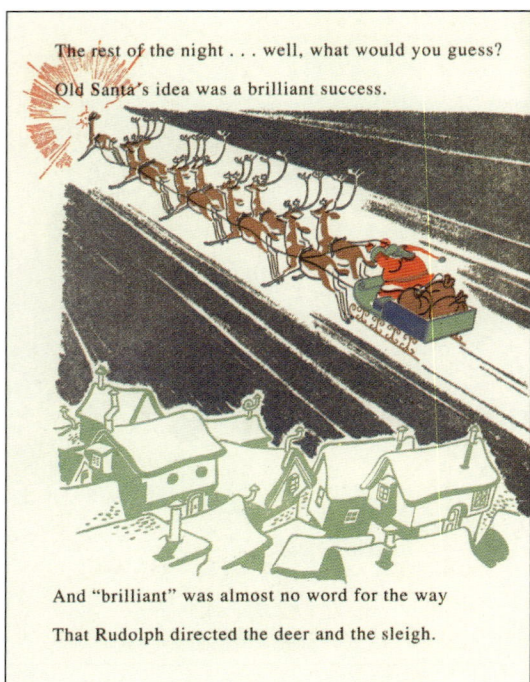

The rest of the night . . . well, what would you guess?

Old Santa's idea was a brilliant success.

And "brilliant" was almost no word for the way

That Rudolph directed the deer and the sleigh.

Robert L. May (1905–1976)
From *Rudolph the Red-Nosed Reindeer*
(United States, 1939)

Rudolph, who has become part of the modern mythology of Christmas, was created for an advertising promotion by the department store Montgomery Ward, which gave away 2.5 million copies of the poem at Christmas 1939, and another 3.5 million in 1945. The influence of Central European artists is clear in the bold and stylized designs. The famous song was written in 1949.

IN spite of the fog, they flew quickly, and low,

And made such good use of the wonderful glow

From Rudolph's . . . er . . . forehead, at each intersection

That not even <u>once</u> did they lose their direction!

His home was not the hot and dangerous plains of Africa
where hunters lie in wait with their guns,
it was a lovely French town with brown tile roofs and gray shutters.
The happy lion had a house in the town zoo, all for himself,
with a large rock garden surrounded by a moat,
in the middle of a park with flower beds and a bandstand.

Roger Duvoisin (1904–1980)
From *The Happy Lion* (United States, 1954)

Written by Roger Duvoisin in collaboration with his wife, Louise Fatio (b. 1904), *The Happy Lion* represents internationalism in children's books: Duvoisin was a Swiss-born illustrator who became a naturalized American, the book has a French setting, and it won the first West German children's book award.

**And when he came to the place where the wild things are
they roared their terrible roars and gnashed their terrible teeth**

MODERN CLASSIC

Maurice Sendak (b. 1928)
From *Where the Wild Things Are* (United States, 1963)

In probably the most-discussed picture book of the twentieth century, Maurice Sendak
expanded the possibilities of the genre. The steadily increasing size of the images and
their bleed from page to page reflect the fantasy and rebellion of the protagonist, Max.
The achievement of depth through shading and cross-hatching and the progressive inten-
sifying of the color are characteristic of Sendak's multilayered work.

and rolled their terrible eyes and showed their terrible claws

One winter morning Peter woke up
and looked out of the window.
Snow had fallen during the night. It
covered everything as far as he could see.

Ezra Jack Keats (1916–1983)
From *The Snowy Day* (United States, 1962)

Keats's technique of collage strikingly depicts the urban scene, which presents a grim contrast with his characters' constant delight and interest in the world. This Caldecott Medal–winner was one of the first picture books to confront the invisibility of black people in children's books, as it provided a black central character—although some critics complained that Keats did not escape stereotypes.

Do you like
green eggs and ham?

11

Dr. Seuss [Theodor Seuss Geisel] (1904–1991)
From *Green Eggs and Ham* (United States, 1960)

Dr. Seuss's surreal and extravagantly undisciplined drawings first appeared in 1937 with *And to Think That I Saw It on Mulberry Street*. *Green Eggs and Ham* is one of the best-loved of his limited vocabulary Beginner Books that began with *The Cat in the Hat* (1957). There is an extremely complex relationship between the simplicity of the words and the extremes of the fluid compositions: the simple, repetitive verbal patterns are in tension with the madness of the pictures. Several of Seuss's books have an underlying political or social critique.

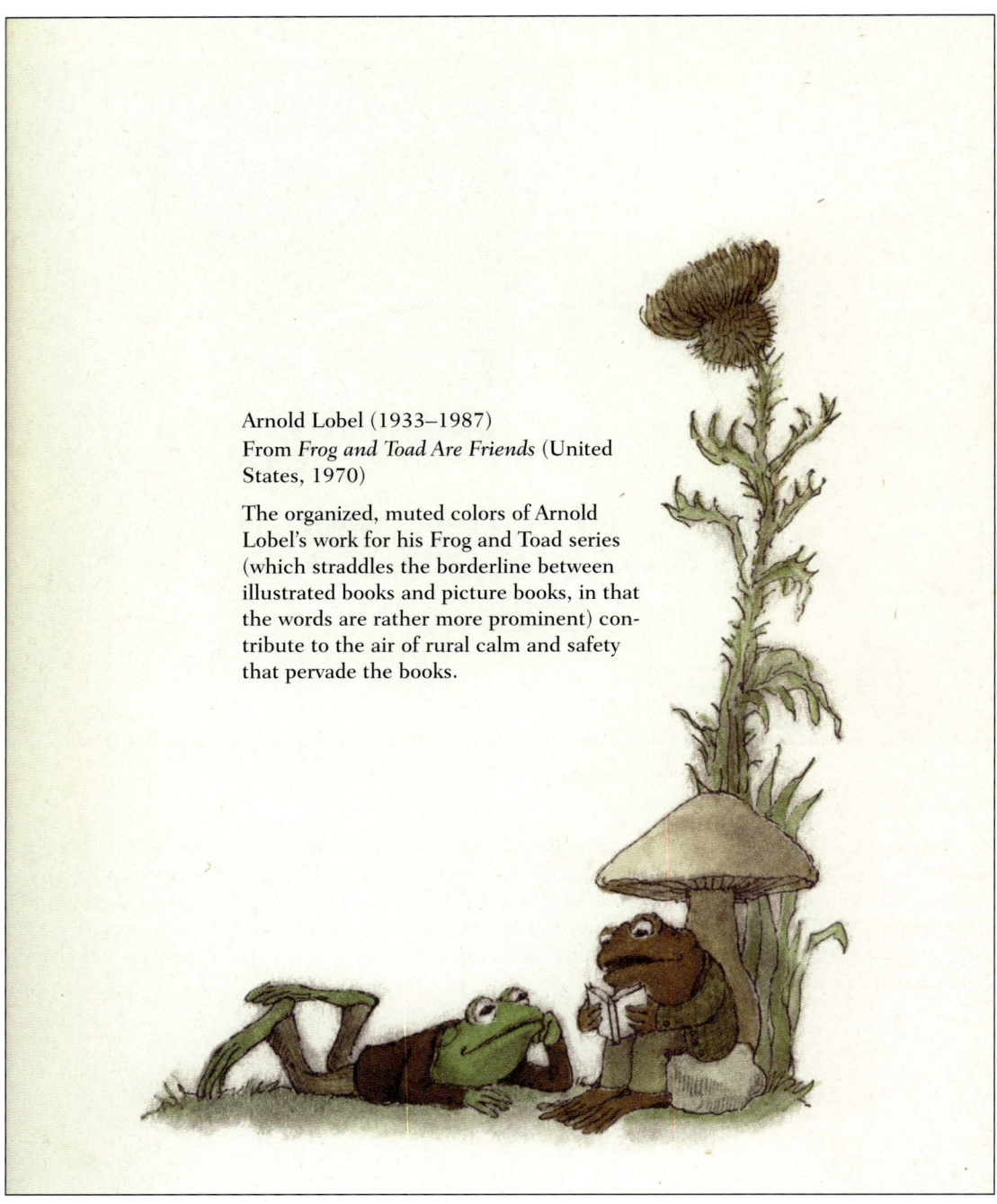

Arnold Lobel (1933–1987)
From *Frog and Toad Are Friends* (United States, 1970)

The organized, muted colors of Arnold Lobel's work for his Frog and Toad series (which straddles the borderline between illustrated books and picture books, in that the words are rather more prominent) contribute to the air of rural calm and safety that pervade the books.

The new aunt's name was Bundlejoy Cosysweet. She had a floppy hat with flowers on it. She had long, long hair. "That sounds fine to me," she said. "We'll have a go."

Tom took his boat and pedalled to the next town down the river. There he advertised in the newspaper for a new aunt. When he found one that he liked, he told her, "No greasy bloaters, no mutton and no cabbage-and-potato sog. No Nautical Almanac. And I do lots of fooling around. Those are my conditions."

Russell Hoban (b.1925), with illustrator Quentin Blake (b. 1932)

From *How Tom Beat Captain Najork and His Hired Sportsmen* (United Kingdom/United States, 1974)

Like *Rosie's Walk*, this Anglo-American collaboration colludes with the child reader against the adult world. Tom, persecuted by his aunt, Miss Fidget Wonkham-Strong, wins incomprehensible games against Captain Najork by being an independent spirit. The apparent casualness of Quentin Blake's highly skilled pen-and-wash illustrations matches the eccentricity and anarchy of Russell Hoban's plot. Blake was named the first British Children's Laureate. He collaborated on Roald Dahl's later children's books, eventually illustrating or reillustrating them all, and his lightness of touch and profound humanitarianism somewhat mute Dahl's undoubted savagery. Hoban is an award-winning writer of novels for both children and adults.

Pat Hutchins (b.1942)

Cover of *Rosie's Walk* (United Kingdom, 1968; this cover is from the U.S. edition)

Rosie's Walk is a rare example of a "single-focus" text. The written text does not mention the most obvious feature of the visual text (the fox that pursues Rosie the hen): the words, in effect, play straight man to the pictures, thus allowing preliterate and just-literate children to "own" the text. Pat Hutchins's "folk art" can be contrasted with the work of Barbara Cooney.

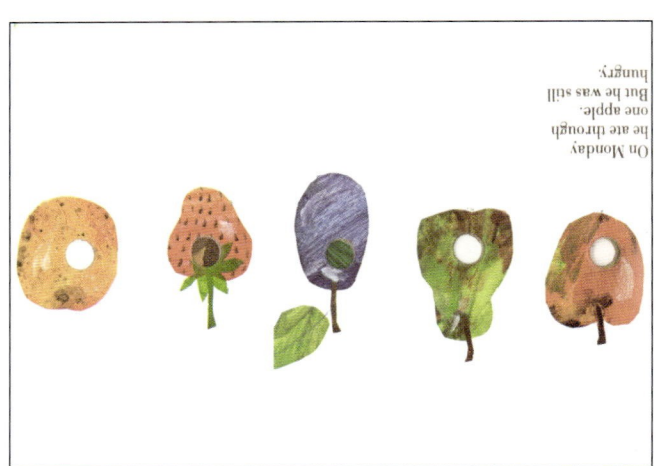

On Monday
he ate through
one apple.
But he was still
hungry.

Eric Carle (b. 1929)
From *The Very Hungry Caterpillar* (United States, 1969)

This is a rudimentary game book: holes are cut through the fruit, through which the caterpillar crawls. The imaginative use of collage and very bright colors are characteristic of the period, and Eric Carle continues to work in this mode. The Eric Carle Museum of Picture Book Art opened in Amherst, Massachusetts, in 2002.

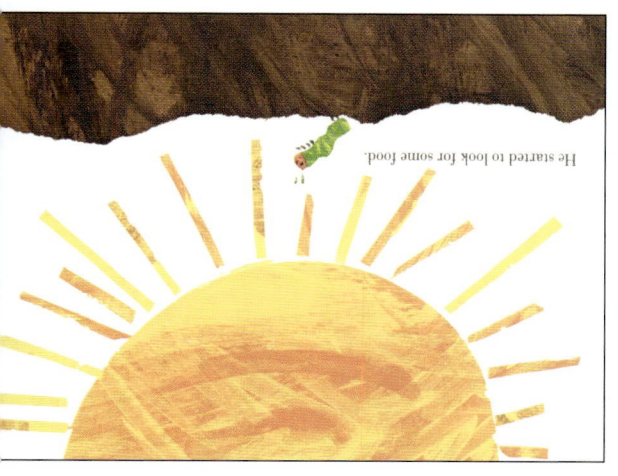

He started to look for some food.

Raymond Briggs (b. 1934)

From *Fungus the Bogeyman* (United Kingdom, 1977)

Raymond Briggs has demonstrated the possibilities of the cartoon strip when adapted to the picture book, exploiting both its wordless (as in *The Snowman*, 1978) and, in this case, its hugely wordy possibilities. *Fungus* is a complex wordy discussion of existence, dense with visual and verbal jokes and intertextual references.

Raymond Briggs (b. 1934)
From *The Snowman* (United Kingdom, 1978)

Here Raymond Briggs has produced a totally wordless text, relying on the conventions of cartooning to move the narrative forward and exploiting a *lack* of color. The book ends with the Snowman melting at daybreak; the 1982 film version was highly sentimentalized. Briggs has a rather bleak approach to the world, and some of his cartoon-strip books—such as *When the Wind Blows* (1982), about the effects of the nuclear bomb—are, despite appearances, for adults.

One night Rose looked out of the window
and saw something move in the garden.

Each Peach Pear Plum
I spy Tom Thumb

'What's that in the garden, John Brown?' she said.
John Brown would not look.

Jenny Wagner (b. 1939), with illustrator Ron Brooks (b. 1948)
From *John Brown, Rose and the Midnight Cat* (Australia, 1977)

Increasingly, fewer subjects have been taboo for children's books, and this one tackles the idea of death, personified as a black cat moving around outside the house. The old lady, Rose, wants to welcome it in; her faithful dog, John Brown, resists. Ron Brooks's illustrations, which won the Australian Picture Book of the Year Award, use a limited palette of somber colors, matching the book's mood of unease.

Allan Ahlberg (b. 1938), with illustrator Janet Ahlberg (1944–1994)
From *Each Peach Pear Plum* (United Kingdom, 1978)

Behind Janet Ahlberg's delicate and nostalgic illustrations is a complex and allusive world that relies on the reader's awareness of other texts. *Each Peach* foreshadows the Ahlbergs' use of multidimensional, interactive media in works such as *The Jolly Postman* (1986), which contains letters and other materials that can be removed from the book. The Ahlbergs assume that their child readers have a wide range of reference, although several of their books, such as *Peepo!* (*Peek-a-Boo!* in the United States, 1981), nostalgically depict a lost England that seems more appropriate for an adult audience.

Picture books often use the two facing pages of an "opening," sometimes called a "spread," as a single picture or as contrasting or connecting pictures.

That's the third and last time I'm asking you whether you want a drink, Shirley

When his cart was full, he waved good-bye to his wife, his daughter, and his son

and he walked at his ox's head ten days

John Burningham (b. 1936)
From *Come Away from the Water, Shirley*
(United Kingdom, 1977)
John Burningham has been a major innovator.
In this book, the left-hand page represents the
washed-out world of adults, with their inhibit-
ing, inhibited, clichéd use of words, while the
right-hand page shows, in bold colors, the isolated child's wordless fantasies of freedom and
adventure.

Donald Hall (b. 1928), with illustrator Barbara Cooney (1917–2000)
From *The Ox-Cart Man* (United States, 1979)

Barbara Cooney uses both a style and a technique (painting on wood) similar to those used by American
"primitive" artists. The luminous colors and the remarkable panoramic use of the spread create an idyllic
view of nineteenth-century New England and of the cycle of the year.

over hills, through valleys, by streams

past farms and villages

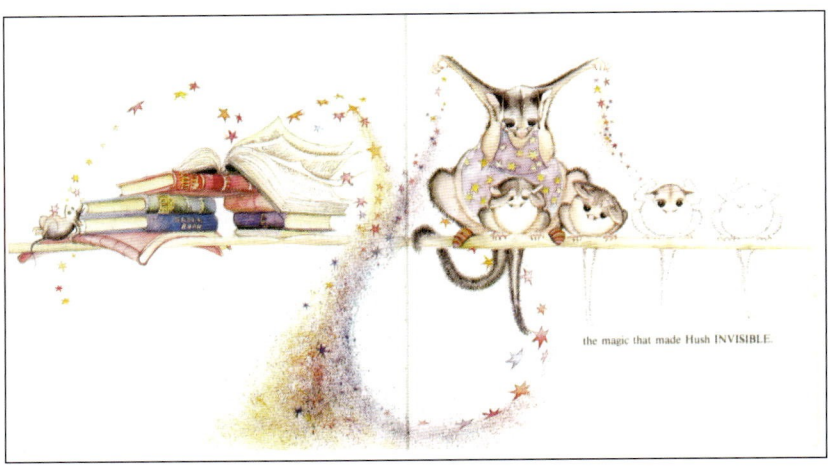

the magic that made Hush INVISIBLE.

Mem Fox (b. 1946), with illustrator Julie Vivas (b. 1947)
From *Possum Magic* (Australia, 1983)

Julie Vivas's startlingly bright colors and rounded style are exploited in this celebration of Australia's animals. *Possum Magic* illustrates the uneasy relationship between Western civilization and the Australian outback. Vivas's
idiosyncratic treatments of subjects such as *The Nativity* (1986)—using a biblical text but featuring (for example) the angel Gabriel in large boots—the happy
death-camp survivors in *Let the Celebrations Begin!* (1991), and the explicitly
portrayed natural birth in *Hello Baby* (1999) have been highly controversial.

"Say yes, Ernest! Say yes!"

"I'm sorry Celestine. Not this year."
"But you promised, Ernest."

Gabrielle Vincent [Monique Martin] (1928–2000)
From *Merry Christmas, Ernest and Celestine* (France, 1983)

Gabrielle Vincent's delicate watercolors look back to a golden age with fascinating local cultural detail. They reflect the simple and affectionate relationship
between adult and child (in a world where all the adults are bears and all the
children are mice).

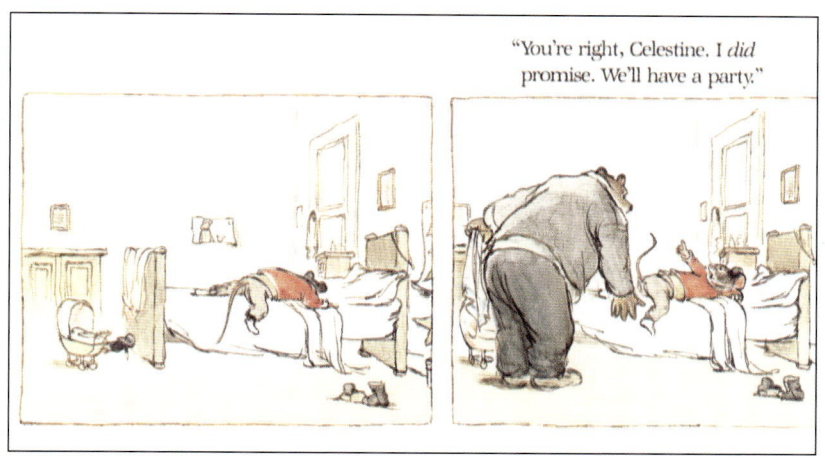

"You're right, Celestine. I *did* promise. We'll have a party."

"Oh, Ernest, isn't this fun?"

David McKee (b. 1935)
From *I Hate My Teddy Bear*
(United Kingdom, 1982)

David McKee's faux-naïf artwork assumes a highly intelligent audience, and he packs his books with postmodern and surreal jokes. The verbal text of this book is no more than a minor quarrel between two children, but in the pictures are fragments of narrative and disjunctions that may, ironically, make more sense to naive readers than to adults.

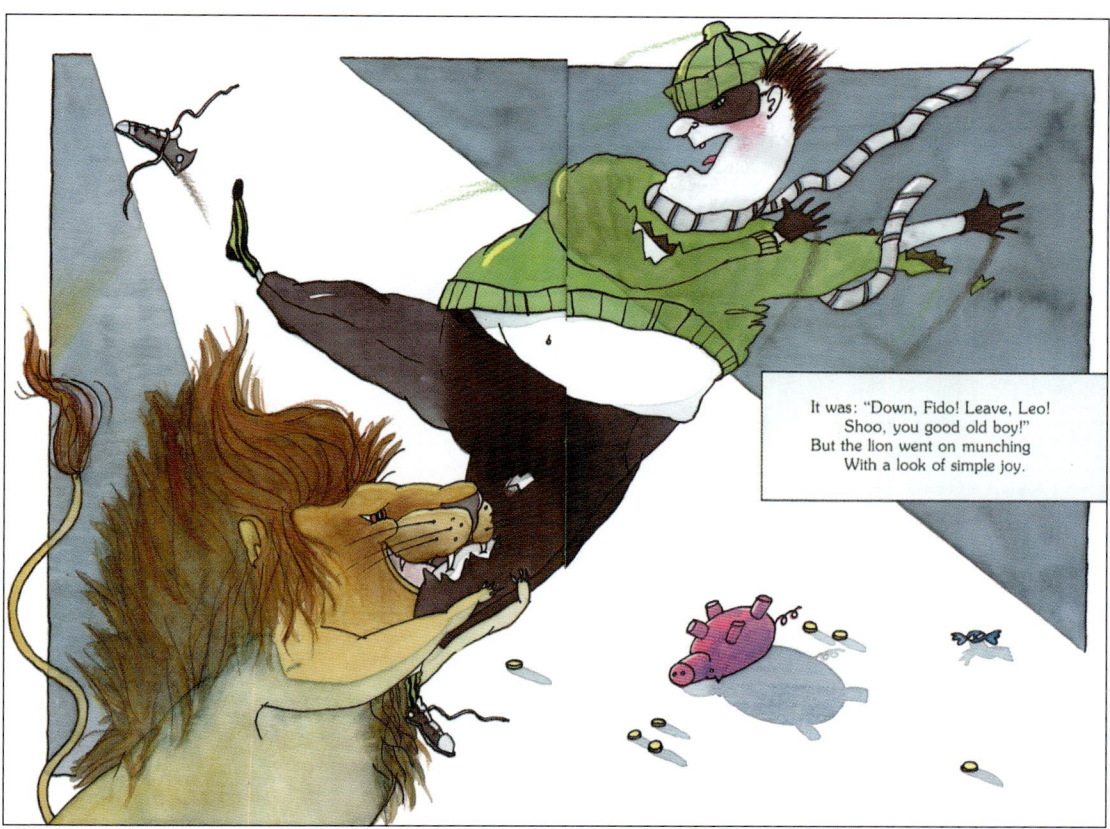

It was: "Down, Fido! Leave, Leo!
Shoo, you good old boy!"
But the lion went on munching
With a look of simple joy.

Dennis Lee (b. 1938), with illustrator Mary-Louise Gay (b. 1952)
From *Lizzy's Lion* (Canada, 1984)

The depiction of the lion tearing the robber to pieces caused some controversy in Canada when *Lizzy's Lion* was first released, but the book endured and became a great favorite. The pen-and-watercolor illustration with the off-kilter robber is cartoonlike and comic, not tragic. The pieces of robber scattered about become part of the general bedroom debris (shown earlier) on the floor of a slightly untidy child.

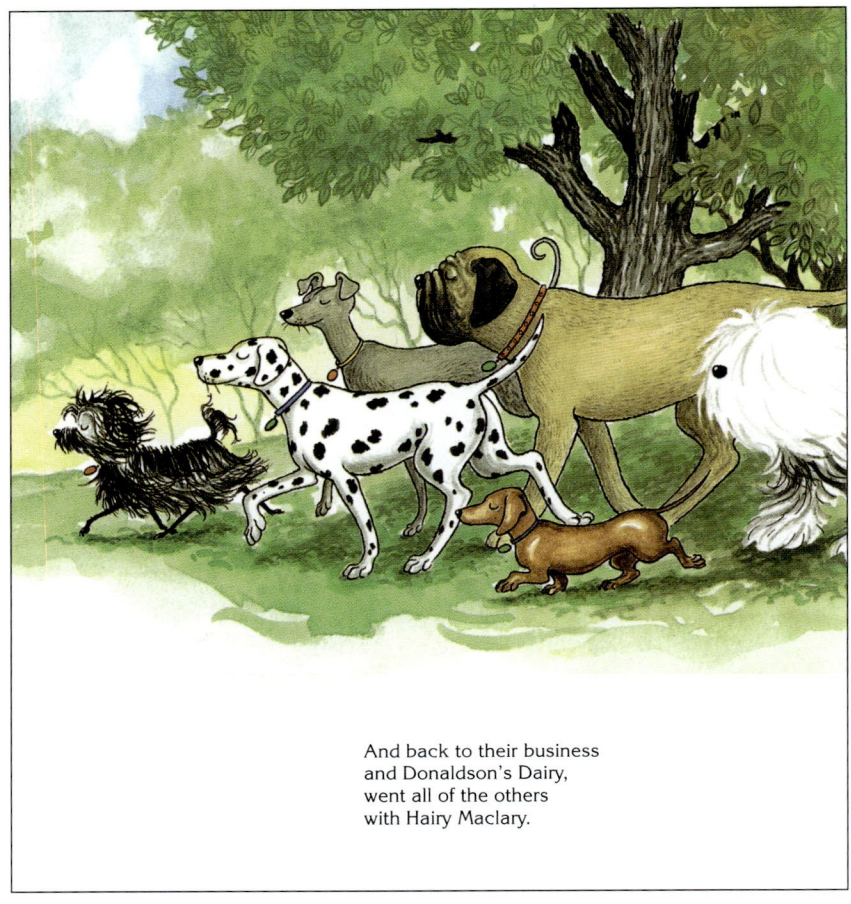

And back to their business
and Donaldson's Dairy,
went all of the others
with Hairy Maclary.

Lynley Dodd (b. 1941)
From *Hairy Maclary's Caterwaul Caper* (New Zealand, 1987)

With excellent draughtsmanship, glowing colors, and an exuberance of spirit, the New Zealander Lynley Dodd represents the mainstream of high-quality picture-book making in the late twentieth century.

Sometime in the early morning hours, the train comes to rest. All is quiet. Suddenly, the door of the compartment slides open. The conductor leans in, announces that something is blocking the tracks, and disappears. A few minutes later, an old woman enters the compartment and sits down opposite the boy. She says nothing.

Every morning at seven o'clock they leave for their offices in the city.

The worst thing about Holstein cows is that if they ever get out of the field, they're almost impossible to find.

David Macaulay (b. 1946)
From *Black and White* (United States, 1990)

David Macaulay has an international reputation for books that lay out the intricate workings of buildings (*Castle*, 1977; *Cathedral*, 1973); here he looks at the intimate workings of narrative. His four parallel but not necessarily concurrent or complementary narratives push the boundaries of multimedia effects within a single medium.

Jon Scieszka (b. 1954), with illustrator Lane Smith (b. 1959)
From *The Stinky Cheese Man and Other Fairly Stupid Tales* (United States, 1992)

As an "advanced" multireferential text, *The Stinky Cheese Man* has not (yet) been bettered. It assumes intertextual skills, its collage medium is deliberately ironic, and its characters try to break the bounds of the book. "The Princess and the Bowling Ball" is a fractured fairy tale that mocks "The Princess and the Pea." The prince, frustrated that successive princesses don't feel the pea beneath the mattresses, substitutes a bowling ball: "And everyone lived happily, though maybe not completely honestly, ever after."

Comics

The Appeal of Comics

Including a section on "comics" in an anthology such as this might seem to be a descent into the trivial. Comics, after all, are not respectable: they are crude, simple-minded, and ephemeral. They are what children buy for themselves to read in private. They are not meant to last long, and they are soon thrown away. In short, they may be fun, but they are not art: they are read by people who don't or can't read "proper" books. And, if that were not enough to disqualify comics from this book, a lot of them are actually for adults, or are read as often by adults as by children.

Many believe that comics are distinguished from picture books in the same way that action and adventure stories are distinguished from the classic realist novel: comics and action stories are only, or primarily, concerned with the story. (This is also why comics are considered inferior to picture books.) It is certainly true that comics invite a certain kind of initial reading in which the reader "consumes" the text rather than reflecting on it, but the comic can be (and is) profitably reread and lingered over. Indeed, only brief reflection is needed for the reader to realize that comics, in their broadest sense, are an extremely interesting and complex form of narrative communication. As the editor of the vast *World Encyclopedia of Comics* (1999), Maurice Horn, stresses,

> the comic strip is emphatically *not* a medium of graphic narration. The narrative in the strip is not conveyed visually, but expressed in both pictures and words. While emphasis may be given to one of the dual aspects of the strip over the other, the interest most often shifts back and forth, according to the demands of the action or the needs of the character.

Comics take several forms. They can be a single panel, delivering a visual or verbal "one-liner"; they can be a four- (or more) panel strip cartoon, telling a joke or making a pointed observation, often with a built-in reaction from the characters. Both of these forms can stand alone, or may depend in whole or part on all the other cartoons about those characters, as in Charles Schulz's *Peanuts* series: if you have never met Snoopy before, you might not know about his fantasies—or even that he is a beagle. Comics can take the form of a daily continuous newspaper strip, telling a story that lasts many months. This in itself is a very skilled art, and a curious phenomenon: what other form of storytelling can sustain interest for such long spans, read for ten seconds every twenty-four hours? They can combine the continuous and the discontinuous: a daily strip in G. B. Trudeau's *Doonesbury* series can work on its own, or as part of a short sequence on the same topic, or as part of the story of characters who have been interacting (with each other and the audience) for forty years. Or they can take the form of short or long stories in weekly or monthly comic papers or comic books; in such works as *Superman* and *The Fantastic Four*, links and elements of story and character can be developed over many years. And comics can take the form of "graphic novels"—long pictorial narratives with all the verbal and psychological complexity and depth of the classic novel.

Similarly, it does not take long to dispel the myth that comics are crude and simple. Over the years, comics have developed a vast range of styles, and they include some examples of the highest-quality visual art, as *The Yellow Kid* and Winsor McCay's *Little Nemo in Slumberland* demonstrate. While there is obviously a great deal of "functional" cartooning—that is, cartooning intended to convey biographical or other facts, such as that in *The Life of Pope John Paul II*—the work of innovative artists such as (among many) Frank Hampson for the U.K. comic *Eagle* and Jack Kirby and Stan Lee for Marvel in the United States is highly original, offering radical perspectives and viewpoints and continuously experimenting with ways of making the dynamic visual and the visual dynamic.

Comics have an affinity to films, using many of the same devices—varied viewpoints and angles, cutting, panning, close-ups, long shots, and so on—together with some unique elements. It says a great deal about the pervasiveness of comics in world culture that many readers do not realize how many visual codes are operating in comics. Some, like the distinction between thought and speech balloons, methods of verbal emphasis (size, boldness, formality of lettering), and movement lines, are (perhaps) obvious. Others are more subtle: as action develops from frame to frame, the "gaps" between frames become significant: in the gaps things happen, which the reader supplies; time can stop or pause or move on. And action is not necessarily confined to the frames, as characters burst through dividing lines and commentary panels explain or reinforce. The verbal and visual syntax is highly complex.

However, some insist that all of this sophistication is being applied to necessarily superficial materials: the "daily joke" does not have any long-term interest, and the superheroes who defeat another would-be master of the universe each month are only pale, repetitive shadows of classical heroes. But there are many strips, from *Tintin* to *Little Orphan Annie*, that deliberately set out to make social and political points, and no comic can escape its own contexts. Maurice Horn argues that "the intellectual limitations of the comics are apparent[;] . . . but . . . by their very inability to sustain for long any lofty and more relevant theme, they retain the virtue of timelessness, thus refusing to become another dreary exercise in ephemeral literature." Furthermore, it can be argued that many comics do sustain complex themes and arguments and that, like picture books, they can be deceptive in their "simplicity."

The History of Comics

Comics—or "sequential art," as the writer and illustrator Scott McLeod has called them—have a very complex and respectable history. Some scholars trace them back to prehistoric cave paintings—to a preliterate world that needed to record stories. In the modern world, the word *comics* refers to different things in different cultures; it can mean strip cartoons appearing in newspapers or collected in books, where the audience is primarily an adult one (this is the primary meaning in the United States);

it can mean strip-cartoon papers (usually weekly) designed for children (this is the primary meaning in England). The principle of the comic—a sequence of linked images—seems quite simple, with each frame or picture (where there is more than one) making sense only in terms of other frames in the sequence, and the relationships between them contributing to their meaning. Nevertheless, the actual terms—*comics, the comics, comic strips, strip cartoons,* and so on—have different connotations in different countries and at different stages of the form's development.

Stories told in pictures that use speech balloons date back to fourteenth-century woodcuts. There have been illustrated magazines from the beginning of the nineteenth century, and in continental Europe there was a tradition of "comic" sheets: single pages with sixteen pictures and accompanying text. The first publisher of these was Jean-Charles Pellerin in Epinal, France, and one of the sheets produced by his company was the first comic sold in the United States, *Impossible Adventures* (probably in the 1880s).

Toward the end of the nineteenth century, in the West, comic strips emerged for the mass market as successors to the cheaply produced, usually densely printed and sensational penny dreadfuls and dime novels. The question of which was the earliest of each type is hard to answer definitively. For example, in 1892 *Little Bears and Tykes* appeared in the *San Francisco Examiner*; it has some claim to being the first American comic strip, though it did not use speech balloons. It consisted of what would now be called "spot gags" rather than an ongoing story, but it used the same characters over a period of time.

The world's first comic paper—a collection of cartoons independent of any other publication—was probably *Funny Folks,* published in the United Kingdom in December 1874. It consisted of single-panel jokes, cartoons, and strips: "A Weekly Budget of Funny Pictures, Funny Notes, Funny Jokes, Funny Stories." The magazine ran only until 1894 but it began a trend, and its successors were increasingly aimed at children. One of these, *Snap-Shots* (from 1890), was composed of strips from American magazines such as *Life* and *Harper's Weekly*.

The first British comic magazine to feature a regular character was *Ally Sloper's Half Holiday* (1884), and from the 1890s onward dozens of cheap comics, often of eight tabloid pages and with circulations exceeding half a million, flooded the market. The most famous were *Comic Cuts, Chips,* and the *Beano.* The last of these, which is still running, featured a character called Dennis the Menace, who first appeared on March 17, 1951, drawn by David Law. By a remarkable coincidence, an American character with the same name, drawn by Hank Ketcham, appeared in U.S. newspapers on March 12, 1951; the two characters today coexist amicably.

The story of the first American comic book is especially complicated. *The Yellow Kid* initially appeared in the Sunday supplement of Joseph Pulitzer's *New York World* in 1895. The artist, Richard F. Outcault, was hired by a rival newspaper magnate, William Randolph Hearst, in 1897 to draw the *Yellow Kid* for the *New York Journal* and as a five-cent comic-book compilation; he then went back to Pulitzer, and then back to Hearst. Outcault finally worked for the *New York Herald,* producing another classic, *Buster Brown.* The first daily strip was the equally famous *Mutt and Jeff,* which began with Augustus Mutt in the *San Francisco Chronicle* in 1907. Most of these strips were single jokes; the first serial strip, *Hairbreadth Harry,* did not appear until 1906. Newspaper syndication of these strips began with Moses Koenigsberg, who founded King Features in 1915.

The newspaper strip had become big business, but in the United States, comic books did not have an independent existence; they were reprints given away in grocery stores or as newspaper supplements. Comic books were first printed in quantity in Japan, in the 1920s. In the United States, after a shaky start with *The Funnies* (1929), followed by a major Proctor and Gamble free book, *Funnies on Parade* (1933), comic books began to boom with books such as *Famous Funnies* (reprints, 1934) and *New Fun* (original material, 1935), usually selling at ten cents. From then on, original comic books led the field—and in June 1938, probably the most important comic-strip hero in the history of world comics appeared. *Superman* was published in *Action Comics* and was then syndicated in newspapers six months later. Sales of both *Superman* and other comics climbed into the millions.

Jerry Siegel and Joe Shuster, both seventeen, had designed *Superman* as a newspaper strip, but it had been rejected several times before the publisher Harry Donnenfeld produced it as a comic book. *Superman*'s appearance in itself changed the history of the American comic book, which from this time forward differed from the newspaper strip in style, audience, and complexity. *Superman* first appeared in a syndicated newspaper strip in 1939, then as a radio show in 1940, and in most other media thereafter. Unlike many of his imitators, Superman does not present the young audience with someone at their own level with whom to empathize: he is an abstract embodiment of goodness and power—of America's vision of itself. The plot lines involved a succession of much-imitated supervillains, and toward the end of the century they became increasingly complex and cosmic; this shift was reflected in highly sophisticated artwork, which clearly demonstrated not only the staying power of Superman but the place of the comic strip as a center of innovation. The international success of American superheroes, who rapidly displaced most local heroes such as the Canadian "Captain Canuk," may reflect the increasing cultural domination by the United States of the rest of the world. These superheroes—Superman, Batman, Captain America, Wonder Woman, and hundreds of others—fought their way through World War II, and the comic book rapidly colonized the world (with particular success in Japan).

In the United States, the quality and popularity of both the newspaper strip and the comic book declined in the early 1950s. One result was an upsurge in "horror comics" depicting extreme violence. A campaign against them culminated in Fredric Wertham's highly influential analysis, *Seduction of the Innocent* (1954), and in hearings in the U.S. Senate. In response, most of the publishers of comics agreed to subscribe to a voluntary "Comics Code." In the United Kingdom, horror comics were banned under the Children and Young Persons (Harmful Publications) Act of 1955. There, too, quality had fallen after World War II. But also in the 1950s the old comic papers—some of which, such as *Chips*, had been running for more than fifty years—were replaced by more contemporary designs, such as *TV Fun*, and four-color, large-format comics, such as *Eagle*.

Through the 1960s, new publishers (notably Marvel Comics Group) using high-quality artwork revived the American comic book; and while the fortunes of individual companies have varied, the output of comic strips in diverse forms has vastly increased around the world. The merchandising of comic-book characters, from Superman and Mickey Mouse to, in Europe, Tintin (Belgium) and Asterix (France), is part of the integration of the comic into the multimedia commercial world. The huge output of Japanese comics—the *manga*, often written for adults—is starting to influence American artists, while in the late twentieth and early twenty-first century we have seen a blurring of the boundaries between film, comics, and computer games. Characters such as Judge Dredd—who first appeared in the U.K. comic

2000AD—and Asterix have appeared in live-action films; blockbuster movies, such as *X-Men, Spiderman, Batman, Superman,* and *The Hulk,* have both borrowed from the comics and contributed to their survival. At the same time, there are comic-book spin-offs from computer games such as *Tomb Raider.* It seems inevitable that these forms will increasingly become indistinguishable, arguably marking a change in concepts of literacy. The crossover between texts for adults and texts for children, which is more and more evident in novels and film, has always been a feature of the comic; George Herriman's *Krazy Kat* (1910–44) is a notable example. In recent years, however, the comic designed primarily for adults has flourished; the "underground comix" of the 1970s and the satirical *Howard the Duck* (1973–81) (from the mainstream publisher Marvel) were highly innovative. Perhaps the most outstanding (of many) practitioners have been writer/artists Neil Gaiman, whose *Sandman* (1989–96) was described by Norman Mailer as "a comic strip for intellectuals," and Art Spiegelman, with his graphic novels (*Maus: A Survivor's Tale* [1986] and *Maus II: From Mauschwitz to the Catskills* [1991], Holocaust allegories, and *In the Shadow of No Towers* [2004], about 9/11). How accessible to children these comics are is a matter for debate.

Comics have become an important—in some countries the dominant—form of popular written culture, and are increasingly being taken seriously as a lively and powerful art form.

From *Funny Folks* (United Kingdom, 1887)

A typical issue of the earliest comic book in Britain, with a characteristically patriotic cover. The caricatures of different races in the background demonstrate British confidence in the superiority of the Empire, as well as the displacement of the "other" to the margins.

From *Impossible Adventures* (France/United States, ca. 1888)

The first comic strip sold in the United States was a translation produced in France by Jean-Charles Pelerin, "Printed expressly for the Humoristic Publishing Co., Kansas City, Mo." *Impossible Adventures* was the first in a successful series; appropriately, it takes the form of a tall tale in the American tradition.

Richard F. Outcault (1863–1928)
From *The Yellow Kid*, No. 1 (United States, 1897)

Probably the first of the nationally recognized comic characters, the Yellow Kid (named from
an experiment in color printing) was the center of a newspaper war—and ultimately lent his
name to the reporting practices of the newspapers involved, "yellow journalism."

Winsor McCay (1869–1934)

From *Little Nemo in Slumberland* (United States, 1908)

The comic strip is immensely varied in its style, and the form has often risen to heights of artistic skill and ingenuity. *Little Nemo* first appeared in the *New York Herald* in 1905, and its art nouveau intricacy opened new doors for cartooning. It was made into a musical in 1908 and an animated film in 1909; some experts view it as representing the pinnacle of comic-strip art.

From *The Funnies*, No. 1 (United States, 1929)

The first comic book to hit American newsstands, and the first product of an important comics publishers, Dell, *The Funnies* ran for only thirty-six issues, probably because it looked too much like a newspaper supplement. But it introduced the form of the comic book as we know it.

Hergé [Georges Rémi] (1907–1993)

From *Tintin in the Land of the Soviets* (France, 1930)

Tintin first appeared in *Le Petit Vingtième*, a supplement to the Belgian daily *Le Vingtième Siecle*; Hergé was a pioneer in the development of the European comic book. *Tintin in the Land of the Soviets* was strong, crude political criticism; in the twenty-two books that followed, the propaganda was replaced by a more indirect satire (see p. 1110).

Sensational developments in the
Tintin story!...
The famous and Friendly reporter re-
appears! Tintin, missing some
days back from a banquet in his
honour, led police to the hideout of
the Central Syndicate of Chicago
Gangsters. Apprehended were 355
suspects, and police collected
hundreds of documents, expected
to lead to many more arrests...
This is a major clean-up for the
city of Chicago... Mr Tintin admitted that the gangsters had been
ruthless enemies, cruel and
desperate men. More than once
he nearly lost his life in the
heat of his fight against crime...
Today is his day of glory.
We know that every American
will wish to show his gratitude,
and honour Tintin the reporter
and his faithful companion
Snowy, heroes who put out of
action the bosses of Chicago's
underworld!

LONG LIVE
TINTIN & SNOWY

After a full round of celebrations,
Tintin and Snowy embark
for Europe...

Pity!... I was almost
beginning to get
used to it!

TOOOOOT

HERGÉ.

Tintin in America (France, 1954)

Tintin's foray into the United States explores many American comics clichés, from
cowboys and Indians to gangsters, in the process painting an image of the country that
is not too complimentary.

Walt Disney (1901–1966) and Floyd Gottfredson (1905–1986)
Mickey Mouse and the Pirate Submarine (United States, 1935)

Probably the first spin-off from an animated cartoon, the original Mickey Mouse newspaper strip, which first appeared in 1930, was written by Walt Disney himself. It ran until the 1950s, taking in Mickey's wartime activities (for example, *The Nazi Submarine*, 1943), largely illustrated by Floyd Gottfredson. Since then, Mickey has appeared in every conceivable format and, like Superman, is an American icon.

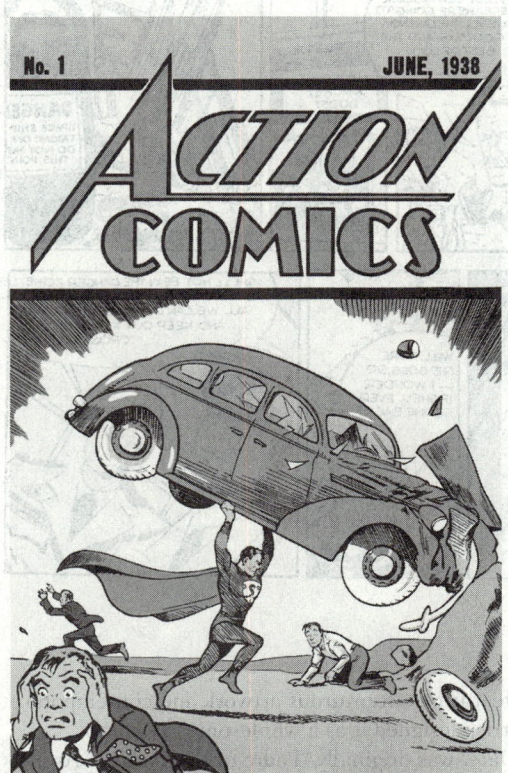

Joe Shuster (1914–1992); text by Jerry Siegel (1914–1996)
Action Comics, No. 1 (United States, 1938)

Superman, the most revolutionary and influential comic-strip character, grew from modest beginnings in 1938 to be a highly sophisticated, integral part of American culture. One of the two creators of this quintessentially U.S. hero, Joe Shuster, was a Canadian, and he drew the cover of the first comic book in a deceptively simple style. Because Shuster and Jerry Siegel had sold their character to Detective Comics, they earned little from *Superman*'s tremendous success; finally, beginning in 1978, the publishers granted them each an annual stipend.

Frank Hampson (1918–1985)
Eagle, No. 1 (United Kingdom, 1950)

Eagle was the first of a new breed of comic, featuring adventurous artwork and contemporary themes. Its editor, the Reverend Marcus Morris, designed it as a wholesome riposte to American horror comics, and its hero, Dan Dare, was originally "Padre of the Future." As "Pilot of the Future" Dan Dare became internationally famous; Frank Hampson won many awards for his inventive use of color and viewpoint, as well as his design of whole pages.

Albert Uderzo (b.1927); text by René Goscinny (1926–1977)

From *Asterix in Britain* (France, 1966; trans. Anthea Bell and Derek Hockridge, 1970)

Asterix first appeared in *Pilote* in 1959. Its continuing popularity—it has been translated into over one hundred languages—led to the Asterix theme park outside Paris (1989), as well as animated and live-action films. The witty and allusive satirical text has taxed many translators, is accompanied by complex and subtle illustrations, and assumes a highly sophisticated audience. *Asterix* demonstrates the increasing fluidity of categories: is this a cartoon, or a picture book, or a graphic novel? This excerpt exploits French prejudices against the British.

MARVEL COMICS

Marvel Comics came to prominence in the 1960s with the outstanding work of Stan Lee, Jack Kirby, and others on superheroes such as the Fantastic Four and Spider-Man. Much of Marvel's output was a team effort, with writers, pencillers, inkers, letterers, and colorists working together in the house's vigorous and distinctive style. Joe Sinnott, a Marvel veteran, inked *The Hulk* (below), which first appeared in 1962; *The Hulk*'s popularity has been sustained for decades, not only by the comic but also by a television series (*The Incredible Hulk*, 1978–82) and a film (2002). Sinnott also worked on the team that created *The Life of Pope John Paul II* (right; others on the team include Steven Grant, John Tartaglione, Jim Novak, and Marie Severin); this 1982 word-and-picture biography demonstrates the surprising range and versatility of the comic book and its creators.

From *The Hulk* (United States, 1982)

From *The Life of Pope John Paul II* (United States, 1982)

Verse

> Hush! Hush! Whisper who dares!
> Christopher Robin is saying his prayers.

In this couplet from "Vespers" (1923), A. A. Milne draws on two characteristic strains of the English tradition of poetry for children: the prayer and the nursery rhyme. When Milne's poem first appeared in *Vanity Fair*, poetry for children was at a turning point, beginning a shift from the religious to the secular, from the rural to the urban, from the white Anglo-Saxon Protestant to the religiously and culturally diverse. "Vespers" was an instant hit. On the one hand, the image of the little blond boy kneeling at the side of his bed saying his prayers is instantly endearing and sentimental. On the other hand, as Ann Thwaite notes in her 1990 biography of Milne, its tone presents "an entirely ironic picture of childhood." In the history of poetry for children, we find the ironic as well as the sentimental. To trace the history of that poetic tradition, its "verbal music" (a phrase from the poet Seamus Heaney's essay "Feeling into Words" [1990]), we must begin with the prayers, hymns, and religious songs of the late seventeenth century.

Religious Verse for Children

Although we today associate children's verse with something light and cheerful, for most of its history it was much more stern. "In Adam's fall / We sinned all" is the couplet that introduced the young Puritan students of *The New-England Primer* (1690) both to the alphabet and to humanity's dreadful state. This rhyming alphabet was a revolutionary pedagogical tool, at once memorable and moral, with a specific religious purpose. The rest of the religious poetry in *The New-England Primer* reinforced the message of sinfulness and mortality. Its famous bedtime prayer first appeared in the 1749 edition:

> Now I lay me down to sleep
> I pray the Lord my soul to keep
> If I should die before I wake
> I pray the Lord my soul to take.

Puritans saw children as necessarily disobedient (like Adam) and needing to be instructed in fear of God and fear for their immortal souls. This view permeates the writings of the two founding fathers of children's poetry, John Bunyan and Isaac Watts. In *The Discovery of Childhood in Puritan England* (1992), C. John Sommerville suggests that the appeal of Puritan doctrine lay largely in its desire to "purify" not only the Church of England but other institutions as well. Various sects urged "reform of the law and the judicial system, of the constitution, of marriage, of business practices, of science and education, of language." All English Dissenters were excluded from their country's major political and educational institutions (including the only universities, Oxford and Cambridge), but they preferred in any case to educate their children without the interference of the state. Education was crucial, for rejection by Dissenters of external authority made the cultivation of individual judgment all the more important. Moreover, they often objected to the contents of the chapbooks that children then read. Poetry, as Bunyan wrote, offered a way to teach and "entice" them "To mount their thoughts from what are childish toys, / To heaven, for that's prepared for girls and boys." Play and entertainment that had genuine appeal to children could stoke their desire to create a "purer" world.

At a time when the Bible was commonly viewed as the only suitable reading for Sundays, Bunyan's *The Pilgrim's Progress* (1678) provided a religious allegory cast as a lively, action-packed adventure story. Bunyan's *A Book for Boys and Girls; or Country Rhimes for Children* (1686), later known as *Divine Emblems*, was one of the earliest collections of poetry written specifically for children. By presenting everyday objects—"temporal things spiritualized," as a later subtitle put it—Bunyan grounds the abstract concepts of virtue and vice in the real sounds of conflicts between parents and children. "Upon the Disobedient Child," for example, ends with the recognition that children "snap and snarl, if Parents them control."

For about 200 years, Isaac Watts's writings, like Bunyan's, were well known to anglophone children. Like Bunyan, Watts was a Dissenter, though far better educated (he had learned Latin, Greek, Hebrew, and French while still young). He also wrote several works on education and educational theory, expressing scathing criticism of rote learning. Watts thought it important that children understand what they were being taught. Only then would they willingly accept precepts that are apparently restrictive. The stakes are high, as Song 12 from his *Divine Songs Attempted in Easy Language for the Use of Children* (1715) indicates:

> Happy the child whose youngest years
> Receive instructions well;
> Who hates the sinner's path, and fears
> The road that leads to hell.

Today Watts's sermons and verse are largely forgotten, but some of the hundreds of hymns he wrote are still familiar to churchgoers—and "Joy to the World" (1719), in its 1848 setting to a melody from Handel's *Messiah*, is heard every Christmas.

The affinity between liturgical music and the earliest composers of children's verse is continued in the work of Anna Laetitia Barbauld, another prominent Dissenting writer and educator (see Primers and Readers, above, for a selection from her *Lessons for Children*, 1778–79). Although she was an accomplished poet, Barbauld deliberately avoided verse in her *Hymns in Prose for Children* (1781); yet the hymns are rhythmic, lyrical, and (according to her preface) "intended to be committed to memory, and recited." Like her lessons, they encourage children to explore the world around them, while making clear the responsibility of the adult teacher:

> Come, let us walk abroad; let us talk of the works of God.
> Take up a handful of the sand; number the grains of it;
>   tell them one by one into your lap
> Try if you can count the blades of grass in the field,
>   or the leaves on the trees.
> You cannot count them, they are innumerable;
>   much more the things which God has made. ("Hymn IX")

The hymn is filled with a sense of wonder and joy at God's creation, which echoes in the opening of William Blake's "Auguries of Innocence" (ca. 1805): "To see a World in a Grain of Sand / And a Heaven in a Wild Flower."

Many generations of children heard the exhortations of Bunyan, Watts, and Barbauld to be obedient and consider their immortal souls. But from the late eighteenth century onward, as a new market for children's books was being developed, a secular and even profane genre of children's verse—known in the United States as "Mother Goose rhymes" and in Great Britain as "nursery verse"—was moving out of the oral tradition and into print.

Nursery Culture and Nursery Verse

Almost everybody knows some nursery verse—that may be its single most distinguishing feature. Yet we rarely recall being taught or learning the rhymes; as children, we seem almost to take them in with the air we breathe. One reason may be that the rhymes we designate as nursery verse come from such a huge rag-bag of human experience, including songs on various themes (war, love, bawdy subjects, drinking), ballads, street cries, rhyming alphabets and counting rhymes, rhymes sung while bouncing a baby on one's knee, riddles, proverbs, and lullabies. According to Iona Opie, the great collector of children's rhymes and games, "brevity and strongly-marked rhythm" are "two of the chief characteristics of nursery rhymes." Such accentual verse has an equal number of strong stresses in a line, providing an easy and regular beat. Almost any rhyme picked at random can demonstrate the point: consider "Ráin, ráin, gó awáy / Come agáin anóther dáy," or "Lóndon Brídge is fálling dówn, / Fálling dówn, fálling dówn." In both cases, each line has four strong stresses.

The ease with which nursery verse is remembered and absorbed makes individual rhymes difficult to study. The oral tradition of songs sung to young children is "as old as the hills where the first human mothers bore children," notes F. J. Harvey Darton in his *Children's Books in England* (1932), and the verses "are of parentage as uncertain as the piebald kitten." Even a historian sees no point in trying to identify a "true source" for oral verses. But their publishing history can be traced, and it is closely aligned with the development of children's literature as a genre in its own right.

Popular American lore holds that "Mother Goose" was a Bostonian—Elizabeth Goose (sometimes Vergoose or Vertigoose)—whose son-in-law, a printer named Thomas Fleet, published the rhymes she incessantly repeated to her grandchildren as *Songs for the Nursery, or, Mother Goose's Melodies for Children* (1719). Unfortunately, it is a ghost volume. There is no evidence that it ever existed anywhere outside the imagination of the printer's great-grandson, John Fleet Eliot, who gave an elaborately detailed account of the book's genesis in an article written in 1860. An alternative view, offered by scholar Michael Joseph in an unpublished paper, "John Fleet Eliot and the American Mother Goose, a Nationalist Icon in Nineteenth-Century America" (given at the Children's Literature Association Conference, Wilkes-Barre, Pennsylvania, 2002), is that the case for the American origin of Mother

Goose was symbolic rather than literal, arising out of a shift in national identity at the end of the Jacksonian period (1829–41). As the youthful spirit of the "age of expansion" receded, the nationalist character of Mother Goose (cast as the historical Elizabeth Vergoose) emerged retrospectively—partly because of the energetic program of printing Mother Goose rhymes during the 1830s and 1840s—as a symbol of a lost national innocence and exuberance. In France, the figure of "Mother Goose" (Mère Oye) had been associated with a teller of children's tales at least as early as the sixteenth century; and as Iona and Peter Opie point out in *The Oxford Dictionary of Nursery Rhymes* (1951), German folklore also has a Fru Gode or Fru Gosen. She appears to have arrived in the English-speaking world with *Tales of Mother Goose* (1729), the first English translation of Charles Perrault.

The first book defined as a collection of nursery verse, *Tommy Thumb's Pretty Song Book* (ca. 1744), is credited to the English publisher Mary Cooper. Like her more successful contemporary John Newbery, whose *A Little Pretty Pocket-Book* (1744) was followed by *Mother Goose's Melody; or, Sonnets for the Cradle* (ca. 1765), Cooper grasped the importance of marketing to children: her *Child's New Plaything* (1743) was an early example of an instructional book packaged as a toy. By assembling scraps of popular songs and verses, drawn largely from an already-existing oral tradition, into a book explicitly for children, she created a genre that has been profitable for publishers ever since.

Most nursery verse is in the public domain, relieving publishers of the need to pay royalties for its use. Generally, the authors of specific rhymes are unknown—and the memory of those that are known tends to be erased from the cultural consciousness once their verse has been successfully absorbed into the genre. Thus, though the accomplished British writer Jane Taylor and the Americans Sarah Hale and Eugene Field are almost entirely forgotten today, their nursery rhymes—"Twinkle, twinkle, little star" ("The Star," 1806), "Mary had a little lamb" ("Mary's Lamb," 1832), and "Wynken, Blynken, and Nod" (1896), respectively—live on, both among children and (usually unattributed) in published collections.

The relationship between poetry ("literature") and nursery verse ("folklore") remains problematic. In *The Oxford Dictionary of Nursery Rhymes*, the Opies quote author Robert Graves: "The best of the older ones [nursery verses] are nearer to poetry than the greater part of *The Oxford Book of English Verse*." Yet most nursery rhymes were not written specifically for children. Instead, many are what the Opies call "survivals of an adult code of joviality," often altered in ways that hide their bawdy origins. For example, an earlier version of "Rub-a-dub-dub, / Three men in a tub" had in its second line "three maids"—whom the butcher, baker, and candlestick maker ogled at a country fair's peep show.

Very few nursery rhymes contain coded references to terrible events or rituals; thus the later verses of "London Bridge is falling down" allude to the practice of burying people alive in the foundations of bridges. More contain attitudes that are just as shocking to modern readers, and in many cases such verses have been quietly dropped from contemporary collections. One example is the counting rhyme "Ten little nigger boys," which was originally a Victorian music hall song, composed in 1869 by Frank Green and popular in what the Opies call "nigger minstrel shows." There were many illustrated editions, including one published by Frederick Warne (Beatrix Potter's publisher) in 1875 whose preface recommends it to the "youthful public" as a source of "innocent mirth." In this poem, like its inspiration "Ten Little Injuns" (by the American songwriter Septimus Winner, 1868), the counting down is accomplished largely through inventive forms of death. "One chopped himself in half," another "got frizzled up" by the sun, and so on. In the twenty-first century, sensitivity to racial epithets has banished niggers and Injuns (and Gollywogs, found in a 1909 adaptation) from the nursery.

Death, however, remains a frequent presence in nursery verse—especially in the lullaby, which is literally a means of soothing a child to sleep. Lullabies are the most singable type of nursery verse; but in those songs, as Marina Warner observes in *No Go the Bogeyman: Scaring, Lulling and Making Mock* (1999), "the minor third dominates," contributing to a feeling of "acute sadness." The mention of death and injury seems to have prophylactic force, as if naming a harm such as falling out of a tree ("Hush-a-bye, baby, on the tree top") or having eyes pecked out ("All the Pretty Little Horses") will guard the baby against it.

In the publishing history of nursery verse, song and image have become inextricably linked. The woodcuts of the first collections became increasingly lavish, perhaps reaching their pinnacle in *The Baby's Opera: A Book of Old Rhymes with New Dresses* (1877), designed by the famous Victorian illustrator Walter Crane. He decorated the verses and the musical settings (arranged by his sister, Lucy Crane) with pictures whose black outlines and flat color were inspired by the Japanese prints then in fashion. Illustrated nursery rhyme collections were successfully packaged with musical scores in the twentieth century as well. Sometimes the verses were traditional collections, as in *Lullabies and Night Songs* (1965), edited by William Engvick, illustrated by Maurice Sendak, and with music by Alec Wilder; sometimes they were original, as in Charles Causley's *Early in the Morning: A Collection of New Poems* (1986), with illustrations by Michael Foreman and music by Anthony Castro.

Some of the pictures have become as canonical as the verses they illustrate. The British illustrator Randolph Caldecott often made individual nursery rhymes into freestanding picture books, with a narrative structure determined by the verse. His version of "Hey Diddle Diddle" (1882) turns the tale of the dish running away with the spoon into a story of a culturally mixed couple doomed to failure as they elope. Kate Greenaway's *Mother Goose; or, The Old Nursery Rhymes* (1881) depicts sweetly dressed little girls in long Empire-waisted dresses and boys in pastel breeches, all playing gracefully in a house or a fenced garden. Arthur Rackham created a more threatening world: in his *Mother Goose: The Old Nursery Rhymes* (1913), Mother Goose is a witch, bent over and hook-nosed. The black-and-white checkerboard on the cover and the art nouveau pastel illustrations within make *The Real Mother Goose* (1916) by the American artist Blanche Fisher Wright instantly recognizable, and her images have become synonymous with American versions of Mother Goose rhymes.

Contemporary artists continue to find new, often complex ways to interpret seemingly transparent and familiar nursery verses. Marina Warner notes the enigmatic qualities of the nursery verse illustrations done in the 1980s by the Portuguese-born British artist Paula Rego: "Marvels mix with the day-to-day, and banality meets mystery in the nursery rhyme." The black sheep in Rego's version of "Baa baa black sheep" (below, p. 1140) is a huge ram holding a young woman in a seductive grasp. Her illustration of "How Many Miles to Babylon" depicts girls and women of various ages jumping over what might be birthday candles, as if they could somehow turn back time.

Poets, too, continue to renew the nursery verse genre. In poems written for children, poets echo phrases and musical ideas they know will be familiar from nursery verse. In the twentieth century, Robert Graves joined with the illustrator Edward Ardizzone to produce two collections of poems for children, *The Penny Fiddle* (1960) and *Ann at Highwood Hall* (1964). The Canadian Dennis Lee produced very successful nursery verse with distinctly Canadian content in *Alligator Pie* (1974),

Garbage Delight (1977), and *Jelly Belly* (1983). And *No Hickory, No Dickory, No Dock: A Collection of Caribbean Nursery Rhymes* (1991), a mixture of new and traditional Caribbean verses written and compiled by Grace Nichols and John Agard and illustrated by Cynthia Jabar, is a joyful entry into the field. It appears that nursery verse today is being remade; as its scope broadens to include a more diverse range of voices, it is returning to its often x-rated origins and relegating the sweet images of the nineteenth century to historical curiosities.

Poetry Written for Children

Throughout the nineteenth century, poetry for children began to break away from its twin traditions of nursery verse and religious verse, becoming lighter and increasingly secular. This move is best demonstrated in the United States by the poem "A Visit from St. Nicholas" (1823), better known as "The Night Before Christmas." The features of the modern American Santa Claus were solidified in the poem. Fat, jolly, and red-suited, he drives a sleigh drawn by eight reindeer (each named) and delivers presents via the chimney. Clement Moore, a professor of Greek and oriental literature, took credit for the poem two decades after its publication; but recently Don Foster, an expert in textual attribution, has argued in *Author Unknown: On the Trail of Anonymous* (2000) that the author was the gentleman-poet Henry Livingston Jr., as his descendants had long claimed.

In England, the heavily instructive verses by Watts and Bunyan were losing their dominance, as gifted poets turned to amusing as well as instructing children. The most eloquent mix of nursery play and religion is found in the poetry of Christina Rossetti, whose *Goblin Market* (1862) is at once a warning against and a headlong rush into sensual pleasure. Though religious instruction is not overt in *Sing-Song: A Nursery Rhyme Book* (1872), it contains strong themes of divine protection ("Angels at the foot, / And Angels at the head") as well as death and resurrection:

> A baby's cradle with no baby in it,
> A baby's grave where autumn leaves drop sere;
> The sweet soul gathered home to Paradise,
> The body waiting here.

The collection also contains riddling and wordplay. Some is amusing, as is "A dumb-bell is no bell, though dumb"; and some is bittersweet: "What are heavy? Sea-sand and sorrow: / What are brief? Today and tomorrow." Around the 1860s, children's poetry began to take on the features familiar to twenty-first-century readers, particularly in the form of its humor. Two men were central in defining the new comic and especially nonsense elements of the changing genre: Lewis Carroll (the pen name of the Oxford mathematics don Charles Dodgson) and Edward Lear.

Carroll established himself as a master of parody and nonsense verse in *Alice's Adventures in Wonderland* (1865) and *Through the Looking-Glass, and What Alice Found There* (1871). Though he was a devout Christian, his writing for children was decidedly secular. Carroll's playful " 'Tis the voice of the Lobster: I heard him declare / 'You have baked me too brown, I must sugar my hair' " is a delicious parody of Watts's "The Sluggard": " 'Tis the voice of the sluggard; I heard him complain, / 'You have waked me too soon, I must slumber again'. " The nineteenth-century children who knew Watts's poem by heart (and were supposed to take its message seriously) must have thrilled at the comic relief of Carroll's parody. Taken together with an earlier parody of Watts's "Against Idleness and Mischief"—"How doth the little busy bee / Improve each shining hour" becomes in Carroll's hands "How doth the little crocodile / Improve his shining tail"—the lines seemed to license childhood playfulness, fantasy, laughter, and even idleness. The change was welcome.

Carroll was not alone in this revolution in children's verse. Whereas he was the master of parody, Edward Lear was the master of caricature—in words and pictures, especially in *A Book of Nonsense* (1846). Both possessed extraordinary powers of linguistic invention. Lear's favorite verse form for caricature was the limerick, which he popularized but did not invent. It originated with a school of Irish poets, Fili na Maighe (poets of Maighe), in County Limerick, Ireland, hence the name. The following example comes from *A Book of Nonsense*:

> There was an Old Man of the South,
> Who had an immoderate mouth;
> But in swallowing a dish,
> That was quite full of fish,
> He was choked, that Old Man of the South.

The words convey the exaggerated features, here a gaping mouth and a grotesque death, characteristic of Lear's nonsense verse caricatures. The illustration shows a man with a mouth as wide as a dinner plate. Anything is possible and can be made amusing in the nonsense world, including violence; nonsense verse can offer children a kind of cathartic "theater of cruelty" (to use a term borrowed from Antonin Artaud's 1933 manifesto).

Though the Romantic image of the child (discussed in the following section) as innocent and in need of protection became dominant in the nineteenth century, the comic grotesque of Lear and some nursery verse remained available to children. Probably the most widely read book in the genre was *Struwwelpeter* (1845). This collection of cautionary tales by Heinrich Hoffmann, a German physician who wrote the book for his three-year-old son, first appeared in English in 1848; *Struwwelpeter* is often translated as *Slovenly Peter*. The subtitle (originally the title), *Cheerful Stories and Funny Pictures for Little Children*, is part of the joke, as both pictures and poems are alarming. The work derives its humor and shock from taking the admonitions of the humorless moralists to their logical and grisly end. Little Conrad, the title character of one poem, who ignores warnings not to suck his thumbs, has them cut off by "the great long-legged scissor man." In another poem, Augustus starves to death because he refuses to eat soup. And Harriet, despite being told not to play with matches, strikes one because "when they burn, it is so pretty." She pays the price:

> So she was burnt, with all her clothes,
> And arms, and hands, and eyes, and nose;
> Till she had nothing more to lose
> Except her little scarlet shoes;
> And nothing else but these was found
> Among her ashes on the ground.

Struwwelpeter remained popular and notorious through the nineteenth and twentieth centuries; Darton calls it "a remarkable freak of acclimatization." It is also in the spirit of Edward Gorey's *The Gashlycrumb Tinies; or, After the Outing* (1963), a contemporary classic of macabre humor best appreciated by adults—as was *Shock-*

headed Peter (1998), the award-winning "junk opera" based on *Struwwelpeter* that was created by the British punk cabaret trio the Tiger Lillies.

Into the Garden

By the middle of the nineteenth century, the conception of children as born in sin—and thus in need of instruction and correction—was fading. In *Pictures of Innocence: The History and Crisis of Ideal Childhood* (1998), the art historian Anne Higonnet traces the change in view by examining the literal images of children in portraits, particularly of the late eighteenth and early nineteenth centuries. She finds an emphasis on features designed to make children appear innocent, vulnerable, and in need of protection. By pointing to portraits in which children appear in costumes of an earlier age, or in pastoral settings (often with animals), or in playful poses as miniature adults, Higonnet gradually builds up a composite set of attributes we associate with a generically Romantic innocent child. Much like the child invented by Jean-Jacques Rousseau in *Emile* (1762), this quintessential Romantic child is naturally good, happily playing, completely charming, and literally the picture of innocence. This is the child "trailing clouds of glory," in William Wordsworth's phrase from "Ode: Intimations of Immortality from Recollections of Early Childhood" (1807). In that poem, the poet mourns what he has lost:

> . . . a time when meadow, grove, and stream,
> The earth, and every common sight,
> To me did seem
> Apparelled in celestial light,
> The glory and the freshness of a dream.

The Romantic child is innocent, associated with nature, and semidivine. Representations of such children became increasingly common in the nineteenth century with the introduction of two new technologies, photography and lithographic reproduction.

Images of children dressed in old-fashioned, delicate clothes and playing in pastoral settings that hinted at an earlier age rapidly proliferated in the late nineteenth and early twentieth centuries not just in paintings, but as posters folded into weekly illustrated newspapers and on everything from playing cards to biscuit boxes. Among the most popular creators of these pretty children were Kate Greenaway and Charles Robinson in Britain and Jessie Willcox Smith in the United States. Supporting the strong market for their works were new printing technologies: for the first time, picture books could be mass-produced. The appeal of the look was so strong that charming children in flowing clothes began to accompany even unlikely texts. Greenaway illustrated a robust adventure story by Bret Harte, *The Queen of the Pirate Isle* (1886), and both Robinson (1895) and Smith (1905) produced idealized illustrations for Robert Louis Stevenson's *A Child's Garden of Verses* (published as text alone in 1885). *A Child's Garden of Verses* marks a turning point in the history of poetry for children, for Stevenson was the first poet to re-create the voice of a real child and portray the world from a child's point of view: the frustration of going to bed before dark, the magic of playing with a shadow, and the pleasures of imaginatively transforming everyday objects.

At about this time, the poetry anthology—a genre originally intended for adults—became increasingly important for children and for the image of the natural child. The most famous Victorian anthology and the model for all to follow was *The* edited by Francis T. Palgrave, a poet and a critic of art and literature. It has never gone out of print, and an expanded update was printed in 1996. With brilliant economy the title suggests the riches within. Palgrave's anthology was a staple of middle-class homes with upper-class pretensions—so it was generally scoffed at by those cultured classes who owned collected works of individual poets and had no need of anthologies. Not surprisingly, the greatest number of selections are by Shakespeare, and a good number of seventeenth- and eighteenth-century lyrics are included; however, the Romantics are particularly well represented—especially Wordsworth, but there are also numerous selections from Sir Walter Scott, Robert Burns, and John Keats (Palgrave deliberately omitted living poets). Often the subjects of the poems were those commonly associated with the Romantic child: the landscape and weather, animals, childhood innocence. Alfred, Lord Tennyson, England's poet laureate and Palgrave's good friend, had suggested the idea of an anthology to him. It turned out to be a form whose success endures.

The anthology *Come Hither: A Collection of Rhymes and Poems for the Young of All Ages* (1923), edited by Walter de la Mare, probably best demonstrates the elusiveness of the boundary between poetry for adults and poetry for children. De la Mare himself, a major literary figure in the early decades of the twentieth century, wrote fiction and poetry for both audiences. *Come Hither*, as the title suggests, was designed to draw children into the intellectual pleasures of English verse. Though de la Mare clearly subscribes to the Romantic tradition of children and childhood, he demonstrates his trust in their intelligence. He includes poets ranging from Geoffrey Chaucer to Robert Graves, Christina Rossetti to Siegfried Sassoon, and John Clare to William Butler Yeats: a catholic list with great bones, though today's reader cannot help noticing his preference for the white, the male, the British.

Through the twentieth century, poetry anthologies for children have tended to be luxurious hardcovers with heavy paper, gilt decorations, and generous illustrations—the sort of books purchased as special gifts. Following Palgrave's model, their titles often included "golden," "treasury," or both. Examples include *The Golden Treasury of Poetry* (1959), edited by Louis Untermeyer (an American poet and prolific anthologist), and *The New Treasury of Poetry* (1990), edited by Neil Philip (a British anthologist and folklorist). An earlier Untermeyer anthology, *Rainbow in the Sky* (1935), with illustrations by Reginald Birch, contains all the features of Romantic poetry for children: the antique feel of the drawings, harking back to a vaguely imagined preindustrial space; poems focusing on the farm, the garden, animals, and weather; riddles; nonsense poems; and lullabies. The introduction develops the central metaphor of the rainbow that ends in a "fabled pot of gold."

The landscapes associated with images of the Romantic child were tame, often domestic; they had the qualities of a well-tended garden or a stage-set forest. For example, in *The Song of Hiawatha* (1855), Henry Wadsworth Longfellow's enormously popular mythic narrative of an Indian hero, the primeval forest is oddly domesticated. As "the little Hiawatha" sat, he

> Heard the whispering of the pine-trees,
> Heard the lapping of the waters,
> Sounds of music, words of wonder.

It is the perfect setting for a child of nature; and nature itself, according to the introduction, is responsible for this tale, which should be listened to by all who

Love the sunshine of the meadow
Love the shadow of the forest,
Love the wind among the branches.

For generations, parts of the poem were recited by both British and American schoolchildren, often from the section "Hiawatha's Childhood" (which includes "By the shores of Gitche Gumee, / By the shining Big-Sea-Water, / Stood the wigwam of Nokomis"). The poem's deliberately chantlike trochaic tetrameter has proved irresistible to parodists: Lewis Carroll's "Hiawatha's Photographing" (1887) begins "From his shoulder Hiawatha / Took the camera of rosewood, / Made of sliding, folding rosewood." Late-twentieth-century contributions by Bill Greenwell ("By the supermarket trollee. In an eezi-fold up buggee") and by John Mole ("These are the shoes / Dad walked about in / When we did jobs / In the garden") can be found, along with Longfellow's original, in *This Poem Doesn't Rhyme* (1990), an anthology edited by Gerard Benson. Taken together, the three poems also illustrate the shift in poetry for children from pastoral innocence to urban knowingness as described by Morag Styles in *From the Garden to the Street: Three Hundred Years of Poetry for Children* (1998). By the 1960s and 1970s, comic, urban poetry specifically written and published for children was the dominant mode. And the tradition of serious nature poetry (often selected, but not necessarily written for children) was in decline—with one significant exception: Ted Hughes (1930–1998), the poet laureate of England from 1984 until his death.

Ted Hughes was prolific and successful, and though roughly half of his works (poetry, fiction, criticism, librettos, and plays) were published for children, he was never marked explicitly as a children's author. His poems frequently migrated, without comment, between collections published for adults and those for children. Yet all his work emerged from a single crucible: out of the clash (as he liked to explain) of titanic forces, at once brutal and compassionate, powerful and gentle, destructive and redemptive. One of his most famous early poems, "The Thought-Fox," published in his first award-winning collection (for adults), *Hawk in the Rain* (1957), has for some time been a set poem for study by schoolchildren. On the other hand, the fox, bat, and hare poems from *What Is the Truth? A Farmyard Fable for the Young* (1984) were published in the *Times Literary Supplement*—without any hint that they were for children. And the donkey poem, from the same collection, was published in the *New Yorker*, again without reference to its placement in a children's collection.

The moment-to-moment observations of life playing itself out to death are at the heart of all Hughes's work, though he explained that, when publishing explicitly for children, he always proceeded "with affection." In "The Birth of a Rainbow" (1978), he celebrates a cow "licking her gawky black calf / Collapsed wet-fresh from the womb, blinking his eyes / In the low morning dazzling washed sun." And in "Sheep," from *Season Songs* (1975), he describes a newborn lamb, born "with everything but the will" to live: "So he died, with the yellow birth-mucus / Still in his cardigan. / He did not survive a warm summer night." Hughes took the position that children had the right to know, and to be inducted into the pains and pleasures of adult knowledge (see above, in Fairy Tales, *The Iron Giant*). His collection of BBC radio talks for children, *Poetry in the Making* (1967), remains one of the most compelling books available on the reading and writing of poetry—for adults and children.

macabre, fantastic, and grotesque. They are often reminiscent of playground verse—especially those that emphasize food and eating. Thus "Jellyfish Stew" (from *The New Kid on the Block*, 1984) is gross: "You're soggy, you're smelly, / you taste like shampoo, / you bog down my belly with oodles of goo." Silverstein began his professional career in 1956 as a cartoonist and then writer for *Playboy*; he also found success as a composer, lyricist, and playwright. Two collections of Silverstein's verse are commonly found on school and library shelves: *Where the Sidewalk Ends* (1974) and *A Light in the Attic* (1982). The plodding metrical structures and predictable jokes ensure that the verse remains denigrated as being solely for children. "Prayer for the Selfish Child," for example, begins with lines familiar from *The New-England Primer*'s "Now I lay me down to sleep," but it ends in a dull thud: "I pray the Lord my toys to break / So none of the other kids can use 'em. Amen."

A number of twentieth-century poets with greater technical skills and range have also written light verse for children including British poets Wendy Cope, John Mole, and Michael Rosen. Wendy Cope (b. 1945), best known for her gently ironic parodies of famous contemporary poets in *Making Cocoa for Kingsley Amis* (1986), applies the same wit to her collection of finger-rhymes for very young children, *Twiddling Your Thumbs* (1988). As a young student at Cambridge, John Mole (b. 1941) received encouragement from Robert Graves, who taught him to combine well-schooled technique with "lightness of being"—as in jazz. Mole is a jazz musician, and it is possible to hear him "riff" on traditional riddle poems in his award-winning 1987 collection *Boo to a Goose*. A prolific and popular poet, Michael Rosen (b. 1945) produces what sounds like artless verse. But it is a trick. His metrically sensitive ear is tuned to the sounds of conversations between adults and children, which he then sharpens into bright comic moments, as in *You Can't Catch Me* (1981) and *Jelly Smelly Fish* (1986). There is a well-established tradition of light verse for children by American poets, including books by David McCord and Myra Cohn Livingston. The fact that E. E. Cummings (1894–1962) eschewed upper-case conventions in his verse has made his poems standard in anthologies for children, though he did not write as a children's poet. David McCord (1897–1997) wrote over forty books of poetry, plays, and essays for both children and adults through his long and productive life. His pleasure in wordplay and games permeates his verse for children, from his first collection, *Far and Few* (1952), to his last, *All Small* (1986). And Myra Cohn Livingston (1926–1996) is important not only for the twenty-three volumes of popular verse for children she published but also for her influence, as a teacher and mentor, on a whole new generation of children's poets. The Australian performance poet Steven Herrick has written a number of verse-novels for young adults, including *Love, Ghosts, and Nose Hair* (1996) and *The Spangled Drongo* (1999). And the whimsical nursery verses of Dennis Lee's *Alligator Pie* have been chanted by generations of young Canadian children since its publication in 1974.

Perhaps the most famous American children's poet of the century was Dr. Seuss (Theodor Seuss Geisel), who before World War II worked first as a freelance cartoonist and then as an ad illustrator. Seuss's first book, *And to Think That I Saw It on Mulberry Street* (1937), contains many of the elements that were to make him a best-selling children's writer: anarchic visual and verbal comedy, the compelling rhythms of nonsense verse, and the triumph of the fantastic over the commonplace. Other enduring early works of verse include *Horton Hatches the Egg* (1940) and *If I Ran the Zoo* (1950). Seuss's lasting importance, however, is less poetic than pedagogical. He revolutionized reading primers with *The Cat in the Hat* (1957), a volume whose success led to the founding of Beginner Books (after 1960, Seuss's company became a division of Random House). At their best, these easy-to-read books are engaging; unlike the Dick and Jane readers that they helped supplant (see Primers and Readers, above), they are not dull despite the inevitable repetitions of their highly limited vocabulary. Many of them, including *Green Eggs and Ham* (1960), remain popular today in print and in musical settings.

Some twentieth-century poets approached children's verse more seriously, though the resulting poems are not themselves necessarily serious. They were poets, and though they often wrote for children, they were not ghettoized as children's poets (as is the case with Silverstein, Prelutsky, and even Seuss). Robert Graves, Charles Causley, and Ted Hughes have already been mentioned; others include Edna St. Vincent Millay, Theodore Roethke, Randall Jarrell, John Ciardi, and Richard Wilbur. Only Jarrell, Causley, and Hughes—who all wrote for both adults and children and who all wrote with passionate concern about both poetry and children—made significant contributions to the developing tradition. Jarrell's untimely death sadly diminished his actual and potential influence on American verse for children; British verse was well served by Hughes and Causley, both of whom produced substantial bodies of intelligent contemporary poetry for children and provided them with access to the best traditions of English verse.

An ambitious effort to help children engage those traditions was the Modern Masters Books for Children, a series of large-format, "portrait"-shaped (that is, tall and narrow) picture books published in the mid-1960s and 1970s by Collier Macmillan in London and Crowell-Collier Press in New York. Robert Graves, Louis Untermeyer, Jay Williams, William Jay Smith, John Ciardi, Eve Merriam, Arthur Miller, William Saroyan, Theodore Roethke, and Richard Wilbur—all major literary figures of the time—contributed texts. For example, Wilbur's *Loudmouse* (1963), illustrated by Don Almquist, offers poems entwined in a narrative that delicately play on earlier monitory works as well as on nursery verse riddles and puns (e.g., on *loudmouth*). Thus the Loudmouse sings "a song to himself":

> If you see a thing
> That's a piece of wood
> And a kind of spring
> And a hook and a bar
> And a bite of cheese
>
> That looks very good,
> Don't touch it, please.
> Stay where you are.
> Take care or—*snap!*—
> You'll be caught in a *trap!*

In part, the development of verse in English for children in the last part of the twentieth century was hampered by a lack of critical attention. There were a few welcome exceptions. In England, between 1979 and 2001, the children's literature journal *Signal* offered a (small) prize for the best book of poetry published each year; more important was the long essay about the year's work in poetry for children that accompanied its announcement. Among the poets whom *Signal* helped achieve recognition are James Berry, Jackie Kay, Grace Nichols, John Mole, Gareth Owen, and Michael Rosen. In 2003, the Centre for Literacy in Primary Education began administering a new annual prize for children's poetry, the CLPE Poetry Award. In the United States, in the final decades of the century, the poets and teachers Kenneth Koch, Myra Cohn Livingston, X. J. Kennedy, and Lee Bennett Hopkins all supported children's verse and those writing it. Hopkins has established two prizes: the annual Lee Bennett Hopkins Award, first given in 1993 and administered since 1991 by Pennsylvania State University, for the outstanding new book of children's poetry published the previous year; and the Lee Bennett Hopkins Promising Poet Award, given every three years to a promising new writer of children's poetry, given since 1995 and administered by the International Reading Association. The *Signal* tradition of publishing an essay on the year's work in poetry for children continues in the United States in the journal *The Lion and the Unicorn*, which gives its first Award for Excellence in North American Poetry in 2005.

New Sounds

The most radical shift in children's poetry occurred in the late twentieth century, when it lost its largely white, Christian look and standard English sounds and found new music. Its proponents in Britain include a thriving group of poets who grew up in the Caribbean: John Agard, Valerie Bloom, James Berry, Jackie Kay, Grace Nichols, and Benjamin Zephaniah provide new music. In the United States, the rhythms of African American spirituals, blues, and jazz—established strains of American music—had already begun to enter mainstream children's poetry, followed by rap, hip-hop, reggae, dub, and the calypso beat of Caribbean culture. It is a music that grafts well onto traditional English ballads and nursery verses. While every group has its own poetry, the acceptance of the legitimacy of the African American tradition within the larger culture started with Langston Hughes. He was soon joined by such accomplished poets for adults and children as Gwendolyn Brooks, Lucille Clifton, Nikki Giovanni, and Marilyn Nelson. And in both countries, these poets have succeeded in revitalizing a poetic tradition that was in danger of stagnating not just in its content but also in its transmission. The performance poets of the 1990s, as they emphasized the physical, dramatic, and musical qualities of their verse, reconnected poetry to its oral and aural core.

The Dream Keeper and Other Poems (1932) by Langston Hughes, with illustrations by Helen Sewell, begins a new musical tradition in children's poetry. At the time of its publication, Hughes, only thirty, had already published four volumes of poetry and a novel and was a towering figure in the Harlem Renaissance—the flowering of African American culture in the 1920s that takes its name from the uptown Manhattan neighborhood that had become a literary and artistic center. His writing was characterized by the rhythms of jazz and the speech patterns of working-class blacks. *Dream Keeper* includes several poems described as being "written in the manner of the Negro folk songs known as the Blues." That means, according to Hughes, that their mood is "almost always despondency, but when they are sung people laugh." Moreover, Hughes explains the typical verse pattern: "one long line, repeated, and a third line to rhyme with the first two." For example,

> Sun's a settin'
> This is what I'm gonna sing.
> Sun's a settin',
> This is what I'm gonna sing:
> I feels de blues a comin,
> Wonder what de blues'll bring. ("Night and Morn")

As the music of African American poetry evolved, its rhythms became more inclusive. An eloquent testament to the variety and range of the poetry developed in and in response to the Harlem Renaissance is offered by the poet Nikki Giovanni's anthology of African American poetry, *Shimmy Shimmy Shimmy Like My Sister Kate: Looking at the Harlem Renaissance through Poems* (1996). Her selections of poems from twenty-three American poets and her often personal commentary clarify the political and artistic trajectory of that development, starting before the Harlem Renaissance with W. E. B. Du Bois, the pioneering sociologist and activist who in 1896 was the first African American scholar to receive a Ph.D. from Harvard, and ending with the poet, novelist, and playwright Ntozake Shange, author of *For Colored Girls Who Have Considered Suicide When the Rainbow Is Enuf* (1975).

Though the Caribbean British poets have much in common with their American counterparts, including the pain of slavery in past generations and of racism, their relationship to colonialism is different, and their language moves to a different beat. They bring their own histories to their poetry and its performance. Benjamin Zephaniah, one of the best-known performance poets and a vegetarian, had a huge success with "Talking Turkeys" (1994), which begins:

> Be nice to yu turkeys dis Christmas
> Cos' turkeys just wanna hav fun
> Turkeys are cool, turkeys are wicked
> And every turkey has a mum.

Zephaniah's empathy with animals may mark another recent change in children's poetry. In Milne's poem "At the Zoo," for example, from *When We Were Very Young* (1924), Christopher Robin seems to have the authority of the British Empire behind his confident assertion: "But *I* gave buns to the elephant when *I* walked down to the zoo." Seventy years later, when Grace Nichols revisits the same zoo, the focus is, instead, on the elephant ("For Dilberta: Biggest of the Elephants at London Zoo," from *Give Yourself a Hug*, 1994):

> But sometimes, in her mind's eye,
> Dilberta gets this idea—She could be a Moth!
> Yes, with the wind stirring behind her ears,
> She could really fly.
>
> Rising above the boundaries of the paddock,
> Making for the dark light of the forest—
>
> Hearing, O once more, the trumpets roar.

To the sound of those trumpets, poetry for children moves out of the garden, out of the cage, and out of whiteness and into songs no longer circumscribed.

LULLABIES AND BABY SONGS

The history of poetry written for children begins in oral tradition: in lullabies, and in the scraps of verse that parents have used since time immemorial with their babies and young children. Lullabies are sleep songs. They are among the oldest verse forms known, and generally the first introductions newborns have to words and music. According to research done by the psychologist Sandra Trehub, lullabies are stable across time and culture, and are instantly recognizable in experiments in which adult subjects are asked to distinguish them from other, similar melodies. The subjects immediately identified characteristic simple pitch contours (i.e., distances between notes), repeated rhythms, and elongated vowels. Trehub's experiments also prove that infants demonstrate a marked preference for lullabies over other types of songs.

Although lullabies soothe and comfort, their lyrics are often threatening. In *No Go the Bogeyman: Scaring, Lulling and Making Mock* (1999), Marina Warner explains that "lullabies dip infants prophylactically in the imaginary future of ordeals and perils; nightmares are uttered in order to chase them from the impending dreamworld—a manoeuvre akin to a blessing in the form of a curse: as in

'Break a leg.'" In the lullabies selected for this section, the balance between harshness and sentimentality changes depending on time and culture. Those authored lullabies from the late nineteenth century, for example, tend to reflect a sentimental attitude toward children that is typical of the period.

The section begins with four variants of a lullaby usually known as "All the Pretty Little Horses," which comes from the African American tradition. In later versions, such as "Go to Sleepy, Little Baby," the bleak realities of slave life—in which a woman must care for her mistress's child rather than her own—are softened or erased altogether. Other traditional lullabies follow; most were first published in the eighteenth or nineteenth century, and most are from England.

The section ends with poems to which (unlike most lullabies) an author's name can be attached. "Lullaby of a Female Convict" by Henry Kirke White, a Romantic poet who died very young, uses the lullaby form to tell a dramatic story. The lullabies by Robert Ellice Mack ("The Little Orphan" and "Sleep, Baby, Sleep") and Eugene Field ("Wynken, Blynken, and Nod") cater to the nineteenth-century preference for sentimental images of innocent children.

All the Pretty Little Horses

Hush-a-bye don't you cry, go to sleep you little
　　baby
When you wake you shall have all the pretty
　　little horses
Blacks and bays, dapples and grays, coach and
　　six-a little horses.

Hush-a-bye don't you cry, go to sleep you little
　　baby,
Way down yonder in the meadow lays a poor
　　little lambie
The bees and the butterflies peckin' out his eyes
The poor little thing cries 'Mammy'.

Go to Sleepy, Little Baby

Go to sleepy, little baby,
Go to sleepy, little baby.
Mammy and daddy have both gone away
And left nobody for to mind you.
So rockaby,
And don't you cry.
And go to sleepy, little baby.
And when you wake
You can ride
All the pretty little ponies.

Paint and bay,
Sorrel and a gray,
And all the pretty little ponies.
So go to sleepy, little baby.
Rockaby
And don't you cry
And go to sleep, my baby.

[A Baby Song]

Go to sleep, little baby,
When you wake
You shall have
All the mulies in the stable.
Buzzards and flies
Picking out its eyes,
Pore little baby crying,
Mamma, mamma!

Rocky Bye Baby

Rocky bye baby, go to sleepy little baby
When you wake I'm gonna cook you a cake
And a whole stew with potatoes

Rocky bye baby, go to sleepy little baby
Mama's gone away (off) and papa's on a stroll
And they left nobody here to hold you

Black sheep, black sheep, where's your mama
　　(mammy)
She way down yonder in the valley
The birds and the flies are peckin' in his eyes
And the poor little baby cryin' mammy (mama)

[Bye, O my baby]

Bye, O my baby,
　　When I was a lady,
O then my baby didn't cry;
　　But my baby is weeping
　　For want of good keeping,
O I fear my poor baby will die.

[Baby, baby, naughty baby]

Baby, baby, naughty baby,
Hush, you squalling thing, I say.
Peace this moment, peace, or maybe
Bonaparte[1] will pass this way.

Baby, baby, he's a giant,
Tall and black as Rouen[2] steeple,
And he breakfasts, dines, rely on't,
Every day on naughty people.

Baby, baby, if he hears you,
As he gallops past the house,
Limb from limb at once he'll tear you,
Just as pussy tears a mouse.

And he'll beat you, beat you, beat you,
And he'll beat you all to pap,
And he'll eat you, eat you, eat you,
Every morsel snap, snap, snap.

[Baby and I]

Baby and I
Were baked in a pie,
The gravy was wonderful hot.
We had nothing to pay
To the baker that day
And so we crept out of the pot.

[Hush-a-bye, baby]

Hush-a-bye, baby,
   Daddy is near,
Mammy's a lady,
   And that's very clear.

[Bye, baby bunting]

Bye, baby bunting,[3]
Daddy's gone a-hunting,
Gone to get a rabbit skin
To wrap the baby bunting in.

[Hush-a-ba, babie, lie still, lie still]

Hush-a-ba, babie, lie still, lie still,
Your mammie's awa to the mill, the mill;
Babie is greeting[4] for want of good keeping—
Hush-a-ba, babie, lie still, lie still!

[Hush-a-bye, lie still and sleep]

Hush-a-bye, lie still and sleep,
It grieves me sore to see thee weep,
For when thou weep'st thou wearies me,
Hush-a-bye, lie still and bye.

---

1. Napoléon Bonaparte (1769–1821), who crowned himself emperor of France in 1804. His attempts to win a larger European empire (until his defeat by the British in 1815 at the Battle of Waterloo) made him a bogeyman of the British nursery.

2. A city in northern France, home to a thirteenth-century cathedral.
3. A term of endearment; also a blanket in which infants are wrapped.
4. Crying.

Cradle Song

Hush-a-bye, baby, on the tree top,
When the wind blows the cradle will rock;
When the bough breaks the cradle will fall,
Down will come baby and cradle and all.

[Hush-a-bye a baa-lamb]

Hush-a-bye a baa-lamb,
Hush-a-bye a milk cow,
We'll find a little stick
To beat the barking bow-wow.

[Norwegian Lullaby][5]

Baby, lullaby!
If thou wilt but sleep and mind me,
Then a sweet cake I will find thee
If there be no cake at hand,
I will let the cradle stand,
Let the baby cry!

Raisins and Almonds

Yiddish lullaby

Under Baby's cradle in the night
Stands a goat so soft and snowy white
The Goat will go to the market
To bring you wonderful treats
He'll bring you raisins and almonds
Sleep, my little one, sleep.

All through the Night

Welsh folk song

Sleep my child and peace attend thee,
All through the night

Guardian angels God will send thee,
All through the night
Soft the drowsy hours are creeping
Hill and vale in slumber sleeping,
I my loving vigil keeping
All through the night.

While the moon her watch is keeping
All through the night
While the weary world is sleeping
All through the night
O'er they spirit gently stealing
Visions of delight revealing
Breathes a pure and holy feeling
All through the night.

Love, to thee my thoughts are turning
All through the night
All for thee my heart is yearning,
All through the night.
Though sad fate our lives may sever
Parting will not last forever,
There's a hope that leaves me never,
All through the night.

1784

[He'll toil for thee the whole day long]

He'll toil for thee the whole day long,
And when the weary work is o'er,
He'll whistle thee a merry song,
And drive the bogies from the door.

5. Translated by Alma Strettel (fl. 1887–1912).

The Little Orphan

by Robert Ellice[6]

Lie still my pretty one,
    Lie still and rest,
You shall be snug and warm,
You are quite safe from harm,
    Safe on my breast.

Though you are motherless,
    Though you are lone,
I will be kind to you,
Temper the wind to you,
    Pretty, my own.

Lie still my pretty one,
    Lie still and rest,
You shall no longer roam,
You shall be safe at home,
    Safe on my breast.

            1884

Lullaby of a Female Convict to Her Child, the Night Previous to Execution

by Henry Kirke White[7]

Sleep, baby mine,[8] enkerchieft on my bosom;
    Thy cries they pierce again my bleeding
        breast;
Sleep, Baby mine, not long thou'lt have a
    mother
    To lull thee fondly in her arms to rest.

Baby, why dost thou keep this sad complaining?
    Long from mine eyes have kindly slumbers
        fled;
Hush, hush, my babe, the night is quickly
    waning,
    And I would fain compose my aching head.

Poor wayward wretch! and who will heed they
    weeping,
    When soon an outcast on the world thou'lt be?
Who then will sooth thee, when thy mother's
    sleeping
    In her low grave of shame and infamy!

Sleep, baby mine!—to-morrow I must leave
    thee,
    And I would snatch an interval of rest:
Sleep these last moments, ere the laws bereave
    thee,
    For never more thou'lt press a mother's breast.

            1807

6. I.e., Robert Ellice Mack (fl. 1884–1902), British author and editor of children's verse.
7. British poet (1785–1806).

8. These three words also begin a song by the English poet Sir Philip Sidney (1554–1586).

[Sleep, baby, sleep!]

by Robert Ellice

Sleep, baby, sleep!
    Thy father guards his sheep,
Thy mother shakes the dreamland tree,
Down falls a little dreams[9] for thee,
    Sleep, baby, sleep!

    Sleep, baby, sleep!
The large stars are the sheep,
The little stars are the lambs, I guess,
The gentle moon is the shepherdess.
    Sleep, baby, sleep!

    Sleep, baby, sleep!
And cry not like a sheep,
Else the sheep-dog will bark and whine,
And bite this naughty child of mine.
    Sleep, baby, sleep!

    Sleep, baby, sleep!
Away to tend the sheep,
Away, thou sheep-dog fierce and wild,
And do not harm my sleeping child.
    Sleep, baby, sleep!

    Sleep, baby, sleep!
Our Saviour loves His sheep;
He is the Lamb of God on high,
Who for our sakes came down to die.
    Sleep, baby, sleep!

1884

Wynken, Blynken, and Nod

by Eugene Field[1]

Wynken, Blynken, and Nod one night
    Sailed off in a wooden shoe—
Sailed on a river of crystal light,
    Into a sea of dew.
"Where are you going, and what do you wish?"
    The old moon asked the three.
"We have come to fish for the herring fish
    That live in this beautiful sea;
    Nets of silver and gold have we!"
        Said Wynken,
        Blynken,
        And Nod.

The old moon laughed and sang a song,
    As they rocked in the wooden shoe,
And the wind that sped them all night long
    Ruffled the waves of dew.
The little stars were the herring fish
    That lived in that beautiful sea—
"Now cast your nets wherever you wish—
    Never afeard are we";
    So cried the stars to the fishermen three:
        Wynken,
        Blynken,
        And Nod.

All night long their nets they threw
    To the stars in the twinkling foam—
Then down from the skies came the wooden
      shoe,
    Bringing the fishermen home;
'Twas all so pretty a sail it seemed
    As if it could not be,
And some folks thought 'twas a dream they'd
      dreamed
    Of sailing that beautiful sea—
    But I shall name you the fishermen three:
        Wynken,
        Blynken,
        And Nod.

---

9. Sadness, gloom.

1. American poet, humorist, and journalist (1850–1895).

Wynken and Blynken are two little eyes,
   And Nod is a little head,
And the wooden shoe that sailed the skies
   Is a wee one's trundle-bed.
So shut your eyes while mother sings
   Of wonderful sights that be,
And you shall see the beautiful things
   As you rock in the misty sea,
Where the old shoe rocked the fishermen
      three:
            Wynken,
            Blynken,
            And Nod.

                           1889

NURSERY VERSE

Whereas lullabies are sleep songs, the poems in this section are waking songs: verses for an adult to sing or chant in a game with a very young child. Many of these anonymous verses have resonated through the generations; we often can find their echoes in collections by later poets.

Nursery verse began to appear in print only in the eighteenth century, when the idea of a special nursery culture—and indeed the idea that infants and young children should have a separate space in the home—started to take hold. In America and England, such verses have become known as Mother Goose rhymes, largely because of a historical accident. When Charles Perrault's 1697 collection of fairy tales, *Histories, ou contes du temps passé* (Stories, or Tales of Past Times), was first translated into English in 1729, the title was taken from its frontispiece: an old woman with a rapt audience that was labeled "Contes de ma Mère l'Oye," or "Tales of Mother Goose." "Mother Goose" had long been associated in France with a teller of children's tales; Perrault himself had titled a smaller collection *Contes de ma Mère l'Oye* (1695). Soon thereafter, British publishers began collecting and printing the bits and pieces of children's songs and poems that

had been circulating orally. The earliest was Mary Cooper's *Tommy Thumb's Pretty Song Book* (ca. 1744); John Newbery offered *Mother Goose's Melody* (ca. 1765), and the name stuck. A few traditional Mother Goose rhymes are lullabies (e.g., "Baby Bunting"), but most are not.

The selections are arranged in loose clusters, moving roughly from verses aimed at the youngest audience to those for older children. They include games an adult might play with a baby, such as "Jeremiah, blow the fire"; delightfully silly rhymes, such as "Dickery, dickery, dare" and "Hickory dickory dock"; commemorations of historical teachers, such as "Blessed be the memory" and "Miss Buss and Miss Beale"; and verses to be recited as part of a cozy bedtime ritual. Many have been selected because they echo forward into the published collections of verse included below. The illustrations demonstrate how open the words of these poems are to interpretation. Some of the earliest illustrators represented, from collections in the nineteenth century, were not named. Artists who did receive credit for their famous works reproduced here include Arthur Rackham (1867–1939), Walter Crane (1845–1915), and Paula Rego (b. 1935).

[How many days has my baby to play?]

How many days has my baby to play?
Saturday, Sunday, Monday,
Tuesday, Wednesday, Thursday, Friday,
Saturday, Sunday, Monday.
Hop away, skip away,
My baby wants to play,
My baby wants to play every day.

[Jeremiah, blow the fire]

Jeremiah, blow the fire,[1]
Puff, puff, puff!
First you blow it gently,
Then you blow it rough.

[Daffy-down-dilly has come up to town]

Daffy-down-dilly[2] has come up to town
In a yellow petticoat and a green gown.

[Lavender's blue, diddle, diddle][3]

Lavender's blue, diddle, diddle,
    Lavender's green;
When I am king, diddle, diddle,
    You shall be queen.

Call up your men, diddle, diddle,
    Set them to work,
Some to the plough, diddle, diddle,
    Some to the cart.

Some to make hay, diddle, diddle,
    Some to thresh corn,
Whilst you and I, diddle, diddle,
    Keep ourselves warm.

[Ride a cock-horse to Banbury Cross]

Ride a cock-horse to Banbury[4] Cross
To see an old woman ride on a white horse;
With rings on her fingers and bells on her toes,
She shall have music wherever she goes.

1. While reciting this poem, the adult blows a baby's hair with the force specified.
2. I.e., daffodil; "daffy-down-dilly" is a playful expansion of the dialectal *daffydilly*.
3. In *The Oxford Dictionary of Nursery Rhymes* (1953), Iona and Peter Opie note that this nursery version derives from a much longer seventeenth-century love song; yet another version—"Lavender Blue (Dilly Dally)" (1945), with lyrics by Larry Morey and music by Eliot Daniel—became a popular dance tune.
4. A town in England, near Oxford; the large cross there was destroyed by Puritans in the early seventeenth century.

[Baa, baa, black sheep]

Baa, baa, black sheep,
   Have you any wool?
Yes, sir, yes, sir,
   Three bags full;
One for the master,
   And one for the dame,
And one for the little boy
   Who lives down the lane.

[Little Bo-peep]

Little Bo-peep has lost her sheep,
   And can't tell where to find them;
Leave them alone, and they'll come home,
   And bring their tails behind them.

Little Bo-peep fell fast asleep,
   And dreamt she heard them bleating;
But when she awoke, she found it a joke,
   For they were still all fleeting.

Then up she took her little crook,
   Determined for to find them;
She found them indeed, but it made her heart
     bleed,
   For they'd left their tails behind them.

It happened one day, as Bo-peep did stray
   Into a meadow hard by,
There she espied their tails side by side,
   All hung on a tree to dry.

She heaved a sigh, and wiped her eye,
   And over the hillocks went rambling,
And tried what she could, as a shepherdess
     should,
   To tack again each to its lambkin.

[Little boy blue]

Little boy blue, come, blow up your horn:
The sheep's in the meadow, the cow's in the
     corn.[5]
Where's the little boy that tends the sheep?
He's under the haycock, fast asleep.
Go wake him, go wake him! Oh, no, not I!
For if I do he will certainly cry.

[Three blind mice]

Three blind mice,
Three blind mice,
See how they run!
See how they run!
They all ran after the farmer's wife,
Who cut off their tails with a carving-knife;
Did you ever see such fun in your life
As three blind mice?

[Four and twenty tailors]

Four and twenty tailors went to kill a snail;
The best man among them durst not touch her
    tail;
She put out her horns like a little Kyloe cow:[6]
Run, tailors, run, or she'll kill you all e'en now.

5. I.e., the wheat.
6. A small breed with long horns, raised on the western coast
and islands of northern Scotland.

[There was an owl]

There was an owl lived in an oak,
  Wisky, wasky, weedle;
And every word he ever spoke
  Was, Fiddle, faddle, feedle.

A gunner chanced to come that way,
  Wisky, wasky, weedle;
Says he, I'll shoot you, silly bird.
  Fiddle, faddle, feedle.

[Dickery, dickery, dare]

Dickery, dickery, dare,
The pig flew up in the air;
The man in brown soon brought him down,
Dickery, dickery, dare.

[The man in the moon]

The man in the moon
Came tumbling down,
And asked the way to Norwich;
He went by the south,
And burnt his mouth
With eating cold pease porridge.[7]

[Pease porridge hot]

Pease porridge hot,
  Pease porridge cold;
Pease porridge in the pot
  Nine days old.
Some like it hot.
  Some like it cold,
Some like it in the pot
  Nine days old.

7. A dish of peas (often dried, either whole or ground into meal) cooked in water or milk.

[Hey diddle diddle]

Hey diddle diddle,
The cat and the fiddle,
The cow jumped over the moon;
The little dog laughed
To see such sport,
And the dish ran away with the spoon.

[Jack and Jill]

Jack and Jill went up the hill
  To fetch a pail of water;
Jack fell down and broke his crown,[8]
  And Jill came tumbling after.

Up Jack got, and home did trot,
  As fast as he could caper,
To old Dame Dob, who patched his nob
  With vinegar and brown paper.

[Little Jack Horner]

Little Jack Horner sat in corner,
Eating a Christmas pie.
He put in his thumb, and pull'd out a plum,
And said "What a good boy am I!"

8. The top of his head.

[There was an old woman called Nothing-at-all]

There was an old woman called Nothing-at-all,
Who rejoiced in a dwelling exceedingly small;
A man stretched his mouth to its utmost extent,
And down at one gulp house and old woman
      went.

[There was an old woman]

There was an old woman
    And nothing she had,
And so this old woman
    Was said to be mad.
She'd nothing to eat
    She'd nothing to wear,
She'd nothing to lose,
    She'd nothing to fear,
She'd nothing to ask,
    And nothing to give,
And when she did die
    She'd nothing to leave.

[There was an old woman who lived in a shoe]

There was an old woman who lived in a shoe,
She had so many children she didn't know what to do;
She gave them some broth without any bread;
She whipped them all soundly and put them to bed.

[Poor old Robinson Crusoe!]

Poor old Robinson Crusoe![9]
Poor old Robinson Crusoe!
They made him a coat
Of an old nanny goat,
I wonder how they could do so!

With a ring a ting tang,
And a ring a ting tang,
Poor old Robinson Crusoe!

[For want of a nail]

For want of a nail the shoe was lost,
For want of a shoe the horse was lost,
For want of a horse the rider was lost,
For want of a rider the battle was lost,
For want of a battle the kingdom was lost,
And all for the want of a horseshoe nail.

[One fine day in the middle of the night]

One fine day in the middle of the night
Two dead men got up to fight.
A blind man came to see fair play,
A dumb man came to shout hurray.

[Doctor Faustus was a good man]

Doctor Faustus[1] was a good man,
He whipt his scholars now and then;
When he whipp'd them he made them dance,
Out of Scotland into France,
Out of France into Spain,
And then he whipp'd them back again!

[Blessed be the memory]

Blessed be the memory
Of good old Thomas Sutton,[2]
Who gave us lodging, learning,
As well as beef and mutton.

9. The title character of Daniel Defoe's 1719 novel. During his years shipwrecked on an island, he made himself many garments from goatskin.

1. Johann Faust (ca. 1480–ca. 1540), a German teacher and magician who became the subject of many stories and folktales.
2. English merchant (1532–1611), founder of the Charterhouse School for boys in London.

[Miss Buss and Miss Beale]

Miss Buss and Miss Beale[4]
Cupid's darts do not feel;
  How different from us
Miss Beale and Miss Buss.

[Three Wise Men of Gotham]

Three Wise Men of Gotham[3]
  Went to sea in a bowl;
If the bowl had been stronger,
My song would have been longer.

[I'll tell you a story]

I'll tell you a story
  About Jack-a-Nory,[5]—
And now my story's begun:
I'll tell you another
  About Jack and his brother,—
And now my story's done.

---

3. A village in north-central England, near Nottingham; from as early as the fifteenth century, Gotham was proverbial for the foolishness of its inhabitants.
4. Two English pioneers of women's education. Frances Mary Buss (1827–1894) founded and became headmistress of the North London Collegiate School for Ladies in 1850; Dorothea Beale (1831–1906) was principal of Cheltenham Ladies' College and founder of St. Hilda's College, Oxford. Neither married.
5. *The Oxford Dictionary of Nursery Verse* explains that the verse is "sometimes used to put off children's demands for a story." *Jackanory* was also the name of a popular British television program (1965–96) that featured storytelling.

[Wee Willie Winkie][6]

Wee Willie Winkie runs through the town,
Upstairs and downstairs in his nightgown,
Rapping at the window, crying through the lock,
"Are the children in their beds,
for now it's eight o'clock?"

6. This nursery rhyme slightly modifies the first verse of an
1841 poem by the Scottish poet William Miller.

RIDDLES AND WORDPLAY

The desire to tell jokes and share in them begins
very early. Even pre-school-age children delight in
knock-knock jokes—especially those that touch on
naughty or forbidden adult pleasures such as sex or
alcohol. For example,

> Knock knock.
> *Who's there?*
> Beryl!
> *Beryl who?*
> Beryl of beer!

A riddle is a verbal puzzle, a trick of words—and
a mental test whose appeal is very ancient. According to Greek mythology, Oedipus saved Thebans
from the Sphinx, who had been killing all those

unable to answer her riddle: "What walks on four
legs in the morning, two in the afternoon, and
three at night?" When he correctly replied, "A
human"—who first crawls, then walks on two legs,
and finally uses a stick in old age—she killed herself in shame. Anglo-Saxon riddles have been preserved from the tenth century.

The two traditional riddles in this section rely
on the same verbal tricks and plays on double
meanings that we find in the riddling verse of
Christina Rossetti's *Sing-Song* (1872). John Cotton's "Totleigh Riddles" are also complex and subtle. They are fully realized poems, providing the
reader with clues in their metaphors as well as in
their wordplay.

[Riddle me, riddle me ree]

Riddle me, riddle me ree,[1]
A little man in a tree;
A stick in his hand,
A stone in his throat,
If you read me this riddle
I'll give you a groat.[2]

1. Interpret my riddle rightly.
2. An old coin worth 4 pennies. The answer, according to
Iona and Peter Opie (*The Oxford Book of Nursery Rhymes*), is
the hawthorne berry.

[Hyder iddle diddle dell]

Hyder iddle diddle dell,
    A yard of pudding's not an ell;[3]
Not forgetting tweedle-dye,
    A tailor's goose[4] will never fly.

3. A unit of length (once used to measure cloth) equal to 45
inches.
4. A heavy iron with a handle shaped like a goose's neck.

Totleigh Riddles

by John Cotton[5]

1

Insubstantial I can fill lives,
Cathedrals, worlds.
I can haunt islands,
Raise passions
Or calm the madness of kings.
I've even fed the affectionate.
I can't be touched or seen,
But I can be noted.[6]

2

We are a crystal zoo,
Wielders of fortunes,
The top of our professions.
Like hard silver nails
Hammered into the dark
We made charts for mariners.[7]

3

I reveal your secrets.
I am your morning enemy,
Though I give reassurance of presence
I can be magic,
Or the judge in beauty contests.
Count Dracula[8] has no use for me.
When you leave
I am left to my own reflections.[9]

4

My tensions and pressures
Are precise if transitory.
Iridescent, I can float
And catch small rainbows,
Beauties luxuriate in me.
I can inhabit ovens
Or sparkle in bottles.
I am filled with that
Which surrounds me.[1]

5

Containing nothing
I can bind people for ever,
Or just hold a finger.
Without end or beginning
I go on to appear in fields,
Ensnare enemies,
Or in another guise
Carry in the air
Messages from tower to tower.[2]

6

Silent I invade cities,
Blur edges, confuse travellers,
My thumb smudging the light.
I drift from rivers
To loiter in early morning fields,
Until constable sun
Moves me on.[3]

7

Rain polishes
My round the year gloss,
Honing my row
Of sharp spears.
In winter I come into my own,
Bearing the crown[4]
And gifts
Of bright beads of blood.[5]

8

I work while you sleep,
Needing no light to etch windows
Or elaborate leaf or branch.
Without colour my wonder is
My patterns within patterns
Growing like crisp stars.
Look, but do not touch.
Your warmth is my end.[6]

---

5. British poet and teacher (1925–2003). Cotton himself supplied the answers to these riddles.
6. I.e., music.
7. I.e., stars.
8. The vampire featured in Bram Stoker's *Dracula* (1897). Though centuries of lore about vampires preceded his novel, Stoker was apparently the first to suggest that they cast no reflection in mirrors.
9. I.e., a mirror.
1. I.e., bubbles.
2. I.e., a ring. "Tower": i.e., a tower carrying telephone lines.
3. I.e., fog.
4. "Of all the trees that are in the wood, / The holly bears the crown" (Christmas carol, "The Holly and the Ivy").
5. I.e., holly.
6. I.e., frost.

9

A great cold cinder,
At year's end I face the sun
Across pale-washed skies,
Outshone but not outpulled.
Ruling tides, blood and calendars,
I float on water, bend minds,
And like knowledge
Illumine but not warm.[7]

10

I am one of an endless family,
My brothers and sisters
Never far behind.
I crash and swirl,
Grind pebbles, growl,
And gnaw the bones of the land
Like a great wet dog.[8]

11

Painted or plain,
Of earth or glass,
Being filled
My purpose is fulfilled.
Water or wine
My being is in holding,
Though I, too, am held
By my unhearing ear.[9]

12

My momentary delights
Are held close
In a paper bud,
I flower best at night,
My petals falling
Like bright showers
When I am fired to beauty.[1]

1981

---

7. I.e., the moon.
8. I.e., a wave.

9. I.e., a jug.
1. I.e., a firework.

TEXTS AND CONTEXTS

Twinkle, Twinkle, Little Star

"Twinkle, twinkle, little star / How I wonder what you are!" The lines are so familiar that we rarely consider answering the compelling question. It is difficult to imagine that the poem once was new or that its author, Jane Taylor, ever imagined that the poem she titled "The Star" would be so ubiquitous two hundred years after it first appeared in *Rhymes for the Nursery* in 1806.

Rhymes for the Nursery was the second collection of verses for children that Jane Taylor published with her sister Ann. The first, *Original Poems for Infant Minds* (1804), is described by F. J. Harvey Darton as "the book that awoke the nurseries of England" (*Children's Books in England: Five Centuries of Social Life*, 1932). The earliest collections of nursery verse from oral tradition had been issued in the latter part of the eighteenth century, and the first bearing the name of an author is thought to be Lucy Aikin's *Poetry for Children* (1801). By the time the Taylor sisters produced their volume of original poetry, the market for books for the nursery was burgeoning.

One mark of the fame of "The Star" is that its first stanza has often been reprinted without attribution. Another is that it suffers from what Darton calls "the obloquy of easy parody." The four variations on the original in this section demonstrate how easily Jane Taylor's verse slips between printed and oral versions as it moves across Anglophone cultures. Lewis Carroll's "Twinkle, twinkle little bat" (in *Alice's Adventures in Wonderland*, 1865) no doubt delighted its original readers as much as it does today's children, for the target of the parody is instantly recognizable. Unk White's Australian nursery rhyme, "Twinkle, Twinkle, Southern Cross" (1943), celebrates the stars of the Southern Hemisphere. "Ringo, Ringo, Ringo Starr" circulated in American school-yards and playgrounds in the 1960s, when the Beatles, with drummer Ringo Starr, were the dominant force in music and popular culture. More recently, John Agard has published a version for the Caribbean, "Twinkle, Twinkle, Firefly" (1991).

The Star

by Jane Taylor[1]

Twinkle, twinkle, little star
How I wonder what you are!
Up above the world so high
Like a diamond in the sky.

When the blazing sun is gone,
When he nothing shines upon,
Then you show your little light,
Twinkle, twinkle, all the night.

Then the traveller in the dark,
Thanks you for your tiny spark,
He could not see which way to go,
If you did not twinkle so.

In the dark blue sky you keep,
And often through my curtains peep,
For you never shut your eye,
Till the sun is in the sky.

As your bright and tiny spark,
Lights the traveller in the dark,—
Though I know not what you are,
Twinkle, twinkle, little star.

1806

[Twinkle, twinkle, little bat]

by Lewis Carroll[2]

"We quarreled last March—just before *he* went mad, you know—" (pointing with his teaspoon at the March Hare) "—it was at the great concert given by the Queen of Hearts, and I[3] had to sing

'Twinkle, twinkle, little bat!
How I wonder what you're at!'

You know the song, perhaps?"
"I've heard something like it," said Alice.
"It goes on, you know," the Hatter continued, "in this way:—

'Up above the world you fly,
Like a tea-tray in the sky.
Twinkle, twinkle—' "

Here the Dormouse shook itself, and began singing in its sleep "*Twinkle, twinkle, twinkle, twinkle*—" and went on so long that they had to pinch it to make it stop.

1865

---

1. British author of books of poetry, essays, and short stories for children (1783–1824), many of which were coauthored with her sister Ann.

2. Pseudonym of Charles Dodgson (1832–1898), British mathematician and author of children's stories and verse.
3. The speaker is the Mad Hatter, in chapter 7 of *Alice's Adventures in Wonderland* (1865), "A Mad Tea-Party."

Twinkle, Twinkle, Southern Cross

by Unk White[4]

Twinkle, Twinkle, Southern Cross[5]
What you are, I'm at a loss

Up above the world so high
You look like diamonds in the sky

When the blazing sun is gone
When he nothing shines upon

Then you show your little stars
Like lights of fairy motor-cars

Then your bright and tiny spark
Lights the swaggie[6] in the dark

Then you show your little beams
To light the way to happy dreams

Now Mrs. Roo[7] in all the dark
Thanks you for a tiny spark

How could she see which way to go
If you did not twinkle so?

On my roof the wombat plays
Basking in your silvery rays

Happy as a lark to be
'Twixt the sky and you and me

One two three—and then two more
At school we learn that's over four

But when you are, I'm at a loss
You've got me thinking, Southern Cross

In the dark blue sky you keep
And often through my curtains peep

For you never shut your eye
'Til the sun is in the sky.

1943

Ringo, Ringo, Ringo Starr

Ringo, Ringo, Ringo Starr,[8]
How I wonder what you are.
Underneath that mop of hair,[9]
Ringo, are you really there?
Ringo, Ringo, Ringo Starr,
How I wonder what you are.

Twinkle Twinkle Firefly

by John Agard[1]

Twinkle
Twinkle
Firefly
In the dark
It's you I spy

Over the river
Over the bush

Twinkle
Twinkle
Firefly
For the traveller
passing by

Over the river
Over the bush

Twinkle
Twinkle
Firefly
Lend the dark
your sparkling eye.

1991

---

4. Cecil John White (1900–1986), New Zealand–born illustrator who worked for Australian journals and in the Australian comics industry.
5. A bright constellation of the Southern Hemisphere.
6. A swagman; a drifter.
7. I.e., a kangaroo.
8. British musician (born Richard Starkey, 1940) who became famous as the drummer for the Beatles. This playground rhyme was published in 1973.

9. In the early coverage of the four Beatles, commentators almost always noted their "mop tops"; at the time, most men kept their hair quite short.
1. British writer of poetry, drama, and fiction (b. 1949); now living in England, he was born in Guyana (then British Guiana).

PLAYGROUND VERSE

Unlike nursery verse, which adults recite to or sing with children, playground verse is passed from child to child. Once children start school, the playground becomes their cultural community, and they teach each other rituals and games. All of this lore is transmitted within a relatively brief span, between about the age of four, when children begin primary school, to about eleven or twelve, before they begin secondary school. It is during this period that they learn verses to be sung while bouncing a ball or jumping rope (e.g., "Little Sally Walker"), or ritual songs to accompany games of hide-and-seek (e.g., "All Hid").

[How many miles to Babylon?][1]

How many miles to Babylon?[2]
Three score and ten.
Can I get there by candlelight?
Yes, and back again.
Open your gates as wide as the sky
And let the king and his men pass by.

[Ear-r-r-r-r-ly in the morning][3]

Ear-r-r-r-r-ly in the morning when the cock
    began to crow,
Ev'rybody take a cock before they go.
Pay two pounds ten[4] before you go,
Pay two pounds ten before you go.

1. This verse accompanies a catching game (sometimes called "thread the needle"), in which children form chains and try to trap those attempting to pass through.
2. An ancient city south of Baghdad.

3. This verse accompanies a clapping song and game, played by children in La Plaine, on the island of Dominica in the Lesser Antilles.
4. I.e., and 10 shillings.

[Down to the carpet you must go][5]

Down to the car<u>pe</u>t you must go,
Like a black<u>bird</u> in the air.
Oh, rise and stand <u>up</u> on your knees,
And choose the one you love the best.
Oh, when you marry, you tell me so,
First a boy, second a girl,
Ten days after, ten days old,
Kiss, kiss and say goodbye.

[Shortenin' bread][6]

CHORUS:

I do love
Shortenin' bread,
I do love
Shortenin' bread.
Mama love
Shortenin' bread,
Papa love
Shortenin' bread,
Everybody love
Shortenin' bread.

1. Two little babies layin' in bed,
   One play sick an' the other'n play dead.
   　I do love
   　Shortenin' bread,
   　I do love
   　Shortenin' bread.

2. Ever' since my dog been dead,
   Hog's been rootin' my 'tater bed.
CHORUS

3. Old Aunt Dinah sick in the bed,
   Sent for the Doctor; Doctor said,
   "All she need's some shortenin' bread."
CHORUS

[Little Sally Water][7]

Little Sally Water,
Sitting in a saucer,
Crying and weeping for someone to come.
Rise, Sally, rise, Sa-la-ly,
Wipe your weeping eyes, Sa-la-ly,
Turn to the East, Sa-la-ly,
Turn to the West, Sa-la-ly,
Turn to the very one that Sally loves the best.

Put your hands on your hips,
Let your backbone shake,
Shake it to the East,
Shake it to the West,
Shake it to the very one that
Sally loves the best.

[Little Sally Walker]

Little Sally Walker,
Sittin' in the saucer,
Rise, rise, little Sally, rise.
Oh, cry, Sally, cry,
Oh, wipe yo' cheek,
Oh, shake it to the east,
Oh, shake it to the west,
Oh, shake it to the very one you love the best.
[*Repeat.*]

---

5. The verse accompanies a ring game that simulates a courtship ritual. When it is sung, the "wrong" syllable (indicated by underlining) is accented.
6. A traditional African American verse, accompanied by a dance as it is sung.

7. A jump rope song (a different version of the same song follows).

[All hid?][8]

CHORUS:

All hid?
All hid?
Five, ten, fifteen, twenty.
'S all hid?

1. Way down yonder by the devil's town.
   Devil knocked my daddy down.
   Is all hid?

CHORUS

2. Six little horses in the stable.
   One jumped out and skinned his nable.[9]
   Is all hid?

CHORUS

3. Old man Ned fell out the bed,
   Cracked his head on a hot piece of lead.
   Is all hid?

CHORUS

8. This verse is sung by children playing hide-and-seek.
9. A nonsense word.

NONSENSE

Nonsense syllables such as "hickory, dickory dock" and "eeny, meeney, miney, mo" abound in nursery verse. They have been used at least since the time of the comedies of ancient Greece—in *The Birds* and *The Frogs*, Aristophanes mimics the animals' calls and croaks. Nonsense has always been about pushing at the boundaries of sense, provoking them, playing with the serious world, and exposing pomposity. But only in the mid-nineteenth century did nonsense verse in English take on its characteristic form, in the writings of Lewis Carroll and Edward Lear. Perhaps both sensed that Victorian culture in some respects was inviting their deflating verbal jabs and attacks on didacticism. And while both are hailed as the creators of a new genre, each also used that genre to reshape unsatisfactory aspects of his life. Charles Dodgson was an Oxford mathematician who stuttered. Lear, as an epileptic, depressed man without formal education created limericks, songs, and pictures that made others laugh out loud. Those carrying on the tradition of nonsense verse include Hilaire Belloc and Colin McNaughton (in England), Shel Silverstein and Nancy Willard (in the United States), and Margaret Mahy (in New Zealand); the latter two are represented here.

EDWARD LEAR
1812–1888

There are two parrots named after Edward Lear: *Anodorhynchus leari* (Bonaparte), also called Lear's macaw, and *Laprochroa leari*, Lear's cockatoo. The recognition was in honor of his first publication: privately printed drawings of parrots in the Gardens of the Zoological Society in Regent's Park in London, *Illustrations of the Family of Psittacidae, or Parrots* (1832). Although Lear's parrots were the faithful renditions of a naturalist, they appeared at the time as fantasies. That's because these and other exotic birds and curiosities from Africa and South America were newly available and fashionable in England in the early nineteenth century. The fantastic creatures and botanies of Lear's later caricatures and nonsense verses seem almost natural extensions of the period's fascination with exotic peoples, places, and things.

As is often the case with comedians, Lear was not a happy man; he was often lonely, insecure, and melancholy. The twentieth and youngest surviving child in a family of twenty-one children, he suffered from both bronchitis and epilepsy (a condition kept secret from all but his family); and when he was a child his family was devastated by his father's financial ruin. Raised primarily by his eldest sister, who encouraged his interest in drawing, he received little formal education. His drawings of birds for a study in the late 1820s led to his parrot book, which won him the attention of Lord Stanley (later the thirteenth Earl of Derby), who in 1832 hired Lear to make an illustrated record of the large collection of exotic birds and animals on his estate near Liverpool. Lear worked at Knowsley Hall until 1837. During this time, he was intro-

duced to the idea of the limerick and began to draw caricatures and make up comic verses for the children in Stanley's extended family. Eventually, under the pseudonym Derry Down Derry, Lear published *A Book of Nonsense* (1846). That work, finally published under Lear's own name (in an expanded edition) in 1861, was very popular, as were the works that followed, though Lear continued to support himself by painting and by writing travel books. He traveled a great deal, and after 1837 he rarely returned to England for long. From 1871 until the end of his life, he lived in San Remo, Italy.

"The Owl and the Pussycat" was composed in 1867 as a gift for a sick three-year-old child, Janet Symonds (the daughter of his friends Catherine and John Addington Symonds). It was published with "The Jumblies," composed a little later, in *Nonsense Songs, Stories, Botany, and Alphabets* (1870).

The Owl and the Pussy-cat

The Owl and the Pussy-cat went to sea
   In a beautiful pea-green boat,
They took some honey, and plenty of money,
   Wrapped up in a five-pound note.
The Owl looked up to the stars above,
   And sang to a small guitar,
'O lovely Pussy! O Pussy, my love,
   What a beautiful Pussy you are,
      You are,
      You are!
What a beautiful Pussy you are!'

Pussy said to the Owl, 'You elegant fowl!
   How charmingly sweet you sing!

O let us be married! too long we have tarried:
   But what shall we do for a ring?'
They sailed away, for a year and a day,
   To the land where the Bong-tree grows,
And there in a wood a Piggy-wig stood,
   With a ring at the end of his nose,
      His nose,
      His nose,
With a ring at the end of his nose.

'Dear Pig, are you willing to sell for one shilling
   Your ring?' Said the Piggy, 'I will.'
So they took it away, and were married next day
   By the Turkey who lives on the hill.
They dinèd on mince, and slices of quince,
   Which they ate with a runcible spoon;[1]
And hand in hand, on the edge of the sand,
   They danced by the light of the moon,
      The moon,
      The moon,
They danced by the light of the moon.

1867   1870

---

1. Though Lear made up the word *runcible*, the phrase "runcible spoon" has come to mean a curved fork with three broad prongs, sharp on one outside edge.

The Jumblies

They went to sea in a Sieve, they did,
  In a Sieve they went to sea:
In spite of all their friends could say,
On a winter's morn, on a stormy day,
  In a Sieve they went to sea!
And when the Sieve turned round and round,
And every one cried, 'You'll all be drowned!'
They called aloud, 'Our Sieve ain't big,
But we don't care a button! we don't care a fig!
  In a Sieve we'll go to sea!'
    Far and few, far and few,
      Are the lands where the Jumblies live;
    Their heads are green, and their hands are
        blue,
    And they went to sea in a Sieve.

They sailed away in a Sieve, they did,
  In a Sieve they sailed so fast,
With only a beautiful pea-green veil
Tied with a riband by way of a sail,
  To a small tobacco-pipe mast;
And every one said, who saw them go,
'O won't they be soon upset, you know!
For the sky is dark, and the voyage is long,
And happen what may, it's extremely wrong
  In a Sieve to sail so fast!'
    Far and few, far and few,
      Are the lands where the Jumblies live;
    Their heads are green, and their hands are
        blue,
    And they went to sea in a Sieve.

The water it soon came in, it did,
  The water it soon came in;
So to keep them dry, they wrapped their feet
In a pinky paper all folded neat,
  And they fastened it down with a pin.
And they passed the night in a crockery-jar,
And each of them said, 'How wise we are!
Though the sky be dark, and the voyage be long,
Yet we never can think we were rash or wrong,
  While round in our Sieve we spin!'
    Far and few, far and few,
      Are the lands where the Jumblies live;
    Their heads are green, and their hands are
        blue,
    And they went to sea in a Sieve.

And all night long they sailed away;
  And when the sun went down,
They whistled and warbled a moony song
To the echoing sound of a coppery gong,
  In the shade of the mountains brown.
'O Timballo! How happy we are,
When we live in a sieve and a crockery-jar,
And all night long in the moonlight pale,
We sail away with a pea-green sail,
  In the shade of the mountains brown!'
    Far and few, far and few,
      Are the lands where the Jumblies live;
    Their heads are green, and their hands are
        blue,
    And they went to sea in a Sieve.

They sailed to the Western Sea, they did,
  To a land all covered with trees,
And they bought an Owl, and a useful Cart,
And a pound of Rice, and a Cranberry Tart,
  And a hive of silvery Bees.
And they bought a Pig, and some green Jack-
    daws,
And a lovely Monkey with lollipop paws,
And forty bottles of Ring-Bo-Ree,
  And no end of Stilton Cheese.
    Far and few, far and few,
      Are the lands where the Jumblies live;
    Their heads are green, and their hands are
        blue,
    And they went to sea in a Sieve.

And in twenty years they all came back,
  In twenty years or more,
And every one said, 'How tall they've grown!
For they've been to the Lakes, and the Torrible
    Zone,
  And the hills of the Chankly Bore!'

1156

And they drank their health, and gave them a
    feast
Of dumplings made of beautiful yeast;
And every one said, 'If we only live,
We too will go to sea in a Sieve,—
    To the hills of the Chankly Bore!'

Far and few, far and few,
    Are the lands where the Jumblies live;
Their heads are green, and their hands are
    blue,
    And they went to sea in a Sieve.

1870

LEWIS CARROLL
1832–1898

As a shy and stuttering lecturer in mathematics and logic, with a keen interest in language and puzzles, Charles Dodgson might have been a footnote in the history of Oxford University. But his writings under the name Lewis Carroll made him one of the best-known authors of children's literature in the world.

The third of eleven children, and the oldest boy (he had seven sisters), Dodgson found pleasure in writing from an early age. As a schoolboy, he began composing illustrated family manuscript magazines, a practice that continued through his studies at Christ Church, Oxford. They often displayed his delight in parody and his wit. While a tutor of mathematics, he contributed poetry, fiction, and nonfiction to a number of newspapers and magazines; with the publication of *Alice's Adventures in Wonderland* in 1865, Carroll's position in literary history was secure.

It is Carroll, along with Edward Lear, who consolidates the inclusion of comedy and levity in children's literature. In creating parodies of sentimental, didactic, and "improving" poetry, including the sacred works of Isaac Watts, Carroll played a critical role in transforming constructions of childhood. "How Doth the Little Crocodile" was included in the earliest written version of *Alice* (created for Alice Liddell), *Alice's Adventures under Ground* (1864). Carroll's mockery of instructional verse, rote learning, and moralizing school curricula helped move the genre from eighteenth-century concerns with the instruction and correction of children toward modern celebrations of play.

Carroll's love of wordplay made him, like Lear, a master of English nonsense poetry. "Jabberwocky" was published in *Through the Looking-Glass, and What Alice Found There* (1871), but its first stanza appeared under the title "Stanza of Anglo-Saxon Poetry" (1855) in his manuscript scrapbook "Misch-masch" as "an obscure, yet deeply-affecting, relic of ancient Poetry" (indeed, the subject of the longer poem—the slaying of a monster—itself recalls the Anglo-Saxon *Beowulf*). Its invented words are solemnly glossed with many of the same meanings later expounded by Humpty Dumpty in *Looking-Glass*. Often they are what Humpty Dumpty calls "portmanteau" words—two meanings packed into one, as into a suitcase with two equal compartments—a notion that Carroll explains at greater length in his preface to another nonsense poem, "The Hunting of the Snark" (1876). One of the more obvious examples is *chortle*, a coinage that has made its way into standard English (as has *galumph*): it combines *chuckle* and *snort*. Other coinages rely on puns; thus the grass that extends a long way before and a long way behind a sundial is the *wabe*. And a few, such as *toves* (they're "something like badgers—they're something like lizards—and they're something like corkscrews," says Humpty Dumpty), are simply absurd.

Two of the Carroll's nonsense verses, "How doth the little crocodile" and " 'Tis the voice of the lobster," are included here because they are parodies of two famous poems by Isaac Watts, "Against Idleness and Mischief" and "The Sluggard," both of which are reprinted in the Religion section of the anthology, on pages 529 and 530. Carroll's poems appear in *Alice's Adventures in Wonderland* (1865). "Against Idleness and Mischief," misremembered as "How doth the little crocodile," is the first of the poems that "all came different" when Alice tried to remember them; the second is "The Sluggard," whose "words came very queer indeed" as Alice began " 'Tis the voice of the Lobster." Victorian children would have known the originals and delighted in the mockery of the familiar.

How doth the little crocodile[1]

How doth the little crocodile
   Improve his shining tail,
And pour the waters of the Nile
   On every golden scale!

How cheerfully he seems to grin,
   How neatly spreads his claws,
And welcomes little fishes in
   With gently smiling jaws!

1864   1865

'Tis the voice of the Lobster[2]

" 'Tis the voice of the Lobster: I heard him declare
'You have baked me too brown, I must sugar my
   hair:'
As a duck with its eyelids, so he with his nose
Trims his belt and his buttons, and turns out his
   toes.
When the sands are all dry, he is gay as a lark
And will talk in contemptuous tones of the
   Shark:
But, when the tide rises and the sharks are around,
His voice has a timid and tremulous sound."

   "That's different from what I used to say when
I was a child," said the Gryphon.

   "Well, I never heard it before," said the Mock
Turtle; "but it sounds uncommon nonsense."

   Alice said nothing: she had sat down with her
face in her hands, wondering if anything would
ever happen in a natural way again.

   "I should like to have it explained," said the
Mock Turtle.

   "She ca'n't explain it," said the Gryphon
hastily. "Go on with the next verse."

   "But about his toes?" the Mock Turtle persisted. "How *could* he turn them out with his
nose, you know?"

   "It's the first position in dancing," Alice said;
but she was dreadfully puzzled by the whole
thing, and longed to change the subject.

   "Go on with the next verse," the Gryphon
repeated: "it begins *I passed by his garden.*'"

   Alice did not dare to disobey, though she felt
sure it would all come wrong, and she went on in
a trembling voice:—

*"I passed by his garden, and marked, with one
   eye,*
How the Owl and the Panther were sharing a pie:
The Panther took pie-crust, and gravy, and meat,
*While the Owl had the dish as its share of the
   treat.*
*When the pie was all finished, the Owl, as a
   boon,*
Was kindly permitted to pocket the spoon:
*While the Panther received knife and fork with a
   growl,*
And concluded the banquet by—"

                           1865

Jabberwocky

'Twas brillig, and the slithy toves[3]
   Did gyre and gimble in the wabe;[4]
All mimsy were the borogoves,[5]
   And the mome raths outgrabe.[6]

---

1. A parody of "Against Idleness and Mischief" (1715), by
Isaac Watts.
2. A parody of "The Sluggard" (1715), by Isaac Watts.
3. Badgerlike animals. "Brillig": the time at which to begin
broiling things for dinner (about 4 P.M.). "Slithy": lithe and
slimy. (The definitions for words in the first stanza are found
in chapter 6 of *Through the Looking-Glass.*)

4. Grass around a sun dial. "Gyre": to move in circles, like a
gyroscope. "Gimble": to make holes like a gimlet.
5. Odd-looking birds. "Mimsy": miserable and flimsy.
6. Made a noise between a bellow and a whistle, with a kind
of sneeze in the middle. "Mome": perhaps, "from home" (so
Humpty Dumpty); also, a blockhead (archaic). "Raths": green
pigs.

'Beware the Jabberwock, my son!
  The jaws that bite, the claws that catch!
Beware the Jubjub bird, and shun
  The frumious[7] Bandersnatch!

He took his vorpal sword in hand:
  Long time the manxome foe he sought—
So rested he by the Tumtum tree,
  And stood awhile in thought.

And as in uffish thought he stood,
  The Jabberwock, with eyes of flame,
Came whiffling through the tulgey wood,
  And burbled as it came!

One, two! One, two! And through and through
  The vorpal blade went snicker-snack![8]
He left it dead, and with its head
  He went galumphing back.

'And hast thou slain the Jabberwock?
  Come to my arms, my beamish boy!
O frabjous day! Callooh! Callay!'
  He chortled in his joy.

'Twas brillig, and the slithy toves
  Did gyre and gimble in the wabe;
All mimsy were the borogoves,
  And the mome raths outgrabe.

                                        1871

---

7. Furious and fuming (Carroll's explanation in the preface to *The Hunting of the Snark*, 1876). This word, like many others in the poem (e.g., uffish, beamish, Jubjub, Bandersnatch), is also found in *Snark*.

8. "Snick" means to cut sharply, and also a "glancing blow." In the Middle English tale of *Sir Gawain and the Green Knight*, the Green Knight "snicked" the neck of Gawain.

NANCY WILLARD
b. 1936

Even as a young child, American author Nancy Willard experienced a sense of wonder in writing stories and drawing pictures for her own amusement and pleasure. The fact that she was influenced early by Lewis Carroll, as well as by fantasists George MacDonald and L. Frank Baum, is visible in the characteristic blends of fantasy and reality, natural and supernatural, which mark her fiction and poetry. Willard, who began teaching creative writing at Vassar in 1965 after earning her Ph.D. at Stanford, initially wrote only for adults. But after her son was born she started to concentrate on writing for children; she has published more than sixty volumes of children's fiction and poetry, as well as literary criticism, poetry, novels, and short stories for adults.

A Visit to William Blake's Inn: Poems for Innocent and Experienced Travelers, from which the three poems included here are taken, was published in 1981 and illustrated by Alice and Martin Provensen. Notably, it was the first book of poetry to be awarded a Newbery Medal. Its poems do not parody Blake's *Songs of Innocence and Experience* (1794), though the first stanza of "The Tiger Asks Blake for Bedtime Story" deliberately echoes "The Tyger." Instead, Willard celebrates the work she first read at age seven by imagining the visionary poet as the keeper of the inn where the imagination rules. In her nonsense verses, the edge of cruelty that marks nineteenth-century nonsense is replaced with a sense of wonder.

William Blake's Inn for Innocent and Experienced Travelers

This inn belongs to William Blake[1]
and many are the beasts[2] he's tamed
and many are the stars[3] he's named
and many those who stop and take
their joyful rest with William Blake.

Two mighty dragons brew and bake
and many are the loaves they've burned
and many are the spits they've turned
and many those who stop and break
their joyful bread with William Blake.

Two patient angels wash and shake
his featherbeds, and far away
snow falls like feathers. That's the day
good children run outside and make
snowmen to honor William Blake

The Wise Cow Makes *Way, Room,* and *Believe*

The Rabbit cried, "Make *Way*!
Make *Way* for William Blake!
Let our good poet pass."
The Wise Cow said, "Alas!
Alack! How shall I make
a thing I've never seen?
To one that lives on grass
what's good is green.
Therefore I must make *Way*
of grass and hay,
a nest where he can nap
like fieldmice in a cap."

The Rabbit cried, "Make *Room*!
Make *Room* for the marmalade man![4]
He is mopping and mapping the floors.

He is tidying cupboards and drawers."
The Wise Cow said, "Can I
make *Room* and *Way* together?
To one that lives outdoors
what's good is weather.
Therefore I must make *Room*
like a bright loom.
The marmalade man can weave
good weather, I believe."

The Rabbit cried, "Make *Believe*,
and make it strong and clear
that I may enter in
with all my kith and kin."
The Wise Cow said, "My dear,
Believe shall be a boat
having both feet and fins.
We'll leave this quiet moat.
We'll welcome great and small
with *Ways* and *Rooms* for all,
and for our captain let us take
the noble poet, William Blake."

Blake Leads a Walk on the Milky Way

He gave silver shoes to the rabbit
and golden gloves to the cat
and emerald boots to the tiger and me
and boots of iron to the rat.

He inquired, "Is everyone ready?
The night is uncommonly cold,
We'll start on our journey as children,
but I fear we will finish it old."

He hurried us to the horizon
where morning and evening meet.
The slippery stars went skipping
under our hapless feet.

"I'm terribly cold," said the rabbit.
My paws are becoming quite blue,

---

1. British poet and engraver (1757–1827); almost all of his works combine text and illustration. This was the method he used for *Songs of Innocence* (1789) and for *Songs of Innocence and of Experience* (1794).
2. Wild beasts in the *Songs* include tigers (notably in "The Tyger," one of Blake's most famous poems), lions, and wolves.
3. Willard may have in mind one of the "Proverbs of Hell" from Blake's *The Marriage of Heaven and Hell* (1790–93), which she quotes on the final page of her book: "He whose face gives no light, will never become a star."
4. This figure was introduced earlier in *William Blake's Inn*, "carr[ying] a bucket and mop," in "The Man in the Marmalade Hat Arrives."

and what will become of my right thumb
while you admire the view?"

"The stars," said the cat, "are abundant
and falling on every side.
Let them carry us back to our comforts.
Let us take the stars for a ride."

"I shall garland my room," said the tiger,
"with a few of these emerald lights."
"I shall give up sleeping forever," I said.
"I shall never part day from night."

The rat was sullen. He grumbled
he ought to have stayed in his bed.
"What's gathered by fools in heaven
will never endure," he said.

Blake gave silver stars to the rabbit
and golden stars to the cat
and emerald stars to the tiger and me
but a handful of dirt to the rat.

1981

MARGARET MAHY
b. 1936

New Zealander Margaret Mahy has written almost two hundred works for young readers. She writes with facility across all genres, from picture books for the very young to novels of social realism for adolescents. One reason her writings succeed is that they convey her strong belief that truths are often best expressed by telling stories—even if those stories contain elements of fairy tales, fantasy, or science fiction.

Whether creating poetry or prose, Mahy displays finely crafted language and a remarkable sense of imagination's possibilities. In her alliterative flights of fancy (e.g., *The Birthday Burglar*, 1984), comic names, and invention of exotic and fantastic creatures, she recalls Edward Lear. In *17 Kings and 42 Elephants* (1972; illustrated by Patricia MacCarthy, 1987), she tells of a joyous journey between points unknown in strongly rhythmic verse filled with words both nonsensical and evocative.

17 Kings and 42 Elephants

Seventeen kings on forty-two elephants
Going on a journey through a wild wet night,

Baggy ears like big umbrellaphants,
Little eyes a-gleaming in the jungle light.

Seventeen kings saw white-toothed crocodiles
Romping in the river where the reeds grow tall,

Green-eyed dragons, rough as rockodiles,
Lying in the mud where the small crabs crawl.

1161

Forty-two elephants—oh, what a lot of 'ums,
Big feet beating in the wet wood shade,

Proud and ponderous hippopotomums
Danced to the music that the marchers made.

Seventeen kings sang loud and happily,
Forty-two elephants swayed to the song.

Tigers at the riverside drinking lappily,
Knew the kings were happy as they marched
   along.

Who joined the singsong? Cranes and pelicans,
Peacocks fluttering their fine fantails,

Flamingos chanting "Ding Dong Bellicans!"
Rosy as a garden in the jungle vales.

Tinkling tunesters, twangling trillicans,
Butterflied and fluttered by the great green trees.

Big baboonsters, black gorillicans
Swinging from the branches by their hairy knees.

Kings in crimson, crowns all crystalline,
Moving to the music of a single gong.

Watchers in the jungle, moist and mistalline,
Bibble-bubble-babbled to the bing-bang-bong!

Seventeen kings—the heavy night swallowed
   them,
Raindrops glistened on the elephants' backs.

Nobody stopped them, nobody followed them—
The deep dark jungle has devoured their tracks.

1972

POETRY COLLECTIONS

The history of poetry published for children begins in 1804, with *Original Poems for Infant Minds*. Although attributed to "Several Young Persons," the authors were Jane (author of "Twinkle, twinkle, little star") and Ann Taylor and their brother Isaac. It was "the book that awoke the nurseries of England," claims children's book historian F. J. Harvey Darton. Although soaked in the traditions of nursery verse and religious moral verse, the volume recognized even in its title the beginning of a new genre: these were "original" poems, composed in the early days of the children's book-publishing industry.

Each collection in this section is something of a staging post in the publishing history of children's poetry. Though traditional nursery and religious verses continue to echo forward into the published collections, other voices gradually make themselves heard. The delicate tunes of Christina Rossetti's verses give way to the sound of a child's voice speaking in Robert Louis Stevenson's *A Child's Garden of Verses*. The imperialist boyishness of Stevenson's poems opens into de la Mare's enigmatic ones. Robert Graves, while still evoking nursery verse, simultaneously engages a newly awake mythic sensibility and a modern, curious child. A. A. Milne's collections from the early 1920s, though not represented here, establish an openly ironic secular character in children's poetry. Randall Jarrell's *The Bat-Poet*, a poetic novel, moves verse for children firmly into the mid-twentieth century, with its focus on the individual struggling against the pressure to conform. Irony and rootedness in landscape and English poetry mark the work of Charles Causley. Ted Hughes, though not included here, re-imagines the Romantic tradition, his verses tipping on the brink between those for children and those for adults. But the most dramatic changes in children's poetry come from the youngest poets. In Lucille Clifton and Marilyn Nelson, the lives and linguistic markers of African Americans begin to alter the Anglophone traditions of children's poetry. Pat Mora brings Hispanic American border cultures into play. And Grace Nichols, with her Creole inflections, injects radical new life into standard English and reawakens children's poetry.

CHRISTINA ROSSETTI
1830–1894

In 1866, Dante Gabriel Rossetti produced a drawing, in colored chalk, of his sister Christina. She appears to have just looked up from the book in front of her, captured in a moment of reflection. Her hair is dark and shining against the voluminous white of her dress, and her features are strong and intelligent. The picture evokes the antithetical characteristics she brought to her life as an artist: darkness and light, gravity and sweetness, intense religious devotion and sensual passion, virtuoso brilliance and artless simplicity.

Christina Rossetti was the youngest of four gifted children born into an intellectual family of modest means. Her father, Gabriele Rossetti, was a political exile from Italy who taught Italian at the University of London; her mother, Frances, was a former governess whose own mother had married another Italian emigré. As Christina was growing up, Italian expatriates frequently gathered at this bilingual and cosmopolitan household. Apparently she was a willful child who loved fairy tales; her father called her his "angelic little demon." She was often ill during adolescence and during this time began her lifelong attachment to a strict form of Anglicanism, one also followed by her mother and sister Maria. At the same time, she shared with her brothers, Gabriel and William, a deep love of art and literature; both brothers were involved in the Pre-Raphaelite movement. Christina's earliest volume of verses was privately published by her grandfather in 1847, and her brothers aided the publication of two poems in the *Athenaeum* in 1848; seven more in the short-lived Pre-Raphaelite journal, the *Germ*, in 1850; and three in *Macmillan's Magazine* in 1861. Although the Rossetti brothers lived a bohemian lifestyle, Christina remained constrained by the Victorian conventions of her day. She broke off her engagement with James Collinson, a painter and member of the Pre-Raphaelite brotherhood, because he became a Roman Catholic; differences of religious faith also

figured in her later refusal of a proposal from the writer Charles Cayley. Some of her best-known poetry, such as "Up-hill" (1861), explores religious themes, and late in her life several volumes of devotional prose and verse were published by the Society for Promoting Christian Knowledge. Virginia Woolf, in an essay written for the hundredth anniversary of Rossetti's birth, describes her at a tea party as a "little woman dressed in black"—but also calls her an "instinctive poet" whom she admired greatly.

In the history of English poetry, Rossetti figures as a study in black and white. On the (white) religious side is the tender hymn "In the Bleak Midwinter." On the dark, erotic side is "Goblin Market," published in Rossetti's first commercial volume, *Goblin Market, and Other Poems* (1862). On its surface, "Goblin Market" is a moral tale, suitable though not written specifically for children. Yet it is a breathless moral fable about desire, temptation, resistance, sisterly love, and redemption. It is likely that Rossetti's experience working as a "sister" in a home for "fallen" women (the St. Mary Magdalene Penitentiary in Highgate, London) at least in part inspired "Goblin Market." After one sister, Laura, has been seduced by the call of "goblin men" to buy their fruits, Lizzie faces them to save her. What follows is a kind of rape, as they

> Tore her gown and soiled her stocking,
> Twitched her hair out by the roots,
> Stamped upon her tender feet,
> Held her hands and squeezed their fruits
> Against her mouth to make her eat.

Refusing to open her mouth, Lizzie carries home, on her own body, her sister's cure, and cries to her, "Hug me, kiss me, suck my juices / Squeezed from goblin fruits for you." The erotic charge of "Goblin Market" and its successful rejection of male control attracted the attention of feminist critics toward the end of the twentieth century.

Rossetti's volume of children's verse, *Sing-Song: A Nursery Rhyme Book* (1872), illustrated by the Pre-Raphaelite artist Arthur Hughes, was well-received when published but later fell out of favor. Though a few of its poems, such as "Mix a pancake," continue to turn up in anthologies, most have long been neglected—perhaps because the Victorian didacticism and sentimentalism in some and the emphasis on infant and maternal mortality in others are jarring to a modern reader. Yet they repay serious consideration. Rossetti herself coyly notes that the book is dedicated "without permission to the baby who suggested them," but Jan Marsh, in her biography of the poet, finds a strong suggestion that Rossetti was addressing the baby she once was. For example, one of the first poems in the collection, "Kookoorookoo," echoes the nursery rhyme her Italian father recited to his infant children. *Sing-Song* is attracting new attention. In "The Cadence in Song" (2002), published in the *Times Literary Supplement,* the poet Tom Paulin praises Rossetti for her "subtly stringent ear, an acoustic imagination that is uninsistently perfect." The 120 poems in *Sing-Song*, all written in a single burst in the autumn of 1869, attest to her perfect pitch.

Sing-Song: A Nursery Rhyme Book

Angels at the foot,
   And Angels at the head,
And like a curly little lamb
   My pretty babe in bed.

Love me,—I love you,
   Love me, my baby;
Sing it high, sing it low,
   Sing it as may be.

Mother's arms under you,
   Her eyes above you
Sing it high, sing it low,
   Love me,—I love you.

My baby has a father and a mother,
   Rich little baby!
Fatherless, motherless, I know another
    Forlorn as may be:
    Poor little baby!

Our little baby fell asleep,
   And may not wake again
For days and days, and weeks and weeks;
   But then he'll wake again,
And come with his own pretty look,
   And kiss Mamma again.

"Kookoorookoo! kookoorookoo!"
   Crows the cock before the morn;
"Kikirikee! kikirikee!"[1]
   Roses in the east are born.

"Kookoorookoo! kookoorookoo!"
   Early birds begin their singing;
"Kikirikee! kikirikee!"
   The day, the day, the day is springing.

---

1. Italian equivalent of "cock-a-doodle-doo" (usually spelled *chicchirichì*).

CHRISTINA ROSSETTI

Baby cry—
Oh fie!—
At the physic[2] in the cup:
    Gulp it twice
    And gulp it thrice,
Baby gulp it up.

———

Eight o'clock;
The postman's knock!
Five letters for Papa;
    One for Lou,
    And none for you,
And three for dear Mamma.

———

Bread and milk for breakfast,
    And woollen frocks to wear,
And a crumb for robin redbreast
    On the cold days of the year.

———

There's snow on the fields,
    And cold in the cottage,
While I sit in the chimney nook
    Supping[3] hot pottage.

My clothes are soft and warm,
    Fold upon fold,
But I'm so sorry for the poor
    Out in the cold.

———

Dead in the cold, a song-singing thrush,
Dead at the foot of a snowberry bush,—
Weave him a coffin of rush,
Dig him a grave where the soft mosses grow,
Raise him a tombstone of snow.

I dug and dug amongst the snow,
And thought the flowers would never grow;
I dug and dug amongst the sand,
And still no green thing came to hand.

Melt, O snow! the warm winds blow
To thaw the flowers and melt the snow;
But all the winds from every land
Will rear no blossom from the sand.

———

A city plum[4] is not a plum;
A dumb-bell is no bell, though dumb;
A statesman's rat[5] is not a rat;
A sailor's cat[6] is not a cat;
A soldier's frog[7] is not a frog;
A captain's log is not a log.

———

Your brother has a falcon,
    Your sister has a flower;
But what is left for mannikin,[8]
    Born within an hour?

I'll nurse you on my knee, my knee,
　My own little son;
I'll rock you, rock you, in my arms,
　My least little one.

————

Hear what the mournful linnets say:
　"We built our nest compact and warm,
But cruel boys came round our way
　And took our summerhouse by storm.

"They crushed the eggs so neatly laid;
　So now we sit with drooping wing,
And watch the ruin they have made,
　Too late to build, too sad to sing."

————

A baby's cradle with no baby in it,
　A baby's grave where autumn leaves drop sere;
The sweet soul gathered home to Paradise,
　The body waiting here.

————

Hop-o'-my-thumb and little Jack Horner,[9]
　What do you mean by tearing and fighting?
Sturdy dog Trot close round the corner,
　I never caught him growling and biting.

————

Hope is like a harebell trembling from its birth,
Love is like a rose the joy of all the earth;
Faith is like a lily lifted high and white,
Love is like a lovely rose the world's delight;
Harebells and sweet lilies show a thornless
　　　growth,
But the rose with all its thorns excels them
　　　both.

————

O wind, why do you never rest,
　Wandering, whistling to and fro,
Bringing rain out of the west,
　From the dim north bringing snow?

————

Crying, my little one, footsore and weary:
　Fall asleep, pretty one, warm on my shoulder:
I must tramp on through the winter night dreary,
　While the snow falls on me colder and colder.

You are my one, and I have not another;
　Sleep soft, my darling, my trouble and
　　　treasure;
Sleep warm and soft in the arms of your mother,
　Dreaming of pretty things, dreaming of
　　　pleasure.

————

Growing in the vale
　By the uplands hilly,
Growing straight and frail,
　Lady Daffadowndilly.[1]

In a golden crown,
And a scant green gown
　While the spring blows chilly,
Lady Daffadown,
　Sweet Daffadowndilly.

————

9. Title character in the nursery rhyme that begins "Little Jack Horner / Sat in a corner." "Hop-o'-my-thumb": also known as Tom Thumb, the thumb-sized character who outwits a giant in Charles Perrault's "Le Petit Poucet" (1697).
1. Daffodil (a playful expansion of the dialectal *daffadilly*).

A linnet in a gilded cage,—
  A linnet on a bough,—
In frosty winter one might doubt
  Which bird is luckier now.

But let the trees burst out in leaf,
  And nests be on the bough,
Which linnet is the luckier bird,
  Oh who could doubt it now?

———

Wrens and robins in the hedge,
  Wrens and robins here and there;
Building, perching, pecking, fluttering,
      Everywhere!

———

My baby has a mottled fist,
  My baby has a neck in creases;
My baby kisses and is kissed,
  For he's the very thing for kisses.

———

Why did baby die,
Making Father sigh,
Mother cry?

Flowers, that bloom to die,
Make no reply
Of "why?"
But bow and die.

———

If all were rain and never sun,
  No bow could span the hill;
If all were sun and never rain,
  There'd be no rainbow still.

———

O wind, where have you been,
  That you blow so sweet?
Among the violets
  Which blossom at your feet.

The honeysuckle waits
  For Summer and for heat.
But violets in the chilly Spring
  Make the turf so sweet.

———

On the grassy banks
Lambkins at their pranks;
Woolly sisters, woolly brothers
  Jumping off their feet
While their woolly mothers
  Watch by them and bleat.

———

Rushes in a watery place,
  And reeds in a hollow;
A soaring skylark in the sky,
  A darting swallow;
And where pale blossom used to hang
  Ripe fruit to follow.

———

Minnie and Mattie
  And fat little May,
Out in the country,
  Spending a day.

Such a bright day,
  With the sun glowing,
And the trees half in leaf,
  And the grass growing.

Pinky white pigling
  Squeals through his snout,
Woolly white lambkin
  Frisks all about.

Cluck! cluck? the nursing hen
  Summons her folk,—
Ducklings all downy soft
  Yellow as yolk.

Cluck! cluck! the mother hen
  Summons her chickens
To peck the dainty bits
  Found in her pickings.

Minnie and Mattie
    And May carry posies,
Half of sweet violets,
    Half of primroses.

Give the sun time enough,
    Glowing and glowing,
He'll rouse the roses
    And bring them blowing.

Don't wait for roses
    Losing to-day,
O Minnie, Mattie,
    And wise little May.

Violets and primroses
    Blossom to-day
For Minnie and Mattie
    And fat little May.

    ———

Heartsease in my garden bed,
    With sweetwilliam white and red,
Honeysuckle on my wall:—
    Heartsease blossoms in my heart
When sweet William comes to call,
    But it withers when we part,
And the honey-trumpets[2] fall.

    ———

If I were a Queen.
    What would I do?
I'd make you King,
    And I'd wait on you.

If I were a King,
    What would I do?
I'd make you Queen,
    For I'd marry you.

    ———

What are heavy? sea-sand and sorrow:
What are brief? to-day and to-morrow:
What are frail? Spring blossoms and youth:
What are deep? the ocean and truth.

There is but one May in the year,
    And sometimes May is wet and cold;
There is but one May in the year
    Before the year grows old.

Yet though it be the chilliest May,
    With least of sun and most of showers,
It's wind and dew, its night and day,
    Bring up the flowers.

    ———

The summer nights are short
    Where northern days are long:
For hours and hours lark after lark
    Thrills out his song.

The summer days are short
    Where southern nights are long:
Yet short the night when nightingales
    Trill out their song.

    ———

The days are clear,
    Day after day,
When April's here,
    That leads to May,
And June
Must follow soon:
    Stay, June, stay!—
If only we could stop the moon
And June!

    ———

Twist me a crown of wind-flowers;[3]
    That I may fly away
To hear the singers at their song,
    And players at their play.

Put on your crown of wind-flowers:
    But whither would you go?
Beyond the surging of the sea
    And the storms that blow.

2. I.e., the flowers of the honeysuckle.

3. Wood anemones.

Alas! your crown of wind-flowers
   Can never make you fly:
I twist them in a crown to-day,
   And to-night they die.

———

Brown and furry
Caterpillar in a hurry,
Take your walk
To the shady leaf, or stalk,
Or what not,
Which may be the chosen spot.
No toad spy you,
Hovering bird of prey pass by you;
Spin and die,
To live again a butterfly.

———

A toadstool comes up in a night,—
   Learn the lesson, little folk:—
An oak grows on a hundred years,
   But then it is an oak.

———

A pocket handkerchief to hem—
   Oh dear, oh dear, oh dear!
How many stitches it will take
   Before it's done, I fear.

Yet set a stitch and then a stitch,
   And stitch and stitch away,
Till stitch by stitch the hem is done—
   And after work is play!

———

If a pig wore a wig,
   What could we say?
Treat him as a gentleman,
   And say "Good day."

If his tail chanced to fail,
   What could we do?
Send him to the tailoress
   To get one new.

———

Seldom "can't,"
   Seldom "don't;"
Never "shan't,'
   Never "won't."

———

1 and 1 are 2—
That's for me and you.

2 and 2 are 4—
That's a couple more.

3 and 3 are 6
Barley-sugar sticks.[4]

4 and 4 are 8
Tumblers at the gate.

5 and 5 are 10
Bluff seafaring men.

6 and 6 are 12
Garden lads who delve.

7 and 7 are 14
Young men bent on sporting.

8 and 8 are 16
Pills the doctor's mixing.

9 and 9 are 18
Passengers kept waiting.

10 and 10 are 20
Roses—pleasant plenty!

11 and 11 are 22
Sums for brother George to do.

12 and 12 are 24
Pretty pictures, and no more.

———

4. Hard candy about the size and shape of a pencil.

How many seconds in a minute?
Sixty, and no more in it.

How many minutes in an hour?
Sixty for sun and shower.

How many hours in a day?
Twenty-four for work and play.

How many days in a week?
Seven both to hear and speak.

How many weeks in a month?
Four, as the swift moon runn'th.

How many months in a year?
Twelve the almanack makes clear.

How many years in an age?
One hundred says the sage.

How many ages in time?
No one knows the rhyme.

———

What will you give me for my pound?
Full twenty shillings round.
What will you give me for my shilling?
Twelve pence to give I'm willing.
What will you give me for my penny?
Four farthings,[5] just so many.

———

January cold desolate;
February all dripping wet;
March wind ranges;
April changes;
Birds sing in tune
　　To flowers of May,
Till sunny June
　　Brings longest day;
In scorched July
The storm-clouds fly
Lightning torn;

August bears corn,[6]
September fruit;
In rough October
Earth must disrobe her;
Stars fall and shoot
In keen November;
And night is long
And cold is strong
In bleak December.

———

What is pink? a rose is pink
By the fountain's brink.
What is red? a poppy's red
In its barley bed.
What is blue? the sky is blue
Where the clouds float thro'.
What is white? a swan is white
Sailing in the light.
What is yellow? pears are yellow,
Rich and ripe and mellow.
What is green? the grass is green,
With small flowers between.
What is violet? clouds are violet
In the summer twilight
What is orange? why, an orange,
Just an orange!

———

Mother shake the cherry-tree,
　　Susan catch a cherry;
Oh how funny that will be,
　　Let's be merry!

One for brother, one for sister,
　　Two for mother more,
Six for father, hot and tired,
　　Knocking at the door.

———

A pin has a head, but has no hair;
A clock has a face, but no mouth there;
Needles have eyes, but they cannot see;

———

5. Coins worth a quarter of a penny. This poem explains the relative value of the most common British currency before decimalization in 1971.
6. Wheat.

A fly has a trunk[7] without lock or key;
A timepiece may lose, but cannot win;
A corn-field dimples without a chin;
A hill has no leg, but has a foot;
A wine-glass a stem, but not a root;
A watch has hands, but no thumb or finger;
A boot has a tongue, but is no singer;
Rivers run, though they have no feet;
A saw has teeth, but it does not eat;
Ash-trees have keys,[8] yet never a lock;
And baby crows, without being a cock.

————————

Hopping frog, hop here and be seen,
    I'll not pelt you with stick or stone:
Your cap is laced and your coat is green;
    Good bye, we'll let each other alone.

Plodding toad, plod here and be looked at,
You the finger of scorn is crooked at:
But though you're lumpish, you're harmless too;
You won't hurt me, and I won't hurt you.

————————

Where innocent bright-eyed daisies are,
    With blades of grass between,
Each daisy stands up like a star
    Out of a sky of green.

————————

The city mouse lives in a house;—
    The garden mouse lives in a bower,
He's friendly with the frogs and toads,
    And sees the pretty plants in flower.

The city mouse eats bread and cheese;—
    The garden mouse eats what he can;
We will not grudge him seeds and stalks,
    Poor little timid furry man.

————————

What does the donkey bray about?
What does the pig grunt through his snout?
What does the goose mean by a hiss?
Oh, Nurse, if you can tell me this,
I'll give you such a kiss.

The cockatoo calls "cockatoo,"
The magpie chatters "how d' ye do?"
The jackdaw bids me "go away,"
Cuckoo cries "cuckoo" half the day:
What do the others say?

————————

Three plum buns
    To eat here at the stile
In the clover meadow,
    For we have walked a mile.

One for you, and one for me,
    And one left over:
Give it to the boy who shouts
    To scare sheep from the clover.

————————

A motherless soft lambkin
    Alone upon a hill;
No mother's fleece to shelter him
    And wrap him from the cold:—
I'll run to him and comfort him,
    I'll fetch him, that I will;
I'll care for him and feed him
    Until he's strong and bold.

————————

Dancing on the hill-tops,
    Singing in the valleys,
Laughing with the echoes,
    Merry little Alice.

Playing games with lambkins
    In the flowering valleys,
Gathering pretty posies,
    Helpful little Alice.

7. I.e., an abdomen. The wordplay rests on understanding *fly* to refer not just to an insect but to a stagecoach, whose luggage compartment (trunk) would presumably be lockable.
8. The ash tree's fruit, so named because it grows in bunches.

If her father's cottage
  Turned into a palace,
And he owned the hill-tops
  And the flowering valleys,
She'd be none the happier,
  Happy little Alice.

———

When fishes set umbrellas up
  If the rain-drops run,
Lizards will want their parasols
  To shade them from the sun.

———

The peacock has a score of eyes.
  With which he cannot see;
The cod-fish has a silent sound,[9]
  However that may be;

No dandelions tell the time,
  Although they turn to clocks;[1]
Cat's-cradle does not hold the cat.
  Nor foxglove fit the fox.

———

Pussy has a whiskered face,
Kitty has such pretty ways;
Doggie scampers when I call,
And has a heart to love us all.

———

The dog lies in his kennel,
  And Puss purrs on the rug,
And baby perches on my knee
  For me to love and hug.

Pat the dog and stroke the cat,
  Each in its degree;
And cuddle and kiss my baby,
  And baby kiss me.

———

If hope grew on a bush,
  And joy grew on a tree,
What a nosegay for the plucking
  There would be!

But oh! in windy autumn,
  When frail flowers wither,
What should we do for hope and joy,
  Fading together?

———

I planted a hand
  And there came up a palm,
I planted a heart
  And there came up balm.

Then I planted a wish,
  But there sprang a thorn,
While heaven frowned with thunder
  And earth sighed forlorn.

———

Under the ivy bush
  One sits sighing,
And under the willow tree
  One sits crying:—

Under the ivy bush
  Cease from your sighing,
But under the willow tree
  Lie down a-dying.

———

There is one that has a head without an eye,
  And there's one that has an eye without a head:
You may find the answer[2] if you try;
  And when all is said,
  Half the answer hangs upon a thread!

———

If a mouse could fly,
  Or if a crow could swim,

9. A fish's air bladder.
1. The downy seeds of dandelion flowers.

2. I.e., a needle.

1172

Or if a sprat could walk and talk,
    I'd like to be like him.

If a mouse could fly,
    He might fly away;
Or if a crow could swim,
    It might turn him grey;
Or if a sprat could walk and talk,
    What would he find to say?

————————

Sing me a song—
    What shall I sing?—
Three merry sisters
    Dancing in a ring,
Light and fleet upon their feet
    As birds upon the wing.

Tell me a tale—
    What shall I tell?—
Two mournful sisters,
    And a tolling knell,
Tolling ding and tolling dong,
    Ding dong bell.

————————

The lily has an air,
    And the snowdrop a grace,
And the sweetpea a way,
    And the heartsease a face,—
Yet there's nothing like the rose
    When she blows.[3]

————————

Margaret has a milking-pail,
    And she rises early;
Thomas has a threshing-flail,
    And he's up betimes.
Sometimes crossing through the grass
    Where the dew lies pearly,
They say "Good morrow" as they pass
    By the leafy limes.

————————

In the meadow—what in the meadow?
Bluebells, buttercups, meadowsweet,
And fairy rings for the children's feet
    In the meadow.

In the garden—what in the garden?
Jacob's-ladder and Solomon's-seal,
And Love-lies-bleeding with none to heal
    In the garden.

A frisky lamb
And a frisky child
Playing their pranks
    In a cowslip meadow:
The sky all blue
And the air all mild
And the fields all sun
    And the lanes half shadow.

Mix a pancake,
Stir a pancake,
    Pop it in the pan;
Fry the pancake,
Toss the pancake,—
    Catch it if you can.

————————

The wind has such a rainy sound
    Moaning through the town,
The sea has such a windy sound,—
    Will the ships go down?

The apples in the orchard
    Tumble from their tree.—
Oh, will the ships go down, go down,
    In the windy sea?

————————

Three little children
    On the wide wide earth
Motherless children—
    Cared for from their birth
        By tender angels.

3. Blossoms.

Three little children
    On the wide wide sea,
Motherless children—
    Safe as safe can be
        With guardian angels.

————

Fly away, fly away over the sea,
    Sun-loving swallow, for summer is done.
Come again, come again, come back to me,
    Bringing the summer and bringing the sun.

————

Minnie bakes oaten cakes,
        Minnie brews ale,
All because her Johnny's coming
        Home from sea.
And she glows like a rose,
        Who was so pale,
And "Are you sure the church clock goes?"
        Says she.

————

A white hen sitting
    On white eggs three:
Next, three speckled chickens
    As plump as plump can be.

An owl, and a hawk,
    And a bat come to see:
But chicks beneath their mother's wing
    Squat safe as safe can be.

————

Currants on a bush,
    And figs upon a stem,
And cherries on a bending bough,
    And Ned to gather them.

————

I have but one rose in the world,
    And my one rose stands a-drooping:
Oh, when my single rose is dead
    There'll be but thorns for stooping.

Rosy maiden Winifred,
With a milkpail on her head,
Tripping through the corn,
    While the dew lies on the wheat
        In the sunny morn.
Scarlet shepherd's-weatherglass
    Spreads wide open at her feet
        As they pass;
Cornflowers give their almond smell
    While she brushes by,
And a lark sings from the sky
        "All is well."

————

When the cows come home the milk is coming
Honey's made while the bees are humming;
Duck and drake on the rushy lake,
And the deer live safe in the breezy brake;
And timid, funny, brisk little bunny,
Winks his nose and sits all sunny.

————

Roses blushing red and white,
        For delight;
Honeysuckle wreaths above,
        For love;
Dim sweet-scented heliotrope,
        For hope;
Shining lilies tall and straight,
        For royal state;
Dusky pansies, let them be
        For memory;
With violets of fragrant breath,
        For death.

————

"Ding a ding,"
The sweet bells sing,
And say:
"Come, all be gay"
For a wedding day.

"Dong a dong,"
The bells sigh long,

And call:
"Weep one, weep all"
For a funeral.

———————

A ring upon her finger,
    Walks the bride,
With the bridegroom tall and handsome
    At her side.

A veil upon her forehead,
    Walks the bride,
With the bridegroom proud and merry
    At her side.

Fling flowers beneath the footsteps
    Of the bride;
Fling flowers before the bridegroom
    At her side.

———————

"Ferry me across the water,
    Do, boatman, do."
"If you've a penny in your purse
    I'll ferry you."

"I have a penny in my purse,
    And my eyes are blue;
So ferry me across the water,
    Do, boatman, do."

"Step into my ferry-boat,
    Be they black or blue,
And for the penny in your purse
    I'll ferry you."

———————

When a mounting skylark sings
    In the sunlit summer morn,
I know that heaven is up on high,
    And on earth are fields of corn.

But when a nightingale sings
    In the moonlit summer even,
I know not if earth is merely earth,
    Only that heaven is heaven.

———————

Who has seen the wind?
    Neither I nor you:
But when the leaves hang trembling
    The wind is passing thro'.

Who has seen the wind?
    Neither you nor I:
But when the trees bow down their heads
    The wind is passing by.

———————

The horses of the sea
    Rear a foaming crest,
But the horses of the land
    Serve us the best.

The horses of the land
    Munch corn and clover,
While the foaming sea-horses
    Toss and turn over.

———————

O sailor, come ashore,
    What have you brought for me?
Red coral, white coral,
    Coral from the sea

I did not dig it from the ground,
    Nor pluck it from a tree;
Feeble insects made it
    In the stormy sea.

———————

A diamond or a coal?
    A diamond, if you please:
Who cares about a clumsy coal
    Beneath the summer trees?

A diamond or a coal?
    A coal, sir, if you please:
One comes to care about the coal
    What time the waters freeze.

———————

An emerald is as green as grass;
    A ruby red as blood;
A sapphire shines as blue as heaven;
    A flint lies in the mud.

A diamond is a brilliant stone,
    To catch the world's desire;
An opal holds a fiery spark;
    But a flint holds fire.

———

Boats sail on the rivers,
    And ships sail on the seas;
But clouds that sail across the sky
    Are prettier far than these.

There are bridges on the rivers,
    As pretty as you please;
But the bow that bridges heaven,
    And overtops the trees,
And builds a road from earth to sky,
    Is prettier far than these.

———

The lily has a smooth stalk,
    Will never hurt your hand;
But the rose upon her briar
    Is lady of the land.

There's sweetness in an apple tree,
    And profit in the corn;
But lady of all beauty
    Is a rose upon a thorn.

When with moss and honey
    She tips her bending briar,
And half unfolds her glowing heart,
    She sets the world on fire.

———

Hurt no living thing:
    Ladybird,[4] nor butterfly,
Nor moth with dusty wing,
    Nor cricket chirping cheerily,
Nor grasshopper so light of leap,
    Nor dancing gnat, nor beetle fat,
Nor harmless worms that creep.

———

I caught a little ladybird
    That flies far away;
I caught a little lady wife
    That is both staid and gay.

———

All the bells were ringing
And all the birds were singing,
When Molly sat down crying
    For her broken doll:
    O you silly Moll!
Sobbing and sighing
    For a broken doll,
When all the bells are ringing,
And all the birds are singing.

———

Wee wee husband,
    Give me some money,
I have no comfits,
    And I have no honey.

Wee wee wifie,
    I have no money,
Milk, nor meat, nor bread to eat,
    Comfits, nor honey.

———

I have a little husband[5]
    And he is gone to sea,
The winds that whistle round his ship
    Fly home to me.

———

4. Ladybug.
5. After the traditional nursery verse: "I had a little husband, / No bigger than my thumb; / I put him in a pint-pot / And there I bade him drum."

CHRISTINA ROSSETTI

The dear old woman in the lane
  Is sick and sore with pains and aches,
We'll go to her this afternoon,
  And take her tea and eggs and cakes.

————

Swift and sure the swallow,
  Slow and sure the snail:
Slow and sure may miss his way,
  Swift and sure may fail.

————

"I dreamt I caught a little owl
  And the bird was blue—"

"But you may hunt for ever
And not find such an one."

"I dreamt I set a sunflower,
  And red as blood it grew—"

"But such a sunflower never
Bloomed beneath the sun."

————

What does the bee do?
  Bring home honey.
And what does Father do?
  Bring home money.
And what does Mother do?
  Lay out the money.
And what does baby do?
  Eat up the honey.

————

I have a Poll parrot,
  And Poll is my doll,
And my nurse is Polly,
  And my sister Poll.

————

A house of cards
  Is neat and small:
Shake the table,
  It must fall.

Find the Court cards
  One by one;
Raise it, roof it,—
  Now it's done:—
Shake the table!
  That's the fun.

————

The rose with such a bonny blush,
  What has the rose to blush about?
If it's the sun that makes her flush,
  What's in the sun to flush about?

————

The rose that blushes rosy red,
  She must hang her head;
The lily that blows spotless white,
  She may stand upright.

————

Oh, fair to see
Bloom-laden cherry tree,
  Arrayed in sunny white;
  An April day's delight,
Oh, fair to see!

Oh, fair to see
Fruit-laden cherry tree,
  With balls of shining red
  Decking a leafy head,
Oh, fair to see!

————

Clever little Willie wee,
  Bright eyed, blue eyed little fellow;
Merry little Margery
  With her hair all yellow.

————

A peach for brothers, one for each,
  A peach for you and a peach for me;
But the biggest, rosiest, downiest peach
  For Grandmamma with her tea.

A rose has thorns as well as honey,
I'll not have her for love or money;
An iris grows so straight and fine,
That she shall be no friend of mine;
Snowdrops like the snow would chill me;
Nightshade would caress and kill me;
Crocus like a spear would fright me;
Dragon's-mouth might bark or bite me;
Convolvulus but blooms to die;
A wind-flower suggests a sigh;
Love-lies-bleeding makes me sad;
And poppy-juice would drive me mad:—
But give me holly, bold and jolly,
Honest, prickly, shining holly;
Pluck me holly leaf and berry
For the day when I make merry.

———

Is the moon tired? she looks so pale
Within her misty veil:
She scales the sky from east to west,
And takes no rest.

Before the coming of the night
The moon shows papery white;
Before the dawning of the day
She fades away.

———

If stars dropped out of heaven,
    And if flowers took their place,
The sky would still look very fair,
    And fair earth's face.

Winged angels might fly down to us
    To pluck the stars,
But we could only long for flowers
    Beyond the cloudy bars.

———

"Goodbye in fear, goodbye in sorrow,
    Goodbye, and all in vain,
Never to meet again, my dear—"
    "Never to part again."

———

"Goodbye to-day, goodbye to-morrow,
    Goodbye till earth shall wane,
Never to meet again, my dear—"
    "Never to part again."

———

If the sun could tell us half
    That he hears and sees,
Sometimes he would make us laugh,
    Sometimes make us cry:
Think of all the birds that make
    Homes among the trees;
Think of cruel boys who take
    Birds that cannot fly.

———

If the moon came from heaven,
    Talking all the way,
What could she have to tell us,
    And what could she say?

———

"I've seen a hundred pretty things,
    And seen a hundred gay;
But only think: I peep by night
    And do not peep by day!"

———

O Lady Moon, your horns point toward the
        east:
    Shine, be increased;
O Lady Moon, your horns point toward the
        west:
    Wane, be at rest.

———

What do the stars do
    Up in the sky,
Higher than the wind can blow,
    Or the clouds can fly?

Each star in its own glory
    Circles, circles still;
As it was lit to shine and set,
    And do its Maker's will.

———

Christina Rossetti

Motherless baby and babyless mother,
Bring them together to love one another.

Crimson curtains round my mother's bed,
  Silken soft as may be;
Cool white curtains round about my bed,
  For I am but a baby.

———

Baby lies so fast asleep
  That we cannot wake her:
Will the Angels clad in white
  Fly from heaven to take her?

———

Baby lies so fast asleep
  That no pain can grieve her;
Put a snowdrop in her hand,
  Kiss her once and leave her.

———

I know a baby, such a baby,—
  Round blue eyes and cheeks of pink,
Such an elbow furrowed with dimples,
  Such a wrist where creases sink.

"Cuddle and love me, cuddle and love me"
  Crows the mouth of coral pink:
Oh, the bald head, and, oh, the sweet lips,
  And, oh, the sleepy eyes that wink!

———

Lullaby, oh, lullaby!
Flowers are closed and lambs are sleeping;
  Lullaby, oh, lullaby!
Stars are up, the moon is peeping;
  Lullaby, oh, lullaby!
While the birds are silence keeping,
  (Lullaby, oh, lullaby!)
Sleep, my baby, fall a-sleeping,
  Lullaby, oh, lullaby!

Lie a-bed,
Sleepy head,
Shut up eyes, bo-peep;
Till daybreak
Never wake:—
Baby, sleep.

1872

ROBERT LOUIS STEVENSON
1850–1894

The publication of *A Child's Garden of Verses* in 1885 marked a turning point in the history of children's poetry: it was the first work to celebrate both the imaginative play of children and children's voices. Robert Louis Stevenson even called the register in which he wrote the verses "a kind of childish treble." The sad irony is that so many of his sunny verses were composed while he lay in bed with hemorrhaging lungs, too weak to write prose. He is quoted as saying, grimly: "when I spit blood I write verses." Throughout his short life, Stevenson was painfully thin, verging sometimes on skeletal, often ill with the kinds of bronchial infections that had tormented him in earliest childhood. His verse reveals the dramatic, internal, life-and-death adventures he played out on a battlefield between delirium and consciousness—not the conventional experiences of a rough-and-tumble boyhood. As James Campbell says in a 2003 review of *The Collected Poems of Robert Louis Stevenson*, the poems "capture little memory-spots of the daily journey to the Land of Play."

The only child of solidly middle-class, Calvinist Scottish parents, Stevenson spent much of his youth confined to his sickroom in Edinburgh, looked after mainly by his much-loved nurse, Alison Cunningham. His formal schooling was intermittent, but he entered the University of Edinburgh in 1867 to study civil engineering. It soon became clear he was more interested in writing than in following his father and grandfather—famous builders of lighthouses—into the family profession. In 1871 he chose the study of law as a respectable compromise, though he never practiced; and his less-than-respectable behavior at the university (drinking, seeking out prostitutes), as well as his newly professed religious agnosticism, for a time threatened to estrange him permanently from his parents.

Even before being called to the bar, Stevenson had already started to write short stories, pieces of literary criticism, and travel essays; some of these appeared only posthumously, but by the mid-1870s he was beginning to publish. He was also beginning to make valuable contacts with figures such as Sidney Colvin and Leslie Stephen, then editor of *Cornhill* (and later the father of Virginia Woolf). As would be true through his life, illness often led him to seek climates more hospitable than Scotland's, and he spent a great deal of time in France. His early books *An Inland Voyage* (1878) and *Travels with a Donkey in the Cévennes* (1879) are outgrowths of his travels.

Stevenson's popular fame rests on three novels written in the 1880s: *Treasure Island* (1883), *Strange Case of Dr. Jekyll and Mr. Hyde* (1886), and *Kidnapped* (1886). All captured a Victorian taste for wildness, darkness, and the bizarre; and all show Stevenson rejecting the idea that fiction should attempt to mimic reality. The characters Stevenson created—Long John Silver, Dr. Jekyll, and Mr. Hyde—have become so integral a part of the public imagination that they are known even to those who have never read his books.

Treasure Island, like other classics of children's literature such as *Alice's Adventures in Wonderland* (1865) by Lewis Carroll and *The Wind in the Willows* (1908) by Kenneth Grahame, was written both out of the author's own childhood experience and out of his experience with a particular child. In Stevenson's case, the child was his stepson, Lloyd. In 1876, while in France, Stevenson had met Fanny Van de Grift Osbourne, a married American who was more than ten years his senior and had two children. It was with Lloyd that the adult Louis played with hundreds of lead soldiers. And it was with paints from Lloyd's paint box that Louis made the map that became the genesis of *Treasure Island*.

Stevenson was highly productive in the 1880s, though he was frequently ill. Many of the poems in *A Child's Garden of Verses* were created when he was at his weakest. The impetus for the volume was *Kate Greenaway's Birthday Book for Children* (1880), which Stevenson's mother showed him in 1881. The verses by Mrs. Sale Barker that accompanied the illustrations were trite, moralistic and forgettable sort. According to Janet Adam Smith, the editor of Stevenson's *Collected Poems* (1971), Stevenson declared that he didn't think "such verses would be difficult to do" and promptly wrote the first fourteen poems. Others quickly followed, and a new genre in poetry for children was created. Stevenson, self-deprecatingly, called his new collection a "ragged regiment," and its appeal to young and adult readers has been lasting: *A Child's Garden of Verses* has remained in print since its first publication in 1885.

Though most of the poems are in the lilting iambic tetrameter and pentameter characteristic of nursery verse, they rarely slip into soft sentimentality. The edges of Stevenson's nightmare battles with illness are often caught in the dark images and metrical variations. Sometimes a line comes to an abrupt, falling-off-the-cliff metrical halt, as in: "All the wicked shadows coming tramp, tramp, tramp, / With the black night overhead," from the "Shadow March" in "North West Passage." Others delight in inner and outer voyages. Thus, in "Pirate Story," Stevenson imagines three children "afloat in the meadow by the swing," who then wonder where, "steering by a star," their adventure will take them: "Shall it be to Africa, a-steering of the boat, / To Providence, or Babylon, or off to Malabar?" Steeped as they are in the glory of the British Empire, many of Stevenson's poems appear to twenty-first-century readers as overly patronizing, masculine, and even racist. That's why it's important to remember Stevenson and his poems in their historical context.

By the late 1880s, Stevenson was financially secure (due to his own success and his inheritance after his father's death in 1886) and so able to indulge both his passion for adventure and his physical need for a tropical climate. A publisher's commission to travel to the South Seas enabled him to cruise the islands for months in the late 1880s with his extended family (which now included his mother). But Stevenson's health remained fragile during this period, and he realized he'd not be able to return to Scotland. By early 1890, Stevenson was able to buy a huge property on Samoa, an estate called Vailima, on the island of Upolu. He grew stronger there, and the family was happy too, often going "native" in bare feet and comfortable clothes. Stevenson himself often wore loose white trousers, a white open shirt, and a red sash to complete his costume. On the day Stevenson died, he'd had a good writing day. He was preparing for a relaxing evening, just helping Fanny prepare dinner, when he realized something had happened. It was a stroke. He died a few hours later.

A CHILD'S GARDEN OF VERSES

To Alison Cunningham[1]

From Her Boy

For the long nights you lay awake
And watched for my unworthy sake:
For your most comfortable hand
That led me through the uneven land:
For all the story-books you read:
For all the pains you comforted:

For all you pitied, all you bore,
In sad and happy days of yore:—
My second Mother, my first Wife,

The angel of my infant life—
From the sick child, now well and old,
Take, nurse, the little book you hold!

And grant it, Heaven, that all who read
May find as dear a nurse at need,
And every child who lists[2] my rhyme,
In the bright, fireside, nursery clime,
May hear it in as kind a voice
As made my childish days rejoice!

R. L. S.

1. Alison Cunningham (1822–1913), or "Cummy," was Stevenson's nurse throughout his childhood.

2. Listens to.

Bed in Summer

In winter I get up at night
And dress by yellow candle-light.
In summer, quite the other way,
I have to go to bed by day.

I have to go to bed and see
The birds still hopping on the tree,
Or hear the grown-up people's feet
Still going past me in the street.

And does it not seem hard to you,
When all the sky is clear and blue,
And I should like so much to play,
To have to go to bed by day?

A Thought

It is very nice to think
The world is full of meat and drink,
With little children saying grace
In every Christian kind of place.

At the Seaside

When I was down beside the sea
A wooden spade they gave to me
    To dig the sandy shore.

My holes were empty like a cup,
In every hole the sea came up,
    Till it could come no more.

Young Night Thought

All night long and every night,
When my mamma puts out the light,
I see the people marching by,
As plain as day, before my eye.

Armies and emperors and kings,
All carrying different kinds of things,
And marching in so grand a way,
You never saw the like by day.

So fine a show was never seen,
At the great circus on the green;
For every kind of beast and man
Is marching in that caravan.

At first they move a little slow,
But still the faster on they go,
And still beside them close I keep
Until we reach the town of Sleep.

Whole Duty of Children

A child should always say what's true
And speak when he is spoken to,
And behave mannerly at table:
At least as far as he is able.

Rain

The rain is raining all around,
    It falls on field and tree,
It rains on the umbrellas here,
    And on the ships at sea.

Pirate Story

Three of us afloat in the meadow by the swing,
    Three of us aboard in the basket on the lea.
Winds are in the air, they are blowing in the spring,
    And waves are on the meadow like the waves
        there are at sea.

Where shall we adventure to-day that we're
        afloat,
    Wary of the weather and steering by a star?
Shall it be to Africa, a-steering of the boat,
    To Providence, or Babylon, or off to
        Malabar?[3]

ROBERT LOUIS STEVENSON

3. A region on the southwest coast of India.

Hi! but here's a squadron a-rowing on the sea—
   Cattle on the meadow a-charging with a roar!
Quick, and we'll escape them, they're as mad as
      they can be,
   The wicket is the harbour and the garden is
      the shore.

Foreign Lands

Up into the cherry tree
Who should climb but little me?
I held the trunk with both my hands
And looked abroad on foreign lands.

I saw the next door garden lie,
Adorned with flowers before my eye,
And many pleasant places more
That I had never seen before.

I saw the dimpling river pass
And be the sky's blue looking-glass;
The dusty roads go up and down
With people tramping in to town.

If I could find a higher tree
Farther and farther I should see,
To where the grown-up river slips
Into the sea among the ships,

To where the roads on either hand
Lead onward into fairy land,
Where all the children dine at five,
And all the playthings come alive.

Windy Nights

Whenever the moon and stars are set,
   Whenever the wind is high,
All night long in the dark and wet,
   A man goes riding by.
Late in the night when the fires are out,
Why does he gallop and gallop about?

Whenever the trees are crying aloud,
   And ships are tossed at sea,
By, on the highway, low and loud,
   By at the gallop goes he;
By at the gallop he goes, and then
By he comes back at the gallop again.

Travels

I should like to rise and go
Where the golden apples[4] grow;—
Where below another sky
Parrot islands anchored lie,
And, watched by cockatoos and goats,
Lonely Crusoes[5] building boats;—
Where in sunshine reaching out
Eastern cities, miles about,
Are with mosque and minaret
Among sandy gardens set,
And the rich goods from near and far
Hang for sale in the bazaar;—
Where the Great Wall round China goes,
And on one side the desert blows,
And with bell and voice and drum,
Cities on the other hum;—
Where are forests, hot as fire,
Wide as England, tall as a spire,
Full of apes and cocoa-nuts
And the negro hunters' huts;—
Where the knotty crocodile
Lies and blinks in the Nile,
And the red flamingo flies
Hunting fish before his eyes;—
Where in jungles near and far,
Man-devouring tigers are,
Lying close and giving ear
Lest the hunt be drawing near,
Or a comer-by be seen
Swinging in a palanquin;—
Where among the desert sands
Some deserted city stands,
All its children, sweep[6] and prince
Grown to manhood ages since,

---

4. In Greek mythology, the garden of the Hesperides (located
in the far west).
5. I.e., shipwrecked sailors, like the hero of Daniel Defoe's
Robinson Crusoe (1719).
6. Chimney sweep.

Not a foot in street or house,
Not a stir of child or mouse,
And when kindly falls the night,
In all the town no spark of light.
There I'll come when I'm a man
With a camel caravan;
Light a fire in the gloom
Of some dusty dining-room;
See the pictures on the walls,
Heroes, fights and festivals;
And in a corner find the toys
Of the old Egyptian boys.

Singing

Of speckled eggs the birdie sings
    And nests among the trees;
The sailor sings of ropes and things
    In ships upon the seas.

The children sing in far Japan,
    The children sing in Spain;
The organ with the organ man
    Is singing in the rain.

Looking Forward

When I am grown to man's estate
I shall be very proud and great,
And tell the other girls and boys
Not to meddle with my toys.

A Good Play

We built a ship upon the stairs
All made of the back-bedroom chairs,
And filled it full of sofa pillows
To go a-sailing on the billows.

We took a saw and several nails,
And water in the nursery pails;
And Tom said, 'Let us also take
An apple and a slice of cake;'—
Which was enough for Tom and me
To go a-sailing on, till tea.

We sailed along for days and days,
And had the very best of plays;
But Tom fell out and hurt his knee,
So there was no one left but me.

Where Go the Boats?

Dark brown is the river,
    Golden is the sand.
It flows along for ever,
    With trees on either hand.

Green leaves a-floating,
    Castles of the foam,
Boats of mine a-boating—
    Where will all come home?

On goes the river
    And out past the mill,
Away down the valley,
    Away down the hill.

Away down the river,
    A hundred miles or more,
Other little children
    Shall bring my boats ashore.

Auntie's Skirts

Whenever Auntie moves around
Her dresses make a curious sound
They trail behind her up the floor,
And trundle after through the door.

Robert Louis Stevenson

The LAND OF COUNTER-PANE

When I was sick and lay a-bed,
I had two pillows at my head,
And all my toys beside me lay
To keep me happy all the day.

And sometimes for an hour or so
I watched my leaden soldiers go,
With different uniforms and drills,
Among the bed-clothes, through the hills;

And sometimes sent my ships in fleets
All up and down among the sheets;
Or brought my trees and houses out,
And planted cities all about.

I was the giant great and still
That sits upon the pillow-hill,
And sees before him, dale and plain,
The pleasant land of counterpane.

The Island of Nod

From breakfast on through all the day
At home among my friends I stay;
But every night I go abroad
Afar into the land of Nod.

All by myself I have to go,
With none to tell me what to do—
All alone beside the streams
And up the mountain-sides of dreams.

The strangest things are there for me,
Both things to eat and things to see,
And many frightening sights abroad
Till morning in the land of Nod.

Try as I like to find the way,
I never can get back by day,
Nor can remember plain and clear
The curious music that I hear.

My Shadow

I have a little shadow that goes in and out with
    me,
And what can be the use of him is more than I
    can see.
He is very, very like me from the heels up to the
    head;
And I see him jump before me, when I jump
    into my bed.

The funniest thing about him is the way he likes
    to grow—
Not at all like proper children, which is always
    very slow;
For he sometimes shoots up taller, like an india-
    rubber ball,
And he sometimes gets so little that there's
    none of him at all.

He hasn't got a notion of how children ought to
    play,
And can only make a fool of me in every sort of
    way.
He stays so close beside me, he's a coward you
    can see;
I'd think shame to stick to nursie as that
    shadow sticks to me!

One morning, very early, before the sun was up,
I rose and found the shining dew on every
    buttercup;
But my lazy little shadow, like an arrant sleepy-
    head,
Had stayed at home behind me and was fast
    asleep in bed.

System

Every night my prayers I say,
And get my dinner every day;
And every day that I've been good,
I get an orange after food.

The child that is not clean and neat,
With lots of toys and things to eat,
He is a naughty child, I'm sure—
Or else his dear papa is poor.

A Good Boy

I woke before the morning, I was happy all the
    day,
I never said an ugly word, but smiled and stuck
    to play.

Robert Louis Stevenson

And now at last the sun is going down behind
    the wood,
And I am very happy, for I know that I've been
    good.

My bed is waiting cool and fresh, with linen
    smooth and fair,
And I must off to sleepsin-by, and not forget my
    prayer.

I know that, till to-morrow I shall see the sun
    arise,
No ugly dream shall fright my mind, no ugly
    sight my eyes,

But slumber hold me tightly till I waken in the
    dawn,
And hear the thrushes singing in the lilacs
    round the lawn.

Escape at Bedtime

The lights from the parlour and kitchen shone out
    Through the blinds and the windows and bars;
And high overhead and all moving about,
    There were thousands of millions of stars.
There ne'er were such thousands of leaves on a
    tree,
    Nor of people in church or the Park,
As the crowds of the stars that looked down
    upon me,
    And that glittered and winked in the dark.

The Dog, and the Plough, and the Hunter,[7] and
    all,
    And the star of the sailor,[8] and Mars,
These shone in the sky, and the pail by the wall,
    Would be half full of water and stars.
They saw me at last, and they chased me with
    cries,
    And they soon had me packed into bed;
But the glory kept shining and bright in my eyes,
    And the stars going round in my head.

7. Constellations: Canis Major, Ursa Major, and Orion.
8. The North Star, or Polaris, by which sailors in the Northern Hemisphere navigate.

Marching Song

Bring the comb and play upon it!
    Marching, here we come!
Willie cocks his highland bonnet,
    Johnnie beats the drum.

Mary Jane commands the party,
    Peter leads the rear;
Fleet in time, alert and hearty,
    Each a Grenadier![9]

All in the most martial manner
    Marching double-quick;
While the napkin like a banner
    Waves upon the stick!

Here's enough of fame and pillage,
    Great commander Jane!
Now that we've been round the village,
    Let's go home again.

The Cow

The friendly cow all red and white,
    I love with all my heart:
She gives me cream with all her might,
    To eat with apple-tart.

She wanders lowing here and there,
    And yet she cannot stray,
All in the pleasant open air,
    The pleasant light of day;

And blown by all the winds that pass
    And wet with all the showers,
She walks among the meadow grass
    And eats the meadow flowers.

Happy Thought

The world is so full of a number of things.
I'm sure we should all be as happy as kings.

9. I.e., a member of an elite British regiment.

The Wind

I saw you toss the kites on high
And blow the birds about the sky;
And all around I heard you pass,
Like ladies' skirts across the grass—
    O wind, a-blowing all day long,
    O wind, that sings so loud a song!

I saw the different things you did,
But always you yourself you hid.
I felt you push, I heard you call,
I could not see yourself at all—
    O wind, a-blowing all day long,
    O wind, that sings so loud a song!

O you that are so strong and cold,
O blower, are you young or old?
Are you a beast of field and tree,
Or just a stronger child than me?
    O wind, a-blowing all day long,
    O wind, that sings so loud a *song!*

Keepsake Mill

Over the borders, a sin without pardon,
    Breaking the branches and crawling below,
Out through the breach in the wall of the
    garden,
    Down by the banks of the river, we go.

Here is the mill with the humming of thunder,
    Here is the weir with the wonder of foam,
Here is the sluice with the race running under—
    Marvellous places, though handy to home!

Sounds of the village grow stiller and stiller,
    Stiller the note of the birds on the hill;
Dusty and dim are the eyes of the miller,
    Deaf are his ears with the moil of the mill.

Years may go by, and the wheel in the river
    Wheel as it wheels for us, children, to-day,
Wheel and keep roaring and foaming for ever
    Long after all of the boys are away.

Home from the Indies and home from the
       ocean,
     Heroes and soldiers we all shall come home;
Still we shall find the old mill wheel in motion,
     Turning and churning that river to foam.

You with the bean that I gave when we
       quarrelled,
     I with your marble of Saturday last,
Honoured and old and all gaily apparelled,
     Here we shall meet and remember the past.

Good and Bad Children

Children, you are very little,
And your bones are very brittle;
If you would grow great and stately,
You must try to walk sedately.

You must still be bright and quiet,
And content with simple diet;
And remain, through all bewild'ring,
Innocent and honest children.

Happy hearts and happy faces,
Happy play in grassy places—
That was how, in ancient ages,
Children grew to kings and sages.

But the unkind and the unruly,
And the sort who eat unduly,
They must never hope for glory—
Theirs is quite a different story!

Cruel children, crying babies,
All grow up as geese and gabies,[1]
Hated, as their age increases,
By their nephews and their nieces.

1. Simpletons.

Foreign Children

Little Indian, Sioux or Crow,
     Little frosty Eskimo,
     Little Turk or Japanee,
O! don't you wish that you were me?

You have seen the scarlet trees
And the lions over seas;
You have eaten ostrich eggs,
And turned the turtles off their legs.

Such a life is very fine,
But it's not so nice as mine:
You must often, as you trod,
Have wearied *not* to be abroad.

You have curious things to eat,
I am fed on proper meat;
You must dwell beyond the foam,
But I am safe and live at home.

Little Indian, Sioux or Crow,
     Little frosty Eskimo,
     Little Turk or Japanee,
O! don't you wish that you were me?

The Sun's Travels

The sun is not a-bed, when I
At night upon my pillow lie;
Still round the earth his way he takes,
And morning after morning makes.

While here at home, in shining day,
We round the sunny garden play,

Each little Indian sleepy-head
Is being kissed and put to bed.

And when at eve I rise from tea,
Day dawns beyond the Atlantic Sea
And all the children in the West
Are getting up and being dressed.

The Lamplighter

My tea is nearly ready and the sun has left the
    sky;
It's time to take the window to see Leerie going
    by;
For every night at tea-time and before you take
    your seat,
With lantern and with ladder he comes posting[2]
    up the street.

Now Tom would be a driver and Maria go to
    sea,
And my papa's a banker and as rich as he can
    be;
But I, when I am stronger and can choose what
    I'm to do,
O Leerie, I'll go round at night and light the
    lamps[3] with you!

For we are very lucky, with a lamp before the
    door,
And Leerie stops to light it as he lights so many
    more;
And O! before you hurry by with ladder and
    with light,
O Leerie, see a little child and nod to him to-
    night!

My Bed Is a Boat

My bed is like a little boat;
    Nurse helps me in when I embark;
She girds me in my sailor's coat
    And starts me in the dark.

2. Hurrying.
3. Gas streetlamps.

At night, I go on board and say
    Good-night to all my friends on shore;
I shut my eyes and sail away
    And see and hear no more.

And sometimes things to bed I take,
    As prudent sailors have to do:
Perhaps a slice of wedding-cake,
    Perhaps a toy or two.

All night across the dark we steer:
    But when the day returns at last,
Safe in my room, beside the pier,
    I find my vessel fast.

The Swing

How do you like to go up in a swing,
    Up in the air so blue?
Oh, I do think it the pleasantest thing
    Ever a child can do!

Up in the air and over the wall,
    Till I can see so wide,
Rivers and trees and cattle and all
    Over the countryside—

Till I look down on the garden green,
    Down on the roof so brown—
Up in the air I go flying again,
    Up in the air and down!

The Moon

The moon has a face like the clock in the hall;
She shines on thieves on the garden wall,
On streets and fields and harbour quays,
And birdies asleep in the forks of the trees.

The squalling cat and the squeaking mouse,
The howling dog by the door of the house,
The bat that lies in bed at noon,
All love to be out by the light of the moon.

But all of the things that belong to the day
Cuddle to sleep to be out of her way;
And flowers and children close their eyes
Till up in the morning the sun shall arise.

Time to Rise

A birdie with a yellow bill
Hopped upon the window sill,
Cocked his shining eye and said:
'Ain't you 'shamed, you sleepy-head?'

Fairy Bread

Come up here, O dusty feet!
   Here is fairy bread to eat.
Here in my retiring room,
   Children you may dine
On the golden smell of broom
   And the shade of pine;
And when you have eaten well,
Fairy stories hear and tell.

Looking-Glass River

Smooth it slides upon its travel,
   Here a wimple,[4] there a gleam—
      O the clean gravel!
      O the smooth stream!

Sailing blossoms, silver fishes,
   Paven pools as clear as air—
      How a child wishes
      To live down there!

We can see our coloured faces
   Floating on the shaken pool
      Down in cool places,
      Dim and very cool;

Till a wind or water wrinkle,
   Dipping marten, plumping trout,
      Spreads in a twinkle
      And blots all out.

4. Curve.

See the rings pursue each other;
   All below grows black as night,
      Just as if mother
      Had blown out the light!

Patience, children, just a minute—
   See the spreading circles die;
      The stream and all in it
      Will clear by-and-by.

From a Railway Carriage

Faster than fairies, faster than witches,
Bridges and houses, hedges and ditches;
And charging along like troops in a battle,
All through the meadows the horses and cattle:
All of the sights of the hill and the plain
Fly as thick as driving rain;
And ever again, in the wink of an eye,
Painted stations whistle by.

Here is a child who clambers and scrambles,
All by himself and gathering brambles;
Here is a tramp who stands and gazes;
And there is the green for stringing the daisies!

Here is a cart run away in the road
Lumping along with man and load;
And here is a mill and there is a river:
Each a glimpse and gone for ever!

Winter-Time

Late lies the wintry sun a-bed,
A frosty, fiery sleepy-head;
Blinks but an hour or two; and then,
A blood-red orange, sets again.

Before the stars have left the skies,
At morning in the dark I rise;
And shivering in my nakedness,
By the cold candle, bathe and dress.

Close by the jolly fire I sit
To warm my frozen bones a bit;

Or, with a reindeer-sled, explore
The colder countries round the door.

When to go out, my nurse doth wrap
Me in my comforter and cap:
The cold wind burns my face, and blows
Its frosty pepper up my nose.

Black are my steps on silver sod;
Thick blows my frosty breath abroad;
And tree and house, and hill and lake,
Are frosted like a wedding-cake.

The Hayloft

Through all the pleasant meadow-side
    The grass grew shoulder-high,
Till the shining scythes went far and wide
    And cut it down to dry.

These green and sweetly smelling crops
    They led in waggons home;
And they piled them here in mountain tops
    For mountaineers to roam.

Here is Mount Clear, Mount Rusty-Nail,
    Mount Eagle and Mount High;—
The mice that in these mountains dwell,
    No happier are than I!

O what a joy to clamber there,
    O what a place for play,
With the sweet, the dim, the *dusty air*,
    The happy hills of hay.

Farewell to the Farm

The coach is at the door at last;
The eager children, mounting fast
And kissing hands, in chorus sing:
Good-bye, good-bye, to everything!

To house and garden, field and lawn,
The meadow-gates we swang upon,
To pump and stable, tree and swing,
Good-bye, good-bye, to everything!

And fare you well for evermore,
O ladder at the hayloft door,
O hayloft, where the cobwebs cling,
Good-bye, good-bye, to everything!

Crack goes the whip, and off we go;
The trees and houses smaller grow;
Last, round the woody turn we swing:
Good-bye, good-bye, to everything!

North-West Passage

1. *Good Night*

When the bright lamp is carried in,
The sunless hours again begin;
O'er all without, in field and lane,
The haunted night returns again.

Now we behold the embers flee
About the firelit hearth; and see
Our faces painted as we pass,
Like pictures, on the window-glass.

Must we to bed, indeed? Well then.
Let us arise and go like men,
And face with an undaunted tread
The long, black passage up to bed.

Farewell, O brother, sister, sire!
O pleasant party round the fire?
The songs you sing, the tales you tell,
Till far to-morrow, fare ye well!

2. *Shadow March*

All round the house is the jet-black night:
    It stares through the window-pane;
It crawls in the corners, hiding from the light,
    And it moves with the moving flame.

Now my little heart goes a-beating like a drum,
    With the breath of the Bogie[5] in my hair;
And all round the candle the crooked shadows
    come
    And go marching along up the stair.

5. I.e., a bogey, an object of terror.

The shadow of the balusters, the shadow of the
lamp,
  The shadow of the child that goes to bed—
All the wicked shadows coming, tramp, tramp,
tramp,
  With the black night overhead.

3. *In Port*

Last, to the chamber where I lie
My fearful footsteps patter nigh,
And come from out the cold and gloom
Into my warm and cheerful room.

There, safe arrived, we turn about
To keep the coming shadows out,
And close the happy door at last
On all the perils that we past.

Then, when mamma goes by to bed,
She shall come in with tip-toe tread,
And see me lying warm and fast
And in the Land of Nod at last.

The Child Alone

The Unseen Playmate

When children are playing alone on the green,
In comes the playmate that never was seen,
When children are happy and lonely and good,
The Friend of the Children comes out of the
wood.

Nobody heard him and nobody saw,
His is a picture you never could draw,
But he's sure to be present, abroad or at home,
When children are happy and playing alone.

He lies in the laurels, he runs on the grass,
He sings when you tinkle the musical glass;
Whene'er you are happy and cannot tell why
The Friend of the Children is sure to be by!

He loves to be little, he hates to be big,
'T is he that inhabits the caves that you dig;

ROBERT LOUIS STEVENSON

1192

'T is he when you play with your soldiers of tin
That sides with the Frenchmen[6] and never can
win.

'T is he, when at night you go off to your bed,
Bids you go to your sleep and not trouble your
head;
For wherever they're lying, in cupboard or shelf,
'T is he will take care of your playthings himself!

My Ship and I

O it's I that am the captain of a tidy little ship,
  Of a ship that goes a-sailing on the pond;
And my ship it keeps a-turning all around and
  all about;
But when I'm a little older, I shall find the
  secret out
  How to send my vessel sailing on beyond.

For I mean to grow as little as the dolly at the
  helm,
  And the dolly I intend to come alive;
And with him beside to help me, it's a-sailing I
  shall go,
It's a-sailing on the water, when the jolly breezes
  blow
  And the vessel goes a divie-divie-dive.

O it's then you'll see me sailing through the
  rushes and the reeds,
  And you'll hear the water singing at the prow;
For beside the dolly sailor, I'm to voyage and
  explore,
To land upon the island where no dolly was
  before,
  And to fire the penny cannon in the bow.

My Kingdom

Down by a shining water well
I found a very little dell,
  No higher than my head.
The heather and the gorse about

6. I.e., against the British. Great Britain and France were
repeatedly at war in the century before Stevenson's birth.

In summer bloom were coming out,
    Some yellow and some red.

I called the little pool a sea;
The little hills were big to me;
    For I am very small.
I made a boat, I made a town,
I searched the caverns up and down,
    And named them one and all.

And all about was mine, I said,
The little sparrows overhead,
    The little minnows too.
This was the world and I was king;
For me the bees came by to sing,
    For me the swallows flew.

I played, there were no deeper seas,
Nor any wider plains than these,
    Nor other kings than me.
At last I heard my mother call
Out from the house at evenfall,
    To call me home to tea.

And I must rise and leave my dell,
And leave my dimpled water well,
    And leave my heather blooms.
Alas! and as my home I neared,
How very big my nurse appeared,
    How great and cool the rooms!

PICTURE BOOKS
IN WINTER

Summer fading, winter comes—
Frosty mornings, tingling thumbs,
Window robins, winter rooks,[7]
And the picture story-books.

Water now is turned to stone
Nurse and I can walk upon;
Still we find the flowing brooks
In the picture story-books.

All the pretty things put by,
Wait upon the children's eye,
Sheep and shepherds, trees and crooks[8]
In the picture story-books.

We may see how all things are,
Seas and cities, near and far,
And the flying fairies' looks,
In the picture story-books.

How am I to sing your praise,
Happy chimney-corner days,
Sitting safe in nursery nooks,
Reading picture story-books?

My Treasures

These nuts, that I keep in the back of the nest
Where all my lead soldiers are lying at rest,
Were gathered in autumn by nursie and me
In a wood with a well by the side of the sea.

This whistle was made (and how clearly it
    sounds!)
By the side of a field at the end of the grounds.
Of a branch of a plane,[9] with a knife of my
    own—
It was nursie who made it, and nursie alone!

The stone, with the white and the yellow and
    grey,
We discovered I cannot tell *how* far away;
And I carried it back although weary and cold,
For though father denies it, I'm sure it is gold.

But of all of my treasures the last is the king,
For there's very few children possess such a
    thing;
And that is a chisel, both handle and blade,
Which a man who was really a carpenter made.

7. Crows.

8. I.e., shepherd's crooks.
9. I.e., a plane tree, or sycamore.

Block City

What are you able to build with your blocks?
Castles and palaces, temples and docks.
Rain may keep raining, and others go roam,
But I can be happy and building at home.

Let the sofa be mountains, the carpet be sea,
There I'll establish a city for me:
A kirk and a mill and a palace beside,
And a harbour as well where my vessels may
        ride.

Great is the palace with pillar and wall,
A sort of a tower on the top of it all,
And steps coming down in an orderly way
To where my toy vessels lie safe in the bay.

This one is sailing and that one is moored:
Hark to the song of the sailors on board!
And see on the steps of my palace, the kings
Coming and going with presents and things!

Now I have done with it, down let it go!
All in a moment the town is laid low.
Block upon block lying scattered and free,
What is there left of my town by the sea?

Yet as I saw it, I see it again,
The kirk and the palace, the ships and the men,
And as long as I live and where'er I may be,
I'll always remember my town by the sea.

The Land of Story-Books

At evening, when the lamp is lit,
Around the fire my parents sit;
They sit at home and talk and sing,
And do not play at anything.

Now, with my little gun, I crawl
All in the dark along the wall,
And follow round the forest track
Away behind the sofa back.

There, in the night, where none can spy,
All in my hunter's camp I lie,
And play at books that I have read
Till it is time to go to bed.

These are the hills, these are the woods,
These are my starry solitudes;
And there the river by whose brink
The roaring lions come to drink.

I see the others far away
As if in firelit camp they lay,
And I, like to an Indian scout,
Around their party prowled about.

So, when my nurse comes in for me,
Home I return across the sea,
And go to bed with backward looks
At my dear land of Story-books.

Armies in the Fire

The lamps now glitter down the street;
Faintly sound the falling feet;
And the blue even slowly falls
About the garden trees and walls.

Now in the falling of the gloom
The red fire paints the empty room:
And warmly on the roof it looks,
And flickers on the backs of books.

Armies march by tower and spire
Of cities blazing, in the fire;
Till as I gaze with staring eyes,
The armies fade, the lustre dies.

Then once again the glow returns;
Again the phantom city burns;
And down the red-hot valley, lo!
The phantom armies marching go!

Blinking embers, tell me true,
Where are those armies marching to,
And what the burning city is
That crumbles in your furnaces!

ROBERT LOUIS STEVENSON

The Little Land

When at home alone I sit
And am very tired of it,
I have just to shut my eyes
To go sailing through the skies—
To go sailing far away
To the pleasant Land of Play;
To the fairy land afar
Where the little people are;
Where the clover-tops are trees,
And the rain-pools are the seas,
And the leaves like little ships
Sail about on tiny trips;
And above the daisy tree
    Through the grasses,
High o'erhead the Bumble Bee
    Hums and passes.

In that forest to and fro
I can wander, I can go;
See the spider and the fly,
And the ants go marching by
Carrying parcels with their feet
Down the green and grassy street.
I can in the sorrel sit
Where the ladybird[1] alit.
I can climb the jointed grass;
    And on high
See the greater swallows pass
    In the sky,
And the round sun rolling by
Heeding no such things as I.

Through that forest I can pass
Till, as in a looking glass,
Humming fly and daisy tree
And my tiny self I see,
Painted very clear and neat
On the rain-pool at my feet.
Should a leaflet come to land
Drifting near to where I stand,
Straight I'll board that tiny boat
Round the rain-pool sea to float.

Little thoughtful creatures sit
On the grassy coasts of it;
Little things with lovely eyes
See me sailing with surprise.
Some are clad in armour green—
(These have sure to battle been!)—
Some are pied with ev'ry hue,
Black and crimson, gold and blue;
Some have wings and swift are gone;—
But they all look kindly on.

When my eyes I once again
Open, and see all things plain:
High bare walls, great bare floor;
Great big knobs on drawer and door;
Great big people perched on chairs,
Stitching tucks and mending tears,
Each a hill that I could climb,
And talking nonsense all the time—
    O dear me,
    That I could be
A sailor on the rain-pool sea,
A climber in the clover-tree,
And just come back, a sleepy head,
Late at night to go to bed.

Garden Days

Night and Day

When the golden day is done,
    Through the closing portal,
Child and garden, flower and sun,
    Vanish all things mortal.

As the blinding shadows fall,
    As the rays diminish,
Under the evening's cloak, they all
    Roll away and vanish.

1. Ladybug.

Garden darkened, daisy shut,
  Child in bed, they slumber—
Glow-worm in the highway rut,
  Mice among the lumber.

In the darkness houses shine,
  Parents move with candles;
Till on all, the night divine
  Turns the bedroom handles.

Till at last the day begins
  In the east a-breaking,
In the hedges and the whins
  Sleeping birds a-waking.

In the darkness shapes of things,
  Houses, trees, and hedges
Clearer grow; and sparrow's wings
  Beat on window ledges.

These shall wake the yawning maid;
  She the door shall open—
Finding dew on garden glade
  And the morning broken.

There my garden grows again
  Green and rosy painted,
As at eve behind the pane
  From my eyes it fainted.

Just as it was shut away,
  Toy-like, in the even,
Here I see it glow with day
  Under glowing heaven.

Every path and every plot,
  Every bush of roses,
Every blue forget-me-not
  Where the dew reposes,

Robert Louis Stevenson

1196

"Up!" they cry, "the day is come
  On the smiling valleys:
We have beat the morning drum;
  Playmate, join your allies!"

Nest Eggs

Birds all the sunny day
  Flutter and quarrel
Here in the arbour-like
  Tent of the laurel.

Here in the fork
  The brown nest is seated;
Four little blue eggs
  The mother keeps heated.

While we stand watching her,
  Staring like gabies,
Safe in each egg are the
  Bird's little babies.

Soon the frail eggs they shall
  Chip, and upspringing
Make all the April woods
  Merry with singing.

Younger than we are,
  O children, and frailer,
Soon in blue air they'll be,
  Singer and sailor.

We, so much older,
  Taller and stronger,
We shall look down on the
  Birdies no longer.

They shall go flying
  With musical speeches
High overhead in the
  Tops of the beeches.

In spite of our wisdom
  And sensible talking,
We on our feet must go
  Plodding and walking.

The Flowers

All the names I know from nurse:
Gardener's garters, Shepherd's purse;
Bachelor's buttons, Lady's smock,
And the Lady Hollyhock.

Fairy places, fairy things,
Fairy woods where the wild bee wings,
Tiny trees for tiny dames—
These must all be fairy names!

Tiny woods below whose boughs
Shady fairies weave a house;
Tiny tree tops, rose or thyme,
Where the braver fairies climb!

Fair are grown-up people's trees,
But the fairest woods are these;
Where, if I were not so tall,
I should live for good and all.

Summer Sun

Great is the sun, and wide he goes
Through empty heaven without repose;
And in the blue and glowing days
More thick than rain he showers his rays.

Though closer still the blinds we pull
To keep the shady parlour cool,
Yet he will find a chink or two
To slip his golden fingers through.

The dusty attic spider-clad
He, through the keyhole, maketh glad;
And through the broken edge of tiles,
Into the laddered hayloft smiles.

Meantime his golden face around
He bares to all the garden ground,
And sheds a warm and glittering look
Among the ivy's inmost nook.

Above the hills, along the blue,
Round the bright air with footing true,
To please the child, to paint the rose,
The gardener of the World, he goes.

The Dumb Soldier

When the grass was closely mown,
Walking on the lawn alone,
In the turf a hole I found
And hid a soldier underground.

Spring and daisies came apace;
Grasses hide my hiding place;
Grasses run like a green sea
O'er the lawn up to my knee.

Under grass alone he lies,
Looking up with leaden eyes,
Scarlet coat and pointed gun,
To the stars and to the sun.

When the grass is ripe like grain,
When the scythe is stoned[2] again,
When the lawn is shaven clear,
Then my hole shall reappear.

I shall find him, never fear,
I shall find my grenadier;
But for all that's gone and come,
I shall find my soldier dumb.

He has lived, a little thing,
In the grassy woods of spring;
Done, if he could tell me true,
Just as I should like to do.

He has seen the starry hours
And the springing of the flowers;
And the fairy things that pass
In the forests of the grass.

In the silence he has heard
Talking bee and ladybird,
And the butterfly has flown
O'er him as he lay alone.

Not a word will he disclose,
Not a word of all he knows.
I must lay him on the shelf,
And make up the tale myself.

2. Sharpened on a whetstone.

1197

Autumn Fires

In the other gardens
    And all up the vale,
From the autumn bonfires
    See the smoke trail!

Pleasant summer over
    And all the summer flowers,
The red fire blazes,
    The grey smoke towers.

Sing a song of seasons!
    Something bright in all!
Flowers in the summer,
    Fires in the fall!

The Gardener

The gardener does not love to talk,
He makes me keep the gravel walk;
And when he puts his tools away,
He locks the door and takes the key.

Away behind the currant row
Where no one else but cook may go,
Far in the plots, I see him dig,
Old and serious, brown and big.

He digs the flowers, green, red and blue,
Nor wishes to be spoken to.
He digs the flowers and cuts the hay,
And never seems to want to play.

Silly gardener! summer goes,
And winter comes with pinching toes,
When in the garden bare and brown
You must lay your barrow down.

Well now, and while the summer stays
To profit by these garden days,
O how much wiser you would be
To play at Indian wars with me!

ROBERT LOUIS STEVENSON

1198

Historical Associations

Dear Uncle Jim, this garden ground
That now you smoke your pipe around,
Has seen immortal actions done
And valiant battles lost and won.

Here we had best on tip-toe tread,
While I for safety march ahead,
For this is that enchanted ground
Where all who loiter slumber sound.

Here is the sea, here is the sand,
Here is simple Shepherd's Land,
Here are the fairy hollyhocks,
And there are Ali Baba's rocks.[3]

But yonder, see! apart and high,
Frozen Siberia lies; where I,
With Robert Bruce and William Tell,[4]
Was bound by an enchanter's spell.

There, then, awhile in chains we lay,
In wintry dungeons, far from day;
But ris'n at length, with might and main,
Our iron fetters burst in twain.

Then all the horns were blown in town;
And to the ramparts clanging down,
All the giants leaped to horse
And charged behind us through the gorse.

On we rode, the others and I,
Over the mountains blue, and by
The Silver River, the sounding sea,
And the robber woods of Tartary.[5]

A thousand miles we galloped fast,
And down the witches' lane we passed,

---

3. An allusion to the tale "Ali Baba and the Forty Thieves," in *The Arabian Nights' Entertainment.*
4. The legendary national hero of Switzerland (14th c.), who is said to have been forced by the Austrian governor of his canton to shoot an apple from the head of his son with his crossbow; he later shot the governor, setting off the rebellion that led to Swiss freedom from Austrian domination. Robert Bruce: Robert I, king of Scotland (r. 1306–29).
5. The Tatar Empire, which at its greatest extent dominated Russia and Siberia; the Tatars were descended from the Mongols, known as fierce warriors.

And rode amain with brandished sword,
Up to the middle, through the ford.

Last we drew rein—a weary three—
Upon the lawn, in time for tea,
And from our steeds alighted down
Before the gates of Babylon.

Envoys

To Willie and Henrietta

If two may read aright
These rhymes of old delight
And house and garden play,
You two, my cousins, and you only, may.

You in a garden green
With me were king and queen,
Were hunter, soldier, tar,[6]
And all the thousand things that children are.

Now in the elders' seat
We rest with quiet feet,
And from the window-bay
We watch the children, our successors, play.

"Time was," the golden head
Irrevocably said;
But time which none can bind,
While flowing fast away, leaves love behind.

To My Mother

You too, my mother, read my rhymes
For love of unforgotten times,
And you may chance to hear once more
The little feet along the floor.

To Auntie

Chief of our aunts—not only I,
But all your dozen of nurslings cry—
What did the other children do?
And what were childhood, wanting you?

To Minnie

The red room with the giant bed
Where none but elders laid their head;
The little room where you and I
Did for awhile together lie
And, simple suitor, I your hand
In decent marriage did demand;
The great day nursery, best of all,
With pictures pasted on the wall
And leaves upon the blind—
A pleasant room wherein to wake
And hear the leafy garden shake
And rustle in the wind—
And pleasant there to lie in bed
And see the pictures overhead—
The wars about Sebastopol,[7]
The grinning guns along the wall,
The daring escalade,[8]
The plunging ships, the bleating sheep,
The happy children ankle-deep
And laughing as they wade:
All these are vanished clean away,
And the old manse[9] is changed to-day;
It wears an altered face
And shields a stranger race.
The river, on from mill to mill,
Flows past our childhood's garden still;
But ah! we children never more
Shall watch it from the water-door!
Below the yew—it still is there—
Our phantom voices haunt the air
As we were still at play,
And I can hear them call and say:
'How far is it to Babylon?'[1]

---

6. Sailor.
7. The Crimean War (1853–56), fought between Russia and a coalition that included Great Britain.
8. The act of scaling a fortification.
9. The house of a minister. As a child, Stevenson spent sum-

mers in the country at the manse of the Reverend Lewis Balfour, his grandfather.
1. A well-known nursery rhyme begins "How many miles to Babylon?"; it also contains the question "Can I get there by candlelight?"

Ah, far enough, my dear,
Far, far enough from here—
Yet you have farther gone!
'Can I get there by candlelight?'
So goes the old refrain.
I do not know—perchance you might—
But only, children, hear it right,
Ah, never to return again!
The eternal dawn, beyond a doubt,
Shall break on hill and plain,
And put all stars and candles out,
Ere we be young again.
To you in distant India, these
I send across the seas,
Nor count it far across.
For which of us forgets
The Indian cabinets,
The bones of antelope, the wings of albatross,
The pied and painted birds and beans,
The junks and bangles, beads and screens,
The gods and sacred bells,
And the loud-humming, twisted shells?
The level of the parlour floor
Was honest, homely,[2] Scottish shore;
But when we climbed upon a chair,
Behold the gorgeous East was there!
Be this a fable; and behold
Me in the parlour as of old,
And Minnie just above me set
In the quaint Indian cabinet!
Smiling and kind, you grace a shelf
Too high for me to reach myself.
Reach down a hand, my dear, and take
These rhymes for old acquaintance' sake.

To My Name-Child

I

Some day soon this rhyming volume, if you
    learn with proper speed,
Little Louis Sanchez[3] will be given you to read.

Then shall you discover that your name was
    printed down
By the English printers, long before, in London
    town.

In the great and busy city where the East and
    West are met,
All the little letters did the English printer set:
    While you thought of nothing, and were still
    too young to play,
Foreign people thought of you in places far
    away.

Ay, and while you slept, a baby, over all the
    English lands
Other little children took the volume in their
    hands;
    Other children questioned, in their homes
    across the seas:
Who was little Louis, won't you tell us, mother,
    please?

2

Now that you have spelt your lesson, lay it
    down and go and play,
Seeking shells and seaweed on the sands of
    Monterey.
    Watching all the mighty whalebones, lying
    buried by the breeze,
Tiny sandy-pipers, and the huge Pacific seas.

And remember in your playing, as the sea-fog
    rolls to you,
Long ere you could read it, how I told you what
    to do;
    And that while you thought of no one, nearly
    half the world away
Some one thought of Louis on the beach of
    Monterey!

To Any Reader

As from the house your mother sees
You playing round the garden trees,
So you may see, if you will look
Through the windows of this book,

---

2. Homelike.
3. Stevenson's nephew (son of his sister-in-law, Nellie Van de
Grift Sanchez), born in California.

Another child, far, far away,
And in another garden, play.
But do not think you can at all,
By knocking on the window, call
That child to hear you. He intent
Is all on his play-business bent.

He does not hear; he will not look,
Nor yet be lured out of this book.
For, long ago, the truth to say,
He has grown up and gone away,
And it is but a child of air
That lingers in the garden there.

1885

WALTER DE LA MARE
1873–1956

There is something very attractive about Walter de la Mare's respect for poems. "Even the simplest ones," he says in the introduction to *Come Hither* (1923), his anthology of poetry for children, "have secrets which will need a pretty close searching out." He might have said the same thing of his own 1913 collection, *Peacock Pie*, which made his name as a poet for children. Readers encounter the invisible secret of "some one" who "came knocking / At my wee, small door." And the narrator observes the "poor old Widow in her weeds," who "Sowed her garden with wild-flower seeds." The characters populating de la Mare's poems are always presented with compassion. "Poor 'Miss 7,'" for example, though "Lone and alone" and "Five steep flights from the earth, / And one from heaven," still finds singing in her memory "clear flowers and tiny wings, / All tender, lovely things." Similarly, an "Old Soldier" who comes to the door asking for "a crust" after "The wars had thinned him very bare" nevertheless sings "The song of youth that never grows old." Illustrated by Edward Ardizzone, haunting poems such as "The Song of the Mad Prince," "The Ruin," and "The Old Stone House" invite readers to search out their secrets.

The son of a civil servant, de la Mare could not afford to attend a university. He spent eighteen years working in the offices of the Anglo-American (Standard) Oil Company in London, though he wrote constantly in his spare time; he published his first story, "Kismet" (1895), when he was just twenty-two. In 1889 he married Constance Elfrida Ingpen; they would have two sons and two daughters. De la Mare's literary distinction—established by his first book of poetry for children (*Songs of Childhood*, 1902), first novel (*Henry Brocken*, 1904), and first collection of poetry for adults (*Poems*, 1906)—won him a Civil List pension that

enabled him to become a full-time writer. He wrote verse and fiction for children and adults, as well as book reviews and essays. His stories for children, including *The Three Mulla-Mulgars* (1910; reprinted in 1935 as *The Three Royal Monkeys*) and *Broomsticks and Other Tales* (1925), were favorites of the Georgian nursery. From the 1930s onward, he concentrated on poetry.

Walter de la Mare was repeatedly honored near the end of his life. He received honorary degrees from a number of universities, including Oxford, Cambridge, and St. Andrews; was made a Companion of Honour by George VI in 1948; and was awarded the Order of Merit by Elizabeth II in 1953. But his reputation had begun to fade decades earlier. Critics such as F. R. Leavis (*New Bearings in English Poetry*, 1932) dismissed de la Mare as not truly "modern," as too imbued with an escapist Victorian romanticism and lacking the kind of allusiveness and formal experimentation then in favor. By the end of the twentieth century, he was viewed as a minor figure.

As twentieth-century modernism fades into the past, so does criticism of de la Mare as not stylistically experimental or fractured—that is, not modernist—enough. And his status appears to be rising again. The archetypal nursery rhythms and psychological dreamscapes of his verses seem increasingly in tune with contemporary sensibilities. Angela Carter provides a clue to the enduring pleasures of de la Mare's apparently old-fashioned forms of storytelling. In her introduction to a 1982 reprint of de la Mare's *Memoirs of a Midget* (1921), she says that, "it may be read with a great deal of simple enjoyment and then it sticks likes a splinter in the mind." The poems stick in exactly the same way, "like a splinter in the mind."

PEACOCK PIE

The Horseman

I heard a horseman
  Ride over the hill;
The moon shone clear,
The night was still;
His helm was silver,
  And pale was he;
And the horse he rode
  Was of ivory.

Alas, Alack!

Ann, Ann!
  Come! quick as you can!
There's a fish that *talks*
  In the frying-pan.
Out of the fat,
  As clear as glass,
He put up his mouth
  And moaned 'Alas!'
Oh, most mournful,
  'Alas, alack!'
Then turned to his sizzling,
  And sank him back

Tired Tim

Poor tired Tim! It's sad for him.
He lags the long bright morning through,
Ever so tired of nothing to do;
He moons and mopes the livelong day,
Nothing to think about, nothing to say;
Up to bed with his candle to creep,
Too tired to yawn, too tired to sleep:
Poor tired Tim! It's sad for him.

Mima

Jemima is my name,
  But oh, I have another;
My father always calls me Meg,
  And so do Bob and my mother;
Only my sister, jealous of
  The strands of my bright hair,
'Jemima—Mima—Mima!'
  Calls, mocking, up the stair.

The Huntsmen

Three jolly gentlemen,
  In coats of red,
Rode their horses
  Up to bed.

Three jolly gentlemen
  Snored till morn,
Their horses champing
  The golden corn.

Three jolly gentlemen,
  At break of day,
Came clitter-clatter down the stairs
  And galloped away.

The Bandog

Has anybody seen my Mopser?——
  A comely dog is he,
With hair of the colour of a Charles the Fifth,
  And teeth like ships at sea,
His tail it curls straight upwards,
  His ears stand two abreast,
And he answers to the simple name of Mopser,
  When civilly addressed.

I Can't Abear

I can't abear a Butcher,
    I can't abide his meat,
The ugliest shop of all is his,
    The ugliest in the street;
Bakers' are warm, cobblers' dark,
    Chemists' burn watery lights;
But oh, the sawdust butcher's shop,
    That ugliest of sights!

The Dunce

Why does he still keep ticking?
    Why does his round white face
Stare at me over the books and ink,
    And mock at my disgrace?
Why does that thrush call, 'Dunce, dunce,
      dunce!'?
    Why does that bluebottle buzz?
Why does the sun so silent shine?——
    And what do I care if it does?

Chicken

Clapping her platter stood plump Bess,
    And all across the green
Came scampering in, on wing and claw,
    Chicken fat and lean:—
Dorking, Spaniard, Cochin China,[1]
    Bantams sleek and small,
Like feathers blown in a great wind,
    They came at Bessie's call.

Some One

Some one came knocking
    At my wee, small door;
Some one came knocking,
    I'm sure—sure—sure;
I listened, I opened,
    I looked to left and right,
But nought there was a-stirring
    In the still dark night;
Only the busy beetle
    Tap-tapping in the wall,
Only from the forest
    The screech-owl's call,
Only the cricket whistling
    While the dewdrops fall,
So I know not who came knocking,
    At all, at all, at all.

Bread and Cherries

'Cherries, ripe cherries!'
    The old woman cried,
In her snowy white apron,
    And basket beside;
And the little boys came,
    Eyes shining, cheeks red,
To buy bags of cherries,
    To eat with their bread.

---

1. Breeds of chickens, as are bantams.

Old Shellover

'Come!' said Old Shellover.[2]
'What?' says Creep.[3]
'The horny[4] old Gardener's fast asleep;
The fat cock Thrush
To his nest has gone;
And the dew shines bright
In the rising Moon;
Old Sallie Worm from her hole cloth peep:
Come!' said Old Shellover.
'Ay!' said Creep.

Hapless

Hapless, hapless, I must be
All the hours of life I see,
Since my foolish nurse did once
Bed me on her leggen bones;
Since my mother did not weel
To snip my nails with blades of steel.
Had they laid me on a pillow
In a cot of water willow,
Had they bitten finger and thumb,
Not to such ill hap I had come.

The Little Bird

My dear Daddie bought a mansion
  For to bring my Mammie to,
In a hat with a long feather,

And a trailing gown of blue;
And a company of fiddlers
  And a rout of maids and men
Danced the clock round to the morning,
  In a gay house-warming then.
And when all the guests were gone—and
  All was still as still can be,
In from the dark ivy hopped a
  Wee small bird. And that was Me.

Mr. Alacadacca

Mr. Alacadacca's
Long strange name
Always filled his heart
With shame.
'I'd much—much—rather
Be called,' said he,
'Plain "Mr. A,"
Or even "Old B";
What can Alacadacca
Mean to me!'
Nobody answered;
Nobody said
Plain 'Mr. A';
'Old B,' instead.
They merely smiled
At his dismay—
A-L-A-C-A-D-A-
C-C-A.

Not I!

As I came out of Wiseman's Street,
The air was thick with driven sleet;
Crossing over Proudman's Square
Cold louring clouds obscured the air;
But as I entered Goodman's Lane
The burning sun came out again;
And on the roofs of Children's Row
In solemn glory shone the snow.
There did I lodge; there hope to die:
Envying no man—no, not I.

2. A garden snail.
3. A garden slug.
4. Calloused.

Cake and Sack

Old King Caraway
    Supped on cake,
And a cup of sack[5]
    His thirst to slake;
Bird in arras
    And hound in hall
Watched very softly
    Or not at all;
Fire in the middle,
    Stone all round
Changed not, heeded not,
    Made no sound;
All by himself
    At the Table High[6]
He'd nibble and sip
    While his dreams slipped by;
And when he had finished,
    He'd nod and say,
'Cake and sack
    For King Caraway!'

Groat nor Tester

No groat[7] for a supper,
No tester[8] for a bed:
Ay, some poor men for taper have
    The light stars shed;
And some poor men for pillow have
    A mossy wayside stone,
Beneath a bough where sits and sings
    The night-bird lone;
And some poor men for coverlid
Lie 'neath the mists of night—
Heavy the dew upon their breasts
    At pierce of morning light;
And some poor men for valance have
    Bracken whose spicy smell
Haunts the thick stillness of the dark
    And brings sweet dreams as well;
And some poor men for bellman have

The farm cocks grey and red—
Who paid no groat for supper
Nor had tester for a bed.

The Ship of Rio

There was a ship of Rio
    Sailed out into the blue,
And nine and ninety monkeys
    Were all her jovial crew.
From bo'sun to the cabin boy,
    From quarter to caboose,[9]
There weren't a stitch of calico
    To breech[1] 'em—tight or loose;
From spar to deck, from deck to keel,
    From barnacle to shroud,[2]
There weren't one pair of reach-me-downs[3]
    To all that jabbering crowd.
But wasn't it a gladsome sight,
    When roared the deep sea gales,
To see them reef her fore and aft,
    A-swinging by their tails!
Oh, wasn't it a gladsome sight,
    When glassy calm did come,
To see them squatting tailor-wise
    Around a keg of rum!
Oh, wasn't it a gladsome sight,
    When in she sailed to land,
To see them all a-scampering skip
    For nuts across the sand!

Tillie

Old Tillie Turveycombe
Sat to sew,
Just where a patch of fern did grow;
There, as she yawned;
And yawn wide did she,
Floated some seed
Down her gull-e-t;

---

5. A white wine imported to England from Spain and the Canary Islands.
6. I.e., high table: the raised table at which the most important individuals eat (in British colleges, the masters and fellows eat there).
7. Both a kind of crushed grain and an old British silver coin (worth four pence).

8. Canopy.
9. Small cook room on deck. "Quarter": the upper part of a ship's side.
1. Clothe with breeches.
2. A rope that helps support the mast.
3. I.e., hand-me-downs.

And look you once,
And look you twice,
Poor old Tillie
Was gone in a trice.
But oh, when the wind
Do a-moaning come,
'Tis poor old Tillie
Sick for home;
And oh, when a voice
In the mist do sigh,
Old Tillie Turveycombe's
Floating by.

Jim Jay

Do diddle di do,
    Poor Jim Jay
Got stuck fast
    In Yesterday.
Squinting he was,
    On cross-legs bent,
Never heeding
    The wind was spent.
Round veered the weathercock,
    The sun drew in——
And stuck was Jim
    Like a rusty pin. . . .
We pulled and we pulled
    From seven till twelve,
Jim, too frightened
    To help himself.
But all in vain.
    The clock struck one,
And there was Jim
    A little bit gone.
At half-past five
    You scarce could see
A glimpse of his flapping
    Handkerchee.
And when came noon,
    And we climbed sky-high,
Jim was a speck
    Slip—slipping by.
Come to-morrow,
    The neighbours say,
He'll be past crying for:
    Poor Jim Jay.

Up and Down

Down the Hill of Ludgate,[4]
    Up the Hill of Fleet,
To and fro and East and West
    With people flows the street;
Even the King of England
    On Temple Bar[5] must beat
For leave to ride to Ludgate
    Down the Hill of Fleet.

Miss T.

It's a very odd thing——
    As odd as can be——
That whatever Miss T. eats
    Turns into Miss T.;
Porridge and apples,
    Mince,[6] muffins and mutton,
Jam, junket, jumbles[7]——
    Not a rap, not a button
It matters; the moment
    They're out of her plate,
Though shared by Miss Butcher
    And sour Mr. Bate;
Tiny and cheerful,
    And neat as can be,
Whatever Miss T. eats
    Turns into Miss T.

The Cupboard

I know a little cupboard,
With a teeny tiny key,
And there's a jar of Lollipops
        For me, me, me.

---

4. Ludgate Hill, like Fleet Street, is in the western part of the City of London.
5. The western entrance to the City of London, where the Strand becomes Fleet Street. By long-standing custom, a king or queen entering the City stops here to request permission to proceed.
6. I.e., mincemeat: a finely chopped mixture of dried fruit, nuts, suet, sugar, etc.
7. Sweet cakes. Junket: sweetened and flavored cream or milk pudding; more generally, any sweet confection.

It has a little shelf, my dear,
As dark as dark can be,
And there's a dish of Banbury Cakes[8]
    For me, me, me.

I have a small fat grandmamma,
With a very slippery knee,
And she's Keeper of the Cupboard,
    With the key, key, key.

And when I'm very good, my dear,
As good as good can be,
There's Banbury Cakes, and Lollipops
    For me, me, me.

The Barber's

Gold locks, and black locks,
    Red locks, and brown,
Topknot to love-curl
    The hair wisps down;
Straight above the clear eyes,
    Rounded round the ears,
Snip-snap and snick-a-snack,
    Clash the Barber's shears;
Us, in the looking-glass,
    Footsteps in the street,
Over, under, to and fro,
    The lean blades meet;
Bay Rum or Bear's Grease,
    A silver groat to pay——
Then out a-shin-shan-shining
    In the bright, blue day.

Hide and Seek

Hide and seek, says the Wind,
    In the shade of the woods;
Hide and seek, says the Moon,
    To the hazel buds;
Hide and seek, says the Cloud,
    Star on to star;
Hide and seek, says the Wave
    At the harbour bar;[9]

Hide and seek, says I,
    To myself, and step
Out of the dream of Wake
    Into the dream of Sleep.

Mrs. Earth

Mrs. Earth makes silver black,
    Mrs. Earth makes iron red,
But Mrs. Earth can not stain gold
    Nor ruby red.
Mrs. Earth the slenderest bone
    Whitens in her bosom cold,
But Mrs. Earth can change my dreams
    No more than ruby or gold.
Mrs. Earth and Mr. Sun
    Can tan my skin, and tire my toes,
But all that I'm thinking of, ever shall think,
    Why, neither knows.

Then

Twenty, forty, sixty, eighty,
    A hundred years ago,
All through the night with lantern bright
    The Watch trudged to and fro.
And little boys tucked snug abed
    Would wake from dreams to hear——
'Two o' the morning by the clock,
    And the stars a-shining clear!'
Or, when across the chimney-tops
    Screamed shrill a North-East gale,
A faint and shaken voice would shout,
    'Three! and a storm of hail!'

The Window

Behind the blinds I sit and watch
The people passing—passing by;
And not a single one can see
    My tiny watching eye.

8. A flaky pastry with currants (a specialty of Banbury, near Oxford).
9. A fully or partly submerged bank.

They cannot see my little room,
All yellowed with the shaded sun,
They do not even know I'm here;
    Nor'll guess when I am gone.

Poor Henry

Thick in its glass
    The physic[1] stands,
Poor Henry lifts
    Distracted hands;
His round cheek wans
    In the candlelight,
To smell that smell!
    To see that sight!

Finger and thumb
    Clinch his small nose.
A gurgle, a gasp,
    And down it goes;
Scowls Henry now;
    But mark that cheek,
Sleek with the bloom
    Of health next week!

Full Moon

One night as Dick lay fast asleep,
    Into his drowsy eyes
A great still light began to creep
    From out the silent skies.
It was the lovely moon's, for when
    He raised his dreamy head,
Her surge of silver filled the pane
    And streamed across his bed.
So, for awhile, each gazed at each——
    Dick and the solemn moon——
Till, climbing slowly on her way,
    She vanished, and was gone.

The Bookworm

'I'm tired—Oh, tired of books,' said Jack,
    'I long for meadows green,
And woods where shadowy violets
    Nod their cool leaves between;
I long to see the ploughman stride
    His darkening acres o'er,
To hear the hoarse sea-waters drive
    Their billows 'gainst the shore;
I long to watch the sea-mew[2] wheel
    Back to her rock-perched mate;
Or, where the breathing cows are housed,
    Lean, dreaming at the gate.
Something has gone, and ink and print
    Will never bring it back;
I long for the green fields again,
    I'm tired of books,' said Jack.

The Quartette

Tom sang for joy and Ned sang for joy and old
    Sam sang for joy;
All we four boys piped up loud, just like one
    boy;
And the ladies that sate with the Squire—their
    cheeks were all wet,
For the noise of the voice of us boys, when we
    sang our Quartette.

Tom he piped low and Ned he piped low and
    old Sam he piped low;
Into a sorrowful fall did our music flow;
And the ladies that sate with the Squire vowed
    they'd never forget,
How the eyes of them cried for delight, when
    we sang our Quartette.

Mistletoe

Sitting under the mistletoe
(Pale-green, fairy mistletoe),
One last candle burning low,
All the sleepy dancers gone,

---

1. Medicine.

2. Seagull.

Just one candle burning on,
Shadows lurking everywhere:
Some one came, and kissed me there.

Tired I was; my head would go
Nodding under the mistletoe
(Pale-green, fairy mistletoe);
No footsteps came, no voice, but only,
Just as I sat there, sleepy, lonely,
Stooped in the still and shadowy air
Lips unseen—and kissed me there.

The Lost Shoe

Poor little Lucy
  By some mischance,
Lost her shoe
  As she did dance:
'Twas not on the stairs,
  Not in the hall;
Not where they sat
  At supper at all.
She looked in the garden,
  But there it was not;
Henhouse, or kennel,
  Or high dovecote.
Dairy and meadow,
  And wild woods through
Showed not a trace
  Of Lucy's shoe.
Bird nor bunny
  Nor glimmering moon
Breathed a whisper
  Of where 'twas gone.
It was cried and cried,
  Oyez and *Oyez!*
In French, Dutch, Latin
  And Portuguese.
Ships the dark seas
  Went plunging through,
But none brought news
  Of Lucy's shoe;
And still she patters,
  In silk and leather,

Snow, sand, shingle,
  In every weather;
Spain, and Africa,
  Hindustan,
Java, China,
  And lamped Japan,
Plain and desert,
  She hops—hops through,
Pernambuco[3]
  To gold Peru;
Mountain and forest,
  And river too,
All the world over
  For her lost shoe.

The Truants

Ere my heart beats too coldly and faintly
  To remember sad things, yet be gay,
I would sing a brief song of the world's little
    children
    Magic hath stolen away.

The primroses scattered by April,
  The stars of the wide Milky Way,
Cannot outnumber the hosts of the children
    Magic hath stolen away.

The buttercup green of the meadows,
  The snow of the blossoming may,
Lovelier are not than the legions of children
    Magic hath stolen away.

The waves tossing surf in the moonbeam,
  The Albatross lone on the spray,
Alone know the tears wept in vain for the
    children
    Magic hath stolen away.

In vain: for at hush of the evening,
  When the stars twinkle into the grey,
Seems to echo the far-away calling of children
    Magic hath stolen away.

---

3. State in eastern Brazil.

The Sea Boy

Peter went—and nobody there—
Down by the sandy sea,
And he danced a jig, while the moon shone big,
All in his lone danced he;
And the surf splashed over his tippeting toes,
And he sang his riddle-cum-ree,
With hair a-dangling,
Moon a-spangling
The bubbles and froth of the sea.
He danced him to, and he danced him fro,
And he twirled himself about,
And now the starry waves tossed in,
And now the waves washed out;
Bare as an acorn, bare as a nut,
Nose and toes and knee,
Peter the sea-boy danced and pranced,
And sang his riddle-cum-ree.

Must and May

Must and May they were two half-brothers,
    And Must—a giant was he:
And May but a wisp of a flibbetigibbet,
    A mere minikin manikinee.

They dwelt in a mansion called Oughtoo, yes,
    Oughtoo,
And a drearisome house was she.
In an hundred great chambers Must wallowed
    in comfort,
    All at his ease to be.

And the hundred and first was a crack of a
    cupboard,
    With nought but a hole for the key,
Where the glint of a glimmer of a quickle of
    sunshine
    Gleamed in about half-past three.

And there our May, smiling up at the window—
    At the place where the window should be;
As he sang to a harp with a top and a bottom
        string—

Walter de la Mare

A—B—C—D—E—F— and G.

But if there was one thing Must could not
    instomach,
    'Twas a treble-shrill fiddlededee,
And he vowed a great vow he would learn May
    his manners,
    And he did—as you'll shortly agree.

Down—down—he collumbered; and with ear to
    the keyhole
    He crouched upon bended knee;
And he roared with a roar that drowned the
    sweet harpstrings,
    He roared like a storm at sea.

And he catched little May by the twist of his
    breeches
    Where the slack is snipped out in a V;
And swallowed him whole; and he scrunched
    up his harp, too,
    He was so an—ga—ree.

Now mutterers say that that Oughtoo is
    haunted,
    Exactly at half-past three,
By the phantom of poor little May to fey harp-
    strings
    Singing A, B, C, D, E. F. G.

Berries

There was an old woman
    Went blackberry picking
Along the hedges
    From Weep to Wicking.
Half a pottle[4]——
    No more she had got,
When out steps a Fairy
    From her green grot;
And says, 'Well, Jill,
    Would 'ee pick 'ee mo?'
And Jill, she curtseys,
    And looks just so.
'Be off,' says the Fairy,
    'As quick as you can,
Over the meadows

---

4. A half gallon.

To the little green lane,
That dips to the hayfields
   Of Farmer Grimes:
I've berried those hedges
   A score of times;
Bushel on bushel
   I'll promise 'ee, Jill,
This side of supper
   If 'ee pick with a will.'
She glints very bright,
   And speaks her fair;
Then lo, and behold!
   She had faded in air.

Be sure Old Goodie
   She trots betimes
Over the meadows
   To Farmer Grimes.
And never was queen
   With jewellery rich
As those same hedges
   From twig to ditch;
Like Dutchmen's coffers,
   Fruit, thorn, and flower——
They shone like William
   And Mary's bower.[5]
And be sure Old Goodie
   Went back to Weep
So tired with her basket
   She scarce could creep.

When she comes in the dusk
   To her cottage door,
There's Towser wagging
   As never before,
To see his Missus
   So glad to be
Come from her fruit-picking
   Back to he.
As soon as next morning
   Dawn was grey,
The pot on the hob
   Was simmering away;
And all in a stew
   And a hugger-mugger
Towser and Jill
   A-boiling of sugar,

And the dark clear fruit
   That from Faërie came,
For syrup and jelly
   And blackberry jam.

Twelve jolly gallipots
   Jill put by;
And one little teeny one,
   One inch high;
And that she's hidden
   A good thumb deep,
Half-way over
   From Wicking to Weep.

Off the Ground

Three jolly Farmers
Once bet a pound
Each dance the others would
Off the ground.

Out of their coats
They slipped right soon,
And neat and nicesome,
Put each his shoon.

One—Two—three!——
And away they go,
Not too fast,
And not too slow;
Out from the elm-tree's
Noonday shadow,
Into the sun
And across the meadow.
Past the schoolroom,
With knees well bent
Fingers a-flicking,
They dancing went.
Up sides and over,
And round and round,
They crossed click-clacking,
The Parish bound.
By Tupman's meadow
They did their mile,
Tee-to-tum
On a three-barred stile.

---

5. Queen Mary's bower is a covered walk in the gardens
at Hampton Court.

Then straight through Whipham,
Downhill to Week,
Footing it lightsome,
But not too quick,
Up fields to Watchet,
And on through Wye,
Till seven fine churches
They'd seen skip by——
Seven fine churches,
And five old mills,
Farms in the valley,
And sheep on the hills;
Old Man's Acre
And Dead Man's Pool
All left behind,
As they danced through Wool
And Wool gone by,
Like tops that seem
To spin in sleep
They danced in dream:
Withy—Wellover——
Wassop—Wo——
Like an old clock
Their heels did go.
A league and a league
And a league they went,
And not one weary,
And not one spent.
And lo, and behold!
Past Willow-cum-Leigh
Stretched with its waters
The great green sea.

Says Farmer Bates,
'I puffs and I blows,
What's under the water,
Why, no man knows!'
Says Farmer Giles,
'My wind comes weak,
And a good man drownded
Is far to seek.'
But Farmer Turvey,
On twirling toes
Up's with his gaiters,
And in he goes:
Down where the mermaids
Pluck and play
On their twangling harps

WALTER DE LA MARE

In a sea-green day;
Down where the mermaids,
Finned and fair,
Sleek with their combs
Their yellow hair. . . .

Bates and Giles——
On the shingle sat,
Gazing at Turvey's
Floating hat.
But never a ripple
Nor bubble told
Where he was supping
Off plates of gold.
Never an echo
Rilled through the sea
Of the feasting and dancing
And minstrelsy.
They called—called—called:
Came no reply:
Nought but the ripples'
Sandy sigh.
Then glum and silent
They sat instead,
Vacantly brooding
On home and bed,
Till both together
Stood up and said:——
'Us knows not, dreams not,
Where you be,
Turvey, unless
In the deep blue sea;
But axcusing silver——
And it comes most willing——
Here's us two paying
Our forty shilling;[6]
For it's sartin sure, Turvey,
Safe and sound,
You danced us square, Turvey;
Off the ground!'

The Thief at Robin's Castle

There came a Thief one night to Robin's Castle,
    He climbed up into a Tree;
And sitting with his head among the branches,
    A wondrous Sight did see.

6. I.e., one pound each.

For there was Robin supping at his table,
  With Candles of pure Wax,
His Dame and his two beauteous little
    Children,
  With Velvet on their backs.

Platters for each there were shin-shining,
  Of Silver many a pound,
And all of beaten Gold, three brimming
    Goblets,
  Standing the table round.

The smell that rose up richly from the Baked
    Meats
  Came thinning amid the boughs,
And much that greedy Thief who snuffed the
    night air—
  His Hunger did arouse.

He watched them eating, drinking, laughing,
    talking,
  Busy with finger and spoon,
While three most cunning Fiddlers, clad in
    crimson,
  Played them a supper-tune.

And he waited in the tree-top like a Starling,
  Till the Moon was gotten low;
When all the windows in the walls were
    darkened,
  He softly in did go.

There Robin and his Dame in bed were
    sleeping,
  And his Children young and fair;
Only Robin's Hounds from their warm kennels
  Yelped as he climbed the stair.

All, all were sleeping, page and fiddler,
  Cook, scullion, free from care;
Only Robin's Stallions from their stables
  Neighed as he climbed the stair.

A wee wan light the Moon did shed him,
  Hanging above the sea,
And he counted into his bag (of beaten Silver)
  Platters thirty-three.

Of Spoons three score; of jolly golden Goblets
  He stowed in four save one,
And six fine three-branched Cupid
    Candlesticks,
  Before his work was done.

Nine bulging bags of Money in a cupboard,
  Two Snuffers and a Dish
He found, the last all studded with great
    Garnets
  And shapen like a Fish.

Then tiptoe up he stole into a Chamber,
  Where on Tasselled Pillows lay
Robin and his Dame in dreaming slumber,
  Tired with the summer's day.

That Thief he mimbled round him in the
    gloaming,
  Their Treasures for to spy,
Combs, Brooches, Chains, and Rings, and Pins
    and Buckles
  All higgledy piggle-dy.

A Watch shaped in the shape of a flat Apple
  In purest Crystal set,
He lifted from the hook where it was ticking
  And crammed in his Pochette.[7]

He heaped the pretty Baubles on the table,
  Trinkets, Knick-knackerie,
Pearls, Diamonds, Sapphires, Topazes, and
    Opals——
  All in his bag put he.

And there in night's pale Gloom was Robin
    dreaming
  He was hunting the mountain Bear,
While his Dame in peaceful slumber in no wise
    heeded
  A greedy Thief was there.

And that ravenous Thief he climbed up even
    higher,
  Till into a chamber small
He crept where lay poor Robin's beauteous
    Children,
  Lovelier in sleep withal.

7. A small pocket.

Oh, fairer was their Hair than Gold of Goblet,
  'Yond Silver their Cheeks did shine,
And their little hands that lay upon the linen
  Made that Thief's hard heart to pine.

But though a moment there his hard heart
    faltered,
  Eftsoons he took the twain,
Slipped them into his Bag with all his Plunder,
  And softly stole down again.

Spoon, Platter, Goblet, Ducats, Dishes,
    Trinkets,
  And those two Children dear,
A-quaking in the clinking and the clanking,
  And half bemused with fear,

He carried down the stairs into the Courtyard,
  But there he made no stay,
He just tied up his Garters, took a deep breath,
  And ran like the wind away.

Past Forest, River, Mountain, River, Forest——
  He coursed the whole night through
Till morning found him come into a Country,
  Where none his bad face knew.

There came a little maid and asked his
    Business;
  A Cobbler dwelt within;
And though she much misliked the Bag he
    carried,
  She led the Bad Man in.

He bargained with the Cobbler for a lodging
  And soft laid down his Sack——
In the Dead of Night, with none to spy or
    listen——
  From off his weary Back.

And he taught the little Chicks to call him
    Father,
  And he sold his stolen Pelf,
And bought a Palace, Horses, Slaves, and
    Peacocks,
  To ease his wicked self.

And though the Children never really loved him,
  He was rich past all belief;
While Robin and his Dame o'er Delf[8] and
    Pewter
  Spent all their Days in Grief.

A Widow's Weeds

A poor old Widow in her weeds[9]
Sowed her garden with wild-flower seeds;
Not too shallow, and not too deep,
And down came April—drip—drip—drip.
Up shone May, like gold, and soon
Green as an arbour grew leafy June.
And now all summer she sits and sews
Where willow-herb, comfrey, and bugloss blows,
Teasel and tansy, meadowsweet,
Campion, toadflax, and rough hawksbit;[1]
Brown bee orchis, and Peals of Bells;
Clover, burnet, and thyme she smells;
Like Oberon's[2] meadows her garden is
Drowsy from dawn till dusk with bees.
Weeps she never, but sometimes sighs,
And peeps at her garden with bright brown eyes;
And all she has is all she needs——
A poor old Widow in her weeds.

'Sooeep!'

Black as a chimney is his face,
And ivory white his teeth,
And in his brass-bound cart he rides,
The chestnut blooms beneath.

'Sooeep, Sooeep!' he cries, and brightly peers
This way and that, to see
With his two light-blue shining eyes
What custom[3] there may be.

And once inside the house, he'll squat,
And drive his rods on high,

---

8. I.e., delft: earthenware made in Delft, in the Netherlands.
9. A black garment worn as a sign of mourning.
1. Hawkbit: an herb with a flower resembling a dandelion's.
2. King of the fairies in *A Midsummer Night's Dream*.
3. Business.

WALTER DE LA MARE

Till twirls his sudden sooty brush
Against the morning sky.

Then, 'mid his bulging bags of soot,
With half the world asleep,
His small cart wheels him off again,
Still hoarsely bawling, 'Sooeep!'

Mrs. MacQueen

With glass like a bull's-eye,
  And shutters of green,
Down on the cobbles
  Lives Mrs. MacQueen.

At six she rises;
  At nine you see
Her candle shine out
  In the linden tree;

And at half-past nine
  Not a sound is nigh,
But the bright moon's creeping
  Across the sky;

Or a far dog baying;
  Or a twittering bird
In its drowsy nest,
  In the darkness stirred;

Or like the roar
  Of a distant sea
A long-drawn S-s-sh!
  In the linden tree.

The Little Green Orchard

Some one is always sitting there,
    In the little green orchard;
  Even when the sun is high,
  In noon's unclouded sky,
  And faintly droning goes
  The bee from rose to rose,
Some one in shadow is sitting there,
    In the little green orchard.

Yes, and when twilight's falling softly
    On the little green orchard;
  When the grey dew distils
  And every flower-cup fills;
  When the last blackbird says,
  'What—what!' and goes her way—ssh!
I have heard voices calling softly
    In the little green orchard.

Not that I am afraid of being there,
    In the little green orchard;
  Why, when the moon's been bright,
  Shedding her lonesome light,
  And moths like ghosties come,
  And the horned snail leaves home:
I've sat there, whispering and listening there,
    In the little green orchard;

Only it's strange to be feeling there,
    In the little green orchard,
  Whether you paint or draw,
  Dig, hammer, chop, or saw;
  When you are most alone,
  All but the silence gone . . .
Some one is waiting and watching there,
    In the little green orchard.

Poor 'Miss 7'

Lone and alone she lies
  Poor Miss 7,
Five steep flights from the earth,
  And one from heaven;
Dark hair and dark brown eyes,——
Not to be sad she tries,
Still—still it's lonely lies
  Poor Miss 7.

One day-long watch hath she,
  Poor Miss 7,
Not in some orchard sweet
  In April Devon,——
Just four blank walls to see,
And dark come shadowily,
No moon, no stars, ah me!
  Poor Miss 7.

And then to wake again,
   Poor Miss 7,
To the cold night—to have
   Sour physic given—
Out of some dream of pain;
Then strive long hours in vain
Deep dreamless sleep to gain:
   Poor Miss 7.

Yet memory softly sings
   Poor Miss 7
Songs full of love and peace
   And gladness even;
Clear flowers and tiny wings,
All tender, lovely things,
Hope to her bosom brings——
   Happy Miss 7.

Sam

When Sam goes back in memory,
   It is to where the sea
Breaks on the shingle, emerald-green,
   In white foam, endlessly;
He says—with small brown eye on mine——
   'I used to keep awake,
And lean from my window in the moon,
   Watching those billows break.
And half a million tiny hands,
   And eyes, like sparks of frost,
Would dance and come tumbling into the
     moon,
   On every breaker tossed.
And all across from star to star,
   I've seen the watery sea,
With not a single ship in sight,
   Just ocean there, and me;
And heard my father snore . . . And once,
   As sure as I'm alive,
Out of those wallowing, moon-flecked waves
   I saw a mermaid dive;
Head and shoulders above the wave,
   Plain as I now see you,
Combing her hair, now back, now front,
   Her two eyes peeping through;

WALTER DE LA MARE

Calling me, "Sam!"—quietlike—"Sam!" . . .
   But me . . . I never went,
Making believe I kind of thought
   'Twas someone else she meant . . .
Wonderful lovely there she sat,
   Singing the night away,
All in the solitudinous[4] sea
   Of that there lonely bay.
P'raps,' and he'd smooth his hairless mouth,
   'P'raps, if 'twere *now*, my son,
P'raps, if I heard a voice say, "Sam!" . . .
   Morning would find me gone.'

Andy Battle's and Nod's Song

Once and there was a young sailor, yeo ho!
   And he sailed out over the say
For the isles where pink coral and palm
     branches blow.
   And the fire-flies turn night into day,
     Yeo ho!
   And the fire-flies turn night into day.

But the *Dolphin* went down in a tempest, yeo ho!
   And with three forsook sailors ashore,
The Portingals[5] took him where sugar-canes grow,
   Their slave for to be evermore.
     Yeo ho!
   Their slave for to be evermore.

With his musket for mother and brother, yeo ho!
   He warred with the Cannibals drear,
In forests where panthers pad soft to and fro,
   And the Pongo[6] shakes noonday with fear,
     Yeo ho!
   And the Pongo shakes noonday with fear.

Now lean with long travail, all wasted with woe,
   With a monkey for messmate and friend,
He sits 'neath the Cross in the cankering snow,
   And waits for his sorrowful end,
     Yeo ho!
   And waits for his sorrowful end.

4. Characterized by solitude.
5. Portuguese (a sixteenth-century term).
6. An ape (usually a chimpanzee or an orangutan).

Late

Three small men in a small house,
    And none to hear them say,
'One for his nob,' and 'One for his noddle,'[7]
    And 'One for his dumb dog Stray!'
'Clubs are trumps—and he's dealt and bluffed':
    'And Jack of diamonds led':
'And perhaps the cullie[8] has dropped a shoe;
    He tarries so late,' they said.

Three small men in a small house,
    And one small empty chair,
One with his moleskin[9] over his brows,
    One with his crany bare,
And one with a dismal cast in his eye,
    Rocking a heavy head . . .
'And perhaps the cullie's at *The Wide World's
    End*;
    He tarries so late,' they said.

Three small men in a small house,
    And a candle guttering low,
One with his cheek on the ace of spades,
    And two on the boards below.
And a window black 'gainst a waste of stars,
    And a moon five dark nights dead . . .
'Who's that a-knocking and a-knocking and
    a-knocking?'
    One stirred in his sleep and said.

The Old Soldier

There came an Old Soldier to my door,
Asked a crust, and asked no more;
The wars had thinned him very bare,
Fighting and marching everywhere,
    With a Fol rol dol rol di do.

With nose stuck out, and cheek sunk in,
A bristling beard upon his chin——
Powder and bullets and wounds and drums
Had come to that Soldier as suchlike comes——
    With a Fol rol dol rol di do.

'Twas sweet and fresh with blossoming May,
Flowers springing from every spray;
And when he had supped the Old Soldier
    trolled[1]
The song of youth that never grows old,
    Called Fol rol dol rol di do.

Most of him rags, and all of him lean,
And the belt round his belly drawn tightly in,
He lifted his peaked old grizzled head,
And these were the very same words he
    said——
    A Fol-rol-dol-rol-*di*-do.

The Picture

Here is a sea-legged sailor,
    Come to this tottering inn,
Just when the bronze on its signboard is fading,
    And the black shades of evening begin.

With his head on his paws sleeps a sheepdog,
    There stoops the shepherd, and see,
All follow-my-leader the ducks waddle
    homeward,
    Under the sycamore tree.

Burned brown is the face of the sailor;
    His bundle is crimson; and green
Are the thick leafy boughs that hang dense o'er
    the tavern;
    And blue the far meadows between.

But the crust, ale and cheese of the sailor,
    His mug and his platter of Delf,
And the crescent to light home the shepherd
    and sheepdog
    The painter has kept to himself.

---

7. Head. "Nob": head.
8. Fellow.
9. I.e., a moleskin hat.

1. Sang.

The Little Old Cupid

'Twas a very small garden;
The paths were of stone,
Scattered with leaves,
With moss overgrown:
And a little old Cupid[2]
Stood under a tree,
With a small broken bow
He stood aiming at me.

The dog-rose in briars
Hung over the weeds,
The air was aflock
With the floating of seeds;
And a little old Cupid
Stood under a tree,
With a small broken bow
He stood aiming at me.

The dovecote was tumbling,
The fountain dry,
A wind in the orchard
Went whispering by;
And a little old Cupid
Stood under a tree,
With a small broken bow
He stood aiming at me.

King David

King David was a sorrowful man:
　　No cause for his sorrow had he:
And he called for the music of a hundred harps,
　　To solace his melancholy.

They played till they all fell silent:
　　Played—and play sweet did they;
But the sorrow that haunted the heart of King
　　David
　　They could not charm away.

He rose; and in his garden
　　Walked by the moon alone,
A nightingale hidden in a cypress-tree
　　Jargoned[3] on and on.

King David lifted his sad eyes
　　Into the dark-boughed tree——
'Tell me, thou little bird that singest,
　　Who taught my grief to thee?'

But the bird in no wise heeded;
　　And the king in the cool of the moon
Hearkened to the nightingale's sorrowfulness,
　　Till all his own was gone.

The Penny Owing

Poor blind Tam, the beggar man,
I'll give a penny to as soon as I can.
Where he stood at the corner in his rags, and
　　cried,
The sun without shadow does now abide.

Safe be my penny till I come some day
To where Tam's waiting. And then I'll say,
'Here is my ghost, Tam, from the fire and dew,
And the penny I grudged kept safe for you.'

Kings and Queens

Eight Henries, one Mary,
　　One Elizabeth;
Crowned and throned Kings and Queens
　　Now lie still in death.

Four Williams, one Stephen,
　　Anne, Victoria, John:
Sceptre and orb[4] are laid aside;
　　All are to quiet gone.
And James and Charles, and Charles's sons—
　　They, too, have journeyed on.

---

2. In Roman mythology, the god of love; his arrows cause the person shot to fall in love.

3. Warbled.
4. Traditional symbols of the monarchy, used in all British coronations since 1661.

Three Richards, seven Edwards
  Their royal hour did thrive;
They sleep with Georges one to four:
  And we praise God for five.[5]

The Old House

A very, very old house I know——
And ever so many people go,
Past the small lodge, forlorn and still,
Under the heavy branches, till
Comes the blank wall, and there's the door.
Go in they do; come out no more.
No voice says aught; no spark of light
Across that threshold cheers the sight;
Only the evening star on high
Less lonely makes a lonely sky,
As, one by one, the people go
Into that very old house I know.

Unstooping

Low on his fours the Lion
  Treads with the surly Bear;
But Men straight upward from the dust
  Walk with their heads in air;
The free sweet winds of heaven,
  The sunlight from on high
Beat on their clear bright cheeks and brows
  As they go striding by;
The doors of all their houses
  They arch so they may go,
Uplifted o'er the four-foot beasts,
  Unstooping, to and fro.

All But Blind

All but blind
  In his chambered hole

Gropes for worms
  The four-clawed Mole.

All but blind
  In the evening sky
The hooded Bat
  Twirls softly by.

All but blind
  In the burning day
The Barn Owl blunders
  On her way.

And blind as are
  These three to me,
So, blind to Some-One
  I must be.

Nicholas Nye

Thistle and darnel and dock grew there,
  And a bush, in the corner, of may,
On the orchard wall I used to sprawl
  In the blazing heat of the day;
Half asleep and half awake,
  While the birds went twittering by,
And nobody there my lone to share
  But Nicholas Nye.

Nicholas Nye was lean and grey,
  Lame of a leg and old,
More than a score of donkey's years[6]
  He had seen since he was foaled;
He munched the thistles, purple and spiked,
  Would sometimes stoop and sigh,
And turn his head, as if he said,
  'Poor Nicholas Nye!'

Alone with his shadow he'd drowse in the meadow,
  Lazily swinging his tail,
At break of day he used to bray,——
  Not much too hearty and hale;
But a wonderful gumption was under his skin,

5. I.e., George V (1865–1936; r. 1910–36), king at the time de la Mare wrote this poem. He here lists kings and queens of England, starting with William I, the Conqueror (ca. 1028–1087; r. 1066–87).

6. Besides its literal sense, *donkey's years* also means "a long time."

PEACOCK PIE

And a clear calm light in his eye,
And once in a while: he'd smile . . . .
   Would Nicholas Nye.

Seem to be smiling at me, he would,
   From his bush in the corner, of may,——
Bony and ownerless, widowed and worn,
   Knobble-kneed, lonely and grey;
And over the grass would seem to pass
   'Neath the deep dark blue of the sky,
Something much better than words between me
   And Nicholas Nye.

But dusk would come in the apple boughs,
   The green of the glow-worm shine,
The birds in nest would crouch to rest,
   And home I'd trudge to mine;
And there, in the moonlight, dark with dew,
   Asking not wherefore nor why,
Would brood like a ghost, and as still as a post,
   Old Nicholas Nye.

The Pigs and the Charcoal-Burner

The old Pig said to the little pigs,
   'In the forest is truffles and mast,[7]
Follow me then, all ye little pigs,
   Follow me fast!'

The Charcoal-burner[8] sat in the shade
   With his chin on his thumb,
And saw the big Pig and the little pigs,
   Chuffling[9] come.

He watched 'neath a green and giant bough,
   And the pigs in the ground
Made a wonderful grizzling and gruzzling
   And greedy sound.

And when, full-fed, they were gone, and Night
   Walked her starry ways,
He stared with his cheeks in his hands
   At his sullen blaze.

Five Eyes

In Hans' old Mill his three black cats
Watch his bins for the thieving rats.
Whisker and claw, they crouch in the night,
Their five eyes smouldering green and bright:
Squeaks from the flour sacks, squeaks from
   where
The cold wind stirs on the empty stair,
Squeaking and scampering, everywhere.
Then down they pounce, now in, now out,
At whisking tail, and sniffing snout;
While lean old Hans he snores away
Till peep of light at break of day;
Then up he climbs to his creaking mill,
Out come his cats all grey with meal——
Jekkel, and Jessup, and one-eyed Jill.

Tit for Tat

Have you been catching of fish, Tom Noddy?
   Have you snared a weeping hare?
Have you whistled, 'No Nunny,' and gunned a
      poor bunny,
   Or a blinded bird of the air?

Have you trod like a murderer through the green
      woods,
   Through the dewy deep dingles and glooms,
While every small creature screamed shrill to
      Dame Nature,
   'He comes—and he comes!'?

Wonder I very much do, Tom Noddy,
   If ever, when off you roam,
An Ogre from space will stoop a lean face
   And lug you home:

Lug you home over his fence, Tom Noddy,
   Of thorn-sticks nine yards high,
With your bent knees strung round his old iron gun
   And your head dan-dangling by:

And hang you up stiff on a hook, Tom Noddy,
   From a stone-cold pantry shelf,
Whence your eyes will glare in an empty stare,
   Till you are cooked yourself!

---

7. Nuts on the forest floor.
8. I.e., one who makes charcoal by partially burning wood.
9. Perhaps chuffing (i.e., puffing) and shuffling.

Earth Folk

The cat she walks on padded claws,
The wolf on the hills lays stealthy paws,
Feathered birds in the rain-sweet sky
At their ease in the air, flit low, flit high.

The oak's blind, tender roots pierce deep,
His green crest towers, dimmed in sleep,
Under the stars whose thrones are set
Where never prince hath journeyed yet.

Grim

Beside the blaze, as of forty fires,
Giant Grim doth sit,
Roasting a thick-woolled mountain sheep
Upon an iron spit.
Above him wheels the winter sky,
Beneath him, fathoms deep,
Lies hidden in the valley mists
A village fast asleep——
Save for one restive hungry dog
That, snuffing towards the height,
Smells Grim's broiled supper-meat, and spies
His watch-fire twinkling bright.

Summer Evening

The sandy cat by the Farmer's chair
Mews at his knee for dainty fare;
Old Rover in his moss-greened house
Mumbles[1] a bone, and barks at a mouse.
In the dewy fields the cattle lie
Chewing the cud 'neath a fading sky;
Dobbin at manger pulls his hay:
Gone is another summer's day.

At the Keyhole

'Grill me some bones,' said the Cobbler,
    'Some bones, my pretty Sue;
I'm tired of my lonesome with heels and soles,
Springsides and uppers too;
A mouse in the wainscot is nibbling;
A wind in the keyhole drones;
And a sheet webbed over my candle, Susie,——
    Grill me some bones!'

'Grill me some bones,' said the Cobbler,
    'I sat at my tic-tac-to;
And a footstep came to my door and stopped,
And a hand groped to and fro;
And I peered up over my boot and last;
And my feet went cold as stones:——
I saw an eye at the keyhole, Susie!——
    Grill me some bones!'

The Old Stone House

Nothing on the grey roof, nothing on the brown,
Only a little greening where the rain drips down;
Nobody at the window, nobody at the door,
Only a little hollow which a foot once wore;
But still I tread on tiptoe, still tiptoe on I go,
Past nettles, porch, and weedy well, for oh, I
    know
A friendless face is peering, and a clear still eye
Peeps closely through the casement as my step
    goes by.

The Ruin

When the last colours of the day
Have from their burning ebbed away,
About that ruin, cold and lone,
The cricket shrills from stone to stone;
And scattering o'er its darkened green,
Bands of the fairies may be seen,
Chattering like grasshoppers, their feet
Dancing a thistledown dance round it:
While the great gold of the mild moon
Tinges their tiny acorn shoon.

PEACOCK PIE

---

1. Chews with his gums.

1221

The Ride-by-Nights

Up on their brooms the Witches stream,
Crooked and black in the crescent's gleam;
One foot high, and one foot low,
Bearded, cloaked, and cowled, they go.
'Neath Charlie's Wain[2] they twitter and tweet,
And away they swarm 'neath the Dragon's[3] feet,
With a whoop and a flutter they swing and sway,
And surge pell-mell down the Milky Way.
Between the legs of the glittering Chair[4]
They hover and squeak in the empty air.
Then round they swoop past the glimmering
    Lion[5]
To where Sirius barks behind huge Orion;[6]
Up, then, and over to wheel amain,
Under the silver, and home again.

Peak and Puke

From his cradle in the glamourie[7]
They have stolen my wee brother,
Housed a changeling[8] in his swaddlings
For to fret my own poor mother.
Pules it in the candle light
Wi' a cheek so lean and white,
Chinkling up its eyne[9] so wee
Wailing shrill at her an' me.
It we'll neither rock nor tend
Till the Silent Silent[1] send,
Lapping in their waesome arms
Him they stole with spells and charms,
Till they take this changeling creature
Back to its own fairy nature——
Cry! Cry! as long as may be,
Ye shall ne'er be woman's baby!

The Changeling

'Ahoy, and ahoy!'
  'Twixt mocking and merry——
'Ahoy and ahoy, there,
  Young man of the ferry!'

She stood on the steps
  In the watery gloom——
That Changeling—'Ahoy, there!'
  She called him to come.
He came on the green wave,
  He came on the grey,
Where stooped that sweet lady
  That still summer's day.
He fell in a dream
  Of her beautiful face,
As she sat on the thwart
  And smiled in her place.

No echo his oar woke,
  Float silent did they,
Past low-grazing cattle
  In the sweet of the hay.
And still in a dream
  At her beauty sat he,
Drifting stern foremost
  Down—down to the sea.
Come you, then: call,
  When the twilight apace
Brings shadow to brood
  On the loveliest face;
You shall hear o'er the water
  Ring faint in the grey——
'Ahoy, and ahoy, there!'
  And tremble away;
'Ahoy, and ahoy! . . .'
  And tremble away.

---

2. The group of stars also known as the Big Dipper.
3. The constellation Draco.
4. The constellation Cassiopeia, or Cassiopeia's Chair.
5. Leo, one of the constellations of the zodiac.
6. The constellation shaped like a hunter. Sirius: the brightest star in Canis Major (one of Orion's hunting dogs).

7. Magic. "Puke": i.e., puck: a malicious spirit or demon.
8. A fairy child left in the place of a human child.
9. Eyes.
1. Fairies are sometimes known as the Silent People.

The Mocking Fairy

'Won't you look out of your window, Mrs. Gill?'
  Quoth the Fairy, nidding, nodding in the
      garden;
'*Can't* you look out of your window, Mrs. Gill?'
  Quoth the Fairy, laughing softly in the
      garden;
But the air was still, the cherry boughs were
      still,
And the ivy-tod[2] 'neath the empty sill,
And never from her window looked out Mrs.
      Gill
  On the Fairy shrilly mocking in the garden.

What have they done with you, you poor Mrs.
      Gill?'
  Quoth the Fairy brightly glancing in the
      garden;
'Where have they hidden you, you poor old Mrs.
      Gill?'
  Quoth the Fairy dancing lightly in the garden;
But night's faint veil now wrapped the hill,
Stark 'neath the stars stood the dead-still Mill,
And out of her cold cottage never answered
      Mrs. Gill
  The Fairy mimbling, mambling[3] in the
      garden.

The Honey Robbers

There were two Fairies, Gimmul and Mel,
Loved Earth Man's honey passing well;
Oft at the hives of his tame bees
They would their sugary thirst appease.

When even began to darken to night,
They would hie along in the fading light,
With elf-locked[4] hair and scarlet lips,
And small stone knives to slit the skeps,
So softly not a bee inside
Should hear the woven straw divide.
And then with sly and greedy thumbs
Would rifle the sweet honeycombs.
And drowsily drone to drone would say,

'A cold, cold wind blows in this way';
And the great Queen would turn her head
From face to face, astonished,
And, though her maids with comb and brush
Would comb and soothe and whisper, 'Hush!'
About the hive would shrilly go
A keening—keening, to and fro;
At which those robbers 'neath the trees
Would taunt and mock the honey-bees,
And through their sticky teeth would buzz
Just as an angry hornet does.

And when this Gimmul and this Mel
Had munched and sucked and swilled their fill,
Or ever Man's first cock should crow
Back to their Faerie Mounds they'd go.
Edging across the twilight air,
Thieves of a guise remotely fair.

Longlegs

Longlegs—he yelled 'Coo-ee!'
  And all across the combe[5]
Shrill and shrill it rang—rang through
  The clear green gloom.
Fairies there were a-spinning,
  And a white tree-maid
Lifted her eyes, and listened
  In her rain-sweet glade.
Bunnie to bunnie stamped; old Wat
  Chin-deep in bracken sate;
A throstle piped, 'I'm by, I'm by!'
  Clear to his timid mate.
And there was Longlegs straddling,
  And hearkening was he,
To distant Echo thrilling back
  A thin 'Coo-ee!'

Bewitched

I have heard a lady this night,
  Lissome and jimp[6] and slim,
Calling me—calling me over the heather,
  'Neath the beech boughs dusk and dim.

2. Ivy-bush (archaic).
3. Muttering, chattering.
4. Tangled, matted.

5. Valley.
6. Graceful.

I have followed a lady this night,
  Followed her far and lone,
Fox and adder and weasel know
  The ways that we have gone.

I sit at my supper 'mid honest faces,
  And crumble my crust and say
Nought in the long-drawn drawl of the voices
  Talking the hours away.

I'll go to my chamber under the gable,
  And the moon will lift her light
In at my lattice from over the moorland
  Hollow and still and bright.

And I know she will shine on a lady of
    witchcraft,
  Gladness and grief to see,
Who has taken my heart with her nimble
    fingers,
  Calls in my dreams to me;

Who has led me a dance by dell and dingle
  My human soul to win,
Made me a changeling to my own, own mother,
  A stranger to my kin.

Melmillo

Three and thirty birds there stood
In an elder in a wood;
Called Melmillo—flew off three,
Leaving thirty in the tree;
Called Melmillo—nine now gone,
And the boughs held twenty-one;
Called Melmillo—and eighteen
Left but three to nod and preen;
Called Melmillo—three—two—one
Now of birds were feathers none.

Then stole slim Melmillo in
To that wood all dusk and green,
And with lean long palms outspread
Softly a strange dance did tread;
Not a note of music she

Had for echoing company;
All the birds were flown to rest
In the hollow of her breast;
In the wood—thorn, elder, willow——
Danced alone—lone danced Melmillo.

Trees

Of all the trees in England,
  Her sweet three corners in,
Only the Ash, the bonnie Ash
  Burns fierce while it is green.

Of all the trees in England,
  From sea to sea again,
The Willow loveliest stoops her boughs
  Beneath the driving rain.

Of all the trees in England,
  Past frankincense and myrrh,
There's none for smell, of bloom and smoke,
  Like Lime and Juniper.

Of all the trees in England,
  Oak, Elder, Elm and Thorn,
The Yew[7] alone burns lamps of peace
  For them that lie forlorn.

Silver

Slowly, silently, now the moon
Walks the night in her silver shoon;
This way, and that, she peers, and sees
Silver fruit upon silver trees;
One by one the casements catch
Her beams beneath the silvery thatch;
Couched in his kennel, like a log,
With paws of silver sleeps the dog;
From their shadowy cote the white breasts peep
Of doves in a silver-feathered sleep;
A harvest mouse goes scampering by,
With silver claws, and silver eye;
And moveless fish in the water gleam,
By silver reeds in a silver stream.

7. The yew is associated with mourning and death.

WALTER DE LA MARE

Nobody Knows

Often I've heard the Wind sigh
  By the ivied orchard wall,
Over the leaves in the dark night,
  Breathe a sighing call,
And faint away in the silence,
  While I, in my bed,
Wondered, 'twixt dreaming and waking,
    What it said.

Nobody knows what the Wind is,
  Under the height of the sky,
Where the hosts of the stars keep far away
      house
  And its wave sweeps by——
Just a great wave of the air,
  Tossing the leaves in its sea,
And foaming under the eaves of the roof
    That covers me.

And so we live under deep water,
  All of us, beasts and men,
And our bodies are buried down under the
      sand,
  When we go again;
And leave, like the fishes, our shells,
  And float on the Wind and away,
To where, o'er the marvellous tides of the air,
    Burns day.

Will Ever?

Will he ever be weary of wandering,
  The flaming sun?
Ever weary of waning in lovelight,
  The white still moon?

Will ever a shepherd come
  With a crook of simple gold,
And lead all the little stars
  Like lambs to the fold?

Will ever the Wanderer sail
  From over the sea,
Up the river of water,
  To the stones to me?

Will he take us all into his ship,
  Dreaming, and waft us far,
To where in the clouds of the West
  The Islands[8] are?

Wanderers

Wide are the meadows of night,
And daisies are shining there,
Tossing their lovely dews,
Lustrous and fair;
And through these sweet fields go,
Wand'rers 'mid the stars[9]——
Venus, Mercury, Uranus, Neptune,
Saturn, Jupiter, Mars.

'Tired in their silver, they move,
And circling, whisper and say,
Fair are the blossoming meads of delight
Through which we stray.

Many a Mickle[1]

A little sound——
Only a little, a little——
The breath in a reed,
A trembling fiddle;
A trumpet's ring,
The shuddering drum;
So all the glory, bravery, hush
Of music come.

A little sound——
Only a stir and a sigh
Of each green leaf
Its fluttering neighbour by;

8. The Islands of the Blessed: mythological islands where the favorites of the gods dwell after death.
9. *Planet* is derived from the Greek word for "wanderer."
1. A great quantity. Compare the proverb "Many a little [or 'a pickle'] makes a mickle."

Oak on to oak,
The wide dark forest through——
So o'er the watery wheeling world
The night winds go.

A little sound,
Only a little, a little——
The thin high drone
Of the simmering kettle,
The gathering frost,
The click of needle and thread;
Mother, the fading wall, the dream,
The drowsy bed.

Snow

No breath of wind,
No gleam of sun—
Still the white snow
Whirls softly down—
Twig and bough
And blade and thorn
All in an icy
Quiet, forlorn.
Whispering, rustling,
Through the air,
On sill and stone,
Roof—everywhere,
It heaps its powdery
Crystal flakes,
Of every tree
A mountain makes;
Till pale and faint
At shut of day,
Stoops from the West
One wintry ray.
And, feathered in fire,
Where ghosts the moon,
A robin shrills
His lonely tune.

The Horseman

There was a Horseman rode so fast
The Sun in heaven stayed still at last.

WALTER DE LA MARE

1226

On, on, and on, his galloping shoon
Gleamed never never beneath the Moon.

The People said, 'Thou must be mad, O
Man with a never-lengthening shadow!

'Mad and bad! Ho! stay thy course,
Thou and thy never-stabled horse!

'Oh, what a wild and wicked sight—
A Horseman never dark with night!

'Depart from us, depart from us,
Thou and thy lank-maned Pegasus!'[2] . . .

They talked into declining day,
Since both were now leagues—leagues away.

The Song of the Secret

Where is beauty?
     Gone, gone:
The cold winds have taken it
     With their faint moan;
The white stars have shaken it,
     Trembling down,
Into the pathless deeps of the sea:
     Gone, gone
     Is beauty from me.

The clear naked flower
     Is faded and dead;
The green-leafed willow,
     Drooping her head,
Whispers low to the shade
     Of her boughs in the stream,
     Sighing a beauty
     Secret as dream.

The Song of Soldiers

As I sat musing by the frozen dyke,
There was one man marching with a bright steel pike,
Marching in the dayshine like a ghost came he,

2. The winged horse of classical mythology.

And behind me was the moaning and the
    murmur of the sea.

As I sat musing, 'twas not one but ten——
Rank on rank of ghostly soldiers marching o'er
    the fen,
Marching in the misty air they showed in
    dreams to me,
And behind me was the shouting and the
    shattering of the sea.

As I sat musing, 'twas a host in dark array,
With their horses and their cannon wheeling
    onward to the fray,
Moving like a shadow to the fate the brave must
    dree,[3]
And behind me roared the drums, rang the
    trumpets of the sea.

The Bees' Song

Thousandz of thornz there be
On the Rozez where gozez
The Zebra of Zee:
Sleek, striped, and hairy,
The steed of the Fairy
Princess of Zee.

Heavy with blossomz be
The Rozez that growzez
In the thickets of Zee,
Where grazez the Zebra
Marked *Abracadeeebra*
Of the Princess of Zee.

And he nozez the poziez
Of the Rozez that growzez
So luvez'm[4] and free,
With an eye, dark and wary,
In search of a Fairy,
Whose Rozez he knowzez
Were not honeyed for he,
But to breathe a sweet incense
To solace the Princess
Of far-away Zzzee.

3. Endure.
4. I.e., lovesome: lovely.

The Song of Enchantment

A Song of Enchantment I sang me there,
In a green—green wood, by waters fair,
Just as the words came up to me
I sang it under the wild wood tree.

Widdershins[5] turned I, singing it low,
Watching the wild birds come and go;
No cloud in the deep dark blue to be seen
Under the thick-thatched branches green.

Twilight came; silence came;
The planet of evening's silver flame;
By darkening paths I wandered through
Thickets trembling with drops of dew.

But the music is lost and the words are gone
Of the song I sang as I sat alone,
Ages and ages have fallen on me——
On the wood and the pool and the elder tree.

Dream-Song

Sunlight, moonlight,
    Twilight, starlight——
Gloaming at the close of day,
    And an owl calling,
    Cool dews falling
In a wood of oak and may.

Lantern-light, taper-light,
    Torchlight, no-light:
Darkness at the shut of day,
    And lions roaring,
    Their wrath pouring
In wild waste places far away.

Elf-light, bat-light,
    Touchwood-light and toad-light,
And the sea a shimmering gloom of grey,
    And a small face smiling
    In a dream's beguiling
In a world of wonders far away.

5. Counterclockwise. Turning opposite the direction of the
sun is often associated with black magic, and also with rituals
of ridding or banishment.

The Song of Shadows

Sweep thy faint strings, Musician,
    With thy long lean hand;
Downward the starry tapers burn,
    Sinks soft the waning sand;
The old hound whimpers couched in sleep,
    The embers smoulder low;
Across the walls the shadows
        Come, and go.

Sweep softly thy strings, Musician,
    The minutes mount to hours;
Frost on the windless casement weaves
    A labyrinth of flowers;
Ghosts linger in the darkening air,
    Hearken at the open door;
Music hath called them, dreaming,
        Home once more.

The Song of the Mad Prince

Who said, 'Peacock Pie'?
    The old King to the sparrow:
Who said, 'Crops are ripe'?
    Rust to the harrow:
Who said, 'Where sleeps she now?
    Where rests she now her head,
Bathed in eve's loveliness'?——
    That's what I said.

Who said, 'Ay, mum's the word'?
    Sexton to willow:
Who said, 'Green dusk for dreams,
    Moss for a pillow'?
Who said, 'All Time's delight
    Hath she for narrow bed;
Life's troubled bubble broken'?——
    That's what I said.

The Song of 'Finis'

At the edge of All the Ages
    A Knight sate on his steed,
His armour red and thin with rust,
    His soul from sorrow freed;
And he lifted up his visor
    From a face of skin and bone,
And his horse turned head and whinnied
    As the twain stood there alone.

No Bird above that steep of time
    Sang of a livelong quest;
No wind breathed,
        Rest:
'Lone for an end!' cried Knight to steed,
    Loosed an eager rein——
Charged with his challenge into Space:
    And quiet did quiet remain.

1913   1916

WALTER DE LA MARE

ROBERT GRAVES
1895–1985

There's a cool web of language winds us in,
Retreat from too much joy or too much fear.
—"The Cool Web"

In his long life, Robert Graves published fifty-five collections of poetry and more than forty major works of nonfiction. A classicist, translator, and critic, he wrote one of the great memoirs of World War I, *Good-bye to All That: An Autobiography* (1929); historical novels, including *I, Claudius* (1933); and one of the twentieth century's most influential studies of myth, *The White Goddess: A Historical Grammar of Poetic Myth* (1948). Although Graves wrote only six books explicitly for children, he remained in touch with the immediacy of a child's fresh experience of the world. Randall Jarrell describes Graves as a poet who "has never forgotten the child's incommensurable joys; nor has he forgotten the child and the man's incommensurable, irreducible agonies."

Graves's experience with children was considerable, for he had eight, born over a thirty-four-year period. In 1918 (back in England after having been wounded so seriously on the Somme that he had been reported dead), he married Nancy Nicholson. In 1919 he took up his war-deferred studies at St. John College, Oxford, writing furiously as he attempted to support a family that by 1924 included four children. Earning a B.Litt. in 1925 enabled him to take a job the following year teaching literature at the Royal Egyptian University in Cairo. The entire family accompanied him—as did Laura Riding, an American whose poetry he admired and whom he had invited to visit them in England. A year later, they all returned to England, and in 1929 Graves and Riding moved to Deyá on Majorca, where he was to make his permanent home for the rest of his life (they were forced out by the Spanish Civil War in 1936, and he returned after the end of World War II, ten years later). Riding had an extraordinarily important influence on him, both as literary partner and as muse. But in 1939, while they were in America, she fell in love

with another man. Once back in England, Graves soon began living with Beryl Hodge; three of their children were born in England, and one on Majorca. They married in 1950.

Most of Graves's books for children were written in the 1960s, when he was Professor of Poetry at Oxford (1961–66). Two, *The Penny Fiddle: Poems for Children* (1960) and *Ann at Highwood Hall: Poems for Children* (1964), were illustrated by Edward Ardizzone, and each of the others, all prose, had a different illustrator: *The Big Green Book* (1963), Maurice Sendak; *Two Wise Children* (1966), Ralph Pinto; and *The Poor Boy Who Followed His Star* (1968), Alice Meyer-Wallace. One of his final works—*An Ancient Castle* (1980), illustrated by his niece Elizabeth Graves—was for children, and many of his writings on classical myth appealed to young readers.

Although Graves is central to any general history of twentieth-century literature, his writings for children have received little critical attention. He was one of a number of serious poets (including Ted Hughes, Randall Jarrell, Theodore Roethke, and Richard Wilbur) writing for children in a short period during the early 1960s. Though Hughes and Jarrell—both of whom acknowledged Graves's influence on their work—became canonical in the field of poetry for children, the others, including Graves did not.

As well as intending to restore the historical trace of Graves's critical line, the inclusion of *The Penny Fiddle* here foregrounds his ability to speak directly while engaging emotional complexity and the traditional tunes of nursery verse. Graves dedicated the volume to his youngest child, Tomás, "on his eighth birthday." In a 1963 interview with the film star Gina Lollobrigida, Graves indirectly explained its appeal: "A child's mind is simple yet complicated," he told her. So is his verse for children.

THE PENNY FIDDLE

The Penny Fiddle

Yesterday I bought a penny fiddle
    And put it to my chin to play,
But I found that the strings were painted,
    So I threw my fiddle away.

A gipsy girl found my penny fiddle
    As it lay abandoned there;
When she asked me if she might keep it,
    I told her I did not care.

Then she drew such music from the fiddle
    With help of a farthing[1] bow,
That I offered five shillings[2] for the secret.
    But, alas, she would not let it go.

Allie

Allie, call the birds in,
    The birds from the sky!
Allie calls, Allie sings,
    Down they all fly:
First there came
Two white doves,
    Then a sparrow from her nest,
Then a clucking bantam hen,
    Then a robin red-breast.

Allie, call the beasts in,
    The beasts, every one!
Allie calls, Allie sings,
    In they all run:
First there came
Two black lambs,
    Then a grunting Berkshire sow,
Then a dog without a tail,
    Then a red and white cow.

Allie, call the fish up,
    The fish from the stream!
Allie calls, Allie sings,
    Up they all swim:
First there came
Two gold fish,
    A minnow and a miller's thumb,
Then a school of little trout,
    Then the twisting eels come.

Allie, call the children,
    Call them from the green!
Allie calls, Allie sings,
    Soon they run in:
First there came
Tom and Madge,
    Kate and I who'll not forget
How we played by the water's edge
    Till the April sun set.

Robinson Crusoe

Robinson Crusoe[3] cut his coats
    Not too narrow, not too big,
From the hides of nanny-goats;
    Yet he longed to keep a pig.

Robinson Crusoe sat in grief,
    All day long he sometimes sat,
Gazing at the coral reef,
    Grumbling to his favourite cat.

'Queen of Pussies,' he would say,
    'Two things I am sure about:
Bacon should begin the day,
    "Pork!" should put the candle out.'

---

1. A coin worth one-quarter of a penny (no longer in circulation).
2. There were 12 pennies in a British shilling.

3. The title character of Daniel Defoe's 1719 novel. During his years shipwrecked on an island, he made himself many garments from goatskin.

The Six Badgers

As I was a-hoeing, a-hoeing my lands,
Six badgers walked up, with white wands in
  their hands.
They formed a ring round me and, bowing, they
  said:
'Hurry home, Farmer George, for the table is
  spread!
There's pie in the oven, there's beef on the
  plate:
Hurry home, Farmer George, if you would not
  be late!'

So homeward went I, but could not understand
Why six fine dog-badgers with white wands in
  hand
Should seek me out hoeing, and bow in a ring,
And all to inform me so common a thing!

One Hard Look

Small gnats that fly
In hot July
And lodge in sleeping ears
Can rouse therein
A trumpet's din
With Day of Judgement fears.

Small mice at night
Can wake more fright
Than lions at midday;
A straw will crack
The camel's back—
There is no easier way.

One smile relieves
A heart that grieves
Though deadly sad it be,
And one hard look
Can close the book
That lovers love to see.

Jock o' Binnorie[4]

King Duncan had a fool called Leery
    And gave him very high pay
To tell him stories after dinner,
    A new one every day;
But if the stories failed him
    (As Leery did agree)
The King would call his merry men all
    And hang him from a tree.

Leery began with Jim o' Binnorie
    Who danced on Stirling Rock
And emptied a peck of pickled eels
    All over his brother Jock;
Yet Jock refrained from unkind words
    That many a lad might use,
And while Jim slept on a load of hay
    Put five live eels in his shoes.

Leery had told nine hundred tales
    And found no others to tell,
He started from the first once more—
    King Duncan knew it well.
'Old friends are best, dear Fool,' he cried,
    'And old yarns heard again.
You may tell me the story of Jock o' Binnorie
    Every night of my reign!'

What Did I Dream?

What did I dream? I do not know—
    The fragments fly like chaff.
Yet, strange, my mind was tickled so
    I cannot help but laugh.

Pull the curtains close again,
    Tuck me grandly in;
Must a world of pleasure wane
    Because birds begin

Chattering in a restless tone,
    Rousing me from sleep:
The finest entertainment known,
    And given rag-cheap?

---

4. Variant of "Jack a Nory," a character in a nursery rhyme that is a circular story (see "I'll tell you a story," above).

Lift-Boy

Let me tell you the story of how I began:
I began as the boot-boy and ended as the boot-
      man,[5]
With nothing in my pockets but a jack-knife and
      a button,
With nothing in my pockets but a jack-knife and
      a button,
With nothing in my pockets.

Let me tell you the story of how I went on:
I began as the lift-boy and ended as the lift-man,[6]
With nothing in my pockets but a jack-knife and
      a button,
With nothing in my pockets but a jack-knife and
      a button,
With nothing in my pockets.

But along came Old Eagle, like Moses or David,
He stopped at the fourth floor and preached me
      Damnation:
'Not a soul shall be savèd, not one shall be
      savèd.
The whole First Creation shall forfeit salvation:
From knife-boy to lift-boy, from ragged to regal,
Not one shall be savèd, not you, not Old Eagle—
No soul on earth escapeth, even if all repent . . .'
So I cut the cords of the lift and down we went,
With nothing in our pockets.

Henry and Mary

Henry was a young king,
      Mary was his queen;
He gave her a snowdrop
      On a stalk of green.

Then all for his kindness
      And all for his care
She gave him a new-laid egg
      In the garden there.

'Love, can you sing?'
            'I cannot sing.'
   'Or tell a tale?'
            'Not one I know.'
'Then let us play at queen and king
   As down the garden walks we go.'

Dicky

Mother: Oh, what a heavy sigh!
            Dicky, are you ailing?

Dicky: Even by the fireside, Mother,
            My heart is failing.

         Tonight across the down,
            Whistling and jolly,
         I sauntered out from town
            With my stick of holly.

         Bounteous and cool from sea
            The wind was blowing,
         Cloud shadows under the moon
            Coming and going.

         I sang old country songs,
            Ran and leaped quick,
         And turned home by St Swithin's
            Twirling my stick.

         And there, as I was passing
            The churchyard gate,
         An old man stopped me: 'Dicky,
            You're walking late.'

         I did not know the man,
            I grew afeared
         At his lean, lolling jaw,
            His spreading beard.

         His garments old and musty,
            Of antique cut,
         His body very frail and bony,
            His eyes tight shut.

---

5. A servant in a hotel who cleans boots.
6. An elevator operator.

1232

Oh, even to tell it now
    My courage ebbs . . .
His face was clay, Mother,
    His beard, cobwebs.

In that long horrid pause
    'Good night,' he said,
Entered and clicked the gate:
    'Each to his bed.'

Mother: Do not sigh or fear, Dicky;
    How is it right
To grudge the dead their ghostly dark
    And wan moonlight?

We have the glorious sun,
    Lamp and fireside.
Grudge not the dead their
    moonbeams
When abroad they ride.

Love Without Hope

Love without hope, as when the young bird-
    catcher
Swept off his tall hat to the Squire's own
    daughter,
So let the imprisoned larks escape and fly
Singing about her head, as she rode by.

The Hills of May

Walking with a virgin heart
    The green hills of May,
Me, the Wind, she took as lover
    By her side to play,

Let me toss her untied hair,
    Let me shake her gown,
Careless though the daisies redden,
    Though the sun frown,

Scorning in her gay habit
    Lesser love than this,
My cool spiritual embracing,
    My secret kiss.

So she walked, the proud lady,
    So danced or ran,
So she loved with a whole heart,
    Neglecting man . . .

Fade, fail, innocent stars
    On the green of May:
She has left our bournes for ever,
    Too fine to stay.

In the Wilderness

He, of his gentleness,
Thirsting and hungering
Walked in the wilderness;
Soft words of grace he spoke
Unto lost desert-folk
That listened wondering.
He heard the bittern call
From ruined palace-wall,
Answered him brotherly;
He held communion
With the she-pelican
Of lonely piety.
Basilisk, cockatrice,
Flocked to his homilies,
With mail[7] of dread device,
With monstrous barbèd stings,
With eager dragon-eyes;
Great bats on leathern wings
And old, blind, broken things
Mean in their miseries.
Then ever with him went,
Of all his wanderings
Comrade, with ragged coat,
Gaunt ribs—poor innocent—
Bleeding foot, burning throat,
The guileless young scapegoat:[8]
For forty nights and days
Followed in Jesus' ways,
Sure guard behind him kept,
Tears like a lover wept.

---

7. Armor.
8. Literally, the goat that, in an annual ceremony described in the Bible, was driven into the wilderness after the sins of the Israelites were placed on its head (see Leviticus 16.8–10).

'The General Elliott'

He fell in victory's fierce pursuit,
    Holed through and through with shot;
A sabre sweep had hacked him deep
    'Twixt neck and shoulder-knot.

The potman[9] cannot well recall,
    The ostler[1] never knew,
Whether that day was Malplaquet,
    The Boyne, or Waterloo.[2]

But there he hangs, a tavern sign,
    With foolish bold regard
For cock and hen and loitering men
    And wagons down the yard.

Raised high above the hayseed world
    He smokes his china pipe;
And now surveys the orchard ways,
    The damsons clustering ripe—

Stares at the churchyard slabs beyond,
    Where country neighbours lie:
Their brief renown set lowly down,
    But his commands the sky.

He grips a tankard of brown ale
    That spills a generous foam:
Often he drinks, they say, and winks
    At drunk men lurching home.

No upstart hero may usurp
    That honoured swinging seat;
His seasons pass with pipe and glass
    Until the tale's complete—

And paint shall keep his buttons bright
    Though all the world's forgot
Whether he died for England's pride
    By battle or by pot.

Vain and Careless

Lady, lovely lady,
    Careless and gay!
Once, when a beggar called,
    She gave her child away.

The beggar took the baby,
    Wrapped it in a shawl—
'Bring him back,' the lady said,
    'Next time you call.'

Hard by lived a vain man,
    So vain and so proud
He would walk on stilts
    To be seen by the crowd

Up above the chimney pots,
    Tall as a mast;
And all the people ran about
    Shouting till he passed.

'A splendid match surely,'
    Neighbours saw it plain,
'Although she is so careless,
    Although he is so vain.'

But the lady played bobcherry,[3]
    Did not see or care,
As the vain man went by her,
    Aloft in the air.

This gentle-born couple
    Lived and died apart—
Water will not mix with oil,
    Nor vain with careless heart.

The Forbidden Play

I'll tell you the truth, Father, though your heart
    bleed:
    To the Play I went,

---

9. Man who serves liquor at a pub.
1. One who attends to horses or mules.
2. Three important battles: at Malplaquet, a town in France near the Belgian border, the French were defeated by allied forces led by the Duke of Marlborough (1709); at the Boyne, a river in Ireland, the Protestant forces of William III of England defeated James II, the Catholic king he had replaced (1690); and at Waterloo, a town in central Belgium, Napoleon suffered his final defeat at the hands of the Duke of Wellington and Gebhard von Blücher (1815).
3. A game in which children try to catch in their teeth cherries tied to a string.

With sixpence for a near seat, money's worth
    indeed,
    The best ever spent.

You forbade me, you threatened me, but here's
    the story
    Of my splendid night:
It was colour, drums, music, a tragic glory,
    Fear with delight.

Hamlet, Prince of Denmark,[4] title of the tale:
    He of that name,
A tall, glum fellow, velvet cloaked, with a shirt
    of mail,
    Two eyes like flame.

All the furies of Hell circled round that man,
    Maddening his heart,
There was old murder done before play began,
    Aye, the ghost took part.

There were grave-diggers delving, they brought
    up bones,
    And with rage and grief
All the players shouted in full, kingly tones,
    Grand, passing belief.

Ah, there were ladies there radiant as day,
    And changing scenes:
Fabulous words were tossed about like hay
    By kings and queens.

I puzzled on the sense of it in vain,
    Yet for pain I cried,
As one and all they faded, poisoned or slain,
    In great agony died.

Drive me out, Father, never to return,
    Though I am your son,
And penniless! But that glory for which I burn
    Shall be soon begun:

I shall wear great boots, shall strut and shout,
    Keep my locks curled;
The fame of my name shall go ringing about
    Over half the world.

4. By William Shakespeare (ca. 1600).
5. In British legend, a giant, as was Magog. After their race
was conquered by Brutus and other Trojans who fled to
England after the fall of Troy, Gog and Magog were forced to
serve as porters at Brutus's palace, on the site where London's

The Bedpost

Sleepy Betsy from her pillow
    Sees the post and ball
Of her sister's wooden bedstead
    Shadowed on the wall.

Now this grave young warrior standing
    With uncovered head
Tells her stories of old battle
    As she lies in bed:

How the Emperor and the Farmer,
    Fighting knee to knee,
Broke their swords but whirled their scabbards
    Till they gained the sea.

How the ruler of that shore
    Foully broke his oath,
Gave them beds in his sea cave,
    Then stabbed them both.

How the daughters of the Emperor,
    Diving boldly through,
Caught and killed their father's murderer
    Old Cro-bar-cru.

How the farmer's sturdy sons
    Fought the Giant Gog,[5]
Threw him into Stony Cataract
    In the land of Og.

Will and Abel were their names,
    Though they went by others:
He could tell ten thousand stories
    Of these brave brothers.

How the Emperor's eldest daughter
    Fell in love with Will
And went with him to the Court of Venus[6]
    Over Hoo Hill;

How Gog's wife encountered Abel
    Whom she hated most,
Stole away his arms and helmet,
    Turned him to a post.

Guildhall was later built; their effigies have stood in the
Guildhall for centuries.
6. Roman goddess of love.

THE PENNY FIDDLE

As a post he shall stay rooted
        For yet many years,
Until a maiden shall release him
        With pitying tears.

But Betsy likes the fiercer stories,
        Clang and clash of fight,
And Abel wanes with the spent candle—
        'Sweetheart, good night!'

The Well-dressed Children

Here's flowery taffeta for Mary's new gown:
        Here's black velvet, all the rage, for Dick's
                birthday coat.
Coral buttons for you, Mary, all the way down;
        Lace ruffles, Dick, for you—you'll be a man
                of note.

For Mary, I have chosen this green gingham
                shade,
        And a silk purse brocaded with roses gold
                and blue—
You'll learn to hold them proudly like colours on
                parade,
        No banker's wife in all the town half so
                grand as you.

For Dick, I have brought a Malacca[7] walking-
                stick,
        And a pair of buckskin gloves by the King's
                glover made—
I'll teach you to flourish them like a lordly Dick,
        Marching beside Mary, your pearl pin
                displayed.

On Sunday to Church you'll go, each with a
                book of prayer:
        Then up the street and down the aisles,
                everywhere you'll see
Of all the honours earned in Town, how small is
                virtue's share,
        How large the share of lordly pride in
                peacock finery.

The Magical Picture

Glinting on the roadway
A broken mirror lay;
Then what did the child say
        Who found it there?
He cried there was a goblin
Looking out as he looked in:
Wild eyes and speckled skin,
        Black, bristling hair!

He brought it to his father
Who, being a simple sailor,
Swore: 'This is a true wonder,
        Deny it who can!
Plain enough to me, for one,
'Tis a picture deftly done
Of Admiral Horatio Nelson[8]
        When a young man.'

The sailor's wife perceiving
Her husband had some pretty thing
At which he was peering,
        Seized it from his hand.
Then tears started and ran free:
'Jack, you have deceived me,
I love you no more,' said she,
        'So understand!'

'But, Mary,' cries the sailor,
'This is a famous treasure;
Admiral Nelson's picture
        Taken in youth.'
'O cruel man,' she cries,
'To trick me with such lies,
Who is this lady with bold eyes?
        Tell me the truth!'

Up rides their parish priest
Mounted on a thin beast.
Grief and anger have not ceased
        Between those two;
Little Tom still weeps for fear:
He has seen Hobgoblin, near—
Ugly face and foul leer
        That pierced him through.

---

7. Made of the stem of an Asian rattan palm (Malacca is a town on the Malay Peninsula, in Southeast Asia).

8. British naval hero of the Napoleonic wars (1758–1805).

Now the old priest lifts his glove
Bidding all, for God's love,
To stand and not to move,
    Lest blood be shed.
'O, O!' cries the urchin,
'I saw the Devil grin,
He glared out as I looked in—
    Like a death's head!'

Mary weeps: 'Ah, Father,
My Jack loves another!
On some voyage he courted her
    In a land afar.'
This, with cursing, Jack denies:
'Father, use your own eyes—
It is Lord Nelson in the guise
    Of a young tar.'

When the priest took the glass,
Fresh marvels came to pass:
'A saint of glory, by the Mass!
    Where got you this?'
He signed him with the good sign;
Be sure the relic was divine,
He would fix it in a shrine
    For pilgrims to kiss.

The *Alice Jean*

One moonlight night a ship drove in,
    A ghost ship from the west,
Drifting with bare mast and lone tiller;
    Like a mermaid drest
In long green weed and barnacles
    She beached and came to rest.

All the watchers of the coast
    Flocked to view the sight;
Men and women, streaming down
    Through the summer night,
Found her standing tall and ragged
    Beached in the moonlight.

Then one old woman stared aghast:
    'The *Alice Jean*? But no!
The ship that took my Ned from me
    Sixty years ago—

Drifted back from the utmost west
    With the ocean's flow?

'Caught and caged in the weedy pool
    Beyond the western brink,
Where crewless vessels lie and rot
    In waters black as ink,
Torn out at last by a sudden gale—
    Is it the *Jean*, you think?'

A hundred women gaped at her,
    The menfolk nudged and laughed,
But none could find a likelier story
    For the strange craft
With fear and death and desolation
    Rigged fore and aft.

The blind ship came forgotten home
    To all but one of these,
Of whom none dared to climb aboard her:
    And by and by the breeze
Veered hard about, and the *Alice Jean*
    Foundered in foaming seas.

A Boy in Church

'Gabble-gabble . . . brethren . . . gabble-gabble!'
    My window frames forest and heather.
I hardly hear the tuneful babble,
    Not knowing nor much caring whether
The text is praise or exhortation,
Harvest thanksgiving or salvation.

Outside it blows wetter and wetter,
    The tossing trees never stay still.
I shift my elbows to catch better
    The full round sweep of heathered hill.
The tortured copse bends to and fro
In silence like a shadow-show.

I add the hymns up, over and over,
    Until there's not the least mistake:
    Seven-seventy-one. (Look! there's a plover!
    It's gone!) Who's that Saint by the lake?
The red glow from his mantle passes
Across the broad memorial brasses.

It's pleasant here for dreams and thinking,
    Lolling and letting reason nod,
With ugly, serious people linking
    Their prayers to a forgiving God . . .
But a dumb blast sets the trees swaying
With furious zeal like madmen praying.

How and Why

How and why
Poets die,
    That's a dismal tale:
Some take a spill
On Guinea Hill,
    Some drown in ale.

ROBERT GRAVES

Some get lost
At sea, or crossed
    In love with cruel witches;
Yet some attain
Long life and reign
    Like Popes among their riches.

Warning to Children

Children, if you dare to think
Of the greatness, rareness, muchness,
Fewness of this precious only
Endless world in which you say
You live, you think of things like this:
Blocks of slate enclosing dappled
Red and green, enclosing tawny
Yellow nets, enclosing white
And black acres of dominoes,
Where a neat brown paper parcel
Tempts you to untie the string.
In the parcel a small island,
On the island a large tree,
On the tree a husky fruit.
Strip the husk and pare the rind off:
In the kernel you will see
Blocks of slate enclosed by dappled
Red and green, enclosed by tawny
Yellow nets, enclosed by white
And black acres of dominoes,
Where the same brown paper parcel—
Children, leave the string alone!
For who dares undo the parcel
Finds himself at once inside it,
On the island, in the fruit,
Blocks of slate about his head,

Finds himself enclosed by dappled
Green and red, enclosed by yellow
Tawny nets, enclosed by black
And white acres of dominoes,
With the same brown paper parcel
Still untied upon his knee.

And, if he then should dare to think
Of the fewness, muchness, rareness,
Greatness of this endless only
Precious world in which he says
He lives—he then unties the string.

1960

RANDALL JARRELL
1914–1965

It was in the Carnegie Public Library in Nashville, Tennessee, that the literary tastes of the child Randall Jarrell were formed, a process he alludes to in "Children Selecting Books in a Library":

> Read meanwhile . . . hunt among the shelves,
>   as dogs do, grasses,
> And find one cure for Everychild's diseases
> Beginning: *Once upon a time there was*
> A wolf that fed, a mouse that warned, a bear
>   that rode
> A boy. Us men, alas! Wolves, mice, bears bore.
> And yet wolves, mice, bears, children, gods
>   and men
> In slow perambulation up and down the shelves
> Of the universe are seeking . . . who knows
>   except themselves?

Jarrell himself was seeking a place to belong; his parents' divorce in 1925 had taken him from California, where he had lived almost his entire life, to Nashville, the home of his mother's family. In one sense, he would find his place in literature, earning an M.A. in English at Vanderbilt (1939, after a B.A. in psychology) and becoming a poet, critic, and inspiring teacher at a number of institutions—most notably the University of North Carolina at Greensboro (then called the Women's College), where he taught from 1947 until his death. In another sense, the quest itself became a part of who he was. The poet Robert Lowell, a lifelong friend, implies as much by calling Jarrell "Child Randall" in an appreciation written after his death. Lowell is evoking Childe Roland and Childe Harold, the questers made famous by Robert Browning and Byron.

By the time Jarrell published his first book for children, *The Gingerbread Rabbit* (1964), he was already a distinguished man of letters: he had received two Guggenheim Fellowships (1946,

1963), published numerous poetry collections, and won a National Book Award for *The Woman at the Washington Zoo* (1961). He had also written a well-received satirical novel of life in the academy (*Pictures from the Institution: A Comedy*, 1954), served as poetry consultant at the Library of Congress (1956–58), and created a substantial body of witty, incisive criticism, often prescient in its judgments (see especially the essays collected in *Poetry and the Age*, 1953).

As a poet, Jarrell remains best known for his often-anthologized "The Death of the Ball Turret Gunner." It was one of his sequence of World War II poems. The punch line, "When I died they washed me out of the turret with a hose," is characteristic of Jarrell at his most powerful: a tiny, painfully straightforward domestic detail caught in a cosmic nightmare. Jarrell had served in the air force as a flight and celestial navigation instructor (1943–46), though he did not see any combat. The image of washing the remains out with a hose is a striking example of Jarrell's capacity for imaginative sympathy, his ability to find the exact physical detail to convey an abstract emotional state. Jarrell described himself as interested in "Gestalt psychology, ethnology and 'folk' literature." Fairy tales were a persistent theme in his writing, reworked and explored in such poems as "Cinderella," "Sleeping Beauty: Variation of the Prince," and "The Märchen." In 1962, at the invitation of the children's book editor Michael di Capua. Jarrell contributed translations to a new edition of the Grimm Brothers' tales; di Capua then urged him to write his own children's stories. While *The Gingerbread Rabbit*, illustrated by Garth Williams, is a new version of the old folktale about the Gingerbread Man, *The Bat-Poet* (1964), illustrated by Maurice Sendak, is a highly original and quasi-autobiographical parable of a poet's development. Sendak, then at the beginning of his career, also illustrated *The Animal Family* (1965), a story of a family created by love rather than blood. There is a lovely autobiographical element in the story: with his marriage to Mary von Schrader in 1952, Jarrell gained two stepdaughters (his first marriage to Mackie Langham had been childless). Sendak also provided the cover illustration for *The Lost World: Last Poems* (1965), published just months before Jarrell's death. And Sendak illustrated Jarrell's posthumously published book for children, *Fly By Night* (1976). All engage, at least partly, Jarrell's quest for childhood's loss and a lost childhood.

Jarrell's books for children, all written in the early 1960s, had been precipitated by a chance gift from his mother in 1962: "an old Christmas card box from the twenties containing the letters he had written her from California when he was twelve" (foreword to *The Lost World*, by Mary Jarrell). Yet there is nothing sentimental or nostalgic about any of Jarrell's children's books.

The Bat-Poet remains Jarrell's most enduring legacy, a book he described as "half for children, half for grownups": a tragicomic quest for both an authentic voice and a responsive audience. The story tracks the attempts of the misfit Bat-Poet (Jarrell's alter-ego) to transform experience into poems (embedded in the prose narrative) and find good listeners. It's a perfect introduction to reading and writing poetry. Jarrell plays the naïve chipmunk (who responds emotionally) against the confident mockingbird—modeled, according to Mary Jarrell, on Frost and Lowell.

Early in 1965, Jarrell was depressed, and was hospitalized after an attempted suicide. He appeared to be recovering, and his last letters are heartbreakingly optimistic and hopeful. But one night when he was walking alone, as he often did, on a country road, he was struck by a car; his death was ruled an accident. Though his books remain, there is an inevitable sense that his critical and poetic voices were silenced much too soon.

The Bat-Poet

Once upon a time there was a bat—a little light brown bat, the color of coffee with cream in it. He looked like a furry mouse with wings. When I'd go in and out my front door, in the daytime, I'd look up over my head and see him hanging upside down from the roof of the porch. He and the others hung there in a bunch, all snuggled together with their wings folded, fast asleep. Sometimes one of them would wake up for a minute and get in a more comfortable position, and then the others would wriggle around in their sleep till they'd got more comfortable too; when they all moved it looked as if a fur wave went over them. At night they'd fly up and down, around and around, and catch insects and eat them; on a rainy night, though, they'd stay snuggled together just as though it were still day. If you pointed a flashlight at them you'd see them screw up their faces to keep the light out of their eyes.

Toward the end of summer all the bats except the little brown one began sleeping in the barn. He missed them, and tried to get them to come back and sleep on the porch with him. "What do you want to sleep in the barn for?" he asked them.

"We don't know," the others said. "What do you want to sleep on the porch for?"

"It's where we always sleep," he said. "If I slept in the barn I'd be homesick. Do come back and sleep with me!" But they wouldn't.

So he had to sleep all alone. He missed the others. They had always felt so warm and furry against him; whenever he'd waked, he'd pushed himself up into the middle of them and gone right back to sleep. Now he'd wake up and, instead of snuggling against the others and going back to sleep, he would just hang there and think. Sometimes he would open his eyes a little and look out into the sunlight. It gave him a queer feeling for it to be daytime and for him to be hanging there looking; he felt the way you would feel if you woke up and went to the window and stayed there for hours, looking out into the moonlight.

It was different in the daytime. The squirrels and the chipmunk, that he had never seen before—at night they were curled up in their nests or holes, fast asleep—ate nuts and acorns and seeds, and ran after each other, playing. And all the birds hopped and sang and flew; at night they had been asleep, except for the mockingbird. The bat had always heard the mockingbird. The mockingbird would sit on the highest branch of a tree, in the moonlight, and sing half the night. The bat loved to listen to him. He could imitate all the other birds—he'd even imitate the way the squirrels chattered when they were angry, like two rocks being knocked together; and he could imitate the milk bottles being put down on the porch and the barn door closing, a long rusty squeak. And he made up songs and words all his own, that nobody else had ever said or sung.

The bat told the other bats about all the things you could see and hear in the daytime. "You'd love them," he said. "The next time you wake up in the daytime, just keep your eyes open for a while and don't go back to sleep."

The other bats were sure they wouldn't like that. "We wish we didn't wake up at all," they said. "When you wake up in the daytime the light hurts your eyes—the thing to do is to close them and go right back to sleep. Day's to sleep in; as soon as it's night we'll open our eyes."

"But won't you even try it?" the little brown bat said. "Just for once, try it."

The bats all said: "No."

"But why not?" asked the little brown bat.

The bats said: "We don't know. We just don't want to."

"At least listen to the mockingbird. When you hear him it's just like the daytime."

The other bats said: "He sounds so queer. If only he squeaked or twittered—but he keeps shouting in that bass voice of his." They said this because the mockingbird's voice sounded terribly loud and deep to them; they always made little high twittering sounds themselves.

"Once you get used to it you'll like it," the little bat said. "Once you get used to it, it sounds wonderful."

"All right," said the others, "we'll try." But they were just being polite; they didn't try.

The little brown bat kept waking up in the daytime, and kept listening to the mockingbird, until one day he thought: "*I could make up a song like the mockingbird's.*" But when he tried, his high notes were all high and his low notes were all high and the notes in between were all high: he couldn't make a tune. So he imitated the mockingbird's words instead. At first his words didn't go together—even the bat could see that they didn't sound a bit like the mockingbird's. But after a while some of them began to sound beautiful, so that the bat said to himself: "If you get the words right you don't need a tune."

The bat went over and over his words till he could say them off by heart. That night he said them to the other bats. "I've made the words like the mockingbird's," he told them, "so you can tell what it's like in the daytime." Then he said to them in a deep voice—he couldn't help imitating the mockingbird—his words about the daytime:

> At dawn, the sun shines like a million moons
> And all the shadows are as bright as moonlight.
> The birds begin to sing with all their might.
> The world awakens and forgets the night.

The black-and-gray turns green-and-gold-and-blue.
The squirrels begin to—

But when he'd got this far the other bats just couldn't keep quiet any longer.

"The sun *hurts*," said one. "It hurts like getting something in your eyes."

"That's right," said another. "And shadows are black—how can a shadow be bright?"

Another one said: "What's green-and-gold-and-blue? When you say things like that we don't know what you mean."

"And it's just not real," the first one said. "When the sun rises the world goes to sleep."

"But go on," said one of the others. "We didn't mean to interrupt you."

"No, we're sorry we interrupted you," all the others said. "Say us the rest."

But when the bat tried to say them the rest he couldn't remember a word. It was hard to say anything at all, but finally he said: "I—I—tomorrow I'll say you the rest." Then he flew back to the porch. There were lots of insects flying around the light, but he didn't catch a one; instead he flew to his rafter, hung there upside down with his wings folded, and after a while went to sleep.

But he kept on making poems like the mockingbird's—only now he didn't say them to the bats. One night he saw a mother possum, with all her little white baby possums holding tight to her, eating the fallen apples under the apple tree; one night an owl swooped down on him and came so close he'd have caught him if the bat hadn't flown into a hole in the old oak by the side of the house; and another time four squirrels spent the whole morning chasing each other up and down trees, across the lawn, and over the roof. He made up poems about them all. Sometimes the poem would make him think: "It's like the mockingbird. This time it's really like the mockingbird!" But sometimes the poem would seem so bad to him that he'd get discouraged and stop in the middle, and by the next day he'd have forgotten it.

When he would wake up in the daytime and hang there looking out at the colors of the world, he would say the poems over to himself. He wanted to say them to the other bats, but then he would remember what had happened when he'd said them before. There was nobody for him to say the poems to.

One day he thought: "I could say them to the mockingbird." It got to be a regular thought of his. It was a long time, though, before he really went to the mockingbird.

The mockingbird had bad days when he would try to drive everything out of the yard, no matter what it was. He always had a peremptory, authoritative look, as if he were more alive than anything else and wanted everything else to know it; on his bad days he'd dive on everything that came into the yard—on cats and dogs, even—and strike at them with his little sharp beak and sharp claws. On his good days he didn't pay so much attention to the world, but just sang.

The day the bat went to him the mockingbird was perched on the highest branch of the big willow by the porch, singing with all his might. He was a clear gray, with white bars across his wings that flashed when he flew; every part of him had a clear, quick, decided look about it. He was standing on tiptoe, singing and singing and singing; sometimes he'd spring up into the air. This time he was singing a song about mockingbirds.

The bat fluttered to the nearest branch, hung upside down from it, and listened; finally when the mockingbird stopped for a moment he said in his little high voice: "It's beautiful, just beautiful!"

"You like poetry?" asked the mockingbird. You could tell from the way he said it that he was surprised.

"I love it," said the bat. "I listen to you every night. Every day too. I—I—"

"It's the last poem I've composed," said the mockingbird. "It's called 'To a Mockingbird.'"

"It's wonderful," the bat said. "Wonderful! Of all the songs I ever heard you sing, it's the best."

This pleased the mockingbird—mockingbirds love to be told that their last song is the best. "I'll sing it for you again," the mockingbird offered.

"Oh, please do sing it again," said the bat. "I'd love to hear it again. Just love to! Only when you've finished could I—"

But the mockingbird had already started. He not only sang it again, he made up new parts, and sang them over and over and over; they were so beautiful that the bat forgot about his own poem and just listened. When the mockingbird had finished, the bat thought: "No, I just can't say him mine. Still, though—" He said to the mockingbird: "It's wonderful to get to hear you. I could listen to you forever."

"It's a pleasure to sing to such a responsive audience," said the mockingbird. "Any time you'd like to hear it again just tell me."

The bat said: "Could—could—"

"Yes?" said the mockingbird.

The bat went on in a shy voice: "Do you suppose that I—that I could—"

The mockingbird said warmly: "That you could hear it again? Of course you can. I'll be delighted." And he sang it all over again. This time it was the best of all.

The bat told him so, and the mockingbird looked pleased but modest; it was easy for him to look pleased but hard for him to look modest, he was so full of himself. The bat asked him: "Do you suppose a bat could make poems like yours?"

"A *bat?*" the mockingbird said. But then he went on politely, "Well, I don't see why not. He couldn't sing them, of course—he simply doesn't have the range; but that's no reason he couldn't make them up. Why, I suppose for bats a bat's poems would be ideal."

The bat said: "Sometimes when I wake up in the daytime I make up poems. Could I—I wonder whether I could say you one of *my* poems?"

A queer look came over the mockingbird's face, but he said cordially: "I'd be delighted to hear one. Go right ahead." He settled himself on his branch with a listening expression.

The bat said:

A shadow is floating through the moonlight.
Its wings don't make a sound.
Its claws are long, its beak is bright.
Its eyes try all the corners of the night.

It calls and calls: all the air swells and heaves
And washes up and down like water.
The ear that listens to the owl believes
In death. The bat beneath the eaves,

The mouse beside the stone are still as death—
The owl's air washes them like water.
The owl goes back and forth inside the night,
And the night holds its breath.

When he'd finished his poem the bat waited for the mockingbird to say something; he didn't know it, but he was holding his breath.

"Why, I like it," said the mockingbird. "Technically it's quite accomplished. The way you change the rhyme-scheme's particularly effective."

The bat said: "It is?"

"Oh yes," said the mockingbird. "And it was clever of you to have that last line two feet short."

The bat said blankly: "Two feet short?"

"It's two feet short," said the mockingbird a little impatiently. "The next-to-the-last line's iambic pentameter, and the last line's iambic trimeter."

The bat looked so bewildered that the mockingbird said in a kind voice: "An iambic foot has one weak syllable and one strong syllable; the weak one comes first. That last line of yours has six syllables and the one before it has ten: when you shorten the last line like that it gets the effect of the night holding its breath."

"I didn't know that," the bat said. "I just made it like holding your breath."

"To be sure, to be sure!" said the mockingbird. "I enjoyed your poem very much. When you've made up some more do come round and say me another."

The bat said that he would, and fluttered home to his rafter. Partly he felt very good—the mockingbird had liked his poem—and partly he felt just terrible. He thought: "Why, I might as well have said it to the bats. What do I care how many feet it has? The owl nearly kills me, and he says he likes the rhyme-scheme!" He hung there upside down, thinking bitterly. After a while he said to himself: "The trouble isn't making poems, the trouble's finding somebody that will listen to them."

Before he went to sleep he said his owl-poem over to himself, and it seemed to him that it was exactly like the owl. "The *owl* would like it," he thought. "If only I could say it to the owl!"

And then he thought: "That's it! I can't say it to the owl, I don't dare get that near him; but if I made up a poem about the chipmunk I could say it to the chipmunk—*he'd* be interested." The bat got so excited his fur stood up straight and he felt warm all over. He thought: "I'll go to the chipmunk and say, 'If you'll give me six crickets I'll make a poem about you.' Really I'd do it for nothing; but they don't respect something if they get it for nothing. I'll say: 'For six crickets I'll do your portrait in verse.'"

The next day, at twilight, the bat flew to the chipmunk's hole. The chipmunk had dozens of holes, but the bat had noticed that there was one he liked best and always slept in. Before long the chipmunk ran up, his cheeks bulging. "Hello," said the bat.

The instant he heard the bat the chipmunk froze; then he dived into his hole. "Wait! Wait!" the bat cried. But the chipmunk had disappeared. "Come back," the bat called. "I won't hurt you." But he had to talk for a long time before the chipmunk came back, and even then he just stuck the tip of his nose out of the hole.

The bat hardly knew how to begin, but he timidly said to the chipmunk, who listened timidly: "I thought of making this offer to—to the animals of the vicinity. You're the first one I've made it to."

The chipmunk didn't say anything. The bat gulped, and said quickly: "For only six crickets I'll do your portrait in verse."

The chipmunk said: "What are crickets?"

The bat felt discouraged. "I knew I might have to tell him about poems," he thought, "but I never thought I'd have to tell him about *crickets.*" He explained: "They're little black things you see on the porch at night, by the light. They're awfully good. But that's all right about them; instead of crickets you could give me— well, this time you don't have to give me anything. It's a—an introductory offer."

The chipmunk said in a friendly voice: "I don't understand."

"I'll make you a poem about yourself," said the bat. "One just about you." He saw from the look in the chipmunk's eyes that the chipmunk didn't understand. The bat said: "I'll say you a poem about the owl, and then you'll see what it's like."

He said his poem and the chipmunk listened intently; when the poem was over the chipmunk gave a big shiver and said, "It's terrible, just terrible! Is there really something like that at night?"

The bat said: "If it weren't for that hole in the oak he'd have got *me*."

The chipmunk said in a determined voice: "I'm going to bed earlier. Sometimes when there're lots of nuts I stay out till it's pretty dark; but believe me, I'm never going to again."

The bat said: "It's a pleasure to say a poem to—to such a responsive audience. Do you want me to start on the poem about you?"

The chipmunk said thoughtfully: "I don't have enough holes. It'd be awfully easy to dig some more holes."

"Shall I start on the poem about you?" asked the bat.

"All right," said the chipmunk. "But could you put in lots of holes? The first thing in the morning I'm going to dig myself another."

"I'll put in a lot," the bat promised. "Is there anything else you'd like to have in it?"

The chipmunk thought for a minute and said, "Well, nuts. And seeds. Those big fat seeds they have in the feeder."

"All right," said the bat. "Tomorrow afternoon I'll be back. Or day after tomorrow—I don't really know how long it will take." He and the chipmunk said good-by to each other and he fluttered home to the porch. As soon as he got comfortably settled he started to work on the poem about the chipmunk. But somehow he kept coming back to the poem about the owl, and what the chipmunk had said, and how he'd looked. "*He* didn't say any of that two-feet-short stuff," the bat thought triumphantly; "*he* was scared!" The bat hung there upside down, trying to work on his new poem. He was happy.

When at last he'd finished the poem—it took him longer than he'd thought—he went looking for the chipmunk. It was a bright afternoon, and the sun blazed in the bat's eyes, so that everything looked blurred and golden. When he met the chipmunk hurrying down the path that ran past the old stump, he thought: "What a beautiful color he is! Why, the fur back by his tail's rosy, almost. And those lovely black and white stripes on his back!"

"Hello," he said.

"Hello," said the chipmunk. "Is it done yet?"

"All done," said the bat happily. "I'll say it to you. It's named 'The Chipmunk's Day.'"

The chipmunk said in a pleased voice: "My day." He sat there and listened while the bat said:

> In and out the bushes, up the ivy,
> Into the hole
> By the old oak stump, the chipmunk flashes.
> Up the pole
>
> To the feeder full of seeds he dashes,
> Stuffs his cheeks.
> The chickadee and titmouse scold him.
> Down he streaks.

Red as the leaves the wind blows off the maple,
Red as a fox,
Striped like a skunk, the chipmunk whistles
Past the love seat, past the mailbox.

Down the path.
Home to his warm hole stuffed with sweet
Things to eat.
Neat and slight and shining, his front feet

Curled at his breast, he sits there while the sun
Stripes the red west
With its last light: the chipmunk
Dives to his rest.

When he'd finished the bat asked: "Do you like it?"

For a moment the chipmunk didn't say anything, then he said in a surprised, pleased voice: "Say it again." The bat said it again. When he'd finished, the chipmunk said: "Oh, it's *nice*. It all goes in and out, doesn't it?"

The bat was so pleased he didn't know what to say. "Am I really as red as that?" asked the chipmunk.

"Oh yes," the bat said.

"You put in the seeds and the hole and everything," exclaimed the chipmunk. "I didn't think you could. I thought you'd make me more like the owl." Then he said: "Say me the one about the owl."

The bat did. The chipmunk said: "It makes me shiver. Why do I like it if it makes me shiver?"

"I don't know. I see why the owl would like it, but I don't see why we like it."

"Who are you going to do now?" asked the chipmunk.

The bat said: "I don't know. I haven't thought about anybody but you. Maybe I could do a bird."

"Why don't you do the cardinal? He's red and black like me, and he eats seeds at the feeder like me—you'd be in practice."

The bat said doubtfully: "I've watched him, but I don't know him."

"I'll ask him," said the chipmunk. "I'll tell him what it's like, and then he's sure to want to."

"That's awfully nice of you," said the bat. "I'd love to do one about him. I like to watch him feed his babies."

The next day, while the bat was hanging from his rafter fast asleep, the chipmunk ran up to the ivy to the porch and called to the bat: "He wants you to." The bat stirred a little and blinked his eyes, and the chipmunk said: "The cardinal wants you to. I had a hard time telling him what a poem was like, but after I did he wanted you to."

"All right," said the bat sleepily. "I'll start it tonight."

The chipmunk said: "What did you say I was as red as? I don't mean a fox, I remember that."

"As maple leaves. As leaves the wind blows off the maple."

"Oh yes, I remember now," the chipmunk said; he ran off contentedly.

When the bat woke up that night he thought, "Now I'll begin on the cardinal." He thought about how red the cardinal was, and how he sang, and what he ate, and how he fed his big brown babies. But somehow he couldn't get started.

All the next day he watched the cardinal. The bat hung from his rafter, a few feet from the feeder, and whenever the cardinal came to the feeder he'd stare at him and hope he'd get an idea. It was queer the way the cardinal cracked the sunflower seeds; instead of standing on them and hammering them open, like a titmouse, he'd turn them over and over in his beak—it gave him a thoughtful look—and all at once the seed would fall open, split in two. While the cardinal was cracking the seed his two babies stood underneath him on tiptoe, fluttering their wings and quivering all over, their mouths wide open. They were a beautiful soft bright brown—even their beaks were brown—and they were already as big as their father. Really they were old enough to feed themselves, and did whenever he wasn't there; but as long as he was there they begged and begged, till the father would fly down by one and stuff the seed in its mouth, while the other quivered and cheeped as if its heart were breaking. The father was such a beautiful clear bright red, with his tall crest the wind rippled like fur, that it didn't seem right for him to be so harried and useful and hard-working: it was like seeing a general in a red uniform washing hundreds and hundreds of dishes. The babies followed him everywhere, and kept sticking their open mouths up by his mouth—they shook all over, they begged so hard—and he never got a bite for himself.

But it was no use: no matter how much the bat watched, he never got an idea. Finally he went to the chipmunk and said in a perplexed voice: "I can't make up a poem about the cardinal."

The chipmunk said: "Why, just say what he's like, the way you did with the owl and me."

"I would if I could," the bat said, "but I can't. I don't know why I can't, but I can't. I watch him and he's just beautiful, he'd make a beautiful poem; but I can't think of anything."

"That's *queer*," the chipmunk said.

The bat said in a discouraged voice: "I guess I can't make portraits of the animals after all."

"What a shame!"

"Oh well," the bat said, "it was just so I'd have somebody to say them to. Now that I've got you I'm all right—when I get a good idea I'll make a poem about it and say it to you."

"I'll tell the cardinal you couldn't," the chipmunk said. "He won't be too disappointed, he never has heard a poem. I tried to tell him what they're like, but I don't think he really understood."

He went off to tell the cardinal, and the bat flew home. He felt relieved; it was wonderful not to have to worry about the cardinal any more.

All morning the mockingbird had been chasing everything out of the yard—he gave you the feeling that having anything else in the world was more than he could bear. Finally he flew up to the porch, sat on the arm of a chair, and began to chirp in a loud, impatient, demanding way, until the lady who lived inside brought him out some raisins. He flew up to a branch, waited impatiently, and as soon as she was gone dived down on the raisins and ate up every one. Then he flew over to the willow and began to sing with all his might.

The bat clung to his rafter, listening drowsily. Sometimes he would open his eyes a little, and the sunlight and the shadows and the red and yellow and orange branches waving in the wind made a kind of blurred pattern, so that he would blink, and let his eyelids steal together, and go contentedly back to sleep. When he woke up it was almost dark; the sunlight was gone, and the red and yellow and orange leaves were all gray, but the mockingbird was still singing.

The porch light was lit, and there were already dozens of insects circling round it. As the bat flew toward them he felt hungry but comfortable.

Just then the mockingbird began to imitate a jay—not the way a jay squawks or scolds but the way he really sings, in a deep soft voice; as he listened the bat remembered how the mockingbird had driven off two jays that morning. He thought: "It's queer the way he drives everything off and then imitates it. You wouldn't think that—"

And at that instant he had an idea for a poem. The insects were still flying around and around the light, the mockingbird was still imitating the jay, but the bat didn't eat and he didn't listen; he flapped slowly and thoughtfully back to his rafter and began to work on the poem.

When he finally finished it—he'd worked on it off and on for two nights—he flew off to find the chipmunk. "I've got a new one," he said happily.

"What's it about?"

"The mockingbird."

"The mockingbird!" the chipmunk repeated. "Say it to me." He was sitting up with his paws on his chest, looking intently at the bat—it was the way he always listened.

The bat said:

> Look one way and the sun is going down.
> Look the other and the moon is rising.
> The sparrow's shadow's longer than the lawn.
> The bats squeak: "Night is here," the birds cheep: "Day is gone."
> On the willow's highest branch, monopolizing
> Day and night, cheeping, squeaking, soaring,
> The mockingbird is imitating life.
>
> All day the mockingbird has owned the yard.
> As light first woke the world, the sparrows trooped
> Onto the seedy lawn: the mockingbird
> Chased them off shrieking. Hour by hour, fighting hard
> To make the world his own, he swooped
> On thrushes, thrashers, jays, and chickadees—
> At noon he drove away a big black cat.
>
> Now, in the moonlight, he sits here and sings.
> A thrush is singing, then a thrasher, then a jay—
> Then, all at once, a cat begins meowing.
> A mockingbird can sound like anything.
> He imitates the world he drove away
> So well that for a minute, in the moonlight,
> Which one's the mockingbird? which one's the world?

When he had finished, the chipmunk didn't say anything; the bat said uneasily, "Did you like it?"

For a minute the chipmunk didn't answer him. Then he said: "It really is like him. You know, he's chased me. And can he imitate me! You wouldn't think he'd drive you away *and* imitate you. You wouldn't think he could."

The bat could see that what the chipmunk said meant that he liked the poem, but he couldn't keep from saying: "You do like it?"

The chipmunk said, "Yes, I like it. But he won't like it."

"You liked the one about you," the bat said.

"Yes," the chipmunk answered. "But he won't like the one about him."

The bat said: "But it *is* like him."

The chipmunk said: "Just like. Why don't you go say it to him? I'll go with you."

When they found the mockingbird—it was one of his good days—the bat told him that he had made up a new poem. "Could I say it to you?" he asked. He sounded timid—guilty almost.

"To be sure, to be sure!" answered the mockingbird, and put on his listening expression.

The bat said, "It's a poem about—well, about mockingbirds."

The mockingbird repeated: "About mockingbirds!" His face had changed, so that he had to look listening all over again. Then the bat repeated to the mockingbird his poem about the mockingbird. The mockingbird listened intently, staring at the bat; the chipmunk listened intently, staring at the mockingbird.

When the bat had finished, nobody said anything. Finally the chipmunk said: "Did it take you long to make it up?"

Before the bat could answer, the mockingbird exclaimed angrily: "You sound as if there were something wrong with imitating things!"

"Oh no," the bat said.

"Well then, you sound as if there were something wrong with driving them off. It's my territory, isn't it? If you can't drive things off your own territory what can you do?"

The bat didn't know what to say; after a minute the chipmunk said uneasily, "He just meant it's odd to drive them all off and then imitate them so well too."

"Odd!" cried the mockingbird. "Odd! If I didn't it really would be odd. Did you ever hear of a mockingbird that didn't?"

The bat said politely: "No indeed. No, it's just what mockingbirds do do. That's really why I made up the poem about it—I admire mockingbirds so much, you know."

The chipmunk said: "He talks about them all the time."

"A mockingbird's *sensitive*," said the mockingbird; when he said *sensitive* his voice went way up and way back down. "They get on my nerves. You just don't understand how much they get on my nerves. Sometimes I think if I can't get rid of them I'll go crazy."

"If they didn't get on your nerves so, maybe you wouldn't be able to imitate them so well," the chipmunk said in a helpful, hopeful voice.

"And the way they sing!" cried the mockingbird. "One two three, one two three— the same thing, the same thing, always the same old thing! If only they'd just once sing something different!"

The bat said: "Yes, I can see how hard on you it must be. I meant for the poem to show that, but I'm afraid I must not have done it right."

"You just haven't any *idea!*" the mockingbird went on, his eyes flashing and his feathers standing up. "Nobody but a mockingbird has any *idea!*"

The bat and the chipmunk were looking at the mockingbird with the same impressed, uneasy look. From then on they were very careful what they said—mostly they just listened, while the mockingbird told them what it was like to be a mockingbird. Toward the end he seemed considerably calmer and more cheerful, and even told the bat he had enjoyed hearing his poem.

The bat looked pleased, and asked the mockingbird: "Did you like the way I rhymed the first lines of the stanzas and then didn't rhyme the last two?"

The mockingbird said shortly: "I didn't notice"; the chipmunk told the mockingbird how much he always enjoyed hearing the mockingbird sing; and, a little later, the bat and the chipmunk told the mockingbird good-by.

When they had left, the two of them looked at each other and the bat said: "You were right."

"Yes," said the chipmunk. Then he said: "I'm glad I'm not a mockingbird."

"I'd like to be because of the poems," the bat said, "but as long as I'm not, I'm glad I'm not."

"He thinks that he's different from everything else," the chipmunk said, "and he is."

The bat said, just as if he hadn't heard the chipmunk: "I wish I could make up a poem about bats."

The chipmunk asked: "Why don't you?"

"If I had one about bats maybe I could say it to the bats."

"That's right."

For weeks he wished that he had the poem. He would hunt all night, and catch and eat hundreds and hundreds of gnats and moths and crickets, and all the time he would be thinking: "If only I could make up a poem about bats!" One day he dreamed that it was done and that he was saying it to them, but when he woke up all he could remember was the way it ended:

> At sunrise, suddenly, the porch was bats:
> A thousand bats were hanging from the rafter.

It had sounded wonderful in his dream, but now it just made him wish that the bats still slept on the porch. He felt cold and lonely. Two squirrels had climbed up in the feeder and were making the same queer noise—a kind of whistling growl—to scare each other away; somewhere on the other side of the house the mockingbird was singing. The bat shut his eyes.

For some reason, he began to think of the first things he could remember. Till a bat is two weeks old he's never alone: the little naked thing—he hasn't even any fur—clings to his mother wherever she goes. After that she leaves him at night; he and the other babies hang there sleeping, till at last their mothers come home to them. Sleepily, almost dreaming, the bat began to make up a poem about a mother and her baby.

It was easier than the other poems, somehow: all he had to do was remember what it had been like and every once in a while put in a rhyme. But easy as it was, he kept getting tired and going to sleep, and would forget parts and have to make them over. When at last he finished he went to say it to the chipmunk.

The trees were all bare, and the wind blew the leaves past the chipmunk's hole; it was cold. When the chipmunk stuck his head out it looked fatter than the bat had ever seen it. The chipmunk said in a slow, dazed voice: "It's all full. My hole's all full." Then he exclaimed surprisedly to the bat: "How fat you are!"

"I?" the bat asked. "I'm fat?" Then he realized it was so; for weeks he had been eating and eating and eating. He said: "I've done my poem about the bats. It's about a mother and her baby."

"Say it to me."

The bat said:

> A bat is born
> Naked and blind and pale.
> His mother makes a pocket of her tail

And catches him. He clings to her long fur
By his thumbs and toes and teeth.
And then the mother dances through the night
Doubling and looping, soaring, somersaulting—
Her baby hangs on underneath.
All night, in happiness, she hunts and flies.
Her high sharp cries
Like shining needlepoints of sound
Go out into the night and, echoing back,
Tell her what they have touched.
She hears how far it is, how big it is.
Which way it's going:
She lives by hearing.
The mother eats the moths and gnats she catches
In full flight; in full flight
The mother drinks the water of the pond
She skims across. Her baby hangs on tight.
Her baby drinks the milk she makes him
In moonlight or starlight, in mid-air.
Their single shadow, printed on the moon
Or fluttering across the stars,
Whirls on all night; at daybreak
The tired mother flaps home to her rafter.
The others all are there.
They hang themselves up by their toes,
They wrap themselves in their brown wings.
Bunched upside down, they sleep in air.
Their sharp ears, their sharp teeth, their quick sharp faces
Are dull and slow and mild.
All the bright day, as the mother sleeps,
She folds her wings about her sleeping child.

When the bat had finished, the chipmunk said: "It's all really so?"

"Why, of course," the bat said.

"And you do all that too? If you shut your eyes and make a noise you can hear where I am and which way I'm going?"

"Of course."

The chipmunk shook his head and said wonderingly: "You bats sleep all day and fly all night, and see with your ears, and sleep upside down, and eat while you're flying and drink while you're flying, and turn somersaults in mid-air with your baby hanging on, and—and—it's really queer."

The bat said: "Did you like the poem?"

"Oh, of course. Except I forgot it was a poem. I just kept thinking how queer it must be to be a bat."

The bat said: "No, it's not queer. It's wonderful to fly all night. And when you sleep all day with the others it feels wonderful."

The chipmunk yawned. "The end of it made me all sleepy," he said. "But I was already sleepy. I'm sleepy all the time now."

The bat thought, "Why, I am too." He said to the chipmunk: "Yes, it's winter. It's almost winter."

"You ought to say the poem to the other bats," the chipmunk said. "They'll like it just the way I liked the one about me."

"Really?"

"I'm sure of it. When it has all the things you do, you can't help liking it."

"Thank you so much for letting me say it to you," the bat said. "I *will* say it to them. I'll go say it to them now."

"Good-by," said the chipmunk. "I'll see you soon. Just as soon as I wake up I'll see you."

"Good-by," the bat said.

The chipmunk went back into his hole. It was strange to have him move so heavily, and to see his quick face so slow. The bat flew slowly off to the barn. In the west, over the gray hills, the sun was red: in a little while the bats would wake up and he could say them the poem.

High up under the roof, in the farthest corner of the barn, the bats were hanging upside down, wrapped in their brown wings. Except for one, they were fast asleep. The one the little brown bat lighted by was asleep; when he felt someone light by him he yawned, and screwed his face up, and snuggled closer to the others. "As soon as he wakes up I'll say it to him," the bat thought. "No, I'll wait till they're all awake." On the other side of him was the bat who was awake: that one gave a big yawn, snuggled closer to the others, and went back to sleep.

The bat said to himself sleepily: "I wish I'd said we sleep all winter. That would have been a good thing to have in." He yawned. He thought: "It's almost dark. As soon as it's dark they'll wake up and I'll say them the poem. The chipmunk said they'd love it." He began to say the poem over to himself; he said in a soft contented whisper,

> A bat is born
> Naked and blind and pale.
> His mother makes a pocket of her tail
> And catches him. He clings—he clings—

He tried to think of what came next, but he couldn't remember. It was about fur, but he couldn't remember the words that went with it. He went back to the beginning. He said,

> A bat is born
> Naked and blind—

but before he could get any further he thought: "I wish I'd said we sleep all winter." His eyes were closed; he yawned, and screwed his face up, and snuggled closer to the others.

1964

CHARLES CAUSLEY
1917–2003

"All poetry is magic," declares Charles Causley in the introduction to *The Puffin Book of Magic Verse* (1974). "It is," he continues, "a spell against insensitivity, failure of imagination, ignorance and barbarism." His belief in the importance of poetry was profound, and that faith was rewarded: he not only won numerous awards in both the United States (including the Ingersoll Foundation's T. S. Eliot Award) and England (including being named a Companion of the British Empire), but he also became one of the best-loved twentieth-century poets in Britain.

Causley was born in Launceston, Cornwall, a town between Dartmoor and Bodmin Moor where he lived all his life except for the years he served in the Royal Navy (1940–46). Because he had left school at fifteen to work, he was largely self-educated. Yet he had always intended to be an author, and in the 1930s he published three plays. When he returned home after World War II, he attended the Peterborough Teacher's Training College, began teaching in the same elementary school he had attended (where he remained until retiring in 1976), and started to write poetry. His first collection, *Farewell, Aggie Weston*, appeared in 1951; dozens more, for children and adults, followed.

Causley's background and aesthetic set him far apart from the dominant strains of modern poetry. While his Oxford- and Cambridge-educated contemporaries favored cosmopolitan free verse and confessional poetry, often delving into their rather messy private lives, the never-married Causley tended to treat his personal experience impersonally, eschewing irony and personal mythography. He embraced narrative poems in traditional forms, drawing particularly on folk songs and ballads. He read, in his own phrase, "absolutely everything," and was strongly influenced by William Blake, William Wordsworth, and the King James Bible. Whether writing nursery rhymes or ballads, sea chanteys or religious sonnets, he was never quaint or sentimental. His intensely honest verse was deeply rooted in the history and geography of his corner of England, and never condescended to the reader. One of his most popular poems, "I Saw a Jolly Hunter" from his first collection described as expressly for children, *Figgie Hobbin* (1970, illustrated by Pat Marriott), begins as a conventional nursery rhyme:

> I saw a jolly hunter
> With a jolly gun
> Walking in the country
> In the jolly sun.

But it ends in black comedy:

> Jolly hunter jolly head
> Over heels gone.
> Jolly old safety-catch
> Not jolly on.
>
> Bang went the jolly gun.
> Hunter jolly dead.
> Jolly hare got clean away.
> Jolly good, I said.

Causley repeatedly returns to British and especially Cornish folklore, the world of nursery rhymes, and the music of strong rhythms. In *Early in the Morning: A Collection of New Poems* (1986), which won the Signal Book Award for children's poetry, the poems are both illustrated (by Michael Foreman) and in many cases set to music (by Anthony Castro). Because his characteristic themes, preoccupations, and freshness of language vary little, it is often difficult to distinguish between his writings for children and those for adults. He himself declared that he did not know whether a given poem was for children or adults as he was writing it, and he included his children's poetry without comment in his collected works. Causley stayed true to what he called his "guiding principle," a comment made by W. H. Auden in his introduction to a selection of verse by Walter de la Mare (both poets to whom Causley was indebted): "while there are some good poems which are only for adults, because they pre-suppose adult experience in their readers, there are no good poems which are only for children."

Early in the Morning
A Collection of New Poems

Early in the Morning

Early in the morning
The water hits the rocks,
The birds are making noises
Like old alarum clocks,
The soldier on the skyline
Fires a golden gun
And over the back of the chimney-stack
Explodes the silent sun.

I Went to Santa Barbara

I went to Santa Barbara,
I saw upon the pier
Four-and-twenty lobster pots
And a barrel of German beer.

The ships in the bay sailed upside-down,
The trees went out with the tide,
The river escaped from the ocean
And over the mountain-side.

High on the hill the Mission[1]
Broke in two in the sun.
The bell fell out of the turning tower
And struck the hour of one.

I heard a hundred fishes fly
Singing across the lake
When I was in Santa Barbara
And the earth began to shake.

My friend Gregor Antonio,
Was with me all that day,
Says it is all inside my head
And there's nothing in what I say.

But I was in Santa Barbara
And in light as bright as snow
I see it as if it were yesterday
Or a hundred years ago.

John Clark

John Clark sat in the park,
Saw the sun jump out of the dark,
Counted one and counted two,
Watched the sky from black to blue,
Counted three and counted four,
Heard a horse and then some more,
Counted five and counted six,
Heard a snapping in the sticks,
Counted seven and counted eight,
Saw a fox and saw his mate,
Counted nine and counted ten.

'Hurry home to your den, your den,
Or you never may see the sun again
For I fear I hear the hunting men,
The hunting men and the hounds that bark!'

Said John Clark as he sat in the park.

Spin Me a Web, Spider

Spin me a web, spider,
Across the window-pane
For I shall never break it
And make you start again.

Cast your net of silver
As soon as it is spun,
And hang it with the morning dew
That glitters in the sun.

---

1. The Santa Barbara Mission Church in California was
founded by the Franciscans in 1786. The existing church
building is famous for its twin bell towers.

It's strung with pearls and diamonds,
The finest ever seen,
Fit for any royal King
Or any royal Queen.

Would you, could you, bring it down
In the dust to lie?
Any day of the week, my dear,
Said the nimble fly.

Tommy Hyde

Tommy Hyde, Tommy Hyde,
What are you doing by the salt-sea side?

Picking up pebbles and smoothing sand
And writing a letter on the ocean strand.

Tommy Hyde, Tommy Hyde,
Why do you wait by the turning tide?

I'm watching for the water to rub it off the shore
And take it to my true-love in Baltimore.

One for the Man

One for the man who lived by the sand,
Two for his son and daughter,
Three for the sea-birds washed so white
That flew across the water.

Four for the sails that brought the ship
About the headland turning.
Five for the jollyboys in her shrouds,[2]
Six for the sea-lamps burning.

Seven for the sacks of silver and gold
They sailed through the winter weather.
Eight for the places set on shore
When they sat down together.

Nine for the songs they sang night-long,
Ten for the candles shining.
Eleven for the lawmen on the hill
As they all were sweetly dining.

Twelve for the hour that struck as they stood
To the Judge so careful and clever.
Twelve for the years that must come and go
And we shall see them never.

Mrs McPhee

Mrs McPhee
Who lived in South Zeal
Roasted a duckling
For every meal.

'Duckling for breakfast
And dinner and tea,
And duckling for supper,'
Said Mrs McPhee.

'It's sweeter than sugar,
It's clean as a nut,
I'm sure and I'm certain
It's good for me—BUT

'I don't like these feathers
That grow on my back,
And my silly webbed feet
And my voice that goes quack.'

As easy and soft
As a ship to the sea,
As a duck to the water
Went Mrs McPhee.

'I think I'll go swim
In the river,' said she;
Said Mrs Mac, Mrs Quack,
Mrs McPhee.

2. Ropes that support a ship's mast.

There Was an Old Woman

There was an old woman of Chester-le-Street
Who chased a policeman all over his beat.

She shattered his helmet and tattered his
    clothes
And knocked his new spectacles clean off his
    nose.

'I'm afraid,' said the Judge, 'I must make it quite
    clear
You can't get away with that sort of thing here.'

'I can and I will,' the old woman she said,
'And I don't give a fig for your water and bread.

'I don't give a hoot for your cold prison cell,
And your bolts and your bars and your
    handcuffs as well.

'I've never been one to do just as I'm bid.
You can put me in jail for a year!'
                So they did.

Daniel Brent

Daniel Brent, a man of Kent,
Went to market without a cent.
He chose an apple, he chose a pear,
He chose a comb for his crooked hair,
He chose a fiddle, he chose a flute,
He chose a rose for his Sunday suit,
He chose some pickles, he chose some ham,
He chose a pot of strawberry jam,
He chose a kite to climb the sky.

How many things did Daniel buy?

But when it came the time to pay,
Daniel Brent he ran away.

Freddie Phipps

Freddie Phipps
Liked fish and chips.
Jesse Pinch liked crime.

Woodrow Waters
Liked dollars and quarters.
Paul Small liked a dime.

Sammy Fink
Liked a lemon drink.
Jeremy Jones liked lime.

Morimer Mills
Liked running down hills.
Jack Jay liked to climb.

Hamilton Hope
Liked water and soap.
Georgie Green liked grime;

But Willy Earls
Liked pretty girls
And had a much better time.

CHARLES CAUSLEY

Charity Chadder

Charity Chadder
Borrowed a ladder,
Leaned it against the moon,
Climbed to the top
Without a stop
On the 31st of June,
Brought down every single star,
Kept them all in a pickle jar.

Jeremiah

Jeremiah
Jumped out of the fire
Into the frying pan;
Went zig and zag
With a sausage and egg
All the way to Japan.

But when he got
To Fuji-san[3]
And saw the mountain smoking,
'Good gracious,' said he.
'This ain't for me';
Ran all the way back to Woking.[4]

High on the Wall

High on the wall
Where the pennywort grows
Polly Penwarden
Is painting her toes.

One is purple
And two are red
And two are the colour
Of her golden head.

One is blue
And two are green
And the others are the colours
They've always been.

Wilbur

Wilbur, Wilbur,
Your bed is made of silver,
Your sheets are Irish linen,
Your pillow soft as snow.
Wilbur, Wilbur,
The girls all look you over,
Look you up and look you down
When into town you go.

Wilbur, Wilbur,
Walking by the river,
Swifter than the sunlight
Is your glancing eye.
Wilbur, Wilbur,
You're the sweetest singer.
You've a pair of dancing legs
That money cannot buy.

Wilbur, Wilbur,
On your little finger
You wear a ring of platinum
Set with a diamond stone.
But Wilbur, Wilbur,
Now the days are colder
You go to bed at six o'clock
And lie there all alone.

My Cat Plumduff

My cat Plumduff
When feeling gruff
Was terribly fond
Of taking snuff,
And his favourite spot
For a sniff and a sneeze
Was a nest at the very
Top of the trees.

And there he'd sit
And sneeze and sniff
With the aid of a gentleman's
Handkerchief;
And he'd look on the world
With a lordly air
As if he was master
Of everything there.

---

3. Mount Fuji, a volcano in Japan dormant since 1708.
4. A town about 20 miles southwest of London.

EARLY IN
THE MORNING

1257

Cried the passers by,
'Just look at that!
He thinks he's a bird,
That silly old cat!'
But my cat Plumduff
Was heard to say,
'How curious people
Are today!'

'Do I think I'm a bird?'
Said my cat Plumduff.
'All smothered in fur
And this whiskery stuff,
With my swishy tail
And my teeth so sharp
And my guinea-gold[5] eyes
That shine in the dark?

'Aren't they peculiar
People—and how!
Whoever has heard
Of a bird with a miaow?
Such ignorant creatures!
What nonsense and stuff!
No wonder I'm grumpy,'
Said my cat Plumduff.

The Owl Looked out of the Ivy Bush

The owl looked out of the ivy bush
And he solemnly said, said he,
'If you want to live an owlish life
Be sure you are not like me.

'When the sun goes down and the moon comes
        up
And the sky turns navy blue,
I'm certain to go tu-whoo tu-whit
Instead of tu-whit tu-whoo.

'And even then nine times out of ten
(And it's absolutely true)
I somehow go out of my owlish mind
With a whit-tu whoo-tu too.'

'There's nothing in water,' said the owl,
'In air or on the ground
With a kindly word for the sort of bird
That sings the wrong way round.'

'I might,' wept the owl in the ivy bush,
'Be just as well buried and dead.
You can bet your boots no one gives two hoots!'
'Do I, friend my,' I said.

Ring Dove

Ring dove, ring dove,
High in the tree,
What are the words
You say to me?

What do you sing
And what do you tell
Loud as the ring
Of a telephone bell?

Take two cows, Davy,
Take them to the shore,
And when you've taken two
Take two cows more.

Baby, Baby

Baby, baby
In the walking water,
Are you my sister's
Darling daughter?

My sister, they said,
Who went to Spain
And vowed she'd never
Come home again?

Her eyes were the self-same
Periwinkle-blue
And she wore a locket
Just like you.

---

5. The guinea, a gold coin no longer in circulation, was worth 21 shillings.

She wore a shawl
Of Honiton[6] lace
Like the one that drifts
About your face.

Baby, don't stray
Where the tall weeds swim.
Fetch the boat, Billy,
And bring the baby in.

At Linkinhorne[7]

At Linkinhorne
Where the devil was born
I met old Mollie Magee.
'Come in,' she said
With a wag of her head,
'For a cup of camomile tea.'
And while the water whistled and winked
I gazed about the gloom
At all the treasures Mollie Magee
Had up and down the room.

With a sort of a smile
A crocodile
Swam under an oaken beam,
And from tail to jaw
It was stuffed with straw
And its eye had an emerald gleam.
In the farthest corner a grandfather clock
Gave a watery tick and a tock
As it told the date and season and state
Of the tide at Falmouth[8] Dock.

She'd a fire of peat
That smelled as sweet
As the wind from the moorland high,
And through the smoke
Of the chimney broke
A silver square of sky.
On the mantelshelf a pair of dogs
Gave a china smile and a frown,

And through the bottle-glass pane there stood
The church tower upside-down.

She'd shelves of books,
And hanging on hooks
Were herbals all to hand,
And shells and stones
And animal bones
And bottles of coloured sand.
And sharp I saw the scritch-owl stare
From underneath the thatch
As Matt her cat came through the door
With never a lifted latch.

At Linkinhorne
Where I was born
I met old Mollie Magee.
She told me this,
She told me that
About my family-tree.
And oh she skipped and ah she danced
And laughed and sang did we,
For Mollie Magee's the finest mother
Was ever given to me.

In My Garden

In my garden
Grows a tree
Dances day
And night for me,
Four in a bar
Or sometimes three
To music secret
As can be.

Nightly to
Its hidden tune
I watch it move
Against the moon,
Dancing to
A silent sound,
One foot planted
In the ground.

---

6. A town in southwest England, famous for its lace.
7. Linkinhorne is a village in south-east Cornwall, and the first two lines of the poem are a well-known local saying [Causley's note].
8. Port in Cornwall, on the English Channel.

Dancing tree,
When may I hear
Day or night
Your music clear?
What the note
And what the song
That you sing
The seasons long?

It is written,
Said the tree,
On the pages
Of the sea;
It is there
At every hand
On the pages
Of the land;

Whether waking
Or in dream:
Voice of meadow-grass
And stream,
And out of
The ringing air
Voice of sun
And moon and star.

It is there
For all to know
As tides shall turn
And wildflowers grow;
There for you
And there for me,
Said the glancing
Dancing tree.

Foxglove

Foxglove purple,
Foxglove white,
Fit for a lady
By day or night.

Foxglove bring
To friend and stranger

CHARLES CAUSLEY

A witches' thimble
For the finger.

Foxglove on
The sailing sea,
Storm and tempest
There shall be.

Foxglove sleeping
Under the sky,
Watch the midnight
With one eye.

Foxglove burning
In the sun,
Ring your bells
And my day is done.

Stone in the Water

Stone in the water,
Stone on the sand,
Whom shall I marry
When I get to land?

Will he be handsome
Or will he be plain,
Strong as the sun
Or rich as the rain?

Will he be dark
Or will he be fair,
And what will be the colour
That shines in his hair?

Will he come late
Or will he come soon,
At morning or midnight
Or afternoon?

What will he say
Or what will he sing,
And will he be holding
A plain gold ring?

Stone in the water
Still and small,
Tell me if he comes,
Or comes not at all.

Round the Corner Comes Jack Fall

Round the corner comes Jack Fall,
Dressed in yellow, dressed in brown.
'Goodbye, summer,' hear him call
As he wanders through the town.

'Give her a kiss and wish her well,
Give her a gold and silver chain.
Tell her you love her,' said Jack Fall.
'And bring her back this way again.'

Said the Clown

Said the clown in the seven-ring circus
As he dived in a bucket of sand,
'Why nobody claps at my quips and my cracks
Is something I can't understand.

'The start of my act's a selection
Of millions and millions of jokes,
Then like wind and like fire I whizz down a wire
On a bike with one wheel and no spokes.

'When I fill up my pockets with water
And paint my face red, white and blue,
Folk stare at the ground and they don't make a
    sound.
I can't think of the reason. Can you?'

Janny Jim Jan

Janny Jim Jan
The Cornish man
Walked out on Bodmin Moor,[9]
A twist of rye
For a collar and tie
And his boots on backsyvore.[1]

'Janny Jim Jan,'
The children sang,
'Here's a letter from the King of Spain.'
But Janny turned nasty,
Hit 'em with a pasty,[2]
Sent 'em home again.

Mistletoe

Mistletoe[3] new,
Mistletoe old,
Cut it down
With a knife of gold.

Mistletoe green,
Mistletoe milk,
Let it fall
On a scarf of silk.

Mistletoe from
The Christmas oak,
Keep my house
From lightning stroke.

Guard from thunder
My roof-tree
And any evil
That there be.

Balloono

Balloono, Balloono,
    What do you bring
Flying from your fingers
    And fifty bits of string?

Is it the sun
    Or is it the moon
Or is it a football[4]
    For Saturday afternoon?

A peach or a melon?
    Tell me, please.
An orange or an apple
    Or a big Dutch cheese?

See them tugging
    In the bright blue air
As if they would wander
    Everywhere!

Come back, Balloono,
    When I draw my pay
And I'll buy them and fly them
    All away.

Take Me to the Water Fair

Take me to the Water Fair,
Row me in your boat,
Whisper with the willow tree
As down the stream we float.

The sky was cold as iron
When we set off from land,
But soon, you say, a day will come
With flowers on either hand.

---

9. Moor in the center of Cornwall, about 100 square miles in area.
1. The wrong way round [Causley's note].
2. A meat pie made with a folded-over circle of pastry dough (traditional in Cornwall).

3. The Druids believed that mistletoe, a parasitic plant that often grows on oaks, was sacred and had great power to ward off evil; it was ritually harvested and distributed to individual households to keep their members safe.
4. I.e., soccer ball.

Let me lie upon your arm
As on the flood we slide
And watch the shining fishes play
Swiftly our boat beside.

And here the lilies lean upon
The waters as we pass,
And there the munching cattle swim
Deep in the meadow grass.

As high above the chestnut burns
Its candles on the sky
You say that summer cannot end—
And you will never lie.

Rebekah

Rebekah, Rebekah,[5]
Wake up from your sleep,
The cattle are thirsty
And so are the sheep
That come with the evening
Down from the high fell
To drink the sweet water
Of Paradise Well.

Rebekah, Rebekah,
The spring rises free
But the well it is locked
And you have the key,
And the sheep and the cattle
Rebekah, are dry
And would drink of the water.
And so would I.

Nicholas Naylor

Nicholas Naylor
The deep-blue sailor
Sailed the sea
As a master-tailor.

He sewed for the Captain,
He sewed for the crew,
He sewed up the kit-bags
And hammocks too.

He sewed up a serpent,
He sewed up a shark,
He sewed up a sailor
In a bag of dark.

How do you like
Your work, master-tailor?
'So, so, so,'
Said Nicholas Naylor.

John, John the Baptist

John, John the Baptist[6]
Lived in a desert of stone,
He had no money,
Ate beans and honey,
And he lived quite on his own.

His coat was made of camel,
His belt was made of leather,
And deep in the gleam
Of a twisting stream
He'd stand in every weather.

John, John the Baptist
Worked without any pay,
But he'd hold your hand
And bring you to land
And wash your fears away.

Tell, Tell the Bees

Tell, tell the bees,[7]
The bees in the hive,
That Jenny Green is gone away,
Or nothing will thrive.

---

5. The wife of Isaac; Abraham's servant chose her to be Isaac's wife after she drew water from a well for the servant and his camels (Genesis 24.12–67).
6. Jewish prophet (d. ca. 30 C.E.), believed by Christians to be the forerunner of Jesus. On his food and clothing in the wilderness, see Matthew 3.1–4.
7. An old custom on farms in Britain and New England was to tell the bees about the death of anyone in the family.

There'll be no honey
And there'll be no comb
If you don't tell the bees
That Jenny's not home.

Tap on their window,
Tap on their door,
Tell them they'll never see
Jenny Green more.

Tell them as true
As you know how
Who is their master
Or mistress now.

Tell all the hives
As they buzz and hum,
Jenny is gone
But another will come.

Tell, tell the bees,
The bees in the hive,
That Jenny Green is gone away,
Or nothing will thrive.

Johnny Come over the Water

Johnny come over the water
And make the sun shine through.
Johnny come over the water
And paint the sky with blue.

Cover the field and the meadow
With flowers of red and gold,
And cover with leaves the simple trees
That stand so bare and cold.

Johnny come over the water,
Turn the white grass to hay.
It's winter, winter all the year
Since you went away.

CHARLES CAUSLEY

I Love My Darling Tractor

I love my darling tractor,
I love its merry din,
Its muscles made of iron and steel,
Its red and yellow skin.

I love to watch its wheels go round
However hard the day,
And from its bed inside the shed
It never thinks to stray.

It saves my arm, it saves my leg,
It saves my back from toil,
And it's merry as a skink[8] when I give it a drink
Of water and diesel oil.

I love my darling tractor
As you can clearly see,
And so, the jolly farmer said,
Would you if you were me.

Let's Go Ride

Let's go ride in a sleigh, Johanna,
Let's go ride in a sleigh,
Through the mountains,
Under the trees,
Over the ice
On Lake Louise.
Let's go ride in a sleigh, Johanna,
          —There's only five dollars to pay.

Let's go ride today, Johanna,
Let's go ride today,
The horses shaking
Their silver traces,
The branches flaking
Snow on our faces.
Let's go ride today, Johanna,
          —There's only five dollars to pay.

Let's go ride while we may, Johanna,
Let's go ride while we may,
By the tall ice-fall
And the frozen spring
As the frail sun shines
And the sleigh-bells ring.
Let's go ride while we may, Johanna,
          —There's only five dollars to pay.

8. One who serves liquor (dialectal).

Here's the Reverend Rundle

Here's the Reverend Rundle
His gear in a bundle,
He has a dog
He has a sled
And thousands of stories
In his head
And coloured pictures
Of the Holy Scriptures
To show, show
The Indians red
Who had picture and story
And saints in glory
And a heavenly throne
Of their very own
But were so well-bred
That they met him like a brother
And they loved each other
It was said,
The Reverend Rundle
And the Indians red
And through the Rockies
They watched him go
Over the ice
And under the snow—
But this was a very long
Time ago,
A long, long, long, long
Time ago.
They loved him from
His heels to his hat
As he rode on the rough
Or walked on the flat
Whether he stood
Or whether he sat,
The Reverend Rundle
His gear in a bundle
And as well as that
His favourite cat
Warm in a poke
Of his sealskin cloak
For fear some son
Of a hungry gun
Ate her for supper
In Edmonton[9]

---

9. The capital of Alberta, Canada. East of the Canadian Rockies, it was established in 1795 as a trading post and fort of the Hudson's Bay colony.

And they loved each other
It was said,
The Reverend Rundle
And the Indians red
And through the Rockies
They watched him go
Over the ice
And under the snow—
But this was a very long
Time ago,
A long, long, long, long
Time ago.

The Money Came in, Came in

My son Sam was a banjo man,
His brother played the spoons,
Willie Waley played the ukelele
And his sister sang the tunes:
    Sometimes sharp,
    Sometimes flat,
    It blew the top
    Off your Sunday hat,
    But no one bothered
    At a thing like that,
    And the money came in, came in.

Gussie Green played a tambourine,
His wife played the mandolin,
Tommy Liddell played a one-string fiddle
He made from a biscuit tin.
    Sometimes flat,
    Sometimes sharp,
    The noise was enough
    To break your heart,
    But nobody thought
    To cavil or carp,
    And the money came in, came in.

Clicketty Jones she played the bones,
Her husband the kettle-drum,
Timothy Tout blew the inside out
Of a brass euphonium.
    Sometimes sharp,
    Sometimes flat,
    It sounded like somebody
    Killing the cat,
    But no one bothered

At a thing like that,
And the money came in, came in.

Samuel Shute he played the flute,
His sister played the fife.
The Reverend Moon played a double bassoon
With the help of his lady wife.
    Sometimes flat,
    Sometimes sharp
    As a pancake
    Or an apple tart,
    But everyone, everyone
    Played a part
    And the money came in, came in.

Good Morning, Mr Croco-doco-dile

Good morning, Mr Croco-doco-dile,
And how are you today?
I like to see you croco-smoco-smile
In your croco-woco-way.

From the tip of your beautiful croco-toco-tail
To your croco-hoco-head
You seem to me so croco-stoco-still
As if you're croco-doco-dead.

Perhaps if I touch your croco-cloco-claw
Or your croco-snoco-snout,
Or get up close to your croco-joco-jaw
I shall very soon find out.

But suddenly I croco-soco-see
In your croco-oco-eye
A curious kind of croco-gloco-gleam,
So I just don't think I'll try.

Forgive me, Mr Croco-doco-dile
But it's time I was away.
Let's talk a little croco-woco-while
Another croco-doco-day.

When I Was a Boy

When I was a boy
On the Isle of Wight
We all had a bath

On Friday night.
The bath was made
Of Cornish tin
And when one got out
Another got in.
    First there was Jenny
    Then there was Jean,
    Then there was Bessie
    Skinny as a bean,
    Then there was Peter,
    Then there was Paul,
    And I was the very last
    One of all.

When mammy boiled the water
We all felt blue
And we lined up like
A cinema queue.
We never had time
To bob or blush
When she went to work
With the scrubbing brush.
    First there was Jenny, etc.

When I was a boy
On the Isle of Wight
My mammy went to work
Like dynamite:
Soap on the ceiling,
Water on the floor,
Mammy put the kettle on
And boil some more!
    First there was Jenny, etc.

I Am the Song

I am the song that sings the bird.
I am the leaf that grows the land.
I am the tide that moves the moon.
I am the stream that halts the sand.
I am the cloud that drives the storm.
I am the earth that lights the sun.
I am the fire that strikes the stone.
I am the clay that shapes the hand.
I am the word[1] that speaks the man.

1986

---

1. Jesus is often identified with "the Word" (see John 1.1).

LUCILLE CLIFTON
b. 1936

At the annual Christmas concert at her church, Lucille Sayles was five—and suffering from stage fright. Unable to remember the poem she was supposed to recite, she stood silently, attempting to hide her embarrassment: "I don' wanna," she said when encouraged to perform by members of the audience. Her mother came to the rescue. " 'Come on, baby,' she smiled, then turned to address the church: 'She don't have to do nothing she don't want to do.' " Lucille Clifton recalls that the gesture made her, at once, "empowered" and "free." That generosity of spirit and sensitivity to language and the nuances of family life clearly inform all Clifton's poetry.

Clifton was born in Depew, New York, a small town near Buffalo, where the family moved when she was about six; she grew up with two half-sisters and a brother. Her father, who worked in a steel mill, loved to read and told her stories he had heard from his great-grandmother, kidnapped from Dahomey by slave traders in 1830; her mother, a launderer, wrote verse, though she (like Clifton's father) had never completed elementary school. At sixteen, Clifton began studying drama at Howard University, and some of the people she met there, such as LeRoi Jones (Amiri Baraka), would later become part of her intellectual community. But after two years she lost her fellowship, and after returning to New York she continued her education at Fredonia State Teachers College (now SUNY Fredonia). Though she was already starting to write, she published little. In 1958 she married Fred Clifton (who died in 1984); he was then teaching philosophy at the University of Buffalo, and they had six children within seven years.

Clifton arrived on the literary scene in spectacular fashion. In 1969, after winning the prestigious Discovery Award from the 92nd St. Y's Poetry Center (bestowed on a poet who had not yet published a book-length manuscript), she won wide acclaim for her first book, *Good Times*. She took up the first of several academic positions in 1971 as poet-in-residence at Coppin State College, Baltimore; universities at which she has taught include Duke and Columbia, and since 1971 she has been Distinguished Professor of Humanities at St. Mary's College in Maryland. She has published a dozen collections of poetry and a memoir for adults, together with more than twenty books of poetry and fiction for children. Among the major prizes she has won are a National Book Award for *Blessing the Boats: New and Selected Poems, 1988–2000* (2000) and an Emmy for her writing in *Free to Be . . . You and Me* (1974).

Clifton's writing blends evocative images, passion, humor, honesty, and hope with a clear-eyed portrayal of black life in America, past and present. Though the tone is conversational, the words seem effortlessly precise and distilled. She celebrates the everyday and especially the strength of family ties. Eight of her children's books feature as their protagonist Everett Anderson—a perfect poetic name, a double dactyl: Ev´-er-ett An´-der-son. The first book in the series, *Some of the Days of Everett Anderson* (1970), illustrated by Evaline Ness, was chosen as one of the *School Library Journal*'s Best Books of the year. Throughout the series, Clifton never averts her gaze from the pain and fear experienced by a young African American boy (see "Saturday Night Late"); for example, in a later volume his family is abandoned by his father. But she remembers to rejoice in tiny moments of satisfaction. In "Friday Mom Is Home Payday," for example, she focuses on a single perfect comforting shared moment between mother and son. Everett Anderson enjoys:

> Swishing one finger
> in the foam
> of Mama's glass
> when she gets home.

SOME OF THE DAYS OF EVERETT ANDERSON

Monday Morning Good Morning

Being six
is full of tricks
and Everett Anderson knows it.

Being a boy
is full of joy
and Everett Anderson shows it.

Tuesday All Day Rain

Everett Anderson
absolutely
refuses to lose his
umbrella.

Everett Anderson
absolutely
is pleased to leave it
at home.

Rain or shine
he doesn't whine
about "catching cold" or
"summer showers."

Sad or merry
he doesn't carry
the thing around for
hours and hours.

Everett Anderson
absolutely
would rather get wet
than to forget.

Everett Anderson
absolutely
refuses to lose his
umbrella.

Wednesday Noon Adventure

Who's black
and runs
and loves to hop?
Everett Anderson does.

Who's black
and was lost
in the candy shop?
Everett Anderson was.

Who's black
and noticed the
peppermint flowers?
Everett Anderson did.

Who's black
and was lost for
hours and hours?
Everett Anderson
                    Hid!

Thursday Evening

Afraid of the dark
is afraid of Mom
and Daddy,
and Papa
and Cousin Tom.

"I'd be as silly
as I could be,
afraid of the dark
is afraid of Me!"

says ebony
Everett
Anderson.

LUCILLE CLIFTON

Friday Waiting for Mom

When I am seven
Mama can stay
from work and play with me
all day.

I won't go to school,
I'll pull up a seat
by her and we can talk
and eat

and we will laugh
at how it ends;
Mama and
Everett Anderson—
Friends.

Friday Mom Is Home Payday

Swishing one finger
in the foam
of Mama's glass
when she gets home
is a very
favorite thing to do.
Mama says
foam is a comfort,
Everett Anderson
says so too.

Saturday Night Late

The siren seems so far away
when people live in 14 A,
they can pretend that all the noise
is just some other girls and boys
running and
laughing and
having fun
instead of whatever it is
whispers
Everett Anderson.

Sunday Morning Lonely

Daddy's back
is broad and black
and Everett Anderson loves to ride it.

Daddy's side
is black and wide
and Everett Anderson sits beside it.

Daddy's cheek
is black and sleek
and Everett Anderson kisses it.

Daddy's space
is a black empty place
and Everett Anderson misses it.

Sunday Night Good

The stars are so near
to 14 A
that after playing outside
all day
Everett Anderson likes to pretend
that stars are where
apartments end.

1970

PAT MORA
b. 1942

In her first essay collection, *Nepantla* (1993), Pat Mora defines herself as a "denizen of *nepantla*," a word in the Native American language Nahuatl that means "the land of the middle." She locates herself spatially in the interior domestic spaces of her family memoir, *House of Houses* (1997), which draws on *The Poetics of Space* (1957) by the French philosopher Gaston Bachelard for its controlling metaphor. She centers her story in a web of family relationships that are explicitly domestic, then paradoxically expands to include family histories that move her ancestors from Spain and Mexico across the border into the English-speaking world of the United States.

Mora identifies borders as places of power. Her works of poetry and prose for children and adults occupy a borderland: moving between desert and urban landscapes, between intimate, domestic family scenes and larger historical contexts, and between English and Spanish. In "Legal Alien," from *Chants* (1984), her first published book, Mora defines Hispanic/American doubleness:

> Bi-lingual. Bi-cultural,
> able to slip from "How's life?"
> to *"Me'stan volviendo loca."*

One of the most significant features of Mora's books for both adults and children is that she slips between English and Spanish; sometimes she offers hints to help monolingual readers puzzle out the meaning within the text, sometimes not. Sometime she offers a glossary, as in *Confetti: Poems for Children* (1996), her first collection for a juvenile audience.

Mora was born in El Paso, Texas. Both sets of her grandparents had fled there in the early twentieth century during the Mexican Revolution. One of four children, she was raised in a warm, extended family that included her maternal grandmother and aunt. She credits them with instilling in her a respect for the power of stories and storytelling.

Mora received all her education in El Paso, earning a B.A. in 1963 at the University of Texas campus (then called Texas Western College). She married William Burnside soon afterward, and they had three children. After teaching public school, she returned to UTEP for a master's in English (1971) and subsequently taught part-time at the college level. In 1981, the same year that she and her husband divorced, she made a career change as well, moving out of the classroom and into administration at UTEP so that she could have time to write. Her first poem was published in 1981; and her first book for children—*A Birthday Basket for Tía*, a picture book partly based on a memory of her own aunt's ninetieth birthday—was published in 1992.

Pat Mora is one of the authors defining the widening context and look of children's literature in the twenty-first century. Since 1989 she has been writing and speaking full-time, and she has published more than twenty books for children and seven for adults, as well as articles and essays. In 1984 she married Vernon Scarborough, an archaeologist who teaches at the University of Cincinnati, so she divides her time between their home in Kentucky and their home in Santa Fe, New Mexico, in her native Southwest—the place central to her writing. Mora, a frequent, popular speaker, has become an important advocate for conserving and appreciating cultures and for supporting multicultural education. She sees herself as someone who campaigns for the rights of people to see themselves, their heritage and culture, in their literature. In her own words, she is able "to foster book joy."

CONFETTI
POEMS FOR CHILDREN

Sun Song

Birds in the branches hear the sun's first song.
Ranitas[1] in the rocks hear the sun's first song.
Bees in the bushes hear the sun's first song.
Wind in the willows hears the sun's first song.

Birds in the branches chirp their morning song.
Ranitas in the rocks croak their morning song.
Bees in the bushes buzz their morning song.
Wind in the willows whirrs its morning song.

Sun song. Sun song. Sun song.

Colors Crackle, Colors Roar

Red shouts a loud, balloon-round sound.
Black crackles like noisy grackles.
Café clickety-clicks its wooden sticks.
Yellow sparks and sizzles, tzz-tzz.
White sings, *Ay*, her high, light note.
Verde rustles leaf-secrets, swhish, swhish.
Gris whis-whis-whispers its kitten whiskers.
Silver ting-ting-a-ling jingles.
Azul coo-coo-coos like *pajaritos* do.
Purple thunders and rum-rum-rumbles.
Oro blares, a brassy, brass tuba.
Orange growls its striped, rolled roar.
Colors Crackel, Colors Roar.

Purple Snake

"It's in there, sleeping,"
Don Luis says and winks.
He knows I want to feel
the animal asleep in a piece of wood,
like he does
turning it this way and that,
listening.

---

1. On p. 1274 is Mora's glossary of Spanish words.

Slowly he strokes the wood,
rough and wrinkled. Like his hands.
He begins to carve his way.
"*Mira*. Its head, its scales, its tail."
Don Luis rubs and strokes
the animal before he paints
its eyes open.
When the paint dries,
I place the purple snake
by the green bull and red frog
that Don Luis found asleep
in a piece of wood.

Can I, Can I Catch the Wind

Can I, can I catch the wind, in the morning,
catch the wind?
Can I, can I catch the wind, in my two hands,
catch the wind?
Can I, can I catch the wind, in my basket,
catch the wind?
Can I, can I catch the wind, in my clay pot,
catch the wind?
Can I, can I catch the wind, in my tin box,
catch the wind?
Can I, can I catch the wind, in my straw hat,
catch the wind?
Can I, can I catch the wind, in my bird cage,
catch the wind?
Wind, Wind, run and spin, dance and spin,
run and spin.

Cloud Dragons

What do you see
in the clouds so high?
What do you see in the sky?

Oh, I see dragons
that curl their tails
as they go slithering by.

What do you see
in the clouds so high?
What do you see? Tell me, do.

Oh, I see *caballitos*
that race the wind
high in the shimmering blue.

Castanet Clicks

Uno, dos
one, two
baskets blue.

Tres, cuatro
three, four
one bell more.

Cinco, seis
five, six
castanet clicks.

Siete, ocho
seven, eight
copper plates.

Nueve, diez
nine, ten
count again.

Mexican Magician

All day the *panadero*,
in white apron and ball cap,
stirs flour, eggs and sugar
then *salsas* with his broom.

His hands brim with sweet secrets,
he folds into thick fillings.
He pushes his huge rolling pin
and sings to make dough rise.

He cuts large *marranitos*
that fatten in his oven,

Pat Mora

1272

chops nuts, raisins and apples,
then *cha-chas* round the room.

With cinnamon and anise,
he flavors spongy dough puffs,
stirs pineapple and pumpkin
he pours in tarts and pies.

He heaps clean shelves and counters
with *pan* and *empanadas*,
pastry so light and flaky,
it sails into warm air.

His hips sway while he sprinkles
cookies with sweet confetti,
dance-dancing *panadero*,
magician with a flair.

Leaf Soup

Leaves sail through the air
like lazy *mariposas*
gliding on warm gusts
and breezes onto my hair.
Leaves spin quiet into puddles,
float on their backs then drift
down
down.

Near the prickly pear,
leaves soften into mush-clumps,
season the soup for brown squirrels
and plump birds quick hopping
to sip green
pools of tasty leaf soup.

I Hear, I Hear

I hear the rhythm of the Tarahumaras
pom, pom,
I hear them hoeing in the cornfields
pom, pom,
I hear them patting tortillas
pom, pom,
I hear them herding their goats
pom, pom,

I hear their bare feet on the land
    pom, pom,
I hear them running, running
    pom, pom,
I hear their steady drumbeats
    pom, pom,
    pom, pom,
    pom, pom.

Dancing Paper

Let's fill the room with laughing
  before our friends arrive.
We'll bring the colored paper.
  The room will come alive.

Let's start with the *piñata*.
The air will sway and swing.
  We'll string *papel picado*
    to start its fluttering.

  I'll fling the *serpentinas*,
    toss coils in the air.
We'll add *marimba* music,
start dancing everywhere.

  Remember *cascarones*,
    to hide will be in vain.
Egg-bursts of bright confetti
  will shower us like rain.

Abuelita's Lap

    I know a place where I can sit
      and tell about my day,
      tell every color that I saw
      from green to cactus gray.

    I know a place where I can sit
      and hear a favorite beat,
  her heart and *cuentos* from the past,
      the rhythms honey-sweet.

    I know a place where I can sit
      and listen to a star,

    listen to its silent song
      gliding from afar.

    I know a place where I can sit
      and hear the wind go by,
hearing it spinning round my house,
      my whirling lullaby.

Words Free As Confetti

Come, words, come in your every color.
I'll toss you in storm or breeze.
I'll say, say, say you,
taste you sweet as plump plums,
bitter as old lemons.
I'll sniff you, words, warm
as almonds or tart as apple-red,
feel you green
and soft as new grass,
lightwhite as dandelion plumes,
or thorngray as cactus,
heavy as black cement,
cold as blue icicles,
warm as *abuelita's* yellowlap.
I'll hear you, words, loud as searoar's
purple crash, hushed
as *gatitos* curled in sleep,
as the last goldlullaby.
I'll see you long and dark as tunnels,
bright as rainbows,
playful as chestnutwind.
I'll watch you, words, rise and dance and spin.
I'll say, say, say you
in English,
in Spanish,
I'll find you.
Hold you.
Toss you.
I'm free too.
I say *yo soy libre*,
I am free
free, free,
free as confetti.

River Voice

In the desert, the river's voice
    is cool, in canyons,
the song of rock and hawk.

In the desert, the *rio's* voice
    is cool, in valleys,
the song of field and owl.

In the desert, the river's voice
    is cool, at dusk,
the song of star-gleam and moon.

In the desert, the *rio's* voice
    is cool, at dawn,
the song of wind and fresh light.

GLOSSARY

abuelita (ah-bweh-LEE-tah): grandmother
azul (ah-ZUHL): blue
caballitos (kah-bah-YEE-toce): little horses
café (kah-FEH): brown
cascarones (kahs-kah-RONE-ehs): painted
    eggshells filled with confetti
cha-cha (CHAH-chah): a Latin American dance
cinco (SEEN-koh): five
cuatro (KWAH-troe): four
cuentos (KWEN-toce): stories
diez (dee-EHS): ten
dos (DOSE): two

empanadas (ehm-pa-NAH-dahs): small pies;
    turnovers
gatitos (gah-TEE-toce): kittens
gris (GREECE): gray
libre (LEE-breh): free
marimba (mah-REEM-bah): a musical instru-
    ment similar to a xylophone
mariposas (mah-ree-POH-sahs): butterflies
marranitos (mah-rah-NEE-toce): cookies
mira (MEE-rah): look
nueve (noo-WEH-veh): nine
ocho (OH-choh): eight
oro (OH-roh): gold
pajaritos (pah-hah-REE-toce): little birds
pan (PAHN): bread
panadero (pah-nah-DEH-roe): baker
papel picado (pah-PEHL-pee-CAH-doe): cut
    paper
piñata (pee-NYAH-tah): piñata
ranitas (rah-NEE-tahs): little frogs
río (REE-oh): river
salsa (SAHL-sah): a Latin American dance
seis (SEHS): six
serpentinas (sehr-pen-TEE-nahs): paper coils
siete (see-EH-teh): seven
Tarahumaras (Tah-rah-hu-MAH-rahs): Indians
    indigenous to northern Mexico
tres (TREHS): three
uno (OO-noe): one
verde (VER-deh): green
yo soy (YOE SOY): I am

1996

MARILYN NELSON
b. 1946

"Abracadabra, alakazam, paz, salaam, shalom, amen": Marilyn Nelson began her speech accepting the Boston Globe–Horn Book Award for *Carver: A Life in Poems* (2001) with this list of "magic words." She had originally composed it with a group of children in a poetry workshop, as "a spell to bring the world peace." There is an eloquent simplicity in this spell, and a faith that words can bring about positive change. That trust in the power of words permeates her work for both children and adults.

Born in Cleveland, Ohio, Nelson was one of three children. Her mother was a teacher, who Nelson recalls telling them "proud stories of her family"; her father was a pilot in the U.S. Air Force. He also wrote poems and plays, and they constantly moved from one air base to another. He was among the first Tuskegee Airmen, the blacks who began to be trained as fighter pilots in 1941. Nelson wrote movingly of their experience in a series of poems in *The Homeplace,* published in 1990 under the name Marilyn Nelson Waniek (as were all her books until 1995; she was married to Erdmann F. Waniek from 1970 to 1979). Works such as "Lonely Eagles"—the nickname of her father's squadron—pay tribute to heroism in the face of racism:

Being black in America
was the Original Catch,
so no one was surprised
by 22:
The segregated airstrips,
separate camps.
They did the jobs
they'd been trained to do.

Although Nelson began writing poetry as a child, she stopped for a decade after college. A B.A. from the University of California, Davis, was followed by an M.A. from the University of Pennsylvania and a Ph.D. from the University of Minnesota. She held several teaching posts before joining the English department of the University of Connecticut in 1978—the same year that her first volume of poetry was published, *For the Body*. In 2002 she left for the University of Delaware. She has two children from her marriage to Roger Wilkenfeld.

Nelson is among the African American poets who are "writing back" (to borrow a term sometimes used of postcolonial literature) to Anglo-Saxon literary traditions. One of her characteristic methods is to re-create traditional forms, such as the villanelle and the sonnet. Several of what Nelson calls "unbuttoned sonnets" appear in the "Still Faith" section of *The Fields of Praise: New and Selected Poems* (1997); "From an Alabama Farmer" is one example from *Carver*. Such poems demonstrate her virtuoso ability to make new the rhythms and

rhymes of that most traditional form, retaining its history while making it speak in a voice imbued with African American language and culture. She has won numerous honors, including a Guggenheim Fellowship and two Pushcart Prizes, in addition to the many awards given to *Carver*.

Though Nelson had co-authored one book of poetry for children (*The Cat Walked through the Casserole and Other Poems for Children*, with Pamela Espeland, 1984) and co-translated another (Halfdan Rasmussen's *Hundreds of Hens and Other Poems for Children*, with Espeland, 1982), she says that she wrote her book about the groundbreaking black scientist George Washington Carver with her usual adult audience in mind. The idea for this verse biography came from a chance visitor, one of the men who had worked with her father years before, when he was stationed in New Hampshire.

The collection begins with Carver an infant slave ("Out of 'Slave's Ransom'") and ends with the dying professor hearing the planes flown by the black aviators from the airfield near Tuskegee, as Nelson's father "makes a sky-roaring victory roll" ("Moton Field"). In her second publication for readers "twelve and up," *Fortune's Bones: The Manumission Requiem* (2004), Nelson clothes the literal bones of a former slave with the story of his life. In *Carver*, she fleshes out the life of an African American hero by placing Carver in the context of American history, conveying what she calls "the best values of humankind" in lyrical and honest verse.

FROM CARVER
A LIFE IN POEMS

Out of "Slave's Ransom"

John Bentley, Diamond Grove, Missouri[1]

There's a story to the name.
Had her since I was a colt myself.
Oh, I was a wild one,
up to my withers in oats, and

when Moses Carver comes to me
and begs me to go after
their slave-girl Mary and her son,
well, I never was one
to turn down good money.
Tracked the bushwhackers[2]
two days south of here
and caught up with them

---

1. **c. 1864** Carver is born in Diamond Grove, Missouri. His mother, Mary, is a slave owned by Moses and Susan Carver; Mary has an older son, Jim. Shortly after George's birth, Mary and George are stolen; Moses Carver hires John Bentley to find them. Bentley finds only the infant [Nelson's note].
2. In the American Civil War, irregular or guerrilla fighters.

down in Arkansas: The girl,
already sold, had left them
holding a bundle of wet rags,
convulsive with fever and shook
by the whooping cough.
They were glad
to be shut of[3] him.

When I handed him to Missus Carver,
you never seen such carrying-on.
All that over a puny black baby.
You'd have thought that Mary
was her sister or something.
Carver give me his best filly
as a reward.

Many's the winnings I've toasted
thanks to her and her colts.
This one's her fifteenth.
Look at the clean lines,
the sleekness, the self-respect.
His dam's a quarter Arabian,[4]
and when you see him run you'll swear
he was sired by the wind.

Prayer of the Ivory-Handled Knife

Susan Carver, 1871

Father, you have given us,
instead of our own children, your
and Mary's orphans, Jim and George.
What would you have us make
of them? What
kind of freedom
can we raise them to?
They will always be strangers
in this strange, hate-filled land.

Jim is a big help to Moses:
Thank you for their joined laughter
like morning mist over new-plowed fields.
And our little plant-doctor:
Now he's crushing leaves and berries
and painting sanded boards.

Thank you
for his profusion of roses
on our bedroom wall,
for his wildflower bouquet
in the sitting room,
his apples and pears beside the stove.

He ran out before breakfast,
saying he'd dreamed last night
of that pocket knife he's been
asking us and praying for.
A few minutes later he ran back up
from the garden, calling
Aunt Sue! Aunt Sue!
He'd found it in a watermelon,
ivory-handled,
exactly as he had dreamed.
Seemed like he all but flew
into my arms.
Oh, Father, gracious Lord:
How shall I thank you?

Washboard Wizard

Highland, Kansas, 1885

All of us take our clothes to Carver.
He's a wizard with a washboard,
a genie of elbow grease and suds.
We'll take you over there next week;
by that time you'll be needing him.
He's a colored boy, a few years older
than we are, real smart. But he stays
in his place. They say
he was offered a scholarship
to the college.[5] I don't know
what happened, but they say
that's why he's here in town.
Lives alone, in a little shack
filled with books
over in Poverty Row.
They say he reads them.
Dried plants, rocks, jars of colors.
A bubbling cauldron of laundry.
Pictures of flowers and landscapes.

---

3. Rid of.
4. A breed of swift horse.

5. Highland College had accepted Carver by mail, but refused him admittance when he arrived because he was black.

They say he
painted them. They say
he was turned away when he got here,
because he's a nigger. I don't know about
all that. But he's the best
washwoman in town.

A Ship Without a Rudder

Helen Milholland, Winterset, Iowa, 1890

A new voice in church. I turned around to look.
A colored boy, high-cheeked and handsome,
his head thrown back, his eyes closed,
a well-groomed mustache. Well, it was love,
so to speak, at first sight. I asked John
to speak to him after the service. He was tall,
slender, shabbily dressed but clean
and well-smelling. He wore a snapdragon,
I remember it was yellow and purple,
in his lapel. When our eyes met,
I knew it was mutual. But he looked
at John, and at everyone else
who welcomed him in the doorway,
with the same forever.
We asked him home,
talked with him. Then John,
my dearest John, I'd never known
such pride in him: *Yes you will
go to college; yes you will
get an education; God
has something big
in store for you; I'll talk
to the president of Simpson College[6]
myself if I have to.*
When my eyes met John's
just after he spoke those words,
that was when I knew,
I mean really, really, truly knew,
I meant what I said when I married him.

Curve-Breaker

for Mrs. W. A. Liston

What broke the ice?
Was it his G.P.A.? The prayer group
he joined and sustained? The Agricultural
Society he founded, his writing
the class poem and painting the class
picture? His good accent in German Club?
Was it the Art Club? Was it his balancing
an unspilled glass of water on a hoop
to raise funds for new football uniforms?
Was it his soft guitar? His impermeable
arguments in debate? Was it the way
he transformed the cafeteria with vines
and autumn leaves for Welsh Eclectic
Society banquets? Was it his
sidesplitting renditions there
of humorous poems? How the hell
should I know? Maybe it was that white
lady who took the train to Ames[7] to eat
at his table. They both laughed
when she said she was his mother.
Anyway, way before Christmas
we were calling him Doc.

My People[8]

Strutting around here acting all humble,
when everybody knows
he's the only one here[9]
got a master's degree
from a white man's college.
Everybody knows his salary
is double ours. He's got two singles
in Rockefeller Hall; the rest of us
bachelors share doubles. The extra room
is for his "collections."
A pile of you-know-what,
if you ask me.

---

6. School in Indianola, Iowa; Carver was admitted in September 1890.
7. Location of the Iowa State College of Agriculture. Carver had transferred there in 1891, after he was persuaded to change his major from art to agriculture, and earned a B.S. (1894) and M.S. (1896).
8. According to the black writer and folklorist Zora Neale Hurston, "My people! My people" is a "sad and satiric expression in the Negro language; sad when a Negro comments on the backwardness of some members of his race; at other times, used for satiric or comic effect" ("Glossary of Harlem Slang," 1942).
9. The Tuskegee Normal and Industrial Institute (now Tuskegee University), in Tuskegee, Alabama, a school for black students founded in 1881. Carver began teaching there in 1897.

All that fake politeness, that white accent.
He thinks he's better than us.
Wears those mismatched suits every day, too:
white men's castoffs with the sleeves too short,
the trousers all bagged out at the knees.
His ties look like something
he made himself.
Always some old weed in his lapel,
like he's trying to be dapper.
It makes you want to laugh.
Talking all those big words,
quoting poems at you
in that womanish voice.
So high and mighty,
he must think he's white.
Wandering around through the fields
like a fool, holding classes in the dump.
Always on his high horse, as if his
wasn't the blackest face on the faculty,
as if he wasn't a nigger.

From an Alabama Farmer

Dere Dr. Carver, I bin folloring
the things I herd you say last planting time.[1]
I give my cow more corn, less cottonseed
and my creme chirns mo better butter. I'm
riting to you today, Sir, jes to tell
you at I furtulize: 800 pounds
to the acur las March. Come harves, well
it were a bompercrop. How did you found
out you coud use swamp mock?[2] I presheate
your anser Dr. Carver by mail soon.
What maid my cotton grow? It do fele grate
to see the swet off your brow com to bloom.
I want to now what maid my miricle.
Your humbel servint, (*name illegible*)

The Sweet-Hearts

Sarah Hunt, rumored suicide[3]

Bright as I was,
I knew Mama would suck her teeth
and shake her head with disgust
if she knew we were courting.
He came to the schoolyard
toward the end of every day,
patted the children's heads as they passed,
let them find the roasted peanuts
hidden in his pockets.
Then he would turn to me,
his tawny eyes grow golden.
He'd hand me a flower.

He in his mismatched
secondhand suits
with the top button always buttoned,
always some kind of a flower
in his faded lapel.

He took my books,
offered his arm,
and as we walked
told me about my flower.
Every day a different Latin name.

I flirted.
He talked about the lilies of the field,
about feeding the multitudes with the miracle
of the peanut and the sweet potato.[4]
My invisible, disapproving family.
With him, I could never again ride
in the white car, or sleep in a decent hotel.
He told me of the vision
he'd had on his first day here:
That the school would flourish,
that Tuskegee was the place for him
to be God's instrument.

I straightened his ties,
told me when
his sleeves and collars

---

1. In his early years at Tuskegee, Carver held conferences to teach black farmers better farming methods, and he spear-headed the development of farm demonstration work and outreach programs.
2. I.e., muck. This fertile soil is rich in decaying vegetable matter.

3. c. 1905   Carver meets Miss Sarah Hunt [Nelson's note]. Hunt was the sister-in-law of the Tuskegee treasurer.
4. Carver was largely responsible for the development of peanuts and sweet potatoes as leading crops in the South. Previously, they had had little commercial use.

needed turning,
suggested he give away
his baggiest trousers,
that there's such a thing
as too much mending.
How he trembled
the first time I took his hand.
That gold light so fierce my shame
was almost burned away.
But our children would be dark,
they might have his hair.
For three years
people smiled at us.
We knew there were whispers:
"The Sweet-Hearts."

He helped my fourth graders
start a garden, talked to them
about growing things.
I wish I'd kept his little notes.
The last one said something like
"Miss Sarah, I believe you care
more about my clothes
than you do about me or my work."
He stopped coming around.
How the children missed him.

I left at the end of the school year
and started a new life. Started you.
Children, you are almost grown,
and I have saved you from Negro shame.
But the man in this clipping
might have been your father.
Charles.—
I can live no longer
this life of a fool.

Dear ones,
forgive me.

The Joy of Sewing

First the threading of the needle,
that eye nearly invisible
held nearer and farther away,
so the tip of the thread
is a camel through a keyhole,
a rich man

carrying all of his belongings
through the Pearly Gates.[5]
But at last, near cussing,
you thread the filament
into the orifice. *Aha!*
The cloth lies on your lap
like an infant in a christening gown,
as smooth under your palm
as your mother's lost skirts.
The needle slow at first,
jackrabbits straight and true.
The making.
The focus.
The stitches your fingers' mantra.

The finished products of contemplation:
the ties Carver always wears
with his secondhand suits.
And the snickers behind his back.

Veil-Raisers

Sometimes one light burned late
in The Oaks, the stately home of the great
Principal, Booker T.[6] He sat and wrote
note after note, controlling faculty,
philanthropists, and family
with spiderweb reins.
When a plank broke and he plunged
into white hopelessness,
he shook himself
and rang up to the third floor,
where a student exchanging service
for tuition sproinged to his feet.

The breathless summons reached
Carver's cluttered rooms
down in Rockefeller Hall,
where he dozed in his easy chair.
He still had lab notes to write,
tomorrow's classes to prepare,
letters, and his Bible reading.
He'd been up, as always,
since that godliest hour
when light is created anew,

---

5. See Matthew 19.24.
6. Booker T. Washington (1856–1915). Born a slave, he founded and was the first principal of the Tuskegee Institute.

and he would wake again
in a few more hours.
Roused, he nodded,
exchanged slippers for brogans.

You saw them sometimes
if you were sneaking in past curfew,
after a tête-à-tête on a town girl's porch:
shoulder to shoulder
and dream to dream,
two veil-raisers.
Walking our people
into history.

How a Dream Dies

It was 1915,[7] the year
of trenches and poison gas,
when Booker T. Washington
rushed home from New Haven
to die in his own bed.
For the first days after the funeral
Carver sat and rocked, sat
and rocked. For months
he could not teach,
would not go into the lab.
He sat in his room, he rocked.
His duties were reduced
to supervising the study hall,
where he sat at the front of the room
staring into his hands.

In a vision the first time they met,
Carver had been shown a lifelong partnership.
He paced the campus. He rocked.
He had seen Washington and Carver together
winning back the birthright of the disinherited.
This is how a dream dies.
In the news Europe's tribal feuds
spread to the colonies,
a conflagration of madness.

As if fifty thousand shot and bayoneted men
strewn in an unplowed field
could make right any righter.
As if might
made wrong any less wrong.
All of the dead are of the same nation.

His presence turned laughter down
to whispers. "He acts like he's lost
his best friend." *Uh-uh: He acts
like he's lost his faith.*

The Wild Garden

c. 1916

Genesis 1:29[8]

The flowers of *Cercis canadensis,*[9]
ovate *Phytolacca decandra* leaves,[1]
the serrate leaves of *Taraxacum officinale,*[2]
Viola species and *Trifolium pratens*[3] flowers
a handful of tulip petals,
a small chopped onion, a splash of vinegar,
a little salt and pepper and oil, and voilà!
Would you like a second helping?
The Creator makes nothing
for which there is no use.
There are choice wild vegetables
which make fine foods.
Lepidium[4] species, a common dooryard pest,
can be cooked up as greens.
Cirsium vulgare[5] stems,
harvested with gloves and scissors
in a roadside ditch
and stripped of thorns,
can be steamed, drizzled,
and pulled through the teeth
so the delicious heart
oozes to the tongue.
Mmmmmmm . . . Oh, excuse me.

7. **1915** Booker T. Washington dies. The monument erected at Tuskegee in his honor depicts him lifting a veil from the eyes of a male slave who is rising from a kneeling position [Nelson's note]. The Germans first used gas against British forces at Ypres in April 1915.
8. And God said, Behold, I have given you every herb bearing seed, which is upon the face of all the earth, and every tree, in the which is the fruit of a tree yielding seed; to you it shall be for meat.

9. Eastern redbud.
1. Pokeweed.
2. Dandelion.
3. Red clover. *"Viola"*: the genus of violets.
4. Cress.
5. Bull thistle.

If all crops perished, the race could survive
on a balanced diet of wild vegetables.
The homeliest, lowest,
torn out by the roots, poisoned;
the "inferior," the "weeds"—
They grow despite our will to kill them,
despite our ignorance
of what their use might be.
We refuse to thank them,
but they keep on coming back
with the Creator's handwritten invitation.
Another *Hemerocallis*[6] fritter?
Try some of this *Potentilla*[7] tea.

Professor Carver's Bible Class

After Alvin D. Smith[8]

I'd always pictured God as a big old
long-bearded white man throned up in the sky,
watching and keeping score. I had been told
we get harps or pitchfork brimstone when we
    die.
Superstitiously, I watched for "signs,"
living in fear of a Great Master's wrath.
Professor Carver's class gave me the means
to liberation from that slavish faith.
He taught us that our Creator lives within,
yearning to speak to us through silent prayer;
that all of nature, if we'll just tune in,
is a vast broadcasting system; that the air
carries a current we can plug into:
Your Creator, he said, *is itching to contact you!*

Friends in the Klan

1923[9]

Black veterans of WWI experienced
such discrimination in veterans' hospitals
that the Veterans' Administration, to save face,
opened in Tuskegee a brand-new hospital,
for Negroes only. Under white control.
(White nurses, who were legally excused
from touching blacks, stood holding their
    elbows
and ordering colored maids around, white shoes
tapping impatiently.)
           The Professor joined
the protest. When the first black doctor arrived
to jubilation, the KKK uncoiled
its length and hissed. *If you want to stay alive
be away Tuesday.* Unsigned. But a familiar hand.
The Professor stayed. And he prayed for his
    friend in the Klan.

Driving Dr. Carver

Al Zissler, 1999[1]

Al Zissler's friend Jim Hardwick offered him
a job. It was Spring 1933,
the Great Depression. So Zissler and Jim
drove Carver through the South for several
    weeks.
At eighty-eight, Zissler recalls picnics:
ham sandwiches, potato chips, sardines
and crackers; Zissler tinkering with the Buick,
Jim reading, Carver gathering salad greens.
They played pranks on each other. Hardwick
    once
said at a lecture that the Professor was deaf,
and everyone addressed him at the top of their
    lungs.

6. Daylily.
7. Cinquefoil.
8. **1913** At the request of students, Carver offers the first of his fifteen-minute Sunday evening Bible classes. The classes meet weekly for the next thirty years [Nelson's note]. Smith wrote *George Washington Carver, Man of God* (1954).
9. **1923** The KKK marches in Tuskegee. Carver receives the Spingarn Medal for Distinguished Service to Science, the first of many such honors [Nelson's note]. The Ku Klux Klan, founded by defeated Confederate soldiers in late 1865 to fight

Reconstruction governments in the southern states, was officially disbanded in 1869 and faded in the 1870s. The white supremacist organization was re-formed in Georgia in 1915 and had gained millions of members by the early 1920s.
1. Both Zissler (an engineer) and Hardwick were whites who had graduated from Iowa State; Hardwick had been inspired by Carver's lectures. A story about the spring they spent chauffeuring Carver on his lecture tour appeared in the ISU alumni magazine, *Visions*, in March/April 1999 (Karol Crosbie, "Driving Dr. Carver").

But Carver was a genius of mischief:
Later, in his trousers pocket, Jim found a toad.
Falera ha ha they sang along the open road.

Baby Carver

Austin Curtis, 1935[2]

Potential assistants strode in
and stumbled out,
repacking their paper credentials.
The Professor, grown more stooped
and now white-haired,
stood a moment beside the door,
then the door slammed.
After all these years of crying out
for another pair of hands
he preferred to work alone,
no young whippersnapper
taking notes over his shoulder.

But young Curtis shook his hand
and disappeared into the student lab.
He resurfaced a couple of weeks later
with six products
from the magnolia seed.
A few weeks later
the Professor wrote to Curtis' father
that Austin seemed to him
more like a son
than an assistant.

Graciously, humbly,
his assistant freed the Professor
from choredom and followed up
on some of his earlier ideas.
Before long Curtis had become
"Baby Carver."
And his children had acquired
a third grandpa.

Last Talk with Jim Hardwick

A *"found" poem*

When I die I will live again.
By nature I am a conserver.
I have found Nature
to be a conserver, too.
Nothing is wasted
or permanently lost
in Nature. Things
change their form,
but they do not cease
to exist. After
I leave this world
I do not believe I am through.
God would be a bigger fool
than even a man
if He did not conserve
the human soul,
which seems to be
the most important thing
He has yet done in the universe.
When you get your grip
on the last rung of the ladder
and look over the wall
as I am now doing,
you don't need their proofs:
You see.
You know
you will not die.

2001

2. **1935** Austin W. Curtis becomes Carver's assistant [Nelson's note].

MARILYN NELSON

GRACE NICHOLS
b. 1950

I have crossed an ocean
I have lost my tongue
from the root of the old one
a new one has sprung
—"I is a long memoried woman" (1983)

The epigraph above is a classic Grace Nichols quatrain: the easy bounce of nursery verse unflinchingly speaking against the harsh history of colonialism. As a Caribbean black woman born and raised in what was then British Guiana, she knows exactly what it means to be silenced doubly, by gender and by race. The image of the lost tongue recalls the classical myth of Philomela, whose brother-in-law cut out her tongue so that she could not say that he had raped her (she told her story by weaving it into a tapestry). But it also reminds the reader of the black slaves who lost their African languages when brought to the New World by white colonists. Nichols celebrates the vibrant hybrid that emerged from that loss, Creole.

Until she was eight, Nichols lived in a village on the coast; then she moved with her family (she has six sisters and one brother) to the principal city, Georgetown. There in the mid-1960s she came of age amid the tumult of the independence movement (Guyana became a sovereign state in 1966), an experience that informs her novel *Whole of a Morning Sky* (1986). Nichols worked first as a teacher and then, after earning a diploma in communications from the University of Guyana in 1971, as a journalist and as a freelance writer. She gave birth to a daughter, and published a short story and a few poems. But it was not until after her 1977 move to England with John Agard, also a Guyana-born poet and writer for children, that her first book—*Trust You, Wriggly* (1981), about the adventures of a seven-year-old girl in a Guyanese village—was published. And only after the appearance of her first collection of poems for adults—*I is a long memoried woman* (1983), which won the Commonwealth poetry prize—did she call herself a poet. She continues to live and write in England, where she had another daughter. Her work is in turn political and erotic, historical and comic. In 2000 she received the Cholmondeley Award, given to a poet in recognition of a distinguished body of work.

Nichols infuses her writing with Creole to reclaim her heritage and ensure its survival. In doing so, she, like Agard and other expatriate Caribbean poets now living in Britain, change the sound and shape of standard English poetry. For example, *No Hickory, No Dickory, No Dock: A Collection of Caribbean Nursery Rhymes* (1992), co-written with Agard and illustrated by Cynthia Jabar, consists largely of original poems that recast Mother Goose in the Caribbean idiom. The Caribbean childhood she depicts in her first verse collection for children, *Come on into My Tropical Garden* (1988, illustrated by Caroline Binch), is compelling and memorable. She celebrates the pleasures of domestic life (combing hair, planting, cooking)—and of disobedience. The book was a strong runner-up for the *Signal* poetry award. Nichols slips easily between the cadences of standard English, Rap, and Creole, remembering the tragedies of colonization but not subdued by them.

Come on into My Tropical Garden

Come on into My Tropical Garden

Come on into my tropical garden
Come on in and have a laugh in
Taste my sugar cake and my pine[1] drink
Come on in please come on in

And yes you can stand up in my hammock
and breeze out in my trees
you can pick my hibiscus
and kiss my chimpanzees

O you can roll up in the grass
and if you pick up a flea
I'll take you down for a quick dip-wash
in the sea
believe me there's nothing better
for getting rid of a flea
than having a quick dip-wash in the sea

Come on into my tropical garden
Come on in please come on in

Alligator

If you want to see an alligator
you must go down to the muddy slushy end
of the old Caroony River

I know an alligator
who's living down there
She's a-big. She's a-mean. She's a-wild.
She's a-fierce.

But if you really want to see an alligator
you must go down to the muddy slushy end
of the old Caroony River

Go down gently to that river and say
'Alligator Mama
Alligator Mama
Alligator Mamaaaaaaaa'

And up she'll rise
but don't stick around
RUN FOR YOUR LIFE

I Like to Stay Up

I like to stay up
and listen
when big people talking
jumbie[2] stories

I does feel
so tingly and excited
inside me

But when my mother say
'Girl, time for bed'

Then is when
I does feel a dread

Then is when
I does jump into me bed

Then is when
I does cover up
from me feet to me head

Then is when
I does wish I didn't listen
to no stupid jumbie story

Then is when
I does wish I did read
me book instead

---

1. Pineapple.

2. *Jumbie* is a Guyanese word for "ghost" [Nichols's note].

GRACE NICHOLS

They Were My People

They were those who cut cane[3]
to the rhythm of the sunbeat

They were those who carried cane
to the rhythm of the sunbeat

They were those who crushed cane
to the rhythm of the sunbeat

They were women weeding, carrying babies
to the rhythm of the sunbeat

They were my people working so hard
to the rhythm of the sunbeat

They were my people, working so hard
to the rhythm of the sunbeat—long ago
to the rhythm of the sunbeat

Poor Grandma

Why this child
so spin-spin spin-spin
Why this child
can't keep still

Why this child
so turn-round
turn-round
Why this child
can't settle down

Why this child
can't eat without getting
up to look through window
Why this child must behave so
I want to know
Why this child
so spin-spin spin-spin
Why this child
can't keep still

Riddle

Me-riddle me-riddle me-ree[4]
Me father got a tree
Tell me what you see
hanging from this tree

You can boil it
you can bake it
you can roast it
you can fry it
it goes lovely in a dish
with flying fish

It's big
it's rough
it's green
it came with old Captain Bligh
from way across the sea

Still can't guess?
well it's a ⁿᴉɐʇuɐlԀ
Me-riddle me-riddle me-ree

Granny Granny Please Comb My Hair

Granny Granny please comb
my hair
you always take your time
you always take such care

You put me on a cushion
between your knees
you rub a little coconut oil
parting gentle as a breeze

Mummy Mummy
she's always in a hurry-hurry
rush
she pulls my hair
sometimes she tugs

But Granny
you have all the time
in the world

---

3. Sugarcane.

4. I.e., riddle me ree: interpret my riddle rightly.

and when you're finished
you always turn my head and say
'Now who's a nice girl'

My Cousin Melda

My Cousin Melda
she don't make fun
she ain't afraid of anyone
even mosquitoes
when they bite her
she does bite them back
and say—
'Now tell me, how you like that?'

Wha Me Mudder Do

Mek me tell you wha me Mudder do
wha me mudder do
wha me mudder do

Me mudder pound plantain mek fufu[5]
Me mudder catch crab mek calaloo stew[6]

Mek me tell you wha me mudder do
wha me mudder do
wha me mudder do

Me mudder beat hammer
Me mudder turn screw
she paint chair red
then she paint it blue

Mek me tell you wha me mudder do
wha me mudder do
wha me mudder do

Me mudder chase bad-cow
with one 'Shoo'
she paddle down river
in she own canoe

Ain't have nothing
dat me mudder can't do
Ain't have nothing
dat me mudder can't do

Mek me tell you

The Fastest Belt in Town

Ma Bella was the fastest belt in town
Ma Bella was the fastest belt
for miles and miles around

In fact Ma Bella was the fastest belt
both in the East and in the West
nobody dared to put Ma Bella to the test

plai-plai[7]
her belt would fly
who don't hear must cry

Milk on the floor
and Ma Bella reaching for—de belt

Slamming the door
and Ma Bella reaching for—de belt

Scribbling on the wall
and Ma Bella reaching for—de belt

Too much back-chat
and yes, Ma Bella reaching for—de belt

plai-plai
her belt would fly
who don't hear must cry

Ma Bella was the fastest belt in town
Ma Bella was the fastest belt
for miles and miles around

In fact Ma Bella was the fastest belt
both in the East and in the West
nobody dared to put Ma Bella to the test

---

5. An accompaniment to stews that is a staple in West Africa.
Fufu is made from plantains or a starchy vegetable such as
yams, which are boiled, pounded, and stirred until thick.

6. A Caribbean stew or soup made with okra and callaloo (the
spinachlike leaves of a kind of taro) or a similar vegetable.
7. A term representing the sharpness of a lash (Creole).

GRACE NICHOLS

Until one day
Ma Bella swished
missed
and lashed her own leg

That was the day Ma Bella got such a welt
That was the day Ma Bella knew exactly how it
    felt
That was the day Ma Bella decided to hang up
    her belt

Moody Mister Sometimish

Mister Sometimish, Mister Sometimish
you too sometimish!

Sometimish you tipping you cap
with a smile

Sometimish you making you face
sour like lime

Sometimish you stopping in for a chat
Sometimish you passing just like that

Sometimish you saying 'how-dee' and you
    waving
Sometimish you putting your head straight
you playing you ain't hearing

when I calling you
but Mister Sometimish I can be sometimish too
because you too sometimish, Mister
    Sometimish
Man you too sometimish.

Mango

Have a mango
sweet rainwashed
sunripe mango
that the birds themselves
woulda pick
if only they had seen it
a rosy miracle
Here
take it from mih hand

Banana Man

I'm a banana man
I just love shaking
those yellow hands
Yes, man
Banana in the morning
Banana in the evening
Banana before I go to bed
at night—that's right
that's how much I love
the banana bite

I'm a banana man
not a superman
or a batman
or a spiderman
No, man
Banana in the morning
Banana in the evening
Banana before I go to bed
at night—that's right
that's how much I love
the banana bite

Drinking Water-coconut

Feeling thirsty
feeling hot
nothing to cool you down
like a water-coconut

With a flick of her cutlass
market-lady will hand you one—
a sweet little hole brimming at the top
when you put it to yuh head
you wouldn't want it to stop

Then you'll be wondering
if there's jelly inside
ask market-lady she wouldn't mind
she'll flick the big nut right open for you
she'll flick you a coconut spoon
to scoop with too

Feeling thirsty
feeling hot
the best thing to spend yuh money on
is a water-coconut

Early Country Village Morning

Cocks crowing
Hens knowing
later they will cluck
their laying song

Houses stirring
a donkey clip-clopping
the first market bus
comes jugging along

Soon the sun
will give a big yawn
and open her eye
pushing the last bit of darkness
out of the sky

Grace Nichols

The Sun

The sun is a glowing spider
that crawls out
from under the earth
to make her way across the sky
warming and weaving
with her bright old fingers
of light

Sky

Tall and blue
true and open

So open my arms have room
for all the world
for sun and moon
for birds and stars

Yet how I wish I had the chance
to come drifting down to earth—
a simple bed sheet
covering some little girl or boy
just for a night
but I am Sky
that's why

I Am the Rain

I am the rain
I like to play games
like sometimes
I pretend
I'm going
to fall
Man that's the time
I don't come at all

Like sometimes
I get these laughing stitches
up my sides
rushing people in
and out
with the clothesline
I just love drip
dropping

down collars
                and spines
Maybe it's a shame
but it's the only way
I get some fame

Lizard

A lean wizard—
watch me slither
up and down
the breadfruit tree
sometimes pausing a while
for a dither in the sunshine

The only thing
that puts a jitter up my spine
is when I think about
my great great great
great great great great
great great grandmother
Dinosaura Diplodocus[8]

She would have the shock of her life
if she were to come back
and see me reduced to lizardsize!

Dinosaurs

Diplodocus
Brontosaurus
Tyrannosaurus
Fabrosaurus

How I love the sound of dinosaurs
even though they were supposed to be
big and ugly and made wars

Dinosaurs O Dinosaurs
you might have been ferocious
but what a loss!

One hundred million years ago
you were the boss

8. A massive herbivorous dinosaur of the late Jurassic.

Cow's Complaint

Somebody calls somebody
a lazy cow
now in my cow's life
I ask you how?

If it wasn't so unfair
I would have to laugh
Dear children, as it is
I can only ask

Who gives you the milk
for your cornflakes
(crispy crunchy yes)
but it's my nice cold milk

that really brings them awake
children make no mistake

Who gets up at the crack of dawn
and works until the set of sun
Who eats up the grass
helping to mow the place for free
tell me who if it isn't me

Who gives you hamburgers
Who gives you steaks
it's my meat they take
it's my meat they take

So the next time
you call anyone a lazy cow
think again, my friend, you'd better
especially if your shoes are made of leather

Old Man's Weary Thoughts

Sun—too much sun
Rain—too much rain
Grass—too much green
Sky—too much blue
'Lord, dis world
ah weigh me down fuh true!'

I'm a Parrot

I am a parrot
I live in a cage
I'm nearly always
in a vex-up rage

I used to fly
all light and free
in the luscious green
forest canopy

I am a parrot
I live in a cage
I'm nearly always
in a vex-up rage

I miss the wind
against my wing
I miss the nut
and the fruit picking

I am a parrot
I live in a cage
I'm nearly always
in a vex-up rage

I squawk I talk
I curse I swear
I repeat the things
I shouldn't hear

So don't come near me
or put out your hand
because I'll pick you
if I can
pickyou
pickyou
if I can

I want to be Free
Can't You Understand

GRACE NICHOLS

Parakeets

Parakeets wheel
            screech
                        scream
in a flash of green
among the forest trees
sunlight smooth their feathers
cool leaves soothe their foreheads
creeks are there for beaks
lucky little parakeets

Doctor Blair[9]

Doctor Blair is the name of a bat
down out in the forest
they call him that

Cause Doctor Blair has a flair
for visiting his patients in the dead of night
his little black sac tucked under his back
his scissors-sharp teeth and his surgical flaps

Even if you don't want to see him
Doctor Blair makes his rounds
and he comes without as much as a sound
to perform a pain free operation

In fact Doctor Blair works with such care
that you'll sleep through
in the morning all you'll see on your leg
is a little line of blue

Where the blood seeped through
Where the blood seeped through

---

9. Remembering Oliver Hunter, Guyana man and one-time
pork knocker who told me about Dr Blair [Nichols's note].
Pork knocker: a gold or diamond prospector.

For Forest

Forest could keep secrets
Forest could keep secrets

Forest tune in every day
to watersound and birdsound

Forest letting her hair down
to the teeming creeping of her forest-ground

But Forest don't broadcast her business
no Forest cover her business down
from sky and fast-eye sun
and when night come
and darkness wrap her like a gown
Forest is a bad dream woman

Forest dreaming about mountain
and when earth was young
Forest dreaming of the caress of gold
Forest rootsing with mysterious Eldorado[1]

and when howler monkey
wake her up with howl
Forest just stretch and stir
to a new day of sound

but coming back to secrets
Forest could keep secrets
Forest could keep secrets

And we must keep Forest

Sea Timeless Song

Hurricane come
and hurricane go
but sea—sea timeless
sea timeless
sea timeless
sea timeless
sea timeless

Hibiscus bloom
then dry wither so
but sea—sea timeless
sea timeless
sea timeless
sea timeless
sea timeless

Tourist come
and tourist go
but sea—sea timeless
sea timeless
sea timeless
sea timeless
sea timeless

Crab Dance

Play moonlight
and the red crabs dance
their scuttle-foot dance
on the mud-packed beach

Play moonlight
and the red crabs dance
their side-ways dance
to the soft-sea beat

Play moonlight
and the red crabs dance
their bulb-eye dance
their last crab dance

1988

1. El Dorado (literally, "the Gilded Man"; Spanish), a legendary country of immense wealth believed to be in South America. Sir Walter Raleigh sought it in Guiana, a northeastern
region that included present-day Guyana.

Plays

Dramas written and acting companies that perform especially for children are largely
a product of the twentieth century in the West, but young people have long participated in and attended performances of all kinds. In ancient Greece, training in
elements of dramatic performance—dancing, singing, music, gymnastics, and recitation—was the mainstay of education. And wherever drama was part of general
community life, children were eager spectators. They delighted in the dramas and
pageants connected with church holidays, in morality plays, in folk festivals, in commedia dell'arte, and in puppet shows.

The first play created in English specifically for children, *A New Interlude for
Children to Play Named Jack Juggler, both Witty and Very Pleasant* (ca. 1553–58),
was a comedy of mistaken identity of the sort familiar to us from Shakespeare. In
Shakespeare's own plays, women's roles were played by boys. Indeed, for a time his
chief dramatic competitors included two companies formed exclusively of boy actors.
Interest in drama among English children and adults alike continued during and
after the closure of public professional theaters under the Puritans (1642–60), as
they turned to the religious theater, folk festivals, and informal performances that
persisted. English colonists carried these forms to America, where all enjoyed them.
It was only in the nineteenth century that signs of a separate theater for and by
children began to appear. This separation, though, never complete, has had effects
both positive (e.g., efforts to cultivate the sensitivities and talents of young people)
and negative (e.g., efforts to limit the subject treated to the "child-appropriate" in
ways that often patronize and exploit children).

When theater became "legitimate" as high culture in the nineteenth century—that
is, gained general approval in a form that observed relevant laws—children and young
adults attended performances. In particular, Christmas pantomimes, classics (especially Shakespeare), and fairy tales were often staged in December and January. Many
plays adapted from fairy tales, legends (e.g., that of Robin Hood), and literary works
that had become part of popular culture (e.g., *Gulliver's Travels*, *A Christmas Carol*,
"Rip Van Winkle," and *Little Women*) were performed in schools, community centers,
or small theaters. Legitimate theater was attended largely by the middle and upper
classes, while popular entertainments including vaudeville and the music hall found
mass audiences. Various skits and performances, including pageants, took place in
families, schools, churches, and other community settings.

By the beginning of the twentieth century, mandatory schooling and a new interest in the educational benefits of drama combined to make plays more accessible to all children. New theaters concentrating wholly on young audiences were established in communities and schools, and commercial theaters began producing plays specifically intended to entertain children. In the nineteenth century, the scripts of such dramas were generally regarded (with some reason) as not worth preserving; in the twentieth century, greater efforts were made to produce high-quality plays that would appeal to more ethnically and economically diverse audiences. Nevertheless, most playwrights were conservative, preferring to reproduce classic children's literature and fairy tales over controversial topics and original stories. The tendency toward mediocrity and homogeneity in live children's theater clearly reflects the moral and cultural imperatives of adults and educators in each theater's community.

Children's theater and drama have taken many forms in Great Britain and the United States (considered separately below), resisting easy definition. In both countries, a separate children's theater initially involved adults producing plays (sometimes with children as actors) so that children might enjoy culture more, learn about national traditions, and gain a sense of community, with material that complemented school curricula. Sensing a new and profitable market, in the early twentieth century commercial theaters began introducing family plays, often large-scale spectacles, as matinees or as features. The separate children's theaters emphasized education, and their work naturally spread to universities, which established theater departments and produced many plays for children.

Eventually, these university departments, as well as independent drama schools and companies, had two important outgrowths. One was creative dramatics, which focuses on nurturing the creative and critical skills of children by introducing them to acting techniques and methods; it relies heavily on improvisation. Approaches to improvisation such as those that Viola Spolin developed and described in *Improvisation for the Theater* (1963) are used in public schools and universities in diverse ways by those who believe that acting can help children develop their individual talents, learn the importance of cooperation, and understand social issues. A second development was theater-in-education groups: they create plays, often with the help of children, to educate young audiences about social problems such as drugs, divorce, racism, violence, and sexism. In addition, they draw on research to stimulate children to think in new ways about the environment, science, history, and more.

United Kingdom

At the beginning of the twentieth century, no distinct theater for children existed. One of the earliest productions specifically for children was *Bluebell in Fairyland* (1901), a musical dream play by the famous actor Seymour Hicks. In fact, it was this play that inspired J. M. Barrie to write *Peter Pan* (1904), produced first in London and a year later in New York—the best-known classic play for children, though Barrie wrote it for adults. These early plays, including Maurice Maeterlinck's *The Blue Bird* (1908; London, 1909); *Where the Rainbow Ends* (1911), a musical fairy play by Clifford Mills, John Ramsey, and Roger Quilter; *Fifinella* (1912), a fairy-tale play by Barry Jackson and Basil Dean; works by Laurence Housman such as *Bethlehem, A Nativity Play* (1902); and adaptations of Christmas stories (notably Charles Dickens's *A Christmas Carol*), were performed in provincial theaters or in London's West End mainly during the Christmas season. They were intended as family spectacles for entertainment and profit; this tradition continued throughout the twentieth century on Broadway and in the West End, especially in musicals adapted from books (e.g.,

The Wiz [1975], from L. Frank Baum's *The Wizard of Oz* [1900]) or even from films (e.g., *The Lion King*, 1997; film, 1994).

Around the same time, another movement emerged that was to have far more significance in promoting dramas performed specifically for children and created with children. The plays of Shakespeare, which were viewed as having particular educational significance, won the support of schools and governmental authorities. As early as 1889, a theatrical company founded by Frank Benson began touring and performing his plays in schools. Before and after his tenure as the Old Vic's theater director (1914–18), Ben Greet produced Shakespeare for schoolchildren, and he began the Old Vic's special matinees for young audiences. His work with Shakespeare was sponsored by the British Board of Education and inspired Nancy Hewin, Bertha Wadell, Peter Slade, and others who prepared the ground for the great flowering of children's theater that took place after World War II. Hewin, who formed the Osiris Players, traveled throughout Great Britain from 1927 to 1968 with "Shakespeare to Schools." Waddell's Scottish Children's Theatre (founded in 1924) brought unusual adaptations (mainly of folk and fairy tales) to many elementary schools in Scotland in the 1930s. Slade's Fen Players brought a variety of plays to children up to 1938, mainly in East Anglia (1930–37); after the war he founded another company, the Pear Tree Players (1945–47), and was active in promoting creative dramatics. His book *Child Drama* (1957) was one of the first significant treatments of children's theater.

Though funds and facilities were scarce, the touring companies and commercial theaters did not stop producing plays for children during World War II. This continuity led to the great postwar rise and spread of children's theater as the general public became more aware of the cultural significance of such performances. Because government support was inadequate, schools, parents, and local boards of educations helped subsidize the many gifted touring companies that traveled throughout the country, including Brian Way's West of England Children's Theatre Company (1944–51), Peter Slade's Pear Tree Players (1945–47), George Devine's Young Vic (1946–51), Caryl Jenner's Amersham Mobile Theatre (which became the Unicorn Theatre in London, 1948–), and John English's Arena Theatre Company (1948–58). For the most part, they produced traditional plays based on fairy tales, familiar fantasies, classic literature, and Shakespeare, often relying on a small group of authors or members of the company for the adaptations.

In 1966, the educational and cultural importance of these plays and workshops was recognized in a governmental report, *The Provision of Theatre for Young People*, which led to subsidies and grants to support productions and projects for young people. The government allocated money both to independent touring companies and to local theaters and groups producing plays that complemented school curricula. Most important, the report led to a special emphasis on theater-in-education, a program devised in 1965 by the Belgrade Theatre of Coventry. The local board of education had paid these actors to train teachers to mount plays by themselves and to use drama and acting in classrooms to develop the creative and critical skills of students. The approach stressed each child's own talents: the process of acting and learning about plays and theater was regarded as more important than the actual performance of a play. The goals of theater-in-education are set forth in Brian Way's *Development through Drama* (1967). Way and many other directors and actors sought both to educate children about social issues through theater projects and to make students, teachers, and parents more aware of professional theater and its role in the cultural life of the community.

As a result of these efforts (which often overlapped), children's theater burgeoned in the second half of the twentieth century. Today, more than thirty companies, based in cities, also tour the country and perform plays in schools and community centers; more than forty professional theater-in-education programs assist schools in training teachers and students; more than seventy puppet companies perform plays for children; and about fifteen young people's touring theater companies encourage youth organizations to produce their own plays.

The almost exclusive focus on traditional children's fare started to shift only in the 1970s. The Young Vic, which is an auxiliary company of the National Theatre, and the Unicorn Theatre began producing plays by authors previously thought unsuitable for young audiences (Samuel Beckett, Bertolt Brecht) and mounting innovative versions of standard children's works such as *The Arabian Nights* and fairy tales by the Brothers Grimm. David Wood, a well-known playwright, founded Whirlygig Theatre, a touring group that aimed at theatrical performances of high quality while introducing novel ideas into the repertoire of regional theaters. A growing number of original plays grappled with sensitive social and political topics. For instance, David Holman, working with different theater-in-education companies, wrote the peace plays *ABC*, *Susummu's Story*, and *Peacemaker* (1981–83), which questioned British imperialism and racism. Other important authors who challenged children in a range of new ways with their plays were Mary Melwood, John Arden, Margaretta D'Arcy, Ken Campbell, Robert Bolt, Ted Hughes, Joan Aiken, Alan Garner, and Nona Shepherd.

Some children's theaters, including the Unicorn Theatre, the Theatre Centre, Belgrade Theatre-in-Education, the Young Vic, and Greenwich People's Theatre, are financially stable, have developed diverse programs, and present a variety of plays. Many other talented groups operate on a shoestring budget, writing and performing their own plays, often with workshops. All rely on organizations such as the Association of Professional Theatre for Children and Young People and the International Association of Theatre for Children and Young People to support their work; national and international theater festivals also create bonds among the groups. This interchange of ideas and projects supported new growth in children's theater in the 1990s that continues into the twenty-first century.

United States

In the early twentieth century, conditions in the United States were very similar to those in Great Britain: commercial and legitimate theaters showed little interest in producing plays specifically for children until after World War II, but they customarily offered some kind of holiday fare at Christmas and Easter. As noted above, commercial theaters' emphasis on lighthearted family fantasies and spectacles, preferably musicals, has lasted to the present.

Beginning in 1899, Franklin Sargent, the director of New York's American Academy of Dramatic Art, offered productions of *Humpty Dumpty*, *Jack the Giant Killer*, *Alice in Wonderland*, and *Oliver Twist*, but attracted only a small audience. He closed his children's theater in 1903—the same year that Alice Minnie Herts founded the Children's Educational Theatre at the Educational Alliance in New York City. Herts was a social worker dedicated to helping immigrants and poor children, and she introduced acting classes, storytelling, puppetry, and performances by adult actors into the program at the Alliance. Her first production was Shakespeare's *The Tempest*; others included adaptations from popular fiction, such as Mark Twain's *The Prince and the Pauper* (1881). In 1910 her program ended, having lost its funding, but by then it had inspired similar theater groups in community centers and settlement houses in Chicago, Cleveland, Boston, San Francisco, Washington, and Detroit. Jane Addams's programs in Chicago's Hull House and Nettie Greenleaf's theater in Boston also helped alter conceptions of the appropriate for children's plays. Their work led to the writing of new dramas by Constance D'Arcy Mackay, Percy MacKaye, Stuart Walker, and Lillian Wald—plays still based on children's classics, fairy tales, and folktales.

The other driving force at the beginning of the twentieth century was Winifred Ward, a professor at Northwestern University and the author of *Creative Dramatics* (1930) and *Theatre for Children* (1939). In many respects, Ward was one of the pioneers of creative dramatics and theater-in-education in America, developing courses on improvisation and creative dramatics for children at schools and at the university that emphasized process, not production. She also persuaded the board of education in Evanston, Illinois, to introduce drama into the school curriculum and in 1944 was one of the founding members of the Children's Theatre Association of America.

Two organizations—the Drama League of America, founded in 1910, and the Association of Junior Leagues of America, a national women's group—also played major roles in the spread of children's theaters throughout the United States. The Junior League had a particularly powerful impact because of its members' commitment to performing dramas. By 1928 more than fifty chapters throughout the United States were producing such children's plays as *The Wizard of Oz*, *A Christmas Carol*, and Frances Hodgson Burnett's *A Little Princess* (1903) and *Racketty-Packetty House* (1912) in community theaters and settlement houses.

As regional and amateur theaters for children and school plays multiplied during the 1920s and 1930s, professional companies began to flourish. In 1921 Clare Tree Major, a British actress who had come to New York five years earlier, formed the Threshold Players, which performed Shakespeare for high school students and fairy tales for younger children. She collaborated with the National Council of Teachers of English and the New York City Board of Education to perform plays that fit the curriculum of schools; she also taught classes for actors in her company, working until her death in 1954.

From its founding in 1924, the Goodman Theatre (associated with the Chicago Institute of Art) produced numerous plays for children, many written by Charlotte Chorpenning. By 1931, when she was made director of children's plays, there was an official Goodman Theatre for Children. For more than twenty years, Chorpenning created adaptations of fairy tales and classic children's literature of high literary quality; many of her plays are still produced. During this period, small nonprofit and commercial companies producing original and traditional works were being founded throughout America. Among the more important was Dorothy McFadden's New Jersey–based Junior Program, which performed plays for children from 1935 to 1942. McFadden's very large company was one of the first commercial ventures to offer musicals, dance, and traditional plays specifically for young audiences. In New York, Monte Meacham founded the Children's World Theatre (1947–55), a nonprofit company that emphasized the educational aspects of children's theater. Other significant groups active during the 1920s, 1930s, and 1940s include the Karamus House Children's Theatre (Cleveland), the House of Play (Washington), the Children's Theatre of San Francisco State Teachers College, the Knickerty Knockerty Players (Pittsburgh), the Seattle Junior Program, the Children's Experimental Theatre (Baltimore), and the King-Coit School (New York).

The Federal Theatre Project, established to assist unemployed actors, directors, and technicians during the Great Depression, created a children's program (1935–39) that supported unusual and provocative plays as well as educational programs in creative dramatics. During the same decade, theater arts programs took firmer root at a wide range of universities and schools, including Emerson College, Mills College, Syracuse University, the University of Iowa, Johns Hopkins University, Denison University, Baylor University, and the University of Denver. In 1936 the American Educational Theatre Association was formed to promote the teaching of drama and creative arts at all educational levels, a task viewed with great seriousness. In 1940 Sara Shakow told members of the National Progressive Education Association in Chicago: "A children's theatre today, if it hopes to justify its right to existence, cannot confine its aims to merely furnishing amusement. A children's theatre today, if it expects to exercise its rightful function as a developmental agency and serve effectively as an instrument of education and culture, must offer more than sheer diversion and clean entertainment."

As in Great Britain, both professional companies concentrating on popular and classic plays for children and programs of theater-in-education thrived after World War II. But American theater for children was more closely connected to universities and colleges, which could produce plays at a minimal cost and train actors to work with children. Despite low pay and poor working conditions—a constant problem—actors eagerly joined children's theaters. Many cities in America could boast of important theater companies by the late 1990s, largely nonprofits relying on municipal and private support. Among the best known are the Children's Theatre Company of Minneapolis, the Empire State Institute for the Performing Arts (Albany), Palo Alto Children's Theatre, the Nashville Academy Theatre, the Wichita Children's Theatre, the Seattle Children's Theatre, Stage One: The Louisville Children's Theatre, and the Honolulu Theatre for Youth. The Paper Bag Players, founded in 1958 in New York, specializes in original fifty-minute plays with the minimal use of costumes and props. By improvising and collaborating with children, the group has created dramas that grow out of the everyday experiences of children; this approach has been used by other theater companies. Another distinguished group is CAT (Creative Arts Team), founded by Nancy Swortzell of New York University. Influenced by the theater-in-education movement in England, CAT has more than sixty members in separate companies in the New York metropolitan area; their plays, dealing with drugs, racism, sexism, and child abuse, are performed not only in schools but also at the Kennedy Center, Lincoln Center, and the New York Shakespeare Festival Public Theatre.

Though numerous authors have been encouraged to write for children's theater, few Americans have distinguished themselves in this field. Even Aurand Harris, regarded as America's foremost playwright for children—his *Androcles and the Lion* (1964) has been performed thousands of times—tends to follow the traditional path of Charlotte Chorpenning. Harris was a fine craftsman, but his adaptations of folktales and children's classics for the stage display little originality. The social ferment of the mid-twentieth century did influence others, such as Joanna Kraus and Suzan Zeder: Kraus's *The Ice Wolf* (1963), based on an Eskimo legend, deals with child abuse and racism; and in *Step on a Crack* (1976) and other plays Zeder deals with difficulties and conflicts within families. In 1989 children's theaters in Honolulu, Seattle, Minneapolis, and Louisville joined forces to commission major American dramatists to create new works that would set high aesthetic standards and directly engage contemporary children. The eight plays that resulted were innovative retellings of traditional tales (Constance Congdon, *Beauty and the Beast*; Tina Howe, *East of the Sun and West of the Moon*) and adaptations of fiction (Len Jenkin, *The Invisible*

Man; Y York, *The Witch of Blackbird Pond*), as well as works of modern fantasy (Mark Medoff, *Kringle's Window*; Eric Overmyer, *Duke Kahanamoku vs. The Surfnappers*; Michael Weller, *Dogbrain*) and realism (Velina Hasu Houston, *Hula Heart*). Though these plays had mixed success, the experiment underscored the need to go beyond the traditional repertoire with more challenging works.

Children's Theater in the Twenty-First Century

Although the rise of cinema and television, along with video games and the Internet, has somewhat undermined the popularity of commercial and professional children's theater and though funding cuts in the United Kingdom and United States have eliminated many theater-in-education projects, national and international collaboration in the field is now on the rise. Even if a major city does not have an established repertory theater for children, commercial theaters continue to produce plays for children, especially during the holiday seasons, and touring companies—bringing ice shows, ballets, musicals, operas, and puppet shows—perform for children. Drama as spectacle and as entertainment is widely available, with traditional favorites and popular new plays dominating the stage. Children are generally accompanied by parents, and most commercial performances avoid anything controversial.

At the same time, theater-in-education and creative dramatics programs in both countries continue to innovate in subject matter, design, and staging, as do some of the more established repertory companies and university groups. They often seek to use the theater to raise political and social awareness with dramas that question traditional pedagogy and aesthetics; very few of these plays ever make it to the main stage of the major theater companies. For children's theater to develop, the established theater companies, which largely serve white, middle-class audiences, must devise means to encourage playwrights to write quality plays, to challenge the conservative notions of theater and entertainment held by most children, and to expand their audience base.

The three plays included here—*Peter Pan, A Christmas Carol*, and *Dragonwings*—are representative of the modern types of dramas for children in Great Britain and the United States. Barrie's *Peter Pan*, like many works originally conceived for older audiences that struck a chord with children, is now largely regarded as a drama for children. Performed in a range of venues, from large commercial theaters to community center to professional children's theaters, *Peter Pan* is the prototype of the family spectacle that nevertheless raises serious questions about family life, the socialization of children, and immortality. The same could be said of Charles Dickens's *A Christmas Carol*, a warmhearted work about poverty and philanthropy. Because the latter has been adapted as a play by scores of authors and is generally performed only during the Christmas holidays—again, in various theaters, in schools, and in churches—it is akin to the traditional morality play. Barbara Field's fine 1975 adaptation, which has been produced annually at the famous Guthrie Theatre in Minneapolis, captures the essence of Dickens's short story.

Unlike the other two plays, which are often-performed classics (several times made into films), *Dragonwings* (1991), originally commissioned by the Berkeley Repertory Theatre, is rarely produced, perhaps because of its more unorthodox style or more sophisticated treatment of a sensitive social issue. This original work by a gifted contemporary writer for children and young adults, Laurence Yep, follows in the tradition of high-quality plays that challenge the preconceptions of young audiences and also change spectators' view of the history and the meaning of theater for children.

J. M. BARRIE
1860–1937

World famous as the creator of the play and stories about Peter Pan, the boy who would not grow up, James Matthew Barrie was born in the Scottish village of Kirriemuir, the ninth of ten children. By the age of thirteen, he had left his village to study at Dumfries Academy, where he became interested in the works of such authors as Jules Verne (1828–1905) and James Fenimore Cooper (1789–1851). After completing his studies at the University of Edinburgh in 1882, he began working as a journalist for the *Nottingham Journal*; in 1885 he departed for London and the life of a freelance writer. With the publication of *Auld Licht Idylls* (1888), sketches of Scottish life, Barrie made a name for himself in London literary society. But it was the sentimental novel *The Little Minister* (1891), adapted for the theater in 1897, that established his fame. From that time on, he wrote almost entirely for the theater.

During this period, in 1894, Barrie met and married the actress Mary Ansell. Their marriage was childless and unhappy (they divorced in 1909); almost as if to compensate for his marital difficulties, Barrie began spending more time with the family of three boys he had met while walking his dog in Kensington Gardens. Arthur Llewelyn and Sylvia DuMaurier Davies would have five sons, and Barrie became very attached to them. He often told them stories, some of which appeared in his novel *The Little White Bird* (1902), about a wealthy retired military officer who befriends a poor young couple and their little boy named David. In particular, six chapters about an eternally youthful boy who could fly became the basis for his play *Peter Pan*, first performed in 1904. Though written for adult audiences, it immediately became a children's classic. It was later published as a novel with the title *Peter and Wendy* (1911), and Barrie continued to revise the play as it was restaged many times; a definitive text was not published until 1928.

Among his other plays, Barrie wrote *A Kiss for Cinderella* (1916), about a girl caring for four war orphans who dreams of attending a ball with the Prince of Wales; *Dear Brutus* (1917), about people who, finding that they have been given a second chance to relive their lives, repeat their past mistakes; and *Mary Rose* (1920), about a mother who both in life and as a ghost searches for her lost son. His next work, the mystery play *Shall We Join the Ladies?* (1921), was successful though unfinished, but Barrie did little subsequent creative work. Some critics point to his depression after the drowning of Michael Davies in 1921; he had become the guardian of the Davies boys after their parents died (Arthur in 1907, Sylvia in 1910). He won many honors in the 1920s and became a well-known public personality; with the help of his secretary, Lady Cynthia Asquith, he began writing and giving autobiographical lectures, as well as attending and hosting social gatherings. He continued to watch over the three surviving Davies boys, Peter, Jack, and Nicholas (the eldest, George, had been killed in World War I). His final play—*The Boy David* (1936), a philosophical drama about David's transition to becoming King of Israel—was not well-received. During the last couple of years of his life his health deteriorated, and he had many bouts of depression. On June 19, 1937, he became seriously ill; he died within a few days and was buried in his hometown of Kirriemuir next to his mother, father, and siblings.

Peter Pan; or, The Boy Who Would Not Grow Up had its premiere at the Duke of York's Theatre, London, in 1904, and during Barrie's lifetime it was performed at Christmas every year. In the United States, the 1905 New York production was a huge hit and toured the country; many other productions followed. Music was always part of the play's spectacle, and a 1924 version contained two songs by Jerome Kern, but *Peter Pan* did not become a full-blown musical until 1954 (starring Mary Martin in the title role, with music by Mark Charlap and Jule Styne, and lyrics by Carolyn Leigh, Betty Comden, and Adolph Green). Both this production and a 1950 adaptation starring Jean Arthur (with less singing, though music and lyrics by Leonard Bernstein) had long runs in New York and London and were taken on tour. The first movie version was in 1924 and the most recent in 2004, though the most familiar is Walt Disney's classic animated film of 1953. Steven Spielberg revisited the story from a different angle in *Hook* (1991), and there have been several television versions. In various media, *Peter Pan* continues to make its presence felt in children's culture throughout the world.

Interpretations of the play often have focused on its effectiveness in expressing a longing for a lost childhood or state of innocence that can never be recaptured by adults, but many recent critics have explored the psychological complexities of its ambivalent representation of mother love, with an eye to the author's biography. Barrie was a very small man (five feet tall), suffered from migraines, and was apparently impotent; his attachment to his mother was excessive if not obsessive, and as a boy he vainly competed for her affection with the memory of her favorite—his older brother who had died at age thirteen. Some have concluded from his interest in the Davies boys and his depictions of the Darling brothers and Lost Boys that Barrie might have been a pedophile. In one of the most important critical studies of children's literature, *The Case of Peter Pan: or, The Impossibility of Children's Fiction* (1984), Jacqueline Rose has provocatively argued from a Lacanian perspective that Barrie and many other authors of children's literature manipulate and exploit the figure of the child to gain control and power over young readers. Whether one agrees with this thesis or not, *Peter Pan* inarguably remains one of the most significant twentieth-century dramas for children.

Peter Pan; or, The Boy Who Would Not Grow Up

A Dedication. To the Five

Some disquieting confessions must be made in printing at last the play of *Peter Pan*; among them this, that I have no recollection of having written it. Of that, however, anon. What I want to do first is to give Peter to the Five[1] without whom he never would have existed. I hope, my dear sirs, that in memory of what we have been to each other you will accept this dedication with your friend's love. The play of Peter is streaky with you still, though none may see this save yourselves. A score of Acts had to be left out, and you were in them all. We first brought Peter down, didn't we, with a blunt-headed arrow in Kensington Gardens?[2] I seem to remember that we believed we had killed him, though he was only winded, and that after a spasm of exultation in our prowess the more soft-hearted among us wept and all of us thought of the police. There was not one of you who would not have sworn as an eye-witness to this occurrence; no doubt I was abetting, but you used to provide corroboration that was never given to you by me. As for myself, I suppose I always knew that I made Peter by rubbing the five of you violently together, as savages with two sticks produce a flame. That is all he is, the spark I got from you.

We had good sport of him before we clipped him small to make him fit the boards.[3] Some of you were not born when the story began and yet were hefty figures before we saw that the game was up. Do you remember a garden at Burpham and the initiation there of No. 4 when he was six weeks old, and three of you grudged letting

---

1. The five Davies brothers, the children to whom Barrie told the stories that became the basis of *Peter Pan*: George (1893–1915), Jack (1894–1959), Peter (1896–1960), Michael (1900–1921), and Nicholas (1903–1980). When this dedication (which refers to them by number) was written in 1928, George and Michael were already dead.
2. A park in central London, separated from Hyde Park by water (the Long Water and the Serpentine). While walking his dog there, Barrie first met the three older Davies boys, who lived nearby. In a story told in Barrie's novel *The Little White Bird* (1902), Peter Pan lives on an island in the Serpentine.
3. I.e., the stage.

him in so young? Have you, No. 3, forgotten the white violets at the Cistercian abbey in which we cassocked[4] our first fairies (all little friends of St Benedict), or your cry to the Gods, 'Do I just kill one pirate all the time?' Do you remember Marooners' Hut in the haunted groves of Waverley, and the St Bernard dog in a tiger's mask who so frequently attacked you, and the literary record of that summer, *The Boy Castaways*,[5] which is so much the best and the rarest of this author's works? What was it that made us eventually give to the public in the thin form of a play that which had been woven for ourselves alone? Alas, I know what it was, I was losing my grip. One by one as you swung monkey-wise from branch to branch in the wood of make-believe you reached the tree of knowledge. Sometimes you swung back into the wood, as the unthinking may at a crossroad take a familiar path that no longer leads to home; or you perched ostentatiously on its boughs to please me, pretending that you still belonged; soon you knew it only as the vanished wood, for it vanishes if one needs to look for it. A time came when I saw that No. 1, the most gallant of you all, ceased to believe that he was ploughing woods incarnadine, and with an apologetic eye for me derided the lingering faith of No. 2; when even No. 3 questioned gloomily whether he did not really spend his nights in bed. There were still two who knew no better, but their day was dawning. In these circumstances, I suppose, was begun the writing of the play of Peter. That was a quarter of a century ago, and I clutch my brows in vain to remember whether it was a last desperate throw to retain the five of you for a little longer, or merely a cold decision to turn you into bread and butter.

This brings us back to my uncomfortable admission that I have no recollection of writing the play of *Peter Pan*, now being published for the first time so long after he made his bow upon the stage. You had played it until you tired of it, and tossed it in the air and gored it and left it derelict in the mud and went on your way singing other songs; and then I stole back and sewed some of the gory fragments together with a pen-nib. That is what must have happened, but I cannot remember doing it. I remember writing the story of *Peter and Wendy*[6] many years after the production of the play, but I might have cribbed that from some typed copy. I can haul back to mind the writing of almost every other assay of mine, however forgotten by the pretty public; but this play of Peter, no. Even my beginning as an amateur playwright, that noble mouthful, *Bandelero the Bandit*,[7] I remember every detail of its composition in my school days at Dumfries. Not less vivid is my first little piece, produced by Mr Toole. It was called *Ibsen's Ghost*,[8] and was a parody of the mightiest craftsman that ever wrote for our kind friends in front. To save the management the cost of typing I wrote out the 'parts', after being told what parts were, and I can still recall my first words, spoken so plaintively by a now famous actress—'To run away from my second husband just as I ran away from my first, it feels quite like old times.' On the first night a man in the pit found *Ibsen's Ghost* so diverting that he had to be removed in hysterics. After that no one seems to have thought of it at all. But what a man to carry about with one! How odd, too, that these trifles should adhere to the mind that cannot remember the long job of writing Peter. It does seem almost suspicious, especially as I have not the original MS of *Peter Pan* (except a few stray pages) with which to support my claim. I have indeed another MS, lately made, but that 'proves

4. I.e., clothed.
5. *The Boy Castaways of Black Lake Island* (1901), a book commemorating the boys' holiday at the Barries' summer cottage. Only two copies were printed: Arthur Davies, the boys' father, left his on a train; Barrie kept his until he died.

6. The 1911 novelized version of the 1904 play.
7. Barrie's first play, produced in 1877 at Dumfries Academy.
8. *Ibsen's Ghost; or, Toole Up-to-Date* (1891), which caricatured the drama of the Norwegian playwright Henrik Ibsen (1828–1906).

nothing'. I know not whether I lost that original MS or destroyed it or happily gave it away. I talk of dedicating the play to you, but how can I prove it is mine? How ought I to act if some other hand, who could also have made a copy, thinks it worth while to contest the cold rights? Cold they are to me now as that laughter of yours in which Peter came into being long before he was caught and written down. There is Peter still, but to me he lies sunk in the gay Black Lake.

Any one of you five brothers has a better claim to the authorship than most, and I would not fight you for it, but you should have launched your case long ago in the days when you most admired me, which were in the first year of the play, owing to a rumour's reaching you that my spoils were one-and-sixpence a night. This was untrue, but it did give me a standing among you. You watched for my next play with peeled eyes, not for entertainment but lest it contained some chance witticism of yours that could be challenged as collaboration; indeed I believe there still exists a legal document, full of the Aforesaid and Henceforward to be called Part-Author, in which for some such snatching I was tied down to pay No. 2 one halfpenny daily throughout the run of the piece.

During the rehearsals of Peter (and it is evidence in my favour that I was admitted to them) a depressed man in overalls, carrying a mug of tea or a paint-pot, used often to appear by my side in the shadowy stalls and say to me, 'the gallery boys won't stand it.' He then mysteriously faded away as if he were the theatre ghost. This hopelessness of his is what all dramatists are said to feel at such times, so perhaps he was the author. Again, a large number of children whom I have seen playing Peter in their homes with careless mastership, constantly putting in better words, could have thrown it off with ease. It was for such as they that after the first production I had to add something to the play at the request of parents (who thus showed that they thought me the responsible person) about no one being able to fly until the fairy dust had been blown on him; so many children having gone home and tried it from their beds and needed surgical attention.

Notwithstanding other possibilities, I think I wrote Peter, and if so it must have been in the usual inky way. Some of it, I like to think, was done in that native place which is the dearest spot on earth to me, though my last heart-beats shall be with my beloved solitary London that was so hard to reach. I must have sat at a table with that great dog waiting for me to stop, not complaining, for he knew it was thus we made our living, but giving me a look when he found he was to be in the play, with his sex changed. In after years when the actor who was Nana had to go to the wars he first taught his wife how to take his place as the dog till he came back, and I am glad that I see nothing funny in this; it seems to me to belong to the play. I offer this obtuseness on my part as my first proof that I am the author.

Some say that we are different people at different periods of our lives, changing not through effort of will, which is a brave affair, but in the easy course of nature every ten years or so. I suppose this theory might explain my present trouble, but I don't hold with it; I think one remains the same person throughout, merely passing, as it were, in these lapses of time from one room to another, but all in the same house. If we unlock the rooms of the far past we can peer in and see ourselves, busily occupied in beginning to become you and me. Thus, if I am the author in question the way he is to go should already be showing in the occupant of my first compartment, at whom I now take the liberty to peep. Here he is at the age of seven or so with his fellow-conspirator Robb, both in glengarry bonnets.[9] They are giving an

9. Scottish woolen caps.

entertainment in a tiny old washing-house that still stands. The charge for admission is preens, a bool, or a peerie[1] (I taught you a good deal of Scotch, so possibly you can follow that), and apparently the culminating Act consists in our trying to put each other into the boiler, though some say that I also addressed the spellbound audience. This washing-house is not only the theatre of my first play, but has a still closer connection with Peter. It is the original of the little house the Lost Boys built in the Never Land for Wendy, the chief difference being that it never wore John's hat as a chimney. If Robb had owned such a hat I have no doubt that it would have been placed on the washing-house.

Here is that boy again some four years older, and the reading he is munching feverishly is about desert islands; he calls them wrecked islands. He buys his sanguinary tales surreptitiously in penny numbers. I see a change coming over him; he is blanching as he reads in the high-class magazine, Chatterbox,[2] a fulmination against such literature, and sees that unless his greed for islands is quenched he is for ever lost. With gloaming he steals out of the house, his library bulging beneath his palpitating waistcoat. I follow like his shadow, as indeed I am, and watch him dig a hole in a field at Pathhead farm and bury his islands in it; it was ages ago, but I could walk straight to that hole in the field now and delve for the remains. I peep into the next compartment. There he is again, ten years older, an undergraduate now and craving to be a real explorer, one of those who do things instead of prating of them, but otherwise unaltered; he might be painted at twenty on top of a mast, in his hand a spy-glass through which he rakes the horizon for an elusive strand. I go from room to room, and he is now a man, real exploration abandoned (though only because no one would have him). Soon he is even concocting other plays, and quaking a little lest some low person counts how many islands there are in them. I note that with the years the islands grow more sinister, but it is only because he has now to write with the left hand, the right having given out; evidently one thinks more darkly down the left arm.[3] Go to the keyhole of the compartment where he and I join up, and you may see us wondering whether they would stand one more island. This journey through the house may not convince any one that I wrote Peter, but it does suggest me as a likely person. I pause to ask myself whether I read Chatterbox again, suffered the old agony, and buried that MS of the play in a hole in a field.

Of course this is over-charged. Perhaps we do change; except a little something in us which is no larger than a mote in the eye, and that, like it, dances in front of us beguiling us all our days. I cannot cut the hair by which it hangs.

The strongest evidence that I am the author is to be found, I think, in a now melancholy volume, the aforementioned The Boy Castaways; so you must excuse me for parading that work here. Officer of the Court, call The Boy Castaways. The witness steps forward and proves to be a book you remember well though you have not glanced at it these many years. I pulled it out of a bookcase just now not without difficulty, for its recent occupation has been to support the shelf above. I suppose, though I am uncertain, that it was I and not you who hammered it into that place of utility. It is a little battered and bent after the manner of those who shoulder burdens, and ought (to our shame) to remind us of the witnesses who sometimes get an hour off from the cells to give evidence before his lordship. I have said that it is the rarest of my printed works, as it must be, for the only edition was limited to two

---

1. I.e., pins, a marble, or a spinning top.
2. An important British magazine for children (1866–1948), which Barrie read enthusiastically.

It contained religious stories, serialized fiction, and nonfiction.
3. In Latin, sinister means "left."

copies, of which one (there was always some devilry in any matter connected with Peter) instantly lost itself in a railway carriage. This is the survivor. The idlers in court may have assumed that it is a handwritten screed, and are impressed by its bulk. It is printed by Constable's (how handsomely you did us, dear Blaikie[4]), it contains thirty-five illustrations and is bound in cloth with a picture stamped on the cover of the three eldest of you 'setting out to be wrecked'. This record is supposed to be edited by the youngest of the three, and I must have granted him that honour to make up for his being so often lifted bodily out of our adventures by his nurse, who kept breaking into them for the fell purpose of giving him a midday rest. No. 4 rested so much at this period that he was merely an honorary member of the band, waving his foot to you for luck when you set off with bow and arrow to shoot his dinner for him; and one may rummage the book in vain for any trace of No. 5. Here is the title-page, except that you are numbered instead of named—

THE BOY
CASTAWAYS
OF BLACK LAKE ISLAND
Being a record of the Terrible
Adventures of Three Brothers
in the summer of 1901
faithfully set forth
by No. 3.

LONDON
Published by J. M. Barrie
in the Gloucester Road
1901

There is a long preface by No. 3 in which we gather your ages at this first flight. 'No. 1 was eight and a month, No. 2 was approaching his seventh lustrum,[5] and I was a good bit past four.' Of his two elders, while commending their fearless dispositions, the editor complains that they wanted to do all the shooting and carried the whole equipment of arrows inside their shirts. He is attractively modest about himself, 'Of No. 3 I prefer to say nothing, hoping that the tale as it is unwound will show that he was a boy of deeds rather than of words,' a quality which he hints did not unduly protrude upon the brows of Nos. 1 and 2. His preface ends on a high note, 'I should say that the work was in the first instance compiled as a record simply at which we could whet our memories, and that it is now published for No. 4's benefit. If it teaches him by example lessons in fortitude and manly endurance we shall consider that we were not wrecked in vain.'

Published to whet your memories. Does it whet them? Do you hear once more, like some long-forgotten whistle beneath your window (Robb at dawn calling me to the fishing!) the not quite mortal blows that still echo in some of the chapter headings?—'Chapter II, No. 1 teaches Wilkinson (his master) a Stern Lesson—We Run away to Sea. Chapter III, A Fearful Hurricane—Wreck of the *Anna Pink*—We go crazy from Want of Food—Proposal to eat No. 3—Land Ahoy'. Such are two chapters

---

4. Walter Biggar Blaikie (1847–1928), head of the printing firm of T. and A. Constable.
5. Though Barrie clearly uses *lustrum* to mean

"year," the term actually refers to a period of five years.

out of sixteen. Are these again your javelins cutting tunes in the blue haze of the pines; do you sweat as you scale the dreadful Valley of Rolling Stones, and cleanse your hands of pirate blood by scouring them carelessly in Mother Earth? Can you still make a fire (you could do it once, Mr Seton-Thompson[6] taught us in, surely an odd place, the Reform Club) by rubbing those sticks together? Was it the travail of hut-building that subsequently advised Peter to find a 'home under the ground'? The bottle and mugs in that lurid picture, 'Last night on the Island', seem to suggest that you had changed from Lost Boys into pirates, which was probably also a tendency of Peter's. Listen again to our stolen sawmill, man's proudest invention; when he made the sawmill he beat the birds for music in a wood.

The illustrations (full-paged) in *The Boy Castaways* are all photographs taken by myself; some of them indeed of phenomena that had to be invented afterwards, for you were always off doing the wrong things when I pressed the button. I see that we combined instruction with amusement; perhaps we had given our kingly word to that effect. How otherwise account for such wording to the pictures as these: 'It is undoubtedly', says No. 1 in a fir tree that is bearing unwonted fruit, recently tied to it, 'the *Cocos nucifera*, for observe the slender columns supporting the crown of leaves which fall with a grace that no art can imitate.' 'Truly,' continues No. 1 under the same tree in another forest as he leans upon his trusty gun, 'though the perils of these happenings are great, yet would I rejoice to endure still greater privations to be thus rewarded by such wondrous studies of Nature.' He is soon back to the practical, however, 'recognising the Mango (*Magnifera indica*) by its lancet-shaped leaves and the cucumber-shaped fruit'. No. 1 was certainly the right sort of voyager to be wrecked with, though if my memory fails me not, No. 2, to whom these strutting observations were addressed, sometimes protested because none of them was given to him. No. 3 being the author is in surprisingly few of the pictures, but this, you may remember, was because the lady already darkly referred to used to pluck him from our midst for his siesta at 12 o'clock, which was the hour that best suited the camera. With a skill on which he has never been complimented the photographer sometimes got No. 3 nominally included in a wild-life picture when he was really in a humdrum house kicking on the sofa. Thus in a scene representing Nos. 1 and 2 sitting scowling outside the hut it is untruly written that they scowled because 'their brother was within singing and playing on a barbaric instrument. The music', the unseen No. 3 is represented as saying (obviously forestalling No. 1), 'is rude and to a cultured ear discordant, but the songs like those of the Arabs are full of poetic imagery.' He was perhaps allowed to say this sulkily on the sofa.

Though *The Boy Castaways* has sixteen chapter headings, there is no other letterpress; an absence which possible purchasers might complain of, though there are surely worse ways of writing a book than this. These headings anticipate much of the play of *Peter Pan*, but there were many incidents of our Kensington Gardens days that never got into the book, such as our Antarctic exploits when we reached the Pole in advance of our friend Captain Scott[7] and cut our initials on it for him to find, a strange foreshadowing of what was really to happen. In *The Boy Castaways* Captain Hook has arrived but is called Captain Swarthy, and he seems from the pictures to have been a black man. This character, as you do not need to be told, is held by those

6. Ernest Thompson Seton (1860–1946), British-born American naturalist and author who founded the Woodcraft Indians (1902) and was instrumental in founding the Boy Scouts of America (1910).

7. Robert Falcon Scott (1868–1912), British naval officer and Antarctic explorer who died on the return from his losing race to the South Pole. He was a close friend of Barrie's.

in the know to be autobiographical. You had many tussles with him (though you never, I think, got his right arm) before you reached the terrible chapter (which might be taken from the play) entitled 'We Board the Pirate Ship at Dawn—A Rakish Craft—No. 1 Hew-them-Down and No. 2 of the Red Hatchet—A Holocaust of Pirates—Rescue of Peter'. (Hullo, Peter rescued instead of rescuing others? I know what that means and so do you, but we are not going to give away all our secrets.) The scene of the Holocaust is the Black Lake (afterwards, when we let women in, the Mermaids' Lagoon). The pirate captain's end was not in the mouth of a crocodile though we had crocodiles on the spot ('while No. 2 was removing the crocodiles from the stream No. 1 shot a few parrots, *Psittacidae*, for our evening meal'). I think our captain had divers deaths owing to unseemly competition among you, each wanting to slay him single-handed. On a special occasion, such as when No. 3 pulled out the tooth himself, you gave the deed to him, but took it from him while he rested. The only pictorial representation in the book of Swarthy's fate is in two parts. In one, called briefly 'We string him up', Nos. 1 and 2, stern as Athos,[8] are hauling him up a tree by a rope, his face snarling as if it were a grinning mask (which indeed it was), and his garments very like some of my own stuffed with bracken. The other, the same scene next day, is called 'The Vultures had Picked him Clean', and tells its own tale.

The dog in *The Boy Castaways* seems never to have been called Nana but was evidently in training for that post. He originally belonged to Swarthy (or to Captain Marryat?[9]), and the first picture of him, lean, skulking, and hunched (how did I get that effect?), 'patrolling the island' in that monster's interests, gives little indication of the domestic paragon he was to become. We lured him away to the better life, and there is, later, a touching picture, a clear forecast of the Darling nursery, entitled 'We trained the dog to watch over us while we slept'. In this he also is sleeping, in a position that is a careful copy of his charges; indeed any trouble we had with him was because, once he knew he was in a story, he thought his safest course was to imitate you in everything you did. How anxious he was to show that he understood the game, and more generous than you, he never pretended that he was the one who killed Captain Swarthy. I must not imply that he was entirely without initiative, for it was his own idea to bark warningly a minute or two before twelve o'clock as a signal to No. 3 that his keeper was probably on her way for him (Disappearance of No. 3); and he became so used to living in the world of Pretend that when we reached the hut of a morning he was often there waiting for us, looking, it is true, rather idiotic, but with a new bark he had invented which puzzled us until we decided that he was demanding the password. He was always willing to do any extra jobs, such as becoming the tiger in mask, and when after a fierce engagement you carried home that mask in triumph, he joined in the procession proudly and never let on that the trophy had ever been part of him. Long afterwards he saw the play from a box in the theatre, and as familiar scenes were unrolled before his eyes I have never seen a dog so bothered. At one matinee we even let him for a moment take the place of the actor who played Nana, and I don't know that any members of the audience ever noticed the change, though he introduced some 'business' that was new to them but old to you and me. Heigh-ho, I suspect that in this reminiscence I am mixing him up with his successor, for such a one there had to be, the loyal Newfoundland who, perhaps

8. One of the adventurers in Alexandre Dumas's *The Three Musketeers* (1844).
9. Frederick Marryat (1792–1848), British naval

commander and prolific author of adventure novels and stories, mostly of sea life. Barrie was very fond of his works.

in the following year, applied, so to say, for the part by bringing hedgehogs to the hut in his mouth as offerings for our evening repasts. The head and coat of him were copied for the Nana of the play.

They do seem to be emerging out of our island, don't they, the little people of the play, all except that sly one, the chief figure, who draws farther and farther into the wood as we advance upon him? He so dislikes being tracked, as if there were something odd about him, that when he dies he means to get up and blow away the particle that will be his ashes.

Wendy has not yet appeared, but she has been trying to come ever since that loyal nurse cast the humorous shadow of woman upon the scene and made us feel that it might be fun to let in a disturbing element. Perhaps she would have bored her way in at last whether we wanted her or not. It may be that even Peter did not really bring her to the Never Land of his free will, but merely pretended to do so because she would not stay away. Even Tinker Bell had reached our island before we left it. It was one evening when we climbed the wood carrying No. 4 to show him what the trail was like by twilight. As our lanterns twinkled among the leaves No. 4 saw a twinkle stand still for a moment and he waved his foot gaily to it, thus creating Tink. It must not be thought, however, that there were any other sentimental passages between No. 4 and Tink; indeed, as he got to know her better he suspected her of frequenting the hut to see what we had been having for supper, and to partake of the same, and he pursued her with malignancy.

A safe but sometimes chilly way of recalling the past is to force open a crammed drawer. If you are searching for anything in particular you don't find it, but something falls out at the back that is often more interesting. It is in this way that I get my desultory reading, which includes the few stray leaves of the original MS of Peter that I have said I do possess, though even they, when returned to the drawer, are gone again, as if that touch of devilry lurked in them still. They show that in early days I hacked at and added to the play. In the drawer I find some scraps of Mr Crook's[1] delightful music, and other incomplete matter relating to Peter. Here is the reply of a boy whom I favoured with a seat in my box and injudiciously asked at the end what he had liked best. 'What I think I liked best', he said, 'was tearing up the programme and dropping the bits on people's heads.' Thus am I often laid low. A copy of my favourite programme of the play is still in the drawer. In the first or second year of Peter No. 4 could not attend through illness, so we took the play to his nursery, far away in the country, an array of vehicles almost as glorious as a travelling circus; the leading parts were played by the youngest children in the London company, and No. 4, aged five, looked on solemnly at the performance from his bed and never smiled once. That was my first and only appearance on the real stage, and this copy of the programme shows I was thought so meanly of as an actor that they printed my name in smaller letters than the others.

I have said little here of Nos. 4 and 5, and it is high time I had finished. They had a long summer day, and I turn round twice and now they are off to school. On Monday, as it seems, I was escorting No. 5 to a children's party and brushing his hair in the ante-room; and by Thursday he is placing me against the wall of an underground station and saying, 'Now I am going to get the tickets; don't move till I come back for you or you'll lose yourself.' No. 4 jumps from being astride my shoulders fishing, I knee-deep in the stream, to becoming, while still a schoolboy, the sternest of my literary critics. Anything he shook his head over I abandoned, and

---

1. John Crook, a London theatrical composer and conductor.

conceivably the world has thus been deprived of masterpieces. There was for instance an unfortunate little tragedy which I liked until I foolishly told No. 4 its subject, when he frowned and said he had better have a look at it. He read it, and then, patting me on the back, as only he and No. 1 could touch me, said, 'You know you can't do this sort of thing.' End of a tragedian. Sometimes, however, No. 4 liked my efforts, and I walked in the azure that day when he returned *Dear Brutus*[2] to me with the comment 'Not so bad.' In earlier days, when he was ten, I offered him the MS of my book *Margaret Ogilvy*.[3] 'Oh, thanks,' he said almost immediately, and added, 'of course my desk is awfully full.' I reminded him that he could take out some of its more ridiculous contents. He said, 'I have read it already in the book.' This I had not known, and I was secretly elated, but I said that people sometimes liked to preserve this kind of thing as a curiosity. He said 'Oh' again. I said tartly that he was not compelled to take it if he didn't want it. He said, 'Of course I want it, but my desk——' Then he wriggled out of the room and came back in a few minutes dragging in No. 5 and announcing triumphantly, 'No. 5 will have it.'

The rebuffs I have got from all of you! They were especially crushing in those early days when one by one you came out of your belief in fairies and lowered on me as the deceiver. My grandest triumph, the best thing in the play of *Peter Pan* (though it is not in it), is that long after No. 4 had ceased to believe, I brought him back to the faith for at least two minutes. We were on our way in a boat to fish the Outer Hebrides (where we caught *Mary Rose*[4]), and though it was a journey of days he wore his fishing basket on his back all the time, so as to be able to begin at once. His one pain was the absence of Johnny Mackay, for Johnny was the loved gillie of the previous summer who had taught him everything that is worth knowing (which is a matter of flies) but could not be with us this time as he would have had to cross and re-cross Scotland to reach us. As the boat drew near the Kyle of Lochalsh pier I told Nos. 4 and 5 it was such a famous wishing pier that they had now but to wish and they should have. No. 5 believed at once and expressed a wish to meet himself (I afterwards found him on the pier searching faces confidently), but No. 4 thought it more of my untimely nonsense and doggedly declined to humour me. 'Whom do you want to see most, No. 4?' 'Of course I would like most to see Johnny Mackay.' 'Well, then, wish for him.' 'Oh, rot.' 'It can't do any harm to wish.' Contemptuously he wished, and as the ropes were thrown on the pier he saw Johnny waiting for him, loaded with angling paraphernalia. I know no one less like a fairy than Johnny Mackay, but for two minutes No. 4 was quivering in another world than ours. When he came to he gave me a smile which meant that we understood each other, and thereafter neglected me for a month, being always with Johnny. As I have said, this episode is not in the play; so though I dedicate *Peter Pan* to you I keep the smile, with the few other broken fragments of immortality that have come my way.

ACT I. THE NURSERY

The night nursery of the Darling family, which is the scene of our opening Act, is at the top of a rather depressed street in Bloomsbury. We have a right to place it where we will, and the reason Bloomsbury is chosen is that Mr Roget[5] *once lived there. So*

2. Barrie's play, first performed in 1917.
3. Barrie's biography of his mother, published in 1896.
4. Barrie's play, first performed in 1920; its heroine disappears on a mysterious Hebridean island,

once for twenty days and once for twenty-five years.
5. Peter Mark Roget (1779–1869), English physician and lexicographer. He worked fifty years on preparing a thesaurus, published as *Thesaurus of English Words and Phrases* (1852). In the late nine-

did we in days when his Thesaurus was our only companion in London; and we whom he has helped to wend our way through life have always wanted to pay him a little compliment. The Darlings therefore lived in Bloomsbury.

It is a corner house whose top window, the important one, looks upon a leafy square from which Peter used to fly up to it, to the delight of three children and no doubt the irritation of passers-by. The street is still there, though the steaming sausage shop has gone; and apparently the same cards perch now as then over the doors, inviting homeless ones to come and stay with the hospitable inhabitants. Since the days of the Darlings, however, a lick of paint has been applied; and our corner house in particular, which has swallowed its neighbour, blooms with awful freshness as if the colours had been discharged upon it through a hose. Its card now says 'No children', meaning maybe that the goings-on of Wendy and her brothers have given the house a bad name. As for ourselves, we have not been in it since we went back to reclaim our old Thesaurus.

That is what we call the Darling house, but you may dump it down anywhere you like, and if you think it was your house you are very probably right. It wanders about London looking for anybody in need of it, like the little house in the Never Land.

The blind (which is what Peter would have called the theatre curtain if he had ever seen one) rises on that top room, a shabby little room if Mrs Darling had not made it the hub of creation by her certainty that such it was, and adorned it to match with a loving heart and all the scrapings of her purse. The door on the right leads into the day nursery, which she has no right to have, but she made it herself with nails in her mouth and a paste-pot in her hand. This is the door the children will come in by. There are three beds and (rather oddly) a large dog-kennel; two of these beds, with the kennel, being on the left and the other on the right. The coverlets of the beds (if visitors are expected) are made out of Mrs Darling's wedding-gown, which was such a grand affair that it still keeps them pinched. Over each bed is a china house, the size of a linnet's nest, containing a night-light. The fire, which is on our right, is burning as discreetly as if it were in custody, which in a sense it is, for supporting the mantelshelf are two wooden soldiers, home-made, begun by Mr Darling, finished by Mrs Darling, repainted (unfortunately) by John Darling. On the fire-guard hang incomplete parts of children's night attire. The door the parents will come in by is on the left. At the back is the bathroom door, with a cuckoo clock over it; and in the centre is the window, which is at present ever so staid and respectable, but half an hour hence (namely at 6.30 P.M.) will be able to tell a very strange tale to the police.

The only occupant of the room at present is Nana the nurse, reclining, not as you might expect on the one soft chair, but on the floor. She is a Newfoundland dog, and though this may shock the grandiose, the not exactly affluent will make allowances. The Darlings could not afford to have a nurse, they could not afford indeed to have children; and now you are beginning to understand how they did it. Of course Nana has been trained by Mrs Darling, but like all treasures she was born to it. In this play we shall see her chiefly inside the house, but she was just as exemplary outside, escorting the two elders to school with an umbrella in her mouth, for instance, and butting them back into line if they strayed.

The cuckoo clock strikes six, and Nana springs into life. This first moment in the play is tremendously important, for if the actor playing Nana does not spring properly we are undone. She will probably be played by a boy, if one clever enough can be found, and must never be on two legs except on those rare occasions when an ordinary nurse

---

teenth century, Bloomsbury—near the British Library and University of London—was not a fashionable neighborhood.

would be on four. This Nana must go about all her duties in a most ordinary manner, so that you know in your bones that she performs them just so every evening at six; naturalness must be her passion; indeed, it should be the aim of everyone in the play, for which she is now setting the pace. All the characters, whether grown-ups or babes, must wear a child's outlook on life as their only important adornment. If they cannot help being funny they are begged to go away. A good motto for all would be 'The little less, and how much it is.'

    Nana, making much use of her mouth, 'turns down' the beds, and carries the various articles on the fire-guard across to them. Then pushing the bathroom door open, she is seen at work on the taps preparing Michael's bath; after which she enters from the day nursery with the youngest of the family on her back.

MICHAEL (*obstreperous*)   I won't go to bed, I won't, I won't. Nana, it isn't six o'clock yet. Two minutes more, please, one minute more? Nana, I won't be bathed, I tell you I will not be bathed.

    (*Here the bathroom door closes on them, and* MRS DARLING, *who has perhaps heard his cry, enters the nursery. She is the loveliest lady in Bloomsbury, with a sweet mocking mouth, and as she is going out to dinner tonight she is already wearing her evening gown because she knows her children like to see her in it. It is a delicious confection made by herself out of nothing and other people's mistakes. She does not often go out to dinner, preferring when the children are in bed to sit beside them tidying up their minds, just as if they were drawers. If Wendy and the boys could keep awake they might see her repacking into their proper places the many articles of the mind that have strayed during the day, lingering humorously over some of their contents, wondering where on earth they picked this thing up, making discoveries sweet and not so sweet, pressing this to her cheek and hurriedly stowing that out of sight. When they wake in the morning the naughtinesses with which they went to bed are not, alas, blown away, but they are placed at the bottom of the drawer; and on the top, beautifully aired, are their prettier thoughts ready for the new day.*

    As she enters the room she is startled to see a strange little face outside the window and a hand groping as if it wanted to come in.)

MRS DARLING   Who are you? (*The unknown disappears; she hurries to the window.*) No one there. And yet I feel sure I saw a face. My children! (*She throws open the bathroom door and Michael's head appears gaily over the bath. He splashes; she throws kisses to him and closes the door. 'Wendy, John,' she cries, and gets reassuring answers from the day nursery. She sits down, relieved, on Wendy's bed; and* WENDY *and* JOHN *come in, looking their smallest size, as children tend to do to a mother suddenly in fear for them.*)

JOHN (*histrionically*)   We are doing an act; we are playing at being you and father. (*He imitates the only father who has come under his special notice.*) A little less noise there.

WENDY   Now let us pretend we have a baby.

JOHN (*good-naturedly*)   I am happy to inform you, Mrs Darling, that you are now a mother. (WENDY *gives way to ecstasy.*) You have missed the chief thing; you haven't asked, 'boy or girl?'

WENDY   I am so glad to have one at all, I don't care which it is.

JOHN (*crushingly*)   That is just the difference between gentlemen and ladies. Now you tell me.

WENDY   I am happy to acquaint you, Mr Darling, you are now a father.

JOHN   Boy or girl?

WENDY   (*presenting herself*)   Girl.

JOHN   Tuts.

WENDY   You horrid.

JOHN   Go on.

WENDY   I am happy to acquaint you, Mr Darling, you are again a father.

JOHN   Boy or girl?

WENDY   Boy. (JOHN *beams*). Mummy, it's hateful of him.

(MICHAEL *emerges from the bathroom in John's old pyjamas and giving his face a last wipe with the towel.*)

MICHAEL   (*expanding*)   Now, John, have me.

JOHN   We don't want any more.

MICHAEL   (*contracting*)   Am I not to be born at all?

JOHN   Two is enough.

MICHAEL   (*wheedling*)   Come, John; boy, John. (*Appalled*) Nobody wants me!

MRS DARLING   I do.

MICHAEL   (*with a glimmer of hope*)   Boy or girl?

MRS DARLING   (*with one of those happy thoughts of hers*)   Boy.

(*Triumph of* MICHAEL; *discomfiture of* JOHN. MR DARLING *arrives, in no mood unfortunately to gloat over this domestic scene. He is really a good man as bread-winners go, and it is hard luck for him to be propelled into the room now, when if we had brought him in a few minutes earlier or later he might have made a fairer impression. In the city where he sits on a stool all day, as fixed as a postage stamp, he is so like all the others on stools that you recognise him not by his face but by his stool, but at home the way to gratify him is to say that he has a distinct personality. He is very conscientious, and in the days when Mrs Darling gave up keeping the house books correctly and drew pictures instead (which he called her guesses), he did all the totting up for her, holding her hand while he calculated whether they could have Wendy or not, and coming down on the right side. It is with regret, therefore, that we introduce him as a tornado, rushing into the nursery in evening dress, but without his coat, and brandishing in his hand a recalcitrant white tie.*)

MR DARLING   (*implying that he has searched for her everywhere and that the nursery is a strange place in which to find her*)   Oh, here you are, Mary.

MRS DARLING   (*knowing at once what is the matter*)   What is the matter, George dear?

MR DARLING   (*as if the word were monstrous*)   Matter! This tie, it will not tie. (*He waxes sarcastic.*) Not round my neck. Round the bedpost, oh yes; twenty times have I made it up round the bedpost, but round my neck, oh dear no; begs to be excused.

MICHAEL   (*in a joyous transport*)   Say it again, father, say it again!

MR DARLING   (*witheringly*)   Thank you. (*Goaded by a suspiciously crooked smile on Mrs Darling's face.*) I warn you, Mary, that unless this tie is round my neck we don't go out to dinner tonight, and if I don't go out to dinner tonight I never go to the office again, and if I don't go to the office again you and I starve, and our children will be thrown into the streets.

(*The children blanch as they grasp the gravity of the situation.*)

MRS DARLING   Let me try, dear.

(*In a terrible silence their progeny cluster round them. Will she succeed? Their fate depends on it. She fails—no, she succeeds. In another moment they are wildly gay, romping round the room on each other's shoulders. Father is even a better horse than mother.* MICHAEL *is dropped upon his bed,* WENDY *retires to prepare for hers,* JOHN *runs from* NANA, *who has reappeared with the bath towel.*)

JOHN (*rebellious*) I won't be bathed. You needn't think it.

MR DARLING (*in the grand manner*) Go and be bathed at once, sir.

(*With bent head* JOHN *follows* NANA *into the bathroom.* MR DARLING *swells.*)

MICHAEL (*as he is put between the sheets*) Mother, how did you get to know me?

MR DARLING A little less noise there.

MICHAEL (*growing solemn*) At what time was I born, mother?

MRS DARLING At two o'clock in the night-time, dearest.

MICHAEL Oh, mother, I hope I didn't wake you.

MRS DARLING They are rather sweet, don't you think, George?

MR DARLING (*doting*) There is not their equal on earth, and they are ours, ours!

(*Unfortunately* NANA *has come from the bathroom for a sponge and she collides with his trousers, the first pair he has ever had with braid on them.*)

MR DARLING Mary, it is too bad; just look at this; covered with hairs. Clumsy, clumsy!

(NANA *goes, a drooping figure.*)

MRS DARLING Let me brush you, dear.

(*Once more she is successful. They are now by the fire, and* MICHAEL *is in bed doing idiotic things with a teddy bear.*)

MR DARLING (*depressed*) I sometimes think, Mary, that it is a mistake to have a dog for a nurse.

MRS DARLING George, Nana is a treasure.

MR DARLING No doubt; but I have an uneasy feeling at times that she looks upon the children as puppies.

MRS DARLING (*rather faintly*) Oh no, dear one, I am sure she knows they have souls.

MR DARLING (*profoundly*) I wonder, I wonder.

(*The opportunity has come for her to tell him of something that is on her mind.*)

MRS DARLING George, we must keep Nana. I will tell you why. (*Her seriousness impresses him.*) My dear, when I came into this room tonight I saw a face at the window.

MR DARLING (*incredulous*) A face at the window, three floors up? Pooh!

MRS DARLING It was the face of a little boy; he was trying to get in. George, this is not the first time I have seen that boy.

MR DARLING (*beginning to think that this may be a man's job*) Oho!

MRS DARLING (*making sure that* MICHAEL *does not hear*) The first time was a week ago. It was Nana's night out, and I had been drowsing here by the fire when suddenly I felt a draught, as if the window were open. I looked round and I saw that boy—in the room.

MR DARLING In the room?

MRS DARLING I screamed. Just then Nana came back and she at once sprang at him. The boy leapt for the window. She pulled down the sash quickly, but was too late to catch him.

MR DARLING (*who knows he would not have been too late*) I thought so!

MRS DARLING Wait. The boy escaped, but his shadow had not time to get out; down came the window and cut it clean off.

MR DARLING (*heavily*) Mary, Mary, why didn't you keep that shadow?

MRS DARLING (*scoring*) I did. I rolled it up, George; and here it is.

(*She produces it from a drawer. They unroll and examine the flimsy thing, which is not more material than a puff of smoke, and if let go would probably float into the ceiling without discolouring it. Yet it has human shape. As they nod their heads over it they present the most satisfying picture on earth, two happy parents conspiring cosily by the fire for the good of their children.)*

MR DARLING   It is nobody I know, but he does look a scoundrel.

MRS DARLING   I think he comes back to get his shadow, George.

MR DARLING (*meaning that the miscreant has now a father to deal with*)   I dare say. (*He sees himself telling the story to the other stools at the office.*) There is money in this, my love. I shall take it to the British Museum tomorrow and have it priced.

(*The shadow is rolled up and replaced in the drawer.*)

MRS DARLING (*like a guilty person*)   George, I have not told you all; I am afraid to.

MR DARLING (*who knows exactly the right moment to treat a woman as a beloved child*)   Cowardy, cowardy custard.

MRS DARLING (*pouting*)   No, I'm not.

MR DARLING   Oh yes, you are.

MRS DARLING   George, I'm not.

MR DARLING   Then why not tell? (*Thus cleverly soothed she goes on.*)

MRS DARLING   The boy was not alone that first time. He was accompanied by—I don't know how to describe it; by a ball of light, not as big as my fist, but it darted about the room like a living thing.

MR DARLING (*though open-minded*)   That is very unusual. It escaped with the boy?

MRS DARLING   Yes. (*Sliding her hand into his.*) George, what can all this mean?

MR DARLING (*ever ready*)   What indeed!

(*This intimate scene is broken by the return of* NANA *with a bottle in her mouth.*)

MRS DARLING (*at once dissembling*)   What is that, Nana? Ah, of course; Michael, it is your medicine.

MICHAEL (*promptly*)   Won't take it.

MR DARLING (*recalling his youth*)   Be a man, Michael.

MICHAEL   Won't.

MRS DARLING (*weakly*)   I'll get you a lovely chocky[6] to take after it.

(*She leaves the room, though her husband calls after her.*)

MR DARLING   Mary, don't pamper him. When I was your age, Michael, I took medicine without a murmur. I said 'Thank you, kind parents, for giving me bottles to make me well.'

(WENDY, *who has appeared in her nightgown, hears this and believes.*)

WENDY   That medicine you sometimes take is much nastier, isn't it, father?

MR DARLING (*valuing her support*)   Ever so much nastier. And as an example to you, Michael, I would take it now (*thankfully*) if I hadn't lost the bottle.

WENDY (*always glad to be of service*)   I know where it is, father. I'll fetch it.

(*She is gone before he can stop her. He turns for help to* JOHN, *who has come from the bathroom attired for bed.*)

MR DARLING   John, it is the most beastly stuff. It is that sticky sweet kind.

JOHN (*who is perhaps still playing at parents*)   Never mind, father, it will soon be over.

(*A spasm of ill-will to* JOHN *cuts through* MR DARLING, *and is gone.* WENDY *returns panting.*)

WENDY   Here it is, father; I have been as quick as I could.

MR DARLING (*with a sarcasm that is completely thrown away on her*)   You have been wonderfully quick, precious quick!

(*He is now at the foot of Michael's bed,* NANA *is by its side, holding the medicine spoon insinuatingly in her mouth.*)

6. A sweet made with chocolate.

WENDY (*proudly, as she pours out Mr Darling's medicine*) Michael, now you will see how father takes it.

MR DARLING (*hedging*) Michael first.

MICHAEL (*full of unworthy suspicions*) Father first.

MR DARLING It will make me sick, you know.

JOHN (*lightly*) Come on, father.

MR DARLING Hold your tongue, sir.

WENDY (*disturbed*) I thought you took it quite easily, father, saying 'Thank you, kind parents, for——'

MR DARLING That is not the point; the point is that there is more in my glass than in Michael's spoon. It isn't fair, I swear though it were with my last breath, it is not fair.

MICHAEL (*coldly*) Father, I'm waiting.

MR DARLING It's all very well to say you are waiting; so am I waiting.

MICHAEL Father's a cowardy custard.

MR DARLING So are you a cowardy custard.

(*They are now glaring at each other.*)

MICHAEL I am not frightened.

MR DARLING Neither am I frightened.

MICHAEL Well, then, take it.

MR DARLING Well, then, you take it.

WENDY (*butting in again*) Why not take it at the same time?

MR DARLING (*haughtily*) Certainly. Are you ready, Michael?

WENDY (*as nothing has happened*) One—two—three.

(MICHAEL *partakes, but* MR DARLING *resorts to hanky-panky.*)

JOHN Father hasn't taken his!

(MICHAEL *howls.*)

WENDY (*inexpressibly pained*) Oh father!

MR DARLING (*who has been hiding the glass behind him*) What do you mean by 'oh father'? Stop that row, Michael. I meant to take mine but I—missed it. (NANA *shakes her head sadly over him, and goes into the bathroom. They are all looking as if they did not admire him, and nothing so dashes a temperamental man.*) I say, I have just thought of a splendid joke. (*They brighten.*) I shall pour my medicine into Nana's bowl, and she will drink it thinking it is milk! (*The pleasantry does not appeal, but he prepares the joke, listening for appreciation.*)

WENDY Poor darling Nana!

MR DARLING You silly little things; to your beds every one of you; I am ashamed of you.

(*They steal to their beds as* MRS DARLING *returns with the chocolate.*)

MRS DARLING Well, is it all over?

MICHAEL Father didn't—— (*Father glares.*)

MR DARLING All over, dear, quite satisfactorily. (NANA *comes back.*) Nana, good dog, good girl; I have put a little milk into your bowl. (*The bowl is by the kennel, and* NANA *begins to lap, only begins. She retreats into the kennel.*)

MRS DARLING What is the matter, Nana?

MR DARLING (*uneasily*) Nothing, nothing.

MRS DARLING (*smelling the bowl*) George, it is your medicine!

(*The children break into lamentation. He gives his wife an imploring look; he is begging for one smile, but does not get it. In consequence he goes from bad to worse.*)

MR DARLING   It was only a joke. Much good my wearing myself to the bone trying to be funny in this house.

WENDY (*on her knees by the kennel*)   Father, Nana is crying.

MR DARLING   Coddle her; nobody coddles me. Oh dear no. I am only the bread-winner, why should I be coddled? Why, why, why?

MRS DARLING   George, not so loud; the servants will hear you.

> (*There is only one maid, absurdly small too, but they have got into the way of calling her the servants.*)

MR DARLING (*defiant*)   Let them hear me; bring in the whole world. (*The desperate man, who has not been in fresh air for days, has now lost all self-control.*) I refuse to allow that dog to lord it in my nursery for one hour longer. (NANA *supplicates him.*) In vain, in vain, the proper place for you is the yard, and there you go to be tied up this instant.

> (NANA *again retreats into the kennel, and the children add their prayers to hers.*)

MRS DARLING (*who knows how contrite he will be for this presently*)   George, George, remember what I told you about that boy.

MR DARLING   Am I master in this house or is she? (*To* NANA *fiercely.*) Come along. (*He thunders at her, but she indicates that she has reasons not worth troubling him with for remaining where she is. He resorts to a false bonhomie.*) There, there, did she think he was angry with her, poor Nana? (*She wriggles a response in the affirmative.*) Good Nana, pretty Nana. (*She has seldom been called pretty, and it has the old effect. She plays rub-a-dub with her paws, which is how a dog blushes.*) She will come to her kind master, won't she? won't she? (*She advances, retreats, waggles her head, her tail, and eventually goes to him. He seizes her collar in an iron grip and amid the cries of his progeny drags her from the room. They listen, for her remonstrances are not inaudible.*)

MRS DARLING   Be brave, my dears.

WENDY   He is chaining Nana up!

> (*This unfortunately is what he is doing, though we cannot see him. Let us hope that he then retires to his study, looks up the word 'temper' in his Thesaurus, and under the influence of those benign pages becomes a better man. In the meantime the children have been put to bed in unwonted silence, and* MRS DARLING *lights the night-lights over the beds.*)

JOHN (*as the barking below goes on*)   She is awfully unhappy.

WENDY   That is not Nana's unhappy bark. That is her bark when she smells danger.

MRS DARLING (*remembering that boy*)   Danger! Are you sure, Wendy?

WENDY (*the one of the family, for there is one in every family, who can be trusted to know or not to know*)   Oh yes.

> (*Her mother looks this way and that from the window.*)

JOHN   Is anything there?

MRS DARLING   All quite quiet and still. Oh, how I wish I was not going out to dinner tonight.

MICHAEL   Can anything harm us, mother, after the night-lights are lit?

MRS DARLING   Nothing, precious. They are the eyes a mother leaves behind her to guard her children.

> (*Nevertheless we may be sure she means to tell Liza, the little maid, to look in on them frequently till she comes home. She goes from bed to bed, after her custom, tucking them in and crooning a lullaby.*)

MICHAEL (*drowsily*)   Mother, I'm glad of you.

MRS DARLING (*with a last look round, her hand on the switch*)   Dear night-lights that protect my sleeping babes, burn clear and steadfast tonight.

(*The nursery darkens and she is gone, intentionally leaving the door ajar. Something uncanny is going to happen, we expect, for a quiver has passed through the room, just sufficient to touch the night-lights. They blink three times one after the other and go out, precisely as children (whom familiarity has made them resemble) fall asleep. There is another light in the room now, no larger than Mrs Darling's fist, and in the time we have taken to say this it has been into the drawers and wardrobe and searched pockets, as it darts about looking for a certain shadow. Then the window is blown open, probably by the smallest and therefore most mischievous star, and* PETER PAN *flies into the room. In so far as he is dressed at all it is in autumn leaves and cobwebs.*)

PETER (*in a whisper*)   Tinker Bell, Tink, are you there? (*A jug lights up.*) Oh, do come out of that jug. (TINK *flashes hither and thither.*) Do you know where they put it? (*The answer comes as of a tinkle of bells; it is the fairy language.* PETER *can speak it, but it bores him.*) Which big box? This one? But which drawer? Yes, do show me. (TINK *pops into the drawer where the shadow is, but before* PETER *can reach it,* WENDY *moves in her sleep. He flies on to the mantelshelf as a hiding-place. Then, as she has not waked, he flutters over the beds as an easy way to observe the occupants, closes the window softly, wafts himself to the drawer and scatters its contents to the floor, as kings on their wedding day toss ha'pence to the crowd. In his joy at finding his shadow he forgets that he has shut up* TINK *in the drawer. He sits on the floor with the shadow, confident that he and it will join like drops of water. Then he tries to stick it on with soap from the bathroom, and this failing also, he subsides dejectedly on the floor. This wakens* WENDY, *who sits up, and is pleasantly interested to see a stranger.*)

WENDY (*courteously*)   Boy, why are you crying?

(*He jumps up, and crossing to the foot of the bed bows to her in the fairy way.* WENDY, *impressed, bows to him from the bed.*)

PETER   What is your name?

WENDY (*well satisfied*)   Wendy Moira Angela Darling. What is yours?

PETER (*finding it lamentably brief*)   Peter Pan.

WENDY   Is that all?

PETER (*biting his lip*)   Yes.

WENDY (*politely*)   I am so sorry.

PETER   It doesn't matter.

WENDY   Where do you live?

PETER   Second to the right and then straight on till morning.[7]

WENDY   What a funny address!

PETER   No, it isn't.

WENDY   I mean, is that what they put on the letters?

PETER   Don't get any letters.

WENDY   But your mother gets letters?

PETER   Don't have a mother.

WENDY   Peter!

(*She leaps out of bed to put her arms round him, but he draws back; he does not know why, but he knows he must draw back.*)

PETER   You mustn't touch me.

7. These directions echo those sent by Robert Louis Stevenson (1850–1894), who invited Barrie to visit him in the South Seas: "Take the boat to San Francisco, and then my place is second to the left."

WENDY   Why?

PETER   No one must ever touch me.

WENDY   Why?

PETER   I don't know.

 (*He is never touched by anyone in the play.*)

WENDY   No wonder you were crying.

PETER   I wasn't crying. But I can't get my shadow to stick on.

WENDY   It has come off! How awful. (*Looking at the spot where he had lain.*) Peter, you have been trying to stick it on with soap!

PETER   (*snappily*)   Well then?

WENDY   It must be sewn on.

PETER   What is 'sewn'?

WENDY   You are dreadfully ignorant.

PETER   No, I'm not.

WENDY   I will sew it on for you, my little man. But we must have more light. (*She touches something, and to his astonishment the room is illuminated.*) Sit here. I dare say it will hurt a little.

PETER   (*a recent remark of hers rankling*)   I never cry. (*She seems to attach the shadow. He tests the combination.*) It isn't quite itself yet.

WENDY   Perhaps I should have ironed it. (*It awakes and is as glad to be back with him as he to have it. He and his shadow dance together. He is showing off now. He crows like a cock. He would fly in order to impress Wendy further if he knew that there is anything unusual in that.*)

PETER   Wendy, look, look; oh the cleverness of me!

WENDY   You conceit; of course I did nothing!

PETER   You did a little.

WENDY   (*wounded*)   A little! If I am no use I can at least withdraw.

 (*With one haughty leap she is again in bed with the sheet over her face. Popping on to the end of the bed the artful one appeals.*)

PETER   Wendy, don't withdraw. I can't help crowing, Wendy, when I'm pleased with myself. Wendy, one girl is worth more than twenty boys.

WENDY   (*peeping over the sheet*)   You really think so, Peter?

PETER   Yes, I do.

WENDY   I think it's perfectly sweet of you, and I shall get up again. (*They sit together on the side of the bed.*) I shall give you a kiss if you like.

PETER   Thank you. (*He holds out his hand.*)

WENDY   (*aghast*)   Don't you know what a kiss is?

PETER   I shall know when you give it me. (*Not to hurt his feelings she gives him her thimble.*) Now shall I give you a kiss?

WENDY   (*primly*)   If you please. (*He pulls an acorn button off his person and bestows it on her. She is shocked but considerate.*) I will wear it on this chain round my neck. Peter, how old are you?

PETER   (*blithely*)   I don't know, but quite young, Wendy. I ran away the day I was born.

WENDY   Ran away, why?

PETER   Because I heard father and mother talking of what I was to be when I became a man. I want always to be a little boy and to have fun; so I ran away to Kensington Gardens and lived a long time among the fairies.

WENDY   (*with great eyes*)   You know fairies, Peter!

PETER   (*surprised that this should be a recommendation*)   Yes, but they are nearly all dead now. (*Baldly*) You see, Wendy, when the first baby laughed for the first time, the laugh broke into a thousand pieces and they all went skipping about, and that was the beginning of fairies. And now when every new baby is born its first laugh becomes a fairy. So there ought to be one fairy for every boy or girl.

WENDY (*breathlessly*) Ought to be? Isn't there?

PETER Oh no. Children know such a lot now. Soon they don't believe in fairies, and every time a child says 'I don't believe in fairies' there is a fairy somewhere that falls down dead. (*He skips about heartlessly.*)

WENDY Poor things!

PETER (*to whom this statement recalls a forgotten friend*) I can't think where she has gone. Tinker Bell, Tink, where are you?

WENDY (*trilling*) Peter, you don't mean to tell me that there is a fairy in this room!

PETER (*flitting about in search*) She came with me. You don't hear anything, do you?

WENDY I hear—the only sound I hear is like a tinkle of bells.

PETER That is the fairy language. I hear it too.

WENDY It seems to come from over there.

PETER (*with shameless glee*) Wendy, I believe I shut her up in that drawer!

(*He releases* TINK, *who darts about in a fury using language it is perhaps as well we don't understand.*)

You needn't say that; I'm very sorry, but how could I know you were in the drawer?

WENDY (*her eyes dancing in pursuit of the delicious creature*) Oh, Peter, if only she would stand still and let me see her!

PETER (*indifferently*) They hardly ever stand still.

(*To show that she can do even this* TINK *pauses between two ticks of the cuckoo clock.*)

WENDY I see her, the lovely! where is she now?

PETER She is behind the clock. Tink, this lady wishes you were her fairy. (*The answer comes immediately.*)

WENDY What does she say?

PETER She is not very polite. She says you are a great ugly girl, and that she is my fairy. You know, Tink, you can't be my fairy because I am a gentleman and you are a lady.

(TINK *replies.*)

WENDY What did she say?

PETER She said 'You silly ass.' She is quite a common girl, you know. She is called Tinker[8] Bell because she mends the fairy pots and kettles.

(*They have reached a chair,* WENDY *in the ordinary way and* PETER *through a hole in the back.*)

WENDY Where do you live now?

PETER With the lost boys.

WENDY Who are they?

PETER They are the children who fall out of their prams when the nurse is looking the other way. If they are not claimed in seven days they are sent far away to the Never Land. I'm captain.

WENDY What fun it must be.

PETER (*craftily*) Yes, but we are rather lonely. You see, Wendy, we have no female companionship.

WENDY Are none of the other children girls?

---

8. Tinkers—those who repaired household utensils—were often itinerant.

PETER   Oh no; girls, you know, are much too clever to fall out of their prams.

WENDY   Peter, it is perfectly lovely the way you talk about girls. John there just despises us.

(PETER, *for the first time, has a good look at* JOHN. *He then neatly tumbles him out of bed.*)

You wicked! you are not captain here. (*She bends over her brother who is prone on the floor.*) After all he hasn't wakened, and you meant to be kind. (*Having now done her duty she forgets* JOHN, *who blissfully sleeps on.*) Peter, you may give me a kiss.

PETER (*cynically*)   I thought you would want it back.

(*He offers her the thimble.*)

WENDY (*artfully*)   Oh dear, I didn't mean a kiss, Peter. I meant a thimble.

PETER (*only half placated*)   What is that?

WENDY   It is like this. (*She leans forward to give a demonstration, but something prevents the meeting of their faces.*)

PETER (*satisfied*)   Now shall I give you a thimble?

WENDY   If you please. (*Before he can even draw near she screams.*)

PETER   What is it?

WENDY   It was exactly as if some one were pulling my hair!

PETER   That must have been Tink. I never knew her so naughty before.

(TINK *speaks. She is in the jug again.*)

WENDY   What does she say?

PETER   She says she will do that every time I give you a thimble.

WENDY   But why?

PETER (*equally nonplussed*)   Why, Tink? (*He has to translate the answer.*) She said 'You silly ass' again.

WENDY   She is very impertinent. (*They are sitting on the floor now.*) Peter, why did you come to our nursery window?

PETER   To try to hear stories. None of us knows any stories.

WENDY   How perfectly awful!

PETER   Do you know why swallows build in the eaves of houses? It is to listen to the stories. Wendy, your mother was telling you such a lovely story.

WENDY   Which story was it?

PETER   About the prince, and he couldn't find the lady who wore the glass slipper.

WENDY   That was Cinderella. Peter, he found her and they were happy ever after.

PETER   I am glad. (*They have worked their way along the floor close to each other, but he now jumps up.*)

WENDY   Where are you going?

PETER (*already on his way to the window*)   To tell the other boys.

WENDY   Don't go, Peter. I know lots of stories. The stories I could tell to the boys!

PETER (*gleaming*)   Come on! We'll fly.

WENDY   Fly? You can fly!

(*How he would like to rip those stories out of her; he is dangerous now.*)

PETER   Wendy, come with me.

WENDY   Oh dear, I mustn't. Think of mother. Besides, I can't fly.

PETER   I'll teach you.

WENDY   How lovely to fly!

PETER   I'll teach you how to jump on the wind's back and then away we go. Wendy, when you are sleeping in your silly bed you might be flying about with me, saying funny things to the stars. There are mermaids, Wendy, with long tails. (*She just succeeds in remaining on the nursery floor.*) Wendy, how we should all respect you. (*At this she strikes her colours.*)

WENDY   Of course it's awfully fas-cin-a-ting! Would you teach John and Michael to fly too?

PETER (*indifferently*)   If you like.

WENDY (*playing rum-tum on* JOHN)   John, wake up; there is a boy here who is to teach us to fly.

JOHN   Is there? Then I shall get up. (*He raises his head from the floor.*) Hullo, I am up!

WENDY   Michael, open your eyes. This boy is to teach us to fly.

(*The sleepers are at once as awake as their father's razor; but before a question can be asked Nana's bark is heard.*)

JOHN   Out with the light, quick, hide!

(*When the maid* LIZA, *who is so small that when she says she will never see ten again one can scarcely believe her, enters with a firm hand on the troubled Nana's chain the room is in comparative darkness.*)

LIZA   There, you suspicious brute, they are perfectly safe, aren't they? Every one of the little angels sound asleep in bed. Listen to their gentle breathing. (*Nana's sense of smell here helps to her undoing instead of hindering it. She knows that they are in the room.* MICHAEL, *who is behind the window curtain, is so encouraged by Liza's last remark that he breathes too loudly.* NANA *knows that kind of breathing and tries to break from her keeper's control.*) No more of it, Nana. (*Wagging a finger at her*) I warn you if you bark again I shall go straight for master and missus and bring them home from the party, and then won't master whip you just! Come along, you naughty dog.

(*The unhappy* NANA *is led away. The children emerge exulting from their various hiding-places. In their brief absence from the scene strange things have been done to them; but it is not for us to reveal a mysterious secret of the stage. They look just the same.*)

JOHN   I say, can you really fly?

PETER   Look! (*He is now over their heads.*)

WENDY   Oh, how sweet!

PETER   I'm sweet, oh, I am sweet!

(*It looks so easy that they try it first from the floor and then from their beds, without encouraging results.*)

JOHN (*rubbing his knees*)   How do you do it?

PETER (*descending*)   You just think lovely wonderful thoughts and they lift you up in the air. (*He is off again.*)

JOHN   You are so nippy at it; couldn't you do it very slowly once? (PETER *does it slowly.*) I've got it now, Wendy. (*He tries; no, he has not got it, poor stay-at-home, though he knows the names of all the counties in England and* PETER *does not know one.*)

PETER   I must blow the fairy dust on you first. (*Fortunately his garments are smeared with it and he blows some dust on each.*) Now, try; try from the bed. Just wriggle your shoulders this way, and then let go.

(*The gallant* MICHAEL *is the first to let go, and is borne across the room.*)

MICHAEL (*with a yell that should have disturbed Liza*)   I flewed!

(JOHN *lets go, and meets* WENDY *near the bathroom door though they had both aimed in an opposite direction.*)

WENDY   Oh, lovely!

JOHN (*tending to be upside down*) How ripping!

MICHAEL (*playing whack on a chair*) I do like it!

THE THREE Look at me, look at me, look at me!

> (*They are not nearly so elegant in the air as* PETER, *but their heads have bumped the ceiling, and there is nothing more delicious than that.*)

JOHN (*who can even go backwards*) I say, why shouldn't we go out?

PETER There are pirates.

JOHN Pirates! (*He grabs his tall Sunday hat.*) Let us go at once!

> (TINK *does not like it. She darts at their hair. From down below in the street the lighted window must present an unwonted spectacle: the shadows of children revolving in the room like a merry-go-round. This is perhaps what* MR *and* MRS DARLING *see as they come hurrying home from the party, brought by* NANA *who, you may be sure, has broken her chain. Peter's accomplice, the little star, has seen them coming, and again the window blows open.*)

PETER (*as if he had heard the star whisper Cave*[9]) Now come!

> (*Breaking the circle he flies out of the window over the trees of the square and over the house-tops, and the others follow like a flight of birds. The broken-hearted father and mother arrive just in time to get a nip from* TINK *as she too sets out for the Never Land.*)

ACT II. THE NEVER LAND

When the blind goes up all is so dark that you scarcely know it has gone up. This is because if you were to see the island bang[1] (as Peter would say) the wonders of it might hurt your eyes. If you all came in spectacles perhaps you could see it bang, but to make a rule of that kind would be a pity. The first thing seen is merely some whitish dots trudging along the sward, and you can guess from their tinkling that they are probably fairies of the commoner sort going home afoot from some party and having a cheery tiff by the way. Then Peter's star wakes up, and in the blink of it, which is much stronger than in our stars, you can make out masses of trees, and you think you see wild beasts stealing past to drink, though what you see is not the beasts themselves but only the shadows of them. They are really out pictorially to greet Peter in the way they think he would like them to greet him; and for the same reason the mermaids basking in the lagoon beyond the trees are carefully combing their hair; and for the same reason the pirates are landing invisibly from the longboat, invisibly to you but not to the red-skins, whom none can see or hear because they are on the war-path. The whole island, in short, which has been having a slack time in Peter's absence, is now in a ferment because the tidings has leaked out that he is on his way back; and everybody and everything know that they will catch it from him if they don't give satisfaction. While you have been told this the sun (another of his servants) has been bestirring himself. Those of you who may have thought it wiser after all to begin this Act in spectacles may now take them off.

What you see is the Never Land. You have often half seen it before, or even three-quarters, after the night-lights were lit, and you might then have beached your coracle on it if you had not always at the great moment fallen asleep. I dare say you have chucked things on to it, the things you can't find in the morning. In the daytime you think the Never Land is only make-believe, and so it is to the likes of you, but this is the Never

---

9. Beware (Latin); schoolboy slang meaning "keep watch."

1. Directly, completely.

Land come true. It is an open-air scene, a forest, with a beautiful lagoon beyond but not really far away, for the Never Land is very compact, not large and sprawly with tedious distances between one adventure and another, but nicely crammed. It is summer time on the trees and on the lagoon but winter on the river, which is not remarkable on Peter's island where all the four seasons may pass while you are filling a jug at the well. Peter's home is at this very spot, but you could not point out the way into it even if you were told which is the entrance, not even if you were told that there are seven of them. You know now because you have just seen one of the lost boys emerge. The holes in these seven great hollow trees are the 'doors' down to Peter's home, and he made seven because, despite his cleverness, he thought seven boys must need seven doors.

The boy who has emerged from his tree is Slightly, who has perhaps been driven from the abode below by companions less musical than himself. Quite possibly a genius, Slightly has with him his homemade whistle to which he capers entrancingly, with no audience save a Never ostrich which is also musically inclined. Unable to imitate Slightly's graces the bird falls so low as to burlesque them and is driven from the entertainment. Other lost boys climb up the trunks or drop from branches, and now we see the six of them, all in the skins of animals they think they have shot, and so round and furry in them that if they fall they roll. Tootles is not the least brave though the most unfortunate of this gallant band. He has been in fewer adventures than any of them because the big things constantly happen while he has stepped round the corner; he will go off, for instance, in some quiet hour to gather firewood, and then when he returns the others will be sweeping up the blood. Instead of souring his nature this has sweetened it and he is the humblest of the band. Nibs is more gay and debonair, Slightly more conceited. Slightly thinks he remembers the days before he was lost, with their manners and customs. Curly is a pickle, and so often has he had to deliver up his person when Peter said sternly, 'Stand forth the one who did this thing,' that now he stands forth whether he has done it or not. The other two are First Twin and Second Twin, who cannot be described because we should probably be describing the wrong one. Hunkering on the ground or peeping out of their holes, the six are not unlike village gossips gathered round the pump.

TOOTLES Has Peter come back yet, Slightly?

SLIGHTLY (*with a solemnity that he thinks suits the occasion*) No, Tootles, no.

(*They are like dogs waiting for the master to tell them that the day has begun.*)

CURLY (*as if Peter might be listening*) I do wish he would come back.

TOOTLES I am always afraid of the pirates when Peter is not here to protect us.

SLIGHTLY I am not afraid of pirates. Nothing frightens me. But I do wish Peter would come back and tell us whether he has heard anything more about Cinderella.

SECOND TWIN (*with diffidence*) Slightly, I dreamt last night that the prince found Cinderella.

FIRST TWIN (*who is intellectually the superior of the two*) Twin, I think you should not have dreamt that, for I didn't, and Peter may say we oughtn't to dream differently, being twins, you know.

TOOTLES I am awfully anxious about Cinderella. You see, not knowing anything about my own mother I am fond of thinking that she was rather like Cinderella.

(*This is received with derision.*)

NIBS All I remember about my mother is that she often said to father, 'Oh how I wish I had a cheque book of my own.' I don't know what a cheque book is, but I should just love to give my mother one.

SLIGHTLY (*as usual*) My mother was fonder of me than your mothers were of you.

(*Uproar.*) Oh yes, she was. Peter had to make up names for you, but my mother had wrote my name on the pinafore I was lost in. 'Slightly Soiled'; that's my name. (*They fall upon him pugnaciously; not that they are really worrying about their mothers, who are now as important to them as a piece of string, but because any excuse is good enough for a shindy.*[2] *Not for long is he belaboured, for a sound is heard that sends them scurrying down their holes: in a second of time the scene is bereft of human life. What they have heard from nearby is a verse of the dreadful song with which on the Never Land the pirates stealthily trumpet their approach—*

Yo ho, yo ho, the pirate life,
The flag of skull and bones,
A merry hour, a hempen rope,
And hey for Davy Jones!*[3]

The pirates appear upon the frozen river dragging a raft, on which reclines among cushions that dark and fearful man, CAPTAIN JAS HOOK. *A more villainous-looking brotherhood of men never hung in a row on Execution Dock. Here, his great arms bare, pieces of eight in his ears as ornaments, is the handsome* CECCO, *who cut his name on the back of the governor of the prison at Gao.*[4] *Heavier in the pull is the gigantic black who has had many names since the first one terrified dusky children on the banks of the Guidjo-mo.* BILL JUKES *comes next, every inch of him tattooed, the same* JUKES *who got six dozen on the* Walrus *from* FLINT. *Following these are* COOKSON, *said to be Black Murphy's brother [but this was never proved]; and* GENTLEMAN STARKEY, *once an usher in a school; and* SKYLIGHTS [*Morgan's Skylights*]; *and* NOODLER, *whose hands are fixed on backwards; and the spectacled boatswain,* SMEE, *the only Nonconformist in Hook's crew; and other ruffians long known and feared on the Spanish main.*

Cruellest jewel in that dark setting is HOOK *himself, cadaverous and black-avised, his hair dressed in long curls which look like black candles about to melt, his eyes blue as the forget-me-not and of a profound insensibility, save when he claws, at which time a red spot appears in them. He has an iron hook instead of a right hand, and it is with this he claws. He is never more sinister than when he is most polite, and the elegance of his diction, the distinction of his demeanour, show him one of a different class from his crew, a solitary among uncultured companions. This courtliness impresses even his victims on the high seas, who note that he always says 'Sorry' when prodding them along the plank. A man of indomitable courage, the only thing at which he flinches is the sight of his own blood, which is thick and of an unusual colour. At his public school*[5] *they said of him that he 'bled yellow'. In dress he apes the dandiacal associated with Charles II, having heard it said in an earlier period of his career that he bore a strange resemblance to the ill-fated Stuarts.*[6] *A holder of his own contrivance is*

2. An altercation or a row, generally in good fun.
3. A personification of the evil spirit of the sea (usually found in the expression "Gone to Davy Jones's locker," i.e., dead).
4. I.e., Goa, a former Portuguese colony in India.
5. I.e., an English private boarding house. In early drafts of the play Hook represented a headmaster and the stuffy British institutions of higher learning. However, as Barrie revised the play, he associated Hook with a satanic if not conflicted aristocrat turned pirate.
6. Members of a Scottish and English royal house, "ill-fated" because, as rulers of England, two were beheaded and one was deposed. They included Charles II (1630–1685; r. 1660–85), whose extravagance set the tone of the Restoration period (i.e., the restoration of the English monarchy) in reaction against the severity of the Puritan Commonwealth that preceded it.

*in his mouth enabling him to smoke two cigars at once. Those, however, who
have seen him in the flesh, which is an inadequate term for his earthly tenement,
agree that the grimmest part of him is his iron claw.*

They continue their distasteful singing as they disembark—

> Avast, belay, yo ho, heave to,
> A-pirating we go,
> And if we're parted by a shot
> We're sure to meet below!

NIBS, *the only one of the boys who has not sought safety in his tree, is seen for
a moment near the lagoon, and Starkey's pistol is at once up-raised. The captain
twists his hook in him.*)

STARKEY (*abject*)   Captain, let go!

HOOK   Put back that pistol, first.

STARKEY   'Twas one of those boys you hate; I could have shot him dead.

HOOK   Ay, and the sound would have brought Tiger Lily's redskins on us. Do you
want to lose your scalp?

SMEE (*wriggling his cutlass pleasantly*)   That is true. Shall I after him, Captain, and
tickle him with Johnny Corkscrew? Johnny is a silent fellow.

HOOK   Not now. He is only one, and I want to mischief all the seven. Scatter and
look for them. (*The boatswain whistles his instructions, and the men disperse on
their frightful errand. With none to hear save* SMEE, HOOK *becomes confidential.*)
Most of all I want their captain, Peter Pan. 'Twas he cut off my arm. I have waited
long to shake his hand with this. (*Luxuriating*) Oh, I'll tear him!

SMEE (*always ready for a chat*)   Yet I have oft heard you say your hook was worth a
score of hands, for combing the hair and other homely[7] uses.

HOOK   If I was a mother I would pray to have my children born with this instead of
that (*his left arm creeps nervously behind him. He has a galling remembrance*).
Smee, Pan flung my arm to a crocodile that happened to be passing by.

SMEE   I have often noticed your strange dread of crocodiles.

HOOK (*pettishly*)   Not of crocodiles but of that one crocodile. (*He lays bare a lacerated
heart.*) The brute liked my arm so much, Smee, that he has followed me ever since,
from sea to sea, and from land to land, licking his lips for the rest of me.

SMEE (*looking for the bright side*)   In a way it is a sort of compliment.

HOOK (*with dignity*)   I want no such compliments; I want Peter Pan, who first gave
the brute his taste for me. Smee, that crocodile would have had me before now,
but by a lucky chance he swallowed a clock, and it goes tick, tick, tick, tick inside
him; and so before he can reach me I hear the tick and bolt. (*He emits a hollow
rumble.*) Once I heard it strike six within him.

SMEE (*sombrely*)   Some day the clock will run down, and then he'll get you.

HOOK (*a broken man*)   Ay, that is the fear that haunts me. (*He rises.*) Smee, this seat
is hot; odds, bobs,[8] hammer and tongs, I am burning.

(*He has been sitting, he thinks, on one of the island mushrooms, which are of
enormous size. But this is a hand-painted one placed here in times of danger to
conceal a chimney. They remove it, and tell-tale smoke issues; also, alas, the
sound of children's voices.*)

SMEE   A chimney!

---

7. Household, domestic.   8. An archaic exclamation.

HOOK (*avidly*) Listen! Smee, 'tis plain they live here, beneath the ground. (*He replaces the mushroom. His brain works tortuously.*)

SMEE (*hopefully*) Unrip your plan, Captain.

HOOK To return to the boat and cook a large rich cake of jolly thickness with sugar on it, green sugar. There can be but one room below, for there is but one chimney. The silly moles had not the sense to see that they did not need a door apiece. We must leave the cake on the shore of the mermaids' lagoon. These boys are always swimming about there, trying to catch the mermaids. They will find the cake and gobble it up, because, having no mother, they don't know how dangerous 'tis to eat rich damp cake. They will die!

SMEE (*fascinated*) It is the wickedest, prettiest policy ever I heard of.

HOOK (*meaning well*) Shake hands on 't.

SMEE No, Captain, no.

(*He has to link with the hook, but he does not join in the song.*)

HOOK   Yo ho, yo ho, when I say 'paw',
                    By fear they're overtook,
                    Naught's left upon your bones when you
                    Have shaken hands with Hook!

(*Frightened by a tug at his hand,* SMEE *is joining in the chorus when another sound stills them both. It is a tick, tick as of a clock, whose significance* HOOK *is, naturally, the first to recognise. 'The crocodile!' he cries, and totters from the scene.* SMEE *follows. A huge crocodile, of one thought compact, passes across, ticking, and oozes after them. The wood is now so silent that you may be sure it is full of redskins.* TIGER LILY *comes first. She is the belle of the Piccaninny⁹ tribe, whose braves would all have her to wife, but she wards them off with a hatchet. She puts her ear to the ground and listens, then beckons, and* GREAT BIG LITTLE PANTHER *and the tribe are around her, carpeting the ground. Far away someone treads on a dry leaf.*)

TIGER LILY Pirates! (*They do not draw their knives; the knives slip into their hands.*) Have um scalps? What you say?

PANTHER Scalp um, oho, velly quick.

THE BRAVES (*in corroboration*) Ugh, ugh, wah.

(*A fire is lit and they dance round and over it till they seem part of the leaping flames.* TIGER LILY *invokes Manitou;¹ the pipe of peace is broken; and they crawl off like a long snake that has not fed for many moons.* TOOTLES *peers after the tail and summons the other boys, who issue from their holes.*)

TOOTLES They are gone.

SLIGHTLY (*almost losing confidence in himself*) I do wish Peter was here.

FIRST TWIN H'sh! What is that? (*He is gazing at the lagoon and shrinks back.*) It is wolves, and they are chasing Nibs!

(*The baying wolves are upon them quicker than any boy can scuttle down his tree.*)

NIBS (*falling among his comrades*) Save me, save me!

TOOTLES What should we do?

SECOND TWIN What would Peter do?

SLIGHTLY Peter would look at them through his legs; let us do what Peter would do.

---

9. Originally, a word used in the West Indies to mean "baby" (probably from the Portuguese *pequenino*, "very small"); an offensive term for a black child.

1. The supernatural power that, according to some Native American traditions, permeates all things (literally, "spirit" in languages in the Algonquian family).

(The boys advance backwards, looking between their legs at the snarling red-eyed enemy, who trot away foiled.)

FIRST TWIN *(swaggering)* We have saved you, Nibs. Did you see the pirates?

NIBS *(sitting up, and agreeably aware that the centre of interest is now to pass to him)* No, but I saw a wonderfuller thing, Twin. *(All mouths open for the information to be dropped into them.)* High over the lagoon I saw the loveliest great white bird. It is flying this way. *(They search the firmament)*.

TOOTLES What kind of a bird, do you think?

NIBS *(awed)* I don't know; but it looked so weary, and as it flies it moans 'Poor Wendy.'

SLIGHTLY *(instantly)* I remember now there are birds called Wendies.

FIRST TWIN *(who has flown to a high branch)* See, it comes, the Wendy! *(They all see it now.)* How white it is! *(A dot of light is pursuing the bird malignantly.)*

TOOTLES That is Tinker Bell. Tink is trying to hurt the Wendy. *(He makes a cup of his hands and calls)* Hullo, Tink! *(A response comes down in the fairy language.)* She says Peter wants us to shoot the Wendy.

NIBS Let us do what Peter wishes.

SLIGHTLY Ay, shoot it; quick, bows and arrows.

TOOTLES *(first with his bow)* Out of the way, Tink; I'll shoot it. *(His bolt goes home, and WENDY, who has been fluttering among the treetops in her white nightgown, falls straight to earth. No one could be more proud than TOOTLES)*. I have shot the Wendy; Peter will be so pleased. *(From some tree on which TINK is roosting comes the tinkle we can now translate, 'You silly ass.' TOOTLE falters.)* Why do you say that? *(The others feel that he may have blundered, and draw away from TOOTLES.)*

SLIGHTLY *(examining the fallen one more minutely)* This is no bird; I think it must be a lady.

NIBS *(who would have preferred it to be a bird)* And Tootles had killed her.

CURLY Now I see, Peter was bringing her to us. *(They wonder for what object.)*

SECOND TWIN To take care of us? *(Undoubtedly for some diverting purpose.)*

OMNES[2] *(although every one of them had wanted to have a shot at her)* Oh, Tootles!

TOOTLES *(gulping)* I did it. When ladies used to come to me in dreams I said 'Pretty mother,' but when she really came I shot her! *(He perceives the necessity of a solitary life for him.)* Friends, goodbye.

SEVERAL *(not very enthusiastic)* Don't go.

TOOTLES I must; I am so afraid of Peter.

(He has gone but a step toward oblivion when he is stopped by a crowing as of some victorious cock.)

OMNES Peter!

(They make a paling of themselves in front of WENDY as PETER skims round the treetops and reaches earth.)

PETER Greetings, boys! *(Their silence chafes him.)* I am back; why do you not cheer? Great news, boys, I have brought at last a mother for us all.

SLIGHTLY *(vaguely)* Ay, ay.

PETER She flew this way; have you not seen her?

SECOND TWIN *(as PETER evidently thinks her important)* Oh mournful day!

TOOTLES *(making a break in the paling)* Peter, I will show her to you.

THE OTHERS *(closing the gap)* No, no.

TOOTLES *(majestically)* Stand back all, and let Peter see.

2. All (Latin).

(*The paling dissolves, and* PETER *sees* WENDY *prone on the ground.*)

PETER   Wendy, with an arrow in her heart! (*He plucks it out.*) Wendy is dead. (*He is not so much pained as puzzled.*)

CURLY   I thought it was only flowers that die.

PETER   Perhaps she is frightened at being dead? (*None of them can say as to that.*) Whose arrow? (*Not one of them looks at* TOOTLES.)

TOOTLES   Mine, Peter.

PETER (*raising it as a dagger*)   Oh, dastard hand!

TOOTLES (*kneeling and baring his breast*)   Strike, Peter; strike true.

PETER (*undergoing a singular experience*)   I cannot strike; there is something stays my hand.

(*In fact* WENDY's *arm has risen.*)

NIBS   'Tis she, the Wendy lady. See, her arm. (*To help a friend.*) I think she said 'Poor Tootles.'

PETER (*investigating*)   She lives!

SLIGHTLY (*authoritatively*)   The Wendy lady lives.

(*The delightful feeling that they have been cleverer than they thought comes over them and they applaud themselves.*)

PETER (*holding up a button that is attached to her chain*)   See, the arrow struck against this. It is a kiss I gave her; it has saved her life.

SLIGHTLY   I remember kisses; let me see it. (*He takes it in his hand.*) Ay, that is a kiss.

PETER   Wendy, get better quickly and I'll take you to see the mermaids. She is awfully anxious to see a mermaid.

(TINKER BELL, *who may have been off visiting her relations, returns to the wood and, under the impression that* WENDY *has been got rid of, is whistling as gaily as a canary. She is not wholly heartless, but is so small that she has only room for one feeling at a time.*)

CURLY   Listen to Tink rejoicing because she thinks the Wendy is dead! (*Regardless of spoiling another's pleasure*) Tink, the Wendy lives.

(TINK *gives expression to fury*)

SECOND TWIN (*tell-tale*)   It was who said that you wanted us to shoot the Wendy.

PETER   She said that? Then listen, Tink, I am your friend no more.

(*There is a note of acerbity in Tink's reply; it may mean 'Who wants you?'*) Begone from me for ever. (*Now it is a very wet tinkle.*)

CURLY   She is crying.

TOOTLES   She says she is your fairy.

PETER (*who knows they are not worth worrying about*)   Oh well, not for ever, but for a whole week.

(TINK *goes off sulking, no doubt with the intention of giving all her friends an entirely false impression of Wendy's appearance.*)

                    Now what shall we do with Wendy?

CURLY   Let us carry her down into the house.

SLIGHTLY   Ay, that is what one does with ladies.

PETER   No, you must not touch her; it wouldn't be sufficiently respectful.

SLIGHTLY   That is what I was thinking.

TOOTLES   But if she lies there she will die.

SLIGHTLY   Ay, she will die. It is a pity, but there is no way out.

PETER   Yes, there is. Let us build a house around her! (*Cheers again, meaning that no difficulty baffles* PETER.) Leave all to me. Bring the best of what we have. Gut our house. Be sharp! (*They race down their trees.*)

> (*While* PETER *is engrossed in measuring* WENDY *so that the house may fit her,* JOHN *and* MICHAEL, *who have probably landed on the island with a bump, wander forward, so draggled and tired that if you were to ask* MICHAEL *whether he is awake or asleep he would probably answer 'I haven't tried yet.'*)

MICHAEL (*bewildered*)   John, John, wake up. Where is Nana, John?

JOHN (*with the help of one eye but not always the same eye*)   It is true, we did fly! (*Thankfully*) And here is Peter. Peter, is this the place?

> (PETER *alas, has already forgotten them, as soon maybe he will forget* WENDY. *The first thing she should do now that she is here is to sew a handkerchief for him, and knot it as a jog to his memory.*)

PETER (*curtly*)   Yes.

MICHAEL   Where is Wendy? (PETER *points.*)

JOHN (*who still wears his hat*)   She is asleep.

MICHAEL   John, let us wake her and get her to make supper for us.

> (*Some of the boys emerge, and he pinches one.*)

John, look at them!

PETER (*still house-building*)   Curly, see that these boys help in the building of the house.

JOHN   Build a house?

CURLY   For the Wendy.

JOHN (*feeling that there must be some mistake here*)   For Wendy? Why, she is only a girl.

CURLY   That is why we are her servants?

JOHN (*dazed*)   Are you Wendy's servants?

PETER   Yes, and you also. Away with them. (*In another moment they are woodsmen hacking at trees, with* CURLY *as overseer.*) Slightly, fetch a doctor. (SLIGHTLY *reels and goes. He returns professionally in John's hat.*) Please, sir, are you a doctor?

SLIGHTLY (*trembling in his desire to give satisfaction*)   Yes, my little man.

PETER   Please, sir, a lady lies very ill.

SLIGHTLY (*taking care not to fall over her*)   Tut, tut, where does she lie?

PETER   In yonder glade. (*It is a variation of a game they play.*)

SLIGHTLY   I will put a glass thing in her mouth. (*He inserts an imaginary thermometer in Wendy's mouth and gives it a moment to record its verdict. He shakes it and then consults it.*)

PETER (*anxiously*)   How is she?

SLIGHTLY   Tut, tut, this has cured her.

PETER (*leaping joyously*)   I am glad.

SLIGHTLY   I will call again in the evening. Give her beef tea[3] out of a cup with a spout to it, tut, tut.

> (*The boys are running up with odd articles of furniture.*)

PETER (*with an already fading recollection of the Darling nursery*)   These are not good enough for Wendy. How I wish I knew the kind of house she would prefer!

FIRST TWIN   Peter, she is moving in her sleep.

TOOTLES (*opening Wendy's mouth and gazing down into the depth.*)   Lovely!

---

3. Beef broth.

PETER   Oh, Wendy, if you could sing the kind of house you would like to have.
            (*It is as if she had heard him.*)
WENDY (*without opening her eyes*)

>   I wish I had a woodland house,
>   The littlest ever seen,
>   With funny little red walls
>   And roof of mossy green.

(*In the time she sings this and two other verses, such is the urgency of Peter's silent orders that they have knocked down trees, laid a foundation and put up the walls and roof, so that she is now hidden from view. 'Windows,' cries* PETER, *and* CURLY *rushes them in, 'Roses,' and* TOOTLES *arrives breathless with a festoon for the door. Thus springs into existence the most delicious little house for beginners.*)

FIRST TWIN   I think it is finished.
PETER   There is no knocker on the door. (TOOTLES *hangs up the sole of his shoe.*)
    There is no chimney; we must have a chimney.
            (*They await his deliberations anxiously.*)
JOHN (*unwisely critical*)   It certainly does need a chimney.
            (*He is again wearing his hat, which* PETER *seizes, knocks the top off it and places on the roof. In the friendliest way smoke begins to come out of the hat.*)
PETER (*with his hand on the knocker*)   All look your best; the first impression is awfully important. (*He knocks, and after a dreadful moment of suspense, in which they cannot help wondering if any one is inside, the door opens and who should come out but* WENDY! *She has evidently been tidying a little. She is quite surprised to find that she has nine children.*)
WENDY (*genteelly*)   Where am I?
SLIGHTLY   Wendy lady, for you we built this house.
NIBS AND TOOTLES   Oh, say you are pleased.
WENDY (*stroking the pretty thing*)   Lovely, darling house!
FIRST TWIN   And we are your children.
WENDY (*affecting surprise*)   Oh?
OMNES (*kneeling, with outstretched arms*)   Wendy lady, be our mother! (*Now that they know it is pretend they acclaim her greedily.*)
WENDY (*not to make herself too cheap*)   Ought I? Of course it is frightfully fascinating; but you see I am only a little girl; I have no real experience.
OMNES   That doesn't matter. What we need is just a nice motherly person.
WENDY   Oh dear, I feel that is just exactly what I am.
OMNES   It is, it is, we saw it at once.
WENDY   Very well then, I will do my best. (*In their glee they go dancing obstreperously round the little house, and she sees she must be firm with them as well as kind.*) Come inside at once, you naughty children, I am sure your feet are damp. And before I put you to bed I have just time to finish the story of Cinderella.
            (*They all troop into the enchanting house, whose not least remarkable feature is that it holds them. A vision of* LIZA *passes, not perhaps because she has any right to be there; but she has so few pleasures and is so young that we just let her have a peep at the little house. By and by* PETER *comes out and marches up and down with drawn sword, for the pirates can be heard carousing far away on the lagoon, and the wolves are on the prowl. The little house, its walls so red*)

and its roof so mossy, looks very cosy and safe, with a bright light showing through the blind, the chimney smoking beautifully, and PETER *on guard. On our last sight of him it is so dark that we just guess he is the little figure who has fallen asleep by the door. Dots of light come and go. They are inquisitive fairies having a look at the house. Any other child in their way they would mischief, but they just tweak Peter's nose and pass on. Fairies, you see, can touch him.)*

ACT III. THE MERMAIDS' LAGOON

It is the end of a long playful day on the lagoon. The sun's rays have persuaded him to give them another five minutes, for one more race over the waters before he gathers them up and lets in the moon. There are many mermaids here, going plop-plop, and one might attempt to count the tails did they not flash and disappear so quickly. At times a lovely girl leaps in the air seeking to get rid of her excess of scales, which fall in a silver shower as she shakes them off. From the coral grottoes beneath the lagoon, where are the mermaids' bed-chambers, comes fitful music.

One of the most bewitching of these blue-eyed creatures is lying lazily on Marooners' Rock, combing her long tresses and noting effects in a transparent shell. Peter and his band are in the water unseen behind the rock, whither they have tracked her as if she were a trout, and at a signal ten pairs of arms come whack upon the mermaid to enclose her. Alas, this is only what was meant to happen, for she hears the signal (which is the crow of a cock) and slips through their arms into the water. It has been such a near thing that there are scales on some of their hands. They climb on to the rock crestfallen.

WENDY *(preserving her scales as carefully as if they were rare postage stamps)*   I did so want to catch a mermaid.

PETER *(getting rid of his)*   It is awfully difficult to catch a mermaid.

  (The mermaids at times find it just as difficult to catch him, though he sometimes joins them in their one game, which consists in lazily blowing their bubbles into the air and seeing who can catch them. The number of bubbles PETER *has flown away with! When the weather grows cold mermaids migrate to the other side of the world, and he once went with a great shoal of them half the way.)*

They are such cruel creatures, Wendy, that they try to pull boys and girls like you into the water and drown them.

WENDY *(too guarded by this time to ask what he means precisely by 'like you', though she is very desirous of knowing)*   How hateful!

  (She is slightly different in appearance now, rather rounder, while JOHN *and* MICHAEL *are not quite so round. The reason is that when new lost children arrive at his underground home* PETER *finds new trees for them to go up and down by, and instead of fitting the tree to them he makes them fit the tree. Sometimes it can be done by adding or removing garments, but if you are bumpy, or the tree is an odd shape, he has things done to you with a roller, and after that you fit.*

  The other boys are now playing King of the Castle, throwing each other into the water, taking headers and so on; but these two continue to talk.)

PETER   Wendy, this is a fearfully important rock. It is called Marooners' Rock. Sailors are marooned, you know, when their captain leaves them on a rock and sails away.

WENDY   Leaves them on this little rock to drown?

PETER *(lightly)*   Oh, they don't live long. Their hands are tied, so that they can't swim. When the tide is full this rock is covered with water, and then the sailor drowns.

(WENDY *is uneasy as she surveys the rock, which is the only one in the lagoon and no larger than a table. Since she last looked around a threatening change has come over the scene. The sun has gone, but the moon has not come. What has come is a cold shiver across the waters which has sent all the wiser mermaids to their coral recesses. They know that evil is creeping over the lagoon. Of the boys* PETER *is of course the first to scent it, and he has leapt to his feet before the words strike the rock—*

'And if we're parted by a shot
We're sure to meet below.'

The games on the rock and around it end so abruptly that several divers are checked in the air. There they hang waiting for the word of command from PETER. *When they get it they strike the water simultaneously, and the rock is at once as bare as if suddenly they had been blown off it. Thus the pirates find it deserted when their dinghy strikes the rock and is nearly stove in by the concussion.*)

SMEE   Luff, you spalpeen,[4] luff! (*They are* SMEE *and* STARKEY, *with* TIGER LILY, *their captive, bound hand and foot.*) What we have got to do is to hoist the redskin on to the rock and leave her there to drown.

(*To one of her race this is an end darker than death by fire or torture, for it is written in the laws of the Piccaninnies that there is no path through water to the happy hunting ground. Yet her face is impassive; she is the daughter of a chief and must die as a chief's daughter; it is enough.*)

STARKEY (*chagrined because she does not mewl*)   No mewling. This is your reward for prowling round the ship with a knife in your mouth.

TIGER LILY (*stoically*)   Enough said.

SMEE (*who would have preferred a farewell palaver*)   So that's it! On to the rock with her, mate.

STARKEY (*experiencing for perhaps the last time the stirrings of a man*)   Not so rough, Smee; roughish, but not so rough.

SMEE (*dragging her on to the rock*)   It is the captain's orders.

(*A stave has in some past time been driven into the rock, probably to mark the burial place of hidden treasure, and to this they moor the dinghy.*)

WENDY (*in the water*)   Poor Tiger Lily!

STARKEY   What was that? (*The children bob.*)

PETER (*who can imitate the captain's voice so perfectly that even the author has a dizzy feeling that at times he was really* HOOK)   Ahoy there, you lubbers!

STARKEY   It is the captain; he must be swimming out to us.

SMEE (*calling*)   We have put the redskin on the rock, Captain.

PETER   Set her free.

SMEE   But, Captain——

PETER   Cut her bonds, or I'll plunge my hook in you.

SMEE   This is queer!

STARKEY (*unmanned*)   Let us follow the captain's orders.

(*They undo the thongs and* TIGER LILY *slides between their legs into the lagoon, forgetting in her haste to utter her war-cry, but* PETER *utters it for her, so naturally that even the lost boys are deceived. It is at this moment that the voice of the true* HOOK *is heard.*)

4. Rascal.

HOOK   Boat ahoy!

SMEE (*relieved*)   It is the captain.

     (HOOK *is swimming, and they help him to scale the rock. He is in gloomy mood.*)

STARKEY   Captain, is all well?

SMEE   He sighs.

STARKEY   He sighs again.

SMEE (*counting*)   And yet a third time he sighs. (*With foreboding*) What's up, Captain?

HOOK (*who has perhaps found the large rich damp cake untouched*)   The game is up. Those boys have found a mother!

STARKEY   Oh evil day!

SMEE   What is a mother?

WENDY (*horrified*)   He doesn't know!

HOOK (*sharply*)   What was that?

     (PETER *makes the splash of a mermaid's tail.*)

STARKEY   One of them mermaids.

HOOK   Dost not know, Smee? A mother is——(*he finds it more difficult to explain than he had expected, and looks about him for an illustration. He finds one in a great bird which drifts past in a nest as large as the roomiest basin.*) There is a lesson in mothers for you! The nest must have fallen into the water, but would the bird desert her eggs? (PETER, *who is now more or less off his head, makes the sound of a bird answering in the negative. The nest is borne out of sight.*)

STARKEY   Maybe she is hanging about here to protect Peter?

     (HOOK's *face clouds still further and* PETER *just manages not to call out that he needs no protection.*)

SMEE (*not usually a man of ideas*)   Captain, could we not kidnap these boys' mother and make her our mother?

HOOK   Obesity and bunions, 'tis a princely scheme. We will seize the children, make them walk the plank, and Wendy shall be our mother!

WENDY   Never! (*Another splash from* PETER.)

HOOK   What say you, bullies?

SMEE   There is my hand on't.

STARKEY   And mine.

HOOK   And there is my hook. Swear. (*All swear.*) But I had forgot; where is the redskin?

SMEE (*shaken*)   That is all right, Captain; we let her go.

HOOK (*terrible*)   Let her go?

SMEE   'Twas your own orders, Captain.

STARKEY (*whimpering*)   You called over the water to us to let her go.

HOOK   Brimstone and gall, what cozening is here? (*Disturbed by their faithful faces*) Lads, I gave no such order.

SMEE   'Tis passing queer.

HOOK (*addressing the immensities*)   Spirit that haunts this dark lagoon tonight, dost hear me?

PETER (*in the same voice*)   Odds, bobs, hammer and tongs, I hear you.

HOOK (*gripping the stave for support*)   Who are you, stranger, speak.

PETER (*who is only too ready to speak*)   I am Jas Hook, Captain of the *Jolly Roger*.

HOOK (*now white to the gills*)   No, no, you are not.

PETER   Brimstone and gall, say that again and I'll cast anchor in you.

HOOK   If you are Hook, come tell me, who am I?

PETER A codfish, only a codfish.

HOOK (*aghast*) A codfish?

SMEE (*drawing back from him*) Have we been captained all this time by a codfish?

STARKEY It's lowering to our pride.

HOOK (*feeling that his ego is slipping from him*) Don't desert me, bullies.[5]

PETER (*top-heavy*) Paw, fish, paw!

> (*There is a touch of the feminine in* HOOK, *as in all the greatest pirates, and it prompts him to try the guessing game.*)

HOOK Have you another name?

PETER (*falling to the lure*) Ay, ay.

HOOK (*thirstily*) Vegetable?

PETER No.

HOOK Mineral?

PETER No.

HOOK Animal?

PETER (*after a hurried consultation with* TOOTLES) Yes.

HOOK Man?

PETER (*with scorn*) No.

HOOK Boy?

PETER Yes.

HOOK Ordinary boy?

PETER No!

HOOK Wonderful boy?

PETER (*to* WENDY's *distress*) Yes!

HOOK Are you in England?

PETER No.

HOOK Are you here?

PETER Yes.

HOOK (*beaten, though he feels he has very nearly got it*) Smee, you ask him some questions.

SMEE (*rummaging his brains*) I can't think of a thing.

PETER Can't guess, can't guess! (*Foundering in his cockiness.*) Do you give it up?

HOOK (*eagerly*) Yes.

PETER All of you?

SMEE AND STARKEY Yes.

PETER (*crowing*) Well, then, I am Peter Pan!

> (*Now they have him.*)

HOOK Pan! Into the water, Smee. Starkey, mind the boat. Take him dead or alive!

PETER (*who still has all his baby teeth*) Boys, lam into the pirates!

> (*For a moment the only two we can see are in the dinghy, where* JOHN *throws himself on* STARKEY. STARKEY *wriggles into the lagoon and* JOHN *leaps so quickly after him that he reaches it first. The impression left on* STARKEY *is that he is being attacked by the* TWINS. *The water becomes stained. The dinghy drifts away. Here and there a head shows in the water, and once it is the head of the crocodile. In the growing gloom some strike at their friends,* SLIGHTLY *getting* TOOTLES *in the fourth rib while he himself is pinked by* CURLY. *It looks as if the boys were getting the worse of it, which is perhaps just as well at this point, because* PETER,

---

5. Mates.

who will be the determining factor in the end, has a perplexing way of changing sides if he is winning too easily. Hook's iron claw makes a circle of black water round him from which opponents flee like fishes. There is only one prepared to enter that dreadful circle. His name is PAN. *Strangely, it is not in the water that they meet.* HOOK *has risen to the rock to breathe, and at the same moment* PETER *scales it on the opposite side. The rock is now wet and as slippery as a ball, and they have to crawl rather than climb. Suddenly they are face to face.* PETER *gnashes his pretty teeth with joy, and is gathering himself for the spring when he sees he is higher up the rock than his foe. Courteously he waits;* HOOK *sees his intention, and taking advantage of it claws twice.* PETER *is untouched, but unfairness is what he never can get used to, and in his bewilderment he rolls off the rock. The crocodile, whose tick has been drowned in the strife, rears its jaws, and* HOOK, *who has almost stepped into them, is pursued by it to land. All is quiet on the lagoon now, not a sound save little waves nibbling at the rock, which is smaller than when we last looked at it. Two boys appear with the dinghy, and the others despite their wounds climb into it. They send the cry 'Peter— Wendy' across the waters, but no answer comes.)*

NIBS   They must be swimming home.

JOHN   Or flying.

FIRST TWIN   Yes, that is it. Let us be off and call to them as we go.

(The dinghy disappears with its load, whose hearts would sink if they knew of the peril of WENDY *and her captain. From near and far away come the cries 'Peter—Wendy' till we no longer hear them.*

Two small figures are now on the rock, but they have fainted. A mermaid who has dared to come back in the stillness stretches up her arms and is slowly pulling WENDY *into the water to drown her.* WENDY *starts up just in time.)*

WENDY   Peter!

(He rouses himself and looks around him.)

Where are we, Peter?

PETER   We are on the rock, but it is getting smaller. Soon the water will be over it. Listen!

(They can hear the wash of the relentless little waves.)

WENDY   We must go.

PETER   Yes.

WENDY   Shall we swim or fly?

PETER   Wendy, do you think you could swim or fly to the island without me?

WENDY   You know I couldn't, Peter; I am just a beginner.

PETER   Hook wounded me twice. *(He believes it; he is so good at pretend that he feels the pain, his arms hang limp.)* I can neither swim nor fly.

WENDY   Do you mean we shall both be drowned?

PETER   Look how the water is rising!

(They cover their faces with their hands. Something touches WENDY *as lightly as a kiss.)*

PETER *(with little interest)*   It must be the tail of the kite we made for Michael; you remember it tore itself out of his hands and floated away. *(He looks up and sees the kite sailing overhead.)* The kite! Why shouldn't it carry you? *(He grips the tail and pulls, and the kite responds.)*

WENDY   Both of us!

PETER   It can't lift two. Michael and Curly tried.

(She knows very well that if it can lift her it can lift him also, for she has been told by the boys as a deadly secret that one of the queer things about him is that he is no weight at all. But it is a forbidden subject.)

WENDY I won't go without you. Let us draw lots which is to stay behind.

PETER And you a lady, never! *(The tail is in her hands, and the kite is tugging hard. She holds out her mouth to* PETER, *but he knows they cannot do that.)* Ready, Wendy!

(The kite draws her out of sight across the lagoon.

The waters are lapping over the rock now, and PETER *knows that it will soon be submerged. Pale rays of light mingle with the moving clouds, and from the coral grottoes is to be heard a sound, at once the most musical and the most melancholy in the Never Land, the mermaids calling to the moon to rise.* PETER *is afraid at last, and a tremor runs through him, like a shudder passing over the lagoon; but on the lagoon one shudder follows another till there are hundreds of them, and he feels just the one.)*

PETER *(with a drum beating in his breast as if he were a real boy at last)*   To die will be an awfully big adventure.

(The blind rises again, and the lagoon is now suffused with moonlight. He is on the rock still, but the water is over his feet. The nest is nearer, and the bird, after cooing a message to him, leaves it and wings her way upwards. PETER, *who knows the bird language, slips into the nest, first removing the two eggs and placing them in Starkey's hat, which has been left on the stave. The hat drifts away from the rock, but he uses the stave as a mast. The wind is driving him toward the open sea. He takes off his shirt, which he had forgotten to remove while bathing, and unfurls it as a sail. His vessel tacks, and he passes from sight, naked and victorious. The bird returns and sits on the hat.)*

ACT IV. THE HOME UNDER THE GROUND

We see simultaneously the home under the ground with the children in it and the wood above ground with the redskins on it. Below, the children are gobbling their evening meal; above, the redskins are squatting in their blankets near the little house guarding the children from the pirates. The only way of communicating between these two parties is by means of the hollow trees.

The home has an earthen floor, which is handy for digging in if you want to go fishing; and owing to there being so many entrances there is not much wall space. The table at which the lost ones are sitting is a board on top of a live tree trunk, which has been cut flat but has such growing pains that the board rises as they eat, and they have sometimes to pause in their meals to cut a bit more off the trunk. Their seats are pumpkins or the large gay mushrooms of which we have seen an imitation one concealing the chimney. There is an enormous fireplace which is in almost any part of the room where you care to light it, and across this Wendy has stretched strings, made of fibre, from which she hangs her washing. There are also various tomfool things in the room of no use whatever.

Michael's basket bed is nailed high up on the wall as if to protect him from the cat, but there is no indication at present of where the others sleep. At the back between two of the tree trunks is a grindstone, and near it is a lovely hole, the size of a band-box, with a gay curtain drawn across so that you cannot see what is inside. This is Tink's withdrawing-room and bed-chamber, and it is just as well that you cannot see inside, for it is so exquisite in its decoration and in the personal apparel spread out on the bed that you could scarcely resist making off with something. Tink is within at present, as one can guess from a glow showing through the chinks. It is her own glow, for though she has a chandelier for the look of the thing, of course she lights her residence herself. She is probably wasting valuable time just now wondering whether to put on the smoky blue or the apple-blossom.

All the boys except Peter are here, and WENDY *has the head of the table, smiling complacently at their captivating ways, but doing her best at the same time to see that they keep the rules about hands-off-the-table, no-two-to-speak-at-once, and so on. She is wearing romantic woodland garments, sewn by herself, with red berries in her hair which go charmingly with her complexion, as she knows; indeed she searched for red berries the morning after she reached the island. The boys are in picturesque attire of her contrivance, and if these don't always fit well the fault is not hers but the wearers', for they constantly put on each other's things when they put on anything at all. Michael is in his cradle on the wall. First Twin is apart on a high stool and wears a dunce's cap, another invention of Wendy's, but not wholly successful because everybody wants to be dunce.*

It is a pretend meal this evening, with nothing whatever on the table, not a mug, nor a crust, nor a spoon. They often have these suppers and like them on occasions as well as the other kind, which consist chiefly of bread-fruit, tappa rolls, yams, mammee apples and banana splash, washed down with calabashes of poe-poe.[6] The pretend meals are not Wendy's idea; indeed she was rather startled to find, on arriving, that Peter knew of no other kind, and she is not absolutely certain even now that he does eat the other kind, though no one appears to do it more heartily. He insists that the pretend meals should be partaken of with gusto, and we see his band doing their best to obey orders.

WENDY (*her fingers to her ears, for their chatter and clatter are deafening*) Si-lence! Is your mug empty, Slightly?

SLIGHTLY (*who would not say this if he had a mug*) Not quite empty, thank you.

NIBS Mummy, he has not even begun to drink his poe-poe.

SLIGHTLY (*seizing his chance, for this is tale-bearing*) I complain of Nibs!

    (JOHN *holds up his hand.*)

WENDY Well, John?

JOHN May I sit in Peter's chair as he is not here?

WENDY In your father's chair? Certainly not.

JOHN He is not really our father. He did not even know how to be a father till I showed him.

    (*This is insubordination.*)

SECOND TWIN I complain of John!

    (*The gentle* TOOTLES *raises his hand.*)

TOOTLES (*who has the poorest opinion of himself*) I don't suppose Michael would let me be baby?

MICHAEL No, I won't.

TOOTLES May I be dunce?

FIRST TWIN (*from his perch*) No. It's awfully difficult to be dunce.

TOOTLES As I can't be anything important would any of you like to see me do a trick?

OMNES No.

TOOTLES (*subsiding*) I hadn't really any hope.

    (*The tale-telling breaks out again.*)

---

6. I.e., poi, a Hawaiian dish made from taro or kalo root (not usually a drink). "Tappa": a kind of unwoven cloth made by Polynesians from bark. "Mammee apples": the fruit of a tropical tree native to America.

NIBS   Slightly is coughing on the table.

CURLY   The twins began with tappa rolls.

SLIGHTLY   I complain of Nibs!

NIBS   I complain of Slightly!

WENDY   Oh dear, I am sure I sometimes think that spinsters are to be envied.

MICHAEL   Wendy, I am too big for a cradle.

WENDY   You are the littlest, and a cradle is such a nice homely thing to have about a house. You others can clear away now. (*She sits down on a pumpkin near the fire to her usual evening occupation, darning.*) Every heel with a hole in it!

> (*The boys clear away with dispatch, washing dishes they don't have in a non-existent sink and stowing them in a cupboard that isn't there. Instead of sawing the table-leg tonight they crush it into the ground like a concertina, and are now ready for play, in which they indulge hilariously.*
>
> *A movement of the Indians draws our attention to the scene above. Hitherto, with the exception of* PANTHER, *who sits on guard on top of the little house, they have been hunkering in their blankets, mute but picturesque; now all rise and prostrate themselves before the majestic figure of* PETER, *who approaches through the forest carrying a gun and game bag. It is not exactly a gun. He often wanders away alone with this weapon, and when he comes back you are never absolutely certain whether he has had an adventure or not. He may have forgotten it so completely that he says nothing about it; and then when you go out you find the body. On the other hand he may say a great deal about it, and yet you never find the body. Sometimes he comes home with his face scratched, and tells* WENDY, *as a thing of no importance, that he got these marks from the little people for cheeking them at a fairy wedding, and she listens politely, but she is never quite sure, you know; indeed the only one who is sure about anything on the island is* PETER.)

PETER   The Great White Father is glad to see the Piccaninny braves protecting his wigwam from the pirates.

TIGER LILY   The Great White Father save me from pirates. Me his velly nice friend now; no let pirates hurt him.

BRAVES   Ugh, ugh, wah!

TIGER LILY   Tiger Lily has spoken.

PANTHER   Loola, loola! Great Big Little Panther has spoken.

PETER   It is well. The Great White Father has spoken.

> (*This has a note of finality about it, with the implied 'And now shut up,' which is never far from the courteous receptions of well-meaning inferiors by born leaders of men. He descends his tree, not unheard by* WENDY.)

WENDY   Children, I hear your father's step. He likes you to meet him at the door. (PETER *scatters pretend nuts among them and watches sharply to see that they crunch with relish.*) Peter, you just spoil them, you know!

JOHN (*who would be incredulous if he dare*)   Any sport, Peter?

PETER   Two tigers and a pirate.

JOHN (*boldly*)   Where are their heads?

PETER (*contracting his little brows*)   In the bag.

JOHN (*No, he doesn't say it. He backs away.*)

WENDY (*peeping into the bag*)   They are beauties! (*She has learned her lesson.*)

FIRST TWIN   Mummy, we all want to dance.

WENDY   The mother of such an armful dance!

     SLIGHTLY   As it is Saturday night?

(*They have long lost count of the days, but always if they want to do anything special they say this is Saturday night, and then they do it.*)

WENDY   Of course it is Saturday night, Peter? (*He shrugs an indifferent assent.*) On with your nighties first.

(*They disappear into various recesses, and PETER and WENDY with her darning are left by the fire to dodder parentally. She emphasises it by humming a verse of 'John Anderson my Jo',*[7] *which has not the desired effect on PETER. She is too loving to be ignorant that he is not loving enough, and she hesitates like one who knows the answer to her question.*)

What is wrong, Peter?

PETER (*scared*)   It is only pretend, isn't it, that I am their father?

WENDY (*drooping*)   Oh yes.

(*His sigh of relief is without consideration for her feelings.*)

But they are ours, Peter, yours and mine.

PETER (*determined to get at facts, the only things that puzzle him*)   But not really?

WENDY   Not if you don't wish it.

PETER   I don't.

WENDY (*knowing she ought not to probe but driven to it by something within*)   What are your exact feelings for me, Peter?

PETER (*in the classroom*)   Those of a devoted son, Wendy.

WENDY (*turning away*)   I thought so.

PETER   You are so puzzling. Tiger Lily is just the same; there is something or other she wants to be to me, but she says it is not my mother.

WENDY (*with spirit*)   No, indeed it isn't.

PETER   Then what is it?

WENDY   It isn't a lady to tell.

(*The curtain of the fairy chamber opens slightly, and TINK, who has doubtless been eavesdropping, tinkles a laugh of scorn.*)

PETER (*badgered*)   I suppose she means that she wants to be my mother.

(*Tink's comment is 'You silly ass.'*)

WENDY (*who has picked up some of the fairy words*)   I almost agree with her!

(*The arrival of the boys in their nightgowns turns Wendy's mind to practical matters, for the children have to be arranged in line and passed or not passed for cleanliness. SLIGHTLY is the worst. At last we see how they sleep, for in a babel the great bed which stands on end by day against the wall is unloosed from custody and lowered to the floor. Though large, it is a tight fit for so many boys, and WENDY has made a rule that there is to be no turning round until one gives the signal, when all turn at once.*

FIRST TWIN is the best dancer and performs mightily on the bed and in it and out of it and over it to an accompaniment of pillow fights by the less agile; and then there is a rush at WENDY.)

NIBS   Now the story you promised to tell us as soon as we were in bed!

WENDY (*severely*)   As far as I can see you are not in bed yet.

(*They scramble into the bed, and the effect is as of a boxful of sardines.*)

WENDY (*drawing up her stool*)   Well, there was once a gentleman——

CURLY   I wish he had been a lady.

NIBS   I wish he had been a white rat.

---

7. Song by the Scottish poet Robert Burns (1759–1796). "Jo": sweetheart.

WENDY   Quiet! There was a lady also. The gentleman's name was Mr Darling and the lady's name was Mrs Darling——

JOHN   I knew them!

MICHAEL (*who has been allowed to join the circle*)   I think I knew them.

WENDY   They were married, you know; and what do you think they had?

NIBS   White rats?

WENDY   No, they had three descendants. White rats are descendants also. Almost everything is a descendant. Now these three children had a faithful nurse called Nana.

MICHAEL (*alas*)   What a funny name!

WENDY   But Mr Darling—(*faltering*) or was it Mrs Darling?—was angry with her and chained her up in the yard; so all the children flew away. They flew away to the Never Land, where the lost boys are.

CURLY   I just thought they did; I don't know how it is, but I just thought they did.

TOOTLES   Oh, Wendy, was one of the lost boys called Tootles?

WENDY   Yes, he was.

TOOTLES (*dazzled*)   Am I in a story? Nibs, I am in a story!

PETER (*who is by the fire making Pan's pipes with his knife, and is determined that* WENDY *shall have fair play, however beastly a story he may think it*)   A little less noise there.

WENDY (*melting over the beauty of her present performance, but without any real qualms*)   Now I want you to consider the feelings of the unhappy parents with all their children flown away. Think, oh think, of the empty beds. (*The heartless ones think of them with glee.*)

FIRST TWIN (*cheerfully*)   It's awfully sad.

WENDY   But our heroine knew that her mother would always leave the window open for her progeny to fly back by; so they stayed away for years and had a lovely time.
        (PETER *is interested at last.*)

FIRST TWIN   Did they ever go back?

WENDY (*comfortably*)   Let us now take a peep into the future. Years have rolled by, and who is this elegant lady of uncertain age alighting at London station?
        (*The tension is unbearable.*)

NIBS   Oh, Wendy, who is she?

WENDY (*swelling*)   Can it be—yes—no—yes, it is the fair Wendy!

TOOTLES   I am glad.

WENDY   Who are the two noble portly figures accompanying her? Can they be John and Michael? They are. (*Pride of* MICHAEL.) 'See, dear brothers,' says Wendy, pointing upward, 'there is the window standing open.' So up they flew to their loving parents, and pen cannot inscribe the happy scene over which we draw a veil. (*Her triumph is spoilt by a groan from* PETER *and she hurries to him.*) Peter, what is it? (*Thinking he is ill, and looking lower than his chest.*) Where is it?

PETER   It isn't that kind of pain. Wendy, you are wrong about mothers. I thought like you about the window, so I stayed away for moons and moons, and then I flew back, but the window was barred, for my mother had forgotten all about me and there was another little boy sleeping in my bed.
        (*This is a general damper.*)

JOHN   Wendy, let us go back!

WENDY   Are you sure mothers are like that?

PETER   Yes.

WENDY   John, Michael! (*She clasps them to her.*)

FIRST TWIN (*alarmed*)   You are not to leave us, Wendy?

WENDY   I must.

NIBS   Not tonight?

WENDY   At once. Perhaps mother is in half-mourning by this time! Peter, will you make the necessary arrangements?
>   (*She asks it in the steely tones women adopt when they are prepared secretly for opposition.*)

PETER (*coolly*)   If you wish it.
>   (*He ascends his tree to give the redskins their instructions. The lost boys gather threateningly round* WENDY.)

CURLY   We won't let you go!

WENDY (*with one of those inspirations women have, in an emergency, to make use of some male who need otherwise have no hope*)   Tootles, I appeal to you.

TOOTLES (*leaping to his death if necessary*)   I am just Tootles and nobody minds me, but the first who does not behave to Wendy I will blood him severely. (PETER *returns.*)

PETER (*with awful serenity*)   Wendy, I told the braves to guide you through the wood as flying tires you so. Then Tinker Bell will take you across the sea. (*A shrill tinkle from the boudoir probably means 'and drop her into it'.*)

NIBS (*fingering the curtain which he is not allowed to open*)   Tink, you are to get up and take Wendy on a journey. (*Star-eyed*) She says she won't!

PETER (*taking a step toward that chamber*)   If you don't get up, Tink, and dress at once—— She is getting up!

WENDY (*quivering now that the time to depart has come*)   Dear ones, if you will all come with me I feel almost sure I can get my father and mother to adopt you.
>   (*There is joy at this, not that they want parents, but novelty is their religion.*)

NIBS   But won't they think us rather a handful?

WENDY (*a swift reckoner*)   Oh no, it will only mean having a few beds in the drawing-room; they can be hidden behind screens on first Thursdays.[8]
>   (*Everything depends on* PETER.)

OMNES   Peter, may we go?

PETER (*carelessly through the pipes to which he is giving a finishing touch*)   All right.
>   (*They scurry off to dress for the adventure.*)

WENDY (*insinuatingly*)   Get your clothes, Peter.

PETER (*skipping about and playing fairy music on his pipes, the only music he knows*)   I am not going with you, Wendy.

WENDY   Yes, Peter.

PETER   No.
>   (*The lost ones run back gaily, each carrying a stick with a bundle on the end of it.*)

WENDY   Peter isn't coming!
>   (*All the faces go blank.*)

JOHN (*even* JOHN)   Peter not coming!

TOOTLES (*overthrown*)   Why, Peter?

PETER (*his pipes more riotous than ever*)   I just want always to be a little boy and to have fun.

---

8. I.e., the day when Mrs. Darling was "at home" to receive visitors.

(There is a general fear that they are perhaps making the mistake of their lives.) Now then, no fuss, no blubbering. *(With dreadful cynicism)* I hope you will like your mothers! Are you ready, Tink? Then lead the way.

(TINK *darts up any tree, but she is the only one. The air above is suddenly rent with shrieks and the clash of steel. Though they cannot see, the boys know that* HOOK *and his crew are upon the Indians. Mouths open and remain open, all in mute appeal to* PETER. *He is the only boy on his feet now, a sword in his hand, the same he slew Barbicue with; and in his eye is the lust of battle.*

We can watch the carnage that is invisible to the children. HOOK *has basely broken the two laws of Indian warfare, which are that the redskins should attack first, and that it should be at dawn. They have known the pirate whereabouts since, early in the night, one of Smee's fingers crackled. The brushwood has closed behind their scouts as silently as the sand on the mole;[9] for hours they have imitated the lonely call of the coyote; no stratagem has been overlooked, but, alas, they have trusted to the pale-faces' honour to await an attack at dawn, when his courage is known to be at the lowest ebb.* HOOK *falls upon them pell-mell, and one cannot withhold a reluctant admiration for the wit that conceived so subtle a scheme and the fell genius with which it is carried out. If the braves would rise quickly they might still have time to scalp, but this they are forbidden to do by the traditions of their race, for it is written that they must never express surprise in the presence of the pale-face. For a brief space they remain recumbent, not a muscle moving, as if the foe were here by invitation. Thus perish the flower of the Piccaninnies, though not unavenged, for with* LEAN WOLF *fall* ALF MASON *and* CANARY ROBB, *while other pirates to bite dust are* BLACK GILMOUR *and* ALAN HERB, *that same* HERB *who is still remembered at Manaos for playing skittles[1] with the mate of the Switch for each other's heads.* CHAY TURLEY, *who laughed with the wrong side of his mouth (having no other), is tomahawked by* PANTHER, *who eventually cuts a way through the shambles with* TIGER LILY *and a remnant of the tribe.*

This onslaught passes and is gone like a fierce wind. The victors wipe their cutlasses, and squint, ferret-eyed, at their leader. He remains, as ever, aloof in spirit and in substance. He signs to them to descend the trees, for he is convinced that PAN *is down there, and though he has smoked the bees it is the honey he wants. There is something in* PETER *that at all times goads this extraordinary man to frenzy; it is the boy's cockiness, which disturbs* HOOK *like an insect. If you have seen a lion in a cage futilely pursuing a sparrow you will know what is meant. The pirates try to do their captain's bidding, but the apertures prove to be not wide enough for them; he cannot even ram them down with a pole. He steals to the mouth of a tree and listens.)*

PETER *(prematurely)* All is over!

WENDY But who has won?

PETER Hst! If the Indians have won they will beat the tom-tom; it is always their signal of victory.

(HOOK *licks his lips at this and signs to* SMEE, *who is sitting on it, to hold up the tom-tom. He beats upon it with his claw, and listens for results.)*

TOOTLES The tom-tom!

PETER *(sheathing his sword)* An Indian victory!

(The cheers from below are music to the black hearts above.)

---

9. Pier, breakwater.
1. A game played by knocking down pins in a wooden frame. Manaos: Manaus, a city in west Brazil.

You are quite safe now, Wendy. Boys, goodbye. (*He resumes his pipes.*)

WENDY Peter, you will remember about changing your flannels,[2] won't you?

PETER Oh, all right!

WENDY And this is your medicine.

(*She puts something into a shell and leaves it on a ledge between two of the trees. It is only water, but she measures it out in drops.*)

PETER I won't forget.

WENDY Peter, what are you to me?

PETER (*through the pipes*) Your son, Wendy.

WENDY Oh, goodbye!

(*The travelers start upon their journey, little witting that* HOOK *has issued his silent orders: a man to the mouth of each tree, and a row of men between the trees and the little house. As the children squeeze up they are plucked from their trees, trussed, thrown like bales of cotton from one pirate to another, and so piled up in the little house. The only one treated differently is* WENDY, *whom* HOOK *escorts to the house on his arm with hateful politeness. He signs to his dogs to be gone, and they depart through the wood, carrying the little house with its strange merchandise and singing their ribald song. The chimney of the little house emits a jet of smoke fitfully, as if not sure what it ought to do just now.*

HOOK *and* PETER *are now, as it were, alone on the island. Below,* PETER *is on the bed, asleep, no weapon near him; above,* HOOK, *armed to the teeth, is searching noiselessly for some tree down which the nastiness of him can descend. Don't be too much alarmed by this; it is precisely the situation* PETER *would have chosen; indeed if the whole thing were pretend——. One of his arms droops over the edge of the bed, a leg is arched, and the mouth is not so tightly closed that we cannot see the little pearls. He is dreaming, and in his dreams he is always in pursuit of a boy who was never here, nor anywhere: the only boy who could beat him.*

HOOK *finds the tree. It is the one set apart for* SLIGHTLY, *who being addicted when hot to the drinking of water has swelled in consequence and surreptitiously scooped his tree for easier descent and egress. Down this the pirate wriggles a passage. In the aperture below his face emerges and goes green as he glares at the sleeping child. Does no feeling of compassion disturb his sombre breast? The man is not wholly evil: he has a Thesaurus in his cabin, and is no mean performer on the flute. What really warps him is a presentiment that he is about to fail. This is not unconnected with a beatific smile on the face of the sleeper, whom he cannot reach owing to being stuck at the foot of the tree. He, however, sees the medicine shell within easy reach, and to Wendy's draught he adds from a bottle five drops of poison distilled when he was weeping from the red in his eye. The expression on Peter's face merely implies that something heavenly is going on.* HOOK *worms his way upwards, and winding his cloak around him, as if to conceal his person from the night of which he is the blackest part, he stalks moodily toward the lagoon.*

A dot of light flashes past him and darts down the nearest tree, looking for PETER, *only for* PETER, *quite indifferent about the others when she finds him safe.*)

PETER (*stirring*) Who is that? (TINK *has to tell her tale, in one long ungrammatical*

<hr />

2. Flannel underwear.

sentence.) The redskins were defeated? Wendy and the boys captured by the pirates! I'll rescue her, I'll rescue her! (*He leaps first at his dagger, and then at his grindstone, to sharpen it.* TINK *alights near the shell, and rings out a warning cry.*) Oh, that is just my medicine. Poisoned? Who could have poisoned it? I promised Wendy to take it, and I will as soon as I have sharpened my dagger. (TINK, *who sees its red colour and remembers the red in the pirate's eye, nobly swallows the draught as Peter's hand is reaching for it.*) Why, Tink, you have drunk my medicine! (*She flutters strangely about the room, answering him now in a very thin tinkle.*) It was poisoned and you drank it to save my life! Tink, dear Tink, are you dying? (*He has never called her dear Tink before, and for a moment she is gay; she alights on his shoulder, gives his chin a loving bite, whispers 'You silly ass,' and falls on her tiny bed. The boudoir, which is lit by her, flickers ominously. He is on his knees by the opening.*)

Her light is growing faint, and if it goes out, that means she is dead! Her voice is so low I can scarcely tell what she is saying. She says—she says she thinks she could get well again if children believed in fairies! (*He rises and throws out his arms he knows not to whom, perhaps to the boys and girls of whom he is not one.*) Do you believe in fairies? Say quick that you believe! If you believe, clap your hands! (*Many clap, some don't, a few hiss. Then perhaps there is a rush of Nanas to the nurseries to see what on earth is happening. But* TINK *is saved.*) Oh, thank you, thank you, thank you! And now to rescue Wendy!

(TINK *is already as merry and impudent as a grig,[3] with not a thought for those who have saved her.* PETER *ascends his tree as if he were shot up it. What he is feeling is 'Hook or me this time!' He is frightfully happy. He soon hits the trail, for the smoke from the little house has lingered here and there to guide him. He takes wing.*)

Act V, Scene 1. The Pirate Ship

The stage directions for the opening of this scene are as follows:—1 Circuit Amber checked to 80. Battens, all Amber checked, 3 ship's lanterns alight, Arcs: prompt perch 1. Open dark amber flooding back, O.P.[4] perch open dark amber flooding upper deck. Arc on tall steps at back of cabin to flood back cloth. Open dark Amber. Warning for slide. Plank ready. Call Hook.

In the strange light thus described we see what is happening on the deck of the Jolly Roger, *which is flying the skull and crossbones and lies low in the water. There is no need to call Hook, for he is here already, and indeed there is not a pirate aboard who would dare to call him. Most of them are at present carousing in the bowels of the vessel, but on the poop Mullins is visible, in the only greatcoat on the ship, raking with his glass the monstrous rocks within which the lagoon is cooped. Such a lookout is supererogatory, for the pirate craft floats immune in the horror of her name.*

From Hook's cabin at the back Starkey appears and leans over the bulwark, silently surveying the sullen waters. He is bare-headed and is perhaps thinking with bitterness of his hat, which he sometimes sees still drifting past him with the Never bird sitting on it. The black pirate is asleep on deck, yet even in his dreams rolling mechanically out of the way when Hook draws near. The only sound to be heard is made by Smee at his sewing-machine, which lends a touch of domesticity to the night.

---

3. A lively person full of frolic and jest (usually appearing in the expression "merry / lively as a grig").

4. Orchestra pit.

Hook is now leaning against the mast, now prowling the deck, the double cigar in his mouth. With Peter surely at last removed from his path we, who know how vain a tabernacle is man, would not be surprised to find him bellied out by the winds of his success, but it is not so; he is still uneasy, looking long and meaninglessly at familiar objects, such as the ship's bell or the Long Tom, like one who may shortly be a stranger to them. It is as if Pan's terrible oath 'Hook or me this time!' had already boarded the ship.

HOOK (*communing with his ego*) How still the night is; nothing sounds alive. Now is the hour when children in their homes are a-bed; their lips bright-browned with the good-night chocolate, and their tongues drowsily searching for belated crumbs housed insecurely on their shining cheeks. Compare with them the children on this boat about to walk the plank. Split my infinitives, but 'tis my hour of triumph! (*Clinging to this fair prospect he dances a few jubilant steps, but they fall below his usual form.*) And yet some disky spirit compels me now to make my dying speech, lest when dying there may be no time for it. All mortals envy me, yet better perhaps for Hook to have had less ambition! O fame, fame, thou glittering bauble, what if the very—— (SMEE, *engrossed in his labours at the sewing-machine, tears a piece of calico with a rending sound which makes the Solitary think for a moment that the untoward has happened to his garments*). No little children love me. I am told they play at Peter Pan, and that the strongest always chooses to be Peter. They would rather be a Twin than Hook; they force the baby to be Hook. The baby! that is where the canker gnaws. (*He contemplates his industrious boatswain.*) 'Tis said they find Smee lovable. But an hour agone I found him letting the youngest of them try on his spectacles. Pathetic Smee, the Nonconformist pirate, a happy smile upon his face because he thinks they fear him! How can I break it to him that they think him lovable? No, bi-carbonate of Soda, no, not even—— (*Another rending of the calico disturbs him, and he has a private consultation with* STARKEY, *who turns him round and evidently assures him that all is well. The peroration of his speech is nevertheless for ever lost, as eight bells strikes and his crew pour forth in bacchanalian orgy. From the poop he watches their dance till it frets him beyond bearing.*) Quiet, you dogs, or I'll cast anchor in you! (*He descends to a barrel on which there are playing-cards, and his crew stand waiting, as ever, like whipped curs.*) Are all the prisoners chained, so that they can't fly away?

JUKES Ay, ay, Captain.

HOOK Then hoist them up.

STARKEY (*raising the door of the hold*) Tumble up, you ungentlemanly lubbers.
　　(*The terrified boys are prodded up and tossed about the deck.* HOOK *seems to have forgotten them; he is sitting by the barrel with his cards.*)

HOOK (*suddenly*) So! Now then, you bullies, six of you walk the plank tonight, but I have room for two cabin-boys. Which of you is it to be? (*He returns to his cards.*)

TOOTLES (*hoping to soothe him by putting the blame on the only person, vaguely remembered, who is always willing to act as a buffer*) You see, sir, I don't think my mother would like me to be a pirate. Would your mother like you to be a pirate, Slightly?

SLIGHTLY (*implying that otherwise it would be a pleasure to him to oblige*) I don't think so. Twin, would your mother like——

HOOK Stow this gab. (*To* JOHN) You boy, you look as if you had a little pluck in you. Didst never want to be a pirate, my hearty?

JOHN (*dazzled by being singled out*) When I was at school I—what do you think, Michael?

MICHAEL (*stepping into prominence*)   What would you call me if I joined?

HOOK   Blackbeard[5] Joe.

MICHAEL   John, what do you think?

JOHN   Stop, should we still be respectful subjects of King George?[6]

HOOK   You would have to swear 'Down with King George.'

JOHN (*grandly*)   Then I refuse!

MICHAEL   And I refuse.

HOOK   That seals your doom. Bring up their mother.

(WENDY *is driven up from the hold and thrown to him. She sees at the first glance that the deck has not been scrubbed for years.*)

So, my beauty, you are to see your children walk the plank.

WENDY (*with noble calmness*)   Are they to die?

HOOK   They are. Silence all, for a mother's last words to her children.

WENDY   These are my last words. Dear boys, I feel that I have a message to you from your real mothers, and it is this, 'We hope our sons will die like English gentlemen.'

(*The boys go on fire.*)

TOOTLES   I am going to do what my mother hopes. What are you to do, Twin?

FIRST TWIN   What my mother hopes. John, what are——

HOOK   Tie her up! Get the plank ready.

(WENDY *is roped to the mast; but no one regards her, for all eyes are fixed upon the plank now protruding from the poop over the ship's side. A great change, however, occurs in the time* HOOK *takes to raise his claw and point to this deadly engine.[7] No one is now looking at the plank: for the tick, tick of the crocodile is heard. Yet it is not to bear on the crocodile that all eyes slew round, it is that they may bear on* HOOK. *Otherwise prisoners and captors are equally inert, like actors in some play who have found themselves 'on' in a scene in which they are not personally concerned. Even the iron claw hangs inactive, as if aware that the crocodile is not coming for it. Affection for their captain, now cowering from view, is not what has given* HOOK *his dominance over the crew, but as the menacing sound draws nearer they close their eyes respectfully.*

There is no crocodile. It is PETER, *who has been circling the pirate ship, ticking as he flies far more superbly than any clock. He drops into the water and climbs aboard, warning the captives with upraised finger (but still ticking) not for the moment to give audible expression to their natural admiration. Only one pirate sees him,* WHIBBLES *of the eye patch, who comes up from below.* JOHN *claps a hand on Whibbles' mouth to stifle the groan; four boys hold him to prevent the thud;* PETER *delivers the blow, and the carrion is thrown overboard. 'One!' says* SLIGHTLY, *beginning to count.*

STARKEY *is the first pirate to open his eyes. The ship seems to him to be precisely as when he closed them. He cannot interpret the sparkle that has come into the faces of the captives, who are cleverly pretending to be as afraid as ever. He little knows that the door of the dark cabin has just closed on one more boy. Indeed it is for* HOOK *alone he looks, and he is a little surprised to see him.*)

STARKEY (*hoarsely*)   It is gone, Captain! There is not a sound.

(*The tenement that is* HOOK *heaves tumultuously and he is himself again.*)

5. Edward Teach (d. 1718), a privateer in the West Indies during the War of the Spanish Succession (1701–14) who then became a brutal pirate, preying on shipping as far north as the Virginia coast.
6. George V (1865–1936; r. 1910–36), king of England. His father, Edward VII (1841–1910; r. 1901–10), was king when *Peter Pan* was first staged.
7. Device, mechanical contrivance.

HOOK (*now convinced that some fair spirit watches over him*)   Then here is to Johnny
   Plank—

> Avast, belay, the English brig
> We took and quickly sank,
> And for a warning to the crew
> We made them walk the plank!

(*As he sings he capers detestably along an imaginary plank and his copy-cats do
likewise, joining in the chorus.*)

> Yo ho, yo ho, the frisky cat,
> You walks along it so,
> Till it goes down and you goes down
> To looral looral lo!

(*The brave children try to stem this monstrous torrent by breaking into the
National Anthem.*[8])

STARKEY (*paling*)   I don't like it, messmates!

HOOK   Stow that, Starkey. Do you boys want a touch of the cat[9] before you walk the
   plank? (*He is more pitiless than ever now that he believes he has a charmed life.*)
   Fetch the cat, Jukes; it is in the cabin.

JUKES   Ay, ay, sir. (*It is one of his commonest remarks, and is only recorded now
   because he never makes another. The stage direction 'Exit* JUKES*' has in this case a
   special significance. But only the children know that someone is awaiting this unfortunate in the cabin, and* HOOK *tramples them down as he resumes his ditty:*)

> Yo ho, yo ho, the scratching cat,
> Its tails are nine you know,
> And when they're writ upon your back,
> You're fit to——

(*The last words will ever remain a matter of conjecture, for from the dark cabin
comes a curdling screech which wails through the ship and dies away. It is
followed by a sound, almost more eerie in the circumstances, that can only be
likened to the crowing of a cock.*)

HOOK   What was that?

SLIGHTLY (*solemnly*)   Two!

(CECCO *swings into the cabin, and in a moment returns, livid.*)

HOOK (*with an effort*)   What is the matter with Bill Jukes, you dog?

CECCO   The matter with him is he is dead—stabbed.

PIRATE   Bill Jukes dead!

CECCO   The cabin is as black as a pit, but there is something terrible in there: the
   thing you heard a-crowing.

HOOK (*slowly*)   Cecco, go back and fetch me out that doodle-doo.

CECCO (*unstrung*)   No, Captain, no. (*He supplicates on his knees, but his master
   advances on him implacably.*)

---

8. "God Save the King" (1745).
9. Cat o' nine tails, a whip with multiple knotted cords fastened to its handle, used to punish sailors.

HOOK (*in his most syrupy voice*) Did you say you would go, Cecco?

(CECCO *goes. All listen. There is one screech, one crow.*)

SLIGHTLY (*as if he were a bell tolling*) Three!

HOOK S'death[1] and oddsfish, who is to bring me out that doodle-doo?

(*No one steps forward.*)

STARKEY (*injudiciously*) Wait till Cecco comes out.

(*The black looks of some others encourage him.*)

HOOK I think I heard you volunteer, Starkey.

STARKEY (*emphatically*) No, by thunder!

HOOK (*in that syrupy voice which might be more engaging when accompanied by his flute*) My hook thinks you did. I wonder if it would not be advisable, Starkey, to humour the hook?

STARKEY I'll swing before I go in there.

HOOK (*gleaming*) Is it mutiny? Starkey is ringleader. Shake hands, Starkey.

(STARKEY *recoils from the claw. It follows him till he leaps overboard.*)

Did any other gentleman say mutiny?

(*They indicate that they did not even know the late* STARKEY.)

SLIGHTLY Four!

HOOK I will bring out that doodle-doo myself.

(*He raises a blunderbuss but casts it from him with a menacing gesture which means that he has more faith in the claw. With a lighted lantern in his hand he enters the cabin. Not a sound is to be heard now on the ship, unless it be* SLIGHTLY *wetting his lips to say 'Five.'* HOOK *staggers out.*)

HOOK (*unsteadily*) Something blew out the light.

MULLINS (*with dark meaning*) Some—thing?

NOODLER What of Cecco?

HOOK He is as dead as Jukes.

(*They are superstitious like all sailors, and* MULLINS *has planted a dire conception in their minds.*)

COOKSON They do say as the surest sign a ship's accurst is when there is one aboard more than can be accounted for.

NOODLER I've heard he allus boards the pirate craft at last. (*With dreadful significance*) Has he a tail, Captain?

MULLINS They say that when he comes it is in the likeness of the wickedest man aboard.

COOKSON (*clinching it*) Has he a hook, Captain?

(*Knives and pistols come to hand, and there is a general cry 'The ship is doomed!' But it is not his dogs that can frighten* JAS HOOK. *Hearing something like a cheer from the boys he wheels round, and his face brings them to their knees.*)

HOOK So you like it, do you! By Caius and Balbus,[2] bullies, here is a notion: open the cabin door and drive them in. Let them fight the doodle-doo for their lives. If they kill him we are so much the better; if he kills them we are none the worse.

(*This masterly stroke restores their confidence; and the boys, affecting fear, are driven into the cabin. Desperadoes though the pirates are, some of them have been boys themselves, and all turn their backs to the cabin and listen, with arms outstretched to it as if to ward off the horrors that are being enacted there.*)

---

1. God's death (an oath).
2. Lucius Cornelius Balbus (fl. 72–40 B.C.E.), a Roman politician who was Caesar's ally and acted as his secretary. "Caius" (Gaius) is a common Roman name; here, perhaps C. Julius Caesar (100–44 B.C.E.), the Roman general and statesman.

Relieved by Peter of their manacles, and armed with such weapons as they can lay their hands on, the boys steal out softly as snowflakes, and under their captain's hushed order find hiding-places on the poop. He releases WENDY; *and now it would be easy for them all to fly away, but it is to be* HOOK *or him this time. He signs to her to join the others, and with awful grimness folding her cloak around him, the hood over his head, he takes her place by the mast, and crows.*)

MULLINS   The doodle-doo has killed them all!

SEVERAL   The ship's bewitched.

(*They are snapping at* HOOK *again.*)

HOOK   I've thought it out, lads; there is a Jonah[3] aboard.

SEVERAL (*advancing upon him*)   Ay, a man with a hook.

(*If he were to withdraw one step their knives would be in him, but he does not flinch.*)

HOOK (*temporising*)   No, lads, no, it is the girl. Never was luck on a pirate ship wi' a woman aboard. We'll right the ship when she has gone.

MULLINS (*lowering his cutlass*)   It's worth trying.

HOOK   Throw the girl overboard.

MULLINS (*jeering*)   There is none can save you now, missy.

PETER   There is one.

MULLINS   Who is that?

PETER (*casting off the cloak*)   Peter Pan, the avenger!

(*He continues standing there to let the effect sink in.*)

HOOK (*throwing out a suggestion*)   Cleave him to the brisket.[4]

(*But he has a sinking feeling that this boy has no brisket.*)

NOODLER   The ship's accurst!

PETER   Down, boys, and at them!

(*The boys leap from their concealment and the clash of arms resounds through the vessel. Man to man the pirates are the stronger, but they are unnerved by the suddenness of the onslaught and they scatter, thus enabling their opponents to hunt in couples and choose their quarry. Some are hurled into the lagoon; others are dragged from dark recesses. There is no boy whose weapon is not reeking save* SLIGHTLY, *who runs about with a lantern, counting, ever counting.*)

WENDY (*meeting* MICHAEL *in a moment's lull*)   Oh, Michael, stay with me, protect me!

MICHAEL (*reeling*)   Wendy, I've killed a pirate!

WENDY   It's awful, awful.

MICHAEL   No, it isn't, I like it, I like it.

(*He casts himself into the group of boys who are encircling* HOOK. *Again and again they close upon him and again and again he hews a clear space.*)

HOOK   Back, back, you mice. It's Hook; do you like him? (*He lifts up* MICHAEL *with his claw and uses him as a buckler. A terrible voice breaks in.*)

PETER   Put up your swords, boys. This man is mine.

(HOOK *shakes* MICHAEL *off his claw as if he were a drop of water, and these two antagonists face each other for their final bout. They measure swords at arms' length, make a sweeping motion with them, and bringing the points to the deck rest their hands upon the hilts.*)

---

3. In the biblical book of Jonah, sailors throw the prophet into the sea because God's anger at him has caused the storm that endangers them all.
4. The breast.

HOOK (*with curling lip*) So, Pan, this is all your doing!

PETER Ay, Jas Hook, it is all my doing.

HOOK Proud and insolent youth, prepare to meet thy doom.

PETER Dark and sinister man, have at thee.

(*Some say that he had to ask* TOOTLES *whether the word was sinister or canister.* HOOK *or* PETER *this time! They fall to without another word.* PETER *is a rare swordsman, and parries with dazzling rapidity, sometimes before the other can make his stroke.* HOOK, *if not quite so nimble in wrist play, has the advantage of a yard or two in reach, but though they close he cannot give the quietus with his claw, which seems to find nothing quite to tear at. He does not, especially in the most heated moments, quite see* PETER, *who to his eyes, now blurred or opened clearly for the first time, is less like a boy than a mote of dust dancing in the sun. By some impalpable stroke Hook's sword is whipped from his grasp, and when he stoops to raise it a little foot is on its blade. There is no deep gash on* HOOK, *but he is suffering torment as from innumerable jags.*)

BOYS (*exulting*) Now, Peter, now!

(PETER *raises the sword by its blade, and with an inclination of the head that is perhaps slightly overdone, presents the hilt to his enemy.*)

HOOK 'Tis some fiend fighting me! Pan, who and what art thou?

(*The children listen eagerly for the answer, none quite as eagerly as* WENDY.)

PETER (*at a venture*) I'm youth, I'm joy, I'm a little bird that has broken out of the egg.

HOOK To 't again!

(*He has now a damp feeling that this boy is the weapon which is to strike him from the lists[5] of man; but the grandeur of his mind still holds and, true to the traditions of his flag, he fights on like a human flail.* PETER *flutters round and through and over these gyrations as if the wind of them blew him out of the danger zone, and again and again he darts in and jags.*)

HOOK (*stung to madness*) I'll fire the powder magazine. (*He disappears they know not where.*)

CHILDREN Peter, save us!

(PETER, *alas, goes the wrong way and* HOOK *returns.*)

HOOK (*sitting on the hold with gloomy satisfaction*) In two minutes the ship will be blown to pieces.

(*They cast themselves before him in entreaty.*)

CHILDREN Mercy, mercy!

HOOK Back, you pewling spawn. I'll show you now the road to dusty death.[6] A holocaust[7] of children, there is something grand in the idea!

(PETER *appears with the smoking bomb in his hand and tosses it overboard.* HOOK *has not really had much hope, and he rushes at his other persecutors with his head down like some exasperated bull in the ring; but with bantering cries they easily elude him by flying among the rigging.*

Where is PETER? *The incredible boy has apparently forgotten the recent doings, and is sitting on a barrel playing upon his pipes. This may surprise others but does not surprise* HOOK. *Lifting a blunderbuss he strikes forlornly not at the boy but at the barrel, which is hurled across the deck.* PETER *remains sitting in*

---

5. The places of combat or contest.
6. An echo of Shakespeare, *Macbeth* (ca. 1606), "The way to dusty death" (5.5.22). "Pewling": i.e.,

puling, or whimpering.
7. Literally, a sacrifice consumed by fire.

the air still playing upon his pipes. At this sight the great heart of HOOK *breaks. That not wholly unheroic figure climbs the bulwarks murmuring 'Floreat Etona',[8] and prostrates himself into the water, where the crocodile is waiting for him open-mouthed.* HOOK *knows the purpose of this yawning cavity, but after what he has gone through he enters it like one greeting a friend.*

The curtain rises to show PETER *a very Napoleon[9] on his ship. It must not rise again lest we see him on the poop in Hook's hat and cigars, and with a small iron claw.*)

ACT V, SCENE 2. THE NURSERY AND THE TREETOPS

The old nursery appears again with everything just as it was at the beginning of the play, except that the kennel has gone and that the window is standing open. So Peter was wrong about mothers; indeed there is no subject on which he is so likely to be wrong.

Mrs Darling is asleep on a chair near the window, her eyes tired with searching the heavens. Nana is stretched out listless on the floor. She is the cynical one, and though custom has made her hang the children's night things on the fire-guard for an airing, she surveys them not hopefully but with some self-contempt.

MRS DARLING (*starting up as if we had whispered to her that her brats are coming back*) Wendy, John, Michael! (NANA *lifts a sympathetic paw to the poor soul's lap.*) I see you have put their night things out again, Nana! It touches my heart to watch you do that night after night. But they will never come back.

(*In trouble the difference of station can be completely ignored, and it is not strange to see these two using the same handkerchief. Enter* LIZA, *who in the gentleness with which the house has been run of late is perhaps a little more masterful than of yore.*)

LIZA (*feeling herself degraded by the announcement*) Nana's dinner is served.

(NANA, *who quite understands what are Liza's feelings, departs for the dining-room with our exasperating leisureliness, instead of running, as we would all do if we followed our instincts.*)

LIZA To think I have a master as have changed places with his dog!

MRS DARLING (*gently*) Out of remorse, Liza.

LIZA (*surely exaggerating*) I am a married woman myself. I don't think it's respectable to go to his office in a kennel, with the street boys running alongside cheering. (*Even this does not rouse her mistress, which may have been the honourable intention.*) There, that is the cab fetching him back! (*Amid interested cheers from the street the kennel is conveyed to its old place by a cabby and friend, and* MR DARLING *scrambles out of it in his office clothes.*)

MR DARLING (*giving her his hat loftily*) If you will be so good, Liza. (*The cheering is resumed.*) It is very gratifying!

LIZA (*contemptuous*) Lot of little boys.

MR DARLING (*with the new sweetness of one who has sworn never to lose his temper again*) There were several adults today.

(*She goes off scornfully with the hat and the two men, but he has not a word of*

---

8. May Eton flourish (Latin), the motto of Eton College, the famous private secondary school founded in 1440.

9. Napoléon Bonaparte (1769–1821), emperor of the French.

reproach for her. It ought to melt us when we see how humbly grateful he is for a kiss from his wife, so much more than he feels he deserves. One may think he is wrong to exchange into the kennel, but sorrow has taught him that he is the kind of man who whatever he does contritely he must do to excess; otherwise he soon abandons doing it.)

MRS DARLING (*who has known this for quite a long time*) What sort of a day have you had, George?

(*He is sitting on the floor by the kennel.*)

MR DARLING There were never less than a hundred running round the cab cheering, and when we passed the Stock Exchange the members came out and waved.

(*He is exultant but uncertain of himself, and with a word she could dispirit him utterly.*)

MRS DARLING (*bravely*) I am so proud, George.

MR DARLING (*commendation from the dearest quarter ever going to his head*) I have been put on a picture postcard, dear.

MRS DARLING (*nobly*) Never!

MR DARLING (*thoughtlessly*) Ah, Mary, we should not be such celebrities if the children hadn't flown away.

MRS DARLING (*startled*) George, you are sure you are not enjoying it?

MR DARLING (*anxiously*) Enjoying it! See my punishment: living in a kennel.

MRS DARLING Forgive me, dear one.

MR DARLING It is I who need forgiveness, always I, never you. And now I feel drowsy. (*He retires into the kennel.*) Won't you play me to sleep on the nursery piano? And shut that window, Mary dearest; I feel a draught.

MRS DARLING Oh, George, never ask me to do that. The window must always be left open for them, always, always.

(*She goes into the day nursery, from which we presently hear her playing the sad song of Margaret.*[1] *She little knows that her last remark has been overheard by a boy crouching at the window. He steals into the room accompanied by a ball of light.*)

PETER Tink, where are you? Quick, close the window. (*It closes.*) Bar it. (*The bar slams down.*) Now when Wendy comes she will think her mother has barred her out, and she will have to come back to me! (TINKER BELL *sulks.*) Now, Tink, you and I must go out by the door. (*Doors, however, are confusing things to those who are used to windows, and he is puzzled when he finds that this one does not open on to the firmament. He tries the other, and sees the piano player.*) It is Wendy's mother! (TINK *pops on to his shoulder and they peep together.*) She is a pretty lady, but not so pretty as my mother. (*This is a pure guess.*) She is making the box say 'Come home, Wendy.' You will never see Wendy again, lady, for the window is barred! (*He flutters about the room joyously like a bird, but has to return to that door.*) She has laid her head down on the box. There are two wet things sitting on her eyes. As soon as they go away another two come and sit on her eyes. (*She is heard moaning 'Wendy, Wendy, Wendy.'*) She wants me to unbar the window. I won't! She is awfully fond of Wendy. I am fond of her too. We can't both have her, lady! (*A funny feeling comes over him.*) Come on, Tink; we don't want any silly mothers. (*He opens the window and they fly out.*)

It is thus that the truants find entrance easy when they alight on the sill, JOHN to his credit having the tired MICHAEL on his shoulders. They have nothing else

---

1. A musical setting of the poem "Margaret's Song" (1808), by Johann Wolfgang von Goethe.

to their credit; no compunction for what they have done, not the tiniest fear that any just person may be awaiting them with a stick. The youngest is in a daze, but the two others are shining virtuously like holy people who are about to give two other people a treat.)

MICHAEL (*looking about him*)   I think I have been here before.

JOHN   It's your home, you stupid.

WENDY   There is your old bed, Michael.

MICHAEL   I had nearly forgotten.

JOHN   I say, the kennel!

WENDY   Perhaps Nana is in it.

JOHN (*peering*)   There is a man asleep in it.

WENDY (*remembering him by the bald patch*)   It's father!

JOHN   So it is!

MICHAEL   Let me see father. (*Disappointed*) He is not as big as the pirate I killed.

JOHN (*perplexed*)   Wendy, surely father didn't use to sleep in the kennel?

WENDY (*with misgivings*)   Perhaps we don't remember the old life as well as we thought we did.

JOHN (*chilled*)   It is very careless of mother not to be here when we come back.

    (*The piano is heard again.*)

WENDY   H'sh! (*She goes to the door and peeps.*) That is her playing!

    (*They all have a peep.*)

MICHAEL   Who is that lady?

JOHN   H'sh! It's mother.

MICHAEL   Then are you not really our mother, Wendy?

WENDY (*with conviction*)   Oh dear, it is quite time to be back!

JOHN   Let us creep in and put our hands over her eyes.

WENDY (*more considerate*)   No, let us break it to her gently.

    (*She slips between the sheets of her bed; and the others, seeing the idea at once, get into their beds. Then when the music stops they cover their heads. There are now three distinct bumps in the beds.* MRS DARLING *sees the bumps as soon as she comes in, but she does not believe she sees them.*)

MRS DARLING   I see them in their beds so often in my dreams that I seem still to see them when I am awake! I'll not look again. (*She sits down and turns away her face from the bumps, though of course they are still reflected in her mind.*) So often their silver voices call me, my little children whom I'll see no more.

    (*Silver voices is a good one, especially about* JOHN; *but the heads pop up.*)

WENDY (*perhaps rather silvery*)   Mother!

MRS DARLING (*without moving*)   That is Wendy.

JOHN (*quite gruff*)   Mother!

MRS DARLING   Now it is John.

MICHAEL (*no better than a squeak*)   Mother!

MRS DARLING   Now Michael. And when they call I stretch out my arms to them, but they never come, they never come!

    (*This time, however, they come, and there is joy once more in the Darling household. The little boy who is crouching at the window sees the joke of the bumps in the beds, but cannot understand what all the rest of the fuss is about.*

    The scene changes from the inside of the house to the outside, and we see MR DARLING *romping in at the door, with the lost boys hanging gaily to his coat-tails. So we may conclude that* WENDY *has told them to wait outside until she explains the situation to her mother, who has then sent* MR DARLING *down to tell them that they are adopted. Of course they could have flown in by the window like a covey of birds, but they think it better fun to enter by a door. There is a moment's trouble about* SLIGHTLY, *who somehow gets shut out. Fortunately* LIZA *finds him.*)

LIZA What is the matter, boy?

SLIGHTLY They have all got a mother except me.

LIZA (*starting back*) Is your name Slightly?

SLIGHTLY Yes'm.

LIZA Then I am your mother.

SLIGHTLY How do you know?

LIZA (*the good-natured creature*) I feel it in my bones.

(*They go into the house and there is none happier now than* SLIGHTLY, *unless it be* NANA *as she passes with the importance of a nurse who will never have another day off.* WENDY *looks out at the nursery window and sees a friend below, who is hovering in the air knocking off tall hats with his feet. The wearers don't see him. They are too old. You can't see* PETER *if you are old. They think he is a draught at the corner.*)

WENDY Peter!

PETER (*looking up casually*) Hullo, Wendy.

(*She flies down to him, to the horror of her mother, who rushes to the window.*)

WENDY (*making a last attempt*) You don't feel you would like to say anything to my parents, Peter, about a very sweet subject?

PETER No, Wendy.

WENDY About me, Peter?

PETER No. (*He gets out his pipes, which she knows is a very bad sign. She appeals with her arms to* MRS DARLING, *who is probably thinking that these children will all need to be tied to their beds at night.*)

MRS DARLING (*from the window*) Peter, where are you? Let me adopt you too.

(*She is the loveliest age for a woman, but too old to see* PETER *clearly.*)

PETER Would you send me to school?

MRS DARLING (*obligingly*) Yes.

PETER And then to an office?

MRS DARLING I suppose so.

PETER Soon I should be a man?

MRS DARLING Very soon.

PETER (*passionately*) I don't want to go to school and learn solemn things. No one is going to catch me, lady, and make me a man. I want always to be a little boy and to have fun.

(*So perhaps he thinks, but it is only his greatest pretend.*)

MRS DARLING (*shivering every time* WENDY *pursues him in the air*) Where are you to live, Peter?

PETER In the house we built for Wendy. The fairies are to put it high up among the treetops where they sleep at night.

WENDY (*rapturously*) To think of it!

MRS DARLING I thought all the fairies were dead.

WENDY (*almost reprovingly*) No indeed! Their mothers drop the babies into the Never birds' nests, all mixed up with the eggs, and the mauve fairies are boys and the white ones are girls, and there are some colours who don't know what they are. The row the children and the birds make at bath time is positively deafening.

PETER   I throw things at them.

WENDY   You will be rather lonely in the evenings, Peter.

PETER   I shall have Tink.

WENDY (*flying up to the window*)   Mother, may I go?

MRS DARLING (*gripping her for ever*)   Certainly not. I have got you home again, and I mean to keep you.

WENDY   But he does so need a mother.

MRS DARLING   So do you, my love.

PETER   Oh, all right.

MRS DARLING (*magnanimously*)   But, Peter, I shall let her go to you once a year for a week to do your spring cleaning.

> (WENDY *revels in this, but* PETER, *who has no notion what a spring cleaning is, waves a rather careless thanks.*)

MRS DARLING   Say good-night, Wendy.

WENDY   I couldn't go down just for a minute?

MRS DARLING   No.

WENDY   Good-night, Peter!

PETER   Good-night, Wendy!

WENDY   Peter, you won't forget me, will you, before spring-cleaning time comes?

> (*There is no answer, for he is already soaring high. For a moment after he is gone we still hear the pipes.* MRS DARLING *closes and bars the window.*)

We are dreaming now of the Never Land a year later. It is bedtime on the island, and the blind goes up to the whispers of the lovely Never music. The blue haze that makes the wood below magical by day comes up to the treetops to sleep, and through it we see numberless nests all lit up, fairies and birds quarrelling for possession, others flying around just for the fun of the thing and perhaps making bets about where the little house will appear tonight. It always comes and snuggles on some treetop, but you can never be sure which; here it is again, you see John's hat first as up comes the house so softly that it knocks some gossips off their perch. When it has settled comfortably it lights up, and out come Peter and Wendy.

Wendy looks a little older, but Peter is just the same. She is cloaked for a journey, and a sad confession must be made about her; she flies so badly now that she has to use a broomstick.

WENDY (*who knows better this time than to be demonstrative at partings*)   Well, good-bye, Peter; and remember not to bite your nails.

PETER   Goodbye, Wendy.

WENDY   I'll tell mother all about the spring cleaning and the house.

PETER (*who sometimes forgets that she has been here before*)   You do like the house?

WENDY   Of course it is small. But most people of our size wouldn't have a house at all. (*She should not have mentioned size, for he has already expressed displeasure at her growth. Another thing, one he has scarcely noticed, though it disturbs her, is that she does not see him quite so clearly now as she used to do.*) When you come for me next year, Peter—you will come, won't you?

PETER   Yes. (*Gloating*) To hear stories about me!

WENDY   It is so queer that the stories you like best should be the ones about yourself.

PETER (*touchy*)   Well, then?

WENDY   Fancy your forgetting the lost boys, and even Captain Hook!

PETER   Well, then?

WENDY   I haven't seen Tink this time.

PETER   Who?

WENDY   Oh dear! I suppose it is because you have so many adventures.

PETER (*relieved*)   'Course it is.

WENDY   If another little girl—if one younger than I am——(*She can't go on.*) Oh, Peter, how I wish I could take you up and squdge you! (*He draws back.*) Yes, I know. (*She gets astride her broomstick.*) Home! (*It carries her from him over the treetops. In a sort of way he understands what she means by 'Yes, I know,' but in most sorts of ways he doesn't. It has something to do with the riddle of his being. If he could get the hang of the thing his cry might become 'To live would be an awfully big adventure!' but he can never quite get the hang of it, and so no one is as gay as he. With rapturous face he produces his pipes, and the Never birds and the fairies gather closer till the roof of the little house is so thick with his admirers that some of them fall down the chimney. He plays on and on till we wake up.*)

THE END

1904   1928

BARBARA FIELD
b. 1933

Devoted to all aspects of theater for children and adults, Barbara Field has worked as educator, dramaturge, and playwright in many theaters throughout the United States. She was born in Buffalo, New York; attended high school in Atlantic City, New Jersey; and received her B.A. in 1955 from the University of Pennsylvania with a major in English. When she moved to Minneapolis the following year, she began studying theater arts, earning an M.A. from the University of Minnesota in 1971.

In 1971 Field became one of the founding members of the Playwrights' Center, which serves as a workshop to help young dramatists. In addition she served as dramaturge and playwright-in-residence at the Guthrie Theater in Minneapolis from 1974 to 1981. During that time she wrote a number of adaptations, notably *A Christmas Carol* (1975; from Charles Dickens), *Pantagleize*; (1977; from Michael de Ghelderode), and *Marriage* (1978; from Nikolai Gogol) for the Guthrie Theater. She wrote *Off the Ice* (1995) and collaborated on a musical, *The Skinflint* (1997), for the Repertory Theatre of St. Louis. Her *Great Expectations* (1986; Dickens) won a Los Angeles Drama Critics' Circle award for best adaptation. In 2003 her production of *Dreams in the Golden Country* premiered at the Kentucky Center's Theatre for Youth and Families, then toured the East Coast.

Field's adaptation of *A Christmas Carol* by Charles Dickens (1812–1870) has been produced by many other theaters in America, including the Goodman Theatre in Chicago, Actors Theatre of Louisville, and the Missouri Repertory Theater of Kansas City. It was revised in 1998 and has become a staple of the Guthrie Theater, which has staged the play every year since 1975. Though there have been numerous cinematic and theatrical adaptations of Dickens's *A Christmas Carol*, often produced at Christmas, Field's play is distinguished by her depiction of Scrooge as absorbed in business without pontification about his lack of social awareness. She follows Dickens's story line carefully and introduces elements of humor in portraying Scrooge's encounters with the ghosts. Dickens envisioned Christmas as a kind of secular celebration of community and of the sharing of wealth and good spirits, and Field manages to capture that spirit in her play.

A Christmas Carol, a story originally published at Christmastime in 1843, became an immediate success. Dickens had been disturbed by reports about the abuse of young people and growing poverty in England, and he intended in great part to remind the rich of their responsibilities to poor and starving people and to underscore the importance of charity. But instead of simply condemning the rich, Dickens depicted the possibility of individual and social transformation, emphasizing the importance of home and family for the moral and economic development of society. Dickens himself, who loved the theater, immediately grasped the dramatic potential of *A Christmas Carol*. He began giving public readings of the story, first for charity—to raise money for hospital treatment of disadvantaged children in London—and later as part of the highly lucrative speaking tours of his last two decades. By the end of the nineteenth century, dramatic adaptations had burgeoned. Christmas in England and America became identified with Dickens and his story, whose persistence in our culture into the twenty-first century, after thousands of presentations on stage and on television and movie screen, attests to the power of its sentiments.

A Christmas Carol

ACT I

Stave One: Marley's Ghost

A quartet sings, a funeral procession with a coffin enters, crosses the stage, as:

NARRATION   Marley was dead to begin with. There is no doubt whatever about that. Seven long years dead.

The death certificate was signed by the clergyman, the clerk, the undertaker, and the chief mourner. Scrooge signed it. And Scrooge's signature was as good as gold, for he was an excellent man of *business*.

Old Marley was as dead as a door-nail.

Mind! We don't mean to say we know of our own knowledge what there is particularly dead about a door-nail. I might have been inclined to regard a coffin-nail as the deadest piece of ironmongery in the trade. But the wisdom of our ancestors is in the simile and I shall not disturb it.

Permit me to repeat emphatically that Marley was dead as a door-nail.

Scrooge knew he was dead? Of course he did. How could it be otherwise? Scrooge and Marley were partners for I don't know how many years. Scrooge was his sole executor, his sole administrator, his sole friend, his sole mourner and his sole heir.

But even Scrooge was not so dreadfully cut up by the sad event, for he proved to be an excellent man of business on the very day of the funeral, for he solemnized it with a fine bargain.

SCROOGE *takes a paper from* MR. SNARKERS, *then exits.*

GRASPER   Wait—didn't he bury Mr. Marley today?

SNARKERS   Yes indeed, old Marley's gone to the devil at last.

GRASPER   And he's holding the wake at the stock exchange? The nerve!

They go.

Afternoon crossover. A throng of people in the street.

NARRATION   There is no doubt Marley was dead—you must understand this or nothing wonderful can come of our story. And yet his name still stood painted on the warehouse door. Scrooge had never bothered to paint it out. 'Scrooge and Marley.'

Oh! But he was a tight-fisted hand at the grindstone, was Scrooge! A squeezing, wrenching, grasping, scraping, clutching, covetous old sinner! Hard and sharp as flint, from which no steel had ever struck out generous fire; secret, and self-contained, and solitary as an oyster.

To edge his way along the crowded paths of life, warning all human sympathy to keep its distance, was the very thing he liked.

A quartet sings a carol as Scrooge's office comes on.

Once upon a time—of all good days in the year, on Christmas Eve—old Scrooge was busy in his counting-house.

It was cold, bleak, biting weather—foggy withal; but Scrooge carried his own low temperature always about with him. He iced his office in the dog days,[1] and didn't thaw it one degree at Christmas. External heat and cold had little influence on him.

Clock strikes three.

Three o'clock, but it was quite dark already. It had not been light all day.

SCROOGE *is at his desk.* CRATCHIT *is at his own counter, scribbling away. His fingers are nearly frozen. He tries to warm them at a candle. Futile.* CRATCHIT *sneezes,* SCROOGE *glares.*

Scrooge kept the coal box in his own room and so surely as the clerk, Bob Cratchit, came in with the shovel, the master predicted that it would be necessary for them to part.

Wherefore the clerk tried to warm himself at his candle, but not being a man of strong imagination, he failed.

Laughter off. FRED *enters.*

FRED   A merry Christmas, Uncle. God save you!

SCROOGE (*paying no attention*)   Bah! Humbug!

FRED   Christmas a humbug, Uncle? You don't mean that, I'm sure.

SCROOGE   I mean it. I mean it! Look at you—what right have you to be merry? You're poor enough.

FRED   What right have you to be dismal? You're rich enough.

SCROOGE   Bah! Humbug.

FRED   Don't be cross, Uncle.

SCROOGE   But I live in a world of fools. Merry Christmas? Out upon 'Merry Christmas!' What's Christmas to you but a time for paying bills without money; a time for finding yourself a year older, and not an hour richer?

FRED   Yes, but—

SCROOGE   If I had my way, every idiot who goes about with a 'Merry Christmas' on his lips should be boiled in his own pudding, and buried with a stake of holly in his heart—

FRED   Uncle!

SCROOGE   Nephew! You keep Christmas in your own way, and let me keep it in mine.

FRED   But you don't keep it.

SCROOGE   Let me leave it alone, then. What profit has it ever brought you?

FRED   It is true, I not have profited from Christmas, but I've always thought it a good time, a kind, forgiving, charitable, pleasant time. The only time in the long calendar of the year, in fact, when men and women open their shut-up hearts freely, and think of people below them as if they really were fellow passengers to the grave, and not another race of creatures bound on other journeys. And so, Uncle, though it has never put a scrap of gold or silver in my pocket, I believe that it *has* done me good, and *will* do me good; and I say, God bless it!

1. The heat of July and August, when Sirius (the Dog Star) is visible above the horizon at dawn.

BOB CRATCHIT *applauds.*

SCROOGE (*to* BOB) Let me hear another sound from *you*, and you'll spend your Christmas looking for a new situation. (*To* FRED.) Stop distracting my clerk, Nephew, or I'll bill you for his time!

FRED Uncle—

SCROOGE You're such a powerful speaker, Nephew, I wonder you don't go into Parliament.

FRED Come to dinner tomorrow, Uncle.

SCROOGE I'll see you in Hell, first—

NARRATION He said it—yes indeed he did. He went the whole length of the expression, and said he would see him in that extremity first.

FRED But why? Why? You have yet to meet my wife. Please, Uncle, come and dine with us—

SCROOGE 'Us.' I see you're still a prisoner of marital bliss. Why did you get married?

FRED Because I fell in love.

SCROOGE Because you fell in love?! Good afternoon!

FRED I want nothing from you; why cannot we be friends? I've never asked you for a penny, sir, and never shall.

SCROOGE Ha!

FRED Why are we enemies? We're family.

SCROOGE Good afternoon.

FRED I'm sorry to find you so resolute against me. But I came here in homage to Christmas, and I *will* keep my Christmas humor to the last. And so . . . a merry Christmas, Uncle—

SCROOGE Good afternoon.

FRED And a happy New Year—!

SCROOGE *hurls his paperweight at* FRED, *who catches it.*

SCROOGE Good afternoon!

FRED Why, thank you, Uncle, I shall treasure this fine paperweight.
        Going, stops at Cratchit's desk.
    Greetings of the season, Bob. And to your good wife.

CRATCHIT And the same to you, Mr. Fred, the same to you!

FRED *exits.*

SCROOGE There's another fellow—my clerk with fifteen shillings a week, and five mouths to feed—

CRATCHIT Six—

SCROOGE Even worse—talking about a merry Christmas. Next year I'll seek refuge in a mad house.

CRATCHIT Yes, sir.

SCROOGE What's that?

CRATCHIT Nothing, sir.
        Two charitable citizens of beatific countenance enter. BLAKELY *is round,* MR.
        FORREST *is lean and deaf as a post.*

CRATCHIT Two visitors, sir.

BLAKELY Scrooge and Marley's, I believe? Have I the pleasure of addressing Mr. Scrooge or Mr. Marley?

SCROOGE Addressing Mr. Marley would be no pleasure. Mr. Marley has been dead these seven years. (*Struck by a thought.*) Seven years ago, this very night.

BLAKELY We have no doubt his generosity has survived in his partner.

SCROOGE Oh? Why?

SCROOGE *resumes scribbling away at work.* MR. FORREST, *who hasn't heard a word, of course, goes on enthusiastically.*

FORREST   Mr. Scrooge, Mr. Marley: at this festive time of year it is with urgency that we provide for the poor and destitute. Many thousands are in want of the basic necessities. Hundreds of thousands are in want of common comforts, sir—

SCROOGE   Are there no prisons?

BLAKELY   Plenty of prisons.

SCROOGE   And the workhouses? They still exist?

BLAKELY   I wish I could say they did not.

SCROOGE   And the Treadmill?[2] The Poorhouse? They're still in full vigor?

BLAKELY   Both very busy, sir.

SCROOGE   Thank heavens—I was afraid they had been stopped in their useful course.

FORREST   We are raising a fund to buy the poor some food and means of warmth, Mr. Marley—

BLAKELY   Mr. Scrooge.

SCROOGE   It doesn't matter.

BLAKELY   At this time of year, want is felt keenly, and abundance rejoices. What shall I put you down for?

SCROOGE   Nothing.

BLAKELY   Ah, you wish to remain anonymous?

SCROOGE   I wish to be left alone. Since you ask me what I wish, gentlemen, that is my answer. I cannot afford the luxury of making idle people merry. I am taxed— outrageously taxed—to support those fine old institutions: the workhouse, the treadmill—

BLAKELY   Many can't go there, sir, and many would rather die than go there—

SCROOGE   If they had rather die, they had better do so, and decrease the surplus population.

　　　BLAKELY *drops his papers in horror.*

Besides, I don't *know* that to be true.

BLAKELY   But you *should* know it, sir.

SCROOGE   It's none of my business, and as mine occupies me profitably enough . . . good afternoon.

　　　BLAKELY *pulls* FORREST *out the door.*
　　　SCROOGE *and* CRATCHIT *resume work.*
　　　A boy stands in the doorway and starts to sing a carol.
　　　SCROOGE *chases him out with a ruler.*
　　　The city clocks strike seven. CRATCHIT *prepares to leave.*

SCROOGE (*mutters*)   Yes, I know it's time to close up.

NARRATION   In the street the fog and darkness thickened, and at length the hour of shutting up the counting-house arrived.

　　　Most shops and businesses had shut up early, and lords and laborers alike commenced their celebrations.

SCROOGE   You'll want all day tomorrow, I suppose?[3]

CRATCHIT   If quite convenient, sir.

---

2. Prisoners sentenced to hard labor might spend hours each day on a treadmill; and residents of poorhouses were also forced to work.

3. In the 1840s, Christmas was often treated as a normal workday.

SCROOGE It's *not* convenient—and it's not fair. If I was to deduct half a crown for your holiday, you'd think yourself ill-used.

CRATCHIT It's only once a year, sir.

SCROOGE A poor excuse for picking my pockets every December 25th. I am a victim—a victim of humbug! Cratchit, take your Christmas, but be here all the earlier next morning.

> SCROOGE *storms out.*

CRATCHIT I shall, sir. Thank you, Mr. Scrooge, and a merry—

> CRATCHIT *wraps his muffler round his neck and races out of the office like a boy released from school.*

> *Street activity. Carol quartet.*

NARRATION Scrooge took his melancholy dinner in his usual melancholy tavern; and having read all the newspapers, he beguiled the rest of the dinner hour with his favorite volume, his banking book.

He lived in a gloomy set of rooms which had once belonged to his deceased partner, Jacob Marley. No one lived there now but Scrooge.

The fog and frost so hung about the house that it seemed the Genius[4] of the Weather sat in mournful meditation on the threshold.

Now it was a fact that there was nothing peculiar about the knocker on the door, except that it was very large.

It was also a fact that Scrooge had seen it night and day during his whole residence in that place. It was also a fact that Scrooge was not a fanciful man.

And then let any man explain, if he can, how it happened that Scrooge saw in the knocker *not* a knocker, but—

> *A face appears in the door knocker.*

SCROOGE Jacob—Jacob Marley! No, it can't be you, you're dead.

NARRATION As Scrooge stared at it . . . it was a knocker once more.

Not being a man to be frightened by echoes, Scrooge entered through the door and slowly climbed the stairs.

> *The door slams shut, echoing loudly.*

NARRATION It was dark, but Scrooge cared not a button for that.

> SCROOGE *starts undressing for bed.*

SCROOGE I like the dark. Darkness is cheap, and cheapness is tonic for the sensible man. I like the cold. It nips the bones and keeps the blood from overheating. I like solitude. It makes me independent. No one can make demands on me, no one can do me injury, there's nothing I need share. I deem solitude to be a state of bliss!

> *He checks the room, locks the door.*

MARLEY'S VOICE Ebenezer . . .

SCROOGE No one behind the curtain, nothing under the bed . . . good.

NARRATION Thus secured against surprise, he put on his dressing gown and slippers, and sat down to eat his gruel.

SCROOGE Mrs. Grigsby—?

> MRS. GRIGSBY *enters, bringing a bowl of gruel. She goes.* SCROOGE *sits in his chair.*

NARRATION But there, floating on the top of the bowl, was the face of his old partner.

MARLEY'S VOICE Ebenezer Scrooge . . .

> SCROOGE *starts, throws the bowl away.*

---

4. Spirit.

SCROOGE Absurd! Humbug!

An old bell begins to ring. He gets up to look at it.
It stops ringing. He sits down.
The bell starts to ring again, joined by a cacophony of bells.

SCROOGE Is a man not to have a decent night's sleep?!

Suddenly, from the cellar comes a horrible clanking and rattling of chains. The cellar trap opens with a boom, and from below appears JACOB MARLEY.

SCROOGE How now, what do you want of me?

MARLEY Much.

SCROOGE Who are you?

MARLEY Ask me who I was.

SCROOGE You're mighty particular for a ghost. Well, who were you?

MARLEY In life I was your partner, Jacob Marley.

SCROOGE Jacob! You don't look at all well. Can you sit down?

MARLEY I can.

SCROOGE Then have a seat, and let me tell you all about our thriving business.

MARLEY *Business!!!*

SCROOGE I see, you haven't come to discuss business.

MARLEY You don't believe in me.

SCROOGE I don't.

MARLEY What evidence would you have of my reality besides your senses?

SCROOGE I don't know.

MARLEY Then why do you doubt your senses?

SCROOGE Because little things affect them. You might be the result of my dinner—
an undigested bit of beef, a blot of mustard, an undercooked potato—there's more
of the gravy than the grave about you, whatever you are!

MARLEY *raises a frightful cry and rattles his chains.*

SCROOGE (*on his knees*) Dreadful apparition, why do you trouble me?

MARLEY Man of the worldly mind, do you believe in me?

SCROOGE I do. I must. But why do spirits walk the earth, and why do they visit me?

MARLEY It is required of every man that his spirit must walk among his fellow man,
and if that spirit goes not forth in life, it is condemned to do so after death. It is
doomed to wander through the world—oh woe is me!—and witness what it might
have changed to happiness.

Again, MARLEY *cries out and rattles his chains.*

SCROOGE But why are you fettered, Jacob?

MARLEY I wear the chain I forged in life. I made it, link by link and yard by yard,
and of my own free will I wore it. Is its pattern strange to you? You have your own
chain, Ebenezer, and yours was as heavy as mine seven Christmas Eves ago . . .
and you have labored on yours since. It will be colder, heavier—

SCROOGE No, no—Jacob—Jacob Marley, speak comfort to me.

MARLEY I have none to give. Comfort is conveyed by other messengers, for other,
better kinds of men.

A bell strikes.

Nor have I time. I cannot stay, I cannot rest, I cannot linger anywhere. Mark me—
in life my spirit never roved beyond the narrow limits of our counting-house. Now
weary journeys lie before me.

SCROOGE Seven years, and traveling all the time?

MARLEY The whole time—no rest, no peace, incessant torture of remorse.

SCROOGE You travel fast?

MARLEY   On the wings of the wind.

SCROOGE   You must have covered a lot of ground in seven years—

MARLEY   Oh fellow-captive, regret alone cannot make amends for opportunities mis-used! Yet such was I, such was I.

SCROOGE   You were always a good man of business, Jacob.

MARLEY   *Business!!* Mankind was my business. The common welfare was my busi-ness. Charity, mercy, forbearance, benevolence were all my business, but I did not heed them. The dealings of my trade were but a drop of water in the comprehensive ocean of my business. Why did I walk through crowds of fellow-beings with my eyes turned away—

He holds up his chains.

Hear me, Ebenezer, my time is nearly gone.

SCROOGE   I will. But don't be hard on me, Jacob, and don't be so flowery—

A gong sounds.

MARLEY   My time is nearly gone. How it is that I appear before you in a shape that you can see, I may not tell. I have sat invisible beside you many and many a day.

SCROOGE *shivers.*

I come tonight to warn you that you have yet a chance and hope of escaping my fate . . . a chance and hope of my procuring.

SCROOGE   You were always a good friend to me, Jacob. Thank'ee.

MARLEY   You will be haunted by three spirits.

Scrooge's countenance falls.

SCROOGE   Is that the chance and hope you mentioned, Jacob?

MARLEY   It is. Expect the first tomorrow night, when the bell tolls one.

SCROOGE   Couldn't I take 'em all at once and have it over with?

MARLEY   Expect the second on the next night at the same hour. The third on the third night, when the last stroke of twelve has ceased to vibrate.

SCROOGE   I . . . think I'd rather not.

MARLEY   Without their visits you cannot hope to shun the path I tread.

Phantoms appear, confused sounds, voices, lights.

See how the air is filled with phantoms? They wander restlessly as I do.

SCROOGE   I—I know some of these ghosts—*knew* them.

MARLEY   The misery with us all is that we seek to interfere for good in human mat-ters, but have lost that power forever. Heed these spirits, Ebenezer Scrooge. Remember what has passed between us, and look to see me no more.

MARLEY *disappears down the trap.* SCROOGE *turns back into the room, checks it out, looks under the bed.*

SCROOGE   H-humbug!

He blows out his candle. It comes on again. Etc.

The bed curtains are closed.

NARRATION   Being much in need of repose, Scrooge fell asleep upon the instant.

Stave Two: The First of the Three Spirits

The stage is dark. Slowly Scrooge's bed comes into relief, and the bells of a nearby church begin to chime. SCROOGE *peeks through his bed curtains.*

SCROOGE   Ten . . . eleven . . . twelve—but it was past two when I went to bed—something's wrong with the clock—it's got an icicle in its works—

It's not possible I've slept through a whole day-and-a-half. It's not possible that it's now twelve noon and something's happened to the sun?!

It was a dream.

Or was it? "Expect the first ghost when the bell tolls one."
The church bell chimes the first quarter.
A quarter past twelve.
The bell chimes the half-hour.
Half past the hour.
The bell chimes the third quarter.
Quarter to it.
The bell chimes the hour.
The hour itself—
A city clock strikes one.
(*triumphant.*) And nothing else!
A light.
The GHOST OF CHRISTMAS PAST *opens the curtains.*

SCROOGE   Are you the spirit whose coming was foretold to me?

PAST   I am.

SCROOGE   Who and what are you?

PAST   I am the Ghost of Christmas Past.

SCROOGE   Long past?

PAST   No, your past. I am your memory, your transport, your history, your gadfly—come walk with me.

SCROOGE   Where are you going—what are you doing? What business brings you here?

PAST   *Business*? Your welfare, your education, your reclamation—

SCROOGE   This reclamation, how much will it cost me?

PAST   Take heed! Beware! Look sharp!
The bed disappears.

SCROOGE   A good night's sleep might have been more beneficial to my welfare. Why don't you run along . . . or float along—

PAST   Shut me out at your peril! I have come about the *business* of your reclamation. Come, and walk with me.
PAST *clasps him by the arm.*

SCROOGE   The weather's not fit for walking. It's freezing outside. I've only my slippers on and I've a head cold. Spirit, I'm a mortal and liable to fall!

PAST   Bear but a touch of my hand there, on your heart, and you shall be upheld.
PAST *leads* SCROOGE *forward.*

PAST   Ah, here we are . . .

NARRATION   The city had vanished and Scrooge found himself in the country.

SCROOGE   Good heavens, I know this place.

PAST   Do you?

SCROOGE   Of course, it's my old school, I was a boy here. I would know it blindfolded.

PAST   Your lip is trembling . . . and what's that on your cheek?

SCROOGE   It is snow . . . snow.

SCHOOLMASTER'S VOICE (*off*)   Hurry, boys, the coach is waiting! Laggards, don't make me punish you for missing your coach!
Sound of sleigh bells, off.

SCHOOLMASTER   Hurry, you lazy brats!
Boys with baggage exit.

SCROOGE   Look, it's Billy, and Thomas, and Jeremiah—
School boys exit with their valises.

BOYS   Merry Christmas, Ebenezer! See you in the New Year. (*Etc.*)
>   SCROOGE *draws back.*

PAST   Don't worry, these are but shadows of the things that have been—they have no consciousness of us. But the school is not quite deserted. A solitary boy is left there still.

SCROOGE   I know. (*He sobs.*)

And look, my books, my dear, dear books. My Robinson Crusoe[5]—such adventures we had together.
>   *He reads over the boy's shoulder.*

Ah, "The Arabian Nights" . . . Ali Baba[6] . . .
>   *A fantastical figure appears.*

Look, it's Ali Baba! Dear old Ali Baba—
>   *Ali Baba brandishes his sword.*

He was always my friend—came whenever I needed him—

YOUNG EBENEZER   Are your band of thieves prepared to rescue the princess?
>   *Another figure appears.*

Robinson Crusoe, and his parrot!

YOUNG EBENEZER   The Sultan has locked the princess in the tower!
>   *A third figure appears.*

SCROOGE   And Puss in Boots[7]—Halloo!
>   *Suddenly his mood changes.*

Poor boy . . . I wish . . .

PAST   What?

SCROOGE   Nothing. Nothing. There was a boy singing a Christmas carol at my door last night. I wish I had given him—
>   FAN *enters.*

Never mind.

NARRATOR   Suddenly the princess appeared.

SCROOGE   Look, Spirit, it's my sister, Fan!
>   SCROOGE *comes close to her, studies her.*

SCROOGE   Fan! Isn't it odd? You're so young and I'm so old—

FAN   I have come to bring you home, little brother. Home, home, home!

EBENEZER   Home, dear Fan?

FAN   Yes, Father is so much kinder than he used to be, and when I asked him if you might come home, he said yes—we'll be together all Christmas long.

EBENEZER   Oh, Fan!

FAN   And you're to be a man! And never come back here. And look, Ebenezer, I've brought you a present.

EBENEZER   What is it, Fan?
>   *She hands him a box; inside is a round globe.*

EBENEZER   What's this?

FAN   A paperweight . . . you put it on top of papers, to keep them from blowing away.

EBENEZER   It's beautiful. Thank you, Fan.

FAN   And look what Father gave me.

---

5. *The Adventures of Robinson Crusoe* (1719–20), by Daniel Defoe.
6. The title character in "Ali Baba and the Forty Thieves," one of the most popular stories in *The*

Arabian Nights' Entertainments, a collection of ancient tales in Arabic (arranged in its present form ca. 1450).
7. The fairy tale.

She opens a music box, which plays 'The Holly and the Ivy.'

PAST Your sister Fan. She was a delicate creature, was she not? But possessed of a generous heart.

SCROOGE So she was, Spirit.

PAST She died a young woman, and had, as I recall, children?

SCROOGE One child.

PAST Your nephew Fred.

SCROOGE Yes. Yes.

SCHOOLMASTER Here is your trunk, Master Scrooge. So . . . I hear you're leaving us? On to better things? Your father writes me that he has found you a situation.

EBENEZER What's a situation?

SCHOOLMASTER A job! Work! Immediately after Christmas you go to London.

EBENEZER London? But where shall I live? I want to stay home. Fan—?

FAN (*she is fading*) Ebenezer . . . dear brother . . .

SCHOOLMASTER / FOREMAN Faster, boy, faster! Elbow grease! Nose to the grindstone! Earn your wages!

He drags LITTLE EBENEZER *off by the ear.*

PAST Six shillings a week was not a bad wage for a ten-year-old boy.

SCROOGE I was abandoned . . . but I learned.

PAST You learned, yes. You learned to save your shillings and pence.

SCROOGE I learned to be self-sufficient. The dark stain of poverty never stuck to me—let us go, Spirit, I have seen enough.

PAST You don't know the meaning of the word 'enough.'

NARRATION The spirit gave Scrooge a wise little nod, and drew him forward through his past. They left the country, and suddenly they were in the busy thoroughfares of London.

A small ice pond. A bench. BELLE *sits watching her charges,* WILLIAM *and* ANNA ROSE, *skating.*

BELLE Come children, it's time to go home, we'll be late for tea.

SCROOGE Belle—it's Belle!

BELLE William, take off your skates. Anna Rose—

EBENEZER, *a young man of twenty, enters with a huge hamper of purchases. He can't see where he's going, and* WILLIAM *crashes into him. They both fall on the ice. Packages fly.*

BELLE Watch out, William—oh dear, look what you've done!

WILLIAM Oops, sorry, sir.

EBENEZER No harm done.

BELLE Oh, please let me help you up, sir—

She lends him a hand, he succeeds in pulling her down as well. They both look around, stunned, then laugh.

EBENEZER I'd ask you to have a seat, madam, but you already have—

They laugh again.

BELLE William, lend a hand to Mr. . . . ?

EBENEZER Scrooge, Ebenezer Scrooge, madam.

WILLIAM *manages to get him up.*

Slowly does it, lad, let me find my footing . . . there.

BELLE Heavens, your bundles are scattered everywhere. I hope nothing's broken.

EBENEZER What's a biscuit or two?

He helps her up off the ice.

Here you go . . . I hope nothing's broken.

BELLE   What's a bone or two? I'm joking, Mr. Scrooge.

> *He seats her on the bench.*

William, since you knocked them down, it's only fair you help Mr. Scrooge collect his bundles.

> *Both children do so.*

It looks like you're planning quite a feast, sir.

EBENEZER   Me? Oh no, no indeed, I'm only the delivery boy. All this belongs to my employer, Mr. Fezziwig. His annual Christmas party is tonight. Old Fezziwig's very open-handed that way.

BELLE   Don't you love Christmas?

EBENEZER   I do. I mean, yes indeed.

BELLE   The warmth, the spirit, the good smells.

EBENEZER   As I said, Mr. Fezziwig's very kind—generous to a fault.

BELLE   Impossible!

EBENEZER   What? Oh, you're absolutely right! Which is why he'd be delighted if I offered you a peppermint.

> *He opens a box, peers inside.*

No, they're chocolates, ordered specially for the occasion.

BELLE   Even better.

> *They each take a piece.*

EBENEZER   May the children—?

BELLE   Yes. (*The children come over. To them.*) One piece each, then home!

CHILDREN   Thank you, sir.

> *They go.*

EBENEZER   You have quite a handsome family, madam. They look like you—

BELLE   Oh! Oh dear! You're quite mistaken, sir, these are not *my* children—

EBENEZER   But—

BELLE   They are my charges. I am their governess. I work for my bread, Mr. Scrooge, just as you do.

EBENEZER   I'm glad—not that you must work, but—I mean that I'm glad to meet—

BELLE   My name is Belle Crawford. Miss Belle Crawford.

EBENEZER   Miss Belle . . . at the risk of appearing impertinent, may I venture to . . . that is, would you consider . . . May I invite you to Mr. Fezziwig's party?

That is . . . he encourages us to bring our special friends, and since I have no friends—

BELLE   I'd like very much to come, Mr. Scrooge.

> *He hands her another chocolate.*

> *The scene fades.*

SCROOGE   Belle, dear Belle—

NARRATION   The stars were particularly bright that night, and the laughter, unable to keep within the confines of the houses, crept beneath the door jambs and echoed in the streets.

And about everything there hung an air of expectation.

PAST   Do you know this place?

> *Fezziwig's warehouse appears.* DICK WILKINS *is readying decorations for a party.*

SCROOGE   Know it? I was apprenticed here!

> FEZZIWIG *enters.*

FEZZIWIG   Hilli ho, Dick! Ebenezer!

SCROOGE   Why, it's old Fezziwig, bless his heart! Old Fezziwig alive again!

> EBENEZER *enters with bundles.*

EBENEZER   Here I am, sir, I've just had the most delightful accident—

FEZZIWIG   Ho, there! Dick! Ebenezer!

SCROOGE   Dick Wilkins . . . he was very much attached to me, was Dick!

FEZZIWIG   Ho, my boys. No more work tonight. It's Christmas Eve, Dick, Christmas Eve, Ebenezer! Finish up, and do it before a man can say Jack Robinson!

NARRATION   The floor was swept and watered.

The lamps were trimmed.

And fuel was heaped upon the fire.

The guests begin to enter, bearing gifts.

In came the fiddler with his fiddle—he turned it like fifty stomach aches, and made a whole orchestra of it.

NARRATION   In came Mrs. Fezziwig, one glorious, substantial smile.

In came the two Misses Fezziwig, beaming and loveable.

In came the two young fellows whose hearts they broke.

In came what seemed like all of London . . .

And in came Belle . . .

They sing 'Deck the Halls.'

FEZZIWIG   My dear friends—my dear neighbors—my dear children—

CHILDREN   Mr. Fezziwig!

FEZZIWIG   Tonight we'll do it! We'll eat and drink and trip the light fantastic. And we'll have music, right, Sam?

The fiddler plays a flourish on his fiddle. All cheer. The socializing is in full swing.

NARRATION   And away they all went.

BELLE   Such a lovely party, Mr. Scrooge.

EBENEZER   Ebenezer. Isn't it grand? I wish my clothes were—

BELLE   Were what?

EBENEZER   A little less worn. And look at my boots—they're brown and clumsy, not black and elegant.

BELLE   Oh dear. Does that mean I must apologize for my shoes as well?

EBENEZER   Of course not. You're a princess in a fairy tale. I've never seen anyone as perfect as you, you're—

BELLE   Cinderella?

EBENEZER   Precisely! And at midnight, does your dress turn to rags?

BELLE   Close enough. I borrowed this gown from my employer. Tomorrow I shall be quite myself again, dressed in plain brown wool.

EBENEZER   It doesn't matter that there's no glass slipper. You'd be quite as splendid in brown wool—

BELLE   Or brown boots? You have a nice smile, Ebenezer.

EBENEZER   Me? Smile? I'm not exactly famous for my smile, Miss Belle. *Trés belle.*

SCROOGE   Love!

PAST   Love, indeed. Romance, hope—a healthy percentage of mortals' time is spent on love. You're a man who respects figures—why do you suppose they do it?

SCROOGE   Because they're fools. It's a useless commodity, love; it produces nothing but excess children . . . and pain. Love's a humbug.

PAST   Pain? Indeed.

FEZZIWIG   Now come, such a feast we'll have, my friends. A blazing haunch of good English beef, and savory meat pies. And pickles, of course!

Cheers

And sweets and puddings!

Cheers.

Hot mulled wine and punch!

The young men cheer.

And Mrs. Fezziwig's rich mince pies—magnificent!

Cheers. The cook enters with a huge goose, covered.

And of course—the Goose!

The goose escapes the carving knife. They all chase it, capture it at last.

NARRATION Scrooge and the Spirit quickly traveled through time to the next Christmas Eve.

And Mr. Fezziwig's annual party.

DICK *and* EBENEZER *enter with a broom, hammer.*

EBENEZER Tonight everything must be perfect—like clockwork! It must all be absolutely perfect.

DICK I wonder who'll be here?

EBENEZER Everyone.

DICK Everyone? Even Belle?

EBENEZER Of course Belle, you fool. Tonight, Dick, I plan to set the date for our wedding.

DICK Congratulations, Ebenezer. By the way, have you mentioned it to the bride?

EBENEZER No, it's a surprise. Why?

DICK I just wondered. They're coming!

The party enters.

FEZZIWIG Christmas Eve! Christmas Eve, dear friends, dear children—tonight we'll do it! We'll make merry, and dance away the night . . . a thorough celebration.

MRS. F. Mr. F. has such a way with words.

FEZZIWIG My wife, my beautiful, bountiful wife—yes, I mean *you*, Mrs. F.—and I bid you welcome. Now don't be modest, Mrs. F., you're as handsome as the day I met you—

MRS. F. Get on with you!

FEZZIWIG Come, give us a song!

MRS. F. Oh no, I couldn't, I couldn't. Oh, very well.

Song.

FEZZIWIG (*in tears*) Beautiful, my dear, simply beautiful. (*He kisses her.*)

And my daughters. You all know my daughters . . . Petunia—she came first.

PETUNIA *enters.*

And Marigold, the baby.

MARIGOLD *enters.*

MRS. F. Don't they look a treat, Mr. F?

FEZZIWIG Blooming, positively blooming!

MRS. F. I laced them in good and tight—they can scarce breathe, but they have *shape!* And I sprinkled them with violet water and I dusted them with rice powder—they near sneezed their heads off! Are they not works of art?

FEZZIWIG Peerless. And last, but not least, our little surprises: Basil and sweet Marjoram.

The little children join them. EBENEZER *enters.*

But none can compare with their dear old mum.

MRS. F. He's such a rake! Tonight, Mr. F., I hope our girls will find—

FEZZIWIG What, Mrs. F?

She giggles, points.

Ah, romance! Girls, your mum wishes you to look sharp tonight and find an eligible suitor each.

PETUNIA and MARIGOLD   Papa! Really, Papa!

MRS. F. (*to* EBENEZER)   Where is Miss Belle, tonight?

EBENEZER   Late, ma'am.

MRS. F.   There, there . . . she'll be along at any time.

EBENEZER   She's careless about time. I'll have to speak to her about that.

MRS. F.   But not on Christmas Eve.

FEZZIWIG   No, Ebenezer, on Christmas Eve time takes a holiday and dances in the streets. Which reminds me—Sam! Music! We must have music!

> *They dance.*
> BELLE *enters.*

FEZZIWIG   Belle, Belle, our Christmas bell.

SCROOGE   Such a splendid party, Spirit.

PAST   A small matter for Mr. Fezziwig, to make these silly folk full of gratitude.

SCROOGE   Small?

PAST   He spends but a few pounds of mortal money. For this does he deserve such praise?

SCROOGE   It's not that, Spirit. The happiness he gives is quite as great as if it cost a fortune . . . oh dear . . .

PAST   What's the matter?

SCROOGE   Nothing . . . in particular.

PAST   Something, I think.

SCROOGE   No. I only wish I could have a word or two with my clerk just now, that's all.

PAST (*indicating* BELLE *and* EBENEZER.)   Listen . . .

BELLE   Goodness, I'm out of breath.

EBENEZER   Dancing puts the roses in your cheeks.

BELLE   Flattery, Mr. Scrooge?

EBENEZER   No, truth. Belle, have you a father?

BELLE   Everyone has a father. Why?

EBENEZER   Because I'm getting on so well at Mr. Fezziwig's warehouse, that tomorrow night I shall go to your father and ask for your hand.

> *They laugh.*

And when we are married, we'll be so rich—

BELLE   So *happy*—

EBENEZER   That you'll have a gown for every day of the week.

BELLE   No need.

EBENEZER   No need? But a rich gown would set you ablaze like a jewel. Clothes make a statement, Belle.

BELLE   I beg your pardon?

EBENEZER   Others judge us by our—

BELLE   Boots? Come, now, Ebenezer . . .

> YOUNG MISTER MARLEY *enters, spots* EBENEZER.

EBENEZER   I have great dreams for us, Belle. Ambitions. I don't intend to stay here much longer. I plan to set up my own business. I've been saving—

MARLEY   Ah! Mr. Scrooge, a word, please.

EBENEZER   Mr. Marley.

BELLE   Ebenezer, it's Christmas—

EBENEZER   Only a minute, Belle, it's business.

BELLE   Need we talk about business at a party?

MARLEY   Good evening, Miss Belle, are you enjoying yourself?

BELLE   I was—

EBENEZER   Belle! Belle, you've met Mr. Marley? A merry Christmas, Jacob.

MARLEY   For us, I think it will be.

EBENEZER   Do I catch your meaning, sir? You've obtained the mortgages?

MARLEY   At a price you'll like.

EBENEZER   All three buildings?

MARLEY   As of this evening, the properties are ours. There'll be great profit, if we
don't let sentiment get in the way.

BELLE   You mean *heart?*

MARLEY   No, I mean good sense, Miss Belle. Common sense. Old Fezziwig thinks I
have no heart at all.

   He starts to go.

EBENEZER   Some feel that he has too much.

MARLEY   Just so.

He exits.

BELLE   Too much heart?

   She turns to go.

EBENEZER   Belle—

SCROOGE   Belle, don't go—

EBENEZER   Come, my dear, you're quite right. We'll join the others.

Everyone dances off.

NARRATION   Young Ebenezer Scrooge devoted himself to work. His business was
lucrative, and that was all that mattered. His pence and shillings quickly grew into
pounds and guineas.

   And by the third Christmas party at the Fezziwig's, he was his own man.

SCROOGE   What's wrong with that?!

   The company enters, singing 'Panpatapan.' They cross over and out.
   FEZZIWIG *spots* BELLE *and* EBENEZER.

FEZZIWIG   Ebenezer, so glad you could join us this year.

EBENEZER   My pleasure, sir.

FEZZIWIG   You've been quite a stranger to us—I hope your business is prospering?

EBENEZER   Indeed. And your own business thrives?

FEZZIWIG   Middling . . . middling. Miss Belle, how lovely you look tonight. Come
have a glass of punch.

   FEZZIWIG *goes off.* BELLE *holds* EBENEZER *back.*

BELLE   I must speak to you, Ebenezer—

EBENEZER   Later, my dear.

BELLE   I cannot wait.

SCROOGE   Spirit, no, take me home. I cannot bear to watch.

PAST   Just one more scene. Our time grows short.

EBENEZER   Your fingers are cold. You've scarcely smiled this evening. If something's
wrong, tell me. I was never very good at guessing.

BELLE   I have been displaced in your heart.

EBENEZER   I don't know what you mean—

SCROOGE (*to* EBENEZER)   Good grief, *listen* to the girl!

BELLE   Your new love cheers and comforts you better than I ever could—

EBENEZER   Are you jealous? Of whom? What love?

BELLE   A golden one. You want to be rich, so rich that no one in the world can hurt you. You fear the world too much.

EBENEZER   Here's irony indeed! There's nothing in the world so cruel as poverty; yet there's nothing the world professes to condemn so severely as the pursuit of wealth!

BELLE   That pursuit is the only passion you permit yourself—

EBENEZER   I've grown wiser, but I've not changed toward you. Have I?

BELLE   Our contract is an old one, made when we were both poor and content to be so. When it was made you were another man—

EBENEZER   I was a boy!

BELLE   Ebenezer, I release you—

SCROOGE   Do something—kiss her, win her back—

EBENEZER   Have I ever sought release?

BELLE   Tell me, if you were free today, would you seek a dowerless girl?

SCROOGE   Yes! Tell her yes, tell her you would!

EBENEZER   You think not?

BELLE   Be honest. Regret would follow and we would spend our lives in misery. And so I release you, with a heart full of love for the man you once were—

SCROOGE   Say something!

   The party dances in.

FEZZIWIG   Ladies and gentlemen—no, my friends, my dear warm friends. The comfort, the cheer of Christmas, and of good friends. I have an announcement to make, a very important . . . (*He begins to weep.*) My daughters, the Misses Fezziwig: my sweet Petunia and my radiant Marigold are . . . are . . . (*Sobs.*)

MRS. F.   Mr. F. is such a sentimentalist. Yes, our daughters are engaged to be married.

   Cheers; couples embrace.

Wedding dates to be announced at the first opportunity. (*Cheers.*) Well done, girls. (*To* FEZZIWIG.) Pull yourself together.

FEZZIWIG   Yes, indeed, let us drink to the happy couples—and, yes, let us also drink to Belle and Ebenezer.

   Cheers.

Where is Belle? Come, Ebenezer—smile . . .

ALL   Smile. Smile. Smile. Smile. Smile.

EBENEZER   Humbug!

ALL   Humbug?

   Mad dance: the music plays with more fire and energy. EBENEZER *pulls* PETUNIA *wildly into the dance, then shoves her away. He grabs* MARIGOLD. *His roughness is frightening, and finally the dancers flee.*

   EBENEZER *is alone on stage with* SCROOGE *and* PAST. EBENEZER *looks around wildly, almost seems to see* SCROOGE. *They stare at each other for an instant, then:*

EBENEZER   It's all . . . humbug!

   He runs off.

SCROOGE   Spirit, show me no more, I beg you. Leave me! Take me home! Haunt me no longer! I cannot bear it, I cannot bear it—

   SCROOGE *runs at* PAST *with a blanket to put out its light, and* PAST *vanishes.* SCROOGE *leaps into his bed.*

   Blackout.

ACT II

Stave Three: The Second of the Three Spirits

SCROOGE *peeks out from behind his bed curtains. The bell tolls one.*

SCROOGE I'm awake. I'm alert. And I'm ready for anything. Nothing scares me, nothing at all, short of a cross between a rhinoceros and a baby!

NARRATION A blaze of ruddy light streamed upon him.

And being only light, it was more alarming than a dozen ghosts.

The light pursues SCROOGE.

And Scrooge was powerless to make out what it meant.

He was apprehensive that he might be at that very moment an interesting case of spontaneous combustion.

At last he thought—as you or I would have thought at first, for it is always the person *not* in the predicament who knows what ought to have been done—

I say, at last he began to think the source and secret of the ghostly light might be from above.

The GHOST OF CHRISTMAS PRESENT *enters on a huge throne, bedecked with fruits and vegetables and sweets.*

SCROOGE Good grief!

PRESENT Come forward, come and know me better. (*He laughs.*)

SCROOGE Who are you?

PRESENT I am the Ghost of Christmas Present. Look upon me, little man, you've never seen the like of me before. (*Laughs.*)

SCROOGE I—

PRESENT Speak up, don't quake—I shan't damage you. Have a peach? Are you ready to go? Last night my comrade took you traveling through time. I'll take you traveling through space.

SCROOGE Have I a choice? (PRESENT *shakes his head.*) I didn't think so. Likely I'll catch my death of cold, tempting providence in my slippers. Catarrh. Lumbago. Pneumonia . . .

Oh, what's the use, Spirit, conduct me where you will. I was forced forth last night and I learnt a lesson which is working now. Tonight, if you have aught to teach me, let me profit from it.

PRESENT Come, little man.

SCROOGE *climbs up onto the throne. It travels.*

Snow crossover. Shoveling, snowballs, busy people.

NARRATOR They looked upon the city streets on Christmas morning.

Smooth white snow on the roofs, much dirtier snow on the ground.

Nothing very cheerful in the climate—and yet there was an air of joy abroad, for the people were jovial and full of glee.

Poor families emerged from scores of bystreets and lanes, carrying their dinners to the bakers' shops to cook in their giant ovens.

So intent in their progress were these humble merry-makers, that at times they tumbled up against each other.

FIRST MAN Ow—hey, you've near broke my foot, you idiot! Crippled me for life, you have.

SECOND MAN Then don't stick your bloomin' foot in the middle of the road, you sod.

They start to argue.

The SPIRIT *sprinkles the contents of his torch on them.*

SECOND MAN   Sorry, mate, didn't mean to offend.

FIRST MAN   My fault entirely, I believe. Merry Christmas, mate.

They go off.

SCROOGE   Spirit, is there something special in your torch?

SCROOGE *and* PRESENT *descend from the throne, which magically leaves the stage.*

PRESENT   Flavor! Zest! My own blend of spices to remind you poor mortals that life is short and must be savored while it lasts. Deliciousness pours from my torch and lights on every table . . . . the poor ones most of all.

SCROOGE   Why the poor?

PRESENT   They need it most of all.

They are now in a small room in Camden Town. A mother and her children are preparing dinner.

SCROOGE   Where are we? Who are these people?

PRESENT   The family of your 'fifteen-shillings-a-week' clerk, Bob Cratchit. That's Mrs. Cratchit, with her daughter Belinda. They both wear threadbare gowns, made brave with ribbons. Ribbons make a good show for a mere sixpence.

PETER *runs in.*

And Master Peter Cratchit, who seems to be swallowed up in a castoff collar of his father's. And here comes Tom—

TOM *enters.*

TOM   Mother—

SCROOGE   Good heavens—too many children!

PETER   The potatoes are almost done, Mother.

TOM   And I smelled it—I stood outside the baker's shop and I smelled our goose!

MRS. CRATCHIT   Tom, how could you tell you were smelling *our* goose? And Peter . . . the potatoes can't be done, I'm not ready for them. You positively can't allow them to be done!

PETER   How can I stop them? Are you teasing me, Mum?

MRS. C.   Of course I'm teasing you. But what's keeping your precious father, and Tim? And where on earth is Martha? She can't still be busy in that millinery shop—

MARTHA *enters.*

MARTHA   Here's Martha, Mum.

CHILDREN   Martha, Martha!

MRS. C.   Bless your heart, how late you are. And your hands—they're like ice.

MARTHA   I got away as soon as I could, believe me. We had to work late last night— Peter! You're as tall as me! And we had to clear away the mess this morning. Tom! Belinda!

MRS. C.   So long as you're here. Come, sit by the fire, girl, and have a good warm. Don't they feed you in that place?

MARTHA   They gave us all day tomorrow off.

MRS. C.   I wish I could say the same for your father. That miserable job is wearing him out.

SCROOGE   These little ruffians are wearing him out!

PETER *looks out the door.*

PETER   Father's coming! He and Tim are coming—hide, Martha! Quick, we'll surprise him! Behind the table!

MARTHA *obliges.*

(*To* TOM.) One squeak from you, Tom, and I'll pound you—

The room grows silent. CRATCHIT *enters with* TIM *on his shoulders.*

CRATCHIT   Mrs. Cratchit, my love; children.

    He sets TIM *down.*

It's cold out there.

    He kisses MRS. C. *on the cheek.*

Still the prettiest girl in Camden Town, I declare. Merry Christmas, my dears—

    He holds out his arms and they run to him. But something is missing. He looks around.

Where's Martha? Mrs. Cratchit, where's our girl?

MRS. C.   Not coming.

CRATCHIT (*crestfallen*)   Not coming, on Christmas Day?!

SCROOGE   She's under the table, Cratchit. Under the *table.*

    (*To* PRESENT.) He never listens to a thing I tell him.

MRS. C.   Isn't it a pity, Bob?

    MARTHA *emerges from beneath the table, creeps up on her father.*

MARTHA   I can't bear teasing him. Surprise! Father, here I am!

CRATCHIT   Martha! Dear girl . . .

MARTHA   Father, you looked as if you might cry.

CRATCHIT   My clever family played a trick on me, eh, Mrs. Cratchit?

    The children climb all over him.

I do believe I am what is called a 'family man.'

SCROOGE   Spirit, they're mauling him. Stop that! He'll have no strength for work tomorrow.

CRATCHIT   Children, do I smell something? Do I hear something bubbling in your mother's laundry boiler?

PETER   The pudding![8] It's steaming away in the wash house—come, have a look, Tim.

SCROOGE   What's wrong with that little one?

CRATCHIT   Be careful, children.

                PETER *and* TOM *gather up* TIM; BELINDA *follows them off.*

MRS. C.   Don't touch—only smell.

CRATCHIT   Ah, Martha, my love.

MRS. C.   That's it, you two have a good stretch-out. Look at you . . . the idle rich. You *shall* be idle this day, that will be my Christmas pleasure. But as for rich—

CRATCHIT   We're rich.

SCROOGE   On fifteen bob[9] a week?

CRATCHIT   We're rich.

MRS. C.   How did little Tim behave in church?

CRATCHIT   As good as gold—better. But he gets so thoughtful sitting by himself so much. He says the strangest things. He told me, coming home, that he hoped people saw him in church, because he was a cripple—

MRS. C.   Bob!

CRATCHIT   Because it might be pleasant for people to remember on Christmas Day, the miracles that made lame beggars walk and blind men see.

    MARTHA *embraces him, but shares a look with her mother.*

But he's growing stronger every day, don't you agree, Martha? Yes, I do believe he's growing hearty and strong.

---

8. A steamed or baked dish, sometimes savory (made with meat, fish, or vegetables) and sometimes sweet. The ingredients of a traditional Christmas pudding include spices, dried fruit, suet, and alcohol; often it is doused with more alcohol and set alight when served.
9. Shillings.

The children come back, singing. TIM *uses his crutch to walk to his father. The others applaud.*

TOM   The pudding will be *gorgeous*.

BELINDA   It smells heavenly.

SCROOGE   Spirit, that little boy—

PRESENT   Tim.

CRATCHIT   Martha, tell us about the milliner's shop.

MARTHA   Well, it's feathers and ribbons and bows and straw—hats and more hats—(*Bitterly.*) Fourteen hours a day.

MRS. C.   It's cruel.

PETER   It must go right to your head.

All laugh; CRATCHIT *regards* PETER *proudly.*

CRATCHIT   Incorrigible!

SCROOGE   'Go right to your head' . . . dreadful boy.

MARTHA   You wouldn't believe the fine customers! In furs! I saw a Countess. And a Lord, day before yesterday—he wasn't an inch bigger than our Peter here.

PETER *straightens up, lords it.*

But it's strange . . . they can never seem to decide what they want.

CRATCHIT   We don't have that problem, do we?

MARTHA   'Do I want the gray velvet with red cherries, or the blue straw with corn-flowers?'

PETER   'Such a crisis, Countess. You mustn't be subjected to the stress. We'll have them both!'

CRATCHIT   My lad's a positive wag.

MARTHA   He's a goose—

MRS. C. *jumps up in shock.*

MRS. C.   Good heavens, the goose! Peter, run to the baker's and fetch the goose! Belinda, mash the potatoes. I'll tend to the gravy.

CRATCHIT   And I'll make the punch.

MRS. C.   Bob, go easy on the gin in that punch of yours . . . remember last year.

There is a flurry of activity. Perhaps a carol?

MARTHA   I do confess, I'm starving.

PETER *and* TOM *come in with the goose.*

PETER   Here it is, it's ready!

CRATCHIT   Now children, settle down.

They get seated, bow their heads.

For that which we are about to receive, may the Lord make us truly thankful.

MRS. C.   Look at your father, children, he's beaming like the man in the moon.

CRATCHIT   Because I'm a rich man.

SCROOGE   He keeps saying that. Not on fifteen shillings a week, you're not!

CRATCHIT (*removing the platter cover*)   And now . . .

PETER   Our goose is cooked!

SCROOGE   Goose . . . cooked? Cheeky lad!

MARTHA   Such a handsome bird!

BELINDA   I can't wait.

CRATCHIT   It's a feast.

SCROOGE   You must be joking, Cratchit, that goose is a humbug!

MRS. C.   Remarkably cheap for the size of it, very generous, isn't it?

SCROOGE   It's scrawny! (*To* PRESENT.) So minute a bird for so many people . . . ?

NARRATION   There never was such a goose. Its tenderness and flavor, size and cheapness elicited universal admiration. And, eked out with applesauce and mashed potatoes, it was a sufficient dinner for the whole family.

TOM   I'm going to burst!

BELINDA   The best we've ever had.

NARRATION   For once everyone had enough. Wonderful word, enough. And the youngest Cratchits in particular were steeped in onion and sage to the eyebrows!

MRS. CRATCHIT *rises nervously.*

NARRATION   But now a moment of high anxiety is at hand!

MRS. C.   I'm so nervous . . . so nervous.

CRATCHIT   Children, it's the annual pudding crisis.

MRS. C.   Don't tease me, Bob. What if it's not thoroughly cooked? What if it should break when I turn it out. (*Horror-struck.*) What if someone climbed over the wall and nicked it while we were busy eating goose?

CRATCHIT   Then I'd make a pudding of the thief! Face the challenge, my dear. Belinda will accompany you.

MRS. C. *and* BELINDA *go out to fetch the pudding.*

CRATCHIT   It happens every Christmas, eh? Oh, my dear family, such a day, such a day! Wait—I smell something.

MRS. C. *and* BELINDA *enter with a blazing pudding.*

Salute the pudding. Salute your mother! It's another triumph, my dear, the greatest triumph since you married me.

MRS. C.   I confess I had my doubts about the quantity of flour.

CRATCHIT   But first, gather round the hearth. It's time for our punch, served in the family crystal.

SCROOGE   Such a small pudding for so large a family.

PRESENT   You think so? Any Cratchit would blush to hint at such a thought. They had enough . . . wonderful word, enough. It means something different to each man.

CRATCHIT   I believe I've outdone myself this year.

He raises his cup.

My lords and ladies, I give you Mr. Scrooge, the Founder of the Feast.

MRS. C.   Founder of the Feast indeed! I wish I had him here, I'd give him a piece of my mind to feast upon, and I hope he'd have a good appetite for it.

CRATCHIT   My dear, it's Christmas Day.

MRS. C.   It should be Christmas Day, I'm sure, on which one drinks the health of such a stingy, odious, hard, unfeeling man as Mr. Scrooge is—you know he is, Robert.

CRATCHIT   My dear—

MRS. C.   You know he is, Robert. But I'll drink his health for your sake, and the day's, not for his. Long life to him. A merry Christmas and a happy New Year— he'll be merry and happy, I've no doubt.

ALL   Mr. Scrooge.

CRATCHIT   And to us—a merry Christmas. God bless us!

They drink.

TIM   God bless us, every one.

PRESENT   Behold them, one of the most fortunate families I visit tonight—

SCROOGE   Fortunate? Their clothing is shabby, their shoes are far from waterproof, and that minuscule goose—

PRESENT   They are happy and grateful, and contented with the time.

SCROOGE   Spirit . . . tell me if Tiny Tim will live?

PRESENT   I see a vacant seat in the chimney corner, and a crutch without its owner—

SCROOGE   No, no, kind Spirit, say he will not die.

PRESENT   If he be like to die, he had better do it and decrease the surplus population.

The Cratchits and their room disappear.

SCROOGE   Spirit—

PRESENT   Man, if man you be at heart, forebear your wickedness. You must discover what the surplus is, and where it is. You would decide which men shall live, which men shall die? It may be that in the sight of heaven you are more worthless and less fit to live than millions like this poor man's crippled child. Oh God, to hear the insect on the leaf pronouncing on the too much life among his hungry brothers in the dust!

Come, the day is waning and you've more to learn.

Carolers, singing in French, German, Italian . . .

NARRATION   They sped through the lonely darkness, over land, over sea, over an unknown abyss whose depths were secrets as profound as death.

Scrooge suddenly saw the planet with great clarity.

He grew to know the 'surplus population.'

He observed, tallied, totaled in his best counting-house way.

He peeked into the soul of humanity, heard the carol on its lips, and understood the memory of bygone Christmases in its heart.

Being a man who respected numbers, the very quantity of human souls preoccupied with Christmas thoughts gave him pause.

He turned in mid-ocean to ask the Spirit to explain . . . and found himself in a bright, dry, warm parlor instead.

The fog drifts away and the lights come up on Fred's house. A party is in progress.

FRED enters with CECIL, laughing, in mid-conversation.

SCROOGE   I recognize that laugh. It belongs to my nephew, Fred.

CECIL   Surely you exaggerate, Fred?

FRED   I swear it's true! He said that Christmas was a humbug—believed it, too.

MRS. FRED   More shame for him, Fred.

SCROOGE (*to* PRESENT)   Is that the wife? (*The* SPIRIT *nods.*) She's poor, you know. Not a ha'penny to her name.

He moves close to her, studies her.

I confess she's what you'd call *provoking*. And satisfactory . . .

PRESENT   Oh, perfectly satisfactory.

CECIL   I hear he's rich, Fred.

SOPHIA   Oodles of money.

MRS. FRED   But you can't prove it by any largesse Fred's received.

FRED (*seating MRS. FRED, who's quite pregnant*)   I don't desire anything—oh, but he has given me a gift—this old paperweight.

He pulls it out of his pocket.

CECIL   That's thoughtful.

FRED   He shied it at me yesterday. I quite treasure it.

As he passes it around, SCROOGE makes a grab for it.

MRS. FRED   I've no patience with him.

DOROTHEA   Neither have I.

FRED   His offense carries its own punishment, my love. He takes it into his head to dislike us and he won't come to dine. The result? He cheats himself—

SCROOGE   What?! How?!

FRED   Well, in truth, I guess he doesn't lose much of a dinner—

MRS. FRED   He loses a very good dinner—

FRED   A repast faultlessly wrought by my wife and her two lovely sisters—

EDWARDS   A feast—

TOPPER   Fit for a king.

SOPHIA   That must be true, for there's not a single bite left.

MRS. FRED   Fred had three servings—

TOPPER (*eyeing* DOROTHEA)   Food, food, another benefit of marriage. A bachelor's a
    wretched outcast of society, underfed and unloved, dependent on others for scraps
    of affection and crumbs of comfort . . . oh, desolation!

MRS. FRED   Wipe your tears, Desolation, before they make the carpets mildew. I
    wish some nice young lady would take pity on Topper and end his misery. Any
    volunteers?

        The others look at DOROTHEA.

FRED   My uncle has missed something far more important that our dinner.

TOPPER   Could anything *be* more important?

FRED   My wife herself.

MRS. FRED   Thank you, my dear.

FRED   He's lost much by not knowing her. She is so altogether . . . satisfactory.
        But I'll try again next year, for I pity him. If my good humor puts him in the
    mood to leave his poor clerk fifty pounds, I'll feel it's worth the effort—

SCROOGE   Fifty pounds—are you mad?

MRS. FRED   Enough about your uncle. Let's have a game! Blind Man's Buff?

FRED   Yes! Topper, you must be the Blind Man.

        Applause. FRED *binds Topper's eyes,* MRS. FRED *twirls him around.*

ALL   One . . . two . . . three!

        Mrs. Fred's sister, DOROTHEA, *is the object of Topper's chase. She really wants
        to be caught, and he's cheating, in order to catch her, but other guests keep
        getting in the way. Shrieks and giggles.*

SCROOGE   Spirit, that man is cheating. I believe he can see perfectly well.

PRESENT   Yes, the game is fixed, I'm afraid.

        Finally TOPPER *catches her and extracts a prize—a kiss, cheers. Then they sing
        'The Holly and the Ivy.' Finally, Mrs. Fred's other sister, the quiet one, speaks
        up.*

SOPHIA   Let's play a quiet game now. Yes and No.

PRESENT   We must be going—

SCROOGE   No, wait, here's another game—

PRESENT   We cannot stay.

                                    PRESENT *leaves, unnoticed by* SCROOGE.

SCROOGE   One half-hour, Spirit. It's so warm and cosy here, and I want to play—

MRS. FRED   Yes and No. Fred, you start it.

FRED   Well then . . . let me see . . . aha. It's an animal.

SOPHIA   A live animal?

FRED   Yes.

TOPPER   Wild or tame?

MRS. FRED   He can only answer yes or no.

TOPPER   Wild, then?

FRED   I'd say . . . yes.

EDWARDS   Is it a cat?

FRED   No.

CECIL   Does it growl?

FRED   Yes. Yes, indeed.

SOPHIA   Is it a tiger?

FRED   No.

DOROTHEA   An insect?

FRED   No.

CECIL   A wolf?

FRED   No.

TOPPER   A wildebeest?

FRED   A wildebeest does *not* growl.

TOPPER   How do you know?

SCROOGE   A lion?

MRS. FRED   Perhaps . . . a lion?

FRED   No.

TOPPER   Is it a bear?

EDWARDS   Does it live in a zoo?

MRS. FRED   In a menagerie?

CECIL   In the desert?

EDWARDS   Is the animal indigenous to Australia?

FRED   Good grief, no. No, no, no and no.

SCROOGE   Is it kept in England?

TOPPER   Can it be found in the streets?

FRED   Yes.

SCROOGE   London! London!

SOPHIA   Could it be . . . . London?

FRED   Yes!

TOPPER   Is it led around by a rope or chain?

FRED   No.

MRS. FRED   Is it a carnivore?

FRED   I suppose so, yes.

CECIL   Does it have spots?

FRED   No spots.

TOPPER and DOROTHEA   Stripes?

FRED   No stripes.

DOROTHEA   I know what it is, Fred! I know!

FRED   Well?

DOROTHEA   It's your Uncle Scro-o-o-ge.

FRED   Aha! Yes!

    Cheers, laughter.

TOPPER   You cheated, old man. When I asked 'is it a bear,' you ought to have answered yes.

    Laughter.

FRED   Ah me, he's given us plenty of merriment this evening. It would be ungrateful not to drink his health.

    They raise their glasses.

I give you Uncle Scrooge.

ALL   Uncle Scrooge.

    They drink.

SCROOGE   Oh dear, I don't know what to say—

    He glances off.

I don't deserve—

The party dances off.

Spirit, wait—where did he go? Spirit, come back.

The party at Fred's has disappeared, and the GHOST OF CHRISTMAS PRESENT *is revealed, looking thinner and smaller.*

SCROOGE   Spirit—you look quite worn. Are spirits' lives so short?

PRESENT   My life upon this globe is very brief. It ends tonight.

SCROOGE   Tonight!

PRESENT   At midnight. Hark, the time is drawing near.

Chimes ring.

SCROOGE   Spirit, I see something strange protruding from your skirt. A foot . . . . or a claw . . .

PRESENT   It might be a claw, for all the flesh there is on it. Look here. Oh man, look down, behold these wretches . . .

PRESENT *reveals two children, who crawl from beneath his robes. They are wretched, abject, miserable.*

SCROOGE   Are these your children?

PRESENT   They are man's. And yet they cling to me. This boy is Ignorance, this girl is Want. Beware them both and all their kind, but most of all beware this boy, for on his brow I see written Doom, unless the writing be erased.

SCROOGE   Have they no refuge? No resource?

PRESENT   Are there no prisons? No workhouses?

The bells toll twelve and the world around SCROOGE *begins to spin.* PRESENT *and the two children are superseded by the phantom: The* GHOST OF CHRISTMAS YET TO COME.

Stave Four: The Last of The Spirits

SCROOGE   Am I in the presence of the Ghost of Christmas Yet to Come?

Ghost of the Future, I fear you more than any specter I have seen, yet will I travel with you, and do it with a grateful heart. Will you speak to me?

Lead on, Spirit. The night is waning fast, and it is precious time to me. Lead on.

SCROOGE *observes a funeral procession, which is led by the undertaker and followed by four men of business.*

GRASPER   Well, Mr. Snarkers, I see Old Scratch has claimed his own at last. The fellow's dead.

SNARKERS   Dead as a door-nail. (*They laugh.*) What do you know about it?

GRASPER   Not much, either way. I only know he *is* dead.

SQUEEZE   When did he die?

GRASPER   Ah, Mr. Squeeze. Last night, I believe.

SNARKERS   I thought he'd *never* die.

SQUEEZE   What did he die of?

KROOKINGS   Hardening of the heart.

They laugh.

SQUEEZE   God knows, he was as tough as the devil himself.

SNARKERS   The devil will be an intimate of his now, eh?

GRASPER   What's he done with his money?

KROOKINGS   He hasn't left it to me, that's all I know.

SQUEEZE   Anyone planning to attend the funeral?

SNARKERS   I don't mind going if a lunch is provided. But I must be fed if I go.

GRASPER   I'll offer to go if everyone else will . . .

KROOKINGS   You know, I'm what you'd call one of his particular friends, Yes, he said 'hello' to me once in the street.

They laugh, exit.

SCROOGE   There's a trivial conversation, don't you think? Evidently someone's died. Jacob Marley? No, no, that happened long ago, and you're all about the future, aren't you?

Well, I'll be guided by you entirely, Spirit. I'm sure it will all become clear in due course, won't it?

Still you say nothing. Won't you answer?

NARRATION   Scrooge felt the phantom's eyes keenly upon him as they traveled to a part of town which Scrooge had never laid eyes on.

The whole place reeked of filth, misery, crime.

In a wretched alley there was a rag and bone shop, where iron, old rags, bottles and greasy offal were bought and sold. And amidst the merchandise was Joe, the proprietor, a grimy rascal.

JOE is expecting customers.

The UNDERTAKER lurks in the shadows.

MRS. GRIMSBY enters with a bundle, followed by the laundress, MRS. DILBER.

GRIMSBY   Good day to ye, Joe.

JOE   If it isn't Mrs. Grimsby, lookin' lovely as ever.

SCROOGE   Spirit, that's my charwoman, Mrs. Grimsby. What's she doing in a sordid place like this?

GRIMSBY   'Ave you met Mrs. Dilber, the laundress?

JOE   Enchanted.

LAUNDRESS   Likewise.

She curtsies as if to royalty, JOE pinches her cheek, and she cringes.

GRIMSBY   Now, Joe, it's her first time here and she's that scared!

The UNDERTAKER clears his throat, steps forward.

JOE   Oh my soul, look who else is 'onoring us with a visit. Mr. Grubb, the undertaker!

The others draw away from the UNDERTAKER.

Ill-met by moonlight, my old friends. What a strange coincidence . . . all of you coming here with merchandise at the same time. It's what I'd call an embarrassment of riches.

They all laugh.

Who's first?

GRIMSBY   I was—

UNDERTAKER   I beg to disagree.

GRIMSBY   You saw me, Joe. I'm to be first, then the laundress, let her be second. And the undertaker *last*; the undertaker is always last, eh?

JOE   As you like. I'll buy it all, whatever you bring, be it linen or lead, candlesticks, nut-picks, old stones . . . or old bones. I do love my trade, don't you know. Happy in my work.

No one moves for a moment.

My, ain't we polite.

GRIMSBY   She's afraid. (*To MRS. DILBER.*) You've a perfect right to look after yourself, love, the dead man always did.

DILBER   True, no man more so, and my little ones never get enough to eat.

GRIMSBY   Then don't stand there quaking. Who'll be the wiser?

UNDERTAKER   No one will be the wiser. If he'd been half human in life, he'd have someone to look after him in death, 'stead of gasping out his last breath all alone—

JOE   Enough pretty sentiment—let's do *business*.

> The UNDERTAKER *steps in front of the two women, thrusts a small package at* JOE.

What have we here? A pencil case, pair o' sleeve buttons, spectacles, a balance wheel . . . and an old paperweight.

SCROOGE   Oh, look—

JOE   Not worth much, any of it. There, ten shillings, and I wouldn't give you sixpence more if you pickled me[1] for it—

UNDERTAKER   I *will* be pickling you, one day soon, in my workroom.

JOE   Very funny. Who's next?

> MRS. DILBER *moves forward cautiously.*

Towels . . . nice pair o' boots, a pair o' wool knickers, with holes in the seats, two pretty little silver teaspoons, sugar tongs . . . and an old copy of *Robinson Crusoe*— You'll do fine in this business.

> *He calculates, hands her a coin, pinches her cheek.*

That's your account, my dear . . . and may I repent of my liberal nature.

> MRS. GRIGSBY *bustles forward.*

GRIGSBY   Now you'll see somethin' Joe, I'm quite the collector.

> *She unfurls her bundle.*

JOE   A splendid bed-curtain—

GRIMSBY   With brass rings an' all, and tassels . . . and fully lined!

DILBER   Cor!

JOE   What'd you do, love, pull them down right in front of the corpse?

GRIMSBY   He didn't object. Here's a woolen blanket—

JOE   With nary a moth hole in sight.

GRIMSBY   'Course not—even the bedbugs couldn't bear to stay in his room, it were that cold!

JOE   Where he's going he won't be needing to keep warm. And what's this? A fine linen shirt?

DILBER   You don't mean you stripped the shirt off his corpse?!

GRIGSBY   (*with a glare at the* UNDERTAKER)   Some fool put it on him to be buried in, but I took it off. Waste not, want not—

> *They roar with laughter.* JOE *counts out coins for her.*

JOE   This is the end of it, ya see. He frightened everyone away from him when he was alive, to profit us now he's dead.

> *They laugh, the scene dissolves.*

SCROOGE   Oh horrible, horrible . . . jackals! Spirit, I see, I see. The case of this unhappy man might be my own. My life tends that way now.

> *He almost bumps into a stripped bed with a sheet-covered corpse.*

Merciful heavens, what's this?

> *Two pallbearers roll on the empty bed (no curtains). A body lies beneath a single sheet on the bed. The* PHANTOM *gestures to the head.* SCROOGE *approaches, but cannot bring himself to lift the sheet.*

SCROOGE   No, Spirit, I cannot—I cannot lift that sheet. If this man could be raised up now, what would be his foremost thought? Avarice? Hard dealing? They have brought him to a fine end, truly. He is quite alone.

---

1. I.e., punished me by rubbing salt into my back after a whipping.

The pallbearers leave with the bed, and there is a dreadful sound of rats scratching and the yowl of a cat.

SCROOGE   What's that? A cat at the door?

A child's coffin is brought on.

Rats gnawing through the baseboard? What do they want?

Oh horrible, horrible. Spirit, I am desolate. Show me some kindness and mercy in death.

The PHANTOM *points again.*

Oh no, no, Spirit—please, it cannot be—

MRS. CRATCHIT, BELINDA, MARTHA, TOM, PETER. *The ladies are sewing on a shroud,* PETER *is reading from the Bible.*

PETER   'And he called to him a little child and set him in the midst of them and said, verily I say unto you: except ye become as little children, ye shall in no wise enter the kingdom of heaven . . .'[2]

MRS. CRATCHIT *wipes her eyes.*

MRS. C.   It's the color of the cloth—it's hard to see, and it hurts my eyes. There, all better. The candle light makes them weak, and I wouldn't want your father to see me with weak eyes, when he comes home . . . not for the world. Peter, isn't he late?

PETER   He walks a little slower than he used to . . . before Tim . . .

MRS. C.   I have known him to walk with Tim upon his shoulders very fast indeed.

BELINDA   And so have I.

MRS. C.   But Tim was light to carry, and your father loved him so—they seemed to float along together.

BOB *enters.*

MRS. C.   Ah, Bob, your tea is ready on the hob.

CRATCHIT   Isn't the sewing coming along nicely. Such nimble fingers.

I've just been to the place where Tim will rest. I wish you all could have seen it, it would have done you good to see how green a place it is. But I'll take you there often—we'll visit every Sunday . . . my little child . . . my little, little child . . .

I met Mr. Scrooge's nephew on my way home, Mr. Fred. When I told him our sad news, he said, 'I'm heartily sorry for it, Mr. Cratchit—' (He knew my name, fancy!) 'And heartily sorry for your good wife.' Now how did he come to know that?

MRS. C.   Know what, dear?

CRATCHIT   That you're a good wife.

The children smile.

And he handed me his card, and offered to be of any service . . . I shouldn't be surprised if he got our Peter a better situation.

MRS. C.   Just think, children . . .

MARTHA   And then Peter will be keeping company with some young lady and setting up for himself—

PETER   Get on with you—!

CRATCHIT   It's as likely as not, Peter. But children, however and whenever we part from one another, I'm sure we shall none of us forget poor Tim, shall we?

CHILDREN   Never, father, never.

The lights fade on the Cratchits.

SCROOGE   Spirit, tell me, are these the shadows of things that will be? Or are they the shadows of things that may be? Answer, Prince of Death, for I know you now and you are He. Death is the subject of your lesson, and that I must study . . .

2. Matthew 18.2–3.

Gravestones appear. The PHANTOM *gestures to one of them.* SCROOGE *approaches it.*

SCROOGE   Here lies the wretched man whose name I now must learn. Before I draw near this stone, Spirit, hear me.

The SPIRIT *gestures to the stone.*

No, Spirit, I am afraid to look—

The name on the stone is revealed.

No, Spirit, no, no, no—Spirit, hear me—I am not the man I was. Why show me this if I am past all hope?

The PHANTOM *starts away.* SCROOGE *follows and falls.*

Good Spirit, assure me that I may yet change these shadows you have shown me.

He kneels.

I will honor Christmas in my heart and try to keep it all the year. The spirits of the past, present and future will strive within me. I shall not shut out the lessons I have learned.

Oh, tell me I may sponge away that name—!

But by now we are back in his bedroom, with his bed, chair, etc. The bed is no longer bare, but fully dressed, curtains and all.

Stave Five: The End of It

SCROOGE *is still on his knees before the bed.*

SCROOGE   I will honor Christmas in . . . my own bed?! Yes! The bedpost's my own! The bed's my own! And Time—Time is my own to make amends in!

Oh Jacob Marley, I say it on my knees, old Jacob, on my knees!

I will honor Christmas in my heart and try to keep it all the year. You'll see, Jacob, my life shall be a celebration!

He rises.

Must get dressed. Where's my shoe? My shirt? Mrs. Grigsby! I can't find a thing.

MRS. GRIGSBY *enters.*

Ah, Mrs. Grigsby, look, my bed curtains, you didn't tear them down rings and all. They're here—I'm here—

She helps him dress.

The bed goes off.

This miserable old sinner has come to his senses at last!

And at long last, I understand my *business* here on earth.

Oh, I am as light as a feather. I'm as happy as an angel. I'm as merry as a school boy. I'm as giddy as a drunken man.

I don't know what day it is! I don't know how long I've been among the Spirits. Mrs. Grigsby, old Jacob came up through there, and the Past opened the curtains on the bed, just *opened* them! And from above . . . .

He finds the peach.

Oh my!

He kisses MRS. GRIGSBY *on the cheek, laughs. She bolts.*

I don't know anything—I'm quite a baby, but I don't care, I'd rather be a baby!

The bells begin to ring at a nearby church.

A ragged boy, SIMON, *appears below.*

SCROOGE   Bells!

He spots SIMON.

Hallo—hallo, there, lad. What's today?

SIMON   Eh?

SCROOGE   What's today, my fine fellow?

SIMON   Today? Why, Christmas Day.

SCROOGE   Christmas Day? I haven't missed it? The Spirits have done it all in one night—they can do anything they like, of course they can!

SIMON   The *what*?

SCROOGE   The Spirits.

SIMON   Spirits? Ha!

SCROOGE   Ha indeed. In fact, ha, ha. Laugh, my lad.

SIMON   I never laugh. As I see it, gov'ner, life is no laughing matter.
        He starts to leave.

SCROOGE   Oh dear, that will never do. Lad, wait—have a peach?

SIMON   What do I have to do for it?

SCROOGE   Nothing, but wait—
        *He hands him a small coin. It's still hard for him to unglue the money from his
        hand, but he does. He smiles, the boy flashes a minute smile back, which fades.*
    Lad, do you know the poulterer's on the next street?

SIMON   I should hope I did.

SCROOGE   An intelligent boy, a remarkable boy. Do you know if they've sold the prize turkey in the window? Not the little prize turkey, the big one.

SIMON   What, the one as big as me?

SCROOGE   Delightful boy! Yes, my buck.

SIMON   It's hanging there now.

SCROOGE   Splendid—go and buy it.

SIMON   Go on!

SCROOGE   No, I'm in earnest. Go and buy it, and tell them to bring it here. Come back with the man and I'll give you a shilling.
        SIMON *starts off.*
    Wait—come back with him in less than five minutes and I'll give you half a crown![3]
        SIMON *runs off like a shot.*
    I'll send it to Bob Cratchit's! It's twice the size of Tiny Tim! Bob shan't know who sent it. I can imagine the look on his face.
        He laughs heartily.

NARRATION   Really, for a man who had been out of practice for so many years, it was splendid laugh, a most illustrious laugh—the father of a long line of laughs.
        SIMON *returns with the poulterer, and a huge bird.*

POULTERER   Here's your prize bird, gov'ner.

SCROOGE   Now *that's* a turkey—it could never have stood on its own two legs, they'd have snapped off. You can't carry that all the way to Camden Town, you must have a cab.
        He distributes coins.
    This is for the turkey. And this is for the cab.

POULTERER   Thank you, sir.

SCROOGE   Oh—the address—Number 7 Delancey Passage. Don't forget—Camden Town.

POULTERER   Right, gov'ner.
                                                                            He goes.

SCROOGE   And a merry Christmas! (*To* SIMON.) And as for you my boy . . .
        He hands him a coin.

SIMON   Name's Simon.
        He smiles.

_____

3. I.e., two and a half shillings.

SCROOGE   Merry Christmas, Simon.

SIMON   Merry Christmas, gov'nor.

The boy runs off.

SCROOGE   I'll visit the foundling homes, the workhouses . . . I shall endeavor to bring food to the hungry and ease to the sick. And I'll buy toys for all the children, and *I'll* play with them too! Such a turkey—I wish I could see Bob's face!

Christmas morning crossover. Various people shout 'Merry Christmas.'

NARRATION   Scrooge said afterward that of all the joyous sounds he had ever heard, those were the most joyful in his ears.

Carolers surround SCROOGE. *They sing, he joins them.*

NARRATION   Scrooge had not gone far, however, when he saw two familiar figures.

He approaches them.

Sir—madam—how do you do?

BLAKELY   Mr. Scrooge?

SCROOGE   Scrooge is my name, although I fear it may not be pleasant to either of you. Allow me to beg your pardon, and will you have the goodness to accept my pledge—

SCROOGE *whispers in Forrest's ear.*

BLAKELY   Lord bless me! My dear Mr. Scrooge, are you serious?

SCROOGE   Not a farthing[4] less. A great many back-payments are included, I assure you.

BLAKELY *speaks into Forrest's earphone.*

FORREST   My dear sir, I don't know what to say to such munificence—

SCROOGE   Don't say anything, but please come and see me. Will you come and see me?

BLAKELY   We will! Merry Christmas!

FORREST   A very merry Christmas, Mr. Marley!

NARRATION   He went to church, and walked about the streets, and watched the people hurrying to and fro, and patted children on the head, and ministered to beggars.

Scrooge never dreamed that any walk—any thing—could give him so much happiness.

He purchases a sprig of mistletoe from a vendor.

In the afternoon, he turned his steps toward his nephew's house.

SCROOGE *knocks on a door. A little maid appears.*

MAID   May I help you, sir?

SCROOGE   Is your master at home, my dear? Nice girl, very . . .

MAID   Yes, sir, in the dining room.

SCROOGE   Thank you, my dear.

He enters.

MAID *(after him)*   I'll show you, if you please.

SCROOGE   Thank'ee, but he knows me.

The party reenters.

SCROOGE *enters from the center door, maid following.*

MRS. FRED   Bless us, are you—

SCROOGE   Your Uncle Scrooge? Yes.

MRS. FRED *(yells)*   Fred!

SCROOGE *(yells)*   Nephew!

FRED   Who is it, dear? Why—Uncle!

---

4. A quarter of a penny.

SCROOGE   Nephew! I believe you've made off with my paperweight!

FRED   Yes, but I—

SCROOGE   Keep it, Nephew, as a memento. It was a gift from your mother. Only could you be so kind as to let me stay?

FRED   Of course.

SCROOGE   You see, I've come to dinner.

MRS. FRED   Yes, indeed, let me take your coat. Come in, come in.

SCROOGE   Young woman, you are provoking . . . bewitching . . . and altogether satisfactory.

> *He steals a kiss.*

FRED   Uncle, I shan't be able to trust you alone with her.

SCROOGE   Will there be games tonight? Blindman's Bluff, I hope. And perhaps Yes and No?

FRED   Of course, of course.

SCROOGE   You see, I know the answer to Yes and No.

NARRATION   He felt at home in five minutes. Wonderful party, wonderful games . . . wonderful unanimity.

Wonderful happiness.

> *The scene fades, Scrooge's office comes on.*

NARRATION   But the crowning delight of the very altered Mr. Ebenezer Scrooge came when he arrived at the office the next morning.

> *The office clock ticks noisily.*

Oh, he was early there! He couldn't wait to catch Bob Cratchit come in late.

SCROOGE   I have my heart set on it!

NARRATION   The clock struck nine. No Bob. A quarter past.

NARRATOR AND SCROOGE   No Bob.

> *The tardy* BOB *tries to sneak in unobserved.*

SCROOGE   Good *afternoon*, Cratchit.

CRATCHIT   I'm very sorry, sir, I am behind my time.

SCROOGE   A full eighteen and a half minutes past your time.

Step this way, if you please.

CRATCHIT   It's only once a year, sir. It shall not be repeated. I was making rather merry, yesterday. Such an unexpected feast we had—

SCROOGE   I cannot stand for this sort of thing any longer. And therefore . . .

> *He pushes* BOB.

Therefore . . . I am about to . . . raise your salary!

> *He pushes* BOB, *who grabs his ruler.*

A merry Christmas, Bob, a merrier Christmas than I have given you for many a year. I shall raise your salary, and we'll discuss your affairs this very afternoon, over a bowl of smoking Bishop![5] Build up the fires, and buy another scuttle of coal before you dot another 'i,' Bob Cratchit.

> *He holds out his hand;* CRATCHIT, *still weak in the knees, shakes it enthusiastically.*

> *Town crossover.*

SCROOGE (*as narrator*)   Scrooge was even better than his word. He did it all, and infinitely more.

> SIMON *comes in, waves at* SCROOGE.

---

5. A sweet drink made of heated red wine, oranges or lemons, sugar, and spices (it is purple, like a bishop's cassock).

SCROOGE (*as narrator*)   He became as good a friend, as good a master, as good a man as the good old city knew.

Some people laughed to see the alteration in him.

But he let them laugh. His own heart laughed, and that was quite enough for him.

He had no further commerce with spirits, but lived upon the Total Abstinence Principle ever afterward.

And to Tiny Tim, who did not die, he was a second father.

And it was always said of him, that he knew how to keep Christmas well, if any man alive possessed the knowledge.

May that be truly said of us, and all of us.

And so, as Tiny Tim observed . . .

TINY TIM   God bless us, every one.

SCROOGE   *Every* one.

1975 — 1998

LAURENCE YEP
b. 1948

The versatile Chinese American writer Laurence Yep is best known for his historical fiction, fantasy, and science fiction for young adults. He has also published two important collections of traditional Chinese tales, as told by immigrants to California (see "The Phantom Heart" in the Fairy Tales section, above, for further biographical information). In the 1980s he began writing plays, a genre he finds particularly challenging. His writings often are examinations of otherness, sharing themes such as alienation, class conflicts, the importance of the family, and the complex negotiations of adolescence; many of them provide a realistic view of the culture and history of both extraordinary and ordinary Chinese Americans.

Because Yep was born in San Francisco, it is perhaps natural that his first work to deal directly with the Chinese immigrant experience was inspired by a long-forgotten piece of the city's history: the successful efforts of the immigrant Fung Joe Guey to design, build, and fly a biplane over Oakland in 1909. *Dragonwings* (1975) is also Yep's most critically acclaimed work, a Newbery Honor Book that has won numerous other awards. This "historical fantasy" (as Yep calls it), which blends Chinese folklore and myth with carefully researched facts, is nar-

rated by Moon Shadow, an eight-year-old boy who leaves China to join his father, Windrider (a kite builder, as was Yep's own father), in turn-of-the-century San Francisco.

A dramatic adaptation of the novel was commissioned by the Berkeley Repertory Theatre; it premiered in 1991 with the Asian American director Phyllis S. K. Look, who was instrumental in its creation. Other productions have been staged at such prestigious venues as New York's Lincoln Center Institute and the Kennedy Center in Washington, D.C. The play, which is very poetic, conveys more than just the determination and courage of one Chinese immigrant. It also demonstrates how he and his son must confront racism and prejudice as they endeavor to find a place for themselves in American culture. In this regard, the drama's specific story of a "Chinese" experience in America can be understood as encompassing a larger critique of prejudice faced by ethnic groups in the United States. Many of Yep's writings concern individuals negotiating two or more cultures, and the play makes a highly effective statement about all immigrant groups in the United States whose important contributions to American culture have often been overlooked and whose voices have often been ignored.

Dragonwings

CAST DESCRIPTION

MOON SHADOW, Chinese boy who grows from five to fourteen in the course of the play.

MOTHER, Chinese woman in her late twenties. Doubles as Miss Whitlaw.

WINDRIDER, Chinese man in his thirties.

UNCLE BRIGHT STAR, Chinese man in his sixties. Doubles as Dragon King and Mr. Alger and perhaps Earthquake Dragon.

BLACK DOG, Chinese teenager. Doubles as Tom and perhaps the Earthquake Dragon.

DRAGON KING, an elderly dragon. Played by Uncle Bright Star.

MR. ALGER, a middle-aged American man. Played by Uncle Bright Star.

MISS WHITLAW, American woman in her sixties. Played by Moon Shadow's mother.

EARTHQUAKE DRAGON, a young dragon. May be played by Uncle Bright Star, Black Dog or a stage assistant.

Two stage assistants. Uncle Bright Star and/or Black Dog can double as one of them depending on the scene.

SCENE 1

The year is 1928 in America. MOON SHADOW *enters from stage right as an adult in a 1920s peaked cap and coat. He wears wire-rim glasses.*

MOON SHADOW   When I was a boy, my father had a special dream.

(*A stage assistant appears from upstage and helps* MOON SHADOW *remove his cap, coat and glasses and exits stage left. Underneath his coat,* MOON SHADOW *wears the simple clothing of a Chinese peasant boy.*)

MOON SHADOW   Then it became mine. This is our story.

(MOON SHADOW *begins a Tai Chi–like movement which segues rhythmically into a mime of flying a kite.*)

(*As* MOON SHADOW *begins to tug at his kite, his mother enters quickly from stage left. She wears a patched peasant costume.*)

MOTHER (*urgently*)   Reel in the slack. Hurry. There. You caught the wind.

MOON SHADOW   Oh, no.

MOTHER (*guiding his hands*)   Don't let the wind take it.

MOON SHADOW   It's like the kite's alive.

MOTHER   The string is your leash. The kite, your dog. Keep hold. (*Stepping away.*) Maybe we'll catch a phoenix.

MOON SHADOW (*letting it fly higher*)   Look at it go.

MOTHER   Not so fast.

MOON SHADOW   It's mine. Papa made it for me.

MOTHER   Not so high. (*Pause.*) Do you remember him?

MOON SHADOW   When's he coming back to China?

MOTHER (*watching the kite anxiously*)   When he's rich. Then he'll leave the land of the Golden Mountain.[1]

MOON SHADOW   Grandmother says it's a big, big mountain. Three thousand miles

_____

1. A name for America, used by the Chinese.

wide and a thousand high. And all you have to do is take a bucket and scoop it up.

MOTHER   The wind's switching.

MOON SHADOW   So if father's sitting on top of a gold mountain, why doesn't he pick up some nuggets and come home? Why does he work in a laundry?

MOTHER (*wistfully*)   I don't know. I've never been there.

(MOTHER *and* MOON SHADOW *remain on stage.* UNCLE BRIGHT STAR *and* WIND-RIDER *enter from upstage. They occupy a part of the stage representing the interior of the Peach Orchard laundry in San Francisco's Chinatown. China and the laundry are staged simultaneously.*)

(UNCLE BRIGHT STAR *is hanging clothes. The sleeves of his collarless shirt are rolled up.* WINDRIDER *is ironing.*)

(BLACK DOG *stumbles in. About eighteen, his dandy-ish clothes are mussed and his face is cut.*)

BLACK DOG   They'll be sorry.

WINDRIDER   What happened to you?

BLACK DOG   I'm going to bust their heads.

UNCLE BRIGHT STAR   Where's your queue?[2]

BLACK DOG   White demons cut it.

UNCLE BRIGHT STAR (*to* WINDRIDER)   They're starting in again.

WINDRIDER (*going to a window*)   Where are they?

BLACK DOG   Left 'em at Union Square.

UNCLE BRIGHT STAR   Stupid! What were you doing outside of Chinatown?

BLACK DOG   Walking.

WINDRIDER   Were they coming this way?

BLACK DOG   They were too drunk to walk far.

UNCLE BRIGHT STAR   You couldn't outrun them?

BLACK DOG   They started it.

UNCLE BRIGHT STAR   And you just stopped and talked?

BLACK DOG   Should've finished it. (*Grabs the iron.*)

WINDRIDER   It's hot.

BLACK DOG   I'll brand them.

(WINDRIDER *grabs Black Dog's arms while* UNCLE *grabs the wrist holding the iron.*)

WINDRIDER   Calm down.

UNCLE BRIGHT STAR   Stupid!

BLACK DOG   Let me go.

(UNCLE *and* WINDRIDER *wrestle* BLACK DOG *to the ground.*)

(MOTHER *is now flying the kite.*)

MOON SHADOW   Why don't you ever talk about the Gold Mountain?

MOTHER   Your grandmother has all the answers.

MOON SHADOW   She says that demons roam up and down the mountain. And they beat anyone they catch taking the gold. With sticks big as trees. But if you do like they say, they let you take a little nugget.

MOTHER   Look at the kite. Like a little rainbow.

MOON SHADOW   Grandmother says that she heard about this man over there. He let a demon touch him. Only the demon had poison on his hand. Knocked the man out. When the man woke up, he was in chains. Is that true?

---

2. A braid worn at the back of the head. Although originally a sign of defeat—the Manchu, victorious in the seventeenth century, forced the native Chinese to wear the queue—it had become a sign of Chinese manhood.

MOTHER   How should I know?

MOON SHADOW   Grandmother heard it from Aunt Piety and she heard it from a man down by Three Willows. And they all swear it's the truth.

MOTHER   Then I guess it is.

MOON SHADOW   Then why did you let Father go there?

MOTHER   We didn't have a choice.

MOON SHADOW   Why didn't we go with him?

MOTHER   The white demons won't let any Chinese women into their country.[3] So the men have to go alone.

MOON SHADOW   Will I have to go when I'm a man?

   (**MOTHER** *turns away as if she is absorbed in flying the kite.*)

   (**WINDRIDER** *and* **UNCLE BRIGHT STAR** *are tending Black Dog's cuts.*)

UNCLE BRIGHT STAR (*applying an antiseptic*)   Stupid bum! It could've been your head. Be cunning. Be silent. But above all be invisible. How can you go home to China without your queue? The first Manchu who sees you will think you're a rebel.

BLACK DOG   By the time I leave, my hair'll be long and gray.

UNCLE BRIGHT STAR   Hunh! Still want to play the prince back in China.

BLACK DOG   Better than here. Demons all around. Why'd you bring me to San Francisco? Up to my waist in dirty clothes. In boiling water. (*Holding up his hands.*) Look at them. Crab claws. Some father. (*As* **UNCLE BRIGHT STAR** *leaves in disgust,* **BLACK DOG** *addresses* **WINDRIDER**.) And now you want to play the big shot. Want to bring your boy to this country. Didn't you learn anything?

   (**BLACK DOG** *exits.* **MOON SHADOW** *waves a letter at his mother.*)

MOON SHADOW   Mother!

MOTHER   Read slow. (*Taps ear and makes fist.*) What my ears hear, my mind holds.

MOON SHADOW   It's to me!

MOTHER   Not to me?

MOON SHADOW   No. (*Reading.*) The sixth day of the second month of the thirty-first year of the era Continuing Enlightenment.[4] Dear boy. So much has happened that I need to share it with you. I wish the Western folk would let your mother come here; but they do not. So you must join me . . . in the land of the Golden Mountain.

WINDRIDER (*simultaneously*)   In the land of the Golden Mountain.

MOTHER   No. You're only ten.

WINDRIDER   It is your time as it once was mine.

MOON SHADOW (*reading*)   It is your time as it once was mine.

MOTHER   It's too dangerous.

   (**WINDRIDER** *stretches out a hand towards* **MOON SHADOW**.)

MOON SHADOW (*to* **MOTHER**)   I want to go.

MOTHER   No.

MOON SHADOW   I'll write.

MOTHER   I'll have every letter read to me right away. Over and over. So what my ears hear, my heart will hold.

   (*They embrace. The stage assistant appears with Moon Shadow's box, containing his worldly possessions, and hands it to* **MOTHER** *who gives it to* **MOON SHADOW**. *Hesitantly* **MOON SHADOW** *begins to circle the stage, representing his passage across the Pacific. He stops at stage center.*)

FIRST VOICE (*voice-over*)   I am with the immigration service of the United States of

---

3. U.S. immigration policy was intended to discourage the Chinese from settling.

4. The rule of the Guongxu emperor began in 1875.

America. We must ask you questions to verify your right to enter this country. You must answer truthfully. Do you understand?

MOON SHADOW (*timidly*) Yes.

FIRST VOICE (*aggressive*) Who are you?

MOON SHADOW Lee Moon Shadow.

FIRST VOICE What is your father's name?

MOON SHADOW Increase.

FIRST VOICE What is your mother's name?

MOON SHADOW Springtime.

FIRST VOICE How many rooms in your house?

MOON SHADOW Three.

FIRST VOICE How many windows does your house have?

MOON SHADOW Two.

FIRST VOICE How many trees outside?

MOON SHADOW One. A plum tree.

FIRST VOICE Any animals?

MOON SHADOW Two chickens and a pig.

SECOND VOICE (*aggressive*) Who are you? What is your father's name? What is your mother's? How many rooms in your house? How many windows does your house have? How many trees outside? Any animals?

THIRD VOICE (*overlapping*) Who are you? What is your father's name? What is your mother's? How many rooms in your house? How many windows does your house have? How many trees outside? Any animals?

FIRST VOICE (*overlapping*) Who are you? What is your father's name? What is your mother's? How many rooms in your house? How many windows does your house have? How many trees outside? Any animals?

MOON SHADOW (*confused*) Moon . . . Increase . . . Spring . . . Two, I mean, three. A pig tree. Plums and chickens.

MOON SHADOW (*increasingly agitated*) Moon-Increase-Spring-three-two-pig-plum-chicken-increase-two-three.

ALL THREE VOICES Who are you?

MOON SHADOW Moon Shadow.

ALL THREE VOICES Who are you? Who are you? Who are you?

MOON SHADOW Moon Shadow!

Scene 2

WINDRIDER *and* UNCLE BRIGHT STAR *enter from upstage and anxiously scan an imaginary crowd for* MOON SHADOW. *When he spots his son,* WINDRIDER *holds out his arms.*

WINDRIDER   Moon Shadow. Hello, boy. I've been waiting a long time to do this. Too long.
>   (*They hug awkwardly.*)

UNCLE BRIGHT STAR   In my day, we didn't go around making public displays of ourselves.

WINDRIDER   This is your Uncle Bright Star.

MOON SHADOW (*bowing*)   So honored.

UNCLE BRIGHT STAR   Hunh. The docks are no place to chat. This way to our palace.

MOON SHADOW   Palace?

WINDRIDER   Our laundry in Chinatown.
>   (*They walk in a large circle.*)

WINDRIDER   Was the trip rough?

MOON SHADOW   I managed.

WINDRIDER   Not even seasick?

MOON SHADOW   A little. (*Looking around.*) What funny houses. Like boxes.[5]

UNCLE BRIGHT STAR   Don't gawk.

MOON SHADOW   Yeuh. What a smell.

WINDRIDER   Saloons aren't perfume factories.

UNCLE BRIGHT STAR   Keep close.

WINDRIDER   Eyes straight.

MOON SHADOW (*breaking the circle*)   Where is the gold mountain?

UNCLE BRIGHT STAR   It's just poetry, boy.

WINDRIDER   You'll learn.
>   (*They finish the circle.*)

UNCLE BRIGHT STAR   Sound the trumpets. The hero has arrived. Enter the Laundry of the Peach Orchard Vow.[6]
>   (MOON SHADOW *sets his box down and investigates the laundry.*)

MOON SHADOW   What are those blue packages?

UNCLE BRIGHT STAR   Witness the treasure vault of shirts, skirts and long johns.

MOON SHADOW   What's in this room?

UNCLE BRIGHT STAR   Behold the grotto of crystal purity.

MOON SHADOW (*looks*)   You could sail back to China in one of those tubs.

WINDRIDER (*to the puzzled* MOON SHADOW)   Here's where we wash the clothes.

UNCLE BRIGHT STAR   And this is the drying room.

WINDRIDER   You'll have to keep the stove well stocked.

UNCLE BRIGHT STAR (*playing it to the hilt*)   Gaze upon the clotheslines: the harp of our livelihood. When the clothes are drying, you can listen to the music—tip, tippy, tip.

---

5. Traditional Chinese houses are built around an internal courtyard.
6. In the novel, Yep explains that this vow was "taken by the man who became the god of war and his sworn brothers, to serve the people and help one another."

WINDRIDER   What about the gifts?

>   (*The stage assistant enters with a pair of boots and hat. After leaving them near Moon Shadow's box, the stage assistant exits.*)

UNCLE BRIGHT STAR (*remembering his dignity*)   Well, a guest of the Gold Mountain has to be properly attired. (*Placing hat on Moon Shadow's head.*) That should keep the sun off that girlish skin. (*Holds up the pair of boots and stamps his own feet.*) And these should keep those farmer's feet from wearing out the Gold Mountain.

MOON SHADOW (*admiring them*)   Just like father's.

>   (UNCLE *fusses over* MOON SHADOW *as he tries on his new hat and boots.*)

UNCLE BRIGHT STAR   What're you waiting for? Fetch your silly toy.

WINDRIDER   There are more important things for the soul.

>   (WINDRIDER *exits.* UNCLE *makes sure he is gone before he takes the Monkey carving from his pocket and gives it to* MOON SHADOW.)

UNCLE BRIGHT STAR   Just a little knickknack. Made it in my spare time.

MOON SHADOW   It's the Monkey King.

UNCLE BRIGHT STAR   Know the story?

MOON SHADOW   He went up to Heaven and almost conquered it.

UNCLE BRIGHT STAR (*strikes an operatic pose like the Monkey King*)   And jumped so high that the sky ran out of blue. And the world ran out of ground. And all that was left to stand on was the hand.

MOON SHADOW   Or when he first learned how to fly. And he did all those funny somersaults.

UNCLE BRIGHT STAR   Have we got an actor for you. Does the Monkey King better than anybody in China. We'll take you to the theater when he puts on that show.

MOON SHADOW   I've never seen an opera.

UNCLE BRIGHT STAR   You're not at the end of the world. So they still teach some of the old stories. (*Hearing* WINDRIDER *returning*) Well, if you don't want it, just chuck it away.

MOON SHADOW (*putting it away*)   Not a chance.

>   (WINDRIDER *enters with a kite whose frame is of bamboo bent into the shape of a butterfly. Rice paper covers the frame and is painted with the colorful markings of a butterfly.*)

WINDRIDER   Well, boy?

MOON SHADOW (*examining it*)   It's the best ever.

>   (*A door slams offstage and* BLACK DOG *enters. He ignores the glaring* UNCLE BRIGHT STAR *and walks over to* MOON SHADOW.)

BLACK DOG   Nice boots. But that hat. (*He snatches the hat from Moon Shadow's head and adjusts the crown and brim.*) Makes you look like the old monument. (*Nods to* UNCLE BRIGHT STAR.) Don't want the pigeons roosting on you. (*Sets the hat back on Moon Shadow's head at a rakish angle.*) Now you're a regular swell.

UNCLE BRIGHT STAR   Where's your gift?

>   (BLACK DOG *has been listening for the mob and hears it faintly in the distance.*)

BLACK DOG   I brought some friends to serenade him. There's a mob coming.

>   (*A curious* MOON SHADOW *moves toward the door but his father pulls him to safety.*)

MOON SHADOW (*dropping the kite offstage*)   My kite!

>   (BLACK DOG *crouches nearby.* WINDRIDER, MOON SHADOW *and* UNCLE *take shelter as if behind the laundry's counter.*)

MOB (*their drunken singing grows in volume as they approach*)
(*To the tune of "Buffalo Gals":*)

> Yellow monkeys,
> Won't you come out tonight?
> Come out tonight, come out tonight.
> Yellow monkeys,
> Won't you come out tonight?
> And dance by the light of the Moon?

(*As the sound of the mob grows,*)

MOB (*variously*)   Hey, Monkeys. Tails, tails. We want your tails. Chop off their tails.

MOON SHADOW   What tails?

(WINDRIDER *silently holds up his own queue.*)

(*A window breaks offstage.*)

MOON SHADOW   Are we going to stay here?

UNCLE BRIGHT STAR   It's safer here in Chinatown. Don't ever forget that.

MOON SHADOW   Does this happen often?

WINDRIDER   Just when they get liquored up.

MOB   Cut your hair for free. Come on out. Chop off their tails.

(*The singing resumes as the mob moves on.*)

UNCLE BRIGHT STAR   Filthy demons. Can't turn your back on any of them.

MOON SHADOW (*fetching broken kite and revealing it*)   Father.

BLACK DOG   Next time the demons won't stop with our hair. Next time they'll go for our heads. (*To* MOON SHADOW.) Welcome to the land of the Gold Mountain. (*Exits.*)

UNCLE BRIGHT STAR (*to* WINDRIDER)   Take your boy upstairs. (*Follows* BLACK DOG *out.*)

SCENE 3

MOON SHADOW *takes his box. He and* WINDRIDER *circle the stage as if they are going upstairs to Windrider's room. They stop center right where there is a table with a large, bulbous electric light and a jerry-rigged pair of telephones. There is also a model of the Wright Brothers' aeroplane[7] hanging overboard.*

MOON SHADOW   Why did that happen?

WINDRIDER   Don't go by those idiots outside. We've got a lot to learn here.

MOON SHADOW   From the demons?

WINDRIDER   Westerners. Only the superstitious call them demons.

MOON SHADOW (*stepping inside into Windrider's room*)   Look at all the toys. (*Putting his box down and setting his hat on top.*)

WINDRIDER   Now you're sounding like Uncle. (*Flips a crude switch on the base of the light.*) This is called the electric light. I made this one myself.

MOON SHADOW (*holding up his hands and squinting*)   That's bright. What makes it go?

WINDRIDER   Ee-lec-tri-ci-ty.

MOON SHADOW   Electricity.

7. The biplane built by Wilbur (1867–1919) and Orville Wright (1871–1948), flown in the first motor-powered flight in 1903.

WINDRIDER   No more candles. No more stinky lanterns. No more gas light. See those little things inside.

MOON SHADOW   Like a bug?

WINDRIDER   Those are bits of bamboo. Burn almost forever. You can have daylight anytime. And this is a telephone.

MOON SHADOW (*softly*)   Tel-e-phone.

WINDRIDER   It's another one of my experiments. You talk into this part and you listen to this.

MOON SHADOW (*speaking into the mouthpiece*)   How've you been eating?

WINDRIDER   Still got some kinks to work out. But one day, you can crank the magneto and get the operator. And he'll get you anyone you want to talk to.

MOON SHADOW   Even Mama?

WINDRIDER   Maybe one day.

MOON SHADOW (*hiding his disappointment*)   That'd be nice. (*Looking around.*) What kind of kite is that?

WINDRIDER (*Taking it down*)   It's not a kite. It's a model of an ae-ro-plane.

MOON SHADOW   Ae-ro-plane.

WINDRIDER   Two Westerners, the Wright brothers, they built the real one. It carries them through the sky. No bumps, no lumps like on the ground. Just riding through the air, smooth and slick and easy.

MOON SHADOW   People can't fly.

WINDRIDER   Now you really do sound like Uncle. The Wright brothers flew, and sooner or later so will I. (*Handing him the model.*)

MOON SHADOW   Really?

WINDRIDER   I have the Dragon King's word.

MOON SHADOW   You spoke to him?

WINDRIDER   My first night here, I tried to sleep, but my mind kept trying to understand all the strange, new things I'd seen that day. But finally I drifted off. (WINDRIDER *begins to move in the style of Chinese opera.*) And woke up on a beach. All shiny blue. And behind me, mountains with steep sides, all of amber. I turned, and I heard this funny noise. I turned again. The same funny noise. It was the sand. Only it wasn't sand. It was tiny sapphires. When you rubbed them together they made this little laughing noise. And suddenly (*a Chinese gong strikes*) these dragon heads burst out of the water. Row after row. Regiment after regiment. And they're carrying this enormous dragon.

DRAGON VOICES (*voice-over*)   His Royal Exaltedness, the Pearly Potentate, Sovereign of the Scaly, Dictator of the Deluge, Suzerain of the Seas—

DRAGON KING   Enough!

(WINDRIDER *stands petrified as the* DRAGON KING *enters from stage right. He wears a beard and a half-mask painted in Chinese operatic colors and is dressed in kingly robes and head dress complete with flags and feathers. On his feet are a pair of Chinese operatic shoes with high platforms. In his hand he carries a spear. He becomes annoyed after regarding* WINDRIDER *for a moment and dances in fury.*)

DRAGON KING (*the dance ends with a grand pose*)   Haven't picked up any manners as a softskin. (*When* WINDRIDER *kowtows, the dragon king inspects him.*) How do you breathe through a snout that small?

WINDRIDER (*looking up slightly*)   Do I know you, Your Exaltedness?

DRAGON KING (*strutting behind* WINDRIDER)   You made terrible puns, cheated at dice and criticized my poetry, but you were a phenomenal healer—though I never would've told you before. You already had a swelled-enough head.

WINDRIDER   Your Exaltedness, I know nothing about healing.

DRAGON KING (*gesturing*)   Before you were reborn as a human, you were given a broth that made you forget. But my spies tell me you've kept your old skills.

WINDRIDER   I tinker with machines.

DRAGON KING (*gesturing*)   What's magic in our kingdom takes other forms in the human worlds. As a dragon you could cut butterflies out of paper and make them come to life. Now as a softskin you make kites.

WINDRIDER   I was a dragon?

DRAGON KING (*angrily swinging his spear overhead as he dances*)   Think I chat with squirrels? Though they do have a bit more sense than softskins.

  (*A gong sounds as* WINDRIDER *straightens up.*)

WINDRIDER   Did you bring me here just to insult me?

DRAGON KING (*approvingly*)   That's my old Windrider! I've missed you.

MOON SHADOW   Windrider.

  (*A stage assistant appears and places a box on stage.*)

DRAGON KING   I've kept it for you. This is the first time anyone else has touched it.

WINDRIDER   What is it?

DRAGON KING   It's your medicine case. Heal me. Your paws—I mean, your hands will remember. And if they don't, have no fear. No harm will come to you. I called you here as an old friend.

WINDRIDER   What seems to be the trouble?

  (*The* DRAGON KING *raises a wing, revealing a deep gash in his side.*)

WINDRIDER   What could cut through that hide?

DRAGON KING   Outlaws. Dragons to the south.

WINDRIDER   I can't work on you when you're this big.

DRAGON KING   A dragon king must be a royal size. (*Trying to swing his spear overhead again, but stops short, wincing at the pain.*)

WINDRIDER   I'm softskin size now.

DRAGON KING (*grumbling*)   I don't see how you can stand it.

  (*The* DRAGON KING *"shrinks."* WINDRIDER *opens the case doubtfully. After a moment's hesitation, he takes out a pair of forceps and begins to work, picking up more confidence as he goes.*)

WINDRIDER   Why was I re-born as a human?

DRAGON KING   You got to showing off. Tried to grow big enough to blow out the sun. Just high spirits. But Heaven didn't see it that way. I tried my best. I begged them to make you into a lizard, a gecko, a skink. But they can be awfully stuffy. Ow!

  (WINDRIDER *has been pulling at something with his forceps. He does a shoulder roll that takes him across stage. He holds up a claw.*)

WINDRIDER   A claw. Made a hole big enough for a window.

DRAGON KING (*thumbing toward in the direction of the outlaws*)   You should see the outlaw. (DRAGON KING *"expands" and sighs as he stretches.*) Ah! How can I ever repay you?

WINDRIDER (*kowtowing*)   Lord, make me a dragon again.

DRAGON KING   I would if I could but my paws are bound. You must live out your allotted span as a softskin. And in that time you must prove yourself worthy of becoming a dragon again. Sometimes you will not even know you are being tested until the test is over.

WINDRIDER   How do I pass?

DRAGON KING   Just follow your heart and you will become a true dragon. (*Thoughtful *pause.*) Maybe I should refresh your memory by showing you about the kingdom. Stand up.

> (*When* WINDRIDER *stands up uncertainly, the* DRAGON KING *gestures three times magically toward Windrider's back as a gong beats.*)

DRAGON KING (*when* WINDRIDER *begins to itch*)   Don't wriggle! And don't scratch!

> (*After a moment,* WINDRIDER *leans forward and falls to his knees.*)

DRAGON KING   You've forgotten how to balance yourself. (*Laughing.*)

> (*The stage assistant runs in behind* WINDRIDER *and tosses two red ribbons ten feet in length into the air.*)

WINDRIDER   Wings. I've grown wings. Like silk over gold wire. Look at the colors. Like a rainbow.

DRAGON KING   Try them if you have the courage.

> (*As* WINDRIDER *begins his dance, the stage assistant manipulates the ribbons in an energetic and yet graceful ribbon dance.*)

WINDRIDER   Just one flap and I was shooting up, up into the air. I floated along so slow and easy. I looped. The world spun away like a top. The beach was just a scrap of paper, the mountains lumpy rags, the sea, broken glass. And there was nothing between me and Heaven but sky—lovely blue sky. Free of the earth. Free of everything. Free.

DRAGON KING (*shouting*)   Is it good to have wings again?

WINDRIDER (*shouting*)   Yes!

> (WINDRIDER *finishes his dance and the stage assistant exits stage right.*)

DRAGON KING   Then here I come.

> (DRAGON KING *does a solo dance.*)

WINDRIDER   And this great, green scaly mountain leapt upward. Ton after ton just pouring itself into the sky. He was old that dragon, but his heart was young. He twisted and curled like he was a piece of ribbon. He wrote his name in the sky.

DRAGON KING   Race you.

> (WINDRIDER *and the* DRAGON KING *dance together.*)
> (*The dance climaxes.*)

DRAGON KING   Time for you to go back.

> (WINDRIDER *sinks to one knee.*)

DRAGON KING (*exiting stage left*)   Be a dragon at heart and you will become a dragon in body.

WINDRIDER   When will I see you again?

> (*Back in his room in the laundry,* WINDRIDER *turns to* MOON SHADOW.)

WINDRIDER   The next morning my back and ribs were all sore. Uncle says it was just a dream. He says I walked in my sleep and fell over something. But I know it was real.

> (MOON SHADOW *nods.*)

SCENE 4

In the laundry six months later. MOON SHADOW *is downstage as he picks up a brush. After dipping it in ink, he begins to write in vertical columns from right to left.*

MOON SHADOW   The eighteenth day of the ninth month of the thirty-first year of the era Continuing Enlightenment. Nineteen-ought-five.

Dear mother. We think of you too. Are you still flying my kite? I have no time for that now. I try to please father, but he asks for much. But that only makes me try harder. (*Crosses out the last two sentences and rewrites.*) Uncle sees to my Chinese lessons. Father sees to my demon . . . (*Crosses out the last word and rewrites.*) my Western ones. After six months, I can talk to the customers myself. I go out with father when he delivers the laundry and picks up the dirty stuff. We ride in Uncle's wagon. It's pulled by Uncle's old horse, Red Rabbit.

(WINDRIDER *enters from upstage and pantomimes handling the reins of a horse.*)

WINDRIDER   Whoa, Red Rabbit.

MOON SHADOW   The other day we were making our rounds when we saw this gasoline carriage. It's a kind of wagon made out of metal with big rubber wheels. No horses pull it. Somehow this powerful engine makes it go. Only this one was stopped. In front of it was this westerner in a big overcoat.

(MR. ALGER *enters from stage left with his car. He is a prosperous, plump middle-aged American. He wears a long, driving coat and goggles. He kicks his Maxwell Runabout. Note: The car repair scene should be done with comic bounce and energy as in* Commedia dell' Arte *or a Chaplin silent movie.*)

MISTER ALGER   (*swearing*)   Ding-dang consarned piece of junk. Oughta make you into a flower box. You hear me? A chicken coop. A horse trough.

WINDRIDER   Need help?

MISTER ALGER   Know where there's a garage, John?

WINDRIDER   (*excited and curious*)   I look. (*Inspecting the engine.*)

MISTER ALGER   I'll take it to a garage. (*Louder as* WINDRIDER *examines the car.*) You sabe[8] me? (*Even louder.*) Garage. Repair my Maxwell Runabout.

WINDRIDER   You got screwdriver? (*Straightening up.*)

MISTER ALGER   Hold on a minute, John. That's an expensive piece of machinery. Cost purt near five hundred dollars.

WINDRIDER   (*fishing a coin from his own pocket*)   Never mind. I got dime. (*Ducking back toward the engine.*)

MISTER ALGER   Hail, Columbia! That's enough, John. Time to surface. Rise and shine.

WINDRIDER   (*straightening up*)   You got wrench?

MISTER ALGER   You've helped enough, John. Now get out of there.

WINDRIDER   Never mind. I got skeleton key. (*Ducking back.*)

MISTER ALGER   This is a very temperamental, complex piece of machinery. H. G. Wells![9] I pay mechanics bushels of money; and they don't understand it. J. D. Maxwell[1] invented the infernal contraption; and even he doesn't understand it! So you couldn't possibly—

WINDRIDER   (*straightening*)   Horseless ready.

MISTER ALGER   —Understand it.

WINDRIDER   (*putting his key away*)   It ready.

(MR. ALGER *skeptically gets behind the wheel. When* WINDRIDER *turns the crank at the front, the motor coughs into life.*)

MISTER ALGER   I'll be jiggered, you did fix it. (*Unbuttoning his coat and taking out his wallet.*) Here, John.

WINDRIDER   No tip. (*Pointing at the automobile.*) Look . . . make me happy.

MISTER ALGER   I can use a honest handyman like you. Got a lot of properties. Got a lot of machines. Always breaking down.

WINDRIDER   (*curious*)   You pay, I fix machines?

8. Understand (from the Spanish *sabe* [*usted*], "[you] know").
9. The British author (1866–1946), some of whose science fiction novels contain complicated

machinery (notably, *The Time Machine*, 1895).
1. A car builder (1864–1928); he began with the Maxwell Runabout in 1904.

MISTER ALGER (*taking a card from his wallet*) You read 'Merican? (*When* WINDRIDER *nods,* MR. ALGER *hands him the card.*) That's got my address. You come around anytime, sabe? Just ask for Oliver Alger.

WINDRIDER I fix, you pay?

(MR. ALGER *exits in his Maxwell Runabout.*)

MOON SHADOW (*finishing writing*) Father kept that card. Every now and then I see him looking at it when he thinks no one is watching.

(WINDRIDER *exits.*)

(*When he hears a thump,* MOON SHADOW *stops writing. A haggard* BLACK DOG *enters from upstage. His hands are in his coat pockets.*)

MOON SHADOW Where were you all night?

BLACK DOG None of your business.

MOON SHADOW (*blocking his way*) Father and Uncle are out looking for you.

BLACK DOG I'm found.

(*As he shoves* MOON SHADOW *out of the way, the opium drops out of his coat pocket. When* BLACK DOG *clumsily fumbles at the floor,* MOON SHADOW *picks it up for him.*)

MOON SHADOW What's this?

BLACK DOG That's mine.

MOON SHADOW (*sniffing*) Yeuh.

BLACK DOG Give it to me. (*Snatching it back.*) Gotta stick your nose in everything, don't you?

MOON SHADOW (*horrified as he realizes*) That's opium.

BLACK DOG Just trying it out.

MOON SHADOW That's poison.

BLACK DOG It just makes you forget for a while. When you've been over here as long as me, you'll understand.

(*As* MOON SHADOW *returns to his letter, a new thought occurs to* BLACK DOG.)

BLACK DOG Gonna squeal, Monkey? (*When* MOON SHADOW *turns his back and tries to walk away,* BLACK DOG *grabs him from behind.*) Squeal and I'll cut off your tail. (*Shows* MOON SHADOW *his knife.*)

(WINDRIDER *and* UNCLE *enter from stage right.*)

MOON SHADOW Father, Uncle, he's got—(BLACK DOG *grabs his queue.*) Ow!

BLACK DOG I mean it. (*Raising the knife threateningly.*)

UNCLE BRIGHT STAR Put that down.

MOON SHADOW He's got opium.

UNCLE BRIGHT STAR (*storming over*) Demon mud? In my house?

BLACK DOG I warned you. (*Cuts off Moon Shadow's queue and throws it down.*)

WINDRIDER Crazy!

UNCLE BRIGHT STAR You can't do that.

(*As* MOON SHADOW *picks up his severed queue,* WINDRIDER *rushes over to him.*)

UNCLE BRIGHT STAR Stupid bum! You're no son of mine.

BLACK DOG Who cares?

UNCLE BRIGHT STAR (*slapping Black Dog's face*) Don't talk back.

WINDRIDER Are you all right, boy?

MOON SHADOW (*holding his severed queue*) I can't go home.

BLACK DOG Everything I do is wrong. Everything he does is right.

UNCLE BRIGHT STAR He's a good boy. He listens. He obeys.

BLACK DOG Play the emperor. Make me a slave. No more.

UNCLE BRIGHT STAR Lazy. You want a roof? You want food? You work!

MOON SHADOW What'll I do?

BLACK DOG (*to* MOON SHADOW) I'll fix you, you little squealer. Next haircut's down to your throat. I got friends.

UNCLE BRIGHT STAR I said you're no son of mine. Get out! And don't ever come back!

BLACK DOG Have it your way. (*Exiting and saying to* MOON SHADOW) I got friends.

WINDRIDER (*pause*) He means it. It won't be safe to leave the laundry.

MOON SHADOW Did you hear what he said?

UNCLE BRIGHT STAR Who? I heard no one.

MOON SHADOW Black Dog.

UNCLE BRIGHT STAR I know no one by that name.

WINDRIDER You may not have a son, but I do. It's safer to go away until he cools off.

UNCLE BRIGHT STAR Where?

WINDRIDER I'll fix machines and this westerner will pay.

(WINDRIDER *produces Mr. Alger's card and hands it to Uncle.*)

UNCLE BRIGHT STAR Work for demons?

WINDRIDER (*taking back the card*) Come on, boy.

(*They exit stage right. Disgusted and amazed,* UNCLE *exits stage left.*)

SCENE 5

MOON SHADOW *re-enters from stage right as an adult in cap, coat and glasses. The stage assistant sets out a pump downstage left and a stained-glass window of St. George[2] slaying a dragon stage right during the following.*

MOON SHADOW So father went to see Mr. Alger and Mr. Alger remembered him. Said it was hard to forget him. He gave father a job and let us have a shack off Polk Street to the west of Chinatown.

Over one block was Van Ness Avenue where all the rich folk lived in big mansions. But Polk Street was where the servants lived. And the grocers and the tailors, the doctors and the dentists, and all the other people the rich folk needed.

So we carried our things eight blocks over the hill. When we got there, everyone was in a hurry. Dodging the horse trolleys. Maids carrying big baskets of groceries. Men with towels strutting to the public baths. I almost lost father twice in the crowd.

(*During the last part of this speech,* TOM *enters. He is about Moon Shadow's age and is dressed in a collarless shirt and derby. He gets to his knees and begins a game of marbles.*)

(*Late afternoon on Polk Street.* WINDRIDER *enters from stage left with a toolbox. The adult* MOON SHADOW *watches his father briefly and then exits stage left.*)

WINDRIDER (*looking around*) There's the octagon house. Mr. Alger said our shack was to the rear. Hurry up, boy. It's over here. Got to be at Mr. Alger's by four.

MOON SHADOW (*offstage*) Coming!

(*As* WINDRIDER *exits right into the shack, the young* MOON SHADOW *staggers in with a stack of boxes from left. The stack is so high, he cannot see over them. As he circles the stage uncertainly,* TOM *stalks* MOON SHADOW. *Finally, looking*

---

2. Patron saint of England; according to legend, he rescued a princess from a dragon, eventually killing it.

from the side, MOON SHADOW *sees the water pump. He crosses to it, sets his boxes down and begins to prime the pump.*)

TOM Hey, John. (*As* MOON SHADOW *ignores him*) I'm talking to you, John. (*Pulling him away from the pump*) You sabe me, John?

MOON SHADOW (*warily*) My name not John.

TOM (*pointing toward the pump*) That pump's Miss Whitlaw's. It's not for your kind.

MOON SHADOW We need water too. (TOM *knocks him over when he tries to return to the pump.*)

TOM Ching Chong Chinaman,
Sitting in a tree
Wanted to pick a berry
But sat on a bee.

(MOON SHADOW *rises in outrage but he is so furious that he is tongue-tied at first.*)

MOON SHADOW I no like you.

TOM You no likee me? I no likee you.

MOON SHADOW Pig! Turtle! I'm going to cut off your head and throw it in the gutter and leave it for the dogs to eat.

TOM (*at same time in mock Chinese*) Hee-yow yo yeah. Nee woo yee yow. Woe yo hay nay. Fay lee low you. [*N.B. These lines are only a suggestion. Tom can improvise the syllables.*]

(MISS WHITLAW *enters from stage right. She is an American woman in her sixties. She claps her hands together loudly to get the attention of the two boys.*)

MISS WHITLAW My stars, what's all that commotion?

TOM He was drinking from your pump, ma'am. All them chinks got the bew-bonicks.[3]

MISS WHITLAW The only plague they have is manners, and God forbid you catch that, or we wouldn't know you.

TOM (*making a fist at* MOON SHADOW) You mind me, John. (*Exits stage left.*)

MISS WHITLAW You drink anytime you want, John.

(WINDRIDER *enters from stage right.*)

MOON SHADOW My name not John.

WINDRIDER Watch your tongue.

MOON SHADOW I Lee Moon-Shadow.

MISS WHITLAW (*chagrined*) I'm so sorry.

WINDRIDER (*joining them*) Lee Windrider.

MISS WHITLAW You must be the new neighbors Mr. Alger told me about. (*Holds out her hand.*) Pleased to meet you. I'm Henrietta Whitlaw.

(MOON SHADOW *grabs his father's arm when* WINDRIDER *tries to shake hands with* MISS WHITLAW.)

MOON SHADOW No!

WINDRIDER What's gotten into you? (*Shaking hands with Miss Whitlaw.*) This is her way of being friendly.

MISS WHITLAW Welcome to our neighborhood. (*Extending a hand to Moon Shadow.*)

WINDRIDER (*to his petrified son*) Take it.

MOON SHADOW Her hand could be poisoned.

WINDRIDER Did your grandmother tell you that? (*When Moon Shadow nods.*) Look. Nothing happened to me. Take her hand.

3. I.e., bubonic plague. An outbreak in San Francisco in 1900 began in Chinatown.

(MOON SHADOW *takes her hand stiffly and gives it a twitch. He then wipes his hands on his clothes.*)

MISS WHITLAW You look a little peaked. I was just going to sit down to tea. Can I offer you some?

WINDRIDER Yes.

MOON SHADOW (*simultaneously in a petrified voice.*) No.
(*They enter Miss Whitlaw's home and cross into her kitchen.*)

MISS WHITLAW The house has eight sides because that was Papa's lucky number. He built it back in '83. He did everything but make the nails. Look at those beams. This house will stand till Gabriel[4] blows the trump of doom.

MISS WHITLAW Please have a seat. (*Pouring tea as they sit.*) How long have you been in this country, Mr. Lee?

WINDRIDER Long time Californ'.

MISS WHITLAW (*holding up a pitcher*) Milk?

MOON SHADOW (*to father*) What's that?

WINDRIDER It comes from cows.

MOON SHADOW You mean cow's urine?

WINDRIDER No, stupid. Milk comes from the cow's udders. (*To* MISS WHITLAW *who has been waiting patiently.*) Yes. Him. Me.

MISS WHITLAW (*pouring the milk and lifting up a spoonful of sugar*) Sugar?

MOON SHADOW (*suspiciously to Miss Whitlaw*) Where that from?

MISS WHITLAW Sugar cane. It's sweet.

MOON SHADOW (*sniffing first*) O-kay.
(*As he opens his mouth, a startled* MISS WHITLAW *diplomatically avoids his mouth and drops it in his cup. When* MISS WHITLAW *lifts another spoonful of sugar and looks at* WINDRIDER, *he nods nervously. As she adds a spoonful of sugar and milk to her tea, they watch the strange ingredients mingle in their cups. Misunderstanding their silence, she gets up.*)

MISS WHITLAW Oh, what's the matter with me. I forgot the teaspoons.
(*She exits upstage.*)
(MOON SHADOW *tries to pick up his cup Chinese style—by the rim and the bottom, but the handle gets in the way.*)

MOON SHADOW (*to father as he traces the the handle's shape with his finger*) What's this stupid thing for?
(WINDRIDER *puzzles over the handle for a moment.*)

WINDRIDER You point it at what you want.
(*He demonstrates.* MOON SHADOW *copies.*)
(MISS WHITLAW *returns with spoons and a plate of gingerbread cookies.*)

MISS WHITLAW And here's some cookies fresh from the oven.
(*She gives* WINDRIDER *and* MOON SHADOW *each a spoon, sets the plate of cookies down and sits. When she picks up her spoon, they copy her self-consciously. When she stirs her cup with her spoon, they imitate her, noisily clinking their spoons.*)

MISS WHITLAW I do hope you like darjeeling.
(*When she lifts up her saucer, her guests concentrate as they imitate her. When she takes her cup by the handle,* WINDRIDER *and* MOON SHADOW *sheepishly pick*

---

4. I.e., the angel Gabriel, often depicted in Christian art with the trumpet he will blow to announce the second coming of Christ.

up their cups by the handles. When she thrusts out her pinkie, WINDRIDER *imitates her and then* MOON SHADOW *does the same.*)

MISS WHITLAW What kind of tea do you drink, Mr. Lee? (*Sipping.*)

MOON SHADOW (*making a face as he smells his teacup*) What died?

WINDRIDER (*to* MOON SHADOW) Drink. (*Drinks his own and says to Miss Whitlaw*) All kind.

(*After* MOON SHADOW *drinks, his cheeks bulge as he looks around for somewhere to spit.*)

WINDRIDER Swallow. (*When* MOON SHADOW *shakes his head*) You heard me.

MOON SHADOW (*choking it down*) You could tan leather with it.

MISS WHITLAW (*to* WINDRIDER) What did your son say?

WINDRIDER (*to* MISS WHITLAW) Too hot.

MISS WHITLAW Have some more milk. (*Reaching for the pitcher.*)

MOON SHADOW (*covering his cup in alarm and saying to* MISS WHITLAW) No!

MISS WHITLAW (*holding up the plate to* MOON SHADOW) Gingerbread?

WINDRIDER Go on. And you better eat it all.

MOON SHADOW They look like dung.

WINDRIDER I don't care. She made it. You eat it.

MOON SHADOW I will if you will.

WINDRIDER (*to* MISS WHITLAW) May I?

MISS WHITLAW Certainly.

(WINDRIDER *takes a cookie and remembers to extend a pinkie. He then takes a bite and chews as* MOON SHADOW *watches him expectantly. When he takes a second bite,* MOON SHADOW *tries one, also sticking out his pinkie. He chews warily at first and looks surprised to find that it tastes good. As soon as he gobbles that one down, he reaches for another.*)

WINDRIDER First you don't want any. Now you want to gobble them all up.

MISS WHITLAW (*as* MOON SHADOW *hesitates*) Please be my guest.

(*When* WINDRIDER *nods his head,* MOON SHADOW *takes another and eats happily.*)

WINDRIDER Look at this boy. He eat like four pig.

MISS WHITLAW There's really only one compliment for a cook and that's for her guests to eat everything.

WINDRIDER Too kind. You make us ashame. (*Kicks* MOON SHADOW *under the table.*)

MOON SHADOW Yes, ashame.

(*A grandfather clock bongs four times.*)

WINDRIDER (*rising*) Must go. See Mr. Alger. Tea good. Gin-gerbread good. Too kind. (*To* MOON SHADOW.) Come on, boy.

MISS WHITLAW Must you? We were just getting acquainted.

(MOON SHADOW *glances uneasily in the direction of the water pump and his boxes. He nervously begins to eat with both hands.*)

MOON SHADOW It wouldn't be polite.

MISS WHITLAW Do you need your son?

WINDRIDER He got boxes. Pick up. Put away.

MISS WHITLAW They can wait a little while longer.

WINDRIDER No, too much.

MISS WHITLAW (*rising to escort* WINDRIDER *to the door*) Fiddlesticks.

WINDRIDER (*as he leaves*) Don't be a pig.

(*He follows* MISS WHITLAW *to stage left where they shake hands and she watches him exit. Momentarily reprieved,* MOON SHADOW *looks around and catches sight of the stained-glass window. As* MISS WHITLAW *rejoins* MOON SHADOW, *he points at the glass.*)

MOON SHADOW   What that?

MISS WHITLAW   The stained glass? My father sent for it. All the way from England. He said no house was complete without one. He also said no one owns it. It's meant to be shared. So you feel free to look.

MOON SHADOW   But what that thing?

MISS WHITLAW   It's a dragon.

MOON SHADOW   But that shiny man kill it!

MISS WHITLAW   Dragons are wicked beasts. They go around burning towns and kid-napping princesses. They would have destroyed everything if St. George hadn't killed them.

MOON SHADOW   No.

MISS WHITLAW   Do you have dragons in China too?

MOON SHADOW   Yes, and maybe some do terrible thing. But most do good thing too. My father, (*pantomiming excessively*) he say they bring rain for rice. All scaly thing, he king. Live in sea. Lake. Pond. (*Pause as a new thought occurs.*) Live in hill too. You make mad. They shake, shake. You make happy. They help.

MISS WHITLAW   Fancy that? I never knew dragons did so much.

MOON SHADOW   Maybe only bad kind live here. You know, outlaw.

MISS WHITLAW   That would explain a lot of things. All the dragons I've read about haven't been very pleasant creatures.

MOON SHADOW   No dragon pleas-sant. A dragon dragonee.

(TOM *enters from stage left. He loudly whistles "I've Been Working on the Rail-road" as he begins to examine the boxes.*)

MISS WHITLAW   That sounds like Tom. Maybe you'd better put your things away.

MOON SHADOW (*nervously gulping down his tea*)   Maybe more tea.

MISS WHITLAW   I thought you didn't like my tea.

MOON SHADOW   I change mind.

MISS WHITLAW (*pouring*)   You know, there's one thing about Tom.

MOON SHADOW   Yes?

MISS WHITLAW   He's the biggest boy in the neighborhood. The strongest too. So sometimes I hire him to do odd jobs for me. One time he was peeling potatoes when he nicked his finger. The next thing I knew he was blubbering like a baby. I thought I'd have to take him to the hospital, but you know what? (MOON SHADOW *shakes his head.*) It was only the tiniest scratch. You know what else? (MOON SHADOW *shakes his head again.*) I think he's scared of the sight of blood. (MOON SHADOW *nods.*) Silly me. You don't take milk. Sugar?

MOON SHADOW   No thank you. I got work. Maybe next time.

MISS WHITLAW   I can't wait to learn more about dragons.

(MISS WHITLAW *escorts him to her door, then exits.*)

MOON SHADOW   You leave box alone. They mine.

TOM   Who made you boss, John?

MOON SHADOW   I not John.

TOM   I'll call you whatever I want. You sabe me? (*Shoving* MOON SHADOW *away.*)

MOON SHADOW   I understand. (*Poking* TOM *in the nose.*)

TOM   You hit me.

MOON SHADOW (*penitent*)   What you expect?

(*When* TOM *puts a hand to his nose and examines his fingers, he begins to panic.*)

TOM   I'm bleeding. (*Goes to the pump and works the handle for some water.*)

MOON SHADOW   You not die.

TOM   I ain't scared. Just don't want my shirt to get dirty. My mom'd skin me alive.

MOON SHADOW   Sure, sure.

TOM   You're pretty scrappy for a Chinaboy.

MOON SHADOW   I not Chinaboy. Moon Shadow.

> (MOON SHADOW *makes a fist again, then thinks better of it. He extends his hand.* TOM *takes it and* MOON SHADOW *helps* TOM *to his feet.* MOON SHADOW *then shakes Tom's hand as if he were priming a pump. After a moment's surprise,* TOM *returns the shake enthusiastically.*)

TOM   Moon Shadow.

> (TOM *exits stage left.*)

SCENE 6

Before dawn in their Polk Street shack six months later. MOON SHADOW *is writing a letter by the light of a kerosene lantern while* WINDRIDER *washes up at the pump.*

MOON SHADOW   April eighteenth, Nineteen-ought-six.

Dear Mother. Do not worry. Father and I are well. We get up before sunrise every morning and go to work. Mr. Alger has many tenements. There is always something to be fixed. At night, I do my lessons and chores while Father works on his plans for the aeroplane. Miss Whitlaw has helped us write to Mister Orville Wright and Mister Wilbur Wright. They are very encouraging. The horizontal stabilizers must be five inches longer. Some day you and I will see father fly. I have never seen him so busy. Or so happy.

> (*Two stage assistants have entered and knelt with the earthquake cloth between them. With the sound of rumbling, they raise the cloth behind* MOON SHADOW *and shake it back and forth.*)

WINDRIDER   Earthquake.

> (MOON SHADOW *staggers to his feet as a mad chorus of bells rings in the distance.*)

MOON SHADOW   What's happening?

WINDRIDER   (*trying to keep his balance*)   The church bells are shaking.

> (*When the shaking stops, the bells gradually diminish. The earthquake cloth subsides.*)

MOON SHADOW   That was like riding a dragon.

> (*More rumbling. The stage assistants lift the cloth again and shake it back and forth. The bells jangle more forcefully.* MOON SHADOW *and* WINDRIDER *fall.*)

WINDRIDER   Miss Whitlaw.

> (WINDRIDER *exits stage left,* MOON SHADOW *tries to stand, but as he scrambles on all fours, he is surprised by the* EARTHQUAKE DRAGON *, who appears suddenly from behind the cloth.* MOON SHADOW *exits. The* DRAGON *dances and then exits.*)

SCENE 7

Golden Gate Park late that afternoon. We hear the giant murmuring of a crowd. MOON SHADOW *and* WINDRIDER *enter with a tent of purple satin sheets sewn together.* MOON SHADOW *takes up a position to the left of the tent,* WINDRIDER *to the right. They pull on the tent's ropes.* MISS WHITLAW *enters from stage right with her trunk. On her head are several hats stacked one on top of the other. She sets the trunk down.* UNCLE *enters from stage left with several boxes.*

UNCLE BRIGHT STAR   The tent's leaning too much to the left. Slacken the left, make it taut on the right.

    (*When* MOON SHADOW *and* WINDRIDER *obey, the tent sags to the right.*)

MISS WHITLAW   Oh, dear. No. A bit more to the left.

UNCLE BRIGHT STAR   Right, right.

MISS WHITLAW   Left please.

UNCLE BRIGHT STAR   Right.

MISS WHITLAW   Left.

UNCLE RIGHT STAR   Right.

MISS WHITLAW   Left.

UNCLE BRIGHT STAR   Right.

MISS WHITLAW   Left.

UNCLE BRIGHT STAR AND MISS WHITLAW   Pull!

    (MOON SHADOW *and* WINDRIDER *struggle to obey both contradictory commands when there is a tearing sound and the tent collapses.*)

UNCLE BRIGHT STAR and MISS WHITLAW (*to one another*)   Now see what you've done.

WINDRIDER (*disgustedly holding up a torn section of tent*)   I go soldier. Get new tent.

MISS WHITLAW   There are an awful lot of people.

UNCLE BRIGHT STAR   Get a needle and thread and maybe we can fix it.

WINDRIDER   You'll tell me to sew one way and she'll tell me to sew the other. (*Exits upstage with the remains of the tent.*)

    (*Tired,* MISS WHITLAW *begins to go through her trunk, looking for brandy.*)

UNCLE BRIGHT STAR (*goes to the boxes at stage left*)   I slave all my life and what do I get? Back to living in the dirt.

MOON SHADOW   It's Golden Gate Park, Uncle. Everybody's here. Even the rich. The earthquake's made us all the same.

UNCLE BRIGHT STAR   Everybody panics just because the ground shakes a little and there are a few fires. Those soldiers chased us here just so they could rob our homes. (*Finding a jar of plum brandy.*) But they won't get my brandy. (*Searching.*) Did you pack any cups?

MOON SHADOW (*searching*)   I'm sorry.

UNCLE BRIGHT STAR (*searching again*)   Stuck in the weeds—Heaven knows for how long. And now we don't even have a tent—thanks to her. No cup.

    (*At that moment,* MISS WHITLAW *straightens up with a tea cup in each hand. She catches sight of the brandy at the same time that* UNCLE *sees the cups. They do a double take.*)

MISS WHITLAW   I have some.

    (UNCLE *grudgingly goes over to her and pours brandy into the cups.*)

UNCLE BRIGHT STAR   This will probably be wasted on her.

MISS WHITLAW   What did your uncle say?

MOON SHADOW   He hope you like it.

MISS WHITLAW (*sniffing the brandy*)   What a wonderful bouquet.

UNCLE BRIGHT STAR (*to* MOON SHADOW)   What'd she say?

MOON SHADOW   She said it smells like flowers.

UNCLE BRIGHT STAR (*correcting her*)   Liquid sunshine.

MISS WHITLAW (*trying to top him*)   It smells like spring.

UNCLE BRIGHT STAR   Like spring long gone.

MISS WHITLAW   Like all the springs that should have been and never were. (*As* UNCLE *hunts for a line to top her.*) Distilled.

UNCLE BRIGHT STAR (*grudging*)   You talk like poet. You should be Chinese.

MOON SHADOW   Maybe she was. In another life. If a dragon can be a human . . .

UNCLE BRIGHT STAR   But what awful thing did she do so she wasn't born Chinese again? She doesn't look like a killer.

MISS WHITLAW   What did you say?

UNCLE BRIGHT STAR   We talk about family.

MISS WHITLAW   Do you have a large family?

UNCLE BRIGHT STAR   Ee-normous family. Grow every time meet someone. Make new friend. Men on railroad. Chinatown. (*Catches himself and grunts as he realizes that logically he ought to include her in the circle now.*)

MISS WHITLAW (*raising her cup*)   To family and friends, here and abroad.

UNCLE BRIGHT STAR (*raising his cup*)   Alive and dead.

(*They drink.*)

UNCLE BRIGHT STAR (*turning his cup upside down*)   Dry cup.

MISS WHITLAW (*turning over hers*)   Dry cup.

WINDRIDER *enters from up right.*

MOON SHADOW   Where's the tent?

WINDRIDER   Didn't get one. (*Going over to* UNCLE.) I overheard the soldiers talking. The general's ordered all the Chinese out of Golden Gate Park and over to the Presidio.

UNCLE BRIGHT STAR   Why pack us all the way over there? Why don't we go back to Chinatown?

WINDRIDER   Chinatown's burning up.

MISS WHITLAW (*to* UNCLE)   Are you all right? (*Helps* UNCLE *to sit on her trunk.*) What's wrong?

UNCLE BRIGHT STAR   Chinatown. All ash.

MISS WHITLAW   You poor man.

WINDRIDER   Polk Street too. You, me, we lose everything.

MISS WHITLAW (*sitting down on her trunk*)   Papa's house? Oh, no!

UNCLE BRIGHT STAR   Fire done. You, me, we build new home, same spot.

WINDRIDER (*speaking English for Miss Whitlaw's sake*)   I hear more gossip. Chinatown land worth too much.[5] After fire, American take over. After fire, Chinese go Hunter Point. Build there.

MISS WHITLAW   They can't grab your homes like that.

UNCLE BRIGHT STAR   I own land.

MISS WHITLAW   Do you have the deed?

UNCLE BRIGHT STAR (*taking deed from basket*)   Here, here. I fight. I got lawyer. Phil-a-del-fee-ah lawyer.[6] We go home. New laundry. (*Indicating* WINDRIDER.) New workshop.

WINDRIDER   Why do you want to make things just like they were? Didn't you learn anything? The next quake will just wreck all our plans. Don't you want something purer, freer in your life?

MOON SHADOW   I don't think there is.

5. Chinatown's location near what had become the heart of the city made the land very valuable.
6. A lawyer of great ability (a term taken from Andrew Hamilton, a Philadelphian who in 1735 successfully defended the New York printer John Peter Zenger against charges of libel for criticizing British policies).

WINDRIDER   I think an aeronaut is free. I think an aeronaut may be the freest of all humanity.

UNCLE BRIGHT STAR   I said you could make your toys.

WINDRIDER   You said. They said. Everyone said. All my life I've done what people wanted. I've worked and worked, and what have I got? Nothing. That earthquake was a sign. Life's too short to waste trying to please everyone. You've got to do what you can.

UNCLE BRIGHT STAR   Not that dream again.

WINDRIDER   Dream or not, I can fly. I can build a flying machine.

FIRST SOLDIER (voice-over)   All you Chinamen, pack it up. Come on.

SECOND SOLDIER (voice-over)   Get your gear together, Chinamen. Move it, move it, move it!

UNCLE BRIGHT STAR   Floating about like a dead leaf. How will your family live? How will your family eat while you're building the machine? A superior person admits the truth.

WINDRIDER   It's time I thought of myself. (Crosses to MOON SHADOW at stage center.) I think this is my final test. The hardest and truest proof that I should be a dragon. Do you understand, Moon Shadow? Do you?

UNCLE BRIGHT STAR   Supposing your father and mother had thought like that? Or suppose their fathers and mothers had been that selfish?

WINDRIDER (beginning to sag)   That's cheating.

(There is a tense silence as WINDRIDER tries to resist his growing sense of guilt.)

UNCLE BRIGHT STAR   You're the one who's cheating. Your family. Your wife. Your son. They need you, and you just walk away.

MOON SHADOW   I want to fly too.

UNCLE BRIGHT STAR   You stay out of this.

MOON SHADOW   I'm sorry, Uncle, but I'm his son. Let's build that flying machine. Maybe we can make a living by selling rides in it. And while we're building it, we'll both get jobs. There's always someone with something to fix. We'll manage somehow.

WINDRIDER   Despite what everyone says?

MOON SHADOW   A superior man can only do what he's meant to do.

UNCLE BRIGHT STAR   Don't give me that nonsense.

WINDRIDER   He's the only one talking sense.

UNCLE BRIGHT STAR   I won't have anything to do with fools. Don't come back.

(As WINDRIDER and MOON SHADOW cross to stage right.)

MISS WHITLAW (to WINDRIDER)   Mr. Lee, where are you going? Aren't you going to wait for your uncle?

WINDRIDER   We go ferry boat. Go Oakland. Build my—build our aeroplane.

UNCLE BRIGHT STAR   Oakland has earthquakes too.

WINDRIDER   That's the chance I'll take. We need room for flying.

(WINDRIDER and MOON SHADOW move down stage right.)

WINDRIDER   I was hoping you'd come along.

MOON SHADOW   Why didn't you ask then?

WINDRIDER   It's not something you can ask.

(They exit.)

FIRST SOLDIER (voice-over)   Hey, you posing for a statue? Yeah, you, the old Chinaman. Out of the park. Or I'll put the boot to your lazy backside.

UNCLE BRIGHT STAR (defiantly to the unseen soldier)   I go. For now. (Holding out the cup to MISS WHITLAW.) Thank you.

MISS WHITLAW (*politely refusing*) You may need it.

FIRST AND SECOND SOLDIER (*variously as voice-overs*) Move it. Come on. Pack it up. Get going.

> (UNCLE *exits stage left with his boxes. After a moment,*
> MISS WHITLAW *exits stage right with her trunk.*)

SCENE 8

MOON SHADOW *as adult in cap and glasses.*

MOON SHADOW We moved across the bay to Piedmont where we got a barn cheap. Oakland was so far away that it looked like a bunch of toy blocks dumped on the edge of the bay. All around us were nothing but brown hills sweeping down to empty flat lands. Not a soul in sight. Not a voice. Just the wind. Like we had jumped beyond the end of the world. Beyond the Buddha's hand.

Father was too busy to feel lonely. He and I worked at odd jobs and every spare cent went into building the aeroplane. We called it *Dragonwings.*

It took us three whole years. And all it was was poles and wire and canvas—big, ugly, clumsy. I didn't think it'd get off the ground.

Three whole years.

It wasn't easy being the son of a dragon.

> (*Three years later outside of their barn in Piedmont. Both* WINDRIDER *and* MOON SHADOW *are a bit scruffier. Their crowns are unshaven and there are patches on Moon Shadow's elbows and knees. His cuffs are also a bit short as if he is beginning to outgrow his clothes. They are both in overalls.* MOON SHADOW *counts the money from a tin can.* WINDRIDER *eats a simple meal of rice and vegetables.*)

MOON SHADOW Eleven ninety. Twelve. Twelve fifty. Thirteen. Thirteen-O-five. Time to go to the bank. (*Pulling off his boot and removing two bills.*) Fourteen. Fourteen-fifty. Fifteen. Fifteen dollars and five cents! Five cents ahead on the rent. We could have meat tomorrow.

> (*From the can,* MOON SHADOW *takes a small envelope and puts the money inside.*)

WINDRIDER Some more wire and Dragonwings would be ready.

MOON SHADOW I thought I saw a coil in the shed.

WINDRIDER I'll check when I'm done. But I think it was pretty old. Don't want Dragonwings to fall apart while I'm in the sky.

MOON SHADOW (*disappointed*) I guess not.

> (*Giving the money to his father, he takes his bowl to the creek and begins to wash it.* WINDRIDER *picks up the plans. As he stands, he looks at his son thoughtfully. He exits upstage.*)

MOON SHADOW (*not realizing* WINDRIDER *has gone*) Look at San Francisco, Father. Sunlight shining off all those windows. Glittering like bits of gold. All those little lights. And every light's a person. Uncle. Miss Whitlaw. Everyone. There really is a gold mountain. Right in front of me. All this time.

> (MOON SHADOW *turns, expecting to find his father, and finds* BLACK DOG *who has skulked in from stage right. He is dirty and unshaven and his clothes are filthy and ragged.*)

BLACK DOG Heard you were over here.

> (*He picks up one of the rice bowls and wolfs down the remains with his fingers.*)

MOON SHADOW We thought you were dead.

BLACK DOG Got any more?

MOON SHADOW   That's all we had. Now get out of here.

BLACK DOG   Wanna see the overgrown kite. Need a laugh.

MOON SHADOW   What you need is back in town.

(MOON SHADOW *helps* BLACK DOG *to his feet, but* BLACK DOG *falls.*)

BLACK DOG   Give me some money.

MOON SHADOW   We're through, hoppy.

BLACK DOG (*taking out his knife*)   No way to talk to your barber.

MOON SHADOW   Look at you. Your hand's shaking.

BLACK DOG (*waving it awkwardly*)   Maybe I'll take an ear this time. Or a nose. I'd like to see you preach with only a stub for a tongue.

MOON SHADOW   Sleep it off, hoppy.

(BLACK DOG *thrusts clumsily at* MOON SHADOW *who grabs his wrist. They struggle.* WINDRIDER *enters from stage right with a large coil of very rusty wire. Distracted,* MOON SHADOW *looks toward* WINDRIDER. BLACK DOG *grabs* MOON SHADOW *from behind and holds the knife to his throat.*)

BLACK DOG   Stand back.

WINDRIDER   Don't harm him. (*Drops the wire.*)

BLACK DOG   You got any money?

WINDRIDER   Yes.

MOON SHADOW   Don't.

WINDRIDER   Let him go. (*Taking the envelope of money from his coveralls.*)

MOON SHADOW   No.

WINDRIDER (*holding the money out in one hand*)   Here.

BLACK DOG   That's all?

WINDRIDER   It's every penny.

BLACK DOG   I ought to slit his throat anyway.

WINDRIDER   You do and I'll hunt you down.

BLACK DOG (*releasing* MOON SHADOW)   You got what you want.

WINDRIDER *tosses the money to* BLACK DOG *who runs off stage right.*

MOON SHADOW   I'm sorry.

(WINDRIDER *puts his hand on Moon Shadow's shoulder and gives it a squeeze before he exits upstage.*)

SCENE 9

Piedmont, later that day outside the stable.

MOON SHADOW   September twenty-second, Nineteen-ought-nine.

Dear Mother. I have bad news. We are going to lose Dragonwings before father can fly it. Black Dog stole all we have, and the landlord will not give us an extension. So we'll have to move and leave Dragonwings behind. We have asked Miss Whitlaw for help, but her new house has taken up all of her money. And even if Uncle would speak to us, he has probably spent all he has on rebuilding his laundry.

(UNCLE *and* MISS WHITLAW *enter from stage left.*)

MISS WHITLAW   I could have gotten down from the wagon by myself.

UNCLE BRIGHT STAR   Watch gopher hole.

MISS WHITLAW   I'm younger than you.

MOON SHADOW   Uncle, Miss Whitlaw!

MISS WHITLAW   How are you? (*Shaking Moon Shadow's hand.*)

(WINDRIDER *enters from upstage with the cap.*)

WINDRIDER   Come to laugh, Uncle?

UNCLE BRIGHT STAR   I came to help you fly your contraption.

MOON SHADOW   But you don't believe in flying machines.

UNCLE BRIGHT STAR   And I'll haul that thing back down when it doesn't fly. Red Rabbit and me were getting fat anyway. But look at how tall you've grown. And how thin. And ragged. (*Pause.*) But you haven't broken your neck which was more than I ever expected.

MISS WHITLAW   As soon as I told your uncle, we hatched the plot together. You ought to get a chance to fly your aeroplane.

UNCLE BRIGHT STAR   Flat purse, strong backs.

WINDRIDER   We need to pull Dragonwings to the very top.

UNCLE BRIGHT STAR   That hill is a very steep hill.

WINDRIDER   It has to be that one. The winds are right.

UNCLE BRIGHT STAR   Ah, well, it's the winds.

WINDRIDER   Take the ropes. (*Pantomimes taking a rope over his shoulder as he faces the audience.*) Got a good grip?

OTHERS (*pantomiming taking the ropes*)   Yes, right, etc.

WINDRIDER   Then pull.

> (*They strain.* MOON SHADOW *stumbles but gets right up. Stamping his feet to get better footing, he keeps tugging.*)

MOON SHADOW (*giving up*)   It's no good.

UNCLE BRIGHT STAR   Pull in rhythm. As we did on the railroad.

> (*In demonstration,* UNCLE *stamps his feet in a slow rhythm to set the beat and the others repeat. The rhythm picks up as they move.*)

UNCLE BRIGHT STAR   Ngúng, ngúng.
> Dew gùng.

OTHERS   Ngúng, ngúng.
> Dew gùng.

UNCLE BRIGHT STAR (*imitating the intonation of the Cantonese*)
Púsh, púsh.
Wòrk, wòrk.

OTHERS   Púsh, púsh.
Wòrk, wòrk.

UNCLE BRIGHT STAR   Seen gà,
> Gee gá. [*high rising tone*]

OTHERS   Seen gà,
> Gee gá. [*high rising tone*]

UNCLE BRIGHT STAR   Get rìch,
> Go hóme.

OTHERS   Gèt rìch,
> Go hóme.

> (MOON SHADOW, WINDRIDER, UNCLE *and* MISS WHITLAW *arrive downstage.*)

MOON SHADOW (*panting*)   We made it. Tramp the grass down in front.

> (WINDRIDER *stands stage center as the others stamp the grass. They can't help smiling and laughing a little.*)

WINDRIDER   That's enough.

MOON SHADOW (*to* MISS WHITLAW)   Take that propeller.

> (MISS WHITLAW *takes her place before the right propeller with her hands resting on the blade.* MOON SHADOW *takes his place beside the left propeller.* WINDRIDER *faces upstage, his back to the audience.*)

MISS WHITLAW   Listen to the wind on the wings.

UNCLE BRIGHT STAR   It's alive.

WINDRIDER   All right.

> (MOON SHADOW *and* MISS WHITLAW *pull down at the propellers and back away quickly. We hear a motor cough into life. Bicycle chains clink musically. Propellers begin to turn with a roar.*)

UNCLE BRIGHT STAR (*slowly turning*)   What's wrong? Is it just going to roll down the hill.

> (MISS WHITLAW *crosses her fingers as they all turn to watch the aeroplane.*)

MISS WHITLAW   He's up!

> (WINDRIDER *starts to do his flight ballet.*)

MOON SHADOW (*pointing*)   He's turning.

UNCLE BRIGHT STAR   He's really flying.

MISS WHITLAW   I never thought I'd see the day. A human up in the sky. Off the ground.

> (*They turn and tilt their heads back.*)

MISS WHITLAW   Free as an eagle.

UNCLE BRIGHT STAR (*correcting her*)   Like dragon.

MOON SHADOW   Father, you did it. (*Wonderingly.*) You did it.

> (*The aeroplane roars loudly overhead.*)

> (MOON SHADOW *as adult steps forward and addresses the audience.*)

MOON SHADOW   I thought he'd fly forever and ever. Up, up to Heaven and never come down. But then some of the guy wires broke, and the right wings separated. Dragonwings came crashing to earth. Father had a few broken bones, but it was nothing serious. Only the aeroplane was wrecked.

Uncle took him back to the laundry to recover. Father didn't say much, just thought a lot—I figured he was busy designing the next aeroplane. But when Father was nearly well, he made me sit down next to him.

WINDRIDER   Uncle says he'll make me a partner if I stay. So the Western officials would have to change my immigration class. I'd be a merchant, and merchants can bring their wives here. Would you like to send for Mother?

MOON SHADOW (*going to* WINDRIDER)   But Dragonwings?

WINDRIDER   When I was up in the air, I tried to find you. You were so small. And getting smaller. Just disappearing from sight. (*Handing his cap to* MOON SHADOW.) Like you were disappearing from my life. (*He begins his ballet again.*) I knew it wasn't the time. The Dragon King said there would be all sorts of tests.

> (MOON SHADOW *turns to audience as an adult.*)

MOON SHADOW   We always talked about flying again. Only we never did. (*Putting on cap.*) But dreams stay with you, and we never forgot.

> (WINDRIDER *takes his final pose. A gong sounds.*)

1991   2001

Books of Instruction

Antarctic. Boats. Computers. Dinosaurs. Elephants. Fish. Greece. Horses. Insects. Jungles. Kites. Life. Mammals. Natural Disasters. Oceans. Planets. Queens of England. Rain Forests. Sex Education. Trees. Underwater Photography. Volcanoes. Weather. X-Rays and Other Medical Technologies. Yeti: The Abominable Snowman of the Himalayas. Zero. The items in this list are all subjects of "information" books, as they are called in North America, or "topic" books in England. Historically, all develop out of a tradition of "books of instruction." All are lumped together by libraries and bookstores as nonfiction: that is, something other than fiction or poetry. When schoolchildren do projects—on rain forests, the solar system, or whatever similar topics the curriculum mandates—they turn to these "finding-out books," as a group of five-year-olds once described them. For children growing up in today's information age, "information" is what they need to know.

Though precisely what it is that children must learn changes from generation to generation, the assumption remains that adults have a moral imperative to instruct—and children to be instructed. That's why "books of instruction" is its own sprawling category, containing everything from books on how to read to books on boatbuilding to books teaching religion and morality. The idea that children's instruction should also be fun comes from the man who is credited with inventing the children's book publishing industry, John Newbery.

On June 18, 1744, Newbery put an advertisement in the *Penny London Morning Advertiser* announcing the publication of *A Little Pretty Pocket-Book*: it is, he says, "intended for the Instruction and Amusement of little Master Tommy and pretty Miss Polly; with an agreeable Letter to each from *Jack the Giant-Killer*; as also a Ball and Pincushion, the Use of which will infallibly make Tommy a good Boy and Polly a good Girl." (For a selection from *A Little Pretty Pocket-Book*, see the Primers and Readers section, above.) By linking instruction, amusement, and toys with the promise that "good" boys and girls will be magically created by the purchase of a book, Newbery laid the foundation for a system of beliefs that permeates children's book publishing to this day.

The details of what children need to know are often put into a curriculum (from the Latin *currere*, "to run"), or course of study, whose makeup has changed over the centuries. A child in the late Middle Ages in England or France might have been given a courtesy book to read (or, more likely, been told to memorize its verses about good behavior). An eighteenth-century child in England or America would have been given a conduct or advice book; in the late eighteenth century and certainly into the nineteenth, a boy might also have been given a book about one of the new technologies of the age, the microscope or the telescope. His little sister might receive *Presents for Good Girls* (1804) or *Tales for Mothers and Daughters* (1807) by Miss Woodland.

By the early twentieth century, parents were buying compendiums of knowledge—often from door-to-door salesmen hawking sets of encyclopedias in residential neighborhoods. These people were the modern equivalents of the sixteenth-century chapmen, or traveling salesmen, who sold chapbooks, though the latter were far less expensive. One popular publication for children was sold in England as *The Children's Encyclopedia* and in the United States as *The Book of Knowledge*. Besides purveying the facts that today's consumer expects from encyclopedias and other information resources, they also—and to us more surprisingly—contained fairy tales, fiction, and poetry. Attempts to simultaneously delight and instruct children in the twenty-first century are likely to involve a multimedia extravaganza combining a book and CD, possibly with stickers, puzzles, and an educational computer game, too—all linked to some subject probably in the school curriculum.

Courtesy Books

Books of instruction now cover a huge pedagogical range, but the earliest examples of the genre, medieval courtesy books, had a narrow focus. Aristocratic young boys preparing to serve at royal courts in England in the fifteenth century were advised:

> Oute ouere youre dysshe your heede yee nat hynge
> And withe fulle mouthe drynke in no wyse;
> Youre nose, your teethe, your naylles, from pykynge.
> (*Babees Book* [ca. 1475])

Behind the puzzling spelling are sentiments shared by twenty-first-century parents: "When you're eating dinner, don't hang your head close to the dish, shoveling in your food; don't drink with your mouth full; and don't pick your nose, teeth, or nails." Such links between the living and generations of parents and children long dead were clear to the Victorian scholar Frederick Furnivall when he assembled and annotated a group of related late medieval manuscripts about manners, published collectively by the Early English Text Society as *The Babees Book* (1868). The title page of his book indicates the general tone of the instruction manuals that would have circulated in the fifteenth century, all aimed at defining the rules of good behavior: *The Babees Book, Aristotle's ABC, Urbanitatis, Stans Puer ad Mensam* [Latin, "The Boy (or Page) Standing at Table"; usually translated "Table Manners for Children"], *The Lytille Childrenes Lytil Boke, The Bokes of Nurture of Hugh Rhodes and John Russell, Wynkn de Worde's Book of Kerveynge, The Book of Demeanor, The Boke of Curtasye, Seager's Schoole of Vertue,*●*c., &c.*

The advice in *The Babees Book* collection covers a lot of territory eerily familiar to a modern reader, despite the distance between fifteenth-century court etiquette and twenty-first-century urban, democratic life. Among the rules we find (here modernized) are "Speak when you are spoken to." "Don't fidget." "Don't spit." "Use a handkerchief when you sneeze." "Don't blow your nose into your hand." "Speak politely." "Don't make stupid faces, especially when you're talking to an adult or a stranger." Desiring that their children be able to function in polite society, parents through the centuries have issued such directions. In the context of the history of books of instruction, however, the codes of behavior that medieval children needed to know seem innocent and easy to follow; rules of conduct would soon become far more complex.

Conduct or Advice Books

By the seventeenth century, the shift in focus from courtesy to conduct, from court to a burgeoning middle class, was beginning to become apparent in the target market for books of instruction. For example, in 1612, a Puritan book whose title proclaimed its focus on "a godly form of household government," outlined gender-specific forms of good behavior:

HUSBAND	WIFE
Get goods	Gather them together and save them
Travel, seek a living	Keep the house
Get money and provisions	Do not vainly spend it
Deal with many men	Talk with few
Be entertaining	Be solitary and withdrawn
Be skillful in talk	Boast of silence
Be a giver	Be a saver
Apparel yourself as you may	Apparel yourself as it becomes you
Dispatch all things out of door	Oversee and give order within

The gendering of conduct books became increasingly explicit through the seventeenth and eighteenth centuries. Middle-class boys were instructed on how to succeed in work, and in social and political life, by such volumes as *The Father's Legacy: or, Faithful Counsels of a Good Father to His Children and Friends* (1678) and *A Present for an Apprentice: or, A Sure Guide to Gain Both Esteem and an Estate* (1749). Middle-class girls, especially by the nineteenth century, were encouraged to focus on cultivating manners, morals, appearance, and codes of behavior—particularly self-control—so that as married women they would submissively accept the authority of their husbands as they had that of their fathers.

The Polite Academy, first published in 1762 and into its tenth edition by 1800, is typical of conduct books for girls. It contains detailed instructions on walking and curtseying (among other things) and was described by the venerable historian of children's book publishing history, F. J. Harvey Darton, as a "magnificent survey of the proper conduct for all possible occasions." The book opens with a firm statement of its benefits:

> A Young Woman of Virtue and good Sense, will never think it beneath her Care and Study to cultivate the Graces of her outward Mien and Figure, which contribute so considerably towards making her Behaviour acceptable: For as from the happy Disposition of the Hands, Feet, and other Parts of the Body, there arises a genteel Deportment; so where we see a young Lady standing in a genteel Position, or adjusting herself properly in Walking, Dancing or Sitting, in a graceful Manner, we never fail to admire that exterior Excellence of Form, and Disposition, suited to the Rules of Decency, Modesty, and good Manners.

Like *A Little Pretty Pocket-Book* and what we now call self-help books, *The Polite Academy* promises its readers happiness and success. That Jane Austen was inti-

The three young women staring sensitively out the window in the frontispiece engraving of *The Young Lady's Own Book* (1832) are posed in the desirable attitude of their day: contentedly locked inside, perfectly dressed and coiffed, languorous but not idle. "The sensitive mind," the anonymous author informs us authoritatively, "discovers poetry everywhere."

mately familiar with such books is clear from the intense scrutiny and critical discussion to which the actions (including reading, dancing, education, and conversation) of her characters are subjected. Even such titles as *Sense and Sensibility* (1811) and *Pride and Prejudice* (1813) convey exactly the concerns of *The Polite Academy*, which are vital to the resolutions of the marriage plots governing Austen's novels. Though the market was so saturated with conduct books by Jane Austen's time that she often subtly mocks their conventions, the genre flourished into the nineteenth century, with the rules on morals and manners continuing to lock into place a rigid social hierarchy and class structure.

Poor people, servants, members of the working class, and children were taught to obey by works like *Duties of a Lady's Maid* (1825). Rich, noble, and upper-class people were taught to take charge, as *Lord Chesterfield's Advice to His Son* (1818) demonstrates. Many of the mid-nineteenth-century conduct books, now found primarily in rare book libraries, tantalize their prospective readers with titles promising a perfect life, or at least a better one. Take, for example, an American book published in 1852: Daniel Wise's *The Young Lady's Counsellor: or, Outlines and Illustrations on the Sphere, the Duties and the Dangers of Young Women. Designed to be a Guide to True Happiness in This Life and to Glory in the Life Which Is to Come.* American men of the time could read Daniel C. Eddy's *The Young Man's Friend: Containing Admo-*

nitions for the Erring, Counsel for the Tempted, Encouragement for the Desponding, Hope for the Fallen (1849).

To some degree, this genre still persists—and is still gendered, though less explicitly so. There are, on the one hand, self-help books on investing, on interview strategies, and assertiveness training, which are aimed primarily at men. On the other hand, books on weight control, makeup and fashion advice, and dating tips have a largely female audience. And in the tradition of encouraging adults to instruct children, manuals on effective child-rearing continue to be published, covering everything from how to teach babies to sleep through the night to how to raise obedient children and how to keep teenagers from engaging in unsafe sex.

Other Books of Instruction

By the middle of the eighteenth century, a distinct children's book publishing and marketing industry was firmly established in England. More children were being exposed to formal schooling, and more attention was being given to establishing a set curriculum that would address what children needed to know in order to function in societies that were becoming increasingly industrialized and democratized, more "rational" (the term often used to describe the period), and more scientific. Books of instruction were now visible in middle-class European and American homes. Publishers capitalized on the desires of middle-class parents for their children to succeed in this new society. Even though Newbery's marketing mantra of instruction, delight, and toys was firmly established by this time, and the Romantic move toward imaginative literature was under way, conduct books were still, as Darton points out, highly "vendible wares" in the "children's-book business."

The burgeoning children's book business of the late eighteenth and early nineteenth centuries employed marketing practices still used in the twenty-first century, including "product placement." In films and television, specific products are prominently featured in the action seen on screen—examples include Reeses Pieces in the film *E.T. the Extra-Terrestrial* (1982) and Ford vehicles in the television program *24* (2002–). Using a similar technique, nineteenth-century publishers plugged their own books.

In Elizabeth Kilner's *A Visit to London*, published by Benjamin Tabart in 1805, the fictional Mrs. Sandby and her daughter Maria make a shopping trip to Tabart's Juvenile Library (the children's bookstore owned by Tabart). Maria urges her mother to spend freely: " 'Oh mamma,' exclaimed she, 'here is a *History of Greece*, and another of *Rome* by Dr. Mavor. Be so good as to buy them for us. You know how much we were pleased with his *History of England*.' " Because her children have "applied the information" from the books she had previously bought them from Tabart's in "the proper manner," Mrs. Sandby is willing to buy more. "You are therefore deserving," she says, "of other histories, and I give you leave to take them."

Among the books purchased are *The Wonders of the Microscope*, which Maria had recommended for her brother: "What a charming book that would be for George, because, you know, he has a microscope at home." That recent publication was apparently a hot seller for Tabart's firm, as was its companion volume, *The Wonders of the Telescope*. Both were marketed to boys, and both exploited widespread excitement about the significance of recent scientific discoveries. *The Wonders of the Microscope* came with four fold-out copperplate engravings, including a wonderful enlargement of a louse, with all its parts marked (making it of value in the teaching of natural history). These engravings had originally appeared in *Micrographia* (1665),

Enlarged engraving of a louse, from *The Wonders of the Microscope* (London: Tabart, 1804). The plate is copied from Robert Hook's *Micrographia* (London: 1665).

a treatise on his microscopic investigations by the pioneering scientist Robert Hooke.

The eighteenth and early nineteenth centuries were marked as a scientific age, an age of reason. Those urging the institutionalization of scientific education relied in part on the approach developed much earlier by Johann Amos Comenius, a Czech theologian and teacher. Although he is famous for books that revolutionized the study of Latin and for creating the earliest picture encyclopedia for children, the *Orbis Sensualium Pictus* (1658; translated as *The Visible World*), Comenius was also important in the history of books of instruction. He developed the idea that children could be encouraged to learn if their senses were stimulated—through pictures, models, and music. For eighteenth-century publishers, the drive to instruct and amuse applied across genres, shaping fiction and courtesy books as well as books of science. Newbery, for example, lists his ten-volume *The Circle of the Sciences* (1745–48) in his catalogue of books of manners and instruction, calling it a "compendious library." To a modern eye, Newbery's eighteenth-century definition of *science* looks suspect, as the work includes volumes on arithmetic, chronology, geography, grammar, logic, poetry, and rhetoric.

Though modern disciplinary divisions between the arts and sciences were still far from stable in the eighteenth and nineteenth centuries, the principle that there was a discrete body of information that children needed to know in order to be well-educated was steadily taking hold. Education began to focus on predetermined bits of information, making it possible to determine the thoroughness of a child's education by testing his or her ability to answer questions that were deemed relevant. And so it came to pass that *Mangnall's Questions* became a familiar part of the fabric of life for generations of nineteenth-century children.

In 1800 the schoolmistress Richmal Mangnall assembled a "must know" body of knowledge. Her *Historical and Miscellaneous Questions for the Use of Young People* was essentially a series of lists of questions covering general knowledge of history and science. They were the sorts of question that might now be posed on television quiz shows featuring high school students, or perhaps in board games such as Trivial Pursuit. Even the education of the young princess Victoria included knowledge of the correct answers to *Mangnall's Questions*. Nineteenth-century novelists alluded to them freely, secure in the knowledge that readers would recognize the reference.

In *Vanity Fair* (1847–48), for example, William Makepeace Thackeray invokes them as part of a generalized character sketch, as he poses a rhetorical question to the reader about the value of a woman:

> What is there in a pair of pink cheeks and blue eyes forsooth? These dear Moralists ask, and hint widely that the gifts of genius, the accomplishments of the mind, the mastery of Mangnall's questions, and a ladylike knowledge of botany and geology, . . . and so forth, are far more valuable endowments for a female, than those fugitive charms which a few years will inevitably tarnish.

Thackeray nicely combines here two aspects of books of instruction: science and conduct. Thirty years later, George Eliot puts *Mangnall's Questions* to more nuanced use in chapter 23 of *Middlemarch* (1871–72). That one character "had been a teacher before her marriage" and was intimate with "Mangnall's *Questions*" makes another woman, of slightly higher class, uneasy: "no woman who was better off needed that sort of thing."

Through the course of the nineteenth century, the increased access to formal schooling for the lower classes narrowed school-defined knowledge considerably. It is Charles Dickens, in *Hard Times* (1854), who most harshly criticizes the restrictiveness of what children were being told they needed to know. The first chapter of *Hard Times* is, in fact, called "The One Thing Needful," and the aptly named Thomas Gradgrind outlines his educational philosophy in the novel's very first words: "Now, what I want is, Facts. Teach these boys and girls nothing but Facts. Facts alone are wanted in life. Plant nothing else, and root out everything else." Rote knowledge of facts, however, turns out to be an achingly oppressive way of understanding the world. A horse, for example, is defined only by its quantifiable characteristics: "Quadruped. Graminivorous. Forty teeth, namely twenty-four grinders, four eye-teeth, and twelve incisive. Sheds coat in the spring; in marshy countries, sheds hoofs, too. Hoofs hard, but requiring to be shod with iron. Age known by marks in mouth."

Dickens made it fashionable to recognize that Gradgrind's facts, like those in *Mangnall's Questions*, were sadly unable to produce the kind of knowledge that equipped children to function in the world. By the late nineteenth century, fact-based knowledge was beginning to look tired and out-of-date. The German educator Friedrich Froebel (1782–1852) had already put forward ideas about the relationships between education and play, opening the first kindergarten in 1837. In Italy, Maria Montessori (1870–1952) developed a new approach to early childhood education, advocating a creative space rich in manipulative materials. By the twentieth century, the time was ripe for a more formal codification of these new kinds of pedagogical practices and new approaches to their implementation. In America the progressive educational philosophy of John Dewey (1859–1952), and his ideas of "child-centered" instead of fact-centered education, began to gain prominence.

Information in the Age of Technology

Dewey stressed a quite different kind of learning, one still very much with us today. Rather than assuming that children should blindly accept facts, Dewey proposed that they proceed like scientists, learning through experimentation. On this principle, children would be encouraged to exercise their curiosity about the world, observe, and so acquire broadly based knowledge.

Even as the range of knowledge to which children might gain access was growing exponentially, the end of the nineteenth century also saw a dramatic improvement in technologies that could bring the world to the child. The camera made it possible to photograph things and places, such as Africa or Antarctica, that had been accessible to only a few. Moreover, for the first time photographs could be reproduced in large quantities, relatively cheaply. In 1888, the National Geographic Society was founded. Photographs of exotic peoples and locations were introduced into the magazine in 1905, and these increasingly became one of its defining features. A little earlier, the *Encyclopaedia Britannica* had introduced photographic plates in its tenth edition (1902–03). Although the first edition had been published in the eighteenth century (1768–71, 3 vols.), it came into its own in the ninth edition (1875–89), which began featuring articles by prominent scholars of the day. By the classic eleventh edition (1910–11), photographs were integrated into the texts—as well as appearing as plates. The children's book and journal editor Sir Arthur Mee produced *The Children's Encyclopedia* (1908–33), or *The Book of Knowledge* as it was known in the United States. These large illustrated storehouses became resources for a pedagogy that encouraged children to learn not just by doing but also by looking things up themselves. Educators were beginning to think that children learned most effectively if they discovered information about subjects on their own. And changes in technology introduced changes in access to information.

For decades a bookcase containing a set of encyclopedias was the first line of access to information for most children; in a television- and computer-dominated age, that is no longer true. Today's culture of 24/7 Internet access has led many to believe that knowledge stored in books dates too quickly to be useful. The encyclopedia seems obsolete, much like the traditional department store that promised one-stop shopping. Specialist, dedicated boutiques now appear to provide the target data (or desired item) more effectively. In the twenty-first century, the Internet search engine Google has increasingly become the first research source to which people turn—so much so that "to google" has become a verb.

Boutique shopping for information takes a variety of forms. High-resolution photographs in glossy, uniform books designed to provide all the information children need to complete a project on a topic in the curriculum fall into one category, movable books into another. By offering three-dimensional views, the latter can convey the dynamic picture necessary to help a child understand, for example, how blood flows and hearts beat. Architectural drawings and floor plans can supply knowledge in two dimensions. And, of course, audiovisual media—provided by the Internet, countless films and videos, and CD-ROMs—offer close-up looks at all facets of the natural world and of space. Information is transformed into edutainment.

Voyages of Discovery

If educators are to act on the belief that children learn best when they rely on their own curiosity to discover the information they need to make sense of the world around them, then innovative pedagogical techniques must be devised. The American psychologist Jerome Bruner (b. 1915), for example, influenced by the theories of Jean Piaget (1896–1980), begins with the idea that "any subject can be taught effectively in some intellectually honest form to any child at any stage of development" (*The Process of Education*, 1960). The key is to present the information in a way that encourages learners to embark on a voyage of discovery. Publishers of nonfiction books know that there is a market for books that help the reader/learner participate in that voyage. Thus books like Robert D. Ballard's *Exploring the Titanic* (1988) succeed because they combine drama and facts. Into the tragic story of the "unsinkable" *Titanic*, Ballard interweaves information about the technology that made it possible for him to find and explore the wreck more than 12,000 feet below the ocean's surface. The genre descends in part from the nineteenth-century adventure stories of Sir Walter Scott, Captain Frederick Marryat, and R. M. Ballantyne.

The voyages taken in such books can be imaginary as well as real, for the structure of a narrative adventure can be imposed on almost any material if the author is sufficiently imaginative. Scholastic's Magic School Bus franchise, whose foundation is a series of books written by Joanne Cole and illustrated by Bruce Degen (1986–2000), uses a fantastic premise to teach science to children. In each book or video, a teacher, Ms. Frizzle, takes her elementary students on the magic school bus that travels into a hurricane, through space, within the human body, and so on, on field trips packed with information and humor.

To be sure, not all information books take the voyage of discovery literally; nor are all branded into standard formats or designed to fit into teachers' lesson plans. Margaret Meek's *Information and Book Learning* (1996) offers a thoughtful discussion of the relationships between knowledge, books of instruction, and education. She recommends the Read and Wonder books, published by Candlewick Press in the United States and Walker Books in England, because they are probably the most innovative in the genre. Because different authors and illustrators create each book, the books all feel distinct, despite having the same size and shape. As the series title suggests, each Read and Wonder book proceeds from the author's sense of curiosity about a given subject, and often unconventional titles result: *All Pigs Are Beautiful* (2001), *A Piece of String Is a Wonderful Thing* (1995), *A Ruined House* (1996), *What Is a Wall, after All?* (1995), *The Wheeling and Whirling-Around Book* (1994), and more. These books encourage the idea that it is possible to be interested in a subject for its own sake, and that there is pleasure in finding out about it, in doing the research, in exploring. Such investigations can go in unexpected directions: for example, *A Ruined House* is interested not just in broken pottery (archaeology) but also in the vegetation that reasserts itself in the abandoned house (botany). This open-endedness is quite unlike the tight focus of those information books designed to present information rather than wonder about it.

Graphic Design and the Information Book

Because school curricula have, since the middle of the twentieth century, focused so much on child-centered learning and on the value of children discovering information on their own, a large market has developed for books specifically designed to help them find out about an assigned subject. But how to assess the quality of such information books is not clear—in part because how children access, synthesize, assimilate, and transform information into knowledge is not well understood. Some books, such as those by the American graphic artist David Macaulay, look like architectural drawings (he did, in fact, study architecture at the Rhode Island School of Design). Macaulay's *Cathedral: The Story of Its Construction* (1973) and *Unbuilding* (1980), about taking apart and moving the Empire State Building, work on the premise that technical information is best assimilated if presented in a narrative. *Cathedral* describes construction and *Unbuilding* chronicles deconstruction. Similarly, Macaulay's *The Way Things Work* (1988; rev. ed. on CD-ROM, 1994) orders the facts it conveys in a narrative sequence, a plot, thereby facilitating understanding and interpretation, as well as enhancing the reader's ability to retain and apply the knowledge.

At the opposite end of the design spectrum are the very successful information books published by Dorling Kindersley. They have the high-resolution, intense color photographs and the glossy look and feel of fashion magazines: captioned pictures dominate the page, generally accompanied by a short descriptive paragraph. *River Life: A Close-Up Look at the Natural World of a River* (1992) opens with a double-page spread of what it presents as generic river life. It contains what look like cut-out pictures of birds and insects, fish, a snake, a bat, and so on; many are not shown to scale, though their actual dimensions are given. This elegant color collage displays what would be found in the environs of a river—if all the animals were in full view. The river itself is indicated only by a line across the spread to represent its surface. No attempt is made at geographical accuracy: Asian minnows swim below a European viperine water snake suspended (head down) from a branch over the water. To the right is a remarkably sharp picture of a rat, with a very general caption: "The young brown rat's (*Rattus norvegicus*) body is 4 in. long and it lives all over the world." An explanatory paragraph that occupies about a quarter of the double-page spread is equally generic, and its beginning strikes the tone of a school essay's topic sentence: "From cold, rushing torrents to warm, sluggish tropical waters, the rivers of the world contain a wealth of wildlife."

Technological improvements, especially in computer-assisted design, have made beautifully produced books for children affordable. But Dorling Kindersley's approach is by no means the only option. Although pop-up and movable books have been around since the nineteenth century, they are today more common; new techniques in paper engineering and access to cheap (overseas) labor to manufacture them have encouraged contemporary artists to try designing information books in three dimensions. A movable book can greatly aid the documentation of a voyage or process. Outstanding examples of this subgenre include *The Human Body* (1983) and *The Facts of Life* (1984), created by Jonathan Miller (a physician as well as an actor and director) and the paper engineer David Pelham. *The Human Body* shows readers how blood flows, for example. And *The Facts of Life*, appropriately, contains a pop-up penis and a cross section of a baby in utero.

Movable books are, by definition, interactive: to understand their contents, the reader has to manipulate their parts. They thus differ strikingly from those information books that depend on direct instruction, on the text telling the reading child what he or she needs to know. It is a shift from what the critic Mikhail Bakhtin describes in "Discourse in the Novel" (1934–35) as a "monologic" form (rendered in a single authoritative voice) to a "dialogic" form (interactive and responsive). *It's Perfectly Normal: A Book about Changing Bodies, Growing Up, Sex, and Sexual Health* (1994), written by Robie Harris and illustrated by Michael Emberley, is a quintessential example of the kind of narrative and graphic shift that can occur in information books. The book begins with a series of juxtapositions: between the cartoon characters that recur throughout and the main narrative, between scientific diagrams and comic drawings. Instead of presenting instruction on the "right" way to behave, the book offers a conversation and a sense that multiple options are available.

More than five hundred years separate *The Babees Book* from *It's Perfectly Normal*, though both are books of instruction, addressing what children "need to know." In one sense *It's Perfectly Normal* is in a direct line of descent from the medieval courtesy book and the eighteenth-century conduct book. But it also illustrates the fundamental change that the genre has undergone. Whereas once knowledge of morals and manners was seen as essential to functioning in the world, by the nineteenth century science and technology increasingly defined what children needed to know. Methods of instruction have also changed. Rather than information passing directly from a person in authority to children who must assimilate it to carry on the values and customs of their society, it is made available to learners to take in what they need to know in order to function in an increasingly complex and information-saturated world.

CONDUCT BOOKS FOR BOYS

The first man-to-man talk that a father has with his son generally occurs when the latter is at the point of transition from dependent boy to independent man. This conversation traditionally covers the responsibilities of manhood, including work, sex, and honorable behavior. While the details vary from generation to generation, the explicit gender-coding is a constant. Men are supposed to earn money, support wives and children, and be pillars of society. The anonymous author of *The Father's Legacy* (1678) characterizes this role with a kind of birth myth, beginning with the unlikely posture assumed by babies heading the right way out into the world: "Think with your self, that your preposterous dropping into the world with your head down and feet upwards, is only to teach you that none come in this posture into the natural place of their abode, and that there you must not expect yours." The "faithful counsel" that the father imparts is advice on how to walk on one's own two feet—like a man. Through the generations, such well-meaning though somewhat trite advice has often provided more satisfaction to the one bestowing it than to its intended recipient.

The selections here from seventeenth- and eighteenth-century conduct books for boys offer directions that have not changed much over the years: work hard, don't gamble, choose your friends carefully, marry well, and stay out of trouble. The illustration from Edward White Benson's *Education at Home* (1824) graphically warns against straying from life's designated path. Because conduct books were also designed to maintain class distinctions, upper-class boys were advised to stay away from lower-class women (especially governesses and servants)—involvements with them were likely to jeopardize the family honor and the secure passage of property.

Although Sir John Barnard (1685–1764) is not identified by name on the title page of *A Present for an Apprentice* (1740), which coyly says only "by a late Lord Mayor of London," he is recognized as its author. He must have been an astonishingly forceful personality. From his apprenticeship in a countinghouse in 1699, at age fourteen, to his appointment as Lord Mayor of London in 1737, he moved from strength to strength, winning renown as a financial wizard of his age. According to the *Dictionary of National Biography*, "public attention was drawn to his talents by the skill which he displayed in guarding the interests of his colleagues in business during the progress in parliament of a measure affecting their trade." Although his book is directed toward an apprentice, the advice is much the same as that given any young man: the hierarchical order is maintained in all spheres, whether master be ranked over apprentice or father over son. Barnard speaks from experience, as a former apprentice, a successful businessman, a father (of a son and two daughters), and a politician. Christian virtue is not too distant from commercial virtue—and, he warns, be especially careful "not to have any familiarity with the Maidservants of the family where you are."

A Present for an Apprentice was influential in its time and went through several editions. Like the other books of instruction excerpted here, it combines self-help and lifestyle management. Its tone—an encouraging "if-I-can-do-it-so-can-you"— and its inherent promise that following all its instructions to the letter will result in

Frontispiece to Edward Benson White's *Education at Home* (1824).

a perfect life are familiar from the time and money management manuals found on today's shelves.

The next excerpt is taken from letters by Philip Dormer Stanhope, fourth Earl of Chesterfield (1694–1773). He was famous in his time and a highly regarded states-man. By all accounts he was a charming and quick-witted man as well as a brilliant diplomat. In an attempt to shape the character of his illegitimate son, Philip Stanhope (1732–1768), he wrote hundreds of letters, beginning in 1736. The letters are filled with instructions, exhortations, disquisitions on social values, and, as Philip became older, reflections on history and philosophy. But Philip was not to have anything like his father's success: he was described by contemporaries as "loutish," and he was hampered by ill health and his illegitimacy. To be sure, Lord Chesterfield's own wife, Melusina de Schulemberg, Countess of Walsingham and Baroness of Aldborough, was illegitimate, but her father was the king and she was wealthy (a consideration that, for women, had great weight). The introduction to the 1818 edition of Lord Chesterfield's letters (cited here) delicately describes his situation: "his Lordship had no issue by his Lady, but he had a natural son by Madame de Bouchet, a French lady with whom he carried on a criminal intercourse for some years, chiefly during his residence at the Hague."

Though arguably ineffective in their primary aim, the letters achieved an independent life. A year after Lord Chesterfield's death, Philip's widow published them in two volumes, originally titled *Lord Chesterfield's Advice to his Son, on Men and Man-*

ners: or, a New system of education in which the principles of politeness, the art of acquiring a knowledge of the world, with every instruction necessary to form a man of honour, virtue, taste and fashion are laid down. The book was hugely popular, quickly going into many editions, usually cited as *Chesterfield's Maxims* or *Chesterfield's Letters*. Its pithy and sometimes cynical advice was often quoted, and dictionaries of quotations still reprint some of Chesterfield's wittier remarks, including "Most people enjoy the inferiority of their best friends" and "Let blockheads read what blockheads wrote." The calculatedness of his advice and his unromantic view of human nature do not appeal to everyone, however.

These advice books for boys and young men imply that hard work, good manners, and a sense of responsibility ensure a good life. Theirs is a masculine story, one that promises success to men and boys. Other stories were told to girls and women—and their success was defined very differently.

From The Father's Legacy; or, Faithful Counsels of a Good Father to His Children and Friends

OF THE DIFFERENCE THAT THERE IS BETWIXT THE PROCREATION OF MAN, AND THE OTHER PRODUCTIONS OF NATURE; AND THE REASON THEREOF.

My child, in the first part of this my Will and Testament, where I have treated of your duty toward God, I have showed you that the knowledge of him must go before your adoration, which is your duty towards him. In this second part, where I propose to speak of your duty towards yourself, I intend to observe the same order, judging it most convenient that you should know what you are, before you be instructed of your duty towards your self; to accomplish my design, I think it necessary to trace nature step by step, and to eye her always as the forerunner of any enterprise.

When I consider her in the first elements of our life, I find nothing but incontinence, fainting, griping pains, and a flood of impurities which accompany your tears. It seems that in the other productions of Nature there is somewhat more happiness, and especially in the procreation of Birds and Plants. Birds bear not as we do their young in their womb, they lay and hatch their eggs in the loveliest season of the year, with so much tranquillity and repose, that many times the same hand that robs the nest of their young, does likewise seize the old. Their harmony and consort[1] during that time sufficiently proves that their birth is fortunate in respect of ours. Plants likewise seem to renew their life when they begin to bud, instead of corrupt blood or unsavory water, a sweet dew does moisten and cherish their fruit. It is not (like us) wrapped in an impure coat, its own flowers encompass it, which in blowing[2] perfume the air, and the very leaves, which are as their after-birth, serve them for cloathing and ornament until they are stript and left naked by the winter.

This advantage, my Son, which plants seem to have above you, hath only been granted them for your sake; the chief end of the production of their fruit, is that they are for your use, and prudent nature who designs them for your sustenance, presents them to you in that manner, lest otherwise you might loath and reject them, do not therefore envy them.

---

1. Agreement. 2. Blooming.

Now if the production and birth of some living creatures seem less painful than your own, and that as soon as they are brought forth, they find clothing at hand and their table covered for both which you must labour with the sweat of your brows, yet are they neither your brethren nor your elders, they come into the world as into their own native country, and their own inheritance, without pretending to any other, and therefore it is just that they should be received as the children of the family: But what hurt is done to you, who are a stranger, and come hither as a pilgrim, to demand of you custom and tole[3] for your passage? The goodness of God who hath placed your inheritance elsewhere, thought fit to deprive you at first of the allurements of this life, that so he might separate from it your affection. Think with your self, that your preposterous dropping into the world with your head down and feet upwards,[4] is only to teach you that none come in this posture into the natural place of their abode, and that here you must not expect yours.

Since then, my Son, you are only as a passenger in this life, it is your chief duty to plain[5] the way to that whither you aspire, and to seek out in this painful passage the most proper means to attain to it, every thing that is superfluous, is but a hindrance to a traveller; it is enough for him to live and to have what is necessary for his journey: and because the first desire which discovers it self in man as soon as he is born, is that of living, and the second, of having every thing that he sees. In treating of the Duty of Man towards himself, I shall begin with the measures that he ought to observe in the moderation of those two first appetites.

1678

---

3. Toll; i.e., duty and payment.
4. I.e., at birth.

5. I.e., to plane: to smooth.

JOHN BARNARD
1685–1764

From A Present for an Apprentice; or, A Sure Guide to Gain Both Esteem and an Estate

Dear Son,

Having been at so much Expense and Care to set you fairly out, to act your part upon the forge of the world; I have considered, what might further be done, to contribute to your successful Performance. And observing that you were gone out from under the Shadow of the Father's Wing, when counsel was at hand on every occasion that offered, and yet are exposed to the danger of a much more slippery Situation, through the abundance of powerful Temptations; I thought proper to send you up a stock of such well-tried advice as might serve for your direction on all occasions.

And though some Fathers, and among them persons of great Distinction, have undertaken to give advice unto their Sons, whose works in that kind have been published and extant, and therefore this my little Labour may seem needless; yet not any (that I know of) hath stoopt so low as to give advice to an Apprentice, but they directed their thoughts to such a pitch, as lay not in the level of the greatest part of Mankind; to whom advice was not less needful. However, you'll find here many things not touched on, by their observations, and such as when tried will be found to deserve your care, and caution. But what concerns you most, is not the Doctrine, but the Use; for 'tis not hard to give good Counsel, but to take it.

* * *

3. Discover[1] not those concerns to any of your acquaintance, which may redound either to your damage, or discredit, if present friendship should be changed into unexpected enmity: Consider 'tis a pitiful and precarious life, which depends upon the secrecy or silence of another who may disclose your counsel, either by a natural talkative humour, or by the power of Wine, or a design to oblige another by betraying you: For besides that there is an impossibility in some tempers to stand out a siege, when closely ply'd, as we see *Sampson*[2] himself twice in this kind routed; so it is a miserable captivity to lye at the mercy of another, and at his discretion. And men generally upon such advantages are as imperious, as a Maid that is heir to her Mistress; and takes pleasure to make that yoke pinch and wring, into which your own folly thrust your head, and from whence you have not confidence enough to pull it out.

4. Reserve to your self always a liberty of breaking company, and give up the pursuit; when the Cry hunts not according to your judgment, or your private concerns oblige you to retreat: For as it is little prudence to buy, by what another bids; so is he as little wise, that will exhaust his purse to keep pace with another's expences. And as I have thought it unjust that another should force me to pledge him in a brimmer,[3] because he began it, without regarding whether my body or head will bear it; so I think 'tis wisdom to leave your friend, when he proves an *Ignis fatuus*,[4] and would lead you into a quagmire, intangle you in contests, or expect that you should lavish your money for company, though possibly he may be much better able to afford it, therefore balance your expences not by those of another person, but by your own abilities.

Be especially advised, not to have any familiarity with the Maidservants of the family where you are, more than what conduceth to the dispatching of general affairs, and such an affability as is common and due to all; for those kind of cattle are as weary of a single life, as Nuns of their Cloisters, and therefore catch at the very appearance of a match; and if you show them any kindness more than ordinary, they interpret it affection, and make no difficulty to challenge you upon that account: wherein if you correspond[5] not, they hate you worse than an old decayed woman doth a young flourishing beauty. And therefore they rake Hell to find out inventions to reek their spite on you, and value not how they wound their own reputation, so that they may murder yours; like *Richard* the Third,[6] who scrupl'd not to make his Mother an whore, that he might prove his Brother Illegitimate. Neither will their malice be satisfied till you be ruined. Of which the City of *London* hath given too many, and too pertinent examples, where Women by false accusations have brought those young men to shameful *exits*, whom they could not bring down to their unworthy designs.

1740

---

1. Disclose.
2. After Samson gave in to Delilah, who had repeatedly begged him to tell her the secret of his great strength, she betrayed him to the Philistines (Judges 16). "Stand out": resist.
3. To drink to his health with a goblet filled to the very top.
4. Foolish light (Latin): the light produced by

marsh gas; something that misleads.
5. Answer in agreement (also, have sexual relations).
6. In Shakespeare's *Richard III* (1592–93), as Richard schemes to seize the throne he sends off an ally to persuade Londoners that his brother, Edward IV, is illegitimate and thus he himself is the rightful king (3.5.83–92).

PHILIP DORMER STANHOPE, EARL OF CHESTERFIELD

1694–1773

From Lord Chesterfield's Advice to His Son

AWKWARDNESS OF DIFFERENT KINDS

Many very worthy and sensible people have certain odd tricks, ill habits, and awkwardness in their behaviour, which excite a disgust to, and dislike of, their persons, that cannot be removed or overcome by any other valuable endowment or merit which they may possess.

Now, awkwardness can proceed but from two causes; either from not having kept good company, or from not having attended to it.

When an awkward fellow first comes into a room, it is highly probable that his sword gets between his legs, and throws him down, or makes him stumble, at least: when he has recovered this accident, he goes and places himself in the very place of the whole room where he should not; there he soon lets his hat fall down, and, in taking it up again, throws down his cane; in recovering his cane, his hat falls the second time; so that he is a quarter of an hour before he is in order again. If he drinks tea or coffee, he certainly scalds his mouth, and lets either the cup or the saucer fall, and spills the tea or coffee in his breeches. At dinner, his awkwardness distinguishes itself particularly, as he has more to do: there he holds his knife, fork, and spoon, differently from other people; eats with his knife to the great danger of his mouth, picks his teeth with his fork, and puts his spoon, which has been in his throat twenty times, into the dishes again. If he is to carve, he can never hit the joint; but, in his vain efforts to cut through the bone, scatters the sauce in everybody's face. He generally daubs himself with soup and grease, though his napkin is commonly stuck through a button-hole, and tickles his chin. When he drinks, he infallibly coughs in his glass, and besprinkles the company. Besides all this, he has strange tricks and gestures; such as snuffing up his nose, making faces, putting his fingers in his nose, or blowing it, and looking afterwards in his handkerchief, so as to make the company sick. His hands are troublesome to him when he has not something in them; and he does not know where to put them; but they are in perpetual motion between his bosom and his breeches: he does not wear his clothes, and, in short, does nothing like other people. All this, I own, is not in any degree criminal; but it is highly disagreeable and ridiculous in company, and ought most carefully to be avoided by whoever desires to please.

From this account of what you should not do, you may easily judge what you should do: and a due attention to the manners of people of fashion, and who have seen the world, will make it habitual and familiar to you.

There is, likewise, an awkwardness of expression and words most carefully to be avoided; such as false English, bad pronunciation, old sayings, and common proverbs; which are so many proofs of having kept bad and low company. For example: If, instead of saying, that "tastes are different, and that every man has his own peculiar one," you should let off a proverb, and say, that "what is one man's meat is another man's poison;" or else, "every one as they like, as the good man said when he kissed his cow;" everybody would be persuaded that you had never kept company with anybody above footmen and housemaids.

There is likewise an awkwardness of the mind, that ought to be, and with care may be, avoided; as, for instance, to mistake or forget names. To speak of Mr. What-d'ye-call-him, or Mrs. Thingum or How-d'ye-call-her, is excessively awkward and ordinary. To call people by improper titles and appellations is so too; as, my lord, for sir; and sir, for my lord. To begin a story or narration when you are not perfect in it, and cannot go through with it, but are forced possibly to say in the middle of it, "I have forgot the rest," is very unpleasant and bungling. One must be extremely exact, clear, and perspicuous, in every thing one says; otherwise, instead of entertaining or informing others, one only tires and puzzles them.

BASHFULNESS

Bashfulness is the distinguishing character of an English booby,[1] who appears frightened out of his wits if people of fashion speak to him, and blushes and stammers without being able to give a proper answer; by which means he becomes truly ridiculous, from the groundless fear of being laughed at.

There is a very material difference between modesty and an aukward bashfulness, which is as ridiculous as true modesty is commendable; it is as absurd to be a simpleton as to be an impudent fellow; and we make ourselves contemptible, if we cannot come into a room, and speak to people, without being out of countenance,[2] or without embarrassment. A man who is really diffident, timid, and bashful, be his merit what it will, never can push himself in the world: his despondency throws him into inaction; and the forward, the bustling, and the petulant, will always precede him. The manner makes the whole difference. What would be impudence in one man, is only a proper and decent assurance in another. A man of sense, and of knowledge of the world, will assert his own rights, and pursue his own objects, as steadily and intrepidly as the most impudent man living, and commonly more so; but then he has art enough to give an outward air of modesty to all he does. This engages and prevails; whilst the very same things shock and fail, from the overbearing or impudent manner only of doing them.

Englishmen, in general, are ashamed of going into company. When we avoid singularity, what should we be ashamed of? and why should not we go into a mixed company with as much ease, and as little concern, as we would go into our own room? Vice and ignorance are the only things we ought to be ashamed of: while we keep clear of them, we may venture anywhere without fear or concern. Nothing sinks a young man into low company so surely as bashfulness. If he thinks that he shall not, he most surely will not, please.

Some, indeed, from feeling the pain and inconveniencies of bashfulness, have rushed into the other extreme, and turned impudent; as cowards sometimes grow desperate from excess of danger: but this is equally to be avoided, there being nothing more generally shocking than impudence. The medium between these two extremes points out the well-bred man, who always feels himself firm and easy in all companies; who is modest without being bashful, and steady without being impudent.

A mean fellow is ashamed and embarrassed when he comes into company, is disconcerted when spoken to, answers with difficulty, and does not know how to dispose

---

1. A fool, a clown.   2. Without losing one's composure.

of his hands; but a gentleman, who is acquainted with the world, appears in company with a graceful and proper assurance, and is perfectly easy and unembarrassed. He is not dazzled by superior rank: he pays all the respect that is due to it, without being disconcerted; and can converse as easily with a king as with any of his subjects. This is the great advantage of being introduced young into good company, and of conversing with our superiors. A well-bred man will converse with his inferiors without insolence, and with his superiors with respect and with ease. Add to this, that a man of a gentleman-like behaviour, though of inferior parts, is better received than a man of superior abilities, who is unacquainted with the world. Modesty, and a polite, easy assurance, should be united.

* * *

MATRIMONY

Another common topic for false wit and cold raillery is matrimony. Every man and his wife hate each other cordially, whatever they may pretend, in public, to the contrary: the husband certainly wishes his wife at the devil, and the wife certainly cuckolds her husband: whereas I presume that men and their wives neither love nor hate each other the more, upon account of the form of matrimony which has been said over them. The co-habitation, indeed, which is the consequence of matrimony, makes them either love or hate more, accordingly as they respectively deserve it: but that would be exactly the same between any man and woman who lived together without being married.

1774   1818

CONDUCT BOOKS FOR GIRLS

Typically, success for girls meant a willing embrace of subservience. For lower-class girls and women, success meant being knowledgeable only about domestic details and the Bible. Ambition, whether intellectual or social, was out of the question. The anonymous author of *Duties of a Lady's Maid* (1825) makes it quite clear that marriages between lower-class servants and their masters are doomed to unhappiness. "Such marriages," she says, "have taken place, but they are seldom, if ever, happy ones, and cannot be; for however high you may estimate your own importance, you must always be considered as an intruder by your husband's friends, while he will, probably, look upon your relatives, let them be ever so respectable, as unfit associates, and will despise perhaps your very parents." Apart from the stern injunction never to rise above her station (and the inclusion of numerous recipes for making skin cream and makeup, and methods of removing stains from clothing), the instructions to the aspiring lady's maid differ little from those offered to the girl destined to be the lady of the manor. She is told of her duties to be polite and deferential, pious and diligent. She is given bewildering details on manners and on the protocols of serving food and eating and drinking and visiting.

The trick for upper-class women, especially through the eighteenth and nineteenth centuries, was to be accomplished—without being too accomplished. It was good to be able speak several languages, know something about the political issues of the day, dance, play an instrument, and paint. But to be too skilled at any one of those things put women at risk of becoming professional. The tables of contents in eighteenth- and nineteenth-century conduct books map out the issues to which girls should attend. Among them are happiness, moderation, economy, temper, drawing, painting, dancing, filial duty, keeping a home, dress, and decorum; to be avoided are peevishness and obstinacy. Even in the ostensibly less class-conscious United States, girls and women are urged to be as self-effacing as servants. An American advice book called *The Wedding Gift* (1851), for example, offers the young bride no advice on sexual relations in marriage but much on the virtue of being silent and keeping her temper. For example, she is told how to deal with moments of domestic discord:

> Should a passing cloud overshadow the sunshine of your happiness, confine the fact within your own bosom, and within your own home, till it is dissipated by the return of reason. Any enlargement upon it to relatives or friends will tend to foment it; and you will be equally degraded in their eyes, as you must ultimately in your own, for having made the circumstances public.

The passage is exactly in tune with the famous scene in Louisa May Alcott's *Little Women* (1868–69) in which Marmee confesses to her own feelings of anger and impatience—and the continuing challenge of keeping her feelings to herself. The lesson Jo is meant to learn, and that women generally do learn, is that anger isn't ladylike. Repress it.

A more up-to-date advice book is *Don'ts for Girls: A Manual of Mistakes* (1903), by the American writer Minna Thomas Antrim (b. 1861). Yet despite the inevitable change in idiom, its substance is much the same as that found in advice manuals of earlier centuries. It relentlessly hectors its reader on the need to respect her elders (don't be ashamed of one's parents), to be prudent (don't chatter), to avoid being a tomboy (don't become masculine), and to follow many other interdictions. Its publication date puts this "don't" manual squarely in the period of one of the most famous shapers of boys and girls in the twentieth century, Robert Baden-Powell (1857–1941).

From Duties of a Lady's Maid

FAMILIARITY WITH SUPERIORS

Your situation as a confidential upper servant, will often bring you into conversations with your employers, and if you have a pleasing and affable manner, they will have you more with them than may perhaps be proper for you. My meaning is, that if you observe yourself respected for your affability, your prudence, or your knowledge, you will be very apt to be put off your guard, and begin to act and talk as if you were amongst those equal to yourself in station and respectability. Now I wish to caution you most anxiously and particularly upon this point, as there is nothing connected with your situation of greater importance to attend to:—if you fail here, your place will soon be forfeited, and you will gain a character for impertinence, which is the worst thing that can stand in your way in procuring another.

It is admitted, that it is very hard for a young person to be consulted about any thing, however, trifling, by ladies of rank or fashion, without feeling a good deal of vanity. Perhaps it is not in human nature not to feel a little of this, under such circumstances. The difficulty is to conceal it when you do feel yourself to be of a little consequence; but if you can succeed in so far subduing your looks and manner as not to appear flattered by the condescension of your superiors, no bad consequences can arise from the mere feeling. It is, indeed, more the showing of it, and appearing elated and conceited which will do you injury.

The feeling yourself of some little consequence to your employers, on account of your knowledge and dexterity, may be very proper, and tend to render your character more respectable, as it will prevent you perhaps from forming any low connexion, or engaging in any improper line of conduct, either to your employers or your fellow-servants. If you have once got a character, indeed, it will operate as a stimulus to make you endeavour to preserve it, by greater exertions of care and assiduity.

What I would particularly caution you against, however, in this respect, is giving advice when you are not asked, or thrusting your opinion upon your mistress, whether she seems desirous of having it or not. This is a fault which many commit from thoughtlessness, trusting to the familiarity with which they may have been treated in other cases; but they are certain to repent it, as nothing is more disliked in a servant, whatever may have been the previous familiarity, than this unbidden giving of opinions and advice. So strictly ought you to guard your behaviour in this respect, even when you are well aware your superiors are wrong upon any point—that you should never thrust in your word unless you are particularly asked. If, also, you observe any mistake committed by your employers or their guests, in things which you understand better than they, you should never take the slightest notice of it, nor afterwards mention it.

The familiarities which I am cautioning you to avoid, are more particularly apt to be contracted, should your mistress have required any little attentions from you during sickness, or on any private family concern, which you may have been entrusted to manage. Sickness, danger, and adversity, usually level distinction of rank; but you must never forget that you are a servant, nor assume the airs and the consequences of a gentlewoman[1] so long as you are in the pay and at the command of another. It may, no doubt, give you the wish to be a lady—to have attentions paid you; but you should strive to subdue in your mind all idle repining that it has not been your fate to be placed in such a rank, and that Providence, undoubtedly, for wise purposes, has ordered it otherwise.

There is another point of great delicacy connected with this subject, which I would not willingly omit. If you have any personal attractions, and most young women have something that is agreeable or pleasing, beware of the least approach to familiarity with any of the gentlemen of the family where you live. Any thing of this kind must lead to improper consequences whatever turn it may take. Reflect on the injury which the whole family and their connexions[2] would accuse you of having done them, should you so far gain the affections of any of the young gentlemen as to induce him to marry you. Such marriages have taken place, but they are seldom, if ever, happy ones, and cannot be; for however high you may estimate your own importance, you must always be considered as an intruder by your husband's friends, while he will, probably, look upon your relatives, let them be ever so respectable, as unfit associates,

---

1. I.e., a woman of high rank, but not a member of the nobility.   2. Relatives by marriage.

and will despise perhaps your very parents. Be firm, therefore, and resolutely check all advances of this sort, at the very first; and if you cannot otherwise avoid the evil which will certainly await you by rashly listening to the importunities of passion, leave the situation at once, without disclosing to any one the reason of your conduct; because the least hint of such a circumstance would soon spread, and be exaggerated much to your disadvantage.

On the other hand, it is much more likely that without greatly injuring the other party, the familiarities to which I have alluded would terminate in your ruin. Unfortunately for the character of our country, it is considered to be a matter of little moment for a gentleman to ruin an unsuspecting and confiding girl; but the very chance of such a dreadful consequence to you, ought to make you firm and determined to give no inlet, even to familiar conversation. Pray that you may be preserved from all such temptations and you will receive strength from above, to resist them according to the Scripture promise, "in trouble I will be with you."[3]

There cannot be a truer maxim than that familiarity breeds contempt. If, therefore, it tend to lessen the dignity of superiors to make companions of their servants, recollect that the very same thing will operate against yourself, by lessening your respectability. I do not mean that you should bear yourself with a haughty demeanour or proud air, but there is a certain respectful distance which it ought to be your study to maintain, and you will do wrong by either swaying from this, towards pride or to great familiarity. A proper sense of the nature of your situation, if you keep that properly in mind, will be the best thing to prevent you from falling into either of those extremes.

You owe to your employers respect and attention, because your engagement implies this, and of course you must never speak disrespectfully of them yourself, or keep company with any who may do so, for it is exposing your good principles to temptation even to listen to any thing improper which may be said of the family whose bread you eat.

Stays and Corsets

Although I am unwilling to condemn altogether an article of dress so universally worn as stays, corsets, or whatever other name may be given to the stiff casing that is employed to compress the upper parts of the body; yet I think it will be of some importance to point out to you the inconveniences and even the danger to which this may lead. I admit most readily that stays sometimes add to the elegance of the shape, but if this is done at the hazard of injuring the health, the sacrifice will be allowed to be too great; that stays, corsets, and tight lacing do so may easily be shown; at the same time it continues, as Madame Voïart[4] well remarks, a barbarous custom, contrary to good taste and human comfort. In our gardens, when an unskilful workman tightens the band which supports a feeble shrub, we see the plant deprived of the free circulation of the sap, languish and die, and the buds formed on its branches wither for want of nourishment. Tight lacing and stiff stays produce similar effects on the human body, and the younger or the more feeble the individual is, these effects are the more certainly and speedily produced.

A popular author has justly remarked, that the upright position of the body is chiefly preserved by a number of strong fleshy bands or ribbons, called muscles,

---

3. Psalm 91.15: "He shall call upon me, and I will answer him: I will be with him in trouble; I will deliver him, and honor him."

4. Elise Voïart (1786–1866), French writer.

which both serve to move the different parts of the body, and to hold the bones firmly in their several positions. Taking this under consideration, medical men lay it down as an invariable rule, that if you cause a pressure on any of those muscular bands by means of dress, it will soon diminish in size, and will consequently lose the power of supporting the bones in the natural position, and its functions of producing easy and natural, or, in other words, graceful movements of the parts to which it is attached. This is strongly exemplified in the case of those impostors, who bandage their limbs till they are diminished, frequently to half their natural size, for the purpose of exciting commisseration and extorting charity. All kinds of dress, therefore, which are made so tight as to compress any part of the body or the limbs, and which, by this means, cramps both the free motion of the muscles, and flattens their natural diameter and plumpness of structure, ought to be carefully avoided. Accordingly, stays, corsets, and bands of every description, as well as tight sleeves or garters, must, infallibly, produce mischief, and there is no possibility of avoiding it. The muscles are squeezed, flattened, and prevented from moving; and their healthy tone and fulness give place to contraction, shrivelling, and emaciation. This has the effect of giving the back a twist, throwing the shoulders out of their natural position, contracting the chest, and causing an ungraceful stoop in walking. The great philosopher Locke,[5] who was a medical man, remarks, and most truly, that whalebone stays often make the chest narrow, and the back crooked; the breath becomes fætid, and consumption probably succeeds; and at best the shape is spoiled rather than made slender and elegant, as has been imagined by the inventors.

5. John Locke (1632–1704), British philosopher.

It is allowed, however, that corsets may be made not only harmless, but beneficial, if they are contrived so as to aid the muscles in support of the body. If they do more than this, and are made to compress the chest and stomach by tight lacing, they become hurtful and destructive.

It has been well remarked in a recent work on the spine, that the unfettered Indian females, and even our own peasant girls in some parts of the country, are strangers to twists and deformities of the shape; and this evidently arises from their having no unnatural dress to restrain their freedom of motion. In conformity with the principles here advocated, M. Portal,[6] a celebrated French physician, found the muscles of the back much larger, redder, and stronger in women who had worn stays, than in those who had never used them. He also remarked, that where women who had worn stays from their youth, leave them off at a certain age for greater comfort, they are sure to become distorted; for the muscles have been so weakened by want of use, that when the artificial props are removed, they are no longer capable of supporting the body. We laugh, says Dr. Gregory,[7] at the folly of the Chinese ladies, who compress their feet till they are unable to walk, and at the Africans, who flatten their noses as an indispensible requisite of beauty; but we are still further from Nature, when we imagine that the female chest is not so elegant as we can make it by the confinement of stays; and Nature, accordingly, shows her resentment, by rendering so many of our fashionable ladies who thus encase themselves in steel and whalebone, deformed either in the chest, the shoulders, or the spine.

Instead of this unnatural practice, we should follow the elegant Greeks, the ease and beauty of whose forms are so much admired. They put no unnatural straps on their young ladies. All their garments are easy, loose, and flowing. The effect is seen in their every limb, and every motion. On the contrary, it is easy to distinguish at once, among thousands, from their stiff starched awkwardness, the females who have from their youth up been pinioned and tortured by shoulder braces, and stays, and other wicked inventions (for such they may well be called) to turn beauty into deformity, and the finest figures into ricketty ugliness. Dr. Macartney,[8] of Dublin, says, he has found the fine proportion of the antique statues only in such busts of women who had never worn such restraints on the shape.

When stays, however, are worn, whalebone and steel ought to be prohibited, as certain to produce injury. The stuff of which they are made should be of the most elastic materials that can be procured, in order that it may yield with ease to every motion of the body, without producing injurious compression. Medical men recommend stays of fine white woolen stocking web, doubled, and cut into forms, and instead of whalebone, stripes of jean[9] stitched closely down on both sides, in the places where the whalebones are usually put. These give sufficient firmness, while the elastic web between them admits of the free motion of the body in all directions. The bosom part may be made of jean, for the purpose of supporting the breasts.

A sort of stays, or corset called *strophium* by the ancient Romans, has been introduced in our times by the French, under the name *cincture de Vénus*,[1] though it is by no means entitled to such an appellation; for, as a foreign author well remarks, by forcing the breasts to remain in a position much higher than natural, it destroys

---

6. Antoine Portal (1742–1832).
7. John Gregory (1724–1773), Scottish physician and professor; he was the author of the popular conduct book *A Father's Legacy to His Daughters* (1774).
8. Probably the anatomist James Macartney

(1770–1843).
9. A twilled cotton cloth. "Stocking web": a strongly woven band made of an elastic material.
1. The girdle (*ceinture*) of Venus. In Roman mythology, Venus was the goddess of love.

their elasticity and spring, and renders them soft and flat. It is distressing to think
that fashion should give currency to an article of dress so injurious, and that the
spirit of rivalry which always comes from an evil service, should lead females to
sacrifice without regret the elegance of their figure, the grace of their carriage, and
their movements, by a dress which renders them at once deformed, ungraceful, and
ridiculous. Young ladies who have followed the injurious fashion, may be seen with
their breasts displaced from being pushed too high, and frightful wrinkles established
between the bosom and the shoulder.

At other times you may see those to whom Nature has denied the roundness of
contour requisite for a fine shape, make themselves still more thin and slender by
tight lacing, recalling the ungraceful costume of Catherine de Medicis[2]—a ridiculous
fashion, by means of which the body, separated into two parts, resembles an ant,
with a slender tube uniting the bust to the haunches, which are stuffed out beyond
all proportion. At that period when this was the rage, every body of good sense
exclaimed against it. The whalebone cases, says a French author, which young ladies
are made to wear to improve their shape, act in a manner precisely opposite, for to
lace up the body in such a *cuirasse civile*,[3] is certain to destroy all natural grace, while
it compresses and greatly injures the internal parts.

Medical men, however, and the writings of philosophers, had no power to put a
stop to the evil, and satire and ridicule were tried in vain. The Emperor Joseph II[4]
tried what an Imperial decree could effect in abolishing whalebone stays in his
dominions. His law prohibited the use of all sorts of corsets in the orphan hospitals,
the convents, and the establishments for the education of young ladies; and to throw
a sort of disgrace upon this article of dress, the Emperor ordered female convicts to
wear them when they were lead to punishment. But even the Imperial decree was
found to have less power than the decrees of fashion, and corsets continued to be
worn.

The fashion, however, which resisted both the voice of reason, the shafts of ridicule, and the authority of a monarch, yielded at last to the love of change. In France
the corset was gradually shortened, till the ladies at last reached the middle, between
two extremes, which is so difficult to hit in the vicissitudes of fashion. Unfortunately
this continued only for a short time, as in the endeavour to imitate the antique, the
costume was exaggerated, and the Grecian cincture was placed higher and higher,
till at length it was worn as high as the armpits.

In England the fashions have been equally varied from the ant-like figures of the
reign of George I., to the bunchy humps and short waists of the reign of George III.,[5]
and the lengthened waists at present in vogue.

PADDING, BANDAGING, &c. TO IMPROVE THE FIGURE

It is justly remarked by D'Israeli, that "the origin of many fashions has been the
endeavour to conceal some deformity of the inventor; hence the cushions,[6] ruffs,
hoops, and other monstrous devices of former times. If a reigning beauty chanced to
have an unequal hip, those who had very handsome ones would load them with that

---

2. Catherine de Médici (1519–1589), wife of
Henry II of France. She made a 13-inch waist the
standard at court.
3. Civilian breastplate (the cuirass is a piece of
armor).
4. Joseph II (1741–1790), King of Germany

(1764–90) and Holy Roman Emperor (1765–90).
5. I.e., 1760–1820; George III was born in 1738.
George I (1660–1727; r. 1714–27).
6. Bustles. Benjamin Disraeli (1804–1881), British statesman and author; prime minister, 1868,
1874–80.

false rump, which the others were compelled, by the unkindness of Nature, to sub-stitute. Patches were invented in England in the reign of Edward VI.[7] by a foreign lady, who in this manner ingeniously covered a wen on her neck. When the Spectator wrote, full bottomed wigs were invented by a French barber, one Duvillier, whose name they perpetuated, for the purpose of concealing an elevation in the shoulder of the Dauphin.[8] Charles VII.[9] of France introduced long coats to hide his ill made legs. Shoes with very long points, full two feet in length, were invented by Henry Plantagenet, Duke of Anjou,[1] to conceal a large excrescence on one of his feet. When Francis I.[2] was obliged to wear his hair short, owing to a wound he received in the head, it became the prevailing fashion at Court. Others, on the contrary, adapted fashions to set off their peculiar beauties, as Isabella, of Bavaria,[3] remarkable for her gallantry, and fairness of her complexion, introduced the fashion of leaving the shoul-ders and part of the neck uncovered.

"Fashions have frequently originated from circumstances as silly as the following one. Isabella, daughter of Phillip II. and wife of the Archduke Albert, vowed not to change her linen till Ostend was taken;[4] this siege, unluckily for her comfort, lasted three years; and the supposed colour of the Archduchess's linen gave rise to a fash-ionable colour, hence called L'Isabeau, or the Isabella; a kind of whitish dingy-yellow. Or sometimes they originate in some temporary event: as after the battle of Steenkirk, where the allies wore large cravats, by which the French frequently seized hold of them, the circumstance was perpetuated on the medals of Louis XIV.;[5] and cravats were called Steenkirks: after the battles of Ramillies,[6] wigs received that denomina-tion.

"Courtiers in all ages, and every country, are the modellers of fashions, so that all the ridicule, of which these are so susceptible, must fall on them, and not upon those servile imitators, the citizens. The complaint is made even so far back as 1586, by Jean Des Caures,[7] an old French moralist, who, in declaiming against the fashions of the day, notices one, of the ladies carrying mirrors fixed to their waists, which seemed to employ their eyes in perpetual activity. From this mode will result, accord-ing to honest Des Caures, their eternal damnation. 'Alas! (he exclaims,) in what an age do we live: to see such depravity, which induces them to bring even into church these scandalous mirrors hanging about their waists. Let all histories, divine, human, and profane be consulted, never will it be found that these objects of vanity were ever brought into public by the most meretricious of their sex. It is true, at present none but ladies of the Court venture to wear them.' Such in all times has been the rise and decline of fashion; and the absurd mimicing of the citizens, even to the lowest classes, to their very ruin, in straining to rival the newest fashion, has mortified

7. I.e., 1547–53; Edward VI was born in 1537. "Patches": decorative pieces of silk worn by women on their faces and necks in the seventeenth and eighteenth centuries, either to hide faults or to pro-vide a contrast with attractively pale skin.
8. The eldest son of a king of France. *The Spec-tator*: a London journal (1711–12), written by Joseph Addison and Richard Steele. "Bottomed wigs": i.e., full-bottomed wigs, known as periwigs or perukes (their popularity in the seventeenth cen-tury in fact predated *The Spectator*).
9. Charles III (1403–1461; r., 1422–61).
1. Henry II of England (1133–1189; r. 1154–89), who became Count of Anjou in 1151.
2. King of France (1494–1547; r. 1515–47).
3. Isabella or Isabeau of Bavaria (1371–1435); she married Charles VI of France in 1385.

4. In the Siege of Ostend (1601–04); Ostend was the last Dutch stronghold in Belgium. Isabella Clara Eugenia (1566–1633), daughter of Philip II of Spain (1527–1598 ; r. 1526–98), married Arch-duke Albert (1559–1621) in 1599; together they ruled the Spanish Netherlands (1598–1621). "Linen": underwear.
5. King of France (1638–1715; r. 1643–1715), known as the Sun King. Battle of Steenkirk: at Steenkirk or Steenkerke in Belgium, the French in 1692 defeated the English, Danes, and Dutch in the War of the Grand Alliance (1688–97), in which Louis was largely successful.
6. Fought in 1706 in Belgium, in the War of Span-ish Succession (1701–14); it was a great victory for the English, Danes, and Dutch over the French.
7. Jean Des Caurres (fl. 1570–85).

and galled the courtier." In these remarks every body must agree with Mr. D'Israeli.

The fashion of supplying deficiencies by art, for the purpose of concealing them, is perhaps more under the control of those principles than any other, as it is in many cases within the reach of all, and only requires the exercise of ingenuity to contrive and apply such devices as may suit individual instances. It cannot be expected, therefore, that I can here give you in detail instructions for the concealment of every peculiar defect, and I shall content myself with giving you one or two examples of the principles applicable to such cases.

As I have just been speaking of the injurious effects of high bosomed stays, I shall take an example of the art of padding, bandaging, &c. as applied to the bosom. Fashion and taste vary as much in respect of the contour of the breasts, as in any other particular. Some of the ancients, it appears, liked the breasts to be small and terminating in a point. The breasts, says a Greek poet, in order to be beautiful, must not be larger than two turtle dove's eggs; and a modern critic remarks, that in the antique statues, the breasts are never represented with too great a protuberance or with too much elevation; and it was the practice to prevent them from growing too large, to make use of a certain stone from the island of Naxos, which they reduced to powder and applied to the bosom. The Greek and Roman ladies made use of a sort of bandage to support their breasts, and thus prevented their shape from being spoiled, or from growing too large. Pliny[8] informs us, that women, whose breasts were large and pendant, applied to them a certain kind of fish, which possessed the property of rendering them as firm and plump as those of young persons. Some authors assert, that mint pounded and applied to the breasts checks their growth, and that it is used with success to prevent their too great expansion.

In the countries of Circassia and Georgia,[9] so celebrated for the beauty of their women, the greatest care is taken of the breasts, which are carefully preserved in youth by inclosing them in a kind of case made of light and flexible wood. By this invention the breasts acquire a firmness rarely met with in other countries. In this particular the Spanish women exhibit an instance of excessive absurdity, by using every means to flatten and destroy the breasts, as, according to a lady of high rank, it is considered a mark of beauty to have no breasts. To produce this unnatural effect, they bind thin pieces of lead upon them with bandages as close as children are swaddled. The Egyptian and Moorish ladies, who have a taste altogether opposite, encourage the growth of their breasts by drugs, diet, and bathing.

At Paris, they recommend for beautifying the breasts, the corsets of Delacroix, which are light, flexible, firm, and elastic, and adapt themselves so perfectly to the shape, as not to compress nor injure any part. To this are fitted such paddings as may be required to fill up any deficiency, which ought always to be of the lightest and most elastic materials.

The great danger incident to padding, wherever it may be applied, is precisely the same as that arising from tight bandages, for pressure will have the same injurious effect as tightness, and increase the evil which it is employed to remedy. For the stuff used in padding will press upon the parts under it, and prevent the circulation of the blood, which is so indispensible to supply nourishment for the daily waste of the body. Because, if the blood is prevented from flowing freely and in a full current through the parts, they must pine and decrease for want of nourishment. This effect will be farther increased by the waste of the parts immediately under a pad, by the augmented perspiration arising from a greater heat being occasioned by it than by

8. Pliny the Elder (23/24–79 C.E.), Roman historian and author of *Natural History*.

9. Regions adjoining the Black Sea (to its northeast and east, respectively).

the usual clothing. These are the inconveniences which you must endeavour to avoid in all your contrivances for remedying deficiencies of shape; and unless you are ingenious in your contrivances, considerable injury may sometimes be produced.

If your mistress should be a married lady, it is of still greater importance to be careful in the use of padding and bandaging, as the consequence will be of a worse description than when the case is different; for during pregnancy, tight lacing and bandaging, in order to conceal it, or to render the shape as slender as possible, has been known to produce dangerous and fatal inflammations, and you ought to be aware of this, and endeavour to prevent it. It is a singular fact indeed, well ascertained by experience, that so far from reducing the size, tight lacing and stays actually increase it; those who dress loosely being uniformly observed to be less incommoded by extraordinary size than those who adopt the opposite plan; Nature, it should seem, being determined to award the punishment of disappointment to those who infringe her laws.

Some married ladies conceiving, most erroneously, that suckling has a tendency to injure the beauty of their breasts, employ a hireling wetnurse for their children; and in such circumstances have recourse to bandages and plasters to stop the secretion of the milk. In this opinion, however, they are altogether wrong; for nothing has a stronger tendency to improve the form of the breast, than the performance of the natural office of a mother. You ought to know these facts, though you may not always be able to persuade your mistress to follow the path pointed out by Nature. It is your duty to mention it, but it would be impertinent to press its adoption.

1825

MINNA THOMAS ANTRIM
b. 1861

Don'ts for Girls: A Manual of Mistakes

Don't be ashamed of your parents. They may be unlearned and dull, but they gave you the chance to become what you are. Honor them before all men.

Don't neglect little deeds, while dreaming of great ones.

Don't be spoiled. Permit none to persuade you there are none so lovely, so witty, or so wise. Be sweetly grateful, but not proud.

Don't be a prig. Girls who are never a little foolish, are always deadly dull.

Don't chatter. Babbling is baneful. Gigglers should be punished by solitary confinement.

Don't regulate your behavior by geography. Be as modest at the sea shore as at home.

Don't be good because you must, but because you should.

Don't form hysterical attachments for other girls. It is silly. Such loves die very suddenly, frequently leaving a trail of ridicule behind. "Adore" only God.

Don't ask God for foolish things. Remember, He is all wisdom.

Don't take acquaintances into your confidence. Some very pleasant young persons are good listeners, but more talented as gossips.

Don't fib about little things. It is futile, and foolish, and inevitably creates distrust.

Don't boast. It is vulgar and invariably cheapens you.

Don't confuse possibility and probability. Floods of tears may follow.

Don't purchase any pleasure at the price of another girl's pain. The tables of Fate are ever revolving.

Don't become masculine if you are a college girl. Fit yourself for a vocation if you choose, but hold fast to your girlish personality.

Don't abuse your strength. Young muscles are delicate. "On the go" all the time, presages "off the go" in later life.

Don't attempt conversational feats. One never knows who may be listening, waiting to trip one up.

Don't pet animals at one time and abuse them at another. They have long memories and sharp teeth.

Don't forget that vanity ruins beauty, and blunts the mind.

Don't flush your tear ducts daily. If there is one unbearable boredom it is to dwell with a chronic weeper.

Don't neglect the domestic virtues. If you are a sister, be also a confidante, and staunch friend.

Don't quarrel by mail. It's very bad policy, and worse form.

1903

DORA LANGLOIS
1865–1940

The Child: A Mother's Advice to Her Daughters (1896) is a rare thing: a well-written, sexually explicit pre-twentieth-century sex education manual, supposedly written by a mother for other mothers interested in initiating their daughters into the mysteries of their adult sexuality. The title page identifies the author as Dora Langlois, the author of the novel *In the Shadow of Pa-menkh*, and in a prefatory note the author invites anyone who has questions to contact her in Chipping Norton (a town near Oxford). Though Langlois does not appear in standard—or even obscure—lists of Victorian and Edwardian authors, she was, in the late nineteenth century, a working actress, a poet, an author, a playwright, and a mother—of four of her own children and two stepchildren.

Langlois was born Dora Fanny Emily Knight on October 15, 1865, in Leamington Warwick, the second of the eight children of Colonel Rice Davis Knight and his wife, Emily Jane (who also published). Knight went bankrupt about 1880, when his investments in the cotton trade failed. Dora was only fifteen. She left home and took up acting, following a precedent set by her older brother, Roy. In 1883, Dora joined the company of Hippolyte Arthur Lan-

glois (who used Lonsdell as his stage name). A widower with two young children, he married Dora on November 17, 1884, soon after her nineteenth birthday and just weeks before the birth of their first child.

When young, Dora Langlois was described as an "actress of sterling comedy and pathetic power," according to a little article about her published in *Illustrated Bits* (September 22, 1894). With her husband she co-wrote sketches and plays that were produced in provincial theaters as well as in London, and she continued writing until well into her old age.

In *The Child* (probably written at the family's semi-permanent home "The Firs" in Over-Norton—near Chipping Norton), Langlois has produced a remarkable work. At a time when only veiled approaches were made to physiological facts that were held to be literally unspeakable, Langlois spells out the changes that overtake a girl's body during puberty. Furthermore, she explicitly warns against the danger of sexual abuse, arguing that safety is possible only through knowledge: managing risk is better than ignorance. Not only is her book much more willing to engage with the lived experience of sexuality than other books of the period, but it is also much better written.

The Child: A Mother's Advice to Her Daughters

PREFACE

Addressed to Those Parents and Guardians Who Have Young Girls Under Their Care.

I have given to this little work a very bold title, in order that the cover of the book might honestly indicate its contents. This is not a pamphlet merely urging on mothers the necessity of imparting certain information to their daughters. (That plain duty I have pointed out in print before now.) It is a work specially designed to help those who agree with me in principle, but do not feel themselves equal to putting that principle into practice; therefore, with the exception of this preface, and the necessary directions for laying the work, chapter by chapter, before the pupil, each at a fit and proper period, every line of this book has been written specially for perusal for young girls.

This statement, I know, will raise a storm of opposition in certain quarters.

When I wrote the article, "Should Children Know Their Origin," which appeared in "Reynolds" newspaper,[1] I got a glimpse of what I might expect; but the favourable comment my article provoked, told me that in spite of all the opposition to be looked for from my prejudice and devotion to long-standing custom, many would hail with pleasure the advent of some such work as this. If, therefore, I can help a few mothers at present in doubt and perplexity, uncertain how to act or what to do, in order to serve the best interests of their little ones, I shall have attained my object.

When I first saw the spirit of enquiry developing itself in my own children, I was forced to admit that I must either explain certain matters to them myself, or leave the affair to chance. I chose the former alternative, knowing by personal experience that reticence on the parents' part does not check the desire for information on the child's, but rather provokes and increases that desire. I say personal experience, because I can well remember that all the information which I have now set down in my chapter for the use of the school girl I myself pieced together for my own enlightenment before I was eleven years of age, out of PASSAGES IN THE BIBLE,[2] translated by the aid of my school dictionary and certain observations of the circumstances attending the advent of my many younger brothers and sisters. Thus I spent hours in clandestine research—excited by unhealthy, because secret curiosity—while had I been given the information I sought, in a frank and matter-of-fact manner, I venture to think that the subject would not have engrossed my mind at all. I give my experience, and I fearlessly ask, is there any woman who can conscientiously say that she never in her youth thought of this subject, or strove in some such manner to obtain light on a matter which she has known her elders to be purposely shrouding in mystery?

Let me quote one other case, that of a young lady who, being snubbed by her grandmother for asking questions, applied to a servant, who afterwards proved to be a prostitute and thief, WHO TOLD HER EVERYTHING in coarse and disgusting language, though she, the child, WAS ONLY NINE YEARS' OLD. What wonder then that I resolved

---

1. *Reynold's Weekly Newspapers* (1821–1923).
2. Though the King James translation of the Bible is considerably less explicit regarding sexual matters than is the Hebrew, a reader could find references to such matters as whoredom (e.g., Ezekiel 16), bestiality (Leviticus 18.23), and genital discharges and menstruation (e.g., Leviticus 15); she could also try to parse the vague but charged language of the Song of Solomon.

my daughters should not run the risk of receiving from the jokes and innuendos of coarse-minded persons, hints on subjects which I might deal with rationally and delicately myself.

But even then, with my resolve firm, and my duty staring me in the face, I did not know how to begin. I asked myself "how to weigh my words: how to make sure of saying just enough and not too much; above all, how to make my disclosures gradually, and yet avoid the danger of prevarication." I acknowledged that if I allowed my own sensitiveness to drive me to the use of subterfuge and deceit in my first essays, later on I should be bound to stultify myself, and so rouse my children's resentment, or weaken their regard for truth. Then it was that the difficulty of carrying out my resolve "viva voce"[3] presented itself to me, and I determined to get over the obstacles in my way by trusting to my pen.

I fortified myself by considering that in reading such a work TO HERSELF the child would not see the author's hesitation (the outcome of semi-obsolete customs and foolish prejudices); she would therefore not be embarrassed nor covered with false shame. Receiving it together with ordinary educational works, she would accept it with child-like compliance as merely another lesson given to improve her mind, by increasing her store of knowledge. Encouraged by these reflections, I wrote this little book, every chapter of which I have used, or shall use, at the proper time for my own daughters.

When my article appeared, I was told that no one would dare to follow my advice, by unfolding certain matters to the growing child.

This little work now presenting itself to the public proves that statement to be incorrect.

I was also told that the thing could not be done decently, and that the idea was altogether nasty and repulsive. I can only reply by asking my severe critics to note that a task may be unpleasant though necessary, without being "NASTY," i.e., INDECENT or REPULSIVE, and I INVITE THEM TO SEARCH THE PAGES OF THIS BOOK CAREFULLY TO SEE IF IT CONTAINS ANY IMMODEST PHRASE OR SUGGESTION; ANYTHING, IN FACT, LIKELY TO TAINT A CHILD'S MORAL CHARACTER.

The main question to be decided by fair and impartial minds is this—Are ignorance and innocence synonymous terms? If they are, and if my opponents can prove that they are, then this little work is condemned at once; but if they cannot prove the synonymy of the terms, then they must admit that there is some excuse for this book's appearance; and they must show that the handling of its subject is coarse and vulgar before they can with any justice claim the right to condemn either the book or its author.

In my treatment of the subjects discussed in these pages for the benefit of the young, I have spared no pains, and have used the utmost discretion.

I never have urged or suggested that EVERYTHING should be told to the young female child, though many people take a delight in misunderstanding me on this important point. Therefore, that there may be no further misapprehension, I have arranged this book so that it may be separated, the leaves of each chapter fastened together, and the chapters given one by one to the pupil at that period of life to which that chapter applies. No one can object to adopt the course I suggest, as in the first place, the book is cheap; in the second, it is quite unsuitable—designedly unsuitable—for the library table or the bookshelf. On the other hand, the advantages of my method seem obvious. The YOUNG CHILD is not interested in the subject of sexual connection; she

---

3. With live voice (Latin); i.e., orally.

forms no theories about it; she NEITHER MAKES NOR DESIRES TO MAKE any enquiries on that head. The questions which nature compels her to propound for solution, as to her own origin and the origin of her brothers and sisters, do not probe so deeply into the subject as to reach that matter. She sees her father and mother living under the same roof; she sees and knows no more, and does not seek to know more. Therefore it is quite unnecessary to give her more information on that head until she has passed the critical period of change. All that is necessary is to prepare her mind step by step for the future reception of the facts as a whole, by imparting them by degrees, giving first explanations of those matters which agitate her mind at an early period. Do not let the reader imagine that I have shirked the handling of the most delicate and difficult portion of the subject, i.e., the one which I declare no mere child to be interested in. I have not sufficient effrontery to ask other mothers to undertake a task I myself am incapable of attempting; therefore I have not evaded the responsibility of dealing with the particular fact about which for so long mothers have seemed to unite in a conspiracy of silence; I have merely left the explanation necessary to my last chapter, though the experienced reader will note that I am leading up to that explanation from my first; and I firmly believe that if mothers will only follow the plain directions I subjoin, they will find that nature itself is working with them in preparing the young mind, by its own gradual development, for a full conception of the truth.

During the discussion provoked by my article in "Reynolds'," one lady who took up arms against me boldly declared that the subjects dealt with in this work ought to be kept from a girl ALTOGETHER; that her husband on her marriage was the fit and proper PERSON to impart such knowledge to her. Now my experience teaches me that NO GIRL OF INTELLECT CAN GROW UP ABSOLUTELY IN IGNORANCE; if she has younger brothers and sisters will she not enquire about their origin? If she reads the Bible will she not seek an explanation of the words contained in it! If her mother refuses to assist her, WILL SHE NOT APPLY TO OTHERS, NOT ONE HALF SO FIT FOR THE TASK? But granted that a girl could grow up in absolute ignorance, what mother would feel herself blameless in handing her to her husband with a mind quite unprepared, quite uninformed, as to the nature of the contract she is making! If the subject is so fearfully delicate that a mother must not breathe a word about it to her own child, the development of whose little limbs she has watched, whose body she has seen uncovered a hundred times in the office of the bath, what about the shock to the girl's delicacy in receiving her first initiation into the mysteries of nature from a member of the opposite sex, who, though he is her husband, is not yet on the intimate footing which should subsist between mother and daughter? I speak plainly, for I feel that the subject demands plain speaking, at the same time excusing it; and I ask what mother loving her child would willingly subject her to such a sudden shock? Nevertheless I wish it to be clearly understood that for those who honestly feel opposition to my views, I have a certain respect. I am ready at any moment to meet them on their own ground and listen to their arguments with more patience than perhaps they will extend to mine; but I would remind my opponents that Florence Nightingale,[4] that bright jewel in English womanhood, always advocated the advisability of imparting to girls and young women that kind of knowledge which serves to hedge innocence from danger. It was her opinion that no virtue was TRUE VIRTUE which was

4. British nurse and hospital reformer (1820–1910), the founder of the modern profession of nursing. Nightingale's work (1854–56) to improve the conditions in army hospitals at Üsküdar and Balaklava during the Crimean War won her widespread fame and admiration; because she often helped soldiers through the night, carrying a lamp, she was nicknamed "the lady of the lamp."

merely a state of protected ignorance: and that as a sudden turn of the wheel of fate may at any time deprive ignorance of its defences, the duty of those concerned is to make those outside defences unnecessary. I therefore ask those mothers who may not care to listen to me, a stranger, to listen through me to the teaching of "the lady of the lamp," a woman whose noble and pure life has made her name dear to the hearts of the whole English-speaking race.

This little work has not been written to show off; it therefore contains no Latin terms, no pseudo scientific jargon. I think it will be found none the worse for that. It is REFINED enough, I hope, to come up to the standard demanded by the fastidious, always excepting those who are too fastidious to tolerate the truth in any form. It is SIMPLE enough to meet the requirements of mothers of the artisan classes. Any child who understands enough English to read the ordinary school primer, say of the fourth or fifth standard[5] is capable of mastering the contents of the first chapters. In the text of the book itself I have carefully avoided all controversial matter, whether religious, social, or political, and have dealt only with facts, which are so palpable that they admit of no variation of opinion. This preface contains controversial matter, of course; but no guardian need fear to find anything of the sort in the chapters for the young.

I have striven to this end because I desire to see this book generally used in the HOMES of Great Britain, and I do not wish to SHUT IT OUT OF ONE SINGLE HOME where it might be of use, by introducing my views on religious or social matters.

DIRECTIONS

For Using This Work in Such a Manner That It May Serve Its Intended Purpose, Together with a Few General Remarks for the Guidance of Young Mothers

As the text of this book has been specially written for young girls who are able to read it to themselves, it naturally contains nothing applicable to the infant. Yet as very tiny children often propound difficult questions apt to take a young mother by surprise, a few hints on what to say and what to avoid, may not be out of place here. In the first place, when the inevitable question is proposed, "Mother, where did I come from?" do not answer as many mothers do, "You were brought by an angel from heaven," for as the child will believe in the actual and visible presence of a spiritual being, such an answer is a direct deception. If you are a member of any religious sect, reply in accordance with your own belief, "You were given to me and your father by God." If you are a freethinker, reply, "You were given to me by your father." Should this not prove entirely satisfactory, the next question will probably be (should you have elected to give the first of the above answers), "But how did I come from God to you?" To this reply, according to circumstances, "A kind doctor helped you to get here because you were so very little, and unable to help yourself. You had no clothes on, so a nurse dressed you in nice white things and handed you to me. Then I sent for your father to show him what a dear little child we had got." Most babes will be satisfied with this, but those of a very enquiring turn of mind will persist after this style, "And where (or how) did God make me?" To this answer, "He made a little seed, and when that little seed was planted you grew." "Where do babies grow?" will naturally be the next question. Answer to this that different people's babies grow in

---

5. Recognized degrees of proficiency in British elementary schools (the sixth standard was the highest that children were ordinarily required to pass).

different places, but that when the child is old enough he or she will no doubt be able to find or choose a place for its own babies to grow in, if it would like to have some.

If your own convictions have led you to make the second answer I have given to the first question, which, by the way, hardly ever varies, a slight alteration of the formula is all that is necessary; for to the question, "And where did my father get me?" you have but to reply, "He planted a little seed, and from it you grew." This may call forth the more awkward query, "Where did my papa get the little seed?" and if it is against your principles to answer by referring the matter to the Deity, you must reply, "He could not buy the seed, because there are no shops which sell them, so he made it himself." And if this provokes the question, "How did he make it," you may with truth reply, "I DO NOT KNOW;" for even the most scientific physiologists may confess to being unable to state with any certainty how or why our internal organs convert the food we assimilate into blood, chyle,[6] etc.

All these answers are of course allegorical, but none of them are false, and as much cannot be said of the usual fables repeated (sometimes reluctantly) by young mothers, because tradition has given them nothing better to offer as satisfaction to the enquiring mind.

In using this book I suggest that when you have separated the chapters from each other, and from these preliminary pages, you should give the first to the schoolgirl of about eleven, on some occasion when she herself refers to the subject, or shows a desire to do so. The absolute age cannot be set down, as a child's mental capacity can only be gaged by the mother herself.

Should the child possess a very active mind and commence to ask questions—not babyish ones—say as early as eight or nine, reply "Oh, you will learn all about that when you have to study physiology; now you have other lessons to learn."

The long word, and the prospect of a new task, will stall off the little inquisitive. After the age I mention, it is better to satisfy her than to leave her to satisfy herself.

The second chapter is for the school girl approaching puberty; by giving it in time a mother saves the child from the risks attendant on an attempt to conceal an infirmity,[7] which ignorance might make her believe peculiar to herself.

The third chapter is merely a lecture on female organisation, intended to prepare the mind of the young maiden who has passed the critical period for the reception of the facts contained in the following chapter, WHICH SETS FORTH ALL THAT THE FULLY DEVELOPED girl-woman need know on the subject of sexual connection.

The fifth and last chapter is for the bride elect.

In some cases it may be superfluous, as most mothers will prefer to act at such a time for themselves; but as it may be useful to widowers whose daughters are about to marry, it has a place in these pages; and even mothers may gain a few useful hints from it.

Here I would like to touch upon another matter, which though it does not concern the origin of the child, is connected with its development. WERE IT WHOLLY UNCONNECTED WITH EITHER, some excuse might be found for its introduction here, on the score of the author's solicitude for the welfare of childhood in general. To be brief, experienced mothers and nurses know that there is among young babes of about two years old and upwards, a tendency to touch and handle certain portions of their person. This we should not call impropriety, as the child acts in ignorance; but if the habit be not checked its results will be very serious. Therefore a reasoning woman

6. A milky fluid found in the intestines.   7. I.e., menstruation.

should not say, "I refuse to believe my child capable of anything so disagreeable," she should rather watch for herself, and warn her nursemaid to do so also. Any husband can explain to his wife what the evil effects on the male child will be should the habit extend and develop with his years. Suffice it to say that no child of either sex can ever grow up bright and energetic in body and mind who has once become a slave to this baneful custom.[8] Also, there are some children—even among the upper classes—who, not having been watched and checked at first, develop a fearful mental bias, prompting them to desire to touch and handle other children. I know I am speaking the truth. At this moment I can vividly recall the case of a pretty child, the grand daughter of a colonel in the army, who was left for a few minutes alone in a drawing-room with a boy of ten, the son of a neighbouring gentleman. A noise attracting the boy's attention, he ran from the room in some confusion, and I MYSELF found the child with blood issuing freely from the vaginal passage. The child was too young to be able to talk, and the young ruffian escaped punishment; but I who saw the child's condition and the mother's grief, resolved to do my best to prevent the occurrence of such an affair in my own circle. Therefore, as soon as my girls have been able to understand me, I have informed them that in a certain portion of their bodies, which I have indicated to them while in the bath (that is to say the vaginal passage), there lies "a little thing like a piece of thin glass, which is very easily broken;"[9] that if broken the child will be very much hurt, blood will come, and a great damage be done her. I have then urged on the child the necessity of not touching the parts surrounding this delicate and fragile thing, for fear of breaking it, adding that should anyone else try to do so, she has but to cry for papa, mamma, or nurse, to frighten such a person away.

I have reason to think that this warning has been beneficial in preventing malpractices into which a child might fall through that ABSOLUTE IGNORANCE which is the ideal of so many mothers. I firmly believe that in any case it has at least on one occasion been of even greater service, if a greater service there can be than that of saving a child from the risk of bringing on itself ill-health, unnatural desires, deterioration of the mental powers, and possible insanity. I do not think I can do better than relate the incident to which I refer. One day, when one of my daughters was about four years old (an age at which a child may justly be supposed incapable of guile), she loudly cried to me for assistance. I ran to the nursery where she was alone with a girl of eleven whom I had temporarily engaged to take her walking, etc. On my appearance, without hesitation or circumlocution, and in the presence of the other party, her face showing signs of agitation such as a baby might feel but could not possibly feign, she accused the elder child of having hurt her by trying to "touch her little glass." This fortunately occurred some months after I had cautioned my child, and no harm was done on this occasion; but who will dare to say that none was meant, or that an injury of a serious nature was impossible? Let mothers picture to themselves the fate of a child cruelly violated in its infancy by a young fellow-creature's mischievous hands, and let them say whether it might not even come to pass that on its marriage that child might find her purity doubted, possibly by an affectionate husband, and her future life clouded by undeserved suspicion.

If the incidents I have related above (the truth of which I would willingly affirm in a law court) are not sufficient to show that I have some excuse for urging on mothers the necessity of protecting their children FROM THE VERY FIRST by giving them that knowledge which will teach them rationally how to protect themselves—then I have

---

8. I.e., masturbation.   9. The hymen.

done. A mind incapable of seeing, or unwilling to see, some force in my arguments—a mind determined to deny me, the author of this work, the right to style myself a right-minded and decent woman—is one which needs a miracle to move it.

DORA LANGLOIS.
WEST END, CHIPPING NORTON.

NOTICE

The authoress will be happy at any time to answer letters addressed to her by those who have perused this work. All such communications will be welcome, whether of a hostile nature or the reverse.

Her position has given her the opportunity of seeing more of the seamy side of life than is usually exposed to married women; and if it is possible to say more than she has said in these pages, to show mothers the priceless value of that mutual confidence which it should be the aim of every woman to establish between her daughters and herself, she is willing to attempt the task, by laying bare, privately, some of the sad pages in the book of life which have been open to her inspection. At the same time, she will greatly appreciate the approval and encouragement of those who may think she has done well.

Letters may be addressed:—

MRS. LANGLOIS, CHIPPING NORTON.

A MOTHER'S LETTERS TO HER DAUGHTER AT SCHOOL

LETTER I

My Dear Child,—You tell me you have been greatly perplexed by the conversation of your school companions on the subject of who made you and how you came on this earth. I am not at all surprised that the information received from your young friends bewildered you, and I can readily believe that no two of them agreed in the explanations they sought to give; in fact, they were merely asserting as facts things which they themselves have been told as parables. Now I suppose the idea you have conceived from their conversation is that you were made in some far away realm, and were then brought here in some strange and mysterious way; but let me tell you at once you had no such long and difficult journey to make.

You were made here on this earth by your father and mother, who were endowed with the power of making you by the Creator, who made all things, who has also given you, under certain circumstances, the power of producing other lives.

Now you must know that everything endowed with life has been made subject to change and death; but, as a sort of compensation, everything which must die has also been given a power termed THE POWER OF REPRODUCTION, which enables it to form and leave behind copies of itself, that is to say, reproductions of its species.

Stones and other minerals having no life, we need pay no attention to them; but the more we learn of the animal and vegetable kingdoms the more plainly we shall see that not only do human beings, beasts, birds, fishes, insects, and flowers all possess this power, but that the way in which they reproduce themselves varies very little.

This will surprise you, of course, for you know that you came into the world smaller than your parents, but no less perfect and complete; while birds, fishes, and insects lay eggs out of which their young ones come, and plants spring from tiny seeds. This difference, however, seems much greater than it really is. To make the matter as simple as possible, I will commence by showing you how the flowers reproduce themselves, and will then let you see how you yourself resemble the seed of the flower. Let us take for example a common field campion, or as some people call it, a mountain daisy. Gather any ordinary stalk, and you are pretty sure to find on it buds, blossoms, and dry looking pods. The buds are, so to speak, the INFANTS, the flowers are the YOUNG PEOPLE, and the dry looking pods are the GROWN PEOPLE, or those who have REACHED MATURITY, for mature simply means ripe, and implies that the thing of which we speak IS IN A FIT AND PROPER CONDITION TO BRING FORTH A REPRODUCTION OR REPRODUCTIONS OF ITSELF.

Now take one of the flowers, pull off the bloom and open the green pod below. You will see that it contains more than fifty tiny unripe seeds, which bear a strong resemblance to those butterfly eggs which you found on a cabbage leaf the other morning. Open one of the buds, and you will find indications of unformed seeds in it also. From these tiny seeds under favourable conditions would spring reproductions of the plant, just as reproductions of the butterfly will come in time from those eggs.

Now open one of the mature pods; you will find hard, ripe, and perfect seeds. Just a little later on in the season those seeds would have become too large to be retained. The pod would have opened of itself and discharged them. THUS YOU SEE HOW THE FLOWER MAKES ITS OWN SEED, and how the seed comes forth into the world in due season. But this you will say has nothing to do with you. Wait a little, and I think you will change your opinion. You have noticed the resemblance between the appearance of the seed of the flower and the egg of the butterfly, have you not? Well, that is only a trifling resemblance; their true likeness to each other lies in the fact that not only do the seed and the egg both contain the germ of life, but both were formed in the same way in the body of their mother.

You, belonging as you do to a much higher order than the butterfly, came into the world in a perfect state; but like the butterfly's egg, like the seed of the flower you too were made and formed in your mother's body.

Having told you this, it is probable that you will think you were made by your mother alone, and not by your mother and father; but there you would be entirely mistaken, for nothing not even the seeds of a humble weed, can be produced without a union of both sexes. Strange as it may appear to you, there are males and females even among the flowers. Some plants have separate blossoms, some male, some female; on other plants the blossoms themselves are combinations of both sexes. The Imperial Lily is one of these. The female, or mother portion of the flower is that near the stalk, for there lie the seeds. The male, or father portion of the flower is that which is covered with golden dust, and it is quite certain that if the flower did not contain that portion the seeds would never ripen, that is to say, become perfect enough to produce future plants. Thus you see in this lily the union of the sexes. In animals and insects the sexes are separate and distinct, but unless they unite they cannot reproduce themselves nor increase their species.

Your father and mother, as you know, were united in marriage; that is the highest of all forms of union. Birds, beasts, and insects unite themselves to each other and have young, the sexes are united on the stems of the plant, but HUMAN BEINGS ALONE MARRY, for marriage is a compact into which two persons enter, both binding themselves to care for and protect the helpless babes who may come into the world; and thus you see that while the kitten, the puppy, the lamb, the colt, etc., have only one protector, namely their mother, you are more fortunate, for you are cared for both by father and mother, to whom in an equal degree you owe your existence.

LETTER II

My Dear Child,—I am indeed sorry to hear of your school friend's illness, and trust she will soon be better, at the same time I do not regret the opportunity it affords me of writing to you on the subject, and of warning you under similar circumstances not to do as she unfortunately has done. There was nothing to cause her shame in the nature of her illness, although, as you tell me, she one day found her under-wear stained and soaked with blood; nor was there any occasion for her to wash her clothes in secret as you say she did, and in putting them on again in their damp condition, the wonder is that she did not kill herself.

Had she possessed that knowledge of herself which it has always been my wish to impart to you, she would not have made so painful and dangerous a mistake. She would have known that there was nothing to be ashamed or afraid of, and that every grown woman has had to pass through this painful ordeal, while the same experience awaits every girl. I do not wish you to be morbidly sensitive as to yourself and your functional construction, so I shall try to explain to you the nature of this discharge of blood,[1] which, however painful and even shocking it may seem at first, is really no more a disgrace to you, than is the common necessity of discharging other waste material, solid and fluid, a disgrace to human beings in general. True this particular discharge cannot be retained at our will and got rid of in the privacy of the cabinet,[2] because the organ from which it flows is not subject to muscular control; but the female friends of a young girl will always provide her with bandages to prevent her having the humiliation of seeing her linen[3] in an improper state, and she may have the comfort of knowing that what is happening to her is known only to those who are in her confidence. I have told you that all women suffer in this way, and though it is always more or less a painful affair, it is in no sense a malady or disease when it is regular, that is to say, when it occurs, as it should, about once a month. However, I need say very little more on this head, as after you have gone through this experience no woman would hesitate to speak freely to you on the subject, or object to show you how to watch your health in order to know if all is going well with you.

If at school, your governess[4] would be the proper person to apply to; and I am sure when the time comes, you will not hesitate to seek her aid, thus avoiding all the risks your young friend incurred; for why should a girl seek to conceal a purely natural occurrence which merely marks an epoch in her life. No doubt you have lately noticed certain changes in your body. In the first place your figure has begun to develop, you are no longer flat-chested like a child, while there are other changes not noticeable to others but which must be very apparent to yourself while in your bath. These latter have no doubt both puzzled and annoyed you. It is even probable that, not having been in the habit of seeing other members of your sex of your own age unclothed, you may suppose that the appearance of hair on some portions of your body is as unnatural as the growth of a beard on your face would be. In this you would be entirely mistaken, for nature is only dealing with you as she deals with others.

All these things point to but one conclusion, namely, that a change is at hand. You

1. Menstruation.
2. A small room.
3. Underwear.
4. Schoolmistress.

are ceasing to be like the bud, you are soon to become a flower. In other words, after this discharge takes place your intimates will know that you are no longer a child but a young woman. Like the flower in bloom, you will still be immature, but you will have taken the first step towards maturity. One word more on the subject, and I have done. I do not think I need point out to you the position of the particular organ from which this discharge is destined to flow; it is quite sufficient for me to say that it is situated in a very private part of your person. Now it would not be surprising if a natural curiosity prompted you to examine that part of your body; but I beg you not to do so on any account. Long ago you were warned that stretched across a certain private passage there is a little thing like a glass, which by touching or handling you might break, and so do yourself infinite harm. You are old enough now to learn that the little thing referred to is a membrane or ligament; you may not understand its purpose, as you do not understand the internal usefulness of many of the intricate parts of your body, which is really a complicated and wonderful machine; but like the other portions of your body, it has its purpose, and any curiosity about the parts adjacent to it, which might cause you to meddle with it, might inflict on you an injury which no doctor could cure. Be guided then in this matter, my dear child, by your own sense of modesty and delicacy, and as regards the rest, remember that at any time of life, when you seek information or assistance, if circumstances prevent your obtaining either from me, it is always wisest to place your confidence only in those whose character you can respect, as knowledge gained from proper sources can never do you harm.

There is one thing which I must warn you against. Never have anything to do with those who show a disposition to make a jest of those matters which I have explained to you, relative to your origin and development.

Life, and death, were both created by the same mighty force, and it is as unseemly to find cause for amusement and idle jokes over the birth of a child, as it would be to laugh at the death of one. Persons who indulge in such jests, show themselves to be the unfortunate possessors of empty and vulgar minds. Intercourse with them can do you no good.

Then again, I do not wish you to talk too freely about these matters with your playmates; for that which is a fit and proper subject for discussion between yourself and a person able to explain matters to you, and give you sound advice, is not a subject which you need discuss with your playmates.

Many schoolmistresses object to such conversations, and even punish the girls who indulge in them—no doubt under the impression that any talk of the kind must be like the idle conversation of those persons against whom I have warned you. Therefore, as discussions with those girls whose mothers have not yet explained matters to them, cannot personally do you any good, it will be best for you to abstain from them.

These are things which we should know, but which we should not talk about; and just as I prefer to tell you myself, rather than leave you to find out from others, so I think it clearly your duty not to explain to other girls, who will no doubt learn all that I have told you when their parents think the proper time has come.

LETTER III

My Dear Child,—You tell me that the change I have been expecting to hear of has taken place, and you add that you could bear your present suffering better if you could see any reason for it. Well, if you will exercise a little patience I will show you the reason for that which at present causes you so much uneasiness both bodily and mental. You say it is very hard that you should be forced by nature to tax your digestive and other powers in order to make blood which you cannot retain to build up your frame; and you speak with envy of the superior health and strength of youths of your own age who have no such suffering to undergo. But consider for a moment the facts I have given you relative to the reproduction of the various species. In what flower, or portion of a flower, are the seeds nourished and brought to perfection? In the female. Do you not know that in your own body, and in that of every woman—as also in the female of every living thing—there is an organ similar to that which you have seen and examined in the flower? Recollect this, then you will understand why nature in its dealings with you has given you the power of forming more of the principle of life than you require to nourish and sustain your own body.

This discharge of which you complain, under the impression that it is both vexatious and useless, comes direct from that organ in the woman which I have pointed out to you in the flower. When it ceases to recur with a married woman, who is otherwise in good health, she knows she is about to become a mother, and that all the strength of her body not necessary to her own existence is going to nourish a new life.

Thus you see that this illness, so-called, not only indicates the girl's approach to maturity, but has other ends to serve in the scheme of organization; and knowing this, I hope you will bear the infirmity natural to you with more patience.

It is very probable that the disclosures I have now made to you will suggest a new train of enquiries. Having told you that this discharge comes from that portion of the female organization in which reproductions of the human race may under certain circumstances be formed through the passage connected with it, you will ask, "Is it possible that a living child could come into the world through that same passage without at once killing its mother? Surely," you will say, "there must be some other way." Truth compels me to answer that, incredible as it may seem to you, there is no other way. I can only explain the matter by saying that that portion of the body is composed of ligaments or muscles of wonderful elasticity or power of expansion and contraction. These muscles are capable of supporting the child until it is fully formed, then they expand and allow it to pass. Thus, though the birth of a child is undoubtedly a very painful affair to the mother, nature has made due provisions to meet the necessity of the case.

LETTER IV

My Dear Child,—Once more you have applied to me to clear your mind on certain matters which perplex you. Your questions do not indicate any want of delicacy, they merely show that as your mind develops, and with it your powers of observation, you seek explanations of the problems which circumstances present to you. You ask me first, "What is a natural child?" The term, you say, is so often mentioned in history that you have discovered that so-called natural children are the offspring of persons who have not been contracted together in marriage; but you add the very reasonable query, "Are the children of marriage then UNNATURAL?" No, certainly not. All children are natural; that is to say, made according to the laws of nature. The terms, a "natural" or "illegitimate" child, are preferred to the term bastard, because they sound less harsh, yet they mean the same thing, and are used to mark the distinction between the legitimate child born in wedlock, and protected by the law, and the child born out of wedlock, who is not protected at all.

Hard and cruel as it appears, it is nevertheless a fact that the poor little bastard child comes into the world with no rights at all in property. He cannot inherit anything, even from his mother, unless she specially leaves it him in her will. Should she die without making a will, everything would pass to some very distant relative, or to the Crown, rather than to her own child. That is the effect, or what is called the STIGMA of bastardy, and a very terrible stigma it is. So great is the contempt felt for the mother of a bastard child, and (rightly or wrongly) so widespread the scorn for the child itself—innocent as it is of any fault—that many women who have fallen into error and find that they will shortly be unable to conceal the fact, prefer to destroy their lives rather than face such public humiliation.

Should the mother, however, live to bring her illegitimate child into the world, the disqualifications under which it is destined to exist do not end with the mere fact that it cannot inherit property except through a properly executed will. The child may grow up, to make a fortune by his own exertions; he may marry some good woman who does not know of the blot upon his name, but should he die intestate, that is to say, without leaving written instructions as to what is to be done with his money, his children, the sons and daughters of his legal marriage, may be deprived of everything in the interest of the Crown, should any one rake up the old shame and scandal by proclaiming that the orphan children are descended from a grandmother who was not married to the father of her son.

I speak plainly to you, because I think you are now quite old enough to thoroughly understand what I hinted at some time ago, namely, that marriage and the union of the sexes are not one and the same thing. It is the latter which causes the reproduction of the human species, that is to say, the birth of children; the former is only the public contract which sanctions the union of two persons of opposite sex, and binds them together according to the laws prevailing in society. Marriage, therefore, is the highest religious and social form of union, but it has nothing directly to do with the making of children, for if it had, there would of course be no illegitimate children in the world.

I tell you all this because I would rather have you able to discern evil from good, and see you choose the latter for yourself, than I would have you IGNORANT in your INNOCENCE leaning entirely on me for that support and guidance which my death would rob you of. You may never be exposed to temptation; but knowledge is power, and that buckler you shall have to shield you, for it is a defence of which fate can never rob you, though it should deprive you of every loving friend you have.

But to return to the information which you have gleaned from the pages of history. The unfortunate Catherine, WIFE of Charles II.,[5] had no children, but that monarch had many by the gay women of his Court. That, you will naturally conclude, was because he united himself to those women by living with them. But, my child, it is as well that you should know that women bear children who have never been united to a man by living under the same roof with him, either with or without the sanction of the law. Unfortunately it is only too true that a brief folly, a short deviation from the right path under strong temptation, is sufficient to engulf a woman in that sea of trouble from which society may never permit her to rise again; for "a woman who has fallen," as we say, will always find the evil-minded ever on the alert to solicit her again to wrong-doing, while the majority of the pure will draw away from her, as though her presence was in itself contamination. You will naturally desire to know

---

5. King of England (1630–1685; r. 1660–85); he had numerous mistresses openly and many illegitimate children, most of whom he acknowledged. He married Catherine of Bragaza (1638–1705) in 1662.

what is the nature of that temptation by yielding to which a woman so utterly loses her place in society; but before explaining the matter to you I must make a few general remarks.

You have observed that by the dispensations of nature all animate objects increase and multiply, but you must note that while flowers do so in a passive sort of way, free from either pleasure or pain, the desire to increase their species is in the brute creation a strong impulse or instinct. This impulse is termed the SEXUAL PASSION to distinguish it from other passions such as rage or grief, all of which passions are common alike to humanity and the brutes. Now I know that our intellectual superiority makes it hard for us to acknowledge that we share any impulses with those creatures below us in the scale of nature; but to deny the fact is impossible, while to be hypersensitive on the subject is folly. There is no shame in any of the impulses of our nature, so long as we do not seek to gratify them by offending against the code of right and wrong which human brains have been working for centuries to define and set up for our guidance.

To return to our review of the system of nature, vegetables have no passions; brutes have passions but no ideals of right and wrong; men and women have passions, but they have also ideals and higher emotions than the brute beasts, and the attraction towards each other which is felt by men and women in its highest and purest form is called love. Love, the emotion felt by a man for the woman of his choice is never separated from the animal instinct or impulse of passion. Unfortunately, so weak is our nature, passion is often felt without love. Understand, I am now dealing with the love of a man for the woman of his choice, in order that I may contrast it with the passion of a bad man for any woman. I am not referring now in any way to the love of a man for a blood relative of the opposite sex. The tie of relationship creates AFFECTION without PASSION, and is a very beautiful thing, but one quite apart.

There are also many other affections which are termed "love," which are really the higher forms of friendship. You will naturally exclaim, "If a man's love for a woman is never without passion, and yet passion can exist without love, how is an inexperienced person to know the one from the other?" My answer must be that complicated as the affair seems, in reality it is simple enough. Passion seeks its own gratification, no matter what the cost to the other party. Love also seeks gratification according to the promptings of nature, but NOT at the risk of bringing suffering and degradation on the object beloved. Love, then, feels true regard, consideration, and respect; passion knows none of these feelings. To you, a pure-minded girl, it will seem almost incredible that any woman should lose herself to gratify the passing desires of a selfish individual. It would indeed be incredible if women were only subject to the temptation WHICH COMES FROM WITHOUT. For ages writers and speakers have made it a custom to throw a false light on these matters. They have "made believe," as it were, that men only are moved by the impulse of which we speak; but it is best and wisest to face the truth, that not men only, but women also have to face the temptation which comes from within.

You will say, "If a woman has such a hard battle to fight being thus exposed to a double temptation, how can she hope for victory?" I reply, only by never placing herself in a position of danger. If she reads those books which imply that she is infinitely purer than man, let her accept them as pretty pictures, not photographs of life. Let her clearly understand also that the battle which a right-minded man must constantly fight against his impulses is indeed a hard one; and as she is herself subject to these impulses IN A MUCH LESS DEGREE, let her avoid offering temptation to him, by never showing such levity of conduct as to lead him to believe, or even hope, that levity on his part would meet with toleration. Remember, I do not wish you to be a prude; there is no reason why you should be constrained, unnatural, or affected in the company of the other sex. Familiarity with upright, honest men is good for a woman. Innocent familiarity with any man can never harm a girl; it is in undue familiarity alone that there is any danger. To explain myself more clearly, I will tell you the story of my poor housemaid Amelia (who has now left me for a time), just as she told it to me in her heartbroken confession. It will show you how the innocent sometimes merges into the harmful, and leads to sin and shame, through the folly of a girl, right-minded at first, but not sufficiently on her guard.

To begin then, I must tell you that on the Bank Holiday[6] some months ago Amelia had my permission to attend a fete in the grounds of our local park. There she met a young man of very respectable appearance, who showed her great attention, and begged her to accompany him for a walk the following Sunday. She consented, and for a time all went well. He treated her with a great show of affection, mingled with respect, and even introduced her to his friends as his future wife. From this we may assume that at that time his intentions were honest and honourable; but his own passions getting the upper hand of his conscience, combined with Amelia's foolish compliance to his will in little matters, led to the unfortunate sequel of the story. No doubt he intended to marry her when convenient to himself, but on the ground that theirs must be a long engagement, he asked her to conceal it from her parents, who live at a distance. Unfortunately she complied. Still, for some time after that he continued to treat her with respect. They walked together twice a week, and he always selected quiet spots. There was no absolute harm in that, for lovers naturally desire to be alone. By degrees, however, he ceased to be contented with merely quiet spots, and chose those entirely secluded. This ought to have been a warning to her, and the day soon came when he showed the first open mark of disrespect. Sitting in one of these secluded spots he had his arm about her waist; to this she was accustomed, and took it for what it may generally be said to be, a mark of affectionate endearment. But he went further. He endeavoured to unfasten her bodice and place his hand upon her bare breast. She resisted, warned by her instinct THAT THIS WAS AN UNDUE FAMILIARITY. He, however, persuaded her that it could do her no harm, and she gave way to him. Of course it could do her no absolute bodily harm, but it could, and did, do her the greatest of all harm, for he perceived that he had only to take her in the proper mood to conquer her resistance altogether, bow her will to his, and by approaching himself to other parts of her person, obtain the entire gratification of his desires and passion, at the cost of her purity. Understand this, the mere fact of his having placed his hand on her bare breast, though sufficient in itself to rob her of her purity of mind (because it would leave a certain sense of shame behind it) could not be said to rob her of the purity of her body, for like a kiss, a pressure of the hand or waist, or other such sign of innocent affection, it could not produce any change in the organs of the body, such as are produced by the last familiarity, by which he became the father of that child which is yet to be born.

You will of course seek to know the nature of that last familiarity. I do not think you can do better than turn to the 18th chapter of Leviticus in the Bible. You will see that the chapter deals with unlawful marriages,[7] and unlawful lusts, which are passions or desires of the flesh. If you will read the verses from the 6th to the 14th, you will find one phrase employed over and over again. It simply describes the union

6. A weekday legal holiday.
7. I.e., sexual relations, including various kinds of incest and relations with a menstruating woman, a neighbor's wife, or an animal.

of two persons of opposite sex as the "approach" of a man to a woman to "uncover her nakedness." That is sufficient for our purpose.

Bearing that expression in mind, you have only to exercise your reasoning faculties to come to a logical conclusion on this subject of the union of the sexes. I have described one familiarity which poor Amelia permitted, which was however not to the full extent what is implied by that expression used in the Bible, though it led up to it. You know where the internal organs of reproduction lie in a woman's body, and you have observed for yourself what are the external parts connected with them. Those are the parts of the human body signified by the word "nakedness" in the passages of Scripture I have pointed out to you. It is any approach to them or uncovering of them by a man, which a single woman who wishes to remain pure must forbid.

Young women do indeed need warning in these matters, and there are some deep thinkers who do not hesitate to say that it is those whose natures are sweetest and best, who stand in the greatest need of the bulwarks of knowledge, which can only be built up by cold common sense. It is hard to explain this to one unacquainted with the workings of human emotions, and the terrible pitfalls into which those emotions (though blameless in themselves) may sometimes lead the unwary. It is my duty to try and explain the matter to you, and I make the effort hoping that you will not only be better able to understand yourself, by the light of my revelations, but that you will be more ready to refrain from judging others whose faults you may know, but whose temptations are concealed from your view.

I have said that many persons consider that the most truly womanly girls are those most liable to error, when in a state of ignorance. The explanation is this. Woman's love has less passion in it than man's, and the deficiency in that respect (a deficiency for which the sex has great reason to be thankful) is for the most part made up by a host of complicated emotions, none of which are discreditable so long as they are kept within bounds. There is the natural vanity which makes women cultivate the gifts of nature; there is the desire for love which renders them tender and winning. Moreover, where women love they trust; and as love exaggerates the good qualities of its object, so they are unable to believe in the possibility of guile on the part of the one to whom they have given their affections. Fortunately it is only the minority who ever find their confidence abused, but as that minority exists, and is often recruited from the ranks of the good and pure, it is as well for girls to apply to themselves the old axiom, "Let him that thinketh he standeth take heed lest he fall;"[8] and that you may do this I have striven to show you how the trustful and loving, in their ignorance, sometimes slip insensibly into a position so dangerous that the mere lack of courage and presence of mind may seal their fate for evil.

Of course, there are depraved girls, just as there are depraved youths, whom no warning can reach. With these we have nothing to do. Let us not think about them, or, if we must, let us regard them with that silent inoffensive pity which we extend to those who by some misfortune have come into the world with malformed bodies and crippled limbs, just as these unfortunates possess malformed brains and defective powers of will.

I speak only of SINGLE women. Men and women were formed by nature for each other, and when their union is morally sanctioned by love, and legally and socially sanctioned by marriage, a woman is none the less pure because she lives on intimate terms with a man. In fact, from time immemorial, in all truly enlightened commu-

8. 1 Corinthians 10.12.

nities, the wives and mothers have held the highest social positions. Therefore a woman who lives with a man in marriage, knowing that her honour is henceforth bound up in his, may be sure that what passes between them will be according to the laws of nature, permitted and approved by our social code.

LETTER V

My Dear Child,—As your wedding day is now close at hand you ask me to give you a few hints, in order that you may know what to expect, and how to order yourself so as to act modestly, at the same time saving both yourself and your husband unnecessary confusion; but you beg me not to comply with your wish if I think your husband would prefer you should remain for the present in a state of semi-ignorance. Honestly I do not think such would be his wish. I incline to the belief that any right-thinking man would prefer to feel that his bride knew the sacrifice she must make of her person to his natural demands, and that her confidence in him was sufficient to enable her to face the necessary ordeal; for surely such knowledge is the best test of affection. In finding a woman in some degree prepared, no good man would draw any conclusions prejudicial to her purity; in fact men, having learnt the mysteries of life at a very early age themselves, are disposed to regard an ABSOLUTELY IGNORANT girl-woman as a person acting a part; which is of course a very great pity for the girl herself, who is in no way to blame. There is, however, very little left for me to say. Had I neglected to form your mind in your school days, my task at the present time would be so much the more difficult and embarrassing for us both.

That you may the more easily understand my meaning, let us return to the subject of the union of the sexes in the flowers of the field, and take my earliest illustration, the Imperial Lily. You are aware that the centres or stamens of the blossoms are the male organs of the plant. The golden dust on them, or pollen, as it is called, is the fecundating, or life-giving principle, the attribute of the male organ. You will find in the flower a hollow tube, which being united with the female organ of the blossom, forms a passage through which the life-giving principle, i.e., in the case in point, the pollen passes. Now being as you are acquainted with the portion of the human body in which the female organ of reproduction lies, and being aware that the male organ is situated in the same portion of the body, though differing in form as much as it does in functions and attributes, you easily understand what I meant when I spoke of the union of the sexes as the approach of the male to the female. When this is accomplished, when the male and female organs have not only approached but have been united as you see in the flower, when the life-giving principle formed by nature in the male organ has passed into the female one, then we say that the marriage has been consummated or completed, as without this consummation marriage is only an empty form.

Now it is the strong natural impulse or desire for this consummation which impels men to marry and charge their fortunes with the care of a woman and her future offspring. To obtain possession of your person, and the privilege of enjoying your society, your husband binds himself to keep you in sickness and in health, to share his worldly goods with you, and make you mistress of all he has; while you in your turn promise to comply with his natural demands. Of the other obligations of marriage, and they are many, we have spoken together often, so though I by no means wish to imply that the surrender of your person to your husband is your only duty, nor even that it is your first or greatest, I shall in this letter deal only with that subject.

I have told you that the sexual union of the flowers is free from either pleasure or pain. That is not so with human beings, you may guess. Mankind having reason, does not strive after anything for which a price must be paid, unless some gratification or reward is expected. Nor is the matter so far as the woman is concerned free from pain. I do not here refer to the pangs and pains of childbearing; I speak of the pain which a woman must suffer on her first union with a man.

The female organ is protected by a thin membrane—which doctors and surgeons can detect in the body of a maid. The first connection, however, breaks that membrane, and it is for ever after absent. It has nothing to do with her bodily health. It has no regular function to perform, therefore we can but conclude that its sole purpose is to serve as a mark of the woman's purity. In marriage it is the husband's right to find this proof of the wife's chastity, and in taking it, as its destruction is called, he does not leave her any the less pure, as what was natural in her single state would be unnatural in the state of matrimony. To the women, of course, it is a painful operation, as the fact that the membrane must be broken implies. The amount of the pain varies, and blood flows in lesser or greater quantities according to the strength of the membrane and the relative tenderness of the surrounding parts; in no case, however, is there cause for alarm, as neither life nor health are in any danger. For any subsequent trouble, such as soreness or tenderness of the parts, nothing is so good as plenty of clean cold water. Never be afraid of that. Cold water used on these parts as regularly as you use it on your face itself, is a woman's best friend, and preserves her from much ill health. Of course at the monthly periods you must cease these ablutions, and after them employ tepid water for a time. In the same manner employ tepid water in the winter, if you cannot bear the shock of cold. Form this habit and you will soon find reason to admit that it is beneficial. This, I think, is all that it is necessary for me to say to you. Should you have more reason later on, when I may not be here to apply to, to think that you are about to become a mother, you will find that any woman herself a mother will be glad to give assistance and counsel to a young married woman in need of both; besides which, doctors' handbooks on the subject are easily procured.

My duty it has been to charge your mind without tainting it. From me you have learnt the plain truths of nature. I have not left you, as many girls are unfortunately left, to pick up stray rags of information from unfit sources, and with those shreds of knowledge, so to speak, some of the garbage of the streets. I have had the satisfaction of seeing you grow up to be no less maidenly and modest, because your innocence has been protected by common sense. Henceforth your knowledge of life will come from other sources, but as your own daughters grow up around you, I hope that in their interests you will remember that the girl's best counsellor and friend is the one which nature gives her—her loving mother.

1896

ROBERT BADEN-POWELL
1857–1941

"Be prepared." The Boy Scout motto rang out loudly through most of the twentieth century, as hundreds of thousands of boys and girls worldwide entered the scouting movement in droves. Though Robert Baden-Powell's initial focus was on teenage boys, the movement spread almost immediately to girls (Girl Guides, in Britain) and then to younger children. Little girls became Brownies, a name taken from the title of a moral tale written in 1870 by Juliana Horatia Ewing. Little boys became Wolf Cubs (a name later changed to Cub Scouts), and much of the program's imaginative framework was drawn from *The Jungle Books* (1894–95) by Baden-Powell's friend Rudyard Kipling. To accommodate older Boy Scouts who wanted to stay in the movement, Rovers were added in 1917—young men prepared by scouting for happy lives of service and doing good, in accord with scout law.

By the century's end, however, the motto "be prepared" looked rather tattered, and it was likely to be heard as the punch line of the kind of joke about sex that Baden-Powell scorned. Yet the existence of such jokes, which depend on recognizing the phrase as the Boy Scout slogan, demonstrated just how familiar a cultural reference it had become. Baden-Powell's vision, his definition of the successful child, shaped childhood for generations. And according to scouting organizations, there are still more than 30 million boys and girls around the world involved in the movement.

Baden-Powell was born in London, the eighth child of ten; his father, a vicar and professor of natural science, died when he was three. After failing to be admitted to Balliol College, Oxford, he performed brilliantly on an open examination for an army commission. He began his very successful army career in India, in 1876, and he first came to national attention during the Boer War. At the siege of Mafeking (1899–1900), he and his men held out against a greatly superior force for 217 days. He returned home to find himself a hero; he also found that his *Aids to Scouting* (1899), intended for the military, was a surprise best seller. Long distressed by his soldiers' ignorance of proper tracking and surveillance, he had written *Reconnaissance and Scouting: A Practical Course of Instruction* in 1884. More generally, reports that large numbers of young recruits for the Boer War were medically unfit for service caused great public concern. Though Baden-Powell remained in the army, he set about devising an entire program to improve boys' mental and physical well-being, less focused on drill and marching than William Smith's Boys Brigade (founded in 1883) but educating youth to be healthy, morally upright, and patriotic. *Scouting for Boys* was first published in six parts in 1908.

Baden-Powell's inspired vision brought together disparate elements: the Woodcraft Indians movement of the British-born and Canadian-raised American naturalist Ernest Thomson Seton (1860–1946), based on the woodland skills of Native Americans and incorporating noncompetitive merit badges; the organizations devoted to conservation, handicrafts, and the outdoor life founded by the American illustrator and author Daniel Beard (1850–1941), and Sons of Daniel Boone and the Boy Pioneers of America. Baden-Powell also fused the "muscular Christianity" of *Tom Brown's School Days* (1857) by Thomas Hughes (with its emphasis on team spirit, physical strength, and endurance, obedience, and moral virtue) with his own experience at Mafeking, when he organized the boys of the town into the Mafeking Cadet Corps. Into the mix, Baden-Powell added the romantic thrill of adventure, the exotic, and the wild he so admired in Kipling, together with an emphasis on learning by doing. The Boy Scout brand of lifestyle marketing fashioned these components into a winning formula that succeeded in swallowing all the other youth movements of the time, including those of Beard and Seton—both of whom became charter members of a newly consolidated organization, the Boy Scouts of America, in 1910 (the same year that Baden-Powell resigned from the army to devote himself full-time to this new endeavor).

From the beginning, Baden-Powell's movement was promoted by a shelf of support manuals that were essentially scouting bibles: *Scouting for Boys: A Handbook for Instruction in Good Citizenship* (1908) was followed by *The Wolf Cub's Handbook* (1916) and *Rovering to Success: A Book of Life-Sport for Young Men* (1922); he also collaborated with his sister, Agnes Baden-Powell, in writing *The Handbook for Girl Guides, or How Girls Can Help Build the Empire* (1912). Such works, together with regular scouting magazines, helped disseminate a lifestyle management system designed to benefit and promote the British Empire.

In *Rovering to Success*, Baden-Powell addresses the older boys in the movement, maturing adolescents and young men. Like all advice books, it focuses on how to be a success. "Rovering," says Baden-Powell, is not "aimless wandering"; rather, it is "finding your way by pleasant paths with a definite object in view, and having an idea of the difficulties and dangers." Throughout the volume, the dangers are treated metaphorically as "rocks and breakers" of the sort a canoeist is likely to encounter in rough waters. Baden-Powell identifies those rocks and breakers "in terms of the old toast": "Horses, Wine and Women, with the addition of Cuckoos and Cant." As always, gambling, alcohol, and women are sources of disaster.

As a self-help guide, *Rovering to Success* looks much like what the government might issue today, promoting a healthy lifestyle, moderate eating, and regular exercise. The one interesting exception is that Baden-Powell's recommendations on alcohol and smoking—complete abstinence and moderate indulgence, respectively—reverse the current medical guidelines. On the subject of sex, Baden-Powell urged his readers to abstain until after marriage, on grounds of health as much as morality. He was fifty-five when he married the twenty-three-year-old Olave St. Clair Soames, who took over the Girl Guides movement from his sister and became "World Chief Guide" in 1930. They had a son and two daughters, who were regularly dressed in the uniforms invented by their father.

Baden-Powell attributed his success to his days as a soldier in South Africa. Because of his failing health, he returned to Africa in 1938, and he died in Nyeri, Kenya. His grave is now a tourist destination, and the epitaph on his headstone reads "Robert Baden-Powell, Chief Scout of the World." Also inscribed on the stone is a dot in the center, the symbol meaning "end of the trail," "gone home."

From Rovering to Success: A Book of Life-Sport for Young Men

WOMEN

The Danger is the risk of forgetting the chivalry due to women.

The Bright Side is the development of the manly and protective attitude to the other sex.

SEX INSTINCTS AND RISKS

The Monarch of the Glen

One of the finest sights that you can see of animal life on the moor or in the forest is a full-grown stag in the pride of life. He is the king of the herd—the Monarch of the Glen, as Landseer[1] has pictured him.

He is a type of courage, strength, and virile beauty, as he stands roaring out his challenge to all rivals to "come on."

In the "rutting" or mating season in autumn it is an exciting sight to watch the stags when they are calling and fighting each other for possession of the hinds.[2] They seem to go off their heads for a time, running hither and thither, restless and excited, for weeks unable to settle down to feed or to sleep till utterly worn out. It is the strongest and finest which come out on top. In the combats that follow, with the rattle and clash of antlers and the grunting of struggling combatants, the weaker give

---

1. Sir Edwin Henry Landseer (1802–1873), famous Victorian painter of animals. The oil painting *The Monarch of the Glen* (1850) is one of the best-known Victorian oil paintings, and was much reproduced in the nineteenth century.
2. Mature female deer.

in, and are pressed backwards by their more powerful opponents, until they are driven off in craven flight, leaving to the victor the choice of wives as lord of the herd.

And he takes his responsibilities, ready at all times—and able—to protect his hinds and fawns against all aggressors.

The defeated weaklings can then only sneak about trying to get what joy they can among the outcasts of the herd. These poor, under-sized creatures, are not thought much of by stalkers, who value rather the finer animals with their greater strength and activity.

The same kind of thing goes on in a greater or lesser degree among other animals of the jungle, among the birds in spring, and even among the fishes in winter.

Even plants, trees, and flowers come under the same law of Nature, and in their mating season, the spring, the sap rises and spreads itself through every branch, leaf and tendril, and the flowers blossom out, so that the female pistil can receive the pollen dust from the male stamens, which is a small germ that unites with the female germ, and they jointly make the young seed for a new plant.

Even the throwing out of beautiful flowers by the plants in springtime is similar to the habits of animals and birds, which put on their brightest plumage in the mating season, and this we see reproduced again among the young bloods,[3] with their bright socks, fancy ties, and well-oiled hair.

Manhood

It is the impulse of Nature and occurs also with man.

But here the difference comes in, that, whereas in most animals there is a definite mating season, in man the instinct is always at work and there is no definite mating season. The woman's "monthly periods" are due to the rhythm of the organism but are not the same as the definite periods of "heat"[4] and so on that we see in other animals.

When the adult sexual instinct shows itself in the growing youth, it brings about emotional changes which often feel upsetting.

Don't forget that these impulses are natural. We all have them and we must all learn how to deal with them. I get lots of letters from young fellows who have never been told what to expect when they are growing into manhood, and consequently they have felt worried by finding it an upsetting time for them. They get nervey and unsettled in their mind without knowing why. They can't settle down properly to their work, they get shy of other people and feel miserable, and often think that they are going off their head.

I am only too glad that in their trouble they have thought of writing to me, because in many cases I have been able to reassure them and to help them to take it calmly. There is nothing in it to be upset about. It all comes from quite natural causes.

When a boy grows into manhood his whole body undergoes a gradual change which anyone can see for himself. His voice becomes deeper, hair grows where it didn't grow before, his muscles become set and hardened, his organs develop, and so on.

Sexual Desire Comes from Perfectly Natural Causes

The change is brought about by the secretions from the organs of sex, which influence the development of the whole body and may be compared to the flow of sap in a tree. It gives the vigour of manhood to his frame, and it builds up his nerves and courage.

3. Dandies.
4. Periods of sexual receptivity experienced by most female mammals.

The actual fluid secreted by the testicles and adjoining glands is called *semen*, which is Latin for seed.

The Way in Which Life Is Reproduced

This fluid contains the male organism, which is responsible for fertilising the female organism called the *ovum*, which is Latin for egg. In order for life to be reproduced throughout the animal kingdom and a large part of the vegetable kingdom too, it is this union of the male organism with the female that starts the process of a new life developing. In man the male organism is called the spermatozoon and there are many thousands of these spermatozoa in a single drop of semen. Nature appears to be extravagant in making so many of these, of which only one actually fertilizes the ovum.

You can get some idea of the process by looking at these pictures[5] of the fertilization of the hen's egg and the growth of the chick which uses up the yolk as it grows. The "white" contains the actual ovum, which is fertilized by the spermatozoon of the cock bird when it "covers" the hen. By a similar process in the human being, from the joint germ there emerges a living, breathing creature of flesh, blood and bones, with eyesight, brain and mind, and even with many points of likeness in appearance and character to both of its parents.

The Germ Is of Vital Importance for Carrying on the Race

And this young creature carries within it again the germs for reproducing further children in its turn, when it has grown to the riper age.

The whole of this marvellous and complicated process is a work of God the Creator. The germ from which you were made was passed down by your father just as he came from the germ of his father before him; and so away back into the Dark Ages.

And you have that germ in you to pass out, when the time comes, to join with that of your wife in making your son.

So it is a sacred trust handed down to you through your father and his fathers from the Creator—The Great Father of all.

Sometimes, when this semen is forming over-rapidly, you may find that you pass some of it out in your dreams while you are asleep. This need not alarm you; it is the natural overflow. If brought on by oneself the act is called "self abuse" or "masturbation."

Masturbation

Young men are sensible enough, and are willing, to take advice if they can only get it, and I am certain that if only these things which I have mentioned above were better understood by them they would avoid many of the distressing and sometimes agonising times they go through. It often used to be taught that self abuse is a very dreadful thing leading to insanity and, at any rate, causing permanent and severe damage to the system. Now this is a grossly exaggerated picture to say the least of it. Self abuse is obviously brought about by unnatural conditions. If we were living in a primitive state of nature, boys would behave about sex matters just as our friend the stag! There would be no moral or social check to sexual intercourse. They cannot do this for moral and social reasons, but that does not take away the primitive sexual instinct which is at the bottom of their desires. No, to have the desire is natural, so don't blame yourself for this and don't waste time in self torture *if* you *have* abused

5. The illustrations are not included here.

yourself. The tension is sometimes so great that many fellows have at times practised masturbation. What is it really? It is the gratifying of the sexual instinct by giving *oneself* the feeling of satisfaction. In other words it is a form of self love, which is obviously not a thing to cultivate.

Now we are members of a community governed by certain moral laws and social conventions. Promiscuous sexual intercourse is forbidden by these moral laws, so here is the dilemma. Primitive desires *versus* moral and social laws. We have granted we cannot escape the desires. If our aim is to lead a healthy decent life for ourselves and others, we shall soon adjust these difficulties. Sex is not everything in life, and other energies take the place of sex and relieve the strain. The energy that the primitive male animal puts almost solely into sex, in the human, is turned into all sorts of other activities, such as art, science and a hundred and one other things. So the more interests you have and the more you follow them with keenness the less will primitive sex urges worry you and when the time comes you will have the delight of sharing them naturally with the woman who will surely be your mate. Now you can see how Rovering comes in. Instead of aimless loafing and smutty talks you will find lots to do in the way of hiking and enjoyment of the out-of-door manly activities. Without knowing it you are putting something in the place of sex.

Venereal Disease

One almost invariable result from loose talk among lads is that they get to talk filth, and in this way lower their ideals and thoughts to a beastly standard, and one which they will be ashamed of later on when they have grown to be men.

It puts them back on their road to happiness, because they will have so much leeway to make up in getting out of the mud into which they have floundered. And mud always sticks to some extent.

Then lads are apt to joke airily about venereal diseases which are sure, sooner or later, to overtake those who indulge their sex desires unwisely.

But these diseases are no joking matter; however slight their first effects, they are desperately dangerous to a man.

There are two principal Venereal Diseases: *Syphilis* ("Pox"). Poisonous infection that can be caught by connection with a person already infected. The disease shows itself in a sore at first; this develops in a few weeks into other sores; then in from one to twenty years it causes diseases of parts of the body or of bones, and frequently of the heart, if not properly treated. *Gonorrhœa* ("Clap"). Nearly always caught by connection in the same way as Syphilis. Shown by discharge of matter from the organ and inflammation of the organ itself. Further inflammation is likely to follow in the bladder, etc.

Syphilis is often inherited by children from diseased parents, with the result that they are blind, or deaf, or paralytic, or insane. It has been estimated that twenty-five per cent of people who are blind from infancy are so as the result of parents' syphilis. The sins of the fathers are indeed visited on their children.

When once syphilis has got hold of you, none of the quack medicines as advertised will save you. The only way is to go at once to a good doctor and tell him straight out what has happened. *If he takes you in time* he will be able to cure you.

But the danger is not one which anyone will joke about once he knows the depth of it, is it? A visit to any Lock hospital[6] will give you such examples of venereal disease

6. A hospital for the treatment of venereal disease (the name is taken from an institution of this kind in Southwark, London, founded in medieval times to treat lepers).

as will persuade you, better than any words of mine, to avoid having anything to do with women of the street if you would save yourself in body as well as soul.

The folly of taking such a risk is largely the result of being carried away by the weaknesses of the herd.

It is like drinking or gambling—a disease which you pick up from letting yourself drift too far without thinking, in the company of a lot of other unthinking young fellows.

Many men come to grief from supposing that if they go with a girl who is not a regular prostitute of the streets, there will be no danger of being infected with the disease. But the reports show that the danger is actually greater. The girl who has once been deceived by some blackguard of a man loses her sense of shame and is willing occasionally to go with other men. But in her ignorance she is more liable than the professional to harbour disease, from not knowing what precautions to take. Therefore, she is all the more dangerous to herself, poor creature, and to others with whom she comes in contact.

A man may be continent and resolve to remain so. He may then by chance, or by boon companions, be led to take that fatal "sixssth" glass, and, with brain and senses clouded, do the very things he meant not to do.

That is where so many a good fellow has come to grief and ruined himself not only morally (in his character) but physically (in his body) as well.

There is a play called "Damaged Goods"[7] which deals with the venereal question in an open, common-sense way, and is a good education for a young man. It tells of a young man's infecting his wife and child, and the child's nurse, through ignorance. The pathetic cry which there comes in, "If I had only known in time!" is one which is echoed in hundreds of cases every day.

Sins of the Fathers Visited Upon the Children

When I was writing this chapter a friend asked me whether it was really true that syphilis was passed on by a father to his children to the extent suggested.

I only had to show him a letter that had appeared in *The Times* that morning from a coroner, dated February 21, 1922, in which he said that the loss of life or of reason and the infection of innocent children from this awful disease "is terrible in the extreme."

MANLINESS

Chivalry

You will, I hope, have gathered from what I have said about this Rock "Women," that it has its dangers for the woman as well as for the man. But it has also its very bright side if you only manœuvre your canoe aright.

The paddle to use for this job is CHIVALRY.

Most of the points which I have suggested as being part of the right path are comprised under chivalry.

The knights of old were bound by their oath to be chivalrous, that is to be protective and helpful to women and children.

This means on the part of the man a deep respect and tender sympathy for them, coupled with a manly strength of mind and strength of body with which to stand up

---

7. The play *Les avariés* (1902) by Eugène Brieux was translated into English as *Damaged Goods* (1911); Upton Sinclair novelized it under the same title (1913).

for them against scandal, cruelty or ridicule, and even, on occasion, to help them against their own failings.

A man without chivalry is no man. A man who has this chivalry and respect for women could never lower himself to behave like a beast, nor would he allow a woman to ruin herself with him by losing her own self-respect and the respect of others. It is up to him to give the lead—and that a right one; and not to be led astray.

I have known such chivalry on the part of a man to give further than this, even to the point of raising a woman who had fallen; where she had expected him to join her in debauchery his courteous respect for her, which overlooked her faults and was given *because* she was a woman, caused her once more to think of her own self-respect and so restored her to her place.

Chivalry, like other points of character, must be developed by thought and practice, but when gained it puts a man on a new footing and a higher one with himself and with the world.

To be chivalrous he must put woman on a pedestal, and see all that is best in her; he must also have sympathy for the weaker folk, the aged and the crippled; and he must give protection to the little ones.

For this he must use his self-control to switch off all that is impure from his mind and ensure that his own ideas are clean and honourable, that his sense of duty is so high that ridicule and chaff will mean nothing to him.

Not My Job

"Not my job" is usually the camouflage under which a coward endeavours to conceal his want of chivalry. But for a *man* anything that can be helpful to anyone is his job.

I don't mean by that that he should therefore poke his nose into other people's business, or ask them, "Are you saved?" and so on.

But if he can lend a hand to a woman who is down, or help a young fellow who is trying to keep up and clean, then he can do a great good through his chivalry. And, moreover, he can be of service to others by the very example he sets of leading a clean, upright life, and by showing that he is not ashamed of so doing.

It Is Up to You to Be Master of Yourself

The thing is to remember, as I have said before, that you are YOU, and you have got to make your own road for yourself if you mean to gain happiness. Come out of the herd and take your own practical steps towards dealing with the desires that come upon you in the course of Nature.

Keep away from loose companions, whether men or girls; take on lots of other occupation and healthy exercise, such as boxing, walking, hikes, football, rowing, etc. Keep your thoughts off lewdness by taking up hobbies and good reading in your spare time; keep off drink and over-smoking, over-eating, sleeping in too warm or soft a bed, since all these help to make the temptation worse.

Athletics are also a great outlet to one's natural forces. They have the elements of struggle and victory by physical force, which accompany war, but they should take its place and not be used as training for turning boys into "Cannon Fodder".

You all know about scouting and the immense value that it has, so we need not go into that any more.

Now one word about tolerance—we are all different and we must not think that because other fellows seem inferior to us, they are to be despised.

For example, you may be a good athlete and Smith may be a poor one, but very good at books. Don't despise him, but "Live and let live".

Now we have taken a pretty good look at the problems of sex as they arise in boyhood. I hope you feel happier about them. Life should be natural and easy, and the healthier a life you lead, the less these problems will arise and bother you.

Remember that if you do get troubles that worry you, the best way is to take them to an older man—your Father, if you can talk to him, or an understanding Doctor or Master.[8]

Brooding over troubles never does any good.

If one really lives up to the Scout's Code, one can't go far wrong.

There is an old tag in Latin, which we might do well to close with:

"Mens sana in corpore Sano".

"A healthy mind in a healthy body".

A good thing to aim at!

Keep yourself clean inside and out by daily washing, and swimming if you can. Constipation and neglect to keep the racial organ cleaned daily are apt to cause slight irritation which leads to trouble.

Above all don't be alarmed by the awful penalties which quack doctors hold out to you. They do it in order to make you buy their rotten medicines; that is one of the tricks of their trade. But go forward with good hope and trust in yourself.

It will be a struggle for you, but if you are determined to win you will come out of it all the better for the experience; you will have strengthened your character and your self-control; you will have come through clean-minded and wholesome; and you will have fortified your body with the full power of manhood.

Remember also that you have done this, not only for your own sake, but because you have a duty to the nation, to the race, that is, to beget strong, healthy children in your turn; and to do this you have to keep yourself pure.

Some fellows seem to think that if they don't let themselves go now and then, they will not be able to perform when they get married later on. This is absolute nonsense. Continence does not weaken your powers.

I have had so many letters from young men on the subject that I quote a reply that I have sent them, as it may meet the anxiety of others:

"I am very glad indeed to hear that you have managed to keep yourself straight in spite of the continued temptation. In reply to your question, I don't think you need have any fear about being able to marry, provided that you go on as you are now doing. Lots of fellows have, to my knowledge, been afraid to marry thinking that they might be impotent, because of their having indulged in self-abuse when young. But they found that they were all right after all, and so I hope and expect it will be in your case."

Auto-Suggestion

Imagination runs off into day-dreams, and these may be suggestive ones which bring on temptation.

Yet imagination is the important part of auto-suggestion or self-cure, and therefore the lad who is given to day-dreams is really the one who has the best power for curing himself if he only sets about it on the lines that I have suggested.

The Parents' Influence

A large proportion of the men who have risen to eminence in the world admit that they have owed very much of their character and success to the influence of their mother.

And this is natural since in any case she has been the one who cared for him and

8. I.e., schoolmaster.

watched over his upbringing from his earliest childhood. She has given of her best for him.

The man owes a debt to his mother such as he can never fully repay. But the best that he can do in this direction is to show that he is grateful and prove himself worthy of and bring success to her efforts.

She has probably dreamed ambitious dreams to herself of what her boy would do in the world, and disappointment, as bitter as it is secret, will overshadow her where he turns out a waster or a failure.

Boys don't think of this enough. They are cruel without intending it; they are apt to forget how much she has done for them and how grateful she would be for the smallest return.

I remember Sir Thomas Lipton[9] telling me the story of his life, and I realised how he made his mother a happy woman when, as a shop-boy, he brought her the first week's wages he had earned. "Why, Thomas," she said, "you will be getting me a carriage and pair[1] next!"

That little remark caught his imagination, and on it he built up his ambition. His whole effort was then devoted to the one aim of making enough money to buy a carriage and pair as a surprise-offering to his mother.

He told me that, among the many exciting incidents of his life, the proudest and happiest moment was that when he was able to actually hand over to her the prize that he had gained for her.

So in making your own way to success remember that as you progress it will not be merely a satisfaction to yourself but it will bring a real happiness in a quarter where it is most deserved—in your mother's heart.

And when some of these difficulties or temptations of which I have spoken are troubling you, turn your thoughts to your mother. Think what her wish would be. Act upon it, and it will pull you through.

If problems arise which you feel you cannot cope with by yourself, talk them over with your father. Remember he has been through the same difficulties as you and will be able to help. If for any reason your father is not available there will be some older man you can trust to whom you can go.

Save Yourself and Help to Preserve the Race.

Now, as I have said before, in giving you these ideas I am only trying to help you to get happiness.

Happiness depends to a large extent on health, though it also depends on knowing that you are aiming to help the general well-being of the country as well as of yourself. It is no use your getting married, indeed in some cases it is a crime to do so, unless you are fit and healthy and able to beget healthy children. And part of your responsibility as a parent will be to teach your children how to grow up healthy.

Well, there is an awful lot of happiness missed in our country through ill-health, and most of that ill-health could be prevented if fellows only took reasonable care of themselves.

Do you know that only one man in three is really healthy, and that one in every ten is an invalid?

Out of eight million young men—young men, mind you, not the old worn-outs—called up for army service in the Great War, over one million were found to be medically unfit for service!

9. Scottish merchant and yachtsman (1850–1931), the inventor of the tea bag.

1. I.e., a pair of horses.

A large proportion of these were born healthy, but were allowed by their parents or they allowed themselves to become weak and feeble.

A further proportion were born defective because of the defects in their fathers or mothers—very largely from venereal disease.

If you added up all the working hours that men lose through sickness in Great Britain every year, it would amount to fourteen million weeks. Just think what this means in trade and wages, and yet that loss is largely preventable if fellows only knew how to take care of themselves and had the sense to do it.

If you are an engine driver or a car driver you know what tremendous care is necessary in keeping the machinery properly lubricated, fed with adequate head of steam or petrol, gentle use of levers, thorough cleaning of all its parts; constant care and attention are necessary, together with a close knowledge of each particular bit of the machinery, if you are to have it in good working order, running smoothly and efficiently.

But in your own body you have a machine more wonderful than any man-made engine and one that needs still closer attention and better understanding if you are to keep it well. And what is more, you can, by taking care of it, improve it and make it bigger and stronger, which is more than the engineer can do with his engine.

Yet how few fellows understand anything about their inside and its wonderful mechanism: they try to drive an engine that they know nothing about, they give it all sorts of wrong treatment and then expect it to keep sound and to work well!

How to Keep Healthy and Strong

When I was serving in the fever jungles,[2] both on the east and the west coasts of Africa, I noticed that many of us were healthy enough so long as we were on the march every day, but that whenever we had a day's halt and rested some of us were sure to get fever.

I argued it out in my own mind that our blood got cleaned and freshened every day through the daily rear[3] sweating out of waste stuff in one's system.

A day of rest meant less perspiring and more feeding than usual and therefore less drainage of one's inside.

So I always made a point of going in for a good bit of exercise on a rest day, and sticking to one's usual small amount of food and drink.

I never had a day's sickness, and at one time averaged twenty miles a day marching for over a week in a pretty soggy atmosphere. Never felt fitter.

I had one white officer with me, but he had to be replaced five times by fresh men owing to sickness.

Well, I put it down to keeping my blood clean and pure. It is pure blood that makes your body, muscle and fibre grow and keep strong.

And the heart that pumps it through the body is the most important organ that you have. The "Scout's Pace," i.e., alternate running and walking for short spells of twenty or thirty paces, saves men from the heart strain of long-distance running, which is not a sport that everyone is physically fitted for.

Fresh Air

The blood needs loads of oxygen—that is fresh air—to keep it fresh. Living indoors without fresh air quickly poisons the blood and makes people feel tired and seedy when they don't know why.

For myself I sleep out of doors in winter as well as summer. I only feel tired or

---

2. Tropical jungles where malaria was prevalent.   3. I.e., daily bowel movement.

seedy when I have been indoors a lot. I only catch cold when I sleep in a room.

The *British Medical Journal* of February, 1922, reports that living in the open air improved the metabolism (There's a word! It means getting the best chemical value from the food we eat) of patients in one hospital to the extent of 40 per cent above the average.

Cleanliness

I have said clean yourself from inside, but also it is important to clean yourself outside if you want to be healthy.

Cavalry soldiers are noted for their cleanliness, the truth is they have learnt from grooming their horses and cleaning them up at least twice a day how very important it is to health and freshness, to have the skin and parts properly cleaned.

A bath cannot always be got every day, but a wet and scrubby towel can always be made available and should be used without fail.

Breathing

"Shut your mouth and save your life." That is the name of a booklet written by Catlin[4] as the result of his experiences with the Red Indians.

They train their children while they are yet babies to breathe through the nose and not through the mouth. This is partly with the idea of teaching them not to snore and so give themselves away to the enemy in the night, but also because they think that an open mouth reflects on the character of the man.

An Englishman wanted to fight a duel with a Red Indian, but with true idea of fair play he declined to use pistols or other weapons that the Red Indian was unaccustomed to. So he suggested that they should strip and be armed with a knife apiece and fight it out in that way. The Indian smiled and said he would fight if the Englishman still wished it, but that it would go badly with the Englishman.

When asked his reasons for this he said that he had noticed the Englishman habitually kept his mouth half open and he had no fear whatever of a man who did that. It was the sign of a weak character.

We also know that it often produces weak health, since a man who breathes through his mouth sucks in poisonous germs from the air, instead of getting them caught up in the moisture inside his nostrils.

The way to catch 'flu or any other disease that is flying about is to breathe with your mouth open.

Teeth

It is said that nearly half the ill-health of the nation may be traced to bad teeth.

Although people start with good teeth as children, there are very few that have a sound set after twenty-five, and this is mainly because of their own want of care of their teeth.

Children are not taught the importance of cleaning their teeth THOROUGHLY after meals; and grown-ups don't bother about it. Diseased teeth and gums not only prevent you from properly chewing your food, but may breed little brutes of germs and microbes in your mouth which go down with your food and give you continual small

---

4. George Catlin (1796–1872), American painter who for much of the 1830s traveled throughout the West painting Native Americans. In *Shut Your Mouth*, originally published as *The Breath of Life*, or, *Mal-Respiration, and Its Effects upon the Enjoyments and Life of Man* (1861), he draws on his observations of various Native groups to emphasize the dangers of mouth breathing.

doses of poison which gradually make you seedy and depressed without your knowing the reason.

If you want to see what you have in the way of germs in your mouth it is an interesting experiment to put some hydrogen peroxide with water in a glass and dip a clean toothbrush into it. Nothing happens.

Brush your teeth over with the toothbrush and dip it again into the glass and you will see myriads of bubbles rising in the water, which means so many germs being knocked out.

I have spoken to you elsewhere in this book on food, on temperance, and smoking, and drinking, and sleeping.

So if you would be strong and well stick to regular daily habits, keeping yourself clean inside and out, give yourself plenty of exercise in the open air, a plain food and not too much of it, moderation in smoking and drinking, breathe through the nose— and you will thank God you're alive.

Exercise

I was asked once by a high authority in education whether I did not think that the cost of erecting gymnasia in every town—though it might amount to millions—would be money well spent because it would develop the health and strength of manhood.

I replied that the two strongest, healthiest races I happened to know were the Zulus and the Bhutani peasants[5] of the Himalayas; but in neither country had I ever noticed a gymnasium. There was plenty of God's fresh air, and lots of walking and running and climbing to be done in the daily work of these people; and I believed that these were good enough tonics for any man.

But both fresh air and exercise are absolutely essential to health, both when you are growing and when you have grown up. I always begin the day with a little bit of body twisting, *in the open*, when I tumble out of bed—but that is only as a start.

Some men go in for physical drill, and some for dumb-bell and other muscle-developing exercises till they come out all over lumps that look fine in a photo when you brace them up, but are not of the slightest practical use to you.

And this work is generally done indoors.

Your exercise must be out of doors in the fresh air, and the very best you can get is at the same time the easiest and cheapest, namely, walking. Week-end walking tours are the very best thing for health of mind as well as of body.

The Ruksack

I know nothing more enjoyable or more cheering and health-giving than a good old tramp every week-end. A knapsack on your back makes you absolutely free and independent. You load it with only the essential things and no luxuries. It is not merely every pound but every ounce of weight that tells on a long march. Nothing can beat the Norwegian type of ruksack with its light wooden or metal frame which holds it securely in position without galling or overheating your back. It will take in addition to your clothing a light little tent that can be set up on your staff or on a tree stem, and your sleeping quilt and waterproof sheet. Thus equipped week-end hikes are possible, and what is more enjoyable all the year round? Weather? Can anything be better than a good long tramp on a cold blowy day? If it is wet, all the better; you get a very real enjoyment out of a good fire and shelter in a snug farmhouse or inn at

---

5. Inhabitants of Bhutan, a kingdom between India and China. Zulus: a Bantu-speaking people of southern Africa.

the end of the day. I tell you, you get so hardened by practice of the out of doors that you really don't notice the weather very much and you mind it less. Whatever it is, hot or cold, rain or shine, you gain strength, vitality and cheeriness by it.

Be a Man

A clean young man in his prime of health and strength is the finest creature God has made in this world.

I once had charge of a party of Swazi[6] chiefs on their visit to England. At the end of their stay, when they had seen most of the interesting sights of the country, I asked them what had struck them as the most wonderful of all that they had seen.

(They were, incidentally, wonderful sights themselves, having discarded their fine native dress for top hats and frock coats!)

They unanimously agreed that the finest thing in England was the London omnibus.[7] They were so taken with its brilliant colours and the idea of its being entirely for joy-riding!

The next best thing in their judgment was the troupe of gymnastic instructors at the Gymnasium at Aldershot.[8]

When they saw these men performing their various exercises they were tremendously taken with them, but they were not fully satisfied until they had had the men stripped and had examined for themselves their muscular development.

And I must say these gymnasts were magnificent specimens of what a man should be, and active and alert in mind as well as in body.

And, mind you, a number of these men came originally from poor homes, but had made themselves into what they now were through taking a pride in their manhood. They judged it too good to part with in exchange for philandering after women, swilling beer, and sucking cigarettes. Swazi savages could therefore appreciate manly strength and beauty.

A white man and a man.

A civilised woman can appreciate all the more a man who is a *man* not only in body, but mind as well, strong and chivalrous.

He is the man for her, and she has no use for the sickly minded, sloppy slacker who talks dirt and has no backbone.

God has given you a body—no, He has lent it to you—to make the best use of; not to soak it in drink, not to make it limp and weak with debauchery, but to take care of, to strengthen and build up into a really fine figure of a man and a father of children.

You can do this if you like. It is up to you. And what a splendid adventure it can be.

6. A people of southeast Africa; in 1906 the region became a territory ruled by a British commissioner.
7. Bus.

8. The site of Britain's largest military training camp; it includes a school of gymnastics. The town is about 34 miles southwest of London.

St. George[9] fighting the dragon won't be in it with you, who fight the dragon of temptation and down him so that you may in the end present yourself a *man*, clean and strong and chivalrous to the girl whom you love. You will also have taken a further step towards happiness, and will have fitted yourself bodily for the service of God in carrying on the race on the best lines.

MARRIAGE

You are bound to have your

Love Adventures

I know the difficulty that you are faced with. There is little enough of romance and excitement in the ordinary life of a town or village, and at your particular age, woman comes into your thoughts in a new and alluring way.

It is a great adventure, therefore, to a young lad to seek out a girl for himself.

Sometimes he likes to show her off before the others as a sign of his manliness, in other cases he prefers to get her all to himself. Don't think this unnatural. It is all in the course of Nature. As I have said above, it is in accordance with the law that governs animals as well as man.

But in the case of man there is this difference. He has a mind and intelligence which the animal does not possess; he sees romance in selecting a mate to whom he can give his admiration, love and devotion. These are far above the mere animal instinct. They form human love instead of animal lust; and the higher he raises himself above the animal instinct the less he is of the beast and the more he is of the man.

A main step to happiness in this direction is to select the right kind of girl. There are women and there are dolls.

Calf-Love

As a *very* young man you will of course go entirely by her face and figure and you may fall in love with one girl after another—desperately in love; and sometimes will have perhaps two or three on your string at a time.

Probably you may think it the most glorious adventure and most probably a few days later the most disastrous tragedy that ever happened to anyone. It comes to most young fellows about this period to feel like committing suicide over a love quarrel— but they don't do it!

You may comfort yourself by knowing that all this is what comes to every lad, and is known as "calf-love." There is no harm in it, and nothing to be ashamed of nor to be depressed about. Indeed in a short time, when the really right girl has come along, you will laugh at your first ideas of love-making.

But in that calf-love period don't forget you are a man and not a beast. Behave like a man. Play fair and square with the girl and remember your future son for whom some day you will be responsible.

And you will be on the right side if you only take on with a girl whom you can bring to your own home without shame, among your mother and sisters.

Remember that whoever she is, she is someone else's sister; think of him and behave to her as you would wish him to behave to your sister.

9. Patron saint of England; according to legend, he rescued a princess from a dragon, eventually killing it.

ROBERT
BADEN-POWELL

The right girl will come along sooner or later—if you have kept your head. Your calf-love will have disappeared. You will find a girl whose character you admire and respect, whose tastes are like your own and whose comradeship you long for. It will not be merely her person that attracts you but her personality.

You will find a new, calmer and deeper form of love that links and binds you to her—one which, if you are wise, will never grow less.

And you will expect her to come to you pure and clean, won't you? But what about yourself? Are you going to expect of her what you cannot offer in return yourself?

That would neither be manly nor fair. No, if you are going to enjoy real happiness in life that is the supreme joy of being married to a really good woman from whom you hope for love and respect.

There are women and women.

Don't begin your married life with a lie, else you will be lying all through it, and there will be an end to trusting each other.

Warning from a Pork-Butcher on Getting Engaged

If you have never read a book called *A Self-made Merchant's Letters to his Son*[1] you've got a treat in store for you. It is a most amusing bit of reading, but at the same time full of jolly sound advice.

The merchant is an American pork-packer, writing to his son who holds a junior post in the business. He hears that his son is hanging about after a certain young lady.

So he says: "I suppose I am fanning the air when I ask you to be guided by my judgment in this matter, because while a young fellow will consult his father about buying a horse, he is cocksure of himself when it comes to picking a wife.

"Marriages may be made in Heaven, but most engagements are made in the back parlour with the gas so low that a fellow really doesn't get a square look at what he's taking. While a man doesn't see much of a girl's family when he is courting, he is apt to see a good deal of it when he is housekeeping.

"Your Ma and I set up housekeeping in one of those cottages you read about in story books, but that you want to shy away from when it is put up to you to live in one of them. There were nice climbing roses on the front porch, but no running water in the kitchen; there were plenty of old-fashioned posies in the front yard and plenty of rats in the cellar; there was half an acre of ground at the back, but so little room inside that I had to sit with my feet out of window. It was just the place to go for a picnic, but it's been my experience that a fellow does most of his picnicking before he is married.

"But one way and another we managed to get a good deal of satisfaction out of it,

---

1. *Letters from a Self-Made Merchant to His Son* (1901), by George Horace Lorimer.

because we had made up our minds to get our fun out of everything as we went along.

"With most people happiness is something that is always just a day off, but I *have made it a rule never to put off being happy till to-morrow.* [I have italicized that.]

"Of course when you are married you've got to make an income, and this is going to take so much time and thought that you won't have a very wide margin left for golf. I simply mention this in passing, because I see in the Chicago papers that you were among the players on the links one afternoon a fortnight ago. Golf's a nice foolish game and there ain't any harm in it so far as I know; but a young fellow who wants to be a boss butcher hasn't much daylight to waste on any kinds of links— except sausage links.

"Of course a man should have a certain amount of play, just as a boy is entitled to a piece of pie at the end of his dinner, but he don't want to make a meal of it.

"Of course your salary isn't a large one yet, but you can buy a whole lot of happiness with fifty dollars a week when you have a right sort of woman for your purchasing agent, and, while I don't go much on love in a cottage, love in a flat with fifty a week as a starter is just about right if the girl is just about right. If she isn't, it doesn't make any special difference how you start out, you're going to end up all wrong.

"Money ought never to be *the* consideration about marriage, but it always ought to be *a* consideration. When a boy and girl don't think about it enough before the ceremony they're going to have to think altogether too much about it after; and when a man is doing sums at home, evenings, it comes kind of awkward for him to try to hold his wife on his lap. . . .

"There is nothing in this talk that two can live cheaper than one. A good wife doubles a man's happiness and doubles his expenses, but it is a pretty good investment if a fellow has got the money to invest. . . .

"A married man is worth more salary than a single one, because his wife makes him work more. He is apt to go to bed a little sooner and to get up a little earlier; to go a little steadier and to work a little harder than the fellow who has got to amuse a different girl every night and can't stay at home to do it.

"That's why I am going to raise your salary to seventy-five dollars a week the day you marry."

On the other hand, in *Enchanter's Nightshade*[2] you find:

"Men all seem to want to make money directly they get to a city."

"Well, they must marry."

"You don't need a deal of money—unless the girl is all wrong."

Income an Important Detail

There is truth in both ideas, but the advice from the old pork-packer is sound, if less romantic, and it is your business before marrying to see that you are in a position to keep a wife and family, otherwise you will be condemning these as well as yourself to a struggle for existence.

Success in business is not a matter of luck or favour or interest, nor even of learning, so much as of ability and character. Expert skill in your work is bound to tell, but for promotion to higher grades, character—that is absolute trustworthiness, tact, and energy—is essential.

This applies practically to every trade or profession. I was asked the other day what I meant by tact, and I could only reply by quoting the old example of the tactful

2. By John Bingham Morton (1921).

plumber who, on entering a bathroom which had carelessly been left unlocked by the lady using the bath, promptly said: "I beg pardon, *Sir*. I didn't know you were here," and strolled out again.

I was in a "Rovers' Den"[3] (*see* final Chapter) when congratulations were being showered on one member on his engagement to be married.

"Who is the girl?"

"Oh, she's a Girl Guide."

"Splendid! What a good idea! You couldn't do better."

But immediately two other men chipped in for part of the congratulations, saying that they also were engaged similarly to Girl Guides.

I see promise in this.

You get wives in this way who can be better pals because they have got the same keenness on camping and the out of doors with all the necessary handiness and resourcefulness, health and good temper that comes of such life. I feel certain that if I came to visit you in your home later on, when thus mated, I should find not only a happy home but a clean one; for the premises of campers, who were accustomed to leave their camp grounds as neat as they found them, would not be lumbered up with piles of old tins, scrap-iron, and other rubbish that are a disgrace to so many of our back gardens and waste lands.

A Man's Duties on Getting Married

Someone once told me my fortune by looking at the lines on the palm of my hand, and he said: "Your line of head is stronger than your line of heart," meaning that I should not be carried off my legs by the first beautiful girl I saw, but that I should think as much about the character of the girl I admired as about her appearance; and that is, I am certain, the way to make your choice. Take care lest, in making your choice, you think too much of what you would require in your future wife and forget her point of view and *what she would like of you* as a husband. Think of that.

When I got married, an old friend, on giving me his congratulations, also gave me a new vision of my future state when he said: "My dear fellow, I have been married over twelve years and it is still a honeymoon with us. Life has gone on getting happier and happier for us."

And in my turn I too have since found the truth of this.

I should hope that it will be the case with you who read this, but it means using your "line of head" as well as heart; it means getting the right girl to start with.

Mind you, it is only a little step to ask a girl to say yes, but on that word depends a life-long sentence to both of you, consigning you both to happiness—or hell.

Then, as I said above, "Be wise"; that is, in taking the girl to be your wife for "better or worse" you are rather apt in the rosy sunshine of it all to forget that "worse."

Clouds may come and you've got to be prepared for them—that's what I mean by being wise.

Have no secrets from your wife and she will have none from you—and all will be plain sailing.

There may be times of trouble, little difficulties in the home which you don't foresee at first. Before you married you only did things for yourself; now that you are married you've got to chuck your *self* and do things for your wife—and later on for your children. You have got to catch yourself up in little bits of selfishness on your

---

3. Baden-Powell's name for a meeting place of Rovers.

part, such, for instance, as grousing at the food because it isn't exactly to your liking, and that sort of thing. Look at things from her point of view.

Grousing won't mend matters. Give instead some of the little love gifts of your courting days, of admiration and praise; give and take and SMILE all the time, but most especially at that time when most women get a little off their usual line, just before the first baby arrives. You've got to show your manliness and chivalry as her comforter and protector then.

If she is a little fractious it is through her love for you that she is so. To such attention she will respond. Women are not only more grateful than men, but their character shapes itself according as it is led by their man.

If he be nasty she will nag; if he be nice then she will be nicer, and then there's love and laughter in the home.

Children

Have you ever read Rudyard Kipling's story *They?*[4] I read it long before I was married, away out in the bush in Africa. The point in that story that went home to me was not the delightful description of English scenery, of the old-world home and garden. etc.; it was where the man imagined that he felt the clinging of little children's fingers in his hand; he only imagined it, but it thrilled him to the core.

And I had that imagination in my mind for parenthood as vividly as in the story. But when it came to pass that I actually felt a tiny hand in mine, the hand of my own little child, it gave me something more than a thrill—a feeling that has never worn off with custom, for it still does so—the heart-filling joy of it never grows less. . . .

But, there! Try it for yourself, in your own home, of your own making—and you will know what happiness is.

There is nothing like it—and it cannot be described, at least not by me.

So, as I have already said before, Heaven is not just a vague something somewhere up in the skies.

It is right here on earth, in your own home. It does not depend on riches or position, but rests with you to make it, in your own way, with your own brain, and heart, and hands. And you can do it if only you like to use these aright.

Responsibilities of Parenthood

But the joy of being a father brings with it a big responsibility. Children learn mainly by the example of their elders.

A grousing, selfish father must not be surprised if one day his son swears at him and goes his own way; the father will get later on what he gives out to-day. Train your children through Love rather than Fear.

A kindly parent gains a loving daughter and devoted sons. As I have suggested before, you will be happier if you aim to leave this world a little better for your being in it.

One step in this direction, and one which is within your reach as a father, is to make your boy a better man than yourself, by teaching him all that you know, what to aim for and what to avoid. Especially he will want your helpful advice when he, in his turn approaches Manhood.

4. Published in the collection *Traffics and Discoveries* (1904). Kipling (1865–1936), Anglo-Indian writer of fiction and poetry.

Think how much or how little your father did for you and go one better with your son.

You will be the happier for it.

But are you prepared for this? You may have been educated, or you may have educated yourself for your profession in life, which after all can only last a certain number of years, but have you gone through any training for this much more important point, on which depends so much the future lives of your children?

Have you had any practice yourself in the training and upbringing of boys? Of knowing their ways, of judging their temperaments, of developing their character?

This is all of grave importance to you in your responsible position as a parent.

I hope in the concluding chapters to give you a few practical suggestions about it.

Many parents object to their sons being told about sex matters and venereal disease. I have heard men curse their parents for not having told them. Personally I don't think that any parent who has seen something of the effects of ignorance, or of what is worse, the wrong notions which boys pick up all too soon from their fellows, would hesitate about warning his sons.

A Final Tip for Happiness

But I warn you that there is still another item needed to make your Heaven complete.

A man came to me who had been a big-game hunter and naturalist in Central Africa; he had been a farmer in British Columbia; he had started a tobacco plantation in East Africa; and he had seen the world in a life of adventure and romance. He had now settled down in an island of his own in the Indian Ocean in a glorious climate of sunshine amongst beautiful and healthy surroundings. One might well have thought, as he did at first, that this was going to be a heavenly haven after all his strenuous wanderings, but he had now come to discover a fly in the ointment.

He realised that he was living comfortably merely for himself. This conviction had now brought him to give up that *Existence* and exchange it for *Life*—that is, for activity in doing something for others.

I had myself gone through much the same experience when I finished my career as a soldier.[5] It had been a pretty varied and strenuous one, bringing a good deal of the rough along with the smooth, and I had loved every minute of it.

At the end my ambition was to settle down in a little farm in some out-of-the-way corner of the world.

I planned it out, but then the second thought arose which made me realise that idleness and indulgence of self did not mean happiness—that true happiness could only be got through Service.

So there is another chapter to this book.

To sum up:

Sex is universal in all forms of life—man, the "lower" animals, birds, fishes and reptiles. It is also found in the vegetable kingdom and in the most primitive forms of living matter. There is no sin in sex. The sin arises when sex is abused.

In primitive, unspoiled man, where sex is simply taken as a matter of course, the same problems do not arise as in "civilised" men. Here there has always been a certain shame and mystery about this matter. This must lead to much guilt and abuse. The problem of prostitution comes in and venereal disease appears. This form of disease is unknown among really primitive, unspoiled races. It is only when these races get contaminated by "civilisation" that such diseases appear. They are indeed dreadful

5. In 1910 Baden-Powell resigned from the army to devote himself wholly to the scouting movement.

afflictions. Syphilis if not promptly and properly treated may not only affect the person who contracts it, but he may pass it on to his offspring. Blindness, paralysis and insanity are all possible after-effects. Gonorrhœa, in the same way, may have lasting effects, and babies who are infected from the mother are often hopelessly blind. It is right that you should know about these diseases and what may be the consequences of promiscuous sex. It happens fairly often that a girl who has been with men and who is not a real prostitute, may have a slight form of venereal disease, which shows so little that she may not even realise she has it. You see how dangerous this sort of thing can be. If by unfortunate folly you or your friends ever acquired any form of venereal disease, the only thing to remember is to go at *once* to your Doctor. With modern methods of treatment these diseases can be cured when taken in time.

Remember that the ideal to aim at is for a man to be as clean as the girl he is going to marry. If there were sex-equality in this matter it would be a great step towards a healthier attitude. However, you cannot expect to solve all these difficult problems which social reformers and others have studied for many years with little result up to the present! You can each one of you, however, do your bit in bringing about a better state of affairs. Sex is often the matter for sly, obscene jokes when there is really nothing funny about it. As we have seen it is part of all living things and only require proper management.

What Others Have Said on the Subject

Men ought to be mighty good to women, for Nature gave them the big end of the log to lift and mighty little strength to do it with (*Abraham Lincoln*).

Have a heart that never hardens, and a temper that never tries, and a touch that never hurts (*Charles Dickens*).[6]

Whoso findeth a wife findeth a good thing and the favour of the Lord (*Proverbs* xviii. 22).

Health is worth more than wealth.

Cleanliness is next to Godliness.

A "Gentleman" is a bloke wot keeps even 'is toenails clean.

Fear of a father does not necessarily mean respect for him.

The cane often makes the coward and the liar.

Men! With the help of God, be MEN (*Heard at St. Gervais Church, Paris*).

As man was created for Health, so was man created for Happiness (*Maeterlinck*).[7]

Let not thy fancy be guided by thine eye, nor let thy will be formed by thy fancy; let thy understanding moderate between thine eye and thy fancy (*F. Quarles*).[8]

Helpful Books

The Care of the Body. F. Cavanagh (Methuen),
That Body of Yours. J. W. Barton (Hodder & Stoughton).

1922

6. British novelist (1812–1870). The quotation is from *Our Mutual Friend* (1864–65).
7. Maurice Maeterlinck (1862–1949), Belgian poet, dramatist, and essayist. The quotation is from *Wisdom and Destiny* (1898).
8. Francis Quarles (1592–1644), British poet.

ROBIE H. HARRIS *and* MICHAEL EMBERLEY
b. 1940   *b. 1960*

Robie Harris and Michael Emberley's message—"it's perfectly normal"—is not entirely new in the history of books on sexuality for children: variants of the refrain reassured readers of *The Child* at the end of the nineteenth century, and early in the twentieth century Robert Baden-Powell even stated that masturbation is natural. The scope of what is declared to be normal has steadily increased, however, and the declaration's tone has changed strikingly. The lecture has given way to reassuring friendly conversation, and high-minded seriousness has been replaced by humor and an emphasis on fun. In addition, the audience is younger. Whereas Baden-Powell wrote *Rovering to Success* for older adolescents and young men, Harris and Emberley address preteens.

Sexuality is only one subject covered by courtesy books, advice books, and books of instruction for children, but changes in its treatment illustrate how larger social changes have dramatically affected what children are expected to know in order to function successfully in society. When most children lived either on farms (raising animals) or in cramped city dwellings, often sharing sleeping spaces and even beds with adults, knowledge about sex was almost unavoidable. As sleeping and living spaces were separated and society became more urbanized, sex became private and secret. Today, when sexual references and representations of sexual activity permeate the media, and when American culture puts unprecedented value on individual choice, the need to convey explicit sexual knowledge to children has become increasingly urgent.

It is that need to which Robie Harris and Michael Emberley have responded. Emberley was born into a household where writing and illustrating children's books was part of daily life: his father, Ed, is a well-known writer and illustrator (sometimes of books by his mother) and he and his sister, Rebecca, followed the same career. His first publication was *Dinosaurs! A Drawing Book* (1980), a book that instructed children how to draw ten different dinosaurs, and his best-known is probably the picture book *Ruby* (1990), a retelling of the Red Riding Hood story (for further biographical information, see *Ruby* in the Fairy Tales section, above).

Robie Harris, the daughter of a physician and a biologist, earned a B.A. from Wheaton College (1962) and a master's degree in teaching from the Bank Street College of Education (1970). She began writing collaboratively in the 1960s as a member of the Bank Street College of Education's Writing Laboratory. A freelance author since 1975—her first book was *Before You Were Three: How You Began to Walk, Talk, Explore, and Have Feelings* (1977, with Elizabeth Levy), aimed at middle graders—she has worked in a Headstart program, directed an afterschool program, been a second-grade master teacher, and coauthored segments of *Captain Kangaroo*, a pioneering educational television show for children (1955–84). Harris has always involved herself in creating conditions in which children can thrive. When she moved to a new community without adequate playground facilities for her young son (the first of two), she helped organize other mothers to design and develop the playground that was eventually built—though too late for Harris's own children. Her collaboration with Michael Emberley, which began when she spotted him signing copies of *Ruby* at a bookstore, has been long and successful.

Their first book together was the award-winning *It's Perfectly Normal: A Book about Changing Bodies, Growing Up, Sex, and Sexual Health* (1994), and other books about sexuality, babies, and growing up followed: *Happy Birth Day!* (1996), *It's So Amazing! A Book about Eggs, Sperm, Birth, Babies, and Families* (1999), and *Hi, New Baby!* (2000). With *Hello Benny! What It's Like to Be a Baby* (2002) they began a new series in which they plan to consider in turn each of the first five years of life. Each book clearly details the physiological and social stages of life, dealing as well with newer concerns such as HIV/AIDS and abortion.

The conversation format of *It's Perfectly Normal* derives in part from the dialogue between writer and artist, as they create a mix of picture and text that appeals to readers in an age in which television is the dominant medium. That conversation succeeds because the collaboration between author and illustrator is so effective.

As Harris and Emberley work together, the narrative acknowledges the tendency of information about sex to become by turn scary or silly or funny or gross. The characters, the boldly curious bird (who wants to know more) and the embarrassed bee (who doesn't), are a comedy team; in their voices, the unspeakable becomes easily sayable. A term like *masturbating* is "just another big word," according to the bee. The book recognizes what Harris calls the "blend of curiosity, disinterest and apprehension" found in most discussions about sex, not just those among children. The cartoons are explicit without being erotic, and they reflect the shapes of real people—neither model-perfect nor grotesque. By mixing narrative exposition, conversations between the bird and the bee, and accurate diagrams, Harris and Emberley present information in the dialogic form appropriate for a twenty-first-century audience.

Introduction
Lots of Questions

Changing Bodies, Growing Up, Sex, and Sexual Health

Sometime between the ages of nine and fifteen, kids' bodies begin to change and grow into adult bodies.

> Gr-r-reat!

> Gr-r-ross!

Most kids wonder about and have lots of questions about what will be happening to them as their bodies change and grow during this time.

> Not me.

> Me.

It's perfectly normal for kids to be curious about and want to know about their changing and growing bodies. Most of the changes—but not all—that take place during this time make it possible for humans to make a baby and give birth to a baby. And making a baby has a lot to do with sex.

> Well, I do know that this stuff is not just about the birds and the bees.

> It's about the facts of life.

Sex is about a lot of things—bodies, growing up, families, babies, love, caring, curiosity, feelings, respect, responsibility, biology, and health. There are times when sickness and danger can be a part of sex, too.

Most kids wonder about and have lots of questions about sex. It's also perfectly normal to want to know about sex.

> Whew! I was feeling weird.

> I was feeling perfectly normal.

You may wonder why it's a good idea to learn some facts about bodies, about growing up, about sex, and about sexual health. It's important because these facts can help you stay healthy, take good care of yourself, and make good decisions about yourself as you are growing up and for the rest of your life.

Besides, learning about these things can be fascinating and fun.

> Doesn't sound like that much fun to me.

> Maybe you are weird.

Life Writing

The story of someone's life begins not "once upon a time," but "in *this* time and place." In life writing for children, the timelessness of the fairy tale is replaced with the magic of uniqueness. Although life writing is in part concerned with facts, its origins—like those of folktales—lie in the oral tradition. The legends, epics, and chivalric romances of the ancient bards and medieval troubadours awakened an interest in tales of individual acts of bravery or treachery, in heroic or tragic figures, that has never waned since ancient times. Interestingly, the biographies, autobiographies, and factual accounts that writers have documented and fixed in script have often been transformed into legend even into the twenty-first century. Ultimately, the truth of life writing depends on art, and writers have employed many original forms of art to represent their lives and the lives of famous and common people.

Definitions

"Life writing" is used here as an umbrella term that covers narratives found in such forms as autobiography, biography, letters, memoir, and personal essays. Much of its appeal is based in the access it seems to offer to the "truth" of a real person's life. Where biography introduces a "self" to the reader by describing public actions and events as well as more private concerns such as relationships, emotions, and motivations, personal life writing (in autobiography and memoir, for example) invites the reader to accompany the author on a significantly more introspective journey. Although aspects of life writing mimic the conventions of the novel or short story— the subject may function as a "character," and the timing of events may be contracted or conversations paraphrased in the retelling—life writing is essentially a form of nonfiction prose that nonetheless offers an argument about the subject to the reader. Maxine Hong Kingston's *The Woman Warrior: Memoirs of a Girlhood among Ghosts* (1976) blends autobiography, myth, and Chinese history with Kingston's personal mythmaking as a means to understand the tensions between gender and generations in midcentury China and America. When the children's author Jean Fritz began to think about her childhood in China, she found that her memory "came out in lumps." She then retold the events of her childhood as a story, contracting her early life into two years, "told as truly as I can tell it."

Life writing found in letters and diaries is wholly private and not meant to be read by anyone other than the recipient or the self. Thus, the intended readership may be an audience of one or it may include readers from all over the globe. The diary that chronicles more than two years in hiding in Amsterdam in a tense, tragicomic eight-person society before Anne Frank's death in a Nazi concentration camp has become one of the most penetrating voices to sound and reject the evils of the Holocaust.

The Development of Life Writing

The wide acceptance of life writing as "true" and therefore more valuable and weighty than fictional forms such as the romance—discredited as false and frivolous, and thus harmful to readers—affected the development of the early English novel. To gain the authority of truth for their character-driven fictions, Daniel Defoe in *Robinson Crusoe* (1719) and Samuel Richardson in *Pamela* (1740–41) used diaries, letters, and journals as they created epistolary and journalistic novels. This generic blending maintained a strong presence into the nineteenth century; in novels such as Charles Dickens's *David Copperfield* (1849–50) and Charlotte Brontë's *Jane Eyre* (1847), the reader is drawn into a personal relationship with a protagonist who tells the story of his or her life from childhood through adulthood—sometimes using direct address, as the narrator of *Jane Eyre* famously does ("Reader, I married him").

In *A Poetics of Women's Autobiography* (1987), the scholar Sidonie Smith comments that the self-conscious autobiographer "joins together facets of remembered experience—descriptive, impressionistic, dramatic, analytic—as she constructs a narrative that promises both to capture the specificities of personal experience and to cast her self-interpretation in a timeless, idealized mold for posterity." Similarly, the biographer sifts, weighs, and combines events and the subject's character into a whole that communicates a coherent "self" to the reader. Contemporary autobiography and biography, which routinely top best-seller lists, have tended to explode the notion of the private, endorsing a reading experience that invites intimate identification with the author.

Early forms of life writing, by contrast, sought neither exposure nor confession but rather aimed to celebrate inspirational lives. The first-century *Lives* by Plutarch, first translated into English by Sir Thomas North in 1579 as *Lives of the Noble Grecians and Romans*, outlined the prowess of men notable for their military and political deeds. The earliest Western autobiographies were medieval and Renaissance narratives of the subject's relationship with God. One example is *The Book of Margery Kempe* (1436), dictated by the illiterate Christian mystic to a scribe. By the eighteenth century, however, the allure of the private becoming public began to color autobiographical life writing. Women such as the cross-dressing Charlotte Charke (daughter of the well-known dramatist Colley Cibber), who wrote the *Narrative of the Life of Mrs Charlotte Charke* (1775), brought the lives of scandalous women into the drawing room. Similarly, the five-volume *Newgate Calendar* (1773; other versions were published into the nineteenth century) appealed to the public's taste for sordid details about notorious criminals. A higher-brow form of biographical compilation could be found in Samuel Johnson's prefaces to the *Lives of the English Poets* (1779–81). Indeed, one of the most famous biographies of the eighteenth century was *The Life of Samuel Johnson* (1791), in which James Boswell raised the standards of the genre through his insights, frankness, intimate detail, and narrative skill. Other important innovations to autobiography include Benjamin Franklin's *Autobiography* (1793), which featured the debut of the self-invented American, and William Wordsworth's *The Prelude: or, Growth of a Poet's Mind* (published posthumously in 1850), the first autobiography in verse.

Gender and Life Writing

Though life writing was originally the province of the culturally or politically significant "great man," works by women gained popularity and prominence in the nineteenth century. Elizabeth Gaskell's 1857 biography of her friend and fellow novelist Charlotte Brontë followed the dictates of Victorian propriety in telling Brontë's life story; at the same time, it heralded a new direction in serious biographical treatment of women's lives. The prolific Scots writer Margaret Oliphant, whose *Autobiography* was published in 1899, was spurred to comment on the difference between male and female autobiography while reading John Addington Symonds's autobiography: "I have been reading the life of Mr. Symonds, and it makes me almost laugh (though little laughing is in my heart) to think of the strange difference between this prosaic little narrative [Oliphant's autobiography], all about the facts of a life so simple as mine, and his elaborate self-discussions." Linda Peterson comments in "Women Writers and Self-Writing" (2001) that the "link between domesticity and authorship or artistry was explicitly made in many women's auto/biographies of the nineteenth century; with a few notable exceptions, most memoirs by women authors and artists turn away from the *chroniques scandaleuses,* with its association of women's self-writing and indecorous self-display, even prostitution, and embrace instead the genre of domestic memoir." The nineteenth-century domestic memoir included diaries of girlhood written by talented but unknown young women such as Emily Shore, an amateur naturalist, "home daughter," and private intellectual, who died of tuberculosis in 1839, at age nineteen. In 1891 her sisters, the poets Arabella Shore and Louisa Shore, edited and published a selection of entries from Emily's diary. The poet Lucy Larcom's autobiography, *A New England Girlhood: Outlined from Memory* (1889), was written for girl readers and described Larcom's early years as a mill girl in a Lowell, Massachusetts, textile factory. Nancy F. Cott's introduction to the 1986 reprint states that Larcom's work both "celebrates the advantages of collectivity, education, and paid work for girls" and upholds the ideals of true womanhood.

Life Writing and Young Readers: Inspiration and Motivation

Life writing directed specifically at the young was intended to inspire child readers to appreciate the great men and women of the past or to emulate their qualities of bravery, loyalty, self-sacrifice, and patriotism. Collective biographies—"role model anthologies," to use Allison Booth's phrase—were popular in nineteenth-century Britain and America. John M. Darton's *Famous Girls Who Have Become Illustrious Women: Forming Models for Imitation for the Young Women of England* (1864) stands as a good example of the genre. Darton reminds his audience that greatness need not attach only to actions of the famous; it can also be achieved through depth of feeling and devotion to duty: "This is the lesson of our little volume: not that we should be mere copyists of the great ones who have emblazoned their names on the roll of fame, but that we should imbibe their spirit, learn of their devotion and endurance, and, as far as in us lies, in the discharge of daily duty obtain that which is of far greater price than fame—the approval of 'the still small voice,' which utters the blessed words—'Well done, thou good and faithful servant.'" In *A Book of Golden Deeds of All Times and All Lands* (1864) by Charlotte Mary Yonge, Yonge tells thrilling stories about actual persons whose Golden Deeds, informed by the "spirit that gives itself for others," are meant to stir her young male and female readers to similar works of unconscious selflessness. By contrast, in their collective biography for girls titled *Girls Who Made Good* (1930), Winifred and Frances Kirkland focus on the ethic of rising to public success through hard work. Lively sketches featured artists (e.g., Rosa Bonheur), politicians (Lady Astor), scientists (Marie Curie), and businesswomen (the New York restaurateur Alice Foote Macdougall), among other contemporaries or near-contemporaries who, through their efforts, improved the lives of others. Although she was a scientist in her own right, the biographical sketch of "assistant astronomer" Caroline Herschel (1750–1848) in Clara L. Balfour's *Women Worth Emulating* (1877) emphasizes Caroline Herschel's sisterly role and her qualities as a self-effacing, helpful, and humble woman. One wonders what additional scientific contributions Herschel might have made if she had received the support from family members and the community of scientists, or the patronage of royalty, that her brother, the astronomer Sir William Herschel, enjoyed.

In *Facts to Correct Fancies* (1840), the wise father corrects the erroneous view asserted by his son that only men performed important deeds or lived lives worthy of admiration. Similarly, the biographical sketches, essays, and photographs of notable African American men, women, and children included in the 1920–21 periodical *The Brownies' Book*—whose founders explicitly saw it as a tool to "uplift the race"—refute the argument (implied by the absence of literature about African Americans) that the only appropriate subjects for biographical treatment were white. The utter absence of this counternarrative from other children's magazines was felt acutely. In a letter printed in "The Grown-Ups' Corner," one New York City mother urges the editors of *The Brownies' Book* to emphasize the accomplishments of "colored men and women of achievement." She concludes, "Our little girl is dark brown, and we want her to be proud of her color and to know that it isn't the kind of skin people have that makes them great." Introducing *The Best of the Brownies' Book* (1996), Marian Wright Edelman comments, "Going out into their 1920s world, black children faced every sign, symbol, slogan, and slight needed to convince them they were second best, at best. But reading an essay by Langston Hughes or Nella Larsen, answering a quiz about the contributions of heroes and heroines of their race, reading profiles of their forebears, and seeing children who looked like them in photos and drawings was a strong antidote."

For adolescents faced with life-changing events—whether the trauma of war or the adventure of a new home—journals and letters have often been a means of preserving or creating an identity. Fourteen-year-old Maryanne Caswell wrote a series of letters to her grandmother between 1887 and 1888 as her family traveled west across Canada from Ontario to Saskatchewan. The letters, which first appeared in the Saskatoon *Star-Phoenix* newspaper, were published in 1964 as a book titled *Pioneer Girl* and have since been reprinted. *The Diary of a Young Girl* by Anne Frank, mentioned above, is perhaps the best-known example of a wartime diary. Initially written as a conventional outlet for a schoolgirl's private thoughts about her parents, friends, and school, Anne Frank's diary quickly became a source of vital comfort as she and her family were forced to flee from Nazi oppression and go into hiding. The diary became a second self for the passionate and confined girl. Later still, after listening to a radio broadcast that suggested that wartime diaries would serve an important purpose after the conflict had ended, Anne decided to rewrite, edit, and shape her diary for eventual publication. Anne's ambition—to become a famous writer—was ultimately realized. *The Diary of a Young Girl* has sold tens of millions of copies worldwide, and has inspired other young writers to confide their private thoughts as well as to imagine the potential for their words to transform the world through those selfsame private thoughts. In her chronicle of living in war-torn Bosnia in the early 1990s, young Zlata Filipović self-consciously invokes Anne Frank when she writes, "Hey Diary! You know what I think? Since Anne Frank called her diary Kitty, maybe I could give you a name too" (*Zlata's Diary: A Child's Life in Sarajevo*, 1994). She chooses "Mimmy." Judith Kerr's *When Hitler Stole Pink Rabbit* (1971), a fictionalized account of Kerr's early years as a refugee in Europe in pre- and postwar Europe, focuses not on losing her home but on positive changes that followed, such as making new friends, learning new languages, and discovering fresh means of expression.

The genre of life writing for children gained recognition when the first such American biography to win an award for excellence featured the famous children's author Louisa May Alcott. Although *Invincible Louisa* (1933) skips rather lightly over the personal repercussions of living a selfless life—Cornelia Meig argues that Alcott's "happy death" resulted from the fulfilled desire to take care of her family members, "the whole of what [Alcott] had wanted from life"—the biography combines admiration for her subject's indomitable spirit and work ethic with accurate details of Alcott's life and times. In the tradition of Meigs's biography of Louisa May Alcott, biographies of American heroes have continued to garner praise and honors. Russell Freedman's award-winning, unsentimental, and lavishly illustrated *Lincoln: A Photobiography* (1987) reveals the sixteenth American president through photographs found on virtually every other page, and through Lincoln's own words. Milton Meltzer, author of more than eighty social histories for young readers—five of which have been nominated for the National Book Award—has dedicated his creative life to writing penetrating and honest nonfiction for children and young adults. In "The Social Responsibility of the Writer" (1989), he remarks: "In writing biography, whether of the famous or the obscure, I want to give young readers vision, hope, energy. . . . My aim is to challenge young Americans to examine the past as they move into their future. And you cannot do that without stirring their feelings so that they live the history of others, as though it were their own personal experience."

Jean Fritz's short biographies, which primarily treat figures from American history, employ a lighthearted style that complements the lightly worn but extensive research that undergirds them. In explaining why the genre attracts her, Fritz writes, "Something about a personality in the past commands a personal response in the present. Not admiration, necessarily; not love. Often, in fact, the relationship that I develop is a love/hate relationship. I grapple with a person as one sometimes does with a member of one's own family, in an attempt to reach a kind of understanding and arrive at acceptance" (*Worlds of Childhood*, 1989). For Fritz, too, the work of the biographer is intimately connected with his or her own autobiography: "Writing biographies for any age becomes a spiraling process, circling away from oneself, circling back with messages from afar, and all the time circling around one's own autobiography." The death of her father at age ninety-six severed an important link to Fritz's childhood, and she was then convinced that it was time to complete a task first contemplated much earlier: she produced a memoir of her childhood in China, *Homesick: My Own Story* (1982).

Homesick is part of a growing genre of children's life writing—the memoir/autobiography of children's book authors, which satisfies the curiosity of children who wonder about the lives of those who create their favorite books. Some notable contemporary additions to this subgenre include Tomie de Paola's series of picture books that feature his child self growing up on 26 Fairmont Avenue; Lois Lowry's "snapshot"-style photo-memoir, *Looking Back: A Book of Memories* (1998); the Australian Mem Fox's whimsically titled memoir of her life and career as a writer for children, *Dear Mem Fox, I Have Read All Your Books Even the Pathetic Ones: And Other Incidents in the Life of a Children's Book Author* (1992); Gary Soto's collection of short essays about his childhood in the barrios of Fresno, California, collected in *A Summer Life* (1990) and *Living up the Street: Narrative Recollections* (1985); and Walter Dean Myers's autobiography of growing up in Harlem, *Bad Boy* (2002). Not all these memoirs seek to inspire or amuse their readers. Autobiography written for a young audience can be as stark and sad as that written for adults. The humorist Roald Dahl's account of his sometimes brutal childhood, titled *Boy: Tales of Childhood* (1984), is marginally softened by the whimsical illustrations by Quentin Blake. Art Spiegelman's *Maus I* (1987) and *Maus II* (1991) recall how the Holocaust affected his family life. Beverly Cleary's *The Girl from Yamhill* (1988) details her lonely childhood and complicated relationship with her mother. The illustrator Anita Lobel's unstinting memoir of the waste and suffering of World War II seen through the eyes of a child, *No Pretty Pictures: A Child of War* (1998), concludes, "In the end, what is there to say? I was born far, far away, on a bloody continent at a terrible time. I lived there for a while. I live [in America] now. . . . Mine is only another story." Gary Paulsen's *Guts: The True Story behind "Hatchet" and the Brian Books* (2001) recounts to readers the events that inform his series of books about surviving in the wilderness.

Contemporary children's biographies and autobiographies feature subjects notable in sports, entertainment, politics, and history. Notwithstanding the works just described, this growing genre is almost always upbeat in tone and intent, urging the child reader to overcome obstacles, to do something splendid with his or her life, to respect the talents of others, or to embrace self-sacrifice. Scholastic's "Dear America" fictional journals (including the "My America" and "My Name Is America" series) function as "creative" life writing; they preserve the intimacy of the diary while at the same time using the experiences of ordinary children to tell stories about important chapters in the development of America, such as the colonial period, the Dust Bowl era, and the years of westward expansion. These books attempt to impart to children the immediacy of history by way of sympathetic identification with the imagined diarist's voice, urging readers to take "the journey back into time through the eyes of the children who lived it." As was demonstrated in the fiction of Samuel Richardson and Daniel Defoe so long ago, life writing can be fictional yet maintain a connection to "truth."

FACTS TO CORRECT FANCIES
1840

The tradition of women writing anonymously or pseudonymously to protect their identities is a long one. Given the prevalence of anonymous publication by both men and women in the early days of printing, it is impossible to tell when works by women began to appear in English. Yet for women the appeal of anonymity continued to be strong, as publication was viewed as an affront to female propriety. At times, British female authors assumed male names in order to professionalize their work as writers—perhaps the most famous example was that of George Eliot (Mary Ann Evans). Nineteenth-century American women writers tended instead to choose feminine names such as "Fanny Fern" or "Pansy" as their noms de plume. Hack writers (male and female) who produced prodigious amounts of work in magazines, newspapers, novels, annuals, and books of poetry could disguise their output through the use of pen names. Often, as in the case of *Facts to Correct Fancies; or, Short Narratives compiled from the Biography of Remarkable Women* (1840), the author would choose a descriptor such

as "A Lady" or "A Mother" both to shield her from indecorous publicity and to support her authority as a writer. In such books for the young, the wisdom of a good parent is sufficient testimony for the educational material contained within the book.

Hannah More (1745–1833), the British Evangelical writer and social reformer, sums up the aims of *Facts to Correct Fancies* on its title page: "Women, in their course of action, describe a smaller circle than men; but the perfection of a circle consists, not in its dimension, but in its correctness." The volume aimed both to rescue Woman from denigration by emphasizing the intelligence, bravery, and loyalty of a few women from history (the most well-known to today's readers are Queen Elizabeth and Joan of Arc) and to underscore the importance of domestic duties to feminine "correctness." The frame tale of the Stanley children's quarrel, while didactic in intention, also creates a narrative thread that helps enliven the history lessons that follow. The illustration to the Lady Jane Grey segment is from an 1845 American edition.

From Facts to Correct Fancies; or, Short Narratives compiled from the Biography of Remarkable Women, written for children, by a Mother

CHAPTER I

"Well, it is very provoking!" exclaimed little Charlotte Stanley, throwing down her doll, with an unusual violence of manner, "well, it is very provoking!"

"What is it that you complain of, Charlotte?" said her father, who had just entered the room where he beheld his two children, Philip, the eldest, a boy of twelve years of age, standing perfectly erect, in the attitude of one who considers he has just made a very wise observation; while the little Charlotte, a rosy faced girl of nine, seated on the floor with the tears rolling down her cheeks, looked so unhappy, that Mr. Stanley was utterly at a loss to imagine what could have occurred, so deeply to affect the merry little girl.

The cause of her uneasiness was, however, quickly made known, as she replied to her father's inquiry. "Philip says, father, that women have not half the sense of men, and that I shall never be fit for anything but to darn stockings and make pies and puddings."

"Well, my dear," said Mr. Stanley, "you need not be so much troubled by such an opinion. Is your dear mother fitted for no other employments than those Philip has mentioned? So far from it, the instances we have on record of those women who have had the opportunity and inclination to cultivate their natural abilities, prove, most clearly, that nature has been by no means so partial in her gifts of intellect as is frequently supposed. In order, however, to bring down Philip's extravagant notions of man's superiority, and for your consolation, I will this evening relate some short histories of a few of those women who have been celebrated for their high acquirements."

But it is necessary to explain how Philip Stanley, possessed of a sensible, well-judging father, should have been led to a conclusion so opposed to gentlemanly feeling, or common sense.

The truth was, that a year before, Philip had been removed from home, and placed at the grammar school at Fairbourne, where, mixing with boys older than himself, he had insensibly been led to affect their manners and opinions, and consequently that contempt for females so general amongst the would-be men of a large school. Philip was neither ill-natured nor wanting in affection towards his mother and sister, but an excessive dread of ridicule often overcame his better feelings, and when the boys at Fairbourne school called him a milksop, and said he had been pinned to his mother's apron strings, he, without considering the subject, at once admitted they were right, and persuaded himself that it was indeed very ridiculous to employ his thoughts so much about a little girl like Charlotte. Accordingly, on his return to his father's house, he considered it necessary to manifest the improvement that had taken place in his opinions, as well as his rapid advance towards manhood, by despising the amusements and occupations of his sister.

The loss of Philip as a playmate was of itself sufficiently vexatious, for Mr. Stanley lived in a very retired situation, and the little girl had no companions of her own age. Her brother had, till the period of his going to school, supplied this deficiency, and Charlotte shed her first bitter tears at his departure, lamenting that she had now no one to assist her in gathering wild flowers, or setting her baby-house in order. Her mother had endeavoured to console her, by leading her to anticipate the arrival of the holidays, when her playfellow would be restored to her. The Christmas vacation was, however, spent by Philip at an uncle's house, and much did Charlotte regret this disappointment; especially when the pond where Philip used to skate was so completely frozen, and the snow lay on the ground, so temptingly drifted into every corner, "just fit," as she expressed herself to her mother, "to make beautiful snowballs."

Time, however, will pass, whether we be merry or sad, and the summer was now come, bringing happiness to the heart of the little girl as the day approached, when Mr. Stanley would go to Fairbourne to bring home her dear Philip.

What then was her grief and dismay at hearing him reply to her request that he would admire the beautiful way in which she had dressed her doll entirely by herself—"Don't torment me, Charlotte; I want to read this newspaper; really you girls have no sense."

Poor Charlotte ventured to remonstrate, saying that Philip did not formerly object to her amusements.

"Yes," replied he, "but that was because I had never been fortunate enough to have boys for companions, and I assure you I was quizzed[1] enough when I first went to Fairbourne, for talking so much of you, Charlotte. However, I soon left off such childish habits, and learned to think with other men, that women are fit for nothing but to darn stockings and make pies and puddings."

Now this was too much for poor Charlotte. She had been accustomed to hear herself called a sensible, intelligent girl, and this bringing down of all her ideas of self-importance, was more than she could patiently endure. Accordingly she vented her indignation in the exclamation recorded at the commencement of this chapter. However, her father's speech had somewhat reassured her, and she impatiently awaited the evening which was to bring a refutation of Philip's reproach.

At length the tea equipage was removed, and the party assembled round the open window; Mrs. Stanley provided with her work, Charlotte engaged in making a new pinafore for her doll, and Philip looking very much as if he wished he were not too old, and too manly to employ himself as formerly, in making nets for his father's fruit-trees. He could not, however, so speedily give up his newly acquired ideas of dignity, and consequently sat patting a favourite little spaniel while Mr. Stanley related.

The History of Lady Jane Grey

"As I am somewhat partial to my own countrywomen," said Mr. Stanley, "I have chosen the history of this most accomplished and unfortunate English lady[2] as my first attack upon Philip's unreasonable prejudices. You have read of her, my boy, although you probably may not have met with some of the particulars I shall relate. Pray do you happen to know who she was?"

"Yes, father, she was the eldest daughter of the Duke of Suffolk, who lived in the reign of Henry the Eighth."

"Good," said Mr. Stanley. "Well, this young lady, although born in a station where pleasure was always at command, yet early manifested an eager thirst for learning. She was educated with her cousin, Edward the Sixth, and learned Greek, Latin, Arabic, and Chaldee, with French and Italian. She was thoroughly acquainted with ancient and modern literature, and devoted herself to the study of philosophy. Do not imagine, however, my dear Charlotte, that, because she was so much more learned than the generality of women, she neglected what may be called the peculiar refinements of female education. It is especially recorded that she wrote a fine hand, understood music, and excelled in all womanly attainments. She is styled by Dr. Burnett in his history of the Reformation, 'the wonder and delight of all who knew her.'

"You may perhaps be surprised, my dear children, that a girl situated as Lady Jane Grey, so far above the necessity of mental exertion, should nevertheless, in her earliest years, have shown that devotion to study which characterized the whole of her short life. In explanation of this, there is a story told of a visit paid to Jane's parents by Roger Ascham, the tutor to the princess Elizabeth.[3]

"Lady Jane was then residing with her family at Bradgate Park, in Leicestershire.

---

1. Ridiculed or mocked.
2. Lady Jane Grey (1537–1554), a grandniece of Henry VIII, was Queen of England for nine days in 1553. At the death of Edward VI (1537–1553; r. 1547–53), a struggle ensued over the succession; it pitted Lady Jane Grey against Mary Tudor (later Mary I, 1516–1558; r. 1553–58), a Catholic daughter of Henry VIII. Mary emerged victorious in this contest and ultimately had Lady Jane Grey beheaded.
3. Future Queen of England (1533–1603; r. 1558–1603), younger daughter of Henry VIII.

On the arrival of Ascham, he found Lady Jane alone, reading Plato with great apparent delight. He expressed his surprise that she was not out hunting with her parents, when she replied, that she had more pleasure in reading than in hunting, adding, 'they know not what true pleasure means.' He then inquired how it happened that she had acquired tastes so unusual at her age. She replied that it was to be attributed to the circumstances in which she had been brought up. 'I have,' said she, 'severe parents and a gentle tutor. My parents expected perfection in everything; and if I did anything wrong, they threatened, rebuked, and have even beaten me. When I went back to my tutor, everything was changed; he instructs so mildly and pleasantly that the hours pass unconsciously; everything but learning brings me sorrow, so study has become a pleasure.'"

"Oh! father, how very unhappy Lady Jane Grey must have been," said Charlotte; "what cruel people her father and mother were!"

"Unnecessarily harsh, my love, they undoubtedly were, but I dare say not intentionally cruel; they wished their daughter to be thoroughly educated, and they pursued the plan that seemed to them most likely to effect their purpose. Great allowance must also be made for them on account of the customs of the age. Parental authority was then far more strictly enforced than it is now, and children were kept in order more by fear than affection. The daughters, even of people of the first rank in society, were obliged to stand at the side of the cupboard, which in those days served the purpose of a side board, when any company was present, unless indeed, through any especial favour, they were permitted to have a cushion to kneel upon, and upon every trifling occasion they were found fault with, and often, even in womanhood, were corrected by their mothers with the large fan it was at that time the fashion to carry. But to return. As I have given you some idea of the character of this gentle and unfortunate young lady, let us hear, Philip, whether you cannot tell Charlotte some particulars of her history."

"Yes, father, I remember that she was executed when she was only eighteen, by the wicked Queen Mary, because she was persuaded by her father and the Duke of Northumberland, whose son she had married, to claim the crown upon the death of Edward the Sixth. But I do not understand, father, how, if she were so very good and fond of learning, she could ever consent to usurp the throne, because, you know, it certainly was Mary's right."

"True, my son, but this circumstance was only one of the misfortunes that seemed to follow Lady Jane through her brief but most eventful career. It is said that when on Edward's death she was informed that he had settled the crown on the Duchess of Suffolk, who resigned her right in favour of her daughter, poor Lady Jane received the news of her advancement with grief and consternation: that she positively rejected the brilliant offer, pleading the superior right of the princess Mary, and ended by declaring that her own principles would not suffer her to agree to the proposal. Accustomed, however, as she had always been, to obey implicitly the commands of her parents, she was unable long to resist, especially as her husband and mother joined their entreaties to those of her father and the Duke of Northumberland. She did not, however, give way without many tears and forebodings of the fearful consequences that afterwards ensued. Indeed, when on her being proclaimed in London, the people rallied round Mary as the rightful heir, Jane immediately resigned, saying, that she gladly returned to her private station, convinced that she had been guilty of a great fault in allowing her principles to be overcome by authority, but that in resigning the crown she had usurped, both her inclination and her judgment concurred. This, however, was not sufficient to satisfy the resentment of Mary, who immediately on her accession, ordered the arrest of Lady Jane Grey and her husband, together with her father, and the Duke of Northumberland. The Duke of Suffolk succeeded in gaining a pardon, but Northumberland, with the Lady Jane, and Guildford Dudley, her husband, were excuted. She was eminently pious, and met her fate with the utmost meekness and resignation. It is said, that on the day fixed for her execution, her husband, to whom she was tenderly attached, expressed a desire to have an interview with her. On his request being made known to Lady Jane, she steadily refused, saying it would destroy the courage of both. She saw from her window her husband led to execution, and on her way to the scaffold met his lifeless body. She was so overcome that she burst into tears, but dried them again directly on hearing of his courage and constancy. When she reached the scaffold, she requested the executioner would despatch her quickly; then kneeling down and saying, 'Lord, into thy hands I commend my spirit,' she meekly bowed her head to the fatal stroke."

When Mr. Stanley had ended his narrative, little Charlotte quitted her seat, and climbing her father's knee, imprinted a kiss of gratitude on his cheek, but she forebore to make any observation, lest Philip, whom she dearly loved, should imagine she was glorying in his defeat.

Mr. Stanley, observing that his son made no remark, turned to him, and guessing the nature of his thoughts from the expression of his countenance, said, "I perceive, Philip, that you consider this an extreme case, and that there are few such women as Lady Jane Grey. It is true, such characters are uncommon, as are the circumstances that called forth her energies; nevertheless, it is somewhat unfair to argue of what women might be, from what they generally are. There is, too often, a degree of frivolity in their habits and pursuits, which obscures the brighter points in their character, and has frequently led the merely superficial observer to a severe and general condemnation. Yet there always have been, and I doubt not always will be, some splendid proofs that such an opinion is unfounded; and I believe, the wisest men are agreed, that with equal advantages, and in equally favourable circumstances, the attainments of women would rank nearly, if not quite, as high as those of men. This, however, is a subject which it is not necessary for us to discuss; I am only anxious to prove to you, Philip, that women are fit for higher occupations than you seem disposed to allot them, and at the same time, I would have my little Charlotte clearly understand that making puddings and darning stockings are by no means such contemptible employments as you have represented them, and may with the utmost propriety be performed by a well-educated woman."

"But, father," said Charlotte, "you surely do not think that Lady Jane Grey ever did such things?"

"I dare say not, my love, because she was in a situation to command the services of others; but there is no doubt that had she been reduced to a lower station in life, she would cheerfully have performed all the duties of her condition, among which these despised occupations might have been classified. But it is time you were in bed, you are now more than half asleep; to-morrow we will try to find another history suited to our purpose."

CLARA L. BALFOUR
1808–1878

Although she is little known today, the temperance activist Clara (Liddell) Balfour combined a life of social work—particularly on women's behalf—with a robust career as an editor and writer. Her publications included moral tracts against drinking, a history of women's participation in the temperance movement, children's books, and sketches of meritorious women, such as *Working Women of the Last Half-Century* (1854). Balfour resolutely believed that arguments about the "rights and wrongs" of women were only distractions from woman's duty to work for the betterment of society; she asserts in the introduction to *Working Women* that "the noble performance of duty is the best assertion of power; the careful development of mind and moral character the best barrier against injustice." In 1877, Balfour was elected president of the British Women's Temperance League.

Women Worth Emulating (1877) belongs to the genre of role-model anthologies offering young female readers examples of virtuous, intelligent, and diligent women who successfully advanced literature and science without sacrificing "womanly" qualities such as piety, domesticity, and family loyalty. In the preface Balfour declares: "Emulation is the spirit most desirable to arouse in the young. . . . It is with this purpose that the following varied selections of womanly worth and wisdom are presented to the young of their own sex; in the hope

that studious habits, intellectual pursuits, domestic industry, and sound religious principles, may be promoted and confirmed by such examples." The biographical sketch reprinted here celebrates and praises the amateur astronomer Caroline Herschel (1750–1848), who herself discovered eight comets and three nebulae (celestial bodies of gases and dust); at the same time, it subordinates her accomplishments to those of her more famous brother, Sir William Herschel (1738–1822), astronomer to King George III. Indeed, Balfour's writing imitated life: Herschel's great honor, the Royal Astronomical Society's gold medal, was awarded to her not for her own discoveries but for her work in arranging her late brother's catalogue of star clusters and nebulae.

A memorial address preached after Balfour's death (and published shortly thereafter) by the Reverend Dr. John Wood Todd similarly argues that Balfour's success in life lay within the blend of the domestic and intellectual: "no one has done more to illustrate and demonstrate the perfect compatibility and harmony of the highest mental culture with all that is comprehended in motherhood and domestic obligation. For in all the home-relationships and responsibilities of her position—as much as in the nurture of her tastes and in her intellectual toil—she was eminently one of those whom she described, as WOMEN WORTH EMULATING."

From Women Worth Emulating

CHAPTER III. MISS CAROLINE HERSCHEL
(Some Sisters of Memorable Men)

There is a hallowed charm in the relationship of sister, when its duties are tenderly felt and faithfully fulfilled. It has often been remarked that young men, who have grown up surrounded by a group of amiable sisters, or even in companionship with only one who possessed a loving heart and gentle mind, are easily known by their superior refinement and their deference to and respect for women. "I knew he must have had nice sisters," is a frequent comment, when the speech and deportment of a young man has led to an inquiry as to his family connections.

I do not say that many a young man has not attained mild, considerate, kindly manners who has never had a sister; but I hold that one of the most refining educational influences is possessed in families where the affection and innocent gaiety of the girls tempers the hardihood and roughness of the boys. The two sexes growing up together in the household do each other good. The sisters gain in frankness, courage, activity, and it may be, in solid intelligence, if the boys are conscientious; while the brothers become more considerate in act and speech, purer and gentler in thought and word and action.

The sweet, strong bond which nature knits at birth between the children of the same parents, nursed at the same bosom, fondled on the same lap, kneeling at the same household altar, ought to be able to defy the changes and vicissitudes of life, although these affect this relationship more than any other. Sons go forth to battle with the world, daughters marry and enter upon other and nearer ties and responsibilities; still the heart cannot be quite right which does not always retain and respond to the first early claims—the associations identified with childhood. Sad is it when the cares of the world obliterate the tender memories of early youth, or the pride of life dries up or diverts the fountains of affection which welled forth in the home of childhood.

To some true hearts this kindred tie, when it has been stretched across wide oceans to far distant lands, has bravely borne the strain, and grown the tighter by the firm clasp with which at each end it has been held. Multitudes might and do echo the kindly words of Goldsmith[1]—

> "Where'er I roam, whate'er new realms I see,
> My heart, untravelled, fondly turns to thee;
> Still to my brother turns, with ceaseless pain,
> And drags at each remove a lengthening chain."

In literary biography there are many memorable sisters of distinguished men. The poet Wordsworth testified as to the softening influence his sister, Miss Deborah Wordsworth,[2] exerted on his mind and manners, and the benefit he derived from her wise criticisms. From his own experience of a relationship that never was interrupted by any newer ties on Miss Wordsworth's part,—for she lived with him until her death, and as long as health permitted, devoted herself to his family,—from tender reverence for this life-long bond of love, so precious in his own case, the poet could deeply appreciate its value; and he said of the quaint essayist and his sister—Charles and Mary Lamb[3]—

> "Thus, 'mid a shifting world,
> Did they together testify of time
> And seasons' difference—a double tree,
> With two collateral stems sprung from one root."[4]

1. Oliver Goldsmith (ca. 1730–1774), Anglo-Irish writer. The quoted lines are from "The Traveller" (1764).
2. Dorothy Wordsworth (1771–1855), diarist and sister of the British Romantic poet William Wordsworth (1770–1850).
3. Sister (1738–1822) of Charles Lamb (1775–1834), British essayist and critic; the two lived together, and Charles cared for Mary during her recurring bouts of violent insanity. They also together adapted Shakespeare's works for children.
4. From "Written after the Death of Charles Lamb" (1835), by William Wordsworth.

In humble life there have been most worthy instances of sisterly affection, by which the welfare of brothers has been so promoted as to aid them in their upward struggle to a higher position of life. Catherine Hutton is a memorable case in point. William Hutton,[5] the successful bookseller, and valued historian of the important town of Birmingham, which now shines like a star in the midst of England, passed through as sad an experience of suffering and hardship in childhood as was ever lived through and triumphed over.

At seven years of age the poor child was put to work in a silk-mill, and being too short for his hands to reach the machinery, he was mounted on high pattens[6] to pursue his toil. Seven years of this slavery passed, and then, the boy being out of his time, trade was bad, and he could not get employment. He was again bound for seven years to the stocking weaving, a relative being his master, or rather his tyrant. Taunts and blows were his portion in his second apprenticeship. His mother was dead, and his father drank; one only heart yearned to the motherless boy, and that was his sister Catherine's. The poor boy made an effort to escape from his tyrant, by running away when he was seventeen years of age; and his narrative of his journey,—the loss of his bundle of clothes containing all he had in the world, his sleeping on a butcher's block at night, and his subsequent famished wanderings, is as affecting as any record of American slavery. His brutal uncle was, however, brought to own the value of the lad's services, and promising to treat him better, William returned and served out his time.

In his few, very few, intervals of leisure, and by subtracting from the hours of sleep in summer mornings, William Hutton managed to cultivate his mind; and growing fond of books, he also began a little traffic in them by buying a book for his own reading and then selling it to obtain another. By tact and shrewdness he managed to make a profit out of his little trading. It was well that he did; for on his being out of his time as a stockinger—though he worked two years as a journeyman—trade was bad and employment uncertain, and so he bought himself an old bookbinder's press, and taught himself enough of the art of bookbinding to renovate the shabby and tattered books which alone he had the means to purchase. He took a little shop, and his sister Catherine came to live with him; and with tender gratitude he recounts:—

"I set off at five every Saturday morning, carried a burden of from three pounds weight to thirty, opened shop (or stall) at ten, starved in it all day upon bread and cheese and half a pint of ale, took from one to six shillings, shut up at four, and by trudging through the solitary night and deep roads five hours, I arrived at Nottingham by nine, where I always found a mess of milk porridge by the fire prepared by my invaluable sister."

We can picture the welcome and the smile that greeted the weary, foot-sore man, as he entered his dwelling, and cannot doubt that to his sister's care and kindness it was due that his health and life were preserved in his hard wrestle with fortune. The tenderness and domestic order of that kind sister kept him from resorting to the public-house, preserved both his health and morals; and he knew and owned in after-life, when he became a thriving and a prosperous man, that his sister had been a true helper, without whose aid he would probably have succumbed to the hardship of his lot.

---

5. Bookseller and publisher (1733–1815), whose shop grew to be the largest in Birmingham. His own works included *History of Birmingham* (1782).

6. Shoes with thick wooden soles to protect the feet from mud or water.

William Hutton was not merely a prosperous man, he was good in all the various relationships of life, and he lived to extreme old age.

On the publication of his "History of Birmingham," which had a very large circulation, he was elected a Fellow of the Antiquarian Society of Edinburgh. Wealth and honours followed; but in wealth as in poverty he retained a humble, kindly, grateful nature, and always delighted to own his great obligations to his sister Catherine.

Certainly the most memorable case in modern biography of sisterly sympathy and help is furnished in the life of Miss Caroline Herschel, of whom incidental mention has been made in the sketch of Mrs. Mary Somerville.[7] The splendour of the name of Herschel, and the scientific distinctions attained by Sir William, and Sir John[8] his son, might throw into complete shade the early history of the family, and thus prevent us from knowing and being instructed by a very impressive and beautiful domestic history, only that the recent publication of the life of Miss Herschel[9] throws the quiet light of home on the narrative of the scientific progress of her distinguished relatives.

In the garrison school[1] at Hanover, from 1739 to 1755, there were a group of pupils ranging from the age of two to fourteen, the elder boys of whom were noted for their talents, particularly in music. Jacob, William, and John had all been well instructed at home in that art by their father, a musician in the Guards' band. But this good father's plans for the education of his family were much hindered by his ill health. He was a martyr to asthma and rheumatism, owing to the hardships he had endured in war-time with the army. But his children were a great compensation. The eldest, Sophia, went away to reside with a family, where she married early a musician named Griesbach; and the three elder boys soon obtained employment—Jacob as an organist, and William and John in the band. Their brightness rather threw into the shade the fifth child of the family, Caroline, a little, quiet, plain-looking girl. By her own account, she was not much cared for in the busy household, some of whom—the eldest sister and brother—were certainly selfish and exacting. But there was one brother, William, to whom the little Caroline always firmly attached herself with all the strength of a loving heart, sadly repressed in its demonstrations. William had always a kind look and word for his little sister, which fell on her heart like dew upon a drooping flower.

There was a younger child than Caroline, who completed the family group, Alexander, a fine boy, the care of whom fell to the lot of the sister five years his elder.

Never was there a harder worked child than Caroline Herschel. She had to do the actual drudgery of the house, and in her life calls herself "Cinderella,"—running errands, nursing the baby, washing up after meals, mending the clothes, filled all the time that she was not at the garrison school, which of course, with all the enforced punctuality of a German child, she attended. It is affecting to read such statements as the following, of her early recollections. The incident occurred before she was seven years of age, and her father was returning home after an absence:—

"My mother being very busy preparing dinner, had suffered me to go alone to the parade[2] to meet my father, but I could not find him anywhere, nor anybody whom I

---

7. Scottish mathematician and scientist (1780–1872).

8. Distinguished British astronomer and innovator in photography (1792–1871). Sir William Herschel (1738–1822), distinguished British astronomer born in Hanover, Germany.

9. "Memoir and Correspondence of Caroline Herschel." By Mrs. John Herschel [Balfour's note]. This work was published in 1876.

1. School at a military post.

2. A promenade of shops, or a muster of troops for ceremonial public display.

knew; so at last, when nearly frozen to death, I came home and found them all at table. My dear brother William threw down his knife and fork, and ran to welcome me, and crouched down to me, which made me forget all my grievances. The rest were so happy at seeing one another again, that my absence had never been perceived."

In another place she says, "I was mostly, when not in school, sent with Alexander to play on the walls, or with the neighbours' children, in which I seldom could join; and often stood freezing on the shore to see my brother skating till he chose to go home. In short, there was no one who cared anything about me."

A sad testimony. This doubtless had the effect of concentrating her affection on the one brother who did care something for her. Her father, too, she always remembered with great tenderness, for he perceived some talent in the child, and taught her a little music and singing,—not with his wife's concurrence. Mrs. Herschel was a toil-worn mother, wearied with her necessary household tasks. She saw that her eldest daughter's education had not made her helpful, but the reverse; that her elder sons' talents were likely to cause them, as they did, to leave their native land in search of a wider sphere; therefore she was resolute to prevent little Caroline having any but the humblest and plainest instruction—what the school laws prescribed, and no more.

Thus there was the greatest impediment to Caroline's mental progress which could possibly exist. A child—a daughter especially—is so influenced by a mother's feelings and prejudices, that it is one of the marvels which real life supplies, more strangely than fiction can do, that this little hard-worked household drudge should have ever emerged from the gloom of her early condition. This it is which makes her life so valuable; what she was, quite as much as what she did, is a rich legacy of instruction to all. This little girl, who was to become the greatest female astronomer of the age, was a capital knitter, and records that she knitted a pair of stockings for one of her brothers, which when done were as long as she was high.

The departure of the two eldest brothers for England on a musical tour was the next important event in the family. This was followed by the death of the good father, to the deep grief of his wife and children, to whom he left "little more than the heritage of a good example, unblemished character, and those musical talents, which he had so carefully educated, and by which he probably hoped the more gifted of his sons would attain to eminence."

The little Caroline was thrown, as she says, into a "state of stupefaction" for many weeks after this bereavement. All hope of intellectual improvement seemed now closed to her. She went for a short time to learn millinery and dressmaking, but this was not continued long. She returned to her household duties, and the toiling mother was constant at her spinning-wheel, while the sons were gaining great reputation in England, particularly at Bath, where William was mostly resident.

It should be noted that from William's earliest years he had shown not merely musical talent, but a great mechanical and inventive faculty. His mind had a wide range, and he could study languages and mathematics, and yet train his hands to skill in mechanics. He was never idle, but always acquiring; indeed, idleness was unknown in the family, though some were more diligent and far more unselfish than others.

Thus some years passed on, until Caroline was twenty-two, when there came a letter from her brother William, proposing that she should join him at Bath. He remembered her voice and singing, and thought by his instruction he might make her useful for his winter concerts at Bath. She was to return to Hanover, if on trial she did not succeed. Her eldest brother Jacob, who, as she said, had never heard her voice except in speaking, turned the whole scheme into ridicule. But stimulated by the hope of doing something to aid her brother and gain a living for herself, she began to study, practise, and prepare herself. Meanwhile, in the expectation of going away, she knitted as many cotton stockings for her mother and youngest brother "as would last two years at least."

In the August of 1772, her brother William came to see his mother, and take Caroline to England. She says, "My mother had consented to my going with him, and the anguish of my leaving her was somewhat alleviated by my brother settling a small annuity on her, by which she would be able to keep an attendant to supply my place."

What a journey she had to England! In these days, the cheapest train and steamer take a passenger to the Continent in comfort in a few hours; then, Miss Herschel travelled six days and nights in an open *postwagen*,[3] and then embarked at Helvoetsluys, on a stormy sea, to the packet-boat, two miles distant; and she and her brother were, she says, "thrown on shore by the English sailors like balls, at Yarmouth, for the vessel was almost a wreck, without a main and another of the masts."

Her troubles were not over on landing; for after a hasty breakfast, brother and sister mounted some sort of cart, to take them to the place where the London coach passed. They were upset into a ditch, fortunately dry, and came off with only a fright; some kind fellow-passengers, who accompanied them to London, helping them.

Poor Caroline entered the metropolis bareheaded, having lost her hat, amid her other troubles of the way. The landlady of the inn in the city lent her a bonnet, and thus equipped, she made one short excursion, to see something of the metropolis. Curiously enough, among all the fine shops she noticed only one with an interested and longing gaze—it was an optician's. But they could not linger. That same night saw them on the way to Bath, where they arrived, she says, "almost annihilated, having been only twice in bed during their twelve days' journey."

It must have been a strange new life to the little German girl at Bath. Her brother William was organist at the Octagon chapel, director of the public concerts, and as a teacher of music he had a large circle of pupils from the first families. All his professional work was, however, with him but means to an end. Every moment of leisure that he could snatch by day from his musical pursuits, and every hour that he could subtract from his sleep at night, were devoted to those astronomical studies to which, by the strong workings of natural genius, he was impelled with a force he had no power or wish to resist.

From the quietude of her retired home, and the monotonous music of her mother's spinning-wheel and her own knitting needles, Caroline was plunged at once into a life of ceaseless activity. She had a purpose quite as strong as her brother's, and that was—to be in all things possible, and some that seemed impossible, his devoted helper. It is said of her, that for ten years she persevered by night and day, "singing when she was told to sing, copying when she was told to copy, lending a hand in the workshop (where her brother manufactured his telescopes), and taking her full share in all the stirring and exciting changes by which the musician ultimately became the king's astronomer and a celebrity."

Besides all these unusual duties, she kept her brother's house, and had a full share of trouble with inefficient and wasteful servants, whose extravagance shocked her thrifty habits and harassed her temper. Yet she never says anything of her own exertions or privations in that arduous time of toil, and only recalled them to her nephew

---

3. Mail coach, stagecoach (German).

in after-days, "to show," as she said, "with what miserable assistance your father made shift to obtain the means of exploring the heavens." Every one but herself would call it most invaluable assistance, every power of her body and mind being devoted to him.

At breakfast times, upon her first arrival, her brother gave her some lessons in English and arithmetic. "By way of relaxation, we talked of astronomy, and the bright constellations with which I had made acquaintance during the fine nights we had spent on the *postwagen*, travelling through Holland." In this desultory way she began the studies in which she ultimately excelled. Had she chosen, there is little doubt she might have had great success as a public singer; but her brother's tastes and pursuits were hers, and no excitement of praise, or hope of emolument, ever interfered with her steady resolve to work for and with him.

The difficulties, fatigues, and dangers of her brother's experiments and first mechanical contrivances were almost innumerable. There was then no optician resident in Bath, and the toil of making tubes for telescopes, polishing mirrors, procuring or inventing tools, took up all the time that could be spared from music. Indeed, Caroline had to watch her brother, and almost put the food in his mouth, so that his health might not suffer by his mind being so absorbed in his scientific pursuits.

As far as a wide reading of biography enables me to judge, I think there is no record of such hard, various, and continued study and work as that which was performed by this remarkable woman. Her brother's career was extraordinary, but he had the advantage of a good, sound, early education, and habits of study fostered by his father's approbation. Caroline had merely been able to gather the crumbs of knowledge that fell around her in her childhood's home, and to devour them in secrecy and fright, being far more likely to have blame than praise. All the deficiencies of her *early mental* training she had now to make up, as well as to pursue tasks wholly unusual to her sex. At night she watched the heavens with her brother, regardless of, yet not without feeling, cold and weariness. Once, on a bitter December night, she records, that in making some alteration in the machinery of the telescope, she slipped on the snowy ground, and was impaled on an iron hook. "My brother's call, 'Make haste,' I could only answer by a pitiful cry, 'I am hooked.' He and the workman were instantly with me; but they could not lift me without leaving nearly two ounces of my flesh behind. The workman's wife was called, but was afraid to do anything; and I was obliged to be my own surgeon, by applying aquabusade (water bandages) and tying kerchiefs about it for some days." The wound was bad for a long time; and a physician told her that had a soldier met with such a hurt he would have been entitled to six weeks' nursing in hospital.

The astronomical discoveries of her brother attracted the attention of the scientific world, and led to George III, his Queen,[4] and the Princesses taking an interest in the astronomer. Royal patronage, and still more, his own strong desire, determined William Herschel to devote himself entirely to his astronomical studies. The brother and sister played and sung professionally for the last time on Whit-Sunday, 1782, at St. Margaret's Chapel, Bath, the anthem for the day being a composition of William Herschel.

The honours which came to the brother were by no means remunerative. He gave up his pupils and musical career at Bath, which had enabled him to spend a large amount of money on scientific instrument and experiments. His salary, when he was

---

4. Queen Charlotte (1744–1818), wife of George III (1738–1820; r. 1760–1820).

appointed Royal Astronomer, was but £200 a year! Well might Sir William Watson[5] say, "Never bought monarch honour so cheap."

This stipend would not have paid the rent of the new Observatory and the expenses of frequent journeys to and fro to the king and queen at Windsor, but for the astronomer's success in making telescopes for sale. He was compelled to pursue this mechanical branch, or he could not have continued his observations of the heavens.

His sister, finding she must qualify herself as assistant astronomer, learned to use the telescope, and, as she called it, "sweep the heavens," in which she soon acquired great skill. In her brother's absences from home, she, to use her own quaint phrase, "Minded the heavens," and with such success that her watching was rewarded in a very wonderful way. On the 1st of August, 1786, she discovered a comet; and, her brother being abroad, she with characteristic promptitude wrote on the following morning an account of her discovery to two eminent men, Dr. Blagden and Alex. Aubert, Esq., who in a few days congratulated her warmly, the latter saying, "You have immortalized your name; and you deserve such a reward from the Being who has ordered all these things to move as we find them, for your assiduity in the business of astronomy, and for your love for so celebrated and deserving a brother."

From this time, Miss Caroline Herschel became what, in her humility, she never desired to be—a celebrity. She rather shrunk from any praise of herself, as if it was taken from her brother. He was to her as the sun, and she merely a shadow called up by his brightness. Surely, it was an absurd and exaggerated humility in her to say, "I did nothing for my brother but what a well-trained puppy-dog would have done. I was a mere tool, which he had the trouble of sharpening."

All the thoughtful people of her own time, and still more since the narrative of her life has been given to the world, will not take her own estimate of herself. She achieved individual, quite as much as relative greatness.

Space will not permit me to follow the career of Miss Herschel as an astronomer, except to remind my young readers that she did not allow herself to become less diligent as she grew more celebrated. A real love of science for its own sake, and not for any praise, still less for pecuniary advantage, possessed and ennobled her mind. She had the small salary of fifty pounds a year awarded her as assistant astronomer, and this was continued as a pension in her old age.

Her discovery of the first comet was followed by that of seven or eight others. After her brother's marriage, which took place late in his life to a very amiable lady, Miss Herschel removed to a small residence near him, and continued to sit up with him in his observatory, note down his observations, and make necessary and difficult calculations for him. She was greatly delighted, with what may be called an almost maternal joy, when a son of that beloved brother was placed in her arms—that son who lived to nobly inherit his father's genius, and uphold and extend the fame of the honoured name of Herschel.

Of course as celebrity came to her she was sought out by the wealthy and distinguished; but whether in the courtly sphere of royalty, or among the *elite* of fashionable and scientific circles, she always retained the unaffected simplicity of her manners, delighting all by her friendliness and entire freedom from assumption. She was a true gentlewoman in heart and manners, thinking always of others rather than of herself.

Miss Herschel reached the age of seventy, and was still toiling on at her celestial studies, when her brother, Sir William, died, full of years and honours, aged eighty-

5. Physician and naturalist (1715–1787).

two. She mourned him with an intensity of sorrow that seemed like the uprooting of her own heart. She felt that she could not live in England now he was gone, and went home to her native land to die. It was not exactly a wise determination. The resolutions we take in sorrow, or in any strong emotion, are more the result of excited feeling than calm judgment; and so it was in this case. The country she returned to, after nearly fifty years' absence, was not at all like the place she had left, or that youthful memory had retained in her mind. All her immediate acquaintance and most of her kinsfolk were gone, or came to her as strangers. She left the most cultured circle in England to find neither companionship for her heart or her mind. Yet deep as the disappointment must have been, she did not say much about it; for at first she thought her life would not last long, and after that she grew more accustomed to the change. Her correspondence with her nephew, Sir John Herschel, to whom she transferred the love she had borne his father, that nephew's success in his scientific career, the letters and tributes she received from eminent people throughout England and the world, and the respect with which she was treated by all at Hanover, from the king[6] and his family, with whom she was a great favourite, to the more accessible circles of intellectual society—all these gradually reconciled her to her residence, and made it less a state of exile.

Moreover, her sincere and cheerful piety sustained her, as year followed year and found her yet remaining, still taking an interest in all that was going on in the scientific world, and deeply sympathising in the greater advantages of education that were coming within the reach of her own sex. She deplored what she thought (and not without reason) the extravagance in modern attire among women. Her own modest income of £50 a year, to which her nephew insisted, against her remonstrance, on adding another £50, was always sufficient for her wants, although she visited and received the visits of royalty. A single maid-servant conducted her frugal household arrangements in her simple apartments; and thus in all the dignity of simplicity and independence her life went on, until it almost seemed as if death had forgotten her.

Sir John Herschel's visit to the Cape[7] (1834), to make astronomical observations, interested her greatly. She was amused when the astronomical societies of England and Dublin elected her a member, and awarded her a medal. She could not believe she had done anything very great, or indeed at all worthy of being called great; and she said, quaintly enough, "To think of their electing me, when I have not discovered a comet for eighteen years!"

She lived to within nearly two years of a hundred. In anticipation of her death, she had long before composed her epitaph, and left memorials to her nephew and a few relatives, and her books and telescopes to friends and learned Societies.

She retained her faculties unclouded, and her will strong and active to the last. It was winter when the end came, and she had reluctantly to keep her bed, but was free from pain, and able to raise herself and converse.

The guns which announced the birth of a child[8] in the royal family struck on her dying ear; she was told the cause. The departing one expressed hopes for the new pilgrim, and then fell gently asleep. With scarcely a struggle, she entered into rest on the 9th of January, 1848. She was buried beside her father and mother, and her tomb bears the following inscription:—

6. Ernst August I (1771–1851; r. 1837–51), son of George III; it was not until 1837 that the crowns of Great Britain and Hanover were separated.
7. I.e., the Cape of Good Hope. This expedition lasted until 1838.
8. Princess Friederika, King Ernst August's granddaughter.

Here rests the earthly exterior of
CAROLINE HERSCHEL,
born at Hanover, March 16th, 1750,
died Jany. 9th, 1848.

The eyes of her who is glorified were here below turned to the starry heavens.
Her own discoveries of comets, and her participation in the immortal labours of
her brother, William Herschel, bear witness of this to future ages.

1877

CHARLOTTE MARY YONGE
1823–1901

The prolific Charlotte Yonge was never satisfied with writing one book at a time. Her biographer Georgina Battiscombe notes that she tended to write manuscripts in three different genres concurrently—generally, a novel, a history, and a religious work (for further biographical information, see the headnote to "A Patchwork Fever" in the Domestic Fiction section, below). She would compose a page of each in turn, only waiting for the ink to dry before repeating the cycle. Although Yonge is chiefly remembered today as a novelist, she wrote in a letter that she was unwilling to contain her writing to fiction alone, as doing so was akin to "eating a long meal of sweets." Writing history, she continued, provided "a rest, for research or narration brings a different part of the mind into play." Yonge's books of history for the schoolroom include *Cameos from History* (ultimately nine volumes) and *Aunt Charlotte's Stories of English History for the Little Ones* (1873).

In the epilogue to her biography of Yonge, perhaps unfairly subtitled *The Story of An Uneventful Life* (1943), Battiscombe argues that reading Yonge's works produces a profound effect within the reader: "the longing to be good." She adds, "Charlotte's particular gift is to make ordinary, everyday goodness appear the most exciting thing in the world." *A Book of Golden Deeds* (1864), by contrast, relates stories of extraordinary merit and self-sacrifice in extreme situations. A "golden deed," as Yonge is eager to point out, consists not simply of bravery, daring, or obedience: rather, "it is the spirit that gives itself for others—the temper that for the sake of religion, of country, of duty, of kindred, nay, of pity even to a stranger, will dare all things, risk all things, endure all things, meet death in one moment, or wear away in slow, persevering tendance [*sic*] and suffering." The selection printed here, "Fathers and Sons," tells tales of death in battle, and Yonge's patriotism is evident. The first short sketch is set during the English Civil War when the Royalists or "Cavaliers," supporters of King Charles and the monarchy, fought against the Parliamentarians or "Roundheads"; the second takes place during the British war against Napoleon and France.

Golden Deeds was a popular inspirational text enjoyed by children and others. For decades it was favored as a school prize book; and according to Alethea Hayter in her biography of Yonge, John Keble, Yonge's beloved spiritual advisor, chose to read *Golden Deeds* as he lay dying after a stroke.

CHARLOTTE
MARY YONGE

From A Book of Golden Deeds of All Times and All Lands

WHAT IS A GOLDEN DEED?

We all of us enjoy a story of battle and adventure. Some of us delight in the anxiety and excitement with which we watch the various strange predicaments, hair-breadth escapes, and ingenious contrivances that are presented to us; and the mere imaginary dread of the dangers thus depicted, stirs our feelings and makes us feel eager and full of suspense.

This taste, though it is the first step above the dulness that cannot be interested in anything beyond its own immediate world, nor care for what it neither sees, touches, tastes, nor puts to any present use, is still the lowest form that such a liking can take. It may be no better than a love of reading about murders in the newspaper, just for the sake of a sort of startled sensation; and it is a taste that becomes unwholesome when it absolutely delights in dwelling on horrors and cruelties for their own sake; or upon shifty, cunning, dishonest stratagems and devices. To learn to take interest in what is evil is always mischievous.

But there is an element in many of such scenes of woe and violence that may well account for our interest in them. It is that which makes the eye gleam and the heart throb, and bears us through the details of suffering, bloodshed, and even barbarity—feeling our spirits moved and elevated by contemplating the courage and endurance that they have called forth. Nay, such is the charm of brilliant valour, that we often are tempted to forget the injustice of the cause that may have called forth the actions that delight us. And this enthusiasm is often united with the utmost tenderness of heart, the very appreciation of suffering only quickening the sense of the heroism that risked the utmost, till the young and ardent learn absolutely to look upon danger as an occasion for evincing the highest qualities.

> "O Life, without thy chequer'd scene
> Of right and wrong, of weal and woe,
> Success and failure, could a ground
> For magnanimity be found?"[1]

The true cause of such enjoyment is perhaps an inherent consciousness that there is nothing so noble as forgetfulness of self. Therefore it is that we are struck by hearing of the exposure of life and limb to the utmost peril, in oblivion, or recklessness of personal safety, in comparison with a higher object.

That object is sometimes unworthy. In the lowest form of courage it is only avoidance of disgrace; but even fear of shame is better than mere love of bodily ease, and from that lowest motive the scale rises to the most noble and precious actions of which human nature is capable—the truly golden and priceless deeds that are the jewels of history, the salt of life.

And it is a chain of Golden Deeds that we seek to lay before our readers; but, ere entering upon them, perhaps we had better clearly understand what it is that to our mind constitutes a Golden Deed.

It is not mere hardihood. There was plenty of hardihood in Pizarro[2] when he led his men through terrible hardships to attack the empire of Peru, but he was actuated

---

1. From "After-Thought" (1822), by William Wordsworth.

2. Francisco Pizarro (ca. 1475–1541), Spanish conqueror of Peru.

by mere greediness for gain, and all the perils he so resolutely endured could not make his courage admirable. It was nothing but insensibility to danger, when set against the wealth and power that he coveted, and to which he sacrificed thousands of helpless Peruvians. Daring for the sake of plunder has been found in every robber, every pirate, and too often in all the lower grade of warriors, from the savage plunderer of a besieged town up to the reckless monarch making war to feed his own ambition.

There is a courage that breaks out in bravado, the exuberance of high spirits, delighting in defying peril for its own sake, not indeed producing deeds which deserve to be called golden, but which, from their heedless grace, their desperation, and absence of all base motives—except perhaps vanity—have an undeniable charm about them, even when we doubt the right of exposing a life in mere gaiety of heart.

Such was the gallantry of the Spanish knight who, while Fernando and Isabel[3] lay before the Moorish city of Granada, galloped out of the camp, in full view of besiegers and besieged, and fastened to the gate of the city with his dagger a copy of the Ave Maria. It was a wildly brave action, and yet not without service in showing the dauntless spirit of the Christian army. But the same can hardly be said of the daring shown by the Emperor Maximilian[4] when he displayed himself to the citizens of Ulm upon the topmost pinnacle of their cathedral spire: or of Alonso de Ojeda,[5] who figured in like manner upon the tower of the Spanish cathedral. The same daring afterwards carried him in the track of Columbus, and there he stained his name with the usual blots of rapacity and cruelty. These deeds, if not tinsel, were little better than gold leaf.

A Golden Deed must be something more than mere display of fearlessness. Grave and resolute fulfilment of duty is required to give it the true weight. Such duty kept the sentinel at his post at the gate of Pompeii, even when the stifling dust of ashes came thicker and thicker from the volcano,[6] and the liquid mud streamed down, and the people fled and struggled on, and still the sentry stood at his post, unflinching, till death had stiffened his limbs; and his bones, in their helmet and breastplate, with the hand still raised to keep the suffocating dust from mouth and nose, have remained even till our own times to show how a Roman soldier did his duty. In like manner the last of the old Spanish infantry originally formed by the Great Captain, Gonzalo de Cordova, were all cut off, standing fast to a man, at the battle of Rocroy, in 1643, not one man breaking his rank. The whole regiment was found lying in regular order upon the field of battle, and their colonel, the old Count de Fuentes, at their head, expiring in a chair, in which he had been carried, because he was too infirm to walk, to this his twentieth battle. The conqueror, the high-spirited young Duke d'Enghien, afterwards prince of Condé, exclaimed, "Were I not a victor, I should have wished thus to die!" and preserved the chair among the relics of the bravest of his own fellow-countrymen.

Such obedience at all costs and all risks is, however, the very essence of a soldier's life. An army could not exist without it, a ship could not sail without it, and millions upon millions of those whose "bones are dust and good swords are rust" have shown

3. King and Queen of Castile and León (r. 1474–1504) and Aragon (r. 1479–1516, 1479–1504), Ferdinand V (1452–1516) and Isabella I (1451–1504) unified Spain with the defeat of Granada in 1492.

4. Maximilian I (1756–1825), first king of Bavaria (r. 1806–1825). His act as a young man in climbing the spire of Ulm Cathedral, the tallest in Europe, was merely reckless.

5. Spanish explorer and colonizer (1468–1515), who began his career in 1493 by sailing in the second voyage to America led by Christopher Columbus (1451–1506).

6. Mount Vesuvius, in southern Italy, erupted in 79 C.E., burying the cities of Pompeii and Herculaneum.

such resolution. It is the solid material, but it has hardly the exceptional brightness, of a Golden Deed.

And yet perhaps it is one of the most remarkable characteristics of a Golden Deed that the doer of it is certain to feel it merely a duty: "I have done that which it was my duty to do" is the natural answer of those capable of such actions. They have been constrained to them by duty, or by pity; have never even deemed it possible to act otherwise, and did not once think of themselves in the matter at all.

For the true metal of a Golden Deed is self-devotion. Selfishness is the dross and alloy that gives the unsound ring to many an act that has been called glorious. And, on the other hand, it is not only the valour, which meets a thousand enemies upon the battle-field, or scales the walls in a forlorn hope, that is of true gold. It may be, but often it is mere greed of fame, fear of shame, or lust of plunder. No, it is the spirit that gives itself for others—the temper that for the sake of religion, of country, of duty, of kindred, nay, of pity even to a stranger, will dare all things, risk all things, endure all things, meet death in one moment, or wear life away in slow, persevering tendance and suffering.

Such a spirit was shown by Leæna, the Athenian woman at whose house the overthrow of the tyranny of the Pisistratids was concerted, and who, when seized and put to the torture that she might disclose the secrets of the conspirators, fearing that the weakness of her frame might overpower her resolution, actually bit off her tongue, that she might be unable to betray the trust placed in her.[7] The Athenians commemorated her truly golden silence by raising in her honour the statue of a lioness without a tongue, in allusion to her name, which signifies a lioness.

Another woman, in 1450, when Sir Gilles of Brittany was savagely imprisoned and starved almost to death by his brother, Duke François, sustained him for several days by bringing wheat in her veil, and dropping it through the grated window, and when poison had been used to hasten his death, she brought a priest to the grating to enable him to make his peace with Heaven.[8] Tender pity made these women venture all things; and surely their doings were full of the gold of love.

So again two Swiss lads, whose father was dangerously ill, found that they could by no means procure the needful medicine, except at a price far beyond their means, and heard that an English traveller had offered a large price for a couple of eaglets. The only eyrie was on a crag supposed to be so inaccessible, that no one ventured to attempt it, till these boys, in their intense anxiety for their father, dared the fearful danger, scaled the precipice, captured the birds, and safely conveyed them to the traveller. Truly this was a deed of gold.

Such was the action of the Russian servant whose master's carriage was pursued by wolves, and who sprang out among the beasts, sacrificing his own life willingly to slake their fury for a few minutes in order that the horses might be untouched, and convey his master to a place of safety. But his act of self-devotion has been so beautifully expanded in the story of "Eric's Grave," in "Tales of Christian Heroism,"[9] that we can only hint at it, as at that of "the Helmsman of Lake Erie," who, with the steamer on fire around him, held fast by the wheel in the very jaws of the flame, so

7. The story of Leæna, tortured and killed by Hippias, who succeeded his father Pisistratus as ruler of Athens (527–510 B.C.E.), is told in Pausanias 1.23.2.
8. This event occurred during the Hundred Years War (1337–1453) between England and France,

an episodic yet drawn-out conflict marked by uneasy truces and fierce battles on the Continent.
9. *The Triumphs of the Cross: Tales and Sketches of Christian Heroism* (1845), by John Mason Neale (a volume in "The Juvenile Englishman's Library").

as to guide the vessel into harbour, and save the many lives within her, at the cost of his own fearful agony, while slowly scorched by the flames.

Memorable, too, was the compassion that kept Dr. Thompson upon the battle-field of the Alma,[1] all alone throughout the night, striving to alleviate the sufferings and attend to the wants, not of our own wounded, but of the enemy, some of whom, if they were not sorely belied, had been known to requite a friendly act of assistance with a pistol-shot. Thus to remain in the darkness, on a battle-field in an enemy's country, among the enemy themselves, all for pity and mercy's sake, was one of the noblest acts that history can show. Yet, it was paralleled in the time of the Indian Mutiny,[2] when every English man and woman was flying from the rage of the Sepoys at Benares, and Dr. Hay alone remained, because he would not desert the patients in the hospital, whose life depended on his care—many of them of those very native corps who were advancing to massacre him. This was the Roman sentry's firmness, more voluntary and more glorious. Nor may we pass by her, our living type of Golden Deeds, who first showed how woman's ministrations of mercy may be carried on, not only within the city, but on the borders of the camp itself—"the lady with the lamp,"[3] whose health and strength were freely devoted to the holy work of softening the after sufferings that render war so hideous; whose very step and shadow carried gladness and healing to the sick soldier, and who has opened a path of like shining light to many another woman who only needed to be shown the way. Fitly, indeed, may the name of Florence Nightingale be given a place at the opening of our roll of Golden Deeds.

What have been here brought together are chiefly cases of self-devotion that stand out remarkably, either from their hopelessness, their courage, or their patience, vary-ing with the character of their age; but with that one essential distinction in all, that the dross of self was cast away.

Among these we cannot forbear mentioning the poor American soldier, who, griev-ously wounded, had just been laid in the middle bed, by far the most comfortable of the three tiers of berths in the ship's cabin in which the wounded were to be conveyed to New York. Still thrilling with the suffering of being carried from the field, and lifted to his place, he saw a comrade in even worse plight brought in, and thinking of the pain it must cost his fellow-soldier to be raised to the bed above him, he surprised his kind lady nurses (daily scatterers of Golden Deeds) by saying, "Put me up there, I reckon I'll bear hoisting better than he will."

And, within living memory, there was an American Railway collision that befell a train on the way to Elmira with prisoners.[4] The engineer, whose name was William Ingram, might have leapt off and saved himself before the shock; but he remained in order to reverse the engine, though with certain death staring him in the face. He was buried in the wreck of the meeting train, and when found, his back was against the boiler—he was jammed in, unable to move, and actually being burnt to death; but even in that extremity of anguish he called out to those who came round to help

---

1. The 1854 battle at the Alma River in Russia during the Crimean War (1853–56), fought between Russia and the allied powers of England, Turkey, France, and Sardinia.
2. Also known as the Sepoy Rebellion (1857–58), an uprising against British rule in India by native troops (sepoys) serving the British East India Com-pany. Assistant-Surgeon John MacDowell Hay was killed by mutineers in 1857.

3. Florence Nightingale (1820–1910), British founder of modern nursing practices who gained this name while nursing soldiers during the Cri-mean War.
4. Confederate prisoners were being transported to Elmira, N.Y.; the accident described—a head-on collision with a coal train—occurred in Pennsyl-vania in 1864.

him to keep away, as he expected the boiler would burst. They disregarded the generous cry, and used every effort to extricate him, but could not succeed until after his sufferings had ended in death.

While men and women still exist who will thus suffer and thus die, losing themselves in the thought of others, surely the many forms of woe and misery with which this earth is spread do but give occasions of working out some of the highest and best qualities of which mankind are capable. And oh, young readers, if your hearts burn within you as you read of these various forms of the truest and deepest glory, and you long for time and place to act in the like devoted way, bethink yourselves that the alloy of such actions is to be constantly worked away in daily life; and that if ever it be your lot to do a Golden Deed, it will probably be in unconsciousness that you are doing anything extraordinary, and that the whole impulse will consist in the having absolutely forgotten self.

FATHERS AND SONS

1642–1798

The story of a brave and devoted son lights up the sadness of our civil wars between Cavaliers and Roundheads[5] in the middle of the seventeenth century. It was soon after King Charles had raised his standard at Nottingham, and set forth on his march for London, that it became evident that the Parliamentary army, under the Earl of Essex, intended to intercept his march. The King himself was with the army, with his two boys, Charles and James; but the General-in-Chief was Robert Bertie, Earl of Lindsay, a brave and experienced old soldier, sixty years of age, godson to Queen Elizabeth, and to her two favourite earls, whose Christian names he bore. He had been in her Essex's expedition to Cambridge, and had afterwards served in the Low Countries, under Prince Maurice of Nassau; for the long Continental wars had throughout King James's peaceful reign[6] been treated by the English nobility as schools of arms, and a few campaigns were considered as a graceful finish to a gentleman's education. As soon as Lord Lindsay had begun to fear that the disputes between the King and Parliament must end in war, he had begun to exercise and train his tenantry in Lincolnshire and Northamptonshire, of whom he had formed a regiment of infantry. With him was his son Montagu Bertie, Lord Willoughby, a noble-looking man of thirty-two, of whom it was said, that he was as "excellent in reality as others in pretence," and that, thinking "that the cross was an ornament to the crown, and much more to the coronet, he satisfied not himself with the mere exercise of virtue, but sublimated it, and made it grace." He had likewise seen some service against the Spaniards in the Netherlands, and after his return had been made a captain in the Lifeguards, and a Gentleman of the Bedchamber. Lindsay was called General-in-Chief, but the King had imprudently exempted the cavalry from his command, its general, Prince Rupert of the Rhine, taking orders only from himself. Rupert was only three-and-twenty, and his education in the wild school of the Thirty Years' War[7] had not taught him to lay aside his arrogance and opinionativeness;

5. During the English Civil War (1642–48), Cavaliers supported Charles I's divine right to rule; Roundheads, or "parliamentarians," fought for the right to govern the nation independent of the crown. The Roundheads were led by Oliver Cromwell, and their victories forced the king to surrender in 1645; he was beheaded for treason in 1649.
6. James I, king of England (1566–1625; r. 1603–

25), also known as James VI of Scotland (r. 1567–1625), succeeded Queen Elizabeth I (r. 1558–1603). "Her Essex" was Robert Devereux, second earl of Essex (1566–1601). His son Robert, the third earl (1591–1646), commanded the Parliamentary army.
7. A series of conflicts (1618–48), fought mainly in Germany, between most of the countries in

indeed, he had shown great petulance at receiving orders from the King through Lord Falkland.

At eight o'clock, on the morning of the 23rd of October, King Charles was riding along the ridge of Edgehill, and looking down into the Vale of Red Horse, a fair meadow land, here and there broken by hedges and copses. His troops were mustering around him, and in the valley he could see with his telescope the various Parliamentary regiments, as they poured out of the town of Keinton and took up their positions in three lines. "I never saw the rebels in a body before," he said, as he gazed sadly at the subjects arrayed against him. "I shall give them battle. God, and the prayers of good men to Him, assist the justice of my cause." The whole of his forces, about 11,000 in number, were not assembled till two o'clock in the afternoon, for the gentlemen who had become officers found it no easy matter to call their farmers and retainers together, and marshal them into any sort of order; but while one troop after another came trampling, clanking, and shouting in, trying to find and take their proper place, there were hot words round the royal standard.

Lord Lindsay, who was an old comrade of the Earl of Essex, the commander of the rebel forces, knew that he would follow the tactics they had both together studied in Holland, little thinking that one day they should be arrayed against the other in their own native England. He had a high opinion of Essex's generalship, and insisted that the situation of the Royal army required the utmost caution. Rupert, on the other hand, had seen the swift fiery charges of the fierce troopers of the Thirty Years' War, and was backed up by Patrick, Lord Ruthven, one of the many Scots who had won honour under the great Swedish King, Gustavus Adolphus.[8] A sudden charge of the Royal horse would, Rupert argued, sweep the Roundheads from the field, and the foot would have nothing to do but to follow up the victory. The great portrait at Windsor shows us exactly how the King must have stood, with his charger by his side, and his grave, melancholy face, sad enough at having to fight at all with his subjects, and never having seen a battle, entirely bewildered between the ardent words of his spirited nephew and the grave replies of the well-seasoned old Earl. At last, as time went on, and some decision was necessary, the perplexed King, willing at least not to irritate Rupert, desired that Ruthven should array the troops in the Swedish fashion.

It was a greater affront to the General-in-Chief than the King was likely to understand, but it could not shake the old soldier's loyalty. He gravely resigned the empty title of General, which only made confusion worse confounded, and rode away to act as colonel of his own Lincoln regiment, pitying his master's perplexity, and resolved that no private pique should hinder him from doing his duty. His regiment was of foot-soldiers, and was just opposite to the standard of the Earl of Essex.

The church bell was ringing for afternoon service when the Royal forces marched down the hill. The last hurried prayer before the charge was stout old Sir Jacob Astley's, "O Lord, Thou knowest how busy I must be this day; if I forget Thee, do not Thou forget me"; then, rising, he said, "March on, boys." And, amid prayer and exhortation, the other side awaited the shock, as men whom a strong and deeply embittered sense of wrong had roused to take up arms. Prince Rupert's charge was, however, fully successful. No one even waited to cross swords with his troopers, but all the Roundhead horse galloped headlong off the field, hotly pursued by the Royalists. But the main body of the army stood firm, and for some time the battle was

western Europe and the Holy Roman Empire. Rupert (1619–1682) was Charles I's nephew.

8. King of Sweden (1594–1632; r. 1611–32).

nearly equal, until a large troop of the enemy's cavalry who had been kept in reserve, wheeled round and fell upon the Royal forces just when their scanty supply of ammunition was exhausted.

Step by step, however, they retreated bravely, and Rupert, who had returned from his charge, sought in vain to collect his scattered troopers, so as to fall again on the rebels; but some were plundering, some chasing the enemy, and none could be got together. Lord Lindsay was shot through the thigh bone, and fell. He was instantly surrounded by the rebels on horseback; but his son, Lord Willoughby, seeing his danger, flung himself alone among the enemy, and forcing his way forward, raised his father in his arms, thinking of nothing else, and unheeding his own peril. The throng of the enemy around called to him to surrender, and, hastily giving up his sword, he carried the Earl into the nearest shed, and laid him on a heap of straw, vainly striving to staunch his blood. It was a bitterly cold night, and the frosty wind came howling through the darkness. Far above, on the ridge of the hill, the fires of the King's army shone with red light, and some way off on the other side twinkled those of the Parliamentary forces. Glimmering lanterns or torches moved about the battle-field, those of the savage plunderers who crept about to despoil the dead. Whether the battle were won or lost, the father and son knew not, and the guard who watched them knew as little. Lord Lindsay himself murmured, "If it please God I should survive, I never will fight in the same field with boys again!"—no doubt deeming that young Rupert had wrought all the mischief. His thoughts were all on the cause, his son's all on him; and piteous was that night, as the blood continued to flow, and nothing availed to check it, nor was any aid near to restore the old man's ebbing strength.

Towards midnight the Earl's old comrade Essex had time to understand his condition, and sent some officers to inquire for him, and promise speedy surgical attendance. Lindsay was still full of spirit, and spoke to them so strongly of their broken faith, and of the sin of disloyalty and rebellion, that they slunk away one by one out of the hut, and dissuaded Essex from coming himself to see his old friend, as he intended. The surgeon, however, arrived, but too late; Lindsay was already so much exhausted by cold and loss of blood, that he died early in the morning of the 24th, all his son's gallant devotion having failed to save him.

The sorrowing son received an affectionate note the next day from the King, full of regret for his father and esteem for himself. Charles made every effort to obtain his exchange, but could not succeed for a whole year. He was afterwards one of the four noblemen who, seven years later, followed the King's white, silent snowy funeral in the dismantled St. George's Chapel; and from first to last he was one of the bravest, purest, and most devoted of those who did honour to the Cavalier cause.

We have another brave son to describe, and for him we must turn away from these sad pages of our history, when we were a house divided against itself, to one of the hours of our brightest glory, when the cause we fought in was the cause of all the oppressed, and nearly alone we upheld the rights of oppressed countries against the invader. And thus it is that the battle of the Nile is one of the exploits to which we look back with the greatest exultation, when we think of the triumph of the British flag.

Let us think of all that was at stake. Napoleon Bonaparte[9] was climbing to power

---

9. Leader of France (1769–1821), who proclaimed himself emperor in 1804 and King of Italy in 1805; by 1806, he had conquered much of the Continent. Military resistance to Napoleon's expansionist ambitions ended with his defeat in 1815 at Waterloo.

in France, by directing her successful arms against the world. He had beaten Germany and conquered Italy; he had threatened England, and his dream was of the conquest of the East. Like another Alexander,[1] he hoped to subdue Asia, and overthrow the hated British power by depriving it of India. Hitherto, his dreams had become earnest by the force of his marvellous genius, and by the ardour which he breathed into the whole French nation; and when he set sail from Toulon, with 40,000 tried and victorious soldiers and a magnificent fleet, all were filled with vague and unbounded expectations of almost fabulous glories. He swept away as it were the degenerate knights of St. John from their rock of Malta[2] and sailed for Alexandria in Egypt, in the latter end of June, 1798.

His intentions had not become known, and the English Mediterranean fleet was watching the course of this great armament. Sir Horatio Nelson was in pursuit, with the English vessels, and wrote to the First Lord of the Admiralty: "Be they bound to the Antipodes,[3] your lordship may rely that I will not lose a moment in bringing them to action."

Nelson had, however, not ships enough to be detached to reconnoitre, and he actually overpassed the French, whom he guessed to be on the way to Egypt; he arrived at the port of Alexandria on the 28th of June, and saw its blue waters and flat coast lying still in their sunny torpor, as if no enemy were on the seas. Back he went to Syracuse, but could learn no more there; he obtained provisions with some difficulty, and then, in great anxiety, sailed for Greece, where at last, on the 28th of July, he learnt that the French fleet had been seen from Candia,[4] steering to the south-east, about four weeks since. In fact, it had actually passed by him in a thick haze, which concealed each fleet from the other, and had arrived at Alexandria on the 1st of July, three days after he had left it.

Every sail was set for the south, and at four o'clock in the afternoon of the 1st of August a very different sight was seen in Aboukir Bay, so solitary a month ago. It was crowded with shipping. Great castle-like men-of-war rose with all their proud calm dignity out of the water, their dark portholes opening in the white bands on their sides, and the tricoloured flag floating as their ensign. There were thirteen ships of the line and four frigates, and, of these, three were 80-gun ships, and one, towering high above the rest, with her three decks, was *L'Orient*, of 120 guns. Look well at her, for three stands the hero for whose sake we have chosen this and no other of Nelson's glorious fights to place among the setting of our Golden Deeds. There he is, a little *cadet de vaisseau*, as the French call a midshipman, only ten years old, with a heart swelling between awe and exultation at the prospect of his first battle; but, fearless and glad, for is he not the son of the brave Casabianca, the flag-captain? And is not this Admiral Brueys' own ship, looking down in scorn on the fourteen little English ships, not one carrying more than 74 guns, and one only 50?

Why Napoleon had kept the ships there was never known. In his usual mean way of disavowing whatever turned out ill, he laid the blame upon Admiral Brueys; but, though dead men could tell no tales, his papers made it plain that the ships had

1. Alexander the Great (356–323 B.C.E.), king of Macedon and greatest general of the ancient world; his empire encompassed Greece, Egypt, and Persia, reaching as far into India as the Punjab.
2. The Hospitallers of St. John, a Catholic order that had taken on a military role protecting lands seized during the Crusades, became sovereign rulers of Malta in 1530. Their "degeneracy" began

soon thereafter, as many knights ignored their vows of celibacy and obedience; the order's grand master treacherously surrendered to Napoleon.
3. The opposite side of the earth. Nelson (1758–1805), British naval admiral and hero of the Napoleonic wars.
4. Crete.

remained in obedience to commands, though they had not been able to enter the harbour of Alexandria. Large rewards had been offered to any pilot who would take them in, but none could be found who would venture to steer into that port a vessel drawing more than twenty feet of water. They had, therefore, remained at anchor outside, in Aboukir Bay, drawn up in a curve along the deepest of the water, with no room to pass them at either end, so that the commissary of the fleet reported that they could bid defiance to a force more than double their number. The admiral believed that Nelson had not ventured to attack him when they had passed by one another a month before, and when the English fleet was signalled, he still supposed that it was too late in the day for an attack to be made.

Nelson had, however, no sooner learnt that the French were in sight than he signalled from his ship, the *Vanguard*, that preparations for battle should be made, and in the meantime summoned up his captains to receive his orders during a hurried meal. He explained that, where there was room for a large French ship to swing, there was room for a small English one to anchor, and, therefore, he designed to bring his ships up to the outer part of the French line and station them close below their adversaries; a plan that he said Lord Hood[5] had once designed, though he had not carried it out.

Captain Berry was delighted, and exclaimed, "If we succeed, what will the world say?"

"There is no *if* in the case," returned Nelson, "that we shall succeed is certain. Who may live to tell the tale is a very different question."

And when they rose and parted, he said, "Before this time to-morrow I shall have gained a peerage or Westminster Abbey."[6]

In the fleet went, through a fierce storm of shot and shell from a French battery on an island in advance. Nelson's own ship, the *Vanguard*, was the first to anchor within half-pistol-shot of the third French ship, the *Spartiate*. The *Vanguard* had six colours flying, in case any should be shot away; and such was the fire that was directed on her, that in a few minutes every man at the six guns in her forepart was killed or wounded, and this happened three times. Nelson himself received a wound in the head, which was thought at first to be mortal, but which proved but slight. He would not allow the surgeon to leave the sailors to attend to him till it came to his turn.

Meantime his ships were doing their work gloriously. The *Bellerophon* was, indeed, overpowered by *L'Orient*, 200 of her crew killed, and all her masts and cables shot away, so that she drifted away as night came on; but the *Swiftsure* came up in her place, and the *Alexander* and *Leander* both poured in their shot. Admiral Brueys received three wounds, but would not quit his post, and at length a fourth shot almost cut him in two. He desired not to be carried below, but that he might die on deck.

About nine o'clock the ship took fire, and blazed up with fearful brightness, lighting up the whole bay, and showing five French ships with their colours hauled down, the others still fighting on. Nelson himself rose and came on deck when this fearful glow came shining from sea and sky into his cabin; and gave orders that the English boats should immediately be put off for *L'Orient*, to save as many lives as possible.

The English sailors rowed up to the burning ship which they had lately been attack-

5. Samuel Hood (1724–1816), British admiral made first viscount Hood.
6. I.e., gain burial in Westminster Abbey among England's monarchs and most distinguished citizens.

ing. The French officers listened to the offer of safety, and called to the little favourite of the ship, the captain's son, to come with them. "No," said the boy; "he was where his father had stationed him, and bidden him not to move save at his call." They told him his father's voice would never call him again, for he lay senseless and mortally wounded on the deck, and that the ship must presently blow up. "No," said the brave child; "he must obey his father." The moment allowed no delay—the boat put off. The flames showed all that passed in a quivering glare more intense than daylight, and the little fellow was then seen on the deck, leaning over the prostrate figure, and presently tying it to one of the spars of the shivered masts.

Just then a thundering explosion shook down to the very hold every ship in the harbour, and burning fragments of *L'Orient* came falling far and wide, plashing heavily into the water, in the dead awful stillness that followed the fearful sound. English boats were plying busily about, picking up those who had leapt overboard in time. Some were dragged in through the lower portholes of the English ships, and about seventy were saved altogether. For one moment a boat's crew had a sight of a helpless figure bound to a spar, and guided by a little childish swimmer, who must have gone overboard with his precious freight just before the explosion. They rowed after the brave little fellow, earnestly desiring to save him; but in darkness, in smoke, in lurid uncertain light, amid hosts of drowning wretches, they lost sight of him again.

> The boy, O where was he?
> Ask of the winds that far around
> With fragments strewed the sea;
> With mast and helm, and pennant fair
> That well had done their part:
> But the noblest thing that perished there
> Was that young faithful heart![7]

By sunrise the victory was complete. Nay, as Nelson said, "It was not a victory, but a conquest." Only four French ships escaped, and Napoleon and his army were cut off from home. These are the glories of our navy, gained by men with hearts as true and obedient as that of the brave child they had tried in vain to save. Yet still, while giving the full meed of thankful, sympathetic honour to our noble sailors, we cannot but feel that the Golden Deed of Aboukir Bay fell to—

"That young faithful heart."

1864

---

7. From "Casabianca" (1826), by Felicia Hemans.

THE BROWNIES' BOOK
1920–1921

To Children, who with eager look
Scanned vainly library shelf and nook,
For History or Song or Story
That told of Colored Peoples' glory—
We dedicate *The Brownies' Book*.

So reads Jessie Redmon Fauset's dedicatory verse to the inaugural issue of *The Brownies' Book* (1920–21), the new monthly publication for African American children created by W. E. B. Du Bois (1868–1963), Augustus Granville Dill (1881–1956), and Fauset (1882–1961). All three were integrally involved in the creation and running of *The Crisis,* the official magazine of the National Association for the Advancement of Colored People (NAACP). The idea for a publication "designed for all children, but especially for *ours*" was first advanced within the 1919 "children's number" of *The Crisis*; it became a reality when Du Bois and Dill formed a publishing company in order to produce *The Brownies' Book.* Du Bois was the editor of the magazine; Dill, the business manager; and Fauset, the literary editor in 1920 and managing editor in 1921.

The Brownies' Book was the first full-length magazine written expressly for African American youth. In its innovations, literary and artistic merit, and sophistication, *The Brownies' Book* was both a product of and contributor to the artistic movement of the 1920s and 1930s known as the Harlem Renaissance. In particular, the magazine highlighted the history and achievements of African American men, women, and children; it also provided stories, poetry, photography, puzzles, readers' responses (from both children and adults), and artwork for the pleasure of its young audience. Rejecting the racist stereotyping, condescension, and cruelty or indifference in such popular magazines as *St. Nicholas,* the editors offered African American role models absent in any other publication intended for children. Dianne Johnson-Feelings, quoting W. E. B. Du Bois, comments that

because of the preponderance of negative black images in the American mass media, the creators of *The Brownies' Book* were concerned that "all of the Negro child's idealism, all his sense of the good, the great and the beautiful is associated with white people.... He unconsciously gets the impression that the Negro has little chance to be great, heroic or beautiful." So, quite consciously, the editors went about their mission of presenting alternative images to Negro youth.

The magazine regularly featured sketches of people from Africa itself or the African diaspora. These brief biographies of figures both living and dead—brave, selfless, dedicated, gifted with genius—were meant to inspire young readers. Some of the sketches were signed (such as "The Story of Harriet Tubman" by Augusta E. Bird, "The Bravest of the Brave" by Lillie Buffum Chace Wyman, and "Benjamin Banneker" by Elizabeth Ross Haynes, below); others appeared anonymously. A representative sample is reprinted here.

Jessie Fauset contributed many of the unsigned pieces in *The Brownies' Book.* A novelist, poet, essayist, and short story writer who earned a B.A. degree from Cornell University and an M.A. from the University of Pennsylvania, Fauset was possibly the first African American woman to be elected to Phi Beta Kappa. She was the literary editor of *The Crisis* from 1919 to 1926 (after 1926 she was a contributing editor) and a major force in promoting the work of African American writers of the Harlem Renaissance, including Jean Toomer, Countee Cullen, Langston Hughes, and Claude McKay. In her capacity as editor, she also encouraged both black and white women writers to publish their work in *The Crisis* and *The Brownies' Book.* The latter, though short-lived (it had too few subscribers to cover the costs of printing a top-quality periodical), was an attractive and progressive magazine that played a key role in the history of American children's literature.

The Brownies' Book

JUNE, 1920

$ 1.50 A YEAR   15 cts. A COPY

Benjamin Banneker

Elizabeth Ross Haynes

One winter evening long ago, everything in Baltimore County, Maryland, was covered with deep snow. Icicles nearly a foot long hung from the roofs of the rough log cabins. And the trees of thick forest which extended for miles around stood like silent ghosts in the stillness, for no one in all that wooded country stirred out on such an evening.

Far away from the other cabins stood the Banneker cabin. Little Benjamin Banneker was busy before a glowing wood fire roasting big, fat chestnuts in the hot embers. His grandmother sat in the corner in a quaint splint-bottom white oak chair. It is true she was sitting there knitting but her thoughts had carried her far away to England, her native country. With the eyes of her mind, she saw the River Thames, the Tower of London, and Westminster Abbey.

All was still except for the moving of Benjamin now and then and the sudden bursting of a chestnut. Benjamin's grandfather, a native African, who was sitting on the left, and whom Benjamin thought was asleep, broke the silence. Said he, "Benjamin, what are you going to be when you are a man, a *chestnut* roaster?" "I am going to be—I am going to be—what is it, Grandmother?—You know you told me a story about the man who knew all the stars," said Benjamin. "An astronomer," replied his grandmother. "That's it, I am going to be an astronomer," answered Benjamin. "You have changed in the last day or two then," said his grandfather. "The day your grandmother told you about the man who could figure so with his head, you said you would be that." "That man was a born mathematician," suggested his grandmother. Benjamin began to bat his eyelids rapidly and to twist and turn for an answer. The minute the answer came to him his mouth flew open saying, "Well, I'll be both; I'll be both."

Just then his grandmother interrupted by saying, "I wonder what has become of my little inventor. Benjamin, you remember what you said when I told you the story about that inventor." Benjamin gave that look which always said, "Well, I am caught." But soon he recovered and with this reply, "I can tell you what I am going to do. I am going to school first to learn to figure. And then while I am farming a little for my living I can stay up at night and watch the stars. And in the afternoon I can study and invent things until I am tired, and then I can go out and watch my bees."

"When are you going to sleep, my boy?" asked his grandmother.

"In the morning," said he.

"And you are going to have a farm and bees, too?" she asked.

"Yes, Grandmother," said Benjamin. "We might just as well have something while we are here. Father says that he will never take mother and me to his native country—Africa—to live. Grandmother, did you and grandfather have any children besides mother?"

"Yes, there were three other children," replied his grandmother.

"When father and mother were married," said Benjamin, "mother didn't change her name at all from Mary Banneker, as the ladies do now. But father changed his name to Robert Banneker. I am glad of it, for you see you are Banneker, grandfather is Banneker, I am Banneker and all of us are Bannekers now."

"My boy," interrupted his grandfather, "I am waiting to hear how you are going to buy a farm."

"Oh, Grandfather," said Benjamin as he rose, "you remember that mother and father gave Mr. Gist seven thousand pounds of tobacco, and Mr. Gist gave them one hundred acres of land here in Baltimore County. Grandfather, don't you think father will give me some of this land? He can not use it all."

"Yes, when you are older, Benjamin. But you must go to school and learn to read first," answered his grandfather.

"Yes, but—ouch, that coal is hot!" cried Benjamin as he shook his hand, danced about the floor and buried his fingers in the pillow. That time he had picked up a hot coal instead of a chestnut. And he had a hot time for a while even after his fingers were doctored up and he was apparently snug in bed for the night.

Benjamin Banneker did retire for the night but he did not sleep twenty years like Rip Van Winkle. He rose the next morning. And a long while after breakfast he began again to roast chestnuts. When the snow had all cleared away he entered a pay school and learned to read, write and do some arithmetic. Then he began to borrow books and teach himself.

When he was about twenty-seven years old his father died. And just as he had prophesied when he was a boy, his father's farm, bought with the tobacco, became his. On this farm was Banneker's house—a log cabin about half a mile from the Patapsco River. Along the banks of this river he could see the near and distant beautiful hills. What he said about his bees when he was a boy came true also. These he kept in his orchard. And in the midst of this orchard a spring which never failed, babbled beneath a large, golden, willow tree. His beautiful garden and his well kept grounds were his delight.

Banneker never married, but lived alone in retirement after the death of his mother. He cooked his own food and washed his own clothes. And yet he lived like a man and was well thought of by all who knew him and especially by those who saw that he was a genius. He was glad to have visitors. And he kept a book in which was written the name of every person by whose visit he felt greatly honored.

Some one who knew him well says that he was a brave looking, pleasant man with something very noble in his face. He was large and somewhat fleshy. And in his old age he wore a broad brimmed hat which covered his thick suit of white hair. He always wore a super-fine, drab broadcloth, plain coat with a straight collar and long waistcoat. His manners were those of a perfect gentleman—kind, generous, hospitable, dignified, pleasing, very modest and unassuming.

He had to work on his farm for his living but he found time to study all the books which he could borrow. He studied the Bible, history, biography, travels, romance and other books.

But his greatest interest was in mathematics. And he became familiar with some of the hardest problems of the time. Like many other scholars of his day, he often amused himself during his leisure by solving hard problems. Scholars from many parts of the country often sent him difficult problems to see if he could work them. It is said that he solved every one and often returned with an answer an original question in rhyme. For example, he sent the following question to Mr. George Ellicott, which was solved by a scholar of Alexandria:

> "A Cooper and Vintner sat down for a talk,
> Both being so groggy that neither could walk;
> Says Cooper to Vintner, 'I'm the first of my trade,
> There's no kind of vessel, but what I have made
> And of any shape, Sir,—just what you will,

And of any size, Sir,—from a ton to a gill!'
'Then,' says the Vintner, 'you're the man for me—
Make me a vessel, if we can agree.
The top and the bottom diameter define,
To bear that proportion as fifteen to nine;
Thirty-five inches are just what I crave,
No more and no less in the depth will I have,
Just thirty-nine gallons this vessel must hold,
Then I will reward you with silver and gold,—
Give me your promise, my honest old friend?'
'I'll make it tomorrow, that you may depend!'
So the next day the Cooper his work to discharge,
Soon made the new vessel, but made it too large;
He took out some staves, which made it too small,
And then cursed the vessel, the Vintner and all.
He beat on his breast, 'By the Powers!' he swore,
He never would work at his trade any more!
Now, my worthy friend, find out, if you can,
The vessel's dimensions and comfort the man."

When Banneker was about thirty-eight years old he made a clock. It was made with his imperfect tools and without a model except a borrowed watch. He had never seen a clock, for there was not one perhaps within fifty miles of him. An article published in London, England, in 1864, says that Banneker's clock was probably the first clock of which every part was made in America. He had to work very hard to make his clock strike on the hour and to make the hands move smoothly. But he succeeded and felt repaid for his hard work.

Time passed, and after some years Mr. George Ellicott's family began to build flour mills, a store and a post office, in a valley adjoining Banneker's farm. He was now fifty-five years old. And he had won the reputation of knowing more than any other person in that country. Mr. Ellicott opened his library to him. He gave him a book which told of the stars. He gave him tables about the moon. He urged him to work problems in astronomy for almanacs.[1] Early every evening now Banneker wrapped himself in a big cloak. He stretched out upon the ground and lay there all night studying the stars and planets. At sunrise he rose and went to his house. He slept and rested all the morning and worked in the afternoon. Because his neighbors saw him resting during the morning, they began to call him a lazy fellow who would come to no good end.

In spite of this he compiled an almanac. His first almanac was published for the year 1792. It so interested one of the great men of the country that he wrote two almanac publishers of Baltimore about it. These publishers gladly published Banneker's almanac. They said that it was the work of a genius, and that it met the hearty approval of distinguished astronomers.

Banneker wrote Thomas Jefferson, then secretary of the United States, on behalf of his people and sent him one of his almanacs. Mr. Jefferson replied:

---

1. Annual publications that include a calendar, the phases of the moon, the times of sunrises and sunsets, and other statistical information.

"Philadelphia, Pa., August 30, 1791. Sir,—

I thank you sincerely for your letter of the 19th inst. and for the almanac it contained. Nobody wishes more than I do to see such proofs as you exhibit, that nature has given to your race talents equal to those of the other races of men.

> "I am with great esteem, Sir,
> "Your most obedient servant,
> "THOS. JEFFERSON."

This strange man, Benjamin Banneker, never went away from home any distance until he was fifty-seven years old. Then he was asked by the commissioner appointed to run the lines of[2] the District of Columbia, to go with him and help in laying off the District of Columbia. He accompanied him and helped to lay off the District of Columbia and he greatly enjoyed the trip.

On his return home he told his friends that during that trip he had not touched strong drink, his one temptation. "For," said he, "I feared to trust myself even with wine, lest it should steal away the little sense I had." In those days wines and liquors were upon the tables of the best families. Therefore wherever he went strong drink was tempting him.

Perhaps no one living knows the exact day of Banneker's death. In the fall probably of 1804, on a beautiful day he walked out on the hills seeking the sunlight as a tonic for his bad feelings. While walking, he met a neighbor to whom he told his condition. He and his neighbor walked along slowly to his house. He lay down at once upon his couch, became speechless and died.

During a previous illness he had asked that all his papers, almanacs, etc., be given at his death to Mr. Ellicott. Just two days after his death and while he was being buried, his house burned to the ground. It burned so rapidly that the clock and all his papers were burned. A feather bed on which he had slept for many years was removed at his death. The sister to whom he gave it opened it some years later and in it was found a purse of money.

Benjamin Banneker was well known on two continents. An article written about him in 1864 by the London Emancipation Society says, "Though no monument marks the spot where he was born and lived a true and high life and was buried, yet history must record that the most original scientific intellect which the South has yet produced was that of the African, Benjamin Banneker."

1920

America's First Martyr-Patriot

A TRUE STORY

Almost every land boasts of some man who has particularly distinguished himself in the service of his country. Sweden has its Gustavus Adolphus, Italy its Garibaldi, Poland its Kosciusko[1] and America its Crispus Attucks.

---

2. I.e., to survey.
1. Tadeusz Kościuszko (1746–1817), Polish general and patriot. Gustavus Adolphus (1594–1632;

r. 1611–32), King of Sweden. Giuseppe Garibaldi (1807–1882), Italian nationalist leader and soldier.

Long ago when these United States were still a part of the British Empire and were known as "colonial possessions," a revolt broke out on the part of the colonists against the mother country. English soldiers who were guarding the province of New England—as it was then known—conducted themselves with such arrogance and swagger that finally the "colonials" could stand it no longer. So one never-to-be-forgotten day, the 5th of March, 1770, a small band of citizens made an attack on some British soldiers who were marching through State Street, Boston, and the affray which has come down to us under the name of the "Boston Massacre" took place.

The leader of this band was Crispus Attucks. He was a tall, splendidly-built fellow, and must have been very impressive as he rushed with his handful of men pell-mell into the armed opposition. He knew only too well how precious a thing is freedom and how no sacrifice is too much for its purchase. For Attucks had been a slave and perhaps still was at this date, though a runaway one. Of this we cannot be sure, for history goes blank at this point, but in any event twenty years earlier in 1750 this advertisement had occurred in *The Boston Gazette* or *Weekly Journal*:

> "Ran away from his master, William Brown of Framingham, on the 30th of September last, a Molatto Fellow, about 27 Years of Age, named Crispas, 6 Feet 2 Inches high, short curl'd Hair, his Knees nearer together than common; had on a light colour'd Bear-skin Coat, plain brown Fustain Jacket, or brown all-Wool one, new Buck-skin Breeches, blue Yarn Stockings, and a checked woolen Shirt.
>
> "Whoever shall take up said Run-away, and convey him to his above-said Master, shall have ten Pounds, old Tenor[2] Reward, and all necessary Charges paid. And all Masters of Vessels and others, are hereby cautioned against concealing or carrying off said Servant on Penalty of the Law. Boston, October 2, 1750."

What had Attucks done in those twenty long years? Certainly whatever else his interests he must have spent some time dwelling on the relationship existing between England and the American colonies. Perhaps he was imaginative enough to feel that if England were so despotic in her treatment now of her colonies, she would be a worse task-mistress than ever as the years rolled by and her authority became more secure. If he had spent his time near Boston, which seems likely, he may have heard the eloquent and fearless assertions of James Otis[3] on the rights of the colonists.

That he was deeply interested in political affairs is shown by this letter which he wrote long before the date of the Boston Massacre to Thomas Hutchinson, Governor of the Province:

> Sir:
> You will hear from us with astonishment. You ought to hear from us with horror. You are chargeable before God and man, with our blood. The soldiers were but passive instruments, mere machines; neither moral nor voluntary agents in our destruction, more than the leaden pellets with which we were wounded. You were a free agent. You acted, coolly, deliberately, with all that

2. I.e., in the paper currency of the Massachusetts colony (which was issued in several different series, of different value).

3. American colonial political leader (1725–1783), member of the Massachusetts legislature.

premeditated malice, not against us in particular, but against the people in general, which, in the sight of the law, is an ingredient in the composition of murder. You will hear further from us hereafter.

CRISPUS ATTUCKS.

Whatever his preparation he was ready on that fateful fifth of March to offer himself up to the holy cause of liberty. At the head of his little host he flung himself on the soldiers of the oppressors shouting: "The way to get rid of these soldiers is to attack the main-guard; strike at the root; this is the nest!"

We are used to terrible descriptions of warfare on a huge plane in these days, but the scene that followed in that quiet street still brings a thrill of horror. For the enraged British soldiers answered the blows and missiles of the American patriots with a deadly shower of bullets. Down fell Crispus Attucks mortally wounded, the first American to die for his Fatherland. And with him fell Samuel Gray and Jonas Caldwell. Afterwards Patrick Carr and Samuel Maverick died also as a result of their wounds received in the fray.

The cost of patriotism had come high.

All down the street, doors and windows flew open. The alarm bells rang and people rushed to the scene from all directions. The bodies of Attucks and Caldwell were carried to Faneuil Hall[4] and laid in state. The other dead and dying were carried to their homes and buried thence. But Attucks and Caldwell, being strangers in the city, were buried from the hall where they had lain. A long procession attended them as a token of respect and appreciation. These two and Gray and Maverick were buried in the same grave and over them was reared a stone on which the inscription read:

> "Long as in Freedom's cause the wise contend,
> Dear to your country shall your fame extend;
> While to the world the lettered stone shall tell
> Where Caldwell, Attucks, Gray and Maverick fell."

Many years later Boston showed afresh her appreciation of Attucks in the shape of a new monument which she raised to his memory on Boston Common.

What patriot of any time has done a nobler deed than that of Attucks? *Dulce et decorum est pro patria mori*,[5] says the Roman proverb. "It is a sweet and fitting thing to die for one's country." That is true and many have done it. But to die as Attucks did for a country which while seeking its own freedom, yet denied his—such an act calls for the highest type of patriotism. I like to think that as his courage was high, so was his faith so abounding that he needs must have believed that America one day would come to realize and put into practice what one of her great statesmen said one famous fourth of July:

> *"All men are born free and equal."*[6]

1920

4. Public hall in Boston, frequently used as a meeting place for American patriots.
5. Horace, *Odes* 3.2.13 (ca. 23 B.C.E.).

6. Paraphrased from the Declaration of Independence, drafted by Thomas Jefferson and adopted on July 4, 1776.

The Story of Phillis Wheatley

A True Story

Somewhere in Africa nearly 175 years ago a band of children were playing on the sea-coast. They were youngsters of seven and eight who were so engrossed in their childish games that they did not notice the appearance of a boat with a number of white men in it. When they did become aware of this it was far too late, for the men had stolen up to them and seizing several had rushed off to the boat in which they were carried to a ship anchored not far away.

Only a few of the children escaped but the rest were borne off to America where they were to be sold as slaves. For these white men were slavers and the waiting ship was a slave-vessel.

Among the children who were captured and led off to such a cruel fate was a little girl of six or seven years. She was a slender, delicate little thing who had never gone far from her mother's side. Picture then her fear and anguish when she found herself torn away from everything and everybody whom she had ever known, on her way to a strange land full of queer looking people who were going to subject her to she knew not what experiences and hardships.

After a long and stormy voyage, during which the little girl was very seasick, she arrived, thin and wretched, with only a piece of carpet about her fragile body, in Boston where she was offered in the streets for sale. This was in 1761.

Of course the best thing that could have happened to this little child of misfortune would have been to be left with her mother in Africa. As that could not be, it is pleasant to realize that the next best lot was hers. A well-to-do tailor, John Wheatley by name, happened to be in that neighborhod that day. He had long been looking for a slave girl to be a special servant for his wife and his twin children, Mary and Nathaniel. He spied the wretched little African maiden, and despite her thinness and her miserable appearance, or maybe on account of it, it occurred to him that this was just the kind of child to whom to give a home. So he bought her for a few dollars and took her to his house to live.

The Wheatley family was a kind one. They received the little stranger gladly, named her Phillis Wheatley and proceeded to make her acquainted with the strange new world to which she had come and to the part which she was to play in it. In particular little Mary Wheatley became very fond of her slave playfellow and between her and Phillis there seems to have developed a strong attachment. At first Phillis' place in the house was simply that of servant, though partly because of her extreme youth and the considerateness of the Wheatleys it seems likely that her duties were not very arduous. But before long, owing to what was considered a remarkable tendency in a slave child of such tender years, her lot became very tolerable indeed.

This was what happened. One day Mary Wheatley came across Phillis busily engaged in making letters on the wall with a piece of charcoal. Phillis had already shown herself apt at picking up the spoken language but that she should display an interest in writing was a new idea to the Wheatleys and gave them much pleasure. From that day on Mary constituted herself Phillis' teacher. They progressed from letters to words and from words to complete sentences. And behold the keys to the treasure-houses of the world were in little Phillis' hands for she had learned to delve into books. Short of granting her her freedom, the Wheatleys could not have bestowed on her a greater gift.

She seems to have been of an extraordinarily studious disposition. Mostly her mind took a literary bent, for she read all kinds of books in English and even mastered Latin enough to become acquainted with some of its masterpieces. It is not surprising then that a mind so eager to take in should at last become desirous of giving out. And so we have the remarkable phenomenon of Phillis the little slave girl totally unversed in the ways and manners of western civilization, passing through a period of study and preparation and developing into Phillis the writer.

Her chosen medium of self-expression was through poetry. In 1767, at the age of 13, she had written a poem to Harvard University which was even then in existence. This was passed about among the "intellectuals" of New England, and was the occasion of much genuine, astonishment and admiration. And well it might be for it was written in a lofty vein and was full of fine sentiments such as one would hardly expect from the pen of a little girl. In 1768 she wrote a poem to His Majesty King George of England[1]—America was still a colony in those days, we must remember—and in 1770 she wrote an elegiac poem or a lament on the death of George Whitefield, a celebrated divine.

As the years went on the number of her poems grew. Their reputation grew, too, not only at home but abroad. In 1772 her health became impaired and the Wheatley household did a wonderful thing. Nathaniel had to go on a business trip to England and it was arranged that Phillis the prodigy and poet should accompany him, for the sake of the sea-voyage. Imagine her astonishment when on arriving in England, she found that her fame had already preceded her! London society took her up and could not make enough of her. She was courted and petted to an extent which might well have turned a less well-balanced head than hers. In particular she was made a special protégée of a Lady Huntingdon and a Lord Dartmouth who at that time was Lord Mayor of London. Through their persuasion and influence she collected a number of verses which she had been writing for the last six years and actually had them published,—to our great good fortune.

The quaint title reads: *"Poems on Various Subjects, Religious and Moral. By Phillis Wheatley, Negro Servant to Mr. Wheatley of Boston. Dedicated to Lady Huntingdon."*[2] The particularly interesting thing about this book is that as so many people doubted the ability of a girl so young and of slave origin to write such verse, it contains a certificate attesting to the authenticity of the poems, and the signatures of many prominent men.

The certificate says in part:

> "We whose Names are under-written, do assure the World that the Poems specified in the following page, were (as we verily believe) written by Phillis, a young Negro Girl, who was but a few Years since, brought an uncultivated Barbarian from Africa, and has ever since been, and now is, under the Disadvantage of serving as a Slave in a family in this Town. She has been examined by some of the best Judges, and is thought qualified to write them."

Those days in London were probably the happiest and brightest of Phillis' brief life. But while yet abroad she received the news of the precarious state of Mrs. Wheatley's health. And so although arrangements had been made for her to meet

---

1. George III (1738–1820; r. 1760–1820).
2. This work (reprinted in America in 1786) was the first published by a black American.

the king, she hastened back to America, just in time to see her mistress once more before she died.

Poor Phillis! After Mrs. Wheatley's death she seems to have fallen on

"Evil times and hard."

For Mary Wheatley was married and of course lived apart from her. Nathaniel Wheatley had his own affairs and here was Phillis all alone in the world. Naturally enough she turned to marriage and became the wife of John Peters, a Negro, "who kept a shop, wore a wig, carried a cane, and felt himself superior to all kinds of labor." Historians disagree on his real calling. Some say he was a grocer, others a baker, a man of all work, a lawyer and a physician. All agree, however, that he lost his property during the War of the Independence and that he and Phillis became very poor. Sad to relate, all agree also that he did not try very hard to relieve their condition. Finally he allowed himself to be arrested for debt, and poor Phillis was in a sorry plight indeed.

She was a proud woman. She would not seek help of either Mary or Nathaniel Wheatley. Nor at their death would she approach their friends. Fortunately at Mrs. Wheatley's death she had been set free and this gave her a chance to earn an independent livelihood. She dragged out a miserable existence in a colored boarding house doing work for which she was little fitted. Her pride and misery made her very retiring. So that when she died in December, 1784, few would have known of her death had it not been for the notice which appeared next day in the *Independent Chronicle*. It read:

"Last Lord's day, died Mrs. Phillis Peters (formerly Phillis Wheatley), aged thirty-one, known to the literary world by her celebrated miscellaneous poems. Her funeral is to be this afternoon at four o'clock, from the house lately improved by Mr. Todd, nearly opposite Dr. Bulfinch's at West Boston, where her friends and acquaintances are desired to attend."

Phillis Wheatley possessed undoubted poetical ability. It is true that viewed from our modern standards she seems stilted, even affected in style, but we must remember that with few exceptions such was the tendency of those days. Undoubtedly she was the possessor of a fine vocabulary and a really broad grasp of classical and literary allusions and figures. But these are hardly in themselves the reasons why colored Americans should hold Phillis Wheatley in such high esteem. There are others more striking. In the first place, she is the first Negro in America to win prestige for purely intellectual attainments. And she won it, oh so well! Secondly, her writings influenced and strengthened anti-slavery feeling. When the friends of slavery made as a reason for holding human beings in bondage the statement that Negroes were mentally inferior, the foes of slavery pointed with pride to the writings of this girl who was certainly the peer of any American poet of those days. Lately, Phillis Wheatley showed by her writings that she favored the cause of the colonists rather than that of England. Thus she proved that the sympathies of Negroes are always enlisted in the fight for freedom even when, as Roscoe Jamison,[3] not her blood but her poetical descendant, wrote

3. American poet (ca. 1886–1918), published posthumously. The quoted line is from "The Negro Soldiers."

In those brief years Phillis made a gallant showing. In all she wrote five volumes of poems and letters and received the recognition of England's peerage, of America's George Washington, and of many other possessors of honored and famous names. We are sensible of a deep gratitude toward this little lonely figure who came from Africa determined to give voice to her precious dower of song, even though she had to express it in a far country and in a stranger's tongue.

1920

"The Bravest of the Brave"

A True Story

Lillie Buffum Chace Wyman

Some great dread of what might happen must have come to a nineteen-year-old girl in the winter of 1849–50 so that she had to decide whether or not she should plunge into other horrors to escape the thing she feared.

I do not know exactly what her trouble was, but one can guess at its nature for she was a mulatto girl named Elizabeth or Betsy Blakesley, and she was a slave in North Carolina. No slaves could be legally married, but slave boys and girls, men and women, did love each other, and they formed unions to which they would often have been glad to be true. Their masters, however, could sell them apart, sell their children from them and they also often forced the slave women to live as wives with men with whom they did not want to live. Betsy had a little baby. We can pity her trouble even though we do not know just what it was then or had been for a long time.

She made up her mind to run away to the North. But she could not take her baby with her. She knew that her own slave mother had never been able to help her in any trouble that grew out of their enslaved condition, and so she knew that she could not make life right for her child if she stayed with it.

Betsy hid herself on a coast vessel which was bound for Boston. Probably some northern sailor helped her to stow herself away, but we have no record of that. Wendell Phillips,[1] the Abolitionist orator, did, however, in one of his speeches say that Betsy was hidden "in the narrow passage between the side of the vessel and partition that formed the cabin." Two feet and eight inches of space—into that she cramped her young, sensitive body. No place for a baby there—and it might have cried and betrayed her presence.

Her master missed her soon after she left for the boat and the vessel was held at the dock while it was searched. She was not found. Her master still felt sure that she was on board, so he had the boat smoked three times over with sulphur and tobacco. Betsy did not crawl forth from that closet of horror, but the baby would have died had it been subjected to such torture.

At last the boat swung out and on to the tossing ocean and day and night the cold

---

1. Boston-born American reformer and orator (1811–1884), president of the Anti-Slavery Society (1865–70).

stiffened her limbs and struck inward like sharp knives, and the rolling waves outside seemed to enter her hiding place and like demons to crush her and bruise her body against the timbers of her prison cell.

Betsy reached Boston in January, 1850. There were many mysterious ways in which the Abolitionists learned whenever a fugitive slave had come into their vicinity. And so Betsy, half frozen and scarcely able to walk, soon found herself among kind friends who ministered unto her.

These friends were so much shocked by her condition that they did a more daring thing than I have ever known any Abolitionist to do at any other time in connection with a fugitive slave. They wanted many Boston people to see Betsy so that a profound feeling of the wickedness of slavery should stir the northern world. As the law then stood they believed that she could be publicly shown for an hour or two, before the legal machinery to arrest her could be brought to bear upon her personally. And Betsy was brave enough to do what her new friends wanted her to,—and she trusted them when they told her, as they must have done, that it would help to make people want to free all the slaves if she would do what they said. Her baby was a slave, you see.

The Abolitionists took Betsy to an anti-slavery meeting in Faneuil Hall. She sat on the platform beside Wendell Phillips, who was a handsome, blonde man, then not quite forty years old.

Frederika Bremer, a renowned Swedish novelist, sat very near the platform beside Charles Sumner,[2] with whom she had come as a sight-seer. At a given moment, Lady Stone,[3] young, fair in the face, and clad in white, led Betsy forward, and holding her hand she told the audience how, driven by unutterable woe, Betsy had come to Boston through brimstone smoke and winter cold. Lucy Stone had one of the sweetest speaking voices that was ever heard in this world. Once, as she spoke, she lifted her hand and placing it on Betsy's head called her "my sister."

Miss Bremer had never before seen an American slave. She was emotionally humane. Wendell Phillips came down from the platform to speak to his very dear friend, Charles Sumner, and to be introduced to Miss Bremer. She gave him a rose to take to Betsy. I wish I knew whether it were a white or a red rose. Then Betsy suddenly and quietly disappeared. She was taken out of the Hall, and started on the so-called Under-Ground Railroad, and she was borne swiftly to Canada and to freedom.

The Fugitive Slave Bill[4] was passed before that year ended. The Abolitionists would not have dared to show Betsy for even two minutes after that.

Lucy Stone remained always the friend of the slave. Frederika Bremer, though never approving of slavery, sentimentalized away much of her objection to it. But Elizabeth Blakesley,—was she not like Joan of Arc in her courage? I think every white child and every colored child in this country should be proud because she was an American girl.

1920

2. Massachusetts senator and abolitionist (1811–1874). Bremer (1801–1865), Swedish novelist who also published a volume of "impressions of America."

3. American abolitionist and leader of the movement for women's suffrage (1818–1893).
4. Federal law of 1850 requiring the return of escaped slaves from free states to slave states.

The Story of Harriet Tubman

Augusta E. Bird

On the eastern shore of Maryland, in Dorchester County, about the year 1821, a wee little baby girl was born, who grew and grew and grew in spirit, as well as in stature, until she was known all over the nation as the greatest and noblest of heroines of anti-slavery. Some will think that it was very extraordinary for such a wonderful woman to be the grand-daughter of a slave imported from Africa. Her parents were Benjamin Ross and Harriet Greene, both slaves, but married and faithful to each other. They named their little baby Araminta, but later she adopted the name Harriet as a Christian name. As she married a man whose surname was Tubman, she is better known as Harriet Tubman.

She had ten brothers and sisters, not less than three of whom she rescued from slavery among the hundreds of other slaves, and in 1857, at a great risk to herself, she also took away to the North her aged father and mother.

When Harriet was six years old (nothing more than a baby herself), she was sent away from her home to another home to take care of a baby. You can imagine how tiny she was when she had to sit down on the floor and have the baby placed in her lap in order to mind it. One morning after breakfast she was standing by the breakfast table while her mistress and her husband were eating, waiting to take the baby. Just by her was a bowl of lump sugar. Now every little girl who knows how tempting lump sugar is, can easily realize how much more tempting it must have been to little Harriet who never had anything nice like most little girls of six have nowadays. So while the baby's mother, who, possessed of a violent temper, was busily engaged in a quarrel with her husband, Harriet thought she would take a lump of sugar without being seen. But the woman turned just in time to see her fingers go into the sugar bowl, and the next minute the raw hide, a whip used—in those days alas!—to beat slaves with, was down from the wall.

Little Harriet saw her coming and gave one jump out of the door. She ran and ran until she passed many houses. She didn't dare to stop and go into any of those houses for she knew they all knew her mistress, and if she appealed to them for protection she would only be sent back. By and by she came to a large pig-pen, which belonged on one of the farms. She was too small to climb into it, so she just tumbled over the high board and for a long time lay where she had fallen, for she was so tired. There with that old sow and eight or ten little pigs Harriet stayed from Friday until the next Tuesday, fighting with those little pigs for the potato peelings and scraps that would come down in the trough, with the old mother sow not so kindly disposed towards her either for taking her children's food. By Tuesday she was so hungry that she decided she would have to go back to her mistress. You see in those days no one had conceived the idea of the Society for the Prevention of Cruelty to Children[1] and Harriet had no other place to go. Harriet knew what was coming but she went back.

It is impossible to give the many accounts of hardships which this little girl went through, but she thinks she was about twenty-five when she decided to make her escape from slavery, and this was in the last year of James K. Polk's administration.[2] From that time until the beginning of the war, her years were spent in journeying

---

1. The New York Society for the Prevention of Cruelty to Children was founded in 1874.

2. Polk (1795–1849) was the eleventh president of the United States (1845–49).

back and forth to rescue her fellow brothers, with intervals between, in which she worked only to spend what her labor availed her in providing for the wants of her next party of fugitives. By night she traveled, many times on foot over mountains, through forests, across rivers, oftentimes sleeping on the cold ground. She traveled amid perils by land, perils by water, perils from enemies, perils among false brethren, but with implicit faith in God she always returned successful.

Sometimes members of her party would become exhausted and footsore, and declare they could not go on; they must stay where they dropped down, and die. Others would think a voluntary return to slavery better than being overtaken and carried back, and would insist on returning; then there was no alternative but force. The revolver carried by this bold and daring pioneer would be pointed at their heads. "Dead niggers tell no tales," said Harriet. "Go on or die." And so she compelled them to drag their weary limbs on their journey north. The babies she managed by drugging them with opium. No wonder a price of $40,000 was put upon her head by the slaveholders. Oftentimes when she and her party were concealed in the woods they saw their pursuers pass, on their horses, down the high road, tacking up the advertisements of the rewards for the capture of her and her fugitives.

"An' den how we laughed," she said. "We was de fools, an' dey was de wise men; but we wasn't fools enough to go down de high road in de broad daylight."

America in particular, as well as humanity, owes Harriet Tubman much. To Colonel Higginson, of Newport, R. I., and Colonel James Montgomery, of Kansas, she was invaluable as a spy and guide during the Civil War.[3] She also rendered great service to our soldiers in the hospitals as well as to the armies in the fields. In this way she worked day after day until late at night. Then she went home to her little cabin and made about fifty pies, a great quantity of gingerbread, and two casks of root beer. These she would hire some contraband[4] to sell for her through the camps, and thus she would provide her support for another day. For this service Harriet never received pay or pension, and never drew for herself but twenty days' rations during the four years of her labors.

At one time she was called away from Hilton Head, by one of our officers, to come to Fernandina, where the men were dying very fast from a certain disease. Harriet had acquired quite a reputation for skill in curing this disease by a medicine which she prepared from roots which grew near the waters which caused the disease. Here she found thousands of sick soldiers and contrabands. She immediately gave up her time and attention to them. At another time, we find her nursing those who were down by hundreds with small-pox and malignant fevers. She had never had these diseases, but she never seemed to fear death in one form more than in another.

"A nobler, higher spirit, or truer, seldom dwells in the human form," was a tribute paid to her by W. H. Seward,[5] one of her many influential friends who tried very hard, although unsuccessfully, to secure for her a pension from her government. So you see how much the government is indebted to Harriet Tubman and her people.

After the war Harriet Tubman made Auburn, N.Y., her home, establishing there a refuge for aged Negroes. She died at a very advanced age on March 10, 1913. On Friday, June 12, 1914, a tablet in her honor was unveiled at the Auditorium in Albany.

---

3. These activities took place in South Carolina, where Col. Thomas Wentworth Higginson (1823–1911) commanded the Union's first black regiment, the First South Carolina, and where Tubman acted as a scout for the Second South Carolina Colored Volunteers, a regiment led by Col. Montgomery (1814–1871).

4. A fugitive or captured slave attached to the Union Army.

5. William Seward (1801–1872), U.S. senator and later secretary of state (1861–69).

It was provided by the Cayuga County Historical Association. Dr. Booker T. Washington[6] was the chief speaker of the occasion, and the ceremonies were attended by a great crowd of people.

The tributes to this woman whose charity embraced the whole human race, the slaveholders as well as the fugitives, were remarkable. Wendell Phillips[7] said of her: "In my opinion there are few captains, perhaps few colonels, who have done more for the loyal cause since the war began, and few men who did before that time more for the colored race than our fearless and most sagacious friend, Harriet." Abraham Lincoln gave her ready audience and lent a willing ear to whatever she had to say. Frederick Douglass[8] wrote to her: "The difference between us is very marked. Most that I have done and suffered in the service of our cause has been in public, and I have received much encouragement at very step of the way. You, on the other hand, have labored in a private way. I have wrought in the day—you in the night. I have had the applause of the crowd and the satisfaction that comes of being approved by the multitude, while the most that you have done has been witnessed by a few trembling, scarred, and footsore bondmen and women, whom you have led out of the house of bondage, and whose heartfelt 'God bless you' has been your only reward."

1920

6. American educator (ca. 1856–1915), born a slave.
7. American reformer and orator (1811–1884), president of the Anti-Slavery Society (1865–70).

8. American abolitionist and social activist (1818–1895) who described his escape from slavery in his 1845 autobiography.

ANNE FRANK
1929–1945

The Diary of a Young Girl is the world's best-known example of life writing. This landmark twentieth-century text details the day-to-day experiences and emotions of a passionate and deeply perceptive German teenager who, with her family and four others, endured two years of fear and deprivation while in hiding in Amsterdam from the Nazi invaders of Holland, where they had fled in 1933. The diary is a remarkable testament to the fortitude of the persecuted Jews and of those who risked their own lives by sheltering them, as well as a record of the characteristic confusion, moods, joys, and sorrows of an adolescent girl who was also a gifted writer.

Anne received the red checkered cloth-bound diary for her thirteenth birthday and began to confide her private thoughts to it. Less than a month later, a letter from the Central Office for Jewish Emigration summoned her older sister, Margot, to labor service and drove the family into hiding. They retreated to the place that Anne's father, Otto, had begun to prepare some time before: a few small rooms on two floors above the warehouse and office of his business. There, Anne decided to treat all her diary entries as letters written to an imaginary girl-friend she called Kitty. The selections printed here range from the first entry begun just as the Frank family entered the "annex" in 1942, through the years of seclusion, to the final entry, dated August 1, 1944. They were betrayed and captured on August 4. Miep Gies, an employee in Otto Frank's business who was one of the family's protectors, returned to the annex immediately after the inhabitants had been seized, and she rescued the diary and Anne's other writings. Anne Frank, Margot, and their mother, Edith, died from disease and starvation at Bergen-Belsen, a German concentration camp. Margot and Anne perished only weeks before the camp was liberated in 1945 by British troops.

After surviving Auschwitz, Otto Frank returned to Amsterdam; Gies gave him the diary, unread.

Anne Frank's diary has been translated widely and popularly adapted for both the stage and film. The text exists in a number of different forms: the original, the version that Anne was working on before her capture for a proposed book she called "The Secret Annex," the somewhat shortened and edited diary that Otto Frank first published in Dutch in 1947 (*Het Achterhuis*, or *The House Behind*, translated into English as *The Diary of a Young Girl* and known the world over), and a "critical edition" of 1989 that combines all three versions.

Anne Frank is arguably the most famous teenager of the twentieth century. As such, Anne Frank the individual has become "Anne Frank" the icon. She has become an inspirational figure of near-worship; her words have been read throughout the world; her story has been dramatized on stage and on television and movie screens; and her "meaning" has been debated since the diary was first published only a few years after her death. Who is the "real" Anne Frank? Although no list can do justice to any person, Anne can be described as a lively and fun-loving teen, talented writer, Jew, daddy's girl, witness, concentration camp victim. Her diary has been asked to represent not just an individual's voice and vision but all Holocaust documents, hope in the face of evil, Jewish suffering, belief in humanity's essential goodness, innocence, even teenage angst. As the diary has been interpreted and adapted into a performance, many of Anne's darker thoughts, her fear and despair, sorrow and rage, have been smoothed over in favor of often-quoted statements of hope and cheer. In her provocative essay "Who Owns Anne Frank?" (1997), published in the *New Yorker*, Cynthia Ozick offers the shocking suggestion (shocking to herself as well) that perhaps the better result for the diary would have been its destruction: "Anne Frank's diary burned, vanished, lost—saved from a world that made of it all things, some of them true, while floating lightly over the heavier truth of named and inhabited evil." The "real" Anne may live on after her death, a wish she fervently expressed in the spring of 1944, only if we read her words in their historical context so that the life can be restored to the legend.

From The Diary of a Young Girl

Saturday, 11 July, 1942

Dear Kitty,

Daddy, Mummy, and Margot can't get used to the sound of the Westertoren clock yet, which tells us the time every quarter of an hour.[1] I can. I loved it from the start, and especially in the night it's like a faithful friend. I expect you will be interested to hear what it feels like to "disappear"; well, all I can say is that I don't know myself yet. I don't think I shall ever feel really at home in this house, but that does not mean that I loathe it here, it is more like being on vacation in a very peculiar boardinghouse. Rather a mad idea, perhaps, but that is how it strikes me. The "Secret Annexe" is an ideal hiding place. Although it leans to one side and is damp, you'd never find such a comfortable hiding place anywhere in Amsterdam, no, perhaps not even in the whole of Holland. Our little room looked very bare at first with nothing on the walls; but thanks to Daddy who had brought my film-star collection and picture postcards on beforehand, and with the aid of paste pot and brush, I have transformed the walls into one gigantic picture. This makes it look much more cheerful, and, when the Van Daans come, we'll get some wood from the attic, and make a

1. Since July 9, 1942, two days before this entry, the Frank family (Otto and Edith Frank and Anne's older sister, Margot) had been in hiding in the "secret annex" at the top of the building that housed Otto's business. They would be joined by the Van Daan family and, later, Mr. Dussel (pseudonyms of Hermann and Auguste van Pels; their son, Peter; and Fritz Pfeffer). The diary was first published in Holland as *Het Achterhuis* (lit., "the house behind").

few little cupboards for the walls and other odds and ends to make it look more lively.

Margot and Mummy are a little bit better now. Mummy felt well enough to cook some soup for the first time yesterday, but then forgot all about it, while she was downstairs talking, so the peas were burned to a cinder and utterly refused to leave the pan. Mr. Koophuis[2] has brought me a book called *Young People's Annual*. The four of us went to the private office yesterday evening and turned on the radio. I was so terribly frightened that someone might hear it that I simply begged Daddy to come upstairs with me. Mummy understood how I felt and came too. We are very nervous in other ways, too, that the neighbors might hear us or see something going on. We made curtains straight away on the first day. Really one can hardly call them curtains, they are just light, loose strips of material, all different shapes, quality, and pattern, which Daddy and I sewed together in a most unprofessional way. These works of art are fixed in position with drawing pins, not to come down until we emerge from here.

There are some large business premises on the right of us, and on the left a furniture workshop; there is no one there after working hours but even so, sounds could travel through the walls. We have forbidden Margot to cough at night, although she has a bad cold, and make her swallow large doses of codeine. I am looking for Tuesday when the Van Daans arrive; it will be much more fun and not so quiet. It is the silence that frightens me so in the evenings and at night. I wish like anything that one of our protectors could sleep here at night. I can't tell you how oppressive it is *never* to be able to go outdoors, also I'm very afraid that we shall be discovered and be shot. That is not exactly a pleasant prospect. We have to whisper and tread lightly during the day, otherwise the people in the warehouse might hear us.

Someone is calling me.

Yours, Anne

Sunday, 11 July, 1943

Dear Kitty,

To return to the "upbringing" theme for the umpteenth time, I must tell you that I really am trying to be helpful, friendly, and good, and to do everything I can so that the rain of rebukes dies down to a light summer drizzle. It is mighty difficult to be on such model behavior with people you can't bear, especially when you don't mean a word of it. But I do really see that I get on better by shamming a bit, instead of my old habit of telling everyone exactly what I think (although no one ever asked my opinion or attached the slightest importance to it).

I often lose my cue and simply can't swallow my rage at some injustice, so that for four long weeks we hear nothing but an everlasting chatter about the cheekiest and most shameless girl on earth. Don't you think that sometimes I've cause for complaint? It's a good thing I'm not a grouser, because then I might get sour and bad-tempered.

I have decided to let my shorthand go a bit, firstly to give me more time for my other subjects and secondly because of my eyes. I'm so miserable and

2. Johannes Kleiman, a manager and bookkeeper in Otto's business.

wretched as I've become very shortsighted and ought to have had glasses for a long time already (phew, what an owl I shall look!) but you know, of course, in hiding one cannot. Yesterday everyone talked of nothing but Anne's eyes, because Mummy had suggested sending me to the oculist with Mrs. Koophuis. I shook in my shoes somewhat at this announcement, for it is no small thing to do. Go out of doors, imagine it, in the street—doesn't bear thinking about! I was petrified at first, then glad. But it doesn't go as easily as that, because all the people who would have to approve such a step could not reach an agreement quickly. All the difficulties and risks had first to be carefully weighed, although Miep[3] would have gone with me straight away.

In the meantime I got out my gray coat from the cupboard, but it was so small that it looked as if it belonged to my younger sister.

I am really curious to know what will come of it all, but I don't think the plan will come off because the British have landed in Sicily now and Daddy is once again hoping for a "quick finish."

Elli[4] gives Margot and me a lot of office work; it makes us both feel quite important and is a great help to her. Anyone can file away correspondence and write in the sales book, but we take special pains.

Miep is just like a pack mule, she fetches and carries so much. Almost every day she manages to get hold of some vegetables for us and brings everything in shopping bags on her bicycle. We always long for Saturdays when our books come. Just like little children receiving a present.

Ordinary people simply don't know what books mean to us, shut up here. Reading, learning, and the radio are our amusements.

Yours, Anne

Sunday, 2 January, 1944

Dear Kitty,

This morning when I had nothing to do I turned over some of the pages of my diary and several times I came across letters dealing with the subject "Mummy" in such a hotheaded way that I was quite shocked, and asked myself: "Anne, is it really you who mentioned hate? Oh, Anne, how could you!" I remained sitting with the open page in my hand, and thought about it and how it came about that I should have been so brimful of rage and really so filled with such a thing as hate that I had to confide it all in you. I have been trying to understand the Anne of a year ago and to excuse her, because my conscience isn't clear as long as I leave you with these accusations, without being able to explain, on looking back, how it happened.

I suffer now—and suffered then—from moods which kept my head under water (so to speak) and only allowed me to see the things subjectively without enabling me to consider quietly the words of the other side, and to answer them as the words of one whom I, with my hotheaded temperament, had offended or made unhappy.

I hid myself within myself, I only considered myself and quietly wrote down

---

3. Hermine "Miep" Gies, an employee of Otto Frank who assisted the family throughout their hiding, visiting them twice a day.

4. Elli Vossen (pseudonym of Elisabeth "Bep" Voskuijl), Miep Gies's assistant in Otto's business.

all my joys, sorrows, and contempt in my diary. This diary is of great value to me, because it has become a book of memoirs in many places, but on a good many pages I could certainly put "past and done with."

I used to be furious with Mummy, and still am sometimes. It's true that she doesn't understand me, but I don't understand her either. She did love me very much and she was tender, but as she landed in so many unpleasant situations through me, and was nervous and irritable because of other worries and difficulties, it is certainly understandable that she snapped at me.

I took it much too seriously, was offended, and was rude and aggravating to Mummy, which, in turn, made her unhappy. So it was really a matter of unpleasantness and misery rebounding all the time. It wasn't nice for either of us, but it is passing.

I just didn't want to see all this, and pitied myself very much; but that, too, is understandable. Those violent outbursts on paper were only giving vent to anger which in a normal life could have been worked off by stamping my feet a couple of times in a locked room, or calling Mummy names behind her back.

The period when I caused Mummy to shed tears is over. I have grown wiser and Mummy's nerves are not so much on edge. I usually keep my mouth shut if I get annoyed, and so does she, so we appear to get on much better together. I can't really love Mummy in a dependent childlike way—I just don't have that feeling.

I soothe my conscience now with the thought that it is better for hard words to be on paper than that Mummy should carry them in her heart.

Yours, Anne

Saturday, 12 February, 1944

Dear Kitty,

The sun is shining, the sky is a deep blue, there is a lovely breeze and I'm longing—so longing—for everything. To talk, for freedom, for friends, to be alone. And I do so long . . . to cry! I feel as if I'm going to burst, and I know that it would get better with crying; but I can't, I'm restless, I go from one room to the other, breathe through the crack of a closed window, feel my heart beating, as if it is saying, "Can't you satisfy my longings at last?"

I believe that it's spring within me, I feel that spring is awakening, I feel it in my whole body and soul. It is an effort to behave normally, I feel utterly confused, don't know what to read, what to write, what to do, I only know that I am longing . . . !

Yours, Anne

Wednesday, 23 February, 1944

Dear Kitty,

It's lovely weather outside and I've quite perked up since yesterday. Nearly every morning I go to the attic where Peter[5] works to blow the stuffy air out of my lungs. From my favorite spot on the floor I look up at the blue sky and the bare chestnut tree, on whose branches little raindrops shine, appearing like

---

5. Peter Van Daan (i.e., Van Pels), who was two years older than Anne.

silver, and at the seagulls and other birds as they glide on the wind.

He stood with his head against a thick beam, and I sat down. We breathed the fresh air, looked outside, and both felt that the spell should not be broken by words. We remained like this for a long time, and when he had to go up to the loft to chop wood, I knew that he was a nice fellow. He climbed the ladder, and I followed; then he chopped wood for about a quarter of an hour, during which time we still remained silent. I watched him from where I stood, he was obviously doing his best to show off his strength. But I looked out of the open window too, over a large area of Amsterdam, over all the roofs and on to the horizon, which was such a pale blue that it was hard to see the dividing line. "As long as this exists," I thought, "and I may live to see it, this sunshine, the cloudless skies, while this lasts, I cannot be unhappy."

The best remedy for those who are afraid, lonely, or unhappy is to go outside, somewhere where they can be quite alone with the heavens, nature, and God. Because only then does one feel that all is as it should be and that God wishes to see people happy, amidst the simple beauty of Nature. As long as this exists, and it certainly always will, I know that then there will always be comfort for every sorrow, whatever the circumstances may be. And I firmly believe that nature brings solace in all troubles.

Oh, who knows, perhaps it won't be long before I can share this overwhelming feeling of bliss with someone who feels the way I do about it.

Yours, Anne

A thought

We miss so much here, so very much and for so long now: I miss it too, just as you do. I'm not talking of outward things, for we are looked after in that way; no, I mean the inward things. Like you, I long for freedom and fresh air, but I believe now that we have ample compensation for our privations. I realized this quite suddenly when I sat in front of the window this morning. I mean inward compensation.

When I looked outside right into the depth of Nature and God, then I was happy, really happy. And Peter, so long as I have that happiness here, the joy in nature, health and a lot more besides, all the while one has that, one can always recapture happiness.

Riches can all be lost, but that happiness in your own heart can only be veiled, and it will still bring you happiness again, as long as you live. As long as you can look fearlessly up into the heavens, as long as you know that you are pure within, and that you will still find happiness.

Tuesday, 1 August, 1944

Dear Kitty,

"Little bundle of contradictions." That's how I ended my last letter[6] and that's how I'm going to begin this one. "A little bundle of contradictions," can you tell me exactly what it is? What does contradiction mean? Like so many words, it can mean two things, contradiction from without and contradiction from within.

The first is the ordinary "not giving in easily, always knowing best, getting in

6. The previous entry ends, "Forgive me, they haven't given me the name 'little bundle of contradictions' all for nothing!"

the last word," *enfin*,[7] all the unpleasant qualities for which I'm renowned. The second nobody knows about, that's my own secret.

I've already told you before that I have, as it were, a dual personality. One half embodies my exuberant cheerfulness, making fun of everything, my high-spiritedness, and above all, the way I take everything lightly. This includes not taking offense at a flirtation, a kiss, an embrace, a dirty joke. This side is usually lying in wait and pushes away the other, which is much better, deeper and purer. You must realize that no one knows Anne's better side and that's why most people find me so insufferable.

Certainly I'm a giddy clown for one afternoon, but then everyone's had enough of me for another month. Really, it's just the same as a love film is for deep-thinking people, simply a diversion, amusing just for once, something which is soon forgotten, not bad, but certainly not good. I loathe having to tell you this, but why shouldn't I, if I know it's true anyway? My lighter superficial side will always be too quick for the deeper side of me and that's why it will always win. You can't imagine how often I've already tried to push this Anne away, to cripple her, to hide her, because after all, she's only half of what's called Anne: but it doesn't work and I know, too, why it doesn't work.

I'm awfully scared that everyone who knows me as I always am will discover that I have another side, a finer and better side. I'm afraid they'll laugh at me, think I'm ridiculous and sentimental, not take me seriously. I'm used to not being taken seriously but it's only the "lighthearted" Anne that's used to it and can bear it; the "deeper" Anne is too frail for it. Sometimes, if I really compel the good Anne to take the stage for a quarter of an hour, she simply shrivels up as soon as she has to speak, and lets Anne number one take over, and before I realize it, she has disappeared.

Therefore, the nice Anne is never present in company, has not appeared one single time so far, but almost always predominates when we're alone. I know exactly how I'd like to be, how I am too . . . inside. But, alas, I'm only like that for myself. And perhaps that's why, no, I'm sure it's the reason why I say I've got a happy nature within and why other people think I've got a happy nature without. I am guided by the pure Anne within, but outside I'm nothing but a frolicsome little goat who's broken loose.

As I've already said, I never utter my real feelings about anything and that's how I've acquired the name of chaser-after-boys, flirt, know-all, reader of love stories. The cheerful Anne laughs about it, gives cheeky answers, shrugs her shoulders indifferently, behaves as if she doesn't care, but, oh dearie me, the quiet Anne's reactions are just the opposite. If I'm to be quite honest, then I must admit that it does hurt me, that I try terribly hard to change myself, but that I'm always fighting against a more powerful enemy.

A voice sobs within me: "There you are, that's what's become of you: you're uncharitable, you look supercilious and peevish, people dislike you and all because you won't listen to the advice given you by your own better half." Oh, I would like to listen, but it doesn't work; if I'm quiet and serious, everyone thinks it's a new comedy and then I have to get out of it by turning it into a joke, not to mention my own family, who are sure to think I'm ill, make me swallow pills for headaches and nerves, feel my neck and my head to see whether I'm

7. In conclusion, in short (French).

running a temperature, ask if I'm constipated and criticize me for being in a bad mood. I can't keep that up: if I'm watched to that extent, I start by getting snappy, then unhappy, and finally I twist my heart round again, so that the bad is on the outside and the good is on the inside and keep on trying to find a way of becoming what I would so like to be, and what I could be, if . . . there weren't any other people living in the world.[8]

Yours, Anne

1942–44   1947

8. This is Anne's last entry in the diary. A Dutch informer (whose identity is a matter of some controversy) betrayed the eight hidden Jews, and on August 4, 1944, Dutch policemen led by a German member of the Gestapo raided the secret annex. All the inhabitants were arrested and sent to German concentration camps; only Otto Frank survived.

JEAN FRITZ
b. 1915

Jean Fritz was born in Hankow (now Wuhan), China, to missionary parents and lived there until she was twelve years old. Although the Yangtze River flowed through Fritz's days (and invaded her dreams once the family left China), Fritz was anxious to become a "real American." When she finally arrived in America, Fritz's feelings of being an outsider both to her native land—China—and to her ancestral home deeply affected her long and distinguished career as an author of children's books. Since the 1950s, Fritz has published more than fifty books, most of them in the genre of life writing.

Fritz is especially known for her biographies of figures from American history (see the excerpt from her "The Double Life of Pocahontas" in the Legends section, above). As Fritz recounts in her second memoir for children, *China Homecoming* (1985), "I could not feel that I truly belonged to my country until I had waded into history and stretched my own American experience into the past." Many of Fritz's accurate and lively biographies have questions in the titles—typical are *And Then What Happened, Paul Revere?* (1973) and *Will You Sign Here, John Hancock?* (1976)—because Fritz believes that "questions imply surprise" and that the power of "surprise" will lead children to both knowledge and pleasure. In her biographies for children, Fritz was determined not to repeat the format of earlier bio-

graphical treatments of heroes and heroines of the American past, which, she explains in *Worlds of Childhood* (1989), were too often "hagiographic, or didactic, or patronizing, or just plain dull." Fritz's elegant books contain the scholarly apparatus expected in a serious biography (notes, sources, direct quotations) as well as the little-known or humorous details of the subject's life that children find fascinating. For example, in *You Want Women to Vote, Lizzie Stanton?* (1995), we learn that while Elizabeth Cady Stanton was conducting a speaking tour with the former governor of Kansas in 1867, rallying support for a proposed amendment to Kansas's state constitution to enact women's suffrage, the two would travel in their mule-drawn carriage at night so that their days could be devoted to gathering audiences. In the deep darkness, Governor Robinson would walk in front of the carriage wearing a white shirt like a beacon guiding Stanton as she drove the mules behind him.

Because Fritz has compressed many of the events of her twelve years in China into one, *Homesick: My Own Story* (1982), a Newbery Honor Book, is not, strictly speaking, an autobiography. In it, Fritz was able to capture for a young audience her love for China, her yearning for an unknown America, and her feelings of dislocation in both worlds.

Homesick: My Own Story

FOREWORD

When I started to write about my childhood in China, I found that my memory came out in lumps. Although I could for the most part arrange them in the proper sequence, I discovered that my preoccupation with time and literal accuracy was squeezing the life out of what I had to say. So I decided to forget about sequence and just get on with it.

Since my childhood feels like a story, I decided to tell it that way, letting the events fall as they would into the shape of a story, lacing them together with fictional bits, adding a piece here and there when memory didn't give me all I needed. I would use conversation freely, for I cannot think of my childhood without hearing voices. So although this book takes place within two years—from October 1925 to September 1927—the events are drawn from the entire period of my childhood, but they are all, except in minor details, basically true. The people are real people; the places are dear to me. But most important, the form I have used has given me the freedom to recreate the emotions that I remember so vividly. Strictly speaking, I have to call this book *fiction*, but it does not feel like fiction to me. It is my story, told as truly as I can tell it.

JEAN FRITZ

DOBBS FERRY, NEW YORK
JANUARY 11, 1982

1

In my father's study there was a large globe with all the countries of the world running around it. I could put my finger on the exact spot where I was and had been ever since I'd been born. And I was on the wrong side of the globe. I was in China in a city named Hankow, a dot on a crooked line that seemed to break the country right in two. The line was really the Yangtse River, but who would know by looking at a map what the Yangtse River really was?

Orange-brown, muddy mustard-colored. And wide, wide, wide. With a river smell that was old and came all the way up from the bottom. Sometimes old women knelt on the riverbank, begging the River God to return a son or grandson who may have drowned. They would wail and beat the earth to make the River God pay attention, but I knew how busy the River God must be. All those people on the Yangtse River! Coolies[1] hauling water. Women washing clothes. Houseboats swarming with old people and young, chickens and pigs. Big crooked-sailed junks[2] with eyes painted on their prows so they could see where they were going. I loved the Yangtse River, but, of course, I belonged on the other side of the world. In America with my grandmother.

Twenty-five fluffy little yellow chicks hatched from our eggs today, my grandmother wrote.

I wrote my grandmother that I had watched a Chinese magician swallow three yards of fire.

---

1. Cheaply employed laborer.
2. Ship used in China with square sails, high sterns, and flat bottoms.

The trouble with living on the wrong side of the world was that I didn't feel like a *real* American.

For instance. I could never be president of the United States. I didn't want to be president; I wanted to be a writer. Still, why should there be a *law* saying that only a person born in the United States could be president? It was as if I wouldn't be American enough.

Actually, I was American every minute of the day, especially during school hours. I went to a British school and every morning we sang "God Save the King." Of course the British children loved singing about their gracious king.[3] Ian Forbes stuck out his chest and sang as if he were saving the king all by himself. Everyone sang. Even Gina Boss who was Italian. And Vera Sebastian who was so Russian she dressed the way Russian girls did long ago before the Revolution[4] when her family had to run away to keep from being killed.

But I wasn't Vera Sebastian. I asked my mother to write an excuse so I wouldn't have to sing, but she wouldn't do it. "When in Rome," she said, "do as the Romans do." What she meant was, "Don't make trouble. Just sing." So for a long time I did. I sang with my fingers crossed but still I felt like a traitor.

Then one day I thought: If my mother and father were really and truly in Rome, they wouldn't do what the Romans did at all. They'd probably try to get the Romans to do what *they* did, just as they were trying to teach the Chinese to do what Americans did. (My mother even gave classes in American manners.)

So that day I quit singing. I kept my mouth locked tight against the king of England. Our teacher, Miss Williams, didn't notice at first. She stood in front of the room, using a ruler for a baton, striking each syllable so hard it was as if she were making up for the times she had nothing to strike.

(Miss Williams was pinch-faced and bossy. Sometimes I wondered what had ever made her come to China. "Maybe to try and catch a husband," my mother said.

---

3. George V (1865–1936; r. 1910–36).   4. That is, the Bolshevik Revolution of 1917.

A husband! Miss Williams!)

"Make him vic-tor-i-ous," the class sang. It was on the strike of "vic" that Miss Williams noticed. Her eyes lighted on my mouth and when we sat down, she pointed her ruler at me.

"Is there something wrong with your voice today, Jean?" she asked.

"No, Miss Williams."

"You weren't singing."

"No, Miss Williams. It is not my national anthem."

"It is the national anthem we sing here," she snapped. "You have always sung. Even Vera sings it."

I looked at Vera with the big blue bow tied on the top of her head. Usually I felt sorry for her but not today. At recess I might even untie that bow, I thought. Just give it a yank. But if I'd been smart, I wouldn't have been looking at Vera. I would have been looking at Ian Forbes and I would have known that, no matter what Miss Williams said, I wasn't through with the king of England.

Recess at the British School was nothing I looked forward to. Every day we played a game called prisoner's base, which was all running and shouting and shoving and catching. I hated the game, yet everyone played except Vera Sebastian. She sat on the sidelines under her blue bow like someone who had been dropped out of a history book. By recess I had forgotten my plans for that bow. While everyone was getting ready for the game, I was as usual trying to look as if I didn't care if I was the last one picked for a team or not. I was leaning against the high stone wall that ran around the schoolyard. I was looking up at a little white cloud skittering across the sky when all at once someone tramped down hard on my right foot. Ian Forbes. Snarling bulldog face. Heel grinding down on my toes. Head thrust forward the way an animal might before it strikes.

"You wouldn't sing it. So say it," he ordered. "Let me hear you say it."

I tried to pull my foot away but he only ground down harder.

"Say what?" I was telling my face please not to show what my foot felt.

"*God save the king.* Say it. Those four words. I want to hear you say it."

Although Ian Forbes was short, he was solid and tough and built for fighting. What was more, he always won. You had only to look at his bare knees between the top of his socks and his short pants to know that he would win. His knees were square. Bony and unbeatable. So of course it was crazy for me to argue with him.

"Why should I?" I asked. "Americans haven't said that since George the Third."[5]

He grabbed my right arm and twisted it behind my back.

"Say it," he hissed.

I felt the tears come to my eyes and I hated myself for the tears. I hated myself for not staying in Rome the way my mother had told me.

"I'll never say it," I whispered.

They were choosing sides now in the schoolyard and Ian's name was being called—among the first as always.

He gave my arm another twist. "You'll sing tomorrow," he snarled, "or you'll be bloody sorry."

As he ran off, I slid to the ground, my head between my knees.

Oh, Grandma, I thought, why can't I be there with you? I'd feed the chickens for you. I'd pump water from the well, the way my father used to do.

It would be almost two years before we'd go to America. I was ten years old now;

5. King during the American Revolution (1738–1820; r. 1760–1820).

I'd be twelve then. But how could I think about *years*? I didn't even dare to think about the next day. After school I ran all the way home, fast so I couldn't think at all.

Our house stood behind a high stone wall which had chips of broken glass sticking up from the top to keep thieves away. I flung open the iron gate and threw myself through the front door.

"I'm home!" I yelled.

Then I remembered that it was Tuesday, the day my mother taught an English class at the Y.M.C.A.[6] where my father was the director.

I stood in the hall, trying to catch my breath, and as always I began to feel small. It was a huge hall with ceilings so high it was as if they would have nothing to do with people. Certainly not with a mere child, not with me—the only child in the house. Once I asked my best friend, Andrea, if the hall made her feel little too. She said no. She was going to be a dancer and she loved space. She did a high kick to show how grand it was to have room.

Andrea Hull was a year older than I was and knew about everything sooner. She told me about commas, for instance, long before I took punctuation seriously. How could I write letters without commas? she asked. She made me so ashamed that for months I hung little wagging comma-tails all over the letters to my grandmother. She told me things that sounded so crazy I had to ask my mother if they were true. Like where babies came from. And that someday the whole world would end. My mother would frown when I asked her, but she always agreed that Andrea was right. It made me furious. How could she know such things and not tell me? What was the matter with grown-ups anyway?

I wished that Andrea were with me now, but she lived out in the country and I didn't see her often. Lin Nai-Nai, my amah,[7] was the only one around, and of course I knew she'd be there. It was her job to stay with me when my parents were out. As soon as she heard me come in, she'd called, "Tsai loushang," which meant that she was upstairs. She might be mending or ironing but most likely she'd be sitting by the window embroidering. And she was. She even had my embroidery laid out, for we had made a bargain. She would teach me to embroider if I would teach her English. I liked embroidering: the cloth stretched tight within my embroidery hoop while I filled in the stamped pattern with cross-stitches and lazy daisy flowers. The trouble was that lazy daisies needed French knots for their centers and I hated making French knots. Mine always fell apart, so I left them to the end. Today I had twenty lazy daisies waiting for their knots.

Lin Nai-Nai had already threaded my needle with embroidery floss.

"Black centers," she said, "for the yellow flowers."

I felt myself glowering. "American flowers don't have centers," I said and gave her back the needle.

Lin Nai-Nai looked at me, puzzled, but she did not argue. She was different from other amahs. She did not even come from the servant class, although this was a secret we had to keep from the other servants who would have made her life miserable, had they known. She had run away from her husband when he had taken a second wife. She would always have been Wife Number One and the Boss no matter how many wives he had, but she would rather be no wife than head of a string of wives. She was modern. She might look old-fashioned, for her feet had been bound

---

6. Young Men's Christian Association, an international community service organization; the first chapter was founded in London in 1844.
7. Nurse, governess.

up tight when she was a little girl so that they would stay small, and now, like many Chinese women, she walked around on little stumps stuffed into tiny cloth shoes. Lin Nai-Nai's were embroidered with butterflies. Still, she believed in true love and one wife for one husband. We were good friends, Lin Nai-Nai and I, so I didn't know why I felt so mean.

She shrugged. "English lesson?" she asked, smiling.

I tested my arm to see if it still hurt from the twisting. It did. My foot too. "What do you want to know?" I asked.

We had been through the polite phrases—Please, Thank you, I beg your pardon, Excuse me, You're welcome, Merry Christmas (which she had practiced but hadn't had a chance to use since this was only October).

"If I meet an American on the street," she asked, "how do I greet him?"

I looked her straight in the eye and nodded my head in a greeting. "Sewing machine," I said. "You say, 'Sew-ing ma-chine.'"

She repeated after me, making the four syllables into four separate words. She got up and walked across the room, bowing and smiling. "Sew Ing Ma Shing."

Part of me wanted to laugh at the thought of Lin Nai-Nai maybe meeting Dr. Carhart, our minister, whose face would surely puff up, the way it always did when he was flustered. But part of me didn't want to laugh at all. I didn't like it when my feelings got tangled, so I ran downstairs and played chopsticks on the piano. Loud and fast. When my sore arm hurt, I just beat on the keys harder.

Then I went out to the kitchen to see if Yang Sze-Fu, the cook, would give me something to eat. I found him reading a Chinese newspaper, his eyes going up and down with the characters. (Chinese words don't march across flat surfaces the way ours do; they drop down cliffs, one cliff after another from right to left across a page.)

"Can I have a piece of cinnamon toast?" I asked. "And a cup of cocoa?"

Yang Sze-Fu grunted. He was smoking a cigarette, which he wasn't supposed to do in the kitchen, but Yang Sze-Fu mostly did what he wanted. He considered himself superior to common workers. You could tell because of the fingernails on his pinkies. They were at least two inches long, which was his way of showing that he didn't have to use his hands for rough or dirty work. He didn't seem to care that his fingernails were dirty, but maybe he couldn't keep such long nails clean.

He made my toast while his cigarette dangled out of the corner of his mouth, collecting a long ash that finally fell on the floor. He wouldn't have kept smoking if my mother had been there, although he didn't always pay attention to my mother. Never about butter pagodas, for instance. No matter how many times my mother told him before a dinner party, "No butter pagoda," it made no difference. As soon as everyone was seated, the serving boy, Wong Sze-Fu, would bring in a pagoda and set it on the table. The guests would "oh" and "ah," for it was a masterpiece: a pagoda molded out of butter, curved roofs rising tier upon tier, but my mother could only think how unsanitary it was. For, of course, Yang Sze-Fu had molded the butter with his hands and carved the decorations with one of his long fingernails. Still, we always used the butter, for if my mother sent it back to the kitchen, Yang Sze-Fu would lose face and quit.

When my toast and cocoa were ready, I took them upstairs to my room (the blue room) and while I ate, I began *Sara Crewe*[8] again. Now there was a girl, I thought, who was worth crying over. I wasn't going to think about myself. Or Ian Forbes. Or the next day. I wasn't. I wasn't.

---

8. Children's story published in 1888 by Frances Hodgson Burnett.

And I didn't. Not all afternoon. Not all evening. Still, I must have decided what I was going to do because the next morning when I started for school and came to the corner where the man sold hot chestnuts, the corner where I always turned to go to school, I didn't turn. I walked straight ahead. I wasn't going to school that day.

I walked toward the Yangtse River. Past the store that sold paper pellets that opened up into flowers when you dropped them in a glass of water. Then up the block where the beggars sat. I never saw anyone give money to a beggar. You couldn't, my father explained, or you'd be mobbed by beggars. They'd follow you everyplace; they'd never leave you alone. I had learned not to look at them when I passed and yet I saw. The running sores, the twisted legs, the mangled faces. What I couldn't get over was that, like me, each one of those beggars had only one life to live. It just happened that they had drawn rotten ones.

Oh, Grandma, I thought, we may be far apart but we're lucky, you and I. Do you even know how lucky? In America do you know?

This part of the city didn't actually belong to the Chinese, even though the beggars sat there, even though upper-class Chinese lived there. A long time ago other countries had just walked into China and divided up part of Hankow (and other cities) into sections, or concessions, which they called their own and used their own rules for governing.[9] We lived in the French concession on Rue de Paris. Then there was the British concession and the Japanese. The Russian and German concessions had been officially returned to China, but the people still called them concessions. The Americans didn't have one, although, like some of the other countries, they had gunboats on the river. In case, my father said. In case what? Just in case. That's all he'd say.

The concessions didn't look like the rest of China. The buildings were solemn and orderly with little plots of grass around them. Not like those in the Chinese part of the city: a jumble of rickety shops with people, vegetables, crates of quacking ducks, yard goods, bamboo baskets, and mangy dogs spilling onto a street so narrow it was hardly there.

The grandest street in Hankow was the Bund,[1] which ran along beside the Yangtse River. When I came to it after passing the beggars, I looked to my left and saw the American flag flying over the American consulate building. I was proud of the flag and I thought maybe today it was proud of me. It flapped in the breeze as if it were saying ha-ha to the king of England.

Then I looked to the right at the Customs House, which stood at the other end of the Bund. The clock on top of the tower said nine-thirty. How would I spend the day?

I crossed the street to the promenade part of the Bund. When people walked here, they weren't usually going anyplace; they were just out for the air. My mother would wear her broad-brimmed beaver hat when we came and my father would swing his cane in that jaunty way that showed how glad he was to be a man. I thought I would just sit on a bench for the morning. I would watch the Customs House clock, and when it was time, I would eat the lunch I had brought along in my schoolbag.

I was the only one sitting on a bench. People did not generally "take the air" on a Wednesday morning and besides, not everyone was allowed here. The British had put a sign on the Bund, NO DOGS, NO CHINESE. This meant that I could never bring

9. Treaties signed with Western powers between 1842 and 1860 opened up Chinese ports to foreign trade and residents. By the provisions of these treaties, foreign residents were granted extraterritori- ality, ensuring that they were subject only to their own country's and not Chinese law.
1. The name often given in the Far East to an embanked street along a river or sea.

Lin Nai-Nai with me. My father couldn't even bring his best friend, Mr. T. K. Hu. Maybe the British wanted a place where they could pretend they weren't in China, I thought. Still, there were always Chinese coolies around. In order to load and unload boats in the river, coolies had to cross the Bund. All day they went back and forth, bent double under their loads, sweating and chanting in a tired, singsong way that seemed to get them from one step to the next.

To pass the time, I decided to recite poetry. The one good thing about Miss Williams was that she made us learn poems by heart and I liked that. There was one particular poem I didn't want to forget. I looked at the Yangtse River and pretended that all the busy people in the boats were my audience.

" 'Breathes there the man, with soul so dead,'" I cried, " 'Who never to himself hath said, This is my own, my native land!'"[2]

I was so carried away by my performance that I didn't notice the policeman until he was right in front of me. Like all policemen in the British concession, he was a bushy-bearded Indian with a red turban wrapped around his head.

He pointed to my schoolbag. "Little miss," he said, "why aren't you in school?"

He was tall and mysterious-looking, more like a character in my Arabian Nights book than a man you expected to talk to. I fumbled for an answer. "I'm going on an errand," I said finally. "I just sat down for a rest." I picked up my schoolbag and walked quickly away. When I looked around, he was back on his corner, directing traffic.

So now they were chasing children away too, I thought angrily. Well, I'd like to show them. Someday I'd like to walk a dog down the whole length of the Bund. A Great Dane. I'd have him on a leash—like this—(I put out my hand as if I were holding a leash right then) and he'd be so big and strong I'd have to strain to hold him back (I strained). Then of course sometimes he'd have to do his business and I'd stop (like this) right in the middle of the sidewalk and let him go to it. I was so busy with my Great Dane I was at the end of the Bund before I knew it. I let go of the leash, clapped my hands, and told my dog to go home. Then I left the Bund and the concessions and walked into the Chinese world.

My mother and father and I had walked here but not for many months. This part near the river was called the Mud Flats. Sometimes it was muddier than others, and when the river flooded, the flats disappeared underwater. Sometimes even the fishermen's huts were washed away, knocked right off their long-legged stilts and swept down the river. But today the river was fairly low and the mud had dried so that it was cracked and cakey. Most of the men who lived here were out fishing, some not far from the shore, poling their sampans[3] through the shallow water. Only a few people were on the flats: a man cleaning fish on a flat rock at the water's edge, a woman spreading clothes on the dirt to dry, a few small children. But behind the huts was something I had never seen before. Even before I came close, I guessed what it was. Even then, I was excited by the strangeness of it.

It was the beginnings of a boat. The skeleton of a large junk, its ribs lying bare, its backbone running straight and true down the bottom. The outline of the prow was already in place, turning up wide and snub-nosed, the way all junks did. I had never thought of boats starting from nothing, of taking on bones under their bodies. The eyes, I supposed, would be the last thing added. Then the junk would have life.

The builders were not there and I was behind the huts where no one could see me

---

2. From "The Lay of the Last Minstrel" (1805), by Sir Walter Scott.

3. Flat-bottomed boats propelled from the stern by one or two oars.

as I walked around and around, marveling. Then I climbed inside and as I did, I knew that something wonderful was happening to me. I was a-tingle, the way a magician must feel when he swallows fire, because suddenly I knew that the boat was mine. No matter who really owned it, it was mine. Even if I never saw it again, it would be my junk sailing up and down the Yangtse River. My junk seeing the river sights with its two eyes, seeing them for me whether I was there or not. Often I had tried to put the Yangtse River into a poem so I could keep it. Sometimes I had tried to draw it, but nothing I did ever came close. But now, *now* I had my junk and somehow that gave me the river too.

I thought I should put my mark on the boat. Perhaps on the side of the spine. Very small. A secret between the boat and me. I opened my schoolbag and took out my folding penknife that I used for sharpening pencils. Very carefully I carved the Chinese character that was our name. Gau. (In China my father was Mr. Gau, my mother was Mrs. Gau, and I was Little Miss Gau.) The builders would paint right over the character, I thought, and never notice. But I would know. Always and forever I would know.

For a long time I dreamed about the boat, imagining it finished, its sails up, its eyes wide. Someday it might sail all the way down the Yangtse to Shanghai, so I told the boat what it would see along the way because I had been there and the boat hadn't. After a while I got hungry and I ate my egg sandwich. I was in the midst of peeling an orange when all at once I had company.

A small boy, not more than four years old, wandered around to the back of the huts, saw me, and stopped still. He was wearing a ragged blue cotton jacket with a red cloth, pincushion-like charm around his neck which was supposed to keep him from getting smallpox. Sticking up straight from the middle of his head was a small pigtail which I knew was to fool the gods and make them think he was a girl. (Gods didn't bother much with girls; it was boys that were important in China.) The weather was still warm so he wore no pants, nothing below the waist. Most small boys went around like this so that when they had to go, they could just let loose and go. He walked slowly up to the boat, stared at me, and then nodded as if he'd already guessed what I was. "Foreign devil," he announced gravely.

I shook my head. "No," I said in Chinese. "American friend." Through the ribs of the boat, I handed him a segment of orange. He ate it slowly, his eyes on the rest of the orange. Segment by segment, I gave it all to him. Then he wiped his hands down the front of his jacket.

"Foreign devil," he repeated.

"American friend," I corrected. Then I asked him about the boat. Who was building it? Where were the builders?

He pointed with his chin upriver. "Not here today. Back tomorrow."

I knew it would only be a question of time before the boy would run off to alert the people in the huts. "Foreign devil, foreign devil," he would cry. So I put my hand on the prow of the boat, wished it luck, and climbing out, I started back toward the Bund. To my surprise the boy walked beside me. When we came to the edge of the Bund, I squatted down so we would be on the same eye level.

"Good-bye," I said. "May the River God protect you."

For a moment the boy stared. When he spoke, it was as if he were trying out a new sound. "American friend," he said slowly.

When I looked back, he was still there, looking soberly toward the foreign world to which I had gone.

The time, according to the Customs House clock, was five after two, which meant that I couldn't go home for two hours. School was dismissed at three-thirty and I was home by three-forty-five unless I had to stay in for talking in class. It took me about fifteen minutes to write "I will not talk in class" fifty times, and so I often came home at four o'clock. (I wrote up and down like the Chinese: fifty "I's," fifty "wills," and right through the sentence so I never had to think what I was writing. It wasn't as if I were making a promise.) Today I planned to arrive home at four, my "staying-in" time, in the hope that I wouldn't meet classmates on the way.

Meanwhile I wandered up and down the streets, in and out of stores. I weighed myself on the big scale in the Hankow Dispensary and found that I was as skinny as ever. I went to the Terminus Hotel and tried out the chairs in the lounge. At first I didn't mind wandering about like this. Half of my mind was still on the river with my junk, but as time went on, my junk began slipping away until I was alone with nothing but questions. Would my mother find out about today? How could I skip school tomorrow? And the next day and the next? Could I get sick? Was there a kind of long lie-abed sickness that didn't hurt?

I arrived home at four, just as I had planned, opened the door, and called out, "I'm home!" Cheery-like and normal. But I was scarcely in the house before Lin Nai-Nai ran to me from one side of the hall and my mother from the other.

"Are you all right? Are you all right?" Lin Nai-Nai felt my arms as if she expected them to be broken. My mother's face was white. "What happened?" she asked.

Then I looked through the open door into the living room and saw Miss Williams sitting there. She had beaten me home and asked about my absence, which of course had scared everyone. But now my mother could see that I was in one piece and for some reason this seemed to make her mad. She took me by the hand and led me into the living room. "Miss Williams said you weren't in school," she said. "Why was that?"

I hung my head, just the way cowards do in books.

My mother dropped my hand. "Jean will be in school tomorrow," she said firmly. She walked Miss Williams to the door. "Thank you for stopping by."

Miss Williams looked satisfied in her mean, pinched way. "Well," she said, "ta-ta." (She always said "ta-ta" instead of "good-bye." Chicken language, it sounded like.)

As soon as Miss Williams was gone and my mother was sitting down again, I burst into tears. Kneeling on the floor, I buried my head in her lap and poured out the whole miserable story. My mother could see that I really wasn't in one piece after all, so she listened quietly, stroking my hair as I talked, but gradually I could feel her stiffen. I knew she was remembering that she was a Mother.

"You better go up to your room," she said, "and think things over. We'll talk about it after supper."

I flung myself on my bed. What was there to think? Either I went to school and got beaten up. Or I quit.

After supper I explained to my mother and father how simple it was. I could stay at home and my mother could teach me, the way Andrea's mother taught her. Maybe I could even go to Andrea's house and study with her.

My mother shook her head. Yes, it was simple, she agreed. I could go back to the British School, be sensible, and start singing about the king again.

I clutched the edge of the table. Couldn't she understand? I couldn't turn back now. It was too late.

So far my father had not said a word. He was leaning back, teetering on the two hind legs of his chair, the way he always did after a meal, the way that drove my mother crazy. But he was not the kind of person to keep all four legs of a chair on the floor just because someone wanted him to. He wasn't a turning-back person so I hoped maybe he would understand. As I watched him, I saw a twinkle start in his eyes and suddenly he brought his chair down slam-bang flat on the floor. He got up and motioned for us to follow him into the living room. He sat down at the piano and began to pick out the tune for "God Save the King."

A big help, I thought. Was he going to make me practice?

Then he began to sing:

"My country 'tis of thee,

Sweet land of liberty, . . ."

Of course! It was the same tune. Why hadn't I thought of that? Who would know what I was singing as long as I moved my lips? I joined in now, loud and strong.

"Of thee I sing."

My mother laughed in spite of herself. "If you sing that loud," she said, "you'll start a revolution."

"Tomorrow I'll sing softly," I promised. "No one will know." But for now I really let freedom ring.

Then all at once I wanted to see Lin Nai-Nai. I ran out back, through the courtyard that separated the house from the servants' quarters, and upstairs to her room.

"It's me," I called through the door and when she opened up, I threw my arms around her. "Oh, Lin Nai-Nai, I love you," I said. "You haven't said it yet, have you?"

"Said what?"

"Sewing machine. You haven't said it?"

"No," she said, "not yet. I'm still practicing."

"Don't say it, Lin Nai-Nai. Say 'Good day.' It's shorter and easier. Besides, it's more polite."

"Good day?" she repeated.

"Yes, that's right. Good day." I hugged her and ran back to the house.

The next day at school when we rose to sing the British national anthem, everyone stared at me, but as soon as I opened my mouth, the class lost interest. All but Ian Forbes. His eyes never left my face, but I sang softly, carefully, proudly. At recess he sauntered over to where I stood against the wall.

He spat on the ground. "You can be bloody glad you sang today," he said. Then he strutted off as if he and those square knees of his had won again.

And, of course, I was bloody glad.

2

I always thought I would feel more American if I'd been named Marjorie. I could picture a girl named Marjorie roller skating in America (I had never roller-skated). Or sled riding (there was neither snow nor hills in Hankow). Or being wild on Halloween night (I had never celebrated Halloween). The name Jean was so short, there didn't seem to be enough room in it for all the things I wanted to do, all the ways I wanted to be. Sometimes I wondered if my mother had picked a short name because she had her heart set on my being just one kind of person. Ever since she'd written in my autograph book, I was afraid that goodness was what she really wanted out of me.

"Be good, sweet child," she had written, "and let who will be clever."[4]

Deep in my heart I knew that goodness didn't come natural to me. If I had to

---

4. Adapted from "A Farewell" (1856), by Charles Kingsley (who wrote "maid" instead of "child").

choose, I would rather be clever, but I didn't understand why anyone had to choose. I wasn't even sure that the people could choose, although my mother was always saying that if they really tried, people could be whatever they wanted to be. But that was just more grown-up talk. As if wanting to be beautiful (like my mother) could make one bit of difference in my looks. As if trying to beat up Ian Forbes could do anything but land me in trouble. As for being good, I had to admit that I didn't always want to be.

Dear Grandma (I wrote in my next letter): I want to warn you so you won't be disappointed. I'm not always good. Sometimes I don't even try.

It was true. I knew I wasn't supposed to go to the Mud Flats alone, but twice I had managed to sneak off for a quick visit. The boat was gone, already at home on the river, I supposed, but my little friend was there. Each time he had run up to greet me and I had given him an orange. Each time he had called me "American friend" and had walked me back to the Bund.

Of course I knew I was wrong to disobey my mother but that hadn't stopped me. Still, I did feel guilty. If my name had been Marjorie, I thought, I would not have been the sort of person to feel guilty. And if it had not been the end of November, with Christmas already in the air, I might not have thought of the perfect way to solve my problem.

"I know what you can give me for Christmas," I told my mother.

"I've already bought your presents." My mother was writing letters at her little black lacquer desk and she didn't look up.

"This wouldn't cost a thing," I explained. "It would be easy."

"Well?" She still didn't look up.

"You could give me a new name. That's what I really want."

Now she did look up. She even put down her pen. "And what, may I ask, is the matter with the name you have?"

"I don't like it. Take it back." I put my arm around her neck because I didn't want her to feel bad about the mistake she'd made. "Give me the name Marjorie. Just write it on a gift card and put it in a box. You see how easy it would be."

My mother shook her head as if she couldn't understand how I'd got into the family. "I wouldn't name a cat Marjorie," she said.

Well, of course not! "Marjorie is not a cat's name," I yelled. And I stamped out of the room.

When I asked my father, he simply changed the subject. "I know one present you are getting for Christmas," he said, "that you've never even thought of."

He was a good subject-changer.

"Animal, vegetable, or mineral?" I asked.

"Vegetable."

"How heavy?"

"As heavy as a pound of butter." He'd give me no more clues, but of course I did give it a lot of thought between then and Christmas.

But I hadn't forgotten about Marjorie. I was going to Andrea's for the weekend and I would see what she thought.

I loved going to the Hulls'. Not only did they have low ceilings and three children (Andrea, Edward, and David, the adopted one), but the Hull family was different from any I had ever known. They must have believed in goodness because, like us, they were a Y.M.C.A. family, but what they stressed was being free and natural. When the family was alone, for instance, they thought nothing of walking around upstairs without any clothes on. The way Andrea spoke, it was as if she hardly noticed if her parents were naked or not. Moreover, the Hulls seemed to talk together about anything, not as if conversation were divided into Adult subjects and You're-Not-Old-Enough-to-Understand subjects. They discussed whether Adam and Eve had been real people or whether there would ever be another world war. Things like that. And Andrea not only knew how babies were born, she knew exactly how she, herself, had been born.

Since Mr. and Mrs. Hull were in such agreement, you would have thought they would have been happy, but they weren't. According to Andrea, her parents did not get along. She was even afraid they might get a divorce. I had never known anyone who'd had a divorce and I had no way of knowing how married people got along, so of course I was interested in hearing the ups and downs of Mr. and Mrs. Hull's married life. Indeed, I never came back from Andrea's without something new to think about.

My mother was going to take me to the Hulls' on Friday and since my father had a committee meeting that night, she would stay for supper and Mr. Hull would drive her home in his Dodge sedan. I would go home when the Hulls came into town for church on Sunday.

So on Friday I put on my middy blouse which, more than any of my clothes, made me feel like a Marjorie, and my mother called for rickshas. The coolies came running, jostling and swearing at each other, each one shouting for us to take *his* ricksha, take *his*, take *his*. I always felt sorry for the coolies who weren't chosen. I knew how few coppers they made and how often they had to go without rice but, on the other hand, I felt sorry for those who were chosen. The harder a coolie ran and the heavier his load, the sooner he would die. Most ricksha coolies didn't live to be thirty, my father said. Of course I was not a heavy load, but even so, by the time we reached the Hulls' house, my coolie was wiping the sweat from his face, using the dirty rag that hung at his waist. It was no use telling a coolie to walk, not run. He'd feel he was a weakling if he didn't run; he'd lose face.

The Hulls' house was red brick and American-looking, not American like the pictures of my grandmother's house which had a front porch and honeysuckle vines and a swing, but American like a picture in a magazine. Mr. Hull had designed it himself, with special features for his family. Andrea's room, for instance, had a bar down one wall for her to use when she practiced dancing. We went straight to her room and I sat down in her white wicker rocking chair and waited for the news.

"Well, I'm afraid they are doomed," she sighed. Her parents had had a terrible fight the week before, she reported, and hadn't spoken for days. "And they won't listen to me. I figured out how we could bring our whole family together but they won't listen."

Andrea was lying flat on the floor because that was good for her posture, but with news like this, I was surprised that she still cared about her posture.

"What did you figure out?" I asked.

"A baby." Andrea gave me time to get used to the idea. "I didn't expect my mother to have the baby," she explained. "That would take too long. I wanted my parents to adopt one from the same place that they adopted David. Then we'd all have someone we could love together." She began pedaling her legs in the air to strengthen her thighs. "Besides," she added, "an adopted baby would be good for David. He wouldn't feel so left out. You know how he is."

I did know. At twelve, David was the oldest of the children. The Hulls had adopted him when they thought they couldn't have children of their own. Then a year later Andrea had come along and afterwards Edward, but Mr. and Mrs. Hull treated David the same as the others and seemed to love him as much. Still, David felt different. He was always wondering who his real mother and father were, even though the Hulls said they didn't know, couldn't find out, and it didn't matter. They didn't even want him to talk about it and he didn't, except sometimes to Andrea and me.

Andrea let her legs drop to the floor and rolled over to look at me. "They weren't even interested in a baby," she said. "But guess what?"

"What?"

"They decided it would be nice to invite an orphan here for Christmas vacation. So they wrote to the orphanage and we heard yesterday. We're going to have a girl. Eleven years old. She'll arrive by boat three days before Christmas and stay through New Year's."

"What's her name?"

"Millie." Andrea screwed up her face. "Ugh."

I agreed that the name was not good. But an orphan! I'd like an orphan sleeping in my house and spending Christmas with me. "Maybe you could call her Lee for short," I suggested.

Later at supper Mrs. Hull told my mother about Millie's coming. As soon as she was finished, I spoke up.

"Why couldn't we . . ." I began, but Mrs. Hull interrupted. She turned to my mother.

"We could share Millie," she said. "She could go to your house for a few days in the middle of her stay. I expect Jean would like that."

That wasn't what I'd had in mind, but still it sounded like a good idea. So it was settled that when the Hulls came to our house for Christmas dinner (which they always did), they would leave Millie with us for three days. (In my mind I was already calling her Lee. She'd be more like a sister, I decided, than a friend.)

I was still thinking about Lee when we went to bed, although I didn't usually bother with private thoughts when I was going to bed at Andrea's. The Hulls believed in fresh air, so they had a sleeping porch where the whole family slept, winter and summer, with the windows wide open around three sides of the room. When I came for a visit, Mr. and Mrs. Hull slept in their own room and I used their bed. Sometimes before going to sleep, David and Andrea and Edward (who was only six) and I played Pioneer. We'd roll the beds into a semicircle and fight off the horse thieves. Sometimes we played War and lined up the beds for the wounded. Maybe because it was later than usual, tonight we didn't play anything. Andrea got under the covers and began right away to shake her head from side to side on the pillow, which was the way she went to sleep. Sometimes she had to shake her head a long time but not tonight. I had decided that I was the only one awake when I saw David sit up.

"Jean?" he whispered. "You awake? I want to ask a favor."

I couldn't imagine what David Hull could want of me. I did understand, however, that it wasn't easy for him to ask. He was a pale, thin-faced, twitchy boy who, I had to admit, seemed out of place in the Hull family with their free and natural ways.

"I want it to be a secret." His whisper had turned hoarse.

I got up, pulled a blanket off my bed, wrapped myself up, and went to sit on his bed.

"You know that Millie," he said.

"Yes."

"Well, she comes from the same orphans' home as I came from. And I was thinking. They must have records in the office of that place." He was looking out the window and shivering as he talked.

"Why couldn't she sneak into that office when she goes back after being here? Why couldn't she find out about me?" He took such a big breath I could feel the favor coming.

"Then she could write you. And you could tell me. That way, Mom and Dad wouldn't have to know anything about it. You know how they are."

The whole idea sounded crazy. "David," I said, "why do you care so much? What difference does it make?"

He turned on me, his face fiercer than I'd known it could be. "How would you like it," he hissed, "if you didn't know whether your father was a crook or what he was? Or whether he was dead or alive? If you didn't know that you were American? You might be Russian or Danish or German or anything. How would you like it?"

Well, of course, I knew I wouldn't like it. "But you're legally an American," I pointed out.

"Legally! What difference does that make?" David's whisper was becoming raspier and raspier. "When you go back to America, you'll know you're home. When you meet your grandmother, you'll know she's your real grandmother. I won't know anything." He spoke so fast it was as if he'd learned his thoughts by heart. "You see?" he asked.

"Yes."

"Well, will you or won't you? Will you make the plans with Millie?"

"Yes," I said, "I will." But as I went back to bed, my feelings were tangled up again. Part of me said that I had to help him; part of me said I couldn't help him. In the first place, the idea wouldn't work; in the second place, David would never be satisfied. No matter what he found out, he would always want to know more.

From across the room came his whisper, quieter now. "Thanks," he said. "But remember. Don't even tell Andrea."

As it turned out, Andrea and I were so busy the next day, I wasn't even tempted to tell. As soon as we got up, she announced that we were going to wash our hair. She had a new rinse made from dried camomile flowers. "It brings out the hidden lights in your hair," she explained. Andrea had different shades of gold already in her hair, but I didn't see what could be hidden in my plain brown hair. Certainly I never dreamed I could have undiscovered red highlights but Andrea said I could; I just needed to encourage them to come out. And of course I was willing to do that. So Andrea dropped the dried, buttonlike flowers in a pitcher of hot water, and while they soaked, we began washing our hair, each of us soaping each other and giving each other a first rinse with ordinary water.

Then for the magic rinse. I poured half the pitcher of camomile mixture over Andrea's head and she poured the other half over mine. I rushed to the mirror.

"Wait until it dries," Andrea said.

So I rubbed my head with a towel, stopping every few minutes for a look. No sign of red yet. I kept rubbing until at last Andrea (whose hair was a-glint) told me to quit. As soon as I'd combed my hair, she inspected it and assured me that there was a change. "Wait until the sun shines on it," she said. "That's when it really shows up." I smiled as I fluffed out my hair. I had never appreciated its possibilities before.

After breakfast we walked on top of the wall that separated the Hulls' property from the Chinese farms. It was an eight-foot-high wall and when you stood on it, you felt as if you owned the world. Today with the air crisp and the sun making highlights on my hair, I felt especially pleased with that world. It was like a picture postcard. Across the background a water buffalo walked with a boy on its back. The rest of the picture was divided neatly into little farm plots, each with its mud hut, each with its creaking well. From this height the people didn't look like poor, over-worked Chinese; they seemed to be toy people going happily about their business. And I felt like a queen, walking the turret of my castle. I waved my arm at the scene below.

"That's our kingdom," I announced to Andrea. "And I am Queen Marjorie. Who are you?"

"You are Queen—who?"

"Marjorie."

Andrea gave me the same kind of withering look as my mother had. "Marjorie is not a name for a queen," she said. "It's not a decent name for anyone."

I felt myself getting mad, so to be safe, I sat down, my feet dangling over the Chinese side of the wall.

"I happen to like the name Marjorie," I said stiffly. "I guess I can be Queen-anything-I-want-to-be. What's your name?"

Andrea was sitting down too. "Queen Zobeide."[5]

I didn't have the chance to tell her what I thought of her name. Actually both of us forgot all about being queens because at that moment an old woman stepped out of a hut and started shrieking and cursing at a man in the next farmyard. She shook her fists. "Egg of a turtle!" she screamed. "May all your children fall sick! May you outlive every one of them! May the gods heap misfortune on your head!" On and on.

At night lying on the sleeping porch, Andrea and I had often heard women carrying on like this. Now we were trying so hard to catch all the language, not to miss a word, that we were surprised when at the height of her rage the woman stopped short. There was a moment of complete silence. The woman had caught sight of us, sitting on our wall, staring. She put her hands on her hips, threw back her head, and called on all the gods and neighbors to come and witness the dog-things in their midst. It was as if now, *now* she had at last found someone worthy of her anger. She could forget the poor pig of a man who lived next door. For us she found new words so bad we couldn't translate them, although our Chinese was as good as our English. As her voice grew more shrill, her neighbors did come to listen and look. Occasionally a man would laugh and add an insult. Young boys began picking up stones and hurling them at the wall. "Foreign devils," they shouted. "Foreign devils."

Andrea and I were used to being called "foreign devil." We were used to insults. Coolies often spat directly in our path, but we had been taught to act as if we didn't see, as if nothing had happened. But today it was different. More people angry all together, angrier than before. We knew the stones wouldn't reach us; still, we couldn't get down from that wall fast enough.

As soon as we were off the ladder, we slid to the ground, out of breath. "I guess it will get worse," Andrea said. "It's the Communists who are doing this. They're the ones who are making the Chinese so mad."

Of course I knew about the Communists who wanted to make a revolution in China like the one in Russia that had driven Vera Sebastian out. Still, I hadn't paid much attention. All my life there had been fighting somewhere in China—warlord against warlord. Grown-ups were constantly talking about these warlords, hoping that one of them would finally bring the country together in peace. When a warlord was a Christian (and one or two were), my father really got his hopes up. But I just thought of the Communists as another group of Chinese. Fighting as always.

But it wasn't like that, Andrea said. If the Communists got the chance, there would

5. Heroine (sometimes called "Zobeida") of one of the tales in *The Arabian Nights*.

be a new kind of war. Farmers against their landlords. Factory workers against factory owners. The poor against the rich. Chinese against foreigners. "The Communists want to get us out," she said. "My father says that one day we may be glad to have those gunboats in the river to protect us."

It all sounded so complicated, I thought of my father when he was discouraged. Sometimes he'd put out his hands in a kind of helpless gesture. "But China's so big," he'd say, as if he were apologizing for having come so far and doing so little. That's the way I felt now. China was too big for me to even imagine all the things that might happen. At the moment all I hoped was that the Communists wouldn't spoil Christmas.

But after the weekend when I got home, I was glad to see that Christmas seemed to be coming on in the usual way. We had mailed our packages to America months ago. (I had sent my grandmother a doily filled with nothing but French knots. It was a "labor of love," I explained.) Now big, bulky packages were arriving from America, pasted over with seals that said, DO NOT OPEN UNTIL DECEMBER 25. Of course I knew what my grandmother had sent me because every year she sent the same thing. I didn't blame her. Without having met me, how could she know that I hated to get clothes for Christmas? Besides, she had made every one of the petticoats she sent, so they were probably labors of love too.

In addition to the American packages, presents were being delivered to my parents from Chinese friends. Almost every day when I came home from school I'd find one or two cakes on the hall table, waiting to be put away. They were all alike—tall, castlelike cakes, each with white icing and pink characters that said LONG LIFE AND HAPPINESS and sprinkled all over with tiny silver pellets that my mother wouldn't let me eat.

I was also buying presents to give away. For Lee I had bought a red pencil box with two drawers in it, like mine. A package of open-up paper flowers. And I had gone into the sandalwood box where I kept my savings and taken out twenty coppers and four twenty-cent pieces. I had them changed into a silver dollar and put it in a velvet-lined jewelry case my mother had. Although it was hard to take so much money out of my savings all at once, I figured that orphans would hardly ever have money of their own, certainly not as much as a whole dollar. My mother, who was positive that Lee would like clothes, was knitting a sweater and a pair of mittens.

I had thought so much about Lee that by Christmas Eve I felt I knew her. I pictured how much more comfortable she'd be with me than with a sleeping porch full of children and with grown-ups who might or might not be speaking to each other. I wished she could have been with us to help decorate the tree and hang the red crepe paper streamers in the dining room, but I knew I shouldn't expect life to be one-hundred-percent perfect. It was enough that she was coming the next day. And if we really became good friends—well, who knew what might happen? After all, orphans could be adopted.

I bargained with my parents about what time we'd get up in the morning. "Six o'clock," I suggested. "Seven," my father countered. "Six-thirty," I offered. He accepted. He even agreed not to shave until after we had opened our presents. Our guests wouldn't be arriving until one o'clock. Eleven guests altogether: the Hulls, Lee, two elderly missionary ladies who would otherwise be alone at Christmas, and three sailors (whom we'd never met) from an American gunboat.

What I liked best about Christmas was that for a whole day grown-ups seemed to agree to take time off from being grown-ups. At six-thirty sharp when I burst into my parents' room, yelling "Merry Christmas!," they both laughed and jumped right up as if six-thirty wasn't an early hour at all. By the time we came downstairs, the servants were lined up in the hall dressed in their best. "Gung-shi." They bowed. "Gung-shi. Gung-shi." This was the way Chinese offered congratulations on special occasions, and the greeting, as it was repeated, sounded like little bells tinkling. Lin Nai-Nai, however, didn't "gung-shi." For months she had been waiting for this day. She stepped forward. "Merry Christmas," she said just as if she could have said anything in English that she wanted to. I was so proud, I took her hand as we all trooped into the living room. My father lighted the tree and he distributed the first gifts of the day—red envelopes filled with money for the servants. After a flurry of more "gung-shis," the servants left and there were the three of us in front of a huge mound of packages. All mysteries.

I kept telling myself that we wanted to make Christmas last but whenever it was my turn to open a package, I yanked at the ribbons and tore off the paper because I couldn't wait. When I had finished, I was sitting inside a circle of presents: four books, a fountain pen, an Uncle Wiggily game,[6] a stamp album, a skipping rope, a pocketbook, a bracelet, a paperweight with snow falling inside, and best of all, the "pound of butter" present—a box of pale blue stationery with my name JEAN GUTTERY and HANKOW, CHINA printed in gold at the top with a little gold pagoda at each side. And of course there were clothes, including the petticoat from my grandmother, one size larger than last year's. But I felt strange when I thought of my grandmother. Here I was in the middle of Christmas and there she was with Christmas not even started in her house. It was only December 24 in America.

I was watching out the window when the Hulls arrived. As soon as the Dodge sedan drew up, a back door flew open and Andrea jumped out. By the time she reached the door, I was there.

"Call her Millie," she whispered. "She hates Lee."

David was behind. "She's shy," he said, whispering too. "And hard to talk to. But remember, you promised."

Edward followed, pushing past to get to the Christmas tree.

Back at the car Mrs. Hull was standing at one side, bending over and looking in. Even from the back she looked like someone who studied American fashion magazines. Mr. Hull was standing on the other side of the car, also bending over. They were obviously talking to Millie. After a few minutes Mr. Hull straightened up and came to the house, carrying Millie's suitcase. Mrs. Hull and Millie followed.

I was surprised at Millie. I guess I expected everyone to look happy on Christmas, but I could tell by the way she walked with her head down that she wasn't happy. When she reached the door and did look up, what struck me was her expression. She had the same secretive, stubborn look that Vera Sebastian had. Well, she was scared, I told myself. I would be scared too if I were in her place.

I grinned in a way that was supposed to show that at least I wasn't anyone to be scared of. "Come on up and see my room," I said.

She followed.

"Bring your suitcase," I suggested.

Her suitcase was standing inside the front door but she didn't turn around. "No," she said. "Not now."

Upstairs I showed her not only my room but all the rooms and each time she said, "Uh-huh." By the end of the tour I was talking so loud, it was as if I thought she was deaf. "Let's go downstairs," I said. "Your presents are under the tree."

---

6. Based on the main character of a series of children's books by Howard R. Garis (1873–1962).

Sitting beside the tree, Millie opened her packages slowly, careful to untie the ribbons, careful not to tear the paper. Each time she said "Thank you" dutifully as if she'd been told to say it. She did seem to like her sweater because she put it on, and I noticed that when she thought no one was looking, she took the silver dollar out of its box and slipped it into her sweater pocket. When she had finally finished, Andrea and I tore open our gifts to each other. A can of camomile flowers for me, a package of fortune-telling cards for her.

The other guests arrived now and at my mother's nod, I made the rounds, dropping a British School curtsy to each one. I only did it to please my mother, but it was a mistake. The missionary ladies tried to be cute and, giggling, they curtsied back. Andrea looked ready to throw up and the sailors, who had obviously not been in a curtsying crowd before, blushed. Fortunately Wong Sze-Fu, the serving boy, saved the day by announcing that dinner was ready, so we trooped into the dining room. The turkey, surrounded by a ring of candied red apples, sat on a silver platter at my father's place. Rising triumphantly from the center of the table was a butter pagoda, unusually tall and splendid. As we sat down, I thought that now things would be better. Once we started eating, people would perk up and be jolly. Maybe even Millie.

What I hadn't counted on was that those three sailors would be quite so shy. I could see that they wanted to be friendly but didn't know how. So my father began talking about Christmas at home in Pennsylvania and before long all the grown-ups were talking about old Christmases. The sailors told about their families in New Jersey and Illinois and Ohio and the missionary ladies chimed in about Michigan and Maryland and Mr. Hull described Christmas in Los Angeles, California, and Mrs. Hull said, no, it wasn't like that at all. Of course this left the children with nothing to talk about. Not one of us had been to a single state in America.

Well, I thought, after dinner we'd go into the living room and sing around the piano. Then things would be better. But when the time came, Millie didn't want to sing. She sat on the couch, and although Andrea and I urged her, she wouldn't even join in for "Deck the Halls," my favorite. She wouldn't come to the piano when Phillip, the sailor from New Jersey, asked her, even though he was the cutest of the three sailors and I didn't see how anyone could turn him down.

Andrea looked at me and shrugged as if she'd given up, but when the missionary ladies and the sailors left, Millie suddenly seemed to come to life. Edward suggested that we children should play hide-and-seek, and right away Millie smiled as if she'd been waiting for something like this. "Let's," she said.

David said he'd be "it," and as the five of us ran into the hall to start the game, I took Millie's hand.

"You can hide with me," I said.

"Thanks, but I'd rather hide by myself." Millie answered in a tone that was almost friendly, so I didn't feel bad. And since I'd shown her the house, I didn't suppose she'd get lost.

While everyone scattered, I crept into my favorite hiding place, the little closet tucked under the stairs. I closed the door and although I could just barely hear David beginning to count, in a few minutes I couldn't even hear that. Scrunched up on the floor in the dark, I planned how Millie and I would play Uncle Wiggily after everyone had left. I suppose the time passed faster than I thought, for suddenly I realized that it had been quite a while since I'd heard anything. Surely I would have heard pounding steps or at least one "Home free!" but when I opened the door and crawled out, I couldn't see any signs of the game.

My mother and father were standing in the hall, looking unhappy.

"Where's everybody?" I asked. Then I noticed that Millie's suitcase that had been standing by the front door was gone.

"Where's Millie?" I shouted.

The way my mother and father led me into the living room, I knew that everything had gone wrong. Everything. My mother explained: As soon as the game had started, Millie had taken her suitcase and run out to the Hulls' car. The grown-ups had heard the front door closing, so they had investigated.

"No one could do anything with her," my mother said. "So they went home."

"How could they?" I was crying. "How could they sneak off like that without even saying good-bye to me?"

"Oh, Jean," my mother sighed, "it happened so quickly. David was trying to pull Millie out of the car and Mrs. Hull was getting mad at Mr. Hull and right in the middle of everything Mr. Hull told everyone to get in the car and he just drove off." She put her arms around me. "I know," she said. "I know."

"Even if Millie had stayed," my father said, "you wouldn't have had a good time."

"She didn't like me," I sniffled.

"She didn't seem to like anyone." My father pulled his handkerchief out of his breast pocket so I could blow my nose. It was then I noticed that Millie's pencil box and paper flowers and Andrea's fortune-telling cards were still under the tree and I began to feel sorry for myself all over again. Oh, I knew the Hulls would feel bad—especially David—but I didn't have room for anyone's feelings but my own. I picked up my snowflake paperweight and I shook it and shook it. I shook until the snow came down in a perfect fury of a storm.

"After supper we'll go upstairs, you and I, and start reading one of your new books together," my mother suggested. "How would you like that?"

"All right."

Usually I loved it when my mother lay down on my bed and we got interested in a new story together, but somehow tonight when my mother kicked off her shoes and stretched out beside me, I didn't want a book. She was still dressed in her black velvet dress and her pearls. She still smelled of lavender sachet and I just wanted her to talk.

"Tell me about when you were a little girl in Washington, P.A.," I said. (My parents always called their hometown in Pennsylvania, Washington, P.A.)

So my mother told me the old stories about her pet cat, Kitty Gray, who had been so mean and about her sister Blanche's pet cat, Big Puss, who had been so sweet. She told how her brother George used to chase her and Blanche out of his tree house and how rough their older sister, Sarah, had been when she gave them their baths.

"And what did you do when she rubbed too hard?" I asked.

My mother laughed. "Why, we splashed her. Yes, until she was wet right through her apron."

"You and Aunt Blanche don't sound as if you were always good."

My mother was still smiling. "I guess we weren't."

"Then how come," I asked, "that you expect me to be one-hundred-percent perfect?"

My mother snapped back from her little-girl time. "All I want you to do is try," she said.

I wished I had never asked. I wished she had never answered. But what I said next came as a surprise even to me. I propped myself up on my elbow.

"Why can't we adopt a baby?" I asked. "Not an eleven-year-old. A baby. Why not?"

Sometimes when my mother was given a hard question, she'd say, "Maybe" or "We'll see." Not tonight.

"Well, we can't," she said. Then quickly she began talking about Washington, P.A., again.

And I began thinking about my grandmother. I wondered if she would put my doily on her dining-room table. After my mother had said "good night" and left the room, I got up and went to my desk. I took out the first sheet of my brand-new stationery.

Dear Grandma, (I wrote): Thank you so much for the petticoat. It is lovely.

I didn't want to spoil my stationery by writing the whole truth about our Christmas, so I just told her what I got and signed my name, along with love and kisses.

Then I added a P.S. on the back.

How do you like the name Marjorie? (I wrote).

I still thought that if my name were Marjorie, things might be different.

3

Once the revolution began in earnest in Hankow, it was impossible to ignore it. Every few days there was a strike of some sort. Student strikes. Worker strikes. Coolie strikes. There were demonstrations and marches and agitators haranguing about how foreigners ought to be kicked out of China and how poor people should take money from the rich. Even our servants listened to the agitators. Once Lin Nai-Nai came home and told my mother that a wonderful thing was going to happen in China. All the money in the country would be gathered up and divided equally so that there would no longer be rich people and poor people.

"If they do that," my mother said, "maybe you won't have as much money as you do now. There are many more poor people in China than there are rich."

But I could tell that Lin Nai-Nai thought that the money dividing would be part of a great new China where men would stick to one wife and women wouldn't bind their feet.

Once an agitator gathered a crowd around him in front of the Y.M.C.A. building. He shouted about the Y.M.C.A. being a foreign organization with a foreigner in charge who should be run out of town. The man in charge, of course, was my father and when he heard what was going on, he slipped quietly out the front door of the building so that he was standing behind the agitator without the agitator seeing him. My father put his hands casually in his pockets and cocked his head as he listened to the man carrying on. Then my father smiled and winked at the crowd as if it were a huge joke that the agitator should be calling my father names while my father was right there behind him. The crowd thought it was a joke too and laughed. Of course the agitator lost face and that was the end of that. My father was lucky, but at the same time he had many Chinese friends, even among the coolies. Some of his friends were for the Communists, some were against, but my father had made up his mind not to take sides. He worked in the Y.M.C.A. so he could help those Chinese who needed help in whatever way they needed it.

Occasionally there were riots. The first time the riot siren blew, we were eating supper. My father, who was a member of the riot squad (organized to help put down riots, with tear bombs if necessary), rushed out of the house and my mother began pacing. She hadn't been feeling well lately and I could tell that she certainly didn't feel well now. She had me sleep in a cot in her room that night, and after I got into bed, she sat down beside me.

"I want to tell you something, Jean," she said. "No matter what I ask you to do tonight, I want you just to do it. No questions. No arguments."

It was on the tip of my tongue to ask, "Like what?" but I realized that was a question in itself. Of course I knew what my mother was afraid of. She thought a mob might burst into the house and she wanted to hide me, but I wasn't sure that she knew the best places or would even think of the closet under the stairs. And I wasn't sure that she was planning to hide with me. Still, I didn't say anything.

She lay down on her bed with her clothes on, but I knew her eyes were open, just as mine were. We were both listening, but all we heard were the usual night sounds. A beggar woman crying for money to bury her dead baby. Dogs howling. Every night ten greyhounds that belonged to the Frenchman across the street wailed as if the world were coming to an end.

But we heard no fighting. I spent the time deciding how I would save my mother instead of letting her save me, but as it turned out, neither of us had to do any saving. About three o'clock in the morning Mr. Hull came into the yard below our window and called to my mother.

Both of us ran out on the balcony.

"Arthur's all right," he said. "It's all over. Everything's under control. He'll be back in about an hour." He talked some more but I didn't listen. I just stood on the balcony, looking up at the night sky, at the crook of the moon, at the spangle of stars—each one in its proper place.

Oh, Grandma, I thought, that is the same moon and the same stars that will be over your grape arbor and your henhouse tomorrow. It was almost too hard to believe.

There was upheaval all around me that spring, and although it was often scary, it was also hazy, like passages in a book that you just skim over. "We're living right in the middle of history," my father would say, but it seemed to me I could understand long-ago history better than history today. All I hoped was that however this revolution turned out, Lin Nai-Nai would get her wishes. And I hoped that all the people who had drawn rotten lives would be given a change of luck.

As for me, I went on with my own life—going to school, learning poetry, reading. Twice I managed to take an orange to my little friend in the Mud Flats. Actually the worst thing that happened to me had nothing to do with the revolution. My father came home one evening with the news that Mr. Hull had been transferred to the Shanghai Y.M.C.A. The whole family would move the next week. I felt as if I'd had the wind knocked out of me and I knew that I wouldn't have time to get it back before they'd be gone.

They came for dinner the night before they left. I hadn't even tried to imagine how the Hulls would feel about the move, but since I felt bad, I took for granted that they would too. But they were excited, all except David. Ever since Christmas, David had stopped getting excited about anything. Sometimes I felt like shaking him and telling him to quit feeling so sorry for himself, but tonight I didn't care how David Hull felt.

As soon as we were alone, Andrea began talking about Shanghai. They were going to live in a house with five modern bathrooms, she said. She was going to take dancing lessons from an Austrian dancer named Hans. And she'd go to the Shanghai American School.

"Shanghai is so much more up-to-date than Hankow," she said. "More like the States."

"Since when have you been calling America 'the States'?" I asked.

Andrea just tossed her head as if that were too silly a question to answer.

"My mother is going to have her hair bobbed[7] when we get there," she said. "And my father says that's all right with him. Ever since we heard about Shanghai, they've been nice to each other."

I could understand why Andrea was excited. I'd be excited just to have the five modern bathrooms, but right then I couldn't think of a single thing to be happy about.

"Well, you've got something to look forward to too," Andrea said.

I couldn't imagine what.

"It won't be long now," she said.

I supposed she must mean summer vacation. It was true. I certainly did look forward to the three months we spent every summer in Peitaiho on the ocean north of Peking. Once we had gone to the mountains in Kuling which was nearer and beautiful too. But not like Peitaiho. The most glorious moment of the whole year was when I first caught sight of the ocean. We'd be riding donkeys from the train station to our house on the beach when, halfway up a hill, the ocean would suddenly come into view. The blueness of it rolling on and on right out to the sky made something inside me leap. Free, I thought. The ocean made me feel free. Free of school and grown-ups, free of goodness and badness and ugliness and loneliness. Sometimes in the winter when I walked past the beggars in Hankow, I would think of Peitaiho and be glad to know that it was in the same world.

"Yes," I told Andrea, "I do look forward to Peitaiho."

"How's your mother feeling?"

I shrugged. It wasn't as if my mother were sick enough to stay in bed. I thought Andrea gave me a funny look but right away she put her hand on my arm.

"We'll write," she said. "Probably sometime you'll visit us and then you can have a bathroom all to yourself."

As soon as Andrea had left town, I began concentrating on Peitaiho. I made pictures in my mind of the summer until the pictures became so real I could leaf through them like pages in an album. A picture of us having a picnic on the Great Wall. (We did this once each summer.) Pictures of my father and me wading at low tide from rock to rock, chipping off oysters for our supper. A picture of us sitting on the porch at sunset, watching the sky flame up and then drift off into pinks and purples. "That's the best one yet," we'd say.

My mother and father were both so busy these days I could never find time for us to go through my pictures together. But one Sunday morning when my father was shaving, I decided that I couldn't keep the summer to myself any longer. I often watched my father shave on Sunday when he was in no hurry. He'd stand in front of the mirror in his trousers, his suspenders loose over his undershirt, and he'd lather up his face until the lather stood in peaks like whipped cream. Since we didn't have a modern bathroom, he'd shave over an enamel basin and use hot water from a pitcher. (The bathtub, round like a big green salad bowl, took so many pitchers of water you never sat in more than a puddle.)

I leaned against the doorframe while my father twisted his face to shave down one side.

"How do you suppose the oysters will be this summer?" I asked. "Do you think this will be the year I'll find a pearl?" (I always hoped.)

My father put down his razor and straightened his face. "I've been meaning to tell

7. I.e., cut in a daringly short style.

you," he said. "We can't go to Peitaiho this summer, Jean. We'll be going to Kuling."

I couldn't believe it. There he was with soap over one half of his face, saying Kuling, not Peitaiho, just as if he were saying cornflakes, not Grape-Nuts.

"What do you mean—*can't?*"

"With all the trouble in Hankow," he said, "I can't be so far away. I'll have to travel back and forth."

"Well, why don't you tell me things?" I shouted. "Why couldn't I have been around while you were still deciding? You think it's easy for me to throw away all my plans just like that?"

"We just decided last week," my father said.

"Then we'll never go to Peitaiho again," I pointed out. We'd be leaving China in April of the next year and we'd be in America the next summer. "Never." I hated the word *never* and hoped that, hearing it, my father might find some way to change our plans.

"Maybe we should put off going to America."

"You know I don't mean that." My father had no business trying to turn this into a joke.

He sighed as he picked up his razor, but the soap on his face had dried and he had to wipe it off and begin again. "I know you're disappointed," he said. "And I'm sorry. But you'll like Kuling. You've just forgotten it."

"I haven't forgotten how you go up the mountain."

"You're older now; you won't be scared."

"Mother is a grown-up," I reminded him, "and she was scared." Who wouldn't be? The only way up the mountain to Kuling was by sedan chair. Two coolies, one in front and one in back (four or even six coolies if the person were heavy), carried the shafts of your chair up a narrow, pebbly, dirt path that twisted its way up the steep mountain. Sometimes going around a sharp corner, your chair would swing right over the edge of the mountain. If a coolie stumbled, there was no place for a person in a chair to go but over and down.

Of course I understood why we had to go to Kuling, but that didn't make me feel any less cross. Since it was Sunday, I felt cross anyway because, as far as I was concerned, Sunday was a lost day. Not only did I have to sit through Sunday School and church, but even after that I couldn't be natural. I wasn't allowed to embroider on Sunday, for instance. Or skip rope. Or play games. The only thing that I liked about the day was singing hymns. When I came to a line like "Fight manfully onward," I could believe that if I held out, one day I might really get to Washington, P.A.

But this Sunday in church we sang no "onward" hymns and needless to say, I didn't listen to Dr. Carhart's sermon. Instead I played my usual climbing game. There were more rafters in that Union Church than I've ever seen in any building. The whole ceiling was a maze of rafters crisscrossing and flying up from wooden columns on the floor. In my mind I would shinny up one of those columns and then work my way from rafter to rafter, figuring out how to make my next move, seeing how far I could get.

Today I was balancing myself just above the altar when I heard Dr. Carhart say that he knew what death was like. I hung tight to the rafter. Of course I wondered about death since grown-ups never talked about it, at least in front of me. Sometimes waking up in the middle of the night, I would think right away about death, as if the idea were just waiting in the dark to pop out of me. Well, Dr. Carhart said that he'd once taken a train from Switzerland to Italy and at the border the train went through a long dark tunnel. Then suddenly it burst out of the tunnel into a blaze of light and you were in Italy. That's what death was like, he said. It was a glory. Nothing to feel sad about.

I had to admit he made it sound interesting. Maybe everyone should travel from Switzerland to Italy, I thought, just for practice. Yet why couldn't I believe Dr. Carhart? He was a grown-up and a preacher; he ought to know what he was talking about. But part of me was never sure about grown-ups.

Personally, I was certain I'd prefer Peitaiho to Italy. Indeed, I never stopped being sorry that we weren't going there, but I did feel better one day in the middle of May when my father said we were going to Kuling early. Before school was over.

On the day before we left, I took a note from my mother to Miss Williams, explaining my absence for the rest of the term.

"But you'll miss your examinations," Miss Williams said after she'd read the note.

"Yes, Miss Williams," I smiled.

"I don't know how I can give you a report card."

I kept smiling.

"You know you have done very poorly in arithmetic."

"Yes, Miss Williams."

"Well, perhaps you'll just have to take the examinations in September and get your report then."

Somehow I couldn't stop smiling. September? Why should I worry about September now?

The next morning when we got on the boat for the trip to Kiukiang where we'd start up the mountain, I thought: Ta-ta, Miss Williams. Ta-ta, Ian Forbes and Vera Sebastian and the king of England. I was off and away! Two whole days and one night on the Yangtse.

Why did I love the river so? It wasn't what you would call beautiful. It wasn't *like* anything. It just *was* and it had always been. When you were on the river or even looking at it, you flowed with time. You were part of forever. At first I looked among all the boats we passed for a new junk that might be mine, but after a while I decided it didn't matter. My boat was somewhere out there. Wide-awake, eyes peeled.

I was so happy on the river that I had put the mountain trip out of my mind until we were actually in Kiukiang and I could see the mountains rearing up in the background. We had made friends on the boat with two young Catholic priests from New Jersey who were also going to Kuling, so we included them in our party. After spending a night in a hotel in Kiukiang, we went by car across the plains (rice fields on either side of us) to the base of the mountain where we rented our sedan chairs.

It was a hot day. We all wore pith helmets to protect us from the sun except Lin Nai-Nai who wore a Chinese straw hat. One of the priests led our procession; my mother came next, then my father, me, the other priest, and Lin Nai-Nai. Behind us came a string of coolies with our luggage strapped on their backs.

I had decided that I would not look to my right over the edge of the mountain at any time. Still, I could tell when the mountain became steep. My chair tilted back; the coolies stopped talking and began grunting. The muscles bulged in the legs of my father's coolies and the sweat poured down their bodies. I knew we were really high when the priest behind me called out to the priest in the front of the line.

"Just look at that, will you?" he yelled. "That must be three thousand feet straight down."

I closed my eyes. Why didn't that priest just shut up and pray? I wondered. But no, he went right on. "What a view! You never saw anything like that in Paterson, did you?"

Pray, I begged him silently as I gripped the arms of my chair.

My coolies slowed down, shifting the shafts of my chair, feeling for their footing, so I knew we were going around a corner. I must be out over the edge.

Oh, God, I prayed, just get me out of here safely and I'll never ask another favor of you.

A few moments later the priest must have been over the edge. And what did he say? "Wow!" That's all. Just—wow. I was surprised he hadn't flunked religion.

I didn't know that we had actually reached Kuling until I felt my chair being thumped down on the ground and I heard the welcoming voices of Mr. and Mrs. Jordan, whose house we'd be sharing. A Y.M.C.A. couple from another city, the Jordans had often visited us in Hankow and I knew I liked them.

I was stiff when I got out of my chair, so while my father was paying the coolies and we were saying good-bye to the priests and hello to the Jordans, I walked about. My mother came and put her arm around my shoulders. She seemed tired and pale after the ride up the mountain, but now that we were here, we both looked at the scenery for the first time. At the violet and blue mountains. At the pink and red azaleas that were scattered with such abandon over the hillsides.

"Isn't the color wonderful?" my mother whispered. She sounded as if she were afraid to raise her voice for fear the color would fade into Hankow gray.

"Yes." I couldn't get enough of looking. My eyes must have been starved for color and I hadn't known it.

"And do you hear that?"

What I heard sounded like a stream and tumbling water.

"That's Rattling Brook," my mother said. "We'll explore tomorrow."

Right now we went into the house and let Mrs. Jordan show us around. The front porch was for warm days and sunsets, she said, and the glassed-in porch was for rainy times. Mrs. Jordan turned to me. "But I think what you are going to like best," she said, "is your room."

Upstairs she opened the door to a room in the back of the house. The first thing I noticed was that the windows faced the mountains so I'd always be looking up and not down. And there was a window seat. And a little desk painted blue with shiny black knobs on the drawers. And a bookcase with books in it.

"Whoever had this room before was crazy about the Bobbsey Twins,"[8] Mrs. Jordan said. "I think that's the whole set there. They may be too young for you but you'll find some old copies of *St. Nicholas* magazine."[9]

At each new discovery, I said "Oh" as if that were the only word for joy that had been invented, but when I looked at my bed, I said, "Ohhh." Right in the middle of the bed, curled up like a cushion, was a tiger cat with a white bib. I sank down on my knees beside the bed and put my hand gently on the cat's fur. She opened her eyes and blinked at me as if she'd just been waiting for me to come along.

"Is she yours?" I asked Mrs. Jordan.

I saw Mrs. Jordan and my mother smile at each other. "She's yours," Mrs. Jordan said. "She just walked in last week and made herself at home." Mrs. Jordan explained that when she'd first come, they'd called her *Ke-ren*, the Chinese word for "guest," but when she made it clear that she was staying, they shortened it to Kurry.

I liked everything about my room so much that I hardly felt I needed an outside to my world, but the next morning when my mother and I went exploring, I could

8. A series of children's books, which began appearing in 1904, by Laura Lee Hope (a pseudonym used by several authors).
9. Children's periodical (1873–1940).

see that the outside was far better than the inside. First, we went behind the house and between two banks of azaleas we found Rattling Brook, gurgling and bouncing topsy-turvy over stones.

"May I put my feet in?"

My mother nodded. The brook was obviously too stony for wading, so when I'd taken off my shoes and socks, I sat on the bank and let the water dance over my bare toes and splash up my legs.

Later we walked up the hill, looking for wild flowers. Actually, we didn't need to look. They were everywhere—buttercups, daisies, wild roses, violets. When my mother came across an unusual one, she would give an "Oh" of joy and tell me its name: daphne, wild heliotrope, pink orchid. Sometimes we'd stop and look up at the mountains and at the scarves of fog they wore around their shoulders. There were eagles up there people said and mountain lions maybe. My mother sat down on the ground and threw her head back to look at the sky. She was wearing her new blue dress, one of the loose dresses she'd made to keep her cool, and I thought I'd never seen her look so pretty. I thought I've never loved her quite so much.

That night I went to sleep listening to Rattling Brook and when I came down to breakfast the next morning, Mrs. Jordan told me that my mother was in the hospital. She had gone in the middle of the night and my father was still there with her. I pushed my plate of fried eggs away from me. "What's wrong?" I asked.

"She had pain in her legs," Mrs. Jordan said.

Later when I asked Lin Nai-Nai what was wrong, she pointed to her middle and shook her head. So there was something wrong with her middle too. I didn't want to think about it. I looked over the Bobbsey Twin books and decided that it didn't matter which one I started since the Bobbsey Twins had been everywhere and done everything. I took the one that told about them on the seashore and went to the front porch. With Kurry on my lap, I began, pretending that life really was the way Bert and Nan[1] found it—one good time after another and nothing ever going very wrong. When it was time for lunch, I put a marker in my place so I could begin again quickly just where I'd left off.

My father was still not home from the hospital.

I had left the seashore and was in the Great West when my father finally came home in the late afternoon. He looked tired.

"She has phlebitis in both legs," he said. "That means she has a clot in the veins so that her legs swell up. She may have to stay in bed a long time."

"What about her middle? Lin Nai-Nai says there's something wrong with her middle."

My father sighed as if he wished Lin Nai-Nai had kept still. "The doctor thinks that is going to be all right."

"Can I see her?"

"Not for a day or two." My father lay down on the sofa and fell right to sleep.

The next day I stayed glued to the Bobbsey Twins. I was glad that there were so many books. I was glad that I didn't have to worry about how any of them would turn out. When my father came back from the hospital, I kept my finger in my place.

"How is she?" I asked.

"She's doing all right." He spoke in a strong voice and smiled as he sat down on the top step of the porch. "And I have a surprise for you."

I closed the book. "Animal, vegetable, or mineral?"

---

1. The older of the two pairs of Bobbsey Twins.

He laughed. "Animal," he said. "Jean, you have a baby sister."

I heard the words all right but they seemed to dangle in the air. I couldn't make them travel all the way into my head.

"Are you joking?" I whispered.

"No, I'm not joking. You have a baby sister."

The word "baby" registered first. "A boy or a girl?" I asked and then the whole sentence hit me. I threw the Bobbsey Twins into the air so they landed in a jumble, pages topsy-turvy. "I have a baby sister," I yelled. I jumped up and threw myself at my father. "I have a baby sister." It was the most wonderful sentence I had ever heard. I ran inside and told Mrs. Jordan. "I have a baby sister." I ran to Lin Nai-Nai's room. "I have a baby sister." I went back to the porch where both Mr. and Mrs. Jordan had joined my father.

"What does she look like?"

"Small," my father said. "Brown hair like you. She was born six weeks early but the doctor says she'll be fine."

Suddenly I realized that my mother and father had known about this baby for a long time. Probably everyone had known but me.

"Why didn't you tell me before?" I asked.

"Mother was having a hard time," my father said. "She didn't want you to worry."

"Did Mrs. Hull know?"

"Yes. Mother told Mrs. Hull."

So Andrea had known too and had probably been told not to tell. But how could I not have noticed? I asked myself. How could I not have seen what was going on under those loose dresses? There was part of me that might have felt cross but I couldn't feel cross today. There wasn't room in me for anything but a wild, tumbling excitement. Just think, I told myself, I would never be alone again. There'd always be another child in the family. Of course there'd be eleven years between us, but my father had a sister, my Aunt Margaret, who was twenty years younger than he was. Who cared about age? I had a sister, oh, I had a sister!

"When can I see her?"

"Tomorrow, I think," my father said.

I couldn't stay still. I raced up the hill in the sunshine, my heart singing. When I ran out of breath, I threw myself down on the grass and before I knew it, I had begun a new picture album. Me reading to my sister. Me walking her to kindergarten the first day of school. Me picking her up when she fell down. And the older she grew, the more we would share.

The next afternoon when I walked down the hill to the hospital with my father, I carried two bunches of daisies, one for my mother, one for my sister.

"Now that the baby has been born," my father said, "we think the worst is over for Mother. But until her legs get well, she'll have to stay in the hospital. Maybe for most of the summer. If she's coming along all right, I'll be going back to Hankow next week for a while."

"Well, I'll visit her," I said. "Every day."

"Yes. You and Mrs. Jordan can go together. Or you and Lin Nai-Nai. But I want you to remember one thing. You mustn't worry Mother. If something goes wrong or if you don't feel well, just don't mention it. We want her to get well fast. All right?"

"All right."

We went to see the baby first. She was in a basket in the doctor's office where he could keep an eye on her. He got up from his desk, all smiles. "She's doing just fine," he said.

She was tiny. And kind of puckered-looking, the way your hands get if they've been in the water a long time, but I knew this was just because she was new. Her hands were folded into two little fists and when I slipped a finger into her fist, she held on. "I'm your sister," I said. Even if she couldn't understand, I wanted to tell her. "I'm your sister, Jean." I put the daisies in a glass beside the basket.

Then we went to see my mother. She smiled when she saw me and held out her hand. "How do you like your sister?" she asked.

"I think she's the most wonderful baby in the whole world."

"We'll have to think of a name for her before your father goes back to Hankow."

Of course I had already decided what her name should be, but I remembered I wasn't supposed to upset my mother. I waited until the Jordans and my father and I were sitting at the supper table.

"I think she should be named Marjorie," I announced.

My father was cutting up his meat. "I don't believe Mother would like that," he said. "You have to think how the first name goes with the last name. Marjorie Guttery. That doesn't sound nice."

"I think it does."

"We've talked about a few names. Ann. Ruth."

I shook my head. "Too short. Like mine, they're both too short."

Every time I saw the baby in the next few days, I thought she looked more and more like a Marjorie, but I knew that was a lost cause. All I hoped was that whatever they called her, she wouldn't sound too good. I didn't want a sister who would be one-hundred-percent perfect.

The night before he left for Hankow, my father told us it was decided. My mother had picked the name.

Miriam.

Straight out of the Bible, I thought. A name for a saint.

"I hate it," I said.

My father looked at me over the rim of his coffee cup. "Well, don't tell Mother."

"Do you want me to lie?"

"I think you're smart enough," he said, "to make her happy without actually telling a lie."

After my father had gone the next day, I went to the hospital with Mrs. Jordan.

"How do you like the baby's name?" my mother asked.

"I think it's a nice Bible name," I said primly.

My mother turned to Mrs. Jordan. "Has Jean been good?" she asked. Now that my father had left, I knew that my mother was worried that I'd be a bother to Mrs. Jordan. I knew that every time we visited, my mother would ask the same question. "Has Jean been good? Has Jean been good?" All summer long. I felt like a coolie who has had a load strapped to his back before going up the mountain.

Later while Mrs. Jordan was talking to the doctor in the hall, I slipped into his office for a private visit with my sister. Someday, I thought, she'd have a load on her back too.

"Listen," I told her, "I don't care what your name is, I just want you to know that I'm not going to worry about your being good. And don't expect too much of me either. We're together, remember. We're sisters." I could hardly wait for her to understand.

My life took on a pattern now. Since I could never stay long at the hospital, there was a lot of time to fill up. Mrs. Jordan introduced me to some other children, and when I wasn't reading in my window seat with Kurry or writing letters at my blue desk, I was often with Peggy Reynolds who lived two houses down. We played tennis and checkers and I lent her the Bobbsey Twins and she lent me the Rosemary[2] books. Once the Jordans took me to the Cave of the Immortals in the West Valley. At the temple inside the cave, I could go up to the altar and talk to the Rain God if I wanted to, but I didn't have a thing to say to him. My prayers had nothing to do with weather.

What I really liked best that summer was going on little breakfast picnics with Lin Nai-Nai. We had found a fish pool in a park not too far away and while the fog was still lifting from the ground, we would sit there in the midst of bluebells and tiger lilies and eat our hard-boiled eggs and bananas and drink the tea we'd brought in a thermos bottle. Sometimes I gave Lin Nai-Nai English lessons while we ate. She could carry on a conversation now about health and one about weather, but she couldn't manage to say "Miriam." So we settled on Mei Mei, the Chinese word for Little Sister, which I liked better anyway.

After three weeks, my father came back, but he could only stay for a few days. We went down together to the hospital and found Mother sitting up in a chair, her legs propped on a stool. The baby had been moved into her room. Miriam had lost her pucker now and when she looked at me, I imagined she knew who I was.

"She had her fingernails cut yesterday," my mother said.

That was wonderful news, I thought. If her fingernails were growing, the rest of her must be hurrying up too. I leaned over the basket to see.

"Would you like to hold her?" my mother said.

I had never supposed that they would trust me to hold her. I sat in a chair and my father placed her gently in my arms. She didn't cry. She just looked up at me and I looked down at her. I'm so lucky, I thought. Who would have dreamed I would be so lucky?

When I went back to the house, I told Lin Nai-Nai about it. The next morning at breakfast I was telling the Jordans when one of the servants came in with a note and gave it to my father. He tore it open and as he read, his shoulders slumped. When he looked up from the note, there was emptiness in his eyes.

"Miriam died last night," he said. "They don't know exactly why." He pushed back his chair. "I must go right down to the hospital."

I didn't recognize my voice when I spoke. "Will you tell Mother?"

"She knows."

"But I thought—" I didn't go on. I thought something awful would happen to my mother if she were even a little bit upset. I was afraid that now she might break in two. Mr. Jordan went out of the house with my father and Mrs. Jordan put her arms around me. I think she expected me to cry, but I didn't feel like crying. I felt numb. Wooden. Oh, I should have known, I told myself. It was too good to be true. I should have known.

Later that morning my father took me to see Mother. She was lying white-faced in bed and she put up her arms to hug me, but she didn't say a word about Miriam. It seemed to me that I would never dare say Miriam's name to my mother for fear of what it might do to her.

In the afternoon Lin Nai-Nai came to me with a little picnic basket in her hand. "We'll go to the blue-bells," she said. "That will be good for you."

Still wooden, I followed her. We sat down by the pool and she spread out the

---

2. Protagonist of a series by Josephine Lawrence (ca. 1890–1978).

picnic. Almond cookies too—my favorite. I tried to eat but I couldn't.

"Cry," Lin Nai-Nai said. "Put your head down," she patted her lap, "and cry. It's the only way."

"I don't feel like crying. I don't feel anything." But suddenly I did feel. Not grief. Anger. It flooded through me. I was furious. At first I couldn't figure out whom I was furious with, but then I knew. I was mad at Dr. Carhart. I picked a daisy and began ripping off the petals. Who did he think he was? What did he know? Standing up in a pulpit and saying death was a glory! Nothing to be sad about! What kind of glory could it be for a little baby who wouldn't know if she was in a dark tunnel or not? I took a bite of hard-boiled egg and chewed it furiously. I ate my whole lunch that way. In a rage. Then we went back to the house.

That night I tried to write to my grandmother but no words came. It would be weeks and weeks before she'd know that Miriam had died. In fact, she was probably still getting used to her being born. She was still happy. I crumpled the paper.

We had a funeral for Miriam in the living room. My mother couldn't leave the hospital, of course, but my father and the Jordans had invited a few friends. The tiny white coffin was set on a table. There was a wreath of flowers on it but no bluebells. I ran out and picked some bluebells and put them in the center of the wreath before the service started. We sang hymns but I didn't sing. There was no song in me. The minister from the Kuling church read the twenty-fourth psalm and said a prayer, but he didn't mention glory, thank goodness. Then because Miriam was to be buried in Hankow, two coolies carried the little coffin down the long narrow path. Standing alone with my father on the porch, I thought I had never seen anything as sad as that tiny coffin winding down that steep mountain, bumping along under two poles that the coolies carried on their shoulders. Every bump was another *never*. Never, never, never, never.

When the coffin was out of sight, my father put his arm around me. "You know, Jean," he said, "you have been very, very good through this."

Suddenly something inside me exploded. I wheeled around at my father. "Good!" I shouted. "That's all anyone can think about. Good! I haven't even thought about being good. I haven't tried to be good. I don't care about being good. I have just been *me*. Doesn't anyone ever look at *me*?"

My father had sat down in a rocking chair and had pulled me onto his lap. I was crying now. All those tears that had been stored up inside were pouring out. My whole body was shaking with them. My father held me close and rocked back and forth.

"You don't understand," I cried. "You and Mother will never understand. I was waiting for Miriam to grow. I knew she'd understand. She was the only one. I was counting on her. I *needed* her."

I looked up at my father. His head was back on the headrest, his eyes were closed. Tears were streaming down his cheeks. "I do understand, Jean," he said. And we went on rocking and rocking together.

4

After my father left this time for Hankow, he didn't come back at all. Communist soldiers had begun to attack Wuchang (the city across the river from Hankow) and he was helping to set up hospitals for the sick and wounded. He wrote that we should come home as soon as Mother was able in case the riverboats stopped running, so in the middle of September, even though Mother could walk only a little, we went back down the mountain. Kurry was shut up tight in a basket on my lap, and the Jordans, who were traveling all the way to Hankow with us, led our procession.

I wasn't sorry to leave Kuling. The bluebells and the tiger lilies had dried up and dropped off their stems. And I was glad to get away from the wind. Every night it came howling down from the mountaintop as if it were looking for something lost. It shook the trees inside out, rattled at doors, banged at shutters. Then it would stop for breath. Not there, it seemed to say. Not there. Then it would begin again. *Whooo, whooo,* going back to all the same places it had been, looking and looking. Some nights it never gave up. Even in a war, I thought, I would be safer in Hankow than in these mountains and with a wind that might, for all I knew, be looking for me. Maybe in Hankow my mother would get well quickly so I wouldn't have to worry about upsetting her. Maybe sometime I could talk out loud about once having had a real baby sister with fingernails that had to be cut.

Not yet, of course. My mother was carried down the mountain on a stretcher, and although she got up for meals on the boat, she spent most of the time lying down in our cabin. When we approached Hankow, she went on deck and stretched out on a long chair.

"It looks just the same, doesn't it?" she said.

And it did. Even from the middle of the river I could see the plane trees marching up the Bund in their white socks. (Their socks were painted on to keep bugs away, my father said.) As we came closer, I saw that there were more coolies on the dock than usual, more jostling, more noise, but I thought nothing of it. Just coolies. There was nothing that looked like war.

Then the gangplank was lowered and my father bounded on the deck in his white panama hat and his white duck suit. He hugged us both, but Mother got the first hug and the longer one because of course she was the one to worry about. He shook hands with the Jordans. "This may be the last boat to get through," he announced triumphantly. My father loved to set records: to be the last, the first, the fastest, to get through what he called Narrow Squeaks.

He explained that he'd borrowed the Hulls' Dodge sedan (which the Y.M.C.A. had bought) and parked it close by on the Bund. Did my mother think she could walk that far?

It really wasn't far and when my mother said yes, she could, my father motioned for coolies to carry our luggage to the car. I think he suspected there might be trouble because he stood on the gangplank and held up four fingers, as if he were trying to keep more coolies from coming on board. Mr. Jordan, a wide man, blocked the gangplank by standing right behind my father.

But suddenly there was a roar from the dock and thirty or more coolies stormed up the gangplank, lifted my father and Mr. Jordan right off their feet and set them down on the deck. They circled around our pile of luggage (ten pieces), shouting, grabbing up suitcases and bundles, even pulling the briefcase out of my father's hand. One coolie, seeing the basket I was holding, tried to pull it away. I clung tight.

"This is not baggage," I shouted. "It's alive." When he didn't let go, I kicked him on the shin. "It's a baby tiger!" I yelled. The coolie glanced at a tall, pockmarked man who stood at the edge of the crowd, each hand tucked, Chinese fashion, up his other sleeve. He was better dressed than the coolies and seemed to be the boss. He motioned for the coolie to leave me alone.

By this time five coolies had taken charge of the baggage. The others had backed off but had not left the boat. "Pay now," they shouted. "Make the foreign devils pay now." The tall, pockmarked man unfolded his arms; in one hand he held a knife.

The cost of carrying a bag had always been five coppers, so for eleven bags (including the briefcase), the total should have been fifty-five cents. Today my father handed a twenty-cent piece to each of the five coolies which was, of course, almost double the normal rate.

"I know you fellows are having hard times," my father said.

The coolies threw the money on the deck as if it were dirt. All the coolies began chanting: "Fifty cents a bag! Fifty cents! Fifty cents!"

I could see my father set his chin in his stubborn, not-giving-in way. Then he glanced at my mother and without another word he opened his wallet and pulled out five single dollars, one for each coolie and an extra fifty cents for the man with the briefcase.

As we followed the coolies off the boat, I thought the trouble was over. Some of the coolies lost interest when we reached the dock and went their own way, but some, including the boss, stayed with us. When we reached the stone steps that led to the Bund, the five coolies plunked the baggage down. That was as far as they went for a dollar, they said. They each needed two dollars more to finish the job.

My father's chin turned hard as stone. He looked at the boss. "We will go on," he said, "or I will call the police." He raised his arm as if he were about to call the police, but the boss pointed his knife at him. Other coolies produced knives.

"If you call the police," the boss said, "you will be dead by the time they get here."

I felt my knees go weak and tremble. I was surprised, because I didn't know that people's knees really shook when they were scared. I had supposed that writers of books just said that in the same way as they made happy endings at the last minute. As I looked at my father's chin and at the men with their knives, I knew no one was going to give in. Only a writer could save us now, I thought.

Suddenly Lin Nai-Nai nudged me and pointed to the Bund which as usual was lined with rickshas parked on both sides of the street, but there were no coolies with the rickshas. All of them, up and down the street, were running toward us. In a moment they had surrounded us.

"This way, Mr. Gau. Hurry. This way," one of the coolies cried. I recognized him. My father had helped him once when he was in trouble and he'd been our friend ever since. He must have seen what was going on and called the others. Forming a double line that led to the Dodge sedan, they hurried us and our baggage into the car while they stood guard. My father and the Jordans slid into the front seat, my mother, Lin Nai-Nai, and I into the back. The ricksha coolies stayed until we had the car started and were off the street. It was a grand rescue. I didn't think there was a writer in the whole world who could have done better.

But I was afraid something terrible might have happened to my mother. My father and the Jordans were all asking how she was and she said she was all right and she did seem to be. I put my hand on her knees and they weren't even shaking. Maybe she was better already.

As soon as we were inside the house, I let poor Kurry out of her basket and we all gave a big sigh, glad to be safe again.

My father leaned against the door. "Well," he said proudly, "that was a Narrow Squeak!" Probably he was already thinking what a good story this would make when he wrote home, but I planned to write first.

Dear Grandma (I would say): We were almost murdered tonight but in the nick of time we were saved by a bunch of ricksha coolies. I was so scared that my knees were shaking, but don't worry about us. Just remember that in China there are always ricksha coolies around.

We went into the living room where my mother stretched out on the sofa and my father began talking about what had been going on in Hankow. Since the Jordans were leaving the next day, he wanted them to hear everything, so he went on and on, the way he did when he was taking Dr. Carhart's place and preaching a sermon. I paid no attention; it was just more Chinese-fighting talk. Who was going to rule China. Who was going to beat whom. It was like a Victrola record that had been playing ever since I was born. Then suddenly my father interrupted the record to speak to me.

"You'll be interested in this news, Jean," he said. "The British School is not going to open this fall and Miss Williams has gone back to England."

"You're joking!" I cried.

"Cross my heart," my father said.

Like all good news, it was hard to believe. I tried to imagine it. No more Miss Williams ever. No more worrying about Ian Forbes or the king of England or prisoner's base.

"We'll have lessons together," my mother said.

I nodded, thinking how I'd study my favorite subjects: poetry and George Washington and the map of America. No complicated math problems, no French. My mother didn't speak French and I had never seen her do anything but add and subtract in her account book. She said we wouldn't start for two or three weeks to give her a chance to rest.

I began to see that this war was going to mean more than just talk, but at first I didn't connect Yang Sze-Fu's fingernails with the war. Of course I was surprised the next morning when I noticed that the long, spiky nails on his pinkies were gone and were now the same length as his other nails.

I asked Lin Nai-Nai. "How come Yang Sze-Fu cut his nails?"

"He's a Communist," Lin Nai-Nai said. "Communists don't believe in long fingernails. They believe all people should be working people, no one pretending to be better than anyone else."

"Are you still interested in being a Communist?" I asked.

"No," she said. "How can I like the Communists when they are attacking my city?"

I had forgotten that Lin Nai-Nai's family lived in Wuchang. Once long ago she had explained to me that she had disgraced her family when she had run away from her husband and they would never want to see her again. Now she was worried about them, and no wonder. My father had told me how Communist soldiers were trying to make the city of Wuchang surrender by starving it to death. It was a city with walls around it, and since the soldiers wouldn't let anyone in or out, eventually the people would run out of food. I had read about sieges like this in my English history book, but in ancient days soldiers had worn armor and ridden horseback and used battering rams against the city walls. These soldiers had only cloth caps and cotton clothes, but they had a cannon which they fired from the hills and they had bombs which they dropped on the city from the one airplane they owned. And they waited.

I took Lin Nai-Nai's hand as she sat in her embroidery chair. "How many brothers and sisters do you have?" I asked.

"Two brothers. One, ten years—Dee Dee. One, twenty-two. Two sisters, sixteen and twenty, but maybe they are married now and moved away. Maybe my parents are dead. Who knows? One thing is sure, anyone alive in Wuchang is hungry."

From that moment the whole war became for me a war against Lin Nai-Nai's family. When I heard the cannon being fired across the river, I thought of Lin Nai-Nai's little brother, Dee Dee, and wondered if his knees were shaking. The first time the Communist airplane flew over Hankow on its way to Wuchang, I ran outside and shook my fist at the pilot and shouted all the Chinese swear words I knew. My mother called me in.

"What would people think if they heard you?" she asked.

"They'd think I was mad at the Communists."

"They'd think you hadn't been brought up right. And I think we'd better start lessons pretty soon."

But we didn't start right away and meanwhile I began to worry about Yang Sze-Fu being a Communist. I couldn't help seeing how he had changed. No butter pagodas now. He just slapped butter on a plate any old way and didn't even try to make our company meals special. He acted as if he hated foreigners, especially me. Sometimes he pretended he didn't hear me when I asked for cocoa.

"I think my father should fire Yang Sze-Fu," I told Lin Nai-Nai, but she shook her head.

"That would be wrong. Then he might become dangerous. He may be rude now, but no foreigners have been harmed by their servants."

But I wasn't so sure about Yang Sze-Fu. One day as I was finishing a bowl of canned cherries, I saw a drop of red at the bottom of my bowl that didn't look one bit like cherry juice. It looked like potassium. In strawberry season we used potassium to kill the germs on fresh berries. Of course before we ate them, we had to wash the potassium off with sterile water because potassium was poisonous. (In China we had to be very careful about germs.) I knew we had potassium in the kitchen and suddenly I knew that if I were writing a story about a Communist cook, I'd have him poison his foreign employers with potassium. The more I thought of it, the more sure I was that was exactly what Yang Sze-Fu was trying to do, so when no one was looking, I spit the cherries I still had in my mouth into my big linen napkin. After that, every meal I picked over my food, looking for traces of red, and sometimes with my mouth full, I'd suddenly get the feeling that I tasted potassium and I'd spit into my napkin again.

After a few days the serving boy, who took care of the napkins, spoke to Lin Nai-Nai about it and Lin Nai-Nai asked me. We were sitting beside the embroidery window.

"Oh, it's nothing," I said. I didn't want her to tell Mother. Grown-ups generally took the truth too seriously or not seriously enough; either way it meant trouble.

"Are you sick?" Lin Nai-Nai asked.

"No. It's just that sometimes when I think about the people in Wuchang, I don't want to swallow my food. I won't do it anymore, so don't tell." I was ashamed of myself for lying, so I ran out of the room to find Kurry who was a comfort to me in my guilty times. She'd purr and blink her eyes as if she were saying, "What's the difference?"

But although I looked all over the house, I couldn't find Kurry. I was always afraid that she'd streak out the front door sometime when it was open, and even though this was Hankow, not Wuchang, I didn't want her outside. (In Wuchang there were no dogs or cats left, my father said; they'd all been eaten.) She was allowed, however, in the enclosed courtyard between the house and the servants' quarters, and when I looked out the glass window in the back door, I saw her in the courtyard, crouching between Yang Sze-Fu and the serving boy, eating from a blue rice bowl. I was the one who fed Kurry. Why was she eating with the servants? More important, *what* was she eating?

I stood still and watched. The two men were squatting on their heels, eating their evening meal, shoveling rice into their mouths with chopsticks, dipping into the large bowl of vegetables and meat that sat between them. Every once in a while Yang Sze-Fu would pick up a bite and drop it into Kurry's bowl. Once he laid down his chopsticks and stroked Kurry on the head and talked to her.

Before the summer I had often squatted in the courtyard with the servants while they ate, so I went out now and joined them.

Yang Sze-Fu seemed embarrassed. "The cat likes Chinese food," he explained.

"You like my cat?" I asked.

He shrugged. "A cat is a cat. There are no foreign cats, no Chinese cats, no capitalist cats, no Communist cats. Just cats."

He picked up a cup of tea and took a loud sip from it. I noticed how, as he held the cup, he tried to hide his pinkie, and I remembered how he used to flourish it as if he felt especially superior when he was drinking tea. Suddenly I saw that no matter how strong a Communist Yang Sze-Fu was, he missed his nails and I felt sorry for him. I decided not to worry about potassium anymore.

When my father came home in the evenings now, the first thing he did was to announce how long the siege had been going on. The twenty-third day, the twenty-fourth day. It was as if this was the only way he could keep track of time. Then he would tell us the news. Sometimes the Communists had allowed a few boatloads of sick and wounded to cross the river to hospitals that the Y.M.C.A. had helped to set up. These refugees had terrible stories to tell: houses destroyed, people sleeping in the streets, children dying, water running low, disease spreading. I listened now because this was Lin Nai-Nai's war and I wanted it to be over. Already I was helping Lin Nai-Nai fill baskets with food to take to Wuchang as soon as the city gates opened. She knew her family might refuse to see her, but she had to try, she said. I bought a big bar of milk chocolate for her little brother, but I didn't always tell her the news that my father brought home.

Sometimes the news was so bad that my father wouldn't even tell us. Instead, he'd go to the piano and pound out the one piece he knew by heart, "Napoleon's Last Charge."[3] I loved the piece, but even more, I liked to watch what it did to my father. He could sit down at the piano, looking as if he had given up on China, but pretty soon his left hand would get the cannon booming and the drums beating. His right hand would say Giddyap to the horses and off they'd go, galloping off to battle. Then both hands would charge faster and faster up and down the keyboard, armor clashing, bugles blowing, and by the end, I knew it didn't matter whether Napoleon ever fought again or not. My father had won.

Still the siege went on. One night at supper I tried to imagine what people in Washington, P.A., talked about at the end of the day.

"What do you suppose they think is news?" I asked.

"Well, they're probably worrying about the first frost now and wondering if they should cover up their tomatoes," my father said.

We all laughed. Suddenly it seemed both wonderful and funny to have nothing more than a frost to worry about.

"Can you imagine us when we get to Washington, P.A.?" I asked.

My father tipped his chair back. "I suppose I'll be watching the papers to see how Pittsburgh is doing in baseball."

---

3. A popular piece by Edwin Ellis, published in 1910. Napoleon Bonaparte (1769–1821), emperor of France; he was defeated by the British in 1815 at the Battle of Waterloo.

"And Blanche and I will be talking about the length of our skirts," my mother added.

"And I'll be roller skating all over the place."

It wouldn't be long now, I thought. We were due to go to America on the twenty-sixth of April and this was the first of October. I counted on my fingers. "Just six more months," I said. "Plus a couple of weeks."

My father brought his chair down slowly. "We hope," he said.

"What do you mean—*hope?*" The date of our going back to America had always been a sure thing. We had our reservations. We knew the name of our ship, the *President Taft*. We had even bought a Dodge car that would be waiting for us in San Francisco so we could drive across the continent to Pennsylvania.

"Well, Jean," my father said, "you can see what war is like. If we were scheduled to leave Hankow next week, for instance, we couldn't do it. I'm needed here."

"But the siege will be over long before spring," I pointed out. "You said yourself you didn't think that Wuchang could hold out much longer."

"Yes, and then we'll have to take care of the people, the living and the dead." But that wasn't all, I found out. Even after Wuchang had fallen, the war wouldn't be over. This was only what my father called a "skirmish." The main part of the Nationalist Army hadn't even arrived.

"Well, for heaven's sake," I exploded, "you don't expect to hang around China until it's all through fighting, do you?"

"No. I expect we'll go to America on schedule. I just thought I'd warn you. Delay is possible."

I should know by this time, I thought, that nothing in the world was sure. Certainly nothing on this side of the world. I felt the tears beginning when Mother put her hand over mine.

"We're going to begin lessons tomorrow morning," she said. "So get your pencils sharpened and your desk in order. School begins at nine o'clock."

My mother was really much better. She was up for most of the day now and her keys hung around her waist, which meant that she was back in charge. (I envied her the keys: desk drawer keys, kitchen cupboard keys, trunk keys, door keys. Foreigners locked up everything.) She was even well enough so that we had visited friends, which was a treat. Since I wasn't allowed out alone now, days often became boring and I was glad that we'd be starting lessons and I thought my mother must be glad too. She had been a Latin teacher before she married and my father said she'd been a whiz-bang.

We began school on the thirty-first day of the siege. I had my pencils, razor-sharp, lined up on my desk with a red pencil for my mother to use for marking papers. I had put a little bell on the desk so she could ring it when a class was over or when it was time for recess. I thought it would be like play-school. Of course I expected to work, but I thought we'd have fun pretending to be teacher and pupil when we were really mother and daughter.

I guess I hadn't understood what it meant to be a whiz-bang. My mother started right off with complicated arithmetic, and since she didn't know French, she said she would teach me Latin.

"*Latin?*" I cried. "No one in America studies Latin until they're in high school. You said so yourself. You were a high school teacher."

"So you'll have a head start." I could see my mother wasn't pretending anything. Even her voice became the kind of teacher voice you didn't argue with. So I learned about dative and ablative cases and I solved problems about how long it would take a train to go from Hankow to Peking if it were going so many miles an hour and stopped five times on the way. I knew that grown-ups never figured out such problems; they just looked at timetables. But when I pointed this out to my mother, she said someone had to make up the timetables. It didn't make a bit of difference that I intended to write stories, not timetables, when I grew up.

Of course I liked some subjects more than others. I learned the capitals of all forty-eight states, and when my mother called out the name of the state, I snapped back the name of the city. I liked reading about explorers planting flags all over the New World and I marveled how they never looked mussed up in their pictures, although I thought exploring must be dirty work. But there was Balboa[4] taking possession of the Pacific Ocean and he was neat as a pin. Still, the best part of every day was when my mother rang the bell which meant that school was over and she could be my mother again.

On the fortieth day (October 10, 1926) the siege was over and my mother declared a school holiday. Lin Nai-Nai and I went to the market to buy fresh food for her baskets because she expected to go to Wuchang the next day with my father. As a member of the relief committee, my father was already there and would be going back and forth for a long time, I supposed.

But when my father came home that night, he looked too sick to go anywhere. He said he wasn't sure if he could even eat supper. As he lowered himself into a chair in the living room, he just shook his head.

"You can't imagine it," he told my mother. I think he'd forgotten I was in the room or he might not have told all that he did. So many dead rotting bodies in the streets! In just one hour he'd counted sixty bodies being wheeled through the city gates in wheelbarrows. "And I figure there are at least fifty thousand sick people that will have to be brought to Hankow." His voice cracked as he spoke, and I guessed he was thinking about sights too pitiful to put into words.

"A bomb went through the roof of the Wuchang Y.M.C.A. building," he went on, "but they continued to give out free rice as long as they had it."

Part of my father still seemed to be in Wuchang, which must have been why he looked so sick and why he didn't seem to hear the knock on the living-room door.

My mother called, "Come in," and there was Lin Nai-Nai.

"Excuse me, Mr. Gau," she said, "but you promised that I might go to Wuchang with you. What time should I be ready tomorrow?"

It was my mother who answered. "Oh, Lin Nai-Nai," she said, "I think you should wait a couple of days until the city has been cleaned up a little."

Lin Nai-Nai stood firm on her little bound feet. "If my family are hungry, they are hungry now."

My father dragged himself back from wherever he'd been, looked at Lin Nai-Nai, and nodded. He told her to be ready at seven o'clock. They would cross the river in the relief committee's launch and he would see that she got as far as the Wuchang "Y." He knew she hoped to stay for a while with her family—that is, if they'd let her.

"Leave a message for me at the 'Y,'" he said, "so we'll know your plans. And when you're ready to return, I'll arrange for it." He pulled out his wallet. "You'll need some money."

The next morning after my father and Lin Nai-Nai had left, my mother suddenly announced that we'd have another school holiday.

"Let's go visiting," she said.

4. Vasco Núñez de Balboa (1475–1519), Spanish explorer.

"Not to the Gales'," I begged. Mr. Gale owned the Dodge agency and Mrs. Gale was my mother's best friend. They had no children but they did have two pet monkeys, Nip and Tuck—disgusting creatures who should have been left in the jungle. They were not housebroken, but for some reason Mrs. Gale thought she was doing me a favor when she dropped one in my lap for me to play with.

"All right," my mother agreed. "How about the Littles in the Episcopalian Mission?"

It was a good choice, one of the few places where I still had friends. Many families had left Hankow and many had sent their children away for their education—to boarding school in Shanghai or to relatives back home in England or America—but at the Episcopalian Mission there were three girls, Nancy Little, Margaret Masters, and Isobel Wilbur, all a little younger but I didn't mind that. What I liked was that there was space to play in the center of their circle of houses. Trees and grass and swings.

When my mother went inside to visit with Mrs. Little, Nancy and I ran to the swings. And how I ran! It was as if my legs had been holding back and holding back without my knowing it. I jumped on a swing and pumped myself right up to the sky. Margaret and Isobel came out and we played tag and climbed trees and shouted until we were out of breath and then we threw ourselves down on Nancy's porch.

We lay there panting for a few minutes and suddenly I heard myself say something I had not planned to say at all.

"Did you know I had a baby sister this summer?" I asked.

Nancy sat up and handed me a piece of gum. "Yeah, I heard."

"If she had lived," I said, "she would be four months old now."

"You keep track?" Nancy was pulling the chewed gum from her mouth and stretching it out with both hands so that it was a flat, rubbery piece punctured with holes. "These are Miss Williams' pants," she laughed.

I didn't want to talk about Miss Williams. "Sure, I keep track," I said. "I know the exact day she would have turned four months."

Nancy stuffed the gum back into her mouth. "Well, let me tell you. Four-month-old babies are a pain in the neck. I know. We've had two."

My mother came out on the porch with a sweater for me to put on. I don't know what got into me but I had started something I didn't want to let go.

"I was just telling everyone about Miriam," I said. "How she would have been four months old now."

My mother looked as if I'd slapped her in the face. She didn't say a word, but as she went back into the house, I knew she would never in her whole life talk about Miriam. It was as if I'd never had a baby sister.

I stretched my gum out the way Nancy had, only I pulled mine so thin it was almost all holes. "These are your pants," I said and I ran back to the swings.

When we got home at about four o'clock, my mother went upstairs to take her afternoon rest. I went into the living room where Wong Sze-Fu was dusting the furniture with a feather duster. He swooped the feathers over the piano keys and as the dust drifted back down, he told me that Lin Nai-Nai was home. She had come about a half hour ago.

Already! But my father wasn't even home!

I ran to the servants' quarters and up to her room. I was so worried that I didn't even knock, just slipped inside. Her back was turned toward me as she sat in a straight chair, swaying to and fro. "Ai-ya," she whispered. "Ai-ya, ai-ya." Her trouser legs were rolled up. The strips of bandage that bound her feet had been taken off and her stumps of feet, hard little hooves with the toes bent under, were soaking in a pan of water on the floor. "Ai-ya," she said.

I threw myself on my knees beside her chair and put my arms around her waist. "What is it?" I whispered. "What happened?"

I had never seen her feet unbound or tears on her face or her sleek black hair straggling out of the bun on the back of her neck. She put an arm around my shoulder as if she welcomed me, as if good friends were supposed to share bad times.

"My father would not allow me in the house," she said. "My mother is sick but he wouldn't let me see her. He would not even take the food. He closed the door in my face."

With her eyes shut, Lin Nai-Nai shook her head back and forth as if the world were more than she could understand.

"I just left the baskets on the doorstep and ran. I ran all the way to the river and rented a sampan to take me across. Then I walked from the Bund."

"Oh, your poor, poor feet," I moaned.

"Yes, my poor feet."

She was quiet for a moment but I knew she had more to tell. "I saw Dee Dee," she went on. "He is the only one home and he is thin. So thin. My sisters are married and in Shanghai. My other brother was killed by a shell." She shut her eyes again.

"Dee Dee told you that?"

"Yes. He ran after me in the street. He told me that when he grows up, I can live with him." She shook her head. "He doesn't know that when he grows up, he will be a man. A different person. Now he is still a boy and when I told him there was chocolate in the basket, he forgot everything else. And when he left, I began running again." She made a small laugh. "Bound feet running. Like a stumbling duck."

I tried to think of something to say that would make Lin Nai-Nai feel better, but I could find nothing. As far as I could see, she had not a single thing in her life to look forward to.

"I'll make you a cup of tea." I went to her little two-burner stove and put water on to boil. When the tea was ready, she drank noisily to show her appreciation. Tomorrow she would feel better, she said. I shouldn't worry.

But I didn't see how she would feel better. That night at supper I asked what would happen to Lin Nai-Nai when we went back to America.

"She'll go to live with Mr. and Mrs. T. K. Hu," my mother said. "We made arrangements months ago, but of course she hoped to go back to her family. Since she can't, I'm sure she'll be happy with the Hus."

Still, I couldn't bear to think of leaving Lin Nai-Nai. "How will we ever know what's happening to each other?" I asked her one day. "You can't write English and I can't read Chinese."

"Mr. Hu can write for me and he can read your letters to me. You can tell me all about your grandmother and how you feed the chickens and how happy you are."

As much as I'd talked, I found it hard to imagine myself actually picking up a pen to write such a letter. Ever since my father had said delay was possible, I hadn't dared to make plans for fear of being disappointed. I had tried to put America right out of my mind. Of course I wrote to my grandmother as usual and we sent off our Christmas packages to Washington, P.A., but I wasn't keeping any album of pictures of what it would be like when we got there. I held out until Christmas and then I couldn't hold out any longer.

It all started when I opened the present from my father. It was a big, soft package and inside there was blue-and-gray-plaid wool that looked like a blanket, but it was not a regular blanket, my father said. It was a steamer rug made especially for ocean voyages. He described how I would sit on a deck chair as we crossed the Pacific and I'd cover myself with the steamer rug and while I looked at the ocean, a steward would bring me a cup of beef tea.[5] That did it. How could I stay put in China when my steamer rug was ready for the high seas?

Then I opened my grandmother's present. Of course she sent me a petticoat but she also sent a calendar for the next year: 1927. She had attached a note: "I have a calender just like this. Beginning January 1st, let's both cross off the days until you're home. That will make the time go faster." She figured that it might be July by the time we had crossed the continent, so at the end of every month she had written down how many days were left. At the end of January: 150 days. At the end of February: 122 days. As I turned the pages, the days seemed to fly past. Then I came to July, and there pasted over the whole month was a picture of my grandmother and my grandfather and my Aunt Margaret.

My grandmother was a large woman who looked as if she did everything in a big way. In the picture, she was laughing so hard I could almost hear her, and her arms were out as if she were waiting for me to run into them. Beside her, my grandfather smiled under his mustache as if he were saying, "How about a game of horseshoes?" (My father said he was a champion.)

On the other side was my Aunt Margaret. I hadn't seen a picture of her since she'd been in high school and now she was twenty-one and taught music and had lots of beaus. I'd been afraid that maybe she had turned into a flapper with spit curls and spike heels and she might not like me. But when I saw her picture, I knew I could get in bed with her on Sunday mornings and tell jokes even if she had been out late the night before with a beau.

"Do you think we really will leave for America on time?" I asked.

"Yes," my mother said. "I feel it in my bones."

That was the best Christmas present of all. I knew that my mother's bones were almost always right.

5

In history books war seemed to be a simple matter of two sides fighting, the right side against the wrong, so I didn't see how this Chinese war was ever going to make it into history. In the first place, there weren't just two sides. There were warlords scattered around, each with his own army, and there was the Nationalist Army (under General Chiang Kai-shek[6]) which was trying to conquer the warlords and unify the country. And there were the Communists who were supposed to be part of the Nationalist movement, but they had their own ideas, my father said, and they didn't always agree with General Chiang Kai-shek. Both the Communists and the Nationalists wanted to make things better in China, he explained, but both did terrible things to people who opposed them. If a man was an enemy, sometimes they'd cut off his head and stick it up on a pole as a warning to others. My father had seen this with his own eyes.

Furthermore, it wasn't armies who made the most trouble in Hankow. Gangs of

---

5. Beef broth.
6. Jiang Jieshi (1887–1975), commander of the Guomindang army and, from 1928 to 1949, head of the Nationalist government; after the Communists gained control of the mainland, he became president of Taiwan (1950–55).

Communist-organized workers were the ones who did the rioting. In January they took over the British concession and returned it to the Chinese. I didn't understand much of what was going on, but it didn't matter since all I cared about was going to America on time. And it looked as if we would. In February we had some of our furniture and all of our Chinese things crated for shipment. We still had our beds and chairs and bureaus and dining-room furniture, so we could get along, but even so, the house was bare and echoey. It was while we were in the midst of this packing that Mr. and Mrs. T. K. Hu came calling. Mr. Hu was carrying a large box which he handed to my father.

"Since you are packing," he said, "we thought this would be the time to give you our remembrance."

My father unwrapped the package and took out a very large ginger jar. Shiny Chinese yellow it was, the happiest color in the world, and it was decorated with bright green characters which wished us long life and health and happiness and lots of money which certainly took care of my wishes. As we stood admiring the jar, Mr. Hu took it from my father's hands and set it on one side of our fireplace.

"A pair of these jars was given us as a wedding gift," he said. "They have always stood one on each side of our fireplace. We will keep one and now you have the other. When we look at ours, we will think of you and when you look at yours, you will think of us."

My mother put her arms around Mrs. Hu. My father took one of Mr. Hu's hands in both of his. "Old friend," he said. "Old friend." He must have been misty-eyed, for he took off his glasses and wiped them. Suddenly I found myself blinking back tears and I didn't know why. I was counting the days on the calendar, wasn't I? Then how could a yellow ginger jar turn everything inside me upside down?

Mr. Hu, a large, merry-faced man whom I'd always liked, turned to me.

"And when you look at that jar, Miss Jean," he said, "you can think: 'I was born in China. Part of me will always be there.'"

I had never planned to think any such thought. I was upset by the idea and changed the subject.

"Mr. Hu," I said, "if I write letters to Lin Nai-Nai in English, will you read them to her in Chinese?"

He smiled as we all sat down. "Yes. And you can be sure that we'll take good care of your Lin Nai-Nai."

There was something else. I knew I should have talked to my mother about this first but she might have said no. "Mr. Hu," I said, "do you think you could take care of my cat too?"

"Jean!" My mother was embarrassed but before she could stop me, I scooped up Kurry who was under the sofa. "She's a gentle cat," I said.

"Of course we'll take her." Mr. Hu smiled and Mrs. Hu scratched Kurry in her favorite spot behind the ears.

Everything was going well. In March my father received word that a new man was being sent to the Y.M.C.A. to take his place, so I didn't see how my father could feel "needed" now. We planned to take the riverboat from Hankow on April 15, arriving in Shanghai on the twentieth. We would stay with the Hulls for six days before the *President Taft* sailed.

We hadn't heard from the Hulls for about a month but the last news had not been good. Mrs. Hull had written that she and Mr. Hull were going to get a divorce and he had moved to an apartment. Andrea wrote that her father was happy in his apartment and maybe this was for the best, after all. The rest of them might go to America.

She didn't know when but she was ready. She had learned the Charleston.[7]

Why would Andrea want to learn the Charleston? I wondered. That was a flapper[8] thing to do and Andrea was only in eighth grade. I asked my mother about it.

"Andrea has always been old for her age," my mother pointed out. "She even looks older than she is." (That was true.) "And in Shanghai, Americans are crazy to keep up with American fads. They don't want to fall behind."

Well, I just hoped that Andrea hadn't grown up so much that she'd forgotten that I was to have a bathroom of my own when we visited.

On the morning of March 26 when I sat down at my desk, I crossed out March 25 on the calendar. Eighty-five days crossed out, ninety-six to go before July. But only twenty before we left for Shanghai, which was really the beginning of our trip home.

At about ten o'clock that morning as my mother was reviewing me in spelling, we heard the front door being flung open. We knew it was my father because of the way he ran up the stairs—two at a time. When he appeared at the door, he had that excited, tense look that meant a Narrow Squeak was on its way.

"All women and children have to leave Hankow today. You have about three hours to pack and get ready." He must have run home because he was still out of breath.

"What's happened?" My mother banged the spelling book shut and stood up as if she were ready to leave that very minute.

The day before yesterday the Nationalist Army had captured Nanking (down the river from Hankow), my father told us, and afterwards the soldiers had gone wild. They had broken into foreign homes, knocked foreigners around, stolen right and left. They were doing such terrible things to people that American and British gunboats had opened fire on them. Foreign gunboats hadn't done this before, my father said, and there was no telling what might happen now. There might be wholesale murder of foreigners up and down the Yangtse. We might find ourselves at war.

I could feel my knees beginning to shake. This time, however, it was not only from being scared but from being mad. Fifteen days left and this crazy war might still spoil everything.

"You'll come with us, won't you?" I asked my father. "You won't wait?" My father shook his head. This boat was for women and children. He'd take the boat on the fifteenth, if all went well.

If! There it was again. That nasty little word that was always snapping at my plans. "Pack as many clothes as you can. Stuff it all in," my father said. "What doesn't fit, I'll bring when I come." He was already on his way to the attic to bring down suitcases and then he was going to the boat to see about our cabin. If he made arrangements for our luggage to be taken to the boat before we went, he said, we could probably avoid trouble.

My mother turned to me. "Get Lin Nai-Nai. I'll need her help."

As I started for the door, I realized that this might be my only chance to give Lin Nai-Nai my good-bye present. My father had framed a picture of Kurry and me and I had wrapped it in red tissue paper. I grabbed it out of my dresser drawer and ran to the servants' quarters.

Lin Nai-Nai was just coming out of her room. She had heard the news.

"I have a present for you," I said.

"I have one for you too." I went into her room and on her bed was a small soft present also wrapped in red tissue paper.

"You mustn't open this," she said, "until you have left China."

7. Popular dance of the 1920s.   8. Unconventional young woman in the 1920s.

"On the ship?"

"Yes. After the ship has sailed."

"Well, open yours at the same time," I said. "April twenty-sixth. That way we'll almost be opening them together." I had planned a private good-bye tea party in her room with almond cookies and rice cakes. Now there wasn't time for anything. I put my arms around her. "Oh, Lin Nai-Nai," I moaned.

Back upstairs my mother was rushing from room to room, her arms full of clothes. Suitcases were open all over the beds.

"May I pack the small green suitcase just for myself?" I asked.

"Yes, but take only what you'll need from here to Shanghai. We'll repack at the Hulls'." As she handed things to Lin Nai-Nai, she would say, "Brown suitcase. Blue." Suddenly she turned back to me. "No books," she said. "But don't forget underwear. And a sweater and socks."

I had put Lin Nai-Nai's present on the bottom of my bag so I wouldn't be separated from it and now I quickly covered the two books I had packed with a bunch of underwear. On top I put everyday clothes and at the last minute I happened to think of "wholesale murder" so I stuck in some first-aid equipment.

At twelve o'clock my father returned. Everything was all set, he said. He'd made private deals with coolies whom he could trust and they were outside now.

"How do you know we won't all be mobbed as we get on the boat?" I asked.

My father waved his hand as if there were no time for silly questions. Then he went along with the baggage to see that it got on the boat. When he came back, he honked the horn on the Dodge sedan to let us know it was time to go.

"We're going to stop for the Gales," he told us as we got in the car. "They found their car this morning with four flat tires."

At the Gales' house my father honked again and out they came—Mr. and Mrs. Gale carrying a cage between them. I couldn't believe it, so I got out of the car to make sure. Yes, Nip and Tuck were inside. Chattering. Making messes.

"You're not taking them, are you?" I asked.

"Of course I'm taking them," Mrs. Gale spoke sharply. "I'm not leaving them for the Communists."

I was furious. Here I'd left a sweet, well-mannered, housebroken cat behind and they were dragging along two disgusting, smelly, flea-covered monkeys. I slid into the front seat with my mother and left the Gales and their dirty animals have the backseat to themselves. I nudged my mother and she nudged me back. She hated those monkeys too.

On the Bund gray-coated soldiers with rifles over their shoulders were stationed all over the place. They were here to keep order, my father said. They knew the gunboats would fire if they had to and they evidently didn't want that to happen. Crowds of Chinese were milling around but they didn't look like organized riot-makers, just ordinary Chinese who had come out of curiosity to laugh at the foreigners scuttling away. The Gales and their monkeys, were, of course, the main attraction, and I couldn't help grinning as the crowd jeered and joked about them.

On the dock I saw that our boat had been fitted all around with huge steel plates. They were meant to stop bullets, but according to Mr. Gale, they'd been put up so clumsily, they'd fall over if a shell hit them.

"Do you really think we'll be fired on?" I asked.

My father gave me a reassuring pat. "Probably the worst thing about your trip will be that those steel plates will cut off your view. You won't be able to see a thing, so you better take a last look now."

Before going up the gangplank, I turned around and looked at Hankow. No one could say it was a pretty city but today with spring in the air, it was at its best. I tried to memorize the Bund. The American flag flying merrily over the consulate. The branches of the plane trees bumpy with buds. The clock on the Customs House looking down, like a great-uncle, on us all.

Then I noticed that not six feet away from me a little boy was jumping up and down, screaming, "Foreign devil!" It was my little friend from the Mud Flats. He had grown taller and his pigtail was gone but he was the same boy. I stepped over to him and leaned down.

"It's me," I said. "Look, it's me. Your American friend."

I could see in his eyes that he recognized me but not for a moment did he stop screaming.

I couldn't bear it. "I gave you oranges," I reminded him.

He spat on the ground. "Foreign devil!" he screamed.

I leaned closer. "Shut up!" I screamed back.

I turned and ran up the gangplank. As soon as I was on the boat, I gave a steel plate a hard kick.

My father was watching. "Who are you mad at?"

"The world," I answered. "The whole world."

With the steel plates up, the deck was dark and dismal and prisonlike. I had the sudden feeling that we were all on an ark, waiting for a flood to begin, but this ark wasn't big enough for two of a kind, so the men would have to get off. Meanwhile we stood about in little family clusters, hugging each other, giving advice, saying good-bye. I called "Hello" to Nancy Little who was standing close by with her family. Then the boat gave a whistle and the men paraded single file down the gangplank while the women and children stood behind the steel plates, not even able to wave good-bye.

As soon as the boat had cleared the dock and was headed downriver, the captain announced over the loudspeaker that all passengers were to assemble in the lounge. When we went in, the room was already crowded—babies, children of all ages, and women of all kinds: nuns, spike-heeled flappers, lame grandmothers, fat mothers and thin ones, brave ones and sniffling ones. Nancy, Margaret, Isobel, and I found each other and sat down on the floor, waiting for the captain to speak, which he was obviously going to do as soon as the room had quieted down.

His speech was about safety. If we heard firing while we were on deck, we were to throw ourselves immediately on the floor. The bullets, he said, would probably just rattle against the plates and fall off, but there were gaps between the plates and there was no telling how heavy the firing might be. He explained all the emergency procedures and told us where the life jackets and lifeboats were. At night we were to pull the black curtain that hung at our portholes so that the boat wouldn't be easily seen. Finally, whenever we heard a bell ring three times, we were to grab our life jackets and hit the deck.

We were busy the rest of the day getting settled in our cabins, but the next morning after breakfast Nancy and I decided we should practice the safety measures. We talked Margaret and Isobel into being the enemy and hiding from us. Then as we strolled around the deck, they were to make rat-a-tat sounds and Nancy and I would fall to the deck. It was a good game and we played all day, improving our speed as we went along. When we got tired of plain falling, we tried different styles of falling. How would the nuns fall? we asked ourselves. And the flappers? We pretended that we were Mrs. Gale walking Nip and Tuck on their leashes, and although we let Mrs. Gale escape the bullets, we made sure that Nip and Tuck got it right in their hearts.

Back in the cabin at the end of the day, my mother told me that I was too old for that kind of game.

"I am?" I hadn't thought of myself as being too old for anything. I looked in the mirror. Of course I had grown taller, up to my mother's shoulders now and too big for any of my grandmother's petticoats. I studied my face to see if it had changed but all I could see was the same old face.

My mother looked over my shoulder. Then she licked her finger and reached around to smooth out my eyebrows. I was dumbfounded. I'd seen her smooth out her own eyebrows but surely it couldn't be time for me to pay attention to mine. Still, she kept looking at my reflection as if she were seeing someone who was not quite there yet.

"I certainly hope you don't have the Guttery eyes," she said. "It would be a shame if you had to wear glasses."

My mother didn't know that I was dying to wear glasses. All writers wore glasses and the sooner I got into them, I figured, the better. I moved away from the mirror because I knew what my mother was really thinking. Now she was hoping that I'd not only be good but that I'd turn pretty. I wanted to tell her to give up, but how could I? I was the only daughter she had.

The next day I told Nancy that I was bored by the falling-down game, so for the rest of the trip Nancy, Margaret, Isobel, and I spent most of our time in the lounge, playing snap and old maid. In any case, all that practice in falling down turned out to be a waste of time. No one had to fall down at all. The only bullets that hit the boat came at night when everyone was flat in bed anyway. I'd wake up with a jerk. Ping! Ping! Ping! And sometimes pingpingpingping. I'd burrow under my covers, wondering if a whole army was shooting at us or just a couple of soldiers on the riverbank. In the end it didn't matter. We got to Shanghai safely and on time.

My father had telegraphed Mrs. Hull about our arrival and she had sent someone to meet us and take care of our luggage. I worried about how much Andrea might have changed since learning the Charleston, and when she came to the door, my heart sank. There she was in silk stockings and there I was in woolen knee socks. There she was with her belt around her hips and there I was with my belt at the same old place around my waist. But as soon as she started to talk, I felt better.

"Guess what? Guess what?" She was full of news as always, but her mother hushed her.

"Later, Andrea," she said. "It will save. Let Jean and her mother take their coats off and settle down first."

My mother couldn't wait to settle down. "Any word from Arthur?" I knew she was hoping that there'd be a telegram, telling us that all was well and he'd see us for sure on the twentieth.

"No word from him. But there was a story in the paper yesterday." As soon as we were in the living room, Mrs. Hull handed my mother a clipping. I could tell it wasn't good news. Over my mother's shoulder I read that there had been rioting in Hankow. All foreign men had been staying overnight on boats where they would be safer.

My mother put the clipping down and looked out the window. "Well," she said, "I'm not going to America until Arthur gets here. No matter how long we have to wait."

I could see that Andrea was impatient. "But the paper doesn't say that people can't leave Hankow," she pointed out. "He better get here. Guess what?" She couldn't hold back her news any longer. "We have reservations on the *President Taft* too. We'll be going with you. David and Edward and Mother and I."

"*Really*? Oh, that's wonderful," I said. "Isn't that wonderful?"

Andrea grinned. "And how!"

"We'll just take for granted that Arthur will be here." Mrs. Hull spoke firmly to my mother. "We'll go right ahead and get ready. You may want to take up the hems on your skirts, Myrtle."

My mother seemed to cheer up as the talk turned to skirt lengths and I leaned over to Andrea. "I have to go to the bathroom," I whispered.

"Sure. Follow me."

I climbed the stairs behind Andrea's silk stockings. At the top she pointed out the rooms: her mother's room with its bath on one side; next to it the guest room (where my mother would be) and its bath; down the hall the boys' room.

I was keeping track. "Do they each have a bathroom?"

"No, they share. And they're not even here now. School is over for us and they're staying with my father in his apartment until we sail." She sighed. "We're having a hard time with David. He doesn't want to go to America."

"Does he have to? Can't he stay with your father?"

Andrea shook her head. "Both my mother and father think that would be bad for him. He'd just keep brooding and hoping. Maybe when he gets to a new country, he'll forget the adoption business."

I was interested in David Hull's troubles and I could see that Andrea wanted to talk about them, but right now I was more interested in the bathroom situation.

"You know," I said, "I'm kind of in a hurry."

"Sorry." Andrea took me into another bedroom. "We'll share my bedroom." She pointed to a door on the right. "My bathroom is there." Then she pointed to a door on the left. "That's yours there."

"My private bathroom?"

"Of course. I told you, didn't I?"

Well, that's all I wanted to know. I went in and shut the door. Right away, as if I'd been touched with a magic wand, I felt like a queen. I'd never dreamed that a bathroom could make so much difference in a person's life. Not only was it private, it was elegant. The basin and pot and tub were pale blue. The toilet paper too. (I'd always supposed all that stuff *had* to be white.) In one corner of the room was a dressing table with a blue-and-white-striped skirt flounced around it. I sat down on a chair in front of the table, picked up a comb, and ran it through my hair. I had never combed my hair sitting down before. Then I opened the door of the medicine cabinet and found little jars and tubes of face cream lined up inside. And a bottle of shampoo. And a big box of bath salts. I wondered if it would be all right for me to try out the bath salts. I flushed the toilet so Andrea would think I'd really had to go, then I went into the bedroom and asked about the bath salts.

"Sure you can use it. Help yourself to anything. I put it there just for you."

I was overwhelmed. "Do you always use bath salts?"

"And how!" Andrea was lying on the floor, just the way she used to, exercising her thighs.

"How come you say 'and how' so much?"

"It's the latest. They say it in the States all the time."

"Maybe when we get there, they'll be saying something different," I pointed out.

Andrea got up. "I can change. Want to see me do the split?" She took off her stockings so she wouldn't get a run and then glided to the floor as if her legs had been built to go in opposite directions.

She jumped up. "Now the back bend." Slowly she went over, all the way until the tips of her fingers touched the floor. Then a little more until her hands were down flat.

"I'm going on the stage," she announced.

She amazed me. She knew just how to get ready for life while all I seemed to do was to wait for life to happen.

That night I took a long, luxurious bath in deep, lilac-scented water. Afterward I sat down at the dressing table and on one side of my face I rubbed night cream that said "For oily skin." On the other side I rubbed cream that said "For dry skin." I'd never noticed what kind of skin I had so I figured this would be a good test. Andrea called to me from the bedroom.

"Did you brush your hair?"

"Now? Why should I brush it now?"

"To keep it in good condition, you should brush fifty strokes every night."

So I brushed. By the time I'd finished my beauty work, it seemed a shame just to go to bed but that was obviously all there was to do. I put on my flannel pajamas and Andrea put on her flowered nightgown and we lay in the dark and talked and talked.

The next day after my mother and Mrs. Hull had gone shopping, Andrea turned on the Victrola. I should learn about popular music, she said. So I listened to "Five Feet Two, Eyes of Blue" and "Gimme a Little Kiss, Will Ya Huh?" I didn't much care for the "Eyes of Blue" song, but I agreed that "Gimme a Little Kiss" had a nice snappy tune. Still, the song I liked best was "I Scream, You Scream, We All Scream for Ice Cream."[9]

"You would," Andrea said.

"What do you mean—'I would'?"

"Well, it's not sophisticated or romantic. Your trouble is that you think America is just feeding your grandmother's chickens. There's a lot more to America than that."

I supposed she was right. Still, I felt silly snapping my fingers and singing "Five Feet Two" the way Andrea did.

"Just remember," Andrea went on, "when you start school in the States next fall, you'll be in eighth grade. Nobody in the eighth grade is going to be singing 'Swanee River.'"[1]

She scared me.

"You don't still curtsy, I hope?"

"No."

"Well, thank goodness for that."

She made me feel so behind the times that when my mother came home and handed me a package of silk stockings, I went right upstairs and put them on, rolling the tops over round garters, the way Andrea did. Then I stretched out my legs to give them the once-over. They didn't look like my legs but I decided they weren't too bad. Still, I kept wondering: How on earth was I going to roller-skate in silk stockings?

The next day when my mother and Mrs. Hull came home from shopping, my mother seemed more lighthearted than she'd been for ages. "Well," she said, "I have a surprise."

She pulled off her hat and her hair was bobbed. I felt sick to my stomach. Andrea told her how stylish she looked, but I knew that she had ruined herself. She didn't look like my mother at all. I knew that my father would feel exactly the way I did. "What will Dad say?"

"Oh, he'll be mad at first," she said gaily, "but he'll get used to it."

---

9. All songs of the 1920s.   1. Song written by Stephen Foster in 1851.

When my father got mad, it was not a laughing matter. When his chin went hard, he was really trying to hold down the lid on a private volcano, but sometimes the lid blew. Sky-high.

"Don't you like it, Jean?" My mother was pirouetting around me.

"Well, you're pretty, no matter what you do." After all, she couldn't stick her hair back on, could she? When I looked at her, I'd just try to skip over her hair.

I had plenty of other things to think about. Mr. Hull was taking all the children to the moving pictures the next afternoon. Andrea was sorry that John Gilbert[2] wasn't playing because she was in love with him, but this was next best, she said. Not a love movie, a scary one. *The Phantom of the Opera* with Lon Chaney.[3] She said that a boy in the Shanghai American School had been so scared, he'd wet his pants. I could see that Andrea thought this movie was a real challenge, a test of how grown-up you were. I pretended to be excited too but secretly I was worried because I didn't know if I could pass the test. To make sure, I'd just close my eyes, I decided, if I felt any danger.

The way my mother and Mrs. Hull were tearing around—packing, shopping, sewing—you wouldn't have thought either one of them would have bothered to ask what we were going to see. But Mrs. Hull did, just as we were leaving. Andrea tried to get over the moment by shrugging and saying a loud good-bye, but David told.

"The Phantom of the Opera," he said.

Mrs. Hull grabbed Andrea's arm. "You are doing no such thing," she announced. She looked at Mr. Hull as if he'd taken leave of his senses. "You can't take children to that. *Rin-Tin-Tin*[4] is playing across the street. Either the children go to that or they stay home."

"That's for babies!" Andrea cried. "Daddy promised us Lon Chaney."

But Mrs. Hull didn't care what Mr. Hull had promised and he didn't argue. After we'd left, Andrea tried to talk him into going to Lon Chaney anyway. "After all," she scoffed, "it's just a movie. How could a movie hurt anyone?"

But Mr. Hull took us to *Rin-Tin-Tin*. Secretly, of course, I was glad, because I knew I could keep my eyes open the whole time.

Actually, we should have gone to the movies the next day, the twentieth, and taken my mother to distract her. It was the day my father was due to arrive, and from the time she got up, my mother was beside herself. She would start a job, look at the clock, forget what she'd been doing, and go to another job. Every time the telephone rang, she jumped. Every time there was a knock at the door, she ran to it. It was never my father. In the evening she called up the boat company. No, they said, the boat from Hankow had not come in and they'd had no word.

The following day my mother paced. Every few hours she'd call up the boat company but there was still no news. I kept thinking of the pingpingpings on our boat; I kept worrying that my father didn't know how to fall down fast enough.

Andrea and I stayed downstairs late that night but at eleven o'clock, just as we were about to give up, there was a bang on the front door. My mother got there first.

And yes, it was my father, triumphant, laughing, happy, brimming with news of Narrow Squeaks. The boat, it seemed, had run aground in that shallow channel of the river that boats were always wary of. It had taken all this time to get clear. He told about the riots in Hankow and was reporting on what had happened to different

---

2. American romantic star of silent movies (1899–1936).
3. American actor who frequently starred in horror movies (1883–1930); *The Phantom of the Opera*

was released in 1925.
4. Two movies starring Rin-Tin-Tin, a German shepherd, were released in 1925.

friends when all at once I noticed that the line of my mother's mouth had gone tight and thin. My father had been here over half an hour, talking steadily about his news, and he hadn't even noticed her hair. After all, my mother had never had her hair cut in her life and of course she expected my father to be startled or shocked. But not even to notice! I was afraid that at any minute my mother might blow her own volcano, and I didn't want to be around, so I kissed them good night and went to bed.

I never did find out what went on between them but the next morning everything seemed to be all right. I was the last one down for breakfast and right away I noticed how happy everyone was.

"The day after the day after tomorrow," Andrea announced.

Suddenly I felt as if a genie had clapped his hands and poof! my "ifs" had vanished. We all seemed to agree that nothing was going to stop us now. So we should celebrate, I thought. We should *do* something. We shouldn't just sit here eating oatmeal.

My father must have had the same feeling because all at once he slapped the table, tipped his chair back, and began singing "Pack Up Your Troubles in Your Old Kitbag and Smile, Smile, Smile."[5] I looked at Andrea to see if she was turning up her nose at such an old-fashioned song, but no, she was grinning and singing along with everyone else.

I never knew grown-ups to stay excited for so long and I wondered when the spell would break. I knew, of course, that once we got on the ship, it would be hard for Andrea and David and Edward to say good-bye to their father, but no one was coming to say good-bye to me so I figured I could go on being happy indefinitely.

On the twenty-sixth, just before we went on the ship, my father sent my grandmother a cablegram: SAILING TODAY. I wanted him to add "Hooray," but every word cost money, he said, and besides she'd recognize the hooray even if it wasn't there. Certainly on board the *President Taft* the hooray feeling was all over the place. On deck the ship's band was playing "California, Here I Come," and people were dancing and singing and laughing. A steward was handing out rolls of paper streamers for passengers to throw over the railing as the ship sailed.

Although my mother, father, and I had spoken to Mr. Hull when he'd first come on board with the boys, we'd left him to visit alone with his children. I tried not to look in their direction so I wouldn't spoil my hooray feeling, but when the whistle blew for visitors to leave, I went to Andrea and stood beside her. Together we threw our streamers as the ship began to pull away from the dock. Everyone threw. Roll after roll until the distance from the ship to the dock was aflutter with paper ribbons—red, yellow, blue, green. Flimsy things, they looked as if they didn't want to let Shanghai go, but of course as the ship moved farther away, they broke, fell into the water, or simply hung bedraggled over the ship's side. Andrea leaned over the railing, waving to her father as long as she could see him. Then suddenly she turned and ran—to her cabin, I supposed.

My mother, father, and Mrs. Hull went into the lounge for tea. Edward went exploring, and I walked to the back of the ship with David trailing behind me. It seemed to me that once we were completely out of sight of land, I would really feel homeward bound. But as I looked at the Shanghai skyline and at the busy waterfront, I had the strange feeling that I wasn't moving away at all. Instead the land was slowly moving away and leaving me. Not just Shanghai but China itself. It was as if I could see the whole country at once: all the jogging rickshas, the pagodas, the squeaking

---

5. A 1912 song that became very popular during World War I.

wells, the chestnut vendors, the water buffaloes, the bluebells, the gray-coated soldiers, the bare-bottomed little boys. And of course the muddy Yangtse with my own
junk looking at me with its wide eyes. I could even smell China, and it was the smell
of food cooking, of steam rising from so many rice bowls it hung in a mist over the
land. But it was slipping away. No matter how hard I squinted, it was fading from
sight. I glanced at David, woebegone as always, but I knew he wasn't sad at leaving
Mr. Hull or at leaving China. He was just feeling sorry for himself in the same old
way.

Suddenly I was mad. "You make me sick, David Hull," I said. "Cry-babying over
something in the past that you can't know a thing about. Don't you know your real
past is right there? Yours and mine both." I pointed at China. "It's been under our
noses the whole time and we've hardly noticed."

I didn't want to talk to David Hull, so I went down to the cabin to open Lin Nai-
Nai's present. That would make me feel better, I thought. I took the red package out
of my suitcase and tore off the tissue paper. Inside was a folded square of cloth that
was obviously a piece of Lin Nai-Nai's embroidery. As I unfolded it, I drew in my
breath. This was no iron-on pattern. This was Lin Nai-Nai's own design: a picture of
a mountain, a thin black line climbing up to a scallop of clouds. In the center of the
picture was a pool with bluebells and tiger lilies growing all around it. I started to
cry—not just a flurry of sniffles but such huge sobs I had to throw myself on my
bunk and bury my head in my pillow.

I heard my mother and father come into the cabin but I kept on crying. My mother
leaned over me. "Whatever is the matter?" she asked.

I couldn't talk. I held up Lin Nai-Nai's embroidery for her to see.

"Of course," my mother said. "You miss Lin Nai-Nai."

That was true, but I was crying for more than that. For more than the memory of
Kuling. For more than I could ever explain.

My mother put her arms around me. "You're just tired," she said. "You'll feel better
after a good night's sleep."

"That's right," my father agreed. "You'll be fine in the morning."

I wasn't tired. I knew I had good reasons for crying even if they were too mixed up
to put into words.

Still, I did feel better the next morning. At eleven o'clock I was stretched out on a
deck chair, my steamer rug over my legs. I was looking at the ocean and waiting for
the steward to bring me a cup of beef tea.

6

It took twenty-eight days to go from Shanghai to San Francisco, and on that first
morning I thought I'd be content to lie on my deck chair and stare at the ocean and
drink beef tea the whole time. Not Andrea. She thought the ocean was one big waste.
We should be watching the people, she said, and sizing them up as they went by. So
we did. We found that mostly they fit into definite types. There were the Counters,
for instance: fast-walking men, red-cheeked women, keeping score of how many
times they walked around the deck, reveling in how fit they were. Then there were
the Stylish Strollers, the Huffers and Puffers, the Lovebirds, leaning on each other,
the Queasy Stomachs who clutched the railing and hoped for the best.

"You notice there's no one our age," Andrea said.

That was true. We had seen young people who were probably in their twenties,
children who were Edward's age, and of course the majority who were our parents'

age or older. But not one who might be in seventh or eighth grade or even high school.

Andrea jumped from her chair. "I'm going to explore."

Normally I would have gone with her but I hadn't had a chance yet to get my fill of the ocean. It was the same ocean as I'd had in Peitaiho and I looked and looked. I walked up to the top deck where I could see the whole circle of water around me. I was smack in the middle of no place, I thought. Not in China, not in America, not in the past, not in the future. In between everything. It was nice.

By the time I went back to my chair, Andrea had returned from her explorations. "There really is no one our age on board," she reported.

"Well, we can play shuffleboard and deck tennis. There are lots of things we can do."

Andrea sighed. "I was hoping for some boys."

I knew that Andrea had begun to like boys. She said everyone at the Shanghai American School had a crush on someone else and when your love was requited— well, that was the cat's.[6] What I couldn't understand was how someone could be in love with John Gilbert and a kid in knickers at the same time.

I suppose Andrea could see that I was trying to figure out the boy business. She gave me a curious look. "Just how do you picture your school in Washington, P.A.?" she asked.

Well, I knew exactly what it would be like, so I told her: I'd be an American in a class with nothing but Americans in it. When we fought the American Revolution, we'd all fight on the same side. When we sang "My country 'tis of thee," we'd yell our heads off. We'd all be the same. I would *belong*.

"There'll be boys in your class," Andrea pointed out.

"Naturally. I've seen boys before. So what?"

"Well, I think you're going to be surprised."

I didn't want to be surprised. For years I'd planned my first day at school in America.

"So how do you picture your school in Los Angeles, California?" I asked.

Andrea looked out at the ocean as if she expected to see her school sitting out there on the water. Then suddenly she shut her eyes and dropped her head in her hands. "Oh, Jean," she whispered, "I can't picture anything anymore. All I keep thinking about is my father. Alone in Shanghai."

This was as close as I'd ever seen Andrea come to crying. I put my hand on her shoulder. "I'm sorry," I said. Sorry! Such a puny word. You'd think the English language could give you something better. "I'm so sorry," I repeated.

Andrea dropped her hands and took a deep breath. "Well, let's play shuffleboard," she said.

From then on we played a lot of shuffleboard. Sometimes David joined us, but mostly he stayed in the ship's library, reading books about boys with real families. Edward kept busy in programs planned for children his age and the grown-ups made friends and talked their usual boring grown-up talk.

On the whole, Andrea and I had a good time on the *President Taft*. In the evenings we often watched movies. In the afternoons we made pigs of ourselves at tea where we had our pick of all kinds of dainty sandwiches, scones, macaroons, chocolate bonbons, and gooey tarts. Actually, I even liked going to bed on shipboard. I'd lie in my bunk and feel the ship's engines throbbing and know that even when I fell asleep

6. I.e., the cat's pajamas or the cat's meow (both slang phrases of the 1920s meaning "great").

I wouldn't be wasting time. I'd still be on the go, moving closer to America every minute.

Still, my "in-between" feeling stayed with me. One evening after supper I took Andrea to the top deck and told her about the feeling. Of course the "in-between-ness" was stronger than ever in the dark with the circle of water rippling below and the night sky above spilling over with stars. I had never seen so many stars. When I looked for a spot where I might stick an extra star if I had one, I couldn't find any space at all. No matter how small, an extra star would be out of place, I decided. The universe was one-hundred-percent perfect just as it was.

And then Andrea began to dance. She had slipped off her shoes and stockings and she was dancing what was obviously an "in-between" dance, leaping up toward the stars, sinking down toward the water, bending back toward China, reaching forward toward America, bending back again and again as if she could not tear herself away, yet each time dancing farther forward, swaying to and fro. Finally, her arms raised, she began twirling around, faster and faster, as if she were trying to outspin time itself. Scarcely breathing, I sat beside a smokestack and watched. She was making a poem and I was inside the poem with her. Under the stars, in the middle of the Pacific Ocean. I would never forget this night, I thought. Not if I lived to be one hundred.

Only when we came to the international date line did my "in-between" feeling disappear. This is the place, a kind of imaginary line in the ocean, where all ships going east add an extra day to that week and all ships going west drop a day. This is so you can keep up with the world turning and make time come out right. We had two Tuesdays in a row when we crossed the line and after that when it was "today" for me, I knew that Lin Nai-Nai was already in "tomorrow." I didn't like to think of Lin Nai-Nai so far ahead of me. It was as if we'd suddenly been tossed on different planets.

On the other hand, this was the first time in my life that I was sharing the same day with my grandmother.

Oh, Grandma, I thought, ready or not, here I come!

It was only a short time later that Edward saw a couple of rocks poking out of the water and yelled for us to come. The rocks could hardly be called land, but we knew they were the beginning of the Hawaiian Islands and we knew that the Hawaiian Islands were a territory belonging to the United States. Of course it wasn't the same as one of the forty-eight states; still, when we stepped off the *President Taft* in Honolulu (where we were to stay a couple of days before going on to San Francisco), we wondered if we could truthfully say we were stepping on American soil. I said no. Since the Hawaiian Islands didn't have a star in the flag, they couldn't be one-hundred-percent American, and I wasn't going to consider myself on American soil until I had put my feet flat down on the state of California.

We had a week to wait. The morning we were due to arrive in San Francisco, all the passengers came on deck early, but I was the first. I skipped breakfast and went to the very front of the ship where the railing comes to a point. That morning I would be the "eyes" of the *President Taft*, searching the horizon for the first speck of land. My private ceremony of greeting, however, would not come until we were closer, until we were sailing through the Golden Gate. For eyes I had heard about the Golden Gate, a narrow stretch of water connecting the Pacific Ocean to San Francisco Bay. And for years I had planned my entrance.

Dressed in my navy skirt, white blouse, and silk stockings, I felt every bit as neat as Columbus or Balboa and every bit as heroic when I finally spotted America in the distance. The decks had filled with passengers by now, and as I watched the land come closer, I had to tell myself over and over that I was HERE. At last.

Then the ship entered the narrow stretch of the Golden Gate and I could see American hills on my left and American houses on my right, and I took a deep breath of American air.

" 'Breathes there the man, with soul so dead,'" I cried,

" 'Who never to himself hath said,

This is my own, my native land!'"

I forgot that there were people behind and around me until I heard a few snickers and a scattering of claps, but I didn't care. I wasn't reciting for anyone's benefit but my own.

Next for my first steps on American soil, but when the time came, I forgot all about them. As soon as we were on the dock, we were jostled from line to line. Believe it or not, after crossing thousands of miles of ocean to get here, we had to prove that it was O.K. for us to come into the U.S.A. We had to show that we were honest-to-goodness citizens and not spies. We had to open our baggage and let inspectors see that we weren't smuggling in opium or anything else illegal. We even had to prove that we were germ-free, that we didn't have smallpox or any dire disease that would infect the country. After we had finally passed the tests, I expected to feel one-hundred-percent American. Instead, stepping from the dock into the city of San Francisco, I felt dizzy and unreal, as if I were a made-up character in a book I had read too many times to believe it wasn't still a book. As we walked the Hulls to the car that their Aunt Kay had driven up from Los Angeles, I told Andrea about my crazy feeling.

"I'm kind of funny in the head," I said. "As if I'm not really me. As if this isn't really happening."

"Me too," Andrea agreed. "I guess our brains haven't caught up to us yet. But my brains better get going. Guess what?"

"What?"

"Aunt Kay says our house in Los Angeles is not far from Hollywood."

Then suddenly the scene speeded up and the Hulls were in the car, ready to leave for Los Angeles, while I was still stuck in a book without having said any of the things I wanted to. I ran after the car as it started.

"Give my love to John Gilbert," I yelled to Andrea.

She stuck her head out the window. "And how!" she yelled back.

My mother, father, and I were going to stay in a hotel overnight and start across the continent the next morning, May 24, in our new Dodge. The first thing we did now was to go to a drugstore where my father ordered three ice-cream sodas. "As tall as you can make them," he said. "We have to make up for lost time."

My first American soda was chocolate and it was a whopper. While we sucked away on our straws, my father read to us from the latest newspaper. The big story was about America's new hero, an aviator named Charles Lindbergh who had just made the first solo flight across the Atlantic Ocean.[7] Of course I admired him for having done such a brave and scary thing, but I bet he wasn't any more surprised to have made it across one ocean than I was to have finally made it across another. I looked at his picture. His goggles were pushed back on his helmet and he was grinning. He had it all over John Gilbert, I decided. I might even consider having a crush on him—that is, if and when I ever felt the urge. Right now I was coming to the

---

7. Lindbergh (1902–1974) flew from New York City to an airfield near Paris, landing May 21, 1927.

bottom of my soda and I was trying to slurp up the last drops when my mother told me to quit; I was making too much noise.

The rest of the afternoon we spent sight-seeing, riding up and down seesaw hills in cable cars, walking in and out of American stores. Every once in a while I found myself smiling at total strangers because I knew that if I were to speak to them in English, they'd answer in English. We were all Americans. Yet I still felt as if I were telling myself a story. America didn't become completely real for me until the next day after we'd left San Francisco and were out in the country.

My father had told my mother and me that since he wasn't used to our new car or to American highways, we should be quiet and let him concentrate. My mother concentrated too. Sitting in the front seat, she flinched every time she saw another car, a crossroad, a stray dog, but she never said a word. I paid no attention to the road. I just kept looking out the window until all at once there on my right was a white picket fence and a meadow, fresh and green as if it had just this minute been created. Two black-and-white cows were grazing slowly over the grass as if they had all the time in the world, as if they knew that no matter how much they ate, there'd always be more, as if in their quiet munching way they understood that they had nothing, nothing whatsoever to worry about. I poked my mother, pointed, and whispered, "Cows." I had never seen cows in China but it was not the cows themselves that impressed me. It was the whole scene. The perfect greenness. The washed-clean look. The peacefulness. Oh, *now!* I thought. Now I was in America. Every last inch of me.

By the second day my father acted as if he'd been driving the car all his life. He not only talked, he sang, and if he felt like hitching up his trousers, he just took his hands off the wheel and hitched. But as my father relaxed, my mother became more tense. "Arthur," she finally said, "you are going forty-five."

My father laughed. "Well, we're headed for the stable, Myrtle. You never heard of a horse that dawdled on its way home, did you?"

My mother's lips went tight and thin. "The whole point of driving across the continent," she said, "was so we could see the country."

"Well, it's all there." My father swept his hand from one side of the car to the other. "All you have to do is to take your eyes off the road and look." He honked his horn at the car in front of him and swung around it.

At the end of the day, after we were settled in an overnight cabin, my father took a new notebook from his pocket. I watched as he wrote: "May 24. 260 miles." Just as I'd suspected, my father was out to break records. I bet that before long we'd be making 300 miles or more a day. I bet we'd be in Washington, P.A., long before July.

The trouble with record breaking is that it can lead to Narrow Squeaks, and while we were still in California we had our first one. Driving along a back road that my father had figured out was a shortcut, we came to a bridge with a barrier across it and a sign in front: THIS BRIDGE CONDEMNED. DO NOT PASS. There was no other road marked DETOUR, so obviously the only thing to do was to turn around and go back about five miles to the last town and take the regular highway. My father stopped the car. "You'd think they'd warn you in advance," he muttered. He slammed the door, jumped over the barrier, and walked onto the bridge. Then he climbed down the riverbank and looked up at the bridge from below. When he came back up the bank, he pushed the barrier aside, got in the car, and started it up. "We can make it," he said.

It hadn't occurred to me that he'd try to drive across. My mother put her hand on his arm. "Please, Arthur," she begged, but I didn't bother with any "pleases." If he wanted to kill himself, he didn't have to kill Mother and me too. "Let Mother and me walk across," I shouted. "Let us out. Let us OUT."

My father had already revved up the motor. "A car can have only one driver," he snapped. "I'm it." He backed up so he could get a flying start and then we whooped across the bridge, our wheels clattering across the loose boards, space gaping below. Well, we did reach the other side and when I looked back, I saw that the bridge was still there.

"You see?" my father crowed. "You see how much time we saved?"

All I could see was that we'd risked our lives because he was so pigheaded. Right then I hated my father. I felt rotten hating someone I really loved but I couldn't help it. I knew the loving would come back but I had to wait several hours.

There were days, however, particularly across the long, flat stretches of Texas, when nothing out-of-the-way happened. We just drove on and on, and although my father reported at the end of the day that we'd gone 350 miles, the scenery was the same at the end as at the beginning, so it didn't feel as if we'd moved at all. Other times we ran into storms or into road construction and we were lucky if we made 200 miles. But the best day of the whole trip, at least as far as my mother and I were concerned, was the day that we had a flat tire in the Ozark Mountains. The spare tire and jack were buried in the trunk under all our luggage, so everything had to be taken out before my father could even begin work on the tire. There was no point in offering to help because my father had a system for loading and unloading which only he understood, so my mother and I set off up the mountainside, looking for wild flowers.

"Watch out for snakes," my mother said, but her voice was so happy, I knew she wasn't thinking about snakes.

As soon as I stepped out of the car, I fell in love with the day. With the sky—fresh, blotting-paper blue. With the mountains, warm and piney and polka-dotted with flowers we would never have seen from the window of a car. We decided to pick one of each kind and press them in my gray geography book which I had in the car. My mother held out her skirt, making a hollow out of it, while I dropped in the flowers and she named them: forget-me-not, wintergreen, pink, wild rose. When we didn't know the name, I'd make one up: pagoda plant, wild confetti, French knot. My mother's skirt was atumble with color when we suddenly realized how far we'd walked. Holding her skirt high, my mother led the way back, running and laughing. We arrived at the car, out of breath, just as my father was loading the last of the luggage into the trunk. He glared at us, his face streaming with perspiration. "I don't have a dry stitch on me," he said, as if it were our fault that he sweat so much. Then he looked at the flowers in Mother's skirt and his face softened. He took out his handkerchief and wiped his face and neck and finally he smiled. "I guess I picked a good place to have a flat tire, didn't I?" he said.

The farther we went, the better mileage we made, so that by the middle of June we were almost to the West Virginia state line. My father said we'd get to Washington, P.A., the day after the next, sometime in the afternoon. He called my grandmother on the phone, grinning because he knew how surprised she'd be. I stood close so I could hear her voice.

"Mother?" he said when she answered. "How about stirring up a batch of flannel cakes?"[8]

8. Pancakes.

"Arthur!" (She sounded just the way I knew she would.) "Well, land's sakes, Arthur, where are you?"

"About ready to cross into West Virginia."

My grandmother was so excited that her words fell over each other as she tried to relay the news to my grandfather and Aunt Margaret and talk over the phone at the same time.

The next day it poured rain and although that didn't slow us down, my mother started worrying. Shirls Avenue, my grandparents' street, apparently turned into a dirt road just before plunging down a steep hill to their house and farm. In wet weather the road became one big sea of mud which, according to my mother, would be "worth your life to drive through."

"If it looks bad," my mother suggested, "we can park at the top of the hill and walk down in our galoshes."

My father sighed. "Myrtle," he said, "we've driven across the Mohave Desert. We've been through thick and thin for over three thousand miles and here you are worrying about Shirls Avenue."

The next day the sun was out, but when we came to Shirls Avenue, I could see that the sun hadn't done a thing to dry up the hill. My father put the car into low, my mother closed her eyes, and down we went, sloshing up to our hubcaps, careening from one rut to another, while my father kept one hand down hard on the horn to announce our arrival.

By the time we were at the bottom of the hill and had parked beside the house, my grandmother, my grandfather, and Aunt Margaret were all outside, looking exactly the way they had in the calendar picture. I ran right into my grandmother's arms as if I'd been doing this every day.

"Welcome home! Oh, welcome home!" my grandmother cried.

I hadn't known it but this was exactly what I'd wanted her to say. I needed to hear it said out loud. I was home.

7

When Aunt Margaret took me to the back of the house to show me around, I found everything so familiar I didn't need to be told what was what. "Here's the grape arbor," I said, and I ran through the long archway that led from the back door to what was once the stable but was now a garage for my grandfather's truck.

"Oh, and there's the pump!"

"We have running water now," Aunt Margaret explained, "so we don't use the pump much."

"But I can pump if I want to, can't I?"

"Sure you can."

Running up the hill on one side of the house was the cornfield. Running down the hill on the other side was the vegetable garden, the rhubarb plot, the dahlia beds. At the bottom of the hill was my grandfather's greenhouse.

"Where are the chickens?" I asked.

"Around the corner."

As we went to the other side of the house, a brown-and-white-speckled rooster came strutting to meet us.

"That's Josh," Aunt Margaret said. "He's such a serious-minded rooster, he can't stand to hear anyone laugh. He ruffles up his feathers and cusses his head off."

I squatted down and tried to force a laugh. "Ha ha-ha ha."

"No," Aunt Margaret said, "he knows you're just pretending."

Not far behind Josh was the chicken house with a big fenced-in yard around it. I ran over and looked at the hens, teetering like plump little ladies on spike heels.

"What are their names?" I asked.

"They don't have names."

"How come?"

"We don't want to become too fond of them."

I'd never heard anything so silly. If I was going to feed them, I ought to know their names. "Why not?" I asked.

"Well, Jean," Aunt Margaret explained, "you know that this is a farm. In the end we eat every one of those chickens."

I felt dumb not to have known. I decided that when I fed the chickens, I'd try not to even look them in the eye.

As we went inside, Aunt Margaret pointed to a pair of roller skates on the back porch. "I dug those out of the attic," she said. "I thought you'd like them." She looked at my legs. "But you can't roller-skate in silk stockings."

"That's O.K.," I grinned. "I have socks."

Of course I wanted to try the roller skates right away but my mother's family was due to arrive for a welcome-home party and all of us had to get dressed up.

"Are we going to have flannel cakes?" I asked.

Aunt Margaret laughed. "That was just a joke. We're going to have potato salad and smearcase[9] and cold chicken and apple pie and lots of other good things. We've been cooking ever since your father called."

My mother's family arrived all at once: Aunt Blanche, Aunt Etta, Aunt Mary L., Aunt Sarah and Uncle Welsh, Uncle George and Aunt Edith, and my four cousins— Elizabeth and Jane who were much older and Katherine and Charlotte who were about three years younger. There were a couple of extra girls, but I couldn't figure out where they fit in. The family parked their cars at the top of the hill, stopped to pull on galoshes, and then picked their way down the grassy side of the road which was fairly dry. When my mother saw them, she ran up the hill, her arms out, and I watched one of her sisters run ahead of the others, her arms out too. I knew it must be Aunt Blanche. They stood beside the road, hugging, stepping back to make sure who they were, then hugging again. When the whole family got to the bottom of the hill where my father and I were waiting, everyone began crying and laughing and kissing and hugging at the same time. I never saw such carrying-on. Not just one kiss apiece, but kiss after kiss while I was still trying to figure out which aunt was which.

My youngest cousin, Charlotte, who was watching all this, suggested that we clear out until the excitement had died down. Those two other girls tagged along as we went to the back of the house where we all sat down on the platform surrounding the pump.

"I can't stand all that kissing business," Charlotte said. "Can you?"

"No," I agreed. "They wouldn't even let me get my breath."

"Let's make a pact," she suggested. "I'll never kiss you if you promise never to kiss me."

We shook on it. But I still wondered about those other two girls, so I whispered to Charlotte, asking if they were related. She said no, they were neighbor kids who had begged to come along because they wanted to see the girl from China. "This is

_____

9. Soft, spreadable cheese, especially cream cheese.

Ruth and this is Marie," she said, but I could tell she wished they were someplace else.

Up to this time Ruth and Marie had just stared at me, but now Ruth nudged Marie and whispered, "You ask."

Marie giggled. "We want to know if you ate rats in China and what they tasted like."

"And if you ate their *tails* too," Ruth added.

Rats! "No one in China eats rats," I said stiffly.

"Oh, you don't need to pretend." Ruth was smuggling her laughter behind her hands. "Everyone knows that people in China eat queer things. Snakes, birds' nests . . ."

"They do not."

The girls were looking at me as if I were some kind of a freak in a circus. As if maybe I had two heads.

"Did you use sticks to eat with?" Marie asked.

"Chopsticks, you mean. Sometimes. Of course."

Both girls lay back on the platform, shrieking with laughter. Josh came tearing around the house, scolding, ruffling his feathers, and I didn't blame him. He wasn't any madder than I was.

"Quit it," I told the girls. "You're upsetting the rooster."

This only set them off again. When they finally got control of themselves, they asked if I could speak Chinese and I said yes, I certainly could.

I turned to Marie and said in Chinese, "Your mother is a big turtle." ("Nide muchin shr ega da wukwei.") Then I looked at Ruth and told her that her mother was a turtle too. I knew that in English it wouldn't sound so bad but in China this was an insult.

The girls were rolling all over the platform in spasms of laughter while Josh croaked and flapped. "Oh, it sounds so funny, say it again," Ruth begged.

So I did. And I added that they were worthless daughters of baboons and they should never have been born.

"What does it mean?" they asked. "Tell us what it means."

"You wouldn't understand," I said coldly. "Come on, Charlotte, let's go back to the party."

That night after everyone had left, I told my mother and father about the crazy questions Ruth and Marie had asked.

"Well, Jean," my father said, "some people in Washington don't know any better. China seems so far away they imagine strange things."

I told myself that only little kids like Ruth and Marie could be so ignorant. Eighth graders would surely know better.

But for a while I didn't worry about eighth grade. I spent the summer doing the things I had dreamed about. Charlotte and I roller-skated, and although it didn't take me long to learn, my knees were skinned most of the time. I didn't care. I was proud of every one of my scabs; they showed that I was having a good time. And there were so many ways to have a good time—so many flavors of ice cream to try, so many treasures to choose at the five-and-ten, so many trees to climb, so many books to borrow from the library, so many relatives willing to stop for a game of dominoes or checkers. My grandfather and I played horseshoes, and although I never beat him, he said I was every bit as good as my father had been at my age.

And I helped my grandmother. Sometimes I spent the whole day working beside her: shelling peas, kneading bread dough, turning the handle of the wringer after she'd washed clothes, feeding the chickens, sweeping the porch. In China I'd had nothing to do with the work of the house. It just went on automatically around me as if it could have been anyone's house, but now suddenly I was a part of what went on. I had a place. For instance, my grandmother might ask me if we had enough sugar in the house or should she get some, and likely as not, I would know.

"The sugar bin is getting low," I would say. "Maybe you should buy another bag."

Then my grandmother would add "sugar" to her shopping list and she'd say she didn't know how she'd ever got along without me. I loved to hear her say that even though I knew she'd done fine without me. But I did have a lot of new accomplishments. I wrote to Lin Nai-Nai and described them to her. I could even do coolie work, I told her. I could mow grass. I could mop floors.

Still, I thought about school. I'd always supposed I knew exactly what an American school would be like, but as the time came near, I wasn't sure. Suppose I didn't fit in? Suppose I wasn't the same as everyone else, after all? Suppose I turned out to be another Vera Sebastian? Suppose eighth graders thought I was a rat eater?

I couldn't forget the first Sunday I'd gone to church in Washington. The other kids in church had poked each other when I'd walked in. "There's the girl from China." I knew by their faces that's what they were thinking. The woman who sat behind me had made no bones about it. I overheard her whispering to her husband. "You can tell she wasn't born in this country," she said. How could she tell? I wondered. If just looking at me made people stare, what would happen when they heard me talk? Suppose I said something silly? I remembered the rainy afternoon at my grandmother's when we were all sitting around reading and I had come to a word that I didn't know.

"What's a silo?" I asked.

The way everyone looked up so surprised, it was as if they were saying, "How on earth did she live this long without knowing what a silo is?" Of course when my father explained, I realized I'd seen silos all over the country; I just hadn't known what they were called. But suppose I had asked that question in school!

I kept pestering Aunt Margaret to tell me if there was anything about eighth grade that I should know and didn't.

"It doesn't matter," she would say. "Not everyone in eighth grade is going to know exactly the same things."

Aunt Margaret had a new beau and I suspected that she wasn't giving my eighth-grade problems enough serious thought, but one day she did ask me if I knew the Pledge of Allegiance.

"What Pledge of Allegiance?"

So she explained that every morning we'd start off by pledging allegiance to the flag and she taught me how to say it, my hand over my heart. After that, I practiced every day while I was feeding the chickens. I'd clap my hand over my heart and tell them about "one nation indivisible." It gave me courage. Surely if the whole class felt strongly about the American flag, I'd fit in all right.

My mother and father would be away when school started. Toward the end of the summer they had begun to give lectures in order to raise money for the Y.M.C.A. and now they were going to Canada for two weeks. Before they left, my mother called the school principal to notify him that I'd be entering eighth grade. She gave Aunt Margaret money to buy me a new dress for school. When she kissed me good-bye, she smoothed out my eyebrows.

"Be good," she whispered.

I stiffened. I wondered if she'd ever forget goodness. Probably the last thing she'd say to me before I walked up the aisle to be married was "Be good."

The next day Aunt Margaret took me to Caldwell's store on Main Street and bought me a red-and-black-plaid gingham dress with a white collar and narrow black patent leather belt that went around my hips. She took me to a beauty parlor and I had my hair shingled.[1]

When I got home, I tried on my dress. "How do I look?" I asked my grandmother.

"As if you'd just stepped out of a bandbox."[2]

I wasn't sure that was the look I was aiming for. "But do I look like a regular eighth grader?"

"As regular as they come," she assured me.

The day before school started, I laid out my new dress and stockings and shoes so I'd be ready. I put aside the loose-leaf notebook Aunt Margaret had given me. I pledged allegiance to the chickens and then I sat down on the back steps next to my grandmother who was shelling peas. I reached into her lap, took a bunch of peas, and began shelling into the pan.

"I wish my name were Marjorie," I said. "I'd feel better starting to school with the name Marjorie."

My grandmother split a pea pod with her thumbnail and sent the peas plummeting into the pan.

"Do you like the name Marjorie?" I asked.

"Not much. It sounds common."

"But that's the idea!" I said. "It would make me fit in with everyone else."

"I thought you were going to be a writer."

"I am."

"Well, my stars! Writers do more than just fit in. Sometimes they don't fit in at all." My grandmother quit shelling and looked straight at me. "You know why I like the name *Jean*?" she asked.

"Why?"

"It's short and to the point; it doesn't fool around. Like my name—Isa. They're both good, strong Scottish names. Spunky."

I'd never known my name was Scottish. I surely had never thought of it as strong.

"Grandma," I said, "do you worry about whether I'm good or not?"

My grandmother threw back her head and hooted. "Never. It hasn't crossed my mind." She gave my knee a slap. "I love you just the way you are."

I leaned against her, wanting to say "thank you" but thinking that this wasn't the kind of thing that you said "thank you" for.

The next morning my grandmother and grandfather watched me start up Shirls Avenue in my new outfit, my notebook under my arm.

"Good luck!" they called. I held up my hand with my fingers crossed.

The school was about four blocks away—a big, red-brick, square building that took care of all grades, kindergarten through the eighth. So, of course, there were all ages milling about, but I looked for the older ones. When I'd spotted some—separate groups of girls and boys laughing and talking—I decided that I didn't look any different, so I went into the building, asked in the office where the eighth grade was, and went upstairs to the first room on the right.

Others were going into the room, and when I saw that they seemed to sit wherever they wanted, I picked a desk about halfway up the row next to the window. I slipped my notebook into the open slot for books and then looked at the teacher who was

---

1. Cut in a short, layered hairstyle.   2. I.e., smart and neat.

standing, her back to us, writing on the blackboard. She had a thick, straight-up, corseted figure and gray hair that had been marcelled into such stiff, even waves I wondered if she dared put her head down on a pillow at night.

"My name is Miss Crofts," she had written.

She didn't smile or say "Good Morning" or "Welcome to eighth grade" or "Did you have a nice summer?" She just looked at the clock on the wall and when it was exactly nine o'clock, she tinkled a bell that was like the one my mother used to call the servants.

"The class will come to order," she said. "I will call the roll." As she sat down and opened the attendance book, she raised her right index finger to her head and very carefully she scratched so she wouldn't disturb the waves. Then she began to roll:

Margaret Bride (*Here*). Donald Burch (*Here*), Andrew Carr (*Present*). Betty Donahue (*Here*).

I knew the G's would be coming pretty soon.

John Goodman (*Here*), Jean Guttery.

Here, I said. Miss Crofts looked up from her book. "Jean Guttery is new to our school," she said. "She has come all the way from China where she lived beside the Yangs-Ta-Zee River. Isn't that right, Jean?"

"It's pronounced *Yang-see*," I corrected. "There are just two syllables."

Miss Crofts looked at me coldly. "In America," she said, "we say Yangs-Ta-Zee."

I wanted to suggest that we look it up in the dictionary, but Miss Crofts was going right on through the roll. She didn't care about being correct or about the Yangtse River or about me and how I felt.

Miss Crofts, I said to myself, your mother is a turtle. A big fat turtle.

I was working myself up, madder by the minute, when I heard Andrew Carr, the boy behind me, shifting his feet on the floor. I guess he must have hunched across his desk, because all at once I heard him whisper over my shoulder:

"Chink, Chink, Chinaman

Sitting on a fence,

Trying to make a dollar

Out of fifteen cents."

I forgot all about where I was. I jumped to my feet, whirled around, and spoke out loud as if there were no Miss Crofts, as if I'd never been in a classroom before, as if I knew nothing about classroom behavior.

"You don't call them Chinamen or Chinks," I cried. "You call them *Chinese*. Even in America you call them *Chinese*."

The class fell absolutely silent, all eyes on me, and for the first time I really looked at Andrew Carr. I think I had expected another Ian Forbes, but he was just a freckle-faced kid who had turned beet-red. He was slouched down in his seat as if he wished he could disappear.

Miss Crofts stood up. "Will someone please explain to me what all this is about?"

The girl beside me spoke up. "Andrew called Jean a Chinaman."

"Well, you don't need to get exercised, Jean," she said. "We all know that you are American."

"But that's not the *point*!" Before I could explain that it was an insult to call Chinese people *Chinamen*, Miss Crofts had tapped her desk with a ruler.

"That will be enough," she said. "All eyes front." Obediently the students stopped staring and turned their attention to Miss Crofts. All but one boy across the room. He caught my eye, grinned, and put his thumb up, the way my father did when he thought I'd done well. I couldn't help it; I grinned back. He looked nice, I thought.

"We will stand now and pledge allegiance," Miss Crofts announced. Even though I still felt shaky, I leaped to attention. I wasn't going to let anything spoil my first official pledge. As I placed my hand on my heart, I glanced around. The girl next to me had her hand on her stomach.

"I pledge allegiance to the flag of the United States of America." The class mumbled, but maybe that was because of the flag. It was the saddest-looking flag I'd ever seen, standing in the corner, its stars and stripes drooping down as if they had never known a proud moment. So as I pledged, I pictured the American flag on the Bund, waving as if it were telling the world that America was the land of the free and the home of the brave. Maybe I made my pledge too loud, because when I sat down, the boy across the room raised his thumb again. I hoped he wasn't making fun of me but he seemed friendly so I smiled back.

When I looked at Miss Crofts, she had her finger in her hair and she was daintily working her way through another wave.

After the commotion I had already made in the class, I decided to be as meek as I possibly could the rest of the morning. Since this was the first day at school, we would be dismissed at noon, and surely things would improve by then.

Miss Crofts put a bunch of history books on the first desk of each row so they could be passed back, student to student. I was glad to see that we'd be studying the history of Pennsylvania. Since both my mother's and father's families had helped to settle Washington County, I was interested to know how they and other pioneers had fared. Opening the book to the first chapter, "From Forest to Farmland," I skimmed through the pages but I couldn't find any mention of people at all. There was talk about dates and square miles and cultivation and population growth and immigration and the Western movement, but it was as if the forests had lain down and given way to farmland without anyone being brave or scared or tired or sad, without babies being born, without people dying. Well, I thought, maybe that would come later.

After history, we had grammar and mathematics, but the most interesting thing that I learned all morning was that the boy across the room was named Donald Burch. He had sandy-colored hair combed straight back and he wore a sky-blue shirt.

The last class was penmanship. I perked up because I knew I was not only good at penmanship, but I enjoyed making my words run across a page, round and neat and happy-looking. At the British School we had always printed, so I had learned to make my letters stand up straight and even, and when I began to connect up my letters for handwriting, I kept that proud, straight-up look.

I took the penmanship workbooks from the girl in front of me, kept my copy, and passed the rest to Andrew Carr. The workbook was called *The Palmer Method*, but the title was not printed; it was handwritten in big, oversized, sober-looking letters, slanting to the right. If you pulled one letter out of a word, I thought, the rest would topple over like a row of dominoes.

"Jean," Miss Crofts said after the workbooks had been distributed, "I expect you have not been exposed to the Palmer method of penmanship. The rest of the class will work on Exercise One, but I want you to come up to my desk while I explain the principle of Palmer penmanship."

Slowly I dragged myself to the front of the room and sat down in the chair that Miss Crofts had pulled up beside her own.

"You see," Miss Crofts said, "in the Palmer method you really write with the underside of your forearm. The fleshy part." She pointed to her own forearm which was quite fleshy and then she put it down on the desk. "You hold your fingers and wrist stiff. All the movement comes from your arm. You begin by rotating the flesh on your arm so that your pen will form slanting circles." She filled a line on the paper with falling-down circles. "When you have mastered the circles," she said, "your arm will be ready for the letters."

As Miss Crofts looked at me to see if I understood, she made a quick dive with her index finger into her waves.

I folded my hands in my lap. "I have very good penmanship," I said. "No one has trouble reading it. I really do not care to change my style."

Miss Crofts pushed a pen and a pad of paper in front of me. "The Palmer method has been proved to be the most efficient system." She had so many years of teaching behind her I could see she wasn't going to fool around. "Just put your arm on the desk, Jean," she said, "and try some circles."

"I don't think I have enough flesh on the underside of my arm," I whispered. "I'm too skinny."

Miss Crofts reached over, picked up my arm, put it on the desk, and pushed a pen in my hand. "Just roll your arm around but keep your fingers stiff. Let your arm do the work."

Sitting in front of the room with everyone peeking up at me from their workbooks, I was afraid I was going to cry. How could I stand to let my letters lean over as if they were too tired to say what they wanted straight out? How could I ever write a poem if I couldn't let the words come out through my fingers and feel their shape? I glanced at Donald Burch who, like everyone else, must have seen how miserable I was. He tapped his forehead to show how crazy Miss Crofts was. Then he shrugged as if he were saying, "What can you do with a nitwit like that?"

I moved my arm halfheartedly and produced a string of sick-looking circles.

"I think you have the idea," Miss Crofts said. "You may go to your seat and practice."

So I went to my seat but I didn't make a single circle unless I saw Miss Crofts watching me. I just hunched over my workbook, promising myself that I would never use the Palmer method outside the classroom. Never. I wouldn't even try hard in the classroom and if I flunked penmanship, so what? I kept looking at the clock, waiting and waiting for the big hand to crawl up and meet the little hand at *Twelve*. When it finally did, Miss Crofts tinkled her bell.

"Class—attention!" she ordered. We all stood up. "First row, march!" Row by row we marched single file out the door, down the stairs, and into the free world where the sun was shining.

Donald Burch was standing on the sidewalk and as I came up, he fell into step beside me.

"She's a real bird, isn't she?" he said.

"You said it!" I glanced up at him. He was two inches taller than I was. "Where do you suppose she dug up the Palmer method?"

"It's not just here," Donald said. "It's all over. Every school in the country uses it."

I stopped in my tracks. "All over *America*?"

"Yep."

I had a sudden picture of schools in every one of the forty-eight states grinding out millions and millions of sheets of paper covered with leaning letters exactly alike. "But what about liberty for all?" I cried. "Why do they want to make us copycats?"

Donald shrugged. "Search me. Grown-ups don't write all the same. Dumb, isn't it?"

As we walked on together, I began to feel better, knowing that Donald felt the same way as I did. Besides, I'd had a good look at him now. When he grew up, he might look a little like Charles Lindbergh, I decided, especially if he wore goggles.

"I guess you never had anyone as bad as Miss Crofts in your school in China, did you?" he asked.

"Well, I had one teacher who was pretty bad, but I think Miss Crofts has her beat."

"Did you like living in China?" Donald asked.

"Yes." (*Oh, please, I prayed, please don't let him ask me if I ate rats.*)

"I bet it was nice. But you know something?"

"What?"

"I'm sure glad you came back to America." He squinted at the sky as if he were trying to figure out the weather. "How about you? Are you glad you came back?"

"And how!" I didn't say it; I breathed it. At the same time I began mentally composing a letter to Andrea.

Dear Andrea: I started school today and there's this boy in my class. Donald Burch. He is the CAT'S!

We had come to Shirls Avenue now. I pointed down the hill. "That's where I live," I said. "That's my grandparents' farm down there. Where do you live?"

Donald pointed over his shoulder. "Back there a few blocks."

He had come out of his way.

"O.K. if I walk with you again tomorrow?" he asked.

I'm sure I said it would be O.K., although all I remember as I ran down the hill was thinking: Oh, I'm in love, I'm in love, and I think it's requited!

When I came to the bottom of the hill, I called out that I was home and my grandmother yoo-hooed from the vegetable garden. I found her among the carrots, standing up in her long white, starched apron, waiting for me, smiling.

"My, you look happy," she said.

I grinned. "I made a friend," I explained.

"Good! That's the best thing that could happen. And how about school?"

I came down to earth with a thump. There was no way I could look happy with a question like that to answer. I just shook my head.

"So it wasn't one-hundred-percent," my grandmother said. "Few things are."

"It was a flop."

"Who's your teacher?"

"Miss Crofts."

"My stars!" My grandmother put her hands on her hips. "Don't tell me she's still hanging around? Why, Margaret had her."

"She's still hanging around," I said.

My grandmother's face took on a sly, comical look. She put her index finger to her head and scratched carefully. "Still scratching, is she?"

Her imitation was so perfect, I burst out laughing.

"Still scratching," I said.

My grandmother and I laughed together and once started, we couldn't seem to stop. We'd let up for a second, then look at each other, and one of us would scratch, and we'd break out again. In fact, it felt so good to laugh, I didn't want to stop.

"She must have cooties,"[3] I gasped.

---

3. Lice.

"She ought to have her head examined." And off we went again!

By this time Josh, who had joined us at the first explosion, was throwing himself about in an outrage, but I couldn't let a rooster spoil the fun. Coming to the surface from my last spasm, I told my grandmother about the Palmer method.

"We're supposed to write with the underside of our arms." I showed her where. "We can't move our fingers or our wrists."

At first my grandmother couldn't believe me, but as I went on about the workbooks and circles, she dissolved into another round of laughter. She turned toward the greenhouse where my grandfather was working. "Will," she called. "Oh, Will! Come and hear this!"

Well, I decided, the only thing a person could do about the Palmer method was to laugh at it. And listening to my grandmother telling it, making up bits as she went along about the imaginary Mr. Palmer who was so set on exercising the underside of children's forearms, I had to laugh again. We all laughed until we were laughed out.

My grandmother turned serious. "You can't move your fingers at all?" she asked, as if she might not have heard right the first time.

"Not at all."

My grandmother shook her head. "They must be preparing you for a crippled old age." She leaned down to comfort Josh. "Sh, sh, sh," she said, smoothing out his feathers. "It's all right, Josh. It's all over. You don't know how funny the world can be, do you? Maybe even a little crazy. There are times when people just *have* to laugh."

"Times when they have to eat too," my grandfather added. "What are we having?"

My grandmother said she'd fixed apple dumplings, and together the three of us walked to the house. Past the cabbages and beans, down the path lined with gold and orange chrysanthemums. We stopped to admire the grapes, dangling in heavy clusters from the vines, fat and purple.

Then I ran ahead to put the plates on the table.

Background of Chinese History, 1913–1927

When my mother and father arrived in China in 1913, China had been a republic with a president for only a year. For thousands of years before this, China had been ruled by emperors and empresses who had tried to seal China off from the rest of the world. Early in the nineteenth century, however, Western nations had gradually been exerting their power and forcing their way into the country. In a series of "unequal" treaties, the foreign nations gained "concessions" in which Western law was practiced and Western police kept order; they put gunboats on the rivers to protect the interests of Western merchants. By 1907 there were thousands of foreign businessmen and foreign missionaries in China (3500 Protestant missionaries alone).

Eventually the Chinese rebelled not only against this Western imposition but against their own internal system which served a ruling class at the expense of millions of farmers and laborers. The leader of the revolutionary movement was a Chinese Christian by the name of Sun Yat-sen who had been educated in both Chinese and British schools. "China is being transformed everywhere," he wrote, "into a colony of foreign powers." Sun Yat-sen was in America when the revolution actually broke out on October 10, 1911, in Wuchang, across the river from Hankow. Sun went back to China and was sworn in as president of the Republic of China on January 1, 1912. But he needed military help to back up his government, so he consented to an agreement with Yuan Shih-k'ai, a military leader in the imperial army. If Yuan completed the overthrow of the old imperial government, Yuan could be president of the new republic.

The trouble was that Yuan Shih-k'ai did not share Sun Yat-sen's ideas for a democratic China. Once he became president, he was interested only in power; he even tried to get himself elected emperor. When he died on June 6, 1916, the country was no further ahead than it had been in 1912.

While warlords fought back and forth, Sun Yat-sen made another attempt at national unity. Although he was head of the Nationalist party, he still did not have the military support he needed to get rid of the warlords and do away with the special privileges of the foreigners. "The only country that shows any sign of helping us," he wrote, "is the Soviet Government of Russia." Beginning in September 1922, he allowed Chinese Communists to join his party, and the following year the Russians began sending advisers to China. Later they sent arms. Sun himself was not a Communist and had he lived, he might have been able to unite China in the way he wanted. Unfortunately, Sun Yat-sen died on March 12, 1925, and was later succeeded by Chiang Kai-shek as party leader. By August 1926, Chiang had marched the National Revolutionary Army north, gathering warlords on the way, and was at the Yangtse River.

Meanwhile Hankow, an industrial city, had become a central point for strikes, agitation, and anti-foreign demonstrations. Behind the scenes Mao Tse-tung[4] was organizing peasants for a Communist uprising, but Chiang was against the idea of peasants taking violent action against their landlords. In order to ensure a united China, Chiang believed he had to make deals with Chinese capitalists, with members of China's underworld, and with foreigners who believed that with Chiang in charge, they could continue business as usual. He eliminated Communists from his party and in April 1927 (after the Nanking Incident[5]), he set up his own government in Nanking. Foreign nations recognized this as the legal government of China. By August the Russians had left China and Mao Tse-tung and his small band of followers were hiding in the hills.

It was during this turbulent period of transition that I was in China. Struggle and civil war (interrupted by a war with Japan) continued for twenty-two years before Mao Tse-tung defeated Chiang Kai-shek and established the People's Republic of China. Chiang, with remnants of his army and many of his followers, took refuge on the island of Taiwan, where they continued a government which they claimed was still the government of all China. America recognized that government as the government of China until December 1978, although it had lost its seat in the United Nations in 1971.

4. Mao Zedong (1893–1976), military leader and theoretician who became chairman of the Chinese Communist Party and of the People's Republic of China after the Nationalists were defeated in 1949; he remained chairman of the Party until his death.
5. In March 1927, Nationalist soldiers who had seized Nanjing attacked foreign consulates and residents of the foreign concessions, killing a number of Westerners; these actions forced the hasty departure of Jean and her mother from Hankow (described in chapter 5, above).

Dear Grandma:

Thank you so much for the petticoat. It is lovely. The thing that I think is nice about it is that it is so much like a grown up petticoat. Everything was perfectly beautiful. Thanks Aunt Margaret and aunt Etta please for the ring. I am wearing it now. And please thank Aunt Margaret for the pocket book. I am so proud of it, that when I take it out with me everyone blooks me and says, What a pretty pocket book where did you get it? Shall I name the presents? Fountain pen, Stamp album (from mother,) Dolls furniture (from Daddy) lovely invitations cards. aunt navy black coat, (aunt ?and,) album, Paper papers beads, letter Angel cake cookers, Book of furnities. Pink silk cloth, Brown satin, White, rubber apron (cousin Margaret,) my petticoat, pocket book, bag, 1 book, 2 book, 3 book, Dolls clothes, gold balls pocketbook, gold bracelet, stocking full of things, teaset, 1 candy box, 2 candy box, hankerchiefs (galore,) skirt, skipping rope 1926 Diary.

With loads of
Love
your Grand daughter
Jean Guley.

1925 Christmas letter from Jean to her grandmother

1982

MILTON MELTZER
b. 1915

When the young Milton Meltzer entered the imposing red stone library building in Worcester, Massachusetts, he was astonished and moved at the appearance of so many books, "treasures" he had been seeking, lined up on tall shelf after tall shelf. In his autobiography, *Starting from Home: A Writer's Beginnings* (1988), Meltzer recalls his insatiable desire to read: "I was like some insect nibbling words to appease an instinctive craving." One book and one insect in particular—and one special high school teacher, Anna Shaughnessy, to whom *Starting from Home* is dedicated—changed Meltzer's life not once, but twice. Shaughnessy suggested that Meltzer read Henry David Thoreau's *Walden* (1854). Though the book was not on the approved syllabus, she thought it would speak to her hungry student. The prose was difficult at first, but Meltzer persisted and ultimately found the work to be deeply satisfying. Many years later, troubled and uneasy about his life, Meltzer returned to *Walden*. On its last page he reread the passage about an insect that had existed dormant in a tree for sixty years, yet finally hatched. Meltzer was moved to tears by Thoreau's larger message of renewal and hope: "The image of a bug emerging into life after all those years in a wooden tomb, touched something deep in me. The tears poured out in relief. . . . I felt like one reborn." Thoreau's work was a book of "revelation" for Meltzer, and he hopes his own writing can have the same effect on readers.

Meltzer grew up in Worcester, the child of Jewish immigrants. While a student at Columbia University he decided to become a writer rather than a teacher. Meltzer wrote for the WPA Federal Theater Project and served in the air force in World War II. Before he began to concentrate on young readers, Meltzer was a journalist and magazine, radio, television, and film writer.

Meltzer has published more than eighty books, most of them focusing on history, biography, and social issues confronting America and other parts of the world. He has written about some of the gravest injustices in world history, including the Holocaust, in *Never to Forget: The Jews of the Holocaust* (1976); slavery, in *Slavery: A World History* (1971, 1972); and child labor, in *Cheap Raw Material: How Our Youngest Workers Are Exploited and Abused* (1994),

as well as histories of generally unsung heroes such as the potato (*The Amazing Potato: A Story in Which the Incas, Conquistadors, Marie Antoinette, Thomas Jefferson, Wars, Famines, Immigrants, and French Fries All Play a Part*, 1992) and the pacifist (*Ain't Gonna Study War No More: The Story of America's Peace-Seekers*, 1985). In his books about injustice, discrimination, peace, poverty, crime, and fascinating personalities, both well-known and forgotten, Meltzer encourages young readers to engage critically with the world around them, to question the past and present, and to construct their own values in dialogue with history.

In "Seeding Vision, Energy and Hope: Writing and Social Responsibility" (1989), Meltzer explains the thread that ties together his biographies—whose subjects range from so-called Founding Fathers such as Thomas Jefferson to twentieth-century authors, social reformers, and artists of distinction such as Langston Hughes (African American poet), Margaret Sanger (leader in the American birth control movement), and Dorothea Lange (American photographer) to forgotten authors such as Lydia Maria Child (nineteenth-century abolitionist): each person fought for unpopular causes. E. Wendy Saul, who edited *Nonfiction for the Classroom* (1994), a book of Meltzer's essays, comments in her introduction that Meltzer's signature as an author is the ability to "situate deep sentiment in context[,] . . . to locate caring in the detached and unbending chronological record." Meltzer's books have been widely recognized, receiving five nominations for the National Book Award as well as such honors as the Golden Kite Award, Carter G. Woodson Book Award, Jane Addams Book Award, Jefferson Cup Award, *Washington Post*'s Children's Book Guild Award, and Olive Branch Award. In 2001, Meltzer won the Laura Ingalls Wilder Award for his substantial and lasting contribution to literature for children.

There were a number of challenges facing Meltzer as he prepared to write a biography of Benjamin Franklin, America's first Renaissance man. Unlike most of Meltzer's subjects, whose talents tend to cluster in one area of achievement, Franklin was an accomplished printer, scientist, publisher, inventor, diplomat, social reformer, and author;

thus a wide range of topics had to be digested and explained. Meltzer has commented, "Benjamin Franklin forces you to march into so much new territory that you fear you will stumble into a deep pit and be unable to climb out" ("Benjamin Franklin," in *Nonfiction for the Classroom*). What his biographer found attractive was Franklin's successful determination to make something of himself despite his lack of formal education or advantages. As Meltzer suggests, in Franklin young readers can see "potentialities for personal growth and development that may lift them out of the rut of their perhaps still narrowly confined world." In this three-chapter excerpt from *Benjamin Franklin: The New American* (1988), readers are introduced to some of the innovations and interests of the adult Franklin, who had become a successful printer, publisher, and social activist in colonial Philadelphia.

From Benjamin Franklin: The New American

CHAPTER 6. IMPROVE YOURSELF, IMPROVE YOUR COMMUNITY

"Improve Yourself" was a motto Ben followed faithfully. Making the most of your abilities, however, could not be done in isolation. We are social creatures, he believed, and we live and grow within a community to which and for which we are responsible. We help ourselves by helping others.

Perhaps the earliest sign of that impulse occurred back in Ben's boyhood in Boston. Recall the time when he tried to improve fishing conditions for his gang by building a wharf into the pond. His interest in improvements was given depth and urgency when he read those essays on social projects by Cotton Mather and Daniel Defoe.[1] In Philadelphia he started the Junto[2] Club as a collective effort at self-improvement. It reached out into the community by starting the first circulating library[3] in America, an idea that was soon copied throughout the colonies. It was followed by many other projects Ben designed for the public benefit.

These would begin when he saw something wrong in his surroundings. Take the condition of Philadelphia's streets. They were broad, straight, and regularly spaced— but unpaved. In wet weather the carriages and wagons plowed them into quagmires, and pedestrians had to wade in mud. In dry weather the dust choked everyone. It had been this way for a very long time, but no one thought to do anything about it— until Ben went into action. He took it one step at a time. First he talked about it. Then he wrote about it in his *Gazette*.[4] When public opinion was ripe, he began with a small enterprise: he got a street in just one busy market block paved with stone. Ah, that was very nice; people noticed the happy difference and appreciated it. Then he found a man who was willing to sweep the pavement twice a week, carry off the dirt and garbage in front of all the houses and shops on that block, and do it for just sixpence per month, to be paid by each house.

Now Ben wrote and printed a leaflet setting out the advantages of such a cleaning system, to be done at small expense, stressing the benefits to the residents, to the shopkeepers and to their customers. He sent the leaflet to each house, and a day or so later went around to see who would consent to the proposal. Everyone signed up for it, and the cleaning job began. The whole town was delighted with the vastly improved condition of the market district, for it was a convenience for all. And, of course, he wrote, "This raised a general desire to have all the streets paved, and made the people more willing to submit to a tax for that purpose." This was the moment he was waiting for. He drew up a bill to pave the city. The Assembly[5] passed it, even adding a provision for lighting as well as for paving the streets.

That is but one example of how Franklin saw the connection between what was good for himself and what was good for the community. He was able to tap the civic spirit of the people to draw them into a public organization of their town that would provide everyone with the decencies of civic life. Today we take these things for granted. But he was among the very first to come up with all kinds of plans and projects for getting something socially useful done.

Many of Franklin's projects were first tested in the Junto. He read a paper to his club on the careless ways houses were set on fire, with proposals for how to avoid such accidents. That led to the formation of a volunteer fire brigade. About thirty men soon joined, each equipped with leather water buckets and strong bags and baskets to carry out endangered furniture, and so on. They met monthly to exchange experience in firefighting and ideas on fire prevention, and, as Ben shrewdly saw, to enjoy a social evening together. The value of this first fire brigade led to one company after another being formed until the whole town was covered, with fire engines, ladders, and all the other necessary equipment stocked by each group. Ben was able

---

1. British author (ca. 1660–1731) whose works include *An Essay upon Projects* (1697), which described a number of different ways to improve England. Among the topics addressed were bankruptcy laws (Defoe had been imprisoned after declaring bankruptcy) and female education. Mather (1663–1728), New England Puritan minister and prolific writer. His *Essays to Do Good* (1710) encouraged readers to perform humanitarian acts and assist their communities.

2. A group united around a common purpose.
3. I.e., a library of books bought by and shared among subscribers.
4. Franklin was the proprietor and editor of *The Pennsylvania Gazette*, established in 1729. It quickly became the major newspaper of the colonies.
5. The Pennsylvania Assembly, the colony's legislative body.

to boast that no other city in the world was better prepared for fires than his Philadelphia.

What about a police force? All the town had was an amateurish watch system. Each ward had a constable who mustered a number of householders to serve with him for the night. You could get out of the civic duty by paying six shillings a year. The money was supposed to be used to hire substitutes, but much of it went into the constables' private purse and the rest bought drinks for "ragamuffins" who were too tipsy to walk their rounds.

Ben saw that the system failed to work. He wrote a paper for the Junto that proposed a more effective watch. Let's hire a full-time police force, he said, and support it by levying a tax on every citizen proportionate to the value of his property. Thus, the better off, who had most to lose by theft, would pay more than the poorer folk. He got the idea talked about, lined up other clubs to support it, and in a few years a law was adopted to carry it out.

A self-educated man, Franklin knew the value of providing a good education for every child. The Quakers ran some elementary schools in Philadelphia, but no college. There were still only three colleges[6] throughout the colonies, none in Philadelphia and not even an academy. Ben discussed his ideas for higher education in the Junto and then wrote a pamphlet to spread his proposals. His views on education were liberal: he wanted to see science and other practical subjects taught, as well as the classical Greek and Latin. But knowing that this desire to change the old system would not be well received by the influential people he hoped to raise money from, he tempered his views to suit them. His pamphlet brought in a large sum of money, and within a year an academy was operating in a big building in the center of town. It met a real need and had plenty of students. Not forgetting his own childhood, Ben arranged for the academy to maintain a free school for poor children. Later the academy obtained a charter from the province and became a college. Today it is the University of Pennsylvania. It might better have been called Franklin University.

The academy was only one of Franklin's many projects to encourage education. He established elementary schools in half a dozen towns in the colony. For a time he chaired a committee devoted to founding schools for Blacks and Indians. He was in advance of his time in advocating better and more widespread education for women. When a printer he had set up as a partner in South Carolina died, and the man's widow took over the business, he was delighted to see her become so successful she was able to buy him out. She was an example he used on others. He thought greater stress on practical education for women so that they could make their own way in the world was better than lessons limited to music and dancing and the arts of catching a husband.

Not all such projects were his own idea. But he knew how to make a reality out of other people's hopes and dreams. A friend, Dr. Thomas Bond, conceived the idea of establishing a hospital in Philadelphia. That was such a novelty in America that Bond got nowhere with it. He came to Ben because he had seen that no public-spirited project was carried through without Franklin behind it. Ben liked the idea and went to work. He kept pushing the need for a hospital in the columns of his *Gazette*, then wrote a pamphlet outlining the proposal and the means to finance it. After some astute political maneuvering, he got the Assembly to provide a grant. He used the device of the matching grant to get backing for the bill. If Philadelphians would subscribe a certain sum of money, the Assembly would match it.

6. Harvard in Massachusetts, William and Mary in Virginia, and Yale in Connecticut.

Once the hospital was established, he kept a close eye on it, publicizing what it offered and presiding over its board. He always made sure to keep Philadelphians informed and involved. They were the hospital's patients, of course, but they were also its patrons and source of support.

What Ben learned as he pursued his public projects was a lesson he thought everyone could profit by. People don't like it, he said, when you put yourself forward as the proposer of any useful project they think might raise your reputation even a tiny degree above theirs. If you need their help, then it is best to keep yourself in the background. Make it appear that the project is the idea of a number of people who asked you to help launch it. That way it will go more smoothly. From his frequent successes with this method, he said he could "heartily recommend it." You may sacrifice your vanity for the moment, but afterward you are amply repaid. People will find out to whom the credit really belongs.

As printer and publisher, Ben was familiar with the most intimate daily dealings of the town. Himself in the center of things, it was inevitable that he quickly became one of Philadelphia's most prominent citizens. Early on, the General Assembly chose him to be its clerk. It was boring to sit through hours of dull speeches. But besides pay for the service, the clerkship put him in close touch with the members. And that brought him business—the printing of votes, laws, paper money, and other public work. All very profitable. The appointment also gave him influence with the Assembly; it helped advance his public projects. He held the position for nearly fifteen years.

In 1737 the postmaster general of the colonies made him deputy postmaster for Philadelphia. It was not a full-time job. He continued doing everything else. The post office was placed alongside his print shop and store. While it meant more work for Debby,[7] she enjoyed getting the news first. In colonial times it was the person who received a letter who paid the postage. If he or she didn't have the money, the postmaster entered the debt on the books and tried to collect it when he could. It was Debby who kept those books.

The postmaster's salary was small, but the position was valuable to Ben. He could gather news for his *Gazette* more easily, and it cost him nothing to distribute the paper through his post-riders.[8] With these advantages his subscriptions increased and so did his advertising.

Now he was very much a public figure: assembly clerk, postmaster, and sponsor of library, hospital, academy, college—all this while in his early thirties. How much money he made in his business enterprises it is hard to tell. It must have been considerable, for he was the most successful printer in British America, doing most of the printing for both the middle and the southern colonies.

During these same years, his mind was busy with scientific as well as civic projects. (More on these shortly.) How much can one man do? And what is the best use to make of your abilities? It is a hard choice that always confronts the talented. Some would say, let your personal preference take you where it will. In Franklin's century strong opinion held that the public welfare came first. To a scientist who wanted badly to retire, Ben wrote: "Had Newton[9] been pilot of but a single ship, the finest of his discoveries would scarce have excused or atoned for his abandoning the helm

7. Deborah Read, Franklin's wife; they married in 1730.
8. The colonial mail delivery system used riders on horseback.

9. Sir Isaac Newton (1642–1727), British mathematician and physicist, perhaps best known for formulating the law of gravity.

one hour in time of danger; how much less if she carried the fate of the common-wealth!" Jefferson[1] disagreed: "Nobody can conceive that nature ever intended to throw away a Newton upon the occupations of a crown."

It was the immediate threat of an invasion that thrust Ben into the center of political affairs. In the 1740s Britain got involved with France in a series of conti-nental battles (King George's War,[2] they called it.) Neither side pushed the war hard in America. But there were some engagements here, with the French and their Span-ish or Indian allies making raids on English towns. In 1747 French and Spanish privateers sailed up the Delaware, sacked two plantations, and threatened Philadel-phia. The Assembly was dominated by Quaker pacifists who refused to pass a bill to establish a militia. The other wealthy merchants were not eager to spend money to protect Quaker property. It made Ben think of the story about the man who "refused to pump in a sinking ship because one on board whom he hated would be saved by it as well as himself."

The town had been lucky up to now: the Quaker policy of friendship with the Indians had saved them from war for over fifty years. But it had left Philadelphia defenseless: no troops and no forts. Ben rushed to press with a pamphlet that argued it was the government's duty to protect the people and the people's duty to obey the government in this crisis. Unlike the Quakers, he didn't believe that man is inherently good and peaceful. But since the Quakers would not drop their religious pacifism and the merchants were selfishly blind to danger, the people must defend themselves. "The way to secure peace is to be prepared for war," he wrote. His call to arms won the governor's backing, and ten thousand men volunteered for a militia. They bought arms, drilled themselves, and elected their own officers. Ten regiments were formed in the town and another hundred in the colony. To finance the defense Ben organized a lottery that paid for the erection of a battery[3] and the purchase of guns from Boston.

The militia asked Ben to be their regimental colonel, but he thought he was not fit, and refused. His boldness and his initiative in rising to the challenge of defense made him immensely popular throughout the colony. Again he showed that good citizenship took cooperative action. If the Assembly would not move, then the people must. The peace treaty of 1748 in Europe soon ended the threat of invasion, and the militia faded away. What Ben did to mobilize the Pennsylvanians foreshadowed how public-minded citizens would act together in a democratic way when their liberties were in danger.

He did all these things with such tact and skill that he made few enemies. But the public man was not yet a public official. That would be the next step.

In 1748 Ben decided to retire from business. At the age of forty-two (it proved to be halfway through his long life), he had made enough to be able to do it. This after working for himself for only twenty years. He brought into partnership his foreman, David Hall. Hall would run the printing and publishing business, now renamed Franklin and Hall, at a salary of £1000 a year. The agreement assured Ben of a comfortable living for the life of the partnership, set at eighteen years, when Hall would become sole owner. During that time, Ben received from the profits an average of £500 per year.

---

1. Thomas Jefferson (1743–1826), American statesman, principal author of the Declaration of Independence (1776), and third president of the United States (1801–09).
2. Known in Europe as the War of Austrian Suc-cession, the conflict began on the Continent in 1740 and was fought between the colonists and the French (with their Indian and Spanish allies) from 1744 to 1748.
3. A military fortification equipped with artillery.

Did that mean he was rich? Yes, if you compare his income with others. In his day, a housemaid was paid £10 a year, a clerk £25, a teacher £60. The chief justice of the colony got £200 per year, and the highest official, the governor, £1,000. Remember that Ben was a partner in print shops in other colonies, too, and had income from the post office and real estate, as well as from financial investments.

He was not a greedy man; business of itself gave him no joy. It was only a means to carry out his other goals. Wealth to him meant freedom to do what he wanted, freedom to be useful to the community. He would not retire from public life, only from private enterprise.

And best of all, he would be able to give much more time to his passion for scientific research.

CHAPTER 7. INVENTOR AND SCIENTIST

To be forty-two in Ben Franklin's time was to be well beyond middle age. Life was much shorter then. He never guessed he would live double those years. Since retirement was not forced upon him, he felt no depression for cutting himself off from his work. He moved his family from Market Street to a more spacious rented house. It was on the northwest corner of Race and Second, a quieter part of town, and nearer to the river. Although he did not live luxuriously, he acquired slaves to help with the household chores and errands.

Now he was ready to plunge headlong into his life as a scientist. Science as a way of exploring and explaining the world was a path he had entered long ago. Recall how his inventiveness was revealed in boyhood when he devised new ways to speed himself through water. At twenty, sailing back from England,[4] he had crammed his notebook with observations of wind and weather and ocean currents and animal life. His scientific curiosity could be aroused by what others brushed off as trivial. Once he found that an open pot of molasses in Debby's pantry was crawling with ants. He removed all of them but one, then tied the pot to a string suspended from the ceiling, led the string across the ceiling and down the wall, and sat by to observe. The one ant gorged itself in the pot, then clambered along the string and down the wall, and disappeared. About thirty minutes later, the pot was once again thick with ants that had crossed over to it on the string. How, Ben asked, had the first ant communicated to the others the feast awaiting them in the pot?

Again and again he saw in everyday aspects of nature questions that demanded answers. Where others before him had noticed nothing interesting or significant, his mind saw something wonderful. He was born to be a "natural philosopher," the term used then for scientists.

It was Sir Francis Bacon[5] who began the turn toward modern science. In 1620— the same year the Puritan dissenters fled England to find refuge in New England— he published the first statement of a new attitude. It would change the way people lived in the world and the way they thought about it. Bacon believed the whole world

---

4. In 1724, at the urging of Sir William Keith, governor of Pennsylvania, Franklin traveled to London to buy printing equipment. Keith had promised to help the young man set up a printing business in Philadelphia. But Keith's support evaporated once Franklin reached London, where he remained for eighteen months—working for a printer, enjoying himself, and saving money to pay for his return passage.

5. British philosopher, essayist, and statesman (1561–1626). In 1620, Bacon published his *Novum Organum*, which set forth an inductive approach to interpreting nature.

was open for genius to explore. The object of knowledge was to increase man's power over nature and to make life better. Only by a true understanding of the physical world could we master our fate.

Later, in 1662, Bacon's followers founded the Royal Society in London "to promote the welfare of the arts and sciences." The great Isaac Newton, one of the Society's original members, had shown that the universe moved by its own laws and that mathematics could chart those movements of the planets. Only a few Americans, Cotton Mather among them, were familiar with science. Mather, when Franklin was fifteen, had published America's first popular book on science. He wanted people to break from stale myths and go out and dig for the truth in the real world of nature. It was an appeal young Ben responded to.

Scientific research back then was vastly different from what it is now. In Ben's time it was an amateur's game. No government, no corporation, no university, no foundation was on hand to pour funds into research. Scientists—the few there were—did not combine their specialized knowledge to work together in large laboratories under ideal conditions. Nor was there any kind of training for them in research. Like Ben, they taught themselves and worked alone, usually at home, funding their own expenses. It was a kind of game, but with an intellectual edge that gave it great excitement, especially when you could claim a discovery.

Several months after he retired, Ben wrote to his friend Cadwallader Colden that he was happy "to make experiments, and converse at large with such ingenious and worthy men as are pleased to honor me with their friendship on such points as may produce something for the common benefit of mankind, uninterrupted by the little cares and fatigues of business."

Years earlier Ben had suggested that people interested in science ought to form an organization "to promote useful knowledge" in the colonies. His notion was to expand the Junto on a continental scale. He had already corresponded with scientists throughout the colonies, as well as with some in England and Europe. He knew how rapidly interest in science was growing and saw that pooling information and ideas would greatly benefit everyone. He wrote out his proposal in 1743 and printed and circulated it. Out of it came the American Philosophical Society. It is the oldest American learned society, and the first to be devoted to science. Ben's desire was to make it a center for exchanging information on all aspects of the natural world and on all experiments that "tend to increase the power of man over matter, and multiply the conveniences or pleasures of life." Franklin became its first president, to be followed later by Thomas Jefferson and other distinguished Americans. Today, as at its founding, it concerns itself with many diverse fields of knowledge—medicine, physics, anthropology, history, literature—and its publications and projects are important to the international world of science.

A look through the pages of Ben's *Gazette* shows how early it began to reflect the range of his scientific curiosity. Esmond Wright[6] has traced his stories of "the weather and waterspouts; why salt dissolves in water; why the sea is sometimes luminous; cures for kidney stones and cancer; mortality rates in Philadelphia; the cause of earthquakes; 'on making rivers navigable'; how many people could stand in an area of 100 square yards."

Ben's voracious appetite for learning made him ask the why and how of everything he came across. When he was still tied down by his business, he did his best to

6. British historian (b. 1915), the author of *Franklin of Philadelphia* (1986).

encourage others in the pursuit of science. For instance, he raised a fund to enable John Bartman, a botanist, to continue his research on the condition that he report his findings to contributors to the fund.

In Franklin's mind there was nothing that could not be improved. Take his invention of the Franklin stove. One of the questions he had posed for the Junto was, "How may smoky chimneys be cured?" How strange it was, he thought, that while chimneys have been so long in use, no workman would pretend he could make one that would carry off all the smoke. Then, too, fireplaces were often too hot to sit near, and when you did, while the heat toasted your front, the cold air nipped your back and legs. It was next to impossible to warm a room with such a fireplace. So in 1739 or 1740 he invented a stove that fitted into the fireplace and radiated the heat outward. It warmed rooms better, and at the same time saved fuel. The important feature was the flue, which doubled back and formed a sort of radiator around which warm air circulated. It cured most smoky chimneys, thus protecting both the eyes and the furniture. He turned over his model to a friend with an iron furnace, who cast the plates for the stoves. They were soon in great demand as people learned about them through a pamphlet Ben wrote and printed.

A profitable invention—but not for him. As with all his inventions, he refused to patent his stove, on the principle "that as we enjoy great advantages from the inventions of others, we should be glad of an opportunity to serve others by any invention of ours, and this we should do freely and generously."

He was as much interested in ventilating rooms as in warming them. He believed it healthier to keep windows open and let in fresh air, a practice that annoyed many of his friends. To keep rooms warmer in cold weather, he developed a damper, a metal plate that fits horizontally into the base of the chimney passage and can completely close it off, or when opened a small distance, creates a slight draft, allowing smoke to go up the chimney while keeping most of the warm air in the room.

To improve the lighting of rooms, he devised a new candle made from whale oil. It gave a clearer and whiter light, could be held in the hand without softening, and its drippings did not make grease spots. His candles lasted much longer and needed little or no snuffing. He also developed a four-sided lamp to light the city streets. The lamps stayed clean much longer and thus gave more light.

When Franklin's scientific fame comes up, most people think of the spectacular kite experiment. That was not his greatest contribution, and it was made well after his international reputation was established. Most important was his experimental approach: it was this that made all his contributions possible. His experiments in so many different fields were completely original and crucial. The way he went about his research displayed his analytic powers and his objectivity. He never rested with merely amplifying what someone else had done.

His work on electricity is the best example. Before he began to think about it, electricity was a mass of uncoordinated observations and confusing theories worded in obscure and puzzling language. Franklin's mind was able to unify what was already known, then to add his own original findings so that he came out with a new and simple theory that would stand the test of time. The very vocabulary of modern electricity originated with him: as he went along he had to invent words like *condenser, conductor, charge, discharge, armature, battery, electrician, electric shock, positive* and *negative* electricity, and concepts of *plus* and *minus* charges.

Few of his contemporaries were equipped to perceive how different and advanced his approach was. Those who did understand his work thought it extraordinary. By the time Ben went abroad on his first diplomatic mission (1757),[7] scientists in England and Europe greeted him as the Newton of electricity.

The Ben Franklin who earned that reputation was not the Franklin we know from the famous portraits of him in later years. These show him as portly or dumpy, stringy haired or bald. The Franklin of his pioneering years in science was a tall, muscular man with chestnut hair and an enigmatic smile. Charming and witty, Ben at that time was equalled by no one in the variety of his accomplishments. A physicist sees Franklin's uniqueness in "an intellect that could penetrate through a morass of detail to the one underlying simplicity. Of all human talents, it is the most uncommon, even though men flatter themselves by calling it common sense."

The first spark to ignite Ben's interest in "the mysterious fluid" called electricity was struck on a visit to Boston in 1743. There he met Dr. Archibald Spencer from Scotland who was traveling around the colonies to display his repertoire of tricks in electrostatics. His most spectacular stunt was to suspend a small boy from the ceiling by silken threads while he drew sparks from the child's hands and feet. The audiences for these shows were both fascinated and frightened. Ben said that what he witnessed had "surprised and pleased" him as a quite new subject. He invited Spencer to display his "shocks" and "magic" in Philadelphia and bought his apparatus. Then, with the help of the Junto and the library company, he tried some experiments. Ben asked the botanist Peter Collinson, a member of the Royal Society, to send him a glass "electric tube," with directions for using it in making experiments. He eagerly set out to repeat what he had learned and then developed new experiments. His house was "continually full for some time with people who came to see these new wonders. . . . I was never before engaged in any study that so totally engrossed my attention and my time," he wrote Collinson as he provided details on what he was trying to do. Already he was transforming the electrical parlor games into a science.

Part of the standard equipment of electrical experiments at that time was the Leyden jar. It was simply a stoppered bottle of water. Through the cork stopper a metal rod hung down into the liquid. Some experiments coated the bottle on the outside with metal foil. When charged, the Leyden jar gave a strong shock to people touching it. In one experiment to enlighten the French court, when a shock was given to a line of 180 guardsmen, all holding hands, they jumped simultaneously into the air as though parading in the sky. The same experiment at a monastery threw seven hundred monks into a whirling convulsion.

Here is how a twentieth-century physicist, Mitchell Wilson,[8] explains the significance of Franklin's Leyden jar experiments:

> Franklin set himself the task of answering a question which no one else had thought of asking: exactly what was it in such an apparently simple arrangement of glass, metal, and water that allowed for such enormous accumulations of electricity? Was it due to the wire, the water or the bottle? Or what combination? In Franklin's day, no one even knew, once the questions had been asked, how to go about finding the answer. Actually, to ask the same question two centuries after Franklin would leave an embarrassingly large number of people looking blank. Franklin's step-by-step approach had the simplicity of genius:
> "To analyze the electrified bottle, in order to find wherein its strength lay, we

---

7. The Pennsylvania Assembly sent Franklin to England to promote their efforts to enforce taxes on proprietary estates.

8. American physicist and writer (1913–1973), whose works include *American Science and Invention* (1954).

placed it on glass and drew out the cork and wire. . . . . Then taking the bottle in one hand, and bringing a finger of the other near the bottle's mouth, a strong spark came from the water . . . which showed that the force did not reside in the wire."

And so one possibility was completely eliminated.

"Then to find if it resided in the water . . . which had been our former opinion, we electrified the bottle again." This time, Franklin and his assistant removed the cork and the wire as before, and then in addition decanted the water from the electrically charged flask into another flask which had not been electrified. If the electric charge actually was in the water alone, then the new flask should give a spark. It did not.

"We judged then, that it must be lost in decanting or remain in the first bottle. The latter we found to be true, for that bottle on trial gave the shock, though filled with fresh, electrified water from a teapot."

Now, having come this far, not one man in a hundred thousand would have gone on to the next question, which was this: did the electrical charge reside in the bottle because it was shaped like a bottle or because it was made of glass? Again, one may well ask how could that be tested? Franklin took glass of a completely different shape: a simple pane of window glass. On either side of the glass, he placed a thin sheet of lead. This arrangement was electrified. Then, one at a time, the sheets of lead were slid away and tested. Neither, when isolated, gave off any spark. The glass pane, standing alone, being touched, gave off a multitude of sparks. Franklin then concluded that "The whole force and power of giving a shock is in the glass itself. . . ."

This proof that the seat of electrostatic action is in the material which insulates a conductor laid the foundation for Maxwell's[9] work a century later when he developed the theory of electromagnetic waves which in turn led to radio. In this one experiment alone, Franklin had invented the electrical condenser, one of the most useful elements in circuit theory, a device that was to be used in every radio, television set, telephone circuit, radar transmitter, cyclotron and cosmotron.

Until Franklin, the prevalent theory had been that there were two different kinds of electricity vaguely distinguished by unanalytical names as resinous and vitreous. He claimed that there was only one kind; that electricity was neither created nor destroyed either by friction or by any other means, but that electricity was simply redistributed throughout matter. Moreover, he stated that electricity had to be composed of "subtile particles" that could penetrate the interior of metals as easily as gas diffused through the atmosphere. J. J. Thomson,[1] who later discovered the electron and laid the foundations of modern electron theory, paid tribute to Franklin as generously as Franklin's own contemporaries.

Ben wrote several letters to Collinson describing his experiments, and the botanist got them read to the Royal Society. Ben's reports took an amusing turn at times:

The hot weather coming on when electrical experiments are not so agreeable, it is proposed to put an end to them for this season [spring 1749], somewhat humorously, in a party of pleasure on the banks of the Schuylkill. Spirits, at the

---

9. James Clerk Maxwell (1831–1879), a Scottish physicist.

1. British physicist (1865–1940), winner of the 1906 Nobel Prize in Physics.

same time, are to be fired by a spark sent from side to side through the river, without any other conductor than the water; an experiment which we some time since performed, to the amazement of many. A turkey is to be killed for our dinner by the electrical shock, and roasted by the electrical jack, before a fire kindled by the electrified bottle; when the healths of all the famous electricians in England, Holland, France and Germany are to be drunk in electrified bumpers, under the discharge of guns from the electrical battery.

Thus, he put his discoveries to use, though in this case only to entertain. Always he believed in a worldwide collaboration of scientists, advancing their common interest by the free exchange of information. He wanted even "short hints and imperfect experiments" to be reported, for anything might lead others to more complete and accurate discoveries. In 1751 Ben's accounts of his experiments were published in London in an eighty-six-page pamphlet called *Experiments and Observations on Electricity Made at Philadelphia in America by Mr. Benjamin Franklin*. He wrote in simple, direct, and clear language so that all could understand. The work was translated into several languages and built his European reputation as a scientist.

What gave Franklin's pamphlet even greater celebrity was the success of one of the experiments he proposed to determine whether or not the clouds that contain lightning are electrified. He suggested that on top of some high tower, a sentry box be placed, big enough to contain a man standing on an insulated platform. "From the middle of the stand let an iron rod rise and pass bending out of the door, and upright 20 or 30 feet pointed very sharp at the end. If the electrical stand be kept clean and dry, a man standing on it when such clouds are passing low might be electrified and draw sparks, the rod drawing fire . . . from a cloud."

This he proposed in July 1750. He planned to perform the lightning experiment after the completion of the spire on Christ Church in Philadelphia. But meantime, his pamphlet was published in France and made a strong impression. Thomas Francis D'Alibard, a scientist, made a secret trial of the sentry box experiment near Paris on May 10, 1752. There was a peal of thunder, and the iron shaft sparkled blue with charge pouring into a Leyden jar, proving that the cloud was electrified. Shortly afterward, the experiment was repeated for the king in Paris, and then again in London. By the time news of the proofs reached Franklin, he had been world famous for months.

For almost fifty years before Franklin, people had been suggesting that lightning and the electric spark were one and the same thing. But no one had ever worked out a way of proving it. Ben not only proposed an actual experiment, but he was also able to explain lightning rationally. No longer could it be viewed as an awesome expression of the supernatural.

Meanwhile, before he knew of the successful experiments in Europe, he decided not to wait for the church spire to be completed. It occurred to him that a common kite would be better able to reach the regions of a thunderstorm. With the help of his son William, then about twenty-two, he built a kite out of a large silk handkerchief and two cross-sticks. To the upright stick of the cross he tied a sharp pointed wire, rising about a foot above the wood. To the end of the string he fastened a silk ribbon and a key. When signs of a storm approached, they walked out into the fields. William ran three times across a pasture to get the kite aloft while Ben watched from a shepherd's hut nearby. With the kite flying, there was an anxious time before any sign came of its being electrified. One promising cloud passed over it without any effect. Then, just as Ben despaired of any result, he saw some loose threads of the hempen string stand erect, avoiding one another as though they had been suspended on a common conductor. Struck with this promising appearance, Ben touched his knuckle to the key at his end of the kite string and—an exquisite moment of pleasure!—perceived an electric spark. His discovery was complete, even before the string was wet. When the rain had soaked the string, he collected a great amount of electric fire.

This happened in June 1752, a month after the French proof of his idea, but before he heard of anything they had done.

Chapter 8. Disarming the Clouds of Heaven

Now that the theory of the sameness of electricity and lightning had been confirmed, Ben did what came naturally: he put the knowledge to immediate use. He proposed the lightning rod as the way to protect structures from the stroke of lightning. By fixing sharply pointed iron rods to the highest part of a structure and extending from them a wire down the outside of the building into the ground, the electricity would be drawn silently out of the cloud before it came near enough to strike, and "thereby secure us from that most sudden and terrible mischief."

He put up a lightning rod on the roof of his own house, and soon they were put up on Philadelphia's new academy and the new State House. Again, he would not patent his invention to draw profit from it. Instead he described how to secure protection through lightning rods in the *Poor Richard*[2] of 1753 so that anyone could do it freely. He was happy to make his idea useful to others. Not everyone approved of "Franklin's rod," as it was called. Even twenty years later someone wrote that "as lightning is one of the means of punishing the sins of mankind and of warning them from the commission of sin, it *is* impious to prevent its full execution."

For a time many hesitated to erect lightning rods for fear they would bring down upon themselves the wrath of the Lord. But the practical success of the invention eventually overcame all resistance. Nothing enlarged Ben's reputation so much as the lightning rod. Because it is more than two hundred years in the past, it is hard for us to realize the impact it had on people of that time. Ben's contemporary, John Adams,[3] can tell us how his world viewed it:

> Nothing, perhaps, that ever occurred upon the earth was so well calculated to give any man an extensive and universal a celebrity as . . . the invention of lightning-rods. The idea was one of the most sublime that ever entered a human imagination, that a mortal should disarm the clouds of heaven. . . . His [lightning rods] erected their heads in all parts of the world, on temples and palaces no less than on cottages of peasants and habitations of ordinary citizens. These visible objects reminded all men of the name and character of their inventor; and in the course of time have not only tranquillized the minds and dissipated the fears of the tender sex and their timorous children, but have almost annihilated that panic, terror and superstitious horror which was once almost universal in violent storms of thunder and lightning.

When others disagreed with Franklin or criticized his research, he would make no reply. He refused to defend his scientific views: "I leave them to take their chance

---

2. Every year from 1733 to 1758, Franklin, under the pen name Richard Saunders, wrote *Poor Richard's Almanack*. Each compendium was filled with humorous sayings and maxims as well as crop predictions, phases of the moon, recipes, and other useful bits of information.
3. Massachusetts lawyer (1735–1826), and second president of the United States (1796–1800).

in the world. If they are right, truth and experience will support them; if wrong, they ought to be refuted and rejected."

Out of his loving investigation of nature came not a single book about science. There were few scientific journals then, and Ben's findings were usually presented through letters to friends with like interests. The public affairs in which he soon became immersed and his long years as diplomat in England and France left him little time for his passion to investigate. But he never stopped observing nature, gathering facts, finding connections, interpreting them, and recording what he learned. Always, it should be noted, in homely language that reads as freshly today as when it was penned. If only a Franklin were here to write the modern textbooks in science!

In 1753 both Harvard and Yale gave Ben honorary degrees, and a year later the Royal Society awarded him the Copley Gold Medal. In the years ahead he would be made a member of thirty-eight learned societies and academies. Today's scientists are no less impressed by Ben's achievements. And he did what he did with no technical training. When the Nobel Laureate Robert Millikan offered his personal rating of the great scientists from the sixteenth century to the twentieth, he placed Franklin fifth, after Copernicus, Galileo, Newton, and Huygens.[4]

While carrying on his own studies, Ben was in frequent correspondence with many other scientists, both in America and Europe. He shared his interests with them and established lifelong friendships with many distinguished men in England and France. Although he valued his scientific honors, he seldom referred to them and even poked fun at them, once calling "a feather in the cap not so useful a thing as a pair of good silk garters." When he was invited to become a corresponding member of the Royal Society, he replied that he esteemed the honor and was not discouraged by the fact that "as yet, the quantity of human knowledge bears no proportion to the quality of human ignorance."

Franklin's contributions were so extensive as to make him the supreme scientist in the American colonies. He was viewed as a Renaissance man. Noting his genius, Charles L. Mee, Jr.,[5] lists a few of his characteristic interests:

> Franklin had always been the sort of man who could, in the space of a single brief letter, cover such topics as linseed oil, hemp land, swamp drainage, variations in climate, northeast storms, the cause of springs on mountains, seashell rocks, grass seed, taxation, and smuggling. He loved facts. He loved the particular. He was able to talk with knowledge and cheerful interest about mastodon tusks, lead poisoning, chimney construction, the reason canal boats move more slowly in low water than in high water, silk culture, Chinese rhubarb seeds, sunspots, magnetism, a new method for making carriage wheels, the electrocution of animals to be eaten, how to heat a church in Boston, the census in China, the vegetable origins of coal, and the good of keeping a window in the bedroom open at night.

Philadelphia was fertile soil for the cultivation of Ben's scientific interests. He was surrounded by ingenious mechanics and artisans eager to perfect their craft and

4. Christiaan Huygens (1629–1695), Dutch mathematician, physicist, and astronomer; he improved telescopes and their lenses and developed a wave theory of light. Milliken (1868–1953), American physicist, best known for his work in atomic physics. Nicolaus Copernicus (Latinized name of Mikolaj Kopernik, 1473–1543), Polish astronomer whose heliocentric theory of planetary motion replaced the Ptolemaic system in which Earth was believed to be the motionless center of the universe. Galileo Galilei (1564–1642), Italian astronomer, mathematician, and physicist who constructed the first astronomical telescope.

5. American popular historian (b. 1938).

improve their product. Their love of tinkering was typical of that era. Several of those men, as we saw, were active in the Junto. Some, like David Rittenhouse, earned reputations as scientists that carried their names across the Atlantic. Rittenhouse, a clock-maker by trade, developed great skill in making mathematical instruments and became a famous astronomer. Ben's own talent for experiment was constantly stimulated by the company of such men. Thomas Jefferson wrote that Franklin, Rittenhouse, and George Washington were proof that America could nurture genius.

To describe in detail Franklin's discoveries needs a book unto itself. But just to list some of them will indicate the range of his observations and experiments. To start with the simpler things—those he made himself. He is credited with clocks, the stove, the lightning rod, astronomical instruments, bifocal eyeglasses, the flexible catheter, a chair that can be converted into a ladder, a clothes-pressing machine, improvements in the printing press, a pole with a manipulable grasp at the end to take down books from high shelves, laboratory equipment, the musical instrument called the "glass harmonica" for which Mozart and Beethoven wrote music. (He could, by the way, play the harp, the guitar, and the violin.)

The qualities of his mind are illustrated by his attention to many aspects of nature. Even the most casual incident was enough to set his mind spinning. In his eight crossings of the Atlantic he recorded things he saw at sea. One of the most important was the existence of the Gulf Stream, which he was the first scientist to study. It began in 1745 when he puzzled over why ships had much shorter voyages from America to England than in returning. Inquiring of sea captains, he learned that they were aware of the Gulf Stream and how it affected voyages. But Ben knew that no notice had been taken of this current upon the navigational charts. So he had a captain mark out the stream for him, adding directions for how to avoid it when sailing from Europe to North America. Then Ben had it engraved upon new charts and sent copies to sea captains who, he said wryly, "ignored it, however."

It was Ben who first suggested that the aurora borealis[6] was an electrical phenomenon. He theorized on the origin of many things from colds to earthquakes. He demonstrated the way dark- or light-colored clothing increased or diminished how hot the wearer felt. His observations on the direction of storms began the modern study of weather. And he was the first to test the use of oil to quiet troubled waters.

One of his more significant innovations was the investigation of population changes that led to the new science of demography. It began with his observations in 1750 of the increase of pigeons. A year later he wrote the essay, "Observations Concerning the Increase of Mankind, Peopling of Countries, etc." Published in America and in London, it showed that population was increasing faster in the colonies than in Britain. Although his data were scanty, he forecast with great accuracy that the American population would shoot up enormously by a doubling of numbers every generation. It meant that in a hundred years there would be more people in America than in the mother country.

What this pointed to, he said, was that the colonies would be a "glorious market" for manufactured goods well beyond the capacity of England to fulfill. And therefore colonial manufacture should not be restricted, as it was under the mercantilist system. He was not seeking a rupture with the home country; he still saw the colonies as part of the British Empire—but a part with a vast potential that "a wise and good mother" would not harm. He foresaw that American manufacturing would have to increase to satisfy the needs of the rapidly growing population. And he predicted that

---

6. The northern lights.

the frontier territory would provide an escape for the poor of the colonies, giving them a place to settle their large families on free and uncrowded land. Ben based his calculations on tables of births and deaths. (There would be no official census in America until 1790, the year of his death.)

One sorry aspect of his views on population is the racism that was common to his time, even among the most enlightened, such as Thomas Jefferson. Franklin was extremely ethnocentric. He did not welcome nonwhites to America, or even whites who were not English. The German settlers in western Pennsylvania upset him. He didn't like the way they clung to their own language and customs, and feared they would become so numerous as to "Germanize us, instead of our Anglifying them." He worried over the fact that white people were a relatively small part of the population of the earth. Why plant in America the dark, the tawny, the swarthy people? he asked. He discouraged their immigration. Then, perhaps feeling a twinge of guilt or shame over this point of view, he added, "But perhaps I am partial to the complexion of my country, for such kind of partiality is natural to mankind."

Among Franklin's many pursuits in science was a lifelong interest in medicine. Its condition in colonial America was far from medicine today. Formal training was almost unknown, and licensing did not exist. In fact, medicine was not yet a profession. Some learned the art by serving as apprentices to established doctors. But many simply declared themselves doctors and set themselves up in practice. Surgeons were thought to be the lowest doctors of all because they worked with their hands.

Experimental medicine, whether in laboratory or clinic, was a rarity. Franklin, always the realist, wanted to test every belief and practice. He looked for practical results, not old wives' tales about medical miracles. If an experiment proved an idea of his was wrong, he was quick to admit it. During his experiments with electricity, he tried applying it to stiff or paralyzed joints, but when no improvement was noted, he stopped the treatment. In his time few people were concerned with personal cleanliness. Ben advised stripping off your clothes and scrubbing yourself clean in a tub of water. Shocking! said his contemporaries. He designed and built his own copper bathtub, with a rack to hold a book so he could read while bathing. He advised moderation in eating and drinking, and regular exercise to keep fit. His ardent demand for fresh air and ventilation made him a nuisance to people who had to share a room with him.

His low view of the medical profession was expressed in some of his sayings: "God heals and the doctor takes the fee." Or, "He is the best physician that knows the worthlessness of most medicines." Yet some of his closest friends in America and in Europe were medical men. Perhaps because they were often radicals? So many doctors were active in the American Revolution that they made up almost an army of doctor-patriots. One estimate holds that nearly twelve thousand were involved in the cause. The reason is uncertain. It may be that they supported revolutionary politics because they were committed to science and reason.

Franklin did not hesitate to expose charlatans in science or quacks in medicine. On the other hand, he gave all the help he could to worthy scientists. In 1745 he aided Peter Kalm, the Swedish naturalist who had come to the colonies to search for botanical specimens unique to America. And in 1779, while Ben was serving as American commissioner to France, he protected the exploring expedition of British Captain James Cook,[7] who was liable to capture at sea because of the war between

---

7. Explorer and officer in the Royal Navy (1728–1779). In the *Endeavor* he sailed around the world and charted the coasts of Australia and New Zea- land (1768–71). Cook is also credited with preserving the health of his crewmen by strictly enforcing hygiene and a proper diet.

Britain and America. Franklin notified all American naval vessels not to consider Cook an enemy or to obstruct his scientific mission in any way.

The list of Franklin's innovations could go on and on. He suggested daylight saving time. He was the first to introduce cartoons and the use of the question-and-answer format into journalism. He advocated adding to the traditional Latin and Greek the teaching of modern foreign languages. To promote the international spread of knowledge, he invented a language of symbols all peoples could use. He figured out a way to put Indian languages into print although the tribes had no written symbols. To get rid of the bewildering confusion of English spelling, he prepared "A Scheme for a New Alphabet and Reformed Mode of Spelling." Calling war a mass form of theft and murder, he advocated the idea of punishing aggressor nations through the organization of a United Nations.

1988

Adventure Stories

The Pattern of Adventure

"To die will be an awfully big adventure," says Peter Pan. Adventure, like death, is implicitly both risky and rewarding. By the time J. M. Barrie used the line in the stage production of *Peter Pan* (first performed in 1904), he knew that his audience would recognize the broad strokes of the genre: the brave hero fighting nature or enemies, and enjoying the possibility of reward at the end. Rooted in the Latin *adventus* (arrival), the word *adventure* came to mean, by the eighteenth century, an enterprise that is physically and financially hazardous.

The general pattern of the adventure can be discerned in many famous stories, ancient and modern, whether based in fact or in fiction: stories of Jesus, Beowulf, and King Arthur, as well as those of Joan of Arc, Superman, and Lara Croft, Tomb Raider. As the scholar and mythologist Joseph Campbell notes in *The Hero with a Thousand Faces* (1949), adventures share a circular shape. First, a "call to adventure" is precipitated by a crisis of some kind at home. Then the adventure begins with the crossing of a threshold, marking the transition into a quest for something that will bring about a better life or a cure or a reward. The quest involves a descent into a series of battles or tests of skill and courage. A crisis at the bottom of the circle—often a major battle—marks the beginning of the return journey upward. Finally, when all tests have been passed and enemies defeated, the threshold of home is crossed again and the victorious quester celebrates and is rewarded. In *Anatomy of Criticism* (1957), the literary critic Northrop Frye adapted Greek terms from Aristotle's *Poetics* to offer elegant labels for key elements of this heroic story pattern: *agon* (the "conflict" that precipitates the launch of the hero into the adventure), *pathos* (the feelings of "pity and fear" aroused by the trials and tests of strength endured by the hero), and *anagnorisis* (the "recognition" that the conflicts have been successfully resolved, that order is restored). Although Campbell's and Frye's shorthand definitions of the adventure genre are helpful, they focus on male heroes and on only a narrow range of the available stories.

Critics often categorize adventure stories as *romances*, formally acknowledging their debt to Arthurian romances—the heroic tales of King Arthur and his knights of the Round Table that flourished from the twelfth to the fifteenth century. These stories celebrate the amazing feats of men whose strength, courage, honor, and nobility are presented as only slightly less than godlike. Some concern quests for the Holy Grail, a vessel that, in Christian legend, was used by Christ at the Last Supper. In others a woman sparks the quest or is its prize. Over the centuries, the heroic deeds of men have faded into the background; the works now called romances are typically regarded as subliterary, popular fiction consumed by a low-brow and largely female audience. Adventure stories sprawl between the medieval Arthurian romance and the sentimental love story available at the supermarket checkout.

The author credited with more or less inventing the genre of the adventure novel is Daniel Defoe. His most famous book, *The Life and Strange Surprizing Adventures of Robinson Crusoe* (1719), a story about a man struggling alone for survival on a desert island, provides the core cluster of features most frequently associated with adventures, both fictional and real: an exotic location, perils from forces of nature and enemy threats, as well as endurance and self-reliance. The faraway settings of adventure stories range from Crusoe's Caribbean island to outer space. Threatening forces of nature include everything from the storms that stranded the fictional Crusoe to the potentially lethal cold endured by polar explorers. Enemies—often, but not always, those categorized as threatening or dangerous when they are simply foreign or "other"—could include the stereotypical cannibals feared by Robinson Crusoe, or the generic "Red Indians" that alarm the whites in cowboy movies.

By the time Barrie staged *Peter Pan* (to huge, instant success) he knew that his audience would recognize immediately his parody of adventure story conventions: the exotic island of Never Land, the blood-thirsty pirates, and the deadly potential of nature. Peter utters his famous line about death being an awfully big adventure while standing on a rock, waiting for the tide to rise above his head and drown him. He doesn't drown, of course; he's rescued by a bird who offers her nest as a boat, and so fights and plays again.

Robinson Crusoe and Robinsonnades

One way to measure the success of a book is by the number of editions and spin-offs it generates. Within four months of its initial publication, *Robinson Crusoe* had appeared in four editions and two reprints. By the end of the eighteenth century, there were dozens of editions as well as adaptations, cheap chapbooks (sold by peddlers who traveled from town to town and city to city), theatrical performances, and translations. In fact, stories bearing *Robinson Crusoe*–like characteristics eventually became so popular in Europe that bibliographers coined terms for them: *Robinsonnades* or *Robinsonades* in French (a name borrowed by English speakers), *Robinsonaden* in German.

The prominence of Robinsonnades in children's literature may be explained in part by *Robinson Crusoe*'s prominent role in *Émile; or, On Education* (1762). In that book, intended to illustrate, step-by-step, the ideal way to bring up a boy, the French philosopher Jean-Jacques Rousseau allowed his fictional pupil (in the early stages of learning) to read only Defoe's novel. Rousseau's innovative emphasis on learning by experience and observation, and on a developmental approach to child rearing, had enormous influence on later pedagogical theory in the West. His choice of reading material no doubt also swayed opinion. But in the end, it is the very narrative flexibility of *Robinson Crusoe*, its openness to a wide range of interpretive possibilities, that has given it such a conspicuous place in children's literature for more than three hundred years.

F. J. Harvey Darton, in *Children's Books in England* (1932), identifies three main types of Crusoe-ish stories that recur in Robinsonnades: "the lonely savage, the mariner of York, and the rational-natural man"—that is, the survivor story, the seafaring adventure story, and the story that supports a "colonial" order (faith in a Christian God and Eurocentric civilization). For example, George Borrow, in his fictionalized memoir, *Lavengro* (1851), recounts being profoundly impressed in early childhood by his encounter with a picture in a book:

> There was a human figure upon the beach, wild and uncouth, clad in the skins of animals, with a huge cap on his head, a hatchet at his girdle, and in his hand a gun; his feet and legs were bare; he stood in an attitude of horror and surprise, his body was bent far back, and his eyes, which seemed starting out of his head, were fixed upon a mark on the sand—a large distinct mark—a human footprint.

Knowing that the description of Crusoe first sighting the footprint would be recognizable, he coyly asks, "Readers, is it necessary to name the book . . . ?" Borrow lavishly credits the "hardy deeds" of the story, "and the spirit of strange and romantic enterprise which it tends to awaken," with shaping both British fiction and the British Empire.

By the mid-nineteenth century, when Borrow wrote his fictionalized memoir, many Robinsannades were in circulation, including *The Swiss Family Robinson* (1812–13), by a Swiss pastor, J. D. Wyss, first published in English in 1814, and *Masterman Ready: or, The Wreck of the Pacific* (1841–42), by the prolific adventure story writer Captain Frederick Marryat. These books featured marooned groups rather than an isolated individual—as did most of the growing number of Robinsonnades, such as *The Canadian Crusoes: A Tale of the Rice Lake Plains* (1852), by Catherine Parr Traill; *The Coral Island: A Tale of the Pacific Ocean* (1858), by R. M. Ballantyne; and *Treasure Island* (1883), by Robert Louis Stevenson. In Ivan Southall's contemporary update, *To the Wild Sky* (1967), a plane crash strands a group of children on a deserted Australian island.

Through all of the nineteenth and much of the twentieth century, Borrow's understanding of *Robinson Crusoe* as a celebration of adventure and endurance in the face of overwhelming odds went unquestioned. Similarly, the book's depiction of Friday was long regarded as completely normal. As cultural norms have changed, so has that reading, yet the story has repeatedly adapted to such shifts.

In a famous episode in the story, Crusoe rescues Friday from certain death at the hands of cannibals, and he describes how Friday expresses his gratitude: he "laid his Head upon the Ground, and taking me by the Foot, set my Foot upon his Head; this it seems was in token of swearing to be my Slave for ever." This scene makes modern readers uneasy, as does Crusoe's implicit belief that non-European peoples are cannibalistic savages who obviously ought to be converted to Christianity. Twentieth-century authors began to recast the story in ways that undercut earlier assumptions. Thus in *Island of the Blue Dolphins* (1960), Scott O'Dell recounts the story (based in Californian history) of a Native American girl alone on an island for eighteen years who survives by developing her ability to coexist with nature. *Foe* (1986), a sophisticated novel for adults by the South African writer J. M. Coetzee, retells and alters Defoe's original tale; it subverts Crusoe's version of his "strange adventures" as it focuses on the racial relationship between master and servant, and on language and colonialism. The title plays on Defoe's own history (his father's name had been Foe) to question his narrative authority. It's a far cry from George Borrow's clear praise: "Hail to thee, spirit of De Foe."

Other aspects of the typical Robinsonnade, as described by Darton, were also rethought. The British author Jane Gardam, recognizing the particularly masculine emphasis on possessions and property in *Robinson Crusoe*, conceived a feminist inversion, *Crusoe's Daughter* (1985). She recasts her heroine, Polly Flint, as the antithesis of Defoe's hero, who carefully and frequently takes stock of his possessions (goats, corn, pots, guns, ammunition, etc.), refers to his home as his "castle," and routinely patrols the perimeter after spotting the lone footprint. Polly, obsessed with Defoe's novel, is isolated not on a desert island but in a house by the sea. To continue to possess it, she must take in strangers (first lodgers, then schoolboys) rather than keep them out. Probably the most famous twentieth-century re-visioning of *Robinson Crusoe* is *Lord of the Flies* (1954). William Golding's obvious target (to which his novel directly refers) is an earlier Robinsonnade featuring marooned schoolboys, *The Coral Island*. Whereas Ballantyne tells a story of survival and success, Golding depicts the defects of human nature in a story that contains a premeditated "savage" murder. Ironically, *Lord of the Flies*, which suggests the failure of schooling to humanize, has become a staple of secondary school English classes. In a different but also highly critical vein, the French writer Michel Tournier has written another stimulating verison of *Robinson Crusoe*, with the title *Vendredi: ou les Limbes du Pacifique* (*Friday; or, the Other Island*, 1967). First published for adults, this metaphysical novel, which depicts Friday resisting Crusoe's attempts to "civilize" him, was rewritten for children as *Vendredi: ou la vie sauvage* (*Friday and Robinson: Life on Esperanza Island*, 1971), and it has become the second-most popular children's book in France after *The Little Prince*.

The Robinsonnade persists into the twenty-first century, though in very different form. Recently it has taken shape in new media not as an inspirational success story but as something between soap opera and situation comedy. In the 1960s, two television series took their place in the genre. *Gilligan's Island* (1964–67) gained a cult following by playing out the comic possibilities of rich, urban Americans shipwrecked without the comforts of home; *Lost in Space* (1965–68) was explicitly a science fiction version of Wyss's *Swiss Family Robinson*, espousing the same kinds of family values as the novel (though the show about these futuristic Robinsons rapidly descended into camp). The latest twist—the "reality" program *Survivor* (which premiered in 2000)—is perhaps the most cartoonish of all. In each season of this game show, participants are left in some isolated spot without the usual comforts of the modern world; they are expected to cooperate in gaining food and shelter when they are not competing in elaborately staged contests. The last of the "tribe" remaining wins $1 million. In its focus on the cash payoff this (ersatz) adventure echoes Defoe's, with its emphasis on risk and reward, and on the accumulation of wealth and material goods.

Venturing Out

The desert island survival story, the founding plot of adventure fiction, continued to be popular in seemingly endless variations. The genre itself, however, escaped the confines of stock location and characters when Sir Walter Scott began writing historical novels in the early nineteenth century. Raised on traditional medieval romances and ballads, and on tales of battles and political power struggles, Scott incorporated these elements into his fiction: locations made exotic by being set in a vanished past, colorful characters, passionate emotional drama, and lots of action. His breakthrough novel, *Waverly; or,'Tis Sixty Years Since,* was published anonymously in 1814, when Scott was already a best-selling narrative poet in his native Scotland (the setting for much of his fiction). The hero of the novel becomes caught up in the rebellion of 1745 on the side of the Young Pretender, Charles Stuart. This hugely successful novel was followed in quick succession by more than twenty others (collectively known as the *Waverly* novels), most of which chronicle the lives of ordinary people at crucial transitional moments in Scotland's history. Scott also mined the late medieval period for a series of novels he characterized as "romances"—notably *Ivanhoe* (1819), which depicts the conflict and reconciliation between Anglo-Saxons and Normans in twelfth-century England. Although Scott's only writings aimed directly at children were the stories collected in *Tales of a Grandfather* (three series dealing with Scotland, one with France; 1827–30), his action-packed historical novels were enormously popular with young readers.

The authors of the nineteenth-century Robinsonnades discussed above were strongly influenced by Scott as they enlarged the geographical and historical scope of their other adventure stories, marketed particularly to boys. For example, Captain Frederick Marryat maroons four children in the English wilderness in *The Children of the New Forest* (1847). R. M. Ballantyne drew on his adventures in the Canadian north in such novels as *Ungava: A Tale of Esquimaux Land* (1857). And Robert Louis Stevenson's varied works include historical adventures such as *Kidnapped* (1886).

The market was steady and large for relentlessly upbeat adventure stories, and many appeared in periodicals that thrived well into the twentieth century. Ballantyne was a regular contributor to one of the most famous and enduring, *The Boy's Own Paper* (1879–1967); published initially by the Religious Tract Society, it was dedicated to promoting a new kind of muscular Christian manhood. Similar magazines, with equally telling titles, included *The Captain: A Magazine for Boys and Old Boys* (1899–1924) and *Boys of England: A Magazine of Sport, Sensation, Fun, and Instruction* (1866–99). The "muscular Christian" was a man who could be counted on as a team player, standing with other men against tyranny and dictatorship in a new, enlightened, republican spirit. This mythic celebration of male moral and physical courage was perfectly realized in the adventure story genre.

For the most part, boys' adventure stories were characterized by a narrative tactic that the critic Dennis Butts calls "the blending of the probable with the extraordinary." The illusion, he points out, is often created in the loving detail: readers drink in the accurate descriptions of the topography, vegetation, and natural world, as well as practical instructions on how to make pots or build fires or kill wild animals. Should you happen to find yourself stranded on a desert island, in the American wilderness, or in the frozen North, you would know what to do.

By the late nineteenth century, the genre had expanded to accommodate not just tales set long ago and far away but also factual narratives of explorations to remote corners of the world. People in Victorian England were fascinated by accounts of David Livingstone's search for the source of the Nile and his "discovery" in 1855 on the border of present-day Zambia and Zimbabwe of a huge waterfall (which he named the Victoria Falls after his queen). The story of his meeting in the jungle with the American journalist H. M. Stanley is memorialized in Stanley's famous greeting: "Dr. Livingstone, I presume." Also chronicled were the expeditions of Robert Peary, the American who was the first to reach the North Pole, in 1909; Roald Amundson, the Norwegian who won the race to the South Pole in 1911; and Ernest Shackleton, the British explorer who managed to survive with all his crew when their ship was crushed in the Antarctic (1914–16). The newspapers regularly covered these exploits, as did *National Geographic*, the American magazine that became synonymous with adventure and exploration stories (founded in 1888 "for the increase and diffusion of geographical knowledge"). By early in the twentieth century, the exploration narrative had become so familiar that A. A. Milne's gentle satire of it was obvious to all when he sent Christopher Robin and Winnie-the-Pooh on their "expotition" to the North Pole in *Winnie-the-Pooh* (1926). The public hunger for real-life adventure continues, as our fascination with stories of both undersea and space exploration demonstrates.

The calamities of the twentieth century—particularly the two world wars—were major sources for new adventure stories. Thus the 102 "Biggles" stories by Captain W. E. Johns (1893–1968), featuring the British flying ace James Bigglesworth, spanned both wars. Like their predecessors, they clearly distinguished good and evil characters, and they appealed to generations of boys. By the end of the century, attitudes toward war expressed in some children's books had become more complex; the shift toward ambiguity can be seen in works by Robert Westall, who grew up in England during World War II (e.g., *The Machine-Gunners*, 1975), and other authors.

Other conventions of adventure stories also began to show new flexibility in the twentieth century. The hero could be a girl, such as the detective Nancy Drew, in the hugely popular series begun in 1930 (written for the Stratemeyer Syndicate by a variety of authors under the name Carolyn Keene). Another heroic girl is Lyra, who quests across time and space in Philip Pullman's extraordinary fantasy trilogy, His Dark Materials (1995–2000). Women can even engage in hand-to-hand combat in video games, as in *Lara Croft: Tomb Raider* (first version issued in 1996, followed, beginning in 2001, by movie adaptations); on television, as in *Xena: Warrior Princess* (1995–2001); and in film, as in Ang Lee's *Crouching Tiger, Hidden Dragon* (2000). And as the last example suggests, it is no longer assumed that heroes are white.

Frontier Adventures and Westerns

Certain kinds of adventure stories have explicitly American roots: the captivity narrative, the frontier story, and the western. Although the categories overlap, especially in today's popular culture, they can be roughly distinguished. Captivity narratives are generally first-person accounts of white people captured by American Indians; the earliest and most famous is *A Narrative of the Captivity and Restoration of Mrs. Mary Rowlandson* (1682). The frontier story is probably the broadest category, and its significance for American history and culture was argued in a highly influential and much-debated 1893 paper by the American historian Frederick Jackson Turner. After identifying the frontier as the boundary between the civilized and the wild, the tame and the savage, Turner focuses on a cluster of what he defines as explicitly American traits: "coarseness and strength combined with acuteness and acquisitiveness," as well as "restless, nervous energy" and "dominant individualism." Those characteristics are precisely those ascribed to an entire class of American heroes that includes Davy Crockett, Daniel Boone, Buffalo Bill Cody, and James Bowie.

The popularity of westerns, which typically feature cowboys fighting Indians, surged in the late nineteenth century and long remained high. The genre easily adapted to a wide range of media, moving from print to radio and television shows and to movies. It was exportable too, turning up both in books (e.g., of the German writer Karl May [1842–1912]) and in Japanese and Italian films, which were so prolific they were known as "spaghetti westerns." Westerns were also part of the culture of non-American children, who played endless games of "cowboys and Indians." Clothes and toys were sold to children as props: plastic guns with holsters, star-shaped sheriff badges, plastic bowie knives, toy bows and arrows, child-sized Stetsons, raccoon-skin hats (like those supposedly worn by Davy Crockett), fringed skirts for girls, and "Indian" headbands.

By the late twentieth century, however, such play had declined, both because of increased sensitivity to how all the peoples involved experienced the "taming" of the American West and because of a growing aversion to toy weapons of any sort. Moreover, those cowboys that remain on the children's shelves of libraries are sensitive, New Age cowboys, no longer necessarily tough, male, or white. In *The Cowboy and the Black-Eyed Pea* (1992) by Tony Johnston (a version of Hans Christian Andersen's

"Princess and the Pea," 1835), a cowboy becomes saddle-sore when a pea is hidden under his saddle—despite a large pile of blankets to reduce the irritation. Nicole Rubel's *A Cowboy Named Ernestine* (2001) offers readers a girl cowboy. African American cowboys were common in the West but invisible in classic western stories, and books such as *Bill Pickett: Rodeo Ridin' Cowboy* (1996) by Andrea Pinkney are correcting the historical record. Stories of Indian cowboys—a seeming oxymoron in a genre that traditionally pits "good" cowboys against "savages"—are also being told, particularly by Native American writers. Thus Virginia Driving Hawk Sneve offers *Grandpa Was a Cowboy and an Indian and Other Stories* (2000). And there are toy cowboys: Woody from *Toy Story* (1995, 1999) is a recent addition. One thing New Age cowboy stories demonstrate is the continuing flexibility of the genre, and its tough, persistent place in American culture and literary history.

The heyday of the working cowboy was historically quite short, lasting from about the late 1860s to the late 1880s, when large herds of cattle were driven from the open grazing ranges of the West and Southwest to railheads for shipment east. This period is the setting for Owen Wister's classic western novel, *The Virginian: A Horseman of the Plains*, published in 1902. Wister, who was born and spent most of his life in the suburbs of Philadelphia, visited Wyoming just as the frontier was closing and trains had almost replaced cowboys in moving cattle long distances. He turns the cowboy into a romantic hero, a noble defender of good in the face of evil— someone who embodies just the "dominant individualism" that Turner found in the frontier character. Multiple film versions and a long-running television adaptation of *The Virginian* (1962–70) further fixed the character type in the American cultural imagination. And the demand for stories of the period was met by a steady supply of cowboy novels by authors such as Zane Grey (1872–1939) and Louis L'Amour (1908–1988).

As a subgenre of adventure stories, the western sits at a crucial juncture in the history of children's literature and children's culture. When Buffalo Bill Cody began staging his cowboy shows in 1883, he was selling a version of the Wild West that was already disappearing. "Buffalo Bill" himself, as public figure, was largely the creation of the prolific writer E. Z. C. Judson, who published a long series on the plainsman in *New York Weekly* (1869–70). His four dime novels on Buffalo Bill were followed by many others, well into the twentieth century. The western as nostalgic spectacle translated easily into visual media, and soon "the western" was most closely associated with films—especially Saturday matinees—and television shows. By 1959 there were dozens of series featuring anachronistic cowboys who loved their mothers and their country, fought bad guys (outlaws or Indians), dressed in buckskins, and wore belts that held guns, knives, or both. Today, they have all but disappeared.

The United States has had a number of frontiers, and not all of them involved cowboys. The archetypal frontiersman was Natty Bumppo, the hero of James Fenimore Cooper's five Leather-Stocking Tales (1823–41); the frontier of his youth was New York State. Natty embodies Turner's ideal of the rugged, resourceful individualist, as do the real frontiersmen Daniel Boone, Davy Crockett, and James Bowie, indelibly associated with the settlement of Kentucky, Tennessee, and Texas, respectively. An influential child's-eye view of the settler's life is offered in the autobiographical novels of Laura Ingalls Wilder (1867–1957), who experienced life on the frontiers of Minnesota, Kansas, and Iowa. The frequent appearance of all these figures in film and television adaptations has kept them alive in American culture.

In the twentieth century, as the spaces of the West increasingly closed, another frontier opened up: the "final frontier," as the familiar voice-over that began each episode of the original *Star Trek* series (1966–69) declared. Science fiction writers for young adults had already imagined colonists as the new pioneers, in novels such as Robert Heinlein's *Farmer in the Sky* (1950). Space is typically presented to viewers of *Star Trek* as offering limitless opportunities for intergalactic encounters with "natives" of other species. In a universe in which good guys are still pitted against bad guys, rough justice and rugged individualism still count as important. Later additions to the Star Trek franchise, on television and in movie theaters, strike a similar note, as does *Star Wars* (especially the first film in the series, 1977)—and even the *Matrix* trilogy (1999–2003), where the frontier lies on the border between the real and the computer-simulated.

Animal Adventures

Animals do not rationalize death as "an awfully big adventure"; they avoid it at all costs. Animal adventure stories—as opposed to stories that detail the life of an animal, such as Anna Sewell's *Black Beauty* (1877), or stories focusing on animal-human relations, such as those in *The Jungle Books* (1894, 1895) of Rudyard Kipling—are about surviving, about cheating death by trickery, by flight, or by a fight. Though their plots are broadly similar, animal adventures vary a great deal depending on the degree to which the characters in the story exhibit human qualities. At one end of the spectrum are anthropomorphic trickster figures, mythical demigods who take both animal and human form; at the other are realistic animals whose stories gain human emotional resonance in the telling. In between are stories that mix animal behavior with human thought, speech, and action—sometimes including the wearing of human clothes—in different blends.

The trickster turns up in myth and folklore all over the world, often but not always as an animal (well-known tricksters include the Greek god Hermes, as well as Jack of the folktale "Jack and the Beanstalk"). In the oral myths of Native Americans, the trickster character shifts seamlessly between human and animal form, with the specific animal varying by place. Thus Coyote is found in myths originating in what is now California, tales of Rabbit and Hare are told in the U.S. Southwest, and Raven appears in the Arctic and sub-Arctic regions. Traditionally the stories of their adventures explain aspects of the teller's culture or of the natural world: why crows are black, why there are days and nights, and so on. Unlike standard literary heroes, who usually are models of exemplary behavior, trickster heroes generally are governed by their appetites (for food, for sex, for control). They act sometimes nobly and sometimes as buffoons, sometimes for the collective good and sometimes not.

In Afro-Caribbean stories, Ananse the spider god is the trickster figure. In Africa he was originally Kwaku Ananse, but as Africans moved to the "new" world he mutated, into Anancy in the Caribbean and sometimes into "Aunt Nancy" in the southern United States. In *A Story, A Story* (1970), Gail E. Haley retells and illustrates an African Ananse story about the origin of storytelling. Ananse "the spider man" first wants to buy the Sky God's stories. The price is "Osebo the leopard of-the-terrible-teeth, Mmboro the hornet who-stings-like-fire, and Mmoatia the fairy whom-men-never-see." Ananse successfully tricks and traps all three, binds them into a web, and takes them to the Sky God—who bestows the reward: " 'From this day and going on forever,' proclaimed the Sky God, 'my stories belong to Ananse and shall be called 'Spider stories.' " And that's how "all the stories scattered to the corners of the world, including this one."

The descendants of mythical tricksters fit naturally into children's literature, because they tend to be small creatures facing bigger and more powerful enemies. In America, probably the best known of these are found in the Uncle Remus stories

(185 altogether) collected by Joel Chandler Harris (1848–1908). The fictional Uncle Remus, an old slave who speaks in dialect, narrates distinctly African American stories, filtering African folktales through the brutal and violent conditions of slavery. The weak must live by their wits—as does Brer Rabbit, who tricks Brer Fox into throwing him into a briar patch (a rabbit's natural refuge), keeping himself alive to fight his enemy another day. Some of these tales have been exquisitely retold in a contemporary idiom by Virginia Hamilton in *The People Could Fly* (1985).

Escape stories within the animal adventure genre often resemble the tales of human explorers. Applying Joseph Campbell's structural divisions, we find that the episodes of crossing the threshold and journeying through dangerous, foreign territory are most significant. One such story is Sheila Burnford's *The Incredible Journey* (1961), in which three family pets—two dogs and a cat—travel across hundreds of miles of Canadian wilderness to return to their home. *Watership Down* (1972) by the British author Richard Adams became against all odds a huge international best seller (it had been rejected by many major publishing houses). Its combination of anthropomorphism and biological realism appealed to adults as well as children. Forced to move by encroaching urban sprawl, the rabbit heroes undertake an epic quest for a safe refuge. In order to find a new home (which will be well-governed and democratic), they have to survive battles with other undemocratic rabbit societies as well as natural and urban enemies. The Silverwing series by the Canadian Kenneth Oppel (begun in 1997) falls into the same quest category. The adventures of Shade, a silverwing bat, begin when he breaks the law of the bats to steal a look at the sun. Although Shade and the others in his colony behave in many respects like bats, they think like people and deal with both emotional and physical challenges.

Realistic animal stories are even more directly concerned with the lives and deaths of their closely observed subjects. Ernest Thompson Seton, who grew up in Canada and founded the precursor of the Boy Scouts in the United States, is generally regarded as having invented the genre with his first collection of stories, *Wild Animals I Have Known* (1898). He was a dedicated naturalist who kept careful field notes, and he wrote sympathetically but not sentimentally of wolves and rabbits, crows and foxes. Other familiar works of this type include, in Canada, Charles G. D. Roberts's *The Kindred of the Wild: A Book of Animal Life* (1902), a collection of stories written from the animals' point of view, and in England, Henry Williamson's *Tarka the Otter* (1927), which follows the life of the playful predator to his death in an otter hunt.

Venturing Within

Traditional adventure stories have featured heroes who leave home and go out into the world, preferably to exotic locations. But in the mid–twentieth century, stories about adventures in civilized rather than savage spaces begin to appear. Instead of boys alone, or in small groups, facing the elements, there are new tales of girls bravely negotiating urban, civilized environments.

Three books set in the densely populated core of New York City typify the genre. In Kay Thompson's *Eloise: A Book for Precocious Grown-Ups* (1955), the rambunctious Eloise pries into everything at the Plaza Hotel, where she lives with her nanny. In Louise Fitzhugh's *Harriet the Spy* (1964), the title character is an upper-middle-class child (residing somewhat more conventionally with her parents in a Manhattan brownstone); she obsessively observes and records the lives of her neighbors and classmates. And in E. L. Konigsburg's *From the Mixed-Up Files of Mrs. Basil E. Frankweiler* (1967), Claudia carefully chooses a comfortable place for her adventure, the museum, as she and her brother run away from their home in the suburbs. In feminine adventures, concrete jungles and thickets of art treasures in well-appointed interior spaces replace rough shelters on traditional tropical islands inhabited by hostile, incomprehensible natives and wild animals. Each heroine employs her considerable wit to establish herself as an intelligent, articulate presence in a community of adults who would otherwise tend to relegate her—unseen and unheard—to the margins. All three New York books accord value to the domestic, the inward, and the familial, in keeping with the rising feminist movement—but striking a tone new to the adventure genre.

Female protagonists in children's adventure stories of the late twentieth century adapted to the genre while retaining the central drama of the heroic quest to restore social order. But whereas male protagonists use brute force, female protagonists exploit their intellectual and psychological strengths. Two books of the 1980s demonstrate the ability of feminine adventure stories to incorporate traditional motifs of the quest romance: *The Root Cellar* (1981), by the Canadian Janet Lunn, and *The Changeover: A Supernatural Romance* (1984), by Margaret Mahy from New Zealand. Both are fantasies that involve girls who simultaneously engage the trappings of the male quest (particularly battles) and seek to restore domestic order.

Rose, the twelve-year-old protagonist of *The Root Cellar,* has been raised by her grandmother very much in Eloise style. The two of them move between an apartment on New York's Upper East Side and hotels in major European cities. After her grandmother dies suddenly in Paris, Rose suffers deep cultural as well as geographic dislocation when she is sent to live with relatives she does not know in a sprawling old farmhouse in rural Ontario. She enters an old root cellar and is transported to the same root cellar in the 1860s. In that time, she meets Will and Susan; and when Will does not return from the American Civil War, Rose ventures on a quest—disguised as a boy—to rescue him. By descending into the root cellar and into the nineteenth century, Rose engages in a series of heroic adventures that enable her to restore domestic order both to the past of the house and to her own present.

As in *The Root Cellar*, the social order in *The Changeover* is restored as a result of the heroic quest taken on by the female protagonist. Desperate to save the life of her young brother, whose vital force is being consumed by an ancient spirit in human form, Laura Chant agrees to be transformed into a witch. The process involves a journey of initiation and passage through a series of tests—much like the quests of medieval knights. But hers is a psychological inner journey, even though the action feels real and external, and though it carries the risk of death. Laura's mission is personal and domestic in that she fights for someone she loves rather than for broad social change. She keeps her success a secret, as is also typical of female heroes—and unlike the heroic pattern sketched by Campbell, which ends with public celebration. Indeed, the protagonists of both *The Root Cellar* and *The Changeover* conform relatively well to a five-phase pattern of female heroic quests suggested by Annis Pratt in *Archetypal Patterns in Women's Fiction* (1981): a splitting off from the family, a green-world guide or token, a green-world lover, confrontation with parental figures, a plunge into the unconscious, and finally an integration with society.

The adventure story is clearly a very flexible genre, maintaining its core across changes in time, space, culture, and gender. Heroes with mysterious births try to return the world to its lost order, and pitched battles provide opportunities for demonstrations of heroic gifts. The contradictions within the genre remain, too: the pull between dreams of wish fulfillment and anxiety and between life and death, that "awfully big adventure."

DANIEL DEFOE
ca. 1660–1731

Daniel Defoe apparently died "of a lethargy" at age seventy—an odd end, given his enormous productivity. By the time he died, he had produced hundreds of books, pamphlets, and religious tracts, including his most famous work, *The Life and Strange Surprizing Adventures of Robinson Crusoe, of York, mariner: who lived eight and twenty years, all alone, in an un-inhabited island on the coast of America, near the mouth of the great river of Oroonoque; having been cast on shore by shipwreck, wherein all the men perished but himself: with an account of how he was at last as strangely deliver'd by pyrates, written by himself*. He was almost sixty when the book was published in 1719, and about to embark on a career as a novelist. Following up on the success of *Robinson Crusoe*, Defoe quickly produced several novels for which he is still remembered: *Moll Flanders* (1722), *A Journal of the Plague Year* (1722), and *Roxana, the Fortunate Mistress* (1724). He is often credited with founding the modern English novel because his original mix of realistic setting, psychologically true characterization, and compelling plot was new in the early eighteenth century.

Born into a middle-class family of Dissenters (those who refused to conform to the Church of England), Defoe was barred from attending an English university and did not receive a gentleman's classical education; he did, however, attend an excellent Dissenting academy. Before becoming a novelist, he had failed as a businessman, had been bankrupt twice, had been arrested for debt and for political writings, had been imprisoned and pilloried for seditious libel, had worked effectively as a spy and political agent for the government, and had almost single-handedly written an influential periodical, the *Review* (1704–13). His companion

through these changes in fortune was Mary Tuffley, whom he married in 1684 but mentions almost as little as Crusoe does his wife (Crusoe's marriage, the birth of three children, and his wife's death take only fifty words in the book's final paragraphs). Six of their children lived to adulthood.

Defoe was a writer of the Enlightenment, an eighteenth-century thinker who applied reason to all areas of life and took a practical approach to social problems. His first book-length work, *An Essay upon Projects* (1697), includes plans to improve the national roads, to provide pensions and insurance, to build an academy for women, and to amend bankruptcy laws. These were the sorts of projects upon which Crusoe himself might have embarked if he had a large population to govern instead of an island of one. Defoe continued to suggest such schemes throughout his life. He also wrote many didactic works, the most popular of which was *The Family Instructor* (1715). This domestic conduct book, which mixed realistic dialogue with narrative, was in its nineteenth edition by 1809 and had outsold all of Defoe's other works except *Robinson Crusoe*.

Robinson Crusoe has been read in various ways—as a spiritual autobiography, a meditation on education and religion, a myth proclaiming the dignity of labor, and more—but its most enduring hold on the imagination of young readers is as an adventure story. The chapbook version printed here pares down the novel to its essence as an adventure tale: a hero who goes against the will of his parents to strike out on his own, his capture by pirates, his dramatic escape then shipwreck, his survival in the wilderness, his encounter with hostile natives, and finally his triumphant, celebrated return home.

The Adventures of Robinson Crusoe

I was born of a good family in the city of York, where my father, who was a native of Bremen, settled, after his having got a handsome estate by merchandise.[1] My heart was very early filled with rambling thoughts; and though, when I grew up, my father persuaded me to settle to some business, while my mother used the tenderest entreaties, yet nothing could prevail upon me to lay aside my desire of going to sea. I at length resolved to gratify my roving disposition, notwithstanding the uneasiness my father and mother showed at my leaving them.

On the 1st of September, 1651, I went on board a ship for London, and, without letting my father know the rout[2] I had taken, set sail; but no sooner was the ship out of the Humber, than the wind began to blow, and the sea to rise in a most terrible manner. Having never been at sea before, I was extremely sick, and my mind was filled with terror. The next day the wind abated, and my companions laughed at my fears, and with a bowl of punch made me half drunk, and thus drowned my repentance and reflections. The weather continued calm several days, and we went into Yarmouth Ronds,[3] where we cast anchor. After riding here four or five days, the wind blew very hard till the eighth day in the morning, when it still increased, and we had all hands at work to strike our topmasts, and at last cast our sheet-anchor.[4]

It now blew a terrible storm; I began to see terror in the faces even of the seamen themselves; and as the master passed by me, I heard him say softly to himself, "Lord, be merciful to us, we shall be all lost!"

I cannot express the horror of mind with which I was seized; I was in ten times more tremor[5] on account of slighting my former convictions, than even at death itself. The storm still increased, and I saw the master, the boatswain,[6] and several others, at prayers, expecting every moment the ship would go to the bottom. One of the men cried out we had sprung a leak, upon which all hands were called to the pump, but the water gained upon us, and it was apparent that the ship would founder; the storm, however, beginning to abate, the master fired guns for help, and a ship which had rode it out just a-head of us, came near with the utmost hazard, venturing their lives to save ours; our men casting a rope over the stern, they, after much hazard, got hold of it, and we with great difficulty got to land, and walked to Yarmouth. On my arrival in that city, I contracted an acquaintance with the master of a ship who had been on the coast of Guinea, and was resolved to go again: he taking a fancy to me, told me I should have liberty of trading for myself. Encouraged by this offer, and the assistance of some of my relations, with whom I still corresponded, I raised £40, which I laid out in such toys and trifles as my friend the captain directed me. I got a competent knowledge of the mathematics, navigation, and how to take an observation.[7] In a word, this voyage made me both a sailor and a merchant, for my adventure yielded me in London, at my return, £300.

I now set up for a Guinea trader, and, my friend dying soon after his arrival, I resolved to go the same voyage again in the same vessel, with one who was his mate in the former voyage, and had now the command of the ship. This was one of the

1. I.e., by being a merchant. Bremen: a major port in northwest Germany.
2. Route.
3. The area between the town of Yarmouth (on the eastern coast of England) and the sandbanks offshore.
4. The largest of a ship's anchors, used only in an emergency.
5. Terror.
6. The officer in charge of sails and rigging, who summons men to their duties.
7. To use an instrument to determine the altitude of heavenly bodies in order to ascertain longitude or latitude.

most unhappy voyages ever made, for, as we were steering about the Canary Islands and the African shore, we were surprised in the morning by a rover of Sallee,[8] who gave chase to us with all the sail she could make. We, finding that the pirate gained upon us, and would come up with us, prepared to fight; our ship having twelve guns, and the pirate eighteen. About three in the afternoon she came up with us, and a very smart engagement ensued; but we were obliged to submit, and were all carried prisoners into Sallee, a port belonging to the Moors.[9]

My master having the long-boat of our English ship, had a little cabin built in the middle of it, like a barge. In this pleasure-boat he frequently went a fishing; and as I was dexterous at catching fish, he never went without me. One day he appointed to go out with two or three Moors of distinction, and he had sent over-night a larger store of provisions than usual, and ordered me to get ready two or three fusils[1] of powder and shot, for that they designed to have sport at the fowling as well as fishing. At this moment the hopes of deliverance darted into my thoughts, and I resolved to furnish myself for a voyage.

Every thing being prepared, we sailed out of the port to fish; but purposely catching none, I told Muley that we must stand further off, which he agreed to, and I having the helm, ran the boat a league out further, and then brought to, as if I would fish, when, giving the boy the helm, I stepped forward, and stooping behind the Moor, took him by surprise, and tossed him overboard; he rose immediately, and called me to take him in, but, fetching one of the fowling-pieces, I presented it, and told him that if he came near I would shoot him, and as the sea was calm, he might easily reach the shore. So he turned about, and I make no doubt but he reached it with ease.

I turned to the boy, whom they called Xury, and said to him, Xury, if you will be faithful to me, I will make you a great man; but if you will not, I must throw you into the sea too. The boy smiled, and spoke so innocently, that I could not mistrust him.

About ten days after, as I was steering out to sea, in order to double a cape,[2] on a sudden Xury called out in a fright, Master, Master, a ship! I jumped out of the cabin, and saw that it was a Portuguese vessel. On my coming near, they asked me what I was, in Portuguese, Spanish, and French; but I understood none of them; at last a Scotch sailor called to me, and I answered I was an Englishman, and had made my escape from the Moors of Sallee. I offered all that I had to the captain of the ship, but he would take nothing from me, and told me that all that I had should be delivered to me when we came to the Brazils. We had a very good voyage to the Brazils, and the good captain recommended me to an honest man who had a plantation and a sugar-house, with whom I lived, and learned the planting and making of sugar; after which I took a piece of land, and became a planter myself. Had I continued in the station I was now in, I might have been happy, but my fellow-planters prevailed on me to make a trial of purchasing negroes on the coast of Guinea. We fitted out a ship, and made sail with the hopes of purchasing slaves to assist in our plantations; we had very good weather for twelve days, but after we had crossed the Line,[3] a violent hurricane drove us quite out of our reckoning. In this distress, one of our men called out "Land!" but the ship struck against a sand-bank. We took to the boat,

8. A slave-trading ship (identified in the complete text as Turkish; during the seventeenth century, Muslims enslaved captured Christians, and vice versa). Sallee: Salé, a port in Morocco that was then an independent republic and a center of the Barbary pirates.

9. North Africans.
1. Flintlock muskets.
2. To sail to the other side of a cape (specified in the original as Cape de Verde, on the West African coast in present-day Senegal).
3. The equator.

and after we had rowed a league and a half, a wave came rolling a-stern of us, and overset the boat at once, so that out of fifteen none escaped but myself. I got upon my feet, and made towards the shore, and got to land, clambering up the cliffs of the shore, and sat me down upon the grass. Being much fatigued, I got up into a tree, and slept comfortably till the morning.

When I awoke, it was broad day, and the storm abated; but what surprised me most was, that in the night the ship had been lifted from the land by the swelling of the tide, and driven almost as far as the place where I landed, and I saw that if we had all staid on board, we had been all safe. I swam to the ship, and found she was bulged,[4] and had a great deal of water in the bold; but, to my great joy, saw that all the provisions were dry; and being well disposed to eat, I filled my pockets, and ate as I went about other things. I found several spare yards[5] and planks, with which I made a raft. I emptied three of the seamen's chests, and let them down upon the raft, and filled them with bread, some dried goats' flesh, and three Dutch cheeses. I also let down the carpenter's chest,[6] two fowling-pieces, two pistols, with some powder, and two rusty swords, all which I placed on my raft, and after much labour got it safely landed. My first raft being too unwieldy, I swam to the ship and made another; on which I placed three bags of nails and spikes, some hatchets, a grindstone, two iron crows,[7] several muskets, and another fowling-piece, two barrels of musket bullets, a large bag of small shot, all the men's clothes I could find, a hammock and some bedding, and, to my great comfort, brought all to land. After I had made five or six of these voyages, and though I had nothing more to expect from the ship worth taking, I found a great hogshead of bread, three large rumlets[8] of rum, a box of fine sugar, a barrel of fine flour, three dozen of good knives and forks. I then went in search of a place where to fix my dwelling.

Before I set up my tent, I drew a half circle before a hollow place, which extended about twenty yards, and drove large piles[9] into the ground, sharpened at the top, and the entrance I made by a short ladder to go over the top, and when I was in, I lifted it over after me, so that I was perfectly secure.

In the midst of my labours, when I was rummaging amongst my things, I found a little bag with a few husks of corn[1] in it, and shook it by the side of my fortification: but how great was my astonishment when I saw ten or twelve ears of barley springing up: with this barley there came up a few stalks of rice, and these were of more worth to me than all the gold in the world.

I then took a view of the island, and at about two miles distant from my habitation, found some fine savannahs,[2] and a little further, a variety of fruit, melons upon the ground, and the trees spread over, and covered with clusters of grapes. I was so enamoured with this place, that I built a bower, fenced by a double hedge; and this country house, as I called it, cost me two months' labour, but the rainy season coming on, I was obliged to retreat to my old one, taking with me grapes, which were now become fine raisins of the sun.

When my corn was ripe, I made me a scythe with a sword, and cut off the ears, which I rubbed out with my hands. At the end of the harvest, I guessed that I had a bushel of rice, and two bushels of barley. I kept all this for seed, and bore the want[3] of bread with patience.

---

4. Had the bottom or sides stove in.
5. Wooden spars, comparatively long and slender.
6. Toolbox.
7. Crowbars.
8. Casks.

9. Pointed stakes.
1. Wheat.
2. Treeless plains.
3. Lack.

When I came to make bread, I had innumerable wants. I wanted a mill to grind it, sieves to dress it, yeast and salt to make it into bread, and an oven to bake it. However, I had six months to contrive all these things in. I made some misshapen pots of clay, that all broke in the sun except two, which I cased in wicker work; but I succeeded better in little pans, flat dishes, and pitchers, which the sun baked surprisingly hard; but they would not bear the fire so as to hold any liquid, and I wanted one to boil my meat.

Certainly a Stoic[4] would have smiled to have seen me at dinner: there was my royal majesty, an absolute prince and ruler of my kingdom, attended by my dutiful subjects, whom, if I pleased, I could either hang, draw or quarter—give liberty, or take it away. When I dined, I seemed a king, eating alone, none daring presume to do so till I had done. Poll[5] was the only person permitted to talk with me. My old but faithful dog, now growing exceeding crazy,[6] continually sat at my right hand; while my two cats sat on each side of the table, expecting a bit from my hand, as a princely mark of my royal favour. Yet these were not the cats I had brought from the ship; they had been dead long before, and interred near my habitation by my own hands; but one of them, as I suppose, generating with a wild cat, these were a couple I had made tame, whereas the rest ran into the woods, and grew so impudent as to return and plunder me of my stores, till such time as I shot a great many, and the rest left me with this attendance. One thing more indeed concerned me, the want of my boat. I knew not which way to get round the island. I resolved one time to go along the shore by land

4. A follower of the Greek philosophy characterized by austerity and freedom from passion.

5. A parrot captured by Crusoe.
6. Broken-down, frail.

to her; but had any one in England met such a figure, it would either have affrighted him, or made him burst into laughter.

One day after I had dressed my dinner, I went to put out my fire, and found a piece of one of my earthenware vessels burnt as hard as a stone, and as red as a tile; this taught me to burn my pipkins,[7] and I soon wanted for no sort of earthenware; but when I found that I had made a pot which would bear the fire, I had hardly patience to stay till it was cold, before I set it on with a piece of a kid, in order to make me some broth—which answered tolerably well.

I used to burn my earthenware in a cave which I found in the wood, and which I made convenient for that purpose; but the principal cause that first brought me here, was to make charcoal, so that I might bake and dress my bread and meat, without any danger. While I was cutting down some wood for this purpose, I perceived a cavity behind a very thick branch of underwood. Curious to look into it, I got to its mouth, and found it sufficient for me to stand upright in it. But when I entered and took a further view, two rolling shining eyes, like flaming stars, seemed to dart themselves at me, so that I made all the haste out that I could, not knowing whether it was a savage, or a monster that had taken up his residence in that place. On recovering a little from my surprise, I resumed all the courage I had, and taking up a flaming firebrand, in I rushed again; when not having proceeded above three steps, I was more affrighted than before; for I heard a very loud sigh, like that of a human creature in the greatest agony, succeeded by a broken noise, resembling words half expressed, and then a broken sigh again. Stepping back, thought I to myself, am I got into some enchanted place, such as is reported to contain miserable captives, till death puts an end to their sorrow? It struck me with a cold sweat; but again, trusting God's protection, I proceeded forward, and, by the light of my firebrand, perceived it to be a monstrous he-goat, lying on the ground, gasping for life, and dying of mere old age. When at first I stirred him, thinking to drive him out, he strove to get upon his feet, but was not able; so I left him there, to fright any one from venturing into the cave.

At the furthermost part of the cave I observed a sort of entrance, but so low as to oblige me to creep upon my hands and knees to get through, but on advancing, I found that it rose in height about twenty feet, and appeared, from the reflection of the light I carried with me, to be a grotto adorned with diamonds and other precious stones. I found it dry and comfortable, therefore determined to make it my principal magazine.[8]

While these things were doing, my thoughts ran many times upon the land I had seen, and I began to make myself a canoe; the most preposterous enterprise that ever man in his senses undertook. I felled a great cedar, about five feet in diameter next the root, but when the impossibility of launching this heavy thing came into my mind, I gave myself this foolish answer; *Let me but once make it, I'll warrant I'll get it along when it is done.* I made it big enough to carry twenty-five men; but all my devices to get it into the water failed me, for I could no more stir it than I could the island. I then determined, since I could not bring my canoe to the water, that I should bring the water to the canoe, and began to dig; but when I calculated the time this canal would take in making, I found that I could not accomplish it in less than twelve years, and therefore gave it over, determining to enjoy what I had, without repining for what I could not get.

---

7. Small earthenware pots. "Burn": to fire, as in a kiln.

8. Storage place.

I had at length a great mind to go to the point of the island to see how the shore lay, and resolved to travel thither by land. And now, reader, I will give you a short sketch of the figure I made. I had a great high shapeless cap, made of a goat's skin, a jacket with the skirts coming down to the middle of my thighs, and a pair of open-kneed breeches[9] of the same, with the goat's hair hanging to the middle of my leg. Stockings and shoes I had none; but I had a pair of somethings, I scarce know what to call them, to slip over my legs like spatterdashes.[1] Under my arm hung two pouches for shot and powder; on my back I carried a basket, on my shoulder a gun, and over my head a great clumsy goat-skin umbrella. My beard was cut short, except what grew on my upper lip; but as for my figure, as I had few to observe me, it was no matter of consequence.

In this attire I went on my new journey, and was out five or six days. In one of my excursions I was exceedingly surprised at the print of a man's naked foot on the shore, which was plain to be seen on the sand. I stood like one thunderstruck; I listened, I looked around, but I could hear nothing, nor see any thing. I went upon a rising ground to look farther; I walked backward and forward on the shore, but I could see only that one impression. I went to look at it again; how it came there I knew not; but I hurried home to my fortifications, looking behind me every two or three steps, and fancied every tree, bush, and stump, to be a man. I had no sleep that night, but my terror gradually wore off, and I ventured down to take measure of the foot by my own, but I found it much larger. This filled me again with ridiculous whimsies, and when I went home, I began to double my fortifications, planted my seven muskets on carriages,[2] in the manner of cannon, and was at the expense of an infinite deal of labour, purely from my apprehensions of this print of a foot.

Rambling more to the western point one day than ever I had done before, I was presently convinced that the seeing the print of a man's foot was not such a strange thing in the island as I had imagined, for, on approaching the shore I was perfectly confounded and amazed, nor is it possible to express the horror I felt, at seeing the shore spread with the skulls, hands, feet, and other bones of human bodies, and particularly a place, where as I supposed, there had been a fire made, and a circle dug in the earth for the savage wretches to sit down to their inhuman feasts, on the bodies of their fellow-creatures.

I had now been twenty-two years in the island, and was so naturalized to the place, that had I been secure as to the savages, I then fancied I could have been contented to have staid in it till I had died of mere old age.

One morning very early, I saw five canoes of the savages on shore. I clambered up a hill, and, by the help of my perspective glass,[3] discovered no less than thirty dancing round a fire. I soon after saw two miserable wretches dragged out of the boats, one of whom was immediately knocked down, but the other starting from them, ran with incredible swiftness along the sands towards me. I confess I was horribly frightened when I saw him come my way, imagining he would be pursued by the whole body; however, I kept my station, and quite lost my apprehension when I found but three followed him. He greatly outran them, and was in a fair way of escaping them all, when, coming to a creek, he plunged into it, landed, and ran as swift as before. Of the three that followed, but two entered the water, the other returning back. I hastily fetched my guns from the foot of my ladder, and, taking a short cut down the hill, I

9. Knee-length pants.
1. Gaiters, spats.
2. Wheeled supports for mounting artillery.

3. Optical instrument for viewing objects at a distance.

clapped[4] myself in the way betwixt the pursued and the pursuers; then rushing at once on the foremost, knocked him down with the stock of my piece; the other stopped as if frightened, but when I advanced towards him, I perceived he was fitting his bow to shoot me, upon which I shot him dead directly. The poor savage who had fled, was so terrified at the noise of my piece, though he saw his enemies fallen, that he stood stock still, but seemed rather inclined to fly than come forwards. However, when I gave him signs of encouragement, he came nearer, kneeling down every ten or twelve steps. I then took him away to my cave at the farther part of the island. Here I gave him bread and a bunch of raisins to eat, and a draught of water, which he wanted much; and, having refreshed him, I made signs for him to lie down on some rice straw, which the poor creature did, and soon went to sleep. After he had slept about half an hour, he waked again, and came running to me in the enclosure just by. Then kneeling down again, he made all possible signs of thankfulness, subjection, and submission. I began to speak to him, and to teach him to speak to me; and first made him know that his name should be *Friday*, which was the day wherein I saved his life. I taught him to say *Master*, and let him know that was to be my name. The next day I gave him clothes, at which he seemed pleased.

Having now more courage, and consequently more curiosity, I took my man *Friday* with me, and marched to the place where his enemies had been. When we came there, my blood ran cold in my veins; the place was covered with human bones, and the ground dyed with blood; great pieces of flesh were left here and there half eaten,

4. Threw.

mangled, and scorched. We saw three skulls, five hands, and the bones of three or four legs and feet; and *Friday*, by his signs, made me understand that they brought over four prisoners to feast upon, and that three of them were eaten up; that he, pointing to himself, was the fourth, and that they had been conquered and taken in war. I caused *Friday* to collect the remains of this horrid carnage, then to light a fire, and burn them to ashes. When this was done, we returned to our castle.

I was now entered into the 27th year of my captivity, and intended soon to set sail, when one morning I bid *Friday* go to the sea shore to see if he could find a turtle; but he had not long been gone, when he came running back like one who felt not the ground on which he trod, and before I had time to speak, cried, *O Master! O Master! O sorrow! O bad!* What's the matter, *Friday*, said I? *O yonder, there*, said he, *one, two, three!* Well, *Friday*, said I, do not be frightened; he was, however, terribly scared, imagining that they were come to look for him, and would cut him in pieces, and eat him.

I then took my perspective glass and went up to the side of the hill, when I saw twenty-one savages, three prisoners, and three canoes. I bid him softly bring me word what they were doing; he did so, and coming back immediately, told me they were all about the fire, eating the flesh of one of their prisoners, and that a bearded man lay bound upon the sand, whom he said they would kill next. The news fired my soul, and filled me with horror, and, going to the tree, I plainly saw a white man clothed, lying on the beach with his hands and feet tied with flags. I had not a moment to lose, for nineteen of the horrid wretches sat huddled together on the ground, and the other two were stooping down to untie the Christian in order to murder him. Now, *Friday*, said I, do as you see me do. I laid the muskets down and took up one, and then we both fired; we then fired again, till seventeen of them were killed; and four of them getting into a canoe, got out to sea.

I resolved to pursue them, lest they should return with a greater force to destroy us, and ran to a canoe, calling to *Friday* to follow me; but I was no sooner in the canoe than I found another poor creature lying there alive, bound hand and foot; I immediately cut the twisted flags, and seeing that he had been bound so tight that he was almost dead, I gave him a dram,[5] and ordered *Friday* to tell him of his deliverance; but when the poor fellow looked in his face, and heard him speak, it would have moved any one to tears, to have seen how he kissed, embraced, hugged him, cried, danced, sang, and then cried again. It was some time before I could make him tell what was the matter, but when he came a little to himself, he said it was his own dear father. He then sat down by him, held the old man's head close to his bosom, and chafed his arms and ankles, which were stiff with binding.

The white man, who was a Spaniard, expressed the utmost gratitude for his deliverance, gave me an account of his shipwreck, and the situation of his companions; when we resolved that *Friday's* father and the *Spaniard* should go in the boat to fetch them over.

About eight days after they were gone, *Friday* awakened me one morning by crying out, *Master, they are come!* I dressed, and hastened to the top of the hill, and plainly discovered an *English* ship lying at anchor. At first I felt in my mind a tumult of joy, which was soon turned into fear; for, though I knew them to be my countrymen, I had reason to dread them as enemies.

They ran the boat ashore on the beach, and eleven men landed, three of them unarmed, who, by their gestures, seemed to be prisoners; and one of them I could

5. I.e., a small amount of alcohol.

perceive using the most passionate gestures of entreaty, affliction, and despair, while the two others, though their grief seemed less extravagant, appeared pleading for mercy. At this instant, I saw a villain lift up his arms to kill one of the prisoners, but he did not strike him. The men having left the prisoners, and gone into the woods, I went up to them with my man *Friday*, and said to them in *Spanish*, What are you, Gentlemen? They started at the noise, but prepared to fly. I then said in *English*, Gentlemen, perhaps you may have a friend near you, whom you would little expect. Tell me your case. I was commander of that ship, replied one of the prisoners; my men have mutinied against me; and if they do not murder me, they intend to leave me and these two gentlemen ashore in this desolate place; they are but in that thicket, and I tremble for fear they shall have seen you and heard us speak. Having concerted matters with the captain, and armed ourselves, we went to the sailors; and the captain reserving his own piece, the two men shot one of the villains dead, and wounded another. He who was wounded cried out for help, and I coming up, gave orders for sparing their lives, on condition of their being bound hand and foot while they staid in the Island.

A little after, another boat with ten men and fire arms approached the shore. We had a full view of them as they came; the captain told me three of them were peaceable fellows, but the rest were desperate wretches. Having formed an ambuscade,[6] I ordered *Friday* and the captain to creep upon their hands and feet, that they might not be seen, and to get very near them before they fired; but one of the principal ringleaders of the mutiny, with two of the crew, came towards us, and the captain was so eager at having him in his power, that he let fly, killing him and another on the spot, the third ran for it. I immediately advanced with my whole army, upon which *Will Atkins*, one of the ringleaders, called out, For God's sake, captain, spare my life, the rest are as bad as I. The captain told him he must lay down his arms at discretion,[7] and trust to the governor's mercy, upon which they all submitted.

It was now determined to seize the ship, which, with the assistance of the faithful part of the crew, the captain effected thus: Atkins and two of the worst were sent fast bound to the cave, and the rest committed to my bower. I sent the captain to tamper with[8] them, in the governor's name, offering them pardon, if they would assist him in recovering the ship; upon which they all agreed to stand by him till their last drop of blood. They were all released on these assurances; and then the captain repaired the other boat, making his passenger captain, with four men well armed; while his mate, himself, and five men more, went in the other. By midnight they came within call of the ship, when the captain ordered Robinson to hail her, and tell them that with great difficulty they had found the men at last. But while they were discoursing, the captain, his mate, and the rest entered, and knocking down the second mate and carpenter, secured those that were upon deck, by putting them under hatches, while the other boat's crew entered, and securing the forecastle, broke into the round-house,[9] where the mate, after some resistance, shot the pirate captain through the head; upon which all the rest yielded themselves prisoners. Thus the ship being recovered, the joyful signal was fired.

When I saw my deliverance thus put into my hands, I was ready to sink with surprise; I was not able to answer one word, but a flood of tears brought me to myself, and a little while after I recovered my speech. I then in my turn embraced the captain

6. Ambush.
7. Unconditionally.
8. Deal with.

9. A cabin or set of cabins on the ship's deck, serving as living quarters. "Forecastle": the forward part of a ship.

as my deliverer, and we rejoiced together. Having brought the prisoners before me, I asked them what they had to say in their own defence, telling them I had power to execute them there.

They pleaded the captain's promise of mercy. I then told them that I intended to go passenger in the ship, with all my men; but that they, if they went, could only go as prisoners; observing, however, that they might, if they chose it, stay in the island. This they gladly accepted, and I prepared to go on board the next day. The captain returning to the ship, got every thing ready for my reception.

When he was gone, I talked to the men, told them my story, how I managed my household business; instructed them in all I knew, and gave them my best advice with regard to their behavior to one another.

I divided the tools among them in this manner; to every man I gave a digging spade, a shovel, and a rake, as having no barrows or ploughs; and to every separate place a pick-axe, a crow, a broad axe, and a saw, with a store for a general supply, should any be broken or worn out. I left them also nails, staples, hinges, hammers, chisels, knives, scissors, and all sorts of tools and iron-work; and for the use of the smith, I gave him three tons of unwrought iron for a supply: and as to arms and ammunition, I stored them sufficiently to equip a little army. The next day I went on board the ship, taking *Friday* with me.

The next morning two of the men came swimming to the ship's side, desiring the captain to take them on board, even if he hung them afterwards, complaining mightily how barbarously the others used them. Upon which I prevailed with the captain to take them in, and, being severely whipped and pickled,[1] they proved more honest for the future. And so I bid farewell to the island, carrying along with me my money, parrot, umbrella, and goatskin-cap, setting sail December 12, 1686, after twenty-eight years, two months, and nineteen days' residence, the same day and month that I escaped from Sallee, landing in England June 11th, 1687, after thirty-five years' absence from my native country, which rendered me altogether a stranger to it. Some time after I went to *Lisbon,* to see after my effects in the *Brazils,* and found the generous captain, who had been so much my friend, still alive, and he put me in the way of recovering the produce of my plantations. And a few months after, there arrived ships in the *Tagus,* with effects for my use, to the amount of £50,000, besides £1000 a-year, which I expected to receive annually for my plantation.

And now resolved to harass myself no more, I am preparing for a longer journey than all those, for I have lived seventy-two years, chequered with infinite variety, and have been taught sufficiently the value of retirement, and the blessing of ending my days in peace, and in the true worship of my Almighty Deliverer.

FINIS.

---

1. Further punished by having salt or salt and vinegar rubbed into their wounds.

ERNEST THOMPSON SETON
1860–1946

"The life of a wild animal," wrote Ernest Thompson Seton, *always has a tragic end.*" Much of Seton's work as a naturalist, author, and illustrator relies on the close observation and detailed recording of those lives and deaths. Seton was born in England, the twelfth of fourteen children. In 1866 financial losses drove his father, who had been a prosperous shipowner, to settle his family first on one hundred acres of forest and farmland in Ontario, then in the city of Toronto. The ravines that still run like veins through the city fostered Seton's early inclinations as a naturalist—and provided sanctuary from his rough school, crowd of siblings, and brutal father. One summer, while in the country (he'd been ill and had been sent there to recover his health), Seton began his serious bird studies and had the adventures he later fictionalized in *Two Little Savages* (1903).

Because his father wanted him to be an illustrator, not a naturalist, Seton studied art, first in Toronto and then in London. Though he won a large scholarship to the Royal Academy of Arts, he took classes for only a few months. He spent most of the next five years in rural Manitoba, where his brothers were homesteading. He began the fieldwork that would lead to his first book, *A List of Mammals of Manitoba* (1886). He also started publishing little illustrated nature studies and stories in such popular periodicals as *Scribner's, St. Nicholas,* and *Century Magazine.* Elements of "Raggylug" appear in a very early nature study, "The True Story of a Little Gray Rabbit," which Seton published in September 1890 in *St. Nicholas,* under the name Ernest E. Thompson. Eventually, Seton published many of his stories in a collection, *Wild Animals I Have Known* (1898). He pursued further studies in art in New York and in Paris, where his realistic paintings of wolves attracted much attention in 1891. He went back to Paris to work on a book of animal anatomy specifically for artists. He returned to New York in 1896 and began a life of traveling through the wilderness, writing and illustrating books of natural history, and publishing animal stories and giving public lectures.

Also in 1896 Seton married Grace Gallatin; they had one child (who became a well-known nov-elist, Anya Seton). Grace collaborated on his publications for more than fifteen years, though they grew apart. In 1935, after they divorced, Seton married his longtime secretary, Julia Moss, who was deeply interested in Indian lore. After their farm property in Connecticut was repeatedly vandalized by local boys, Seton devised a response that had a lasting effect on children's culture. He invited the boys to learn woodcraft and what he called "Indian ways"; he celebrated and idealized Native Americans' ties to nature as he drew on boys' love of glory and group loyalty to shape their behavior. The Woodcraft Indians movement took off with the publication of *American Woodcraft for Boys* in 1902 and then a handbook, *The Birch-Bark Roll of the Wood-craft Indians* (1906). Sir Robert Baden-Powell borrowed heavily from Seton in his *Scouting for Boys* (1908), though Baden-Powell's model was military and not Indian. Seton was one of the founders of the Boy Scouts of America—becoming "Chief Scout" and writing *Boy Scouts of America: A Handbook of Woodcraft, Scouting, and Life-Craft* (1910). The Woodcraft Indians were incorporated into the larger organization, but Seton resigned in 1915 to protest its shift away from camping and woodcraft to uniforms and calls to arms.

Seton's instrumental role in the scouting movement may be largely forgotten, but as an originator of the realistic animal story, his place in the history of children's literature is secure. *Wild Animals I Have Known* was an instant international best-seller, bringing him fame and wealth; a story from it, "Raggylug: The Story of a Cottontail Rabbit," is included here. Seton received praise from other authors, including Rudyard Kipling, whose *Jungle Books* (1894, 1895) offered a different kind of animal story. By focusing on animals' struggle to survive, Seton created a significant new genre. The emphasis on how animals actually live in nature made his animals seem much more real than those of his contemporaries. He portrayed them as having human feelings and even, as in "Raggylug," a language that he claims to "translate." The Canadian novelist Margaret Atwood remembers her own childhood fascination with the animal tracks that Seton drew on the pages of his books, and she credits him with defining something characteristic in the national imagination. "The main thing," says Atwood in *Survival* (1972), a guide to Canadian literature, "was to avoid dying, and only by a mixture of cunning, experience and narrow escapes could the animal—or the human relying on his own resources—manage that." The reprieve is likely to be only temporary.

Raggylug: The Story of a Cottontail Rabbit

Raggylug, or Rag, was the name of a young cottontail rabbit. It was given him from his torn and ragged ear, a life-mark that he got in his first adventure. He lived with his mother in Olifant's swamp, where I made their acquaintance and gathered, in a hundred different ways, the little bits of proof and scraps of truth that at length enabled me to write this history.

Those who do not know the animals well may think I have humanized them, but those who have lived so near them as to know somewhat of their ways and their minds will not think so.

Truly rabbits have no speech as we understand it, but they have a way of conveying ideas by a system of sounds, signs, scents, whisker-touches, movements, and example that answers the purpose of speech; and it must be remembered that though in telling this story I freely translate from rabbit into English, *I repeat nothing that they did not say*.

I

The rank swamp grass bent over and concealed the snug nest where Raggylug's mother had hidden him. She had partly covered him with some of the bedding, and, as always, her last warning was to 'lay low and say nothing, whatever happens.' Though tucked in bed, he was wide awake and his bright eyes were taking in that part of his little green world that was straight above. A bluejay and a red-squirrel, two notorious thieves, were loudly berating each other for stealing, and at one time Rag's home bush was the centre of their fight; a yellow warbler caught a blue butterfly but six inches from his nose, and a scarlet and black ladybug, serenely waving her knobbed feelers, took a long walk up one grassblade, down another, and across the nest and over Rag's face—and yet he never moved nor even winked.

After a while he heard a strange rustling of the leaves in the near thicket. It was an odd, continuous sound, and though it went this way and that way and came ever nearer, there was no patter of feet with it. Rag had lived his whole life in the Swamp (he was three weeks old) and yet had never heard anything like this. Of course his curiosity was greatly aroused. His mother had cautioned him to lay low, but that was understood to be in case of danger, and this strange sound without footfalls could not be anything to fear.

The low rasping went past close at hand, then to the right, then back, and seemed going away. Rag felt he knew what he was about; he wasn't a baby; it was his duty to learn what it was. He slowly raised his roly-poly body on his short fluffy legs, lifted his little round head above the covering of his nest and peeped out into the woods. The sound had ceased as soon as he moved. He saw nothing, so took one step forward to a clear view, and instantly found himself face to face with an enormous Black Serpent.

"Mammy," he screamed in mortal terror as the monster darted at him. With all the strength of his tiny limbs he tried to run. But in a flash the Snake had him by one ear and whipped around him with his coils to gloat over the helpless little baby bunny he had secured for dinner.

"Mam-my—Mam-my," gasped poor little Raggylug as the cruel monster began slowly choking him to death. Very soon the little one's cry would have ceased, but bounding through the woods straight as an arrow came Mammy. No longer a shy, helpless little Molly Cottontail, ready to fly from a shadow: the mother's love was strong in her. The cry of her baby had filled her with the courage of a hero, and— hop, she went over that horrible reptile. Whack, she struck down at him with her sharp hind claws as she passed, giving him such a stinging blow that he squirmed with pain and hissed with anger.

"M-a-m-m-y," came feebly from the little one. And Mammy came leaping again and again and struck harder and fiercer until the loathsome reptile let go the little one's ear and tried to bite the old one as she leaped over. But all he got was a mouthful of wool each time, and Molly's fierce blows began to tell, as long bloody rips were torn in the Black Snake's scaly armor.

Things were now looking bad for the Snake; and bracing himself for the next charge, he lost his tight hold on Baby Bunny, who at once wriggled out of the coils and away into the underbrush, breathless and terribly frightened, but unhurt save that his left ear was much torn by the teeth of that dreadful Serpent.

Molly now had gained all she wanted. She had no notion of fighting for glory or revenge. Away she went into the woods and the little one followed the shining beacon of her snow-white tail until she led him to a safe corner of the Swamp.

II

Old Olifant's Swamp was a rough, brambly tract of second-growth woods, with a marshy pond and a stream through the middle. A few ragged remnants of the old forest still stood in it and a few of the still older trunks were lying about as dead logs in the brushwood. The land about the pond was of that willow-grown sedgy kind that cats and horses avoid, but that cattle do not fear. The drier zones were overgrown with briars and young trees. The outermost belt of all, that next the fields, was of thrifty, gummy-trunked young pines whose living needles in air and dead ones on earth offer so delicious an odor to the nostrils of the passer-by, and so deadly a breath to those seedlings that would compete with them for the worthless waste they grow on.

All around for a long way were smooth fields, and the only wild tracks that ever crossed these fields were those of a thoroughly bad and unscrupulous fox that lived only too near.

The chief indwellers of the swamp were Molly and Rag. Their nearest neighbors were far away, and their nearest kin were dead. This was their home, and here they lived together, and here Rag received the training that made his success in life.

Molly was a good little mother and gave him a careful bringing up. The first thing he learned was 'to lay low and say nothing.' His adventure with the snake taught him the wisdom of this. Rag never forgot that lesson; afterward he did as he was told, and it made the other things come more easily.

The second lesson he learned was 'freeze.' It grows out of the first, and Rag was taught it as soon as he could run.

'Freezing' is simply doing nothing, turning into a statue. As soon as he finds a foe near, no matter what he is doing, a well-trained Cottontail keeps just as he is and stops all movement, for the creatures of the woods are of the same color as the things in the woods and catch the eye only while moving. So when enemies chance together, the one who first sees the other can keep himself unseen by 'freezing' and thus have all the advantage of choosing the time for attack or escape. Only those who live in the woods know the importance of this; every wild creature and every hunter must learn it; all learn to do it well, but not one of them can beat Molly Cottontail in the doing. Rag's mother taught him this trick by example. When the white cotton cushion that she always carried to sit on went bobbing away through the woods, of course Rag ran his hardest to keep up. But when Molly stopped and 'froze,' the natural wish to copy made him do the same.

But the best lesson of all that Rag learned from his mother was the secret of the Brierbrush. It is a very old secret now, and to make it plain you must first hear why the Brierbrush quarrelled with the beasts.

Long ago the Roses used to grow on bushes that had no thorns. But the Squirrels and Mice used to climb after them, the Cattle used to knock them off with their horns, the Possum[1] would twitch them off with his long tail, and the Deer, with his sharp hoofs, would break them down. So the Brierbrush armed itself with spikes to protect its roses and declared eternal war on all creatures that climbed trees, or had horns, or hoofs, or long tails. This left the Brierbrush at peace with none but Molly Cottontail, who could not climb, was hornless, hoofless, and had scarcely any tail at all.

In truth the Cottontail had never harmed a Brierrose, and having now so many enemies the Rose took the Rabbit into especial friendship, and when dangers are threatening poor Bunny he flies to the nearest Brierbrush, certain that it is ready with a million keen and poisoned daggers to defend him.

So the secret that Rag learned from his mother was, 'The Brierbush is your best friend.'

Much of the time that season was spent in learning the lay of the land, and the

---

1. I.e., an opossum.

bramble and brier mazes. And Rag learned them so well that he could go all around the swamp by two different ways and never leave the friendly briers at any place for more than five hops.

It is not long since the foes of the Cottontails were disgusted to find that man had brought a new kind of bramble and planted it in long lines throughout the country. It was so strong that no creatures could break it down, and so sharp that the toughest skin was torn by it. Each year there was more of it and each year it became a more serious matter to the wild creatures. But Molly Cottontail had no fear of it. She was not brought up in the briers for nothing. Dogs and foxes, cattle and sheep, and even man himself might be torn by those fearful spikes: but Molly understands it and lives and thrives under it. And the further it spreads the more safe country there is for the Cottontail. And the name of this new and dreaded bramble is—*the barbed-wire fence.*

III

Molly had no other children to look after now, so Rag had all her care. He was unusually quick and bright as well as strong, and he had uncommonly good chances; so he got on remarkably well.

All the season she kept him busy learning the tricks of the trail, and what to eat and drink and what not to touch. Day by day she worked to train him; little by little she taught him, putting into his mind hundreds of ideas that her own life or early training had stored in hers, and so equipped him with the knowledge that makes life possible to their kind.

Close by her side in the clover-field or the thicket he would sit and copy her when she wobbled her nose 'to keep her smeller clear,' and pull the bite from her mouth or taste her lips to make sure he was getting the same kind of fodder. Still copying her, he learned to comb his ears with his claws and to dress[2] his coat and to bite the burrs out of his vest and socks. He learned, too, that nothing but clear dewdrops from the briers were fit for a rabbit to drink, as water which has once touched the earth must surely bear some taint. Thus he began the study of woodcraft, the oldest of all sciences.

As soon as Rag was big enough to go out alone, his mother taught him the signal

code. Rabbits telegraph each other by thumping on the ground with their hind feet. Along the ground sound carries far; a thump that at six feet from the earth is not heard at twenty yards will, near the ground, be heard at least one hundred yards. Rabbits have very keen hearing, and so might hear this same thump at two hundred yards, and that would reach from end to end of Olifant's Swamp. A single *thump* means 'look out' or 'freeze.' A slow *thump thump* means 'come.' A fast *thump thump* means 'danger;' and a very fast *thump thump thump* means 'run for dear life.'

At another time, when the weather was fine and the bluejays were quarreling among themselves, a sure sign that no dangerous foe was

2. Groom.

about, Rag began a new study. Molly, by flattening her ears, gave the sign to squat. Then she ran far away in the thicket and gave the thumping signal for 'come.' Rag set out at a run to the place but could not find Molly. He thumped, but got no reply. Setting carefully about his search he found her foot-scent and following this strange guide, that the beasts all know so well and man does not know at all, he worked out the trail and found her where she was hidden. Thus he got his first lesson in trailing, and thus it was that the games of hide and seek they played became the schooling for the serious chase of which there was so much in his after life.

Before that first season of schooling was over he had learnt all the principal tricks by which a rabbit lives and in not a few problems showed himself a veritable genius.

He was an adept at 'tree,' 'dodge,' and 'squat,' he could play 'log-lump,' with 'wind' and 'baulk' with 'back-track' so well that he scarcely needed any other tricks. He had not yet tried it, but he knew just how to play 'barb-wire,' which is a new trick of the brilliant order; he had made a special study of 'sand,' which burns up all scent, and he was deeply versed in 'change-off,' 'fence,' and 'double' as well as 'hole-up,' which is a trick requiring longer notice, and yet he never forgot that 'lay-low' is the beginning of all wisdom and 'brierbush' the only trick that is always safe.

He was taught the signs by which to know all his foes and then the way to baffle them. For hawks, owls, foxes, hounds, curs, minks, weasels, cats, skunks, coons,[3] and men, each have a different plan of pursuit, and for each and all of these evils he was taught a remedy.

And for knowledge of the enemy's approach he learnt to depend first on himself and his mother, and then on the bluejay. "Never neglect the bluejay's warning," said Molly; "he is a mischief-maker, a marplot,[4] and a thief all the time, but nothing escapes him. He wouldn't mind harming us, but he cannot, thanks to the briers, and his enemies are ours, so it is well to heed him. If the woodpecker cries a warning you can trust him, he is honest; but he is a fool beside the bluejay, and though the bluejay often tells lies for mischief you are safe to believe him when he brings ill news."

The barb-wire trick takes a deal of nerve and the best of legs. It was long before Rag ventured to play it, but as he came to his full powers it became one of his favorites.

"It's fine play for those who can do it," said Molly. "First you lead off your dog on a straightaway and warm him up a bit by nearly letting him catch you. Then keeping just one hop ahead, you lead him at a long slant full tilt into a breast-high barb-wire. I've seen many a dog and fox crippled, and one big hound killed outright this way. But I've also seen more than one rabbit lose his life in trying it."

Rag early learnt what some rabbits never learn at all, that 'hole-up' is not such a fine ruse as it seems; it may be the certain safety of a wise rabbit, but soon or late is a sure death-trap to a fool. A young rabbit always thinks of it first, an old rabbit never tries it till all others fail. It means escape from a man or dog, a fox or a bird of prey, but it means sudden death if the foe is a ferret, mink, skunk, or weasel.

There were but two ground-holes in the Swamp. One on the Sunning Bank, which was a dry sheltered knoll in the South-end. It was open and sloping to the sun, and here on fine days the Cottontails took their sunbaths. They stretched out among the fragrant pine needles and winter-green in odd cat-like positions, and turned slowly over as though roasting and wishing all sides well done. And they blinked and panted,

---

3. I.e., raccoons.
4. One who deliberately interferes with or frustrates a plot.

and squirmed as if in dreadful pain; yet this was one of the keenest enjoyments they knew.

Just over the brow of the knoll was a large pine stump. Its grotesque roots wriggled out above the yellow sandbank like dragons, and under their protecting claws a sulky old woodchuck had digged a den long ago. He became more sour and ill-tempered as weeks went by, and one day waited to quarrel with Olifant's dog instead of going in so that Molly Cottontail was able to take possession of the den an hour later.

This, the pine-root hole, was afterward very coolly taken by a self-sufficient young skunk who with less valor might have enjoyed greater longevity, for he imagined that even man with a gun would fly from him. Instead of keeping Molly from the den for good, therefore, his reign, like that of a certain Hebrew king,[5] was over in seven days.

The other, the fern-hole, was in a fern thicket next the clover field. It was small and damp, and useless except as a last retreat. It also was the work of a woodchuck, a well-meaning friendly neighbor, but a hare-brained youngster whose skin in the form of a whip-lash[6] was now developing higher horse-power in the Olifant working team.

"Simple justice," said the old man, "for that hide was raised on stolen feed that the team would a' turned into horse-power anyway."

The Cottontails were now sole owners of the holes, and did not go near them when they could help it, lest anything like a path should be made that might betray these last retreats to an enemy.

There was also the hollow hickory, which, though nearly fallen, was still green, and had the great advantage of being open at both ends. This had long been the residence of one Lotor, a solitary old coon whose ostensible calling was frog-hunting, and who, like the monks of old, was supposed to abstain from all flesh food. But it was shrewdly suspected that he needed but a chance to indulge in a diet of rabbit. When at last one dark night he was killed while raiding Olifant's hen-house, Molly, so far from feeling a pang of regret, took possession of his cosy nest with a sense of unbounded relief.

IV

Bright August sunlight was flooding the Swamp in the morning. Everything seemed soaking in the warm radiance. A little brown swamp-sparrow was teetering on a long rush in the pond. Beneath him there were open spaces of dirty water that brought down a few scraps of the blue sky, and worked it and the yellow duckweed into an exquisite mosaic, with a little wrong-side picture[7] of the bird in the middle. On the bank behind was a great vigorous growth of golden green skunk-cabbage, that cast dense shadow over the brown swamp tussocks.[8]

The eyes of the swamp-sparrow were not trained to take in the color glories, but he saw what we might have missed; that two of the numberless leafy brown bumps under the broad cabbage-leaves were furry living things, with noses that never ceased to move up and down whatever else was still.

It was Molly and Rag. They were stretched under the skunk-cabbage, not because they liked its rank smell, but because the winged ticks could not stand it at all and so left them in peace.

---

5. I.e., Zimri, a servant who conspired and killed a king; the people rose up against him (1 Kings 16.8–25).

6. I.e., a whip made out of the woodchuck's skin.

7. I.e., a reflection in the water.

8. A dense tuft of vegetation, or an area of solid ground in a marsh.

Rabbits have no set time for lessons, they are always learning; but what the lesson is depends on the present stress, and that must arrive before it is known. They went to this place for a quiet rest, but had not been long there when suddenly a warning note from the ever-watchful bluejay caused Molly's nose and ears to go up and her tail to tighten to her back. Away across the Swamp was Olifant's big black and white dog, coming straight toward them.

"Now," said Molly, "squat while I go and keep that fool out of mischief." Away she went to meet him and she fearlessly dashed across the dog's path.

"Bow-ow-ow," he fairly yelled as he bounded after Molly, but she kept just beyond his reach and led him where the million daggers struck fast and deep, till his tender ears were scratched raw, and guided him at last plump into a hidden barbed-wire fence, where he got such a gashing that he went homeward howling with pain. After making a short double, a loop and a baulk in case the dog should come back, Molly returned to find that Rag in his eagerness was standing bolt upright and craning his neck to see the sport.

This disobedience made her so angry that she struck him with her hind foot and knocked him over in the mud.

One day as they fed on the near clover field a red-tailed hawk came swooping after them. Molly kicked up her hind legs to make fun of him and skipped into the briers along one of their old pathways, where of course the hawk could not follow. It was the main path from the Creekside Thicket to the Stove-pipe brush-pile. Several creepers had grown across it, and Molly, keeping one eye on the hawk, set to work and cut the creepers off. Rag watched her, then ran on ahead, and cut some more that were across the path. "That's right," said Molly, "always keep the runways clear, you will need them often enough. Not wide, but clear. Cut everything like a creeper across them and some day you will find you have cut a snare. "A what?" asked Rag, as he scratched his right ear with his left hind foot.

"A snare is something that looks like a creeper, but it doesn't grow and it's worse than all the hawks in the world," said Molly, glancing at the now far-away red-tail, "for there it hides night and day in the runway till the chance to catch you comes."

"I don't believe it could catch me," said Rag, with the pride of youth as he rose on his heels to rub his chin and whiskers high up on a smooth sapling. Rag did not know he was doing this, but his mother saw and knew it was a sign, like the changing of a boy's voice, that her little one was no longer a baby but would soon be a grown-up Cottontail.

V

There is magic in running water. Who does not know it and feel it? The railroad builder fearlessly throws his bank across the wide bog or lake, or the sea itself, but the tiniest rill of running water he treats with great respect, studies its wish and its way and gives it all it seems to ask. The thirst-parched traveller in the poisonous alkali deserts[9] holds back in deadly fear from the sedgy ponds till he finds one down whose centre is a thin, clear line, and a faint flow, the sign of running, living water, and joyfully he drinks.

There is magic in running water, no evil spell can cross it. Tam O'Shanter[1] proved

9. Deserts containing mineral salts that form strongly basic solutions in water.
1. In "Tam O'Shanter" (1790), a poem by Robert Burns, Tam saves himself from witches by managing to get to the middle of the river—a safe zone—before they reach him.

its potency in time of sorest need. The wild-wood creature with its deadly foe follow-ing tireless on the trail scent, realizes its nearing doom and feels an awful spell. Its strength is spent, its every trick is tried in vain till the good Angel leads it to the water, the running, living water, and dashing in it follows the cooling stream, and then with force renewed takes to the woods again.

There is magic in running water. The hounds come to the very spot and halt and cast about; and halt and cast in vain. Their spell is broken by the merry stream, and the wild thing lives its life.

And this was one of the great secrets that Raggylug learned from his mother—"after the Brierrose, the Water is your friend."

One hot, muggy night in August, Molly led Rag through the woods. The cotton-white cushion she wore under her tail twinkled ahead and was his guiding lantern, though it went out as soon as she stopped and sat on it. After a few runs and stops to listen, they came to the edge of the pond. The hylas[2] in the trees above them were singing 'sleep, sleep,' and away out on a sunken log in the deep water, up to his chin in the cooling bath, a bloated bullfrog was singing the praises of a 'jug o' rum.'

"Follow me still," said Molly, in rabbit, and 'flop' she went into the pond and struck out for the sunken log in the middle. Rag flinched but plunged with a little 'ouch,' gasping and wobbling his nose very fast but still copying his mother. The same move-ments as on land sent him through the water, and thus he found he could swim. On he went till he reached the sunken log and scrambled up by his dripping mother on the high dry end, with a rushy screen around them and the Water that tells no tales. After this in warm black nights when that old fox from Springfield came prowling through the Swamp, Rag would note the place of the bullfrog's voice, for in case of direst need it might be a guide to safety. And thenceforth the words of the song that the bullfrog sang were, 'Come, come, in danger come.'

This was the latest study that Rag took up with his mother—it was really a post-graduate course, for many little rabbits never learn it at all.

VI

No wild animal dies of old age. Its life has soon or late a tragic end. It is only a question of how long it can hold out against its foes. But Rag's life was proof that once a rabbit passes out of his youth he is likely to outlive his prime and be killed only in the last third of life, the downhill third we call old age.

The Cottontails had enemies on every side. Their daily life was a series of escapes. For dogs, foxes, cats, skunks, coons, weasels, minks, snakes, hawks, owls, and men, and even insects were all plotting to kill them. They had hundreds of adventures, and at least once a day they had to fly for their lives and save themselves by their legs and wits.

More than once that hateful fox from Springfield drove them to taking refuge under the wreck of a barbed-wire hog-pen by the spring. But once there they could look calmly at him while he spiked his legs in vain attempts to reach them.

Once or twice Rag when hunted had played off the hound against a skunk that had seemed likely to be quite as dangerous as the dog.

Once he was caught alive by a hunter who had a hound and a ferret to help him. But Rag had the luck to escape next day, with a yet deeper distrust of ground holes. He was several times run into the water by the cat, and many times was chased by hawks and owls, but for each kind of danger there was a safeguard. His mother taught

2. Tree frogs (*Hyla* is their genus).

him the principal dodges, and he improved on them and made many new ones as he grew older. And the older and wiser he grew the less he trusted to his legs, and the more to his wits for safety.

Ranger was the name of a young hound in the neighborhood. To train him his master used to put him on the trail of one of the Cottontails. It was nearly always Rag that they ran, for the young buck enjoyed the runs as much as they did, the spice of danger in them being just enough for zest. He would say:

"Oh, mother! here comes the dog again, I must have a run to-day."

"You are too bold, Raggy, my son!" she might reply. "I fear you will run once too often."

"But, mother, it is such glorious fun to tease that fool dog, and it's all good training. I'll thump if I am too hard pressed, then you can come and change off while I get my second wind."

Oh he would come, and Ranger would take the trail and follow till Rag got tired of it. Then he either sent a thumping telegram for help, which brought Molly to take charge of the dog, or he got rid of the dog by some clever trick. A description of one of these shows how well Rag had learned the arts of the woods.

He knew that his scent lay best near the ground, and was strongest when he was warm. So if he could get off the ground, and be left in peace for half an hour to cool off, and for the trail to stale, he knew he would be safe. When, therefore, he tired of the chase, he made for the Creekside brier-patch, where he 'wound'—that is, zig-zagged—till he left a course so crooked that the dog was sure to be greatly delayed in working it out.[3] He then went straight to D in the woods, passing one hop to windward of the high log E. Stopping at D, he followed his back trail to F, here he leaped aside and ran toward G. Then, returning on his trail to J, he waited till the hound passed on his trail at I. Rag then got back on his old trail at H, and followed it to E, where, with a scent-baulk or great leap aside, he reached the high log, and running to its higher end, he sat like a bump.

Ranger lost much time in the bramble maze, and the scent was very poor when he got it straightened out, and came to D. Here he began to circle to pick it up, and after losing much time, struck the trail which ended suddenly at G. Again he was at fault, and had to circle to find the trail. Wider and wider the circles, until at last, he passed right under the log Rag was on. But a cold scent, on a cold day, does not go downward much. Rag never budged nor winked, and the hound passed.

Again the dog came round. This time he crossed the low part of the log, and stopped to smell it. 'Yes, clearly it was rabbity,' but it was a stale scent now; still he mounted the log.

It was a trying moment for Rag, as the great hound came sniff-sniffing along the log. But his nerve did not forsake him; the wind was right; he had his mind made up to bolt as soon as Ranger came half way up. But he didn't come. A yellow cur would have seen the rabbit sitting there, but the hound did not, and the scent seemed stale, so he leaped off the log, and Rag had won.

VII

Rag had never seen any other rabbit than his mother. Indeed he had scarcely thought about there being any other. He was more and more away from her now, and yet he never felt lonely, for rabbits do not hanker for company. But one day in December, while he was among the red dogwood brush, cutting a new path to the great Creekside

---

3. A small map of the woods, showing points A–J, accompanies the text in *Wild Animals I Have Known*.

thicket, he saw all at once against the sky over the Sunning Rank the head and ears of a strange rabbit. The newcomer had the air of a well-pleased discoverer and soon came hopping Rag's way along one of *his* paths into *his* Swamp. A new feeling rushed over him, that boiling mixture of anger and hatred called jealousy.

The stranger stopped at one of Rag's rubbing-trees—that is, a tree against which he used to stand on his heels and rub his chin as far up as he could reach. He thought he did this simply because he liked it; but all buck-rabbits do so, and several ends are served. It makes the tree rabbity, so that other rabbits know that this swamp already belongs to a rabbit family and is not open for settlement. It also lets the next one know by the scent if the last caller was an acquaintance, and the height from the ground of the rubbing-places shows how tall the rabbit is.

Now to his disgust Rag noticed that the newcomer was a head taller than himself, and a big, stout buck at that. This was a wholly new experience and filled Rag with a wholly new feeling. The spirit of murder entered his heart; he chewed very hard with nothing in his mouth, and hopping forward onto a smooth piece of hard ground he struck slowly:

'Thump—thump—thump,' which is a rabbit telegram for, 'Get out of my swamp, or fight.'

The new-comer made a big V with his ears, sat upright for a few seconds, then, dropping on his fore-feet, sent along the ground a louder, stronger, 'Thump—thump—thump.'

And so war was declared.

They came together by short runs side-wise, each one trying to get the wind of the other and watching for a chance advantage. The stranger was a big, heavy buck with plenty of muscle, but one or two trifles such as treading on a turnover and failing to close when Rag was on low ground showed that he had not much cunning and counted on winning his battles by his weight. On he came at last and Rag met him like a little fury. As they came together they leaped up and struck out with their hind feet. *Thud, thud* they came, and down went poor little Rag. In a moment the stranger was on him with his teeth and Rag was bitten, and lost several tufts of hair before he could get up. But he was swift of foot and got out of reach. Again he charged and again he was knocked down and bitten severely. He was no match for his foe, and it soon became a question of saving his own life.

Hurt as he was he sprang away, with the stranger in full chase, and bound to kill him as well as to oust him from the Swamp where he was born. Rag's legs were good and so was his wind. The stranger was big and so heavy that he soon gave up the chase, and it was well for poor Rag that he did, for he was getting stiff from his wounds as well as tired. From that day began a reign of terror for Rag. His training had been against owls, dogs, weasels, men, and so on, but what to do when chased by another rabbit, he did not know. All he knew was to lay low till he was found, then run.

Poor little Molly was completely terrorized; she could not help Rag and sought only to hide. But the big buck soon found her out. She tried to run from him, but she was not now so swift as Rag. The stranger made no attempt to kill her, but he made love to her, and because she hated him and tried to get away, he treated her shamefully. Day after day he worried her by following her about, and often, furious at her lasting hatred, he would knock her down and tear out mouthfuls of her soft fur till his rage cooled somewhat, when he would let her go for a while. But his fixed purpose was to kill Rag, whose escape seemed hopeless. There was no other swamp he could go to, and whenever he took a nap now he had to be ready at any moment to dash for his life. A dozen times a day the big stranger came creeping up to where he slept, but each time the watchful Rag awoke in time to escape. To escape yet not to escape. He saved his life indeed, but oh! what a miserable life it had become. How maddening to be thus helpless, to see his little mother daily beaten and torn, as well as to see all his favorite feeding-grounds, the cosy nooks, and the pathways he had made with so much labor, forced from him by this hateful brute. Unhappy Rag realized that to the victor belong the spoils, and he hated him more than ever he did fox or ferret.

How was it to end? He was wearing out with running and watching and bad food, and little Molly's strength and spirit were breaking down under the long persecution. The stranger was ready to go to all lengths to destroy poor Rag, and at last stooped to the worst crime known among rabbits. However much they may hate each other, all good rabbits forget their feuds when their common enemy appears. Yet one day when a great goshawk came swooping over the Swamp, the stranger, keeping well under cover himself, tried again and again to drive Rag into the open.

Once or twice the hawk nearly had him, but still the briers saved him, and it was only when the big buck himself came near being caught that he gave it up. And again Rag escaped, but was no better off. He made up his mind to leave, with his mother, if possible, next night and go into the world in quest of some new home when he heard old Thunder, the hound, sniffing and searching about the outskirts of the swamp, and he resolved on playing a desperate game. He deliberately crossed the hound's view, and the chase that then began was fast and furious. Thrice around the Swamp they went till Rag had made sure that his mother was hidden safely and that his hated foe was in his usual nest. Then right into that nest and plump over him he jumped, giving him a rap with one hind foot as he passed over his head.

"You miserable fool, I kill you yet," cried the stranger, and up he jumped only to find himself between Rag and the dog and heir to all the peril of the chase.

On came the hound baying hotly on the straight-away scent. The buck's weight and size were great advantages in a rabbit fight, but now they were fatal. He did not know many tricks. Just the simple ones like 'double,' 'wind,' and 'hole-up,' that every baby Bunny knows. But the chase was too close for doubling and winding, and he didn't know where the holes were.

It was a straight race. The brier-rose, kind to all rabbits alike, did its best, but it was no use. The baying of the hound was fast and steady. The crashing of the brush and the yelping of the hound each time the briers tore his tender ears were borne to the two rabbits where they crouched in hiding. But suddenly these sounds stopped, there was a scuffle, then loud and terrible screaming.

Rag knew what it meant and it sent a shiver through him, but he soon forgot that when all was over and rejoiced to be once more the master of the dear old Swamp.

VIII

Old Olifant had doubtless a right to burn all those brush-piles in the east and south of the Swamp and to clear up the wreck of the old barbed-wire hog-pen just below the spring. But it was none the less hard on Rag and his mother. The first were their various residences and outposts, and the second their grand fastness and safe retreat.

They had so long held the Swamp and felt it to be their very own in every part and suburb,—including Olifant's grounds and buildings—that they would have resented the appearance of another rabbit even about the adjoining barnyard.

Their claim, that of long, successful occupancy, was exactly the same as that by which most nations hold their land, and it would be hard to find a better right.

During the time of the January thaw the Olifants had cut the rest of the large wood about the pond and curtailed the Cottontails' domain on all sides. But they still clung to the dwindling Swamp, for it was their home and they were loath to move to foreign parts. Their life of daily perils went on, but they were still fleet of foot, long of wind, and bright of wit. Of late they had been somewhat troubled by a mink that had wandered up-stream to their quiet nook. A little judicious guidance had transferred the uncomfortable visitor to Olifant's hen-house. But they were not yet quite sure that he had been properly looked after. So for the present they gave up using the ground-holes, which were, of course, dangerous blind-alleys, and stuck closer than ever to the briers and the brush-piles that were left.

That first snow had quite gone and the weather was bright and warm until now. Molly, feeling a touch of rheumatism, was somewhere in the lower thicket seeking a teaberry tonic. Rag was sitting in the weak sunlight on a bank in the east side. The smoke from the familiar gable chimney of Olifant's house came fitfully drifting a pale blue haze through the underwoods and showing as a dull brown against the brightness of the sky. The sun-gilt gable was cut off midway by the banks of brier-brush, that purple in shadow shone like rods of blazing crimson and gold in the light. Beyond the house the barn with its gable and roof, new gilt as the house, stood up like a Noah's ark.

The sounds that came from it, and yet more the delicious smell that mingled with the smoke, told Rag that the animals were being fed cabbage in the yard. Rag's mouth watered at the idea of the feast. He blinked and blinked as he snuffed its odorous promises, for he loved cabbage dearly. But then he had been to the barnyard the night before after a few paltry clover-tops, and no wise rabbit would go two nights running to the same place.

Therefore he did the wise thing. He moved across where he could not smell the cabbage and made his supper of a bundle of hay that had been blown from the stack. Later, when about to settle for the night, he was joined by Molly, who had taken her teaberry and then eaten her frugal meal of sweet birch near the Sunning Bank.

Meanwhile the sun had gone about his business elsewhere, taking all his gold and glory with him. Off in the east a big black shutter came pushing up and rising higher and higher; it spread over the whole sky, shut out all light and left the world a very gloomy place indeed. Then another mischief-maker, the wind, taking advantage of the sun's absence, came on the scene and set about brewing trouble. The weather turned colder and colder; it seemed worse than when the ground had been covered with snow.

"Isn't this terribly cold? How I wish we had our stove-pipe brush-pile," said Rag.

"A good night for the pine-root hole," replied Molly, "but we have not yet seen the pelt of that mink on the end of the barn, and it is not safe till we do."

The hollow hickory was gone—in fact at this very moment its trunk, lying in the wood-yard, was harboring the mink they feared. So the Cottontails hopped to the south side of the pond and, choosing a brush-pile, they crept under and snuggled down for the night, facing the wind but with their noses in different directions so as to go out different ways in case of alarm. The wind blew harder and colder as the hours went by, and about midnight a fine icy snow came ticking down on the dead leaves and hissing through the brush heap. It might seem a poor night for hunting, but that old fox from Springfield was out. He came pointing up the wind in the shelter of the Swamp and chanced in the lee of the brush-pile, where he scented the sleeping Cottontails. He halted for a moment, then came stealthily sneaking up toward the brush under which his nose told him the rabbits were crouching. The noise of the wind and the sleet enabled him to come quite close before Molly heard the faint crunch of a dry leaf under his paw. She touched Rag's whiskers, and both were fully awake just as the fox sprang on them; but they always slept with their legs ready for a jump. Molly darted out into the blinding storm. The fox missed his spring but followed like a racer, while Rag dashed off to one side.

There was only one road for Molly; that was straight up the wind, and bounding for her life she gained a little over the unfrozen mud that would not carry the fox, till she reached the margin of the pond. No chance to turn now, on she must go.

Splash! splash! through the weeds she went, then plunge into the deep water.

And plunge went the fox close behind. But it was too much for Reynard[4] on such a night. He turned back, and Molly, seeing only one course, struggled through the reeds into the deep water and struck out for the other shore. But there was a strong headwind. The little waves, icy cold, broke over her head as she swam, and the water was full of snow that blocked her way like soft ice, or floating mud. The dark line of the other shore seemed far, far away, with perhaps the fox waiting for her there.

But she laid her ears flat to be out of the gale, and bravely put forth all her strength with wind and tide against her. After a long, weary swim in the cold water, she had nearly reached the farther reeds when a great mass of floating snow barred her road; then the wind on the bank made strange, fox-like sounds that robbed her of all force, and she was drifted far backward before she could get free from the floating bar.

Again she struck out, but slowly—oh so slowly now. And when at last she reached the lee[5] of the tall reeds, her limbs were numbed, her strength spent, her brave little heart was sinking, and she cared no more whether the fox were there or not. Through the reeds she did indeed pass, but once in the weeds her course wavered and slowed, her feeble strokes no longer sent her landward, the ice forming around her, stopped her altogether. In a little while the cold, weak limbs ceased to move, the furry nose-tip of the little mother Cottontail wobbled no more, and the soft brown eyes were closed in death.

But there was no fox waiting to tear her with ravenous jaws. Rag had escaped the first onset of the foe, and as soon as he regained his wits he came running back to change-off and so help his mother. He met the old fox going round the pond to meet Molly and led him far and away, then dismissed him with a barbed-wire gash on his head, and came to the bank and sought about and trailed and thumped, but all his searching was in vain; he could not find his little mother. He never saw her again, and he never knew whither she went, for she slept her never-waking sleep in the ice-arms of her friend the Water that tells no tales.

Poor little Molly Cottontail! She was a true heroine, yet only one of unnumbered millions that without a thought of heroism have lived and done their best in their little world, and died. She fought a good fight in the battle of life. She was good stuff; the stuff that never dies. For flesh of her flesh and brain of her brain was Rag. She lives in him, and through him transmits a finer fibre to her race.

And Rag still lives in the Swamp. Old Olifant died that winter, and the unthrifty sons ceased to clear the Swamp or mend the wire fences. Within a single year it was a wilder place than ever; fresh trees and brambles grew, and falling wires made many Cottontail castles and last retreats that dogs and foxes dared not storm. And there to this day lives Rag. He is a big strong buck now and fears no rivals. He has a large

4. The fox, after the fox-hero of the 14th-century French epic *Roman de Renart*.   5. Shelter.

family of his own, and a pretty brown wife that he got I know not where. There, no doubt, he and his children's children will flourish for many years to come, and there you may see them any sunny evening if you have learnt their signal code, and choosing a good spot on the ground, know just how and when to thump it.

1898

A. A. MILNE
1882–1956

For children growing up in the twenty-first century, the world of Christopher Robin, Winnie-the-Pooh, and the inhabitants of the Hundred Acre Wood is likely to begin with *The Tigger Movie*, an animated film released in 2000 by the Walt Disney Company, which owns the rights to Pooh and his friends. Although the words of A. A. Milne and the illustrations of E. H. Shepard are fixed in the twentieth-century imagination, the traces of that world are being buried by the new images, the upper-class English edges airbrushed into Disney-esque shape. It is possible to buy several Pooh books—with titles such as *Fun with Manners*—but they are only tangentially related to Milne's compositions. Milne was the product of a much more witty, subtle, elegant, and graceful time and culture. He was also a lot less didactic than Disney.

Alan Alexander Milne grew up in the last years of Queen Victoria's reign, in a loving, erudite household. He was the youngest and easily the cleverist of the three sons of John Vine Milne—which made things a little awkward for the older two boys. Milne proceeded smoothly through boyhood, moving from Westminster School in London to Trinity College, Cambridge, from which he graduated with a degree in mathematics in 1903. He then embraced the career of a successful man-about-town in Edwardian London and soon became an assistant editor of *Punch* (1906–14), a venerable magazine (estab-

lished in 1841) that published humorous sketches, poems, satire, and cartoons. In 1913 he married Dorothy de Sélincourt, and their son, Christopher Robin, was born in 1920.

Milne was prolific. He wrote six novels and more than thirty plays, as well as short stories, screenplays, and adaptations, also publishing collections of his *Punch* sketches and verses. By the 1920s he was one of England's most popular and successful playwrights. But the books Milne wrote for Christopher Robin's childhood are the ones that have survived into the twenty-first century. There are just four: two linked sets of stories, *Winnie-the-Pooh* (1926) and *The House at Pooh Corner* (1928), and two collections of poetry, *When We Were Very Young* (1924) and *Now We Are Six* (1927).

By the time Milne sent Christopher Robin, Pooh, and a brave band of followers on an "expotition" to the North Pole (in the excerpt from *Winnie-the-Pooh* reprinted here), the extensive coverage in magazines and newspapers of the real expeditions to the North and South Poles undertaken by Robert Scott, Sir Ernest Shackleton, Robert Peary, and others had made the narrative pattern of exploration stories familiar to the popular imagination. These accounts emphasized courage and endurance under extreme conditions as well as the thrill of discovery. Milne's gentle satire of the genre is instantly recognizable.

From Winnie-the-Pooh

CHAPTER VIII.
IN WHICH
CHRISTOPHER ROBIN LEADS AN EXPOTITION
TO THE NORTH POLE

One fine day Pooh had stumped up to the top of the Forest to see if his friend Christopher Robin was interested in Bears at all. At breakfast that morning (a simple meal of marmalade spread lightly over a honeycomb or two) he had suddenly thought of a new song. It began like this:

"Sing Ho! for the life of a Bear!"

When he had got as far as this, he stretched his head, and thought to himself "That's a very good start for a song, but what about the second line?" He tried singing "Ho," two or three times, but it didn't seem to help. "Perhaps it would be better," he thought, "if I sang Hi for the life of a Bear." So he sang it . . . but it wasn't. "Very well, then," he said, "I shall sing that first line twice, and perhaps if I sing it very quickly, I shall find myself singing the third and fourth lines before I have time to think of them, and that will be a Good Song. Now then:"

Sing Ho! for the life of a Bear!
Sing Ho! for the life of a Bear!
I don't much mind if it rains or snows,
'Cos I've got a lot of honey on my nice new nose,
I don't much care if it snows or thaws,
'Cos I've got a lot of honey on my nice clean paws!
Sing Ho! for a Bear!
Sing Ho! for a Pooh!
And I'll have a little something in an hour or two!

He was so pleased with this song that he sang it all the way to the top of the Forest, "and if I go on singing it much longer," he thought, "it will be time for the little something, and then the last line won't be true." So he turned it into a hum instead.

Christopher Robin was sitting outside his door, putting on his Big Boots. As soon as he saw the Big Boots, Pooh knew that an Adventure was going to happen, and he brushed the honey off his nose with the back of his paw, and spruced himself up as well as he could, so as to look Ready for Anything.

"Good-morning, Christopher Robin," he called out.

"Hallo, Pooh Bear. I can't get this boot on."

"That's bad," said Pooh.

"Do you think you could very kindly lean against me, 'cos I keep pulling so hard that I fall over backyards."

Pooh sat down, dug his feet into the ground, and pushed hard against Christopher Robin's back, and Christopher Robin pushed hard against his, and pulled and pulled at his boot until he had got it on.

"And that's that," said Pooh. "What do we do next?"

"We are all going on an Expedition,"[1] said Christopher Robin, as he got up and brushed himself. "Thank you, Pooh."

"Going on an Expotition?" said Pooh eagerly. "I don't think I've ever been on one of those. Where are we going to on this Expotition?"

"Expedition, silly old Bear. It's got an 'x' in it."

"Oh!" said Pooh. "I know." But he didn't really.

"We're going to discover the North Pole."

"Oh!" said Pooh again. "What *is* the North Pole?" he asked.

"It's just a thing you discover," said Christopher Robin carelessly, not being quite sure himself.

"Oh! I see," said Pooh. "Are bears any good at discovering it?"

"Of course they are. And Rabbit and Kanga and all of you. It's an Expedition. That's what an Expedition means. A long line of everybody. You'd better tell the others to get ready, while I see if my gun's all right. And we must all bring Provisions."

"Bring what?"

"Things to eat."

"Oh!" said Pooh happily. "I thought you said Provisions. I'll go and tell them." And he stumped off.

The first person he met was Rabbit.

"Hallo, Rabbit," he said, "is that you?"

"Let's pretend it isn't," said Rabbit, "and see what happens."

"I've got a message for you."

"I'll give it to him."

"We're all going on an Expotition with Christopher Robin!"

"What is it when we're on it?"

"A sort of boat, I think," said Pooh.

"Oh! that sort."

"Yes. And we're going to discover a Pole or something. Or was it a Mole? Anyhow we're going to discover it."

"We are, are we?" said Rabbit.

"Yes. And we've got to bring Po—things to eat with us. In case we want to eat them. Now I'm going down to Piglet's. Tell Kanga, will you?"

He left Rabbit and hurried down to Piglet's house. The Piglet was sitting on the ground at the door of his house blowing happily at a dandelion, and wondering whether it would be this year, next year, sometime or never. He had just discovered

1. In the first two decades of the twentieth century, there were several well-documented polar expeditions. That Robert Peary, credited with being the first to reach the North Pole, had to defend his claim against skeptics adds to the joke.

that it would be never, and was trying to remember what "it" was, and hoping it wasn't anything nice, when Pooh came up.

"Oh! Piglet," said Pooh excitedly, "we're going on an Expotition, all of us, with things to eat. To discover something."

"To discover what?" said Piglet anxiously.

"Oh! just something."

"Nothing fierce?"

"Christopher Robin didn't say anything about fierce. He just said it had an 'x'."

"It isn't their necks I mind," said Piglet earnestly. "It's their teeth. But if Christopher Robin is coming I don't mind anything."

In a little while they were all ready at the top of the Forest, and the Expotition started. First came Christopher Robin and Rabbit, then Piglet and Pooh; then Kanga, with Roo in her pocket, and Owl; then Eeyore; and, at the end, in a long line, all Rabbit's friends-and-relations.

"I didn't ask them," explained Rabbit carelessly. "They just came. They always do. They can march at the end, after Eeyore."

"What I say," said Eeyore, "is that it's unsettling. I didn't want to come on this Expo—what Pooh said. I only came to oblige. But here I am; and if I am the end of the Expo—what we're talking about—then let me *be* the end. But if, every time I want to sit down for a little rest, I have to brush away half a dozen of Rabbit's smaller friends-and-relations first, then this isn't an Expo—whatever it is—at all, it's simply a Confused Noise. That's what *I* say."

"I see what Eeyore means," said Owl. "If you ask me——"

"I'm not asking anybody," said Eeyore. "I'm just telling everybody. We can look for the North Pole, or we can play 'Here we go gathering Nuts and May' with the end part of an ant's nest. It's all the same to me."

There was a shout from the top of the line.

"Come on!" called Christopher Robin.

"Come on!" called Pooh and Piglet.

"Come on!" called Owl.

"We're starting," said Rabbit. "I must go." And he hurried off to the front of the Expotition with Christopher Robin.

"All right," said Eeyore. "We're going. Only Don't Blame Me."

So off they all went to discover the Pole. And as they walked, they chattered to each other of this and that, all except Pooh, who was making up a song.

"This is the first verse," he said to Piglet, when he was ready with it.

"First verse of what?"

"My song."

"What song?"

"This one."

"Which one?"

"Well, if you listen, Piglet, you'll hear it."

"How do you know I'm not listening?"

Pooh couldn't answer that one, so he began to sing.

> They all went off to discover the Pole,
>   Owl and Piglet and Rabbit and all;
>   It's a Thing you Discover, as I've been tole
>   By Owl and Piglet and Rabbit and all.
> Eeyore, Christopher Robin and Pooh

> And Rabbit's relations all went too——
> And where the Pole was none of them knew. . . .
> Sing Hey! for Owl and Rabbit and all!

"Hush!" said Christopher Robin turning round to Pooh, "we're just coming to a Dangerous Place."

"Hush!" said Pooh turning round quickly to Piglet.

"Hush!" said Piglet to Kanga.

"Hush!" said Kanga to Owl, while Roo said "Hush!" several times to himself very quietly.

"Hush!" said Owl to Eeyore.

"*Hush!*" said Eeyore in a terrible voice to all Rabbit's friends-and-relations, and "Hush!" they said hastily to each other all down the line, until it got to the last one of all. And the last and smallest friend-and-relations was so upset to find that the whole Expotition was saying "Hush!" to *him*, that he buried himself head downwards in a crack in the ground, and stayed there for two days until the danger was over, and then went home in a great hurry, and lived quietly with his Aunt ever-afterwards. His name was Alexander Beetle.

They had come to a stream which twisted and tumbled between high rocky banks, and Christopher Robin saw at once how dangerous it was.

"It's just the place," he explained, "for an Ambush."

"What sort of bush?" whispered Pooh to Piglet. "A gorse-bush?"

"My dear Pooh," said Owl in his superior way, "don't you know what an Ambush is?"

"Owl," said Piglet, looking round at him severely, "Pooh's whisper was a perfectly private whisper, and there was no need——"

"An Ambush," said Owl, "is a sort of Surprise."

"So is a gorse-bush sometimes," said Pooh.

"An Ambush, as I was about to explain to Pooh," said Piglet, "is a sort of Surprise."

"If people jump out at you suddenly, that's an Ambush," said Owl.

"It's an Ambush, Pooh, when people jump at you suddenly," explained Piglet.

Pooh, who now knew what an Ambush was, said that a gorse-bush had sprung at him suddenly one day when he fell off a tree, and he had taken six days to get all the prickles out of himself.

"We are not *talking* about gorse-bushes," said Owl a little crossly.

"I am," said Pooh.

They were climbing very cautiously up the stream now, going from rock to rock, and after they had gone a little way they came to a place where the banks widened out at each side, so that on each side of the water there was a level strip of grass on which they could sit down and rest. As soon as he saw this, Christopher Robin called "Halt!" and they all sat down and rested.

"I think," said Christopher Robin, "that we ought to eat all our Provisions now, so that we shan't have so much to carry."

"Eat all our what?" said Pooh.

"All that we've brought," said Piglet, getting to work.

"That's a good idea," said Pooh, and he got to work too.

"Have you all got something?" asked Christopher Robin with his mouth full.

"All except me," said Eeyore. "As Usual." He looked round at them in his melancholy way. "I suppose none of you are sitting on a thistle by any chance?"

"I believe I am," said Pooh. "Ow!" He got up, and looked behind him. "Yes, I was. I thought so."

"Thank you, Pooh. If you've quite finished with it." He moved across to Pooh's place, and began to eat.

"It don't do them any Good, you know, sitting on them," he went on, as he looked up munching. "Takes all the Life out of them. Remember that another time, all of you. A little Consideration, a little Thought for Others, makes all the difference."

As soon as he had finished his lunch Christopher Robin whispered to Rabbit, and Rabbit said, "Yes, yes, of course," and they walked a little way up the stream together.

"I didn't want the others to hear," said Christopher Robin.

"Quite so," said Rabbit, looking important.

"It's—I wondered—It's only—Rabbit, I suppose *you* don't know, What does the North Pole *look* like."

"Well," said Rabbit, stroking his whiskers. "Now you're asking me."

"I did know once, only I've sort of forgotten," said Christopher Robin carelessly.

"It's a funny thing," said Rabbit, "but I've sort of forgotten too, although I did know *once*."

"I suppose it's just a pole stuck in the ground?"

"Sure to be a pole," said Rabbit, "because of calling a pole, and if it's a pole, well, I should think it would be sticking in the ground, shouldn't you, because there'd be nowhere else to stick it."

"Yes, that's what I thought."

"The only thing," said Rabbit, "is, *where is it sticking?*"

"That's what we're looking for," said Christopher Robin.

They went back to the others. Piglet was lying on his back, sleeping peacefully. Roo was washing his face and paws in the stream, while Kanga explained to everybody proudly that this was the first time he had ever washed his face himself, and Owl was telling Kanga an Interesting Anecdote full of long words like Encyclopædia and Rhododendron to which Kanga wasn't listening.

"I don't hold with all this washing," grumbled Eeyore. "This modern Behind-the-ears nonsense. What do *you* think, Pooh?"

"Well," said Pooh, "I think——"

But we shall never know what Pooh thought, for there came a sudden squeak from Roo, a splash, and a loud cry of alarm from Kanga.

"So much for *washing*," said Eeyore.

"Roo's fallen in!" cried Rabbit, and he and Christopher Robin came rushing down to the rescue.

"Look at me swimming!" squeaked Roo from the middle of his pool, and was hurried down a waterfall into the next pool.

"Are you all right, Roo dear?" called Kanga anxiously.

"Yes!" said Roo. "Look at me sw——" and down he went over the next waterfall into another pool.

Everybody was doing something to help. Piglet, wide awake suddenly, was jumping up and down and making "Oo, I say" noises; Owl was explaining that in a case of Sudden and Temporary Immersion the Important Thing was to keep the Head Above Water; Kanga was jumping along the bank, saying "Are you *sure* you're all right, Roo dear?" to which Roo, from whatever pool he was in at the moment, was answering "Look at me swimming!" Eeyore had turned round and hung his tail over the first pool into which Roo fell, and with his back to the accident was grumbling quietly to himself, and saying, "All this washing; but catch on to my tail, little Roo, and you'll be all right"; and, Christopher Robin and Rabbit came hurrying past Eeyore, and were calling out to the others in front of them.

"All right, Roo, I'm coming," called Christopher Robin.

"Get something across the stream lower down, some of you fellows," called Rabbit.

But Pooh was getting something. Two pools below Roo he was standing with a long pole in his paws, and Kanga came up and took one end of it, and between them they held it across the lower part of the pool; and Roo, still bubbling proudly, "Look at me swimming," drifted up against it, and climbed out.

"Did you see me swimming?" squeaked Roo excitedly, while Kanga scolded him and rubbed him down. "Pooh, did you see me swimming? That's called swimming, what I was doing. Rabbit, did you see what I was doing? Swimming. Hallo, Piglet! I say, Piglet! What do you think I was doing! Swimming! Christopher Robin, did you see me——"

But Christopher Robin wasn't listening. He was looking at Pooh.

"Pooh," he said, "where did you find that pole?"

Pooh looked at the pole in his hands.

"I just found it," he said. "I thought it ought to be useful. I just picked it up."

"Pooh," said Christopher Robin solemnly, "the Expedition is over. You have found the North Pole!"

"Oh!" said Pooh.

Eeyore was sitting with his tail in the water when they all got back to him.

"Tell Roo to be quick, somebody," he said. "My tail's getting cold. I don't want to mention it, but I just mention it. I don't want to complain but there it is. My tail's cold."

"Here I am!" squeaked Roo.

"Oh, there you are."

"Did you see me swimming?"

Eeyore took his tail out of the water, and swished it from side to side.

"As I expected," he said. "Lost all feeling. Numbed it. That's what it's done. Numbed it. Well, as long as nobody minds, I suppose it's all right."

"Poor old Eeyore. I'll dry it for you," said Christopher Robin, and he took out his handkerchief and rubbed it up.

"Thank you, Christopher Robin. You're the only one who seems to understand about tails. They don't think—that's what the matter with some of these others. They've no imagination. A tail isn't a tail to *them*, it's just a Little Bit Extra at the back."

"Never mind, Eeyore," said Christopher Robin, rubbing his hardest. "Is *that* better?"

"It's feeling more like a tail perhaps. It Belongs again, if you know what I mean."

"Hullo, Eeyore," said Pooh, coming up to them with his pole.

"Hullo, Pooh. Thank you for asking, but I shall be able to use it again in a day or two."

"Use what?" said Pooh.

"What we are talking about."

"I wasn't talking about anything," said Pooh, looking puzzled.

"My mistake again. I thought you were saying how sorry you were about my tail, being all numb, and could you do anything to help?"

"No," said Pooh. "That wasn't me," he said. He thought for a little and then suggested helpfully, "Perhaps it was somebody else."

"Well, thank him for me when you see him."

Pooh looked anxiously at Christopher Robin.

"Pooh's found the North Pole," said Christopher Robin. "Isn't that lovely?"

Pooh looked modestly down.

"Is that it?" said Eeyore.

"Yes," said Christopher Robin.

"Is that what we were looking for?"

"Yes," said Pooh.

"Oh!" said Eeyore. "Well, anyhow—it didn't rain," he said.

They stuck the pole in the ground, and Christopher Robin tied a message on to it.

NORTH POLE
DISCOVERED BY POOH
POOH FOUND IT.

Then they all went home again. And I think, but I am not quite sure, that Roo had a hot bath and went straight to bed. But Pooh went back to his own house, and feeling very proud of what he had done, had a little something to revive himself.

1926

SHANNON GARST
1894–1981

James Bowie and His Famous Knife (1955) tells the kind of story about killer cowboys popular in the United States in the middle of the twentieth century. Between 1938 and 1970, Doris Shannon Garst wrote almost fifty books, mostly on various cowboy subjects, usually churning out two a year. Born in Michigan and educated in Denver and Oregon, she married an attorney, Joseph Garst, and moved to Wyoming. There, as she raised her three children, she began writing in response to their request for bedtime stories; she soon abandoned her earlier career as a teacher to become a full-time author. It was while living in Wyoming, she says, that she found herself "in a gold field of material for western writing."

During her lifetime, Garst's work was translated into several languages, widely reviewed, and prominently advertised by her publishers (primarily Julian Messner of New York). Many of her books were fictionalized biographies of famous western characters, including Buffalo Bill, Sitting Bull, Crazy Horse, and Daniel Boone. She also wrote a biography of the author and illustrator Ernest Thompson Seton (see above), focusing on his work as a naturalist. Her inclusion in the first volume of *Something about the Author* (1971)—a standard, regularly updated reference work featuring biographical and bibliographic information on writers for children and young adults—marks her success in the field, though she is almost completely unknown today; all her books are out of print.

In writing juvenile fiction (marketed mainly to children in grades four to nine), Garst was filling an important mid-twentieth-century demand for cowboy books in America—even if it meant making the definition of "cowboy book" fit the kind of hack writ-

ing at which she excelled. The books are of the type deemed especially good for boys, and all follow the same pattern: slightly unusual boyhood marked by expertise in manly skills, good relations with mothers and families, a sudden event that pushes the hero out of the nest, a few redeeming exploits, and a final blaze of glory. Shannon Garst herself put her reason for writing westerns very simply: "I strive to make my work a real contribution by bringing to life the heroes who helped make our country—and by recreating a picture of the times in which they lived." The rough frontier justice, the loving description of the bowie knife as a murder weapon, the "cushiony Negress," and the "dumb Indian" in Garst's book were unremarkable in the America of the 1950s but are unspeakable now. Though books such as *James Bowie and His Famous Knife* were once abundant in the children's section of libraries, today they have all but disappeared; and when a volume is removed, so too is its record in a library's catalog. It is thus impossible to know what was on the shelves with Garst's book in 1955—and that is why its entire text is reproduced here. If we do not know the historical record, then we cannot grasp the reasons for changes in adventure stories and in cultural values more generally.

James Bowie and His Famous Knife

Chapter 1. A Thrilling Ride

Jim stepped light footed as a deer through the tangled underbrush along the edge of the beautiful Bayou Teche.[1] Sunlight seeping through the tangled bearded moss which draped the live oaks glistened on his tousled red hair. His blue eyes were alert, for danger lurked in this swampy, jungle country.

He was dressed in a suit of soft buckskin with long fringes, which served not only as decoration but could be cut off and used for numerous tying or mending jobs. In one hand he carried a cloth sack. His other hand, by force of habit, rested on the knife he always wore in a sheath at his belt.

He had left Rezin, his older brother, back a ways sitting on the edge of the bayou fishing. Fishing was not an exciting enough sport for Jim's restless spirit. So he had wandered along the bayou catching turtles sunning themselves on the rocks. Mammy Lou could use them for soup or gumbo.[2]

But the turtles were too easy to catch to suit him, so he took the lariat from his belt. Like his knife, this was standard equipment wherever he went. Constant prac-

1. A stream in Louisiana, about 125 miles long; it flows into the Atchafalaya River. According to a Native American legend, a huge snake (*teche*) once inhabited that bayou.

2. A stew thickened with okra or filé (powdered sassafras leaves).

tice had made him unusually adept in the throwing of both the lasso and the knife.

In this wild Teche country a man's life depended upon these skills. Jim was a good marksman, too. His father had seen to it that his sons could handle a rifle, but guns were cumbersome and ammunition scarce and expensive, so the boys' preference was for a rope or a knife.

Jim shook out his loop and sent it spinning to where an old granddaddy turtle basked upon a stump. His lasso found its mark, but the turtle slipped through the noose and splashed into the water.

"Guess they aren't the right shape for roping." Jim spoke aloud and chuckled at the eerie, hollow sound of his voice in this lonely swampland.

He stopped when he came to a river, sluggish and choked with water hyacinths.

"Why don't we build a canoe?" He again spoke aloud as he often did on his lonely wanderings. His imagination raced ahead to the wonderful exploring jaunts he and Rezin could have paddling up the numerous lagoons and creeks which fed the Bayou Teche. John might come along sometimes, too, although he was seven years older than Jim and was not so adventurous as his two younger brothers. Surely in the back country would be Cajun villages and farther on camps of the half-wild Caddo[3] Indians.

The more he thought about it, the more enthusiastic he became about having a pirogue—a dugout canoe. They could make it from a cypress log, as the Indians did, burning out the inside. He and Rezin had ranged far on horseback, but they could not ride in the swampy ground along the bayous. In a pirogue they could explore parts of the country beyond their reach.

A queer-looking log half covered by the water hyacinths caught Jim's eye. Almost automatically his rope began to twirl. It snaked out and fell neatly about the point of the log. As he tightened the noose, the "log" thrashed and churned the water. He had roped an alligator! He dug his heels into the soft ground and pulled hard on the rope, choking the great creature into submission. Then with a whoop Jim splashed through the water. Throwing himself upon the back of the gator, he loosened the rope a trifle to give the creature enough air to enable it to give him an interesting ride.

"Jim! Jim!" It was Rezin's voice shrill with alarm. "What on earth are you doing?"

"Yipee!" Jim shouted. A wide grin split his handsome face. "I've tamed me a gator. He's going to take me swamp riding."

"You crazy loon!" Rezin shouted. "Get off before he flops over and takes off an arm or leg."

The idea sobered Jim slightly. Anyway, by this time the thrill was lessening. He had ridden a gator—a feat that would certainly make John sit up and take notice.

He gave his rope a jerk to tighten it, leaped off and splashed to shore as fast as his long legs would take him. Shaking his rope from the monster he made it into a neat coil which he tucked into his belt. As soon as it was free the alligator rolled over on its back.

"See!" Rezin said, his eyes still large with alarm. "If he'd rolled with you on him, you wouldn't have had a chance. Haven't you any sense?"

"Sure." Jim grinned. "Sense enough to keep the rope so tight he couldn't bite me."

Rezin shook his head. "It's the craziest thing I ever heard of."

3. A Native American tribe that originally lived in present-day northern Louisiana, southwestern Arkansas, eastern Texas, and eastern Oklahoma. "Cajun": a Louisianan descended from the French colonists driven out of Acadia (the francophone communities in Nova Scotia, Prince Edward Island, and New Brunswick) by the British (1755–63). *Cajun* is a corruption of *Acadian*.

"It's fun," Jim insisted. "Try it sometime."

Jim strutted a bit as he and Rezin strode along the trail toward home. He was glad that he had tried this alligator riding stunt first. "Those wild Bowie boys" their neighboring Acadian and Spanish neighbors called them. There was always good-natured rivalry between the brothers in doing dangerous and exciting things and in excelling in markmanship and roping.

"We're going to make us a pirogue," Jim announced as they swung along in step with each other.

"Zat so?"

"Yeh. I've got a hankering to explore the back country of the Cajuns and the Caddo."

"There are plenty of Acadians all around us," his brother pointed out. "And Caddo come in to Opelousas[4] to trade every Saturday."

"Yes. But those are tame ones. I want to see how they live in their villages. I hear tell that some of the Cajuns in the back country have never come near a town. And I've never seen an Indian village."

"It might be just as well to stay away from them," Rezin said sensibly. "And I suppose the backwoods Cajuns are just like the backwoods Tennesseans, where we used to live."

"But I never saw them," Jim said. "We left Tennessee before I was knee high to a grasshopper."

"That's right. You weren't born till the spring of '96. What a noise you made! And you've kept it up ever since."

Jim chuckled. "You were only two when I was born. You can't remember. But Mom says the reason we left Tennessee and moved to Kentucky was because I yelled so loud it drew the Indians to our plantation. But I think the reason we moved from Kentucky to Georgia, then here to Louisiana, is because Dad likes moving. I hope we stay here, though. I like it!"

They trudged in silence for a time. Jim looked around in deep content at the gigantic Spanish moss-bearded live oaks, at the great cypress spraddled in the lagoons. It was a peaceful yet mysterious country which cast a spell upon the imagination. Ever since the first day they arrived Jim had felt quite at home in this tranquil land of the Acadians.

His father, the elder Rezin Pleasant Bowie, had brought along about a dozen slaves from his Tennessee plantation. He had built a rambling farmhouse and began raising sugar cane in the rich bottom lands near Opelousas—the town named after the Opelousas Indians.

Reaching home, Rezin lost no time in telling about Jim's latest exploit to the Bowie children gathered in the shade of the magnolia. David and Stephen, the younger brothers, frowned in envy, obviously wishing they were old enough to join in such wild activities. Sarah and Mary squealed over such daring and John, the steady, sober one of the three older boys, shook his head and said, "Such show off doings are just plain silly."

"But I wasn't showing off." Quick anger blazed in Jim's blue eyes. "There wasn't anyone there to see—at first. Eat those words, John Bowie, or I'll ram 'em down your throat."

---

4. Town in south-central Louisiana, named after a small Native American tribe that had almost disappeared by the early nineteenth century.

"Yes?" John's tone was contemptuous, which only added fuel to Jim's flaring anger. He leaped at John with pounding knuckles.

One blow from John's great fist sent the lighter boy reeling. Seeing his younger brother getting the worst of it, Rezin loyally jumped into the battle to help—and from then on it was so mixed up no one could tell who was who.

A figure in wide ruffled skirts raced from the house. "Boys! Stop it. Stop it this instant I say."

Slowly the three brothers straightened up and wiped their bloody noses.

"For shame!" the little woman cried. "How many times do I have to tell you that I will not tolerate fighting among you? I'm trying to teach you to behave like gentlemen."

"I'm sorry, Mom." The three boys spoke as one.

"Now shake hands and apologize to each other." Her voice was low, but it held the note of authority which commanded instant obedience. They turned and gripped hands and grinned as they sheepishly said a brief, "Sorry!"

"Jimmy rode a gator, Mom," Stevie shrilled.

"Jimmy what?" Mrs. Bowie turned with a shocked expression on her delicate features.

"Rode a gator," the boy repeated.

"Your father shall hear of this," she threatened, as she whisked into the house.

The boys looked at each other apprehensively as they washed for supper at the long bench outside the kitchen. Soberly they filed inside to wait until Mammy Lou had the meal ready to serve. Mrs. Bowie was back at the spinning wheel where she spent most of her time. With six children to clothe the pleasant whirr of the wheel could be heard at any time of day, and often it lulled the boys to sleep at night.

When Mr. Bowie came in from the fields, the evening meal was served.

"Jimmy rode an alligator today," his wife said. "I'd thank you, Rezin, to put a stop once and for all to such foolhardiness."

He turned his dark gaze on Jim. "Is that right, son?"

Jim nodded. "Yes, suh."

"I admire bravery," his father said slowly. "But you're mighty reckless, seems to me."

"It was fun." Jim knew that this was a pretty feeble excuse, but he could think of nothing better.

"I'm not going to forbid you to do it again," his father said. "I know that forbidden fruit always tastes sweetest. I don't want to tempt you to disobey me. But to survive on the frontier, you need good old common horse sense. I ask you to try to cultivate it."

"Yes, suh," Jim said meekly. For a few moments they were all silent, then Jim burst into an explosive snicker.

"What are you laughing at?" his mother demanded.

"I was thinking of the time back in Tennessee when you got Pa out of jail by pointing a pistol at the sheriff."

Everyone burst into laughter. The story was an old one often told but gained savor by each repetition. Mr. Bowie had been bothered by a squatter who settled on a choice plot of his land and who refused to move until the elder Rezin backed up his threats with a rifle load of bird shot. He was arrested. Whereupon Elvira, his wife, had one of the slaves drive her to the jail where she informed the sheriff that she had come to visit her husband. Shortly man and wife confronted the officer, each armed with a pistol which the little woman had concealed under her full skirts.

"You haven't any business holding my husband for defending his rights," she told the sheriff. "He's needed at home and I'm taking him."

"I was about to let him go," the man said meekly.

Mr. Bowie laughed as heartily as his children over this story. "Jim's right, Elvie," he chuckled. "Shows where he gets his reckless nature."

"I wonder where he gets his wanderlust—his hankering to be always on the move exploring new places," she remarked, with a toss of her blonde head.

CHAPTER 2. HOW TO TRAP A BEAR

Jim's bare feet hit the rough plank floor with a smack. The narrow slit of sunlight entering at the edge of the oiled hide at the window had wakened him. Always the first one up, he never lost much time in rousing his brothers. The boys slept in the attic on bunks built against the walls, their mattresses and pillows stuffed with Spanish moss.

Jim liked to get up early in order to practice roping or throwing the knife at some tree stump or having a horse race with Rezin and John.

There was continuous excitement and adventure to be found in the Louisiana bayou country—possum[5] hunting with hound dogs, fishing, turtle catching, hunting wild turkeys, geese, ducks, partridges and deer. Besides the wealth of wild game there were persimmons, grapes, wild figs and muscadines to eat. This was the life for a red-blooded, adventure-loving boy! Yet there were less pleasant sides to it, for Mrs. Bowie was determined that her lively brood should be as well educated as she herself.

Mr. Bowie had been too busy either fighting Indians or in the Revolutionary War[6] to get much education. Nevertheless he was a highly intelligent man and commanded the respect both of his children and the community. His spelling, though, showed lack of schooling. His own name bore witness to this. He has been christened Reason Pleasant Bowie, but he always signed his first name as it sounded—Rezin. And his son and namesake used the same spelling.

After a rousing race to the edge of the bayou John, Rezin and Jim handed their horses over to Jeb, one of the slave boys. They washed up hastily and went in to devour hoecakes, hominy grits, corn pone and roast bass, washing it down with steaming chicory[7] from gourd cups. When the meal was over Mammy Lou removed the dishes but the children, with the exception of the toddlers, remained in their places.

Jim sighed deeply as he brought the schoolbooks, tossing them on the table with a lack of grace and willingness which brought a frown of disapproval from his mother.

"Sorry, Mom. They slipped." He flashed his wide grin which he had already learned could quite disarm not only cross parents but other people, too.

He slid into his place on the long bench and picked up the arithmetic book. There was an hour of silent study, the children taking turns with the grammar, the Latin primer, the Bible, *Pilgrim's Progress*[8] and a battered copy of Shakespeare's plays. During this time Elvira Bowie bustled about her household duties. Then for another hour she listened to recitations.

---

5. I.e., opossum.
6. I.e., the American Revolution, fought for independence from the British (1775–83).
7. An herb whose root (dried, ground, and roasted) serves as a coffee substitute. "Hoecakes": pancakes made of cornmeal. "Hominy grits": corn coarsely ground, soaked in lye, and hulled. "Corn pone": a plain cornbread.
8. The allegory (1678) by John Bunyan, one of the most widely read books in English; simplified versions were often given to young children (see in the Religion section, above).

Jim resented this time of inaction, but he had learned the uselessness of shirking his lessons; he would only have to sit in the house longer and study, while the others were whooping outside. So he had learned to apply his fine intelligence to the task at hand, and through concentration he learned quickly.

After lessons the girls were set to spinning or carding wool or working on their samplers.[9] The older boys went to help their father. Although there were slaves to do the labor, Mr. Bowie was determined that his sons should know how to run a plantation. So they helped with the cane, the cotton, the tobacco, and the mule-drawn sugar presses,[1] or worked in the sawmill in which Mr. Bowie had an interest. In the afternoons they were free to do as they pleased.

Their "parish"—as a Louisiana county is called—of St. Landry was populated mainly by French- and Spanish-speaking people. The Bowie boys quickly learned to speak these languages.

The afternoons were never long enough for all the exciting things they wanted to do. Now Rezin and Jim were building a pirogue, but before they got it finished a new project had to be undertaken. Bears were raiding the sugar cane and their father told the boys to take rifles and lie in wait for the intruders.

"We could wait for days," Jim cried impatiently, "and never catch them. I've a better plan than that. John and Rezin, you can come and help me this afternoon—that is, if Pa'll let me borrow a mule and some long spikes."

"Anything you like," his father agreed. "Just so you get rid of those bears."

"Follow me!" Jim cried as he mounted his favorite horse—Fleetfoot.

His brothers were also mounted and armed with axes. Jim led a big gray mule called Molasses, because he was so slow. Now, however, the mule sensed the excitement in the air and trotted along with the horses.

They followed Jim into the woods to a bee tree, which was hollow about halfway up. The boys dismounted and built a brush fire beneath the tree. Dipping Spanish moss from the live oaks into the near-by stream, they made a smudge[2] which nearly choked them as well as the bees.

When the bees had been smoked from their home the boys set to work with their axes and brought down the tree with its precious store of honey. Jim chained the log to the mule and led the way to the edge of the sugar cane field where tracks showed that the bears had been entering.

He and his brothers drove spikes into the log on a slant. Then Jim spread a generous gob of honey on a flat leaf and thrust it as far back into the log as he could reach.

"Now," he said, waving his hand with a flourish, "please step into my parlor, Mr. Bear. A feast is waiting."

"You're clever," John said. "I never would have thought of such a trap. The bears will be able to get his head in easily when he goes after the honey. But he won't be able to draw it out because the spikes are slanted inward."

"Just a nice collar for Bruin." Jim chuckled, well pleased with himself.

Next morning the three boys rode out to look at their trap. Sure enough, a bear was snorting and growling his disapproval of the "collar" he had acquired.

"Dibs on[3] the hide," Jim said as John raised his rifle to shoot the marauding beast. "That will be one less bear to raid our sugar field."

9. Pieces of needlework that display different kinds of stitches, often containing alphabets or mottoes. "Carding": preparing fibers for spinning by pulling them between two paddle-shaped implements set with teeth.

1. Mangles for pressing juice out of the sugarcane to make sugar.
2. A suffocating smoke to drive away or repel insects.
3. I.e., "I claim."

After several bears were caught in this fashion the raiding stopped.

Rezin and Jim went back to finishing their pirogue. John spent most of his time working with their father. He felt himself too old for many of the activities of his younger brothers. Between Rezin and Jim, however, there was an extraordinarily strong bond. They liked the same things and could laugh and chat or enjoy each other's company without a word for long periods of time.

Finally the pirogue was finished and they spent many happy afternoons poling through the numerous bayous of the half-drowned land. Although they drifted along with little sound, blue herons and white egrets rose at their approach. Now and then a gator moved or opened enormous jaws, but they felt fairly safe in the pirogue.

When Jim was twelve years old his father took him, with John and Rezin, to Natchez to sell the cotton. It was a slow but exciting trip over boggy country, where often pine boughs had to be cut to make a solid enough bottom for the wagons loaded with cotton bales and driven by the slaves. The boys rode beside or ahead of the wagons, each carrying a pistol and a knife thrust in his belt, for often thieves or Indians waylaid the caravans.

Finally, without meeting a single robber or Indian, they came in sight of Natchez. Brown bluffs two hundred feet high rose on each bank of the Mississippi. On one side stood the white, columned mansions of Natchez-on-the-Hill, which took Jim's breath away with their grandeur.

He went to the levee and saw the mountains of baled cotton heaped on the slow-moving barges floating down the mighty river on the way to New Orleans. He saw his first cotton engine,[4] which deafened him with its hurried chugging and clattering.

"Engine! Gin," he shouted above the noise. "I see now why they call it a cotton gin. Why don't we get one on our place?"

"Maybe we will one of these days." His father bent down to shout in Jim's ear.

The three boys roamed along the water front of Natchez-under-the-Hill where the houses were tumble-down shacks.

"Keep your hands on your knives, my pardners," Jim said. "I hear these water-front toughs will cut your throat for a silver dollar. I've already spent mine, so I don't need to worry."

"You'd better worry," John said. "The scum around here would kill you first and search your pockets afterward."

They spent half a day wandering up and down the shore, watching the barges being loaded. Half-naked Negroes heaved bales of cotton as though they were pillows. There was tobacco, too, and cattle and hogs—all bound for New Orleans.

"That's a place I must see someday," Jim said, speaking softly, as though to himself.

"I've got a feeling that you'll see a lot of places in your lifetime," Rezin told him.

"I hope so. Now we'd better go find Pa or he'll tan our britches[5] for being gone so long."

They found their father at the Bristol House where they had taken lodgings for the night. He was talking to several men. Jim heard him say, "I can hardly believe it. You say that Fulton[6] actually made a boat sail by means of steam—without sails?"

One of the men nodded. "Up the Hudson.[7] I saw it with my own eyes. Fulton's

---

4. The cotton gin, a machine whose ability to rapidly separate cotton seeds from the fibers (a slow job when done by hand) made large-scale production of cotton economical; it was invented in 1793 by Eli Whitney.
5. Spank us.

6. Robert Fulton (1765–1815), an American inventor and engineer who built the first commercial steamboat in 1807.
7. A river in New York that runs south from the Adirondack Mountains to its mouth at New York City.

Folly, men called it, while he was working on it. But Fulton had the last laugh."

"I'll be glad when we have steamboats on the Mississippi," Mr. Bowie said.

He turned and saw his sons. "I was beginning to wonder about you lads," he said. "How about supper?"

Jim was relieved to see that his father had not had time to worry about them. Evidently his day's business had been successful for he was in a jovial mood and ordered a whopping meal for the hungry boys.

CHAPTER 3. "OUR FORTUNES FOR TO SEEK!"

It had been a long time since Jim had slept in a real bed. At first he rather missed the crisp crackle of the Spanish moss which filled his mattress at home, but he was so tired he soon fell asleep. It seemed that he had scarcely closed his eyes when his father was shaking his shoulder, ordering him to get up.

"'Tisn't light yet, suh," the boy protested.

"We're starting anyway," his father said in a low tone. "I sold the crop for a good price and I've got two bags of money. A couple of mean-looking fellows were watching me last night as though they were planning some evil. I want to be well on our way before they're up."

Jim got into his linsey[8] jeans, shirt and fringed buckskin jacket in no time.

"I've some food in my pouch," his father said. "We'll eat on the way."

Zeb had their horses saddled and ready by the time they stepped out into the cool air. They set out slowly so as not to awaken those still asleep on the hill, but away from the lodging house they urged their horses into a fast gallop.

"Where're the wagons?" Jim asked.

"I sent Tom and the other men out to sleep in them on the edge of town. They were to get up early and start. We'll overtake them."

Jim was relieved to hear this. If they were to be waylaid by highwaymen they might need a strong force. His heart was beating fast.

"Slow down," his father said.

Jim obeyed.

Mr. Bowie shifted his own saddlebags to the front of Jim's saddle. "These hold the money," he said quietly. "You're just a boy. Thieves won't expect you to have it. You have the fastest horse. If we're attacked, let Fleetfoot feel your heels. Keep going as fast as you can. Don't stop to fight. Understand?"

Jim nodded, not too happily. Already he had imagined himself the hero of a bandit attack, fighting like a demon with knife and pistol. It seemed not a bit heroic to be singled out as the one to run away when the battle started.

They finally overtook the empty wagons. At noon they rested their horses and ate lunch. While they waited Jim grew restless and drew out his knife for some practice throwing.

"Why, Jim!" his father exclaimed. "You're very good at handling a knife!"

"He practices all the time," Rez said. "When he isn't swinging the lariat he's throwing that knife of his."

"That's a good skill for a frontiersman." Mr. Bowie nodded approvingly. "A knife is quicker than a gun and often more useful. I'm glad to see you boys learn skills which might someday save your lives. You've got a good head on your shoulders, Jim. I've a notion you'll do all right."

8. Linsey-woolsey, a coarse cloth made of linen or cotton and wool.

Jim was so set up by his father's praise that when they set forth again he wanted a few bandits to appear so that he could send his knife straight through the heart of the leader. But the return trip was quite uneventful.

The pleasant days raced by. When no excitement offered itself, Jim and Rezin made it. Now they were closer to each other than ever, for John was a grown man and had gone into business for himself, buying and selling land. To add excitement to their hunting expeditions they roped deer, then one of the boys would leap from his horse and cut the throat of the captured animal. They also caught wild horses, just for the fun of it. Sometimes they let the animals go, or they would pull some promising steed home for the Negro boys to break.

One day, however, Rezin's knife slipped and gashed the palm of his hand to the bone.

"Drat it!" Rezin cried, wrapping his handkerchief around his hand to stop the flow of blood. "That's no way for a knife to behave. I've got to figure out a way to make one that won't slip. This will stop me from hunting for a while."

"I'm afraid it will!" Jim cried. "Let's get home quick so Mom can fix up your hand to keep you from getting blood poisoning."

While waiting for his hand to heal Rezin made drawings of a knife which would prevent a man's hand from slipping down upon the blade.

When he had finally drawn one to scale which suited him, he took it to Jesse Cliff, the plantation blacksmith. "Can you make me a knife like this, Jesse?" he asked.

"I'll do my best," the smithy promised.

A few days later Rezin proudly showed Jim his new weapon. It was an ordinary, single-edged hunting knife with a wooden handle, but with a straight bar between handle and blade.

"It's a dandy," Jim said admiringly, taking the knife in his hand. "Your hand won't slip onto the blade with this. That's sure. But is it balanced in throwing?"

"Try it and see."

Jim flipped the blade back over his shoulder and with a swift snap of the wrist sent the knife hurtling toward a knot in a log of the fence. The blade made a singing sound as it flew and a clink as it hit.

The brothers looked at each other in triumph. It took considerable strength to wrench the knife loose from its mark.

"Wow!" Jim cried. "What a knife!"

"Get the smithy to make you one," Rezin said, tucking his weapon into a sheath at his belt. All his life he would carry the scar on his palm which led to the making of the first crude Bowie knife.

Jim intended to go to the blacksmith, but cane-cutting time had come. Every hand on the place, including himself and Rezin, were busy from daylight until dark in the canebrake.[9] Jim was wielding a knife, but not in a way he enjoyed.

He hacked away with rhythmic strokes. He had taken off his shirt and the strong muscles rippled under his bronzed skin. He was over six feet tall now and "strong as a young steer," his father proudly said. This work was not especially wearying, just monotonous. Jim's thoughts roamed. He was seventeen. A man. What would he do with his life?

His father was prospering on the plantation. Now there was a large new house

9. The thicket of sugarcane.

with glass windows instead of oiled skins. Elvie Bowie had her own carriage to take her to Opelousas to shop or visit friends on near-by plantations. Life was pleasant here, but it was becoming too peaceful. He and Rez had to roam far afield to find excitement. Besides, it was time they were getting out on their own. Jim had no desire to carry on this business which his father had built up. Merely riding a fine horse over acres of plantation to oversee the work held no attraction for him.

He and Rezin had not discussed the future at any great length. Yet each knew pretty well what was in the other's mind.

The bell clanged from the big house summoning the Bowie men to the noon meal. When Jim and Rez reached the house they stood under the great live oak and pumped water from the well, drinking deep and throwing gourdfuls of the cool liquid on each other's heads. They pulled on their linsey shirts before going in to eat.

A strange carriage stood in front of the house, the horse tied to the hitching post.

"Mom's got company again," Rezin remarked.

"Evidently," Jim said. "It would be a dreary day if no callers came to the Bowie plantation. I don't feel up to company manners today. Besides, I smell sweaty as a horse. Let's get Mammy Lou to fill our plates and bring 'em out here and eat under the magnolia tree."

"Good idea." Rez grinned.

"Fill our plates heaping full," Jim directed Mammy Lou. "We're hungry and want to eat outdoors. Please tell Mom that we're too dirty to come to the table."

The cushiony Negress chuckled. "Mammy Lou'll give you plenty to eat and make excuses to yore ma. Seems to me, though, that since you have to stoop to come in the door, yore too grown up to keep tied to Mammy Lou's apron strings any more."

Jim patted her shoulder. "You know you love having us young'uns underfoot. You're going to miss it terribly when we cut loose. And it won't be too long."

Mammy Lou began to sniff. "It's the Lawd's trufe. So it is. Marsa[1] John's already growed up and moved away. Miss Sarah married. Now you and Marsa Rez growed up—talkin' about leavin'. Ain't been no babies at this house for a long time. The rest will be leavin'. . . ." She picked up the corner of her apron to wipe her eyes.

"Now, now, Mammy Lou!" Jim said. "We're not gone yet, and Dave and Stevie'll be around for a long time. You'd better hurry and get the meal on the table. I heard Mom's bell tinkle a bit impatiently. Here, I'll fill our plates. You go and take care of the folks in the dining room."

When the two brothers had gorged themselves on Mammy Lou's fried chicken and biscuits, with yams, fresh peas and grape jelly topped by peach pie, they lay back with their hands under their heads.

They were under the open dining room window and the sound of voices reached them. They paid little attention until they heard their own names.

Their mother was speaking. "I wish you could have met my sons," she said. "Mr. Bowie and I are very proud of them. John, the eldest, is the steady one of the family— a successful business man. Rezin is the most brilliant. He can sit down and dash off an exceptional speech or bit of writing. Jim, two years younger, is a born leader. He's inclined to be bold and reckless though. Not afraid of anything in the world. However, I suppose time will steady him."

Jim and Rez looked at each other and grinned. "Eavesdroppers are supposed never to hear good of themselves." Jim chuckled.

1. Master.

"Unless," Rez drawled, "it's their mothers who happen to be doing the talking. It's a good thing mothers see the best in their children. The world at large won't be so kind in its judgment, I reckon."

"I suppose not," Jim answered. "When are we going out on our own, Rez? It's about time."

"I've been thinking the same thing. Funny how we always seem to have the same thoughts. How shall we set out to conquer the world?"

"There's a small sawmill for sale down on Bayou Beouf," Jim said slowly, "with a world of cypress and pine all around. The way this country's building up, there'll be a big demand for lumber. And merchants at New Orleans are clamoring for it. We can raft our logs through the bayous to the Mississippi. We ought to make good money. I'm sure that Pa'll back us and we can have him paid back in no time."

"Got it all thought out, haven't you?" Rez said, smiling. "When do we start being lumber barons?"

CHAPTER 4. A RUGGED LIFE

While on a business trip, John came to spend the weekend with his family. During the long lazy Sunday afternoon the brothers talked. When he heard of Jim and Rezin's plan to operate a sawmill on Bayou Beouf, John said, "You weren't planning to leave me out, were you? I thought we were a threesome."

"We used to be," Jim said. "But you're doing all right on your own now. After all, you're older than we are. We'll both have to start from scratch, just as you did. We'd planned to ask Pa to stake us."

"No need of that," John insisted. "I've done right well on land deals. I've got money to invest. I'll go in with you and finance the deal. As you know, I'm pretty hard-headed so I expect to get my money back with interest in a short time. You boys, though, have enough energy and ambition to make it go."

Not only did John back his younger brothers financially, he also helped clear a patch of land and fell and saw timber for a comfortable but simple cabin. It was backbreaking labor in the languid southern air, with the sun beating down mercilessly.

This primitive life was well suited to the temperaments of "those wild Bowie boys." The arm of the bayou reached far into the backwoods in real wilderness area, yet it was an easy day's ride to Alexandria.[2] The only humans the boys saw were the Acadian boatmen, called Cajuns for short. These Frenchmen were *couer du bois*[3] and usually their approach on the rafts or long pirogues was heralded by song ringing through the forests. Then John, Rezin and Jim stopped working and waved to the happy *voyageurs*.[4] Sometimes they hired the Cajuns to raft their lumber to some market, but as yet they were not so overwhelmed with business that they were pushed to fill orders.

They cut thousands of feet of cypress, oak and ash and finally the boatmen made a regular habit of stopping to take on the lumber for Baton Rouge, New Orleans or other markets. They charged such a large commission, however, that the Bowies were dissatisfied and decided to find their own markets. One of them must go to New Orleans. John said he was too busy with his various land deals. Rezin was the logical one to go.

2. Town in central Louisiana.
3. Woodsmen; i.e., trappers and traders (the proper French is *coureur de bois*).

4. Travelers. The term is used specifically of French Canadians who traveled by canoe.

"You have a way with you," Jim said earnestly as he and Rezin paused to mop their sweaty brows. "You're the best talker and have the most polished manners."

"As if any son of Elvie Bowie would grow up without polished manners!" Rezin remarked. "You have a magnetic personality, Jim, whether you realize it or not. You're the one to go."

Jim's heart missed a beat. It had long been his dream to visit that exciting city, yet he did not want to appear too eager for fear Rezin cherished a similar wish.

"Ho!" he scoffed. "You're afraid you'll miss a Sunday with the lovely Miss Margaret Neville."

Rezin grinned. "You've guessed it," he admitted. "I'd really like to take in the sights of New Orleans with you, but we can't afford to have both of us go anyway. And right now I seem to be making some headway with Miss Maggie, although the beaux buzz around her like bees around a honey tree. But who can blame them? Isn't she the prettiest young lady you ever saw?"

"She's pretty all right." Jim tried to sound enthusiastic. "I don't blame you a bit if you've fallen in love. I wish you luck. . . ." His voice trailed off. His heart wasn't in what he was saying. Since Rez had taken up courting he was detached and Jim felt out and lonely.

Although hewing down trees and sawing them into lumber with a whipsaw was the hardest sort of physical labor, the Bowie boys still had enough energy for wresting, gator riding and wild steer roping. Whenever they needed game for food they would not consider getting it by so dull a method as shooting it. No. They must mount horses and chase the game, then rope it, after which Rezin would gallop up, slide from his horse and neatly cut the animal's throat with his new knife.

Thus danger lent spice to the food they ate. The Cajun boatmen who chanced upon the "wild Bowie boys" riding roped gators stared goggle eyed at such crazy sport.

Now and then Elvie Bowie rode in her carriage to the small clearing on the bayou, bringing Mammy Lou with baskets of civilized food. Then the old Negress cleaned up the cabin to make it "fitten for young gentlemen."

John was gone for longer and longer periods of time, for his business was growing. Rez and Jim were still unusually comradely and evidently it was only Jim who noticed the widening breach in their relationship. He knew that when Rezin married things could never be the same again. Naturally his main interest would be in his bride and later in his own family. Jim tried to suppress his jealousy, but he had long moments of silence when he was morose and almost bitter. At such times he wandered off alone into the woods, or got into the pirogue and poled his way through shadowy caverns of foliage.

One day, smoothly and silently, he was making his way up a stream he had never before traveled. Although he tried to make no sound with his pole to disturb the birds or the deer which came to the water's edge, his passing awoke a napping alligator. It gave an angry flip of its tail before it sank to the bottom of the stream.

The splash caused a beautiful egret to fly into the air. Immediately a man leaped up at the water's edge and shook angry fists at Jim. "*Mon Dieu! Sacrébleu!*[5] Awkward oaf! Why for do you disturb the holy silence of the forest? You spoil my loveliest picture."

Jim rested his pole against the bottom of the water to stop the pirogue while he stared in amazement at this small and angry man.

---

5. My God! Damn it! (mild oaths that might be recognized by English speakers).

"Don't sit there looking so stupid. Why do you not explain?" the stranger demanded.

Jim suppressed a chuckle and said politely, "Please pardon me. I did not realize that you owned this wilderness."

The man's anger seemed to evaporate. "You will pardon me, please," he said contritely. "Of course I do not own this wilderness. It belongs to God. And to the birds— the beautiful, wonderful birds. I was painting the one that just flew away. I was almost finished."

"I'm terribly sorry, suh," Jim said. "I didn't know there was another human being within miles. I certainly didn't expect to find a painter here."

"Come and see what you have spoiled."

Jim clambered out of the pirogue. The little man led him to an easel under a spreading oak tree.

Jim whistled in sincere admiration. "Am I seeing a painting or an actual bird?" he asked. "If that one on canvas should take off and fly away, I wouldn't be the least bit surprised."

The painter grinned. "You like, then?"

Jim nodded. "It's amazingly lifelike!"

"Look. I show you the others." The stranger picked up a portfolio and proudly leafed through pictures of various birds, all done with exquisite detail.

"You are a fine artist," Jim said sincerely. "What is your name, suh?"

"John James Audubon.[6] And yours?"

"James Bowie. But surely you don't live about here or I would have heard of you. You must be famous."

Audubon sighed and closed his portfolio. "Alas no! The public has little interest in birds. They want anyone who can wield a brush to paint their vain, simpering women in satins and laces. That I have to do in order to eat. My Lucy[7] and I teach the young ladies and gentlemen how to dance." He held up an imaginary skirt and pointed his toes daintily and bowed and pranced until Jim roared with laughter.

"And all I want is to paint birds. I leave my lovely Lucy and my young Victor at home whenever we have a few pennies ahead. She teaches the dancing while I wander the forest—painting, painting, painting. It is for this I live. It drives me." He clasped his head dramatically as though the something which drove him caused intense pain.

"You are a genius, suh," Bowie said. "My brothers and I would be proud if you would accept the hospitality of our cabin while you are in this region. You didn't tell me where you are from."

"New Orleans. The Queen City."

"Fine!" Jim exclaimed. "You can tell me about it. I plan to make a trip there soon to try to find a market for our lumber."

The artist stayed several days as the guest of the Bowies, using their pirogue to go into the waterways in search of birds. His flimsy clothes were neat but patched in several places. He was extremely thin and from the way he devoured the food it was evident that he had not had enough to eat for some time. It did the generous-hearted Bowies good to stuff him with fish, fowl and wild game.

Jim and the artist set out early one morning on horseback. They planned to ride

6. American ornithologist and artist (1785–1851), born in Haiti.

7. Audubon's wife, Lucy Bakewell; they married in 1807 and had two sons, Victor and John.

across country until they reached the Mississippi where they would take a boat. While they jogged along Audubon told Jim about New Orleans.

"It is a strange and wonderful city," he said. "Like no other American city, for it is a mixture of French and Spanish. Americans are regarded as foreigners. First founded by the French in 1718, it became the capital of the immense colonial empire of Louisiana.

"Most of the population had come from France," he continued, "and they retained the French language and customs. The city was isolated from the rest of the country and the citizens scarcely knew or cared when the American Revolution was fought.

"Then in 1769 the people of New Orleans received a terrible shock. They learned that six years earlier France had sold Louisiana to Spain. The first intimation the New Orleanians had of this transaction was when twenty-four Spanish men-of-war appeared in the harbor, carrying the officials who had come to occupy and govern the city.

"The Spanish rule was not strict and for the most part the people went on living much the same as before," Audubon said, as they jogged along the shady trail. "French language and customs still prevailed, although some Spanish was spoken.

"It was during the Spanish rule that smuggling was introduced," he went on. "The Spanish rulers tried to put severe rules about trading into effect, but the French loved to fool their masters and so smuggling became a game in which everyone indulged. Privateers[8] who raided Spanish ships were looked upon as heroes and merchants vied to buy their merchandise.

"You know, of course, that Napoleon,[9] desperate for money, sold all of Louisiana to the United States in 1803. Although now an American city, the citizens of French or Spanish blood, called Creoles, look down upon all Americans as crude savages. Quarrels are frequent between the two factions. And, according to the code of the day, dueling is the accepted and only honorable way to settle such quarrels."

"What about this pirate Lafitte?"[1] Jim asked. "I've heard about him. He must be a daring fellow."

"My dear friend!" Audubon said in mock horror. "Never call the great Lafitte a pirate. He's a privateer, he'll have you know. He has letters of marque from the Columbians[2] allowing him to raid enemy Spanish ships wherever he finds them. And he does. With amazing daring. He is the most famous privateer of the day. It's a well-known fact that the blacksmith shop his brother Pierre runs is a hangout for smugglers who trade in his merchandise. His main hangout, though, is down on Barataria,[3] below the swamplands. There, they say, he lives like a king."

"That," vowed Jim Bowie, "is a place I must see."

CHAPTER 5. MEETING WITH THE PIRATE JEAN LAFITTE

Audubon insisted that Jim Bowie be his guest at his New Orleans home. He met the artist's sweet, cheery wife Lucy, and his lively, dark-eyed son Victor. They lived in a

8. Private ships with government-issued licenses to attack enemy shipping; also, those serving on such ships.
9. Napoléon Bonaparte (1769–1821), who effectively became dictator in France in 1799 and crowned himself emperor in 1804. Impending war with England and a costly slave revolt in Haiti helped persuade him to sell Louisiana—the area between the Mississipi River and the Rockies,

extending as far north as Canada—to the United States for $15 million.
1. Jean Lafitte (ca. 1780–ca. 1826), a French pirate active in the Gulf of Mexico.
2. I.e., Colombians. "Letters of marque": written authorization to fit out a privateer.
3. Bayou of southeast Louisiana, west of the mouth of the Mississippi.

modest, one-story log house, the walls of which were decorated with Audubon's wonderful bird pictures at which Jim would stare by the hour.

"My husband is a very great genius," Lucy said proudly. "The world does not yet appreciate him. In time it will—but alas, perhaps not until after he is buried! His pictures, though, will live forever. For that I work myself to such skinniness teaching the rich Creole belles to dance so that we will not starve while my James paints."

"Your husband seems to be in great demand as a portrait painter," Bowie remarked.

She shrugged. "At that he might become rich—but it is not so important. There are many who can paint portraits, but only one Audubon, the bird painter."

Bowie found that his friendship with the artist opened doors to him in New Orleans that would otherwise have remained closed. To the haughty Creoles he was a "foreigner," ignorant and uncultured like all Americans.

But he went about with Audubon on his portrait commissions to plantations and homes and so met the upper classes, although scarcely as a social equal. Jim discovered that his clothes were all wrong. When he saw the finely clad Creole dandies looking down their noses at him he went to the finest tailor in New Orleans and ordered skin-fitting trousers of soft tan wool, a long-tailed waistcoat and satin vest imprinted with roses. He added to this outfit a high collar, wide flowing cravat and white beaver hat, and felt he was ready to meet the young Creole gentlemen on their own grounds.

He went with Audubon to a great plantation[4] where the artist was to do the portrait of the seventeen-year-old daughter Eliza Pirrie.

Miss Eliza acknowledged the introduction with a graceful curtsy and a beguiling display of dimples. Her blue eyes frankly admired Jim's wide shoulders and great height. She looked disappointed when he said he was an American.

"I had hoped you were French," she said, giving him an arch look.

"Is it such a disgrace to be an American?" he asked a trifle stiffly. "I'm very proud that I am."

"But of course," she said. "I have no doubt there are many well-born Americans, too."

He shrugged. "We consider a countryman well born if he's a good citizen."

She broke into delighted, tinkling laughter. "You big American!" she cried. "You are so different. You make the dainty Creole gentlemen I know seem silly."

This was a new experience for Bowie. He had not met many young ladies and none who gave him such an excited, important feeling.

"Shall we go on with the sitting?" Audubon threw a chill over the little flirtation.

Bowie watched for a while, but at last he grew restless and strolled about, admiring the beautiful curved stairway which joined two galleries, the rich carpeting, the high ceilings, the brocaded satin draperies, the gleaming silver and the glittering crystal chandeliers. Beautiful gardens and smooth lawns surrounded the house. An air of serenity, peacefulness and gracious living hung about the plantation.

It was the same in the city. Jim had already wandered through the fascinating *Vieux Carré*,[5] or French quarter, where the houses were built flush with the banguette, or sidewalk. Negro women shuffled along balancing huge bundles on their heads. Housemaids saved themselves steps by doing their shopping for groceries by means of a bucket and rope. Numerous peddlers of pralines and other sweets wan-

4. Oakley Plantation in St. Francisville, where in 1821 Audubon came to tutor the daughter of the owners; he painted some of his bird paintings there.

5. Literally, "old square."

dered through the streets with their wares on boards hung around their necks. He admired the lace ironwork which adorned most of the fine homes. Now and then he caught a glimpse through a partly opened gateway of sunny courtyards beautiful with flowers and foliage. He was eager to see inside the tantalizing paradises.

At length Jim got the opportunity to visit two of the finest homes when Audubon went to paint portraits. In both places the elders greeted him coldly, making him feel like an intruder. The young Creole dandies looked him over critically, although Jim had a notion that they envied his broad shoulders and great height. Most of them were short with absurdly small hands and feet. The young ladies of the families, however, stared at him with frank admiration. Everywhere he went he was impressed by the easygoing air, unhurried and relaxed. Here indeed was gracious living.

"I'm enjoying myself immensely," Bowie said one day as they returned home after a day of portrait painting. "But I must get about my business, and find a market for my lumber."

The artist spread his hands in a hopeless gesture. "Alas, my friend! There I cannot help you. I know no purchasers of lumber. I gain entry to the homes of the rich Creoles merely to paint the empty faces of their empty women. Bah! What a waste of time! My birds are waiting in the forests, wondering why I neglect them. But my Lucy and Victor must eat. And somehow I must earn money to publish my book of bird paintings."

"I wish I were rich," Bowie said. "I'd publish it for you."

"Ah, my generous friend! And I cannot even find anyone to buy your lumber."

"Don't worry, suh," Bowie told him. "I'll stir myself and find a buyer. You've been showing me such a good time that I've been neglecting the business I came for."

Early next day Jim went to the water front to try to find someone to buy his lumber. On his way he passed through the *Vieux Carré* and upon numerous lamp posts he saw this sign in big letters:

PROCLAMATION

I DO SOLEMNLY CAUTION ALL AND SINGULAR AGAINST GIVING ANY KIND OF SUCCOR AGAINST[6] *Jean Lafitte* & HIS ASSOCIATES: BUT TO THE AIDING & ABETTING IN ARREST-ING HIM & THEM, AND ALL OTHER IN LIKE MANNER OFFENDING, & DO FURTHER-MORE, IN THE NAME OF THE STATE, OFFER A REWARD OF $500 WHICH WILL BE PAID OUT OF THE TREASURY TO ANY PERSON DELIVERING *Jean Lafitte* TO THE SHERIFF OF THE PARISH OF NEW ORLEANS, OR TO ANY OTHER SHERIFF IN THE STATE, SO THAT *Jean Lafitte* MAY BE BROUGHT TO JUSTICE.

GOVERNOR W. C. C. CLAIBORNE[7]

Jim saw a man with a wide grin on his face standing under one of the signs. His arms were folded across his chest and his whole attitude was one of open defiance. A group of men stood watching him and whispering among themselves.

"Well, here I am," the man said. "Why doesn't someone go tell Claiborne that I, Jean Lafitte, dare him to arrest me?"

No one moved. So this was the famous Jean Lafitte! Jim saw a slim man with broad shoulders. His dark eyes were restless and the lid of one of them drooped, as though in a half wink. His hair was dark and glossy. His high-cheekboned face was handsome

6. Aid to. "Singular": each.
7. William Charles Coles Claiborne (1775–1817),

Virginia-born American politician who was the first governor of Louisiana (1812–16).

and he looked more a gentleman than a pirate. There was a forceful, arrogant manner about him, and Jim instantly sensed a spirit dynamic and untamed.

Bowie stepped up boldly and held out his hand. "I've wanted to meet you, suh," he said. "I've a feeling that we might be kindred spirits."

Lafitte's keen eyes swept over him. Finally he thrust out a hand and Jim's hand was squeezed in a warm grip. "I like your looks, young man. You have force. What is your business?"

"I'm in the lumber business, suh. I came to New Orleans to see if I could find a buyer. But I don't know anyone here."

"Look up Martin Bel on the water front," Lafitte told him. "Say that Jean Lafitte sent you. He's contracting to build many of the fine mansions in the American section, and is in the market for hardwood. I'm sure he'll buy from you."

"Thanks, suh. I'm very grateful."

The piercing gray eyes narrowed. "You say you cut this wood yourself—you and your brothers?"

Bowie nodded.

"It must be hard work."

"It is."

"You are too intelligent to work like a slave. Do you want to make a great deal of money quickly?"

"Yes. Of course, suh."

"Then come to see me at my place at Barataria. We can do business. I should like you to be my guest."

"Thank you, suh. I'll plan to do that."

"Do so. Very soon."

He moved away from his post beneath the sign toward the Lafitte blacksmith shop. Bowie hurried to the water front to look up Martin Bel, who agreed to buy all the cypress and oak the Bowie brothers could deliver within the next year.

The following day Jim went back to the *Vieux Carré* on his way to the Lafitte blacksmith shop hoping to find the privateer in order to thank him for the favor. He noticed that the signs offering five hundred dollars for Lafitte's arrest had been torn down and in their places were other notices offering fifteen hundred dollars for the arrest and delivery of Governor Claiborne to Jean Lafitte.

Everyone was laughing over the placards and Jim himself was amused. He vowed that he would certainly accept Lafitte's invitation. The man interested him. Besides, he was burning with curiosity to know what sort of business deal Lafitte had in mind. Probably something along the order of smuggling which, though illegal according to the governor's edict, had become an accepted sport indulged in by the most respectable citizens of New Orleans.

Chapter 6. Visit to the Privateer Stronghold

John and Rezin were pleased with the success of their brother's trip to New Orleans. With a market for all the hardwood that could be cut, they were ready to plunge into the labor of procuring it. But Jim was restless and dissatisfied and hated the work more every day.

One day he loosened his hold on his end of the whipsaw and mopped his forehead. "There must be some easier way than this!" he burst out.

"Easier than what?" Rez asked.

Jim waved a hand at the boards they had sawed and the hated tool with which they had done the work. "To make money. We work harder than any slaves we know. In New Orleans I saw a new way of life. People living in beautiful homes, wearing fine clothes and having time to enjoy life. That's what I want. And I don't want to wait until I'm an old man. Rez, we've got to figure out some way to make a lot of money in a hurry."

Rez shrugged and drawled. "I'm with you, Jim. Start figuring. Got anything in mind?"

"Nothing definite yet." Jim's tone was impatient. "But I've made up my mind. Nothing'll stop me."

"John's been doing well buying and selling land," Rezin pointed out.

Jim nodded. "That may be the answer. To the west of us are millions of acres which can be bought cheap. I'm sure there's going to be a strong, steady expansion to the west since President Jefferson[8] bought all of Louisiana from Napoleon. He sent Lewis and Clark[9] out to make a report on the new territory, you know. I've also got a hankering to see Texas. I'll use my wits to buy up likely sections[1] and sell them at a profit as civilization moves westward."

His eyes held a faraway expression. "But first," he went on, "I want to pay a visit to Jean Lafitte's hideout. When he invited me he hinted that he might have some money-making deal for me."

With a chuckle he sank to a log to rest and motioned his brother to sit beside him as he told how the New Orleaneans delighted in outwitting those in authority by dealing in smuggled goods. The Lafittes were the leaders in this sort of business.

Jim said, "I wouldn't care to engage in smuggling myself. But I can see how a man of Lafitte's caliber would find delight in outsmarting a man like Claiborne. I've an overpowering curiosity to see Lafitte's hideout."

"Then let's go," Rez said.

"First," Jim responded, "let's get rid of this place. We'll ship our lumber off to Martin Bel, according to my agreement. Then we'll put our sawmill and the acres we've cleared up for sale. That should give us a nice nest egg of working capital to go on."

Jim knew of the mysterious Barataria country south of New Orleans, where Lafitte's headquarters had been located. In his pirogue he had explored portions of this watery area, the haunt of wild things. From Louis Gasperon, a Baratarian who sometimes worked at the Bowie sawmill, Jim learned more of the region and of the activities of Jean Lafitte.

Louis himself greatly amused Jim and Rezin. He wore a bright red head scarf and large brass earrings. Although actually a mild-mannered man he tried hard to look like a pirate. He was proud of the fact that he often worked for Jean Lafitte, as many of the Baratarians did. For many years Spanish, French and Portuguese people had lived quietly along the waterways of the Barataria in small fishing villages. They were for the most part gentle, religious folk, although the swamplands formed ideal hiding places for those who wanted to escape the law. When the Lafittes adopted Grand Isle and Grande-Terre as their headquarters, the Baratarians took up smuggling, too, along with trapping and fishing.

Jim well knew the circumstances which made this a ripe time for privateering to

8. Thomas Jefferson (1743–1826; third U.S. president, 1801–09) oversaw the 1803 purchase of Louisiana from France.
9. Meriwether Lewis (1774–1809) and William Clark (1770–1838), leaders of an expedition (1804–06) from St. Louis to the Pacific Ocean in search of a navigable water passage to the west.
1. Allotments of land, each 1 square mile (640 acres) in area.

thrive. Mexico, Central America and South America were all in revolt against Spain. The republic of Cartagena, a seaport of Colombia, accommodatingly issued letters of marque against Spanish shipping. The Baratarians, armed with cannons and cutlasses and with these letters to give legality to their actions, then sailed from the numerous byways of the swamplands to capture and loot Spanish ships. And right at their back yard was New Orleans with a wealthy population of about thirty thousand. It was also the gateway to commerce of the whole Mississippi Valley.

Early in 1813 the New Orleans merchants became so disturbed over the inroads the smugglers were making in their business that they appealed to the naval authorities for help. Louisiana's Governor Claiborne meantime posted the proclamation which branded Jean and Pierre Lafitte as "banditti and pirates."

Yet within a few months desperate New Orleaneans would be begging those same "banditti" and pirates to help them. Jim chuckled when he heard the story. In 1812 the United States declared war upon Great Britain.[2] The Louisianians, however, felt remote from the battle until 1814 when two English officials boldly went to Jean Lafitte's headquarters at Grande-Terre and offered him thirty thousand dollars cash, a captaincy in the British navy and an opportunity for each of his men to enlist if he would organize the Baratarians to help capture New Orleans.

Jean Lafitte asked for time to consider the proposition. Then he straightway sent a message to the American officials informing them that the British were planning to besiege New Orleans and telling of their offer to him. He furthermore offered to organize the Baratarians in defense of the city.

When Andrew Jackson[3] reached New Orleans and saw the desperate situation, he immediately called upon Jean Lafitte and the Baratarians, who joined forces with the Americans and swung victory to their side.

"To think," Jim told Rezin, "that I had to miss all that excitement! I'm more determined than ever to accept Lafitte's invitation to visit him."

"If this deal to sell our place goes through, I'll certainly go with you," Rezin said eagerly.

The place was sold and the Bowie brothers made a profit which amazed them.

"Maybe we've found the secret for quick wealth," Jim chuckled as he counted the money. "Buy a piece of uncleared land for a song, improve it a bit, then sell it for several times what we paid for it."

They engaged Louis Gasperon to guide them, since they wanted to travel by pirogue through the Barataria to the Gulf. Louis was sure that he could get them passage on some ship going to Galvez-town,[4] Lafitte's present headquarters.

They followed one waterway after another, through many bayous and marshes, a strangely wild and beautiful region.

"The trembling prairie," Louis called it. It was difficult to tell where dry land left off and water began. Mostly it was swampland with a jungle growth of high grass and shrubbery. A blue mist hung over the place, giving it a strange, eerie look.

"What a wonderful place to get lost!" Jim shuddered slightly as he saw a water moccasin slither into the water from the tall grass.

He and Rezin were both alert, trying to memorize landmarks in case they wanted to make their way here again without a guide.

2. The War of 1812 (1812–15) ended in a stalemate but left Americans feeling more secure about the prospects of their young nation.
3. Politician and soldier (1767–1845), born in South Carolina, and the seventh president of the United States (1829–37). He became a national hero after defeating the British in the Battle of New Orleans (1814–15).
4. Now Galveston, on the eastern coast of Texas.

"The Temple." Louis' waving hand indicated one island much larger than any others they had seen. Great oaks circled a central clear space. "Lafitte held his auctions there for smuggled goods and slaves. Many merchants and planters from New Orleans came to bid for his goods."

Jim laughed. "The New Orleaneans love to break the laws the American officials make. Ever since it was made illegal,[5] traffic in slaves boomed more than ever. Blackbirding[6] became an accepted way of making a living, just as smuggling did."

"A silly law if there ever was one," Rezin said hotly. "How can men run plantations—raise cotton and sugar and tobacco without slaves? And the black men are better off on fine plantations where they receive good care and are taught and trained as Christian, civilized beings."

Jim nodded. "Often when we were working the whipsaw I envied Father's slaves. It makes me tired to hear these narrow-minded Yankees carry on about the evils of slavery. Most of the slaves we know are very well treated."

"Louis," Jim asked, "why is Jean Lafitte so bitter against the Spaniards? I believe him when he says that he is a privateer, not a pirate; that he has a letter of marque from Cartagena making it legal for him to prey upon Spanish ships. But he does it with such relish. Why does he hate them so much?"

"That is a story to wring your heart," Louis said. "Once he was rich enough to buy and outfit his own ship with merchandise. About the same time he fell in love with and married a beautiful French girl. They set out to sea for the American coast but were captured by a Spanish man-of-war which took over his ship and set Lafitte adrift in a small boat. He was later picked up half dead from starvation and thirst by Baratarian fishermen who nursed him back to health. Later he learned the sad fate of his lovely wife. Believing that Lafitte had a fortune hidden somewhere, they put the young woman to the torture and she died as a result. So-o, who can blame our captain for carrying on unceasing war against the Spanish?"

"That explains it," said Jim. "No wonder Lafitte hates the Spanish."

Now it was easy enough to distinguish water from land. They had reached Barataria Bay which was sprinkled with little islands. The largest, Grande-Terre, had been Lafitte's headquarters and a large house, now deserted, still stood there.

Louis learned from his fisherman friends that a boat would embark for Galveztown, or "Campeachy" (Campeche), as Lafitte called the island port of the Mexican state of Coahuila.

Coming in sight of Campeche around the curve of the Gulf of Mexico, Rezin and Jim stared eagerly at the amazing tall red house surrounded by as motley a collection of dwellings as could be imagined. Some were made of palmetto, others of canvas and a few of stone or wood. Ships and small boats were anchored in the harbor.

"The Maison Rouge,"[7] Louis said, pointing to the bright red building, the second story bristling with cannon. It was on a high dune at the back of the town and obviously served as a fortress as well as a dwelling.

"Since he moved from Barataria, the scum of the earth have taken up with our Captain Lafitte, men who would murder you for gold."

"Fortunately we haven't any gold," Jim said calmly. But he thought of the six thousand dollars he and Rezin carried in their money belts, and involuntarily put his hand on his knife.

---

5. The importation of slaves was outlawed in 1808, though their ownership and sale within the United States continued to be legal.

6. Engaging in the slave trade.
7. Literally, the "Red House."

Louis did not miss the gesture. "You'll be safe enough with Jean Lafitte," he said. "The men respect and fear him."

As they approached the large house an immensely fat man, with a long black pigtail hanging between his shoulders, waddled down the walk. At his ears dangled enormous earrings. About his monstrous middle was a sash of bright red and in it was thrust a huge, ivory-handled knife. A sword in a sheath hung beside it.

"Dominique You," Louis Gasperon said, "this is Jim Bowie and his brother. Jean Lafitte met Mr. Bowie in New Orleans and asked him to be his guest."

Dominique You gave them a genial smile and tried to bow but was prevented by his too-fat stomach. "Follow me," he said, walking ahead and up the steps onto the wide veranda and into the house. "Wait here. I'll call the captain," he said, and he waddled from the room.

The Bowie brothers stared around in amazement. Here was a room with heavy timbers of weathered mahogany. On the walls were beautiful tapestries and at the windows hung the finest of brocaded draperies. The floor was covered with rich rugs. Silver and crystal glistened on tables and shelves.

"Are we in some sultan's palace?" Jim whispered.

Then quickly both were on their feet for Jean Lafitte had entered, his footsteps silent on the thick rugs.

"Ah, Mister James Bowie!" he called cordially. "How nice of you to accept my invitation and to bring your handsome brother. I am most happy to have you as my guests."

He turned to the three men who had followed him. "You have met Dominique You," he said. His clipped speech held only the slightest trace of French accent. "This is Beluche and here is Nez Coupe,[8] who was most unfortunate to lose his nose in a saber duel. His opponent, needless to say, met a much worse fate."

While the Bowies were acknowledging the introductions to the lieutenants, Lafitte pulled a bell rope and almost instantly a servant entered bearing a tray of sparkling cool wine which the Bowies found most refreshing.

"René," Lafitte said, "show my guests to the front bedroom. After you wash up, gentlemen, join me here and we will dine."

Jim and Rezin found their room as fine as the rest of the house.

"The houses I saw in New Orleans were furnished no better than this," Jim said, speaking in a whisper for fear someone might be spying.

"No doubt the loot from many a ship has gone into these furnishings," Rezin likewise spoke softly. "It's all very luxurious, but I don't exactly feel at home here."

Their luggage had been brought up and the two guests changed into their best garments, for Lafitte was garbed in fawn-colored breeches and waistcoat and brocaded vest.

Lafitte led them into a long dining room where a mahogany table gleamed beneath the light of numerous candles in silver holders. They dined on roast wild turkey and on a delicious mixture something like a dish Jim had tasted in New Orleans called "bouillabaisse,"[9] and on candied fruits. Never had Jim tasted such a meal.

"You live in great comfort here," he remarked.

"Why not?" said Lafitte. "The comforts of life were made for those who have the perceptions to enjoy them. You . . ."—his sharp eyes bored into Jim's—"are, I discern, such a person. And your brother, too. Tonight we will chat. You will rest. Tomorrow we will tour the island. See the sights—such as they are."

---

8. Literally, "Cut Nose."

9. A French stew made from a variety of fish.

Again Jim was conscious of that boring look, as though Lafitte were trying to pry into his soul. It made him slightly uncomfortable.

CHAPTER 7. BLACK GOLD

In the morning after a sumptuous breakfast Lafitte said to his guests, "Gentlemen, do you care to join me in a walk about my premises?"

"We will be pleased to," Jim replied.

Nez Coupe and Dominique You followed. They seemed always to be with their captain.

A weird sound as of mournful singing came from the upper end of the island. Rounding a bend Jim saw an enclosure built of high logs.

"The barracoon," Lafitte said. "I presumed you gentlemen would like to see it."

"The slave pen?" Jim was conscious that again the captain was giving him that strange, questioning look. "Do you have slaves there now?"

"A ship brought some yesterday," Lafitte replied, his tone casual.

"Do you have trouble disposing of them now that the law has made their traffic illegal?" Rezin asked.

Lafitte laughed. "The Louisianians like nothing better than breaking Yankee-made laws. No. It's very simple to sell slaves. And immensely profitable. I sell them at a dollar a pound. Whoever buys them takes them to the settlements and informs the official that he found someone dealing in slaves. Then they are auctioned off and the informer is given half of whatever they bring. Usually he or his agents bid them in. Then whoever bought them from me originally sells them to the planters."

Again Jim met Lafitte's crafty stare. He was beginning to understand what sort of business deal the privateer had in mind for him.

When they reached the barracoon, an overseer turned the key in a great padlock and the gate swung open. Jim could scarcely suppress a gasp at what he saw—the most miserable human beings he could possibly imagine. They sat against the fence, chained to its logs, although Jim could not see why they should be, for certainly they had neither the strength nor the energy to try to escape. They had stopped their mournful singing at the sight of the man who owned them, and sat staring at the ground.

"These are in bad shape," Lafitte admitted. "As I said, they just came in yesterday. I haven't had time to fatten them. Poor creatures. They evidently suffered in the hands of their captors—the Spanish dogs."

The pen was indescribably filthy and a sickening stench rose in the hot enclosure.

"I've seen enough," Jim said curtly, turning away.

"They often arrive in this condition," Lafitte said. "Don't be shocked. In a few weeks they will be fat and sleek on some rich man's sugar plantation. You have seen how they fare."

"If the poor creatures live that long." Jim bit the words off shortly.

"They'll live, if they get out in the open soon enough," Lafitte said. "That's the trouble. They aren't used to being penned up. If they have to be kept that way long after an ocean trip during which they are half starved, it's just too bad."

"How much do you want for them?" Jim stopped in his tracks and stared at Lafitte. Rezin had caught up with them.

"A dollar a pound," Lafitte replied. "To simplify matters and make it round numbers, I estimate an average of one hundred and forty pounds per slave."

"I'll buy the lot," Jim snapped. "At your price. If you will also sell me supplies for the poor devils to live on until we can get them into the hands of humane owners."

"Mr. Bowie! Do you mean to imply that I'm not humane?" Lafitte's eyelid came down in that queer wink, and Jim did not know whether he had actually taken offense or was laughing at him.

"You're in this business for what you can get out of it," Jim replied shortly. "I realize that you aren't responsible for the condition of those creatures. And you haven't room here to turn them out."

Lafitte shrugged. "I consider I'm doing the poor devils a favor by taking them from the Spanish dogs and turning them over to men who will treat them humanely." Again the wink.

"Jim!" Rezin broke in. "Do you realize if you do this you will be a blackbirder?"

"Aren't you with me, Rez?"

"Well, I'm not sure that I like the idea too well."

Jim turned to Lafitte. "Do you mind if my brother and I discuss this matter alone for a moment?"

"Of course not. You gentlemen join me at Maison Rouge when you have reached your decision."

"I don't like the idea of being a blackbirder, either," Jim said. "But it would haunt me forever to go away from here and leave those black people in that filthy hole. I'm going through with it. I'd like to have you with me, but if you aren't I'll go it alone."

"You know I'm with you," Rezin said.

The business transaction was completed after the Bowie brothers went to their room and took the needed cash from their money belts. Lafitte had his men outfit some small boats at the mouth of the Calcasieu. Jim, Rezin and Louis Gasperon transported their "black gold" by water to Calcasieu Lake, then marched them overland.

It was early morning when this land trek began. Each Negro was clad in cheap linsey breeches and carried on his head a week's supply of food, wrapped in sacking. Louis walked at the head of the procession, leading the way. Rezin and Jim brought up the rear, each with a rifle cradled in his arm. The slaves gave them no trouble. They seemed relieved to be on the move and in the open where the air was clean and fresh.

Arriving at the border of the United States, Jim found that it was as ridiculously easy as Lafitte had promised. He reported that he had discovered a camp of slaves in a near-by forest and led the officials to the spot. Of course the captors were nowhere to be found. The slaves except for the six they kept for themselves were sold at auction and Jim and Rezin Bowie were given half the amount, eighteen thousand dollars.

They bought a new plantation in Rapides Parish, near Alexandria. With the slaves to clear the land they built a house, for Rezin was engaged to Margaret Neville and eager to be married.

Soon Jim received word from Lafitte that another load of slaves awaited him. He asked Rezin to go with him to get them.

"I've got all I want, Jim," his brother said. "Maggie's against this sort of thing, and I wouldn't risk losing her for all the money in the world. We've a fine plantation here. Or it will be in time."

"That way takes too long!" Jim cried. "I haven't your patience. Besides, I haven't any Maggie to lose. I'm going it alone, Rez."

"Good luck to you!" Rezin said.

Jim turned away. So their paths were finally separating. Rez wanted to settle down to being a family man and to the humdrum work of running a plantation. Well, such a tame life wasn't for Jim.

Louis went with him to Galvez-town and again Jim bought forty blacks. Now, even more than on the first trip, he realized that every foot of the way was fraught with danger. He and Louis each had a rifle and a knife, but two men would have little chance against forty Negroes if they decided to turn on them. He chained them at night; otherwise the slaves were free to plod single file through the tall grass and marshy ground. They were completely docile, however, and gave him no trouble.

Three times he traveled to Campeche and brought back slaves. And strangely enough, each time he was gone tragedy struck the Bowie home. The first time his brother David was seized with cramps while in swimming and drowned. Next, his sister Sarah died in childbirth. The third time he returned home to find the family mourning the death of his father.

Mrs. Bowie had gone to live with Rezin, Maggie and their two small daughters at Arcadia. She called Jim before her.

"What is this I hear about you, Jim?" she asked, staring up at his six-foot-two.

"I don't know. What do you hear?"

"That you have turned blackbirder. Is it true?"

He felt like a small boy about to be chastised for some wrongdoing.

"It's true," he said. "Don't tell me, Mom, that you have turned against slavery."

"It's an economic necessity for the South," she said. "But what you're doing is illegal. I raised my sons to be gentlemen. I will not have you doing something which will brand you as less than one."

"Are you ashamed of me, Mom?"

"Yes, I am. So ashamed that I can't hold up my head among my friends." She put her hand before her face and wept. That was the undoing of Jim Bowie. He had been about to tease her about her inconsistency. But he had made her ashamed and the knowledge turned like a knife in his heart.

He put his arms around her. "Don't cry, Mom! Please. I'll never do it again. I wouldn't humiliate you for the world."

"Oh, Jim!" she sobbed. "I do so want to be proud of my sons. And you—the one I expected the most of. I was always sure that you'd make me proud of you."

"And I'll do it, too, Mom," he promised. "You'll never be ashamed of me again."

CHAPTER 8. A LEGEND GROWS

Jim Bowie was on his way to becoming a legend. Already he looked like the sort of person of whom one would expect heroic deeds. Handsome and dynamic, he towered head and shoulders above the average man. Wherever he went, eyes turned his way. His work at the whipsaw had made his shoulders massive. His hands were huge and incredibly strong. His reddish hair, always slightly tousled, gave him the look of a man in a hurry to do important things. His eyes, sometimes gray, sometimes blue, according to his mood, had a compelling look.

He had made over sixty-five thousand dollars running slaves and at twenty-five was considered rich. With his brothers he owned three prosperous plantations and had numerous other land holdings. They had set up the first engine for making sugar from cane.

Having given up trading in slaves to please his mother, he returned to Alexandria, now a booming town crowded with land speculators. Cotton and sugar were bringing swift wealth and the westward expansion Jim had prophesied had begun.

He and Rezin sold one of the plantations and immediately bought other land with the proceeds, then borrowed more money for more land.

Jim was welcome at the finest homes. Now there were many mansions similar to those on the plantations around New Orleans. He was continually on the go, traveling on horseback or by stagecoach, buying or selling lands or playing the gallant gentleman at social functions.

With characteristic wholeheartedness he threw himself into the political dissensions which were then bubbling with white-hot fury in Rapides Parish. Two factions had sprung up and were fighting each other with deadly rivalry: the Old-Timers, who had conquered the wilderness and therefore considered it their right to rule it; and the New-Comers, whom the former considered upstarts but who seemed determined to take the reins of government into their own hands. The southerners' regard for background and tradition and the New-Comers' lack of such regard was to bring about an inevitable clash.

Norris Wright, a frail-looking young man, came from Baltimore to work as clerk in the general merchandise store. In spite of his appearance, he was a man to fear. Already he had fought five duels and killed two of his adversaries, seriously wounding the others. He was shrewd, calculating and ruthless.

The Old-Timer sheriff of Rapides Parish died in office. Before citizens realized what was happening young Norris Wright was appointed to fill the vacancy. When Wright was up for election Bowie campaigned zealously against him, agreeing with his friends that it would not do to allow the upstarts to gain the political saddle. Wright, however, was elected. In no time at all he became the political leader of the New-Comers. He helped organize a new bank and was elected to its board of directors.

"Seems to me," Jim remarked ironically to Rezin, when he heard this, "that for a young man, comparatively new to the community, he's coming up mighty fast. And there are indications that there was skulduggery about the election."

Rezin nodded. "I wonder how that will affect our standing at the bank."

"It shouldn't matter much." Jim shrugged.

He stooped down to kiss his mother. "Take care of yourself, Mom," he said. "I'm riding to the sugar plantation. Some trouble has developed with the new steam engine. Then I have business in Natchez."

He mounted his fine blooded horse and galloped through the rows of trees, delighting to see the improvements on all sides. It gave him great satisfaction to realize that he had had a very active part in developing this lovely country.

Passing one of the newer plantations he slowed down so that he could see what had been done there. The mansion was nearing completion. Jim nodded approvingly. The tall pillars rising from ground to balustrade[1] were in the traditional southern style, the proportions of the great white house were correct and pleasing. He wondered what sort of person the owner was.

He was not long in finding out. Rounding a clump of bushes he came upon a sight which sent him into one of his swift rages. A Negro was tied to a tree and a brawny white man was beating him unmercifully, although the unfortunate slave seemed near unconsciousness—or death—with blood streaming down his back.

Jim leaped from his horse and, snatching the whip from the man's hands, started laying it onto the erstwhile flogger. "Anyone who would treat a defenseless slave like that should be shot!" he cried.

---

1. Railing with its supporting posts.

The man, who was nearly as tall as Bowie, managed to seize the lash and the two stood panting and glaring at each other, pulling at opposite ends of the whip.

"What business is it of yours what I do to my own slave?" the man demanded.

"I make it my business when I see a human being mistreated," Jim replied.

"This slave's no good," the man blustered. "He deserved a flogging."

"No creature on earth could deserve such a beating as that." Jim let go of the whip. "You would have killed him before long. I'll buy him from you. How much do you want for him?"

"He's not for sale."

"You say he's no good. If that's the case, you should be glad to get rid of him."

A shrewd gleam came into the man's eyes. "Twelve hundred dollars will buy him," he said.

Jim whistled. "A pretty price for a slave that's no good."

He drew out his wallet and wrote a check for the amount. The man accepted it. "So you're Jim Bowie," he said. "I've heard about you. My friend Norris Wright has often mentioned you."

"Indeed?" Jim said, stepping over to untie the bonds of his newly acquired slave. He made no further comment, realizing that probably whatever Norris Wright said about him was not complimentary.

He led the Negro over to his horse. The black man could scarcely walk. Bowie half lifted him behind the saddle before he mounted.

"My horse is strong enough to carry double the short way back to the plantation," he said.

"God bless you, massa!" the Negro murmured. "I'll make you a good slave, as God is my witness."

"What's your name, boy?"

"Sam, suh. Big Sam, they calls me."

"All right, Big Sam. Do your best for me and we'll get along."

He rode back to the home plantation and left Big Sam in Rezin's care, to have his wounds treated. He did not know it then, but he had acquired more than a slave; he had gained a man who would worship his rescuer all his life.

Jim continued his trip toward Natchez, stopping to visit various friends on their plantations. One of these was Dr. William Lattimore, an owner of a large estate and a highly respected citizen.

"By the way," Jim said as he was preparing to leave, "where's young Bill? I missed him."

Dr. Lattimore chuckled with indulgent pride. "Bill's getting to be quite a man. My political duties take me away so much I'm training him to take over. I sent him to Natchez the other day to sell the cotton. Time he took some responsibility."

"Good idea," Jim said, mounting his horse. "Bill's a fine lad. He won't disappoint you. Good-by until next time I see you."

"Look Bill up when you get to Natchez," Dr. Lattimore said. "He'll be disappointed to have missed you. He is stopping at Roseleigh Manor."

"I'll make it a point to do that," Bowie promised.

It was late at night when he reached Natchez. Arriving at the inn he inquired about young Lattimore, but was told that he had not yet come in. On his return from supper, Jim saw a tall figure walking ahead of him with an unsteady gait.

Catching up with the man, he saw that it was Bill Lattimore. "Why, Bill Lattimore! What luck! I've been looking for you."

"Oh, Jim Bowie! It's good to meet a friend after being in a den of thieves." The young man moaned and would have fallen if Jim had not caught him.

"What's the matter, Bill? Are you sick—or drunk?"

"Both—I guess. Oh, Jim! I've done a terrible thing."

"Suppose we sit here on the inn steps and you tell me about it," Jim suggested.

The young man sank down and put his head in his hands. "I can never go home. I've disgraced my father."

"Come now!" Jim said, "things can't be that bad! Tell me what happened."

"I lost my father's crop money. Every cent of it. He trusted me. Depended upon me . . ."

"You've been to Natchez-Under-the-Hill." Jim hazarded a guess.

The young man nodded.

"I can take up your story from there," Jim went on. "You stopped somewhere to buy a drink. You met a friendly, likable chap who bought you another drink, then suggested that the two of you see the sights. Feeling in an adventurous mood you agreed. Your new acquaintance then led you to one of the dives under the hill. You were offered more drinks. Then you were neatly fleeced by experienced crooks. I've heard that story many times."

"What a fool I was—the farmer boy out to see the sights. I'll never face my father after this, Jim."

"That's nonsense." Jim rose. "Come with me, Bill. Take me to this place where you got fleeced."

"Oh, no, Jim! I won't have you doing that."

"Won't have me doing what? You don't even know what I have in mind—if anything."

"I—I was afraid you planned to go there and try to make them give my money back. You might get hurt. They're a rough lot."

"Why don't you just leave things to me, Bill? After all, I'm rather experienced. I've been around Natchez a bit and know it 'on' and 'under' the hill. I'd really like to see this particular place and I promise you that Jim Bowie can take care of himself."

"Well, if you insist." Bill got to his feet reluctantly.

"I do insist. However, I'll bet I know which dive it was. Did you happen to hear the name Sturdivant mentioned?"

"Yes!" Bill cried. "That's it. They called it Sturdivant's place."

Jim groaned inwardly. John Sturdivant was the most notorious of the desperadoes who made Natchez-Under-the-Hill their haunt, and his henchmen were the toughest there were. Yet it was considered the thing to do by fashionable gentlemen on the hill to frequent these gambling dens from time to time. Jim had followed the fad with his young friends, so knew the various houses, although he did not care for such amusement.

He knew that Sturdivant was a dangerous man. Called "Bloody Sturdivant," he was one of those who used the then-prevalent dueling code as a pretext for getting rid of his enemies. He was deadly with both pistol and knife and had several killings to his credit. Besides, it was known he had burned to the ground the homes of four of his political enemies.

Jim Bowie strode into Sturdivant's gambling house with white-faced Bill Lattimore at his heels. At one of the tables Jim pushed Bill into a chair and pulled out a roll of money. "Play this as if it were your own," he whispered into his young friend's ear.

Jim stood watching with a nonchalant air while the game went on. Bill won, then lost, won slightly, then began to lose steadily. Jim's eyes were half closed as though he were about to fall asleep, but he was not missing a movement of the dealer's fluid hands.

Finally he yawned, stretched and nudged Bill. "Give me your place for a while or I'll fall asleep."

The game went on silently for a time, Jim winning then losing. Suddenly he reached across and seized the dealer's hand. "Put that card back!" he said in a threatening tone. "I saw you palm that ace."

He rose, pushed back his chair and calmly pulled the money on the table toward him and put it in his pockets.

"Hey there!" John Sturdivant bellowed. "You can't do that in my house."

"Yes I can," Jim said calmly. "I caught your man cheating. A little while ago one of your confederates brought this man here and robbed him of all of his father's crop money. I don't stand for that sort of thing being done to my friends—here, or anywhere else."

"Put that money back!" Sturdivant roared.

"I took only enough to repay my friend for what you stole."

"You can't call me a thief."

Jim stared the gambler straight in the eye. "I did call you one, suh," he said in a gentle voice, but there was nothing gentle in his eyes.

"You won't leave here with that money without fighting for it," Sturdivant's voice quivered with anger.

"Then we'll fight. What weapon do you choose?"

Sturdivant jerked out a knife. Bowie took his from its sheath.

"We'll fight with our wrists strapped together," Sturdivant declared.

"Very well." Jim shrugged.

While the chairs and tables were pushed back the two contenders had their left wrists bound with a buckskin cord. All color was drained from Bill Lattimore's face as he watched.

Complete silence fell over the room while the antagonists faced each other. Then one of the croupiers started counting slowly, "One, two. . . ." When he said "three," knives clashed and there was the sound of shuffling feet as the men thrust and parried. Bowie made a sudden lunge and Sturdivant's knife clattered to the floor. Jim's thrust had cut the tendons of his wrist.

Sturdivant's face turned white. He tensed, bracing himself for the death blow. Instead Jim slashed through the buckskin bond. "I'm not killing you," he said. "I wouldn't kill a defenseless man. I reckon, though, that I've cured you of knifing men for a while at least, Sturdivant."

Pushing Bill Lattimore before him, he left the room in a deliberate manner, but as the door was closing behind him he heard Sturdivant's vicious tone, "Get that man, Bowie! Do you hear me! You three get him—or you'll be accountable to me."

Jim opened the door and peered inside. "I promise," he said in a level tone, "that I won't be so generous to whatever poor devils you're sending after me, Sturdivant. I've never yet provoked a fight and never will. But I'm ready for those who come after me."

He and Bill were allowed to ascend the hill safely.

Young Lattimore lost no time in spreading the tale of Jim Bowie's first duel. And the tale lost nothing in the retellings. From it sprang absurd variations, for James Bowie was the sort of personage about whom legends gathered.

CHAPTER 9. THE BLOODIEST DUEL

After his fight with Bloody Sturdivant people called Jim Bowie the Young Lion. He laughed at the name, but it so fitted his courageous and fiery personality that it stuck.

For several years Jim and Rezin had been making money from everything they touched. Then a streak of ill fortune hit them. For three years in a row crops were bad. The following year their lands were flooded.

"What shall we do, Jim?" Rezin asked, as he stared at the inundated land.

"Our credit has always been good," Jim said reassuringly. "We'll go to Alexandria and borrow money to tide us over until we get good crops again."

"I hope you're right." Rezin's worried frown eased a bit. "You go and attend to it, Jim. I'll stay on the plantation and see about things here."

Next day Jim rode to Alexandria and asked for the loan. He thought he noticed the bank president, long a friend, hesitate as though embarrassed. "I'll have to take it up with the board of directors, you know, Jim," he said.

Bowie nodded. "I'll drop in tomorrow and get the money."

He was not prepared for the shock he received when he stepped cheerily into the bank next morning.

"I'm sorry, Jim," the banker said. "But the directors turned down your application."

"Turned it down!" Jim's tone was incredulous.

"I was in favor of it, of course," the banker went on. "But I couldn't swing enough of the other directors."

"Who opposed me?"

"I'd rather not say."

Jim's brows met in a deep frown. "You don't need to tell me. I know. It was Norris Wright, wasn't it?"

The banker nodded.

"I would expect him to be against me. But since when and how has he got so much power that he overrules the rest of you? Some of you are my friends."

"I don't understand it myself," the banker said unhappily. "That man does wield power. And it is growing."

"It's going too far." Jim rose and gripped the back of the chair until the knuckles of his great hands showed white. "The man's a rascal. I'm satisfied he bought the election which made him sheriff. And a man who steals votes will steal money. Not only that. His friends are allowed to commit murder safe in the knowledge that they won't be arrested."

The banker nodded. "You refer to the scandalous Crain affair, of course. I agree with you, Jim, that things are going too far. The feud that's been simmering so long between the Old-Timers and the New-Comers is bound to come to a head someday. And I'm afraid that someone will be killed."

The Crain affair to which Jim had referred had added considerable fuel to the smoldering feud between the two factions. Colonel Robert Crain from Virginia had rented a plantation on Bayou Rapides. He straightway took sides with Norris Wright and proceeded to cut quite a swath in and about Alexandria, both socially and politically. Despite his exaggerated southern gallantry, he ignored his debts. When any creditor attempted to collect an overdue account he flew into a rage and instantly challenged him to a duel.

When his landlord went to collect the rent, the colonel offered to give him a note.

"I prefer cash," the landlord said.

Thereupon Colonel Crain pulled out his pistol and shot the man for "insulting a gentleman from Virginia."

The Virginia "gentleman" was accused of stealing a neighbor's slaves and taking them from the state. It looked as if the colonel was about to be indicted, but Norris Wright pulled political strings and quashed the proceedings against his friend. There were many similar incidents.

Jim Bowie happened to be in Alexandria on business during this tense time. Dressed in a suit of fine broadcloth and wearing a high beaver hat he was unarmed. Rounding a corner he came face to face with Norris Wright.

He bowed slightly and would have hurried by, but Norris seized his arm. "I've heard the things you've been saying about me." His usually pale face was flushed with anger. "You wouldn't dare say them to my face."

"You're wrong," Jim replied calmly. "I'm willing to say anything to your face that I'd say behind your back. I said that you stole the election which put you in the sheriff's office. I said that anyone who would steal votes would steal money."

Wright whipped out his pistol and fired. Jim saw the blaze and knew that for a moment he was slightly off balance but he felt no pain. Suddenly all of the enmity for this unprincipled man that he had been holding in leash bubbled to the surface. With a bellow he threw himself at Wright and seized his throat between his strong fingers.

Friends jerked at his arms, but his grip held.

He heard Rezin shout, "Stop, Jim! You're killing him."

After he had been pulled away, he saw two men supporting Norris Wright. Jim's anger drained from him and he turned away—shocked at what he had almost done.

His own knees nearly buckled and his friend Dr. Denny came to help Rezin bolster him up. Jim put his hand to his side, then drew it away covered with blood. "Looks like he hurt me more than I thought."

"Come to my office," the doctor said.

They found a flattened silver dollar in Jim's vest pocket, which had deflected the bullet. It had only grazed Jim's ribs, making a painful but not serious wound.

"Of course you'll call Wright out for this," the doctor said.

Jim shook his head.

"Don't you believe in the code of honor?" the doctor asked.

"Not to the extent of provoking fights," Jim said. "I nearly killed Wright with my bare hands. So far as I'm concerned, that evens up things between us."

"If he challenges you, though, Jim, you'll have to fight," Rezin said.

"I suppose so, or be branded a coward for the rest of my life. But I've got a feeling he won't be too anxious to meet me again."

Jim was right. No challenge came from Norris Wright, yet the Alexandria street fight between them fanned the white-hot embers of the feud.

Rezin gave Jim his knife—the one with the guard between handle and blade. "Wear this always when you go away from the house," he said seriously. "After what happened, you would be a fool to go about unarmed. A knife is more dependable than a gun. Sometimes a gun doesn't go off, but a knife will never fail you if you're quick enough."

Then into the tense atmosphere was dropped an explosive morsel of scandal regarding General Montford Wells, a prominent citizen. He traced the origin of the gossip back to Dr. Maddox, also prominent in the Wright faction. Naturally the gossip-monger was challenged to a duel.

Elaborate preparations were made for this "medley," as duels were often called.

The Vidalia sand bar, a long, heavily wooded peninsula reaching into the Mississippi, was chosen as the dueling ground. In the center was a barren circle whose sands had already been drenched with the blood of those who believed in the "code of honor" to settle personal differences.

Dr. Maddox chose as his seconds Major Norris Wright, Colonel Crain, who settled his debts with bullets, Crain's son-in-law Alfred Blanchard and Alfred's brother Cary. Dr. Denny would go along as his surgeon.

Sam Wells selected his brother Tom; Jim Bowie chose General Cuny and George McWhorter, a prominent planter. His surgeon was Dr. Dick Cuny.

Never were the potentials for serious trouble so neatly gathered. Tom Wells had been shot by Alfred Blanchard. Jim Bowie had been shot by Norris Wright and in self-defense had nearly strangled him. General Sam Cuny had shot Colonel Crain in the arm when the latter was trying to collect a defaulted note.[2]

At dawn on September 18, 1827, the two groups of grim-faced men walked quietly up the dark street and boarded the ferry to Vidalia. Walking in pairs they reached the sand bar just as the sun was rising. The trees were tipped with rosy gold. Birds sang. Otherwise there was no sound but their footsteps crunching through sand.

The seconds of each side withdrew to opposite positions behind clumps of bushes. Jim found a place where he could peer between branches and see what was going on.

Dr. Maddox and Sam Wells, the two principals, stood facing each other at ten paces. At the count of three both pistols blazed. Neither man was hit. Once more both weapons spat fire. Again no one was hit. Sam Wells stepped forward, hand outstretched. Honor had been satisfied.

Jim bit back an impulse to laugh. He had been keyed up for so long that the idea of a bloodless duel after so much tension struck him as deliciously funny.

He emerged from behind the bushes and stepped up beside General Cuny. "A fortunate ending for a duel." He grinned.

Cuny put a hand on Jim's arm. "I'm not so sure it's over," he gasped. "Look!"

Jim stared in the direction toward which Cuny pointed and saw Colonel Crain striding toward them, a black look of hatred on his face. His hand lowered toward his pistol. He drew and fired at Cuny, but missed. Jim felt a blazing pain in his hip. He had no gun, but drew the big knife Rezin had told him to wear and advanced toward Crain, who had drawn another pistol. The colonel fired again, this time killing General Cuny.

Seeing his friend fall, Jim's grip tightened on his knife handle. Dragging his injured leg, he continued his advance. Crain brought his pistol down on Jim's head.

The world broke apart in blinding pain. Blood from a gash in his scalp poured into his eyes. He wiped it away with his coat sleeve and struggled to his feet, the knife held menacingly before him. The sight was too much for the "gentleman from Virginia." He turned and ran into the bushes.

Still dizzy and unsteady from the blow on the head, Jim mopped the blood again from his eyes just in time to see Norris Wright coming at him with a sword cane upheld. Bitter hatred was graven on those foxlike features.

Wright lunged. Jim tried to parry the blow with his knife blade. He missed then, felt the sharp blade rip through his chest. He fell on his back, but struggled to rise. Wright put one foot on Jim's chest in an effort to pull out his sword. The blade broke.

2. An unpaid debt.

Jim reached up and gripped Wright's arm, as he tugged at the sword. Just as the handle broke off, Jim's knife came up, slashing Wright's abdomen, and the Wright-Bowie feud was over. Jim tried to rise, but a bullet from another direction hit him in the arm. He fell again and consciousness was blotted out.

Jim Bowie felt as though part of him were floating in space, yet pain gripped every inch of his body.

"He'll be dead before morning," he heard a voice say.

Were they talking about him?

"Four serious wounds," the voice went on. "He lost more blood than any man can stand to lose and live. That sword just missed his heart." Jim Bowie heard the words, but he was too tired to open his eyes. Nothing seemed to matter.

"What a medley!"[3] the voice went on. "Norris Wright and Sam Cuny dead. Jim here as good as dead. Crain and Blanchard wounded. That's the bloodiest duel ever. One that'll go down in history."

"It should be a duel to end all duels." It was Rezin's voice with a bitter note in it. Jim recognized it. Yet he could not summon sufficient strength to move or speak.

"Jim won't die, Dick," Rezin's voice said. "You aren't reckoning on that marvelous stamina of his."

Good old Rez! Jim thought as he slowly sank again into unconsciousness. Of course he wouldn't die! He would fool that prophet of doom whose voice seemed so far away.

CHAPTER 10. A MAN AND HIS KNIFE

James Bowie did not die, but there were weeks of delirium while his pain-wracked, blood-drained body lay in a friend's home in Natchez and his life hung in the balance. Later Dr. Cuny told him it was a miracle that he was alive.

Rezin was there, as he had been nearly every day since the historic duel on the Vidalia sand bar.

Jim chuckled. "I was half dead when I heard you and Rez discussing me. You said I couldn't live. Rez said I would. And I made up my own mind right then that it would be a good joke to fool you, Doctor."

"I was never happier to be mistaken," his friend replied.

"Never forget," Rezin's tone was deadly serious, "that it was a knife that saved your life. The knife that I gave you. Never be without it."

"I won't." Jim's seriousness matched his brother's. "I've been doing a lot of thinking while I lay here. And much of that thinking was about your knife. I worked out a design for improving the knife. I hope I never have to kill another man. But I intend to be ready to defend my own life if need be."

Soon he was strong enough to return with Rezin in the carriage to Arcadia. It was spring and the air was heavy with the fragrance of the waxy magnolia blossoms. He strolled about the lovely gardens with Rezin's pretty little daughters. Later he was able to ride a horse. Always Big Sam rode at his side. Each day the rides were longer until he could sit for an hour or so in the saddle without breaking out into a cold sweat from weakness.

Now that he had begun to mend, his tremendous vitality reasserted itself.

Every day he whittled models of the knife he had designed in his mind while convalescing in Natchez. Finally he had one that suited him. He showed it to Rezin.

3. Melee.

His brother turned it in his hand, critically studying every detail.

Finally he nodded approvingly. "It's good," he said. "I'll take it to Jesse Cliff in the morning and have him make it in metal."

Jim shook his head. "This isn't a job for our plantation smithy. This knife must be made by an expert craftsman, with a genius for working metals. It will be something special." His long fingers caressed the wooden model.

"Where will you find such a metalworker?" Rez asked.

Jim stared off into space, a dreamy look in his gray eyes. "There is such a man," he said. "I heard about him in Natchez. He served an apprenticeship as a silversmith, went west and settled at Washington in Arkansas where he set up a blacksmith shop. His partner takes care of the rough work of the Southwest Trail, while he tends to mending guns and making knives. His name's James Black."

"That's quite a distance to go to get a knife made."

"I'll stop on my way," Jim said. "I'm planning to take to the Chihuahua Trail soon. I want to look into the land deals that are opening up there in Arkansas. Texas still appeals to me. I want to take a look-see out there. I've sat around here being lazy long enough."

Rezin looked at him and sighed. "I figured that the wanderlust had you again. Wish I could go with you. But I can't go traipsing off and leave Maggie and the girls. But of course John and I are with you financially. We Bowie boys will stick together always. And if anything extra exciting comes up, I might manage to be with you for a time."

Jim grinned. "I'll make it a point to find some venture to hold you to that promise."

"I suppose you have in mind buying up some Spanish land grants," Rez said.

Jim nodded. "Why not? It's more or less of a gamble, I suppose. But not too much of one. The population is pushing westward. If we buy up land cheap and then sell at a profit, how can we lose?"

"I'll always hold Arcadia as our stronghold," Rezin promised. "I've got a feeling that you'll make money for all of us. But in case you don't, there'll be Arcadia to come back to. Consider it your home as long as you live."

A mist blurred Jim's eyes. "That's mighty good of you. But somehow the wide open spaces pull me mighty strong. I aim to take Sam along, and we'll take our time and look the places over. It's plenty wide. It should give a man room to grow."

Within a week Jim was on his way, galloping along on a fine chestnut horse with Big Sam followed him on another and leading a pack animal.

Jim felt the powerful animal under him and the wind brushing his face. This was Living—to be traveling once again the Adventure Trail! Strength and zest raced through his veins. He was glad to be putting behind him the artificial plantation existence. It held no challenge. The slaves did all of the work while the gentlemen and ladies, dressed in fine clothes, gave balls and hunts and gossiped in the Natchez or Alexandria coffee shops. It was all very well for a time. Jim grinned when he remembered how he had once envied that sort of life and had bent every effort toward achieving it. But when that goal was won it seemed tame and flavorless.

Would it always be that way? he wondered. Would he always be dashing off toward some new goal only to find it dull and tasteless once his aim was achieved? At any rate, there was a thrill in pitting his abilities toward new attainments.

They rode at a good clip over a well-defined trail which divided Arkansas into two sections. The southeastern part was level and neatly plotted off into cotton planta-tions. To the north lay thickly timbered hills where gaunt men and women lived in miserable cabins clinging to the hillsides. The condition of the trail showed the heavy travel of people pushing westward. He hoped he wouldn't be too late to get in on some good land deals.

Washington, he found, was quite a civilized town with substantial buildings and an air of prosperity. There was a better-than-average inn with good food and clean, comfortable beds.

After supper Jim lounged about the narrow lobby and asked the innkeeper if he knew of an ironworker named Black.

"Sure do," the man replied. "Has a shop right at the end of the street. He's busier than a cat on a tin roof in a hail storm. Can't keep up with the business coming over the trail. Keeps five slaves turning out knives, axes, plowshares, and the like. Mighty clever man. Works all day and sometimes into the night."

The following morning Jim strolled to the end of the street where he saw a big sign:

JAMES BLACK
IRONWORKER

Jim strode inside and stared around curiously at the three large forges where slaves, naked from the waist up, were blowing up the blazes with bellows or hammering metal on one of the several anvils. The place bustled with activity, yet there was neatness and order in the conglomeration of wagon wheels, tools, horseshoes and various articles to be mended.

He told one of the slaves that he would like to see Mr. Black.

"Yessuh. I go tell him," the Negro answering, disappearing behind a black curtain. In a moment he came out followed by a slim man who moved with quick steps.

"I'm James Bowie from Alexandria way. Even in Natchez your fame as an expert in tempering steel is known. I understand that you have a special method . . ."

Jim stopped, realizing that he must have said the wrong thing, for it was as though the man had drawn a mask over his face.

"I do my best always," Black said. "But my methods are my own. In fact, not even my partner knows my secret. I work behind this curtain."

"Pardon me, suh. I have no wish to pry into your secrets. But I have a special job for you to do. I want you to make a particular knife. I've come many long miles to ask you to do this."

He drew the wooden model from his pocket. After examining it, Black said, "Come with me." He held aside the curtain so that Jim could enter into the space where he had a desk. Adorning the wall was a collection of finely wrought knives which made Jim's eyes sparkle.

Then his glance was drawn to the ironworker whose thin face was bent over the model. Jim noticed his long-fingered hands—the hands of an artist.

"Yes—yes!" Black said eagerly. "It is good. I will do it. I enjoy making fine knives. This I shall strive to make a masterpiece."

Jim drew out the knife Rezin had given him. "This weapon saved my life," he said. "But it's just an ordinary hunting knife with a guard. It's not good for defense. It's clumsy. As you can see, I want an extra thick heel to give the blade strength so it will not snap. The point must come at the precise center of the width of the blade, for balance. Notice that the blade curves to the point from both front and back. Both of these curves must be as sharp as the edge of the blade itself—which must be sharper than any knife you have ever made before."

"You leave it to me," Black said impatiently. "You will be satisfied, Mr. Bowie. Come back in two weeks."

"I must have it sooner than that, suh." Jim thought of the thick money belt he wore. He needed the improved knife as protection from border ruffians and highwaymen.

Black shook his head. "You ask for perfection, Mr. Bowie. I cannot do such a job in less time."

"I shall be back in two weeks." Jim bowed and let the curtain drop behind him.

Jim put in the time buying land grants. In two weeks he was back at James Black's shop, admiring the gleaming knife which the master cutler[4] proudly placed in his hand. He tested the balance. But when he was about to check the keenness of the blade with moistened finger Black warned, "You'll cut yourself. Here, test it like this." He pulled out one of his own brown hairs, held it up and with a quick stroke neatly cut the slender hair in two.

"Well, I never!" Jim exclaimed.

He reached for the knife again, turning it in his hands, admiring the workmanship. The blade was fourteen inches long, single edged to the curve of the point, where both sides had been sharpened to a razorlike edge. The curve started two inches from the point. On the back of the blade was a parrying guard of hardened brass.

Jim's fingers stroked this guard which had been Rezin's invention.

"Hardened brass is a much softer metal than tempered steel," the ironworker explained. "So I made the guard of brass so it would catch and hold a blow. Otherwise your opponent's blade might slide and cut you."

Jim nodded and studied the two-pronged cross guard which was about three inches long. He noted that even the handle was a work of art, being of buckhorn[5] dressed smooth where his hand would clasp it. On one side was a small silver plate with his name crudely engraved upon it.

"Mr. Black," Jim said. "This weapon is a masterpiece. I shall feel safe with it. I think that you've made a knife that will go down in history."

Black laughed, obviously well pleased with his work, but neither man had any idea how true those words would prove to be.

Jim found several land deals to his liking while in Arkansas and invested all the money he had with him, making it necessary for him to return to Alexandria to raise more funds. One evening he and Sam continued riding after nightfall in order to reach Rezin's plantation so that they would not have to sleep on the trail. Suddenly Jim's horse shied violently.

"Whoa, boy!" Jim spoke soothingly. He leaned forward and slid a hand along his mount's neck. He felt a coarse coat sleeve and realized that someone was holding the bridle. A shot rang out and sharp pain stabbed his leg.

Rough hands pulled him from the saddle and pushed him to the ground. Jim jerked his knife from the sheath and slashed upward. There was a cry of agony, then a great sigh and the hands eased from his shoulders.

Again someone seized him in the darkness. Again the knife slashed. Then there was silence except for the snorting of the frightened horses. Jim felt around for the reins and climbed into the saddle.

"Where are you, Sam?" He kept his voice low.

---

4. One who makes, deals in, or repairs knives.   5. The horn of a buck.

"Right here, massa." Jim could hear the thankful relief in his slave's voice. "Oh, praise the Lawd, you's all right, suh!"

"Follow me. Hurry!" Jim set his horse to a gallop.

Not until the following afternoon when he went to Natchez did Jim know that he was thought to be dead—killed on the trail by unknown highwaymen.

"That's strange!" Jim said after several friends had been amazed to see him limping around the streets. The shot he had received in the fleshy part of the leg was painful but not serious. "I can't understand why it should be known in Natchez that I was waylaid—unless whoever attacked me came from here."

Later in the afternoon word was brought that the bodies of two men, recognized as Bloody Sturdivant's hoodlums, had been found beside the trail.

"It's plain now," Jim told Dr. Cuny, who was dressing his leg. "Sturdivant hasn't forgotten his threat to get even with me. But he boasted too soon that I was dead."

Later he went looking for Sturdivant, but the gambler was nowhere to be found.

Friends clamored to see the "Bowie knife" as it immediately was called. From that day on, cutlers were besieged with orders for copies. As for James Black, his reputation was made. He could not keep up with orders for this new weapon of the frontier—the knife which would carve for itself a niche in history.

Chapter 11. Texas Adventure

Following his complete recovery from the terrible wounds suffered in the sand bar duel, Bowie felt a greater rush of ambition and energy than he had ever known. Nothing seemed impossible. He and faithful Big Sam rode back and forth between Alexandria and Arkansas, buying and selling land, or promoting land deals in Louisiana.

It was an exciting, adventurous era—one well suited to his temperament. As he had foreseen, already by 1829 the American tide had spilled over into Texas. The Mexican government at that time welcomed the energetic American settlers, stipulating only that they become Catholics and Mexican citizens. Stephen Austin's efforts at colonization were a success[6] and prospects for ambitious settlers were bright.

Bowie perceived the shrewdness of the Mexican government's action in encouraging American settlement in Texas. The Mexicans themselves had been unable to cope with the Indian problem. Over those wide acres roamed the fiercest and cruelest Indians of the whole hemisphere: the Comanche, Waco, Caddo and the cannibalistic Karankahau. The very names of such tribes struck terror to men's hearts. Yet when did danger ever hold back Americans from seeking new goals? To Bowie it only served to lend spice to his ventures in Texas.

The early Spaniards, as he knew, had been brave enough, yet they had failed to establish permanent settlements. Except for those at Nacogdoches and San Antonio de Bexar, their missions and presidios[7] had been wiped out. No wonder the wily Mexicans decided to let the savages throw themselves against the Americans, who might subdue them to such an extent that the Mexicans would dare move in.

Jim found the Mississippi at Natchez crowded with great steamers, loaded to the gunwales with cargoes and settlers. There were immigrants fresh from Europe, and

6. Austin (1793–1836), born in Virginia and raised in the Missouri territory, oversaw a settlement of Americans on land purchased by his father between the Brazos and Colorado rivers in the Mexican territory of Tejas.

7. Forts, fortresses (Spanish).

Americans whose fathers had pioneered the frontier and who were again pushing westward to new, uncrowded lands. Naturally Jim Bowie wanted to be with these adventurers on the trail blazed not so long ago by Davy Crockett and other Kentuckians like Daniel Boone, moving from "cramped quarters" looking for new "b'ar kentry."[8]

There were gentlemen from the South in that crowd—many of education and culture. There were gamblers and river pirates, too, and others seeking to escape the consequences of a lawless past.

It was 1830 when Jim Bowie reached Texas—still a Mexican state, but where already the seeds of revolt had been sown. He had left Sam behind at Arcadia. Old age and "rheumatiz" had put misery in Sam's big bones and he could no longer keep up with his master.

Jim Bowie took his time looking over the land—the woods and streams and hills— the vast open spaces alive with buffalo and wild horses. Here was room enough for all he decided—Mexicans, Americans and Indians. His heart quickened with the realization that this was a region where many men would make fortunes. And he was in at the beginning! Certainly he would become rich—and a leader.

He rode to San Antonio de Bexar, the largest town in Texas. Established by the Catholic fathers in the days of the Spanish Conquest, the Spanish influence still predominated. It was the capital of the province, and Bowie found himself in a new world of leisurely living and charming customs. Strangers spoke to him smilingly as though he were a friend.

The city had two main squares, the Plaza de la Constitution which the *palacio*[9] of the vice-governor faced, and the Plaza Militar where the soldiers' barracks were located. Jim was amused by the lack of military bearing of the Mexican soldiers. Their chief function seemed to be standing guard before the *palacio* of Juan Martin de Veramendi.[1]

He wandered about the streets enjoying the sights. It was spring. The sun was warm and the flower gardens in bloom. There was an other-world charm about Bexar. The tree-lined San Antonio River wound through the city where Mexican women bent over the water, washing clothes. He was delighted by the pastel-colored houses built of thick adobe walls, the huge carved doors and barred windows of the *palacios*. Many of the finer homes were built around courtyards, as were the homes along the *Vieux Carré* in New Orleans. Now and then the great carved gates swung ajar showing gardens with gracious shade trees and tropical flowers.

He soon grew used to the groan of ungreased, solid wooden wheels drawing the overloaded *carettas*,[2] and the clang of the church bells summoning worshipers to services nearly every hour of the day.

He roamed through the markets with their spreading awnings beneath which peddlers lounged beside their wares.

He succumbed to the *mañana*[3] atmosphere and found it restful for a time to let matters drift from day to day. *Mañana* would be soon enough to decide what he would eventually do. This much he knew: he liked Texas and intended to stay.

---

8. Bear country. Crockett (1786–1836), who was born and spent most of his life in Tennessee, and Boone (ca. 1734–1820), who was born in Pennsylvania and spent most of his life in Kentucky, were America's most famous frontiersmen.
9. Palace, imposing residence.

1. Juan Martín de Veramendi (1778–1833), born in Bexar; he was elected vice governor of Coahila and Texas in 1830, and assumed the office of governor in 1832.
2. Carts.
3. Tomorrow.

It surprised him that now and then men or boys he met on the street called him by name and some of the bolder youngsters asked to see his knife. He wondered how these people had learned who he was or about the Bowie knife. He did not realize that he was a famous person, or that the knife was already a symbol of heroism and daring and that schools for training men in the use of the Bowie knife had sprung up in New Orleans.

One day a soldier brought a note to his room. The paper was heavy with important-looking seals.

Written in Spanish, it was an invitation to visit Vice-governor Veramendi at his *palacio* the following morning.

"Tell the vice-governor that I shall be there," Jim said in Spanish.

After the messenger left, Jim asked himself what it meant? Obviously it was a command, but was it merely a social courtesy—or something more?

In the morning he got out his gray broadcloth suit, linen shirt, brocaded waistcoat and fine beaver hat. Although the *palacio* was only a short walk from his *fonda*,[4] he rode horseback, for the Spanish were horsemen before all else. They had little respect for a man afoot.

The Veramendi *palacio* was a two-story stone building built around three sides of a patio which gave upon the river. Bowie was ushered into a large room with massive dark furniture and great oak beams across the ceiling. A man with glossy black hair, handsome features and piercing dark eyes rose as Bowie entered.

The vice-governor bowed in a courtly manner. "I am honored by your visit," he said.

"I was honored to receive your invitation." Jim's courtliness was a match for Veramendi's.

"Be seated. We will talk." The vice-governor motioned to a huge carved chair.

"You have been a visitor in Bexar for two weeks now." It was not a question but a statement of fact.

Bowie raised his eyebrows and merely nodded.

"You were a friend—or shall I say a business associate—of Jean Lafitte. You were victor in a famous duel. You invented the knife named for you and which has become the chosen weapon of nearly every man in the country."

A smile tugged at Jim's lips. "You know much about me, suh. I'm honored at your interest."

"What are your intentions in Texas, Mr. Bowie?"

The curtness of the question after such preliminary courtesy startled Jim. At first he resented such directness. After all, his business was his own. Veramendi didn't own Texas, he reflected, but it occurred to him also that the vice-governor was very powerful and could by a mere nod of the head cause him a great deal of trouble in a strange land.

"I haven't exactly made up my mind, suh." Jim decided to be perfectly frank. "Texas is a wonderful place with a great future. I want to become part of it. I want to help develop her riches and resources. On my way here I noticed vast cotton fields. In Louisiana my brothers and I set up on one of our plantations the first steam engine for making sugar. I wondered why something like that couldn't be used here—to make cloth without shipping it away."

Veramendi slapped his hand on the polished desk top and his face broke into a

4. An inn, a small hotel.

delighted smile. "I knew it!" he cried. "I knew you were that sort of man. When you entered my room, I said to myself, 'There stands a leader of men.' You will be good for Texas. I will help you."

"You are very kind."

"But you must swear to protect the Mexican government, and enter the Catholic church. Are you willing?"

Jim nodded. "I had understood those things. I am willing to uphold the Mexican government. And, although I was brought up a Presbyterian, I believe that every church has the same goal—toward God. I would feel privileged to become a member of your church."

"You must take instruction from our padre before the church will accept you."

"Of course."

Veramendi rose and Jim did also, believing this was his cue that the interview was over. However, the vice-governor motioned him to remain seated. He pulled a bell rope and a servant appeared.

"Señor Bowie will do us the honor of lunching with us," the vice-governor said. "Please see that a place is set for him."

"You are too kind." Jim was amused by Veramendi's imperious manner of announcing that he was eating with them, without first inviting him.

His word is law in this land, I see, Bowie said to himself. Soon a gong sounded and Veramendi led the way to a long dining room where even at midday candles glowed over smooth white damask and gleaming silver.

A handsome woman with dark hair slightly marked with silver stood at the doorway, her arm across the shoulders of a slim boy of about ten.

"Your son," Jim said to the vice-governor. "The resemblance is striking."

"Sí. And my wife." The pride in the man's face was unmistakable. "Querida,[5] may I present Señor James Bowie, a very great American? Señor Bowie, my wife Señora Maria Josefa Navarro Veramendi."

"It is our pleasure to have you dine with us," she said with charming grace.

"And this rascal is Carlos, my one and only son."

"Can I see your knife, Señor Bowie?" Carlos piped up.

"This is a friendly visit." Jim's eyes twinkled. "I came unarmed. Some other time, Carlos."

He heard high heels clicking on the hallway and turned to see two lovely girls enter the room.

"This is Teresa," Juan Veramendi said. "Our youngest daughter."

Jim guessed her age at about fourteen.

"And this, our elder daughter, is Urselita."

The girl raised her eyes and held out dainty finger tips to him. For a long moment while their eyes met, Jim's breath stopped. When she looked down quickly he realized that it was not the way for a Spanish maiden to give such a full glance to a man upon first acquaintance. Evidently she was as surprised by her boldness as he, for a flush spread over her olive skin. Creole women were famous for beauty, so he had not been starved in this respect. But this was the most beautiful girl Bowie had ever seen.

"Will you come this way," Señora Veramendi's gentle voice brought Jim Bowie back to earth. "I insist that you sit at my right so that you two men will not talk

___

5. Darling. "Sí": yes.

politics during the whole meal. We would all like to share the attention of so distinguished and famous a gentleman."

CHAPTER 12. A YELLOW ROSE ON THE RIVERBANK

His acquaintanceship with the Veramendi family speedily opened doors for James Bowie, throwing him into a social whirl unrivaled in graciousness and luxury by any that he had experienced in Louisiana. The fine Spanish families of José Navarro, Señora Veramendi's parents, Francisco Ruiz, Juan Seguin, Placido Benavidos, the Flores, the De la Garzas were cultivated people who welcomed Bowie to their elaborate dinners and balls. Although he fitted easily into such a life, it was not for this he had come to Texas.

He threw himself vigorously into buying lands which seemed to promise a good investment and working with Juan Veramendi on plans to establish a textile mill. He also organized other energetic young Americans into a group which he called Rangers,[6] but which the Mexicans called *Los Leonidas*—the Young Lions. The purpose of this organization was to discourage the raids of the Comanche on outlying ranches and settlements around Bexar. It took only a few counterraids by this vigorous, sharpshooting group to put a stop to the Indians' depredations.

It never ceased to surprise Jim to be pointed out as the "man who had invented the Bowie knife" and to see copies of the weapon in use wherever he went.

Now there was a song about it, sung everywhere:

> "If you ever monkey with my Lulu gal,
> I'll tell you what I'll do;
> I'll carve you with my Bowie knife
> And shoot you with my pistol, too."

Jim's lodgings were only a brief stroll from the Veramendi *palacio* and since he and the vice-governor had become partners in the textile mill project, it was natural that he was a frequent dinner guest at the Veramendi home. Soon he began to feel like one of the family. In the evenings after dinner it was extremely pleasant to sit or walk in the patio giving upon the willow-lined river.

As the lazy, pleasant days slid by, Jim was aware that the lovely Urselita was occupying his thoughts more and more. The picture of her beautiful eyes, her smooth olive skin, glossy black hair, the graceful movements of her hands, the quality of her voice were ever with him. He tried to push the thought of her away, telling himself that she was just a child—only eighteen to his thirty-five. How utterly absurd to be thinking of her so constantly, like a romantic schoolboy!

His plans were beginning to shape up well. He had purchased numerous tracts of land and was already recognized as a man of property and importance.

Now a new interest absorbed his attention. It was inevitable that he should hear tales of lost mines which have passed from generation to generation since the times of the early Spanish missions—stories of silver bars hidden in caves, of rich lodes lost to record because of the death, usually violent, of the key person who knew their location.

---

6. There is no evidence that Bowie created the Texas Rangers (generally dated to 1823), though he was a colonel in a Ranger company in 1830.

Several times Bowie was offered the opportunity to buy a "secret" map to some such treasure. He told Juan Veramendi of such offers, but the vice-governor only scoffed. "Lost mines! Pouff!" he cried. "Don't waste time or thought on them!"

"But when the Lipan[7] come to Bexar to trade," Bowie insisted, "they bring silver nuggets to buy goods with. Where does that come from?"

Veramendi shrugged. "Who knows? I do not doubt that silver exists back in the mountains. But white men could find it only at great peril. The Comanche will resist to the last man further invasion into their mountain fastnesses. Many others have attempted to find the lost mines. Most of them never return."

"No! No! Jaime!" Urselita's voice broke in with a shrill note of alarm. "Do not try to find the lost mines. It is too dangerous."

She had been sitting at the table silently listening to this talk and her sudden outburst caused everyone to stare at her in surprise. Tears filled her eyes. She put her hands to her cheeks to hide their telltale color and ran from the room.

Jim gave Don Juan a questioning look. He found a quizzical expression on the face of the vice-governor.

"I—I did not mean to offend her," Jim said lamely. "She seemed ready to burst into tears. Why?"

"I leave that for you to solve."

"But—but—!" Never had Jim Bowie been so at a loss for words. "She is only a child. It couldn't be that—that—"

"She is nearly nineteen," the vice-governor said gently. "Our girls mature early. She is a woman."

"But I am old enough to be her father. She is the most popular girl in Bexar. Surely she wouldn't be interested in me!"

"Who can fathom the heart of a young woman?" Doña Josefa murmured.

Jim rose suddenly and started to pace the floor. "Urselita's image has been in my heart from the moment I first saw her," he said. "She's the most beautiful—the loveliest person I've ever seen. I'm in love with her. But I didn't dare hope. . . ."

"When did Los Leoncitos not have the courage to dare try to win the heart of a woman? You, the bravest of men!" Veramendi's voice was tinged with amusement.

"But you? How do you and Doña Josefa feel about it? Would you favor my suit?"

Don Juan seemed to ponder the matter, but there was a twinkle in his eyes. "How about it, *querida*," he finally said. "Would you favor Don Jaime as a son-in-law?"

She raised her large dark eyes and smiled. "Do not tease Don Jaime," she said. "You know we would both be most happy. But Urselita will have to decide for herself."

However, if Jim thought that the preliminaries to his courtship of Urselita Veramendi were settled he was to find himself very much mistaken. He found the girl elusive, even cool at times. At parties she seemed to avoid him and paid special attention to a handsome young Flores scion who had been courting her.

Jim began to believe that the Veramendis had been mistaken about their daughter's interest in him.

He joined the Catholic church, under the sponsorship of Veramendi, and so removed the religious obstacle, but Urselita remained aloof.

He went ahead trying to cultivate the friendship of the Lipan—the friendly Indians who came to San Antonio de Bexar to trade. He had managed to make slight headway with Chief Zolic, who always had a few nuggets of silver in a worn leather pouch

---

7. One of the more important subgroups of Apaches in Texas.

tucked in his sash. Jim gave him a Bowie knife and so made an entering wedge into his friendship. Now Zolic looked him up when he came to trade.

There were no doubts in Bowie's mind that his future lay in Texas where opportunities were as vast as her acres. He made plans to return to Louisiana to dispose of his holdings there so that he could transfer his finances to his adopted home.

He was eager to get this over with for he had met an interesting character—Cephas Hamm, a hunter who had wandered far and wide throughout the Southwest.

"Once I went to live with a Lipan chief—just for the adventure of it," Cephas told Bowie. "A certain warrior often hunted with me. One time he pointed to a hill where he said there was a rich silver mine. I asked him to take me to it. He said that if we could manage to go hunting alone, he would, but that if the other Indians discovered what we were doing they would kill us both."

"Did you find the mine?" Jim asked eagerly.

Cephas shook his head. "Nope. The Lipan got into a fight with another tribe and my warrior friend was killed. I always intended to go looking on my own, but never got around to it."

"I must go back to Louisiana to wind up some business," Jim said. "Maybe when I get back we can go together."

"Maybe," Cephas agreed.

Jim was invited to dine with the Veramendis the evening before he was to leave for his old home. When Jim rose to make his farewells, he told the family how much he had enjoyed their hospitality.

"We will miss you," Doña Josefa said graciously.

"That we will," Don Juan agreed. "Don't forget to attend to all of the details of the textile mill."

"Oh, business! Business!" Doña Josefa broke in with what was for her exceptional impatience. "Have we not had enough of it? Urselita, that lovely pale yellow rose is in bloom at the river's edge. I am sure Don Jaime will want to see it before he leaves so that he can tell his friends in New Orleans what lovely roses we have here."

"I will be happy to show it to you, Jaime," the girl said demurely.

He walked beside her over the flagstone path. The yellow rosebush was conveniently located behind a willow. They could hear the voices of Don Juan and Doña Josefa not a stone's throw away, so they were properly chaperoned, yet out of sight.

Urselita cupped a perfect blossom in her graceful hands and her lovely head bent over it.

"It is beautiful." Jim's voice was husky and low. "But not nearly so beautiful as you, Urselita."

She raised her head and her great eyes stared into his. "Oh, Jaime!" she cried softly. "You are going away! Will you ever come back?"

"Do you want me to, Urselita?"

"If you don't, I would want to die." Her voice came in a half sob.

Then she was in his arms. When he raised his head from their first kiss he knew that never again would there be doubt in his heart. They loved each other truly and for all time. She was no child, but a woman, full blown as the rose at which they had just been looking.

"I will be back, Urselita," he promised, "bringing a ring to bind our troth."

"Hurry, Jaime. Please hurry!" she murmured.

CHAPTER 13. JIM BOWIE MEETS SAM HOUSTON

Before Bowie set out to return to the Bayou Teche country he bought from Chief Zolic numerous gifts of silver to take to his family and friends. It was fall when he started. He rode by way of the Stephen Austin settlement of San Felipe on the Brazos. It would make a welcome break in his long journey, and he hoped to meet Austin who had made such a success of colonizing Texas.

At San Felipe, Jim stayed at the Peyton Tavern for several days, enjoying the rest and the company of these energetic Americans and their simple, easy-going way of life. These colonists, selected for their industry and integrity, had few comforts, but seemed not to mind the hardships. Most of them raised cattle, hogs, cotton and corn which they exported to Mexico or the States. Living mainly on salt pork, venison and corn pone, they got along with almost no cash, doing business by barter.

Jim went to call upon Stephen Austin, a tall, thin man, who worked hard and carried responsibility. He dealt with the central government at Mexico City and with his own state government at Saltillo. Both were as unstable as they were unpredictable. He was military and civilian chief to his colonists, besides being broker, banker, merchant and adviser in personal and business matters. And they were all completely devoted to him.

Jim's keen eyes took in the worn homespun suit, the lean body, the haggard, fine features. He told himself that here was a man unfitted by temperament to the hardships of frontier life. Bowie had heard that Austin liked the quiet pleasures of cultivated society, yet he was wearing himself to the bone carrying out the colonizing dream of his father Moses Austin, who had died before he himself could bring them to realization.

At the end of the brief visit, Jim said, "You are certainly to be congratulated upon your success in bringing civilization to this wilderness."

Jim returned to Arcadia and to bounteous southern hospitality.

Although his mother's hair was whiter and she seemed to have shrunk in size, she was still vigorous and spirited.

"What's this I hear about your selling out here and transferring all of your assets to Texas?" she asked, obviously not in favor of the idea.

Jim leaned forward in his chair and took her thin hands in his enormous strong ones. "It's true," he said. "There's something exciting about that country. It's a place of opportunity for the likes of me."

"But you're a gentleman," she protested. "Why should such a wild primitive land appeal to you?"

He smiled down on her fondly. "You were reared a lady—a gracious southern belle," he replied. "Yet you came here as a pioneer and fitted yourself into the harsh way of living and liked it."

Understanding came into her eyes. "I did like it," she said thoughtfully. "Perhaps because it was a challenge to my resourcefulness. But it was from your father that you inherited this wanderlust that is always driving you. Yet you fit in so beautifully with the gracious way of life that we helped establish in this region. When you first went to New Orleans and tasted this mode of living you couldn't rest until you made enough money to make it possible here."

"I still like it," he admitted. "But not as a steady diet. It's not exciting enough. But don't think that gracious living does not prevail in San Antonio de Bexar. The well-born Spanish people live every bit as luxuriously as we do on our plantation and in New Orleans and Natchez. They are cultivated, charming people—as you will see when I bring home Urselita, my beautiful bride-to-be."

Her eyes widened. "Jim!" she cried. "You aren't going to marry a Mexican girl?"

"Urselita de Veramendi is from an aristocratic Spanish family," he told her. "You'll love her. Wait and see."

"If she's the girl you've chosen for your wife, of course I'll love her." She smiled up at him.

Rezin was excited by what Jim told him about the lost mines of the Southwest. "If you find anything that looks promising, I'd like to join you on such an adventure," he cried eagerly.

Jim explained his plan of deliberately cultivating the friendship of the Lipan chief, hoping that he might gain some definite information. Rezin examined the beautiful silver belt Jim had brought him, his eyes alight with interest.

At Natchez Jim selected a rifle with elaborately engraved silver decorations to take back for a gift to Zolic.

"The old boy's claws will reach out to grab this," Jim told Rezin. "It should help me locate the famed San Saba mine. You can be sure that I'll send for you if anything exciting develops. Those southwestern mountains pull me. There's something about them—mystery, fascination."

"Not to speak of adventure—and the chance of a great fortune," Rezin added. "It would be fun to have one more topnotch adventure with you, Jim, before we settle down to being solid citizens for the rest of our lives."

"I'll try to work it out so that we can, Rez," Jim promised.

He went to Helena, Arkansas, to visit John and to dispose of his land holdings there. John had put on considerable weight and looked like the prosperous businessman he was. He was also a member of the legislature, and accustomed to being looked upon as a man of importance. But when it became known that Jim Bowie was in town, brother John played second fiddle. Men and boys crowded about to stare at Jim, and invariably they asked to see "the knife."

"Jim, you're famous!" John said. "I hope you don't get conceited."

"No danger." Jim's reply was abrupt. "I hope that I can someday do something which will be a more desirable claim to fame than being the originator of a symbol of bloodshed."

"You will," John assured him. "But the knife is more than a symbol of bloodshed. It's a symbol of man's right to protect himself against the heavy odds of a pioneer life. It's helping to carve civilization out of the wilderness."

"I hadn't thought of it that way," Jim said.

"Another thing you haven't thought of." John smiled. "You're a symbol yourself."

Jim looked surprised. "How do you mean?"

"Everyone loves a hero. You look like one. There's something about you, Jim. You stand out in any crowd. When you walk down the street people turn to look at you. Haven't you noticed?"

"Yes," Jim admitted. "And it bothers me. Makes me wonder if I look queer or forgot to put on my pants or something."

"It's because of a certain quality you have. That—and your reputation for utter fearlessness. Most men have to die before they gain such prominence."

"You're trying to inflate me." Jim laughed.

They strolled down to the boat landing on the Mississippi. Except for some Negroes loading cotton bales on a steamship docked at the wharf, no one was there. They were about to turn away when they saw a flatboat coming from up the river and waited for it to come to shore.

Two men leaned against the boat's cabin, staring at the town. One of them was bearded and it was he who drew Jim's eye. As the flatboat bumped against the wharf, he straightened up and Jim drew in his breath. The man was a giant! He wore the typical frontier garb—stained buckskin suit with fringes half gone and a wide-brimmed woolen hat. There was something about the set of his magnificent head which told him that here was a remarkable man.

"Sam!" John cried out. "Sam Houston.[8] I didn't recognize you under all that foliage."

"Hello, John Bowie." The man's voice was deep enough to match his physical proportions.

He stepped ashore and shook John's hand. Immediately John introduced him to Jim.

Jim Bowie wasn't in the habit of looking up to many men, being six feet, two himself, but Sam Houston towered over him.

"Jim Bowie," Houston said, gripping his hand. "I've heard of you. You're a legend, you know—you and your knife."

"I'm afraid that some of the reports you've heard were exaggerated," Jim said.

As they walked toward a tavern, Jim remembered what he had heard about this man. Once he had been the favorite of Andrew Jackson and had been governor of Tennessee. Later he had had the presidency of the United States practically in the palm of his hand. He had married the daughter of a prominent family, but within a few weeks he took her back to her father's home, resigned the governorship and disappeared into the wilderness to live among the Indians. He had become a man of mystery, but no one could forget his strange history. And Jim was certain he would never forget his strangely compelling personality, either.

Jim returned to Natchez to complete some business, then set off on horseback for Texas.

He reached San Antonio de Bexar just in time for the Christmas celebrations, of which the Mexicans made a great deal. He was all eagerness to see Urselita alone, but here he ran against the Spanish taboo in such matters. It was not proper for even engaged couples to be unchaperoned. Besides, there was all this uproar about the celebrations.

So Jim had to content himself with being part of the audience and enjoying the singing.

After the music the children broke into an excited clamor. "The *piñata!* The *piñata!*" they cried.

Jim had no idea what the word meant, but he soon learned. Servants came in bearing a large, brightly colored clay jar[9] in the form of a peacock. This was hoisted by a rope over a beam in the center of the ballroom. A child was blindfolded and handed a stick, then whirled around several times. He tried to strike the piñata with his stick. Each youngster was allowed three strikes, then he handed the stick to someone of his own choice who went through a similar performance. Every time someone missed, the rafters rang with shouts of delight from the spectators.

---

8. Virginia-born soldier and politician (1793–1863), elected first president of Republic of Texas (1836–38); after Texas became a state, he was elected U.S. senator (1846–59) and governor (1859–61).

9. Modern piñatas are often made of papier-mâché.

Finally the stick was passed to young Carlos de Veramendi. After he had been whirled around Jim saw him brace his sturdy legs, then stand still for a long moment as though to get his bearings. He struck twice and missed, but the third time he hit the piñata squarely. It broke and from it burst a shower of *dulces*—candies wrapped in bright paper. Then began an excited and noisy scramble, as each child fought for his share of the goodies.

This concluded the children's part of the performance. An orchestra moved into a corner of the long room where the grownups were to dance.

At once Urselita was surrounded by eager partners. Bowie's heart sank. He had not been quick enough, or could he bring himself to hurry in so undignified a manner. Yet he longed for a word with her. Then he saw her looking over the heads of the young men. Their eyes met, and Jim knew that hers were summoning him. Forgetting his precious dignity, he took long strides until he reached her side. "Our dance," he said and they glided over the floor in a quadrille.[1]

She was feather light and graceful as a hummingbird. Dancing with her was sheer delight, but he wanted to speak to her alone.

"It has seemed so long," he whispered close to her ear.

"*Si.*" Her long eyelashes swept her cheeks.

"I must get you alone," he said.

"But no. It would be scandalous."

"We are engaged," he insisted. "Step into the garden with me. I must show you something."

"When the dance takes us near the door," she said.

Reaching the patio, Jim and Urselita strolled over to the place beneath the weeping willow tree, beside the yellow rose, where they had plighted their troth.

"Are you still sure, Urselita?" he asked.

"*Si!* Jaime. So sure."

He wanted to take her in his arms, but not so publicly.

"But you could have any man in Texas," he said. "I am older. I love you so dearly, Urselita. But I still can't believe that you really love me."

Soft laughter tinkled on her lips. "You are older. *Si.* But you make all the others seem such boys. Ah, Jaime. You do not see yourself as you are. When you come into the room—everything at once comes alive. The other men are pale—without character."

He drew from his pocket the ring he had purchased in Natchez and slipped it upon her finger. "In my country, this means that we are promised to each other for all time," he whispered. "Now please, darling, hurry the wedding date so that we can get away from this mob."

CHAPTER 14. A TREASURE FOUND AND A TREASURE WON

Jim Bowie was to find that nothing could be rushed in Texas-Coahuila, especially the wedding of a daughter of a high-born Spanish family. Custom decreed that such arrangements should be very elaborate. Linens for numerous and varied uses must be embroidered, and it would take months to assemble a fitting trousseau for such a young lady. And during all this time the couple must never be unchaperoned.

Meanwhile Jim was building a fine home for his lovely Urselita, besides attending to the business details of installing the textile mill at Saltillo. Also, he was tracing to

1. A formal square dance for four couples.

their sources the numerous fascinating tales of lost mines. The story which most interested him, because it obviously was based most firmly on fact, was about the lost San Saba mine.

Although not enthusiastic about his prospective son-in-law's interest in the subject, Don Juan made available to him the Miranda report, which sent Jim's adventurous blood coursing through his veins with excitement.

In 1756, according to the report, the governor of the province of Texas sent Lieutenant General de Miranda out with a small force to investigate the long persistent tales of a lost mine. He rode eight days to the northwest, setting up camp on the Arroyo San Miguel. Only a short distance ahead lay the Cerre del Almagre (Red Hill). On the far side of this hill he came across a cave, which he named the Cave of St. Joseph of Alcasar.

Bowie read, "The mines are numerous. . . . The principal vein is more than two *varas*[2] in width and in its westward lead appears to be of immeasurable thickness. . . . Fuel and water for mining operations are available near by."

The report further stated that Miranda, on his return to San Antonio de Bexar, met an Indian whom he trusted, who reported that more and richer mines were at Los Dos Almagres, close to the headwaters of the Colorado River. He said that his people were there to get solid silver with which to make *conchas*[3] and other ornaments. Miranda offered his Indian friend a butcher knife and a red blanket to guide him there, but the Indian refused, saying that the Comanche were too numerous. They would all be tortured to death. *"Mañana,"* he said, "I will lead you there, when the Comanche are far away."

Later on Jim learned the Mexican government had built a fort on the San Saba River. They had also established a mission three miles to the south. However, in 1758 the mission was overrun by two thousand Comanche and completely destroyed. The fort was so undermanned that it afforded little protection. Digging further into the records, Bowie found evidence that mining and smelting operations were carried on before the Indians drove the Mexicans from their diggings.

After reading the report Bowie waited impatiently for Zolic and his people to come to Bexar to trade. As the Veramendis had moved to their summer home in the mountains at Montaclava to escape the heat, Jim was more eager than ever for the chief to appear.

At last the Lipan came. Jim took the handsome silver-plated rifle and strolled casually down the street to the market place where the Lipan had spread out their wares.

He found old Zolic dozing in the shade of a pecan tree and quietly sat down beside him. The chief opened his eyes.

"Hola,"[4] Jim said.

He suppressed a grin at the way the Indian looked at the weapon lying across his lap. He saw the talonlike fingers curl and uncurl as if he could scarcely keep from grabbing it.

"Buena.[5] Good gun," Zolic said finally.

"Yes, it is," Bowie drawled. "The finest rifle I've ever handled. Want to look at it?" He laid the gleaming weapon in Zolic's lap.

---

2. A little less than 2 yards.
3. Literally, "shells" (Spanish)—disks used to decorate clothing or tack.

4. Hello (Spanish).
5. Good (Spanish).

The chief examined it from every angle, stroking the muzzle, eying the exquisite silver mounting.

"Will give you blanket, hides for it," he said. Although he tried to speak casually, there was a greedy gleam in the Indian's eyes.

"No," Jim said.

"Two blankets. Much silver."

Jim shook his head.

"Much, much silver—*conchas*, belts, bracelets."

"No," Jim repeated. "The rifle is not for trade. I brought it to you as a gift, because you are my brother."

"You give to me?" His tone was incredulous.

"Yes, my brother."

"I will give you gift in exchange. It is the Lipan way."

Bowie shook his head. "No. I would like to hunt with you, my brother."

The old chief nodded slowly. "*Buena*. You will come to my camp. Live in my lodge. We are brothers. Will hunt together."

Three days later Jim Bowie and Zolic rode side by side toward the mysterious blue mountains. It was late evening when they reached the Lipan village. As they rode in they were surrounded by warriors who gave the visitor frowning scrutiny, but when Zolic spoke to them their frowns vanished.

Jim was led into the chief's lodge—the largest in the village.

While he lived among the Lipan, Jim became one of them as much as possible. He ate the dog stew and other concoctions they enjoyed, learned to shoot the bow and arrow as skillfully as any brave, taught them how to throw the Bowie knife. Soon his skin took on an Indian copper color, although his gray-blue eyes and red hair set him apart from the others. The Lipan called him *Cuchillo Grande*, Big Knife.

Every day when they went out to hunt, Jim kept his eyes open, but took care not to excite suspicion. He was looking for a red hill. It was nearly time for him to return to Bexar before he saw it one day when he and Zolic were hunting far from camp. He had shot and wounded a deer which disappeared over a rise. Jim put his horse to the gallop trying to overtake the wounded animal. At last he brought it down near a clump of brush.

He rode over and drew his knife to slit its throat. He was straightening up when something strange about the appearance of the area behind the bushes caused him to pull some branches aside. He caught his breath. Here was a well-concealed cave! He entered the cave and when his eyes grew accustomed to the dim light he saw stacks of bar silver and chunks of loose nuggets on the ground.

Stepping outside he started dressing the deer, but while he worked he made mental notes of the landmarks. He saw that this hill was definitely reddish in color. Near by were the ruins of a stone wall and close to it was a large slab with a trace of silver sticking to it. His heart beat fast. He had discovered the lost San Saba mine! Would his luck hold, now that great treasure was within his grasp? There had been many others who had come far only to fail in the end.

He heard hoofbeats. Zolic was riding up. Jim knelt beside the deer with his back to the bushes which concealed the cave. He looked up and grinned. "I almost lost this buck," he said. "But I finally brought him down. I must practice my marksmanship more."

Zolic looked at him with a trace of suspicion, but Jim acted innocent. He hated to deceive this fine man who had befriended him, but he realized it would be better if

Zolic did not know that he had discovered the silver. Then the chief could always truthfully tell his tribesmen that he had not led *Cuchillo Grande* to it.

They loaded the deer carcass onto the pack horse, and rode silently to camp.

Bowie managed to restrain his impatience to return to Bexar, now that he had found what he was looking for. He stayed another week in camp, then left for San Antonio to make ready for his approaching marriage.

The bells of San Fernado Parish Church rang out a vibrant summons. Jim Bowie had heard them hundreds of times, but now their clanging was summoning him to his wedding. He was dressed in a new dark broadcloth suit with a dove-colored brocaded vest and wide flowing black tie. His shirt was of finest linen and his shoes, polished to reflect like a mirror, were of glove-soft leather. He moistened his dry lips nervously, then squared his shoulders and made his way to the church across the square. Carriages lined the streets as far as he could see. Well-dressed men and their mantilla-draped wives were entering the church. The thought of facing all those people and of the elaborate Catholic marriage ceremony gave him stage fright.

But when he stood before the altar and saw Urselita coming up the aisle on the arm of her father, all his panic evaporated. She wore a dress of creamy satin and her face was veiled. But through the veil he saw that beloved face, those madonnalike eyes radiant, and his heart was filled with an overwhelming joy.

After the wedding there was a reception at the Veramendi *palacio*, with the inevitable feasting and dancing which lasted three days. Then finally the young couple were allowed to go to their own home.

In a week they set out in a carriage for the Bayou Teche country.

Elvira Bowie looked at her new daughter-in-law for a long moment, then took her in her arms. "She is even lovelier than you said," his mother remarked over the bride's shoulder. "I love her dearly."

Jim nearly burst with pride over Urselita's social success. Her beauty and charm won every heart. And even in this land famed for beautiful and charming women, she stood out like some rare, exotic flower.

Jim took her to New Orleans where he looked up his old friend James Audubon, now famous since the publication of his book of bird paintings.[6]

"I know that you'd rather paint portraits of birds than of people," Jim said. "But as a special favor I'd like to have you paint a portrait of my lovely Urselita."

"This commission will be a joy," Audubon said. "If I could always paint such beauty in human face and form, I might forsake my precious birds. Hers is beauty not just on the surface. It comes from a lovely soul within."

"I want my Jaime's portrait painted, too," Urselita insisted.

"Oh, no!" Jim protested. "Audubon is a very great artist and he is particular about his subjects."

Audubon shrugged. "I will paint my friend James also—because his lovely bride wishes me to. But I could be better employed out in the swamps." His eyes twinkled at Jim.

6. *The Birds of America*, published in parts between 1827 and 1838.

Before Jim and Urselita returned to Texas, he told Rezin all about his finding evidence of the old mine. So Rez made plans to join his brother in November.

By the time Rezin reached San Antonio de Bexar, Jim had won Urselita's consent to his setting out to search for the mine on the San Saba. At first she had raised a great outcry about the danger of such a venture.

Jim had laughed at her fears. "Give Rezin and me a handful of Texans," he scoffed, "and we'll be the match of any Indians we meet."

"But the Comanche are so fierce—so cruel," she cried.

But when she saw his jaw set, she said, "The saints will protect you. You love the spice of danger. I love you for what you are. I would not change you."

When news of the project leaked out the members of Los Leoncitos clamored to go. Rezin was in favor of a strong force. Jim, however, said a handful of men could travel and maneuver much faster. So, besides the two leaders and their two servants, only seven men were picked for the treasure hunt, one of whom was Cephas Hamm.

Bowie led his small force over much the same route as Zolic had taken him. Later he would branch off toward the Red Hill.

He told the men that the ruins of an old fort lay about thirty miles ahead on the San Saba River. They should be able to reach it by nightfall and it would afford good protection in case a battle with any Indians developed. The route was so crisscrossed by rocky arroyos that the horses' hoofs were badly damaged and they found it impossible to reach the fort that night.

Jim had picked a place to set up camp on a slight elevation where a small timber island of about thirty live oaks grew. On the northern rim was a thicket of bushes and below was a stream of running water.

Everything we need, Jim thought.

The men cleared the prickly pear from the thicket, making a circle where the horses could be hobbled. A trail was slashed through to the stream. Guards were placed for the night.

Morning dawned clear and calm. Cephas Hamm climbed the tallest tree and looked over the country but reported that he saw no signs of any Indians.

"The fort is only about six miles farther on," Jim said. "It will be better protection if Indians do strike. And we'll be that much nearer our goal."

Since many of the horses had gone lame it was necessary to rearrange the supplies, so it was nearly eight o'clock when they were ready to set out.

Cephas climbed his tree for another look. He came scrambling down quickly. "Injuns to the east!" he cried. "One of 'em has his face to the ground as if he was sniffing our trail."

"Dismount! Prepare for defense!" Jim's voice snapped.

The saddle and pack horses were tethered. The men stationed themselves behind the trunks of the largest trees. Soon bloodcurdling war whoops split the air. The Indians could be seen stripping and then daubing war paint on their bodies.

A man named Buchanan, who knew a smattering of Caddo, offered to go out and parley with the Indians if someone would accompany him.

"I know a bit of Indian," Jim said. "I'll go. Keep us covered, Rez. Since they are about a hundred and sixty-four to our eleven I hope we can talk them out of fighting."

The two men strode forward boldly.

"Send out your chief," Buchanan shouted in Caddo. "We want to talk to him."

"Howdy do! Howdy do!" the Indians replied. Evidently this was the extent of their English.

Their next greeting was a barrage of shot, one of which broke Buchanan's leg. Jim returned their fire with a double-barreled shotgun and a pistol. Then he reached down and lifted Buchanan over his shoulder.

As he staggered back toward the encampment he was surrounded by heavy fire. Two more shots hit Buchanan. Seeing that their gunfire did not bring down Jim Bowie, eight warriors came at him with upraised tomahawks. But Rezin and several others rushed to Jim's rescue and sent the Indians running, after killing four of them. Buchanan was laid in the shade of a tree where Rezin dressed his wounds.

The men discovered that a hill to the northeast, about sixty yards away, was swarming with Indians. They began a heavy fire accompanied by shrill war whoops. Their chief was at the front, urging his men to charge.

"Get that Indian on horseback. He's the chief," Jim shouted.

Several shots were fired and he was brought down. His warriors rushed forward to carry him from the battlefield, and then went over the hill out of sight, giving the white men a chance to reload.

Soon the Indians reappeared firing bows and arrows. The Texans took deadly aim with their rifles. Now another chief began haranguing his warriors.

Jim aimed, fired and the second chief fell to the ground. He, too, was caught up by his men and carried off.

"If we keep picking off their chiefs we'll soon have them plumb discouraged." Cephas Hamm laughed.

"We must plan better, though," Jim said, "so every shot will count. Only five men fire at one time. Then there will always be five guns loaded."

While the attention of the treasure seekers was taken up by the attack from the Indians on the hill, twenty of the Caddo crept under the bank at the rear and opened fire. Soon the Indians had completely encircled Bowie's handful of men, concealing themselves behind the shrubbery.

"We're too exposed," Jim shouted. "To the bushes, men."

Crouching low, the Bowie men scampered into the bushes in which the small clearing had been made. Although they were not as well protected as they had been by the oak trunks, the men had an advantage here, for they could see the enemy without being seen.

"Move every time you fire," Bowie ordered.

This strategy proved sound, for the Indians' only target was the smoke from the rifles. For two long hours the fighting went on with only one other Bowie man being wounded. The Indians on the other hand were losing heavily from the deadly aim of the Texans.

Now the Indians adopted a more dangerous tactic. They set fire to the dry grass which lay near the Bowie camp, and under cover of the smoke were able to carry off their dead and wounded. The wind from the west whipped the fire into black billows of smoke from which darted forked tongues of flame. The grass shriveled, then leaped into blaze. The white men were gasping and choking and could not see their enemy.

Behind the curtain of smoke the Indians whooped as though already celebrating a victory.

"Work, boys, work!" Jim shouted, himself a fury of energy as he piled rocks for a breastwork,[7] scraped dead grass from around the wounded and beat out creeping flames with blankets.

It was like the inside of a furnace. Sparks filled the air and fell on their faces. But they beat the licking flames and labored with knives or bare hands to heighten the breastwork and dig a trench. Outside the ring of fire the Indians kept up their incessant whooping and yelling.

"The red devils must think we're already roasting at the stake," Jim growled as he and Rezin worked shoulder to shoulder.

Then the flames ran into bare ground and died on one side of the camp and on the other side the fire was checked by the stream.

Having failed to burn the white men out, the Indians again occupied the point of rocks and began a fierce attack. The wind veered, blowing strongly from the north. Jim bade the two servants scrape away the dry leaves and grass from their side of the encampment. It was too much to hope that the redskins would fail to notice the advantage this change in wind direction gave them.

Soon one of them was seen crawling to the creek with a firebrand in his hand. He managed to fire the grass on the side near the camp and shortly the flames, ten feet high, raced toward the white men.

Should they remain in this spot and be cooked or go out onto the prairie where they would certainly fall into the hands of the Indians?

The men gathered about Bowie. "Keep your powder horns closed," he ordered, "or we'll be blown to bits. We each have one load apiece to use on the red devils. When they charge, let them have it. Then we'll stand back to back and use our knives as long as possible. We must all fight the fire with buffalo robes, deerskins and blankets, and protect our wounded."

As the brush burned, the circle became smaller and smaller. But evidently the flames were too hot for the Indians, so the men had time to build their breastwork higher and dig a trench with knives and sticks.

With the setting of the sun, the clamor around the camp died down, as did the wind. The fire died, too, when it reached the ground which the trapped men had scraped bare.

They had been fighting furiously since sunrise, and now that the battle was over they realized how exhausted they were. The Indians withdrew beyond rifle fire and set up a mournful wailing over their dead.

But the Bowie men did not waste time. They buried the one man who had been killed and attended to the three wounded as best they could. They filled their canteens, cups and cooking pans with water and soaked the blankets in case the fire broke out again. Then they worked feverishly until long into the night, raising and strengthening the breastwork, getting ready for the attack all were sure would come with the dawn.

However, the expected attack did not develop. When it was light enough to see, Bowie peered toward the hill where the Indians had been camped, but they had vanished. Later Jim and Cephas Hamm rode out to reconnoiter. They counted forty-eight telltale red spots on the ground. Three of those killed had been chiefs.

"It's sure as the sun shines that a third of their number was wiped out," Cephas said triumphantly. "I believe they're plumb discouraged with fighting an outfit like ours."

"I hope they stay discouraged," Jim said.

7. A temporary defensive wall.

They did. The white men remained in the comparative safety of their little fortress for eight days, waiting for the wounded men and horses to recover sufficiently to be moved—and to see if the Indians showed any further inclination to fight.

Jim and Rezin did not know then that this fight was to go down in history as the fiercest ever recorded in Indian warfare. They were not much concerned with their historic battle. They were heartsick that their treasure hunt had failed.

"We'll try again, won't we, Jim?" Rez said as they were riding back toward Bexar.

"Of course," his brother said confidently. "As soon as we can reorganize."

But when he reached home Urselita had news for him which changed his mind.

"I'm sorry, Rez," he said. "We'll have to postpone our plans—perhaps until next fall. You see," his chest swelled, "I'm going to be a father. I couldn't leave Urselita now."

CHAPTER 16. STORM CLOUDS GATHERING

News of the extraordinary victory at San Saba against the Indians added to the growing prestige of James Bowie.

Now the Bowie knife was the preferred weapon of all frontiersmen. Powder and lead were expensive, and precious time was lost in reloading after each shot. But the Bowie knife was always ready for quick action and a dozen uses.

Many of these knives were manufactured in England. There was some variation in both the length and breadth of the blade, but otherwise the weapons were nearly exact copies of the original one made by James Black.

Many of Jim's friends tried in vain to pry from him the location of the San Saba mine, but he refused to disclose the secret.

Although plans for another treasure hunt were still very active in his mind, Jim's main interest was in Urselita and their coming child.

Usually restless to be on the go, Jim now resented the need to travel back and forth to Saltillo and other places to attend to the many business affairs in which he and his father-in-law were involved. He was afraid he might be absent at the time of the child's birth.

However, he was at home when it took place. But he found himself reduced to maddening uselessness when Doña Josefa took affairs in her capable hands and shooed Jim from the room.

"This is no place for a man," she said firmly. "You're in the way."

At last Doña Josefa called him inside and placed in his arms a blanket-wrapped bundle.

"Your daughter," Doña Josefa said proudly.[8]

For the first time in his life Jim Bowie wanted to remain at home, but the press of business and events made it more imperative than ever that he spend most of his days in the saddle.

Political affairs were now in such a ferment that Don Juan's constant presence at his desk in Bexar was required. So Jim had to ride back and forth to Saltillo to keep the steam factory for manufacturing cotton goods running smoothly. He and Veramendi were also involved in numerous real estate deals. Then, too, as Bowie had become an important person in Texas, he was expected to assume heavy responsibilities during this critical time.

A new president, Bustamante,[9] had risen to power, and immediately trouble began.

8. Biographers disagree over the number of children Jim Bowie had—if any.

9. Anastasio Bustamante (1780–1853), general and politician who as vice president of the Mexican republic led a revolt against and took the place of the president in 1830.

He promptly forbade further immigration from the United States, imposed heavy taxes and duties on the colonists and decreed that from now on Texas was to be colonized only by Mexicans who would also administer all affairs.

There were feelings of ill will on both sides. The well-founded rumor that the American government planned to annex Texas—had, in fact, offered to buy the province for one million dollars—alarmed Mexico. Some American statesmen considered that by the terms of the Louisiana Purchase, Texas belonged to the United States. The colonists, in turn, feared that they might lose the holdings for which they had labored so hard.

Austin called a convention to meet in October, 1832, at San Felipe, to discuss the new crisis and to ask for greater liberties under the Mexican law. Of course Jim Bowie was there. But Mexico City completely ignored the resolutions passed at the meeting. As the Bustamente regime grew more harsh, trouble-breeding incidents between the colonists and the Mexicans increased.

The following year Austin called for another convention to meet in December.

"You don't have to go this time, Jaime!" Urselita protested when she heard her father and husband discussing the matter.

"Of course he must go, *muchacha*,"[1] Don Juan said. "Don Jaime is an important man. His words bear weight in such meetings."

"But it will mean that he will be away from us during the Nativity celebrations," she said.

Bowie drew her close. "I always suffer when I am away from you, *querida*," he said tenderly, "and it will be worse to be separated from you and the baby during the Christmas season. Perhaps we can get the convention over quickly so I can be with you."

She shook her head. "You men with your tiresome politics! You talk, talk, talk—and get nowhere."

Jim chuckled. "We should be stingy with words, as the women are, eh? You may depend upon it, *novia*,[2] I shall be back with you as soon as possible."

Arriving at San Felipe de Austin, Bowie sought lodging at Peyton Tavern. When he entered the long room he saw a giant of a man standing before the great fireplace. There was something familiar about the set of the magnificent head on those massive shoulders. Then, as though drawn by Bowie's stare, the man turned and his stern features broke into a smile of welcome.

"Jim Bowie!" he cried, seizing Jim's hand in a bone-crushing grip. "How lucky to run into you!"

At first Jim did not recognize this man who was so vastly changed since their chance meeting at the river landing in Arkansas. Now he was clean shaven save for the bushy sideburns, and his clothing was well tailored.

"Sam Houston!" Jim cried. "I didn't expect to find you here."

Houston grinned. "President Jackson sent me with a message to Steve Austin. But I reckon I would've come anyway. Seems as if things are about to pop wide open here in Texas—and Sam Houston's the man to be in the middle of any scrap."

"We must be kindred spirits, suh," Bowie remarked. "I used to tell my brother Rezin that I aimed to live to the hilt during my prime, then go out in a blaze of glory."

These two men, both giants in stature as well as spirit, stood measuring each other.

---

1. Girl (a term of affection). 2. Sweetheart.

It seemed as though this was a fateful moment—that these two natural leaders of men had come together for a special purpose.

The convention of 1833 proposed a state constitution and asked for separation from the Mexican state of Coahuila, with free immigration and some minor reforms. It denied any wish for independence.

Word came from Mexico City that Santa Anna[3] had overthrown Bustamente. The Texans were sure that the new president would be friendly to their cause, and Stephen Austin volunteered to carry their message in person to the Mexican capital.

There was an air of jubilance among the settlers when the convention was adjourned. They believed that their problems were over.

Bowie and Houston, who had become well acquainted during the meetings, drew together at their close.

Bowie sighed. "I had hoped to be with my family on Christmas Day. What do you say we dine here together, suh? You say you plan to ride to Bexar. I should be proud to have you as my guest there, but I suppose that my father-in-law will snatch you from me."

"I'll enjoy riding with you," Houston said. "I'd planned to talk to Veramendi. You can bring me up to date on Texas affairs as we travel."

Jim longed to be with Urselita, enjoying the special celebration the Veramendis made of Christmas. He therefore welcomed the company of Sam Houston, a fascinating conversationalist and good companion.

One thing, though, which Houston told him made Jim shudder. Bowie had mentioned that he might have to make a business trip back to the States the following summer.

"I trust," Houston said, "the plague will have run its course by then."

"What plague?"

"Asiatic cholera. An epidemic has been raging through the whole Mississippi Valley. It was probably brought in by some sailor from the Black Sea. In New Orleans alone, five thousand have died in less than two weeks. Doctors work day and night until they themselves lie down to die. Bodies are piled like corkwood and buried in great trenches. It has spread upriver to all the towns. Fur traders carried it to the Indians and whole tribes were wiped out."

Jim's face had turned pale. He thought of his family back in Louisiana and his loved ones here in Texas. "We heard nothing of the pestilence here," he said. "I pray that it doesn't strike this part of the country."

"Texas is too sparsely settled for it to take hold here," Houston's words were faintly reassuring.

While they ate a well-cooked Christmas dinner, Jim told Houston of the factors which had brought about the present crisis in Texas.

"As you probably know, suh, the trouble started in 1830 when Mexico passed a law checking further immigration into Texas."

Houston nodded.

Jim went on. "There was fault on both sides, I reckon. The Bustamante regime has been too harsh for the high-spirited Texans. We look for an improvement now that Santa Anna is in power. And naturally Mexico grew alarmed over the zeal of the United States government to buy Texas.

"But the biggest trouble," Jim added seriously, "arose when Bradburn—a Ken-

---

3. Antonio López de Santa Anna (1794–1876), who removed Bustamante from office in 1832; as president (1833–36), he led the Mexican army against the Texans.

tuckian, mind you, but in the paid service of the Mexicans—arrested William Travis[4]
and other Anglo-Americans on some trivial charge. Of course the Texans would not
stand for that and one hundred and sixty armed colonists marched to Anáhuac to
their rescue. Travis and the others were soon freed, but there was a fierce, short
battle at Velasco. A small Mexican force surrendered there, but were released upon
their promise that they would not again attack Texans."

"General Jackson wonders if Travis' friends did not go too far," Houston said
thoughtfully.

"Some of the colonists think so, too. This little incident, trivial as it may seem,
might be the tinder to set off a real explosion in Texas affairs."

"It's often little things like that which start big wars," Houston said sagely.

Next day they set out for San Antonio de Bexar. As soon as they arrived Jim introduced Houston to Vice-president de Veramendi. Although his father-in-law seemed
to regard Don Samuel, as he called Houston, with some suspicion, he insisted that
Houston be his guest during his stay in Bexar.

Jim, too, thought there was some mystery connected with Houston's presence in
Texas. The matter was somewhat clarified just before Houston was to return to Nacogdoches, Texas.

As they were talking together, Houston suddenly threw out a challenging remark,
"How do you stand on the Texas question, Jim?"

"What do you mean?"

"Like the other Texans, you became a Mexican citizen in order to hold lands here.
By marriage you're tied to the highest in the Mexican government. But you're American born. If it comes to a showdown of Texans' fighting for independence, where
will you stand?"

"Suh, I consider your question premature!"

"And impertinent?" Sam threw in with a laugh. "Forgive me, Jim. That was a very
personal question and you've a right to resent it. Yet I've reasons for asking. You're
a leader—will be whichever side you're on."

"Whatever influence I may have," Jim said stiffly, "I am trying to use to avert trouble
among my people, both Mexican and American."

Houston nodded understandingly. "And you're doing a good job of it. Yet I'm afraid
the fat's in the fire. Because I consider you my friend, I'm going to confide in you.
But I ask you to keep this matter between us. Here's a report I'm sending to my
president from Nacogdoches as soon as I get there."

He handed a paper to Jim.

Bowie read the communication addressed to General Jackson, in which Houston
reported that nineteen twentieths of the population of Texas wanted the United
States to acquire the province; that Mexico was involved in civil war; that the people
of Texas were determined to form a state government; and that Mexico's want of
money, taken in connection with the course which Texas "*must* and *will* adopt" would
render a transfer of Texas to some power inevitable.

He concluded with these words: "My opinion is that Texas, by her members in
convention, will, by the first of April, declare all that country (north of the Rio
Grande) as Texas proper, and form a state constitution. I expect to be present at that

---

4. A leader of the party favoring war (1809–1836),
born in South Carolina; he came to Texas in 1831
and established a law practice at Anáhuac, a port
on the eastern end of Galveston Bay. John David
Bradburn (17787–1842), commander of the Mexican garrison at Anáhuac; he had been in Texas in
the Mexican army since 1821.

convention, and will apprise you of the course adopted. I may make Texas my abiding place, but I will never forget the country of my birth." The letter was signed, "Your friend and obedient servant, Sam Houston."

Jim handed the document back to Houston. "I believe, suh, that you've summed the matter up very neatly. And if so, as you said, the fat *is* in the fire. Perhaps you have a better perspective on affairs than we have who are so close to it."

"I think so," Houston answered. "And if a crisis comes, as I'm sure it must, be sure, Jim Bowie, that you're on the side of right. For you're a big man, and we'll need you."

"When the time comes—if it does—I'll let my conscience be my guide," Jim said, holding out his hand to bid his strangely fascinating friend farewell.

CHAPTER 17. HEARTBREAK

Bowie's divided loyalties did not prove to be as troublesome as he had feared. Most of the highborn Mexicans to whom he was tied by marriage or friendship were as fervently against the oppressive rule of Bustamante as were the colonists. When it was learned that the hated president had been overthrown by Santa Anna, Texans and Mexicans alike cheered, believing that the crisis in Texas affairs had passed safely.

Yet when month after month went by and Stephen Austin did not return, the colonists grew suspicious. It was rumored that Austin had been thrown into prison, but no one knew if this were true.

Meantime Jim Bowie had other matters to worry about. He received a frantic letter from Maggie, Rezin's wife, saying that his brother was going blind. Could Jim come and take care of his business matters?

"No! No!" Urselita clung to him. "The plague! The terrible plague. I will not allow you to go where it is raging."

"But I must go, *mi querida*. Rezin is my other self. He needs me."

Urselita's beautiful dark eyes flashed. "But what about me? I am your wife. It is *I* who is your other self. You know that I am with child again. I need you, too."

Jim took her in his arms tenderly. "Try to understand," he said gently. "You are my wife—my very soul, closer than my other self. But you will be here with your family. You will be cared for. At the moment Rezin's need for me is greater. I must see that he has the best doctors. He's a brilliant man. It's unthinkable that he should spend the rest of his days in darkness. I will not let it happen. I'll sell Arcadia and see that he and his family and my mother are comfortably settled in a smaller place. And I shall hurry back to you, *novia*. I shall be here before our child is born."

"Then go," she said with a sigh. "I would not be so selfish as to hold you—but take care of yourself—my beloved. *Voya con Dios!*"[5]

Three times Rezin had represented his parish in the state legislature, greatly distinguishing himself. Jim was determined that his brother's career should not be blighted by blindness.

Jim found Rezin's condition as serious as Maggie had said. He promptly took his brother to Baltimore where the best eye specialist in the country practiced. Later Jim left Rezin there for treatment while he returned to Louisiana to sell his brother's widely scattered lands.

---

5. Go with God.

The work of disposing of Rezin's land holdings could not be done hurriedly. So it was October before Jim was free to set out for home—and the child had been expected in September. He would make Urselita understand, for she was the kindest, most unselfish of women.

Before he left Jim saw Rezin and his family and his mother comfortably established in a lovely home in Avoyelles Parish.

Gripping Rezin's hand at parting, Jim said, huskily, "Take care of yourself now, Rez. Get those eyes well so we can have another go at our silver mine."

"I'm planning on it." Rezin smiled. "I hope to make it next spring."

"I'll have all the arrangements made. You'd better bring Mom and Maggie and the girls. I want them to meet my children. There are two of them by now. And I haven't even met my son yet."

"That's a long, hard journey for an old lady," Elvie said. "Better bring your family here."

"You're as spry as any girl of twenty," he told her.

Jim took with him a sturdy Negro named Ham as his servant. As he rode the long miles through forests and plains, fording wild rivers, sleeping under the stars, he dreamed of San Antonio de Bexar drowsing in the sun, and of his own home where Urselita would welcome him, her madonnalike eyes full of love. Now she would be holding the new baby.

Finally they reached San Felipe. When Jim, exhausted by the journey, stumbled into Peyton Tavern the proprietor stared at him strangely.

"What's the matter?" Jim asked a trifle testily.

"Nothing at present. Eat your supper. Then I have news for you."

"Tell me now. I insist."

"No." Mr. Peyton shook his head. "I can see you're worn out. You need food. Meet me in my office after you've eaten."

Jim shrugged. Probably the news had something to do with Texas politics. At the moment he did not want to hear about it, for he was dead tired. He wanted to eat, fall into bed, then set out at dawn for home.

The meal made him more drowsy than ever. He was tempted to pass the office and go straight to his room, but Mr. Peyton was waiting by the door and beckoned to him.

With a yawn Jim sank into a chair.

"Brace yourself, Mr. Bowie," the innkeeper said. "I have bad news. You've probably heard that the cholera has taken heavy toll in Texas?"

Jim gasped. His heart stopped beating for a moment. "My family? Not Urselita or the child."

Peyton nodded.

"Which one? Not both of them. For God's sake, man, tell me!"

"I have a letter here from your brother-in-law. You'd better read it."

Jim rose to his feet. "Tell me what it says. Quickly!"

"When the cholera hit Bexar," Peyton said, "Veramendi fled with his family, including your wife, little daughter and your newborn son, to his mountain home in Montaclava. But it was too late. Veramendi—every member of your family and his died of the plague."

A roar of anguish came from Jim Bowie's throat. "It can't be!" he cried. "I don't believe it. What hideous lie are you telling?"

"It is true. I am more sorry than I can say."

Jim seized the letter, read and reread the terrible news. "Then it's true," he moaned. "It is Navarro's[6] writing. What have I done to deserve this?"

He stumbled from the office. Loungers in the tavern stared at him—frightened at the wild look in his eyes.

"Call my boy Ham," Bowie cried in a hoarse voice. "Tell him to saddle the horses."

"You're not setting out tonight, I hope," Mr. Peyton said. "You're exhausted. It's storming."

"How could I rest?" Bowie whirled on him. "How can I ever rest? My Urselita gone! My daughter! The son I never saw. . . ."

Sobs choked him. He staggered from the tavern, out into the night where strong wind and cold, drenching rain beat upon him.

Jim Bowie did not want to go on living. Existence had lost all meaning for him. He could not bear to go back to the home where Urselita had always run to meet him with a smile of joy and where his little daughter had toddled toward him with out-stretched arms. He stayed at an inn and roamed the streets aimlessly, trying to find relief for the grief which was devouring him.

He blamed himself. Perhaps if he had not gone to Louisiana, this terrible thing might not have happened. Oh, if only he could have died with his loved ones!

He went back to his family in Louisiana, hoping to find relief, but decided he was more miserable there than in Texas. Rezin's condition was somewhat improved. There was no business with which Jim could occupy himself. The days dragged unbearably.

"I reckon I'll be better off in Texas," he finally told his mother. "Things are going bad for the colonists. I can be useful there."

Mrs. Bowie nodded. "I think you're wise," she said. "Lock this sorrow in your heart. Throw your great energies into some work or some cause. You'll be happier."

"I can never be happy again," he said bitterly.

"You can at least be useful." There was a snap to her voice and in her eyes. "No son of mine will sit back and feel sorry for himself. There's no use blaming yourself. You couldn't have held off the plague from hitting your loved ones if you'd been there."

"I could have died with them then."

"But you didn't. You're alive and must keep on living and carrying your weight in the world. Perhaps fate had a hand in this. You know"—her eyes took on a strange, faraway look—"I've always had a feeling about you. That destiny had singled you out for a special purpose. Few men get to be legends during their lifetime."

"Because of a bloodstained knife! What a road to glory!"

"Stop being bitter. Get hold of yourself. Go out with head up to meet whatever lies in your path."

For the first time in months a smile quirked at his lips. "You're good for me, Mother Elvie," he said patting her shoulder. "I'll brace up and take anything life hands me without crying."

"That sounds like my son," she said proudly.

When Ham brought around the horses Rezin clasped Jim's hand and said, "Get ready for that treasure hunt. As soon as my eyes are better I'll come out to join you."

"I'll be waiting," Jim responded, although he now had no interest in the silver mine. Of what use was wealth to a man without a family?

---

6. José Antonio Navarro (1795–1871), one of the three Mexican signers of the Texas Declaration of Independence. He was Ursula Veramendi's cousin.

Back in San Antonio, Bowie tried to take up the broken threads of his life. He put the big white house up for sale and also sold his interest in the textile mill in Saltillo.

He found the political affairs of Texas still as unsettled as when he had left. The fact that nothing had been heard from Stephen Austin did not ease the strained relations between the colonists and Mexico.

The Texans had hoped that with the reins of government in the hands of Santa Anna restrictions would be eased, but so far nothing like that had happened.

Jim Bowie went back to dealing in land. He had brought a number of commissions from Louisiana friends who wished to speculate in Texas real estate. Although he made a nice profit on these transactions, he had little interest in money.

That spring the people in San Antonio were talking about a new development in Texas political affairs. Usually the Mexican government kept only a small garrison at Bexar, but suddenly Colonel Domingo de Ugartecha,[7] the new commandant, had brought his military up to over four hundred men. Added to that came a rumor that Santa Anna was about to march upon Texas with strong military forces. The new dictator had given himself the title, "Napoleon of the West."

Upon hearing this Bowie said to his friends, "Santa Anna is proving himself an even worse tyrant than Bustamante."

The news spread rapidly, and almost as speedily Texas split into two factions, the War party and the Peace party, with constant bickering between them. As the Mexican custom laws became more strict and the troops more arrogant and overbearing, the War party grew in strength and more and more talk about Texas independence was heard.

Bowie did not join in this futile quarreling, but he longed for some action which would take his mind from his tragic loss. He rode to Matamoros, the great Mexican port at the mouth of the Rio Grande, to do a little private spying. Although he was dressed as a Mexican and could speak the language fluently, there was little he could do to disguise his red hair and blue eyes, except keep his wide hat pulled low to shade his face.

No particular spying was necessary to sense war in the air, however. Matamoros, usually a sleepy town, was now bustling with activity. Over the cobbled streets strode *zapadores*, dragoons and lancers,[8] dressed in new uniforms.

Bowie slipped in and out of the smoky *cantinas*[9] and heard the loud boasts of the coming expedition to subdue the Texans. More important, he discovered that every sort of craft in the river's mouth was being made ready to transport troops.

He had felt fairly safe until the second day when he saw signs posted on the walls forbidding all foreigners to leave the city.

After nightfall he slipped out of town and quietly rode away. When he was far enough from the city, he set his horse to a gallop and rode all night, hiding in groves of trees during the day. He traveled up the Texas coast until he arrived at Hatch's Plantation on the Lavaca River. From there he promptly dispatched a letter to the political chief of the Brazos department, reporting about the vessels at Matamoros and of the orders issued by Commandant General Cos,[1] forbidding foreigners to leave the city. He further stated that three thousand troops had reached Saltillo on their

---

7. I.e., Ugartechea, Mexican army officer.
8. Light cavalry. "*Zapadores*": sappers (military engineers, whose work includes building fortifications). "Dragoons": heavily armed cavalry.

9. Bars.
1. Martín Perfecto de Cos (1800–1854), Mexican general.

way to Texas. And he promised to be with the chief in a few days' time.

Then Jim rode on to San Felipe. Event piled on event. President Santa Anna dissolved the legislatures of Cohuila and Texas and demanded that all provinces reduce their militia to one man for each five hundred inhabitants. Not only did this arouse the anger of the Texans, but many of the former members of the Mexican governing party joined with them in shouting for war against Santa Anna.

Impetuous William Barrett Travis, a lawyer who aspired to leadership of the War party, led a band of Americans to Anáhuac, captured the customs house with its store of arms and ammunition and forced Captain Antonio Tenorio and forty-four Mexican troops to surrender. He afterward released them upon their promise never to take up arms against Texas again.

Bowie was visiting Sam Houston when he heard this news. Both men groaned. "Travis will get us into war now, I'm afraid," Houston said.

Bowie nodded. These two intelligent men had been cautioning their countrymen to avoid action which would plunge them into revolution for which they were ill prepared, since Texas was divided by the war and peace factions and was without leadership.

At this critical time Austin, who had been imprisoned in Mexico City for many months, was released and returned to Texas. Though broken in health, he was still dedicated to the cause of his colonists.

Early in September of 1835 he arrived at Velasco. Texas turned out to give him a wholehearted welcome. At a banquet held in his honor he said, "Texas needs peace and local government. Its inhabitants are farmers. They need a calm and quiet life. But how can anyone now remain indifferent when our right, our all, appear to be in jeopardy?"

Austin said he could see no choice except for drastic measures, and advocated that a general consultation be held as soon as possible. Four days later this meeting was held.

Austin had sent a message to Ugartecha deploring the impetuous action of Travis at Anáhuac. The Mexican commander at San Antonio demanded the arrest of Travis and his followers. This, of course, the Texans would not tolerate, but before the election could be held, Texas was plunged into war with Mexico.

Now Jim Bowie did not have time to think about his own tragedy. During September new crises arose. General Cos, Santa Anna's brother-in-law, landed on the southern coast of Copano with five hundred troops and immediately began a march by way of Goliad toward San Antonio. From San Felipe came notices warning "every man of Texas who cherishes liberty to prepare for war. All hope of peaceful settlement is gone."

Santa Anna made no secret of his aims to overrun Texas. In one of his frenzies he shouted, "If the Americans do not beware I shall march through their own country and plant the Mexican flag in Washington."

At another time he declared his intention of disarming the people and driving out every American who had entered Texas since 1830, as well as punishing those who had not obeyed the regulations of the president.

Jim was riding between Nacogdoches and San Felipe when the first real clash of the Texas struggle took place at DeWitt's settlement of Gonzales.[2] In 1831 the colonists of this place had been given a brass cannon as defense against the Indians. As

2. Established by Green DeWitt (1787–1835) and his surveyor, James Kerr (1790–1850), in 1825.

their first effort to disarm the Americans, the Mexicans sent Captain Castenada from Bexar with two hundred men, demanding the cannon.

The Texans sent back the answer, "Come and take it."

The news spread quickly and volunteers gathered, armed with squirrel guns, rifles and the inevitable Bowie knife.

Just before the battle DeWitt's daughter made a flag from a sheet and painted upon it a black cannon surrounded by the words, "COME AND TAKE IT," which was placed on the cannon.

The brass cannon was turned on those who had come to take it, and within a short time the Mexican force was routed with serious losses. Not a man of the Texas band was scratched.

The victorious Texans gave a wild "yipee" as they wheeled the cannon back to the settlement, their banner proudly flying above their heads. This Battle of Gonzales, fought October 2, 1835, was the first blow for independence.

Bowie's heart beat fast when he heard the news at San Felipe. He had not wanted his countrymen to become involved in war, but ever since his secret visit to Matamoros he knew that a clash was inevitable. The mounting tension, added to his grief, had him keyed up to the bursting point. It was a relief to have the thing settled—to know where he stood. Of course he would fight with his countrymen!

Austin sent messengers to the various settlements to carry the news of the "Come and Take It" victory. Colonists rode toward Gonzales from all directions.

Meantime fifty volunteers, sparked by Bowie's friend Old Ben Milam,[3] aged forty-four, stormed the Mexican fort of Goliad and seized about ten thousand dollars' worth of military supplies—material sorely needed by the Texans.

Bowie rode with all haste toward Gonzales to join the Texans. He overtook the army where it was encamped on the banks of the Guadalupe River awaiting reinforcements. Stephen Austin and Sam Houston were both there.

Austin had already been elected commander in chief of the Volunteer Army of Texas—the "People's Army." Also the vote had been cast to march on Bexar and attack.

Houston spoke against such impetuous action. "We aren't ready," he said. "Our men are untrained, undisciplined. Cos's army is trained, experienced, strong and well armed."

"Also well entrenched behind strong walls at Bexar," Jim added.

But those who advised caution were shouted down.

Jim went to Austin and offered his services.

"We need men of your caliber, Bowie," Austin said. "I appoint you volunteer aide, carrying the honorary rank of colonel."

Jim wished that Sam Houston had been chosen leader, for Austin was no warrior and was ill, besides. But Houston was new in Texas and had expressed himself against hasty action. Such a point of view was unpopular with the Texans who were sure they could easily whip the Mexican army and wanted to get on with the job.

On October 12th the People's Army started the march on San Antonio de Bexar. Bowie had to suppress a smile as he saw them set out. They were as ragtag an army as had ever marched to battle. Some of them were in buckskin, like himself; some in linsey-woolsey. Some wore wool hats, others coonskin[4] caps or handkerchiefs

---

3. Benjamin Rush Milam (1788–1835), Kentucky-born soldier and entrepreneur; he first came to

Texas in 1818.
4. I.e., raccoon skin.

around their heads. They were armed with old-fashioned muskets, horse pistols, double-barreled fowling pieces, broadswords—any sort of weapon they could lay hands on. But nearly every man carried a Bowie knife at his belt. Some were mounted; many walked. But there was no lack of fighting spirit.

The straggling army marched to San Francisco de la Espada, one of the abandoned early Spanish missions. There they rested while Bowie was sent in command of two companies to choose a suitable spot to establish a camp as close as possible to Bexar.

With ninety-two horsemen, Bowie set out over country he knew well. His men had confidence in him, for they knew of his victory on the San Saba River. They rode first to the San Juan Capistrano Mission. But Jim could see no favorable military positions here, so he continued on.

Two miles south of Bexar he selected a bend in the San Antonio River, about five hundred yards from the towered Concepción Mission.

Well pleased with the natural advantages of the site, Bowie placed guards in the cupola of the mission house which overlooked the whole country.

At dawn next day, such a heavy mist lay over the land that Henry Karnes, who had just been relieved of duty in one of the towers, had to pick his way back to camp. Although he could detect no movement in the mesquite,[5] the sound of rifle fire drew him up short. It seemed to come from the tower. A shot cracked from the plains in front of the river. Then, through the mist, Karnes detected shadowy forms and felt something slap his side.

He dashed toward camp yelling, "They're here, boys! And the danged rascals've shot out the bottom of my powder horn!"

At the first shot the Texans fired into the mist, although they could not sight their targets.

Bowie ran along the river bottom shouting, "Wait until you can see what you're shooting at and make every shot count. Keep your heads down. We haven't a man to lose."

He set them to clearing away the bushes and vines under the hill and along the edge of the bluff. At the steepest places he had steps dug in the side of the bluff so that they could ascend to fire, then drop below the bank to reload.

The rising sun dispelled the mist and revealed the advancing Mexican infantry, supported by five companies of cavalry—about four hundred Mexican soldiers, to Bowie's ninety-two men.

The harsh crack of rifle fire opened the battle about eight o'clock that chilly morning. At once the firing became general. From the Mexican side it presented a steady sheet of flame. The Texans fired with deadly accuracy, then ducked below the bank to reload.

A Texas sharpshooter picked off the mule driver in charge of the caisson carrying the ammunition. The team raced through the Mexican lines creating great confusion.

The battle had scarcely begun when the enemy brought up a big brass cannon which they trained on the American line.

"Pick off the cannon, men!" Bowie shouted.

One by one the artillerymen manning the cannon were killed, only to be replaced by others. Another charge from the four-pounder blasted through the timber. At the same time the cavalry charged, but so deadly was the Texans' aim that they were repelled.

5. A shrub that forms extensive thickets.

Three times foot soldiers attempted to charge across the plains, but each time they were forced to fall back, leaving the prairie littered with bodies.

Finally Jim roared, "Let's take the cannon, boys! Follow me! The cannon and victory."

He dashed from the thicket, pistol in hand, a band of his men right at his heels, their guns spitting fire. The Mexicans ran. With a yell the Bowie men seized the cannon and turned it on the fleeing enemy. Someone grabbed the brand from the hand of a dead Mexican and applied it to the vent.

With triumphant shouts the other Americans poured over the edge of the bluff. Seeing them, the Mexicans broke and ran toward Bexar. The entire Battle of Concepción had lasted only half an hour, but it was a smashing victory which greatly cheered the Americans and did much to enhance Jim Bowie's glory.

There were sixteen bodies around the captured cannon. One hundred more Mexican soldiers lost their lives, against only one casualty for the Texans.

CHAPTER 19. FALSE VICTORY

Austin rode to join the main troops at Concepción. James Bowie and Captains Fannin and Briscoe[6] rode out to meet him. If they expected any praise for their smashing victory they were disappointed.

"You should have followed them," Austin said peevishly. "With the enemy so demoralized, you could have smashed into San Antonio."

Bowie stared at him in surprise. "You seem to have forgotten, suh, that you gave me written orders not to do so."

Austin ignored him. "With our combined forces we should push on without delay. Drive them from Bexar."

"Such a course would be foolhardy," Bowie said. "I do not wish to dispute your authority as commander in chief, suh. But as a long-time resident of Bexar I know the fortifications of the city. They have been greatly altered during the two years you were a prisoner in Mexico. Our men are brave fighters, but it would be folly to send a small force against such strongly entrenched enemies."

Austin's thin lips tightened. "What do you think about it, Fannin?"

"I agree with Bowie," the captain said.

While he was speaking Briscoe nodded.

"Nonsense! Sheer nonsense!" Austin put heel to his horse. His subordinates said nothing, but Bowie knew what was in their minds. Austin had been dedicated to the interests of his colonists, but he was a misfit as a military leader and had as little heart as ability for his present role.

Jim was dumfounded the following morning when Austin announced his intention of skirting around Bexar and entrenching the main army at the Old Mill, about a mile north of the Alamo—on the opposite side of San Antonio from Concepción.

"I consider it a more strategic point," he said. "Bowie, you and your command will remain here and daily demonstrate before the enemy position. I have reason to think that many Mexicans will desert to our side with a little show of force."

Jim clamped his mouth shut tight so that he would not voice further criticism of

6. Andrew Briscoe (1810–1849), a merchant born in Mississippi who settled in Texas in 1833; after independence, he became a judge and a railroad promoter. James Walker Fannin (1804–1836), Georgia-born agitator for the Texas Revolution who moved to Texas in 1834.

his commander in chief. He realized that Austin was not used to being contradicted and that although he did not relish his present position, he took it very seriously. Also, Jim knew that Austin greatly resented his friendship with Sam Houston, who was rapidly growing more powerful.

Every day Bowie went through the ridiculous farce of making a "show of force" before the enemy with his ninety men. And nearly every day he dispatched a message to Austin expressing his opinion that the forces should be united.

Nothing happened. His men became bored. One or two at a time they drifted away.

"It's time for a showdown," Jim told Fannin. "I'm sending in my resignation to Austin."

"You can't do that," Fannin said. "The men have confidence in you."

"I can and have done so," Bowie said. He handed Fannin the letter he had just finished writing. After tendering his resignation, Jim had written:

> I deem it of the utmost importance for you to effect a union of the army as soon as practicable. Great dissatisfaction now exists in this division, and unless counteracted by the measure suggested, I seriously apprehend the dissolution of it.

Before this letter reached Austin, however, Jim received instructions from him to march his detachment and join with the main force at the Old Mill.

As soon as the Bowie-Fannin division reached them, Austin called a council of war and again brought up his demand for an immediate assault on Bexar. Again his officers voted him down. Finally they prevailed upon him to leave a small company at the mill and take the main force to the strategic location at Concepción to await reinforcements and the arrival of an eighteen-pound cannon reported to be on the way.

Then, while the colonists in San Felipe argued endlessly about drafting plans for a provisional government, the restless volunteers lay around Concepción grumbling.

"How can Austin talk of taking Bexar," one lanky fellow complained to Bowie. "We haven't even any ammunition for the one dinky four-pounder we took from the Mexicans."

Jim chuckled. "We can fix that. And liven things up a bit for you fellows, too. Follow me!"

A handful of curious volunteers mounted their horses and rode behind Bowie, who whooped and fired his pistol close to the enemy line.

He got the desired result. The Mexicans, evidently believing an attack had started, fired their cannon, while Jim led his daring companions out of danger. Later they went out and gathered up the cannon balls. Every day they eased their boredom by this sport until the Mexicans grew wise to their strategy and ceased firing. However, the volunteers had gained something to feed their four-pounder when the time came to use it against its former owners.

Once more boredom settled over the little army of less than six hundred. At this time, however, new hope was injected into the ranks by the arrival of two companies of New Orleans Grays, dapper in new uniforms, with cocky flat caps and gleaming side arms. Outfitted at their own expense they had come to join the Texas fight for independence.

As they displayed their superiority over the ragtag volunteer army, its ranks continued to diminish. Yet two other companies joined: one from Mississippi and another from eastern Texas. Lanky weatherbeaten Ben Milam came riding in, saying if there was any excitement brewing he hankered to be in the middle of it.

Jim grinned at his old friend. "There's not much excitement right now," he said. "But it may start any time."

On November 18th Austin appeared in the doorway of the mission to make an announcement.

"I have a communication from San Felipe," he said. "Plans for a provisional government were drawn up on the 12th. Henry Smith[7] was elected governor; Sam Houston, commander in chief of the army. I have been chosen to serve as commissioner to the United States. General Burleson replaces me in command here until Houston arrives. I am ready at all times to serve Texas in any station where it is considered I can be useful."

Then his head snapped up and his eyes looked coldly over the shocked volunteers as though forbidding them to show pity.

After being dismissed, his men gathered in small groups to discuss this new shift.

Bowie turned to Ben Milam. "There have been times when I wanted to wring Austin's neck. He's no military man. But now I admire him. He took his demotion like a man. He should be president of the provisional government. There wouldn't be any Texas if it weren't for him! What has Smith ever done?"

Jim walked away puzzling over the inconsistencies of political fortunes. He believed, though, that Sam Houston was the right man to be commander in chief.

Volunteers continued to straggle into camp from the States. Some recruits brought in two small artillery pieces to add to the four-pounder Bowie had captured at the Battle of Concepción. Bowie established contact with some of Urselita's kin in the city who informed him that Cos was expecting Ugartecha with money to pay the eight hundred Mexican soldiers.

Bowie planned to head off the Ugartecha force. He sent his old friend Deaf Smith[8] out to scout.

On the morning of the 26th Deaf Smith galloped into camp on a lather-flecked horse. "It's them," he cried. "The money train. Ugartecha with a strong force."

"Bowie!" Burleson shouted. "Take as many men as you need and go out and intercept the train. I'll follow up with the infantry."

Bowie strode through the camp, choosing forty men. As they went over the old Presidio Road the men shouted to each other that they were going to sink their arms to the elbows in Mexican money.

Four miles beyond they spied the Mexican column. Bowie ordered his men to dismount, tie their horses in clumps of mesquite and take cover in a near-by arroyo.

When the Mexicans came within gunshot Bowie gave the signal to fire. Several dragoons were brought down. The Mexicans promptly took refuge behind the bank of a dry creek bed. Both sides banged away without doing any harm. Then the firing ceased. During this interval Bowie saw Burleson leading the infantry across the open plain.

"Go back! You fools!" he shouted.

Burleson had led his division directly between the two lines. The Mexicans opened fire. The Texas infantry scattered over the prairie.

"Let's get 'em, boys!" Jim shouted.

---

7. A leader of the party favoring war (1788–1851); born in Kentucky, he spent most of his youth in Missouri and came to Texas in 1827.

8. Erastus Smith (1787–1837), born in New York and raised in the Mississippi Territory (he lost his hearing in childhood); he settled in Texas in 1821.

He scrambled from the ravine, followed by his forty men. They were joined by about fifty of the infantrymen who had by this time collected their wits. Without the loss of a single man, they routed the Mexicans from their creek bed, leaving about thirty dead.

The whooping Texans gleefully gathered the sixty horses and burros with their precious packs.

"Mexican money!" some of the volunteers cried. "Let's divide the loot."

Chuckling, Jim yanked out his knife and slit open one of the sacks. Freshly cut grass slipped out upon the ground. The men stared openmouthed while Jim slit open another sack. More grass! He repeated the performance three more times. Then it dawned on everyone that this was not Ugartecha with the pay roll from Laredo, but merely a foraging party carrying grass to Bexar to feed Cos's livestock.

The Texans whooped with laughter, shouting, slapping each other on the shoulders, rolling on the ground. Jim forced himself to laugh with them, but he felt that this attack had made him ridiculous. The men wouldn't forget it for a long time. Nor did they. Jokes about the "Grass Fight" relieved the tedium around camp until Jim Bowie was heartily sick of it.

On December 3rd, Burleson called for a general council of war to decide whether to attack Bexar or retire to winter quarters at Goliad or Gonzales. The decision was made to go into winter quarters. Bowie spoke up in meeting for this plan, feeling sure that Sam Houston, their commander in chief, was raising reinforcements, and they should await word from him.

Next day, while baggage was being packed for the evacuation, a Mexican deserter rode into camp, reporting that the defenses at Bexar were weak and that the Americans could easily take the place.

Burleson put no stock in the report but fiery Ben Milam shouted, "Now's the time! Who'll go with Old Ben Milam into San Antonio!"

Two hundred men stepped out to follow. General Burleson gave grudging permission for Milam to take whatever men wished to volunteer and make the attack. He would hold the remainder in readiness for whatever support might be needed.

Milam set out with three hundred volunteers armed with crowbars as well as firearms. Bowie was sorry now that he had spoken so strongly for waiting. He was like an old war horse champing at the bit to get into battle. But he hesitated to go back on his own statement.

However, he directed a steady firing on the Alamo to divert the attention of the Mexicans while Milam led his brave men in a house-to-house attack toward Military Plaza where Cos had his main defenses.

For four long days Bowie kept up his blasting while listening to gunshots and shouts within the city.

Then on the morning of December 9th the Mexicans raised the white flag. Bexar was won, but Ben Milam had paid for it with his life.

Bowie rode with Burleson to the Alamo where Cos had retired to accept the surrender and sign the papers stating that he agreed to withdraw all Mexican military beyond the Rio Grande and to swear that he would never again oppose the re-establishment of the Constitution of 1824[9] in Texas.

The triumph of the Texans knew no bounds. They had cleared the province of all

---

9. Mexico's Constitution of 1824 established a federal government. It limited the power of the president and provided the states with a great deal of autonomy; Santa Anna sought to centralize control.

Mexican soldiers. Now, they believed, they could go home and enjoy Christmas with their families, plant their crops in the spring and settle down to normal living.

Bowie went into Bexar to visit the Navarros. "I'm afraid this is only the beginning," he told his uncle.[1] "Santa Anna won't take this defeat. We should dig in and really prepare for war."

"That Santa Anna is the Devil incarnate," Navarro said. "I'm afraid there will be more and bloodier war than any we've yet seen."

"Tomorrow," Jim went on, "I'm going to ride to San Felipe to talk with Sam Houston. I want a commission to raise a regiment of troops and train them myself."

But on the next day, Bowie found himself confronted with a new emergency. Many of the Texans thought that when Cos was driven from Bexar the war was over and had gone home. Yet there was a scheme afoot which appealed to the imaginations of most of the adventurers who had come to fight for Texas independence and who felt they were being cheated of the excitement they had expected to find.

CHAPTER 20. GATHERING STORM CLOUDS

James Bowie had mistrusted Dr. Grant when he first joined the Army of the People. The Mexicans had taken over his country estate in Coahuila, so it was natural that he should seek vengeance. He had been with the command only a few days when he began urging an attack upon Matamoros—to cut the Mexicans off at their source of supply.

Bowie shrugged the plan off as so much visionary talk. If the Texans had sufficient force they could carry it out, but weak and divided as they were, it was too impracticable. Yet after the defeat of Cos, Jim was alarmed to see that many of the volunteers were paying attention to the doctor. Even Fannin had joined his ranks and since Fannin was a West Point man,[2] the recruits from the States threw in their lot with him.

One morning Bowie found a proclamation stuck to the wall of one of the buildings at Goliad stating that volunteers with Grant and Fannin would be paid "out of the first spoils taken from the enemy." It was boldly signed by Colonel J. W. Fannin, "acting commander in chief."

Despite Jim's protests that they were acting without authority from the real commander in chief, the cream of the army rode off. One of the arrogant young adventurers from Louisiana threw over his shoulder, "Go find another grass fight, Jim Bowie," and laughter swept through the ranks. Jim had led two victorious charges against overwhelming numbers, yet it was this one humiliating mistake that his comrades remembered.

He turned and called for his servant Ham to bring his horse. He had no definite plan of action; he merely wanted to get away from this nearly deserted post where only thirty men remained.

On the road leading from town he saw a rider coming from the east. He gave a shout of joy—"Sam Houston! Never have my eyes seen a more welcome sight."

"Where are they?" Houston demanded.

"Who do you mean?"

"That rascal Grant and those he's trying to lead to attack Matamoros solely for the purpose of getting back his own property."

---

1. José Angel Navarro (1784–1836), a native of San Antonio.

2. I.e., well-trained in warfare as a graduate of the United States Military Academy.

"They rode away this morning."

"Then I must hurry and overtake them."

"You'll need a fresh horse," Bowie pointed out. "And some food and rest yourself."

"I'll eat. And beg a fresh mount," Houston agreed. "Then I must be on my way."

"Everything is in a mess," Houston said as they rode into Goliad. "At a time when we should stand united, everyone is pulling in different directions. Governor Smith has no hold over the people. They should have elected Austin. The settlers respected and obeyed him."

"Then tossed him out when they needed him most." There was bitterness in Jim's tone. "I had hoped for a commission from you to recruit and train a force."

"No one deserves it more," Houston said. "You're the best fighting man we have, Jim Bowie. Oh, I know how you feel about it! Buck Travis was made a colonel because he captured a herd of wild horses."

"He was Austin's favorite," Jim said quietly.

"Fannin was promoted because of your brilliant work at Concepción when he was your aide. Yet you still have a kind word for Austin. You're a big man, Jim. You see how it is. Those men were settlers, whereas you married a highborn Mexican girl. So a cloud of suspicion still clings to you."

"I'm heart and soul for Texas in her fight for independence from Santa Anna," Jim said. "Tell me what to do, Sam."

"I wish that there were more like you," Houston said. "I had a desperate letter from Colonel Neill[3] at the Alamo, saying that Santa Anna has four thousand men at Laredo. Neill has only one hundred men and you have thirty here. May God save Texas! Oh, Bowie, what am I to do? I should be galloping toward the runaway army and persuading it to come back. Did any commander in chief ever have his army stolen from under his nose?"

"I doubt it," Jim responded.

"Neill pleads for help. I should be in San Felipe trying to help hold the government together and to muster troops. I could do it, Jim, if I just had more time!"

"Tell me how I can best serve you," Jim repeated.

"Ride to the Alamo. If Santa Anna is really in Laredo we'll need all our forces to stop him along the way. Evacuate the troops from the Alamo, remove the cannon and blow up the place. But use your own judgment. I trust you, Jim."

The men rode off in different directions. Bowie ordered his thirty men to follow him to Bexar.

He rode straight to the Alamo, to confer with Colonel Neill, an impatient man.

"You say you're bringing only thirty men?" he asked pettishly.

"That's every man there was at Goliad." Jim's tone was calm.

"I tell you the Mexicans are already on the march. What can we do with a mere handful of men?"

"Let me study the situation here. I want to look over the Alamo."

"Do so," Neill snapped. "You will see that a thousand men could not hold the place."

Jim had, of course, seen the ancient mission many times, but he had never before looked at it as a possible military fortification. The vast extent of the outer wall was its worst weakness. Neill was right. At least a thousand men would be required to defend it.

---

3. James Clinton Neill (1790–1845), an artillery officer in the Texas militia. Born in North Carolina, he settled in Texas in 1831.

The Alamo was in the same condition that General Cos had left it at his surrender the previous December. The rear wall of the chapel—the building known today as the Alamo—had crumbled. Only at the front was any of the flat roof left. Jim decided that this would serve as a platform for a cannon. The inside of the chapel was piled high with debris, yet its thick walls might lend protection for a last-ditch stand.

As there were no loopholes the riflemen would have to stand on earthen platforms to shoot over the top, with their heads, shoulders, and arms exposed.

Mounds would have to be erected for the emplacement of the cannon. A feeling of hopelessness seized Jim when he saw there were no structural features to aid in defense.

With sufficient men willing to work, the place eventually might be made into an adequate fortification. But like Houston, Jim felt the desperate need for time—more time.

Before conferring again with Colonel Neill he rode into Bexar. A lump came into his throat when he passed the Veramendi *palacio*. The huge carved cedar door hung open, half torn from its hinges. The white adobe walls were pock-marked with rifle bullets and there was a great wound in the side wall where the Texans had crashed through with their crowbars.

He went to the Navarro home and Don José seized his arm with a cry of welcome as he drew him inside the house.

"I have a grave decision to make," Bowie told him. "I have instructions from Sam Houston to clear the Alamo and blow it up. But he told me to act at my discretion. What do you think? Do you believe that Santa Anna has a force already on Texas soil?"

"I know he has," Navarro answered.

"What do you and others in Bexar think of the matter?"

"Need you ask?" Don José said reprovingly. "Within a few days I leave for San Felipe as a delegate to the convention summoned to meet March 1st to declare independence, elect a president and adopt a constitution. As you know, your old friend Juan Seguin[4] is a captain with Neill. His nephew Blaz Herraera is at this moment doing valuable duty as a scout."

"Will the common people help us fight Santa Anna?" Jim asked.

Navarro shook his head and smiled ruefully. "They have a horrible fear of that devil. They have heard of his massacre of the people of Zacatecas,[5] when he stood hundreds against a wall and slaughtered them in cold blood. If Santa Anna comes, the people of Bexar will run, not fight—and who can blame them?"

Bowie stood up. His jaw was set and his eyes blazed. "Thank you, Don José," he said. "You have helped me make up my mind."

"And what is your decision, nephew?"

"To hold the Alamo at all costs. It is the keystone of Texas—the only bulwark to hold Santa Anna from storming through the province, burning and slaughtering, as he did in Zacatecas."

Jim rode back to the Alamo and told Colonel Neill his plan.

"Hold the Alamo with so few men?" Neill scoffed. "Are you crazy, man?"

Jim shook his head. "I was never more sane in my life. I *know* this is what we must

---

4. Juan Nepomuceno Seguín (1806–1890), a native of San Antonio who played an important political and military role in Texas in the 1830s.

5. A state of central Mexico where an attempt by liberals to defy Santa Anna's authority was crushed in 1835.

do. Every hour that we can delay Santa Anna gives Houston that much more time to muster an army to reinforce us."

Bowie spoke with such conviction that Neill finally agreed.

Jim thereupon wrote to Governor Henry Smith that the salvation of Texas depended on keeping Bexar out of enemy hands. And that both he and Colonel Neill would "rather die in these ditches than give up to the enemy." He asked for relief, stating that they had only one hundred and twenty men against the enemy's thousands.

A few days after Bowie dispatched this letter, Buck Travis rode into Bexar at the head of thirty men. Neill greeted him with such enthusiasm that Bowie was surprised, although he had suspected that the colonel had definitely cooled off in his desire to "die in these ditches."

Next day Neill announced that he had received news that a member of his family was gravely ill and he must leave immediately. As he rode off he threw over his shoulder, "I leave you in charge, Travis."

Bowie flushed angrily. "He has no right to turn the command over to you," he said hoarsely. "Sam Houston considers that I am in charge."

"Neill and I are regular army," Travis said, arrogantly.

"And I am only a volunteer, eh?" Jim roared. "Well, if you are so set on military procedure, I outrank you a long way by right of seniority. I remind you that I am forty-one and you can't be more than twenty-eight. Until our commander in chief sends word that I am to be relieved, I remain in command here."

Still fuming, Bowie called for his horse and rode into Bexar. He strode into one of the *cantinas* where he saw a buckskin-clad fellow sprawled at one of the tables. The eyes of the two men met. Although Jim had never seen this weatherbeaten face before, there was something about that humorous, sly expression and the shrewd look in the gray eyes that attracted him.

"I'll bet you be Jim Bowie," the stranger said.

"That's right. And you?"

"Davy Crockett from Tennessee. I heard about the ruckus here in Texas, so I took old Betsey"—he put his hand affectionately on the barrel of his long rifle—"and gathered up a band of twelve scrappers and trekked out here to get on the fun."

"I can assure you that you're more than welcome," Jim said, laughing.

"Let me see that knife of yourn I've heard so much about."

Jim laid his knife on the table.

Crockett picked it up and examined it, turning it over and over. "Tarnation!" he exclaimed. "The very sight of this is enough to give a man a squeamish stomach—'specially afore breakfast!"

Crockett handed the weapon back and drew his own knife from its sheath. "Mine was made in Bristol, England. Pretty good copy, I'd say. Every man in my company's got one like it."

"Good!" Jim said. "I'm mighty glad you've come to help us. I've a feeling that before long you and your men will find all the excitement you want."

Jim Bowie was not the only one disturbed by Neill's appointment of Travis to take command of the defense of the Alamo. The volunteers took up the quarrel in earnest, and the matter created such a hubbub that Travis was forced to put it to a vote. Jim Bowie won by an overwhelming margin.

Travis took his defeat with such bad grace that the force which should have been readying the Alamo for battle continued to spend valuable time quarreling.

Finally Jim went to Travis. "This won't do," he said. "Unity between us is more important than personal ambition. I suggest that you take charge of the regular army, while I command the volunteers. Then I believe our men will pull together."

So the matter was finally settled agreeably and the forces at last began to work at the tremendous task of fortifying the Alamo.

CHAPTER 21. BLAZE OF GLORY

Bowie and Travis built barricades of earth tamped between cowhides, opening into the various rooms which would serve as barracks. Platforms of earth lined the inner walls to provide places for the riflemen to stand. Although a ditch flowed through the grounds, there was danger that the Mexicans would cut off the water supply, and so a well was dug.

Jim worked feverishly to set the fourteen cannon, left behind by Cos after his surrender, in the best position for defense. All ammunition was stored in the sacristy of the chapel. Over the rampart waved the Mexican flag of 1824, showing that the Texans would still abide by the constitution of that year.

On the morning of February 23rd, 1836, the bell in the tower of the San Fernando Church, where a sentinel had been posted, clanged violently.

Soon a messenger galloped from Bexar with the news that the Mexican troops were on the heights of Alazan. Deaf Smith and Dr. John Sutherland[6] were sent out to scout. In a short time they came back shouting that the Mexican army was in sight.

Then the exodus from Bexar began. Frightened householders piled personal belongings on clumsy two-wheeled carts and joined the long lines clogging the roads leading to the country. Volunteers of the People's Army hurried to the Alamo. Even one woman joined them there, the wife of Almaron Dickerson,[7] with her infant daughter.

Jim Bowie was standing on a cedar platform supervising the mounting of a large cannon above the gate. The pulley screeched; the cannon commenced to swing dangerously.

"Look out!" someone shouted from below.

Bowie stepped back—into nothingness. His arms flailed, searching for something to grasp. His body struck the ground. There was a blinding flash, then blackness.

The worried face of Dr. Edward Mitchason bent over Jim, while skilled fingers probed gently, yet sent stabs of pain through his chest. Bowie choked, coughed and glanced up at the doctor in alarm when he saw a blot of red stain the ground.

"I've broken something, Doc," he said.

"I'm afraid that a rib has penetrated the lung," Mitchason said with deep concern.

Bowie struggled to his feet. "I can't be bothered with a little thing like that now," he gasped.

"I've taped your chest," the doctor said. "It's all I can do. Any strenuous action, however, will only worsen your condition—prolong your recovery."

Jim laughed as he swayed to his feet. "Santa Anna won't wait for my recovery. I'll keep going as long as I can."

And keep going he did, for a time, although every movement was agony.

Santa Anna sent a message demanding unconditional surrender. The answer was a cannon shot directed at an enemy group gathered at the main plaza. This shot

---

6. Virginia-born physician (1792–1867) who moved to the Austin colony in Texas in 1829; he was sent away from the Alamo to bring help from Gonzales.

7. A Pennsylvanian (ca. 1800–1836) who eloped with Susanna Wilkerson in 1829; the couple settled in Texas in 1831, and their daughter, Angelina, was born in 1834.

opened that epic struggle on February 23, 1836. All day long as cannon boomed and rifles cracked, Bowie managed to stay on his feet directing operations. But by night he sank to his cot, coughing and shaking with chills.

Next morning he tried to rise, but the world whirled crazily. Worse than the terrible pain was the spiritual agony because at this critical hour he was unable to take part in the fighting. It had been his decision to take this stand and hold the Alamo at all costs. Therefore he should be directing its defense.

He sent his servant Ham to summon Travis. "I won't be much use to you now," he gasped. "I pass my command on to you."

Travis leaned over and grasped his hand. "You'll be better in a day or so," he said. "By then, perhaps we'll have reinforcements. I'd like to have you read this letter which I'm sending out by courier after dark tonight."

Jim read:

Commandancy of the Alamo, Bexar
Feb'y 24, 1836

To the People of Texas and all Americans in the World:
FELLOW CITIZENS AND COMPATRIOTS: I am besieged by a thousand or more Mexicans under Santa Anna. I have sustained continual bombardment for 24 hours and have not lost a man. The enemy has demanded surrender at discretion; otherwise the garrison are to be put to the sword,[8] if the fort is taken. I have answered the demand with a cannon shot, and our flag still flies proudly from the walls. I shall never surrender or retreat. Then, I call on you in the name of Liberty, of Patriotism, and everything dear to the American character, to come to our aid with all dispatch. The enemy is receiving reinforcements of daily and will no doubt increase to three or four thousand in four or five days. If this call is neglected, I am determined to sustain myself as long as possible and die like a soldier who never forgets what is due to his own honor and that of his country. Victory or Death!

WILLIAM BARRETT TRAVIS,
Lt. Col. Comdt.

"Noble words," Bowie gasped. "Words that will go down in history."

"I feel sure," Travis said, "that if reinforcements come in time, we can hold the Alamo indefinitely, even with only fourteen pieces of artillery. But the scarcity of ball and powder worries me."

"When Fannin sees this letter," Bowie said, "he will come at once to our aid."

Travis sent frantic messages to Fannin, who had most of Texas' military strength under his control at Goliad. One courier came back with the discouraging word that Fannin had set out toward the Alamo, but because one supply train had broken down he had turned back.

The lookouts stared in vain toward the east, hoping to see a cloud of dust which would mean Fannin's army was coming. Day after day dragged by, bringing only disappointment.

At night Davy Crockett played his fiddle and pranced about, clowning to try to cheer "the boys."

The fighting went on day and night. The deadly aim of the Texas sharpshooters

---

8. Slaughtered with the sword. "At discretion": unconditionally.

was taking heavy toll of Santa Anna's forces, but he had replacements to fill the gaps, for he had emptied the Mexican prisons and had taken every available man.

The doctor tried to keep Bowie in a small room above the chapel for comparative quiet from the everlasting booming, but Jim asked Ham and Davy Crockett to carry his cot down into the chapel where he could encourage the weary men as they passed back and forth to the sacristy for ammunition.

On the first of March the Alamo defenders were cheered when thirty-two men from Gonzales slipped into the fortress.

Bowie heard Travis tell them, "You've given our hearts a lift, boys. We thought the world had forgotten us. We'll hold out. Santa Anna has fired over two hundred cannon balls into the Alamo, but we haven't lost a man. We fire the balls right back at them. What's Sam Houston doing? Why doesn't he send us some help?"

Jim was shocked when he heard one of the newcomers say, "Sam Houston's off dickering with the Cherokee to keep them from attacking the settlements. Santa Anna's been egging them on to do that very thing. The council kicked both Smith and Houston out. Right now Texas has no government at all—and no commander in chief. All the council does is squabble."

Jim groaned and turned his face away. He had struggled so hard to hold this Texas keystone in order to give Sam Houston time. Now those fools in San Felipe were spoiling everything by their everlasting bickering.

Bowie was determined to get well quickly. But for once he had met something he could not conquer. Every breath he drew was like a knife gashing the inside of his chest. Most of the time he either burned with fever or shook with chills. There were times of wild delirium during which he was soothed by the gentle hands of Mrs. Dickerson as she bathed his face.

Awaking from a restless sleep, he found that an ominous silence had fallen.

Davy Crockett loomed in the doorway. "How ye doing, Jim? Me and Betsey's been too busy pickin' off Mexicans to pay you much attention."

"I wish I could have been with you," Bowie said in a faint voice. "I'm not gaining very fast, Davy. What's happening out there? Why is it so quiet?"

"Don't rightly know. Maybe the Mexicans are tired."

Jim shook his head. Perhaps this was the lull before the real storm, he thought. Now and then he heard voices, and the tramping of feet.

"I want to be out where I can see what's going on," he said.

Crockett yelled for three of his comrades to help carry Jim's cot to where the troops had assembled. The men were unshaven, dirty, haggard—obviously bone weary, starved for sleep.

"What's the date?" Bowie asked Crockett.

"March 3rd." Crockett replied.

"Has the battle been going on for ten days?" Jim was incredulous.

Crockett nodded. "Day and night. Ain't one of us has had a bit of sleep except what we could grab between rifle shots."

"How can human beings endure it?" Bowie wondered aloud.

"We can bear it all right," Davy said. "The rations get kind of tiresome, though, nothing but beef and corn. But I reckon we're lucky to have that—and plenty of water. The Mexicans tried to dam up the ditch, but the well gives us all we need for drinkin'. Ain't got time to wash nohow."

Travis' voice rang out. "Gather around, men, I want to speak to you."

Bowie was shocked at the change in the leader. His face was haggard; his mouth bracketed by lines of fatigue.

"My brave companions," Travis said in a voice husky with emotion, "I am compelled to tell you that within a few days—perhaps hours—we must all be in eternity. We cannot avoid it. It is our certain doom.

"We are surrounded by an enemy that could almost eat us for breakfast, from whose arms our lives are, for the present, protected by these stone walls. We have no hope of help, for no force could get through the strong ranks of these Mexicans. We dare not surrender, for we know what fate we would meet at the hands of our enemies. If we attempt to escape we would all be slain in less than ten minutes. Nothing remains but to stay within this fort and fight to the last moment. Sooner or later we must all be killed, for I am sure that Santa Anna will storm the fort and take it, at whatever it may cost in the lives of his own men.

"Then we must die! Our business is not to make a fruitless effort to save our lives, but to choose the manner of our death by which we may best serve our country. The Mexican army is strong enough to march through the land and exterminate its inhabitants. Our countrymen are not able to oppose them in open field. My choice, then, is to remain in this fort, to resist every assault and to sell our lives as dearly as possible."

"Hurray!" Bowie's voice was weak, although he put all his strength into this cheer. Instantly it was taken up by the men until the walls echoed.

Travis went on: "Then let us band together as brothers and vow to die together. Let us resolve to withstand our enemies to the last, and at each advance to kill as many of them as possible. Let us kill them as they scale our walls! Kill them as they leap within! Kill them as they raise their weapons and as they use them! And continue to kill them as long as one of us shall remain alive!

"By this policy I trust that we shall so weaken our enemies that our countrymen at home can meet them on fair terms, cut them up, expel them from our country and thus establish their own independence.

"But I leave every man to his own choice. Should any man prefer to surrender or to attempt to escape, he is at liberty to do so.

"My choice is to stay here and die for my country, fighting as long as breath remains in my body. This I will do, even if you leave me alone."

A great wave of emotion swept through Bowie as Travis concluded his speech. He looked over the grave faces of the men as they stood in line. It was apparent that those inspired words had put new energy into them.

Travis drew a line with his sword on the ground before the volunteers. "I now want every man who is determined to stay here and die with me to come across this line. Who will be first?"

Bowie's spirits rose when he saw young Tapley Holland[9] leap across the line shouting, "I am ready to die for my country!"

In a moment all save Bowie and William Rose were standing on Travis' side of the line.

Jim mustered all his strength and called, "Hey, Davy, I want to be with you. Lift me across the line."

Four pairs of willing hands seized the corners of his cot and bore him across. Now everyone was on the side of Travis but William Rose, a trader who had fought well enough.

"What's the matter, man?" New strength had come to Bowie's voice. "You aren't afraid to fight with your comrades, are you?"

9. Artilleryman (1810–1836), born in Ohio, whose family settled in Texas in 1822.

There was a long silence and then Rose said, "I'm willing to fight, but not to die and I won't if I can help it. I'm dark enough to pass for a Mexican and I speak their dialect. I think I have a chance to escape."

"Nonsense," Crockett's nasal twang broke out. "You'd better stay with us, old man. Escape ain't possible."

Rose stared wildly at the top of the wall. Then he ran and scrambled up and over.

"Anyone want to follow him?" Travis' curt voice broke the stunned silence.

A resounding chorus of "noes" was his reply.

"Clean your rifles, reload them and back to your posts," Travis said. "The attack may recommence at any moment."

Then after a pause, he said, "I charge the last man left alive to fire the powder magazine—blow up the Alamo."

Not a shot was fired during the entire night. Santa Anna could not have devised a more fiendish and effective method of catching the gallant defenders off guard. They had been keyed up to battle pitch for so long that under pressure they could have carried on indefinitely. But with the lull came the overpowering desire to sleep, and when they gave way they were as though drugged.

Bowie had asked to be left beside the wall with the other sick and wounded. He woke now and then with a start, wondering about the unwonted stillness.

Two hours before dawn the attack started again, but this time above the roar of gunfire came a bloodcurdling sound—the bands playing the dread *deguello*[1]—which meant: "No quarter. Slaughter the enemy."

Jim Bowie, helpless on his cot, knew its meaning, as did every man on the walls.

Ham told him that Santa Anna had run up a blood red flag over the San Fernando Church.

"This is the end, Ham," Bowie said calmly. "Load four pistols and lay them and my knife close to my hand. Go where you can see what's going on and come and tell me."

Soon Ham reported that the Mexicans had surrounded three sides of the Alamo—that they were carrying scaling ladders but that two attempts to climb the walls had been driven back.

"The ground out there is covered with dead men," Ham said. "It's the worst slaughter you could dream of. Someone says the officers are slapping the soldiers with their swords to keep 'em coming on."

"His victory will cost Santa Anna dearer than defeat," Bowie said.

Lying helpless on his cot, Jim was aware of the unceasing pounding and cracking of artillery, of the acrid smell of powder, of dust and sweat. He knew when the enemy was driven back by the triumphant shouts of the Texans.

Although there was little strength in his body, his senses were keener than they had ever been. He felt his cot being lifted. He opened his eyes and looked up in amazement. Ham, Davy Crockett and two others were carrying his cot into a small room.

"They've broken through," Crockett panted. "They're tumbling over the north wall. Now they'll have to take the Alamo room by room."

"Don't stick me off like this," Bowie protested. "I want to fight, too."

"Take care of him, Ham," was Davy's reply as he slammed the heavy door of the little room.

1. Literally, "beheading, slaughter."

It was dark and chill inside. "Drag my cot to that corner facing the door," Bowie said. "Then crouch against the wall out of sight. Hand me the pistols. I'll use them as long as I can. Then I'll use the knife."

It seemed that he lay there waiting for hours listening to the continuous booms, bangs and yells which went on all through the inner wall and the chapel. He had heard Travis order the last man left alive to blow up the powder magazine. He waited for the explosion which did not come.

Finally the noise died down. The only shouting he heard was in Mexican dialect. Were all his comrades dead then? Was he the last one left?

The door burst open and he saw savage, wild-eyed faces staring in. He raised a pistol, pulled the trigger. One man fell. He reached for another pistol, then another and another in quick succession. Weakness had fled. New energy flowed into his wasted muscles. His deadly aim claimed four enemy lives. Now he reached for the knife as he stared up into evil faces and saw the glint of bayonets over him. His knife ripped up. There was a terrible cry and a heavy body fell across him. But Jim Bowie did not know it, for with that knife blow he gave his last ounce of energy.

And so the famous knife did its work for the final time. Fittingly enough, James Bowie, whose momentous decision it was to make that epic stand at the Alamo, delivered the last blow for freedom and was the last of her defenders to die there.

CHAPTER 22. THE RECKONING

And so Jim Bowie's wish to "live to the hilt during the best years of my life, then go out in a blaze of glory" was fulfilled.

Santa Anna strode through the Alamo asking his guide from Bexar to point out to him the bodies of Travis, Bowie and Crockett—the "bravest of the brave." Then he ordered his men to bring wood to make a gigantic funeral pyre outside the walls for these bodies.

The lives of Mrs. Dickerson and her child and the servants of Travis and Bowie were spared. But Santa Anna had a purpose in such mercy.

"Tell everyone you meet," he said to Mrs. Dickerson as he sent them riding eastward, "that we will deal in this manner with anyone who opposes our march through Texas."

Meanwhile the convention to organize a new government had met at San Felipe, and the bickering broke out anew. But when Travis' brave and pathetic message reached the meeting and was read aloud, a hubbub arose to adjourn and march at once to the rescue of the Alamo.

"Don't talk like fools!" Sam Houston roared. "Precious time has already been lost. The first thing we must do is organize a government so that Texas will have leadership. Then our men will flock to her defense. I will ride to the front, raising troops as I go and interpose them between the enemy and our seat of government. Then if mortal power can avail I will relieve the brave men in the Alamo."

He left the convention, clad as he had come from his meeting with the Cherokee. He mounted a fast horse and with only four men rode toward Gonzales after sending a messenger to Goliad with word for Fannin to bring his troops and meet him.

On the afternoon of March 11th, Houston was heartened to find at Gonzales a volunteer force of three hundred and seventy-four men, with two cannon, who were awaiting a leader. Still nothing was heard from Fannin.

Houston was organizing the force into companies when Deaf Smith rode in with Mrs. Dickerson, her little daughter and the two Negro servants.

In a matter of moments came the news of the fall of the Alamo. Then reports were circulated that the Mexican army was in sight. Only a man of Houston's forcefulness could have stemmed the tide of panic.

He prepared for a midnight retreat, with a rear guard to protect the refugees who would swell as the army moved east.

Houston had no way of knowing that Santa Anna was still in Bexar licking his wounds from the terrific mauling the heroes of the Alamo had given his army. Sixteen hundred of the pick of the Mexican troops had been killed, and hundreds more wounded. Before he could do further damage he must completely reorganize his forces. Bowie's decision to defend the Alamo had given Texas twelve precious days.

The tremendous sacrifices of the defenders of the Alamo were not in vain. This delay saved the American colonies in Texas from Santa Anna's threat to conquer.

The fateful news from the Alamo finally spurred the convention at San Felipe into declaring for the independence of Texas and putting into motion the machinery of government.

As Sam Houston moved eastward he gathered both refugees and little groups of men willing to fight. Finally a courier on a lathered horse caught up with him, reporting that Santa Anna had moved on to Goliad and demanded the surrender of Fannin—under "honorable terms of war." Upon receiving this, Santa Anna ordered Fannin and his army taken out onto the plains and killed.

While Houston moved to the Colorado River, Santa Anna stormed across the country, pillaging and burning the deserted farms and towns. The runaway army threatened to depose Houston as commander in chief if he did not take a stand. Yet he managed to hold them together while he moved across the Colorado and on to the Brazos, then still farther to the Buffalo Bayou which flowed into the San Jacinto River.

Houston hustled his army into a grove of live oaks which fringed the bayou, placing the two cannon, which the men called the "Twin Sisters," so that they commanded the grassy plains over which Santa Anna must come if he attacked.

Deaf Smith came in to report that the Mexicans were massed across the bayou. They had been reinforced by Cos, which raised Santa Anna's number to fourteen hundred against eight hundred Texans.

In the middle of the afternoon Houston formed his volunteers to attack.

"Victory is certain," he said. "Trust in God and fear not." Then he raised his right hand aloft. His eyes blazed as he cried, "Remember the Alamo!"

From the ranks came the resounding echo, "Remember the Alamo!"

The Twin Sisters boomed. Their battle fervor aroused by that cry, "Remember the Alamo," the Texans swept forward with such force that Santa Anna's army turned and fled in terror. The Mexicans were caught completely off guard. The surprise had been complete.

When the Texans ran out of ammunition they pulled out their knives. And so, although James Bowie was not there, the knives which bore his name finally slashed the fetters of despotism which bound Texas. The battle of San Jacinto freed her forever from Mexican tyranny.

SHANNON GARST

James Bowie: 1796–1836

1796:	Born in Tennessee. Parents moved from Georgia few years before he was born.
1802:	Moved to Spanish province of Louisiana, in what is now Catahoula Parish, afterward moving south to vicinity of Opelousas, a region of small prairies, great swamps and vast forests. Land extremely rich. Bowie plantation prospered. James Bowie's boyhood unusual.
1803:	Louisiana is purchased by the United States.
1814:	James Bowie and his brothers establish a sawmill on Bayou Boeuf. Battle of New Orleans.
1817–21:	Jean Lafitte, privateer, operates on "Galvez-town" Island.
1818:	James and Rezin Bowie deal in slave trade with Lafitte.
1819–21:	Dr. James Long, filibusterer,[2] leads an expedition into Texas.
1820:	Moses Austin secures permission to colonize three hundred Anglo-American families.
1821:	The Austin colony, first Anglo-American settlement in Texas, is founded by Stephen Austin.
	Mexico gains freedom from Spain, and Texas becomes a Mexican state.
1824–32:	Mexico grants colonization contracts to *emprasarios*.[3] Towns of Victoria and Gonzales, founded.
1828:	Estimated Anglo-American population, two thousand and twenty.
	James Bowie goes to Texas. Takes steps to become a citizen.
1830:	April 6th. Mexico passes law checking further immigration of Anglo-Americans into Texas. James Bowie weds Urselita Veramendi, daughter of the Mexican vice-governor.
1831:	Estimated population, exclusive of Indians, twenty thousand.
1832:	Texans and Mexicans clash at Anáhuac and Velasco. Convention at San Felipe petitions for political separation of Texas from Coahuila.
1834:	Stephen Austin imprisoned in Mexico. After death of his wife and children, Bowie becomes involved in Texas Revolution.
1835:	June 30. Mexican troops driven from Anáhuac.
	Oct. 2. Settlers win battle of Gonzales, first battle of Texas revolution.
	Oct. 9. Texans capture Goliad.
	Oct. 12. Volunteer Texas army, called the People's Army, under Stephen Austin marches on San Antonio de Bexar, Mexican stronghold.
	Oct. 28. Battle of Concepción, led by James Bowie aided by James Fannin, is won by Texans.
	Nov. 3. Provisional government drafted under Governor Henry Smith. Sam Houston made commander in chief of the Armies.
	Dec. 5. Concluding siege of San Antonio led by Ben Milam.
	Dec. 9. San Antonio is captured.
	Dec. 10. Cos, the Mexican general, surrenders.
	Dec. 14. General Cos and his army depart from Texas, leaving it freed of Mexican soldiers.

---

2. One who carries out military insurrections in foreign countries.

3. Land agents, land contractors (*empresarios*).

1836:	Feb. 15.	Bowie decides to defend the Alamo in order to allow time for Texas to strengthen her defenses. General Santa Anna and Mexican army arrive in San Antonio to lay siege to the Alamo.
	Mar. 2.	Declaration of Independence issued at Washington on the Brazos.
	Mar. 6.	The Alamo falls; every defender dies.
	Mar. 13.	General Sam Houston, commanding Texas army begins eastward retreat. Gonzales is burned.
	Mar. 17.	Texas Constitution is adopted at Washington on the Brazos.
	Mar. 20.	Battle of Coleto ends in surrender of Col. James Fannin and his command.
	Mar. 27.	Fannin and his men are massacred at Goliad.
	April 21.	The People's Army, under General Sam Houston, defeats Santa Anna and his army at San Jacinto, thus winning the Texas Revolution and ending Latin domination.

1955

E. L. KONIGSBURG
b. 1930

"My office looks more like a laboratory than an office," observes Mrs. Basil E. Frankweiler toward the end of the novel bearing her name. She's quoting an observation made by her lawyer—to whom the entire story is addressed as she explains the changes he is to make in her will. The reference to her place of "research" is an inside joke: although Elaine Lobel Konigsburg is famous now as an author of witty, sophisticated urban novels for preteen readers, she first studied chemistry, earning a B.S. from the Carnegie Institute of Technology and then undertaking graduate work at the University of Pittsburgh. Her husband David joked that "she began to think of other occupations" after she had suffered "a few minor explosions, burned hair, and stained and torn clothes."

All of Konigsburg's novels to some extent seem to bear the marks of that early desire to experiment and to find secrets hidden in material things. The search may be for the historical trace, as in the novel printed here. In *From the Mixed-Up Files of Mrs. Basil E. Frankweiler* (1967), Konigsburg's second novel and first Newbery Medal winner, Claudia and her young brother Jamie set out to trace the history of a marble angel attributed to Michelangelo. In a historical novel, *The Second Mrs. Giaconda* (1975), Konigsburg explores the mystery of the Mona Lisa's smile and of Leonardo da Vinci's character. But in these novels, as in her others, the secrets that Konigsburg cares most about are connected to family and identity: the kinds of secrets often critical to children on the verge of adolescence.

Jennifer, Hecate, Macbeth, William McKinley, and Me, Elizabeth (1967), Konigsburg's first novel, addresses lying, telling the truth, and the value of fitting in. *Silent to the Bone* (2000) examines child abuse, unraveling the mysterious web of emotions within a blended family. But not all the secrets that Konigsburg explores are dark. In her second Newbery Medal–winning novel, *The View from Saturday* (1996), interwoven first-person narratives reveal just who the sixth-grade champions of a quiz bowl team are and why they are so successful.

Like many middle-class mothers of baby boomers, Konigsburg stopped working while her three children, born between 1955 and 1959, were infants; she returned to her job teaching science in a girls' school in 1960 but left the profession for good when her husband's career in industrial psychology took the family from Florida to New York (they returned to Jacksonville in 1968). There she attended weekend art classes—most of her books are self-illustrated—and began collecting her material in what she calls the "dailiness" of the everyday: "the corn-flakes, worn-out sneakers way of life" that she depicts in *From the Mixed-Up Files*. As she continues to write, she remains keenly aware of contemporary sensibilities, both depicting and questioning the widespread obsession with material things in such works as *Journey to an 800 Number* (1982) and *Amy Elizabeth Explores Bloomingdale's* (1992).

In almost a score of novels characterized by wit, respect for children, and tireless experimentation, Elaine Konigsburg has tracked shifting definitions of childhood into a new millennium. *From the Mixed-Up Files* sets forth an enduring theme of her writing, as protected suburban children seek to balance what is safe but suffocating against what is dangerous but full of potential, the usual against the unexpected. Instead of seeking adventure in the outdoor wilderness, her characters find their adventures within themselves. These children, like real children, are not Romantic innocents: they are urban, urbane, and knowing.

From the Mixed-Up Files of Mrs. Basil E. Frankweiler

To my lawyer, Saxonberg:
   I can't say that I enjoyed your last visit. It was obvious that you had too much on your mind to pay any attention to what I was trying to say. Perhaps, if you had some interest in this world besides law, taxes, and your grandchildren, you could almost be a fascinating person. Almost. That last visit was the worst bore. I won't risk another dull visit for a while, so I'm having Sheldon, my chauffeur, deliver this account to your home. I've written it to explain certain changes I want made in my last will and testament. You'll understand those changes (and a lot of other things) much better after reading it. I'm sending you a carbon copy. I'll keep the original in my files. I don't come in until much later, but never mind. You'll find enough to interest you until I do.
   You never knew that I could write this well, did you? Of course, you don't actually know yet, but you soon will. I've spent a lot of time on this file. I listened. I investigated, and I fitted all the pieces together like a jigsaw puzzle. It leaves no doubts. Well, Saxonberg, read and discover.

Mrs. Basil E. Frankweiler

1

Claudia knew that she could never pull off the old-fashioned kind of running away. That is, running away in the heat of anger with a knapsack on her back. She didn't like discomfort; even picnics were untidy and inconvenient: all those insects and the sun melting the icing on the cupcakes. Therefore, she decided that her leaving home would not be just running from somewhere but would be running to somewhere. To a large place, a comfortable place, an indoor place, and preferably a beautiful place. And that's why she decided upon the Metropolitan Museum of Art in New York City.[1]

---

1. One of New York's premier museums, founded in 1870; it contains art from around the world, from ancient through modern times, and is located on Fifth Avenue at 82nd Street.

1747

FROM THE MIXED-
UP FILES OF
MRS. BASIL E.
FRANKWEILER,
CH. 1

She planned very carefully; she saved her allowance and she chose her companion. She chose Jamie, the second youngest of her three younger brothers. He could be counted on to be quiet, and now and then he was good for a laugh. Besides, he was rich; unlike most boys his age, he had never even begun collecting baseball cards. He saved almost every penny he got.

But Claudia waited to tell Jamie that she had decided upon him. She couldn't count on him to be *that* quiet for *that* long. And she calculated needing *that* long to save her weekly allowances. It seemed senseless to run away without money. Living in the suburbs had taught her that everything costs.

She had to save enough for train fare and a few expenses before she could tell Jamie or make final plans. In the meantime she almost forgot why she was running away. But not entirely. Claudia knew that it had to do with injustice. She was the oldest child and the only girl and was subject to a lot of injustice. Perhaps it was because she had to both empty the dishwasher and set the table on the same night while her brothers got out of everything. And, perhaps, there was another reason more clear to me than to Claudia. A reason that had to do with the sameness of each and every week. She was bored with simply being straight-A's Claudia Kincaid. She was tired of arguing about whose turn it was to choose the Sunday night seven-thirty television show, of injustice, and of the monotony of everything.

The fact that her allowance was so small that it took her more than three weeks of skipping hot fudge sundaes to save enough for train fare was another example of injustice. (Since you always drive to the city, Saxonberg, you probably don't know the cost of train fare. I'll tell you. Full fare one way costs one dollar and sixty cents. Claudia and Jamie could each travel for half of that since she was one month under twelve, and Jamie was well under twelve—being only nine.) Since she intended to return home after everyone had learned a lesson in Claudia appreciation, she had to save money for her return trip, too, which was like full fare one way. Claudia knew that hundreds of people who lived in her town worked in offices in New York City and could afford to pay full fare both ways every day. Like her father. After all, Greenwich[2] was considered an actual suburb of New York, a commuting suburb.

Even though Claudia knew that New York City was not far away, certainly not far enough to go considering the size and number of the injustices done to her, she knew that it was a good place to get lost. Her mother's Mah-Jong[3] club ladies called it *the* city. Most of them never ventured there; it was exhausting, and it made them nervous. When she was in the fourth grade, her class had gone on a trip to visit historical places in Manhattan. Johnathan Richter's mother hadn't let him go for fear he'd get separated from the group in all the jostling that goes on in New York. Mrs. Richter, who was something of a character, had said that she was certain that he would "come home lost." And she considered the air very bad for him to breathe.

Claudia loved the city because it was elegant; it was important; and busy. The best place in the world to hide. She studied maps and the Tourguide book of the American Automobile Association and reviewed every field trip her class had ever taken. She made a specialized geography course for herself. There were even some pamphlets about the museum around the house, which she quietly researched.

Claudia also decided that she must get accustomed to giving up things. Learning

---

2. Greenwich, Connecticut, an affluent town less than 30 miles from New York City.
3. A Chinese game in which four players vie to complete their hands with tiles of different suits. The introduction into the United States of an English-language version in the 1920s began a short-lived craze for it. By the 1930s and 1940s, mahjong was most popular among urban women.

to do without hot fudge sundaes was good practice for her. She made do with the Good Humor bars[4] her mother always kept in their freezer. Normally, Claudia's hot fudge expenses were forty cents per week. Before her decision to run away, deciding what to do with the ten cents left over from her allowance had been the biggest adventure she had had each week. Sometimes she didn't even have ten cents, for she lost a nickel every time she broke one of the household rules like forgetting to make her bed in the morning. She was certain that her allowance was the smallest in her class. And most of the other sixth graders never lost part of their pay since they had full-time maids to do the chores instead of a cleaning lady only twice a week. Once after she had started saving, the drug store had a special. HOT FUDGE, 27¢, the sign in the window said. She bought one. It would postpone her running away only twenty-seven cents worth. Besides, once she made up her mind to go, she enjoyed the planning almost as much as she enjoyed spending money. Planning long and well was one of her special talents.

Jamie, the chosen brother, didn't even care for hot fudge sundaes although he could have bought one at least every other week. A year and a half before, Jamie had made a big purchase; he had spent his birthday money and part of his Christmas money on a transistor radio, made in Japan, purchased from Woolworth's.[5] Occasionally, he bought a battery for it. They would probably need the radio; that made another good reason for choosing Jamie.

On Saturdays Claudia emptied the wastebaskets, a task she despised. There were so many of them. Everyone in her family had his own bedroom and wastebasket except her mother and father who shared both—with each other. Almost every Saturday Steve emptied his pencil sharpener into his. She knew he made his basket messy on purpose.

One Saturday as she was carrying the basket from her parent's room, she jiggled it a little so that the contents would sift down and not spill out as she walked. Their basket was always so full since there were two of them using it. She managed to shift a shallow layer of Kleenex, which her mother had used for blotting lipstick, and thus exposed the corner of a red ticket. Using the tips of her forefinger and thumb like a pair of forceps, she pulled at it and discovered a ten ride pass for the New York, New Haven, and Hartford Railroad.[6] Used train passes normally do not appear in suburban wastebaskets; they appear in the pockets of train conductors. Nine rides on a pass are marked off in little squares along the bottom edge, and they are punched one at a time as they are used; for the tenth ride the conductor collects the pass. Their cleaning lady who had come on Friday must have thought that the pass was all used up since rides one through nine were already punched. The cleaning lady never went to New York, and Claudia's dad never kept close track of his pocket change or his train passes.

Both she and Jamie could travel on the leftover pass since two half fares equal one whole. Now they could board the train without having to purchase tickets. They would avoid the station master and any stupid questions he might ask. What a find! From a litter of lipstick kisses, Claudia had plucked a free ride. She regarded it as an invitation. They would leave on Wednesday.

On Monday afternoon Claudia told Jamie at the school bus stop that she wanted him to sit with her because she had something important to tell him. Usually, the

---

4. A brand of chocolate-covered ice cream bars.
5. A chain of retail stores carrying inexpensive

notions and household goods.
6. A commuter line.

1749

FROM THE MIXED-
UP FILES OF
MRS. BASIL E.
FRANKWEILER,
CH. 1

four Kincaid children neither waited for each other nor walked together, except for Kevin who was somebody's charge each week. School had begun on the Wednesday after Labor Day. Therefore, their "fiscal week" as Claudia chose to call it began always on Wednesday. Kevin was only six and in the first grade and was made much over by everyone, especially by Mrs. Kincaid, Claudia thought. Claudia also thought that he was terribly babied and impossibly spoiled. You would think that her parents would know something about raising children by the time Kevin, their fourth, came along. But her parents hadn't learned. She couldn't remember being anyone's charge when she was in the first grade. Her mother had simply met her at the bus stop every day.

Jamie wanted to sit with his buddy, Bruce. They played cards on the bus; each day meant a continuation of the day before. (The game was nothing very complicated, Saxonberg. Nothing terribly refined. They played *war*, that simple game where each player puts down a card, and the higher card takes both. If the cards are the same, there is a war which involves putting down more cards; winner then takes all the war cards.) Every night when Bruce got off at his stop, he'd take his stack of cards home with him. Jamie would do the same. They always took a vow not to shuffle. At the stop before Bruce's house, they would stop playing, wrap a rubber band around each pile, hold the stack under each other's chin and spit on each other's deck saying, "Thou shalt not shuffle." Then each tapped his deck and put it in his pocket.

Claudia found the whole procedure disgusting, so she suffered no feelings of guilt when she pulled Jamie away from his precious game. Jamie was mad, though. He was in no mood to listen to Claudia. He sat slumped in his seat with his lips pooched out and his eyebrows pulled down on top of his eyes. He looked like a miniature, clean-shaven Neanderthal man.[7] Claudia didn't say anything. She waited for him to cool off.

Jamie spoke first, "Gosh, Claude, why don't you pick on Steve?"

Claudia answered, "I thought, Jamie, that you'd see that it's obvious I don't want Steve."

"Well," Jamie pleaded, "want him! Want him!"

Claudia had planned her speech. "I want you, Jamie, for the greatest adventure in our lives."

Jamie muttered. "Well, I wouldn't mind if you'd pick on someone else."

Claudia looked out the window and didn't answer. Jamie said, "As long as you've got me here, tell me."

Claudia still said nothing and still looked out the window. Jamie became impatient. "I said that as long as you've got me here, you may as well tell me."

Claudia remained silent. Jamie erupted, "What's the matter with you, Claude? First you bust up my card game, then you don't tell me. It's undecent."

"Break up, not bust up. Indecent, not undecent," Claudia corrected.

"Oh, boloney! You know what I mean. Now tell me," he demanded.

"I've picked you to accompany me on the greatest adventure of our mutual lives," Claudia repeated.

"You said that." He clenched his teeth. "Now tell me."

"I've decided to run away from home, and I've chosen you to accompany me."

"Why pick on me? Why not pick on Steve?" he asked.

---

7. A hominid that existed from about 130,000 to 25,000 years ago (overlapping with modern humans); Neanderthals are popularly represented with heavy brow ridges and a great deal of hair.

Claudia sighed, "I don't want Steve. Steve is one of the things in my life that I'm running away from. I want you."

Despite himself, Jamie felt flattered. (Flattery is as important a machine as the lever, isn't it, Saxonberg? Give it a proper place to rest, and it can move the world.[8]) It moved Jamie. He stopped thinking, "Why pick on me?" and started thinking, "I am chosen." He sat up in his seat, unzipped his jacket, put one foot up on the seat, placed his hands over his bent knee and said out of the corner of his mouth, "O.K., Claude, when do we bust out of here? And how?"

Claudia stifled the urge to correct his grammar again. "On Wednesday. Here's the plan. Listen carefully."

Jamie squinted his eyes and said, "Make it complicated, Claude. I like complications."

Claudia laughed. "It's got to be simple to work. We'll go on Wednesday because Wednesday is music lesson day. I'm taking my violin out of its case and am packing it full of clothes. You do the same with your trumpet case. Take as much clean underwear as possible and socks and at least one other shirt with you."

"All in a trumpet case? I should have taken up the bass fiddle."

"You can use some of the room in my case. Also use your book bag. Take your transistor radio."

"Can I wear sneakers?" Jamie asked.

Claudia answered. "Of course. Wearing shoes all the time is one of the tyrannies you'll escape by coming with me."

Jamie smiled, and Claudia knew that now was the correct time to ask. She almost managed to sound casual. "And bring all your money." She cleared her throat. "By the way, how much money do you have?"

Jamie put his foot back down on the floor, looked out the window and said, "Why do you want to know?"

"For goodness' sake, Jamie, if we're in this together, then we're together. I've got to know. How much do you have?"

"Can I trust you not to talk?" he asked.

Claudia was getting mad. "Did *I* ask *you* if I could trust you not to talk?" She clamped her mouth shut and let out twin whiffs of air through her nostrils; had she done it any harder or any louder, it would have been called a snort.

"Well, you see, Claude," Jamie whispered, "I have quite a lot of money."

Claudia thought that old Jamie would end up being a business tycoon someday. Or at least a tax attorney like their grandfather. She said nothing to Jamie.

Jamie continued, "Claude, don't tell Mom or Dad, but I gamble. I play those card games with Bruce for money. Every Friday we count our cards, and he pays me. Two cents for every card I have more than he has and five cents for every ace. And I always have more cards than he has and at least one more ace."

Claudia lost all patience. "Tell me how much you have! Four dollars? Five? How much?"

Jamie nuzzled himself further into the corner of the bus seat and sang, "Twenty-four dollars and forty-three cents." Claudia gasped, and Jamie, enjoying her reaction, added, "Hang around until Friday and I'll make it twenty-five even."

"How can you do that? Your allowance is only twenty-five cents. Twenty-four forty-

8. An allusion to the famous claim of the Greek mathematician and inventor Archimedes (287–212 B.C.E.), who set forth the principle of the lever: "Give me a place to stand and I will move the earth."

three plus twenty-five cents makes only twenty-four dollars and sixty-eight cents."
Details never escaped Claudia.

1751

FROM THE MIXED-
UP FILES OF
MRS. BASIL E.
FRANKWEILER,
CH. 2

"I'll win the rest from Bruce."

"C'mon now, James, how can you know on Monday that you'll win on Friday?"

"I just know that I will," he answered.

"How do you know?"

"I'll never tell." He looked straight at Claudia to see her reaction. She looked puzzled. He smiled, and so did she, for she then felt more certain than ever that she had chosen the correct brother for a partner in escape. They complemented each other perfectly. She was cautious (about everything but money) and poor, he was adventurous (about everything but money) and rich. More than twenty-four dollars. That would be quite a nice boodle[9] to put in their knapsacks if they were using knapsacks instead of instrument cases. She already had four dollars and eighteen cents. They would escape in comfort.

Jamie waited while she thought. "Well? What do you say? Want to wait until Friday?"

Claudia hesitated only a minute more before deciding, "No, we have to go on Wednesday. I'll write you full details of my plan. You must show the plan to no one. Memorize all the details; then destroy my note."

"Do I have to eat it?" Jamie asked.

"Tearing it up and putting it in the trash would be much simpler. No one in our family but me ever goes through the trash. And I only do if it is not sloppy and not full of pencil sharpener shavings. Or ashes."

"I'll eat it. I like complications," Jamie said.

"You must also like wood pulp," Claudia said. "That's what paper is made of, you know."

"I know. I know," Jamie answered. They spoke no more until they got off the bus at their stop. Steve got off the bus after Jamie and Claudia.

Steve yelled, "Claude! Claude! It's your turn to take Kevin. I'll tell Mom if you forget."

Claudia who had been walking up ahead with Jamie stopped short, ran back, grabbed Kevin's hand and started retracing her steps, pulling him along to the side and slightly behind.

"I wanna walk with Stevie," Kevin cried.

"That would be just fine with me, Kevin Brat," Claudia answered. "But today you happen to be my responsibility."

"Whose 'sponsibility am I next?" he asked.

"Wednesday starts Steve's turn," Claudia answered.

"I wish it could be Steve's turn every week," Kevin whined.

"You just may get your wish."

Kevin never realized then or ever that he had been given a clue, and he pouted all the way home.

2

On Tuesday night Jamie found his list of instructions under his pillow pinned to his pajamas. His first instruction was to forget his homework; get ready for the trip

9. A large amount of money.

instead. I wholeheartedly admire Claudia's thoroughness. Her concern for delicate details is as well developed as mine. Her note to Jamie even included a suggestion for hiding his trumpet when he took it out of its case. He was to roll it up in his extra blanket, which was always placed at the foot of his bed.

After he had followed all the instructions on the list, Jamie took a big glass of water from the bathroom and sat cross-legged on the bed. He bit off a large corner of the list. The paper tasted like the bubble gum he had once saved and chewed for five days; it was just as tasteless and only slightly harder. Since the ink was not waterproof, it turned his teeth blue. He tried only one more bite before he tore up the note, crumpled the pieces, and threw them into the trash. Then he brushed his teeth.

The next morning Claudia and Jamie boarded the school bus as usual, according to plan. They sat together in the back and continued sitting there when they arrived at school and everyone got out of the bus. No one was supposed to notice this, and no one did. There was so much jostling and searching for homework papers and mittens that no one paid any attention to anything except personal possessions until they were well up the walk to school. Claudia had instructed Jamie to pull his feet up and crouch his head down so that Herbert, the driver, couldn't see him. He did, and she did the same. If they were spotted, the plan was to go to school and fake out their schedules as best they could, having neither books in their bags nor musical instruments in their cases.

They lay over their book bags and over the trumpet and violin cases. Each held his breath for a long time, and each resisted at least four temptations to peek up and see what was going on. Claudia pretended that she was blind and had to depend upon her senses of hearing, touch, and smell. When they heard the last of the feet going down the steps and the motor start again, they lifted their chins slightly and smiled—at each other.

Herbert would now take the bus to the lot on the Boston Post Road where the school buses parked. Then he would get out of the bus and get into his car and go wherever else he always went. James and Claudia practiced silence all during the ragged ride to the parking lot. The bus bounced along like an empty cracker box on wheels—almost empty. Fortunately, the bumps made it noisy. Otherwise, Claudia would have worried for fear the driver could hear her heart, for it sounded to her like their electric percolator brewing the morning's coffee. She didn't like keeping her head down so long. Perspiration was causing her cheek to stick to the plastic seat; she was convinced that she would develop a medium-serious skin disease within five minutes after she got off the bus.

The bus came to a stop. They heard the door open. Just a few backward steps by Herbert, and they would be discovered. They held their breath until they heard him walk down the steps and out of the bus. Then they heard the door close. After he got out, Herbert reached in from the small side window to operate the lever that closed the door.

Claudia slowly pulled her arm in front of her and glanced at her watch. She would give Herbert seven minutes before she would lift her head. When the time was up, both of them knew that they could get up, but both wanted to see if they could hold out a little bit longer, and they did. They stayed crouched down for about forty-five more seconds, but being cramped and uncomfortable, it seemed like forty-five more minutes.

When they got up, both were grinning. They peeked out of the window of the bus,

1753

FROM THE MIXED-
UP FILES OF
MRS. BASIL E.
FRANKWEILER,
CH. 2

and saw that the coast was clear. There was no need to hurry so they slowly made their way up to the front, Claudia leading. The door lever was left of the driver's seat, and as she walked toward it, she heard an awful racket behind her.

"Jamie," she whispered, "what's all that racket?"

Jamie stopped, and so did the noise. "What racket?" he demanded.

"You," she said. "You are the racket. What in the world are you wearing? Chain mail?"

"I'm just wearing my usual. Starting from the bottom, I have B.V.D. briefs, size ten, one tee shirt . . ."

"Oh, for goodness' sake, I know all that. What are you wearing that makes so much noise?"

"Twenty-four dollars and forty-three cents."

Claudia saw then that his pockets were so heavy they were pulling his pants down. There was a gap of an inch and a half between the bottom hem of his shirt and the top of his pants. A line of winter white skin was punctuated by his navel.

"How come all your money is in change? It rattles."

"Bruce pays off in pennies and nickels. What did you expect him to pay me in? Traveler's checks?"

"O.K. O.K.," Claudia said. "What's that hanging from your belt?"

"My compass. Got it for my birthday last year."

"Why did you bother bringing that? You're carrying enough weight around already."

"You need a compass to find your way in the woods. Out of the woods, too. Everyone uses a compass for that."

"What woods?" Claudia asked.

"The woods we'll be hiding out in," Jamie answered.

"Hiding *out* in? What kind of language is that?"

"English language. That's what kind."

"Who ever told you that we were going to hide out in the woods?" Claudia demanded.

"There! You said it. You said it!" Jamie shrieked.

"Said what? I never said we're going to hide out in the woods." Now Claudia was yelling, too.

"No! you said '*hide out in.*'"

"I did not!"

Jamie exploded. "You did, too. You said, 'Who ever told you that we're going to *hide out in* the woods?' You said that."

"O.K. O.K." Claudia replied. She was trying hard to remain calm, for she knew that a group leader must never lose control of herself, even if the group she leads consists of only herself and one brother brat. "O.K.," she repeated. "I *may* have said hide *out in*, but I didn't say *the woods.*"

"Yes, sir. You said, 'Who ever told you that . . .'"

Claudia didn't give him a chance to finish. "I know. I know. Now, let's begin by my saying that we are going to hide out in the Metropolitan Museum of Art in New York City."

Jamie said, "See! See! you said it again."

"I did not! I said, 'The Metropolitan Museum of Art.'"

"You said *hide out in* again."

"All right. Let's forget the English language lessons. We are going to the Metropolitan Museum of Art in Manhattan."

For the first time, the meaning instead of the grammar of what Claudia had said penetrated.

"The Metropolitan Museum of Art! Boloney!" he exclaimed. "What kind of crazy idea is that?"

Claudia now felt that she had control of herself and Jamie and the situation. For the past few minutes they had forgotten that they were stowaways on the school bus and had behaved as they always did at home. She said, "Let's get off this bus and on the train, and I'll tell you about it."

Once again James Kincaid felt cheated. "The train! Can't we even hitchhike to New York?"

"Hitchhike? and take a chance of getting kidnapped or robbed? Or we could even get mugged," Claudia replied.

"Robbed? Why are you worried about that? It's mostly my money," Jamie told her.

"We're in this together. Its mostly your money we're using, but it's all my idea we're using. We'll take the train."

"Of all the sissy ways to run away and of all the sissy places to run away to. . . ." Jamie mumbled.

He didn't mumble quite softly enough. Claudia turned on him, "Run *away to*? How can you run *away* and *to*? What kind of language is that?" Claudia asked.

"The American language," Jamie answered. "American James Kincaidian language." And they both left the bus forgetting caution and remembering only their quarrel.

They were not discovered.

On the way to the train station Claudia mailed two letters.

"What were those?" Jamie asked.

"One was a note to Mom and Dad to tell them that we are leaving home and not to call the FBI. They'll get it tomorrow or the day after."

"And the other?"

"The other was two box tops from corn flakes. They send you twenty-five cents if you mail them two box tops with stars on the tops. For milk money,[1] it said."

"You should have sent that in before. We could use twenty-five cents more."

"We just finished eating the second box of corn flakes this morning," Claudia informed him.

They arrived at the Greenwich station in time to catch the 10:42 local. The train was not filled with either commuters or lady shoppers, so Claudia walked up the aisles of one car and then another until she found a pair of chairs that dissatisfied her the least with regard to the amount of dust and lint on the blue velvet mohair covers. Jamie spent seven of the twenty-eight-and-a-half railroad miles trying to convince his sister that they should try hiding in Central Park. Claudia appointed him treasurer; he would not only hold all the money, he would also keep track of it and pass judgment on all expenditures. Then Jamie began to feel that the Metropolitan offered several advantages and would provide adventure enough.

And in the course of those miles Claudia stopped regretting bringing Jamie along. In fact when they emerged from the train at Grand Central into the underworld of cement and steel that leads to the terminal, Claudia felt that having Jamie there was important. (Ah, how well I know those feelings of hot and hollow that come from that dimly lit concrete ramp.) And his money and radio were not the only reasons. Manhattan called for the courage of at least two Kincaids.

---

1. I.e., money for purchasing milk at school.

1755

FROM THE MIXED-
UP FILES OF
MRS. BASIL E.
FRANKWEILER,
CH. 3

As soon as they reached the sidewalk, Jamie made his first decision as treasurer. "We'll walk from here to the museum."

"Walk?" Claudia asked. "Do you realize that it is over forty blocks[2] from here?"

"Well, how much does the bus cost?"

"The bus!" Claudia exclaimed. "Who said anything about taking a bus? I want to take a taxi."

"Claudia," Jamie said, "you are quietly out of your mind. How can you even think of a taxi? We have no more allowance. No more income. You can't be extravagant any longer. It's not my money we're spending. It's *our* money. We're in this together, remember?"

"You're right," Claudia answered. "A taxi is expensive. The bus is cheaper. It's only twenty cents each. We'll take the bus."

"*Only* twenty cents each. That's forty cents total. No bus. We'll walk."

"We'll wear out forty cents worth of shoe leather," Claudia mumbled. "You're sure we have to walk?"

"Positive," Jamie answered. "Which way do we go."

"Sure you won't change your mind?" The look on Jamie's face gave her the answer. She sighed. No wonder Jamie had more than twenty-four dollars; he was a gambler and a cheapskate. If that's the way he wants to be, she thought, I'll never again ask him for bus fare; I'll suffer and never, never let him know about it. But he'll regret it when I simply collapse from exhaustion. I'll collapse quietly.

"We'd better walk up Madison Avenue," she told her brother. "I'll see too many ways to spend *our* precious money if we walk on Fifth Avenue. All those gorgeous stores."

She and Jamie did not walk exactly side by side. Her violin case kept bumping him, and he began to walk a few steps ahead of her. As Claudia's pace slowed down from what she was sure was an accumulation of carbon dioxide in her system (she had not yet learned about muscle fatigue in science class even though she was in the sixth grade honors class), Jamie's pace quickened. Soon he was walking a block and a half ahead of her. They would meet when a red light held him up. At one of these mutual stops Claudia instructed Jamie to wait for her on the corner of Madison Avenue and 80th Street, for there they would turn left to Fifth Avenue.

She found Jamie standing on that corner, probably one of the most civilized street corners in the whole world, consulting a compass and announcing that when they turned left, they would be heading "due northwest." Claudia was tired and cold at the tips; her fingers, her toes, her nose were all cold while the rest of her was perspiring under the weight of her winter clothes. She never liked feeling either very hot or very cold, and she hated feeling both at the same time. "Head due northwest. Head due northwest," she mimicked. "Can't you simply say turn right or turn left as everyone else does? Who do you think you are? Daniel Boone?[3] I'll bet no one's used a compass in Manhattan since Henry Hudson."[4]

Jamie didn't answer. He briskly rounded the corner of 80th Street and made his hand into a sun visor as he peered down the street. Claudia needed an argument.

2. There are twenty north–south blocks to a mile (Grand Central Terminal is at Park Ave. and 42nd St.). Generally, streets in Manhattan run east–west, while avenues run north–south.
3. American frontiersman (1734–1820) who guided settlers into Kentucky; *Daniel Boone* was also a popular television series (1964–70).
4. English navigator (d. 1611); in 1609 he discovered and explored the Hudson River, which has New York City at its mouth.

Her internal heat, the heat of anger, was cooking that accumulated carbon dioxide. It would soon explode out of her if she didn't give it some vent. "Don't you realize that we must try to be inconspicuous?" she demanded of her brother.

"What's inconspicuous?"

"Un-noticeable."

Jamie looked all around. "I think you're brilliant, Claude. New York is a great place to hide out. No one notices no one."

"Anyone," Claudia corrected. She looked at Jamie and found him smiling. She softened. She had to agree with her brother. She was brilliant. New York was a great place, and being called brilliant had cooled her down. The bubbles dissolved. By the time they reached the museum, she no longer needed an argument.

As they entered the main door on Fifth Avenue, the guard clicked off two numbers on his people counter. Guards always count the people going into the museum, but they don't count them going out. (My chauffeur, Sheldon, has a friend named Morris who is a guard at the Metropolitan. I've kept Sheldon busy getting information from Morris. It's not hard to do since Morris loves to talk about his work. He'll tell about anything except security. Ask him a question he won't or can't answer, and he says, "I'm not at liberty to tell. Security.")

By the time Claudia and Jamie reached their destination, it was one o'clock, and the museum was busy. On any ordinary Wednesday over 26,000 people come. They spread out over the twenty acres of floor space; they roam from room to room to room to room to room. On Wednesday come the gentle old ladies who are using the time before the Broadway matinee begins. They walk around in pairs. You can tell they are a set because they wear matching pairs of orthopedic shoes, the kind that lace on the side. Tourists visit the museum on Wednesdays. You can tell them because the men carry cameras, and the women look as if their feet hurt; they wear high heeled shoes. (I always say that those who wear 'em deserve 'em.) And there are art students. Any day of the week. They also walk around in pairs. You can tell that they are a set because they carry matching black sketchbooks.

(You've missed all this, Saxonberg. Shame on you! You've never set your well-polished shoe inside that museum. More than a quarter of a million people come to that museum every week. They come from Mankato, Kansas where they have no museums and from Paris, France, where they have lots. And they all enter free of charge because that's what the museum is: great and large and wonderful and free to all. And complicated. Complicated enough even for Jamie Kincaid.)

No one thought it strange that a boy and a girl, each carrying a book bag and an instrument case and who would normally be in school, were visiting a museum. After all, about a thousand school children visit the museum every day. The guard at the entrance merely stopped them and told them to check their cases and book bags. A museum rule: no bags, food, or umbrellas. None that the guards can see. Rule or no rule, Claudia decided it was a good idea. A big sign in the checking room said NO TIPPING, so she knew that Jamie couldn't object. Jamie did object, however; he pulled his sister aside and asked her how she expected him to change into his pajamas. His pajamas, he explained, were rolled into a tiny ball in his trumpet case.

Claudia told him that she fully expected to check out at 4:30. They would then leave the museum by the front door and within five minutes would re-enter from the back, through the door that leads from the parking lot to the Children's Museum. After all, didn't that solve all their problems? (1) They would be seen leaving the museum. (2) They would be free of their baggage while they scouted around for a place to spend the night. And (3) it was free.

1757

FROM THE MIXED-
UP FILES OF
MRS. BASIL E.
FRANKWEILER,
CH. 3

Claudia checked her coat as well as her packages. Jamie was condemned to walking around in his ski jacket. When the jacket was on and zipped, it covered up that exposed strip of skin. Besides, the orlon plush lining did a great deal to muffle his twenty-four-dollar rattle. Claudia would never have permitted herself to become so overheated, but Jamie liked perspiration, a little bit of dirt, and complications.

Right now, however, he wanted lunch. Claudia wished to eat in the restaurant on the main floor, but Jamie wished to eat in the snack bar downstairs; he thought it would be less glamorous, but cheaper, and as chancellor of the exchequer, as holder of the veto power, and as tightwad of the year, he got his wish. Claudia didn't really mind too much when she saw the snack bar. It was plain but clean.

James was dismayed at the prices. They had $28.61 when they went into the cafeteria, and only $27.11 when they came out still feeling hungry. "Claudia," he demanded, "did you know food would cost so much? Now, aren't you glad that we didn't take a bus?"

Claudia was no such thing. She was not glad that they hadn't taken a bus. She was merely furious that her parents, and Jamie's too, had been so stingy that she had been away from home for less than one whole day and was already worried about survival money. She chose not to answer Jamie. Jamie didn't notice; he was completely wrapped up in problems of finance.

"Do you think I could get one of the guards to play me a game of war?" he asked.

"That's ridiculous," Claudia said.

"Why? I brought my cards along. A whole deck."

Claudia said, "*Inconspicuous* is exactly the opposite of that. Even a guard at the Metropolitan who sees thousands of people every day would remember a boy who played him a game of cards."

Jamie's pride was involved. "I cheated Bruce through all second grade and through all third grade so far, and he still isn't wise."

"Jamie! Is that how you knew you'd win?"

Jamie bowed his head and answered, "Well, yeah. Besides, Brucie has trouble keeping straight the jacks, queens, and kings. He gets mixed up."

"Why do you cheat your best friend?"

"I sure don't know. I guess I like complications."

"Well, quit worrying about money now. Worry about where we're going to hide while they're locking up this place."

They took a map from the information stand; for free. Claudia selected where they would hide during that dangerous time immediately after the museum was closed to the public and before all the guards and helpers left. She decided that she would go to the ladies' room, and Jamie would go to the men's room just before the museum closed. "Go to the one near the restaurant on the main floor," she told Jamie.

"I'm not spending a night in a men's room. All that tile. It's cold. And, besides, men's rooms make noises sound louder. And I rattle enough now."

Claudia explained to Jamie that he was to enter a booth in the men's room. "And then stand on it," she continued.

"Stand on it? Stand on what?" Jamie demanded.

"You know," Claudia insisted. "Stand on it!"

"You mean stand on the toilet?" Jamie needed everything spelled out.

"Well, what else would I mean? What else is there in a booth in the men's room? And keep your head down. And keep the door to the booth very slightly open," Claudia finished.

"Feet up. Head down. Door open. Why?"

"Because I'm certain that when they check the ladies' room and the men's room, they peek under the door and check only to see if there are feet. We must stay there until we're sure all the people and guards have gone home."

"How about the night watchman?" Jamie asked.

Claudia displayed a lot more confidence than she really felt. "Oh! there'll be a night watchman, I'm sure. But he mostly walks around the roof trying to keep people from breaking in. We'll already be in. They call what he walks, a cat walk. We'll learn his habits soon enough. They must mostly use burglar alarms in the inside. We'll just never touch a window, a door, or a valuable painting. Now, let's find a place to spend the night."

They wandered back to the rooms of fine French and English furniture. It was here Claudia knew for sure that she had chosen the most elegant place in the world to hide. She wanted to sit on the lounge chair that had been made for Marie Antoinette[5] or at least sit at her writing table. But signs everywhere said not to step on the platform. And some of the chairs had silken ropes strung across the arms to keep you from even trying to sit down. She would have to wait until after lights out to be Marie Antoinette.

At last she found a bed that she considered perfectly wonderful, and she told Jamie that they would spend the night there. The bed had a tall canopy, supported by an ornately carved headboard at one end and by two gigantic posts at the other. (I'm familiar with that bed, Saxonberg. It is as enormous and fussy as mine. And it dates from the sixteenth century like mine. I once considered donating my bed to the museum, but Mr. Untermyer[6] gave them this one first. I was somewhat relieved when he did. Now I can enjoy my bed without feeling guilty because the museum doesn't have one. Besides, I'm not that fond of donating things.)

Claudia had always known that she was meant for such fine things. Jamie, on the other hand, thought that running away from home to sleep in just another bed was really no challenge at all. He, James, would rather sleep on the bathroom floor, after all. Claudia then pulled him around to the foot of the bed and told him to read what the card said.

Jamie read, "Please do not step on the platform."

Claudia knew that he was being difficult on purpose; therefore, she read for him, "State bed—scene of the alleged murder of Amy Robsart, first wife of Lord Robert Dudley,[7] later Earl of . . ."

Jamie couldn't control his smile. He said, "You know, Claude, for a sister and a fussbudget, you're not too bad."

Claudia replied, "You know, Jamie, for a brother and a cheapskate, you're not too bad."

Something happened at precisely that moment. Both Claudia and Jamie tried to explain to me about it, but they couldn't quite. I know what happened, though I never told them. Having words and explanations for everything is too modern. I especially wouldn't tell Claudia. She has too many explanations already.

What happened was: they became a team, a family of two. There had been times before they ran away when they had acted like a team, but those were very different

---

5. Queen of France (1755–1793), the wife of King Louis XVI. She was known for her extravagance and love of luxury.
6. Irwin Untermyer (1886–1973), a N.Y. judge whose father had amassed a great fortune as a lawyer and financial advisor; he had an extensive col-

lection of antique furniture and other art. (This bed is no longer on display at the museum.)
7. The first Earl of Leicester (ca. 1532–1588); a favorite of Queen Elizabeth, Dudley was rumored to have killed his wife (1560).

from *feeling* like a team. Becoming a team didn't mean the end of their arguments. But it did mean that the arguments became a part of the adventure, became discussions not threats. To an outsider the arguments would appear to be the same because feeling like part of a team is something that happens invisibly. You might call it *caring*. You could even call it *love*. And it is very rarely, indeed, that it happens to two people at the same time—especially a brother and a sister who had always spent more time with activities than they had with each other.

1759

FROM THE MIXED-
UP FILES OF
MRS. BASIL E.
FRANKWEILER,
CH. 3

They followed their plan: checked out of the museum and re-entered through a back door. When the guard at that entrance told them to check their instrument cases, Claudia told him that they were just passing through on their way to meet their mother. The guard let them go, knowing that if they went very far, some other guard would stop them again. However, they managed to avoid other guards for the remaining minutes until the bell rang. The bell meant that the museum was closing in five minutes. They then entered the booths of the rest rooms.

They waited in the booths until five-thirty, when they felt certain that everyone had gone. Then they came out and met. Five-thirty in winter is dark, but nowhere seems as dark as the Metropolitan Museum of Art. The ceilings are so high that they fill up with a lot of darkness. It seemed to Jamie and Claudia that they walked through miles of corridors. Fortunately, the corridors were wide, and they were spared bumping into things.

At last they came to the hall of the English Renaissance.[8] Jamie quickly threw himself upon the bed forgetting that it was only about six o'clock and thinking that he would be so exhausted that he would immediately fall asleep. He didn't. He was hungry. That was one reason he didn't fall asleep immediately. He was uncomfortable, too. So he got up from bed, changed into his pajamas and got back into bed. He felt a little better. Claudia had already changed into her pajamas. She, too, was hungry, and she, too, was uncomfortable. How could so elegant and romantic a bed smell so musty? She would have liked to wash everything in a good, strong, sweet-smelling detergent.

As Jamie got into bed, he still felt uneasy, and it wasn't because he was worried about being caught. Claudia had planned everything so well that he didn't concern himself about that. The strange way he felt had little to do with the strange place in which they were sleeping. Claudia felt it, too. Jamie lay there thinking. Finally, realization came.

"You know, Claude," he whispered, "I didn't brush my teeth."

Claudia answered, "Well, Jamie, you can't always brush after every meal." They both laughed very quietly. "Tomorrow," Claudia reassured him, "we'll be even better organized."

It was much earlier than her bedtime at home, but still Claudia felt tired. She thought she might have an iron deficiency anemia: tired blood. Perhaps, the pressures of everyday stress and strain had gotten her down. Maybe she was light-headed from hunger; her brain cells were being robbed of vitally needed oxygen for good growth and, and . . . yawn.

She shouldn't have worried. It had been an unusually busy day. A busy and unusual day. So she lay there in the great quiet of the museum next to the warm quiet of her brother and allowed the soft stillness to settle around them: a comforter of quiet. The silence seeped from their heads to their soles and into their souls. They stretched out and relaxed. Instead of oxygen and stress, Claudia thought now of hushed and

8. This hall contains artifacts mainly from the sixteenth century.

quiet words: glide, fur, banana, peace. Even the footsteps of the night watchman added only an accented quarter-note to the silence that had become a hum, a lullaby.

They lay perfectly still even long after he passed. Then they whispered good night to each other and fell asleep. They were quiet sleepers and hidden by the heaviness of the dark, they were easily not discovered.

(Of course, Saxonberg, the draperies of that bed helped, too.)

4

Claudia and Jamie awoke very early the next morning. It was still dark. Their stomachs felt like tubes of toothpaste that had been all squeezed out. Giant economy-sized tubes. They had to be out of bed and out of sight before the museum staff came on duty. Neither was accustomed to getting up so early, to feeling so unwashed, or feeling so hungry.

They dressed in silence. Each felt that peculiar chill that comes from getting up in the early morning. The chill that must come from one's own bloodstream, for it comes in summer as well as winter, from some inside part of you that knows it is early morning. Claudia always dreaded that brief moment when her pajamas were shed and her underwear was not yet on. Even before she began undressing, she always had her underwear laid out on the bed in the right direction, right for getting into as quickly as possible. She did this now, too. But she hurried less pulling her petticoat down over her head. She took good long whiffs of the wonderful essence of detergent and clean dacron[9]-cotton which floated down with the petticoat. Next to any kind of elegance, Claudia loved good clean smells.

After they were dressed, Claudia whispered to Jamie, "Let's stash our book bags and instrument cases before we man our stations."

They agreed to scatter their belongings. Thus, if the museum officials found one thing, they wouldn't necessarily find all. While still at home they had removed all identification on their cases as well as their clothing. Any child who has watched only one month's worth of television knows to do that much.

Claudia hid her violin case in a sarcophagus that had no lid. It was well above eye level, and Jamie helped hoist her up so that she could reach it. It was a beautiful carved Roman marble sarcophagus. She hid her book bag behind a tapestry screen in the rooms of French furniture. Jamie wanted to hide his things in a mummy case, but Claudia said that that would be unnecessarily complicated. The Egyptian wing of the Metropolitan was too far away from their bedroom; for the number of risks involved, it might as well be in Egypt. So the trumpet case was hidden inside a huge urn and Jamie's book bag was neatly tucked behind a drape that was behind a statue from the Middle Ages. Unfortunately, the museum people had fastened all the drawers of their furniture so that they couldn't be opened. They had never given a thought to the convenience of Jamie Kincaid.

"Manning their stations" meant climbing back into the booths and waiting during the perilous time when the museum was open to the staff but not to visitors. They washed up, combed their hair, and even brushed their teeth. Then began those long moments. That first morning they weren't quite sure when the staff would arrive, so they hid good and early. While Claudia stood crouched down waiting, the emptiness and the hollowness of all the museum corridors filled her stomach. She was starved. She spent her time trying not to remember delicious things to eat.

9. A trademark for polyester.

1761

FROM THE MIXED-
UP FILES OF
MRS. BASIL E.
FRANKWEILER,
CH. 4

Jamie made one slight error that morning. It was almost enough to be caught. When he heard the sound of running water, he assumed that some male visitor was using the men's room to wash up. He checked his watch and saw that it was five past ten; he knew that the museum officially opened at ten o'clock, so he stepped down to walk out of his booth. It was not, however, a museum visitor who had turned on the water tap. It was a janitor filling his bucket. He was leaning down in the act of wringing out his mop when he saw Jamie's legs appear from nowhere and then saw Jamie emerge.

"Where did you come from?" he asked.

Jamie smiled and nodded. "Mother always says that I came from Heaven." He bowed politely and walked out, delighted with his brush with danger. He could hardly wait to tell Claudia. Claudia chose not to be amused on so empty a stomach.

The museum restaurant wouldn't open until eleven thirty and the snack bar wouldn't open until after that, so they left the museum to get breakfast. They went to the automat[1] and used up a dollar's worth of Bruce's nickels. Jamie allotted ten nickels to Claudia and kept ten for himself. Jamie bought a cheese sandwich and coffee. After eating these he still felt hungry and told Claudia she could have twenty-five cents more for pie if she wished. Claudia, who had eaten cereal and drunk pineapple juice, scolded him about the need to eat properly. Breakfast food for breakfast, and lunch food for lunch. Jamie countered with complaints about Claudia's narrow-mindedness.

They were better organized that second day. Knowing that they could not afford more than two meals a day, they stopped at a grocery and bought small packages of peanut butter crackers for the night; they hid them in various pockets in their clothing. They decided to join a school group for lunch at the snack bar. There were certainly enough to choose from. That way their faces would always be just part of the crowd.

Upon their return to the museum, Claudia informed Jamie that they should take advantage of the wonderful opportunity they had to learn and to study. No other children in all the world since the world began had had such an opportunity. So she set forth for herself and for her brother the task of learning everything about the museum. One thing at a time. (Claudia probably didn't realize that the museum has over 365,000 works of art. Even if she had, she could not have been convinced that learning everything about everything was not possible; her ambitions were as enormous and as multi-directional as the museum itself.) Every day they would pick a different gallery about which they would learn everything. He could pick first. She would pick second; he, third; and so on. Just like the television schedule at home. Jamie considered learning something every day outrageous. It was not only outrageous; it was unnecessary. Claudia simply did not know how to escape. He thought he would put a quick end to this part of their runaway career. He chose the galleries of the Italian Renaissance.[2] He didn't even know what the Renaissance was except that it sounded important and there seemed to be an awful lot of it. He figured that Claudia would soon give up in despair.

When she gave Jamie first pick, Claudia had been certain that he would choose Arms and Armor. She herself found these interesting. There was probably two days' worth of learning there. Perhaps, she might even choose the same on the second day.

---

1. A cafeteria in which all the food is dispensed from vending machines.

2. In art, the Renaissance began first in Italy, in the mid-fourteenth century.

1763

From the Mixed-
Up Files of
Mrs. Basil E.
Frankweiler,
Ch. 4

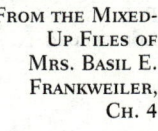

Claudia was surprised at Jamie's choice. But she thought she knew why he chose the Italian Renaissance. She thought she knew because along with tennis, ballet, and diving lessons at the "Y",[3] she had taken art appreciation lessons last year. Her art teacher had said that the Renaissance was a period of glorification of the human form; as best she could figure out, that meant bare bodies. Many painters of the Italian Renaissance had painted huge billowy, bosomy naked ladies. She was amazed at Jamie; she thought he was too young for that. He was. She never even considered the possibility that he wanted her to be bored. She had given him first choice, and she was stuck with it. So she marched with him toward the long wide stairway straight in from the main entrance, which leads directly to the Hall of the Italian Renaissance.

If you think of doing something in New York City, you can be certain that at least two thousand other people have that same thought. And of the two thousand who do, about one thousand will be standing in line waiting to do it. That day was no exception. There were at least a thousand people waiting in line to see things in the Hall of the Italian Renaissance.

Claudia and Jamie did not think that there was anything unusual about the size of the crowd. This was New York. *Crowded* was part of the definition of New York. (To many art experts, Saxonberg, *crowded* is part of the definition of the Italian Renaissance, too. It was a time much like this: artistic activity was everywhere. Keeping track of the artists of the fifteenth and sixteenth centuries in Italy is as difficult as keeping track of the tax laws in the nineteen fifties and sixties in the United States. And almost as complicated.)

As they reached the top of the stairs, a guard said, "Line forms to the right. Single file, please." They did as they were told, partly because they didn't want to offend any guard or even attract his attention and partly because the crowd made them. Ladies' arms draped with pocketbooks and men's arms draped with coats formed a barrier as difficult to get through as barbed wire. Claudia and Jamie stood in the manner of all children who are standing in line. They stood leaning back with their necks stretched and their heads tilted away, way back, making a vain effort to see over the shoulders of the tall adult who always appears in front of them. Jamie could see nothing but the coat of the man in front of him. Claudia could see nothing but a piece of Jamie's head plus the coat of the man in front of Jamie.

They realized that they were approaching something out of the ordinary when they saw a newspaper cameraman walking along the edge of the crowd. The newsman carried a large, black, flash camera which had *TIMES* stenciled in white on its case. Jamie tried to slow down to the pace of the photographer. He didn't know what he was having his picture taken for, but he liked getting his picture taken—especially for a newspaper. Once when his class had visited the fire department, his picture had been in the paper at home. He had bought seven copies of the paper and used that page for bookcovers. When the bookcovers began to tear, he covered the covers with Saran wrap. They were still in his bookcase at home.

Claudia sensed danger. At least *she* remembered that they had run away from home, and she didn't want any New York paper advertising her whereabouts. Or Jamie's either. Especially if her parents happened to be looking for her. Someone in Greenwich was bound to read the *New York Times* and tell her folks. It would be more than a clue; it would be like booking anyone looking for them on a chartered bus ride straight to the hideaway. Wouldn't her brother ever learn inconspicuous? She shoved him.

---

3. I.e., the YMCA (Young Men's Christian Association), whose facilities offer various recreational activities.

He almost fell into the man in the coat. Jamie turned to Claudia and gave her an awful look. Claudia paid no attention, for now they reached what everyone was standing in line to see. A statue of an angel; her arms were folded, and she was looking holy. As Claudia passed by, she thought that that angel was the most beautiful, most graceful little statue she had ever seen; she wanted to stop and stare; she almost did, but the crowd wouldn't let her. As Jamie passed by, he thought that he would get even with Claudia for shoving him.

1765

FROM THE MIXED-
UP FILES OF
MRS. BASIL E.
FRANKWEILER,
CH. 4

They followed the line to the end of the Renaissance Hall. When the velvet ropes that had guided the crowd by creating a narrow street within the room ended, they found themselves going down a staircase to the main floor. Claudia was lost in remembrance of the beautiful angel she had seen. Why did she seem so important; and why was she so special? Of course, she was beautiful. Graceful. Polished. But so were many other things at the museum. Her sarcophagus, for example: the one in which her violin case was hidden. And why was there all that commotion about her? The man had come to take pictures. There would be something about it in tomorrow's paper. They could find out from the newspapers.

She spoke to Jamie, "We'll have to buy a *New York Times* tomorrow to see the picture."

Jamie was still mad about that shove. Why would he want to buy the paper? He wouldn't be in the picture. He chose to fight Claudia with the one weapon he had—the power of the purse. He answered, "We can't afford a *New York Times*. It costs a dime."

"We've got to get one, Jamie. Don't you want to know what's so important about that statue? Why everyone is standing in line to see it?"

Jamie felt that letting Claudia know that she couldn't get away with shoving him in public was more important than his curiosity. "Well, perhaps, tomorrow you can push someone down and grab his paper while he's trying to get up. I'm afraid, though, that our budget won't allow this expense."

They walked for a short while before Claudia said, "I'll find out some way." She was determined about that.

She was also determined about learning; they wouldn't skip a lesson so easily. "Since we can't learn everything about the Italian Renaissance today, let's learn everything about the Egyptian rooms. That will be our lesson instead."

Jamie liked the mummies even if he didn't like lessons, so they walked together to the Egyptian wing. There they encountered a class that was also touring the halls. Each child in the class wore a round circle of blue construction paper on which was written in magic marker: Gr. 6, W.P.S. The class was seated on little rubber mats around a glass case within which was a mummy case within which was the mummy they were talking about. The teacher sat on a folding stool. Both Claudia and Jamie wandered over toward the class and soon became part of it—almost. They listened to the guide, a very pretty young lady who worked for the museum, and they learned a lot. They didn't even mind. They were surprised that they could actually learn something when they weren't in class. The guide told them how mummies were prepared and how Egypt's dry climate helped to preserve them. She told them about digging for tombs, and she told them about the beautiful princess Sit Hat-Hor Yunet whose jewelry they would see in another room. Before they left this room, however, she wanted to know if there were any questions. Since I'm sure this group was typical of all the school groups that I've observed at the museum, I can tell you what they were doing. At least twelve members of Gr. 6, W.P.S. were busy poking at each other. Twelve were wondering when they would eat; four were worried about how long it would be before they could get a drink of water.

Only Jamie had a question: "How much did it cost to become a mummy?"

The pretty guide thought he was part of the class; the teacher thought that he was planted in the audience to pep up the discussion; the class knew that he was an impostor. When they bothered to notice Claudia, they knew that she was one, also. But the class had the good manners that come with not caring; they would leave the impostors alone. The question, however, would have caused at least ten of them to stop poking at each other; six to forget about eating and three others to find the need for drink suddenly less urgent. It caused Claudia to want to embalm Jamie in a vat of mummy fluid right that minute. That would teach him *inconspicuous*.

The guide told Jamie that some people saved all their lives so that they could become mummies; it was indeed expensive.

One of the students called out, "You might even say it costs him his life."

Everyone laughed. Then they picked up their rubber mats and walked to the next room. Claudia was ready to pull Jamie out of line and make him learn another part of the museum today, but she got a glimpse of the room they were to go to next. It was filled with jewelry: case after case of it. So they followed the class into that hall. After a short talk there, the guide bid them good-bye and mentioned that they might enjoy buying some of the museum pamphlets on Egypt. Jamie asked if *they* were expensive.

The guide answered, "Some are as inexpensive as a copy of the Sunday *New York Times*. Others cost much more."

Jamie looked over at Claudia; he shouldn't have. Claudia looked as satisfied as the bronze statue of the Egyptian cat she was standing near. The only real difference between them was that the cat wore tiny golden earrings and looked a trifle less smug.

They got the *New York Times* the next day. Neither Claudia nor Jamie bought it. The man who left it on the counter while he was looking at the reproductions of antique jewelry bought it. The Kincaids stole it from him. They left the museum immediately thereafter.

Claudia read the paper while they ate breakfast at Horn and Hardart's.[4] That morning she didn't eat breakfast food for breakfast. Crackers and roasted chestnuts in bed at night satisfied only a small corner of her hunger. Being hungry was the most inconvenient part of running away. She meant to eat heartily for every cent Jamie gave her. She bought macaroni and cheese casserole, baked beans, and coffee that morning. Jamie got the same.

The information they wanted was on the first page of the second section of the *Times*. The headline said: RECORD CROWD VIEWS MUSEUM "BARGAIN." There were three pictures: one of the record crowd standing in line; one of the statue itself; and one of the director of the museum with an assistant. The article was as follows: (Saxonberg you can find an original of the newspaper in my files. It's in one of the seventeen cabinets that line the north wall of my office.)

> Officials of the Metropolitan Museum of Art report that 100,000 people climbed the great stairway to catch a glimpse of one of its newest acquisitions, a twenty four inch statue called "Angel." Interest in the marble piece arises from the unusual circumstances attending its acquisition by the museum and from

4. The best-known chain of automats (founded in Philadelphia in 1902 by Joseph Horn and Frank Hardart).

1767

FROM THE MIXED-
UP FILES OF
MRS. BASIL E.
FRANKWEILER,
CH. 4

the belief that it may be the work of the Italian Renaissance master, Michelangelo.[5] If proof is found that it is an early work of Michelangelo, the museum will have purchased the greatest bargain in art history; it was purchased at an auction last year for $225.00. Considering that recently Prince Franz Josef II accepted an offer of $5 million for a small painting by Leonardo da Vinci,[6] an artist of the same period and of similar merit, will give some idea of how great a bargain this is.

The museum purchased the statue last year when one of its curators spotted it during a preview showing of works to be auctioned by the Parke-Bernet Galleries.[7] His initial suspicion that it might be the work of Michelangelo was confirmed by several other museum officials, all of whom kept their thoughts quiet in a successful effort to keep the bidding from being driven higher. The statue has been the subject of exhaustive tests and study by the museum staff as well as art experts from abroad. Most believe it to have been done about 470 years ago when Michelangelo was in his early twenties.

The statue was acquired by the Parke-Bernet Galleries from the collection of Mrs. Basil E. Frankweiler. She claims to have purchased it from a dealer in Bologna, Italy before World War II. Mrs. Frankweiler's residence on East 63rd Street was long a Manhattan showplace for what many considered one of the finest private collections of art in the Western Hemisphere. Others considered it a gigantic hodgepodge of the great and the mediocre. Mrs. Frankweiler closed her Manhattan residence three years ago; important pieces from its contents have found their way to various auctions and galleries since that time.

Mr. Frankweiler amassed a fortune from the corn oil industry and from developing many corn products. He died in 1947. Mrs. Frankweiler now lives on her country estate in Farmington, Connecticut. Her home, which at one time was open to the greats in the worlds of art, business, and politics, is now closed to all but her staff, her advisors, and a few close friends. The Frankweilers had no children.

A museum spokesman said yesterday, "Whether or not conclusive proof will be found that this was the work of Michelangelo, we are pleased with our purchase." Although Michelangelo Buonarroti is perhaps best known for his paintings of the Sistine Chapel[8] in Rome, he always considered himself a sculptor, and primarily a sculptor of marble. The question of whether the museum has acquired one of his lesser known masterpieces still awaits a final answer."

If Claudia's interests had been a little broader, if she had started with the national news on page one and had then read the continuations on page twenty-eight, she might have noticed a small article on that page, one column wide, that would have interested her. The date line was Greenwich, Connecticut, and it stated that two children of Mr. and Mrs. Steven C. Kincaid, Sr. had been missing since Wednesday. The article didn't mention any clues like Claudia's letter. It said that the children were last seen wearing nylon quilted ski jackets. Small help. Fourteen out of fifteen kids in the U.S.A. wear those. It went on to describe Claudia as brunette and pretty

---

5. Michelangelo Buonarroti (1475–1564), Italian sculptor, painter, and architect; born in Caprese (near Florence), he was active mainly in Florence and Rome.
6. Italian painter, sculptor, inventor, architect, and scientist (1452–1519); born in Vinci, he was active mainly in Florence and Milan. Prince Franz

Josef II (1906–1989; r. 1938–89), of Liechtenstein.
7. The largest U.S. fine art auction house (purchased in 1964 by Sotheby's).
8. I.e., the chapel's ceiling (painted 1508–12) and end wall (1536–41).

and Jamie as brunette and brown eyed. Police in the neighboring towns of Darien and Stamford in Connecticut and Port Chester, New York, had been alerted. (You see, Saxonberg, Claudia had found the article about the statue too easily. She didn't even look at the first section of the paper. I keep telling you that often the search proves more profitable than the goal. Keep that in mind when you're looking for something in my files.)

Claudia and Jamie read about the statue with great interest. Claudia read the article twice so that she could memorize it all. She decided that the statue was not only the most beautiful in the world but also the most mysterious.

Jamie said, "I don't think $225 is cheap. I've never had that much money in my whole life. Totaling up all my birthday and Christmas presents since I was born nine long years ago wouldn't make $225."

Claudia said, "You wouldn't consider two and a quarter cents very much, would you?"

Jamie answered, "I might."

"That's right. *You* might, but most people wouldn't. Well, if this statue is by Michelangelo, it's worth about $2,250,000 instead of $225. That's the same as saying that suddenly two and a quarter cents is worth $225."

Jamie thought this over a minute. He was impressed. "When I grow up, I'm going to find a way to know for certain who did a statue."

This was all Claudia needed. Something that had been smoldering inside her since she first saw the statue, that had been fed by the *Times* article, now flared into an idea.

"Jamie, let's do it now. Let's skip learning everything about everything in the museum. Let's concentrate on the statue."

"Can we still take class tours as we did yesterday?"

Claudia answered, "Of course. We don't have to skip learning *something* about everything. We just won't learn everything about everything. We'll concentrate on Michelangelo."

Jamie snapped his fingers. "I've got it!" he exclaimed. He held up his hands for Claudia to see.

"What does that mean?"

"Fingerprints, silly. If Michelangelo worked on that statue, his fingerprints would be on it."

"Fingerprints? Almost five-hundred-year-old fingerprints? How would you know that they belonged to Michelangelo? He didn't have a police record. I don't suppose he did. As a matter of fact, I'm not sure people were fingerprinted in those days even if they did."

"But what if we were to find identical fingerprints on something they knew that he did? We could compare them."

Claudia kept looking at the picture of the statue as she finished eating her baked beans.

"Jamie," she said, "do you think the statue looks like anyone special?" She folded her arms and gazed into the distance.

"No one I know looks like an angel."

"Think a minute." She cleared her throat and lifted her chin slightly and gazed into the distance. "Don't think about the hair style or the clothes or anything. Just think about the face." She nudged the page of the *New York Times* closer under Jamie's nose and resumed her pose. Jamie looked at the picture.

"Nope," he said looking up.

1769

From the Mixed-
Up Files of
Mrs. Basil E.
Frankweiler,
Ch. 4

"Can't you see any resemblance?"

"Nope." He looked at the picture again. "Who do you think it looks like?"

"Oh, I don't know," she stammered.

Jamie noticed Claudia blushing. "What's the matter? You getting a fever?"

"Don't be silly. I just feel that the statue looks like someone in our family."

"You sure you don't have a fever? You're talking out of your head."

Claudia unfolded her arms and lowered her distant gaze. "I wonder who posed for it," she said half aloud.

"Probably some fat old lady. Then the chisel slipped, so he made a skinny angel instead."

"Jamie, you have as much romance in you as the wolf in Little Red Riding Hood."[9]

"Romance! Boloney! But I do like the mystery part."

"So do I!" Claudia answered. "But I like more than that about Angel."

"We going to look for fingerprints then?"

Claudia reconsidered, "Well, we might look for fingerprints. That's one way. For a start." She looked at Jamie and sniffed, "But I'm sure it won't work. We'll look tomorrow. Even though it won't work." And she looked some more at the picture.

On the second day the crowd going up the broad staircase to see the little Angel was even greater. The newspaper article had made people curious. Besides, it was a cloudy day, and museum attendance always improves in bad weather. Some people who had not been to the Metropolitan Museum for years came. Some people who had never been there ever, came; they got directions from maps, subway conductors, and police. (I'm surprised, Saxonberg, that seeing my name in the paper in connection with Michelangelo didn't bring even you to the museum. You would have profited more than you would have thought by that trip. Are photo albums of your grandchildren the only pictures you look at? Are you altogether unconscious of the magic of the name of Michelangelo? I truly believe that his name has magic even now; the best kind of magic because it comes from true greatness. Claudia sensed it as she again stood in line. The mystery only intrigued her; the magic trapped her.)

Both children were annoyed when the guards plus the push of the crowd hurried them past the Angel. How could they possibly look for fingerprints when they were so rushed? After this hurried visit to the statue, they decided to do their research when they had the statue and the museum to themselves. Claudia especially wanted to make herself important to the statue. She would solve its mystery; and it, in turn, would do something important to her, though what this was, she didn't quite know.

As they once again reached the back stairs, Claudia asked Jamie, "With whom shall we dine today, Sir James?"

Jamie answered, "Oh, I don't know, dear Lady Claudia. Shall we find a good and proper group?"

"Yes, let us, Sir James."

Thereupon, Jamie held out his arm, Claudia rested the tips of her fingers on the top of his hand, and they descended the stairs. They proved to be as fussy in their selection as Goldilocks.[1] This group was too old; that group, too young; this, too small; that, all girls. But they found a good and proper group in the American wing where they spent a lovely and informative hour and a half learning about the arts

---

9. I.e., none at all.
1. In "Goldilocks and the Three Bears," Goldilocks

is very particular about what food and which bed belonging to the bears she takes.

and crafts of colonial days. They dined with the group, staying always at the rear of the line, always slightly apart. Both Jamie and Claudia had acquired a talent for being near but never part of a group. (Some people, Saxonberg, never learn to do that all their lives, and some learn it all too well.)

5

They had been gone from home for three days now. Claudia insisted on a fresh change of underwear every day. That was the way she had been brought up. She insisted for Jamie, too. No question about it; their laundry was becoming a problem. They had to get to a laundromat. That night they removed all their dirty clothes from their instrument cases and stuffed those that would fit into various pockets. Those that didn't fit, they wore. A double layer of clothes never hurts anyone in winter, as long as the clean ones are worn closest to the skin.

Saturday seemed a good day for housekeeping chores. There would be no school groups for them to join. Claudia suggested that they eat both meals outside the museum. Jamie agreed. Claudia next suggested a real sit-down restaurant with table-cloths on the tables and waiters to serve you. Jamie said "NO" with such force that Claudia didn't try to persuade him.

From breakfast at the automat they went to laundry at the laundromat. They emptied their pockets of underwear and removed the layer of soiled socks. No one stared. Someone before them had probably done the same thing some time that week. They bought soap from a machine for ten cents and deposited a quarter into the slot in the washer. Through the glass in the door they watched their assorted clothing spill and splash over and over and around and around. Drying cost ten cents for ten minutes, but it took twenty cents worth of minutes to dry everything. When all was done, they were disappointed; all of it looked dismally gray. Very unelegant. Claudia had thought that their white underwear should not have been washed with the red and navy blue socks, but she would not have considered asking for more money for anything as unglamorous as dirty socks.

"Oh, well," she moaned, "at least they smell clean."

Jamie said, "Let's go to the TV department of Bloomingdale's and watch TV."

"Not today. We've got to work on the mystery of the statue all morning tomorrow, because tomorrow the museum doesn't open until one o'clock. Today we must learn all about the Renaissance and Michelangelo to prepare ourselves. We'll do research at the big library at 42nd Street."[2]

"How about the TV department of Macy's instead?"

"To the library, Sir James."

"Gimbels?"[3]

"Library."

They packed their gray-looking laundry back into their pockets and walked to the door of the laundromat. At the door Claudia turned to Jamie and asked, "Can we . . . ?"

Jamie didn't let her finish, "No, dear Lady Claudia. We have not the funds for taxis, buses, or subways. "Shall we walk?" He extended his arm. Claudia placed her gloved fingertips on top of Jamie's mittened ones. Thus they began their long walk to the library.

---

2. The New York Public Library, whose main branch is at 5th Avenue and 42nd Street.

3. The New York department store (now closed) that was Macy's main rival.

Once there, they asked the lady at the information booth where they could find books on Michelangelo. She directed them first to the children's room, but when the librarian there found out what they wanted to know, she advised them to go to the Donnell Branch Library on Fifty-third Street. Jamie hoped this would discourage Claudia, but it didn't. She didn't even seem to mind back-tracking up Fifth Avenue. Her determination convinced Jamie that Saturday should be spent just this way. Once at the library, they examined the directory which told what was available where and when the library was open. In the downstairs Art Room the librarian helped them find the books which Claudia selected from the card catalogue. She even brought them some others. Claudia liked that part. She always enjoyed being waited on.

Claudia began her studies never doubting that she could become an authority that morning. She had neither pencil nor paper to make notes. And she knew she wouldn't have a lot of time to read. So she decided that she would simply remember everything, absolutely everything she read. Her net profit, therefore, would be as great as that of someone who read a great deal but remembered very little.

Claudia showed the executive ability of a corporation president. She assigned to Jamie the task of looking through the books of photographs of Michelangelo's work to find pictures of Angel. She would do the reading. She glanced through several thick books with thin pages and tiny print. After reading twelve pages, she looked to the end to see how many more pages there were to go: more than two hundred. The book also had footnotes. She read a few more pages and then busied herself with studying some of Jamie's picture books.

"You're supposed to do the reading!"

"I'm just using these pictures for relief," Claudia whispered. "I have to rest my eyes sometime."

"Well, I don't see any pictures that look like that statue," Jamie sighed.

"Keep looking. I'll do some more reading."

A few minutes later Jamie interrupted her. "Here he is," he said.

"That doesn't look anything like the statue. That's not even a girl," Claudia said.

"Of course not. That's Michelangelo himself."

Claudia replied, "I knew that."

"Two minutes ago you didn't. You thought I was showing you a picture of the statue."

"Oh, I meant . . . I meant. Well . . . there's his broken nose." She pointed to the nose in the picture. "He got in a fight and had his nose broken when he was a teenager."

"Was he a juvenile delinquent? Maybe they do have his fingerprints on file."

"No, silly," Claudia said. "He was a hot-tempered genius. Did you know he was famous even when he was alive?"

"Is that so? I thought that artists don't become famous until after they're dead. Like mummies."

They studied a while longer before Jamie's next interruption. "You know, a lot of his works were lost. They say *lost* in parentheses under the picture."

"How can that be? A statue isn't something like an umbrella that you leave in a taxi and lose. That is, those people who actually ride taxis, something you wouldn't know about."

"Well, they weren't lost in taxis. They were lost track of."

"What kind of a sentence is that? Lost track of?"

"Oh, boloney! There are whole long books about the lost works of Michelangelo. Picture works and sculptor works that people lost track of."

Claudia softened. "Is the little angel one of them?"

"What's the difference between an angel and a cupid?"[4] Jamie inquired.

"Why?" Claudia asked.

"Because there's a lost cupid for sure."

"Angels wear clothes and wings and are Christian. Cupids wear bows and arrows; they are naked and pagan."

"What's pagan?" Jamie asked. "Boy or girl?"

"How would I know?" Claudia answered.

"You said they are naked."

"Well, pagan has nothing to do with that. It means worshipping idols instead of God."

"Oh," Jamie nodded. "The statue in the museum is an angel. It's dressed in its altogether. I don't know yet if an angel was lost . . ." Then he glanced over at his sister and muttered, "track of."

Claudia had begun her research confident that a morning's study would make her completely an expert; but Michelangelo had humbled her, and humility was not an emotion with which she felt comfortable; she was irritable. Jamie ended his research where Claudia had begun: very confident and happy. He felt that his morning had been well spent; he had seen a lot of pictures and he had learned about pagan. He leaned back and yawned; he was becoming bored with pictures of David and Moses[5] and the Sistine Ceiling; he wanted to find clues. Already he knew enough to tell if Michelangelo had sculptured the little angel. All he needed was a chance to investigate. Without the guards hurrying him. He would know, but would his opinion be accepted by the experts?

"I think we should find out how the experts decide whether or not the statue belongs to Michelangelo. That will be better than finding out about Michelangelo himself," Jamie said.

"I know how they find out. They gather evidence like sketches he did and diaries and records of sales. And they examine the statue to see what kind of tools were used and how they were used. Like no one living in the fifteenth century would use an electric drill. How come you didn't take art appreciation lessons with me?"

"The summer before last?"

"Yes. Before school started."

"Well, the summer before last, I had just finished the second half of first grade."

"So what?"

"So boloney! It was all I could do to sound out the name of Dick and Jane's dog."[6]

Claudia had no answer for Jamie's logic. Besides, Jamie agreed with her, "I guess it is better to look for clues. After all, we're doing something that none of the experts can do."

Claudia's impatience surfaced. She had to pick a fight with Jamie. "Don't be silly. They can read all this stuff, too. There's certainly plenty of it."

"Oh, I don't mean that. I mean that we're living with the statue. You know what they always say: The only two ways to get to know someone are to live with him or play cards with him."

"Well, at least the little statue can't cheat at cards like someone else I know."

---

4. A statue representing Cupid, the Roman god of erotic love.
5. Two of Michelangelo's most famous sculptures, completed in 1504 and about 1515, respectively (now in Florence and in Rome).

6. I.e., Spot. Books in the Dick and Jane series (published 1930–65) were the dominant U.S. primers in the 1940s and 1950s (see the Primers and Readers section, above).

1773

FROM THE MIXED-
UP FILES OF
MRS. BASIL E.
FRANKWEILER,
CH. 5

"Claudia, dear, I'm no angel. Statue or otherwise."

Claudia sighed, "O.K. Sir James, let's go." And they did.

As they were walking up the steps, Jamie spied a Hershey's almond bar still in its wrapper lying in the corner of the landing. He picked it up and tore open one corner.

"Was it bitten into?" asked Claudia.

"No," Jamie smiled. "Want half?"

"You better not touch it," Claudia warned. "It's probably poisoned or filled with marijuana, so you'll eat it and become either dead or a dope addict."

Jamie was irritated. "Couldn't it just happen that someone dropped it?"

"I doubt that. Who would drop a whole candy bar and not know it? That's like leaving a statue in a taxi. Someone put it there on purpose. Someone who pushed dope. I read once that they feed dope in chocolates to little kids, and then the kids become dope addicts, then these people sell them dope at very high prices which they just can't help but buy because when you're addicted you have to have your dope. High prices and all. And Jamie, we don't have that kind of money."

Jamie said, "Oh, well, bottoms up." He took a big bite of the candy, chewed and swallowed. Then he closed his eyes, leaned against the wall and slid to the floor. Claudia stood with her mouth open, stunned. She was on the verge of screaming for help when Jamie opened his eyes and smiled. "It's delicious. Want a bite?"

Claudia not only refused the bite, she also refused to talk to Jamie until they got to the restaurant. Lunch cheered her. She suggested that they play in Central Park[7] for a while, and they did. They bought peanuts, chestnuts, and pretzels from the vendor outside the museum. They knew that since the museum opened late on Sunday, they would accumulate a lot of hunger before they got out. Their bulging pockets were now full of the staples of life: food and clothing.

Jamie entered the men's room. He had arrived, as was his custom, shortly before the first bell rang, the bell that warned everyone that the museum would close in five minutes. He waited; the bell rang. He got into a booth. First bell, second bell, it was routine just as boarding the school bus had once been routine. After the first day, they had learned that the staff worked from nine A.M. until five P.M., a work schedule just like their father's. Routine, routine. The wait from nine when the staff came until ten when the public came seemed long. Claudia and Jamie had decided that the washrooms were good for the shorter evening wait when the help left at the same time as the visitors, but the washrooms were less satisfactory for the long morning wait . . . especially after Jamie's close call that first morning. So time from eight forty-five until some safe time after ten in the mornings was spent under various beds. They always checked for dust under the bed first. And for once Claudia's fussiness was not the reason. Reason was the reason. A dustless floor meant that it had been cleaned very recently, and they stood less chance of being caught by a mop.

Jamie stood on the toilet seat waiting. He leaned his head against the wall of the booth and braced himself for what would happen next. The guard would come in and make a quick check of his station. Jamie still felt a ping during that short inspection; that was the only part that still wasn't quite routine, and that's why he braced himself. Then the lights would be turned out. Jamie would wait twelve minutes (lag time, Claudia called it) and emerge from hiding.

Except.

Except the guard didn't come, and Jamie couldn't relax until after he felt that final ping. And the lights stayed on, stayed on. Jamie checked his watch ten times within

7. New York City's largest park; the Metropolitan Museum of Art is located on its eastern edge.

five minutes; he shook his arm and held the watch up to his ear. It was ticking slower than his heart and much more softly. What was wrong? They had caught Claudia! Now they would look for him! He'd pretend he didn't speak English. He wouldn't answer any questions.

Then he heard the door open. Footsteps. More footsteps than usual. What was happening? The hardest part was that every corpuscle of Jamie's nine-year-old self was throbbing with readiness to run, and he had to bind up all that energy into a quiet lump. It was like trying to wrap a loose peck of potatoes into a neat four-cornered package. But he managed to freeze. He heard the voices of two men talking over the sound of water running in the sink.

"I guess they expect even more people tomorrow."

"Yeah. Sundays are always jammed up anyway."

"It'll be easier to move the people in and out of the Great Hall."

"Yeah. Two feet of marble. What do you figure it weighs?"

"I dunno. Whatever it weighs, it has to be handled delicate. Like it was a real angel."

"C'mon. They probably have the new pedestal ready. We can start."

"Do you think they'll have as many people as they had for the Mona Lisa?"[8]

"Naw! The Mona Lisa was here for a short time only. Besides it was the real McCoy."

"I think this one's. . ."

The men left, turning off the lights as they did so. Jamie heard the door close before he melted. Legs first. He sat down on the seat as he allowed the familiar darkness as well as new realization to fill him.

They were moving Angel. Did Claudia know? They wouldn't have women moving the statue. There would be no one in the ladies' room washing up. Who would give her the information? He would. By mental telepathy. He would think a message to Claudia. He folded his hands across his forehead and concentrated. "Stay put, Claudia, stay put. Stay put. Stay put. Claudia, stay put." He thought that Claudia would not approve of the grammar in his mental telegram; she would want him to think *stay in place*. But he didn't want to weaken his message by varying it one bit. He continued thinking STAY PUT.

He must have thought STAY PUT exactly hard enough, for Claudia did just that. They never knew exactly why she did, but she did. Perhaps she sensed some sounds that told her that the museum was not yet empty. Maybe she was just too tired from running around in Central Park. Maybe they were not meant to get caught. Maybe they were meant to make the discovery they made.

They waited for miles and miles of time before they came out of hiding. At last they met in their bedroom. Claudia was sorting the laundry when Jamie got there. In the dark, mostly by feel. Although there is no real difference between boys' stretch socks and girls', neither ever considered wearing the other's. Children who have always had separate bedrooms don't.

Claudia turned when she heard Jamie come up and said, "They moved the statue."

"How did you know? Did you get my message?"

"Message? I saw the statue on my way here. They have a dim light on it. I guess so that the night guard won't trip over it."

---

8. One of the most famous portraits in the world (1503–06), by Leonardo da Vinci. When the painting was on loan to the Metropolitan Museum in 1963, more than 1 million visitors saw it in less than a month.

Jamie replied, "We're lucky we didn't get caught."

1775

FROM THE MIXED-
UP FILES OF
MRS. BASIL E.
FRANKWEILER,
CH. 5

Claudia never thought very hard about the plus-luck she had; she concentrated on the minus-luck. "But they held us up terribly. I planned on our taking baths tonight. I really can't stand one night more without a bath."

"I don't mind," Jamie said.

"Come along, Sir James. To our bath. Bring your most elegant pajamas. The ones embroidered in gold with silver tassels will do."

"Where, dear Lady Claudia, dost thou expect to bathe?"

"In the fountain, Sir James. In the fountain."

Jamie extended his arm, which was draped with his striped flannel pajamas, and said, "Lady Claudia, I knew that sooner or later you would get me to that restaurant."

(It makes me furious to think that I must explain that restaurant to you, Saxonberg. I'm going to make you take me to lunch in there one day soon. I just this minute became determined to get you into the museum. You'll see later how I'm going to do it. Now about the restaurant. It is built around a gigantic fountain.[9] Water in the fountain is sprayed from dolphins sculptured in bronze. The dolphins appear to be leaping out of the water. On their backs are figures representing the arts, figures that look like water sprites. It is a joy to sit around that wonderful fountain and to snack petit fours and sip espresso coffee. I'll bet that you'd even forget your blasted ulcer while you ate there.)

Lady Claudia and Sir James quietly walked to the entrance of the restaurant. They easily climbed under the velvet rope that meant that the restaurant was closed to the public. Of course they were not the public. They shed their clothes and waded into the fountain. Claudia had taken powdered soap from the restroom. She had ground it out into a paper towel that morning. Even though it was freezing cold, she enjoyed her bath. Jamie, too, enjoyed his bath. For a different reason.

When he got into the pool, he found bumps on the bottom; smooth bumps. When he reached down to feel one, he found that it moved! He could even pick it up. He felt its cool roundness and splashed his way over to Claudia. "Income, Claudia, income!" he whispered.

Claudia understood immediately and began to scoop up bumps she had felt on the bottom of the fountain. The bumps were pennies and nickels people had pitched into the fountain to make a wish. At least four people had thrown in dimes and one had tossed in a quarter.

"Some one very rich must have tossed in this quarter," Jamie whispered.

"Some one very poor," Claudia corrected. "Rich people have only penny wishes."

Together they collected $2.87. They couldn't hold more in their hands. They were shivering when they got out. Drying themselves as best they could with paper towels (also taken from the restroom), they hurried into their pajamas and shoes.

They finished their preparations for the night, took a small snack and decided it was safe to wander back into the Great Hall to look again at their Angel.

"I wish I could hug her," Claudia whispered.

"They probably bugged her already. Maybe that light is part of the alarm. Better not touch. You'll set it off."

"I said 'hug' not 'bug!' Why would I want to bug her?"

"That makes more sense than to hug her."

"Silly. Shows how much you know. When you hug someone, you learn something else about them. An important something else."

9. This fountain is no longer in the museum restaurant.

Jamie shrugged his shoulders.

Both looked at Angel a long time. "What do you think?" Jamie asked. "Did he or didn't he?"

Claudia answered, "A scientist doesn't make up his mind until he's examined all the evidence."

"You sure don't sound like a scientist. What kind of scientist would want to hug a statue?"

Claudia was embarrassed, so she spoke sternly, "We'll go to bed now, and we'll think about the statue very hard. Don't fall asleep until you've really thought about the statue and Michelangelo and the entire Italian Renaissance."

And so they went to bed. But lying in bed just before going to sleep is the worst time for *organized* thinking; it is the best time for free thinking. Ideas drift like clouds in an undecided breeze, taking first this direction and then that. It was very difficult for Jamie to control his thoughts when he was tired, sleepy, and lying on his back. He never liked to get involved just before falling asleep. But Claudia had planned on their thinking, and she was good at planning. So think he did. Clouds bearing thoughts of the Italian Renaissance drifted away. Thoughts of home, and more thoughts of home settled down.

"Do you miss home?" he asked Claudia.

"Not too much," she confessed. "I haven't thought about it much."

Jamie was quiet for a minute; then he said, "We probably have no conscience. I think we ought to be homesick. Do you think Mom and Dad raised us wrong? They're not very mean, you know; don't you think that should make us miss them?"

Claudia was silent. Jamie waited. "Did you hear my question, Claude?"

"Yes. I heard your question. I'm thinking." She was quiet a while longer. Then she asked, "Have you ever been homesick?"

"Sure."

"When was the last time?"

"That day Dad dropped us off at Aunt Zell's when he took Mom to the hospital to get Kevin."

"Me, too. That day," Claudia admitted. "But, of course, I was much younger then."

"Why do you suppose we were homesick that day? We've been gone much longer than that now."

Claudia thought. "I guess we were worried. Boy, had I known then that she was going to end up with Kevin, I would have known why we were worried. I remember you sucked your thumb and carried around that old blanket the whole day. Aunt Zell kept trying to get the blanket away from you so that she could wash it. It stank."

Jamie giggled, "Yeah, I guess homesickness is like sucking your thumb. It's what happens when you're not very sure of yourself."

"Or not very well trained," Claudia added. "Heaven knows, we're well trained. Just look how nicely we've managed. It's really their fault if we're not homesick."

Jamie was satisfied. Claudia was more. "I'm glad you asked that about homesickness, Jamie. Somehow, I feel older now. But, of course, that's mostly because I've been the oldest child forever. And I'm extremely well adjusted."

They went to sleep then. Michelangelo, Angel, and the entire Italian Renaissance waited for them until morning.

6

It was still dark when they awoke the next morning, but it was later than usual. The museum wouldn't open until one. Claudia was up first. She was getting dressed when Jamie opened his eyes.

"You know," he said, "Sunday is still Sunday. It *feels* like Sunday. Even here."

Claudia answered, "I noticed that. Do you think we ought to try to go to church when we go out?"

Jamie thought a minute before answering, "Well, let's say a prayer in that little room of the Middle Ages. The part with the pretty stained glass window."

They dressed and walked to the little chapel and knelt and said *The Lord's Prayer*.[1] Jamie reminded Claudia to say she was sorry for stealing the newspaper. That made it officially Sunday.

"C'mon," Claudia said as she was rising, "let's go to the statue."

They walked over to Angel and looked very closely. It was difficult to look for clues. Even after their research. They were accustomed to having all the clues neatly laid out on a diagram placed in front of the exhibit. "See the clues where the..."

"I still say that it's too bad we can't touch her," Claudia complained.

"At least we're living with it. We're the only two people in the whole world who live with it."

"Mrs. Frankweiler did, too. She could touch . . ."

"And hug it," Jamie teased.

1. Matthew 6.9–13.

"I'll bet she knows for sure if Michelangelo did it."

"Sure she does," Jamie said. He then threw his arms around himself, leaned his head way back, closed his eyes, and murmured, "Every morning when she got up, Mrs. Frankweiler would throw her arms about the statue, peer into its eyes, and say, 'speak to me, baby.' One morning the statue ans . . ."

Claudia was furious. "The men who moved it last night hugged it when they moved it. There's all kinds of hugging."

She refused to look at Jamie again and instead stared at the statue. The sound of footsteps broke the silence and her concentration. Footsteps from the Italian Renaissance were descending upon them! The guard was coming down the steps. Oh, boloney! thought Jamie. There was just too much time before the museum opened on Sundays. They should have been in hiding already. Here they were out in the open with a light on!

Jamie grabbed Claudia's hand and pulled her behind the booth where they rent walkie-talkies for a tour of the museum. Even though they were well hidden by the dark as they squatted there, they felt as exposed as that great bare lady in the painting upstairs.

The footsteps stopped in front of Angel. Jamie sent another mental telegram: Get going, get going, get going. Of course it worked. The guard moved on toward the Egyptian wing to cover the rest of his tour. The two children wouldn't even allow themselves a sigh of relief. They were that well disciplined.

After ten minutes lag time, Jamie tugged the hem of Claudia's jacket, and they cautiously got up. Jamie led the way back up the great stairway. As he did so, his logic became clear to Claudia. Thank goodness Jamie thought so clearly so fast, and thank goodness for those twenty acres of floor space. It would take the watchman more than an hour before he passed that way again.

They stealthily climbed the wide stairway, staying close to the rail. Step, pause. Step, pause. All the way to the top until they found themselves in front of the pedestal on which Angel had stood just the day before. Claudia paused to look; partly from habit and partly because anything associated with Angel was precious. Jamie paused to catch his breath.

"Why do you think they changed the velvet under her from blue to gold?" Claudia whispered.

"This blue probably got dirty. C'mon, let's hide."

Claudia looked again at the velvet. Light was beginning to seep into the museum. Something on top of the velvet caught her eye. "One of the workmen must have been drinking beer when he moved the statue."

"Most people drink beer," Jamie said. "What's so unusual about that?"

"They don't let visitors bring in beer," answered Claudia. "I wonder why they allow the workers to do it? What if he had spilled it on Angel? See where he must have put his beer can on that platform." She pointed to the blue velvet covering the pedestal. "See the rings where the pile of the velvet isn't crushed."

Jamie said, "Yeah, Ballantine beer. Those three rings."[2] Then he began humming a commercial that he had heard during the baseball game on television last spring.

Claudia interrupted, "Those are the marks of the beer can itself. After all, the emblem on the can is flat against the can. It could have been any kind of beer. Schlitz, Rheingold."

Jamie stared at the blue velvet. "You're right, Claude. Except for one thing."

2. The brand's logo is three interlocking rings.

1779

FROM THE MIXED-
UP FILES OF
MRS. BASIL E.
FRANKWEILER,
CH. 6

"What's that?" she asked.

"The rings the beer cans made would have crushed the plush of the velvet *down* . . . and the plush of this velvet is crushed *up*."

"What kind of a sentence is that? Crushed *up*!"

"Oh, boloney! You just go ahead and pick on my grammar. Go ahead pick on my grammar. But you can't pick on my logic. The weight of the statue crushed all the velvet down except where the marble was chipped away and the plush was crushed up. Claudia, there's a crushed-up *W* in one of those circles that is also crushed up."

"For goodness' sake, Jamie. That's not a *W*; that's an *M*." She looked at Jamie, and her eyes widened, "*M* for Michelangelo!"

Jamie was rubbing his eyes. "You know, Claude, I saw that symbol yesterday on the cover of one of the books I looked at."

"What was it, Jamie? What was it?"

"How should I know? You were supposed to be doing the reading! I was just supposed to be looking for pictures and clues."

"James Kincaid, you are *something*. You are *absolutely* something. As if it would have hurt you to read one little thing. Just one little thing!"

Jamie said, "Well, we have a clue."

"We could know already."

"We have an important clue. I'll bet they never even looked at the bottom of the statue."

"Now we have to go back to the library today to find out what that symbol means. But we can't! That library is closed on Sundays. Oh, Jamie, I've got to know."

"We'll check the museum bookshop. Don't worry, Claude; I'll recognize the book. Right now, we better hide."

Claudia glanced at her watch. "Where are we going to hide up here? There's no furniture. We can't risk going downstairs again."

Jamie picked up a corner of the blue velvet drape. "Be my guest," he said indicating the floor under the platform with an elegant sweep of his hand.

Jamie and Claudia squatted under the platform waiting. It was close quarters under there. Jamie needed only to point his fingers to poke his sister in the ribs. "I say, Lady Claudia, I do believe we're safe and onto something really great."

"Perhaps, Sir James, perhaps."

Claudia didn't think about their close calls. They were unimportant; they wouldn't matter in the end, the end having something to do with Michelangelo, Angel, history, and herself. She thought about the history test she had had on Monday at school. There had been a question on the test that she couldn't answer. She had studied hard and read the chapter thoroughly. She knew where the answer was—the second paragraph in the right hand column of page 157. In her mind she could actually see *where* the *answer* was, but she couldn't think of *what* it was.

Angel was that way. An answer to running away, and also to going home again, lay in Angel. She knew it was there, but she didn't know what it was. It was just escaping her as the answer to the question on the test had . . . except this was even harder, for she wasn't exactly certain of the question she was trying to answer. The question had something to do with why Angel had become more important than having run away or even being safe, at the museum. Oh! she was right back where she had started. It was too stuffy under that velvet. How could anyone think straight? No wonder her thinking came out in circles. She knew one thing for sure: maybe they had a clue.

A crowd formed in front of the museum before it opened. The guard who was to have removed the pedestal and drape was called outside to set up sawhorses and make orderly rows out of the mass of people. The museum couldn't spare Morris until after the police had sent help for the sidewalk traffic. When he finally moved the platform and drape and took them to the basement for storage, Claudia and Jamie had already left and were browsing around the crowded bookshop peeking under the dust jackets of books about Michelangelo.

They found the book with the mark on the cover! The crushed-up mark on the dark blue velvet was Michelangelo's stonemason's mark. He had chipped it into the base of the marble to identify himself as owner, much as brands are burned into the hides of cattle to identify their owners.

They emerged from the bookshop feeling triumphant. And hungry.

"C'mon," Claudia shouted as soon as they got out, "Let's grab a taxi to the Automat."

"We'll walk," Jamie said.

"We have income now. All we have to do is take a bath whenever we need money." Jamie thought a second. "O.K. I'll allow a bus."

Claudia smiled. "Thank you, Mr. Pinchpenny."

"You call me Pinchpenny, and I'll call you . . ."

"Call me a taxi," she laughed, running toward the bus stop in front of the museum.

Jamie was feeling so satisfied that he gave Claudia seventy-five cents for brunch. He allowed himself the same. As they ate, they discussed what they should do about the awesome information they had.

"Let's call the *New York Times*," Jamie suggested.

"All that publicity! They'll want to know how we found out."

"Let's call the head of the Metropolitan."

"*He'll* want to know how we found out."

"We'll tell him," Jamie said.

"Are you out of your mind?" Claudia asked. "Tell him we've been living there?"

"Don't you think we ought to tell the museum about the crushed-up mark on the velvet?"

"We owe it to them," Claudia answered. "We've been their guests all this time."

"Then you figure out how we can let them know without getting caught. I'll bet you already have it all worked out."

"As a matter of fact, I do." Claudia leaned across the table and spoke to Jamie in her best secret agent fashion. "We'll write them a letter and tell them to look at the base of the statue for an important clue."

"What if they can't figure out what the clue is?"

"We'll help them with that when they need help. We'll reveal ourselves then. And they'll be very happy to have been our hosts," Claudia said. She paused long enough for Jamie to begin to get impatient, but just begin. "Here's the plan: we rent a post office box in Grand Central. Like when you send in box tops, you always send them to P.O. Box Number So-and-so. We write a letter and tell them to answer us at the box number. After they tell us that they need help, we reveal ourselves. As heroes."

"Can't we go home and wait? That was rough last night and this morning. Besides, then we can be heroes twice. Once when we return home and once when we reveal ourselves."

"No!" Claudia screeched. "We have to know about Angel first. We have to be right."

1781

FROM THE MIXED-
UP FILES OF
MRS. BASIL E.
FRANKWEILER,
CH. 6

"Wow! What's the matter with you, Claude? You know you planned on going home sometime."

"Yes," she answered, "sometime. But not just anytime." Her voice was becoming high pitched again.

"Anytime we come home—from a visit to Grandpa's or from summer camp— they're always glad to see us."

"But it never makes any difference. Going home without knowing about Angel for sure will be the same as going home from camp. It won't be any different. After one day, maybe two, we'll be back to the same old thing. And I didn't run away to come home the same."

"Well, this has been more fun than camp. Even the food's been better. There's that difference."

"But, Jamie, it's not enough."

"Yeah, I know, it's not enough. I'm hungry most of the time."

"I mean the difference is not enough. Like being born with perfect pitch, or being born very ordinary and then winning the Congressional Medal of Honor or getting an Academy Award.[3] Those are differences that will last a lifetime. Finding out about Angel will be that kind of difference.

"I think you're different already, Claude."

"Do you?" she asked. She was smiling and her eyes were modestly lowered, ready for a compliment.

"Yes. We're all sane, and you're *insane*."

"Jamie Kincaid!"

"O.K. O.K. I'm insane, too. I'll go along with you. Besides some of the complications are getting interesting, even though some are dull. How will you disguise your handwriting?"

"No need to do that. I'll use a typewriter."

Claudia waited for Jamie's look of surprise.

She got it. "Where are you going to get a typewriter?"

"In front of the Olivetti[4] place on Fifth Avenue. We passed it twice yesterday. Once when you made us walk from the laundromat. And again when we walked from library to library. It's bolted to a stand outside the building for everyone to use. You know, sort of a sample of their product. It's free."

Jamie smiled, "It's a good thing that I'm insane about walking. Otherwise, you would never have found that typewriter."

"And it's a good thing that I'm an excellent observer," Claudia added.

They marched up Fifth Avenue and were delighted to find a piece of paper already in the typewriter. Across the top of the page someone had typed: Now is the time for all good men to come to the aid of their party. Claudia didn't know that this sentence was a common one used in practice typing. She thought it appeared appropriate to their message and would add a proper note of mystery besides. (Here, Saxonberg, is a copy of the letter Claudia typed. You can see that her typing needed a great deal of improvement.)

---

3. Award given annually (in various categories) by the Academy of Motion Picture Arts and Sciences. "Medal of Honor": the highest American military decoration, awarded to individuals for valor in action against an enemy force.
4. A brand of typewriter; the showroom was on Fifth Avenue at 47th Street.

Now is the time for all good men to come to the aid of their party;

Dear Museum Head,

We think that you should examine the bottom of the statue for an important clue. The statue we mean is the ~~sea~~ one you bought for $225.00. And the clue is that you will find Michelangelo's stone mason's mark on the bottom. If you need help about this clue, you may write to us at Grand Central Post Office. Box 847 in Manhanttan.

Sincerely,
Friends of the Museum

Pleased with their effort, they felt that they could take the rest of the day off. They wandered around Rockefeller Center[5] and watched the skaters for a short while. They watched the crowd watching the skaters for a while longer. When they returned to the museum filled with satisfaction and with snacks for their supper, they saw a long line of Sunday people waiting to climb the museum steps. Knowing that everyone in that line would be shepherded in and out, in front of and past the statue in a matter of minutes, they decided to enter through the rear entrance. Instead the guard at that door told them that they would have to use the Fifth Avenue entrance if they wished to see Angel.

"Oh, we've already seen that!" Jamie said.

The guard from friendliness, helpfulness or, perhaps, sheer loneliness (very few people had entered through his door that day) asked Jamie what he thought of it.

"Well, we need to do more research, but it seems to me that . . ."

Claudia pulled Jamie's arm. "Come along, *Albert,*" she urged.

On their way to the rooms containing Greek vases, they again observed the enormous crowd passing by the statue.

"As I was about to tell that guard, it seems to me that they should try to get to the *bottom* of the mystery."

Claudia giggled; Jamie joined in. They spent exactly enough time among the vases of ancient Greece to be able to man their waiting stations and not be discovered.

7

When they left the museum on Monday morning, Claudia walked to the bus stop without even consulting Jamie.

"Don't you think we ought to get breakfast first?" he asked.

"Mail early in the day," Claudia answered. "Besides, we want them to get this letter as soon as possible."

"It will get there faster if we deliver it by hand," Jamie suggested.

"Good idea. We'll get our mailbox number, write it in, and then take it to the museum office."

Since Jamie was official treasurer of the team, it was he who approached the man behind the cage window at the post office.

"I would like to rent a post office box," he declared.

"For how long?" the man inquired.

"For about two days."

5. An enormous complex of office buildings and stores, located between 5th and 6th Avenues and 48th and 51st Streets; its sunken plaza contains a popular outdoor skating rink.

1783

FROM THE MIXED-
UP FILES OF
MRS. BASIL E.
FRANKWEILER,
CH. 7

"Sorry," the man said, "we rent them quarterly."

"All right, then. I'll take eight quarterlies. That makes two days."

"Quarter of a year," the man said. "That makes three months."

"Just a minute," Jamie said. He held a whispered conference with Claudia.

"Go ahead. Rent it," she urged.

"It'll cost a stack of money."

"Why don't you find out instead of arguing about it now?" Claudia's whisper began to sound like cold water hitting a hot frying pan.

"How much will a quarter of a year be?" he asked the postman.

"Four dollars and fifty cents."

Jamie scowled at Claudia. "See. I told you a stack."

Claudia shrugged her shoulders, "We'll take a long, long bath tonight."

The postman hardly looked puzzled. People working at the Grand Central Post Office grow used to strange remarks. They hear so many. They never stop hearing them; they simply stop sending the messages to their brains. Like talking into a telephone with no one on the receiver end. "Do you or don't you want it?" he asked.

"I'll take it."

Jamie paid the rent, signed a form using the name Angelo Michaels and gave his address as Marblehead, Massachusetts. He received a key to Box Number 847. Jamie-Angelo-Kincaid-Michaels felt important having a key to his own mailbox. He found his box and opened the little door.

"You know," he remarked to Claudia, "it's a lot like Horn and Hardart's. Except that we could have a complete spaghetti dinner for both of us coming out of the little door instead of just empty, empty space.

Paying four dollars and fifty cents for empty space had been hard on Jamie. Claudia knew they wouldn't take a bus back to the museum. They didn't.

Both Claudia and Jamie wanted to deliver the letter, but neither thought he should. Too risky. They decided to ask someone to deliver it for them. Someone with a bad memory for faces. Someone their own age would be best; someone who might be nosey but who wouldn't really care about them. It would be easiest to find a school group and select their messenger. They began their search for the group of the day by looking in the usual places: Arms and Armor, the Costume Institute, and Egyptian Art. As they approached the Egyptian wing, they heard the shuffling of feet and a sound they recognized as the folding of chairs and the gathering up of rubber mats. They weren't anxious to hear the talk about mummies again; they never watched repeats on television, either. But they decided to look the group over. So they waited inside the tomb.

(Now, Saxonberg, I must tell you about that Egyptian tomb called a mastaba. It is not a whole one; it is the beginning of one. You can walk into it. You can spend a lot of time in it, or you can spend very little time in it. You can try to read the picture writing on the walls. Or you can read nothing at all. Whether you read or not, whether you spend a lot of time or a little in that piece of Ancient Egypt, you will have changed climate for at least that part of your day. It is not a hard place to wait in at all.)

The group was moving past the entrance. Claudia and Jamie were relaxed and waiting—wrapped up in the vacuum of time created by those warm stone walls. Puffs of conversation broke the silence of their tomb.

"Sarah looks like pharaoh.[6] Pass it on."

---

6. Literally, "great house": the title given to ancient Egyptian rulers, who are often depicted with headgear falling squarely around their faces.

"When are we gonna eat?"

"Man, what a lot of walking."

The conversation rained in softly and comfortably and told the two stowaways that they had the correct age group. That was the way kids in their classes always talked. Words continued to drizzle into their shelter.

"Hey, Rube, look at this."

"C'mon, Bruce, let me borrow it."

Something else now showered down upon them. Something much less comfortable. *Familiarity!* The names, Sarah, Bruce, Rube, were familiar . . . Ages ago, in time well outside the mastaba, they had heard these names—in a classroom, on a school bus . . .

Closer, louder, the sounds poured in. Then one small cloud burst right outside their door.

"Hey, let's go back in here."

Jamie's eyes caught Claudia's. He opened his mouth. Claudia didn't wait to discover whether he opened it in surprise or to say something. She clamped her hand over his mouth as fast as she could.

An adult voice urged, "Come on, boys. We have to stay with the group."

Claudia took her hand from Jamie's mouth. She looked at him solemnly and nodded *yes*. The "come-on-boys" voice belonged to Miss Clendennan, Jamie's third grade teacher. Rube was Reuben Hearst, and Bruce was Bruce Lansing. Sarah was Sarah Sawhill, and unfortunately, she did look a great deal like pharaoh. Believe it or not, the mountain had come to Mohammed;[7] their school had come to them. At least, Jamie's class had.

Jamie was furious. Why had Claudia muzzled him? Did she think he had no sense at all? He pulled his eyebrows down and made his best possible scowl. Claudia held her finger up to her lips and signaled him to stay quiet yet. The sounds of third grade shuffling and third grade jostling faded from their shelter. The quiet of the ages returned to the tomb.

But not to Jamie. He couldn't contain himself another minute. He could still feel the pressure of Claudia's hand over his mouth. "I have half a mind to join that group and go back with them and just be mysterious about where I came from."

"If you do that, it'll show that you have half a mind. Exactly half. Only half. Something I've suspected for a long time. You can't even see that this is perfect."

"How perfect?"

Claudia slowed down. "You go to the museum office. Deliver the letter. Tell them you are in the third grade group that is visiting from Greenwich and someone asked you to deliver the letter. The teacher said it would be O.K. If they ask you your name, say Bruce Lansing. But only if they ask."

"You know, Claude, when I'm not wishing I could give you a sock right in the nose, I'm glad you're on my team. You're smart even if you're hard to live with."

"You'll do it then?" Claudia asked.

"Yeah, I'll do it. It *is* perfect."

"Let's hurry before they come back."

Jamie entered the museum office, and Claudia stood guard outside the door. She intended to step inside the office if she spotted the class returning. Jamie wasn't gone long. Everything had gone well, and they hadn't asked his name. Claudia grabbed

---

7. An allusion to the proverb "If the mountain will not come to Mohammed, then Mohammed must go to the mountain."

1785

FROM THE MIXED-
UP FILES OF
MRS. BASIL E.
FRANKWEILER,
CH. 8

his arm as he came out. All the energy of Jamie's wound up nerves let loose. He collapsed as hard as if Claudia had suddenly jumped off the down end of a teeter-totter while he was still sitting on the up end.

"Yikes!" he yelled. Claudia was tempted to muzzle him again, but didn't. Instead she led him out the door into the Fifth Avenue crowd and began walking uptown with him as fast as she could go.

8

On Tuesday they again did their laundry. The product of their efforts this time looked only slightly grayer than it had the time before. Claudia's sweater was considerably shrunken.

They knew that it was too early to get an answer to their letter, but they couldn't resist starting down to Grand Central Post Office to take a look anyway. It was noon by the time they stopped and ate breakfast at a Chock Full O'Nuts[8] on Madison Avenue. They dragged it out beyond the patience of the people who were standing waiting to occupy their seats. Both Claudia and Jamie almost didn't want to look at their box in the post office. As long as they didn't look, they still had hopes that they could find a letter there.

They didn't. They strolled along the streets and found themselves near the United Nations building.[9] Claudia suggested to Jamie that they take the guided tour she had read about when she was studying the Tourguide Book of the American Automobile Association.

"Today we can learn everything about the U.N."

Jamie's first question was, "How much?"

Claudia challenged him to walk in and find out. Fifty cents. Each. They could go if Claudia was willing to skip dessert that afternoon.

Jamie added, "You know, you can't have your cake and take tours, too."

"How about having tours and hot fudge sundaes, too?" Claudia asked.

They stood in line and got tickets for a tour. The girl selling tickets smiled down at them. "No school today?" she asked casually.

"No," Jamie answered. "The boiler on the furnace broke. No heat. They had to dismiss school. You should have heard the explosion! All the windows rattled. We thought it was an earthquake. Fourteen kids got cuts and abrasions, and their parents are suing the school to pay for their medical expenses. Well, it was about ten in the morning. We had just finished our spelling lesson when . . ."

The man behind Jamie who was dressed in a derby hat and who looked more as if he belonged in the U.N. than visiting it said, "I say, what's holding up this line? *I repeat*, what is *holding* up this line?"

The girl gave Jamie the two tickets. As she did so, the man in the derby hat was already pushing his money onto the counter. The girl looked after Jamie and Claudia as they were leaving and said, "Where is . . ."

She couldn't finish her question. The man in the derby hat was scolding the girl. "No wonder it takes the U.N. forever to get something done. I've never seen a line move more slowly." He only looked as if he belonged; he certainly didn't act it.

The girl blushed as she gave the man his ticket. "I hope you enjoy your tour, sir." She acted as if she belonged.

8. A chain of coffee shops.
9. The headquarters of the United Nations is located between 42nd and 47th Streets and First Avenue and the East River.

Jamie and Claudia sat with other ticket holders waiting for their numbers to be called.

Claudia spoke softly to Jamie, "You sure are a fast thinker. Where did you cook up that story about the furnace?"

"I've had it ready and waiting ever since we left home. First chance I've had to use it," he answered.

"I thought I had thought of everything," Claudia said.

"That's O.K."

"You're quite a kid."

"Thanks." Jamie smiled.

The guide who was calling the numbers finally said, "Will the people holding tickets number 106 to 121 please go to the double doors on the wall opposite this desk. There your guide will begin your tour."

Jamie and Claudia went. Their guide was an Indian girl who wore a sari[1] and whose long hair was bound into a single braid that hung down her back to well below her waist. With one hand she lifted the folds of her sari; her walk was flavored by her costume: her steps were short and light and there appeared to be great movement around her knees. Claudia looked at her guide's skin and thought of smoky topaz: November, her mother's birthstone. She listened to her guide's accent and formed the sounds in her mind without listening to what the sounds said.

Thus, when the tour was finished, Claudia was no expert on the United Nations, but she had discovered something: saris are a way of being different. She could do two things, she decided. When she was grown, she could stay the way she was and move to some place like India where no one dressed as she did, or she could dress like someone else—the Indian guide even—and still live in an ordinary place like Greenwich.

"How did you like those ear phones[2] where you can tune in almost any old language at all?" Jamie asked his sister. "Pretty keen, huh?"

Claudia seemed to have a far away look in her eye.

"Yes," she answered. It sounded like "yah-ess." Jamie inspected Claudia closely. She was holding one arm crooked and the other pressed against her stomach. Her steps seemed shorter than usual and lighter than usual, and there appeared to be great movement around her knees.

"What's the matter with you?" he asked. "You got stomach cramps or something?"

Claudia lowered her eyes to him and said, "Jamie, you know, you could go clear around the world and still come home wondering if the tuna fish sandwiches at Chock Full O'Nuts still cost thirty-five cents."

"Is that what gave you stomach cramps?" he asked.

"Oh, just skip it! Just skip it." Claudia knew she would have to discover some other way to be different. Angel *would* help her somehow.

Her hopes centered more than ever on Box 847 in the post office, and the following day when they peeked through its little window, they saw an envelope. Claudia was prepared to be the discoverer of great truths, Greenwich's own heroine of the statue—and only twelve years old. Jamie was so excited that he could hardly get the key into the lock to open the box. Claudia waited while he opened it and the envelope,

---

1. A garment traditionally worn by women of southern Asia; it consists of several yards of light cloth draped around the body.

2. Used to provide simultaneous translation into the six official languages of the United Nations.

too. He held the letter unfolded and off-center so that they could read it together. In silence.

Saxonberg, I have here attached a copy of the actual letter which I have in my files:

1787

FROM THE MIXED-
UP FILES OF
MRS. BASIL E.
FRANKWEILER,
CH. 8

> *Dear Friends of the Museum:*
>
> *We sincerely thank you for your interest in trying to help us solve the mystery of the statue. We have long known of the clue you mention; in fact, that clue remains our strongest one in attributing this work to the master, Michelangelo Buonarroti. Other evidence, however, is necessary, for it is known that Michelangelo did not carve all the marble blocks which were quarried for him and which bore his mark. We cannot ignore the possibility that the work may have been done by someone else, or that someone counterfeited the mark into the stone much later. We summarize the possibilities as follows:*
>
> 1. *The work was designed and done by Michelangelo himself.*
> 2. *The work was designed by Michelangelo but done by someone else.*
> 3. *The work was neither designed nor done by Michelangelo.*
>
> *Our hope, of course, is to find evidence to support the first of these three possibilities.*
>
> *Neither Condivi nor Vasari,[3] Michelangelo's biographers who knew him personally mention the master carving this little angel; they mention only the angel carved for the altar in Siena.[4] However, in a letter he wrote to his father from Rome on August 19, 1497, Michelangelo mentions ". . . I bought a piece of marble . . . I keep to myself, and I am sculpturing an image for my own pleasure." In the past experts have believed the image which he sculptured for his own pleasure to be a cupid. Now, we must examine the possibility that it was an angel.*
>
> *The problem of Angel has now become a matter for consensus. Four Americans, two Englishmen, and one German, all of whom are experts on the techniques of Michelangelo have thus far examined the statue. We are presently awaiting the arrival of two more experts from Florence,[5] Italy. After all of these experts have examined the statue, we will write a summary of their opinions which we will release to the press.*
>
> *We greatly appreciate your interest and would enjoy your disclosing further clues to us if you find them.*
>
> Sincerely,
>
> Harold C. Lowery
Public Relations,
The Metropolitan Museum of Art

Claudia and Jamie walked from the post office to Grand Central Terminal and sat down in the waiting room. They sat perfectly quiet. Disappointed beyond words.

---

3. Georgio Vasari (1511–1574), an Italian painter (a student of Michelangelo), architect, and art historian, best-known for his *Lives* (1550; rev. 1568) of Italian artists. Ascanio Condivi (ca. 1520–ca. 1574), an Italian painter; he published his *Life of Michelangelo* in 1553.

4. A city in Tuscany, about 35 miles south of Florence.

5. Because a number of Michelangelo's sculptures (including *David*, now in the Uffizi Gallery) are in Florence, it is natural that experts on his work would be based there.

Claudia would have felt better if the letter had not been so polite. A nasty letter or a sarcastic one can make you righteously angry, but what can you do about a polite letter of rejection? Nothing, really, except cry. So she did.

Jamie let her cry for a while. He sat there and fidgeted and counted the number of benches. She still cried; he counted the number of people on the benches. She was still at it; he calculated the number of people per bench.

After the big blobs of tears stopped, he said, "At least they treated us like grown-ups. That letter is full of big words and all."

"Big deal," Claudia sobbed. "For all they know, we *are* grown-ups." She was trying to find a corner of her shredded Kleenex that she could use.

Jamie let her sniff some, then he quietly asked, "What do we do now? Go home?"

"What? Go home now? We haven't even got our clothes. And your radio is in the violin case. We'd have to go home absolutely empty handed."

"We could leave our clothes; they're all gray anyway."

"But we never even used your radio. How can we face them at home? Without the radio and all. With nothing." She paused for a minute and repeated, "With nothing. We've accomplished nothing."

"We accomplished having fun," Jamie suggested. "Wasn't that what you wanted when we started out, Claude? I always thought it was."

Claudia began big tears again. "But that was then," she sobbed.

"You said you'd go home after you knew about Angel. Now you know."

"That's it," she sobbed. "I do not know."

"You know that you don't know. Just as the people at the museum don't know. C'mon," he pleaded, "we'll enjoy telling them about how we lived in the museum. The violin case can be evidence. Do you realize that we've lived there a whole week?"

"Yes," Claudia sighed. "Just a week. I feel as if I jumped into a lake to rescue a boy, and what I thought was a boy turned out to be a wet, fat log. Some heroine that makes. All wet for nothing." The tears flowed again.

"You sure are getting wet. You started this adventure just running away. Comfortably. Then the day before yesterday you decided you had to be a hero, too."

"Heroine. And how should I have known that I wanted to be a heroine when I had no idea I wanted to be a heroine? The statue just gave me a chance . . . almost gave me a chance. We need to make more of a discovery."

"So do the people at the museum. What more of discovery do you think that you, Claudia Kincaid, girl runaway, can make? A tape recording of Michelangelo saying, 'I did it?' Well, I'll clue you in. They didn't have tape recorders 470 years ago."

"I know that. But if we make a real discovery, I'll know *how* to go back to Greenwich."

"You take the New Haven, silly. Same way as we got here." Jamie was losing patience.

"That's not what I mean. I want to know how to go back to Greenwich different."

Jamie shook his head. "If you want to go different, you can take a subway to 125th Street and then take the train."

"I didn't say *differently*, I said *different*. I want to go back different. I, Claudia Kincaid, want to be different when I go back. Like being a heroine is being different."

"Claudia, I'll tell you one thing you can do different . . ."

"Differently," Claudia interrupted.

"Oh, boloney, Claude. That's exactly it. You can stop ending every single discussion with an argument about grammar."

"I'll try," Claudia said quietly.

1789

FROM THE MIXED-
UP FILES OF
MRS. BASIL E.
FRANKWEILER,
CH. 8

Jamie was surprised at her quiet manner, but he continued to be businesslike, "Now about this discovery."

"Jamie, I want to know if Michelangelo did it. I can't explain why exactly. But I feel that I've got to know. For sure. One way or the other. A real discovery is going to help me."

"If the experts don't know for sure, I don't mind not knowing. Let's get tickets for home." Jamie started toward the New Haven ticket window. Claudia stayed behind. Jamie realized that she was not following, returned to her, and lectured, "You're never satisfied, Claude. If you get all A's, you wonder where are the pluses. You start out just running away, and you end up wanting to know everything. Wanting to be Joan of Arc, Clara Barton, and Florence Nightingown[6] all in one."

"Nightingale," Claudia sighed. She got up then and followed slowly behind her brother. But she was feeling too low to go home. She couldn't. She just couldn't. It just wasn't right.

There were only two windows that didn't say, "Closed." They waited a short while as the man in front of them purchased a red commuter's pass like the one that had brought them to Manhattan.

Jamie addressed the man behind the counter and said, "Two half-fare tickets for . . ."

"FARMINGTON, CONNECTICUT," Claudia broke in.

"To get to Farmington, you have to go to Hartford and take a bus," the ticket agent said.

Jamie nodded to the man and said, "Just a minute, please." He stepped away from the window, grabbing Claudia's arm. He pulled her away.

Claudia whispered, "Mrs. Basil E. Frankweiler."

"What about Mrs. Basil E. Frankweiler?"

"She lives in Farmington."

"So what?" Jamie said. "The paper said that her house was closed."

"Her New York house was closed. Can't you read anything right?"

"You talk that way, Claude, and . . ."

"All right, Jamie. All right. I shouldn't talk that way. But, please let's go to Farmington. Jamie, please. Can't you see how badly I need to find out about Angel? I just have a hunch she'll see us and that she knows."

"I've never known you to have a hunch before, Claude. You usually plan everything."

"I have, too, had a hunch before."

"When?"

"That night they moved the statue and I stayed in the washroom and didn't get caught. That was a hunch. Even if I didn't know it was a hunch at the time."

"O.K. We'll go to Farmington," Jamie said. He marched to the ticket window and bought passage to Hartford.

They were waiting at track twenty-seven when Claudia said to Jamie, "That's a first for you, too."

"What is?" he asked.

6. Florence Nightingale (1820–1910), the British nurse and hospital reformer who gained fame for her work during the Crimean War (1853–56); she founded the first institution for the training of nurses (1860). Joan of Arc (ca. 1412–1431), the French national heroine (ultimately canonized as a saint) who, claiming divine guidance, successfully led a small army against the English. Barton (1821–1912), an American humanitarian who was largely responsible for founding the American Red Cross and served as its first president (1882–1904). All three women were characterized by single-minded determination.

"Buying something without asking the price first."

"Oh, I must have done that before now," he answered.

"When? Name one time."

"I can't think of it right now." He thought a minute then said, "I haven't been a tightwad all my life, have I?"

"As long as I've known you," Claudia answered.

"Well, you've known me for as long as I've known me," he said smiling.

"Yes," Claudia said, "I've been the oldest child since before you were born."

The enjoyed the train ride. A large portion of it went over track they had never before seen. Claudia arrived in Hartford feeling much happier than she had since they received the morning's mail. Her self-assurance had returned to her.

The Hartford station was on Farmington Avenue. Claudia reasoned that they could not be far from Farmington itself. Why take a bus and worry about which stop to get off? Without consulting Jamie she hailed a cab. When it stopped, she got in; Jamie followed. Claudia told the driver to take them to the house of Mrs. Basil E. Frankweiler in Farmington, Connecticut. Claudia sat back. In a taxi at last.

(And that, Saxonberg, is how I enter the story. Claudia and Jamie Kincaid came to see me about Angel.)

9

Up the entire length of my long, wide, tree-lined road they came.

"Do you suppose that Mrs. Frankweiler owns the highway?" Jamie asked.

The taxi driver answered, "This ain't no highway. It's all her propitty. I tell ya, this dame's loaded. In front of the house this here begins to resemble wattcha call a *normal* driveway."

Claudia discovered that indeed it does. My tree-lined avenue circles in front of my house. Jamie looked up at my house and said, "Another museum."

Claudia answered, "Then we should feel very much at home."

Jamie paid the taxi driver. Claudia pulled his arm and whispered, "Tip him."

Jamie shrugged his shoulders and gave the driver some money. The driver smiled, took off his hat, bowed from the waist, and said, "Thank you, sir."

After he drove away Claudia asked, "How much did you give him?"

Jamie answered, "All I had."

"That was stupid," Claudia said. "Now, how are we going to get back?"

Jamie sighed, "I gave him seventeen cents. So it wasn't such a great trip. Also, it would never be enough to get us back. We're broke. How do you feel about that, Miss Taxi Rider?"

"Pretty uncomfortable," she murmured. "There's something nice and safe about having money."

"Well, Claude, we just traded safety for adventure. Come along, Lady Claudia."

"You can't call me Lady Claudia anymore. We're paupers now."

They ascended the low, wide steps of my porch. Jamie rang the bell. Parks, my butler, answered.

"We'd like to see Mrs. Basil E. Frankweiler," Jamie told him.

"Whom shall I say is calling?"

Claudia cleared her throat, "Claudia and James Kincaid."

"Just one moment, please."

They were left standing in the reception hall more than "one-moment-please" before Parks returned.

1791

FROM THE MIXED-
UP FILES OF
MRS. BASIL E.
FRANKWEILER,
CH. 8

"Mrs. Frankweiler says she doesn't know you."

"We would like her to," Claudia insisted.

"What is the nature of your business?" he asked. Parks always asks that.

Both hesitated. Jamie decided on an answer first, "Please tell Mrs. Basil E. Frankweiler that we are seeking information about the Italian Renaissance."

Parks was gone a full ten minutes before his second return. "Follow me," he commanded. "Mrs. Frankweiler will see you in her office."

Jamie winked at Claudia. He felt certain that mentioning the Italian Renaissance had intrigued me.

They walked behind Parks through my living room, drawing room, and library. Rooms so filled with antique furniture, Oriental rugs, and heavy chandeliers that you complain that they are also filled with antique air. Well, when a house is as old as mine, you can expect everything in it to be thickened by time. Even the air. My office surprised them after all this. It surprises everyone. (You once told me, Saxonberg, that my office looks more like a laboratory than an office. That's why I call what I do there *research*.) I suppose it does look like a lab furnished as it is with steel, Formica,[7] vinyl and lit by fluorescence. You must admit though that there's one feature of the room that looks like an office. That's the rows and rows of filing cabinets that line the walls.

I was sitting at one of the tables wearing my customary white lab coat and my baroque pearl necklace when the children were brought in.

"Claudia and James Kincaid," Parks announced.

I allowed them to wait a good long while. Parks had cleared his throat at least six times before I turned around. (Of course, Saxonberg, you know that I hadn't wasted the time between Parks's announcement that Claudia and James Kincaid wanted to see me and the time they appeared at the office. I was busy doing research. That was also when I called you. You sounded like anything but a lawyer when I called. Disgusting!) I could hear the children shuffling back and forth impatiently. The importance of Parks's manner is what kept them from interrupting me. They shuffled and scratched, and Jamie even emitted two very false sneezes to attract my attention. It's particularly easy for me to ignore fake sneezes, and I went on with my research.

I don't like to waste time, so when I at last turned around, I did so abruptly and asked directly, "Are you the children who have been missing from Greenwich for a week?" (You must admit, Saxonberg, that when the need arises, I have a finely developed sense of theatrics.)

They had become so used to not being discovered that they had entirely forgotten that they were runaways. Now their reaction was one of amazement. They both looked as if their hearts had been pushed through funnels.

"All right," I said. "You don't have to tell me. I know the answer."

"How did you know about us?" Jamie asked.

"Did you call the police?" Claudia asked at the same time.

"From the newspapers," I replied, pointing to Jamie. "And no," I replied pointing to Claudia. "Now both of you sit down here and talk about the Italian Renaissance."

Jamie glanced at the newspapers I had been researching. "We're in the newspapers?" He seemed pleased.

"Even your pictures," I nodded.

"I'd like to see that," Claudia said. "I haven't had a decent picture taken since I've been able to walk."

---

7. A laminated plastic product, often used for countertops because it is heat resistant (trademark).

"Here you are." I held out several papers. "Two days before yesterday you were on the fifth page in Hartford, the second page in Stamford and the front page in Greenwich."

"The front page in Greenwich?" Claudia asked.

"That's my school picture from the first grade!" Jamie exclaimed. "See, I don't have one of my front teeth."

"Goodness! This picture of me is three years old. Mother never even bought my school pictures the last two years." Claudia held her picture up for Jamie to see. "Do you think I still look like this?"

"Enough!" I said. "Now, what do you want to tell me about the Italian Renaissance?"

"Is your butler calling the police while you stall us here?" Jamie asked.

"No," I answered. "And I refuse to keep reassuring you. If you keep on with this kind of talk, I shall find you so dull that I shall call your parents as well as the police to get rid of you. Is that clear, young man?"

"Yes," Jamie muttered.

"Young lady?"

Claudia nodded yes. They both stood with bowed heads. Then I asked Jamie, "Do I frighten you, young man?"

Jamie looked up. "No, ma'am. I'm quite used to frightening things. And you're really not so bad looking."

"So bad looking? I wasn't referring to the way I look." Actually, I never think much about that any more. I rang for Parks. When he arrived I told him to please bring me a mirror. Everyone waited in silence until Parks returned with the mirror. Silence continued as I picked it up and began a very long and close inspection of my face.

It's not a bad face except that lately my nose seems to have grown longer, and my upper lip appears to have collapsed against my teeth. These things happen when people get older. And I am getting just that. I ought to do something about my hair besides have Parks cut it for me. It's altogether white now and looks like frayed nylon thread. Maybe, I'll take time out and get a permanent wave, except that I hate beauty parlors.

"My nose has gotten longer. Like Pinocchio.[8] But not for the same reason. Well, not most of the time," I said as I put down the mirror. Claudia gasped, and I laughed. "Oh, so you were thinking the same thing? No matter. I never really look past my eyes. That way I always feel pretty. Windows of the soul, you know."

Claudia took a step closer to me. "You really do have beautiful eyes. They're like looking into a kaleidoscope—the way those golden flecks in them keep catching the light."

She was quite close to me now and actually peering into my face. It was uncomfortable. I put a stop to that.

"Do you spend much time looking in mirrors, Claudia?"

"Some days I do. Some days I don't."

"Would you care to look now?"

"No, thank you," she said.

"Well, then," I said, "we'll continue. Parks, please return this mirror. We want to talk about the Italian Renaissance. James, you haven't said one word since you told me that I look frightening. Speak now."

"We want to know about the statue," Jamie stammered.

---

8. The title character in Carlo Collodi's *The Adventures of Pinocchio* (1883) is a wooden puppet who wants to be a real boy. When he lies, his nose grows longer.

1793

FROM THE MIXED-
UP FILES OF
MRS. BASIL E.
FRANKWEILER,
CH. 9

"Speak up, boy," I commanded. "What statue?"

"The statue in the Metropolitan Museum in New York City. In Manhattan. The one of the angel."

"The one you sold for $225," Claudia added.

I walked over to my files of newspaper clippings and pulled out a manila folder, the one which has all the newspaper clippings about the auction and the museum buying the statue. It also contains the article about the crowds going to see the statue.

"Why did you sell her?" Claudia asked pointing to the picture of Angel.

"Because I don't like to donate things."

"If I owned such a lovely statue, I'd never sell it. Or donate it either. I'd cherish it like a member of my own family," Claudia preached.

"Considering all the trouble you've caused your family, that isn't saying very much."

"Have they been worried?" she asked.

"If you hadn't been so busy looking at your picture in the paper, you could have read that they are nearly frantic."

Claudia blushed. "But I wrote them a letter. I told them not to worry."

"Evidently your letter didn't work. Everyone is worried."

"I told them not to," she repeated. "We're going home anyway as soon as you tell us if Michelangelo carved Angel. Did he do it?"

"That's my secret," I answered. "Where have you been all week?"

"That's our secret," Claudia answered, lifting her chin high.

"Good for you!" I cheered. Now I was certain that I liked these two children. "Let's go to lunch." Examining the two of them in that bright light I saw that they looked wrinkled, dusty, and gray. I instructed them to wash up while I told the cook to prepare for two more.

Parks led Jamie to one bathroom; my maid, Hortense, led Claudia to another. Apparently, Claudia had never enjoyed washing up so much. She took forever doing it. She spent a great deal of time looking into all the mirrors. Examining her eyes very carefully, she decided that she, too, was beautiful. But mostly her thoughts were about the beautiful black marble bathtub in that bathroom.

(Even in this very elegant house of mine, that bathroom is especially grand. All the walls are black marble except for one that is mirrored entirely. The faucets are gold, and the spigot is shaped like a dragon's head. The tub looks like a black marble swimming pool sunken into the floor; there are two steps down to the bottom.)

There was nothing she wanted more than to take a bath in that tub. She examined her eyes a little longer and then spoke to her image in the mirror, "You'll never have a better chance, Lady Claudia. Go ahead. Do it." So she did. She opened the taps and began undressing as the tub was filling up.

Meanwhile, Jamie had done his customary job of washing up. That is, he had washed the palms but not backs of his hands, his mouth but not the eyes of his face. He emerged from the bathroom long before Claudia and growing impatient, began wandering through rooms until he found Hortense and asked her the whereabouts of his sister. He followed directions to Claudia's bathroom where he heard the water still running. It takes a lot of water to fill that tub.

"Suicide!" he thought. "She's going to drown herself because we're caught." He tried the door; it was locked.

"Claudia," he yelled, "is anything the matter?"

"No," she answered. "I'll be right there."

"What's taking you so long?"

"I'm taking a bath," she called.

"Oh, boloney," Jamie answered. He walked away to find me. I was waiting in the dining room. I'm accustomed to eating on time, and I was hungry.

"That nutty sister of mine is taking a bath. Don't mind her. She even takes baths when she comes in from swimming. She even made us take baths while we were hiding at the Metropolitan Museum. I think we should start without her."

I smiled, "I think, James, that you already have."

I rang for Parks, and he appeared with the salad and began serving.

"How did Claudia manage to take a bath in the museum?" I asked casually.

"In the fountain. It was cold, but I didn't mind when we found . . . Uh oh. Uuuuh. Ooooh. I did it. I told. I did it." He rested his elbow on the table and his chin on his hand. He slowly shook his head "Sometimes I stink at keeping secrets. Don't tell Claudia I told. Please."

"I'm curious to know how you managed." I *was* curious, and you know that I can be absolutely charming when I want information.

"Let Claude tell you all that. She did the planning. I managed the money. She's big on ideas, but she's also big on spending money. I managed fine until today. Now we're broke. Not one cent left to get back to Greenwich."

"You can walk or hitchhike."

"Try telling that to Claude."

"Or you can turn yourselves in. The police will take you back, or your parents will come and get you."

"Maybe that will appeal to Claudia, but I doubt it. Even though she sure doesn't approve of making herself walk."

"Perhaps we can work out a deal. You give me some details, and I'll give you a ride back."

1795

FROM THE MIXED-
UP FILES OF
MRS. BASIL E.
FRANKWEILER,
CH. 9

Jamie shook his head. "You'll have to work that out with Claude. The only kind of deal I can make concerns money, and we don't have any more of that."

"You are poor, indeed, if that's the only kind of a deal you can make."

Jamie brightened. "Would you like a game of cards?"

"Which game?" I asked.

"War."

"I assume you cheat."

"Yeah," he sighed.

"I may decide to play after lunch anyway."

"Can we start eating now?" Jamie asked.

"You don't worry about manners too much do you?"

"Oh," he replied, "I don't worry about them too much when I'm this hungry."

"You're honest about some things."

Jamie shrugged his shoulders. "You might say that I'm honest about everything except cards. For some reason I'm helpless about cheating at cards."

"Let's eat," I said. I was anxious, for I do enjoy a good game of cards, and Jamie promised to provide just that.

Claudia appeared as we were finishing our soup. I saw that she was annoyed that we had not waited for her. She was all bound up in concern for good manners, and she wanted very much to let us know that she was annoyed and why. She acted cool. I pretended I didn't notice. Jamie didn't pretend; he simply did not notice.

"I'll skip the soup," Claudia announced.

"It's good," Jamie said. "Sure you don't want to try it?"

"No, thank you," Claudia said. Still cool.

I summoned Parks; he appeared bearing a silver casserole.

"What's that?" Jamie asked.

"*Nouilles et fromage en casserole,*"[9] Parks answered.

Claudia showed interest. "I'll have some, please. Sounds like something special."

Parks served. Claudia looked down at her plate, looked up at me and moaned, "Why, it's nothing but macaroni and cheese."

"You see," I laughed, "under the fancy trappings, I'm just a plain lady."

Claudia laughed then. We all did, and we began enjoying our lunch. I asked Claudia what she would like to do while Jamie and I played cards. She said that she would like to just watch us and think.

"Think about what?"

"About how we're going to get back home."

"Call up your family," I suggested. "They'll come for you."

"Oh, it's so hard to explain over the phone. It will cause so much commotion."

I was astounded. "You still don't think you've caused any commotion so far?"

"I haven't really thought about it very hard. I've been so busy worrying about Michelangelo and avoiding getting caught. If only you'd tell me if the statue was done by Michelangelo. Then I would feel that I could go home again."

"Why would that make a difference?" I asked.

"It would because . . . because . . ."

"Because you found that running away from home didn't make a real difference? You were still the same Greenwich Claudia, planning and washing and keeping things in order?"

"I guess that's right," Claudia said quietly.

9. Noodles and cheese in a casserole (French).

"Then why did you run away?"

Claudia's words came slowly; she was forming thoughts into the shape of words for the first time in a long time. "I got the idea because I was mad at my parents. That was getting the idea. Then I started planning it. I thought that I had to think of everything, and I thought of an awful lot. Didn't I, Jamie?" She looked over at her brother, and he nodded. "I enjoyed the planning. Without anyone knowing that I was doing it. I am very good at planning."

"And the more plans you made, the more it became like living at home away from home." I interrupted.

"That's true," she said. "But we did enjoy living away from home in a mild kind of way."

(Notice that Claudia is still being very careful not to reveal to me where she and Jamie stayed. I wasn't ready to push yet. I felt I had to help the child. Don't laugh as you read this, Saxonberg; I do have some charity in me.)

"What part of living away from home did you like the best?"

Jamie answered first, "Not having a schedule."

Claudia became impatient, "But, Jamie, we did have a schedule. Sort of. The best that I could manage under the circumstances. *That* wasn't the most fun part of running away."

"What was the most fun part for you, Claudia?"

"First, it was hiding. Not being discovered. And after hiding became easy, there was Angel. Somehow, Angel became more important than running away."

"How did Angel become involved with your running away?" I purred.

"I won't tell you," Claudia answered.

I put on my surprised look and asked, "Why not?"

"Because if I tell you how Angel got involved, it will be telling you too much else."

"Like telling me where you've been all week?"

"Maybe," she answered coolly.

"Why don't you want to tell me that?"

"I told you before; that's *our* secret."

"Oho! You don't want to lose your bargaining weapon," I crowed. "Is that why you're not telling me where you stayed?"

"That's part of the reason," she said. "The other part is—I think the other part is— that if I tell, then I know for sure that my adventure is over. And I don't want it to be over until I'm sure I've had enough."

"The adventure is over. Everything gets over, and nothing is ever enough. Except the part you carry with you. It's the same as going on a vacation. Some people spend all their time on a vacation taking pictures so that when they get home they can show their friends evidence that they had a good time. They don't pause to let the vacation enter inside of them and take that home."

"Well, I don't really want to tell you where we've been."

"I know," I answered.

Claudia looked at me. "Do you know I don't want to tell you, or do you know where we've been? Which do you mean?"

"Both," I told her quietly. I resumed eating *nouilles et fromage en casserole*.

Claudia looked over at Jamie. Jamie had slipped down in his seat and had thrown his napkin over his face. Claudia jumped up from her seat, grabbed the napkin off Jamie's face. Jamie quickly threw his forearms where the napkin had been.

"It slipped, Claude; it slipped out." Jamie's voice was muted since his forearms were protecting his mouth.

"Jamie! Jamie! That was all I had. All we had. The only thing we had left."

"I just forgot, Claude. It's been so long since I've had a conversation with anyone but you."

"You shouldn't have told her. You heard me say to her that that was our secret. Twice. Now everything is lost. How can I get her to tell? You had to go and blab it all. Blabbermouth!"

Jamie looked at me for sympathy, "She does get emotional."

"Claudia," I said, "be seated."

She obeyed. I continued. "All is not lost. I'm going to make a bargain with you. Both of you. First of all, stop referring to me as *her*. I am Mrs. Basil E. Frankweiler. Then if you give me all the details of your running away, if you tell me everything— *everything*—I'll give you a ride home. I'll have Sheldon, my chauffeur, drive you home."

Claudia nodded "no."

"A Rolls Royce, Claudia. And a chauffeur. That's a very fine offer," I teased.

Jamie said, "How about it, Claude? It beats walking."

Claudia squinted her eyes and crossed her arms over her chest. "It's not enough. I want to know about Angel."

I was glad that I wasn't dealing with a stupid child. I admired her spirit; but more, I wanted to help her see the value of her adventure. She still saw it as buying her something: appreciation first, information now. Nevertheless, Claudia was tiptoeing into the grown-up world. And I decided to give her a little shove. "Claudia. James. Both of you. Come with me."

We walked single file through several rooms to my office. For a minute I thought I was leader in a game of follow-the-leader.

Jamie caught up with me and said, "For an old lady you sure can walk fast."

Claudia then caught up with Jamie and kicked him.

We arrived at my office, and I motioned for them to sit down.

"Do you see those filing cabinets along that wall?" I asked pointing to the south wall. "Those are my secrets. In one of them is the secret of Michelangelo's Angel. I'll share that secret with you as the rest of my bargain. But now my information is more important than yours. So you must have a handicap. The handicap is that you must find the secret file yourselves, and you have one hour to do it in." I turned to leave, then remembered, "And I don't want my files messed up or placed out of order. They're in a special order that makes sense only to me. If you move things around, I won't be able to find anything. And our whole arrangement will be off."

Jamie spoke, "You sure know how to nervous a guy."

I laughed and left the room. I tiptoed into the large closet I have next to my office. From there I watched and listened to all they did.

Jamie got up immediately and began opening file drawers. Claudia shouted, "STOP!" He did.

"What's the matter with you, Claude? We have only one hour."

"Five minutes of planning are worth fifteen minutes of just looking. Quick, give me the pencil and note pad from that table." Jamie ran to get them. Claudia immediately began making a list. "Here's what we'll look up. I'll take the odd numbers; you take the even."

"I want odd."

"For goodness' sake, Jamie, take odds then."

Here's the list Claudia wrote:

1797

FROM THE MIXED-
UP FILES OF
MRS. BASIL E.
FRANKWEILER,
CH. 9

1. Michelangelo
2. Buonarroti
3. Angel
4. Parke Bernet Galleries
5. Metropolitan Museum of Art
6. Italian Renaissance
7. Auctions
8. Sculptor
9. Marble
10. Florence, Italy
11. Rome, Italy

Jamie looked over the list. "I changed my mind. I'll take evens. There's one less."

"Talk about wasting time!" Claudia screamed. "Take evens then, but get to it."

They began to work very rapidly. Claudia once or twice cautioned Jamie not to make a mess. They had exhausted the list, odds as well as evens. There were folders on most of the categories they looked up, but upon examining them, they found not one hint of Angel. Claudia was feeling depressed. She looked at the clock. Six minutes to go.

"Think, Jamie, think. What else can we look up?"

Jamie squinted his eyes, a sign that he was thinking hard. "Look him up under . . ."

"What kind of language is that? Look him *up under* . . ."

"Oh, boloney, Claude. Why do you always pick on my gra . . ."

"Boloney, boloney! That's it, Jamie. She bought Angel in Bologna, Italy. The paper said so. Look up Bologna." Both ran back to the files and pulled out a file folder fat with papers and documents. It was labeled: BOLOGNA, ITALY. They knew even before opening it that it was the right one. I knew, too. They had found the file that held the secret.

Claudia was no longer in a hurry; she sauntered over to a table, carefully laid down the file, smoothed her skirt under her, and sat in a chair. Jamie was jumping up and down, "Hurry up, Claude. The hour is almost over."

Claudia was not to be hurried. She carefully opened the folder, almost afraid of what she would find. The evidence was sealed between two sheets of glass. The evidence was a very special, very old piece of paper. On one side was written a poem, a sonnet. Since it was written in Italian, neither Claudia nor Jamie could read it. But they could see that the handwriting was angular and beautiful, in itself almost a work of art. And there was a signature: Michelangelo. The other side of the paper needed no translation. For there, in the midst of sketches of hands and torsos was a sketch of someone they knew: Angel. There were the first lines of a thought that was to become a museum mystery 470 years later. There on that piece of old paper was the idea just as it had come from Michelangelo's head to his hand, and he had jotted it down.

Claudia looked at the sketch until its image became blurred. She was crying. At first she said nothing. She simply sat on the chair with tears slowly streaming down her face, hugging the glass frame and shaking her head back and forth. When at last she found her voice, it was a hushed voice, the voice she used for church. "Just think, Jamie, Michelangelo himself touched this. Over four hundred years ago."

Jamie was looking through the rest of the folder. "The glass," he said. "I'll bet he didn't touch the glass. Are his fingerprints on it?" He didn't wait for an answer before asking something else. "What do you suppose the rest of these papers are?"

"They are my research on Angel," I answered as I emerged from my hiding place in the closet. "He did it in Rome, you know. I just file it under *B* for Bologna to make it hard."

1799

FROM THE MIXED-
UP FILES OF
MRS. BASIL E.
FRANKWEILER,
CH. 9

Both children looked up at me startled. Just as they had lost all their feelings of urgency, they had also lost all thoughts of me. Finding a secret can make everything else unimportant, you know.

Claudia said nothing and nothing and nothing. She continued clutching the drawing to her chest and rocking it back and forth. She appeared to be in a trance. Jamie and I stared at her until she felt our eyes focused on her like four laser beams. She looked up at us then and smiled.

"Michelangelo did sculpture the statue, didn't he, Mrs. Frankweiler?"

"Of course. I've known for a long time that he did. Ever since I got that sketch."

"How did you get the sketch?" Jamie asked.

"I got it after the war. . . ."

"Which war?" Jamie interrupted.

"World War II. Which war did you think I meant? The American Revolution?"

"Are you that old?" Jamie asked.

"I'm not even going to answer that."

Claudia said, "Hush, Jamie. Let her tell us." But she couldn't hush either. She rushed in with an explanation, "I'll bet you helped some rich Italian nobleman or some descendant of Michelangelo's to escape, and he gave you the sketch out of his undying gratitude."

"That's one explanation. But not the correct one. There was a rich Italian nobleman involved. That part is right."

"Did he sell it to you?" Jamie asked.

Claudia rushed in again with another explanation, "He had this beautiful daughter and she needed this operation very badly and you . . ."

Jamie interrupted. "Hush, Claudia." Then he asked me, "Why did he give it to you?"

"Because he was a very, very bad poker player, and I am a very good one."

"You won it at cards?" I could see admiration grow in Jamie's eyes.

"Yes I did."

"Did you cheat?" he asked.

"Jamie, when the stakes are high, I never cheat. I consider myself too important to do that."

Jamie asked, "How come you don't sell the sketch? You could get quite a boodle for it. Being that it matches up with the statue and all."

"I need having the secret more than I need the money," I told him.

I knew that Claudia understood. Jamie looked puzzled.

"Thank you for sharing your secret with us," Claudia whispered.

"How do you know that we'll keep your secret?" Jamie asked.

"Now, now, a boy who cheats at cards should be able to answer that."

Jamie's face broke into a huge grin. "Bribery!" he exclaimed. "You're going to bribe us. Hallelujah! Tell me. I'm ready. What's the deal?"

I laughed. "The deal is this: you give me the details of your running away, and I'll give you the sketch."

Jamie gasped. "That doesn't sound like bribery. That doesn't even sound like you, Mrs. Frankweiler. You're smarter than that. How do you know that I won't slip about your secret as I did about the museum?"

That boy really amused me. "You're right, Jamie. I am smarter than that. I've got a method to keep you slip-proof about the sketch."

"What's that?"

"I'm not going to give you the sketch outright. I'm going to leave it to you in my will. You won't tell my secret because if you do, I'll write you out of my will. You would lose all that money. You said that the sketch was worth quite a boodle. So you're going to be very good about keeping this secret. Claudia will keep quiet for a different reason. Her reason happens to be the same as mine."

"Which is what?" Jamie asked.

"Simply because it is a secret. It will enable her to return to Greenwich *different*."

Claudia looked at Jamie and nodded. Something I had just said made sense.

I continued, "Returning with a secret is what she really wants. Angel had a secret and that made her exciting, important. Claudia doesn't want adventure. She likes baths and feeling comfortable too much for that kind of thing. Secrets are the kind of adventure she needs. Secrets are safe, and they do much to make you different. On the inside where it counts. I won't actually be getting a secret from you; I'll be getting details. I'm a collector of all kinds of things besides art," I said pointing to my files.

"If all those files are secrets, and if secrets make you different on the inside, then your insides, Mrs. Frankweiler, must be the most mixed-up, the most different insides I've ever seen. Or any doctor has ever seen, either."

I grinned. "There's a lifetime of secrets in those files. But there's also just a lot of newspaper clippings. Junk. It's a hodgepodge. Like my art collection. Now, you'll tell me all about your running away, and I'll add that to my files."

Whereas Jamie's excitement bubbled out of him in grins and spurts of jittering around the room, Claudia's excitement flowed not bubbled. I could see that she was a little surprised. She had known that Angel would have the answer, but she had expected it to be a loud bang, not a quiet soaking in. Of course secrets make a difference. That was why planning the runaway had been such fun; it was a secret. And hiding in the museum had been a secret. But they weren't permanent; they had to come to an end. Angel wouldn't. She could carry the secret of Angel inside her for twenty years just as I had. Now she wouldn't have to be a heroine when she returned home . . . except to herself. And now she knew something about secrets that she hadn't known before.

I could tell that she felt happy. Happiness is excitement that has found a settling down place, but there is always a little corner that keeps flapping around. Claudia could have kept her doubts to herself, but she was an honest child, an honorable child.

"Mrs. Frankweiler," she said swallowing hard, "I really love the sketch. I really do. I love it. Just love, love, love it. But don't you think you ought to give it to the museum. They're just dying to find out whether the statue is real or not."

"Nonsense! What a conscience you suddenly have. I want to give it to you. In exchange. If you and Jamie want to give it to the museum after you inherit it, then you give it to the museum. I won't let the museum people near here. If I could keep them out of Connecticut altogether, I would. I don't want them to have it while I'm alive."

Claudia wiped her forehead with the sleeve of her sweater and asked, "Why not?"

"I've thought about that for a long time, and I've decided 'why not?' What they'll do is start investigating the authenticity of the sketch. They'll call in authorities from all over the world. They'll analyze the ink. And the paper. They'll research all his illustrated notes and compare, compare, compare. In short, they'll make a science of it. Some will say 'yes.' Some will say 'no.' Scholars will debate about it. They'll poll all the authorities, and probably the majority will agree that the note and the statue are really the work of Michelangelo. At least that's what they should conclude. But

1801

FROM THE MIXED-
UP FILES OF
MRS. BASIL E.
FRANKWEILER,
CH. 10

some stubborn ones won't agree, and thereafter the statue and the sketch will appear in books with a big question mark. The experts don't believe in coincidence as much as I do, and I don't want them to throw doubt on something that I've felt always, and actually known for about twenty years."

Claudia's eyes widened, "But, Mrs. Frankweiler, if there is the slightest doubt that either the statue or the sketch is a forgery, don't you want to know? Don't you want the last little bit of doubt cleared up?"

"No," I answered abruptly.

"Why not?"

"Because I'm eighty-two years old. That's why. There now, Jamie, you see, I slip too. Now I've told you how old I am."

Jamie looked at his sister and asked, "What's that got to do with anything, Claude?" Claudia shrugged.

"I'll tell you what it's got to do with it," I said. "I'm satisfied with my own research on the subject. I'm not in the mood to learn anything new."

Claudia said, "But, Mrs. Frankweiler, you should want to learn one new thing every day. We did even at the museum."

"No," I answered, "I don't agree with that. I think you should learn, of course, and some days you must learn a great deal. But you should also have days when you allow what is already in you to swell up inside of you until it touches everything. And you can feel it inside you. If you never take time out to let that happen, then you just accumulate facts, and they begin to rattle around inside of you. You can make noise with them, but never really feel anything with them. It's hollow."

Both children were quiet, and I continued. "I've gathered a lot of facts about Michelangelo and Angel. And I've let them grow inside me for a long time. Now I feel that I know. That's enough for that. But there is one new thing that I'd like to experience. Not know. Experience. And that one thing is impossible."

"Nothing is impossible," Claudia said. She sounded to me exactly like a bad actress in a bad play—unreal.

"Claudia," I said patiently, "when one is eighty-two years old, one doesn't have to learn one new thing every day, and one knows that some things are impossible."

"What would you like to experience that is impossible?" Jamie asked.

"Right now, I'd like to know how your mother feels."

"You keep saying that she's frantic. Why do you want to feel frantic?" This came from Claudia. Now she sounded like the real Claudia Kincaid.

"It's an experience I would like to have because it's part of a bigger experience I want."

Claudia said, "You mean you'd like to be a mother?"

Jamie leaned toward Claudia and whispered in the loudest, wettest whisper I have ever heard, "Of course that's impossible. Her husband is dead. You can't be a mother without a husband."

Claudia poked Jamie, "Never call people *dead*; it makes others feel bad. Say 'deceased' or 'passed away.'"

"Come now, children. Put away the file. You must tell me all about your adventure. All, all, all about it. What you thought and what you said and how you managed to carry off the whole crazy caper."

10

I kept the children up late getting the details. Jamie and I played war while Claudia talked into the tape recorder. Jamie ended up with two aces and twelve cards more than I; the game cost me thirty-four cents. I still don't know how he does it. It was my deck of cards; but I was somewhat preoccupied listening to Claudia and interrupting her with questions. And then there was that telephone call from the children's parents. I knew you'd tell them, Saxonberg. I knew it! What a combination you are: soft heart and hard head. It was all I could do to persuade them to stay home and let me deliver the children in the morning. Mrs. Kincaid kept asking if they were bruised or maimed. I think she has read too many accounts of lost children in the newspapers. You realize now why I insisted that they stay overnight. I wanted all sides of the bargain kept, and I had to get my information. Besides I had promised them a ride home in the Rolls Royce, and I never cheat when the stakes are high.

When it came to be Jamie's turn to talk into the tape recorder, I thought that I would never get him to quit fussing with the switches. He enjoyed saying something and then erasing it. Finally, I scolded him, "You're not Sir Lawrence Olivier[1] playing Hamlet, you know. All I want are the facts and how you felt. Not a theatrical production."

"You want me to be accurate, don't you?"

"Yes, but I also want you to finish."

Claudia asked for a tour of the house while Jamie told his story. She asked about everything. We rode the elevator up to the third floor, and she went from one room to the next. I hadn't been through the entire house for a long time, so I enjoyed the tour, too. We talked; we both enjoyed that also. Claudia told me about her routine at home. When we came back to the black marble bathroom, she told me how she came to take a bath there earlier. I allowed her to pick the bedroom where she would sleep that night.

Very early the next morning I had Sheldon drive them to Greenwich. I'm enclosing a copy of his report for your amusement, Saxonberg; you ought to be in a mood to laugh now.

> The boy, madam, spent the first five minutes of the trip pushing every button in the back seat. I transported them in the Rolls Royce as you requested. He pushed some buttons at least twelve times; others I stopped counting at five. He seemed to regard the button panel, madam, as some sort of typewriter or piano or I.B.M. computer. Without realizing it he pushed the button to the intercom *on* and neglected to push it *off*. In this way I overheard all their conversation; they thought they were privately sealed behind the glass screen that divides the front seat from the back. The girl was quiet while the other tested things. Everything, I might add.
>
> Finally, the girl remarked to the other, "Why do you suppose she sold Angel in the first place? Why didn't she just donate it to the museum?"
>
> "Because she's tight. That's why. She said so," the boy answered.
>
> "That's not the reason. If she were tight, and she knew it was worth so much, she would never have sold it for $225."
>
> Thank goodness the girl interested him in conversation. He stopped pushing buttons. Besides neglecting to turn off the intercom, he also neglected to turn off the windshield wipers on the rear window. I might add, madam, that it was not raining.
>
> "Well, she sold it at auction, silly. At an auction you have to sell it to the

---

1. British actor and director (1907–1989), especially renowned for his performances of Shakespeare; he starred in *Hamlet* both on stage (1937, 1963) and in a 1948 film that he also directed and produced.

1803

FROM THE MIXED-
UP FILES OF
MRS. BASIL E.
FRANKWEILER,
CH. 10

highest bidder. No one bid higher than $225. It's that simple."

The girl replied, "She didn't sell it for the money. She would have shown her evidence if she really wanted a big price. She sold it for the fun of it. For excitement."

"Maybe she didn't have room for it anymore."

"In that museum of a house? There's rooms upstairs that . . . oh! Jamie, the statue is only two feet tall. She could have tucked it into any corner."

"Why do *you* think she sold it?"

The girl thought a minute. (I was hoping she would answer soon, madam. Before the boy got interested in the buttons again.) "Because after a time having a secret and nobody knowing you have a secret is no fun. And although you don't want others to know what the secret is, you want them to at least know you have one."

I observed from the rear view mirror, madam, that the little boy grew quiet. He looked at the girl and said, "You know, Claude, I'm going to save my money and my winnings, and I'm going to visit Mrs. Frankweiler again." A long pause, then, "There's something about our running away that I forgot to say into the tape recorder."

The girl said nothing.

"Wanna come, Claude? We won't tell anyone."

"How much did you win last night?" the girl asked.

"Only thirty-four cents. She's a lot sharper than Bruce."

"Maybe my twenty-five cents from the cornflakes came already. That would make fifty-nine." The girl was silent for a few minutes before she asked, "Do you think she meant that stuff about motherhood?"

The boy shrugged his shoulders. "Let's visit her every time we save enough money. We won't tell anyone. We won't stay overnight. We'll just tell Mom and Dad that we're going bowling or something, and we'll take a train up instead."

"We'll adopt her," the girl suggested. "We'll become her kids, sort of."

"She's too old to be a mother. She said so herself. Besides, we already have one."

"She'll become our grandmother, then, since ours are deceased."

"And that will be our secret that we won't even share with her. She'll be the only woman in the world to become a grandmother with never becoming a mother first."

I drove the car to the address they gave me, madam. The shades were up, and I could see a quite handsome man and a young matron watching by the window. I also thought I saw our own Mr. Saxonberg. The boy had opened the doors even before I had completely stopped. That is a very dangerous thing to do. A much younger creature, also a boy, came running out of the house immediately ahead of the others. As I drove away, this younger one was saying, "Boy! what a car. Hey, Claude, I'll be your *sponsibility* the rest of . . ."

The children, madam, neglected to say thank you.

Well, Saxonberg, that's why I'm leaving the drawing of Angel to Claudia and Jamie Kincaid, your two lost grandchildren that you were so worried about. Since they intend to make me their grandmother, and you already are their grandfather, that makes us—oh, well, I won't even think about that. You're not that good a poker player.

Rewrite my will with a clause about my bequeathing the drawing to them. Also put in a clause about that bed I mentioned, too. I guess I ought to donate it to the Metropolitan Museum. I haven't really begun to like donating things. You'll notice that everyone is getting these things after I'm dead. I should say *passed away*. After you have all those things written into my will, I'll sign the new version. Sheldon and Parks can be witnesses. The signing of the will will take place in the restaurant of the Metropolitan Museum of Art in New York City. You'll come there with me, dear Saxonberg, or lose me, your best client.

I wonder if Claudia and Jamie will come visit me again. I wouldn't mind if they did. You see, I still have an edge; I know one bit more of a secret than they do. They don't know that their grandfather has been my lawyer for forty-one years. (And I recommend that for your own good, you not tell them, Saxonberg.)

By the way I heard a radio interview by the new Commissioner of Parks in New York City. He said that his budget had been cut. When asked by a reporter where the money that should have been spent for the parks was going, the commissioner replied that most of it was going towards increased security for the Metropolitan Museum. Suspecting that something special had prompted this move, I asked Sheldon to call his friend, Morris the guard, to find out if anything unusual had been discovered lately.

Morris reported that a violin case was found in a sarcophagus last week. A trumpet case was found two days later. Morris says that guards who have worked at the museum for a year have seen everything; those who have worked there for six months have seen half of everything. They once discovered a set of false teeth on the seat of an Etruscan chariot. They sent the children's cases to Lost and Found. They are still there. Full of gray-washed underwear and a cheap transistor radio. No one has claimed them yet.

1967

School Stories

The inherent relationship between youth and education, between books written for children and the desire to teach lessons through narrative, makes the connection between children's literature and school a natural one. It is not surprising that school stories are among the earliest forms of children's literature. Although the recurring plot devices found in many school stories can make them formulaic, the contours of the genre have changed dramatically over time as educational theory, the roles of schools in society, and interpretations of children's natures and of children's needs have altered. In moral tales set at school, dating from the eighteenth century, the school and its members function as substitutes for the family; teachers act as surrogate parents, imparting wisdom and counsel. Boarding school tales for boys and girls emphasize independence from parental controls and the importance of self-reliance and loyalty to peers. In contemporary school fiction, the school might be a place of corruption, a microcosm of the fallen world that surrounds it. Such tales rarely concern curriculum, address pedagogy, or impart information; from the earliest examples of Anglo-American school stories onward, the focus has been on the emotional (sometimes physical), psychological, and social development of the child character apart from the family's influence.

Leaving the family while still a child to become a schoolboy was a rite of passage for the elite male youth of Great Britain. The school story essentially emerged from the exclusive world of the English public school. The statement attributed to the Duke of Wellington and well-known today, that the 1815 Battle of Waterloo was "won on the playing fields of Eton," points to the long-standing belief that wealth and social position produce the statesmen, soldiers, and financiers who will one day run the world. Many nineteenth-century British school stories, written for boys and later adapted for girls, can be traced to this selfsame fascination with the camaraderie and rituals that emerge from the exclusive environment of the boarding school. Though school stories are almost always set in a world of privilege (even as scholarship pupils often "intrude"), their readership tended to be young people whose school lives were very different from that presented in the books. Indeed, Talbot Baines Reed (1852–1893), credited with popularizing the boys' public (i.e., boarding) school novel in books first serialized in the Religious Tract Society's magazine *Boy's Own Paper*, never himself attended public school.

The genre of the school story became popular in nineteenth-century England, although some isolated early examples, such as Sarah Fielding's *The Governess; or,*

Little Female Academy (1749) and Maria Edgeworth's story "The Barring Out" (1796), used a school setting as a frame for moral tales. Harriet Martineau's *The Crofton Boys* (1841) created a fully rounded world of school, complete with bullies, masters, friendships, and moral dilemmas, that sketched the generic characteristics later built on by writers such as Thomas Hughes in *Tom Brown's Schooldays* (1857). School stories were typically written for either boys or girls, reflecting the distinction between male and female education found in most schools, whether sex-segregated or not. The profusion of school stories in novels and weekly papers from the later nineteenth century for boys' fiction, and the 1920s through '30s for girls', confirmed the conventions of character—for example, the manly boy, misfit child, sporty girl, scholarship pupil, tomboy, bully—and plot that would come to distinguish the genre. Stock scenes found in the Anglo-American school story from the nineteenth century forward include the big game, the midnight feast, the inspiring teacher's speech, the new boy beating the school bully, the dramatic rescue, the showdown in the principal's office. Significant differences exist between the school stories written before and after World War II, as the school story becomes more grounded in realistic portrayals of adults and children at school.

Early Educational Theories and British Schooling

Theories about education have always informed the school story. Early writing about education was dominated by authors such as John Locke (*Some Thoughts Concerning Education*, 1693) and Jean-Jacques Rousseau (*Emile, or On Education*, 1762), two philosophers whose theories about child nature and education proved to be very influential. Locke believed that the child was a *tabula rasa*, a "blank slate" upon which knowledge could be impressed. He also believed that the most effective instruction combined learning with amusement. In Rousseau's philosophy, the child's innate nature was to be tampered with as little as possible and the best education was a "natural" one defined by the child's needs. For some educators and child advocates (including rationalist authors such as Maria Edgeworth), the theories of Locke and Rousseau provided a new way of thinking about the child as a reasonable and intelligent being rather than as inherently evil. The needs and abilities of the individual child entered discussions about child rearing and education, and earlier practices such as physical punishment for imperfectly learned lessons or an overreliance on rote memorization were questioned in literature written for and about children. Although contemporary educational philosophies of course differ from these early models, the faint traces of these theories in both educational practices and school fiction remain visible today.

It is important to note, however, that for Locke and Rousseau, "child" meant "boy." Rousseau's position on girls' education, detailed at length in *Emile* and encapsulated in the following quotation, is perhaps extreme in degree, but suspicion of the learned female was widespread throughout the eighteenth and early nineteenth centuries: "the whole education of women ought to relate to men. To please men, to be useful to them, to make herself loved and honored by them, to raise them when young, to care for them when grown, to counsel them, to console them, to make their lives agreeable and sweet—these are the duties of women at all times and they ought to be taught from childhood." Even in the late nineteenth century, as educational opportunities for women were slowly increasing, theories positing the inferiority of the female intellect persisted. One example, "Mental Differences between Men and Women" (1887), written by George J. Romanes—a Canadian naturalist and friend of Charles Darwin, who was generally in favor of "appropriate" higher education for women—held that women's smaller average brain weight (about 5 ounces less than that of men), delicate physiques, "comparative absence of originality [of thought]," and weakness of will, among other reasons, proved them to be less intelligent than men. Many believed women's education to be a dangerous fad; others—such as Mary Wollstonecraft in *A Vindication of the Rights of Woman* (1792)—believed that educational equality was the cornerstone of sexual equality and thus of the utmost importance. Still others understood "equal education" as requiring separate education for boys and girls because each sex was expected to play very distinct roles in society. These attitudes against equality in education were implicitly countered by late-nineteenth- and early-twentieth-century girls' school stories through their emphasis on the intelligence and high moral character of the heroines. In other works, traces of these debates can be seen in the educational sacrifices many a worthy girl must undertake in order to help her family. These "womanly" sacrifices are generally acknowledged through a beneficial "softening" of the girl's character and the gratitude of the helpless relative, as well as rewarded through the benefaction of an outsider impressed by the girl's selflessness.

In the sixteenth through early nineteenth centuries, poor British children who were not working themselves might attend dame schools (in which a schooldame would look after children and teach them their letters and perhaps numbers) or village schools. In the earliest years, boys might be taught to read, write, and figure, while girls would be taught to read as well as useful crafts such as sewing, knitting, and spinning. Schooling was by no means universal for poor children, but as Margaret Spufford points out in her study of Cambridgeshire, "Women Teaching Reading to Poor Children in the Sixteenth and Seventeenth Centuries" (1997), "Schooling was available within walking distance all over much of the country of Cambridgeshire." The Sunday School Movement, first established in the late eighteenth century by Protestant clergy and others interested in keeping poor children productively occupied, stepped in to help educate slum children and, eventually, poor children who lived outside urban areas. It was hoped that religious instruction and literacy would assist the youngest poor in maintaining godliness, cleanliness, honesty, contentment in their station, and sobriety. In the 1830s, the English government began to support some church schools with government grants. Effective child labor laws and the advent of (secular) government-sponsored board schools (in the Elementary Education Act of 1870, for example) dramatically increased the number of boys and girls who could attend regulated institutions of learning. By 1880, elementary education was compulsory for children between seven and ten years old; and by 1891, schools were free.

Early British Boys' School Stories

The wide gulf separating male and female, lower- and upper-class education, directly informed the development of the British school story, which dominated the development of the genre in English. Only sons of the wealthy could be sent to public schools (costly boarding schools for gentlemen's sons) such as Eton and Winchester. Public school fiction contained very little about intellectual education and very much about physical, moral, and character education. *Tom Brown's Schooldays* is perhaps the best-known example of a nineteenth-century English school story written for boys. The novel is set at Rugby School during the tutelage of Dr. Arnold, its most famous headmaster. Hughes himself went to Rugby in 1833, after Dr. Arnold had been headmaster for five years. Rugby had fallen into disorder and lawlessness until Arnold, acting as the moral center of the school, instituted a number of reforms to restore Christian character-building to the school's mission. The hero of the novel, Tom Brown, is gradually transformed—by the nearly invisible hand of Dr. Arnold and the gentling influence of his "feminine" and devout friend Arthur—from a genial scapegrace and indifferent scholar into an honest, upstanding leader of the school on both the moral high ground and the cricket pitch. *Eric, or, Little by Little* (1858) by F. W. Farrar is the most notorious moral boys' school story. (Rudyard Kipling, most notably, mocked the maudlin story relentlessly in his Stalky stories and later apologized to Farrar.) *Eric* is a cautionary tale, however, as young Eric—at first only a weak and heedless, rather than bad, boy—succumbs to ever-escalating temptations (from cheating on his Greek translation to drunkenness and theft) and leaves school after being framed for a deed he did not do. After running away to sea, he becomes mortally ill, is brutally treated, and returns to his aunt's house and dies there, repentant, having learned that his mother was expiring from grief over his behavior. Talbot Baines Reed's stories such as *The Fifth Form at St. Dominic's* (1887; first serialized in the *Boy's Own Paper*, 1881–82), published later in the century, tended to downplay religion and emphasize sports.

At the turn of the century, Rudyard Kipling's *Stalky and Co.* (1899)—based on his experiences at the United Services College in Devon, an institution for boys who would one day enter army or colonial service—offered an unusually cynical view of the boys' academy. The corruption of the school's masters and many of its students serves to help Stalky and his friends cohere into a loyal band against the brutish and harsh authority all around them. Notably, one of the boys receives Farrar's *Eric*, much to everyone's disgust. The three friends survive and triumph in the school by exercising their wit, exacting revenge, and breaking rules. One purpose of Kipling's book was to emphasize that ultimately, the cruel, unfair, demanding, petty world of the academy is closer to the real world of war and empire than the enclosed, essentially comic, worlds offered in conventional school stories. Though similarly freed from the boundaries of the boarding school tales, the Canadian Lucy Maud Montgomery's books about schooling indulge a romantic sensibility and childlike humor far removed from the hard-edged *Stalky*. *Anne of Avonlea* (1909), the sequel to *Anne of Green Gables* (1908), concerns Anne Shirley's short tenure as a teacher in a rural Prince Edward Island school before going off to college to further her education, as described in *Anne of the Island* (1915).

Early British Girls' School Stories

School stories for girls first emerged within a culture that devalued female education. In the eighteenth and early nineteenth centuries, formal and rigorous educational opportunities for middle- and upper-class girls were rare. Informal education—provided privately by mothers or governesses—although well-intentioned, tended to be irregular and to focus on polite accomplishments (e.g., music and drawing), Bible study, and "feminine" subjects such as history and modern languages (as opposed to the classical languages). But attitudes about the inferiority of girls and women held by many women as well as men notwithstanding, female education captured the interest of social reformers and educators alike in midcentury. The first academic day school for girls, the North London Collegiate School, was established in 1850 by Frances Mary Buss, an activist in the suffrage movement among other causes. It quickly developed a reputation for providing an excellent education for its students, and it remains in operation today. Cheltenham Ladies' College, socially selective and admitting some boarders, was led by Buss's friend and fellow educational pioneer, Dorothea Beale, who became principal of the school in 1858. Beale founded St. Hilda's College (for women) at Oxford University while still the principal at Cheltenham.

Boarding schools such as St. Leonard's (1877) and Wycombe Abbey (1896) were modeled after boys' public schools and became the prototypes for many fictional schools in popular school stories. The school story for girls by English authors such as L. T. Meade (her most famous book is titled *A World of Girls*, 1886) burgeoned in the later nineteenth century, and it self-consciously adopted some of the successful ingredients of the school stories for boys as it added elements particular to girls and education. Meade's books are prototypical of late-nineteenth-century girls' school stories. In "Children's Reading and the Culture of Girlhood: The Case of L. T. Meade" (1989), the critic Sally Mitchell maintains,

> Just as the boys' public school was seen as a model of the adult male world—politics, the army, the empire—for girls, only the older small "family" boarding school provides a parallel model. . . . [A]s the formula developed, [L. T. Meade] took the organizational structure of the "men's world" and grafted onto it the emotional content of the "woman's world" of friendship, feelings, and the care and development of relationships.

Although sentimental, Meade's works were often filled with "New Girls": athletic, lively, intelligent but not "grinds," and loyal friends eager to buck authority. These kinds of stories offer fuel for fantasizing independence and adventure for girls of all classes.

The schoolgirl ethic and code of conduct were delineated in the boarding school fiction of Angela Brazil as well as in the numerous weekly papers, such as *The School Friend* (1919–29), *Schoolgirls' Own* (1921–36), and *Schoolgirls Weekly* (1922–39), designed for middle- and lower-class girl readers. Girls who would almost certainly never attend the kind of school described in the stories were nevertheless their audience. The independence and freedom of the girl characters, and their friendships, emotions, and adventures all described from the girl's perspective, help explain the fascination of these stories for girls whose lives were so different from those of the characters. Wildly popular fiction about girls in boarding school includes the long-running Chalet School series by Elinor Brent-Dyer (1925–1970) and Enid Blyton's school story series Malory Towers (six books published from 1946 to 1951), featuring one of her best-loved heroines, Darrell Rivers.

Imitation and Innovation: The School Story in America, Canada, and Australia

Louisa May Alcott's *Little Men: Life at Plumfield with Jo's Boys* (1871) serves as a kind of bridge between the boys' school story and those written for girls. *Little Men*, though about boys at a fictional New England boarding school and including familiar character types such as the "bad boy" with a good heart, is far removed from the world of Tom Brown and Eric. Indebted to the educational theories of Alcott's father, Amos Bronson Alcott (1799–1888), Plumfield School is a nurturing place, generally disregarding sports and welcoming a few female scholars as well. Bronson, a Transcendentalist and an educational philosopher, believed in the importance of children's self-expression. He encouraged his students to ask questions and to study art, nature, and music, while he rejected traditional educational methods still in play such as rote memorization and corporal punishment.

"New World" educational systems and practices reveal the desire to maintain old traditions as well as to adopt new strategies appropriate for living far beyond England's borders. Indeed, Australian schooling remained deeply connected to Great Britain even well into the twentieth century, as Jill Ker Conway (b. 1934) recalls in her autobiography *The Road from Coorain* (1989): "We might have been born in Sussex for all the attention we paid to Australian poetry and prose. It did not count. We, for our part, dutifully learned Shakespeare's imagery drawn from the English landscape and from English horticulture." In America, Canada, and Australia, the school story both imitated British precursors and departed from their conventional framework. Yet the relative paucity of school stories set in these countries published before 1870 or so reflects the lack of boarding schools that had become a typical setting for the genre. In Australia, Louise Mack published a successful series of books for girls beginning with *Teens: A Story of Australian Schoolgirls* (1897), but the boarding school genre never really thrived outside of Britain. In America, the first boarding schools were established in the New England states and modeled on British schools. Thus, in Susan Coolidge's *What Katy Did at School* (1873), Katy Carr, the tomboy-turned-"light-of-the-home" heroine of the popular What Katy Did series for girls, must be sent to school "in the East" so that she can learn to be "girlish."

The American common school (grammar schools open to all white children in a district), unlike the British boarding school that seemingly institutionalized class hierarchies, was designed as part of a sweeping social reform agenda meant to encourage civic virtues such as honesty, hard work, and moral uprightness. It also underscored the "meritocracy" (albeit a limited one, given slavery and prejudice against Catholics, Jews, and foreigners) on which the new republic had been built. These common school democratic ideals existed side by side with other, less high-minded purposes, however: one driving force behind the movement was the desire to "Americanize" the growing number of immigrants (many of them non-Protestant) through a "common" educational system.

As America was settled, rough, country schools sprang up to serve the growing populations of the west. Schools spread rapidly from the New England states west-ward, as rural, usually one-room common schools were established for boys and girls in the expanding territories. These schools were unregulated, and there was little curricular uniformity; schoolbooks and teacher expertise could vary significantly from school to school. In Edward Eggleston's *The Hoosier School-Boy* (1883), the conditions in such schools are largely condemned; the novel is about a rural village school in Indiana in 1850 that is run by a tyrannical teacher. Standardization and attendance were twin goals of the flourishing educational system, and inroads were made in attaining them. By the 1870s, approximately 60 percent of white children received some schooling, and by the end of the century more than 70 percent had attended school.

Character building was of paramount importance for American schoolchildren, and the heroes of the early republic, such as George Washington, were served up as the models for American children to follow. In one early American didactic school story—*Rollo at School* (1839), one of a series of books written by Jacob Abbott—the gentle and upright teacher Miss Mary explains to her students that "Children are sent [to school] partly to be cured of their faults and improved in character. If any children have bad characters, they may be said to be morally diseased or sick, and I want to cure them." Horace Mann (1796–1859), secretary of the Massachusetts state board of education and a U.S. representative (1848–53), energetically supported educational reform; he was at the forefront of the movement to institute free, universal, coeducational, and nonsectarian public schools. After the Civil War, the Freedman's Bureau (1865–72), a federal agency designed to aid former slaves in the transition to life after slavery, built hospitals and more than a thousand schools for African American children. (The agency was short-lived because of pressure from white southerners.) The 1896 U.S. Supreme Court decision in *Plessy v. Ferguson* determined that segregation in schools was legal if the schools were "separate but equal." This position was not reversed until 1954, with *Brown v. Board of Education*; then integration became the law, although many public schools remained segregated for a decade or more, and some were never integrated.

Extending the focus on the growth of the individual child advanced by Rousseau and Alcott in particular, the American Progressive educational ideas promoted by John Dewey (1859–1952)—notably, the necessity for children to learn by experience, in a hands-on manner, and to bring their experiences from home *to* school and thus to connect the two halves of their lives—inflected school story fiction. That fiction began to blend with the family story and explore the child character's development both at home and at school. Dewey's ideas, in particular, cohered and spoke in the 1950s and '60s to those both appalled and inspired by the traumas and triumphs, optimism and opportunism that attended the wake of two world wars, struggles for civil rights and women's rights, the sexual revolution, the rise of the suburbs, an increase in divorce, and the disillusion of the Vietnam War era. Individual responsibility and action became the focus of progressive American educational philosophy, as put forth in such works as Dewey's *Experience and Education* (1938): "There is . . . no point in the philosophy of progressive education which is sounder than its emphasis upon the importance of the participation of the learner in the formation of the purposes which direct his activities in the learning process." "How do we educate the children?" was clearly a pressing political and philosophical question— in large part because the population constituting "the children" had expanded to include girls, nonwhites, and lower-class youth.

Recentering Authority in the Twentieth Century

The rise of the school story in nineteenth-century Britain in particular, but also in North America, attested to an increasingly literate population, growing numbers of schooling opportunities for (white) girls and the lower classes, and the appealing nature of stories about idealized schools and teachers. Adult nostalgia for school life can be located in those books that tend to glorify school days as the happiest days of one's life and to view teachers and school chums—rather than family—as having the most influence on character formation and ultimate success in later life.

Yet the ordered and comfortable world in which fairness ultimately triumphs, honor is upheld, and pleasure is found in games and loyal friendship stood in stark contrast to the chaos of World Wars I and II and the social changes that ensued. In particular, the popularity of girls' school story fiction between the wars may be evidence of a wish to escape a depressing reality and shifting social mores by reading about youthful high spirits and successes. In the long period of rebuilding after World War II, children's school stories reflected both the desire for heroes and the distrust of authority. Although wise instructors had played an important role in many of the earliest school stories, the love affair with the inspirational and often misunderstood teacher is particularly evident in children's and young adult school stories written in English from this period forward. Bel Kaufman's best-seller *Up the Down Staircase* (1965), about an urban American high school, uses realistic dialogue and the documents of the school day (notes, memorandums, etc.) to defend with pathos and humor the position of teachers and good teaching. Paula Danziger's first novel, *The Cat Ate My Gymsuit* (1974), describes a heroic young English teacher, Ms. Finney, who inspires her students to learn about books, language, and other people through unconventional teaching methods. When Ms. Finney's refusal to say the Pledge of Allegiance is brought before the school board in an attempt to fire her, students and parents defend her approach to teaching and mobilize to try to save her job. Along the way, both Marcy Lewis—who had always referred to herself as a worthless "baby blimp"—and her mother, president of the PTA but doormat to her boorish and harsh husband, learn to stand up for themselves and to speak out against mindless authoritarians and for progressive and feminist values. Similarly, the social outcast Bradley Chalkers in Louis Sachar's *There's a Boy in the Girls' Bathroom* (1987) learns how to control his anger and fear of rejection at school and at home through the intervention of a caring school counselor who helps him to think for himself (yet who is also run out of the school). Kirkpatrick Hill's *The Year of Miss Agnes* (2000) is about a young Englishwoman who begins teaching in an Alaskan village school in 1948 and who inspires the children through her unorthodox teaching methods and dedication to treating each child as an individual.

But teachers are sometimes human, weak, and flawed, and school stories increasingly include unflinching looks at the corruption of teachers and school leaders. J. D. Salinger's *The Catcher in the Rye* (1951) opens with Holden Caulfield running away from Pencey Prep, an exclusive private school in Agerstown, Pennsylvania, in part to avoid the "phonies" who surround him at school. He visits Mr. Spenser, in an attempt to find some answers, but can see only the pathetic nature of his aging teacher. Robert Cormier's *The Chocolate War* (1974) presents perhaps the most damning condemnation of authority figures in schools. Behind the ivy-covered walls of Trinity, a New England prep school for boys, resides a bullying teacher thirsty for power and the Vigils, a secret society of upperclassmen who devise cruel initiations for selected victims. Conflict arises around the chocolate sale, an annual fund-raising tradition, when Jerry Renault refuses to participate and defies the Vigils. Jerry suffers, yet he is able to withstand the targeted viciousness of individual teachers and students until finally he is physically and emotionally beaten by the realization that self-interest, conformity, and the anonymity of the mob are all stronger and more effective than any individual action.

In Andrew Clements's *The Landry News* (1999), written for younger readers, a fifth-grade student, Cara Landry, takes on her burned-out teacher (who refuses to teach and just reads the newspaper every day) by exposing his failures in an editorial. The short novel has a happy ending, however. Mr. Larson recognizes his failings and begins to teach his students in earnest again, starting with a unit on the First Amendment in conjunction with the disciplinary hearing he must undergo before the school board (the case is ultimately dismissed). Tom Perrota's *Election* (1998; made into a film starring Matthew Broderick and Reese Witherspoon in 1999) reveals the corruption of both teachers and students in a large public school during an election for student body president. The naked ambition, lust, indifference, and pettiness of both faculty and students are exposed through the changing first-person narratives that form the structure of the book. Ultimately, the previously popular and admired government teacher, Mr. McAllister, is brought down by his snap decision to destroy two ballots in order to favor the only sincere candidate running for student body president.

Making and Marking Transitions and Differences

Although the ideal of the American common school and ultimately of integration may have been to erase or minimize the importance of "differences" in the student body, schools have always been places of unrest and social unease for many children and young adults. Twentieth-century school stories reflect the growing awareness that school—or, indeed, home—may fail to support or nurture children. Leaving home (even to return at the end of the day), while considered liberating in the British school stories of old, often presents a troubling passage for contemporary characters.

Successfully negotiating the transition from home to school is the plot of many contemporary school stories, especially those written for younger children. In Beverly Cleary's *Ramona the Pest* (1968), the irrepressible Ramona conquers kindergarten, with some familiar low points along the way (being misunderstood, having to sit out a game, etc.). This transition can be made more difficult when conflicts arising from race, class, gender, and disability shape the school experience. One complaint made about the school story is that it has, historically, tended to be concerned with upper- and middle-class white children, though there are exceptions and the genre is changing. Eleanor Estes's *The Hundred Dresses* (1944), for example, concerns a Polish immigrant child who is kept out of the inner circle of girls at school because of her obvious poverty. She draws their attention only as an object of curiosity and a source of amusement after she claims to have a hundred beautiful dresses at home. Given the universal anxiety attendant on being "new," readers of the opening to Alma Flor Ada's novella *My Name Is María Isabel* (1993) will likely sympathize with third-grader María Isabel's growing despair as she anticipates her first day at a new school. María Isabel's integration into the classroom is delayed by her well-meaning but insensitive teacher's erasure of her real name for the English equivalent, "Mary." In the British author Anne Fine's *Bill's New Frock* (1989), Bill awakens one morning to find that he has turned into a girl. His experiences at school—from the way that teachers respond to him to the books he is encouraged to read and the restrictions placed on him by his clothes—are all determined by his gender transformation. Issues of race, ethnicity, religion, and disability at school are confronted in the African American author Virginia Hamilton's *Bluish* (1999), an honest portrayal of the fears that many children have when confronted with differences related to disability and illness. Jack Gantos's novel about a boy who suffers from attention deficit hyperactivity disorder (ADHD), *Joey Pigza Swallowed the Key* (1998), takes the reader on a wild ride through Joey's mind as he careens around school. Reading about Joey, a child who has lived in an abusive, dysfunctional family and who is consistently undermedicated and punished for his inability to control himself, is painful, and his successes, in keeping with the realistic nature of the book, are moderate.

At times, overcoming differences is not the key to success in school, or to making the leap between safe home and alienating school. Although formulaic plots in which the scholarship pupil becomes the most popular student in school have always been well-received, choosing whether or not to fit in is more complicated—and it is a decision that many children must make. In Jacqueline Woodson's *Maizon at Blue Hill* (1992), for example, Maizon's discomfort in an exclusive and primarily white boarding school makes her rethink what success in school means to her.

Peer Relationships

Adults have consistently feared and attempted to regulate the strong attachments children and young adults make in school. As peers replace family as the young person's primary social objects, adults grow anxious about losing their influence over the child, and perhaps about the rapid changes that take place within him or her seemingly overnight. Parents and other authority figures are kept to the margins of contemporary school fiction, and virtually all school stories focus on the intense peer relationships that children form at school. In Nikki Grimes's *Bronx Masquerade* (2002), for example, a group of high school classmates, previously closed off to each other, participate in "open mike" poetry events and reveal their inner selves through performing their poetry. In sharing their poems, the students form a close-knit community based on trust and mutual respect. Peer relationships are often nourishing, yet increasingly in contemporary fiction friendships have the potential to be devastating. John Knowles's *A Separate Peace* (1960), often taught in American secondary schools, is set in 1942 at a New England prep school and explores the close and complex relationship that develops between two classmates. For the narrator Gene Forrester, the "confusions of [his] own character" are revealed in his intense relationship with his best friend, Phineas. In the Canadian author Kit Pearson's boarding school novel *The Daring Game* (1986), eleven-year old Eliza chooses to attend Ashdown Academy in Vancouver in part because she has enjoyed British school stories. At Ashdown, however, Eliza's loyal friendship with the unhappy girl who institutes the "daring game" threatens her own happiness and balance.

The petty or profound cruelties children inflict—either unintentionally or willingly—on other children at school is a consistent theme in nineteenth- to twentieth-century school stories. In Frances Hodgson Burnett's *A Little Princess* (1905), once the "princess" Sara Crewe loses her fortune, she is treated abominably by the headmistress and most of the girls, who take their cues from the cruel school leader (although a core of other students continue to love her for her selflessness and quick imagination). Contemporary stories tend to explore the psychological dimension of the bully or to focus on the peer pressure that pushes children to hurt each other, rather than simply punishing the antisocial character. The heroine of Louise Fitzhugh's *Harriet the Spy* (1964) is quite understandably ostracized and humiliated by her classmates after her journal filled with truthful but terribly unkind commentary is discovered. Harriet learns that it's sometimes necessary to lie to others—but never to herself. The characters Margalo and Mikey in Cynthia Voigt's *Bad Girls* (1996) are true inheritors of Harriet M. Welsch. Voigt's novel is set entirely in a fifth-grade class run by the strictest teacher in Washington Street Elementary School. Margalo and Mikey are both new to the school and become united—though they don't entirely trust each other—through a general interest in disrupting the class, upsetting the status quo, and fighting for position and power in the classroom. The point of the book is not to redeem these characters or to reform them, but to examine why they act in certain ways and to celebrate their "bad" attitudes.

The problem of bullying in school, which has always been an alarming issue for some children, parents, and school officials, has lately become a topic of some interest to educational theorists, psychologists, and lawmakers. Aidan Chambers's novel *The Present Takers* (1983) depicts a female bully who makes life miserable for her selected victims at a coeducational school in England. Significantly, the bullying does not stop at the intervention of adults—children know that this kind of top-down action never really works—but is resolved through the problem solving of the children themselves. There is pain and anxiety involved and no fairy-tale magic ending. Yet in such works the effect for the characters is usually hard-won wisdom and sometimes empathy for the harassing student.

Humorous School Stories

Children spend most of their days in school, and life's pleasures and pains are primarily experienced there. The school day as framework for the interaction of a host of characters that range across schoolbus driver, teacher, principal, best friend, bully, nemesis, and god or goddess classmate provides the material for unlimited scenes of rueful pathos and humor. Humorous books about contemporary school experiences often run in series and invert, mock, or exaggerate the day-to-day challenges and rewards, generally of early school days. The short story "Tweedledum and Tweedledead" (1993) by the Canadian author Tim Wynne-Jones sends up the kind of stultifying, creativity-deadening homework assignment that every schoolchild will recognize. The absurdity in Louis Sachar's first short story collection about Wayside School (built "sideways," so that the thirty classrooms in the school are stacked on top of one another), *Sideways Stories from Wayside School* (1978), runs the gamut from John, who is in the highest reading group but who can only read upside down, to Dana, who scratches her many mosquito bites and can't concentrate on her arithmetic until the mosquito bites turn into numbers and are counted. Sachar's Marvin Redpost series and Barbara Park's Junie B. Jones series are child-centered easy-to-read books that combine the kind of humor children enjoy (often gross or mildly crass) with frank attention to their concerns about being popular and succeeding at school. The "classroom" setting for the Australian author Elizabeth Honey's *Don't Pat the Wombat!* (1996) is the Australian outback. A raucous group of sixth-grade children spend a week at school camp to learn about pioneer ways. The book is illustrated with joyful and silly cartoons and photographs of children at camp, yet this hilarious and fast-paced narrative also contains a serious story about the inability to belong to the group, the cruelties of an unpopular and unjust teacher, and the corresponding insensitivity of children toward an adult with problems. Certainly, in her Harry Potter books (whose publication began in Britain in 1997) J. K. Rowling uses the school story conventions described above, while combining fantasy and humor to create the wildly popular series.

Many young adult novels about school—or popular television programs that use high school as a backdrop, such as the Canadian *Degrassi Junior High* and *Degrassi High* series (1987–91; see also the current show, *Degrassi: The Next Generation*) or the American *Beverly Hills 90210* (1990–2000)—no longer attempt to teach anything heavy-handedly "moral." In these books, students, teachers, and parents are all flawed. Contemporary books about the bad decisions teen characters make as a result of their boredom, high spirits, lust, and loneliness often highlight the personal growth and self-knowledge that can ensue from such mistakes, rather than their negative effects. High schoolers have sex without serious consequences, drink and take drugs, lie and skip school as a part of "normal" high school life. For example, Rob Thomas's linked short stories in *Doing Time: Notes from the Undergrad* (1997) contain first-person narratives of nine American secondary school students who attend a school that requires 200 hours of community service before graduation. The stories transcend what this plot conceit may seem to promise: tales of do-gooder students who learn about the underprivileged and come to a greater understanding of themselves. Although in a number of stories the characters' forced efforts to help others result in positive, mutual benefits for the teen and the "objects" of his or her community service, many reveal the narrators' cynicism, betrayal, intolerance, and self-centeredness.

A look at today's schools in Britain and North America can tell us quite a bit about the societies that support them (or fail to do so), as they change because of the demands of and new conditions in a fast-paced, diverse, and ever-changing world. Accommodations that schools have made in response to political and social pressures, whether voluntarily or by legislative dictate, include the provision of breakfast, often subsidized for low-income students; the institution of required technology and keyboarding courses, coupled with the virtual disappearance of home economics and shop; the ever-increasing presence of national standards, ascertained by standardized testing, in grade-level curriculum; rules and laws banning hate speech and sexual harassment; and in some U.S. schools, a mandatory moment of silence and the required recitation of the Pledge of Allegiance. Unlike the school stories of the past that were about self-contained worlds, children's books written about children in schools today reflect both the negative and positive of what lies outside the classroom. The basic requirements for a "good" school—a safe place where all children can learn and succeed both academically and socially—often fail to be met. Many schools are impersonal, violent, and oppressive places. But even the most bleak school stories written for teens generally express a belief in the resilience of youth and in the value of gaining knowledge of self and the world, however hard-won. Sally Mitchell argues that the success of the formulaic school story of the past is due, in part, to its creation of "a community where the important rules are the children's own ethics and mores." This element remains crucial in contemporary school stories, though the ethics have changed somewhat. School stories designed for either younger or older readers tend to be deeply reassuring; even if school is a scary, boring, or alienating place, the ultimate message they convey is that you are not alone.

SARAH FIELDING
1710–1768

As the first full-length story written expressly for the amusement of girls, *The Governess; or, Little Female Academy* (1749) marks a milestone in children's literature. In the preface to *The Governess*, Sarah Fielding makes clear that her intention in writing a book for girls is to encourage them to find happiness through virtue: "The Design of the following Sheets is to prove to you, that Pride, Stubbornness, Malice, Envy, and, in short, all manner of Wickedness, is the greatest Folly we can be possessed of. . . . Certainly, Love and Affection for each other make the Happiness of all Societies; and therefore Love and Affection (if we would be happy) are what we should chiefly encourage and cherish in our Minds." By the time of Fielding's death in 1768, *The Governess* had gone into its fifth English edition, and its success may well have inspired the educationalists Ann Murray in *Mentoria, or the Young Lady's Instructor* (1778) and Mary Wollstonecraft in *Thoughts on the Education of Daughters* (1787) to write their works on female education. Mary Sherwood, an Evangelical author of numerous children's tales and tracts, was so convinced that the moral fairy tales embedded within *The Governess* were harmful to children that she rewrote Fielding's story and published it in 1820 under her own name. Charlotte Yonge, a bestselling novelist of domestic life and the editor of *The Monthly Packet*, a magazine for girls, reunited the text with its true author by republishing Fielding's original in 1870.

Sarah Fielding, sister of the novelist Henry Fielding (1707–1754), was born on a country estate in Dorset and lived happily there with her five siblings until her mother died when she was seven years old. Very soon after her mother's death, Fielding's father married a Roman Catholic woman and the family was split up, with the girls sent to boarding school. Attending school was atypical for young females of any social class, and Fielding would later use this unusual yet positive experience as the basis for one of her most popular works, *The Governess; or, Little Female Academy*. Fielding lived quietly but without financial security in London or Bath with her brother Henry and his family, with sisters and friends, or alone, surviving by her pen and by the kindness of others. Fielding's first and most successful novel, *The Adventures of David Simple* (1744), promoted prudent friendship, a topic carried through many of her works. The printer and moralist Samuel Richardson, author of the popular epistolary novel *Pamela, or Virtue Rewarded* (1740–41), encouraged Fielding's literary efforts and printed *The Governess*, her third book. Among other works, the learned Fielding published a translation of Xenophon's *Memoirs of Socrates* (1761).

The audience, setting, and subject of *The Governess* are worth remarking: writing for girls about female friendship, community, moral development, and self-respect, Fielding also included entertaining tales of wonder as a strategy of instruction for her middle-class readers, even though at this time fantasy was considered to be dangerous for children to read. The body of the story, which focuses on the nine pupils enrolled at Mrs. Teachum's Academy, takes place over eleven days. Eight of the girls quarrel bitterly and it is up to Jenny Peace, the eldest girl, to help the students reconcile and learn the difficult lesson that happiness resides in self-denial and generosity. By imitating Jenny's good example, confessing their faults, telling their life stories, and listening to persuasive moral tales about the consequences of right and wrong conduct, the students gain self-knowledge and valuable social skills. The selection printed here includes the preface and first two days of the narrative. Jenny Peace's story about the rewards of patience and kindness, "The Story of the Cruel Giant Barbarico, the Good Giant Benefico, and the Little Pretty Dwarf Mignon," is reprinted in the Fairy Tale section, above. Our text is from the revised and corrected 1759 edition.

From The Governess; or, The Little Female Academy

PREFACE

My Young Readers,

Before you begin the following Sheets, I beg you will stop a Moment at this Preface, to consider with me what is the true Use of Reading; and if you can once fix this Truth in your Minds, namely, that the true Use of Books is to make you wiser and better, you will then have both Profit and Pleasure from what you read.

One Thing quite necessary to make any Instructions that come either from your Governors, or your Books, of any Use to you, is to attend with a Desire of Learning, and not to be apt to fansy yourselves too wise to be taught. For this Spirit will keep you ignorant as long as you live, and you will be like the Birds in the following Fable:

The *Magpye* alone, of all the Birds, had the Art of building a Nest, the Form of which was with a Covering over Head, and only a small Hole to creep out at.—The rest of the Birds, being without Houses, desired the *Pye* to teach them how to build one.—A Day is appointed, and they all meet.—The *Pye* then says, "You must lay Two Sticks across, thus."—"Aye, says the *Crow*, I thought that was the way to begin.—Then lay a little Straw and Moss.—Certainly, says the *Jack-Daw*, I knew that must follow.—Then place more Straw, Moss, and Feathers, in such a Manner as this.—Aye, without doubt, cries the *Starling*, that must necessarily follow; any one could tell how to do that."—When the *Pye* had gone on teaching them till the Nest was built half way, and every Bird in his Turn had known either one thing or another, he left off, and said, "Gentlemen, I find you all understand building Nests as well, if not better, than I do; therefore you cannot want any more of my Instructions."——So saying, he flew away, and left them to upbraid each other with their Folly; which is visible to this Day, as no Bird but the *Magpye* knows how to build more than half a Nest.

The Reason these foolish Birds never knew how to build more than half a Nest, was, that instead of trying to learn what the *Pye* told them, they would boast of knowing more already than he could teach them: And this same Fate will certainly attend all those, who had rather please themselves with the Vanity of fansying they are already wise, than take Pains to become so.

But take care, that, instead of being really humble in your own Hearts, you do not, by a fansied Humility, run into an Error of the other Extreme, and say that you are incapable of understanding it at all; and therefore, from Laziness, and sooner than take any Pains, sit yourselves down contented to be ignorant, and think, by confessing your Ignorance, to make full Amends for your Folly. This is being as contemptible as the *Owl*, who hates the Light of the Sun; and therefore often makes use of the Power he has, of drawing a Film over his Eyes, to keep himself in his beloved Darkness.

When you run thro' Numbers of Books, only for the sake of saying, you have read them, without making any Advantage of the Knowledge got thereby, remember this Saying, "That a Head, like a House, when crammed too full, and no regular Order observed in the placing what is there, is only littered instead of being furnished." And that you may the better understand the Force of this Observation, I will tell you a Story.

Mr. *Thomas Watkins* had Two Daughters, Miss *Hannah* and Miss *Fanny*. Their Father and Mother assigned them a very pretty Apartment for their own Use, allowed them all Things in great Plenty, and only desired them to keep their Cloaths, Linen, and all their Things, in such a proper Order, that they might have the Use of them. But these Two foolish Girls, fansying themselves wiser than their Parents, disobeyed their Commands, and threw all their Things about in such irregular Heaps, that whenever they were to be dressed, they found themselves more at a Loss, than any poor Girl would have been, who had not had half their Plenty allowed her. Whenever their Mamma sent them Word she would take them abroad,[1] they were in the greatest Confusion that can be imagined: 'Oh! Sister *Hannah* (cries Miss *Fanny*), can you tell where I put my Cap?' No, indeed (answers Miss *Hannah*) nor can I find my own, nor my Gloves, nor my Hood. Well, what shall I do? My Mamma is in such a Hurry, she will not stay for us.'——Then would these Two Girls tumble all the Things in their Drawers; but in that Confusion could find nothing, till their Mamma was drove from the Door, leaving them at home as they deserved: Whilst, looking ashamed at each other, they were laughed at by the rest of the Family.

Thus will those foolish Children be served, who heap into their Heads a great deal, and yet never observe what they put there, either to mend their Practice, or increase their Knowledge. Their Heads will be in as much Confusion, as were Miss *Watkins*'s Chests of Drawers. And when in Company they endeavour to find out something to say to the Purpose, they will be hunting in the midst of a Heap of Rubbish, whilst they expose themselves, and become a Laughing-stock to their Companions.

The Design of the following Sheets is to prove to you, that Pride, Stubbornness, Malice, Envy, and, in short, all manner of Wickedness, is the greatest Folly we can be possessed of; and constantly turns on the Head of that foolish Person who does not conquer and get the better of all Inclinations to such Wickedness. Certainly, Love and Affection for each other make the Happiness of all Societies; and therefore Love and Affection (if we would be happy) are what we should chiefly encourage and cherish in our Minds.

I depend on the Goodness of all my little Readers, to acknowledge this to be true. But there is one Caution to be used, namely, That you are not led into many Inconveniences,[2] and even Faults, by this Love and Affection: For this Disposition will naturally lead you to delight in Friendship; and this Delight in Friendship may lead you into all manner of Errors, unless you take care not to be partial to any of your Companions, only because they are agreeable, without first considering whether they are good enough to deserve your Love: And there is one Mark in which you can never be deceived; namely, That whoever tempts you to fail in your Duty, or justifies you in so doing, is not your real Friend. And if you cannot have Resolution enough to break from such pretended Friends, you will nourish in your Bosoms Serpents, that in the End will sting you to Death.

THE GOVERNESS; OR, THE LITTLE FEMALE ACADEMY

There lived in the Northern Parts of *England*, a Gentlewoman who undertook the Education of young Ladies; and this Trust she endeavour'd faithfully to discharge, by instructing those committed to her Care in Reading, Writing, Working, and in all proper Forms of Behaviour. And tho' her principal Aim was to improve their Minds

---

1. Out of the house.　　　　　　　　2. Improprieties.

in all useful Knowledge; to render them obedient to their Superiors, and gentle, kind, and affectionate to each other; yet did she not omit teaching them an exact Neatness in their Persons and Dress, and a perfect Gentility in their whole Carriage.

This Gentlewoman, whose Name was *Teachum*, was the Widow of a Clergyman, with whom she had lived nine Years, in all the Harmony and Concord which form the only satisfactory Happiness in the married State. Two little Girls (the youngest of which was born before the second Year of their Marriage was expired) took up a great Part of their Thoughts; and it was their mutual Design to spare no Pains or Trouble in their Education.

Mr. *Teachum* was a very sensible Man, and took great Delight in improving his Wife; as she also placed her chief Pleasure in receiving his Instructions. One of his constant Subjects of Discourse to her was concerning the Education of Children: So that, when in his last Illness his Physicians pronounced him beyond the Power of their Art to relieve him, he expressed great Satisfaction in the Thought of leaving his Children to the Care of so prudent a Mother.

Mrs. *Teachum*, tho' exceedingly afflicted by such a Loss, yet thought it her Duty to call forth all her Resolution to conquer her Grief, in order to apply herself to the Care of these her dear Husband's Children. But her Misfortunes were not here to end: For within a Twelvemonth after the Death of her Husband, she was deprived of both her Children by a violent Fever, that then raged in the Country; and about the same time, by the unforeseen Breaking[3] of a Banker, in whose Hands almost all her Fortune was just then placed, she was bereft of the Means of her future Support.

The Christian Fortitude with which (thro' her Husband's Instructions) she had armed her Mind, had not left it in the Power of any outward Accident to bereave her of her Understanding, or to make her incapable of doing what was proper on all Occasions. Therefore, by the Advice of all her Friends, she undertook what she was so well qualified for; namely, the Education of Children. But as she was moderate in her Desires, and did not seek to raise a great Fortune, she was resolved to take no more Scholars than she could have an Eye to herself, without the Help of other Teachers; and, instead of making Interest[4] to fill her School, it was looked upon as a great Favour when she would take any Girl: And as her Number was fixed to Nine, which she on no Account would be prevailed on to increase, great Application was made, when any Scholar went away, to have her Place supplied; and happy were they who could get a Promise for the next Vacancy.

Mrs. *Teachum* was about Forty Years old, tall and genteel in her Person, tho' somewhat inclined to Fat. She had a lively and commanding Eye, insomuch that she naturally created an Awe in all her little Scholars; except when she condescended to smile, and talk familiarly to them; and then she had something perfectly kind and tender in her Manner. Her Temper was so extremely calm and good, that tho' she never omitted reprehending, and that pretty severely, any Girl that was guilty of the smallest Fault proceeding from an evil Disposition; yet for no Cause whatsoever was she provoked to be in a Passion: But she kept up such a Dignity and Authority, by her steady Behaviour, that the Girls greatly feared to incur her Displeasure by disobeying her Commands; and were equally pleased with her Approbation, when they had done anything worthy [of] her Commendation.

At the Time of the ensuing History, the School (being full) consisted of the Nine following young Ladies:

---

3. Financial failure, bankruptcy.   4. Bringing personal interest to bear.

Miss *Jenny Peace*,

Miss *Sukey Jennett*,	Miss *Nanney* [sic] *Spruce*,
Miss *Dolly Friendly*,	Miss *Betty Ford*,
Miss *Lucy Sly*,	Miss *Henny Fret*,
Miss *Patty Lockit*,	Miss *Polly Suckling*.

The eldest of these was but fourteen Years old, and none of the rest had yet attained their twelfth Year.

AN ACCOUNT OF A FRAY, BEGUN AND CARRIED ON FOR THE SAKE OF AN APPLE: IN WHICH ARE SHEWN THE SAD EFFECTS OF RAGE AND ANGER.

It was on a fine Summer's Evening, when the School-hours were at an End, and the young Ladies were admitted to divert themselves for some time, as they thought proper, in a pleasant Garden adjoining to the House, that their Governess, who delighted in pleasing them, brought out a little Basket of Apples, which were intended to be divided equally amongst them: But Mrs. *Teachum* being hastily called away (one of her poor Neighbours having had an Accident which wanted her Assistance), she left the Fruit in the Hands of Miss *Jenny Peace*, the eldest of her Scholars, with a strict Charge to see that every one had an equal Share of her Gift.

But here a perverse Accident turned good Mrs. *Teachum*'s Design of giving them Pleasure into their Sorrow, and raised in their little Hearts nothing but Strife and Anger: For, alas! there happened to be one Apple something larger than the rest, on which the whole Company immediately placed their desiring Eyes, and all at once cried out, 'Pray, Miss *Jenny*, give me 'that Apple.' Each gave her Reasons why she had the best Title to it: The youngest pleaded her Youth, and the eldest her Age; one insisted on her Goodness, another from her Meekness claimed a Title to Preference; and one, in Confidence of her Strength, said positively, she would have it: but all speaking together, it was difficult to distinguish who said this, or who said that.

Miss *Jenny* begg'd them all to be quiet: But in vain; for she could not be heard: They had all set their Hearts on that fine Apple, looking upon those she had given them as nothing. She told them, they had better be contented with what they had, than be thus seeking what it was impossible for her to give to them all. She offered to divide it into Eight Parts, or to do any thing to satisfy them: But she might as well have been silent; for they were all talking, and had no time to hear. At last, as a Means to quiet the Disturbance, she threw this Apple, the Cause of their Contention, with her utmost Force, over a Hedge, into another Garden, where they could not come at it.

At first they were all silent, as if they were struck dumb with Astonishment with the Loss of this one poor Apple, tho' at the same time they had Plenty before them.

But this did not bring to pass Miss *Jenny*'s Design: For now they all began again to quarrel which had the most Right to it, and which *ought* to have had it, with as much Vehemence as they had before contended for the Possession of it: And their Anger by degrees became so high, that Words could not vent half their Rage; and they fell to pulling of Caps, tearing of Hair, and dragging the Cloaths off one another's Backs: Though they did not so much strike, as endeavour to scratch and pinch their Enemies.

Miss *Dolly Friendly* as yet was not engaged in the Battle: But on hearing her Friend Miss *Nanny Spruce* scream out, that she was hurt by a sly Pinch from one of the

Girls, she flew on this sly Pincher, as she called her, like an enraged Lion on its Prey; and not content only to return the Harm her Friend had received, she struck with such Force, as felled her Enemy to the Ground. And now they could not distinguish between Friend and Enemy; but fought, scratch'd, and tore, like so many Cats, when they extend their Claws to fix them in their Rival's Heart.

Miss *Jenny* was employed in endeavouring to part them.

In the Midst of this Confusion, appeared Mrs. *Teachum*, who was returned, in Hopes to see them happy with the Fruit she had given them: But she was some time there before either her Voice or Presence could awaken them from their Attention to the Fight; when on a sudden they all faced her, and Fear of Punishment began now a little to abate their Rage. Each of the Misses held in her Right-hand, fast clenched, some Marks of Victory; for they beat and were beaten by Turns. One of them held a little Lock of Hair, torn from the Head of her Enemy: Another grasped a Piece of a Cap, which, in aiming at her Rival's Hair, had deceived[5] her Hand, and was all the Spoils she could gain: A third clenched a Piece of an Apron; a fourth, of a Frock. In short, every one unfortunately held in her Hand a Proof of having been engaged in the Battle. And the Ground was spread with Rags and Tatters, torn from the Backs of the little inveterate Combatants.

Mrs. *Teachum* stood for some time astonished at the Sight: But at last she required Miss *Jenny Peace*, who was the only Person disengaged, to tell her the whole Truth, and to inform her of the Cause of all this Confusion.

Miss *Jenny* was obliged to obey the Commands of her Governess; tho' she was so good-natured, that she did it in the mildest Terms; and endeavoured all she could to lessen, rather than increase, Mrs. *Teachum*'s Anger. The guilty Persons now began all to excuse themselves as fast as Tears and Sobs would permit them.

One said, "Indeed, Madam, it was none of my Fault; for I did not begin; for Miss *Sukey Jennett*, without any Cause in the World (for I did nothing to provoke her), hit me a great Slap in the Face, and made my Tooth ach: The Pain *did* make me angry; and then, indeed, I hit her a little Tap; but it was on her Back; and I am sure it was the smallest Tap in the World; and could not possibly hurt her half so much as her great Blow did me."

"Law, Miss! replied Miss *Jennett*, How can you say so? when you know that you struck me first, and that yours was the great Blow, and mine the little Tap; for I only went to defend myself from your monstrous Blows."

Such-like Defences they would all have made for themselves, each insisting on not being in Fault, and throwing the Blame on her Companion: But Mrs. *Teachum* silenced them by a positive Command; and told them, that she saw they were all equally guilty, and as such she would treat them.

Mrs. *Teachum*'s Method of punishing I never could find out. But this is certain, the most severe Punishment she had ever inflicted on any Misses, since she had kept a School, was now laid on these wicked Girls, who had been thus fighting, and pulling one another to Pieces, for a sorry Apple.

The first thing she did, was to take away all the Apples; telling them, that before they had any more instances of such kindness from her, they should give her Proofs of their deserving them better. And when she had punished them as much as she thought proper, she made them all embrace one another, and promise to be Friends for the future; which, in Obedience to her Commands, they were forced to comply with, tho' there remained a Grudge and Ill-will in their Bosoms; every one thinking

5. Frustrated; cheated.

she was punished most, altho' she would have it, that she deserved to be punished least; and they contrived all the sly Tricks they could think on to vex and teaze each other.

A Dialogue between Miss JENNY PEACE, and Miss SUKEY JENNETT; wherein the latter is at last convinced of her own Folly in being so quarrelsome; and, by her Example, all her Companions are brought to see and confess their Fault.

The next Morning Miss *Jenny Peace* used her utmost Endeavours to bring her School-fellows to be heartily reconciled; but in vain: For each insisted on it, that she was not to blame; but that the whole Quarrel arose from the Faults of others. At last ensued the following Dialogue between Miss *Jenny Peace* and Miss *Sukey Jennett*, which brought about Miss *Jenny*'s Designs; and which we recommend to the Consideration of all our young Readers.

Miss *Jenny*.   Now pray, Miss *Sukey*, tell me, What did you get by your Contention and Quarrel about that foolish Apple?

Miss *Sukey*.   Indeed, Ma'am, I shall not answer you. I know that you only want to prove, that you are wiser than I, because you are older. But I don't know but some People may understand as much at Eleven Years old, as others at Thirteen: But, because you are the oldest in the School, you always want to be tutoring and governing. I don't like to have more than one Governess; and if I obey my Mistress, I think that is enough.

Miss *Jenny*.   Indeed, my Dear, I don't want to govern you, nor to prove myself wiser than you: I only, want, that, instead of quarreling, and making yourself miserable, you should live at Peace, and be happy. Therefore, pray do, answer my Question, Whether you got any-thing by your Quarrel?

Miss *Sukey*.   No! I cannot say I got any-thing by it: For my Mistress was angry, and punished me; and my Hair was pulled off, and my Cloaths torn, in the Scuffle: Neither did I value the Apple: But yet I have too much Spirit to be imposed on. I am sure I had as good a Right to it as any of the others: And I would not give up my Right to any one.

Miss *Jenny*.   But don't you know, Miss *Sukey*, it would have shewn much more Spirit to have yielded the Apple to another, than to have fought about it? Then, indeed, you would have proved your Sense; for you would have shewn, that you had too much Understanding to fight about a Trifle. Then your Cloaths had been whole, your Hair not torn from your Head, your Mistress had not been angry, nor had your Fruit been taken away from you.

Miss *Sukey*.   And so, Miss, you would fain prove, that it is wisest to submit to every-body that would impose upon one? But I will not believe it, say what you will.

Miss *Jenny*.   But is not what I say true? If you had not been in the Battle, would not your Cloaths have been whole, your Hair not torn, your Mistress pleased with you, and the Apples your own?

Here Miss *Sukey* paused for some time: For as Miss *Jenny* was in the Right, and had Truth on her Side, it was difficult for Miss *Sukey* to know what to answer. For it is impossible, without being very silly, to contradict Truth; And yet Miss *Sukey* was so foolish, that she did not care to own herself in the Wrong; tho' nothing could have been so great a Sign of her Understanding.

When Miss *Jenny* saw her thus at a Loss for an Answer, she was in Hopes of making her Companion happy; for, as she had as much Good-nature as Understanding, that was her Design. She therefore pursued her Discourse in the following Manner:

Miss *Jenny*.   Pray, Miss *Sukey*, do answer me one Question more. Don't you lie awake at Nights, and fret and vex yourself, because you are angry with your School-fellows? Are not you restless and uneasy, because you cannot find a safe Method to be revenged on them, without being punished yourself? Do tell me truly, Is not this your Case?

Miss *Sukey*.   Yes, it is. For if I could but hurt my Enemies, without being hurt myself, it would be the greatest Pleasure I could have in the World.

Miss *Jenny*.   Oh, fy, Miss *Sukey!* What you have now said is wicked. Don't you consider what you say every Day in your Prayers? And this Way of Thinking will make you lead a very uneasy Life. If you would hearken to me, I could put you into a Method of being very happy, and making all those Misses you call your Enemies, become your Friends.

Miss *Sukey*.   You could tell me a Method, Miss! Do you think I don't know as well as you what is fit to be done? I believe I am as capable of finding the Way to be happy, as you are of teaching me.

Here Miss *Sukey* burst into Tears, that any-body should presume to tell her the Way to be happy.

Miss *Jenny*.   Upon my Word, my Dear, I don't mean to vex you; but only, instead of tormenting yourself all Night in laying Plots to revenge yourself, I would have you employ this one Night in thinking of what I have said. Nothing will shew your Sense so much, as to own that you have been in the Wrong: Nor will any-thing prove a right Spirit so much, as to confess your Fault. All the Misses will be your Friends, and perhaps follow your Example. Then you will have the Pleasure of having caused the Quiet of the whole School; your Governess will love you; and you will be at Peace in your Mind, and never have any more foolish Quarrels, in which you all get nothing but Blows and Uneasiness.

Miss *Sukey* began now to find, that Miss *Jenny* was in the Right, and she herself in the Wrong; but yet she was so proud she would not own it. Nothing could be so foolish as this Pride; because it would have been both good and wise in her to confess the Truth the Moment she saw it. However, Miss *Jenny* was so discreet as not to press her any farther that Night; but begged her to consider seriously on what she had said, and to let her know her Thoughts the next Morning. And then left her.

When Miss *Sukey* was alone, she stood some time in great Confusion. She could not help seeing how much hitherto she had been in the Wrong; and that Thought stung her to the Heart. She cried, stamped, and was in as great an Agony as if some sad Misfortune had befallen her. At last, when she had somewhat vented her Passion by Tears, she burst forth into the following Speech:

"It is very true what Miss *Jenny Peace* says; for I am always uneasy. I don't sleep in quiet; because I am always thinking, either that I have not my Share of what is given us, or that I cannot be revenged on any of the Girls that offend me. And when

I quarrel with them, I am scratched and bruised, or reproached. And what do I get by all this? Why, I scratch, bruise, and reproach them in my Turn. Is not that Gain enough? I warrant I hurt them as much as they hurt me. But then, indeed, as Miss *Jenny* says, if I could make these Girls my Friends, and did not wish to hurt them, I certainly might live a quieter, and perhaps a happier Life.—But what, then, have I been always in the Wrong all my Life-time? for I always quarreled and hated every one who had offended me.—Oh! I cannot bear that Thought! It is enough to make me mad! when I imagined myself so wise and so sensible, to find out that I have been always a Fool. If I think a Moment longer about it, I shall die with Grief and Shame. I must think myself in the Right; and I will too.—But, as Miss *Jenny* says, I really am unhappy; for I hate all my School-fellows: And yet I dare not do them any Mischief; for my Mistress will punish me severely if I do. I should not so much mind that neither: But then those I intend to hurt will triumph over me, to see me punished for their sakes. In short, the more I reflect, the more I am afraid Miss *Jenny* is in the Right; and yet it breaks my Heart to think so."

Here the poor Girl wept so bitterly, and was so heartily grieved, that she could not utter one Word more; but sat herself down, reclining her Head upon her Hand, in the most melancholy Posture that could be: Nor could she close her Eyes all Night; but lay tossing and raving with the Thought how she should act, and what she should say to Miss *Jenny* the next Day.

When the Morning came, Miss *Sukey* dreaded every Moment, as the Time drew nearer when she must meet Miss *Jenny*. She knew it would not be possible to resist her Arguments; and yet Shame for having been in Fault overcame her.

As soon as Miss *Jenny* saw Miss *Sukey* with her Eyes cast down, and confessing, by a Look of Sorrow, that she would take her Advice, she embraced her kindly; and, without giving her the Trouble to speak, took it for granted, that she would leave off quarreling, be reconciled to her School-fellows, and make herself happy.

Miss *Sukey* did indeed stammer out some Words, which implied a Confession of her Fault; but they were spoke so low they could hardly be heard: Only Miss *Jenny*, who always chose to look at the fairest Side of her Companions Actions, by Miss *Sukey*'s Look and Manner, guessed her Meaning.

In the same manner did this good Girl, *Jenny*, persuade, one by one, all her Schoolfellows to be reconciled to each with Sincerity and Love.

Miss *Dolly Friendly*, who had too much Sense to engage in the Battle for the sake of an Apple, and who was provoked to strike a Blow only for Friendship's Sake, easily saw the Truth of what Miss *Jenny* said; and was therefore presently convinced, that the best Part she could have acted for her Friend, would have been withdrawing her from the Scuffle.

A Scene of Love and Friendship, quite the Reverse of the Battle: Wherein are shewn the different Effects of Love and Goodness from those attending Anger, Strife, and Wickedness: With the Life of Miss *Jenny Peace*.

After Miss *Jenny* had completed the good Work of making all her Companions Friends, she drew them round her in a little Arbour, in that very Garden which had been the Scene of their Strife, and consequently of their Misery; and then spoke to them the following Speech; which she delivered in so mild a Voice, that it was sufficient to charm her Hearers into Attention, and to persuade them to be led by her Advice, and to follow her Example, in the Paths of Goodness.

"My dear Friends and School-fellows, you cannot imagine the Happiness it gives me to see you thus all so heartily reconciled. You will find the joyful Fruits of it. Nothing can shew so much Sense, as thus to own yourselves in Fault: For could anything have been so foolish, as to spend all your Time in Misery, rather than at once to make use of the Power you have of making yourselves happy? Now if you will use as many Endeavours to love, as you have hitherto done to hate each other, you will find, that every one amongst you, whenever you have any-thing given you, will have double, nay, I may say, Eight times (as there are Eight of you) the Pleasure, in considering that your Companions are happy. What is the End of Quarrels, but that every-one is fretted and vexed, and no one gains any-thing? Whereas by endeavouring to please and love each other, the End is Happiness to ourselves, and Joy to every one around us. I am sure, if you will speak the Truth, none of you have been so easy since you quarreled, as you are now you are reconciled. Answer me honestly, if this is not Truth."

Here Miss *Jenny* was silent, and waited for an Answer. But the poor Girls, who had in them the Seeds of Good-will to each other, altho' those Seeds were choaked and over-run with the Weeds of Envy and Pride; as in a Garden the finest Strawberries will be spoiled by rank Weeds, if Care is not taken to root them out: These poor Girls, I say, now struck with the Force of Truth, and sorry for what they had done, let drop some Tears, which trickled down their Cheeks, and were Signs of Meekness, and Sorrow for their Fault. Not like those Tears which bursted from their swoln Eyes, when Anger and Hatred choaked their Words, and their proud Hearts laboured with Stubbornness and Folly; when their Skins reddened, and all their Features were changed and distorted by the Violence of Passion, which made them frightful to the Beholders, and miserable to themselves:—No! Far other Cause had they now for Tears, and far different were the Tears they shed: Their Eyes, melting with Sorrow for their Faults, let fall some Drops, as Tokens of their Repentance: But, as soon as they could recover themselves to speak, they all with one Voice cried out, Indeed, Miss *Jenny*, we are sorry for our Fault, and will follow your Advice; which we now see is owing to your Goodness.

Miss *Jenny* now produced a Basket of Apples, which she had purchased out of the little Pocket money she was allowed, in order to prove, that the same Things may be a Pleasure, or a Pain, according as the Persons to whom they are given, are good or bad.

These she placed in the Midst of her Companions, and desired them to eat, and enjoy themselves; and now they were so changed, that each helped her next Neighbour before she would touch any for herself: And the Moment they were grown thus good-natured and friendly, they were as well-bred, and as polite, as it is possible to describe.

Miss *Jenny*'s Joy was inexpressible, that she had caused this happy Change: Nor less was the Joy of her Companions, who now began to taste Pleasures, from which their Animosity to each other had hitherto debarred them. They all sat looking pleased on their Companions: Their Faces borrowed Beauty from the Calmness and Goodness of their Minds: And all those ugly Frowns, and all that ill-natured Sourness, which when they were angry and cross, were but too plain in their Faces, were now intirely fled: Jessamine and Honeysuckles surrounded their Seats, and played round their Heads, of which they gathered Nosegays to present each other with. They now enjoyed all the Pleasure and Happiness that attend those who are innocent and good.

Miss *Jenny*, with her Heart overflowing with Joy at this happy Change, said, "Now, my dear Companions, that you may be convinced what I have said and done was not occasioned by any Desire of proving myself wiser than you, as Miss *Sukey* hinted while she was yet in her Anger, I will, if you please, relate to you the History of my past Life; by which you will see in what manner I came by this Way of thinking; and as you will perceive it was chiefly owing to the Instructions of a kind Mamma, you may all likewise reap the same Advantage under good Mrs. *Teachum*, if you will obey her Commands, and attend to her Precepts: And after I have given you the Particulars of my Life, I must beg that every one of you will, some Day or other, when you have reflected upon it, declare all that you can remember of your own; for, should you not be able to relate any-thing worth remembering as an Example, yet there is nothing more likely to amend the future Part of any one's Life, than the recollecting and confessing the Faults of the past."

All our little Company highly approved of Miss *Jenny*'s Proposal, and promised, in their Turns, to relate their own Lives; and Miss *Polly Suckling* cried out, "Yes indeed, Miss *Jenny*, I'll tell all, when it comes to my Turn: So pray begin; for I long to hear what you did, when you was no bigger than I am now." Miss *Jenny* then kissed little *Polly*, and said, she would instantly begin.

But as, in the reading any one's Story, it is an additional Pleasure to have some Acquaintance with their Persons; and as I delight in giving my little Readers every Pleasure that is in my Power; I shall endeavour, as justly as I can, by Description, to set before their Eyes the Picture of this good young Creature: And the same of every one of our young Company, as they begin their Lives.

The *Description* of Miss *Jenny Peace*.

Miss *Jenny Peace* was just turned of Fourteen, and could be called neither tall nor short of her Age: But her whole Person was the most agreeable that can be imagined. She had an exceeding fine Complexion, with as much Colour in her Cheeks as is the natural Effect of perfect Health. Her Hair was light-brown, and curled in so regular and yet easy a manner, as never to want any Assistance from Art.[6] Her Eye-brows (which were not of that correct Turn, as to look as if they were drawn with a Pencil), and her Eye-lashes, were both darker than her Hair; and the latter being very long, gave such a Shade to her Eyes, as made them often mistaken for black, tho' they were only a dark Hazle. To give any Description of her Eyes beyond the Colour and Size, which was perfectly the Medium, would be impossible; except by saying they were expressive of every-thing that is amiable and good: For thro' them might be read every single Thought of the Mind; from whence they had such a Brightness and Chearfulness, as seemed to cast a Lustre over her whole Face. She had fine Teeth, and a Mouth answering to the most correct Rules of Beauty; and when she spoke (tho' you were at too great a Distance to hear what she said), there appeared so much Sweetness, Mildness, Modesty, and Good-nature, that you found yourself filled more with Pleasure than Admiration in beholding her. The Delight which every one took in looking on Miss *Jenny* was evident in this; That tho' Miss *Sukey Jennett*, and Miss *Patty Lockit*, were both what might be called handsomer Girls; and if you asked any Persons in Company their Opinion, they would tell you so; yet their Eyes were a direct Contradiction to their Tongues, by being continually fixed on Miss *Jenny*: For, while *She* was in the Room, it was impossible to fix them any-where else. She had a

6. I.e., to need any artificial means to curl hair.

natural Ease and Gentility in her Shape; and all her Motions were more pleasing, tho' less striking, than what is commonly acquired by the Instruction of Dancing-Masters.

Such was the agreeable Person of Miss *Jenny Peace*; who, in her usual obliging Manner, and with an Air pleasing beyond my Power to express, at the Request of her Companions, began to relate the History of her Life, as follows:

The *Life* of Miss *Jenny Peace*.

"My Father dying when I was but half a Year old, I was left to the Care of my Mamma; who was the best Woman in the World, and to whose Memory I shall ever pay the most grateful Honour. From the time she had any Children, she made it the whole Study of her Life to promote their Welfare, and form their Minds in the manner she thought would best answer her Purpose of making them both good and happy: For it was her constant Maxim, that Goodness and Happiness dwelt in the same Bosoms, and were generally found to live so much together, that they could not easily be separated.

"My Mother had six Children born alive; but could preserve none beyond the first Year, except my Brother *Harry Peace* and myself. She made it one of her chief Cares to cultivate and preserve the most perfect Love and Harmony between us. My Brother is but a Twelvemonth older than I: So that, till I was Six Years old (for Seven was the Age in which he was sent to School) he remained at home with me; in which time we often had little childish Quarrels: But my Mother always took care to convince us of our Error in wrangling and fighting about nothing, and to teach us how much more Pleasure we enjoyed whilst we agreed. She shewed no Partiality to either, but endeavoured to make us equal in all Things, any otherwise than that she taught me I owed a Respect to my Brother, as the eldest.

"Before my Brother went to School, we had set Hours appointed us, in which we regularly attended to learn whatever was thought necessary for our Improvement; my Mamma herself daily watching the opening of our Minds, and taking great Care to instruct us in what manner to make the best Use of the Knowledge we attained. Whatever we read she explained to us, and made us understand, that we might be the better for our Lessons. When we were capable of thinking, we made it so much a Rule to obey our Parent, the Moment she signified her Pleasure, that by that means we avoided many Accidents and Misfortunes: For Example; My Brother was running one Day giddily round the Brink of a Well; and if he had made the least false Step, he must have fallen to the Bottom, and been drowned; my Mamma, by a Sign with her Finger that called him to her, preserved him from the imminent Danger he was in of losing his Life; and then she took care that we should both be the better for this little Incident, by laying before us, how much our Safety and Happiness, as well as our Duty, were concerned in being obedient.

"My Brother and I once had a Quarrel about something as trifling as your Apple of Contention;[7] and, tho' we both heartily wished to be reconciled to each other, yet did our little Hearts swell so much with Stubbornness and Pride, that neither of us would speak first: By which means we were so silly as to be both uneasy, and yet would not use the Remedy that was in our own Power to remove that Uneasiness. My Mamma found it out, and sent for me into her Closet,[8] and said, 'She was sorry

---

7. An allusion to the mythological Apple of Discord, which indirectly caused the Trojan War (because it was awarded to Aphrodite, who prom-ised Helen to Paris if he would judge Aphrodite the most beautiful).

8. Private inner chamber.

to see her Instructions had no better Effect on me: For, continued she, indeed, *Jenny*, I am ashamed of your Folly, as well as Wickedness, in thus contending with your Brother.' A Tear which I believe flowed from Shame, started from my Eyes at this Reproof; and I fixed them on the Ground, being too much overwhelmed with Confusion to dare to lift them up on my Mamma. On which she kindly said, 'She hoped my Confusion was a Sign of my Amendment: That she might indeed have used another Method, by commanding me to seek a Reconciliation with my Brother; for she did not imagine I was already so far gone in Perverseness, as not to hold her Commands as inviolable; but she was willing, for my Good, first to convince me of my Folly.' As soon as my Confusion would give me Leave to speak, on my Knees I gave her a thousand Thanks for her Goodness, and went immediately to seek my Brother. He joyfully embraced the first Opportunity of being reconciled to me: And this was one of the pleasantest Hours of my Life. This Quarrel happened when my Brother came home at Breaking-up,[9] and I was Nine Years old.

"My Mamma's principal Care was to keep up a perfect Amity between me and my Brother. I remember once, when *Harry* and I were playing in the Fields, there was a small Rivulet stopped me in my Way. My Brother being nimbler and better able to jump than myself, with one Spring leaped over, and left me on the other Side of it; but seeing me uneasy that I could not get over to him, his Good-nature prompted him to come back and to assist me; and, by the Help of his Hand, I easily passed over. On this my good Mamma bid me remember how much my Brother's superior Strength might assist me in his being my Protector; and that I ought in return to use my utmost Endeavours to oblige him; and that then we should be mutual Assistants to each other throughout Life. Thus every-thing that passed was made use of to improve my Understanding, and amend my Heart.

"I believe no Child ever spent her Time more agreeably than I did; for I not only enjoyed my own Pleasures, but also of those others. And when my Brother was carried abroad, and I was left at home, that *he* was pleased, made me full Amends for the Loss of any Diversion. The Contentions between us (where our Parent's Commands did not interfere) were always exerted in Endeavours each to prefer the other's Pleasures to our own. My Mind was easy, and free from Anxiety: For as I always took care to speak Truth, I had nothing to conceal from my Mamma, and consequently had never any Fears of being found in a Lye: For one Lye obliges us to tell a thousand others to conceal it; and I have no Notion of any Condition's being so miserable, as to live in a continual Fear of Detection. Most particularly, my Mamma instructed me to beware of all Sorts of Deceit: So that I was accustomed, not only in Words to speak Truth, but also not to endeavour by any means to deceive.

"But tho' the Friendship between my Brother and me was so strongly cultivated, yet we were taught, that lying for each other, or praising each other, when it was not deserved, was not only a Fault, but a very great Crime: For this, my Mamma used to tell us, was not Love, but Hatred; as it was encouraging one another in Folly and Wickedness: And though my natural Disposition inclined me to be very tender of every thing in my Power, yet was I not suffered to give way even to *this* in an unreasonable Degree: One Instance of which I remember;

"When I was about Eleven Years old, I had a Cat that I had bred up from a little Kitten, that used to play round me, till I had indulged for the poor Animal a Fondness that made me delight to have it continually with me where-ever I went; and, in return for my Indulgence, the Cat seemed to have changed its Nature, and assumed the

9. Dismissal from school for vacation.

Manner that more properly belongs to Dogs than Cats; for it would follow me about the House and Gardens, mourn for my Absence, and rejoice at my Presence: And, what was very remarkable, the poor Animal would, when fed by my Hand, lose that Caution which Cats are known to be possessed of, and eat whatever I gave it, as it could reflect, that I meant only its Good, and no Harm could come from me.

"I was at last so accustomed to see this little *Frisk* (for so I called it) playing round me, that I seemed to miss Part of myself in its Absence. But one Day the poor little Creature followed me to the Door; when a Parcel of School-boys coming by, one of them catched her up in his Arms, and ran away with her. All my Cries were to no Purpose; for he was out of Sight with her in a Moment, and there was no Method to trace his Steps. The cruel Wretches for Sport, as they called it, hunted it the next Day from one to the other, in the most barbarous manner; till at last it took Shelter in that House that used to be its Protection, and came and expired at my Feet.

"I was so struck with the Sight of the little Animal dying in that manner, that the great Grief of my Heart overflowed at my Eyes, and I was for some time inconsolable.

"My indulgent Mamma comforted without blaming me, till she thought I had sufficient time to vent my Grief; and then sending for me into her Chamber, spoke as follows:

'*Jenny*, I have watched you ever since the Death of your little favourite Cat; and have been in Hopes daily, that your Lamenting and Melancholy on that Account would be at an End: But I find you still persist in grieving, as if such a Loss was irreparable. Now tho' I have always encouraged you in all Sentiments of Good-nature and Compassion, and am sensible, that where those Sentiments are strongly implanted, they will extend their Influence even to the least Animal; yet you are to consider, my Child; that you are not to give way to any Passions that interfere with your Duty: For whenever there is any Contention between your Duty and your Inclinations, you must conquer the latter, or become wicked and contemptible. If, therefore, you give way to this Melancholy, how will you be able to perform your Duty towards me, in chearfully obeying my Commands, and endeavouring, by your lively Prattle, and innocent Gaiety of Heart, to be my Companion and Delight? Nor will you be fit to converse with your Brother, whom (as you lost your good Papa when you was too young to know that Loss) I have endeavoured to educate in such a manner, that I hope he will be a Father to you, if you deserve his Love and Protection. In short, if you do not keep Command enough of yourself to prevent being ruffled by every Accident, you will be unfit for all the social Offices[1] of Life, and be despised by all those whose Regard and Love is worth your seeking. I treat you, my Girl, as capable of considering what is for your own Good: For tho' you are but Eleven Years of Age, yet I hope the Pains I have taken in explaining all you read, and in answering all your Questions in Search of Knowledge, has not been so much thrown away, but that you are more capable of judging, than those unhappy Children are, whose Parents have neglected to instruct them: And therefore, farther to enforce what I say, remember that repining at any Accident that happens to you, is an Offence to that God, to whom I have taught you daily to pray for all the Blessings you can receive, and to whom you are to return humble Thanks for every Blessing.

'I expect therefore *Jenny*, that you now dry up your Tears, and resume your usual Chearfulness. I do not doubt but your Obedience to me will make you at least put on the Appearance of Chearfulness in my Sight: But you will deceive yourself, if you think that is performing your Duty; for if you would obey me as you ought, you must

---

1. Functions, duties.

try heartily to root from your Mind all Sorrow and Gloominess. You may depend upon it, this Command is in your Power to obey; for you know I never require any thing of you that is impossible.'

"After my Mamma had made this Speech, she went out to take a Walk in the Garden, and left me to consider of what she had said.

"The Moment I came to reflect seriously, I found it was indeed in my Power to root all Melancholy from my Heart, when I considered it was necessary, in order to perform my Duty to God, to obey the best of Mothers, and to make myself a Blessing and a chearful Companion to her, rather than a Burden, and the Cause of her Uneasiness, by my foolish Melancholy.

"This little Accident, as managed by my Mamma, has been a Lesson to me in governing my Passions ever since.

'It would be endless to repeat all the Methods this good Mother invented for my Instruction, Amendment, and Improvement. It is sufficient to acquaint you, that she contrived that every new Day should open to me some new Scene of Knowlege; and no Girl could be happier than I was during her Life. But, alas! when I was Thirteen Years of Age, the Scene changed. My dear Mamma was taken ill of a Scarlet-Fever. I attended her Day and Night whilst she lay ill, my Eyes starting with Tears to see her in that Condition; and yet I did not dare to give my Sorrows vent, for fear of increasing her Pain."

Here a trickling Tear stole from Miss *Jenny*'s Eyes. She suppressed some rising Sobs that interrupted her Speech; and was about to proceed in her Story; when casting her Eyes on her Companions, she saw her Sorrow had such an Effect upon them all, that there was not one of her Hearers who could refrain from shedding a sympathizing Tear. She therefore thought it was more strictly following her Mamma's Precepts to pass this Part of her Story in Silence, rather than to grieve her Friends; and having wiped away her Tears, she hastened to conclude her Story: Which she did as follows:

"After my Mamma's Death, my Aunt *Newman*, my Father's Sister, took the Care of me: But being obliged to go to *Jamaica* to settle some Affairs relating to an Estate she is possessed of there, she took with her my Cousin *Harriot* her only Daughter, and left me under the Care of good Mrs. *Teachum* till her Return: And since I have been here, you all know as much of my History as I do myself."

As Miss *Jenny* spoke these Words, the Bell summoned them to Supper, and to the Presence of their Governess, who having narrowly watched their Looks ever since the Fray, had hitherto plainly perceived, that tho' they did not dare to break out again into an open Quarrel, yet their Hearts had still harboured unkind Thoughts of one another. She was surprised *now*, as she stood at a Window in the Hall that overlooked the Garden, to see all her Scholars walk towards her Hand in Hand, with such chearful Countenances, as plainly shewed their inward good Humour: And as she thought proper to mention to them her Pleasure in seeing them thus altered, Miss *Jenny Peace* related to her Governess all that had passed in the Arbour, with their general Reconciliation. Mrs. *Teachum* gave Miss *Jenny* all the Applause due to her Goodness, saying, "She herself had only waited a little while, to see if their Anger would subside, and Love take its place in their Bosoms, without her interfering again; for *that* she certainly should otherwise have done, to have brought about what Miss *Jenny* had so happily effected."

Miss *Jenny* thanked her Governess for her kind Approbation, and said, "That if she would give them Leave, they would spend what Time she was pleased to allow them from School in this little Arbour, in reading Stories, and such Things as she should think a proper and innocent Amusement."

Mrs. *Teachum* not only gave Leave, but very much approved of this Proposal; and desired Miss *Jenny*, as a Reward for what she had already done, to preside over these Diversions, and to give her an Account in what manner they proceeded. Miss *Jenny* promised in all Things to be guided by good Mrs. *Teachum*. And now, soon after Supper, they retired to Rest, free from those uneasy Passions which used to prevent their Quiet; and as they had passed the Day in Pleasure, at Night they sunk in soft and sweet Repose.

MONDAY

The First Day after their Repentance: And, consequently, the First Day of the Happiness of Miss JENNY PEACE *and her Companions.*

Early in the Morning, as soon as Miss *Jenny* arose, all her Companions flocked round her; for they now looked on her as the best Friend they had in the World; and they agreed, when they came out of School, to adjourn into their Arbour, and divert themselves till Dinner-time; which they accordingly did. When Miss *Jenny* proposed, if it was agreeable to them to hear it, to read them a Story, which she had put in her Pocket for that Purpose; and as they now began to look upon her as the most proper Person to direct them in their Amusements, they all replied, "What was most agreeable to her would please them best." She then began to read the following Story, with which we shall open their First Day's Amusement.[2]

* * *

Thus ended the Story of the Two Giants: And Miss *Jenny* being tired with reading, her little Company left the Arbour for that Night, and agreed to meet there again the next Day.

As soon as they had supp'd, Mrs. *Teachum* sent for Miss *Jenny Peace* into her Closet, and desired an exact Account from her of this their First Day's Amusement, that she might judge from thence how far they might be trusted with the Liberty she had given them.

Miss *Jenny* shewed her Governess the Story she had read; and said, "I hope, Madam, you will not think it an improper one; for it was given me by my Mamma; and she told me, that she thought it contained a very excellent Moral."

Mrs. *Teachum* having looked it over, thus spoke: "I have no Objection, Miss *Jenny*, to your reading any Stories to amuse you, provided you read them with the Disposition of a Mind not to be hurt by them. A very good Moral may indeed be drawn from the Whole, and likewise from almost every Part of it; and as you had this Story from your Mamma, I doubt not but you are very well qualified to make the proper Remarks yourself upon the Moral of it to your Companions. But here let me observe to you (which I would have you communicate to your little Friends) that Giants, Magic, Fairies, and all Sorts of supernatural Assistance in a Story, are introduced only to amuse and divert: For a Giant is called so only to express a Man of great Power; and the magic Fillet round the Statue was intended only to shew you, that by Patience you will overcome all Difficulties. Therefore by no means let the Notion of Giants or Magic dwell upon your Minds. And you may farther observe, that there

2. Jenny Peace's didactic tale, "The Story of the Cruel Giant Barbarico, the Good Giant Benefico, and the Little Dwarf Mignon," is reprinted in the Fairy Tales section of this anthology, above.

is a different Stile adapted to every Sort of Writing; and the various sounding Epithets given to *Barbarico* are proper to express the raging Cruelty of his wicked Mind. But neither this high-founding Language, nor the supernatural Contrivances in this Story, do I so thoroughly approve, as to recommend them much to your Reading; except, as I said before, great Care is taken to prevent your being carried away, by these high-flown Things, from that Simplicity of Taste and Manners which is my chief Study to inculcate."

Here Miss *Jenny* looked a little confounded; and, by her down-cast Eye, shewed a Fear that she had incurred the Disapprobation, if not the Displeasure, of her Governess: Upon which Mrs. *Teachum* thus proceeded:

"I do not intend by this, my Dear, to blame you for what you have done; but only to instruct you how to make the best Use of even the most trifling Things: And if you have any more Stories of this kind, with an equally good Moral, when you are not better employed, I shall not be against your reading them; always remembering the Cautions I have this Evening been giving you."

Miss *Jenny* thanked her Governess for her Instructions, and kind Indulgence to her, and promised to give her an exact Account of their daily Amusements; and, taking Leave, retired to her Rest.

* * *

1749, 1759

THOMAS HUGHES
1822–1896

Thomas Hughes once wrote, "The years from ten to eighteen are the most important in a boy's life." In fact, Hughes believed that careful attention to these years was essential for the good of the nation's—as much as any individual's—emotional and spiritual health. Hughes became famous for writing *Tom Brown's Schooldays* (1857), a *Bildungsroman* that locates the essence of English manliness and Christian moral courage in the games, camaraderie, and insularity afforded by the public school (a costly boarding school for gentlemen's sons). Hughes is credited with popularizing the public school novel and influencing British authors of children's literature such as F. W. Farrar and Talbot Baines Reed (writing for boys) and L. T. Meade, Angela Brazil, and Antonia Fraser (writing for girls). Hughes wrote *Tom Brown's Schooldays* for his eight-year-old son, Maurice; he based it on his own experiences at Rugby, a famous English public school, during its heyday in the 1830s when the institution was under the reformist tutelage of Dr. Thomas Arnold (1795–1842), a clergyman, historian, and man of high moral character and suasion. The book was pub-

lished anonymously under the pseudonym "An Old Boy," but Hughes's identity was soon discovered. Well-received by the public and professional reviewers alike, within a year the book had gone into six printings. *Tom Brown's Schooldays* remains in print today and has been translated into a number of different languages, has been adapted in three different film versions, and has provided the basis for two television programs. In their biography of Hughes, Edward C. Mack and W. H. G. Armytage attribute the book's enduring popularity to Hughes's ability to transcribe a "real" boy's life with sincerity and enthusiasm: "*Tom Brown's Schooldays* has about it the zest and joy of happy memory, the love of frosty mornings and endurance, and the eager anticipation of life."

Thomas Hughes's own early days growing up sixty miles west of London in a small town in the Berkshire Downs were carefree and filled with the delights of a simple, country life. From his window he could see the enormous White Horse—an ancient and mysterious chalk figure carved out of the side of White Horse Hill some two miles away.

This countryside would provide the setting for some of his fiction. The young Tom Hughes enjoyed the rough-and-tumble world of Rugby, where he made friends, excelled at games, and managed to scrape by in his Latin and Greek studies. (Hughes believed his aptitude for literature and history made up for some of his failings in the classics.) In his first year at Oriel College of Oxford University he was intellectually idle, choosing to concentrate on sports and pleasure outings rather than his studies. He dramatized this wasted year in *Tom Brown at Oxford* (serialized in *Macmillan's Magazine* from 1859 to 1861 and published as a novel in 1861), the sequel to *Tom Brown's Schooldays*. After Hughes fell in love with seventeen-year-old Frances (Fanny) Ford in 1843, he became serious and reflective: his religious feelings deepened, and he became more sensitive to plight of the working class. He decided to become a barrister, graduated from Oxford, and married Fanny in 1847. Their happy marriage would produce nine children over the years.

Early in 1848 Hughes was called to the bar and began to work as a lawyer, although a clergyman's vocation had always appealed to him. While studying for the bar, he had come under the influence of Frederick Denison Maurice (1805–1872), a clergyman and social reformer. With Maurice as leader, Charles Kingsley (1819–1875), Hughes, and others turned to the Christian Socialist movement as an avenue for their spiritual and reformist energies. The Christian Socialist movement actively supported and helped institute working men's associations, trade unions, cooperative enterprises, and the Working Men's College (where Hughes taught boxing), among other causes. Because their strenuous work on behalf of the workingman was informed by Christian doctrines of brotherhood and self-sacrifice, these reformers were sometimes called "muscular Christians" (a term first used in a 1857 review of one of Kingsley's books). In 1865 Hughes was elected to the House of Commons; he remained in Parliament for nine years. In his literary biography of Hughes, George J. Worth comments, "Being the man he was, Hughes was bound to use his position as a Member of Parliament to promote his religious, moral, and social beliefs and his vision of a nation in which greed and misery would be abol-

ished when Christian cooperation became a reality." In addition to his three novels, Hughes published many nonfiction works, including *The Manliness of Christ* (1879) and a number of biographies.

Long an admirer of North American pluck and industry, and concerned about England's overcrowding and social problems, Hughes was inspired by a trip to the United States and Canada to plan an English colony in Tennessee. The cooperative settlement was established in 1880: he called it "Rugby," and his mother emigrated there to live out her final days. The settlement failed, however, leaving Hughes—who had been rapidly spending his money on various social experiments—financially ruined. Hughes lost his home and had to give up his legal practice in London. To economize, he and Fanny moved to Chester, where Hughes became a county judge. He continued to be very active in social and educational causes, speaking out in favor of progressive social, political, educational, and religious movements until his death, at age seventy-four.

Squire Brown, Tom's father (a romanticized version of Hughes's father), decides to send his son to Rugby so that he will become, in the course of his time at school, "a brave, helpful, truth-telling Englishman, and a gentleman, and a Christian." The classical education he will receive is of secondary importance to Squire Brown (as it had been for Hughes himself). Of the thirteen chapters of *Tom Brown's Schooldays* that are set at Rugby during Tom's nine years there, two are dedicated to his first day at school. As the years pass, the good-natured and mischievous Tom is in some danger of becoming intellectually lazy, superficial, and self-absorbed. The headmaster, Dr. Arnold, steps in and assigns Tom a project that he believes (though he keeps this motive secret) will aid Tom's moral development: the care and guidance of a new boy, the delicate and feminine George Arthur. Although Tom resists the charge at first, Arthur and Tom become fast friends, and Arthur's sober and pious nature influences Tom for the better. By the time he graduates, Tom is a responsible, honest, and generous young man and captain of the cricket team. His education in manliness, self-reliance, and Christian self-sacrifice has been completed.

From Tom Brown's Schooldays

CHAPTER V. RUGBY AND FOOTBALL

"—Foot and eye opposed
In dubious strife."[1]

—Scott.

nd so here's Rugby, sir, at last, and you'll be in plenty of time for dinner at the School-house,[2] as I tell'd you," said the old guard, pulling his horn out of its case, and tootle-tooing away; while the coachman shook up his horses, and carried them along the side of the school close, round Deadman's corner, past the school gates, and down the High Street to the Spread Eagle; the wheelers in a spanking trot, and leaders cantering, in a style which would not have disgraced "Cherry Bob," "ramping, stamping, tearing, swearing Billy Harwood," or any other of the old coaching heroes.[3]

Tom's heart beat quick as he passed the great school field or close, with its noble elms, in which several games at football[4] were going on, and tried to take in at once the long line of grey buildings, beginning with the chapel, and ending with the School-house, the residence of the head-master, where the great flag was lazily waving from the highest round tower. And he began already to be proud of being a Rugby boy, as he passed the school-gates, with the oriel-window[5] above, and saw the boys standing there, looking as if the town belonged to them, and nodding in a familiar manner to the coachman, as if any one of them would be quite equal to getting on the box, and working the team down street as well as he.

One of the young heroes, however, ran out from the rest, and scrambled up behind; where, having righted himself, and nodded to the guard, with "How do, Jem?" he turned short round to Tom, and, after looking him over for a minute, began—

"I say, you fellow, is your name Brown?"

"Yes," said Tom, in considerable astonishment; glad, however, to have lighted on some one already who seemed to know him.

"Ah, I thought so: you know my old aunt, Miss East, she lives somewhere down

1. Slightly misquoted from *The Lady of the Lake* (1810), by the Scottish poet and novelist Sir Walter Scott (1771–1832): "Then foot, and point, and eye opposed / In dubious strife they darkly closed" (5.14).
 Previous chapters have told of the headstrong Tom's early years and the events that lead up to his father's decision to send him to Rugby. The two chapters printed here recount Tom's first day at school.
2. Name of one of the "houses" at Rugby (specif-

ically, the headmaster's house). As each student enters the school, he is assigned to a house, a specific living quarters that helps foster group identity and loyalty.
3. "Heroes," because driving a four-horse coach was considered a manly skill and sport in nineteenth-century England.
4. I.e., rugby (the game was invented at Rugby School in the nineteenth century).
5. Projecting window in an upper story.

your way in Berkshire. She wrote to me that you were coming to-day, and asked me to give you a lift."[6]

Tom was somewhat inclined to resent the patronising air of his new friend, a boy of just about his own height and age, but gifted with the most transcendent coolness and assurance, which Tom felt to be aggravating and hard to bear, but couldn't for the life of him help admiring and envying—especially when young my lord begins hectoring two or three long loafing fellows, half porter half stableman, with a strong touch of the blackguard; and in the end arranges with one of them, nicknamed Cooey, to carry Tom's luggage up to the School-house for sixpence.

"And heark'ee, Cooey, it must be up in ten minutes, or no more jobs from me. Come along, Brown." And away swaggers the young potentate, with his hands in his pockets, and Tom at his side.

"All right, sir," says Cooey, touching his hat, with a leer and a wink at his companions.

"Hullo tho'," says East, pulling up, and taking another look at Tom, "this'll never do—haven't you got a hat?—we never wear caps here. Only the louts wear caps. Bless you, if you were to go into the quadrangle with that thing on, I——don't know what'd happen." The very idea was quite beyond young Master East, and he looked unutterable things.

Tom thought his cap a very knowing affair, but confessed that he had a hat in his hat-box; which was accordingly at once extracted from the hind boot,[7] and Tom equipped in his go-to-meeting roof, as his new friend called it. But this didn't quite suit his fastidious taste in another minute, being too shiny; so, as they walk up the town, they dive into Nixon's the hatter's, and Tom is arrayed, to his utter astonishment and without paying for it, in a regulation cat-skin at seven-and-sixpence;[8] Nixon undertaking to send the best hat up to the matron's room, School-house, in half an hour.

"You can send in a note for a tile[9] on Monday, and make it all right, you know," said Mentor; "we're allowed two seven-and-sixers a half, besides what we bring from home."

Tom by this time began to be conscious of his new social position and dignities, and to luxuriate in the realized ambition of being a public-school boy at last, with a vested right of spoiling two seven-and-sixers in half a year.

"You see," said his friend, as they strolled up towards the school-gates, in explanation of his conduct, "a great deal depends on how a fellow cuts up[1] at first. If he's got nothing odd about him, and answers straightforward, and holds his head up, he gets on. Now you'll do very well as to rig, all but that cap. You see I'm doing the handsome thing by you, because my father knows yours; besides, I want to please the old lady. She gave me half-a-sov[2] this half, and perhaps'll double it next, if I keep in her good books."

There's nothing for candour like a lower-school boy, and East was a genuine specimen—frank, hearty, and good-natured, well satisfied with himself and his position, and chock full of life and spirits, and all the Rugby prejudices and traditions which he had been able to get together, in the long course of one half year, during which he had been at the School-house.

And Tom, notwithstanding his bumptiousness, felt friends with him at once, and

6. To give you a helping hand.
7. The outside compartment behind the body of the coach.
8. Seven and a half shillings. "Cat-skin": inferior

kind of silk hat.
9. Hat.
1. Behaves.
2. A sovereign was a gold coin worth a pound.

began sucking in all his ways and prejudices, as fast as he could understand them.

East was great in the character of cicerone;[3] he carried Tom through the great gates, where were only two or three boys. These satisfied themselves with the stock questions,—"You fellow, what's your name? Where do you come from? How old are you? Where do you board? and, What form[4] are you in?"—and so they passed on through the quadrangle and a small courtyard, upon which looked down a lot of little windows (belonging, as his guide informed him, to some of the School-house studies), into the matron's room, where East introduced Tom to that dignitary; made him give up the key of his trunk, that the matron might unpack his linen, and told the story of the hat and of his own presence of mind: upon the relation whereof the matron laughingly scolded him, for the coolest new boy in the house; and East indignant at the accusation of newness, marched Tom off into the quadrangle, and began showing him the schools,[5] and examining him as to his literary attainments; the result of which was a prophecy that they would be in the same form and could do their lessons together.

"And now come in and see my study; we shall have just time before dinner; and afterwards, before calling over,[6] we'll do the close."

Tom followed his guide through the School-house hall, which opens into the quadrangle. It is a great room thirty feet long and eighteen high, or thereabouts, with two great tables running the whole length, and two large fire-places at the side, with blazing fires in them, at one of which some dozen boys were standing and lounging, some of whom shouted to East to stop; but he shot through with his convoy, and landed him in the long dark passages, with large fire at the end of each, upon which the studies opened. Into one of these, in the bottom passage, East bolted with our hero, slamming and bolting the door behind them, in case of pursuit from the hall, and Tom was for the first time in a Rugby boy's citadel.

He hadn't been prepared for separate studies, and was not a little astonished and delighted with the palace in question.

It wasn't very large certainly, being about six feet long by four broad. It couldn't be called light, as there were bars and a grating to the window; which little precautions were necessary in the studies on the ground-floor looking out into the close, to prevent the exit of small boys after locking-up, and the entrance of contraband articles. But it was uncommonly comfortable to look at, Tom thought. The space under the window at the further end was occupied by a square table covered with a reasonably clean and whole red and blue check tablecloth; a hard-seated sofa covered with red stuff occupied one side, running up to the end, and making a seat for one, or by sitting close, for two, at the table; and a good stout wooden chair afforded a seat to another boy, so that three could sit and work together. The walls were wainscoted half-way up, the wainscot being covered with green baize, the remainder with a bright patterned paper, on which hung three or four prints, of dogs' heads, Grimaldi winning the Aylesbury steeple-chase, Amy Robsart, the reigning Waverley beauty of the day, and Tom Crib[7] in a posture of defence, which did no credit to the science of that hero, if truly represented. Over the door were a row of hat-pegs, and on each

---

3. A guide who shows and explains the antiquities or curiosities of a place to strangers.
4. Grade.
5. School buildings.
6. Roll call.
7. Champion boxer (1781–1848). "Green baize": fabric used to cover office or gaming tables. Gri-

maldi: famous racehorse. Amy Robsart: heroine of Walter Scott's *Kenilworth* (1821); collectively, Scott's volumes of fiction were published as the "Waverley Novels," because they first appeared anonymously as "by the author of *Waverley*" (his first novel).

side bookcases with cupboards at the bottom; shelves and cupboards being filled indiscriminately with school-books, a cup or two, a mousetrap, and candlesticks, leather straps, a fustian bag, and some curious-looking articles, which puzzled Tom not a little, until his friend explained that they were climbing irons,[8] and showed their use. A cricket bat and small fishing-rod stood up in one corner.

This was the residence of East and another boy in the same form, and had more interest for Tom than Windsor Castle,[9] or any other residence in the British Isles. For was he not about to become the joint owner of a similar home, the first place he could call his own? One's own—what a charm there is in the words! How long it takes boy and man to find out their worth! how fast most of us holds on to them! faster and more jealously, the nearer we are to that general home, into which we can take nothing, but must go naked as we came into the world. When shall we learn that he who multiplieth possession multiplieth troubles, and that the one single use of things which we call our own is that they may be his who hath need of them?

"And shall I have a study like this, too?" said Tom.

"Yes, of course, you'll be chummed[1] with some fellow on Monday, and you can sit here till then."

"What nice places!"

"They're well enough," answered East patronisingly, "only uncommon cold at

8. Crampons.
9. A residence of the British sovereign (about 20 miles west of London).
1. Share chambers.

nights sometimes. Gower—that's my chum—and I make a fire with paper on the floor after supper generally, only that makes it so smoky."

"But there's a big fire out in the passage," said Tom.

"Precious little we get out of that tho'," said East; "Jones the præpostor[2] has the study at the fire end, and he has rigged up an iron rod and green baize curtains across the passage, which he draws at night, and sits there with his door open, so he gets all the fire, and hears if we come out of our studies after eight, or make a noise. However, he's taken to sitting in the fifth-form room lately, so we do get a bit of fire now sometimes; only to keep a sharp look-out that he don't catch you behind his curtain when he comes down—that's all."

A quarter past one now struck, and the bell began tolling for dinner, so they went into the hall and took their places, Tom at the very bottom of the second table, next to the præpostor (who sat at the end to keep order there), and East a few paces higher. And now Tom for the first time saw his future schoolfellows in a body. In they came, some hot and ruddy from football or long walks, some pale and chilly from hard reading in their studies, some from loitering over the fire at the pastry-cook's, dainty mortals, bringing with them pickles[3] and sauce-bottles to help them with their dinners. And a great big-bearded man, whom Tom took for a master, began calling over the names, while the great joints were being rapidly carved on the third table in the corner by the old verger[4] and the housekeeper. Tom's turn came last, and meanwhile he was all eyes, looking first with awe at the great man who sat close to him, and was helped first, and who read a hard-looking book all the time he was eating; and when he got up and walked off to the fire, at the small boys round him, some of whom were reading, and the rest talking in whispers to one another, or stealing one another's bread, or shooting pellets, or digging their forks through the tablecloth. However, notwithstanding his curiosity, he managed to make a capital dinner by the time the big man called "Stand up!" and said grace.

As soon as dinner was over, and Tom had been questioned by such of his neighbours as were curious as to his birth parentage, education, and other like matters, East, who evidently enjoyed his new dignity of patron and Mentor,[5] proposed having a look at the close, which Tom, athirst for knowledge, gladly assented to, and they went out through the quadrangle and past the big fives' court, into the great playground.

"That's the chapel, you see," said East, "and there just behind it is the place for fights; you see it's most out of the way of the masters, who all live on the other side and don't come by here after the first lesson or callings-over. That's when the fights come off. And all this part where we are is the little side ground, right up to the trees, and on the other side of the trees is the big side ground, where the great matches are played. And there's the island in the furthest corner; you'll know that well enough next half, when there's island fagging.[6] I say, it's horrid cold, let's have a run across;" and away went East, Tom close behind him. East was evidently putting his best foot

2. I.e., prefect (a senior pupil given the authority to manage and control other pupils).
3. Relishes.
4. Attendant.
5. In Homer's *Odyssey* (ca. 8th c. B.C.E.), an old friend of Odysseus whose form Athena took when giving advice to his son, Telemachus; thus, a wise counselor or guide.
6. In the late 1820s, the sixth form's gardens were lost to new boardinghouses. Garden plots were assigned on the "island," separated from the school grounds by water-filled ditches. "Island fags" were eighty or ninety younger boys forced to line up and race across the bridge to the island; only the first six boys across were excused from the task of digging the garden plots without tools. This custom ceased in 1835.

foremost, and Tom, who was mighty proud of his running, and not a little anxious to show his friend that although a new boy he was no milksop, laid himself down to work in his very best style. Right across the close they went, each doing all he knew, and there wasn't a yard between them when they pulled up at the island moat.

"I say," said East, as soon as he got his wind, looking with much increased respect at Tom, "you ain't a bad scud,[7] not by no means. Well, I'm as warm as toast now."

"But why do you wear white trousers in November?" said Tom. He had been struck by this peculiarity in the costume of almost all the School-house boys.

"Why, bless us, don't you know?—No, I forgot. Why, to-day's the School-house match. Our house plays the whole of the School at football. And we all wear white trousers, to show 'em we don't care for hacks.[8] You're in luck to come to-day. You just will see a match; and Brooke's going to let me play in quarters. That's more than he'll do for any other lower-school boy, except James, and he's fourteen."

"Who's Brooke?"

"Why, that big fellow who called over at dinner, to be sure. He's cock of the School, and head of the School-house side, and the best kick and charger in Rugby."

"Oh, but do show me where they play. And tell me about it. I love football so, and have played all my life. Won't Brooke let me play?"

"Not he," said East, with some indignation; "why, you don't know the rules—you'll be a month learning them. And then it's no joke playing-up in a match, I can tell you. Quite another thing from your private school games. Why, there's been two collar-bones broken this half, and a dozen fellows lamed. And last year a fellow had his leg broken."

Tom listened with the profoundest respect to this chapter of accidents, and followed East across the level ground till they came to a sort of gigantic gallows of two poles eighteen feet high, fixed upright in the ground some fourteen feet apart, with a cross bar running from one to the other at the height of ten feet or thereabouts.

"This is one of the goals," said East, "and you see the other, across there, right opposite, under the Doctor's[9] wall. Well, the match is for the best of three goals; whichever side kicks two goals wins: and it won't do, you see, just to kick the ball through these posts, it must go over the cross bar; any height'll do, so long as it's between the posts. You'll have to stay in goal to touch the ball when it rolls behind the posts, because if the other side touch it they have a try at goal. Then we fellows in quarters, we play just about in front of goal here, and have to turn the ball and kick it back before the big fellows on the other side can follow it up. And in front of us all the big fellows play, and that's where the scrummages[1] are mostly."

Tom's respect increased as he struggled to make out his friend's technicalities, and the other set to work to explain the mysteries of "off your side," "drop-kicks," "punts," "places," and the other intricacies of the great science of football.

"But how do you keep the ball between the goals?" said he; "I can't see why it mightn't go right down to the chapel."

"Why, that's out of play," answered East. "You see this gravel-walk running down all along this side of the playing-ground, and the line of elms opposite on the other? Well, they're the bounds. As soon as the ball gets past them, it's in touch, and out of play. And then whoever first touches it, has to knock it straight out amongst the players-up, who make two lines with a space between them, every fellow going on

---

7. A swift runner (school slang).
8. Cuts caused by kicks.
9. I.e., Dr. Arnold's. Thomas Arnold (1797–1842) was appointed headmaster of Rugby in 1828.

1. I.e., scrums—at this early stage of rugby football, confused struggles for control of the ball involving large numbers of players.

his own side. Ain't there just fine scrummages then! and the three trees you see there which come out into the play, that's a tremendous place when the ball hangs there, for you get thrown against the trees, and that's worse than any hack."

Tom wondered within himself, as they strolled back again towards the fives' court, whether the matches were really such break-neck affairs as East represented, and whether, if they were, he should ever get to like them and play-up well.

He hadn't long to wonder, however, for next minute East cried out, "Hurra! here's the punt-about,—come along and try your hand at a kick." The punt-about is the practice ball, which is just brought out and kicked about anyhow from one boy to another before callings-over and dinner, and at other odd times. They joined the boys who brought it out, all small School-house fellows, friends of East; and Tom had the pleasure of trying his skill, and performed very creditably, after first driving his foot three inches into the ground, and then nearly kicking his leg into the air, in vigorous efforts to accomplish a drop-kick after the manner of East.

Presently more boys and bigger came out, and boys from other houses on their way to calling-over, and more balls were sent for. The crowd thickened as three o'clock approached; and when the hour struck, one hundred and fifty boys were hard at work. Then the balls were held, the master of the week came down in cap and gown to calling-over, and the whole school of three hundred boys swept into the big school to answer to their names.

"I may come in, mayn't I?" said Tom, catching East by the arm and longing to feel one of them.

"Yes, come along, nobody'll say anything. You won't be so eager to get into calling-over after a month," replied his friend; and they marched into the big school together and up to the further end, where that illustrious form, the lower fourth, which had the honour of East's patronage for the time being, stood.

The master mounted into the high desk by the door, and one of the præpostors of the week stood by him on the steps, the other three marching up and down the middle of the school with their canes, calling out "Silence, silence!" The sixth form stood close by the door on the left, some thirty in number, mostly great big grown men, as Tom thought, surveying them from a distance with awe. The fifth form behind them, twice their number, and not quite so big. These on the left; and on the right the lower fifth, shell, and all the junior forms in order; while up the middle marched the three præpostors.

Then the præpostor who stands by the master calls out the names, beginning with the sixth form; and as he calls, each boy answers "here" to his name, and walks out. Some of the sixth stop at the door to turn the whole string of boys into the close; it is a great match day, and every boy in the School, will-he, nill-he, must be there. The rest of the sixth go forwards into the close, to see that no one escapes by any of the side gates.

To-day, however, being the School-house match, none of the School-house præpostors stay by the door to watch for truants of their side; there is *carte blanche* to the School-house fags to go where they like: "They trust to our honour," as East proudly informs Tom; "they know very well that no School-house boy would cut[2] the match. If he did, we'd very soon cut him, I can tell you."

The master of the week being short-sighted, and the præpostors of the week small, and not well up to their work, the lower school boys employ the ten minutes which elapse before their names are called, in pelting one another vigorously with acorns,

---

2. Ignore. "Fags": junior students who perform drudge work for upperclassmen.

which fly about in all directions. The small præpostors dash in every now and then, and generally chastise some quiet, timid boy, who is equally afraid of acorns and canes, while the principal performers get dexterously out of the way; and so calling-over rolls on somehow, much like the big world, punishments lighting on wrong shoulders, and matters going generally in a queer, cross-grained way, but the end coming somehow, which is after all the great point. And now the master of the week has finished, and locked up the big school; and the præpostors of the week come out, sweeping the last remnant of the School fags—who had been loafing about the corners by the fives' court, in hopes of a chance of bolting—before them into the close.

"Hold the punt-about!" "To the goals!" are the cries, and all stray balls are impounded by the authorities; and the whole mass of boys moves up towards the two goals dividing as they go into three bodies. That little band on the left, consisting of from fifteen to twenty boys, Tom amongst them, who are making for the goal under the School-house wall, are the School-house boys who are not to play-up, and have to stay in goal. The larger body moving to the island goal are the School boys in a like predicament. The great mass in the middle are the players-up, both sides mingled together; they are hanging their jackets, and all who mean real work, their hats, waistcoats, neck-handkerchiefs, and braces,[3] on the railings round the small trees; and there they go by twos and threes up to their respective grounds. There is none of the colour and tastiness of get-up, you will perceive, which lends such a life to the present game at Rugby, making the dullest and worst fought match a pretty sight. Now each house has its own uniform of cap and jersey, of some lively colour: but at the time we are speaking of, plush caps have not yet come in, or uniforms of any sort, except the School-house white trousers, which are abominably cold to-day; let us get to work, bare-headed and girded with our plain leather straps—but we mean business, gentlemen.

And now that the two sides have fairly sundered, and each occupies its own ground, and we get a good look at them, what absurdity is this? You don't mean to say that

3. Suspenders.

those fifty or sixty boys in white trousers, many of them quite small, are going to play that huge mass opposite? Indeed I do, gentlemen; they're going to try at any rate, and won't make such a bad fight of it either, mark my word; for hasn't old Brooke won the toss, with his lucky halfpenny, and got choice of goals and kick-off? The new ball you may see lie there quite by itself, in the middle, pointing towards the School or island goal, in another minute it will be well on its way there. Use that minute in remarking how the School-house side is drilled. You will see, in the first place, that the sixth-form boy who has the charge of goal has spread his force (the goal-keepers) so as to occupy the whole space behind the goal-posts, at distances of about five yards apart; a safe and well-kept goal is the foundation of all good play. Old Brooke is talking to the captain of quarters; and now he moves away. See how that youngster spreads his men (the light brigade) carefully over the ground, half-way between their own goal and the body of their own players-up (the heavy brigade). These again play in several bodies; there is young Brooke and the bull-dogs—mark them well—they are the "fighting brigade," the "die-hards," larking about at leap-frog to keep themselves warm, and playing tricks on one another. And on each side of old Brooke, who is now standing in the middle of the ground and just going to kick-off, you see a separate wing of players-up, each with a boy of acknowledged prowess to look to—here Warner, and there Hedge; but over all is old Brooke, absolute as he of Russia,[4] but wisely and bravely ruling over willing and worshipping subjects, a true football king. His face is earnest and careful as he glances a last time over his array, but full of pluck and hope, the sort of look I hope to see in my general when I go out to fight.

The School side is not organized in the same way. The goal-keepers are all in lumps, any-how and no-how; you can't distinguish between the players-up and the boys in quarters, and there is divided leadership; but with such odds in strength and weight it must take more than that to hinder them from winning; and so their leaders seem to think, for they let the players-up manage themselves.

But now look, there is a slight move forward of the School-house wings; a shout of "Are you ready?" and loud affirmative reply. Old Brooke takes half-a-dozen quick steps, and away goes the ball spinning towards the School goal; seventy yards before it touches ground, and at no point above twelve or fifteen feet high, a model kick-off; and the School-house cheer and rush on; the ball is returned, and they meet it and drive it back amongst the masses of the School already in motion. Then the two sides close, and you can see nothing for minutes but a swaying crowd of boys, at one point violently agitated. That is where the ball is, and there are the keen players to be met, and the glory and the hard knocks to be got: you hear the dull thud thud of the ball, and the shouts of "Off your side," "Down with him," "Put him over," "Bravo." This is what we call "a scrummage," gentlemen, and the first scrummage in a School-house match was no joke in the consulship of Plancus.[5]

But see! it has broken; the ball is driven out on the School-house side, and a rush of the School carries it past the School-house players-up. "Look out in quarters," Brooke's and twenty other voices ring out. No need to call though: the School-house captain of quarters has caught it on the bound, dodges the foremost School boys who are heading the rush, and sends it back with a good drop-kick well into the

4. I.e., the czar, an absolute despot.
5. The Roman statesman Lucius Munatius Plancus, who was consul with Lepidus in 42 B.C.E.

enemy's country. And then follows rush upon rush, and scrummage upon scrummage, the ball now driven through into the School-house quarters, and now into the School goal; for the School-house have not lost the advantage which the kick-off and a slight wind gave them at the outset, and are slightly "penning"[6] their adversaries. You say, you don't see much in it all; nothing but a struggling mass of boys, and a leather ball, which seems to excite them all to great fury, as a red rag does a bull. My dear sir, a battle would look much the same to you, except that the boys would be men, and the balls iron; but a battle would be worth your looking at for all that, and so is a football match. You can't be expected to appreciate the delicate strokes of play, the turns by which a game is lost and won,—it takes an old player to do that, but the broad philosophy of football you can understand if you will. Come along with me a little nearer, and let us consider it together.

The ball has just fallen again where the two sides are thickest, and they close rapidly around it in a scrummage, it must be driven through now by force or skill, till it flies out on one side or the other. Look how differently the boys face it! Here come two of the bull-dogs, bursting through the outsiders; in they go, straight to the heart of the scrummage; bent on driving that ball out on the opposite side. That is what they mean to do. My sons, my sons! you are too hot; you have gone past the ball, and must struggle now right through the scrummage, and get round and back again to your own side, before you can be of any further use. Here comes young Brooke; he goes in as straight as you, but keeps his head, and backs and bends, holding himself still behind the ball, and driving it furiously when he gets the chance. Take a leaf out of his book, you young chargers. Here come Speedicut, and Flashman the School-house bully, with shouts and great action. Won't you two come up to young Brooke, after locking-up, by the School-house fire, with "Old fellow, wasn't that just a splendid scrummage by the three trees!" But he knows you, and so do we. You don't really want to drive that ball through that scrummage, chancing all hurt for the glory of the School-house—but to make us think that's what you want—a vastly different thing; and fellows of your kidney will never go through more than the skirts of a scrummage, where it's all push and no kicking. We respect boys who keep out of it, and don't sham going in; but you—we had rather not say what we think of you.

Then the boys who are bending and watching on the outside, mark them—they are most useful players, the dodgers; who seize on the ball the moment it rolls out from amongst the chargers, and away with it across to the opposite goal; they seldom go into the scrummage, but must have more coolness than the chargers: as endless as are boys' characters, so are their ways of facing or not facing a scrummage at football.

Three-quarters of an hour are gone; first winds are failing, and weight and numbers beginning to tell. Yard by yard the School-house have been driven back, contesting every inch of ground. The bull-dogs are the colour of mother earth from shoulder to ankle, except young Brooke, who has a marvellous knack of keeping his legs. The School-house are being penned in their turn, and now the ball is behind their goal, under the Doctor's wall. The Doctor and some of his family are there looking on, and seem as anxious as any boy for the success of the School-house. We get a minute's breathing time before old Brooke kicks out, and he gives the word to play strongly for touch, by the three trees. Away goes the ball, and the bull-dogs after it,

6. Confining.

and in another minute there is shout of "In touch," "Our ball." Now's your time, old Brooke, while your men are still fresh. He stands with the ball in his hand, while the two sides form in deep lines opposite one another: he must strike it straight out between them. The lines are thickest close to him, but young Brooke and two or three of his men are shifting up further, where the opposite line is weak. Old Brooke strikes it out straight and strong, and it falls opposite his brother. Hurra! that rush has taken it right through the School line, and away past the three trees, far into their quarters, and young Brooke and the bull-dogs are close upon it. The School leaders rush back, shouting "Look out in goal," and strain every nerve to catch him, but they are after the fleetest foot in Rugby. There they go straight for the School goal-posts, quarters scattering before them. One after another the bull-dogs go down, but young Brooke holds on. "He is down." No! a long stagger, but the danger is past; that was the shock of Crew, the most dangerous of dodgers. And now he is close to the School goal, the ball not three yards before him. There is a hurried rush of the School fags to the spot, but no one throws himself on the ball, the only chance, and young Brooke has touched it right under the School goal-posts.

The School leaders come up furious, and administer toco to the wretched fags nearest at hand; they may well be angry, for it is all Lombard-street to a china orange[7] that the School-house kick a goal with the ball touched in such a good place. Old Brooke of course will kick it out, but who shall catch and place it? Call Crab Jones. Here he comes, sauntering along with a straw in his mouth, the queerest, coolest fish in Rugby: if he were tumbled into the moon this minute, he would just pick himself up without taking his hands out of his pockets or turning a hair. But it is a moment when the boldest charger's heart beats quick. Old Brooke stands with the ball under his arm motioning the School back; he will not kick-out till they are all in goal, behind the posts; they are all edging forwards, inch by inch, to get nearer for the rush at Crab Jones, who stands there in front of old Brooke to catch the ball. If they can reach and destroy him before he catches, the danger is over; and with one and the same rush they will carry it right away to the School-house goal. Fond hope! it is kicked out and caught beautifully. Crab strikes his heel into the ground, to mark the spot where the ball was caught, beyond which the School line may not advance; but there they stand, five deep, ready to rush the moment the ball touches the ground. Take plenty of room! don't give the rush a chance of reaching you! place it true and steady! Trust Crab Jones—he has made a small hole with his heel for the ball to lie on, by which he is resting on one knee, with his eye on old Brooke. "Now!" Crab places the ball at the word, old Brooke kicks, and it rises slowly and truly as the School rush forward.

Then a moment's pause, while both sides look up at the spinning ball. There it flies, straight between the two posts, some five feet above the cross-bar, an unquestioned goal; and a shout of real genuine joy rings out from the School-house players-up, and a faint echo of it comes over the close from the goal-keepers under the Doctor's wall. A goal in the first hour—such a thing hasn't been done in the School-house match these five years.

"Over!" is the cry: the two sides change goals, and the School-house goal-keepers come threading their way across through the masses of the School; the most openly triumphant of them, amongst whom is Tom, a School-house boy of two hours' standing, getting their ears boxed in the transit. Tom indeed is excited beyond measure,

---

7. I.e., it is a safe bet. "Toco": corporal punishment.

and it is all the sixth-form boy, kindest and safest of goal-keepers, has been able to do, to keep him from rushing out whenever the ball has been near their goal. So he holds him by his side, and instructs him in the science of touching.

At this moment Griffith, the itinerant vendor of oranges from Hill Morton, enters the close with his heavy baskets; there is a rush of small boys upon the little pale-faced man, the two sides mingling together, subdued by the great Goddess Thirst, like the English and French by the streams in the Pyrenees.[8] The leaders are past oranges and apples, but some of them visit their coats, and apply innocent-looking ginger-beer bottles to their mouths. It is no ginger-beer though, I fear, and will do you no good. One short mad rush, and then a stitch in the side, and no more honest play; that's what comes of those bottles.

But now Griffith's baskets are empty, the ball is placed again midway, and the School are going to kick off. Their leaders have sent their lumber into goal, and rated the rest soundly, and one hundred and twenty picked players-up are there, bent on retrieving the game. They are to keep the ball in front of the School-house goal, and then to drive it in by sheer strength and weight. They mean heavy play and no mistake, and so old Brooke sees; and places Crab Jones in quarters just before the goal, with four or five picked players, who are to keep the ball away to the sides, where a try at goal, if obtained, will be less dangerous than in front. He himself, and Warner and Hedge, who have saved themselves till now, will lead the charges.

"Are you ready?" "Yes." And away comes the ball kicked high in the air, to give the School time to rush on and catch it as it falls. And here they are amongst us. Meet them like Englishmen, you School-house boys, and charge them home. Now is the time to show what mettle is in you—and there shall be a warm seat by the hall fire, and honour, and lots of bottled beer to-night, for him who does his duty in the next half-hour. And they are well met. Again and again the cloud of their players-up gathers before our goal, and comes threatening on, and Warner or Hedge, with young Brooke and the relics of the bull-dogs, break through and carry the ball back: and old Brooke ranges the field like Job's war-horse;[9] the thickest scrummage parts asunder before his rush, like the waves before a clipper's bows; his cheery voice rings over the field, and his eye is everywhere. And if these miss the ball, and it rolls dangerously in front of our goal, Crab Jones and his men have seized it and sent it away towards the sides with the unerring drop-kick. This is worth living for; the whole sum of school-boy existence gathered up into one straining, struggling half-hour, a half-hour worth a year of common life.

The quarter to five has struck, and the play slackens for a minute before goal; but there is Crew, the artful dodger, driving the ball in behind our goal, on the island side, where our quarters are weakest. Is there no one to meet him? Yes! look at little East! the ball is just at equal distances between the two, and they rush together, the young man of seventeen and the boy of twelve, and kick it at the same moment. Crew passes on without a stagger; East is hurled forward by the shock, and plunges on his shoulder, as if he would bury himself in the ground; but the ball rises straight into the air, and falls behind Crew's back, while the "bravos" of the School-house attest the pluckiest charge of all that hard-fought day. Warner picks East up lame and half stunned, and he hobbles back into goal, conscious of having played the man.

And now the last minutes are come, and the School gather for their last rush every

---

8. During the Peninsular War (1808–14), the Pyrenees were the scene of a battle between the English and French in 1813.

9. I.e., fearlessly rejoicing in battle (Job 39.19–25).

boy of the hundred and twenty who has a run left in him. Reckless of the defence of their own goal, on they come across the level big-side ground, the ball well down amongst them, straight for our goal, like the column of the Old Guard up the slope at Waterloo.[1] All former charges have been child's play to this. Warner and Hedge have met them, but still on they come. The bull-dogs rush in for the last time; they are hurled over or carried back, striving hand, foot, and eyelids. Old Brooke comes sweeping round the skirts of the play, and, turning short round, picks out the very heart of the scrummage, and plunges in. It wavers for a moment—he has the ball! No, it has passed him, and his voice rings out clear over the advancing tide, "Look out in goal." Crab Jones catches it for a moment; but before he can kick, the rush is upon him and passes over him; and he picks himself up behind them with his straw in his mouth, a little dirtier, but as cool as ever.

The ball rolls slowly in behind the School-house goal not three yards in front of a dozen of the biggest School players-up.

There stand the School-house præpostor, safest of goal-keepers, and Tom Brown by his side, who has learned his trade by this time. Now is your time, Tom. The blood of the Browns is up, and the two rush in together, and throw themselves on the ball, under the very feet of the advancing column; the præpostor on his hands and knees arching his back, and Tom all along on his face. Over them topple the leaders of the rush, shooting over the back of the præpostor, but falling flat on Tom, and knocking all the wind out of his small carcase. "Our ball," says the præpostor, rising with his prize, "but get up there, there's a little fellow under you." They are hauled and roll off him, and Tom is discovered a motionless body.

Old Brooke picks him up. "Stand back, give him air," he says; and then feeling his limbs, adds, "No bones broken. How do you feel, young un?" "Hah-hah," gasps Tom as his wind comes back, "pretty well, thank you—all right."

"Who is he?" says Brooke. "Oh, it's Brown, he's a new boy; I know him," says East, coming up. "Well, he is a plucky youngster, and will make a player," says Brooke.

And five o'clock strikes. "No side" is called, and the first day of the School-house match is over.

1. Final battle of the Napoleonic Wars, fought on June 18, 1815, near Waterloo (in Belgium); Napoleon and the French were soundly defeated. Old Guard: trusted veterans in Napoleon's army.

CHAPTER VI. AFTER THE MATCH

"——Some food we had."
—*Shakspere.*

ἧς πότος ἁδύς.[2]

THEOCR. *Id.*

s the boys scattered away from the ground, and East leaning on Tom's arm and limping along, was beginning to consider what luxury they should go and buy for tea to celebrate that glorious victory, the two Brookes came striding by. Old Brooke caught sight of East, and stopped; put his hand kindly on his shoulder and said, "Bravo, youngster, you played famously; not much the matter, I hope?"

"No, nothing at all," said East, "only a little twist from that charge."

"Well, mind and get all right for next Saturday;" and the leader passed on, leaving East better for those few words than all the opodeldoc[3] in England would have made him, and Tom ready to give one of his ears for as much notice. Ah! light words of those whom we love and honour, what a power ye are, and how carelessly wielded by those who can use you! Surely for these things also God will ask an account.

"Tea's directly after looking-up, you see," said East, hobbling along as fast as he could, "so you come along down to Sally Harrowell's; that's our School-house tuck shop—she bakes such stunning murphies,[4] we'll have a penn'orth each for tea; come along, or they'll all be gone."

Tom's new purse and money burnt in his pocket; he wondered, as they toddled through the quadrangle and along the street, whether East would be insulted if he suggested further extravagance, as he had not sufficient faith in a penny-worth of potatoes. At last he blurted out,—

"I say, East, can't we get something else besides potatoes? I've got lots of money, you know."

"Bless us, yes, I forgot," said East, "you've only just come. You see all my tin's been gone this twelve weeks: it hardly ever lasts beyond the first fortnight; and our allowances were all stopped this morning for broken windows, so I havn't got a penny. I've got a tick[5] at Sally's, of course; but then I hate running it high, you see, towards the end of the half, 'cause one has to shell out for it all directly one comes back, and that's a bore."

Tom didn't understand much of this talk, but seized on the fact that East had no

2. It was a sweet drinking bout; *Idyl* 14.17, by the Greek poet Theocritus (ca. 300–ca. 260 B.C.E.). The Shakespeare quoted is from *The Tempest* (1511), 1.2.

3. Liniment, medicinal salve.
4. Potatoes. "Tuck": food.
5. Line of credit. "Tin": money, cash.

money, and was denying himself some little pet luxury in consequence. "Well, what shall I buy?" said he; "I'm uncommon hungry."

"I say," said East, stopping to look at him and rest his leg, "you're a trump, Brown. I'll do the same by you next half. Let's have a pound of sausages, then; that's the best grub for tea I know of."

"Very well," said Tom, as pleased as possible; "where do they sell them?"

"Oh, over here, just opposite;" and they crossed the street and walked into the cleanest little front room of a small house, half parlour, half shop, and bought a pound of most particular sausages; East talking pleasantly to Mrs. Porter while she put them in paper, and Tom doing the paying part.

From Porter's they adjourned to Sally Harrowell's, where they found a lot of School-house boys waiting for the roast potatoes, and relating their own exploits in the day's match at the top of their voices. The street opened at once into Sally's kitchen, a low brick-floored room, with large recess for fire, and chimney-corner seats. Poor little Sally, the most good-natured and much enduring of womankind, was bustling about with a napkin in her hand, from her own oven to those of the neighbours' cottages, up the yard at the back of the house. Stumps, her husband, a short easy-going shoemaker, with a beery humorous eye and ponderous calves, who lived mostly on his wife's earnings, stood in a corner of the room, exchanging shots of the roughest description of repartee with every boy in turn. "Stumps, you lout, you've had too much beer again to-day." " 'Twasn't of your paying for, then."— "Stumps's calves are running down into his ankles; they want to get to grass." "Better be doing that, than gone altogether like yours," &c. &c. Very poor stuff it was, but it served to make time pass; and every now and then Sally arrived in the middle with a smoking tin of potatoes, which was cleared off in a few seconds, each boy as he seized his lot running off to the house with "Put me down two-penn'orth, Sally;" "Put down three-penn'orth between me and Davis," &c. How she ever kept the accounts so straight as she did, in her head and on her slate, was a perfect wonder.

East and Tom got served at last, and started back for the School-house just as the locking-up bell began to ring; East on the way recounting the life and adventures of Stumps, who was a character. Amongst his other small avocations, he was the hind carrier of a sedan-chair, the last of its race, in which the Rugby ladies still went out to tea, and in which, when he was fairly harnessed and carrying a load, it was the delight of small and mischievous boys to follow him and whip his calves. This was too much for the temper even of Stumps, and he would pursue his tormentors in a vindictive and apoplectic manner when released, but was easily pacified by twopence to buy beer with.

The lower schoolboys of the School-house, some fifteen in number, had tea in the lower-fifth school, and were presided over by the old verger or head-porter. Each boy had a quarter of a loaf of bread and pat of butter, and as much tea as he pleased; and there was scarcely one who didn't add to this some further luxury, such as baked potatoes, a herring, sprats, or something of the sort; but few, at this period of the half-year, could live up to a pound of Porter's sausages, and East was in great magnificence upon the strength of theirs. He had produced a toasting-fork from his study, and set Tom to toast the sausages, while he mounted guard over their butter and potatoes; " 'cause," as he explained, "you're a new boy, and they'll play you some trick and get our butter, but you can toast just as well as I." So Tom, in the midst of three or four more urchins similarly employed, toasted his face and the sausages at the same time before the huge fire, till the latter cracked; when East from his watch-tower shouted that they were done, and then the feast proceeded, and the festive cups of tea were filled and emptied, and Tom imparted of the sausages in small bits to many neighbours, and thought he had never tasted such good potatoes or seen such jolly boys. They on their parts waived all ceremony, and pegged away at the sausages and potatoes, and, remembering Tom's performance in goal, voted East's new crony a brick. After tea, and while the things were being cleared away, they gathered round the fire, and the talk on the match still went on; and those who had them to show, pulled up their trousers and showed the hacks they had received in the good cause.

They were soon however all turned out of the school, and East conducted Tom up to his bedroom, that he might get on clean things and wash himself before singing.

"What's singing?" said Tom, taking his head out of his basin, where he had been plunging it in cold water.

"Well, you are jolly green," answered his friend from a neighbouring basin. "Why, the last six Saturdays of every half, we sing of course: and this is the first of them. No first lesson to do, you know, and lie in bed to-morrow morning."

"But who sings?"

"Why, everybody, of course; you'll see soon enough. We begin directly after supper, and sing till bed-time. It ain't such good fun now tho' as in the summer half, 'cause then we sing in the little fives' court, under the library, you know. We take out tables, and the big boys sit round, and drink beer; double allowance on Saturday nights; and we cut about the quadrangle between the songs, and it looks like a lot of robbers in a cave. And the louts come and pound at the great gates, and we pound back again, and shout at them. But this half we only sing in the hall. Come along down to my study."

Their principal employment in the study was to clear out East's table, removing the drawers and ornaments and tablecloth: for he lived in the bottom passage, and his table was in requisition for the singing.

Supper came in due course at seven o'clock, consisting of bread and cheese and beer, which was all saved for the singing; and directly afterwards the fags went to work to prepare the hall. The School-house hall, as has been said, is a great long high room, with two large fires on one side, and two large iron-bound tables, one running down the middle, and the other along the wall opposite the fire-places. Around the upper fire the fags placed the tables in the form of a horse-shoe, and upon them the jugs with the Saturday night's allowance of beer. Then the big boys used to drop in and take their seats, bringing with them bottled beer and song-books; for although they all knew the songs by heart, it was the thing to have an old man-uscript book descended from some departed hero, in which they were all carefully written out.

The sixth-form boys had not yet appeared: so to fill up the gap, an interesting and time-honoured ceremony was gone through. Each new boy was placed on the table in turn, and made to sing a solo, under the penalty of drinking a large mug of salt and water if he resisted or broke down. However, the new boys all sing like night-ingales to-night, and the salt water is not in requisition; Tom, as his part, performing the old west-country song of "The Leather Bottèl" with considerable applause. And at the half-hour down come the sixth and fifth form boys, and take their places at the tables, which are filled up by the next biggest boys; the rest, for whom there is no room at the table, standing round outside.

The glasses and mugs are filled, and then the fugle-man strikes up the old sea-song—

> "A wet sheet and a flowing sea,
> And a wind that follows fast," &c.

which is the invariable first song in the School-house, and all the seventy voices join in, not mindful of harmony, but bent on noise, which they attain decidedly, but the general effect isn't bad. And then follow the "British Grenadiers," "Billy Taylor," "The Siege of Seringapatam," "Three Jolly Post-boys," and other vociferous songs in rapid succession, including the "Chesapeake and Shannon," a song lately introduced in honour of old Brooke: and when they come to the words—

> "Brave Broke he waved his sword, crying, Now, my lads, aboard,
> And we'll stop their playing Yandee-doodle-dandy oh!"

you expect the roof to come down. The sixth and fifth know that "brave Broke" of the Shannon was no sort of relation to our old Brooke. The fourth form are uncertain in their belief, but for the most part hold that old Brooke *was* a midshipman then on board his uncle's ship. And the lower school never doubt for a moment that it was our old Brooke who led the boarders, in what capacity they care not a straw. During the pauses the bottled-beer corks fly rapidly, and the talk is fast and merry, and the big boys, at least all of them who have a fellow-feeling for dry throats, hand their mugs over their shoulders to be emptied by the small ones who stand round behind.

Then Warner, the head of the house, gets up and wants to speak, but he can't, for every boy knows what's coming; and the big boys who sit at the tables pound them and cheer; and the small boys who stand behind pound one another, and cheer, and rush about the hall cheering. Then silence being made, Warner reminds them of the old School-house custom of drinking the healths, on the first night of singing, of those who are going to leave at the end of the half. "He sees that they know what he is going to say already—(loud cheers)—and so won't keep them, but only ask them to treat the toast as it deserves. It is the head of the eleven, the head of big-side football, their leader on this glorious day—Pater[6] Brooke!"

And away goes the pounding and cheering again, becoming deafening when old Brooke gets on his legs: till, a table having broken down, and a gallon or so of beer been upset, and all throats getting dry, silence ensues, and the hero speaks, leaning his hands on the table, and bending a little forwards. No action, no tricks of oratory; plain, strong, and straight, like his play.

"Gentlemen of the School-house! I am very proud of the way in which you have received my name, and I wish I could say all I should like in return. But I know I shan't. However, I'll do the best I can to say what seems to me ought to be said by a fellow who's just going to leave, and who has spent a good slice of his life here. Eight years it is, and eight such years as I can never hope to have again. So now I hope you'll all listen to me—(loud cheers of 'that we will')—for I'm going to talk seriously. You're bound to listen to me, for what's the use of calling me 'pater,' and all that, if you don't mind what I say? And I'm going to talk seriously, because I feel so. It's a jolly time, too, getting to the end of the half, and a goal kicked by us first day—(tremendous applause)—after one of the hardest and fiercest day's play I can remember in eight years—(frantic shoutings). The School played splendidly, too, I will say, and kept it up to the last. That last charge of theirs would have carried away a house.

6. Father (Latin).

I never thought to see anything again of old Crab there, except little pieces, when I saw him tumbled over by it—(laughter and shouting, and great slapping on the back of Jones by the boys nearest him). Well, but we beat 'em—(cheers). Ay, but why did we beat 'em? answer me that—(shouts of 'your play'). Nonsense! 'Twasn't the wind and kick-off either—that wouldn't do it. 'Twasn't because we've half-a-dozen of the best players in the school, as we have. I wouldn't change Warner, and Hedge, and Crab, and the young un, for any six on their side—(violent cheers). But half-a-dozen fellows can't keep it up for two hours against two hundred. Why is it, then? I'll tell you what I think. It's because we've more reliance on one another, more of a house feeling, more fellowship than the School can have. Each of us knows and can depend on his next hand man better—that's why we beat 'em to-day. We've union, they've division—there's the secret—(cheers). But how's this to be kept up? How's it to be improved? That's the question. For I take it, we're all in earnest about beating the School, whatever else we care about. I know I'd sooner win two School-house matches running than get the Balliol scholarship[7] any day—(frantic cheers).

"Now, I'm as proud of the house as any one. I believe it's the best house in the school, out-and-out—(cheers). But it's a long way from what I want to see it. First, there's a deal of bullying going on. I know it well. I don't pry about and interfere; that only makes it more underhand, and encourages the small boys to come to us with their fingers in their eyes telling tales, and so we should be worse off than ever. It's very little kindness for the sixth to meddle generally—you youngsters, mind that. You'll be all the better football players for learning to stand it, and to take your own parts, and fight it through. But depend on it, there's nothing breaks up a house like bullying. Bullies are cowards, and one coward makes many; so good-bye to the School-house match if bullying gets ahead here. (Loud applause from the small boys, who look meaningly at Flashman and other boys at the tables.) Then there's fuddling[8] about in the public-house, and drinking bad spirits, and punch, and such rot-gut stuff. That won't make good drop-kicks or chargers of you, take my word for it. You get plenty of good beer here, and that's enough for you; and drinking isn't fine or manly, whatever some of you may think of it.

"One other thing I must have a word about. A lot of you think and say, for I've heard you, 'There's this new Doctor hasn't been here so long as some of us, and he's changing all the old customs. Rugby, and the School-house especially, are going to the dogs. Stand up for the good old ways, and down with the Doctor!' Now I'm as fond of old Rugby customs and ways as any of you, and I've been here longer than any of you, and I'll give you a word of advice in time, for I shouldn't like to see any of you getting sacked. 'Down with the Doctor's' easier said than done. You'll find him pretty tight on his perch, I take it, and an awkwardish customer to handle in that line. Besides now, what customs has he put down? There was the good old custom of taking the linchpins out of the farmers' and bagmen's gigs at the fairs, and a cowardly blackguard custom it was. We all know what came of it, and no wonder the Doctor objected to it. But, come now, any of you, name a custom that he has put down."

"The hounds," calls out a fifth-form boy, clad in a green cutaway with brass buttons and cord trousers, the leader of the sporting interest, and reputed a great rider and keen hand generally.

"Well, we had six or seven mangey harriers and beagles belonging to the house,

---

7. Coveted scholarship to Oxford University's Balliol College, then reputed to be the most intellec-

tually prestigious of the colleges.
8. Tippling, boozing.

I'll allow, and had had them for years, and that the Doctor put them down. But what good ever came of them? Only rows with all the keepers for ten miles round; and big-side Hare and Hounds[9] is better fun ten times over. What else?"

No answer.

"Well, I won't go on. Think it over for yourselves: you'll find, I believe, that he don't meddle with any one that's worth keeping. And mind now, I say again, look out for squalls, if you will go your own way, and that way ain't the Doctor's, for it'll lead to grief. You all know that I'm not the fellow to back a master through thick and thin. If I saw him stopping football, or cricket, or bathing, or sparring, I'd be as ready as any fellow to stand up about it. But he don't—he encourages them; didn't you see him out to-day for half-an-hour watching us?—(loud cheers for the Doctor)—and he's a strong true man, and a wise one too, and a public-school man too." (Cheers.) "And so let's stick to him, and talk no more rot, and drink his health as the head of the house. (Loud cheers.) And now I've done blowing up,[1] and very glad I am to have done. But it's a solemn thing to be thinking of leaving a place which one has lived in and loved for eight years; and if one can say a word for the good of the old house at such a time, why, it should be said, whether bitter or sweet. If I hadn't been proud of the house and you—ay, no one knows how proud—I shouldn't be blowing you up. And now let's get to singing. But before I sit down I must give you a toast to be drunk with three-times-three and all the honours. It's a toast which I hope every one of us, wherever he may go hereafter, will never fail to drink when he thinks of the brave bright days of his boyhood. It's a toast which should bind us all together, and to those who've gone before, and who'll come after us here. It is the dear old School-house— the best house of the best school in England!"

My dear boys, old and young, you who have belonged, or do belong, to other schools and other houses, don't begin throwing my poor little book about the room, and abusing me and it, and vowing you'll read no more when you get to this point. I allow you've provocation for it. But, come now—would you, any of you, give a fig for a fellow who didn't believe in, and stand up for, his own house and his own school? You know you wouldn't. Then don't object to me cracking up[2] the old School-house, Rugby. Haven't I a right to do it, when I'm taking all the trouble of writing this true history for all of your benefits? If you ain't satisfied, go and write the history of your own houses in your own times, and say all you know for your own schools and houses, provided it's true, and I'll read it without abusing you.

The last few words hit the audience in their weakest place; they had been not altogether enthusiastic at several parts of old Brooke's speech; but "the best house of the best school in England" was too much for them all, and carried even the sporting and drinking interests off their legs into rapturous applause, and (it is to be hoped) resolutions to lead a new life and remember old Brooke's words; which how- ever they didn't altogether do, as will appear hereafter.

But it required all old Brooke's popularity to carry down parts of his speech; espe- cially that relating to the Doctor. For there are no such bigoted holders by established forms and customs, be they never so foolish or meaningless, as English schoolboys, at least as the schoolboy of our generation. We magnified into heroes every boy who had left, and looked upon him with awe and reverence, when he revisited the place a year or so afterwards, on his way to or from Oxford or Cambridge; and happy was

---

9. Sport in which one person, the "hare," lays the "scent" (usually paper torn into fragments) and others (the "hounds") follow. The game is also called *paper chase*. "Keepers": gamekeepers.
1. Scolding.
2. Eulogizing.

the boy who remembered him, and sure of an audience as he expounded what he used to do and say, though it were sad enough stuff to make angels, not to say headmasters weep.

We looked upon every trumpery little custom and habit which had obtained in the school as though it had been a law of the Medes and Persians,[3] and regarded the infringement or variation of it as a sort of sacrilege. And the Doctor, than whom no man or boy had a stronger liking for old school customs, which were good and sensible, had, as has already been hinted, come into most decided collision with several which were neither the one nor the other. And as old Brooke had said, when he came into collision with boys or customs, there was nothing for them but to give in or take themselves off; because what he said had to be done, and no mistake about it. And this was beginning to be pretty clearly understood; the boys felt that there was a strong man over them, who would have things his own way; and hadn't yet learned that he was a wise and loving man also. His personal character and influence had not had time to make itself felt, except by a very few of the bigger boys with whom he came more directly in contact; and he was looked upon with great fear and dislike by the great majority even of his own house. For he had found School, and Schoolhouse, in a state of monstrous licence and misrule, and was still employed in the necessary but unpopular work of setting up order with a strong hand.

However, as has been said, old Brooke triumphed, and the boys cheered him, and then the Doctor. And then more songs came, and the healths of the other boys about to leave, who each made a speech, one flowery, another maudlin, a third prosy, and so on, which are not necessary to be here recorded.

Half-past nine struck in the middle of the performance of "Auld Lang Syne,"[4] a most obstreperous proceeding; during which there was an immense amount of standing with one foot on the table, knocking mugs together and shaking hands, without which accompaniments it seems impossible for the youth of Britain to take part in that famous old song. The under-porter of the School-house entered during the performance, bearing five or six long wooden candlesticks, with lighted dips in them, which he proceeded to stick into their holes in such part of the great tables as he could get at; and then stood outside the ring till the end of the song, when he was hailed with shouts.

"Bill, you old muff, the half-hour hasn't struck."

"Here, Bill, drink some cocktail," "Sing us a song, old boy," "Don't you wish you may get the table?" Bill drank the proffered cocktail not unwillingly, and putting down the empty glass, remonstrated, "Now, gentlemen, there's only ten minutes to prayers, and we must get the hall straight."

Shouts of "No, no!" and a violent effort to strike up "Billy Taylor" for the third time. Bill looked appealingly to old Brooke, who got up and stopped the noise. "Now then, lend a hand, you youngsters, and get the tables back, clear away the jugs and glasses. Bill's right. Open the windows, Warner." The boy addressed, who sat by the long ropes, proceeded to pull up the great windows, and let in a clear fresh rush of night air, which made the candles flicker and gutter, and the fires roar. The circle broke up, each collaring his own jug, glass, and song-book; Bill pounced on the big table, and began to rattle it away to its place outside the buttery-door. The lower-passage boys carried off their small tables, aided by their friends, while above all,

3. I.e., unalterable (see Daniel 6.8).
4. This song, whose lyrics by the Scottish poet Robert Burns were first published in 1796, is traditional at leave-taking (the title means "Long Ago").

standing on the great hall-table, a knot of untiring sons of harmony made night doleful by a prolonged performance of "God save the King." His Majesty King William IV.[5] then reigned over us, a monarch deservedly popular amongst the boys addicted to melody, to whom he was chiefly known from the beginning of that excellent, if slightly vulgar song in which they much delighted—

> "Come, neighbours all, both great and small,
> Perform your duties here,
> And loudly sing 'live Billy our king,'
> For bating the tax upon beer."[6]

Others of the more learned in songs also celebrated his praises in a sort of ballad, which I take to have been written by some Irish loyalist. I have forgotten all but the chorus, which ran—

> "God save our good King William, be his name for ever blest,
> He's the father of all his people, and the guardian of all the rest."

In troth we were loyal subjects in those days, in a rough way. I trust that our successors make as much of her present Majesty,[7] and, having regard to the greater refinement of the times, have adopted or written other songs equally hearty, but more civilized, in her honour.

Then the quarter to ten struck, and the prayer-bell rang. The sixth and fifth form boys ranged themselves in their school order along the wall, on either side of the great fires, the middle fifth and upper school boys round the long table in the middle of the hall, and the lower-school boys round the upper part of the second long table, which ran down the side of the hall furthest from the fires. Here Tom found himself at the bottom of all, in a state of mind and body not at all fit for prayers, as he thought; and so tried hard to make himself serious, but couldn't, for the life of him, do anything but repeat in his head the choruses of some of the songs, and stare at all the boys opposite, wondering at the brilliancy of their waistcoats, and speculating what sort of fellows they were. The steps of the head-porter are heard on the stairs, and a light gleams at the door. "Hush!" from the fifth form boys who stand there, and then in strides the Doctor, cap on head, book in one hand, and gathering up his gown in the other. He walks up the middle, and takes his post by Warner, who begins calling over the names. The Doctor takes no notice of anything, but quietly turns over his book, and finds the place, and then stands, cap in hand and finger in book, looking straight before his nose. He knows better than any one when to look, and when to see nothing; to-night is singing night, and there's been lots of noise, and no harm done; nothing but beer drunk, and nobody the worse for it; though some of them do look hot and excited. So the Doctor sees nothing, but fascinates Tom in a horrible manner, as he stands there, and reads out the Psalm in that deep, ringing, searching voice of his. Prayers are over, and Tom still stares open-mouthed after the Doctor's retiring figure, when he feels a pull at his sleeve, and turning round, sees East.

"I say, were you ever tossed in a blanket?"

"No," said Tom; "why?"

---

5. King of England (1765–1837; r. 1830–37).
6. The tax on beer was removed in 1830.

7. Queen Victoria (1819–1901; r. 1837–1901), niece of William IV.

" 'Cause there'll be tossing to-night, most likely, before the sixth come up to bed. So if you funk,[8] you just come along and hide, or else they'll catch you and toss you."

"Were you ever tossed? Does it hurt?" inquired Tom.

"Oh yes, bless you, a dozen times," said East, as he hobbled along by Tom's side up-stairs. "It don't hurt unless you fall on the floor. But most fellows don't like it."

They stopped at the fireplace in the top passage, where were a crowd of small boys whispering together, and evidently unwilling to go up into the bed-rooms. In a minute, however, a study door opened, and a sixth-form boy came out, and off they all scuttled up the stairs, and then noiselessly dispersed to their different rooms. Tom's heart beat rather quick as he and East reached their room, but he had made up his mind. "I shan't hide, East," said he.

"Very well, old fellow," replied East, evidently pleased; "no more shall I—they'll be here for us directly."

The room was a great big one with a dozen beds in it, but not a boy that Tom could see, except East and himself. East pulled off his coat and waistcoat, and then sat on the bottom of his bed, whistling, and pulling off his boots; Tom followed his example.

A noise and steps are heard in the passage, the door opens, and in rush four or five great fifth-form boys, headed by Flashman in his glory.

Tom and East slept in the further corner of the room, and were not seen at first.

"Gone to ground, eh?" roared Flashman; "push 'em out then, boys! look under the beds:" and he pulled up the little white curtain of the one nearest him. "Who-o-op," he roared, pulling away at the leg of a small boy, who held on tight to the leg of the bed, and sung out lustily for mercy.

"Here, lend a hand, one of you, and help me pull out this young howling brute. Hold your tongue, sir, or I'll kill you."

"Oh, please, Flashman, please, Walker, don't toss me! I'll fag for you, I'll do anything, only don't toss me."

"You be hanged," said Flashman, lugging the wretched boy along, " 'twon't hurt you,——you! Come along, boys, here he is."

"I say, Flashey," sung out another of the big boys, "drop that; you heard what old Pater Brooke said to-night. I'll be hanged if we'll toss any one against their will—no more bullying. Let him go, I say."

Flashman, with an oath and a kick, released his prey, who rushed headlong under his bed again, for fear they should change their minds, and crept along underneath the other beds, till he got under that of the sixth-form boy, which he knew they daren't disturb.

"There's plenty of youngsters don't care about it," said Walker. "Here, here's Scud East—you'll be tossed, won't you, young un?" Scud was East's nickname, or Black, as we called it, gained by his fleetness of foot.

"Yes," said East, "if you like, only mind my foot."

"And here's another who didn't hide. Hullo! new boy; what's your name, sir?"

"Brown."

"Well, Whitey Brown, you don't mind being tossed?"

"No," said Tom, setting his teeth.

"Come along then, boys," sung out Walker, and away they all went, carrying along Tom and East, to the intense relief of four or five other small boys, who crept out from under the beds and behind them.

8. Flinch or shrink out of fear; try to back out of something.

"What a trump Scud is!" said one. "They won't come back here now."

"And that new boy, too; he must be a good plucked[9] one."

"Ah! wait till he has been tossed on to the floor; see how he'll like it then!"

Meantime the procession went down the passage to No. 7, the largest room, and the scene of the tossing, in the middle of which was a great open space. Here they joined other parties of the bigger boys, each with a captive or two, some willing to be tossed, some sullen, and some frightened to death. At Walker's suggestion all who were afraid were let off, in honour of Pater Brooke's speech.

Then a dozen big boys seized hold of a blanket, dragged from one of the beds. "In with Scud, quick, there's no time to lose." East was chucked into the blanket. "Once, twice, thrice, and away;" up he went like a shuttlecock, but not quite up to the ceiling.

"Now, boys, with a will," cried Walker, "once, twice, thrice, and away!" This time he went clean up, and kept himself from touching the ceiling with his hand, and so again a third time, when he was turned out, and up went another boy. And then came Tom's turn. He lay quite still, by East's advice, and didn't dislike the "once, twice, thrice;" but the "away" wasn't so pleasant. They were in good wind now, and sent him slap up to the ceiling first time, against which his knees came rather sharply. But the moment's pause before descending was the rub, the feeling of utter help-lessness, and of leaving his whole inside behind him sticking to the ceiling. Tom was very near shouting to be set down, when he found himself back in the blanket, but thought of East, and didn't; and so took his three tosses without a kick or a cry, and was called a young trump for his pains.

He and East, having earned it, stood now looking on. No catastrophe happened, as all the captives were cool hands, and didn't struggle. This didn't suit Flashman. What your real bully likes in tossing, is when the boys kick and struggle, or hold on to one side of the blanket, and so get pitched bodily on to the floor; it's no fun to him when no one is hurt or frightened.

"Let's toss two of them together, Walker," suggested he. "What a cursed bully you are, Flashey!" rejoined the other. "Up with another one."

And so no two boys were tossed together, the peculiar hardship of which is, that it's too much for human nature to lie still then and share troubles; and so the wretched pair of small boys struggle in the air which shall fall a-top in the descent, to the no small risk of both falling out of the blanket, and the huge delight of brutes like Flashman.

But now there's a cry that the præpostor of the room is coming; so the tossing stops, and all scatter to their different rooms: and Tom is left to turn in, with the first day's experience of a public school to meditate upon.

9. Having pluck or courage.

RUDYARD KIPLING
1865–1936

Although still called "Giggers" (shortened from "gig-lamps") for wearing glasses, and rather hopeless at the sports that consumed a large portion of a typical nineteenth-century British schoolboy's life, the fourteen-year-old Rudyard Kipling found that his sudden strength and surprising whiskers protected him from the bullying that had characterized his first eighteen months at boarding school. Kipling based the three boys at the center of *Stalky & Co.* (1899) on the school experiences of himself and his two best friends. Stalky (in real life, a future major-general) was chosen the "commander-in-chief" of the Triple Alliance, Kipling relates in his autobiographical fragment *Something of Myself* (1936), for his "executive capacity [in the] . . . organization of raids, reprisals and retreats." Hints of the later Kipling—his conservative political views, clipped and sardonic tone, and appreciation of a British manliness of empire and antagonism—can be found in *Stalky & Co.* Another important aspect of the man and writer also comes through: his love for children. Angus Wilson, one of Kipling's biographers, argues that this affection and respect for children and what they imagine is at the heart of his best work. Indeed, Kipling's literary reputation today rests primarily on his books for the young, including the animal fables in *The Jungle Books* (1894, 1895) and the playful *Just So Stories* (1902); two books about England's deep historical past, *Puck of Pook's Hill* (1906) and *Rewards and Fairies* (1910); and his novel *Kim* (1901) about an Anglo-Indian boy in colonial India.

Kipling was born in Bombay, India. His father, a mason, was a craftsman who believed in the artistic principles of the author and designer William Morris (1834–1896). Lockwood Kipling was appointed in 1864 to the Art School of Bombay to teach molding, the manufacture and design of terra-cotta pottery, and architectural sculpture. After a bucolic six years spent primarily in India, the spoiled and "rumbustious" Rudyard, with his younger sister Trix, were brought to England. The children were left for five years with a couple from Southsea who had advertised in a newspaper as caretakers. Although it was not unusual to send Anglo-Indian children to England to maintain or improve their health (thought to be threatened by India's climate) and to ensure that they developed "English" characters and received proper schooling, Rudyard's abandonment to complete, and often unkind, strangers traumatized him. After his eyesight and spirits began to fail in 1877, his worried mother, Alice Kipling, returned to England to remove Rudyard from the "House of Desolation," as he called it in "Baa, Baa, Black Sheep" (1888), an autobiographical story recounting those days.

Kipling was next sent, at age eleven, to the United Services College, established in Southwest England in 1874 to cater to army and navy officers' sons, with an eye to their own future military careers. Kipling ultimately blossomed at the rough school, editing the school magazine and reading and writing poetry. At sixteen he went back to India and his parents and became a journalist. For the next seven years Kipling worked at minor newspapers, first the *Civil and Military Gazette* and then the *Pioneer*. He began publishing stories, sketches, and poems—reprinted in *Plain Tales from the Hills* (1888)—that found an instant readership in India and made him a celebrity when he returned to England in 1889. In 1892 Kipling married Carrie Balestier, an American and the sister of a close friend, Wolcott Balestier. The couple moved to Vermont to be near her family. There Kipling wrote his two *Jungle Books*, dedicated to his beloved first child, Josephine.

Kipling became friends with such notable Americans as Theodore Roosevelt, then undersecretary of the navy, yet he was never entirely comfortable in Vermont. After an embarrassing falling-out with one of his brothers-in-law, the famous author, his wife, and their three children moved back to England. Although he never again lived in India it continued to inspire him, and he began to work on a novel featuring it. When the Kiplings visited the United States in the summer of 1899 to visit Carrie's mother, tragedy struck: the entire family became ill with bronchial infections, and Josephine died. The grief-stricken Kipling threw himself into his work and returned to colonial India in his imagination; the resulting novel was *Kim*, considered by many to be his best work.

In 1902 the Kipling family settled at Bateman's, a beautiful Jacobean house of stone in East Sussex. Just before they moved he published *Just So Stories*, the series of read-aloud stories of humorous explanation—such as "The Elephant's Child," which reveals how the elephant's trunk was formed ("How the Camel Got His Hump" is included in Animal Fables, above). Kipling had long been wildly popular with the common reader; his reputation among the highbrow increased after he received the Nobel Prize for literature in 1907, the first writer in English to be so honored.

Though Bateman's secluded location seemed to promise peace, it shielded Kipling from neither mundane disturbances (eager celebrity hounds) nor the global cataclysm of World War I—in 1915 his only son was reported missing in action. In 1917, the year that John Kipling was confirmed dead, Kipling began working for the Imperial War Graves Commission. The increasingly bitter yet still-prolific author declined honors from his own government but accepted them from other nations. He became notorious for his support of English imperialism and for paternalistic and jingoistic views proclaiming Anglo-Saxon racial superiority (notably in the 1899 poem "The White Man's Burden"). Kipling died at age seventy-one and was buried at Poet's Corner in Westminster Abbey.

Kipling's work has been compared with that of Robert Louis Stevenson (1850–1894) and J. M. Barrie (1860–1937), two other popular late-Victorian British writers of books about boys and boyishness. The stories in Stalky & Co., many of which had first appeared in periodicals, create an often brutal schoolboys' world in which pulling pranks and punishing bullies offer the character training in justice and honor that Kipling believed essential to create men who could sustain the British Empire. Kipling's school story is partially indebted to the public school ideologies of loyalty and commitment to the group first described in Thomas Hughes's Tom Brown Schooldays (1857), yet Stalky & Co. never achieved the popular or commercial success of its forerunner. Kipling's cynical view of school life as a "game" to be won through craft and stealth and through subverting authority figures contrasts with the sunnier picture promoted by Hughes. Fifteen-year-old Beetle (Kipling) and his two friends, McTurk and Stalky, are targets of teasing and abuse from the students and masters of other houses (the dormitories that foster group identity within the school) primarily because they eschew sports and heartily congenial activities. In "An Unsavory Interlude," first published in The Windsor Magazine and McClure's Magazine, the eccentric and quick-witted three strike back at their enemies in a typically clever caper that turns the tables on their tormentors and confirms their belief in their own superiority.

From Stalky & Co.

AN UNSAVORY INTERLUDE

It was a maiden aunt of Stalky who sent him both books, with the inscription, "To dearest Artie, on his sixteenth birthday;" it was McTurk who ordered their hypothecation; and it was Beetle, returned from Bideford, who flung them on the windowsill of Number Five study with news that Bastable would advance but ninepence on the two; "Eric; or, Little by Little," being almost as great a drug as "St. Winifred's."[1] "An' I don't think much of your aunt. We're nearly out of cartridges, too—Artie, dear."

Whereupon Stalky rose up to grapple with him, but McTurk sat on Stalky's head, calling him a "pure-minded boy" till peace was declared. As they were grievously in arrears with a Latin prose, as it was a blazing July afternoon, and as they ought to have been at a house cricket-match, they began to renew their acquaintance, intimate and unholy, with the volumes.

"Here we are!" said McTurk. " 'Corporal punishment produced on Eric the worst effects. He burned *not* with remorse or regret'—make a note o' that, Beetle—'but

1. Famous moral school stories, published in 1858 and 1862, respectively, by F. W. Farrar. "Hypothecation": pawning. "Advance but ninepence on the two": i.e., pay very little for the books. "Drug": a commodity that has become unsellable.

with shame and violent indignation. He glared'—oh, naughty Eric! Let's get to where he goes in for drink."

"Hold on half a shake. Here's another sample. 'The Sixth,' he says, 'is the palladium[2] of all public schools.' But this lot"—Stalky rapped the gilded book—"can't prevent fellows drinkin' and stealin', an' lettin' fags[3] out of window at night, an'—an' doin' what they please. Golly, what we've missed—not goin' to St. Winifred's! . . ."

"I'm sorry to see any boys of my house taking so little interest in their matches."

Mr. Prout[4] could move very silently if he pleased, though that is no merit in a boy's eyes. He had flung open the study-door without knocking—another sin—and looked at them suspiciously. "Very sorry, indeed, I am to see you frowsting[5] in your studies."

"We've been out ever since dinner, sir," said McTurk wearily. One house-match is just like another, and their "ploy" of that week happened to be rabbit-shooting with saloon-pistols.[6]

"I can't see a ball when it's coming, sir," said Beetle. "I've had my gig-lamps[7] smashed at the Nets till I got excused. I wasn't any good even as a fag, then, sir."

"Tuck[8] is probably your form. Tuck and brewing. Why can't you three take any interest in the honor of your house?"[9]

They had heard that phrase till they were wearied. The "honor of the house" was Prout's weak point, and they knew well how to flick him on the raw.

"If you order us to go down, sir, of course we'll go," said Stalky, with maddening politeness. But Prout knew better than that. He had tried the experiment once at a big match, when the three, self-isolated, stood to attention for half an hour in full view of all the visitors, to whom fags, subsidized for that end, pointed them out as victims of Prout's tyranny. And Prout was a sensitive man.

In the infinitely petty confederacies of the Common-room, King and Macrea, fellow house-masters, had borne it in upon him that by games, and games alone, was salvation wrought. Boys neglected were boys lost. They must be disciplined. Left to himself, Prout would have made a sympathetic house-master; but he was never so left, and with the devilish insight of youth, the boys knew to whom they were indebted for his zeal.

"Must we go down, sir?" said McTurk.

"I don't want to order you to do what a right-thinking boy should do gladly. I'm sorry." And he lurched out with some hazy impression that he had sown good seed on poor ground.

"Now what does he suppose is the use of that?" said Beetle.

"Oh, he's cracked. King jaws him in Common-room about not keepin' us up to the mark, an' Macrea burbles about 'dithcipline,' an' old Heffy sits between 'em sweatin' big drops. I heard Oke (the Common-room butler) talking to Richards (Prout's house-servant) about it down in the basement the other day when I went down to bag some bread," said Stalky.

"What did Oke say?" demanded McTurk, throwing "Eric" into a corner.

"Oh, he said, 'They make more nise nor a nest full o' jackdaws, an' half of it like we'd no ears to our heads that waited on 'em. They talks over old Prout—what he've done an' left undone about his boys. An' how their boys be fine boys, an' his'n be dom bad.' Well, Oke talked like that, you know, and Richards got awf'ly wrathy. He has a down on King for something or other. Wonder why?"

"Why, King talks about Prout in form-room—makes allusions, an' all that—only half the chaps are such asses they can't see what he's drivin' at. And d'you remember what he said about the 'Casual House' last Tuesday? He meant us. They say he says perfectly beastly things to his own house, making fun of Prout's," said Beetle.

"Well, we didn't come here to mix up in their rows," McTurk said wrathfully. "Who'll bathe after call-over?[1] King's takin' it in the cricket-field. Come on." Turkey seized his straw[2] and led the way.

They reached the sun-blistered pavilion over against the gray Pebbleridge just before roll-call, and, asking no questions, gathered from King's voice and manner that his house was on the road to victory.

"Ah, ha!" said he, turning to show the light of his countenance. "Here we have the ornaments of the Casual House at last. You consider cricket beneath you, I believe"—the crowd, flannelled,[3] sniggered—"and from what I have seen this afternoon, I fancy many others of your house hold the same view. And may I ask what you purpose to do with your noble selves till tea-time?"

"Going down to bathe, sir," said Stalky.

"And whence this sudden zeal for cleanliness? There is nothing about you that particularly suggests it. Indeed, so far as I remember—I may be at fault—but a short time ago——"

"Five years, sir," said Beetle hotly.

King scowled. "*One* of you was that thing called a water-funk.[4] Yes, a water-funk. So now you wish to wash? It is well. Cleanliness never injured a boy or—a house. We will proceed to business," and he addressed himself to the call-over board.

"What the deuce did you say anything to him for, Beetle?" said McTurk angrily, as they strolled towards the big, open sea-baths.

" 'Twasn't fair—remindin' one of bein' a water-funk. My first term, too. Heaps of chaps are—when they can't swim."

"Yes, you ass; but he saw he'd fetched[5] you. You ought never to answer King."

"But it wasn't fair, Stalky."

"My Hat! You've been here six years, and you expect fairness. Well, you *are* a dithering idiot."

A knot of King's boys, also bound for the baths, hailed them, beseeching them to wash—for the honor of their house.

"That's what comes of King's jawin' and messin'. Those young animals wouldn't have thought of it unless he'd put it into their heads. Now they'll be funny about it for weeks," said Stalky. "Don't take any notice."

The boys came nearer, shouting an opprobrious word. At last they moved to windward, ostentatiously holding their noses.

"That's pretty," said Beetle. "They'll be sayin' our house stinks next."

When they returned from the baths, damp-headed, languid, at peace with the world, Beetle's forecast came only too true. They were met in the corridor by a fag—a common, Lower-Second fag—who at arm's length handed them a carefully wrapped piece of soap "with the compliments of King's house."

"Hold on," said Stalky, checking immediate attack. "Who put you up to this, Nixon?

---

1. Roll call.
2. I.e., his hat, boater.
3. Cricket is traditionally played in long white flan-

nel trousers.
4. A person who is afraid to go in the water.
5. I.e., gotten to, or scored off.

Rattray and White? (Those were two leaders in King's house.) Thank you. There's no answer."

"Oh, it's too sickening to have this kind o' rot shoved on to a chap. What's the sense of it? What's the fun of it?" said McTurk.

"It will go on to the end of the term, though," Beetle wagged his head sorrowfully. He had worn many jests threadbare on his own account.

In a few days it became an established legend of the school that Prout's house did not wash and were therefore noisome. Mr. King was pleased to smile succulently in form when one of his boys drew aside from Beetle with certain gestures.

"There seems to be some disability attaching to you, my Beetle, or else why should Burton major[6] withdraw, so to speak, the hem of his garments? I confess I am still in the dark. Will some one be good enough to enlighten me?"

Naturally, he was enlightened by half the form.

"Extraordinary! Most extraordinary! However, each house has its traditions, with which I would not for the world interfere. *We* have a prejudice in favor of washing. Go on, Beetle—from '*jugurtha tamen*'[7]—and, if you can, avoid the more flagrant forms of guessing."

Prout's house was furious because Macrea's and Hartopp's houses joined King's to insult them. They called a house-meeting after dinner—an excited and angry meeting of all save the prefects, whose dignity, though they sympathized, did not allow them to attend. They read ungrammatical resolutions, and made speeches beginning, "Gentlemen, we have met on this occasion," and ending with, "It's a beastly shame," precisely as houses have done since time and schools began.

Number Five study attended, with its usual air of bland patronage. At last McTurk, of the lanthorn jaws,[8] delivered himself:

"You jabber and jaw and burble, and that's about all you can do. What's the good of it? King's house'll only gloat because they've drawn you, and King will gloat, too. Besides, that resolution of Orrin's is chock-full of bad grammar, and King'll gloat over *that*."

"I thought you an' Beetle would put it right, an'—an' we'd post it in the corridor," said the composer meekly.

"*Par si je le connai*.[9] I'm not goin' to meddle with the biznai," said Beetle. "It's a gloat for King's house. Turkey's quite right."

"Well, won't Stalky, then?"

But Stalky puffed out his cheeks and squinted down his nose in the style of Panurge,[1] and all he said was, "Oh, you abject burblers!"

"You're three beastly scabs!"[2] was the instant retort of the democracy, and they went out amid execrations.

"This is piffling," said McTurk. "Let's get our sallies, and go and shoot bunnies."

Three saloon-pistols, with a supply of bulleted breech-caps, were stored in Stalky's trunk, and this trunk was in their dormitory, and their dormitory was a three-bed attic one, opening out of a ten-bed establishment, which, in turn, communicated with the great range of dormitories that ran practically from one end of the College

---

6. The elder Burton (two brothers at school were distinguished by the Latin *major* and *minor*, literally "larger" and "smaller").
7. Jugurtha, however (Latin). The boys are reading the Roman historian Sallust (ca. 86–35 B.C.E.).
8. Undershot jaws.

9. *Pas si je le connais*, "Not if I know it" (French).
1. Rogue who was a companion of Pantagruel in François Rabelais's *Gargantua and Pantagruel* (1532–64).
2. Scoundrels.

to the other. Macrea's house lay next to Prout's, King's next to Macrea's, and Hartopp's beyond that again. Carefully locked doors divided house from house, but each house, in its internal arrangements—the College had originally been a terrace of twelve large houses—was a replica of the next; one straight roof covering all.

They found Stalky's bed drawn out from the wall to the left of the dormer window, and the latter end of Richards protruding from a two-foot-square cupboard in the wall.

"What's all this? I've never noticed it before. What are you tryin' to do, Fatty?"

"Fillin' basins, Muster Corkran." Richards's voice was hollow and muffled. "They've been savin' me trouble. Yiss."

" 'Looks like it," said McTurk. "Hi! You'll stick if you don't take care."

Richards backed puffing.

"I can't rache un. Yiss, 'tess a turncock, Muster McTurk. They've took an' runned all the watter-pipes a storey higher in the houses—runned 'em all along under the 'ang of the heaves, like. Runned 'em in last holidays. *I* can't rache the turncock."

"Let me try," said Stalky, diving into the aperture.

"Slip 'ee to the left, then, Muster Corkran. Slip 'ee to the left, an' feel in the dark."

To the left Stalky wriggled, and saw a long line of lead pipe disappearing up a triangular tunnel, whose roof was the rafters and boarding of the college roof, whose floor was sharp-edged joists, and whose side was the rough studding of the lath and plaster wall under the dormer.

"Rummy show. How far does it go?"

"Right along, Muster Corkran—right along from end to end. Her runs under the 'ang of the heaves. Have 'ee rached the stopcock yet? Mr. King got un put in to save us carryin' watter from downstairs to fill the basins. No place for a lusty[3] man like old Richards. I'm tu thickabout to go ferritin'. Thank 'ee, Muster Corkran."

The water squirted through the tap just inside the cupboard, and, having filled the basins, the grateful Richards waddled away.

The boys sat round-eyed on their beds considering the possibilities of this trove. Two floors below them they could hear the hum of the angry house; for nothing is so still as a dormitory in mid-afternoon of a midsummer term.

"It has been papered over till now." McTurk examined the little door. "If we'd only known before!"

"I vote we go down and explore. No one will come up this time o' day. We needn't keep *cavé*."[4]

They crawled in, Stalky leading, drew the door behind them, and on all fours embarked on a dark and dirty road full of plaster, odd shavings, and all the raffle that builders leave in the waste room of a house. The passage was perhaps three feet wide, and, except for the struggling light round the edges of the cupboards (there was one to each dormer), almost pitchy dark.

"Here's Macrea's house," said Stalky, his eye at the crack of the third cupboard. "I can see Barnes's name on his trunk. Don't make such a row, Beetle! We can get right to the end of the Coll. Come on! . . . We're in King's house now—I can see a bit of Rattray's trunk. How these beastly boards hurt one's knees!" They heard his nails scraping on plaster.

"That's the ceiling below. Look out! If we smashed that the plaster 'ud fall down in the lower dormitory," said Beetle.

3. Stout, fat.   4. Keep watch (literally, "beware"; Latin).

"Let's," whispered McTurk.

"An' be collared first thing? Not much. Why, I can shove my hand ever so far up between these boards."

Stalky thrust an arm to the elbow between the joists.

"No good stayin' here. I vote we go back and talk it over. It's a crummy place. 'Must say I'm grateful to King for his water-works."

They crawled out, brushed one another clean, slid the saloon-pistols down a trouser-leg, and hurried forth to a deep and solitary Devonshire lane in whose flanks a boy might sometimes slay a young rabbit. They threw themselves down under the rank elder bushes, and began to think aloud.

"You know," said Stalky at last, sighting at a distant sparrow, "we could hide our sallies in there like anything."

"Huh!" Beetle snorted, choked, and gurgled. He had been silent since they left the dormitory. "Did you ever read a book called 'The History of a House' or something? I got it out of the library the other day. A French woman wrote it—Violet somebody.[5] But it's translated, you know; and it's very interestin'. Tells you how a house is built."

"Well, if you're in a sweat to find out *that*, you can go down to the new cottages they're building for the coastguard."

"My Hat! I will." He felt in his pockets. "Give me tuppence, some one."

"Rot! Stay here, and don't mess about in the sun."

"Gi' me tuppence."

"I say, Beetle, you aren't stuffy[6] about anything, are you?" said McTurk, handing over the coppers. His tone was serious, for though Stalky often, and McTurk occasionally, manœuvred on his own account, Beetle had never been known to do so in all the history of the confederacy.[7]

"No, I'm not. I'm thinking."

"Well, we'll come, too," said Stalky, with a general's suspicion of his aides.

"Don't want you."

"Oh, leave him alone. He's been taken worse with a poem," said McTurk. "He'll go burbling down to the Pebbleridge and spit it all up in the study when he comes back."

"Then why did he want the tuppence, Turkey? He's gettin' too beastly independent. Hi! There's a bunny. No, it ain't. It's a cat, by Jove! You plug[8] first."

Twenty minutes later a boy with a straw hat at the back of his head, and his hands in his pockets, was staring at workmen as they moved about a half-finished cottage. He produced some ferocious tobacco, and was passed from the forecourt into the interior, where he asked many questions.

"Well, let's have your beastly epic," said Turkey, as they burst into the study, to find Beetle deep in Viollet-le-Duc and some drawings. "We've had no end of a lark."

"Epic? What epic? I've been down to the coastguard."

"No epic? Then we will slay you, O Beatle,"[9] said Stalky, moving to the attack. "You've got something up your sleeve. *I* know, when you talk in that tone!"

"Your Uncle Beetle"—with an attempt to imitate Stalky's war-voice—"is a great man."

5. Eugène-Emmanuel Viollet-le-Duc (1814–1879), the (male) French scholar, architect, and author of *L'histoire d'une maison* (*The Story of a House*, 1873).
6. Angry, sulky.
7. I.e., their friendship.
8. Shoot.
9. Misquotation of "There was an old man of Quebec" (1846) by Edward Lear ("With a needle, / I'll slay you, O beadle!").

"Oh, no; he jolly well isn't anything of the kind. You deceive yourself, Beetle. Scrag[1] him, Turkey!"

"A great man," Beetle gurgled from the floor. "*You* are futile—look out for my tie!—futile burblers. I am the Great Man. I gloat. Ouch! Hear me!"

"Beetle, de-ah"—Stalky dropped unreservedly on Beetle's chest—"we love you, an' you're a poet. If I ever said you were a doggaroo, I apologize; but you know as well as we do that you can't do anything by yourself without mucking it."

"I've got a notion."

"And you'll spoil the whole show if you don't tell your Uncle Stalky. Cough it up, ducky, and we'll see what we can do. Notion, you fat impostor—I knew you had a notion when you went away! Turkey said it was a poem."

"I've found out how houses are built. Le' me get up. The floor-joists of one room are the ceiling-joists of the room below."

"Don't be so filthy technical."

"Well, the man told me. The floor is laid on top of those joists—those boards on edge that we crawled over—but the floor stops at a partition. Well, if you get behind a partition, same as you did in the attic, don't you see that you can shove anything you please under the floor between the floor-boards and the lath and plaster of the ceiling below? Look here. I've drawn it."

He produced a rude sketch, sufficient to enlighten the allies. There is no part of the modern school curriculum that deals with architecture, and none of them had yet reflected whether floors and ceilings were hollow or solid. Outside his own immediate interests the boy is as ignorant as the savage he so admires; but he has also the savage's resource.

"I see," said Stalky. "I shoved my hand there. An' then?"

"An' then . . . They've been calling us stinkers, you know. We might shove somethin' under—sulphur, or something that stunk pretty bad—an' stink 'em out. I know it can be done somehow." Beetle's eyes turned to Stalky handling the diagrams.

"Stinks?" said Stalky interrogatively. Then his face grew luminous with delight. "By gum! I've got it. Horrid stinks! Turkey!" He leaped at the Irishman. "This afternoon—just after Beetle went away! *She's* the very thing!"

"Come to my arms, my beamish boy," caroled McTurk, and they fell into each other's arms dancing. "Oh, frabjous day! Calloo, callay![2] She will! She will!"

"Hold on," said Beetle. "I don't understand."

"Dearr man! It shall, though. Oh, Artie, my pure-souled youth, let us tell our darling Reggie about Pestiferous Stinkadores."

"Not until after call-over. Come on!"

"I say," said Orrin, stiffly, as they fell into their places along the walls of the gymnasium. "The house are goin' to hold another meeting."

"Hold away, then." Stalky's mind was elsewhere.

"It's about you three this time."

"All right, give 'em my love . . . *Here, sir,*" and he tore down the corridor.

Gamboling like kids at play, with bounds and sidestarts, with caperings and curvetings, they led the almost bursting Beetle to the rabbit-lane, and from under a pile of stones drew forth the new-slain corpse of a cat. Then did Beetle see the inner meaning of what had gone before, and lifted up his voice in thanksgiving for that the world held warriors so wise as Stalky and McTurk.

---

1. Manhandle, rough up.
2. From the nonsense poem "Jabberwocky" by Lewis Carroll, included in *Through the Looking-Glass and What Alice Found There* (1871).

"Well-nourished old lady, ain't she?" said Stalky. "How long d'you suppose it'll take her to get a bit whiff in a confined space?"

"Bit whiff! What a coarse brute you are!" said McTurk. "Can't a poor pussy-cat get under King's dormitory floor to die without your pursuin' her with your foul innuendoes?"

"What did she die under the floor for?" said Beetle, looking to the future.

"Oh, they won't worry about *that* when they find her," said Stalky.

"A cat may look at a king."[3] McTurk rolled down the bank at his own jest. "Pussy, you don't know how useful you're goin' to be to three pure-souled, high-minded boys."

"They'll have to take up the floor for her, same as they did in Number Nine when the rat croaked. Big medicine—heap big medicine! Phew! Oh, Lord, I wish I could stop laughin'," said Beetle.

"Stinks! Hi, stinks! Clammy ones!" McTurk gasped as he regained his place. "And"—the exquisite humor of it brought them sliding down together in a tangle—"it's all for the honor of the house, too!"

"An' they're holdin' another meetin'—on us," Stalky panted, his knees in the ditch and his face in the long grass. "Well, let's get the bullet out of her and hurry up. The sooner she's bedded out the better."

Between them they did some grisly work with a penknife; between them (ask not who buttoned her to his bosom) they took up the corpse and hastened back, Stalky arranging their plan of action at the full trot.

The afternoon sun, lying in broad patches on the bed-rugs, saw three boys and an umbrella disappear into a dormitory wall. In five minutes they emerged, brushed themselves all over, washed their hands, combed their hair, and descended.

"Are you sure you shoved her far enough under?" said McTurk suddenly.

"Hang it, man, I shoved her the full length of my arm and Beetle's brolly. That must be about six feet. She's bung in the middle of King's big upper ten-bedder. Eligible central situation, *I* call it. She'll stink out his chaps, and Hartopp's and Macrea's, when she really begins to fume. I swear your Uncle Stalky is a great man. Do you realize what a great man he is, Beetle?"

"Well, I had the notion first, hadn't I—? only—"

"You couldn't do it without your Uncle Stalky, could you?"

"They've been calling us stinkers for a week now," said McTurk. "Oh, *won't* they catch it!"

"Stinker! Yah! Stink-ah!" rang down the corridor.

"And she's there," said Stalky, a hand on either boy's shoulder. "She—is—there, gettin' ready to surprise 'em. Presently she'll begin to whisper to 'em in their dreams. Then she'll whiff. Golly, how she'll whiff! Oblige me by thinkin' of it for two minutes."

They went to their study in more or less of silence. There they began to laugh—laugh as only boys can. They laughed with their foreheads on the tables, or on the floor; laughed at length, curled over the backs of chairs or clinging to a book-shelf; laughed themselves limp.

And in the middle of it Orrin entered on behalf of the house.

"Don't mind us, Orrin; sit down. You don't know how we respect and admire you. There's something about your pure, high young forehead, full of the dreams of innocent boyhood, that's no end fetchin'. It is, indeed."

---

3. A sixteenth-century proverb, meaning that the lower orders have some rights; it is quoted in Lewis Carroll's *Alice's Adventures in Wonderland* (1865).

"The house sent me to give you this." He laid a folded sheet of paper on the table and retired with an awful front.

"It's the resolution! Oh, read it, some one. I'm too silly-sick with laughin' to see," said Beetle.

Stalky jerked it open with a precautionary sniff.

"Phew! Phew! Listen. *'The house notices with pain and contempt the attitude of indiference'*—how many f's in indifference, Beetle?"

"Two for choice."[4]

"Only one here—*'adopted by the occupants of Number Five study in relation to the insults offered to Mr. Prout's house at the recent meeting in Number Twelve form-room, and the house hereby pass a vote of censure on the said study.'* That's all."

"And she bled all down my shirt, too!" said Beetle.

"An' I'm catty all over," said McTurk, "though I washed twice."

"An' I nearly broke Beetle's brolly plantin' her where she would blossom!"

The situation was beyond speech, but not laughter. There was some attempt that night to demonstrate against the three in their dormitory; so they came forth.

"You see," Beetle began suavely as he loosened his braces, "the trouble with you is that you're a set of unthinkin' asses. You've no more brains than spidgers.[5] We've told you that heaps of times, haven't we?"

"We'll give all three of you a dormitory lickin'. You always jaw at us as if you were prefects," cried one.

"Oh, no, you won't," said Stalky, "because you know that if you did you'd get the worst of it sooner or later. *We* aren't in any hurry. *We* can afford to wait for our little revenges. You've made howlin' asses of yourselves, and just as soon as King gets hold of your precious resolutions to-morrow you'll find that out. If you aren't sick an' sorry by to-morrow night, I'll—I'll eat my hat."

But or ever the dinner-bell rang the next day Prout's were sadly aware of their error. King received stray members of that house with an exaggerated attitude of fear. Did they purpose to cause him to be dismissed from the College by unanimous resolution? What were their views concerning the government of the school, that he might hasten to give effect to them? He would not offend them for worlds; but he feared—he sadly feared—that his own house, who did not pass resolutions (but washed), might somewhat deride.

King was a happy man, and his house, basking in the favor of his smile, made that afternoon a long penance to the misled Prouts. And Prout himself, with a dull and lowering visage, tried to think out the rights and wrongs of it all, only plunging deeper into bewilderment. Why should his house be called "Stinkers"? Truly, it was a small thing, but he had been trained to believe that straws show which way the wind blows, and that there is no smoke without fire. He approached King in Common-room with a sense of injustice, but King was pleased to be full of airy persiflage[6] that tide, and brilliantly danced dialectical rings round Prout.

"Now," said Stalky at bedtime, making pilgrimage through the dormitories before the prefects came up, "*now* what have you got to say for yourselves? Foster, Carton, Finch, Longbridge, Marlin, Brett! I heard you chaps catchin' it from King—he made hay of you—an' all you could do was to wriggle an' grin an' say, 'Yes, sir,' an' 'No, sir,' an' 'O, sir,' an' 'Please, sir'! You an' your resolution! Urh!"

4. By preference.
5. Spadgers, or sparrows.

6. Bantering, frivolous talk.

"Oh, shut up, Stalky."

"Not a bit of it. You're a gaudy lot of resolutionists, you are! You've made a sweet mess of it. Perhaps you'll have the decency to leave us alone next time."

Here the house grew angry, and in many voices pointed out how this blunder would never have come to pass if Number Five study had helped them from the first.

"But you chaps are so beastly conceited, an'—an' you swaggered into the meetin' as if we were a lot of idiots," growled Orrin of the resolution.

"That's precisely what you *are!* That's what we've been tryin' to hammer into your thick heads all this time," said Stalky. "Never mind, we'll forgive you. Cheer up. You can't help bein' asses, you know," and, the enemy's flank deftly turned, Stalky hopped into bed.

That night was the first of sorrow among the jubilant King's. By some accident of under-floor drafts the cat did not vex the dormitory beneath which she lay, but the next one to the right; stealing on the air rather as a pale-blue sensation than as any poignant offense. But the mere adumbration of an odor is enough for the sensitive nose and clean tongue of youth. Decency demands that we draw several carbolized[7] sheets over what the dormitory said to Mr. King and what Mr. King replied. He was genuinely proud of his house and fastidious in all that concerned their well-being. He came; he sniffed; he said things. Next morning a boy in that dormitory confided to his bosom friend, a fag of Macrea's, that there was trouble in their midst which King would fain keep secret.

But Macrea's boy had also a bosom friend in Prout's, a shock-headed fag of malignant disposition, who, when he had wormed out the secret, told—told it in a high-pitched treble that rang along the corridor like a bat's squeak.

"An'—an' they've been calling us 'stinkers' all this week. Why, Harland minor says they simply can't sleep in his dormitory for the stink. Come on!"

"With one shout and with one cry"[8] Prout's juniors hurled themselves into the war, and through the interval between first and second lesson some fifty twelve-year-olds were embroiled on the gravel outside King's windows to a tune whose *leit-motif* was the word "stinker."

"Hark to the minute-gun[9] at sea!" said Stalky. They were in their study collecting books for second lesson—Latin, with King. "I thought his azure brow was a bit cloudy at prayers. 'She is comin', sister Mary. She is——'"

"If they make such a row now, what *will* they do when she really begins to look up an' take notice?"

"Well, no vulgar repartee, Beetle. All we want is to keep out of this row like gentlemen."

" 'Tis but a little faded flower.'[1] Where's my Horace?[2] Look here, I don't understand what she means by stinkin' out Rattray's dormitory first. We holed in under White's, didn't we?" asked McTurk, with a wrinkled brow.

"Skittish little thing. She's rompin' about all over the place, I suppose."

"My Aunt! King'll be a cheerful customer at second lesson. I haven't prepared my Horace one little bit, either," said Beetle. "Come on!"

---

7. Impregnated with carbolic acid (a common disinfectant).
8. Misquoted from "The Armada" (1832) by Thomas Babington Macaulay ("And with one start, and with one cry, the royal city woke").

9. The firing of a gun every minute.
1. The first line of a poem by the American poet Ellen Clementine Howarth (1827–1899).
2. Roman poet (65–8 B.C.E.) whose works often appear in school texts.

They were outside the form-room door now. It was within five minutes of the bell, and King might arrive at any moment.

Turkey elbowed into a cohort of scuffling fags, cut out Thornton tertius[3] (he that had been Harland's bosom friend), and bade him tell his tale.

It was a simple one, interrupted by tears. Many of King's house had already battered him for libel.

"Oh, it's nothing," McTurk cried. "He says that King's house stinks. That's all."

"Stale!" Stalky shouted. "We knew that years ago, only we didn't choose to run about shoutin' 'stinker.' We've got some manners, if they haven't. Catch a fag, Turkey, and make sure of it."

Turkey's long arm closed on a hurried and anxious ornament of the Lower Second. "Oh, McTurk, please let me go. I don't stink—I swear I don't!"

"Guilty conscience!" cried Beetle. "Who said you did?"

"What d'you make of it?" Stalky punted the small boy into Beetle's arms.

"Snf! Snf! He does, though. I think it's leprosy—or thrush.[4] P'raps it's both. Take it away."

"Indeed, Master Beetle"—King generally came to the house-door for a minute or two as the bell rang—"we are vastly indebted to you for your diagnosis, which seems to reflect almost as much credit on the natural unwholesomeness of your mind as it does upon your pitiful ignorance of the diseases of which you discourse so glibly. We will, however, test your knowledge in other directions."

That was a merry lesson, but, in his haste to scarify Beetle, King clean neglected to give him an imposition,[5] and since at the same time he supplied him with many priceless adjectives for later use, Beetle was well content, and applied himself most seriously throughout third lesson (algebra with little Hartopp) to composing a poem entitled "The Lazar-house."[6]

After dinner King took his house to bathe in the sea off the Pebbleridge. It was an old promise; but he wished he could have evaded it, for all Prout's lined up by the Fives Court and cheered with intention. In his absence not less than half the school invaded the infected dormitory to draw their own conclusions. The cat had gained in the last twelve hours, but a battlefield of the fifth day could not have been so flamboyant as the spies reported.

"My word, she *is* doin' herself proud," said Stalky. "Did you ever smell anything like it? Ah, an' she isn't under White's dormitory at all yet."

"But she will be. Give her time," said Beetle. "She'll twine like a giddy honeysuckle. What howlin' Lazarites they are! No house is justified in makin' itself a stench in the nostrils of decent——"

"High-minded, pure-souled boys. *Do* you burn with remorse and regret?" said McTurk, as they hastened to meet the house coming up from the sea. King had deserted it, so speech was unfettered. Round its front played a crowd of skirmishers— all houses mixed—flying, reforming, shrieking insults. On its tortured flanks marched the Hoplites,[7] seniors hurling jests one after another—simple and primitive jests of the Stone Age. To these the three added themselves, dispassionately, with an air of aloofness, almost sadly.

"And they look all right, too," said Stalky. "It can't be Rattray, can it? Rattray?"

---

3. Third (Latin), applied to the youngest of three brothers at school.
4. A minor fungal disease (which bears no resemblance to leprosy).

5. A task imposed as a punishment at school.
6. I.e., "Leper House."
7. Among the Greeks, infantry in heavy armor (and thus contrasted here with "the skirmishers").

No answer.

"Rattray, dear? He seems stuffy about something or other. Look here, old man, *we* don't bear any malice about your sending that soap to us last week, do we? Be cheerful, Rat. You can live this down all right. I dare say it's only a few fags. Your house is so beastly slack, though."

"You aren't going back to the house, are you?" said McTurk. The victims desired nothing better. "You've simply no conception of the reek up there. Of course, frowzin' as you do, you wouldn't notice it; but, after this nice wash and the clean, fresh air, even *you'd* be upset. 'Much better camp on the Burrows. We'll get you some straw. Shall we?" The house hurried in to the tune of "John Brown's body,"[8] sung by loving schoolmates, and barricaded themselves in their form-room. Straightway Stalky chalked a large cross, with "Lord, have mercy upon us," on the door,[9] and left King to find it.

The wind shifted that night and wafted a carrion-reek into Macrea's dormitories; so that boys in nightgowns pounded on the locked door between the houses, entreating King's to wash. Number Five study went to second lesson with not more than half a pound of camphor apiece in their clothing; and King, too wary to ask for explanations, gibbered a while and hurled them forth. So Beetle finished yet another poem at peace in the study.

"They're usin' carbolic now. Malpas told me," said Stalky. "King thinks it's the drains."

"She'll need a lot o' carbolic," said McTurk. "No harm tryin', I suppose. It keeps King out of mischief."

"I swear I thought he was goin' to kill me when I sniffed just now. He didn't mind Burton major sniffin' at me the other day, though. He never stopped Alexander howlin' 'Stinker!' into our form-room before—before we doctored 'em. He just grinned," said Stalky. "What was he frothing over you for, Beetle?"

"Aha! That was my subtle jape. I had him on toast. You know he always jaws about the learned Lipsius."[1]

" 'Who at the age of four'—*that* chap?" said McTurk.

"Yes. Whenever he hears I've written a poem. Well, just as I was sittin' down, I whispered, 'How is our learned Lepsius?' to Burton major. Old Butt grinned like an owl. *He* didn't know what I was drivin' at; but King jolly well did. That was really why he hove us out. Ain't you grateful? Now shut up. I'm goin' to write the 'Ballad of the Learned Lipsius.'"

"Keep clear of anything coarse, then," said Stalky. "I shouldn't like to be coarse on this happy occasion."

"Not for wo-orlds. What rhymes to 'stenches,' some one?"

In Common-room at lunch King discoursed acridly to Prout of boys with prurient minds, who perverted their few and baleful talents to sap discipline and corrupt their equals, to deal in foul imagery and destroy reverence.

"But you didn't seem to consider this when your house called us—ah—stinkers. If you hadn't assured me that you never interfere with another man's house, I should almost believe that it was a few casual remarks of yours that started all this nonsense."

Prout had endured much, for King always took his temper to meals.

---

8. This popular song of the American Civil War begins, "John Brown's body lies a-mouldring in the grave."
9. Steps taken to identify infected houses in times of plague (e.g., London's Great Plague of 1665).
1. Justus Lipsius (1547–1606), an eminent humanist who was also known as a child prodigy.

"You spoke to Beetle yourself, didn't you? Something about not bathing, and being a water-funk?" the school chaplain put in. "I was scoring in the pavilion[2] that day."

"I may have—jestingly. I really don't pretend to remember every remark I let fall among small boys; and full well I know the Beetle has no feelings to be hurt."

"May be; but he, or they—it comes to the same thing—have the fiend's own knack of discovering a man's weak place. I confess I rather go out of my way to conciliate Number Five study. It may be soft, but so far, I believe, I am the only man here whom they haven't maddened by their—well—attentions."

"That is all beside the point. I flatter myself I can deal with them alone as occasion arises. But if they feel themselves morally supported by those who should wield an absolute and open-handed justice, then I say that my lot is indeed a hard one. Of all things I detest, I admit that anything verging on disloyalty among ourselves is the first."

The Common-room looked at one another out of the corners of their eyes, and Prout blushed.

"I deny it absolutely," he said. "Er—in fact, I own that I personally object to all three of them. It is not fair, therefore, to——"

"How long do you propose to allow it?" said King.

"But surely," said Macrae, deserting his usual ally, "the blame, if there be any, rests with you, King. You can't hold them responsible for the—you prefer the good old Anglo-Saxon, I believe—stink in your house. My boys are complaining of it now."

"What can you expect? You know what boys are. Naturally they take advantage of what to them is a heaven-sent opportunity," said little Hartopp. "What *is* the trouble in your dormitories, King?"

Mr. King explained that as he had made it the one rule of his life never to interfere with another man's house, so he expected not to be too patently interfered with. They might be interested to learn—here the chaplain heaved a weary sigh—that he had taken all steps that, in his poor judgment, would meet the needs of the case. Nay, further, he had himself expended, with no thought of reimbursement, sums, the amount of which he would not specify, on disinfectants. This he had done because he knew by bitter—by most bitter—experience that the management of the college was slack, dilatory, and inefficient. He might even add, almost as slack as the administration of certain houses which now thought fit to sit in judgment on his actions. With a short summary of his scholastic career, and a précis of his qualifications, including his degrees, he withdrew, slamming the door.

"Heigho!" said the chaplain. "Ours is a dwarfing life—a belittling life, my brethren. God help all schoolmasters! They need it."

"I don't like the boys, I own"—Prout dug viciously with his fork into the table-cloth—"and I don't pretend to be a strong man, as you know. But I confess I can't see any reason why I should take steps against Stalky and the others because King happens to be annoyed by—by——"

"Falling into the pit he has digged,"[3] said little Hartopp. "Certainly not, Prout. No one accuses *you* of setting one house against another through sheer idleness."

"A belittling life—a belittling life." The chaplain rose. "I go to correct French exercises. By dinner King will have scored off some unlucky child of thirteen; he will repeat to us every word of his brilliant repartees, and all will be well."

"But about those three. Are they so prurient-minded?"

2. I.e., keeping score during the cricket match.　　　3. See Ecclesiastes 10.8.

"Nonsense," said little Hartopp. "If you thought for a minute, Prout, you would see that the 'precocious flow of fetid imagery,' that King complains of, is borrowed wholesale from King. *He* 'nursed the pinion that impelled the steel.'[4] Naturally he does not approve. Come into the smoking-room for a minute. It isn't fair to listen to boys; but they should be now rubbing it into King's house outside. Little things please little minds."

The dingy den off the Common-room was never used for anything except gowns. Its windows were ground glass; one could not see out of it, but one could hear almost every word on the gravel outside. A light and wary footstep came up from Number Five.

"Rattray!" in a subdued voice—Rattray's study fronted that way. "D'you know if Mr. King's anywhere about? I've got a——" McTurk discreetly left the end of the sentence open.

"No. He's gone out," said Rattray unguardedly.

"Ah! The learned Lipsius is airing himself, is he? His Royal Highness has gone to fumigate." McTurk climbed on the railings, where he held forth like the never-wearied rook.

"Now in all the Coll, there was no stink like the stink of King's house, for it stank vehemently and none knew what to make of it. Save King. And he washed the fags *privatim et seriatim.*[5] In the fishpools of Hesbon[6] washed he them, with an apron about his loins."

"Shut up, you mad Irishman!" There was the sound of a golf-ball spurting up gravel.

"It's no good getting wrathy, Rattray. We've come to jape with you. Come on, Beetle. They're all at home. You can wind 'em."

"Where's the Pomposo Stinkadore? 'Tisn't safe for a pure-souled, high-minded boy to be seen round his house these days. Gone out, has he? Never mind. I'll do the best I can, Rattray. I'm *in loco parentis* just now."

("One for you, Prout," whispered Macrea, for this was Mr. Prout's pet phrase.)

"I have a few words to impart to you, my young friend. We will discourse together a while."

Here the listening Prout sputtered: Beetle, in a strained voice, had chosen a favorite gambit of King's.

"I repeat, Master Rattray, we will confer, and the matter of our discourse shall not be stinks, for that is a loathsome and obscene word. We will, with your good leave— granted, I trust, Master Rattray, granted, I trust—study this—this scabrous upheaval of latent demoralization. What impresses me most is not so much the blatant indecency with which you swagger abroad under your load of putrescence" (you must imagine this discourse punctuated with golf-balls, but old Rattray was ever a bad shot) "as the cynical immorality with which you revel in your abhorrent aromas. Far be it from me to interfere with another's house——"

("Good Lord!" said Prout, "but this *is* King.")

"Line for line, letter for letter; listen," said little Hartopp.)

"But to say that you stink, as certain lewd fellows of the baser sort[7] aver, is to say nothing—less than nothing. In the absence of your beloved house-master, for whom no one has a higher regard than myself, I will, if you will allow me, explain the

4. From Byron's "English Bards and Scotch Reviewers" (1809).
5. Privately and one after another (Latin).
6. I.e., "the fishpools in Heshbon" (Song of Solomon 7.4).
7. A phrase from Acts 17.5.

grossness—the unparalleled enormity—the appalling fetor of the stenches (I believe in the good old Anglo-Saxon word), stenches, sir, with which you have seen fit to infect your house . . . Oh, bother! I've forgotten the rest, but it was very beautiful. Aren't you grateful to us for laborin' with you this way, Rattray? Lots of chaps 'ud never have taken the trouble, but we're grateful, Rattray."

"Yes, we're horrid grateful," grunted McTurk. "We don't forget that soap. We're polite. Why ain't you polite, Rat?"

"Hallo!" Stalky cantered up, his cap over one eye. "Exhortin' the Whiffers, eh? I'm afraid they're too far gone to repent. Rattray! White! Perowne! Malpas! No answer. This is distressin'. This is truly distressin'. Bring out your dead,[8] you glandered lepers!"

"You think yourself funny, don't you?" said Rattray, stung from his dignity by this last. "It's only a rat or something under the floor. We're going to have it up tomorrow."

"Don't try to shuffle it off on a poor dumb animal, and dead, too. I loathe prevarication. 'Pon my soul, Rattray——"

"Hold on. The Hartoffles never said, ' 'Pon my soul' in all his little life," said Beetle critically.

("Ah!" said Prout to little Hartopp.)

"Upon my word, sir, upon my word, sir, I expected better things of you, Rattray. Why can you not own up to your misdeeds like a man? Have I ever shown any lack of confidence in you?"

("It's not brutality," murmured little Hartopp, as though answering a question no one had asked. "It's boy; only boy.")

"And this was the house," Stalky changed from a pecking, fluttering voice to tragic earnestness. "This was the—the—open cesspit that dared to call us 'stinkers.' And now—and now, it tries to shelter itself behind a dead rat. You annoy me, Rattray. You disgust me! You irritate me unspeakably! Thank Heaven, I am a man of equable temper——"

("This is to your address, Macrea," said Prout.

"I fear so, I fear so.")

"Or I should scarcely be able to contain myself before your mocking visage."

"Cavé!" in an undertone. Beetle had spied King sailing down the corridor.

"And what may you be doing here, my little friends?" the house-master began. "I had a fleeting notion—correct me if I am wrong" (the listeners with one accord choked)—"that if I found you outside my house I should visit you with dire pains and penalties."

"We were just goin' for a walk, sir," said Beetle.

"And you stopped to speak to Rattray en route?"

"Yes, sir. We've been throwing golf-balls," said Rattray, coming out of the study.

("Old Rat is more of a diplomat than I thought. So far he is strictly within the truth," said little Hartopp. "Observe the ethics of it, Prout.")

"Oh, you were sporting with them, were you? I must say I do not envy you your choice of associates. I fancied they might have been engaged in some of the prurient discourse with which they have been so disgustingly free of late. I should strongly advise you to direct your steps most carefully in the future. Pick up those golf-balls." He passed on.

---

8. The cry of those collecting corpses in London during the Great Plague.

Next day Richards, who had been a carpenter in the Navy, and to whom odd jobs were confided, was ordered to take up a dormitory floor; for Mr. King held that something must have died there.

"We need not neglect all our work for a trumpery incident of this nature; though I am quite aware that little things please little minds. Yes, I have decreed the boards to be taken up after lunch under Richards's auspices. I have no doubt it will be vastly interesting to a certain type of so-called intellect; but any boy of my house or another's found on the dormitory stairs will *ipso facto* render himself liable to three hundred lines."[9]

The boys did not collect on the stairs, but most of them waited outside King's. Richards had been bound to cry the news from the attic window, and, if possible, to exhibit the corpse.

" 'Tis a cat, a dead cat!" Richards's face showed purple at the window. He had been in the chamber of death and on his knees for some time.

"Cat be blowed!" cried McTurk. "It's a dead fag left over from last term. Three cheers for King's dead fag!"

They cheered lustily.

"Show it, show it! Let's have a squint at it!" yelled the juniors. "Give her to the Bug-hunters." (This was the Natural History Society). "The cat looked at the King—and died of it! Hoosh! Yai! Yaow! Maiow! Ftzz!" were some of the cries that followed.

Again Richards appeared.

"She've been"—he checked himself suddenly—"dead a long taime."

The school roared.

"Well, come on out for a walk," said Stalky in a well-chosen pause. "It's all very disgustin', and I do hope the Lazar-house won't do it again."

"Do what?" a King's boy cried furiously.

"Kill a poor innocent cat every time you want to get off washing. It's awfully hard to distinguish between you as it is. I prefer the cat, I must say. She isn't quite so whiff. What are you goin' to do, Beetle?"

"*Je vais gloater. Je vais gloater tout le blessed afternoon. Jamais j'ai gloaté comme je gloaterai aujourd'hui. Nous bunkerons aux bunkers.*"[1]

And it seemed good to them so to do.

Down in the basement, where the gas flickers and the boots stand in racks, Richards, amid his blacking-brushes, held forth to Oke of the Common-room, Gumbly of the dining-halls, and fair Lena of the laundry.

"Yiss. Her were in a shockin' staate an' condition. Her nigh made me sick, I tal 'ee. But I rowted un out, and I rowted un out, an' I made all shipshape, though her smelt like to bilges."

"Her died mousin', I rackon, poor thing," said Lena.

"Then her moused different to any made cat o' God's world, Lena. I up with the top-board, an' she were lying on her back, an' I turned un ovver with the brume-handle, an' 'twas her back was all covered with the plaster from 'twixt the lathin'. Yiss, I tal 'ee. An' under her head there lay, like, so's to say, a little pillow o' plaster druv up in front of her by raison of her slidin' along on her back. No cat niver went mousin' on her back, Lena. Some one had shoved her along right underneath, so far

9. I.e., an assignment to translate three hundred lines of Greek or Latin poetry.
1. "I am going to gloat. I am going to gloat all the blessed afternoon. I have never gloated as I will gloat today. We will make our escape to the bunkers" (mock French).

as they could shove un. Cats don't make theyselves pillows for to die on. Shoved along, she were, when she was settin' for to be cold, laike."

'Oh, yeou'm too clever to live, Fatty. Yeou go get wed an' taught some sense," said Lena, the affianced of Gumbly.

"Larned a little 'fore iver some maidens was born. Sarved in the Queen's Navy, I have, where yeou'm taught to use your eyes. Yeou go 'tend your own business, Lena."

"Do 'ee mean what you'm been tellin' us?" said Oke.

"Ask me no questions, I'll give 'ee no lies. Bullet-hole clane thru from side to side, an' tu heart-ribs broke like withies.[2] I seed un when I turned un ovver. They'm clever, oh, they'm clever, but they'm not too clever for old Richards! 'Twas on the born tip o' my tongue to tell, tu, but . . . he said us niver washed, he did. Let his dom boys call us 'stinkers,' he did. Sarve un dom well raight, I say!"

Richards spat on a fresh boot and fell to his work, chuckling.

2. Twigs.

EVELYN SHARP
1869–1955

Evelyn Sharp may have been a rebel devoted to social and political causes, but she also always kept her promises. In 1906 she joined the Women's Social and Political Union, a group that advocated militant action in support of workingwomen's causes, including suffrage; but she promised her mother that she wouldn't do anything that might land her in prison. When her mother released her from that promise in 1911, Sharp promptly participated in breaking government office building windows—"provoked," as she wrote in her autobiography *Unfinished Adventure* (1933), "by a more than usually cynical postponement of the Women's Bill, which was implied in a Government forecast of manhood suffrage." She was sentenced to fourteen days in Holloway Prison for her role in the demonstration. Two years later, as an active member of the Women Writers Suffrage League, Sharp and others from that group attempted to meet with the home secretary about the Prisoner's Temporary Discharge of Ill Health Act (legislation meant to control imprisoned hunger-striking suffragists by releasing them as they became ill and then returning them to prison once they recovered; it was dubbed by the suffragists the "Cat and Mouse Act"). When he refused to meet with the delegation and the women declined to

decamp, Sharp and another woman were arrested and sent again to Holloway; two others were physically ejected from the House of Commons.

Sharp was born in London, the ninth of eleven children, and was educated at home until she was twelve years old; she spent the next four years as a day-boarder (eating dinner at the school but returning home to sleep) at the Strathallan House school. Although women at university were rare, Sharp strongly desired further formal education. Unfortunately, her family could not afford it. She studied on her own until 1894, when she left home to earn her living. Sharp joined a group of London writers and artists known as the *Yellow Book* set because of their loose connection with the avant-garde illustrated quarterly of that title (1894–97) edited by Henry Harland and Aubrey Beardsley. Her first novel was issued by John Lane, the journal's publisher. Sharp wrote about a dozen books for children, as well as novels for adults and two opera librettos. She was also a journalist whose work appeared in a variety of newspapers, including the *Daily Chronicle*, the *Pall Mall Gazette*, and the *Manchester Guardian*, a left-leaning newspaper that published her work for more than thirty years.

A pacifist and member of the Women's International League for Peace, Sharp continued to fight for women's causes during World War I, though many feminists suspended their work during this period. She traveled widely after the war and the passage of the Suffrage Bill in 1918 (which granted voting rights to women age thirty and older). In 1922 she worked in Russia as part of a famine relief project sponsored by the Quakers. Sharp also turned her attention to the plight of the poor in England and published *The London Child* (1927), which described their day-to-day living conditions. At age sixty-four Sharp married Henry Nevinson, the widower of her friend Margaret Nevinson, himself a feminist and member of the Men's League for Women's Suffrage. She remained active in political and social causes throughout her life, working for the Labour Party, the National Council for Civil Liberties, and the Council for the Abolition of the Death Penalty.

Sharp's school story for girls, "In School" (1896–97), was first serialized in the British girls' magazine *Atalanta* (1887–98); it was later published as a novel titled *The Making of a Schoolgirl* (1897). The story covers only young Becky's anticipation of and first term at a London girls' school. Becky's preconceptions about her boarding school come from her own reading in popular literature and her much-admired older brother's dismissal of anything "girlish." Despite her fears and a few humorous missteps, the down-to-earth Becky adapts to schoolgirl codes of behavior and manages to find a niche for herself at school. Sharp's ironic tale—revealing assumptions made about women's roles and the poor, and subverting traditional expectations of girls' abilities—resembles the boys' school story in its focus on classmates, hierarchies, and rules, yet it diverges in important ways as well. The girls' exploits and growth are not connected to games or outdoors activities, but instead take place indoors and within the self. The girls are encouraged to think for themselves, as the young and innovative composition teacher urges them to "Say what you mean. . . . Try to forget what other people think, and find out what you think yourselves." Through her struggles and successes at school, Becky learns that to be a girl is not such an awful fate after all.

In School

I. Anticipations

I was overjoyed when I heard that I was to go to school. At last, I should have some one to play with, in the absence of Jack; at last, the ignominy of a nursery dinner would be wiped away, and I should dine with my equals, where distinctions of age and sex did not exist; and all elderly tyranny, except the mysterious domination of a head-mistress, would cease to exist. The head-mistress, in my mind, was going to dislike me very much at first, after the manner of head-mistresses in story-books; but later on, when I had rescued her life in a fire, or something like that, she would suddenly acknowledge my true value, and become my greatest friend and protector for the rest of my days. I had raced through several dreams of this sort, by the time I arrived at the top of the house, and rushed into the nursery to seek the manly sympathy of Jack.

But Jack's scorn was immense.

"You don't call a girl's school *school*, do you?" he said. "How poor!"

"Why not?" I asked. "I am going to take a cake, and two pots of jam, and ten shillings. If that isn't school, what is?"

"Don't care a hang about that," retorted Jack. "I know what girl's schools are; no studies of their own, no fags, no gym.,[1] no anything. Call *that* school?"

---

1. Gymnastics, athletic exercises. "Fags": junior students who perform drudge work for upperclassmen.

"There's a half-term holiday," I said, timidly.

"*Suppose* you mean an *exeat*,"[2] he replied with contempt. "But of course girls never know these things. Where does your rubbishy school hang out, Becky?"

When I told him it was only on the other side of London, he scoffed more than ever.

"Then you won't even go by train?" he exclaimed. "And you won't have a river, or a bath, or a fives' court?[3] It's going to be a rotten show, any way; and I'm jolly glad I'm not a girl."

I felt it was no use arguing any further with Jack, so I turned to the more ready sympathy of Nurse. Nurse never failed me in situations of this kind; she had an indifference to facts that made her a most valuable ally.

"School's school," she said, in her decided manner. "Boys *or* girls, it don't make much difference to speak of, excepting that the one is much more noisier and masterfuller than the other. Don't you tease your sister, Master Jack, or I shall go straight to your Papa."

In spite of Jack's scorn for feminine argument, and all the other unpleasant notions he had acquired at school, nursery authority still had its terrors for him; and he dropped his aggressive attitude, and even condescended to show some interest in the coming crisis of my life. I at once began to draw vivid pictures, founded partly on a slender knowledge of Miss Strangways' school, and coloured largely by my own imaginations, of the glorious time I was going to have; until I had succeeded, not only in impressing Jack a little, but even in rousing his jealousy.

"Girls are jolly lucky chaps," he grumbled, "*I* don't have such a high old time as all that, I know. Working all day long, and two cheap half holidays a week!"

"And saints' days," I put in, carefully.

"Precious few saints," said Jack, with unconscious cynicism. "Seems to me that girls get all the fun, and none of the solid grind. Beastly hard, I call it."

"Yes," I observed, feeling that my turn had come. "For some things, I am almost glad I am not a boy."

Jack gave me a withering look.

"Oh, it's quite worth it. Don't you trouble to be cocky about that," he said, in an airy way; and my temporary triumph was over.

I was surprised to find that what appeared to me such a happy change in my fortunes merely aroused everybody's pity. All sorts of people, who had never taken the least interest in me before, suddenly sent me presents, or wrote me sympathetic letters, for the express purpose of telling me that I should soon "get over the worst of it," and that it would not be long before the holidays came round again. Even the drawing-room visitors, of whose race Jack and I had a deeply rooted distrust, which was mainly founded on their habit of talking French before us, behaved all at once as though they were quite human, instead of being merely drawing-room visitors, who lived on afternoon tea, and never had any second-best clothes.

"So you are going to school for the first time?" said one of them, in the caressing tone that drawing-room visitors always put on when they talk to children. "Poor little mite! that's terribly sad, is it not? Do you feel dreadfully unhappy?"

"I'm going to have a cake, and ten shillings, and two pots of jam," I hastened to explain.

But the drawing-room visitor did not mean to admit that any alleviation of my

---

2. Permission for temporary absence (literally, "let him or her depart"; Latin).

3. In the game of fives, a ball is struck by the hand against the front wall of a three-sided court.

situation was possible; and I began to think, in time, that everybody must be right, and that I had made an absurd mistake in thinking that I was happy at all.

"Hullo! Why I thought you were so beastly glad," said Jack when he discovered me in tears, on the nursery floor, the day before the term began.

"So I was," I said, mournfully. "But I'm not, now. I'm m-miserable. So would you be, if you were going to a horrid strict school, with horrid strict rules, and horrid strict mistresses and people, and nothing but girls to play with. It's—it's frightening!"

To do Jack justice, he could be very sympathetic sometimes, if I was really in trouble, and no one was listening.

"It must be rather awful," he admitted. "Just imagine, all girls! You bet they play cricket with a soft ball, too—so poor! Perhaps they don't play at all, though; and if they did, they would be 'leg before'[4] all the time, wouldn't they? Girls are always 'leg before'; its their silly skirts or something. Never mind, Becky! It mayn't be so bad, after all; and you will have *me* in the holidays, don't you know. Besides, you are a girl yourself, aren't you?"

I had to own sorrowfully that this was the case, but as it had always been my greatest trouble, it was not calculated to raise my spirits now; and Jack hastily corrected himself, and said that of course I couldn't help it, if I was, and that nobody would know it if it came to being longstop,[5] which made me prouder than anything else he could possibly have said.

When the great day came at last, I drove to school with mother, in the lowest depths of depression. Even the knowledge of the cake that was packed in the crown of my Sunday hat, and the two pots of jam that were wedged among my stockings, and the ten shillings that lay in my new purse, together with three hot pennies from Jack's pocket, did not bring me courage or consolation when I found myself in a crowded drawing-room, with no occupation but to try and distinguish the dread headmistress from her visitors. I believe mother shook hands with someone; and two or three people kissed me, among them a voluble dark lady, who talked French, without reminding me of our drawing-room visitors, and then went off to bewilder some one else in the same manner. But I was too shy to notice much, and I found myself, presently, on a couch in the middle of the room, with a sea of other mothers and other daughters all round me. It was very hot, and very dismal, and I began to feel sleepy, as well as neglected.

"Dear me, how sorry I feel for you poor children who have never been to school before!" said some one, who had just dropped into the seat beside me. The voice had so much feeling in it, that I turned as to a comrade, and was surprised to find quite a grown-up person, who was smiling at me, just as though she had known me all my life. She had none of the patronising ways of the ordinary grown-up person, however, and I smiled back at her and felt we were friends.

"It wouldn't be so bad," I said, "if *only* they were not all girls. Don't you call it rather a bore?"

"That is only because you have always had boys to play with," said the strange lady. "Perhaps, when you get used to girls, you will find that they are just as nice in their own way. And after all, your brothers are only home in the holidays, are they?"

Now whatever made her guess that I had been used to boys? But she was evidently not one of those stupid people who never seem to know anything that is really impor-

---

4. I.e., "leg before wicket": in cricket, the act of using the leg to stop a straight-pitched ball that would otherwise have hit the wicket.

5. In cricket, the player who stands behind the wicketkeeper to stop any ball that might get by.

tant, and ask interminable questions, so I grew quite confidential.

"I have only one brother," I explained, "but we are great chums, don't you know. And then, it isn't only the girls I mind, it's the head-mistress. She is going to mis-understand me, you see; and then she will dislike me very much, at least, until some-thing dreadful happens, like a fire, or perhaps a burglary. And it isn't pleasant to be disliked very much by anyone, is it? And, you see, it may be months before there is a fire."

"I see," said my friend, sympathetically. "But why will she cease to dislike you when there is a fire? I am afraid I don't *quite* understand."

"Oh," I said, with enthusiasm, "of course, I shall rush into the heat of the flames, just where the wall is going to fall in with a crash and every one else is too frightened to go, and the head-mistress will be there sound asleep, and the next moment she is going to be smothered up! Only, *I* shall save her life, and she will like me for ever after. You couldn't very well go on disliking any one, after she had saved your life, could you?"

"It would be difficult," said the strange lady. "But I should very much like to meet this terrible head-mistress, who is going to dislike you so much. Can you tell me if she is in the room?"

"She must be somewhere about," I replied, sadly, "because mother came on pur-pose to put me in her charge. I think it must be that awful old lady over there, with spectacles. Don't you think she looks head-mistressy?"

"I should hardly think so," said my companion, doubtfully. "A head-mistress would not wear a bonnet in her own house, would she?"

"I don't know, I'm sure. You never know what a head-mistress might do," I said, emphatically. "Besides, there isn't any one in the room without a bonnet, except you."

"Now I come to think of it," said the strange lady, smiling; "there certainly isn't."

"I know it isn't polite to ask questions," I went on; "but I do *so* want to know why you haven't got a bonnet on. Are you staying in the house, or anything?"

"Well, yes," she replied, smiling still more. "I have been staying here a good long time."

"Oh," I said, with awe in my voice. "As long as Miss Strangways?"

"Just about as long as Miss Strangways," she said, after appearing to reflect for an instant. I was burning to know why she had been there so long, but the stern visage of Nurse, the inventor of manners, rose in my mind, and I restrained the impulse to ask her another question.

"I'm just frightfully glad you are here," I said, instead. "Perhaps, I shall see you again?"

"There is no doubt about that," said the strange lady.

"And if the head-mistress is very unkind to me, you will be nice to me when she isn't looking?" I pursued, anxiously. For, in the story-books, the poor, persecuted, misjudged child always had one champion in the camp of the enemy.

"It won't be very easy," she said, gravely. "But I will see what I can do."

My spirits began to rise. Everything was turning out in accordance with all the known canons of fiction. Nothing was wanting, now, except the fire—and the head-mistress.

"I am not a bit sorry I have come to school, after all," I exclaimed.

"That's right," said my friend. And I wondered why she looked so pleased.

Presently, mother came to bid me good-bye. In obedience to tradition, I ought to have sobbed in her arms, and refused to be comforted. But I did nothing of the sort.

"I'm awfully glad I'm here," I told her, cheerfully. "I think school is an immensely jolly place. And, oh, mother, there is a perfectly splendid lady over there, who is staying in the house, too, and she is going to be nice to me when the head-mistress isn't looking. She promised me she would. Isn't that beautiful?"

Just then, my new friend came up to shake hands with mother.

"You will look after my little girl, won't you, dear Miss Strangways?" said my mother, fervently.

"I am afraid," said the head-mistress, smiling, "that we shall have to wait until there is a fire."

II. THE GIRLS

Until I went to school, I had never had anything to do with girls. My idea of them was entirely founded upon what Jack said about them, and as Jack had no definite opinions at all, but merely regarded the whole sex vaguely as inferior and not worth troubling about, I naturally had a good deal to learn, when Miss Strangways took me into the class-room and left me with my future schoolfellows. There seemed to be masses of girls everywhere, all apparently older than myself; not one of them took the least notice of me, and I wondered whether I had done anything to offend them, as I looked round in vain to try and find a friendly face. I had always imagined, from Jack's conversation, that girls spent their time in "fagging over their rotten lessons, just to spite their brothers," so that the irate parent might hold them up as examples to their more lazy sons, who, according to Jack, "knew better than to play so poorly, when there was something really decent to be done, such as"—here Jack usually became confused, "such as, *not* fagging over them, for instance." But here were girls innumerable, and their only occupation seemed to be incessant talking. I stared at them in complete bewilderment, and wondered what the world contained that could be discussed in so many words, and by so many people, amongst whom was not the leavening influence of a single boy. I was amazed, too, by the affection they showed for one another; girls walked about with their arms round one another's waists; girls called one another "dearest" and "*darling*"—there was always a strong accent on the "darling"—girls threw themselves with shouts of welcome upon every fresh arrival who came into the room, and the fresh arrival at once began kissing every one within reach, two kisses to each person, until I blushed to think what Jack would have said of it all, Jack who only kissed me three times in the year, when he went back to school, and would shirk that if Nurse were not there to enforce the brotherly attention. Neglected and strange as I felt, I was at least glad I was not expected to kiss anybody, and I wondered if the day would ever come, when I should have the courage to call one of those dreadfully superior girls "dearest," and walk about with my arm linked in hers, and pretend that the new girls were not there at all.

"I say, what's your name?" suddenly asked one of the older girls, detaching herself from her particular group, and strolling up to me. The tone was aggressive, but I welcomed the friendliness of the intention, and faltered out my name apologetically.

"Been to school before?" was the next question.

"No," I said, still more apologetically.

"Governess?" said the girl.

"No, I have always been taught by my sister."

"Oh," in a tone of gentle approval. "Then you don't know much, do you?"

"Oh no," I assured her, heartily. I could quite understand her attitude of contempt towards the acquisition of knowledge, for it was precisely the same as Jack's. And my questioner actually condescended to smile, when she received my assurance.

"Got any brothers? Is he at school? Where?" she proceeded rapidly. "And what is he going to be?"

"He isn't quite sure" I answered, doubtfully. As a matter of fact, Jack's future vocation was a different one, every holiday. "Either an engine driver or a cowboy, I think."

She seemed a little surprised, and I took advantage of the temporary lull in the questions, to ask her for her own name. This she apparently regarded as a piece of great presumption on my part, for she resumed her aggressive manner, jerked out "Dorothy Pearson," and went back to her companions, who were waiting curiously to hear the result of her inquiries. I thought it would have saved a good deal of bother if they had asked me themselves, but after all, I reflected, something must be allowed for the stupidity of girls when left entirely to themselves. And I did not know until afterwards, that Dorothy, as head girl, was the only one present who could have been seen speaking to a new girl, without danger of losing caste.

Then a bell rang, and there was a murmur of "Strangles" round the room, and every one again began kissing every one else with great vigour; and Miss Strangways came and stood by the open door, and the girls filed upstairs to prayers. She, too, kissed them all as they passed out, and much as I pitied her for being obliged to do so, I supposed that she was grown up, and therefore used to kissing people, in which case she might not mind it quite so much.

"Well, are the girls at all like what you expected to find?" she asked, when my turn came.

"I don't know, yet," I replied, cautiously. "They seem to do a great lot of kissing, but I suppose they can't help it. They're just girls, you see."

"Yes," she said, gravely. "We must not forget that, must we?"

I wrote to Jack in pencil, with the bed for a writing-table, when I was left for the night in one of four curtained compartments in a large bed-room. And in the fulness of my heart, I wrote to him as follows:—

"There are awful lots of girls everywhere, and I do wish you were here. Miss Strang-ways is not a bit like a head-mistress, and she hasn't got horrid patronising ways, and she doesn't laugh when you say things that are not funny. The girls all talk without stopping, and they kiss one another for nothing at all, even when they haven't had a present given them, or anything. Isn't it rum? All the same, I think they are not *quite* like the girls you seem to know. None of them scream, or giggle, or anything like that, and I haven't seen one of them with a book, and they don't gas about lessons, as you said they would. They just kiss and talk, that's all, so, of course, they might be much worse. I will write every day. Give my love to Simpson, and Wilkins minor, and tell Boston terts[6] I have thought of a new name for his ferret."

As I crept sleepily into bed, a whispered conversation in the other part of the room caught my ear.

"It's all very well for you to be so high and mighty about rules," grumbled a muffled voice from one side of me, "you talk every afternoon at prep., and that's against the rules too, isn't it?"

"Nancy is always so fond of talking about her honour," said another muffled voice, from the opposite corner. "How about the day Maddy took us for a walk, and you cut all the crossings, and swung your arms, and got a conduct-mark, and Strangles lectured you before the whole school about the example to the younger ones?"

---

6. *Tertius*, "third" (Latin); applied to the youngest of three boys at school. Two brothers were distinguished by *major* and *minor* (literally, "larger" and "smaller").

"That's different," said a third voice, which was not muffled at all. "I don't care two-pence about the *rules*. It doesn't matter how often you break the rules, if there is a very good chance of your being caught; that's only fair. But we are put on our honour not to talk in our bedrooms, and they'd never find us out if we did, and I don't like the feel of it. So shut up, can't you?"

I was too tired to listen any longer, but I went off to sleep, meaning to add a postscript to Jack's letter, telling him that, in spite of the general inferiority of the sex, there actually seemed to be a sense of honour among girls, as well as boys.

I made many more startling discoveries about girls, as the days went on. For instance, the very morning after my arrival, I was unexpectedly addressed by a particularly cheerful looking girl, not much older than myself, who asked me if I would do her a great favour; and when I assented, feeling flattered at being noticed by anybody at all, she proceeded to draw a three-cornered note from her apron pocket.

"I shall be much obliged," she said, very impressively, "If you will give that to Nancy Waterhouse, and tell her that I don't expect an answer."

"Nancy Waterhouse? Why, she's over there, isn't she?" I exclaimed. "Won't it do if you tell her yourself?"

It evidently would not do at all, to judge from her expression, when I, a new girl, presumed to offer a suggestion; so I hastily did as I was told, and conveyed the note to Nancy Waterhouse.

"Who gave you this?" she demanded, in a sharp tone, as though I were somehow to blame for it.

"The girl with the big nose and the red hands," I explained carefully, recalling the most distinctive features of the girl who had employed me as her messenger.

"I *suppose*," said Nancy emphatically, "that you mean Madge Smith. And her nose isn't big, and her hands are white enough for most people."

"Yes," I said submissively, though I wondered how Nancy had identified her from my description, in that case.

"And you can tell her," continued Nancy, "that I decline to hold any communication with her whatever."

"Yes," I said again, and trotted back with the three-cornered note.

"Well?" said Madge, eagerly.

"She says she doesn't want the rotten thing," was my rather free translation of the message that had been entrusted to me.

"Horrid, mean thing," cried Madge. "She might at least read my explanation. Go and tell her it is to explain everything, and she must read it at once."

"Wouldn't it save time," I suggested once more, "if you were to go and say all that yourself? It's such a stupid thing to do, to go backwards and forwards like this all the morning, when——"

But Madge's infuriated expression sent me hastily on my fruitless errand again; and, as I expected, Nancy Waterhouse was as serenely indifferent as before.

"I require no formal explanation. Tell her that nothing can ever be the same again, and that all is henceforth over between us," she said loftily, and the three-cornered note travelled across the room once more.

"It is too bad," declared the outraged Madge, when I had done my best to reproduce the elegant language of Nancy Waterhouse. "It is a beautiful explanation, and it took me the whole of French lesson to write. Read it yourself, and see if it isn't."

As this was what I had been longing to do all the time, I hastily unfolded the three-cornered note, and, in obedience to the request of the proud writer, I read it aloud.

"My own darling," it ran; "it was *not* my fault that I did not hear what you said at the history class. Strangles was talking so much that it was impossible to hear one's self speak. Please forgive me, and be nice once more, as you used to be. If you smile at me in the German lesson, and say, 'All right,' I shall understand. But please believe that it was *not* my fault, and that there is *nothing* to forgive. Your heart-broken, Madge."

"But," I objected, when I folded it up again, "if there is nothing to forgive, what is the use of making all this fuss about it?"

Madge Smith stared at me in dumb amazement.

"I should like to know," she said at last, "who asked for *your* opinion?"

"It wasn't meant for an opinion," I hastened to explain. "I only thought it was rather silly—"

"You only *thought*, did you?" cried Madge, with a withering scorn. "I'm sorry we're all too *silly* for you. May I ask when you are going to be moved up into the first class?"

"Come along, Madge," said the voice of an unexpected ally. "That babe isn't worth squashing." And to my astonishment, the enemy was at once subdued and led off affectionately, by Nancy Waterhouse herself.

"Well, kiddy, what are you meditating about?" asked the abrupt voice of Dorothy Pearson. I was still looking blankly after the two friends.

"I was thinking how awfully stupid it was to quarrel about nothing at all, and to say all those long words about it, and then to behave as though nothing had happened" I returned, promptly.

"I wouldn't criticise quite so much if I were you," said Dorothy crushingly. "You'll get yourself disliked, if you do."

"What's criticising?" I asked in a puzzled tone.

"Eh, what?" said Dorothy, slightly taken aback. "Well, it's criticising, of course; saying what you think about people, don't you know."

"Then, have I got to say what I *don't* think about them?" I asked in astonishment.

"If you'll take my advice, you won't say anything at all. And you'd better remember you're the youngest kid here," said Dorothy severely; and then she went away too, and I wondered if I should ever be able to propitiate all these perfect people, who were so ready and anxious to tell me of my deficiencies.

After all, I soon found that my chief offence was the fact of my being a new girl, and as that was a defect that necessarily wore off with time, my companions gradually began to treat me with a condescension that even ripened into endurance. I felt that my last claim to their acknowledgment was established, when Dorothy Pearson admitted me to the ranks of her slaves, and allowed me to put away her books for her, and to perform sundry other offices of a servile nature, the doing of which was much coveted by her other and less favoured admirers. But the one barrier that still remained between us, and prevented me from enjoying the full confidence of my companions, was my staunchness to Miss Strangways. Of course, it was not to be supposed that I could learn all at once every detail of the school girl's code, or else I should have known that it is never considered etiquette to profess anything more than a kindly tolerance for those in authority. But to me, it seemed quite ridiculous not to like some one, just because the making of my report happened to be in her hands, and I therefore remained faithful, in the face of much opposition, to my early friendship for her.

"It isn't as though she was like the ordinary grown up person, who talks French before you," I represented to them. "But she's as reasonable as a jolly sort of boy; and she doesn't always look, when you drop your books and things; and she only pulls you up *sometimes*, when you say 'awfully' or 'rotten.' *I* think she's nice."

"She's Strangles, all the same," objected Madge Smith. "You can't get over that. And if she was as nice as you make out, she wouldn't be a head-mistress at all; she'd be something jolly and kind, like a mother, or a widow, or—or—"

The lack of vocations for women, who were jolly and kind, brought Madge's eloquence to an abrupt end, and I repeated my defence of Miss Strangways, stolidly.

"I think she's nice, all the same, and I'm going to stick to her," I said.

"Wait till you have been lectured by her, that's all," replied Madge. But at the moment, I could imagine nothing more delightful than to be lectured by Miss Strangways.

The state of my spirits may best be gathered from a letter I received from Jack, when I had been at school about a fortnight.

"You are only a girl, after all," he wrote, gloomily. "It is very rotten of you to give in so easily, and I did think you'd hold out for one term at least. I knew you would only make a girl in the end, but you might have shown fight a little longer I do think. I know what it will be now, you will be always writing long letters to the other rotten girls; what they find to write about I don't know, but they always do write rot by the yard. And you'll be afraid of getting your feet wet, and all those poor things girls make such a fuss about, and you won't be any fun at all. Wilkins minor says *his* sister won't do a thing for him since she went to school, girls are never any more good, he says, when they've once been to school; it makes them so independent, he says. And Wilkins minor *knows*. There are those dormice of mine, perhaps Nurse will feed them for me in future? Of course, she's only a woman, but even that is better than being a girl. I have left off counting the days to the holidays; if you are only going to be a cheap *girl* all the time, I might just as well stop here, though it is such a beastly hole, and we have to grind all day without stopping. Girls don't know the meaning of hard work, Boston terts says. And Boston terts says he doesn't want any more names for his ferret now that you've gone to school; he says he couldn't feel sure now that you hadn't swotted them out of a rotten history book or something. Simpson sends you his love, it's beastly poor of him, and he actually says he knows some girls who are quite nice though they *are* at a girls' school. But, of course, Simpson hasn't got any sisters. Your disappointed Jack."

I felt rather hurt when I read Jack's letter for, as I wrote to him immediately, he did not know how difficult it was to keep free from the taint of femininity, when there was nothing but girls in the house, when a bad mark was the penalty for whistling, and when one was not even allowed to make friends with the boot-boy. But, in spite of the base defection of Jack, and Wilkins minor, and Boston terts, there was a measure of comfort in the loyalty of Simpson, even although it was mainly founded on his ignorance of sisters.

And when Miss Strangways glanced over our letters on the following Sunday, to see if they were tidy, I was called upon to give a full and satisfactory explanation of the identity of one Master Thomas Simpson.

III. WORK

Much to my surprise, I was put into the second class. I knew that my spelling had none of the quaint originality of Jack's, and I was equally conscious of a certain superiority over him in minor matters of French and history, for which he loved to profess a sincere contempt, based on rudimentary Latin and ignorance; but, for all that, I was quite unprepared to be found worthy of ranking with Nancy Waterhouse and Madge Smith, and all the other superior people, who had treated me like a mere child ever since my arrival. Nor were they backward in letting me know, that their surprise was quite equal to mine.

"Hullo! what are *you* doing here?" asked Madge, ungraciously, when I presented myself, nervously, at my first arithmetic lesson. It was another surprise to me, to find that Nancy, the patronising, overbearing Nancy, was at the bottom of her class, and, in consequence, sat next to me. Clearly, my school-fellows did not base their supremacy on anything so trivial as talent or ability, and I made another note in their favour, for the edification of Jack in my next letter.

"I'm not doing anything yet," I replied, humbly and truthfully. "I didn't know there was anything to do, until Miss Poland came."

"I didn't mean *sums*, stupid!" retorted Madge, with brusqueness. "But why on earth aren't you in the third, with all the other kids?"

"I didn't know there was a third," I said, a little assertively. "Did *you* always know things before you were told, when you were a new girl?"

I quite forgot, until I saw Madge's face, that, of course, she never had been a new girl at all; but the arrival of Miss Poland, or, as the girls more familiarly termed her, "Roley-poley," put an end to our conversation.

Miss Poland was an eminently cheerful, little person. She taught arithmetic as though it were some delightful new game, which we were all pining to know; and she showed a gentle endurance for the absurdities of recurring decimals, and compound interest, which gave them quite a personal significance. How anyone could teach arithmetic, and remain human, was a mystery to me; but I felt that Roley-poley was the exceptional person who could, and I mentally calculated the possibilities of buying her a bunch of violets, when the opportunity should occur. Violets, at the moment, seemed the only adequate expression of my gratitude for her tolerance of my home-taught arithmetic, and it was not very long before my intended gift reached the dimensions of several bunches. For arithmetic had always been my weak point. Even when I was alone, I was never very brilliant over it; but the presence of fifteen other girls, who worked out their answers with maddening rapidity, and never seemed to ink their fingers in the process, sent my opinion of myself down to its lowest ebb. The knowledge that every one of those fifteen girls considered, that I ought to have been placed in the third class, did not make me any happier, and I sighed miserably, as I delivered up my note-book for the inspection of Roley-poley. She looked at it thoughtfully. I felt she had every reason to be meditative. I knew what masses of badly-formed figures covered those two pages of my note-book; and I wondered, wretchedly, why anyone should take all that trouble, to discover the price of one pound of brown sugar, when there were grocers in every street who knew it without any arithmetic at all.

"The answer is—is not quite clear," she observed. Fifteen pairs of remorseless eyes were witnessing my discomfiture, and fifteen pairs of ears awaited my trembling reply.

"Three hundred pounds, seven shillings, and eightpence, and ninety-five ninety-sixths," I said, sadly. "It seems rather a lot of money for brown sugar, doesn't it?"

Astonishment pervaded the fifteen faces beyond me, and Roley-poley looked at me, sharply. Apparently, my expression saved me, for she returned to the sum; and I, who had not, of course, tried to be funny at all, felt slightly comforted on finding that Roley-poley, at least, had more sense than all those other fifteen, who did their sums correctly, but did not know a bad joke from a good one. I felt almost convinced, that Jack would have approved of Miss Poland.

"There, I said you ought to have been in the third," remarked Madge, cheerfully, when we met again at the history class. The discovery that I was as stupid as she expected to find me, seemed to have improved her spirits wonderfully.

"It's not my fault," I complained. I was not in a position to contradict her, after my recent exposure over the brown sugar sum, but I felt a vague grudge against Miss Strangways, all the same, for not having had as much perception as Madge Smith, in which case I should have been placed, where I ought to have been—"with the other kids, in the third."

"Nobody said it was," replied Madge, most unreasonably. "You shouldn't talk so much."

I was quite willing to relapse into silence, and studied my history carefully. But this did not seem to please her any better.

"I wish you wouldn't *grind* so," she grumbled, presently. "It's very dull to sit next to anyone who never opens her mouth, even when there *isn't* a class going on."

I shut up the book, hastily, and said the first thing that came into my head.

"Do you like Charles I. or Cromwell[7] best?" I inquired, in the most obliging manner I could assume.

"*Like* them?" exclaimed Madge. "Why, who ever thought of liking anyone in a history book? How awfully queer you are!"

"But you must know which one you like best," I persisted. "They're so different, don't you know."

"I don't see it myself," said Madge. "They're not people at all, to begin with; and you can't like somebody who isn't there, can you? Besides, they are alike. They're both dead, for one thing, and they're both in the history book, for another. Real people, like us, never get into history books at all; it's only musty, slow, old fogeys—"

"Elizabeth wasn't a bit slow, or Henry VIII," I interrupted. "You couldn't call Henry VIII slow, could you? Then, there was Richard I;[8] don't you like Richard I? I do. He killed such a lot of people, and never got killed himself. He could sing, too; don't you remember how he got out of prison, just because he knew how to sing, when What's-his-name came along, and—oh! no, Richard I wasn't a bit slow. His wife had beautiful long hair, too. It would be heaps jollier if people were like that now, wouldn't it? Nobody ever has any excitement now; if you're grown up, you turn into a drawing-room visitor, and go to dances, and that's all."

"I'd much sooner go to dances than be inside a stuffy history-book," retorted Madge. "So would you, really; only you pretend you wouldn't, just to look different. I had a new evening dress, last holidays, white silk with chiffon sleeves; I'm going to wear it at the break-up party. That's better than being in a history-book, isn't it?"

"Nobody can be in a history-book, *now*," I explained, hastily. "Nobody ever is. And mine is pink crepon,[9] with—"

The voice of Miss Strangways broke in upon our interesting discussion. The rival merits of Cromwell and Charles I, of white silk and pink crepon, had been sufficiently engrossing to cover her entrance into the room; and we buried our heads in our note-books, and assumed the necessary expression of meek indifference, when she looked in our direction.

But, the most interesting of all our lessons was the weekly lecture on composition. This was a recent innovation; and, for the first time, I felt on a level with my com-

---

7. Oliver Cromwell (1599–1658), leader of the Puritan forces who overthrew and executed Charles I (1600–1649; r. 1625–49) in the English Civil War; he was installed as "lord protector" in 1653.
8. Richard the Lion-Hearted (1157–1199; r. 1189–99); according to legend, when he was imprisoned by Leopold V, Duke of Austria, he heard his troubadour Blondel singing and made his whereabouts known by responding with a song that both of them knew. Both Elizabeth I (1533–1603; r. 1558–1603) and her father, Henry VIII (1491–1574; r. 1509–74), were highly educated.
9. A fine fabric resembling crepe, but heavier.

panions, as I raised my voice with theirs in eloquent protest against all innovations, and against this particular one, most of all. But, in spite of ourselves, our new lecturer began to make some sort of an impression on our unwilling minds, before she was half through her first lecture. There was something completely new about her, something that nettled us, and something that fascinated us. She was very young, and very contemptuous, and very enthusiastic. She talked to us as though we had nothing to do all the week, except write compositions for her; and she seemed to take it for granted, that we all wanted to be authors some day, but were too foolish to know how to begin now. And, as hardly any writer, past or present, seemed good enough for her, we naturally had little hope of being able to please her. And the curious thing was, that, partly goaded by her contempt for our foolishness, and partly inspired by her turgid enthusiasm, we really did feel constrained to do our very best, in writing those compositions of ours.

"Say what you mean," she urged. "Half the time, you are only echoing what hundreds of other people think they mean. Try to forget what other people think, and find out what you think yourselves. Very likely, you never have thought before. Very well, then; think *now*. Don't cultivate your memory, cultivate your observation; the world will become a different place for you, if you do. There are myriads of things, pregnant with interest, all round you, at this moment, and you don't even know they are there. Try and find them out. Discover your own sense of humour; you all have it, somewhere; you will find, that it is often only a trick of circumstance, that makes you laugh at a thing you might otherwise have cried at. Don't be afraid of putting *yourselves* into your compositions; we are all so ridiculously afraid of giving ourselves away. What does it matter, if we do? It is all we have to give, most of us, and it is not very much at the most. Besides, what else do you suppose we are here for?" And so on, all through the lecture. We had never heard anything like it, before; our youthful schoolgirls' hearts beat warmly in response to the extreme youthfulness of our lecturer; our minds were filled with ideas for the composition we were going to write for her. The subject was to be "Life in a Country Lane," and, for the next week, we talked of little else but our composition, and our composition lecturer. But, when Thursday came round again, and we sat in our places before her, the misgiving crept into the hearts of many of us, that we had not entirely expressed what Miss Ashwood expected of us. Nor did Miss Ashwood's manner, as she read one after another of our papers, re-assure us in any way. She began with the head-girl's.

"The 'Life in a Country Lane' is very varied," it began. "Very few of us, perhaps, have noticed how very varied it is, but then very few of us notice anything at all. Most of us only notice what somebody else has noticed before, and that is because our memory is good, but our observation is bad. So it is in a country lane. Many of us can remember all the books that have been written about country lanes, but can one of us remember what there really is to be seen in a country lane? Alas, no! Perhaps, it is because we have no sense of humour, and that is why we often laugh at things that ought to make us cry. Ah, indeed, the life in a country lane teaches us how many things there are, all round us on every side, which we have never noticed before, and this is most interesting. There are flowers to begin with; convolvulus, and crocuses, and briar roses, and wild thyme, and others as well. Perhaps, Shakespeare was thinking of the life in a country lane when he wrote, 'I know a bank whereon the wild thyme grows.'"[1]

---

1. Misquoted from *A Midsummer Night's Dream* (1594–96), 2.1 ("I know a bank where the wild thyme blows").

We waited, breathlessly, for the lecturer's comment on the essay of our head girl; so much observation and erudition should not, we felt, be without its meed of praise. She did not say very much, however; indeed, her enthusiasm seemed to have greatly declined, since last week. She just glanced over it, and remarked, casually, "Even Shakespeare, I think, would not make crocuses and briar roses bloom together." And then, she passed on to the next paper, and Dorothy Pearson looked surprised.

Gradually, a distinct gloom began to settle down on the composition class. If we had all put ourselves into our essays, as we had been recommended to do, there was evidently a certain monotony about our personalities; and our lecturer's comments grew fewer and fewer, as she laid down paper after paper. We could not make much of her expression, as the lesson dragged on its weary way, but we noticed, that she did not tell us any longer to think for ourselves. There was a momentary diversion when she came to Nancy Waterhouse's. It certainly had a style of its own, if the matter was slightly familiar to us, and we listened with great admiration to the flowing phrases, and the strings of adjectives.

"The life in a country lane," it began (this being, by the way, the unvarying way in which all the thirty-eight essays began) "may be seen in any country lane you like to mention. We will take a very beautiful one as an example. I can see it before me as I write; it is verdantly green, and romantically sequestered. It is luxuriantly full of exquisite flowers with the most delicious rainbow hues and the sweetest of alluring perfumes. Here are majestic poppies and nodding violets, there is the humble pansy and the rich westeria; tropical creepers hang in rank profusion from the tree ferns and the cocoa-nut palms, while the banyans stand in solitary dignity among the dear old oaks and elms of merry England. It is a wonderful little country lane, remarkable at once for its rich beauty and its glorious simplicity. Our gentle Will loved to sing of 'sweet musk roses and eglantine,' while our beloved Wordsworth[2]———."

The lecturer sighed, and did not finish the elegant composition of Nancy Waterhouse. "It is well," she suggested, "to avoid familiarity with the poets." The rest of us wondered why Nancy had put the advanced Geography Reader into her essay, instead of herself.

At last, my turn came. I had never felt so frightened in my life. If the other compositions had not satisfied the expectations of Miss Ashwood, what would she think of mine? For, my knowledge of the poets was confined to Edmund Lear, and the great Strewelpeter;[3] and my only experience of country lanes had been gained in the summer holidays, when Jack and I had gone beetle-hunting. And, my adjectives were limited, and—colloquial. So I sat with lowered eyes and burning cheeks, while my paper was read, and my schoolfellows tittered.

"The life in a country lane is very lively," I had written. "There are lots of jolly things you can't get in London, or any of those moggy places[4] where there isn't any life at all. The best thing to do is to put your head down on the ground, and listen; it is just beautiful, you hear all the sounds that are worth hearing, all sorts of beetles whirring, and bees humming, and gnats singing, and they are all as different as anything, and after a little while you can tell one from another, and it is like being in an awfully jolly new place where you never were before. And if you look up through the hedge, you don't see people or dull things like that, but you see thousands of

2. William Wordsworth (1770–1850), British poet. The phrase quoted from William Shakespeare appears in the passage of *A Midsummer Night's Dream* cited above (2.1).
3. "Slovenly Peter" (1844), a children's story by Heinrich Hoffmann. Lear (1812–1888), British nonsense poet and artist.
4. I.e., places where "moggies," or alley cats, would congregate. Later in the story, Becky refers to London as full of cats.

green branches and twigs that look as though they were roads going away somewhere. I am sure they do go somewhere, but some people say they don't. I like catching beetles, and letting them crawl over my hand; some people like putting them into boiling water and then sticking them with pins for his collection, but I don't. Some people say it is stupid to mind because it doesn't hurt them, and he says he supposes I can't help it because I am a girl, but sometimes I think he is wrong and I don't half mind being a girl. And we both think that the life in a country lane is the jolliest kind of life in the whole world."

Everybody was giggling. I wished I could get away, and hide somewhere. Of course, I was ignorant and foolish; of course, my composition was ill-written and disgraceful; but, was it my fault that I had not read any poetry, and did not know the names of flowers? The lecturer spoke at last.

"Will the writer of the last composition kindly stand up?" she was saying. I staggered to my feet, and fought desperately to keep back my tears. I could see, through a sort of mist, that she was smiling at me.

"So you wrote this, all by yourself?" she said. "Then, take my advice, and try to improve your language and style. I want you to try very hard, if you will, for everyone can do that much; and you have something else already, that neither I nor any one else could ever teach you. And that is the great thing."

I sat down, with my head whirling. I could not have said what her exact meaning was, but I had grasped this much, that she was not laughing at me, and that she thought I might write as elegantly as the head girl, some day. My schoolfellows were no longer tittering, and some of them nodded encouragingly at me. My period of probation was over, and no one said anything more about my not being in the third. I wished I had not spent so much of my pocket-money on Miss Poland's violets, until I reflected that all the violets in the London streets would not have expressed the state of my emotions at that moment. In a kind of dream, I heard the subject given out for next week's composition; I did not hear what the lecturer was saying, but I noticed that her expression had saddened considerably, since she came into the room.

And I do not think she ever again recommended us, to put *ourselves* into our compositions.

IV. The "Decagon"

I suppose it was owing to the composition lectures, that the whole school fell a prey to the literary fever, that term. For the moment, it eclipsed all the permanent and legitimate hobbies in which we indulged, such as, the aimless collection of current penny stamps, in the strange and wild hope, which was never realised, of making a fortune out of them, some day; or the condensing of silver chocolate paper into a large and weighty ball, with no end in view at all, except the unprincipled one of making it the largest and most important silver ball in the school. These, however, were our regular pastimes, and necessary to the social standing of every schoolgirl among us; whereas, the literary fever was quite ephemeral, and the limit of its endurance was that of the "Decagon." And the "Decagon" never survived its first issue. It was the opinion of the girls, that the "Decagon" owed its collapse to me, an opinion I still resent, on looking back, for it would be equally true to say, that, if it had not been for me, the "Decagon" would never have appeared at all. But this was a subtle view that could not be expected to appeal to them; and they refused to allow, with the uncompromising judgment of their kind, that the real cause of its failure was the sudden decline of the literary fever.

Now, although the head girl and her own particular clique were by no means unaffected by the literary fever, and were guilty of more than one poem, and even, it was whispered, of a novelette or two, it was left for the second class to distinguish itself by issuing a paper of its own. We of the second class claimed, that the girls in the first never originated anything at all; they were too occupied, we said in our envy and contempt, in thinking about the hair they had just turned up, and the frocks they had just let down. Be that as it may, this particular inspiration was taken up at once by the whole sixteen of us, and we all clamoured eagerly for a place in its columns, until Audrey Thomson, who had become editor by virtue of being top of the class, looked hopelessly bewildered. Audrey Thomson, by the way, was not a born leader; she was painstaking, good-natured, and submissive, in consequence of which we all liked her, and nobody showed her any respect. So the first meeting, that was held on the subject, was a very stormy one. It took place in one of the music rooms, on a wet afternoon, and all the noise we did not make ourselves was contributed by envoys from the third class, who kept on demanding through the keyhole, what we meant by "sitting up in a stupid room where there wasn't anything to sit on," when there were games of blindman's buff—and the third class—downstairs. The potent truth of these remarks failed, however, to convince us, and we continued to sit with cheerful faces, and some ingenuity, on the shining lid of the walnut-wood piano, while our editor occupied the music-stool, and looked placid.

"If you would only stop talking for a minute," she began, for the third time, only to be interrupted once more—this time by Winifred Hill, who, as a day-girl, at once commanded our attention. The day-girls were never popular with us as companions, and it was an unwritten law that they should keep more or less to themselves. But they represented the outer world to us, and they always knew when anybody important died, or when the country was going to war; and we submitted to them as authorities on all matters of this kind. And it was obvious that literature, and therefore newspapers, belonged to the outer world, and not to us; so Winifred had no difficulty in making herself heard.

"We must elect a staff," she began, with the air of one who knows. Silence immediately fell upon us, for we had not the remotest idea of what her meaning might be.

"A what?" asked Madge Smith, at last.

"Don't you know?" I said, with easy indifference. "It's what the pilgrims always—"

"*Pilgrims!*" echoed Winifred, scornfully. "Who's talking about pilgrims? If you want to turn the thing into a lesson, I won't have anything more to do with it."

Amid the blackening looks of my companions, I apologised humbly for seeming to know something; and Winifred was coaxed into proceeding.

"You see," she resumed, with a gentle air of patronage, "you must have a staff, to make sure of getting enough things to fill the paper. The staff's the people who write the paper, don't you know; the whole class can't expect to be in it, can it?"

The whole class did, to judge from its rebellious attitude, when Winifred had delivered her definition of a staff; and she condescended to try and propitiate us a little.

"Of course," she said, "everybody *may* send in something, and the editor can take it, if she likes; but the staff has got to write the paper, practically, or else there wouldn't be a paper at all. Don't you see?"

Nobody seemed to see; and Audrey interposed, timidly, and with apology in her tone.

"I think," she suggested, hurriedly, "that Winifred had better be editor instead of me." But everybody objected to this; we felt that nothing would ever be accepted at

all, if Winifred were made editor; and we were just beginning to realise the importance of having an editor, who would be open to the wishes of her contributors. So
Audrey retained, with a sigh, the position we all envied her; and Winifred was
quenched for the moment. Not for long, however, for she soon had a new idea for
our edification, and her own possible advancement.

"You must have a sub-editor, too," she announced.

The editor looked more unhappy than before.

"Must I?" she said. "What for?"

"Oh, to do things," said Winifred, vaguely. "Editors always have a sub-editor, and
she has to go round and bully the staff to write their things in time, and all that. Sub-
editors have the most fun, really; I shouldn't mind being one, myself. And you can
choose your own sub-editor," she added, suggestively, and began humming a tune.

There was a pause. Even the editor did not take very kindly to the notion of Winifred Hill as a colleague.

"I suppose I ought to choose the one who writes the best compositions and things,"
she said, looking along the row of literary aspirants, as it wavered uncertainly on the
slanting lid of the cottage piano. None of us gave her any help in her unwelcome
task; we all hummed tunes instead, and looked up at the rain-washed skylight, and
the dull, colourless bit of atmosphere beyond; and we made a great show of preserving
our equilibrium in our perilous position, and nobody would have suspected that the
vacant appointment was of the least interest to any one of us. Madge spoke at last,
in the blunt, direct manner she always put on, when she was going to do something
that was rather nice.

"I vote for Becky," she said. "Of course, she's the youngest kid here, but she did
the best composition in the whole school."

I lost my balance on the spot, and plunged on to the shoulders of the editor, who
was sitting with her back to me, at the moment. Any one else would have felt annoyed;
but Audrey only smiled.

"I don't mind," she said, referring to the appointment and not to my reception of
it. "She'll do as well as any one, won't she?"

"Oh, no," I said, with becoming modesty, and a throbbing heart. "I think Madge
would do much better."

But, to my intense joy, no notice was taken of my perfunctory sacrifice, and sub-
editor I accordingly became. After that, owing perhaps to a natural ebb in our wild
enthusiasm, business proceeded more peaceably, and, when it came to electing the
staff, the eight, who joined it, actually needed persuasion to induce them to take
office. For, after all, the meeting had lasted more than an hour; and it was a wet
afternoon.

The question of a name revived our interest a little.

"I think," said the editor, with her customary timidity, "that the 'Weekly Record'
is rather good."

"But it isn't weekly, it's monthly," objected Winifred, who was not averse, at this
stage of the proceedings, to a tussle with the editor. The editor, as usual, was unconscious of her intention. Nancy Waterhouse yawned, and proposed "Our Society Journal," which received no more support than the editor's suggestion.

"Call it 'Strangles Scraps,'" cried Madge; and everybody laughed.

"Why?" I asked, in a puzzled tone. But my desire for information was, as usual,
misinterpreted.

"Why not?" retorted Madge. "You needn't think you're everybody, just because you
have got yourself made sub-editor. It's nothing to make such a fuss about."

"I didn't think I was everybody," I cried, hotly. But the inexorable bell rang us down to preparation; and, for the next couple of hours, the new and temporary distinctions we had acquired in the music-room were forgotten, in the common aim of getting through as much work with as little trouble as possible, and as much conversation as the inattention of Mademoiselle and our own ingenuity would permit. And, as I sat and laboriously absorbed the names of the great-uncles and god-mothers and other relationships, that exist for the torture of the beginner in the French conversation book, I watched the passage of a scrap of paper down the row of desks, and concealed it deftly under my hand, when it reached me at last. I buried my head in a ponderous French dictionary, and galloped through columns of words, until it was safe to read my missive.

"Will the 'Decagon' do?" wrote Nancy Waterhouse, who had Latin lessons on Wednesdays.

"What does it mean?" wrote I, who did not have Latin lessons on Wednesdays.

"Stupid! It means a thing with ten sides," was the reply that reached me, after the necessary interval. And I, who failed to see how the paper, or the editor, or the staff had any connection with a thing that had ten sides, wrote back: "All right; I will tell the editor after prep., and don't write any more rot, because Maddy is getting so sharp."

Of course, the editor was as agreeable to Nancy's suggestion as to everything else that had been proposed, and as the staff was not consulted at all, the "Decagon" it accordingly remained. And, about a week later, the following notice was pinned up, surreptitiously, in the music-rooms, and the bedrooms, and in any other place that might be reasonably expected to evade the eyes of authority:—

"On Saturday, December 15th, will appear a new and literary journal called the 'Decagon.' The editor of this amusing and literary journal is Audrey Thomson. There is also a sub-editor, and a staff of eight contributors. (N.B.—That is why it is called the 'Decagon,' because a decagon has ten sides.) This fashionable and literary journal will only cost twopence. (N.B.—That means you pay twopence to be allowed to read it.) And only the second class is in it. (N.B.—Please burn this.)"

Needless to say, the editor had nothing to do with this announcement, which was the unaided handiwork of the sub-editor and her boon companion, Madge Smith. Indeed, for the first time, the editor showed a little spirit.

"What's the good of putting up a notice about the stupid thing?" she asked, gloomily. I was surprised at her putting it that way, for I was as yet unacquainted with the attitude of editors towards their own papers.

"That's to announce it," I explained. "You always have to announce a paper, Winifred says, or else no one buys it."

"What's the good of announcing a thing that's never going to happen?" retorted the editor, in the same tone of pessimism. "Nobody has sent in a single thing yet, and we shall all be working for the exams. directly. The botany exam. is on the same day, and that's ever so much more important than the 'Decagon.'"

"Oh, it's all right," I assured her, confidently. "There's a whole week before the 15th, and you can do a lot in a week. Besides, we have got one thing already; Madge has just given me her comic poem, and it's awfully good. Shall I read it to you?"

The editor, true to her rôle, wore an air of gentle resignation, as I read Madge's comic poem aloud:—

"There's a lady we all know as Strangles,
Who's mixed up in all sorts of tangles,

> Her fondness for history
> To me is a mystery,
> That preposterous lady called Strangles."

"What does it mean?" asked Audrey.

"Oh, I don't think it means anything particular," I replied, doubtfully. "But then, you see, it is a comic poem."

"Is it?" said the editor, sceptically. "I don't see anything funny in it myself. And I seem to have heard something like it before. But it will take up five lines, that's one thing. Anything else?"

"Not yet. But I'm going round to wake them all up," I replied, still confidently.

"You don't know what exam. week is," said the editor, discouragingly, as I started on my mission of waking up the staff of the "Decagon." I found that her words were true; any one would have thought, from the cold way in which I was received, that none of them had ever heard of the "Decagon." And, as the week crept on, and none of the promised contributions seemed to be forthcoming, I began to feel a little uneasy myself. But nothing would have induced me to show it. I was determined, and so was Madge, that the "Decagon" should appear on the 15th. Jack's scornful reply, when I wrote him an account of the meeting in the music-room, only made me more determined; although it was accompanied by a copy of *his* school magazine, which was in every way a very superior publication. It was printed and uncut; and it looked dull. There was an article on Christopher Columbus by the fifth form master, and a poem on Spring by X. Y. Z., and long columns of names relating to football[5] matches, and extracts from other papers about bicycling; and I believe firmly that nobody ever read it, except the boys' sisters at home. But still, there it was, sleek and prosperous looking; and of the "Decagon," two days before the date of publication, there still only existed the comic poem, that had not made the editor laugh.

"Have you tried them *all*?" asked Madge, anxiously, as we met for five minutes before dinner, on the 13th of December.

"Every one, except Nancy; and she always scoots when she sees me coming. If we only had her sentimental poem on Love, it would be something." I sighed. A little way off, sat the editor, with a book on her lap, and her fingers over her ears. Clearly, there was no help to be expected from her. "The others are hopeless," I continued, sadly. "When I asked Winifred Hill for her essay on London, she said, 'What essay on London?' and told me not to interfere. I'm always being told not to interfere. It's so poor, isn't it?"

"It's all because you don't know how to attack them," said Madge, rather unjustly. "You let them see you're afraid of them; and you talk too much, too. Now, if I'd done the asking—hullo, there's Nancy. Now's your chance, Becky! You don't mind if I go and brush my hair, do you?"

Nancy was the same as all the others, only a little worse. She told me she knew nothing about sentimental poems, or love either, and that I was becoming a perfect little nuisance, and that there wasn't going to be a "Decagon" at all. And, leaving her first two statements undisputed, I told myself that there *was* going to be a "Decagon," and that it was going to contain all the contributions originally promised, under the names of the contributors who had promised them, and that they should be written entirely by Madge and myself.

5. I.e., soccer. Christopher Columbus (1451–1506), Italian-born Spanish explorer. "Form": grade (the sixth form was the highest).

"How about the Botany exam.?" asked Madge, when I unfolded my stupendous scheme to her. "We shall have to write all prep. time, as well as in bed, shan't we?"

"Oh, we must chance the Botany exam.," I replied, airily. "You can always think of *something* to say, when there's nothing else to be done."

So the Botany exam. was "chanced," and the "Decagon" appeared, as had been announced, on the 15th. And half of it was in Madge's handwriting, and the other half was in mine. On the front page was her comic poem; being the only real contribution, we felt it deserved the best place. Following that, was an essay on London, said to be by Winifred Hill. I give one paragraph of it, to show how unfounded was the anger of the real Winifred, when she read it:—

"London is a city on the Thames. It is full of people, and cats, and organs, and schools. I live in London myself, because all great writers always begin by coming to London, Dick Whittington[6] for example. Ordinary people, who are not so great, and are never going to be great writers, live in the country, &c., &c."

Madge explained, that of course she thought Winifred would like to be described as great. But Winifred said she had no business to think, and various other remarks of that nature, so we apologised for our mistake, and pitied her.

Then, there was a column of "Advice from the Editor to her little readers."

"As we hover trembling on the brink of our exam. week," it began, "let me make a last earnest appeal to you all. Do not linger at lunch-time to eat dry and dusty biscuits, and to drink the milk of the London cow; follow my example, dear children, and retire to a quiet corner with your book, and do not answer when you are spoken to, even if you get called names for it. Why am I top of the class, dear children? I am top of the class, dear children, because I know how to give up the dry luncheon biscuit for the still drier lesson book; if you would all learn to exchange the dryness of the luncheon biscuit for the dryness of the lesson book, &c., &c."

I had been convinced, that so exact a fac-simile of the editor's sentiments and language could not fail to be pleasing to her, but she was just as injured as Winifred; and, for the first time, they had a natural bond of sympathy. My own signed contribution was called "Friendship." It ran as follows:—

"To study friendship properly, we must go to school, and see nothing but girls. Friendship means kissing, and writing letters about nothing at all, and quarrelling so that you can make it up again. Friendship is a very beautiful and touching thing, but being chummy is ever so much jollier. Chumminess means liking the same sort of things, and keeping the same sort of animals, and it means that one of you generally does the fagging, and the other does the other part. But you don't say you are fond of one another, because of course that's granted, and you don't kiss at all, at least not often. It is boys who understand being chums, and the only kind of boy who kisses, is the boy who hasn't got any sisters, I think. Girls don't understand chumminess at all; they would if they were boys. But they can't help being girls; I wish they could."

I never understood why my views about friendship gave so much offence to the rest of the school. I had only said just what I thought, and it seemed ridiculous that anyone should object to that. But girls were incomprehensible, as I had to own to myself for the twentieth time that term, and it was some days before any of them would speak to me again—always with the exception of Madge, who had brothers of

6. British merchant (ca. 1358–1423) who became lord mayor of London; several legends were attached to his rise to prominence (e.g., see "The History of Sir Richard Whittington and His Cat" in the Chapbooks section, above), often told in the play and pantomime *Dick Whittington*.

her own, and only kissed me four times a day—twice in the morning, and twice at bed-time—which was quite reasonable—for a girl at school.

But, nothing raised such a storm of anger about my head as the sentimental poem on Love, which I had inserted under the name of Nancy Waterhouse. I will give that also, in all its naïve simplicity, to show how unnecessary the fuss was. I was ready to own, that there might be too many adjectives for some people's taste; but then, if it had really been written by Nancy Waterhouse, there would have been ever so many more. At all events, here it is:—

How sweet is love!
Like some white dove
Dropped from above—
O Love! O Dove!

This dove is white,
Is glorious bright,
And beauteous quite—
O wondrous sight!

Love waits for me,
As you shall see;
When I'm twenty-three
I'll married be.

I should still be glad to know why Nancy never forgave me for that poem on Love. But, most of the events of my first term at school were inexplicable to me, and none more so, than the cold reception of my first essay in journalism.

And Madge and I figured, as we deserved, at the bottom of the list in the Botany examination. But the "Decagon" had appeared, as we had promised it should.

V. The Break-up

"I don't understand a bit," I complained, for the fiftieth time that term.

"That's because you're only half alive," retorted Madge, also not for the first time. "You never understand anything; you're asleep all the time, or something. You've only got to ask any infant in the third why she is glad the holidays are coming, and you won't have to ask twice. Fancy not knowing!"

I sighed, and felt just as perplexed as ever. For, as the term drew to a close, the picture of the average schoolgirl, as Jack had painted her, gradually faded from my mind. I had come to school, expecting to find girls who minced their language and minded their clothes, girls who put lessons before larks, girls who told tales, and girls who giggled, and all of them incipient drawing-room visitors. Instead of which, I had tumbled upon Madge Smith, a real, human person, who hated pretence as much as Jack had taught me to do, someone who honestly liked her fun even if she had more than a sneaking regard for the value of lessons. It is true that Madge Smith had more untidiness marks against her name than any other girl in the school; but she was a fair type, on the whole, of the average schoolgirl, and she was not at all like the picture that Jack had drawn of her.

"But," I protested, "it isn't as though we were miserable here——"

"Isn't it, though!" interrupted Madge. "How awfully funny you are, Becky! I suppose you'd rather walk along dull London streets like this, than go to pantomimes and things with brothers and all sorts of jolly people, wouldn't you?"

She looked along the human crocodile[7] of which we formed a humble pair, and gave an impatient stamp as a message came up from Mademoiselle that she was not to swing her arm.

"Look at that," she said in an injured tone. "They never leave you alone, for a moment. Why shouldn't I swing my arm if I like?"

"My mother never lets me swing my arm," I observed.

"No more does mine," rejoined Madge. "But that's altogether different."

I did not see it myself, so I returned to the original subject. "Of course, I like the holidays for some things," I said, thoughtfully. "It's nice to see everybody again, and the dormice, and Jack, and the new kittens. But being here is very jolly too; and I shall miss the gymnasium classes awfully. And then, there's you, and Miss Strangways."

"Yes, there's me," she allowed. "But nobody could possibly mind leaving Miss Strangways. Just think how she lectures us, and starves us, and makes us grind. I wonder any of us can stand it."

I looked at her round plump face, and thought she stood it very well.

"She doesn't starve us, exactly," I objected. "There's lots to eat; and I'm never so hungry anywhere else, I know."

"Oh, there's lots to eat, right enough; but that isn't *eating*," replied Madge, making the unconscious definition of the epicure.

"And we don't grind very hard, even if she does make us," I added, a little illogically.

"I don't know about that. I don't, of course. But *you* won't be bottom of the class any more; I heard Nancy Waterhouse say, only this morning, that you are sure to go up, this term. So you must have ground, some time or other."

"Oh no," I said deprecatingly, although my voice trembled with pride at what Nancy had said, "you are much more likely to go up than I am."

We disputed the point politely, at some length, but were unanimous in arriving at the conclusion that we much preferred to remain where we were, at the bottom of the class.

"They don't pitch on you to be monitress, or to look after the younger ones, if you're at the bottom," said Madge, going out of her way as she spoke to step in a tempting puddle. "And Strangles doesn't lecture you after prayers in the evening, about the responsibilities of your position."

"And Jack won't be able to chaff,"[8] I murmured.

I was obliged to own, as the days went on, that there was some cause to look forward to the end of the term, when it was going to be marked on the day of the break-up party, by so many exciting events. For one thing, there was the prize giving; and although I as a new girl ran no chance of winning one, there was at least the fun of speculating as to the lucky ones. Madge and I both agreed that the gymnasium prize was the only one worth having, though, to use her own words, "of course, your own people always like you to get a musty prize, for German, or tidiness, or something like that."

"I wouldn't get the tidiness prize for anything in the whole world," I declared.

"Well, you won't," remarked Madge. "It isn't meant for people like us. Audrey Thomson is going to get it. *She* never puts her hat into the linen drawer, or forgets

7. A line of people (usually schoolchildren) walk-   8. Banter, tease.
ing in pairs.

to fold up her dressing gown. If it wasn't for girls like Audrey Thomson there wouldn't be a tidiness prize at all."

"What's the good of having prizes, then?" I asked doubtfully. It seemed a little quaint, I thought, that there should have to be a winner before there could be a prize.

"Well, of course, they aren't any good, are they? You always want to know such stupid things," said Madge, which brought the conversation to an abrupt end.

Besides the prize-giving there were going to be selected scenes from the "Tempest," and the whole school was going to take part in a cantata called, "The Ocean Wave," in which we were announced to appear "in costume." Nobody knew, two days before the party, what the "costume" was going to be, but this did not seem to concern anyone in the least.

"They'll leave your hair loose, and wrap you in art muslin, and stick seaweed and shells all over the place," said Winifred Hill, with the *blasé* air of one who has assisted at many break-up parties. And the whole entertainment was going to conclude with a "Sculpture Gallery," in which, to our mingled pride and apprehension, Madge and I found we were to figure respectively as "Diana" and a "Head of Mercury."[9]

"How am I to be a head?" I asked, in an amazed voice, of Dorothy Pearson.

"Wait and see, and don't ask so many questions," she replied, in the crushing manner that endeared her to all the younger ones. "You're anything but a *head* now," she added, with unnecessary severity.

"But none of the dresses are made yet, and we haven't had a single rehearsal, and the party is on Thursday," I exclaimed.

"Well, what of that?" said Dorothy calmly. "You don't know Miss Strangways. There is never more than one rehearsal, and none of them ever know their parts before the day, and the dresses are generally being finished when the people are waiting for the curtain to go up. But it's always all right, and everybody goes away pleased, and you hear Strangles telling everyone that the school work hasn't been interrupted. Do you see, now? Of course," she concluded with the sarcasm that belongs of right to the head girl, "I have no doubt that it will be done much better, now that you are here."

In spite of Dorothy's assurance, it really seemed as though nothing was going to be ready in time. The only thing Miss Strangways took any trouble to prepare was the programme, and that was printed with a charming design, and passed round the breakfast table for inspection quite a fortnight before the event.

"They are quite excellent, those new printers of mine," she observed with enthusiasm to Miss Poland. "They saw my idea at once, and they've actually done exactly what I told them. It's quite delightful to find printers who have no views of their own."

But if Miss Strangways seemed unduly casual at first about the rehearsals, it was a very different matter when the last examination was finished, and we all filed out of the lecture-room on the morning before the day of the break-up, and knew that we had done with books and pencil boxes for four whole weeks. The carpenters were putting up the platform in a trice, the French class-room was transformed by a multitude of gaily coloured fabrics, and Miss Strangways, bristling with energy and ideas, seemed to be in half a-dozen places at once.

"We are getting on capitally!" she exclaimed to Mademoiselle, when the confusion was at its height.

9. Roman messenger god, portrayed with winged cap and winged sandals. Diana: Roman virgin goddess of the hunt. "Sculpture Gallery": a silent and motionless performance in which participants dress to resemble famous sculptures.

Mademoiselle looked dubious.

"There are forty-five dresses to be made by to-morrow," she observed.

"And forty-five girls to make them," retorted Miss Strangways. Then, raising her voice, she continued, "Who is going to make me a cavern on the seashore? That's a good girl! How are you to make it? Oh, that's quite simple, You take a sofa——."

I heard no more, for I fled into the next room, in fear lest I should be called upon to help in making the school-room sofa into a cavern on the seashore. But I was not allowed to escape, for the next minute came a hue and cry after me.

"Becky! Where's Becky? Come along, childie; I want you to take some brown paper and make a rock, will you? Oh, it's quite simple; you must have a foundation of some sort, the coal-scuttle, or a foot-stool, or the fender, or something like that. And you get some shells from the glass case in the drawing-room——What is it, Madge? How are you to get a bow and arrows? Why, make them of course! There's some gold thread in the basket, and——now, where are all the sea-maidens? Will all the sea-maidens kindly take down their hair and put on muslin smocks? I am going to hear you sing the cantata once through. Come here, Ferdinand and Miranda,[1] and do your scene while they are getting ready. And every one who is going to take a man's part must go and put on her gymnasium dress[2] at once, etc., etc."

"Am I a man or a woman?" Madge asked me, in an anxious tone.

"I don't know," I replied, miserably, as I busied myself in making the footstool into a neat brown paper parcel. "Mercury is a man, I suppose, so I must go and put on mine. I do wish to-morrow was over."

"It will never be over," said Madge, despairingly, and we separated in search of our gymnasium costumes.

But even that was not right.

"What's this for?" said Miss Strangways, when we presented ourselves in blue serge and white braid. "I said those who were going to take men's parts."

"I thought Diana was a man," stammered Madge.

"And Mercury surely isn't a woman?" I added in a perplexed tone. Miss Strangways smiled in a tolerant manner.

"You don't wear your gymnasium dress on your head, do you?" she said, and I crept away reduced in spirits.

The confusion seemed to increase rather than to lessen as the day went on. There were hasty rehearsals at intervals on the platform, when sundry girls in gymnasium dresses and others in unfinished court dress of no period in particular, struggled through their parts and tried to copy the vigorous action of Miss Strangways, who directed them from below. Dorothy Pearson sat in a dejected attitude, with blue serge and white braid peeping out from below a gorgeous green satin coat, and studied the part of Ferdinand with the desperation born of stern necessity. Nancy sat a little way off, stitching away at the white nun's veiling that was to suggest the simplicity of Miranda. Sea-maidens assisted one another in the suppression of obtrusive winter clothing, which insisted on asserting itself through the diaphonous green muslin that was supposed to cover it. And at the end of the evening, after a dress rehearsal in which nobody knew her part except Audrey Thomson, and not a single dress had proved wholly satisfactory, Miss Strangways turned with a cheerful smile to Miss Poland, and said, "I think we are more forward than we have ever been before. They

1. Characters in Shakespeare's *The Tempest* (1611).   2. Comfortable outfit worn in gymnastics classes.

can go to bed now, and to-morrow morning we will run through everything once more, just to make it quite perfect."

Somebody said something about the Sculpture Gallery, which had not even been rehearsed once. But Miss Strangways only smiled again. "I can dress them at the time," she said. "I have got it all in my head."

Miss Strangways' head must have been remarkably full, for there were fifteen characters in the Sculpture Gallery, and nothing was ready for it except Diana's bow and arrows. And yet, when the time came for the representation, everybody agreed that the Sculpture Gallery was the greatest success of the evening. And nobody who applauded the wonderful group of white clad figures guessed that the head of Mercury was myself down to the shoulders, or that the pedestal on which it stood was the rest of me wrapped in linoleum, or that the winged hat on his head was the whitened crown of an old felt hat, and the white wings on it were torn out of Miss Strangways' Sunday bonnet. And the people who congratulated their stately hostess, as she stood at the door to bid them farewell, later on in the evening, would have been a little astonished if they had seen her just before in the green-room, with streaks of white across her face and the flour-dredger[3] in her hand, surrounded by fifteen helpless schoolgirls in undraped sheets.

For some reason or another, the prize-giving had to be postponed till the end of the evening. Dramatically, this was the right moment for it, but the effect was curious as the girls stepped on the platform one by one, with the powder still clinging to their hair and face, and with every appearance of having hastily exchanged the classic linen sheet for the modern evening dress. Madge and I stood together far away at the back, and clapped the prize-winners till our hands were sore, and managed to enjoy ourselves immensely, although our disappointment when Winifred Hill, a mere day girl, carried off the gymnasium prize, was extreme.

"She doesn't do Indian clubs[4] half so well as you do, Becky, and anyone can beat her over the bar," whispered Madge, while the prize-giver, a celebrated and prosy barrister, was saying something about the ancient Greeks and physical exercise; and Winifred Hill, in book muslin and pink ribbons was carrying off "The Conquest of Mexico"[5] in red morocco.

"She isn't in it with you when it comes to swinging on the rings," I replied, loyally. But I was suppressed hastily by my other neighbour, for Miss Strangways had risen to her feet and was beginning to speak.

"A kind friend," she was saying, "whose name I have been requested to keep secret, has offered a prize for history in each of the three classes. The girls have known nothing of this, and I have awarded it in each case to the one who has done the best work, both during the term and in the examination. In the first class it falls to our head girl, Dorothy Pearson."

A burst of applause came from us all as our idol and our tyrant walked in her disdainful and nonchalant way towards the platform.

"Doesn't she look splendid?" whispered Madge.

"Oh, she's all right," I replied, indifferently.

For, up to this time, Dorothy Pearson had only played the tyrant to me, and I had not yet reached the stage of idolatry. Madge, of course, replied with some warmth,

---

3. A container with a perforated lid.
4. Heavy clubs, shaped like large bottles, for use in gymnastic exercises.

5. William Hickling Prescott's *History of the Conquest of Mexico* (1843), reprinted in many editions through the nineteenth century.

and in the dispute that followed we lost Miss Strangways' next speech. We became gradually aware of a pause in the proceedings, however, and when we looked up to discover the reason, we found, to our horror, that everybody's eyes were turned in our direction. We had evidently been overheard, and we turned hot all over at the enormity of our behaviour.

"Go *on!*" said the girls around me, in frantic whispers. They seemed to have made a pathway in front of me, and I felt myself being pushed forward from behind. I was certainly expected to do something, and an instinct of self-preservation made me shrink backwards. Then Miss Strangways raised her voice, and said my name a little impatiently.

"What is it?" I cried, desperately. "What have I done?"

A burst of laughter from everyone in the room drowned the words in which Miss Strangways tried to explain the situation; and, without knowing how I got there, I found myself on the platform, receiving the second prize for history at the hands of the learned barrister, who even forgot to be prosy, and merely smiled at me in an indulgent manner.

That evening I went to bed in a confused whirl of many emotions. It was the end of my first term at school, and I could never again be a new girl. I had won a history prize and gone up three places in my class, and nobody would call me stupid any more, or tell me that I ought to be in the third. I had also acquired the easy familiarity with the rest of my school-fellows which allowed me to kiss them all indifferently, and even to walk about with my arm round the waist of one or another of them. I behaved like everybody else, and gave flowers to my favourite teachers when no one was looking, and was happy for a week afterwards if they kissed me in return for them. I had, moreover, a real friend of my own, with whom I quarrelled nearly every day of my life, and I had come to know that an ardent admiration for those in author-ity had better be concealed, and that it was always well to grumble vigorously when-ever there was the least occasion for doing so. And next term, I knew that I should be the first to ignore all the new girls, and should expect them to know everything without being told. In all respects I had become a school-girl. And yet, when I tried to persuade myself that I was glad of the fact, I felt doubtful.

Miss Strangways came to turn out the gas, that night; and she found me sitting disconsolately on the edge of the bed.

"What is it, child?" she asked, and sat down on the edge of the bed, too. And at the sound of her voice, I completely forgot the schoolgirl's code I had been at so much pains to acquire, and I weakly gave in to her charms, and began to cry.

"I didn't mean to change, and—and get different," I sobbed. "I told Jack I wouldn't; and now—now, he will tease so, and perhaps he won't like me so much; and there's the history prize, and I shall not dare to tell him about it, and—and—oh! why didn't I get the gymnasium prize instead?"

Miss Strangways did not smile.

"Poor child," she said. "Did you expect to stop in the same place, always? That would never do, you know, for the people we are fond of would just pass on, and we should be left behind by ourselves. We must always be going on, always. Did you find Jack unaltered, when he came back from his first term at school?"

"Oh, no," I replied. "But he is a boy, and boys are different; at least, Jack always says they are. But he always expects me to be the same, because I am a girl. It is much harder to be a girl than a boy, isn't it? If you are a boy you can change as much as you please, and nobody says anything. And then, I promised Jack I would not get to like girls; but I do! And the worst of it is, I have asked Madge Smith to stay with me in the holidays, and if he doesn't like her——"

"Does he *never* like girls?" asked Miss Strangways. I hesitated a moment.

"There was Wilkins minor's sister," I began, and remembered the awful jealousy I had cherished for her, during the brief period in which she had usurped my place in Jack's affections.

"Ah," said Miss Strangways, nodding wisely. "I should most certainly ask Madge to stay with you in the holidays. And I shouldn't worry about Jack, if I were you."

VI. THE HOLIDAYS

School had been full of surprises to me, but it was something of a shock to me on my return home, to find that all the old things had somehow grown unfamiliar, while the new ones had no place there. The dormice had become sleek and unresponsive, with too much food and too little affection; and the new kittens, at the instigation of their mother, treated me as an intruder. The discovery, too, that the name of our head girl contained neither charm nor terror for any one in the house damped my early efforts at conversation; and when I found that people were not in the least surprised at my getting the history prize, spoke of it indeed with a forced interest which was worse than indifference, I felt that the kittens had only anticipated the feelings of their betters, and that I was of no more consequence here than I had been at school on my first arrival there. It was rather hard to understand why one should have to be for ever accommodating one's self to something fresh; it had taken me three whole months to get used to school, and here I was again feeling just as much of a stranger as ever in my own home. It was very perplexing, but when I mentioned it to Jack he only treated it in the philosophical manner Nurse used to call his "unfeelingness."

"If it isn't one chap, it's another. Girls are different, of course, because it doesn't matter what they do think. I shouldn't bother about *them*, if I were you."

I reflected that if he knew Winifred Hill, and Nancy Waterhouse, and a few more girls like that, he would have to allow that it did sometimes matter what they thought. But I had reasons of my own for wishing to propitiate Jack just then, and I refrained from argument.

"Some girls are all right," I said mildly.

"They all *think* they are," responded Jack. "But they're a poor show anyhow. Don't matter to me though," he added indifferently.

"It's all very well," I exclaimed; "but I am a girl myself, and you always seem to forget that."

"Yes," said Jack, looking at me pityingly, "I suppose you are. But you know you never used to be. It's that rotten school."

I thought of the history prize, and felt that I had burnt all my ships. So I led up the subject gently to what I wanted to say.

"Madge Smith is a girl," I said. "And Madge is awfully jolly. She's not a bit like a girl."

"I'm sick of hearing about Madge Smith," said Jack.

"All the same, you'd like her," I protested.

"Pooh!" said Jack. "Like a girl! Jolly glad I don't have to know any."

"You will have to know Madge," I cried; "because she is coming to stay here next week."

I waited nervously for his reply, which was a long time coming. It surprised me very much when it came.

"Next week?" he said, digging his knife into the sleek and varnished neck of the rocking-horse. "That's when Boston terts is coming."

"Boston terts!" I exclaimed. "Why didn't you tell me before?"

"Oh, hang!" said Jack, still working away at the paint on the rocking-horse. "You didn't tell me about Madge Smith, did you?"

We had evidently a common ground of complaint, so it was no use feeling hurt. And I could hardly object to sharing Jack with someone else, when I was going to ask him to share me with Madge Smith. In fact, the only immediate result of our conversation was that he became much more affectionate to me than usual, and I half wished, when the day for Madge's arrival came round, that she had not been coming at all. But still, if she had not been coming it might never have occurred to him to be affectionate, and this reflection so complicated the matter in my mind that I had to give it up. Jack, as usual, accepted the situation gloomily.

"I wish Boston terts was coming to-day instead of Wednesday," he observed, as we waited for Madge to arrive. "Two whole days by myself, while you and she are rotting together! Poor, I call it."

"But you needn't leave us alone," I said. "You won't, will you? It won't be any fun at all if you keep to yourself. Besides," I added timidly, "you—you *might* like her, you know."

Jack laughed incredulously.

"Never liked a girl yet," he said.

"How about Wilkins minor's sister?" I cried.

"Well, what of her? I never *liked* her; who said I did? Besides, she was an awfully decent little girl, and she *could* run; you should just have seen her. It reminded you of that Greek Johnny with short skirts and a bow and arrows—yes, Diana, that's the chap—but other girls are not like that. Besides, I didn't *like* her; she wasn't bad for a girl, that's all. And Wilkins says she is quite different now she's gone to school. Doesn't matter to *me* what she's like, of course."

And he began to whistle airily, to show how little the alteration in the sister of Wilkins minor mattered to him.

When Madge really came, I am afraid I did forget everything else including Jack for the first half-hour, while I ran her through all the rooms in the house, pressed dormice and kittens upon her in dangerous proximity, and tried to tell her everything that had happened since we last met, just fifteen days ago. And in the middle of it all Jack strolled into the nursery, looking very disconsolate, and would have gone away again when he saw us if I had not cried after him, and made him come back.

"This—this is Jack," I said anxiously, and watched the effect of the introduction. I seemed to remember in that instant all the remarks Jack had made about the girls he had never seen—all the scorn and contempt he had poured upon their heads, all the views he had held concerning their manners, their frailty, and their inferiority generally, and I hoped he would remember at any rate that Madge was our guest. My only consolation was the recollection I had of Madge's frank and boyish way with strangers, and I hoped that it would even disarm Jack.

There was the briefest pause, and then she blushed hotly. I had never seen her blush before, and I naturally felt disappointed at her display of feminine weakness. I could vaguely imagine Jack's reflections. But, to my surprise, he spoke first.

"How do you do?" he said awkwardly.

"Oh, I—I'm all all right, thanks," said Madge, and blushed a little more. "I'm always all right," she added inconsequently.

Jack brightened a good deal.

"I'm glad of that," he said. "Some girls are always having colds in their head, don't you know? I'm awfully glad you don't."

"I don't either," I observed. But they did not seem to notice me at all.

"The girls at school are always pretending they've got colds," said Madge. "But that's only because they want to get out of going for walks and things. *You'd* pretend to be ill if you had to go out two and two, and walk like a snail."

"Guess I should," said Jack. And the conversation slackened. "What do you like doing best?" he asked her, presently.

"Reading jolly books, I think," she replied without the least hesitation. And I trembled again for the opinion Jack was certain to form of her. But he did not seem in the least disconcerted.

"I'll show you some bound numbers of the 'Boys' Own Paper,'[6] if you'll come with me," he said.

And they went off together at once. I was left behind; but they did not seem to notice that either. Indeed, for the whole of the two days which elapsed before the arrival of Boston terts I spent most of my time alone, while Jack and Madge talked together, romped together, and even read together. I had never seen Jack spend more than five minutes with a book in my whole life; but now he suddenly developed an extraordinary taste for reading, and would sit with Madge Smith for an hour at a time, with a large volume open in front of him, resenting bitterly any interruption I might try to make for my own selfish reasons. Those were the dullest two days I had ever spent; and to think that my own particular friend, to whose visit I had so looked forward, was to answer for it, was the most annoying thought of all.

"Hullo! What's the matter?" asked Jack, coming upon me in a corner of the nursery, after breakfast. He was swinging his skates about in the most aggravating manner, and I knew quite well he was going to take Madge to the Serpentine.[7]

"Nothing," I said, very crossly. So much was the matter that this seemed the only appropriate answer.

"That's all right then, isn't it?" rejoined Jack, quite cheerfully.

"No, it isn't; you know it isn't," said, still crossly.

"That's just like a girl," cried Jack. "First you say—"

"Oh, don't," I interrupted. "Of course I'm like a girl, or else I shouldn't be a girl, should I, stupid? Why don't you go out and leave me alone?"

"Why don't *you* come out, instead of sticking in a corner and grumping?"

"Because I haven't been asked. And I'm not grumping; it's all you," I said, becoming incoherent. Jack assumed a virtuous air of patience.

"Girls are the most unreasonable creatures," he began, in a superior tone.

"You seem to find it very easy to put up with one of them, anyhow," I retorted, choking with the tears I would not allow to fall.

"I like that! Why, it was you who *wanted* me to be friendly with her two days ago," exclaimed Jack. "And now that I'm doing my best—"

"Oh, yes! Easy for you to pretend you're only doing it to please me. It's so likely, isn't it?"

6. A periodical (1879–1967), published by the Religious Tract Society.

7. Lake of a winding shape in London's Hyde Park.

"Of course I'm not. It's quite impossible to please you, you're so beastly unreasonable," complained Jack, beginning to show signs of repentance. But I seized the opportunity to become dignified; and when Madge came in, also swinging her skates in an aggravating manner, I was gazing out of one window and Jack out of the other, and neither of us was speaking a word.

"Isn't Becky coming?" she asked, when Jack hailed her with much relief.

"I don't know. Are you, Becky? She doesn't know how to skate," he said, rather lamely.

"No," I said, without turning round. "I'm not coming. I wouldn't come for *anything*."

"All right," they said, evidently much relieved. "You'll be all right, won't you? And this afternoon we'll do something jolly."

And I was left to meditate on my unreasonableness in wanting to learn to skate instead of spending the morning alone.

That afternoon Boston terts arrived. He was rather small and very square, with flat red hair, and a round, freckled face, and he had a very polite manner—although how much of it was shyness it was difficult to say at first—and he was altogether quite unlike the important person I had been led to expect, who hated everything feminine, and was not going to notice me at all. As it happened we were thrown very much together, for Madge and Jack continued to go about with one another, and there was nothing left for me to do but to meet the half shy advances of Boston terts. And there was something comforting to my wounded feelings in the knowledge that this doughty champion of football, this avowed hater of my sex and leader of his own, should want to be friends with a mere girl. But Jack's friends were always so very unlike his own descriptions of them, that I soon got over my surprise at the gentleness of Boston terts, and set to work to arouse the same jealousy in Jack that was still torturing myself. For all through that week of the holidays I never ceased to feel hurt that Jack had so readily thrown me over for Madge Smith; and although I concealed my injured feelings before our two visitors, I never felt wholly natural with him as long as they were there. But Jack seemed quite unconscious of my desire to annoy him, and went about as cheerfully as ever. He was always like that. I sometimes wished he had not been so good-tempered; it would have made it so much easier to quarrel with him.

"Where's Jack?" Boston terts asked, soon after his arrival.

"Oh, he's down in the schoolroom, reading," I replied. Boston stopped tickling the dormouse with a piece of string, and stared at me incredulously.

"Jack *reading*?" he exclaimed. I nodded. "He's always reading now. It's awfully slow; I wish he wouldn't," I volunteered further. My companion was silent for a moment or two, and I tried to think of something to say that should honour the capacity of Boston terts. But he spoke first, and saved me the trouble.

"I say, do you like swotting[8] at story-books all the holidays?" he asked suddenly.

"Oh no; at least, only sometimes. I like *doing* things best, if they're jolly things; and I don't often read in the holidays—there isn't time, and Jack never would let me. Besides, I don't want to, *much*; I don't really," I said hurriedly. The desire to please Boston terts was very strong within me at the moment, and I was much divided between common truthfulness and the sore feeling of my loneliness.

"Good for you," said Boston approvingly. "Can you slide down the balusters? And does anyone kick up a row if you do?"

8. Grinding, studying hard.

"*Rather*," I replied, to both questions. "But you have to watch them out of the house first, and then it's all right. They're out now," I added suggestively. Boston terts gave me an answering look, and we raced out on to the landing.

"Look here, Becky," he cried, as we landed with a thump, one after the other, at the bottom of the first flight of stairs; "we'll go down and rot[9] Jack, shall we? And I say, you are *great*, aren't you?"

I glowed with pride, and we accomplished the next flight with the same success.

"I tell you what's much better," I said, as we paused again, "and that's tobogganing down on a tea tray. You can only do it on the bottom flight, because it's straight, and it's rather dangerous, because there might be a caller. But still, it's *ripping*."

"You bet," was the eloquent response of Boston terts, as he went sailing off again. When we reached the ground floor, and sat on the bottom stair to recover our breath before going in to "rot" Jack, we felt that our friendship was a thing accomplished. Then I blurted out the question I had been wanting to put to him ever since we began to grow intimate, ten minutes ago, on the nursery landing.

"I say, do you like to be called Boston terts every time, or is Boston enough?" I asked him, anxiously.

"Terts is all right," he said. "Nobody says Boston; it's confusing when there are three of us, don't you see?" It was the first time I *had* seen why terts was tacked on to his name, but I did not say so, and watched him silently while he doubled himself up at what seemed to me a very acute angle, and fumbled away at his shoe lace, which was already tied twice over.

"My other name is Dick," he then emitted in an apoplectic voice. And, of course, I understood.

All the same, as I said before, I was not really happy once during the whole of that week. And although I was quite sorry when Boston terts drove away in a cab, I was cheered by the thought that Madge had also left an hour or two ago, and so Jack and I would be alone again for the last few days of the holidays. All the same, I rather dreaded his return from the station, and wondered whether he would feel as uncomfortable as I should when we met for the first time without the protection of our two friends. But I might have known he had completely forgotten our little quarrel, and I was vaguely disappointed when he came whistling into the nursery just as though nothing had happened.

"I suppose you'll find it awfully stale without Madge," I could not help saying.

"Oh no," said Jack, with the most provoking density. "You're there, aren't you?"

I fired up angrily. This was too much, considering the soreness of my heart at his neglect.

"If you think I'm going to amuse you when there's no one else, you're mistaken," I cried passionately. Jack stood and stared at me. I know he had literally no idea what I meant; and I have no doubt I merely appeared to him in the light of an extremely disagreeable person. And yet, it was not altogether my fault that I had a better memory than he.

"If you're going to be in a wax[1] for nothing," he remarked, "I'm sure I am not going to stay here."

And then I cried. I had not cried before Jack since I was about six, and I verily believe he had not thought me capable of tears. But I had been miserable about him

---

9. Abuse, denigrate.   1. A fit of anger.

for a whole week, and Boston terts had failed to satisfy me as Madge had satisfied him, and I could not help it. I thought his scorn would have been intense. But instead of that, he came and looked at me, and grew very red, and touched me on the cheek very gently.

"I say, Becky, don't," he said, and looked round to see if anyone was listening. "Of course, it's all my fault, no rotting;[2] only do dry up, there's a brick. I'll do anything you like if you'll only stop crying, and tell me what I've done. I never meant to do it, honour bright I didn't, and of course I'll never do it again. I say, Becky, buck up, dear old girl; there's no one half so fit as you anywhere, you know that don't you? Madge is all right in her way, but she's awfully tiring, and she funks[3] lots of things. I shouldn't care about seeing much of her, don't you know. There, you're all right now, aren't you, old chap?"

I was all right, as he said. And that moment quite made up for all my misery when I thought Jack did not care for me any more. And I think Jack, in spite of his good temper, and his density, and his bad memory, really understood me that afternoon.

Of course, we quarrelled again lots of times before school began. But that didn't matter.

1896–97

2. Joking.   3. Tries to shirk or evade.

ELEANOR ESTES
1906–1988

Twice in a decade, the New York Public Library children's librarian Eleanor Estes fell ill with tuberculosis and was forced to stop working in order to recuperate. While she rested her body in an attempt to regain her health, Estes was busy creating the memorable child characters that would animate her most famous books: Janey Moffat in *The Moffats* (1941) and Maddie from *The Hundred Dresses* (1944). After Harcourt Brace accepted *The Moffats* for publication, Estes decided to leave her position and become a full-time writer. Estes wrote eighteen books in all, most of them works of domestic fiction that celebrate the simple joys and sorrows of family life, including the well-loved Moffat series of four books and the self-illustrated *Ginger Pye* (1951). She set these books in Cranbury, Connecticut, a fictional locale based on her own hometown of West Haven, Connecticut.

After graduating from high school, Estes entered the New Haven Free Public Library training class and eventually became head of the children's department there. In 1931 she won a scholarship that enabled her to leave Connecticut to attend the Pratt Institute Library School in New York City. She met her future husband, Rice Estes, at Pratt, and they married in 1932. The Estes had one child, Helena, born in 1948 while they were living in California. Estes based Janey Moffat on herself; other of her fictional heroines, such as Helena in *A Little Oven* (1954) and Amy in *The Witch Family* (1960), drew on her daughter and their family experiences. In the later 1950s and the 1960s, the Esteses traveled frequently, spending most of their summers in Europe. In the summer of 1957, Eleanor and Rice went to England and met Edward Ardizzone (1900–1979), a famous war artist, author, and illustrator; he would eventually illustrate five of Estes's books. Estes died of a stroke in 1988.

The Hundred Dresses is one of the first American children's books to confront the problem of prejudice against immigrant or "different" children. Estes's novella, illustrated by the noted American sculptor and children's author Louis Slobodkin (1903–1975), details the development of a child's ethical consciousness. A poor, Polish immigrant girl, Wanda Petronski, who wears the same faded dress to school day after day, is ignored by her schoolmates. After she makes a boast that the popular children find ridiculous, Wanda is teased and consistently made a figure of fun. Maddie, whose family is also financially insecure, fails to stop her schoolfriends from ridiculing Wanda because she is afraid of becoming ostracized herself. Maddie's feelings of guilt for her cowardice, and the fantasies of atonement that she devises, supply the tension in this carefully crafted and powerful story.

In addition to winning the Newbery Medal for *Ginger Pye*, Estes received in 1961 the Certificate of Award for Outstanding Contribution to Children's Literature from the New York Association for Supervision of Curriculum Development and in 1970 was nominated, along with Rebecca Caudill, James Daugherty, and E. B. White, for the Laura Ingalls Wilder Award from the American Library Association. Writing for the Gale Literary Database, Virginia L. Wolf has praised her work for its "emphasis on the positive, her celebration of the child's spirit, her faith in the family, her fondness for daily events and details [and] her wonder over the miraculous tricks life plays." Estes herself once wrote, "I like to feel that I am holding up a mirror and I hope that what is reflected in it is a true image of childhood." Although the time of *The Hundred Dresses* may seem far distant to readers today, the emotions evoked in Estes's moving portrait of psychological distress suffered by both the ridiculed child and her tormentors surely continue to resonate.

The Hundred Dresses

1. WANDA

Today, Monday, Wanda Petronski was not in her seat. But nobody, not even Peggy and Madeline, the girls who started all the fun, noticed her absence.

Usually Wanda sat in the next to the last seat in the last row in Room 13. She sat in the corner of the room where the rough boys who did not make good marks on their report cards sat; the corner of the room where there was most scuffling of feet, most roars of laughter when anything funny was said, and most mud and dirt on the floor.

Wanda did not sit there because she was rough and noisy. On the contrary she was very quiet and rarely said anything at all. And nobody had ever heard her laugh out loud. Sometimes she twisted her mouth into a crooked sort of smile, but that was all.

Nobody knew exactly why Wanda sat in that seat unless it was because she came all the way from Boggins Heights, and her feet were usually caked with dry mud that she picked up coming down the country roads. Maybe the teacher liked to keep all the children who were apt to come in with dirty shoes in one corner of the room. But no one really thought much about Wanda Petronski once she was in the classroom. The time they thought about her was outside of school hours, at noontime when they were coming back to school, or in the morning early before school began, when groups of two or three or even more would be talking and laughing on their way to the school yard.

Then sometimes they waited for Wanda—to have fun with her.

The next day, Tuesday, Wanda was not in school either. And nobody noticed her absence again, except the teacher and probably big Bill Byron, who sat in the seat behind Wanda's and who could now put his long legs around her empty desk, one on each side, and sit there like a frog, to the great entertainment of all in his corner of the room.

But on Wednesday, Peggy and Maddie, who sat in the front row along with other children who got good marks and didn't track in a whole lot of mud, did notice that Wanda wasn't there. Peggy was the most popular girl in school. She was pretty; she had many pretty clothes and her auburn hair was curly. Maddie was her closest friend.

The reason Peggy and Maddie noticed Wanda's absence was because Wanda had made them late to school. They had waited and waited for Wanda—to have some fun with her—and she just hadn't come. They kept thinking she'd come any minute. They saw Jack Beggles running to school, his necktie askew and his cap at a precarious tilt. They knew it must be late, for he always managed to slide into his chair exactly when the bell rang as though he were making a touchdown. Still they waited one minute more and one minute more, hoping she'd come. But finally they had to race off without seeing her.

The two girls reached their classroom after the doors had been closed. The children were reciting in unison the Gettysburg Address,[1] for that was the way Miss Mason always began the session. Peggy and Maddie slipped into their seats just as the class was saying the last lines . . . "that these dead shall not have died in vain; that the nation shall, under God, have a new birth of freedom, and that government of the people, by the people, for the people, shall not perish from the earth."

2. THE DRESSES GAME

After Peggy and Maddie stopped feeling like intruders in a class that had already begun, they looked across the room and noticed that Wanda was not in her seat. Furthermore her desk was dusty and looked as though she hadn't been there yesterday either. Come to think of it, they hadn't seen her yesterday. They had waited for her a little while but had forgotten about her when they reached school.

They often waited for Wanda Petronski—to have fun with her.

Wanda lived way up on Boggins Heights, and Boggins Heights was no place to live. It was a good place to go and pick wild flowers in the summer, but you always held your breath till you got safely past old man Svenson's yellow house. People in the town said old man Svenson was no good. He didn't work and, worse still, his house and yard were disgracefully dirty, with rusty tin cans strewn about and even an old straw hat. He lived alone with his dog and his cat. No wonder, said the people of the town. Who would live with him? And many stories circulated about him and the stories were the kind that made people scurry past his house even in broad daylight and hope not to meet him.

Beyond Svenson's there were a few small scattered frame houses, and in one of these Wanda Petronski lived with her father and her brother Jake.

Wanda Petronski. Most of the children in Room 13 didn't have names like that. They had names easy to say, like Thomas, Smith, or Allen. There was one boy named Bounce, Willie Bounce, and people thought that was funny but not funny in the same way that Petronski was.

Wanda didn't have any friends. She came to school alone and went home alone. She always wore a faded blue dress that didn't hang right. It was clean, but it looked as though it had never been ironed properly. She didn't have any friends, but a lot of girls talked to her. They waited for her under the maple trees on the corner of

1. Delivered by Abraham Lincoln on November 19, 1863, at the dedication of the national cemetery at Gettysburg battlefield.

Oliver Street. Or they surrounded her in the school yard as she stood watching some little girls play hopscotch on the worn hard ground.

"Wanda," Peggy would say in a most courteous manner, as though she were talking to Miss Mason or to the principal perhaps. "Wanda," she'd say, giving one of her friends a nudge, "tell us. How many dresses did you say you had hanging up in your closet?"

"A hundred," said Wanda.

"A hundred!" exclaimed all the girls incredulously, and the little girls would stop playing hopscotch and listen.

"Yeah, a hundred, all lined up," said Wanda. Then her thin lips drew together in silence.

"What are they like? All silk, I bet," said Peggy.

"Yeah, all silk, all colors."

"Velvet too?"

"Yeah, velvet too. A hundred dresses," repeated Wanda stolidly. "All lined up in my closet."

Then they'd let her go. And then before she'd gone very far, they couldn't help bursting into shrieks and peals of laughter.

A hundred dresses! Obviously the only dress Wanda had was the blue one she wore every day. So what did she say she had a hundred for? What a story! And the girls laughed derisively, while Wanda moved over to the sunny place by the ivy-covered brick wall of the school building where she usually stood and waited for the bell to ring.

But if the girls had met her at the corner of Oliver Street, they'd carry her along with them for a way, stopping every few feet for more incredulous questions. And it wasn't always dresses they talked about. Sometimes it was hats, or coats, or even shoes.

"How many shoes did you say you had?"

"Sixty."

"Sixty! Sixty pairs or sixty shoes?"

"Sixty pairs. All lined up in my closet."

"Yesterday you said fifty."

"Now I got sixty."

Cries of exaggerated politeness greeted this.

"All alike?" said the girls.

"Oh, no. Every pair is different. All colors. All lined up." And Wanda would shift her eyes quickly from Peggy to a distant spot, as though she were looking far ahead, looking but not seeing anything.

Then the outer fringe of the crowd of girls would break away gradually, laughing, and little by little, in pairs, the group would disperse. Peggy, who had thought up this game, and Maddie, her inseparable friend, were always the last to leave. And finally Wanda would move up the street, her eyes dull and her mouth closed tight, hitching her left shoulder every now and then in the funny way she had, finishing the walk to school alone.

Peggy was not really cruel. She protected small children from bullies. And she cried for hours if she saw an animal mistreated. If anybody had said to her, "Don't you think that is a cruel way to treat Wanda?" she would have been very surprised. Cruel? What did the girl want to go and say she had a hundred dresses for? Anybody could tell that was a lie. Why did she want to lie? And she wasn't just an ordinary person, else why would she have a name like that? Anyway, they never made her cry.

As for Maddie, this business of asking Wanda every day how many dresses and how many hats and how many this and that she had was bothering her. Maddie was poor herself. She usually wore somebody's hand-me-down clothes. Thank goodness, she didn't live up on Boggins Heights or have a funny name. And her forehead didn't shine the way Wanda's round one did. What did she use on it? Sapolio?[2] That's what all the girls wanted to know.

Sometimes when Peggy was asking Wanda those questions in that mock polite voice, Maddie felt embarrassed and studied the marbles in the palm of her hand, rolling them around and saying nothing herself. Not that she felt sorry for Wanda exactly. She would never have paid any attention to Wanda if Peggy hadn't invented the dresses game. But suppose Peggy and all the others started in on her next! She wasn't as poor as Wanda perhaps, but she was poor. Of course she would have more sense than to say a hundred dresses. Still she would not like them to begin on her. Not at all! Oh, dear! She did wish Peggy would stop teasing Wanda Petronski.

3. A BRIGHT BLUE DAY

Somehow Maddie could not buckle down to work.

She sharpened her pencil, turning it around carefully in the little red sharpener, letting the shavings fall in a neat heap on a piece of scrap paper, and trying not to get any of the dust from the lead on her clean arithmetic paper.

A slight frown puckered her forehead. In the first place she didn't like being late to school. And in the second place she kept thinking about Wanda. Somehow Wanda's desk, though empty, seemed to be the only thing she saw when she looked over to that side of the room.

How had the hundred dresses game begun in the first place, she asked herself impatiently. It was hard to remember the time when they hadn't played that game with Wanda; hard to think all the way back from now, when the hundred dresses was like the daily dozen,[3] to then, when everything seemed much nicer. Oh, yes. She remembered. It had begun that day when Cecile first wore her new red dress. Suddenly the whole scene flashed swiftly and vividly before Maddie's eyes.

It was a bright blue day in September. No, it must have been October, because when she and Peggy were coming to school, arms around each other and singing, Peggy had said, "You know what? This must be the kind of day they mean when they say, 'October's bright blue weather.'"[4]

Maddie remembered that because afterwards it didn't seem like bright blue weather any more, although the weather had not changed in the slightest.

As they turned from shady Oliver Street into Maple, they both blinked. For now the morning sun shone straight in their eyes. Besides that, bright flashes of color came from a group of a half-dozen or more girls across the street. Their sweaters and jackets and dresses, blues and golds and reds, and one crimson one in particular, caught the sun's rays like bright pieces of glass.

A crisp, fresh wind was blowing, swishing their skirts and blowing their hair in their eyes. The girls were all exclaiming and shouting and each one was trying to talk louder than the others. Maddie and Peggy joined the group, and the laughing, and the talking.

2. Hand soap made by Enoch Morgan's Sons.
3. Physical exercises performed each day upon rising.
4. Title of (and repeated line in) a poem by the American writer Helen Hunt Jackson (1830–1885).

"Hi, Peg! Hi, Maddie!" they were greeted warmly. "Look at Cecile!"

What they were all exclaiming about was the dress that Cecile had on—a crimson dress with cap and socks to match. It was a bright new dress and very pretty. Everyone was admiring it and admiring Cecile. For long, slender Cecile was a toe-dancer[5] and wore fancier clothes than most of them. And she had her black satin bag with her precious white satin ballet slippers slung over her shoulders. Today was the day for her dancing lesson.

Maddie sat down on the granite curbstone to tie her shoelaces. She listened happily to what they were saying. They all seemed especially jolly today, probably because it was such a bright day. Everything sparkled. Way down at the end of the street the sun shimmered and turned to silver the blue water of the bay. Maddie picked up a piece of broken mirror and flashed a small circle of light edged with rainbow colors onto the houses, the trees, and the top of the telegraph pole.

And it was then that Wanda had come along with her brother Jake.

They didn't often come to school together. Jake had to get to school very early because he helped old Mr. Heany, the school janitor, with the furnace, or raking up the dry leaves, or other odd jobs before school opened. Today he must be late.

Even Wanda looked pretty in this sunshine, and her pale blue dress looked like a piece of the sky in summer; and that old gray toboggan cap[6] she wore—it must be something Jake had found—looked almost jaunty. Maddie watched them absent-mindedly as she flashed her piece of broken mirror here and there. And only absent-mindedly she noticed Wanda stop short when they reached the crowd of laughing and shouting girls.

"Come on," Maddie heard Jake say. "I gotta hurry. I gotta get the doors open and ring the bell."

"You go the rest of the way," said Wanda. "I want to stay here."

Jake shrugged and went on up Maple Street. Wanda slowly approached the group of girls. With each step forward, before she put her foot down she seemed to hesitate for a long, long time. She approached the group as a timid animal might, ready to run if anything alarmed it.

Even so, Wanda's mouth was twisted into the vaguest suggestion of a smile. She must feel happy too because everybody must feel happy on such a day.

As Wanda joined the outside fringe of girls, Maddie stood up too and went over close to Peggy to get a good look at Cecile's new dress herself. She forgot about Wanda, and more girls kept coming up, enlarging the group and all exclaiming about Cecile's new dress.

"Isn't it lovely!" said one.

"Yeah, I have a new blue dress, but it's not as pretty as that," said another.

"My mother just bought me a plaid, one of the Stuart plaids."

"I got a new dress for dancing school."

"I'm gonna make my mother get me one just like Cecile's."

Everyone was talking to everybody else. Nobody said anything to Wanda, but there she was, a part of the crowd. The girls closed in a tighter circle around Cecile, still talking all at once and admiring her, and Wanda was somehow enveloped in the group. Nobody talked to Wanda, but nobody even thought about her being there.

Maybe, thought Maddie, remembering what had happened next, maybe she figured all she'd have to do was say something and she'd really be one of the girls. And

---

5. I.e., a ballet dancer who stands on pointe. 6. A long woolen cap.

this would be an easy thing to do because all they were doing was talking about dresses.

Maddie was standing next to Peggy. Wanda was standing next to Peggy on the other side. All of a sudden, Wanda impulsively touched Peggy's arm and said something. Her light blue eyes were shining and she looked excited like the rest of the girls.

"What?" asked Peggy. For Wanda had spoken very softly.

Wanda hesitated a moment and then she repeated her words firmly.

"I got a hundred dresses home."

"That's what I thought you said. A hundred dresses. A hundred!" Peggy's voice raised itself higher and higher.

"Hey, kids!" she yelled. "This girl's got a hundred dresses."

Silence greeted this, and the crowd which had centered around Cecile and her new finery now centered curiously around Wanda and Peggy. The girls eyed Wanda, first incredulously, then suspiciously.

"A hundred dresses?" they said. "Nobody could have a hundred dresses."

"I have though."

"Wanda has a hundred dresses."

"Where are they then?"

"In my closet."

"Oh, you don't wear them to school."

"No. For parties."

"Oh, you mean you don't have any everyday dresses."

"Yes, I have all kinds of dresses."

"Why don't you wear them to school?"

For a moment Wanda was silent to this. Her lips drew together. Then she repeated stolidly as though it were a lesson learned in school, "A hundred of them. All lined up in my closet."

"Oh, I see," said Peggy, talking like a grown-up person. "The child has a hundred dresses, but she wouldn't wear them to school. Perhaps she's worried of getting ink or chalk on them."

With this everybody fell to laughing and talking at once. Wanda looked stolidly at them, pursing her lips together, wrinkling her forehead up so that the gray toboggan slipped way down on her brow. Suddenly from down the street the school gong rang its first warning.

"Oh, come on, hurry," said Maddie, relieved. "We'll be late."

"Good-by, Wanda," said Peggy. "Your hundred dresses sound bee-you-tiful."

More shouts of laughter greeted this, and off the girls ran, laughing and talking and forgetting Wanda and her hundred dresses. Forgetting until tomorrow and the next day and the next, when Peggy, seeing her coming to school, would remember and ask her about the hundred dresses. For now Peggy seemed to think a day was lost if she had not had some fun with Wanda, winning the approving laughter of the girls.

Yes, that was the way it had all begun, the game of the hundred dresses. It all happened so suddenly and unexpectedly, with everybody falling right in, that even if you felt uncomfortable as Maddie had there wasn't anything you could do about it. Maddie wagged her head up and down. Yes, she repeated to herself, that was the way it began, that day, that bright blue day.

And she wrapped up her shavings and went to the front of the room to empty them in the teacher's basket.

4. THE CONTEST

Now today, even though she and Peggy had been late to school, Maddie was glad she had not had to make fun of Wanda. She worked her arithmetic problems absent-mindedly. Eight times eight . . . let's see . . . nothing she could do about making fun of Wanda. She wished she had the nerve to write Peggy a note, because she knew she'd never have the courage to speak right out to Peggy, to say, "Hey, Peg, let's stop asking Wanda how many dresses she has."

When she finished her arithmetic, she did start a note to Peggy. Suddenly she paused and shuddered. She pictured herself in the school yard, a new target for Peggy and the girls. Peggy might ask her where she got the dress she had on, and Maddie would have to say that it was one of Peggy's old ones that Maddie's mother had tried to disguise with new trimmings so that no one in Room 13 would recognize it.

If only Peggy would decide of her own accord to stop having fun with Wanda. Oh, well! Maddie ran her hand through her short blonde hair as though to push the uncomfortable thoughts away. What difference did it make? Slowly Maddie tore the note she had started into bits. She was Peggy's best friend, and Peggy was the best-liked girl in the whole room. Peggy could not possibly do anything that was really wrong, she thought.

As for Wanda, she was just some girl who lived up on Boggins Heights and stood alone in the school yard. Nobody in the room thought about Wanda at all except when it was her turn to stand up for oral reading. Then they all hoped she would hurry up and finish and sit down, because it took her forever to read a paragraph. Sometimes she stood up and just looked at her book and couldn't, or wouldn't, read at all. The teacher tried to help her, but she'd just stand there until the teacher told her to sit down. Was she dumb or what? Maybe she was just timid. The only time she talked was in the school yard about her hundred dresses. Maddie remembered her telling about one of her dresses, a pale blue one with cerise-colored[7] trimmings. And she remembered another that was brilliant jungle green with a red sash. "You'd look like a Christmas tree in that," the girls had said in pretended admiration.

Thinking about Wanda and her hundred dresses all lined up in the closet, Maddie began to wonder who was going to win the drawing and color contest. For girls, this contest consisted of designing dresses, and for boys, of designing motor boats. Probably Peggy would win the girls' medal. Peggy drew better than anyone else in the room. At least that's what everybody thought. You should see the way she could copy a picture in a magazine or some film star's head. You could almost tell who it was. Oh, Maddie did hope Peggy would win. Hope so? She was sure Peggy would win. Well, tomorrow the teacher was going to announce the winners. Then they'd know.

Thoughts of Wanda sank further and further from Maddie's mind, and by the time the history lesson began she had forgotten all about her.

5. THE HUNDRED DRESSES

The next day it was drizzling. Maddie and Peggy hurried to school under Peggy's umbrella. Naturally on a day like this they didn't wait for Wanda Petronski on the corner of Oliver Street, the street that far, far away, under the railroad tracks and up the hill, led to Boggins Heights. Anyway they weren't taking chances on being late today, because today was important.

---

7. Cherry red.

"Do you think Miss Mason will surely announce the winners today?" asked Peggy.

"Oh, I hope so, the minute we get in," said Maddie, and added, "Of course you'll win, Peg."

"Hope so," said Peggy eagerly.

The minute they entered the classroom they stopped short and gasped. There were drawings all over the room, on every ledge and window sill, tacked to the tops of the blackboards, spread over the bird charts, dazzling colors and brilliant lavish designs, all drawn on great sheets of wrapping paper.

There must have been a hundred of them all lined up!

These must be the drawings for the contest. They were! Everybody stopped and whistled or murmured admiringly.

As soon as the class had assembled Miss Mason announced the winners. Jack Beggles had won for the boys, she said, and his design of an outboard motor boat was on exhibition in Room 12, along with the sketches by all the other boys.

"As for the girls," she said, "although just one or two sketches were submitted by most, one girl—and Room 13 should be very proud of her—this one girl actually drew one hundred designs—all different and all beautiful. In the opinion of the judges, any one of her drawings is worthy of winning the prize. I am happy to say that Wanda Petronski is the winner of the girls' medal. Unfortunately Wanda has been absent from school for some days and is not here to receive the applause that is due her. Let us hope she will be back tomorrow. Now, class, you may file around the room quietly and look at her exquisite drawings."

The children burst into applause, and even the boys were glad to have a chance to stamp on the floor, put their fingers in their mouths and whistle, though they were not interested in dresses. Maddie and Peggy were among the first to reach the black-board to look at the drawings.

"Look, Peg," whispered Maddie, "there's that blue one she told us about. Isn't it beautiful?"

"Yeah," said Peggy, "and here's that green one. Boy, and I thought I could draw!"

While the class was circling the room, the monitor from the principal's office brought Miss Mason a note. Miss Mason read it several times and studied it thought-fully for a while. Then she clapped her hands and said, "Attention, class. Everyone back to his seat."

When the shuffling of feet had stopped and the room was still and quiet, Miss Mason said, "I have a letter from Wanda's father that I want to read to you."

Miss Mason stood there a moment and the silence in the room grew tense and expectant. The teacher adjusted her glasses slowly and deliberately. Her manner indicated that what was coming—this letter from Wanda's father—was a matter of great importance. Everybody listened closely as Miss Mason read the brief note:

> "Dear teacher: My Wanda will not come to your school any more. Jake also. Now we move away to big city. No more holler Polack. No more ask why funny name. Plenty of funny names in the big city. Yours truly,
>
> Jan Petronski."

A deep silence met the reading of this letter. Miss Mason took her glasses off, blew on them and wiped them on her soft white handkerchief. Then she put them on again and looked at the class. When she spoke her voice was very low.

"I am sure none of my boys and girls in Room 13 would purposely and deliberately hurt anyone's feelings because his name happened to be a long unfamiliar one. I prefer to think that what was said was said in thoughtlessness. I know that all of you feel the way I do, that this is a very unfortunate thing to have happen. Unfortunate and sad, both. And I want you all to think about it."

The first period was a study period. Maddie tried to prepare her lessons, but she could not put her mind on her work. She had a very sick feeling in the bottom of her stomach. True, she had not enjoyed listening to Peggy ask Wanda how many dresses she had in her closet, but she had said nothing. She had stood by silently, and that was just as bad as what Peggy had done. Worse. She was a coward. At least Peggy hadn't considered they were being mean, but she, Maddie, had thought they were doing wrong. She had thought, supposing she was the one being made fun of. She could put herself in Wanda's shoes. But she had done just as much as Peggy to make life miserable for Wanda by simply standing by and saying nothing. She had helped to make someone so unhappy that she had had to move away from town.

Goodness! Wasn't there anything she could do? If only she could tell Wanda she hadn't meant to hurt her feelings. She turned around and stole a glance at Peggy, but Peggy did not look up. She seemed to be studying hard.

Well, whether Peggy felt badly or not, she, Maddie, had to do something. She had to find Wanda Petronski. Maybe she had not yet moved away. Maybe Peggy would climb the Heights with her and they would tell Wanda she had won the contest. And that they thought she was smart and the hundred dresses were beautiful.

When school was dismissed in the afternoon, Peggy said with pretended casualness, "Hey, let's go and see if that kid has left town or not."

So Peggy had had the same idea as Maddie had had! Maddie glowed. Peggy was really all right, just as she always thought. Peg was really all right. She was o.k.

6. Up on Boggins Heights

The two girls hurried out of the building, up the street toward Boggins Heights, the part of town that wore such a forbidding air on this kind of a November afternoon, drizzly, damp, and dismal.

"Well, at least," said Peggy gruffly, "I never did call her a foreigner or make fun of her name. I never thought she had the sense to know we were making fun of her anyway. I thought she was too dumb. And gee, look how she can draw! And I thought I could draw."

Maddie could say nothing. All she hoped was that they would find Wanda. Just so she'd be able to tell her they were sorry they had all picked on her. And just to say how wonderful the whole school thought she was, and please not to move away and everybody would be nice. She and Peggy would fight anybody who was not nice.

Maddie fell to imagining a story in which she and Peggy assailed any bully who might be going to pick on Wanda. "Petronski—Onski!" somebody would yell, and she and Peggy would pounce on the guilty one. For a time Maddie consoled herself with these thoughts, but they soon vanished and again she felt unhappy and wished everything could be nice the way it was before any of them had made fun of Wanda.

Br-r-r! How drab and cold and cheerless it was up here on the Heights! In the summer time the woods, the sumac, and the ferns that grew along the brook on the side of the road were lush and made this a beautiful walk on Sunday afternoons. But now it did not seem beautiful. The brook had shrunk to the merest trickle, and today's drizzle sharpened the outlines of the rusty tin cans, old shoes, and forlorn remnants of a big black umbrella in the bed of the brook.

The two girls hurried on. They hoped to get to the top of the hill before dark.

Otherwise they were not certain they could find Wanda's house. At last, puffing and panting, they rounded the top of the hill. The first house, that old rickety one, belonged to old man Svenson. Peggy and Maddie hurried past it almost on tiptoe. Somebody said once that old man Svenson had shot a man. Others said "Nonsense! He's an old good-for-nothing. Wouldn't hurt a flea."

But, false or true, the girls breathed more freely as they rounded the corner. It was too cold and drizzly for old man Svenson to be in his customary chair tilted against the house, chewing and spitting tobacco juice. Even his dog was nowhere in sight and had not barked at the girls from wherever he might be.

"I think that's where the Petronskis live," said Maddie, pointing to a little white house with lots of chicken coops at the side of it. Wisps of old grass stuck up here and there along the pathway like thin wet kittens. The house and its sparse little yard looked shabby but clean. It reminded Maddie of Wanda's one dress, her faded blue cotton dress, shabby but clean.

There was not a sign of life about the house except for a yellow cat, half grown, crouching on the one small step close to the front door. It leapt timidly with a small cry half way up a tree when the girls came into the yard. Peggy knocked firmly on the door, but there was no answer. She and Maddie went around to the back yard and knocked there. Still there was no answer.

"Wanda!" called Peggy. They listened sharply, but only a deep silence pressed against their eardrums. There was no doubt about it. The Petronskis were gone.

"Maybe they just went away for a little while and haven't really left with their furniture yet," suggested Maddie hopefully. Maddie was beginning to wonder how she could bear the hard fact that Wanda had actually gone and that she might never be able to make amends.

"Well," said Peggy, "let's see if the door is open."

They cautiously turned the knob of the front door. It opened easily, for it was a light thing and looked as though it furnished but frail protection against the cold winds that blew up here in the winter time. The little square room that the door opened into was empty. There was absolutely nothing left in it, and in the corner a closet with its door wide open was empty too. Maddie wondered what it had held before the Petronskis moved out. And she thought of Wanda saying, "Sure, a hundred dresses . . . all lined up in the closet."

Well, anyway, real and imaginary dresses alike were gone. The Petronskis were gone. And now how could she and Peggy tell Wanda anything? Maybe the teacher knew where she had moved to. Maybe old man Svenson knew. They might knock on his door and ask on the way down. Or the post office might know. If they wrote a letter, Wanda might get it because the post office might forward it. Feeling very downcast and discouraged, the girls closed the door and started for home. Coming down the road, way, way off in the distance, through the drizzle they could see the water of the bay, gray and cold.

"Do you suppose that was their cat and they forgot her?" asked Peggy. But the cat wasn't anywhere around now, and as the girls turned the bend they saw her crouching under the dilapidated wooden chair in front of old man Svenson's house. So perhaps the cat belonged to him. They lost their courage about knocking on his door and asking when the Petronskis had left and anyway, goodness! here was old man Svenson himself coming up the road. Everything about Svenson was yellow; his house, his cat, his trousers, his drooping mustache and tangled hair, his hound loping behind him, and the long streams of tobacco juice he expertly shot from between his scattered yellow teeth. The two girls drew over to the side of the path as they hurried by. When they were a good way past, they stopped.

"Hey, Mr. Svenson!" yelled Peggy. "When did the Petronskis move?"

Old man Svenson turned around, but said nothing. Finally he did answer, but his words were unintelligible, and the two girls turned and ran down the hill as fast as they could. Old man Svenson looked after them for a moment and then went on up the hill, muttering to himself and scratching his head.

When they were back down on Oliver Street again, the girls stopped running. They still felt disconsolate, and Maddie wondered if she were going to be unhappy about Wanda and the hundred dresses forever. Nothing would ever seem good to her again, because just when she was about to enjoy something—like going for a hike with Peggy to look for bayberries or sliding down Barley Hill—she'd bump right smack into the thought that she had made Wanda Petronski move away.

"Well, anyway," said Peggy, "she's gone now, so what can we do? Besides, when I was asking her about all of her dresses she probably was getting good ideas for her drawings. She might not even have won the contest otherwise."

Maddie carefully turned this idea over in her head, for if there were anything in it she would not have to feel so bad. But that night she could not get to sleep. She thought about Wanda and her faded blue dress and the little house she had lived in; and old man Svenson living a few steps away. And she thought of the glowing picture those hundred dresses made—all lined up in the classroom.

At last Maddie sat up in bed and pressed her forehead tight in her hands and really thought. This was the hardest thinking she had ever done. After a long, long time she reached an important conclusion.

She was never going to stand by and say nothing again.

If she ever heard anybody picking on someone because they were funny looking or because they had strange names, she'd speak up. Even if it meant losing Peggy's friendship. She had no way of making things right with Wanda, but from now on she would never make anybody else so unhappy again. Finally, all tired out, Maddie fell asleep.

7. THE LETTER TO ROOM 13

On Saturday Maddie spent the afternoon with Peggy. They were writing a letter to Wanda Petronski.

It was just a friendly letter telling about the contest and telling Wanda she had won. They told her how pretty her drawings were, and that now they were studying about Winfield Scott[8] in school. And they asked her if she liked where she was living now and if she liked her new teacher. They had meant to say they were sorry, but it ended up with their just writing a friendly letter, the kind they would have written to any good friend, and they signed it with lots of X's for love.

They mailed the letter to Boggins Heights, writing "Please Forward" on the envelope. The teacher had not known where Wanda had moved to, so their only hope was that the post office knew. The minute they dropped the letter in the mail box they both felt happier and more carefree.

8. American army officer (1786–1866) who was acclaimed as a hero of the War of 1812; he was named general-in-chief of the U.S. Army in 1847 and commanded U.S. forces in Mexico in the Mexican War (1846–48).

Days passed and there was no answer, but the letter did not come back so maybe Wanda had received it. Perhaps she was so hurt and angry she was not going to answer. You could not blame her. And Maddie remembered the way she hitched her left shoulder up as she walked off to school alone, and how the girls always said, "Why does her dress always hang funny like that, and why does she wear those queer, high, laced shoes?"

They knew she didn't have any mother, but they hadn't thought about it. They hadn't thought she had to do her own washing and ironing. She only had one dress and she must have had to wash and iron it overnight. Maybe sometimes it wasn't dry when it was time to put it on in the morning. But it was always clean.

Several weeks went by and still Wanda did not answer. Peggy had begun to forget the whole business, and Maddie put herself to sleep at night making speeches about Wanda, defending her from great crowds of girls who were trying to tease her with, "How many dresses have you got?" Before Wanda could press her lips together in a tight line the way she did before answering, Maddie would cry out, "Stop! This girl is just a girl just like you are . . ." And then everybody would feel ashamed the way she used to feel. Sometimes she rescued Wanda from a sinking ship or the hoofs of a runaway horse. "Oh, that's all right," she'd say when Wanda thanked her with dull pained eyes.

Now it was Christmas time and there was snow on the ground. Christmas bells and a small tree decorated the classroom. And on one narrow blackboard Jack Beggles had drawn a jolly fat Santa Claus in red and white chalk. On the last day of school before the holidays, the children in Peggy's and Maddie's class had a Christmas party. The teacher's desk was rolled back and a piano rolled in. First the children had acted the story of Tiny Tim.[9] Then they had sung songs and Cecile had done some dances in different costumes. The dance called the "Passing of Autumn" in which she whirled and spun like a red and golden autumn leaf was the favorite.

After the party the teacher said she had a surprise, and she showed the class a letter she had received that morning.

"Guess who this is from," she said. "You remember Wanda Petronski? The bright little artist who won the drawing contest? Well, she has written me and I am glad to know where she lives because now I can send her medal. And I hope it gets there for Christmas. I want to read her letter to you."

The class sat up with a sudden interest, and listened intently to Miss Mason as she read the letter.

"Dear Miss Mason: How are you and Room 13? Please tell the girls they can keep those hundred dresses because in my new house I have a hundred new ones all lined up in my closet. I'd like that girl Peggy to have the drawing of the green dress with the red trimming and her friend Maddie to have the blue one. For Christmas. I miss that school and my new teacher does not equalize with you. Merry Christmas to you and everybody. Yours truly, Wanda Petronski."

The teacher passed the letter around the room for everybody to see. It was pretty, decorated with a picture of a Christmas tree lighted up in the night in a park surrounded by high buildings.

On the way home from school Maddie and Peggy held their drawings very carefully. They had stayed late to help straighten up after the play and it was getting dark. The houses looked warm and inviting with wreaths and holly and lighted trees in their windows. Outside the grocery store hundreds of Christmas trees were stacked, and

---

9. Crippled child in *A Christmas Carol* (1843) by Charles Dickens.

in the window candy peppermint canes and cornucopias of shiny bright transparent paper were strung. The air smelled like Christmas and bright lights everywhere reflected different colors on the snow.

"The colors are like the colors in Wanda's hundred dresses," said Maddie.

"Yes," said Peggy, holding her drawing out to look at it under the street lamp. "And boy! This shows she really liked us. It shows she got our letter and this is her way of saying that everything's all right. And that's that," she said with finality.

Peggy felt happy and relieved. It was Christmas and everything was fine.

"I hope so," said Maddie sadly. She felt sad because she knew she would never see the little tight-lipped Polish girl again and couldn't ever really make things right between them.

She went home and she pinned her drawing over a torn place in the pink-flowered wall-paper in the bedroom. The shabby room came alive from the brilliancy of the colors. Maddie sat down on the edge of her bed and looked at the drawing. She had stood by and said nothing, but Wanda had been nice to her anyway.

Tears blurred her eyes and she gazed for a long time at the picture. Then hastily she rubbed her eyes and studied it intently. The colors in the dress were so vivid she had scarcely noticed the face and head of the drawing. But it looked like her, Maddie! It really did. The same short blonde hair, blue eyes, and wide straight mouth. Why, it really looked like her own self! Wanda had really drawn this for her. Wanda had drawn her! In excitement she ran over to Peggy's.

"Peg!" she said. "Let me see your picture."

"What's the matter?" asked Peggy as they clattered up the stairs to her room, where Wanda's drawing was lying face down on the bed. Maddie carefully lifted it up.

"Look! She drew you. That's you!" she exclaimed. And the head and face of this picture did look like the auburn-haired Peggy.

"What did I say!" said Peggy. "She must have really liked us anyway."

"Yes, she must have," agreed Maddie, and she blinked away the tears that came every time she thought of Wanda standing alone in that sunny spot in the school yard close to the wall, looking stolidly over at the group of laughing girls after she had walked off, after she had said, "Sure, a hundred of them—all lined up . . ."

1944

AIDAN CHAMBERS
b. 1934

For Aidan Chambers, writing and adolescence have always been connected. He began to write at age fifteen because, he says, he "couldn't help it." And he explains his concentration on adolescence as an adult, "Because it is in adolescence that we face for the first time all the great questions of life and deal with them freshly. Because adolescence is about beginnings not ends."

Chambers jokes that his own earliest beginning— he was born two weeks before his due date—helped shape his character: "I have been a slow learner and early for appointments ever since." He grew up in northeastern England, where the dedication and inspiration of a secondary school English teacher helped him blossom intellectually; he went on to become a teacher of English himself in 1957.

Chambers spent most of the turbulent 1960s as an Anglican Franciscan monk, and he began to write plays and novels that portrayed characters and issues familiar and interesting to his working-class students. After he left the religious order in 1967, he was employed as a reviewer, public speaker on literature and education, instructor of teacher-training courses, journalist, and editor of a series of books for teens. Together with his wife Nancy, a former editor of *Children's Book News*, he started Thimble Press, dedicated to publishing a wide range of critical writing about children's literature. That same focus characterized the journal *Signal*, which Chambers and his wife founded in 1970; it ran until 2003.

Aidan Chambers was working full-time as a freelance writer and publisher when he published *Breaktime* (1979), his first novel for teens in his Dance Sequence—a loosely related series of realistic, suspenseful, and intricate novels about various manifestations of "ordinary courage" found in young adults. *Postcards from No Man's Land* (1999), the fifth novel in the sequence, has won awards around the world, including Britain's Carnegie Medal and the Michael Printz Award (given by the American Library Association for excellence in young adult literature). In 2002 Chambers's career was honored by the International Board of Books for the Young with the Hans Christian Andersen Award. Chambers is also an advocate of engaging young people in literary discourse, or "booktalk," as he calls this exchange; his *Tell Me: Children, Reading and Talk* (1993) has become a classic of literacy education.

Even preadolescents sometimes must face and deal with life's harsh realities. *The Present Takers* (1983) is based on actual events in the life of a friend's daughter who was being bullied at school. Chambers unflinchingly portrays the despair and alienation that result from being the target of a classmate's cruelty. The novel acknowledges the conditions that can create abusive children; it also offers a creative solution to the problem of harassment that eschews adult intervention, drawing instead on the power of children working together.

The Present Takers

1

LUCY BEWARE MELANIE PROSSER SHE IS OUT
TO GET YOU
Angus x x x

How do you know? And stop sending me notes.

I HERD x x x Angus

"Wait here," Melanie Prosser said at the school gate. "Then we won't miss her."

"In her daddy's posh car," Sally-Ann Simpson said. "Show-off pig."

"I'll put an armlock on her," Vicky Farrant said. "I'm amazing at armlocks."

"Not till we've got her behind the cycle shed," Melanie said. "Be all smarmy smiles till then."

From the corner of the school hall Angus Burns watched the three girls hanging about by the gate.

He knew they'd wait for her today, being her birthday. Just like Prosser to think of that. He also knew what he would like to do to Prosser: kick her fat teeth in.

Angus swept the hair out of his face and scanned the road, the school field, and then the drive right up into what he could see of the playground, looking for Clare Tonks. They'd be giving her a day off today while they had a go at Lucy. Poor old

Clare, all she ever got was days off when they were bored with her, and were giving themselves a change by tormenting somebody else.

Angus spotted Clare at last. He could hardly miss her if she was in sight, she was so big in every direction. Tonks the tank. She was standing inside the cycle shed just out of view of the gate, and watching Angus.

"A new pencil case will do for me first time," Sally-Ann said. "My old one is grotty."[1]

"Could put a neat half nelson on her," Vicky said. "With a wrist-lever to screw on the agony."

"Save something for another day," Melanie said, as patient as a granny.

"Or put her down with a hip throw, do a step-over toe hold, and really make the silly witch scream."

Melanie yawned.

Sally-Ann giggled. "You and that wrestling. I reckon you're a bit loopy."

Lucy Hall came downstairs wearing her new blue birthday shoes. She could hear her father backing the car out of the garage.

"Is it such a good idea to wear those?" Sarah Hall said, meeting Lucy at the door to say good-bye.

"Stop fussing, Mum." Lucy gathered her things into her schoolbag.

"Don't complain if they get scuffed."

"They won't."

Jack Hall blew the car horn.

" 'Bye, Mum, see you this afternoon."

They kissed before Lucy ran to the waiting car.

Last five weeks, Sarah thought, then the holidays and after that she goes to the High. Seems only yesterday she started at Infants. Where does it go?

She waved as the car drove off.

"Morning, Mrs. Harris," Melanie said as the teacher hurried through the gate.

"Morning, girls," Mrs. Harris called, stopping to look. "What are you doing here? Can't you play in the yard?"

"Lucy's birthday, Miss," Melanie said, sweet as candy floss.

"Got a surprise for her," Sally-Ann said, simpering. She was good at simpering, because she thought she was right in every way to play Annie in the musical,[2] and had practiced a special simper so that she would be ready when the call came.

"I'd forgotten," Mrs. Harris said. "And, heavens, isn't she on hamster duty today? I'd better see to them myself. Have you a nice surprise?"

"Smashing," Vicky said flatly, her eyes on the road.

"How thoughtful of you." Mrs. Harris strode away up the drive.

"Old bat," Sally-Ann muttered.

"Shut it," Melanie said.

"Mrs. Harris," Angus said, stepping into the teacher's path.

"Hello, Angus. Early for a change."

"Lucy's birthday."

---

1. Shabby, dirty.
2. I.e., perform the lead in the musical *Annie* (by Charles Strouse, Martin Charnin, and Thomas Meehan; it opened on Broadway in 1977).

"So I gather." Mrs. Harris glanced back at the group by the gate. "She's popular all of a sudden."

"I thought—"

Mrs. Harris waited. "Come on then, dear. I haven't all day."

"—I thought you might meet her."

"Meet her?"

"Her birthday and that."

"At the gate, you mean?" Mrs. Harris laughed. "No, couldn't do that, Angus. I'd have to meet every one of you on your birthdays if I did. I'd never be done. Anyway, Melanie and Sally-Ann and, what's her name, Vicky Farrant are there with a surprise. We'll all sing 'Happy Birthday' after registration[3] as usual, so the occasion will be properly celebrated, won't it? She isn't royalty after all."

"It's just—"

"Yes?"

Angus blushed. Or, at least, what little of him Mrs. Harris could see blushed. His face was mostly hidden by his hair. Luxurious you might call it; long certainly.

Mrs. Harris laughed again, louder this time. "Well, I never! You of all people, Angus Burns! A dark horse, you are. You've good taste though, I'll give you that."

She stepped around him, about to go inside leaving Angus staked to the spot with embarrassment, but stopped.

"There is something you can do that would help Lucy, and me as well, if you want."

Angus brushed the hair out of his eyes and managed to look at the teacher. "Miss?"

"Feed the hamsters. Lucy's meant to—"

"But, Miss, I—"

"You'll see her later. And think how pleased she'll be."

Mrs. Harris took Angus by the shoulder and drew him with her into school. Angus looked back furiously at the group by the gate as he went inside.

Jack Hall stopped the car a safe distance from the gate.

"Friends of yours?" he asked, nodding in the direction of the three girls who had come out onto the pavement.

"Same class," Lucy said, busying herself unnecessarily with her bag.

"Pleased to see you from the way they're waving."

"Just being silly. 'Bye, Dad."

"Happy birthday again, sweetheart."

They leaned together and kissed, Lucy pulling away quickly and getting out.

"See you later," Jack said.

" 'Bye." Lucy slammed the car door and watched her father drive away. She would rather he were out of sight before she faced Melanie. Till that moment she had pretended to herself that it wouldn't happen. Not to her.

But Melanie and the others came pelting toward her.

"Hi, Lucy!" Melanie called, breathless with gush, grabbing Lucy's spare hand in what might have been a friendly grip if, looking on, you didn't know better. She gave Lucy an awkward hug.

Sally-Ann and Vicky frisked and stomped on either side.

"Sure," they said. "Happy birthday!"

---

3. Attendance.

"Ten today!" Melanie said, an announcement to the world.

"Eleven, if you have to," Lucy said, trying to pull her hand away.

"*Eleven!*" Melanie's eyebrows rose and her grip tightened. "Isn't that great, everybody! Lucy's *eleven* today!"

Sally-Ann giggled.

Other children, passing by, gave them a wide berth.

"All growed up," Vicky said.

"Give us your bag, then." Sally-Ann snatched it. "I'll carry it for you today. What an honor!"

Lucy swung her hand to snatch her bag back, but found instead that her arm was grabbed by Vicky and twisted up behind her.

"Let me go!" she shouted, trying to wriggle free. She had heard people shouting like that before as the same thing was done to them, but she had never interfered, as nobody did now.

"Run!" Melanie ordered, and she and Vicky towed Lucy along the pavement, through the gates, and took her stumbling up the drive, across the playground, all unhindered, and round behind the cycle shed, where they were out of sight of the school building.

All the way Melanie and Vicky, and Sally-Ann bringing up the rear with Lucy's bag hugged to her like something precious, laughed and whooped.

From the classroom where he was feeding the hamsters Angus heard their noisy progress. He threw the rest of the food into the cage and dodged across the room to the windows overlooking the playground. He was just in time to spot tail-end Sally-Ann disappearing behind the shed.

Some of the other kids were watching, but no one was following. Angus searched for Clare Tonks, at first could not find her, then saw her shadow looming at the back of the shed, leaning against the wall. Only the bricks, Angus thought, were separating her from what was happening on the other side. She could probably hear every word Prosser and her goons were saying. He'd ask her later.

Angus turned from the window. Mrs. Harris was paying no attention, busy with work at her desk.

"Can I go now, Miss?"

"All done?"

"Think so."

"The fish?"

"Yes, Miss," he lied. He'd see to them at break. They wouldn't die before. Lucy was more important.

"All right."

He sped away.

"We only want to *talk* to you," Melanie was saying.

Sally-Ann had thrown Lucy's bag at her feet. She and Vicky held Lucy's arms out, pinning them against the cycle shed wall. To avoid Melanie's eyes, Lucy stared across the field at the houses on the other side of the road.

"Want to hear all about the fabulous prezzies you got this morning," Sally-Ann said.

"Some fancy stuff, I bet," Vicky said, "your dad owning a shop and that."

Melanie nudged Lucy's bag with a foot. "What've you brought to show off?"

"Nothing!" Lucy's reply was a note too triumphant.

Melanie's face lost its grin. "Must have." She crouched and slowly unzipped the bag, watching Lucy's face all the time.

Lucy forced herself to keep quiet.

"Best make sure," Sally-Ann said. "Don't mind, do you, Luce?"

Melanie started rummaging.

Her temper fraying, Lucy could not help crying out, "Leave my things alone!"

"Shut up, Whining Winnie," Vicky Farrant said between clenched teeth, and gave Lucy's arm a sharp nip that made her catch her breath.

Running feet echoed round the shed. Angus burst into view, skidding to a stop at the corner. He glared at the little group frozen into statues by his arrival. But the hair closed over his face at once. Melanie stood up, glaring back. "Had an eyeful?" she said, hands on hips.

"Leave her alone," Angus said unimpressively.

"What's it to you, you hairy beanpole?" Sally-Ann said. She had a voice that sliced your ears when she wanted it to.

"Just leave her, that's all."

"He do fancy her," Vicky said, matter-of-fact.

"Oooo—d'you think so!" Sally-Ann hooted.

"No, I don't!" Angus said too quickly.

"Yes, you do," Melanie said, not even smiling. "Well, you needn't worry. We're only talking. No harm in *talking*, is there? So you can just bug off, Angus Burns, because what we're having with your *sweetheart*"—she paused, challenging him—"is a *private* conversation."

There was silence. Angus opened his mouth, then shut it. He looked sideways as if someone out of sight round the corner were talking to him.

"Have you got some of your stinky friends with you?" Sally-Ann shouted. "They don't scare us. You know what'll happen if we tell Mr. Hunt you boys have been bothering us girls."

Angus shifted on his feet, looking back and away. Finally he brushed the hair out of his face and said, "Just watch it, Prosser, that's all."

"I'd rather not watch your ugly mug at all, if you don't mind," Melanie said. "*Yuk!* Put your hair over it again!"

"I'm warning you," Angus said, straining against his anger.

"Don't forget old Hunt," Melanie said.

Angus hesitated; then, seething, slowly backed away round the shed corner.

As soon as he was gone, Melanie turned on Lucy. "Rotten friends you've got. No bottle."[4]

"Not half as rotten as yours," Lucy said, unable to restrain herself. "And Angus Burns isn't my friend."

"Not good enough for you, eh?" Vicky said.

Sally-Ann said, "Never mind all that. What about the prezzies?"

"Nothing much in her bag, just the usual stuff," Melanie said, her eyes not moving from Lucy's. She had unsettling eyes, like a cat's, gray, and they didn't blink much.

"I told you!" Lucy said.

"Funny what you notice though," Melanie said, "when you get down to earth."

"What she on about?" Vicky said to Sally-Ann.

Sally-Ann looked down, and hooted, "Ooooo, yes!"

---

4. No good.

"Eh?" Vicky said.

Melanie, her eyes still unblinkingly on Lucy's, pointed with a finger. "We'll have to teach Pukey Lukey some manners," she said. "No prezzies, but show-off new shoes."

"So she has!" Vicky said. Lucy felt the grip on her arm tighten.

"Happy birthday, Lukey," Melanie said, and, moving very close, pushed her lips, exaggeratedly wet and pursed, into Lucy's face. Lucy twisted her head to avoid the soggy kiss. Melanie's lips landed, squelching, on her ear.

Melanie stepped back. "All right, little Miss Stuckup, we'll just have to show you what happens to people who won't be friendly."

"It shouldn't be bad *this* time," Sally-Ann said, like a nurse comforting a patient before an operation.

"Ready," Melanie said.

Vicky and Sally-Ann each raised a foot above one of Lucy's.

"Stamp!" Melanie ordered.

The hovering feet pounded down onto Lucy's toes, screwed this way and that, and lifted off.

Lucy cried out, and instinctively tried to bend down to grasp her feet and comfort them. But Vicky and Sally-Ann pinned her against the wall; all she could do was squirm, and shift her feet about inside her shoes, trying to wriggle the hurt out of them. Tears filled her eyes. Through them, as she bent her head to hide her face, she saw the scuffed and dented surface of her birthday shoes.

She had been wanting them for weeks. Her father had made a special trip to Gloucester to buy them for her, and this morning, longing to wear them, she could not resist the temptation. Now the pain in her toes was nothing to the distress she felt for her ruined gift. She hated Melanie for that.

As soon as she recovered her breath and could see properly again, she glared her hatred at Melanie, who laughed, as if pleased by such passionate dislike.

"Come on, Pukey," Melanie said. "Tell us all about your other presents."

Lucy shook her head.

"You must have millions," Sally-Ann said. "Stuck-ups like you always do."

Lucy shook her head again, fighting herself to say nothing.

"Think you're something, you do," Vicky said. "Coming to school in that poncy car."

"Other people come in their parents' cars." She could not help herself. Why should they get away with saying such stupid things about her?

"I don't," Vicky said, twisting Lucy's arm a turn.

"And not in show-off big ones like your dad's," Sally-Ann said.

"He has a big car for his work. He has to carry a lot."

"Work!" Vicky sneered. "Call what he do *work*? Owning a shop."

"Doesn't own it. He manages it."

"Same difference. Up the workers."

"What do you know, Farrant!"

"Here," Vicky said, "don't get fresh with me." And she banged her forehead against Lucy's.

Lucy's eyes swam again.

Vicky observed the results with close interest. "Head butt," she said. "Might make it my speciality."

Sally-Ann said, "Vicky's going to be a wrestler, aren't you, Vick?"

"As if we didn't know!" Lucy said.

"She watches it every Saturday on telly and even goes and sees them live when they're at the Leisure Center, don't you, Vick? She's going to be the first woman champion of the world. Over the men as well as the women, of course. Aren't you, Vick?"

"As you've no prezzies with you," Melanie said, "you can invite us to your party tonight."

"Not having one," Lucy said, still battling her tears.

"Too mean," Vicky said.

"Having it in the holidays, if you must know." Lucy was furious at herself for letting them provoke her into telling them anything.

"Can't wait till the holidays," Melanie said. "You'd better bring me a present tomorrow to make up for it."

"Me as well," Sally-Ann said.

"And for Vicky," Melanie added.

"Something nice," Sally-Ann said. "Something lovely and new." She placed a fingertip on the end of Lucy's runny nose and began pressing slowly.

"Like a squashed tomato," she said.

"You won't forget, will you, Lukey, dear?" Melanie said. At that moment Mrs. Harris came striding round the corner.

"Now, girls, what are you doing here?" she called.

Melanie stood back; the others let go; Lucy wiped at her face with the back of a stiffening hand.

"Nothing, Mrs. Harris," Melanie said brightly. "Just a game. Lucy is a robot that's broken down and we're repairing her."

"Well, I'm sorry to spoil your fun, but you should be inside. You'll be late. Quickly."

Melanie snatched up Lucy's bag and ran off. Sally-Ann and Vicky grabbed Lucy's hands again and pulled her along with them. All friends together.

They let go as they entered the building and made for the cloakroom.

"Don't forget," Melanie said cheerfully, "see you tomorrow before school."

2

Mrs. Harris led the class in singing "Happy Birthday." Lucy pretended to be pleased but was really too upset to care. One or two of her friends gave her cards, but more diffidently than they might have done, knowing what had just happened outside. Samantha Ling gave her a little brooch made of something that looked like red fruit gum with yellow Chinese writing on it.

"Your name," Sam said. "Hope you like it."

"It's pretty. Thanks, Sam." Lucy looked round to see if Melanie had noticed, but luckily she and Vicky and Sally-Ann had their heads together round their corner table. Plotting, Lucy thought.

Samantha said quietly, "What were they doing to you?"

Lucy, looking closely at Sam's present to avoid her eyes, said, "Nothing."

"They weren't getting onto you, were they?"

Lucy shook her head, though she couldn't think why she lied. "I don't want to talk about it."

"If they were, you should go straight to Mr. Hunt."

Lucy kept quiet.

"You're not going to be friends, are you?"

"Course not."

"What was going on then?"

"Nothing."

Sam waited.

"Look," Lucy said, "I've told you. I don't want to talk about it, that's all." She turned away.

Samantha sniffed. "All right," she said, "be like that!" And she went off and made noisy conversation with Mary Gardiner, who, as usual, was busy organizing Mrs. Harris.

Halfway through the morning Angus came gangling over to Lucy.

"Borrow us a needle, Loo," he said, leaning his spiky elbows on her table and talking through his cascading hair.

"My name is Lucy, if you don't mind," Lucy said, not stopping her work.

"I've got some paper to stitch for that book we're making." He waited but got no reply. "I hate stitching."

Lucy said at last, "You should have brought your own needle."

Angus had a scrappy piece of paper held between his fingers. He dandled it between Lucy's eyes and her work.

"I had one," he said. "But I lost him."

"You would," Lucy said, pushing his dandling hand away with her pen. "Being stupid."

"Can't all be geniuses," Angus said, putting the piece of paper on the table and fiddling about with it. "Did the hamsters for you though, didn't I?"

"The hamsters!" Lucy said, hand over mouth. "I clean forgot."

"Birthday present," Angus said, pleased. "Sort of, anyway."

"Thanks," Lucy said, but not sounding grateful. "I'll do it when it's your turn."

"Borrow us a needle, then." He flipped the piece of paper onto the page where she was writing.

Anything to get rid of him. "Here," she said, fishing one out from her bag. "Now go away."

Angus took the needle and ambled back to his place.

"Dropped her a note, I think," Sally-Ann whispered to Melanie, who made no move to look.

"One throat chop, he'd be out like a light," Vicky said. "He's a weed."

"Is she reading it?" Melanie asked, working away.

Sally-Ann bobbed up from her seat, pretending to ease her skirt. "Letting it lie."

"He's not that bad, I expect," Melanie said. "Under all that hair."

Sally-Ann leaned closer. "Don't fancy him, do you, Mel?"

Melanie looked up from her math and winked.

Five minutes later Lucy could not help herself. She poked at the grubby scrap with her pen.

It had to be another of Angus's notes. She was half fed up, and half amused by them. He'd been giving her one every day for the last two weeks. The first she had discovered sticking out of one of her shoes when she got back from a games lesson. The second had been glued to the bottom of her pencil case with a piece of chewing gum. The third had been delivered to her home; written on the envelope in large red letters were the words: SECRET AND PRIVAT AND CONFIDENSHAL. There was no stamp, so he must have brought it himself, either very early, or late the night before.

But today's note—the tenth—was the only one he had almost handed to her. Must be getting brave, Lucy thought. Or desperate. And she had to admit that she was keen to know what this one said.

As casually as she could manage, she unfolded the scruffy page.

> TODAY 1700 RAILWAY CROSSING
> GOT PLAN TO STOP PROSSER
> xxx Angus

Lucy smiled for the first time since arriving at school. All Angus's notes were attempts to get her to meet him, but were never subtle. PLEASE MEET ME AFTER SCHOOL OUTSIDE GATE—that kind of message. One of them, the eighth, had begun U R THE GREATEST and was the first to finish with an x. Lucy thought them so funny she had kept them, safely tucked away in a small pocket inside her bag so that she could read them and cheer herself up when she was bored.

Twice she had taken him at his word, and met him. The first time to satisfy her curiosity; the second, after his note about her being the greatest, because she took pity on him. Both times she went home afterward wishing she hadn't bothered. Angus had done nothing but bumble about, paying her hardly any attention, and dragging her across muddy fields between school and Whiteshill. There he abandoned her outside his house with hardly a word. This was not Lucy's idea of a date.

Not that she had ever had a proper date. Melanie Prosser had, of course. Several, if what Sally-Ann said was true. All of them with much older boys from the High School, which all the other girls seemed to think was very daring. And judging by what Sally-Ann said happened, Lucy's meetings with Angus did not count as dates at all. They were just mucking about. Kids' stuff.

Lucy glanced across at Melanie's table and met Sally-Ann's eyes gazing back at her over the top of Melanie's bent head. Spying, as usual. Sally-Ann twinkled her fingers in a brazen wave.

Lucy looked away, and pushed Angus's note into her bag with the others.

What was all this 1700 nonsense and having a plan to stop Melanie? Was it just a dodge to get her to meet him again? And she wished he'd just forget about Prosser and what had happened this morning. She wished they all would; everybody would be talking about it. She hated the thought; the whole thing made her feel unclean. Small. A mutt. She couldn't find the right word.

And anyway, Prosser could eat Angus for breakfast and still feel hungry. Angus. Aberdeen Angus. A kind of cattle they make steaks out of. Angus Steak Houses. She had seen them in London. Her father would not take her to eat there because he said he wanted fish and somewhere quieter.

Aberdeen Angus. A rather stupid bull. Hardly a bull yet, though, more like a skinny calf. A long streak of steakless stupidity. She found herself smiling again. But he was good for a laugh, and that was something.

Though you only had to look at him and then straightaway look at Melanie (who was still bent over her work, chewing the ends of her hair as she often did when she was trying to concentrate) and you could tell that Melanie knew about a thousand times more than Angus about everything to do with the hardest parts of life. Like making other people do what you wanted, and how to be nasty without really trying.

They were both the same age and both in the same class, but Angus looked like a boy and mostly behaved like a boy, whereas Melanie—well, Melanie wasn't exactly a woman yet but you could tell she knew what it meant.

Not that she, Lucy, was any better than Angus. Beside Melanie she felt like a rake. She had hoped being eleven might make a difference. But of course it hadn't. And what Melanie had done this morning only made her feel more like a kid than ever. Some birthday present—being made to feel more childish just when you were wanting to feel grown up.

"What's this, Lucy?" Mrs. Harris said, coming up from behind. "You don't seem to have done much."

"Thinking about my project, Miss," Lucy said, pulling herself together.

"You look very glum for a birthday girl. Are you all right?"

Dragging energy from the pit of her stomach, Lucy managed a birthday-girl smile. Mrs. Harris gave her a studied look, but left her to get on.

At the end of afternoon school Mrs. Harris clapped her hands for silence.

"Mary tells me you want to hold a meeting," she said, "and I gather I'm not wanted. I don't know what this is all about but here's what I'm going to do. You're all on your honor to behave. Mary is in charge. I'll go off to the staff room for, let's see"—she consulted her wristwatch—"for about ten minutes. That should do. Then I'll come back and see you off home."

She went, closing the door firmly behind her. Mary Gardiner was already at the front, standing behind Mrs. Harris's desk.

"Some of us have been talking," she said. "These are our last few weeks in this school. Some of us thought we'd like to give a present to Mrs. Harris because she's been so terrific. We wondered if the rest of you would like to join in. Everybody would give money and we would buy something with it. What do you think?"

There was a brief pause while the suggestion sank in. Then, as usual, some of the boys jeered. After that people started chattering all at once, till Mary broke in and made them put their hands up if they wanted to say anything. After that the usual few did all the arguing.

Lucy said nothing. She sat at her table, chin in hands, half listening. She had heard enough about presents for one day.

Samantha came over and sat next to her.

"Don't know how she does it," Sam said. "Nobody would let me hold a meeting."

"Nor me," Lucy said. "Not that I want to."

"Nor me neither," Sam said. "Nobody else could do it," she went on, full of admiration at Mary's command. "There'd be a riot if anybody tried."

"Melanie could," Lucy said.

"Sure," Sam said. "Except she'd do all the talking and we'd have to sit and listen." She gave Lucy a sideways glance. "You certain you aren't being friends?"

Lucy couldn't even be bothered to reply. Sam, rebuffed again, moved back to her own place.

In a way, Lucy thought, Mary and Melanie were two of a kind. Only Melanie used whatever it was they both had to bully and squash people, so they did as she said and hated her for it, while everybody liked Mary (except Melanie and her hangers-on of course) and elected her class leader every time.

It was sickening, Lucy grumbled to herself as the discussion heated up around her, how Mary seemed to know exactly what to do and exactly how to do it, and was good-looking as well. If one person in the class could stop Melanie, it was Mary. But of course they both made sure to keep out of each other's way. Almost as if they had a secret agreement.

"Okay," Mary was saying, "I think we've decided that we'll give as much as we want. Anybody who doesn't want to doesn't have to. The present will be from the class, but we'll put in a special card that only those who have given some money will sign. Those in favor put up a hand."

Lucy held up hers because it was obvious you would have to.

"Against," Mary said.

Roland Oliver raised a hand, but he would, just as a joke, Roland having elected himself class comedian. Sally-Ann put hers up too, turned, grinning, expecting to see Melanie's in the air as well, was surprised that it wasn't, and rather sheepishly let her own drop again.

"Only Roland against," Mary said. "Great. There's one more thing. I don't mind collecting the money but I think someone else should buy the present. Any suggestions?"

Silence.

Then Melanie's voice: "Lucy Hall."

Lucy braced, startled out of her dumps. "No!" she called. "I don't want to. Why me?"

Melanie said, "Your dad owns a shop. You'd be good at picking presents."

"Hear, hear!" Gordon James shouted, mocking.

"Good idea," Mary said.

"But—" Lucy spluttered.

Before she could say anything more, Mary asked, "Who agrees?"

A forest of hands. Cheers from the usual boys.

Mrs. Harris came in. "Sounds like you've had a good time."

"Thanks, Mrs. Harris," Mary said. "We've just finished."

And that was that. They all scattered for home, leaving Lucy trying to gather herself together again.

"See you tomorrow, present picker," Melanie muttered into Lucy's ear as she brushed by on her way to the door.

Lucy wanted to scream.

3

Sarah Hall sat cross-legged on the living-room floor surrounded by a clutter of bills and invoices and checks and account books. Her fingers flicked over the keys of a pocket calculator lying at her side. The remains of her lunch—scraps of cheese, a bread crust, and an apple core turning brown—lay on a plate behind her.

Stopping in the doorway, Lucy thought: she'll have forgotten the plate is behind her and she'll either sit on it or knock it over. Why does she have to be so untidy? And why does she have to work with her stuff all over the floor?

Sarah glanced up quickly. "Hello, sweetheart. Wishing you'd had a party after all?" Her fingers didn't pause on the keys. Lucy always admired the speed her mother could tap the keys; when she tried it, the calculator went crazy and the answers were billions wrong. "We could still do something to celebrate if you want."

Lucy shook her head. "No. It'll be better in the holidays."

"Can't say I'm sorry," Sarah said. "The tax man threatens. Got to finish this before supper. Could you make yourself some tea today?"

Lucy nodded.

"Okay at school?"

"Average boring," Lucy said, turning away and crossing the passage into the kitchen.

"Never mind," her mother called, "soon be holidays. Then the High. You'll enjoy that."

Maybe. Weeks away. So who cared? Melanie Prosser was tomorrow.

Lucy had rushed home meaning to talk to her mother about what had happened. Usually she talked to her mother about everything. Sarah was that kind of mum. Which some were not, Lucy knew. A few of her friends came and talked to her mother quite often because they couldn't talk to their own.

But today, when she saw Sarah sitting in the middle of the floor poring over the shop accounts, Lucy felt for the first time that she did not want to talk to her about something important. Not only did she not want to, but could not. It was as if what she wanted to say was too private, even to tell her mother.

Important? Private? Standing in the kitchen surrounded by so many familiar things all higgledy-piggledy as usual, the whole thing seemed silly. Three girls teasing a fourth for a bit of fun. That's what the story would sound like, wouldn't it? Who would take it seriously?

For a few seconds Lucy wondered if the scene behind the cycle shed had really happened. Or at least had been as bad as she remembered. It couldn't have been, could it?

One glance at her wounded shoes and she knew.

But if she told her mother, she'd want to know all the stupid details, all the ridiculous chat. (Sarah was a great one for knowing what everybody said, and as a rule Lucy enjoyed telling her.) And certain sure she would be stomping-mad. She would want to do something drastic about Prosser. Dad would have to be told, and Lucy couldn't bear the thought of his hearing about it. She knew he would feel more hurt than she felt herself—he always was when anything unpleasant happened to her. And this he would say was not just unpleasant; it was sordid. Sordid was one of his biggest hate words. And hearing him say it would only make her mother even more agitated.

No, she wouldn't tell them. Interfering parents she could do without. Anyway, tomorrow might be different. Prosser might only have been trying to scare her today because it was her birthday.

Lucy realized with a start that she had been staring into the cluttered sink for five minutes without moving. She gave herself a glass of iced milk and five Tango biscuits[5]—her favorites but banned at teatime—as a reward and comfort for having survived horrible, rubbishy Prosser, and for keeping her mouth shut, instead of blurting everything all out straightaway to her mum.

On the third biscuit, it occurred to her that, if her mother saw the state of her shoes, keeping her mouth shut would end then and there. Sarah was also a first-rate interrogator. So she flipped the shoes off, stuffed them into her bag, and as coolly as possible made for her room upstairs, clutching her now bulging bag, her half-finished glass of milk and the two remaining biscuits.

With her room door safely shut, she transferred her shoes, after a close, regretful

5. Cookies.

examination of their scars, to a box where she kept old toys hidden at the back of her clothes cupboard.

Looking carefully at her shoes had brought vividly to mind every second of her ordeal behind the cycle shed. Instead of feeling relieved, she felt sick. Sick with Prosser's disease, otherwise known as The Nasties. So far not thought to be deadly. But there was always a first time.

It was as if even her clothes were contaminated. She pulled off her skirt, her blouse, her socks, threw them all into her laundry bag, and put on a favorite red sweater and knockabout jeans and sneakers.

This made her feel a little better; but not knowing what to do next—as if she were standing in a waiting room with nothing to do but wait—she sat on her bed and stared at herself in her mirror. Short hair curling round her head, framing a thin triangular face. A nose she always thought was stubby. Thin long neck. Square shoulders showing bonily through her jumper. Flat chest. Flat, flat chest. How could anybody like her? Even Angus, the steakless wonder?

Lucy stared herself defiantly in her green eyes. "I will not cry," she told herself.

Sarah Hall finished the accounts and sat back onto her plate of leftovers. "Blast!" she said, and cleared up.

Finding no Lucy in the kitchen, she went to the bottom of the stairs and called. A faint and delayed reply.

"Want to help with supper?"

No answer, but sounds of movement.

Lucy wasn't herself, Sarah decided. It wasn't like her to mope. There had been something wrong when she came in. But what?

Sarah went back to the kitchen and set about preparing food.

Lucy arrived looking pale, even perhaps a hint weepy.

"Clean some lettuce?" Sarah suggested.

Lucy stood at the sink, where Sarah had dumped a head of lettuce fresh from the garden, its milky juice still oozing from the stem.

Sarah peeled and chopped and mixed.

"No gossip?" she asked when they were well started.

Lucy shrugged. "They did the usual. Some of them gave me cards. Sam gave me a brooch with my name on in Chinese."

"Nice of her. Can I see?"

"It's upstairs." With surprise, Lucy realized she hadn't even bothered to look at it or the cards since she had been given them that morning. Prosser's disease really did things to you.

"Show us when Daddy gets in."

"Okay."

"What are you going to do with the five pounds Uncle Bob sent?"

"Don't know yet."

They worked for a while in silence but for the clack of the kitchen clock. Twenty to five. Sixteen forty!

"Angus Burns gave me another of his silly notes."

Sarah laughed, glad of something to lighten the conversation. "Probably his idea of a present."

"Wants to meet me at the crossing at five."

"How romantic."

"Mum!"

"Well, it is. Crossroads of life. Trains rushing by to exotic places like Swindon.[6] Two beautiful people keeping a secret tryst."

"Yuk!" Lucy was cheering up again. "I'm beautiful, naturally. But Angus Burns . . . !"

"You I'm not so sure about. Angus—I think he's gorgeous."

"You've only seen him once. When you picked me up from school the other day."

Sarah gave her daughter a glancing kiss on the brow as she went by to a cupboard. "Know-all. I've seen him more than that."

"When?"

"In the shop. Buys screws, gardening stuff, tools now and then. Quite the handyman. Can't be for him. For his dad I should think."

"You didn't tell me."

"Didn't think you wanted to know. Always grumbling about how boring he is."

"Well, he is. He's stupid and skinny and all floppy hair, which I'm sure isn't clean, and he's clumsy."

"You wait. In a year or two bumbling Angus will metamorphose into a knockout."

"You do talk rubbish, Mum. And he isn't getting better, he's getting worse. This year he's got really scruffy."

"Have it your own way."

"I don't see how you can tell. Mostly he's just hair and mud anyway."

"Let's say it's something you know when you're me that you still can't know when you're you." Sarah took away the lettuce and plonked a bowl of potatoes and a peeler in their place. "Exercise your fingers on those."

"Do I have to?"

"Do I have to?"

"Okay, okay, don't start! What's left for Dad?"

"Washing up the breakfast things, clearing out the waste bin—"

"All right!"

"—bringing in the laundry, plus he wants to mow the lawn because it hasn't been done for five weeks and there are probably elephants lost in it."

"You needn't go on, Mum—I'm sorry I asked."

"Want to help him?"

"No thanks." Lucy jabbed at a potato eye. "Is most of being grown up so boring?"

"Is boring today's word?"

"Forget it."

Ten minutes to five. Sixteen fifty. Could he really have a plan?

"I might as well go and meet Angus if that's okay. I might catch him at it."

"At what?"

"Meta-what-you-said."

"Metamorphosing."

"Could be fun."

"Is he less boring than the spuds?"

"Oh, Mum!"

"As it's your non-birthday birthday I'll finish them. But don't be long."

"Thanks. I won't. He never has much to say."

6. A town about 70 miles west of London; it gained prominence in the nineteenth century as a junction of the Great Western Railway.

"Hello, is that you?" Mrs. Prosser shouted from upstairs.

Melanie switched on the television and flopped onto the sofa. "No," she said, "it's the milkman."

Her mother's voice went on, "Your tea's in the kitchen." Then the noise of her clopping feet on the stairs and the smell of her scent coming before her like fog. "You'll be all right, won't you?"

Melanie glanced up. Her mother had tipped the contents of her everyday handbag onto the top of the drinks cabinet and was selecting the few things she wanted in her funbag.

"There's some of your favorite ice cream in the fridge and a new video I bought specially for you on the table." She stopped sorting and looked across the room at her daughter. "I did tell you, didn't I? I'm meeting your dad after work and we're off to a new club in Bristol. I did say, didn't I, I do remember saying something, and I'm running a bit late. You know how he goes on if I'm late."

Melanie turned back to the television. "Go on, shove off."

Cynthia Prosser grabbed up her funbag, glared at her daughter, said, "Ungrateful brat," and left, slamming the front door behind her, and over-revving the car.

As Lucy strolled up the lane to the railway crossing she saw Angus sitting on the top bar of the gate. A spaghetti-style gnome.

"Thought you weren't coming," he said. "Again."

"I'm only having a walk before supper, so don't excite yourself," Lucy said, stopping in front of him.

An old woman carrying a loaded shopping basket came plodding across the tracks and stood making faces. Lucy nodded towards her, Angus saw at last, and all but fell off the gate. The old woman edged through, eyeing them both suspiciously.

Lucy said, "Are you going to keep me here long? I'm not sure it's safe to be seen with you."

"We could walk along the line. There's some interesting stuff, birds and plants and that."

"I'd rather stay alive, if it's all the same to you."

Angus hitched his jeans and stared sideways across the railway.

Lucy could not at all see what her mother was talking about. No sign of any metamorphosing that she could see. He was a head taller than she, which meant he was tall for his age, and he was so slim his grubby blue T-shirt was slack on his body, though this could also be from losing its shape because of needing a good wash. As for his jeans, they might well have no legs inside them for all she could see, except for worn and bony points where his knees must be, one of which, the left, had a hole torn just above it.

Angus glanced at Lucy, aware that she was staring at him. With his right hand he flicked his hair from his face, a habit almost as irritating as his hair hanging there in the first place. But only with his hair pushed back could Lucy see that he had big brown eyes that gave her a shock, they were so unexpected. His hands, however, were long-fingered and filthy, and to hide her surprise she said, "Your dad a coalman?"

"No, why?"

"You look like you've been digging coal."

Angus inspected his hands as if he had never seen them before. "Been planting lettuce," he said, rubbing them down the sides of his jeans, where they had clearly been rubbed many times before. "For my rabbit," he went on. "He works at Daniels."[7]

"Your rabbit works at Daniels?"

Angus grinned. "No. My dad. He's a fitter. On the night shift." He examined his hands again, which on the whole looked worse than before. He stuffed them into his pockets. "Don't see him much. Weekends mostly. He's a bit grumpy sometimes when I get in from school. He's just got up, you see, and sorting himself out for work. He was like that this afternoon, so I put off asking him."

"About the lettuce?"

"About Prosser."

Wary of that name, Lucy said, "What about Prosser?"

"He'll know what to do."

"Angus Burns!" Lucy said, rearing. "Was that your plan? Is that why you dragged me out here to meet you?"

"I thought you were just having a walk."

"What if I don't want you asking your rotten dad about Prosser, or about anything to do with me?"

"He's not rotten and—"

"Maybe I'm going to ask my own dad. Maybe he knows more than your dad about anything you care to mention."

Furious, Lucy was about to stalk off when Angus said, as if reaching a difficult decision, "Yeah, he might."

Lucy swung back, hands on hips. "Who might what?"

"Your dad."

"Just be careful what you say about my dad, Angus Burns!" She wagged a finger at him. "You don't know anything about him. You haven't even met him."

"Yes, I have. In his shop. I often ask him about things I have to buy for my dad. My dad says your dad has the best shop in town for tools and gardening gear and stuff like that and knows about them—"

"Oh, shut up!" Lucy plonked herself down on the grass verge and leaned her back against the fence. The things parents didn't tell you! "I don't want to talk to anybody about Prosser, if you must know," she said. "So I think your plan is a real *futt.*"

The warning bell above the gate started clanging, preventing speech with its deafening harshness. The five nineteen to Gloucester went rattling by. When the bell stopped, the silence itself was a sound for a few seconds.

Melanie picked up the telephone and dialed.

"Hi," she said. "Guess what! Want to come over?"

She listened.

"A new viddy. You'd think she'd left the crown jewels. A rubbishy one as well. Bring one of yours."

More listening. She giggled.

"You aren't half rude!"

She listened again.

"Not till late. After your bedtime anyway."

She laughed.

"See you," she said, and put the receiver down.

7. A department store.

"Wasn't going to talk to my dad about *you*," Angus said, sitting an arm's length from Lucy. "If you'd only listen."

"I am listening. Get on with it."

"I wouldn't have said it was you. I'm not that stupid. And I didn't say that was my plan."

"So?"

Angus shuffled. "I was reading this book—"

Lucy chortled. "You—read a book!"

"Why not?"

"What sort of book?"

"A story sort of book, why?"

"You never read books."

"Yes, I do. All the time."

"I've never seen you."

"You're not there all the time."

"When then?"

"In the evenings mostly. After my dad's gone to work."

"Storybooks?"

Angus rounded on her. "I thought you wanted to know my plan."

Reading storybooks—Angus Burns? Lucy stared at him: another surprise. And which books? She was dying to know. But she said, "All right, get on with it."

"In this story," Angus began, and sounding, Lucy thought, as if he were going to tell her every word of it exactly as in the book, "three boys were getting on to another boy—"

"I'm not a boy."

"I know you aren't, but who cares?"

"I do. And I thought you did too, Angus Burns."

"I only meant—"

What Lucy could see of him went red. He turned away, bending his head to look at the ground between his knees, his hair falling like a curtain over his face.

Why don't I keep my big mouth shut, Lucy thought, but said brightly, as if nothing had happened, "Go on, then."

Angus hitched, brushed the curtain open, picked at the hole in his jeans. "The kid they were after kept running and hiding and everything." He paused while he watched a stray scallywag dog pottering by, sniffing at garbage on the other side of the lane.

"And?" Lucy said, nursing her patience. With Angus, she was realizing, you needed lots of patience.

"They kept after him. He kept imagining how he might get rid of them, and his friend wouldn't help, and his mother wouldn't listen, and his dad was away, and there was nobody he could turn to, so in the end—"

"At last!"

"—he decided he just had to stand up to them whatever they did to him, so he and the biggest of the bullies had a punch-up, and the kid got a busted nose, but he hurt the bully as well, and in the story it said how the bully didn't seem as big after that, and didn't bother the kid anymore."

Angus glanced at Lucy, waiting for her reaction.

"Yuk!" Lucy said.

Having reached the railway tracks, the litter-hunting dog turned back and came trotting down the lane, paying no attention to Lucy and Angus sitting against the fence.

Angus said, "I haven't told it very good, but the book's okay and funny as well. I'll borrow you it, if you want."

"No, thanks. Are you trying to tell me that your plan is for me to have a fight with Prosser?"

"I'm only suggesting."

"Then don't. Because what you're suggesting, Angus Burns, is that I get myself duffed up.[8] Prosser and Farrant and that creepy Simpson would mince me into little pieces. Look what they do to Clare Tonks."

"They wouldn't if she stood up to them."

"How can she? What could she do?"

"The kid in the story did."

"You and that silly story! It doesn't happen like that. Haven't you noticed? To start with, the big bully probably wouldn't have fought him on his own. The three of them would have got onto the kid all at once. Then where would he be?"

Angus said nothing, but kicked at the grass with a foot. Which, Lucy noticed, wore a running shoe caked in mud and split along the toes.

"He'd have been okay if his friend had helped."

"Nobody helps Clare, or any of the others Prosser goes after. None of my friends helped me."

Angus muttered, "I tried."

"You call that help! And who said you're my friend?"

"Clare Tonks was trying to help."

"Clare Tonks?"

"Yeah, she was standing by the wall and going, 'Don't, don't, you'll only make it worse for Lucy.' And I listened. But she was wrong."

Lucy sniffed. "She was right."

"No, she wasn't." Angus startled Lucy with his sudden anger. "I've been thinking." He stubbed at the grass so hard a tuft went skipping across the lane. "I should have kicked them to death."

Lucy could not help herself feeling pleased at his vehemence on her behalf. "It wouldn't have worked," she said quietly. "They'd only have got you in trouble with Mr. Hunt."

Angus pushed himself to his feet. "I hate Prosser," he said. "She's sick."

Above their heads, the warning bell started clanging again. The five forty-four from Gloucester to Swindon.

Lucy got up and brushed herself off while the train clattered by. Angus leaned on the gate, chin on hands, watching it pass.

In the after-silence Lucy said, "They probably won't bother me again."

"Yes, they will," Angus said, not turning round. "And next time I'll pile in."

"No, don't," Lucy said, feeling panic in her stomach. "You won't stop Prosser and everybody will laugh at you. At me as well."

Angus said nothing.

"Do you hear, Angus Burns?"

He turned at last and leaned back against the gate, his hands jammed into his pockets. "Yeah, I hear," he muttered, staring, as far as Lucy could tell, at his feet.

"I've got to go," she said.

The hair nodded.

8. Hit repeatedly, beaten up.

"Angus Burns," Lucy said, exasperated. "Do me a favor."

"Yeah, what," Angus said, too eagerly pushing the curtain out of his eyes.

"If we have to be friends, at least wash your hair and get it cut. It's *awful.*"

Angus, unthinking, put a hand to his head.

"That's right," Lucy said. "The stuff that grows on your noddle."

And she set off down the lane.

Melanie answered the door. She had changed into a pair of tight red jeans and a clingy white T-shirt with ZAP printed across the front in zappy black letters.

"Hi," she said. "Come in quick. There's a right old nosey next door."

"For someone who's boring, you talk a lot about him," Lucy's father said at supper.

"It's just that he's so weird," Lucy said.

"Doesn't seem a bit weird to me," Jack said.

"Nor to me," Sarah said.

Lucy ignored them. "And he's so scruffy. Why doesn't his mother do something about him?"

Sarah laughed. "Why doesn't his dad?"

"His dad works night shift all the time. Angus hardly sees him. Except at weekends. You'd do something about me if I got into the state he's in."

Jack helped himself to more salad. "You must like him or you wouldn't go on so much."

Lucy said, trying to laugh this off, "I do not, Dad. I'm just curious, that's all. Like a scientist who's found a new kind of gruesome maggot."

Sarah and Jack grinned at each other across the table.

As soon as his father had cycled off to work, Angus took the scissors from his mother's workbox and went up to the bathroom. He studied himself in the mirror from as many angles as he could manage. Then he started clipping.

"She sounds a right nurd."

Curling up on the sofa, Melanie said, "She is."

"Just asking for it."

"That lovey-dovey father and that know-all stuck-up mother."

"Vomit-making."

"I called her Pukey Lukey this morning. She could have killed me."

"She might try."

"With Farrant around! Farrant's as thick as frozen porridge but she has her uses." Melanie pulled a gormless[9] face and flexed her biceps like a body-builder.

"Hey, that's nice! Do it again."

"Fink!" Melanie said and kicked out.

They both laughed.

"We've got a terrific thing going."

"Tell us, then," Melanie said.

Not altogether sure about his evening's work, Angus checked the doors were locked, that the stove was safely off, found his book, turned off the television, and went to bed, forgetting, as usual, to wash.

9. Stupid-looking.

Lucy lay in the dark of her room. She could hear her parents two floors below and a background of music playing not quite loudly enough for her to pick out the tune.

She couldn't sleep. Melanie Prosser kept invading her thoughts. She broke out into a cold sweat each time.

Since coming to bed she had been trying to decide what to do. Hope Melanie wouldn't bother her again? Take some small presents and hope that would end it?

Or maybe Angus was right: Prosser wouldn't forget or give up. But what would Prosser do if she didn't take anything tomorrow? Hurt her a bit? Say vile things? Not much else. That was the trouble. Most kids gave in straightaway, just at the thought of what Prosser was supposed to do to you. All because of the stories that went around about her. But take nothing the first time, and more than likely Prosser would find someone else to pick on, wouldn't she?

It was worth a try.

Lucy squirmed onto her back, sighed, and tried to settle down again.

The front door slammed, shutting in arguing voices.

Melanie scrambled to her feet. "Cripes, they're back early!"

She tore round the room, tidying it and herself.

The sitting-room door flew open: Bill Prosser came with it.

"It was lousy!" he was shouting over his shoulder. But was stopped short. "What's all this?" he said, his tone changing to danger. "Who the devil are you?"

"A friend of Mel's."

"Mel's? You mean Melanie, don't you? And who said you could be here at this hour of night?" Bill Prosser glanced at the clock above the fireplace. "Quarter past eleven!"

"Oh, Dad," Melanie protested.

"Don't Oh, Dad, me, madam! And you—" Bill said, pointing, "—out!"

"We weren't doing anything," Melanie shouted.

"And you—" Bill pointed at his affronted daughter, "—bed. Now!"

Melanie stomped from the room, her friend careering ahead of her.

Cynthia Prosser appeared in the doorway. "What are you going on about now, you great lump."

"I hope you've seen to her, that's all," her husband said, marching around the room.

"Stop yelling," Cynthia said, opening the drinks cabinet and pouring herself a large tumbler full.

Melanie's bedroom door slammed, shaking the house.

"You'll have to talk to her," Bill Prosser said, slumping into his chair.

"Talk to her yourself." Cynthia Prosser poured a glass for her husband. "She might listen to you. She doesn't listen to me, that's for sure." She handed him the glass. "Here, swill this down and shut your face."

"And next time," Bill Prosser said, "find somewhere more exciting than that dead hole."

4

Next morning Lucy contrived to be late for school. Sarah was cross with her for not having her things ready. Jack grumbled that she was making him late for the shop. But one way and another she managed to delay leaving the house long enough to be sure that the bell would have gone by the time Jack dropped her off at the school gate. As they arrived, she saw with relief that the playground was deserted.

"Not like you to be late," Mrs. Harris said.

"Couldn't find my games things," Lucy said. "Sorry."

She carefully avoided glancing in Melanie's direction, but saw at once that Angus was not in his place. As she settled in her seat, Samantha smiled across at her, repairing yesterday's breach. Lucy smiled back vaguely. Not because she wanted to put Sam off, but because her thoughts, she found to her surprise, were on Angus. Why was he so late?

A few minutes later a note arrived in front of her. She thought for a second that Angus must be there after all and looked quickly round. Only to realize that the note couldn't be his; it was clean and too neatly folded. At once her eyes met Melanie's coolly looking back from her corner table.

Trying not to appear disturbed or much interested, Lucy unfolded the note.

10:30 PENS REST

She had to puzzle at it for a while before she understood what it meant. And then the day closed in, as though she had been shut into a box. Melanie was not going to give up.

Angus arrived at ten past ten. He was wearing his winter anorak with the fur-lined hood up and its drawstrings pulled tight round his face.

"So you've decided to grace us with your presence," Mrs. Harris said. "Late even by your standards."

Angus stood by the teacher's desk. There were titters from various parts of the room. Melanie Prosser coughed significantly.

Mrs. Harris went on, "It's not raining, is it?"

"No, Miss," Angus said.

Warily, knowing Angus of old, Mrs. Harris said, "Then why the anorak? And the hood? You'd think we were in January instead of June."

Angus did not reply, just gazed back. Expectant faces waited.

"Well," Mrs. Harris said, "take it off and get to work."

"I don't want to, Miss."

With heavy patience, Mrs. Harris said, "You don't want to take it off, or you don't want to start work?"

"Take it off, Miss."

"Why ever not?"

"I've got a note." Angus handed over a crumpled envelope.

Mrs. Harris took it gingerly, peered at it, smoothed it out, decided it wouldn't explode, sliced it open with her red pen, and took a page from inside. As Mrs. Harris read the letter, Lucy was sure she saw a smile flicker in the corners of the teacher's mouth. But when Mrs. Harris looked at Angus again, her mouth was as unsmiling as usual.

"Does Mr. Hunt know about this?"

Angus shook his hooded head.

"Never mind now." Mrs. Harris folded the letter again and put it into her handbag. "But he'll have to be told. I'll take you to him at playtime."

She surveyed the ear-flapping faces.

"Angus has had a slight accident," she announced in her no-nonsense voice. "You might as well hear about it now so we can get it over. Don't you agree, Angus?"

Angus looked as though Mrs. Harris were suggesting she pull out all his teeth with a pair of pliers and no anaesthetic.

"Just remember," Mrs. Harris said to them all, "about people who live in glass houses. Anyone—*anyone* can have an accident."

Roland Oliver chuckled. Mrs. Harris glared him into silence.

"Now, Angus," she said when she was sure everyone was subdued and ready, "off with that anorak."

Unwillingly, Angus untied the drawstrings, bent forward, and began tugging at the clinging garment. Once it was over his head so that he couldn't see, his hands got tangled in his sleeves. Lucy wanted to rush out and help him, but as it was, Mrs. Harris came to his rescue. She took hold of the anorak by the shoulders and with one strong pull emptied Angus out.

There was a moment's suspended pause before everyone, even Mrs. Harris, burst into squalls of laughter. Unprotected, Angus forlornly braved the storm.

The accident had happened, of course, to his head. In place of the lank curtain of unruly hair, there was now a dome of short and spiky tufts, looking, Lucy thought, like an old brush that's been chewed by a dog.

But this was not all. From having been a muddy sort of brown, Angus's hair had changed to brightly colored blotches of various shades of yellow. And the shades ran into each other in a melting sort of pattern.

Once they had taken it in, most of the boys cheered, as if Angus had scored a goal. The girls went on roaring with laughter.

"Looks like a frightened hedgehog!" Priscilla Moulton yelled.

"He's fallen in the Flash!" Sue Dodson shouted.

Angus blinked unhappily at them.

But Lucy all of a sudden was not laughing anymore. Angus, she knew now, was not at all what she had thought. He was quite a different person. Her mother was right. Only the metamorphosing hadn't taken a year or two; it seemed to have happened overnight. Now that drooping hair no longer blurred his features, she could see his nose and mouth and chin. They were firmly shaped, with clean, neat lines. But what caught her attention most were the eyes. Large, appealing brown eyes she had first caught a proper glimpse of last night at the railway crossing. Now they were glancing here and there, pained with embarrassment. And his embarrassment became hers because she knew why his hair was in such a state.

She wanted to scream at them all to shut up and leave him alone. That it was all her fault.

"It seems," Mrs. Harris said at last, quietening the class, "that last night Angus decided to cut his own hair. And as if that wasn't enough, he tried to shampoo it with what turned out to be a sachet of color rinse. How anyone can possibly manage such a stunning feat of ineptitude, I cannot imagine. But, Angus, if anyone can, you will."

There was more laughter, though of the exhausted kind this time. Laughter for laughter's sake.

Mrs. Harris let it blow itself out before saying firmly, "I hope we can all forget Angus's little mishap now, and get back to work. Go and sit down, Angus. Maybe after school this afternoon you'll do something to put right last night's disaster, eh?"

Angus trailed to his place, and fiddled distractedly with his gear, carefully avoiding his friends' eyes. He looked, Lucy thought, on the outside as she felt for him in her inside.

The bell went for playtime soon after.

Angus was at once set upon by a chattering, cheering, questioning mob.

In the crush Melanie, Vicky and Sally-Ann hustled Lucy out into the yard, and round behind the cycle shed. Only Clare Tonks paid any heed, and followed.

Meanwhile, Mrs. Harris shooed the mob away from Angus, arrested him by the shoulder, and led him off to Mr. Hunt's room. A small band of determined and ebullient boys tagged along at a safe distance, only to be waylaid by Mrs. Fletcher, patrolling the corridor on duty; she herded them, bleating protests, into the playground.

"*Nothing!*" Melanie's eyes narrowed. "Didn't ask for nothing, Pukey."

"Asked for *presents*," Sally-Ann said, nipping Lucy's thigh so painfully she cried out.

"What's in her bag?" Vicky said, shifting her grip swiftly from an armlock to a half nelson, making a hand free to snatch a hank of Lucy's hair.

Sally-Ann tipped Lucy's bag upside down on the ground. The contents spilled at Lucy's feet. She squirmed to break free.

"Wouldn't jump about if I was you," Melanie said. "You'll only tread on your own rubbish." She squatted beside Sally-Ann and the pair of them picked through Lucy's belongings.

"Get your filthy hands off my things!" Lucy cried, struggling against Vicky's grip even though it hurt.

"Shut up, stinky," Vicky growled, yanking at the handful of hair.

Lucy screeched. Tears came, which she couldn't stop. They seemed to have been poised, ready to flow. Anger at their coming added to the insult that was causing them.

At this moment Clare Tonks drifted round the corner. Lucy tried to hide her face.

"Push off, Tonks," Vicky yelled.

Clare did not budge, but watched from a safe distance.

Melanie glanced up. "Forget her," she said. "She doesn't matter. She'll pay later."

"This pencil sharpener isn't bad," Sally-Ann said, matter-of-fact, as if choosing goods in a shop. "There's a fairly okay key ring with Snoopy on it. And there's a nice felt tip in green. You'd like that, Vick. Green's your color. And, oooo, look at these, Mel!"

Sally-Ann held up some scraps of scruffy paper. At the sight of them Lucy went wild. She writhed, and tugged, and twisted, and wrenched. She tried to kick; she even tried to bite. But Vicky held on, seeming to enjoy the tussle. Until, panting and trembling with rage, Lucy gave up.

"You haven't had enough practice," Vicky said.

"Beast!" Lucy gasped. "Pig!"

Vicky laughed and gave Lucy's arm a sharp twist that sent pain shooting into her shoulder, making her cry out again.

Melanie said, with mocking pleasure, "They're little love letters from her boyfriend."

"Angus Burns," Sally-Ann said, jigging on her toes. "Yellow mop. Read them out, Mel."

Melanie performed, an actress reading a script: " 'Outside the gate after school.' 'You are the greatest.' "

Sally-Ann, peering over Melanie's shoulder, said, "Oooo—kisses!" and swooned dramatically against the wall. "Tell us all about it, Lucy. I bet you had a fab time outside the gate after school. Is that what made his hair shrink and change color? You must be *dynamite*! All his strength went into snogging.[1] Wasn't an accident at all!"

"Witch!" Lucy shouted.

"Snob!" Sally-Ann yelled, piercingly, back.

"Creep!"

"Smelly, toe-jammy, nitty sow!"

Lucy blustered, but could think just then of nothing really insulting to say.

Vicky muttered into her ear, "You haven't had enough practice at that either."

Melanie said, "Don't know whether he can kiss but he definitely can't spell." She was unfolding the last of the notes. Her face broke into a wide grin. "Listen to this. 'Lucy, beware Melanie Prosser, she is out to get you. Angus, ex ex ex.'"

"The nerk!" Sally-Ann sneered.

Melanie went on, " 'Today seventeen hundred. Railway crossing. Got plan to stop Prosser. Ex ex ex, Angus.'"

"The worm!" Sally-Ann said. "That must be the one he dropped her yesterday."

"What was the plan, Pukey?" Melanie came close up. "Going to blab about us, was he?"

"No, he wasn't," Lucy said. "And I wouldn't tell you anyway."

Melanie tried to outstare her, but couldn't. "Don't matter," she said, turning away. "Hopeless Hunt never does anything anyway."

Sally-Ann performed a twirling dance step. "We say we didn't do it, it's all lies, and he gives up."

"But you'll have to give us extra presents to pay for chatting about us behind our backs," Melanie added.

"Yes," Sally-Ann said. "We'll want really great prezzies tomorrow. Specially as you've brought nothing today."

Lucy said, "I haven't been chatting about you and I won't bring you anything."

"Yes, you will," Melanie said, holding Angus's notes up and waving them under Lucy's nose. "If you want these back."

Sally-Ann giggled. "Otherwise, we might have to stick them up in school for other people to have a good laugh at as well."

"You wouldn't dare!" Lucy exploded with a fresh assault of rage.

"Yes, we would," Melanie said flatly. And she walked away. "Let her go," she ordered without turning when she was well out of range.

Vicky released her grip and she and Sally-Ann ran after Melanie, and all three disappeared round the corner.

Mrs. Harris followed Angus out of Mr. Hunt's room, closing the door behind her.

"Don't forget what Mr. Hunt told you," she said. "That awful hair has to be seen to by tomorrow or you're not to come to school. Tell your father. We can't have a rash of yellow scrubbing brushes among the boys. If you do things like that now, heaven knows what you'll do when you're a few years older. But it won't be my problem, then, thank heaven."

"Yes, Miss," Angus muttered, his mind on Lucy and what they might be doing to her. He saw from the school clock that playtime was nearly over. He'd be too late to help.

1. Kissing and cuddling.

"And you're to stay in the classroom at dinnertime and go straight home after school—"

"But, Miss—"

"—I don't want any more scenes like this morning. False heroes I can do without, thank you. Now, go along and catch up with the work you missed. I'll just get my coffee and I'll be there to see to you."

Lucy gathered her scattered belongings and carefully repacked her bag.

Clare Tonks sidled up on feet the size of dinner plates and just as flat.

"You shouldn't let them see you cry," she said.

Lucy sniffed, but did not look up. "What are you on about, Clare?"

"They like it, you see. If you cry they treat you worse."

Lucy stood up, still not able to look Clare in the face.

"Couldn't help it," she said. "They're such—" There wasn't a word bad enough.

"Next time," Clare said, "look at me. It'll help, honest."

Lucy had never had a conversation with Clare before. But she had watched her suffering the same treatment that she herself had just received. She felt guilty about that now.

"Why should looking at you help?" she said.

"Having someone who knows what it's like."

"How do you know there'll be a next time?" Lucy said irritably.

"There will be," Clare said. "You haven't given them anything yet. And them notes—"

"Shut up, Clare. You dare even mention those to anybody— Anyway, I'm not going to give them anything. Rotten thieves."

"They'll go on till you do."

Lucy stared fiercely at her. Tonks the tank. But she still wasn't big enough to stop Melanie. So what could Clare know?

The bell rang for the end of playtime.

Lucy turned away and hurried into school alone.

5

"But it *was* an accident."

Angus had appeared from behind a tree as Lucy walked home. He was encased again in his anorak. Looking, Lucy thought, like a rumpled stick insect. He might be successfully hiding his hair, but he was also making himself more conspicuous in the warm afternoon sun. And if there was anything Lucy disliked, it was being the object of attention from strangers. So she was refusing to stop and talk.

"No one can have an accident like that," she said, not turning to look at Angus and hoping that people on the street wouldn't think they were together. "You wanted to look big in front of the other boys, that's all."

"I didn't. There was these packet things—"

"Sachets."

"—Sachets, and I thought they were all shampoo but they weren't. Some were dyes. Rinses. I dunno. Hair color stuff."

"Learn to read."

"I can read. I keep saying—it was an accident."

Angus trudged along for a while in silence. Lucy hoped he had given up and would go away. But no.

"It's all your fault," he said morosely.

Lucy stopped in her tracks and swung on him. "What did you say?"

Angus stopped short and took a step back. "You told me to cut my hair and get it washed. I did it for you."

"Don't blame me, Angus Burns, for *that* mess," Lucy said all the more vehemently for knowing she was in the wrong. "I did *not* ask you to cut your hair with the lawn mower and wash it in custard powder."

"If you hadn't of told me, I wouldn't of tried."

"Then please do not do anything I tell you ever again, thanks very much." Lucy swung on her heel and set off once more. All she wanted was to get back to the safe comfort of home, away from beasts like Prosser and apes (even metamorphosing ones) like Angus. She had had enough of everybody for today.

But Angus followed doggedly behind as if towed by an invisible rope. She tried to pretend he wasn't there.

At last, however, by the corner of her own road she could bear it no longer. And she didn't want him following her all the way home, because her mother might ask him in. So she stopped, took a deep breath for patience, and said, "Why don't you go home?"

"I daren't go yet."

"Are you trying to annoy me?"

"No," Angus said with genuine surprise. "I thought after yesterday—"

"What about yesterday?"

"—you know. At the crossing."

With warning in her voice, Lucy said, "What about the crossing?"

"Well—" Angus swallowed. "That we—" He shifted on his feet, watched the traffic, shrugged. "Nothing."

"Then go home," Lucy said.

"I've told you. I *daren't*."

"I'm getting fed up of you."

"It's my dad," Angus said, as though Lucy ought to understand. "When he saw my hair this morning he went mad. I was really scared, honest. He said if I didn't have it right by this afternoon, he'd skin me, he'd cut it all off himself. And old Hunt said it wasn't the school's job to see to it and I had to tell my dad to do it. But he'll go wild again, and he always does what he says, my dad, so he will, he'll shave it all off. I'll be bald, honest."

"Don't be silly," Lucy said. "Your mother won't let him."

"How can she stop him?"

"Well, she isn't going to stand there and let your dad make you bald, is she? Mine wouldn't."

For a moment Angus looked suspiciously at Lucy, before he said, "But my mum doesn't live with us."

"Oh!" Lucy said, and, feeling the need of support, leaned against the corner wall.

"She went," Angus said, "before Christmas. With a friend of my dad's. They used to go fishing together. My dad and him. I thought everybody knew."

Lucy shook her head, unable to think of anything to say.

"It was funny, she didn't take anything, only some of her own stuff in a case. Just went. When I got up in the morning she wasn't there. She'd been okay when I went to bed. She didn't say about going or anything. Just left a letter on the mantelpiece with Dad's name on it. I haven't seen her since. I don't even know where she is. And my dad, he won't say much about it. Says I won't understand."

Angus was talking so quietly now that Lucy could hardly hear him above the noise of the traffic. Suddenly standing there seemed all wrong. And she was noticing again how much Angus had metamorphosed, and how nicely.

"If you want," she said, "you can come home with me. I expect Mum will know what to do about that hair."

"They're staying in," Melanie said quietly into the telephone, "and some of their twitty friends are coming. They'll be drinking and viddying all night."

She played nervously with the telephone cord while she listened.

"We could go down the park."

Clattering sounds from the kitchen told her she was still safe.

"But why not? . . . I couldn't help last night."

She did not pause for long but her face crumpled at what she heard.

"Just because of that?" she said then, almost shouting. "You know what you are? You're a spotty-faced, horrible creep is what you are!"

She slammed the receiver down, ran upstairs, and locked herself in her room.

Hearing the commotion, Cynthia Prosser flung open the kitchen door and scurried to the bottom of the stairs, steaming saucepan in hand.

"Melanie!" she shouted. "Were you on that phone? You know what your dad said. Stay off it!"

No reply.

"Talk to yourself, Cynthia," she shouted up the stairs, and scurried back into the kitchen, shoving the door closed with her backside and attacking her pans again.

Douglas Burns waited with his bicycle at the garden gate. He had been there ten minutes, looking anxiously up and down the road.

David Waller came along the pavement on his skates.

"Here, Davey," Mr. Burns shouted after him.

David freewheeled back.

"Seen our Angus at all?"

"Not since school," David said, wanting to be off.

"Did he seem all right?"

David grinned. "Got a right going over for his hair."

"But you didn't see where he went after school?"

"Ran off Cainscross way. Everybody was ribbing him, but Mrs. Harris made him go. She didn't want us talking to him about his hair."

"And you haven't seen him since?"

David shook his head.

"Okay, thanks."

David scurled away.

Douglas glanced up and down the road again. Thought for a moment. Then swung his bike round, pushed it to the back door, leaned it against the wall, and went inside.

"It'll have to have another rinse later," Sarah Hall said.

"You'll wash my head away soon," Angus said, his voice sounding hollow in the basin, "and I'm whacked."

"Serves you right," Lucy said. She was sitting on the edge of the bathtub, watching.

Sarah said, "Wrap this towel round your head and come downstairs."

They drank Coke in the kitchen while Angus dried out. Sarah snipped at his hair until it was an even length all over.

"They used to call that a crew cut," she said.

Angus looked scrubbed and polished, and his hair was neat and soft and a sun-bleached brown instead of custard yellow.

He's metamorphosing even more, Lucy thought, hardly able to take her eyes off him. She smiled to herself but then thought of Angus's notes, which reminded her of Melanie, and of tomorrow, and the inside smile evaporated. She'd die if the notes were put up for everyone to read.

Sarah said, "I think he should keep his hair the color it is now. Suits him."

"Not bad," Lucy said, sipping her Coke.

She and Sarah sat in silence regarding Angus. Then Sarah looked at Lucy, grinned, and said, "Told you."

Lucy smiled back and shrugged, not daring to say anything.

Angus, unaware of what all this meant, said, "My dad probably wouldn't let me keep it like this."

Sarah plonked her scissors down in panic. "Oh, my goodness! Does he know where you are?"

Angus looked startled. "Dunno."

"The poor man'll be worried to death." Sarah glanced at the kitchen clock. Five forty.

"He'll have gone to work by now," Angus said. "Night shift at Daniels." His face paled, the new-scrubbed bloom gone.

"I'll phone him there," Sarah said. "Just in case."

She was out of the room before Angus or Lucy could stop her.

Now that they were alone, Lucy found she couldn't look at Angus. She stared with restless eyes at the crockery littering the table and the wreckage of that morning's breakfast. She heard Angus sniff urgently. She gave him a sideways look; their eyes met and Angus raised his eyebrows as if to say "O Lord!"

From the hall outside they heard the carefully calm sound of Sarah's voice. But she put the phone down much too soon for everything to be all right.

"Apparently," Sarah said when she came back, "he hasn't turned up yet."

They studied one another with closed faces.

"He'll be at home, waiting," Angus said bleakly.

Sarah said, "Lucy's dad has the car. He won't be in till six thirty. I think I'd better walk home with you."

Resigned, Angus nodded.

Sarah went fussing around the kitchen setting switches on the oven and absent-mindedly moving things from one place to another. Angus dressed himself ready to leave, discarding the towel and pulling on his T-shirt, which looked more drab than ever now that his face and hands were so clean and his hair so trim.

"I'll come too," Lucy said, but knowing.

Sarah shook her head.

"Why not?" Lucy asked, unnecessarily.

"Wouldn't help," Sarah said, a hand on Angus's shoulder to guide him ahead of her. "Daddy will want to know what's happened. While you wait, sort out things for supper, there's a good girl." She paused at the door and gave Lucy a brief kiss. "Won't be long. Best for Angus this way."

They left the house at a busy pace, Angus casting a regretful look back at Lucy, who, watching them go, felt deserted. Jealous for both of them.

"Let me in, you hear me, girl!" Bill Prosser shouted, losing his temper, which never took him long, and hammering on Melanie's door with his fist.

"No!" Melanie yelled back. Apart from the lock, she had wedged a chairback under the door handle.

"I'm telling you, Melanie," Bill Prosser said, "open this blasted door or you'll stay there for the rest of the day."

"Don't care."

From the bottom of the stairs, Cynthia Prosser shouted, "Leave the silly twit. Come and eat your meal."

Bill Prosser fumed.

"She'll come off worst," his wife shouted. "She's the one who'll get nothing."

Her husband rattled at the door handle again. The door shuddered.

"Stupid witch," he bellowed, and stormed off into his bedroom, slamming the door behind him.

Cynthia Prosser went into the sitting room and poured herself another drink. "One's as bad as the other," she grumbled to herself. "Let them rot, Cynthia."

"Thanks for fetching him," Douglas Burns said.

Sarah said, "No bother. Enjoyed having him. Hope we see him again. 'Bye, Angus."

Angus waved, disconsolately.

When Sarah had gone, Douglas shut the front door. By then Angus was in the living room trying to look normal, and not managing.

Douglas came in and leaned on the corner of the sideboard. Defeated by his father's angry gaze, Angus gave up pretending to be normal, hitched up onto the edge of the sofa, and looked uncertainly across the room at his father.

But the storm didn't come. Instead, Douglas said quietly, "Might of come home first."

Angus said, shamefaced, "You said I hadn't to till my hair was right."

"Aye well, but couldn't you have gone to the barber's?"

"I tried. Straightaway this morning. I walked all the way into town. But they wanted five pounds twenty just to change the color. I didn't have more than seventy pence. I had to walk all the way back to school. I was late."

"How late?"

"Ten past ten."

"One mess after another," Douglas said.

"But I did try, Dad."

"You should have asked. I'd have given you enough."

"How could I?"

"What d'you mean, how could you?" Douglas was getting worked up again: the storm perhaps after all. "Are we not speaking or something?"

"After last night," Angus said weakly.

There was very little between anger and tears.

"Last night," Douglas said, coming to the center of the room and standing over his son. "I got a bit upset, that's all."

"Worse than before."

"Good heavens, Angus, you'll have to buck up, you know. Life isn't easy. You're growing up now. People aren't always nice to you. You'll have to get used to that."

"It wasn't people. It was you." Angus bit his lip. His breath catching. "You've never hit me before. I thought—"

His voice choked.

Douglas took a deep breath.

Angus sniffed, wiped his nose on the back of his hand.

"Now then," his father said, quiet again. He took hold of Angus and, drawing him to his feet, hugged him. "We're both a bit on edge these days."

Neither said anything for a while.

"Not been easy since Christmas," Douglas said at last. They sat together on the sofa.

"Your hair looks better this way." Douglas stroked his hand over it. "One good thing."

"Is she never coming back?" Angus said.

He felt his father go tense. "That's what she says."

"I don't understand."

"No," Douglas said. "It's hard."

"Can't you explain?"

Douglas shook his head. "Another day, maybe. Not today."

There was silence again.

"This morning," Douglas said, "when I saw you with that hair. You reminded me of her."

Angus waited, tense himself now.

"But I shouldn't take it out on you," Douglas said.

Lucy in bed, Sarah and Jack cleared up for the night before settling to watch television.

"She's been in a funny mood the last couple of days," Sarah was saying.

"Maybe it's just her age," Jack said.

"Maybe."

"Angus what's-his-name."

"Burns. Nice lad."

"Well then."

"She says she doesn't like him."

"You didn't like me to start with."

Sarah laughed. "Not sure I do yet."

"Thanks!"

"But there's something else. She's moody. That's not like her."

"Growing pains."

They looked at each other, wondering.

"Should we encourage this Angus thing or not?" Jack asked.

Sarah thought before saying, "He's probably just a phase. Bound to happen sometime soon."

"And at least he's bearable."

They smiled at each other.

Their chores done, they switched on the television and sat together to watch.

Lying in bed, Lucy prayed for rain. Rain, she had decided, was her only hope. Preferably with lashings of thunder and lightning as well. And arrange, please, she asked God, for it to happen just before school, during playtime, all through dinner, and again at home time. Then everybody will be kept inside and Prosser won't have a chance.

If He did all that, Lucy promised God, she would not grumble one word, even if she got soaked, just about drowned in fact, all four times, so long as the storms came when required. She wouldn't even grumble at having to do things like helping in the kitchen or cleaning her room on Friday evenings.

And if for some reason known only to God this was not possible, could Prosser please be made to twist her ankle by falling off a wall while showing off on the way to school tomorrow and have to be taken straight back home for a week in bed. And by the way, she added, a wall is not absolutely necessary; anything high enough to fall off will do.

Not that she had found God entirely reliable in the past, she reminded herself, giving up the Almighty as an ally. And there were, now she came to think of it, other ways of getting the better of someone like Melanie. By cunning, for example.

Perhaps she could smarm up to Prosser and offer to share a fizzy lemon drink from her Snoopy vacuum flask. Tomorrow would be bound to be hot, God deliberately not having provided the required storms as asked, so Prosser would be thirsty. But—ha ha—the lemon fizz would be mostly Andrews liver salts, or some other bog-booster[2] diluted in lemon squash. Prosser being so greedy would glug it all down before realizing the fizz was not altogether what it appeared to be. The resulting lurgy[3] would keep Melanie occupied for one day at least; she'd be too busy pooping to bother anybody at all.

But there was also the business of Angus's notes. She'd have to get them away from Prosser somehow. Maybe she could do a trade. A good swig of lemon drink in return for the notes?

Lucy fell asleep rehearsing to herself a satisfying drama in which Melanie took the bait, became bedridden for days on end from weakness because of Lucy's poop bomb, and never bothered anyone ever again.

6

God did not answer Lucy's prayers next day—not the way she wanted Him to at any rate. Nor did she go off to school armed with lethal lemonade. She had not really expected anything better of God, but her own timidity depressed her. And the thought of Melanie letting everybody see Angus's notes was the worst prospect of all.

The day stretched ahead gloomily. As she got out of the car it seemed as if an army of Melanies stood between her and the moment when she would arrive back in the safety of home. She would have given anything to be able to jump back into the car and be driven away to be with her father all day. But the car drove off, Jack giving a cheery wave, leaving Lucy feeling abandoned and helpless at the school gate—a fearful kind of loneliness she had never felt before: a desolation.

Halfway up the drive Melanie waited, with Vicky and Sally-Ann on either side, a barrier of bodies blocking her path. Had Lucy known just how awful that day would be, she would have run off home regardless.

"Tie her up," Melanie ordered.

They must have planned it, for they were well prepared. Or maybe they went around prepared all the time. Sally-Ann produced a length of pink ribbon from under her skirt and tied Lucy's hands behind her back, while Vicky held Lucy in a headlock.

Lucy didn't struggle or call out. There was no use making a fuss. She had decided that from the moment Melanie waved Angus's notes at her as she came through the gate. And anyway, Clare was right: they enjoyed themselves more if you resisted. So let them get on with it, she thought; they would have to stop when the bell went.

This time they had not taken her behind the cycle shed, but stayed openly in the

2. A laxative, such as Andrews Liver Salts (long popular in Britain as a "tonic" for the digestion).   3. Any unspecified illness.

middle of the playground, as if they wanted everyone to see. Which is just what they did want, as it turned out. Clare Tonks hovered about a few paces away, making sure she could see Lucy's face. This time, Lucy stared back at her, and in some unexpected way it did help, like holding hands in the dark, only it was eyes and minds that were being held now.

A small crowd gathered like a ring of spectators at a circus. They knew they were in for some kind of show. "They're yellow," Angus said later. "You weren't kicking up a row so they thought they were safe and they could have some fun watching what Prosser did to you."

But what Melanie did was not what anyone expected.

Angus was not in the playground to watch because he was in Mr. Hunt's room having his hair inspected. (He told Lucy afterward that he was being given a wigging,[4] which Angus thought a great joke.)

Mr. Hunt was saying, "I suppose it's an improvement."

Angus did not reply but squinted at the head teacher from under furrowed brows.

Mr. Hunt picked through as if looking for nasties. "Is it likely to make further changes overnight," he asked tartly, "or can we hope for time to recover from the shock of this latest hue?"

No reply.

"Well?"

"Don't know, Sir."

Mr. Hunt wiped his fingers on his handkerchief with elaborate care and sat himself at his desk, regarding Angus with a resigned smile.

From somewhere outside a jeering cheer went up.

"Ladies and gentlemen," Melanie repeated as the cheer that greeted her first show-biz announcement died away. She paraded like a ringmaster. "We 'ave 'ere a speci-woman of that strange and 'orrible h-animile—a Diddicums."

She paused, hand and arm dramatically pointing at Lucy. On cue, the crowd cheered again, as they knew they were meant to. Wasn't it all part of the game?

Melanie went on, "The name of this per-ticlar Diddicums is—Pukey Lukey!"

Most of the crowd laughed; some of the boys gave shrill whistles and clapped.

"This speci-woman, Diddicums Lukey, 'as been captured and brought 'ere at great h-expense for your per-ticlar h-entertainment."

More cheers and clapping. Lucy took a deep breath, as though about to dive under water for a long time, and hung her head. Clare's eyes weren't strong enough to save her any longer.

Melanie, grinning, held up her hands for silence. "But before we see Pukey per-form, 'ere with a lyric specially composed for the h-occasion, is the very loverly, the very wonderful, the talented Saucy Songstress—Sally-Ann Simpson."

Louder cheers and shriller whistles and more clapping. The crowd, warmed up now and in the spirit of things, was totally absorbed.

Enter Sally-Ann. She had slipped away behind the cycle shed and made a quick change while Melanie was gathering the crowd; now she appeared in a flouncy pink blouse and slippery wet-look bright-red jeans and white tap-dancing shoes.

At the sight of her the cheers became deafening. They brought Mr. Jenkins, the duty teacher, into the yard. He peered over the heads of the spectators. "What's going on?" he asked the nearest girl.

4. A scolding.

"Some sort of game, Sir. They're pretending to give a show."

Mr. Jenkins assured himself that nothing untoward was happening, looked at his watch, said, "Not long before the bell anyway," and went back inside.

Sally-Ann, making the most of every second of her big opportunity center stage, acted the acclaimed star with practiced confidence.

Tired at last of applauding, the crowd fell silent.

Sally-Ann waited, smiling sweetly. And at the very second when some impatient spectator might have been tempted to catcall, she suddenly let rip.

Not even Melanie, knowing what was coming, expected such a performance. Some girls in the crowd jumped, and had to ram their hands over their mouths to stop themselves gagging from shock. The usually jeery boys, never having seen anything like it before, were silenced by amazement. None of them could take their eyes from the parcel of irresistible energy that was Sally-Ann Simpson The Saucy Songstress. Only Vicky, standing guard over Lucy, was unaffected. The evening before she had watched Sally-Ann rehearse in the garage of Sally's house.

Sally-Ann not only sang, she also clapped, danced, gyrated like a star from *Top of the Pops*:[5] the showgirl of showgirls.

"*Yeeee-ow!*" she began with ear-splitting force.

"*Yeeee-ow!*" she repeated, pirouetting recklessly.

"*O—yeah!*" she sang.

"*O—yeah!—Let's hear it now!*"

"Let's hear it!" shouted back some of the boys.

And hear it they did, a song-and-dance routine that went:

> "This is the story
> Of a Diddicum girl,
> Sweet as sugar—
> Keeps her daddy in a whirl.
> O—yeah! (two three)—
> O—yeah!"

> (*Turn, kick, spin, a quick tap-dance rhythm, clap.*)

> "Name of Pukey Lukey—
> Jus' look at her smile—
> Makes everybody
> Want to throw up all the while.
> O—yeah! (ain't it right?)
> O—yeah!"

> (*Gyrations from Sally-Ann. Loud guffaws from
> some of the crowd. More high kicks, spins, taps,
> and accompanying hand claps from Sally-Ann.*)

> "This is how she walks—
> I'll show you if you wish.
> Nose in the air
> And tail out like a fish.

5. British television show featuring pop music stars.

O—yeah! (bump! bump!)
O—yeah! (Want to see?)"

Some of the boys shout, "Go, Sally! Go!"

And now, encouraged by Melanie, almost everyone is clapping in time.

"SHALL I DO IT?" Sally-Ann yells.

"Yes—DO IT! DO IT!" they yell back.

Submitting to popular acclaim, as every great artiste must, Sally-Ann goosesteps up to Lucy. Stops. Eyes the crowd. Turns sideways to Lucy. Takes up an exaggerated posture, nose stuck in the air, chest thrust forward, bottom poking out backward. Then, keeping to the rhythm of the clapping, sets off round the circle in a stiff-kneed, waddling strut that tickles everyone into gales of laughter.

"O—yeah!" she sings at bellow-pitch as she goes, "O—yeah!"

She returns again to the center. Pauses. Makes come-here gestures to the crowd who, like well-trained dogs, edge closer. And she sings very quietly:

"Tell you what it is
Makes Lukey such a puke.
Got a mammy who's a walker[6]
And a daddy who's a fluke."

Roars of laughter. Through which, breaking into her high-kicking, spinning, tap-dancing, clapping routine again, she sings:

"O—yeah! (That's so)
O—yeah! (Ho ho)
O—yeah! O—yeah!—yeah!
O—o—o—o—yeah . . . ! (Man!)"

The end of the song is greeted with wild cheers, whistles, applause, foot-stomping. Sally-Ann bows, curtsies, does an encore of high kicks for good measure. Would have started again, but Melanie joins her. They bow together. First to one side, then to the other. Then, the deepest bows of all, toward Lucy.

Shouts of "More! More! Sing it again!"

But Melanie turns and walks slowly toward tethered and guarded Lucy.

Instinctively, the crowd knows this means a new turn of events, a different excitement. The ovation drains away.

Melanie stops, hands on hips, square in front of Lucy. Only then does most of the crowd notice that tears are running down Lucy's cheeks, and dripping from the end of her chin. The crowd shuffles into a tighter circle, the better to see and hear.

Melanie waits, as Sally-Ann had waited, smiling.

When the crowd is still, she says quietly, "Not clapping, Lukey? Didn't you enjoy it?"

She pauses for an answer. Tears or not, Lucy forces herself to say nothing, nor to make any movement that might suggest a reply.

"Everybody else loved it," Melanie says. And then with sudden understanding, "Oh, but you've got your hands tied. No wonder you weren't clapping! Untie her hands, Vicky."

6. Streetwalker, prostitute.

Vicky undoes Sally-Ann's tight little knots.

The bell for school goes, but no one pays attention.

Vicky steps back. Lucy's arms fall to her sides.

Melanie says, "Well—go on, Lukey. Now you can clap. You wouldn't like to be *the odd one out*—would you?"

Somehow, in the way Melanie says those few simple words, Lucy hears a terrible message. And when Melanie takes from her jeans pocket Angus's crumpled notes and holds them up, Lucy's will fails. She finds her eyes flicking away, not wanting even to see the scraps of paper. It is as though she is dazzled by a sharp light. Tears come freely and fast now. Her eyes drown; she can see only blurred faces surrounding her. Her thoughts drown too in waves of unhappiness.

"Go on, Pukey," Melanie orders without any pretense of friendliness now. "Clap!"

With torturing shame, Lucy claps.

"They're having a great time out there," Mr. Hunt said to Mr. Jenkins as he released Angus from his room. "But better call them in."

Mr. Jenkins went out into the yard again and bellowed to the crowd, "All right, everybody, let's be having you. Bell's gone."

Angus tried to dodge past, but Mr. Jenkins grabbed his arm and hauled him back. "Too late, Burns. Fun's over. Back inside."

In ones and twos the silent crowd broke up and drifted, still silent, into school.

"Gone quiet all of a sudden," Mr. Jenkins said as some of his class went by. "Makes a change."

But no one replied. All he got from a few brasher spirits were sheepish grins and quickly averted eyes.

"Too much excitement," Mr. Jenkins said. "Not good before school."

Halfway through the morning, sitting distractedly at her work, Lucy felt a nudge and saw a note lying on the table in front of her.

THATS FOR STARTERS
PENS REST TOMORROW OR ELSE

7

That night, in bed, Lucy reviewed her day. Since arriving home she had shut school and Prosser out of her mind. Even Angus as well, who had waylaid her again from behind his tree.

But now, lying in bed with summer evening light still glazing the sky outside her window, everything came sickeningly back.

Her stomach clenched. Though covered only by a sheet, she suddenly felt too hot, and threw the sheet off. Then she felt exposed, defenseless, and pulled it back over her again.

The hot flush turned into a cold sweat. She curled up on her side and tried to lie completely still, hoping this might help her get to sleep. But scraps of her day floated through her mind like flotsam in a stream, the fragments all belonging to one broken object, but jostling by in any old order and swirling away before they could be rescued.

Angus stalking along beside her after school.

"*Tomorrow I'll be there. They won't keep me in tomorrow. I'll get there early, really early, and hide somewhere. Just let Prosser start on you!*"

Lucy replying desperately, "You can't do anything."

Pens rest tomorrow or else.

Clapping.

Mrs. Harris checking Lucy's sums. Most of them wrong.

"*You don't usually make such silly mistakes, Lucy. It looks like carelessness to me. Were you paying attention?*"

And Melanie, moments later, grinning round at the class in a glow of self-satisfaction as Mrs. Harris, marking, says, "Very good. Excellent. One thing you do well, Melanie, is your math."

Lucy standing in a hidden corner behind the school kitchen during dinnertime. How could a warm summer day feel so cold? No one playing with her; but she didn't want anyone.

Clare Tonks plodding into view.

"*You shouldn't cry, Lucy. I tried to be where you could see me. But you stopped looking.*"

Clapping.

Lucy clapping.

Everybody standing silent around her, watching.

And Lucy alone clapping.

She turned from one side to the other.

She could not bear anything like that again, she just knew it.

She could have stood Farrant's stupid pinching and twisting and ridiculous wrestling. And witchy Simpson's twitting talk. She could even stand Prosser's threats, and mean, jealous, spiteful tricks.

But she could not stand being made a fool of in front of everyone, and hearing them all laugh at idiot things being said about her mother and father. And worst of all she could not stand the thought of Angus's notes on show. It wasn't that Angus had written them, or that they were from a boy—she was secretly pleased at that. It was that they were private. They had nothing to do with anyone else. They were hers. For herself. Not for others to read and say things about. And it was because they were private that everyone would laugh if they were put on show, and make fun of her.

She loathed Melanie for that.

Afternoon school. Sally-Ann flouncing up to Lucy during games on the field, saying, "If you don't bring prezzies tomorrow, Pukey, we'll put your silly notes up, and tell everybody that you go with Angus Burns after school every day and do filthy things in Randwick woods."

Lucy saying, "You dare and I'll kill you, Simpson."

Sally-Ann going on cheerfully, "And I'll tell everybody the reason Angus Burns cut his hair so short is that he's got plaguey nits and the color is really the stuff they use to kill them."

"You're vile, Simpson."

"Which means, you know, that you've got nits as well, because nobody can do what you two do after school and not catch each other's nits, can they?"

"I'm not listening to you anymore, Simpson."

"And besides, Melanie's got something reeeally terrific lined up for you tomorrow, Pukey, you'll see. Reeeally ace. Everybody will be amazed."

Sally-Ann ran off to rejoin her own team.

"We've got to get tough," Angus was saying. "Somebody has to stop her."

"What's this about we, Angus Burns! I'm the only one that's being picked on. And nobody has stopped her yet. Not even teachers."

"Well, somebody ought to stand up to her."

"It shouldn't depend on just one person to stop a gang like Prosser's."

"Then we should gang up on her."

"Sure! You and whose army?"

"A few of us might. Olly and Gordon and Samantha."

"Like today, you mean. Who did they all gang up on today?"

"It wasn't against you."

"It felt like it."

"They thought Simpson was funny. There were laughing at her. What Prosser did at the end—they didn't like that."

"How do you know?"

"We were talking about it this afternoon."

"Talking behind my back?"

"No!"

"You're on their side now."

"I'm not! I'm just explaining."

"Don't explain to me, Angus Burns. It was me it all happened to, remember? I don't need telling. You weren't even there. How do you know what they were laughing at!"

"I was just saying—"

"Don't say! All you do is say."

"But I've got a plan—"

"And don't tell me about your plans, Angus. I know all about your plans, Angus. They're drippy. Stupid. Fliddy. Okay? Now leave me alone. I'm going home."

Lucy turned onto her back and shook her head to banish the memory.

Now the sky was dark. The patch of acid orange glow from a streetlamp was reflecting on the wall in its usual place.

What might Melanie be planning for tomorrow?

Lucy wished tomorrow would never come. But could not sleep for worrying about what it would bring. Prosser wasn't going to give up, she knew that for sure now. How could she, after today?

Tomorrow was Friday. Get through tomorrow and for two days she wouldn't have to worry about Prosser or any of them. She would be at home. Do what she liked.

She longed for Friday evening to come.

In twenty-four hours she would be lying in her bed, just as she was now, only she would not be feeling so awful. She would lie here and remember tonight, and how she felt now, and know that tomorrow was done with, was over. Tomorrow would be today and finished. And perhaps by Monday, after two days of not having her to pick on, Melanie would lose interest and get fed up and decide to find a fresh victim.

But tomorrow still had to happen.

Her skin broke out again in a sweat. And inside, her body prickled as though her blood had turned to fizzy bubbles, and her bones were splintering into needles.

No one could help. That was the truth of it. So there was only one thing to do and she would do it.

8

"What've you got?" Melanie demanded next morning.

"Better be something sensational," Sally-Ann said.

"Carbohydrate," Vicky said.

"You what?" Sally-Ann said.

"Carbohydrate," Vicky said. "Got to eat more of it."

"But what is it?"

"Bread and spuds and that."

"Why?"

"Training. Body needs it."

Sally-Ann said to Lucy, "Is that what you've brought—carbonflybait?"

"No," Lucy said.

"Thank goodness," Sally-Ann said with relief.

"Get on with it," Melanie said. The prospect of actually receiving a present at last seemed to make her irritable.

Lucy took an old envelope out of her pocket and handed it over halfheartedly. Melanie might have been given a filthy handkerchief. "What's this?"

"Having us on." Vicky flexed her muscles.

"Give it here," Sally-Ann said, snatching the envelope from Melanie's disdainful fingers and tearing it open.

Melanie snatched it back before Sally-Ann could look inside. "I'll do it." She fished inside, cautiously, as though it might be contagious, and drew out a five-pound note.

There was a silence.

Then: "Money!" Sally-Ann said flatly as she might have said "Cabbage" or "Toothpaste" or anything else she thought dull.

"Five quid," Melanie said. "That isn't any good, Pukey."

"Oh, I dunno—" Vicky started to say.

"Shut it!" Melanie snapped.

Another silence. Melanie crinkled the note between her fingers.

"It's all I've got," Lucy said at last.

Sally-Ann said, "Money doesn't count."

Vicky laughed.

"What's so funny?" Sally-Ann asked sourly.

"Money," Vicky said, "not counting."

"That's funny?"

"Yeah. Counting. Sums. You know."

Sally-Ann ignored her.

Vicky spat at Lucy's feet.

Melanie said, "Money isn't presents. You don't give money to friends." She sounded hurt.

Lucy said, "My uncle sent it for my birthday."

"He must have a really vivid imagination," Sally-Ann said.

"Anyway," Lucy said defiantly, "you're not my friends, and that's all you're going to get."

Sally-Ann went rigid. "You're going to give us some nice prezzies, pigface," she said through clenched teeth, "or next week we're really going to get nasty with you."

She gave Lucy a vicious nip on the arm. Lucy cried out and tried to push away but Vicky grabbed her from behind.

"Twit," Sally-Ann went on, nip-nip. "Noddy. Bean pole. Smelly-nelly." At every word she pinched Lucy again, now on the body, now on the leg, now on the arm, faster and faster. "Squirt. Goofy-creep."

"Stop it!" Lucy cried. "Stop it! Let me alone!"

Tears came again, though she had determined they would not, and shame, and most weakening of all, despair. She was soon sobbing breathlessly as she struggled to break free.

"Let her go," Melanie ordered at last when it seemed that Lucy might become hysterical.

Vicky stood back. Lucy raced away up the path and into school.

"Blubber mouth!" Sally-Ann shouted shrilly after her.

The other two laughed but without amusement.

When Lucy was out of sight, Melanie said, "I'll keep this," and stuffed the five-pound note into her jeans pocket. "Not a proper present, so it's no use to you two, is it?"

> WANT 2 TALK 2 U
> *No*
> Y
> *Stop sending stupid notes.*

Having avoided Angus all day, Lucy was determined not to be ambushed by him after school. She knew if she talked about Prosser and his notes she would not be able to control herself. All she wanted was to be at home on her own. She was starting to hate everybody, not just Prosser and her lot. Except her father; and her mother of course.

As soon as school was over she slipped out of the side gate and walked home the long way round.

Angus waited behind his usual tree. Not having a watch he couldn't tell how long he had been there; but longer than on the other days, he knew. He kept spying round the tree trunk, but still no Lucy.

Then suddenly beside him, having come from a direction he wasn't watching, there was Melanie Prosser.

"Hi, Angus. Been stood up?"

He swung round, scowling. "Push off, Prosser."

Melanie smiled as if Angus were being as friendly as anyone could want. "She won't come now."

"Who won't?"

"You heard what happened this morning?"

"The sun rose."

"Very witty." Melanie enjoyed the joke. " 'Morning has broken',"[7] she sang, mocking Mr. Hunt's favorite hymn at assembly. And then said, not able to hide her gloating, "And so has she."

Angus kept quiet, but only with an effort.

"She didn't give us prezzies. You heard? But she did give us this," Melanie fingered in her jeans pocket and pulled out the corner of the five-pound note.

"Liar!" Angus said.

Melanie tossed her hair. "Ask her, then."

Angus stared at Melanie, who smoothed her hair and gazed idly down the street, posing herself.

She said, "Mind, I don't care whether you believe me or not. You'll soon find out." She gave Angus a wide smile. "She's just like the rest. Nothing, really."

Angus leaned back against the tree.

"Nobody likes being made to look a fool." Melanie was still relishing the memory. "Specially stuck-ups like her."

"Yesterday, you mean?"

"That was just for starters."

"I don't get you."

Melanie gave him a sly glance. "That'd be telling."

"So?"

"You'd tell her."

"Can't, can I. She isn't speaking."

"But you're still friends."

"Might be." Angus shrugged. "Might not."

"You send her notes. Wait for her here."

"Been spying, have you?"

"Watching *you*." Melanie tossed her hair again.

Angus regarded her silently.

"Anyway," Melanie said, "I only tell things to friends."

Angus laughed. "And you haven't many of them."

"Shows what you know, Angus Burns. Only they're not drippos from our crummy school. They're older. From the High actually."

Angus sniffed.

Melanie took the five-pound note from her pocket and crackled it between her fingers. "We could do all sorts with this."

"Like what?"

"Movies."

"Here!"

"Gloucester. It'd pay the fare as well."

"You're full of bright ideas."

"*The Murder of Dracula* is on at the Odeon."

"So?"

"Think I'll go." She gave him a sideways glance. "Want to come?" And she added with a grin, "After all, your girlfriend is paying."

Angus thought a moment. "What about all them friends from the High?"

"What about them?"

"Won't they be jealous?"

7. This hymn is a poem by the British children's author Eleanor Farjeon (1881–1965), "A Morning Song (For the First Day of Spring)," set to the music of an old Gaelic hymn.

Melanie screamed with laughter.

"Oh well," Angus said, "let them suffer, eh?"

Which sent Melanie into a fresh bout.

"Hey," Angus said, apparently enjoying himself, "reckon I should be on telly."

Lucy stayed in her room most of that evening, listening to her transistor[8] and rearranging her books on their bookcase. They had been in order of the ones she liked most. But from time to time the order changed because she decided she liked others better.

Tomorrow there would have been two more; she had planned to spend some of the money she had given Melanie on new ones. Now there wouldn't be.

She sat on the edge of her bed and stared at her books till the memory faded.

Last night she had lain in bed thinking that by this time today she would be free from Prosser and feeling happy. But she wasn't; not free or happy. The thought depressed her even more.

She switched off her radio. The noise was replaced by the sound of the vacuum cleaner coming from downstairs. The Friday-night house clean. She thought Friday evenings should be for having fun. Going out; enjoying not having school for the next two days. Not for dusting and polishing and tidying. But her parents said that Friday evenings were the only time in the week they could do it.

Tonight though, Lucy somehow found the activity comforting. She went onto the landing and called down.

"Dad."

"Hallo?"

"If you fetch the vacuum up, I'll do my room."

"Good heavens! Can this be true? Are my ears deceiving me?" Jack climbed the stairs with the cleaner. "You're not ill, are you?"

Lucy laughed, a relief in itself.

In the interval Melanie bought two ice creams with the last of Lucy's money.

"You could have a great time," she went on as soon as she sat down again, "with your dad out at work every night."

"You reckon?" Angus slurped his ice cream.

"I do when mine are out. Which is most nights. My dad's a builder. Has to socialize with his customers."

"Must be loaded."

"Mountains."

"Doesn't pass it on though."

"He does! Whatever I want."

"Why d'you have to take stuff from other kids then?"

Melanie gave him one of her sly glances, and grinned. "Fun, cloth head."

"Don't seem fun to me."

"Try it and see."

"On Lucy?"

Melanie laughed. "She's starting to bore me. Not that she isn't boring all the time, wouldn't you say?"

"Why bother with her then?"

"Probably won't much longer. Just a couple of times. Till she's got used to the idea. Then you can have a go if you want."

8. I.e., radio.

"You're dead generous."

Melanie chuckled. "Bighearted, that's me."

The lights dimmed. She flipped her empty carton into the air over the heads of the people in front and slunk down in her seat.

Sarah answered the telephone.

"Hello?"

"It's Douglas Burns here, Mrs. Hall."

"Oh, yes, hello, Mr. Burns."

"I'm sorry to bother you, but I wondered—have you seen Angus? He's not with you, is he?"

"He isn't, I'm afraid."

"It's just—well, he hasn't come home."

"You mean, not even from school?"

"No."

"Goodness! Just a minute, I'll ask Lucy."

Sarah called upstairs. Lucy came to the banister. "Did you see Angus after school?"

"No, why?"

"But he was in school?"

"Yes. What's the matter?"

Sarah went back to the telephone. Lucy hurried downstairs and sat on the bottom step listening to Sarah's end of the conversation.

"No," Sarah said, "I'm sorry. Lucy didn't see him after school."

"It's not like him to be so late," Douglas said. "Not without telling me. Half past eight."

"Is there anything we can do?"

"No, no. I'll give him a few more minutes, thanks, Mrs. Hall, then I'll ring the police."

"Dear me! Seems a bit drastic. Get in touch again if we can help."

Lucy could hardly contain herself. "What's happening? What's he done?"

"Calm down," Sarah said, replacing the receiver. "I thought you didn't like him."

"Oh, Mum, not that now. What's *happening*?"

"He's late home and his dad's worried, that's all."

"Can't we go looking? He'll be picking stuff for his rabbit or up in the fields playing. He forgets things. Time and things."

"How do you know?"

"I just know. Mum, can't we look?"

"No, no, he'll be all right. He'll turn up, you'll see."

"You're hard, Mum, honest."

"Hard!"

Lucy stomped upstairs to her room.

Sarah watched from below, wondering what on earth had brought on such an outburst. Surely not the news about Angus? Not that alone? Something was upsetting her these days, Sarah could sense it. But whatever it was was something more than first-boy trouble.

Jack, hearing the row, came into the hall. Sarah took him back into the living room to give him the news.

Douglas Burns decided to give Angus till ten o'clock.

Five minutes before the deadline Angus came rushing in, breathless.

"I thought you'd be at work," he panted.

"Never mind where I should be. Where the devil have you been?" Having kept his patience all this time, Douglas was seething now as much from relief as from anger.

"Pictures," Angus said, knowing he was for it.

"The pictures! Couldn't you have come home first? Or telephoned even?"

"Couldn't."

"What are you talking about? Couldn't ring your own father? Who were you with?"

"Just somebody."

"Don't you somebody me. Who?"

"You don't know her."

"Oh, it was a her was it? Is that why you couldn't ring?"

Angus nodded.

"Or didn't dare?"

"No, no! It was just— I can't explain."

Douglas laughed dryly. "I'll bet you can't. So who was she? It wasn't the Hall girl, that I know."

"How?"

"Telephoned and asked, that's how."

"Oh, Dad!"

"Who was it?"

Angus mumbled, "Melanie Prosser."

"Prosser? Prosser the builder? His girl?"

"Suppose."

"You suppose! Must have had a lot to talk about if you didn't find that out. And here—where did you get the money for the pictures? You hadn't enough this morning."

Angus stared at his father, speechless.

Douglas couldn't believe it. "You didn't let her pay for you, did you?" He sank heavily into his chair. "I don't know what's got into you lately, Angus. This is the second night this week I've missed work, you know. They'll be sacking me next."

Angus sat on the edge of his chair across the hearth from his father, hugging himself. "I'm sorry, Dad."

Douglas sighed. "I shall have to go on days. It's no good me being on nights. You on your own."

Angus said nothing. He had been wishing his father would make the change, but he knew this was not the moment to say so.

"If they'll wear it," his father went on, "jobs the way they are at present. They'll not be keen."

Douglas and Angus looked at each other. So much to say. But how to say it?

"I nearly had the police out." Douglas smiled.

"You never!"

"Five more minutes."

"Yikes!" Angus went weak at the thought.

"So mind—never again."

Angus shook his head.

"Time you were in bed," Douglas said, standing.

Angus got up, agitated, remembering. "I've just got to ring Lucy—"

"Lucy? Now? This time of night? No you don't!"

"But it's important."

"Rubbish! One girl takes you to the pictures and as soon as you get in you're wanting to ring another."

"But, Dad, it's not like that—"

"Don't care what it's like—bed for you."

"But it's about tomorrow."

"Let's get tonight's fuss over before you start wrecking tomorrow."

"But, Dad, Prosser is going to do something terrible to Lucy tomorrow. I have to warn her."

"Lucy can look after herself. All you've to do is go to bed. NOW."

"But I've got to tell her," Angus shouted.

Exasperated, Douglas took his struggling son by the shoulders and propelled him upstairs, saying, "Enough! I've had all I can stand for one night. You're tired and you're going to bed this second and that's the end of it."

And for Angus, for that night, it was. Douglas stayed home from work to make sure.

9

On Saturday mornings Lucy earned extra pocket money by helping at the shop. While Sarah and Jack looked after customers and staff in the shop itself, Lucy worked in the storeroom behind, tidying, opening new deliveries, doing whatever odd jobs she was given.

She was there that Saturday morning when Sarah came looking for her.

"There's a girl asking for you," Sarah said.

"For me?"

"She said to tell you it's Melanie."

"Melanie! What does she want?"

"How should I know, sweetheart? The shop's busy so whatever it is, don't hang about in there."

Sarah hurried back to work.

Lucy fumed. How dare Melanie come here? For a second she thought of ignoring her, of letting her wait till she got fed up and went away. But at once Lucy knew this was not a good idea; Melanie would do something embarrassing to attract attention. She might just as well go out and see her, and get rid of her somehow.

It was nine thirty before Angus woke up.

Furious with himself, he ran downstairs to telephone Lucy. No answer, of course.

"Oh—knickers!" he swore, and scrambled back to his room to dress.

"Hi, Lucy," Melanie called in loud friendliness as Lucy approached through the busy shop.

"What do you want?" Lucy kept her voice down and was as unwelcoming as she could be.

But Melanie lost none of her cheeriness. "Thought I'd come and see you, that's all."

"Come outside." Lucy led the way.

Angus had washed and was almost dressed when it occurred to him that Lucy might be at the shop. He almost fell over himself in his rush back to the telephone. But first he had to find the number. This seemed to take decades. Then a hurried woman's voice he did not recognize said, "Handy Hardware."

"Is Lucy there, please?"

"Lucy? Who's this, please?"

"It's Angus Burns. She'll know."

"I'd better get Mr. Hall."

"No . . . no!"

But the voice was gone with a clatter of the receiver.

Angus champed. Centuries went by.

"Hello, Angus. This is Lucy's dad."

"Is she there, Mr. Hall? It's sort of important."

"She was just now. Hang on."

Clatter again. A millennium passed.

Then: "Sorry. Apparently a friend called for her."

"Who was the friend, Mr. Hall?"

"Didn't see, sorry."

"Was it a girl or a boy?"

"Girl, I think. We're a bit busy, Angus. . . ."

Angus desperately wanted to tell, struggled with himself, took a deep breath to keep it all in. "Thanks," he said, and straightaway decided he would have to cycle into town to find them. He might just be in time.

"What do you want?" Lucy asked when she and Melanie were away from the shop.

"Nothing."

"Makes a change."

"Just being friendly."

"After this week?"

"Oh, come on. Just a bit of fun."

"Not for me."

"You shouldn't take things so serious."

"You shouldn't take things."

"Very witty." Melanie said, sharp as a knife. "Like your boyfriend, you mean?"

Lucy stopped and faced Melanie. "What are you on about, Prosser?"

"Hasn't Angus told you?"

"Told me what?"

"We went to the movies last night. Had a *great* time."

"Don't believe you."

"Oh, but I nearly forgot. *You* paid for the seats, didn't you." Melanie was bubbling with such enthusiastic gratitude that passersby turned and looked. "*And* for the train fare. Thanks a million, Luce."

She leaned forward and pecked a kiss at Lucy's cheek.

"I still don't believe you," Lucy said, pushing Melanie away, but believing every horrifying word. She felt weak from the shock of such betrayal.

"Ask him yourself," Melanie said, and launched into a loud song right there on the pavement, words and movements.

Lucy turned on her heel and set off back to the shop.

"Hey," Melanie called after her, "hang on. What about this morning?"

Lucy marched on doggedly, refusing to answer.

"I haven't had today's prezzie." Melanie might have been pleading.

Lucy stopped dead in her tracks.

Melanie dodged round her, blocking her path. She took Angus's notes from her jeans pocket and held them up in Lucy's face. "Today," she said encouragingly, "I know what I want."

Lucy sucked in her breath.

"Not money," Melanie went on. "Money's so boring." She grinned. "Well, usually. Not last night though." She waited for Lucy to say something. When she didn't,

Melanie pushed the notes at her. "By the way, here's your love letters. You can have them back."

Lucy might have been made of stone. Melanie shrugged and dropped the notes into the gutter.

Lucy watched them fall among the litter of ice-cream wrappers and orange peels and disgusting cigarette ends and used bus tickets. Was that all they were: bits of rubbish to be thrown carelessly away? And was that all she meant to Angus?

The thought of his betrayal drove all the fight out of her. And yet, it was only at this moment, staring at his notes abandoned in the gutter, that she realized how much she liked him.

"Come on, Luce, let's go." Melanie tugged at her sleeve. "After all, he's only a boy! Who cares? You and me can be real friends."

What point was there in resisting? Might as well get it over with. Just as Clare Tonks gave in day after day. Clare Tonks, whom Lucy had always thought of as someone pitiful, even ridiculous, for allowing herself to be picked on. But now here she was herself, standing in a busy street outside her own parents' shop, being picked on in just the same way and behaving exactly like poor Clare Tonks.

Poor Clare Tonks? Then poor Lucy Hall. Ridiculous Clare Tonks? Then ridiculous Lucy Hall.

In a mood of deep self-loathing, Lucy said, "Okay, show me."

There was no mistaking the look of triumph on Melanie's face.

As Angus stood on his pedals and pumped his bike up Rowcroft hill he saw Melanie, with Lucy trailing after, cross the road ahead and go into Woolworths.

Sprinting the last stretch, he threw himself off his bike and dumped it beside others against the wall outside, but then got stuck behind a large man and his wife encumbered with loaded shopping bags, and had to follow them slowly into the store. Inside, the crowd was so thick he couldn't see where Melanie and Lucy had gone.

They were standing in front of the music counter. On the wall above was a huge poster of The Pits, top of the charts this week. Oil-smeared skin showing through ripped and tight-fitting garage-mechanics' gear, screaming hair dyed blue, pink and green, the group was swarming over an old banger of a car and threatening the viewer with hammers and pliers, their faces fixed in mocking snarls.

"Aren't they hypnotic!" Melanie was raving. "But I mean *explosive!*"

"No," Lucy said flatly.

"But they're fabulous ace. I could eat them, Luce, honest."

She might too, Lucy thought, from the way she was drooling. This was a Melanie she had never seen before. Not cool, sharp, and in command. But pop-fizzy, just like everybody else.

"I'm dying for their latest album," Melanie said as she scrabbled through cassettes banked on the counter. "Here it is. *Rev, Baby, Rev.*" She turned to Lucy, her fizzy-bubble frozen to dry ice. "This is what I want."

Lucy shrugged. "Don't have any money."

Melanie laughed. "You are thick. Don't want you to buy it, Pukey. No fun in that."

Lucy went as cold as Melanie looked.

"It's easy," Melanie said.

Lucy shook her head, her stomach clenching now in panic.

"You'll have to learn sometime." Melanie was as matter-of-fact as if she were explaining a math problem.

"That's the way we get all our best prezzies."

"No," Lucy managed to say.

Melanie chuckled humorlessly. "Got news for you."

"If you want it," Lucy muttered, "you take it."

"Don't be twitty, Puke. Then it wouldn't be a prezzie, would it? And you'd best be quick or somebody is going to start wondering why we're hanging about."

Lucy did not, could not, move.

At which Melanie lost her temper. "Honest, you're so *wet!*[9] There's nothing to it. This time I'll help. But next time you're on your own."

And suddenly, another quick change, Melanie was all smiles and loud talk, giving a performance as a Saturday morning shopper. "Oh, look, Luce," she sang in a bright honest voice, "there's a new one from Sweet'n'Sour. Aren't they just terrif!" Aside she muttered in Lucy's ear, "Stay close." And all the time her hands were rapidly picking up cassettes and putting them down. "*And* from Charlie Chase. I just loved his last one, didn't you? Ooo, and Hector Protector. I just don't know which to buy. There's too much choice this week. What d'you think, Luce?"

Melanie stopped. Looked back along the counter. Looked round the rest of the store, quite unable to make up her mind, sighed, and said, "Let's go round town while we think about it and come back in a while."

She hooked an arm firmly through Lucy's and guided her with unhurried steps toward the exit. As they threaded through the crowd, Lucy felt something being tucked into the waistband of her jeans.

"What are you doing?" she protested.

"Shut up and keep going," Melanie said, tightening her grip.

But Lucy used her free hand to remove the object. A cassette of The Pits' album.

They had almost reached the doors. Lucy tried to pull her arm free. Melanie said, "Stop it, stupid nellie!"

And suddenly there was Angus, bursting through the crowd right in front of them, waving his hands.

"Don't go, Lucy," he was saying. "Don't leave, you'll get caught, stay inside."

At once, trembling with rage, Melanie snapped back at him, "Don't you dare, Burns, you pig!"

A laden shopper squeezed by. "Now then, you kids," he said, "go and play outside."

Lucy was confused. What on earth was happening? What was Angus doing here? Why was he flapping his hands about and shouting mad things at her?

But when she opened her mouth to ask, what came out in flat mechanical tones was a quite different question.

"Did you go to the pictures with her last night?"

At which they began shouting at each other all at once.

ANGUS:	LUCY:	MELANIE:
I'll tell you in a minute. But you mustn't leave. Have you taken anything? She said she was going to make you take something. Has she? Have you pinched anything?	If you did, I never want to speak to you again, Angus Burns. You said you wanted to help me and all you've done is make things worse, and now she's trying to make me *steal*.	I'll get you for this Angus Burns! You just wait! Think you're clever, don't you. But you aren't clever enough. When I start on you, you—you rotten, stinking, brick head!

9. Feeble.

It was the word *steal* that ended the row. The sound of it seemed to go off like an explosion around their heads so that everybody must hear it. Though, in fact, no one stopped, or even looked.

But Melanie wasn't waiting to find out. "I'll get you two," she said, letting go of Lucy's arm. "You wait till Monday!"

And she was gone.

"Have you taken anything?" Angus repeated urgently, paying no attention to Melanie.

"What?" Lucy said, still trying to gather her senses.

"Have you taken anything?"

"No—but—"

"But *what* . . . ?"

"This—" Lucy showed the cassette clasped tightly in her sweating hand. "She stuffed it in my jeans."

"Give it here." Angus snatched it from her.

"What are you doing?"

"Putting it back."

And he was away, weaving through the crowd before Lucy could say anything more. She glimpsed him as he approached the music counter, then her view was blocked by shoppers.

As Angus reached out to put the cassette back a man's hand grabbed his wrist and held it tightly enough to hurt.

"All right, young feller, you'd better come with me."

Angus was swung round, and found himself facing a towering man in shirt sleeves, who might have been any other shopper.

"I was only putting it back," he said, squirming.

"I've heard that one before, old lad," the man said, grinning wryly.

When the music counter came into view again, Lucy could not see Angus.

But then, her heart sinking for she knew what it meant, she saw him being led by a tall, heavy, shirt-sleeved man through a door marked STAFF ONLY.

Later, thinking back over all that happened, Lucy realized this was the moment when she made her decision. She had had enough of Melanie Prosser. She had had enough of her life being spoiled, of giving in, of doing nothing in the hope that all the nastiness would go away. And she knew she liked Angus enough to be upset if he got hurt, or bothered with another girl, or was in trouble.

She was determined to do something about it. All of it: her own life, and Angus. Starting now.

None of this went through her head then. What she felt was a surge of energy.

She spotted the sales supervisor standing by a checkout and made for her.

"Excuse me," she said in the politest voice she could muster.

"Yes?"

"A friend of mine has just been taken through that door by a man. Could I speak to him, please?"

"Oh?" The supervisor looked at her closely, suspicion sharpening her eyes.

"All right," the manager said, glowering across his desk while the detective guarded the door. "So you were only putting it back. What proof have you?"

Silence from Angus.

The manager leaned forward. "Do you know that shoplifting is the country's biggest crime? Do you know that stores like this lose millions every year because of it? Do you know it is a crime of epidemic proportions among young people like you?"

Angus shook his head. From the fierceness of the manager's gaze, he felt he himself must have thieved all the millions of pounds' worth of goods and be so contagious he ought to be in an isolation ward.

"If," the manager went on, "*if* you were only putting this cassette back, why did you take it away in the first place?"

"I didn't," Angus said before he had time to think what his answer meant.

But the manager knew and pounced. "So there *was* someone else!"

"No!" Angus said, fearful now, but realized where this would lead, decided the truth would be best, and added: "Well—yes."

"Ah!" The manager nodded at the detective.

"But she wasn't taking it. Not stealing it, I mean."

"She? The plot thickens." The manager was becoming quite jaunty with success. "Look, lad, I haven't time to mess about. Let's have the truth and get this over. Otherwise, it'll be the police and your parents and maybe even a court case."

Angus felt himself turn sickly white.

The manager's telephone rang. He picked it up crossly. "I'm busy, Peggy, what is it?" As he listened he began to smile. "Is that right? Well, well! Bring her in, will you." He replaced the receiver. "Your accomplice, I gather, young man. Given herself up apparently."

The door opened; Lucy was led in by the supervisor.

Lucy and Angus stared balefully at each other while the three adults, heads together, held a whispered conversation.

When the manager sat down again he said, "Should I expect more of you?"

No answer.

"Well, who's going to begin?"

"It was all my fault," Angus and Lucy said together. Which made them break into giggles; even the detective smiled.

The manager, though, was busy giving Lucy a closer examination. "Aren't you—" he said, searching for a name, "—yes, Jack Hall's girl, what's your name—?"

"Lucy." The giggles vanished.

"Lucy Hall, that's it. Well, well!"

There was a shocked silence. Lucy's mouth went dry.

"Thanks, Mrs. Wilson," the manager said to the supervisor. "You get back to the floor. You too, Bill. I'll cope with this. Thanks for your trouble, both."

The supervisor and the detective left the room.

"Now then," the manager said. "I'll have the story straight, please. No frills. Then we'd better get your dad over here, Lucy."

10

They were sitting in the Halls' living room: Lucy, Angus, Douglas, Sarah and Jack.

Everything had come out and been discussed over and over till Lucy was sick of it. Melanie, the bullying, Angus and his hair, Lucy and her birthday money, Angus and the pictures, even Angus's notes, and finally this morning's episode in Woolworth's.

Sarah had taken it hardest. Or at least had said most. Jack had been frostily silent.

Which Lucy knew meant he was deeply upset. Douglas was fuming, but restraining himself from saying too much because of the company he was in.

"I knew there was something wrong," Sarah was saying, not for the first time that afternoon. "These last few days you haven't been at all yourself. I wish you'd told me, Lucy."

Lucy, weary, stared at her hands clasped in her lap and kept quiet.

"You can't tell," Angus said, answering for her.

"Usually she tells me everything." Sarah sounded hurt.

"Not this. Only makes it worse," Angus mumbled.

Douglas laughed ruefully. "Oh, aye," he said, "so this isn't bad enough?"

Jack spoke his first words for more than half an hour. "I know what Angus means. It was the same when we were kids. But something will have to be done."

"You're telling me!" Douglas said. "What those young devils are up to isn't just a bit of bullying. We've all had some of that. It's an organized protection racket. If I had my way, they'd be given a present they'd never forget."

A heavy silence settled on the room.

Then Jack's anger boiled over. "It isn't just presents that that wretched girl is taking from them. Not just *things*. It's now. The present moment. All they've got, damn it! Taking that is the real crime."

He stood up, unable to sit still any longer, paced to the window, looked blindly out, turned, saw four pained faces gazing back at him, and could bear it no more.

"I'm going to make some tea," he said, and left the room.

Half an hour later they were all sitting together again, just as they had been earlier, but calmer now, refreshed by Jack's tea.

Finally Jack hitched himself forward in his chair, put his cup down on the floor, and said in his shop manager's voice, "We can't sit here all day. We'd better decide what's to be done."

Douglas said, "Doesn't that depend a bit on Woolworth's?"

"The manager agreed to wait and see what we can do," Jack said. "Nothing was actually stolen and the kids owned up to what was going on."

"That's a help anyway."

"I suppose I'd better go and see Mr. Hunt," Jack said.

Which brought Lucy back to life, protesting loudly. "No, Daddy, no! You'll only make it worse."

Angus too: "He's hopeless! Other parents have tried, honest."

Douglas said, irritably, "Don't be stupid, Angus. He'll have to do something. He'll have to have a go at that Prosser girl for a start."

"He sees her," Angus said, "but she always gets off. There's never any proof."

Sarah burst out: "Well, there's proof this time. There's the two of you. You both know what happened. It isn't just one person's word against another's."

"She'll get out of it somehow," Lucy said.

"I didn't see her take anything," Angus said desperately. "I only stopped them leaving the shop. By then she'd slipped the cassette to Lucy. So that's no proof, is it?"

"You see?" Lucy wailed. "You'll go and see Mr. Hunt, he'll make a fuss, but nothing will happen. Except Prosser will pick on me worse than before."

"No she won't." Sarah said. "It might even scare her off."

"It won't! It won't!" Lucy shouted, despairing now, and tears welling up. "You don't understand. It isn't like you think. She gets worse if anybody tells. Like it was a competition between her and the grown-ups." And the tears flowed. "Oh, I just wish you'd *listen*. I just wish you'd leave me alone."

She jumped up, fumbling for her handkerchief and, not finding it, ran sobbing from the room.

Sarah stood up to go and comfort her. But Jack said, "Leave her. She'll be better by herself for a minute." Sarah sighed, decided Jack was right, and sat down again.

An awkward silence. They all stared hard at anything except each other.

Then, her turn to lose patience, Sarah erupted: "We can't just sit here while that— that little thug abuses our daughter. Nobody is going to make my daughter's life a misery and turn her into a thief. Not if I can do anything about it. So we've got to do something. I mean it, Jack. I don't care what Lucy says."

Jack leaned towards her, speaking quietly. "But we've got to be careful. Maybe the kids are right. We might make things a lot worse instead of better. In a day or two the Prosser girl will get tired of Lucy and that'll be the end of it."

Sarah was furious by now. "She'll leave Lucy alone and turn her obscene attentions onto some other poor child instead. Is that what you mean? It isn't only Lucy, is it? She's obviously torturing one girl after another. Well, that's not good enough for me, Jack."

Jack sat back, giving in. He glanced at Angus, who was slumped unhappily on the sofa beside Sarah, and thought there was no use in him being put through a row among the adults.

"Angus," Jack said, trying to smile, "why not go up and see how Lucy is?"

Angus, keen to but hesitant, looked at his father, who nodded.

"I don't know where she is."

"In her room, I expect," Jack said. "Up the stairs, top floor, first door."

With Angus gone, the adults relaxed.

Douglas said, "It's the parents I blame. Don't they know what their daughter is up to?"

Sarah said, "Douglas is right, Jack. If they don't know they ought to. And if they do know, it's time they put a stop to it."

"Maybe," Jack said. "But—"

"Never mind the buts," Sarah insisted. "At least if I can't do anything about the school I can do something about the parents. I can go and talk to them. Tell them what's happening. Ask what they're going to do about it."

Jack pulled a doubtful face. "Maybe they know. Maybe there are some parents who couldn't care less what their children get up to. What then?"

But Sarah, adamant, said, "Then they'll just have to be persuaded. At least they should be faced with the problem."

The discussion raged on for another quarter of an hour. But Sarah was stubborn; whatever Jack said, she remained convinced she was right. And with Douglas and Sarah agreeing, Jack had at last to give in.

"I'll telephone and fix to see them tomorrow," Sarah said, feeling much better now there was something to be done, rather than just talked about. "Don't tell the children, it would only worry them. Jack, why don't you take them for a visit to Slimbridge[1]

---

1. Town in Gloucestershire along the River Severn, well known for migrating waterbirds and wetland landscapes.

tomorrow while I'm seeing the Prossers? It'll get them out of the way, and they'll enjoy the birds. Take their minds off all this."

Against his better judgement, Jack agreed.

Angus stood outside Lucy's bedroom door and called uncertainly, "Lucy?"

No reply.

"Your dad told me to come up."

Stirrings on a bed. Then Lucy's voice: "Okay, come in if you want."

The room was flooded in late afternoon sun. Lucy was perched uneasily on the edge of her bed, the coverlet rumpled where she had been lying. Her eyes were weepy-red.

Not knowing quite where to put himself, Angus stood awkwardly at the foot of the bed, as if he were visiting someone sick in hospital. But his eyes wandered, curious about Lucy's private things. Her row of big dolls—Paddington Bear, Snoopy, Gonzo Muppet—sitting in a small armchair. Her bookcase with, he guessed, twice as many books as he owned. Her bedside cabinet with its digital clock-lamp on top. Her posters on the wall above the bed, some of animals (a snarling tiger face filled one) and a couple of TV actors to whom Angus took an instant dislike. Her blue wall unit of drawers and clothes cupboard. A long mirror, reflecting himself, ungainly, looking round, and Lucy, watching him from her bed. The whole room neat and trim and bright.

"Better not go into my room," he said, as much for something to say as for any other reason.

"Why?" Lucy asked without enthusiasm, Angus's room not being the most important topic on her mind just then.

"Bit messy." He hitched his jeans.

"I'm made to clean mine up," Lucy said.

"My rabbit's the real trouble," Angus went on.

"Your rabbit?"

Angus nodded. "Clive."

"Clive?"

"He sleeps under my bed."

"You keep your rabbit in your bedroom?"

"Best place. Safe and warm."

"I don't think I'd like that."

Angus shrugged. "He doesn't seem to mind."

Lucy thought it best to change the subject. And there was something else nagging at her she wanted to ask before they went any further. She had to be sure.

"Did you really go with Prosser just to find out what she was going to do to me?"

"I told you."

"But with everybody there. The manager and our parents— Didn't know whether to believe you."

Angus sat cautiously on the corner of the bed. "Look," he said. "I was waiting for you by the tree. She came up. Started wittering on,[2] showing off, boasting. She showed me your five pounds, and said about the pictures. I thought I'd go with her. To find out why she goes on like she does. When we were in the pictures she started hinting about today. I thought if I could find out I could warn you. But when I got back home and was going to ring you, my dad was all worked up and wouldn't let

2. Talking at length about unimportant things.

me. And this morning I didn't wake up and you'd gone to the shop and I had to belt off into town to find you." Angus took a breath before adding, "That's all there was."

Lucy observed him closely, making sure before saying, "And you're not friends with her?"

Angus looked at her, aghast. "With her! Yikes, no! I told you, she's sick."

Lucy smiled inside herself. "Still want to be friends with me?"

"Course." Shyness overtook him again. He looked away. "Why did I write them notes?"

"Boys do that."

"I don't. Least, not that sort."

"Do you still like me even though Prosser made me look stupid?" Thinking of the scene in the playground still made Lucy feel tearful.

"Got nothing to do with it."

"Just thought it might have—well, put you off."

"Well, it hasn't," Angus said, leaning elbows on sharp knees and regarding his feet. His short blond hair made his blushes seem all the brighter.

"If you want then," Lucy said quietly, "you can go with me."

Angus nodded.

Lucy waited for some other reply. But as none came, she leaned forward and kissed him quickly, lightly, on the cheek, then sat back hurriedly, cross-legged against the wall.

The red of Angus's blushes deepened, his toes tapped on the floor in a brief little tattoo, he coughed to clear his throat, and nodded again.

Hoping to cover their confusion, Lucy said, "I was glad you turned up in Woolies when you did."

Angus shrugged. "She'll be waiting on Monday," he said. "And she'll be raving mad."

Lucy sighed. "I don't care now," she said, speaking aloud her new determination for the first time, and trembling a little at the sound of her courage. "She's got to be stopped, that's all." Her courage faded a little in the face of itself, and she had to add, "Not that I know how though."

Angus stretched his pencil length across the bed, supporting himself on an elbow. "I've got a sort of idea."

Lucy laughed, as much because of him as at what he was saying. "Not another of your plans, Angus!"

He smiled and shook his head. "Got it off Clare Tonks."

"Clare Tonks? Why were you talking to her?" Lucy's nervousness for Angus and herself put an edge on her voice.

Angus, knowing, grinned. "She's not that bad when you get to know her," he said.

Lucy, recovering herself, wagged a finger at him. "Angus Burns, you just watch it!"

"I mean to talk to, that's all." They laughed together. "Anyway," Angus went on, "it was her talked to me, really. She said you were the nicest person in our class, and she wanted to help, only you wouldn't let her. She said how if everybody who hated Prosser because of what she'd done to them got together and made a fool of her like she makes fools of them, she would stop picking on other people."

"Did she really say that?"

"Yeah."

"About me, I mean?"

"Yeah. Well, you are really, aren't you? I mean, you're not pushy or anything, like Mary, and you look all right."

"Oh, thanks!"

"And like Clare said, you're always good at thinking things up."

"Did she say that as well?"

"Yeah."

"Honest?"

"Hope to die."

Lucy indulged in a secret glow of pleasure, but said, "Well, she's wrong about me knowing what to do, isn't she, because I don't."

"But she's right about you having ideas. In drama and when we write stories and that, you're always pretty good."

The secret glow warmed up even more.

Angus sat up, his mind on plans. "You were right. The other day, I mean. About fighting Prosser."

"What about it?" She was always having to jump about in her mind to keep track of him.

"She would. She and her lot."

"Would what?"

"Pulverize you if you tried to fight her."

"So?"

"Even if you did beat her up, I was thinking—that would be just as bad as her beating you up, wouldn't it? It would be bullying her instead of her bullying you. Right?"

"Right." Had she said that? She couldn't remember now. But it didn't matter; Angus was obviously following some idea. "Go on, then."

"Well, that means you have to find a way of showing her up, something she hates, but that isn't bad, like beating her up."

"*I* have to?"

"Yeah. Like Clare says, you're good at that sort of thing."

"And what are you going to do?"

"I'll help."

"Thanks!"

"We all will."

"All?"

"Clare and Olly, and Sam and some others. You can do it, Lucy, honest."

Lucy looked at him, his eyes blazing, and laughed. "Talk about Prosser!" she said. "You're even worse."

From downstairs came a shout from Jack. "Angus, your dad's going."

"Rats!" Angus said.

"You can't go now," Lucy wailed.

"I'll have to."

"But we're just getting started."

"I know."

They stared at each other, wishing. But another shout, this time from Douglas, proved they weren't going to be left alone any longer.

Angus opened the door and shouted back, "Coming." Turning, he whispered to Lucy, "You'll think of something. Give us a ring if you do before Monday."

"Okay," Lucy said from her bed, sulky at Angus having to leave.

But when he had closed the door and she heard him clattering down the stairs, she found herself grinning, and hugging herself at a new kind of pleasure.

AIDAN CHAMBERS

Cynthia Prosser showed Sarah Hall into a sitting room furnished with black vinyl easy chairs and wall units made of chromium steel tubes and smoky glass. All very sharp and bright and Sunday color-magazine modern. Or at least, Sarah thought, modern as modern had been about ten years ago.

She was not invited to sit down.

"Well," Cynthia Prosser said in a no-nonsense voice, "what about our Melanie?"

Sarah put herself out to be extra polite. "I hope you don't mind me asking, Mrs. Prosser, but are you worried about Melanie at all?"

Cynthia flushed. "Worried? Why should I be?"

"She hasn't been in any trouble lately?"

"Trouble?" There was a warning in Cynthia's tone. "What kind of trouble?"

"There's been some bullying at school."

Cynthia went dangerously still, like an animal, Sarah thought, before it strikes.

"My daughter, Lucy, has been a victim of it."

"Has she?"

"Along with a number of other girls, I gather." Sarah struggled to keep her temper. "I wondered whether you had heard anything about it?"

"Can't say I have." Cynthia was straining to sound offhand. "If anybody's been bullying our Melanie, I'm sure she'd have told me."

Sarah knew now there was no hope of a reasonable conversation. "I'm sorry," she said, "but Melanie seems to be the one responsible."

Cynthia Prosser's chin trembled, her lips tightened, a little muscle under one of her eyes flickered. "Just you be careful what you're saying," she said, tight-mouthed, tight-voiced.

Sarah thought: What a hard, hurt woman. And wondered what kind of life was lived in this house. Was it buckled and steely, all glossy surface but hollow inside, like the furniture?

"Melanie and two of her friends have been forcing other girls to bring them presents," Sarah said. "In my daughter's case, Melanie took money as well. And yesterday they went to Woolworth's, where Melanie tried to make Lucy steal a music cassette."

"Rubbish."

"I beg your pardon?"

"Rubbish."

"Are you saying I'm lying?"

"Somebody is. Who did you get all this from?"

"My daughter."

"There you are then."

"Mrs. Prosser, are you saying my daughter is lying?"

"Are you saying mine is?"

"Well—"

"Yes, you might well say well! Coming here, accusing our Melanie."

"I've told you, my daughter—"

"Your daughter! She gets caught pinching from Woolies and makes up this cock-and-bull story about Melanie to try and get out of it."

"That's not true!"

"Isn't it? If it's not true, why are you here and not the police? And why hasn't Woolworth's been on to me? Have they been on to you?"

"Of course, that's how it all came out."

"There you are then. Caught red-handed was your daughter, wasn't she, and you believed her pack of lies because you're afraid your prissy reputation might get tarnished. You stuck-up, self-righteous prig!"

"Now just a minute, Mrs. Prosser—"

"Get out of my house, d'you hear!" Cynthia Prosser was shouting now. "How dare you come here bad-mouthing my daughter. Put your own child in order first before you preach to other people about theirs. Hypocrite! Go on—scat!"

Sarah, shouted into silence, retreated with as much dignity as her upset emotions would allow.

The Prossers' door slammed behind her.

From upstairs, sitting on the landing outside her room, Melanie heard everything, and smiled with satisfaction.

Her mother's angry face appeared at the bottom of the stairs. "Don't you ever drop me in it like that again. You hear, you stupid cow? And this time I'm telling your father about it."

When Lucy and Jack arrived back from their afternoon at Slimbridge having dropped Angus off at his house, Sarah was still so distraught that she could not help telling them both about her visit to Cynthia Prosser at once.

Lucy was appalled. Melanie really had, like a disease, infected her own home, the one place she had felt was safe, a refuge. Now nowhere was safe anymore.

The whole lovely afternoon, the fun she had had with Angus and her father, evaporated, might never have been. The awfulness of the past week flooded back to take its place. And her mother's unconcealed distress became a new oppression.

She sat in the kitchen listening and watching as Jack tried to comfort and reassure Sarah. And even this seemed like another theft, another unwilling present Lucy had to give at Melanie's command.

She was jealous. Jealous of her father for giving such attention to her mother, when it was she, Lucy, who would suffer the consequences of Sarah's foolishness. Why couldn't her father see that? Why didn't he say it?

In the end, Lucy could bear it no longer. With deliberate quietness she got up and went slowly to her room, secretly hoping all the time that her father would call after her, bring her back, console her as she was consoling Sarah.

But he did not; and she closed her bedroom door on the murmur of her parents' voices from the kitchen below.

An hour later, Sarah came into Lucy's room, bearing a tray with beans and toast, a glass of Coke, and three Tango biscuits.

Lucy was huddled in bed, as if from winter cold. Sarah waited for her to sit up and take the peace offering, but she remained determinedly still.

Sarah put the tray down on the bedside cabinet and paused for a moment, hoping her daughter might say the first words. But no. Sarah would have to.

Drawing in her breath, she said, "I've bodged[3] it, haven't I?"

Lucy gave a hint of a nod.

"I'm sorry, sweetheart."

For Lucy to have replied in any way would have meant a deluge of tears. She froze herself against it.

Sarah stood by the bed another moment looking down at her unhappy daughter,

3. Botched.

then said, with resignation, "Try to eat something," bent, kissed Lucy's cheek, and went back downstairs.

Two hours later Jack came in. By then, feeling hungry, Lucy had eaten the biscuits and drunk the Coke with a rebellious kind of pleasure.

Now she was sitting up reading *Carrie's War*[4] and finding consolation in it, as well as fellow feeling. Carrie, the girl in the story, sometimes felt embattled too.

Her father sat by her side on the bed and, smiling, took her hand. "Okay?" he asked.

Lucy nodded.

"Good book?"

"Not bad."

"Want me to read it to you?"

She shook her head.

"Want me to go away again?"

She shook her head again. Managed a faint smile.

"Better," Jack said, leaning forward and kissing her brow.

They sat in silence. Outside, dusk was falling. Framed in the window, the sun's last rays haloed the valley top. The room glowed in reflected light.

After a while, Jack said, "It'll pass, you know. It's bad now, but it'll pass."

"But it won't be gone by tomorrow," Lucy said.

"No," Jack sighed. "Can't promise that." After a pause, he added, "Want to stay home for a day or two? Let things blow over."

"No," Lucy said. "I've got to go."

Jack nodded.

Lucy said, "Why are people so awful?"

"Are they? All of them, all the time?"

"Melanie is."

"Maybe you only see her at her worst."

"Why do you always take the other people's side?"

"Do I?"

"You're always saying *maybe*. Maybe they didn't mean it. Maybe they couldn't help it. Maybe they weren't feeling well."

"I take your side too."

"But you always do say maybe."

Jack chuckled. "Maybe because I don't believe anybody is bad all the time."

"Not even Melanie?"

"Not even Melanie, hard though it is to believe."

Lucy was rueful. "She could have fooled me."

"I know. Especially when you're on the receiving end. And I'm not excusing what Melanie has done, you know."

"What are you doing then?"

"Trying to explain. Trying to understand."

"She's rotten, that's all. Angus says she's sick."

"Maybe."

"There!"

They laughed.

"But maybe," Jack said, "well—maybe she's taking out on you something that other people have done to her."

4. A 1973 children's novel by the British author Nina Bawden.

"Like her mother, you mean?"

"Sounds a bit like it from what your mum says."

"Then why doesn't her dad do something? You would if Mum was horrible to me, wouldn't you?"

"Course."

"Well then."

"Maybe—sorry!—but maybe her dad's as bad."

"Or worse."

"Think of that."

"Yuk! I'd rather not."

"We just don't know. That's what I mean, you see? No one ever really knows why someone is bad."

"Not even the person herself?"

"Least of all sometimes."

Lucy thought for a moment. "Still doesn't make it any better."

"No. Not for you this minute. But later maybe."

"Maybe!"

They laughed again.

"Two things you do know though," Jack said.

"What?"

"Stealing won't help."

Glum again, Lucy shook her head. "I won't. I didn't."

"No, I know. But I'm just saying. For the record, eh?"

"What's the second thing?"

Jack smiled. "Something Mum learned the hard way."

Lucy said, "That you and she can't do much to help?"

"Right. Not at present anyway. If there's a solution—"

"I have to find it myself."

"Afraid so."

"I decided that yesterday."

"Told you you knew already."

"Apart from sticking it out till Melanie gets fed up, you mean?"

"Yes. And that's the hard thing I'm having to learn."

"What?"

"That there comes a moment when parents can't always help their children to sort out their lives."

"But you do try," Lucy said with mock generosity.

Jack bowed, smiling. "Thanks, O Queen."

They laughed again.

"Though mind you," Jack said, "talking about it to Mum and me might help. A bit anyway. And we like to know what you're thinking and what's happening to you. Not to pry, but just because we love you."

Lucy looked away, through the window at the fading sky. "Maybe," she said, "I'll just get up for a while and watch TV, if that's okay."

Jack, matter-of-fact, said, "Good idea. Make you sleepy for the night after lazing in bed all evening."

12

On Monday morning Jack drove Lucy up to the school gate as near to starting time as he could manage.

Angus was leaning against the railings as if he had been there all night.

"Sure you don't want me to come in?" Jack said.

"No, thanks," Lucy said, kissing him good-bye.

She got out and joined Angus, and they both waved as Jack drove off.

But Lucy's eyes were already searching for Melanie.

"Hasn't turned up yet," Angus said. "Least, I haven't seen her, and I've been here ages."

"Probably one of her stupid tricks," Lucy said. Having nerved herself for a confrontation, she was on tenterhooks again, once more being made to wait and wonder while Melanie chose the moment.

The bell went.

"I was just ready for her." Angus said, quite disgruntled.

"Me too."

They grinned at each other.

Melanie was not in class by registration either. Sally-Ann and Vicky were there, but subdued without Melanie to direct them. No one knew why she was absent—or rather, no one admitted knowing. But from the way Sally-Ann kept her head down when Mrs. Harris asked, Lucy and Angus both decided she did know but was too scared to tell.

With registration over, Mrs. Harris set about the day's work. She suggested that as the end of term this summer was not just the end of the term but the end of their time in this school, they might like to make a wall newspaper. It would be about their lives here—the things they remembered, some of the funnier ones, and some of the sadder ones too perhaps, though Mrs. Harris hoped there hadn't been too many sad times. There could be poems, and real-life stories, and drawings. They might even like to bring photographs and include those.

"In fact, it would be the autobiography of your last five years."

"Auto-what, Miss?" Brian Webster said, to be awkward.

"*Auto* means self, Brian, as you well know, and biography means—?"

"An account of a person's life," they all called back, except Brian, of course, who was determined to appear as stupid as possible this morning, being Monday, because he knew it tried Mrs. Harris's patience.

"Can we do jokes?" Roland Oliver shouted.

"Yes, Roland," Mrs. Harris said. "I suppose you can do jokes. Though yours I can usually do without."

General agreement on that score gave Roland considerable pleasure and his friends a chance to cheer.

"What about puzzles and quizzes and that?" Hector Sims wanted to know.

"The puzzles and quizzes are all right," Mrs. Harris said. "I'm not so sure about the *and that*."

"We'll need an editor, Miss," Mary said (expecting the job for herself, Lucy thought).

"We will," Mrs. Harris said. "But I'll deal with that high office when you've all done your author and artist work."

Mary subsided with as much apparent enthusiasm as she could muster.

"All right, get busy," Mrs. Harris said.

There was a general stirring and a lot of chatter at first, while they sorted themselves out, and discussed ideas, and while some of them had a quiet moan at such a soppy idea. But gradually they all got started and even began to enjoy the hard work of writing and drawing rough drafts.

It was during playtime, out in the yard, that Angus brought Clare Tonks over to Lucy.

"Tell her what you just said to me," Angus said to Clare.

Talking to Lucy but looking at Angus, Clare said, "I was wondering what you were doing for the newspaper."

Lucy thought, as she waited for Clare to go on: Why do I always feel she's going to roll over and flatten me to death.

"Because—" Angus prompted.

"Because you might be writing about Prosser."

"Prosser!" Lucy said. "Not likely! I don't even want to talk about her, thanks very much. Why should I write about her?"

Clare said into her chest, "So other people would know."

"Know what?"

"What it's like."

Lucy said, "Write about it yourself then. You know more about what it's like than I do."

Clare stood stock-still, staring at her feet.

Unable to keep quiet any longer, Angus said, "She will if you will, that's what she wanted to say, and so will I."

Lucy looked at them both, and pretended to laugh this off as a silly idea. But she said to Angus, "Whatever could you write?"

"I could do the biography of a bully, like Mrs. Harris said."

"She said do *auto*biography."

"Forget the auto," Angus said dramatically.

"But if you wrote about her, she'd really start on you, wouldn't she? We want to stop her, not make her worse."

"But you don't see what Clare means," Angus said, irritated. "Tell her, Clare."

Clare never said anything much, in class or out, and was plainly not keen to have a try now. She took a deep breath and let it out loudly. "It's what I tried to tell you before, Lucy. About making fools of people. It's not the nipping and the spitting or that Vicky. Well, that hurts. But it doesn't matter, not really. It's making fun of you, calling you awful names, and what they say about your mother, and everybody laughing at you. That's the worst—"

She ran out of words; gave Angus a sideways look, appealing for help.

"About laughing at her," Angus said, smiling and nodding encouragement.

Clare even smiled back. "I just thought, if she was made to look a fool, if people laughed at her, she would know what it was like, and that might stop her."

Lucy said nothing. Clare couldn't go on.

Angus said, "She thought you might write something that would make people laugh at Prosser. She says you could do that, but she couldn't."

They looked at each other. Now he had said it briefly like that, the idea no longer sounded convincing. Angus shrugged. "Sorry, Clare. Forget it." And he was turning away to run off and join his friends kicking a football around the field when Lucy said, "No, Angus, wait."

It wasn't so much that Lucy saw now exactly what to do or how to do it, but only that, as Clare and Angus were talking, everything she had worried about and suffered over the last few days, and all her thoughts about how to deal with Melanie, seemed to fall into place. Like a jigsaw puzzle you've stared at for ages that suddenly makes sense, and you realize how the pieces fit together.

For Lucy the important piece that made all the other pieces fit was Angus's notes. Of all that Melanie had done, her threat to display the notes was the worst. Lucy had given money, ashamed of doing so though she had been, just to avoid this happening. And she would have gone on giving presents to stop it, if Melanie hadn't got rid of the notes on Saturday.

Angus's notes would have been on view for everyone to see and laugh at day after day. Everyone would have known; that was the point. Things put in writing for everybody to see were different from things that were only said.

"Clare's right," Lucy said. Clare blinked in surprise. "But it isn't just making them laugh. And it can't be just me. Not just the three of us. That won't stop Prosser. It has to be everybody."

"Everybody!" Angus said, knowing how hopeless that would be to manage.

"Well, not *everybody*, but enough of us who Prosser has bullied to write about what she's done. What she is. And put it all in the newspaper. Then everybody will know."

"They know already," Angus said.

"But not that way. She picks on us one at a time, doesn't she? And no one ever tells, not to us all at once. And we don't ever do anything about her at once."

"But how is writing about it any different?" Angus said.

"Because nobody has to take her on in a fight that way. It isn't bullying—like you said on Saturday. It's not bullying to write down what's happened to you, is it? Writing it down, I mean, so that everybody can read it. But Prosser would hate it, I just know she would. I would if I was her."

"Me as well," Clare said. She was getting so excited she was weaving back and forth on her feet.

Angus said, catching on, "And if Olly did some of his jokes, and Hector did some of his puzzles, and we get kids from other classes to come and look, Prosser wouldn't hear the last of it, would she?"

"That's what I mean, that's what I meant!" Clare said, and, unable to bear the excitement any longer, had to rush off to the toilet.

The bell went for end of playtime.

"Trouble is," Lucy said as she and Angus walked into school, "none of the others will listen to me."

Angus said, "They'll listen to Mary though."

Lucy nodded and sighed; a problem already.

"We'll just have to get her to join in," Angus said.

Lucy shook her head. "Don't think she would, just for me." And she added a little regretfully, "She might if you asked her with me though."

Angus grinned at her with a glance that betrayed a hint of triumph. "Okay," he said. "We'll grab her in a minute."

They cornered Mary as soon as everyone was settled to work again.

"If it's about Mrs. Harris's present," Mary said, "I've got money from nearly everybody now. You could buy it this weekend, I expect."

"It's something else," Angus said, acting as go-between a little too keenly, Lucy felt. "We've got this idea."

"About Melanie," Lucy said, jumping in before Angus could blurt everything out.

"She was rotten to you the other day," Mary said.

"We think she should be stopped," Angus said.

"What he means is," Lucy said quickly, "that it isn't fair what she does. Making fun of people and taking things from kids, and—and—" She could not bring herself to say the word.

"Shoplifting," Angus said straightly.

Mary glanced up to see if Mrs. Harris had heard. But she was over at the other side of the room helping Colin Langport, who was always needing help.

"What's your idea?" she asked cautiously.

Between them Lucy and Angus explained. "Really show Prosser up," Angus said when they had done.

Mary shook her head. "Don't like it. Naming her, I mean. It would be like telling."

"But why not?" Angus said, indignant. "Why should she get away with it? Look what she's done to stacks of kids this year. And it wouldn't be telling, just describing. That's different."

"If you want to do it, go on, do it," Mary said. "But I won't." She looked at Lucy. "It's a great idea, Lucy, but sorry."

"It won't work without you," Angus said.

"Well, I won't join in if you put names."

"Well, we can't do it without saying who it is, can we?"

Lucy said, "Yes, we can." She had been thinking hard. "It can be a game. We all write about Melanie *without* saying who we mean, but so anybody who thinks about it knows who it must be."

"Puzzles?" Angus said. "Mysteries? Guess-who jokes?"

Lucy nodded.

"Would you go along with that?" Angus said to Mary.

Mary thought a moment, then, smiling, said, "Sure. That would be fun."

By the end of the morning Angus had—without too much difficulty—recruited Roland and Gordon. Lucy had started on her "Guess Who?" biography and had managed to persuade Samantha and Hyacinth Johnson to write something as well because they were friends of hers.

Mary had quietly gone round some of the others who had been on the receiving end of Melanie's attentions and talked them into doing something. She had even had a chat with Mrs. Harris and convinced her that part of the newspaper should be what Mary called a "Feature Special" on bullying.

"Sounds depressing to me," Mrs. Harris said. "And we don't get much of it here, do we?"

"Not much," Mary said. "But sometimes. And a few of us thought there should be something about it, because it is part of school life, isn't it? Just like in that book you read us last term."

"I remember," Mrs. Harris said. "But that was quite funny, wasn't it?"

"Well, we'll be having jokes and puzzles," Mary said, "so it won't be terrible or anything."

"I should think that would be all right then," Mrs. Harris said. "Nothing unpleasant though, and you can be editor of that section, seeing it's your idea."

At the end of the day, Mrs. Harris said, "We're getting on very well. All sorts of surprises in store. Finish what you're doing for homework, and we'll put the newspaper up tomorrow."

That evening Angus came to Lucy's house after tea and they worked together on their contributions.

They told Sarah and Jack this was secret homework, and that they would show the results later in the week.

Happy that Lucy was more like her old self again, Sarah left them to get on uninterrupted.

There was certainly plenty of laughter coming from the dining room, where they were working. Which, had any of them known it, would be an odd contrast with events at school next day.

13

Extracts from a wall newspaper by Class 4H

??? GUESS WHO ???

She has a habit of biteing her finger nails, kicking, pinching, black mailing & pulling hair. *Mary Gardiner.*

SHE HAS A GANG. THIS GANG HAS 2 IN IT AS WELL AS HERSELF (= 3). THE OTHER 2 ARE VERY FUNNY (U DON'T SAY!!!) AND SILLY-AND-SOPPY (IF U KNOW WHAT I MEAN). *Angus Burns.*

?

She bullys people by making them do her homework and makes you bring presents for her every day and she likes to make you cry. Lucy Hall.

?

She comes to school very early and creeps into class and leaves nasty things in other children's boxes, like spiders and slugs and many other horrible things. She also takes posseshions from other children. *Samantha Ling.*

?

She called me bootpolish and made her gang try to wash me off in the toilet and made some others write stuff on the walls about me which said Go Home. But this is where I live. Hyacinth Johnson.

?

Her hobbies are pulling hair, taking people's things, demanding presents, telling rude lies. She has long dark hair she sometimes chews when she is working. She is clever and good at math and soon will be twelve and is five feet tall. Her hobbies are also pulling my earrings and smashing my glasses. Prescilla Moulton.

?

She is tall and I watched her saunter through the playground in her skin tight jeans with her frilly blouse with gold sequins and her wine color swade boots. Her long brown hair was frizzed (it isn't anymore) and she had eye shadow on (which Mr. Hunt banned—hate hate). I saw the dominating figure coming toward me. I felt a tug pull me backwards. Her friend had hold of my hair. (I wish my mum wouldn't put ribbons in then maybe she wouldn't notice me.) "Your gonna do my classroom duties, arn't ya." "Yes," I said and with that her friend twisted my arm and all three of them stalked off like chuffed[5] lions. *Maxine Blair.*

THE PRESENT
TAKERS, CH. 14

?

SHE RUNS AWFULLY FAST AND ITS IMPOSSIBLE TO GET AWAY FROM HER. SHE IS A PERFECT NUSANCE. SHE HAS GREEN EYES A BIG MOUTH AND SHE IS AWFULLY TALL FOR HER AGE. SOMETIMES SHE WEARS A MINISKIRT AND A T SHIRT AND A JACKET AND SOME OF THE LADS WHISTLE AT HER (BUT NOT ME!!) *Gordon Sims.*

?

A Joke
(By Roland Oliver, the World's Greatest Comedian)
Q. What did one bully say to the other bully?
A. I get a kick out of you.

?

FATE
A Puzzle Poem
by Clare Tonks

Many a time I've come to school
Eager for the day ahead. But there,
Leaning on the gate, a bully waits
Alone with her two friends.
No one can ever escape them,
I know that for sure. Then,
Eagerness, like mist, soon vanishes,
Puffed away by fear, when,
Round behind the cycle shed,
Orders are given for your fate:
　"See you've prezzies for us tomorrow,
　See they are just like new,
　Else we'll give you something really nasty.
　Remember, we've got our claws in you."

14

"I said no names!" Mary was brittle with anger.

Angus said, grinning, "It's not names. It's a puzzle."

"Rubbish," Mary said. "Everybody can see. Even Mrs. Harris will."

"Tell Clare," Lucy said. "It's her poem. She must have stuck it up after we'd all gone out."

"Anyway," Angus said, "I think it's a terrific poem. Wish I could do something as good."

"Didn't know she had it in her," Lucy said.

---

5. Pleased, satisfied.

Mary was haughty. "She better look out when Prosser sees it, that's all."

"*If* she sees it," Angus said. "She's not back yet."

"Won't work if she doesn't," Lucy said. "Then we'll have wasted all that effort."

Mary, knowing everything, could not help saying, "She fell off her bike. Sally-Ann told me. They kept her home to make sure she's okay."

"Serves her right," Angus said, and left them to join his friends, who were giggling and pointing at the "Special Feature" in the newspaper, which had a title made by Angus in large letters at the top:

BULLIES.

"Fell off her bike?" Lucy said. She had to sit down; a sudden terrible guilt made her feel weak.

Please, God, she prayed, you didn't did you? I'll never, never, never pray for anyone to fall off anything again, if you'll only make Melanie all right.

She felt dizzy at the prospect that God might actually have been listening all the time. She wondered what else He might have heard that she would rather He hadn't.

Half an hour later Melanie arrived.

"Good heavens, Melanie, what have you done to yourself?" Mrs. Harris exclaimed.

Melanie had a fierce black-and-blue bruise circling one eye and a large dressing plastered over her forehead.

She handed Mrs. Harris a letter.

The wall newspaper lost its interest at once, of course; all eyes were fixed on Melanie. There were surreptitious mutterings at the sight of her.

Meanwhile, Mrs. Harris shook her head sorrowfully as she read, and then announced briskly: "Melanie met with an accident. But apparently her wounds are only superficial." She inspected Melanie at close quarters. "Though I must say, you do look dreadful, dear."

"I'm all right!" Melanie said sharply enough to make Mrs. Harris bridle.

"Are you sure?"

Melanie nodded sheepishly, and, looking away, caught sight of the newspaper, picking out at once, Lucy noticed, Angus's headline: BULLIES. But she turned away pretending not to have seen.

Mrs. Harris said, "Very well. But perhaps we'd better let you take things quietly today."

As soon as Melanie was settled in her place, Sally-Ann, perking up, whispered, "Have you seen what they've done?"

"Your name and all," Vicky said. "Need sorting, they do. A few throat chops."

"Wait till you read it," Sally-Ann said with smug satisfaction. "You'll just die."

Melanie ignored them, giving such a good performance of being relaxed, offhand, unaware, that everyone could see she was acting.

"There!" Lucy called to Angus as they sped into the playground after lunch. "Making straight for Clare. Told you!"

They ran and caught up just as Melanie said, "You put them up to this, didn't you, fatso!"

"No!" Clare said, with a new defiance.

"Liar. And it's your poem, isn't it, and it has my name in."

"Leave her alone," Lucy said pushing between them.

At the same time, Angus was shouting, "Olly, Gordon, Sam, Hyacinth!" and waving them over.

Sally-Ann and Vicky let go of Clare to deal with Lucy. But she struggled, and slipped, and found herself sitting down with a bump. The other two, empty-handed, didn't know what to do, so turned their attentions back to Clare. Which made Lucy realize what an advantage it was being on the ground.

"Sit!" she shouted at Clare, who only stared back, not comprehending. "Sit!" Lucy yelled, sounding as bad as the awful woman on television who barked at dogs.

Obediently, unthinking, Clare sat, plonk, as if her legs had been knocked from under her. Sally-Ann and Vicky fumbled, trying to force her up; but Clare was dead weight, even for Vicky.

"Get up!" Melanie bellowed.

But by now Angus and the others were crowding round, distracting her. She surveyed them in a rapid turn, and forced a grin. "Ganging up, is it," she said.

Angus, seeing what Lucy was up to (or down to) said, "We're not ganging up on anybody, Prosser," and he jackknifed, sitting cross-legged on the ground. "I'm just watching the show." He looked up at Roland and Sam and the others.

"Yeah," they said, catching on, "yeah, we're just sitting here to watch what you're doing." And they joined Lucy and Angus, sitting on the ground in a circle round Melanie.

Lucy leaned back on her hands, feeling exhilarated at the turn of events: Melanie was not at all comfortable with what was going on. "What were you saying, Melanie, dear?" she said.

"Terrific poem, eh?" Angus said. "Clare's I mean."

Sally-Ann screeched, "Go and crawl back down your hole, Burns!"

"Shut it!" Melanie said. "Can't you see what they're trying to do?"

Sally-Ann apparently couldn't: her brow furrowed.

Lucy said, "*We're* not doing anything. You're the one who's doing things."

It was an odd sight: Melanie, Sally-Ann and Vicky standing in a triangle, almost back to back, surrounded by a circle of five or six lounging on the ground. Other kids, curious, came wandering across. "What's on?" they asked. "Another of Mel's shows?" So a second, larger crowd was very soon standing round the first. But everyone was unaccustomedly quiet. Nothing seemed to be happening, yet plainly something was. Or was going to.

For a start, no one could mistake that Melanie was seething with fury. Not just angry. But raging. And all her rage was churning inside her like steam locked inside a boiler. The bruise round her eye had turned a vivid, glowing purple; her mouth became a tight, lipless line across her face.

Lucy, sitting in range of Melanie's feet, wondered if she might lose her temper and lash out.

"I'll get you, Tonks!" Melanie said. "Pukey and Burns won't be with you all the time."

"Maybe not, Prosser," Lucy said, "but every time you do anything to one of us, we're going to put something up about it on the wall. We'll keep *notes* about your bullying, and let *everybody* read them."

"Yeah," Angus added, "even if it's just the names of kids you pick on."

After which, to everyone's surprise, Clare said, "And we'll list the presents you take."

"That's right," Lucy said. "A list of names, a list of things you do, and a list of the things you *steal*."

"Where everybody can read them," Angus said.

A silence hung in the air. Melanie looked from one to the next.

Then her rage exploded: the boiler burst, and she screamed with a force that made them all flinch: "You dare! You just dare!"

Her body went rigid, her fists, clenched, beat against her thighs.

Only Angus managed to reply. "Why?" he shouted back. "What'll you do? Take us all on? Make us all shoplift? Not all of us at once, you can't. And we'll be watching. And whatever you do, we'll still write the lists."

Melanie glared at him with deep loathing. "I'll show you if I care about your stupid notes!" she said, hissing at him like a cornered animal. "I'll show you what I think of her poem, and your pukey newspaper." She turned, taking them all in. "I'll show you what I think of all you CREEPS!"

And she set off, like a runner from starting blocks, scattering bodies out of her way, running through the crowd and across the playground toward the school door.

Lucy and Angus scrambled to their feet, Clare struggling up after them.

"She's making for our room," Lucy said.

Others had thought of this too and were already racing, first after Melanie, then, realizing they might get stopped inside, swinging toward the windows of 4H's classroom, whose blank eyes were open against the heat.

Lucy and Angus chased after, Clare pounding along behind.

Sally-Ann and Vicky could not at once decide what to do: follow Melanie, stay where they were, or follow the crowd. But finding themselves alone, hesitated no longer and dashed off after the others.

Lucy, Angus and Clare reached the windows as Melanie came panting into the room. From outside, they watched as she crashed through chairs and against tables, scattering belongings and half-finished work and interrupted books. She made straight for the wall newspaper, reaching out as she got to it, and clawing at Angus's bold headline. She tore at it. BULLIES came ripping down in a streamer of wounded letters. Melanie tore it again and again and again, shredding it into confetti that she scattered around her feet.

Then she reached up again and again in a fever of passion so violent it almost took Lucy's breath away. She ripped and tore and shredded: the Guess Who descriptions, the jokes and puzzles and finally Clare's poem.

Clare's poem sent her into the climax of her rage. She ripped it into smaller and smaller pieces, panting, crying, grunting as she did so.

And then, coming to the window, tossed the pieces out at Lucy and Angus and Clare, on whose heads they fell like ragged snowflakes.

"That's what I care!" she tried to shout, but had no breath for it. "That's what I care!"

And Lucy and Angus and Clare, the rest of the school crowding round, watched with silent, saddened faces.

15

No one saw Melanie again that term. She had been taken for an early holiday, Mrs. Harris said: but Sally-Ann babbled about Melanie being taken into a foster home because of trouble with her dad.

"He do poke her in the eye again," Vicky said, laughing.

"Serves her right," Angus said, but felt ashamed.

The Saturday before end of term, Lucy and Angus met Mary in town and they chose Mrs. Harris's present. Lucy already knew what she wanted to buy, but guessed that Mary would like to be consulted.

"What about a set of felt tips for marking?" Lucy said.

"Uses gallons of red on me every day," Angus said.

At the stationer's they picked out three: a red, a green and a black, each with a new kind of tip. They were so cheap there was money left for something else.

"Have you a tray for keeping the pens, please?" Lucy asked.

"How about this?" the assistant said. "There's a place for paper clips, and for an eraser, and the pens rest here."

Lucy and Angus exchanged startled glances.

"That'll be just right," Mary said, taking charge again.

There was a party on the last day. Mrs. Harris was delighted with her present. "You've been a pleasure to teach," she said, sniffling.

No one even mentioned Melanie, but Lucy couldn't help remembering. To cheer herself up, she looked again at the note clutched in her hand. She had found it a few minutes ago stuck to an ice cream Angus had brought her.

W8 4 U RLY XING 1630 A xxx

1983

ALMA FLOR ADA
b. 1938

Alma Flor Ada was born and raised in Cuba; her extended family lived in a big, old house called La Quinta Simoni (named for its original occupants). The neighbors thought the family of freethinkers and intellectuals eccentric and believed their house to be haunted, but it contains Ada's fondest early memories. Before she was three years old, Ada was taught to read by her grandmother. As a child she especially enjoyed taking her books up into a tall tree, delighted both to read in nature and to watch the river wildlife below. In *Where the Flame Trees Bloom* (1994) and *Under the Royal Palms: A Childhood in Cuba* (1998), she recounts family stories and memories of her happy childhood.

Ada was educated in universities in Spain and Peru, receiving a Ph.D. in Spanish literature; she moved to the United States in 1970. Since 1976 she has been a professor in the Department of International and Multicultural Education at the University of San Francisco, where she also directs the Center for Multicultural Literature for Children and Young Adults. Though she had dreamed about

writing for children since childhood, Ada credits her own children for inspiring her to write creatively. Her then three-year-old daughter Rosalma Zubizarreta (herself an author, who now collaborates with her mother by translating her books into Spanish or English) told Ada that the scholarly works she was writing were "ugly books." Ada took that criticism to heart and began to publish books in Spanish for young children. Ada's children's books have been widely recognized by such groups as the American Folklore Association, the Parents' Choice Foundation, and the American Library Association. Many of Ada's picture books and books for young readers are retellings of Latin American folktales or are set in Latin America. Ada's popular *Dear Peter Rabbit* (1994, translated into Spanish as *Querido Pedrín*), and its sequel *Yours Truly, Goldilocks* (1998), uses an epistolary format to bring various characters from numerous children's stories together.

In *Me Llamo María Isabel* (*My Name Is María Isabel*, 1993), Alma Flor Ada confronts a teacher's insensitivity to cultural difference and the pain of misused names that causes a young student to withdraw. The experience she narrates comes from working with parents, teachers, and children in schools; it also recalls her own experiences of being the new girl in class and her difficulties in getting people to understand that her first name is actually "Alma Flor."

A translator and editor as well as an author and academic, Ada is strongly committed to bilingual education; she was founder and first editor in chief of the *Journal of the National Association for Bilingual Education*, and she supports bilingualism in the schools and home in her many books for children—most of which are written in Spanish and later translated into English. *Gathering the Sun: An Alphabet in Spanish and English* (1997, with translations by Rosa Zubizarreta) celebrates the lives of farmworkers through the perspective of a child. Each poem in Spanish about nature, fieldwork, and cultural pride is linked to a letter in the Spanish alphabet. An English translation accompanies each poem.

My Name Is María Isabel

1. ON THE WAY TO SCHOOL

María Isabel looked at the cup of coffee with milk and the buttered toast in front of her. But she couldn't bring herself to eat.

Her mother said, "Maribel, *cariño*,[1] hurry up."

Her father added, "You don't want to be late on your first day, do you?"

But instead of finishing her breakfast, María Isabel just kept staring at the butter as it slowly melted into the toast, and at the cloud of steam that floated over her cup.

"You'll see, you'll like your new school," her mother said. But her mother's soft, reassuring voice didn't seem to convince María Isabel. María Isabel knew it wasn't going to be easy starting at a new school, especially when the school year had already begun. She was probably the only new student. She kept thinking what bad luck it was that they had had to move two months after school had started. And she had had so many plans to spend her winter vacation playing with Clara and Virginia.

"You'll make new friends soon," said María Isabel's father, as if he could read her thoughts.

María Isabel kept staring at the cup. But when her brother, Antonio, chimed in, "Come on, Belita, hurry up. You're going to make me late," she gulped down her coffee, even though it burned her tongue. María Isabel shook her head, trying to shake the nervous thoughts from her head.

She got up and grabbed her blue backpack. María Isabel had always wanted a backpack, and at the store last Saturday, this seemed to be just the right one. She had been so happy when her mother decided to buy it, even though it was more expensive than the red one. Later that day, when María Isabel was alone in the apartment, she had walked back and forth with the pack on her shoulders and had even climbed up onto the toilet seat to see how she looked in the bathroom mirror. But now it just seemed heavy, and María Isabel couldn't understand why she had liked it so much.

"Good-bye, Mami," María Isabel said softly to her mother, who was already washing the glasses and cups from breakfast.

1. Love (Spanish).

"See you later, my love. May God be with you," her mother answered back, giving María Isabel a kiss on the forehead. Then she dunked her hands back into the soapy water.

"Good-bye, honey," her father said. "Be good at school and listen to your teacher. You know that your teacher at school is like your mother here at home."

"Yes, Papi. Good-bye," said María Isabel, and she got up on her tiptoes to hug her father. Then she took from the table the lunch bag her mother had prepared. María Isabel would have loved to stay in their warm kitchen with its smell of freshly brewed coffee. If only she could sit there all morning hugging her father, who always made her feel safe and secure. But a sudden blast of cold air told her that Antonio was waiting for her at the door.

By the time Antonio and María Isabel got to the front door of their apartment building, the yellow school bus was almost at the bus stop. "Come on, Belita. Run," Antonio called out.

María Isabel started to run. Her new boots, a present for her ninth birthday, made the dry leaves on the sidewalk crunch beneath her feet. In her rush to keep up with her brother, María Isabel did not see a section of sidewalk that, was jutting up because of a tree root. Before she knew what had happened, she had tripped and fallen.

The first thing she heard was laughter. She didn't even realize that Antonio was talking to her. "Are you all right?" he asked her as he helped María Isabel off the ground.

María Isabel didn't answer him. She just bent down to pick up her smushed-up lunch bag. Her knee hurt a lot, but María Isabel was determined to walk to the bus without stopping to look at it. What she couldn't help but notice was the dress her mother had washed and ironed so carefully the night before, and that was now streaked with dirt.

It was her favorite yellow dress, the dress that Aunt Aurea had made especially for her. María Isabel's grandmother had given her the fabric as a gift the last time they had gone to Puerto Rico to visit. María Isabel only wore the dress for special occasions. She had decided to wear it today for good luck on her first day of school. She had hoped the dress would help her feel a little less out of place with these new kids, the same new kids who were now laughing and chattering away on the bus while all María Isabel could do was look down at her bloody knee.

2. Names and Surnames

"Good morning," whispered María Isabel, standing in front of her new teacher's desk. Antonio had gone with her to the principal's office and then left to go to his own school, which was a block away. The secretary had given María Isabel a pink slip and then asked a boy to show her where Room 17 was. And now that she was there, María Isabel didn't know what would happen next.

The other kids had already taken their seats. Some were taking out their books and binders while others just seemed to be waiting for class to start. Many of them were smiling and talking to each other.

María Isabel looked up at an enormous turkey made of construction paper on the wall behind the teacher's desk. She started to read the names that were on each of the tail feathers: Jonathan, Eric, Michelle, Solomon, Laurie, Freddie, Marta, Ricardo, María Sánchez . . .

The teacher had not looked up yet. She was making notes in a large folder where

María Isabel could see a list of names. María Isabel heard quiet laughter behind her. The teacher looked up only when the noise got louder.

"Why, hello," she said, giving María Isabel a warm smile. But it didn't seem to make María Isabel feel more comfortable. "So you are . . . ."

"María Isabel Salazar López," she replied. In Spanish she would have added, "para servirle,"[2] but she didn't know how to say that in English. So María Isabel kept quiet and handed the pink slip to her teacher.

"Ah, María Lopez," the teacher said as she read the card. "We already have two Marías in this class. Why don't we call you Mary instead? Take a seat over there by Marta Pérez, and I'll give you your books later."

María Isabel quietly headed for her seat. Marta Pérez looked up from her book as María Isabel came toward her. She had short hair and bangs. María Isabel lowered her eyes, and neither girl said a word.

A little while later, the teacher came over holding a thick book with a green cover. The book was brand-new and had a picture of a dolphin on the front. María Isabel wondered what the book was about, and if she would be able to read it. She loved the sea and had always dreamed of seeing a real dolphin, so she opened the book eagerly. On the inside cover the teacher had written the name Mary Lopez.

María Isabel stared at the words. Her teacher's handwriting was so neat and pretty. It seemed almost impossible to María Isabel that anyone could write so beautifully. As she looked at that strange name, Mary Lopez, María Isabel thought about her old schoolbooks. She had always enjoyed looking at the first page of a new book. Her mother's handwriting wasn't as pretty as her teacher's. But as they both sat at the kitchen table, her mother would write María Isabel's name in her new books, saying " 'María' is for your grandmother María, who you never knew but would have loved you so; 'Isabel' is for your grandmother Chabela, who loves you so dearly; 'Salazar' is for your father and, of course, for your grandfather Antonio; 'López' is for me and for your grandfather Manuel. You were very small when he died, but you would have loved him. Oh, the stories he would tell!"

María Isabel was proud of being named after her two grandmothers. Grandmother María was only a name to her, but she had often gazed at the picture that her father kept and cherished. Each time they moved, it was always the last thing to be packed, wrapped up neatly so it wouldn't get damaged. Later it would always be the first thing to be hung up on the wall of their new apartment.

And she liked being named after her grandmother Chabela, her sweet, smiling grandmother who lived in Puerto Rico and always seemed to smell of camomile, anisette, and cinnamon. Her sweets were so tasty that everyone would come by and try some. Grandmother Chabela kept the money she made selling her sweets in a tin cookie jar, and would tell María Isabel, "This is so you can study someday, my child, and not spend your whole life in a kitchen." She was the same Grandmother Chabela who had given her the fabric for the dress she was wearing, now streaked with blood and dirt.

"Mary. Mary Lopez. Mary *Lopeeez*," her teacher called out, her voice rising higher and higher. María Isabel's thoughts vanished like a puff of smoke. But it wasn't her teacher's shrill voice that shook her out of her daydreams but the silence that had followed in its wake.

"I'm talking to you, Mary." The teacher was now right by her desk, looking at María

2. [I am here] to serve you (idiomatic expression of polite deference).

Isabel with a mix of surprise and impatience. María Isabel slumped down in her seat and looked at the dolphin that leaped across the cover of her book. She didn't know how to tell the teacher that she just didn't recognize herself in that strange new name.

3. RECESS

When the bell rang for recess, María Isabel waited for the rest of the kids to leave the class first. She wanted to see what they were going to do. María Isabel had started school in Puerto Rico. Then, when her family moved to the mainland, she had started going to another school. Her classes there had been in Spanish, and María Isabel had liked her teachers very much. Miss Herrera, who taught second grade, always praised her for her math, and she had started to teach María Isabel English. María

Isabel especially liked Miss Peyrellade, her third grade teacher, who read wonderful stories and would teach the class outdoors on warm, sunny days.

María Isabel missed her old friends. She didn't know anyone at this new school yet. So she just walked behind the other kids until they reached the schoolyard, and stood in a corner once she got there. After a few minutes, Marta Pérez came over and took her by the hand.

"Come on, let's go jump rope," Marta said, tugging on María Isabel's arm. María Isabel hesitated, and Marta tugged again. "Come on," she urged.

María Isabel followed Marta to the middle of the yard where she held one end of the jump rope as a girl in plaid jumped up and down. The rhythm of the jump rope as it brushed the ground was soothing. It reminded María Isabel of her grandmother Chabela's rocking chair, the one her grandmother would rock her to sleep in, or of the ebb and flow of the waves in front of her grandfather Antonio's house. The waves would gently roll up the beach in the small bay and wash over the sand where the fishing nets were drying on top of the boats.

María Isabel loved that beach. She loved to go out for a walk early in the morning, picking up treasures the sea had left behind the night before: shells that looked like mother-of-pearl; bits of white coral; maybe even a sand dollar or two. And she liked to go swimming at midday, jumping in the waves and playing with the sea spray, feeling the coolness of the clear water beneath the hot sun.

"Go on, it's your turn," the girl in plaid shouted to María Isabel, bringing her back from her daydream.

"No, no," she answered in a low voice. "Not now." María Isabel didn't want the other girls to think she didn't know how to jump rope, but her knee still hurt from her fall. The girl in plaid jumped into the middle again. María Isabel thought, It would be so great to get in the middle and let the rope go back and forth; over and under me. My feet wouldn't touch the rope even once. But she didn't think she would be able to jump well with her hurt knee, and soon the bell rang. Recess was over.

María Isabel followed the two other girls. They hadn't spoken much, and she didn't know the name of the girl in plaid. But they had asked her to jump with them. Tomorrow, when her knee didn't hurt so much, she would show them how well she could jump. And as she limped slightly back to class, María Isabel thought this new school wasn't going to be so bad after all. If only her teacher would not insist on calling her Mary!

4. MARY LÓPEZ

The next day, María Isabel found out that the girl in the plaid dress was one of the Marías in the class, María Fernández. The other María, María Sánchez, had very long braids and spent all her time at recess with her older sister.

María Isabel, on the other hand, began spending recess with María Fernández and Marta Pérez. She even jumped rope when they asked her to, even though her knee still hurt a little.

Over the next few days, she also got used to the rhythm of the school day. There was reading and math in the morning. Their teacher stressed doing well in math, and this was fine with María Isabel. She never had a problem working with numbers.

But best of all, Marta Pérez came up to her during lunch one day and said, "Come with me. I'll show you where the library is. They have tons of magazines!"

"Can we go without the teacher?" asked María Isabel.

"Sure. We can go in whenever we want to at lunchtime," replied Marta, pointing at an open door down the hall.

"Great!" said María Isabel. "At my other school, we could only go to the library when the teacher took the class."

The librarian was sitting at her desk behind some piles of books. She looked up as the girls came in, and smiled warmly. María Isabel felt that her smile was an invitation to feel at home.

Marta went straight to the magazines and grabbed a pile. She sat down on the rug, crossed her legs, and started to read a Batman comic.

María Isabel wandered between the stacks of books. She had never been left alone with so many books before, and she wasn't sure which one to pick. She looked at the titles carefully. Every now and then, she took a book off the shelf to look at the cover. She was holding a book in her hand when she realized the librarian was standing right next to her. María Isabel was surprised because she had not heard the librarian walk up to her, but she felt at ease looking into the woman's sparkling eyes. The librarian bent down and said quietly, as if she and María Isabel were sharing a secret, "Take it. You'll really like it."

As she walked out of the library, María Isabel thought, This new school really isn't so bad. It isn't so hard having classes only in English, and Marta Pérez is really nice. It's too bad Virginia and Clara aren't here, though.

But María Isabel's teacher lost her patience again that afternoon. The teacher asked if anyone knew who the Pilgrims were. Eric said they were sailors who had made a very long trip. Then the teacher turned to María Isabel and said, "Would Mary López tell us what she knows about the Pilgrims?"

María Isabel didn't answer. Again she didn't realize the teacher was calling on her. If she had known, she would have said that the Pilgrims had come to America looking for a better way of life, and that many others came here after them. Perhaps she would even have dared to say that everyone was a Pilgrim in some way. That was what Miss Peyrellade had said.

But María Isabel didn't say anything, and her teacher was getting angry. She glared at María Isabel and said, "When I ask you something, you have to answer, Mary." She turned away and nodded at Solomon, who had raised his hand.

"The Pilgrims came to America to have freedom to practice their religion," Solomon answered.

María Isabel hung her head low for the rest of the afternoon. She worried that all the other kids would think that she was dumb for not having answered the teacher's question. The next day, she had trouble eating her breakfast again, and Antonio was annoyed with her.

"I don't want to have to run to the bus today, Belita," he complained. "Make her hurry, Mamá. Doesn't she care if she's late for school?"

Her mother didn't pay attention to Antonio, but she did help María Isabel put on her jacket and gave her her backpack and lunch bag.

While they were having a snack that afternoon, María Isabel's mother finally asked, "How was school today, Maribel?"

María Isabel said, "Fine." She didn't know what else to say. She felt she couldn't tell her mother that her math class was going well, but that she had forgotten to answer when her teacher called her Mary again that afternoon. And her teacher always seemed to be upset with her.

Antonio, on the other hand, couldn't stop talking about his new friends and about the great band his school had. Or about the baseball team. But even though Antonio talked on and on, their mother didn't really seem to listen. She seemed to have a lot on her mind lately.

The family had moved because Mr. Salazar had a new job cleaning and maintaining a small group of apartment buildings. And as a part of the job, his family could live in one of the apartments. María Isabel's parents had been happy about the move because now they wouldn't have to pay rent anymore. Antonio was happy because the apartment had three bedrooms, and he would finally have a room of his own. And Antonio always liked new things.

But Mrs. Salazar was having trouble getting used to the new neighborhood. She couldn't find the ingredients she used in her cooking. She would try to substitute new things, but she wasn't happy with the results. And even though they didn't have to pay rent for the apartment, Mr. Salazar's pay didn't seem to go far enough to make ends meet.

At dinner that night, Mrs. Salazar announced, "I'm going to look for a job tomorrow. I'll try to be home when you children get home from school, but here is a key to the door in case I'm not." María Isabel's mother handed her a key attached to a long pink ribbon. "Come straight home from school and wait for me here. Don't leave the house, and don't open the door to anyone."

María Isabel felt a little strange the next day, walking around with the pink ribbon around her neck. In one way, it wasn't that unusual. She had always worn something around her neck. First, it had been a pendant with the image of the Virgin Mary, a baptism present from her godmother. Then she had worn a cross that her godfather had given her when she was seven years old. María Isabel was so used to wearing something around her neck that she usually forgot it was there. But the key was different. At times, it made her feel important and grown up. María Isabel noticed that some of the other girls also wore keys, and she felt that they all had something in common. Most of the day, though, the key just made her feel sad.

When she finally got home and opened the door, all María Isabel found was silence. Her mother wasn't there. Antonio had stayed after school for band practice. Ever since he learned to play the drums, Antonio spent all his free time practicing.

The apartment felt like an empty box. María Isabel sat down at the kitchen table. She took out a piece of paper and a pencil from her backpack and started to write: *María Isabel Salazar López, María Isabel Salazar López, María Isabel Salazar López.* Each time she wrote her name, the letters got bigger and bigger until she reached the bottom of the page. María Isabel crumpled the paper up into a ball and threw it at the garbage can, but she missed. She thought about how Antonio would tease her about her aim if he were here and, for a moment, she was glad to be alone. She got up and put the crumpled page in the trash. Then she went to see what there was to eat in the kitchen cabinet.

María Isabel had set the table by the time her father got home from work. Dinner was almost ready. A large bowl of salad sat in the center of the table, while the rice and beans on the stove top were ready to be served. The only thing left to do was to cook the meat.

Mrs. Salazar was exhausted when she got home. She plopped down into a chair and took off her shoes. She smiled when she saw the food and the table.

After they had all sat down to eat, father said, "You've done a wonderful job of helping your mother, María Isabel."

Her mother quickly added, "The rice is delicious! We did the right thing naming you María Isabel. You are as good a cook as your grandmother Chabela."

Antonio didn't say anything, but he did help himself to more beans.

María Isabel wanted to smile and be happy. She liked pleasing her parents, and she knew she had done a good job making dinner. But the same thought kept running through her head, over and over again: How can I feel proud of being named María Isabel when I have to listen so carefully every time the teacher calls for "Mary Lopez"?

5. THE FIRST SNOWFALL

The city was covered by a beautiful blanket of snow. María Isabel couldn't tear herself away from her bedroom window. The snow had covered up all the trash cans and had turned the alleyway her room faced into an enchanted tunnel. The city seemed to be wrapped in silence.

María Isabel tried to step in Antonio's boot prints as they walked to the bus stop. She didn't want to do anything to disturb the wonderful, newly fallen snow. Once she was at school, she kept thinking about the snow all during math. María Isabel wondered if there was enough snow in the alleyway to make a snowman, and if she would be able to see it from her window.

Suddenly she remembered that she hadn't finished her multiplication exercises, and hurried to complete her work. María Isabel was so busy trying to finish the page that she didn't hear the teacher call out, in an irritated tone of voice, "Mary Lopez!" When at last she realized that the teacher was waiting for an answer from her, María Isabel had no idea what the question had been.

"Well, it looks like Mary doesn't want to take part in our Winter Pageant," the teacher said. "That's all right. You can help Tony and Jonathan greet the parents at the door and show them where they can put the food and hang up their coats."

The Winter Pageant . . . María Isabel couldn't think about anything else on the ride home from school. The teacher had told them they would be staging *Amahl and the Night Visitors*.[3] María Isabel remembered seeing the story on television once and liking it very much. I know I wouldn't have gotten to play Mary, she thought, because Ann would be so much better for that part, with her long hair and all. But I would have loved to be a shepherd. I could have used Mama's straw basket, and it would have been so wonderful . . .

María Isabel turned toward the window of the school bus so that no one would see her wiping a tear. When she looked out, she saw that the morning's bright, clean snow had been shoveled and trampled, and was now covered with soot and grime. She wished that she could be with her friend Clara. Clara would understand how María Isabel felt.

María Isabel took out her library book and started to read. She didn't want to look at the dirty snow or think about the pageant anymore. The book was titled *Charlotte's Web*.[4] Fern's life on the farm seemed so simple and carefree to María Isabel. She would have liked to live that way, surrounded by farm animals. She would have plenty of time to sit in the barn and listen to them talk. María Isabel wondered, Why can't real life be more like the books I read?

3. A short opera by Gian-Carlo Menotti, commissioned for television in 1951; in this version of the Christmas story, the crippled boy Amahl and his mother are visited by the three wise men, or kings, on their way to bring gifts to the infant Jesus.
4. The classic 1952 children's novel by E. B. White.

6. THANKSGIVING

On Thanksgiving Day, Mr. and Mrs. Salazar decided to visit their friends in the old neighborhood. It was a last-minute decision they made after dinner was over, when it felt to everyone that there was something missing. The Salazar family had known a lot of people in their old apartment building, and there was always someone to say hello to or to invite in for some coffee and conversation.

Antonio and María Isabel were delighted. On the long subway ride, María Isabel thought about all the things she'd tell Clara and Virginia about her new school.

As soon as they got to the Hernández apartment, María Isabel asked if she could go and visit her friends. She ran upstairs to the third floor to Virginia's apartment. Her next-door neighbor said Virginia had gone to have Thanksgiving dinner at her grandparents'. So María Isabel went to see if Clara was home. When Clara opened the door, her face broke into a big smile, and she hugged María Isabel. María Isabel thought Clara had changed a lot. Then she realized that her friend was wearing makeup. Clara wanted María Isabel to meet her cousin who lived next door. She had just arrived from Puerto Rico.

"Her name is Carmen. And she's thirteen! I know you'll like her," Clara said as she rang the doorbell.

Carmen answered the door. "What a pretty friend you have!" she exclaimed as she led the two girls into the apartment. She looked at María Isabel and added, "Come with me. I'll make you even prettier."

Carmen went into her room and came back with a plastic box full of makeup. She sat María Isabel down in front of a mirror and started to work on her face. Carmen painted María Isabel's lips, put some blush on her cheeks, and applied some eye shadow. Then she brushed María Isabel's hair back and pinned it with a flowered barrette.

"Carmen is going to be a hairdresser," said Clara. "Isn't she good?"

"And a makeup artist," Carmen added. "Someday I'm going to work in Hollywood and do the makeup for all the big stars."

"And you'll know them all!" Clara said excitedly.

Carmen went back into her room to get some magazines. She told the girls all sorts of things about the movie stars in the magazines, and about how she would make up each one.

An hour had gone by before María Isabel knew it. "I have to wash my face," she said. "My mother doesn't want me to wear makeup yet."

"No, don't wash your face," said Carmen. "I'll take most of it off with a tissue." Carmen wiped off the makeup, leaving only a trace behind. María Isabel got up to leave.

"Wait, don't go yet," Carmen said, and she'd dabbed some perfume on María Isabel's wrists.

"Thanks a lot, Carmen. I hope I'll see you again before you go to Hollywood." Clara walked María Isabel back to the Hernández apartment. They walked slowly, trying to stretch their remaining time together.

"How come you never call me? Or Virginia either?" Clara finally asked her.

"Mamá doesn't want us to use the phone unless we have to. But I'll ask if I can call you Sunday," she replied.

"And I'll call you on the Sunday after that," Clara said as they reached the Hernándezes' door.

On the way home, María Isabel thought of all the things that she didn't tell Clara about her new school, especially about her teacher, who always seemed to be so angry with her. They'd had such a good time that she had forgotten all about school. She was already looking forward to calling Clara on Sunday. María Isabel was smiling quietly to herself when suddenly Antonio said, "It looks like your friends think it's Carnaval[5] instead of Thanksgiving."

María Isabel tried to bury her face in her coat. She should have washed her face after all. But her father just laughed. "Leave your sister alone, Antonio. Chabelita is going to be a very pretty young woman someday."

Mr. Salazar leaned over and hugged his daughter. "But that day hasn't come yet. Right, Chabelita?"

María Isabel saw that her mother was smiling too, and then she knew that there really were good reasons to be thankful on this Thanksgiving.

7. THE WINTER PAGEANT

Everything at school now revolved around plans for the Winter Pageant. The class was making wreaths and lanterns. The teacher explained to the class that Christmas is celebrated differently in different countries, and that many people don't celebrate Christmas at all. They talked about Santa Claus, and how he is called Saint Nicholas in some countries and Father Christmas in others. The class also talked about the Jewish feast of Hanukkah that celebrates the rededication of the Temple of Jerusalem, and about the special meaning of the nine candles of the Hanukkah menorah.

The teacher had asked everyone to bring in pictures or other things having to do with the holidays. A lot of kids brought in photographs of their families by their Christmas trees. Mayra brought in pictures of New Year's Day in Santo Domingo. Michelle brought in a picture of herself sitting on Santa's lap when she was little. Gabriel brought in photos of the Three Kings' Day[6] parade in Miami, Florida. He had been there last year, when he went to visit his Cuban grandmother. Marcos brought in a piñata shaped like a green parrot that his uncle had brought back from Mexico. Emmanuel showed everyone a photo album of his family's trip to Israel, and Esther brought in cards her grandfather had sent her from Jerusalem.

One day, Suni Paz[7] came to the school. She sang Christmas songs from different countries and taught the class to sing a Hanukkah song, "The Candles of Hanukkah." María Isabel went home humming softly "Hanukkah . . . Hanukkah . . . Let us celebrate." The bus trip seemed a lot shorter as the song ran through her head. It almost felt as if she had traveled to all those different countries and had celebrated all those different holidays.

María Isabel was still singing while she made dinner and set the table:

"With our menorah,
Fine potato latkes,
Our clay trumpets,
Let us celebrate."

---

5. The most popular festival in Spanish culture, held before Ash Wednesday as a counterweight to the coming austerity of Lent.
6. Epiphany (January 6), a holiday throughout the Hispanic world; it celebrates the revelation of Jesus as King of the Jews, as signaled by the coming of

the three wise men (see Matthew 2.1–12).
7. A writer and performer of folk music and children's music; born in Argentina before World War II, she has been living in the United States since 1965. She began collaborating with Alma Flor Ada in 1984.

Her voice filled the empty kitchen. María Isabel was so pleased she promised herself that she'd make a snowman the next time it snowed. And she'd get it finished before the garbage men picked up the trash and dirtied up the snow.

But after Suni Paz's visit to the school, the days seemed to drag by more and more slowly. María Isabel didn't have anything to do during rehearsals, since she didn't have a part in *Amahl*.

The teacher decided that after the play the actors would sing some holiday songs, including María Isabel's favorite about the Hanukkah candles. Since she didn't have a part, María Isabel wouldn't be asked to sing either.

It didn't seem to matter much to Tony and Jonathan, the other two kids who weren't in the play. They spent rehearsal time reading comics or whispering to each other. Neither boy spoke to María Isabel, and she was too shy to say anything to them.

The only fun she had was reading her library book. Somehow her problems seemed so small compared to Wilbur the pig's. He was in danger of becoming the holiday dinner. María Isabel felt the only difference was that the characters in books always seemed to find answers to their problems, while she couldn't figure out what to do about her own.

As she cut out bells and stars for decorations, María Isabel daydreamed about being a famous singer. Someday she would sing in front of a large audience, and her teacher would feel guilty that she had not let María Isabel sing in the Winter Pageant.

But later María Isabel thought, My teacher isn't so bad. It's all a big misunderstanding . . . If only there was some way I could let her know. Even if I'm not a great singer someday, it doesn't matter. All I really want is to be myself and not make the teacher angry all the time. I just want to be in the play and to be called María Isabel Salazar López.

8. TRAPPED IN A SPIDER'S WEB

"I've asked my boss if I can leave work early the day of the school pageant," María Isabel's mother said one evening as she served the soup. "Papá is also going to leave work early. That way we'll be able to bring the rice and beans."

"And best of all, we can hear María Isabel sing," her father added.

María Isabel looked down at her soup. She had not told her parents anything. She knew they were going to be very disappointed when they saw the other kids in her class taking part in the play. She could just hear her mother asking, "Why didn't you sing? Doesn't the teacher know what a lovely voice you have?" María Isabel ate her soup in silence. What could she say?

"Don't you have anything to say, Chabelita?" asked her father. "Aren't you glad we're coming?"

"Sure, Papá, sure I am," said María Isabel, and she got up to take her empty bowl to the sink.

After helping her mother with the dishes, María Isabel went straight to her room. She put on her pajamas and got into bed. But she couldn't sleep, so she turned the light on and continued reading *Charlotte's Web*. María Isabel felt that she was caught in a sticky, troublesome spider's web of her own, and the more she tried to break loose, the more trapped she became.

When the librarian had told her that she would like the book, María Isabel had felt that they were sharing a secret. Now as she turned the pages, she thought that maybe the secret was that *everyone* has problems. She felt close to poor little Wilbur, being fattened up for Christmas dinner without even knowing it. He was a little like her parents, who were so eager to go to the pageant, not knowing what was waiting for them.

"It just isn't fair that this can't be a happy time for all of us!" María Isabel said out loud. She sighed. Then she turned off the light, snuggled under her blanket, and fell asleep trying to figure out a way to save Wilbur from becoming Christmas dinner.

9. My Greatest Wish

Two days were left until the pageant. The morning was cloudy and gray. On the way to school, María Isabel wondered if it was going to snow. Maybe she would be able to make that snowman. But shortly after she got to school, it started to drizzle.

Since they couldn't go outside, the students spent their time rehearsing. No one made a mistake. Melchior[8] didn't forget what he had to say to Amahl's mother. Amahl dropped his crutch only once. Best of all, though, the shepherds remembered when they were supposed to enter, without bumping into the Three Kings.

Even Tony and Jonathan seemed interested in the play. They volunteered to help carry the manger and the shepherds' baskets on- and offstage.

Satisfied with the final rehearsal, the teacher decided there was time for one last class exercise before vacation. "It's been a couple of days since we've done some writing," she said when the students returned to class. "The new year is a time for wishes. Sometimes wishes come true; sometimes they don't. But it's important to have wishes and, most of all, to know what you really want. I'd like you all to take out some paper and write an essay titled 'My Greatest Wish.'"

María Isabel sighed and put away *Charlotte's Web*. Charlotte had just died, and María Isabel wondered what was going to happen to the sack of eggs that Wilbur had saved, and when Charlotte's babies would be born. But María Isabel would have to wait to find out. She bit down on her pencil and wrote: "My greatest wish . . ."

This shouldn't be so hard, María Isabel thought. If I finish writing early, I can probably finish my book. She started to write: "My greatest wish is to make a snow-man. . . ."

María Isabel read over what she had just written, and realized that it wasn't what she really wanted. She put the paper aside, took out a new sheet, and wrote down the title again. "My greatest wish is to have a part in *Amahl*. . . ."

María Isabel stopped writing again. She thought, Would Charlotte have said that her greatest wish was to save Wilbur? Or would she have wished for something impossible, like living until the next spring and getting to know her children? The teacher just said that wishes don't always come true. If I'm going to wish for something, it should be something really worth wishing for.

María Isabel took out a third sheet of paper and wrote down the title again. This time, she didn't stop writing until she got to the bottom of the page.

My Greatest Wish

When I started to write I thought my greatest wish was to make a snowman. Then I thought my greatest wish was to have a part in the Winter Pageant. But I think my greatest wish is to be called María Isabel Salazar López. When that was my name, I felt proud of being named María like my papá's mother, and Isabel, like my grandmother Chabela. She is saving money so that I can study and not have to spend my whole life in a kitchen like her. I was Salazar like my papá and my

---

8. One of the three kings in the opera.

grandpa Antonio, and López, like my grandfather Manuel. I never knew him but he could really tell stories. I know because my mother told me.

If I was called María Isabel Salazar López, I could listen better in class because it's easier to hear than Mary López. Then I could have said that I wanted a part in the play. And when the rest of the kids sing, my mother and father wouldn't have to ask me why I didn't sing, even though I like the song about the Hanukkah candles so much.

The rest of the class had already handed in their essays and were cleaning out their desks to go home when María Isabel got up. She quietly went to the front of the room and put her essay on the teacher's desk. María Isabel didn't look up at the teacher, so she didn't see the woman smiling at her. She hurried back to her desk to get her things and leave.

Holiday spirit was everywhere at school the next day. The paper wreaths and lanterns the class had made were hung up all over the room. The teacher had put the "greatest wish" essays up on the bulletin board, next to the cutouts of Santa Claus, the Three Kings, and a menorah.

All the students were restless. Marta Pérez smiled when María Isabel sat down next to her. "Look at the pretty Christmas card I got from my cousin in Santo Domingo," she said excitedly. María Isabel looked at the tropical Christmas scene, all trimmed in flowers. But she couldn't answer Marta because the teacher had started to speak.

"We're going to do one last rehearsal because there's a small change in the program."

The rest of the kids listened attentively, but María Isabel just kept looking down at her desk. After all, she had nothing to do with the pageant.

Then she heard the teacher say, "María Isabel, María Isabel Salazar López . . ." María Isabel looked up in amazement.

"Wouldn't you like to lead the song about the Hanukkah candles?" the teacher said with a wide grin. "Why don't you start by yourself, and then everyone else can join in. Go ahead and start when you're ready."

María Isabel walked nervously up to the front of the room and stood next to the teacher, who was strumming her guitar. Then she took a deep breath and began to sing her favorite holiday song.

While her mother was getting the rice and beans ready that night, Mr. Salazar called María Isabel over to him. "Since you can't wear makeup yet, Chabelita, I've brought you something else that I think you'll like." In the palm of his hand were two barrettes for her hair. They were shaped like butterflies and gleamed with tiny stones.

"Oh, Papi. They're so pretty! Thank you!" María Isabel exclaimed. She hugged her father and ran to her room to put them on.

At school the next day, María Isabel stood in the center of the stage. She was wearing her special yellow dress, a pair of new shoes, and the shining butterflies. She spoke clearly to the audience. "My name is María Isabel Salazar López. I'm going to sing a song about the Jewish feast of Hanukkah, that celebrates the rededication of the Temple in Jerusalem." The music started, and María Isabel began to sing:

The Candles of Hanukkah

One little candle,
Two little candles,
Three little candles,
Let us celebrate.
Four little candles,
Five little candles,
Six little candles,
Let us celebrate.
Hanukkah, Hanukkah,
Let us celebrate.
Seven little candles,

Eight little candles,
Nine little candles,
Let us celebrate.
Hanukkah, Hanukkah,
Let us celebrate.
With our menorah,
Fine potato latkes,
Our clay trumpets,
Let us celebrate.
With our family,
With our friends,
With our presents,
Let us celebrate.

And the butterflies in María Isabel's hair sparkled under the stage lights so much that it seemed that they might just take off and fly.

1993

TIM WYNNE-JONES
b. 1948

Tim Wynne-Jones moved frequently as a child. He was born in England, and at the age of three moved with his family to the remote town of Kitimat, in British Columbia. By the time he graduated from high school, he had lived in twelve different houses in both western and eastern Canada. These frequent relocations made Wynne-Jones adept at making friends as well as comfortable at being alone, reading. In keeping with his family's roving ways, Wynne-Jones tried a number of vocations after high school, ranging from architecture student at the University of Waterloo and rock-and-roll singer to book designer and performance artist. Along the way he married and received a master's degree in visual arts from York University. Wynne-Jones first tried his hand at writing one summer when his wife was away on a trip driving across America. He rented a typewriter and in six weeks banged out a mystery thriller for adults. The book, *Odd's End* (1980), won an important first novel competition, and Wynne-Jones's career as a writer was launched. He and his wife and family of three children lived in Toronto for many years; they now live near Perth, Ontario.

Wynne-Jones's first successful book for children was the picture book *Zoom at Sea* (1983) about an adventurous cat and the pleasures of the imagination. He has written two sequels about Zoom (*Zoom Away*, 1985; *Zoom Upstream*, 1992). Although Wynne-Jones has written novels for adults, his publications are primarily for children and young adults—quirky picture books, short stories, and novels. His works have won numerous awards from Canada and the United States, including the Governor General's Award (twice), the Canadian Library Association's Children's Book of the Year Award (three times), and the Boston Globe–Horn Book Award. He has written radio plays for the Canadian Broadcasting Corporation (CBC) and a children's opera. Wynne-Jones is also a songwriter (he co-wrote a number of songs for Jim Henson's television show *Fraggle Rock*) and has been known to play rock and roll with his favorite band, the Usual Suspects. Wynne-Jones is on the faculty of Vermont College's Writing for Children and Young Adults MFA Program.

Wynne-Jones found writing *Some of the Kinder Planets* (1993), a book of short stories, his happiest writing experience ever, because "I came to realize when I was working on *Planets* that I would never be anyone else. . . . It is important to emulate writers you respect; they are like trainer wheels on your bike. But at some time the trainer wheels have to come off. I felt, when I was writing *Planets*, that I was riding on my own at last." This is a freedom that characters in the stories, such as Toby in "Tweedledum and Tweedledead," are willing to fight for. Wynne-Jones's comic take on a ubiquitous childhood school experience—writing an essay about what one did on summer vacation—both pays tribute to a classic children's text and promotes the importance of being true to yourself in writing.

Tweedledum and Tweedledead

"It's a commando raid on Wonderland," said Tobias.

Peach rolled her eyes. "This is your assignment?" she asked. "You're going to hand this in?"

Tobias looked at his notebook. Maybe he shouldn't have shown the story to Peach before it was finished. Something in him had said to keep it under his hat, but he had to show someone. Someone he trusted.

Now that someone had handed his story back without finishing the first page.

"It's this guy—"

"Sergeant Steele."

"Yeah. And he hates *Alice in Wonderland*.[1] At the end you find out that his parents forced the book down his throat when he was a kid. He really wanted to play outside, but they made him read instead. So now he has found out by grilling this weasely counterspy that there is a Wonderland. It actually exists. It's Top Secret. So he gets these guys together—"

"The Desperate Throng," said Peach. "I like that. It's good." Peach said "throng" a few times, throwing it off her teeth with her tongue. "The-wrong, the-wrong, the-wrong."

"Right," said Tobias, "and they plan this raid."

Peach rolled her eyes again. That was part of the reason she liked Tobias. No one gave her more reason to roll her eyes, and it was her best trick.

"Just tell me this," she said. "Does Alice live?"

Toby's eyes gave him away. Peach panicked. "No! Don't say it!" She snatched the notebook out of his hands and, holding it up in front of his eyes, prepared to tear it in half.

"What are you doing?"

"Alice has to live!" said Peach. "Maybe this Steele guy doesn't realize it, but he's in love with her, or something, so he saves her life."

"And if he doesn't?" said Tobias, trying to say it the way Sergeant Steele would say it—spitting it out like a piece of gristle.

"Then you end up with two *short* stories, Toby," said Peach. There was menace in her voice.

Tobias smiled like Steele. "Since when could you rip a notebook in half?"

---

1. *Alice's Adventures in Wonderland* (1865), by Lewis Carroll; many of the characters in Tobias's story (Tweedledum and Tweedledee, the playing-card soldiers, etc.) are drawn from this work and from *Through the Looking Glass and What Alice Found There* (1871).

"Since my uncle Mike showed me," said Peach, stepping out of reach. "It's all in the wrists. You just tear one page at a time—that's the trick of it. Mike can rip a phone book in half this way. It's going to become my new best trick."

Tobias took a step towards her and she started to tear. He stopped dead in his tracks.

"All I need is a bit of practice," said Peach. Tobias retreated, holding up his hands like a guy in a movie to show he had no weapons on him.

Peach shook her head. "You can't go around shooting people and bombing them," she said.

"It's just a story."

"It's more like a dumb video game. Alice is special, Toby."

"I know."

"No, you don't. She's not all syrupy like in the Disney movie.[2] That's all you know. She's tough. She doesn't take anything from anybody. You'd like her if you knew her. I seriously don't think you want to trash her, okay?"

Toby knew a threat when he heard one. He gave in. And Peach handed him back the notebook.

"Read *Alice in Wonderland* sometime," she said. Tobias didn't promise anything.

The assignment topic was "What I did on my summer vacation." Amelia had petted a stingray in the Monterey Aquarium. Graham had caught a foul ball at a Blue Jays game. He had the ball to prove it.

Then it was time for Tobias to read about his summer vacation adventure. He read "Tweedledum and Tweedledead: An Eyewitness Report." In only two pages, Sergeant Steele and the Desperate Throng wiped out Wonderland without a hitch. It was brutal. They turned the caterpillar into caterpillar dust, stuffed the Mad Hatter into his own hat and left the rabbit who had started the whole thing twitching in a ditch. Steele kept the rabbit's gold watch. Tweedledum and Tweedledee tried to round up some help from beyond the looking-glass, but they got wasted by one of the commandos, Mad Clyde and his flame-thrower. Alice was spared. She was carried home in a basket by the Desperate Throng and put in a special zoo with Winnie-the-Pooh, Wilbur the pig and the Cat in the Hat.[3]

Nervously, Tobias looked at Ms. Julia Peach to see if she approved of his revised ending. She gave him the thumbs up.

Ms. Knieppe, however, did not. She invited Tobias to the front, took the story from him and reread it to herself.

She said she was appalled.

She asked if anyone knew what appalled meant. The class nodded its head. They could tell what she meant from the look on her face. But Ms. Knieppe didn't stop there. With Tobias still standing at the front, she got the class to try to spell it.

Amelia got it right. Amelia got to look it up in the dictionary: *appall v.t. to fill with dismay or horror; terrify; shock.*

Which was exactly what the class had seen on Ms. Knieppe's face.

Ms. Knieppe scribbled a note and invited Tobias to take his story to Mrs. Armitage,

2. *Alice in Wonderland* (1951); Disney's animated movie also includes elements of Carroll's *Through the Looking Glass* (1871).
3. The main characters, respectively, of *Winnie-*the-*Pooh* (1926), by A. A. Milne; *Charlotte's Web* (1952), by E. B. White; and *The Cat in the Hat* (1957), by Dr. Seuss.

the principal, to see what she thought of it. Tobias snuck a peek at Peach as he left the room. She was rolling her eyes to beat the band.

Tobias sat outside the principal's office in a little dead-end hallway off the main office. In the main office the fall sun streamed through the window. One of the secretaries, Mrs. Devlin, was chatting to a man in a uniform who had delivered some packages. She was having a coffee and telling him about the trouble she was having with her K-Car.[4] It turned out that the man in the uniform had had the same kind of trouble.

The school nurse smiled at Tobias as she got some stuff from her mailbox. And Ms. Rowanook of the orange hair was typing something with a Sony Walkman on, bobbing her head to the music.

It gave Tobias a nice cheery feeling to see everybody having a good time. It gave him hope.

Mrs. Armitage, meanwhile, was on the phone. Tobias could just make her out through the pebbled glass of her door. He could hear bits and pieces of what she was saying. Mrs. Devlin had taken in "Tweedledum and Tweedledead" with the note from Ms. Knieppe, and right away Mrs. Armitage had got on the phone.

At first Tobias thought she was phoning his parents or the cops or something, but the phone call didn't seem to have anything to do with him. So he waited in the dead-end hall, just out of the sunshine, until finally Mrs. Armitage hung up.

His waiting changed then. His ears filled up with the silence of her reading his story. He was Sergeant Steele holding his breath, hiding in a bush as a troop of playing-card soldiers marched by, a fistful of leaves away. Then he heard the scrape of the principal's chair and watched her ghostly, pebbly figure come towards him and invite him in, invite him to sit down.

Tobias sat. Mrs. Armitage sat down, too, and thumbed through the story.

"Wilbur," she said. "From *Charlotte's Web*?"

Tobias nodded hesitantly. Sweet talk. She was going to engage him in conversation before she brought out the thumb screws.

"So how did Sergeant Steele end up with Wilbur and Winnie-the-Pooh and the others?" she asked. "Has he been raiding all the imaginary places?"

Tobias looked for the trap. "The zoo doesn't actually belong to Sergeant Steele," he said.

"Who does it belong to?"

Tobias scratched his head. "I don't know."

Mrs. Armitage frowned. "The writer must be sovereign over the worlds he creates," she said.

Tobias would have liked the chance to write that down. It sounded like a handy thing to know. But Mrs. Armitage was not finished.

She looked over her glasses at Tobias. "I think part of the problem here, Toby, is that Ms. Knieppe was hoping her students would recount events that had really happened to them this summer."

Tobias nodded. "I know," he said. "She heard me telling someone about wrestling with a tiger on my way to the cottage. She said it sounded really interesting and she hoped I would write about it." He didn't go on.

"And?" said Mrs. Armitage.

---

4. Boxy, inexpensive sedan sold by Chrysler in the 1980s.

"And I tried," said Tobias. "But it wouldn't come."

"Tell me about it," said Mrs. Armitage, leaning back in her chair. She seemed to want to hear about wrestling the tiger. But Tobias shrugged and was silent.

"Did it really happen?"

"Yes," said Tobias.

"Then why don't you want to share it with me, with your classmates?"

Through Mrs. Armitage's window, Tobias could see the man in the uniform getting into his truck. The truck was silver and said *Mercury*[5] *Messenger Service* on its side. There was a picture of a guy with wings on his heels running like a halfback with a package in his hands. The man in the uniform was whistling.

"Tobias?"

"I already told them!" said Tobias. "We were going to the cottage and we stopped to get gas and they had a tiger cub in a cage. The man at the gas station said I could go in the cage with him if I wanted, so I went in. It was cute. We wrestled a bit and my mom took a picture. I can show you the picture if you don't believe me."

"I do believe you," said Mrs. Armitage sincerely. "It sounds like a great story. Don't you think that's why Ms. Knieppe wanted you to write it down? Don't you feel that's why she was disappointed?"

Tobias watched the Mercury Messenger Service truck pull out of the school driveway onto Alta Vista Drive. He wondered where the next stop was and what all those packages contained.

Mrs. Armitage turned to see what Tobias was looking at, but the truck was already gone.

"She already knew the story," said Toby. "Everybody in class knew the story. It just wasn't worth writing it out."

"I see," said Mrs. Armitage, nodding. "So instead you decided to fire-bomb Wonderland."

"It was sort of a joke," said Tobias. "The class liked it."

"I'm sure they did," said Mrs. Armitage in a disapproving voice. The end of her sentence was like the bony end of a chicken drumstick. Mrs. Armitage bit down on the word and Tobias figured the sweet talk was over and the lecture was coming. But he was wrong again.

"It is funny," she said. "Tweedledum and Tweedledead, I mean. I'm not 'appalled' by it, Tobias, in case you're wondering. I think it is very imaginative."

"Thank you," said Tobias.

"Ms. Knieppe, however, is correct in thinking that the content of this story is inappropriate for the assignment, and I agree with her on that. But my guess is that you knew it was inappropriate and that's why you wrote it. Am I correct?"

Tobias shrugged.

"This was written purely for its shock value," said Mrs. Armitage.

"No," said Tobias. "It was fun."

Mrs. Armitage didn't look at the clock or anything, but she suddenly looked like someone who had a lot of other things to do and not a lot of time.

"I mean," said Tobias, "I wrote it for a laugh. That was part of it . . ."

"Yes?"

"And I guess I was a little mad, that was part of it . . ."

"Mad?"

---

5. Roman messenger god, portrayed with winged cap and winged sandals.

"About having to write the tiger story."

"I see. And . . . ."

"And . . . ." Tobias stopped short as if at a chasm. Chased by the playing-card soldiers through a minefield, he was now at the brink of Dead Man's Leap. The enemy was right behind him and down below he could see the mangled bodies of kids who had tried to raid Wonderland before and failed. Where had it all gone wrong?

"And it just came to me," he said.

"It just came to you," said Mrs. Armitage.

It didn't seem much of an answer.

Peach was waiting for him after school. "Let me guess," she said. "You have to clean the gym floor with a toothbrush, right?"

"I wish!" said Tobias, falling in beside her. She waited for him to tell her. It wasn't that she actually stopped talking—Peach never stopped talking—but she didn't press him. She talked about a stamp her great-aunt had sent her from Guyana for the stamp collection her great-aunt seemed to think she had. And then she went on about how at her riding class the past Wednesday, Amelia, the girl who touched manta rays and spelled so well, had fallen off her pony.

"No way," said Tobias, grinning.

"Okay," said Peach. "She didn't fall, but she rode appallingly."

Then they talked about a bunch of appalling things until they were suddenly standing at Peach's driveway.

"So?" she said.

Tobias kicked at some fallen leaves. "I've got to write the tiger essay," he said.

"Is that all?" said Peach. "You got off easy."

Tobias looked at her. "I won't do it," he said. "I can't."

Tobias's mother was in the backyard putting her garden to bed. He gave her the news, all of it.

"Why won't you do it?" she said. "Is it a matter of principle or something?"

Tobias tried to think why he couldn't write the essay. "There's no surprise to it," he said.

"Well, this is a fine kettle of fish," said his mother.

She made him carry the lawn chairs to the garage and then help with dinner. She made him roll out the perogi[6] dough while she read his story and the notes on it from Ms. Knieppe and Mrs. Armitage. His mother laughed at something, but Tobias wasn't sure if it was the story or the notes she was laughing at.

"Couldn't you talk to them?" he asked.

His mother patted him on the shoulder and shook her head. She started frying onions.

"I'm not doing it," said Tobias. His mother said nothing. Tobias rolled and rolled. His wrists ached. There is nothing tougher than perogi dough.

Peach phoned right after dinner. "You gonna do it?"

"Nope," said Tobias. "They can throw me to the tigers, as far as I'm concerned."

"But it's easy," said Peach. "You could write it with your eyes tied behind your back."

"I just can't make myself do it," said Tobias.

---

6. I.e., pierogi (Polish filled dumplings).

Peach was silent on the other end, but Tobias waited. Sometimes she was just hitching up her sock or reading the newspaper—her mother said she had very poor telephone manners—but Tobias was used to it. Sometimes she was thinking. That was what it was this time.

"Can you come over?" she said.

"What about your assignment?" said his mom. Tobias lied. He promised he would get right to it when he got back. Since he didn't say that he refused to do it, which is what he had said all through dinner, she let him go.

Peach was at her kitchen table writing on a pad of foolscap. An untouched piece of chocolate cake sat beside her. A dollop of ice cream melted by its side. Peach's mother cut a piece of cake for Tobias. Tobias sat down and watched. Peach kept writing.

"Your manners, young lady," said her mother, but she didn't go on about it and left the two of them alone in the silence of melting ice cream.

Finally Peach stopped writing. She sat up straight and held out the pad of paper in front of her to look it over.

"Exceptional," she whispered.

"What's going on?" said Tobias.

Peach said, "Are you absolutely sure you won't write the tiger story?"

Tobias gritted his teeth. He looked as if he was going to scream.

"Good," said Peach. "Because I've written it for you."

She handed him the foolscap pad.

The Summer of the Tiger
by Tobias Green

> *Every summer we go up to our cottage. I really look forward to swimming and waterskiing. Also my two cousins Terry and Dave live up there all year round and we do lots of things together like going to the antique boat show and fishing. But little did I know that this summer the best part of the trip was going to be the getting there!*

"What?" said Tobias. "This is gross."

"No," said Peach. "It's appalling. And it gets worse."

So, while she helped herself to her much deserved piece of cake, Tobias read on.

> *We always stop at the Kritchmar Esso[7] on our way north. There's an old pop bottle cooler there and Mom and Dad let us choose whatever soft drink we want. They also have a big cage out back of the old service station where there is sometimes an orphaned deer or bear cub. Once there was even an eagle which sat on this dead tree in the cage yelling at everybody. The Kritchmars just keep the animals for a week or two, then they let them go. Imagine our surprise when we arrived this time to find a real tiger cub!*

_____

7. Gas station (Esso was the parent company of Exxon).

"Imagine our surprise." Tobias wrinkled his nose. "It sounds just like Amelia's story about petting the manta rays."

"I'm glad you noticed," said Peach.

Tobias read on. He stopped and looked at Peach again. "How do you know all this stuff, anyway?"

Peach rolled her eyes. "I've heard the story about a hundred times," she said.

Tobias read in silence, shaking his head in disbelief. "She'll never believe I did this," he said when he had finished. "It's got A+ written all over it."

"That's the beauty of it," said Peach, finishing her cake and taking a forkful of Tobias's. "Ms. Knieppe thinks you are very creative. That's why she gets so disappointed with you. This will just prove to her that she was right all along. Teachers like that. Of course, you'll have to write it out again in your own ugly scrawl. And don't tell me you can't do it because it would be wrong or unethical or something. This isn't some sit-com. This is life or death."

Tobias pushed his own piece of cake towards Peach. "Thanks," he said. She took another forkful and pushed it back.

"It's going to cost more than a piece of cake," she said.

Tobias looked worried. Peach got up, left the room and ran upstairs. She came down a minute later with her hands behind her back.

"What?" said Tobias.

"You can have the A+ essay," she said, "but in return I want you to read this." Then, from behind her back, she brought out a copy of *Alice in Wonderland*.

Tobias grimaced.

"Read it," she said. She was about to hand him the book but instead she grabbed a tea towel and made him wipe his hands. The book was a beautiful edition with a clear plastic cover and gold lettering.

"What do you mean?"

Peach grabbed the book from him and opened it at random. "The-players-all-played-at-once-without-waiting-for-turns," she read. "They're called 'words,' Toby. *Read* them."

"But why?" said Tobias. "I know the story."

Peach sighed. "Well, then I guess you won't be needing this," she said. She picked up the foolscap essay and, rolling it up, she took it firmly in two fists and slowly started to tear.

"Hold it!" said Tobias. "Give me a chance to think!"

Peach waited. Tobias looked miserable. She looked away. Then she sighed again, unrolled the essay, smoothed it out and handed it to him. "Sorry," she said. "Jeez, I sounded just like Ms. Knieppe."

Tobias took the essay. Then he reached out and took the book, too.

"It's okay," said Peach. "I'm not going to make you read it."

"I'll read it," he said. "Really."

Peach's eyes lit up. "Tonight?" she asked.

"Tonight!"

"It's only 140 pages of big type and you don't have to read the last three or four pages where she wakes up, because that's garbage."

"Okay, okay!" said Tobias. "It's a deal."

Peach smiled triumphantly.

Tobias shook his head. "You're the worst best friend a guy ever had," he said.

He copied out her essay without changing a word. He wrote it in his best hand-writing. Then, while his folks watched "Unsolved Mysteries,"[8] Tobias settled into the task of reading *Alice in Wonderland*. He knew Peach would quiz him on it and even though he remembered the movie, she would catch him out some way or other if he tried to fake it.

He read late. And he stayed up still later.

The next morning he showed Peach what he had done. "The Summer of the Tiger" was nicely bound with a cover made from torn strips of orange construc-tion paper glued onto black. Very tigerish. There was a plastic dust jacket with gold lettering. It was pretty impressive. He also presented Peach with a little something he had written in his notebook.

"Tweedledum and Tweedledead: The Return." Peach looked dubious. She read it in silence.

The first paragraph showed no signs of improvement. Sergeant Steele and his Desperate Throng throttled the weasely counterspy, found the old map and dug out the rabbit hole just as they had done in the earlier version. They parachuted down the hole and gave themselves hypodermic needles full of Smallness just like before. But having blasted down the door—bazookas blazing—and entered the lovely garden, everything changed.

In the new version, the Desperate Throng couldn't find anybody to annihilate. Wonderland was deserted, or so it seemed. Then, suddenly, the whole deadly group was trapped. It was an elaborate trap, too, the best thing Tobias had ever thought of. They were led before her royal majesty the Queen of Hearts who rolled her eyes magnificently. "Sentence first—Verdict afterwards," roared the queen, and then, despite the protestations of Steele and company, her majesty roared again, "Off with their heads!" The next thing Sergeant Steele and his surly crew knew, they were all just little boys in short pants being kissed awake by a bunch of nice sisters at a picnic.

Peach loved it.

It was his gift to her, but Tobias borrowed it back right away. "Just for a minute," he promised.

In the office he persuaded Ms. Rowanook of the orange hair to make a copy of both stories for the principal. Tobias left them in her mailbox with a note explaining who had written what. He said in the note that he wasn't going to tell Ms. Knieppe about Peach writing the essay for him, but that if the principal needed to tell her, he would understand. As far as he could tell, Mrs. Armitage never did tell, either. Ms. Knieppe seemed altogether pleased with "The Summer of the Tiger." She said it was just what she was looking for.

She gave him a B+. After all, the assignment was a day late.

---

8. A network television series (1988–99) that featured reenactments of crimes and other mysteries; viewers helped solve the cases.

NIKKI GRIMES

b. 1950

A voracious reader as a youth, the poet and novelist Nikki Grimes spent hours in the public libraries of New York City. Although books provided Grimes's greatest delight, she also felt betrayed by them as an African American child because all but a few failed to reflect her image back to her. Grimes vowed to someday write about children who looked and felt as she did.

Grimes's inspiration indeed comes from her own childhood, as she sets most of her work in New York City or in another urban landscape. She moved often within the boroughs of the city during her early years, and she has never forgotten the struggles of settling in and making friends in a new neighborhood. From her first book written for children, *Growin'* (1977), to recent works such as *Meet Danitra Brown* (1994), making and keeping friends is a common theme in Grimes's work.

Grimes has held a number of different jobs, including instructor in writing and applied sociolinguistics, writer and producer of radio programs, and translator of Swedish/English computer manuals, and has both traveled widely around the world and lived abroad. She spent a year in Tanzania and six years in Sweden, where she hosted a radio program for immigrants and another program on Swedish Educational Radio. Yet it is writing, especially poetry, that Grimes calls her favorite activity. She has worked exclusively as a freelance writer since 1991 and has published scores of books for young people, including poetry, novels, picture books, and biographies. Her biography of Malcolm X, *Malcolm X: A Force for Change* (1992), was an NAACP Image Award Finalist for 1993, and *Talkin' about Bessie: The Story of Aviator Elizabeth Coleman* (2001), a picture-book biography of the first African American female aviator, was a Coretta Scott King Honor Book for 2002.

Grimes's school story *Bronx Masquerade* (2002)— an unusual hybrid novel set in a New York City high school classroom—combines poetry with monologue and won the Coretta Scott King Award for 2002. In accepting this award, Grimes called the novel "the most challenging work I had ever attempted. It felt like a high-wire act." Grimes based its situation, a series of "open mike" poetry readings, on the classroom of her friend Drew Ward, a gifted teacher from California who inspired his students to excel in writing and in understanding by sharing personal poetry. Grimes concluded her acceptance speech, "I love to talk about the power of poetry. *Bronx Masquerade* allowed me to display that power—the power poetry has to shape lives, to create community, and to underscore the vital truth that the most important common denominator in our universe is the human heart."

Bronx Masquerade

WESLEY "BAD BOY" BOONE

I ain't particular about doing homework, you understand. My teachers practically faint whenever I turn something in. Matter of fact, I probably got the longest list of excuses for missing homework of anyone alive. Except for my homey[1] Tyrone. He tries to act like he's not even interested in school, like there's no point in studying hard, or dreaming about tomorrow, or bothering to graduate. He's got his reasons. I keep on him about going to school, though, saying I need the company. Besides, I tell him, if he drops out and gets a J.O.B., he won't have any time to work on his

1. Homeboy, close friend.

songs. That always gets to him. Tyrone might convince everybody else that he's all through with dreaming, but I know he wants to be a big hip-hop star. He's just afraid he won't live long enough to do it. Me, I hardly ever think about checking out. I'm more worried about figuring what I want to do if I live.

Anyway, I haven't had to drag Tyrone off to school lately, or make excuses for not having my homework done, because I've been doing it. It's the Harlem Renaissance[2] stuff that's got us both going.

We spent a month reading poetry from the Harlem Renaissance in our English class. Then Mr. Ward—that's our teacher—asked us to write an essay about it. Make sense to you? Me neither. I mean, what's the point of studying *poetry* and then writing *essays*? So I wrote a bunch of poems instead. They weren't too shabby, considering I'd only done a few rap pieces before. My favorite was about Langston Hughes.[3] How was I to know Teach would ask me to read it out loud? But I did. Knees knocking like a skeleton on Halloween, embarrassment bleaching my black cheeks red, eyes stapled to the page in front of me. But I did it, I read my poem.

Guess what. Nobody laughed. In fact, everybody thought it was cool. By the time I got back to my seat, other kids were shouting out: "Mr. Ward, I got a poem too. Can I bring it in to read?"

Teach cocked his head to the side, like he was hearing something nobody else did. "How many people here have poems they'd like to read?" he asked. Three hands shot up. Mr. Ward rubbed his chin for a minute. "Okay," he said. "Bring them with you tomorrow."

After class Teach came over to my desk. "Great poem," said Mr. Ward. "But I still expect to see an essay from you. I'll give you another week." So much for creative expression.

LONG LIVE LANGSTON

By Wesley Boone

Trumpeter of Lenox and 7th
through Jesse B. Semple,[4]
you simply celebrated
Blues and Be-bop
and being Black before
it was considered hip.
You dipped into
the muddy waters
of the Harlem River
and shouted "taste and see"
that we Black folk be good
at fanning hope
and stoking the fires

---

2. The African American cultural movement of the 1920s and 1930s, centered in Harlem, in New York City. Also known as the "New Negro" movement, it encompassed literature, art, music, dance, and social commentary.
3. African American poet (1902–1967), who also wrote fiction, dramas, and essays and was the first black to support himself through his writing.
4. Hughes's streetwise fictional character, nicknamed Simple, whose monologues on race began appearing in 1943.

of dreams deferred.[5]
You made sure
the world heard
about the beauty of
maple sugar children, and the
artfully tattooed backs of Black
sailors venturing out
to foreign places.

Your Sweet Flypaper of Life[6]
led us past the Apollo[7] and on
through 125th and all the other
Harlem streets you knew like
the black of your hand.
You were a pied-piper,[8] brother man
with poetry as your flute.
It's my honor and pleasure to salute
You, a true Renaissance man
of Harlem.

TYRONE BITTINGS

School ain't nothin' but a joke. My moms don't want to hear that, but if it weren't for Wesley and my other homeys, I wouldn't even be here, aiight? These white folk talking 'bout some future, telling me I need to be planning for some future—like I got one! And Raynard agreeing, like he's smart enough to know. From what I hear, that boy can't hardly read! Anyway, it's them white folk that get me with this *future* mess. Like Steve, all hopped up about working on Broadway and telling me I should think about getting with it too. Asked me if I ever thought about writing plays. "Fool! What kinda question is that?" I said. He threw his hands up and backed off a few steps. "All I'm saying is, you're a walking drama, man. You got that down pat, so maybe you should think about putting it on paper." When that boy dyed his hair, I b'lieve some of that bleach must've seeped right into his brain. I grind my teeth and lower my voice. "Boy, get out my face," I tell him. He finally gets the message and splits. I'm ticked off that he even got me *thinking* about such nonsense as Broadway.

White folk! Who they think they kidding? They might as well go blow smoke up somebody else's you-know-what, 'cause a Black man's got no chance in this country. I be lucky if I make it to twenty-one with all these fools running round with AK-47s. Here I am one of the few kids I know whose daddy *didn't* skip out on him, and he didn't even make it to thirty. He was doing okay 'til he got blown away on a Saturday. Blam! Another statistic in a long line of drive-bys. Life is cold. Future? What I got is right now, right here, spending time with my homeys. Wish there was some future to talk about. I could use me some future.

5. "Dream Deferred" (1951) is one of Hughes's best-known poems.
6. A book portraying everyday life in Harlem (1955), with text by Hughes and photographs by Ray DeCarava.
7. A famous theater in Harlem, on 125th Street, that since 1934 has presented black entertainers to mixed audiences.
8. I.e., like the Pied Piper of Hamelin (see in Legends section, above), enticing listeners to follow him.

I'm just about ready to sleep off the whole year when this teacher starts talking about poetry. And he rattles off a poem by some white guy named Dylan Thomas[9] that sounds an awful lot like rap. Now, I know me some rap, and I start to thinking I should show Mr. Ward what rap is really all about. So I tell him I've got a poem I'd like to read. "Bring it on Friday," he says. "As a matter of fact, from now on, I'll leave time for poetry readings at the end of every month. We'll call them Open Mike Fridays." Next thing I know, I'm digging my old rap poems out of my dresser drawer and bringing them to school. I'm thinking it can't hurt to share them, even if there's no chance I'll ever get to be a songwriter. After all, it's the one thing I could see myself doing if there really was a future. And I'm thinking that maybe there could be if I wanted it bad enough. And all of a sudden, I realize I do.

Open Mike

ATTENDANCE

By Tyrone Bittings

We are all here,
Leslie and Bad Boy, Lupe and Raul,
Here, here and here.
Dear Mr. Ward
with his wards and wardettes.
Let's have a show of hands today.
Is Porscha here? Is Diondra here?
Where oh where is Sheila?
It's me, Tyrone,
up here all alone
rapping into a microphone
'cause I've got something to say:
MTV is here, Mir[1] and
morning space-walks are here,
terrorism is here
lurking at the bus stop.
Can't hop on the subway
without thinkin' of Tokyo—
we all know poison gas
does not discriminate.[2]

It's too late to worry
about my innocence
since fear is here.
Why is it a weekend visit
to your local Mickey D's[3]
may be deadly?
Why hasn't somebody
censored death?

---

9. Welsh poet (1914–1953).
1. Russia's space station. MTV: the first music video channel, which went on the air in 1981.
2. On March 20, 1995, members of the Japanese cult Aum Shinrikyo released sarin gas in the Tokyo subways; twelve died and thousands were injured.
3. I.e., McDonald's.

Don't hold your breath waiting.
Still you can chill and celebrate
all that's great about life, like music
and the tick-tick-tick of time
which is equal parts yours and mine
to make of the world what we will.
But first, say no to coke, and smoke.
Say no to police brutality
and causing fatality.
Say no to race hate.
Don't underestimate
the power of love.
But most of all
take two poems
and call me
in the morning.

CHANKARA TROUPE

I am not in the mood for Tyrone's sorry "Baby, gimme some loving" routine, so when I see him in the hall, I storm past as if he's not even there. Eventually, he'll figure out why.

I come to school sporting shades and a johnny-print across my left cheek, Johnny being the name of the idiot who smacked me last night. Naturally, Porscha is the first person who notices my new tattoo. She walks straight up to me and says, "You deserve better, girlfriend. And you know it." No hello. No how are you. Just: "You deserve better." Then she turns away and walks into the classroom. Typical Porscha. No nonsense. That's why we get along.

Then here comes Sheila Gamberoni. The minute she sees me, she demands to know the name of the guy who gave me my shiner, like she's gonna send her brothers after him or something. I keep his name to myself, just in case. She commences to call the guy everything but a child of God, which makes her feel better, I think, then gives me a hug and says she'll see me later. Sheila is a bit over the top with this sister act, as if she's trying to make up for being white, but she means well. I can do without some of the other girls who stare at me, though. I know they're just looking for something to talk about, so I rip off my sunglasses, let them get a better look. *Might as well stare all you want. This is the first and last time you'll ever see me like this.*

Of course, that's what they all say. Nobody knows that better than me. My sister's boyfriends have been beating on her for years. I made up my mind a long time ago, I'm not having none of that.

Last night I tried telling this to Johnny, who seems to be hard of hearing. He'd brought me home from a movie. He came in for a while, got comfortable since Mom was working overtime and we had the apartment to ourselves. We locked lips for a few minutes. Next thing I know, he's fingering my shirt buttons. I push him away, gently at first. "I think we better slow down," I say. "No, no," he says, voice all husky. "It's just getting good." This time, his hands shoots up my skirt. Bad move. I jump off the sofa like it's on fire. "Maybe it's time for you to go." He grabbed my skirt and tried pulling me back down, which is right about when I hauled off and smacked him. He leaped up and smacked me back.

My jaw dropped from shock, and I looked in his eyes and saw my sister's reflection. I turned away, strode to the door, unlocked it, and held it open for him.

"I hope you enjoyed yourself," I said, " 'cause that's the last time you'll ever lay a hand on me. Now get out!" He actually looked like he was studying on staying, so I stepped out into the hall and screamed at the top of my lungs, "I said get out!" Fearing trouble, he left.

Now I've got this ugly tattoo on my cheek. I thought about skipping school today, but I hate to miss English. Besides, the bruise is temporary and so is the pain. Still, I'd rather not have kids gawking at me all period, so I park myself in the back of the room and wait for Mr. Ward to call our English class to attention.

Mr. Ward is funny. Sometimes he asks us a question with no warning, and tells us to answer quick, without stopping to think about it. The truth is always right on the tip of your tongue, he says. It's the fabrications that take a lot of time. Yesterday he asked us: "What do you know?" Yesterday I said my name, but today would be different. Today I'd tell him a woman ain't no punching bag. That's what I know.

Open Mike
BRUISED LOVE

By Chankara Troupe

A midnight thirst sent me
padding to the kitchen
for a jelly-jar of water
and an accidental run-in
with my sister.
She tiptoed in, late
and limping, her cheek
raw as red-brown meat.
I caught a quick glance
in the chilly glow
of the refrigerator
before she had
a chance to hide
the latest souvenir
her boyfriend gave her.
"I bruise easily"
is one of the lies
she sprinkles like sugar.
But I'm fifteen,
not brainless. Besides,
I knew the truth at ten.

"He'll never do it again,"
she swears.
But he will, because
she'll let him.
Now, me?

I've got no use
for lame excuses
or imitation love
that packs
a punch.

TYRONE

My pops used to hit my moms like that.

When I was little, I used to hide under my bed and cry, scared he was coming for
me next. Damn, I ain't thought about that in years. How could you do that, Pops? I
don't get it. Is that why he hung around? So he'd have somebody smaller than him
to beat up on? I don't even want to go there. I'm just glad he finally stopped drinking
and cleaned up his act before he checked out. It gave us a chance to have some good
times together.

Chankara was the third one up today. Her stuff was so deep, nobody wanted to
follow her. There weren't but two more people planning to read anyway, including
me. We both decided to bag it 'til the next Open Mike.

Meanwhile, I'm going to be busy writing me a rap about dudes beatin' on women.
I'll call it "Little Men," 'cause that's what they are.

RAUL RAMIREZ

Lunch is a memory of indigestion. Chankara sat across from me in the cafeteria and
I couldn't help staring at her. Her bruises are almost gone, but I can still see the
shadows they left behind. If she was my *hermanita*,[4] I'd squash the cockroach who
messed her up like that. That's what I was thinking when I remembered it ain't nice
to stare. So I ate too fast and got out of there before she could catch me.

Only twenty minutes 'til class starts, and Mr. Ward don't like it if I leave a mess
on his desk, so that's eighteen minutes to paint, plus two more for cleaning up and
washing the paintbrushes. If Raynard gets here early, he'll help. He always does, I
don't know why. Tyrone's another story. He checks in early lots of times when I'm
here, but he keeps his distance, usually. Once he came up behind me and watched
over my shoulder while I worked. Made me kinda nervous, if you must know. The
Ricans and the brothers[5] don't always hit it off. Anyway, he stood there for the longest. Then he grunted and said, "You good, man, I'll give you that."

"Thanks," I said.

"You wasting your time, though. You know you ain't gonna make no money doing
this."

"Maybe. Maybe not," I said. "But some things ain't about money."

"You tripping, man," said Tyrone. "Money is the alpha and omega. Ask anybody."

I just shrugged and gave him my *"No hablo ingles"*[6] look, like I didn't get what he
was talking about. It was the quickest way to end the conversation.

People just don't get it. Even if I never make a dime—which, by the way, ain't
gonna happen—I'd still have to paint.

Don't get me wrong. Money is useful. I'm lucky Mr. Ward leaves brushes and

---

4. Little sister (Spanish).
5. I.e., the Puerto Ricans and the blacks.

6. I don't speak English (Spanish).

watercolor paper for me to use, though I ain't gonna tell him that. It's none of his business I can't afford fancy brushes and watercolor paper at home. Anyway, it's good for him to help out the future Diego Rivera.[7] He knows I'm the real deal. Didn't he come to me for advice on how to decorate the classroom? The paper frames were my idea. Good work belongs in a gallery, I told him. Especially if it's mine.

I never thought about writing poetry before, but Mr. Ward said he's going to start videotaping our Friday sessions. Guess who's going to be the first one in front of the camera. Of course, that means I have to write a poem, so I better get busy. Even if it's hard, I'll do it. I don't mind working hard. Whatever it takes, ¿entiendes?[8] Raul Ramirez, painter-poet. Yeah. I like the sound of that.

Someday I'll have a poetry reading and a one-man show at the Nuyorican Poets Cafe on the Lower East Side. I'll hand out tokens[9] to all my friends so they got no excuse not to take the ride downtown, okay?

My brothers laugh at me just 'cause they've been in the world a little longer. They say I'm *loco en la cabeza*,[1] that ain't no spic gonna be no big-time artist in America. "First off," I tell them, "I ain't no spic. And second, watch me."

Abuelita[2] says my talent is as old as her bones. She says I got it, and my stubbornness, from her father. He never did nothing with his talent, though. I asked her why not. "*Porque la familia*[3] could not eat paint," she said. So I will be the first painter in the family. That's fine with me.

I've been drawing pictures all my life. I used to make my sister model for me. I'd bribe her with whatever I could scrounge up from returning soda bottles to the grocery. Eventually, I got tired of digging through trash for bottles, and she got bored modeling. Now it's easier. My girlfriend sits for me. Every painter needs a model, right? Anyway, she knows if she's nice to me, one day I'll make her famous. Even if she's not nice, I'll probably paint her because she's beautiful.

I want to show the beauty of our people, that we are not all *banditos* like they show on TV, munching *cuchfritos*[4] and sipping beer through chipped teeth. I will paint *los niños*[5] scooping up laughter in the sunshine and splashing in the temporary pool of a fire hydrant. I will paint my cousins, turning the sidewalk into a dance floor when *salsa* or *la bamba* spills from the third-floor window. I will paint Mami, standing at the ironing board late in the evening, after a day of piecework in the factory, sweat pouring off her, steam rising from a pot in the background, me tugging at her skirt while she irons. I will paint the way she used to smile down at me, the love in her eyes saying "I only do this for you." Mami's beauty is better than a movie star's. It survives a kind of life where pamper is a noun,[6] not a verb. I will capture that beauty on canvas, someday, when I am good enough.

For now, I draw in my sketchbook and paint portraits of myself for practice. But it's not so bad. I'm handsome, after all.

---

7. Mexican Social Realist muralist (1886–1957).
8. Do you understand? (Spanish).
9. Until 2003, tokens were used in New York City to pay bus and subway fare.
1. Crazy in the head (Spanish).
2. Grandma (Spanish).

3. Because the family (Spanish).
4. *Cuchifritos*, a generic term used by Puerto Ricans to designate offal snacks from the pig (pig's tongue, crackling, etc.).
5. The children (Spanish).
6. I.e., Pampers, a brand of disposable diapers.

ZORRO

By Raul Ramirez

Call me Zorro,[7] all swash and buckle while the cam-
eras roll, cape swinging in the breeze, teeth show-
ing as expected. I lunge on cue, save the damsel in
distress. I understand my role. I've studied all
those scripts and comic books. I used to pose for
close-ups, knew how to dutifully disappear

when the script said:
"Fade to black." Then
I'd wait uncomfort-
ably between the lines
of my own story 'til
someone with skin like
milk yelled "Action!"
But I'm done. I'm too
old for comic heros. It's
time to lose the cape,

step off the page, except I think I'll keep the mask.
Why make it easy for you to choose whether I am
Zorro or el bandito when I am neither? Your cate-
gories are too confining. The fact is, you're more com-
fortable with myth than man. But I am here to help. First
off, put down your camera. Second, give me your hand.

TYRONE

Raul is on the money. You gotta make your own rules, Jack. That's the real 411.[8]
Forget who white folks think you are, 'cause they ain't got a *clue.*

That's some strong stuff Raul be writin'. That "Z" thing was cool too. He was
working it.

Frankly, I didn't know Raul had it in him. Matter of fact, I didn't know he knew
that much English!

DIONDRA JORDAN

If only I was as bold as Raul. The other day, he left one of his paintings out on Mr.
Ward's desk where anybody could see it. Which was the point. He sometimes works
at Mr. Ward's desk during lunch. The wet paintbrushes sticking up out of the jar are
always a sign that he's been at it again. So of course, anybody who glances over in
that direction will be tempted to stop by and look.

---

7. The legend of the masked hero Zorro, defender
of the weak and oppressed in Spanish California,
was popularized in a 1919 short story; the earliest
of many film versions was *The Mask of Zorro*
(1920). The story is best known today from a television series, *Zorro* (1957–59), and a recent film,
The Mask of Zorro (1998).
8. Information (rap slang).

This particular painting was rough, but anyone could tell it was Raul. A self-portrait. He'll probably hang it in class. Back in September, Mr. Ward covered two of the classroom walls with black construction paper and then scattered paper frames up and down the walls, each one a different size and color. Now half the room looks sort of like an art gallery, which was the idea. We're supposed to use the paper frames for our work. Whether we put up poems or photographs or even paintings is up to us, so long as the work is ours and we can tie it in with our study of the Harlem Renaissance. I guess Raul's self-portrait fits, since we've been talking a lot about identity. He'll probably put it up next to his poem. You should have seen him hang that thing. You'd think he was handling a million-dollar masterpiece the way he took his time placing it just so. If you look close, you can see the smudges where he erased a word or two and rewrote it. Mr. Ward must be in shock. He can never get Raul to rewrite a lick of homework or anything else. And don't even talk to him about checking his spelling! He'll launch into a tirade on you in a minute. "What?" he'll snap. "You think Puerto Ricans can't spell?" Forget it. Anyway, I dare you to find one misspelled word in that poem of his! Maybe it's a visual thing. Maybe he wants his poem to look as good as his self-portrait. And it is good.

I've never tried doing a self-portrait, but why not? I could maybe do one in charcoal. I like drawing faces in charcoal. I've been drawing since I can't remember when. Not that anyone here knows that, except Tanisha, and she found out by accident when she came to my house to study once and saw a couple of drawings hanging in my room. Mom loves my watercolors and she hung one in the living room, but it isn't signed. Nobody ever mentions it, especially not my father. He's not too wild about my art. Mostly, he's disappointed, first off that I wasn't born a boy, and second that I won't play ball like one. I'm six feet tall, almost as tall as he, and he figures the height is wasted on me since I don't share his dreams of me going to the WNBA. I keep telling him not to hold his breath.

I hate always being the tallest girl in school. Everybody expects me to play basketball, so they pick me for their team, throw me the ball, and wait for me to shoot. Big mistake. I fumble it every time. Then they have the nerve to get mad at me, like I did it on purpose! But basketball is not my game. I have no game. I'm an artist, like Raul. The difference is, I don't tell anybody. I refuse to give them new reasons to laugh at me. The Jolly Green Giant[9] jokes are bad enough.

Yeah, it's definitely time to try a self-portrait. I think I'll paint myself in front of an easel. With a basketball jersey sticking up out of the trash. Then I could hang it in Mr. Ward's class. See if anybody notices.

Open Mike

If

By Diondra Jordan

If I stood on tiptoe
reached up and sculpted
mountains from clouds
would you laugh out loud?

---

9. Since 1928, a giant has appeared in advertisements for Green Giant processed vegetables.

If I dipped my brush in starlight
painted a ribbon of night
on your windowsill
would you still laugh?

If I drew you adrift
in a pen and ink sea
in a raging storm
would you laugh at me?

If I planted watercolor roses
in your garden
would you laugh then?
Or would you breathe deep
to sample their scent?
I wonder.

TYRONE

If the sista read any faster, I'd be looking for her Supergirl cape. Talk about nervous! Diondra's hands were shaking the whole time she was holding that poem. She sure spooks easy for somebody so tall.

"Yo!" I said. "Take a deep breath. Ain't nobody going to hurt you here." She smiled a little and tried to slow down. But I swear that girl burned rubber getting back to her seat when she was through. I guess she's not exactly used to the limelight.

She's got plenty of company. Four more kids read their poetry for the first time today. They were shaking in their boots, but it was all good. I only had to tell one of them to loosen up. Guess you could call that progress!

DEVON HOPE

Jump Shot. What kind of name is that? Not mine, but try telling that to the brothers at school. That's all they ever call me.

You'd think it was written somewhere. Tall guys must be jocks. No. Make that tall *people,* 'cause Diondra's got the same problem. Everybody expects her to shoot hoops. The difference is, she's got no talent in that direction. Ask me, she's got no business playing b-ball. That's my game.

I've got good height and good hands, and that's a fact. But what about the rest of me? Forget who I really am, who I really want to be. The law is be cool, be tough, play ball, and use books for weight training—not reading. Otherwise, everybody gives you grief. Don't ask me why I care, especially when the grief is coming from a punk like Wesley. Judging from the company he keeps, he's a gangsta in sheep's clothing. I don't even know why he and Tyrone bother coming to school. It's clear they don't take it seriously, although maybe they're starting to. That's according to Sterling, who believes in praying for everybody and giving them the benefit of the doubt. I love the preacher-man, but I think he may be giving these brothers too much credit. Anyway, when I hang around after school and any of the guys ask me: "Yo, Devon, where you going?" I tell them I'm heading for the gym to meet Coach and work on my layup. Then once they're out the door, I cut upstairs to the library to sneak a read.

It's not much better at home. My older brother's always after me to hit the streets with him, calls me a girly man for loving books and jazz.

Don't get me wrong. B-ball is all right. Girls like you, for one thing. But it's not *you* they like. It's Mr. Basketball. And if that's not who you are inside, then it's not you they're liking. So what's the point? Still, I don't mind playing, just not all the time.

This year is looking better. My English teacher has got us studying the Harlem Renaissance, which means we have to read a lot of poetry. That suits me just fine, gives me a reason to drag around my beat-up volumes of Langston Hughes and Claude McKay.[1] Whenever anybody bugs me about it, all I have to say is "Homework." Even so, I'd rather the brothers not catch me with my head in a book.

The other day, I duck into the library, snare a corner table, and hunker down with *3000 Years of Black Poetry*.[2] Raynard sees me, but it's not like he's going to tell anybody. He hardly speaks, and he never hangs with any of the brothers I know. So I breathe easy. I'm sure no one else has spotted me until a head pops up from behind the stacks. It's Janelle Battle from my English class. I freeze and wait for the snickers I'm used to. Wait for her to say something like: "What? Coach got you *reading* now? Afraid you're gonna flunk out and drop off the team?" But all she does is smile and wave. Like it's no big deal for me to be in a library reading. Like I have a right to be there if I want. Then she pads over, slips a copy of *The Panther & the Lash*[3] on my table, and walks away without saying a word. It's one of my favorite books by Langston Hughes. How could she know? Seems like she's noticed me in the library more often than I thought.

Janelle is all right. So what if she's a little plump? At least when you turn the light on upstairs, somebody's at home. She's smart, and she doesn't try hiding it. Which gets me thinking. Maybe it's time I quit sneaking in and out of the library like some thief. Maybe it's time I just started being who I am.

Open Mike

BRONX MASQUERADE

By Devon Hope

I woke up this morning
exhausted from hiding
the me of me
so I stand here confiding
there's more to Devon
than jump shot and rim.
I'm more than tall
and lengthy of limb.
I dare you to peep
behind these eyes,
discover the poet
in tough-guy disguise.
Don't call me Jump Shot.
My name is Surprise.

---

1. Jamaican-born American poet (1890–1948), a leading figure in the Harlem Renaissance.
2. An anthology edited by Alan Lomax and Raoul Abdul (1970).
3. A 1967 collection of poems by Langston Hughes.

Shoot. If I had moves like Devon, I'd be cruising crosscourt with Scotty Pippin![4] That's probably what the brotha's gonna end up doing, anyway, 'cause he ain't half the word-man I am. 'Course, I probably been at it longer.

He might get better. I said *might*. And who knows? Muhammad Ali[5] was a boxer *and* a poet. Maybe it's time for another hoop-man to rise to the occasion and show Shaquille[6] he ain't the only word-man on the court.

LUPE ALGARIN

Janelle's got a thing for Devon, but she ain't the only one. Last week I seen some girl named Beth in here staring at him like he was chocolate ice cream she couldn't wait to spoon up. She don't even belong in this class. Come to think of it, a lot of extra kids been showing up in our class on Open Mike Fridays. They heard about the poetry and they been coming to check it out. A bunch of teachers are getting mad at Mr. Ward with all these kids skipping their classes. Everybody's talking about it.

Poor Mr. Ward. He sends students back where they belong—when he catches them. Our class is big, though, and it's easy to duck down behind someone in the back of the room and hide. Sometimes we're halfway through the period before he notices someone who doesn't belong. But he caught Beth last week, and I saw Janelle grinning. She don't have Devon yet, but still she wants him all to herself. I know that feeling, when you love somebody like that. And not just a guy.

I love my Rosa.

Rosa is so beautiful. I wish I could bring her to school. Mr. Ward would love her. Her toes are like tiny *churros*[7] you want to nibble all the time. And I do, whenever my big sister, Christina, has me over to baby-sit. She smiles more than she did before she had Rosa. Or maybe she's just happy to be out of the house. I would be. There's nothing for me there, that's for sure.

My brother, Tito, left long ago, and then Christina. So it's just me now, with Mami and her husband, Berto. Besides her factory job, all she cares about is him. As for Berto, he's got no use for nobody's kids, even Mami's.

Why does she put up with him? All he does is belch beer and scream at her to bring him and his buddies more while they sit around playing dominos or watching fights on TV.

"I bet Papi doesn't guzzle beer all the time," I often say to Mami.

"You don't know what he does, Lupe," she always says. "How could you? You were only five when he left. And he left on his own, Lupe. *Pero*, what did I expect? He was a *jíbaro*[8] through and through. He couldn't *wait* to get back to his precious mountains! And this is the man you love? But Berto, who puts food in your mouth, him you despise. *¡Dios mio!*"

I hate it when she calls Papi a hick, the way she spits the word out.

I used to write him. So many letters. But he never wrote back. Why, Papi? There's

---

4. Scottie Pippin (b. 1965), star basketball player with the Chicago Bulls for most of his career.
5. American heavyweight boxer (born Cassius Clay, 1942), champion 1964–67, 1975–78, 1978–79. Many of his poems were rhyming couplets written before fights to celebrate his imminent victory.
6. Shaquille O'Neal (b. 1972), basketball star; he also has appeared in films and released rap albums.
7. Sugared fried dough (Spanish).
8. In Puerto Rico, a poor man from the mountains. *Pero*: but, yet (Spanish).

nobody here to love me now. Mami has Berto, Tito has his *carnales*[9] on the streets, Christina has Chooch and Rosa. And me? Raul's been giving me the eye lately, but he can forget it. He's too much in love with himself, always drawing pictures of his own face. What's that about? Besides, I already got a man. My Marco. Except, Marco hardly has time for me, even though he claims I'm his woman, his one and only.

Sometimes I say my rosaries and beg for someone to love. I lay in bed under the crucifix and pray 'til my fingers go numb on the beads.

Lately when I look at Rosa, I think I should do like my friend Gloria Martinez. I should make a baby of my own. Maybe that's the answer.

I like Marco good enough. I don't want to marry him, but he's cute. We'd make pretty babies together, I think.

I've always loved babies. When I was younger, I would wrap my doll in the lace from my first Communion and I'd show her off to all my neighbors. *"Mira, mira,"*[1] I'd say. "See my baby. Isn't she perfect?" And she loved me better than anybody, because I was her mother. It was only pretend, of course. But if I had a real baby, she would love me like that. The way Gloria's baby loves her. The way Rosa loves Christina.

I saw Gloria and her baby in the grocery last night. I waved to them and all the time, I'm thinking, Gloria, you have no idea how lucky you are.

Open Mike

Brown Hands

By Lupe Algarin

You, macho soledad,[2]
the secret I whisper in the night,
you fill your eyes with me
like a mirror
I see myself in.
Our twin hearts beat
like congas, the rhythm
churning our blood
to salsa.
Our brown hands entwine
beneath moonshine,
clasping all the love
we'll ever need—

Tyrone

So, the daydreamer speaks.

Every time I look at Lupe, she seems like she's somewhere else. Or maybe she just wants to be. Maybe she's thinkin' about the guy in that poem. But if she is, how come she never smiles?

9. I.e., friends, brothers (Chicano street slang).
1. Look, look (Spanish).

2. Manly loneliness (Spanish).

GLORIA MARTINEZ

Pampers. Apple sauce. Strained peas. I look up for a minute, see Lupe smiling at me. I nod, then go back to making my list. *Orange juice. Baby powder. Soy milk.* I didn't even know what soy milk *was* a year ago.

"Gloria." Raynard pokes me in the arm, gestures toward the front of the room. Mr. Ward is heading in my direction. I put my shopping list away before he can ask me what soy milk has to do with Zora Neale Hurston and the book he's been reading to us, *Their Eyes Were Watching God.*[3] I turn to Raynard and nod thanks. He doesn't say much, but he always looks out for me.

I shoulda made a shopping list before I left the house this morning, but I barely got out as it is. Angel spit up on my shirt right when I was headed out the door. It's like he *picks* the time to do it. Like he doesn't want me to leave. It took me ten minutes to clean him up and find myself another shirt. If Mami hadn't done the laundry for me yesterday, I wouldn't even have a clean one to wear.

I was stupid to think I could do this on my own. Even with Mami's help, I hardly have time to study or do my homework. Last week, Lupe asked if I could hang out with her after school and I just about laughed in her face. *"Chica,"*[4] I wanted to say, "them days are over for me." I go straight home now, except for maybe stopping at the grocery. It's no more *Gloria Loca*, party girl. Fun ain't even in my vocabulary anymore.

Once you have a kid, everything changes.

If I could go back, do things over . . . but I can't. No sense dreaming about it.

I love my Angel, and that's no lie. But I wish he didn't cry so much. He always wants something—his bottle, a new diaper, the teddy he dropped on the floor for the sixteenth time in a row. Or else he wants me to hold him, like I can rock a baby and write a paper at the same time! And forget about sleep. He wakes me up in the middle of the night so much, I practically wake up on my own now.

Two weeks ago, he wakes up crying with a fever. I don't know what to do. I rub him with cold washcloths, and then I take his temperature. I give him baby Tylenol, walk him up and down, and I take his temperature. I sing to him, I rock him, I give him a bottle of water, and take his temperature. I must've taken his temperature ten times before his fever finally broke. Then I put him in bed with me so I can watch him. By the time I close my eyes, the clock radio says 3:16 A.M. The next day, I have a math test. Which I flunk, of course. I keep nodding off between reading the problems and working out the solutions. I was a mess. Lucky for me, when I explained what happened, the teacher let me take the test over.

I still got two years to go before I graduate. But I've got to make it, and I've got to go to college. Period. Angel's father already told me straight-up he ain't having nothing to do with this baby, so it's on me. Mami says she'll help, but it's me who has to make a good life for Angel. It's like she says, my life ain't about just me anymore. It's about my son.

Lupe has no idea how lucky she is.

How can I get through to her?

---

3. Best-known novel (1937) by Hurston (1891– 1960), African American writer of fiction, drama- tist, and anthropologist.

4. Little girl, girlfriend (Spanish slang).

Open Mike

MESSAGE TO A FRIEND

By Gloria Martinez

That girl in the mirror,
daughter of San Juan,[5]
made of sunshine and sugarcane,
looks like me.
She used to run, weightless,
Time a perfumed bottle
hanging from her neck,
mañana[6] a song
she made up the words to
while she skipped—
until the day she stopped,
caught the toothless, squirming bundle
heaven dropped into her arms
and gravity kicked in.
Her life took a new spin.
This screaming gift did not
lead her to dream places
or fill all her empty spaces
like she thought.
Silly chica. She bought into
Hollywood's lie,
that love is mostly what you get
instead of what you give,
and what it costs,
like the perfumed bottle
ripped from her neck
and sent flying to the ground.
The crashing sound
of years lost
shattered in her ears,
and new fears emerged
from the looking glass.
Sometimes I wonder
if she'll ever sing again.

TYRONE

Girl's got a lot of heart, coming back to school after havin' a baby. I saw her around
here last year. Man, did she get big! She shrunk right back down, though. She's fine,
so I can see why a guy would want to give her a child. Not like any other guy will get
the chance, the way she steers clear and keeps to herself.

Fine as she is, the girl ain't no dummy. Not writing poetry like that.

She should put it up on the wall. If you ask me, it belongs there.

---

5. The capital of Puerto Rico.   6. Tomorrow (Spanish).

JANELLE BATTLE

"Janelle Hope. Mrs. Janelle Hope. Mrs. Devon Hope." Dream on, fool. You can stand here in the girls' room and practice saying that name 'til your tongue falls out, or the change bell rings, whichever comes first, and it still won't ever be true. Face it. Devon is Denzel Washington,[7] and you are Thighs "R" Us.

I can hear Lupe now. "Stop putting yourself down. You have a very pretty face. Besides, you have a lot more going for you." Yeah, well, I guess that's true. I mean, I am smart and funny, and I know I'm a good person. But this is high school, and nobody seems to care about that. Why couldn't I be tall and elegant like Diondra, or have Judianne's perfect complexion, all smooth, super-rich fudge? Better yet, why couldn't I look like Tanisha, or Gloria? Then I might have a chance with somebody like Devon. But I don't, so forget it.

Devon is different from the other jocks, though. How many guys you know read Claude McKay for fun? Seems like every time I go to the library, I catch him squeezed into a corner like he's got something to hide. He smiled at me last time I saw him there. That's something, isn't it? He didn't have to smile, even if I did smile and wave first. And he seemed to like the poem I read at the last Open Mike Friday.

I can't believe I'm getting up in front of people and talking about personal stuff, and liking it. I'm saying things that I would never tell anybody, usually. But, I don't know. There's something about reading poetry. It's almost like acting. The room is kind of set up like a stage, anyway. Mr. Ward turns most of the lights out, and we stand in a spot in front of the video camera. Once he switches it on, it's like you become somebody else, and you can say anything, as long as it's in a poem. Then, when you're finished, you just disappear into the dark and sit down, and you're back to being your own self. Gloria says it's the same for her.

"Hey, Janelle."

Oh, no. It's Miss Big Mouth Fifth Avenue[8] in another one of her original getups. Where'd she come from?

"Hey, Judianne." I thought the bathroom was empty. How long was she there? I hope she didn't hear me talking to the mirror. That's all I need, to have the whole school laughing about me having a crush on Devon. Lord, please don't let that happen. It's bad enough they call me Battle of the Bulge behind my back.

I wish, I wish, I wish. God, I wish people could see me on the inside. I know I'm beautiful there.

Open Mike

INSIDE

By Janelle Battle

Daily
I notice you frown
at my thick casing,
feel you poke me
with the sharp tip
of your booted words.
You laugh,

---

7. African American movie star (b. 1954).
8. The major street in Manhattan for clothes shopping.

rap my woody shell
with wicked whispers shaped
like knuckles,
then toss me aside.
Lucky for me,
I don't bruise easily.
Besides,
your loss
is someone else's gain
for I am coconut,
and the heart of me
is sweeter
than you know.

TYRONE

You never think other folks got feelings. Like Janelle. I must've cracked wise a hundred times about her weight. Never even thought about it. It was just something I did for a laugh. Listening to her now, it don't seem all that funny.

LESLIE LUCAS

I'm starting to feel like I know Janelle, at least a little. And Lupe. And Gloria. And Raynard. Before Open Mike Fridays, I hardly knew anybody in this school at all. Big surprise.

What could I possibly have in common with these kids? I must've asked myself that question a million times a day when I moved here. I'm white, they're Black and Hispanic. I grew up in Westchester County.[9] They grew up in New York City. I like Sheryl Crow, they like Lauryn Hill.[1] Except for Raynard and Devon, who are into jazz. It's like we come from two different planets. But hey, it's not my fault. I didn't choose to be here. If it weren't for Mom up and dying on me, I'd still be back in Ossining with my friends.

I miss my friends. That's mostly why I hated moving here. I knew I wouldn't have anybody to talk to when it hurts, and it hurts all the time. Missing Mom, I mean. I was full up with loneliness for her a few weeks ago. It was one of those moments that come from outta nowhere, when you all of a sudden feel something reach inside your chest, grab your heart, and squeeze 'til you can hardly breathe. I was in the girls' locker room at the time, and for a minute, I wheeled around like Uncle Donny does when he's drunk. That's when I bumped into Porscha Johnson.

Porscha Johnson has the reputation for being a little touched in the head. In freshman year, she'd beaten the snot out of a girl who'd pushed her too far. They say it took four people to pull her off of the other girl. Everybody had pretty much steered clear of her since then. This is who I bump into.

"Hey! Watch it," she said.

"Sorry," I told her.

"You got that right. Why don't you sorry yourself on outta here?" Usually, this

9. Wealthy New York county; Ossining is about 30 miles north of New York City.
1. Hill (b. 1975) is an African American singer whose musical roots are Motown and hip-hop;

Crow (b. 1962) is a white rock singer (both have won multiple Grammy awards for their solo albums).

would be the cue for me to make myself invisible, but I was hurting too bad, and I was not in the mood. I flung my locker door open and spoke between my teeth.

"I said I was sorry. Now why don't you just leave me alone?"

"Leave you alone? Look, if you wanted to be left alone, why the hell did you invade *my* space?"

By space, I thought she meant neighborhood. That's when I felt my head spin off. "My mom died, all right? And I was sent to live with my grandmother, who lives in this neighborhood, and I had no choice. Not that it's any of your business."

The split second those last words flew out, I wanted to take them back, but I couldn't. I swallowed hard and waited for Porscha to shove me against the lockers, or to punch me in the stomach, or to whip out a knife like I'd seen kids do on TV. Instead, she stepped back, lowered herself to the bench, and said, "Sorry about your mom. My mom died too."

Turns out we both live with our grandmothers. For a long time, she put off telling me what her mom died from. My mom died of cancer, which was no big secret, but hers died from a drug overdose. Porscha thought that would make a difference, but when I found out, I told her it made no difference at all. Dead is dead, and lonely is lonely, and they both stink. All that matters, I told her, is that we're friends. And we are.

I'm lucky. I was on my way to being like Amy Moscowitz, the one girl in class almost nobody knows anything about. She cuts herself off, hardly ever speaks, or lets anyone in. She seems to be happy by herself, but I need to hear somebody's voice besides my own. I'm not as strong as she is, and now I don't have to pretend that I am.

Open Mike Fridays help. We kind of have our own little clique now. The whole school knows who we are, that we're "the poets." It's weird. For the first time in my life, I'm part of a group that's cool. Who would believe it?

Last month, Mr. Ward gave our class an assignment to write a poem about what frightens us most, in honor of Halloween. A year ago, I might have written about something silly, like ghosts, which I don't even believe in, and even if I did, ghosts would not be at the top of my list. The scariest thing I can think of now is being all alone in the world.

Open Mike

COMMON GROUND

By Leslie Lucas

On the dark side of the moon
where death comes sooner
than expected;
at the edge of heartbreak
we both take
a leap
into the unknown;
at the center of loneliness
we dip into a pool
of tears
and thrash around
desperate not to drown;
we both reach out

for a life preserver,
something to hold on to
something sturdy
something new.
That's when we see it,
a buoy called friendship
bobbing up between us
and we swim toward it
for all we are worth
and we meet there,
somewhere
in the middle.

Tyrone

Man, that little white girl be getting pretty deep. I figured her for something lame
like "Roses are red, violets are blue." Glad I didn't have a bet on that action.

More than half the class wanted to read today, but most of them were girls. I wish
a few more of the brothas would step up to the mike, even this thing out a little.
Know what I'm saying?

Judianne Alexander

Good thing Leslie's cough woke me in class this morning. I nodded off three times.
Once more and Mr. Ward said he'd be bringing me a pillow. That's what I get for
staying up late. Again.

What choice did I have? Open Mike Friday is today and I am not about to stand
in front of the class in some funky old outfit. I didn't realize it would take me half
the night to finish something new. I hope I can stay awake long enough to read my
poem when my turn comes.

Me, writing poetry! What a scream. I'm not smart enough to be writing poetry in
the first place, though Mr. Ward says I'm smarter than I know. Yeah, well, I wouldn't
have bothered trying to write anything except that Open Mike Friday is one time I
know I can get Tyrone Bitting's attention, and I've got a thing for Tyrone. Of course,
he's got a thing for Tanisha Scott—like every other boy in school.

Too bad we can't all have good hair[2] and light skin.

Who am I kidding? She's more than that. She's pretty. Which I'm not, as my
stepfather reminds me ten times a day. Like I don't know that from looking in the
mirror, or from having kids tease me about my blue-black skin all the way through
school. But my body's good. Nothing wrong with me in that department. That's why
I got to show it off, wear clothes that accentuate the positive. The shorter, the better.
And I don't even have to buy them. I can make them myself. It ain't much, but that's
one thing I learned from my mother. How to sew.

Last week, I wore my patchwork denim skirt and vest with the red leather pockets
that just about broke my sewing machine needle. Sheila was all up in my face, telling
me how cool I looked, like I needed her opinion. Why she's always trying to kiss up
to Black people is beyond me. Anyway, it was Lupe's compliment I listened to. She
took one look at my outfit and told me she was jealous. Said she wished she could

---

2. I.e., hair that is straight or wavy, not tightly curled.

sew like me. Honey, I thought to myself, give me some of that pretty skin and hair of yours, and I'll trade.

Lupe has no idea how pretty she is. You should see Raul and some of the other guys—Black *and* white—sniffing round her. And does she notice? Don't look like it to me. Except for Raul. It's hard not to notice Mr. Latin Loverboy. Anyway, Lupe says she already has a boyfriend. I'm thinking he's invisible, though. I never see him. He goes to another school, she says. Others say he doesn't go to school at all, that he dropped out a long time ago, that he's eight years older than Lupe. Eight years! But hey, it's none of my business. At least she's got somebody. I'm still working on that one. Meanwhile, I spend my weekends alone, holed up in a room with my Singer sewing machine.

I've been helping Mom mark and cut out patterns for as long as I can remember. I even helped her draw a few that Vogue[3] never thought of. They should take a look at my sketch pad! Now, if I could just figure out how to design poetry as well as I design clothing, I could turn myself into somebody special. Wouldn't that be a neat trick?

It wouldn't hurt if I could come up with something deep to write about, like Chankara. I wouldn't want to have the experience of someone beating up on me, though. It's bad enough my stepfather talks about me like a dog. The few times my mother gets on him about it, he laughs it off and says he's just joking. I should cut his tongue out, see how funny he thinks that is, 'cause there's sure nothing funny about being called ugly. So why does Mom let him do it? Sometimes I think she loves him more than me. Otherwise, she wouldn't let him tear me down like that.

One of these days, he's going to call me ugly, and I'm going to ugly myself on outta there. I don't know where I'll go, but it'll be far away from him. Then Mom won't have to worry about defending me. And I won't have to waste energy being angry because she hardly ever does.

She's all right in private, though. She tells me to ignore my stepfather, says I've got a lot to work with, that I can make myself over with hair and makeup. When I'm older. For now, I can barely get out of the house with lipstick. Meanwhile, I sit at my sewing machine and dream about the great transformation I'm going to make someday. As if I could use pinking shears to cut out a new face for myself.

Right. Dream on.

Open Mike

COCOON

By Judianne Alexander

Her cocoon is see-through.
Inside, she is busy
with pattern and pinking shears.
If the ears are too long,
she'll snip them.
If the mouth is too wide,
she'll stitch up the corners.
Her needle and thread
hold more magic
than any wand.

---

3. Vogue's are the dressiest sewing patterns produced by the McCall Pattern Company (Vogue originally was an independent company).

With her chalk,
she can outline
a fine and voluptuous shape.
The nape of the neck
is a perfect place
to tuck and fold.
Her straight pins hold
the skin together, just so.
A quick basting stitch
lets her know where
to set her seams,
her cuffs, her hem.
After all, her arms and legs
mustn't be too long.
She mustn't stand too tall.
Perfect beauty is what
she's after.
She's already had enough
laughter in her life.
The day she clips her way
out of her cocoon,
the only sound
she plans to hear
is a deafening cheer.

TYRONE

Don't none of these girls like the way they look? I don't get it. Guys don't have that
problem. Not the guys I know. Would somebody clue me in?

LUPE

Judianne tapped me on the shoulder this morning and passed me a note real quick
before Mr. Ward could see. It was from Leslie. "Are you okay?" it said. I turned and
flashed her my "okay" smile. The smile was for real. I'm fine today. *Pero,* last night?
Forget it. I broke up with Marco and I was a mess.

It was so silly. I been planning to break up with him for weeks. I mean, I hardly
ever seen him anyways. Plus, I've been thinking, if I'm ever going to have a baby, I
need to find a better father than Marco, somebody who's got time for me, at least. I
don't want my baby and me to be alone, like Gloria and Angel. She got it harder than
I thought. Still, I wasn't in no hurry to break up with Marco, because that would
make it official: Lupe Algarin is alone. I can't hardly breathe thinking about it.

I busted up with Marco over the phone, which is good because, right after I hung
up, I felt this big hole rip open inside of me, and I started crying like little Rosa does
when she's hungry and her bottle is empty and her mom has just left the room. Once
I calmed down, I called Leslie. But as soon as I heard her voice, the tears started
coming again.

"I'm sorry," I said, trying to hide my sniffles. "I shouldn't have called."

"Lupe, what's wrong?"

"I don't want to bother you."

"You're not bothering me. Anyway, that's what friends are for. Now, what happened?"

I told her about Marco, and how I left him, and how he didn't even seem to care that much, and how I was all alone now. She was quiet for a minute. Then she said, "Lupe, sounds to me like you were already alone."

"I know, but—"

"Never mind. It's okay. You're not really alone, anyhow. You have friends. You have me."

"Yeah. I guess."

Leslie said she feels lonely sometimes too. She told me about how it was right after her mom died. I really listened because she doesn't talk about her mother much. She said that after the funeral, and even months after she moved in with her grandmother, her world felt so empty and hollow, she could hold it at one end and ring it like a bell. It's better now, she said.

We must've talked for an hour. I can't remember half of what we talked about, except that Leslie said friends can be like *familia*. Only she pronounced it *fama-lea*. It took me a minute to figure out what she meant. Anyway, she was right.

So I don't have a boyfriend now. So what? Neither does Janelle. Or Gloria. Or Leslie. But we have each other.

Maybe we can all be alone together.

Open Mike

El Noche

By Lupe Algarin

I stand out in the cold
el noche[4] and I
both too lonely for whispers.
Only the wind
shatters this silence.
I have been here before
choking in solitude,
but this time
when all the earth
is hollow as a bell,
I hold one end,
ring it,
and you come—
a pale-skinned surprise,
a friend.

Tyrone

Her voice is so soft, I close my eyes every time she reads, trying to hold in the sound a little longer. I'm glad Mr. Ward asked her to read her piece over again. She says it like a whisper, but it's powerful stuff. That's one thing these ladies know how to do. Be soft and strong at the same time. Like my moms.

---

4. The night (Spanish).

JANELLE

Tyrone said something to me today, but I didn't hear him. I'm having trouble getting Judianne's poem out of my head. Even Lupe said it was a surprise. We all thought Miss Fifth Avenue was self-confidence with a capital S, but her poem was all about wishing she could make herself over. I know what that's like. Which is what I tried telling Judianne the other day. Boy, was *that* a mistake!

I ran into her in the bathroom. That seems to be our place to meet. Anyway, I decided to take advantage of the meeting.

"I've been meaning to tell you, I really liked the poem you read for Open Mike Friday."

"Yeah? Well, thanks. I'm not used to writing poetry."

"Well, nobody could tell it. You know, I could really get into what you were saying about trying to make yourself over, wishing you could be perfect and all. I mean, I feel like that every time I look in the mirror."

Judianne nodded, and her tight mouth softened a little. She was about to say something, but then a toilet flushed and she realized we were not alone. Sheila Gamberoni came out of the stall, and the minute she did, Judianne slipped back behind her usual scowl and turned mean.

"Look, I am nothing like you, okay?" she spit out. "In case you haven't noticed, you're fat and I'm not. And you're wrong about my poem. It was just words. It didn't mean anything. You got that?" And she slammed out of the bathroom and left me there, stinging from the inside out.

I bit my lip to keep the tears back. I turned the faucet on and washed my hands a few times, staring at the sink until I heard Sheila step out into the hall. I glanced up at the mirror before I left. "You're wrong, Judianne," I said to the mirror. "They weren't just words, and you know it."

I haven't tried talking with her since. I don't want to give her an excuse to be mean to me again. I'm not mad at her, though. I know there's a part of her that's as scared to look in the mirror as I am. I saw that person for a few seconds, even if she wants to deny it. Calling me names won't change the way she feels inside. One of these days, she's going to find that out.

Open Mike
MIRROR, MIRROR

By Janelle Battle

Sisters under the skin,
we meet in the mirror,
our images superimposed
for one split second.
Ready or not,
I peer into your soul
and dive deep,
splash-landing
in a pool of pain
as salty and familiar
as the tears on my cheek.
Your eyes don't like
what I see.

You don't want to be me.
So you curse
and smash the mirror,
which gets you what?
A bit of blood,
a handful of glass splinters,
another source of pain.

TYRONE

Mm, mm, mm. Janelle is working it. Seems like her pieces are getting tighter. Actually, I think everybody's getting better. Practice makes perfect, I guess, and we be getting plenty of practice these days. Mr. Ward had to switch Open Mike from once a month to once a week 'cause so many people be wanting to read their work.

I b'lieve there's more to this thing than Mr. Ward planned on. But he's cool. He keeps rolling with it.

TANISHA SCOTT

If Tyrone calls me "caramel cutie" one more time, I'll scream. I turn to cut my eyes at him and find Judianne staring at me again. Even after I turn away, I can feel her eyes stroking the back of my head. I'm so sick of people making a big deal over my "good hair."

I caught her pawing my hair just last week. I reached back and grabbed a finger before she had a chance to pull away. I spun around, more aggravated than angry, and said, "Look, it's just hair. It's not magic, so don't go rubbing it for good luck. Trust me, it hasn't brought me any." Raynard stifled a laugh. You never know when that boy is paying attention. Of course, Judianne made out like she didn't know what I was talking about, swearing up and down she hadn't touched a single hair on my head. But I'd seen that hungry look in her eyes, like I had something she wanted. It was the same look my cousin Faith always gives me just before she says "I sure wish I had good hair like yours" or "I wish I was light like you," followed by "then boys would like me better." Which isn't true, if you ask me. But try telling that to my cousin. Or to Judianne. If she doesn't quit bugging me, I'm gonna ask Mr. Ward to change my seat.

She's why I chopped all my hair off last year. Well, people like her.

My mother freaked when she saw me. My bangs were cut straight across my brow and the sides were sort of squared at the neck. I looked like a clown minus the red nose. It was the best I could do on my own. And it looked better than that time I washed it in detergent to kink it up so I could have an Afro like my cousins. Anyway, Mom hated it so much, she finally forked over money for a visit to a hair salon to have it cut professionally.

Served her right. I'd begged her to let me cut it off before. "But your hair is so beautiful," she'd say. "Why would you want to cut it?"

My mind flashed to the school cafeteria that afternoon. I'd walked past a group of would-be girlfriends who sucked their teeth at me and said my name like it was curdled milk they couldn't wait to spit out. "Here come Miss High-Yella, thinkin' she's all that, with her so-called 'good hair,'" said one. "Far's I'm concerned, she ain't nothin'," said another. "Less than nothin'," said a third. I shook off the memory.

"Look, Mom," I said. "You don't understand." But she wasn't listening.

"Most girls you know would kill to have your hair," she said.

"That's just it, Mom. They hate me for it and they hate my skin. I can't do anything about my skin, okay, but my hair I can fix." I lost the argument, of course. Then, three weeks later, I cut it anyway.

It's growing back now and I've decided to let it. I mean, it's not like I can win, you know? I've tried dressing down in T-shirts and baggy pants, with no makeup, and it's still either "Come here, pretty mama" from cocky boys like Wesley who I have absolutely no use for, or getting grief from girls I used to want as friends. I even thought about getting brown contact lenses once, to cover up my green eyes, but my friend Sterling talked me out of it. He's light-skinned too, so he knows where I'm coming from. He said he used to twist himself into a pretzel over it until he realized God loves him just the way he is. Besides, he told me, if I did start wearing colored contacts, those girls would only say I was trying to be something I'm not, and he's right. So I give up. Let 'em say what they want. I am not a skin color or a hank of wavy hair. I am a person, and if they don't get that, it's their problem, not mine.

I'm better off with friends like Diondra and Janelle who know I'm more than what I look like. They know I've got a brain, and I know how to use it. They're no dummies either. That's why I asked Mr. Ward if the three of us could do a group project on Women of the Harlem Renaissance for extra credit. We had our first meeting at my house.

"Can we do Zora Neale Hurston?" asked Janelle. "I know we read *Their Eyes Were Watching God* in class, but she wrote a bunch of other stuff too."

"You're right," I said. "Good idea." I picked up my pad and wrote Z. Hurston at the top. "Okay. That's a good start, but I think we should cover some women you don't hear so much about."

"Like?"

"Georgia Douglas Johnson.[5] I read some of her work in a book called *3000 Years of Black Poetry*. I'd never heard of her before, and I bet nobody else in class has either."

"Cool," said Diondra. "Maybe I should read that book and see if I can get a couple of ideas."

"You can borrow it from the library," I said. "Soon as I return it, that is." We all laughed. I'm notorious for turning library books in late. "Meanwhile, Diondra, you can start working on portraits of these sisters so we can use them for our report covers when we're done."

I didn't wait for her to volunteer, because I knew she wouldn't. For somebody who has talent, she spends an awful lot of energy hiding it. But I figure if enough people tell her she's good, she'll start believing it. That means people actually have to see her work. I'm going to make sure they do, even if I have to keep volunteering her for projects 'til we graduate. She's not about to say no to me. She knows I'm stubborn when I want something.

"Fine," says Diondra. "I'll do the portraits, but don't look at me when Mr. Ward sees those report covers and busts out laughing."

"Laughing? What do you mean, laughing?" Janelle and I looked at each other. I nodded, and on the count of three, we jumped on Diondra and tickled her 'til tears of laughter squirted out of her eyes.

Them's my girls. They don't care what I look like. They know the only difference

5. African American poet and playwright (1886–1966), who from 1909 on lived and worked in Washington, D.C.

between my color and theirs is that the slave master who owned my family raped my great-great-grandma instead of theirs. And like my dad says, that ain't nothing to celebrate or be stuck up about.

Open Mike

FOR THE RECORD

By Tanisha Scott

It's the blood that tells:
slaves black as Mississippi mud
ring the trunk
of my family tree.
They speak through me
Black as they want to be.
The slaver's white drop
couldn't stop the spread
of African cells.
They're bred
in the bone,
past the slick hair,
the too-fair skin.
So don't tell me
I can't fit in.
My heart beats
like a talking drum,
my mom hums to Bessie[6]
just like yours,
the brothers in my dreams
are pure ebony,
and blue-black grandmother arms
like the ones
that cradled my ancestors
have often cradled me.

TYRONE

Now I know why the sista hisses every time I call her "caramel cutie." That'd be the last thing she wants to hear! She's proud of her African self, and I'm down with that. That's why I be wearing my *kufi*[7] every chance I get.

I wonder if the sista's into African music. I gotta ask her about that sometime. Maybe I could hook up some African drum music to go with her poetry for the assembly Teach told us about. She could read her stuff, and I could play DJ. Yeah! I could get into that.

DEVON

I look up from my lunch tray and catch Tanisha's eye while she stands in the cafeteria line. We nod.

6. Bessie Smith (1894–1937), an African American singer known as the "Empress of the Blues."

7. A close-fitting, brimless round hat worn by African Muslims.

"Yo, brotha," says Tyrone, thinking I'm nodding to him. I wave and turn away.

Tanisha is one fine sister, but I never say that to her face. She gets tired of hearing it from all the other guys. They look at her and that's all they see, what's on the surface. That's what she told me when we talked once after Open Mike Friday. We talked about superficial judgments, how people look at you and think they know who you are, what you are, how they put you in a box: jock, china doll, whatever. That's one thing me and Tanisha got in common. We know all about being put in a box. I feel like I'm gonna be climbing out of the one marked "dumb jock" all my life.

"Hey, Jump Shot," I hear somebody call me from behind. It's Mike from the basketball team. I nod, then go back to reading Imamu Amiri Baraka's *Preface to a Twenty Volume Suicide Note*.[8] Mike slams his tray down beside me and sits.

"What's that you reading?"

"Baraka," I tell him. "Poetry."

"Oh. Right. You got that class."

At first I don't say anything. Then I decide. "No, man. It's not for class. I'm reading it for me, actually."

"You gots to be kiddin'."

"No."

"That's so lame, man."

I keep my finger in the book and turn to face him.

"You ever read Baraka?" No answer. "You should check him out."

"Hey, do what you want, man. I ain't interested." Mike picks up his tray and moves to another table, shaking his head. I go back to my reading, seeing as how he'd given me *permission* and all.

Forget this. Tonight our team plays Bronx Science.[9] When I get on the bus with the rest of the guys, I'm taking a copy of Baraka's book with me to read, and I'm gonna make sure everybody sees it. Especially Mike.

Open Mike

Black Box

By Devon Hope

In case I forgot to tell you,
I'm allergic to boxes:
Black boxes, shoe boxes
New boxes, You boxes—
Even cereal boxes
Boasting champions.[1]
(It's all a lie.
I've peeked inside
And what I found
Were flakes.)
Make no mistake,
I make no exceptions

---

8. The first collection of poetry (1961) published by Baraka (b. 1934), African American poet, playwright, and controversial political activist. Born LeRoi Jones, he took the name Ameer ("prince," later Amiri) Baraka ("the blessed one") in 1968; he then also assumed the title Imamu ("spiritual leader"), which he dropped in 1974.

9. The Bronx High School of Science, to which students from all five boroughs of New York City are admitted by competitive examination.
1. The makers of Wheaties cereal began marketing it as "the breakfast of champions" in 1933, and the first athlete appeared on the cereal box in 1934.

For Cracker Jack
Or Christmas glitter.
Haven't you noticed?
I'm made of skeleton,
Muscle and skin.
My body is the only box
I belong in.
But you like your boxes
So keep them.
Mark them geek, wimp, bully.
Mark them china doll, brainiac,
Or plain dumb jock.
Choose whatever
Box you like, Mike.
Just don't put me
In one, son.
Believe me,
I won't fit.

TYRONE

The brotha's right. I look around this class and nobody I see fits into the box I used to put them in. Startin' with Mr. Ward. I figured him for a lightweight do-gooder who would last about five minutes in this neighborhood. But he stuck, and he got this poetry thing going. He even reads his own stuff sometimes. He's okay.

Devon's okay too. I don't know how bright the other jocks are, but there's nothing dumb about this brotha. Mr. Ward says you have to take people one at a time, check out what's in their head and heart before you judge.

Word.[2]

STERLING S. HUGHES

Devon shook his head when he saw me standing in the lunch line yesterday, fingering an imaginary fret, making the appropriate sound effects. Friend or not, he thinks I'm crazy, but the brother behind me got into it, snapping his fingers to the rhythm I set. "Yeah!" he said. "Preacher got it goin' on."

My name is Sterling Samson, but everyone calls me Preacher. I intend to become a science teacher, not a preacher, but I don't mind being called one. Just so long as you don't call me Samson. I'm hoping to end up in a little better shape than he did.[3]

I turned to the brother behind me and eased into a smile. "I play a real guitar at church every Sunday. You ought to come by and check me out sometime." Judging by the way the brother cut his eyes at me, his appearance on the steps of First Baptist Church seemed highly unlikely. Still, you never know.

I went back to my invisible string playing to keep my fingers limber for later. I had promised to hold the bass line for some of the brothers reading at this week's Open

---

2. Truth; an affirmative interjection (rap slang).
3. I.e., than the biblical Samson (Judges 13–16); he is betrayed to the Philistines when he reveals to Delilah, whom he loves, that his uncut hair is the source of the great strength. When the blinded Samson is brought to a feast to be mocked by his enemies, he prays for a return of his strength and then pulls down the pillars of the temple of Dagon, killing thousands of Philistines and himself.

Mike. Mr. Ward was kind enough to lock my guitar up in his office in the morning so I wouldn't have to worry about it walking away before then.

Assuming I made it to his class without any trouble.

A brother named Leon "accidentally" bumped into me as I approached the cashier. He spilled, or should I say poured, a cupful of honey on my shoes. My *new* shoes.

"Oops! Looks like Mr. Goody Two-shoes got a mess to clean up," he said, laughing. His buddies joined in.

I stared down at my shoes, counting. *One. Two. Three. Four.* By the time I reached ten, I realized counting was not going to suffice.

I need you, Lord. Hold back the Samson in me. I may not have his strength, but you know I have his temper.

I counted backward from ten, felt my breath slowly evening out. A still, small voice[4] reminded me to return good for evil, reminded me that my plans for the future do not include fisticuffs or expulsion. I am college-bound and nothing is going to keep me from it. Besides, these poor fools are only trying to get a rise out of me. They're only trying to prove that the peace of God is nonexistent. But how can they?

I looked up at Leon and shook my head. Then I grabbed him by the shoulders, kissed him loudly on both cheeks, and gave him a bear hug.

"Get off me, man!" he said, trying to pull away.

When I finally let him go, I whispered, "Leon, I forgive you." Fear blotted out the pupils in his eyes.

"Man," he yelled, "you some kind of freak!"

I smiled, strummed my imaginary guitar, and sang, "I'll be a fool for Christ,[5] not just once, but twice." Leon and his friends backed away as if I'd set a match to them. They put as much distance between us as possible.

"You sick, man," Leon called over his shoulder. "Stay away from me!"

It's always something with these guys. Either they're trying to draw me into an infantile game of The Dozens so we can trade insults left and right, or they're slapping porno pictures inside my locker hoping to set me off. If they had some direction in their lives like Raul, Devon, or Raynard, they wouldn't have time to worry about me one way or the other. Which is precisely why I want to teach, to give young brothers like Leon some direction. Even Wesley has direction, although the brother could clean up his language. Sometimes he sounds like a thug in training. Leon's not much better.

If only Leon and his friends knew how lame their antics are. As if any of that could stop me from believing in God.

All my life, I've seen my mother pray, and all my life, I've seen her prayers answered. There was the time my baby brother was dying of pneumonia and the doctors had given up, but she prayed until the fever broke. There was the time she was laid off from her job, and the refrigerator was empty, and she bowed her head over an empty pot and prayed for God to fill it. That night, a woman upstairs begged her to accept a bag of frozen meats and vegetables, because she was moving the next day, and she hated to see good food go to waste. We had steaks that night, and we *never* have steaks. There were lots of times like that. "See there," Mom would say. "That's God's hand. If you have God's hand on your life, everything will be all right." So of course I believe. And I believe big. I'm believing God's going to get me and my three brothers

---

4. An allusion to 1 Kings 19.12.
5. See 1 Corinthians 4.10: "We are fools for Christ's sake."

into manhood, into college, and off of these streets—with no more than maybe a couple of black eyes between us. How's that for believing?

The change bell rang and I was still cleaning off my shoes. I could've used a few extra minutes to work on my own poem. It took me a while to get into this whole poetry thing, not that I don't like it. I read *God's Trombones* by James Weldon Johnson, and some of the work by Countee Cullen, like "Simon the Cyrenian Speaks,"[6] and I liked what the brothers had to say, but their styles don't suit me. Then Mr. Ward turned me onto Rev. Pedro Pietri,[7] who is more my speed, even if he is kind of old. He knows how to put God and the street in the same sentence, and I figured if I'm going to write poetry at all, that's what I want to do. So I put together a few. I couldn't tell if they were any good, but I decided to read one anyway. If I get a laugh, it won't be the first time.

The bell rang one last time. I took a few bites of my sandwich, wrapped up the rest, and tossed it in my book case for later. I told my growling stomach to be quiet and headed to Mr. Ward's office for my guitar.

Open Mike

D-TRAIN

By Sterling S. Hughes

He squeezed through the subway doors
a young gun, thirsty for the kind of coke
you can't sip through a straw.
He sized up the passengers,
chose his prey:
a wrinkled woman at the tail end
of her Geritol[8] years
who fears her own shadow
with good reason.
He lunged at her,
demanded her cash
to replenish his stash
of powdered death.
No one blinked or came
to her aid, at first.
Then, in He beamed.
Light streamed from His fingers,
singed anyone caught without
a robe of righteousness
across his back.
The lack of goodness
in the young gun's heart
was oxygen to the fire, and so
he burned a good long while

6. Poem by Cullen (1903–1946), whose lyrical poetry made him a central figure in the Harlem Renaissance; Johnson (1871–1938), an African American civil rights leader and man of letters whose career ranged from diplomat to songwriter, published *God's Trombones: Seven Negro Sermons in Verse* in 1927.
7. Puerto Rico–born poet and dramatist (1943–2004).
8. A vitamin supplement marketed to the elderly.

before I woke.
The dream stoked my faith
in the judgment and justice
that will come someday
or this afternoon.
Soon. I turn up the collar
of my white robe,
relieved to know
God's got me covered
'cause I'm good,
but not that good.

TYRONE

The brotha took me to a whole other place. I'm not sure I got all of it, but I got that he don't call himself no angel. 'Course, if Mr. Goody Two-shoes ain't no angel, what does that make me? Never mind.

He sure worked that rhythm. I know that much. He snuck a little rhyme in there too. I like that. Go on, Preacher! Look like God got hisself a poet!

DIONDRA

I spent way too long yakking with Tanisha over lunch. She couldn't stop talking about Pedro Pietri, the poet Mr. Ward had invited to visit our class. He was coming in a couple of weeks and Tanisha said he was gonna rock the house. He was the only poet Mr. Ward had us read who we were actually going to meet, which was pretty cool. Tanisha could hardly wait to check him out. I had other things on my mind, though, so I was glad Tyrone came over and broke up the conversation. He started hitting on Tanisha as usual. I whispered, "Sorry," and took off.

Ten more minutes and Mr. Ward will be in here. I flip my sketchbook open to a fresh page, clip my father's photo to the corner, and get busy. A few strokes of my pencil and the oval of his face is done. Then I start with his chin, I don't know why. Maybe because the hardness is there and I want to get it out of the way, hurry on to the softer parts of his face. The parts that show love. I've never done a portrait from the bottom to the top before, but why not? As long as it looks like my father when I'm done.

The first bell rings. I lift my head and there's Sterling, staring over my shoulder. "Hey."

"Hey." I lean back so he can get a better look. "I just started this one," I tell him. Other kids file in, so I gather up my charcoal pencils.

Raul swirls his brushes in a jar of water and finishes straightening up Mr. Ward's desk. I catch his eye and we smile at each other. He's part of the reason I don't mind people looking at my drawings anymore. I guess I should give Tanisha some credit too. It was her bright idea to have me do those book report covers.

The day we got our reports back, Mr. Ward held mine up so everyone could see the cover. I tried evaporating on the spot, I swear. The last thing I wanted was extra attention. Too late! When class was over, I ran out of the room before anyone had a chance to laugh in my face, but Raul caught me in the hall and snatched the report from me quicker than a subway door slamming shut. He said he wanted to get a better look at it. I bit my tongue and stared at the floor.

"This is good!" he said. "Especially the eyes. They look right through you. You gotta show me how you do the eyes."

My jaw dropped. "You think they're that good?"

"You're kidding, right?" Raul didn't wait for an answer. He handed me back the report, shaking his head. "Wish I could do eyes like that. Anyway, see you later."

I looked down at my book cover as if I was seeing it for the first time. Raul was right. The drawing *was* good. The eyes *did* look right through you. Maybe I should try working on the rest of the face, I thought. I could do studies of mouths and noses and chins. I could try different kinds of faces, different shapes. I could get Mom to model for me. Or Tanisha. Or I could use pictures. We only have a bazillion photo albums around my house. Maybe I could bring one of them to school with me. Or I could just borrow a few of the pictures and then put them back later. Maybe . . .

I had a hard time concentrating on my classes that afternoon.

The next day, I wolfed down my lunch and half ran to Mr. Ward's room with a sketch pad and charcoal pencils. By the time Raul arrived, I was already at work. Nowadays I'm in here two, three times a week. I'd come more often, but I gotta make time for my friends.

I shade in my father's jawline just as Mr. Ward enters the room, then put my pencil down and look up in case he tries to catch my eye.

"Mr. Ramirez," says Mr. Ward, "may I have my desk, please?" Raul bows deep, like some actor in an old-time movie, then struts to his seat. He passes me on the way, leans down, eyes my rough sketch, and whispers, "Let me know when you get to the eyes."

My smile is so wide, my cheeks hurt.

Open Mike

HIGH DIVE

By Diondra Jordan

A trip to the city pool
ain't what it used to be.
I left the kiddy pool behind
many moons ago.
I know how to float
how to dog paddle
how to hold my breath
between breaststrokes.
I know the stench and sting
of chlorine.
It's no big thing.
But this,
scaling the ladder
for the high dive
drives me to distraction.
What if
I forget to swim?
What if
there's no water in the pool?
But wait.
Is it really water

I'm after?
I reach the top,
pad to the edge of the board,
and peek.
There it is,
swirls of blue, purple,
and periwinkle watercolor.
The perfect palette.
I take a deep breath,
dip the tip of my brush
into sky,
take one long leap
and . . .
To be continued.

TYRONE

I've been thinking we should plan on having a poetry slam next year. I ran the idea past Diondra. She's one of the shyest sistas in our class. At least, she was when school got started. Anyway, I figure if she's into the idea, everybody else should be down with it.

Next thing I need to do is pitch it to Mr. Ward, see if he can get the principal to go for it. Man, I would love to get in some guys from Bronx Science, or one of them other special schools, and turn them into toast at a poetry slam. There's no *way* they'd beat us. They wouldn't even know what hit 'em!

AMY MOSCOWITZ

Amy. The name is petite, like me. It's also soft. I'm not. Just ask Tyrone. Or Diondra. Or Sterling. Better yet, ask my father. He thinks I'm so tough, I don't need anybody. Not even him. He didn't always treat me that way. He used to handle me more like china. But then Mom left to start another family—without us. After the divorce, Dad decided we both needed to toughen up, that we needed to learn to stand on our own. I thought he meant together.

Two years ago I got sick at school and he was called in to take me to the hospital. Apparently I had appendicitis. I was doubled over with pain, tears streaming down my face, and he wouldn't even put his arm around me. He just walked beside me, stiff as a two-by-four, asking "Are you okay?" every couple of minutes. Jerk.

Would it have killed him to touch me? To help me up the hospital stairs? Never mind. I won't bother needing anyone like that again.

Too bad my father's not more like Mr. Ward. His daughter goes to this school, and I saw the two of them in the cafeteria the other day. I hear they have lunch together three times a week. Anyhow, there they were in the lunch line, him with his arm draped over her shoulder, the two of them blabbing away like old buddies. She was bent over a little, from the weight of her backpack I guess, and when he noticed, he slipped it off and carried it for her. She smiled up at him and gave his waist a squeeze, and I felt my stomach turn.

For about a minute, I hated that girl.

Sterling says jealousy is a waste of energy, that I should focus on what I have, not what I don't. That's what I get for opening my big mouth and telling him how I feel. But he's so easy to talk to, sometimes I let things slip before I even realize my mouth is open. Anyway, he's too busy trying to save my Jewish soul to think about betraying my secrets. He knows I'd never forgive him, and then where would he be? He could pretty much forget about preaching love and forgiveness around me after that. Not that all his preaching will get him anywhere, seeing as I'm an atheist. Still, his trying doesn't bother me, he's so up front about it.

He's right about the jealousy, though. I seem to be jealous of everyone and everything. Especially the friendships I see all around me. Leslie and Porscha, Lupe and Gloria, Tanisha and Diondra. It's enough to make me ill.

It's been forever since I had a best friend, let alone a boyfriend.

"Friendships don't just happen," Sterling tells me whenever I complain. "You have to reach out and make them."

"How?" I ask him.

"Just be yourself."

Myself. That's a laugh. If I were to show anyone who I really am inside, how cold my heart is, they'd probably run in the opposite direction. I tell Sterling this and he says, "Maybe. Maybe not. You won't know unless you try."

Sterling's right. I haven't been trying. Not since my parents divorced. I've been afraid to get close to anyone. When my mom left, I was suddenly out of orbit. It's like she was the sun, and when she took off, the only thing left was a big black hole where she used to be. Now the idea of letting somebody else get that close . . . I don't know. I'm just not ready. I wonder if I ever will be.

Open Mike

ODE TO STONE

By Amy Moscowitz

One day at Far Rockaway[9]
is all it took.
One look at rocks in water
decided me:
I want to be stone.
I want to be marble.
Dressed up limestone
never looked so good.
Let me be granite
and I promise
I'll show you how to take
a shellacking.
Yes, I'll risk sunburn.
Just let me be rock
wedged into the earth or sea
tidal waves crashing over me
while I remain intact—
no split at the core,
more buffed than bruised.
Forget the pillar of salt.[1]
I'll look back at the count of three

---

9. A residential area, with a well-known beach, on the south shore of Long Island; it is on the southeastern edge of New York City.
1. An allusion to Genesis 19.26: as Lot, with his wife and two daughters, was fleeing the destruction of the corrupt cities of Sodom and Gomorrah, his wife was turned into a pillar of salt after she disobeyed God's command and looked back.

and you can turn me into stone.
Go on.
I'm half rock
already.

TYRONE

Man! That girl is as cold as the snow on the ground. Somebody must've put a hurting on her. "I want to be stone." Can you get next to that? I've felt that way a couple of times. Once, when the undertaker carried my pops out of here. Another time when my girlfriend left me for my supposed-to-be homey. Both times I remember wishing I couldn't feel the hurt, wishing I could just cut my heart out and be done with it. But I like the way Amy said it. Let me be stone.

SHEILA GAMBERONI

Amy Moscowitz looked at me like I had two heads. Why? Just because I wanted to change my name.

When Mr. Ward took attendance this morning and got to me, I raised my hand and interrupted.

"Please don't call me Sheila," I said. "I prefer Natalina, my Africana name."

"Excuse me?" said Mr. Ward.

I cleared my throat, and spoke a little louder. "Please call me Natalina from now on."

Mr. Ward looked puzzled. "I'm sorry. I don't understand. Why would you—never mind, Sheila. Just see me after class."

I nodded. Diondra Jordan caught my eye and shook her head. Then she turned back to the charcoal portrait I saw her working on when I got to class. She slipped it into her notebook and shook her head again. I looked away just in time to catch Amy rolling her eyes in my direction. It was obvious she didn't understand, but since there are only four white people in this class, I was hoping for some support. So sue me.

"*Africana* name. *Puh-leeze!* Ain't nothing African about Natalina," said Judianne, the girl behind me. We used to call her Short Skirt. I know one thing, her clothes fit her better than my name fits me. But try telling her that. "Why don't you just keep the name your mama gave you?" she said.

"Leave the girl alone," said Porscha. "If she wants to change her name, I'm sure she has a reason. People always have reasons for what they do, even if we don't know what they are."

"I know one thing," said Judianne. "She can call herself whatever she wants. It still ain't gonna make her Black." Tanisha shot her a look of disapproval. Judianne lowered her eyes. "Sorry," she said, but it was too late.

I knew someone would misunderstand.

I'm proud to be an Italian. I *love* being Italian. Not that anybody can tell I *am* one, with this blond hair and pale skin of mine.

Everybody else in my family looks typical. Olive complexion, dark hair, dark eyes. Then there's me, sticking out like the proverbial sore thumb. But hey, I might as well. I'm the black sheep, anyway. The only girl in the family who wants a career instead of babies. The only cousin who likes to hang out with Blacks and Latinos. The only one who doesn't think they're all lazy and shiftless. Never mind that they've been discriminated against and shoved to the bottom of the economic rung since they've been here. Try telling that to my father. And don't even mention slavery, he throws his hands up and walks away. So of course he thinks I'm an idiot for wanting to go into social work to help minorities. He might understand better if he knew any.

It's ten years since Dad took over the neighborhood pizza parlor from Uncle Tony. You'd think by now he and my mother would've taken time to get to know most of their customers, not just the white ones. Maybe they're afraid to get too close to someone who might actually hug them, heaven forbid. It seems the only Gamberoni willing to show affection is me. How weird is that?

Some days I wake up wondering if I'm adopted. I try my life on like a dress, and it doesn't fit. I know this life is mine because the label has my name on it, but what kind of name is Sheila? It doesn't tell you who I am, or where I came from. Sheila could be anybody. That's why I wanted something more Africana. Okay, so maybe Africana isn't the right word. But I definitely want something more ethnic. A name that tells a story. A name with roots. That's what I want people to understand.

After English, I met with Mr. Ward and explained all of that, or enough of it to satisfy him, anyway. "Okay," he said. "Then I'll see you tomorrow. Natalina." It was all I could do not to give him a hug.

Open Mike
WHAT'S IN A NAME?
By Natalina Gamberoni

When strangers meet
they hurry past hello and seek
each other's designation.
"My name is ———.
And who are you?"
is the spade we sink
into this foreign, hue-man soil
to see what nuggets
we can dig up
what history
what ethnic derivation
what concentration of
cultural genes we can use
to weigh and measure each other.
Some will, no doubt
come up wanting
requiring a change
of designation.
"Hello!
My name is Natalina.
Will that do?"

TYRONE

That classroom sounded like a tomb after she read. I'm sitting there studying the video camera, and I'm wondering what Sheila would think if she could hear herself on that tape, if she could watch those words coming out her own mouth.

Judianne's right. There's something wrong with that girl. Hey, lots of peeps[2] change their names, I ain't got no problem with that. Some have to, the names their folks gave them are such dogs. But that girl sound like she wants to change her *race*. What's that about? She feeling guilty 'cause her family's got it good? I don't get it, but I'm gonna leave that one alone.

"Hey, Mr. Ward," I said. "What you planning to do with all them videotapes you're making?"

"I'm going to keep them, maybe show them to my students next year to introduce them to the idea of open-mike readings. If that's okay with you."

"Yeah, that works for me," I said. "Just make sure you show them mine."

STEVE ERICSON

Sheila may have identity problems, but I don't. I know exactly who I am, and no matter what anybody says, I know I was born in New York City for a reason. Where else does the sidewalk tremble under your feet from the rumble of subways underground, and trucks and city buses up top? Where else do cabbies and garbagemen, bankers and businessmen all walk with a beat? Where else can you find grade A, top of the line characters roaming the streets spouting Shakespeare in the middle of a blizzard? And where else can you find Broadway?

The first time my folks set me down in front of a Broadway stage to watch a musical, and I saw walls rising into the ceiling and staircases disappearing into the floor, I knew: I wanted to be a set designer, and I wanted to work on Broadway.

If you come to my house, there's hardly anywhere to sit in my bedroom, or to step, for that matter, because the whole place is cluttered with hand-painted miniature cardboard sets I designed for imaginary plays. I'll work on real ones as soon as I get to college, because I figure there'll be plenty of opportunities to sharpen my skills working on college productions, especially down at NYU,[3] where I plan to go. If I get in. *When* I get in. I have to get in. I have to get back to the city.

Two months ago, my father announced that we're leaving. We're moving out. The city is getting too rough, he said. Mom's not sure she wants to go on teaching in public schools. She has decided to take a break, so this is a good time to move, he said. As for him, he'll keep his job in publishing and just commute. From *Yorktown Heights*.[4]

I tried to pretend like the move is no big deal, since Mom and Dad are so hot on it, especially Mom, who's been wanting her own house forever. But man, I'm dying. I got friends here that I've grown up and gone to school with all my life, and I fit in here, and you can't tell me there are guys with bleach-blond buzz cuts and earrings in Yorktown. And what about the theater? There's no Broadway in *Yorktown*.

But maybe that's the point. Mom's not too keen on my plans to work in the theater, which is no surprise. She's still trying to get over my wearing an earring, even though I bought the smallest one I could find. (She freaked anyway.) I don't think Dad is too stoked about my plans either, although he doesn't say it because he knows I remember him telling me how he used to want to be an entertainer. He played drums in a band when he was my age, and had big-time plans of hitting the road like Ringo Starr[5] and the Beatles, and doing shows across the country. Then his family moved

---

2. People (rap slang).
3. New York University, located in Greenwich Village, is "down" from (i.e., south of) the Bronx.

4. Town in Westchester County, New York, about 40 miles north of New York City.
5. Drummer and singer (born Richard Starkey,

to Binghamton,[6] away from all his band mates, and eventually, his dream faded away.

Is that why they're moving? Is that what they're hoping happens to me?

Just the thought of maybe never working in the theater makes me crazy, and one day, I tell this story about my father to Raul and I tell him I don't understand how my father's dream could just die like that, when what I really want to know is, can mine. And Raul says something that sticks with me. "Maybe your father's dream wasn't really in his heart. If a dream is in your heart, you never lose it."

After we had that conversation, I kicked my doubts to the back of the closet. (Well, almost. I still go in there now and then.) Part of me continues to be afraid of following in my father's footsteps. These days, though, I try to concentrate on keeping my grades up so I can get into NYU when the time comes, because one thing I know for sure is that my dream is in my heart.

I've got two more years of school to go. Two more years to hold on to my dream, and two more years of Open Mike Fridays. Well, one year and a couple of months—this year's going by so fast. I hope I'll still have a chance to do Open Mike next year. They're so popular now, every kid in school wishes they were in Mr. Ward's class. I can't blame them. We got a good thing going here, and people need to know about it. We're sick of the negative press teenagers get all the time. Apparently somebody at *The Bronx Insider* agreed. Mr. Ward said they're sending a reporter to cover our next Open Mike Friday, and it should be a monster. Mr. Ward invited a real poet to come speak to us and to read some of his work. It's not an assembly exactly, but Mr. Ward is having us meet together in the multipurpose room for the special presentation. Pedro Pietri is the poet's name. He's in this book called *The United States of Poetry*[7] and somebody said he's a reverend. Sterling must be stoked! Anyway, I'm looking forward to hearing him. Poetry is the coolest thing we got going on in this school now. Maybe I'll still be around next year to enjoy it.

Whether I finish up school here, or in Yorktown Heights depends on my folks. Either way, there's a set designer's job on Broadway with my name on it, and I'm not giving it up for anybody.

Open Mike

DOUBTLESS

By Steve Ericson

When I was seven,
I looked to heaven
and dreamed
of going to the moon
but pretty soon
somebody came along
to change
my tune.
They put me down.
Bang! There my dream lay
on the ground.

1940) for the British rock band the Beatles (1962–70) and later on solo albums.
6. City in upstate New York, about 180 miles northwest of New York City.
7. Compiled by Joshua Blum, Bob Holman, and Mark Pellington (1996).

Thank God, eventually
I came around
and dreamed
another dream.

At first, it seemed
a good idea to hide it,
confide it
to absolutely no one.

But that was no fun,
besides, I realized
I couldn't. The joy it gave me
just wouldn't
be stopped up. It popped up
at the most
inconvenient times,
effervesced
in all my rhymes.
But, hey! Joy
is not a crime, though
some people
make it seem so.
Does anybody here know
what I mean?
You share your dream
and right away
people laugh,
try to dissuade you,
do what they can to
plant a seed of doubt.
Listen: you've got to
root it out,
laugh last, push past,
pursue. Be you—
whoever that is—
dream intact.
And don't look back.

Don't look back.
Don't look back.
And if you move,
remember: Pack your dreams,
They're portable.

TYRONE

Either that boy's been hanging out with some brothas, or he wish he had. He must've grown up round here, the way he talks. But I hope he ain't studying on hanging out with me. We can peacefully coexist, but I don't have no white boys in my crew.

He ain't half bad, though. Pedro Pietri must've thought so too, the way he clapped when Steve was done. It was kinda cool having a published poet in the audience. First he read to us, then we read to him. He really listened to us too, like we were equals.

I bet Pietri's partly why that reporter came out to our school. Not that the *Insider* is the *Times* or *Daily News*. But hey, it's better than nothing. At least they're interested in the good stuff going on in our neighborhood. Of course, I thought they would send in a brotha, but they sent this white guy. Ain't no telling what kind of piece he'll write about our stuff. Somebody should have told him it's a long way from Shakespeare!

He talked to Rev. Pietri and Mr. Ward, mostly, but he took notes the whole time we were reading, and his photographer snapped a bunch of pictures. He definitely got one of me. He didn't say which ones they'd be using, though. He got down everybody's name, just in case, so he'd have them for the captions. Hope he spells my name right. Be just my luck, I get in the paper for something *good* and they misspell my name.

The paper comes out next week. See if I ain't the first one at the newsstand.

RAYNARD PATTERSON

Finish what you start. That's my mother's favorite saying, and she's earned a right to it. She had me when she was a teenager, but that didn't stop her from finishing high school, and she moved more times than Steve could even dream of! Every now and then, when I consider dropping out, I take a good, long look at my mother and think again.

This year certainly gave me plenty of opportunities to practice.

Homework was a nightmare. Essay questions in history *and* English. What are they trying to do, kill me? All those words swirling around the page gave me a headache I'm still trying to get rid of. If only they could give homework a beat and put it on a CD. Now *that* would work for me. Then they'd be speaking my language. Chords. Melodies. Homework in the key of G. Oh, yeah.

Music has always come easier to me than words. My mother says I used to beat out rhythms on my high chair with a spoon. I don't know if the story's true, but she's told it so often, everyone believes it. The one thing I know for certain is that I eat, sleep, and dream music. Man, when I see myself in the future, it's on a bandstand, fingering my alto. I may not be much of a talker, but hey, give me a sax and I'll talk all night long. My cousin Sterling says one day the whole world will hear what I have to say.

Last week, my English class was the world.

It was Open Mike Friday and I'd shown up with my saxophone case in one hand and a folded-up poem in the other. Not that I needed a copy of the poem. Besides the other kids, I knew we'd have a living, published poet in the audience, so I'd spent a week memorizing and rehearsing my poem in front of a mirror, if you can believe that. Even so, I still thought about maybe skipping the poem and just playing a piece on my sax. But there'd been too much skipping this year for me already. I'd skipped participating in every other Open Mike Friday, and Mr. Ward had skipped over me in class whenever it was time to read aloud. Which is why everybody thought I was three degrees below a moron. Not that I blame them. Even I used to think I was an idiot. Of course, now I know better. So does my English teacher.

Mr. Ward and I had discussed my problem back in September. He'd agreed to keep my secret, although he thought I should share it with the class. As for me, I didn't think they'd understand, and I didn't want anybody treating me as if I was diseased or mentally ill. It seemed easier to let them think I was stupid, so long as I knew I wasn't. But after last Friday, I realized Mr. Ward was right. It's only been a week and already I feel lighter. That's not the way I felt when he called my name, though.

"Okay, Raynard," he said. "You're on."

All my second thoughts rushed forward, causing a traffic jam in my mind. But Gloria caught my eye. "Go on," she whispered. "Do it, Cuz," said Sterling. "Yeah," said Wesley. "Show us what you got."

I nodded thanks and took a deep breath. I shoved the poem in my pocket, grabbed my sax, and went to the front of the room.

Open Mike

DYSLEXIA

By Raynard Patterson

Onion skin, acid-free linen,
80% recycled fiber—
the paper content
doesn't much matter.
My eyes see
letters dancing backward
across whatever page
they're printed on.
The why is a mystery to me.
Could it be I'm one gigabyte short?
Or maybe I was born feet first?
When the doctor smacked my bottom
did I laugh instead of cry?
Do my thoughts trade places
like letters, on the sly?
Such questions are enough
to make you crazy if
you're not.
"Dyslexia is a minor disturbance,
nothing major once you learn
your way around it," says the doc
as if he's a radio jock
announcing a fender-bender.
Steer clear of the wreck ahead.
Try the Triborough[8]
for smoother traffic the next time
you take your mind
for a spin.
Neurological distinction
notwithstanding,
something in me whispers Freak
every time I wriggle out

---

8. A bridge (opened in 1936) that connects three boroughs of New York City: the Bronx, Queens, and Manhattan.

of reading aloud,
or have to ask a stranger
"Excuse me, but
what does that sign say?"
Read me any way you choose.
Only please, stop asking
"What's his problem?"

TYRONE

The world ain't but one big surprise after another. Just look at Raynard. Or look at *Steve*. That white boy got more up his sleeve than anyone would guess. I ain't lying.

Yesterday me, Wesley, and Sterling got up to do a cipher for Open Mike Friday and here come Steve, jumping up to join us. I laughed out loud. Didn't even try to hide it. I ain't never seen no white boy do no free-style poem. You know how hard that is? One person starts a poem, then the next guy has to step into the rhythm, pick up the poem where the first guy left off, and keep it going. Then, after a while, the third guy steps in, if there is a third guy, and he takes over, and then the fourth guy, and so on. You go round and round and round like that, long as you can keep it tight, or until somebody finishes off the poem, or you get tired. Whatever.

Me and Wesley usually team up, going back and forth, with Sterling on guitar layin' down the beat. Sometimes we let Chankara jump in. She ain't half bad either, but then, she's a sister. What you expect? But Steve? Please. So of course I laughed.

"Boy," I said. "Sit your white butt back down before you hurt yo'self."

"Give the guy some slack," said Sterling. See why we call him Preacher?

"Yeah, brother," said Steve.

"You hear this white boy?" I said. I'm thinking he must like to take his life in his hands.

Wesley studied Steve a minute. "The question is, do you flow?"[9] I figured that would be the end of it, 'cause I was sure Steve wouldn't even know what the brotha was talking about. How could he?

"Yeah," said Steve. "I flow."

"Guys?" said Mr. Ward. "Today?"

I shook my head. "Yeah, okay, Teach." I cut my eyes at Steve, betting this boy had never done a cipher in his life.

"Just try to keep up," I told him. "Y'all ready?"

Preacher set up the beat, and we took off.

And guess what? That white boy can *flow*. Makes you kinda wonder 'bout his family tree, now don't it?

What else can that boy do that I don't know about?

Open Mike

NEWS AT FIVE

By Tyrone Bittings, Steve Ericson, and Wesley "Bad Boy" Boone

There be people in this land who want to take me out
But I will not leave the planet earth without a shout.
You may think you know me well, but let me set you straight.
Let me strip away the lies before it gets too late.

9. Continue in the same rhyme scheme without stopping (rap slang).

News at Five has got you thinking I was born to steal.
Blacks are menacing, they say, as if their talk's for real.
Brothas packing 45s work hard to prove them right.
Thanks to them, nobody's granny can go out at night.
But if Five-O[1] checks my pocket, they will find no piece.
I'm a rapper, not a shooter. Words are my release.
I believe in Martin's power, though the King[2] is gone.
But the last I heard, "I Have a Dream" keeps living on.
So will I, because no matter what the papers say,
I will hold on to tomorrow. I am here to stay.

I am here to stay, yo. I am here to play, yo.

Well, the ball is in my court, because I've come to play.
I am Steve, although they call me Dough Boy every day.
I will not apologize because my eyes are blue.
I am cool with being me just like you're cool with you.
By the way, just 'cause you brothers put the H in hip
doesn't mean some of us white boys can't pick up a tip,
I can get down on the get-down. I know how to flow.
I be checking out Dr. Dre[3] too, if you must know.
But enough of that, 'cause I've got something on my mind.
I have seen the News at Five and here is what I find:
There ain't nothing good on teens, don't matter where you look.
Black or white, screen time is strictly for the teenage crook.
Hear them tell it, drugs and violence is our only song.
For myself, I think it's time that we all prove them wrong.

I am here to stay, yo, I am here to play, yo.

Now it's my turn 'cause you always save the best for last.
Mr. Ward just eyed the clock. I better make this fast.
Listen up, my peeps, because I've got the 411.
News at Five is infotainment. That's the game they run.
So forget about those gray heads with their slanted views.
Come tomorrow, we will be the ones to write the news.
Starting now, we can create ourselves a whole new crew.
We can't do no worse than Nixon,[4] I don't think. Do you?
I am not a politician, but I know what's right.
It's high time we knocked the wall down between Black and white.
So what's say we end this thing with Steven and Tyrone
shaking hands and sharing hugs. Let's leave these two alone!

I am here to stay, yo. I am here to play, yo.

Peace.

---

1. A police officer (rap slang).
2. Martin Luther King Jr. (1929–1968), African American civil rights leader; he delivered his "I Have a Dream Speech" at the March on Washington for Jobs and Freedom on August 28, 1963.

3. African American rap musician (born Andre Ramelle Young, 1965).
4. Richard Milhous Nixon (1913–1994), thirty-seventh president of the United States (1969–74) and the first to resign from office.

If anybody had to catch me, I guess I'm glad it was Wesley.

I was in the doorway of a classroom watching Porscha as she walked by. No. That's not right. I wasn't watching Porscha, I was watching the way she *walked*, trying to study it. Then, once she turned the corner, I stepped into the hall and walked just like her. That's when Wesley caught me.

"Girl, what is your problem?"

That's the same question my mother and father keep asking me, although they don't use the exact same words. "What's wrong with you? Why can't you be like your sisters?" I want to know that too. Why *can't* I be like them, be like *somebody*? I hate sticking out.

Everybody around me is dark and ethnic. Which is in, by the way. Look at all the supermodels. They're from places like Venezuela and Africa and Puerto Rico. Then there's me, white bread and pale as the moon. I can't even tan without burning myself. I look around my neighborhood and this school, and nobody looks like me. I keep thinking if I could just stick out *less*, if I could learn to walk and talk like the kids around me, maybe I would fit in more. I don't know. Maybe it's a dumb idea. Wesley sure thinks so. When he pulled me aside in the school hall and I tried to explain why I was copying Porscha's walk, stupid was the word he used. The minute he said it, I felt my cheeks go red. That's not the color I was after. I jerked away from Wesley and avoided his eyes.

"Okay, maybe it was stupid. But I just want to fit in. I'm tired of being different, all right?" Suddenly I thought, Why am I trying to explain this to Wesley? He's Black. He already fits in. "Forget it," I said, beginning to walk away. "You don't understand."

"Oh, get a clue, girl! Everybody's different. It don't matter what your skin color is, or what name you call yourself. Everybody is different inside, anyway. We're all trying to fit in. Ain't nothing new about that."

"Great!" I said. "Since you're so smart, tell me what I'm supposed to do!"

Wesley shrugged. "Hey, I don't know what to tell you, except be yourself."

"Wonderful! Pearls of wisdom. Thanks a lot."

Wesley put his hand on my shoulder. "Sheila," he said, "you want to hang with brothas and sistas, it ain't no big thing. Just don't try to *be* them. Keep your name, change it—whatever. A name is a personal thing and I'm not going to get into that. But why you want to change who you are? Soon as you get out of here, you're going to go to a college or get a job where everybody else is as blond and blue-eyed as you. They walk like you and talk like you. What're you going to do, then? Change yourself back?"

The truth of his words pinned me to the wall. I never even stopped to think about the future, about leaving this school, this neighborhood, maybe even this city. All I ever think about is now, because now hurts so bad.

"I guess you're right," I said.

"Yeah, well." A couple of sisters passed by and threw us a dirty look. Wesley dropped his hand from my shoulder and shifted from one foot to another, suddenly uncomfortable.

"Look, at least in Mr. Ward's class, we make it easy. You want to hang, you want to fit in? It ain't no big secret. Just bring your poetry every Open Mike Friday and share right along with the rest of us. It's that simple."

"Yeah, I guess I can do that. I did it that one time."

"Yes, you did. Hey, I'm out of here," said Wesley. He jogged down the hall to his next class before I could thank him. Halfway there, he turned back and yelled, "By the way, forget Porscha's walk. It ain't working for you."

I don't know where it came from, but somewhere inside myself, I found a smile.

Open Mike

PRIVATE PUZZLE

By Sheila Gamberoni

God must love puzzles
the way he scatters our pieces
across the table of the world.
Here, squares bathed in shadow
appear to be the same
though each bears a different name.
It's only on closer examination
I learn that no two pieces
are alike.
Is that the plan?
To force confrontation?
Investigation?
Communication?
I raise my hand to ask
but am told
to move along.
So I nudge through the crowd,
scrape my shins,
feel the crush of bone,
moan a little,
then cry loud enough
for anyone to hear.
But still I go on seeking
an angular slot
to slip myself into,
someplace that feels
like home.
A friend points me
to the podium.
There!
For a moment,
the puzzle is done.
We are one now—
Eighteen syllables.
A single poem.

TYRONE

That girl's threatening to be a regular feature. This is the second week in a row she's brought something to read for Open Mike Friday. Except for me and Wesley, I don't think anybody's read two times in a row. But hey, she can read all she wants. Least she ain't talking that Africana mess no more. Good thing too. Now even Judianne can stand to have her in the same room.

If that girl ain't careful, somebody might actually end up liking her.

JANELLE

Jojo asked me to marry him yesterday. When Tyrone heard me telling Lupe that, he laughed his head off.

Jojo is eight years old. He's one of the kids I tutor at the public library. I was there yesterday helping him prepare for a math test when he suddenly cocked his head, looked up at me and said, "Miss Janelle, you're the most beautifulest lady on this whole planet."

"Thanks, Jojo."

"I been thinkin', Miss Janelle. Maybe we should get married."

Just like that! Out of the blue. Jojo sounded so serious, it was hard not to laugh. I didn't want to hurt his feelings though, so I pretended to cough a couple of times and covered my face.

"Well! I'll have to think about that," I said. "But first, we have to get you into the fourth grade. Deal?"

"Deal," he said. Jojo's such a cutie.

I'm glad somebody finds me beautiful, even if he is just eight years old! But maybe he's not the only one, though. Not anymore. The kids in Mr. Ward's class sure look at me differently these days. I noticed that at the last Open Mike Friday.

When I first got up to read, I was my usual self. I sucked in my stomach, walked slow to make sure nothing jiggled, and tugged down on my shirt, like I could really hide my extra pounds under there. I waited for Mr. Ward to switch on the video and then started to read.

I looked up from the page a few times and noticed kids in the front row with their eyes closed, smiling. Amy and Tanisha nodded every now and then, like I'd said something familiar, something they understood. Judianne, Leslie, and Porscha leaned forward so they could hear every word. Everybody really listened to what I had to say, even the guys. Tyrone, Wesley, Steve, Raul, Devon—they all stared at me like I was someone special. And nobody cared about the size of my body. Not even me.

Open Mike
THE DOOR

By Janelle Battle
I've been busy lately
carving a door of words
without a lock in sight.
Your ear is the key
that lets you into me.

(I am a secret
I want to share.
I swing my door open
and say a prayer.)

Look around.
Take the tour.
Fear hangs on the wall
and shame, sometimes.
Emotional dislocation too.
But I am brave
in my admission.
Are you?

When no one is looking
I check to see
if anyone else seems
as scared as me,
or lonely, or shy,
or insecure.
Is it just me?
I'm not so sure.

Is your heart
like an onion too?
Show me yours,
I'll show you mine
we used to say.
Your turn.
Peel away.

TYRONE

Janelle made it into the paper. I did too—in the group shot, looking all fuzzy. Devon was the only one got a close-up. They just love them pretty boys. That's okay. I got my name in there.

Mr. Ward brought the paper to school and held it up for the class to see. "Look at this headline," he said. " 'Student Poets Bloom in the Bronx.' That's you guys!"

I don't know who was prouder, us or Mr. Ward.

He brought a few extra copies of the paper for the class, and passed them around for anyone who hadn't seen it. I'd already bought my own, though. I had to, 'specially since they quoted what I said about how our poetry gives us a release, how it helps us relate to one another. They said our stuff was "energetic" and "rich in positive social messages." My moms will frame this puppy, for sure.

I called the reporter this afternoon and thanked him for writing such a nice piece. I told him about our assembly. "We'll be jamming," I told him. "Why don't you come check us out?" He said he'd try to make it.

Maybe we can get us another write-up out of this. You never know.

LUPE

I went to Janelle's this afternoon to study. Of course, before we could get started, she wanted to dish about Raul. Him and me had our first date over the weekend and, as far as Janelle's concerned, it's the biggest news since we all had our pictures splashed across the local paper. I know she's been dying to find out what happened. She called me twice, but I was at the library. She left a message asking if we planned on doing a love poem duet for assembly in a few weeks. That girl's crazy! I am looking forward to our last Open Mike Friday, though.

"So. You finally went out with him," said Janelle.

"Yeah."

"Well?"

"Well what?" I bite my tongue to keep from laughing. I know this is killing her.

"What did you and Latin Loverboy do?"

"We went to a movie."

"And?"

"And what? We watched it and he took me home."

"And?"

"And *nothing*. Now, can we please get to work?"

"Girl, you are no fun anymore. All you want to do is work, work, work."

"Yeah, well, fun ain't going to get me through history or trig."

Janelle stuck her tongue out at me and cracked open her history book, looking all disappointed. I balled up a piece of paper and threw it at her. She looked up, surprised, and threw it back, laughing. Then we settled down.

It's great having somebody to study with, even though I do okay on my own. Mr. Ward says if I keep pulling up all my other grades the way I've pulled up my grade in English, I should be able to get into a decent college when I graduate. That's what I'm planning on.

I want to go somewhere out of state, somewhere away from home, away from Berto and his drinking buddies. I'll miss my sister, Christina, and her little Rosa, though. But I don't see them as much as I used to, anyway. I'm too busy with school.

I'm not sure what I want to major in at college. I know I want to do something with kids, though. Maybe become a kindergarten teacher, or a pediatrician. Gloria says I still got time to figure that out. Keeping my grades up so I can get into a good school—that's the main thing.

Christina says I'm the smart one. "I envy you, Lupe," she told me last night. I could hardly believe my ears. "I wish I had gone to college," she said.

Getting to college takes more than wishing, I can tell you that much.

I've got an exam tomorrow, so I better put in an extra hour of study. I don't know what the questions are going to be, but I want to make sure I'm ready for whatever they throw at me.

Open Mike

IMAGINE

By Lupe Algarin

I walk by a mirror,
catch my eye,
wonder at the universe
behind it.
Past the flashing eyes
is a file
for yesterday's sunset

> *dripping mango light,*
> *for Papi's laughter*
> *tinkling in my*
> *five-year-old ears*
> *so many years gone by,*
> *for tears*
> *shed below a crucifix*
> *on my wall.*
> *I sort it all out,*
> *store it under*
> *"been there, done that"*
> *and open a clean drawer*
> *labeled* Mañana,
> *a place to store adventures*
> *I'm still learning*
> *to imagine.*

TYRONE

Something's different about Lupe's voice. It's still soft, but it's like there's steel running through it now. I don't think I'm making that up. Anyway, I know one thing for sure. I don't catch her staring off the way I used to. She's always looking straight up now, paying attention to whatever the teacher is saying, like she's afraid to miss a word. I see her running off to the library a lot lately too. Something new is definitely up with that girl.

DIONDRA

It was an accident. I didn't mean to leave them out for my father to find. At least, I don't think I did. That's what I told Lupe when she asked me what was wrong this morning. I was still upset about my father throwing a fit when he found my art school brochures last night. You'd think I'd stabbed him in the heart, the way he looked at me.

I'm sorry he feels so bad, but there's nothing I can do about it. I've made up my mind. If I can get into an art school, I'm going. Mr. Ward thinks I have a good chance of getting a scholarship. We'll see. Mom says my dad will come around. Eventually. I'm not so sure. Before I left home today, I slipped a poem and a drawing of Michael Jordan[5] in my father's easy chair, under the remote. That way, he wouldn't miss them. I was planning to give him the drawing for his birthday, but after seeing those brochures, he looked like he needed a transfusion, so why wait? Maybe a drawing of his hero will make him feel better. Besides, doing basketball portraits is the closest I'll ever get to my father's dreams for me, so I might as well let him enjoy one now.

I hope Mom's right, though. I hope he does come around. I'm just not holding my breath.

---

5. African American basketball star (b. 1963), with the Chicago Bulls for most of his career.

SELF-PORTRAIT: A POEM FOR MY FATHER

By Diondra Jordan

I've told you this before
but I guess it bears repeating.
Love is not me being
who you want.
Your definition
is a whirlpool
trying to suck me in
and I'm drowning.
Don't you see?
Don't you hear?
I'm gurgling,
battling for air,
wishing you cared about
what matters to me.
But you can't,
or won't.
Either way, I dip into
my imagination,
grab a rail
and pull myself free.
It's time, Dad.
Time you stop telling me
who to be,
how to live.
This is my portrait.
You chose your canvas.
Let me choose mine.

TYRONE

I didn't get her first few poems, but I dig this one.

The future is ours. Let us have it. That's what she's saying. That's what we're all saying. But I'm lucky. These days my moms ain't trying to push me in one direction or another. She's just glad I have one.

I read her this poem I wrote called "Dream" about doing hip-hop with my own band, and she started crying. My moms don't cry easy, so I felt bad. But she said they were happy tears. "You keep writing, baby," she said. "You're doing good."

I love my moms.

PORSCHA JOHNSON

I slam my lunch tray down on the table across from Leslie and Chankara. Diondra looks up, startled, from the next table, then turns back to her lasagna.

"The minute I turn twenty-one, I'm changing my name," I say to no one in particular. "I mean it."

"Why wait?" says Chankara. We've had this conversation before. "Why not change it now?"

I shake my head. "Too complicated."

"Fine, then. Count to ten, and try this." She slices off a square of pizza from her plate and shoves it in my mouth.

Chankara's a problem solver. She has no patience for talking a thing to death. Do something about it or shut up is her motto. I guess she's right. But one of these days, the name Porscha will have to go. I'm tired of providing oversized boys with the raw material for adolescent jokes about my being a high-maintenance mama, or some sort of luxury item. Then there are those oily, leering, dirty old men on my block who drool or wink at me when I pass by on my way home, asking if they can take me for a test drive. Please. But for now, I'm stuck with Porscha. I can live with it a while longer, though.

It's amazing how easy it is to get a bad reputation. My whole life, I ran around letting people pick on me, laughing it off when they teased me, fast-talking my way out of fights. They'd call me four eyes, or stuck-up, or Miss Bug-eyed Bookworm, and I'd pretend their words were water and let them roll off of my back. Now, I'm nobody's duck, and their words stung a whole lot more than water, but I held my temper. It took a bully nine straight months of riding me to cause my thermometer to boil. And once I lost it, did anybody blame it on the bully? No. They start calling me crazy, whispering it behind my back. It was as if that other Porscha, the easygoing, even-tempered one, never existed. Truth is, she always did, always will.

Diondra and Chankara know that. And now, so does Leslie. If only the other kids knew the truth. I could never beat anybody the way I beat Charmayne last year. I'd be afraid to. What if I couldn't stop? What if there was no one around to pull me off? I could kill somebody. I know it's in me. I've got Mama's blood running in my veins, haven't I? She came close enough to killing me, more than once.

When I was twelve, she went on one of her tears and punched me from one side of the room to the other because I didn't wash the dishes. I don't think that was the real reason, though. She was probably just stressed out from working overtime, from dealing with a hard-to-please new boss, or from juggling bills, and I caught the hard end of it. But who cares about the real reasons? The thing is, the same kind of ugly anger lives in me. I couldn't really see that until Charmayne brought it out. I have to make sure that monster never shows her face again, no matter what.

So I find ways to keep her in check. When anger rips a hole in me now, I punch a wall, or run 'til the wind cuts my breath off. Once, I sat on a curb running a piece of broken bottle across my fingertips. Lucky for me the shard had a dull edge that left a jigsaw of scratches on me, but not a whole lot of blood. I know it was a stupid thing to do, but anything's better than allowing those fingers to hurt somebody else. I couldn't live with that. Not again. Not ever.

No, these kids have nothing to fear from me. They just don't know it.

Leslie says I've got to learn to let people in, and I know she's right. Poetry just may be a way to do that. I mean, it worked for Devon, didn't it? And Tyrone. We all got to see another side of them. Even Janelle gets up there—Miss Shyness herself! I've never seen her turn so bold, although the boldness only seems to last as long as she's up front reading her poems. Still, that's something. Tyrone was the biggest surprise, though. Who would have guessed he wrote poetry? And he knows his poems by heart, no less. Every Friday there he is, the first one to raise his hand when Mr. Ward asks who's got something they want to read. And he's always the first one up, if Mr. Ward gives him the chance. No goofing around like he usually does either. He's all business. He takes center stage, clears his throat, and smoothly launches into his rhyme.

The first time he got up there, I rolled my eyes like half the sisters in class, certain he was going to spout something lame or nasty about girls and sex, or gangsters. I mean, that's all we ever heard him talk about, right? But there was nothing lame about this poem, and none of it was about sex. It was about what's going on in the world, and about trying to make sense of it. It was a poem by somebody who really thinks about things, and that somebody turned out to be Tyrone. He made me change my mind about him that day. Maybe I can change people's minds about me too. It's worth a shot. I better do it quick, though. There are only a few Open Mike Fridays left before school's out, and the last one will be at assembly, and I don't plan on getting up in front of a whole group of strangers my first time out.

Friday is two days away, and I know exactly what poem I'm going to read.

Open Mike

A LETTER TO MY MOTHER

By Porscha Johnson

Dear Mom,
You with the hypodermic needle in your arm,
I never said good-bye, or joined your funeral procession
because I was too angry at the time.

Leaving me seemed to be your choice.
Why make it? Was it something that I did or said?
Weeks after you were dead, those questions
hammered me until I thought my heart would shatter.

But then, as my friend told me, the why of your absence
doesn't really matter. Besides, I'm older now
and understand a little about pain, and the crazy things
it drives us to. So, even though this may be overdue
(remember: Some things are better late than never)—
Mom, I finally forgive you.

Love,
Porscha.

P.S.
Good-bye.

TYRONE

Now I know school's almost over. We came to our English class yesterday and found our poems and drawings gone from the wall. Porscha was about to freak, along with everybody else, 'til Mr. Ward surprised us with a class anthology. He'd gone to some quick-copy place and made up books for each of us with copies of our work. It was pretty cool the way he hooked it up. I can't wait to show my moms.

It was kinda sad seeing the walls all bare. But hey, today was our last Open Mike Friday, so it was time for our stuff to come down. Besides, we were only in there long enough to take attendance. Then we headed for the auditorium to have Open Mike there as part of assembly, just like Mr. Ward planned.

The hall was crowded by the time I got there. I looked around for that reporter, but I don't think he made it. Yeah, well, I thought. His loss.

I slipped into a seat in the front row just as the principal called everybody to attention. Sitting up front ain't my thing, but this assembly was different. Our whole class was there so we could reach the stage quicker to read our work. I was down with that.

The principal made a couple of announcements, but don't ask me about what. Nobody was interested. We all sat up, though, when he called Teach to the stage.

Mr. Ward explained what Open Mike Friday was about and how we got started. (Wesley yelling, "Y'all got me to thank! Remember that!") I was only half listening 'cause I was waiting 'til Teach got to the good stuff, meaning when we finally got to read.

"Before we get started," he said, "I thought it would be good if one or two of the students who have participated in Open Mike this year would say a few words about what it has meant to them." I checked down the row real quick.

"I'll pass," said Leslie.

Amy and Sheila had "Don't look at me" stamped all over their faces. Raul didn't look much better.

Sterling rose outta his seat, but then sat back down. Cracked me up. Everybody was suddenly shy. Not me. I stood, headed for the podium.

I cleared my throat, rolled my shoulders a few times to get relaxed.

"Today, Tyrone," said Mr. Ward.

"Yeah, my brotha," chimed in Porscha.

"I'm getting there," I said, taking a second to adjust the microphone. "Hello? Can you hear me?"

"Yeah, fool, but you ain't saying nothing," said Chankara.

"Aiight. Just give me a minute." Everybody laughed.

"Okay. I just wanted to say I'm really glad I got to do this poetry thing because I feel like, even though the people in our class are all different colors and some of you speak a different language and everything, I feel like we connected. I feel like I know you now. You know what I'm saying? I feel like we're not as different as I thought."

I looked out at Raul, Janelle, Gloria, Devon, my homey Wesley—my whole crew— and felt something deep inside my chest, something that made me swallow hard.

"You guys are okay," I said. "Even you, Steve, with your skinny, bleach-blond self." Steve grinned. Raynard patted him on the back and everybody else tee-heed for a hot second. Then I went back to my seat.

When I sat down, our whole crew was clapping. Tanisha and Judianne whistled. Nobody said it, but it was like I had spoken for all of us. You know what I'm saying? And that don't happen every day.

I'm glad I didn't choke up there, 'cause now the whole school's talking about that assembly. Probably be talking about it all summer, we was so hot. We sizzled! Chankara read, Raul did his Zorro thing, my man Wesley and me did a new cipher with a little sax from Raynard, and I even got Porscha to read her piece again. I never did come up with any African drum music for Tanisha, but the sista did fine all by herself.

Except for Wesley and me, we all pretty much did our old poems. The kids in our class were the only ones who'd already heard them. Besides, most of the kids want to wait 'til next year to break out the new stuff, 'cause Mr. Ward already told us he plans to have Open Mike in all his classes then. Cool, huh?

After assembly, Mr. Ward came up and clapped me on the back. "I like what you had to say, Tyrone. And I loved your cipher," he told me. "Any chance I'll see you next year?"

"I don't know, Mr. Ward," I said. "I've been thinking about hooking up with some guys who want to start a band. I might have to skip school and go on tour, you know what I'm saying? So I can't make no promises." I'm blowing smoke about this tour and Teach knows it, but that's the game.

"I understand. But I did want to let you know, we'll be hosting a poetry slam here next year," said Mr. Ward.

And guess what. All of a sudden, the man's got my attention.

EPILOGUE

My mother says I'm lucky. She thinks I should be thrilled to go to an American school every day. I pretend I'm happy, for her sake. She doesn't understand what it's like for me. Nobody does.

My name is Mai Tren. I'm half Black, half Vietnamese. You try being me for a week, see how well you fit into this world. "Go back where you came from," kids say to me sometimes. And I think, Go where exactly? We left the village my mother grew up in many years ago, right after my father died. He was American, so my mother was able to bring our family to the United States. I have as much right to be here as anyone. But no one hears me. No one cares about that. They can't see past my slanted eyes. Not even the Black kids. Never mind that we're all people of color, that most of us live in single-parent homes, that we catch the same amount of grief from the white world. It's ridiculous.

I'll be all right, though. I'll finish high school, go to college, get my law degree, and be out of here. I just can't count on having too many friends along the way.

Black people keep reminding me that I'm not one of them. Asians shun me because my blood is not "pure." And whites are still making up their minds, although some want me to be their friend so I can help them with their math! Which is a joke, because I don't like math. So where does that leave me? I look around this class, with Black kids, Latinos, Jews, and Italians, and I wonder how I'm ever supposed to connect with any of them.

But then we had an assembly yesterday with all these kids reading poetry. They seemed to get along with each other, almost like a family. They said it was the poems that brought them together. It can't be that simple, can it?

Their teacher is supposed to be doing poetry again next year. Maybe I'll get his class. Who knows? I can think of worse things.

1002

Domestic Fiction

Essential Elements of Domestic Fiction

Domestic fictions are "inside" stories. Unlike narratives of adventure, fantasy, and school life, in which the child character's maturation often occurs outside the home and away from the familiar, in domestic fiction the home and family remain central to the narrative. The home provides the setting of the story; its drama and conflicts take place between family members within the household, as well as within the self. Thus, for example, in Louisa May Alcott's *Little Women* (1868–69), a story about flawed and self-centered girls learning to be cheerful, fulfilled, hardworking women, the essential action occurs within the parlor and within each girl as her characteristic flaws are named and then negotiated and conquered through the course of the novel.

Little Women is a touchstone text, encompassing all of the most significant aspects of domestic fiction: a focus on family relationships, the primacy of home, and lessons taught through both instruction and experience. In the novel's first chapter, a letter to his wife from Mr. March, away from home doing his Civil War duty as a chaplain for the Union soldiers, sets the terms for the work that his daughters must accomplish before their girlhood ends. The girls nestle into a close group around Marmee as she reads: "A year seems very long to wait before I see them, but remind them that while we wait we may all work, so that these hard days need not be wasted. I know they will remember all I said to them, that they will be loving children to you, will do their duty faithfully, fight their bosom enemies bravely, and conquer themselves so beautifully that when I come back to them I may be fonder and prouder than ever of my little women." The girls absorb this message and, with the help of their mother, learn to school their ambitions and desires so as to honor home values—close affective relationships and duty to others—above all else.

Alcott's popular children's books set a new standard for domestic fiction and inspired other nineteenth- and early-twentieth-century writers for girls, including Ethel Turner in Australia and Lucy Maud Montgomery in Canada. Alcott felt that the nuclear family provided the bountiful nourishment that fed the character and enabled affective bonds to form. The rewards of extrafamilial life offered by experiences in work, society, and politics were no more than tasteless substitutes. This core belief is reflected in Alcott's conduct toward her own family members—she remained close to them throughout her life and saw meeting their physical and emotional needs as her principal duty—as well as in the plots and settings of her novels. When, at the end of the second part of *Little Women*, a middle-aged, domestic Jo March Bhaer proclaims, "I do think that families are the most beautiful things in all the world!," she gives voice to a sentiment demonstrated repeatedly throughout the novel: maternal love creates home and provides shelter from the insults and harshness of the world outside.

Domestic fiction so dominates children's literature from the eighteenth century onward that it cannot be easily separated from children's literature generally. Almost every genre of children's literature—realistic fiction, fantasy, poetry, animal stories, life writing, adventure, and so forth—concerns a child or an anthropomorphized animal within a family setting. If no family exists, as in the popular "orphan child" narratives of the nineteenth century, a surrogate is sought and generally found. "Where does the child belong?" is an important question that much of children's literature attempts to answer through narrative. One response can be found in an essential premise of realistic domestic fiction: the best place for a child to grow up is within a loving family.

Yet the family is an amorphous and protean institution that has changed dramatically over time. Michael Cart, in the introduction to his edited collection *Necessary Noise: Stories about Our Families As They Really Are* (2003), cites a number of statistics in sketching what *family* means to contemporary American teenagers:

> Americans are now less likely to marry than at any time in our nation's history. A total of 32 percent of adult Americans are unmarried and childless. Twelve percent are unmarried but have children. The remaining 56 percent—those who do marry—are divorcing in near record numbers (almost 50 percent of marriages now end in divorce, compared to 30 percent as recently as 1970). As a result, more than half of America's young people now grow up in single-parent households; 24 percent of children live in mother-only households, while 2 percent live with their fathers; . . . others are being raised by older siblings or by grandparents (or by a single grandparent). Still others turn to peers or to gangs to provide a surrogate experience of family love and support. No wonder that the once-upon-a-time nuclear family is now routinely described as "fractured," "blended," "at risk," and "in transition."

Such changes within the contemporary family are by no means confined to the United States; patterns in other Western industrialized countries are similar. Yet despite this historical alteration in the nature of the family, the core belief that the child is best raised in a family setting has not wavered in practice or in fiction. Though the specific actions it entails vary significantly, this belief has never been seriously challenged for the more than two hundred years since the first domestic fiction was published in the late eighteenth century. The early examples of the genre in the eighteenth and early nineteenth centuries were overtly didactic—teaching moral lessons at every turn of the plot. But in every age, domestic fiction is especially concerned with communicating life lessons that the child character learns from, or with the assistance of, family members—lessons that will help him or her become a happy and well-adjusted person, however those terms are understood. In the late eighteenth century through the mid-twentieth century in particular, these lessons might delimit or explore good conduct in terms of personal responsibility, social consciousness, gender roles, or religious feeling; in every instance, the purpose behind *didactic* domestic fiction is to demonstrate the proper methods of raising the child to be a moral, social, kind, and responsible adult who will fit into a certain class and gender mold.

While the need for such lessons does not change over time, the lessons themselves do, often shifting their focus from locating and eradicating faults within the self to learning how to negotiate and overcome the fears associated with growing up. In Beverly Cleary's *Ramona and Her Father* (1977), for example, a minor incident—the cat Picky-picky, rejecting the cheaper food newly forced on him by the family's straitened circumstances, eats and ruins a newly carved jack-o-lantern—becomes an opportunity to raise more serious concerns about family finances and, most significantly, about the effects of smoking cigarettes. As a troubled Ramona settles back into bed after the quarrel ends, she wonders, "Didn't grown-ups think children worried about anything but jack-o'-lanterns? Didn't they know children worried about grown-ups?" In contemporary domestic fiction about realistic families, the adult-mandated strict codes of behavior and punishments for error tend to be replaced by the child's greater participation in his or her own maturation.

Home, and what transpires within it, is at the center of domestic fiction. The orphan tale was especially resonant in the nineteenth century, but the story of the lonely child searching for a home and a family to go with it—or accepting the home and family on offer—still appeals to children today. Charles Dickens's novels about child characters, though published for a family audience rather than for young readers alone, define the genre. These novels are filled with memorable characters who, together with orphaned youth, form unusual family groups: examples include the formidable Betsey Trotwood, the confused Mr. Dick, and the orphan David Copperfield (*David Copperfield*, 1849–50); the gentle blacksmith Joe, the apoplectic Mrs. Joe Gargery, and the orphan Pip (*Great Expectations*, 1861); Little Nell Trent and her grandfather (*The Old Curiosity Shop*, 1841); and, of course, the oft-maligned and long-suffering orphan Oliver Twist (*Oliver Twist*, 1838), whose "family" radically shifts from the highly inappropriate (a gang of thieves) to, finally, the perfectly suitable (Oliver's previously unknown relatives).

In Christopher Paul Curtis's *Bud, Not Buddy* (1999), a powerful contemporary orphan tale set in Michigan in the 1930s, ten-year-old Bud runs away from an orphanage in search of his father, convinced that the flier announcing the appearance in Flint of the jazz trio "Herman E. Calloway and the Dusky Devastators of the Depression" holds the key to his father's identity. Although at the end of his quest a grateful Bud finds both a grandfather and a family in the form of his grandfather's jazz band, just as important is his realization that his mother resides not within the mementos he has carried with him in a battered suitcase but within his memory of her loving presence: "I was carrying Momma inside me and there wasn't anyone or anything that could take away from that or add to it either." Unlike in Dickens's versions, in contemporary orphan tales emotional epiphanies rather than some exterior social benefit bestowed by a "legitimate" family assuage the child's feelings of abandonment and betrayal.

Learning Lessons within the Home: Religion and Moral Authority

Early domestic fiction focuses on teaching the child to avoid being "childish"; more recent works celebrate childishness as natural, at the same time demonstrating from the child's perspective—often using humor—how the pains and joys of childhood can be overcome or appreciated. This difference in the treatment of child characters within the family and in the lessons they learn arises directly from fundamentally different attitudes toward children, viewed at one extreme as fallen and imbued with original sin and at the other as innocent and pure. Didactic domestic fiction communicates its lessons through disciplining the child; the discipline can be exerted by external forces (God, parents, neighbors, the law, clergy, and death) or can be self-inflicted (as illness or as feelings of guilt, shame, and fear).

In the Evangelical writer Mary Martha Sherwood's *The History of the Fairchild Family* (1818), the family members—father, mother, and their three young children, Lucy, Emily, and Henry—live together with their two servants far from the wicked city. Their idyllic life is nonetheless punctuated by the physical and emotional conflicts that arise within and among the children or their neighbors. In this family story, every thought and action is directly related to human sinfulness and depravity, heavenly reward or punishment. The father's sermons and moralizing, which all take place within the home, help underscore that the domestic setting is ideal for learning lessons. The function of the nuclear family in early examples of domestic fiction, as this heavily didactic work demonstrates, is to mirror the paternal relationship between God and humanity: the deity (or father) possesses ultimate control over his creation (or children), and a religious answer can be provided for any earthly exigency. The Fairchild children are essentially very good children, but sometimes, as is natural, they behave badly. They feel envious of others' good fortune, sneak treats from the pantry, and argue and physically fight. Emily refuses to let Henry play with her beloved doll a second time, for example, after he hangs the toy by the neck with a piece of string and calls it a thief.

Childhood disobedience is a particular focus of the text; Mr. Fairchild reminds Henry that fathers stand in the place of God to their children and must be obeyed. And as the novel demonstrates, the consequences for failing to obey parental dicta such as "you will learn Latin" or "you will not play with matches" are dire: the first leads to a flogging with a small horsewhip, the silent treatment, and a bread-and-water diet; the second, to death. As the Fairchild children learn from experience, from personal histories related by their parents or neighbors, and from the negative or positive example of others, their inherent wickedness can never be overcome. The "happy" death of young Charles Trueman and Augusta Noble's death by fire impress them mightily, highlighting important distinctions between the two families and the fate of each child. The poor and close-knit Trueman family is suffused with the domestic virtues of hard work, modesty, piety, and affection, and their child dies with his soul guaranteed to God; the wealthy Nobles leave their child in the care of a servant while they pursue worldly pleasures, and their child dies an unrepentant sinner. The Fairchild children are taught that through obedience, charity, mindfulness, faith in Jesus Christ, and constant prayer, they can hope to be happy in this world and the next.

Less rigorously and religiously didactic stories from the nineteenth century also maintain a focus on disciplining the child. While a delirious Beth March lies dangerously ill from scarlet fever in Alcott's *Little Women*, her older sister Jo paces and frets. Jo closely identifies with Beth and confides to Laurie that her loss will be greater than anyone else's in the family if Beth dies: "Beth is my conscience, and I *can't* give her up; I can't! I can't!" Jo's conscience is externalized in the figure of her quiet sister whose meekness and self-sacrifices make her a moral exemplar to everyone around her. Although Beth recovers, her health is forever compromised; by the time she dies, some years later, Jo has internalized Beth's lessons through suffering and thus can let her go.

Female Authority and Domestic Pedagogy

Although the importance of the father's role in maintaining discipline within the home is never questioned, the center of the domestic world was acknowledged as female, especially in domestic fictions that were less overtly religious. Rationalist educators such as Maria Edgeworth set their stories for children within the home and family, just as Sherwood and the Evangelicals would do a bit later, yet these works stress maternal rather than paternal elements in the family. In other examples of domestic fiction—in particular those that rely on a maternal preceptor, such as Mary Wollstonecraft's *Original Stories from Real Life; With Conversations, Calculated to Regulate the Affections, and Form the Mind to Truth and Goodness* (1788; illustrated, 1791)—the family group functions as a microcosm of both the social and the spiritual world. Wollstonecraft joined other women writers, including Madame de Genlis, Lady Eleanor Fenn, Sarah Trimmer, Dorothy Kilner, and Hannah More, in penning stories about girls that foreground female experiences and such conventional strengths as nurturing, empathy, and caretaking. Mrs. Mason, the mother/governess stand-in of Wollstonecraft's *Original Stories*, modeled on such figures as the Baroness d'Almane and the Marquise de Clémire in Madame de Genlis's *Adelaide and Theodore* (3 vols., 1782) and *Tales of the Castle* (3 vols., 1784), does more than educate and guide her pupils Mary and Caroline as a maternal educator; she also, through her honesty, acts of charity, and resignation, serves as an upright and righteous example that the community as a whole would do well to emulate.

Indeed, the community-as-family is an ideal promoted in much domestic fiction for children. In late-eighteenth- and early-nineteenth-century family stories such as Edgeworth's "Lazy Lawrence" (1796), Sherwood's *Fairchild Family*, and Thomas Day's *The History of Sandford and Merton* (3 vols., 1783–89), the poor or lower-class families are often well-scrubbed, orderly, sober, pious, and competent, earning social respect in part because they are content in their place and grateful to their "betters." Thus, the happy village functions as a family in which the squire, his benevolent lady, and the villagers are assigned the roles, respectively, of *pater-* and *materfamilias* and of dependent children.

Although parents and parent figures are often the mouthpieces of moral lessons in the earliest examples of didactic domestic fiction, sometimes it is the child or childlike figure—such as Beth March, or any of the pious children who populate Mary Louisa Charlesworth's best-selling *Ministering Children: A Tale Dedicated to Childhood* (1854), or Frances Hodgson Burnett's Editha in "Editha's Burglar" (1880)—whose wisdom, selflessness, and sensitive behavior reveal the weaknesses of those who surround him or her—especially the adults. Sentimental tales that showcase the power of the saintly or perfectly innocent child to convert faulty adults, or to compensate for their corrupt worldliness, had a particular vogue at the beginning of the twentieth century, though their roots are in much earlier literature. L. M. Montgomery, best-known for her series of domestic novels about Anne Shirley, the unconventional and lively Prince Edward Island orphan first introduced in *Anne of Green Gables* (1908), carries on this tradition in her short story "Each in His Own Tongue" (1912), in which a severe minister misguidedly attempts to prevent his grandson from performing music. Presiding over a deathbed at which he can offer no consolation, in the face of a faith and generosity vastly superior to his own, the minister bows to his feminized grandson's greater abilities to provide comfort to the suffering. The secular yet pure souls of Anne Shirley and Pollyanna Whittier (the title character of Eleanor H. Porter's novel *Pollyanna*, 1913) similarly enliven and instruct everyone around them.

The series of stories, poems, and dialogues meant for "the instruction and amusement of young persons," *Evenings at Home* (16 vols., 1792–96), written by John Aikin with the assistance of his sister, Anna Laetitia Barbauld, set a standard for domestic moral tales. These popular stories about domestic life and scientific inquiry conducted within a home setting were intended to be read aloud to a multigenerational audience. Barbauld became well-known for her early readers for children (a genre she helped create) called *Lessons for Children* (4 vols., 1778–79), as well as for *Hymns in Prose for Children* (1781), a work also suited for the youngest children, who, it was presumed, would learn to read at their mother's knee. Mary Louisa Molesworth, one of the most prolific British Victorian children's book writers of domestic fiction and fantasy, remembered *Evenings at Home* as a favorite book from her own childhood. By expanding its audience to include the entire family circle and demonstrating that learning and inquiry emerged from within the home rather than in spite of or outside it, Aikin's and Barbauld's work functions as an aid to domestic pedagogy. This child-centered theory, advocated by some of the most influential educational theorists of the late eighteenth century—such as Richard Lovell Edgeworth and his daughter Maria—influenced domestic fiction well into the nineteenth century and even beyond.

In searching for suitable reading for their growing family, the Anglo-Irish Edgeworth and his second wife found little that satisfied them beyond Mrs. Barbauld's work. It would be up to Edgeworth's eldest daughter, Maria, to extend Barbauld's writing with lively moral tales about family life. Maria Edgeworth was something of a professional sister. The eldest daughter of twenty-one children, and responsible for the education of many of her younger siblings, she knew well the contours of busy family life. Possessing a natural affinity for children and following the example of the first of her three stepmothers, Honora Sneyd Edgeworth, who put the children's education at the center of her life, Edgeworth directly observed her siblings and transformed the stories she told, conversations she overheard, and learning processes she witnessed into fiction and educational philosophy. In works such as *Practical Education* (2 vols., 1798), co-written with her father, Edgeworth successfully rethought "education from the child's level up . . . rather than from the theoretician's precepts down" (Mitzi Myers, " 'Anecdotes from the Nursery' in Maria Edgeworth's *Practical Education*," 1999). Influenced by Jean-Jacques Rousseau's *Émile, or, On Education* (1762), an educational treatise in the form of a novel that depicted the natural child learning through experience far from the corrupting influence of society, Edgeworth refined the domestic pedagogy offered by Aikin, Barbauld, and de Genlis. Edgeworth's tales, such as those that feature the lively and likable child Rosamond, demonstrate how parents and others can use rational principles to instruct children in moral behavior. In her tale "The Birthday Present" (1796), Rosamond's mother and father rely on careful dialogue to lead their young daughter to understand usefulness and thrift; at the same time, the actions of her older sister demonstrate the true meaning of generosity.

Gender and Domestic Fiction in the Nineteenth Century

Mid- and late-nineteenth-century domestic fiction emphasizes the importance of home and family to the child by featuring first scenes of naughty or erring children running away from home and then their inevitable return. Especially in America and Australia, rambunctious protagonists became the norm in domestic fiction, learning "lessons" that were not obviously didactic or cautionary in intention; yet many conventional gender expectations remain. Normative boyhood required that young male characters spend less time in the home or engaged in introspection than nineteenth-century female characters such as the March sisters. The ideals of domesticity trump gender, however. Even "bad boy" novels, such as Mark Twain's *The Adventures of*

Tom Sawyer (1876) about the scamp Tom and his escapades on the Mississippi frontier or Thomas Bailey Aldrich's *The Story of a Bad Boy* (1869), offer some of the same messages about honoring family ties and affective relationships while at the same time self-consciously and humorously poking fun at sober-minded moral tales for children.

The narrator of *The Story of a Bad Boy*, for example, first clearly sets his boyhood self apart from the heroes of typical children's fare: "I call my story the story of a bad boy, partly to distinguish myself from those faultless young gentlemen who generally figure in narratives of this kind, and partly because I really was not a cherub. . . . I didn't want to be an angel and with the angels stand. . . . In short, I was a real human boy, such as you may meet anywhere in New England, and no more like the impossible boy in a storybook than a sound orange is like one that has been sucked dry." Ethel Turner's *Seven Little Australians* (1894) similarly begins, "If you imagine you are going to read of model children, with perhaps a naughtily-inclined one to point a moral, you had better lay down the book immediately and betake yourself to *Sandford and Merton*, or similar standard juvenile works. Not one of the seven is really good, for the very excellent reason that Australian children never are." Tom Bailey and Tom Sawyer both run away from home—to be met, on their return by scenes of death (the tragic death of Tom Bailey's beloved father, whom Tom had not seen in two years, and the comic funeral of Tom Sawyer himself); in *Seven Little Australians*, by contrast, the tomboy Judy runs away *from* school *to* home and must be hidden from her tyrannical father, who would send her back. The illness she suffers, brought on by exhaustion after she walks hundreds of miles, prefigures her death later in the novel.

From the late nineteenth century until today, domestic fiction has become the special province, both in its emphasis on female characters and in its readership, of girls. In the Victorian domestic novel for girls, the happiness and comforts of life are circumscribed by the domestic and everyday. Other possible goods—ambition, wealth, fame—are not worth pursuing, as their delights are revealed to be transient or illusory. The parameters of morally salubrious girls' fiction emerge from and are underscored by domestic fiction itself. Turner's opening disclaimer in *Seven Little Australians* notwithstanding, her refreshingly unsentimental novel (the father is a bully, the stepmother is just out of childhood herself, and Judy's tragic death serves no religious or moral purpose) also conforms to conventional expectations of "good" gendered behavior. When Meg, the eldest of the seven children, disdains the "wholesome fare" that to that point had constituted her literary education—the works of the British writer Charlotte Yonge and the Americans Alcott and Elizabeth Wetherell (the pseudonym of Susan Warner, author of the sentimental, best-selling *The Wide, Wide World*, 1850)—in favor of the romance stories supplied by her new "fast" companion, the reader realizes that Meg's reputation as a virtuous and sexually innocent girl is in some danger. Yonge's morally upright novels are similarly admired in Alcott's March family chronicles; as Gillian Avery observes in *Childhood's Pattern*, Yonge's girls, with their "ardent dutifulness, their self-sacrificing devotion to parents, and the happiness they feel in the companionship of their brothers and sisters," helped formulate an inspiring ideal of middle-class girlhood that held sway throughout the nineteenth century.

In her 1869 review "Children's Literature of the Last Century," published in *Macmillan's Magazine*, Yonge disparaged the "Rational Dame," well known from tales by Edgeworth and Wollstonecraft, as "intolerably dull and dreary" to "modern eyes." Yet her family stories, celebrating homelike feminine arts such as cooking, child care, and housework and those character strengths (selflessness, self-reliance, piety) that lead to hard work on behalf of others, owe much to these selfsame "mentorias"—to use the term from Ann Murry's popular conduct book for girls, *Mentoria: or, the Young Ladies Instructor in Familiar Conversations on Moral and Entertaining Subjects* (1778). Yonge published scores of domestic novels, histories, and biographies for children, as well as editing *The Monthly Packet of Evening Readings for Members of the Church of England* (1851–90), a popular and long-running periodical for girls. Her most famous novel, *The Daisy Chain* (1856), the saga of a family of eleven children, prominently features the struggles of Ethel May, a headstrong and intelligent girl who is caught between the pleasures of scholarship and the duties of helping to care for numerous younger siblings, an invalid older sister, and a distracted father in the wake of her mother's death. Ethel's desires finally find a productive outlet in tireless work organizing every aspect of building a church for the poor.

Although Ethel never becomes fully domesticated, in "Patchwork Fever" (1883), Yonge's short story of village life aimed at female readers younger and perhaps in a lower class than those of *The Daisy Chain*, properly executed domestic work not only maintains the individual household but also protects the moral characters of its members and even undergirds an orderly society. The house and three younger children are left to the care of thirteen-year-old Frances Gage while her mother is away. Frances's failure to make their home pleasant and happy is blamed for driving the oldest boy, Gilbert, out of the house and into antisocial antics that anger the Squire and threaten to compromise Mr. Gage's position with him. The Squire expects his "family" (the households in "his" town) to be well-run, neat, orderly, polite, and deferential. Gilbert fears the physical punishment that his father might inflict, although the promised horsewhipping in fact consists of only a few light strokes. Frances's punishment, by contrast, will leave lasting emotional scars. Her profound feelings of guilt over neglecting her family—she has concentrated instead on creating a beautiful patchwork piece for her mother, thereby endangering her sister's physical health and her brother's moral health—lead her to renounce creative endeavors and embrace wholesome housework.

Such renunciations exact a high cost from girls in autonomy and independence. In Alcott's life as in the fiction she wrote idealizing her girlhood and family, choosing the domestic meant sublimating other desires. Alcott's ambitious novels and complexly plotted sensation tales for adults found only moderate success, and Jo March, Alcott's alter ego, puts aside her soaring aspirations for literary fame once she marries and becomes a kind of housemother/schoolmarm/wife to Professor Bhaer and the boys enrolled at Plumfield Academy. In "Psyche's Art" (1868), an early story published in the same month that Alcott was asked by a publisher to try her hand at a girls' novel, Psyche puts aside her artistic ambitions in order to care for a dying sister; when she takes up sculpture again, it is out of grief. As Elizabeth Lennox Keyser notes in "'The Most Beautiful Things in All the World'? Families in *Little Women*" (1992),"The lesson of these female artists, then, appears to be the lesson that Alcott supposedly learned: to subordinate their needs for artistic expression to the needs of their families and to use their artistic talents for the benefit not only of their own families but of the family as an institution."

The acknowledgment of the essential functions performed by girls within the family and potentially within a wider community is a theme that unites the work, spanning nearly a hundred years, of Edgeworth, Yonge, and Alcott. Their texts argue that girls should never be merely ornamental in their persons or in their actions, or seek to gain attention for their charity or generosity or cleverness. In these moral family tales, time spent making the fragile basket, the beautiful patchwork, or the work of art is stolen from domestic duties. The cost of this inattention proves too high for these girl characters as they learn through experience to embrace various domestic virtues and to be happier for limiting their ambitions to the home.

Happy Families in Series Fiction

To their readers' and publishers' delight, many of the most successful nineteenth- and early-twentieth-century authors of domestic fiction continued the stories of their beloved protagonists or families in book after book. American authors of series include Louisa May Alcott, with four works centered on the March girls (1868–86); Harriet M. Lothrop (writing as Margaret Sidney), who chronicled the exploits of the fatherless Pepper family in twelve books (1881–1916); Martha Finley (writing as Martha Farquharson), who traced the life of Elsie Dinsmore from girl to grandmother in twenty-eight books (1867–1905); and Sarah Chauncey Woolsey (writing as Susan Coolidge), with the five-book What Katy Did series (1873–90). Probably the longest-running series in children's literature, which includes more than a hundred titles published between 1904 and 1992, features the Bobbsey Twins. Created by the master of syndicated fiction, Edward Stratemeyer (who wrote the first volume), these books about two sets of twins, written by a number of authors but always appearing under the name of Laura Lee Hope, have been periodically updated and revised. Everyday events and mild mysteries fill these bland yet comforting volumes about sibling relationships and family life.

Series were equally popular outside the United States. Mary Grant Bruce, an Australian, wrote fifteen Billabong novels about the Linton family, set on a remote sheep station (1910–42); in Canada, L. M. Montgomery wrote two series in addition to her ten volumes about Anne Shirley (1908–39). Similarly, in Britain, the prolific Enid Blyton, who has been called the best-selling children's author of all time, wrote about stereotypical (white) middle-class children in popular series such as the Secret Seven (1949–63) and the Famous Five (1942–63). Though the children generally leave their actual home, their domestic life style travels with them and is replicated wherever they go. Blyton's exciting, fast-paced stories create a kind of domestic fantasy world in which children eat, play, squabble, solve mysteries, and enjoy adventures with little interference from adults.

Indeed, in this limited space it is possible only to touch on the many well-written series so popular and prominent within twentieth-century children's literature. A few of the characters who inhabit the make-believe neighborhoods of these beloved happy families are Eleanor Estes's Moffats, Maud Hart Lovelace's Betsy Ray and her friends Tacy and Tib, Lois Lowry's Anastasia Krupnik, and Paula Danziger's Amber Brown. The spunky, annoying, and creative Ramona of Beverly Cleary's long-running series deserves special mention. She first appeared as a minor character in Cleary's books about a suburban boy, Henry Huggins, but in Beezus and Ramona (1955) Ramona became the star of her own seriocomic series. Ramona's World, probably its final installment, was published in 1999, forty-four years after the first, demonstrating that the constitution of the twentieth-century happy American family has changed little over time.

Conventionally, the domestic story series has showcased white middle- or upper-class families. However, the genre has come to reflect ethnic, racial, and class diversity—though still more change would be welcome here. The Ramona books, for example, offer a steady look at the hurdles that unemployment and underemployment present for a growing family and at the compromises the family must make together in order to get through a difficult time. The All-of-a-Kind Family series of five books (1951–78) by Sydney Taylor concerns a large Jewish immigrant family living on New York City's Lower East Side during the early twentieth century. The five sisters and their baby brother encounter numerous small troubles against a background of Jewish culture, holidays, and traditions. Mildred Taylor's award-winning cycle of books is set during the Depression in a Mississippi community deeply divided by racism, suspicion, and jealousy; it focuses on the Logans, a close-knit African American family that survives every challenge mounted by the unjust world of white privilege.

Families and Society: New Views

Fiction such as Mildred Taylor's books about the Logans emphasize the family's role as a haven from the pressures and injustices of the world. As they share hurts and celebrate victories, however small and hard-won, family members draw together and become better able to handle race- or class-based conflict with a wider community that rejects them. Many children's books focus on the insults of the past and how they affected individual families. For example, Joy Kogawa's *Naomi's Road* (1986) narrates the story of a Japanese Canadian girl and the fracture of her family during World War II, when Japanese Canadians were sent to internment camps and made to work on farms and on construction crews building roads through the Rocky Mountains.

Some novels draw on aspects of history overlooked in mainstream accounts. Pam Muñoz Ryan's *Esperanza Rising* (2000) is set against the backdrop of Mexican "repatriation," which sent 450,000 unwilling Mexicans and Mexican Americans to Mexico in a futile attempt to solve the problem of rampant unemployment in California during the Depression. Esperanza is a spoiled young teen who faces first tragedy in Mexico—her wealthy father's death by bandits—and then multiple hardships in California, where she flees with her mother and joins other Mexicans living hand to mouth as field workers. Esperanza's fall in social status leads ultimately to rising self-satisfaction and the respect of her loving extended family. Other works personalize well-known events. Christopher Paul Curtis combines humor with a serious history lesson in *The Watsons Go to Birmingham—1963* (1995). When the lively, squabbling Watson family of Flint, Michigan, travels to Alabama to spend the summer with Grandma Sands, its members are unwillingly thrust into the middle of one of the most dramatic and tragic events of the civil rights era: the bombing of the Sixteenth Street Baptist Church, which killed four girls and injured twenty others. The family—especially the middle child, Kenny—like the African American community more generally, is traumatized by the deaths and the violence that followed. Yet with the help of his older brother, Kenny rejects the role of victim and attempts to heal the wounds that hatred creates. These novels stress that the nuclear family and the family formed by the wider community united in its struggle for freedom are crucial to the development of individual strength and to growth.

Even in those works of family fiction that include such serious themes as cultural conflict, alienation, and assimilation, humor often remains an important ingredient. In Roch Carrier's autobiographical short story "The Hockey Sweater" (1979), originally published in French, young Roch's dignified French Canadian mother refuses to bow to pressures to conform, whether they come from her son or from the dominant English-speaking culture. Roch's response is another moment of humorous cultural resistance. Cross-cultural conflict is at the center of Lensey Namioka's *Yang the Youngest and His Terrible Ear* (1992). Neither the novel's narrator, Yingtao Yang, nor his best friend, Matthew Connor, fit easily within their respective families; in particular, neither father understands or values his son's passion for baseball or for music, respectively. Yet this conflict and the misunderstandings that inevitably arise as the immigrant Yang family adjusts to American suburban life and the Connor family learns about Chinese culture are resolved through funny scenes described with sensitivity and good humor.

Some family stories focus on the child's desire to blend—in appearance, traditions, and abilities—into the majority around them. Ten-year-old Miguel, in *How Tia Lola Came to (Visit) Stay* (2001) by Julia Alvarez, already in pain because of his parents' decision to divorce and the difficulty of adjusting to a new school, is at first embarrassed by his colorful aunt with an outsize personality. But along with the chilly Vermonters, Miguel soon learns to appreciate his aunt's warmth and his Dominican heritage.

Although the images of the family promoted by Western popular culture are powerful and narrowly defined—a loving domestic (white) mother and a stable providing (white) father, raising two children together in the suburbs—this single version is of course an illusion. Families everywhere have always been more flexible, troubled, and complicated than the fantasies offered up on television and in advertisements. In many examples of domestic literature from the past, as Suzanne Bunkers points out in " 'We are *not* the Cleavers': Images of Nontraditional Families in Children's Literature" (1992), the successful conclusion of the plot relies on the restoration of the "model" family by reconstituting the "heterosexual, marital, nuclear family"; but contemporary children's literature, especially from the 1970s onward, has increasingly reflected the realities of family life in stories about children living with single parents, divorced parents, gay parents, or parents of different races. Indeed, as the demographics cited above make clear, most children today do not grow up within "traditional" families.

The initial impetus behind publishing books about divorce, stepfamilies, or adoption was to help children understand that a broad range of families are "normal." Yet the titles of some of these early books reveal the ideology of "difference" undergirding their earnest stories: for example, Helen F. Daringer's *Adopted Jane* (1947), Beth Goff's *Where Is Daddy? The Story of a Divorce* (1969), and Peggy Mann's *My Dad Lives in a Downtown Hotel* (1973). While more recent books may maintain a bibliotherapeutic function for some young readers, they are less self-conscious; rather than actively defending the legitimacy of the nontraditional family, they tend to set forth a variety of family structures without comment or judgment.

Domestic fiction that features, or includes as a matter of course, homosexual youth or parents is more often intended for young adults than for younger readers or prereaders; yet Lesléa Newman's picture book *Heather Has Two Mommies* (1989, rev. ed. 2000), whose protagonist, conceived by means of artificial insemination, is born to a lesbian couple, remains perhaps the most widely known (or infamous) example of domestic fiction with a gay theme. Other picture books and novels have followed *Heather*'s example. Francesca Lia Block's fairy tale for young adults, *Weetzie Bat* (1989), describes the creation of a large Los Angeles family that eventually includes the punk teen Weetzie; her lover; Dirk and Duck, their gay best friends; Weetzie's baby, Cherokee, whose father is probably Dirk or Duck; and her lover's baby with another woman. As the novel ends, Weetzie surveys her family around the dinner table and thinks, "But love and disease are both like electricity. . . . They are always there—you can't see or smell or hear, touch, or taste them, but you know they are there like a current in the air. We can choose . . . we can choose to plug into the love current instead." She concludes, "I don't know about happily ever after . . . but I know about happily."

Despite continuing attacks on *Heather* and similar books from conservative American groups such as Focus on the Family and the Heritage Foundation, which view them as a threat to what they call traditional American values, there are today no real taboos in domestic fiction for young adults, and few in books for the youngest readers. Family stories now tackle every painful issue imaginable. Whereas in earlier novels parents dispensed measured counsel and acted as admirable role models, in contemporary fiction they are not always heroic or wise or even competent; in fact, the dangerous frailties and all-too-human qualities of the adults in their lives often create the problems that lead the children in the books to suffer and that they only sometimes overcome.

For example, in Jacqueline Woodson's *I Hadn't Meant to Tell You This* (1994), twelve-year-old Marie, a popular girl, befriends Lena, a lonely and bedraggled white girl who moves into Marie's prosperous black neighborhood. Soon inseparable, Marie and Lena share their grief over the mothers they have lost; Marie's mother abandoned her family and Lena's mother died of breast cancer. Lena also shares a secret with Marie: her father has sexually abused her repeatedly since her mother's death. Once her father begins to touch Lena's eight-year-old sister, the girls vanish and Marie is left to wonder and mourn and carry on with her life. Vera B. Williams's hybrid picture book/poetry collection *Amber Was Brave, Essie Was Smart* (2001) sketches in drawings and verse the lives of two children who spend many hours alone while their mother works and their father serves a jail sentence for forgery. Evoking the many scenes from children's literature and film—from Alcott's *Little Women* to Disney's animated feature *Mulan* (1998)—of a daughter's sacrifice of her hair in order to prove her love for her father, Amber cuts off her braids so that her father can have a memento of her:

> Only I had to cut [my braids] off,
> Amber said,
> to send to Daddy
> so he'll be sure to remember me
> I had to

And the melodic yet horrifying opening sentence of Carolyn Coman's *What Jamie Saw* (1995) unblinkingly conveys the reality and banality of child abuse: "When Jamie saw him throw the baby, saw Van throw the little baby, saw Van throw his little sister Nin, when Jamie saw Van throw his baby sister Nin, then they moved." Jamie's mother, Patty, who miraculously catches Nin, flees with her children that night to a friend who lets them stay in his tiny trailer on a logging road. Jamie and Patty remain nervous, angry, and terrified—of Van's reappearance and of their own seeming powerlessness. They realize they must get past their fear if they are to survive, and they do, but their progress is incremental. Jamie accepts a teacher's concern, learns to ice skate, performs magic tricks, and finally, when Van finds the trailer, realizes that "he was able to *see* Van" as he is, not magnified by fears; Jamie stands by Patty as she orders Van to go away forever. Stories about dysfunctional and troubled families in late-twentieth- and twenty-first-century domestic fiction reaffirm the sanctity of home and the stable and loving family as ideals worth striving for, as Louisa May Alcott and others had suggested so long ago.

Unlike stories such as *What Jamie Saw* or Bruce Brooks's "Out" (1992), in which instability, suspicion, and emotional manipulation permeate the relationship between a stepfather and stepson and create tension, happy domestic fiction emphasizes familial unity and the safety and comfort that can be found within the home. In accepting the 2003 Boston Globe–Horn Book Award for *The Jamie and Angus Stories* (2002), her warm story of a young boy, his stuffed animal, and his loving family, Anne Fine—a British author best known for such truthful and emotionally demanding novels as *Step by Wicked Step* (1995) and *The Tulip Touch* (1996)—praised literature for offering children hope and life choices. Fine explained, "Perhaps you drew the short straw with your own family, surroundings, and supports. But maybe, once you can read or find someone to read to you, learning about a family like Jamie's can offer the shaft of light that shows the way out of a dark place. We know from our own experience, and that of others, how very often even the unspoken 'I wish things were like that for me' has been translated, by sheer human grit and determination over years, into 'but I have made things very different for my own children.'" As the literary critic Mitzi Myers thoughtfully argued in "Anecdotes from the Nursery," all serious writers for children, no matter their time or genre, "understand that childhood is about power, balancing the young person's need for autonomy and world-knowledge . . . and the need for home, for a haven to return to: the conflicting yet interrelated juvenile rights to individual agency and communal protection that we still struggle to resolve." Thus, these inside stories that reflect the protean shape of home, family, and self provide both comfort and challenges for young readers. Moreover, they reveal cultural as well as deeply personal anxieties and arguments about the nature of childhood, parenting, and community responsibility for the young.

MARY WOLLSTONECRAFT
1759–1797

A *Vindication of the Rights of Woman* (1792), a defense of education for women rooted in a claim for women's equality and an attack on social institutions that construct them as inferior, passive, and vain, drew immediate fire from conservative writers such as Horace Walpole, who called its author "a hyena in petticoats." The denunciations of Mary Wollstonecraft grew much fiercer after her death, when her husband, William Godwin, published his candid *Memoirs of the Author of 'Vindication of the Rights of Woman'* (1798) and revealed intimate and painful details of her unconventional relationships. Today, with the opprobrium once attached to her name long forgotten, we can appreciate the justice of Godwin's assessment of her groundbreaking feminist manifesto: "when we consider the importance of [*Vindication*'s] doctrines, and the eminence of genius it displays, it seems not very improbable that it will be read as long as the English language endures."

Much of the pain recorded by Godwin resulted from Wollstonecraft's lifelong difficulty in balancing her belief in women's independence with her desire for emotional support, her political and intellectual ideals with her wish for social acceptance. Moreover, she experienced from childhood the injustice of women's traditional position. The second of seven children and the first daughter born, she watched her older brother monopolize her parents' concern. Her father was a violent man who squandered his inherited fortune on a series of farming ventures; following each failure, the family would move. In 1774 they returned to London, where Wollstonecraft formed an intense friendship with Frances (Fanny) Blood, two years her senior, whose good taste, accomplishments, and intellectual curiosity inspired Wollstonecraft. It was to be one of the most important relationships of her life, and would later provide the basis for her only complete novel, *Mary, A Fiction* (1788). Wollstonecraft was with Fanny in Lisbon when she died in 1785, shortly after childbirth.

Wollstonecraft worked at all the (few) jobs thought suitable for a middle-class woman. She spent two years in Bath as a lady's companion, until at age twenty-one she was called home to nurse her dying mother. After her mother's death in 1783, she moved in with the Bloods and did needlework. Next she established a school in the London suburbs, first in Islington and then (with her two sisters and Fanny) in Newington Green, where she met Dr. Richard Price and other Dissenting intellectuals. Finally, after the school failed—her sisters proved unable to run it while she was in Lisbon—from October 1786 to August 1787 Wollstonecraft was a governess for the two daughters of Robert King, Viscount Kingsborough, and Caroline Fitzgerald, Lady Kingsborough, who lived in Ireland.

Before leaving for Ireland, Wollstonecraft had quickly written her first book, the well-received *Thoughts on the Education of Daughters* (1787). It was printed by the radical publisher and bookseller Joseph Johnson, who had a particular interest in the children's and educational market and in the advancement of women. Johnson, who published all Wollstonecraft's works, was crucial to her in two ways. First, when she returned to London, he offered her a position as a reviewer for his new journal, the *Analytic Review*, and solicited translations of French and German works; this patronage, together with the great success of her book for children, *Original Stories from Real Life* (1788), enabled her to live by her pen. Second, he introduced her to a group of writers, painters, and professionals that included the successful and socially well-placed children's author Anna Laetitia Barbauld; John Bonnycastle, a mathematics professor; George Fordyce, a physician; William Godwin, a radical philosopher and novelist; William Blake, the visionary poet and printmaker whom Johnson commissioned to illustrate the second edition (1791) of *Original Stories from Real Life*; and Henry Fuseli, a Swiss painter and writer. Most in the circle supported the French Revolution and its ideals (liberty, equality, and fraternity); and when Edmund Burke condemned not just the events in France but also Wollstonecraft's friend Richard Price in his *Reflections on the Revolution in France* (1790), she responded with *A Vindication of the Rights of Men* (1790), which appeared anonymously. The pamphlet was the first published rebuttal of Burke's attack, and a second edition with Wollstonecraft's name on it was printed within a month. Suddenly, she was a public figure.

Wollstonecraft was decidedly less successful in her personal life. She had fallen in love with Fuseli, and in 1792 she suggested to him and his wife that she should live with them. After they rejected her proposal, she decided to travel to France. In Paris she met Gilbert Imlay, an American former army captain and speculator, and soon fell in love; for her safety, she registered as his wife at the American embassy. In May 1794 their daughter, Frances, was born; later that year, Wollstonecraft published *A Historical and Moral View of the Origins and Progress of the French Revolution*, composed during the Reign of Terror. Imlay returned to London, followed months later by Wollstonecraft and Fanny. She was in despair over their relationship, and he thwarted her attempted suicide. Imlay persuaded her to attend to some business dealings of his in Scandinavia, where she, Fanny, and a French maid traveled in the summer of 1795. One result was Wollstonecraft's very successful *Letters Written During a Short Residence in Sweden, Norway, and Denmark* (1796), derived from her journal and letters written to Imlay during that trip. On her return in October 1795, after finding that Imlay was living with an actress, she tried to kill herself by jumping into the Thames.

Over the next months, as Wollstonecraft resigned herself to Imlay's loss, she once again became part of Johnson's circle, writing for the *Analytic Review* and making new acquaintances, such as the writers Elizabeth Inchbald, Mary Hays, and Mary Robinson. She also became reacquainted with Godwin, who coyly describes in his memoir of Wollstonecraft how their friendship "melted into love." Although both Wollstonecraft and Godwin opposed marriage, scorning relationships based on tradition and property, they married in March 1797 after Wollstone-

craft became pregnant, for they wished to spare their child the burden of illegitimacy. They maintained separate residences, however, thereby (in Godwin's words) allowing "the novelty and lively sensation of a visit, with the more delicious and heart-felt pleasures of domestic life." On August 30, 1797, the thirty-six-year-old Wollstonecraft gave birth to their daughter, Mary (who in 1814 would elope with Percy Bysshe Shelley and in 1818 would publish *Frankenstein*). She died less than two weeks later of puerperal fever. In addition to husband and children, Wollstonecraft left behind an unfinished manuscript of a novel, published posthumously as a fragment: *Maria; or, The Wrongs of Women* (1798).

Wollstonecraft's reformist energies and strong belief that society could be improved through persuasion, passion, and careful thinking have inspired feminists since the late eighteenth century. In her biography *The Life and Death of Mary Wollstonecraft* (1974), Claire Tomalin writes that Wollstonecraft "had embodied the spirit of the age faithfully, its political optimism, its faith in willpower, self-improvement, education. She had hoped that courage and good intentions might triumph over dead convention and that the whole structure of society might be reformed and renewed by philosophers." This belief in a social revolution that might be made possible by the rigorous moral training of girls—training that never questioned their intelligence and their potential for rational thought and charitable action—underlies *Original Stories from Real Life*, a work based in part on Wollstonecraft's time as a governess. Mrs. Mason, who has taken on the education of twelve-year-old Caroline and fourteen-year-old Mary, is stern, morally tendentious, and unlovable, but she has shouldered a great responsibility. In following her moral lead, Wollstonecraft argues, a new generation of intelligent, purposeful, and strong women would rise.

The excerpt of *Original Stories from Real Life* included here comprises the first five chapters of the text; the final chapter, in which Mrs. Mason departs from her young charges; and one of six engravings that William Blake created for the second edition of 1791.

From Original Stories from Real Life

INTRODUCTION

Mary and Caroline, though the children of wealthy parents, were, in their infancy, left entirely to the management of servants, or people equally ignorant. Their mother died suddenly, and their father, who found them very troublesome at home, placed them under the tuition of a woman of tenderness and discernment, a near relation, who was induced to take on herself the important charge through motives of compassion.

They were shamefully ignorant, considering that Mary had been fourteen, and Caroline twelve years in the world. If they had been merely ignorant, the task would not have appeared so arduous; but they had caught every prejudice that the vulgar casually instil. In order to eradicate their prejudices, and substitute good habits instead of those they had carelessly contracted, Mrs. Mason never suffered them to be out of her sight. They were allowed to ask questions on all occasions, a method she would not have adopted, had she educated them from the first, according to the suggestions of her own reason, and to which experience had given its sanction.

They had tolerable capacities. Mary had a turn for ridicule, and Caroline was vain of her person; she was indeed very handsome, and the inconsiderate[1] encomiums, that had, in her presence, been lavished on her beauty, made her, even at that early age, affected.

MORAL CONVERSATIONS AND STORIES. CHAP. I.

The treatment of animals—The ant—The bee—Goodness—The lark's nest—The Asses.

One fine morning in spring, some time after Mary and Caroline were settled in their new abode, Mrs. Mason proposed a walk before breakfast, a custom she wished to teach them, by rendering it amusing to them.

The sun had scarcely dispelled the dew which hung on every blade of grass, and filled the half-shut flowers; every prospect smiled, and the freshness of the air conveyed the most pleasing sensations to Mrs. Mason's mind; but the children were regardless of the surrounding beauties, and ran eagerly after some insects to destroy them. Mrs. Mason silently observed them, without appearing to do it; and stepped suddenly out of the foot-path into the long grass. Her buckle was caught in it, and striving to disentangle herself, she wet her feet; a thing the children knew she wished to avoid, as she had been lately sick. This circumstance roused their attention; and they forgot their amusement to enquire *why* she had left the path; and Mary could hardly restrain a laugh, when she was informed that it was to avoid treading on some snails that were creeping across the narrow footway. Surely, said Mary, you do not think there is any harm in killing a snail, or any of those nasty creatures that crawl on the ground? I hate them, and should scream if any one of them was to find its way from my clothes to my neck! With great gravity, Mrs. Mason asked how she dared to kill any thing, but to prevent its hurting her? Then, resuming a smiling face, she said, You have been neglected, my child; as we walk along attend to what I say,

1. Thoughtless, imprudent.

Look what a fine morning it is.—Insects, Birds, & Animals are all enjoying existence.

and make the best answers you can; and do you, Caroline, join in the conversation.

You have already heard that God created the world, and every inhabitant of it. He is then called the Father of all creatures; and all are made to be happy. He made those snails you despise, and caterpillars, and spiders; and when he made them, did not leave them to perish, but placed them where the food that is most proper to nourish them is easily found. They do not live long, but *their* Father, as well as your's, directs them to deposit their eggs on the plants that are fit to support the young, when they are not able to get food for themselves. And when such a great and wise Being has taken care to provide every thing necessary for the meanest creature, would you dare to kill it, merely because it appears, as you think, ugly? Mary began to be attentive, and followed Mrs. Mason's example, who allowed a caterpillar and a spider to creep on her hand. You find them very harmless; but too great a quantity would destroy our vegetables and fruit: to prevent this mischief, birds are permitted to eat them, and in spring there are always more than at any other time of the year, to furnish food for the young birds. —Half-convinced, Mary said, but worms are of little consequence in the world. Yet, replied Mrs. Mason, God cares for them, and gives them every thing that is necessary to render their existence comfortable. You are often troublesome—I am stronger than you—yet I do not kill you.

Observe those ants; they have a little habitation in yonder hillock; they carry food to it for the winter, and live very snug in it during the cold weather. The bees, too, have comfortable towns, and lay in a store of honey to support them when the flowers die, and snow covers the ground: and this forecast is as much the gift of God, as any quality you possess.

Do you know the meaning of the word Goodness? I see you are unwilling to answer. I will tell you. It is, first, to avoid hurting any thing; and then, to contrive to give as much pleasure as you can. If any insects are to be destroyed, to preserve my garden from desolation, I have it done in the quickest way. Domestic animals that I keep, I provide the best food for, and never suffer them to be tormented; and this caution arises from two motives:—I wish to make them happy; and, as I love my fellow-creatures still better than them, I would not allow those I have any influence over, to grow habitually thoughtless and cruel, and by these means lose the greatest pleasure life affords,—that of resembling God, by doing good.

A lark now began to sing, as it soared aloft. The children watched it, and listened to its melody. They wondered what it was thinking of—of its young family, they concluded: it flew over the hedge, and drawing near, they heard the young ones chirp. Very soon both the old birds took their flight together, to look for food to satisfy their craving young, who were almost fledged. An idle boy, who had borrowed a gun, fired at them—they fell: and before he could take up the wounded pair, he saw Mrs. Mason; and expecting a very severe reprimand, ran away. They drew near; one was not much hurt; but the other, the cock, had one leg broke, and both its wings shattered; and its little eyes seemed starting out of their sockets, it was in such exquisite pain. The children turned from it. Look at it, said Mrs. Mason; do you not see it suffers as much, and more than you did when you had the small-pox; then you were tenderly nursed. Take up the hen; I will bind her wing together; perhaps it will heal. As to the other, though I hate to kill it, I must put it out of pain; to leave it in its present state would be cruel; and avoiding an unpleasant sensation myself, I should allow the bird to die by inches, and call this treatment tenderness, when it would be weakness or selfishness. Saying so, she put her foot on the bird's head, turning her own another way.

They walked on; when Caroline remarked, that the nestlings, deprived of their parents, would not perish; and the mother began to flutter in her hand as they drew near the hedge, but the poor creature could not fly, though she tried to do it. The girls, with one voice, begged to take the nest, and provide food in a cage; and try if the mother could not contrive to hop about to feed them. The nest and the old mother were instantly in Mary's handkerchief, and a little opening left to admit the air; and Caroline peeped into it every moment to see how they looked. I give you leave, said Mrs. Mason, to take those birds, because an accident has rendered them helpless; if that had not been the case, they should not have been confined.

They had scarcely reached the next field, when they met another boy with a nest in his hand, and on a tree near him saw the mother, who, forgetting her natural timidity, followed the spoiler;[2] and her intelligible tones of anguish reached the ears of the children, whose hearts now first felt the emotions of humanity. Caroline called him, and taking sixpence out of her little purse, offered to give it to him for the nest, if he would shew her where he took it from. The boy consented, and away ran Car-

2. Despoiler, robber.

oline to replace it,—crying all the way, how delighted the old bird will be to find her brood again. The pleasure that the parent-bird would feel was talked of till they came to a large common,[3] and heard some young asses, at the door of an hovel, making a most dreadful noise. Mrs. Mason had ordered the old ones to be confined, lest the young should suck before the necessary quantity had been saved for the sick. After milking them, the thoughtless boy left them still in confinement, and the young in vain implored the food nature designed for them. Open the hatch, said Mrs. Mason, the mothers have still enough left to satisfy their young. It was opened, and they saw them suck.

Now we will return to breakfast; give me your hands, my little girls, you have done good this morning, you are my fellow-creatures. Look, what a fine morning it is. Insects, birds, and animals, are all enjoying the day. Thank God for permitting you to see it, and to imitate himself by doing good. Other creatures only think of themselves; but man is allowed to *retrace* the image that God first implanted in him; he feels disinterested love; every part of the creation affords an exercise for virtue, and a *consequent* source of pleasure.

CHAP. II.

The treatment of animals—The difference between them and men—
Parental affection of a dog—Brutality punished.

After breakfast Mrs. Mason gave the children *Mrs. Trimmer's Fabulous Histories;*[4] and the subject still turned on animals, and the wanton cruelty of those who treated them improperly. The little girls were eager to express their detestation, and begged leave to feed the chickens. They were allowed to do it; only one condition was annexed to the permission, that they did it regularly. When you wait for your food, you learn patience, and you can mention your wants; but those helpless creatures cannot complain. The country people frequently say,—How can you treat a poor dumb beast ill; and a stress is very properly laid on the word dumb;—dumb they appear to those who do not observe; but God, who takes care of every thing, understands their language; and so did Caroline this morning, when she ran with such eagerness to re-place the nest which the thoughtless boy stole, heedless of the mother's agonizing cries!

Mary interrupted her, to ask, if insects and animals were not inferior to men? Certainly, answered Mrs. Mason; and men are inferior to angels; yet we have reason to believe, that those exalted beings delight to do us good. You have heard in a book, that I seldom permit you to read, because you are not of an age to understand it, that angels, when they sung glory to God on high, in the same angelic strain wished for peace on earth, as a proof of the good will they felt towards men. And all the glad tidings that have been sent to men, angels have proclaimed: indeed, the word angel signifies a messenger. In order to please God, and our happiness arises from pleasing him, we must do good. This is what is called virtue; we exercise every benevolent affection to enjoy comfort here, and to fit ourselves to be angels hereafter. When we have acquired human virtues, we shall have a nobler employment in our Father's kingdom. But angels and men have a much greater resemblance, than there is between men and the brute creation; as the two former seem capable of improvement.

---

3. Undivided land belonging to the members of a local community as a whole; usually a patch of unenclosed land.

4. Moral tale that contains a family of talking robins (1786) by the British educator and Sunday school founder Sarah Trimmer (1741–1810).

The birds you saw to-day do not improve—or their improvement only tends to self-preservation; the first nest and the last are exactly the same; though in their flights they must see many other nests, and, had they reason, would observe that some of them are much more convenient than others; and, of course, they would take pattern by the best; but this is not the case. You saw the hen tear the down from her breast to make a nest for her eggs; you saw her beat the grain with her bill, and not swallow a bit, till the young ones were satisfied; and afterwards she covered them with her wings, and seemed perfectly happy; if any one approached, she was ready to defend them, to the hazard of her life: yet, a fortnight after, you may see the same hen drive them from the corn,[5] and forget the fondness that seemed to be stronger than the first impulse of nature.

Animals have not the affections which arise from reason, nor can they do good, or acquire virtue. Every affection, and impulse, I have observed in them, are like our inferior ones (which do not depend entirely on our will, but are involuntary); they preserve the species, and make them grateful for actual kindness. If you caress and feed them, they will love you, as children do, without knowing why; but we neither see imagination nor wisdom in them; and, what principally exalts man, friendship and devotion, they seem incapable of forming any conception of. Friendship flows from knowledge and virtue, and devotion prepares us to be angels; as, when we pray to God, we offer an affront to him, if we do not strive to imitate the perfections He displays every where for our imitation, that we may grow better and happier.

The children eargerly enquired in what manner they were to behave, to prove that they were superior to animals? The answer was short,—be tender-hearted; and let your superior endowments ward off the ills they cannot foresee. It is only to animals that children *can* do good, men are their superiors. When I was a child, added their tender friend, I always made it my study and delight, to feed all the dumb family; and when I could be of use to any one of them I was happy. This employment humanized my heart, while, like wax, it took every impression, and Providence has since made me an instrument of good—I have been useful to my fellow-creatures. I, who never wantonly trod on an insect, or disregarded the plaint of the speechless beast, can now give bread to the hungry, physic[6] to the sick, comfort to the afflicted, and, above all, am preparing you, who are to live for ever, to be fit for the society of angels, and good men made perfect. This world, I told you, was a road to a better—a preparation for it; if we suffer, we grow humbler and wiser: but animals have not this advantage, and man should not prevent their enjoying all the happiness of which they are capable.

A she cat or dog have such strong parental affection, that if you take away all their young, it almost kills them; some have actually died of grief; though they do not seem to miss the greatest part.

A dog had once all her litter taken from her, and drowned in a neighbouring brook: she sought them out, and brought them one by one, and laid them at the feet of her cruel master;—and looking wistfully at them for some time, in dumb anguish, she turned her eyes on the destroyer—and expired!

I myself knew a man who had hardened his heart to such a degree, that he found pleasure in tormenting every thing he had in his power. I saw him let two guinea-pigs roll down sloping tiles, to see if the fall would kill them. And were they killed? cried Caroline. Certainly; and it is well they were, or he would have found some other

5. Wheat.   6. Medicine.

way of tormenting them. When he became a father, he not only neglected to educate his children, and set them a good example, but he taught them to be cruel while he tormented them: the consequence was, that they neglected him when he was old and feeble; and he died in a ditch.

You may now go and feed your birds, and tie some of the straggling flowers round the sticks. After dinner, if the weather continues fine, we will walk to the wood, and I will shew you the hole in the lime-stone mountain (a mountain whose bowels, as we call them, are lime-stones) in which poor crazy Robin and his dog lived.

CHAP. III.

The treatment of animals—The story of crazy Robin—The man confined in the bastile.[7]

In the afternoon the children bounded over the short grass of the common, and walked under the shadow of the mountain till they came to a craggy part; where a stream broke out, and ran down the declivity, struggling with the huge stones which impeded its progress, and occasioned a noise that did not unpleasantly interrupt the solemn silence of the place. The brook was soon lost in the neighbouring wood, and the children turned their eyes to the broken side of the mountain, over which ivy grew in great profusion. Mrs. Mason pointed out a little cave, and desired them to sit down on some stumps of trees, while she told them the promised story.

In yonder cave lived a poor man, who generally went by the name of crazy Robin. In his youth he was very industrious, and married my father's dairy-maid; a girl deserving of such a good husband. For some time they continued to live very comfortably; their daily labour procured their daily bread; but Robin, finding it was likely he should have a large family, borrowed a trifle, to add to the small pittance they had saved in service, and took a little farm in a neighbouring county. I was then a child.

Ten or twelve years after, I heard that a crazy man, who appeared very harmless, had by the side of the brook piled a great number of stones; he would wade into the river for them, followed by a cur dog,[8] whom he would frequently call his Jacky, and even his Nancy; and then mumble to himself,—thou wilt not leave me—we will dwell with the owl in the ivy. —A number of owls had taken shelter in it. The stones he waded for he carried to the mouth of the hole, and only left just room enough to go in. Some of the neighbours at last recollected him; and I sent to enquire what misfortune had reduced him to such a deplorable state.

The information I received from different persons, I will communicate to you in as few words as I can.

Several of his children died in their infancy; and, two years before he came to his native place, he had been overwhelmed by a torrent of misery. Through unavoidable misfortunes he was long in arrears to his landlord; who, feeing that he was an honest man, and endeavoured to bring up his family, did not distress him; but when his wife was lying-in of her last child, the landlord died, and his heir sent and seized the stock for the rent; and the person he had borrowed some money of, exasperated to see all gone, arrested him, and he was hurried to gaol.[9] The poor woman, endeavouring to assist her family before she had gained sufficient strength, found herself very ill; and the illness, through neglect and the want of proper nourishment, turned to a putrid

7. Prison.
8. A mongrel dog.

9. I.e., jail.

fever; which two of the children caught from her, and died with her. The two who were left, Jacky and Nancy, went to their father, and took with them a cur dog, that had long shared their frugal meals.

The children begged in the day, and at night slept with their wretched father. Poverty and dirt soon robbed their cheeks of the roses which the country air made bloom with a peculiar freshness. Their blood had been tainted by the putrid complaint that destroyed their mother; in short, they caught the small-pox, and died. The poor father, who was now bereft of all his children, hung over their bed in speechless anguish; not a groan or a tear escaped from him; while he stood, two or three hours, in the same attitude, looking at the dead bodies of his little darlings. The dog licked his hands, and strove to attract his attention; but for awhile he seemed not to observe his caresses;—when he did, he said, mournfully, thou wilt not leave me—and then he began to laugh. The bodies were removed; and he remained in an unsettled state, often frantic; at length the phrenzy subsided, and he grew melancholy and harmless. He was not then so closely watched; and one day he contrived to make his escape, the dog followed him, and came directly to his native village.

After I received this account, I determined he should live in the place he had chosen, undisturbed. I sent some conveniences, all of which he rejected, except a mat; on which he sometimes slept—the dog always did. I tried to induce him to eat, but he constantly gave the dog whatever I sent him, and lived on haws[1] and blackberries, and every kind of trash. I used to call frequently on him; and he sometimes followed me to the house I now live in, and in winter he would come of his own accord, and take a crust of bread. He gathered water-cresses out of the pool, and would bring them to me, with nose-gays of wild-thyme, which he plucked from the sides of the mountain. I mentioned before, that the dog was a cur; it had the tricks of curs, and would run after horses heels, and bark. One day, when his master was gathering water-cresses, the dog ran after a young gentleman's horse, and made it start, and almost throw the rider. Though he knew it was the poor madman's dog, he levelled his gun at it—shot it,—and instantly rode off. Robin came to him, he looked at his wounds, and not sensible that he was dead, called him to follow him; but when he found that he could not, he took him to the pool, and washed off the blood before it began to clot and then brought him home, and laid him on the mat.

I observed that I had not seen him pacing up the hills, and sent to enquire about him. He was found sitting by the dog, and no entreaties could prevail on him to quit it, or receive any refreshment. I went to him myself, hoping, as I had always been a favourite, that I should be able to persuade him. When I came to him, I found the hand of death was upon him. He was still melancholy; but there was not such a mixture of wildness in it. I pressed him to take some food; but, instead of answering me, or turning away, he burst into tears,—a thing I had never seen him do before, and, in inarticulate accents, he said, Will any one be kind to me!—you will kill me!—I saw not my wife die—no!—they dragged me from her—but I saw Jacky and Nancy die—and who pitied me, but my dog? He turned his eyes to the body—I wept with him. He would then have taken some nourishment, but nature was exhausted—and he expired. Was that the cave? said Mary. They ran to it. Poor Robin! Did you ever hear of any thing so cruel? Yes, answered Mrs. Mason; and as we walk home I will give you another instance of much greater barbarity.

I told you, Robin was confined in a gaol. In France they have a dreadful one.[2] The

---

1. The fruit of the hawthorn (berries).
2. I.e., the Bastille, the prison fortress in Paris that was captured and destroyed by a mob in 1789, at the beginning of the French Revolution.

poor wretches who are confined in it live entirely alone; have not the pleasure of seeing men or animals; nor are they allowed books.—They live in comfortless solitude. Some have amused themselves by making figures on the wall; and others have laid straws in rows. One miserable captive found a spider, he nourished it for two or three years; it grew tame, and partook of his lonely meal. His keeper observed it, and mentioned the circumstance to a superior, who ordered him to crush it. In vain did the man beg to have his spider spared. You find, Mary, it was a comfort in solitude. The keeper obeyed the cruel commands; and the unhappy wretch felt more pain from the crush, than he had experienced during his long confinement. He looked round a dreary apartment, and the small portion of light that the grated bars admitted, only served to shew him, that he breathed where nothing else drew breath.

CHAP. IV.

Anger.—History of Jane B—

A few days after these walks and conversations, Mrs. Mason heard a great noise in the play-room. She ran hastily to enquire the cause, and found the children crying, and near them, on the floor, lay one of the young birds dead. With great eagerness each of them tried to exculpate herself, and prove that the other had killed the bird. Mrs. Mason commanded them to be silent; and, at the same time, called an orphan she had educated, and desired her to take care of the nest.

The cause of the dispute was easily gathered from what they both let fall. They contested which had the best right to feed the birds. Mary insisted she was the eldest; and Caroline, that she took the nest. Snatching it from one side of the room to the other, the bird fell, and was trod on before they were aware.

When they were a little composed, Mrs. Mason calmly thus addressed them:—I perceive you are ashamed of your behaviour, and sorry for the consequence; I will not severely reprehend you, and add bitterness to the self-reproach you must both feel, because I pity you. You are now inferior to the animals that graze on the common; reason only serves to render your folly more conspicuous and inexcusable. I despise anger: its selfish emotions banish compassion, and undermine every other virtue. It is easy to conquer another; but noble to subdue ones-self. Had you, Mary, given way to your sister's humour, you would have proved that you were not only older, but wiser than her. And you, Caroline, would have saved your charge, if you had for the time waved[3] your right.

It is always a proof of superior sense to bear with slight inconveniences, and even trifling injuries, without complaining or contesting about them. The soul reserves its firmness for great occasions, and then it acts a decided part. It is just the contrary mode of thinking, and the conduct it produces, which occasions all those trivial disputes that slowly corrode domestic peace, and insensibly destroy what a great misfortune could not sweep away.

I will tell you a story, that will take stronger hold on your memory than mere remarks.

Jane B. was an only child. Her fond weak mother would not allow her to be contradicted on any occasion. The child had some tenderness of heart; but so accustomed was she to see every thing give way to her humour, that she imagined the world was made for her. If any of her playfellows had toys, that struck her capricious

---

3. I.e., waived.

sickly fancy, she would cry for them; and substitutes were in vain offered to quiet her, she would have the identical ones, or fly into the most violent passion. When she was an infant, if she fell down, her nurse made her beat the floor: she continued the practice afterwards, and would kick the chairs and tables, or any senseless piece of furniture, if they came in her way when she was angry. I have seen her throw her cap into the fire, because some of her acquaintance had a prettier one.

Continual passions weakened her constitution; besides, she would not eat the common wholsome food that children, who are subject to the small-pox and worms,[4] ought to eat, and which is necessary when they grow so fast, to make them strong and handsome. Instead of being a comfort to her tender, though mistaken, mother, she was her greatest torment. The servants all disliked her; she loved none but herself; and the consequence was, she never inspired love; even the pity good-natured people felt, was nearly allied to contempt.

A lady, who visited her mother, brought with her a pretty little dog. Jane was delighted with it; and the lady, with great reluctance, parted with it to oblige her friend. For some time she fondled, and really felt something like an affection for it: but, one day, it happened to snatch a cake she was going to eat, and though there were twenty within reach, she flew into a violent passion, and threw a stool at the dog, who was big with pup. It fell down; I can scarce tell the rest; it received so severe a blow, all the young were killed, and the poor wretch languished two days, suffering the most excruciating torture.

Jane, who was now angry with herself, sat holding it all the time, and every look the miserable animal gave her stung her to the heart. After its death she was very unhappy, but did not try to conquer her temper. All the blessings of life were thrown away on her; and, without any real misfortune, she was continually miserable.

If she had planned out a party of pleasure, and the weather proved unfavourable, the whole day was spent in fruitless repining, or venting her ill-humour on those who depended on her. If no disappointment of that kind occurred, she could not catch pleasure; something always disconcerted her; the horses went too fast, or too slow; the dinner was ill-dressed, or some of the company contradicted her.

She was, when a child, very beautiful; but anger soon distorted her regular features, and gave a forbidding fierceness to her eyes. If for a moment she looked pleased, she still resembled a heap of combustible matter, to which an accidental spark would set fire; of course quiet people were afraid to converse with her. If she ever did a good or a humane action, her ridiculous anger soon rendered it an intolerable burden, if it did not entirely cancel it.

At last she broke her mother's heart, or hastened her death, by her want of duty, and her many other faults, all proceeding from violent unrestrained anger.

The death of her mother, which affected her very much, left her without a friend. She would sometimes say, Ah! my poor mother, if you were now alive, I would not teaze you—I would give the world to let you know that I am sorry for what I have done: you died, thinking me ungrateful; and lamenting that I did not die when you gave me suck. I shall never—oh! never see you more.

This thought, and her temper, preyed on her impaired constitution. She had not, by doing good, prepared her soul for another state, or cherished any hopes that could disarm death of its terrors, or render that last sleep sweet—its approach was dreadful!—and she hastened her end, scolding the physician for not curing her. Her lifeless countenance displayed the marks of convulsive anger; and she left an ample fortune

4. Intestinal parasites.

behind her to those who did not regret her loss. They followed her to the grave, on which no one shed a tear. She was soon forgotten; and I only remember her, to warn you to shun her errors.

CHAP. V.

Lying—Honor—Truth—Small Duties—History of Lady L. and Mr. B—
Mrs. Trimmer's Fabulous Histories.

The little girls were very assiduous to regain Mrs. Mason's good opinion; and, by the mildness of their behaviour, to prove that they were ashamed of themselves. It was a rule with her, when they offended her, that is, behaved improperly, to treat them civilly; but to avoid giving them those marks of affection which they were particularly delighted to receive.

Yesterday, said she to them, I only mentioned to you one fault, though I observed two. You very readily guess I mean the lie you both told. Nay, look up, I wish to see you blush; the confusion I perceive in your faces gives me pleasure; as it convinces me it is not a confirmed habit: and, indeed, my children, I should be sorry such a mean one had taken root in your infant minds.

When I speak of falsehood, I mean every kind; whatever tends to deceive, though not said in direct terms. Tones of voice, motions of the hand or head, if they make another believe what they ought not to believe, are lies, and of the worst kind; as the contrivance aggravates the guilt. I would much sooner forgive a lie told directly, when perhaps fear entirely occupied the thoughts, and the presence of God was not felt: it is Him you affront by telling an untruth.

How so? enquired Mary.

Because you hope to conceal it from every human creature: but, if you consider a moment, you must recollect, that the Searcher of hearts reads your very thoughts; that nothing is hid from him.

You would blush if I discovered it; yet forfeit His favour to screen yourselves from correction or reproof, or, what is still worse, to purchase some trifling gratification, the pleasure of which would last but a moment.

You heard the gentleman who visited me this morning, very frequently use the word Honour. Honour consists in respecting yourself; in doing as you would be done by; and the foundation of it is Truth.

When I can depend on the veracity of people, that is to say, am certain they adhere to truth, I rely on them; am certain they have courage, because I know they will bear any inconvenience rather than tell a lie, and despise themselves. Besides, it is not then necessary to consider what you intend to say, when you have done right. Always determine, on every occasion, to speak the truth, and you will never be at a loss for words. If your character for this scrupulous attention is once fixed, your acquaintance will be courted; and those who are not particularly pleased with you, will respect your honourable principles.

It is impossible to form friendships without making truth the basis; it is indeed the essence of devotion, the employment of the understanding, and the support of every other duty.

I govern my servants, and you, by attending strictly to it, and this observance keeps my head clear and my heart pure; and I am ever ready to pray to the Author of good, the Fountain of truth.

While I am discussing the subject, let me point out to you another branch of this virtue, *Sincerity*, and remember I every day set you an example, for I never, to please for the moment, pay unmeaning compliments, or permit any words to drop from my tongue, that my heart does not dictate; and when I relate any matter of fact, I carefully avoid embellishing it, in order to render it a more entertaining story; not that I think such a practice absolutely criminal; but as it contributes insensibly to wear away a respect for truth, I guard against the vain impulse, lest I lose the chief strength, and even ornament, of my mind, and become like a wave of the sea, drifted about by every gust of passion.

You must in life observe the most *apparently* insignificant duties—the great ones are the pillars of virtue; but the constant concurrence of trifling things, makes it necessary that reason and conscience should always preside, to keep the heart steady. Many people make promises, and appointments, which they scruple not to break, if some other more inviting pleasure occurs. Always remember, that the slightest duty should be performed before a mere amusement is pursued—for any neglect of this kind embitters play. Nothing can long be pleasant that is not innocent!

As I usually endeavour to recollect some persons of my acquaintance, who have suffered by the faults, or follies, I wish you to avoid; I will describe two characters, that, if I mistake not, will very strongly enforce what I have been saying.

Last week you saw Lady L. who came to pay me a morning visit. Did you ever see such a fine carriage, or such beautiful horses? How they pawed the ground, and displayed their rich harnesses! Her servants wore elegant liveries,[5] and her own clothes suited the equipage. Her house is equal to her carriage; the rooms are lofty, and hung with silk; noble glasses and pictures adorn them: and the pleasure-grounds are large and well laid out; besides the trees and shrubs, they contain a variety of summer-houses and temples, as they are called.—Yet my young friends, this is *state* not *dignity*.

This woman has a little soul, she never attended to truth, great part of her fortune she obtained by falsehood, and it has blighted all her enjoyments. She inhabits that superb house, wears the gayest clothes, and rides in that beautiful carriage, without feeling pleasure. Suspicion, and the cares it has given birth to, have wrinkled her countenance, and banished every trace of beauty, which paint in vain endeavours to repair. Her suspicious temper arises from a knowledge of her own heart, and the manner she has employed her understanding.

She imagines that every person she converses with, means to deceive her; and when she leaves the company, supposes all the ill they will say of her, because this is her own practice with others. She listens about her house, expecting to discover the designs of her servants, none of whom she can trust; in consequence of her anxiety her sleep is unfound, and her food tasteless. She walks in her paradise of a garden, and smells not the flowers, nor do the birds inspire her with cheerfulness: these pleasures are true and simple, they lead to the love of God, and all the creatures He has made—and cannot warm a heart which a malicious story can please.

She cannot pray to God, He hates a liar. She is neglected by her husband, whose only motive for marrying her was to clear an incumbered estate.[6] Her son, her only child, is undutiful; the poor never have cause to bless her; nor does she contribute to the happiness of any human being.

To kill time, and drive away the pangs of guilt, she goes from one house to another, collecting and propagating scandalous tales, to bring others on a level with herself.

---

5. Servants' uniforms distinct to their household.
6. I.e., to raise money through marriage, to rein-

state the ownership of an estate by paying off debts.

Even those who resemble her are afraid of her; she lives alone in the world, its good things are poisoned by her vices, and neither inspire joy nor gratitude.

Before I tell you how she acquired these vicious habits, and enlarged her fortune by disregarding truth, I must desire you to think of Mrs. B. the curate's wife, who lives in yonder white house, close to the church; it is a small one, yet the woodbines and jessamins give it a pretty appearance. Her voice is sweet, her manners not only easy, but elegant; and her simple dress makes her person appear to the greatest advantage.

She walks to visit me, and her little ones hang on her hands, and cling to her clothes, they are so fond of her. If any thing terrifies them, they run under her apron, and she looks like the hen taking care of her young brood. The animals play with the children, and find her a mild attentive mistress; and out of her scanty fortune she contrives to feed and clothe many a hungry shivering wretch; who bless her as she passes along.

Though she has not any outward decorations, she appears superior to her neighbors, who call her the *gentlewoman*; indeed every gesture shews an accomplished and dignified mind, that acts from itself; when deprived of the fortune which contributed to polish and give it consequence.

Drawings in the best style, the amusement of her youth, ornament her neat parlor, in one corner stand some musical instruments, she plays with taste, and sings sweetly.

All the furniture, not forgetting a book-case, full of well-chosen books, speaks the refinement of the owner, and the pleasures a cultivated mind has within its grasp, independent of prosperity.

Her husband, a man of taste and learning, reads to her, while she makes clothes for her children, whom she teaches in the tenderest, most persuasive manner, important truths and elegant accomplishments.

When you have been some time good you shall visit her, and ramble in her little garden; there are several pretty seats in it, and the nightingales warble their sweetest songs, undisturbed, in the shade.

I have now given you an account of the present situation of both, and of their characters; listen to me while I relate in what manner these characters were formed, and the consequence of each adhering to a different mode of conduct.

Lady L. when she was a child, used to say pert things, which the injudicious people about her laughed at, and called very witty. Finding that her prattle was approved, she talked incessantly, and invented stories, when adding to those that had some foundation, was not sufficient to entertain the company. If she stole sweetmeats,[7] or broke any thing, the cat, or the dog, was blamed, and the poor animals were corrected for her faults; nay, sometimes the servants lost their places in consequence of her assertions. Her parents died and left her a large fortune, and an aunt, who had a still larger one, adopted her.

Mrs. B. her cousin, was, some years after, adopted by the same lady; but her parents could not leave their estate to her, as it descended to the male heir. She had received the most liberal education, and was, in every respect, the reverse of her cousin; who envied her merit, and could not bear to think of her dividing the fortune she expected to inherit entirely herself. She practiced every mean art to prejudice her aunt against her, and succeeded.

A faithful old servant endeavored to open her mistress's eyes; but the cunning niece, contrived to invent the most infamous story of the old domestic, who was

7. Any sugary pastries, candied fruits, or sugared nuts.

dismissed. Mrs. B. supported her, when she could not succeed in vindicating her, and suffered for her generosity; her aunt dying soon after, left only five hundred pounds to this amiable woman, and fifty thousand to Lady L.

They both of them married shortly after. One, the profligate Lord L. and the other a respectable clergyman, who had been disappointed in his hopes of preferment.[8] This last couple, in spite of their mutual disappointments, are contented with their lot; and are preparing themselves and children for another world, where truth, virtue and happiness dwell together.

Whatever happiness we attain in this life, must faintly resemble what God Himself enjoys, whose truth and goodness produces a sublime degree, such as we cannot conceive, it is so far above our limited capacities.

I did not intend to detain you so long, said Mrs. Mason; have you finished *Mrs. Trimmer's Fabulous Histories?* Indeed we have, answered Caroline, mournfully, and I was very sorry to come to the end. I never read such a pretty book, may I read it over again to Mrs. B's little Fanny? Certainly, said Mrs. Mason, if you can make her understand that birds never talk. Go and run about the garden, and remember the next liar I detect, I shall punish; because lying is a vice; I ought to punish you if you are guilty of it, to prevent your feeling Lady L's misery.

* * *

CHAP. XXV.

Mrs. Mason's farewell Advice to her young Friends.

The day before Mrs. Mason was to leave her pupils, she took a hand of each, and pressing them tenderly in her own, tears started into her eyes—I tremble for you, my dear girls, you must practice by yourselves some of the virtues I have been endeavoring to inculcate; and I shall anxiously wait for the summer, to see the progress you have made.

We have conversed on several very important subjects; do not forget the conclusions I have drawn. I now, as my last present, give you a book, in which I have written the subjects we have discussed; recur frequently to it, the stories will illustrate the instruction it contains, and you will not feel the want of my personal advice. Some of the reasoning you may not thoroughly comprehend, but, as your understandings ripen, you will feel its full force.

Avoid anger; exercise compassion, and love truth. Recollect, that from religion your chief comfort must spring, and never neglect the duty of prayer; the honor of making known your wants and sorrows to the wisest and best of Beings, in whose hands are the issues,[9] not only of this life, but of that which is to come.

Your father will allow you a certain stipend; you have already *felt* the pleasure of doing good; ever recollect that fancy must be conquered, if you wish to gratify benevolence; and practice economy to enable you to be generous. The good you intend to do, do quickly, for know a trifling duty neglected, is a great fault, and the present time only is at your command.

You are now candidates for my friendship, and on your advancement in virtue my regard will depend. Write often to me, and I will punctually answer your letters; and

---

8. I.e., had not been promoted to a high and secure position within the church.

9. Outcomes.

let me have the genuine sentiments of your hearts. In expressions of affection and
respect, do not deviate from truth to turn a period[1] prettily.

Adieu! when you think of your friend, observe her precepts; and let the recollection
of my affection, give additional weight to the truths I have endeavoured to instil.

FINIS.

1788

1. A well-structured sentence.

MARIA EDGEWORTH
1768–1849

In a 1794 letter to her cousin Sophy Ruxton, Maria Edgeworth described with satisfaction the active child-centered household in which she lived, and the many experiments and activities that filled their days: "There are, an' it please you, ma'am, a great many good things here. There is a balloon hanging up, and another going to be put on the stocks. There is soap made, and making from a receipt in Nicholson's *Chemistry*: there is excellent ink made, and to be made by the same book: There is a cake of roses just squeezed in a vice, by my father." The domestic scene and her Irish homeland provided not only the stuff and pleasure of Edgeworth's daily life but also the material for her literary and educational writing. Arguably the most important educationalist and British writer for children of the Romantic era (roughly 1770–1848), Edgeworth is known as well for her innovative novels of Irish life and British manners written for an adult audience. Though modest and unassuming, especially in public, she had a passionate nature and an intelligent wit, partially revealed in her writing and fully expressed within her large and loving family circle.

Within that circle, Edgeworth's father, the Anglo-Irish inventor and educationalist Richard Lovell Edgeworth (1744–1817), had the greatest influence on her writing—reading her work, commenting on it, and, at times, inserting his own words—and on her life. He married Anna Maria Elers when very young; Maria was their second surviving child. For a time R. L. Edgeworth took Maria's older brother, Richard, to France in an attempt to raise him according to the educational method outlined in Jean-Jacques Rousseau's *Émile, or On Education*

(1762), while Maria and her mother remained in England. Anna died in childbirth in 1773, and within four months Edgeworth had married Honora Sneyd, whom he had loved for years. From the age of eight to fourteen, Maria spent most of each year at boarding school, first in Derby and then for a final year in London. She was still at school when Honora died of consumption in 1780, having borne two children. Following Honora's wishes, Edgeworth married her sister Elizabeth, and the entire family moved in 1782 to Edgeworthstown, his large, tenanted estate in the Irish Midlands (County Longford). There Elizabeth created a happy home for her stepchildren and growing number of children (she would have nine). "I do not think one tear per month is shed in this house, nor the voice of reproof heard, nor the hand of restraint felt," R. L. Edgeworth proudly related to a friend.

Maria Edgeworth was essential to the smooth running of the household. At fifteen, she was assisting her father in managing his property, functioning as his accountant and agent. Within the home, she helped raise the children—Henry, Elizabeth's eldest (born in 1782), was Maria's special project. In the summer of 1791, she alone was in charge of their education while her parents went to England. To that end, she wrote onto a slate stories that she read aloud in the evening; her listeners' response determined whether she saved them or destroyed them. In this way, Edgeworth began to select the tales eventually collected in *The Parent's Assistant* (3 vols., 1796; 6 vols., 1800). Her first publication was *Letters to Literary Ladies* (1795), a defense of female education, which was a cause dear to her father; she published steadily for the next forty years.

Edgeworth's early works appeared against a backdrop of great turmoil within the family and the nation. In 1797, her beloved stepmother died, and within six months R. L. Edgeworth married his fourth wife, Frances Beaufort, the daughter of an acquaintance. She was slightly younger than Maria, and the two became very close. Just after the marriage, the Rebellion of 1798 broke out, led by the Society of United Irishmen. Initially a reformist organization containing Protestants, Catholics, and Dissenters who sought change in the Irish Parliament and greater rights for Catholics, it was forced underground and came to advocate Irish independence. The result instead was the 1801 Act of Union, which tied Ireland even more tightly to Britain. Though the uprising was put down fairly quickly, it was bloody, and some skirmishes took place on the estate of the Edgeworths (who supported Catholic emancipation but not revolution). That same tumultuous year saw the publication of *Practical Education* (2 vols.), a theoretical treatise that Edgeworth and her father wrote together. Its educational theories were inspired in part by John Locke and Rousseau—emphasizing the importance of letting the child's curiosity direct his or her education and of appealing to the child's reason rather than fancy—and in part by personal observation of how children learn. Edgeworth called her literary partnership with her father "the joy and pride of my life."

Edgeworth's individual voice was established with the *Castle Rackrent: An Hibernian Tale* (1800). First published anonymously, this novel set in Ireland's recent past was narrated by an old Irish steward. Edgeworth used dialect and humor to sympathetically illustrate a national character, a method carefully noted by Sir Walter Scott. In 1814 Edgeworth wrote to Scott, congratulating him on the publication of *Waverley*, and in the postscript of his response he acknowledged his desire in that novel "in some distant degree to emulate the admirable Irish portraits drawn by Miss Edgeworth." By the end of 1801, Edgeworth's works included two more editions of *Castle Rackrent*; *Belinda*, a novel of manners; and *Early Lessons*, educational tales

published in ten "parts" (two for *Harry and Lucy*, three for *Rosamond*, four for *Frank*, and one devoted to three individual stories), and she became a celebrity.

Edgeworth, her father, and other family members spent some months traveling in England, France, and Scotland in late 1802 to early 1803. Their stay in Paris was cut short, because the renewal of war between France and Britain seemed likely; but before they left, Edgeworth received and rejected a marriage proposal from Abraham Edelcrantz, private secretary to the King of Sweden. Edgeworth's fame increased with her two sets of *Tales of Fashionable Life* (1809, 1812), especially *The Absentee* (in the second series). By 1815, she was the best-known and best-paid novelist in Britain, and she corresponded with major literary figures such as Scott and the playwright Joanna Baillie. In 1816, Jane Austen sent Edgeworth a copy of her novel *Emma*.

The death of Edgeworth's father in 1817 was a great blow, and she wrote relatively little for the rest of her life. As she had promised him, she finished and published *Memoirs of Richard Lovell Edgeworth* (1820); she also wrote sequels to her children's stories about Rosamond (1821), Frank (1822), and Harry and Lucy (1825). In 1826, Edgeworth took over the family estate, which her brother Lovell had mismanaged, in the end quietly buying it from him so that he could pay his debts. She completed one more book for adults, the society novel *Helen* (3 vols., 1834); her last work, *Orlandino* (1848), was a story for children. After Edgeworth's death at age eighty-one, her stepmother wrote: "Much as she was gratified by her 'success' in the society of her celebrated contemporaries, she never varied in her love for Home."

The two tales from *The Parent's Assistant* printed here showcase Edgeworth's primary literary and educational strategy in her writing for young readers. She uses lively tales that feature engaging and well-developed child characters—whether perfectly good, lazy, or faulty—to demonstrate the rational pleasures of choosing hard work, generosity, self-reflection, and duty over selfishness, carelessness, or self-indulgence.

Lazy Lawrence

In the pleasant valley of Ashton there lived an elderly woman of the name of Preston; she had a small neat cottage, and there was not a weed to be seen in her garden. It was upon her garden that she chiefly depended for support; it consisted of strawberry beds, and one small border for flowers. The pinks and roses she tied up in nice nosegays, and sent either to Clifton or Bristol[1] to be sold; as to her strawberries, she did not send them to market, because it was the custom for numbers of people to come from Clifton, in the summer time, to eat strawberries and cream at the gardens in Ashton.

Now the widow Preston was so obliging, active, and good-humoured, that every one who came to see her was pleased. She lived happily in this manner for several years; but, alas! one autumn she fell sick, and, during her illness, every thing went wrong; her garden was neglected, her cow died, and all the money which she had saved was spent in paying for medicines. The winter passed away, while she was so weak that she could earn but little by her work; and, when the summer came, her rent was called for, and the rent was not ready in her little purse as usual. She begged a few months delay, and they were granted to her; but at the end of that time there was no resource but to sell her horse Lightfoot. Now Lightfoot, though perhaps he had seen his best days, was a very great favourite: in his youth he had always carried the dame to market behind her husband; and it was now her little son Jem's turn to ride him. It was Jem's business to feed Lightfoot, and to take care of him; a charge which he never neglected, for, besides being a very good-natured, he was a very industrious boy.

"It will go near to break my Jem's heart," said dame Preston to herself, as she sat one evening beside the fire, stirring the embers, and considering how she had best open the matter to her son, who stood opposite to her, eating a dry crust of bread very heartily for supper.

"Jem," said the old woman, "what, ar't hungry?"

"That I am, brave and hungry!"

"Aye! no wonder, you've been brave[2] hard at work—Eh?"

"Brave hard! I wish it was not so dark, mother, that you might just step out and see the great bed I've dug; I know you'd say it was no bad day's work—and, oh mother! I've good news; Farmer Truck will give us the giant-strawberries, and I'm to go for 'em tomorrow morning, and I'll be back afore breakfast."

"God bless the boy! how he talks!—Four mile there, and four mile back again, afore breakfast."

"Aye, upon Lightfoot you know, mother, very easily, mayn't I?"

"Aye, child!"

"Why do you sigh, mother?"

"Finish thy supper, child."

"I've done!" cried Jem, swallowing the last mouthful hastily, as if he thought he had been too long at supper—"and now for the great needle; I must see and mend Lightfoot's bridle afore I go to bed."—To work he set, by the light of the fire, and the dame having once more stirred it, began again with "Jem, dear, does he go lame

---

1. Cities in the southwest of England.   2. Excellently, worthily.

at all now?"—"What Lightfoot! Oh la, no, not he!—never was so well of his lameness in all his life—he's grown quite young again, I think, and then he's so fat he can hardly wag."[3]—"God bless him—that's right—we must see, Jem, and keep him fat."

"For what, mother?"

"For Monday fortnight at the fair. He's to be—sold!"

"Lightfoot!" cried Jem, and let the bridle fall from his hand; "and *will* mother sell Lightfoot?"

"*Will*; no: but I *must*, Jem."

"Must; who says you *must*? why *must* you, mother?"

"I must, I say, child—Why, must not I pay my debts honestly—and must not I pay my rent; and was not it called for long and long ago; and have not I had time; and did not I promise to pay it for certain Monday fortnight, and am not I two guineas[4] short—and where am I to get two guineas? So what signifies talking, child," said the widow, leaning her head upon her arm, "Lightfoot must go."

Jem was silent for a few minutes.—"Two guineas; that's a great, great deal.—If I worked, and worked, and worked ever so hard, I could no ways earn two guineas *afore* Monday fortnight—could I, mother?"

"Lord help thee, no; not an' work thyself to death."

"But I could earn something, though, I say," cried Jem proudly; "and I *will* earn *something*—if it be ever so little, it will be *something*—and I shall do my very best; so I will."

"That I'm sure of, my child," said his mother, drawing him towards her, and kissing him; "you were always a good industrious lad, *that* I will say afore your face or behind your back;—but it won't do now—Lightfoot *must* go."

Jem turned away, struggling to hide his tears, and went to bed without saying a word more. But he knew that crying would do no good, so he presently wiped his eyes, and lay awake, considering what he could possibly do to save the horse.—"If I get ever so little," he still said to himself, "it will be *something*; and who knows but Landlord might then wait a bit longer? and we might make it all up in time; for a penny a day might come to two guineas in time."[5]

But how to get the first penny was the question.—Then he recollected, that one day, when he had been sent to Clifton to sell some flowers, he had seen an old woman with a board beside her covered with various sparkling stones, which people stopped to look at as they passed, and he remembered that some people bought the stones; one paid twopence, another threepence, and another six-pence for them; and Jem heard her say that she got them amongst the neighbouring rocks: so he thought that if he tried he might find some too, and sell them as she had done.

Early in the morning he wakened full of this scheme, jumped up, dressed himself, and, having given one look at poor Lightfoot in his stable, set off to Clifton in search of the old woman, to inquire where she found her sparkling stones. But it was too early in the morning, the old woman was not at her seat; so he turned back again disappointed.—He did not waste his time waiting for her, but saddled and bridled Lightfoot, and went to farmer Truck's for the giant-strawberries. A great part of the morning was spent in putting them into the ground; and, as soon as that was finished, he set out again in quest of the old woman, whom, to his great joy, he spied sitting at her corner of the street with her board before her. But this old woman was deaf and cross; and when at last Jem made her hear his questions, he could get no answer from her, but that she found the fossils where he would never find any more. "But

---

3. Move or stir.

4. English gold coins, worth 21 shillings each.

5. In 504 days (there were 12 pennies in a shilling).

can't I look where you looked?"—"Look away, nobody hinders you," replied the old woman; and these were the only words she would say.—Jem was not, however, a boy to be easily discouraged; he went to the rocks, and walked slowly along, looking at all the stones as he passed. Presently he came to a place where a number of men were at work loosening some large rocks, and one amongst the workmen was stooping down looking for something very eagerly; Jem ran up, and asked if he could help him. "Yes," said the man, "you can; I've just dropped, amongst this heap of rubbish, a fine piece of crystal that I got to-day."—"What kind of a looking thing is it?" said Jem. "White, and like glass," said the man, and went on working whilst Jem looked very carefully over the heap of rubbish for a great while. "Come," said the man, "it's gone for ever; don't trouble yourself any more, my boy."—"It's no trouble; I'll look a little longer; we'll not give it up so soon," said Jem; and, after he had looked a little longer, he found the piece of crystal. "Thank'e," said the man, "you are a fine little industrious fellow." Jem, encouraged by the tone of voice in which the man spoke this, ventured to ask him the same questions which he had asked the old woman. "One good turn deserves another," said the man; "we are going to dinner just now, and shall leave off work—wait for me here, and I'll make it worth your while."

Jem waited; and, as he was very attentively observing how the workmen went on with their work, he heard somebody near him give a great yawn, and, turning round, he saw stretched upon the grass, beside the river, a boy about his own age, who he knew very well went in the village of Ashton by the name of Lazy Lawrence; a name which he most justly deserved, for he never did any thing from morning to night; he neither worked nor played, but sauntered or lounged about restless and yawning. His father was an alehouse-keeper, and being generally drunk, could take no care of his son, so that Lazy Lawrence grew every day worse and worse. However, some of the neighbours said that he was a good-natured poor fellow enough, and would never do any one harm but himself; whilst others, who were wiser, often shook their heads, and told him, that idleness was the root of all evil.

"What, Lawrence!" cried Jem to him, when he saw him lying upon the grass— "what, are you asleep?"—"Not quite."—"Are you awake?"—"Not quite."—"What are you doing there?"—"Nothing."—"What are you thinking of?"—"Nothing."—"What makes you lie there?"—"I don't know—because I can't find any body to play with me to-day—Will you come and play?"—"No, I can't; I'm busy."—"Busy," cried Lawrence, stretching himself, "you are always busy—I would not be you for the world, to have so much to do always."—"And I," said Jem, laughing, "would not be you for the world, to have nothing to do." So they parted, for the workman just then called Jem to follow him. He took him home to his own house, and shewed him a parcel of fossils, which he had gathered, he said, on purpose to sell, but had never had time yet to sort them. He set about it however now, and having picked out those which he judged to be the best, he put them into a small basket, and gave them to Jem to sell, upon condition that he should bring him half of what he got. Jem, pleased to be employed, was ready to agree to what the man proposed, provided his mother had no objection to it. When he went home to dinner, he told his mother his scheme, and she smiled and said he might do as he pleased, for she was not afraid of his being from home. "You are not an idle boy," said she, "so there is little danger of your getting into any mischief."

Accordingly Jem that evening took his stand, with his little basket, upon the bank of the river, just at the place where people land from a ferry-boat, and where the walk turns to the wells, where numbers of people perpetually pass to drink the waters. He chose his place well, and waited almost all evening, offering his fossils with great assiduity to every passenger; but not one person bought any. "Holla!" cried some sailors, who had just rowed a boat to land, "bear a hand here, will you, my little fellow! and carry these parcels for us into yonder house." Jem ran down immediately for the parcels, and did what he was asked to do so quickly, and with so much good will, that the master of the boat took notice of him, and, when he was going away, stopped to ask him what he had got in his little basket; and when he saw that they were fossils, he immediately told Jem to follow him, for that he was going to carry some shells he had brought from abroad to a lady in the neighbourhood who was making a grotto.[6] "She will very likely buy your stones into the bargain; come along, my lad, we can but try."

The lady lived but a very little way off, so that they were soon at her house. She was alone in her parlour, and was sorting a bundle of feathers of different colours; they lay on a sheet of paste-board upon a window-seat, and it happened that as the sailor was bustling round the table to shew off his shells, he knocked down the sheet of paste-board, and scattered all the feathers.

The lady looked very sorry, which Jem observing, he took the opportunity, whilst she was busy looking over the sailor's bag of shells, to gather together all the feathers, and sort them according to their different colours, as he had seen them sorted when he first came into the room.

"Where is the little boy you brought with you? I thought I saw him here just now."—"And here I am, ma'am," cried Jem, creeping from under the table with some few remaining feathers which he had picked from the carpet; "I thought," added he, pointing to the others, "I had better be doing something than standing idle, ma'am." She smiled, and, pleased with his activity and simplicity, began to ask him several questions; such as, who he was, where he lived, what employment he had, and how much a day he earned by gathering fossils. "This is the first day I ever tried," said Jem; "I never sold any yet, and, if you don't buy 'em now, ma'am, I'm afraid nobody else will, for I've asked every body else."—"Come then," said the lady, laughing, "if that is the case I think I had better buy them all." So emptying all the fossils out of his basket, she put half a crown[7] into it. Jem's eyes sparkled with joy. "Oh, thank you, ma'am," said he, "I will be sure and bring you as many more to-morrow."—"Yes, but I don't promise you," said she, "to give you half a crown to-morrow."—"But, perhaps, though you don't promise it, you will."—"No," said the lady, "do not deceive yourself; I assure you that I will not. *That*, instead of encouraging you to be industrious, would teach you to be idle." Jem did not quite understand what she meant by this, but answered, "I'm sure I don't wish to be idle; what I want is to earn something every day, if I knew how: I'm sure I don't wish to be idle. If you knew all, you'd know I did not."—"How do you mean, *if I knew all?*"—"Why I mean, if you knew about Lightfoot."—"Who's Lightfoot?"—"Why, mammy's horse," added Jem, looking out of the window; "I must make haste home and feed him, afore it get dark; he'll wonder what's gone with me."—"Let him wonder a few minutes longer," said the lady, "and tell me the rest of your story."—"I've no story, ma'am, to tell, but as how mammy says he must go to the fair Monday fortnight to be sold, if she can't get the two guineas for her rent; and I should be main[8] sorry to part with him, for I love him, and he loves me; so I'll work for him, I will, all I can: to be sure, as mammy says, I have no chance, such a little fellow as I am, of earning two guineas afore Monday fortnight."—"But are you in earnest willing to work," said the lady; "you know there

6. An excavation or structure made to imitate a rocky cave, often adorned with shellwork; it was placed in the gardens of the wealthy to serve as a cool retreat.
7. A coin worth 2½ shillings.
8. Very, exceedingly.

is a great deal of difference between picking up a few stones, and working steadily every day, and all day long."—"But," said Jem, "I would work every day, and all day long."—"Then," said the lady, "I will give you work. Come here to-morrow morning, and my gardener will set you to weed the shrubberies, and I will pay you sixpence a day. Remember you must be at the gates by six o'clock." Jem bowed, thanked her, and went away. It was late in the evening, and he was impatient to get home to feed Lightfoot; yet he recollected that he had promised the man who had trusted him to sell the fossils that he would bring him half of what he got for them; so he thought that he had better go to him directly; and away he went, running along by the water side about a quarter of a mile, till he came to the man's house. He was just come home from work, and was surprised when Jem shewed him the half-crown, saying, "Look what I got for the stones; you are to have half, you know."—"No," said the man, when he had heard his story, "I shall not take half of that; it was given to you. I expected but a shilling at the most, and the half of that is but sixpence, and that I'll take.—Wife! give the lad two shillings, and take this half-crown." So wife opened an old glove, and took out two shillings; and the man, as she opened the glove, put in his fingers, and took out a little silver penny.[9]—There, he shall have that into the bargain for his honesty—Honesty is the best policy—There's a lucky penny for you, that I've kept ever since I can remember."—"Don't you ever go to part with it, do ye hear!" cried the woman. "Let him do what he will with it, wife," said the man. "But," argued the wife, "another penny would do just as well to buy gingerbread, and that's what it will go for."—"No, that it shall not, I promise you," said Jem; and so he ran away home, fed Lightfoot, stroked him, went to bed, jumped up at five o'clock in the morning, and went singing to work as gay as a lark.

Four days he worked "every day and all day long"; and the lady every evening, when she came out to walk in her gardens, looked at his work. At last she said to her gardener, "This little boy works very hard."—"Never had so good a little boy about the grounds," said the gardener; "he's always at his work, let me come by when I will, and he has got twice as much done as another would do; yes, twice as much, ma'am; for look here—he began at this here rose bush, and now he's got to where you stand, ma'am; and here is the day's work that t'other boy, and he's three years older too, did to-day—I say, measure Jem's fairly, and it's twice as much, I'm sure."—"Well, said the lady to her gardener, shew me how much is a fair good day's work for a boy of his age."—"Come at six o'clock, and go at six? why, about this much, ma'am," said the gardener, marking off a piece of the border with his spade. "Then, little boy," said the lady, "so much shall be your task every day; the gardener will mark it off for you: and when you've done, the rest of the day you may do what you please." Jem was extremely glad of this; and the next day he had finished his task by four o'clock, so that he had all the rest of the evening to himself. Jem was as fond of play as any little boy could be, and, when he was at it, played with all the eagerness and gaiety imaginable: so as soon as he had finished his task, fed Lightfoot, and put by the sixpence he had earned that day, he ran to the play ground in the village, where he found a party of boys playing, and amongst them Lazy Lawrence, who indeed was not playing, but lounging upon a gate with his thumb in his mouth. The rest were playing at cricket. Jem joined them, and was the merriest and most active amongst them; till, at last, when quite out of breath with running, he was obliged to give up to rest himself, and sat down upon the stile,[1] close to the gate on which Lazy Lawrence was swinging. "And why don't you play, Lawrence?" said he—"I'm tired,"

---

9. Most pennies were made of copper.

1. Steps for easy passage over a fence or wall.

said Lawrence.—"Tired of what?"—"I don't know well what tires me; grandmother says I'm ill, and I must take something—I don't know what ails me."—"Oh, pugh! take a good race, one, two, three, and away, and you'll find yourself as well as ever. Come, run—one, two, three, and away."—"Ah, no, I can't run indeed," said he, hanging back heavily; "you know I can play all day long if I like it, so I don't mind play as you do, who have only one hour for it."—"So much the worse for you. Come now, I'm quite fresh again, will you have one game at ball; do."—"No, I tell you I can't; I'm as tired as if I had been working all day long as hard as a horse."—"Ten times more," said Jem, "for I have been working all day long as hard as a horse, and yet you see I'm not a bit tired; only a little out of breath just now."—"That's very odd," said Lawrence, and yawned, for want of some better answer; then taking out a handful of halfpence—"See what I got from father to-day, because I asked him just at the right time, when he had drunk a glass or two; then I can get any thing I want out of him—see! a penny, two-pence, three-pence, four-pence—there's eight-pence in all; would not you be happy if you had *eight-pence?*"—"Why, I don't know," said Jem laughing, "for you don't seem happy, and you *have eight-pence.*"—"That does not signify though—I'm sure you only say that because you envy me—you don't know what it is to have eight-pence—you never had more than two-pence or three-pence at a time in all your life." Jem smiled. "Oh, as to that," said he, "you are mistaken, for I have at this very time more than two-pence, three-pence, or eight-pence either; I have—let me see—stones, two shillings; then five day's work, that's five sixpences, that's two shillings and sixpence, in all makes four shillings and six-pence, and my silver penny, is four and seven-pence. Four and seven-pence!"—"You have not!" said Lawrence, roused so as absolutely to stand upright; "four and seven-pence! have you? Shew it me, and then I'll believe you."—"Follow me then," cried Jem, "and I'll soon make you believe me; come."—"Is it far?" said Lawrence, following half running, half hobbling, till he came to the stable, where Jem shewed him his treasure. "And how did you come by it? honestly?"—"Honestly; to be sure I did; I earned it all."—"Lord bless me, earned it! well, I've a great mind to work; but then it's such hot weather; besides grandmother says I'm not strong enough yet for hard work; and besides, I know how to coax daddy out of money when I want it, so I need not work.—But four and seven-pence; let's see, what will you do with it all?"—"That's a secret," said Jem, looking great.[2] "I can guess; I know what I'd do with it if it was mine—First, I'd buy pockets full of gingerbread; then I'd buy ever so many apples and nuts; don't you love nuts? I'd buy nuts enough to last me from this time to Christmas, and I'd make little Newton crack 'em for me, for that's the worst of nuts, there's the trouble of cracking 'em."—"Well, you never deserve to have a nut."—"But you'll give me some of yours," said Lawrence in a fawning tone, for he thought it easier to coax than to work—"you'll give me some of your good things, won't you?"—"I shall not have any of those good things," said Jem. "Then what will you do with all your money?"—"Oh, I know very well what to do with it; but, as I told you, that's a secret, and I shan't tell it any body—Come now, let's go back and play—their game's up, I dare say."— Lawrence went back with him full of curiosity, and out of humour with himself and his eight-pence.—"If I had four and seven-pence," said he to himself, "I certainly should be happy!"

The next day, as usual, Jem jumped up before six o'clock and went to his work, whilst Lazy Lawrence sauntered about without knowing what to do with himself. In the course of two days he laid out six-pence of his money in apples and gingerbread,

2. Dignified.

and as long as these lasted he found himself well received by his companions; but at length the third day he spent his last halfpenny, and when it was gone, unfortunately some nuts tempted him very much, but he had no money to pay for them; so he ran home to coax his father, as he called it. When he got home, he heard his father talking very loud, and at first he thought he was drunk; but when he opened the kitchen door, he saw that he was not drunk, but angry.

"You lazy dog!" cried he, turning suddenly upon Lawrence, and gave him such a violent box on the ear as made the light flash from his eyes; "you lazy dog! see what you've done for me—look!—look, look, I say!" Lawrence looked as soon as he came to the use of his senses, and, with fear, amazement, and remorse, beheld at least a dozen bottles burst, and the fine Worcestershire cyder[3] streaming over the floor. "Now, did not I order you three days ago to carry these bottles to the cellar; and did not I charge you to wire the corks?[4] answer me, you lazy rascal; did not I?"—"Yes," said Lawrence, scratching his head. "And why was it not done? I ask you," cried his father with renewed anger, as another bottle burst at the moment. "What do you stand there for, you lazy brat? why don't you move? I say—No, no," catching hold of him, "I believe you can't move; but I'll make you." And he shook him, till Lawrence was so giddy he could not stand. "What had you to think of? what had you to do all day long, that you could not carry my cyder, my Worcestershire cyder to the cellar when I bid you? But go, you'll never be good for any thing, you are such a lazy rascal— get out of my sight!" So saying, he pushed him out of the house door, and Lawrence sneaked off, seeing that this was no time to make his petition for halfpence.

The next day he saw the nuts again, and, wishing for them more than ever, went home in hopes that his father, as he said to himself, would be in a better humour. But the cyder was still fresh in his recollection, and the moment Lawrence began to whisper the word "halfpenny" in his ear, his father swore, with a loud oath, "I will not give you a halfpenny, no, not a farthing,[5] for a month to come; if you want money, go work for it; I've had enough of your laziness—Go work!" At these terrible words Lawrence burst into tears, and, going to the side of a ditch, sat down and cried for an hour; and when he had cried till he could cry no more, he exerted himself so far as to empty his pockets, to see whether there might not happen to be one halfpenny left; and, to his great joy, in the farthest corner of his pocket one halfpenny was found. With this he proceeded to the fruit woman's stall. She was busy weighing out some plums, so he was obliged to wait; and, whilst he was waiting, he heard some people near him talking and laughing very loud. The fruit woman's stall was at the gate of an inn-yard; and peeping through the gate in this yard, Lawrence saw a postilion and stable-boy about his own size playing at pitch-farthing.[6] He stood by watching them for a few minutes. "I begun but with one halfpenny," cried the stable-boy with an oath, "and now I've got two-pence!" added he, jingling the halfpence in his waistcoat pocket. Lawrence was moved at the sound, and said to himself. "If I begin with one halfpenny, I may end like him with having two-pence; and it is easier to play at pitch-farthing than to work."

So he stepped forward, presenting his halfpenny, offering to toss up with the stable-boy, who, after looking him full in the face, accepted the proposal, and threw his halfpenny into the air. "Head or tail!" cried he. "Head," replied Lawrence, and it

3. I.e., hard or alcoholic cider. Worcestershire is a county in west central England.
4. I.e., to securely close the bottle.
5. A quarter of a penny.
6. A game played with coins; usually, unlike the tossing for heads or tails described here, it involved skill in pitching coins toward a hole. "Postilion": a postboy or messenger, or one who rides one of the horses pulling a coach or post chaise.

came up head. He seized the penny, surprised at his own success, and would have gone instantly to have laid it out in nuts; but the stable-boy stopped him, and tempted him to throw again. This time he lost; he threw again and won; and so he went on, sometimes losing, but most frequently winning, till half the morning was gone. At last, however, he chanced to win twice running, and, finding himself master of three halfpence, said he would play no more. The stable-boy, grumbling, swore he would have his revenge another time, and Lawrence went and bought the nuts. "It is a good thing," said he to himself, "to play at pitch-farthing: the next time I want a halfpenny I'll not ask my father for it, nor go to work neither." Satisfied with this resolution, he sat down to crack his nuts at his leisure, upon the horse-block[7] in the inn-yard. Here, whilst he eat, he overheard the conversation of the stable-boys and postillions. At first their shocking oaths and loud wrangling frightened and shocked him; for Lawrence, though a *lazy*, had not yet learned to be a *wicked* boy. But, by degrees, he was accustomed to their swearing and quarrelling, and took a delight and interest in their disputes and battles. As this was an amusement which he could enjoy without any sort of exertion on his part, he soon grew so fond of it, that every day he returned to the stable-yard, and the horse-block became his constant seat. Here he found some relief from the insupportable fatigue of doing nothing, and here, hour after hour, with his elbows on his knees, and his head on his hands, he sat the spectator of wickedness. Gaming, cheating, and lying, soon became familiar to him; and, to complete his ruin, he formed a sudden and close intimacy with the stable-boy with whom he had first began to game—a very bad boy. The consequences of this intimacy we shall presently see. But it is now time to inquire what little Jem has been doing all this while.

One day, after he had finished his task, the gardener asked him to stay a little while, to help him to carry some geranium pots into the hall. Jem, always active and obliging, readily stayed from play, and was carrying in a heavy flower-pot, when his mistress crossed the hall. "What a terrible litter!" said she, "you are making here— why don't you wipe your shoes upon the mat?" Jem turned round to look for the mat, but he saw none. "Oh," said the lady, recollecting herself, "I can't blame you, for there is no mat."—"No, ma'am," said the gardener, "nor I don't know when, if ever, the man will bring home those mats you bespoke,[8] ma'am."—"I am very sorry to hear that," said the lady, "I wish we could find somebody who would do them, if he can't—I should not care what sort of mats they were, so that one could wipe one's feet on them." Jem, as he was sweeping away the litter, when he heard these last words, said to himself, "perhaps I could make a mat." And all the way home, as he trudged along whistling, he was thinking over a scheme for making mats, which, however bold it may appear, he did not despair of executing, with patience and industry. Many were the difficulties which his "*prophetic eye*" foresaw; but he felt within himself that spirit, which spurs men on to great enterprizes, and makes them, "trample on impossibilities."[9]

He recollected, in the first place, that he had seen Lazy Lawrence, whilst he lounged upon the gate, twist a bit of heath[1] into different shapes, and he thought, that if he could find some way of plaiting heath firmly together, it would make a very pretty green, soft mat, which would do very well for one to wipe one's shoes on. About a mile from his mother's house, on the common[2] which Jem rode over when he went to farmer Truck's for the giant-strawberries, he remembered to have seen a great quantity of this heath; and, as it was now only six o'clock in the evening, he knew that he should have time to feed Lightfoot, stroak him, go to the common, return, and make one trial of his skill before he went to bed.

Lightfoot carried him swiftly to the common, and there Jem gathered as much of the heath as he thought he should want. But, what toil, what time, what pains did it cost him, before he could make any thing like a mat! Twenty times he was ready to throw aside the heath, and give up his project, from impatience of repeated disappointments. But still he persevered. Nothing *truly great* can be accomplished without toil and time. Two hours he worked before he went to bed. All his play hours the next day he spent at his mat; which, in all, made five hours of fruitless attempts— The sixth, however, repaid him for the labours of the other five; he conquered his grand difficulty of fastening the heath substantially together, and at length completely finished a mat, which far surpassed his most sanguine expectations. He was extremely happy—sung, danced round it—whistled—looked at it again and again, and could hardly leave off looking at it when it was time to go to bed. He laid it by his bed-side, that he might see it the moment he awoke in the morning.

And now came the grand pleasure of carrying it to his mistress. She looked full as much surprised as he expected, when she saw it, and when she heard who made it. After having duly admired it, she asked him how much he expected for his mat. "Expect!—Nothing, ma'am," said Jem; "I meant to give it you, if you'd have it; I did not mean to sell it. I made it at my play hours, and I was very happy making it; and I'm very glad too that you like it; and if you please to keep it, ma'am—that's all."— "But that's not all," said the lady. "Spend your time no more in weeding in my garden, you can employ yourself much better; you shall have the reward of your ingenuity as well as of your industry. Make as many more such mats as you can, and I will take care and dispose of them for you."—"Thank'e, ma'am," said Jem, making his best bow, for he thought by the lady's looks that she meant to do him a favour, though he repeated to himself, "dispose of them, what does that mean?"

The next day he went to work to make more mats, and he soon learned to make them so well and quickly, that he was surprised at his own success. In every one he made he found less difficulty, so that, instead of making two, he could soon make four, in a day. In a fortnight he made eighteen. It was Saturday night when he finished, and he carried, at three journeys, his eighteen mats to his mistress's house; piled them all up in the hall, and stood with his hat off, with a look of proud humility, beside the pile, waiting for his mistress's appearance. Presently a folding door, at one end of the hall, opened, and he saw his mistress, with a great many gentlemen and ladies, rising from several tables.

"Oh! there is my little boy, and his mats," cried the lady; and, followed by all the rest of the company, she came into the hall. Jem modestly retired whilst they looked at his mats; but in a minute or two his mistress beckoned to him, and, when he came into the middle of the circle, he saw that his pile of mats had disappeared. "Well," said the lady smiling, "what do you see that makes you look so surprised?"—"That all my mats are gone," said Jem; "but you are very welcome."—"Are we?" said the lady; "well, take up your hat, and go home then, for you see that it is getting late, and you know Lightfoot will wonder what's become of you." Jem turned round to take up his hat, which he had left on the floor.

But how his countenance changed! the hat was heavy with shillings. Every one who had taken a mat had put in two shillings; so that for the eighteen mats he had got thirty-six shillings. "Thirty-six shillings!" said the lady; "five and seven-pence I think you told me you had earned already—how much does that make? I must add, I believe, one other six-pence to make out your two guineas."—"Two guineas!" exclaimed Jem, now quite conquering his bashfulness, for at the moment he forgot where he was, and saw nobody that was by: "Two guineas!" cried he, clapping his hands together—"Oh Lightfoot!—oh mother!" Then, recollecting himself, he saw his mistress, whom he now looked up to quite as a friend. "Will *you* thank them all," said he, scarcely daring to glance his eye round upon the company, "will *you* thank 'em, for you know I don't know how to thank 'em *rightly*." Every body thought, however, that they had been thanked *rightly*.

"Now we won't keep you any longer—only," said his mistress, "I have one thing to ask you, that I may be by when you shew your treasure to your mother."—"Come, then," said Jem, "come with me now."—"Not now," said the lady laughing, "but I will come to Ashton to-morrow evening; perhaps your mother can find me a few strawberries."

"That she will," said Jem; "I'll search the garden myself." He now went home, but felt it a great restraint to wait till to-morrow evening before he told his mother. To console himself he flew to the stable: "Lightfoot, you're not to be sold tomorrow! poor fellow!" said he, patting him, and then could not refrain from counting out his money. Whilst he was intent upon this, Jem was startled by a noise at the door: somebody was trying to pull up the latch. It opened, and there came in Lazy Lawrence, with a boy in a red jacket, who had a cock under his arm. They started when they got into the middle of the stable, and when they saw Jem, who had been at first hidden by the horse.

"We—we—we came"—stammered Lazy Lawrence—"I mean, I came to—to—to—" "To ask you," continued the stable-boy in a bold tone, "whether you will go with us to the cock-fight on Monday? See, I've a fine cock here, and Lawrence told me you were a great friend of his, so I came."

Lawrence now attempted to say something in praise of the pleasures of cock-fighting, and in recommendation of his new companion. But Jem looked at the stable-boy with dislike, and a sort of dread; then turning his eyes upon the cock with a look of compassion, said in a low voice to Lawrence, "Shall you like to stand by and see its eyes pecked out?"—"I don't know," said Lawrence, "as to that; but they say a cock-fight's a fine sight, and it's no more cruel in me to go than another; and a great many go; and I've nothing else to do, so I shall go."—"But I have something else to do," said Jem, laughing, "so I shall not go."—"But," continued Lawrence, "you know Monday is the great Bristol fair, and one must be merry then, of all days in the year."— "One day in the year, sure there's no harm in being merry," said the stable-boy. "I hope not," said Jem; "for I know, for my part, I am merry every day in the year."— "That's very odd," said Lawrence; "but I know, for my part, I would not for all the world miss going to the fair, for at least it will be something to talk of for half a year after—come, you'll go, won't you?"—"No," said Jem, still looking as if he did not like to talk before the ill-looking stranger. "Then what will you do with all your money?"— "I'll tell you about that another time," whispered Jem; "and don't you go to see that cock's eyes pecked out; it won't make you merry, I'm sure."—"If I had any thing else to divert me," said Lawrence, hesitating and yawning.—"Come," cried the stable-boy, seizing his stretching arm, "come along," cried he; and, pulling him away from Jem, upon whom he cast a look of extreme contempt, "leave him alone, he's not the sort."—"What a fool you are," said he to Lawrence, the moment he got him out of the stable, "you might have known he would not go—else we should soon have trimmed him out of his four and seven-pence. But how came you to talk of four and seven-pence; I saw in the manger a hat full of silver."—"Indeed!" exclaimed Lawrence. "Yes, indeed—but why did you stammer so when we first got in? you had like to have blown us all up."[3]—"I was so ashamed," said Lawrence, hanging down his head. "Ashamed! but you must not talk of shame now you are in for it, and I shan't let you off: you owe us half a crown, recollect, and I must be paid to-night; so see and get the money some how or other." After a considerable pause he added, "I'll answer for it he'd never miss half a crown out of all that silver."—"But to steal," said Lawrence, drawing back with horror—"I never thought I should come to that—and from poor Jem too—the money that he has worked so hard for too."—"But it is not stealing; we don't mean to steal; only to borrow it: and, if we win, as we certainly shall, at the cock-fight, pay it back again, and he'll never know any thing of the matter; and what harm will it do him? Besides, what signifies talking, you can't go to the cock-fight, or the fair either, if you don't; and I tell ye we don't mean to steal it; we'll pay it again on Monday night." Lawrence made no reply, and they parted without his coming to any determination.

Here let us pause in our story—we are almost afraid to go on—the rest is very shocking—our little readers will shudder as they read. But it is better that they should know the truth, and see what the idle boy came to at last.

In the dead of the night Lawrence heard somebody tap at his window. He knew well who it was, for this was the signal agreed upon between him and his wicked companion. He trembled at the thoughts of what he was about to do, and lay quite still, with his head under the bed-clothes, till he heard the second tap. Then he got up, dressed himself, and opened his window. It was almost even with the ground. His companion said to him in a hollow voice, "Are you ready." He made no answer, but got out of the window and followed. When he got to the stable, a black cloud was just passing over the moon, and it was quite dark. "Where are you?" whispered Lawrence, groping about, "where are you? Speak to me." "I am here; give me your hand." Lawrence stretched out his hand. "Is that your hand?" said the wicked boy, as Lawrence laid hold of him; "how cold it felt."—"Let us go back," said Lawrence; "it is time yet."—"It is no time to go back," replied the other opening the door; "you've gone too far now to go back:" and he pushed Lawrence into the stable.—"Have you found it—take care of the horse—have you done?—what are you about?—make haste, I hear a noise," said the stable-boy, who watched at the door. "I am feeling for the half crown, but I can't find it."—"Bring all together." He brought Jem's broken flower-pot, with all the money in it, to the door.

The black cloud was now passed over the moon, and the light shone full upon them.—"What do we stand here for?" said the stable-boy, snatching the flower-pot out of Lawrence's trembling hands, and pulled him away from the door. "Good God!" cried Lawrence, "you won't take all—you said you'd only take half a crown, and pay it back on Monday—you said you'd only take half a crown!"—"Hold your tongue," replied the other walking on, deaf to all remonstrances—"if I am to be hanged ever, it sha'n't be for half a crown." Lawrence's blood ran cold in his veins, and he felt as if all his hair stood on end. Not another word passed. His accomplice carried off the money, and Lawrence crept, with all the horrors of guilt upon him, to his restless bed. All night he was starting from frightful dreams; or else, broad awake, he lay listening to every small noise, unable to stir, and scarcely daring to breathe—tormented by that most dreadful of all kinds of fear, that fear which is the constant companion of an evil conscience. He thought the morning would never come; but

---

3. I.e., betrayed us.

when it was day, when he heard the birds sing, and saw every thing look cheerful as usual, he felt still more miserable. It was Sunday morning, and the bell rang for church. All the children of the village, dressed in their Sunday clothes, innocent and gay, and little Jem, the best and gayest amongst them, went flocking by his door to church. "Well, Lawrence," said Jem, pulling his coat as he passed, and saw Lawrence leaning against his father's door, "what makes you look so black?" "I!" said Lawrence, starting, "why do you say that I look black?"—"Nay then," said Jem, "you look white enough now, if that will please you; for you're turned as pale as death."—"Pale!" replied Lawrence, not knowing what he said; and turned abruptly away, for he dared not stand another look of Jem's; conscious that guilt was written in his face, he shunned every eye. He would now have given the world to have thrown off the load of guilt which lay upon his mind; he longed to follow Jem, to fall upon his knees, and confess all; dreading the moment when Jem should discover his loss, Lawrence dared not stay at home, and not knowing what to do, or where to go, he mechanically went to his old haunt at the stable-yard, and lurked thereabouts all day, with his accomplice, who tried in vain to quiet his fears and raise his spirits, by talking of the next day's cock-fight. It was agreed, that, as soon as the dusk of the evening came on, they should go together into a certain lonely field, and there divide their booty.

In the mean time Jem, when he returned from church, was very full of business, preparing for the reception of his mistress, of whose intended visit he had informed his mother; and, whilst she was arranging the kitchen and their little parlour, he ran to search the strawberry-beds. "Why, my Jem, how merry you are to-day!" said his mother when he came in with the strawberries, and was jumping about the room playfully. "Now keep those spirits of yours, Jem, till you want 'em, and don't let it come upon you all at once. Have it in mind that to-morrow's fair day, and Lightfoot must go. I bid farmer Truck call for him to-night; he said he'd take him along with his own, and he'll be here just now—and then I know how it will be with you, Jem!"— "So do I!" cried Jem, swallowing his secret with great difficulty, and then tumbling head over heels four times running. A carriage passed the window and stopped at the door. Jem ran out; it was his mistress. She came in smiling, and soon made the old woman smile too, by praising the neatness of every thing in the house. But we shall pass over, however important they were deemed at the time, the praises of the strawberries, and of "my grandmother's china plate."[4] Another knock was heard at the door. "Run, Jem," said his mother, "I hope it's our milk-woman with cream for the lady."—No; it was farmer Truck come for Lightfoot. The old woman's countenance fell. "Fetch him out, dear," said she, turning to her son; but Jem was gone; he flew out to the stable the moment he saw the flap of farmer Truck's great-coat.— "Sit ye down, farmer," said the old woman, after they had waited about five minutes in expectation of Jem's return. "You'd best sit down, if the lady will give you leave; for he'll not hurry himself back again. My boy's a fool, madam, about that there horse." Trying to laugh, she added, "I knew how Lightfoot and he would be loath enough to part—he won't bring him out till the last minute; so do sit ye down, neighbour." The farmer had scarcely sat down, when Jem, with a pale wild countenance, came back. "What's the matter?" said his mistress. "God bless the boy!" said his mother, looking at him quite frightened, whilst he tried to speak, but could not. She went up to him, and then leaning his head against her, he cried, "It's gone!— it's all gone!" and, bursting into tears, he sobbed as if his little heart would break. "What's gone, love?" said his mother. "My two guineas—Lightfoot's two guineas. I

---

4. I.e., dishes.

went to fetch 'em to give you, mammy; but the broken flower-pot that I put them in, and all's gone!—quite gone!" repeated he, checking his sobs. "I saw them safe last night, and was shewing 'em to Lightfoot; and I was so glad to think I had earned them all myself; and I thought how surprised you'd look, and how glad you'd be, and how you'd kiss me, and all!"

His mother listened to him with the greatest surprise, whilst his mistress stood in silence, looking first at the old woman, and then at Jem with a penetrating eye, as if she suspected[5] the truth of his story, and was afraid of becoming the dupe of her own compassion. "This is a very strange thing!" said she gravely. "How came you to leave all your money in a broken flower-pot in the stable? How came you not to give it to your mother to take care of?"—"Why, don't you remember," said Jem, looking up in the midst of his tears; "why, don't you remember you your own self bid me not tell her about it till you were by."—"And did you not tell her?"—"Nay, ask mammy," said Jem, a little offended; and, when afterwards the lady went on questioning him in a severe manner, as if she did not believe him, he at last made no answer. "Oh, Jem! Jem! why don't you speak to the lady?" said his mother. "I have spoke, and spoke the truth," said Jem, proudly, "and she did not believe me."

Still the lady, who had lived too long in the world to be without suspicion, maintained a cold manner, and determined to wait the event[6] without interfering, saying only, that she hoped the money would be found; and advised Jem to have done crying. "I have done," said Jem, "I shall cry no more." And as he had the greatest command over himself, he actually did not shed another tear, not even when the farmer got up to go, saying, he could wait no longer. Jem silently went to bring out Lightfoot.— The lady now took her seat where she could see all that passed at the open parlour window.—The old woman stood at the door, and several idle people of the village, who had gathered round the lady's carriage examining it, turned about to listen. In a minute or two Jem appeared, with a steady countenance, leading Lightfoot; and, when he came up, without saying a word, put the bridle into farmer Truck's hand. "He *has been* a good horse," said the farmer. "He *is* a good horse!" cried Jem, and threw his arm over Lightfoot's neck, hiding his own face as he leaned upon him.

At this instant a party of milkwomen went by; and one of them having set down her pail, came behind Jem, and gave him a pretty smart blow upon the back.—He looked up.—"And don't you know me?" said she. "I forget," said Jem; "I think I have seen your face before, but I forget."—"Do you so? and you'll tell me just now," said she, half opening her hand, "that you forgot who gave you this, and who charged you not to part with it too." Here she quite opened her large hand, and on the palm of it appeared Jem's silver penny. "Where?" exclaimed Jem, seizing it, "oh where did you find it? and have you?—oh tell me, have you got the rest of my money?"—"I know nothing of your money—I don't know what you would be at," said the milkwoman. "But where, pray tell me where, did you find this"—"With them that you gave it to, I suppose," said the milkwoman, turning away suddenly to take up her milk-pail. But now Jem's mistress called to her through the window, begging her to stop, and joining in his entreaties to know how she came by the silver penny.

"Why, madam," said she, taking up the corner of her apron, "I came by it in an odd way too—You must know my Betty is sick, so I come with the milk myself, though it's not what I'm used to; for my Betty—you know my Betty," said she, turning round to the old woman, "my Betty serves you, and she's a tight and stirring lassy,[7] ma'am,

---

5. Had doubts about.
6. Outcome.

7. A neat and hardworking girl.

I can assure—" "Yes, I don't doubt it," said the lady impatiently; "but about the silver penny?"—"Why, that's true; as I was coming along all alone, for the rest came a round, and I came a short cut across yon field—No, you can't see it, madam, where you stand—but if you were here—" "I see it—I know it," said Jem, out of breath with anxiety. "Well—well—I rested my pail upon the stile, and sets me down awhile, and there comes out of the hedge—I don't know well how, for they startled me so I'd like to have thrown down my milk—two boys, one about the size of he," said she, pointing to Jem, "and one a matter taller, but ill-looking like, so I did not think to stir to make way for them, and they were like in a desperate hurry: so, without waiting for the stile, one of 'em pulled at the gate, and when it would not open (for it was tied with a pretty stout cord) one of 'em whips out with his knife and cuts it——

"Now have you a knife about you, Sir?" continued the milk-woman to the farmer. He gave her his knife.

"Here now, ma'am, just sticking as it were here, between the blade and the haft, was the silver penny. He took no notice, but when he opened it, out it falls; still he takes no heed, but cuts the cord, as I said before, and through the gate they went, and out of sight in half a minute. I picks up the penny, for my heart misgave me that it was the very one husband had had a long time, and had given against my voice to he," pointing to Jem; "and I charged him not to part with it; and, ma'am, when I looked I knew it by the mark, so I thought I would shew it to *he*," again pointing to Jem, "and let him give it back to those it belongs to."—"It belongs to me," said Jem, "I never gave it to any body—but—" "But," cried the farmer, "those boys have robbed him—it is they who have all his money."—"Oh, which way did they go?" cried Jem, "I'll run after them."

"No, no," said the lady, calling to her servant; and she desired him to take his horse and ride after them. "Aye," added farmer Truck, "do you take the road, and I'll take the field-way, and I'll be bound we'll have 'em presently."

Whilst they were gone in pursuit of the thieves, the lady, who was now thoroughly convinced of Jem's truth, desired her coachman would produce what she had ordered him to bring with him that evening. Out of the boot[8] of the carriage the coachman immediately produced a new saddle and bridle.

How Jem's eyes sparkled when the saddle was thrown upon Lightfoot's back! "Put it on your horse yourself, Jem," said the lady—"it is yours."

Confused reports of Lightfoot's splendid accoutrements, of the pursuit of thieves, and of the fine and generous lady, who was standing at dame Preston's window, quickly spread through the village, and drew every body from their houses. They crouded round Jem to hear the story. The children especially, who were all fond of him, expressed the strongest indignation against the thieves. Every eye was on the stretch; and now some, who had run down the lane, came back shouting, "Here they are! they've got the thieves!"

The footman on horseback carried one boy before him; and the farmer, striding along, dragged another. The latter had on a red jacket, which little Jem immediately recollected, and scarcely dared lift his eyes to look at the boy on horseback. "Good God!" said he to himself, "it must be—yet surely it can't be Lawrence!" The footman rode on as fast as the people would let him. The boy's hat was slouched, and his head hung down, so that nobody could see his face.

At this instant there was a disturbance in the crowd. A man who was half drunk pushed his way forwards, swearing that nobody should stop him; that he had a right to see; and he *would* see. And so he did; for, forcing through all resistance, he stag-

8. A receptacle for storing luggage, located behind the body of the carriage or under the coachman's seat.

gered up to the footman just as he was lifting down the boy he had carried before him. "I *will*—I tell you I *will* see the thief!" cried the drunken man, pushing up the boy's hat.—It was his own son.—"Lawrence!" exclaimed the wretched father. The shock sobered him at once, and he hid his face in his hands.

There was an awful silence. Lawrence fell on his knees, and in a voice that could scarcely be heard, made a full confession of all the circumstances of his guilt. "Such a young creature so wicked! What could put such wickedness into your head?"—"Bad company," said Lawrence. "And how came you—what brought you into bad company?"—"I don't know—except it was idleness." While this was saying, the farmer was emptying Lazy Lawrence's pockets; and when the money appeared, all his former companions in the village looked at each other with astonishment and terror. Their parents grasped their little hands closer, and cried, "Thank God! he is not my son—how often, when he was little, we used, as he lounged about, to tell him that idleness was the root of all evil."

As for the hardened wretch his accomplice, every one, every one was impatient to have him sent to gaol.[9] He had put on a bold, insolent countenance, till he heard Lawrence's confession; till the money was found upon him; and he heard the milk-woman declare, that she would swear to the silver penny which he had dropped. Then he turned pale, and betrayed the strongest signs of fear. "We must take him before the justice," said the farmer, "and he'll be lodged in Bristol gaol. "Oh!" said Jem, springing forwards when Lawrence's hands were going to be tied, "let him go—won't you—can't you let him go?"—"Yes, madam, for mercy's sake," said Jem's mother to the lady, "think what a disgrace to his family to be sent to gaol." His father stood by wringing his hands in an agony of despair. "It's all my fault," cried he; "I brought him up in *idleness*."—"But he'll never be idle any more," said Jem; "won't you speak for him, ma'am?"—"Don't ask the lady to speak for him," said the farmer; "it's better he should go to bridewell[1] now, than to the gallows by and by."

Nothing more was said, for every body felt the truth of the farmer's speech. Lawrence was sent to bridewell for a month, and the stable-boy was transported to Botany Bay.[2]

During Lawrence's confinement, Jem often visited him, and carried him such little presents as he could afford to give; and Jem could afford to be *generous* because he was *industrious*. Lawrence's heart was touched by his kindness, and his example struck him so forcibly, that, when his confinement was ended, he resolved to set immediately to work; and, to the astonishment of all who knew him, soon became remarkable for industry; he was found early and late at his work, established a new character, and for ever lost the name of *Lazy Lawrence*.

The Birth-day Present

"Mamma," said Rosamond, after a long silence, "do you know, what I have been thinking of all this time?"

"No, my dear.—What?"

"Why, mamma, about my cousin Bell's birth-day; do you know what day it is?"

"No, I don't remember."

9. I.e., jail.
1. A prison or house of correction.
2. An inlet of the Tasman Sea in southeast Australia, and the common name of Australia's first penal colony (actually located at nearby Sydney Harbor). Between 1787 and 1853, tens of thousands of British convicts were sent there to labor.

"Dear mother! don't you remember it's the 22d of December; and her birth-day is the day after to-morrow?—Don't you recollect now? But you never remember about birth-days, mamma: that was just what I was thinking of, that you never remember my sister Laura's birth-day, or—or—or *mine*, mamma?"

"What do you mean, my dear? I remember your birth-day perfectly well."

"Indeed! but you never *keep* it though."

"What do you mean by keeping your birth-day?"

"Oh, mamma, you know very well—as Bell's birth-day is kept.—In the first place there is a great dinner."

"And can Bell eat more upon her birth-day than upon any other day?"

"No; nor I should not mind about the dinner, except the mince pies.[3] But Bell has a great many nice things; I don't mean nice eatable things, but nice new playthings given to her always on her birth-day; and every body drinks her health, and she's so happy."

"But stay, Rosamond, how you jumble things together! Is it every body's drinking her health, that makes her so happy; or the new playthings, or the nice mince pies? I can easily believe, that she is happy whilst she is eating a mince pie, or whilst she is playing; but how does every body's drinking her health at dinner make her happy?"

Rosamond paused, and then said she did not know. "But," added she, "the *nice new* playthings mother!"

"But why the nice new playthings? Do you like them only because they are *new?*"

"Not *only*—I do not like playthings *only* because they are new, but Bell *does* I believe—for that puts me in mind—Do you know, mother, she had a great drawerfull of *old* playthings that she never used, and she said that they were good for nothing, because they were *old*; but I thought many of them were good for a great deal more than the new ones.—Now you shall be judge, mamma; I'll tell you all that was in the drawer."

"Nay, Rosamond, thank you, not just now; I have not time to listen to you."

"Well then, mamma, the day after to-morrow I can shew you the drawer: I want you to be judge very much, because I am sure I was in the right.—And, mother," added Rosamond, stopping her as she was going out of the room, "will you—not now, but when you've time—will you tell me why you never keep my birth-day—why you never make any difference between that day and any other day?"

"And will you, Rosamond—not now, but when you have time to think about it— tell me why I should make any difference between your birth-day and any other day?"

Rosamond thought—but she could not find out any reason: besides, she suddenly recollected, that she had not time to think any longer, for there was a certain work basket to be finished, which she was making for her cousin Bell, as a present upon her birth-day. The work was at a stand for want of some filigree paper,[4] and as her mother was going out she asked her to take her with her, that she might buy some. Her sister Laura went with them.

"Sister," said Rosamond, as they were walking along, "what have you done with your half-guinea?"[5]

"I have it in my pocket."

"Dear! you will keep it for ever in your pocket: you know my god-mother, when she gave it to you, said you would keep it longer than I should keep mine; and I know

---

3. I.e., mincemeat pies, made with a finely chopped mixture of dried fruit, nuts, suet, etc.
4. Delicate paper made with threads and beads.

"Stand": standstill.
5. English gold coin worth 10½ shillings.

what she thought by her look at the time. I heard her say something to my mother."

"Yes," said Laura, smiling, "she whispered so loud, that I could not help hearing her too: she said I was a little miser."

"But did not you hear her say that I was very *generous?* and she'll see that she was not mistaken. I hope she'll be by when I give my basket to Bell—won't it be beautiful?—there is to be a wreath of myrtle, you know, round the handle, and a frost ground, and then the medallions[6]——"

"Stay," interrupted her sister; for Rosamond, anticipating the glories of her work-basket, talked and walked so fast, that she had passed, without perceiving it, the shop where the filigree paper was to be bought. They turned back. Now it happened, that the shop was the corner house of a street, and one of the windows looked out into a narrow lane: a coach full of ladies stopped at the door just before they went in, so that no one had time immediately to think of Rosamond and her filigree paper, and she went to the window, where she saw, that her sister Laura was looking earnestly at something that was passing in the lane.

Opposite to the window, at the door of a poor looking house, there was sitting a little girl weaving lace. Her bobbins[7] moved as quick as lightning, and she never once looked up from her work.

"Is not she very industrious?" said Laura; "and very honest too," added she in a minute afterwards; for just then, a baker with a basket of rolls on his head passed, and by accident one of the rolls fell close to the little girl: she took it up eagerly, looked at it as if she was very hungry, then put aside her work, and ran after the baker to return it to him.

Whilst she was gone, a footman in a livery laced with silver, who belonged to the coach that stood at the shop door, as he was lounging with one of his companions, chanced to spy the weaving pillow,[8] which she had left upon a stone before the door. To divert himself (for idle people do mischief often to divert themselves) he took up the pillow, and entangled all the bobbins. The little girl came back out of breath to her work; but what was her surprize and sorrow to find it spoiled: she twisted and untwisted, placed and replaced the bobbins, while the footman stood laughing at her distress. She got up gently, and was retiring into the house, when the silver-laced footman stopped her, saying insolently—"Sit still, child."

"I must go to my mother, sir," said the child; "besides, you have spoiled all my lace—I can't stay."

"Can't you," said the brutal footman, snatching her weaving pillow again, "I'll teach you to complain of me." And he broke off, one after another, all the bobbins, put them into his pocket, rolled her weaving pillow down the dirty lane, then jumped up behind his mistress's coach, and was out of sight in an instant.

"Poor girl!" exclaimed Rosamond, no longer able to restrain her indignation at this injustice: "Poor little girl!"

At this instant her mother said to Rosamond—"Come now, my dear, if you want this filigree paper, buy it."

"Yes, madam," said Rosamond; and the idea of what her godmother and her cousin Bell would think of her generosity rushed again upon her imagination. All her feelings of pity were immediately suppressed. Satisfied with bestowing another exclamation upon the "*Poor little girl,*" she went to spend her half-guinea upon her filigree basket.

---

6. Medals. "Frost ground": silver-gray underlying surface.

7. Reels or spools used in making lace.

8. A padded or stuffed support or ground upon which fine linen lace is made. "Livery": a servant's uniform, distinct to each household.

In the mean time, she that was called the *little miser*, beckoned to the poor girl, and opening the window said, pointing to the cushion, "Is it quite spoiled?"

"Quite! quite spoiled! and I can't, nor mother neither, buy another; and I can't do any thing else for my bread."—A few, but very few, tears fell as she said this.

"How much would another cost?" said Laura.

"Oh, a great—*great* deal."

"More than that?" said Laura, holding up her half-guinea.

"Oh, no."

"Then you can buy another with that," said Laura, dropping the half-guinea into her hand, and she shut the window before the child could find words to thank her; but not before she saw a look of joy and gratitude, which gave Laura more pleasure probably than all the praise, which could have been bestowed upon her generosity.

Late on the morning of her cousin's birth-day, Rosamond finished her work-basket. The carriage was at the door—Laura came running to call her; her father's voice was heard at the same instant; so she was obliged to go down with her basket but half wrapped up in silver paper, a circumstance at which she was a good deal disconcerted; for the pleasure of surprising Bell would be utterly lost, if one bit of the filigree should peep out before the proper time. As the carriage went on, Rosamond pulled the paper to one side and to the other, and by each of the four corners.

"It will never do, my dear," said her father, who had been watching her operations; "I am afraid you will never make a sheet of paper cover a box, which is twice as large as itself."

"It is not a box, father," said Rosamond, a little peevishly; "it's a basket."

"Let us look at this basket," said he, taking it out of her unwilling hands; for she knew of what frail materials it was made, and she dreaded its coming to pieces under her father's examination.

He took hold of the handle rather roughly, and starting off the coach seat, she cried—

"Oh, sir! father! sir! you will spoil it indeed!" said she with increased vehemence, when, after drawing aside the veil of silver paper, she saw him grasp the myrtle-wreathed handle.

"Indeed, sir, you will spoil the poor handle."

"But what is the use of *the poor handle*," said her father, "if we are not to take hold of it? And pray," continued he, turning the basket round with his finger and thumb, rather in a disrespectful manner—"pray is this the thing you have been about all this week? I have seen you all this week dabbling with paste and rags; I could not conceive what you were about—Is this the thing?"

"Yes, sir—You think then that I have wasted my time, because the basket is of no use: but then it is for a present for my cousin Bell."

"Your cousin Bell will be very much obliged to you for a present that is of no use; you had better have given her the purple jar."[9]

"Oh, father! I thought you had forgotten that—it was two years ago; I'm not so silly now. But Bell will like the basket I know, though it is of no use."

"Then you think Bell is sillier *now*, than you were two years ago.—Well, perhaps that is true; but how comes it, Rosamond, now that you are so wise, that you are fond of such a silly person?"

9. See *Early Lessons*, published by J. Johnson. The allusion is to one of Edgeworth's most famous stories, "Rosamond and the Purple Jar" (1801), first published in *The Parent's Assistant* in 1796, omitted from the 1800 edition, and transferred to *Early Lessons* in 1801.

"I, father?" said Rosamond, hesitating; "I don't think I am *very* fond of her."

"I did not say *very* fond."

"Well, but I don't think I am at all fond of her."

"But you have spent a whole week in making this thing for her."

"Yes, and all my half-guinea besides."

"Yet you think her silly, and you are not fond of her at all; and you say you know this thing will be of no use to her."

"But it is her birth-day, sir; and I am sure she will *expect* something, and every body else will give her something."

"Then your reason for giving is because she expects you to give her something. And will you, or can you, or should you always give, merely because others *expect*, or because somebody else gives?"

"Always!—no, not always."

"Oh, only on birth-days."

Rosamond, laughing, "Now you are making a joke of me, papa, I see; but I thought you liked that people should be generous—my godmother said that she did."

"So do I, full as well as your godmother; but we have not yet quite settled what it is to be generous."

"Why, is it not generous to make presents?" said Rosamond.

"That is a question, which it would take up a great deal of time to answer. But, for instance, to make a present of a thing, that you know can be of no use, to a person you neither love nor esteem, because it is her birth-day, and because every body gives her something, and because she expects something, and because your godmother says she likes that people should be generous, seems to me, my dear Rosamond, to be, since I must say it, rather more like folly than generosity."

Rosamond looked down upon the basket, and was silent.

"Then I am a fool! am I?" said she, looking up at last.

"Because you have made *one* mistake?—No. If you have sense enough to see your own mistakes, and can afterwards avoid them, you will never be a fool."

Here the carriage stopped, and Rosamond recollected, that the basket was uncovered.

Now we must observe, that Rosamond's father had not been too severe upon Bell, when he called her a silly girl. From her infancy she had been humoured; and at eight years old she had the misfortune to be a spoiled child: she was idle, fretful, and selfish, so that nothing could make her happy. On her birth-day she expected, however, to be perfectly happy. Every body in the house tried to please her, and they succeeded so well, that between breakfast and dinner she had only six fits of crying. The cause of five of these fits no one could discover; but the last, and most lamentable, was occasioned by a disappointment about a worked muslin frock,[1] and accordingly at dressing-time her maid brought it to her, exclaiming—"See here miss! what your mamma has sent you on your birth-day—Here's a frock fit for a queen—if it had but lace round the cuffs."

"And why has not it lace round the cuffs? mamma said it should."

"Yes, but mistress was disappointed about the lace; it is not come home."[2]

"Not come home, indeed! and didn't they know it was my birth-day? But then I say I won't wear it without the lace—I can't wear it without the lace—and I won't."

---

1. A long muslin dress ornamented with needle-work or embroidery. 2. I.e., has not yet been delivered.

The lace, however, could not be had; and Bell at length submitted to let the frock be put on. "Come, Miss Bell, dry your eyes," said the maid who *educated* her; "dry your eyes, and I'll tell you something, that will please you."

"What, then?" said the child, pouting and sobbing.

"Why——but you must not tell, that I told you."

"No—but if I am asked?"

"Why, if you are asked, you must tell the truth to be sure.—So I'll hold my tongue, miss."

"Nay, tell me though, and I'll never tell—if I *am* asked."

"Well, then," said the maid, "your cousin Rosamond is come, and has brought you the most *beautifullest* thing you ever saw in your life; but you are not to know any thing about it till after dinner, because she wants to surprise you; and mistress has put it into her wardrobe till after dinner."

"Till after dinner!" repeated Bell, impatiently; "I can't wait till then, I must see it this minute."

The maid refused her several times, till Bell burst into another fit of crying, and the maid, fearing that her mistress would be angry with *her*, if Bell's eyes were red at dinner-time, consented to shew her the basket.

"How pretty!—But let me have it in my own hands," said Bell, as the maid held the basket up out of her reach.

"Oh no, you must not touch it; for if you should spoil it, what would become of me?"

"Become of you indeed!" exclaimed the spoiled child, who never considered any thing but her own immediate gratification—"Become of *you*, indeed! what signifies that—I shan't spoil it; and I will have it in my own hands.—If you don't hold it down for me directly, I'll tell that you shewed it to me."

"Then you won't snatch it?"

"No, no, I won't indeed," said Bell; but she had learned from her maid a total disregard of truth.—She snatched the basket the moment it was within her reach; a struggle ensued, in which the handle and lid were torn off, and one of the medallions crushed inwards, before the little fury returned to her senses. Calmed at this sight, the next question was, how she should conceal the mischief, which she had done. After many attempts, the handle and lid were replaced, the basket was put exactly in the same spot in which it had stood before, and the maid charged the child, "*to look as if nothing was the matter.*"

We hope that both children and parents will here pause for a moment to reflect.— The habits of tyranny, meanness, and falsehood, which children acquire from living with bad servants, are scarcely ever conquered in the whole course of their future lives.

After shutting up the basket they left the room, and in the adjoining passage they found a poor girl waiting with a small parcel in her hand.

"What's your business?" said the maid.

"I have brought home the lace, madam, that was bespoke for the young lady."

"Oh, you have, have you, at last?" said Bell; "and pray why didn't you bring it sooner?"

The girl was going to answer, but the maid interrupted her, saying—"Come, come, none of your excuses; you are a little idle good for nothing thing, to disappoint Miss Bell upon her birth-day.—But now you have brought it, let us look at it?" The little girl gave the lace without reply, and the maid desired her to go about her business, and not to expect to be paid; for that her mistress could not see any body, *because* she was in a room full of company.

"May I call[3] again, madam, this afternoon?" said the child, timidly.

"Lord bless my stars!" replied the maid, "what makes people so poor, I *wonders!* I wish mistress would buy her lace at the warehouse,[4] as I told her, and not of these folks.—Call again! yes, to be sure—I believe you'd call, call, call twenty times for two-pence."

However ungraciously the permission to call again was granted, it was received with gratitude: the little girl departed with a chearful countenance: and Bell teized her maid till she got her to sew the long wished for lace upon her cuffs.

Unfortunate Bell!—All dinner-time passed, and people were so hungry, so busy, or so stupid, that not an eye observed her favourite piece of finery. Till at length she was no longer able to conceal her impatience, and turning to Laura, who sat next to her, she said—"You have no lace upon your cuffs; look how beautiful mine is!—Is not it? Don't you wish your mamma could afford to give you some like it?—But you can't get any if she would, for this was made on purpose for me on my birth-day, and nobody can get a bit more any where, if they would give the world for it."

"But cannot the person who made it," said Laura, "make any more like it?"

"No, no, no!" cried Bell; for she had already learned, either from her maid or her mother, the mean pride, which values things not for being really pretty or useful, but for being such as nobody else can procure.

"Nobody can get any like it, I say," repeated Bell; "Nobody in all London can make it but one person, and that person will never make a bit for any body but me, I am sure—mamma won't let her, if I ask her not."

"Very well," said Laura, coolly, "I do not want any of it; you need not be so violent:[5] I assure you that I don't want any of it."

"Yes, but you do though," said Bell, more angrily.

"No, indeed," said Laura, smiling.

"You do in the bottom of your heart; but you say you don't to plague me, I know," cried Bell, swelling with disappointed vanity.—"It is pretty for all that, and it cost a great deal of money too, and nobody shall have any like it if, they cried their eyes out."

Laura received this sentence in silence—Rosamond smiled. And at her smile the ill-suppressed rage of the spoiled child burst forth into the seventh and loudest fit of crying, which had been heard upon her birth-day.

"What's the matter, my pet?" cried her mother; "Come to me, and tell me what's the matter."

Bell ran roaring to her mother; but no otherwise explained the cause of her sorrow than by tearing the fine lace, with frantic gestures, from her cuffs, and throwing the fragments into her mother's lap.

"Oh! the lace, child!—are you mad?" said her mother, catching hold of both her hands. "Your beautiful lace, my dear love—do you know how much it cost?"

"I don't care how much it cost—it is not beautiful, and I'll have none of it," replied Bell, sobbing—"for it is not beautiful."

"But it is beautiful," retorted her mother; "I chose the pattern myself. Who has put it into your head, child, to dislike it?—Was it Nancy?"

3. I.e., return to be paid.
4. Shop.

5. Vehement.

"No, not Nancy, but *them*, mamma," said Bell, pointing to Laura and Rosamond.

"Oh fie! don't *point*," said her mother, putting down her stubborn finger; "nor say *them*, like Nancy; I am sure you misunderstood.—Miss Laura, I am sure, did not mean any such thing."

"No, madam; and I did not say any such thing, that I recollect," said Laura, gently.

"Oh no, indeed!" cried Rosamond, warmly rising in her sister's defence. But no defence or explanation was to be heard, for every body had now gathered round Bell, to dry her tears, and to comfort her for the mischief she had done to her own cuffs.

They succeeded so well, that in about a quarter of an hour the young lady's eyes, and the reddened arches over her eyebrows came to their natural colour; and the business being thus happily hushed up, the mother, as a reward to her daughter for her good humour, begged that Rosamond would now be so good as to produce her "charming present."

Rosamond, followed by all the company, amongst whom, to her great joy, was her godmother, proceeded to the dressing-room.[6]

"Now I am sure," thought she, "Bell will be surprised, and my godmother will see she was right about my generosity."

The doors of the wardrobe were opened with due ceremony, and the filigree basket appeared in all its glory.

"Well, this is a charming present indeed!" said the godmother, who was one of the company; "*My* Rosamond knows how to make presents." And as she spoke she took hold of the basket, to lift it down to the admiring audience. Scarcely had she touched it when, lo! the myrtle wreath, the medallions, all dropped—the basket fell to the ground, and only the handle remained in her hand.

All eyes were fixed upon the wreck. Exclamations of sorrow were heard in various tones; and "Who can have done this?" was all that Rosamond could say. Bell stood in sullen silence, which she obstinately preserved in the midst of the enquiries, which were made about the disaster. At length the servants were summoned, and amongst them Nancy, Miss Bell's maid and governess: she affected much surprise, when she saw what had befallen the basket, and declared that she knew nothing of the matter, but that she had seen her mistress in the morning put it quite safe into the wardrobe; and that, for her part, she had never touched it, or thought of touching it, in her born days—"Nor Miss Bell neither, ma'am, I can answer for her; for she never knew of its being there, because I never so much as mentioned it to her, that there was such a thing in the house, because I knew Miss Rosamond wanted to surprise her with the secret—so I never mentioned a sentence of it—Did I, Miss Bell?"

Bell, putting on the deceitful look which her maid had taught her, answered boldly, *No*; but she had hold of Rosamond's hand, and at the instant she uttered this falsehood she squeezed it terribly.

"Why do you squeeze my hand so?" said Rosamond, in a low voice; "What are you afraid of?"

"Afraid of!" cried Bell, turning angrily; "I'm not afraid of any thing—I've nothing to be afraid about."

"Nay, I did not say you had," whispered Rosamond; "But only if you did by accident—You know what I mean—I should not be angry if you did—Only say so."

"I say I did not!" cried Bell, furiously; "Mamma!—Mamma!—Nancy! my cousin Rosamond won't believe me! that's very hard—It's very rude! and I won't bear it—I won't."

6. A room for dressing and washing, usually connected to the bedroom.

"Don't be angry, love—don't;" said the maid.

"Nobody suspects you, darling;" said her mother.——"But she has too much sensibility.[7]——Don't cry, love, nobody suspected you."

"But you know," continued she, turning to the maid, "somebody must have done this, and I must know how it was done; Miss Rosamond's charming present must not be spoiled in this way, in my house, without my taking proper notice of it.——I assure you I am very angry about it, Rosamond."

Rosamond did not rejoice in her anger, and had nearly made a sad mistake, by speaking loud her thoughts—"*I was very foolish*——" she began and stopped.

"Ma'am," cried the maid, suddenly, "I'll venture to say I know who did it."

"Who?" said every one eagerly.

"Who?" said Bell, trembling.

"Why, Miss, don't you recollect that little girl with the lace, that we saw peeping about in the passage: I'm sure she must have done it, for here she was by herself half an hour or more, and not another creature has been in mistress's dressing-room, to my certain knowledge, since morning. Those sort of people have so much curiosity, I'm sure she must have been meddling with it;" added the maid.

"Oh yes, that's the thing," said the mistress, decidedly.——"Well, Miss Rosamond, for your comfort, she shall never come into my house again."

"Oh, that would not comfort me at all," said Rosamond; "besides, we are not sure that she did it; and if——" A single knock at the door was heard at this instant: it was the little girl, who came to be paid for her lace.

"Call her in," said the lady of the house; "let us see her directly."

The maid, who was afraid that the girl's innocence would appear if she were produced, hesitated; but upon her mistress's repeating her commands, she was forced to obey.

The child came in with a look of simplicity; but when she saw the room full of company she was a little abashed. Rosamond and Laura looked at her, and at one another with surprise; for it was the same little girl whom they had seen weaving lace.

"Is not it she?" whispered Rosamond to her sister.

"Yes it is; but hush," said Laura, "she does not know us.—Don't say a word, let us hear what she will say." Laura got behind the rest of the company as she spoke, so that the little girl could not see her.

"Vastly well!" said Bell's mother; "I am waiting to see how long you will have the assurance to stand there with that innocent look. Did you ever see that basket before?"

"Yes; ma'am," said the girl.

"*Yes, ma'am*," cried the maid, "and what else do you know about it?—You had better confess it at once, and Mistress perhaps will say no more about it."

"Yes, do confess it;" added Bell, earnestly.

"Confess what, madam?" said the little girl; "I never touched the basket, madam."

"You never *touched* it; but you confess," interrupted Bell's mother, "that you *did* see it before—And pray how came you to see it? you must have opened my wardrobe."

"No indeed, ma'am," said the little girl; "but I was waiting in the passage, ma'am, and this door was partly open; and looking at the maid, you know, I could not help seeing it."

"Why, how could you see it through the doors of my wardrobe?" rejoined the lady.

The maid, frightened, pulled the little girl by the sleeve.

"Answer me," said the lady, "where did you see this basket?"

Another stronger pull.

"I saw it, madam, in her hands," looking at the maid; "and——"

"Well, and what became of it afterwards?"

"Ma'am," hesitating, "Miss pulled, and by accident——I believe, I saw, ma'am—— Miss, you know what I saw."

"I do not know—I do not know: and if I did you had no business there—and mamma won't believe you, I am sure."

But every body else did, and their eyes were fixed upon Bell in a manner which made her feel rather ashamed.

"What do you all look at me so for?—Why do you all look so?—And am I to be shamed upon my birth-day?" cried she, bursting into a roar of passion; "and all for this nasty thing!" added she, pushing away the remains of the basket, and looking angrily at Rosamond.

"Bell! Bell! Oh fie! fie! now I *am* ashamed of you—that's quite rude to your cousin," said her mother, who was more shocked at her daughter's want of politeness than at her falsehood. "Take her away, Nancy, till she has done crying;" added she to the maid, who accordingly carried off her pupil.

Rosamond, during this scene, especially at the moment when her present was pushed away with such disdain, had been making reflections upon the nature of true generosity. A smile from her father, who stood by, a silent spectator of the catastrophe of the filigree basket, gave rise to these reflections; nor were they entirely dissipated by the condolence of the rest of the company, nor even by the praises of her godmother, who to condole her said—"Well, my dear Rosamond, I admire your generous spirit. You know I prophecied that your half-guinea would be gone the soonest—Did I not, Laura?" said she, appealing in a sarcastic tone to where she thought Laura was.—"Where is Laura? I don't see her."

Laura came forward.

"You are too *prudent* to throw away your money like your sister; your half-guinea, I'll answer for it, is snug in your pocket—Is it not?"

"No, madam;" answered she in a low voice. But low as the voice was, the poor little lace-girl heard it; and now, for the first time, fixing her eyes upon Laura, recollected her benefactress.

"Oh, that's the young lady!" she exclaimed, in a tone of joyful gratitude—"The good!—good young lady, who gave me the half-guinea, and would not stay to be thanked for it—but I *will* thank her now."

"The half-guinea, Laura!" said her godmother——"What is all this?"

"I'll tell you, madam, if you please," said the little girl.

It was not in expectation of being praised for it, that Laura had been generous, and therefore every body was really touched with the history of the weaving-pillow; and whilst they praised, felt a certain degree of respect, which is not always felt by those who pour forth eulogiums. *Respect* is not an improper word, even applied to a child of Laura's age; for let the age or situation of the person be what it may, they command respect who deserve it.

"Ah, madam!" said Rosamond to her godmother, "now you see—you see she is *not* a little miser: I'm sure that's better than wasting half-a-guinea upon a filigree basket— Is it not, ma'am?" said she, with an eagerness which shewed that she had forgotten all her own misfortunes in sympathy with her sister.—"This is being *really generous* father, is it not?"

"Yes, Rosamond," said her father, and he kissed her—"this *is* being really generous. It is not only by giving away money that we can shew generosity, it is by giving up to others any thing that we like ourselves: and therefore," added he, smiling, "it is really generous of you to give your sister the thing you like best of all others."

"The thing I like the best of all others, father," said Rosamond, half pleased, half vexed; "what is that I wonder?—You don't mean *praise*, do you, sir?"

"Nay, you must decide that, Rosamond."

"Why, sir," said she, ingenuously, "perhaps it *was* ONCE the thing I liked best; but the pleasure I have just felt, makes me like something else better."

1800

MARY MARTHA SHERWOOD
1775–1851

The best-selling author Mary Martha Sherwood, better known to the readers of her hundreds of titles as "Mrs. Sherwood," was one of the most important and prolific writers for children of the first half of the nineteenth century. Her tales and tracts—and their Evangelical context more generally—greatly influenced generations of Victorians. The Evangelical movement revitalized Anglican congregations in the late eighteenth and early nineteenth centuries by stressing the authority of the Bible and the importance of a personal, emotional relationship with Jesus Christ. Moreover, its emphasis on doing work for others drove Evangelicals' extensive involvement in causes such as missionary work, abolition, and various social ministries at home and abroad. According to M. Nancy Cutt, Evangelicalism "insisted upon individual acceptance of vital religion: its agonizing assessment of the evil at every human heart; the necessity of self-abasement and repentance which alone could culminate in the joyous assurance of salvation" (*Mrs. Sherwood and Her Books for Children: A Study*, 1974). The movement's growth created an enormous market for tracts and moral tales, and Sherwood's Evangelical beliefs permeate her fiction for children. The story of the long popularity, slow decline, and ultimate rejection of Sherwood's *The History of the Fairchild Family* and of her style of writing illuminates both the history of children's literature, particularly domestic fiction, and the broader development of early-nineteenth-century culture and literary traditions.

Mary Butt was the second child and first daughter of the Reverend George Butt, a learned clergyman in a parish near Worcester whose close friends included such notable writers and intellectuals as Anna Seward, Fanny Burney, Thomas Day, and Richard Lovell Edgeworth. Mary's childhood was happy, and her education was in some ways liberal (she was permitted to learn Latin and Greek with her brother), but her upbringing was very strict: from the ages of six to thirteen, she was often forced to wear a backboard and iron collar to correct her posture; she ate only plain, bland food; and she was never allowed to sit in the presence of her mother. She and her sister Lucy, who later would publish many Evangelical tales and tracts under the name Mrs. Cameron, would often make up stories to tell each other. Her schooling was completed at the Abbey School in Reading, a private school for the daughters of clergymen and gentlemen. Jane Austen and her sister Cassandra preceded her as pupils at this school. Mary enjoyed both school and the balls and other social entertainments she began to attend after leaving it. At the same time, she began to write seriously.

The success of her first novel, *The Traditions* (2 vols., 1795), was overshadowed by the sudden death of her father, which changed her life significantly. With her godmother Mary moved to Bath, where she fell into a dalliance with a young gentleman who did not share her Christian principles. Her guilt over this indiscretion, coupled with her family's straitened circumstances and the gift of a Bible from her brother, helped foster her religious seriousness. She and Lucy became involved in the Sunday school movement in Bridgnorth, where the family settled, as both began to teach and to write moral tales. Mary's *The History of Susan Gray* (1802), a popular tractlike novel, told the sentimental and romantic story of a young servant girl who so steadfastly refuses the advances of a military captain that she goes into a decline and dies.

In 1803, Mary married Henry Sherwood, a cousin to whom she had become engaged in 1798. When his regiment was posted to India in 1805, she left England, and their infant daughter, behind. More than a decade would pass before their return. Sherwood would bear six children in India, of whom four survived (her youngest child, born in England, died in infancy); she and her husband also adopted three orphans from the regiment. Distressed to find that no provision had been made to educate the children of British soldiers, she took on the task herself. Over the years, she established schools at four different British army posts, teaching the "half-caste" children of soldiers and Indian women as well as whites.

At the same time, Sherwood continued to write Evangelical tracts and fiction. *The Indian Pilgrim* (written 1811–12; published 1818), a religious allegory, was intended to win and educate Indian converts to Christianity. In 1814 she published one of her most popular books, *The History of Little Henry and His Bearer*; before dying, its saintly eight-year-old hero converts his Indian servant, Boosy, to Christianity.

During the long voyage home to England in 1816, Sherwood began to write the book for which she would become best-known: *The History of the Fairchild Family: or, The Child's Manual* (1818; the second and third parts of this family saga, gentler in tone, were published in 1842 and 1847). On her return, she also published religious stories and tracts at a furious pace. With their finances uncertain following her husband's discharge from the army, she had to make money, and she opened a boarding school near Worcester that quickly prospered. She began writing schoolbooks as well, presenting information within a framework of Evangelical doctrine and Scriptures in such works as *An Introduction to Astronomy: Intended for Little Children* (1817) and *An Introduction to Geography: Intended for Little Children* (1818). In 1820 she rewrote a popular children's tale from 1749, Sarah

Fielding's *The Governess, or The Little Female Academy*, "correcting" its doctrine to conform to Evangelical belief, deleting the didactic fairy stories, and replacing Fielding's name with her own.

The success of Sherwood's school enabled her to retire from teaching at age fifty-five in order to fully devote herself to writing. After her youngest child's death in 1830, the famous author and her family went abroad for two years and toured the Continent. During that decade, she was almost as popular in America as in Britain: Harper and Brothers began to bring out the *Works of Mrs. Sherwood* (16 vols., 1834–58), which remained in print past 1870. Near the end of Sherwood's life she began publishing books with one of her daughters, Sophia, who would later compose and edit *The Life of Mrs. Sherwood, Chiefly Autobiographical* (1854), relying primarily on her mother's journals. Sherwood continued to write until a few days before her death.

Although various later editions of *The History of the Fairchild Family* up to 1902 significantly changed the text by removing the sermons, hymns, and prayers and deleting some key episodes, the original 1818 text remained in print to the end of the nineteenth century; the altered version was available even longer. We reprint below the introduction to the book together with four representative chapters, including the most infamous scene in the book: the Fairchild children's visit, for punishment and edification, to a rotting corpse hanging on a gibbet. That scene helps illustrate why one of the enduring best sellers among children's books written in English—a book whose dramatic episodes, strong emotions, stark justice, and ordered world struck a chord with many children as well as adults—eventually came to be viewed as inappropriate for young readers. As Evangelicalism gave way to other movements during the High Victorian era, its unrelenting and unforgiving worldview, emphasizing childhood depravity and punishment, gradually fell out of favor. But the effects of Evangelicalism, and of Sherwood's writings, were lasting. Their offshoots, Cutt argues, include the force behind the relentless Victorian drive to act and to better oneself and others, along with such movements and institutions as the Tractarians and the Salvation Army; and, "what is more important in the history of children's books, Evangelicalism helped to create the Victorian belief in the family."

From The History of the Fairchild Family;
or, The Child's Manual

INTRODUCTION.

Mr. and Mrs. Fairchild lived very far from any town: their house stood in the midst of a garden, which in the summer time was full of fruit and sweet flowers. Mr. Fairchild kept only two servants, Betty and John: Betty's business was to clean the house, cook the dinner, and milk the cow; and John waited at table, worked in the garden, fed the pig, and took care of the meadow in which the cow grazed.

Mr. and Mrs. Fairchild had three children; Lucy, who was about eight years old when these stories began; Emily, who was next in age; and Henry, who was between five and six. These little children never went to school; Mrs. Fairchild taught Lucy and Emily, and Mr. Fairchild taught little Henry. Lucy and Emily learned to read, and to do various kinds of needle-work. Lucy had begun to write, and took great pains with her writing: their mamma also taught them to sing psalms and hymns, and they could sing several very sweetly. Little Henry, too, had a great notion of singing.

Besides working and reading, the little girls could do many useful things: they made their beds, rubbed the chairs and tables in their rooms, fed the fowls; and, when John was busy, they laid the cloth for dinner, and waited upon their papa and mamma whilst they were eating.

Mr. Fairchild taught Henry every thing that was proper for little boys in his station to learn: and when he had finished his lessons in a morning, his papa used to take him very often to work in the garden; for Mr. Fairchild had great pleasure in helping John to keep the garden clean. Henry had a little basket, and he used to carry the weeds and rubbish in this basket out of the garden, and do many such other little things as his papa set him to.

I must not forget to say, that Mr. Fairchild had a school for poor boys in the next village, and Mrs. Fairchild one for girls. I do not mean that they taught the children entirely themselves, but they paid a master and mistress to teach them; and they used to take a walk, two or three times a week, to see the children, and to give rewards to those who had behaved well. When Lucy, and Emily, and Henry were obedient, their papa and mamma were so kind as to let them go with them to see the schools; and then they always contrived to have some little thing ready to carry with them, as presents to the good children.

Mr. and Mrs. Fairchild loved and feared God, and had done so, by the mercy of God, ever since their younger days. They knew that their hearts were very bad, and that they could not be saved by any good thing they could do: on the contrary, that they were by nature fitted only for everlasting punishment: but they believed in the Lord Jesus Christ, and loved him for having died for them; and they knew that he would save them, because he saves all those people who trust in him. They believed also in the Holy Spirit of God—that it enters into the wicked hearts of men, and makes them good: and they knew that they could not do any thing well without the help of this Holy Spirit; therefore they used to pray for the Holy Spirit every day: and their prayers were heard, for they were helped to be good every day.

Mr. and Mrs. Fairchild loved their little children dearly; but they did not wish them to be handsome, rich, or great: all they desired for them was, that they might be the children of God, and go to heaven when they died. You would, perhaps, like to hear the prayer which Mr. and Mrs. Fairchild used to offer up for their children, as they knelt down in a morning, with the three little ones kneeling before them.

The Father and Mother's Prayer for their dear Children.

O Lord Jesus Christ! we are great sinners, and not worthy to pray for these dear children, whom God hath given us: we, therefore, humbly beseech thee, our glorious Saviour, to offer up for us, before thy heavenly Father, our humble and hearty prayer. Thou, O blessed Saviour, wast sent into this world to die for these dear children: we humbly ask for them faith, that they may believe and be saved. We also implore thy Holy Spirit, that it may come into their sinful hearts, and change them, and make them holy. We do not wish them to be rich, or handsome, or great in this world; but we pray that they may love thee, and live and die beloved by thee.

O glorious Saviour! offer up this prayer for us. We give up our little ones to thee, either to take them now to thyself, or to give them longer life, as it pleaseth thee best: but, oh! intercede for them, that they may be the children of the Holy One; and that of these little ones whom thou hast given us we may be able to say, at the last day, "Of them which thou gavest us, have we lost none." (John xviii. 9.)

Now to God the Father, God the Son, and God the Holy Ghost, be all glory, honour, and praise now and for evermore. *Amen.*

FIRST HYMN.[1]

See Israel's gentle Shepherd stand
With all-engaging charms!
Hark how he calls the tender lambs,
And folds them in his arms!

"Permit them to approach," he cries,
"Nor scorn their humble name;
For 'twas to bless such souls as these
The Lord of angels came."

We bring them, Lord, by fervent prayer,
And bring them up to Thee;
Joyful that we ourselves are thine,
Thine let our children be.

Ye little babes, with pleasure hear;
Ye children, seek His face,
And fly with transport to receive
The blessings of his grace.

If orphans they are left behind.
Thy Guardian Care we trust;
That Care shall heal our bleeding hearts,
If weeping o'er their dust.

---

1. From Philip Doddridge's *Hymns Founded on Various Texts in the Holy Scriptures* (1755).

STORY ON THE SIXTH COMMANDMENT.

One morning, as Mr. Fairchild was coming down stairs, he heard the little ones quarreling in the parlour; and he stood still to hearken to what they said.

"You are very ill-natured, Lucy," said Henry: "why won't you let me play with the doll?"

"What have boys to do with dolls?" said Lucy: "you shan't have it."

"But he shall," said Emily.

And Mr. Fairchild saw her, through the parlour door, snatch the doll from her sister, and give it to Henry, who ran with it behind the sofa. Lucy tried to get the doll away from her brother; but Emily ran in between them, and the two sisters began to fight. Lucy bit Emily's arm, and Emily scratched her sister's face; and, if Mr. Fairchild had not run in and seized hold of them, I do not know what they would have done to each other; for, when Emily felt the bite, she cried out,

"I hate you! I hate you with all my heart, you ill-natured girl!"

And Lucy answered,

"And I hate you too; that I do!"

And they looked as if what they said was true too; for their faces were as red as fire, and their eyes full of anger. Mr. Fairchild took the doll away from Henry; and, taking a rod out of the cupboard, he whipped the hands of all the three children till they smarted again, saying:

"Let dogs delight to bark and bite,
     For God has made them so;
Let bears and lions growl and fight,
     For 'tis their nature too:

But children, you should never let
     Such angry passions rise:
Your little hands were never made
     To tear each other's eyes."[2]

After which he made them stand in a corner of the room, without their breakfasts; neither did they get any thing to eat all the morning; and what was worse, their papa and mamma looked very gravely at them. When John came in to lay the cloth for dinner, Mr. Fairchild called the three children to him, and asked them if they were sorry for the wicked things which they had done.

"Oh! yes, Papa! yes, Papa! we are sorry," they said.

"Do you remember, Lucy—do you remember, Emily," said Mr. Fairchild, "what words you used to each other?"

"Yes, Papa," they answered; "we said that we hated each other; but we did not mean what we said."

"Yes," answered Mr. Fairchild; "you did mean what you said at the time; or else why did you bite and scratch each other with all your might, when you spoke?"

"Oh, Papa!" answered Lucy, "because we were angry then."

---

2. From "Against quarrelling and fighting," Song 16 in *Divine Songs in Easy Language for the Use of Children* (1715), by Isaac Watts. This work was later often reprinted under the title *Divine and Moral Songs for Children*.

"And suppose," said Mr. Fairchild, "that you had had a knife in your hand, Lucy: in your anger you would have struck your sister with it, and perhaps have killed her."

"Oh! no, Papa! no, Papa!" said Lucy: "I would not kill my poor sister for all the world."

Mr. Fairchild. "You would not kill her now. I am sure, for all the world, because you are not now angry with her; nor would you bite her now, I am sure: but when hatred and anger seize upon persons, they do many shocking things which they would not think of at another time. Have you not read how wicked Cain, in his anger, killed his brother Abel?[3] and do you not remember the verse in 1 John iii. 15: 'Whosoever hateth his brother is a murderer, and ye know that no murderer hath eternal life abiding in him?'"

"Oh! Papa, Papa!" said Emily; "we will never be angry again."

"My dear Emily," said Mr. Fairchild, "you must not say that you never will be angry again; but that you will pray to God, in the name of the Lord Jesus Christ, your dear Redeemer, to send his Holy Spirit into your heart, to take away these wicked passions."

"Papa," said Lucy, "when the Spirit of God is in me, shall I never hate any more, or be in wicked passions any more?"

"My dear child," answered Mr. Fairchild, "the Lord Jesus Christ says, 'By this shall all men know that ye are my disciples, if ye have love one towards another.' (John xiii. 31.) Therefore, if you are followers of the Lord Jesus Christ, and the Spirit of God is in you, you will love every body, even those who hate you and use you ill."

Then Mr. Fairchild kissed his children, and forgave them; and they kissed each other; and Mr. Fairchild gave them leave to dine with him as usual. After dinner, Mr. Fairchild said to his wife:

"I will take the children this evening to Blackwood, and shew them something there which, I think, they will remember as long as they live: and I hope they will take warning from it, and pray more earnestly for new hearts, that they may love each other with perfect and heavenly love."

"If you are going to Blackwood," said Mrs. Fairchild, "I cannot go with you, my dear, though I approve of your taking the children. Let John go with you to carry Henry part of the way; for it is too far for him to walk."

"What is there at Blackwood, Papa?" cried the children.

"Something very shocking," said Mr. Fairchild. "There is one there," said Mr. Fairchild, looking very grave, "who hated his brother."

"Will he hurt us, Papa?" said Henry.

"No," said Mr. Fairchild; "he cannot hurt you now."

When the children and John were ready, Mr. Fairchild set out. They went down the lane nearly as far as the village; and then, crossing over a long field, they came to the side of a very thick wood.

"This is Blackwood," said Mr. Fairchild, getting over the stile:[4] "the pathway is almost grown up; nobody likes to come here now."

"What is here, Papa?" added the children: "is it very shocking? We are afraid to go on."

"There is nothing here that will hurt you, my dear children," said Mr. Fairchild. "Am not I with you; and do you think I would lead my children into danger?"

"No, Papa," said the children; "but Mamma said there was something very dreadful in this wood."

---

3. See Genesis 4.8.

4. A set of steps for passing over a fence or wall.

Then Lucy and Emily drew behind Mr. Fairchild, and walked close together; and little Henry asked John to carry him. The wood was very thick and dark; and they walked on for half a mile, going down hill all the way. At last they saw, by the light through the trees, that they were come near to the end of the wood; and, as they went further on, they saw an old garden wall; some parts of which being broken down, they could see beyond a large brick house, which, from the fashion of it, seemed as if it might have stood there some hundred years, and now was fallen to ruin. The garden was overgrown with grass and weeds, the fruit-trees wanted pruning, and it was hardly to be seen where the walks had been. One of the old chimneys had fallen down, breaking through the roof of the house in one or two places; and the glass windows were broken near the place where the garden wall had fallen. Just between that and the wood stood a gibbet, on which the body of a man hung in chains: it had not yet fallen to pieces, although it had hung there some years. The body had on a blue coat, a silk handkerchief round the neck, with shoes and stockings, and every other part of the dress still entire: but the face of the corpse was so shocking, that the children could not look at it.

"Oh! Papa, Papa! what is that?" cried the children.

"That is a gibbet," said Mr. Fairchild; "and the man who hangs upon it is a murderer—one who first hated, and afterwards killed his brother! When people are found guilty of stealing, they are hanged upon a gallows, and taken down as soon as they are dead; but when a man commits a murder, he is hanged in iron chains upon a gibbet, till his body falls to pieces, that all who pass by may take warning by the example."

Whilst Mr. Fairchild was speaking, the wind blew strong and shook the body upon the gibbet, rattling the chains by which it hung.

"Oh! let us go, Papa!" said the children, pulling Mr. Fairchild's coat.

"Not yet," said Mr. Fairchild: "I must tell you the history of that wretched man before we go from this place."

So saying, he sat down on the stump of an old tree, and the children gathered close round him.

"When I first came into this country, before any of you, my children, were born," said Mr. Fairchild, "there lived, in that old house which you see before you, a widow lady, who had two sons. The place then, though old-fashioned, was neat and flourishing; the garden being full of fine old fruit-trees, and the flower-beds in beautiful order. The old lady kept an excellent table, and was glad to see any of her neighbours who called in upon her. Your mamma and I used often to go; and should have gone oftener, only we could not bear to see the manner in which she brought up her sons. She never sent them to school, lest the master should correct them, but hired a person to teach them reading and writing at home; but this man was forbidden to punish them. They were allowed to be with the servants in the stable and kitchen, but the servants were ordered not to deny them any thing: so they used to call them names, swear at them, and even strike them; and the servants did not dare to answer them, lest they should lose their places: the consequence of which was, that no good servant would stay, to be abused by wicked children.

"From quarreling with the servants, these angry boys went on to quarrel with each other. James, the eldest, despised his brother Roger, because he, as eldest, was to have the house and land; and Roger, in his turn, hated his brother James. As they grew bigger, they became more and more wicked, proud and stubborn, sullen and undutiful. Their poor mother still loved them so foolishly, that she could not see their faults, and would not suffer them to be checked. At length, when they became young men, their hatred of each other rose to such a height that they often would not speak to each other for days together; and sometimes they would quarrel, and almost come to blows, before their mother's face.

"One evening in autumn, after one of these quarrels, James met his brother Roger returning from shooting,[5] just in the place where the gibbet now stands: they were alone, and it was nearly dark. Nobody knows what words passed between them; but the wicked Roger stabbed his brother with a case-knife,[6] and hid the body in a ditch under the garden, well covering it with dry leaves. A year or more passed before it was discovered by whom this dreadful murder was committed. Roger was condemned, and hung upon that gibbet; and the poor old lady, being thus deprived of both her sons, went quite mad, and is shut up in a place where such people are confined. Since that time no one has lived in the house, and, indeed, nobody likes to come this way."

"O what a shocking story!" said the children: "and that poor wretch who hangs there is Roger, who murdered his brother? Pray let us go, Papa."

"We will go immediately," said Mr. Fairchild; "but I wish first to point out to you, my dear children, that these brothers, when they first began to quarrel in their play, as you did this morning, did not think that death and hell would be the end of their quarrels. Our hearts by nature, my dear children," continued Mr. Fairchild, "are full of hatred. People who have not got new hearts do not love any body but themselves; and they hate those who have offended them, or those whom they think any way better than themselves. By nature, I should hate Sir Charles Noble, because he is a greater man than myself; and you would hate his children, because they are higher than you. By nature, too, I should hate Farmer Greenfield, because he is ten times richer than I am; and even poor John Trueman, because of all the men in this country, high or low, he is the most esteemed. And take me with my natural heart to heaven, and I should hate every angel and every archangel above myself; and even the glory of the Almighty God would be hateful to me. But when, through faith in my dying Redeemer, I receive a new heart, by the inspiration of the Holy Spirit of God, my hatred of God and of my fellow-creatures will be turned into love: then I shall 'love my enemies, bless them that curse me, do good to them that hate me, and pray for them that despitefully use me and persecute me,' (Matt. v. 44); like my beloved Redeemer, who prayed upon the cross for his enemies, saying, 'Father, forgive them, for they know not what they do.' (Luke xxiii. 34.)"

"Papa," said Lucy, "let us kneel down in this place, and pray for new hearts."

"Willingly, my child," said Mr. Fairchild. So he knelt upon the grass, and his children round him; and afterwards they all went home.

A Prayer for Love towards God and our Neighbours, which may be used by any Child who has been angry with his Companion.

O Lord God, who sent thy dear Son to die upon the cross for us, who by nature hate thee; hear our prayers, for our dear Redeemer's sake. Thou hast commanded us to love every body; but we have such wicked hearts, that we do not love any body but ourselves. O Lord, send thy Holy Spirit to cleanse our wicked hearts; and make us to love thee, O Lord God, and to love each other. Let us not despise poor people, but love them and help them; and let us not envy people who are greater or better than ourselves, but love them also, and bless them, and do good to them. If any body is kind to us, give us hearts to be thankful to them, and to love them; and if any body

5. I.e., hunting.   6. A hunter's knife.

is unkind to us, give us hearts to forgive them, and love them too: for the Lord Jesus Christ prayed for the wicked people who nailed him upon the cross. And, above all, make us to love our dear father and mother, and every body who teaches us any good thing; and our dear brothers and sisters, and all the little children we play with: and may we never quarrel, as wicked men and devils do; but live in love, like the angels of God in heaven.

O Lord God, if thy Holy Spirit is in our hearts, we shall do well; but if it is not in our hearts, we shall do evil. Come, then, O Holy Spirit, come into our young hearts, and fill them with holy love.

"Our Father,"[7] &c. &c.

HYMN VIII.[8]

Whatever brawls disturb the street,
    There should be peace at home:
Where sisters dwell, and brothers meet
    Quarrels should never come.

Birds in their little nests agree;
    And 'tis a shameful sight,
When children of one family
    Fall out, and chide and fight.

Hard names at first, and threat'ning words,
    That are but noisy breath,
May grow to clubs and naked swords,
    To murder and to death.

The devil tempts one mother's son
    To rage against another:
So wicked Cain was hurried on,
    Till he had kill'd his brother.

The wise will make their anger cool,
    At least before the night;
But in the bosom of a fool
    It burns till morning light.

Pardon, O Lord, our childish rage;
    Our little brawls remove;
That, as we grow to riper age,
    Our hearts may all be love.

* * *

THE ALL-SEEING GOD.

I must now tell you of a sad temptation into which Emily fell about this time. It is a long story, but you shall have it all.

---

7. Matthew 6.9–13 ("the Lord's Prayer").   8. From Watts's *Divine Songs.*

There was a room in Mrs. Fairchild's house which was not often used: in this room was a closet full of shelves, where Mrs. Fairchild used to keep her sugar, and tea, and sweatmeats,[9] and pickles, and many other things. Now as Betty was very honest, and John too, Mrs. Fairchild would often leave this closet unlocked for weeks together, and never missed any thing out of it. One day, at the time that damascenes[1] were ripe, Mrs. Fairchild and Betty boiled up a great many damascenes in sugar, to use in the winter; and when they had put them in jars, and tied them down, they put them in the closet I before spoke of. Emily and Lucy saw their mamma do the damascenes, and helped Betty to cover them and carry them to the closet. As Emily was carrying one of the jars, she perceived that it was tied down so loosely that she could put in her finger and get at the fruit. Accordingly she took out one of the damascenes, and ate it: it was so nice that she was tempted to take another; and was going even to take a third, when she heard Betty coming up: she covered the jar in haste, and came away. Some months after this, one evening, just about the time that it was getting dark, she was passing by the room where these sweetmeats were kept, and she observed that the door was open: she looked round to see if any body was near, but there was no one: her mamma and papa, and her brother and sister, were in the parlour, and Betty was in the kitchen, and John was in the garden: no eye was looking at her, but the eye of God, who sees every thing we do, and knows even the secret thoughts of the heart; but Emily, just at that moment, did not think of God. She passed through the open door, and went up to the closet: there she stood still again, and looked round, but saw no one. She then opened the closet door, and took two or three damascenes, which she ate in great haste. She then went to her own room, and washed her hands and mouth, and went down into the parlour, where her papa and mamma were just going to tea.

Although her mamma and papa never suspected what naughty thing Emily had been doing, and behaved just as usual to her, yet Emily felt frightened and uneasy before them; and every time they spoke to her, though it was only to ask her the commonest question, she stared and looked frightened, making out the words of King Solomon; "The wicked flee when no man pursueth, but the righteous are bold as a lion." (Prov. xxviii. 1.)

I am sorry to say, that the next day, when it was beginning to get dark, Emily went again to the closet, and took some more damascenes; and so she did for several days, though she knew she was doing wrong.

On the Sunday following, it happened to be so rainy that nobody could go to church: in consequence of which, Mr. Fairchild called all the family into the parlour, and read the Morning Service,[2] and a sermon. Some sermons are hard, and difficult for children to understand; but this was a very plain, easy sermon; even Henry could tell his mamma a great deal about it. The text was from Psalm cxxxix. 7th to 12th verses: "Whither shall I go from thy Spirit? or whither shall I flee from thy presence? If I ascend up into heaven, thou art there: if I make my bed in hell, behold, thou art there: if I take the wings of the morning, and dwell in the uttermost parts of the sea, even there shall thy hand lead me, and thy right hand shall hold me: if I say, Surely the darkness shall cover me, even the night shall be light about me; yea, the darkness

9. Any sugary pastries, candied fruits, or sugared nuts.
1. Damson plums.
2. The Anglican Book of Common Prayer, which orders the conduct of all services and ceremonies (weddings, funerals, etc.), and sets out the prayers to be read at morning and evening services. These include two "lessons," or Bible verses—one from the Old and one from the New Testament; specific verses are assigned to every Sunday of the year.

hideth not from thee, but the night shineth as the day: the darkness and the light are both alike to thee."

The meaning of these verses were explained in the sermon at full length. It was first shewn that God is a spirit: he has no body like us, no hands, or legs, or arms. Secondly, that there is no place where God is not: that if a person could go up into heaven, he would find God there; if he were to go down to hell, there also he would find God: that God is in every part of the earth, and of the sea, and of the sky; and that, being always present in every place, he knows every thing we do, and every thing we say, and even every thought of our heart, however secret we may think it. Then the sermon went on to shew how foolish and mad it is for people to do wicked things in secret and dark places, trusting that God will not know it. "If I say, Surely the darkness shall cover me, even the night shall be light about me:" for no night is dark unto God: "He will surely bring to light the hidden things of darkness, and will make manifest the counsels of the heart." (1 Cor. iv. 5.) Therefore "woe unto them that seek deep to hide their counsel from the Lord, and their works are in the dark, and they say, Who seeth us? and who knoweth us?" (Isa. xxix. 15.)

All the time that Mr. Fairchild was reading, Emily felt frightened and unhappy, thinking of the wickedness she was guilty of every day; and she even thought that she never would be guilty again of the same sin: but when the evening came, all her good resolutions left her, for she had not prayed to the Lord Jesus Christ to strengthen them; and she went again to the room, where the damascenes were kept. When she came to the door of the closet, she thought of the sermon which her papa had read in the morning, and she stood still a few moments, to consider what she should do. "There is nobody in this room," she said; "and nobody sees me, it is true; but God is in this room: he sees me; his eye is now upon me: I cannot hide what I am going to do from him: he knows every thing, and he has power to cast me into hell. I will not take any more damascenes; I will go back, I think. But yet, as I am come so far, and am just got to the closet, I will just take one damascene—it shall be the last; I will never come here again, without mamma's leave." So she opened the closet door, and took one damascene, and then another, and then two more. Whilst she was taking the last, she heard the cat mew: she did not know that the cat had followed her into the room, and she was so frightened that she spilt some of the red juice upon her frock, but she did not perceive it at the time; as it is said, "The way of the wicked is darkness: they know not at what they stumble." (Prov. iv. 19.) She then left the closet, and went, as usual, to wash her hands and mouth, and went down into the parlour.

When Emily got into the parlour, she immediately saw the red stain on her frock. She did not stay till it was observed, but ran out again instantly, and went up stairs, and washed her frock. As the stain had not dried in, it came out with very little trouble; but not till Emily had wet all the bosom of her frock, and sleeves; and that so much, that all her inner clothes were thoroughly wet, even to the skin: to hide this, she put her pinafore on, to go down to tea. When she came down; "Where have you been, Emily?" said her mamma:"we have almost done tea."

"I have been playing with the cat, up stairs, Mamma," said Emily. But when she told this lie, she felt very unhappy, and her complexion changed once or twice from red to pale.

It was a cold evening, and Emily kept as much from the fire and candle as she could, lest any spots should be left in her frock, and her mamma should see them. She had no opportunity, therefore, of drying or warming herself, and she began to feel quite chilled and trembling: soon after a burning heat came in the palms of her hands, and a soreness about her throat: however, she did not dare to complain, but sat till bed-time, getting every minute more and more uncomfortable.

It was some time after she was in bed, and even after her mamma and papa came to bed, before she could sleep: at last she fell asleep; but her sleep was disturbed by dreadful dreams, such as she never had had before in her life. She fancied she had been doing something wrong, though her head was so confused that she did not know what, and that a dreadful Eye was looking upon her from above. Wherever she went, she thought this Eye followed her with angry looks, and she could not hide herself from it. It was her troubled conscience, together with an uneasy body, which gave her these dreadful dreams; and so horrible were they, that at length she awoke, screaming violently. Her mamma and papa heard her cry, and came running in to her, bringing a light; but she was in such a terror, that at first she did not know them, but kept looking up as if she saw something very horrible.

"Oh, my dear!" said Mrs. Fairchild, "this child is in a burning fever; only feel her hands."

It was true, indeed; and when Mr. Fairchild felt her, he was so much frightened that he resolved to watch by her all night, and in the morning, as soon as it was light, to send John for the doctor.—And what do you think Emily felt all this time; knowing, as she did, how she had brought on this illness, and how she had deceived for many days this dear papa and mamma, who gave up their own rest to attend her; knowing also, as she did, how she had offended God by continuing so many days in sin, and particularly in committing the sin again, after having been warned of the greatness of it in the sermon which her papa had read in the morning?

Emily continued to get worse during the night; neither was the doctor able, when he came, to stop the fever, though he did all he could. It would have grieved you to have seen poor Lucy and Henry. They could neither read nor play, they missed their dear sister so much. They kept crying to each other, "Oh, Emily! dear Emily! there is no pleasure without our dear Emily!"

When the doctor came on the third morning, he found Emily so much worse, that, although he tried to hide it from Mr. and Mrs. Fairchild, he could not. He ordered her to be moved away from her brother and sister, for fear they should catch the fever. Accordingly she was taken into the very room where the sweetmeats were kept: the doctor chose that room, because it was very airy, and separate from the rest of the house.

For some hours Emily had not seemed to notice any thing that passed; neither did she seem to know that they were moving her: but when she came into the room, and saw the closet door (for the bed on which they laid her was just opposite the closet door), she looked this way, and that way, and tried to speak; but was so ill, and her head so confused, that she could not make any body understand what she wanted to say.

The next day, when the doctor came, Emily was so very ill that he thought it right that Lucy and Henry should be sent out of the house. Accordingly, John got the horse ready, and took them to Mrs. Goodwill's. Poor Lucy and Henry! how they cried when they went out of the gate, thinking that perhaps they might never see their dear Emily any more! It was a terrible time for poor Mr. and Mrs. Fairchild: they had no comfort, but in praying and watching by poor Emily's bed. And all this grief Emily brought upon her friends by her own naughtiness! "Woe unto them that seek deep to hide their counsel from the Lord, and their works are in the dark; and they say, Who seeth us? and who knoweth us?" (Isa. xxix.15).

Emily had been exceedingly ill for nine days, and every one feared that if her fever continued a few days longer she must die, when, by the mercy of God, her fever suddenly left her, and she fell asleep, and continued sleeping for many hours. O how did her dear papa and mamma rejoice, when they found her sleeping so sweetly! They went into another room, and fell on their knees, and blessed and praised God. And Mr. Fairchild pointed out these words to his wife: "For the Lord will not cast off for ever; but though he cause grief, yet will he have compassion, according to the multitude of his mercies: for he doth not afflict willingly, nor grieve the children of men." (Lament. iii. 31–33.)

When Emily awoke, she was very weak; but her fever was gone: she kissed her papa and mamma, and wanted to tell them of the naughty things she had done, which had been the cause of her fever; but they would not allow her to speak. How kindly did Mr. and Mrs. Fairchild watch over their dear little girl, and provide her with every thing that was thought good for her!

From that day she got better; and at the end of a week, from the time her fever left her, she was so well, that she was able to sit up, and tell her mamma all the history of her stealing the damascenes, and of the sad way in which she had got the fever. "Oh! Mamma!" said Emily, "what a wicked girl have I been! what trouble have I given to you, and to Papa, and to the Doctor, and to Betty! I thought that God would take no notice of my sin. I thought he did not see me when I was stealing in the dark: but I was much mistaken; his eye was upon me all the time, and he made me feel his anger. And yet how good, how very good it was of Him not to send me to hell for my wickedness! When I was ill, I might have died; and, oh! Mamma, Mamma! what would have become of me then!"

Mrs. Fairchild cried very much when she heard her little girl talk in this way: she kissed her, and held her in her arms. "My beloved child," said Mrs. Fairchild, "God has been very good indeed to you: he has brought you through a dreadful illness, and, what is better than this, he has brought you to a knowledge of your wickedness betimes.[3] You might have gone on in your wickedness for many years, till you became a hardened sinner; and when you died, you would have gone to hell; but God, like a tender Father, has chastised you, my child."—Then Mr. Fairchild shewed Emily these verses: "And ye have forgotten the exhortation, which speaketh unto you as unto children: My son, despise not thou the chastening of the Lord, nor faint when thou art rebuked of him; for whom the Lord loveth he chasteneth, and scourgeth every son whom he receiveth. If ye endure chastening, God dealeth with you as with sons; for what son is he whom the father chasteneth not? But if ye be without chastisement, whereof all are partakers, then are ye bastards, and not sons. Furthermore, we have had fathers of our flesh, which corrected us; and we gave them reverence: shall we not much rather be in subjection unto the Father of spirits, and live? For they verily for a few days chastened us after their own pleasure; but he for our profit, that we might be partakers of his holiness. Now no chastening for the present seemeth to be joyous, but grievous: nevertheless, afterward it yieldeth the peaceable fruit of righteousness unto them which are exercised thereby." (Heb. xii. 5—11.)

"Oh, Mamma!" said Emily, "these are pretty verses; and when I am able, I will learn them, and I hope I shall never forget them."

Mrs. Fairchild then knelt down by Emily's bed, and prayed; after which, she sung a hymn. This prayer and hymn I shall put down in this place, that you may make use

---

3. Early in life; before it is too late.

of it at any time when you may have been tempted to do any thing wrong, trusting that God could not see it.

The Prayer.

O Lord, the great and dreadful God! who seest every thing, and knowest every thing; from whom I cannot hide even one thought of my heart; whose eye can go down into the deepest and darkest place! how wicked have I been! O how wicked have I been! I thought that God would not know the evil thing that I did; I thought that it was hid from him: but his eye was upon me, (his eye, so dreadful to the wicked!) his eye followed me wherever I went: he knew all I did, and he marked it in his book. O God, I thank thee for having brought me to the knowledge of my sin! O Holy Spirit, this is thy glorious work. And now, O Holy Spirit, fill me with the fear of God; that I may know and feel that he is with me, and his eye upon me, wherever I go; and, though my parents may not be with me, yet one more to be feared, even God, is looking upon me.

O God! thou hast the power of death, and the power to cast me into hell, into the place which burns for ever with fire and brimstone: O save me, save me from hell! save me, save me from eternal death! Fill my heart with holy fear, that I may have thee, my God, always in my thoughts.

Oh, Thou that art all fair, in whom is no spot or stain of sin! Thou, O bleeding Lamb! offer up unto God the prayer of a sinful child; and obtain for me, in thy holy name and for thy dear sake, that fear of God which is the beginning of wisdom!

And now to God the Father, God the Son, and God the Holy Ghost, be all glory, and honour, and power, now and for ever. *Amen.*

"Our Father," &c.

HYMN XIV.[4]

Almighty God, thy piercing eye
    Shines through the shades of night;
And our most secret actions lie
    All open to thy sight.

There's not a sin that we commit,
    Nor wicked word we say,
But in the dreadful Book is writ,
    Against the Judgment Day.

And must the crimes that I have done
    Be read and publish'd there;
Be all expos'd before the sun,
    While men and angels hear?

Lord, at thy feet asham'd I lie;
    Upward I dare not look:
Pardon my sins before I die,
    And blot them from thy book.

---

4. From Watts's *Divine Songs.*

Remember all the dying pains
That my Redeemer felt;
And let his blood wash out my stains,
And answer for my guilt.

O may I now for ever fear
T' indulge a sinful thought!
Since the great God can see and hear,
And write down ev'ry thought.

* * *

FATAL EFFECTS OF DISOBEDIENCE TO PARENTS.

When Mr. and Mrs. Fairchild returned from the old gardener's, they found John ready with the cart; so, wishing Mrs. Goodwill a good evening, and thanking her for all her kindness, they returned home.

The next morning Mr. Fairchild got up early, and went down to the village. Breakfast was ready, and Mrs. Fairchild and the children waiting at the table, when he came back. "Get your breakfast, my dear," said he to Mrs. Fairchild; "don't wait for me." So saying, he went into his study, and shut the door: Mrs. Fairchild, supposing that he had some letters to write, got her breakfast quietly: after which, she sent Lucy to ask her Papa if he would not choose any breakfast. When Mr. Fairchild heard Lucy's voice at the study door, he came out, and followed her into the parlour.

When Mrs. Fairchild looked at her husband's face, she saw that something had grieved him very much. She was frightened, and said, "My dear, I am sure something is the matter: what is it? Tell me the worst at once: pray do?"

"Indeed, my dear," said Mr. Fairchild, "I have heard something this morning which has shocked me dreadfully. I was not willing to tell you before you had breakfasted. I know what you will feel when you hear it."

"Do, do, tell it me," said Mrs. Fairchild, turning quite white.

"Poor Augusta Noble!" said Mr. Fairchild.

"What! Papa?" said Lucy and Emily and Henry.

"She is dead!" said Mr. Fairchild.

The children turned as pale as their mother; and poor Mrs. Fairchild would have dropped off her chair, if Betty, guessing what was the matter (for she had heard the news too, though she had not chosen to tell it), had not run in, and held her in her arms.

"Oh! poor Lady Noble! poor Lady Noble!" said Mrs. Fairchild, as soon as she could speak. "Poor Lady Noble!"

As soon as their mamma spoke, the children all together began to cry and sob, which affected Mr. Fairchild so much that he hastened into his study again, and shut the door.

Whilst the children were crying, and Betty holding Mrs. Fairchild, for she continued very faint and sick, Mrs. Barker came into the parlour. Mrs. Barker was a kind woman; and as she lived by herself, was always at liberty to go amongst her neighbours in times of trouble. "Ah, Mrs. Fairchild!" she said, "I know what troubles you: we are all in grief, through the whole village."

When Mrs. Fairchild saw Mrs. Barker, she began to shed tears, which did her much good; after which she was able to ask Mrs. Barker what was the cause of the poor child's death, "as," said she, "I never heard that she was ill."

"Ah, Mrs. Fairchild, the manner of her death is the worst part of the story, and that which must grieve her parents' hearts. You know that poor Miss Augusta was always the darling of her mother, who brought her up in great pride, without fear of God or knowledge of religion: nay, Lady Noble would even mock at religion and religious people in her presence; and she chose a governess for her who had no more of God about her than herself."

"I never thought much of that governess," said Mrs. Fairchild.

"As Miss Augusta was brought up without the fear of God," continued Mrs. Barker, "she had, of course, no notion of obedience to her parents, farther than just striving to please them in their presence: she lived in the constant practice of disobeying them; and the governess continually concealed her disobedience from Lady Noble. And what is the consequence? The poor child has lost her life, and the governess is turned out of doors in disgrace."

"But," said Mrs. Fairchild, "how did she lose her life through disobedience to her parents? Pray tell me, Mrs. Barker."

"The story is so shocking I hardly dare tell it you," answered Mrs. Barker: "but you must know it.—Miss Augusta had a custom of playing with fire, and carrying candles about, though Lady Noble had often warned her of the danger of this, and had strictly charged the governess to prevent it. But it seems that the governess, being afraid of offending, had suffered her very often to be guilty of this piece of disobedience, without telling Lady Noble. And the night before last, when Lady Noble was playing at cards in the drawing-room, with some visitors, Miss Augusta took a candle off the hall table, and carried it up stairs to the governess's room. The governess was not in the room. Miss Augusta went to the closet, and it is supposed was looking in the glass,[5] with the candle in her hand: but this is not known. Lady Noble's maid, who was in a room not far off, was frightened by dreadful screamings: she ran into the governess's room, and there found poor Augusta all in a blaze, from head to foot! The maid burnt herself very much in putting out the fire; and poor Miss Augusta was so dreadfully burnt, that she never spoke afterwards, but died in agonies last night—a warning to all children how they presume to disobey their parents! 'The eye that mocketh at his father, and refuses to obey his mother, the ravens of the valley shall pick it out, and the young eagles shall eat it.' (Prov. xxx. 17)."

When Mrs. Fairchild and the children heard this dreadful story, they were very much grieved. Mrs. Barker staid with them all day; and it was, indeed, a day of mourning through all the house. This was Wednesday; and on Saturday poor Miss Augusta was to be buried. Mr. Fairchild was invited to attend the funeral; and the children also were desired to go, as they had been sometimes the play-fellows of poor Miss Augusta. Mrs. Fairchild dressed them in white; and at four o'clock in the afternoon a coach covered with black cloth came to the door of Mr. Fairchild's house, to take them to Sir Charles Noble's.

When Lucy and Emily and Henry got into the coach, with their papa, they felt very sorrowful; and not one of them spoke one word all the while the coachman was driving to Sir Charles Noble's. When they came into the park, they saw a hearse, and a great many coaches and other carriages, standing at the door of the house, besides many persons on horseback in black clothes with white scarfs and hat-bands. The hearse was hung with black, and so were several of the coaches; and at the top of the hearse were plumes of white feathers.—Perhaps you may never have seen a hearse: in case you have not, I shall try to describe it to you. It is a long close coach,

5. Mirror.

without windows, used for carrying the dead from their houses to their graves. Sometimes black and sometimes white plumes of feathers are fixed at the top of these hearses, according to the age of the person to be borne. Hearses are always painted or hung with black, and are in general drawn by black horses: so that they make a very dismal appearance.

When the children came near to Sir Charles's house, and saw all the people and carriages waiting to accompany their poor little playmate to her grave, they began to cry afresh, and Mr. Fairchild himself looked very sad. "The eye of him that hath seen me shall see me no more: thine eyes are upon me, and I am not." (Job vii. 8.)

When the coach came to the house-door, a footman came out, dressed in black, and took them into the hall, where white gloves and scarfs[6] were given to them, and they were led into the dining-room. There, upon a large table covered with black cloth, was the coffin of poor Augusta, covered with white velvet, and ornamented with silver. Almost all the gentlemen and ladies of the neighbourhood were in the room; but Sir Charles and Lady Noble were not there. When Emily and Lucy saw the coffin, they began to cry more and more; and little Henry too cried, though he rubbed his eyes, and tried to hide his tears.

When every thing was ready, the coffin was lifted up, and put into the hearse; the company got into the coaches; and they all moved slowly to the parish church, which was close to the village, about two miles distant. As the children passed back through the park in the mourning-coach, they saw many places where they had walked and played with poor Augusta; and this made them the more sorrowful. As for man, "all flesh is grass, and all the goodliness thereof as the flower of the field." (Isa. xl. 6.)— When they passed through the park gate, they could hear the church bell tolling very plainly. The carriages moved on very slowly, so that it was between five and six when the funeral reached the church. The church-yard was full of people. The coffin was taken out of the hearse and carried into the church, the clergyman going before and all the people following. The coffin was placed on a bier in the middle of the church whilst the clergyman read the first part of the Funeral Service. Lucy and Emily and Henry stood all the time close to the coffin, crying very bitterly.——Perhaps you have never read the Funeral Service with attention: if you have not, I would advise you to read it immediately, and consider it well; for there are many things in it which may make you wise unto salvation.——Poor Augusta's coffin was then lifted up, and carried, not into the church-yard, but to the door of a vault under the church, which was the burying-place of all the Nobles: and as the people were letting down the coffin into the vault, earth was cast upon it, and the clergyman repeated these words: "Forasmuch as it hath pleased Almighty God of his great mercy to take unto himself the soul of our dear sister here departed, we therefore commit her body to the ground; earth to earth, ashes to ashes, dust to dust; in sure and certain hope of the resurrection to eternal life, through our Lord Jesus Christ; who shall change our vile body, that it may be like his glorious body, according to the mighty working whereby he is able to subdue all things to himself." The coffin then was removed into a dark place in the vault, and Lucy and Emily and Henry saw it no more.

When the service was done, Mr. Fairchild returned sorrowfully to the coach, with his children; but before the coachman drove away, the clergyman himself came to the door, and said, "Mr. Fairchild, if you are going home, I will take a seat with you in the coach, and drink a dish of tea with Mrs. Fairchild this evening; for I feel in want of a little Christian society." Mr. Fairchild gladly made room for Mr. Somers—

6. Worn as mourning dress.

for that was the clergyman's name—and the coach drove back to Mr. Fairchild's house.

As they were going along, they talked of nothing but poor Miss Augusta and her parents; and Mr. Fairchild asked Mr. Somers if he knew in what state of mind the poor child died. "Ah, sir!" said Mr. Somers, "you have touched upon the very worst part of the whole business. From the time of the accident till the time that the breath left her body, she was insensible: she had not one moment for thought or repentance; and it is well known that Lady Noble never taught her any thing concerning God and her Redeemer, and never would let any body else: nay, she was taught to mock at religion and pious people. She knew nothing of the evil of her own heart, and nothing of the Redeemer, nor of the sin of disobedience to her parents."

"Oh, Mr. Somers!" said Mr. Fairchild, "what a dreadful story is this! Had this poor child been brought up in the fear of God, she might now have been living, a blessing to her parents and the delight of their eyes. 'Withhold not correction from the child; for if thou beatest him with the rod, he shall not die: thou shalt beat him with the rod, and shalt deliver his soul from hell.' (Prov. xxiii. 13, 14)."

"Poor little Augusta!" said Mr. Somers: "Lady Noble would never hearken to me, when I spoke to her on the duty of bringing up her children in the fear of God. I believe she thought me very impertinent, to speak to her upon the subject."

By this time the coach was arrived at Mr. Fairchild's door. Mrs. Fairchild and Mrs. Barker were waiting tea for them: they had both been crying, as might be seen by their eyes. After tea, Mr. Somers gave out a hymn, and prayed. I shall put down both the hymn and the prayer in this place; altering only a few words, to suit any little child who wishes to use the prayer by himself.

A Prayer against the Sin of Disobedience to Parents.

O Almighty Father! thou who didst command all children to honour their parents, and didst promise to bless those who obeyed this Commandment, give me a heart to keep this law. I know that I ought to do all that my father and mother and masters bid me do, if they do not order me to do any thing wicked; and yet my heart, O Lord God, is so bad, that I do not like to obey them. Sometimes, when they give me an order, I am obstinate and passionate, and refuse to do it even in their sight, and would rather be punished than obey them; and sometimes I try to disobey them slily, when I think that they do not see me: forgetting that thine eye, O Lord God, is always upon me; and though thou, O Lord God, mayest not punish me immediately, yet thou markest all my sins in a book: and I know that the dreadful day will come, when the dead shall be raised, and the books shall be opened; and all I have done, unless I repent and turn unto the Lord, will be read aloud before men and angels, and I shall be cast into hell fire for my sins.

O holy Father! I am sorry for my disobedience. O make me more and more sorry for it; and send thy Holy Spirit to give me a clean heart, that I may obey this thy Commandment. I know that disobedient children, unless they repent, always come to an ill end: there is no blessing on such as do not honour their parents. O then, dear Saviour, hear my prayer! Thou, that diedst for poor sinners, save a wicked child! Give me a new heart; teach me to be obedient to my parents, and to honour and respect them; that I may be blessed in this present life, and may, through the merits of my dying Redeemer, be received into everlasting glory in the world to come.

Now to God the Father, God the Son, and God the Holy Ghost, be all glory and honour, for ever and ever. *Amen.* "Our Father," &c.

Let children that would fear the Lord
 Hear what their teachers say,
With rev'rence meet their parents' word,
 And with delight obey.

Have you not heard what dreadful plagues
 Are threat'ned by the Lord
To him that breaks his father's law,
 Or mocks his mother's word?

What heavy guilt upon him lies?
 How cursed is his name?
The ravens shall pick out his eyes,
 And eagles eat the same!

But those who worship God, and give
 Their parents honour due,
Here on this earth they long shall live,
 And live hereafter too.

*   *   *

A HAPPY DEATH.

Mrs. Fairchild had invited little Charles[8] and his grandmother, Mary Bush, to dine with her the next day, which was Sunday; but the next day it rained so hard that Mrs. Bush could not come out: and it continued to be very rainy all the week, so that Henry did not see Charles Trueman till the Sunday afterwards, when he and his grandmother came in just before dinner. In the mean time, Mrs. Fairchild had prepared a warm greatcoat,[9] of coarse but soft grey cloth, for little Charles, and two pairs of woollen stockings; and Mrs. Barker, who had seen Mrs. Fairchild and Lucy knitting the stockings, had added to the present a pair of comfortable thick shoes. All these things were ready when Mrs. Bush and Charles came into Mrs. Fairchild's kitchen, just as Betty and John were dishing the dinner to take into the parlour.

As soon as Mrs. Fairchild and the children and Mrs. Barker (for Mrs. Barker was at Mrs. Fairchild's that day) heard that Mary Bush was come, they came into the kitchen to welcome her, and to inquire into Charles's health, and to give him the present they had got ready for him. When Charles received his coat and shoes and stockings, he first thanked God, and then his friends, and then, looking at his grandmother, he said, "I shall be warm now, Grandmother." "God is good, my child!" said Mary Bush: "I have always found him so. These were the very things my little lad wanted. Kind Ladies," (she added, looking at Mrs. Fairchild and Mrs. Barker), "I and his father had begun to put a little money together to buy these things for him; but the goodness of God, through your means, hath provided us with them already, making out Saint Peter's words; 'Cast all your care upon him, for he careth for you.' (1 Peter v. 7.)"

7. From Watts's *Divine Songs.*
8. Charles Trueman, the pious son of a local   laborer.
                9. Heavy overcoat.

After dinner, as there was no evening service in the church, Mr. Fairchild read the Evening Service, in his kitchen, to all the family. After which, Mrs. Barker and Mrs. Fairchild sat talking awhile to Mary Bush, and Henry took Charles up into his little room to talk with him.

"Charles," said Henry, "since I met you that day in the coppice, I have thought a great deal about you. I am sorry you are so ill, and I don't like to think of your dying. I hope you won't die."

"Master Henry," answered Charles, "to be sure God only knows what is to be; but I certainly think that I am not long for this world. Since I saw you, I have at times become very full of pain just about my heart; and the pain is sometimes so bad that I cannot help crying out; and my grandmother told my father, that she thought I never should get quit of that pain till death."

"Is the pain very bad?" said Henry.

"Oh, very bad, Master Henry! very bad indeed! it pulls me, as it were, quite double," said Charles. "God give me grace to bear it with patience, and to cry 'Thy will be done,' till the happy time comes, when, through my blessed Saviour's death, I hope to be set free from all pain."

"Then you really wish to die?" said Henry.

"Yes, Master Henry, I do," answered Charles; "and for this reason, because I know myself to be a grievous sinner, and one that cannot live a day without doing that which is evil: therefore why should I grieve because God is pleased to take me so soon from this state of sin and sorrow?"

"But still," said Henry, "it is sad to feel so much pain as you say you do."

"Pain is hard to bear, Master Henry, to be sure," answered Charles; "but, then, my father tells me that whatever is God's will it is our duty to bear; and, more than that, He will help us to bear it; for he will not tempt us above what we are able to bear."

"I do not quite understand you," said Henry.

"What I mean is this," answered Charles; "God made you and me, and therefore he has a right to do what he will with us. If it is his will that I should die very soon, and you live a long time, we ought to be content with what he orders. Our business is to look which way God leads, and follow on as closely and quietly as we can, being sure that 'our light afflictions, which are but for a moment, will work for us an eternal and exceeding weight of glory.' (2 Cor. iv. 17)."

"Charles," said Henry, "I should like to see you very often; and, if my papa will give me leave, I will meet you in the coppice every day, after I have done my lesson. I like to hear you talk."

"It is not much good that I can say, Master Henry," answered Charles; "for I am a poor sinful child: yet I shall always be glad to meet you in the coppice, for you have always been kind to me, and so has good Madam and Master."

In the evening little Charles and his grandmother went home; and from that time Henry used to go every day, when he had learnt his lessons, and the weather would allow him, to see little Charles. Sometimes, when it was not very cold, they met and walked in the coppice; but as the winter came on, and little Charles grew weaker, they oftener met and sat by Mrs. Bush's fire. As the time of Charles's death drew nearer, and the pains of his body became greater, his faith and trust in his Redeemer grew more lively; his thoughts of himself, in like manner, became more lowly and humble. One morning, not long before he died, Mrs. Bush was cutting some apples to make a pie, and one of the apples was quite rotten all through, although the outside was quite smooth and looked well. "That apple," said Charles, speaking to Henry, "is like my heart by nature, all bad to the very core, not one bit good in it; and yet I remember the time when I thought myself a good boy."

"Why, even now," said Henry, "I don't like to be thought a sinner, although I know that I am one; but you are not ashamed to be thought a sinner, Charles: you do not seem to wish to hide your faults from any body."

"Why, Master Henry," answered Charles, "it is no time for me to be playing the hypocrite when I am going to die. I feel that I have not many days to live: this world is departing fast from me, and the next coming nearer my view: the grave is before me, and heaven and hell beyond, as it were but a step: and though I might deceive my father and mother and other people, and pretend to be better than I am, yet I cannot deceive God. No! I am a miserable sinner, Master Henry; one in whose heart sin has lived and ruled, abiding continually, growing and flourishing, and that from the time of my birth till God humbled me and opposed it by his Holy Spirit."

"What do you mean by sin abiding and flourishing in your heart always?" said Henry.

"Why, Master Henry," answered Charles, "I don't know how to make you understand what I mean; but I will try to explain myself. When I was a little child, the first thoughts I had about good and bad people were, that some men were good and would go to heaven, and that some were bad. I thought my father was good, and my mother, and my grandmother, and Mrs. Fairchild, and Mr. Somers, and Mrs. Barker, and such; and I thought that Farmer Freeman, and 'Squire Collins, and he that was hanged on the gibbet at Blackwood, and such folks, were bad men. As to myself, I thought that I was a very good little boy; and my brothers and sisters, not quite so good to be sure—but I had no idea of their sinful natures, or of my own. As I got older, I became sensible that I had some faults: and then my father taught me about Adam eating the forbidden fruit,[1] and I got some kind of notion that there was evil in my heart; but I thought there was good in my heart too, as well as evil, and a great deal of good too: but since God has been pleased to touch my heart, particularly since my sickness, I have become sensible that by nature there is no manner of good at all in any man's heart: nay, that sin is so strong in us that we can no more stop from sinning than we can from breathing."

"Charles," said Henry, "I know that you understand these things better than I do, yet I do not quite understand what you mean when you say we cannot stop from sinning. Now, here have I been sitting this half hour talking to you—I don't think I have said any bad—how then have I been sinning?"

"Master Henry," answered Charles, "I trust and hope that your heart is not altogether in its natural state, but that the Spirit of God has already begun to work a change in it; so that you are not altogether under the power and dominion of sin: yet I know that sin is not dead in you, nor ever will be, until that blessed time, when, in the morning of the resurrection, your sinful body will awake in the likeness of your Redeemer."

"But," said Henry, "how have I sinned since I came here? Explain it to me, Charles."

"Why," answered Charles, "there is one way in which we all sin continually, and that is, in loving and pleasing ourselves more than God. In all our thoughts we ourselves come foremost, and God (if he comes at all) afterwards, and this with the best of people. The love of ourselves is always present with us, always mixing itself with every thought; so that we may be said to worship ourselves in the place of God; and from this sin, Master Henry, we never cease."

"When you are dead, Charles," said Henry, "I shall often think of you, and go to

1. The fruit of the tree that gives knowledge of good and evil (Genesis 3.3–6).

see your grave. You have taught me many things which I never knew before."

"God bless you! my dear little boys," said Mary Bush; "living or dying, God bless you both!"

A few days before Christmas the weather became very cold, and a great change at the same time took place in little Charles. Mr. and Mrs. Fairchild, and Mr. Somers, notwithstanding the hard frost, often went to see him as he drew nearer his end, and were much pleased with the happy state of mind in which he was, for he seemed to have no desire but to be with Him who died for him, even that Lamb of God which was slain for the sins of the world. Early one Wednesday morning, in the beginning of the month of December, Margery Grey came over in haste to Mr. Fairchild's to call Henry: "Little Charley is dying," she said, "and asks for young Master." As soon as Mr. Fairchild and the family heard the news, they all set off in haste to Mary Bush's. Emily and Lucy were crying all the way as they went; but Henry tried not to cry, which made him only feel the more, for his cheeks were quite pale, and he could scarcely speak, for Henry loved little Charles very much. When they came to the cottage, they found Nurse and Joan, with all John Trueman's little children, in Margery Grey's room. Poor little Charley was lying on a bed in his grandmother's room. His head was lying on a pillow, supported by his mother, who sat upon the bed looking at her dying child, whilst her tears ran down her cheeks. John Trueman was kneeling on one side of the bed, holding one of Charles's hands. Mr. Somers stood looking silently on, sometimes lifting up his eyes and repeating something to himself, as if in prayer: and Mary Bush, and poor Charles's elder brother and sister, were crying in different parts of the room.

When Mr. and Mrs. Fairchild with the children came in, Charles's eyes were shut, and he lay as if sleeping. He was much changed since the day before: his eyes were sunk, his face become deadly pale, and his mouth drawn close. When Henry looked at him, he could keep his tears back no longer; they overflowed his eyes, and ran fast down his cheeks. After a few minutes Charles opened his eyes, and looked round him at every one. At length, perceiving Henry, he smiled, and put his hand towards him.

"Dear, dear Charles!" said Henry, sobbing.

"Do not cry, Master Henry," said Charles, speaking in a low voice; "I am happy."

"And what makes you happy now, my dear boy?" said Mr. Somers; "speak and tell us, that we may all here present lay fast hold of the same Hope, which is able to make a dying bed so easy."

Charles turned his dying eyes towards Mr. Somers, and answered: "I know that my Redeemer liveth; and though after my skin worms shall destroy this body, yet in my flesh I shall see God." (Job xix. 25, 26.)

The little boy spoke these words with difficulty; and indeed the latter part was rather guessed at than heard distinctly: then, as if quite worn out, he shut his eyes, and lay as much as an hour as if asleep, though his frequent startings and convulsions, with his slow and solemn breathings, shewed that death was coming on apace. At length he awoke, and his mother and Mr. Somers spoke to him, but he took no notice of them. The manner of his breathing changed: he looked round the room eagerly; then, suddenly looking upwards, and fixing his eyes on one corner of the room, the appearance of his countenance changed to a kind of heavenly and glorious expression, the like of which no one present ever before had seen; and every one looked towards the place on which his eyes were fixed, but they could see nothing extraordinary. After a while his eyes half shut, and he fell into the agonies of death.

Death, even the death of those whose souls are redeemed, is a dreadful sight; for the sinful body struggles hard with it. Satan then does his worst: but it is written, "He that is with us is stronger than he that is against us;"[2] and he will surely deliver those, whom he hath purchased with his precious blood, even from the power of death and hell.

After several convulsive pangs, little Charles stretched himself; he breathed slower, and slower, and slower; then, fetching a deep sigh, his features became fixed in death. Nurse, who had come into the room some time before, perceiving that the soul of the dear child was departed, came up to the bed-side, and gently closed the eyes, and bound up with a handkerchief the mouth of the corpse; and having laid the arms and feet straight upon the bed, she stepped back to wipe away the tears that were running fast down her cheeks. All this while no one spoke, but all stood silently looking on the features of the dear child as they settled in death. After a few moments, Mr. Somers gave notice that he was going to pray, and every one knelt down around the bed. Mr. Somers's prayer was short, but it was very solemn; he first gave God thanks for the happy departure of the dear child, now with Christ his Redeemer; and, secondly, he earnestly prayed that God would, in his appointed time, grant unto all then present an equally happy death. His prayer finished with these words; "May we die the death of the righteous, and may our latter end be like his!"

Before Mr. Somers left the house, he took John Trueman apart, and asked him if it would be convenient for him that the child should be buried on the next Sunday morning at the hour of Morning Service? John Trueman answered, that he hoped to have every thing ready for the burial by that time. "Then," said Mr. Somers, "I will, with God's help, preach a sermon on the occasion." John Trueman bowed, but his heart was so full he could not speak; and Mr. Somers, and Mr. and Mrs. Fairchild, and the children, left the cottage.

The next morning Mr. Somers sent his clerk from house to house, through all the parish, to give notice that he meant to preach a sermon on the occasion of the death of Charles Trueman the next Sunday, and to request that all parents and masters would be kind enough to see that the younger part of their families came to church. Accordingly, the next Sunday, at Morning Service, the church was crowded: for not only all the young folks in the parish, but from all the country round—from Hill Top way, and Brookside way, and Blackwood way, and from Underhill village, (that is the place where Mrs. Goodwill lived)—as many as were able, came to see the funeral and to hear Mr. Somers's sermon. Mrs. Goodwill herself, too, was present; for she borrowed a horse which carried double, and came to Mr. Fairchild's on the Saturday evening, riding behind young Roberts the gardener, the son of John Roberts whom I spoke of before, and so was ready to go with Mrs. Fairchild to church on the Sunday morning.

The day proved fine, dry, and frosty: the sun just broke through the white clouds, with which the heavens had been overcast, when the bell began to ring for church; and at the same Henry set out to attend little Charles's funeral from Mary Bush's house to the church.——I will tell you the order of the funeral. The coffin was borne by six stout men, day-labourers in the parish: it was quite a plain coffin, marked with the name and age of the corpse. After the coffin walked the father, John Trueman, and old Goodman Grey; and then Henry, and Thomas Trueman; and then came Mary Trueman and Mary Bush, Nurse and Joan, and Trueman's little children, with some other persons, friends and neighbours. It was but a plain funeral: but there were none there who had not loved the departed child; and most persons present,

---

2. Perhaps an allusion to Romans 8.31.

both men and women, were such as lived in the fear of God: for since Mr. and Mrs. Fairchild, and Mr. Somers, had lived in that parish, by God's grace godliness had mightily grown and prospered thereabouts—by God's grace, I say; for Paul may plant, and Apollos water, but God giveth the increase.[3]

When the funeral came up to the church, the church and church-yard were quite full. Mr. Somers directed that the corpse should be brought into the church and set in the middle aisle, and he himself walked in before it, saying the words appointed in the Burial Service: 'I am the Resurrection and the Life, saith the Lord: he that believeth in me, though he were dead, yet shall he live; and whosoever liveth, and believeth in me, shall never die.' (John xi. 25, 26). 'I know that my Redeemer liveth, and that he shall stand at the latter day upon the earth: and though, after my skin, worms destroy this body, yet in my flesh shall I see God: whom I shall see for myself, and mine eyes shall behold, and not another.' (Job xix. 25–27). 'We brought nothing into this world, and it is certain we can carry nothing out. The Lord gave, and the Lord hath taken away; blessed be the name of the Lord.' (1 Tim. vi. 7; Job i. 21). Mr. Somers then went through the Burial Service in a slow and distinct manner: after which he preached a sermon, the substance of which I shall endeavour to lay before you.

Mr. Somers's text was from Matt. xiii. 41–43; 'The Son of man shall send forth his angels, and they shall gather out of his kingdom all things that offend, and them which do iniquity; and shall cast them into a furnace of fire: there shall be wailing and gnashing of teeth. Then shall the righteous shine forth as the sun, in the kingdom of their Father. Who hath ears to hear, let him hear.'——From this text Mr. Somers went on to point out to the young people gathered about him (for, as I said before, the young people from all the villages round about were gathered together that day), that after death there are two places, and only two, appointed; the one for the redeemed, and the other for the damned; namely, heaven and hell. "All who are here present," added he, looking round him, "every one of you, must after death go to one of these places, there to remain for ever and ever: so that it may be asked, 'Who amongst us shall dwell with a devouring fire? who amongst us shall dwell with everlasting burnings?' (Isa. xxxiii. 14)." He then went on to describe the happy state of the blessed, and the misery of the damned, from the Bible. I shall put down some of the most remarkable texts that he quoted: " 'My sheep hear my voice, and I know them, and they follow me: and I give unto them eternal life; and they shall never perish, neither shall any one pluck them out of my hand.' (John x. 27, 28). 'Henceforth there is laid up for me a crown of righteousness, which the Lord the righteous Judge shall give me at that day; and not to me only, but unto all them also that love his appearing.' (2 Tim. iv. 8). 'Ear hath not heard, nor eye seen, neither hath it entered into the heart of man to conceive the things that God hath prepared for them that love him.' (1 Cor. ii. 9). 'For the Lamb, which is in the midst of the throne, shall feed them, and shall lead them unto living fountains of waters; and God shall wipe away all tears from their eyes.' (Rev. vii. 17).—Mr. Somers then went on to describe the place of torment. " 'The fire that never shall be quenched: where their worm dieth not, and their fire is not quenched.' (Mark ix. 45, 46). 'The wicked shall be turned into hell, and all the nations that forget God.' (Psalm ix. 17). 'Upon the wicked he shall rain fire and brimstone, and an horrible tempest.' (Psalm xi. 6). 'But . . . the unbelieving, and the abominable, and murderers, and whoremongers, and sorcerers, and idolaters, and all liars, shall have their part in the lake that burneth with fire and

3. See 1 Corinthians 3.7.

brimstone: which is the second death.' (Rev. xxi. 8)."——When Mr. Somers had finished repeating these promises and threatenings from Scripture, he went on to point out to all present, that, through the sin of Adam, every one of his children had become unfit for heaven, and were by nature children of wrath and heirs of death and hell; having inherited from their father hearts so wholly and entirely filthy and corrupt, that they could not of themselves turn unto any good, or so much as wish to do well. He then spoke of the goodness of God, who, when miserable man had lost heaven by his transgression, sent his only Son to die for us upon the cross: thus was God "manifest in the flesh, justified in the spirit, seen of angels, preached unto the gentiles, believed on in the world, received up into glory."[4]——Mr. Somers then eagerly begged the young people to note his words: "I have shewn you," he said, "that you have lost heaven by nature, being through sin altogether unfit for it; and now, my dear children, I proceed to point out to you how you may recover it, and escape hell. There is One Name, and but One Name under heaven, by which men can be saved: and this Name, this blessed Name, is JESUS: on this Foundation if any man buildeth, he shall be saved. Oh, therefore, my beloved children, as you love your immortal souls, as you dread eternal fire and everlasting darkness and despair, hold fast to the cross of Christ, and count all things as nothing when compared with him."——Mr. Somers then explained unto the young people, that our Saviour by his death obtained three benefits for the redeemed: First, justification, which includes forgiveness of their sins through his death; Secondly, sanctification, which is the changing and cleansing their vile natures by the Holy Spirit; and, Finally, glorification, which no man will receive till after death: as it is written in the 17th Psalm, 'As for me, I will behold thy face in righteousness; I will be satisfied when I awake in thy likeness.'——Mr. Somers then spoke of Charles Trueman; of his state before death, and of his exceedingly happy death. He pointed out that there were two things which had been most remarkable in him, and which gave assurance of his now being blessed: the first was, his great humility and low thoughts of himself; so that, for many months before his death, he was never heard to speak of himself but as a sinner; and that not vainly and lightly, as some will do, but with deep sorrow and shame: and, secondly, his firm trust and joyful confidence in his Redeemer; so that his love seemed to have cast off all fear of death. "Oh, happy state! Oh, blessed death!" said Mr. Somers: "May all here present be found in faith at the hour of death, as this dear child was."——Mr. Somers finished his sermon by a few words to such parents as were present, recommending them, from the example then before them, to give a religious education to their children, and went over, one by one, all the means appointed by God for parents to use towards their children; to wit, bringing them in infancy to receive the sacrament of Baptism, and, in their due course and order, making them to attend and observe all Divine ordinances, such as public and private prayer, hearing of sermons, reading the Bible; setting before them the example of simple and holy living——Mr. Somers, I say, set all these things in order before the parents, and then concluded by urging them to seek from God, by diligent and earnest prayer presented in the name of the Redeemer, a Divine blessing upon their endeavours; "for, without God's grace and blessing, I may preach unto my dying day, and you may labour to instruct your children, rising up early and late taking rest, but all will be to no purpose: the work must be of God: therefore in all things let us give God the glory; ascribing to the Father, and to the Son, and to the Holy Ghost, all glory and honour for ever and ever. Amen."

4. 1 Timothy 3.16.

After the sermon, every one went to his own home. Mr. and Mrs. Fairchild and their children, with Mrs. Goodwill, thought and talked much of little Charles and his happy death, all day. In the evening, after tea, Mr. Fairchild prayed with his family, and they all sang a hymn together. You will, perhaps, like to hear Mr. Fairchild's prayer: I shall therefore put it down here, with the hymn.

A Prayer to be used by the Father or Master of a Family for his Children or Servants.

O Lord God, Thou by whom we hope to be justified, to be sanctified, and glorified; hear the prayer of a father, who, in the name of our blessed Saviour, intercedes for his children and his servants. O Lord, how dreadful would it be to me, at the last day, to see any one of these my dear children, or poor servants, condemned to everlasting fire! Oh! the thought is horrible! O Almighty God, give me grace, then, faithfully, humbly, and in simplicity, to use the means appointed to me for the good of my children. And, O holy Father, for thy dear Son's sake, for the sake of Him who died for us, grant thy grace, grant thy blessing, to this my dear family, from the greatest to the least. Pour thy Holy Spirit upon them. And, O enable me always, and at all times, to give unto thee the glory if my family do well. Unto thee, O Lord, be the glory; unto thee, O Father, unto thee, O Son, unto thee, O Holy Ghost, for ever and ever. *Amen.*

"Our Father, which art in heaven," &c. &c.

HYMN XXVII.[5]

Great God! now condescend
To bless our rising race:
Soon may their willing spirits bend
To thy victorious grace.

Oh, what a vast delight
Their happiness to see!
Our warmest wishes all unite
To lead their souls to thee.

Dear Lord! thy Spirit pour
Upon our infant seed:
Oh, bring the long'd-for happy hour
That makes them thine indeed!

FINIS.

1818

---

5. From Watts's *Divine Songs.*

CHARLOTTE MARY YONGE
1823–1901

A contemporary reviewer of Charlotte Yonge's work once grumbled about the primacy of the domestic in her books: "you have all the small life as well as the eventful; you sit down to nearly every breakfast, you are admitted to almost every room." Indeed, the "small life" was *all* life to her. Although she was a household name during the Victorian era, the shy, modest, and deeply religious Yonge shunned publicity and preferment. She lived her entire life in the Hampshire village of Otterbourne, first in Otterbourne House and then, a few years after her younger brother (her only sibling) brought his new bride to the family home, in a house with her mother a few hundred yards away. She herself never married, and was dedicated to church, family, and village, before all else. Over a span of nearly sixty years, Yonge wrote more than 160 books, including novels, histories, biographies, lesson books, and a pioneering work of onomastics, *History of Christian Names* (2 vols., 1863), but she described herself as a Sunday school teacher. She led her first Sunday school class at the age of seven, and thereafter rarely missed a week for seventy-one years.

Yonge is generally classed as a novelist of the Oxford Movement—the revitalizing movement, begun in 1833 at Oxford University by John Keble and other Anglican clergy, that urged the Church of England to return to older doctrines and rituals, bringing them closer to their Roman Catholic origins. The Oxford Movement reverberated within British life through its emphasis on the role of the church in society, education, church-building, and the revival of Anglican religious communities. The two greatest influences on Yonge's life were her father, who taught her at home, and Keble, who left Oxford to become the vicar of Hursley, a neighboring parish. The lessons of Yonge's confirmation at age fifteen under the spiritual guidance of Keble would guide both the tenor and conduct of her life in all the years of fame to come.

Yonge's great talent lay in creating memorable, lifelike personalities and in writing realistic dialogue. Indeed, conversations create much of the plots of her domestic stories. Yonge's most famous work of domestic realism for young readers, *The Daisy Chain* (1856), chronicles the family life, parish work, and emotional and spiritual crises of Dr.

May and his eleven children. Although its audience was primarily adolescent girls, George Eliot was among those who found the long novel to be both absorbing and satisfying. The enthusiastic, intelligent, and clumsy Ethel May—a precursor to Louisa May Alcott's Jo March in *Little Women* (1868–69; Alcott admired Yonge, to whose works she alluded in her own writings), and similarly semi-autobiographical—is one of Yonge's most beloved characters. Yonge funded missionary ventures in the Melanesian Islands and New Zealand with the considerable profits from her books; *The Daisy Chain*, for example, was in its ninth edition by 1868. She also helped support her brother's family.

As the first editor of and a contributor to *The Monthly Packet of Evening Readings for Members of the Church of England* between 1851 and 1890, Charlotte Yonge played a crucial role in constructing the reading of middle- and upper-class girls through two generations. Lacking office or staff, this periodical ran on a shoestring and never had more than 1,500 subscribers, yet Yonge's creation, in Georgina Battiscombe's words in her 1943 biography of Yonge, "helped to mould the character of innumerable young ladies" through its serials, articles on such subjects as history and botany, and papers on parish work and foreign missions. One enthusiastic set of Yonge's admirers formed a circle called the Goslings, who sought to improve their minds and model themselves after the virtuous heroines found in her fiction. For fifteen years Yonge guided this group of girls (including the future novelist Mrs. Humphry Ward) and oversaw their manuscript magazine, *The Barnacle*.

Other writings by Yonge were intended not for a middle-class audience but for the enjoyment and edification of working-class children and featured working-class characters. Among these were the Langley stories, based on Yonge's own village of Otterbourne and collected in such books as *Langley School* (1850), *Lads and Lasses of Langley* (1881), and *Langley Little Ones: Six Stories* (1882). "A Patchwork Fever," from *Langley Adventures* (1883), is one of these linked stories. (In 1967 Gillian Avery published a selection of Langley stories, including "A Patchwork Fever," as *Village Children*.) Yonge's belief—found in all of her work—in the twin duties of moderation and domesticity can be traced in "A Patchwork Fever" through the trials of studious thirteen-year-old Frances Gale, who is eager "to make everyone own that a girl who was good at her books could also be good at household matters." Frances's good intentions go awry, however, as her obsession with creating an ornamental patchwork tablecloth for her mother's birthday interferes with her duties to her family and with managing the household.

In both her books and her life, Yonge demonstrated the heroism of the domestic virtues. Rather than being "uneventful," her long life was filled with tireless work for her village school, her church, her family, and her readers. Charlotte Yonge was buried on March 29, 1901—the thirty-fifth anniversary of the death of her great mentor, John Keble.

A Patchwork Fever

CHAPTER I

"How long are your Christmas holidays to be, Fancy?" asked Mrs Gale. "A week or a fortnight?"

"A fortnight mother," answered Frances, "because Miss Bolton wants to go home, and there's to be a very grand Christmas tree one of the nights that week."

"Then I shall be able to go and see your granny. It didn't seem worth while to go for a day or two at the end of the week—just coming and going—to worrit the poor old soul, but if I go on Boxing Day with an excursion return,[1] I could come home Thursday or Friday the week after, time to get things round before Sunday, and you are quite old enough now to do for your father and the children for a bit while I'm away."

"Oh, but you'll never be away on your birthday, mother!" cried Frances.

"Which day of the week is it? The seventh? That is Saturday. I shall certainly be at home by that time, please God, and it will be no bad time to leave you with the boys, for Gilbert will be a good deal taken up with all that's going on—practising for the penny reading,[2] and the choir supper and all—and he will be up at the stables all day with father. But you will do your best, like a good girl, to keep him contented at home in the evenings if father has to be out. That's all that troubles me in going away just now, for fear Gilbert should get about with Ben Grant and all that lot, and father be vexed, but you see I must go now. What with one thing and another, I have not seen poor mother since Leonard was a baby, and that's six years ago now. And your aunt Lizzie writes that she's failing, and I'd never forgive myself if I did not go to see her once more, poor dear. And I can trust you, Fancy, to keep things straight at home."

"Yes, indeed, mother, I'll do my best," said Frances. "I can always tackle little Lenny and Clary, and what with his drawing and his book, and all that is going on, I am sure that Gilbert will be a good boy while you are away."

Mr Gale was coachman at Langley Hall, and lived at one of the lodges. There were four children, who had come in pairs, first Frances and Gilbert, now thirteen and twelve years old, and then, after an interval of four years, Leonard and Clara, who were eight and seven. Frances was a bright, quick girl, glad to be able to stay on at school, and with hopes of succeeding Margaret Roller as pupil teacher, a wish

---

1. I.e., a round-trip ticket. Boxing Day: the day after Christmas, observed as a holiday on which servants of various kinds receive a Christmas gift from their employers.

2. An inexpensive entertainment meant for the working classes, at which pieces from literature are recited and music performed.

that rather surprised her mother, who would rather wash all day than even look at one of Frances' long sums or analysed sentences; while Gilbert, instead of being grateful, thought it a great hardship to have to stay on at least another year after passing the sixth standard;[3] not that he was either stupid or idle, but he was tired of books and wanted to be free, and as much of a man as his comrades, and he did not take into his mind what his father told him, that every additional year of schooling ought to fit him for a better place in life.

Amos, the stable-boy at the Hall, was going home for Christmas, and Mr Gale had asked leave to let Gilbert do his work in the holidays, so as to judge whether he would be fit for such a situation. Indeed, Gilbert greatly hoped that Amos would "better himself" and leave the jacket and broom for him at the Hall.

Frances was proud and pleased at being left in authority, though she knew that she should thus have less fun than her companions during the holidays. But how nice it would be to make every one own that a girl who was good at her books could also be good at household matters. Her father sometimes laughed when she talked about the domestic economy she learnt at school, and declared that his own old mother, who had brought up thirteen children on ten shillings a week, without relief from the parish, knew more of it than ever was to be got out of books. Frances had really been taught by her mother how to make herself useful, though rather against her will, and thus, being sharp-witted and neat in her ways, was quite as handy as any girl of her age in the parish.

Mrs Gale put everything in order for her, and told her over and over again how much bread and butter to take in, and what meat she had better get for the pie for the Sunday's dinner, and how all the rest of the week was to be provided for.

"And, Fancy, you and Clara are not to wear your white frocks to the school tea and Christmas-tree. When the young ladies have you up to tea in the nursery on Tuesday, that's a different thing; but in the school you'd only be messing them about. There will be Miss Mary and Miss Hilda trying to pour out tea and upsetting it all over you."

"That will be worse for our claret merinos[4] than for our white frocks," said Fancy, who rather liked coming out in white among her schoolfellows, as only a few of them could do the same, and liked still more setting off little Clara with her blue sash and bows.

"What is the girl thinking of? Your claret dresses, indeed! No, your serges[5] are quite good enough for the school tea. Mind, I'll not have little Clary catching her death of cold in her white! And mind, when father is out late with the carriage, that when you go to bed you lay the things ready for him, and make up the fire with the ashes and one of the big coals at the top, and put the kettle by it so that he can boil it up in a moment. That's the worst of going out just now, there are so many parties, and the carriage will be out so late! Dear, dear, if I had not writ to poor mother that I am coming, I think I should stay at home after all."

"I'll do my best, mother," said Frances.

And she meant it, and when she had seen her father and mother drive off in the dogcart[6] with Clara between them, she set herself heartily to peeling potatoes, in readiness to eat with the cold goose remaining from the Christmas dinner, which had come out of a goose club.[7]

3. The highest degree of proficiency in elementary school, assessed by examination. "Pupil teacher": an apprentice teacher.
4. Light-red fine woolen garments.
5. Clothing of inexpensive woolen fabric.

6. A light, two-wheeled carriage drawn by one horse.
7. A working-class association: subscribers would pay a small weekly sum for thirteen weeks and receive a goose for Christmas Eve.

All went well that day. Father was to have supper with the servants, Gilbert joined the rest of the choir in their rounds, ending with supper at the Hall, and Frances and the two children, as well as Emma Nowell, drank tea in the nursery, and played at games till they were tired. And Miss Manners came up and told them the story of Cinderella, which lasted till the choir began to sing carols in the hall, and then, what fun it was to stand on the broad stairs, and peep down at Gilbert and all the rest as if they were strangers!

Frances, however, was more used to this than were the younger ones, and she presently wandered back to the nursery, where Nurse Grey was sitting, not liking to leave the two youngest children, in case they should be wakened by the unusual sounds.

What attracted Fancy was the sight of a silk patchwork table-cover, which Mrs Grey was lining as she sat at the table. It was very pretty, in a regular pattern of six-sided patches, like a honeycomb, set in black ones, and it was not very large. Mrs Grey had made it at odd times for a new year's gift to her brother's wife, and she was quite ready to let Fancy look at it, and to lend her the pattern cut out in zinc.[8]

Fancy had a large bundle of pieces of silk and ribbon given her by her aunt, a dressmaker, to persuade her to be more fond of her needle than of her book, and it struck her that such a cover as this, for her mother's little round table in the parlour, would be a most beautiful birthday present, and could be made for a surprise while she was away.

"You are very welcome, I am sure," said Mrs Grey; "I only hope you will be able to find time for it in these short days, with your mother away."

"Oh yes," said Fancy. "Mother being away is the beauty of it, or it would not be a surprise. Luckily I've got ever so much black for the ground—and a figured ribbon with little roses that will just make one of the centre pieces. Won't mother be delighted?"

"Yes," said Mrs Grey, with a little doubt in her tone; "that is, if you don't neglect other things that are of more importance for it."

"Oh! I'll take care not to do that," said Fancy; "mother has fixed everything. We are to have the giblet pie tomorrow, she made it all, and I have only to warm it up. Next day, there's a piece of the salt pork, and I'm to see what the butcher can let us have! Let me see, there are—one—two—three—"

"Forty-two stars, if that is what you mean," said Mrs Grey, "besides the halves, but I don't know if your table is the same size as mine, and you must be very careful to keep the pattern straight and even, or it will not look well. I think I have one pretty star left over."

She had, and it was a charming one, made out of some shaded ribbon of soft geranium colour so managed that all the light parts joined exactly round the centre, which was a rose-bud on a straw-coloured ground.

Frances was delighted, and could think of nothing but patches all the way home. Before going up to put Clara to bed, she looked at the little table in the parlour and decided that it would not need quite so large a cover as Mrs Grey's.

---

8. I.e., a stencil guide of thin zinc.

Chapter III

The patchwork was her first thought in the morning, and she hoped to get a great deal of housework done before breakfast, so as to be able to begin the sooner at her delightful undertaking. Her father and Gilbert went off to the stables quite early, before she was dressed, and she must have the fire lighted and the kettle boiling before they came home, the room tidy and breakfast set out. The children could dress themselves, but they must be attended to, if they were to be fit to be seen. Frances, however, trusted to squeeze out a few moments, in which to look out the bundle of patches from the corner of her chest of drawers.

But the fire was provokingly slow in burning up, and kept Frances over it many minutes longer than she had reckoned. Then, just as she had set on the kettle, which could at least take care of itself, there came a voice down stairs, "Fancy, Fancy, I can't find my stockings."

And by the time Leonard's every-day stockings had been routed out of the corner where they had gone, when he dressed for the Hall, there was another call, "Fancy, Fancy, I can't undo this horrid knot."

And by the time the knot in Clara's petticoat string was untied, the kettle was boiling over, and she had to rush down to it in haste. She had only just put on the table-cloth when her father and Gilbert came home, so that she had to make the coffee and toast her father's rasher[9] in the greatest haste; and then Gilbert declared that he must have a rasher too, since he had been up and out at work like a man. Clara and Leonard came tumbling down stairs with very rough[1] heads, and immediately begging for bacon too, upon which their father divided his between them, never thinking—said Fancy to herself—how much more work he made for her, as of course she had to do another for him.

She swallowed her own breakfast in haste, and to her great relief, her father let Leonard come up to the stables, his great treat. When all the men-folk were safe out of the house, Fancy thought she might indulge herself with a rummage for her bundle of silks, since Clara was always proud to be allowed to wash up the breakfast things and could do it very nicely.

But to wash them all alone was a very different thing from doing so with mother's eye upon her, and mother's voice to say "good girl", or "take care", whenever a cup or saucer was safely wiped, and Fancy was roused from reckoning whether she could get six blue spots all into the middle of her hexagons by Clara pattering up the stairs.

"Have you broken anything, you naughty girl?" exclaimed Frances with a great start.

"Oh, no! Only you were so long, I thought I would come and see! Oh, Fancy, how lovely! Do pray give me a bit for my dolly's frock!"

This made Frances roll her bundle up in a hurry, and say: "I'll see, Clary, but I want to make mother a table-cover for a secret for her birthday present, like Mrs Grey's."

"Oh! and I'll help! Let me help, and then it will be both of us," cried the child.

"Very well, we will see," said Frances, thinking that she might please the child and make her useful in cutting out the papers to be covered. "Only you must be a good girl now and help me to get things tidy."

So the two sisters set to work to make the beds and put away the dresses that had been worn last evening, Clara chattering happily all the time, and well pleased to assist, as it was a pleasant change from school work. But when this was done, and

9. A thin slice of bacon or ham.   1. Shaggy, unkempt.

the windows set open, and the sisters down stairs again, Fancy was dismayed to see a great slop[2] on the table, only two tea cups and saucers washed, and the rest still reposing in the bowl.

"Oh, you idle child, why did you leave off before you had done?"

"I didn't like being by myself," said Clara.

"How foolish! Well! now you go on and finish like a good maid."

"No, you do it, Fancy, I'll peel the potatoes."

Fancy could not suffer this, as it was sure to end in the pig getting a great deal too much potato, if not a slice of finger into the bargain, so she ordered Clara back to her work rather crossly, and Clara in a pet upset the bowl all over herself, breaking the handle off her own favourite cup. She cried, and when her sister scolded her, and said it was all her fault; she cried so much more bitterly that there was nothing for it but to give up work to kiss and comfort her, and hang the pinafore upon the back of a chair to dry. All this took up time, and though the giblet-pie was ready made and baked, and required no cooking, Frances could not finish enough of the morning's work to make the house feel moderately respectable till twelve o'clock, and even then she had not dusted the parlour, which she knew ought to be done every day; but she thought that might wait for once, she did so long to set about her patchwork.

She tidied up Clara's hair, for father would not endure that the little one should look shaggy and uncombed, and she was very proud herself of the pretty, glossy, flaxen locks. Then she hunted up an old copybook, and set Clara to cut out the papers on which the patches were to be tacked, after she had cut out the first seven herself, so as to be able to make a beginning.

"Please, Fancy, let me cut the silk," was the cry.

"O dear no, Clary; you could not manage it. It takes ever so much contriving to get it the right way of the stuff—"

"I'm sure I could cut that," said Clara, pouting.

"Don't be so tiresome—I tell you you can't. Why, see how you have done that one. Look, one side is ever so much longer than the other—you must hold the pattern steady."

"I don't like it. It hurts my fingers," said Clara, laying down the scissors; and indeed the little fingers were hardly firm enough to produce the necessary exactness, without which the whole would be spoilt.

"Well, then, you can lay the table for dinner, and be useful."

But every one knows how children like to help as they think, when nobody wants them, but if they can be really useful, always insist on doing something else. Clara did not fancy laying the cloth, but went off in search of her dolls, of which she had three, named after the young ladies at the Hall, Edith, Alice, and Hilda. And she began again on the entreaty for one of the beautiful scraps for Hilda's frock. "Only one, and just see how dirty it is, Fancy!"

That was undeniable, since Hilda had just been discovered reposing in an empty flowerpot under the stairs, and Frances, to prevent the fingering of all her precious bits, consented to give up a piece of pink gauzy material, much too thin to be made into patchwork, though it was very pretty. Clara accepted it, finding it vain to beg for the beautiful piece of blue and white brocade on which she had set her heart.

But after twisting the piece about and crumpling it, she began to beg for help, and Frances soon found that her only chance of being left at peace was to cut out Hilda's

_____
2. A quantity of spilled liquid.

princess dress, and fix it for being made up; and by the time that was done, it was needful to begin preparations for dinner, which had to be over early in case father was wanted to ride out with one of the young ladies.

It was only just ready in time, and when all had been done and put away, Frances trusted that she had obtained a little quiet by sending out Leonard and Clara to pick up fir-cones in the plantations. Gilbert sometimes would amuse himself with gluing fir-cones upon old baskets and boxes, and she hoped to persuade him and Leonard to set in hand a very nice birthday present for mother, in the shape of a case for the pot of her favourite lemon geranium plant.

She really had two hours of comfortable work, in which she made a charming beginning, with a little Chinaman in a broad hat in her central patch, and in the six pieces round him three brown stripes on a grey ground, with a broader one down the middle of each hexagon, so that he looked as if he were in the middle of a brown paling.[3] It was done with beautiful neatness and regularity, and took a very long time, so that Fancy had only just tacked the patches for her second star, a white lily on a crimson ground, with six blue spots round it, when there were the children back again, their baskets full of cones. But, oh dear! oh dear! why was Clara shrinking out of sight? There was a terrible three-cornered rent in her serge frock, a rent that would take all the evening to darn properly.

"Oh, Clara, Clara! how could you be such a naughty girl," she cried.

"It was a nasty stake in the hedge that did it, Fancy," she said.

"Nonsense. Doesn't mother always tell you not to say things did it? The stake wouldn't have done it, if you had let it alone. Now you shall sit down this instant and mend it yourself, and then you will think before you tear your clothes next time."

"I can't mend that, Fancy," said Clara, beginning to cry.

Fancy knew that the child could not really make such a darn, but it might be run up enough to hold together till she had time to do it properly, and it would be good discipline for Clara. And were not Mr Somers and Miss Bolton always talking about discipline?

"But I want to do my dolly's frock," mourned Clara.

"Then, you should not have torn your own," said Frances, who was all the more cross because she knew—at the bottom of her mind—that she had been in too great a hurry to get rid of the children to dress Clara in the old, old frock which was given up to wet days and scrambles.

Clara was by no means a naughty child, and she would have done at once what her mother or her school-mistress desired, but when Frances put upon her a piece of work that she knew her mother would not have given her, and that was very disagreeable besides, she began to fret.

Then Fancy, in a fierce voice which she fancied like her mother's in authority, exclaimed, "None of that, you naughty girl! Sit down directly, and mend your frock."

Clara was rather awed; she began to believe herself naughty and sat down by the window, while Frances sent off Leonard to fetch the milk which they were always allowed from the dairy.

Presently Frances's needle broke, and she had to go up stairs to look out another. When she came down she found Clara and the kitten at high romps with one of the pieces of old copybook from from which she had been cutting out her papers. The remains formed a sort of stiff network, into which Pussy had poked its little paws, and Clara was dancing about holding them, and making the kitten frolic with her on

3. Fence.

its hind legs. Just as Frances came to the room door, over went the little round table she had been working at, and away went all her patches on the floor.

"You very naughty, idle, mischievous child—how dare you?" cried Frances, flying at Clara, and giving her a good shake.

And at that very moment, while Clara was screaming and sobbing, the door opened, and there stood her father, asking, with great displeasure, what this meant, and what Frances was about with her sister. She was still too angry to be frightened, and hotly exclaimed, "She's been a very naughty girl! She's been and torn her frock, and when I told her to mend it, she jumps up, the very moment my back is turned to play with the cat, and goes and upsets all my work—just to spoil it."

"Fancy was so cross," sobbed Clara, now that she had a defender, "and she's hurt my shoulder."

"Don't you know, Frances," said her father, "that mother never will have you hit the little ones?"

"I didn't hit her," cried Fancy, "I only gave her a little shake."

"That's worse," said her father, sitting down and taking Clara up on his knee, while she leant against him, letting her sobs wear themselves down. He did not go into the rights of the question at all, and Frances was left to pick up all her odds and ends from the floor, feeling very much hurt at having the child petted and set up against her, after having really done mischief. And before she had found all her precious bits, her father called her to look alive and get his tea, for he was to drive the little ladies to a children's party, and had to start early.

Gilbert would be wanted in the choir on all these Saints' Day evenings, so that he was safely disposed of, and Fancy hoped to have a nice clear time for her work. But, alas! there was *that* frock. She knew how to mend it properly; nay, it would be a fine field for practising all that fine sewing she had learnt at school, and it might be done so beautifully that the vexation of the rent might be forgotten by her mother in satisfaction at seeing how beautifully her elder daughter could work. But that would be a two or three hours business, and Fancy thought it might wait till the patchwork was finished, if she just ran it up so that it would hold together till she had time.

Leonard and Clara were happily kept quiet most of the evening by picking over the basket of fir-cones, choosing out the perfect, handsome, straight scaly ones that were fit to use, and putting them in one basket, while the shabbier ones were first laid out in a row on the hearth to dry, and well patted by the kitten, and then they were put into the hottest place in the fire, where the bright white flame licked them over, flickered and went out, having painted each scale black with a red edge. Thus thrust in one by one, and each singly watched and admired, the fir-cones lasted a long time, and Frances was only disturbed by calls upon her to look at some specially bright one or some sulky black one that would not light up properly. It was quite the children's bedtime when the last was poked into the fire, and if the clock had not struck eight just then they might even have broken into the basket of good cones!

Frances put them to bed, and had just come down again, when Gilbert tumbled in, tired and sleepy enough to go off to bed as soon as he had had his supper, and after that, she had a good time over her work, which was so interesting that she did not know how time went, and was quite startled to hear her father's step on the gravel outside the door when he came home at half-past ten, after having driven the little misses home, and settled his horses for the night.

"What, up still, Fancy! Mother never meant that, my maid."

"I didn't know it was so late, father," she said, bustling about to clear the table and get his supper.

"Whatever are you about with all those rags?" asked her father.

"Making a surprise for mother for her birthday, father," returned Fancy, holding up her central star with a border of black silk patches round it, and two more of delicate rose-colour and of green stripes beyond.

"Very pretty, no doubt," said Mr Gale, "but don't you get too much taken up with it, Fancy, and neglect other things, or may be mother will have a surprise of the wrong sort."

"Oh, I'll take care of that, father," said Fancy, and if her conscience pricked her as she spoke, she satisfied herself by thinking that she would do everything all right tomorrow.

Chapter IV

This was the first of Fancy's days of management, and the others went on in the same fashion. The silk patchwork grew more interesting as its beauty developed, and the quantity of contrivance it required was wonderful. Emma Nowell came in and admired it very much, and even contributed a precious scrap of her mother's wedding gown, which, being peach-coloured, was better for a dress than a table-cover, so that it was lucky that there was so little of it that it could only go into the half stars that would come at the edge.

Every spare moment did Frances spend on that work, and some moments that could hardly be called spare. She durst not neglect her father's meals, and she kept the rooms tidy and the children neat so far as he could see, so that she did not draw on herself another reproof from him, or else he would probably have made her throw up the work altogether.

But as she became more anxious to finish it off, she put off and left aside more, thinking that when once the table-cover was done, one hard day's work would clear everything up before her mother came home and it made her cross to be interrupted or obliged to do anything else.

Her father was at home on Innocents' Day[4] evening and went to church. The children were always delighted to go on a late weekday evening in the winter; the dark walk, the bright windows, were so delightful; outside and inside the service and the hymns somehow sounded quite different, when all the lamps were shining and the wind swung them as the door was opened, and made all the shadows move in a strange way. And Mr Somers' head was traced upon the wall behind him like a black giant's side face. It was a great treat when father said he could take them. However, tonight Frances was seized with a fit of prudence about the house. She said she could not lock it up and leave it empty when so many Christmas folk were about.

She thought, or fancied she thought, that was her reason, and she was greatly nettled when her father laughed a little to himself and said: "Well, have it your own way;" for well he knew that if Frances had had any real dread of rough tipsy folk coming about, she would ten times rather be anywhere with him than alone in the house.

Certainly it would have served her right to have had a fright, but none came, and she had the full benefit of the quiet hour so that the middle star had the six surrounding ones complete in their black ground, and arranged in a manner that did great credit to her taste and contrivance. There was the Chinaman in the middle, surrounded by his brown paling. A butterfly, which Fancy had cruelly surrounded

4. December 28, also called Childermas; observed by a mass or festival, it commemorates the infants slain by Herod at Bethlehem.

with a cobweb of narrow white and purple stripes, was opposite to another butterfly within patches half black, half yellow. Another pair of stars placed opposite, bore in the centre pieces roses set within white, spotted deep blue. There were two flower-baskets upon a black ground, surrounded by purple and white check, and a couple of little Chinese pagodas were set off by an odd pattern of scarlet and black dashes. The effect was charming, and the middle being now complete, Frances meant to use her plainer silks, which would take much less contrivance and time, but the beginning was so beautiful that she quite hovered over it, thinking how lovely it would be, and how every one would praise her taste and neatness—all the pieces going the right way of the silk, not one of them askew, except one butterfly which could not have been got in otherwise.

She was more in love with it than ever, and less willing to be called off for anything else. She made the family eat baked apples at dinner because a pudding would have taken so long to make; and she cut short blind man's holiday[5] by lighting the lamp, when the children wanted her to have a game and play with them.

They went off with Gilbert into the back kitchen, where they made a prodigious noise and ended by upsetting a crock in the dark and breaking it. And Gilbert said it was all Fancy's fault for being so tiresome!

She thought him the tiresome one, though his father's coming in to tea kept him in some order. But Mr and Mrs Manners were going out to dinner, and Mr Gale would of course drive them, so that the children would be left to themselves that evening.

He told them to behave themselves, and off he went. As soon as he was gone, Gilbert declared they would have some fun—they would put the table out of the way and play at puss-in-the-corner.[6] Then, as Fancy looked in utter contempt, and said, "I can't spare the table, I ain't such a baby," he caught up a bit of the paper which she had cut out, looked through the holes like a pair of spectacles, fitted them on to his nose, laid hold of her, and dragged her dancing round the room, while she screamed and struggled till they all but upset the table, lamp and all. That startled them a little, for they knew that upsetting a paraffin lamp was a dangerous thing. Fancy scolded a little, and then offered to go off into the parlour with the light, and work there with the door open.

"Ho! ho! my Lady Frances; nothing but the parlour for her," hooted Gilbert; and Leonard joined him, and all the children pulled Fancy down on the floor. Leonard, getting hold of her plaited tail of hair, pulled it till she shrieked with pain and anger.

"You naughty boys! You never go on like this when mother's at home!"

"You ain't mother," said Leonard, preparing for a fresh tug.

Poor Frances felt herself in their power, so she made a bargain with them. "Now look here, Gilly and Lenny. If I play with you till the clock strikes the half hour, will you be quiet then and let me do my work?"

They agreed, and the tug of war began, Fancy and Leonard on one side and Gilbert and Clara on the other.

It was an equal match for strength of body, only Fancy's hands never could bear as much strain as Gilbert's, and so she was pulled over. Then came puss-in-the-corner, very merry and good humoured, but the instant the church clock chimed the half hour, Fancy walked gravely out of her corner, put Clara aside when the child ran full tilt against her, and began setting up the flap of the table again. They all

5. Dusk, when it is too dark to work but candles are not yet lit.
6. A children's game (also called *puss-puss*); the

"puss" stands in the center of the room and tries to catch the "mice" as they leave the safety of their corners and change position.

howled at her, and begged for a little more time, but she said, "You promised," and sat herself down.

Gilbert knew he had promised, and the healthy merry sport was stopped, but the boy's idle hands began to find mischief in pinching Clara, and pulling her hair, till she whined and nearly cried.

"Come now," said Frances, "why can't you sit down and learn your lessons[7] for Sunday school. I'm sure you don't know a word of them."

"You don't know them yourself, miss governess," retorted Gilbert.

"I sha'n't go to school on Sunday, there's dinner to get."

"You ought to learn them all the same."

"That's no business of yours. Come, Lenny, get your book."

"I sha'n't."

"There, you see, Gilly, how naughty you are making the children! Come, sit down, and let the fire alone."

"I sha'n't stay here to be worrited.[8] I shall go and see what the other chaps are after."

"Now, Gilbert, you know father won't have you larking about with all the worst fellows in Langley."

"Who told you they were the worst fellows in Langley?" returned Gilbert.

"But he won't have you going out at night."

"This ain't night!" and off he went, shutting the door with a bang.

Frances was too angry with his disobedience to have any notion that it was her own fault, and now that he was gone, she found the hymns for Leonard and Clara, ordered them to down on their stools, and said they *should* learn their lessons. When Leonard declared that he should not learn them till Gilly did, Frances said that they *must* learn or else go to bed; and she looked so determined that the little things were both rather cowed; and as they also knew that mother would have made them learn a piece each evening in the week, they submitted to sit down with books in their hands, and Fancy lost herself again in piecing out her remnant of a geranium-coloured necktie so as to make it surround a patch of pale blue with an odd thing in the middle like the tails of two wasps joined together. She never looked at the children, who had a very comfortable game at 'Handy Spandy Jack a dandy,'[9] under the table, peeping up now and then under their eyelids to see if she was attending to them, and then grinning at each other in triumph, as they saw how little she was likely to enforce their learning.

When the clock struck seven she asked them if they knew the collect.[1]

"Not yet," said Leonard boldly, while Clara grew somewhat redder, but Fancy was only glad not to be obliged to hear them try to repeat it.

It was quite troublesome enough to have to go through the washing and putting to bed, which was always half an hour's work, and looked much larger when they were inclined to be playful and troublesome, as they were tonight, splashing the water about, blowing soap bubbles between their hands, and doing every thing that could possibly tease a sister in a hurry. At last, when it came to dancing round the table with bare feet, and nothing on but a night gown, Fancy could bear it no longer, but caught Leonard by the arm and gave him a sharp slap which made him cry out, while Clara burst forth, "Father said you were never to hit us."

---

7. I.e., memorize Bible verses.
8. Pestered.
9. A game, in which one player shakes an object between his or her hands while reciting this nurs-ery rhyme; once the hands are closed, the other children guess which holds the object.
1. A short prayer in the Anglican service that varies according to specific day.

"To hit *you!*" said Frances. "He didn't know what naughty bad children you could be, going on like this just because you know I'm busy."

They were tired out by this time, and they were not at all audacious children, being generally kept in good order. Leonard began to cry, and Frances was ready to comfort him, till she got them both safely into bed at last. But their prayers had been very oddly muttered by the tired agitated little things, and Frances was still too full of her scheme, to have room in her head for the thought that most of the naughtiness of the evening might have been hindered if she had tried to make things pleasant to the others. She was a little uneasy about Gilbert, but he came in about nine o'clock, hungry, tired, and cross. He would not tell her where he had been, saying, "Girls were always badgering," and he helped himself to a tumbler of beer, from the little cask. She reminded him that he was never allowed it for supper, to which he answered that he wasn't a little chap now. And when she persisted he said, "he wasn't going to be nagged by a girl."

He drank up the beer, set down the tumbler, as if on purpose, upon one of her best pieces of silk, skimmed his hat across the table so as to send everything flying, and stumped up to bed without first taking off his boots, as if on purpose to leave a fringe of clay on the edge of every step. Frances thought what a horrid bad boy he was, but her head was too full to consider how to help him to be better; besides, this was only once in a way.[2]

CHAPTER V

It was true that between parish festivities and evenings that father was at home, there were not many times when Gilbert was on his sister's hands, but still there were two nights when Mr Gale was wanted to take the carriage out. Gilbert glued fir-cones and worked at the window box quite contentedly when his father was at home; or, when he was tired of that, he read *Slaves and Cruisers* or the *Boy's Own Paper*.[3] But when Mr Gale went out of the house, Gilbert found it impossible to go on with anything quietly. He must have some fun, he said. If Fancy would get out the draught-board[4]—Leonard could not play well enough—and play with him—

No! Fancy had had hardly any time for her patches among the many needs of a Saturday; she could not possibly lay them down now. "Bother your work," he said, and flung out of doors again.

That was on Saturday night, and on Sunday Clara and Leonard lost their marks[5] because they could not say their lessons; Fancy had fully meant to teach them on Sunday morning, but she had put off too much from Saturday, and there was nothing but a hurry all the forenoon. And after all, the baked shoulder of mutton with potatoes was not done enough! Father was angry, and said going to school spoilt girls, and it was very odd that a big maid of thirteen like her couldn't have a bit of sense. She would have to go out to service as a scullery maid, or she would be good for nothing all her life.

Frances cried a good deal and had red eyes when she went to church in the afternoon. But then she thought, when people saw what a beautiful piece of work she had done, they would forgive and forget all that was past, and though she said with her lips that she had "followed *too much* the devices and desires of her own heart,"[6]

---

2. I.e., this was exceptional.
3. Weekly boys' magazine (1879–1967), published by the Religious Tract Society. *Slavers and Cruisers*: a tale by Samuel Whitchurch Sadler (1881), published by the Christian Knowledge Society.

4. Checkerboard.
5. Lost their high place in their Sunday school class.
6. Part of the introduction to morning and evening prayer from the Anglican Book of Common Prayer.

she never thought about the meaning of it, or laid to heart that it concerned herself, though at school, or in the senior scholars' examination she could have given an excellent explanation of the whole confession. But all the time she was counting the remaining patches that had to be done. It was very provoking, too, that while playing with Clara in getting over the stile as they came home, Leonard managed to catch his foot in that little girl's frock, and tear the kilting[7] off nearly half way round. It was the best, the claret-coloured Sunday dress, new at Christmas; Frances scolded till Clara cried, and Leonard ran away from her. They had both grown so rough and unruly that they were not like the same children, who used to be so easily managed, and never were known to cry.

However, the dress itself was not torn, and as it was only worn on Sunday there would be plenty of time to mend it after the great work was finished! Frances almost grudged the time that would be taken up by Tuesday's Christmas-tree, when a letter came from Mrs Gale saying that she should come home on Thursday. "That's right!" said father, slapping his knee, "now we shall be something like[8] again!"

Poor man! The kettle had not boiled when he wanted his breakfast in a hurry, and the coffee had been horrible, and there was no butter, because Fancy had forgotten to send for it! To be sure the children made a worse fuss about that than he did, at least it lasted longer, for he and Gilbert had to go off to the stables at once.

But Leonard kicked and cried over his dry bread, till he drove Fancy into getting down the jar of treacle[9] that was only kept for a treat, to keep him quiet while she was upstairs making the beds. Her peace did not last long, there were two howls of dismay: "You did it!" "No, you did it." Down she rushed. Behold the treacle all over the table, floor, and children! For Leonard had wanted more, and Clara thought he had had enough—there was a fight and a struggle, and over went the jar.

Fancy was very angry now, and ready to cry as she scolded right and left, and the children were so frightened at what they had done, that they submitted to be put into opposite corners, while Fancy tried to wash out the treacle from Clara's frock and Leonard's jacket, heartily regretting that they had had no pinafores on. For she had only discovered that very morning that the last clean ones were gone—the messing of the last week had been so much more than usual, and she had put off all the washing.

The cat had had her share of the overthrow but she was better off than the children, as no one objected to her licking herself by the fire, whereas poor Clara stood with bare shoulders in the farthest corner of the kitchen, with the back kitchen doors, inner and outer, open behind her, till at last she began to shiver, and a piteous little voice said,

"Mayn't I come and warm myself, Fancy, I'll be good?"

Fancy relented and let her prisoners out, and having done all that she could to the frock in the way of washing out, she let the child put it on again, and cower over the fire to warm herself. But what was Clara to wear that evening? The serge was clearly in no condition to be put on, for not only was the treacle mark visible all over the front, but the place, so hastily botched up by Fancy, had become incurably worse, and could only be made tolerable by a patch. And Fancy did not believe there were pieces enough to make one, nor was she quite sure where they were! So the serge was out of the question! And as to the claret dress—well, she had no thread of the proper colour, and she really did not think she could make a good job of it without

---

7. Pleats. "Stile": a set of steps for passing over a fence or wall.

8. I.e., something like we ought to be.

9. A light molasses.

mother to tell her how to manage all those great plaits of the kilting, and mother would be sure to say she had better have let it alone. Would all these difficulties have occurred to Frances, if there had not been only the corners of the table-cover crying out to be finished, and if she had not been glad of an excuse for the white frocks?

They wanted ironing, but that did not take long (at least Fancy took care it should not), and mother could not blame her for disobedience, when she knew there was really nothing else to wear!

Clara was well pleased, for she liked her white frock much better than her dark ones, and Fancy made her look very nice, tying her hair with blue ribbons to match her sash. It was a fine moonlight frosty night, and the girls put on their ulsters and clouds[1] for the walk to the school, so that they looked quite warm enough, as they started.

Fancy was quite proud of little Clara at the tea-table with her out-of-door things off, her pink cheeks, her white frock, and her pretty curls. She thought none of the children, not even Fanny Hill with the big brown eyes, about whom a strange visitor once had whispered in school, nor the young ladies themselves, looked better or prettier.

Every one knows school Christmas-trees. How beautiful the tapers and lamps look reflected like gold spangles on the dark glass balls, how the cottonwool[2] lies like snow on the branches and golden fir-cones and walnuts dangle down amid oranges that want no gilding, and wonderful birds' nests with still more wonderful birds sitting by them—yellow canaries and flaming-breasted robins, whose heads come off and disclose sugar plums. And then the paper drums, the crackers, the baskets, the boxes, the twists[3] that all hold sweets, the fairy dolls, the knives, the monkeys, the eggs and nuts with thimbles in them, the endless contrivances for funny presents.

Mr Gale was there, though not at first; he had driven down the younger children from the Hall and would in due time take them back. Meanwhile, he exchanged glances with his own flock and came up to the tree to help Mr Lamb in guarding against anything catching fire, as the branches sprang up after the heavier things were taken off from them by the younger ladies.

Mrs Somers and the elder Misses Manners were looking after the children and bringing them forward in turn, so that each might have a present and some sweets without pushing or scrambling, and they did all behave very well, and stood in their places in three happy rings, 'concentric circles,' as the pupil teacher would have called them; the tiny infants innermost, then the younger ones of the upper school, and lastly the big boys and girls, who got knives and neckties, and photographs and book markers, and scissors like birds, and thimbles in walnuts, and all sorts of unexpected and delightful things. Clara had first a sugar oyster, Leonard a rasher of bacon, both so like the real things that Frances hoped they would not be eaten till mother had been taken in by them, but that the family would be contented with the bullfinch full of sugar plums that had fallen to her share. The chocolate cockchafer[4] that was handed to Gilbert was even more comical, and was enough to make any timid person jump. The next round brought to Clara a doll's kitchen range and to Leonard a box of soldiers, but when Miss Mary handed Frances a little shell stamp box, Miss Manners noticed that Clara looked red and dull, and was coughing.

"Has she a cold?" she asked Frances.

"Not as I know of, ma'am," said Frances; "she has seemed very well all day."

---

1. Light, loosely knitted woolen scarves worn by ladies. "Ulsters": long, loose overcoats.
2. Raw cotton (here, for decoration). "Tapers": candles.

3. Conical wrappers made by twisting paper. "Crackers": small parcels that explode when pulled sharply at both ends.
4. Beetle.

"But this is a thin frock to have brought her out in," said Miss Manners.

"Please, ma'am, she walked down in her ulster," said Frances.

"I'm afraid she has a cold," said the lady. And after a word to her eldest niece, Gale was desired to bring the carriage which was to take home the nursery children, but first to set little Clara down, and Miss Manners advised Frances to put the child into bed at once and give her some warm tea or milk as soon as she was there. Unluckily that was more easily said than done. Fancy had been in too great a hurry to remember to make up the fire properly before she went out, and the tiny red spark that could just be seen on entering the dark cold house went quite out, or only turned to smoke when she tried to feed it with sticks and wood. Clara cried, and said her head ached and her throat was rough; and Frances took her up to bed at once, while Gilbert and Leonard did their best to get the fire up, in time to boil the kettle for their father. They liked the business, but did not do it very cleverly, and Clara had gone to sleep and was snoring when Frances was able to bring her the hot cup of tea.

CHAPTER VI

Miss Manners and all her elder nieces went out for a long day to some of their friends on the morrow, where there was to be a party in the evening, and thus Mr Gale had to be out driving them. Nor could Miss Manners look in to see how little Clara was. The child certainly had a bad cold, and was cross and listless, quarrelling with Leonard and crying as soon as they started any play together, and making herself more troublesome than ever, by asking for pieces of silk for her doll. Fancy had made all her coloured patches now, and could spare some bits, but she must work as fast as possible really to finish off and put in the lining. And she really could not cut out and fix a doll's cloak, which was the next thing Clara expected of her. So she answered sharply, on which the child cried and curled herself up with the doll rolled in the silk, and with her head on a chair, and went to sleep till she was waked by coughing.

She could eat very little dinner, but that was the less surprising since Frances had taken advantage of father being out to make them all dine on bread, cold bacon, and cheese. Gilbert declared that if mother was not coming home tomorrow he should cut. Leonard asked what he would cut, and Fancy scolded him for teaching the little ones bad words, for she did not know the difference between foolish ones and bad ones. Gilbert retorted that he had heard 'our Edmund' talk of cutting when he meant running away, and Fancy had further to observe that the young gentleman ought not to have done so; and likewise that Gilbert had no call to speak of him as 'our Edmund.' On which Gilbert made a face at her and went off.

Presently Jem and Emma Nowell came to fetch Clara and Leonard to spend the afternoon and drink tea with them. Frances was very glad to be freed from them. She had only to finish up the edges of her piece of work and put in the lining, and she trusted to do this in peace, and meet her mother triumphantly the next day.

Nobody came home to tea, but she was so busy that she hardly heeded this, and did not leave off to get her own till the blind man's holiday moment, when she could no longer see to thread her needle. She had just finished, and was going to light the lamp, when there was a knock at the door, and Mrs Nowell came in, leading Clara muffled up to the eyes in a shawl, and with a cloud over her usual wraps. "I've brought the child home, Frances Gale. She isn't well, and she wants care. She hadn't ought to have gone out at all today—and to let her go to that there Tree last night with nothing but a white rag of a frock on! Why what would your poor mother have said to see it."

"She had her ulster," said Fancy, feeling much offended.

"Ulster, indeed," said Mrs Nowell, pinching it up contemptuously in her fingers; "and nothing under, on such a night as that, to keep the wind off her poor little chest. I'm sorry for Mrs Gale when she comes home—I am."

At which Clara burst out crying, and Frances said in as grown up and stand-offish a manner as she could, "She has only got a cold."

"*Only!*" and Mrs Nowell threw up her hands.

Fancy's displeasure began to give way to fright. "You don't think there's much the matter, do you?"

"I don't know what you call much, Frances Gale, I only know that if she was mine, I'd put her to bed with a linseed poultice on her little chest, and give her plenty of hot kettle broth,[5] and if she didn't seem better by the morning, light a fire in her room, unless you wishes your mother to find her with an attack of bronchitis. I only hope it may be taken in time."

"But I haven't any linseed," said Fancy, looking bewildered.

"I thought you wouldn't," said Mrs Nowell; "so I just brought some down that was left after Nowell had his bad throat last October. It always comes in handy. Now, you take the little dear upstairs, and put her warm to bed, and I'll make up the poultice by the time you're done."

Fancy was quite alarmed enough to do what she was told, though with a certain feeling that was less like gratitude than vexation at being interfered with. Clara moaned a little for mother, but she was not so ill as not to enjoy being nursed and made much of; and Mrs Nowell did make her very comfortable. There was a fireplace in the room she shared with Fancy, while Leonard's little bed was by the side of his mother's, and Gilbert had an odd little den in the very pointed roof, with a window in the gable.

Mrs Nowell had left Leonard to play with her Jem, and undertook to send or bring him home by bed-time. And as father was not likely to come home till the middle of the night, and there were no signs of Gilbert, Fancy thought she had better let out the kitchen fire, light the one upstairs, and sit there, as thus she could both finish her work, attend to Clara, and keep the kettle broth going.

It was hard work to get the fire to burn, for the chimney had not been used since— Fancy could not recollect when. It smoked a good deal, and made Clara cough, but at last the room cleared, and it would not have been an uncomfortable evening if Fancy had not been uneasy at Gilbert's not coming in. And as she pieced out the edges and prepared to pull out her tacking threads, some misgivings seized her that her mother would rather have gone without her birthday present than find Clara poorly, Gilbert disobedient and father uncomfortable.

She was beginning to recover[6] her patchwork fever. And even when she spread the whole complete over the bed, and Clara cried out, "Oh! lovely," somehow the little Chinaman in his paling did not look half so charming to her as when she had first sewn him in!

By and by Mrs Nowell came in to see how Clara was going on, bringing Leonard home to bed. The first thing the boy said was, "Oh, Fancy, there's been ever such a row on the hill. All the big boys that go about holloaing out carols and shouting, jumped out of the lane at a trap with squibs and crackers,[7] and made the horse start right into the ditch. And who should it be but the Squire himself."

5. Stale bread, sprinkled with salt and pepper and well moistened with boiling water.

6. I.e., recover from.

7. Firecrackers.

"Not hurt!" exclaimed Fancy.

"Oh, no," said Mrs Nowell, "not a bit. You see he had come home in a trap from the station, and so those idle fellows didn't know him. But policeman, he was watching after them, and he got hold of one of them, so their names will all be known, and a good thing too, for it's a perfect disgrace the way they've been going about holloaing and bellowing all these Christmas nights. We don't hear so much of it up here at the Park, but Mrs Hollis tells me that it's a shame the way they goes about, whenever there's no night school on a moonlight night, molesting quiet folks—"

She was interrupted by Gilbert growling at the door, "Why, Fancy, here! wherever have you put the light to?"

Fancy ran down in a hurry, but he scarcely let her explain that Clara was poorly and Mrs Nowell upstairs with her. He would not come into Clara's room, and said he wanted no supper, he had had his, and snatching the candle from her, he went up to bed.

Frances's mind misgave her, but she said nothing to Mrs Nowell, who had been busy feeding the little patient with some arrowroot[8] she had brought, and attending to the poultice. She told Fancy not to let the child get up till she had seen her, bade them good night, and went home.

CHAPTER VII

Fancy and Clara were both fast asleep when their father came back, and though once or twice the child awoke, coughing and choking, she had a tolerable night; but in the morning she could not speak above a whisper.

Her father was vexed and anxious, and told Frances to ask Mrs Nowell whether to send for the doctor. "It was very odd," he said, "that a big maid like her couldn't look after a child better than that. And here was the house," he added, looking round, "in a pretty mess for mother to come home to. She wouldn't be for going out again in a hurry!"

Fancy's tears came fast, but she knew it would only make her father more angry if she gave in to them, so she only said, "I'm so sorry, father."

Gilbert all the time looked very glum and sulky, not at all as if mother was expected that day by one o'clock, but Fancy had her head and thoughts too full to attend to him. Mr Gale was obliged to go up to the stables before Mrs Nowell could come, but he told Frances to send Leonard up with a note to tell him what Mrs Nowell thought of the child, and whether he should ask the doctor to come and see her when he drove into Ellerby to fetch mother; and he gave some hopes of taking the little boy with him.

Mrs Nowell soon came, and comforted Frances so far as her little sister was concerned. She said she thought there was no need for doctors if the child was kept warm in bed all the morning, and seeing that Frances had a great deal on her hands, and no one to run up and down stairs for her, she sent Emma with her doll and the big picture book which the young ladies had made for her to amuse the little patient.

That was lucky for Fancy, who had gone into a great fright as she looked at the untidy state of the house, and began by a furious scrubbing, putting everything out of place everywhere, turning up her sleeves and tying herself up in a great rough apron. She was on her knees, with a flood of soapsuds before her, and all the chairs

---

8. A bland, nutritious starch.

in one another's laps, when Gilbert came in looking as black as night. "There! you've done for me," he said; "and there ain't a place to sit down in!"

"What have I done? Oh, Gilly!" cried Frances, starting to her feet.

"Got me out of the stables, and very like out of the choir—that's all!" said Gilbert, sitting down on the table, and kicking his heels.

"But what have I done? What has happened?" asked Frances, standing up and gazing at him in consternation.

Then, as he did not answer at once, she went on. "You weren't ever in that row last night, Gilbert?"

"I wasn't. I mean I wasn't half as bad as some of 'em, and Squire never would have known it if that there Black Jack hadn't been a rascal of a sneak. I should like to give it to him well, that I should, he knew it would do me more harm than any of 'em, so he must needs put in my name. I'll give it to him well, I can tell him; I'll never speak to him again."

"I should think that was the best thing," said Fancy, but this made Gilbert turn on her.

"A pretty one you are to preach to me, when you know it was all your doing."

"Mine! oh, Gilbert! I never made you go and holloa at the squire!"

"Didn't you, though, driving a fellow right out of the house with your fads and rags and nonsense!"

"I'm sure I never drove you then," cried Frances.

"I call it driving when you make a place not fit to stay in!" said Gilbert. "I wouldn't be your husband, I know! You'd send him to the public[9] in no time;" and he banged his heels against the leaf of the table.

"Oh, Gilly dear, if I'd only thought of it!"

"Come, don't whine, or I shall go into the coal-hole out of the way. I wouldn't be here now if father hadn't said I should stay till he comes home to give me a flogging. Father's properly mad, I can tell you, for Squire jawed us both so as you never heard. I suppose that little cock sparrow, Pickle's Page, Miss Manners's Robert will have the place after all! Bother him!"

Gradually Gilbert told more. Angry as he was with his sister, he found it a sort of comfort to pour out his troubles to her, more especially as she did not justify herself, nor say, as she might reasonably have done, that if it was dull at home, it did not make it needful for him to run into bad company when he might have found a welcome at the Nowells, or the Braynes, or other safe places.

The truth was, that there were a set of big boys, who either did not go to the night school,[1] or who felt themselves loose on their own hands when it was not open. They were tired of quiet company at the club room, and happily had not money enough for the public house, where indeed Mr Cray would not have made them welcome. So, on moonlight nights, they were apt to roam up and down the hill, bawling and shouting and pushing one another about, not exactly doing much harm, as they thought, but teasing and hunting any young woman or girl who happened to come out, holloaing at any one who rode or drove a donkey, talking in bad language among themselves, and altogether making themselves a nuisance.

This Christmas fortnight they were worse than usual. They would not submit to be trained for the proper regular carolling with Mr Lamb at its head, but went about on their own account, getting, as they said, much less money but much more fun. There was no night school, as the weeks were so broken by Saints' days and festivals,

9. I.e., the public house (pub).   1. Evening classes for working-class adults.

and as the weather was fine they were out every night and worked themselves up to be more riotous and daring than ever before. It was into this lot that Gilbert had fallen the first night he had gone out in a pet with Frances, and the amusement of rushing about and shouting in the dark had quite carried him away. He had helped them considerably in the carol singing, as he knew all the tunes much better than they did, and he had thought little or nothing of the irreverence, or, if he had, the sense of wildness and breaking out had made him enjoy it the more. So the two evenings had passed when he was free from other employments and his father out. The lads had got together enough to buy themselves a supper of meat and mince[2] pies, and bread and cheese bought at Ellerby, and beer from the Hut tap. They ate it after the moon had risen just by the old barn where, on the ground in front, they made a fire, using gunpowder to light it, and the fun and mirth were great. Then the beer, perhaps, making them somewhat uproarious, though Gilbert declared nobody was to be called the worse for it, they set out singing, holloaing, firing off powder, squibbing,[3] up to any mischief that might come in the way, hardly knowing what they were about, so that when they saw a little dog cart going swiftly along in the moonlight there was a general rush to screech "Whip behind," and fire off squibs at it. The horse swerved violently, but was pulled up before any harm was done; one of the persons, however, jumped out, and at the same moment the policeman, who had been determined to put a stop to these noisy doings, hurried up in time to catch one of the lads, who, to his horror, found himself face to face with Mr Manners, exceedingly angry, to find that this was the way that travellers were used at his orderly Langley. He was rather glad that it had happened to himself, since otherwise he might never have known of the boys' pranks till serious damage had been done.

Black Jack, otherwise John Ripley, was one of the loudest and most mischievous of the boys, and also the greatest coward among them. He cried and bellowed and begged for mercy like a baby, and declared that all the others were worse than himself, and he poured out all their names, as if that would excuse himself, Gilbert Gale among them!

The squire scarcely believed his ears. "Gilbert Gale!" said he.

"O yes! sir! 'Twas he as bought the squibs. 'Twarn't me, sir."

Gilbert, however, had known nothing of Jack's information, when he had scampered home last night, only aware that somebody was in the policeman's clutches, but not expecting to be betrayed, for most of the boys were ready to stand by one another, and not get other people into trouble. So he had been taken quite by surprise when he was called up to where his father stood before Mr Manners in the study, and called to account for behaviour, which amazed and shocked Mr Gale quite as much, or more, than the squire. He was a truthful boy and never attempted to deny that he had been about with the other fellows. All he tried to say in his own defence was, "Please, sir, we didn't know as 'twas you"; but of course this did him no good, for Mr Manners only said the shame was in bawling at anybody. It was a disgrace to the parish, said the squire; a disgrace to the family, felt the coachman; and both of them were very severe on the boy, who certainly had not gone wrong, like most of his comrades, for want of careful training.

Mr Manners said he certainly could not have a lad who showed such a want of steadiness about his stables, and since he chose such a set of friends, it would be no

---

2. I.e., mincemeat: a finely chopped mixture of dried fruit, nuts, suet, sugar, etc.

3. Setting off firecrackers

kindness to keep him among them; and Mr Gale only assented, that his master was quite right, and he could not expect anything else.

"And father never said a word for you," said Fancy, with her eyes full of tears. "He never said 'twas all because mother was away, and I was so nasty to you!"

"Bless you, no. Father went on at me when we was gone out worse than Squire himself! Charles came in at last to say that Mrs Riley and Mrs Grant, and all the mothers of 'em were come to speak to master, to beg 'em off, no doubt, but not a word had father to say for me. He ordered me home just like a dog, not to stir out of the house till he gets back to give me a right good flogging. I saw him take down the big old horsewhip."

"Oh! but he sha'n't! he sha'n't," exclaimed Fancy sobbing; "or else he must flog me too! Didn't you tell him how it was all my fault, and that nasty horrid piece of work that I wish I'd never set eyes on. Why didn't you tell him?"

"What good would that have done?" said Gilbert.

The brother and sister in their trouble hardly knew how time went, and there they were still, Gilbert on the table, Frances standing disconsolate by him, the legs of the tables and chairs in the air, and the floor all over soap and water, when the dog cart stopped at the door, and Fancy flew out wildly. "Oh! father, father, you mustn't beat him, for it was all my fault."

"Hold your tongue, Fancy, you're startling Corsair. Help your mother down and be quiet."

"And how's my little Clary?" was of course the first question.

But it was wonderful what a difference it made to know mother was in the house. Of course she satisfied herself about Clara first, but her next thought was to get the place fit for father to sit down in, before he came back from the stables, and setting both Gilbert and Frances to work, it was decent in a wonderfully short time, and as for the dinner, which Fancy in her trouble had quite forgotten, Mrs Gale sent Leonard off to the shop for some red herrings, of which father was always fond, and set Fancy to mash yesterday's potatoes to go with them.

All this was done before there was time for any talk—also a little broth was to be made for Clara out of some scraps of meat.

The little girl seemed so much better that her mother said she should get up to dinner, and that they would have a fire in the parlour, as the kitchen was too damp to sit in. As to listening to either of the elder children, that was impossible, and indeed Gilbert never asked her to do so. His spirit was too sturdy to beg off, and too generous to accuse his sister, however he might grumble at her. He knew his father was a man of his word, so that he should not get off, and he also knew that he had behaved very ill, and deserved to be punished; and that if he took it bravely, he should be forgiven all the sooner. So, though his flesh quailed at the thought of the big whip, which was brought out only to punish a very vicious horse, he would not say anything. Perhaps he would rather have had the flogging than see his mother go bustling about, looking pale and sorrowful, with all the joy of her coming home spoilt; he knew that though Fancy had been to blame, there was a good deal of difference between their faults—for she had cared for her mother's pleasure, and he, only for his own.

Mr Gale was rather late in coming in, and Frances from the window saw, to her great relief, that he had not brought the big whip, and Leonard was trotting down, holding his hand, and looking quite happy.

"Now, Fancy," said her mother, laying hold of her, "don't you go crying and begging, and vexing father about Gilbert. You know very well that what father says he'll do, and he will be much less likely to be hard on him if you don't worry him and make a fuss."

"But 'twas me," said Frances.

"We'll see about that," answered her mother; and by that time father was at the door.

He was much less angry than when he had ordered Gilbert home in the morning, while the knowledge of the boy's misbehaviour and the sting of his master's displeasure had been fresh on him. He had had time to think it over and see what excuse there was, and when he came into the house, the first thing he did after satisfying himself that Clara was better, was to say, "Come, my lad, out into the wood shed, and we'll have it over while mother is dishing up."

He did not speak at all in a terrible voice, and Gilbert followed obediently. Little hardhearted Leonard was running after, out of curiosity, to see what a flogging was like, but his mother caught him up, and ordered him back pretty sharply, and Fancy and Clara both cried bitterly all the time. Even Mrs Gale had tears in her eyes, though she knew that her husband was really only beating the boy because he felt himself bound by his word.

And it was soon over; he only gave his son six strokes over the shoulders with the old gig whip, which stung but was quite bearable, and then said, in a relieved voice.

"There, that will do, old chap. It's for your good, you know."

"I don't bear malice," said Gilbert, which sounded odd, but both knew what it meant. "I didn't ought to have done it."

That was so real a confession of sorrow that his father was quite pleased, and said, "That's right, Gil. I like a lad that will own when he's been to blame. Mind you, womenfolk will have their little ways, but 'tis better to put up with them than to be running off after the roughs. Now, we won't say no more about it at home, you've had your punishment, for you've missed a good situation under me—and I don't know what the vicar may say. But we'll let bygones be bygones."

"Only, father, how about the other chaps?" asked Gilbert anxiously, as they entered the house.

"Well, policeman let 'em all know that they might all have a summons for an assault. And if they had, you must have been had up too, Gil. But most likely master only meant to give 'em a fright. Anyway, all their mothers, seven of them, came up and brought all the young ones that don't go out to work to beg master to let 'em off. Mr Bolton, he told me there was such a crying and lamenting they could hear it in the servants' hall, and he was glad he wasn't master! But master, he gave it well to the boys, and made them promise never to do such a thing again to no one; and when he had sent them off, he gave it still stronger to the mothers that let them get about, and were ruining 'em. And the worse and more gad-about the mothers were, the more they promised the fathers would give 'em the stick. I wonder how many of them will get it," finished Mr Gale, with a dry satisfaction in having done his duty.

Frances knew, when she heard him speak in that voice, that the storm was over, and her brother forgiven. She rolled up her wet handkerchief in a ball and put it in her pocket; but she had no appetite for dinner, and though Gilbert whispered to her that she was a silly, he was not exactly angry with her.

Later in the afternoon, the vicar came in. Gilbert had done what was against all the choir boys' rules by going about with the roughs singing for money. Therefore he certainly must not sing at church on this Epiphany[4] evening, nor come to the choir supper that was to take place afterwards. He was just now gone out on an errand, but Mrs Gale was to send him to the Vicarage as soon as he came in, to be spoken to by Mr Somers.

"Please, mother, tell him," whispered Fancy.

"Well, sir," said Mrs Gale, "my Frances here wants me to tell you she thinks 'twas in part her fault. You see, I was gone out, and she got a piece of work in hand to be a surprise to me tomorrow on my birthday, and, as girls will do, sir, she got so took up with it that she didn't take heed to amuse her brother in the evening. Menfolk take such a lot of attention," added Mrs Gale, quite forgetting that she was talking to one of them, "and so father and me both being out, the children quarrelled, and Gilbert went out, as she thinks he would never have done if she had heeded him more at home."

"And I didn't mind Clary, and let her catch cold; and messed everything," said Frances, in a sad whisper.

"And yet it seems hard to blame her, sir, when she just wanted to make me a nice present. 'Twas a pretty thought of her."

"Only she feels that she put duties aside for it," said Mr Somers. "Isn't that it, Frances?"

"Yes, sir."

"You see, Frances, the devices and desires of our hearts may often be good and right, only if we follow them *too much* instead of the duty, which is the will of God, they lead us astray, and do others harm as well as ourselves. You will think of that when you say the confession tonight?"

"Yes, sir," said Frances again, and she was surprised that the vicar said a grave "God bless you, my child." For he felt that it was real repentance when she only thought of shielding her brother from blame.

Frances hated her poor table-cover by that time, and would have liked to have put it into the fire, but her mother would not hear of that, and it was brought out the next morning with father's present of a pair of fur-lined gloves, and Clara's of "Helen's babies"[5] in china, and Leonard's of a little pig from the same shop, and Gilbert's fir-cone box, nearly but not quite finished, as it would have been had he been wise enough to stay at home. The piece of work was so nicely done that Mrs Gale admired it extremely, and was proud of its neatness and beauty. Fancy begged her to put it out of sight, but she would not hear of this, and it was placed in honour on the little table in the parlour. But Frances never sees it, nor hears it admired without a thought of that unhappy morning, and dreading to follow too much the devices and desires of her own heart.

1883, 1967

---

4. January 6, a holiday celebrating the baptism of Jesus and the visit of the Magi.
5. Figurines of the two little boys featured in the best-selling children's novel (1876) of that title by John Habberton.

LOUISA MAY ALCOTT
1832–1888

Louisa May Alcott once wrote in her childhood journal that she wished to be as famous as the singer Jenny Lind. With fame, she thought, would come happiness. Although the moody and hardworking Alcott found contentment difficult to achieve, her name and life became known the world over after the publication of her best-selling novel for girls based largely on her own family, *Little Women* (1868–69). Because of her ability to create memorable characters, lively dialogue, and realistic domestic plots, Alcott stands as the most significant nineteenth-century American writer of domestic fiction for the young.

The second of four daughters of the eccentric philosopher and educationalist Amos Bronson Alcott, who was a member of the Concord, Massachusetts, Transcendentalist circle and a friend of Henry David Thoreau, Ralph Waldo Emerson, and Nathaniel Hawthorne, Alcott grew up in an atmosphere in which writing and thinking were valued above social prestige or money. Her father, though much admired by the other Transcendentalists, struggled without much success to provide adequately for his family; his radical approach to education made his tenures as schoolmaster brief. When Louisa was ten years old, Bronson and two English mystics founded Fruitlands, a communal farm in Harvard, Massachusetts, on which all were to live as a "consociate family." With a greater emphasis on ideals than on the practicalities of farming—and with much of the actual work left to Louisa's mother, Abigail (Abba)—the venture failed by winter, forcing the Alcotts once again to fall back on the charity of Abba's wealthy Boston relatives and their many friends.

Although this utopian commune was gently parodied in Alcott's "Transcendental Wild Oats" (1873), the experience persuaded her that she would have to find a way to support the family. Beginning in the late 1840s, she took any job she could, including work as a seamstress, domestic servant, and teacher (experiences she turned to fiction in *Work: A Story of Experience*, 1873), and also began publishing stories. Much of her fiction both offers a sentimentalized version of her family life and embodies her father's ideals of temperance, educational reform, women's rights, and abolitionism.

Alcott's first published book was *Flower Fables* (1854), a collection of mostly unremarkable fairy stories originally told to Emerson's daughter Ellen. Her second, the humorous and realistic *Hospital Sketches* (1863), won critical and popular acclaim. Alcott drew on her work as a Civil War nurse at the Union Hotel Hospital in Washington, D.C. Her stay there was brief, for she contracted typhoid fever, then pneumonia; the mercury-based purgative with which she was treated damaged her health for the rest of her life. She continued to write, however. Many of what she called "blood and thunder" sensation tales, published pseudonymously and not attributed to her for almost a hundred years, appeared during the 1860s, and under her own name the adult novel *Moods* (1864) was issued. In 1868 Alcott acceded reluctantly to the request of Thomas Niles, a partner at the publisher Roberts Brothers, that she write a "girls' book." She grumbled in her journal, "Never liked girls or knew many, except my sisters, but our queer plays and experiences may prove interesting, though I doubt it." Alcott completed a manuscript in a matter of weeks, and a few girls who read *Little Women* before publication pronounced it "splendid."

Others agreed; the book rapidly sold out the first printing of 2,000, and by the time of Alcott's death nearly 200,000 copies had been purchased in the United States. The family saga of the four high-spirited March sisters—each a well-rounded character who, helped by the wisdom of their mother, overcomes her own distinctive fault—has never been out of print. Its first readers clamored for a sequel that would take the girls through marriage. Alcott wrote *Good Wives* in two months (1869; the two volumes are conventionally published together under the title *Little Women*). The fortunes of her remaining family members were made. One sister, Elizabeth, had died in 1857; another, Anna, had married in 1860, and Louisa helped support her and her two sons after she was widowed in 1870.

In addition to her sequels to *Little Women* (*Little Men: Life at Plumfield with Jo's Boys*, 1871; *Jo's Boys, and How They Turned Out*, 1886), Alcott wrote other girls' novels in a similar style (including *An Old-Fashioned Girl*, 1870, and *Eight Cousins; or The Aunt-Hill*, 1875) and numerous short stories.

She also published *Work*, the adult novel she had begun drafting in 1861, and *The Modern Mephistopheles* (1877), a sensation novel whose authorship she acknowledged ten years later. Alcott might dismiss her children's works in a journal entry as "moral pap for the young," but the reading public had difficulty accepting her as anyone other than the "Children's Friend," a sobriquet she disliked. Collections of new and reprinted pieces under the title *Aunt Jo's Scrap-Bag* (6 vols., 1872–82) sold well. Indeed it is the tomboy and writer Jo March, based on Alcott herself, who remains her most successful and memorable creation. Generations of young readers have identified with Jo's struggles with anger and pride, and her desires for independence and a career.

In her fiction and journalism, and through personal activism, Alcott herself never flagged in her support for social justice in reforms such as women's suffrage and abolition. Nor did her responsibilities as the family's breadwinner lessen. As she nursed her mother in Abba's final illness, she wrote a book (*Under the Lilacs*, 1878) to help cover the extra expenses; in 1880 she took in the daughter of her youngest sister, May, who had died in Paris only a year and a half after marrying a Swiss businessman; and in 1882 she began to care for her father, who had suffered a debilitating stroke. She established a home for him in Boston with her niece, Lulu (Louisa May Nieriker); her sister Anna; and

Anna's sons, John and Fred Pratt. After her father's death on March 4, 1888, the exhausted Alcott, whose own health had been failing for years, wrote that she wondered if she could find time to die. She did, two days later. The father and daughter, who shared a birthday, also shared a funeral, and they were buried on the same day in Sleepy Hollow Cemetery in Concord. So that she might continue to provide for her family even after death, she had adopted her nephew John, enabling him to renew the copyrights of her works.

Alcott generally avoided the preaching common in many children's books of the later nineteenth century—for example, in Martha Farquharson Finley's twenty-five books (beginning with *Elsie Dinsmore*, 1867) that follow their meek and pious heroine from childhood to old age. Yet although she allows her characters more realistic imperfections, Alcott's fiction, including the short story "Psyche's Art" (1868), maintains a moral center and demonstrates that selflessness leads to happiness. Boys' books of the period, such as Thomas Bailey Aldrich's *Story of a Bad Boy* (1869) or James Otis's *Toby Tyler, or Ten Weeks with a Circus* (1881), emphasize adventure; in contrast, the domestic novels of Alcott and her imitators, such as Susan Coolidge's series that began with *What Katy Did* (1872), depict both the larks of the tomboy and her eventual acceptance of traditional gender roles.

Psyche's Art

"Handsome is that handsome does."

I.

Once upon a time there raged in a certain city one of those fashionable epidemics which occasionally attack our youthful population. It wasn't the music mania, nor gymnastic convulsions, nor that wide-spread malady, croquet. Neither was it one of the new dances which, like a tarantula-bite,[1] set every one a-twirling, nor stage madness, nor yet that American lecturing influenza which yearly sweeps over the land. No, it was a new disease called the Art fever, and it attacked the young women of the community with great violence.

Nothing but time could cure it, and it ran its course to the dismay, amusement, or edification of the beholders, for its victims did all manner of queer things in their delirium. They besieged potteries for clay, drove Italian plaster-workers out of their

1. Popularly thought to cause an uncontrollable urge to dance.

wits with unexecutable orders, got neuralgia and rheumatism sketching perched on fences and trees like artistic hens, and caused a rise in the price of bread, paper, and charcoal, by their order in crayoning. They covered canvas with the expedition of scene-painters, had classes, lectures, receptions, and exhibitions, made models of each other, and rendered their walls hideous with bad likenesses of all their friends. Their conversation ceased to be intelligible to the uninitiated, and they prattled prettily of "chiaro-oscuro, French sauce, refraction of the angle of the eye, seventh spinus process,[2] depth and juiciness of color, tender touch, and a good tone." Even in dress the artistic disorder was visible; some cast aside crinoline altogether, and stalked about with a severe simplicity of outline worthy of Flaxman.[3] Others flushed themselves with scarlet, that no landscape which they adorned should be without some touch of Turner's[4] favorite tint. Some were *blue* in every sense of the word, and the heads of all were adorned with classic braids, curls tied Hebe-wise,[5] or hair dressed à la hurricane.

It was found impossible to keep them safe at home, and, as the fever grew, these harmless maniacs invaded the sacred retreats where artists of the other sex did congregate, startling those anchorites with visions of large-eyed damsels bearing portfolios in hands delicately begrimed with crayon, chalk, and clay, gliding through the corridors hitherto haunted only by shabby paletots,[6] shadowy hats, and cigar smoke. This irruption was borne with manly fortitude, not to say cheerfulness, for studio doors stood hospitably open as the fair invaders passed, and studies from life were generously offered them in glimpses of picturesque gentlemen posed before easels, brooding over master-pieces in "a divine despair,"[7] or attitudinizing upon couches as if exhausted by the soarings of genius.

An atmosphere of romance began to pervade the old buildings when the girls came, and nature and art took turns. There were peepings and whisperings, much stifled laughter and whisking in and out; not to mention the accidental rencontres, small services, and eye telegrams, which somewhat lightened the severe studies of all parties.

Half-a-dozen young victims of this malady met daily in one of the cells of a great art beehive called "Raphel's Rooms," and devoted their shining hours to modelling fancy heads, gossiping the while; for the poor things found the road to fame rather dull and dusty without such verbal sprinklings.

"Psyche Dean, you've had an adventure! I see it in your face; so tell it at once, for we are as stupid as owls here to-day," cried one of the sisterhood, as a bright-eyed girl entered with some precipitation.

"I dropped my portfolio, and a man picked it up, that's all," replied Psyche, hurrying on her gray linen pinafore.

"That won't do; I know something interesting happened, for you've been blushing, and you look brisker than usual this morning," said the first speaker, polishing off the massive nose of her Homer.[8]

"It wasn't anything," began Psyche, a little reluctantly. "I was coming up in a hurry when I ran against a man coming down in a hurry. My portfolio slipped, and my

2. The lowest of the neck vertebrae. "Chiaro-oscuro": chiaroscuro, the treatment of light and shade in pictorial representation.
3. John Flaxman (1755–1826), English neoclassical sculptor.
4. J. M. W. Turner. (1775–1851), English Romantic painter.
5. I.e., as represented in the famous (lost) statue of the goddess of youth by Naucydes (5th c. B.C.E.).
6. Loose outer garments.
7. A phrase from "Tears, Idle Tears," in *The Princess* (1847), by Alfred, Lord Tennyson.
8. I.e., a clay head of the blind Greek poet to whom the *Iliad* and the *Odyssey* (ca. 8th c. B.C.E.) are attributed.

papers went flying all about the landing. Of course we both laughed and begged pardon, and I began to pick them up, but he wouldn't let me; so I held the book while he collected the sketches. I saw him glance at them as he did so, and that made me blush, for they are wretched things, you know."

"Not a bit of it; they are capital, and you are a regular genius, as we all agree," cut in the Homeric Miss Cutter.

"Never tell people they are geniuses unless you wish to spoil them," returned Psyche, severely. "Well, when the portfolio was put to rights I was going on, but he fell to picking up a little bunch of violets I had dropped; you know I always wear a posy into town to give me inspiration. I didn't care for the dusty flowers, and told him so, and scrambled away before any one came. At the top of the stairs I peeped over the railing, and there he was, gathering up every one of those half-dead violets as carefully as if they had been tea-roses."

"Psyche Dean, you have met your fate this day!" exclaimed a third damsel, with straw-colored tresses, and a good deal of weedy shrubbery in her hat, which gave an Ophelia-like expression[9] to her sentimental countenance.

Psyche frowned and shook her head as if half sorry she had told her little story.

"Was he handsome?" asked Miss Larkins, the believer in fate.

_____

9. An appearance like that of William Shakespeare's Ophelia (in *Hamlet*, ca. 1600) after she has gone mad and decorated herself with flowers.

"I didn't particularly observe."

"It was the red-headed man, whom we call Titian;[1] he's always on the stairs."

"No, it wasn't; his hair was brown and curly," cried Psyche, innocently falling into the trap.

"Like Peerybingle's baby when its cap was taken off,"[2] quoted Miss Dickenson, who pined to drop the last two letters of her name.

"Was it Murillo,[3] the black-eyed one?" asked the fair Cutter, for the girls had a name for all the attitudinizers and promenaders whom they oftenest met.

"No, he had gray eyes, and very fine ones they were too," answered Psyche, adding, as if to herself, "he looked as I imagine Michael Angelo[4] might have looked when young."

"Had he a broken nose like the great Mike?" asked an irreverent damsel.

"If he had, no one would mind it, for his head is splendid; he took his hat off, so I had a fine view. He isn't handsome, but he'll *do* something," said Psyche, prophetically, as she recalled the strong, ambitious face which she had often observed, but never mentioned before.

"Well, dear, considering that you didn't 'particularly look' at the man, you've given us a very good idea of his appearance. We'll call him Michael Angelo, and he shall be your idol. I prefer stout old Rembrandt myself, and Larkie adores that dandefied Raphael,"[5] said the lively Cutter, slapping away at Homer's bald pate energetically, as she spoke.

"Raphael is a dear, but Rubens[6] is more to my taste now," returned Miss Larkins. "He was in the hall yesterday talking with Sir Joshua,[7] who had his inevitable umbrella, like a true Englishman. Just as I came up, the umbrella fell right before me. I started back; Sir Joshua laughed, but Rubens said, 'Deuce take it!' and caught up the umbrella, giving me a never-to-be-forgotten look. It was perfectly thrilling."

"Which,—the umbrella, the speech, or the look?" asked Psyche, who was not sentimental.

"Ah, you have no soul for art in nature, and nature in art," sighed the amber-tressed Larkins. "I have, for I feed upon a glance, a tint, a curve, with exquisite delight. Rubens is adorable (*as a study*); that lustrous eye, that night of hair, that sumptuous cheek, are perfect. He only needs a cloak, lace collar, and slouching hat to be the genuine thing."

"This isn't the genuine thing by any means. What *does* it need?" said Psyche, looking with a despondent air at the head on her stand.

Many would have pronounced it a clever thing; the nose was strictly Greek, the chin curved upward gracefully, the mouth was sweetly haughty, the brow classically smooth and low, and the breezy hair well done. But something was wanting; Psyche felt that, and could have taken her Venus[8] by the dimpled shoulders, and given her a hearty shake, if that would have put strength and spirit into the lifeless face.

"Now *I* am perfectly satisfied with my Apollo,[9] though you all insist that it is the

---

1. Tiziano Vecelli (ca. 1488–1576), Venetian painter and portraitist.
2. A quotation from Charles Dickens's *The Cricket on the Hearth* (1845).
3. Bartolomé Esteban Murillo (1617–1682), Spanish painter.
4. Michelangelo di Lodovico Buonarroti Simoni (1475–1565), Italian painter, sculptor, and architect.
5. Raffaello Sanzio (1483–1520), Italian painter and architect. Rembrandt Harmensz van Rijn

(1606–1669), Dutch painter and etcher.
6. Peter Paul Rubens (1577–1640), Flemish painter.
7. Sir Joshua Reynolds (1723–1792), English portrait painter.
8. The Roman goddess of love.
9. The Greek god of prophecy and music, and in art the ideal of young male beauty. As god of light, he was worshiped as Phoebus (lit., "bright"; Greek) Apollo.

image of Theodore Smythe. He says so himself, and assures me it will make a sensation when we exhibit," remarked Miss Larkins, complacently caressing the ambrosial locks of her Smythified Phebus.

"What shall you do if it don't?" asked Miss Cutter, with elegance.

"I shall feel that I have mistaken my sphere, shall drop my tools, veil my bust, and cast myself into the arms of Nature, since Art rejects me," replied Miss Larkins, with a tragic gesture and an expression which strongly suggested that in her eyes Nature meant Theodore.

"She must have capacious arms if she is to receive all Art's rejected admirers. Shall I be one of them?"

Psyche put the question to herself as she turned to work, but somehow ambitious aspirations were not in a flourishing condition that morning; her heart was not in tune, and head and hands sympathized. Nothing went well, for certain neglected home-duties had dogged her into town, and now worried her more than dust, or heat, or the ceaseless clatter of tongues. Tom, Dick, and Harry's unmended hose persisted in dancing a spectral jig before her mental eye, mother's querulous complaints spoilt the song she hummed to cheer herself, and little May's wistful face put the goddess of beauty entirely out of countenance.

"It's no use; I can't work till the clay is wet again. Where is Giovanni?" she asked, throwing down her tools with a petulant gesture and a dejected air.

"He is probably playing truant in the empty upper rooms as usual. I can't wait for him any longer, so I'm doing his work myself," answered Miss Dickenson, who was tenderly winding a wet bandage round her Juno's face, one side of which was so much plumper than the other that it looked as if the Queen of Olympus was being hydropathically treated for a severe fit of ague.[1]

"I'll go and find the little scamp; a run will do me good; so will a breath of air and a view of the park from the upper windows."

Doffing her apron, Psyche strolled away up an unfrequented staircase to the empty apartments, which seemed to be too high even for the lovers of High Art. On the western side they were shady and cool, and, leaning from one of the windows, Psyche watched the feathery treetops ruffled by the balmy wind, that brought spring odors from the hills, lying green and sunny far away. Silence and solitude were such pleasant companions that the girl forgot herself, till a shrill whistle disturbed her daydreams, and reminded her what she came for. Following the sound she found the little Italian errand-boy busily uncovering a clay model which stood in the middle of a scantily furnished room near by.

"He is not here; come and look; it is greatly beautiful," cried Giovanni, beckoning with an air of importance.

Psyche did look and speedily forgot both her errand and herself. It was the figure of a man, standing erect, and looking straight before him with a wonderfully life-like expression. It was neither a mythological nor a historical character, Psyche thought, and was glad of it, being tired to death of gods and heroes. She soon ceased to wonder what it was, feeling only the indescribable charm of something higher than beauty. Small as her knowledge was, she could see and enjoy the power visible in every part of it; the accurate anatomy of the vigorous limbs, the grace of the pose, the strength and spirit in the countenance, clay though it was. A majestic figure, but the spell lay

1. A violent fever. Juno: in Roman mythology, the queen of the gods, wife of Jupiter. Olympus: in Greek and Roman mythology, the home of the gods; Olympus is a mountain range in northeast Greece (Thessaly).

in the face, which, while it suggested the divine, was full of human truth and tenderness, for pain and passion seemed to have passed over it and a humility half-pathetic, a courage half-heroic, seemed to have been born from some great loss or woe.

How long she stood there Psyche did not know. Giovanni went away unseen, to fill his water-pail, and in the silence she just stood and looked. Her eyes kindled, her color rose, despondency and discontent vanished, and her soul was in her face, for she loved beauty passionately, and all that was best and truest in her did honor to the genius of the unknown worker.

"If I could do a thing like that I'd die happy!" she exclaimed, impetuously, as a feeling of despair came over her at the thought of her own poor attempts.

"Who did it, Giovanni?" she asked, still looking up at the grand face with unsatisfied eyes.

"Paul Gage."

It was not the boy's voice, and, with a start, Psyche turned to see her Michael Angelo, standing in the door-way attentively observing her. Being too full of artless admiration to think of herself just yet, she neither blushed nor apologized, but looked straight at him, saying heartily:—

"You have done a wonderful piece of work, and I envy you more than I can tell."

The enthusiasm in her face, the frankness of her manner, seemed to please him, for there was no affectation about either. He gave her a keen, kind glance out of the "fine gray eyes," a little bow, and a grateful smile, saying quietly:—

"Then my Adam is not a failure in spite of his fall?"

Psyche turned from the sculptor to his model with increased admiration in her face, and earnestness in her voice, as she exclaimed, delighted:—

"Adam! I might have known it was he. O sir, you have indeed succeeded, for you have given that figure the power and pathos of the first man who sinned and suffered, and began again."

"Then I am satisfied." That was all he said, but the look he gave his work was a very eloquent one, for it betrayed that he had paid the price of success in patience and privation, labor and hope.

"What can one do to learn your secret?" asked the girl wistfully, for there was nothing in the man's manner to disturb her self-forgetful mood, but much to foster it, because to the solitary worker this confiding guest was as welcome as the doves who often hopped in at his window.

"Work and wait, and meantime feed heart, soul, and imagination with the best food one can get," he answered slowly, finding it impossible to give a receipt[2] for genius.

"I can work and wait a long time to gain my end; but I don't know where to find the food you speak of," she answered, looking at him like a hungry child.

"I wish I could tell you, but each needs different fare, and each must look for it in different places."

The kindly tone and the sympathizing look, as well as the lines in his forehead, and a few gray hairs among the brown, gave Psyche courage to say more.

"I love beauty so much that I not only want to possess it myself, but to gain the power of seeing it in all things, and the art of reproducing it with truth. I have tried very hard to do it, but something is wanting; and in spite of my intense desire I never get on."

2. A recipe.

As she spoke the girl's eyes filled and fell in spite of herself, and turning a little with sudden shamefacedness she saw, lying on the table beside her among other scraps in manuscript and print, the well-known lines:—

> "I slept, and dreamed that life was beauty;
> I woke, and found that life was duty.
> Was thy dream then a shadowy lie?
> Toil on, sad heart, courageously,
> And thou shalt find thy dream to be
> A noonday light and truth to thee."[3]

She knew them at a glance, had read them many times, but now they came home to her with sudden force, and, seeing that his eye had followed hers, she said in her impulsive fashion:—

"Is doing one's duty a good way to feed heart, soul, and imagination?"

As if he had caught a glimpse of what was going on in her mind, Paul answered emphatically:—

"Excellent; for if one is good, one is happy, and if happy, one can work well. Moulding character is the highest sort of sculpture, and all of us should learn that art before we touch clay or marble."

He spoke with the energy of a man who believed what he said, and did his best to be worthy of the rich gift bestowed upon him. The sight of her violets in a glass of water, and Giovanni staring at her with round eyes, suddenly recalled Psyche to a sense of the proprieties which she had been innocently outraging for the last ten minutes. A sort of panic seized her; she blushed deeply, retreated precipitately to the door, and vanished murmuring thanks and apologies as she went.

"Did you find him? I thought you had forgotten," said Miss Dickenson, now hard at work.

"Yes, I found him. No, I shall not forget," returned Psyche, thinking of Gage, not Giovanni.

She stood before her work eying it intently for several minutes; then, with an expression of great contempt for the whole thing, she suddenly tilted her cherished Venus on to the floor, gave the classical face a finishing crunch, and put on her hat in a decisive manner, saying briefly to the dismayed damsels:—

"Good-by, girls; I shan't come any more, for I'm going to work at home hereafter."

II.

The prospect of pursuing artistic studies at home was not brilliant, as one may imagine when I mention that Psyche's father was a painfully prosaic man, wrapt in flannel, so to speak; for his woollen mills left him no time for anything but sleep, food, and newspapers. Mrs. Dean was one of those exasperating women who pervade their mansions like a domestic steam-engine one week and take to their sofas the next, absorbed by fidgets and foot-stoves,[4] shawls and lamentations. There were three riotous and robust young brothers, whom it is unnecessary to describe except by stating that they were *boys* in the broadest sense of that delightful word. There was a feeble

---

3. From "Beauty and Duty" (1840), by Ellen Sturgis Hooper.

4. I.e., foot warmers (holding hot coals).

little sister, whose patient, suffering face demanded constant love and care to mitigate the weariness of a life of pain. And last, but not least by any means, there were two Irish ladies, who, with the best intentions imaginable, produced a universal state of topsy-turvyness when left to themselves for a moment.

But being very much in earnest about doing her duty, not because it *was* her duty, but as a means toward an end, Psyche fell to work with a will, hoping to serve both masters at once. So she might have done, perhaps, if flesh and blood had been as plastic as clay, but the live models were so exacting in their demands upon her time and strength, that the poor statues went to the wall. Sculpture and sewing, calls and crayons, Ruskin[5] and receipt-books, didn't work well together, and poor Psyche found duties and desires desperately antagonistic. Take a day as a sample.

"The washing and ironing is well over, thank goodness, ma used up and quiet, the boys out of the way, and May comfortable, so I'll indulge myself in a blissful day after my own heart," Psyche said, as she shut herself into her little studio, and prepared to enjoy a few hours of hard study and happy day-dreams.

With a book on her lap, and her own round, white arm going through all manner of queer evolutions, she was placidly repeating, "Deltoids, Biceps, Triceps, Pronator, Supinator, Palmanis, Flexor carpi ulnaris[6]—"

"Here's Flexis what-you-call-ums for you," interrupted a voice, which began in a shrill falsetto and ended in a gruff bass, as a flushed, dusty, long-legged boy burst in, with a bleeding hand obligingly extended for inspection.

"Mercy on us, Harry, what have you done to yourself now? Split your fingers with a cricket-ball again?" cried Psyche, as her arms went up and her book went down.

"No, sir. I just pitched into one of the fellows because he got mad and said pa was going to fail."

"O Harry, is he?"

"Course he isn't! It's hard times for every one, but pa will pull through like a brick. No use to try and explain it all; girls can't understand business; so you just tie me up, and don't bother," was the characteristic reply of the young man, who, being three years her junior, of course treated the weaker vessel with lordly condescension.

"What a dreadful wound! I hope nothing is broken, for I haven't studied the hand much yet, and may do mischief doing it up," said Psyche, examining the great grimy paw with tender solicitude.

"Much good your biceps, and deltoids, and things do you, if you can't right up a little cut like that," squeaked the ungrateful hero.

"I'm not going to be a surgeon, thank Heaven; I intend to make perfect hands and arms, not mend damaged ones," retorted Psyche, in a dignified tone, somewhat marred by a great piece of court-plaster on her tongue.

"I should say a surgeon could improve *that* perfect thing, if he didn't die a-laughing before he began," growled Harry, pointing with a scornful grin at a clay arm humpy with muscles all carefully developed in the wrong places.

"Don't hoot, Hal, for you don't know anything about it. Wait a few years and see if you're not proud of me."

"Sculp away then, do your prettiest, and I'll hurrah for your mud-pies like a good one;" with which cheering promise the youth departed, having effectually disturbed his sister's peaceful mood.

5. John Ruskin (1819–1900), English writer and art critic.

6. Arm muscles and tendons ("Palmanus" should be *Palmaris*).

Anxious thoughts of her father rendered "biceps, deltoids, and things" uninterest-ing, and, hoping to compose her mind, she took up The Old Painters and went on with the story of Claude Lorraine.[7] She had just reached the tender scene where:—

"Calista gazed with enthusiasm, while she looked like a being of heaven rather than earth. 'My friend,' she cried, 'I read in thy picture thy immortality!' As she spoke, her head sunk upon his bosom, and it was several moments before Claude perceived that he supported a lifeless form."

"How sweet!" said Psyche, with a romantic sigh.

"Faith, and swate it is thin!" echoed Katy, whose red head had just appeared round the half-opened door. "It's gingybread I'm making the day, miss, and will I be puttin' purlash or sallyrathis[8] into it, if ye plase?"

"Purlash by all means," returned the girl, keeping her countenance, fearing to enrage Katy by a laugh; for the angry passions of the red-haired one rose more quickly than her bread. As she departed with alacrity to add a spoonful of starch and a pinch of whiting[9] to her cake, Psyche, feeling better for her story and her smile, put on her bib and paper cap and fell to work on the deformed arm. An hour of bliss, then came a ring at the door-bell, followed by Biddy to announce callers, and add that as "the mistress was in her bed, miss must go and take care of 'em." Whereat "miss" cast down her tools in despair, threw her cap one way, her bib another, and went in to her guests with anything but a rapturous welcome.

Dinner being accomplished after much rushing up and down stairs with trays and messages for Mrs. Dean, Psyche fled again to her studio, ordering no one to approach under pain of a scolding. All went well till, going in search of something, she found her little sister sitting on the floor with her cheek against the studio door.

"I didn't mean to be naughty, Sy, but ma's asleep, and the boys all gone, so I just came to be near you; it's so lonely everywhere," she said, apologetically, as she lifted up the heavy head that always ached.

"The boys are very thoughtless. Come in and stay with me; you are such a mouse you won't disturb me. Wouldn't you like to play be a model, and let me draw your arm, and tell you all about the nice little bones and muscles?" asked Psyche, who had the fever very strong upon her just then.

May didn't look as if the proposed amusement overwhelmed her with delight, but meekly consented to be perched upon a high stool with one arm propped up by a dropsical plaster cherub, while Psyche drew busily, feeling that duty and pleasure were being delightfully combined.

"Can't you hold your arm still, child? It shakes so I can't get it right," she said, rather impatiently.

"No, it will tremble, 'cause it's weak. I try hard, Sy, but there don't seem to be any strongness in me lately."

"That's better; keep it so a few minutes and I'll be done," cried the artist, forgetting that a few minutes may seem ages.

"My arm is so thin you can see the bunches nicely,—can't you?"

"Yes, dear."

Psyche glanced up at the wasted limb and when she drew again there was a blur before her eyes for a minute.

7. Claude Gellée (1600–1682), French landscape painter. "The Old Painters": *Historical Sketches of the Old Painters* (1838), by Hannah Farnham Sawyer Lee.

8. Two leavening agents: pearl-ash (potassium car-bonate) and saleratus (sodium bicarbonate, or baking soda).

9. Chalk powder (usually an adulterating agent in food).

"I wish I was as fat as this white boy; but I get thinner every day somehow, and pretty soon there won't be any of me left but my little bones," said the child, looking at the winged cherub with sorrowful envy.

"Don't, my darling; don't say that," cried Psyche, dropping her work with a sudden pang at her heart. "I'm a sinful, selfish girl to keep you here; you're weak for want of air; come out and see the chickens, and pick dandelions, and have a good romp with the boys."

The weak arms were strong enough to clasp Psyche's neck, and the tired face brightened beautifully as the child exclaimed, with grateful delight:—

"Oh, I'd like it very much! I wanted to go dreadfully; but everybody is so busy all the time. I don't want to play, Sy; but just to lie on the grass with my head in your lap while you tell stories and draw me pretty things as you used to."

The studio was deserted all that afternoon, for Psyche sat in the orchard drawing squirrels on the wall, pert robbins hopping by, buttercups and mosses, elves and angels; while May lay contentedly enjoying sun and air, sisterly care, and the "pretty things" she loved so well. Psyche did not find the task a hard one; for this time her heart was in it, and if she needed any reward she surely found it; for the little face on her knee lost its weary look, and the peace and beauty of nature soothed her own troubled spirit, cheered her heart, and did her more good than hours of solitary study.

Finding, much to her own surprise, that her fancy was teeming with lovely conceits, she did hope for a quiet evening. But ma wanted a dish of gossip, pa must have his papers read to him, the boys had lessons and rips and grievances to be attended to, May's lullaby could not be forgotten, and the maids had to be looked after, lest burly "cousins"[1] should be hidden in the boiler, or lucifer matches among the shavings. So Psyche's day ended, leaving her very tired, rather discouraged, and almost heart-sick with the shadow of a coming sorrow.

All summer she did her best, but accomplished very little as she thought; yet this was the teaching she most needed, and in time she came to see it. In the autumn May died, whispering with her arms about her sister's neck:—

"You make me so happy, Sy, I wouldn't mind the pain if I could stay a little longer. But if I can't, good-by, dear, good-by."

Her last look and word and kiss were all for Psyche, who felt then with grateful tears that her summer had not been wasted; for the smile upon the little dead face was more to her than any marble perfection her hands could have carved.

In the solemn pause which death makes in every family, Psyche said, with the sweet self-forgetfulness of a strong yet tender nature:—

"I must not think of myself, but try to comfort them;" and with this resolution she gave herself heart and soul to duty, never thinking of reward.

A busy, anxious, humdrum winter, for, as Harry said, "it was hard times for every one." Mr. Dean grew gray with the weight of business cares about which he never spoke; Mrs. Dean, laboring under the delusion that an invalid was a necessary appendage to the family, installed herself in the place the child's death left vacant, and the boys needed much comforting, for the poor lads never knew how much they loved "the baby" till the little chair stood empty. All turned to Sy for help and consolation, and her strength seemed to increase with the demand upon it. Patience and cheerfulness, courage and skill, came at her call like good fairies who had bided their time. House-keeping ceased to be hateful, and peace reigned in parlor and kitchen,

---

1. I.e., a rattlesnake's cousins: copperhead snakes.

while Mrs. Dean, shrouded in shawls, read Hahnemann's Lesser Writings[2] on her sofa. Mr. Dean sometimes forgot his mills when a bright face came to meet him, a gentle hand smoothed the wrinkles out of his anxious forehead, and a daughterly heart sympathized with all his cares. The boys found home very pleasant with Sy always there ready to "lend a hand," whether it was to make fancy ties, help conjugate "a confounded verb," pull candy,[3] or sing sweetly in the twilight when all thought of little May and grew quiet.

The studio door remained locked till her brothers begged Psyche to open it and make a bust of the child. A flush of joy swept over her face at the request, and her patient eyes grew bright and eager, as a thirsty traveller's might at the sight or sound of water. Then it faded as she shook her head, saying, with a regretful sigh, "I'm afraid I've lost the little skill I ever had."

But she tried, and with great wonder and delight discovered that she could work as she had never done before. She thought the newly found power lay in her longing to see the little face again; for it grew like magic under her loving hands, while every tender memory, sweet thought, and devout hope she had ever cherished, seemed to lend their aid. But when it was done and welcomed with tears and smiles, and praise more precious than any the world could give, then Psyche said within herself like one who saw light at last:—

"He was right; doing one's duty *is* the way to feed heart, soul, and imagination; for if one is good, one is happy, and if happy, one can work well."

III.

"She broke her head, and went home to come no more," was Giovanni's somewhat startling answer when Paul asked about Psyche, finding that he no longer met her on the stairs or in the halls. He understood what the boy meant, and with an approving nod turned to his work again, saying, "I like that! If there is any power in her, she has taken the right way to find it out, I suspect."

How she prospered he never asked; for, though he met her more than once that year, the interviews were brief ones in street, concert-room, or picture-gallery, and she carefully avoided speaking of herself. But, possessing the gifted eyes which can look below the surface of things, he detected in the girl's face something better than beauty, though each time he saw it, it looked older and more thoughtful, often anxious and sad.

"She is getting on," he said to himself with a cordial satisfaction which gave his manner a friendliness as grateful[4] to Psyche as his wise reticence.

Adam was finished at last, proved a genuine success, and Paul heartily enjoyed the well-earned reward for years of honest work. One blithe May morning, he slipped early into the art-gallery, where the statue now stood, to look at his creation with paternal pride. He was quite alone with the stately figure that shone white against the purple draperies and seemed to offer him a voiceless welcome from its marble lips. He gave it one loving look, and then forgot it, for at the feet of his Adam lay a handful of wild violets, with the dew still on them. A sudden smile broke over his face as he took them up, with the thought, "She has been here and found my work good."

---

2. *The Lesser Writings of Samuel Hahnemann* (1852). Hahnemann (1755–1843), a German physician, was the founder of homeopathic medicine.

3. Make taffy. "Help conjugate": i.e., in Latin.
4. Agreeable, pleasing.

For several moments he stood thoughtfully turning the flowers to and fro in his hands; then, as if deciding some question within himself, he said, still smiling:—

"It is just a year since she went home; she must have accomplished something in that time; I'll take the violets as a sign that I may go and ask her what."

He knew she lived just out of the city, between the river and the mills, and as he left the streets behind him, he found more violets blooming all along the way like flowery guides to lead him right. Greener grew the road, balmier blew the wind, and blither sang the birds, as he went on enjoying his holiday with the zest of a boy, until he reached a most attractive little path winding away across the fields. The gate swung invitingly open, and all the ground before it was blue with violets. Still following their guidance he took the narrow path, till, coming to a mossy stone beside a brook, he sat down to listen to the blackbirds singing deliciously in the willows overhead. Close by the stone, half hidden in the grass lay a little book, and, taking it up, he found it was a pocket-diary. No name appeared on the fly-leaf, and, turning the pages to find some clue to its owner, he read here and there enough to give him glimpses into an innocent and earnest heart which seemed to be learning some hard lesson patiently. Only near the end did he find the clue in words of his own, spoken long ago, and a name. Then, though longing intensely to know more, he shut the little book and went on, showing by his altered face that the simple record of a girl's life had touched him deeply.

Soon an old house appeared nestling to the hillside with the river shining in the low green meadows just before it.

"She lives there," he said, with as much certainty as if the pansies by the door-stone spelt her name, and, knocking, he asked for Psyche.

"She's gone to town, but I expect her home every minute." "Ask the gentleman to walk in and wait, Katy," cried a voice from above, where the whisk of skirts was followed by the appearance of an inquiring eye over the banisters.

The gentleman did walk in, and while he waited looked about him. The room, though very simply furnished, had a good deal of beauty in it, for the pictures were few and well chosen, the books such as never grow old, the music lying on the well-worn piano of the sort which is never out of fashion, and standing somewhat apart was one small statue in a recess full of flowers. Lovely in its simple grace and truth was the figure of a child looking upward as if watching the airy flight of some butterfly which had evidently escaped from the chrysalis still lying in the little hand.

Paul was looking at it with approving eyes when Mrs. Dean appeared with his card in her hand, three shawls on her shoulders, and in her face a somewhat startled expression, as if she expected some novel demonstration from the man whose genius her daughter so much admired.

"I hope Miss Psyche is well," began Paul, with great discrimination if not originality.

The delightfully commonplace remark tranquillized Mrs. Dean at once, and, taking off the upper shawl with a fussy gesture, she settled herself for a chat.

"Yes, thank Heaven, Sy is well. I don't know what would become of us if she wasn't. It has been a hard and sorrowful year for us with Mr. Dean's business embarrassments, my feeble health, and May's death. I don't know that you were aware of our loss, sir;" and unaffected maternal grief gave sudden dignity to the faded, fretful face of the speaker.

Paul murmured his regrets, understanding better now the pathetic words on a certain tear-stained page of the little book still in his pocket.

"Poor dear, she suffered everything, and it came very hard upon Sy, for the child wasn't happy with any one else, and almost lived in her arms," continued Mrs. Dean, dropping the second shawl to get her handkerchief.

"Miss Psyche has not had much time for art-studies this year, I suppose?" said Paul, hoping to arrest the shower natural as it was.

"How could she, with two invalids, the house-keeping, pa and the boys to attend to? No, she gave that up last spring, and though it was a great disappointment to her at the time, she has got over it now, and is happier than she ever was before, I think," added her mother, remembering as she spoke that Psyche even now went about the house sometimes pale and silent, with a hungry look in her eyes.

"I am glad to hear it," though a little shadow passed over his face as Paul spoke, for he was too true an artist to believe that any work could be as happy as that which he loved and lived for. "I thought there was much promise in Miss Psyche, and I sincerely believe that time will prove me a true prophet," he said with mingled regret and hope in his voice as he glanced about the room, which betrayed the tastes still cherished by the girl.

"I'm afraid ambition isn't good for women; I mean the sort that makes 'em known by coming before the public in any way. But Sy deserves some reward, I'm sure, and I know she'll have it, for a better daughter never lived."

Here the third shawl was cast off, as if the thought of Psyche, or the presence of a genial guest, had touched Mrs. Dean's chilly nature with a comfortable warmth.

Further conversation was interrupted by the avalanche of boys, which came tumbling down the front stairs as Tom, Dick, and Harry shouted in a sort of chorus:—

"Sy, my balloon has got away; lend us a hand at catching him!"

"Sy, I want a lot of paste made, right off."

"Sy, I've split my jacket down the back; come sew me up, there's a dear!"

On beholding a stranger the young gentlemen suddenly lost their voices, found their manners, and with nods and grins took themselves away as quietly as could be expected of six clumping boots and an unlimited quantity of animal spirits in a high state of effervescence. As they trooped off an unmistakable odor of burnt milk pervaded the air, and the crash of china, followed by an Irish wail, caused Mrs. Dean to clap on her three shawls again and excuse herself in visible trepidation.

Paul laughed quietly to himself, then turned sober and said, "Poor Psyche!" with a sympathetic sigh. He roamed about the room impatiently till the sound of voices drew him to the window to behold the girl coming up the walk with her clumsy old father leaning on one arm, the other loaded with baskets and bundles, and her hands occupied by a remarkably ugly turtle.

"Here we are!" cried a cheery voice, as they entered without observing the newcomer. "I've done all my errands and had a lovely time. There is Tom's gunpowder, Dick's fishhooks, and one of Professor Gazzy's famous turtles for Harry. Here are your bundles, mother dear, and, best of all, here's pa, home in time for a good rest before dinner. I went to the mill and got him."

Psyche spoke as if she had brought a treasure; and so she had, for though Mr. Dean's face usually was about as expressive as the turtle's, it woke and warmed with the affection which his daughter had fostered till no amount of flannel could extinguish it. His big hand patted her cheek very gently as he said, in a tone of fatherly love and pride:—

"My little Sy never forgets old pa, does she?"

"Good gracious me, my dear, there's *such* a mess in the kitchen! Katy's burnt up the pudding, put castor-oil[5] instead of olive in the salad, smashed the best meat-dish,

---

5. An oil used as a laxative, skin softener, and lubricant.

and here's Mr. Gage come to dinner," cried Mrs. Dean in accents of despair as she tied up her head in a fourth shawl.

"Oh, I'm so glad; I'll go in and see him a few minutes, and then I'll come and attend to everything; so don't worry, mother."

"How did you find me out?" asked Psyche as she shook hands with her guest and stood looking up at him with all the old confiding frankness in her face and manner.

"The violets showed me the way."

She glanced at the posy in his button-hole and smiled.

"Yes, I gave them to Adam, but I didn't think you would guess. I enjoyed your work for an hour to-day, and I have no words strong enough to express my admiration."

"There is no need of any. Tell me about yourself; what have you been doing all this year?" he asked, watching with genuine satisfaction the serene and sunny face before him, for discontent, anxiety, and sadness were no longer visible there.

"I've been working and waiting," she began.

"And succeeding, if I may believe what I see and hear and read," he said with an expressive little wave of the book as he laid it down before her.

"My diary! I didn't know I had lost it. Where did you find it?"

"By the brook where I stopped to rest. The moment I saw your name I shut it up. Forgive me, but I can't ask pardon for reading a few pages of that little gospel of patience, love, and self-denial."

She gave him a reproachful look and hurried the telltale book out of sight as she said, with a momentary shadow on her face:—

"It has been a hard task; but I think I have learned it, and am just beginning to find that my dream *is* 'a noonday light and truth,' to me."

"Then you do not relinquish your hopes and lay down your tools?" he asked with some eagerness.

"Never! I thought at first that I could not serve two masters; but in trying to be faithful to one I find I am nearer and dearer to the other. My cares and duties are growing lighter every day (or I have learned to bear them better), and when my leisure does come I shall know how to use it, for my head is full of ambitious plans, and I feel that I can do something *now*."

All the old enthusiasm shone in her eyes, and a sense of power betrayed itself in voice and gesture as she spoke.

"I believe it," he said heartily. "You have learned the secret, as that proves."

Psyche looked at the childish image as he pointed to it, and into her face there came a motherly expression that made it very sweet.

"That little sister was so dear to me I could not fail to make her lovely, for I put my heart into my work. The year has gone, but I don't regret it, though this is all I have done."

"You forgot your three wishes; I think the year has granted them."

"What were they?"

"To possess beauty in yourself, the power of seeing it in all things, and the art of reproducing it with truth."

She colored deeply under the glance which accompanied the threefold compliment, and answered with grateful humility,—

"You are very kind to say so; I wish I could believe it." Then, as if anxious to forget herself, she added rather abruptly,—

"I hear you think of giving your Adam a mate,—have you begun yet?"

"Yes, my design is finished, all but the face."

"I should think you could image Eve's beauty since you have succeeded so well with Adam's."

"The features perhaps, but not the expression. That is the charm of feminine faces, a charm so subtle that few can catch and keep it. I want a truly womanly face, one that shall be sweet and strong without being either weak or hard. A hopeful, loving, earnest face, with a tender touch of motherliness in it, and perhaps the shadow of a grief that has softened but not saddened it."

"It will be hard to find a face like that."

"I don't expect to find it in perfection; but one sometimes sees faces which suggest all this, and in rare moments give glimpses of a lovely possibility."

"I sincerely hope you will find one then," said Psyche, thinking of the dinner.

"Thank you; *I* think I have."

Now, in order that every one may be suited, we will stop here, and leave our readers to finish the story as they like. Those who prefer the good old fashion may believe that the hero and heroine fell in love, were married and lived happily ever afterward. But those who can conceive of a world outside of a wedding-ring may believe that the friends remained faithful friends all their lives, while Paul won fame and fortune, and Psyche grew beautiful with the beauty of a serene and sunny nature, happy in duties which became pleasures, rich in the art which made life lovely to herself and others.

1868

FRANCES HODGSON BURNETT
1849–1924

In *Waiting for the Party* (1974), a biography of Frances Hodgson Burnett, Ann Thwaite concludes that in her life and in her works Burnett "tried to make dreams come true." Many of her books provide satisfying fairy-tale plots of transformation and wish fulfillment, demonstrating the very real power of innocence. Her great success came at a time when the division between works for children and for adults was not sharply drawn. Six of the seven best-selling books in English during 1884 to 1886 would now be considered children's literature: *Heidi* (1880–81; trans. 1884), by Johanna Spyri; *Treasure Island* (1883) and *A Child's Garden of Verses* (1885), by Robert Louis Stevenson; *The Adventures of Huckleberry Finn* (1884), by Mark Twain; *King Solomon's Mines* (1885), by H. Rider Haggard; and *Little Lord Fauntleroy* (1886), by Burnett. Burnett's novel had been serialized in 1885 in the popular children's periodical *St. Nicholas*, but William Gladstone, the prime minister of England, and the American poet James Russell Lowell were among the adults who admired the book about a charming American boy, Cedric Errol, whose innocence and loving nature convert his irascible grandfather, the Earl of Dorincourt, to generosity and republican values.

Like her famous hero Cedric (based, in part, on her younger son, Vivian), Frances Hodgson Burnett was an Anglo-American whose fortunes changed radically. She was born in Manchester, England, the middle child of five. The family's relative prosperity ended with the death of her father when she was nearly four: her mother was unable to manage his home furnishings business, and their circumstances grew worse as Manchester's mill-dominated economy slumped during the American Civil War. In 1865 Eliza Hodgson moved with her children to rural Tennessee, where her brother was living. Though they continued to struggle, Frances was delighted to exchange the filth and damp of Manchester for the open skies and promise of Tennessee. To contribute to her family's income, she drew on her love of reading and long practice in writing stories for her own pleasure: the very first story she submitted to *Godey's Lady's Book* was accepted in 1868, and almost immediately she began publishing widely in American women's magazines. In 1870, following the death of her mother, Frances became largely responsible for supporting her younger sisters; in 1871 she broke into the literary market by landing a story at *Scribner's Monthly*.

By 1872 Frances was successful enough to finance an extended trip to England (during which she continued to write stories for American periodicals). On her return in 1873, she married a local doctor, Swan Burnett. Through his advanced studies in ophthalmology in Paris, the birth of two sons, and his setting up a practice in Washington, D.C., in 1876, Burnett's writings helped support her family. Along with many stories, Burnett published several well-received realistic novels, including *That Lass o' Lowrie's* (1877), set in Lancashire, and *Through One Administration* (1883), set in Washington. She also wrote popular lighthearted works such as *A Fair Barbarian* (1881), closer in tone to her later writings for children. By the mid-1880s, Burnett was a well-known writer and had met such important literary figures as Ralph Waldo Emerson, Louisa May Alcott, and Oscar Wilde. But the publication of the wildly popular *Little Lord Fauntleroy* (1886) changed her life dramatically.

Previously, Burnett had published a few children's stories in *St. Nicholas*, the earliest in 1880; the best-selling *Little Lord Fauntleroy* not only brought her great wealth and fame but also changed the focus of her literary efforts. Rather than works of realism she published stories of fashionable life and of almost magical transformation, pleasing adult readers and establishing a reputation as a skillful and popular writer for the young. Burnett's successful adaptation of *Fauntleroy* for the stage—a formula she followed often with her works—increased its sales even further. Her earnings enabled her in effect to end a marriage that had long been unhappy, and she spent a good deal of time in Europe. It was to Europe that Burnett took her older son, Lionel, in 1890 after he was diagnosed with tuberculosis; he died later that year. Grieving, Burnett wrote a number of melancholy stories, many featuring dead or dying children, published in *Children I Have Known and Giovanni and the Other* (1892) and *Piccino and Other Child Stories* (1894). She also wrote *The One I Knew Best of All: A Memory in the Mind of a Child* (1893), her memoir of her childhood up to the beginning of her literary career.

Frances Hodgson Burnett's divorce from Swan Burnett in 1898 drew public criticism, and her marriage two years later to Stephen Townesend, her playwriting collaborator and a man ten years her junior, provided more fodder for gossip—as did their separation in 1902. Such notoriety affected neither her productivity nor her book sales, however. Between 1898 and 1907 (when it was sold), Burnett rented Maytham Hall, a country estate in Kent. She began to write outside in its rose garden, as well as to plant and weed and to make friends with a robin who would eat crumbs from her hand. This garden helped inspire *The Secret Garden* (1911), considered by many critics to be one of the great children's novels of all time. *The Secret Garden*, Thwaite argues, "is a book of the new century. Far from encouraging the attitudes instilled in Frances as a child ('Speak when you're spoken to, come when you're called . . . '), it suggested children should be self-reliant and have faith in themselves, that they should listen not to their elders and betters, but to their own hearts and consciences." This theme can also be traced in an early popular children's tale, "Sara Crewe." Burnett's third reworking of the story (first published as a short story in 1888, then adapted as a play in late 1902) was expanded and published as a novel, *A Little Princess*, in 1905.

In 1905 Burnett also became an American citizen, and after she left Maytham Hall she built a house on Long Island, where she lived and wrote from 1909 until her death. Her last major work for children was *The Lost Prince* (1915), a romantic political fantasy; her final publication, appearing posthumously, was *In the Garden* (1925), an essay on the joys of gardening. Today, despite her many best-selling novels for adults, Burnett is remembered only as a children's writer. In particular, the numerous television, film, and musical versions of *A Little Princess* and *The Secret Garden* have won them new audiences of all ages.

"Editha's Burglar," first published in *St. Nicholas* in 1880 and reprinted in a book in 1888 (the same year that a successful dramatized version, *Nixie*, was staged), is one of Burnett's best-known stories. That its sentimental plot of a selfless, innocent child confronting a wayward adult bent on stealing was mocked by other writers—including O. Henry, F. Anstey, and E. Nesbit—demonstrates the power and pleasure of such stories of redemption and childhood agency. Peter Hunt has called "Editha's Burglar" "an object-lesson in how to walk the fine line between whimsical fantasy and dangerous realism. It shows clearly how Burnett could manipulate a fashionable and sentimental view of childhood—that innocence could overcome evil—within a reasonably realist context."

Editha's Burglar

FRANCES
HODGSON
BURNETT

I will begin, by saying that Editha was always rather a queer little girl, and not much like other children. She was not a strong, healthy little girl, and had never been able to run about and play; and, as she had no sisters or brothers, or companions of her own size, she was rather old-fashioned, as her aunts used to call it. She had always been very fond of books, and had learned to read when she was such a tiny child, that I should almost be afraid to say how tiny she was when she read her first volume through. Her papa wrote books himself, and was also the editor of a newspaper; and, as he had a large library, Editha perhaps read more than was quite good for her. She lived in London; and, as her mamma was very young and pretty, and went out a great deal, and her papa was so busy, and her governess only came in the morning, she was left to herself a good many hours in the day, and when she was left to herself, she spent the greater part of her time in the library reading her papa's big books, and even his newspapers.

She was very fond of the newspapers, because she found so many curious things in them,—stories, for instance, of strange events which happened every day in the great city of London, and yet never seemed to happen anywhere near where she lived. Through the newspapers, she found that there were actually men who lived by breaking into peoples' houses and stealing all the nice things they could carry away, and she read that such men were called burglars. When she first began to read about burglars, she was very much troubled. In the first place, she felt rather timid about going to bed at night, and, in the second place, she felt rather sorry for the burglars.

"I suppose no one ever taught them any better," she thought.

In fact, she thought so much about the matter, that she could not help asking her papa some questions one morning when he was at breakfast. He was reading his paper and eating his chops both at once when she spoke to him.

"Papa," she said, in a solemn little voice, and looking at him in a very solemn manner, "papa dear, what do you think of burglars—as a class?" (She said "as a class," because she had heard one of her papa's friends say it, and as he was a gentleman she admired very much, she liked to talk as he did.) Her papa gave a little jump in his chair, as if she had startled him, and then he pushed his hair off his forehead and stared at her.

"Burglars! As a class!" he said, and then he stared at her a minute again in rather a puzzled way. "Bless my soul!" he said. "As a class, Nixie!" (that was his queer pet name for her.) "Nixie, where is your mother?"

"She is in bed, papa dear, and we mustn't disturb her," said Editha. "The party last night tired her out. I peeped into her room softly as I came down. She looks so pretty when she is asleep. What *do* you think of burglars, papa?"

"I think they're a bad lot, Nixie," said her papa, "a bad lot."

"Are there no good burglars, papa?"

"Well, Nixie," answered papa, "I should say not. As a rule you know,—" and here he began to smile, as people often smiled at Editha when she asked questions—"As a rule burglars are not distinguished for moral perspicuity and blameless character."

But Editha did not understand what moral perspicuity meant, and besides she was thinking again.

"Miss Lane was talking to me the other day, about some poor children who had never been taught anything; they had never had any French or music lessons, and scarcely knew how to read, and she said they had never had any advantages. Perhaps that is the way with the burglars, papa,—perhaps they have never had any advantages,—perhaps if they had had advantages they mightn't have been burglars."

"Lessons in French and music are very elevating to the mind, my dear Nixie," papa began in his laughing way, which was always a trial to Editha, but suddenly he stopped, and looked at her rather sadly.

"How old are you, Nixie?" he asked.

"I am seven," answered Editha, "seven years, going on eight."

Papa sighed.

"Come here, little one," he said, holding out his strong white hand to her.

She left her chair and went to him, and he put his arms around her, and kissed her, and stroked her long brown hair.

"Don't puzzle your little brain too much," he said, "never mind about the burglars, Nixie."

"Well," said Editha, "I can't help thinking about them a little, and it seems to me that there must be, perhaps, one good burglar among all the bad ones, and I can't help being rather sorry, even for the bad ones. You see, they must have to be up all night, and out in the rain sometimes, and they can't help not having had advantages."

It was strange that the first thing she heard, when she went up to her mamma's room, was something about burglars.

She was very, very fond of her mamma, and very proud of her. She even tried to take care of her in her small way; she never disturbed her when she was asleep, and she always helped her to dress, bringing her things to her, buttoning her little shoes and gloves, putting the perfume on her handkerchiefs, and holding her wraps until she wanted them.

This morning, when she went into the dressing room, she found the chamber-maid there before her, and her dear little mamma looking very pale.

"Ah mem! if you please mem!" the chamber-maid was saying, "what a blessing it was they didn't come here!"

"Who, Janet?" Editha asked.

"The burglars, Miss, that broke into Number Eighteen last night, and carried off all the silver, and the missus's jewelry."

"If burglars ever do break in here," said mamma, "I hope none of us will hear them, though it would almost break my heart to have my things taken. If I should waken in the night, and find a burglar in my room, I think it would kill me, and I know I should scream, and then there is no knowing what they might do. If ever you think there is a burglar in the house, Nixie, whatever you do, don't scream or make any noise. It would be better to have one's things stolen, than to be killed by burglars for screaming."

She was not a very wise little mamma, and often said rather thoughtless things; but she was very gentle and loving, and Editha was so fond of her that she put her arms round her waist and said to her:

"Mamma, dearest, I will never let any burglars hurt you or frighten you if I can help it. I do believe I could persuade them not to. I should think even a burglar would listen to reason."

That made her mamma laugh, so that she forgot all about the burglars and began to get her color again, and it was not long before she was quite gay, and was singing a song she had heard at the opera, while Editha was helping her to dress.

But that very night Editha met a burglar.

Just before dinner, her papa came up from the city in a great hurry. He dashed up to the front door in a cab, and, jumping out, ran upstairs to mamma, who was sitting in the drawing room, while Editha read aloud to her.

"Kitty, my dear," he said, "I am obliged to go to Glasgow by the 'five' train. I must throw a few things into a portmanteau and go at once."

"Oh, Francis!" said mamma. "And just after that burglary at the Norris's! I don't like to be left alone."

"The servants are here," said papa, "and Nixie will take care of you; won't you, Nixie? Nixie is interested in burglars."

"I am sure Nixie could do more than the servants," said mamma. "All three of them sleep in one room at the top of the house when you are away, and even if they awakened they would only scream."

"Nixie wouldn't scream," said papa, laughing; "Nixie would do something heroic. I will leave you in her hands."

He was only joking, but Editha did not think of what he said as a joke; she felt that her mamma was really left in her care, and that it was a very serious matter.

She thought about it so seriously that she hardly talked at all at dinner, and was so quiet afterward that her mamma said, "Dear me, Nixie, what *are* you thinking of? You look as solemn as a little owl."

"I am thinking of you, mamma," the child answered.

And then her mamma laughed and kissed her, and said: "Well, I must say I don't see why you should look so grave about me. I didn't think I was such a solemn subject."

At last bed-time came, and the little girl went to her mother's room, because she was to sleep there.

"I am glad I have you with me, Nixie," said mamma, with a rather nervous little laugh. "I am sure I shouldn't like to sleep in this big room alone."

But, after she was in bed, she soon fell asleep, and lay looking so happy and sweet and comfortable that Editha thought it was lovely to see her.

Editha did not go to sleep for a long time. She thought of her papa trying to sleep on the train, rushing through the dark night on its way to Scotland; she thought of a new book she had just begun to read; she thought of a child she had once heard singing in the street; and when her eyes closed at length, her mind had just gone back to the burglars at Number Eighteen. She slept until midnight, and then something wakened her. At first she did not know what it was, but in a few minutes she found that it was a queer little sound coming from down-stairs,—a sound like a stealthy filing of iron.

She understood in a moment then, because she had heard the chamber-maid say that the burglars broke into Number Eighteen by filing through the bars of the shutters.

"It is a burglar," she thought, "and he will awaken mamma."

If she had been older, and had known more of the habits of burglars, she might have been more frightened than she was. She did not think of herself at all, however, but of her mother.

She began to reason the matter over as quickly as possible, and she made up her mind that the burglar must not be allowed to make a noise.

"I'll go down and ask him to please be as quiet as he can," she said to herself, "and I'll tell him why."

Certainly, this was a queer thing to think of doing, but I told you when I began my story that she was a queer little girl.

She slipped out of bed so quietly that she scarcely stirred the clothes, and then slipped just as quietly out of the room and down the stairs.

The filing had ceased, but she heard a sound of stealthy feet in the kitchen; and, though it must be confessed her heart beat rather faster than usual, she made her way to the kitchen and opened the door.

Imagine the astonishment of that burglar when, on hearing the door open, he turned round and found himself looking at a slender little girl, in a white frilled night-gown, and with bare feet,—a little girl whose large brown eyes rested on him in a by no means unfriendly way.

"I'll be polite to him," Editha had said, as she was coming down-stairs. "I am sure he'll be more obliging if I am very polite. Miss Lane says politeness always wins its way."

So the first words she spoke were as polite as she could make them.

"Don't be frightened," she said, in a soft voice. "I don't want to hurt you; I came to ask a favor of you."

The burglar was so amazed that he actually forgot he was a burglar, and staggered back against the wall. I think he thought at first that Editha was a little ghost. "You see I couldn't hurt you if I wanted to," she went on, wishing to encourage him. "I'm too little. I'm only seven,—and a little over,—and I'm not going to scream, because that would waken mamma, and that's just what I don't want to do."

That did encourage the burglar, but still he was so astonished that he did not know what to do.

"Well, I'm blowed," he said in a whisper, "if this ain't a rummy go!"[1] which was extremely vulgar language; but, unfortunately, he was one of those burglars who, as Miss Lane said, "had not had any advantages," which is indeed the case with the majority of the burglars of my acquaintance.

Then he began to laugh,—in a whisper also, if one can be said to laugh in a whisper. He put his hand over his mouth, and made no noise, but he laughed so hard that he doubled up and rocked himself to and fro.

"The rummiest go!" he said, in his uneducated way. "An she haint agoin' to 'urt me. Oh, my heye!"

He was evidently very badly educated, indeed, for he not only used singular words, but sounded his h's all in the wrong places. Editha noticed this, even in the midst of her surprise at his laughter. She could not understand what he was laughing at. Then it occurred to her that she might have made a mistake.

"If you please," she said with great delicacy, "are you really a burglar?"

He stopped laughing just long enough to answer her.

"Lor' no, miss," he said, "by no manner o' means. I'm a dear friend o' yer Par's, come to make a evenin' call, an' not a wishin' to trouble the servants, I stepped in through the winder."

"Ah!" said Editha, looking very gravely at him; "I see you are joking with me, as papa does sometimes. But what I wanted to say to you was this: Papa has gone to Scotland, and all our servants are women, and mamma would be so frightened if you were to waken her, that I am sure it would make her ill. And if you are going to burgle, would you please burgle as quietly as you can, so that you wont disturb her?"

The burglar stopped laughing, and, staring at her, once more uttered his vulgar exclamation:

_____

1. An odd incident.

"Don't be frightened," she said, "I don't want to hurt you."

"Well, I'll be blowed!"

"Why don't you say 'I'll be blown?'" asked Editha. "I'm sure it isn't correct to say you'll be blowed."

She thought he was going off into one of his unaccountable fits of laughter again, but he did not; he seemed to check himself with an effort.

"There haint no time to waste," she heard him mutter.

"No, I suppose there isn't," she answered, "Mamma might wake and miss me. What are you going to burgle first?"

"You'd better go upstairs to yer mar," he said, rather sulkily.

Editha thought deeply for a few seconds.

"You oughtn't to burgle anything," she said. "Of course you know that, but if you have really made up your mind to do it, I would like to show you the things you'd better take."

"What, fer instance?" said the burglar, with interest.

"You mustn't take any of mamma's things," said Editha, "because they are all in her room, and you would waken her, and besides, she said it would break her heart; and don't take any of the things papa is fond of. I'll tell you what," turning rather pale, "you can take my things."

"What kind o' things?" asked the burglar.

"My locket, and the little watch papa gave me, and the necklace and bracelets my grandmamma left me—they are worth a great deal of money, and they are very pretty, and I was to wear them when I grew to be a young lady, but—you can take them. And—then—" very slowly, and with a deep sigh, "there are—my books. I'm very fond of them, but——"

"I don't want no books," said the burglar.

"Don't you?" exclaimed she, "Ah, thank you."

"Well," said the burglar, as if to himself, and staring hard at her brightening face, "I never see no sich a start afore."

"Shall I go upstairs and get the other things?" said Editha.

"No," he said. "You stay where you are—or stay, come along o' me inter the pantry, an' sit down while I'm occupied."

He led the way into the pantry, and pushed her down on a step, and then began to open the drawers where the silver was kept.

"It's curious that you should know just where to look for things, and that your key should fit, isn't it?" said Editha.

"Yes," he answered, "It's werry sing'lar, indeed. There's a good deal in bein' eddicated."

"Are you educated?" asked Editha with a look of surprise.

"Did yer think I wasn't ?" said the burglar.

"Well," said Editha, not wishing to offend him, "you see, you pronounce your words so very strangely."

"It's all a matter o' taste," interrupted the burglar. "Oxford an' Cambridge 'as different vocabillaries."

"Did you go to Oxford?" asked Editha politely.

"No," said he, "nor yet to Cambridge."

Then he laughed again, and seemed to be quite enjoying himself as he made some forks and spoons up into a bundle. "I 'ope there haint no plated stuff 'ere," he said. "Plate's wulgar, an' I 'ope yer parents haint wulgar, cos that'd be settin' yer a werry bad example an' sp'ilin' yer morals."

"I am sure papa and mamma are not vulgar," said Editha.

The burglar opened another drawer, and chuckled again, and this suggested to Editha's mind another question.

"Is your business a good one?" she suddenly inquired of him.

" 'Taint as good as it ought to be, by no manner o' means," said the burglar. "Every one haint as hobligin' as you, my little dear."

"Oh!" said Editha. "You know you obliged me by not making a noise."

"Well," said the burglar, "as a rule, we don't make a practice o' makin' no more noise than we can help. It haint considered 'ealthy in the perfession."

"Would you mind leaving us a few forks and spoons to eat with, if you please? I beg pardon for interrupting you, but I'm afraid we shall not have any to use at breakfast."

"Haint yer got no steel uns?" inquired the burglar.

"Mamma wouldn't like to use steel ones, I'm sure," Editha answered. "I'll tell you what you can do: please leave out enough for mamma, and I can use steel. I don't care about myself, much."

The man seemed to think a moment, and then he was really so accommodating as to do as she asked, and even went to the length of leaving out her own little fork and knife and spoon.

"Oh! you are very kind," said Editha, when she saw him do this.

"That's a reward o' merit, cos yer didn't squeal," said the burglar.

He was so busy for the next few minutes that he did not speak, though now and then he broke into a low laugh, as if he was thinking of something very funny, indeed. During the silence, Editha sat holding her little feet in her night-gown, and watching him very curiously. A great many new thoughts came into her active brain, and at last she could not help asking some more questions.

"Would you really rather be a burglar than anything else?" she inquired, respectfully.

"Well," said the man, "p'r'aps I'd prefer to be Lord Mayor, or a member o' the 'Ouse o' Lords, or heven the Prince o' Wales,[2] honly for there bein' hobstacles in the way of it."

"Oh!" said Editha; "you couldn't be the Prince of Wales, you know. I meant wouldn't you rather be in some other profession? My papa is an editor," she added. "How would you like to be an editor."

"Well," said the burglar, "hif yer par ud change with me, or hif he chanced to know hany heditor with a roarin' trade as ud be so hobligin' as to 'and it hover, hits wot I've allers 'ad a leanin' to."

"I am sure papa would not like to be a burglar," said Editha, thoughtfully; "but perhaps he might speak to his friends about you, if you would give me your name and address, and if I were to tell him how obliging you were, and if I told him you really didn't like being a burglar."

The burglar put his hand to his pocket and gave a start of great surprise.

"To think o' me a forgettin' my card-case," he said, "an' a leavin' it on the pianner when I come hout. I'm sich a bloomin' forgetful cove.[3] I might hev knowed I'd hev wanted it."

"It is a pity," said Editha; "but if you told me your name and your number, I think I could remember it."

"I'm afeared yer couldn't," said the burglar, regretfully, "but I'll try yer. Lord Halgernon Hedward Halbert de Pentonville, YdePark.[4] Can you think o' that?"

"Are you a lord?" exclaimed Editha. "Dear me, how strange!"

"It is sing'lar," said the burglar, shaking his head. "I've hoften thought so myself. But not wishin' to detain a lady no longer than can be 'elped, s'pose we take a turn in the lib'ery among yer respected par's things."

"Don't make a noise," said Editha, as she led the way.

But when they reached the library her loving little heart failed her. All the things her father valued most were there, and he would be sure to be so sorry if one thing was missing when he returned. She stood on the threshold a moment and looked about her.

"Oh," she whispered, "please do me another favor, wont you? Please let me slip quietly upstairs and bring down my own things instead. They will be so easy to carry away, and they are very valuable and—and I will make you a present of them if you will not touch anything that belongs to papa. He is so fond of his things and, besides that, he is so good."

The burglar gave a rather strange and disturbed look at her.

"Go an' get yer gimcracks," he said in a somewhat grumbling voice.

Her treasures were in her own room, and her bare feet made no sound as she crept slowly up the staircase and then down again. But when she handed the little box to the burglar her eyes were wet.

"Papa gave me the watch, and mamma gave me the locket," she whispered, tremulously; "and the pearls were grandmamma's, and grandmamma is in heaven."

It would not be easy to know what the burglar thought; he looked queerer than ever. Perhaps he was not quite so bad as some burglars, and felt rather ashamed of taking her treasures from a little girl who loved other people so much better than she loved herself. But he did not touch any of papa's belongings, and, indeed, did not remain much longer. He grumbled a little when he looked into the drawing-room, saying something to himself about "folks never 'avin' no consideration for a cove, an' leavin' nothin' portable 'andy, a expectin' of him to carry off seventy-five pound bronze clocks an' marble stattoos"; but though Editha was sorry to see that he appeared annoyed, she did not understand him.

After that, he returned to the pantry and helped himself to some cold game pie, and seemed to enjoy it, and then poured out a tumbler of wine, which Editha thought a great deal to drink at once.

"Yer 'e'lth, my dear," he said, "an' 'appy returns, an' many on 'em. May yer grow up a hornyment to yer sect, an' a comfort to yer respected mar an' par."

And he threw his head very far back, and drank the very last drop in the glass, which was vulgar, to say the least of it.

Then he took up his bundles of silver and the other articles he had appropriated, and seeing that he was going away, Editha rose from the pantry step.

"Are you going out through the window?" she asked.

"Yes, my dear," he answered with a chuckle, "it's a little 'abit I've got into. I prefers 'em to doors."

"Well, good-by," she said, holding out her hand politely. "And thank you, my lord."

She felt it only respectable to say that, even if he had fallen into bad habits and become a burglar.

He shook hands with her in quite a friendly manner, and even made a bow.

"Yer welcome, my dear," he said. "An' I must hadd that if I ever see a queerer or better behaved little kid, may I be blowed—or, as yer told me it would be more correcter to say, I'll be blown."

Editha did not know he was joking; she thought he was improving, and that if he had had advantages he might have been a very nice man.

It was astonishing how neatly he slipped through the window; he was gone in a second, and Editha found herself standing alone in the dark, as he had taken his lantern with him.

She groped her way out and up the stairs, and then, for the first time, she began to feel cold and rather weak and strange; it was more like being frightened than any feeling she had had while the burglar was in the house.

"Perhaps, if he had been a very bad burglar, he might have killed me," she said to herself, trembling a little. "I am very glad he did not kill me for—for it would have hurt mamma so, and papa too, when he came back, and they told him."

Her mamma wakened in the morning with a bright smile.

"Nobody hurt us, Nixie" she said. "We are all right, arn't we?"

"Yes, mamma dear," said Editha.

She did not want to startle her just then, so she said nothing more, and she even said nothing all through the excitement that followed the discovery of the robbery, and indeed, said nothing until her papa came home, and then he wondered so at her pale face, and petted her so tenderly, and thought it so strange that nothing but her treasures had been taken from upstairs, that she could keep her secret no longer.

"Papa," she cried out all at once in a trembling voice, "I gave them to him myself."

"You, Nixie! You!" exclaimed her papa, looking alarmed. "Kitty, the fright has made the poor little thing ill."

"No, papa," said Editha, her hands shaking, and the tears rushing into her eyes, she did not know why. "I heard him, and—I knew mamma would be so frightened,—and it came into my mind to ask him—not to waken her,—and I crept down stairs—and asked him;—and he was not at all unkind though he laughed. And I stayed with him, and—and told him I would give him all my things if he would not touch yours nor mamma's. He—he wasn't such a bad burglar, papa,—and he told me he would rather be something more respectable."

And she hid her face on her papa's shoulder.

"Kitty!" papa cried out. "Oh, Kitty!"

Then her mamma flew to her and knelt down by her, kissing her, and crying aloud: "Oh, Nixie! if he had hurt you,—if he had hurt you."

"He knew I was not going to scream, mamma," said Editha. "And he knew I was too little to hurt him. I told him so."

She scarcely understood why mamma cried so much more at this, and why even papa's eyes were wet as he held her close up to his breast.

"It is my fault, Francis," wept the poor little mamma. "I have left her too much to herself, and I have not been a wise mother. Oh, to think of her risking her dear little life just to save me from being frightened, and to think of her giving up the things she loves for our sakes. I will be a better mother to her, after this, and take care of her more."

But I am happy to say that the watch and locket and pearls were not altogether lost, and came back to their gentle little owner in time. About six months after, the burglar was caught, as burglars are apt to be, and, after being tried and sentenced to transportation to the penal settlements (which means that he was to be sent away to be a prisoner in a far country),[5] a police officer came one day to see Editha's papa, and he actually came from that burglar, who was in jail and wanted to see Editha for a special reason. Editha's papa took her to see him, and the moment she entered his cell she knew him.

"How do you do, my lord?" she said, in a gentle tone.

"Not as lively as common,[6] miss," he answered, "in consequence o' the confinement not bein' good fer my 'e'lth."

"None of your chaff," said the police officer. "Say what you have to say."

And then, strange to say, the burglar brought forth from under his mattress a box, which he handed to the little girl.

"One o' my wisitors brought 'em in to me this mornin'," he said. "I thought yer might as well hev 'em. I kep' 'em partly 'cos it was more convenienter, an' partly 'cos I took a fancy to yer. I've seed a many curi's things, sir," he said to Editha's papa, "but never nothin' as bloomin' queer as that little kid a-comin' in an' tellin' me she wont 'urt me, nor yet wont scream, and please wont I burgle quietly so as to not disturb her mar. It brought my 'art in my mouth when first I see her, an' then, lor', how I larft. I almost made up my mind to give her things back to her afore I left, but I didn't quite do that—it was agin human natur'."

But they were in the box now, and Editha was so glad to see them that she could scarcely speak for a few seconds. Then she thanked the burglar politely.

5. Australia. 6. Usual.

"To think of her risking her dear little life to save me!"

"I am much obliged to you," she said, "and I'm really very sorry you are to be sent so far away. I am sure papa would have tried to help you if he could, though he says he is afraid you would not do for an editor."

The burglar closed one eye and made a very singular grimace at the police officer, who turned away suddenly and did not look round until Editha had bidden her acquaintance good-bye.

And even this was not quite all. A few weeks later, a box was left for Editha by a very shabby, queer-looking man, who quickly disappeared as soon as he had given it to the servant at the door; and in this box was a very large, old-fashioned silver watch, almost as big as a turnip, and inside the lid were scratched these words:

> To the little Kid,
> From 'er fr'end and wel wisher,
> Lord halgernon hedward halbert
> de pentonwill, ide park.

1880, 1888

L. M. MONTGOMERY
1874–1942

Lucy Maud Montgomery, the best-selling author of the Anne of Green Gables series of books for girls, is inextricably linked to Canada's smallest province. Montgomery was born on Prince Edward Island, located just off the mainland's northeastern coast, in 1874, and she lived there for all but three of the first thirty-seven years of her life. The island landscape and farming community inspired her fiction throughout her long writing career: nineteen of her twenty novels are set wholly or in part on Prince Edward Island. Although from 1911 onward she lived on the mainland in Ontario, returning only for visits, Montgomery was buried on the island.

Montgomery's literary career had its seeds in the town of Cavendish, her first home, and in the large family circle of aunts, uncles, and cousins—many of them gifted storytellers—who inhabited her world. Maud was raised by her maternal grandparents, the Macneills; her mother had died of tuberculosis before she was two, and her father left the island and moved ever westward, finally settling in Saskatchewan. Her primary childhood home was also the district post office, and young Maud would sit under the post office table listening to and storing up the gossip and tales of her neighbors. Some of these anecdotes would later appear in her fiction. At age nine, Montgomery began to write poetry and keep a journal, a practice she would continue throughout her life. During a mostly unsatisfactory year spent with her father and stepmother when she was fifteen, Montgomery filled her diary with impressions, dialogues, and ruminations; her earliest publications—poems, an essay, and an extended prose narrative—date from the early 1890s. She was determined to be a writer.

Back home in Prince Edward Island, Montgomery yearned for further schooling; she also needed to make a living. At Prince of Wales College in Charlottetown, the province's capital, she condensed a two-year teacher's training course into one year. In 1894 Montgomery began her first teaching job in Bideford, and early in the morning she wrote poems and stories that she regularly published in Canadian and American magazines. She was able to save enough money for only one year at Dalhousie University (then College) in Halifax, Nova Scotia,

before she had to return to teaching on the island. She stopped in 1898, moving back in with her grandmother after her grandfather's death; even as she attended to housekeeping and the post office, her determination to become a full-time writer grew. In 1903, Montgomery wrote to George Boyd Mac-Millan, a younger Scotsman with whom she long corresponded, "But I am frankly in literature to make my living out of it. . . . My aspiration is limited to this—I want to be a *good workman* in my chosen profession" (*My Dear Mr. M: Letters to G. B. Mac-Millan*, 1980).

By then, she was making a modest income from her periodical publications. A new level of success was achieved when Montgomery's first novel, *Anne of Green Gables*, which she had set aside after several publishers had rejected it in 1905, was issued in 1908. This novel and its sequels about Anne Shirley, a quirky and imaginative red-haired orphan who enlivens a dull household and farming community, would make Montgomery Canada's most celebrated author. She herself modestly described the first Anne book to MacMillan as "a juvenilish story of and for girls, but I rather hope some grown-ups will like it, too," explaining that "the character of the little heroine is the motif of the book." The public fell in love with this heroine—called by enthusiastic reviewers "vivid," "original," and "one of the most delightful characters in juvenile fiction"—and the book sold wonderfully well. It went into a fourth edition only a few months after its first printing and was translated into many languages; the publisher immediately requested a sequel.

In fact, the public's desire for more books about Anne was so insatiable that Montgomery—much like Louisa May Alcott as she spun out the March family saga—felt forced to meet her readers' demands for the rest of her writing life. As a result, she was typecast as the author of cheerful, humorous, and sentimental books for girls, even when her topics and characters were more complex than such a label would imply. Montgomery published seven more novels about Anne and her family, as well as two collections of short stories that include some of the same settings and characters. In addition to other books for girls—including *The Story Girl*

(1911) and its sequel, *The Golden Road* (1913); three books (her most autobiographical) about Emily Byrd Starr, who longs to be a writer (1923–27); and *Jane of Lantern Hill* (1937)—Montgomery published two novels intended for adults, *The Blue Castle* (1926) and *A Tangled Web* (1931). Montgomery was very responsive to the many fans who wrote to her, personally answering every letter she received.

In 1911, four months after her grandmother's death, Montgomery married the Reverend Ewan Macdonald in a quiet ceremony; they had been engaged since 1906. She had had an earlier engagement, and had been in love with a second man, but she apparently chose to emphasize affection and perceived compatibility rather than passion when she married. After honeymooning in Scotland, the land of her forebears, they settled about 60 miles northeast of Toronto, as Ewan became Leaskdale's Presbyterian minister. There she bore two sons and wrote eleven books, but was often unhappy: her husband suffered from chronic depression and frequent debilitating breakdowns, and she, too, often went through periods of depression, contributed to by the strain of hiding the nature of Ewan's illnesses from the congregation, her sorrow for a third son, who was stillborn, the complications of a lengthy lawsuit against her publisher, and her deep disturbance at the violence and turmoil of World War I. Nevertheless, Montgomery continued to find pleasure and satisfaction in her children, in her many friendships, and especially in her writing. She once wrote to MacMillan that maintaining a separation between her ideal world and the real one enabled her to maintain a hopeful nature in the midst of disappointments: "no matter what was missing outwardly,

I could find all in my own peculiar kingdom." In 1926, after a schism within the church at Leaskdale, the family moved to Norval, a parish closer to Toronto. In 1935, after Ewan could no longer continue in the ministry, the couple moved to Toronto and to a home Montgomery named "Journey's End." Montgomery continued to publish until two years before her death. Her final stories involving Anne were published posthumously, in 1974, as *The Road to Yesterday*.

During her lifetime, Montgomery's *Anne of Green Gables* was twice made into a film, and many film and television versions of the novels and spin-offs featuring the characters have been produced since. In 1935 she was made a Companion of the Order of the British Empire, a special award given in celebration of King George V's silver jubilee. The Anne series has become an enduring classic of children's literature and the first introduction, for many, to Montgomery's beloved Prince Edward Island. In 1936 the Canadian government designated part of Cavendish as a national park, enshrining many of the places Montgomery had immortalized, and Green Gables House now draws hundreds of thousands of visitors every year. Montgomery was buried in Cavendish cemetery after her death in 1942.

"Each in His Own Tongue," a kind of parable of charity and forgiveness, was first published in the magazine *Delineator* in 1910 and later included in *Chronicles of Avonlea* (1912), a collection of short stories revised to tie them to the character of Anne. Montgomery noted in her 1930 journal that a British critic called it one of the finest stories ever written in English (quoted in *My Dear Mr. M*).

Each in His Own Tongue

The honey-tinted autumn sunshine was falling thickly over the crimson and amber maples around old Abel Blair's door. There was only one outer door in old Abel's house, and it almost always stood wide open. A little black dog, with one ear missing and a lame forepaw, almost always slept on the worn red sandstone slab which served old Abel for a doorstep; and on the still more worn sill above it a large gray cat almost always slept. Just inside the door, on a bandy-legged chair of elder days, old Abel almost always sat.

He was sitting there this afternoon—a little old man, sadly twisted with rheumatism; his head was abnormally large, thatched with long, wiry black hair; his face was heavily lined and swarthily sunburned; his eyes were deep-set and black, with occasional peculiar golden flashes in them. A strange looking man was old Abel Blair; and as strange was he as he looked, Lower Carmody[1] people would have told you.

Old Abel was almost always sober in these, his later years. He was sober to-day. He liked to bask in that ripe sunlight as well as his dog and cat did; and in such baskings he almost always looked out of his doorway at the far, fine blue sky over the tops of the crowding maples. But to-day he was not looking at the sky; instead, he was staring at the black, dusty rafters of his kitchen, where hung dried meats and strings of onions and bunches of herbs and fishing tackle and guns and skins.

But old Abel saw not these things; his face was the face of a man who beholds visions, compact of heavenly pleasure and hellish pain, for old Abel was seeing what he might have been—and what he was; as he always saw when Felix Moore played to him on the violin. And the awful joy of dreaming that he was young again, with unspoiled life before him, was so great and compelling that it counterbalanced the agony in the realization of a dishonoured old age, following years in which he had squandered the wealth of his soul in ways where Wisdom lifted not her voice.

Felix Moore was standing opposite to him, before an untidy stove, where the noon fire had died down into pallid, scattered ashes. Under his chin he held old Abel's brown, battered fiddle; his eyes, too, were fixed on the ceiling; and he, too, saw things not lawful to be uttered in any language save that of music; and of all music, only that given forth by the anguished, enraptured spirit of the violin. And yet this Felix was little more than twelve years old, and his face was still the face of a child who knows nothing of either sorrow or sin or failure or remorse. Only in his large, gray-black eyes was there something not of the child—something that spoke of an inheritance from many hearts, now ashes, which had aforetime[2] grieved and joyed, and struggled and failed, and succeeded and grovelled. The inarticulate cries of their longings had passed into this child's soul, and transmuted themselves into the expression of his music.

Felix was a beautiful child. Carmody people, who stayed at home, thought so; and old Abel Blair, who had roamed afar in many lands, thought so; and even the Rev. Stephen Leonard, who taught, and tried to believe, that favour is deceitful and beauty is vain, thought so.

He was a slight lad, with sloping shoulders, a slim brown neck, and a head set on it with stag-like grace and uplift. His hair, cut straight across his brow and falling over his ears, after some caprice of Janet Andrews, the minister's housekeeper, was a glossy blue-black. The skin of his face and hands was like ivory; his eyes were large and beautifully tinted—gray, with dilating pupils; his features had the outlines of a cameo. Carmody mothers considered him delicate, and had long foretold that the minister would never bring him up; but old Abel pulled his grizzled moustache when he heard such forebodings and smiled.

"Felix Moore will live," he said positively. "You can't kill that kind until their work is done. He's got a work to do—if the minister'll let him do it. And if the minister don't let him do it, then I wouldn't be in that minister's shoes when he comes to the judgment—no, I'd rather be in my own. It's an awful thing to cross the purposes of the Almighty, either in your own life or anybody else's. Sometimes I think it's what's meant by the unpardonable sin[3]—ay, that I do!"

---

1. The fictional Prince Edward Island town, based on Stanley Bridge, described in the books about Anne of Green Gables.

2. Formerly.
3. I.e., blasphemy against the Holy Spirit (Matthew 12.31).

Carmody people never asked what old Abel meant. They had long ago given up such vain questioning. When a man had lived as old Abel had lived for the greater part of his life, was it any wonder he said crazy things? And as for hinting that Mr. Leonard, a man who was really almost too good to live, was guilty of any sin, much less an unpardonable one—well, there now! what use was it to be taking any account of old Abel's queer speeches? Though, to be sure, there was no great harm in a fiddle, and maybe Mr. Leonard was a mite too strict that way with the child. But then, could you wonder at it? There was his father, you see.

Felix finally lowered the violin, and came back to old Abel's kitchen with a long sigh. Old Abel smiled drearily at him—the smile of a man who has been in the hands of the tormentors.

"It's awful the way you play—it's awful," he said with a shudder. "I never heard anything like it—and you that never had any teaching since you were nine years old, and not much practice, except what you could get here now and then on my old, battered fiddle. And to think you make it up yourself as you go along! I suppose your grandfather would never hear to your studying music—would he now?"

Felix shook his head.

"I know he wouldn't, Abel. He wants me to be a minister. Ministers are good things to be, but I'm afraid I can't be a minister."

"Not a pulpit minister. There's different kinds of ministers, and each must talk to men in his own tongue if he's going to do 'em any real good," said old Abel meditatively. "*Your* tongue is music. Strange that your grandfather can't see that for himself, and him such a broad-minded man! He's the only minister I ever had much use for. He's God's own if ever a man was. And he loves you—yes, sir, he loves you like the apple of his eye."

"And I love him," said Felix warmly. "I love him so much that I'll even try to be a minister for his sake, though I don't want to be."

"What do you want to be?"

"A great violinist," answered the child, his ivory-hued face suddenly warming into living rose. "I want to play to thousands—and see their eyes look as yours do when I play. Sometimes your eyes frighten me, but oh, it's a splendid fright! If I had father's violin I could do better. I remember that he once said it had a soul that was doing purgatory for its sins when it had lived on earth. I don't know what he meant, but it did seem to me that *his* violin was alive. He taught me to play on it as soon as I was big enough to hold it."

"Did you love your father?" asked old Abel, with a keen look.

Again Felix crimsoned; but he looked straightly and steadily into his old friend's face.

"No," he said, "I didn't; but," he added, gravely and deliberately, "I don't think you should have asked me such a question."

It was old Abel's turn to blush. Carmody people would not have believed he could blush; and perhaps no living being could have called that deepening hue into his weather-beaten cheek save only this gray-eyed child of the rebuking face.

"No, I guess I shouldn't," he said. "But I'm always making mistakes. I've never made anything else. That's why I'm nothing more than 'Old Abel' to the Carmody people. Nobody but you and your grandfather ever calls me 'Mr. Blair.' Yet William Blair at the store up there, rich and respected as he is, wasn't half as clever a man as I was when we started in life: you mayn't believe that, but it's true. And the worst of it is, young Felix, that most of the time I don't care whether I'm Mr. Blair or old

Abel. Only when you play I care. It makes me feel just as a look I saw in a little girl's eyes some years ago made me feel. Her name was Anne Shirley[4] and she lived with the Cuthberts down at Avonlea. We got into a conversation at Blair's store. She could talk a blue streak to anyone, that girl could. I happened to say about something that it didn't matter to a battered old hulk of sixty odd like me. She looked at me with her big, innocent eyes, a little reproachful like, as if I'd said something awful heretical. 'Don't you think, Mr. Blair,' she says, 'that the older we get the more things ought to matter to us?'—as grave as if she'd been a hundred instead of eleven. 'Things matter so much to me now,' she says, clasping her hands thisaway, 'and I'm sure that when I'm sixty they'll matter just five times as much to me.' Well, the way she looked and the way she spoke made me feel downright ashamed of myself because things had stopped mattering with me. But never mind all that. My miserable old feelings don't count for much. What come of your father's fiddle?"

"Grandfather took it away when I came here. I think he burned it. And I long for it so often."

"Well, you've always got my old brown fiddle to come to when you must."

"Yes, I know. And I'm glad for that. But I'm hungry for a violin all the time. And I only come here when the hunger gets too much to bear. I feel as if I oughtn't to come even then—I'm always saying I won't do it again, because I know grandfather wouldn't like it, if he knew."

"He has never forbidden it, has he?"

"No, but that is because he doesn't know I come here for that. He never thinks of such a thing. I feel sure he *would* forbid it, if he knew. And that makes me very wretched. And yet I *have* to come. Mr. Blair, do you know why grandfather can't bear to have me play on the violin? He loves music, and he doesn't mind my playing on the organ, if I don't neglect other things. I can't understand it, can you?"

"I have a pretty good idea, but I can't tell you. It isn't my secret. Maybe he'll tell you himself some day. But, mark you, young Felix, he has got good reasons for it all. Knowing what I know, I can't blame him over much, though I think he's mistaken. Come now, play something more for me before you go—something that's bright and happy this time, so as to leave me with a good taste in my mouth. That last thing you played took me straight to heaven,—but heaven's awful near to hell, and at the last you tipped me in."

"I don't understand you," said Felix, drawing his fine, narrow black brows together in a perplexed frown.

"No—and I wouldn't want you to. You couldn't understand unless you was an old man who had it in him once to do something and be a *man*, and just went and made himself a devilish fool. But there must be something in you that understands things—all kinds of things—or you couldn't put it all into music the way you do. How do you do it? How in—how *do* you do it, young Felix?"

"I don't know. But I play differently to different people. I don't know how that is. When I'm alone with you I have to play one way; and when Janet comes over here to listen I feel quite another way—not so thrilling, but happier and lonelier. And that day when Jessie Blair was here listening I felt as if I wanted to laugh and sing—as if the violin wanted to laugh and sing all the time."

The strange, golden gleam flashed through old Abel's sunken eyes.

"God," he muttered under his breath, "I believe the boy can get into other folk's souls somehow, and play out what *his* soul sees there."

---

4. The main character of *Anne of Green Gables* (1908).

"What's that you say?" inquired Felix, petting his fiddle.

"Nothing—never mind—go on. Something lively now, young Felix. Stop probing into my soul, where you haven't no business to be, you infant, and play me something out of your own—something sweet and happy and pure."

"I'll play the way I feel on sunshiny mornings, when the birds are singing and I forget I have to be a minister," said Felix simply.

A witching, gurgling, mirthful strain, like mingled bird and brook song, floated out on the still air, along the path where the red and golden maple leaves were falling very softly, one by one. The Reverend Stephen Leonard heard it, as he came along the way, and the Reverend Stephen Leonard smiled. Now, when Stephen Leonard smiled, children ran to him, and grown people felt as if they looked from Pisgah[5] over to some fair land of promise beyond the fret and worry of their care-dimmed earthly lives.

Mr. Leonard loved music, as he loved all things beautiful, whether in the material or the spiritual world, though he did not realize how much he loved them for their beauty alone, or he would have been shocked and remorseful. He himself was beautiful. His figure was erect and youthful, despite seventy years. His face was as mobile and charming as a woman's, yet with all a man's tried strength and firmness in it, and his dark blue eyes flashed with the brilliance of one and twenty; even his silken silvery hair could not make an old man of him. He was worshipped by everyone who knew him, and he was, in so far as mortal man may be, worthy of that worship.

"Old Abel is amusing himself with his violin again," he thought. "What a delicious thing he is playing! He has quite a gift for the violin. But how can he play such a thing as that,—a battered old hulk of a man who has, at one time or another, wallowed in almost every sin to which human nature can sink? He was on one of his sprees three days ago—the first one for over a year—lying dead-drunk in the market square in Charlottetown[6] among the dogs; and now he is playing something that only a young archangel on the hills of heaven ought to be able to play. Well, it will make my task all the easier. Abel is always repentant by the time he is able to play on his fiddle."

Mr. Leonard was on the door-stone. The little black dog had frisked down to meet him, and the gray cat rubbed her head against his leg. Old Abel did not notice him; he was beating time with uplifted hand and smiling face to Felix's music, and his eyes were young again, glowing with laughter and sheer happiness.

"Felix! what does this mean?"

The violin bow clattered from Felix's hand upon the floor; he swung around and faced his grandfather. As he met the passion of grief and hurt in the old man's eyes his own clouded with an agony of repentance.

"Grandfather—I'm sorry," he cried brokenly.

"Now, now!" Old Abel had risen deprecatingly. "It's all my fault, Mr. Leonard. Don't you blame the boy. I coaxed him to play a bit for me. I didn't feel fit to touch the fiddle yet myself—too soon after Friday, you see. So I coaxed him on—wouldn't give him no peace till he played. It's all my fault."

"No," said Felix, throwing back his head. His face was as white as marble, yet it seemed ablaze with desperate truth and scorn of old Abel's shielding lie. "No, grandfather, it isn't Abel's fault. I came over here on purpose to play, because I thought

---

5. The mountain east of Jordan from which Moses viewed the promised land (Deuteronomy 3.27).

6. The largest town in Prince Edward Island and the province's capital.

you had gone to the harbour. I have come here often, ever since I have lived with you."

"Ever since you have lived with me you have been deceiving me like this, Felix?"

There was no anger in Mr. Leonard's tone—only measureless sorrow. The boy's sensitive lips quivered.

"Forgive me, grandfather," he whispered beseechingly.

"You never forbid him to come," old Abel broke in angrily. "Be just, Mr. Leonard—be just."

"I *am* just. Felix knows that he has disobeyed me, in the spirit if not in the letter. Do you not know it, Felix?"

"Yes, grandfather, I have done wrong—I've known that I was doing wrong every time I came. Forgive me, grandfather."

"Felix, I forgive you, but I ask you to promise me, here and now, that you will never again, as long as you live, touch a violin."

Dusky crimson rushed madly over the boy's face. He gave a cry as if he had been lashed with a whip. Old Abel sprang to his feet.

"Don't you ask such a promise of him, Mr. Leonard," he cried furiously. "It's a sin, that's what it is. Man, man, what blinds you? You *are* blind. Can't you see what is in the boy? His soul is full of music. It'll torture him to death—or to worse—if you don't let it have way."

"There is a devil in such music," said Mr. Leonard hotly.

"Ay, there may be, but don't forget that there's a Christ in it, too," retorted old Abel in a low tense tone.

Mr. Leonard looked shocked; he considered that old Abel had uttered blasphemy. He turned away from him rebukingly.

"Felix, promise me."

There was no relenting in his face or tone. He was merciless in the use of the power he possessed over that young, loving spirit. Felix understood that there was no escape; but his lips were very white as he said,

"I promise, grandfather."

Mr. Leonard drew a long breath of relief. He knew that promise would be kept. So did old Abel. The latter crossed the floor and sullenly took the violin from Felix's relaxed hand. Without a word or look he went into the little bedroom off the kitchen and shut the door with a slam of righteous indignation. But from its window he stealthily watched his visitors go away. Just as they entered on the maple path Mr. Leonard laid his hand on Felix's head and looked down at him. Instantly the boy flung his arm up over the old man's shoulder and smiled at him. In the look they exchanged there was boundless love and trust—ay, and good-fellowship. Old Abel's scornful eyes again held the golden flash.

"How those two love each other!" he muttered enviously. "And how they torture each other!"

Mr. Leonard went to his study to pray when he got home. He knew that Felix had run for comforting to Janet Andrews, the little thin, sweet-faced, rigid-lipped woman who kept house for them. Mr. Leonard knew that Janet would disapprove of his action as deeply as old Abel had done. She would say nothing, she would only look at him with reproachful eyes over the teacups at suppertime. But Mr. Leonard believed he had done what was best and his conscience did not trouble him, though his heart did.

Thirteen years before this, his daughter Margaret had almost broken that heart by marrying a man of whom he could not approve. Martin Moore was a professional violinist. He was a popular performer, though not in any sense a great one. He met the slim, golden-haired daughter of the manse[7] at the house of a college friend she was visiting in Toronto, and fell straightway in love with her. Margaret had loved him with all her virginal heart in return, and married him, despite her father's disapproval. It was not to Martin Moore's profession that Mr. Leonard objected, but to the man himself. He knew that the violinist's past life had not been such as became a suitor for Margaret Leonard; and his insight into character warned him that Martin Moore could never make any woman lastingly happy.

Margaret Leonard did not believe this. She married Martin Moore and lived one year in paradise. Perhaps that atoned for the three bitter years which followed—that, and her child. At all events, she died as she had lived, loyal and uncomplaining. She died alone, for her husband was away on a concert tour, and her illness was so brief that her father had not time to reach her before the end. Her body was taken home to be buried beside her mother in the little Carmody churchyard. Mr. Leonard wished to take the child, but Martin Moore refused to give him up.

Six years later Moore, too, died, and at last Mr. Leonard had his heart's desire— the possession of Margaret's son. The grandfather awaited the child's coming with mingled feelings. His heart yearned for him, yet he dreaded to meet a second edition of Martin Moore. Suppose Margaret's son resembled his handsome vagabond of a father! Or, worse still, suppose he were cursed with his father's lack of principle, his instability, his Bohemian instincts. Thus Mr. Leonard tortured himself wretchedly before the coming of Felix.

The child did not look like either father or mother. Instead, Mr. Leonard found himself looking into a face which he had put away under the grasses thirty years before,—the face of his girl bride, who had died at Margaret's birth. Here again were her lustrous gray-black eyes, her ivory outlines, her fine-traced arch of brow; and here, looking out of those eyes, seemed her very spirit again. From that moment the soul of the old man was knit to the soul of the child, and they loved each other with a love surpassing that of women.[8]

Felix's only inheritance from his father was his love of music. But the child had genius, where his father had possessed only talent. To Martin Moore's outward mastery of the violin was added the mystery and intensity of his mother's nature, with some more subtle quality still, which had perhaps come to him from the grandmother he so strongly resembled. Moore had understood what a career was naturally before the child, and he had trained him in the technique of his art from the time the slight fingers could first grasp the bow. When nine-year-old Felix came to the Carmody manse he had mastered as much of the science of the violin as nine out of ten musicians acquire in a lifetime; and he brought with him his father's violin; it was all Martin Moore had to leave his son—but it was an Amati,[9] the commercial value of which nobody in Carmody suspected. Mr. Leonard had taken possession of it and Felix had never seen it since. He cried himself to sleep many a night for the loss of it. Mr. Leonard did not know this, and if Janet Andrews suspected it she held her tongue—an art in which she excelled. She "saw no harm in a fiddle," herself, and thought Mr. Leonard absurdly strict in the matter, though it would not have been well for the luckless outsider who might have ventured to say as much to her. She

7. The residence of a minister.
8. An allusion to David's lamentation over the death of Jonathan (2 Samuel 1.26).

9. A violin created by a member of an Italian family of violin makers; the most famous was Nicolò Amati (1590–1684).

had connived at Felix's visits to old Abel Blair, squaring the matter with her Presbyterian conscience by some peculiar process known only to herself.

When Janet heard of the promise which Mr. Leonard had exacted from Felix she seethed with indignation; and, though she "knew her place" better than say anything to Mr. Leonard about it, she made her disapproval so plainly manifest in her bearing that the stern, gentle old man found the atmosphere of his hitherto peaceful manse unpleasantly chill and hostile for a time.

It was the wish of his heart that Felix should be a minister, as he would have wished his own son to be, had one been born to him. Mr. Leonard thought rightly that the highest work to which any man could be called was a life of service to his fellows; but he made the mistake of supposing the field of service much narrower than it is—of failing to see that a man may minister to the needs of humanity in many different but equally effective ways.

Janet hoped that Mr. Leonard might not exact the fulfilment of Felix's promise; but Felix himself, with the instinctive understanding of perfect love, knew that it was vain to hope for any change of viewpoint in his grandfather. He addressed himself to the keeping of his promise in letter and in spirit. He never went again to old Abel's; he did not even play on the organ, though this was not forbidden, because any music wakened in him a passion of longing and ecstasy which demanded expression with an intensity not to be borne. He flung himself grimly into his studies and conned[1] Latin and Greek verbs with a persistency which soon placed him at the head of all competitors.

Only once in the long winter did he come near to breaking his promise. One evening, when March was melting into April, and the pulses of spring were stirring under the lingering snow, he was walking home from school alone. As he descended into the little hollow below the manse a lively lilt of music drifted up to meet him. It was only the product of a mouth-organ, manipulated by a little black-eyed, French-Canadian hired boy, sitting on the fence by the brook; but there was music in the ragged urchin and it came out through his simple toy. It tingled over Felix from head to foot; and, when Leon held out the mouth-organ with a fraternal grin of invitation, he snatched at it as a famished creature might snatch at food.

Then, with it half way to his lips, he paused. True, it was only the violin he had promised never to touch; but he felt that if he gave way ever so little to the desire that was in him, it would sweep everything before it. If he played on Leon Buote's mouth-organ, there in that misty spring dale, he would go to old Abel's that evening; he *knew* he would go. To Leon's amazement, Felix threw the mouth-organ back at him and ran up the hill as if he were pursued. There was something in his boyish face that frightened Leon; and it frightened Janet Andrews as Felix rushed past her in the hall of the manse.

"Child, what's the matter with you?" she cried. "Are you sick? Have you been scared?"

"No, no. Leave me alone, Janet," said Felix chokingly, dashing up the stairs to his own room.

He was quite composed when he came down to tea, an hour later, though he was unusually pale and had purple shadows under his large eyes.

Mr. Leonard scrutinized him somewhat anxiously; it suddenly occurred to the old minister that Felix was looking more delicate than his wont this spring. Well, he had

---

1. Committed to memory.

studied hard all winter, and he was certainly growing very fast. When vacation came he must be sent away for a visit.

"They tell me Naomi Clark is real sick," said Janet. "She has been ailing all winter, and now she's fast to her bed. Mrs. Murphy says she believes the woman is dying, but nobody dares tell her so. She won't give in she's sick, nor take medicine. And there's nobody to wait on her except that simple creature, Maggie Peterson."

"I wonder if I ought to go and see her," said Mr. Leonard uneasily.

"What use would it be to bother yourself? You know she wouldn't see you—she'd shut the door in your face like she did before. She's an awful wicked woman—but it's kind of terrible to think of her lying there sick, with no responsible person to tend her."

"Naomi Clark is a bad woman and she lived a life of shame, but I like her, for all that," remarked Felix, in the grave, meditative tone in which he occasionally said rather startling things.

Mr. Leonard looked somewhat reproachfully at Janet Andrews, as if to ask her why Felix should have attained to this dubious knowledge of good and evil under her care; and Janet shot a dour look back which, being interpreted, meant that if Felix went to the district school she could not and would not be held responsible if he learned more there than arithmetic and Latin.

"What do you know of Naomi Clark to like or dislike?" she asked curiously. "Did you ever see her?"

"Oh, yes," Felix replied, addressing himself to his cherry preserve with considerable gusto. "I was down at Spruce Cove one night last summer when a big thunderstorm came up. I went to Naomi's house for shelter. The door was open, so I walked right in, because nobody answered my knock. Naomi Clark was at the window, watching the cloud coming up over the sea. She just looked at me once, but didn't say anything, and then went on watching the cloud. I didn't like to sit down because she hadn't asked me to, so I went to the window by her and watched it, too. It was a dreadful sight—the cloud was so black and the water so green, and there was such a strange light between the cloud and the water; yet there was something splendid in it, too. Part of the time I watched the storm, and the other part I watched Naomi's face. It was dreadful to see, like the storm, and yet I liked to see it.

"After the thunder was over it rained a while longer, and Naomi sat down and talked to me. She asked me who I was, and when I told her she asked me to play something for her on her violin,"—Felix shot a deprecating glance at Mr. Leonard—"because, she said, she'd heard I was a great hand at it. She wanted something lively, and I tried just as hard as I could to play something that was terrible—it just played itself—it seemed as if something was lost that could never be found again. And before I got through Naomi came at me, and tore the violin from me, and—*swore*. And she said, 'You big-eyed brat, how did you know *that?*' Then she took me by the arm—and she hurt me, too, I can tell you—and she put me right out in the rain and slammed the door."

"The rude, unmannerly creature!" said Janet indignantly.

"Oh, no, she was quite in the right," said Felix composedly. "It served me right for what I played. You see, she didn't know I couldn't help playing it. I suppose she thought I did it on purpose."

"What on earth did you play, child?"

"I don't know." Felix shivered. "It was awful—it was dreadful. It was fit to break your heart. But it *had* to be played, if I played anything at all."

"I don't understand what you mean—I declare I don't," said Janet in bewilderment.

"I think we'll change the subject of conversation," said Mr. Leonard.

It was a month later when "the simple creature, Maggie" appeared at the manse door one evening and asked for the preacher.

"Naomi wants ter see yer," she mumbled. "Naomi sent Maggie ter tell yer ter come at onct."

"I shall go, certainly," said Mr. Leonard gently. "Is she very ill?"

"Her's dying," said Maggie with a broad grin. "And her's awful skeered of hell. Her just knew ter-day her was dying. Maggie told her—her wouldn't believe the harbour women, but her believed Maggie. Her yelled awful."

Maggie chuckled to herself over the gruesome remembrance. Mr. Leonard, his heart filled with pity, called Janet and told her to give the poor creature some refreshment. But Maggie shook her head.

"No, no, preacher, Maggie must get right back to Naomi. Maggie'll tell her the preacher's coming ter save her from hell."

She uttered an eerie cry, and ran at full speed shoreward through the spruce woods.

"The Lord save us!" said Janet in an awed tone. "I knew the poor girl was simple, but I didn't know she was like *that*. And are you going, sir?"

"Yes, of course. I pray God I may be able to help the poor soul," said Mr. Leonard sincerely. He was a man who never shirked what he believed to be his duty; but duty had sometimes presented itself to him in pleasanter guise than this summons to Naomi Clark's death-bed.

The woman had been the plague spot of Lower Carmody and Carmody Harbour for a generation. In the earlier days of his ministry to the congregation he had tried to reclaim her, and Naomi had mocked and flouted him to his face. Then, for the sake of those to whom she was a snare or a heart-break, he had endeavoured to set the law in motion against her, and Naomi had laughed the law to scorn. Finally, he had been compelled to let her alone.

Yet Naomi had not always been an outcast. Her girlhood had been innocent; but she was the possessor of a dangerous beauty, and her mother was dead. Her father was a man notorious for his harshness and violence of temper. When Naomi made the fatal mistake of trusting to a false love that betrayed and deserted, he drove her from his door with taunts and curses.

Naomi took up her quarters in a little deserted house at Spruce Cove. Had her child lived it might have saved her. But it died at birth, and with its little life went her last chance of worldly redemption. From that time forth her feet were set in the way that takes hold on hell.

For the past five years, however, Naomi had lived a tolerably respectable life. When Janet Peterson had died, her idiot daughter, Maggie, had been left with no kith or kin in the world. Nobody knew what was to be done with her, for nobody wanted to be bothered with her. Naomi Clark went to the girl and offered her a home. People said she was no fit person to have charge of Maggie, but everybody shirked the unpleasant task of interfering in the matter, except Mr. Leonard, who went to expostulate with Naomi, and, as Janet said, for his pains got her door shut in his face.

But from the day when Maggie Peterson went to live with her, Naomi ceased to be the harbour Magdalen.[2]

The sun had set when Mr. Leonard reached Spruce Cove, and the harbour was veiling itself in a wondrous twilight splendour. Afar out, the sea lay throbbing and purple, and the moan of the bar came through the sweet, chill spring air with its burden of hopeless, endless longing and seeking. The sky was blossoming into stars

2. I.e., prostitute.

above the afterglow; out to the east the moon was rising, and the sea beneath it was a thing of radiance and silver and glamour; and a little harbour boat that went sailing across it was transmuted into an elfin shallop from the coast of fairyland.

Mr. Leonard sighed as he turned from the sinless beauty of the sea and sky to the threshold of Naomi Clark's house. It was very small—one room below, and a sleeping-loft above; but a bed had been made up for the sick woman by the down-stairs window looking out on the harbour; and Naomi lay on it, with a lamp burning at her head and another at her side, although it was not yet dark. A great dread of darkness had always been one of Naomi's peculiarities.

She was tossing restlessly on her poor couch, while Maggie crouched on a box at the foot. Mr. Leonard had not seen her for five years, and he was shocked at the change in her. She was much wasted; her clear-cut, aquiline features had been of the type which becomes indescribably witch-like in old age, and, though Naomi Clark was barely sixty, she looked as if she might be a hundred. Her hair streamed over the pillow in white, uncared-for tresses, and the hands that plucked at the bed-clothes were like wrinkled claws. Only her eyes were unchanged; they were as blue and brilliant as ever, but now filled with such agonized terror and appeal that Mr. Leonard's gentle heart almost stood still with the horror of them. They were the eyes of a creature driven wild with torture, hounded by furies, clutched by unutterable fear.

Naomi sat up and dragged at his arm.

"Can you help me? Can you help me?" she gasped imploringly. "Oh, I thought you'd never come! I was skeered I'd die before you got here—die and go to hell. I didn't know before today that I was dying. None of those cowards would tell me. Can you help me?"

"If I cannot, God can," said Mr. Leonard gently. He felt himself very helpless and inefficient before this awful terror and frenzy. He had seen sad death-beds—troubled death-beds—ay, and despairing death-beds, but never anything like this.

"God!" Naomi's voice shrilled terribly as she uttered the name. "I can't go to God for help. Oh, I'm skeered of hell, but I'm skeereder still of God. I'd rather go to hell a thousand times over than face God after the life I've lived. I tell you I'm sorry for living wicked—I was always sorry for it all the time. There ain't never been a moment I wasn't sorry, though nobody would believe it. I was driven on by fiends of hell. Oh, you don't understand—you *can't* understand—but I was always sorry!"

"If you repent, that is all that is necessary. God will forgive you if you ask Him."

"No, He can't! Sins like mine can't be forgiven. He can't—and He won't."

"He can and He will. He is a God of love, Naomi."

"No," said Naomi with stubborn conviction. "He isn't a God of love at all. That's why I'm skeered of him. No, no. He's a God of wrath and justice and punishment. Love! There ain't no such thing as love! I've never found it on earth, and I don't believe it's to be found in God."

"Naomi, God loves us like a father."

"Like *my* father?" Naomi's shrill laughter, pealing through the still room, was hideous to hear.

The old minister shuddered.

"No—no! As a kind, tender, all-wise father, Naomi—as you would have loved your little child if it had lived."

Naomi cowered and moaned.

"Oh, I wish I could believe *that*. I wouldn't be frightened if I could believe that. *Make* me believe it. Surely you can make me believe that there's love and forgiveness in God if you believe it yourself."

"Jesus Christ forgave and loved the Magdalen, Naomi."

"Jesus Christ? Oh, I ain't afraid of *Him*. Yes, *He* could understand and forgive. He was half human. I tell you it's God I'm skeered of."

"They are one and the same," said Mr. Leonard helplessly. He knew he could not make Naomi realize it. This anguished death-bed was no place for a theological exposition on the mysteries of the Trinity.

"Christ died for you, Naomi. He bore your sins in His own body on the cross."

"We bear our own sins," said Naomi fiercely. "I've borne mine all my life—and I'll bear them for all eternity. I can't believe anything else. I *can't* believe God can forgive me. I've ruined people body and soul—I've broken hearts and poisoned homes—I'm worse than a murderess. No—no—no, there's no hope for me." Her voice rose again into that shrill, intolerable shriek. "I've got to go to hell. It ain't so much the fire I'm skeered of as the outer darkness. I've always been so skeered of darkness—it's so full of awful things and thoughts. Oh, there ain't nobody to help me! Man ain't no good and I'm too skeered of God."

She wrung her hands. Mr. Leonard walked up and down the room in the keenest anguish of spirit he had ever known. What could he do? What could he say? There was healing and peace in his religion for this woman as for all others, but he could express it in no language which this tortured soul could understand. He looked at her writhing face; he looked at the idiot girl chuckling to herself at the foot of the bed; he looked through the open door to the remote, starlit night—and a horrible sense of utter helplessness overcame him. He could do nothing—nothing! In all his life he had never known such bitterness of soul as the realization brought home to him.

"What is the good of you if you can't help me?" moaned the dying woman. "Pray—pray—pray!" she shrilled suddenly.

Mr. Leonard dropped on his knees by the bed. He did not know what to say. No prayer that he had ever prayed was of use here. The old, beautiful formulas, which had soothed and helped the passing of many a soul, were naught save idle, empty words to Naomi Clark. In his anguish of mind Stephen Leonard gasped out the briefest and sincerest prayer his lips had ever uttered.

"O, God, our Father! Help this woman. Speak to her in a tongue which she can understand."

A beautiful, white face appeared for a moment in the light that streamed out of the doorway into the darkness of the night. No one noticed it, and it quickly drew back into the shadow. Suddenly Naomi fell back on her pillow, her lips blue, her face horribly pinched, her eyes rolled up in her head. Maggie started up, pushed Mr. Leonard aside, and proceeded to administer some remedy with surprising skill and deftness. Mr. Leonard, believing Naomi to be dying, went to the door, feeling sick and bruised in soul.

Presently a figure stole out into the light.

"Felix, is that you?" said Mr. Leonard in a startled tone.

"Yes, sir." Felix came up to the stone step. "Janet got frightened that you might fall on that rough road after dark, so she made me come after you with a lantern. I've been waiting behind the point, but at last I thought I'd better come and see if you would be staying much longer. If you will be, I'll go back to Janet and leave the lantern here with you."

"Yes, that will be the best thing to do. I may not be ready to go home for some time yet," said Mr. Leonard, thinking that the death-bed of sin behind him was no sight for Felix's young eyes.

"Is that your grandson you're talking to?" Naomi spoke clearly and strongly. The spasm had passed. "If it is, bring him in. I want to see him."

Reluctantly Mr. Leonard signed Felix to enter. The boy stood by Naomi's bed and looked down at her with sympathetic eyes. But at first she did not look at him—she looked past him at the minister.

"I might have died in that spell," she said, with sullen reproach in her voice, "and if I had I'd been in hell now. You can't help me—I'm done with you. There ain't any hope for me, and I know it now."

She turned to Felix.

"Take down that fiddle on the wall and play something for me," she said imperiously. "I'm dying—and I'm going to hell—and I don't want to think of it. Play me something to take my thoughts off it—I don't care what you play. I was always fond of music—there was always something in it for me I never found anywhere else."

Felix looked at his grandfather. The old man nodded; he felt too ashamed to speak; he sat with his fine silver head in his hands, while Felix took down and tuned the old violin, on which so many godless lilts had been played in many a wild revel. Mr. Leonard felt that he had failed his religion. He could not give Naomi the help that was in it for her.

Felix drew the bow softly, perplexedly over the strings. He had no idea what he should play. Then his eyes were caught and held by Naomi's burning, mesmeric, blue gaze as she lay on her crumpled pillow. A strange, inspired look came over the boy's face. He began to play as if it were not he who played, but some mightier power, of which he was but the passive instrument.

Sweet and soft and wonderful was the music that stole through the room. Mr. Leonard forgot his heart-break and listened to it in puzzled amazement. He had never heard anything like it before. How could the child play like that? He looked at Naomi and marvelled at the change in her face. The fear and frenzy were going out of it; she listened breathlessly, never taking her eyes from Felix. At the foot of the bed the idiot girl sat with tears on her cheeks.

In that strange music was the joy of innocent, mirthful childhood, blent with the laughter of waves and the call of glad winds. Then it held the wild, wayward dreams of youth, sweet and pure in all their wildness and waywardness. They were followed by a rapture of young love—all-surrendering, all-sacrificing love.

The music changed. It held the torture of unshed tears, the anguish of a heart deceived and desolate. Mr. Leonard almost put his hands over his ears to shut out its intolerable poignancy. But on the dying woman's face was only a strange relief; as if some dumb, long-hidden pain had at last won to the healing of utterance.

The sullen indifference of despair came next, the bitterness of smouldering revolt and misery, the reckless casting away of all good. There was something indescribably evil in the music now—so evil that Mr. Leonard's white soul shuddered away in loathing, and Maggie cowered and whined like a frightened animal.

Again the music changed. And in it now there was agony and fear—and repentance and a cry for pardon. To Mr. Leonard there was something strangely familiar in it. He struggled to recall where he had heard it before; then he suddenly knew—he had heard it before Felix came in Naomi's terrible words! He looked at his grandson with something like awe. Here was a power of which he knew nothing—a strange and dreadful power. Was it of God! Or of Satan?

For the last time the music changed. And now it was not music at all—it was a great, infinite forgiveness, an all-comprehending love. It was healing for a sick soul; it was light and hope and peace. A Bible text, seemingly incongruous, came into Mr.

Leonard's mind—"This is the house of God; this is the gate of heaven."[3]

Felix lowered the violin and dropped wearily on a chair by the bed. The inspired light faded from his face; once more he was only a tired boy. But Stephen Leonard was on his knees, sobbing like a child; and Naomi Clark was lying still, with her hands clasped over her breast.

"I understand now," she said very softly. "I couldn't see it before—and now it's so plain. I just *feel* it. God *is* a God of love. He can forgive anybody—even me—even me. He knows all about it. I ain't skeered any more. He just loves me and forgives me as I'd have loved and forgiven my baby if she'd lived, no matter how bad she was, or what she did. The minister told me that but I couldn't believe it. I *know* it now. And He sent you here to-night, boy, to tell it to me in a way that I could feel it."

Naomi Clark died just as the dawn came up over the sea. Mr. Leonard rose from his watch at her bedside and went to the door. Before him spread the harbour, gray and austere in the faint light, but afar out the sun was rending asunder the milk-white mists in which the sea was scarfed, and under it was a virgin glow of sparkling water.

The fir trees on the point moved softly and whispered together. The whole world sang of spring and resurrection and life; and behind him Naomi Clark's dead face took on the peace that passes understanding.[4]

The old minister and his grandson walked home together in a silence that neither wished to break. Janet Andrews gave them a good scolding and an excellent breakfast. Then she ordered them both to bed; but Mr. Leonard, smiling at her, said:

"Presently, Janet, presently. But now take this key, go up to the black chest in the garret, and bring me what you will find there."

When Janet had gone he turned to Felix.

"Felix, would you like to study music as your life-work?"

Felix looked up, with a transfiguring flush on his wan face.

"Oh, grandfather! Oh, grandfather!"

"You may do so, my child. After this night I dare not hinder you. Go with my blessing, and may God guide and keep you, and make you strong to do His work and tell His message to humanity in your own appointed way. It is not the way I desired for you—but I see that I was mistaken. Old Abel spoke truly when he said there was a Christ in your violin as well as a devil. I understand what he meant now."

He turned to meet Janet, who came into the study with a violin. Felix's heart throbbed; he recognized it. Mr. Leonard took it from Janet and held it out to the boy.

"This is your father's violin, Felix. See to it that you never make your music the servant of the power of evil—never debase it to unworthy ends. For your responsibility is as your gift, and God will exact the accounting of it from you. Speak to the world in your own tongue through it, with truth and sincerity; and all I have hoped for you will be abundantly fulfilled."

1910, 1912

---

3. Genesis 28.17; the words are spoken by Jacob after he dreams of the ladder and the founding of Israel.

4. "The peace of God, which passeth all understanding" (Philippians 4.7).

BEVERLY CLEARY
b. 1916

When Fernwood School's librarian and reading teacher suggested to Beverly Bunn that she should write children's stories when she grew up, the seventh grader immediately embraced the idea. As a child struggling with reading, Beverly looked in vain in her library's children's section for books that would interest her, books about typical children. And after reading became a joy, she wondered why authors didn't write books about ordinary kids, books that were filled with action instead of description, books that were funny. Years later, when she herself was a children's librarian in Yakima, Washington, and readers asked for funny stories about "real" children, she found few books to recommend. She has filled that gap by providing young readers with realistic and humorous family stories for more than half a century.

When she was six, Beverly Cleary and her parents moved from a farm in Yamhill, Oregon, to the Portland neighborhood where most of her books would be set. Though she had decided to write, she followed her mother's advice that she hold a steady job as well, earning a B.A. in library science from the University of Washington, Seattle, in 1939 after receiving a degree in English from the University of California, Berkeley. She spent a year in Yakima before marrying Clarence Cleary, whom she had met at Berkeley, and moving to Oakland, California; ten years later, having worked as a librarian at the Oakland Army Hospital and then, after World War II, in the children's department of a bookstore, she finally picked up a pencil and wrote *Henry Huggins* (1950), a novel about an ordinary Oregon boy. Cleary's own twins, born in 1955, inspired her to write picture books, and her teen romance stories, such as *Fifteen* (1956), and charming fantasies about Ralph S. Mouse (beginning with *The Mouse and the Motorcycle*, 1965), have remained popular; but it is her realistic series books about family life that best showcase her talent for capturing childhood's subtle sensibilities with timeless sympathy and humor. A two-time Newbery Honor Book win-ner (for *Ramona and Her Father*, 1977, and *Ramona Quimby, Age Eight*, 1981), Clearly was awarded the Newbery Medal in 1984 for *Dear Mr. Henshaw* (1983), a novel structured around diary entries and letters from a lonely boy of divorced parents—"the mediumist boy in the class"—to his favorite author of children's books. Her many other honors include the Laura Ingalls Wilder Award from the American Library Association, given for lasting contributions to children's literature (1975). Cleary has written two memoirs intended for young readers, *A Girl from Yamhill* (1988) and *My Own Two Feet* (1995).

Irrepressible yet sensitive Ramona Quimby, Cleary's most famous heroine, is based, in part, on Cleary's child-self. She appeared as a minor character in Cleary's first novel about Henry Huggins, then came to dominate a series of her own. Like Cleary, Ramona plays on tin-can stilts and names her doll after a car. (Ramona's doll, in *Ramona the Pest* [1968], was Chevrolet; Cleary had named hers Fordson-Lafayette after a neighbor's tractor.) *Ramona and Her Father* (illustrated by Alan Tiegreen)—the fourth of eight Ramona books—focuses on the father-daughter relationship during the emotional and financial difficulties experienced by the Quimby family after Mr. Quimby loses his job. Cleary's own father had been forced to seek work in Portland by the low income of their farm and had later faced unemployment during the Depression. The comic episodes and gentle wisdom of *Ramona and Her Father* entertain young readers as well as reassure them that hardships can be endured and that even imperfect family relationships are more valuable than money.

By penning books about likable characters, such as the slightly anxious Henry Huggins, the prim Beezus Quimby, and the mischievous and creative Ramona, and by drawing their day-to-day concerns and crises with care, Cleary succeeds in writing the kind of books she wanted to read when she was a child—books that make reading fun.

Ramona and Her Father

1. PAYDAY

"Ye-e-ep!" sang Ramona Quimby one warm September afternoon, as she knelt on a chair at the kitchen table to make out her Christmas list. She had enjoyed a good day in second grade, and she looked forward to working on her list. For Ramona a Christmas list was a list of presents she hoped to receive, not presents she planned to give. "Ye-e-ep!" she sang again.

"Thank goodness today is payday," remarked Mrs. Quimby, as she opened the refrigerator to see what she could find for supper.

"Ye-e-ep!" sang Ramona, as she printed *mice or ginny pig* on her list with purple crayon. Next to Christmas and her birthday, her father's payday was her favorite day. His payday meant treats. Her mother's payday from her part-time job in a doctor's office meant they could make payments on the bedroom the Quimbys had added to their house when Ramona was in first grade.

"What's all this yeeping about?" asked Mrs. Quimby.

"I'm making a joyful noise until the Lord[1] like they say in Sunday school," Ramona explained. "Only they don't tell us what the joyful noise sounds like so I made up my own." *Hooray* and *wow*, joyful noises to Ramona, had not sounded right, so she had settled on *yeep* because it sounded happy but not rowdy. "Isn't that all right?" she asked, as she began to add *myna bird that talks* to her list.

"Yeep is fine if that's the way you feel about it," reassured Mrs. Quimby.

Ramona printed *coocoo clock* on her list while she wondered what the treat would be this payday. Maybe, since this was Friday, they could all go to a movie if her parents could find one suitable. Both Ramona and her big sister, Beezus, christened Beatrice, wondered what went on in all those other movies. They planned to find out the minute they were grown-up. That was one thing they agreed on. Or maybe their father would bring presents, a package of colored paper for Ramona, a paperback book for Beezus.

"I wish I could think of something interesting to do with leftover pot roast and creamed cauliflower," remarked Mrs. Quimby.

Leftovers—yuck!, thought Ramona. "Maybe Daddy will take us to the Whopper-burger for supper for payday," she said. A soft, juicy hamburger spiced with relish, French fries crisp on the outside and mealy inside, a little paper cup of cole slaw at the Whopperburger Restaurant were Ramona's favorite payday treat. Eating close together in a booth made Ramona feel snug and cozy. She and Beezus never quarreled at the Whopperburger.

"Good idea." Mrs. Quimby closed the refrigerator door. "I'll see what I can do."

Then Beezus came into the kitchen through the back door, dropped her books on the table, and flopped down on a chair with a gusty sigh.

"What was that all about?" asked Mrs. Quimby, not at all worried.

"Nobody is any fun anymore," complained Beezus. "Henry[2] spends all his time running around the track over at the high school getting ready for the Olympics in eight or twelve years, or he and Robert study a book of world records trying to find a record to break, and Mary Jane practices the piano all the time." Beezus sighed again. "And Mrs. Mester says we are going to do lots of creative writing, and I hate

---

1. "Make a joyful noise unto the Lord" (Psalms 100.1).

2. Henry Huggins, the hero of Cleary's first novel (*Henry Huggins*, 1950) and of several sequels.

creative writing. I don't see why I had to get Mrs. Mester for seventh grade anyway."

"Creative writing can't be as bad as all that," said Mrs. Quimby.

"You just don't understand," complained Beezus. "I can never think of stories, and my poems are stuff like, 'See the bird in the tree. He is singing to me.'"

"Tee-hee, tee-hee," added Ramona without thinking.

"Ramona," said Mrs. Quimby, "that was not necessary."

Because Beezus had been so grouchy lately, Ramona could manage to be only medium sorry.

"Pest!" said Beezus. Noticing Ramona's work, she added, "Making out a Christmas list in September is silly."

Ramona calmly selected an orange crayon. She was used to being called a pest. "If I am a pest, you are a rotten dinosaur egg," she informed her sister.

"Mother, make her stop," said Beezus.

When Beezus said this, Ramona knew she had won. The time had come to change the subject. "Today's payday," she told her sister. "Maybe we'll get to go to the Whopperburger for supper."

"Oh, Mother, will we?" Beezus's unhappy mood disappeared as she swooped up Picky-picky, the Quimbys' shabby old cat, who had strolled into the kitchen. He purred a rusty purr as she rubbed her cheek against his yellow fur.

"I'll see what I can do," said Mrs. Quimby.

Smiling, Beezus dropped Picky-picky, gathered up her books, and went off to her room. Beezus was the kind of girl who did her homework on Friday instead of waiting until the last minute on Sunday.

Ramona asked in a quiet voice, "Mother, why is Beezus so cross lately?" Letting her sister overhear such a question would lead to real trouble.

"You mustn't mind her," whispered Mrs. Quimby. "She's reached a difficult age."

Ramona thought such an all-purpose excuse for bad behavior would be a handy thing to have. "So have I," she confided to her mother.

Mrs. Quimby dropped a kiss on the top of Ramona's head. "Silly girl," she said. "It's just a phase Beezus is going through. She'll outgrow it."

A contented silence fell over the house as three members of the family looked forward to supper at the Whopperburger, where they would eat, close and cozy in a booth, their food brought to them by a friendly waitress who always said, "There you go," as she set down their hamburgers and French fries.

Ramona had decided to order a cheeseburger when she heard the sound of her father's key in the front door. "Daddy, Daddy!" she shrieked, scrambling down from the chair and running to meet her father as he opened the door. "Guess what?"

Beezus, who had come from her room, answered before her father had a chance to guess. "Mother said maybe we could go to the Whopperburger for dinner!"

Mr. Quimby smiled and kissed his daughters before he held out a small white paper bag. "Here, I brought you a little present." Somehow he did not look as happy as usual. Maybe he had had a hard day at the office of the van-and-storage company where he worked.

His daughters pounced and opened the bag together. "Gummybears!" was their joyful cry. The chewy little bears were the most popular sweet at Glenwood School this fall. Last spring powdered Jell-o eaten from the package had been the fad. Mr. Quimby always remembered these things.

"Run along and divide them between you," said Mr. Quimby. "I want to talk to your mother."

"Don't spoil your dinner," said Mrs. Quimby.

The girls bore the bag off to Beezus's room, where they dumped the gummybears onto the bedspread. First they divided the cinnamon-flavored red bears, one for Beezus, one for Ramona. Then they divided the orange bears and the green, and as they were about to divide the yellow bears, both girls were suddenly aware that their mother and father were no longer talking. Silence filled the house. The sisters looked at one another. There was something unnatural about this silence. Uneasy, they waited for some sound, and then their parents began to speak in whispers. Beezus tiptoed to the door to listen.

Ramona bit the head off a red gummybear. She always ate toes last. "Maybe they're planning a big surprise," she suggested, refusing to worry.

"I don't think so," whispered Beezus, "but I can't hear what they are saying."

"Try listening through the furnace pipes," whispered Ramona.

"That won't work here. The living room is too far away." Beezus strained to catch her parents' words. "I think something's wrong."

Ramona divided her gummybears, one heap to eat at home, the other to take to school to share with friends if they were nice to her.

"Something is wrong. Something awful," whispered Beezus. "I can tell by the way they are talking."

Beezus looked so frightened that Ramona became frightened, too. What could be wrong? She tried to think what she might have done to make her parents whisper this way, but she had stayed out of trouble lately. She could not think of a single thing that could be wrong. This frightened her even more. She no longer felt like eating chewy little bears. She wanted to know why her mother and father were whispering in a way that alarmed Beezus.

Finally the girls heard their father say in a normal voice, "I think I'll take a shower before supper." This remark was reassuring to Ramona.

"What'll we do now?" whispered Beezus. "I'm scared to go out."

Worry and curiosity, however, urged Beezus and Ramona into the hall.

Trying to pretend they were not concerned about their family, the girls walked into the kitchen where Mrs. Quimby was removing leftovers from the refrigerator. "I think we'll eat at home after all," she said, looking sad and anxious.

Without being asked, Ramona began to deal four place mats around the dining-room table, laying them all right side up. When she was cross with Beezus, she laid her sister's place mat face down.

Mrs. Quimby looked at the cold creamed cauliflower with distaste, returned it to the refrigerator, and reached for a can of green beans before she noticed her silent and worried daughters watching her for clues as to what might be wrong.

Mrs. Quimby turned and faced Beezus and Ramona. "Girls, you might as well know. Your father has lost his job."

"But he liked his job," said Ramona, regretting the loss of that hamburger and those French fries eaten in the coziness of a booth. She had known her father to change jobs because he had not liked his work, but she had never heard of him losing a job.

"Was he fired?" asked Beezus, shocked at the news.

Mrs. Quimby opened the green beans and dumped them into a saucepan before she explained. "Losing his job was not your father's fault. He worked for a little company. A big company bought the little company and let out most of the people who worked for the little company."

"But we won't have enough money." Beezus understood these things better than Ramona.

"Mother works," Ramona reminded her sister.

"Only part time," said Mrs. Quimby. "And we have to make payments to the bank for the new room. That's why I went to work."

"What will we do?" asked Ramona, alarmed at last. Would they go hungry? Would the men from the bank come and tear down the new room if they couldn't pay for it? She had never thought what it might be like not to have enough money—not that the Quimbys ever had money to spare. Although Ramona had often heard her mother say that house payments, car payments, taxes, and groceries seemed to eat up money, Mrs. Quimby somehow managed to make their money pay for all they really needed with a little treat now and then besides.

"We will have to manage as best we can until your father finds work," said Mrs. Quimby. "It may not be easy."

"Maybe I could baby-sit," volunteered Beezus.

As she laid out knives and forks, Ramona wondered how she could earn money, too. She could have a lemonade stand in front of the house, except nobody ever bought lemonade but her father and her friend Howie. She thought about pounding rose petals and soaking them in water to make perfume to sell. Unfortunately, the perfume she tried to make always smelled like rotten rose petals, and anyway the roses were almost gone.

"And girls," said Mrs. Quimby, lowering her voice as if she was about to share a secret, "you mustn't do anything to annoy your father. He is worried enough right now."

But he remembered to bring gummybears, thought Ramona, who never wanted to annoy her father or her mother either, just Beezus, although sometimes, without even trying, she succeeded in annoying her whole family. Ramona felt sad and somehow lonely, as if she were left out of something important, because her family was in trouble and there was nothing she could do to help. When she had finished setting the table, she returned to the list she had begun, it now seemed, a long time ago. "But what about Christmas?" she asked her mother.

"Right now Christmas is the least of our worries." Mrs. Quimby looked sadder than Ramona had ever seen her look. "Taxes are due in November. And we have to buy groceries and make car payments and a lot of other things."

"Don't we have any money in the bank?" asked Beezus.

"Not much," admitted Mrs. Quimby, "but your father was given two weeks' pay."

Ramona looked at the list she had begun so happily and wondered how much the presents she had listed would cost. Too much, she knew. Mice were free if you knew the right person, the owner of a mother mouse, so she might get some mice.

Slowly Ramona crossed out *ginny pig* and the other presents she had listed. As she made black lines through each item, she thought about her family. She did not want her father to be worried, her mother sad, or her sister cross. She wanted her whole family, including Picky-picky, to be happy.

Ramona studied her crayons, chose a pinky-red one because it seemed the happiest color, and printed one more item on her Christmas list to make up for all she had crossed out. *One happy family*. Beside the words she drew four smiling faces and beside them, the face of a yellow cat, also smiling.

2. RAMONA AND THE MILLION DOLLARS

Ramona wished she had a million dollars so her father would be fun again. There had been many changes in the Quimby household since Mr. Quimby had lost his job, but the biggest change was in Mr. Quimby himself.

First of all, Mrs. Quimby found a full-time job working for another doctor, which was good news. However, even a second-grader could understand that one paycheck would not stretch as far as two paychecks, especially when there was so much talk of taxes, whatever they were. Mrs. Quimby's new job meant that Mr. Quimby had to be home when Ramona returned from school.

Ramona and her father saw a lot of one another. At first she thought having her father to herself for an hour or two every day would be fun, but when she came home, she found him running the vacuum cleaner, filling out job applications, or sitting on the couch, smoking and staring into space. He could not take her to the park because he had to stay near the telephone. Someone might call to offer him a job. Ramona grew uneasy. Maybe he was too worried to love her anymore.

One day Ramona came home to find her father in the living room drinking warmed-over coffee, smoking, and staring at the television set. On the screen a boy a couple of years younger than Ramona was singing:

> Forget your pots, forget your pans.
> It's not too late to change your plans.
> Spend a little, eat a lot,
> Big fat burgers, nice and hot
> At your nearest Whopperburger!

Ramona watched him open his mouth wide to bite into a fat cheeseburger with lettuce and tomato spilling out of the bun and thought wistfully of the good old days when the family used to go to the restaurant on payday and when her mother used to bring home little treats—stuffed olives, cinnamon buns for Sunday breakfast, a bag of potato chips.

"That kid must be earning a million dollars." Mr. Quimby snuffed out his cigarette in a loaded ashtray. "He's singing that commercial every time I turn on television."

A boy Ramona's age earning a million dollars? Ramona was all interest. "How's he earning a million dollars?" she asked. She had often thought of all the things they could do if they had a million dollars, beginning with turning up the thermostat so they wouldn't have to wear sweaters in the house to save fuel oil.

Mr. Quimby explained. "They make a movie of him singing the commercial, and every time the movie is shown on television he gets paid. It all adds up."

Well! This was a new idea to Ramona. She thought it over as she got out her crayons and paper and knelt on a chair at the kitchen table. Singing a song about hamburgers would not be hard to do. She could do it herself. Maybe she could earn a million dollars like that boy so her father would be fun again, and everyone at school would watch her on television and say, "There's Ramona Quimby. She goes to our school." A million dollars would buy a cuckoo clock for every room in the house, her father wouldn't need a job, the family could go to Disneyland.[3] . . .

"Forget your pots, forget your pans," Ramona began to sing, as she drew a picture of a hamburger and stabbed yellow dots across the top of the bun for sesame seeds. With a million dollars the Quimbys could eat in a restaurant every day if they wanted to.

After that Ramona began to watch for children on television commercials. She saw a boy eating bread and margarine when a crown suddenly appeared on his head with a fanfare—ta *da*!—of music. She saw a girl who asked, "Mommy, wouldn't it be nice if caramel apples grew on trees?" and another girl who took a bite of cereal said, "It's good, hm-um," and giggled. There was a boy who asked at the end of a weiner commercial, "Dad, how do you tell a boy hot dog from a girl hot dog?" and a girl who tipped her head to one side and said, "Pop-pop-pop," as she listened to her cereal. Children crunched potato chips, chomped on pickles, gnawed at fried chicken. Ramona grew particularly fond of the curly-haired little girl saying to her mother at the zoo, "Look, Mommy, the elephant's legs are wrinkled just like your pantyhose." Ramona could say all those things.

Ramona began to practice. Maybe someone would see her and offer her a million dollars to make a television commercial. On her way to school, if her friend Howie did not walk with her, she tipped her head to one side and said, "Pop-pop-pop." She said to herself, "M-m-m, it's good," and giggled. Giggling wasn't easy when she didn't have anything to giggle about, but she worked at it. Once she practiced on her mother by asking, "Mommy, wouldn't it be nice if caramel apples grew on trees?" She had taken to calling her mother Mommy lately, because children on commercials always called their mothers Mommy.

Mrs. Quimby's absentminded answer was, "Not really. Caramel is bad for your teeth." She was wearing slacks so Ramona could not say the line about pantyhose.

Since the Quimbys no longer bought potato chips or pickles, Ramona found other foods—toast and apples and carrot sticks—to practice good loud crunching on. When they had chicken for dinner, she smacked and licked her fingers.

"Ramona," said Mr. Quimby, "your table manners grow worse and worse. Don't eat so noisily. My grandmother used to say, 'A smack at the table is worth a smack on the bottom.'"

Ramona, who did not think she would have liked her father's grandmother, was embarrassed. She had been practicing to be on television, and she had forgotten her family could hear.

Ramona continued to practice until she began to feel as if a television camera was

3. Theme park in Anaheim, California; it opened in 1955.

watching her wherever she went. She smiled a lot and skipped, feeling that she was cute and lovable. She felt as if she had fluffy blond curls, even though in real life her hair was brown and straight.

One morning, smiling prettily, she thought, and swinging her lunch box, Ramona skipped to school. Today someone might notice her because she was wearing her red tights. She was happy because this was a special day, the day of Ramona's parent-teacher conference. Since Mrs. Quimby was at work, Mr. Quimby was going to meet with Mrs. Rogers, her second-grade teacher. Ramona was proud to have a father who would come to school.

Feeling dainty, curly-haired, and adorable, Ramona skipped into her classroom, and what did she see but Mrs. Rogers with wrinkles around her ankles. Ramona did not hesitate. She skipped right over to her teacher and, since there did not happen to be an elephant in Room 2, turned the words around and said, "Mrs. Rogers, your pantyhose are wrinkled like an elephant's legs."

Mrs. Rogers looked surprised, and the boys and girls who had already taken their seats giggled. All the teacher said was, "Thank you, Ramona, for telling me. And remember, we do not skip inside the school building."

Ramona had an uneasy feeling she had displeased her teacher.

She was sure of it when Howie said, "Ramona, you sure weren't very polite to Mrs. Rogers." Howie, a serious thinker, was usually right.

Suddenly Ramona was no longer an adorable little fluffy-haired girl on television. She was plain old Ramona, a second-grader whose own red tights bagged at the knee and wrinkled at the ankle. This wasn't the way things turned out on television. On television grownups always smiled at everything children said.

During recess Ramona went to the girls' bathroom and rolled her tights up at the waist to stretch them up at the knee and ankle. Mrs. Rogers must have done the same thing to her pantyhose, because after recess her ankles were smooth. Ramona felt better.

That afternoon, when the lower grades had been dismissed from their classrooms, Ramona found her father, along with Davy's mother, waiting outside the door of Room 2 for their conferences with Mrs. Rogers. Davy's mother's appointment was first, so Mr. Quimby sat down on a chair outside the door with a folder of Ramona's schoolwork to look over. Davy stood close to the door, hoping to hear what his teacher was saying about him. Everybody in Room 2 was anxious to learn what the teacher said.

Mr. Quimby opened Ramona's folder. "Run along and play on the playground until I'm through," he told his daughter.

"Promise you'll tell me what Mrs. Rogers says about me," said Ramona.

Mr. Quimby understood. He smiled and gave his promise.

Outside, the playground was chilly and damp. The only children who lingered were those whose parents had conferences, and they were more interested in what was going on inside the building than outside. Bored, Ramona looked around for something to do, and because she could find nothing better, she followed a traffic boy across the street. On the opposite side, near the market that had been built when she was in kindergarten, she decided she had time to explore. In a weedy space at the side of the market building, she discovered several burdock plants that bore a prickly crop of brown burs, each covered with sharp, little hooks.

Ramona saw at once that burs had all sorts of interesting possibilities. She picked two and stuck them together. She added another and another. They were better than

Tinker-toys.[4] She would have to tell Howie about them. When she had a string of burs, each clinging to the next, she bent it into a circle and stuck the ends together. A crown! She could make a crown. She picked more burs and built up the circle by making peaks all the way around like the crown the boy wore in the magarine commercial. There was only one thing to do with a crown like that. Ramona crowned herself—ta-*da!*—like the boy on television.

Prickly though it was, Ramona enjoyed wearing the crown. She practiced looking surprised, like the boy who ate the margarine, and pretended she was rich and famous and about to meet her father, who would be driving a big shiny car bought with the million dollars she had earned.

The traffic boys had gone off duty. Ramona remembered to look both ways before she crossed the street, and as she crossed she pretended people were saying, "There goes that rich girl. She earned a million dollars eating margarine on TV."

Mr. Quimby was standing on the playground, looking for Ramona. Forgetting all she had been pretending, Ramona ran to him. "What did Mrs. Rogers say about me?" she demanded.

"That's some crown you've got there," Mr. Quimby remarked.

"Daddy, what did she *say?*" Ramona could not contain her impatience.

Mr. Quimby grinned. "She said you were impatient."

Oh, that. People were always telling Ramona not to be so impatient. "What else?" asked Ramona, as she and her father walked toward home.

"You are a good reader, but you are careless about spelling."

Ramona knew this. Unlike Beezus, who was an excellent speller, Ramona could not believe spelling was important as long as people could understand what she meant. "What else?"

"She said you draw unusually well for a second-grader and your printing is the best in the class."

"What else?"

Mr. Quimby raised one eyebrow as he looked down at Ramona. "She said you were inclined to show off and you sometimes forget your manners."

Ramona was indignant at this criticism. "I do not! She's just making that up." Then she remembered what she had said about her teacher's pantyhose and felt subdued. She hoped her teacher had not repeated her remark to her father.

"I remember my manners most of the time," said Ramona, wondering what her teacher had meant by showing off. Being first to raise her hand when she knew the answer?

"Of course you do," agreed Mr. Quimby. "After all, you are my daughter. Now tell me, how are you going to get that crown off?"

Using both hands, Ramona tried to lift her crown but only succeeded in pulling her hair. The tiny hooks clung fast. Ramona tugged. Ow! That hurt. She looked helplessly up at her father.

Mr. Quimby appeared amused. "Who do you think you are? A Rose Festival[5] Queen?"

Ramona pretended to ignore her father's question. How silly to act like someone on television when she was a plain old second-grader whose tights bagged at the

---

4. A construction toy, made of wood; sets originally consisted of round wooden wheels with holes on all sides into which wooden sticks could fit. They were introduced at a toy fair in 1913.

5. The Portland Rose Festival has been held annually since 1907.

knees again. She hoped her father would not guess. He might. He was good at guessing.

By then Ramona and her father were home. As Mr. Quimby unlocked the front door, he said, "We'll have to see what we can do about getting you uncrowned before your mother gets home. Any ideas?"

Ramona had no answer, although she was eager to part with the crown before her father guessed what she had been doing. In the kitchen, Mr. Quimby picked off the top of the crown, the part that did not touch Ramona's hair. That was easy. Now came the hard part.

"Yow!" said Ramona, when her father tried to lift the crown.

"That won't work," said her father. "Let's try one bur at a time." He went to work on one bur, carefully trying to untangle it from Ramona's hair, one strand at a time. To Ramona, who did not like to stand still, this process took forever. Each bur was snarled in a hundred hairs, and each hair had to be pulled before the bur was loosened. After a very long time, Mr. Quimby handed a hair-entangled bur to Ramona.

"Yow! Yipe! Leave me some hair," said Ramona, picturing a bald circle around her head.

"I'm trying," said Mr. Quimby and began on the next bur.

Ramona sighed. Standing still doing nothing was tiresome.

After what seemed like a long time, Beezus came home from school. She took one look at Ramona and began to laugh.

"I don't suppose you ever did anything dumb," said Ramona, short of patience and anxious lest her sister guess why she was wearing the remains of a crown. "What about the time you—"

"No arguments," said Mr. Quimby. "We have a problem to solve, and it might be a good idea if we solved it before your mother comes home from work."

Much to Ramona's annoyance, her sister sat down to watch. "How about soaking?" suggested Beezus. "It might soften all those millions of little hooks."

"Yow! Yipe!" said Ramona. "You're pulling too hard."

Mr. Quimby laid another hair-filled bur on the table. "Maybe we should try. This isn't working."

"It's about time she washed her hair anyway," said Beezus, a remark Ramona felt was entirely unnecessary. Nobody could shampoo hair full of burs.

Ramona knelt on a chair with her head in a sinkful of warm water for what seemed like hours until her knees ached and she had a crick in her neck. "Now, Daddy?" she asked at least once a minute.

"Not yet," Mr. Quimby answered, feeling a bur. "Nope," he said at last. "This isn't going to work."

Ramona lifted her dripping head from the sink. When her father tried to dry her hair, the bur hooks clung to the towel. He jerked the towel loose and draped it around Ramona's shoulders.

"Well, live and learn," said Mr. Quimby. "Beezus, scrub some potatoes and throw them in the oven. We can't have your mother come home and find we haven't started supper."

When Mrs. Quimby arrived, she took one look at her husband trying to untangle Ramona's wet hair from the burs, groaned, sank limply onto a kitchen chair, and began to laugh.

By now Ramona was tired, cross, and hungry. "I don't see anything funny," she said sullenly.

Mrs. Quimby managed to stop laughing. "What on earth got into you?" she asked.

Ramona considered. Was this a question grown-ups asked just to be asking a question, or did her mother expect an answer? "Nothing," was a safe reply. She would never tell her family how she happened to be wearing a crown of burs. Never, not even if they threw her into a dungeon.

"Beezus, bring me the scissors," said Mrs. Quimby.

Ramona clapped her hands over the burs. "No!" she shrieked and stamped her foot. "I won't let you cut off my hair! I won't! I won't! I won't!"

Beezus handed her mother the scissors and gave her sister some advice. "Stop yelling. If you go to bed with burs in your hair, you'll really get messed up."

Ramona had to face the wisdom of Beezus's words. She stopped yelling to consider the problem once more. "All right," she said, as if she were granting a favor, "but I want Daddy to do it." Her father would work with care while her mother, always in a hurry since she was working full time, would go *snip-snip-snip* and be done with it. Besides, supper would be prepared faster and would taste better if her mother did the cooking.

"I am honored," said Mr. Quimby. "Deeply honored."

Mrs. Quimby did not seem sorry to hand over the scissors. "Why don't you go someplace else to work while Beezus and I get supper on the table?"

Mr. Quimby led Ramona into the living room, where he turned on the television set. "This may take time," he explained, as he went to work. "We might as well watch the news."

Ramona was still anxious. "Don't cut any more than you have to, Daddy," she begged, praying the margarine boy would not appear on the screen. "I don't want everyone at school to make fun of me." The newscaster was talking about strikes and a lot of things Ramona did not understand.

"The merest smidgin," promised her father. *Snip. Snip. Snip.* He laid a hair-ensnarled bur in an ashtray. *Snip. Snip. Snip.* He laid another bur beside the first.

"Does it look awful?" asked Ramona.

"As my grandmother would say, 'It will never be noticed from a trotting horse.'"

Ramona let out a long, shuddery sigh, the closest thing to crying without really crying. *Snip. Snip. Snip.* Ramona touched the side of her head. She still had hair there. More hair than she expected. She felt a little better.

The newscaster disappeared from the television screen, and there was that boy again singing:

> Forget your pots, forget your pans.
> It's not too late to change your plans.

Ramona thought longingly of the days before her father lost his job, when they could forget their pots and pans and change their plans. She watched the boy open his mouth wide and sink his teeth into that fat hamburger with lettuce, tomato, and cheese hanging out of the bun. She swallowed and said, "I bet that boy has a lot of fun with his million dollars." She felt so sad. The Quimbys really needed a million dollars. Even one dollar would help.

Snip. Snip. Snip. "Oh, I don't know," said Mr. Quimby. "Money is handy, but it isn't everything."

"I wish I could earn a million dollars like that boy," said Ramona. This was the closest she would ever come to telling how she happened to set a crown of burs on her head.

"You know something?" said Mr. Quimby. "I don't care how much that kid or any other kid earns. I wouldn't trade you for a million dollars."

"Really, Daddy?" That remark about any other kid—Ramona wondered if her father had guessed her reason for the crown, but she would never ask. Never. "Really? Do you mean it?"

"Really." Mr. Quimby continued his careful snipping. "I'll bet that boy's father wishes he had a little girl who finger-painted and wiped her hands on the cat when she was little and who once cut her own hair so she would be bald like her uncle and who then grew up to be seven years old and crowned herself with burs. Not every father is lucky enough to have a daughter like that."

Ramona giggled. "Daddy, you're being silly!" She was happier than she had been in a long time.

3. The Night of the Jack-O'-Lantern

"Please pass the tommy-toes," said Ramona, hoping to make somone in the family smile. She felt good when her father smiled as he passed her the bowl of stewed tomatoes. He smiled less and less as the days went by and he had not found work. Too often he was just plain cross. Ramona had learned not to rush home from school and ask, "Did you find a job today, Daddy?" Mrs. Quimby always seemed to look anxious these days, either over the cost of groceries or money the family owed. Beezus had turned into a regular old grouch, because she dreaded Creative Writing and perhaps because she had reached that difficult age Mrs. Quimby was always talking about, although Ramona found this hard to believe.

Even Picky-picky was not himself. He lashed his tail and stalked angrily away from his dish when Beezus served him Puss-puddy, the cheapest brand of cat food Mrs. Quimby could find in the market.

All this worried Ramona. She wanted her father to smile and joke, her mother to look happy, her sister to be cheerful, and Picky-picky to eat his food, wash his whiskers, and purr the way he used to.

"And so," Mr. Quimby was saying, "at the end of the interview for the job, the man said he would let me know if anything turned up."

Mrs. Quimby sighed. "Let's hope you hear from him. Oh, by the way, the car has been making a funny noise. A sort of *tappety-tappety* sound."

"It's Murphy's Law," said Mr. Quimby. "Anything that can go wrong will."

Ramona knew her father was not joking this time. Last week, when the washing machine refused to work, the Quimbys had been horrified by the size of the repair bill.

"I like tommy-toes," said Ramona, hoping her little joke would work a second time. This was not exactly true, but she was willing to sacrifice truth for a smile.

Since no one paid any attention, Ramona spoke louder as she lifted the bowl of stewed tomatoes. "Does anybody want any tommy-toes?" she asked. The bowl tipped. Mrs. Quimby silently reached over and wiped spilled juice from the table with her napkin. Crestfallen, Ramona set the bowl down. No one had smiled.

"Ramona," said Mr. Quimby, "my grandmother used to have a saying. 'First time is funny, second time is silly, third time is a spanking.'"

Ramona looked down at her place mat. Nothing seemed to go right lately. Picky-picky must have felt the same way. He sat down beside Beezus and meowed his crossest meow.

Mr. Quimby lit a cigarette and asked his older daughter, "Haven't you fed that cat yet?"

Beezus rose to clear the table. "It wouldn't do any good. He hasn't eaten his breakfast. He won't eat that cheap Puss-puddy."

"Too bad about him." Mr. Quimby blew a cloud of smoke toward the ceiling.

"He goes next door and mews as if we never give him anything to eat," said Beezus. "It's embarrassing."

"He'll just have to learn to eat what we can afford," said Mr. Quimby. "Or we will get rid of him."

This statement shocked Ramona. Picky-picky had been a member of the family since before she was born.

"Well, I don't blame him," said Beezus, picking up the cat and pressing her cheek against his fur. "Puss-puddy stinks."

Mr. Quimby ground out his cigarette.

"Guess what?" said Mrs. Quimby, as if to change the subject. "Howie's grandmother drove out to visit her sister, who lives on a farm, and her sister sent in a lot of pumpkins for jack-o'-lanterns for the neighborhood children. Mrs. Kemp gave us a big one, and it's down in the basement now, waiting to be carved."

"Me! Me!" cried Ramona. "Let me get it!"

"Let's give it a real scary face," said Beezus, no longer difficult.

"I'll have to sharpen my knife," said Mr. Quimby.

"Run along and bring it up, Ramona," said Mrs. Quimby with a real smile.

Relief flooded through Ramona. Her family had returned to normal. She snapped on the basement light, thumped down the stairs, and there in the shadow of the furnace pipes, which reached out like ghostly arms, was a big, round pumpkin. Ramona grasped its scratchy stem, found the pumpkin too big to lift that way, bent over, hugged it in both arms, and raised it from the cement floor. The pumpkin was heavier than she had expected, and she must not let it drop and smash all over the concrete floor.

"Need some help, Ramona?" Mrs. Quimby called down the stairs.

"I can do it." Ramona felt for each step with her feet and emerged, victorious, into the kitchen.

"Wow! That *is* a big one." Mr. Quimby was sharpening his jackknife on a whetstone while Beezus and her mother hurried through the dishes.

"A pumpkin that size would cost a lot at the market," Mrs. Quimby remarked. "A couple of dollars, at least."

"Let's give it eyebrows like last year," said Ramona.

"And ears," said Beezus.

"And lots of teeth," added Ramona. There would be no jack-o'-lantern with one tooth and three triangles for eyes and nose in the Quimbys' front window on Halloween. Mr. Quimby was the best pumpkin carver on Klickitat Street. Everybody knew that.

"Hmm. Let's see now." Mr. Quimby studied the pumpkin, turning it to find the best side for the face. "I think the nose should go about here. With a pencil he sketched a nose-shaped nose, not a triangle, while his daughters leaned on their elbows to watch.

"Shall we have it smile or frown?" he asked.

"Smile!" said Ramona, who had had enough of frowning.

"Frown!" said Beezus.

The mouth turned up on one side and down on the other. Eyes were sketched and eyebrows. "Very expressive," said Mr. Quimby. "Something between a leer and a sneer." He cut a circle around the top of the pumpkin and lifted it off for a lid.

Without being asked, Ramona found a big spoon for scooping out the seeds.

Picky-picky came into the kitchen to see if something beside Puss-puddy had been placed in his dish. When he found that it had not, he paused, sniffed the unfamiliar pumpkin smell, and with his tail twitching angrily stalked out of the kitchen. Ramona was glad Beezus did not notice.

"If we don't let the candle burn the jack-o'-lantern, we can have pumpkin pie," said Mrs. Quimby. "I can even freeze some of the pumpkin for Thanksgiving."

Mr. Quimby began to whistle as he carved with skill and care, first a mouthful of teeth, each one neat and square, then eyes and jagged, ferocious eyebrows. He was working on two ears shaped like question marks, when Mrs. Quimby said, "Bedtime, Ramona."

"I am going to stay up until Daddy finishes," Ramona informed her family. "No ifs, ands, or buts."

"Run along and take your bath," said Mrs. Quimby, "and you can watch awhile longer."

Because her family was happy once more, Ramona did not protest. She returned quickly, however, still damp under her pajamas, to see what her father had thought of next. Hair, that's what he had thought of, something he could carve because the pumpkin was so big. He cut a few C-shaped curls around the hole in the top of the pumpkin before he reached inside and hollowed out a candle holder in the bottom.

"There," he said and rinsed his jackknife under the kitchen faucet. "A work of art."

Mrs. Quimby found a candle stub, inserted it in the pumpkin, lit it, and set the lid in place. Ramona switched off the light. The jack-o'-lantern leered and sneered with a flickering flame.

"Oh, Daddy!" Ramona threw her arms around her father. "It's the wickedest jack-o'-lantern in the whole world."

Mr. Quimby kissed the top of Ramona's head. "Thank you. I take that as a compliment. Now run along to bed."

Ramona could tell by the sound of her father's voice that he was smiling. She ran off to her room without thinking up excuses for staying up just five more minutes, added a postscript to her prayers thanking God for the big pumpkin, and another asking him to find her father a job, and fell asleep at once, not bothering to tuck her panda bear in beside her for comfort.

In the middle of the night Ramona found herself suddenly awake without knowing why she was awake. Had she heard a noise? Yes, she had. Tense, she listened hard. There it was again, a sort of thumping, scuffling noise, not very loud but there just the same. Silence. Then she heard it again. Inside the house. In the kitchen. Something was in the kitchen, and it was moving.

Ramona's mouth was so dry she could barely whisper, "Daddy!" No answer. More thumping. Someone bumped against the wall. Someone, something was coming to get them. Ramona thought about the leering, sneering face on the kitchen table. All the ghost stories she had ever heard, all the ghostly pictures she had ever seen flew through her mind. Could the jack-o'-lantern have come to life? Of course not. It was only a pumpkin, but still— A bodyless, leering head was too horrifying to think about.

Ramona sat up in bed and shrieked, "Daddy!"

A light came on in her parents' room, feet thumped to the floor, Ramona's tousled father in rumpled pajamas was silhouetted in Ramona's doorway, followed by her mother tugging a robe on over her short nightgown.

"What is it, Baby?" asked Mr. Quimby. Both Ramona's parents called her Baby when they were worried about her, and tonight Ramona was so relieved to see them she did not mind.

"Was it a bad dream?" asked Mrs. Quimby.

"Th-there's something in the kitchen." Ramona's voice quavered.

Beezus, only half-awake, joined the family. "What's happening?" she asked. "What's going on?"

"There's something in the kitchen," said Ramona, feeling braver. "Something moving."

"Sh-h!" commanded Mr. Quimby.

Tense, the family listened to silence.

"You just had a bad dream." Mrs. Quimby came into the room, kissed Ramona, and started to tuck her in.

Ramona pushed the blanket away. "It was *not* a bad dream," she insisted. "I did too hear something. Something spooky."

"All we have to do is look," said Mr. Quimby, reasonably—and bravely, Ramona thought. Nobody would get her into that kitchen.

Ramona waited, scarcely breathing, fearing for her father's safety as he walked down the hall and flipped on the kitchen light. No shout, no yell came from that part of the house. Instead her father laughed, and Ramona felt brave enough to follow the rest of the family to see what was funny.

There was a strong smell of cat food in the kitchen. What Ramona saw, and what Beezus saw, did not strike them as one bit funny. Their jack-o'-lantern, the jack-o'-lantern their father had worked so hard to carve, no longer had a whole face. Part of its forehead, one ferocious eyebrow, one eye, and part of its nose were gone, replaced by a jagged hole edged by little teeth marks. Picky-picky was crouched in guilt under the kitchen table.

The nerve of that cat. "Bad cat! Bad cat!" shrieked Ramona, stamping her bare foot on the cold linoleum. The old yellow cat fled to the dining room, where he crouched under the table, his eyes glittering out of the darkness.

Mrs. Quimby laughed a small rueful laugh. "I knew he liked canteloupe, but I had no idea he liked pumpkin, too." With a butcher's knife she began to cut up the remains of the jack-o'-lantern, carefully removing, Ramona noticed, the parts with teeth marks.

"I *told* you he wouldn't eat that awful Puss-puddy." Beezus was accusing her father of denying their cat. "Of course he had to eat our jack-o'-lantern. He's starving."

"Beezus, dear," said Mrs. Quimby. "We simply cannot afford the brand of food Picky-picky used to eat. Now be reasonable."

Beezus was in no mood to be reasonable. "Then how come Daddy can afford to smoke?" she demanded to know.

Ramona was astonished to hear her sister speak this way to her mother.

Mr. Quimby looked angry. "Young lady," he said, and when he called Beezus young lady, Ramona knew her sister had better watch out. "Young lady, I've heard enough about that old tom cat and his food. My cigarettes are none of your business."

Ramona expected Beezus to say she was sorry or maybe burst into tears and run to her room. Instead she pulled Picky-picky out from under the table and held him to her chest as if she were shielding him from danger. "They are too my business," she informed her father. "Cigarettes can kill you. Your lungs will turn black and you'll *die!* We made posters about it at school. And besides, cigarettes pollute the air!"

Ramona was horrified by her sister's daring, and at the same time she was a tiny bit pleased. Beezus was usually well-behaved while Ramona was the one who had tantrums. Then she was struck by the meaning of her sister's angry words and was frightened.

"That's enough out of you," Mr. Quimby told Beezus, "and let me remind you that if you had shut that cat in the basement as you were supposed to, this would never have happened."

Mrs. Quimby quietly stowed the remains of the jack-o'-lantern in a plastic bag in the refrigerator.

Beezus opened the basement door and gently set Picky-picky on the top step. "Nighty-night," she said tenderly.

"Young lady," began Mr. Quimby. Young lady again! Now Beezus was really going to catch it. "You are getting altogether too big for your britches lately. Just be careful how you talk around this house."

Still Beezus did not say she was sorry. She did not burst into tears. She simply stalked off to her room.

Ramona was the one who burst into tears. She didn't mind when she and Beezus quarreled. She even enjoyed a good fight now and then to clear the air, but she could not bear it when anyone else in the family quarreled, and those awful things Beezus said—were they true?

"Don't cry, Ramona." Mrs. Quimby put her arm around her younger daughter. "We'll get another pumpkin."

"B-but it won't be as big," sobbed Ramona, who wasn't crying about the pumpkin at all. She was crying about important things like her father being cross so much now that he wasn't working and his lungs turning black and Beezus being so disagreeable when before she had always been so polite (to grown-ups) and anxious to do the right thing.

"Come on, let's all go to bed and things will look brighter in the morning," said Mrs. Quimby.

"In a few minutes." Mr. Quimby picked up a package of cigarettes he had left on the kitchen table, shook one out, lit it, and sat down, still looking angry.

Were his lungs turning black this very minute? Ramona wondered. How would anybody know, when his lungs were inside him? She let her mother guide her to her room and tuck her in bed.

"Now don't worry about your jack-o'-lantern. We'll get another pumpkin. It won't be as big, but you'll have your jack-o'-lantern." Mrs. Quimby kissed Ramona goodnight.

"Nighty-night," said Ramona in a muffled voice. As soon as her mother left, she hopped out of bed and pulled her old panda bear out from under the bed and tucked it under the covers beside her for comfort. The bear must have been dusty because Ramona sneezed.

"*Gesundheit!*" said Mr. Quimby, passing by her door. "We'll carve another jack-o'-lantern tomorrow. Don't worry." He was not angry with Ramona.

Ramona snuggled down with her dusty bear. Didn't grown-ups think children worried about anything but jack-o'-lanterns? Didn't they know children worried about grown-ups?

4 · RAMONA TO THE RESCUE

The Quimbys said very little at breakfast the next morning. Beezus was moody and silent. Mrs. Quimby, in her white uniform, was in a hurry to leave for work. Picky-picky resentfully ate a few bites of Puss-puddy. Mr. Quimby did not say, "I told you he would eat it when he was really hungry," but the whole family was thinking it. He might as well have said it.

Ramona wished her family would cheer up. When they had finished eating, she found herself alone with her father.

"Bring me an ashtray, please," said Mr. Quimby. "That's a good girl."

Reluctantly Ramona brought the ashtray and, with her face rigid with disapproval, watched her father light his after-breakfast cigarette.

"Why so solemn?" he asked as he shook out the flame of the match.

"Is it true what Beezus said?" Ramona demanded.

"About what?" asked Mr. Quimby.

Ramona had a feeling her father really knew what she meant. "About smoking will make your lungs turn black," she answered.

Mr. Quimby blew a puff of smoke toward the ceiling. "I expect to be one of those old men with a long gray beard who has his picture in the paper on his hundredth birthday and who tells reporters he owes his long life to cigarettes and whiskey."

Ramona was not amused. "Daddy"—her voice was stern—"you are just being silly again."

Her father took a deep breath and blew three smoke rings across the table, a most unsatisfactory answer to Ramona.

On the way to school Ramona cut across the lawn for the pleasure of leaving footprints in the dew and then did not bother to look back to see where she had walked. Instead of running or skipping, she trudged. Nothing was much fun anymore when her family quarreled and then was silent at breakfast and her father's lungs were turning black from smoke.

Even though Mrs. Rogers announced, "Today our second grade is going to have fun learning," as she wrote the date on the blackboard, school turned out to be dreary because the class was having Review again. Review meant boredom for some, like Ramona, because they had to repeat what they already knew, and worry for others, like Davy, because they had to try again what they could not do in the first place. Review was the worst part of school. Ramona passed the morning looking through her workbook for words with double o's like *book* and *cook*. She carefully drew eyebrows over the o's and dots within, making the o's look like crossed eyes. Then she drew mouths with the ends turned down under the eyes. When she finished, she had a cross-looking workbook that matched her feelings.

She was in no hurry to leave the building at recess, but when she did, Davy yelled, "Look out! Here comes Ramona!" and began to run, so of course Ramona had to chase him around and around the playground until time to go inside again.

Running until she was hot and panting made Ramona feel so much better that she was filled with sudden determination. Her father's lungs were not going to turn black. She would not let them. Ramona made up her mind, right then and there in the middle of arithmetic, that she was going to save her father's life.

That afternoon after school Ramona gathered up her crayons and papers from the kitchen table, took them into her room, and shut the door. She got down on her hands and knees and went to work on the bedroom floor, printing a sign in big letters.

Unfortunately, she did not plan ahead and soon reached the edge of the paper. She could not find the Scotch tape to fasten two pieces of paper together, so she had to continue on another line. When she finished, her sign read:

NO SMO KING

It would do. Ramona found a pin and fastened her sign to the living-room curtains, where her father could not miss it. Then she waited, frightened by her daring.

Mr. Quimby, although he must have seen the sign, said nothing until after dinner when he had finished his pumpkin pie. He asked for an ashtray and then inquired, "Say, who is this Mr. King?"

"What Mr. King?" asked Ramona, walking into his trap.

"Nosmo King," answered her father without cracking a smile.

Chagrined, Ramona tore down her sign, crumpled it, threw it into the fireplace, and stalked out of the room, resolving to do better the next time.

The next day after school Ramona found the Scotch tape and disappeared into her room to continue work on her plan to save her father's life. While she was working, she heard the phone ring and waited, tense, as the whole family now waited whenever the telephone rang. She heard her father clear his throat before he answered. "Hello?" After a pause he said, "Just a minute, Howie. I'll call her." There was disappointment in his voice. No one was calling to offer him a job after all.

"Ramona, can you come over and play?" Howie asked, when Ramona went to the telephone.

Ramona considered. Of course they would have to put up with Howie's messy little sister, Willa Jean, but she and Howie would have fun building things if they could think of something to build. Yes, she would like to play with Howie, but saving her father's life was more important. "No, thank you. Not today," she said. "I have important work to do."

Just before dinner she taped to the refrigerator door a picture of a cigarette so long she had to fasten three pieces of paper together to draw it. After drawing the cigarette, she had crossed it out with a big black X and under it she had printed in big letters the word *BAD*. Beezus giggled when she saw it, and Mrs. Quimby smiled as if she were trying not to smile. Ramona was filled with fresh courage. She had allies. Her father had better watch out.

When Mr. Quimby saw the picture, he stopped and looked while Ramona waited. "Hmm," he said, backing away for a better view. "An excellent likeness. The artist shows talent." And that was all he said.

Ramona felt let down, although she was not sure what she had expected. Anger, perhaps? Punishment? A promise to give up smoking?

The next morning the sign was gone, and that afternoon Ramona had to wait until Beezus came home from school to ask, "How do you spell *pollution?*" When Beezus printed it out on a piece of paper, Ramona went to work making a sign that said, *Stop Air Pollution*.

"Let me help," said Beezus, and the two girls, kneeling on the floor, printed a dozen signs. *Smoking Stinks. Cigarettes Start Forest Fires. Smoking Is Hazardous to Your Health.* Ramona learned new words that afternoon.

Fortunately Mr. Quimby went out to examine the car, which was still making the *tappety-tappety* noise. This gave the girls a chance to tape the signs to the mantle, the refrigerator, the dining-room curtains, the door of the hall closet, and every other conspicuous place they could think of.

This time Mr. Quimby simply ignored the signs. Ramona and Beezus might as well have saved themselves a lot of work for all he seemed to notice. But how could he miss so many signs? He must be pretending. He had to be pretending. Obviously the girls would have to step up their campaign. By now they were running out of big pieces of paper, and they knew better than to ask their parents to buy more, not when the family was so short of money.

"We can make little signs on scraps of paper," said Ramona, and that was what they did. Together they made tiny signs that said, *No Smoking, Stop Air Pollution, Smoking Is Bad for Your Health*, and *Stamp Out Cigarettes*. On some Ramona drew stick figures of people stretched out flat and dead, and on one, a cat on his back with his feet in the air. These they hid wherever their father was sure to find them—in his bathrobe pocket, fastened around the handle of his toothbrush with a rubber band, inside his shoes, under his electric razor.

Then they waited. And waited. Mr. Quimby said nothing while he continued to smoke. Ramona held her nose whenever she saw her father with a cigarette. He appeared not to notice. The girls felt discouraged and let down.

Once more Ramona and Beezus devised a plan, the most daring plan of all because they had to get hold of their father's cigarettes just before dinner. Fortunately he had tinkered with the car, still trying to find the reason for the *tappety-tappety-tap*, and had to take a shower before dinner, which gave the girls barely enough time to carry out their plan.

All through dinner the girls exchanged excited glances, and by the time her father asked her to fetch an ashtray, Ramona could hardly sit still she was so excited.

As usual her father pulled his cigarettes out of his shirt pocket. As usual he tapped the package against his hand, and as usual a cigarete, or what appeared to be a cigarette, slid out. Mr. Quimby must have sensed that what he thought was a cigarette was lighter than it should be, because he paused to look at it. While Ramona held her breath, he frowned, looked more closely, unrolled the paper, and discovered it was a tiny sign that said, *Smoking Is Bad!* Without a word, he crumpled it and pulled out another—he thought—cigarette, which turned out to be a sign saying, *Stamp Out Cigarettes!* Mr. Quimby crumpled it and tossed it onto the table along with the first sign.

"Ramona." Mr. Quimby's voice was stern. "My grandmother used to say, 'First time is funny, second time is silly—'" Mr. Quimby's grandmother's wisdom was interrupted by a fit of coughing.

Ramona was frightened. Maybe her father's lungs already had begun to turn black.

Beezus looked triumphant. See, we told you smoking was bad for you, she was clearly thinking.

Mrs. Quimby looked both amused and concerned.

Mr. Quimby looked embarrassed, pounded himself on the chest with his fist, took a sip of coffee, and said, "Something must have caught in my throat." When his family remained silent, he said, "All right, Ramona. As I was saying, enough is enough."

Ramona scowled and slid down in her chair. Nothing was ever fair for second-graders. Beezus helped, but Ramona was getting all the blame. She also felt defeated. Nobody ever paid any attention to second-graders except to scold them. No matter how hard she tried to save her father's life, he was not going to let her save it.

Ramona gave up, and soon found she missed the excitement of planning the next step in her campaign against her father's smoking. Her afternoons after school seemed empty. Howie was home with tonsillitis, and she had no one to play with. She wished there were more children her age in her neighborhood. She was so lonely she picked up the telephone and dialed the Quimbys' telephone number to see if she could answer herself. All she got was a busy signal and a reprimand from her father for playing with the telephone when someone might be trying to reach him about a job.

On top of all this, the family had pumpkin pie for dinner.

"Not *again!*" protested Beezus. The family had eaten pumpkin pie and pumpkin custard since the night the cat ate part of the jack-o'-lantern. Beezus had once told Ramona that she thought her mother had tried to hide pumpkin in the meat loaf, but she wasn't sure because everything was all ground up together.

"I'm sorry, but there aren't many pumpkin recipes. I can't bear to waste good food," said Mrs. Quimby. "But I do remember seeing a recipe for pumpkin soup some-place—"

"No!" Her family was unanimous.

Ramona was so disappointed because her father had ignored all her little signs that she did not feel much like eating, and especially not pumpkin pie for what seemed like the hundredth time. She eyed her triangle of pie and knew she could not make it go down. She was sick of pumpkin. "Are you sure you cut off all the parts with cat spit on them?" she asked her mother.

"Ramona!" Mr. Quimby, who had been stirring his coffee, dropped his spoon. "Please! We are eating."

They had been eating, but after Ramona's remark no one ate a bite of pie.

Mr. Quimby continued to smoke, and Ramona continued to worry. Then one after-noon, when Ramona came home from school, she found the back door locked. When she pounded on it with her fist, no one answered. She went to the front door, rang the doorbell, and waited. Silence. Lonely silence. She tried the door even though she knew it was locked. More silence. Nothing like this had ever happened to Ramona before. Someone was always waiting when she came home from school.

Ramona was frightened. Tears filled her eyes as she sat down on the cold concrete steps to think. Where could her father be? She thought of her friends at school, Davy and Sharon, who did not have fathers. Where had their fathers gone? Everybody had a father sometime. Where could they go?

Ramona's insides tightened with fear. Maybe her father was angry with her. Maybe he had gone away because she tried to make him stop smoking. She thought she was saving his life, but maybe she was being mean to him. Her mother said she must not annoy her father, because he was worried about being out of work. Maybe she had made him so angry he did not love her anymore. Maybe he had gone away because he did not love her. She thought of all the scary things she had seen on television—

houses that had fallen down in earthquakes, people shooting people, big hairy men on motorcycles—and knew she needed her father to keep her safe.

The cold from the concrete seeped through Ramona's clothes. She wrapped her arms around her knees to keep warm as she watched a dried leaf scratch along the driveway in the autumn wind. She listened to the honking of a flock of wild geese flying through the gray clouds on their way south for the winter. They came from Canada, her father had once told her, but that was before he had gone away. Raindrops began to dot the driveway, and tears dotted Ramona's skirt. She put her head down on her knees and cried. Why had she been so mean to her father? If he ever came back he could smoke all he wanted, fill the ashtrays and turn the air blue, and she wouldn't say a single word. She just wanted her father back, black lungs and all.

And suddenly there he was, scrunching through the leaves on the driveway with the collar of his windbreaker turned up against the wind and his old fishing hat pulled down over his eyes. "Sorry I'm late," he said, as he got out his key. "Is that what all this boohoo-ing is about?"

Ramona wiped her sweater sleeve across her nose and stood up. She was so glad to see her father and so relieved that he had not gone away, that anger blazed up. Her tears became angry tears. Fathers were not supposed to worry their little girls. "Where have you been?" she demanded. "You're supposed to be here when I come home from school! I thought you had gone away and left me."

"Take it easy. I wouldn't go off and leave you. Why would I do a thing like that?" Mr. Quimby unlocked the door and, with a hand on Ramona's shoulder, guided her into the living room. "I'm sorry I had to worry you. I was collecting my unemployment insurance, and I had to wait in a long line."

Ramona's anger faded. She knew all about long lines and understood how difficult they were. She had waited in lines for her turn at the slides in the park, she had waited in lines in the school lunchroom back in the days when her family could spare lunch money once in a while, she had waited in lines with her mother at the check-out counter in the market, when she was little she had waited in long, long lines to see Santa Claus in the department store, and—these were the worst, most boring lines of all—she had waited in lines with her mother in the bank. She felt bad because her father had had to wait in line, and she also understood that collecting unemployment insurance did not make him happy.

"Did somebody try to push ahead of you?" Ramona was wise in the ways of lines.

"No. The line was unusually long today." Mr. Quimby went into the kitchen to make himself a cup of instant coffee. While he waited for the water to heat, he poured Ramona a glass of milk and gave her a graham cracker.

"Feeling better?" he asked.

Ramona looked at her father over the rim of her glass and nodded, spilling milk down her front. Silently he handed her a dish towel to wipe up while he poured hot water over the instant coffee in his mug. Then he reached into his shirt pocket, pulled out a package of cigarettes, looked at it a moment, and tossed it onto the counter. Ramona had never seen her father do this before. Could it be. . . .

Mr. Quimby leaned against the counter and took a sip of coffee. "What would you like to do?" he asked Ramona.

Ramona considered before she answered. "Something big and important." But what? she wondered. Break a record in that book of records Beezus talked about? Climb Mount Hood?[6]

---

6. The highest mountain in Oregon, about 50 miles east of Portland.

"Such as?" her father asked.

Ramona finished scrubbing the front of her sweater with the dish towel. "Well—" she said, thinking. "You know that big bridge across the Columbia River?"

"Yes. The Interstate Bridge. The one we cross when we drive to Vancouver."

"I've always wanted to stop on that bridge and get out of the car and stand with one foot in Oregon and one foot in Washington."

"A good idea, but not practical," said Mr. Quimby. "Your mother has the car, and I doubt if cars are allowed to stop on the bridge. What else?"

"It's not exactly important, but I always like to crayon," said Ramona. How long would her father leave his cigarettes on the counter?

Mr. Quimby set his cup down. "I have a great idea! Let's draw the longest picture in the world." He opened a drawer and pulled out a roll of shelf paper. When he tried to unroll it on the kitchen floor, the paper rolled itself up again. Ramona quickly solved that problem by Scotch-taping the end of the roll to the floor. Together she and her father unrolled the paper across the kitchen and knelt with a box of crayons between them.

"What shall we draw?" she asked.

"How about the state of Oregon?" he suggested. "That's big enough."

Ramona's imagination was excited. "I'll begin with the Interstate Bridge," she said.

"And I'll tackle Mount Hood," said her father.

Together they went to work, Ramona on the end of the shelf paper and her father halfway across the kitchen. With crayons Ramona drew a long black bridge with a girl standing astride a line in the center. She drew blue water under the bridge, even though the Columbia River always looked gray. She added gray clouds, gray dots for raindrops, and all the while she was drawing she was trying to find courage to tell her father something.

Ramona glanced at her father's picture, and sure enough he had drawn Mount Hood peaked with a hump on the south side exactly the way it looked in real life on the days when the clouds lifted.

"I think you draw better than anybody in the whole world," said Ramona.

Mr. Quimby smiled. "Not quite," he said.

"Daddy—" Ramona summoned courage. "I'm sorry I was mean to you."

"You weren't mean." Mr. Quimby was adding trees at the base of the mountain. "You're right, you know."

"Am I?" Ramona wanted to be sure.

"Yes."

This answer gave Ramona even more courage. "Is that why you didn't have a cigarette with your coffee? Are you going to stop smoking?"

"I'll try," answered Mr. Quimby, his eyes on his drawing. "I'll try."

Ramona was filled with joy, enthusiasm, and relief. "You can do it, Daddy! I know you can do it."

Her father seemed less positive. "I hope so," he answered, "but if I succeed, Picky-picky will still have to eat Puss-puddy."

"He can try, too," said Ramona and slashed dark V's across her gray sky to represent a flock of geese flying south for the winter.

5. Beezus's Creative Writing

The Quimby women, as Mr. Quimby referred to his wife and daughters, were enthusiastic about Mr. Quimby's decision to give up smoking. He was less enthusiastic because, after all, he was the one who had to break the habit.

Ramona took charge. She collected all her father's cigarettes and threw them in the garbage, slamming down the lid of the can with a satisfying crash, a crash much less satisfying to her father, who looked as if he wanted those cigarettes back.

"I was planning to cut down gradually," he said. "One less cigarette each day."

"That's not what you said," Ramona informed him. "You said you would try to give up smoking, not try to cut down gradually."

There followed an even more trying time in the Quimby household. Out of habit Mr. Quimby frequently reached for cigarettes that were no longer in his pocket. He made repeated trips to the refrigerator, looking for something to nibble on. He thought he was gaining weight. Worst of all, he was even crosser than when he first lost his job.

With a cross father, a tired mother, a sister who worried about creative writing, and a cat who grudgingly ate his Puss-puddy, Ramona felt she was the only happy member of the family left. Even she had run out of ways to amuse herself. She continued to add to the longest picture in the world, but she really wanted to run and yell and make a lot of noise to show how relieved she was that her father was giving up smoking.

One afternoon Ramona was on her knees on the kitchen floor working on her picture when Beezus came home from school, dropped her books on the kitchen table, and said, "Well, it's come."

Ramona looked up from the picture of Glenwood School she was drawing on the roll of shelf paper taped to the floor. Mr. Quimby, who had a dish towel tucked into his belt for an apron, turned from the kitchen sink. "What's come?" he asked. Although it was late in the afternoon, he was washing the breakfast dishes. He had been interviewed for two different jobs that morning.

"Creative writing." Beezus's voice was filled with gloom.

"You make it sound like a calamity," said her father.

Beezus sighed. "Well—maybe it won't be so bad this time. We aren't supposed to write stories or poems after all."

"Then what does Mrs. Mester mean by creative?"

"Oh, you know. . . ." Beezus twirled around on one toe to define creative.

"What are you supposed to write if you don't write a story or a poem?" asked Ramona. "Arithmetic problems?"

Beezus continued to twirl as if spinning might inspire her. "She said we should interview some old person and ask questions about something they did when they were our age. She said she would run off what we wrote on the ditto machine,[7] and we could make a book." She stopped twirling to catch the dish towel her father tossed to her. "Do we know anyone who helped build a log cabin or something like that?"

"I'm afraid not," said Mr. Quimby. "We don't know anybody who skinned buffalo either. How old is old?"

"The older the better," said Beezus.

"Mrs. Swink is pretty old," volunteered Ramona. Mrs. Swink was a widow who lived in the house on the corner and drove an old sedan that Mr. Quimby admiringly called a real collector's item.

"Yes, but she wears polyester pant suits," said Beezus, who had grown critical of clothing lately. She did not approve of polyester pant suits, white shoes, or Ramona's T-shirt with Rockaway Beach[8] printed on the front.

---

7. A spirit duplicator, used to make copies (the process involved special paper on which the text to be duplicated was typed or written).

8. A beachfront town on the northern coast of Oregon, about 12 miles north of Tillamook.

"Mrs. Swink is old inside the pant suits," Ramona pointed out.

Beezus made a face. "I can't go barging in on her all by myself and ask her a bunch of questions." Beezus was the kind of girl who never wanted to go next door to borrow an egg and who dreaded having to sell mints for the Campfire Girls.[9]

"I'll come," said Ramona, who was always eager to go next door to borrow an egg and looked forward to being old enough to sell mints.

"You don't barge in," said Mr. Quimby, wringing out the dishcloth. "You phone and make an appointment. Go on. Phone her now and get it over."

Beezus put her hand on the telephone book. "But what'll I say?" she asked.

"Just explain what you want and see what she says," said Mr. Quimby. "She can't bite you over the telephone."

Beezus appeared to be thinking hard. "OK," she said with some reluctance, "but you don't have to listen."

Ramona and her father went into the living room and turned on the television so they couldn't overhear Beezus. When Ramona noticed her father reached for the cigarettes that were not there, she gave him a stern look.

In a moment Beezus appeared, looking flustered. "I meant sometime in a day or so, but she said to come right now because in a little while she has to take a molded salad to her lodge for a potluck supper. Dad, what'll I *say?* I haven't had time to think."

"Just play it by ear," he advised. "Something will come to you."

"I'm going too," Ramona said, and Beezus did not object.

Mrs. Swink saw the sisters coming and opened the door for them as they climbed the front steps. "Come on in, girls, and sit down," she said briskly. "Now what is it you want to interview me about?"

Beezus seemed unable to say anything, and Ramona could understand how it might be hard to ask someone wearing a polyester pant suit questions about building a log cabin. Someone had to say something so Ramona spoke up. "My sister wants to know what you used to do when you were a little girl."

Beezus found her tongue. "Like I said over the phone. It's for creative writing."

Mrs. Swink looked thoughtful. "Let's see. Nothing very exciting, I'm afraid. I helped with the dishes and read a lot of books from the library. The *Red Fairy Book* and *Blue Fairy Book*[1] and all the rest."

Beezus looked worried, and Ramona could see that she was trying to figure out what she could write about dishes and library books. Ramona ended another awkward silence by asking, "Didn't you make anything?" She had noticed that Mrs. Swink's living room was decorated with mosaics made of dried peas and beans and with owls made out of pinecones. The dining-room table was strewn with old Christmas cards, scissors, and paste, a sure sign of a craft project.

"Let's see now. . . ." Mrs. Swink looked thoughtful. "We made fudge, and—oh, I know—tin-can stilts." She smiled to herself. "I had forgotten all about tin-can stilts until this very minute."

At last Beezus could ask a question. "How did you make tin-can stilts?"

Mrs. Swink laughed, remembering. "We took two tall cans. Two-pound coffee cans were best. We turned them upside down and punched two holes near what had once been the bottom of each. The holes had to be opposite one another on each can.

---

9. The first nonsectarian, interracial organization for girls in the United States, founded in 1910. Since 1975, Camp Fire has included boys as well.

1. Two volumes (published in 1890 and 1889, respectively) of the "colored" fairy-tale collections edited by Andrew Lang.

Then we poked about four feet of heavy twine through each pair of holes and knotted the ends to make a loop. We set one foot on each can, took hold of a loop of twine in each hand, and began to walk. We had to remember to lift each can by the loop of twine as we raised a foot or we fell off—my knees were always skinned. Little girls wore dresses instead of slacks in those days, and I always had dreadful scabs on my knees."

Maybe this was why Mrs. Swink always wore pant suits now, thought Ramona. She didn't want scabs on her knees in case she fell down.

"And the noise those hollow tin cans made on the sidewalk!" continued Mrs. Swink, enjoying the memory. "All the kids in the neighborhood went clanking up and down. Sometimes the cans would cut through the twine, and we would go sprawling on the sidewalk. I became expert at walking on tin-can stilts and used to go clanking around the block yelling, 'Pieface!' at all the younger children."

Ramona and Beezus both giggled. They were surprised that someone as old as Mrs. Swink had once called younger children by a name they sometimes called one another.

"There." Mrs. Swink ended the interview. "Does that help?"

"Yes, thank you." Beezus stood up, and so did Ramona, although she wanted to ask Mrs. Swink about the craft project on the dining-room table.

"Good," Mrs. Swink opened the front door. "I hope you get an *A* on your composition."

"Tin-can stilts weren't exactly what I expected," said Beezus, as the girls started home. "But I guess I can make them do."

Do! Ramona couldn't wait to get to Howie's house to tell him about the tin-can stilts. And so, as Beezus went home to labor over her creative writing, Ramona ran over to the Kemps' house. Just as she thought, Howie listened to her excited description and said, "I could make some of those." Good old Howie. Ramona and Howie spent the rest of the afternoon finding four two-pound coffee cans. The search involved persuading Howie's mother to empty out her coffee into mayonnaise jars and calling on neighbors to see if they had any empty cans.

The next day after school Howie arrived on the Quimby doorstep with two sets of tin-can stilts. "I made them!" he announced, proud of his work. "And Willa Jean wanted some, so I made her a pair out of tuna cans so she wouldn't have far to fall."

"I knew you could do it!" Ramona, who had already changed to her playclothes, stepped onto two of the cans and pulled the twine loops up tight before she took a cautious step, lifting a can as she lifted her foot. First the left foot, then the right foot. *Clank, clank.* They worked! Howie clanked along beside her. They clanked carefully down the driveway to the sidewalk, where Ramona tried to pick up speed, forgot to lift a can at the same time she lifted her foot, and, as Mrs. Swink had recalled, fell off her stilts. She caught herself before she tumbled to the sidewalk and climbed back on.

Clank, clank. Clank, clank. Ramona found deep satisfaction in making so much noise, and so did Howie. Mrs. Swink, turning into her driveway in her dignified old sedan, smiled and waved. In a moment of daring, Ramona yelled, "Pieface!" at her.

"Pieface yourself!" Mrs. Swink called back, understanding Ramona's joke.

Howie did not approve. "You aren't supposed to call grown-ups pieface," he said. "Just kids."

"I can call Mrs. Swink pieface," boasted Ramona. "I can call her pieface any old time I want to." *Clank, clank. Clank, clank.* Ramona was having such a good time she began to sing at the top of her voice, "Ninety-nine bottles of beer on the wall, ninety-nine bottles of beer. You take one down and pass it around. Ninety-eight bottles of beer on the wall. . . ."

Howie joined the singing. "Ninety-eight bottles of beer on the wall. You take one down and pass it around. Ninety-seven bottles of beer. . . ."

Clank, clank. Clank, clank. Ninety-six bottle of beer, ninety-five bottles of beer on the wall. Sometimes Ramona and Howie tripped, sometimes they stumbled, and once in a while they fell, muddying the knees of their corduroy pants on the wet sidewalk. Progress was slow, but what their stilts lost in speed they made up in noise.

Eighty-nine bottles of beer, eighty-six. . . . Ramona was happier than than she had been in a long time. She loved making noise, and she was proud of being able to count backwards. Neighbors looked out their windows to see what all the racket was about while Ramona and Howie clanked determinedly on. "Eighty-one bottles of beer on the wall. . . ." As Mrs. Swink had predicted, one of the twine loops broke, tumbling Ramona to the sidewalk. Howie knotted the ends together, and they clanked on until suppertime.

"That was some racket you two made," remarked Mr. Quimby.

Mrs. Quimby asked, "Where on earth did you two pick up that song about bottles of beer?"

"From Beezus," said Ramona virtuously. "Howie and I are going to count backwards all the way to one bottle of beer."

Beezus, doing homework in her room, had not missed out on the conversation. "We used to sing it at camp when the counselors weren't around," she called out.

"When I used to go to camp, we sang about the teeny-weeny 'pider who went up the water 'pout," said Mrs. Quimby.

The teeny-weeny 'pider song was a favorite of Ramona's too, but it was not so satisfying as "Ninety-nine Bottles of Beer," which was a much louder song.

"I wonder what the neighbors think," said Mrs. Quimby. "Wouldn't some other song do?"

"No," said Ramona. Only a noisy song would do.

"By the way, Ramona," said Mr. Quimby. "Did you straighten your room today?"

Ramona was not much interested in the question. "Sort of," she answered truthfully, because she had shoved a lot of old school artwork and several pairs of dirty socks under the bed.

The next afternoon after school was even better, because Ramona and Howie had mastered walking on the tin-can stilts without falling off. "Sixty-one bottles of beer on the wall. Take one down and pass it around," they sang, as they clanked around the block. Ramona grew hot and sweaty, and when rain began to fall, she enjoyed the cold drops against her flushed face. On and on they clanked, singing at the top of their voices. Ramona's hair grew stringy, and Howie's blond curls tightened in the rain. "Forty-one bottles of beer on the wall. . . ." *Clank, crash, clank.* "Thirty-seven bottles of beer. . . ." *Clank, crash, clank.* Ramona forgot about her father being out of a job, she forgot about how cross he had been since he gave up smoking, she forgot about her mother coming home tired from work and about Beezus being grouchy lately. She was filled with joy.

The early winter darkness had fallen and the streetlights had come on by the time Ramona and Howie had clanked and crashed and sung their way down to that last bottle of beer. Filled with a proud feeling that they had accomplished something big, they jumped off their stilts and ran home with their coffee cans banging and clashing behind them.

Ramona burst in through the back door, dropped her wet stilts with a crash on the linoleum, and announced hoarsely, "We did it! We sang all the way down to one bottle of beer!" She waited for her family to share her triumph.

Instead her father said, "Ramona, you know you are supposed to be home before dark. It was a good thing I could hear where you were, or I would have had to go out after you."

Mrs. Quimby said, "Ramona, you're sopping wet. Go change quickly before you catch cold."

Beezus, who was often embarrassed by her little sister, said, "The neighbors will think we're a bunch of beer guzzlers."

Well! thought Ramona. Some family! She stood dripping on the linoleum a moment, expecting hurt feelings to take over, perhaps even to make her cry a little so her family would be sorry they had been mean to her. To her wonder, no heavy feeling weighed her down, no sad expression came to her face, no tears. She simply stood there, cold, dripping, and feeling *good*. She felt good from making a lot of noise, she felt good from the hard work of walking so far on her tin-can stilts, she felt good from calling a grown-up pieface and from the triumph of singing backwards from ninety-nine to one. She felt good from being out after dark with rain on her face and the streetlights shining down on her. Her feelings were not hurt at all.

"Don't just stand there sogging," said Beezus. "You're supposed to set the table."

Bossy old Beezus, thought Ramona. She squelched off to her room in her wet sneakers, and as she left the kitchen she began to sing, "Ninety-nine bottles of beer on the wall. . . ."

"Oh, no!" groaned her father.

6. THE SHEEP SUIT

Ramona did not expect trouble to start in Sunday school of all places, but that was where it was touched off one Sunday early in December. Sunday school began as usual. Ramona sat on a little chair between Davy and Howie with the rest of their class in the basement of the gray stone church. Mrs. Russo, the superintendent, clapped her hands for attention.

"Let's have quiet, boys and girls," she said. "It's time to make plans for our Christmas-carol program and Nativity scene."

Bored, Ramona hooked her heels on the rung of her little chair. She knew what her part would be—to put on a white choir robe and walk in singing carols with the rest of the second-grade class, which would follow the kindergarten and first grade. The congregation always murmured and smiled at the kindergarteners in their wobbly line, but nobody paid much attention to second-graders. Ramona knew she would have to wait years to be old enough for a chance at a part in the Nativity scene.

Ramona only half listened until Mrs. Russo asked Beezus's friend Henry Huggins if he would like to be Joseph. Ramona expected him to say no, because he was so busy training for the Olympics in about eight or twelve years. He surprised her by saying, "I guess so."

"And Beatrice Quimby," said Mrs. Russo, "would you like to be Mary?"

This question made Ramona unhook her heels and sit up. Her sister, grouchy old Beezus—Mary? Ramona searched out Beezus, who was looking pink, embarrassed, and pleased at the same time.

"Yes," answered Beezus.

Ramona couldn't get over it. Her sister playing the part of Mary, mother of the baby Jesus, and getting to sit up there on the chancel[2] with that manger they got out every year.

Mrs. Russo had to call on a number of older boys before she found three who were willing to be wise men. Shepherds were easier. Three sixth-grade boys were willing to be shepherds.

While the planning was going on, a little voice inside Ramona was saying, "Me! Me! What about me?" until it could be hushed no longer. Ramona spoke up. "Mrs. Russo, I could be a sheep. If you have shepherds, you need a sheep."

"Ramona, that's a splendid idea," said Mrs. Russo, getting Ramona's hopes up, "but I'm afraid the church does not have any sheep costumes."

Ramona was not a girl to abandon her hopes if she could help it. "My mother could make me a sheep costume," she said. "She's made me lots of costumes." Maybe "lots" was stretching the truth a bit. Mrs. Quimby had made Ramona a witch costume that had lasted three Halloweens, and when Ramona was in nursery school she had made her a little red devil suit.

Now Mrs. Russo was in a difficult position because she had told Ramona her idea was splendid.

"Well . . . yes, Ramona, you may be a sheep if your mother will make you a costume."

Howie had been thinking things over. "Mrs. Russo," he said in that serious way of his, "wouldn't it look silly for three shepherds to herd just one sheep? My grandmother could make me a sheep costume, too."

"And my mother could make me one," said Davy.

Sunday school was suddenly full of volunteer sheep, enough for a large flock. Mrs. Russo clapped her hands for silence. "Quiet, boys and girls! There isn't room on the chancel for so many sheep, but I think we can squeeze in one sheep per shepherd. Ramona, Howie, and Davy, since you asked first, you may be sheep if someone will make you costumes."

Ramona smiled across the room at Beezus. They would be in the Nativity scene together.

When Sunday school was over, Beezus found Ramona and asked, "Where's Mother going to find time to make a sheep costume?"

"After work, I guess." This problem was something Ramona had not considered.

Beezus looked doubtful. "I'm glad the church already has my costume," she said. Ramona began to worry.

Mrs. Quimby always washed her hair after church on Sunday morning. Ramona waited until her mother had taken her head out from under the kitchen faucet and was rubbing her hair on a bath towel. "Guess what!" said Ramona. "I get to be a sheep in the Nativity scene this year."

"That's nice," said Mrs. Quimby. "I'm glad they are going to do something a little different this year."

"And I get to be Mary," said Beezus.

"Good!" said Mrs. Quimby, still rubbing.

"I'll need a sheep costume," said Ramona.

"The church has my costume," said Beezus.

Ramona gave her sister a you-shut-up look. Beezus smiled serenely. Ramona hoped she wasn't going to start acting like Mary already.

---

2. The area of the church that contains the altar.

Mrs. Quimby stopped rubbing to look at Ramona. "And where are you going to get this sheep costume?" she asked.

Ramona felt very small. "I—I thought you could make me a sheep suit."

"When?"

Ramona felt even smaller. "After work?"

Mrs. Quimby sighed. "Ramona, I don't like to disappoint you, but I'm tired when I come home from work. I don't have time to do a lot of sewing. A sheep suit would be a lot of work and mean a lot of little pieces to put together, and I don't even know if I could find a sheep pattern."

Mr. Quimby joined in the conversation. That was the trouble with a father with time on his hands. He always had time for other people's arguments. "Ramona," he said, "you know better than to involve other people in work without asking first."

Ramona wished her father could sew. He had plenty of time. "Maybe Howie's grandmother could make me a costume, too," she suggested.

"We can't ask favors like that," said Mrs. Quimby, "and besides material costs money, and with Christmas coming and all we don't have a nickel to spare."

Ramona knew all this. She simply hadn't thought; she had wanted to be a sheep so much. She gulped and sniffed and tried to wiggle her toes inside her shoes. Her feet were growing and her shoes felt tight. She was glad she had not mentioned this to her mother. She would never get a costume if they had to buy shoes.

Mrs. Quimby draped the towel around her shoulders and reached for her comb.

"I can't be a sheep without a costume." Ramona sniffed again. She would gladly suffer tight shoes if she could have a costume instead.

"It's your own fault," said Mr. Quimby. "You should have thought."

Ramona now wished she had waited until after Christmas to persuade her father to give up smoking. Then maybe he would be nice to his little girl when she needed a sheep costume.

Mrs. Quimby pulled the comb through her tangled hair. "I'll see what I can do," she said. "We have that old white terry-cloth bathrobe with the sleeve seams that pulled out. It's pretty shabby, but if I bleached it, I might be able to do something with it."

Ramona stopped sniffing. Her mother would try to make everything all right, but Ramona was not going to risk telling about her tight shoes in case she couldn't make a costume out of the bathrobe and needed to buy material.

That evening, after Ramona had gone to bed, she heard her mother and father in their bedroom talking in those low, serious voices that so often meant that they were talking about her. She slipped out of bed and knelt on the floor with her ear against the furnace outlet to see if she could catch their words.

Her father's voice, coming through the furnace pipes, sounded hollow and far away.

"Why did you give in to her?" he was asking. "She had no business saying you would make her a sheep costume without asking first. She has to learn sometime."

I have learned, thought Ramona indignantly. Her father did not have to talk this way about her behind her back.

"I know," answered Ramona's mother in a voice also sounding hollow and far away. "But she's little, and these things are so important to her. I'll manage somehow."

"We don't want a spoiled brat on our hands," said Ramona's father.

"But it's Christmas," said Mrs. Quimby, "and Christmas is going to be slim enough this year."

Comforted by her mother but angry at her father, Ramona climbed back into bed. Spoiled brat! So that was what her father thought of her.

The days that followed were difficult for Ramona, who was now cross with her cross father. He was *mean*, talking about her behind her back that way.

"Well, what's eating you?" he finally asked Ramona.

"Nothing." Ramona scowled. She could not tell him why she was angry without admitting she had eavesdropped.

And then there was Beezus, who went around smiling and looking serene, perhaps because Mrs. Mester had given her an A on her creative-writing composition and read it aloud to the class, but more likely because she was practicing for her part as Mary. Having a sister who tried to act like the Virgin Mary was not easy for a girl who felt as Ramona did.

And the costume. Mrs. Quimby found time to bleach the old bathrobe in the washing machine, but after that nothing happened. The doctor she worked for was so busy because of all the earaches, sore throats, and flu that came with winter weather that she was late coming home every evening.

On top of that, Ramona had to spend two afternoons watching Howie's grandmother sew on his sheep suit, because arrangements had now been made for Ramona to go to Howie's house if Mr. Quimby could not be home after school. This week he had to collect unemployment insurance and take a civil-service examination for a job in the post office.

Ramona studied Howie's sheep suit, which was made out of fluffy white acrylic. The ears were lined with pink, and Mrs. Kemp was going to put a zipper down the front. The costume was beautiful, soft and furry. Ramona longed to rub her cheek against it, hug it, take it to bed with her.

"And when I finish Howie's costume, I am going to make another for Willa Jean," said Mrs. Kemp. "Willa Jean wants one, too."

This was almost too much for Ramona to bear. Besides, her shoes felt tighter than ever. She looked at Willa Jean, who was clomping around the house on her little tuna-can stilts. Messy little Willa Jean in a beautiful sheep suit she didn't even need. She would only spoil the furry cloth by dribbling apple juice down the front and spilling graham-cracker crumbs all over it. People said Willa Jean behaved just the way Ramona used to, but Ramona could not believe them.

A week before the Christmas program Mrs. Quimby managed to find time to buy a pattern during her lunch hour, but she did not find time to sew for Ramona.

Mr. Quimby, on the other hand, had plenty of time for Ramona. Too much, she was begining to think. He nagged. Ramona should sit up closer to the table so she wouldn't spill so much. She should stop making rivers in her mashed potatoes. She should wring out her washcloth instead of leaving it sopping in the tub. Look at the circle of rust her tin-can stilts had left on the kitchen floor. Couldn't she be more careful? She should fold her bath towel in half and hang it up straight. How did she expect it to dry when it was all wadded up, for Pete's sake? She found a sign in her room that said, *A Messy Room Is Hazardous to Your Health*. That was too much.

Ramona marched out to the garage where her father was oiling the lawnmower so it would be ready when spring came and said, "A messy room is not hazardous to my health. It's not the same as smoking."

"You could trip and break your arm," her father pointed out.

Ramona had an answer. "I always turn on the light or sort of feel along the floor with my feet."

"You could smother in old school papers, stuffed animals, and hula hoops if the mess gets deep enough," said her father and added, "Miss Radar Feet."

Ramona smiled. "Daddy, you're just being silly again. Nobody ever smothered in a hula hoop."

"You never can tell," said her father. "There is always a first time."

Ramona and her father got along better for a while after that, and then came the terrible afternoon when Ramona came home from school to find her father closing the living-room windows, which had been wide open even though the day was raw and windy. There was a faint smell of cigarette smoke in the room.

"Why there's Henry running down the street," said Mr. Quimby, his back to Ramona. "He may make it to the Olympics, but that old dog of his won't."

"Daddy," said Ramona. Her father turned. Ramona looked him in the eye. "You *cheated!*"

Mr. Quimby closed the last window. "What are you talking about?"

"You smoked and you *promised* you wouldn't!" Ramona felt as if she were the grown-up and he were the child.

Mr. Quimby sat down on the couch and leaned back as if he were very, very tired, which made some of the anger drain out of Ramona. "Ramona," he said, "it isn't easy to break a bad habit. I ran across one cigarette, an old stale cigarette, in my raincoat pocket and thought it might help if I smoked just one. I'm trying. I'm really trying."

Hearing her father speak this way, as if she really was a grown-up, melted the last of Ramona's anger. She turned into a seven-year-old again and climbed on the couch to lean against her father. After a few moments of silence, she whispered, "I love you, Daddy."

He tousled her hair affectionately and said, "I know you do. That's why you want me to stop smoking, and I love you, too."

"Even if I'm a brat sometimes?"

"Even if you're a brat sometimes."

Ramona thought awhile before she sat up and said, "Then why can't we be a happy family?"

For some reason Mr. Quimby smiled. "I have news for you, Ramona," he said. "We *are* a happy family."

"We are?" Ramona was skeptical.

"Yes, we are." Mr. Quimby was positive. "No family is perfect. Get that idea out of your head. And nobody is perfect either. All we can do is work at it. And we do."

Ramona tried to wiggle her toes inside her shoes and considered what her father had said. Lots of fathers wouldn't draw pictures with their little girls. Her father bought her paper and crayons when he could afford them. Lots of mothers wouldn't step over a picture that spread across the kitchen floor while cooking supper. Ramona knew mothers who would scold and say, "Pick that up. Can't you see I'm trying to get supper?" Lots of big sisters wouldn't let their little sister go along when they interviewed someone for creative writing. They would take more than their fair share of gummybears because they were bigger and . . .

Ramona decided her father was probably right, but she couldn't help feeling they would be a happier family if her mother could find time to sew that sheep costume. There wasn't much time left.

7. RAMONA AND THE THREE WISE PERSONS

Suddenly, a few days before Christmas when the Quimby family least expected it, the telephone rang for Ramona's father. He had a job! The morning after New Year's Day he was to report for training as a checker in a chain of supermarkets. The pay was good, he would have to work some evenings, and maybe someday he would get to manage a market!

After that telephone call Mr. Quimby stopped reaching for cigarettes that were not there and began to whistle as he ran the vacuum cleaner and folded the clothes from the dryer. The worried frown disappeared from Mrs. Quimby's forehead. Beezus looked even more calm and serene. Ramona, however, made a mistake. She told her mother about her tight shoes. Mrs. Quimby then wasted a Saturday afternoon shopping for shoes when she could have been sewing on Ramona's costume. As a result, when they drove to church the night of the Christmas-carol program, Ramona was the only unhappy member of the family.

Mr. Quimby sang as he drove:

"There's a little wheel a-turning in my heart.
There's a little wheel a-turning in my heart."

Ramona loved that song because it made her think of Howie, who liked machines. Tonight, however, she was determined not to enjoy her father's singing.

Rain blew against the car, headlights shone on the pavement, the windshield wipers *splip-splopped*. Mrs. Quimby leaned back, tired but relaxed. Beezus smiled her gentle Virgin Mary smile that Ramona had found so annoying for the past three weeks.

Ramona sulked. Someplace above those cold, wet clouds the very same star was shining that had guided the Three Wise Men to Bethlehem. On a night like this they never would have made it.

Mr. Quimby sang on, "Oh, I feel like shouting in my heart. . . ."

Ramona interrupted her father's song. "I don't care what anybody says," she burst out. "If I can't be a good sheep, I am not going to be a sheep at all." She yanked off the white terry-cloth headdress with pink-lined ears that she was wearing and stuffed it into the pocket of her car coat.[3] She started to pull her father's rolled-down socks from her hands because they didn't really look like hooves, but then she decided they kept her hands warm. She squirmed on the lumpy terry-cloth tail sewn to the seat of her pajamas. Ramona could not pretend that faded pajamas printed with an army of pink rabbits, half of them upside down, made her look like a sheep, and Ramona was usually good at pretending.

Mrs. Quimby's voice was tired. "Ramona, your tail and headdress were all I could manage, and I had to stay up late last night to finish those. I simply don't have time for complicated sewing."

Ramona knew that. Her family had been telling her so for the past three weeks.

"A sheep should be wooly," said Ramona. "A sheep should not be printed with pink bunnies."

"You can be a sheep that has been shorn," said Mr. Quimby, who was full of jokes now that he was going to work again. "Or how about a wolf in sheep's clothing?"

"You just want me to be miserable," said Ramona, not appreciating her father's humor and feeling that everyone in her family should be miserable because she was.

"She's worn out," said Mrs. Quimby, as if Ramona could not hear. "It's so hard to wait for Christmas at her age."

Ramona raised her voice. "I am *not* worn out! You know sheep don't wear pajamas."

"That's show biz," said Mr. Quimby.

"Daddy!" Beezus-Mary was shocked. "It's church!"

"And don't forget, Ramona," said Mr. Quimby, "as my grandmother would have said, 'Those pink bunnies will never be noticed from a trotting horse.'"

Ramona disliked her father's grandmother even more. Besides, nobody rode trotting horses in church.

The sight of light shining through the stained-glass window of the big stone church diverted Ramona for a moment. The window looked beautiful, as if it were made of jewels.

Mr. Quimby backed the car into a parking space. "Ho-ho-ho!" he said, as he turned off the ignition. " 'Tis the season to be jolly."

Jolly was the last thing Ramona was going to be. Leaving the car, she stooped down inside her car coat to hide as many rabbits as possible. Black branches clawed at the sky, and the wind was raw.

"Stand up straight," said Ramona's heartless father.

"I'll get wet," said Ramona. "I might catch cold, and then you'd be sorry."

"Run between the drops," said Mr. Quimby.

"They're too close together," answered Ramona.

"Oh, you two," said Mrs. Quimby with a tired little laugh, as she backed out of the car and tried to open her umbrella at the same time.

"I will not be in it," Ramona defied her family once and for all. "They can give the program without me."

Her father's answer was a surprise. "Suit yourself," he said. "You're not going to spoil our evening."

Mrs. Quimby gave the seat of Ramona's pajamas an affectionate pat. "Run along, little lamb, wagging your tail behind you."

Ramona walked stiff-legged so that her tail would not wag.

At the church door the family parted, the girls going downstairs to the Sunday-school room, which was a confusion of chattering children piling coats and raincoats on chairs. Ramona found a corner behind the Christmas tree, where Santa would

3. A hip-length coat.

pass out candy canes after the program. She sat down on the floor with her car coat pulled over her bent knees.

Through the branches Ramona watched carolers putting on their white robes. Girls were tying tinsel around one another's heads while Mrs. Russo searched out boys and tied tinsel around their heads, too. "It's all right for boys to wear tinsel," Mrs. Russo assured them. Some looked as if they were not certain they believed her.

One boy climbed on a chair. "I'm an angel. Watch me fly," he announced and jumped off, flapping the wide sleeves of his choir robe. All the carolers turned into flapping angels.

Nobody noticed Ramona. Everyone was having too much fun. Shepherds found their cloaks, which were made from old cotton bedspreads. Beezus's friend, Henry Huggins, arrived and put on the dark robe he was to wear in the part of Joseph.

The other two sheep appeared. Howie's acrylic sheep suit, with the zipper on the front, was thick and as fluffy as Ramona knew it would be. Ramona longed to pet Howie; he looked so soft. Davy's flannel suit was fastened with safety pins, and there was something wrong about the ears. If his tail had been longer, he could have passed for a kitten, but he did not seem to mind. Both boys wore brown mittens. Davy, who was a thin little sheep, jumped up and down to make his tail wag, which surprised Ramona. At school he was always so shy. Maybe he felt brave inside his sheep suit. Howie, a chunky sheep, made his tail wag, too. My ears are as good as theirs, Ramona told herself. The floor felt cold through the seat of her thin pajamas.

"Look at the little lambs!" cried an angel. "Aren't they darling?"

"Ba-a, ba-a!" bleated Davy and Howie.

Ramona longed to be there with them, jumping and ba-a-ing and wagging her tail, too. Maybe the faded rabbits didn't show as much as she had thought. She sat hunched and miserable. She had told her father she would *not* be a sheep, and she couldn't back down now. She hoped God was too busy to notice her, and then she changed her mind. Please, God, prayed Ramona, in case He wasn't too busy to listen to a miserable little sheep, I don't really mean to be horrid. It just works out that way. She was frightened, she discovered, for when the program began, she would be left alone in the church basement. The lights might even be turned out, a scary thought, for the big stone church filled Ramona with awe, and she did not want to be left alone in the dark with her awe. Please, God, prayed Ramona, get me out of this mess.

Beezus, in a long blue robe with a white scarf over her head and carrying a baby's blanket and a big flashlight, found her little sister. "Come out, Ramona," she coaxed. "Nobody will notice your costume. You know Mother would have made you a whole sheep suit if she had time. Be a good sport. Please."

Ramona shook her head and blinked to keep tears from falling. "I told Daddy I wouldn't be in the program, and I won't."

"Well, OK, if that's the way you feel," said Beezus, forgetting to act like Mary. She left her little sister to her misery.

Ramona sniffed and wiped her eyes on her hoof. Why didn't some grown-up come along and *make* her join the other sheep? No grown-up came. No one seemed to remember there were supposed to be three sheep, not even Howie, who played with her almost every day.

Ramona's eye caught the reflection of her face distorted in a green Christmas ornament. She was shocked to see her nose look huge, her mouth and red-rimmed eyes tiny. I can't really look like that, thought Ramona in despair. I'm really a nice person. It's just that nobody understands.

Ramona mopped her eyes on her hoof again, and as she did she noticed three big girls, so tall they were probably in the eighth grade, putting on robes made from better bedspreads than the shepherd's robes. That's funny, she thought. Nothing she had learned in Sunday school told her anything about girls in long robes in the Nativity scene. Could they be Jesus's aunts?

One of the girls began to dab tan cream from a little jar on her face and to smear it around while another girl held up a pocket mirror. The third girl, holding her own mirror, used an eyebrow pencil to give herself heavy brows.

Makeup, thought Ramona with interest, wishing she could wear it. The girls took turns darkening their faces and brows. They looked like different people. Ramona got to her knees and peered over the lower branches of the Christmas tree for a better view.

One of the girls noticed her. "Hi, there," she said. "Why are you hiding back there?"

"Because," was Ramona's all-purpose answer. "Are you Jesus's aunts?" she asked.

The girls found the question funny. "No," answered one. "We're the Three Wise Persons."

Ramona was puzzled. "I thought they were supposed to be wise *men*," she said.

"The boys backed out at the last minute," explained the girl with the blackest eyebrows. "Mrs. Russo said women can be wise too, so tonight we are the Three Wise Persons."

This idea seemed like a good one to Ramona, who wished she were big enough to be a wise person hiding behind makeup so nobody would know who she was.

"Are you supposed to be in the program?" asked one of the girls.

"I was supposed to be a sheep, but I changed my mind," said Ramona, changing it back again. She pulled out her sheep headdress and put it on.

"Isn't she adorable?" said one of the wise persons.

Ramona was surprised. She had never been called adorable before. Bright, lively, yes; adorable, no. She smiled and felt more lovable. Maybe pink-lined ears helped.

"Why don't you want to be a sheep?" asked a wise person.

Ramona had an inspiration. "Because I don't have any makeup."

"Makeup on a *sheep!*" exclaimed a wise person and giggled.

Ramona persisted. "Sheep have black noses," she hinted. "Maybe I could have a black nose."

The girls looked at one another. "Don't tell my mother," said one, "but I have some mascara. We could make her nose black."

"Please!" begged Ramona, getting to her feet and coming out from behind the Christmas tree.

The owner of the mascara fumbled in her shoulder bag, which was hanging on a chair, and brought out a tiny box. "Let's go in the kitchen where there's a sink," she said, and when Ramona followed her, she moistened an elf-sized brush, which she rubbed on the mascara in the box. Then she began to brush it onto Ramona's nose. It tickled, but Ramona held still. "It feels like brushing my teeth only on my nose," she remarked. The wise person stood back to look at her work and then applied another coat of mascara to Ramona's nose. "There," she said at last. "Now you look like a real sheep."

Ramona felt like a real sheep. "Ba-a-a," she bleated, a sheep's way of saying thank you. Ramona felt so much better, she could almost pretend she was woolly. She peeled off her coat and found that the faded pink rabbits really didn't show much in the dim light. She pranced off among the angels, who had been handed little flashlights, which they were supposed to hold like candles. Instead they were shining them into their mouths to show one another how weird they looked with light showing through their cheeks. The other two sheep stopped jumping when they saw her.

"You don't look like Ramona," said Howie.

"B-a-a. I'm not Ramona. I'm a sheep." The boys did not say one word about Ramona's pajamas. They wanted black noses too, and when Ramona told them where she got hers, they ran off to find the wise persons. When they returned, they no longer looked like Howie and Davy in sheep suits. They looked like strangers in sheep suits. So I must really look like somebody else, thought Ramona with increasing happiness. Now she could be in the program, and her parents wouldn't know because they wouldn't recognize her.

"B-a-a!" bleated three prancing, black-nosed sheep. "B-a-a, b-a-a."

Mrs. Russo clapped her hands. "Quiet, everybody!" she ordered. "All right, Mary and Joseph, up by the front stairs. Shepherds and sheep next and then wise persons. Angels line up by the back stairs."

The three sheep pranced over to the shepherds, one of whom said, "Look what we get to herd," and nudged Ramona with his crook.

"You cut that out," said Ramona.

"Quietly, everyone," said Mrs. Russo.

Ramona's heart began to pound as if something exciting were about to happen. Up the stairs she tiptoed and through the arched door. The only light came from candelabra on either side of the chancel and from a streetlight shining through a stained-glass window. Ramona had never seen the church look so beautiful or so mysterious.

Beezus sat down on a low stool in the center of the chancel and arranged the baby's blanket around the flashlight. Henry stood behind her. The sheep got down on their hands and knees in front of the shepherds, and the Three Wise Persons stood off to one side, holding bath-salts jars that looked as if they really could hold frankincense and myrhh. An electric star suspended above the organ began to shine. Beezus turned on the big flashlight inside the baby's blanket and light shone up on her face, making her look like a picture of Mary on a Christmas card. From the rear door a wobbly procession of kindergarten angels, holding their small flashlights like candles, led the way, glimmering, two by two. "Ah . . ." breathed the congregation.

"Hark, the herald angels sing," the advancing angels caroled. They looked nothing like the jumping, flapping mob with flashlights shining through their cheeks that Ramona had watched downstairs. They looked good and serious and . . . holy.

A shivery feeling ran down Ramona's backbone, as if magic were taking place. She looked up at Beezus, smiling tenderly down at the flashlight, and it seemed as if Baby Jesus really could be inside the blanket. Why, thought Ramona with a feeling of shock, Beezus looks nice. Kind and—sort of pretty. Ramona had never thought of her sister as anything but—well, a plain old big sister, who got to do everything first. Ramona was suddenly proud of Beezus. Maybe they did fight a lot when Beezus wasn't going around acting like Mary, but Beezus was never really mean.

As the carolers bore more light into the church, Ramona found her parents in the second row. They were smiling gently, proud of Beezus, too. This gave Ramona an aching feeling inside. They would not know her in her makeup. Maybe they would think she was some other sheep, and she didn't want to be some other sheep. She wanted to be their sheep. She wanted them to be proud of her, too.

Ramona saw her father look away from Beezus and look directly at her. Did he recognize her? Yes, he did. Mr. Quimby winked. Ramona was shocked. Winking in church! How could her father do such a thing? He winked again and this time held up his thumb and forefinger in a circle. Ramona understood. Her father was telling her he was proud of her, too.

"Joy to the newborn King!" sang the angels, as they mounted the steps on either side of the chancel.

Ramona was filled with joy. Christmas was the most beautiful, magic time of the whole year. Her parents loved her, and she loved them, and Beezus, too. At home there was a Christmas tree and under it, presents, fewer than at past Christmases, but presents all the same. Ramona could not contain her feelings. "B-a-a," she bleated joyfully.

She felt the nudge of a shepherd's crook on the seat of her pajamas and heard her shepherd whisper through clenched teeth, "You be quiet!" Ramona did not bleat again. She wiggled her seat to make her tail wag.

1977

LENSEY NAMIOKA
b. 1929

Lensey Namioka comes from a long line of outsiders, and the need for outsiders to make adjustments to a new culture constitutes an important theme in both her domestic fiction series about the Chinese immigrant Yang family in contemporary Seattle and her mystery-adventure books about two samurai in sixteenth-century Japan. Both her parents were educated outside of China—her father, Yuen Ren, was a linguist who went to college in America, and her mother, Buwei Yang Chao, was a physician who studied medicine in Japan—and moved often, in China as well as in the United States (Namioka's two older sisters were born in Boston). Namioka and her three sisters were thus outsiders even within China, where they lived in a number of regions that had dialects and customs markedly different from what she was accustomed to in her native Beijing; then, shortly before World War II, the family immigrated to America.

In 1957 Lensey Chao married another outsider: Isaac Namioka, the grandson of a Christian Japanese man and a French woman, whom she met while earning her M.A. in mathematics at the University of California, Berkeley (1952). Though she taught college mathematics for several years, she decided that she liked writing better. In 1963 she moved to Seattle, where Isaac had received an appointment in the mathematics department of the University of Washington and where they raised two girls. Namioka notes that she and her husband "don't belong completely to either the Chinese or the Japanese ethnic groups. In a sense, we are still outsiders. And, like Mary Yang in *Yang the Third and Her Impossible Family* [1998], we have learned to be content."

The Yang children are obvious outsiders to American culture when they arrive from China with their parents and settle in Seattle, and the misunderstandings and mistakes that can result from cross-cultural meetings are the source of much humor. Yet in the Yang books and in novels such as *Who's Hu?* (1981) and *April and the Dragon Lady* (1994), Namioka also urges the importance of celebrating cultural diversity and exploring one's cultural heritage. Her series about Zenta and Matsuzo, traveling unemployed samurai in feudal Japan, also focuses on outsiders who are newcomers to each community they enter. These seven books reflect Namioka's continued interest in the action and adventure stories that had constituted the bulk of her childhood reading. Each novel is a mystery as well. The tales of sword fighting, suspense, courage, and adventure begin with *The Samurai and the Long-Nosed Devils* and *White Serpent Castle* (both published in 1976).

Namioka suggests that her training in mathematics, which emphasizes elegance and economy in proving theorems, informs her desire for spare and economic prose. Music, too, which was the main leisure entertainment for the four Chao daughters and their father, figures importantly in many of Namioka's books for children. Like Yingtao Yang, the young narrator in *Yang the Youngest and His Ter-*

rible Ear (1992, illustrated by Kees de Kiefte), Namioka had the worst ear in a family of gifted musicians but a keen sense of rhythm and the ability to sight-read music. The challenges of making music—an activity she continues to enjoy—under such circumstances, as well as the stresses Namioka witnessed at the recitals of her own children, are depicted with humor in the first of her four novels about the Yang siblings.

Yang the Youngest and His Terrible Ear

1

Yang the Eldest drew his bow across his violin strings, and a shower of sparkling notes fell over the room.

Yang the Second Eldest drew her bow across her viola strings, and a rainbow of notes hung brightly in the air.

Yang the Third Eldest drew her bow across her cello strings, and a wave of deep, mellow notes washed over us.

Yang the Youngest—that's me—drew my bow across my violin strings, and it went *SCREECH*.

I'm the youngest child in our Yang family of four children. According to our Chinese custom, I'm not allowed to call my elder brother and my two sisters by their given names. Instead, I have to address them as Eldest Brother, Second Sister, and Third Sister. They call me Fourth Brother.

My parents are both musicians. Father was a violinist in the Shanghai Philharmonic Orchestra until a few months ago, when we left China and came to live in America. Now he has a job with the Seattle Symphony Orchestra.

Mother is a pianist; she used to accompany Father when he gave concerts. But she hasn't been able to find a job since coming to America. Orchestras can use many violinists, but they don't need more than one pianist. So these days Mother spends most of her time shopping and cooking to feed all of us.

It isn't easy to feed a family of six on Father's salary. He is what's called an alternate, which means he gets to play only when one of the other violinists is absent.

Father also makes some money giving private lessons. At first he didn't get many students. Parents didn't want to bring their children to a music teacher who spoke so little English and had such a strong Chinese accent.

But music is music in any language, and Father doesn't have to say much during the lessons. When one of his students plays well, he smiles. And when a student plays a sour note, Father just puts on a look of great suffering.

I know that look: when Father gives me my music lesson, it never leaves his face. I started playing the violin when I was five, and now, four years later, Father's expression is still the same.

I don't exactly enjoy the lessons, either, but I don't suffer as much as he does. That's because I can't hear what I'm doing wrong. In fact that's my problem: I have a *terrible* ear.

My parents didn't believe that could happen to one of their children. They both had good ears, and so did Eldest Brother, Second Sister, and Third Sister.

Eldest Brother was humming tunes even before he could talk. Mother taught him both Chinese and American songs. Soon he was singing "Old McDonald Had a Farm," right on pitch, even on the "oink oink" and the "quack quack" parts.

On Eldest Brother's fourth birthday, my parents gave him a violin that was one-eighth the size of a regular one. He is fifteen now, and he has been right on pitch ever since.

Second Sister, two years younger than Eldest Brother, started singing along during his violin lessons. So she got a viola, one-eighth size.

Third Sister, who is three years younger than Second Sister, started by playing the viola that had become too small for Second Sister. But she was so short that she had to stand up and hold the instrument on its end, like a cello. She got a real cello as soon as she grew tall enough.

When I was born my parents were pleased, because now they could have a complete string quartet: two violins, a viola, and a cello. They never imagined that the second violin would turn out to be so bad.

But *I* knew. I began to suspect something was wrong, because whenever I started singing, people would move away from me. I loved songs—at least I loved the words. In China, we often sang American songs, and the most popular one was "Oh Susanna." But *my* favorite song was the one about the farmer and his animals, which Eldest Brother had taught me.

"Fourth Brother is singing 'Old McDonald Had a Farm,'" Third Sister announced proudly one day.

"No, he's not!" said Father. "The tune he's singing is quite different."

"Well, at least he's doing the oinks and the quacks," she said.

Third Sister has always been closest to me. It's not just that we're close in age (she's only a year older than I am), but when everyone else thought I wasn't really trying hard enough to play in tune, she was the only one who knew that I was doing the best I could.

The trouble is that except for the oinks and the quacks, "Old McDonald Had a Farm" sounds to me a lot like "Mary Had a Little Lamb." I am what they call "tone-deaf."

You'd think that being Chinese and tone-deaf could be a real problem, because the Chinese language is full of tones. If you make the same sounds, but with different tones, you change the meaning completely.

Luckily, things aren't that bad for me, because the tones in Chinese slide up and down, and I *can* hear the difference between a sound sliding up and a sound sliding down. My problem is that I don't know *how much* to slide up or down. This is not good when you have to play the violin.

At least I didn't have to worry about rhythm. Having a terrible ear means I have a problem with pitch. But I can count as well as any of the Yangs, and I always come in on time. The others probably wished I wouldn't come in on time. Sometimes I suspected they wished I wouldn't come in at all.

So there I was, coming in on time, sliding up and down, doing the best I could. And as usual, my best wasn't good enough.

Eldest Brother rolled his eyes. "You have to *listen* harder, Fourth Brother!"

"Before you play, sing the notes in your head first," ordered Second Sister.

That's easy for her to say. I couldn't even sing the notes in my throat.

"Maybe he's a mutant," said Third Sister.

"A mutant?" asked Second Sister. "Don't you mean a mute? He certainly needs an extra-size mute."

A *mute* is a little button-like thing you put on your violin when you want to sound softer. Second Sister had once suggested permanent mutes on my violin.

Third Sister giggled. She's the giggler of the family because she knows her dimples are cute.

We all have our own ways of learning English, and Third Sister's is to make a list of five new words every day and memorize them. *Mutant* was on her list today.

"*Mutant* means you turn out really different from your parents," she explained. "Fourth Brother isn't Lazy; he was just born different. There's nothing he can do about it."

"Nonsense," said Second Sister. She was thirteen and a young lady. Young ladies didn't giggle and didn't put up with nonsense.

"Let's stop talking and get back to practicing," said Eldest Brother. As the eldest of the family, he was more serious than the rest of us. Whenever we started to waste time, he quickly got us back to work.

We immediately picked up our instruments again. We weren't scared of Eldest Brother—not very much, anyway—but we knew we had to practice.

A very important recital was being planned. For Father's sake, for the sake of the Yang family, we had to make a good impression.

At a recital, all the students play a piece of music, and their families and friends are invited to hear them. This was the first recital Father had organized since he started giving music lessons here in Seattle. If his students did well, their parents would tell other parents. Then Father would get a lot more students.

"At the end," announced Father, "the four of you will be playing a portion from a string quartet. It will be the grand finale of the whole recital."

We all knew the last piece on the program was the most important one. That was the one the audience would remember best when they went home. If we could impress the audience with our skill, we would really show them what a great teacher Father was.

Normally, I didn't suffer much during my lessons. I just ran through the piece as best as I could, and if other people suffered, too bad for them.

But this recital worried me. When they heard me playing so badly, the parents in the audience would say to themselves, "If Mr. Yang can't even teach his own son to play, how can he teach our children?"

Now as we practiced, I found myself sweating with nervousness. My hand felt unsteady, and I couldn't get a good grip on the violin bow. It slid around on the string, and produced those terrible screeches. This got on everybody's nerves.

Even Eldest Brother finally lost his patience. "It's bad enough that you play out of tune! Do you have to keep screeching, too?"

"I'm sorry," I mumbled. I wiped my hands on my pants, then wiped my brow, which was streaming. This made my hands wet again, and I had to borrow Third Sister's handkerchief.

Eldest Brother sighed deeply and put his violin under his chin. "Let's try those last four bars again."

Second Sister picked up her bow, and Third Sister bent over her cello.

One by one, the other three Yangs started playing their sparkling notes. When my entrance came, I pressed harder, to keep my bowing hand from wobbling. But all I got was an extra loud *SCREECH*.

A look of deep suffering came over Eldest Brother's face. At times like these, he looks a lot like Father. He has the same long face, and the same wide mouth that curves down at the corners when he is in pain.

"Fourth Brother," he said, fixing me with his sternest look, "I know that music doesn't mean as much to you as it does to the rest of us. But you really have to try harder. You know the saying, that hard work can overcome ten thousand problems."

"He just doesn't *care* about playing in tune," said Second Sister. "I don't think there's any use practicing until his attitude is better."

She put her instrument back in its case, firmly closed the lid, and snapped the catch.

I tried not to show it, but I was hurt. I admired Eldest Brother and Second Sister deeply for being so dedicated to music, even if I couldn't share their dedication. It must be wonderful to know exactly what you wanted to do. I didn't know what I wanted to do. All I knew was that I didn't want to be a miserable second violin.

After Eldest Brother and Second Sister had left, Third Sister came over and put her arms around me. "Don't feel so bad," she said softly. "I know you're doing your best."

Her kindness only made me feel like crying. "I'll spoil everything. I'll ruin the recital."

"Maybe we can think of something," she said. "Maybe we can fix it so that Eldest Brother plays most of your notes."

"The only way to save the recital is for Eldest Brother to play *all* of my notes," I muttered.

In a string quartet, the second violin—me—usually has the least important part. But even playing the least important part, I could still ruin things. And Eldest Brother couldn't always cover for me. He had his own notes to play.

There was no way, absolutely no way, that I could play in the recital without sounding awful. And if I sounded awful, the whole quartet was going to sound awful. And since our quartet was the last piece, the audience would go home with an awful impression of the recital.

I wanted so much to please my family, but it seemed hopeless. Maybe Third Sister was right: I was a mutant. I would never be one of the musical Yangs.

What if I got so sick that I couldn't play? When the others saw me in pain, they'd feel sorry for criticizing me. I'd be lying, pale and suffering, in bed, and I wouldn't be around for them to pick on anymore.

But maybe they wouldn't be sorry. I was no good. My parents might even be glad if they could exchange me for someone else. Someone with a good musical ear.

Then I realized that I was wallowing in self-pity, and I became disgusted with myself.

I remembered Father's anxious face as he counted heads when we boarded the plane coming to America. I remembered his big smile when he saw all four of us safely strapped in our seats. I remembered Mother carefully dividing a Hershey chocolate bar with almonds into four exactly equal pieces. My parents did love me as much as the others, I knew that.

But what could I do to prevent the recital from being a disaster? I had managed to get out of tight spots before. When I was singing in the chorus of my Chinese school, I always looked around at the person behind me whenever the music teacher scowled in my direction. But this wasn't so simple.

I had to think of something to save the recital. I just had to.

2

Our family arrived in America in the winter, and the school year was almost half over. So when I started school, the other students in my class already knew each other. To make things worse, I didn't even know enough English to try to make friends.

But language was only one of my problems. American kids scared me at first. They yelled terribly loud and ran fast in the hallways.

For the first few weeks, I found myself hugging the walls. It was like the time in

China when I learned to swim. I was afraid to let go of the side of the pool because in the middle were other swimmers splashing around like sharks.

Once when I was walking in the hallway at school, I turned a corner and bumped into a boy. He was running so fast that he knocked me off my feet.

He pulled me upright and shook me a little. Maybe he wanted to see if any parts were rattling loose. When he saw that I wasn't hurt, he winked at me, laughed, and said, "Hey, no sweat!"

He looked so cheerful that I laughed, too. "No sweat" sounded like a good phrase, and I told Third Sister about it. She added it to her list.

In a few weeks I learned to walk just as fast and shove my way just as hard as the other kids.

My parents even complained about it. "You're becoming too rough, Yingtao. Why do you have to stomp your feet so hard?"

Before I got used to the American school, the other kids laughed at some of the things I did. Each morning, as soon as the teacher came into the room, I jumped to my feet and stood stiffly at attention. That was how we showed our respect to the teacher in China.

The first time I did it here, the teacher asked me whether I needed something. I looked around and saw that nobody else was standing up. Feeling foolish, I shook my head and sat down.

When I did it again the next day, a couple of kids behind me started to snigger. After that, I remembered not to jump up, but I half rose a few times. One boy used to watch me, and if he saw my bottom leave my seat, he would whisper, "Down, Fido!"

Third Sister was a great help during those early days. While the other kids were busy talking or playing games at recess, she and I stood in a corner and kept each other company.

Every day we walked together to our elementary school, which was not far from our house. Eldest Brother and Second Sister took a big yellow bus to a school that was farther away.

If Eldest Brother had trouble making friends, it didn't seem to bother him. Music was the only thing he really cared about.

I think Second Sister felt the loneliest. In China, people always said she would turn out to be a real beauty. She had been popular at school there, always surrounded by friends. But in America not many people told her she was beautiful. These days she was often cranky and sad. Mother told the rest of us that we just had to be patient with Second Sister.

Third Sister had no trouble at all making friends. Even before she could speak much English, she began chatting with other kids. She could always fill in the gaps with laughter.

During lunch she and I sat at a table with mostly Asian-Americans. At first we didn't understand what Asian-Americans were. When we were filling out registration forms at school, we put down "Chinese" in the space marked "race."

The secretary at the school told us to change it to "Asian-American." With a big smile, she said, "We have a number of Asian-Americans at this school, so you'll be able to make friends easily."

My teacher must have felt the same because on my first day in class, she seated me next to a girl who was also Asian-American.

I greeted her in Chinese, but she just shook her head. "I'm afraid I don't understand Japanese," she said in English.

"I wasn't speaking Japanese," I told her. "I was speaking Chinese."

"Sorry. I don't understand that, either. My family is from Korea."

I didn't know much about Korea, except that my country had once invaded her country. I hoped she didn't hold it against me.

"You speak good English," I said. "When did you arrive?"

"I was born in America," she said. "So were my parents."

In spite of this bad start, she tried to be helpful to me. But we never became close friends.

So I was lonely. After Third Sister made friends in her class, she began to spend less and less time with me.

Then I met Matthew. During recess one day, Third Sister was busy talking to some new friends, and I was looking wistfully at some boys playing catch and wondering if I could find the nerve to join them.

Suddenly I felt someone pluck my pen from my pocket. This was a ballpoint pen I had brought with me from China, with a picture of a panda on the side of it. Whenever I thought about China and missed the friends I had left behind, I would take out the pen and look at the picture.

The boy who had taken the pen was running away, laughing. I ran after him, shouting. The teacher came up and asked me what the trouble was.

"He took my . . . my . . ." I stopped, because I didn't know the English word for pen. In Chinese we have the same word, *bi*, for pen, pencil, and brush. "He took my writing stick," I finished lamely.

The boy who'd taken the pen stood there and grinned, while the teacher looked puzzled.

"Jake took his ballpoint pen," said a tall, freckled boy with curly brown hair. "I saw the whole thing."

The teacher turned and frowned at Jake. "Is this true?"

"Aw, I was just teasing him a little," said Jake, quickly handing the pen back to me. "He's always playing with it, so I got curious."

I thanked the boy with the curly hair. "Don't mind Jake," he said. "He didn't mean anything."

"My name is Yang Yingtao," I introduced myself. Then I remembered that in America people said their family name last and their given name first.

"Yingtao is my last name," I told him. "Except that in America my last name is really my first name and my first name is my last name. So I'm Yang Yingtao in China and Yingtao Yang in America."

The boy looked confused. Just then the bell rang. "I'm Matthew Conner," he said quickly. "See you around!"

I began to feel a little less lonely.

We discovered that our school had an after-school orchestra, which met twice a week. My parents thought that Third Sister and I were very lucky, and they signed us up for the orchestra right away. They never even asked us whether we wanted to join.

Before Third Sister and I could play in the orchestra, the conductor gave us an audition; that is, he asked each of us to play a few bars of music alone.

He looked pleased when he heard Third Sister play the cello. He immediately put her near the front of the orchestra.

Then it was my turn to play the violin. He stopped me after only four measures and looked at me thoughtfully. "Would you like to try the triangle instead?"

Maybe I should have felt insulted, but in fact I was tempted to accept. You don't need a good ear to play the triangle, since all you do is just hit it with a stick. You only need to come in on time, and I was good at that. And besides, the triangle makes only a small tinkle, so you can't do much harm.

But I knew my parents would be upset. "I have my own violin," I told the conductor unhappily. "My parents will expect me to play it."

He sighed. "Very well. I know what parents are like." He put me in the very last row of the violin section—as far away from the audience as possible.

When I took my place, the boy sharing a music stand with me said, "Hi, looks like I'll be your stand partner."

It was Matthew, the boy who had gotten my pen back. I was very glad to see him. Then the conductor raised his stick and the orchestra began to play.

When playing together with other people, my trick was to draw my bow back and forth, without quite touching the strings. This helped everybody. It helped me; it helped the other players; it helped the conductor; and most of all, it helped the audience.

After a few bars we stopped playing while the conductor tried to cheer up the trombone player, who was making bubbling sounds when he tried to blow.

Matthew turned to me. "You don't play very loudly, do you? I couldn't hear you at all."

"You're lucky," I told him.

He looked puzzled, but I had no time to explain because the conductor raised his stick again.

Matthew played with a dreamy look on his face. I couldn't tell if he was good or not, but he certainly seemed to be enjoying himself.

After the rehearsal the conductor asked Third Sister to stay behind and play a short piece for him. I waited for her outside so we could go home together.

Matthew came up to me while I was waiting. "I heard your sister tell the conductor that your father is a violin teacher."

"Yes, he is," I answered. Maybe this was a chance to get Father another student? "Do you want to take lessons?"

Matthew looked very uncomfortable. "I'd really like to, but my folks can't afford it."

"My father is cheap," I said eagerly, although I didn't actually know how much Father charged. But I felt sure he would love to have a new student, especially someone who really liked music.

When Third Sister came out, she was smiling. "The conductor wants me to play a solo for our first concert!"

I was very happy for her, and even Matthew looked glad. "Hey, that's great!" he said.

"This is my stand partner, Matthew," I said. "And this is my third sister—"

"Hi, my name is Mary," interrupted Third Sister.

I stared at her. I didn't even know she had an American name. She must have picked it without telling the rest of the family. Maybe she felt it would be easier for her new friends to remember.

I'd noticed that many Americans had trouble with Chinese names. When I told people my name was Yingtao, they always asked me to spell it. Even after I spelled it, they had trouble remembering it.

"I heard you play just now," Matthew said to Third Sister. "You're really good!"

Third Sister dimpled again. "I'm terrible. You're just saying that to be nice."

She didn't mean it, of course. That's the way my parents taught us to answer when someone praises us.

"Well, I guess I'd better run," said Matthew. But he didn't seem in a hurry to go.

Neither was Third Sister eager to have him go—not when he had just told her how much he admired her playing. "Would you like to come to our house and meet my elder brother and sister? They also play musical instruments."

Matthew grinned. "Sure, if it's okay with your folks."

"My parents would be glad to meet one of Fourth Brother's friends," she told him.

I liked the way she said that—as if Matthew was really my friend, as if I had lots of other friends.

My parents weren't home, but we found Second Sister in the kitchen, cutting tea bags. "This is my other sister," I told him. "She plays the viola."

Second Sister looked a little moody but not too moody to greet Matthew politely with "Hello."

I waited to see if she had chosen an American name, too. But she just picked up her scissors again.

As we went up the stairs, Matthew looked at me. "What was your sister doing in the kitchen? It looked like she was cutting up tea bags."

"She was."

At the landing Matthew stopped and looked at me again. "What for?"

I was used to seeing Second Sister cutting tea bags, and it had never occurred to me that it might look funny. "When we make tea, we put some tea leaves in the bottom of the cup, and pour hot water over them," I said. "It's ready to drink when all the leaves are wet and sink to the bottom."

"But why do you need to cut the bags?"

"Well, my mother saw some tea for sale at the market one day, and she bought a big box. But it turned out to be all tea bags, not loose tea. So Second Sister cuts up a few bags every day and pours the loose tea into a jar."

It was perfectly obvious to me that tea would steep better when it's loose than when it's tightly packed into a tiny bag.

But I guess Matthew didn't think so. He was still shaking his head and looking puzzled.

I opened the door to the room I shared with Eldest Brother. He was inside, sitting on the floor and screwing knobs into the ends of orange crates. Beside him were a couple of boards and some bricks.

I introduced Matthew, who looked wide-eyed at the crates and boards. "What are you making?"

"I'm making a chest of drawers," said Eldest Brother. "The boards will sit over the piles of bricks to make a top, and the orange crates are the drawers. The knobs make it easier to pull them out."

Matthew peered into one of the crates, which already contained my shirts and underwear. "Why don't you put your clothes in a regular dresser?"

"We don't have enough money to buy much furniture," explained Eldest Brother.

"Gee, I'm sorry," Matthew said, turning red. "I didn't mean to sound rude or nosy." For some reason, he was very sensitive about money.

I had to show Matthew that we didn't mind. Chinese people aren't at all embarrassed to talk about money. When we meet someone, we often ask him how much money he makes.

"That's okay," I told Matthew. "I don't think you're rude or nosy at all."

"My mother was glad when she found all these orange crates she could have for free," Elder Brother said.

As he continued to put the knobs in, I told him that Matthew loved music.

Elder Brother looked pleased. "Are you in the school orchestra?"

"I play the violin," answered Matthew. "I'm Yingtao's stand partner."

Eldest Brother stopped smiling. "Did the conductor put you there after the audition?"

I knew why he asked that. He was trying to find out if Matthew was my stand partner because he played as badly as I did.

"I'm a beginner," said Matthew. "I only started playing the violin last fall. The school had an extra violin that nobody else was using, so I asked if I could borrow it."

"Do you take lessons?" asked Eldest Brother.

Again Matthew turned red. "My parents can't afford them," he mumbled. "My father is out of work right now."

I suddenly had an idea. "Maybe you can give him some free lessons," I said to Eldest Brother. "They don't have to be more than fifteen minutes, just long enough to show him what he's doing wrong."

Eldest Brother looked thoughtful. Finally he got up and went to his violin case. "Play something," he said, taking out the instrument and handing it to Matthew.

Matthew swallowed and wiped his hands on his pants. Then he took the violin carefully and looked at it with wide eyes. "Wow," he breathed. "This is beautiful!"

He closed his eyes for a minute and then began to play. From the expression on Eldest Brother's face, I knew that he liked the sound of what he was hearing.

When Matthew finished, Eldest Brother stood silent and then smiled. "It's certainly clear that you have not been playing very long. But you have a nice feel for the violin."

Matthew looked almost scared. "Then . . . then . . ."

Eldest Brother smiled more widely. "All right, I'll give you lessons. We can start after dinner tonight, if you want. Why don't you stay and eat with us?"

Matthew accepted and went to phone his parents for permission. When he came back he asked if he could go to the bathroom.

I was surprised. Did Americans always take a bath before dinner?

"Is it all right if you didn't take a bath just now?" I asked him. "Our tub has something in it."

It was Matthew's turn to look surprised. "I don't need a bath."

"Then why did you tell me you wanted one?" I demanded.

"I just want to go to the toilet," he explained. He began to laugh. "And you thought I actually asked to take a bath? Without someone making me?"

I laughed, too. This was not like Jake and the others laughing at me for standing at attention when the teacher came in. We were laughing together because we were sharing a joke. I began to like Matthew very much.

When he came out of the bathroom, he looked shocked. "Was I seeing things, or were there really fish swimming in your bathtub?"

"That's just some carp my mother bought in Chinatown today. We're having them for dinner tonight."

"But they're alive!"

"Of course they're alive!" I snorted. "My mother would never buy dead fish. They're not fresh."

"I've never had live fish," Matthew said, as we went downstairs. "The fish I eat are nice and dead. They come in a can, or they're frozen sticks covered with bread crumbs."

When we came into the dining room, Matthew was muttering, "... cut-up tea bags, knobs on orange crates, fish in the bathtub ...."

"Does your friend always talk to himself?" whispered Second Sister as I helped her set the table.

I just smiled. It was a good thing that Second Sister couldn't hear what he was saying.

Matthew was our first American dinner guest. Father nodded approval when Eldest Brother introduced him as my friend and said he had a very good ear.

When we eat dinner, we normally help ourselves to food from the platters in the middle of the table. But since Matthew was my guest, I acted as a host and served him with food.

After a while I noticed that he wasn't eating much. He spent most of the time staring at the chopsticks in my right hand.

"What's wrong?" I asked.

"I've never used chopsticks before," he admitted sheepishly.

"Why don't you give him a fork, Yingtao?" suggested Mother.

"No, please," Matthew said quickly. "I really want to learn how to use chopsticks."

So I taught him. I showed him how to grip one of the two sticks steady and jiggle the other stick to close down on a piece of meat.

He managed to eat most of the food I served him, but I noticed he didn't eat much of the fish. "I'm not used to eating someone I saw swimming just a little while ago," he whispered apologetically.

Matthew learned fast, and by the end of the meal he was using chopsticks pretty well. "Hey, this is good finger exercise!" he joked. "I bet it's going to help my violin playing."

"If that's true, then why doesn't Fourth Brother play a little better?" sniffed Second Sister. "He's been using chopsticks since he was two years old!"

Matthew gave me a sympathetic smile. I was used to remarks from the family about my violin playing, but it was still nice to have someone who was on my side.

From that day on Matthew was my best friend. I didn't have to stand by myself at recess anymore, and we helped each other a lot in school.

I was able to help Matthew with his math homework. Chinese schools are ahead of American schools in math, so everybody thought I was a math genius when I always finished my work long before anyone else. Matthew told me that most kids hated math, except those who were geniuses.

I'm certainly no genius, and Third Sister is much better at math than I am. But I was happy to have people think I was good at something, so I didn't say anything.

Matthew helped me with spelling. I had a lot of trouble because English just didn't sound the way it looked. So Matthew drilled me on tough words like "cough," "enough," and "dough."

I was getting used to American schools. Not only did I stop jumping to attention when the teacher came into the room, I began to slouch in my seat like the other kids. Once I even interrupted to ask a question. In China, the only time we would interrupt the teacher would be if the building was on fire or one of the students was having a fit.

I began to eat lunch with Matthew and his friends. Third Sister looked relieved, because now she could sit and eat with her own friends.

Some of the boys made fun of my lunch, because I'd bring sandwiches with fillings like stir-fried bean sprouts. At first Matthew got angry when his friends laughed, but he soon saw that I didn't mind too much.

"Doesn't it bother you that those guys are always bugging you?" he asked afterward.

"No, it's okay," I said. "I'm used to it. I get a lot of it at home."

"You know, you're tough, Yingtao—a lot tougher than you look."

There was real admiration in his voice, and I suddenly felt twice as tall. There I was, Yang the scrawny, Yang the youngest, and my friend was telling me I was tough.

Just before our spring vacation, we had an assembly. All the classes in the school went into a huge auditorium, and we heard speeches by public officials. We had a lot of speeches in China, too, but they were different. Once I tried to tell Matthew, Jake and the others about the political speeches we had in China. But they didn't understand when I tried to explain. Maybe it was because I didn't understand, myself.

Our orchestra also played some pieces, and several players had solos, including Third Sister. But what I liked best on the program were the funny skits put on by the fifth grade students. In one of them, a tall boy sang a song in a high voice, just like a girl's. Then it turned out that he was only moving his lips, while a girl hiding behind a screen was doing the real singing. Matthew told me afterward that this was called lip sync.

After school one day, Matthew took me to a field nearby to watch him play baseball with the neighborhood boys' team. Before they started playing the game, they spent some time throwing the ball around. Matthew suddenly turned and threw the ball at me.

Without even thinking, I stretched out my arm and caught it. I loved the feeling of the ball smacking against my hand.

"Great catch!" cried the other boys.

I was so happy that I just stood there with a big grin on my face.

The coach came up to us and said, "Matthew, why don't you ask your friend if he'd like to play? Jerry can't come today."

"Sure," said Matthew happily. "I think Yingtao is dying to play." He turned to me. "Here, take my bat and go up to the plate."

For a second I just stared at him.

A bat is a small flying animal that is supposed to bring good luck, I thought. I looked at the big stick Matthew held out to me. Was this a bat, too?

I took the stick and looked around for the plate. We didn't use dinner plates in China, but I had eaten Western meals before, and I knew what plates looked like: big, flat, shiny, round things made of china (but not always from China).

"What are you waiting for?" asked the boy who was catcher. "Get over here!" He pointed to a spot in front of him on the ground, which was outlined in white chalk.

So that was the plate. It was hard enough to learn English, and now I was discovering that English words meant something completely different in baseball language. But I had to learn it if I wanted to play.

The pitcher stared at me for a moment, raised one leg high in the air, and suddenly threw the ball hard at me.

The ball shrank in size and looked no bigger than a walnut. How could I possibly hit that tiny thing?

Trying to remember what the other batters had done, I swung my bat furiously. I missed completely, and nearly lost my balance.

"Strike!" called the man who seemed to be acting as judge.

Strike? Why did he call it a strike? I hadn't struck the ball at all. I had missed. It didn't make sense at all.

The pitcher threw again. I could see that the ball was coming too low for me to hit it well, so I didn't even try to swing the bat.

"Ball!" called the judge.

Of course it was a ball. It was round, and besides, what else did you use in baseball? The judge didn't have to tell me. While I was still trying to make sense out of what was happening, the pitcher threw a ball at me again.

"Strike!" said the judge.

Did the judge have trouble with his eyes? Maybe he needed glasses. But to my surprise, everybody else seemed to agree with him. I was totally confused.

Again the pitcher threw while I was not ready, and again the judge yelled "Ball!"

I pulled myself together, and when the next ball came, I swung my bat hard. I heard a beautiful crack and knew that I had hit the ball at last. But the ball flew high up in the air and was caught by one of the players on the other team.

"Out!" cried the judge. I didn't need to be told what that meant.

Matthew came over and, to my surprise, told me that I had done well. "You could tell that ball was low, couldn't you?" he said. "I bet you'll make a great batter someday."

"Yeah, all he needs is a little practice," said another boy. Suddenly I found myself surrounded by people who actually approved of me. For an instant, I even thought I saw Eldest Brother among the others. But it turned out to be just an American boy who was slender and had black hair.

It was still wonderful to have people smiling at something I had done, instead of screwing up their faces with pain. I felt like floating away into the sky. I had often seen a happy, floating-away look on Eldest Brother's face when he played a piece he really liked. I had never thought I'd feel it myself.

From that day on, instead of walking home after school with Third Sister, I began to stop by the field with Matthew and practice baseball as often as I could. I felt a little guilty about it, because I knew I should have been spending the time practicing my violin. But I didn't feel *too* guilty, because I knew that it didn't make much difference whether I practiced or not. Third Sister knew how much I enjoyed baseball, and she didn't tell on me.

But I couldn't keep the baseball playing a secret. During one of my lessons with Father, he noticed that I was holding my bow differently. "What happened to your hand?" he asked, pointing to my knuckles, which were raw.

"I scraped my hand sliding on the ground," I mumbled. One of the other players had taught me how to slide in the dirt and to touch the home plate before the ball could reach the catcher.

Father frowned. "And just why have you been sliding on the ground?"

Bit by bit the truth came out. I had to tell him about baseball, about going to the field after school and playing on the neighborhood team.

I was afraid Father would be very angry. Instead, he looked sad. "Yingtao, your mother and I both know that you are less fond of music than your brother and sisters. It's clear that your heart isn't in your playing. But why don't you at least try harder— just this once, just for the recital? It's very important to me. It's important to our whole family."

He was begging. I hated to see Father like this. I'd rather have him shouting at me.

How could I tell him that with or without scraped knuckles, I would play miserably—that no matter how hard I tried, I simply could not play in tune? In our string quartet, I was about as useful as a rickshaw with one wheel.

It wouldn't be so bad if we weren't playing a string quartet. When I played in the orchestra or sang in a chorus, I had my usual ways to escape. But in a string quartet, there was no escape, no way for me to cover up.

"Father, why do you make us play a string quartet in the recital?" I asked. "Why can't you just have Eldest Brother play a solo?"

Father thought for a moment before answering my question. "I'll tell you why, Yingtao. When you're playing a solo piece, you care only about yourself. When you're playing in a large orchestra, you do what everyone else is doing. But in a quartet, you have to cooperate with the others, and at the same time you speak out for yourself. Each voice is heard. That's why I love string quartets best of all the different kinds of music."

I knew that he believed in letting each person speak out, in letting each voice be heard. We had heard him say it often. In China not everybody agreed with him. Once I overheard Mother telling him to be careful when he said that.

In most Chinese families, usually the father makes all the decisions and the rest silently accept them. But in our house Father would encourage us to speak out and let each voice in the family be heard. We loved him for it.

But it was because I loved him so much that I couldn't speak out. I knew that if I told him I hated the violin, it would hurt him deeply. The trouble is, in this case we would really be better off if the voice of my violin *couldn't* be heard.

After he started lessons from Eldest Brother, Matthew improved very fast. But in the school orchestra, he still sat with me in the back row, where the worst players were. The conductor was too busy to notice Matthew's improvement, and until there was another audition for all the players, Matthew would have to stay where he was.

He didn't say anything about it, but I knew he wanted some proof that he was getting better.

"My brother says that after only one month of lessons, you're already playing better than I did after four years of lessons," I told him.

He didn't look convinced. "Your brother was just being nice. My folks still hate the sound of my fiddle."

My family was getting used to having Matthew eat with us. By the time his lesson with Elder Brother was finished, it was often dinnertime already.

Matthew began to be embarrassed. "I'm eating dinner at your house a lot, lately. And I'm getting free music lessons, too."

"That's all right," I said. "We often have guests for dinner. We just set some extra plates and chopsticks and add water to the soup."

"But how do you know if you'll have enough food to go around?"

"Everybody just eats a little less. We can always fill up on rice."

"You must run out of rice a lot then," said Matthew.

He was right. We needed more rice that very afternoon. Usually, Second Sister went shopping with Mother, but she was in one of her moods today.

"Matthew and I can go and carry for you," I said to Mother.

Looking first at me and then at Matthew, Mother smiled. "Since there are two of you to help carry, I'll buy a big sack of rice this time—a fifty-pound bag."

Even with the two of us, we were panting hard when we finally heaved the sack of rice into the bus. Matthew didn't believe me at first when I told him that we would eat up all the rice in about two months.

"Gee, I don't know how you stay so skinny when you eat so much!" he said.

"Hey, Matthew!" somebody yelled when we had entered the bus and arranged the sack of rice at our feet. "What have you got there? Cement?"

It was Jake, the boy who had taken my pen during recess at school. He came over to look at the sack. "Phoenix Brand Fragrant Rice, fifty pounds," he said, reading the label.

Then he grinned. "If you eat all this, Matthew, the curl will go out of your hair, and you'll have straight black hair like your Chinese friend here."

Jake went back to his friends at the back of the bus, and I heard laughter.

Matthew pretended not to hear, but his face turned a little red. For the first time, I realized that being friends with me could be embarrassing for him.

But that didn't stop Matthew from staying to dinner that evening. He was using chopsticks pretty well by now, and he only dropped a few things on the table. He even ate a little fish.

Matthew looked up from his fish bones. "Can I stay around and listen to the quartet practice tonight?" he asked Father.

"Of course you can!" said Father, looking pleased. He turned to me. "See how serious your friend is about music, Yingtao. You can learn from his example."

"Maybe he can even play your part in the quartet for a little while," suggested Mother. "Then you can hear how it's *supposed* to sound."

Mother didn't say this to be cruel. She really thought it would improve my "attitude." Except for Third Sister, everybody in the family had been saying things like this for years. I should have been used to it, but somehow it felt worse when they said it in front of my friend.

So Matthew stayed in the living room with us while we set up the stands and put out the music for the quartet.

As usual we had to stop after playing only a few bars, and the place where we stopped was the place where I started playing. Eldest Brother screwed up his face. He looked like someone who had bitten into a green persimmon.

I glanced at Matthew and saw the same suffering on his face, although he tried not to show it. For a moment I felt bad. Even my best friend couldn't stand my playing.

Oh, well, if my own brother and sisters couldn't bear to listen, how could I expect a friend to?

Then, Second Sister remembered Mother's suggestion. "Fourth Brother, why don't you let Matthew play the second violin part? Just so that you get an idea."

I got up and let him take my seat. Standing by myself in a corner, I watched the four of them start to play.

At first Matthew made some mistakes, mostly in counting time. The music was new to him, after all. But he learned quickly, and soon he was playing away. I saw Eldest Brother nod. Even his fussy ear was satisfied.

It was true that Matthew's curly brown hair looked funny, surrounded by the straight black hair of the Yangs. But as Jake had said in the bus, maybe if he ate enough rice . . .

Suddenly I felt an ache in my chest. I wasn't exactly jealous of Matthew—after all, he was my best friend, and I was the one who had invited him over. But I felt left out.

After that, Matthew came regularly to our rehearsals. Second Sister would stop the playing after about ten bars into the quartet. "Why don't you let Matthew take over, Fourth Brother," she would say. "Then you can hear how your part is supposed to sound."

So Matthew ended up playing the second violin part most of the time. None of the others objected.

Then one day, he told me in school that he wouldn't be able to come to my house that afternoon for his lesson with Elder Brother.

"My parents think that I'm spending too much time at your house," he said.

"What's wrong with that?" I asked. Then an uncomfortable thought struck me. "Is it because we're Chinese?"

"No, of course not!" Matthew said quickly—maybe too quickly? "See, I'm eating dinner with you a couple of times a week already, and my mom is embarrassed about that."

"She doesn't have to be," I told him. "We still have about thirty pounds of rice left. And you can help me carry another fifty-pound sack if we run out."

Matthew shook his head. "I don't know. But I'll work on my mom and try to change her mind."

A couple of days later he said his parents had invited me over to dinner at his house.

I suspected they wanted to look me over. I knew that when I went to Matthew's house that evening, I had to make a really good impression.

4

Mr. Conner, Matthew's father, opened the door. "Hello, you must be . . . uh . . ." He turned to Matthew.

"This is Yingtao," said Matthew.

"Sorry," said Mr. Conner. "I have a hard time with Chinese names."

"That's okay," I told him. "I have a hard time with American names."

Mr. Conner looked startled. Maybe he wasn't expecting me to speak whole sentences.

"Your mom's getting some groceries," he said to Matthew. "Supper will be a little late."

"Come on, let's go to my room," Matthew said to me.

"Shouldn't we go to the store and help your mother carry the groceries home?" I asked.

"It's all right," said Matthew. "Mom's driving."

I was surprised. Since Matthew had told me that his father had lost his job and couldn't afford to pay for music lessons, I expected the Conner family to be really poor. "Your family can afford to drive a car?" I asked.

Now Matthew looked surprised. "Of course. Everybody drives."

"In China, only officials and executives of big companies have cars," I told him.

The Conners certainly didn't look poor. Their house was made of wood, painted in a nice light blue color, and it had a yard both in front and in back, with neatly cut lawns.

"Do you share your house with another family?" I asked.

Matthew shook his head. "Nope. We have it all to ourselves. Eric and I each have our own room."

I looked around in wonder at the spacious living room with its matching sofa and armchairs, and at the dining room, which had a table, matching dining chairs, and cupboards.

"I really like your house," I told Matthew.

Matthew looked pleased. "Dad bought this house cheap and fixed it up. Eric and I helped him."

I was impressed. "You really helped him with the carpentry work?"

"Well, we mostly handed him his tools," admitted Matthew. "But he did let us pound a few nails."

I couldn't imagine Father working on a house. In China, when something needed to be done in our apartment, we just called in a carpenter. We even had a carpenter come in to make beds for us. It was cheaper than buying ready-made beds. After we came to America, Eldest Brother got a hammer and did a little repair work, but I didn't think he would ask me to help him.

"It must be nice to help your father fix up your own house," I said wistfully. "We're renting, and we can afford only half of a house. We all have to double up in the bedrooms."

"Well, that's because you're newcomers to this country," said Matthew. "I bet you had more room back in China."

I nearly laughed. "In China, all four of us had to share one bedroom. We ate our meals in the living room, and that's where my parents slept at night. At least we were lucky and had our own kitchen."

"You mean some apartments don't have their own kitchens?" asked Matthew, surprised.

"Most of them don't. Many of our friends had to share a kitchen with two or even four other families. We had to share a bathroom and toilet with our neighbors across the hall."

Matthew looked stunned. "But . . . but . . . your brother has that beautiful violin. You all have expensive instruments. Your family can't be that hard up!"

"We *have* to have good instruments," I said. "According to Father, you can't make good music without good instruments."

But you can have a good instrument and still make terrible music, I said to myself. Matthew was silent and thoughtful as we went up the stairs to his room.

I found his room filled with furniture. Besides a bed, he had a bookshelf, a desk, and a chest with six drawers. The windows even had cloth curtains with ruffles.

In the room I shared with Elder Brother, there were only rolled shades. We pulled them down when the sun was in our eyes, but they would roll up with a loud snap, especially when I was practicing. I still couldn't get used to them.

I went around, admiring Matthew's room. The walls were almost completely covered with photographs. They were divided into two kinds: pictures of baseball players and pictures of violinists.

It was funny, seeing the photo of a ballplayer in his uniform holding a bat, and next to it the photo of a musician in a tuxedo holding a violin and a bow. I laughed.

"You're just like my brother Eric," grumbled Matthew. "He thinks you can't be a baseball fan and a music fan at the same time."

Matthew looked annoyed, so I changed the subject and asked him about his father. "What did your father do before he lost his job?"

"He was a machinist," said Matthew. "He got laid off when his company shut down one of their plants here."

"Laid off? Was he hurt badly?"

Matthew looked puzzled. "I didn't say he was hurt."

"But . . . but . . . I thought he was laid off on a stretcher or something."

"Oh boy, here we go again," said Matthew. He took a deep breath. " 'Laid off' doesn't have anything to do with lying down. It's another way of saying he lost his job."

"Oh. That's too bad. How long ago did he get . . . er . . . laid off?"

"It's been more than two months now."

"No wonder you don't have money for music lessons," I said. Matthew had been surprised because we had expensive instruments, but no money for furniture. The Conners had a big, beautiful house full of furniture, but no money for music lessons. Did they have money for food?

I started to worry about dinner. Somehow I didn't think the Conners bought fifty-pound bags of rice. "Will you have enough food tonight if I eat here?"

"Look, we're not exactly starving around here!" Matthew looked a little offended by my question, and also by my reminder that he didn't have enough money for music lessons.

"I'm sorry," I said quickly. "I didn't mean . . ."

"No, that's okay. Dad has unemployment benefits, and Mom has a part-time job. Besides, both Eric and I have paper routes."

"A paper route." I chewed over the words. Sometimes, if I say the words very, very slowly, they begin to make sense. But not this time.

Matthew explained. "A paper route means delivering newspapers. Every morning we go around and throw newspapers on people's front porches. We do it before going to school."

"That means you have to get up early in the morning," I said, feeling sorry for him. I felt sorry for anyone who had to get up early.

Matthew shrugged. "It's not too bad. Eric and I make good money. We earn enough to buy our own clothes and games and stuff."

He looked at me curiously. "Don't you guys work? How about your sisters? Do they make any money baby-sitting?"

"Baby-sitting?"

"You know, sit babies, when their parents go out," Matthew said patiently—maybe too patiently.

Talking to Americans is like walking along a country footpath in China. You think the path is nice and firm, but your foot suddenly slips on a muddy stretch and you land with a big splash in a wet rice paddy.

My family tries hard to study English. Whenever we come across a strange word, we look it up in a dictionary. But knowing what each word means isn't always enough.

"You mean sit a baby down on a chair?" I finally asked Matthew. "Why should my sisters earn any money doing that?"

Matthew tugged at his hair. He did this a lot when we talked together. Another thing he did was to take a few deep breaths. He did this now. "Forget it. Do you and your brother and sisters earn any money?"

"Why should we?" I asked, puzzled. "We've got enough to eat, and we have a nice apartment. It's not as nice as your house, but it's good enough for us."

Matthew looked really shocked.

"Everybody needs some spending money! I mean, you can't beg your parents for money every time you go to the movies, or something."

I began to feel uncomfortable. "It's true we ask our parents for money if we want to go to the movies. But we don't go a lot, and we don't really go down on our knees to beg."

"In America, most kids get a job and earn their own pocket money. Besides, it helps their parents out."

"We can't get a job," I said. "We're still going to school."

"Yeah? Well, Eric and I go to school, too. I mean, don't you earn money in your extra time?"

"We spend all our extra time studying and practicing music. We don't have any time left for jobs."

Matthew frowned. "I guess that's why my dad doesn't want me to take music lessons. It's not just the money. Maybe he thinks practicing music wastes too much time."

My parents believed that practicing music was never a waste of time. In my case they were wrong, but nothing could change their minds.

Before we could say any more, a boy's voice called, "Supper's ready!"

We ran downstairs. I was introduced to Mrs. Conner, who looked tired. She brushed a damp curl from her forehead, smiled quickly, and began to carry dishes of food from the kitchen.

"Aw, not tuna casserole again!" said Eric, Matthew's older brother.

"Say hello to Matthew's friend," growled Mr. Conner.

Eric rolled his eyes, but he did say "Hi" to me. Then he went back to glaring at the tuna dish in the middle of the table.

I couldn't understand why Eric didn't like tuna. I found it delicious. Seafood is expensive in China, and I like it better than meat. I hoped that Mrs. Conner didn't have to spend a lot of money on the dinner—not when Mr. Conner was out of work, not when Matthew didn't have money for music lessons.

There wasn't much talk at the dinner table. Mr. Conner ate slowly but deliberately. I remembered that Matthew had said his father was a machinist. Maybe he liked things to work smoothly. Mrs. Conner was busy passing the dishes of food around.

I felt the eyes of the whole Conner family on me, and I knew they were waiting to see if I'd do something funny, like bringing the salad bowl to my mouth and drinking up the dressing left at the bottom.

In fact that was what I had tried to do the first time we went to McDonald's and had their salad. But Mother had stopped me. When we got home, she gave us all a lesson in the proper way to eat in America. She also bought us a book on etiquette.

At least learning to eat in America was a lot easier than learning to talk. We learned how to use a knife and fork, not to slurp the spaghetti, not to hunch over the dinner plate, and so on. We just followed the rules. It's not like talking, when you carefully look up new words in a dictionary, and still fall into traps about being laid off and baby-sitting.

At first the Conners looked a little disappointed when I didn't do anything strange. But after a while I saw them relax, and soon they began to chat.

Eric picked out the green peas in the tuna dish. "Matthew told me you ate live fish," he said to me. "This tuna probably looks pretty tame to you."

"Live fish?" I didn't know what he meant.

"Live carp," he said, "that you scoop up from your bathtub."

"Eric, the carp was alive in the tub, but they cooked it afterward," said Matthew, his face turning red. "Why don't you ever listen?"

I enjoyed hearing the phrase "Why don't you ever listen?" being said to somebody else for a change. Did Eric have a terrible ear, too?

I was also a little surprised that Matthew had spoken that way to Eric, his elder brother. In our family, I had to speak respectfully to Eldest Brother, Second Sister, and Third Sister, although they could all be insulting to me, the youngest Yang.

But Eric only scowled at his younger brother and went back to picking out peas.

Mr. Conner turned to me. "Matthew says your family is really musical."

"Not me," I said. "I'm terrible at music."

"I'm sure you're just being modest," said Mrs. Conner.

"No, he really is awful," said Matthew. "He's probably the worst player in our orchestra—and that's saying a lot!"

"Matthew!" said his mother. "That's no way to talk about your friend!"

I had to show them I wasn't angry. "Matthew is right. I have a terrible ear. I wish I never had to touch my violin again."

Mr. Conner looked up from his plate. "Is that a fact? Then why do you play?"

"My parents make me," I mumbled.

"Oh, you poor thing," said Mrs. Conner. Her eyes were warm with sympathy. "Here, have some more tuna casserole."

Even Eric seemed more friendly. "If you don't like music, what do you like?"

"When I went to school in China, what I liked best was gymnastics."

I had never said this to my family. And here, on my very first visit, I was telling the Conners.

Eric made a face. "Gymnastics? It's mostly girls who go in for that."

"I like other sports, too," I said. "Matthew took me to watch him and his friends play baseball. I even play sometimes. It's really fun."

Mr. Conner smiled. "Hey, that's great. Baseball is our national sport. If you like baseball, you'll be right at home here."

He turned to Matthew. "I'm glad you made friends with . . . uh. . . ."

"Yingtao," I supplied.

"Yeah, with Yingtao. A boy should have lots of different interests and not spend all his time on music."

Mrs. Conner smiled, too. "We were getting embarrassed because Matthew was eating dinner at your house so much. I'm glad you could come over here for a change."

"Maybe we can go out in the yard and hit a few balls later," Eric said to me.

After dinner Matthew helped his mother wash the dishes. I started to join them. "Guests don't have to do the dishes," said Eric. "Come on, let's go outside."

Eric brought his baseball out into the yard, and we began to practice throwing.

"Hey, not bad!" he said, when I jumped up to catch a throw that almost sailed into the neighbor's yard.

"Matthew taught me how to do that," I said.

At the mention of his brother, Eric made a face. "Matthew is no fun anymore, now that he's into music."

I wasn't quite sure what he meant. "Why not? You mean he's too busy to play with you?"

Eric looked at his feet. "He looks like such a nerd, carrying that violin case around!"

"What's a nerd?" This word hadn't come up on any of Third Sister's lists.

"A nerd is . . . well, a wimp."

"What's a wimp?" That was another word not on Third Sister's lists.

Eric tugged at his hair. Maybe this was a habit that ran in the Conner family. "It's . . . it's kind of a sissy."

Finally a word I knew. A sissy was someone who was afraid of everything. Matthew was one of the bigger boys in our class, and I had never seen him looking afraid. "I don't think Matthew is a sissy at all."

"The other kids laugh and call him Matthew the Boy Genius," muttered Eric.

"I'm sure what the other kids say doesn't bother Matthew," I told Eric.

"Well, it bothers *me*," grumbled Eric. "And it bothers my dad, too."

I had learned something. In America, it seemed that playing a violin made a boy a nerd, a wimp, a sissy.

"My elder brother and I both play the violin," I said.

Eric shuffled his feet. "That's different. You're Chinese. Everybody knows Chinese kids do that kind of thing—you know—study hard, play the violin."

"Does that mean Chinese kids are all nerds?"

"Not you!" Eric said quickly. "You're all right."

"My folks liked you," Matthew told me later as I was getting ready to leave. "Now that they've met you, they aren't worried anymore."

I was puzzled. "Why were they worried?"

Matthew looked away. "I guess they were afraid that I'd get even more involved with music if I went to your house so much. But you told them you liked sports, so now they think you're okay."

I had passed the test. Matthew's parents thought I was good for him.

"You know, you're really lucky!" Matthew said suddenly.

I was surprised. "You're the one who's lucky. You're musical. My brother says so, and so does my father."

"But at *your* house, people are happy when you make music," Matthew said in a low voice. "At *my* house, people say, 'Oh, not that again!' when I play my violin."

"At my house, people are *not* happy when I make music," I said. "People say, 'Oh, not that again!' when *I'm* the one who is playing the violin."

We looked at each other. "Too bad we can't trade places," sighed Matthew.

That was when I had my brilliant idea. "Maybe," I said slowly, "we can."

Lip sync, that was the idea. Only it wouldn't be lip sync, but bow sync. Matthew would hide behind a screen at the recital and play my part while I moved my bow back and forth silently.

Matthew was shocked when I told him about my idea. "Sure, I want to help you, Yingtao, but this is crazy! We'll never get away with it!"

"It's not crazy," I insisted. "I've had lots of practice moving my bow in time to the music. Don't you want to play in the quartet? This is your chance."

It took a while, but I finally convinced him.

He even began to look excited. "If I can perform with your brother and sister in a real recital, it'll prove that I'm good," he said softly. Lately Matthew had sounded discouraged because in the school orchestra he was still seated next to me, in the very last row.

"You must know by now that you're talented," I said. "My brother and sisters all say so."

"They're just saying that to be nice," he muttered.

"Then why can't they tell *me* I'm talented and be nice to me, too?" I demanded.

Matthew grinned. "Because they know you wouldn't believe them." He became serious. "Maybe they keep saying how good I am to make you work harder, to improve your so-called attitude."

"Well, if that's what you believe," I said quickly, "then you should certainly play in the recital. It will be a test, sort of." I added, "But you can't tell anyone."

"No, but I'll prove something to *myself*," he said. "That's all I care about."

Looking at his shining eyes, I knew that Matthew really loved music. He didn't play to impress an audience, to hear people clapping for him. He would play his heart out even if nobody could see him.

This was what a real music lover was like. I remembered the times when Eldest Brother played a piece alone in his room, not to practice for a lesson or a recital—just because he enjoyed playing.

Since Matthew had already been practicing the second violin part of the quartet, he didn't even need to rehearse with the others. All we had to do was arrange for him to play in the recital itself.

First, we needed a screen to hide him—and I knew just what we could use. Mother had bought an old folding screen at a garage sale, and she was planning to fix it up and use it to divide our dining area from the living room.

"You know the screen you bought last week?" I said to Mother. "Can we use it for the recital?"

"What for?" she asked. "It needs paint, and one of the hinges is broken."

"It'll look more like a stage that way," I said. "Don't we want things to look nice?"

Second Sister sniffed. "Why don't you worry less about the look of the recital and more about the sound?"

When I told Matthew about using the screen, he thought for a moment. "Maybe Mary can help us sell the idea of a screen to your family," he said finally.

"Who's Mary?" I asked, puzzled.

He stared at me. "Who's Mary? How can you forget your own sister's name?"

In fact I had forgotten my sister's name. Third Sister hadn't told the rest of the family that she had chosen the English name of Mary, and she was called that only by her friends at school.

I guess Second Sister was too proud to change her name in order to join the crowd. Unlike Third Sister, who had already changed her haircut to look more like the other girls in school, Second Sister still wore her hair in two long braids, exactly the way she had done in China.

I agreed with Matthew that it would be a good idea to get Third Sister's help. The very next day after school, we talked to her about our plan. As we had hoped, she approved.

"You're right, this is our only way to save the recital." Then she added, "You can't make a silk purse out of a sow's ear."

These days Third Sister wasn't satisfied with learning five new words every day. She was beginning to make lists of whole new sentences that would be useful.

I didn't understand, and she had to explain that she meant we could never make a tone-deaf person (a sow's ear) into a violinist (a silk purse).

Maybe I had a terrible ear, but I thought that comparing me to a sow was not very kind.

The important thing, though, was that Third Sister helped us to convince the family. She announced that we should have a pair of Chinese scenes painted on the folding screen.

That got Second Sister interested. She was the best one in the family with the Chinese brush, and she offered to do some brush paintings.

Even Mother liked the idea. "Some Chinese pictures would make a fine background. If we do a good job, we can use the screen for all our future recitals."

Using a thick Chinese brush and black ink, Second Sister painted two long and narrow pictures, one for each panel of the screen. The first one showed some rocky mountains covered with pine trees, and the second one showed a little boat going down the river.

I was surprised at how much time she spent on the paintings. After school one day, I saw her bent over the dining table, with a long piece of paper spread out in front of her. By her elbow was the inkstone, which we had brought with us from China. It's a flat piece of carved stone, with a depression in the middle. You put a few drops of water in and rub an ink stick against the bottom of the depression until you get a pool of thick, black ink.

Second Sister was holding her brush over the pool of ink, and suddenly I saw a drop of water splash down. It didn't come from the brush. It came from higher up. Another drop plopped into the ink. Second Sister was crying!

Of all the Yangs, she was the most homesick for China. Father was too busy working to support the family, and Mother spent all her time trying to feed us. Eldest Brother was totally wrapped up in his music, and I had Matthew's friendship and baseball to console me. Third Sister already felt at home in America. But Second Sister still missed her old country and her old friends.

She must have heard me come in. She quickly put down her brush and took out a handkerchief to blow her nose.

I tried to find something comforting to say. "I like that picture of the little boat. It reminds me of the time when we went to see the canals in Changzhou."[1]

Second Sister cleared her throat. "I'm surprised you still remember China."

"Of course I do!" I looked away, while she wiped her eyes. "I'm glad you're painting those pictures. Now we'll always have them to remind us of our old life."

---

1. A city in eastern China, slightly northwest of Shanghai and on the Grand Canal.

I heard some snuffles. After a moment, Second Sister said huskily, "You're actually a pretty nice boy, Fourth Brother . . ."

Was this the start of a new relationship between us? Would she pick on me a little less from now on?

". . . when you don't have a violin under your chin," she finished.

Oh, well.

After the paintings were done, we all got to work. Eldest Brother put some new screws into the hinges holding the two panels of the screen together. Third Sister and I pasted Second Sister's paintings on the frame.

I had to make sure that Matthew, sitting behind the screen, could see Eldest Brother through the crack where the two panels were joined. He had to be able to see so he could come in together with the others.

Third Sister and I tried out the screen in the living room, and I was glad to find that I could see through the crack.

Matthew said he knew his part and expected to have no trouble with it. Everything seemed to be going well until our parents started to complain.

The trouble was that Matthew and I were spending a lot of time together, both in and out of school. Almost every afternoon, I went to practice baseball after school, and when I was finally accepted as a regular member of the team, it was the proudest moment of my life.

One day Mr. Conner came to the playfield after school. He was substituting for our baseball coach, who was out of town.

"I almost got to play professionally," he told me. "Missed by a hair getting into one of the minor leagues."

He looked so happy, throwing the ball into the air, that I couldn't help grinning. "I'm glad you're here, Mr. Conner."

"Haven't got anything else to do, now that I'm out of work," he growled.

"I hope you can help me with my batting," I said quickly.

"You bet . . . uh . . ."

"Yingtao," I said.

"Yeah, Yingtao. You're keen, and that's what counts. You'll make a great batter someday."

He showed me how to hold my shoulders so I could put all my strength into the swing. I was smaller than the other players, and not as strong, so I could not hit the ball as far as the rest.

But I soon found that I had one talent. I could see exactly how a ball was coming at me: whether it was high, low, off to one side, and whether it was turning as it came—had a spin, as the others said.

This helped me a lot in deciding whether to hit the ball and how to hit it. That's why I was able to get some base hits, although I seldom got a double or a triple. As for a home run, it was an impossible dream.

Matthew's room had pictures of great home run hitters of the past, like Babe Ruth,[2] the Sultan of Swat. But they were mythical figures to me, like the Monkey King[3] in my favorite Chinese story.

Still, even getting just one-base hits, I was counted as a definite plus on our team.

2. George Herman Ruth (1895–1948), a baseball player who spent most of his career with the New York Yankees (1920–35); his record of 714 home runs stood for 39 years.

3. Mischievous protagonist from the Chinese folktale *Journey to the West* (1553), by Wu Cheng-en.

The best part was when I came up to bat in the game and saw that the people were looking at me hopefully instead of cringing.

Mr. Conner was delighted when I got a hit that not only put me on first base but sent the boy on third base home. "Good work!" he yelled, and almost jumped up and down in his excitement.

Our team tied the score and needed only one more run to win. Two men were out already, but we had one man on first and one on second.

Matthew came up to bat. He was a good hitter, so we had a real chance to make that run.

The pitcher wound up and threw. Even from where I stood, I could see the ball was high. I wanted to shout to Matthew, "Don't hit it!"

But he swung hard, and the ball flew high into the air. The boy in the outfield caught it easily, and our side was retired.

In the last inning, the other team made another run and won the game. The person who felt the loss most was Mr. Conner.

"Aw, come on, Dad," said Matthew, patting his father on the back. "It's not the end of the world! We've lost before, and we'll probably lose again. We'll probably win again, too."

Mr. Conner shook Matthew's hand off. "Not if you keep on playing like that! You popped that fly because you weren't paying attention! Anybody could've seen that ball was high! Anybody except my musical genius son!"

I tried to distract him. "Is that why Babe Ruth is called the Sultan of Swat? Because he hit flies?"

Some of the boys laughed, and after a moment, even Mr. Conner had to smile. "A wise guy, huh? Besides making base hits, you make jokes, too?"

But Mr. Conner soon went back to his grumbling. "You know what's wrong with you?" he said to his son. "You're not concentrating."

Walking behind the Conners, I had a strange feeling as I listened to the tone of Mr. Conner's voice. Suddenly it reminded me of *my* father.

The Saturday before the recital, the Conners invited me to go with them to a Mariners[4] game at the Kingdome. My brother and sisters were going to spend the whole weekend practicing, but since practicing wouldn't do me any good, I immediately accepted. Father was at the Seattle Symphony playing in an afternoon concert, and Mother was off shopping. So without asking for permission, I just went.

I enjoyed the game too much to think about the rest of them busy practicing at home. Even though the Mariners lost, it was great to see real professionals playing. This must be how Eldest Brother felt that time in China when he got to hear Isaac Stern[5] play in a concert.

I eagerly watched how the pitcher warmed up, how the batter tested the weight of the bat, how the outfielder ran backward to catch a fly ball.

When I told Mr. Conner afterward how much I loved the game, he was very pleased. "You know how to keep your eyes open, kid. I bet you learned a few things today."

The wonderful feeling from the game disappeared when I walked in our front door. Father had returned and was waiting for me with a stony face. "Where

---

4. The American League baseball team in Seattle; from the inception of the franchise in 1977 until 1999, the Mariners played in the Kingdome.

5. Russian-born American violinist (1920–2001), one of the great virtuosos of the twentieth century.

have you been?" he demanded. "Have you forgotten that the recital is only one week away?"

I couldn't meet his eyes. "The Conners invited me to go with them to a baseball game."

Father took a deep breath. "Yingtao," he said finally, "you must know by now that you need the practice more than your brother and your sisters. Don't you care about the recital at all?" He didn't look angry, only terribly sad.

I wanted to tell him that I did care about the recital, that I cared a lot. But he went on. "From now on, there will be no more baseball for you until your violin playing improves."

I crept up to my room. "Until your violin playing improves . . ." This meant that I might never play baseball again.

Matthew was having problems, too. Everybody started calling him "Matthew the Musical Genius." Once Jake said, "Hey, Matthew, why don't you play on street corners, so people can throw coins in your violin case? Think how much money you can make!"

Usually Matthew turned red when he was embarrassed. But this time he turned white. I knew that he was sensitive about money and was very upset because his father wasn't working.

Also, practicing in the quartet cut into his time for baseball. By the time he finally got his homework done, he always went to bed late. Then he had to get up early in the morning to deliver papers.

This made him so sleepy that when he was up at bat, he kept striking out.

"Hey, Matthew, wake up!" the coach would yell at him.

There was worse to come. The team had an important game coming up, and Matthew had forgotten even to show up for practice. I wouldn't have forgotten—ever—but I wasn't there to remind him.

Mr. Conner was furious when Eric told him what had happened. He said that Matthew could not go to our house for more music until his baseball improved.

Since Father had forbidden me to play baseball, I had to get news about the team from Matthew during lunch hour.

"What are we going to do?" asked Matthew. He looked tired, and there were circles under his eyes. I knew he was working too hard. This recital meant as much to him as it did to me. If he didn't get to play, he would be crushed. If he played and played badly, he would be even more crushed.

"You're not getting enough sleep," I said. "Maybe if you didn't have to get up so early in the morning . . ."

"I need the paper route," Matthew said in a low voice. "Our family needs the money."

I knew it upset him to admit that. But why should it? It wasn't his fault, and he couldn't do anything about it.

Or could he? With the money they earned, Matthew and Eric paid for their own clothes and school supplies. So they could help their parents quite a lot.

What Matthew had said about his paper route made me thoughtful. Could I earn some money and help my family, too?

Whenever I went grocery shopping with my mother, I noticed that she had to count up all the nickels and dimes carefully. She was always trying to find bargains.

One day she noticed the grocer pulling the green leaves from the broccoli stalks. "What are you going to do with these leaves?" she asked him.

The grocer turned around. "These leaves? We throw them away. They just take up space in the bin, and our customers don't eat them, anyway."

"Then can you give them to me?" asked Mother.

"Sure. You got rabbits or guinea pigs to feed?"

"I've got my family to feed," replied Mother. "These leaves are delicious, and they're full of vitamins."

The grocer was a huge man, and when he looked down at Mother, who was tiny, he grinned. "Tell you what. From now on, I'll save these leaves. Any time you come in, I'll have a bag waiting for you. And if I'm not here, just tell the other grocer that Al wants you to have the broccoli leaves."

Mother had a soft voice, but she somehow got people to do what she wanted. We've been eating free broccoli leaves ever since. To me they taste better than the stalks.

But once when I was helping Mother carry away her usual bags of leaves, I overheard two women talking by the fruit bins.

"Look at those Chinese over there taking away those huge bags of broccoli leaves," said one of them. "Are they really going to eat all that stuff?"

The other one giggled. "I hear that the Chinese will eat almost anything."

It's true that since there are too many people in China and not enough food, we would eat everything that's not a deadly poison. But the two women obviously thought that eating broccoli leaves was something shameful.

I stole a look at Mother and saw that she was biting her lips. For a couple of weeks afterward, we had other vegetables for dinner. But in the end we went back to broccoli leaves.

Sometimes, when I looked at Mother spending so much time cooking, I felt very sorry for her. Her fine pianist's hands, which used to spend so much time over the keyboard, were now rough from washing vegetables and scaling fish.

If I could earn some money like Matthew and his brother, then Mother wouldn't have to work quite so hard trying to save money. Maybe I could deliver newspapers, too.

"Can I go with you on your paper round next time?" I asked him during school orchestra.

By now Matthew was getting used to my brand of English. "Paper route, you mean," he corrected. "Sure. But you have to get up early."

I could hardly believe it when he told me just how early. No wonder he was so sleepy. At five o'clock the next morning, I was struggling to put my clothes on in the darkness.

"Is it time to get up already?" mumbled Eldest Brother.

"No, it's early. I'm getting up because I'm going out with Matthew on his paper road."

"You're crazy," groaned Eldest Brother, burying his head under the covers again.

In Shanghai, we sometimes got up very early on summer mornings because it was so hot that morning was the only comfortable time. But this wasn't summer. I shivered as I hurried to Matthew's house.

He was already waiting for me at the front door. "What kept you?" he asked. "We've got to hurry, since we have to fold the papers first."

My fingers were stiff with cold when I started to help Matthew fold the papers, but they soon warmed up. Then I watched Matthew throw papers at the houses along his route. "Do you want to try?" he asked after a while.

In the beginning I missed a few times, and some of the papers fell short or landed in bushes. I had to pick them up and throw all over again.

But my aim improved, and soon I was throwing the papers as accurately as thew. "It's just like throwing the ball from first base to the pitcher!" I exclaimed.

By the time we reached the end of Matthew's paper road—route—it was daylight, and I was starving.

Matthew looked at me gratefully. "I got through a lot sooner because you were helping. You're really good at throwing. I bet you can get a job delivering papers if you want."

When he told me how much he earned, I was amazed. If I could get a job like this, it would really help our family. But would my parents let me?

I wasn't the only one in the family thinking about getting a job. Third Sister looked thoughtful at dinner that evening. She finally cleared her throat. "My shoes are wearing out. I saw some running shoes on sale at the store today. All the girls in school are wearing them."

Mother sighed. "You know we can't afford to buy you new shoes right now. You'll just have to have the old ones repaired."

"Maybe I can get a job and earn some money," Third Sister said brightly.

"A young girl like you, getting a job?" asked Mother, looking surprised. "What could you possibly do?"

"She can baby-sit," I said. I turned to Second Sister. "You can do it, too. Baby-sitting doesn't mean just sitting the baby in a chair. It means taking care of somebody's baby while the parents go out."

"You don't have to give me a lecture," snapped Second Sister. "I know what baby-sitting means. My friends in school told me about it."

I was surprised. It seems that Second Sister did not spend all her time brooding and longing for the old days in China. She had even made friends.

Second Sister turned to Mother. "Some of the girls earn a lot of money baby-sitting. If Third Sister and I do it every weekend, we can really help with the expenses. I think Mrs. Schultz might give me a job."

Mrs. Schultz was the mother of Father's youngest violin student, Peter. Second Sister often played with him until his mother came to pick him up. Once she was teaching him some Chinese children's games, and Mrs. Schultz was impressed.

Mother looked doubtful. "I can't imagine that parents will want to trust their babies to strange young girls." Then she added in a soft voice, "Especially Chinese girls."

The tone of Mother's voice was a shock. Had someone jeered at her because she was Chinese? She had never mentioned any unpleasant experiences before.

Then I thought of the two women in the grocery store who had laughed at her for taking away big bags of broccoli greens. For some minutes we ate in uncomfortable silence.

Finally Father broke the silence. "No! I will not have any of my children earning money with little jobs outside the house! Young people should concentrate on what is important. You should not sacrifice your schoolwork and your music just to earn money for a pair of shoes."

"But . . ." Third Sister began.

Father was firm. "Music is more important than money."

We went back to eating dinner in silence. I was getting sleepy, and when I put down my rice bowl, I smothered a yawn.

Eldest Brother looked at me. "You got up too early this morning. What were you doing out of bed at five?"

This was not the time to tell everybody that I went out with Matthew because I was hoping to earn some money delivering newspapers. So I just mumbled something.

But that didn't stop everybody from staring at me. Father frowned. "If you have the energy to get up at five o'clock, you can surely spare some of it for your music! It's just a matter of channeling your energies into something worthwhile. You're a healthy, lively boy, Yingtao. Stop frittering yourself away on frivolous activities! Have you forgotten that the recital is coming up?"

Matthew and I saw less of each other, now that I had stopped playing baseball, and he had stopped coming over to our house for quartet practice. I was getting more and more worried about the recital.

"Will you still be able to play?" I asked Matthew, first thing on Monday.

"Yeah, sure, I try to get some practicing done when nobody's home," he replied quickly. But I couldn't tell if he was just saying that to stop me from worrying.

At my house, tempers were getting short. I was playing the second violin part all the time now, and the sound got on everyone's nerves.

One night, after some particularly hard measures, Eldest Brother threw his bow down. "We were doing so well for a while! What's wrong with you, Fourth Brother?"

Eldest Brother rarely lost his temper. We knew things were really getting serious.

Even Third Sister looked worried. She pulled me aside when we finished playing. "The recital is only a couple of days away," she whispered. "What's happened to Matthew? Does this mean he won't be playing after all?" She looked sick at the prospect.

"Matthew will play," I said with more confidence than I felt.

Then on Friday, the day before the recital, my parents did something that would make it quite impossible for Matthew to play.

6

It happened at dinner.

"The quartet sounds just awful," Second Sister said gloomily. "It was much better when Matthew sat in with us. I think Fourth Brother always improved when his friend was around to encourage him."

"What's happened to Matthew?" Eldest Brother asked me. "Why hasn't he been coming lately? He didn't even show up for his lessons."

I stared down into my rice bowl. "His father got mad at him because he was spending too much time on music and not enough time on his baseball. So he won't let Matthew come to our house anymore."

I looked up and saw the Yang family in shock. Father's hand was suspended in air as he reached for a piece of fish. Mother's chopsticks were frozen halfway to her mouth. Eldest Brother's spoon was dripping soup on the table. Second Sister and Third Sister sat with their mouths opening and closing, like a pair of goldfish.

Our family could not imagine a father scolding his son for spending *too much* time on music.

Father recovered himself. "Maybe I should have a talk with the boy's father to convince him that his son has talent and should be encouraged."

"I have a better idea," said Mother. "Why don't we invite Matthew's family to the recital? Then they can see all the other young people happily playing their instruments. It might change their minds about music."

Across the table I met Third Sister's eyes, and I knew she was thinking the same thing I was. If the Conners came to the recital, Matthew would be sitting in the audience; he wouldn't be playing the second violin part.

"I don't think Mr. Conner would accept," I said carefully. "He hates the sound of the violin. He says the screeching hurts his ears."

"Then we'll have to convince him he's wrong," said Father.

Not with this recital, you won't, I thought to myself. I made another effort. "Father, your students are having their first recital. They're going to be nervous, so they'll screech more than usual. Why not invite the Conners to the next recital?"

Father looked offended. "My students don't screech!"

Then Third Sister tried. "Maybe we can just invite Mr. and Mrs. Conner and let Matthew and his brother stay home and practice their baseball."

"Of course not!" said Mother. "Having Matthew here would help Yingtao's morale!"

"And besides," added Father, "Matthew has been helping Yingtao so much, it's only fair that he should come for the recital."

Third Sister and I knew that to argue any more would make our parents suspicious. We watched Mother go to the telephone to call up the Conners. I hoped desperately that they would be out or that they would refuse the invitation.

My hopes were dashed when Mother came back beaming. "I had to work pretty hard to persuade them, but they finally accepted." She turned to me. "Aren't you glad, Yingtao? I know you'll be doing your best, now that your friend will be here to hear you play."

That night, as Third Sister and I did the dishes, we tried to think what to do.

"Why don't you tell Father about your plan?" she whispered. "Tell him how much you want the recital to be a success, and that's why you want Matthew to play your part."

I thought of Father's sad face last week when I went to the baseball game with the Conners instead of practicing. "I can't do that," I said miserably. "He'll just think I'm not playing because I want to spend all my time on baseball."

"I guess you'll just have to play in the quartet," sighed Third Sister. "Anyway, it's more honest that way, and you'll feel better about it."

"It's more honest," I admitted, "but I won't feel better about it."

"Well, Matthew is smart," said Third Sister. "I'm sure he'll think of a way to play."

But maybe she was saying this just to calm my nerves, in case I had to play the next day.

Saturday came. I still hadn't heard from Matthew. I wanted to go over to his house to talk with him, but Father was keeping an eye on me, making sure I was staying home to practice.

Then I thought of calling Matthew up, but every time I went into the kitchen to call, someone was there. Second Sister was cutting up tea bags, or Mother was preparing the refreshments for the recital.

As the hour for the recital approached, I spent my time looking out the window, hoping for a sign from him. There was nothing.

The recital was being held in our living room, and it was to begin at two in the afternoon. Since Father had only six students, we could easily squeeze everybody in. The audience were mostly relatives—close relatives—of the young players, and we expected about twenty-five people.

Mother was going to serve orange soda to the young people and tea to the adults. She also planned to serve fortune cookies. We had actually never seen fortune cookies until we came to America. After Father got his first paycheck, he treated the family to a dinner in Chinatown. Although Mother was a good cook, we were glad to have a change. The food was Cantonese,[6] which was a little different from the Shanghai food we had at home, but it was good and not totally strange.

The one strange item came at the end. When the waiter presented the bill, he also handed us a small plate with six funny-looking cookies. They were shaped like a small, round cake, folded in half, with the corners bent back.

"What are these?" asked Father.

"They are fortune cookies," said the waiter. "Each cookie has a piece of paper with your fortune on it." He showed us how to break the crisp cookie open and get at the tiny slip of paper with a message.

We excitedly broke open our cookies and read the messages. Mine said, "Listen carefully, and your inner voice will tell you what to do." Even my fortune cookie was telling me to listen carefully.

Everyone liked the fortune cookies very much. From that time on, Mother bought them for special celebrations. For the recital, she bought the largest package in the store.

"When the recital is finished, we'll really have something to celebrate," she said. She was smiling bravely as she spoke, but her voice trembled a little.

The only problem was how to get everyone seated. We finally borrowed enough chairs from our neighbors for the grown-ups. The kids in the audience would just have to sit on the floor.

Eldest Brother set up the screen in the living room. While he wasn't looking, I moved the screen a little so that it stood right in front of the door to the kitchen. This way Matthew could move to his place behind the screen without being seen.

If he came.

I could hardly swallow my lunch, I was so anxious about Matthew. Of course, the rest of the family thought I was just suffering from stage fright.

"You'll be all right if you just concentrate, Yingtao," Father said heartily.

"Don't finish your rice if you don't feel like it," said Mother. In our family—in any Chinese family—not finishing your bowl of rice is a terrible thing. So Mother was really trying to be kind.

"Once you get the first few measures right, the rest will come easily," said Eldest Brother. "I know you can do it."

Even Second Sister had a kind word to say. "You have a good sense of rhythm, Fourth Brother. We all have confidence in you."

Could they be right? Maybe if I concentrated, maybe if I got the first few measures right . . . Maybe there was just a chance that I might not disgrace the Yang family after all.

---

6. I.e., characteristic of the region near Guangzhou (Canton), the main port and city of south China and the capital of Guangdong province.

For once, Third Sister was the only one who didn't say anything to cheer me up. Probably because she knew how hopeless it was.

After lunch Mother looked at the living room one last time and nodded. Then her eyes went to Second Sister's pictures of the Chinese scenes. "You've done a good job," she said softly.

We were still putting out the refreshments when the first of Father's students arrived with their parents. They were not only on time; they were early. I guess the parents were curious about how a Chinese family lived.

The kids probably just wanted to get it over with. Most of them didn't look happy about playing in front of people. I knew how they felt.

But stage fright was the least of my worries today. I hung around the backdoor, waiting and hoping for Matthew to arrive. When it was nearly two o'clock and most of the guests had arrived, there was still no sign of him. Slowly, reluctantly, I went to my room and got my violin out. Even the instrument seemed unwilling to leave its case.

"He's here!" It was Third Sister's voice. "He sneaked in through the backdoor without anyone seeing him!"

I spun around, and there, standing behind her, was Matthew.

For a moment we just stood there looking at each other. Neither of us could speak. I was too relieved to say anything, and Matthew too happy.

Then he grinned and made a thumbs-up sign. "I told my folks that I was coming down with something. I said it was better if I didn't go, in case the other kids caught it."

"Come on, we have to hurry down," whispered Third Sister. She was right. The others would be suspicious if we didn't show up soon.

I copied Matthew's thumbs-up sign, and hurried after Third Sister. According to our plan, Matthew was to wait in my room until it was time for the quartet, and then he would come downstairs, go through the kitchen, and get to his place behind the screen.

The program began right on time. Father had arranged the recital in order of age. His youngest student would play first, and then the next youngest, and so on. The last number was our quartet.

First on the program was Peter Schultz, who was five years old and the only boy among Father's students. Maybe he was too young to worry about being called a nerd, a wimp, or a sissy.

I was the same age as Peter when I got my first violin. But unlike me, Peter was not tone-deaf. His problem was that he couldn't count time. He didn't care if he played his notes too soon or too late, as long as he played them all. Mother accompanied Peter on the piano, and she had to scramble to stay with him.

At the end of the piece Peter bowed and beamed until his face almost split in two. We all clapped hard.

The rest of Father's students were girls. Four of them studied the violin and one of them the viola.

The string players in our school orchestra, the violinists, violists, and cellists, were almost all girls. But for some reason it was all right for boys to play wind instruments, like the trumpet and the clarinet. It couldn't have been easy for Matthew to keep on playing the violin, when the other boys teased him about it.

The girl who played next in the recital was terribly nervous. She was biting her lip as she played, and I found myself biting my lip, too. Once she had to stop in the middle of the piece because she had lost her place.

She looked ready to cry, but Father went over and talked softly to her for a minute. She started the piece over again, and this time she finished it. We clapped extra hard.

One of the older girls played a piece with a lot of fast notes. Some of the little kids in the audience said, "Ooh!"

At the end of the piece the girl bowed and quickly ran back to her parents. They hugged her, and I could hear them telling her how proud they were of her playing.

My parents had never told me they were proud of my playing. They never would, either.

I began to look over the other parents in the audience. Suddenly I recognized a couple sitting in the back row. It was Matthew's parents. When Mr. Conner caught my eye, he gave me a big wink. Eric wasn't with them, so he had managed to find an excuse to stay away.

The next three pieces seemed to pass very quickly. Much sooner than I expected, it was time for our quartet.

I jumped up and rushed over to help set up the music stands. As I was putting out the sheet music for the quartet, I noticed that the edge of one of Second Sister's paintings had come loose. There was a big gap, and I could see through it. If I could see through it, so could the audience.

"What's the matter?" Eldest Brother asked me. "Why are you taking so long?"

"The painting is coming loose here," I said. "I'll try to glue it back."

"Never mind!" hissed Second Sister. She seemed in a hurry to get the quartet over with. "Come on, let's get started."

"I won't be a minute," I muttered, and rushed into the kitchen.

Matthew was standing beside the refrigerator. "What's happened?"

"Haven't got time to explain," I gasped. "The glue! Where is the glue?"

Third Sister had used a tube of glue to put up the paintings, and I didn't know where she had put it. Then I saw my bowl of leftover rice on the counter. I grabbed a bit of it and kneaded it together with my fingers until it became a sticky paste. Then I rushed back to the screen and quickly dabbed at the loose edge of the painting with my homemade paste. Third Sister soon saw what I was doing and helped me smooth the paper down.

"I didn't know that painting was so important to you," growled Second Sister. But she looked pleased.

The audience was getting restless, especially the children. We finally settled down in our seats. One of the mothers gave a "shush," and the children quieted. I heard a faint rustling behind the screen.

I glanced at Third Sister to see if she had also heard the rustle. She smiled at me, and her dimples flashed.

When I see her smile like that, I know she's thinking of some mischief. Now she was probably smiling because we were playing a trick on the audience.

Eldest Brother lifted his bow and began to play. Second Sister followed with her entrance, then Third Sister. As she played the deep notes of her cello, it was nearly time for my entrance. I lifted my bow. My fingers were sticky from the rice paste, but at least it gave me a better grip on the bow.

Eldest Brother gritted his teeth and Second Sister stiffened her shoulders as they prepared themselves for the sour notes they expected me to produce.

Then I drew my bow across the strings—or I pretended to. By now, I was really good at keeping my bow just a tiny bit above the strings. I was an expert at bow sync.

A ripple of notes came out as I moved my bow back and forth. Eldest Brother and

Second Sister were so surprised that they both stopped playing for a moment. Only Third Sister's cello kept on going smoothly.

But Eldest Brother and Second Sister recovered quickly. They had both played in a lot of recitals back in China. Unexpected things often happen during a performance. They found their places again, and the quartet went ahead. To my great relief, Matthew was keeping up perfectly with the others.

It didn't take long for Eldest Brother to figure out what was going on. From his seat, he could tell the second violin part wasn't coming from me. And soon he knew it was coming from behind the screen.

I saw Second Sister look at me. She had also figured out what was happening. She probably recognized Matthew's way of playing. But there was nothing she could do except continue to play, and play beautifully.

Everything was fine, until I took hold of the corner of the music to turn it over. The rice paste made my fingers stick to the paper. I broke out in a sweat as I tried to shake the paper loose.

Meanwhile the second violin part continued to issue smoothly from behind the screen. Did the audience notice that while I was struggling with the sheet music, my violin was playing by itself?

Maybe not. A lot of notes were flying around, and the audience couldn't always tell exactly which notes were coming from which player. Only the composer, Haydn,[7] would know exactly, and he had been dead for almost two hundred years.

By the time I finally got my fingers free, my eyes were almost blinded by salty sweat. I wiped my brow and went back to swishing my bow back and forth.

I gave the audience a quick peek and saw that they all looked quite content. Mother smiled, and Father looked pleasantly surprised. They were proud of me.

My mouth filled with a bitter taste. My parents were proud of me for something I didn't do.

Suddenly I wished I had never thought of the trick. Third Sister was right. It would have been better for me to play the second violin part, even if I sounded terrible. At least that would have been honest.

But it was too late to change. Besides, Matthew was in this, too. The quartet kept on playing, and I went on moving my bow back and forth—silently.

The music became faster and louder as we got near the end. Eldest Brother had a short solo part with a dazzling swirl of notes that climbed higher and higher. After that, all four of us—all five of us?—played together, and we finished with a big, crashing chord.

The audience burst out clapping, even the little kids. I stole a look at Matthew's parents. They were clapping as hard as everybody else.

It was time for the four of us to stand up and take a bow. Third Sister seemed to be having some trouble. We were crowded together, and she had to get her cello out of the way before she could bow properly.

Third Sister stepped back a little to give herself more room. She moved her cello to her left, and bumped hard against the screen.

Crash! In full view of the audience stood Matthew, with his violin still in his hands.

There was dead silence. I could see the audience trying to understand what was going on. Father and Mother were the first to suspect the truth. Their eyes went from me to Matthew and then back to me again. I swallowed hard, wanting to melt into a puddle and sink into the ground with shame.

---

7. Franz Joseph Haydn (1732–1809), Austrian composer.

Why was Matthew still standing there? He had promised to steal away as soon as the quartet was over! But I couldn't really blame him for staying. I think he wanted to hear the clapping. After all, he had earned it.

Father broke the silence. "So that's why the quartet sounded so different!" Shock was being replaced by anger on his face.

Mr. and Mrs. Conner just stood stunned, with their mouths open. Finally Mrs. Conner found her voice. "Matthew? What are you doing there? I thought you were sick!"

Matthew grinned sheepishly but didn't say anything.

Third Sister cleared her throat. "I'm glad you all liked the quartet," she said and smiled at the audience.

That was when I realized she had knocked over the screen on purpose. She must have planned on doing it all along.

"Matthew isn't one of my father's regular students," she continued, "but we wanted to show you what a talented musician he is. So we played this little trick on you. We hope you enjoyed it."

She looked at me shyly, silently apologizing. I quickly smiled, letting her know that I wasn't angry at her.

There was a murmuring as the audience finally understood what had happened, that Matthew had been playing behind the screen. The kids loved the whole thing. They started cheering and clapping. After a while their parents joined in.

My parents were the only ones not cheering.

7

I was terrified of facing Father. He looked very angry, and I knew he would be having a stern talk with me at any moment.

But he didn't have a chance to talk to me at first. The recital turned out to a huge hit, much more successful than we had dared to hope. The parents crowded up to Father and congratulated him.

"To be frank with you, I didn't want to come to the recital," confessed the father of the girl who had been nervous. "These things can be a real pain in the . . . ow!"

His wife had kicked him. "We all had such a good time this afternoon!" she said. "After her other recitals, Alison would come home in tears. But today, she actually seems to be enjoying herself."

They looked around for Alison and found her with a group of other children reading their fortune cookie messages. We heard bursts of laughter.

The father of Peter Schultz, the little boy who had played first, felt the same way. "Your recital was as good as a show," he said. "It was a terrific idea to hide that boy behind the screen!"

Mrs. Schultz was talking to Second Sister. "I thought your quartet was beautiful! You must all practice an awful lot."

Second Sister glanced at me. "Yes, we practice long and hard, all five of us," she said darkly. Then she turned back to Peter's mother and smiled. "You're very kind."

A thoughtful look came over the face of Mrs. Schultz. "I wonder, do you do any baby-sitting? Peter seems to like you a lot. Do you think . . ."

Second Sister looked pleased. "I'll have to talk to my mother about it first."

When Second Sister told Mother what Mrs. Schultz had said, Mother looked surprised. "Are you sure you'd trust your son to a stranger?" She asked Mrs. Schultz. "A young girl like my daughter?"

"But your daughter isn't a stranger," protested Mrs. Schultz. "She's good with Peter. Besides, I can tell she is a serious, responsible girl."

While Mother went off to talk to another parent, Mrs. Schultz and Second Sister began to talk about hours and rates.

Several of the parents came up to Father and said they knew people whose children would be interested in taking lessons. "You have such talented children!" said another parent. "You must be really proud."

Father looked more embarrassed than proud. When still another parent congratulated him on his talented children, he started to protest. "Actually, my youngest son isn't—"

Third Sister quickly interrupted. "Your daughter is pretty talented herself," she said to the parent.

I could see that Father was torn. He felt he should confess the shameful truth about Yang the Youngest and his terrible ear. But things were going so well—the parents were very pleased, and the children were all having a good time. Why spoil this nice party?

While the other guests were busy chatting, the Conners just stood there looking dazed. Nobody in the audience had been more amazed than his own parents when Matthew had been revealed behind the screen.

Third Sister brought some refreshments over to them and introduced herself. Mr. and Mrs. Conner still seemed to have trouble finding words.

Matthew finished putting away his violin and came to join his parents. "So it's true?" demanded Mr. Conner. "You were playing all those notes?"

Matthew grinned. "Not all of them, just some of them. In fact I played less than the others, because the second violin has the smallest part."

"But you kept up with the others," said Mr. Conner. There was awe in his voice. "They were all going a mile a minute, and you kept up!"

Mrs. Conner put her arm around Matthew. "I've never been so surprised in my life!"

Father, who was going around greeting all the parents, finally came to the Conners. Mr. Conner cleared his throat. "When your wife invited us, I was going to refuse. Didn't know you were planning this surprise for us."

Father shook Mr. Conner's hand. "You must be very proud of Matthew."

"We didn't know that the boy was any good," admitted Mr. Conner. "All we knew was that he spent a lot of time playing his violin."

"Matthew has a gift for music," Father said. "When someone has a gift for music, he will find a way to play, whether you want him to or not."

"You've certainly opened our eyes," said Mrs. Conner. "That must have been why Mary bumped into that screen. She did it on purpose, to let us know that it was Matthew who was playing."

Father looked bewildered. "Who's Mary?"

Mrs. Conner looked bewildered, too. She pointed to Third Sister, who was putting away orange soda bottles. "Isn't that Mary over there? Your daughter?"

"She means Third Sister," I told Father.

Mr. Conner grinned. "Kids can be real devils, can't they? I bet Mary and . . . er . . ."

"Yingtao," supplied Matthew.

"Yeah, Yingtao," said Mr. Conner. "I bet the two of them cooked up the scheme between them."

"Cooked up?" repeated Father faintly.

"I think what Mr. Conner means is that Third Sister and I planned everything together," I told Father.

But clearly Third Sister had her own ideas about how the recital should end.

I was glad she did it. I was glad that everybody now knew it was Matthew, not me, who had played the second violin part.

Mr. Conner's face became serious. "Do you think you could take Matthew as one of your students?" he asked Father.

Father looked uncomfortable. "I thought . . . I thought my eldest son told me you are not working right now. He was giving Matthew some free lessons, and he would be glad to continue."

"We don't need charity," Mr. Conner said stiffly. "We'll find the money to pay you."

"Matthew earns some money himself," added Mrs. Conner. "He can help pay for his lessons."

"I'll be glad to pay for my lessons," Matthew said. "I mean it."

"He earns a lot of money delivering newspapers," I told Father. "He says I can do it, too, if you'll let me."

"You don't have time for a job," said Father. "You need to study and practice your violin."

"Aw, come on," said Mr. Conner. "Nobody needs to spend *all* his time studying and practicing. Besides, holding a job is good for a kid. Teaches him the value of money."

Father did not look convinced. "I have seen too many American youngsters earning money just to buy something trivial, like a pair of running shoes. Meanwhile their studies suffer."

"Not always," said Mr. Conner. "Take Matthew here. He delivers papers every morning, but he still gets decent grades in school." He added shyly, "And you could see he also did okay with his fiddle."

When Father didn't reply at first, Mr. Conner turned serious. "You just said yourself that when a kid has a gift for music, he'll play whether you want him to or not. Seems to me the opposite is true, too. If he *doesn't* have a gift for music, making him practice won't do much good."

Father winced. Even Mr. Conner saw that his words were not very tactful. "Ouch! I shouldn't have said that. What I really mean is that people are all different. Now, Yangto . . ."

"Yingtao," corrected Matthew.

"Yeah, Yingtao. He's a great kid. And I really mean it."

"Yingtao is welcome at our house anytime," said Mrs. Conner. "He's a good influence on Matthew."

"You bet," said Mr. Conner. "I've never seen anyone pick up baseball so fast. If we're talking about gifts, he's got a real gift for baseball, your . . . er . . . Yingtao."

Father stared at Mr. and Mrs. Conner and then at me. "He's got a real gift? Yingtao?"

He had had a great number of surprises this afternoon, but this was the greatest surprise of all.

"That's right," said Mr. Conner. "You ought to come see him play sometime—then you'll see for yourself how talented he is."

When the door closed behind the Conner family, Father looked very thoughtful.

Mother and Third Sister were cleaning up, while Eldest Brother and Second Sister went around returning chairs to our neighbors.

On her way back Second Sister drew me aside. "I'm proud of you, Fourth Brother."

All this praise was making me light-headed. First, it was the Conners, and now Second Sister, who had always been the most impatient with me.

"What do you mean?" I asked.

"You don't have to pretend," she said. "I know what you did. You gave up your place in the quartet so your friend could play. It was very generous of you, Fourth Brother."

"I just wanted the quartet to sound good," I muttered, embarrassed. "I didn't want to ruin the recital."

"That, too, was noble of you," she said. "You were sacrificing yourself for the good of the family."

Well, if she thought it had been a great sacrifice on my part, I wasn't going to try to change her mind.

That evening, as usual, we all went to practice. Eldest Brother practiced violin scales in our bedroom. Second Sister started a new viola piece in the living room.

Third Sister went into the bathroom and sat down on the toilet seat with her cello. She liked the way the sound bounced off the tiled walls. She also claimed that the carp in the bathtub splashed their tails to show they liked the music.

In the kitchen I sighed and took up my violin. I didn't try to tune it. What was the use?

But before I could tuck the violin under my chin, Father came in. "Yingtao, I want to talk to you."

My heart began to beat faster. It had come, at last, our talk. He was going to tell me I had disgraced the Yang family.

He sat down on a kitchen chair and made me sit facing him. "For years," he began, "your mother and I believed that you did not have the right attitude toward music, that you were simply not trying hard enough."

"I really do try hard," I protested desperately.

Father nodded. "After listening to the quartet this afternoon, I now believe you."

"But I didn't play this afternoon!"

"Precisely," said Father. "Day after day, I've had to listen to the four of you rehearsing, and always, the second violin part sounded . . ."

He stopped. At the thought of how the second violin had sounded, a look of deep suffering came over his face, and the corners of his lips curled down.

"Then this afternoon," he continued, "I heard the quartet play as it had never played before. I was astonished. I never knew the second violin could sound like that."

"Because it wasn't me," I mumbled.

"Because it wasn't you," said Father. He took a deep breath. "I'm afraid you will never sound like that. You have to face the truth, Yingtao, even if it's very painful. You will never become a good violinist."

This was an important moment, and I tried to keep my face serious. But it was hard not to burst out laughing.

"I guess you can't make a silk ear out of a sow's purse," I said, quoting Third Sister.

Father looked puzzled. Maybe I had mixed up Third Sister's sentence.

"I'm glad you're taking this so well," said Father. "I'm proud of you."

8

In the days that followed, the family went out of their way to be nice to me. Actually, the nicest thing they did was to stop making me practice the violin.

I went around looking brave. Third Sister sometimes smiled at me as if we shared a secret. But I knew she wouldn't tell on me.

Matthew now came to our house to take lessons from Father. He insisted on paying, so Father charged him one dollar for each lesson.

I loaned Matthew my violin. He needed a better instrument than the school violin. The news about our recital got around, and when our orchestra conductor heard about it, he decided to give Matthew another audition. After the audition, the conductor moved Matthew to the front row, where the audience could hear him.

As for me, I told the conductor I wanted to give up the violin and play the triangle instead. He looked very relieved.

Matthew still plays quartets with my brother and sisters sometimes. On these days, Second Sister always asks me whether I mind being left out.

Of course I tell her I don't mind. But sometimes when I look at the four of them so wrapped up in the music, I remember a story I used to hear in China about a blind boy.

He was born blind, so he never knew what it was like to see colors. "Tell me again about the sunset," he would ask.

And people would try to tell him. They would describe the orange sky deepening into crimson and the edges of the rooftops lined with gold.

He would thank them politely, but they knew they had not been able to make him see how beautiful it was.

I felt like that blind boy as I listened to Matthew and the rest of the Yangs talking about a certain piece of music.

In the end, Father forgave me for not being able to play the violin. He even bought me my own baseball bat. But the best part was when Mr. Conner finally persuaded our family to attend a game our neighborhood team was playing.

It wasn't easy. "I have to practice," said Eldest Brother, shaking his head. "There's still one passage where I can't seem to get the fingering right."

"We don't know anything about baseball," complained Second Sister. "We'll be bored to death."

"I can explain what's happening," offered Mr. Conner.

Third Sister saw how wistful I was. "Fourth Brother listened patiently to music all these years, and he never complained about being bored. The least we can do is go to the game, just this once."

"All right, let's go," said Father. "I'm curious. I want to know what it is that makes Yingtao work so hard."

The game started badly. The other team was good, and they got two runs right in the first inning.

In the fourth inning, they got a man on first base, and one of their best hitters came up to bat. He could hit hard, so our outfielders got themselves ready for a line drive.

I was the shortstop, and I was close to the batter. From the way his eyes moved around, I guessed that he was going to try to bunt.

I was right. He swung his bat, and the ball bounced on the ground in front of me. I was already running for it. I scooped up the ball and threw it at the first baseman in a single unbroken movement. The batter was out, and the other side was retired.

In the cheers of the crowd, I thought I heard a girl's high, shrill voice. It was probably Third Sister. She could pick up American cheers faster than anybody.

Things began to get better. Our side made a run in the sixth inning. When I came up to bat in the seventh inning, we already had one man on first base and Matthew was on third.

I carefully wiped my hands on my pants. Something made me look up at the stands, where my family was sitting.

They were way up front, and Mr. Conner was leaning over, probably explaining the game to them. Eldest Brother looked bewildered, and Second Sister looked bored. Mother was frowning, but Third Sister was smiling. Father's face was expressionless.

I took a deep breath and faced the pitcher.

The first pitch was low and the second one way too high. I didn't even jerk my bat.

The third one seemed to be outside, but it curved a little at the last minute. By then it was too late to swing.

"Strike!" said the umpire. There was a murmuring from the spectators.

Another throw, this one definitely outside.

Was the pitcher going to walk me? The bases would be loaded then. But our side already had two men out, so the next hitter would have to make a hit.

Should I accept a walk, or should I try for a hit, even if the pitch was not a good one?

I glanced up at the stands, and my eyes met Father's. He nodded. Of course he understood nothing about baseball, but I knew what he wanted.

When the ball came, I swung at it with everything I had. It cracked against the bat and sent a shock up my arms like electricity.

I didn't wait to see where the ball went. I just threw the bat down, lowered my head, and ran like mad.

It wasn't a home run. Maybe I'll never live to hit a home run. But from the screams of the crowd, I knew that Matthew had got home safely.

The roaring got louder. I slid into first base, picked myself up, and looked around. The boy who had been on first base had also made it home.

After that nothing could stop us. Our team got another run in the ninth, and we won the game. We filed off the field to the sound of cheers.

As I passed my family, I heard a tapping noise. I looked back and saw that Eldest Brother and Second Sister were smiling at me and tapping their bench with their pencils.

Suddenly I understood what they were doing. During a rehearsal, the string players sometimes want to tell a soloist or a guest conductor that they think he did well. They show their appreciation by lightly tapping their instruments with their bows.

Eric stared at Eldest Brother and Second Sister. "What are they doing that for?" he asked.

My throat was tight, and I couldn't answer. Matthew answered for me. "It's their way of telling Yingtao he did a good job."

"I'll say he did!" said Eric. "You could see that hitter was going to bunt, couldn't you, Yingtao? You've got a great eye!"

It made up for having a terrible ear.

1992

ROCH CARRIER
b. 1937

When Roch Carrier was growing up in the 1940s, his tiny village of Sainte-Justine, Quebec, had no library. Now, the village has a library named after its famous son. Carrier has made a literal mark on Canadian life in others ways: since 2002, an excerpt from "The Hockey Sweater" (1979), one of his most famous stories for children, has accompanied a representation of children playing winter sports on the back of the Canadian $5 bill.

These marks of distinction reflect the high regard Carrier enjoys in the world of Canadian letters. He is one of the most prolific and important of the country's francophone writers, and the translation of many of his works into English has won him a broad readership in and outside of Canada. Carrier began publishing poems and short stories in the 1950s, and his first book of fiction—a collection of contes or tales, *Jolis deuils, petites tragédies* (*Pretty Bereavements, Small Tragedies*, 1964)—was awarded the Prix Littéraire de la Province de Québec. He gained widespread recognition with *La Guerre, Yes Sir!* (1968; trans. 1970), a hugely popular book and the first in a trilogy of novels that cover some fifty years of Quebec's history with a blend of humor, violence, and grotesquerie.

For much of his professional life, Carrier was based in the academy. He began his studies at the Collège Saint-Louis (in New Brunswick), then earned an M.A. degree from the Université de Montréal and a doctorate in literature from the Sorbonne in Paris. In 1964 he began teaching literature at the Collège militaire royal de Saint-Jean in Quebec, where later he became an administrator and was ultimately appointed rector in 1990; he also taught at the Université de Montréal. He left education to become secretary-general of the Théâtre du Nou-

veau Monde (1970–75) and again when he was named the director of the Canada Council for the Arts (1994–97); since 1999, he has been the National Librarian of Canada. He married Diane Gosselin in 1959, and they have two daughters.

For more than three decades, Carrier has also continued to write steadily: novels, short stories, poetry, plays (most adapted from his novels), screenplays, and essays. His first publication for children was *Les Enfants du bonhomme dans la lune* (1979; *The Hockey Sweater, and Other Stories*, 1979), and many more followed. Carrier received the Stephen Leacock Award for Humour for *Prières d'un enfant très très sage* (1988; *Prayers of a Very Wise Child*, 1991), a novel set in rural Quebec with a nine-year-old protagonist. His other distinctions include several honorary doctorates, and he is a Fellow of the Royal Society of Canada.

"The Hockey Sweater," like many of Carrier's works for children, uses wry humor and a light touch to highlight some of the challenges experienced and loyalties displayed by French Canadian children living within a society dominated by English speakers. This autobiographical story, the first in a series that features young Roch, has become a well-loved classic across Canada. Its companion volumes include *Une Bonne et heureuse année* (1988; *A Happy New Year's Day*, 1991), *Un Champion* (1991; *The Boxing Champion*, 1991), and *Le Joueur de basket-ball* (1996; *The Basketball Player*, 1996). Years after publishing "The Hockey Sweater," Carrier returned to the subject of his boyhood idol in *Our Life with the Rocket: The Maurice Richard Story* (2001). It is fitting that before he died, Maurice Richard gave one of his sweaters to Roch Carrier.

The Hockey Sweater

I remember very well the winter of 1946. We all wore the same uniform as Maurice Richard,[1] the red, white and blue uniform of the Montreal Canadiens, the best

---

1. One of the greatest ice hockey players of all time (1921–2000); Richard played exclusively for the Canadiens (1942–60).

hockey team in the world. We all combed our hair like Maurice Richard, and to keep it in place we used a kind of glue—a great deal of glue. We laced our skates like Maurice Richard, we taped our sticks like Maurice Richard. We cut his pictures out of all the newspapers. Truly, we knew everything there was to know about him.

On the ice, when the referee blew his whistle the two teams would rush at the puck: we were five Maurice Richards against five other Maurice Richards, throwing themselves on the puck. We were ten players all wearing the uniform of the Montreal Canadiens, all with the same burning enthusiasm. We all wore the famous number 9 on our backs.

How could we forget that!

One day, my Montreal Canadiens sweater was too small for me; and it was ripped in several places. My mother said: "If you wear that old sweater, people are going to think we are poor!"

Then she did what she did whenever we needed new clothes. She started to look through the catalogue that the Eaton company[2] in Montreal sent us in the mail every year. My mother was proud. She never wanted to buy our clothes at the general store. The only clothes that were good enough for us were the latest styles from Eaton's catalogue. My mother did not like the order forms included in the catalogue. They were written in English and she did not understand a single word of it. To order my hockey sweater, she did what she always did. She took out her writing pad and wrote in her fine schoolteacher's hand: "Dear Monsieur Eaton, Would you be so kind as to send me a Canadiens' hockey sweater for my son, Roch, who is ten years old and a little bit tall for his age? Docteur Robitaille thinks he is a little too thin. I am sending you three dollars. Please send me the change if there is any. I hope your packing will be better than it was last time."

Monsieur Eaton answered my mother's letter promptly. Two weeks later we received the sweater.

That day I had one of the greatest disappointments of my life! Instead of the red, white and blue Montreal Canadiens sweater, Monsieur Eaton had sent the blue and white sweater of the Toronto Maple Leafs. I had always worn the red, white and blue sweater of the Montreal Canadiens. All my friends wore the red, white and blue sweater. Never had anyone in my village worn the Toronto sweater. Besides, the Toronto team was always being beaten by the Canadiens.

With tears in my eyes, I found the strength to say: "I'll never wear that uniform."

"My boy," said my mother, "first you're going to try it on! If you make up your mind about something before you try it, you won't go very far in this life."

My mother had pulled the blue and white Toronto Maple Leafs sweater over my head and put my arms into the sleeves. She pulled the sweater down and carefully smoothed the maple leaf right in the middle of my chest.

I was crying: "I can't wear that."

"Why not? This sweater is a perfect fit."

"Maurice Richard would never wear it."

"You're not Maurice Richard! Besides, it's not what you put on your back that matters, it's what you put inside your head."

"You'll never make me put in my head to wear a Toronto Maple Leafs sweater."

My mother sighed in despair and explained to me: "If you don't keep this sweater which fits you perfectly I'll have to write to Monsieur Eaton and explain that you don't want to wear the Toronto sweater. Monsieur Eaton understands French per-

---

2. Large Canadian department store, founded in 1869 and based in Toronto.

fectly, but he's English and he's going to be insulted because he likes the Maple Leafs. If he's insulted, do you think he'll be in a hurry to answer us? Spring will come before you play a single game, just because you don't want to wear that nice blue sweater."

So, I had to wear the Toronto Maple Leafs sweater.

When I arrived at the skating rink in my blue sweater, all the Maurice Richards in red, white and blue came, one by one, and looked at me. The referee blew his whistle and I went to take my usual position. The coach came over and told me I would be on the second line. A few minutes later the second line was called; I jumped onto the ice. The Maple Leafs sweater weighed on my shoulders like a mountain. The captain came and told me to wait: he'd need me later, on defense.

By the third period I still had not played.

Then one of the defensemen was hit on the nose with a stick and it started to bleed. I jumped onto the ice. My moment had come!

The referee blew his whistle and gave me a penalty. He said there were already five players on the ice. That was too much! It was too unfair! "This is persecution!" I shouted. "It's just because of my blue sweater!"

I crashed my stick against the ice so hard that it broke.

I bent down to pick up the pieces. When I got up, the young curate, on skates, was standing in front of me.

"My child," he said, "just because you're wearing a new Toronto Maple Leafs sweater, it doesn't mean you're going to make the laws around here. A good boy never loses his temper. Take off your skates and go to the church and ask God to forgive you."

Wearing my Maple Leafs sweater I went to the church, where I prayed to God.

I asked God to send me right away, a hundred million moths that would eat up my Toronto Maple Leafs sweater.

1979

MILDRED D. TAYLOR
b. 1943

In her series of books about the Logan family, Mildred D. Taylor retells the stories that make up the history of her family and of black America: "From *Song of the Trees* to *The Well* I have attempted to present a true picture of life in America as older members of my family remember it, and as I remember it in the days before the civil rights movement. In all of the books I have recounted not only the joy of growing up in a large and supportive family, but my own feelings of being faced with segregation and bigotry." Taylor credits her father's stories and his personal example of dignity, self-respect, and high standards with inspiring her to become a writer and

a voice of truth about African American families, American history, and race relations.

Taylor came of age during a time of great conflict, which she experienced in both the North and the South. Soon after Taylor's birth, her parents took her and her older sister from Jackson, Mississippi, to Toledo, Ohio. When she was ten years old they moved to a different neighborhood and she found herself the only African American child in her class. For the first time, she became acutely aware that the dominant culture treated her as lesser. And when Taylor realized that they drove without stopping on their visits to Mississippi because no establishment would serve them food or let them stay overnight, these trips stopped seeming like extended picnics and became more like journeys to a dangerous foreign country. Yet the South was also a place in which family love, joy, and pride were warmly expressed and celebrated—and it is to that South that her books have returned again and again.

After graduating from high school, Taylor enrolled in the University of Toledo and in 1965 earned a B.Ed. in education. She spent two years in Ethiopia working for the Peace Corps, and then a year back home as a Peace Corps recruiter before deciding to focus on developing her writing. While studying journalism at the University of Colorado (M.A., 1969), she became actively involved in the Black Student Alliance; after she earned her degree, she helped establish the university's black studies program. In 1971 she moved to Los Angeles and began writing in earnest, supporting herself by working as a proofreader and editor for a tax firm. She married Errol Zea-Daly in 1972, and they were divorced in 1975.

Although she had entered a number of writing contests as a student, she had never won any. But in 1973, a short, quickly drafted manuscript won in the African American category of a contest sponsored by the Council on Interracial Books for Children. It became her first book, *Song of the Trees*; the suspenseful story about a confrontation over valuable and beloved trees was based on an event from Taylor's family history. It introduced the Logan clan, as Taylor found her voice in that of eight-year-old Cassie.

Taylor has won many more awards with the six additional books she has written to date about the Logans and people associated with them. Two are prequels to *Song of the Trees*—*The Well: David's Story* (1995), which focuses on Cassie's father, and *The Land* (2001), whose central character is her grandfather who (like Taylor's own great-grandfather)

purchased the Mississippi farmland so important to later generations in the family. Taylor's most acclaimed and best-known work is *Roll of Thunder, Hear My Cry* (1976), in which Cassie, a spunky nine-year-old, both experiences the discrimination and threat of deadly violence that her family and neighbors face because of their color and comes to understand that they nevertheless can maintain their pride and dignity. According to Taylor, the defiant song that begins chapter 11 and that gave the novel its title came to her while she was doing some laundry in the basement of her parents' house, after she had returned to Toledo to help care for them. At that moment, she says, she knew her book would win the Newbery Medal. In accepting the award she dedicated it to her father, who had died a few months before its presentation; she explained that "without his teachings, without his words, my words would not have been." In 2003 she was awarded the first NSK Neustadt Prize for Children's Literature, largely because of the impact of *Roll of Thunder*.

In the note to the reader that prefaces her 2001 book about the Logans, *The Land*, Taylor writes: "Since writing my first book, *Song of the Trees*, it has been my wish to have readers walk in the shoes of the Logan family, who are based on my family, and to feel what they felt. It has been my wish that by understanding this family and what they endured, there would be a further understanding of what millions of families endured, and there would also be a further understanding of why there was a Civil Rights Movement, a movement that changed our nation." April 2, 2004, was declared Mildred D. Taylor Day in Mississippi; in the words of the governor's proclamation, she "return[ed] to the place her life and work began, to a Mississippi that no longer celebrates prejudice, but embraces her works, and honors her life and her family."

Roll of Thunder, Hear My Cry

1

"Little Man, would you come on? You keep it up and you're gonna make us late."
My youngest brother paid no attention to me. Grasping more firmly his newspaper-wrapped notebook and his tin-can lunch of cornbread and oil sausages,[1] he continued

1. Dried sausages packed in oil for preservation without refrigeration.

to concentrate on the dusty road. He lagged several feet behind my other brothers, Stacey and Christopher-John, and me, attempting to keep the rusty Mississippi dust from swelling with each step and drifting back upon his shiny black shoes and the cuffs of his corduroy pants by lifting each foot high before setting it gently down again. Always meticulously neat, six-year-old Little Man never allowed dirt or tears or stains to mar anything he owned. Today was no exception.

"You keep it up and make us late for school, Mama's gonna wear you out," I threatened, pulling with exasperation at the high collar of the Sunday dress Mama had made me wear for the first day of school—as if that event were something special. It seemed to me that showing up at school at all on a bright August-like October morning made for running the cool forest trails and wading barefoot in the forest pond was concession enough; Sunday clothing was asking too much. Christopher-John and Stacey were not too pleased about the clothing or school either. Only Little Man, just beginning his school career, found the prospects of both intriguing.

"Y'all go ahead and get dirty if y'all wanna," he replied without even looking up from his studied steps. "Me, I'm gonna stay clean."

"I betcha Mama's gonna 'clean' you, you keep it up," I grumbled.

"Ah, Cassie, leave him be," Stacey admonished, frowning and kicking testily at the road.

"I ain't said nothing but—"

Stacey cut me a wicked look and I grew silent. His disposition had been irritatingly sour lately. If I hadn't known the cause of it, I could have forgotten very easily that he was, at twelve, bigger than I, and that I had promised Mama to arrive at school looking clean and ladylike. "Shoot," I mumbled finally, unable to restrain myself from further comment, "it ain't my fault you gotta be in Mama's class this year."

Stacey's frown deepened and he jammed his fists into his pockets, but said nothing.

Christopher-John, walking between Stacey and me, glanced uneasily at both of us but did not interfere. A short, round boy of seven, he took little interest in troublesome things, preferring to remain on good terms with everyone. Yet he was always sensitive to others and now, shifting the handle of his lunch can from his right hand to his right wrist and his smudged notebook from his left hand to his left armpit, he stuffed his free hands into his pockets and attempted to make his face as moody as Stacey's and as cranky as mine. But after a few moments he seemed to forget that he was supposed to be grouchy and began whistling cheerfully. There was little that could make Christopher-John unhappy for very long, not even the thought of school.

I tugged again at my collar and dragged my feet in the dust, allowing it to sift back onto my socks and shoes like gritty red snow. I hated the dress. And the shoes. There was little I could do in a dress, and as for shoes, they imprisoned freedom-loving feet accustomed to the feel of the warm earth.

"Cassie, stop that," Stacey snapped as the dust billowed in swirling clouds around my feet. I looked up sharply, ready to protest. Christopher-John's whistling increased to a raucous, nervous shrill, and grudgingly I let the matter drop and trudged along in moody silence, my brothers growing as pensively quiet as I.

Before us the narrow, sun-splotched road wound like a lazy red serpent dividing the high forest bank of quiet, old trees on the left from the cotton field, forested by giant green-and purple stalks, on the right. A barbed-wire fence ran the length of the deep field, stretching eastward for over a quarter of a mile until it met the sloping green pasture that signaled the end of our family's four hundred acres. An ancient oak tree on the slope, visible even now, was the official dividing mark between Logan land and the beginning of a dense forest. Beyond the protective fencing of the forest, vast farming fields, worked by a multitude of sharecropping families, covered two thirds of a ten-square-mile plantation. That was Harlan Granger land.

Once our land had been Granger land too, but the Grangers had sold it during Reconstruction[2] to a Yankee for tax money. In 1887, when the land was up for sell again, Grandpa had bought two hundred acres of it, and in 1918, after the first two hundred acres had been paid off, he had bought another two hundred. It was good rich land, much of it still virgin forest, and there was no debt on half of it. But there was a mortgage on the two hundred acres bought in 1918 and there were taxes on the full four hundred, and for the past three years there had not been enough money from the cotton to pay both and live on too.

That was why Papa had gone to work on the railroad.

In 1930 the price of cotton dropped. And so, in the spring of 1931, Papa set out looking for work, going as far north as Memphis and as far south as the Delta country.[3] He had gone west too, into Louisiana. It was there he found work laying track for the railroad. He worked the remainder of the year away from us, not returning until the deep winter when the ground was cold and barren. The following spring after the planting was finished, he did the same. Now it was 1933, and Papa was again in Louisiana laying track.

I asked him once why he had to go away, why the land was so important. He took my hand and said in his quiet way: "Look out there, Cassie girl. All that belongs to you. You ain't never had to live on nobody's place but your own and long as I live and the family survives, you'll never have to. That's important. You may not understand that now, but one day you will. Then you'll see."

I looked at Papa strangely when he said that, for I knew that all the land did not belong to me. Some of it belonged to Stacey, Christopher-John, and Little Man, not to mention the part that belonged to Big Ma, Mama, and Uncle Hammer, Papa's older brother who lived in Chicago. But Papa never divided the land in his mind; it was simply Logan land. For it he would work the long, hot summer pounding steel; Mama would teach and run the farm; Big Ma, in her sixties, would work like a woman of twenty in the fields and keep the house; and the boys and I would wear threadbare clothing washed to dishwater color; but always, the taxes and the mortgage would be paid. Papa said that one day I would understand.

I wondered.

When the fields ended and the Granger forest fanned both sides of the road with long overhanging branches, a tall, emaciated-looking boy popped suddenly from a forest trail and swung a thin arm around Stacey. It was T.J. Avery. His younger brother Claude emerged a moment later, smiling weakly as if it pained him to do so. Neither boy had on shoes, and their Sunday clothing, patched and worn, hung loosely upon their frail frames. The Avery family share-cropped on Granger land.

"Well," said T.J., jauntily swinging into step with Stacey, "here we go again startin' another school year."

"Yeah," sighed Stacey.

"Ah, man, don't look so down," T.J. said cheerfully. "Your mama's really one great teacher. I should know." He certainly should. He had failed Mama's class last year and was now returning for a second try.

2. The period (1865–77) during which the federal government, following the Civil War, attempted to reshape the social, economic, and political order in the former Confederate states.
3. The flood plain of the Mississippi River, on the western edge of the state.

"Shoot! You can say that," exclaimed Stacey. "You don't have to spend all day in a classroom with your mama."

"Look on the bright side," said T.J. "Jus' think of the advantage you've got. You'll be learnin' all sorts of stuff 'fore the rest of us. . . ." He smiled slyly. "Like what's on all them tests."

Stacey thrust T.J.'s arm from his shoulders. "If that's what you think, you don't know Mama."

"Ain't no need gettin' mad," T.J. replied undaunted. "Jus' an idea." He was quiet for a moment, then announced, "I betcha I could give y'all an earful 'bout that burnin' last night."

"Burning? What burning?" asked Stacey.

"Man, don't y'all know nothin'? The Berrys' burnin'. I thought y'all's grandmother went over there last night to see 'bout 'em."

Of course we knew that Big Ma had gone to a sick house last night. She was good at medicines and people often called her instead of a doctor when they were sick. But we didn't know anything about any burnings, and I certainly didn't know anything about any Berrys either.

"What Berrys he talking 'bout, Stacey?" I asked. "I don't know no Berrys."

"They live way over on the other side of Smellings Creek. They come up to church sometimes," said Stacey absently. Then he turned back to T.J. "Mr. Lanier come by real late and got Big Ma. Said Mr. Berry was low sick and needed her to help nurse him, but he ain't said nothing 'bout no burning."

"He's low sick all right—'cause he got burnt near to death. Him and his two nephews. And you know who done it?"

"Who?" Stacey and I asked together.

"Well, since y'all don't seem to know nothin'," said T.J., in his usual sickening way of nursing a tidbit of information to death, "maybe I ought not tell y'all. It might hurt y'all's little ears."

"Ah, boy," I said, "don't start that mess again." I didn't like T.J. very much and his stalling around didn't help.

"Come on, T.J.," said Stacey, "out with it."

"Well . . ." T.J. murmured, then grew silent as if considering whether or not he should talk.

We reached the first of two crossroads and turned north; another mile and we would approach the second crossroads and turn east again.

Finally T.J. said, "Okay. See, them Berrys' burnin' wasn't no accident. Some white men took a match to 'em."

"Y-you mean just lit 'em up like a piece of wood?" stammered Christopher-John, his eyes growing big with disbelief.

"But why?" asked Stacey.

T.J. shrugged. "Don't know why. Jus' know they done it, that's all."

"How you know?" I questioned suspiciously.

He smiled smugly. " 'Cause your mama come down on her way to school and talked to my mama 'bout it."

"She did?"

"Yeah, and you should've seen the way she look when she come outa that house."

"How'd she look?" inquired Little Man, interested enough to glance up from the road for the first time.

T.J. looked around grimly and whispered, "Like . . . death." He waited a moment for his words to be appropriately shocking, but the effect was spoiled by Little Man, who asked lightly, "What does death look like?"

T.J. turned in annoyance. "Don't he know nothin'?"

"Well, what does it look like?" Little Man demanded to know. He didn't like T.J. either.

"Like my grandfather looked jus' 'fore they buried him," T.J. described all-knowingly.

"Oh," replied Little Man, losing interest and concentrating on the road again.

"I tell ya, Stacey, man," said T.J. morosely, shaking his head, "sometimes I jus' don't know 'bout that family of yours."

Stacey pulled back, considering whether or not T.J.'s words were offensive, but T.J. immediately erased the question by continuing amiably. "Don't get me wrong, Stacey. They some real swell kids, but that Cassie 'bout got me whipped this mornin'."

"Good!" I said.

"Now how'd she do that?" Stacey laughed.

"You wouldn't be laughin' if it'd've happened to you. She up and told your mama 'bout me goin' up to that Wallace store dancin' room and Miz Logan told Mama." He eyed me disdainfully then went on. "But don't worry, I got out of it though. When Mama asked me 'bout it, I jus' said ole Claude was always sneakin' up there to get some of that free candy Mr. Kaleb give out sometimes and I had to go and get him 'cause I knowed good and well she didn't want us up there. Boy, did he get it!" T.J. laughed. "Mama 'bout wore him out."

I stared at quiet Claude. "You let him do that?" I exclaimed. But Claude only smiled in that sickly way of his and I knew that he had. He was more afraid of T.J. than of his mother.

Again Little Man glanced up and I could see his dislike for T.J. growing. Friendly Christopher-John glared at T.J., and putting his short arm around Claude's shoulder said, "Come on, Claude, let's go on ahead." Then he and Claude hurried up the road, away from T.J.

Stacey, who generally overlooked T.J.'s underhanded stunts, shook his head. "That was dirty."

"Well, what'd ya expect me to do? I couldn't let her think I was goin' up there 'cause I like to, could I? She'd've killed me!"

"And good riddance," I thought, promising myself that if he ever pulled anything like that on me, I'd knock his block off.

We were nearing the second crossroads, where deep gullies lined both sides of the road and the dense forest crept to the very edges of high, jagged, clay-walled banks. Suddenly, Stacey turned. "Quick!" he cried. "Off the road!" Without another word, all of us but Little Man scrambled up the steep right bank into the forest.

"Get up here, Man," Stacey ordered, but Little Man only gazed at the ragged red bank sparsely covered with scraggly brown briars and kept on walking. "Come on, do like I say."

"But I'll get my clothes dirty!" protested Little Man.

"You're gonna get them a whole lot dirtier you stay down there. Look!"

Little Man turned around and watched saucer-eyed as a bus bore down on him spewing clouds of red dust like a huge yellow dragon breathing fire. Little Man headed toward the bank, but it was too steep. He ran frantically along the road looking for a foothold and, finding one, hopped onto the bank, but not before the bus had sped past enveloping him in a scarlet haze while laughing white faces pressed against the bus windows.

Little Man shook a threatening fist into the thick air, then looked dismally down at himself.

"Well, ole Little Man done got his Sunday clothes dirty," T.J. laughed as we jumped down from the bank. Angry tears welled in Little Man's eyes but he quickly brushed them away before T.J. could see them.

"Ah, shut up, T.J.," Stacey snapped.

"Yeah, shut up, T.J.," I echoed.

"Come on, Man," Stacey said, "and next time do like I tell ya."

Little Man hopped down from the bank. "How's come they did that, Stacey, huh?" he asked, dusting himself off. "How's come they didn't even stop for us?"

" 'Cause they like to see us run and it ain't our bus," Stacey said, balling his fists and jamming them tightly into his pockets.

"Well, where's our bus?" demanded Little Man.

"We ain't got one."

"Well, why not?"

"Ask Mama," Stacey replied as a towheaded boy, barefooted and pale, came running down a forest path toward us. The boy quickly caught up and fell in stride with Stacey and T.J.

"Hey, Stacey," he said shyly.

"Hey, Jeremy," Stacey said.

There was an awkward silence.

"Y'all jus' startin' school today?"

"Yeah," replied Stacey.

"I wishin' ours was jus' startin'," sighed Jeremy. "Ours been goin' since the end of August." Jeremy's eyes were a whitewashed blue and they seemed to weep when he spoke.

"Yeah," said Stacey again.

Jeremy kicked the dust briskly and looked toward the north. He was a strange boy. Ever since I had begun school, he had walked with us as far as the crossroads in the morning, and met us there in the afternoon. He was often ridiculed by the other children at his school and had shown up more than once with wide red welts on his arms which Lillian Jean, his older sister, had revealed with satisfaction were the result of his associating with us. Still, Jeremy continued to meet us.

When we reached the crossroads, three more children, a girl of twelve or thirteen and two boys, all looking very much like Jeremy, rushed past. The girl was Lillian Jean. "Jeremy, come on," she said without a backward glance, and Jeremy, smiling sheepishly, waved a timid good-bye and slowly followed her.

We stood in the crossing gazing after them. Jeremy looked back once but then Lillian Jean yelled shrilly at him and he did not look back again. They were headed for the Jefferson Davis County School,[4] a long white wooden building looming in the distance. Behind the building was a wide sports field around which were scattered rows of tiered gray-looking benches. In front of it were two yellow buses, our own tormentor and one that brought students from the other direction, and loitering students awaiting the knell of the morning bell. In the very center of the expansive front lawn, waving red, white, and blue with the emblem of the Confederacy emblazoned in its upper left-hand corner, was the Mississippi flag. Directly below it was

---

4. Named for Jefferson Davis (1808–1889), the president of the Confederate States of America (1861–65).

the American flag. As Jeremy and his sister and brothers hurried toward those trans-posed flags,[5] we turned eastward toward our own school.

The Great Faith Elementary and Secondary School, one of the largest black schools in the county, was a dismal end to an hour's journey. Consisting of four weather-beaten wooden houses on stilts of brick, 320 students, seven teachers, a principal, a caretaker, and the caretaker's cow, which kept the wide crabgrass lawn sufficiently clipped in spring and summer, the school was located near three plantations, the largest and closest by far being the Granger plantation. Most of the students were from families that sharecropped on Granger land, and the others mainly from Montier and Harrison plantation families. Because the students were needed in the fields from early spring when the cotton was planted until after most of the cotton had been picked in the fall, the school adjusted its terms accordingly, beginning in October and dismissing in March. But even so, after today a number of the older students would not be seen again for a month or two, not until the last puff of cotton had been gleaned from the fields, and eventually most would drop out of school altogether. Because of this the classes in the higher grades grew smaller with each passing year.

The class buildings, with their backs practically against the forest wall, formed a semicircle facing a small one-room church at the opposite edge of the compound. It was to this church that many of the school's students and their parents belonged. As we arrived, the enormous iron bell in the church belfry was ringing vigorously, warning the milling students that only five minutes of freedom remained.

Little Man immediately pushed his way across the lawn to the well. Stacey and T.J., ignoring the rest of us now that they were on the school grounds, wandered off to be with the other seventh-grade boys, and Christopher-John and Claude rushed to reunite with their classmates of last year. Left alone, I dragged slowly to the building that held the first four grades and sat on the bottom step. Plopping my pencils and notebook into the dirt, I propped my elbows on my knees and rested my chin in the palms of my hands.

"Hey, Cassie," said Mary Lou Wellever, the principal's daughter, as she flounced by in a new yellow dress.

"Hey, yourself," I said, scowling so ferociously that she kept on walking. I stared after her a moment noting that she *would* have on a new dress. Certainly no one else did. Patches on faded pants and dresses abounded on boys and girls come so recently from the heat of the cotton fields. Girls stood awkwardly, afraid to sit, and boys pulled restlessly at starched, high-buttoned collars. Those students fortunate enough to have shoes hopped from one pinched foot to the other. Tonight the Sunday clothes would be wrapped in newspaper and hung for Sunday and the shoes would be packed away to be brought out again only when the weather turned so cold that bare feet could no longer traverse the frozen roads; but for today we all suffered.

On the far side of the lawn I spied Moe Turner speeding toward the seventh-grade-class building, and wondered at his energy. Moe was one of Stacey's friends. He lived on the Montier plantation, a three-and-a-half-hour walk from the school. Because of the distance, many children from the Montier plantation did not come to Great Faith after they had finished the four-year school near Smellings Creek. But there were some girls and boys like Moe who made the trek daily, leaving their homes while

5. The U.S. flag should always fly above all others.

the sky was black and not returning until all was blackness again. I for one was certainly glad that I didn't live that far away. I don't think my feet would have wanted that badly for me to be educated.

The chiming of the second bell began. I stood up dusting my bottom as the first, second, third, and fourth graders crowded up the stairs into the hallway. Little Man flashed proudly past, his face and hands clean and his black shoes shining again. I glanced down at my own shoes powdered red and, raising my right foot, rubbed it against the back of my left leg, then reversed the procedure. As the last gong of the bell reverberated across the compound, I swooped up my pencils and notebook and ran inside.

A hallway extended from the front to the back door of the building. On either side of the hallway were two doorways, both leading into the same large room which was divided into two classrooms by a heavy canvas curtain. The second and third grades were on the left, the first and fourth grades on the right. I hurried to the rear of the building, turned to the right, and slid into a third-row bench occupied by Gracey Pearson and Alma Scott.

"You can't sit here," objected Gracey. "I'm saving it for Mary Lou."

I glanced back at Mary Lou Wellever depositing her lunch pail on a shelf in the back of the room and said, "Not any more you ain't."

Miss Daisy Crocker, yellow and buckeyed, glared down at me from the middle of the room with a look that said, "Soooooooo, it's you, Cassie Logan." Then she pursed her lips and drew the curtain along the rusted iron rod and tucked it into a wide loop in the back wall. With the curtain drawn back, the first graders gazed quizzically at us. Little Man sat by a window, his hands folded, patiently waiting for Miss Crocker to speak.

Mary Lou nudged me. "That's my seat, Cassie Logan."

"Mary Lou Wellever," Miss Crocker called primly, "have a seat."

"Yes, ma'am," said Mary Lou, eyeing me with a look of pure hate before turning away.

Miss Crocker walked stiffly to her desk, which was set on a tiny platform and piled high with bulky objects covered by a tarpaulin. She rapped the desk with a ruler, although the room was perfectly still, and said, "Welcome, children, to Great Faith Elementary School." Turning slightly so that she stared squarely at the left side of the room, she continued, "To all of you fourth graders, it's good to have you in my class. I'll be expecting many good and wonderful things from you." Then addressing the right side of the room, she said, "And to all our little first grade friends only today starting on the road to knowledge and education, may your tiny feet find the pathways of learning steady and forever before you."

Already bored, I stretched my right arm on the desk and rested my head in my upraised hand.

Miss Crocker smiled mechanically, then rapped on her desk again. "Now, little ones," she said, still talking to the first grade, "your teacher, Miss Davis, has been held up in Jackson for a few days so I'll have the pleasure of sprinkling your little minds with the first rays of knowledge." She beamed down upon them as if she expected to be applauded for this bit of news, then with a swoop of her large eyes to include the fourth graders, she went on.

"Now since there's only one of me, we shall have to sacrifice for the next few days. We shall work, work, work, but we shall have to work like little Christian boys and girls and share, share, share. Now are we willing to do that?"

"YES'M, MIZ CROCKER," the children chorused.

But I remained silent. I never did approve of group responses. Adjusting my head in my hand, I sighed heavily, my mind on the burning of the Berrys.

"Cassie Logan?"

I looked up, startled.

"Cassie Logan!"

"Yes, ma'am?" I jumped up quickly to face Miss Crocker.

"Aren't you willing to work and share?"

"Yes'm."

"Then say so!"

"Yes'm," I murmured, sliding back into my seat as Mary Lou, Gracey, and Alma giggled. Here it was only five minutes into the new school year and already I was in trouble.

By ten o'clock, Miss Crocker had rearranged our seating and written our names on her seating chart. I was still sitting beside Gracey and Alma but we had been moved from the third to the first row in front of a small potbellied stove. Although being eyeball to eyeball with Miss Crocker was nothing to look forward to, the prospect of being warm once the cold weather set in was nothing to be sneezed at either, so I resolved to make the best of my rather dubious position.

Now Miss Crocker made a startling announcement: This year we would all have books.

Everyone gasped, for most of the students had never handled a book at all besides the family Bible. I admit that even I was somewhat excited. Although Mama had several books, I had never had one of my very own.

"Now we're very fortunate to get these readers," Miss Crocker explained while we eagerly awaited the unveiling. "The county superintendent of schools himself brought these books down here for our use and we must take extra-good care of them." She moved toward her desk. "So let's all promise that we'll take the best care possible of these new books." She stared down, expecting our response. "All right, all together, let's repeat, 'We promise to take good care of our new books.'" She looked sharply at me as she spoke.

"WE PROMISE TO TAKE GOOD CARE OF OUR NEW BOOKS!"

"Fine," Miss Crocker beamed, then proudly threw back the tarpaulin.

Sitting so close to the desk, I could see that the covers of the books, a motley red, were badly worn and that the gray edges of the pages had been marred by pencils, crayons, and ink. My anticipation at having my own book ebbed to a sinking disappointment. But Miss Crocker continued to beam as she called each fourth grader to her desk and, recording a number in her roll book, handed him or her a book.

As I returned from my trip to her desk, I noticed the first graders anxiously watching the disappearing pile. Miss Crocker must have noticed them too, for as I sat down she said, "Don't worry, little ones, there are plenty of readers for you too. See there on Miss Davis's desk." Wide eyes turned to the covered teacher's platform directly in front of them and an audible sigh of relief swelled in the room.

I glanced across at Little Man, his face lit in eager excitement. I knew that he could not see the soiled covers or the marred pages from where he sat, and even though his penchant for cleanliness was often annoying, I did not like to think of his disappointment when he saw the books as they really were. But there was nothing that I could do about it, so I opened my book to its center and began browsing through the spotted pages. Girls with blond braids and boys with blue eyes stared up at me. I found a story about a boy and his dog lost in a cave and began reading while Miss Crocker's voice droned on monotonously.

Suddenly I grew conscious of a break in that monotonous tone and I looked up. Miss Crocker was sitting at Miss Davis's desk with the first-grade books stacked before her, staring fiercely down at Little Man, who was pushing a book back upon the desk.

"What's that you said, Clayton Chester Logan?" she asked.

The room became gravely silent. Everyone knew that Little Man was in big trouble for no one, but no one, ever called Little Man "Clayton Chester" unless she or he meant serious business.

Little Man knew this too. His lips parted slightly as he took his hands from the book. He quivered, but he did not take his eyes from Miss Crocker. "I—I said may I have another book please, ma'am," he squeaked. "That one's dirty."

"Dirty!" Miss Crocker echoed, appalled by such temerity. She stood up, gazing down upon Little Man like a bony giant, but Little Man raised his head and continued to look into her eyes. "Dirty! And just who do you think you are, Clayton Chester? Here the county is giving us these wonderful books during these hard times and you're going to stand there and tell me that the book's too dirty? Now you take that book or get nothing at all!"

Little Man lowered his eyes and said nothing as he stared at the book. For several moments he stood there, his face barely visible above the desk, then he turned and looked at the few remaining books and, seeming to realize that they were as badly soiled as the one Miss Crocker had given him, he looked across the room at me. I nodded and Little Man, glancing up again at Miss Crocker, slid the book from the edge of the desk, and with his back straight and his head up returned to his seat.

Miss Crocker sat down again. "Some people around here seem to be giving themselves airs. I'll tolerate no more of that," she scowled. "Sharon Lake, come get your book."

I watched Little Man as he scooted into his seat beside two other little boys. He sat for a while with a stony face looking out the window; then, evidently accepting the fact that the book in front of him was the best that he could expect, he turned and opened it. But as he stared at the book's inside cover, his face clouded, changing from sulky acceptance to puzzlement. His brows furrowed. Then his eyes grew wide, and suddenly he sucked in his breath and sprang from his chair like a wounded animal, flinging the book onto the floor and stomping madly upon it.

Miss Crocker rushed to Little Man and grabbed him up in powerful hands. She shook him vigorously, then set him on the floor again. "Now, just what's gotten into you, Clayton Chester?"

But Little Man said nothing. He just stood staring down at the open book, shivering with indignant anger.

"Pick it up," she ordered.

"No!" defied Little Man.

"No? I'll give you ten seconds to pick up that book, boy, or I'm going to get my switch."

Little Man bit his lower lip, and I knew that he was not going to pick up the book. Rapidly, I turned to the inside cover of my own book and saw immediately what had made Little Man so furious. Stamped on the inside cover was a chart which read:

PROPERTY OF THE BOARD OF EDUCATION
Spokane County, Mississippi
September, 1922

CHRONOLOGICAL ISSUANCE	DATE OF ISSUANCE	CONDITION OF BOOK	RACE OF STUDENT
1	September 1922	New	White
2	September 1923	Excellent	White
3	September 1924	Excellent	White
4	September 1925	Very Good	White
5	September 1926	Good	White
6	September 1927	Good	White
7	September 1928	Average	White
8	September 1929	Average	White
9	September 1930	Average	White
10	September 1931	Poor	White
11	September 1932	Poor	White
12	September 1933	Very Poor	nigra
13			
14			
15			

The blank lines continued down to line 20 and I knew that they had all been reserved for black students. A knot of anger swelled in my throat and held there. But as Miss Crocker directed Little Man to bend over the "whipping" chair, I put aside my anger and jumped up.

"Miz Crocker, don't, please!" I cried. Miss Crocker's dark eyes warned me not to say another word. "I know why he done it!"

"You want part of this switch, Cassie?"

"No'm," I said hastily. "I just wanna tell you how come Little Man done what he done."

"Sit down!" she ordered as I hurried toward her with the open book in my hand.

Holding the book up to her, I said, "See, Miz Crocker, see what it says. They give us these ole books when they didn't want 'em no more."

She regarded me impatiently, but did not look at the book. "Now how could he know what it says? He can't read."

"Yes'm, he can. He been reading since he was four. He can't read all them big words, but he can read them columns. See what's in the last row. Please look, Miz Crocker."

This time Miss Crocker did look, but her face did not change. Then, holding up her head, she gazed unblinkingly down at me.

"S-see what they called us," I said, afraid she had not seen.

"That's what you are," she said coldly. "Now go sit down."

I shook my head, realizing now that Miss Crocker did not even know what I was talking about. She had looked at the page and had understood nothing.

"I said sit down, Cassie!"

I started slowly toward my desk, but as the hickory stick sliced the tense air, I turned back around. "Miz Crocker," I said, "I don't want my book neither."

The switch landed hard upon Little Man's upturned bottom. Miss Crocker looked questioningly at me as I reached up to her desk and placed the book upon it. Then she swung the switch five more times and, discovering that Little Man had no intention of crying, ordered him up.

"All right, Cassie," she sighed, turning to me, "come on and get yours."

By the end of the school day I had decided that I would tell Mama everything before Miss Crocker had a chance to do so. From nine years of trial and error, I had learned that punishment was always less severe when I poured out the whole truth to Mama on my own before she had heard anything from anyone else. I knew that Miss Crocker had not spoken to Mama during the lunch period, for she had spent the whole hour in the classroom preparing for the afternoon session.

As soon as class was dismissed I sped from the room, weaving a path through throngs of students happy to be free. But before I could reach the seventh-grade-class building, I had the misfortune to collide with Mary Lou's father. Mr. Wellever looked down on me with surprise that I would actually bump into him, then proceeded to lecture me on the virtues of watching where one was going. Meanwhile Miss Crocker briskly crossed the lawn to Mama's class building. By the time I escaped Mr. Wellever, she had already disappeared into the darkness of the hallway.

Mama's classroom was in the back. I crept silently along the quiet hall and peeped cautiously into the open doorway. Mama, pushing a strand of her long, crinkly hair back into the chignon at the base of her slender neck, was seated at her desk watching Miss Crocker thrust a book before her. "Just look at that, Mary," Miss Crocker said, thumping the book twice with her forefinger. "A perfectly good book ruined. Look at that broken binding and those foot marks all over it."

Mama did not speak as she studied the book.

"And here's the one Cassie wouldn't take," she said, placing a second book on Mama's desk with an outraged slam. "At least she didn't have a tantrum and stomp all over hers. I tell you, Mary, I just don't know what got into those children today. I always knew Cassie was rather high-strung, but Little Man! He's always such a perfect little gentleman."

Mama glanced at the book I had rejected and opened the front cover so that the offensive pages of both books faced her. "You say Cassie said it was because of this front page that she and Little Man didn't want the books?" Mama asked quietly.

"Yes, ain't that something?" Miss Crocker said, forgetting her teacher-training-school diction in her indignation. "The very idea! That's on all the books, and why they got so upset about it I'll never know."

"You punish them?" asked Mama, glancing up at Miss Crocker.

"Well, I certainly did! Whipped both of them good with my hickory stick. Wouldn't you have?" When Mama did not reply, she added defensively, "I had a perfect right to."

"Of course you did, Daisy," Mama said, turning back to the books again. "They disobeyed you." But her tone was so quiet and noncommittal that I knew Miss Crocker was not satisfied with her reaction.

"Well, I thought you would've wanted to know, Mary, in case you wanted to give them a piece of your mind also."

Mama smiled up at Miss Crocker and said rather absently, "Yes, of course, Daisy. Thank you." Then she opened her desk drawer and pulled out some paper, a pair of scissors, and a small brown bottle.

Miss Crocker, dismayed by Mama's seeming unconcern for the seriousness of the matter, thrust her shoulders back and began moving away from the desk. "You understand that if they don't have those books to study from, I'll have to fail them in both reading and composition, since I plan to base all my lessons around—" She stopped abruptly and stared in amazement at Mama. "Mary, what in the world are you doing?"

Mama did not answer. She had trimmed the paper to the size of the books and was now dipping a gray-looking glue from the brown bottle onto the inside cover of one of the books. Then she took the paper and placed it over the glue.

"Mary Logan, do you know what you're doing? That book belongs to the county. If somebody from the superintendent's office ever comes down here and sees that book, you'll be in real trouble."

Mama laughed and picked up the other book. "In the first place no one cares enough to come down here, and in the second place if anyone should come, maybe he could see all the things we need—current books for all of our subjects, not just somebody's old throwaways, desks, paper, blackboards, erasers, maps, chalk . . ." Her voice trailed off as she glued the second book.

"Biting the hand that feeds you. That's what you're doing, Mary Logan, biting the hand that feeds you."

Again, Mama laughed. "If that's the case, Daisy, I don't think I need that little bit of food." With the second book finished, she stared at a small pile of seventh-grade books on her desk.

"Well, I just think you're spoiling those children, Mary. They've got to learn how things are sometime."

"Maybe so," said Mama, "but that doesn't mean they have to accept them . . . and maybe we don't either."

Miss Crocker gazed suspiciously at Mama. Although Mama had been a teacher at Great Faith for fourteen years, ever since she had graduated from the Crandon Teacher Training School at nineteen, she was still considered by many of the other teachers as a disrupting maverick. Her ideas were always a bit too radical and her statements a bit too pointed. The fact that she had not grown up in Spokane County but in the Delta made her even more suspect, and the more traditional thinkers like Miss Crocker were wary of her. "Well, if anyone ever does come from the county and sees Cassie's and Little Man's books messed up like that," she said, "I certainly won't accept the responsibility for them."

"It will be easy enough for anyone to see whose responsibility it is, Daisy, by opening any seventh-grade book. Because tomorrow I'm going to 'mess them up' too."

Miss Crocker, finding nothing else to say, turned imperiously and headed for the door. I dashed across the hall and awaited her exit, then crept back.

Mama remained at her desk, sitting very still. For a long time she did not move. When she did, she picked up one of the seventh-grade books and began to glue again. I wanted to go and help her, but something warned me that now was not the time to make my presence known, and I left.

I would wait until the evening to talk to her; there was no rush now. She understood.

2

"Cassie, you better watch yourself, girl," Big Ma cautioned, putting one rough, large hand against my back to make sure I didn't fall.

I looked down at my grandmother from midway up one of the wooden poles Papa had set out to mark the length of the cotton field. Big Ma was Papa's mother, and like him she was tall and strongly built. Her clear, smooth skin was the color of a pecan shell. "Ah, Big Ma, I ain't gonna fall," I scoffed, then climbed onto the next strong spike and reached for a fibrous puff at the top of a tall cotton stalk.

"You sho' better not fall, girl," grumbled Big Ma. "Sometimes I wish we had more low cotton like down 'round Vicksburg. I don't like y'all children climbin' them things." She looked around, her hand on her hip. Christopher-John and Little Man farther down the field balanced skillfully on lower spikes of their own poles plucking the last of the cotton, but Stacey, too heavy now to climb the poles, was forced to remain on the ground. Big Ma eyed us all again, then with a burlap bag slung across her right shoulder and dangling at the left side of her waist she moved down the row toward Mama. "Mary, child, I think with what we picked today we oughta have ourselves another bale."

Mama was stooped over a low cotton branch. She stuffed one last puff into her bag and straightened. She was tawny-colored, thin and sinewy, with delicate features in a strong-jawed face, and though almost as tall as Big Ma, she seemed somewhat dwarfed beside her. "I expect you're right, Mama," she said. "Come Monday, we'd better haul it up to the Granger place and have it ginned. Then we can—Cassie, what's the matter?"

I didn't answer Mama. I had moved to the very top of my pole and could now see above the field to the road where two figures, one much taller than the other, were walking briskly. As the men rounded a curve in the road, they became more distinct. There was in the easy fluid gait of the shorter man a familiarity that made me gasp. I squinted, shadowing my eyes from the sun, then slipped like lightning down the pole.

"Cassie?"

"It's Papa!"

"David?" Mama questioned unbelievingly as Christopher-John and Little Man descended eagerly and dashed after Stacey and me toward the barbed-wire fence.

"Don't y'all go through that fence!" Big Ma called after us. But we pretended not to hear. We held the second and third rows of the prickly wire wide for each other to climb through: then all four of us sped down the road toward Papa.

When Papa saw us, he began running swiftly, easily, like the wind. Little Man, the first to reach him, was swept lightly upward in Papa's strong hands as Christopher-John, Stacey, and I crowded around.

"Papa, what you doing home?" asked Little Man.

Putting Little Man down, Papa said, "Just had to come home and see 'bout my babies." He hugged and kissed each of us, then stood back. "Just look at y'all," he said proudly. "Ain't y'all something? Can't hardly call y'all babies no more." He turned. "Mr. Morrison, what you think 'bout these children of mine?"

In our excitement, we had taken no notice of the other man standing quietly at the side of the road. But now, gazing upward at the most formidable-looking being we had ever encountered, we huddled closer to Papa.

The man was a human tree in height, towering high above Papa's six feet two inches. The long trunk of his massive body bulged with muscles, and his skin, of the deepest ebony, was partially scarred upon his face and neck, as if by fire. Deep lifelines were cut into his face and his hair was splotched with gray, but his eyes were clear and penetrating. I glanced at the boys and it was obvious to me that they were wondering the same thing as I: Where had such a being come from?

"Children," said Papa, "meet Mr. L.T. Morrison."

Each of us whispered a faint hello to the giant, then the six of us started up the road toward home. Before we reached the house, Mama and Big Ma met us. When Papa saw Mama, his square, high-cheekboned face opened to a wide smile and, lifting Mama with spirited gusto, he swung her around twice before setting her down and kissing her.

"David, is something the matter?" she asked.

Papa laughed. "Something gotta be wrong, woman, for me to come see 'bout you?"

"You got my letter?"

He nodded, then hugged and kissed Big Ma before introducing them both to Mr. Morrison.

When we reached the house we climbed the long, sloping lawn to the porch and went into Mama and Papa's room, which also served as the living area. Mama offered Mr. Morrison Grandpa Logan's chair, a cushioned oak rocker skillfully crafted by Grandpa himself; but Mr. Morrison did not sit down immediately. Instead, he stood gazing at the room.

It was a warm, comfortable room of doors and wood and pictures. From it a person could reach the front or the side porch, the kitchen, and the two other bedrooms. Its walls were made of smooth oak, and on them hung gigantic photographs of Grandpa and Big Ma, Papa and Uncle Hammer when they were boys, Papa's two eldest brothers, who were now dead, and pictures of Mama's family. The furniture, a mixture of Logan-crafted walnut and oak, included a walnut bed whose ornate headboard rose halfway up the wall toward the high ceiling, a grand chiffonier with a floor-length mirror, a large rolltop desk which had once been Grandpa's but now belonged to Mama, and the four oak chairs, two of them rockers, which Grandpa had made for Big Ma as a wedding present.

Mr. Morrison nodded when he had taken it all in, as if he approved, then sat across from Papa in front of the unlit fireplace. The boys and I pulled up straight-backed chairs near Papa as Big Ma asked, "How long you gonna be home, son?"

Papa looked across at her. "Till Sunday evening," he said quietly.

"Sunday?" Mama exclaimed. "Why, today's already Saturday."

"I know, baby," Papa said, taking her hand, "but I gotta get that night train out of Vicksburg so I can get back to work by Monday morning."

Christopher-John, Little Man, and I groaned loudly, and Papa turned to us. "Papa, can't you stay no longer than that? Last time you come home, you stayed a week," I said.

Papa gently pulled one of my pigtails. "Sorry, Cassie girl, but I stay any longer, I might lose my job."

"But, Papa—"

"Listen, all of y'all," he said, looking from me to the boys to Mama and Big Ma, "I come home special so I could bring Mr. Morrison. He's gonna stay with us awhile."

If Mama and Big Ma were surprised by Papa's words, they did not show it, but the boys and I looked with wide eyes at each other, then at the giant.

"Mr. Morrison lost his job on the railroad a while back," Papa continued, "and he ain't been able to find anything else. When I asked him if he wanted to come work here as a hired hand, he said he would. I told him we couldn't afford much—food and shelter and a few dollars in cash when I come home in the winter."

Mama turned to Mr. Morrison, studied him for a moment, and said, "Welcome to our home, Mr. Morrison."

"Miz Logan," said Mr. Morrison in a deep, quiet voice like the roll of low thunder, "I think you oughta know I got fired off my job. Got in a fight with some men . . . beat 'em up pretty bad."

Mama stared into Mr. Morrison's deep eyes. "Whose fault was it?"

Mr. Morrison stared back. "I'd say theirs."

"Did the other men get fired?"

"No, ma'am," answered Mr. Morrison. "They was white."

Mama nodded and stood. "Thank you for telling me, Mr. Morrison. You're lucky no worse happened and we're glad to have you here . . . especially now." Then she turned and went into the kitchen with Big Ma to prepare supper, leaving the boys and me to wonder about her last words.

"Stacey, what you think?" I asked as we milked the cows in the evening. "How come Papa come home and brung Mr. Morrison?"

Stacey shrugged. "Like he said, I guess."

I thought on that a moment. "Papa ain't never brung nobody here before."

Stacey did not reply.

"You think . . . Stacey, you think it's cause of them burnings T.J. was talking 'bout?"

"Burnings?" piped Little Man, who had interrupted his feeding of the chickens to visit with Lady, our golden mare. "What's burnings gotta do with anything?"

"That happened way over by Smellings Creek," said Stacey slowly, ignoring Little Man. "Papa got no need to think . . ." His voice trailed off and he stopped milking.

"Think what?" I asked.

"Nothin'," he muttered, turning back to the cow. "Don't worry 'bout it."

I glared at him. "I ain't worrying. I just wanna know, that's all, and I betcha anything Mr. Morrison come here to do more'n work. Sure wish I knew for sure."

Stacey made no reply, but Christopher-John, his pudgy hands filled with dried corn for the chickens and his lower lip quivering, said, "I—I know what I wish. I wish P-Papa didn't never have to go 'way no more. I wish he could just stay . . . and stay. . . ."

At church the next morning, Mrs. Silas Lanier leaned across me and whispered to Big Ma, "John Henry Berry died last night." When the announcement was made to the congregation, the deacons prayed for the soul of John Henry Berry and the recovery of his brother, Beacon, and his uncle, Mr. Samuel Berry. But after church, when some of the members stopped by the house to visit, angry hopeless words were spoken.

"The way I hears it," said Mr. Lanier, "they been after John Henry ever since he come back from the war and settled on his daddy's place up by Smellings Creek. Had a nice little place up there too, and was doing pretty well. Left a wife and six children."

Big Ma shook her head. "Just in the wrong place at the wrong time."

The boys and I sat at our study table pretending not to listen, but listening still.

"Henrietta Toggins," said Mrs. Lanier, "you know, Clara Davis's sister that live up there in Strawberry? Well, she's kin to the Berrys and she was with John Henry and Beacon when the trouble got started. They was gonna drop her off at home—you know John Henry had him one of them old Model-T pickups—but they needed some gas so they stopped by that fillin' station up there in Strawberry. They was waitin' there for they gas when some white men come up messin' with them—been drinkin', you know. And Henrietta heard 'em say, 'That's the nigger Sallie Ann said was flirtin' with her.' And when she heard that, she said to John Henry, 'Let's get on outa here.'

He wanted to wait for the gas, but she made him and Beacon get in that car, and them men jus' watched them drive off and didn't mess with 'em right then.

"John Henry, he took her on home then headed back for his own place, but evidently them men caught up with him and Beacon again and starts rammin' the back of they car—least that's what Beacon and John Henry told they aunt and uncle when they seed 'em. John Henry knowed he was runnin' outa gas and he was 'fraid he couldn't make it to his own place, so he stopped at his uncle's. But them men dragged him and Beacon both outa that house, and when old man Berry tried to stop it, they lit him afire with them boys."

"It's sho' a shame, all right," said T.J.'s father, a frail, sickly man with a hacking cough. "These folks gettin' so bad in here. Heard tell they lynched a boy a few days ago at Crosston."

"And ain't a thing gonna be done 'bout it," said Mr. Lanier. "That's what's so terrible! When Henrietta went to the sheriff and told him what she'd seed, he called her a liar and sent her on home. Now I hear tells that some of them men that done it been 'round braggin' 'bout it. Sayin' they'd do it again if some other uppity nigger get out of line."

Mrs. Avery tisked, "Lord have mercy!"

Papa sat very quietly while the Laniers and the Averys talked, studying them with serious eyes. Finally, he took the pipe from his mouth and made a statement that seemed to the boys and me to be totally disconnected with the conversation. "In this family, we don't shop at the Wallace store."

The room became silent. The boys and I stared at the adults wondering why. The Laniers and the Averys looked uneasily about them and when the silence was broken, the subject had changed to the sermon of the day.

After the Laniers and the Averys had left, Papa called us to him. "Your mama tells me that a lot of the older children been going up to that Wallace store after school to dance and buy their bootleg liquor[6] and smoke cigarettes. Now she said she's already told y'all this, but I'm gonna tell y'all again, so listen good. We don't want y'all going to that place. Children going there are gonna get themselves in a whole lot of trouble one day. There's drinking up there and I don't like it—and I don't like them Wallaces either. If I ever find out y'all been up there, for any reason, I'm gonna wear y'all out. Y'all hear me?"

"Yessir, Papa," piped Christopher-John readily. "I ain't never going up there."

The rest of us agreed; Papa always meant what he said—and he swung a mean switch.

3

By the end of October the rain had come, falling heavily upon the six-inch layer of dust which had had its own way for more than two months. At first the rain had merely splotched the dust, which seemed to be rejoicing in its own resiliency and laughing at the heavy drops thudding against it; but eventually the dust was forced to surrender to the mastery of the rain and it churned into a fine red mud that oozed between our toes and slopped against our ankles as we marched miserably to and from school.

To shield us from the rain, Mama issued us dried calf-skins which we flung over our heads and shoulders like stiff cloaks. We were not very fond of the skins, for once they were wet they emitted a musty odor which seeped into our clothing and

6. In the United States, Prohibition lasted from 1917 until late in 1933.

clung to our skins. We preferred to do without them; unfortunately, Mama cared very little about what we preferred.

Since we usually left for school after Mama, we solved this problem by dutifully cloaking ourselves with the skins before leaving home. As soon as we were beyond Big Ma's eagle eyes, we threw off the cloaks and depended upon the overhanging limbs of the forest trees to keep us dry. Once at school, we donned the cloaks again and marched into our respective classrooms properly attired.

If we had been faced only with the prospect of the rain soaking through our clothing each morning and evening, we could have more easily endured the journey between home and school. But as it was, we also had to worry about the Jefferson Davis school bus zooming from behind and splashing us with the murky waters of the road. Knowing that the bus driver liked to entertain his passengers by sending us slipping along the road to the almost inaccessible forest banks washed to a smooth baldness by the constant rains, we continuously looked over our shoulders when we were between the two crossroads so that we could reach the bank before the bus was upon us. But sometimes the rain pounded so heavily that it was all we could do to stay upright, and we did not look back as often nor listen as carefully as we should; we consequently found ourselves comical objects to cruel eyes that gave no thought to our misery.

No one was more angered by this humiliation than Little Man. Although he had asked Mama after the first day of school why Jefferson Davis had two buses and Great Faith had none, he had never been totally satisfied by her answer. She had explained to him, as she had explained to Christopher-John the year before and to me two years before that, that the county did not provide buses for its black students. In fact, she said, the county provided very little and much of the money which supported the black schools came from the black churches. Great Faith Church just could not afford a bus, so therefore we had to walk.

This information cut deeply into Little Man's brain, and each day when he found his clean clothes splashed red by the school bus, he became more and more embittered until finally one day he stomped angrily into the kitchen and exploded, "They done it again, Big Ma! Just look at my clothes!"

Big Ma clucked her tongue as she surveyed us. "Well, go on and get out of 'em, honey, and wash 'em out. All of y'all, get out of them clothes and dry yo'selves," she said, turning back to the huge iron-bellied stove to stir her stew.

"But, Big Ma, it ain't fair!" wailed Little Man. "It just ain't fair."

Stacey and Christopher-John left to change into their work clothes, but Little Man sat on the side bench looking totally dejected as he gazed at his pale-blue pants crusted with mud from the knees down. Although each night Big Ma prepared a pot of hot soapy water for him to wash out his clothing, each day he arrived home looking as if his pants had not been washed in more than a month.

Big Ma was not one for coddling any of us, but now she turned from the stove and, wiping her hands on her long white apron, sat down on the bench and put her arm around Little Man. "Now, look here, baby, it ain't the end of the world. Lord, child, don't you know one day the sun'll shine again and you won't get muddy no more?"

"But, Big Ma," Little Man protested, "ifn that ole bus driver would slow down, I wouldn't get muddy!" Then he frowned deeply and added, "Or ifn we had a bus like theirs."

"Well, he don't and you don't," Big Ma said, getting up. "So ain't no use frettin' 'bout it. One day you'll have a plenty of clothes and maybe even a car of yo' own to ride 'round in, so don't you pay no mind to them ignorant white folks. You jus' keep on studyin' and get yo'self a good education and you'll be all right. Now, go on and wash out yo' clothes and hang 'em by the fire so's I can iron 'em 'fore I go to bed."

Turning, she spied me. "Cassie, what you want, girl? Go change into yo' pants and hurry on back here so's you can help me get this supper on the table time yo' mama get home."

That night when I was snug in the deep feathery bed beside Big Ma, the tat-tat of the rain against the tin roof changed to a deafening roar that sounded as if thousands of giant rocks were being hurled against the earth. By morning the heavy rain had become a drizzle, but the earth was badly sodden from the night's downpour. High rivers of muddy water flowed in the deep gullies, and wide lakes shimmered on the roads.

As we set out for school the whiteness of the sun attempted to penetrate the storm clouds, but by the time we had turned north toward the second crossing it had given up, slinking meekly behind the blackening clouds. Soon the thunder rolled across the sky, and the rain fell like hail upon our bent heads.

"Ah, shoot! I sure am gettin' tired of this mess," complained T.J.

But no one else said a word. We were listening for the bus. Although we had left home earlier than usual to cover the northern road before the bus came, we were not overly confident that we would miss it, for we had tried this strategy before. Sometimes it worked; most times it didn't. It was as if the bus were a living thing, plaguing and defeating us at every turn. We could not outwit it.

We plodded along feeling the cold mud against our feet, walking faster and faster to reach the crossroads. Then Christopher-John stopped. "Hey, y'all, I think I hear it," he warned.

We looked around, but saw nothing.

"Ain't nothin' yet," I said.

We walked on.

"Wait a minute," said Christopher-John, stopping a second time. "There it is again."

We turned but still there was nothing.

"Why don't you clean out your ears?" T.J. exclaimed.

"Wait," said Stacey, "I think I hear it too."

We hastened up the road to where the gully was narrower and we could easily swing up the bank into the forest.

Soon the purr of a motor came closer and Mr. Granger's sleek silver Packard eased into view. It was a grand car with chrome shining even in the rain, and the only one like it in the county, so it was said.

We groaned. "Jus' ole Harlan," said T.J. flippantly as the expensive car rounded a curve and disappeared, then he and Claude started down the bank.

Stacey stopped them. "Long as we're already up here, why don't we wait awhile," he suggested. "The bus oughta be here soon and it'll be harder to get up on the bank further down the road."

"Ah, man, that bus ain't comin' for a while yet," said T.J. "We left early this mornin', remember?"

Stacey looked to the south, thinking. Little Man, Christopher-John and I waited for his decision.

"Come on, man," T.J. persuaded. "Why stay up here waitin' for that devilish bus when we could be at school outa this mess?"

"Well . . ."

T.J. and Claude jumped from the bank. Then Stacey, frowning as if he were doing this against his better judgment, jumped down too. Little Man, Christopher-John, and I followed.

Five minutes later we were skidding like frightened puppies toward the bank again as the bus accelerated and barreled down the narrow rain-soaked road; but there was no place to which we could run, for Stacey had been right. Here the gullies were too wide, filled almost to overflowing, and there were no briars or bushes by which we could swing up onto the bank.

Finally, when the bus was less than fifty feet behind us, it veered dangerously close to the right edge of the road where we were running, forcing us to attempt the jump to the bank; but all of us fell short and landed in the slime of the gully.

Little Man, chest-deep in water, scooped up a handful of mud and in an uncontrollable rage scrambled up to the road and ran after the retreating bus. As moronic rolls of laughter and cries of "Nigger! Nigger! Mud eater!" wafted from the open windows, Little Man threw his mudball, missing the wheels by several feet. Then, totally dismayed by what had happened, he buried his face in his hands and cried.

T.J. climbed from the gully grinning at Little Man, but Stacey, his face burning red beneath his dark skin, glared so fiercely at T.J. that he fell back. "Just one word outa you, T.J.," he said tightly. "Just one word."

Christopher-John and I looked at each other. We had never seen Stacey look like this, and neither had T.J.

"Hey, man, I ain't said nothin'! I'm jus' as burnt as you are."

Stacey glowered at T.J. a moment longer, then walked swiftly to Little Man and put his long arm around his shoulders, saying softly, "Come on, Man. It ain't gonna happen no more, least not for a long while. I promise you that."

Again, Christopher-John and I looked questioningly at each other, wondering how Stacey could make such a rash promise. Then, shrugging, we hurried after him.

When Jeremy Simms spied us from his high perch on the forest path, he ran hastily down and joined us.

"Hey," he said, his face lighting into a friendly grin. But no one spoke to him.

The smile faded and, noticing our mud-covered clothing, he asked, "Hey, St-Stacey, wh-what happened?"

Stacey turned, stared into his blue eyes and said coldly, "Why don't you leave us alone? How come you always hanging 'round us anyway?"

Jeremy grew even more pale. "C-cause I just likes y'all," he stammered. Then he whispered, "W-was it the bus again?"

No one answered him and he said no more. When we reached the crossroads, he looked hopefully at us as if we might relent and say good-bye. But we did not relent and as I glanced back at him standing alone in the middle of the crossing, he looked as if the world itself was slung around his neck. It was only then that I realized that Jeremy never rode the bus, no matter how bad the weather.

As we crossed the school lawn, Stacey beckoned Christopher-John, Little Man, and me aside. "Look," he whispered, "meet me at the toolshed right at noon."

"Why?" we asked.

He eyed us conspiratorily. "I'll show y'all how we're gonna stop that bus from splashing us."

"How?" asked Little Man, eager for revenge.

"Don't have time to explain now. Just meet me. And be on time. It's gonna take us all lunch hour."

"Y-you mean we ain't gonna eat no lunch!" Christopher-John cried in dismay.

"You can miss lunch for one day," said Stacey, moving away. But Christopher-John looked sourly after him as if he greatly questioned the wisdom of a plan so drastic that it could exclude lunch.

"You gonna tell T.J. and Claude?" I asked.

Stacey shook his head. "T.J.'s my best friend, but he's got no stomach for this kinda thing. He talks too much, and we couldn't include Claude without T.J."

"Good," said Little Man.

At noon, we met as planned and ducked into the unlocked toolshed where all the church and school garden tools were kept. Stacey studied the tools available while the rest of us watched. Then, grabbing the only shovels, he handed one to me, holding on to the other himself, and directed Little Man and Christopher-John to each take two buckets.

Stealthily emerging from the toolshed into the drizzle, we eased along the forest edge behind the class buildings to avoid being seen. Once on the road, Stacey began to run. "Come on, hurry," he ordered. "We ain't got much time."

"Where we going?" asked Christopher-John, still not quite adjusted to the prospect of missing lunch.

"Up to where that bus forced us off the road. Be careful now," he said to Christopher-John, already puffing to keep up.

When we reached the place where we had fallen into the gully, Stacey halted. "All right," he said, "start digging." Without another word, he put his bare foot upon the top edge of the shovel and sank it deep into the soft road. "Come on, come on," he ordered, glancing up at Christopher-John, Little Man and me, who were wondering whether he had finally gone mad.

"Cassie, you start digging over there on that side of the road right across from me. That's right, don't get too near the edge. It's gotta look like it's been washed out. Christopher-John, you and Little Man start scooping out mud from the middle of the road. Quick now," he said, still digging as we began to carry out his commands. "We only got 'bout thirty minutes so's we can get back to school on time."

We asked no more questions. While Stacey and I shoveled ragged holes almost a yard wide and a foot deep toward each other, dumping the excess mud into the water-filled gullies, Little Man and Christopher-John scooped bucketfuls of the red earth from the road's center. And for once in his life, Little Man was happily oblivious to the mud spattering upon him.

When Stacey's and my holes merged into one big hole with Little Man's and Christopher-John's, Stacey and I threw down our shovels and grabbed the extra buckets. Then the four of us ran back and forth to the gullies, hastily filling the buckets with the murky water and dumping it into the hole.

Now understanding Stacey's plan, we worked wordlessly until the water lay at the same level as the road. Then Stacey waded into the gully water and pulled himself up onto the forest bank. Finding three rocks, he stacked them to identify the spot.

"It might look different this afternoon," he explained, jumping down again.

Christopher-John looked up at the sky. "Looks like it's gonna rain real hard some more."

"Let's hope so," said Stacey. "The more rain, the better. That'll make it seem more likely that the road could've been washed away like that. It'll also keep cars and wagons away." He looked around, surveying the road. "And let's hope don't nothin' come along 'fore that bus. Let's go."

Quickly we gathered our buckets and shovels and hurried back to school. After returning the tools to the toolshed, we stopped at the well to wash the mud from our arms and feet, then rushed into our classes, hoping that the mud caked on our clothes would go unnoticed. As I slipped into my seat Miss Crocker looked at me oddly and shook her head, but when she did the same thing as Mary Lou and Alma sat down, I decided that my mud was no more noticeable than anyone else's.

Soon after I had settled down to the boredom of Miss Crocker, the rain began to pound down again, hammering with great intensity upon the tin roof. After school it was still raining as the boys and I, avoiding T.J. and Claude, rushed along the slippery road recklessly bypassing more cautious students.

"You think we'll get there in time to see, Stacey?" I asked.

"We should. They stay in school fifteen minutes longer than we do and it always takes them a few minutes to load up."

When we reached the crossing, we glanced toward Jefferson Davis. The buses were there but the students had not been dismissed. We hastened on.

Expecting to see the yard-wide ditch we had dug at noon, we were not prepared for the twelve-foot lake which glimmered up at us.

"Holy smokes! What happened?" I exclaimed.

"The rain," said Stacey. "Quick, up on the bank." Eagerly, we settled onto the muddy forest floor and waited.

"Hey, Stacey," I said, "won't that big a puddle make that ole driver cautious?"

Stacey frowned, then said uncertainly, "I don't know. Hope not. There's big puddles down the road that ain't deep, just water heavy."

"If I was to be walking out there when the bus comes, that ole bus driver would be sure to speed up so's he could splash me," I suggested.

"Or maybe me," Little Man volunteered, ready to do anything for his revenge.

Stacey thought a moment, but decided against it. "Naw. It's better none of us be on the road when it happens. It might give 'em ideas."

"Stacey, what if they find out we done it?" asked Christopher-John nervously.

"Don't worry, they won't," assured Stacey.

"Hey, I think it's coming," whispered Little Man.

We flattened ourselves completely and peered through the low bushes.

The bus rattled up the road, though not as quickly as we had hoped. It rolled cautiously through a wide puddle some twenty feet ahead; then, seeming to grow bolder as it approached our man-made lake, it speeded up, spraying the water in high sheets of backward waterfalls into the forest. We could hear the students squealing with delight. But instead of the graceful glide through the puddle that its occupants were expecting, the bus emitted a tremendous crack and careened drunkenly into our trap. For a moment it swayed and we held our breath, afraid that it would topple over. Then it sputtered a last murmuring protest and died, its left front wheel in our ditch, its right wheel in the gully, like a lopsided billy goat on its knees.

We covered our mouths and shook with silent laughter.

As the dismayed driver opened the rear emergency exit, the rain poured down upon him in sharp-needled darts. He stood in the doorway looking down with disbelief at his sunken charge; then, holding on to the bus, he poked one foot into the water until it was on solid ground before gingerly stepping down. He looked under the bus. He looked at the steaming hood. He looked at the water. Then he scratched his head and cursed.

"How bad is it, Mr. Grimes?" a large, freckle-faced boy asked, pushing up one of the cracked windows and sticking out his head. "Can we push it out and fix it?"

"Push it out? Fix it?" the bus driver echoed angrily. "I got me a broken axle here an' a water-logged engine no doubt and no tellin' what-all else and you talkin' 'bout fixin' it! Y'all come on, get outa there! Y'all gonna have to walk home."

"Mister Grimes," a girl ventured, stepping hesitantly from the rear of the bus, "you gonna be able to pick us up in the mornin'?"

The bus driver stared at her in total disbelief. "Girl, all y'all gonna be walkin' for at least two weeks by the time we get this thing hauled outa here and up to Strawberry to get fixed. Now y'all get on home." He kicked a back tire, and added, "And get y'all's daddies to come on up here and give me a hand with this thing."

The students turned dismally from the bus. They didn't know how wide the hole actually was. Some of them took a wild guess and tried to jump it; but most of them miscalculated and fell in, to our everlasting delight. Others attempted to hop over the gullies to the forest to bypass the hole; however, we knew from much experience that they would not make it.

By the time most of the students managed to get to the other side of the ditch, their clothes were dripping with the weight of the muddy water. No longer laughing, they moved spiritlessly toward their homes while a disgruntled Mr. Grimes leaned moodily against the raised rear end of the bus.

Oh, how sweet was well-maneuvered revenge!

With that thought in mind, we quietly eased away and picked our way through the dense forest toward home.

At supper Mama told Big Ma of the Jefferson Davis bus being stuck in the ditch. "It's funny, you know, such a wide ditch in one day. I didn't even notice the beginning of it this morning—did you, children?"

"No'm," we chorused.

"You didn't fall in, did you?"

"We jumped onto the bank when we thought the bus would be coming," said Stacey truthfully.

"Well, good for you," approved Mama. "If that bus hadn't been there when I came along, I'd probably have fallen in myself."

The boys and I looked at each other. We hadn't thought about that.

"How'd you get across, Mama?" Stacey asked.

"Somebody decided to put a board across the washout."

"They gonna haul that bus outa there tonight?" Big Ma inquired.

"No, ma'am," said Mama. "I heard Mr. Granger telling Ted Grimes—the bus driver—that they won't be able to get it out until after the rain stops and it dries up a bit. It's just too muddy now."

We put our hands to our mouths to hide happy grins. I even made a secret wish that it would rain until Christmas.

Mama smiled. "You know I'm glad no one was hurt—could've been too with such a deep ditch—but I'm also rather glad it happened."

"Mary!" Big Ma exclaimed.

"Well, I am," Mama said defiantly, smiling smugly to herself and looking very much like a young girl. "I really am."

Big Ma began to grin. "You know somethin'? I am too."

Then all of us began to laugh and were deliciously happy.

Later that evening the boys and I sat at the study table in Mama and Papa's room attempting to concentrate on our lessons; but none of us could succeed for more than a few minutes without letting out a triumphant giggle. More than once Mama scolded us, telling us to get down to business. Each time she did, we set our faces into looks of great seriousness, resolved that we would be adult about the matter and not gloat in our hour of victory. Yet just one glance at each other and we were lost, slumping on the table in helpless, contagious laughter.

"All right," Mama said finally. "I don't know what's going on here, but I suppose I'd better do something about it or you'll never get any work done."

It occurred to us that Mama might be preparing to whip us and we shot each other warning glances. But even that thought couldn't dampen our laughter, now uncontrollable, welling up from the pits of our stomachs and forcing streams of laughter tears down our faces. Stacey, holding his sides, turned to the wall in an attempt to bring himself under control. Little Man put his head under the table. But Christopher-John and I just doubled up and fell upon the floor.

Mama took my arm and pulled me up. "Over here, Cassie," she said, directing me to a chair next to the fireplace and behind Big Ma, who was ironing our clothes for the next day.

I peeped around Big Ma's long skirts and saw Mama guiding Stacey to her own desk. Then back she went for Little Man and, picking him up bodily, set him in the chair beside her rocker. Christopher-John she left alone at the study table. Then she gathered all our study materials and brought them to us along with a look that said she would tolerate no more of this foolishness.

With Big Ma before me, I could see nothing else and I grew serious enough to complete my arithmetic assignment. When that was finished, I lingered before opening my reader, watching Big Ma as she hung up my ironed dress, then placed her heavy iron on a small pile of embers burning in a corner of the fireplace and picked up a second iron already warming there. She tested the iron with a tap of her finger and put it back again.

While Big Ma waited for the iron to get hot, I could see Mama bending over outspread newspapers scraping the dried mud off the old field shoes of Papa's which she wore daily, stuffed with wads of newspaper, over her own shoes to protect them from the mud and rain. Little Man beside her was deep into his first-grade reader, his eyebrows furrowed in concentration. Ever since Mama had brought the reader home with the offensive inside cover no longer visible, Little Man had accepted the book as a necessary tool for passing the first grade. But he took no pride in it. Looking up, he noticed that Big Ma was now preparing to iron his clothes, and he smiled happily. Then his eyes met mine and silent laughter creased his face. I muffled a giggle and Mama looked up.

"Cassie, you start up again and I'm sending you to the kitchen to study," she warned.

"Yes'm," I said, settling back in my chair and beginning to read. I certainly did not want to go to the kitchen. Now that the fire no longer burned in the stove, it was cold in there.

The room grew quiet again, except for the earthy humming of Big Ma's rich alto voice, the crackle of the hickory fire, and the patter of rain on the roof. Engrossed in a mystery, I was startled when the comfortable sounds were shattered by three rapid knocks on the side door.

Rising quickly, Mama went to the door and called, "Who is it?"

"It's me, ma'am," came a man's gravelly voice. "Joe Avery."

Mama opened the door and Mr. Avery stepped dripping into the room.

"Why, Brother Avery," Mama said, "what are you doing out on a night like this? Come on in. Take off your coat and sit by the fire. Stacey, get Mr. Avery a chair."

"No'm," said Mr. Avery, looking rather nervously over his shoulder into the night. "I ain't got but a minute." He stepped far enough into the room so that he could close the door, then nodded to the rest of us. "Evenin', Miz Caroline, how you t'night?"

"Oh, I'll do, I reckon," said Big Ma, still ironing. "How's Miz Fannie?"

"She's fine," he said without dwelling on his wife. "Miz Logan . . . uh, I come to tell you somethin' . . . somethin' important—Mr. Morrison here?"

Mama stiffened. "David. You heard something about David?"

"Oh, no'm," replied Mr. Avery hastily. "Ain't heard nothin' 'bout yo' husband, ma'am."

Mama regarded him quizzically.

"It's . . . it's them again. They's ridin' t'night."

Mama, her face pale and frightened, glanced back at Big Ma; Big Ma held her iron in midair.

"Uh . . . children," Mama said, "I think it's your bedtime."

"But, Mama—" we chorused in protest, wanting to stay and hear who was riding.

"Hush," Mama said sternly. "I said it was time to go to bed. Now go!"

Groaning loudly enough to voice our displeasure, but not loudly enough to arouse Mama's anger, we stacked our books upon the study table and started toward the boys' room.

"Cassie, I said go to bed. That's not your room."

"But, Mama, it's cold in there," I pouted. Usually, we were allowed to build small fires in the other rooms an hour before bedtime to warm them up.

"You'll be warm once you're under the covers. Stacey, take the flashlight with you and light the lantern in your room. Cassie, take the lamp from the desk with you."

I went back and got the kerosene lamp, then entered my bedroom, leaving the door slightly ajar.

"Close that door, Cassie!"

Immediately, the door was closed.

I put the lamp on the dresser, then silently slid the latch off the outside door and slipped onto the wet front porch. I crossed to the boys' room. Tapping lightly, I whispered, "Hey, let me in."

The door creaked open and I darted in. The room was bathed in darkness.

"What they say?" I asked.

"Shhhhh!" came the answer.

I crept to the door leading into Mama's room and huddled beside the boys.

The rain softened upon the roof and we could hear Mama asking, "But why? Why are they riding? What's happened?"

"I don't rightly know," said Mr. Avery. "But y'all knows how they is. Anytime they thinks we steppin' outa our *place*, they feels like they gotta stop us. You know what some of 'em done to the Berrys." He paused, then went on bitterly, "It don't take but a little of nothin' to set them devilish night men off."

"But somethin' musta happened," Big Ma said. "How you know 'bout it?"

"All's I can tell ya, Miz Caroline, is what Fannie heard when she was leavin' the Grangers' this evenin'. She'd just finished cleanin' up the supper dishes when Mr. Granger come home with Mr. Grimes—ya know, that white school's bus driver— and two other mens. . . ."

A clap of deafening thunder drowned Mr. Avery's words, then the rain quickened and the conversation was lost.

I grabbed Stacey's arm. "Stacey, they're coming after *us*!"

"What!" squeaked Christopher-John.

"Hush," Stacey said harshly. "And Cassie, let go. That hurts."

"Stacey, somebody musta seen and told on us," I persisted.

"No . . ." Stacey replied unconvincingly. "It couldn't be."

"Couldn't be?" cried Christopher-John in a panic. "Whaddaya mean it couldn't be?"

"Stacey," said Little Man excitedly, "whaddaya think they gonna do to us? Burn us up?"

"Nothin'!" Stacey exclaimed, standing up suddenly. "Now why don't y'all go to bed like y'all s'pose to?"

We were stunned by his attitude. He sounded like Mama and I told him so.

He collapsed in silence by the door, breathing hard, and although I could not see him, I knew that his face was drawn and that his eyes had taken on a haggard look. I touched his arm lightly. "Ain't no call to go blaming yourself," I said. "We all done it."

"But I got us into it," he said listlessly.

"But we all wanted to do it," I comforted.

"Not me!" denied Christopher-John. "All I wanted to do was eat my lunch!"

"Shhhhh," hissed Little Man. "I can hear 'em again."

"I'd better go tell Mr. Morrison," Mr. Avery was saying. "He out back?"

"I'll tell him," said Mama.

We could hear the side door open and we scrambled up.

"Cassie, get back to your room quick," Stacey whispered. "They'll probably come check on us now."

"But what'll we do?"

"Nothin' now, Cassie. Them men probably won't even come near here."

"Ya really believe that?" asked Christopher-John hopefully.

"But shouldn't we tell Mama?" I asked.

"No! We can't ever tell nobody!" declared Stacey adamantly. "Now go on, hurry!"

Footsteps neared the door. I dashed onto the porch and hastened back to my own room, where I jumped under the bedcovers with my clothes still on. Shivering, I pulled the heavy patchwork quilts up to my chin.

A few moments later Big Ma came in, leaving the door to Mama's room open. Knowing that she would be suspicious of such an early surrender to sleep, I sighed softly and, making sleepy little sounds, turned onto my stomach, careful not to expose my shirt sleeves. Obviously satisfied by my performance, Big Ma tucked the covers more closely around me and smoothed my hair gently. Then she stooped and started fishing for something under our bed.

I opened my eyes. Now what the devil was she looking for down there? While she was searching, I heard Mama approaching and I closed my eyes again.

"Mama?"

"Stacey, what're you doing up?"

"Let me help."

"Help with what?"

"With . . . with whatever's the matter."

Mama was silent a moment, then said softly, "Thank you, Stacey, but Big Ma and I can handle it."

"But Papa told me to help you!"

"And you do, more than you know. But right now you could help me most by going back to bed. It's a school day tomorrow, remember?"

"But, Mama—"

"If I need you, I'll call you. I promise."

I heard Stacey walk slowly away, then Mama whispering in the doorway, "Cassie asleep?"

"Yeah, honey," Big Ma said. "Go on and sit back down. I'll be out in a minute."

Then Big Ma stood up and turned down the wick of the kerosene lamp. As she left the room, my eyes popped open again and I saw her outlined in the doorway, a rifle in her hands. Then she closed the door and I was left to the darkness.

For long minutes I waited, wide awake, wondering what my next move should be. Finally deciding that I should again consult with the boys, I swung my legs over the edge of the bed, but immediately had to swing them back again as Big Ma reentered the room. She passed the bed and pulled a straight-backed chair up to the window. Parting the curtains so that the blackness of the night mixed with the blackness of the room, she sat down without a sound.

I heard the door to the boys' room open and close and I knew that Mama had gone in. I waited for the sound of the door opening again, but it did not come. Soon the chill of the cotton sheets beneath me began to fade and as Big Ma's presence lulled me into a security I did not really feel, I fell asleep.

When I awoke, it was still nightly dark. "Big Ma?" I called. "Big Ma, you there?" But there was no reply from the chair by the window. Thinking that Big Ma had fallen asleep, I climbed from the bed and felt my way to her chair.

She wasn't there.

Outside, an owl hooted into the night, quiet now except for the drip-drap of water falling from the roof. I stood transfixed by the chair, afraid to move.

Then I heard a noise on the porch. I could not control my trembling. Again the noise, this time close to the door, and it occurred to me that it was probably the boys coming to confer with me. No doubt Mama had left them alone too.

Laughing silently at myself, I hurried onto the porch. "Stacey," I whispered. "Christopher-John?" There was a sudden movement near the end of the porch and I headed toward it, feeling along the wall of the house. "Little Man? Hey, y'all, stop fooling 'round and answer me."

I crept precariously near the edge of the high porch, my eyes attempting to penetrate the blackness of the night. From below, a scratchy bristlyness sprang upon me, and I lost my balance and tumbled with a thud into the muddy flower bed. I lay paralyzed with fear. Then a long wet tongue licked my face.

"Jason? Jason, that you?"

Our hound dog whined his reply.

I hugged him, then instantly let him go. "Was that you all the time? Look what you gone and done," I fussed, thinking of the mess I was in with mud all over me.

Jason whined again and I got up.

I started to climb back up onto the porch but froze as a caravan of headlights appeared suddenly in the east, coming fast along the rain-soaked road like cat eyes in the night. Jason whined loudly, growing skittish as the lights approached, and when they slowed and braked before the house he slunk beneath the porch. I wanted to follow, but I couldn't. My legs would not move.

The lead car swung into the muddy driveway and a shadowy figure outlined by the headlights of the car behind him stepped out. The man walked slowly up the drive.

I stopped breathing.

The driver of the next car got out, waiting. The first man stopped and stared at the house for several long moments as if uncertain whether it was the correct destination. Then he shook his head, and without a word returned to his car. With a wave of his hand he sent the other driver back inside, and in less than a minute the lead car had backed into the road, its headlights facing the other cars. Each of the cars used the driveway to turn around, then the caravan sped away as swiftly as it had come, its seven pairs of rear lights glowing like distant red embers until they were swallowed from view by the Granger forest.

Jason began barking now that the danger had passed, but he did not come out. As I reached for the porch to steady myself, there was a sense of quiet movement in the darkness. The moon slid from its dark covers, cloaking the earth in a shadowy white light, and I could see Mr. Morrison clearly, moving silently, like a jungle cat, from the side of the house to the road, a shotgun in his hand. Feeling sick, I crawled onto the porch and crept trembling toward the door.

Once inside the house, I leaned against the latch while waves of sick terror swept over me. Realizing that I must get into bed before Mama or Big Ma came from the other room, I pulled off my muddy clothes, turning them inside out to wipe the mud from my body, and put on my night clothes. Then I climbed into the softness of the bed. I lay very still for a while, not allowing myself to think. But soon, against my will, the vision of ghostly headlights soaked into my mind and an uncontrollable trembling racked my body. And it remained until the dawn, when I fell into a restless sleep.

4

"Cassie, what's the matter with you, girl?" Big Ma asked as she thrust three sticks of dried pine into the stove to rekindle the dying morning fire. "You sure are takin' a sorrowful long time to churn that butter."

"Nothin'," I muttered.

"Nothin'?" Big Ma turned and looked directly at me. "You been mopin' 'round here for the past week like you got the whoopin' cough, flu, and measles all put together."

I sighed deeply and continued to churn.

Big Ma reached out and felt my forehead, then my cheeks. Frowning, she pulled her hand away as Mama entered the kitchen. "Mary, feel this child's face," she said. "She seem warm to you?"

Mama cupped my face in her thin hands. "You feel sick, Cassie?"

"No'm."

"How do you feel?"

"All right," I said, still churning.

Mama studied me with the same disturbed look Big Ma wore and a tiny frown line appeared on her brow. "Cassie," she said softly, fixing her dark eyes upon me, "is there something you want to tell me?"

I was on the verge of blurting out the awful truth about the bus and the men in the night, but then I remembered the pact Stacey had made us all swear to when I had told him, Christopher-John, and Little Man about the caravan and I said instead, "No, ma'am," and began to churn again. Abruptly, Mama took hold of the churning stick, her eyes searching mine. As she studied me, she seemed about to ask me something, then the question faded and she pulled away, lifting the lid of the churn. "It looks ready now," she said with a sigh. "Dip out the butter like I showed you and wash it down. I'll take care of the milk."

I scooped the butter from the churning lid onto a plate and went through the curtain to the small pantry off the kitchen to get the molding dish.[7] It had been placed on a high shelf under several other dishes and I had to stand on a stool to get it. As I eased it out, Mama and Big Ma spoke softly in worried tones on the other side of the curtain.

"Somethin' the matter with that child, Mary."

7. A dish used to form butter into a regular shape.

"She's not sick, Mama."

"There's all sorts of sickness. She ain't ate right for goin' on over a week. She ain't sleepin' right neither. Restless and murmurin' in her sleep all night long. And she won't hardly even go out and play, rather be in here helpin' us. Now you know that ain't like that child."

There was a moment's pause, then Mama whispered so I could hardly hear her. "You think . . . Mama, you think she could've seen—"

"Oh, Lord, no, child," Big Ma exclaimed hastily. "I checked in there right after they passed and she was sound asleep. She couldn't've seen them ole devils. The boys neither."

Mama sighed. "The boys, they're not themselves either. All of them, too quiet. Here it is Saturday morning and they're quiet as church mice. I don't like it, and I can't shake the feeling it's got something to do with— Cassie!"

Without warning, I had lost my balance and with an absurd topple from the knee-high stool crashed upon the floor with the molding dish. "Cassie, you hurt?" Mama asked, stooping beside me.

"No'm," I mumbled, feeling very clumsy and close to tears. I knew that if I let the tears fall, Mama's suspicion that something was wrong would be confirmed for I never cried about such a silly thing as a fall; in fact, I seldom ever cried. So instead of crying, I jumped up quickly and began to pick up the broken pieces of the dish.

"I'm sorry, Mama," I said.

"That's all right," she said, helping me. When we had swept the chips away with the long field-straw broom, she told me, "Leave the butter, Cassie, and go on in with the boys."

"But, Mama—"

"I'll do the butter. Now go on, do like I say."

I stared up at Mama, wondering if she would ever know what we had done, then joined the boys who were sitting listlessly around the fire absently listening to T.J.

"See, fellows, there's a system to getting out of work," T.J. was expounding as I sat down. "Jus' don't be 'round when it's got to be done. Only thing is, you can't let your folks know that's what you're doin'. See, you should do like me. Like this mornin' when Mama wanted to bring back them scissors she borrowed from Miz Logan, I ups and volunteers so she don't have to make this long trip down here, she bein' so busy and all. And naturally when I got here, y'all wanted me to stay awhile and talk to y'all, so what could I do? I couldn't be impolite, could I? And by the time I finally convince y'all I gotta go, all the work'll be done at home." T.J. chuckled with satisfaction. "Yeah, you just have to use the old brain, that's all."

He was quiet a moment, expecting some comment on his discourse, but no one said a word.

T.J.'s eyes roamed the length of the room, then he admonished, "See, if you was smart like me, Stacey, you'd use the old brain to get the questions on that big test comin' up. Just think, they probably jus' sittin' right here in this very room waitin' to be discovered."

Stacey cast T.J. an annoyed look, but did not speak.

"Y'all sure are a sorry lot this mornin'," T.J. observed. "A fellow's just wastin' his know-how talkin' to y'all."

"Ain't nobody asked you to give it," said Stacey.

"Well, you don't have to get snippety about it," replied T.J. haughtily. Again, silence prevailed; but that would not do for T.J. "Say, how 'bout we sneak down to that ole Wallace store and learn how to do them new dances?"

"Mama told us not to go down there," Stacey said.

"You some mama's boy or somethin' you gotta do everything your mama tells—"

"You go on if you wanna," said Stacey quietly, not rising to T.J.'s bait, "but we staying here."

Again, silence.

Then T.J. said: "Say, y'all hear the latest 'bout them night men?" Suddenly, all eyes turned from the fire and riveted themselves upon him. Our faces were eager question marks; we were totally in T.J's power.

"What 'bout them?" Stacey asked, almost evenly.

T.J., of course, intended to nurse the moment for as long as he could. "You see when a fellow's as smart as me, he gets to know things that other folks don't. Now, this kind of information ain't for the ears of little kids so I really shouldn't even tell y'all—"

"Then don't!" said Stacey with smooth finality, turning back toward the fire as if he cared not at all about the night men. Taking his cue, I nudged Christopher-John and Christopher-John nudged Little Man, and the three of us forced ourselves to stare into the fire in feigned disinterest.

Without a captive audience, T.J. had to reinterest us by getting to the point. "Well, 'bout a week ago, they rode down to Mr. Sam Tatum's place—you know, down the Jackson Road toward Strawberry—and you know what they done?"

Stacey, Little Man, and I kept our eyes upon the fire, but Christopher-John piped eagerly, "What?"

I poked Christopher-John and he turned guiltily around, but T.J., triumphant with an assured audience of one, settled back in his chair ready to prolong the suspense. "You know Mama'd kill me if she knowed I was tellin' this. I heard her and Miz Claire Thompson talkin' 'bout it. They was real scared. Don't know why though. Them ole night men sure wouldn't scare me none. Like I told Claude—"

"Hey, y'all," Stacey said, standing and motioning us up. "Mama said she wanted us to take some milk and butter down to Miz Jackson before noon. We'd better get started."

I nodded, and Christopher-John, Little Man, and I got up.

"Tarred and feathered him!" T.J. announced hastily. "Poured the blackest tar they could find all over him, then plastered him with chicken feathers." T.J. laughed. "Can you imagine that?"

"But why?" asked Little Man, forgetting our ploy.

This time T.J. did not slow down. "I dunno if y'all's little ears should hear this, but it seems he called Mr. Jim Lee Barnett a liar—he's the man who runs the Mercantile down in Strawberry. Mr. Tatum's s'pose to done told him that he ain't ordered up all them things Mr. Barnett done charged him for. Mr. Barnett said he had all them things Mr. Tatum ordered writ down and when Mr. Tatum asked to see that list of his, Mr. Barnett says, 'You callin' me a liar, boy?' And Mr. Tatum says, 'Yessuh, I guess I is!' That done it!"

"Then it wasn't 'cause of the bus?" Christopher-John blurted out.

"Bus? What's a bus got to do with it?"

"Nothin'," said Stacey quickly. "Nothin' at all."

"Well, if anybody said them night men was down in here 'cause of some stupid bus, they crazy," said T.J. authoritatively. " 'Cause my information come direct from Miz Claire Thompson who seen Mr. Tatum herself."

"You sure?" Stacey asked.

"Sure? Sure, I'm sure. When do I ever say anythin' when I ain't sure?"

Stacey smiled with relief. "Come on, let's get the milk."

All of us went into the kitchen, then to the bedrooms to get our coats. When we got outside, T.J. remembered that he had left his cap by the fire and ran back to retrieve it. As soon as we were alone, Little Man asked, "Stacey, you really think them night men put tar and feathers all over Mr. Tatum?"

"I s'pose so," said Stacey.

Little Man frowned, but it was Christopher-John who spoke, whispering shrilly as if a stray morning ghost might overhear. "If they ever find out 'bout the bus, you think they gonna put tar and feathers all over us?"

Little Man's frown deepened and he observed gravely, "If they did, we'd never get clean again."

"Cassie," said Christopher-John, his eyes wide, "w-was you real s-scared when you seen 'em?"

Little Man shivered with excitement. "I wish I could've seen 'em."

"Well, I don't," declared Christopher-John. "In fact, I wish I'd never heard of no night men or buses or secrets or holes in the road!" And with that outburst, he stuffed his pudgy hands into his thin jacket, pressed his lips firmly together, and refused to say another word.

After a few moments, Stacey said, "What's keeping T.J.?" The rest of us shrugged, then followed Stacey back up the porch into Mama's room. As we entered, T.J. jumped. He was standing at the desk with Mama's W. E. B. Du Bois's *The Negro*[8] in his hands.

"That don't look like your cap," said Stacey.

"Aw, man, I ain't done nothin'. Jus' lookin' at Miz Logan's history book, that's all. I'm mighty interested in that place called Egypt she been tellin' us 'bout and them black kings that was rulin' back then." Still talking, he casually put down the book and picked up his cap.

All four of us looked accusingly at T.J. and he halted. "Say, what is this? What's the meanin' of sneakin' up on me like that anyway? Y'all think I was lookin' for them test questions or somethin'? Shoot, a fellow'd think you didn't trust him." Then, thrusting his arm around Stacey's shoulders, he chided, "Friends gotta trust each other, Stacey, 'cause ain't nothin' like a true friend." And with those words of wisdom he left the room, leaving us to wonder how he had managed to slink out of this one.

The Monday after his arrival Mr. Morrison had moved into the deserted tenant shack that stood in the south pasture. It was a sorry mess, that house. Its door hung sadly from a broken hinge; its porch floorboards were rotted; and its one-room interior was densely occupied by rats, spiders, and other field creatures. But Mr. Morrison was a quiet man, almost shy, and although Mama had offered him lodging in our house, he preferred the old shack. Mama sensed that Mr. Morrison was a private person and she did not object to the move, but she did send the boys and me to the house to help clean it.

Little Man, Christopher-John, and I took to Mr. Morrison immediately and had no objections to the cleaning. Anybody who was a friend of Papa's was all right in our book; besides, when he was near, night men and burnings and midnight tarrings faded into a hazy distance. But Stacey remained aloof and had little to do with him.

8. A global history of people of African descent (1915). Du Bois (1863–1953) was a pioneering sociologist and civil rights leader.

After the cleaning I asked Mama if Christopher-John, Little Man, and I could go visit Mr. Morrison, but she said no.

"But, Mama, I wanna know more 'bout him," I explained. "I just wanna know how come he's so big."

"You know about as much as you need to know," she decided. "And long as Mr. Morrison stays here, that's his house. If he wants you down there, he'll ask you."

"Don't know how come y'all wanna go down there no-way," Stacey said moodily when Mama was out of hearing.

" 'Cause we like him, that's why," I answered, tired of his distant attitude toward Mr. Morrison. Then, as discreetly as I could, I said, "What's the matter with you, boy, not liking Mr. Morrison?"

Stacey shrugged. "I like him all right."

"Don't act that way."

Stacey looked away from me. "Don't need him here. All that work he doing, I could've done it myself."

"Ah, you couldn't've done no such thing. Besides"—I looked around to be certain that Big Ma and Mama were not near—"besides, Papa didn't just bring him here to do no work. You know how come he really here."

Stacey turned toward me haughtily. "I could've taken care of that too."

I rolled my eyes at him, but held my peace. I didn't feel like a fight, and as long as Mr. Morrison was within hollering distance of the back porch, it made little difference to me what Stacey *thought* he could do.

"I sure wouldn't want that big ole man stayin' at my place," said T.J. on the way to school. "I betcha he get mad one time, he'd take ole Little Man and swing him over that tree yonder like he wasn't nothin' but a twig." He laughed then as Little Man set his lips and stared angrily up. "Course, I could probably 'bout do that myself."

"Couldn't neither!" denied Little Man.

"Hush, Man," said Stacey. "T.J., leave Man alone."

"Aw, I ain't botherin' him. Little Man's my buddy, ain't ya, Man?" Little Man scowled, but didn't reply. T.J. turned back to Stacey. "You ready for that history test?"

"Hope so," said Stacey. "But I keep forgetting them dates."

"Betcha I could help ya, if you be nice."

"How? You worse than I am 'bout dates."

T.J. grinned, then slyly pulled a folded sheet of paper from his pocket and handed it to Stacey. Stacey unfolded it, looked at it curiously, then frowned. "You planning on cheating?"

"Well, naw, I ain't plannin' on it," said T.J. seriously. "Jus' if I gotta."

"Well, you ain't gonna," said Stacey, tearing the paper in two.

"Hey, what's the matter with you, man!" cried T.J. grabbing for the paper. But Stacey turned his back to him and tore the paper into bits, then deposited them in the gully. "Man, that sho' ain't right! I wouldn't do you that way!"

"Maybe not," replied Stacey. "But at least this way you won't get into no trouble."

T.J. mumbled, "If failin' ain't trouble, I don't know what is."

Little Man, Christopher-John, Claude, and I were sitting on the bottom step of the seventh-grade-class building after school waiting for Stacey and T.J. when the front door banged open and T.J. shot out and tore across the yard. "What's the matter with him?" asked Christopher-John. "Ain't he gonna wait for Stacey?"

The rest of the seventh grade, led by Little Willie Wiggins and Moe Turner, spilled from the building. "There he go!" cried Little Willie as T.J. disappeared on the forest road. Moe Turner yelled, "Let's see where he goin'!" Then he and three other boys dashed away in pursuit of T.J. But the others stood restlessly near the steps as if school had not yet ended.

"Hey, what's going on?" I asked Little Willie. "What's everybody waiting 'round for?"

"And where's Stacey?" demanded Little Man.

Little Willie smiled. "Stacey inside with Miz Logan. He got whipped today."

"Whipped!" I cried. "Why, can't nobody whip Stacey. Who done it?"

"Your mama," laughed Little Willie.

"Mama!" Christopher-John, Little Man, and I exclaimed.

Little Willie nodded. "Yep. In front of everybody."

I swallowed hard, feeling very sorry for my older brother. It was bad enough to be whipped in front of thirty others by a teacher, but to get it by one's own mother— now that was downright embarrassing.

"Why'd Mama do that?" asked Christopher-John.

"She caught him with cheat notes during the history examination."

"Mama knows Stacey wouldn't cheat!" I declared.

Little Willie shrugged. "Well, whether she knowed it or not, she sho' 'nough whipped him. . . . Course, now, she give him a chance to get out of it when he said he wasn't cheatin' and she asked him how he got them cheat notes. But Stacey wouldn't tell on ole T.J., and you know good and well ole T.J. wasn't 'bout to say them notes was his."

"Cheat notes! But how'd T.J. get cheat notes? Stacey got rid of them things this morning!"

"Come noontime though," replied Little Willie, "T.J. was in them woods busy writing himself another set. Me and Moe seen him."

"Well, what the devil was Stacey doing with 'em?"

"Well, we was in the middle of the examination and ole T.J. slips out these cheat notes—me and Clarence here was sittin' right behind him and T.J. and seen the whole thing. Stacey was sittin' right side of T.J. and when he seen them notes, he motioned T.J. to put 'em away. At first T.J. wouldn't do it, but then he seen Miz Logan startin' toward 'em and he slipped Stacey the notes. Well, Stacey didn't see Miz Logan comin' when he took them notes, and by the time he saw her it was too late to get rid of 'em. Wasn't nothin' Miz Logan could do but whip him. Failed him too."

"And ole T.J. just sat there and ain't said a word," interjected Clarence, laughing.

"But knowin' Stacey, I betcha ole T.J. ain't gonna get away with it," chuckled Little Willie. "And T.J. know it too. That's why he lit outa here like he done, and I betcha— Hey, Stacey!"

Everyone turned as Stacey bounded down the steps. His square face was unsmiling, but there was no anger in his voice when he asked quietly, "Anybody seen T.J.?" All the students answered at once, indicating that T.J. had headed west toward home, then surrounded Stacey as he started across the lawn. Christopher-John, Little Man, Claude, and I followed.

When we reached the crossroads, Moe Turner was waiting. "T.J. went down to the Wallace store," he announced.

Stacey stopped and so did everyone else. Stacey stared past Jefferson Davis, then back down the road toward Great Faith. Looking over his shoulder, he found me and ordered, "Cassie, you and Christopher-John and Man go on home."

"You come too," I said, afraid of where he was going.

"Got something to take care of first," he said, walking away.

"Mama gonna take care of you, too!" I hollered after him. "You know she said we wasn't to go down there, and she find out, she gonna wear you out again! Papa too!" But Stacey did not come back. For a moment, Little Man, Christopher-John, Claude, and I stood watching Stacey and the others heading swiftly northward. Then Little Man said, "I wanna see what he gonna do."

"I don't," declared Christopher-John.

"Come on," I said, starting after Stacey with Little Man and Claude beside me.

"I don't want no whipping!" objected Christopher-John, standing alone in the crossroads. But when he saw that we were not coming back, he puffed to join us, grumbling all the while.

The Wallace store stood almost a half mile beyond Jefferson Davis, on a triangular lot that faced the Soldiers Bridge crossroads. Once the Granger plantation store, it had been run by the Wallaces for as long as I could remember, and most of the people within the forty-mile stretch between Smellings Creek and Strawberry shopped there. The other three corners of the crossroads were forest land, black and dense. The store consisted of a small building with a gas pump in front and a storage house in back. Beyond the store, against the forest edge, were two gray clapboard houses and a small garden. But there were no fields; the Wallaces did not farm.

Stacey and the other students were standing in the doorway of the store when Little Man, Christopher-John, Claude, and I ran up. We squeezed through so we could see inside. A man we all knew was Kaleb Wallace stood behind the counter. A few other men sat around a stove playing checkers, and Jeremy's older brothers, R.W. and Melvin, who had dropped out of school long ago, leaned sleepy-eyed against the counter staring at us.

"Y'all go on to the back," said Kaleb Wallace, "lessn y'all wanna buy something. Mr. Dewberry got the music goin' already."

As we turned away from the entrance, Melvin Simms said, "Just look at all the little niggers come to dance," and the laughter of the men filled the room.

Christopher-John tugged at my arm. "I don't like this place, Cassie. Let's go on home."

"We can't leave without Stacey," I said.

Music beckoned from the storage room where Dewberry Wallace was placing round brown bottles on a small table as we crowded in. Aside from the table, there was no furniture in the room. Boxes lined the walls and the center floor had been cleared for dancing—several older couples from Great Faith were already engaged in movements I had never seen before.

"What they doing?" asked Little Man.

I shrugged. "I guess that's what they call dancing."

"There he go!" someone shouted as the back door of the storeroom slammed shut. Stacey turned quickly and sped to the back of the building. T.J. was fleeing straight toward Soldiers Road. Stacey tore across the Wallace yard and, leaping high like a forest fox, fell upon T.J., knocking him down. The two boys rolled toward the road, each trying to keep the other's back pinned to the ground, but then Stacey, who was stronger, gained the advantage and T.J., finding that he could not budge him, cried, "Hey, wait a minute, man, let me explain—"

Stacey did not let him finish. Jumping up, he pulled T.J. up too and hit him squarely in the face. T.J. staggered back holding his eyes as if he were badly hurt, and Stacey momentarily let down his guard. At that moment, T.J. rammed into Stacey, forcing the fight to the ground again.

Little Man, Christopher-John, and I, with the others, circled the fighters, chanting loudly as they rolled back and forth punching at each other. All of us were so engrossed in the battle that no one saw a mule wagon halt on the road and a giant man step out. It wasn't until I realized that the shouting had stopped behind us and that the girls and boys beside me were falling back that I looked up.

Mr. Morrison towered above us.

He did not look at me or Christopher-John or Little Man, although I knew he had seen us, but walked straight to the fighters and lifted a still-swinging Stacey off T.J. After a long, tense moment, he said to Stacey, "You and your sister and brothers get on in the wagon."

We walked through the now-silent crowd. Kaleb and Dewberry Wallace, standing on the front porch of the store with the Simmses, stared at Mr. Morrison as we passed, but Mr. Morrison looked through them as if they were not there. Stacey sat in front of the wagon with Mr. Morrison; the rest of us climbed into the back. "Now we gonna get it," shuddered Christopher-John. "I told y'all we shoulda gone on home."

Before Mr. Morrison took the reins, he handed Stacey a handkerchief in which to wrap his bruised right hand, but he did not say a word and it wasn't until we had passed the crossroads leading to Great Faith that the silence was broken.

"Mr. Morrison . . . you gonna tell Mama?" Stacey asked huskily.

Mr. Morrison was very quiet as Jack the mule clopped noisily along the dry road. "Seems I heard your mama tell y'all not to go up to that Wallace store," he said at last.

"Y-yessir," said Stacey, glancing nervously at Mr. Morrison. Then he blurted out, "But I had good reason!"

"Ain't never no reason good enough to go disobey your mama."

The boys and I looked woefully at each other and my bottom stung from the awful thought of Mama's leather strap against it. "But Mr. Morrison," I cried anxiously, "T.J. was hiding there 'cause he thought Stacey wouldn't never come down there to get him. But Stacey had to go down there cause T.J. was cheating and—"

"Hush, Cassie," Stacey ordered, turning sharply around.

I faltered for only a moment before deciding that my bottom was more important than Stacey's code of honor "—and Stacey had to take the blame for it and Mama whipped him right in front of God and everybody!" Once the truth had been disclosed, I waited with dry throat and nauseous stomach for Mr. Morrison to say something. When he did, all of us strained tensely forward.

"I ain't gonna tell her," he said quietly.

Christopher-John sighed with relief. "Ain't going down there no more neither," he promised. Little Man and I agreed. But Stacey stared long and hard at Mr. Morrison.

"How come, Mr. Morrison?" he asked. "How come you ain't gonna tell Mama?"

Mr. Morrison slowed Jack as we turned into the road leading home. " 'Cause I'm leaving it up to you to tell her."

"What!" we exclaimed together.

"Sometimes a person's gotta fight," he said slowly. "But that store ain't the place to be doing it. From what I hear, folks like them Wallaces got no respect at all for colored folks and they just think it's funny when we fight each other. Your mama knowed them Wallaces ain't good folks, that's why she don't want y'all down there, and y'all owe it to her and y'allselves to tell her. But I'm gonna leave it up to y'all to decide."

Stacey nodded thoughtfully and wound the handkerchief tighter around his wounded hand. His face was not scarred, so if he could just figure out a way to explain the bruises on his hand to Mama without lying he was in the clear, for Mr. Morrison had not said that he *had* to tell her. But for some reason I could not understand he said, "All right, Mr. Morrison, I'll tell her."

"Boy, you crazy!" I cried as Christopher-John and Little Man speedily came to the same conclusion. If he did not care about his own skin, he could at least consider ours.

But he seemed not to hear us as his eyes met Mr. Morrison's and the two of them smiled in subtle understanding, the distance between them fading.

As we neared the house, Mr. Granger's Packard rolled from the dusty driveway. Mr. Morrison directed Jack to the side of the road until the big car had passed, then swung the wagon back into the road's center and up the drive. Big Ma was standing by the yard gate that led onto the drive, gazing across the road at the forest.

"Big Ma, what was Mr. Granger doing here?" Stacey asked, jumping from the wagon and going to her. Little Man, Christopher-John, and I hopped down and followed him.

"Nothin'," Big Ma replied absently, her eyes still on the forest. "Just worryin' me 'bout this land again."

"Oh," said Stacey, his tone indicating that he considered the visit of no importance. Mr. Granger had always wanted the land. He turned and went to help Mr. Morrison. Little Man and Christopher-John went with him, but I remained by the gate with Big Ma.

"Big Ma," I said, "what Mr. Granger need more land for?"

"Don't need it," Big Ma said flatly. "Got more land now than he know what to do with."

"Well, what he want with ours then?"

"Just like to have it, that's all."

"Well, seems to me he's just being greedy. You ain't gonna sell it to him, are you?"

Big Ma did not answer me. Instead, she pushed open the gate and walked down the drive and across the road into the forest. I ran after her. We walked in silence down the narrow cow path which wound through the old forest to the pond. As we neared the pond, the forest gapped open into a wide, brown glade, man-made by the felling of many trees, some of them still on the ground. They had been cut during the summer after Mr. Andersen came from Strawberry with an offer to buy the trees. The offer was backed with a threat, and Big Ma was afraid. So Andersen's lumbermen came, chopping and sawing, destroying the fine old trees. Papa was away on the railroad then but Mama sent Stacey for him. He returned and stopped the cutting, but not before many of the trees had already fallen.

Big Ma surveyed the clearing without a word, then, stepping around the rotting trees, she made her way to the pond and sat down on one of them. I sat close beside her and waited for her to speak. After a while she shook her head and said: "I'm sho' glad your grandpa never had to see none of this. He dearly loved these here old trees. Him and me, we used to come down here early mornin's or just 'fore the sun was 'bout to set and just sit and talk. He used to call this place his thinkin' spot and he called that old pond there Caroline, after me."

She smiled vaguely, but not at me.

"You know, I . . . I wasn't hardly eighteen when Paul Edward married me and brung me here. He was older than me by 'bout eight years and he was smart. Ow-ow, my Lord, that was one smart man! He had himself a mind like a steel trap. Anything he seen done, he could do it. He had done learned carpentry back up there near Macon, Georgia, where he was born. Born into slavery he was, two years 'fore freedom come, and him and his mama stayed on at that plantation after the fightin' was finished. But then when he got to be fourteen and his mama died, he left that place and worked his way 'cross here up to Vicksburg."

"That's where he met you, ain't it, Big Ma?" I asked, already knowing the answer.

Big Ma nodded, smiling. "Sho' was. He was carpenterin' up there and my papa took me in with him to Vicksburg—we was tenant farmin' 'bout thirty miles from there—to see 'bout gettin' a store-bought rocker for my mama, and there was ole Paul Edward workin' in that furniture shop just as big. Had himself a good job, but that ole job wasn't what he wanted. He wanted himself some land. Kept on and kept on talkin' 'bout land, and then this place come up for sell."

"And he bought himself two hundred acres from that Yankee, didn't he?"

Big Ma chuckled. "That man went right on over to see Mr. Hollenbeck and said, 'Mr. Hollenbeck, I understand you got land to sell and I'd be interested in buyin' me 'bout two hundred acres if yo' price is right.' Ole Mr. Hollenbeck questioned him good 'bout where he was gonna get the money to pay him, but Paul Edward just said, 'Don't seem to me it's your worry 'bout how I'm gonna get the money just long as you get paid your price.' Didn't nothin' scare that man!" She beamed proudly. "And Mr. Hollenbeck went on and let him have it. Course now, he was just 'bout as eager to sell this land as Paul Edward was to buy. He'd had it for goin' on nigh twenty years—bought it during Reconstruction from the Grangers—"

" 'Cause they didn't have no money to pay their taxes—"

"Not only didn't have tax money, didn't have no money at all! That war left them plumb broke. Their ole Confederate money wasn't worth nothin' and both Northern and Southern soldiers had done ransacked their place. Them Grangers didn't have nothin' but they land left and they had to sell two thousand acres of it to get money to pay them taxes and rebuild the rest of it, and that Yankee bought the whole two thousand—"

"Then he turned 'round and tried to sell it back to 'em, huh, Big Ma?"

"Sho' did . . . but not till eighty-seven, when your grandpa bought himself that two hundred acres. As I hears it, that Yankee offered to sell all two thousand acres back to Harlan Granger's daddy for less'n the land was worth, but that old Filmore Granger was just 'bout as tight with a penny as anybody ever lived and he wouldn't buy it back. So Mr. Hollenbeck just let other folks know he was sellin', and it didn't take long 'fore he sold all of it 'cause it was some mighty fine land. Besides your grandpa, a bunch of other small farmers bought up eight hundred acres and Mr. Jamison bought the rest."

"But that wasn't *our* Mr. Jamison," I supplied knowingly. "That was his daddy."

"Charles Jamison was his name," Big Ma said. "A fine old gentleman, too. He was a good neighbor and he always treated us fair . . . just like his son. The Jamisons was what folks call 'Old South' from up in Vicksburg, and as I understands it, before the war they had as much money as anybody and even after the war they managed better than some other folks 'cause they had made themselves some Northern money. Anyways, old Mr. Jamison got it into his mind that he wanted to farm and he moved his family from Vicksburg down in here. Mr. Wade Jamison wasn't but 'bout eight years old then."

"But he didn't like to farm," I said.

"Oh, he liked it all right. Just wasn't never much hand at it though, and after he went up North to law school and all he just felt he oughta practice his law."

"Is that how come he sold Grandpa them other two hundred acres?"

"Sho' is . . . and it was mighty good of him to do it, too. My Paul Edward had been eyein' that two hundred acres ever since 1910 when he done paid off the bank for them first two hundred, but ole Mr. Jamison didn't wanna sell. 'Bout that same time, Harlan Granger 'come head of the Granger plantation—you know, him and Wade Jamison 'bout the same year's children—and he wanted to buy back every inch of land that used to belong to the Grangers. That man crazy 'bout anythin' that was before that war and he wantin' his land to be every bit like it was then. Already had more'n four thousand acres, but he just itchin' to have back them other two thousand his granddaddy sold. Got back eight hundred of 'em, too, from them other farmers that bought from Mr. Hollenbeck—"

"But Grandpa and old Mr. Jamison wasn't interested in selling, period, was they, Big Ma? They didn't care how much money Mr. Granger offered 'em!" I declared with an emphatic nod.

"That's the truth of it all right," agreed Big Ma. "But when Mr. Jamison died in 1918 and Wade 'come head of the family, he sold them two hundred acres to Paul Edward and the rest of his land to Harlan Granger, and moved his family into Strawberry. He could've just as easy sold the full thousand acres to the Grangers and gotten more money, but he didn't . . . and till this day Harlan Granger still hold it 'gainst him 'cause he didn't. . . ."

The soft swish of falling leaves made Big Ma look up from the pond and at the trees again. Her lips curved into a tender smile as she looked around thoughtfully. "You know," she said, "I can still see my Paul Edward's face the day Mr. Jamison sold him them two hundred acres. He put his arms 'round me and looked out at his new piece of land, then he said 'zactly the same thing he said when he grabbed himself that first two hundred acres. Said, 'Pretty Caroline, how you like to work this fine piece of earth with me?' Sho' did . . . said the 'zact same thing."

She grew quiet then and rubbed the wrinkles down one hand as if to smooth them away. I gazed at the pond, glassy gray and calm, until she was ready to go on. I had learned that at times like these it was better to just sit and wait than to go asking disrupting questions which might vex her.

"So long ago now," she said eventually, in a voice that was almost a whisper. "We worked real hard gettin' them crops sown, gettin' 'em reaped. We had us a time. . . . But there was good times too. We was young and strong when we started out and we liked to work. Neither one of us, I'm proud to say, never was lazy and we didn't raise us no lazy children neither. Had ourselves six fine children. Lost our girls when they was babies, though. . . . I s'pose that's one of the reasons I love your sweet mama so much. . . . But them boys grew strong and all of 'em loved this place as much as Paul Edward and me. They go away, they always come back to it. Couldn't leave it."

She shook her head and sighed. "Then Mitchell, he got killed in the war and Kevin got drowned. . . ." Her voice faded completely, but when she spoke again it had hardened and there was a determined glint in her eyes. "Now all the boys I got is my baby boys, your papa and your Uncle Hammer, and this they place as much as it is mine. They blood's in this land, and here that Harlan Granger always talkin' 'bout buyin' it. He pestered Paul Edward to death 'bout buyin' it, now he pesterin' me. Humph!" she grumped angrily. "He don't know nothin' 'bout me or this land, he think I'm gonna sell!"

She became silent again.

A cold wind rose, biting through my jacket, and I shivered. Big Ma looked down at me for the first time. "You cold?"

"No-no, ma'am," I stuttered, not ready to leave the forest.

"Don't you be lyin' to me girl!" she snapped, putting out her hand. "It's time we was goin' back to the house anyways. Your mama'll be home soon."

I took her hand, and together we left the Caroline.

Despite our every effort to persuade Stacey otherwise, when Mama came home he confessed that he had been fighting T.J. at the Wallace store and that Mr. Morrison had stopped it. He stood awkwardly before her, disclosing only those things which he could honorably mention. He said nothing of T.J.'s cheating or that Christopher-John, Little Man, and I had been with him, and when Mama asked him a question he could not answer honestly, he simply looked at his feet and refused to speak. The rest of us sat fidgeting nervously throughout the interview and when Mama looked our way, we swiftly found somewhere else to rest our eyes.

Finally, seeing that she had gotten all the information she was going to get from Stacey, Mama turned to us. "I suppose you three went to the store too, huh?" But before any of us could squeak an answer, she exclaimed, "That does it!" and began to pace the floor, her arms folded, her face cross.

Although she scolded us severely, she did not whip us. We were sent to bed early but we didn't consider that a punishment, and we doubted that Mama did either. How we had managed to escape a whipping we couldn't fathom until Saturday, when Mama woke us before dawn and piled us into the wagon. Taking us southwest toward Smellings Creek, she said, "Where we're going the man is very sick and he doesn't look like other people. But I don't want you to be afraid or uncomfortable when you see him. Just be yourselves."

We rode for almost two hours before turning onto a backwoods trail. We were jarred and bounced over the rough road until we entered a clearing where a small weather-grayed house stood and fields stretched barren beyond it. As Mama pulled up on the reins and ordered us down, the front door cracked warily open, but no one appeared. Then Mama said, "Good morning, Mrs. Berry. It's Mary Logan, David's wife."

The door swung wide then and an elderly woman, frail and toothless, stepped out. Her left arm hung crazily at her side as if it had been broken long ago but had not mended properly, and she walked with a limp; yet she smiled widely, throwing her good arm around Mama and hugging her. "Land sakes, child, ain't you somethin'!" she exclaimed. "Comin' to see 'bout these old bones. I jus' sez to Sam, I sez, 'Who you reckon comin' to see old folks like us?' These yo' babies, ain't they? Lord a'mighty, ain't they fine! Sho' is!" She hugged each of us and ushered us into the house.

The interior was dark, lit only by the narrow slat of gray daylight allowed in by the open door. Stacey and I carried cans of milk and butter, and Christopher-John and Little Man each had a jar of beef and a jar of crowder peas[9] which Mama and Big Ma had canned. Mrs. Berry took the food, her thanks intermingled with questions about Big Ma, Papa, and others. When she had put the food away, she pulled stools from the darkness and motioned us to sit down, then she went to the blackest corner and said, "Daddy, who you s'pose done come to see 'bout us?"

There was no recognizable answer, only an inhuman guttural wheezing. But Mrs.

---

9. Legumes similar to black-eyed peas, but with a more robust flavor.

Berry seemed to accept it and went on. "Miz Logan and her babies. Ain't that some-thin'?" She took a sheet from a nearby table. "Gots to cover him," she explained. "He can't hardly stand to have nothin' touch him." When she was visible again, she picked up a candle stump and felt around a table for matches. "He can't speak no more. The fire burned him too bad. But he understands all right." Finding the matches, she lit the candle and turned once more to the corner.

A still form lay there staring at us with glittering eyes. The face had no nose, and the head no hair; the skin was scarred, burned, and the lips were wizened black, like charcoal. As the wheezing sound echoed from the opening that was a mouth, Mama said, "Say good morning to Mrs. Berry's husband, children."

The boys and I stammered a greeting, then sat silently trying not to stare at Mr. Berry during the hour that we remained in the small house. But Mama talked softly to both Mr. and Mrs. Berry, telling them news of the community as if Mr. Berry were as normal as anyone else.

After we were on the main road again, having ridden in thoughtful silence over the wooded trail, Mama said quietly, "The Wallaces did that, children. They poured kerosene over Mr. Berry and his nephews and lit them afire. One of the nephews died, the other one is just like Mr. Berry." She allowed this information to penetrate the silence, then went on. "Everyone knows they did it, and the Wallaces even laugh about it, but nothing was ever done. They're bad people, the Wallaces. That's why I don't want you to ever go to their store again—for any reason. You understand?"

We nodded, unable to speak as we thought of the disfigured man lying in the darkness.

On the way home we stopped at the homes of some of Mama's students, where families poured out of tenant shacks to greet us. At each farm Mama spoke of the bad influence of the Wallaces, of the smoking and drinking permitted at their store, and asked that the family's children not be allowed to go there.

The people nodded and said she was right.

She also spoke of finding another store to patronize, one where the proprietors were more concerned about the welfare of the community. But she did not speak directly of what the Wallaces had done to the Berrys for, as she explained later, that was something that wavered between the known and the unknown and to mention it outright to anyone outside of those with whom you were closest was not wise. There were too many ears that listened for others besides themselves, and too many tongues that wagged to those they shouldn't.

The people only nodded, and Mama left.

When we reached the Turner farm, Moe's widowed father rubbed his stubbled chin and squinted across the room at Mama. "Miz Logan," he said, "you know I feels the same way you do 'bout them low-down Wallaces, but it ain't easy to jus' stop shoppin' there. They overcharges me and I has to pay them high interest, but I gots credit there 'cause Mr. Montier signs for me. Now you know most folks 'round here sharecroppin' on Montier, Granger, or Harrison land and most of them jus' 'bout got to shop at that Wallace store or up at the mercantile in Strawberry, which is jus' 'bout as bad. Can't go no place else."

Mama nodded solemnly, showing she understood, then she said, "For the past year now, our family's been shopping down at Vicksburg. There are a number of stores down there and we've found several that treat us well."

"Vicksburg?" Mr. Turner echoed, shaking his head. "Lord, Miz Logan, you ain't expectin' me to go all the way to Vicksburg? That's an overnight journey in a wagon down there and back."

Mama thought on that a moment. "What if someone would be willing to make the trip for you? Go all the way to Vicksburg and bring back what you need?"

"Won't do no good," retorted Mr. Turner. "I got no cash money. Mr. Montier signs for me up at that Wallace store so's I can get my tools, my mule, my seed, my fertilizer, my food, and what few clothes I needs to keep my children from runnin' plumb naked. When cotton-pickin' time comes, he sells my cotton, takes half of it, pays my debt up at that store and my interest for they credit, then charges me ten to fifteen percent more as 'risk' money for signin' for me in the first place. This year I earned me near two hundred dollars after Mr. Montier took his half of the crop money, but I ain't seen a penny of it. In fact, if I manages to come out even without owin' that man nothin', I figures I've had a good year. Now, who way down in Vicksburg gonna give a man like me credit?"

Mama was very quiet and did not answer.

"I sho' sorry, Miz Logan. I'm gonna keep my younguns from up at that store, but I gots to live. Y'all got it better'n most the folks 'round here 'cause y'all gots your own place and y'all ain't gotta cowtail[1] to a lot of this stuff. But you gotta understand it ain't easy for sharecroppin' folks to do what you askin'."

"Mr. Turner," Mama said in a whisper, "what if someone backed your signature? Would you shop up in Vicksburg then?"

Mr. Turner looked at Mama strangely. "Now, who'd sign for me?"

"If someone would, would you do it?"

Mr. Turner gazed into the fire, burning to a low ash, then got up and put another log on it, taking his time as he watched the fire shoot upward and suck in the log. Without turning around he said, "When I was a wee little boy, I got burnt real bad. It healed over but I ain't never forgot the pain of it. . . . It's an awful way to die." Then, turning, he faced Mama. "Miz Logan, you find someone to sign my credit, and I'll consider it deeply."

After we left the Turners', Stacey asked, "Mama, who you gonna get to sign?" But Mama, her brow furrowed, did not reply. I started to repeat the question, but Stacey shook his head and I settled back wondering, then fell asleep.

5

The blue-black shine that had so nicely encircled T.J.'s left eye for over a week had almost completely faded by the morning T.J. hopped into the back of the wagon beside Stacey and snuggled in a corner not occupied by the butter, milk, and eggs Big Ma was taking to sell at the market in Strawberry. I sat up front beside Big Ma, still sandy-eyed and not believing that I was actually going.

The second Saturday of every month was market day in Strawberry, and for as far back as I could remember the boys and I had been begging Big Ma to take us to it. Stacey had actually gone once, but Christopher-John, Little Man, and I had always been flatly denied the experience. We had, in fact, been denied so often that our pestering now occurred more out of habit than from any real belief that we would be allowed to go. But this morning, while the world lay black, Big Ma called: "Cassie, get up, child, if you gonna go to town with me, and be quiet 'bout it. You wake up Christopher-John or Little Man and I'll leave you here. I don't want them cryin' all over the place 'cause they can't go."

As Jack swept the wagon into the gray road, Big Ma pulled tightly on the reins and

---

1. I.e., kowtow: accept with servile deference.

grumbled, "Hold on! You, Jack, hold on! I ain't got no time to be putting up with both you and T.J.'s foolishness."

"T.J.!" Stacey and I exclaimed together. "He going?"

Big Ma didn't answer immediately; she was occupied in a test of wills with Jack. When hers had prevailed and Jack had settled into a moderate trot, she replied moodily, "Mr. Avery come by after y'all was asleep last night wanting T.J. to go to Strawberry to do some shopping for a few things he couldn't get at the Wallace store. Lord, that's all I need with all the trouble about is for that child to talk me to death for twenty-two miles."

Big Ma didn't need to say any more and she didn't. T.J. was far from her favorite person and it was quite obvious that Stacey and I owed our good fortune entirely to T.J.'s obnoxious personality.

T.J., however, was surprisingly subdued when he settled into the wagon; I suppose that at three-thirty in the morning even T.J.'s mouth was tired. But by dawn, when the December sun was creeping warily upward shooting pale streams of buff-colored light through the forest, he was fully awake and chattering like a cockatoo. His endless talk made me wish that he had not managed to wheedle his way so speedily back into Stacey's good graces, but Big Ma, her face furrowed in distant thoughts, did not hush him. He talked the rest of the way into Strawberry, announcing as we arrived, "Well, children, open your eyes and take in Strawberry, Mississippi!"

"Is this it?" I cried, a gutting disappointment enveloping me as we entered the town. Strawberry was nothing like the tough, sprawling bigness I had envisioned. It was instead a sad, red place. As far as I could see, the only things modern about it were a paved road which cut through its center and fled northward, away from it, and a spindly row of electrical lines. Lining the road were strips of red dirt splotched with patches of brown grass and drying mud puddles, and beyond the dirt and the mud puddles, gloomy store buildings set behind raised wooden sidewalks and sagging verandas.

"Shoot!" I grumbled. "It sure ain't nothing to shout about."

"Hush up, Cassie," Big Ma said. "You, too, T.J. Y'all in town now and I expects y'all to act like it. In another hour this place'll be teeming up with folks from all over the county and I don't want no trouble."

As the stores gave way to houses still sleeping, we turned onto a dirt road which led past more shops and beyond to a wide field dotted with wooden stalls. Near the field entrance several farm wagons and pickups were already parked, but Big Ma drove to the other side of the field where only two wagons were stationed. Climbing from the wagon, she said, "Don't seem like too many folks ahead of us. In the summer, I'd've had to come on Friday and spend the night to get a spot like this." She headed toward the back of the wagon. "Stacey, you and T.J. stay up there a minute and push them milk cans over here so's I can reach 'em."

"Big Ma," I said, following her, "all them folks up there selling milk and eggs too?"

"Not all, I reckon. Some of 'em gots meats and vegetables, quilts and sewing and such. But I guess a good piece of 'em sellin' the same as us."

I studied the wagons parked at the field entrance, then exclaimed, "Well, what the devil we doing way back here then! Can't nobody see us."

"You watch your mouth, girl," warned Big Ma. Then, arranging the milk cans and baskets of eggs near the wagon's edge, she softened her voice and promised, "We'll do all right. I got me some regular customers and they'll check to see if I'm here 'fore they buy."

"Not back here they won't," I grumbled. Maybe Big Ma knew what she was doing, but it made absolutely no sense to me to be so far from the entrance. Most of the other farmers seemed to have the right idea, and I couldn't help but try to make her see the business sense in moving the wagon forward. "Why don't we move our wagon up there with them other wagons, Big Ma? There's plenty of room, and we could sell more."

"Them's white folks' wagons, Cassie," Big Ma said gruffly, as if that explained everything. "Now, hush up and help me get this food out."

"Shoot," I mumbled, taking one of the buckets from Stacey, "by the time a body walk way back here, they'll have bunions on their soles and corns on their toes."

By noon the crowd which had covered the field during the early morning had thinned noticeably, and wagons and trucks began to pack up and head for town. After we had eaten our cold lunch of oil sausages and cornbread washed down with clabber milk,[2] we did the same.

On the main street of Strawberry once more, Big Ma parked the wagon in front of a building where four shingles hung from a rusted post. One of the shingles read: "Wade W. Jamison, Attorney-at-Law."

"Mr. Jamison live here?" I cried, scrambling down. "I wanna see him."

"He don't live here," said Big Ma, opening her large purse. She pulled out a long manila envelope, checked inside, then gingerly put it back again. "This here's his office and I got some business with him. You get on back in the wagon." Big Ma climbed down, but I didn't get back in. "Can't I just go up and say 'Hey'?" I persisted.

"I'm gonna 'Hey' you," Big Ma said, "you keep pesterin' me." She glanced over at Stacey and T.J. "Y'all wait here for me and soon's I get back, we'll go do that shoppin' so's we can get on home 'fore it gets dark."

When she had gone inside, T.J. said, "What you wanna see that ole white man for anyway, Cassie? What you and him got to talk 'bout?"

"I just wanted to see him, that's all," I said, going to the raised sidewalk and taking a seat. I liked Mr. Jamison and I didn't mind admitting it. He came to see us several times a year, mainly on business, and although the boys and I were somewhat shy of him, we were always glad to see him. He was the only white man I had ever heard address Mama and Big Ma as "Missus," and I liked him for it. Besides that, in his way he was like Papa: Ask him a question and he would give it to you straight with none of this pussyfooting-around business. I liked that.

After several minutes of watching farmers in faded overalls and their women in flour-sack-cut dresses promenading under the verandas, T.J. said, "Why don't we go on down to the mercantile and look around?"

Stacey hesitated. "I don't know. I think Big Ma wanted to go with us."

"Ah, shoot, man, we'll be doin' her a favor. We go on down to the mercantile now and order up our stuff, we'll save her some time so when she come from seein' that lawyer, we can jus' go on home. Besides, I got somethin' to show ya."

Stacey pondered the suggestion for a long moment. "Well, I guess it'll be all right," he said finally.

"Big Ma said stay here!" I objected, hoping that Mr. Jamison would come out with Big Ma.

"Stay here then," Stacey called over his shoulder as he crossed the street with T.J.

I dashed after them. I wasn't about to stay on that sidewalk by myself.

The Barnett Mercantile had everything. Its shelves, counters, and floor space

2. Sour, curdled milk; also called *thick milk*.

boasted items from ladies' ribbons to burlap bags of seeds; from babies' bottles to brand-new pot-bellied stoves. T.J., who had been to the store several times before, wove his way among the farmers and led us to a counter at the far corner of the room. The counter had a glass top, and beneath the glass were handguns artfully displayed on a bolt of red velvet.

"Jus' look at it," T.J. said dreamily. "Ain't she somethin'?"

"What?" I said.

"That pearl-handled one. Stacey, man, you ever seen a gun like that before in your whole life? I'd sell my life for that gun. One of these days I'm gonna have it, too."

"I reckon I ain't," said Stacey politely. "It's a nice-looking gun all right."

I stared down at the gun. A price tag of $35.95 stared back at me. "Thirty-five dollars and ninety-five cents!" I almost screamed. "Just for an ole gun? What the devil you gonna use it for? Can't hunt with it."

T.J. looked at me with disgust. "Ain't s'pose to hunt with it. It's for protection."

"Protection of what?" I asked, thinking of Papa's sturdy shotgun that hung over his and Mama's bed, and the sleek Winchester rifle which Big Ma kept locked in the trunk beneath our own bed. "That thing couldn't hardly kill a rattlesnake."

"There's other things a body needs protectin' from more than a rattlesnake," he said haughtily. "I get me that gun and ain't nobody gonna mess with me. I wouldn't need nobody."

Stacey backed away from the counter. He seemed nervous being in the store. "We better get those things you need and get on outa here 'fore Big Ma comes looking for us."

"Ah, man, there's plenty of time," said T.J., looking longingly at the gun. "Sure wish I could jus' hold it, jus' once."

"Come on, T.J.," ordered Stacey, "or me and Cassie's gonna go on back outside."

"Oh, all right." T.J. turned reluctantly away and went to a counter where a man was measuring nails onto a scale. We stood patiently waiting behind the people in front of us and when our turn came, T.J. handed his list to the man. "Mr. Barnett, sir," he said, "I got me this here list of things my mama want."

The storekeeper studied the list and without looking up asked, "You one of Mr. Granger's people?"

"Yessir," answered T.J.

Mr. Barnett walked to another counter and began filling the order, but before he finished a white woman called, "Mr. Barnett, you waiting on anybody just now?"

Mr. Barnett turned around. "Just them," he said, indicating us with a wave of his hand. "What can I do for you, Miz Emmaline?" The woman handed him a list twice as long as T.J.'s and the storekeeper, without a word of apology to us, proceeded to fill it.

"What's he doing?" I objected.

"Hush, Cassie," said Stacey, looking very embarrassed and uncomfortable. T.J.'s face was totally bland, as if nothing at all had happened.

When the woman's order was finally filled, Mr. Barnett again picked up T.J.'s list, but before he had gotten the next item his wife called, "Jim Lee, these folks needing help over here and I got my hands full." And as if we were not even there, he walked away.

"Where's he going?" I cried.

"He'll be back," said T.J., wandering away.

After waiting several minutes for Mr. Barnett's return, Stacey said, "Come on, Cassie, let's go." He started toward the door and I followed. But as we passed one of the counters, I spied Mr. Barnett wrapping an order of pork chops for a white girl. Adults were one thing; I could almost understand that. They ruled things and there was nothing that could be done about them. But some kid who was no bigger than me was something else again. Certainly Mr. Barnett had simply forgotten about T.J.'s order. I decided to remind him and, without saying anything to Stacey, I turned around and marched over to Mr. Barnett.

"Uh . . . 'scuse me, Mr. Barnett," I said as politely as I could, waiting a moment for him to look up from his wrapping. "I think you forgot, but you was waiting on us 'fore you was waiting on this girl here, and we been waiting a good while now for you to get back."

The girl gazed at me strangely, but Mr. Barnett did not look up. I assumed that he had not heard me. I was near the end of the counter so I merely went to the other side of it and tugged on his shirt sleeve to get his attention.

He recoiled as if I had struck him.

"Y-you was helping us," I said, backing to the front of the counter again.

"Well, you just get your little black self back over there and wait some more," he said in a low, tight voice.

I was hot. I had been as nice as I could be to him and here he was talking like this. "We been waiting on you for near an hour," I hissed, "while you 'round here waiting on everybody else. And it ain't fair. You got no right—"

"Whose little nigger is this!" bellowed Mr. Barnett.

Everyone in the store turned and stared at me. "I ain't nobody's little nigger!" I screamed, angry and humiliated. "And you ought not be waiting on everybody 'fore you wait on us."

"Hush up, child, hush up," someone whispered behind me. I looked around. A woman who had occupied the wagon next to ours at the market looked down upon me. Mr. Barnett, his face red and eyes bulging, immediately pounced on her.

"This gal yourn, Hazel?"

"No, suh," answered the woman meekly, stepping hastily away to show she had nothing to do with me. As I watched her turn her back on me, Stacey emerged and took my hand.

"Come on, Cassie, let's get out of here."

"Stacey!" I exclaimed, relieved to see him by my side. "Tell him! You know he ain't fair making us wait—"

"She your sister, boy?" Mr. Barnett spat across the counter.

Stacey bit his lower lip and gazed into Mr. Barnett's eyes. "Yessir."

"Then you get her out of here," he said with hateful force. "And make sure she don't come back till yo' mammy teach her what she is."

"I already know what I am!" I retaliated. "But I betcha you don't know what you are! And I could sure tell you, too, you ole—"

Stacey jerked me forward, crushing my hand in the effort, and whispered angrily, "Shut up, Cassie!" His dark eyes flashed malevolently as he pushed me in front of him through the crowd.

As soon as we were outside, I whipped my hand from his. "What's the matter with you? You know he was wrong!"

Stacey swallowed to flush his anger, then said gruffly, "I know it and you know it, but he don't know it, and that's where the trouble is. Now come on 'fore you get us into a real mess. I'm going up to Mr. Jamison's to see what's keeping Big Ma."

"What 'bout T.J.?" I called as he stepped into the street.

Stacey laughed wryly. "Don't worry 'bout T.J. He knows exactly how to act." He crossed the street sullenly then, his hands jammed in his pockets.

I watched him go, but did not follow. Instead, I ambled along the sidewalk trying to understand why Mr. Barnett had acted the way he had. More than once I stopped and gazed over my shoulder at the mercantile. I had a good mind to go back in and find out what had made Mr. Barnett so mad. I actually turned once and headed toward the store, then remembering what Mr. Barnett had said about my returning, I swung back around, kicking at the sidewalk, my head bowed.

It was then that I bumped into Lillian Jean Simms.

"Why don't you look where you're going?" she asked huffily. Jeremy and her two younger brothers were with her. "Hey, Cassie," said Jeremy.

"Hey, Jeremy," I said solemnly, keeping my eyes on Lillian Jean.

"Well, apologize," she ordered.

"What?"

"You bumped into me. Now you apologize."

I did not feel like messing with Lillian Jean. I had other things on my mind. "Okay," I said, starting past, "I'm sorry."

Lillian Jean sidestepped in front of me. "That ain't enough. Get down in the road."

I looked up at her. "You crazy?"

"You can't watch where you going, get in the road. Maybe that way you won't be bumping into decent white folks with your little nasty self."

This second insult of the day was almost more than I could bear. Only the thought of Big Ma up in Mr. Jamison's office saved Lillian Jean's lip. "I ain't nasty," I said, properly holding my temper in check, "and if you're so afraid of getting bumped, walk down there yourself."

I started past her again, and again she got in my way. "Ah, let her pass, Lillian Jean," said Jeremy. "She ain't done nothin' to you."

"She done something to me just standing in front of me." With that, she reached for my arm and attempted to push me off the sidewalk. I braced myself and swept my arm backward, out of Lillian Jean's reach. But someone caught it from behind, painfully twisting it, and shoved me off the sidewalk into the road. I landed bottom first on the ground.

Mr. Simms glared down at me. "When my gal Lillian Jean says for you to get yo'self off the sidewalk, you get, you hear?"

Behind him were his sons R.W. and Melvin. People from the store began to ring the Simmses. "Ain't that the same little nigger was cuttin' up back there at Jim Lee's?" someone asked.

"Yeah, she the one," answered Mr. Simms. "You hear me talkin' to you, gal? You 'pologize to Miz Lillian Jean this minute."

I stared up at Mr. Simms, frightened. Jeremy appeared frightened too. "I—I apologized already."

Jeremy seemed relieved that I had spoken. "She d-did, Pa. R-right now, 'fore y'all come, she did—"

Mr. Simms turned an angry gaze upon his son and Jeremy faltered, looked at me, and hung his head.

Then Mr. Simms jumped into the street. I moved away from him, trying to get up. He was a mean-looking man, red in the face and bearded. I was afraid he was going to hit me before I could get to my feet, but he didn't. I scrambled up and ran blindly for the wagon. Someone grabbed me and I fought wildly, attempting to pull loose. "Stop, Cassie!" Big Ma said. "Stop, it's me. We're going home now."

"Not 'fore she 'pologizes to my gal, y'all ain't," said Mr. Simms.

Big Ma gazed down at me, fear in her eyes, then back at the growing crowd. "She jus' a child—"

"Tell her, Aunty—"

Big Ma looked at me again, her voice cracking as she spoke. "Go on, child . . . apologize."

"But, Big Ma—"

Her voice hardened. "Do like I say."

I swallowed hard.

"Go on!"

"I'm sorry," I mumbled.

"I'm sorry, *Miz* Lillian Jean," demanded Mr. Simms.

"Big Ma!" I balked.

"Say it, child."

A painful tear slid down my cheek and my lips trembled. "I'm sorry . . . M-Miz . . . Lillian Jean."

When the words had been spoken, I turned and fled crying into the back of the wagon. No day in all my life had ever been as cruel as this one.

6

The ride home was long and silent. None of us felt like talking, not even T.J. Big Ma had informed him shortly after leaving Strawberry that she did not want to hear another word out of him before we reached home. He sulked for a while with a few audible grumbles which no one paid any attention to, but finally he fell asleep and did not awaken until we had driven up the Granger road and stopped in front of the Avery house.

By the time Jack pulled into our own yard, the night was a thick blackness and smelled of a coming rain. Big Ma climbed wearily down from the wagon and went into the house without a word. I stayed with Stacey to help him put the wagon inside the barn and unhitch and feed Jack. While I held the flashlight on the barn doors, Stacey slowly slid aside the plank of wood that held the doors fastened. "Cassie," he said, in a quiet, thoughtful voice, "don't go blaming Big Ma for what she done."

"Why not?" I asked angrily. "She made me apologize to that ole ugly Lillian Jean 'bout something wasn't even my fault. She took them ole Simmses' side without even hearing mine."

"Well, maybe she couldn't help it, Cassie. Maybe she had to do it."

"Had to do it!" I practically screamed. "She didn't have to do nothin'! She's grown just like that Mr. Simms and she should've stood up for me. I wouldn't've done her that way."

Stacey put the plank on the ground and leaned against the barn. "There's things you don't understand, Cassie—"

"And I s'pose you do, huh? Ever since you went down into Louisiana to get Papa last summer you think you know so doggone much! Well, I betcha I know one thing. If that had been Papa, he wouldn't've made me apologize! He would've listened to me!"

Stacey sighed and swung open the barn doors. "Well, Papa . . . that's different. But Big Ma ain't Papa and you can't expect . . ." His voice trailed off as he peered into the barn. Suddenly he cried, "Cassie, give me that flashlight!" Then, before I could object, he tore the flashlight from my hand and shone it into the barn.

"What's Mr. Granger's car doing in our barn?" I exclaimed as the silver Packard was unveiled by the light. Without answering me, Stacey swiftly turned and ran toward the house. I followed closely behind. Throwing open the door to Mama's room, we stood dumbfounded in the doorway. Instead of Mr. Granger, a tall, handsome man, nattily dressed in a gray pin-striped suit and vest, stood by the fire with his arm around Big Ma. For a moment we swayed with excitement, then as if by signal we both cried, "Uncle Hammer!" and dashed into his arms.

Uncle Hammer was two years older than Papa and, unmarried, he came every winter to spend the Christmas season with us. Like Papa, he had dark, red-brown skin, a square-jawed face, and high cheekbones; yet there was a great difference between them somehow. His eyes, which showed a great warmth as he hugged and kissed us now, often had a cold, distant glaze, and there was an aloofness in him which the boys and I could never quite bridge.

When he let us go, Stacey and I both grew consciously shy, and we backed away. I sat down beside Christopher-John and Little Man, who were silently gazing up at Uncle Hammer, but Stacey stammered, "Wh-what's Mr. Granger's car doing in our barn?"

"That's your Uncle Hammer's car," Mama said. "Did you unhitch Jack?"

"Uncle Hammer's!" Stacey exclaimed, exchanging shocked glances with me. "No kidding?"

Big Ma stammered, "Hammer, you—you went and got a car like Harlan Granger's?"

Uncle Hammer smiled a strange, wry smile. "Well, not exactly like it, Mama. Mine's a few months newer. Last year when I come down here, I was right impressed with that big ole Packard of Mr. Harlan Filmore Granger's and I thought I'd like to own one myself. It seems that me and Harlan Granger just got the same taste." He winked slyly at Stacey. "Don't it, Stacey?"

Stacey grinned.

"You like, maybe we'll all go riding in it one day. If it's all right with your mama."

"Oh, boy!" cried Little Man.

"You mean it, Uncle Hammer?" I asked. "Mama, can we?"

"We'll see," Mama said. "But in any case, not tonight. Stacey, go take care of Jack and draw up a bucket of water for the kitchen. We've done the other chores."

Since no one told me to help Stacey, I forgot all about Jack and settled back to listen to Uncle Hammer. Christopher-John and Little Man, who Big Ma had feared would be moping because they had not been allowed to go to town, seemed not at all concerned that Stacey and I had gone. They were awestruck by Uncle Hammer, and compared to his arrival a day in Strawberry was a minor matter.

For a while Uncle Hammer talked only to Mama and Big Ma, laughing from deep down inside himself like Papa, but then to my surprise he turned from them and addressed me. "I understand you had your first trip to Strawberry today, Cassie," he said. "What did you think?"

Big Ma stiffened, but I was pleased to have this opportunity to air my side of the Strawberry affair. "I didn't like it," I said. "Them ole Simmses—"

"Mary, I feel a bit hungry," Big Ma interrupted abruptly. "Supper still warm?"

"Yes, ma'am," said Mama standing. "I'll set it on the table for you."

As Mama stood up, I started again. "Them ole Simmses—"

"Let Cassie get it, Mary," said Big Ma nervously. "You must be tired."

I looked strangely at Big Ma, then up at Mama.

"Oh, I don't mind," said Mama, heading for the kitchen. "Go ahead, Cassie, and tell your uncle about Strawberry."

"That ole Lillian Jean Simms made me so mad I could just spit. I admit that I bumped into her, but that was 'cause I was thinking 'bout that ole Mr. Barnett waiting on everybody else in his ole store 'fore he waited on us—"

"Jim Lee Barnett?" asked Uncle Hammer, turning toward Big Ma. "That ole devil still living?"

Big Ma nodded mutely, and I went on. "But I told him he shouldn't've been 'round there waiting on everybody else 'fore he got to us—"

"Cassie!" Big Ma exclaimed, hearing this bit of news for the first time.

Uncle Hammer laughed. "You told him that!"

"Yessir," I said softly, wondering why he was laughing.

"Oh, that's great! Then what happened?"

"Stacey made me leave and Mr. Barnett told me I couldn't come back no more and then I bumped into that confounded Lillian Jean and she tried to make me get off the sidewalk and then her daddy come along and he—"

Big Ma's eyes grew large and she whispered hoarsely, "Cassie, I don't think—"

"—and he twisted my arm and knocked me off the sidewalk!" I exclaimed, unwilling to muffle what Mr. Simms had done. I glanced triumphantly at Big Ma, but she wasn't looking at me. Her eyes, frightened and nervous, were on Uncle Hammer. I turned and looked at him too.

His dark eyes had narrowed to thin, angry slits. He said: "He knocked you off the sidewalk, Cassie? A grown man knocked you off the sidewalk?"

"Y-yessir."

"This Lillian Jean Simms, her daddy wouldn't be Charlie Simms, would it?"

"Y-yessir."

Uncle Hammer grasped my shoulders. "What else he do to you?"

"N-nothin'," I said, frightened by his eyes. " 'Cepting he wanted me to apologize to Lillian Jean 'cause I wouldn't get in the road when she told me to."

"And you did?"

"Big Ma said I had to."

Uncle Hammer released me and sat very still. No one said a word. Then he stood slowly, his eyes icing into that cold distant way they could, and he started toward the door, limping slightly on his left leg. Christopher-John, Little Man, and I stared after him wonderingly, but Big Ma jumped up from her chair, knocking it over in her haste, and dashed after him. She grabbed his arm. "Let it be, son!" she cried. "That child ain't hurt!"

"Not hurt! You look into her eyes and tell me she ain't hurt!"

Mama came back from the kitchen with Stacey behind her. "What is it?" she asked, looking from Big Ma to Uncle Hammer.

"Charlie Simms knocked Cassie off the sidewalk in Strawberry and the child just told Hammer," said Big Ma in one breath, still holding on to Uncle Hammer's arm.

"Oh, Lord," Mama groaned. "Stacey, get Mr. Morrison. Quick, now!" As Stacey sped from the room, Mama's eyes darted to the shotgun over the bed, and she edged between it and Uncle Hammer. Uncle Hammer was watching her and he said quietly, "Don't worry. I ain't gotta use David's gun. . . . I got my own."

Suddenly Mama lunged to the side door, blocking it with her slender body. "Hammer, now you listen to me—"

But Uncle Hammer gently but firmly pushed her to one side and, brushing Big Ma from his arm, opened the door and bounded down the steps into the light rain.

Little Man, Christopher-John, and I dashed to the door as Big Ma and Mama ran after him. "Get back inside," Mama called over her shoulder, but she was too busy trying to grab Uncle Hammer to see to it that we obeyed, and we did not move. "Hammer, Cassie's all right," she cried. "Don't go making unnecessary trouble!"

"Unnecessary trouble! You think my brother died and I got my leg half blown off in their German war to have some red-neck knock Cassie around anytime it suits him? If I'd've knocked his girl down, you know what'd've happened to me? Yeah, you know all right. Right now I'd be hanging from that oak over yonder. Let go of me, Mary."

Mama and Big Ma could not keep him from reaching the car. But just as the Packard roared to life, a huge figure loomed from the darkness and jumped into the other side, and the car zoomed angrily down the drive into the blackness of the Mississippi night.

"Where'd he go?" I asked as Mama slowly climbed the steps. Her face under the glow of the lamp was tired, drained. "He went up to the Simmses', didn't he? Didn't he, Mama?"

"He's not going anywhere," Mama said, stepping aside and waiting until both Big Ma and Stacey were inside; then she locked the door.

"Mr. Morrison'll bring him back," said Christopher-John confidently, although he looked somewhat bewildered by all that had happened.

"If he don't," said Little Man ominously, "I betcha Uncle Hammer'll teach that ole Mr. Simms a thing or two. 'Round here hitting on Cassie."

"I hope he knocks his block off," I said.

Mama's gaze blazed down upon us. "I think little mouths that have so much to say must be very tired."

"No, ma'am, Mama, we ain't—"

"Go to bed."

"Mama, it ain't but—" Mama's face hardened, and I knew that it would not be in my best interest to argue further; I turned and did as I was told. Christopher-John and Little Man did the same. When I got to my door, I asked, "Ain't Stacey coming?"

Mama glanced down at Stacey sitting by the fire. "I don't recall his mouth working so hard, do you?"

"No'm," I muttered and went into my room. After a few minutes Mama came in. Without a word of reprimand, she picked up my clothes from where I had tossed them at the foot of the bed, and absently draping them over the back of a chair, she said, "Stacey tells me you blame Big Ma for what happened today. Is that right?"

I thought over her question and answered, "Not for all of it. Just for making me apologize to that ole dumb Lillian Jean Simms. She oughtn't've done that, Mama. Papa wouldn't've—"

"I don't want to hear what Papa wouldn't have done!" Mama snapped. "Or what Mr. Morrison wouldn't have done or Uncle Hammer! You were with Big Ma and she did what she had to do and believe me, young lady, she didn't like doing it one bit more than you did."

"Well," I muttered, "maybe so, but—"

"There's no maybe to it."

"Yes'm," I said softly, deciding that it was better to study the patchwork pattern on the quilt until the anger left Mama's eyes and I could talk to her again. After a moment she sat beside me on the bed and raised my chin with the tip of her forefinger. "Big Ma didn't want you to be hurt," she said. "That was the only thing on her mind . . . making sure Mr. Simms didn't hurt you."

"Yes'm," I murmured, then flared, "But, Mama, that Lillian Jean ain't got the brains of a flea! How come I gotta go 'round calling her 'Miz' like she grown or something?"

Mama's voice grew hard. "Because that's the way of things, Cassie."

"The way of what things?" I asked warily.

"Baby, you had to grow up a little today. I wish . . . well, no matter what I wish. It happened and you have to accept the fact that in the world outside this house, things are not always as we would have them to be."

"But, Mama, it ain't fair. I didn't do nothin' to that confounded Lillian Jean. How come Mr. Simms went and pushed me like he did?"

Mama's eyes looked deeply into mine, locked into them, and she said in a tight, clear voice, "Because he thinks Lillian Jean is better than you are, Cassie, and when you—"

"That ole scrawny, chicken-legged, snaggle-toothed, cross—"

"Cassie." Mama did not raise her voice, but the quiet force of my name silenced me. "Now," she said, folding my hand in hers, "I didn't say that Lillian Jean *is* better than you. I said Mr. Simms only *thinks* she is. In fact, he thinks she's better than Stacey or Little Man or Christopher-John—"

"Just 'cause she's his daughter?" I asked, beginning to think Mr. Simms was a bit touched in the head.

"No, baby, because she's white."

Mama's hold tightened on mine, but I exclaimed, "Ah, shoot! White ain't nothin'!"

Mama's grip did not lessen. "It is something, Cassie. White is something just like black is something. Everybody born on this earth is something and nobody, no matter what color, is better than anybody else."

"Then how come Mr. Simms don't know that?"

"Because he's one of those people who has to believe that white people are better than black people to make himself feel big." I stared questioningly at Mama, not really understanding. Mama squeezed my hand and explained further. "You see, Cassie, many years ago when our people were first brought from Africa in chains to work as slaves in this country—"

"Like Big Ma's papa and mama?"

Mama nodded. "Yes, baby, like Papa Luke and Mama Rachel, except they were born right here in Mississippi. But their grandparents were born in Africa, and when they came there were some white people who thought that it was wrong for any people to be slaves; so the people who needed slaves to work in their fields and the people who were making money bringing slaves from Africa preached that black people weren't really people like white people were, so slavery was all right.

"They also said that slavery was good for us because it taught us to be good Christians—like the white people." She sighed deeply, her voice fading into a distant whisper. "But they didn't teach us Christianity to save our souls, but to teach us obedience. They were afraid of slave revolts and they wanted us to learn the Bible's teachings about slaves being loyal to their masters. But even teaching us Christianity didn't make us stop wanting to be free, and many slaves ran away—"

"Papa Luke ran away," I reminded her, thinking of the story of how Great-Grandpa had run away three times. He had been caught and punished for his disobedience, but his owners had not tried to break him, for he had had a knowledge of herbs and cures. He had tended both the slaves and the animals of the plantation, and it was from him that Big Ma had learned medicines.

Mama nodded again. "That's right, honey. He was hiding in a cave when freedom came, so I understand." She was silent a moment, then went on. "Well, after a while, slavery became so profitable to people who had slaves and even to those who didn't that most folks decided to believe that black people really weren't people like everybody else. And when the Civil War was fought and Mama Rachel and Papa Luke and all the other slaves were freed, people continued to think that way. Even the Northerners who fought the war didn't really see us equal to white people. So now, even though seventy years have passed since slavery, most white people still think of us as they did then—that we're not as good as they are—and people like Mr. Simms hold on to that belief harder than some other folks because they have little else to hold on to. For him to believe that he is better than we are makes him think that he's important, simply because he's white."

Mama relaxed her grip. I knew that she was waiting for me to speak. There was a sinking feeling in my stomach and I felt as if the world had turned itself upside down with me in it. Then I thought of Lillian Jean and a surging anger gurgled upward and I retaliated, "Well, they ain't!" But I leaned closer to Mama, anxiously hoping that she would agree with me.

"Of course they aren't," Mama said. "White people may demand our respect, but what we give them is not respect but fear. What we give to our own people is far more important because it's given freely. Now you may have to call Lillian Jean 'Miss' because the white people say so, but you'll also call our own young ladies at church 'Miss' because you really do respect them.

"Baby, we have no choice of what color we're born or who our parents are or whether we're rich or poor. What we do have is some choice over what we make of our lives once we're here." Mama cupped my face in her hands. "And I pray to God you'll make the best of yours." She hugged me warmly then and motioned me under the covers.

As she turned the lamp down low, I asked, "Mama, Uncle Hammer. If Mr. Morrison can't stop him, what'll happen?"

"Mr. Morrison will bring him back."

"But just what if he can't and Uncle Hammer gets to Mr. Simms?"

A shadowy fear fleeted across her face, but disappeared with the dimming light. "I think . . . I think you've done enough growing up for one day, Cassie," she said without answering my question. "Uncle Hammer'll be all right. Now go to sleep."

Mama had been right about Uncle Hammer. When I awoke the next morning and followed the smell of frying ham and baking biscuits into the kitchen, there he sat at the table drinking coffee with Mr. Morrison. He was unshaven and looked a bit bleary-eyed, but he was all right; I wondered if Mr. Simms looked so good. I didn't get a chance to ask, because as soon as I had said good morning, Mama called me into her room, where a tub of hot water was waiting by the fireplace.

"Hurry up," she said. "Uncle Hammer's going to take us to church."

"In his car?"

Mama's brow furrowed. "Well, I just don't know. He did say something about hitching up Jack . . ."

My smile faded, but then I caught the teasing glint in her eyes, and she began to laugh. "Ah, Mama!" I laughed, and splashed into the water.

After my bath I went into my room to dress. When I rejoined Mama she was combing her hair, which fanned her head like an enormous black halo. As I watched, she shaped the long thickness into a large chignon at the nape of her neck and stuck six sturdy hairpins into it. Then, giving the chignon a pat, she reached for her pale-blue cotton dress sprinkled with tiny yellow-and-white flowers and polished white buttons running from top to bottom along its front. She glanced down at me. "You didn't comb your hair."

"No'm. I want you to fix me my grown-up hairdo."

Mama began buttoning the top of her dress with long, flying fingers as I slowly fastened the lower buttons. I loved to help Mama dress. She always smelled of sunshine and soap. When the last button had slipped into place, she buckled a darkblue patent-leather belt around her tiny waist and stood ready except for her shoes. She looked very pretty.

"Where's your brush?"

"Right here," I said, picking up the brush from where I had laid it on the chair.

Mama sat down in Papa's rocker and I sat on the deerskin rug in front of her. Mama divided my hair from ear to ear into two sections and braided the front section to one side and the back section right in the center. Then she wound each braid into a flat chignon against my head. My hair was too thick and long for me to do it well myself, but Mama could do it perfectly. I figured I looked my very best that way.

When Mama finished, I ran to the mirror, then turned, facing her with a grin. She grinned back and shook her head at my vanity.

"One day, Mama, you gonna fix my hair like yours?"

"That'll be a few years yet," she answered, readjusting the cardboard lining she had placed in her shoes to protect her feet from the dirt and gravel which could easily seep through the large holes in the soles. She set the shoes on the floor and stepped into them. Now, with the soles facing downward and Mama's feet in them, no one could tell what the shiny exteriors hid; yet I felt uncomfortable for Mama and wished that we had enough money for her to have her shoes fixed or, better still, buy new ones.

After breakfast Stacey, Christopher-John, Little Man, and I sat impatiently by the dying morning fire waiting for Mama, Big Ma, and Uncle Hammer. Uncle Hammer was dressing in the boys' room and Mama was in with Big Ma. I checked to make sure none of them was about to appear, then leaned toward Stacey and whispered, "You think Uncle Hammer whipped Mr. Simms?"

"No," said Stacey quietly.

"No!" cried Little Man.

"Y-you don't mean Mr. Simms whipped Uncle Hammer?" stammered an unbelieving Christopher-John.

"Nothin' happened," said Stacey in explanation as he tugged irritably at his collar.

"Nothin'?" I repeated, disappointed.

"Nothin'."

"How you know?" asked Little Man suspiciously.

"Mama said so. I asked her straight out this morning."

"Oh," replied Little Man, resigned.

"But something must've happened," I said. "I mean Uncle Hammer and Mr. Morrison look like they haven't even been to bed. How come they look like that if nothin' happened?"

"Mama said Mr. Morrison talked all night to Uncle Hammer. Talked him tired and wouldn't let him go up to the Simmses'."

"Ah, shoot!" I exclaimed, my dream of revenge against the Simmses vanishing as Stacey talked. I propped my elbows on my knees, then settled my head in my upraised hands and stared into the glowing embers. A burning knot formed in my throat and I felt as if my body was not large enough to hold the frustration I felt, nor deep enough to drown the rising anger.

"It ain't fair," Christopher-John sympathized, patting me lightly with his pudgy hand.

"Sho' ain't," agreed Little Man.

"Cassie," Stacey said softly. At first I didn't look at him, thinking he would go ahead and say what he had to say. But when he didn't, I turned toward him. He leaned forward secretively and automatically Christopher-John and Little Man did the same. "Y'all better be glad nothin' happened," he said in a whisper. " 'Cause I heard Big Ma tell Mama last night that if Mr. Morrison didn't stop Uncle Hammer, Uncle Hammer might get killed."

"Killed?" we echoed as the fire sputtered and died. "Who'd do that?" I cried. "Not one of them puny Simmses?"

Stacey started to speak, but then Mama and Big Ma entered, and he cautioned us into silence.

When Uncle Hammer joined us, freshly shaven and in another suit, the boys and I put on our coats and headed for the door; Uncle Hammer stopped us. "Stacey, that the only coat you got, son?" he asked.

Stacey looked down at his faded cotton jacket. Everyone else did too. The jacket was too small for him, that was obvious, and compared to Little Man's and Christopher-John's and mine, it was admittedly in sadder shape. Yet we were all surprised that Uncle Hammer would ask about it, for he knew as well as anyone that Mama had to buy our clothes in shifts, which meant that we each had to wait our turn for new clothes. Stacey looked up at Mama, then back at Uncle Hammer. "Y-yessir," he answered.

Uncle Hammer stared at him, then waving his hand ordered, "Take it off." Before Stacey could question why, Uncle Hammer disappeared into the boys' room.

Again Stacey looked at Mama. "You'd better do like he says," she said.

Uncle Hammer returned with a long box, store wrapped in shiny red Christmas paper and a fancy green ribbon. He handed the package to Stacey. "It was supposed to be your Christmas present, but I think I'd better give it to you now. It's cold out there."

Gingerly, Stacey took the box and opened it.

"A coat!" cried Little Man joyously, clapping his hands.

"Wool," Mama said reverently. "Go ahead, Stacey. Try it on."

Stacey eagerly slipped on the coat; it was much too big for him, but Mama said that she could take up the sleeves and that he would grow into it in another year. Stacey beamed down at the coat, then up at Uncle Hammer. A year ago he would have shot into Uncle Hammer's arms and hugged his thanks, but now at the manly age of twelve he held out his hand, and Uncle Hammer shook it.

"Come on, we'd better go," said Mama.

The morning was gray as we stepped outside, but the rain had stopped. We followed the path of bedded rocks that led to the barn, careful not to slip into the mud, and got into the Packard, shining clean and bright from the washing Uncle Hammer and Mr. Morrison had given it after breakfast. Inside the Packard, the world was a wine-colored luxury. The boys and I, in the back, ran our hands over the rich felt seats, tenderly fingered the fancy door handles and window knobs, and peered down amazed at the plush carpet peeping out on either side of the rubber mats. Mr. Morrison, who was not a churchgoing man, waved good-bye from the barn and we sped away.

As we drove onto the school grounds and parked, the people milling in front of the church turned, staring at the Packard. Then Uncle Hammer stepped from the car and someone cried, "Well, I'll be doggone! It's our Hammer! Hammer Logan!" And in a body, the crowd engulfed us.

T.J. ran up with Moe Turner and Little Willie Wiggins to admire the car. "It's Uncle Hammer's," said Stacey proudly. But before the boys could sufficiently admire the car, Mama and Big Ma shooed us toward the church for the service. It was then that T.J. noticed Stacey's new coat.

"Uncle Hammer gave it to him," I said. "Ain't it something?"

T.J. ran his long fingers over the lapels, and shrugged. "It's all right, I guess, if you like that sort of thing."

"All right!" I cried, indignant at his casual reaction to the coat. "Boy, that's the finest coat you ever did lay eyes on and you know it!"

T.J. sighed. "Like I said, it's all right . . . if you like lookin' like a fat preacher." Then he and Little Willie and Moe laughed, and went on ahead.

Stacey looked down at the coat with its long sleeves and wide shoulders. His smile faded. "He don't know what he's talking 'bout," I said. "He's just jealous, that's all."

"I know it," snapped Stacey sourly.

As we slid into the pew in front of T.J., T.J. whispered, "Here comes the preacher," then leaned forward and said snidely, "How do you do, Reverend Logan?"

Stacey turned on T.J., but I poked him hard. "Mama's looking," I whispered, and he turned back around.

After church, as T.J. and the others looked longingly at the car, Mama said, "Stacey, maybe T.J. wants to ride."

Before Stacey could reply, I spoke up hurriedly. "No, ma'am, Mama, he got something else he gotta do." Then under my breath so that I would not be guilty of a lie, I added, "He gotta walk home like he always do."

"That'll teach him," whispered Little Man.

"Yeah," agreed Christopher-John, but Stacey sulked by the window and said nothing.

The sun was out now and Uncle Hammer suggested that we take a real ride before going home. He drove us the full twenty-two miles up to Strawberry by way of the Jackson Road, one of two roads leading to the town. But Mama and Big Ma objected so much to going through Strawberry that he turned the big car around and headed back toward home, taking the old Soldiers Road. Supposedly, Rebel soldiers had once marched up the road and across Soldiers Bridge to keep the town from falling into the hands of the Yankee Army, but I had my doubts about that. After all, who in his right mind would want to capture Strawberry . . . or defend it either for that matter?

The road was hilly and curving, and as we sped over it scattered road stones hit sharply against the car's underbelly and the dust swelled up in rolls of billowing clouds behind us. Little Man, Christopher-John, and I shrieked with delight each time the car climbed a hill and dropped suddenly downward, fluttering our stomachs. Eventually, the road intersected with the Jefferson Davis School Road. Uncle Hammer stopped the car at the intersection and, leaning his right arm heavily over the steering wheel, motioned languidly at the Wallace store. "Got me a good mind to burn that place out," he said.

"Hammer, hush that kind of talk!" ordered Big Ma, her eyes growing wide.

"Me and John Henry and David grew up together. And John Henry and me even fought in their war together. What good was it? A black man's life ain't worth the life of a cowfly[3] down here."

"I know that, son, but that kinda talk get you hung and you know it."

_____
3. I.e., a deerfly.

Mama touched Uncle Hammer's arm. "There might be another way, Hammer . . . like I told you. Now don't go do something foolish. Wait for David—talk to him."

Uncle Hammer looked glassy-eyed at the store, then sighed and eased the Packard across the road toward Soldiers Bridge. We were taking the long way home.

Soldiers Bridge was built before the Civil War. It was spindly and wooden, and each time I had to cross it I held my breath until I was safely on the other side. Only one vehicle could cross at a time, and whoever was on the bridge first was supposed to have the right of way, although it didn't always work that way. More than once when I had been in the wagon with Mama or Big Ma, we had had to back off the bridge when a white family started across after we were already on it.

As the bridge came into view the other side of the river was clearly visible, and it was obvious to everyone that an old Model-T truck, overflowing with redheaded children, had reached the bridge first and was about to cross, but suddenly Uncle Hammer gassed the Packard and sped onto the creaking structure. The driver of the truck stopped, and for no more than a second hesitated on the bridge, then without a single honk of protest backed off so that we could pass.

"Hammer!" Big Ma cried. "They think you're Mr. Granger."

"Well, now, won't they be surprised when we reach the other side," said Uncle Hammer.

As we came off the bridge, we could see the Wallaces, all three of them—Dewberry, Thurston, and Kaleb—touch their hats respectfully, then immediately freeze as they saw who we were. Uncle Hammer, straight-faced and totally calm, touched the brim of his own hat in polite response and without a backward glance sped away, leaving the Wallaces gaping silently after us.

Stacey, Christopher-John, Little Man, and I laughed, but Mama's cold glance made us stop. "You shouldn't have done that, Hammer," she said quietly.

"The opportunity, dear sister, was too much to resist."

"But one day we'll have to pay for it. Believe me," she said, "one day we'll pay."

7

"Stacey, go bring me your coat," Mama said a few days later as we gathered around the fire after supper. "I've got time to take up the sleeves now."

"Uh-oh!" exclaimed Christopher-John, then immediately opened his reader as Mama looked down at him.

Little Man cupped his hand and whispered to me, "Boy now he's gonna get it!"

"Uh . . . th-that's all right, Mama," stuttered Stacey. "The c-coat's all right like it is."

Mama opened her sewing box. "It's not all right. Now go get it for me."

Stacey stood up and started slowly toward his room. Little Man, Christopher-John, and I watched him closely, wondering what he was going to do. He actually went into the room, but was gone only a moment before he reappeared and nervously clutched the back of his chair. "I ain't got the coat, Mama," he said.

"Not got the coat!" cried Big Ma. Uncle Hammer looked up sharply from his paper, but remained silent.

"Stacey," Mama said irritably, "bring me that coat, boy."

"But, Mama, I really ain't got it! I gave it to T.J."

"T.J.!" Mama exclaimed.

"Yes, ma'am, Mama," Stacey answered, then went on hurriedly as Mama's eyes glittered with rising anger. "The coat was too big for me and . . . and T.J. said it made me look like . . . like a preacher . . . and he said since it fit him just right, he'd . . . he'd take it off my hands till I grow into it, then thataway all the guys would stop laughing at me and calling me preacher." He paused, waiting for someone to speak; but the only sound was a heavy breathing and the crackle of burning hickory. Then, seeming more afraid of the silence than putting his neck further into the noose, he added, "But I didn't give it to him for good, Mama—just lent it to him till I get big enough for it and then . . ."

Stacey's voice faded into an inaudible whisper as Mama slowly put the sewing box on the table behind her. I thought she was headed for the wide leather strap hanging in the kitchen, but she did not rise. In quiet anger she glared at Stacey and admonished, "In this house we do not give away what loved ones give to us. Now go bring me that coat."

Backing away from her anger, Stacey turned to leave, but Uncle Hammer stopped him. "No," he said, "leave the coat where it is."

Mama turned bewildered toward Uncle Hammer. "Hammer, what're you saying? That's the best coat Stacey's ever had and probably ever will have as long as he lives in this house. David and I can't afford a coat like that."

Uncle Hammer leaned back in his chair, his eyes cold on Stacey. "Seems to me if Stacey's not smart enough to hold on to a good coat, he don't deserve it. As far as I'm concerned, T.J. can just keep that coat permanently. At least he knows a good thing when he sees it."

"Hammer," Big Ma said, "let the boy go get the coat. That T.J. probably done told him all sorts—"

"Well, ain't Stacey got a brain? What the devil should he care what T.J. thinks or T.J. says? Who is this T.J. anyway? Does he put clothes on Stacey's back or food in front of him?" Uncle Hammer stood and walked over to Stacey as Little Man, Christopher-John, and I followed him fearfully with our eyes. "I suppose if T.J. told you it was summertime out there and you should run buck naked down the road because everybody else was doing it, you'd do that too, huh?"

"N-no sir," Stacey replied, looking at the floor.

"Now you hear me good on this—look at me when I talk to you, boy!" Immediately Stacey raised his head and looked at Uncle Hammer. "If you ain't got the brains of a flea to see that this T.J. fellow made a fool of you, then you'll never get anywhere in this world. It's tough out there, boy, and as long as there are people, there's gonna be somebody trying to take what you got and trying to drag you down. It's up to you whether you let them or not. Now it seems to me you wanted that coat when I gave it to you, ain't that right?"

Stacey managed a shaky "Yessir."

"And anybody with any sense would know it's a good thing, ain't that right?"

This time Stacey could only nod.

"Then if you want something and it's a good thing and you got it in the right way, you better hang on to it and don't let nobody talk you out of it. You care what a lot of useless people say 'bout you you'll never get anywhere, 'cause there's a lotta folks don't want you to make it. You understand what I'm telling you?"

"Y-yessir, Uncle Hammer," Stacey stammered. Uncle Hammer turned then and went back to his paper without having laid a hand on Stacey, but Stacey shook visibly from the encounter.

Christopher-John, Little Man, and I exchanged apprehensive glances. I don't know what they were thinking, but I for one was deciding right then and there not to do anything to rub Uncle Hammer the wrong way; I had no intention of ever facing a tongue-lashing like that. Papa's bottom-warming whippings were quite enough for me, thank you.

The last days of school before Christmas seemed interminable. Each night I fell asleep with the hope that the morning would bring Papa, and each morning when he wasn't there I trudged to school consoling myself that he would be home when I returned. But the days passed prickly cold and windy, and he did not come.

Added to the misery of the waiting and the cold was Lillian Jean, who managed to flounce past me with a superior smirk twice that week. I had already decided that she had had two flounces too many, but since I hadn't yet decided how to handle the matter, I postponed doing anything until after I had had a chance to talk with Papa about the whole Strawberry business. I knew perfectly well that he would not tear out of the house after Mr. Simms as Uncle Hammer had done, for he always took time to think through any move he made, but he would certainly advise me on how to handle Lillian Jean.

Then too there was T.J., who, although not really my problem, was so obnoxiously flaunting Stacey's wool coat during these cold days that I had just about decided to deflate him at the same time I took care of Lillian Jean. Ever since the night Mr. Avery had brought him to the house to return the coat and he had been told by Uncle Hammer and a faltering Stacey that the coat was his, T.J. had been more unbearable than usual. He now praised the coat from the wide tips of its lapels to the very edges of its deep hem. No one had ever had a finer coat; no one had ever looked better in such a coat; no one could ever hope to have such a coat again.

Stacey was restrained from plugging T.J.'s mouth by Uncle Hammer's principle that a man did not blame others for his own stupidity; he learned from his mistake and became stronger for it. I, however, was not so restrained and as far as I was concerned, if T.J. kept up with this coat business, he could just hit the dirt at the same time as "Miss" Lillian Jean.

The day before Christmas I awoke to the soft murmuring of quiet voices gathered in the midnight blackness of morning. Big Ma was not beside me, and without a moment's doubt I knew why she was gone. Jumping from the bed, my feet barely hitting the deerskin rug, I rushed into Mama's room.

"Oh, Papa!" I cried. "I knew it was you!"

"Ah, there's my Cassie girl!" Papa laughed, standing to catch me as I leapt into his arms.

By the dawn, the house smelled of Sunday: chicken frying, bacon sizzling, and smoke sausages baking. By evening, it reeked of Christmas. In the kitchen sweet-potato pies, egg-custard pies, and rich butter pound cakes cooled; a gigantic coon which Mr. Morrison, Uncle Hammer, and Stacey had secured in a night's hunt baked in a sea of onions, garlic, and fat orange-yellow yams; and a choice sugar-cured ham brought from the smokehouse awaited its turn in the oven. In the heart of the house, where we had gathered after supper, freshly cut branches of long-needled pines lay over the fireplace mantle adorned by winding vines of winter holly and bright red Christmas berries. And in the fireplace itself, in a black pan set on a high wire rack, peanuts roasted over the hickory fire as the waning light of day swiftly deepened into a fine velvet night speckled with white forerunners of a coming snow, and the warm sound of husky voices and rising laughter mingled in tales of sorrow and happiness of days past but not forgotten.

". . . Them watermelons of old man Ellis' seemed like they just naturally tasted better than anybody else's," said Papa, "and ole Hammer and me, we used to sneak up there whenever it'd get so hot you couldn't hardly move and take a couple of them melons on down to the pond and let them get real chilled. Then, talking 'bout eating! We did some kind of good eating."

"Papa, you was stealing?" asked an astonished Little Man. Although he usually strongly disapproved of being held, he was now reclining comfortably in Papa's lap.

"Well . . ." Papa said, "not exactly. What we'd do was exchange one of the melons from our patch for his. Course it was still wrong for us to do it, but at the time it seemed all right—"

"Problem was, though," laughed Uncle Hammer, "old man Ellis grew them ole fat green round watermelons and ours was long and striped—"

"And Mr. Ellis was always right particular 'bout his melons," interjected Papa. "He took the longest time to figure out what we was up to, but, Lord, Lord, when he did—"

"—You should've seen us run," Uncle Hammer said, standing. He shot one hand against and past the other. "Ma—an! We was gone! And that ole man was right behind us with a hickory stick hitting us up side the head—"

"Ow—weee! That ole man could run!" cried Papa. "I didn't know nobody's legs could move that fast."

Big Ma chuckled. "And as I recalls, your Papa 'bout wore y'all out when Mr. Ellis told him what y'all'd been up to. Course, you know all them Ellises was natural-born runners. Y'all remember Mr. Ellis' brother, Tom Lee? Well, one time he . . ."

Through the evening Papa and Uncle Hammer and Big Ma and Mr. Morrison and Mama lent us their memories, acting out their tales with stageworthy skills, imitating the characters in voice, manner, and action so well that the listeners held their sides with laughter. It was a good warm time. But as the night deepened and the peanuts in the pan grew shallow, the voices grew hushed, and Mr. Morrison said:

". . . They come down like ghosts that Christmas of seventy-six. Them was hard times like now and my family was living in a shantytown right outside Shreveport. Reconstruction was just 'bout over then, and them Northern soldiers was tired of being in the South and they didn't hardly care 'bout no black folks in shantytown. And them Southern whites, they was tired of the Northern soldiers and free Negroes, and they was trying to turn things back 'round to how they used to be. And the colored folks . . . well, we was just tired. Warn't hardly no work, and during them years I s'pose it was jus' 'bout as hard being free as it was being a slave. . . .

"That night they come—I can remember just as good—it was cold, so cold we had to huddle all 'gainst each other just trying to keep warm, and two boys—'bout eighteen or nineteen, I reckon—come knocking on my daddy's door. They was scairt, clean out of their heads with fright. They'd just come back from Shreveport. Some white woman done accused them of molestin' her and they didn't know nowhere to run so they come up to my daddy's 'cause he had a good head and he was big, bigger than me. He was strong too. So strong he could break a man's leg easy as if he was snapping a twig—I seen him do it that night. And the white folks was scairt of him. But my daddy didn't hardly have time to finish hearing them boys' story when them devilish night men swept down—"

"Night men!" I echoed in a shrill, dry whisper. Stacey sitting beside me on the floor stiffened; Christopher-John nudged me knowingly; Little Man leaned forward on Papa's lap.

"David . . ." Mama started, but Papa enfolded her slender hand in his and said quietly, "These are things they need to hear, baby. It's their history."

Mama sat back, her hand still in Papa's, her eyes wary. But Mr. Morrison seemed not to notice. ". . . swept down like locusts," he continued in a faraway voice. "Burst in on us with their Rebel sabers, hacking and killing, burning us out. Didn't care who they kilt. We warn't nothing to them. No better than dogs. Kilt babies and old women. Didn't matter."

He gazed into the fire.

"My sisters got kilt in they fire, but my Mama got me out. . . ." His voice faded and he touched the scars on his neck. "She tried to get back into the house to save the girls, but she couldn't. Them night men was all over her and she threw me—just threw me like I was a ball—hard as she could, trying to get me away from them. Then she fought. Fought like a wild thing right 'side my daddy. They was both of them from breeded stock and they was strong like bulls—"

"Breeded stock?" I said. "What's that?"

"Cassie, don't interrupt Mr. Morrison," said Mama, but Mr. Morrison turned from the fire and explained. "Well, Cassie, during slavery there was some farms that mated folks like animals to produce more slaves. Breeding slaves brought a lot of money for them slave owners, 'specially after the government said they couldn't bring no more slaves from Africa,[4] and they produced all kinds of slaves to sell on the block. And folks with enough money, white men and even free black men, could buy 'zactly what they wanted. My folks was bred for strength like they folks and they grandfolks 'fore 'em. Didn't matter none what they thought 'bout the idea. Didn't nobody care.

"But my mama and daddy they loved each other and they loved us children, and that Christmas they fought them demons out of hell like avenging angels of the Lord." He turned back toward the fire and grew very quiet; then he raised his head and looked at us. "They died that night. Them night men kilt 'em. Some folks tell me I can't remember what happened that Christmas—I warn't hardly six years old—but I remembers all right. I makes myself remember."

He grew silent again and no one spoke. Big Ma poked absently at the red-eyed logs with the poker, but no one else stirred. Finally Mr. Morrison stood, wished us a good night, and left.

Uncle Hammer stood also. "Guess I'll turn in too. It's near one o'clock."

"Wait awhile, Hammer," said Big Ma. "Now you and David both home, I gotta talk to y'all—'bout the land. . . ."

Visions of night men and fire mixed in a caldron of fear awakened me long before dawn. Automatically, I rolled toward the comforting presence of Big Ma, but she was not beside me.

A soft light still crept under the door from Mama and Papa's room and I immediately hurried toward it. As I opened the door and stepped into the shadowy room, lit now only by the flickering yellow of the low fire, Big Ma was saying, ". . . y'all start messin' with these folks down in here, no telling what'll happen."

"Is it better to just sit back and complain about how they do us?" Mama snapped, her voice rising. "Everybody from Smellings Creek to Strawberry knows it was them but what do we do about it? We line their pockets with our few pennies and send our children up to their store to learn things they've got no business learning. The older children are drinking regularly there now, even though they don't have any money to pay, and the Wallaces are simply adding the liquor charges to the family bill . . . just more money for them as they ruin our young people. As I see it the least

---

4. The importation of slaves into the United States was outlawed in 1808.

we can do is stop shopping there. It may not be real justice, but it'll hurt them and we'll have done something. Mr. Turner and the Averys and the Laniers and over two dozen other families, and perhaps even more, say they'll think about not shopping there if they can get credit somewhere else. We owe it to the Berrys—"

"Frankly," interrupted Uncle Hammer, "I'd rather burn them out myself."

"Hammer, you go to burning and we'll have nothing," Mama retorted.

"Ain't gonna have nothing noway," replied Uncle Hammer. "You think by shopping up at Vicksburg you gonna drive them Wallaces out, then you got no idea of how things work down here. You forgetting Harlan Granger backs that store?"

"Mary, child, Hammer's right," Big Ma said. "I'm doing what I told y'all 'bout this land 'cause I don't want some legal thing to come up after I'm gone that let that Harlan Granger get this place. But we go backing folks' credit with our land, we'd lose it sure; and we do that, I couldn't face Paul Edward—"

"I didn't say we should back it," Mama said, "but we're just about the only family with any collateral at all."

Papa looked up from the fire. "That may be, honey, but we put up this land to back this thing and it'll be just like giving it away. Times like they are, it ain't likely that any of these people can pay the bills they make—as much as they might mean to—and if they can't pay, where would we be? We've got no cash money to pay other folks' debts." He shook his head. "No . . . we'll have to find another way. . . . Go to Vicksburg maybe and see what we can arrange—" His eyes fell upon me in the shadows and he leaned forward. "Cassie? What is it, sugar?"

"Nothin', Papa," I mumbled. "I just woke up, that's all."

Mama started to rise but Papa motioned her down and got up himself. Escorting me back to bed, he said gently. "Got no cause for bad dreams, Cassie girl. Not tonight anyway."

"Papa," I said, snuggling under the warm quilts as he tucked them around me, "we gonna lose our land?"

Papa reached out and softly touched my face in the darkness. "If you remember nothing else in your whole life, Cassie girl, remember this: We ain't never gonna lose this land. You believe that?"

"Yessir, Papa."

"Then go to sleep. Christmas is coming."

"Books!" cried Little Man on Christmas morning.

For Stacey there was *The Count of Monte Cristo*; for me, *The Three Musketeers*;[5] and for Christopher-John and Little Man, two different volumes of *Aesop's Fables*. On the inside cover of each book in Mama's fine hand was written the name of the owner. Mine read: "This book is the property of Miss Cassie Deborah Logan. Christmas, 1933."

"Man sold me them books told me these two was written by a black man," Papa said, opening my book and pointing to a picture of a man in a long, fancy coat and a wigful of curly hair that fell to his shoulders. "Name of Alexander Du—mas, a French fellow. His daddy was a mulatto and his grandmama was a slave down on one of them islands—Mar-ti-nique, it says here. Man said to me, they right hard reading for children, but I told him he didn't know my babies. They can't read 'em now, I said, they'll grow into 'em."

---

5. Novels (both published in 1844) by the French author and playwright Alexandre Dumas (1802–1870).

In addition to the books there was a sockful of once-a-year store-bought licorice, oranges, and bananas for each of us and from Uncle Hammer a dress and a sweater for me, and a sweater and a pair of pants each for Christopher-John and Little Man. But nothing compared to the books. Little Man, who treasured clothes above all else, carefully laid his new pants and sweater aside and dashed for a clean sheet of brown paper to make a cover for his book, and throughout the day as he lay upon the deerskin rug looking at the bright, shining pictures of faraway places, turning each page as if it were gold, he would suddenly squint down at his hands, glance at the page he had just turned, then dash into the kitchen to wash again—just to make sure.

After the church services, the Averys returned home with us for Christmas dinner. All eight of the Avery children, including the four pre-schoolers, crowded into the kitchen with the boys and me, smelling the delicious aromas and awaiting the call to eat. But only the eldest girls, who were helping Mama, Big Ma, and Mrs. Avery prepare the finishing touches to the meal, were allowed to remain. The rest of us were continuously being shooed out by Big Ma. Finally, the announcement we were all waiting for was made and we were allowed to begin the Christmas feast.

The meal lasted for over two hours through firsts, seconds, and thirds, talk and laughter, and finally dessert. When we were finished the boys and I, with Claude and T.J., went outside, but the half-inch layer of snow made everything sloppy, so we soon went back in and joined the adults by the fire. Shortly afterward, there was a timid knock on the front door. Stacey opened the door and found Jeremy Simms standing there looking frozen and very frightened as he peered into the bright room. Everyone turned to stare at him. Stacey glanced around at Papa, the back at Jeremy. "You—you wanna come in?" he asked awkwardly.

Jeremy nodded and stepped hesitantly inside. As Stacey motioned him toward the fire, Uncle Hammer's eyes narrowed, and he said to Papa, "He looks like a Simms."

"I believe he is," agreed Papa.

"Then what the devil—"

"Let me handle it," Papa said.

Jeremy, who had heard, flushed a deep red and quickly handed Mama a small burlap bag. "I—I brung them for y'all." Mama took the bag. As she opened it, I peeped over her shoulder; the bag was full of nuts.

"Nuts?" I questioned. "Nuts! Why we got more nuts now than we know what—"

"Cassie!" Mama scowled. "What have I told you about that mouth of yours?" Then she turned to Jeremy. "This is very thoughtful of you, Jeremy, and we appreciate them. Thank you."

Jeremy nodded slightly as if he did not know how to accept her thanks, and stiffly handed a slender, paper-wrapped object to Stacey. "Made this for ya," he said.

Stacey looked at Papa to see if he should take it. For a long moment Papa studied Jeremy, then he nodded. "It—it ain't much," stammered Jeremy as Stacey tore off the wrapping. "M-made it myself." Stacey slid his fingers down the smooth, sanded back of a wooden flute. "Go 'head and try it," said a pleased Jeremy. "It blows real nice."

Again Stacey looked at Papa, but this time Papa gave him no indication what he should do. "Thanks, Jeremy, it's real nice," he said finally. Then, flute in hand, he stood uncomfortably by the door waiting for Jeremy to leave.

When Jeremy did not move, Papa asked, "You Charlie Simms's boy?"

Jeremy nodded. "Y-yessir."

"Your daddy know you here?"

Jeremy bit his lower lip, and looked at his feet. "N-no sir, I reckon not."

"Then I expect you'd better be getting on home, son, 'fore he come looking for you."

"Yessir," said Jeremy, backing away.

As he reached the door, I cried after him, "Merry Christmas, Jeremy!" Jeremy looked back and smiled shyly. "Merry Christmas to y'all too."

T.J. made no comment on Jeremy's visit until both Papa and Uncle Hammer had left the room. He was afraid of Papa and downright terrified of Uncle Hammer, so he never had much to say when either was around, but now that they had gone outside with Mr. Avery, he said, "You ain't gonna keep that thing, are you?"

Stacey looked malevolently at T.J. and I knew that he was thinking of the coat. "Yeah, I'm gonna keep it. Why?"

T.J. shrugged. "Nothin'. 'Ceptin' I sure wouldn't want no whistle some ole white boy been blowin' on."

I watched Stacey closely to see if he was going to allow himself to be goaded by T.J.; he was not. "Ah, stuff it, T.J.," he ordered.

"Ah, man, don't get me wrong," said T.J. quickly. "You wanna keep the ole thing, it's up to you. But for me, somebody give me something, I want it to be something fine—like that pretty little pearl-handled pistol. . . ."

When the Averys had left, Stacey asked, "Papa, how come Jeremy give me this flute? I mean, I didn't give him nothin'."

"Maybe you did give him something," said Papa, lighting his pipe.

"No sir, Papa. I ain't never give him nothin'!"

"Not even your friendship?"

"Well . . . not really. I mean . . . he's a crazy kid and he likes to walk to school with us, but—"

"You like him?"

Stacey frowned, thinking. "I told him I didn't want him walking with us, but he keeps on anyway and the white kids laugh at him 'cause he do. But he don't seem to let it bother him none. . . . I s'pose I like him all right. Is that wrong?"

"No," Papa said carefully. "That ain't wrong."

"Actually, he's much easier to get along with than T.J.," Stacey went on. "And I s'pose if I let him, he could be a better friend than T.J."

Papa took the pipe from his mouth, rubbed his moustache and spoke quietly. "Far as I'm concerned, friendship between black and white don't mean that much 'cause it usually ain't on a equal basis. Right now you and Jeremy might get along fine, but in a few years he'll think of himself as a man but you'll probably still be a boy to him. And if he feels that way, he'll turn on you in a minute."

"But Papa, I don't think Jeremy'd be that way."

Papa's eyes narrowed and his resemblance to Uncle Hammer increased. "We Logans don't have much to do with white folks. You know why? 'Cause white folks mean trouble. You see blacks hanging 'round with whites, they're headed for trouble. Maybe one day whites and blacks can be real friends, but right now the country ain't built that way. Now you could be right 'bout Jeremy making a much finer friend than T.J. ever will be. The trouble is, down here in Mississippi, it costs too much to find out. . . . So I think you'd better not try."

Stacey looked full into Papa's face and read his meaning.

On my way to bed, I stopped by the boys' room to retrieve an orange Christopher-

John had swiped from my stocking and spied Stacey fingering the flute. As I stood in the doorway, he lingered over it, then, carefully rewrapping it, placed it in his box of treasured things. I never saw the flute again.

The day after Christmas Papa summoned Stacey, Christopher-John, Little Man, and me into the barn. We had hoped against hope that Mama would not tell him about our trip to the Wallace store or, if she did, that he would forget what he had promised. We should have known better. Mama always told Papa everything, and Papa never forgot anything.

After we had received our punishment, we emerged sore and teary-eyed and watched Papa, Uncle Hammer, and Mr. Morrison climb into the Packard and speed away. Mama said they were going to Vicksburg.

"Why Vicksburg, Mama?" asked Stacey.

"They've got some business to attend to," she said shortly. "Come on now, get busy. We've got chores to do."

In the late afternoon, shortly after the men had returned, Mr. Jamison arrived. He brought with him a fruit cake sent by Mrs. Jamison and a bag of lemon drops for each of the boys and me. Mama allowed us to say our thanks, then sent us outside. We played for a while in the patches of snow that remained, but when that grew tiresome, I popped into the house to see what was happening; Mama ordered me to pop back out again.

"What they doing?" asked Little Man.

"Looking at a whole bunch of papers," I said. "And Uncle Hammer was signing something."

"What kind of papers?" asked Stacey.

I shrugged. "I dunno. But Mr. Jamison was saying something 'bout selling the land."

"Selling the land?" questioned Stacey. "You sure?"

I nodded. "He said: 'Y'all sign them papers and Miz Caroline got no more legal right to this land. Can't sell it, can't sign on it. It'll be in y'all's name and it'll take both of y'all to do anything with it.'"

"Both of who?"

I shrugged again. "Papa and Uncle Hammer, I guess."

After a while it grew chilly and we went inside. Mr. Jamison, sitting next to Big Ma, was putting some papers into his briefcase. "I hope you feel better now that that's done, Miz Caroline," he said, his voice a soft mixture of Southern aristocracy and Northern schooling.

"Hammer and David, they been takin' care of things a long time now," Big Ma said. "Them and Mary works hard to pay the taxes and mortgage on this here place and I been wantin' to make sure while I'm still breathin' that they gets title to this place under the law without no trouble. I ain't wantin' a whole lot of problems after I'm gone 'bout who gots rights to this land." She paused a moment, then added, "That happens sometimes, you know."

Mr. Jamison nodded. He was a long, thin man in his mid-fifties with a perfect lawyer face, so placid that it was difficult to guess what thoughts lay behind it.

The boys and I sat down silently at the study table, and the silence allowed us to stay. I figured that Mr. Jamison would be leaving now. His business was evidently finished and despite the fact that the family thought well of him, he was not considered a friend in the usual sense, and there seemed no reason for him to stay longer.

But now Mr. Jamison put his briefcase back on the floor, indicating that he was not leaving, and looked first at Big Ma and Mama, then across at Papa and Uncle Hammer.

"There's talk that some of the people around here are looking to shop in Vicksburg," he said.

Big Ma looked around at Papa and Uncle Hammer, but neither of them acknowledged her glance; their eyes were pinned on Mr. Jamison.

"There's talk too why folks are looking to shop there." He paused, met Papa's eyes, then Uncle Hammer's, and went on. "As you know, my family has roots in Vicksburg—we've a number of friends there still. I got a call from one of them this morning. Said you were looking to find credit for about thirty families."

Papa and Uncle Hammer neither affirmed nor denied this. "You know as well as I do that credit doesn't come easy these days," continued Mr. Jamison. "You expect to get any, you'll need something to back it."

"I reckon we know that," said Uncle Hammer.

Mr. Jamison glanced at Uncle Hammer and nodded. "I reckoned you did. But as far as I can see, the only thing any of you got to back that credit with is this land . . . and I'd hate to see you put it up."

"Why's that?" asked Uncle Hammer, wary of his interest.

"Because you'd lose it."

The fire popped and the room grew silent. Then Papa said, "What you getting at?"

"I'll back the credit."

Again, silence. Mr. Jamison allowed Papa and Uncle Hammer several moments to search for a motive behind his masklike face. "I'm a Southerner, born and bred, but that doesn't mean I approve of all that goes on here, and there are a lot of other white people who feel the same."

"If you and so many others feel that way," said Uncle Hammer with a wry sneer, "then how come them Wallaces ain't in jail?"

"Hammer—" Big Ma started.

"Because," answered Mr. Jamison candidly, "there aren't enough of those same white people who would admit how they feel, or even if they did, would hang a white man for killing a black one. It's as simple as that."

Uncle Hammer smiled slightly and shook his head, but his eyes showed a grudging respect for Mr. Jamison.

"Backing the loan will be strictly a business matter. In the fall when the crops are in, those people who've bought the goods in Vicksburg will have to pay for them. If they don't, then I'll have to. Of course, as a businessman, I'm hoping that I won't have to put out a penny—my own cash box isn't exactly overflowing—so there'll have to be a credit limit. Still, it would lend me a great deal of satisfaction to know that I was a part of all this." He looked around. "What do you think?"

"You know it ain't hardly likely," Papa said, "that after accounts are figured, there'll be any money to pay any debts at all, except those up at that Wallace store."

Mr. Jamison nodded knowingly. "But the offer still stands."

Papa inhaled deeply. "Well, then, I'd say it's up to those people who'd be buying on your signature. They want to do it, then we got no say in it. We always pay cash."

"You know if you sign that credit," said Uncle Hammer, "you won't be the most popular man down in here. You thought about that?"

"Yes," said Mr. Jamison thoughtfully, "my wife and I discussed it fully. We realize what could happen. . . . But I'm just wondering if you do. Besides the fact that a number of white folks around here resent this land you've got and your independent attitude, there's Harlan Granger. Now I've known Harlan all my life, and he's not going to like this."

I wanted to ask what Mr. Granger had to do with anything, but common sense told me that I would only earn eviction by asking. But then Mr. Jamison went on and explained without any prodding from me.

"Ever since we were boys, Harlan's lived in the past. His grandmother filled him with all kinds of tales about the glory of the South before the war. You know, back then the Grangers had one of the biggest plantations in the state and Spokane County practically belonged to them . . . and they thought it did too. They were consulted about everything concerning this area and they felt it was up to them to see that things worked smoothly, according to the law—a law basically for whites. Well, Harlan feels the same now as his grandmother did back then. He also feels strongly about this land and he resents the fact that you won't sell it back to him. You back the credit with it now and he'll seize this opportunity to take it away from you. You can count on it."

He paused, and when he spoke again his voice had grown so quiet I had to lean forward to hear his next words. "And if you continue to encourage people not to shop at the Wallace store, you could still lose it. Don't forget that Harlan leases that store land to the Wallaces and gets a hefty percentage of its revenue. Before he let the Wallaces set up storekeeping, he was only getting his sharecroppers' money. Now he gets a nice bit of Montier's and Harrison's sharecroppers' money too since both of those plantations are too small to have a store, and he's not hardly going to stand for your interfering with it.

"But even more important than all that, you're pointing a finger right at the Wallaces with this boycott business. You're not only accusing them of murder, which in this case would be only a minor consideration because the man killed was black, but you're saying they should be punished for it. That they should be punished just as if they had killed a white man, and punishment of a white man for a wrong done to a black man would denote equality. Now *that* is what Harlan Granger absolutely will not permit."

Mr. Jamison was silent, waiting; no one else spoke and he went on again.

"What John Henry Berry and his brother were accused of—making advances to a white woman—goes against the grain of Harlan Granger and most other white folks in this community more than anything else, you know that. Harlan may not believe in the methods of the Wallaces, but he'll definitely support them. Believe me on that."

Mr. Jamison picked up his briefcase, ran his fingers through his graying hair, and met Papa's eyes. "The sad thing is, you know in the end you can't beat him or the Wallaces."

Papa looked down at the boys and me awaiting his reply, then nodded slightly, as if he agreed. "Still," he said, "I want these children to know we tried, and what we can't do now, maybe one day they will."

"I do hope that's so, David," murmured Mr. Jamison going to the door. "I truly hope that's so."

In the days that followed Mr. Jamison's visit, Papa, Mama, and Uncle Hammer went to the houses of those families who were considering shopping in Vicksburg. On the fourth day Papa and Uncle Hammer again went to Vicksburg, but this time in the wagon with Mr. Morrison. Their journey took two days and when they returned, the wagon was loaded with store-bought goods.

"What's all that?" I asked Papa as he jumped from the wagon. "That for us?"

"No, Cassie girl. It's things folks ordered from Vicksburg."

I wanted to ask more questions about the trip, but Papa seemed in a hurry to be off again and my questions went unanswered until the following day, when Mr. Granger arrived. Christopher-John and I were drawing water from the well when the silver Packard glided to a smooth stop in the drive and Mr. Granger stepped out. He stared sour-faced at Uncle Hammer's Packard in the barn, then opened the gate to the front yard and stepped briskly across the lawn to the house.

Hastily Christopher-John and I tugged on the well rope, pulled up the water tube, and poured the water into the bucket. Each of us gripping a side of the heavy bucket, we hurried to the back porch where we deposited it, then tiptoed silently through the empty kitchen to the door leading to Mama and Papa's room. Little Man and Stacey, just leaving the room under Mama's orders, allowed the door to remain slightly cracked, and all four of us huddled against it stepladder fashion.

"You sure giving folks something to talk 'bout with that car of yours, Hammer," Mr. Granger said in his folksy dialect as he sat down with a grunt across from Papa. In spite of his college education he always spoke this way. "What they got you doing up North? Bootlegging whiskey?" He laughed dryly, indicating that the question was to be taken lightly, but his eyes tight on Uncle Hammer showed that he intended to have an answer.

Uncle Hammer, leaning against the fireplace mantel, did not laugh. "Don't need to bootleg," he said sullenly. "Up there I got me a man's job and they pay me a man's wages for it."

Mr. Granger studied Uncle Hammer. Uncle Hammer wore, as he had every day since he had arrived, sharply creased pants, a vest over a snow-white shirt, and shoes that shone like midnight. "You right citified, ain't you? Course you always did think you was too good to work in the fields like other folks."

"Naw, that ain't it," said Uncle Hammer. "I just ain't never figured fifty cents a day was worth a child's time, let alone a man's wages." Uncle Hammer said nothing else; he didn't need to. Everyone knew that fifty cents was the top price paid to any day laborer, man, woman, or child, hired to work in the Granger fields.

Mr. Granger ran his tongue around his teeth, making his lips protrude in odd half circles, then he turned from Uncle Hammer to Papa. "Some folks tell me y'all running a regular traveling store up here. Hear tell a fellow can get just 'bout anything he wants from up at Tate's in Vicksburg if he just lets y'all know."

Papa met Mr. Granger's eyes, but did not speak.

Mr. Granger shook his head. "Seems to me you folks are just stirring up something. Y'all got roots in this community. Even got yourselves that loan Paul Edward made from the First National Bank up in Strawberry for that eastern two hundred acres. Course now with times like they are, that mortgage could come due anytime . . . and if it comes due and y'all ain't got the money to pay it, y'all could lose this place."

"Ain't gonna lose it," said Uncle Hammer flatly.

Mr. Granger glanced up at Uncle Hammer, then back to Papa. He took a cigar from his pocket, then a knife to cut off the tip. After he had thrown the tip into the fire, he settled back in his chair and lit the cigar while Papa, Mama, Uncle Hammer, and Big Ma waited for him to get on. Then he said: "This is a fine community. Got fine folks in it—both white and colored. Whatever's bothering you people, y'all just tell me. We'll get it straightened out without all this big to-do."

Uncle Hammer laughed outright. Mr. Granger looked up sharply, but Uncle Hammer eyed him insolently, a smile still on his lips. Mr. Granger, watching him, cautioned sternly, "I don't like trouble here. This is a quiet and peaceful place. . . . I aim to see it stays that way." Turning back to Papa, he continued. "Whatever problems we have, we can work them out. I ain't gonna hide that I think y'all making a big mistake, both for the community and for yourselves going all the way down to Vicksburg to do your shopping. That don't seem very neighborly—"

"Neither does burning," said Uncle Hammer.

Mr. Granger puffed deeply on his cigar and did not look at Uncle Hammer. When he spoke again it was to Big Ma. His voice was harsh, but he made no comment on what Uncle Hammer had said. "I don't think your Paul Edward would've condoned something like this and risked losing this place. How come you let your boys go do it?"

Big Ma smoothed the lap of her dress with her hands. "They grown and it's they land. I got no more say in it."

Mr. Granger's eyes showed no surprise, but he pursed his lips again and ran his tongue around his teeth. "The price of cotton's mighty low, y'all know that," he said finally. "Could be that I'll have to charge my people more of their crops next summer just to make ends meet. . . . I'd hate to do it, 'cause if I did my people wouldn't hardly have enough to buy winter stores, let alone be able to pay their debts . . ."

There was a tense, waiting silence before his glance slid to Papa again.

"Mr. Joe Higgins up at First National told me that he couldn't hardly honor a loan to folks who go around stirring up a lot of bad feelings in the community—"

"And especially stirring the colored folks out of their place," interjected Uncle Hammer calmly.

Mr. Granger paled, but did not turn to Uncle Hammer. "Money's too scarce," he continued as if he had not heard, "and folks like that are a poor risk. You ready to lose your land, David, because of this thing?"

Papa was lighting his pipe. He did not look up until the flame had caught in the tobacco and held there. Then he turned to Mr. Granger. "Two hundred acres of this place been Logan land for almost fifty years now, the other two hundred for fifteen. We've been through bad times and good times but we ain't never lost none of it. Ain't gonna start now."

Mr. Granger said quietly, "It was Granger land before it was Logan."

"Slave land," said Papa.

Mr. Granger nodded. "Wouldn't have lost this section if it hadn't been stolen by your Yankee carpetbaggers after the war. But y'all keep on playing Santa Claus and I'm gonna get it back—real easy. I want you to know that I plan to do whatever I need to, to keep peace down in here."

Papa took the pipe from his mouth and stared into the fire. When he faced Mr. Granger again his voice was very quiet, very distinct, very sure. "You being white, you can just 'bout plan on anything you want. But I tell you this one thing: You plan on getting this land, you're planning on the wrong thing."

Mama's hand crossed almost unseen to Papa's arm.

Mr. Granger looked up slyly. "There's lots of ways of stopping you, David."

Papa impaled Mr. Granger with an icy stare. "Then you'd better make them good," he said.

Mr. Granger stood to go, a smile creeping smugly over his lips as if he knew a secret but refused to tell. He glanced at Uncle Hammer, then turned and left, leaving the silence behind him.

8

"Uh . . . Miz Lillian Jean, wouldja wait up a minute, please?"

"Cassie, you cracked?" cried Stacey. "Cassie, where you . . . get back here! Cassie!"

Stacey's words faded into the gray stillness of the January morning as I turned deaf ears to him and hurried after Lillian Jean. "Thanks for waiting up," I said when I caught up with her.

She stared down at me irritably. "What you want?"

"Well," I said, walking beside her, "I been thinking 'bout what happened in Strawberry back last month."

"Yeah?" commented Lillian Jean suspiciously.

"Well, to tell you the truth, I was real upset for a while there. But my papa told me it don't do no good sitting around being mad. Then I seen how things was. I mean I should've seen it all along. After all, I'm who I am and you're who you are."

Lillian Jean looked at me with astonishment that I could see the matter so clearly. "Well, I'm glad you finally learned the way of things."

"Oh, I did," I piped readily. "The way I see it—here, let me take them books for you, Miz Lillian Jean—the way I see it, we all gotta do what we gotta do. And that's what I'm gonna do from now on. Just what I gotta."

"Good for you, Cassie," replied Lillian Jean enthusiastically. "God'll bless you for it."

"You think so?"

"Why, of course!" she exclaimed. "God wants all his children to do what's right."

"I'm glad you think so . . . Miz Lillian Jean."

When we reached the crossroads, I waved good-bye to Lillian Jean and waited for the others. Before they reached me, Little Man exclaimed, "Owwww, I'm gonna tell Mama! Carrying that ole dumb Lillian Jean's books!"

"Cassie, whatja do that for?" questioned Christopher-John, his round face pained.

"Ah, shoot," laughed T.J. "Ole Cassie jus' learned she better do what's good for her if she don't want no more of Mr. Simms's back hand."

I clinched my fists behind me, and narrowed my eyes in the Logan gaze, but managed to hold my tongue.

Stacey stared at me strangely, then turned and said, "We'd better get on to school."

As I followed, Jeremy touched my arm timidly. "C-Cassie, you didn't have to do that. That—that ole Lillian Jean, she ain't worth it."

I stared at Jeremy, trying to understand him. But he shied away from me and ran down the road after his sister.

"Mama gonna whip you good, too," said prideful Little Man, still fuming as we approached the school. " 'Cause I'm gonna sure tell it."

"Naw you ain't," said Stacey. There was a shocked silence as all heads turned to him. "This here thing's between Cassie and Lillian Jean and ain't nobody telling nobody nothin' 'bout this." He stared directly at T.J., caught his eye, and repeated, "Nobody."

"Ah, man!" cried T.J. "It ain't none of my business." Then, after a moment's silence, he added, "I got too many worries of my own to worry 'bout Cassie Uncle Tomming[6] Lillian Jean."

My temper almost flew out of my mouth, but I pressed my lips tightly together, forcing it to stay inside.

6. Being overeager to win the approval of whites. Uncle Tom was a saintly and obedient black slave in Harriet Beecher Stowe's novel *Uncle Tom's Cabin* (1852).

"Them final examinations comin' up in two weeks, man, and ain't no way I can afford to fail them things again," T.J. continued.

"Then you won't," said Stacey.

"Shoot, that's what I thought last year. But your mama makes up the hardest examinations she know how." He paused, sighed, and ventured, "Bet though if you kind asked her 'bout what kind of questions—"

"T.J., don't you come talking to me 'bout no more cheating!" cried Stacey angrily. "After all that trouble I got in the last time 'count of you. You got questions, you ask Mama yourself, but you say one more word to me 'bout them tests, I'm gonna—"

"All right, all right." T.J. smiled in feigned apology. "It's just that I'm gonna have to figure out somethin'."

"I got a solution," I said, unable to resist just one bit of friendly advice.

"What's that?"

"Try studying."

After Uncle Hammer left on New Year's Day, Papa and I had gone into the forest, down the cow path, and to the misty hollow where the trees lay fallen. For a while we stood looking again at the destruction, then, sitting on one of our fallen friends, we talked in quiet, respectful tones, observing the soft mourning of the forest.

When I had explained the whole Strawberry business to Papa, he said slowly, "You know the Bible says you're s'pose to forgive these things."

"Yessir," I agreed, waiting.

"S'pose to turn the other cheek."

"Yessir."

Papa rubbed his moustache and looked up at the trees standing like sentinels on the edge of the hollow, listening. But the way I see it, the Bible didn't mean for you to be no fool. Now one day, maybe I can forgive John Andersen for what he done to these trees, but I ain't gonna forget it. I figure forgiving is not letting something nag at you—rotting you out. Now if I hadn't done what I done, then I couldn't've forgiven myself, and that's the truth of it."[7]

I nodded gravely and he looked down at me. "You're a lot like me, Cassie girl, but you got yourself a bad temper like your Uncle Hammer. That temper can get you in trouble."

"Yessir."

"Now this thing between you and Lillian Jean, most folks would think you should go around doing what she tell you . . . and maybe you should—"

"Papa!"

"Cassie, there'll be a whole lot of things you ain't gonna wanna do but you'll have to do in this life just so you can survive. Now I don't like the idea of what Charlie Simms did to you no more than your Uncle Hammer, but I had to weigh the hurt of what happened to you to what could've happened if I went after him. If I'd've gone after Charlie Simms and given him a good thrashing like I felt like doing, the hurt to all of us would've been a whole lot more than the hurt you received, so I let it be. I don't like letting it be, but I can live with that decision.

7. In *The Song of the Trees*, Mr. Andersen, an unscrupulous white man, takes advantage of David Logan's absence and the Logan family's financial need and coerces Big Ma into selling some of their valuable timber. When the children learn that Andersen is planning to cut down all of the trees, Stacey is sent to fetch his father. David Logan forces a showdown with Andersen by wiring the forest with dynamite and threatening to blow it and everyone in it up if Andersen does not stop cutting the trees. Andersen backs down and some of the trees are salvaged, though many are felled.

"But there are other things, Cassie, that if I'd let be, they'd eat away at me and destroy me in the end. And it's the same with you, baby. There are things you can't back down on, things you gotta take a stand on. But it's up to you to decide what them things are. You have to demand respect in this world, ain't nobody just gonna hand it to you. How you carry yourself, what you stand for—that's how you gain respect. But, little one, ain't nobody's respect worth more than your own. You understand that?"

"Yessir."

"Now, there ain't no sense in going around being mad. You clear your head so you can think sensibly. Then I want you to think real hard on whether or not Lillian Jean's worth taking a stand about, but keep in mind that Lillian Jean probably won't be the last white person to treat you this way." He turned toward me so that he looked me full in the face, and the seriousness of his eyes startled me. He held my chin up with the wide flat of his hard hand. "This here's an important decision, Cassie, very important—I want you to understand that—but I think you can handle it. Now, you listen to me, and you listen good. This thing, if you make the wrong decision and Charlie Simms gets involved, then I get involved and there'll be trouble."

"B-big trouble?" I whispered. "Like the trees?"

"Don't know," said Papa. "But it could be bad."

I pondered his words, then I promised, "Mr. Simms ain't never gonna hear 'bout it, Papa."

Papa studied me. "I'll count on that, Cassie girl. I'll count real hard on that."

For the month of January I was Lillian Jean's slave and she thoroughly enjoyed it. She even took to waiting for me in the morning with Jeremy so that I could carry her books. When friends of hers walked with us, she bragged about her little colored friend and almost hugged herself with pleasure when I called her "Miz" Lillian Jean. When we were alone, she confided her secrets to me: the boy she had passionately loved for the past year and the things she had done to attract his attention (with no success, I might add); the secrets of the girls she couldn't stand as well as those she could; and even a tidbit or two about her elder brothers' romantic adventures. All I had to do to prime the gossip pump was smile nicely and whisper a "Miz Lillian Jean" every now and then. I *almost* hated to see the source dry up.

At the end of examination day, I shot out of Miss Crocker's class and hurried into the yard. I was eager to get to the crossroads to meet Lillian Jean; I had promised myself to first take care of the examinations and then . . .

"Little Man! Claude! Christopher-John! Come on, y'all!" I cried. "There's Stacey!" The four of us dashed across the yard trailing Stacey and T.J. to the road. When we caught up with them, it was obvious that the jovial mask T.J. always wore had been stripped away.

"She did it on purpose!" T.J. accused, a nasty scowl twisting his face.

"Man, you was cheating!" Stacey pointed out. "What you 'spect for her to do?"

"She could've give me a break. Warn't nothin' but a couple bits of ole paper. Didn't need 'em nohow."

"Well, whatja have them for?"

"Ah, man, leave me be! All y'all Logans think y'all so doggone much with y'all's new coats and books and shiny new Packards!" He swirled around, glaring down at Christopher-John, Little Man, and me. "I'm sick of all y'all. Your mama and your papa, too!" Then he turned and fled angrily up the road.

"T.J.! Hey, man, where you going?" Stacey yelled after him. T.J. did not answer.

The road swelled into a small hill and he disappeared on the other side of it. When we reached the crossroads and saw no sign of him on the southern road leading home, Stacey asked Claude, "Where he go?"

Claude looked shame-faced and rubbed one badly worn shoe against the other. "Down to that ole store, I reckon."

Stacey sighed. "Come on then, we'd better get on home. He'll be all right by tomorrow."

"Y'all go on," I said. "I gotta wait for Lillian Jean."

"Cassie—"

"I'll catch up with ya," I said before Stacey could lecture me. "Here, take my books, will ya?" He looked at me as if he should say something else, but deciding not to, he pushed the younger boys on and followed them.

When Lillian Jean appeared, I sighed thankfully that only Jeremy was with her; it could be today for sure. Jeremy, who seemed to be as disappointed in me as Little Man, hurried on to catch Stacey. That was fine, too; I knew he would. I took Lillian Jean's books, and as we sauntered down the road, I only half listened to her; I was sweeping the road, looking for the deep wooded trail I had selected earlier in the week. When I saw it, I interrupted Lillian Jean apologetically. " 'Scuse me, Miz Lillian Jean, but I got a real nice surprise for you . . . found it just the other day down in the woods."

"For me?" questioned Lillian Jean. "Ah, you is a sweet thing, Cassie. Where you say it is?"

"Come on. I'll show you."

I stepped into the dry gully and scrambled onto the bank. Lillian Jean hung back. "It's all right," I assured her. "It ain't far. You just gotta see it, Miz Lillian Jean."

That did it. Grinning like a Cheshire cat,[8] she crossed the gully and hopped onto the bank. Following me up the overgrown trail into the deep forest, she asked, "You sure this is the way, little Cassie?"

"Just a bit further . . . up ahead there. Ah, here it is."

We entered a small dark clearing with hanging forest vines, totally hidden from the road.

"Well? Where's the surprise?"

"Right here," I said, smashing Lillian Jean's books on the ground.

"Why, what you do that for?" Lillian Jean asked, more startled than angry.

"I got tired of carrying 'em," I said.

"This what you brought me all the way down here for! Well, you just best get untired and pick 'em up again." Then, expecting that her will would be done with no more than that from her, she turned to leave the glade.

"Make me," I said quietly.

"What?" The shock on her face was almost comical.

"Said make me."

Her face paled. Then, red with anger, she stepped daintily across the clearing and struck me hard across the face. For the record, she had hit me first; I didn't plan on her hitting me again.

I flailed into her, tackling her with such force that we both fell. After the first shock of my actually laying hands on her, she fought as best she could, but she was no match for me. I was calm and knew just where to strike. I punched her in the stomach

---

8. The disappearing cat in Lewis Carroll's *Alice's Adventures in Wonderland* (1865); the last bit of him to vanish was his broad grin.

and buttocks, and twisted her hair, but not once did I touch her face; she, expending her energy in angry, nasty name-calling, clawed at mine, managing to scratch twice. She tried to pull my hair but couldn't, for I had purposely asked Big Ma to braid it into flat braids against my head.

When I had pinned Lillian Jean securely beneath me, I yanked unmercifully on her long, loose hair and demanded an apology for all the names she had called me, and for the incident in Strawberry. At first she tried to be cute—"Ain't gonna 'pologize to no nigger!" she sassed.

"You wanna be bald, girl?"

And she apologized. For herself and for her father. For her brothers and her mother. For Strawberry and Mississippi, and by the time I finished jerking at her head, I think she would have apologized for the world being round had I demanded it. But when I let her go and she had sped safely to the other side of the clearing with the trail in front of her, she threatened to tell her father.

"You do that, Lillian Jean. You just do that and I'm gonna make sure all your fancy friends know how you keeps a secret. Bet you won't be learning no more secrets after that."

"Cassie! You wouldn't do that. Not after I trusted you—"

"You mutter one word of this to anybody, Lillian Jean," I said, attempting to narrow my eyes like Papa's, "just one person and everybody at Jefferson Davis is gonna know who you crazy 'bout and all your other business . . . and you know I know. Besides, if anybody ever did find out 'bout this fight, you'd be laughed clear up to Jackson. You here going on thirteen, getting beat up by a nine-year-old."

I was starting up the trail, feeling good about myself, when Lillian Jean asked, bewildered, "But, Cassie, why? You was such a nice little girl. . . ."

I stared at her astonished. Then I turned and left the forest, not wanting to believe that Lillian Jean didn't even realize it had all been just a game.

"Cassie Logan!"

"Yes'm, Miz Crocker?"

"That's the third time I've caught you daydreaming this morning. Just because you managed to come in first on the examinations last week doesn't mean a thing this week. We're in a new quarter and everyone's slate is clean. You make no A's by daydreaming. You understand that?"

"Yes'm," I said, not bothering to add that she repeated herself so much that all a body had to do was listen to the first few minutes of her lesson to be free to daydream to her heart's content.

"I think you'd just better sit in the back where you're not so comfortable," she said. "Then maybe you'll pay more attention."

"But—"

Miss Crocker raised her hand, indicating that she did not want to hear another word, and banished me to the very last row in front of the window. I slid onto the cold seat after former occupant had eagerly left it for my warm quarters by the stove. As soon as Miss Crocker turned away, I mumbled a few indignant phrases, then hugged my Christmas sweater to me. I tried to pay attention to Miss Crocker but the cold creeping under the windowsill made it impossible. Unable to bear the draft, I decided to line the sill with paper from my notebook. I ripped out the paper, then turned the window. As I did, a man passed under it and disappeared.

The man was Kaleb Wallace.

I raised my hand. "Uh, Miz Crocker, may I be excused please, ma'am? I gotta . . . well, you know . . ."

As soon as I had escaped Miss Crocker, I dashed to the front of the building. Kaleb Wallace was standing in front of the seventh-grade-class building talking to Mr. Wellever and two white men whom I couldn't make out from where I stood. When the men entered the building, I turned and sped to the rear and carefully climbed onto the woodpile stacked behind it. I peeked cautiously through a broken window into Mama's classroom. The men were just entering, Kaleb Wallace first, followed by a man I didn't know and Mr. Harlan Granger.

Mama seemed startled to see the men, but when Mr. Granger said, "Been hearing 'bout your teaching, Mary, so as members of the school board we thought we'd come by and learn something," she merely nodded and went on with her lesson. Mr. Wellever left the room, returning shortly with three folding chairs for the visitors; he himself remained standing.

Mama was in the middle of history and I knew that was bad. I could tell Stacey knew it too; he sat tense near the back of the room, his lips very tight, his eyes on the men. But Mama did not flinch; she always started her history class the first thing in the morning when the students were most alert; and I knew that the hour was not yet up. To make matters worse, her lesson for the day was slavery. She spoke on the cruelty of it; of the rich economic cycle it generated as slaves produced the raw products for the factories of the North and Europe; how the country profited and grew from the free labor of a people still not free.

Before she had finished, Mr. Granger picked up a student's book, flipped it open to the pasted-over front cover, and pursed his lips. "Thought these books belonged to the county," he said, interrupting her. Mama glanced over at him, but did not reply. Mr. Granger turned the pages, stopped, and read something. "I don't see all them things you're teaching in here."

"That's because they're not in there," Mama said.

"Well, if it ain't in here, then you got no right teaching it. This book's approved by the Board of Education and you're expected to teach what's in it."

"I can't do that."

"And why not?"

Mama, her back straight and her eyes fixed on the men, answered, "Because all that's in that book isn't true."

Mr. Granger stood. He laid the book back on the student's desk and headed for the door. The other board member and Kaleb Wallace followed. At the door Mr. Granger stopped and pointed at Mama. "You must be some kind of smart, Mary, to know more than the fellow who wrote that book. Smarter than the school board, too, I reckon."

Mama remained silent, and Mr. Wellever gave her no support.

"In fact," Mr. Granger continued, putting on his hat, "you so smart I expect you'd best just forget about teaching altogether . . . then thataway you'll have plenty of time to write your own book." With that he turned his back on her, glanced at Mr. Wellever to make sure his meaning was clear, and left with the others behind him.

We waited for Mama after school was out. Stacey had sent T.J. and Claude on, and the four of us, silent and patient, were sitting on the steps when Mama emerged. She smiled down at us, seemingly not surprised that we were there.

I looked up at her, but I couldn't speak. I had never really thought much about Mama's teaching before; that was just a part of her being Mama. But now that she could not teach, I felt resentful and angry, and I hated Mr. Granger.

"You all know?" she asked. We nodded as she slowly descended the stairs. Stacey took one handle of her heavy black satchel and I took the other. Christopher-John and Little Man each took one of her hands, and we started across the lawn.

"M-Mama," said Christopher-John when we reached the road, "can't you ever teach no more?"

Mama did not answer immediately. When she did, her voice was muffled. "Somewhere else maybe, but not here—at least not for a while."

"But how's come, Mama?" demanded Little Man. "How's come?"

Mama bit into her lower lip and gazed at the road. "Because, baby," she said finally, "I taught things some folks just didn't want to hear."

When we reached home, Papa and Mr. Morrison were both in the kitchen with Big Ma drinking coffee. As we entered, Papa searched our faces. His eyes settled on Mama; the pain was in her face. "What's wrong?" he asked.

Mama sat down beside him. She pushed back a strand of hair that had worked its way free of the chignon, but it fell back into her face again and she left it there. "I got fired."

Big Ma put down her cup weakly without a word.

Papa reached out and touched Mama. She said, "Harlan Granger came to the school with Kaleb Wallace and one of the school-board members. Somebody had told them about those books I'd pasted over . . . but that was only an excuse. They're just getting at us any way they can because of shopping in Vicksburg." Her voice cracked. "What'll we do, David? We needed that job."

Papa gently pushed the stray hair back over her ear. "We'll get by. . . . Plant more cotton maybe. But we'll get by." There was quiet reassurance in his voice.

Mama nodded and stood.

"Where you goin', child?" Big Ma asked.

"Outside. I want to walk for a bit."

Christopher-John, Little Man, and I turned to follow her, but Papa called us back. "Leave your mama be," he said.

As we watched her slowly cross the backyard to the barren garden and head toward the south pasture, Mr. Morrison said, "You know with you here, Mr. Logan, you got no need of me. Maybe there's work to be had around here. . . . Maybe I could get something . . . help you out."

Papa stared across at Mr. Morrison. "There's no call for you to do that," he said. "I'm not paying you anything as it is."

Mr. Morrison said softly, "I got me a nice house to live in, the best cooking a man could want, and for the first time in a long time I got me a family. That's right good pay, I'd say."

Papa nodded. "You're a good man, Mr. Morrison, and I thank you for the offer, but I'll be leaving in a few weeks and I'd rather you was here." His eyes focused on Mama again, a tiny figure in the distance now.

"Papa," rasped Christopher-John, moving close to him, "M-Mama gonna be all right?"

Papa turned and, putting his arms around Christopher-John, drew him even nearer. "Son, your mama . . . she's born to teaching like the sun is born to shine. And it's gonna be hard on her not teaching anymore. It's gonna be real hard 'cause ever since she was a wee bitty girl down in the Delta she wanted to be a teacher."

"And Grandpa wanted her to be one, too, didn't he, Papa?" said Christopher-John.

Papa nodded. "Your mama was his baby child and every penny he'd get his hands on he'd put it aside for her schooling . . . and that wasn't easy for him either cause he was a tenant farmer and he didn't see much cash money. But he'd promised your grandmama 'fore she died to see that your mama got an education, and when your mama 'come high-school age, he sent her up to Jackson to school, then on to teacher training school. It was just 'cause he died her last year of schooling that she come on up here to teach 'stead of going back to the Delta."

"And y'all got married and she ain't gone back down there no more," interjected Little Man.

Papa smiled faintly at Little Man and stood up. "That's right, son. She was too smart and pretty to let get away." He stooped and looked out the window again, then back at us. "She's a strong, fine woman, your mama, and this thing won't keep her down . . . but it's hurt her bad. So I want y'all to be extra thoughtful for the next few days—and remember what I told you, you hear?"

"Yessir, Papa," we answered.

Papa left us then and went onto the back porch. There he leaned against the porch pillar for several minutes staring out toward the pasture; but after a while he stepped into the yard and crossed the garden to join Mama.

"T.J.? You sure?" Stacey asked Little Willie Wiggins at recess the next day. Little Willie nodded morosely and answered, "Heard it myself. Clarence, too. Was standin' right up 'side him at the store when he told Mr. Kaleb. Come talkin' 'bout how Miz Logan failed him on purpose and then said she wasn't a good teacher and that she the one stopped everybody from comin' up to they store. Said she even was destroyin' school property—talkin' 'bout them books, you know."

"Who's gonna take him?" I cried.

"Hush, Cassie," said Stacey. "How come you just telling this now, Little Willie?"

Little Willie shrugged. "Guess I got fooled by ole T.J. Clarence and me, we told him we was gonna tell it soon as we left the store, but T.J. asked us not to do it. Said he was goin' right back and tell them it wasn't nothin' but a joke, what he said. And he went back too, and I thought nothin' was gonna come of it." He hesitated, then confessed, "Didn't say nothin' 'bout it before 'cause me and Clarence wasn't s'pose to be up there ourselves . . . but then here come Mr. Granger yesterday and fires Miz Logan. I figure that's T.J.'s doin'."

"He probably figured it too," I said. "That's why he ain't in school today."

"Talking 'bout he sick," said Christopher-John.

"If he ain't now, he gonna be," prophesied Little Man, his tiny fists balled for action. " 'Round here telling on Mama."

After school when Claude turned up the forest trail leading to the Avery house, we went with him. As we emerged from the forest into the Avery yard, the house appeared deserted, but then we spied T.J., lazily swinging straddle-legged atop an inner tube hanging from an old oak in the front yard. Stacey immediately charged toward him, and when T.J. saw him coming he tried to swing his long right leg over the tube to escape. He didn't make it. Stacey jumped up on the inner tube, giving them both a jerky ride before they landed hard on Mrs. Avery's azalea bush.

"Man, what's the matter with you?" T.J. cried as he rolled from under Stacey to glance back at the flattened bush. "My mama gonna kill me when she see that bush."

Stacey jumped up and jerked at T.J.'s collar. "Was you the one? Did you do it?"

T.J. looked completely bewildered. "Do what? What you talkin' 'bout?"

"Didja tell it? You tell them Wallaces 'bout Mama?"

"Me?" asked T.J. "Me? Why, man, you oughta know me better'n that."

"He do know you," I said. "How come you think we up here?"

"Hey, now, wait a minute," objected T.J. "I don't know what somebody been tellin' y'all, but I ain't told them Wallaces nothin'."

"You was down there," Stacey accused. "The day Mama caught you cheating, you went down to them Wallaces."

"Well, that don't mean nothin'," said T.J., jerking away from Stacey's grip and hopping to his feet. "My daddy says I can go down there if I wanna. Don't mean I told them ole folks nothin' though."

"Heard you told them all sorts of things . . . like Mama didn't know nothin' and she wasn't even teaching what she s'pose to—"

"Didn't neither!" denied T.J. "Ain't never said that! All I said was that it was her that . . ." His voice trailed off as he realized he had said too much, and he began to laugh uneasily. "Hey, look, y'all, I don't know how come Miz Logan got fired, but I ain't said nothin' to make nobody fire her. All I said was that she failed me again. A fellow got a right to be mad 'bout somethin' like that, ain't he?"

Stacey's eyes narrowed upon T.J. "Maybe," he said. "But he ain't got no right to go running his mouth off 'bout things that ain't s'pose to be told."

T.J. stepped backward and looked nervously over his shoulder to the south, where the fields lay fallow. The rutted wagon trail which cut through the fields leading from the distant Granger mansion revealed a thin woman stepping briskly toward us. T.J. seemed to take heart from the figure and grew cocky again. "Don't know who's been tellin', but it ain't been me."

A moment's silence passed, and then Stacey, his eyes cold and condemning, said quietly, "It was you all right, T.J. It was you." Then, turning, he motioned us back toward the forest.

"Ain't you gonna beat him up?" cried a disappointed Little Man.

"What he got coming to him is worse than a beating," replied Stacey.

"What could be worse than that?" asked Christopher-John.

"You'll see," said Stacey. "And so will T.J."

T.J.'s first day back at school after almost a week's absence was less than successful. Avoiding us in the morning, he arrived late, only to be shunned by the other students. At first he pretended that the students' attitude didn't matter, but by the afternoon when school was out, he hurried after us, attempting to convince us that he was merely a victim of circumstances.

"Hey, y'all ain't gonna hold what Little Willie said against me, are you?" he asked.

"You still saying what Little Willie said ain't true?" questioned Stacey.

"Why, shoot, yeah!" he exclaimed. "When I catch up with that little rascal, I'm gonna beat him to a pulp, 'round here tellin' everybody I got Miz Logan fired. Ain't nobody even speakin' to me no more. Little Willie probably told them Wallaces that hisself, so he figures to get out of it by tellin' everybody it was—"

"Ah, stop lying, T.J.," I said testily. "Don't nobody believe you."

"Well, I should've known you wouldn't, Cassie. You never liked me noway."

"Well, anyway, that's the truth," I agreed.

"But," said T.J., grinning again and turning toward Little Man and Christopher-John, "my little buddy Christopher-John believes me, don't you, fellow? And you still my pal, ain't you, Little Man?"

An indignant Little Man looked up at T.J., but before he could speak, easygoing Christopher-John said, "You told on Mama, T.J. Now she all unhappy 'cause she can't teach school no more and it's all your fault, and we don't like you no more!"

"Yeah!" added Little Man in agreement.

T.J. stared down at Christopher-John, not believing that he had said that. Then he laughed uneasily. "I don't know what's got into folks. Everybody's gone crazy—"

"Look," Stacey said, stopping, "first you run off with the mouth to them Wallaces and now you blaming Little Willie for what you done. Why don't you just admit it was you?"

"Hey, man!" T.J. exclaimed, grinning his easy grin. But then, finding that the grin and the smooth words no longer worked, his face dropped. "Oh, all right. All right. So maybe what if I did say somethin' 'bout Miz Logan? I can't even remember saying nothin' 'bout it, but if both Little Willie and Clarence said I did then maybe I did. Anyways, I'm real sorry 'bout your mama losin' her job and—"

All of us, including Claude, stared distastefully at T.J. and walked away from him.

"Hey, wait. . . . I said I was sorry, didn't I?" he asked, following us. "Look, what's a fellow got to do anyway? Hey, y'all, look, this here is still ole T.J.! I ain't changed. Y'all can't turn on me just 'cause—"

"You the one turned, T.J.," Stacey called over his shoulder. "Now leave us alone. We don't want no more to do with you."

T.J., for the first time comprehending that we were no longer his friends, stopped. Then, standing alone in the middle of the road, he screamed after us, "Who needs y'all anyway? I been tired of y'all always hangin' 'round for a long while now, but I been too nice to tell ya . . . I should've known better. What I look like, havin' a bunch of little kids 'round all the time and me here fourteen, near grown . . ."

We walked on, not stopping.

"Got me better friends than y'all! They give me things and treat me like I'm a man and . . . and they white too. . . ."

His voice faded into the wind as we left him and we heard no more.

9

Spring. It seeped unseen into the waiting red earth in early March, softening the hard ground for the coming plow and awakening life that had lain gently sleeping through the cold winter. But by the end of March it was evident everywhere: in the barn where three new calves bellowed and chicks the color of soft pale sunlight chirped; in the yard where the wisteria and English dogwood bushes readied themselves for their annual Easter bloom, and the fig tree budded producing the forerunners of juicy, brown fruit for which the boys and I would have to do battle with fig-loving Jack; and in the smell of the earth itself. Rain-drenched, fresh, vital, full of life, spring enveloped all of us.

I was eager to be in the fields again, to feel the furrowed rows of damp, soft earth beneath my feet; eager to walk barefooted through the cool forest, hug the trees, and sit under their protective shadow. But although every living thing knew it was spring, Miss Crocker and the other teachers evidently did not, for school lingered on indefinitely. In the last week of March when Papa and Mr. Morrison began to plow the east field, I volunteered to sacrifice school and help them. My offer was refused and I trudged wearily to school for another week.

"I guess I won't be seein' much of y'all after next Friday," said Jeremy one evening as we neared his forest trail.

"Guess not," said Stacey.

"Be nice if our schools ended at the same time."

"You crazy!" I cried, remembering that Jefferson Davis didn't dismiss until mid-May.

Jeremy stammered an apology. "I—I just meant we could still see each other." He was silent a moment, then brightened. "Maybe I can come over to see y'all sometime."

Stacey shook his head. "Don't think Papa would like that."

"Well . . . I just thought . . ." He shrugged. "It'll sure be lonely without y'all."

"Lonely?" I asked. "With all them brothers and sisters you got?"

Jeremy frowned. "The little ones, they too young to play with, and the older ones . . . Lillian Jean and R.W. and Melvin, I guess I don't like them very much."

"What you saying?" asked Stacey. "You can't not like your own sister and brothers."

"Well, I can understand that," I said soberly. "I sure don't like them."

"But they're his kin. A fellow's gotta like his own kin."

Jeremy thought about that. "Well, Lillian Jean's all right, I guess. She ain't so persnickety since Cassie stopped bein' her friend." He smiled a secret smile to himself. "But that R.W. and Melvin, they ain't very nice. You oughta see how they treat T.J. . . ." He halted, looked up embarrassed, and was quiet.

Stacey stopped. "How they treat him?"

Jeremy stopped too. "I don't know," he said as if he was sorry he had mentioned it. "They just don't do him right."

"How?" asked Stacey.

"Thought you didn't like him no more."

"Well . . . I don't," replied Stacey defensively. "But I heard he was running 'round with R.W. and Melvin. I wondered why. Them brothers of yours must be eighteen or nineteen."

Jeremy looked up at the sun, squinted, then glanced up his forest trail a few feet ahead. "They brung T.J. by the house a couple of times when Pa wasn't home. They treated him almost friendly like, but when he left they laughed and talked 'bout him—called him names." He squinted again at the trail and said hurriedly, "I better go. . . . See y'all tomorrow."

"Mama, how come you suppose R.W. and Melvin putting in time with T.J.?" I asked as I measured out two heaping tablespoons of flour for the cornbread.

Mama frowned down into the flour barrel. "Only one tablespoon, Cassie, and not so heaping."

"But, Mama, we always use two."

"That barrel will have to last us until Papa goes back to the railroad. Now put it back."

As I returned one tablespoon of flour to the barrel, I again asked, "What you think, Mama? How come them Simmses running 'round with T.J.?"

Mama measured out the baking powder and gave it to me. It was a teaspoon less than we had been using, but I didn't ask her about it. It was running low too.

"I don't really know, Cassie," she said, turning to the stove to stir milk into the butter beans. "They may just want him around because it makes them feel good."

"When T.J.'s around me, he don't make me feel good."

"Well, you told me Jeremy said they were laughing at T.J. behind his back. Some folks just like to keep other folks around to laugh at them . . . use them."

"I wonder how come T.J. don't know they laughing at him? You s'pose he's that dumb?"

"T.J.'s not 'dumb,' Cassie. He just wants attention, but he's going after it the wrong way."

I was going to ask what use T.J. could possibly be to anyone, but I was interrupted by Little Man running into the kitchen. "Mama!" he cried. "Mr. Jamison just drove up!" He had been in the barn cleaning the chicken coop with Christopher-John and stubby particles of straw still clung to his head. I grinned at his mussed appearance but didn't have time to tease him before he was gone again.

Mama looked at Big Ma, a question in her eyes, then followed Little Man outside. I decided that the cornbread could wait and dashed after them.

"Girl, get back in here and finish mixin' this cornbread!" ordered Big Ma.

"Yes'm," I said. "I'll be right back." Before Big Ma could reach me, I was out the back door running across the yard to the drive.

Mr. Jamison touched his hat as Mama approached. "How you doing, Miz Logan?" he asked.

"Just fine, Mr. Jamison," Mama answered. "And yourself?"

"Fine. Fine," he said absently. "Is David here?"

"He's over in the east field." Mama studied Mr. Jamison. "Anything wrong?"

"Oh, no . . . no. Just wanted to speak to him."

"Little Man," Mama said, turning, "go get Papa."

"Oh, no—don't do that. I'll just walk on over there if that's all right. I need the exercise." Mama nodded, and after he had spoken to me Mr. Jamison crossed the yard to the field. Little Man and I started to follow after him but Mama called us back and returned us to our jobs.

Mr. Jamison did not stay long. A few minutes later he emerged from the field alone, got into his car, and left.

When supper was ready, I eagerly grabbed the iron bell before Christopher-John or Little Man could claim it, and ran onto the back porch to summon Papa, Mr. Morrison, and Stacey from the fields. As the three of them washed up on the back porch, Mama went to the end of the porch where Papa stood alone. "What did Mr. Jamison want?" she asked, her voice barely audible.

Papa took the towel Mama handed him, but did not reply immediately. I was just inside the kitchen dipping out the butter beans. I moved closer to the window so that I could hear his answer.

"Don't keep anything from me, David. If there's trouble, I want to know."

Papa looked down at her. "Nothing to worry 'bout, honey. . . . Just seems that Thurston Wallace been in town talking 'bout how he's not gonna let a few smart colored folks ruin his business. Says he's gonna put a stop to this shopping in Vicksburg. That's all."

Mama sighed and stared out across the plowed field to the sloping pasture land. "I'm feeling scared, David," she said.

Papa put down the towel. "Not yet, Mary. It's not time to be scared yet. They're just talking."

Mama turned and faced him. "And when they stop talking?"

"Then . . . then maybe it'll be time. But right now, pretty lady," he said, leading her by the hand toward the kitchen door, "right now I've got better things to think about."

Quickly I poured the rest of the butter beans into the bowl and hurried across the kitchen to the table. As Mama and Papa entered, I slid onto the bench beside Little Man and Christopher-John. Papa beamed down at the table.

"Well, look-a-here!" he exclaimed. "Good ole butter beans and cornbread! You better come on, Mr. Morrison! You too, son!" he called. "These womenfolks done gone and fixed us a feast."

After school was out, spring drooped quickly toward summer; yet Papa had not left for the railroad. He seemed to be waiting for something, and I secretly hoped that whatever that something was, it would never come so that he would not leave. But one evening as he, Mama, Big Ma, Mr. Morrison, and Stacey sat on the front porch while Christopher-John, Little Man, and I dashed around the yard chasing fireflies, I overheard him say, "Sunday I'm gonna have to go. Don't want to though. I got this gut feeling it ain't over yet. It's too easy."

I released the firefly imprisoned in my hand and sat beside Papa and Stacey on the steps. "Papa, please," I said, leaning against his leg, "don't go this year." Stacey looked out into the falling night, his face resigned, and said nothing.

Papa put out his large hand and caressed my face. "Got to, Cassie girl," he said softly. "Baby, there's bills to pay and ain't no money coming in. Your mama's got no job come fall and there's the mortgage and next year's taxes to think of."

"But, Papa, we planted more cotton this year. Won't that pay the taxes?"

Papa shook his head. "With Mr. Morrison here we was able to plant more, but that cotton is for living on; the railroad money is for the taxes and the mortgage."

I looked back at Mama wanting her to speak, to persuade him to stay, but when I saw her face I knew that she would not. She had known he would leave, just as we all had known.

"Papa, just another week or two, couldn't you—"

"I can't, baby. May have lost my job already."

"But Papa—"

"Cassie, that's enough now," Mama said from the deepening shadows.

I grew quiet and Papa put his arms around Stacey and me, his hands falling casually over our shoulders. From the edge of the lawn where Little Man and Christopher-John had ventured after lightning bugs, Little Man called, "Somebody's coming!" A few minutes later Mr. Avery and Mr. Lanier emerged from the dusk and walked up the sloping lawn. Mama sent Stacey and me to get more chairs for the porch, then we settled back beside Papa still sitting on the steps, his back propped against a pillar facing the visitors.

"You goin' up to the store tomorrow, David?" Mr. Avery asked after all the amenities had been said. Since the first trip in January, Mr. Morrison had made one other trip to Vicksburg, but Papa had not gone with him.

Papa motioned to Mr. Morrison. "Mr. Morrison and me going the day after tomorrow. Your wife brought down that list of things you need yesterday."

Mr. Avery cleared his throat nervously. "It's—it's that list I come 'bout, David. . . . I don't want them things no more."

The porch grew silent.

When no one said anything, Mr. Avery glanced at Mr. Lanier, and Mr. Lanier shook his head and continued. "Mr. Granger making it hard on us, David. Said we gonna have to give him sixty percent of the cotton, 'stead of fifty . . . now that the cotton's planted and it's too late to plant more. . . . Don't s'pose though that it makes much difference. The way cotton sells these days, seems the more we plant, the less money we gets anyways—"

Mr. Avery's coughing interrupted him and he waited patiently until the coughing had stopped before he went on. "I'm gonna be hard put to pay that debt in Vicksburg, David, but I'm gonna. . . . I want you to know that."

Papa nodded, looking toward the road. "I suppose Montier and Harrison raised their percentages too," he said.

"Montier did," replied Mr. Avery, "but far as I know Mr. Harrison ain't. He's a decent man."

"That does it," Mama sighed wearily.

Papa kept looking out into the darkness. "Forty percent. I expect a man used to living on fifty could live on forty . . . if he wanted to hard enough."

Mr. Avery shook his head. "Times too hard."

"Times are hard for everybody," Papa said.

Mr. Avery cleared his throat. "I know. I—I feel real bad 'bout what T.J. done—"

"I wasn't talking 'bout that," said Papa flatly.

Mr. Avery nodded self-consciously, then leaned forward in his chair and looked out into the forest. "But—but that ain't all Mr. Granger said. Said, too, we don't give up this shoppin' in Vicksburg, we can jus' get off his land. Says he tired of us stirrin' up trouble 'gainst decent white folks. Then them Wallaces, they come by my place, Brother Lanier's, and everybody's on this thing that owes them money. Said we can't pay our debts, they gonna have the sheriff out to get us . . . put us on the chain gang to work it off."

"Oh, good Lord!" exclaimed Big Ma.

Mr. Lanier nodded and added, "Gotta go up to that store by tomorrow to show good faith."

Mr. Avery's coughing started again and for a while there was only the coughing and the silence. But when the coughing ceased, Mr. Lanier said, "I pray to God there was a way we could stay in this thing, but we can't go on no chain gang, David."

Papa nodded. "Don't expect you to, Silas."

Mr. Avery laughed softly. "We sure had 'em goin' for a time though, didn't we?"

"Yes," agreed Papa quietly, "we sure did."

When the men had left, Stacey snapped, "They got no right pulling out! Just 'cause them Wallaces threaten them one time they go jumping all over themselves to get out like a bunch of scared jackrabbits—"

Papa stood suddenly and grabbed Stacey upward. "You, boy, don't you get so grown you go to talking 'bout more than you know. Them men, they doing what they've gotta do. You got any idea what a risk they took just to go shopping in Vicksburg in the first place? They go on that chain gang and their families got nothing. They'll get kicked off that plot of land they tend and there'll be no place for them to go. You understand that?"

"Y-yessir," said Stacey. Papa released him and stared moodily into the night. "You were born blessed, boy, with land of your own. If you hadn't been, you'd cry out for it while you try to survive . . . like Mr. Lanier and Mr. Avery. Maybe even do what they doing now. It's hard on a man to give up, but sometimes it seems there just ain't nothing else he can do."

"I . . . I'm sorry, Papa," Stacey muttered.

After a moment, Papa reached out and draped his arm over Stacey's shoulder.

"Papa," I said, standing to join them, "we giving up too?"

Papa looked down at me and brought me closer, then waved his hand toward the drive. "You see that fig tree over yonder, Cassie? Them other trees all around . . . that oak and walnut, they're a lot bigger and they take up more room and give so much shade they almost overshadow that little ole fig. But that fig tree's got roots that run deep, and it belongs in that yard as much as that oak and walnut. It keeps on blooming, bearing good fruit year after year, knowing all the time it'll never get as big as them other trees. Just keeps on growing and doing what it gotta do. It don't give up.

It give up, it'll die. There's a lesson to be learned from that little tree, Cassie girl, 'cause we're like it. We keep doing what we gotta, and we don't give up. We can't."

After Mr. Morrison had retired to his own house and Big Ma, the boys, and I had gone to bed, Papa and Mama remained on the porch, talking in hushed whispers. It was comforting listening to them, Mama's voice a warm, lilting murmur, Papa's a quiet, easy-flowing hum. After a few minutes they left the porch and their voices grew faint. I climbed from the bed, careful not to awaken Big Ma, and went to the window. They were walking slowly across the moon-soaked grass, their arms around each other.

"First thing tomorrow, I'm gonna go 'round and see how many folks are still in this thing," Papa said, stopping under the oak near the house. "I wanna know before we make that trip to Vicksburg."

Mama was quiet a moment. "I don't think you and Mr. Morrison should go to Vicksburg right now, David. Not with the Wallaces threatening people like they are. Wait awhile."

Papa reached into the tree and broke off a twig. "We can't just stop taking care of business 'cause of them Wallaces, Mary. You know that."

Mama did not reply.

Papa leaned against the tree. "I think I'll take Stacey with me."

"Now, David, no—"

"He'll be thirteen next month, honey, and he needs to be with me more. I can't take him with me on the railroad, but I can take him with me where I go 'round here. And I want him to know business . . . how to take care of it, how to take care of things when I ain't around."

"David, he's just a boy."

"Baby, a boy get as big as Stacey down here and he's near a man. He's gotta know a man's things. He gotta know how to handle himself."

"I know, but—"

"Mary, I want him strong . . . not a fool like T.J."

"He's got more brains and learning than that," Mama snapped.

"I know," Papa said quietly. "Still it worries me, seeing T.J. turning like he is."

"Seems to me it isn't bothering Joe Avery much. He doesn't seem to be doing anything about it."

Papa allowed the silence to seep between them before he said, "It's not like you, honey, to be bitter."

"I'm not bitter," said Mama, folding her arms across her chest. "It's just that the boy's gotten out of hand, and doesn't seem like anybody's doing anything about it."

"The other day Joe told me he couldn't do nothing with T.J. anymore. That's a hard thing for a man to admit."

"He can still put a good strip of leather against his bottom, can't he?" It was clear that Mama was unsympathetic to Mr. Avery's problem.

"Said he tried, but his health's so poor, he ended up with a bad coughing spell. Got so sick from it, he had to go to bed. Said after that Fannie tried to whip the boy, but T.J.'s stronger than her, and it didn't do no good." Papa paused, then added, "He's gotten pretty sassy, too, I understand."

"Well, sassy or not," Mama grumbled, "they'd better figure out some way of getting that boy back on the right track because he's headed for a whole lot of trouble."

Papa sighed heavily and left the tree. "We'd better go in. I've gotta get an early start if I'm gonna get 'round to everybody."

"You're still set on going to Vicksburg?"

"I told you I was."

Mama laughed lightly in exasperation. "Sometimes, David Logan, I wonder why I didn't marry sweet, quiet Ronald Carter or nice, mild Harold Davis."

"Because, woman," Papa said, putting his arm around her, "you took one look at big, handsome me and no one else would do." Then they both laughed, and together moved slowly to the side of the house.

Seven families, including ours, still refused to shop at the Wallace store even with the threat of the chain gang. Mama said that the number was not significant enough to hurt the Wallaces, only enough to rile them, and she worried, afraid for Papa, Stacey, and Mr. Morrison to make the trip. But nothing she could say could change Papa's mind and they left as planned on Wednesday morning long before dawn.

On Thursday, when they were to return, it began to rain, a hard, swelling summer rain which brought a premature green darkness to the land and forced us to leave our hoeing of the cotton field and return to the house. As the thunder rumbled overhead, Mama peered out the window at the dark road. "Wonder what's keeping them," she said, more to herself than anyone else.

"Probably got held up someplace," said Big Ma. "Could've stopped to get out of this storm."

Mama turned from the window. "You're most likely right," she agreed, picking up a pair of Christopher-John's pants to mend.

As the evening fell into total darkness, we grew silent, the boys and I saying very little, Mama and Big Ma concentrating on their sewing, their brows furrowed. My throat grew tight, and without knowing why I was afraid, I was. "Mama," I said, "they all right, ain't they?"

Mama stared down at me. "Course they're all right. They're just late, that's all."

"But, Mama, you s'pose maybe somebody done—"

"I think you children better go on to bed," Mama said sharply without letting me finish.

"But I wanna wait up for Papa," objected Little Man.

"Me, too," said sleepy Christopher-John.

"You'll see him in the morning. Now get to bed!"

Since there was nothing we could do but obey, we went to bed. But I could not sleep. A cold fear crept up my body, churning my stomach and tightening its grip on my throat. Finally, when I felt that I was going to be sick from it, I rose and padded silently into Mama and Papa's room.

Mama was standing with her back to me, her arms folded and Big Ma was still patching. Neither one of them heard the door swing open. I started to speak, but Mama was talking and I decided not to interrupt her. ". . . I've got a good mind to saddle Lady and go looking for them," she said.

"Now, Mary, what good would that do?" Big Ma questioned. "You runnin' 'round out there on that mare by yo'self in this darkness and rain?"

"But something's happened to them! I can feel it."

"It's just in yo' mind, child," Big Ma scoffed unconvincingly. "Them menfolks all right."

"No . . . no," said Mama shaking her head. "The Wallaces aren't just in my mind, they—" She stopped suddenly and stood very still.

"Mary—"

"Thought I heard something." The dogs started barking and she turned, half running, across the room. Pushing up the lock in a mad haste, she swung the door open and cried to the storm, "David! David!"

Unable to stay put, I dashed across the room. "Cassie, what you doin' up, girl?" asked Big Ma, swatting me as I passed her. But Mama, staring into the wet night, said nothing when I reached her side.

"Is it them?" I asked.

Out of the darkness a round light appeared, moving slowly across the drive, and Mr. Morrison's voice drifted softly to us. "Go on, Stacey," he said, "I got him." Then Stacey, a flashlight in his hand, came into sight, followed by Mr. Morrison carrying Papa.

"David!" Mama gasped, her voice a frightened whisper.

Big Ma standing behind me stepped back, pulling me with her. She stripped the bed to its sheets and ordered, "Put him right here, Mr. Morrison."

As Mr. Morrison climbed the stairs, we could see that Papa's left leg stuck straight out, immobilized by his shotgun strapped to it with a rope. His head was wrapped in a rag through which the dark redness of his blood had seeped. Mr. Morrison eased Papa through the doorway, careful not to hit the strapped leg, and laid him gently on the bed. Mama went immediately to the bed and took Papa's hand.

"Hey, baby . . ." Papa said faintly, "I'm . . . all right. Just got my leg broke, that's all. . . ."

"Wagon rolled over it," said Mr. Morrison, avoiding Mama's eyes. "We better get that leg set. Didn't have time on the road."

"But his head—" Mama said, her eyes questioning Mr. Morrison. But Mr. Morrison said nothing further and Mama turned to Stacey. "You all right, son?"

"Yes'm," Stacey said, his face strangely ashen, his eyes on Papa.

"Then get out of those wet things. Don't want you catching pneumonia. Cassie, you go to bed."

"I'll get a fire started," said Big Ma disappearing into the kitchen as Mama turned to the closet to find sheets for making a cast. But Stacey and I remained rooted, watching Papa, and did not move until Christopher-John and Little Man made a sleepy entrance.

"What's going on?" asked Little Man, frowning into the light.

"Go back to bed, children," Mama said, rushing to keep them from coming farther into the room, but before she could reach them Christopher-John spied Papa on the bed and shot past her. "Papa, you got back!"

Mr. Morrison swung him upward before he could jar the bed.

"Wh-what's the matter?" asked Christopher-John, wide awake now. "Papa, what's the matter? How come you got that thing on your head?"

"Your Papa's asleep," said Mama as Mr. Morrison set Christopher-John back down. "Stacey, take them back to bed . . . and get out of those clothes." None of us stirred. "Move when I tell you!" Mama hissed impatiently, her face more worried than angry.

Stacey herded us into the boys' room.

As soon as the door closed behind us, I asked, "Stacey, how bad Papa hurt?" Stacey felt around for the lamp, lit it, then plopped wearily on the side of the bed. We huddled around him. "Well?"

Stacey shook his head. "I dunno. His leg's busted up by the wagon . . . and he's shot."

"Shot!" Christopher-John and Little Man exclaimed fearfully, but I was silent, too afraid now to speak, to think.

"Mr. Morrison says he don't think the bullet hurt him much. Says he thinks it just hit his skin . . . here." Stacey ran his forefinger along his right temple. "And didn't sink in nowhere."

"But who'd shoot Papa?" asked Little Man, greatly agitated. "Can't nobody just shoot Papa!"

Stacey stood then and motioned Christopher-John and Little Man under the covers. "I've said too much already. Cassie, go on to bed."

I continued to sit, my mind unable to move.

"Cassie, go on now like Mama said."

"How the wagon roll over him? How he get shot?" I blurted out angrily, already plotting revenge against whoever had dared hurt my father.

"Cassie . . . you go on to bed!"

"Ain't moving till you tell me!"

"I'll call Mama," he threatened.

"She too busy," I said, folding my arms and feeling confident that he would tell the story.

He went to the door and opened it. Christopher-John, Little Man, and I watched him eagerly. But he soon closed the door and came back to the bed.

"What was they doing?" asked Little Man.

"Big Ma's tending Papa's head."

"Well, what happened out there?" I repeated.

Stacey sighed despairingly and sat down. "We was coming back from Vicksburg when the back wheels come off," he said, his voice a hollow whisper. "It was already dark and it was raining too, and Papa and Mr. Morrison, they thought somebody done messed with them wheels for both of them to come off at the same time like they did. Then when I told them I'd seen two boys near the wagon when we was in Vicksburg, Papa said we didn't have time to unhitch and unload the wagon like we should to put them wheels back on. He thought somebody was coming after us.

"So after we found the wheels and the bolts, Papa told me to hold the reins real tight on Jack to keep him still. . . . Jack, he was real skittish 'cause of the storm. Then Mr. Morrison went and lifted that wagon all by himself. And it was heavy too, but Mr. Morrison lifted it like it wasn't nothing. Then Papa slipped the first wheel on. . . . That's when he got shot—"

"But who—" I started.

"A truck come up the road and stopped behind us while we was trying to get that wheel on, but didn't none of us hear it coming 'cause of the rain and the thunder and all, and they didn't put their lights on till the truck stopped. Anyways, there was three men in that truck and soon as Papa seen 'em, he reached for his shotgun. That's when they shot him and he fell back with his left leg under the wagon. Then . . . then Jack reared up, scared by the shot, and I—I couldn't hold him . . . and . . . and the wagon rolled over Papa's leg." His voice cracked sharply, and he exploded guiltily, "It's m-my fault his leg's busted!"

I thought on what he had said and, laying my hand on his shoulder, I said, "Naw, it ain't. It's them men's."

Stacey did not speak for a while and I did not prod him to go on. Finally, he cleared his throat and continued huskily. "Soon's I could, I . . . I tied Jack to a tree and run back to Papa, but Papa told me not to move him and to get down in the gully. After them men shot Papa, they come down trying to get Mr. Morrison, but he was too fast and strong for 'em. I couldn't see everything that happened 'cause they didn't always stay in front of them headlights, but I did see Mr. Morrison pick up one of them men like he wasn't nothing but a sack of chicken feathers and fling him down on the ground so hard it must've broke his back. Ain't never seen nothin' like it before in my whole life. Then one of them other two that had a gun shot at Mr. Morrison, but he didn't hit him. Mr. Morrison, he ducked away from the headlights into the darkness and they went after him.

"Couldn't see nothin' then," he said, glancing toward the door where Papa lay. "Heard bones cracking. Heard somebody cursing and crying. Then I couldn't hear nothin' but the rain, and I was real scared. 'Fraid they'd killed Mr. Morrison."

"But they didn't," reminded Little Man, his eyes bright with excitement.

Stacey nodded. "Next thing I seen was a man coming real slow-like into the head-lights and pick up the man lying in the middle of the road—the one Mr. Morrison thrown down. He got him into the truck, then come back and helped the other one. That one looked like he had a broke arm. It was hanging all crazy-like at his side. Then they turned the truck around and drove away."

"Then what?" Little Man inquired.

Stacey shrugged. "Nothin'. We put on the other wheel and come on home."

"Who was it?" I rasped, holding my breath.

Stacey looked at me and said flatly, "The Wallaces, I think."

There was a fearful moment's silence, then Christopher-John, tears in his dark eyes, asked, "Stacey, is . . . is Papa gonna die?"

"No! Course not!" denied Stacey too quickly.

"But he was so still—"

"I don't want Papa to die!" wailed Little Man.

"He was just sleeping—like Mama said. That's all."

"Well, when he gonna wake up?" cried Christopher-John, the tears escaping down his plump cheeks.

"In—in the morning," said Stacey, putting a comforting arm around both Christopher-John and Little Man. "Jus' you wait and see. He'll be jus' fine come morning."

Stacey, still in his wet, muddy clothes, said nothing else, and neither did the rest of us. All the questions had been answered, yet we feared, and we sat silently listening to the rain, soft now upon the roof, and watching the door behind which Papa lay, and wished for morning.

10

"How does it look?" asked Papa as I passed through the sitting room on my way out the side door. Over a week had passed since he had been injured, and this was his first morning up. He was seated by the cold fireplace, his head still bandaged, his broken leg resting on a wooden chair. His eyes were on Mama at her desk.

Mama put down her pencil and frowned at the open ledger before her. She glanced at me absently and waited until I had closed the screen door behind me, then she said, "David, do you think we should go into this now? You're still not well—"

"I'm well enough to know there's not much left. Now tell me."

I hopped down the steps and sat on the bottom one.

Mama was silent a moment before she answered him. "With Hammer's half of the mortgage money, we've got enough to meet the June payment."

"Nothing more?"

"A couple of dollars, but that's all."

They were both silent.

"You think we should write Hammer and borrow some money?" Mama asked.

Papa did not answer right away. "No . . ." he said finally. "I still don't want him to know 'bout this thing. If he knows I'm not on the railroad, he'll wanna know why not, and I don't wanna risk that temper of his when he finds out what the Wallaces done."

Mama sighed. "I guess you're right."

"I know I am," said Papa. "Things like they are, he come down here wild and angry, he'll get himself hung. Long as things don't get no worse, we can make it without him. We'll meet that June note with the money we got there." He paused a moment. "We'll probably have to sell a couple of the cows and their calves to make them July and August notes . . . maybe even that ole sow. But by the end of August we should have enough cotton to make that September payment. . . . Course we'll probably have to go all the way to Vicksburg to get it ginned.[9] Can't hardly use Harlan Granger's gin this year."

There was silence again, then Mama said, "David, Mama's been talking about going into Strawberry to the market next—"

"No," Papa said, not letting her finish. "Too much bad feeling there."

"I told her that."

"I'll talk to her. . . . Anything we just gotta have before the first cotton come in?"

"Well . . . you picked up batteries and kerosene on that last trip . . . but what we're going to need more than anything is some insecticide to spray the cotton. The bugs are getting pretty bad. . . ."

"What 'bout food?"

"Our flour and sugar and baking powder and such are low, but we'll make out— we don't have to have biscuits and cornbread every day. We're out of pepper and there's not much salt, but we don't just have to have those either. And the coffee's all gone. . . . The garden's coming along nicely, though. There's no worry there."

"No worry," Papa muttered as both of them grew quiet. Then suddenly there was a sharp explosion as if something had been struck with an angry force. "If only this leg wasn't busted!"

"Don't let Stacey hear you saying that, David," Mama cautioned softly. "You know he blames himself about your leg."

"I told the boy it wasn't his fault. He just wasn't strong enough to hold Jack."

"I know that, but still he blames himself."

Papa laughed strangely. "Ain't this something? Them Wallaces aim a gun at my head and I get my leg broke, and my boy's blaming himself for it. Why, I feel like taking a bullwhip to all three of them Wallaces and not stopping till my arm get so tired I can't raise it one more time."

"You're sounding like Hammer."

"Am I? Well, a lot of times I feel like doing things Hammer's way. I think I'd get a powerful lot of satisfaction from whipping Kaleb Wallace and them brothers of his."

"Hammer's way would get you killed and you know it, so stop talking like that. Don't we already have enough to worry about? Besides, both Thurston and Dewberry Wallace are still laid up, so I hear. Some folks even say that Dewberry's back is broken. In any case, Mr. Morrison must have hurt them pretty bad."

"Where is he, by the way? I haven't seen him this morning."

There was an instant of silence before Mama answered. "Out looking for work again since dawn."

9. To have the seeds in the cotton removed with a cotton gin.

"He ain't gonna find nothing 'round here. I told him that."

"I know," agreed Mama. "But he says he's got to try. David . . ." Mama stopped, and when she spoke again her voice had grown faint, as if she hesitated to say what was on her mind. "David, don't you think he ought to go? I don't want him to, but after what he did to the Wallaces, I'm afraid for him."

"He knows what could happen, Mary, but he wants to stay—and, frankly, we need him here. Don't pester him about it."

"But, David, if—"

Before Mama finished, I spied Mr. Morrison coming west from Smellings Creek. I left the step and hurried to meet him.

"Hello, Mr. Morrison!" I shouted as Jack pulled the wagon up the drive.

"Hello, Cassie," Mr. Morrison greeted me. "Your papa awake?"

"Yessir. He's sitting out of bed this morning."

"Didn't I tell you nothin' could keep him down?"

"Yessir, you did."

He stepped from the wagon and walked toward the house.

"Mr. Morrison, you want me to unhitch Jack for ya?"

"No, Cassie, leave him be. I gotta talk to your papa then I'll be back."

"Hey, ole Jack," I said, patting the mule as I watched Mr. Morrison enter the side door. I thought of returning to my seat on the steps, but decided against it. Instead I remained with Jack, thoughtfully digesting all I had heard, until Mr. Morrison came from the house. He went into the barn, then reappeared with the planter, a plowlike tool with a small round container for dropping seeds attached to its middle. He put the planter into the back of the wagon.

"Where you going now, Mr. Morrison?"

"Down to Mr. Wiggins' place. I seen Mr. Wiggins this morning and he asked to use your Papa's planter. He ain't got no wagon so I told him I'd ask your Papa and if it was all right, I'd bring it to him."

"Ain't it kinda late for seeding?"

"Well, not for what he got in mind. He thought he'd plant himself some summer corn. It'll be ready come September."

"Mr. Morrison, can I go with ya?" I asked as he climbed up on the wagon.

"Well, I'd be right pleased for your company, Cassie. But you'll have to ask your mama."

I ran back to the house. The boys were now in Mama and Papa's room, and when I asked if I could go up to Little Willie's with Mr. Morrison, Little Man and Christopher-John, of course, wanted to go too.

"Mr. Morrison said it'd be all right, Mama."

"Well, don't you get in his way. Stacey, you going?"

Stacey sat across from Papa looking despondently at the broken leg. "Go on, son," said Papa gently. "There's nothing to do here. Give you a chance to talk to Little Willie."

"You sure there ain't something I can do for you, Papa?"

"Just go and have yourself a good ride over to Little Willie's."

Since it had been my idea to ask to go, I claimed the seat beside Mr. Morrison, and the boys climbed in back. Little Willie's family lived on their own forty acres about two miles east of Great Faith. It was a fine morning for a ride and the six miles there sped by quickly with Mr. Morrison singing in his bassest of bass voices and Christopher-John, Little Man, and me joining in wherever we could as we passed cotton fields abloom in flowers of white and red and pink. Stacey being in one of his moods did not sing and we let him be.

We stayed less than an hour at the Wiggins farm, then headed home again. We had just passed Great Faith and were approaching the Jefferson Davis School Road when a ragged pickup came into view. Very quietly Mr. Morrison said, "Cassie, get in back."

"But why, Mr. Mor—"

"Do quick, Cassie, like I say." His voice was barely above a friendly whisper, but there was an urgency in it and I obeyed, scrambling over the seat to join the boys. "Y'all stay down now."

The truck braked noisily with a grating shriek of steel. We stopped. The boys and I peeped over the edge of the wagon. The truck had veered across the road, blocking us. The truck door swung open and Kaleb Wallace stepped out, pointing a long condemning finger at Mr. Morrison.

He swayed unspeaking for a long, terrible moment, then sputtered, "You big black nigger, I oughta cut your heart out for what you done! My brothers laid up like they is and you still runnin' 'round free as a white man. Downright sinful, that's what it is! Why, I oughta gun you down right where you sit—"

"You gonna move your truck?"

Kaleb Wallace gazed up at Mr. Morrison, then at the truck as if trying to comprehend the connection between the two. "That truck in your way, boy?"

"You gonna move it?"

"I'll move it all right . . . when I get good and ready—" He stopped abruptly, his eyes bulging in a terrified stare as Mr. Morrison climbed down from the wagon. Mr. Morrison's long shadow fell over him and for a breathless second, Mr. Morrison towered dangerously near him. But as the fear grew white on Kaleb Wallace's face, Mr. Morrison turned without a word and peered into the truck.

"What's he looking for?" I whispered.

"Probably a gun," said Stacey.

Mr. Morrison circled the truck, studying it closely. Then he returned to its front and, bending at the knees with his back against the grill, he positioned his large hands beneath the bumper. Slowly, his muscles flexing tightly against his thin shirt and the sweat popping off his skin like oil on water, he lifted the truck in one fluid, powerful motion until the front was several inches off the ground and slowly walked it to the left of the road, where he set it down as gently as a sleeping child. Then he moved to the rear of the truck and repeated the feat.

Kaleb Wallace was mute. Christopher-John, Little Man, and I stared open-mouthed, and even Stacey, who had witnessed Mr. Morrison's phenomenal strength before, gazed in wonder.

It took Kaleb Wallace several minutes to regain his voice. We were far down the road, almost out of hearing, when his frenzied cry of hate reached us. "One of these nights, you watch, nigger! I'm gonna come get you for what you done! You just watch! One night real soon . . ."

When we reached home and told Mama and Papa and Big Ma what had happened, Mama said to Mr. Morrison, "I told you before I was afraid for you. And today, Kaleb Wallace could've hurt you . . . and the children."

Mr. Morrison looked squarely into Mama's eyes. "Miz Logan, Kaleb Wallace is one of them folks who can't do nothing by himself. He got to have a lot of other folks backing him up plus a loaded gun . . . and I knew there wasn't no gun, leastways not in the truck. I checked."

"But if you stay, he'll get somebody and they'll try to take you, like he said—"

"Miz Logan, don't ask me to go."

Mama reached out, laying a slender hand on Mr. Morrison's. "Mr. Morrison, you're a part of us now. I don't want you hurt because of us."

Mr. Morrison lowered his eyes and looked around the room until his gaze rested on the boys and me. "I ain't never had no children of my own. I think sometimes if I had, I'd've wanted a son and daughter just like you and Mr. Logan . . . and grandbabies like these babies of yours. . . ."

"But, Mr. Morrison, the Wallaces—"

"Mary," said Papa quietly, "let it be."

Mama looked at Papa, her lips still poised to speak. Then she said no more; but the worry lines remained creased upon her brow.

August dawned blue and hot. The heat swooped low over the land clinging like an invisible shroud, and through it people moved slowly, lethargically, as if under water. In the ripening fields the drying cotton and corn stretched tiredly skyward awaiting the coolness of a rain that occasionally threatened but did not come, and the land took on a baked, brown look.

To escape the heat, the boys and I often ambled into the coolness of the forest after the chores were done. There, while the cows and their calves grazed nearby, we sat on the banks of the pond, our backs propped against an old hickory or pine or walnut, our feet dangling lazily in the cool water, and waited for a watermelon brought from the garden to chill. Sometimes Jeremy joined us there, making his way through the deep forest land from his own farm over a mile away, but the meetings were never planned; none of our parents would have liked that.

"How's your papa?" he asked one day as he plopped down beside us.

"He's all right," said Stacey, " 'cepting his leg's bothering him in this heat. Itching a lot. But Mama says that's a sign it's getting well."

"That's good," murmured Jeremy. "Too bad he had to get hurt when he done so's he couldn't go back on the railroad."

Stacey stirred uneasily, looked at Christopher-John, Little Man, and me, reminding us with his eyes that we were not to speak about the Wallaces' part in Papa's injury, and said only, "Uh-huh."

Jeremy was silent a moment, then stuttered, "S-some folks sayin' they glad he got hurt. G-glad he can't go make that railroad money."

"Who said that?" I cried, jumping up from the bank. "Just tell me who said it and I'll ram—"

"Cassie! Sit down and be quiet," Stacey ordered. Reluctantly, I did as I was told, wishing that this business about the Wallaces and Papa's injuries were not so complex. It seemed to me that since the Wallaces had attacked Papa and Mr. Morrison, the simplest thing to do would be to tell the sheriff and have them put in jail, but Mama said things didn't work that way. She explained that as long as the Wallaces, embarrassed by their injuries at the hands of Mr. Morrison, did not make an official complaint about the incident, then we must remain silent also. If we did not, Mr. Morrison could be charged with attacking white men, which could possibly end in his being sentenced to the chain gang, or worse.

"I—I ain't the one said it, Cassie," stammered Jeremy by way of apology.

"Well, whoever saying it ought not be," I said huffily.

Jeremy nodded thoughtfully and changed the subject. "Y'all seen T.J. lately?"

Stacey frowned, considering whether or not he should answer. There had been much talk concerning T.J. and the Simms brothers, all of it bad. Moe Turner's father had told Papa that T.J. had stopped by with the Simmses once, and after they had left he had discovered his watch missing; the Laniers had had the same experience with a locket. "That T.J. done turned real bad," Mr. Lanier had said, "and I don't want nothin' to do with no thief . . . 'specially no thief runnin' 'round with white boys."

Finally Stacey said, "Don't see him much no more."

Jeremy pulled at his lip. "I see him all the time."

"Too bad," I sympathized.

Stacey glanced reproachfully at me, then lay flat upon the ground, his head resting in the cushion of his hands clasped under his head. "It sure is beautiful up there," he said, pointedly changing the subject again.

The rest of us lay back too. Overhead, the branches of the walnut and hickory trees met like long green fans sheltering us. Several feet away the persistent sun made amber roads of shimmering sunlight upon the pond. A stillness hovered in the high air, soft, quiet, peaceful.

"I think when I grow up I'm gonna build me a house in some trees and jus' live there all the time," said Jeremy.

"How you gonna do that?" asked Little Man.

"Oh, I'll find me some real strong trees and just build. I figure I'll have the trunk of one tree in the bedroom and the other in the kitchen."

"How come you wanna live in a tree for?" Christopher-John inquired.

"It's so peaceful up there . . . and quiet. Cool, too," answered Jeremy. " 'Specially at night."

"How you know how cool it is at night?" I said.

Jeremy's face brightened. " 'Cause I got my bedroom up there."

We looked at him unbelieving.

"I-I do—really. Built it myself and I sleeps up there. Come these hot nights, I just climbs in my tree and it's like going into another world. Why, I can see and hear things up there that I betcha only the squirrels and the birds can see and hear. Sometimes I think I can even see all the way over to y'all's place."

"Ah, shoot, boy, you're a story," I said. "Your place too far away and you know it."

Jeremy's face dropped. "Well . . . maybe I can't see it, but that don't keep me from pretending I do." He was silent a second, then hopped up suddenly, his face bright again. "Hey, why don't y'all come on over and see it? My pa's gonna be gone all day and it'd be lots of fun and I could show y'all—"

"No," said Stacey quietly, his eyes still on the trees overhead.

Jeremy sat back down, deflated. "J-jus' wanted y'all to see it, that's all. . . ." For a while he looked hurt by Stacey's cold refusal; then, seeming to accept it as part of the things that were, he again took up his position and volunteered good-naturedly, "If y'all ever get a chance to build y'all-selves a tree house, just let me know and I'll help ya. It's just as cool . . ."

Papa sat on a bench in the barn, his broken leg stretched awkwardly before him, mending one of Jack's harnesses. He had been there since early morning, a frown line carved deep into his forehead, quietly mending those things which needed mending. Mama told us not to bother him and we stayed away from the barn as long as we could, but by late afternoon we drifted naturally to it and began our chores. Papa had disappeared within himself and he took no notice of us at first, but shortly afterward he looked up, watching us closely.

When the chores were almost finished, Mr. Morrison arrived from Strawberry, where he had gone to make the August mortgage payment. He entered the barn slowly and handed Papa an envelope. Papa glanced up questioningly, then ripped it open. As he read the letter, his jaw set tightly, and when he finished he smashed his fist so hard against the bench that the boys and I stopped what we were doing, aware that something was terribly wrong.

"They tell you?" he asked of Mr. Morrison, his voice curt, angry.

Mr. Morrison nodded. "I tried to get them to wait till after cotton picking, but they told me it was due and payable immediately. Them's they words."

"Harlan Granger," said Papa quietly. He reached for his cane and stood up. "You feel up to going back to Strawberry . . . tonight?"

"I can make it, but I don't know if this ole mule can."

"Then hitch Lady to it," he said motioning to the mare. He turned then and went to the house. The boys and I followed, not quite sure of what was happening. Papa entered the kitchen; we stayed on the porch peering through the screen.

"David, something the matter, son?"

"The bank called up the note. I'm going to Strawberry."

"Called up the note?" echoed Big Ma. "Oh, Lord, not that too."

Mama stared at Papa, fear in her eyes. "You going now?"

"Now," he said, leaving the kitchen for their room.

Mama's voice trailed him. "David, it's too late. The bank's closed by now. You can't see anyone until morning. . . ."

We could not hear Papa's reply, but Mama's voice rose sharply. "You want to be out on that road again in the middle of the night after what happened? You want us worried to death about you?"

"Mary, don't you understand they're trying to take the land?" Papa said, his voice rising too so that we heard.

"Don't you understand I don't want you dead?"

We could hear nothing else. But a few minutes later Papa came out and told Mr. Morrison to unhitch Lady. They would go to Strawberry in the morning.

The next day Papa and Mr. Morrison were gone before I arose. When they returned in the late afternoon, Papa sat wearily down at the kitchen table with Mr. Morrison beside him. Rubbing his hand over his thick hair, he said, "I called Hammer."

"What did you tell him?" Mama asked.

"Just that the note's been called. He said he'd get the money."

"How?"

"He didn't say and I didn't ask. Just said he'd get it."

"And Mr. Higgins at the bank, David," said Big Ma. "What he have to say?"

"Said our credit's no good anymore."

"We aren't even hurting the Wallaces now," Mama said with acid anger. "Harlan Granger's got no need—"

"Baby, you know he's got a need," Papa said, pulling her to him. "He's got a need to show us where we stand in the scheme of things. He's got a powerful need to do that. Besides, he still wants this place."

"But son, that mortgage give us four more years."

Papa laughed dryly. "Mama, you want me to take it to court?"

Big Ma sighed and placed her hand on Papa's. "What if Hammer can't get the money?"

Papa did not look at her, but at Mr. Morrison instead. "Don't worry, Mama. We ain't gonna lose the land. . . . Trust me."

On the third Sunday of August the annual revival began. Revivals were always very serious, yet gay and long-planned-for, affairs which brought pots and pans from out-of-the-way shelves, mothball-packed dresses and creased pants from hidden chests, and all the people from the community and the neighboring communities up the winding red school road to Great Faith Church. The revival ran for seven days and it was an occasion everyone looked forward to, for it was more than just church services; it was the year's only planned social event, disrupting the humdrum of everyday country life. Teenagers courted openly, adults met with relatives and friends they had not seen since the previous year's "big meeting," and children ran almost free.

As far as I was concerned, the best part of the revival was the very first day. After the first of three services was dismissed, the mass of humanity which had squished its way into the sweltering interior of the small church poured onto the school grounds, and the women proudly set out their dinners in the backs of wagons and on the long tables circling the church.

Then it was a feast to remember.

Brimming bowls of turnip greens and black-eyed peas with ham hocks, thick slices of last winter's sugar-cured ham and strips of broiled ribs, crisply fried chicken and morsels of golden squirrel and rabbit, flaky buttermilk biscuits and crusty cornbread, fat slabs of sweet-potato pie and butter pound cakes, and so much more were all for the taking. No matter how low the pantry supplies, each family always managed to contribute something, and as the churchgoers made the rounds from table to table, hard times were forgotten at least for the day.

The boys and I had just loaded our plates for the first time and taken seats under an old walnut when Stacey put down his plate and stood up again. "What's the matter?" I asked, stuffing my mouth with cornbread.

Stacey frowned into the sun. "That man walking up the road . . ."

I took a moment to look up, then picked up my drumstick. "So?"

"He looks like . . . Uncle Hammer!" he cried and dashed away. I hesitated, watching him, reluctant to leave my plate unless it really was Uncle Hammer. When Stacey reached the man and hugged him, I put the plate down and ran across the lawn to the road. Christopher-John, with his plate still in hand, and Little Man ran after me.

"Uncle Hammer, where's your car?" Little Man asked after we all had hugged him.

"Sold it," he said.

"Sold it!" we cried in unison.

"B-but why?" asked Stacey.

"Needed the money," Uncle Hammer said flatly.

As we neared the church, Papa met us and embraced Uncle Hammer. "I wasn't expecting you to come all the way down here."

"You expecting me to send that much money by mail?"

"Could've wired it."

"Don't trust that either."

"How'd you get it?"

"Borrowed some of it, sold a few things," he said with a shrug. Then he nodded toward Papa's leg. "How'd you do that?"

Papa's eyes met Uncle Hammer's and he smiled faintly. "I was sort of hoping you wouldn't ask that."

"Uh-huh."

"Papa," I said, "Uncle Hammer sold the Packard."

Papa's smile faded. "I didn't mean for that to happen, Hammer."

Uncle Hammer put his arm around Papa. "What good's a car? It can't grow cotton. You can't build a home on it. And you can't raise four fine babies in it."

Papa nodded, understanding.

"Now, you gonna tell me 'bout that leg?"

Papa stared at the milling throng of people around the dinner tables. "Let's get you something to eat first," he said, "then I'll tell you. Maybe it'll set better with some of this good food in your stomach."

Because Uncle Hammer was leaving early Monday morning, the boys and I were allowed to stay up much later than usual to be with him. Long hours after we should have been in bed, we sat on the front porch lit only by the whiteness of the full moon and listened to the comforting sounds of Papa's and Uncle Hammer's voices mingling once again.

"We'll go up to Strawberry and make the payment first thing tomorrow," said Papa. "I don't think I'd better go all the way to Vicksburg with this leg, but Mr. Morrison'll take you there—see you to the train."

"He don't have to do that," replied Uncle Hammer. "I can make it to Vicksburg all right."

"But I'd rest easier if I _knew_ you was on that train headed due north . . . not off getting yourself ready to do something foolish."

Uncle Hammer grunted. "There ain't a thing foolish to what I'd like to do to them Wallaces. . . . Harlan Granger either."

There was nothing to say to how he felt, and no one tried.

"What you plan to do for money?" Uncle Hammer asked after a while.

"The cotton looks good," said Papa. "We do well on it, we'll make out all right."

Uncle Hammer was quiet a moment before he observed, "Just tightening the belt some more, huh?"

When Papa did not answer, Uncle Hammer said, "Maybe I better stay."

"No," said Papa adamantly, "You do better in Chicago."

"May do better but I worry a lot." He paused, pulling at his ear. "Come through Strawberry with a fellow from up in Vicksburg. Things seemed worse than usual up there. It gets hot like this and folks get dissatisfied with life, they start looking 'round for somebody to take it out on. . . . I don't want it to be you."

"I don't think it will be . . ." said Papa, ". . . unless you stay."

In the morning after the men had gone, Big Ma said to Mama, "I sure wish Hammer could've stayed longer."

"It's better he went," said Mama.

Big Ma nodded. "I know. Things like they is, it don't take but a little of nothin' to set things off, and Hammer with that temper he got could do it. Still," she murmured wistfully, "I sho' wish he could've stayed. . . ."

On the last night of the revival the sky took on a strange yellowish cast. The air felt close, suffocating, and no wind stirred.

"What do you think, David?" Mama asked as she and Papa stood on the front porch looking at the sky. "You think we should go?"

Papa leaned against his cane. "It's gonna storm all right . . . but it may not come till late on over in the night."

They decided we would go. Most other families had come to the same decision, for the church grounds were crowded with wagons when we arrived. "Brother Logan," one of the deacons called as Papa stepped awkwardly down from the wagon, "Reverend Gabson wants us to get the meeting started soon as we can so we can dismiss early and get on home 'fore this storm hits."

"All right," Papa said, directing us toward the church. But as we neared the building, we were stopped by the Laniers. As the grown-ups talked, Little Willie Wiggins and Moe Turner, standing with several other boys, motioned to Stacey from the road. Stacey wandered away to speak to them and Christopher-John, Little Man, and I went too.

"Guess who we seen?" said Little Willie as Stacey walked up. But before Stacey could venture a guess, Little Willie answered his own question. "T.J. and them Simms brothers."

"Where?" asked Stacey.

"Over there," Little Willie pointed. "They parked by the classrooms. Look, here they come."

All eyes followed the direction of Little Willie's finger. Through the settling dusk three figures ambled with assurance across the wide lawn, the two Simmses on the outside, T.J. in the middle.

"How come he bringin' them here?" asked Moe Turner angrily.

Stacey shrugged. "Dunno, but I guess we'll find out."

"He looks different," I remarked when I could see T.J. more distinctly. He was dressed in a pair of long, unpatched trousers and, as sticky hot as it was, he wore a suit coat and a tie, and a hat cocked jauntily to one side.

"I s'pose he do look different," murmured Moe bitterly. "I'd look different too, if I'd been busy stealin' other folkses' stuff."

"Well, well, well! What we got here?" exclaimed T.J. loudly as he approached. "Y'all gonna welcome us to y'all's revival services?"

"What you doing here, T.J.?" Stacey asked.

T.J. laughed. "I got a right to come to my own church, ain't I? See all my old friends?" His eyes wandered over the group, but no one showed signs of being glad to see him. His wide grin shrank a little, then spying me he patted my face with his moist hand. "Hey, Cassie girl, how you doin'?"

I slapped his hand away. "Don't you come messing with me, T.J.!" I warned.

Again he laughed, then said soberly, "Well, this is a fine how-do-you-do. I come all the way over here to introduce my friends, R.W. and Melvin, to y'all and y'all actin' like y'all ain't got no manners at all. Yeah, ole R.W. and Melvin," he said, rolling the Simmses' names slowly off his tongue to bring to our attention that he had not bothered to place a "Mister" before either, "they been mighty fine friends to me. Better than any of y'all. Look, see here what they give me." Proudly he tugged at the suit coat. "Pretty nice stuff, eh? Everything I want they give me 'cause they really likes me. I'm they best friend."

He turned to the Simmses. "Ain't that right, R.W. and Melvin?"

Melvin nodded, a condescending smirk on his face which was lost on T.J.

"Anything—just anything at all I want—they'll get it for me, including—" He hesitated as if he were unsure whether or not he was going too far, then plunged on. "Including that pearl-handled pistol in Barnett's Mercantile."

R.W. stepped forward and slapped a reassuring hand on T.J.'s shoulder. "That's right, T.J. You name it and you've got it."

T.J. grinned widely. Stacey turned away in disgust. "Come on," he said, "service is 'bout to start."

"Hey, what's the matter with y'all?" T.J. yelled as the group turned en masse and headed for the church. I glanced back at him. Was he really such a fool?

"All right, T.J.," said Melvin as we walked away, "we come down here like you asked. Now you come on into Strawberry with us like you promised."

"It—it didn't even make no difference," muttered T.J.

"What?" said R.W. "You comin', ain't you? You still want that pearl-handled pistol, don't you?"

"Yeah, but—"

"Then come on," he ordered, turning with Melvin and heading for the pickup.

But T.J. did not follow immediately. He remained standing in the middle of the compound, his face puzzled and undecided. I had never seen him look more desolately alone, and for a fleeting second I felt almost sorry for him.

When I reached the church steps, I looked back again. T.J. was still there, an indistinct blur blending into the gathering dusk, and I began to think that perhaps he would not go with the Simmses. But then the rude squawk of the truck's horn blasted the quiet evening, and T.J. turned his back on us and fled across the field.

11

Roll of thunder
hear my cry
Over the water
bye and bye
Ole man comin'
down the line
Whip in hand to
beat me down
But I ain't
gonna let him
Turn me 'round[1]

The night whispered of distant thunder. It was muggy, hot, a miserable night for sleeping. Twice I had awakened hoping that it was time to be up, but each time the night had been total blackness with no hint of a graying dawn. On the front porch Mr. Morrison sat singing soft and low into the long night, chanting to the approaching thunder. He had been there since the house had darkened after church, watching and waiting as he had done every night since Papa had been injured. No one had ever explained why he watched and waited, but I knew. It had to do with the Wallaces.

Mr. Morrison's song faded and I guessed he was on his way to the rear of the house. He would stay there for a while, walking on cat's feet through the quiet yard, then eventually return to the front porch again. Unable to sleep, I resigned myself to await his return by counting states. Miss Crocker had had a big thing about states, and I sometimes found that if I pretended that she was naming them off I could fall asleep. I decided to count the states geographically rather than alphabetically; that was more of a challenge. I had gotten as far west as the Dakotas when my silent recitation was disturbed by a tapping on the porch. I lay very still. Mr. Morrison never made sounds like that.

There it was again.

Cautiously, I climbed from the bed, careful not to awaken Big Ma, who was still snoring soundly, and crept to the door. I pressed my ear against the door and listened, then slipped the latch furiously and darted outside. "Boy, what you doing here?" I hissed.

"Hey, Cassie, wouldja keep it down?" whispered T.J., invisible in the darkness.

---

1. A song composed by Taylor.

Then he tapped lightly on the boys' door again, calling softly, "Hey, Stacey, come on and wake up, will ya? Let me in."

The door swung open and T.J. slipped inside. I pulled my own door closed and followed him. "I-I'm in trouble, Stacey," he said. "I mean I'm r-really in trouble."

"That ain't nothing new," I remarked.

"What you coming here for?" whispered Stacey icily. "Go get R.W. and Melvin to get you out of it."

In the darkness there was a low sob and T.J., hardly sounding like T.J., mumbled, "They the ones got me in it. Where's the bed? I gotta sit down."

In the darkness he groped for the bed, his feet dragging as if he could hardly lift them. "I ain't no bed!" I exclaimed as his hands fell on me.

There was a deep sigh. Stacey clicked on the flashlight and T.J. found the bed, sitting down slowly and holding his stomach as if he were hurt.

"What's the matter?" Stacey asked, his voice wary.

"R.W. and Melvin," whispered T.J., "they hurt me bad." He looked up, expecting sympathy. But our faces, grim behind the light Stacey held, showed no compassion. T.J.'s eyes dimmed, then, undoing the buttons to his shirt, he pulled the shirt open and stared down at his stomach.

I grimaced and shook my head at the sight. "Lord, T.J.!" Stacey exclaimed in a whisper. "What happened?"

T.J. did not answer at first, staring in horror at the deep blue-black swelling of his stomach and chest. "I think something's busted," he gasped finally. "I hurt something awful."

"Why'd they do it?" asked Stacey.

T.J. looked up into the bright light. "Help me, Stacey. Help me get home. . . . I can't make it by myself."

"Tell me how come they did this to you."

" 'Cause . . . 'cause I said I was gonna tell what happened."

Stacey and I looked at each other, then together leaned closer to T.J. "Tell what?" we asked.

T.J. gulped and leaned over, his head between his legs. "I . . . I'm sick, Stacey. I gotta get home 'fore my daddy wake up. . . . He say I stay 'way from that house one more night, he gonna put me out, and he mean it, too. He put me out, I got no place to go. You gotta help me."

"Tell us what happened."

T.J. began to cry. "But they said they'd do worse than this if I ever told!"

"Well, I ain't about to go nowhere unless I know what happened," said Stacey with finality.

T.J. searched Stacey's face in the rim of ghostly light cast by the flashlight. Then he told his story.

After he and the Simmses left Great Faith, they went directly into Strawberry to get the pearl-handled pistol, but when they arrived the mercantile was already closed. The Simmses said that there was no sense in coming back for the pistol; they would simply go in and take it. T.J. was frightened at the thought, but the Simmses assured him that there was no danger. If they were caught, they would simply say that they needed the pistol that night but intended to pay for it on Monday.

In the storage room at the back of the store was a small open window through which a child or a person as thin as T.J. could wiggle. After waiting almost an hour after the lights had gone out in the Barnetts' living quarters on the second floor, T.J. slipped through the window and opened the door, and the Simmses entered, their faces masked with stockings and their hands gloved. T.J., now afraid that they had something else in mind, wanted to leave without the pistol, but R.W. had insisted that he have it. R.W. broke the lock of the gun case with an axe and gave T.J. the much longed-for gun.

Then R.W. and Melvin went over to a wall cabinet and tried to break off the brass lock. After several unsuccessful minutes, R.W. swung the axe sharply against the lock and it gave. But as Melvin reached for the metal box inside, Mr. Barnett appeared on the stairs, a flashlight in his hand his wife behind him.

For a long moment no one moved or said a word as Mr. Barnett shone the light directly on T.J., then on R.W. and Melvin, their faces darkened by the stockings. But when Mr. Barnett saw the cabinet lock busted, he flew into frenzied action, hopping madly down the stairs and trying to grab the metal box from Melvin. They struggled, with Mr. Barnett getting the better of Melvin, until R.W. whopped Mr. Barnett solidly on the head from behind with the flat of the axe, and Mr. Barnett slumped into a heap upon the floor as if dead.

When Mrs. Barnett saw her husband fall, she dashed across the room and flailed into R.W., crying "You niggers done killed Jim Lee! You done killed him!" R.W., trying to escape her grasp, slapped at her and she fell back, hitting her head against one of the stoves, and did not move.

Once they were outside T.J. wanted to come straight home, but the Simmses said they had business to take care of and told him to wait in the back of the truck. When T.J. objected and said that he was going to tell everybody it was R.W. and Melvin who had hurt the Barnetts unless they took him home, the two of them lit into him, beating him with savage blows until he could not stand, then flung him into the back of the truck and went down the street to the pool hall. T.J. lay there for what he thought must have been an hour before crawling from the truck and starting home. About a mile outside of town, he got a ride with a farmer headed for Smellings Creek by way of Soldiers Road. Not wanting to walk past the Simmses' place for fear R.W. and Melvin had taken the Jackson Road home, he did not get out at the Jefferson Davis School Road intersection, but instead crossed Soldiers Bridge with the farmer and got out at the intersection beyond the bridge and walked around, coming from the west to our house.

"T.J., was . . . was them Barnetts dead?" asked Stacey when T.J. grew quiet.

T.J. shook his head. "I dunno. They sure looked dead. Stacey, anybody find out, you know what they'd do to me?" He stood up, his face grimacing with pain. "Stacey, help me get home," he pleaded. "I'm afraid to go there by myself. . . . R.W. and Melvin might be waitin'. . . ."

"You sure you ain't lying, T.J.?" I asked suspiciously.

"I swear everything I told y'all is the truth. I . . . I admit I lied 'bout tellin' on your mama, but I ain't lyin' now, I ain't!"

Stacey thought a moment. "Why don't you stay here tonight? Papa'll tell your daddy what happened and he won't put—"

"No!" cried T.J., his eyes big with terror. "Can't tell nobody! I gotta go!" He headed for the door, holding his side. But before he could reach it, his legs gave way and Stacey caught him and guided him back to the bed.

I studied T.J. closely under the light, sure that he was pulling another fast one. But then he coughed and blood spurted from his mouth; his eyes glazed, his face paled, and I knew that this time T.J. was not faking.

"You're bad hurt," Stacey said. "Let me get Big Ma—she'll know what to do."

T.J. shook his head weakly. "My mama . . . I'll just tell her them white boys beat me for no reason and she'll believe it . . . she'll take care of me. But you go wakin' your grandmama and your daddy'll be in it. Stacey, please! You my only friend . . . ain't never really had no true friend but you. . . ."

"Stacey?" I whispered, afraid of what he might do. As far back as I could remember, Stacey had felt a responsibility for T.J. I had never really understood why. Perhaps he felt that even a person as despicable as T.J. needed someone he could call "friend," or perhaps he sensed T.J.'s vulnerability better than T.J. did himself. "Stacey, you ain't going, are you?"

Stacey wet his lips, thinking. Then he looked at me. "You go on back to bed, Cassie. I'll be all right."

"Yeah, I know you gonna be all right 'cause I'm gonna tell Papa!" I cried, turning to dash for the other room. But Stacey reached into the darkness and caught me. "Look, Cassie, it won't take me but twenty-five or thirty minutes to run down there and back. Really, it's all right."

"You as big a fool as he is then," I accused frantically. "You don't owe him nothin', 'specially after what he done to Mama."

Stacey released me. "He's hurt bad, Cassie. I gotta get him home." He turned away from me and grabbed his pants.

I stared after him; then I said, "Well, you ain't going without me." If Stacey was going to be a fool and go running out into the night to take an even bigger fool home, the least I could do was make sure he got back in one piece.

"Cassie, you can't go—"

"Go where?" piped Little Man, sitting up. Christopher-John sat up too, yawning sleepily. "Is it morning? What y'all doing up?" Little Man questioned. He blinked into the light and rubbed his eyes. "T.J., that you? What you doing here? Where y'all going?"

"Nowhere. I'm just gonna walk T.J. home," Stacey said. "Now go on back to sleep."

Little Man jumped out of bed and pulled his clothes from the hanger where he had neatly hung them. "I'm going too," he squealed.

"Not me," said Christopher-John, lying back down again.

While Stacey attempted to put Little Man back to bed, I checked the porch to make sure that Mr. Morrison wasn't around, then slipped back to my own room to change. When I emerged again, the boys were on the porch and Christopher-John, his pants over his arm, was murmuring a strong protest against this middle-of-the-night stroll. Stacey attempted to persuade both him and Little Man back inside, but Little Man would not budge and Christopher-John, as much as he protested, would not be left behind. Finally Stacey gave up and with T.J. leaning heavily against him hurried across the lawn. The rest of us followed.

Once on the road, Christopher-John struggled into his pants and we became part of the night. Quiet, frightened, and wishing just to dump T.J. on his front porch and get back to the safety of our own beds, we hastened along the invisible road, brightened only by the round of the flashlight.

The thunder was creeping closer now, rolling angrily over the forest depths and bringing the lightning with it, as we emerged from the path into the deserted Avery yard. "W-wait till I get inside, will ya?" requested T.J.

"Ain't nobody here," I said sourly. "What you need us to wait for?"

"Go on, T.J.," said Stacey. "We'll wait."

"Th-thanks, y'all," T.J. said, then he limped to the side of the house and slipped awkwardly into his room through an open window.

"Come on, let's get out of here," said Stacey, herding us back to the path. But as we neared the forest, Little Man turned. "Hey, y'all, look over yonder! What's that?"

Beyond the Avery house bright lights appeared far away on the road near the Granger mansion. For a breathless second they lingered there, then plunged suddenly downward toward the Averys'. The first set of lights was followed by a second, then a third, until there were half a dozen sets of headlights beaming over the trail.

"Wh-what's happening?" cried Christopher-John.

For what seemed an interminable wait, we stood watching those lights drawing nearer and nearer before Stacey clicked off the flashlight and ordered us into the forest. Silently, we slipped into the brush and fell flat to the ground. Two pickups and four cars rattled into the yard, their lights focused like spotlights on the Avery front porch. Noisy, angry men leaped from the cars and surrounded the house.

Kaleb Wallace and his brother Thurston, his left arm hanging akimbo at his side, pounded the front door with their rifle butts. "Y'all come on outa there!" called Kaleb. "We want that thieving, murdering nigger of y'all's."

"St-Stacey," I stammered, feeling the same nauseous fear I had felt when the night men had passed and when Papa had come home shot and broken, "wh-what they gonna do?"

"I—I dunno," Stacey whispered as two more men joined the Wallaces at the door.

"Why, ain't . . . ain't that R.W. and Melvin?" I exclaimed. "What the devil they doing—"

Stacey quickly muffled me with the palm of his hand as Melvin thrust himself against the door in an attempt to break it open and R.W. smashed a window with his gun. At the side of the house, several men were climbing through the same window T.J. had entered only a few minutes before. Soon, the front door was flung open from the inside and Mr. and Mrs. Avery were dragged savagely by their feet from the house. The Avery girls were thrown through the open windows. The older girls, attempting to gather the younger children to them, were slapped back and spat upon. Then quiet, gentle Claude was hauled out, knocked to the ground and kicked.

"C-Claude!" whimpered Christopher-John, trying to rise. But Stacey hushed him and held him down.

"W-we gotta get help," Stacey rasped, but none of us could move. I watched the world from outside myself.

Then T.J. emerged, dragged from the house on his knees. His face was bloody and when he tried to speak he cried with pain, mumbling his words as if his jaw were broken. Mr. Avery tried to rise to get to him, but was knocked back.

"Look what we got here!" one of the men said, holding up a gun. "That pearl-handled pistol from Jim Lee's store."

"Oh, Lord," Stacey groaned. "Why didn't he get rid of that thing?"

T.J. mumbled something we could not hear and Kaleb Wallace thundered, "Stop lyin', boy, 'cause you in a whole lot of trouble. You was in there—Miz Barnett, when she come to and got help, said three black boys robbed their store and knocked out her and her husband. And R.W. and Melvin Simms seen you and them two other boys running from behind that store when they come in town to shoot some pool—"

"But it was R.W. and Melvin—" I started before Stacey clasped his hand over my mouth again.

"—Now who was them other two and where's that money y'all took?"

Whatever T.J.'s reply, it obviously was not what Kaleb Wallace wanted to hear, for he pulled his leg back and kicked T.J.'s swollen stomach with such force that T.J. emitted a cry of awful pain and fell prone upon the ground.

"Lord Jesus! Lord Jesus!" cried Mrs. Avery, wrenching herself free from the men who held her and rushing toward her son. "Don't let 'em hurt my baby no more! Kill me, Lord, but not my child!" But before she could reach T.J., she was caught by the arm and flung so ferociously against the house that she fell, dazed, and Mr. Avery, struggling to reach her, was helpless to save either her or T.J.

Christopher-John was sobbing distinctly now. "Cassie," Stacey whispered, "you take Little Man and Christopher-John and y'all—"

The headlights of two more cars appeared in the distance and Stacey immediately hushed. One of the cars halted on the Granger Road, its lights beaming aimlessly into the blackness of the cotton fields, but the lead car came crazy and fast along the rutted trail toward the Avery house, and before it had rolled to a complete stop Mr. Jamison leaped out. But once out of the car, he stood very still surveying the scene; then he stared at each of the men as if preparing to charge them in the courtroom and said softly, "Y'all decide to hold court out here tonight?"

There was an embarrassed silence. Then Kaleb Wallace spoke up. "Now look here, Mr. Jamison, don't you come messin' in this thing."

"You do," warned Thurston hotly, "we just likely to take care of ourselves a nigger lover too tonight."

An electric tenseness filled the air, but Mr. Jamison's placid face was unchanged by the threat. "Jim Lee Barnett and his wife are still alive. Y'all let the sheriff and me take the boy. Let the law decide whether or not he's guilty."

"Where's Hank?" someone asked. "I don't see no law."

"That's him up at Harlan Granger's," Mr. Jamison said with a wave of his hand over his shoulder. "He'll be down in a minute. Now leave the boy be."

"For my money, I say let's do it now," a voice cried. "Ain't no need to waste good time and money tryin' no thievin' nigger!"

A crescendo of ugly hate rose from the men as the second car approached. They grew momentarily quiet as the sheriff stepped out. The sheriff looked uneasily at the crowd as if he would rather not be here at all, then at Mr. Jamison.

"Where's Harlan?" asked Mr. Jamison.

The sheriff turned from Mr. Jamison to the crowd without answering him. Then he spoke to the men: "Mr. Granger sent word by me that he ain't gonna stand for no hanging on *his* place. He say y'all touch one hair on that boy's head while he on *this* land, he's gonna hold every man here responsible."

The men took the news in grim silence.

Then Kaleb Wallace cried: "Then why don't we go somewhere else? I say what we oughta do is take him on down the road and take care of that big black giant of a nigger at the same time!"

"And why not that boy he working for too?" yelled Thurston.

"Stacey!" I gasped.

"Hush!"

A welling affirmation rose from the men. "I got me three new ropes!" exclaimed Kaleb.

"New? How come you wanna waste a new rope on a nigger?" asked Melvin Simms.

"Big as that one nigger is, an old one might break!"

There was chilling laughter and the men moved toward their cars, dragging T.J. with them.

"No!" cried Mr. Jamison, rushing to shield T.J. with his own body.

"Cassie," Stacey whispered hoarsely, "Cassie, you gotta get Papa now. Tell him what happened. I don't think Mr. Jamison can hold them—"

"You come too."

"No, I'll wait here."

"I ain't going without you!" I declared, afraid that he would do something stupid like trying to rescue T.J. alone.

"Look, Cassie, go on, will ya please? Papa'll know what to do. Somebody's gotta stay here case they take T.J. off into the woods somewhere. I'll be all right."

"Well . . ."

"Please, Cassie? Trust me, will ya?"

I hesitated. "Y-you promise you won't go down there by yourself?"

"Yeah, I promise. Just get Papa and Mr. Morrison 'fore they—'fore they hurt them some more." He placed the unlit flashlight in my hand and pushed me up. Clutching Little Man's hand, I told him to grab Christopher-John's, and together the three of us picked our way along the black path, afraid to turn on the flashlight for fear of its light being seen.

Thunder crashed against the corners of the world and lightning split the sky as we reached the road, but we did not stop. We dared not. We had to reach Papa.

12

When we neared the house, the dull glow of a kerosene lamp was shining faintly from the boys' room. "Y-you s'pose they already know?" Christopher-John asked breathlessly as we ran up the lawn. "Dunno 'bout that," I said, "but they know we ain't where we s'pose to be."

We ran noisily up onto the porch and flung open the unlatched door. Mama and Big Ma, standing with Mr. Morrison near the foot of the bed, turned as we entered and Big Ma cried, "Lord, there they is!"

"Where have you been?" Mama demanded, her face strangely stricken. "What do you mean running around out there this time of night?"

Before we could answer either question, Papa appeared in the doorway, dressed, his wide leather strap in hand.

"Papa—" I began.

"Where's Stacey?"

"He-he down to T.J.'s Papa—"

"That boy's gotten mighty grown," Papa said, clearly angry. "I'm gonna teach all of y'all 'bout traipsing off in the middle of the night . . . and especially Stacey. He should know better. If Mr. Morrison hadn't seen this door open, I suppose you would've thought you was getting away with something—like T.J. Well, y'all gonna learn right here and now there ain't gonna be no T.J.s in this house—"

"But, Papa, they h-hurt Claude!" Christopher-John cried, tears streaming down his cheeks for his injured friend.

"And T.J., too," echoed Little Man, trembling.

"What?" Papa asked, his eyes narrowing. "What y'all talking 'bout?"

"Papa, they hurt 'em real bad and . . . and . . ." I could not finish. Papa came to me and took my face in his hands. "What is it, Cassie girl? Tell me."

Everything. I poured out everything. About T.J.'s breaking into the mercantile with the Simmses, about his coming in the night fleeing the Simmses, about the coming of the men and what they had done to the Averys. About Mr. Jamison and the threat of the men to come to the house to get him and Mr. Morrison.

"And Stacey's still down there?" Papa asked when I had finished.

"Yessir. But he hid in the forest. They don't know he's there."

Papa spun around suddenly. "Gotta get him out of there," he said, moving quicker than I had thought possible with his bad leg. Mama followed him into their room, and the boys and I followed her. From over the bed Papa pulled his shotgun.

"David, not with the shotgun. You can't stop them like that."

"Got no other way," he said, stuffing a box of shells into his shirt pocket.

"You fire on them and they'll hang you for sure. They'd like nothing better."

"If I don't, they'll hang T.J. This thing's been coming a long time, baby, and T.J. just happened to be the one foolish enough to trigger it. But, fool or not, I can't just sit by and let them kill the boy. And if they find Stacey—"

"I know, David, I know. But there's got to be another way. Some way they won't kill you too!"

"Seems like they might be planning to do that anyway," Papa said, turning from her. "They come here, no telling what'll happen, and I'll use every bullet I got 'fore I let them hurt anybody in this house."

Mama grabbed his arm. "Get Harlan Granger to stop it. If he says so, they'll go on home."

Papa shook his head. "Them cars had to come right past his house to get to the Averys', and if he'd intended to stop them, he'd stop them without me telling him so."

"Then," said Mama, "force him to stop it."

"How?" asked Papa dryly. "Hold a gun to his head?" He left her then, going back into the boys' room. "You coming, Mr. Morrison?"

Mr. Morrison nodded and followed Papa onto the porch, a rifle in his hand. Like a cat Mama sprang after them and grabbed Papa again. "David, don't . . . don't use the gun."

Papa stared out as a bolt of lightning splintered the night into a dazzling brilliance. The wind was blowing softly, gently toward the east. "Perhaps . . ." he started, then was quiet.

"David?"

Papa touched Mama's face tenderly with the tips of his fingers and said, "I'll do what I have to do, Mary . . . and so will you." Then he turned from her, and with Mr. Morrison disappeared into the night.

Mama pushed us back into her room, where Big Ma fell upon her knees and prayed a powerful prayer. Afterward both Mama and Big Ma changed their clothes, then we sat, very quiet, as the heat crept sticky and wet through our clothing and the thunder banged menacingly overhead. Mama, her knuckles tight against her skin as she gripped the arms of her chair, looked down upon Christopher-John, Little Man, and me, our eyes wide awake with fear. "I don't suppose it would do any good to put you to bed," she said quietly. We looked up at her. She did not mean to have an answer; we gave none, and nothing else was said as the night minutes crept past and the waiting pressed as heavily upon us as the heat.

Then Mama stiffened. She sniffed the air and got up.

"What is it, child?" Big Ma asked.

"You smell smoke?" Mama said, going to the front door and opening it. Little Man, Christopher-John, and I followed, peeping around her in the doorway. From deep in the field where the land sloped upward toward the Granger forest, a fire billowed, carried eastward by the wind.

"Mama, the cotton!" I cried. "It's on fire!"

"Oh, good Lord!" Big Ma exclaimed, hurrying to join us. "That lightning done that!"

"If it reaches those trees, it'll burn everything from here to Strawberry," Mama said. She turned quickly and ran across the room to the side door. "Stay here," she ordered, opening the door and fleeing across the yard to the barn. "Mama, you'd better get some water!" she yelled over her shoulder.

Big Ma hurried into the kitchen with Christopher-John, Little Man, and me at her heels. "What we gonna do, Big Ma?" I asked.

Big Ma stepped onto the back porch and brought in the washtub and began filling it with water. "We gotta fight that fire and try and stop it 'fore it reach them trees. Stand back now out the way so y'all don't get wet."

In a few minutes Mama returned, her arms loaded with sacks of burlap. She quickly threw the sacks into the water and ran back out again. When she returned, she carried two shovels and several more sacks.

"Mama, what you gonna do with all that?" asked Little Man.

"It's for fighting the fire," she replied hastily.

"Oh," said Little Man, grabbing for one of the shovels as I started to take the other.

"No," Mama said. "You're going to stay here."

Big Ma straightened from where she was bent dunking the sacks into the water. "Mary, child, you don't think it'd be better to take them with us?"

Mama studied us closely and bit her lower lip. She was silent for several moments, then she shook her head. "Can't anyone get to the house from the Grangers' without our seeing them. I'd rather they stay here than risk them near the fire."

Then she charged each of us, a strange glint in her eyes. "Cassie, Christopher-John, Clayton Chester, hear me good. I don't want you near that fire. You set one foot from this house and I'm going to skin you alive . . . do you hear me now?"

We nodded solemnly. "Yes ma'am, Mama."

"And stay inside. That lightning's dangerous."

"B-but, Mama," cried Christopher-John, "y'all going out there in that lightning!"

"It can't be helped, baby," she said. "The fire's got to be stopped."

Then she and Big Ma laid the shovels across the top of the tub and each took a handle of it. As they stepped out the back door, Mama looked back at us, her eyes uncertain, as if she did not want to leave us. "Y'all be sure to mind now," ordered Big Ma gruffly, and the two of them carrying the heavy tub crossed the yard toward the garden. From the garden they would cut through the south pasture and up to where the cotton blazed. We watched until they were swallowed by the blackness that lay between the house and the fire, then dashed back to the front porch where the view was clearer. There we gazed transfixed as the flames gobbled the cotton and crept dangerously near the forest edge.

"Th-that fire, Cassie," said Christopher-John, "it gonna burn us up?"

"No . . . it's going the other way. Toward the forest."

"Then it's gonna burn up the trees," said Christopher-John sadly.

Little Man tugged at my arm. "Papa and Stacey and Mr. Morrison, Cassie! They in them trees!" Then iron-willed Little Man began to cry. And Christopher-John too. And the three of us huddled together, all alone.

"Hey, y'all all right?"

I gazed out into the night, seeing nothing but the gray smoke and the red rim of the fire in the east. "Who's that?"

"It's me," said Jeremy Simms, running up the lawn.

"Jeremy, what you doing out this time of night?" I questioned, taken aback to see him.

"It ain't night no more, Cassie. It's near dawn."

"But what you doing here?" repeated Little Man with a sniffle.

"I was sleepin' up in my tree like I always do—"

"On a night like this?" I exclaimed. "Boy, you *are* crazy!"

Jeremy looked rather shamefaced, and shrugged. "Well, anyway, I was and I smelled smoke. I knew it was comin' from thisaway and I was 'fraid it was y'all's place, so I run in and told my pa, and him and me we come on up here over an hour ago."

"You mean you been out there fighting that fire?"

Jeremy nodded. "My pa, and R.W. and Melvin too."

"R.W. and Melvin?" Little Man, Christopher-John, and I exclaimed together.

"But they was—" I poked Christopher-John into silence.

"Yeah, they got there 'fore us. And there's a whole lot of men from the town out there too." He looked puzzled. "I wonder what they all was doin' out here?"

"How bad is it?" I asked, ignoring his wonderings. "It get much of the cotton?"

Jeremy nodded absently. "Funny thing. That fire come up from that lightning and struck one of them wooden fence posts, I reckon, and sparked that cotton. Must've burned a good quarter of it. . . . Y'all lucky it ain't headed this way."

"But the trees," said Christopher-John. "It gonna get the trees, ain't it?"

Jeremy looked out across the field, shielding his eyes against the brilliance of the fire. "They tryin' like everything to stop it. Your papa and Mr. Granger, they got—"

"Papa? You seen Papa? He all right?" cried Christopher-John breathlessly.

Jeremy nodded, looking down at him strangely. "Yeah, he's fine—"

"And Stacey, you seen him?" inquired Little Man.

Again, Jeremy nodded. "Yeah, he out there too."

Little Man, Christopher-John, and I glanced at each other, relieved just a bit, and Jeremy went on, though eyeing us somewhat suspiciously. "Your papa and Mr. Granger, they got them men diggin' a deep trench 'cross that slope and they say they gonna burn that pasture grass from the trench back to the cotton—"

"You think that'll stop it?" I asked.

Jeremy stared blankly at the fire and shook his head. "Dunno," he said finally. "Sure hope so, though." There was a violent clap of thunder, and lightning flooded the field. "One thing would sure help though is if that ole rain would only come on down."

All four of us looked up at the sky and waited a minute for the rain to fall. When nothing happened, Jeremy turned and sighed. "I better be gettin' back now. Miz Logan said she left y'all here so I just come to see 'bout ya." Then he ran down the slope, waving back at us as he went. When he got to the road, he stopped suddenly and stood very still; then he put out his hands, hesitated a moment, and spun around wildly as if he were mad.

"It's rainin', y'all!" he cried. "That ole rain a-comin' down!"

Little Man, Christopher-John, and I jumped from the porch and ran barefooted onto the lawn, feeling the rain fine and cool upon our faces. And we laughed, whooping joyously into the thundering night, forgetting for the moment that we still did not know what had happened to T.J.

When the dawn came peeping yellow-gray and sooted over the horizon, the fire was out and the thunderstorm had shifted eastward after an hour of heavy rain. I stood up stiffly, my eyes tearing from the acrid smoke, and looked out across the cotton to the slope, barely visible in the smoggish dawn. Near the slope where once cotton stalks had stood, their brown bolls popping with tiny puffs of cotton, the land was charred, desolate, black, still steaming from the night.

I wanted to go and take a closer look, but for once Christopher-John would not budge. "No!" he repeated over and over. "I ain't going!"

"But what Mama *meant* was that she didn't want us near the fire, and it's out now."

Christopher-John set his lips firmly together, folded his plump arms across his chest and was adamant. When I saw that he would not be persuaded, I gazed again at the field and decided that I could not wait any longer. "Okay, you stay here then. We'll be right back." Ignoring his protests, Little Man and I ran down to the wet road.

"He really ain't coming," said Little Man, amazed, looking back over his shoulder.

"I guess not," I said, searching for signs of the fire in the cotton. Farther up the road the stalks were singed, and the fine gray ash of the fire lay thick upon them and the road and the forest trees.

When we reached the burnt-out section of the field, we surveyed the destruction. As far as we could see, the fire line had extended midway up the slope, but had been stopped at the trench. The old oak was untouched. Moving across the field, slowly, mechanically, as if sleepwalking, was a flood of men and women dumping shovels of dirt on fire patches which refused to die. They wore wide handkerchiefs over their faces and many wore hats, making it difficult to identify who was who, but it was obvious that the ranks of the fire fighters had swelled from the two dozen townsmen to include nearby farmers. I recognized Mr. Lanier by his floppy blue hat working side by side with Mr. Simms, each oblivious of the other, and Papa near the slope waving orders to two of the townsmen. Mr. Granger, hammering down smoldering stalks with the flat of his shovel, was near the south pasture where Mr. Morrison and Mama were swatting the burning ground.

Nearer the fence a stocky man, masked like the others, searched the field in robot fashion for hidden fire under the charred skeletons of broken stalks. When he reached the fence, he leaned tiredly against it, taking off his handkerchief to wipe the sweat and soot from his face. He coughed and looked around blankly. His eyes fell on Little Man and me staring up at him. But Kaleb Wallace seemed not to recognize us, and after a moment he picked up his shovel and started back toward the slope without a word.

Then Little Man nudged me. "Look over there, Cassie. There go Mama and Big Ma!" I followed his pointing finger. Mama and Big Ma were headed home across the field.

"Come on," I said, sprinting back up the road.

When we reached the house, we dragged our feet across the wet lawn to clean them and rejoined Christopher-John on the porch. He looked a bit frightened sitting there all alone and was obviously glad we were back. "Y'all all right?" he asked.

"Course we're all right," I said, plopping on the porch and trying to catch my breath. "What'd it look like?"

Before either Little Man or I could answer, Mama and Big Ma emerged from the field with Stacey, the sacks now blackened remnants in their hands. We ran to them eagerly.

"Stacey, you all right?" I cried. "What 'bout T.J.?"

"And C-Claude?" stammered Christopher-John.

And Little Man asked, "Papa and Mr. Morrison, ain't they coming?"

Mama held up her hand wearily. "Babies! Babies!" Then she put her arm around Christopher-John. "Claude's fine, honey. And," she said, looking down at Little Man, "Papa and Mr. Morrison, they'll be coming soon."

"But T.J., Mama," I persisted. "What 'bout T.J.?"

Mama sighed and sat down on the steps, laying the sacks on the ground. The boys and I sat beside her.

"I'm gonna go on in and change, Mary," Big Ma said, climbing the steps and opening our bedroom door. "Miz Fannie gonna need somebody."

Mama nodded. "Tell her I'll be down soon as I get the children to bed and things straightened out here." Then she turned and looked down at Little Man, Christopher-John, and me, eager to know what had happened. She smiled slightly, but there was no happiness in it. "T.J.'s all right. The sheriff and Mr. Jamison took him into Strawberry."

"But why, Mama?" asked Little Man. "He done something bad?"

"They think he did, baby. They think he did."

"Then—then they didn't hurt him no more?" I asked.

Stacey looked across at Mama to see if she intended to answer; then, his voice hollow and strained, he said, "Mr. Granger stopped them and sent them up to fight the fire."

I sensed that there was more, but before I could ask what, Christopher-John piped, "And—and Papa and Mr. Morrison, they didn't have to fight them ole men? They didn't have to use the guns?"

"Thank the Lord, no," said Mama. "They didn't."

"The fire come up," said Stacey, "and Mr. Morrison come and got me and then them men come down here to fight the fire and didn't nobody have to fight nobody."

"Mr. Morrison come get you alone?" I asked, puzzled. "Where was Papa?"

Stacey again looked at Mama and for a moment they both were silent. Then Stacey said, "Y'all know he couldn't make that slope with that bad leg of his."

I looked at him suspiciously. I had seen Papa move on that leg. He could have made the slope if he wanted to.

"All right now," Mama said, rising. "It's been a long, tiring night and it's time you all were in bed."

I reached for her arm. "Mama, how bad is it really? I mean, is there enough cotton left to pay the taxes?"

Mama looked at me oddly. "Since when did you start worrying about taxes?" I shrugged, then leaned closer toward her, wanting an answer, yet afraid to hear it. "The taxes will get paid, don't you worry," was all the answer she gave. "Now, let's get to bed."

"But I wanna wait for Papa and Mr. Morrison!" protested Little Man.

"Me too!" yawned Christopher-John.

"Inside!"

All of us went in but Stacey, and Mama did not make him. But as soon as she had disappeared into the boys' room to make sure Little Man and Christopher-John got to bed, I returned to the porch and sat beside him. "I thought you went to bed," he said.

"I wanna know what happened over there."

"I told you, Mr. Granger—"

"I come and got Papa and Mr. Morrison like you asked," I reminded him. "Now I wanna know everything happened after I left."

Stacey sighed and rubbed his left temple absently, as if his head were hurting. "Ain't much happened 'cepting Mr. Jamison tried talking to them men some more, and after a bit they pushed him out the way and stuffed T.J. into one of their cars.

But Mr. Jamison, he jumped into his car and lit out ahead of them and drove up to Mr. Granger's and swung his car smack across the road so couldn't nobody get past him. Then he starts laying on his horn.

"You go over there?"

He nodded. "By the time I got 'cross the field to where I could hear what was going on, Mr. Granger was standing on his porch and Mr. Jamison was telling him that the sheriff or nobody else was 'bout to stop a hanging on that flimsy message he'd sent up to the Averys'. But Mr. Granger, he just stood there on his porch looking sleepy and bored, and finally he told the sheriff, 'Hank, you take care of this. That's what folks elected you for.'

"Then Kaleb Wallace, he leaps out of his car and tries to grab Mr. Jamison's keys. But Mr. Jamison threw them keys right into Mrs. Granger's flower bed and couldn't nobody find them, so Melvin and R.W. come up and pushed Mr. Jamison's car off the road. Then them cars was 'bout to take off again when Mr. Granger comes running off the porch hollering like he's lost his mind. 'There's smoke coming from my forest yonder!' he yells. 'Dry as that timber is, a fire catch hold it won't stop burning for a week. Give that boy to Wade like he wants and get on up there!' And folks started running all over the place for shovels and things, then all of them cut back down the road to the Averys' and through them woods over to our place."

"And that's when Mr. Morrison come got you?"

Stacey nodded. "He found me when I followed them men back up to the woods."

I sat very still, listening to the soft sounds of the early morning, my eyes on the field. There was something which I still did not understand.

Stacey nodded toward the road. "Here come Papa and Mr. Morrison." They were walking with slow, exhausted steps toward the drive.

The two of us ran down the lawn, but before we reached the road a car approached and stopped directly behind them. Mr. Jamison was driving. Stacey and I stood curiously on the lawn, far enough away not to be noticed, but close enough to hear.

"David, I thought you should know . . ." said Mr. Jamison. "I just come from Strawberry to see the Averys—"

"How bad is it?"

Mr. Jamison stared straight out at the road. "Jim Lee Barnett . . . he died at four o'clock this morning."

Papa hit the roof of the car hard with his clenched fist and turned toward the field, his head bowed.

For a long, long minute, none of the men spoke; then Mr. Morrison said softly, "The boy, how is he?"

"Doc Crandon says he's got a couple of broken ribs and his jaw's broken, but he'll be all right . . . for now. I'm going to his folks to tell them and take them to town. Just thought I'd tell you first."

Papa said, "I'll go in with them."

Mr. Jamison pulled off his hat and ran his fingers through his hair, damp against his forehead. Then, squinting, he looked over his shoulder at the field. "Folks thinking," he said slowly, as if he did not want to say what he was about to say, "folks thinking that lightning struck that fence of yours and started the fire. . . ." He pulled at his ear. "It's better, I think, that you stay clear of this whole thing now, David, and don't give anybody cause to think about you at all, except that you got what was coming to you by losing a quarter of your cotton. . . ."

There was a cautious silence as he gazed up at Papa and Mr. Morrison, their faces set in grim, tired lines. ". . . Or somebody might just get to wondering about that fire. . . ."

"Stacey," I whispered, "what's he talking 'bout?"

"Hush, Cassie," Stacey said, his eyes intent on the men.

"But I wanna know—"

Stacey looked around at me sharply, his face drawn, his eyes anxious, and without even a murmur from him I suddenly did know. I knew why Mr. Morrison had come for him alone. Why Mr. Jamison was afraid for Papa to go into town. Papa had found a way, as Mama had asked, to make Mr. Granger stop the hanging: He had started the fire.

And it came to me that this was one of those known and unknown things, something never to be spoken, not even to each other. I glanced at Stacey, and he saw in my eyes that I knew, and understood the meaning of what I knew, and he said simply, "Mr. Jamison's going now."

Mr. Jamison turned around in the driveway and headed back toward the Averys'. Papa and Mr. Morrison watched him leave, then Mr. Morrison walked silently up the drive to do the morning chores and Papa, noticing us for the first time, stared down at us, his eyes bloodshot and unsmiling. "I thought y'all would've been in bed by now," he said.

"Papa," Stacey whispered hoarsely, "what's gonna happen to T.J. now?"

Papa looked out at the climbing sun, a round, red shadow behind the smoggish heat. He didn't answer immediately, and it seemed as if he were debating whether or not he should. Finally, very slowly, he looked down, first at me, then at Stacey. He said quietly, "He's in jail right now."

"And—and what then?" asked Stacey.

Papa studied us. "He could possibly go on the chain gang. . . ."

"Papa, could he . . . could he die?" asked Stacey, hardly breathing.

"Son—"

"Papa, could he?"

Papa put a strong hand on each of us and watched us closely. "I ain't never lied to y'all, y'all know that."

"Yessir."

He waited, his eyes on us. "Well, I . . . I wish I could lie to y'all now."

"No! Oh, Papa, no!" I cried. "They wouldn't do that to ole T.J.! He can talk his way outa just 'bout anything! Besides, he ain't done nothing *that* bad. It was them Simmses! Tell them that!"

Stacey, shaking his head, backed away, silent, not wanting to believe, but believing still. His eyes filled with heavy tears, then he turned and fled down the lawn and across the road into the shelter of the forest.

Papa stared after him, holding me tightly to him. "Oh, P-Papa, d-does it have to be?"

Papa tilted my chin and gazed softly down at me. "All I can say, Cassie girl . . . is that it shouldn't be." Then, glancing back toward the forest, he took my hand and led me to the house.

Mama was waiting for us as we climbed the steps, her face wan and strained. Little Man and Christopher-John were already in bed, and after Mama had felt my forehead and asked if I was all right she sent me to bed too. Big Ma had already gone to the Averys' and I climbed into bed alone. A few minutes later both Mama and Papa came to tuck me in, talking softly in fragile, gentle words that seemed about to break. Their presence softened the hurt and I did not cry. But after they had left and I saw Papa through the open window disappear into the forest after Stacey, the tears began to run fast and heavy down my cheeks.

In the afternoon when I awakened, or tomorrow or the next day, the boys and I would still be free to run the red road, to wander through the old forest and sprawl lazily on the banks of the pond. Come October, we would trudge to school as always, barefooted and grumbling, fighting the dust and the mud and the Jefferson Davis school bus. But T.J. never would again.

I had never liked T.J., but he had always been there, a part of me, a part of my life, just like the mud and the rain, and I had thought that he always would be. Yet the mud and the rain and the dust would all pass. I knew and understood that. What had happened to T.J. in the night I did not understand, but I knew that it would not pass. And I cried for those things which had happened in the night and would not pass.

I cried for T.J. For T.J. and the land.

1976

BRUCE BROOKS
b. 1950

Bruce Brooks does not write books *for* children and young adults. Rather, as he explained in a 1990 interview for *Publishers Weekly*, he writes for "intelligent people. I write *about* kids because my own childhood is still something that I am very much wondering about." Brooks's award-winning books confront the pain that can be caused when adults fail to parent appropriately, whether by falling victim to an illness such as alcoholism or by abusing or abandoning children. Brooks's own childhood was defined, in part, by his constant moves between his divorced parents. As the southern kid in the North and the Yankee kid in the South, Brooks found that he never fit in completely, whether with his father in Washington, D.C., or his mother in North Carolina. This awareness of difference, and especially of a difference that kept changing, may have been one thing that led Brooks to become, as he once wrote, "very watchful."

That watchfulness served him well as he explored his interest in writing. After graduating from the University of North Carolina at Chapel Hill in 1972, he supported himself by working as a printer and journalist, but he continued to write fiction. In 1978, he married Penelope Winslow; in the late 1970s he attended the Iowa Writer's Workshop,

earning his M.F.A. in 1982. He drew on his own childhood observations of racial relations in the South in his first book, *The Moves Make the Man* (1984). The African American boy who narrates the story attempts to help a white boy, unhappy because his mother has suffered a nervous breakdown and his stepfather is abusive, by teaching him basketball. The novel garnered much praise and many awards, including being named a Newbery Honor book. By then, Brooks's family included a young son; but the novel's success persuaded him to take the risk of becoming a full-time writer.

Brooks has published more than thirty books, acclaimed for their intelligence and humor. They include several volumes on nature; a collection of essays, *Boys Will Be* (1993), which one reviewer called "part parenting book for fathers, part self-help book for boys"; and the Wolfbay Wings series of books aimed at nine- to twelve-year-old readers, in which Brooks combines his love of ice hockey with thoughtful depiction of each team member. Though the excellence of his writing about sports is generally acknowledged, the backgrounds of his complex and challenging novels for young adults vary widely. For example, *Midnight Hour Encores* (1986) concerns a cello prodigy, her father, and the mother she meets only when she is sixteen; *No Kidding* (1989) is set in an imagined twenty-first-century Washington, D.C., in which most people are alcoholic; and in *Vanishing* (1999), two eleven-year-olds—one dying from cancer, the other escaping her unhappy home life by refusing to eat—share a hospital room.

What Hearts (1992) is a collection of four linked short stories, each focused on a momentous occasion in the protagonist's life. The reader shares Asa's thoughts as a seven-year-old, when his mother remarries and takes him from the home he had known; at age twelve, when he falls in love; during a long, fierce, yet subtle conflict with his stepfather, Dave; and, finally, during their departure from Dave as he and his mother begin a new life, yet again. According to Brooks, it is the most autobiographical of his books, and it won him a second Newbery Honor award. In the story "Out," Asa's negotiations of the tensions within his family—his mother is brittle but loving, and his stepfather is inscrutable and sometimes cruel—bring him pain and reflect a maturity seemingly beyond his years. Yet Brooks cautions his readers not to insist on a wide separation between child and adult; by so doing, he believes, we misunderstand and misremember childhood and do a disservice to children: "What I discovered, by finding it so natural to write in the voice of a thirteen-year-old kid, was that we are missing more than we think. By investing in this illusion of distance, we not only push away and forget the moments of awkwardness, we also push away and forget a lot of insight, intelligence, and sensitivity."

Out

1

The dew was falling. Asa frowned and scuffed the grass with his right foot. In twenty minutes it would be slick as wet tile. He sighed. This was the peril of playing in the second game of the evening: the dew always fell.

Far away at home plate, the batter swung. Asa jumped as he always did when the ball sprang off the bat. This time it was not sailing to him in center field; it lifted straight up in front of home plate. Asa kept moving anyway, his feet keeping pace with the choices his intuition made. He watched the catcher, looking straight up, spin and stagger in a rough circle as the ball peaked and began to drop. Asa trotted low and quiet along a curved shadow that ran between left and center, where the pools of light from the high spots did not quite meet.

The ball came down just as the catcher, in mid-step, was recovering from a dizzy half turn, two feet inside the first baseline. The ball glanced off the heel of his mitt like a waterfall off a rock. The kid who had hit it and run looked back as he rounded first. He hesitated a second while the catcher whirled his head around in confusion, looking for the ball the way a dog does when someone stands on it for a joke; then the runner lit out for second. The catcher found the ball, looked up, saw the runner, and, swaddled by his heavy gear and strained by his panic at the infielders' screams, unleashed a wild throw that disappeared into the black sky fifteen feet over the shortstop's head. The runner, grinning, kept right on running, around second, lightly and surely for third.

Forty feet beyond the shortstop, however, stood Asa, unnoticed. He hollered the third baseman's name, calmly caught the catcher's wild ball on the fly, turned, and fired it—tamed and orderly now—on one hop to third. The third baseman, alerted by the holler, caught it and neatly tagged the runner, who was so surprised by the sight of the ball arriving in front of him that he went into his slide six feet early and never even reached the base.

The umpire jerked his hand. The runner howled. Infielders strutted, slapped hands. The catcher, standing tall, jutted his jaw, jammed his mask on with a warning glare at the next batter, as if to say he hoped the kid had watched carefully and learned not to try to fox *him* with any twisty pop-ups. Asa trotted back to his position in center. Inside, his sense of right and wrong registered once again the justness of baseball: it was too fine a game to allow a triple off a dippy pop five feet from home plate.

The grass was wet now. Asa had to straighten his knees and jog on his heels, more upright, slower. He hated slowing down. Asa liked a challenge, but a dew slick was not a challenge. A challenge allowed solutions without sacrifices; adjustments, yes, but not sacrifices. Sacrificing speed was cheap and easy. *Anyone* could slow down.

The third batter of the inning swung too hard at an inside pitch and dribbled a grounder to the second baseman, who bobbled it but had plenty of time to throw it in the direction of first. The first baseman caught it, looked around for the bag, and stomped on it an instant before the runner arrived. Three outs. Time to bat.

Asa knew he batted fourth this inning; he could get his cuts if one of his teammates got on base. This, he also knew, was unlikely. It was equally unlikely that *he* would reach base when *his* turn came. The Quik-E-Freeze Cool Guys had not scored a single run in the first four games of the season.

Asa watched the boys assemble on the bench, rowdy and happy in relief that another spell amidst the mysteries of defense had somehow been brought to an end. For them, playing in the field was a bad dream—fielding frantic grounders that seemed to pick up speed as they kicked closer, and fly balls that vanished on the way up, only to reappear suddenly coming fast as cars; remembering which base to throw to when there was one out instead of two, or two on base instead of three. They tried to survive until the moment when three outs had miraculously accumulated, then— hooray!—it was off to the dugout to jostle and laugh and spray insect repellent in each other's ears until Coach told you were on deck.

Mack and Jeff, who Asa knew were scheduled to bat first and second this inning, sat along with the rest, waiting without a clue. Only Tim, the third baseman, up third, seemed to know his spot: his batting helmet was already on.

"Mack up, Jeff on deck, Timmy in the hole," said Coach Henderson. The boys scrambled eagerly. Asa listened for the slightest sound of disappointment in the coach's voice, but there was nothing but warmth and ease. He never seemed to expect them to keep up with the game. Watching him, you would think he barely paid attention himself: he seemed committed more to making the kids all feel good than to building a ball team.

Mack hit a line drive back to the pitcher. This boy, whose height and clear jawline revealed he was nearer 13 than 12 (the league's upper age limit), ducked and stuck up his mitt sideways without taking the extra second to try to open it for a catch. The ball caromed off the glove to the shortstop, who threw Mack out.

"Good hustle," said Coach Henderson as Mack returned, full of pep, no regrets, happy with the feel of the decent smack he had given the ball. Jeff stood in and the coach clapped. "Little bingle,[1] Jefferoo." Inspired, Jeff swung early at three high pitches in a row. Out two.

"Good cuts," said the coach.

"Yeah," said Jeff, eyes aglow. "I almost *fouled* that second one!"

---

1. Base hit.

"Attaboy." The coach and Asa watched Tim move out to the plate. Asa waited a moment, then stepped over to the on-deck circle.

He loved being on deck. He loved swinging two bats in a leisurely, patient way, as if this were all there was to it, lulling his arms to stretch and strengthen to handle the big weight. It was a trick, of course. When he went to the plate with only one bat and clicked into the quick intensity of the swing, his arms would find they were able to whip the wood around as if it were a hickory switch. It always worked: his arms never learned. This was a miracle to him—one part of him could remain innocent while another knew perfectly well what was happening.

He was delighted. All of this made him feel mysterious to himself, capable of doing things he could not foresee, with a power that reversed the usual cycle of observation, analysis, understanding, practice, action. *This* power came from *not* knowing, *not* understanding.

Tim took a couple of high ones, then scythed at a low pitch. The ball looped high over first and landed halfway out to right field, just on the line. The right fielder charged hard, scooped it up, and cocked his arm; but instead of firing a throw by instinct, he looked up at Tim rounding first. Tim was ready with a scowl that gave the fielder just a moment's uncertainty, and by the time the boy recovered, his throw was too late to beat Tim.

Good. Runner in scoring position. Asa clapped. He liked the way Tim played offense (though he was careless and impatient with his mitt on); now they might actually score a run, against all odds. The other team, Table Talk Bakery, was one of the best in the league. Their last game against Asa's team had ended 9-0, even with the Table Talk scrubs playing the final three innings.

Asa walked to the plate and took his stance. The Table Talk catcher, an ebullient All-Star named James Neal, chattered at him with a stream of good-natured taunts that were taunts nonetheless.

Asa ignored him and began what he called his "checkup," going over his positioning limb by limb, using a special perception trick: he pretended he was his stepfather in the stands behind home plate. His stepfather *was* there, along with his mother; Asa knew this, though he never looked up at them during a game. And Asa knew his stepfather was scrutinizing his every move, holding the set of each elbow or eye against the technically determined ideal adopted when they practiced together. Dave knew *everything* about baseball, and was a patient, precise teacher. If Asa bent his knees too little, sat back on his heels too much, moved his head during the swing, or failed to roll his wrists all the way in his follow-through, he would hear about it next time they took the field together.

Now he was ready. The pitcher, looking bored, flipped a pitch that caught the outside corner in a hurry. His next one was in the dirt in front of the plate, and his third was high. Asa hated batting against a pitcher who wasn't taking the job seriously: it was impossible to fox someone who had no strategy. He stepped out of the batter's box, took a practice swing to refocus, then stepped back in. The pitcher, impatient, threw quickly.

The ball flicked toward the plate, and without deciding to swing Asa swung—it just looked like a good one. He hit it flush and it flew away. As he dropped the bat and ran, excitement fluttered in his chest. The ball soared high over center field; he willed it to keep going away, not to peak, not to begin its fall. He had never hit a home run; he had never hit a ball this hard. But as he touched first and watched, the ball faltered in its flight. He knew it would stay in the park—his center fielder's eye would not deceive him, no matter what his hopes. He kept running dutifully, in case of an error, but the excitement turned to a sigh. The outfielder, running back, slowed, turned, reached up, and caught the ball snugly. Asa, too, slowed down and stopped. He could hit okay, but he was small. Talent and technique could not create power.

2

When they moved into the big two-story house, Dave did not seem to want to let Asa have one of the two second-floor bedrooms to himself. The master bedroom, with its own bathroom, was on the first floor, in the rear of the house; the room that seemed logical for Asa was in the front of the second floor, over the living room. It was a nice room, with three dormer windows, a peaked ceiling, and a walk-in closet. Asa gravitated toward it as if he had been born there. But then, he was getting to be pretty quick about finding his spot in a new house: this was his tenth move and he was barely eleven.

On the day they moved in—the first time Asa saw the place—he raced up the stairs with the large box containing his comic-book collection, which he had carried on his lap from their old house. Dave grumbled, "Not so fast now," and Asa froze on the landing.

"What's the matter?" Asa's mother asked. Asa heard in her voice something warning, dangerous, tired.

Dave said, "Well, I don't know that the boy should have that room."

"And why not?"

For the first time Dave noticed the dangerous tone. He looked at her and frowned. "Well, it's a big room. An awfully nice room."

"Ah," she said, nodding. "*Too* nice, you mean. For him to just *get*."

"Well—"

"He should have to go through some hardship first, or something. Have to share it, maybe—the way you did, of course, with your two brothers." She made a show of looking around earnestly. "Trouble is, see, there are no other kids."

Dave cocked his head to the side and pushed his chin out a smidgeon, a sign that he was just about to be inclined to begin to get a little tough. "Now, be careful."

"And," said Asa's mother, "as for hardships—well, it's a bit late to come up with some task to make him earn the right to a room in our house, since we're moving in right now and all, but maybe we can think of something. What could we have him do? We don't want anything to be too *easy* for him, do we? Got to keep it *rugged*. Let's see—he could refinish the floors up there. We said they needed it. How about that?"

"Look—"

"No? Well, how about he slates the roof? Too wet today. Besides, we really don't want it to be some simple one-time job, do we? To get yourself a nice room, you should have to go through something long and twisty. He's already done a divorce and a remarriage and seven moves in three years, so we can't let him repeat any of that. Just be going through the motions. Well hey, *I* know!"

She snapped her fingers. Dave just glared at her. Asa watched from the landing, stooping to see their faces under the ceiling. His mother took a step up to Dave and put a hand on his chest. She smiled. He scowled, unmoving.

"*I* know," she repeated. "If we can't think of anything to get out of him, well, then, we can just reserve the right to task him whenever we feel like it in the future!" She gave a fake gay laugh that made even Asa wince. But Dave took it without a flinch, right in his face. She went on, patting him on the chest fondly. "We can just give him a hard time every now and then on general principles, because he's got this nice room he doesn't really deserve. How about that? Solves a *lot* of our problems. Honey!" she called up the stairs to Asa. Her voice was strong now, natural and direct, without sarcasm. "Go ahead and pick your room and carry your stuff up and arrange it however you like. Leave room for your bed." Then she returned Dave's glare, took her hand slowly off his chest, and went out the door to get another load from the rented truck.

In the next couple of months Asa decided that what bothered Dave about his room was not so much that it was nice, but that it was far away: he could really be alone there. There were several things about this that could not fail to aggravate Dave, Asa knew. First, Dave did not trust the state of solitude. He clearly did not think anything good could come of someone being by himself; Asa could not speculate about exactly which evils Dave believed arose from such isolation, but it was obvious that bad things were supposed to happen when you let a kid think too much, or play by himself, or read. Second, Dave did not trust Asa. Again Asa was unable to come up with ideas of what specific sins he was capable of committing up there—but he knew it wasn't really a matter of specifics. Something about him made Dave suspicious.

So he was never all that surprised when Dave came quietly up the stairs and popped into the room without knocking. Asa *did* keep his door closed. Dave always asked him why—implying that anyone who shut his door must have something to hide—and Asa always replied that he liked being "snug." This was true. Also, Asa liked listening to rhythm and blues at low volume on his radio and did not want the music to intrude on the television shows Dave and his mother watched downstairs. These reasons never seemed quite to mollify Dave, who looked suspiciously around the room from a step or two inside the doorway. Asa was usually reading, or drawing, or building a model car, so after his snap check Dave always withdrew without explaining the visit by so much as a feigned message.

One Saturday morning in early October Asa was sitting on the floor in a dormer, reading *Treasure Island*[2] beneath the window, when Dave opened the door and stepped in. Asa looked up. Something was different. Dave was wearing sneakers, thick-soled black hightops. Asa had never seen them before. Even stranger, Dave was holding a football in his right hand.

"It's sunny," he said. He snuck a quick look around the room, but he seemed to be trying to keep his eye on Asa this time.

"Yes," said Asa. He held up his book. "I'm reading by it."

Dave started to say something but stopped his mouth. Then, with an underhand snap of the wrist, he flicked the football across the room in a whirling spiral. Without thinking, Asa dropped *Treasure Island* and caught it.

Dave grinned. "Good," he said.

Asa stared at the ball gripped unmoving in his hands. He was amazed: A second ago it had been whizzing two ways at once. "How did you make it go like that?" he said.

"Come on out and I'll teach you," Dave said.

So they went out and threw the football to each other for almost three hours. During that time, Dave taught Asa quite a few very specific things—grip, arm motion, foot placement, the shifting of weight, the rotating of hips. How to plot a path for the throw to drop just where the running receiver would be. Dave did not instruct

---

2. The 1883 adventure novel by the British author Robert Louis Stevenson.

so much as show, perhaps—"Watch my wrist," he would say, (instead of an analytical explanation)—but Asa knew how to learn things.

He was thrilled by the whole day: the cool edge in the air, the dry detachment with which Dave offered simple expertise, the thin yellow of the light, and the passing itself, especially the eerie connection he felt between the hand that had just released the ball arcing into space and the hands that caught and carried it away on an unchecked run. But there was more going on than just the sport. After a half hour Asa realized quite clearly that for the first time he and Dave were giving free play to the natural tendencies that usually brought them into tight-lipped contention: Dave was being an authority, and Asa was being intelligent.

During their first couple of years as fake father and fake son, Dave had tried to make Asa do many things—but he was terrible at it, like a bulldog sergeant major crushing the recruit in a bad army movie. As for Asa, he tried to make Dave respect his ability to think—but he was a bit of a show-off, snapping out uncanny perceptions about things he knew were supposed to be beyond his reach, racing ahead of both his mother and Dave to note the end points of ramifications just opening before them. When the family considered anything at all together, from dinner at a particular restaurant to a drive in a rainstorm, Asa rattled off the string of consequences attendant on each alternative choice. At eleven he was already a pedant. Dave, at thirty, was still a bully.

They both knew the terms of their life together. But sports, it appeared, was different—perhaps it was not really a part of life. Dave could show him how to let a football slip off his fingertips without the chippy force that usually pushed his commands, and Asa could accept the instruction without feeling belittled, without having to show that he had already figured it out alone. Asa asked himself: Why? Was it because sports did not "matter" (the way saying "Sir" and "Ma'am" in exactly the right tone of voice mattered, or having a short enough haircut, or any of the other things that Dave demanded)? Or was it because sports—clearly a male domain—never brought Asa's mother into play between them? Asa thought about it a lot, as he and Dave expanded on this newfound opportunity to enjoy, if not harmony, at least cooperative neutrality, by playing football and then basketball throughout the fall and winter.

One day they were shooting foul shots and Dave missed five in a row. Without thinking (he *never* spoke to Dave without thinking; the slightest carelessness could be a step into a red elevator shaft of wrath) Asa said, "You're not bending your knees before you shoot. So you're standing up too straight and your shots are flat and long." He added, as if suddenly aware of his temerity, "Maybe we're tired."

Dave stared at him. His eyes narrowed for a moment. Then he looked at the basket, bent his knees, and bobbed a couple of times, spinning the ball in his hands as he eyed the rim. He hit three shots in a row, then said, "Let's go." On the way home he patted Asa once on the shoulder and said, "You're learning good." Asa *felt* good— cold, appraising, alert only to the technicalities of form and result: he was relieved of emotion. This was sports: action without emotion, liberty from putting anything on the line.

Or so it seemed, for a long time over the winter. Certainly there was less tension in the house, and Asa equated less tension with less emotion. He and Dave would return home at dusk, and his mother would be happily setting out the family dinner; they would eat quietly while she talked nonstop; Dave would take his second cup of coffee into the den to watch television, and Asa would scoot upstairs. Often he snuck back down a little later, after Dave had fallen asleep in front of *The Beverly Hillbillies* or *77 Sunset Strip*,[3] to help his mother wash dishes. Oddly, this was a household job Dave had never assigned to him; Asa was certain it was because he did not like the idea of the two of them alone together.

One night as he was scrubbing a glass casserole dish, his mother said, "I'm sure glad to see my boys getting along so good."

He hesitated; when she expressed herself in this girlish-whimsy way, complete with grammatical mistakes—he couldn't convince himself she was being genuine. How could she be so shrewd and resolute sometimes, then so content with cuteness at others? He sensed a huge longing in his mother, a catalogue of keen needs that were beyond him and Dave, even together, even with his long-gone father thrown in for good measure. And often when he suspected her of playing a part, he sensed behind it a desperate will to sincerity; she was trying out a way of being someone people could readily understand. It was not the kind of acting he held in contempt. It was a sadder, nobler performance.

"We're kind of having fun," he said to his casserole dish.

His mother sighed happily and rubbed brisk circles into a dinner plate with her towel. "Fun," she said.

Asa tried to keep it going. He said, "Dave's teaching me a lot."

His mother said nothing for a moment, and he imagined she was putting the plate away. But then her arms closed around him from behind. "Maybe," she said, her mouth pressed against his ear. "Maybe so, baby doll. But 'fun,' now—well, I think my boy has just as much to teach *him*. And *that's* what I like."

One day in late March, he and Dave were walking along a cinder path that wound through woods to the basketball court outside his school. Buds were poised everywhere, as if waiting for a cue; a sweeping glance took in the sight of a misty green below the surface of everything, but focusing on a single branch showed nothing especially verdant. Asa drew a happy sigh and announced that he wanted to play Little League baseball.

Dave frowned. "Well," he said. "Not much of a game."

Asa was ready for this; perhaps the weather made him quick, even funny. "I think baseball's got everything," he said with a smile, "including dullness."

Dave grunted. They walked on. Around them the sumac was sending up its antennalike shoots. Dave said, "It's complicated, baseball. Too many things to do—catch, throw, swing a bat, run bases. Two months, you can barely shoot a jump shot. Too hard for you."

Asa amazed himself by laughing. "Hey, but you're a *great* teacher," he said, going so far as to clap Dave on the back. "And I'm a fantastic student."

There wasn't much Dave could say to that. So, reluctantly, he agreed. But from that moment, Asa felt their cool detachment begin to clench into some sort of grip. Starting the next day, they practiced baseball—not all those complicated parts of the game, but just the elemental art of hitting the ball. However, Dave's instruction lost its air of indifference, took on an edge; and Asa found himself more and more determined to show his stepfather something unexpected and strong. It was still spring, and in the paths and fields fern tendrils unwound and hot new leaves splayed outward. But he and Dave turned away from the green and tightened up.

---

3. Two television programs (on the air 1962–71 and 1958–64, respectively).

3

Somehow the great Table Talk team could not score. In the fourth inning two men reached base with no one down, but the next two hitters struck out on terrible pitches, and the third lashed a line drive that Asa outran to right center and caught one-handed over his shoulder. In the fifth the Cool Guy on the mound walked the bases full, and as he came out of the game, his teammates looked at each other almost with relief: "Ah, *this* is more like it, *this* is where we lose." The next hitter chopped a grounder the new pitcher scooped at and missed—but his mitt knocked it back to home, where the catcher was waiting with his foot on the plate for the force-out. Feeling better, the pitcher threw hard down the pipe to the following batter, who hit the ball on the nose right back at him. It smacked into his glove, spinning him half around; the base runners thought he was watching the ball sail in a flash into center field, so they ran. Grinning, the pitcher trotted to first and tagged the base for the easiest of double plays.

As the innings passed, the facts began to sink in to the Cool Guys: they were not being clobbered. Hits started to fall in. In the top of the fifth they got three base runners, and only a pickoff and a double play kept them off the scoreboard. In the top of the sixth, the last inning, Tim led off with a sharp single to center. Asa, swinging down at a low pitch, crushed it into the infield. Spraying dirt, the ball bounded over the ducking second baseman, and Tim hustled to third. Freddie struck out trying to uppercut a sacrifice fly to the outfield, but everyone hollered happily from the dugout. Asa, on first, saw three of the Table Talk infielders glance fretfully at the hopeful Cool Guys jumping up and down. Then, he, too, knew Quik-E-Freeze had a chance.

Pete, the catcher, was up. Catchers, according to Coach Henderson, were supposed to be the smartest hitters, because they knew all the tricks a pitcher could call upon. Pete, failing to notice that at this level of baseball there were no tricks, believed him, and Asa could tell that for this at bat Pete thought himself cunning as a raccoon. He waggled his bat, cocked his head, relaxed his hands, and shot beams of daring at the pitcher. It was unnerving, apparently: the first two pitches scudded in the dirt. Pete didn't even watch them.

As he leaned into his lead at first base, Asa thought: How could this be? How could we all know what is about to happen? For it was clear that everyone did know. The Table Talk bench, usually as cute and mechanical in its cheering as a Baptist child choir on TV, now slunk forward in gloomy foreboding. The fielders, brows wrinkled, kicked at pebbles between pitches, sometimes not looking up until the ball was on the way to the plate. The pitcher sucked in breaths as if they were cough syrup. But the Cool Guys—hey, life was great! Tim stood on third with his hand on his hips and blew a large pink bubble that did not pop. Asa's legs tingled with speed-to-be. The boys in the dugout laughed. It was as if Pete had already hit the ball somewhere far away. There was no doubt.

The pitcher decided it was time to get it over with. He threw an easy pitch that floated to the plate at the level of the FREEZE logo on Pete's chest, and Pete stepped and swung. The ball was in the sky before anyone heard the solid *tock* of impact. Asa held back, waiting to see it land, but Tim streaked home and hit the plate at the same instant the ball dropped onto the grass way beyond the running boys in left center. Now Asa swept around second and burned toward third. The "coach" there—a third-string infielder—was too busy cheering with two hands in the air, his eyes on the ball, to give Asa a sign to stop or go, so Asa cut across the base and sped on toward home. As he bore down on the catcher, his universe shrank: he was running in a tunnel and the opening at the end got smaller as he got nearer. There, the last thing in the world, was the All-Star catcher, his mask off, his face sweaty and red, crouched with his weight on both legs, blocking the plate; his eyes flashed over Asa's head, pleading for the ball; his mitt, as Asa watched, began to turn and reach. Asa slid without slackening his speed, shooting his right foot between the catcher's legs at the plate and kicking out with his left at one of the boy's planted legs. He scooted almost entirely through before the catcher fell heavily onto him. Beneath his left hip he felt the hard rubber of the plate.

The umpire above him yelled something, but Asa did not pay attention. He was too busy trying to untangle himself from James Neal and stand up; now, finally, it seemed to be his turn to hoot and holler and leap about, and he wanted to strike while the urge was on—deep in his chest he was ready to be delivered of the strange, cool restraint that always kept him apart from his teammates' ups and downs. Up at last, he shook free and spun toward the dugout with a wordless whoop, a scream of joy, waving his fists in front of him as if he had caught something wild in each. But his teammates stood with their mouths open, watching someone large who was at that moment bustling past Asa toward home plate, making noise. Asa, after a glance at the stunned boys, turned to follow their stare.

What had rushed past him was Coach Henderson. It was hard to recognize him. The crisply mannered, fine-featured man was now hunched and flailing, his face like a plum-colored knot squeezed out from his humpy shoulders. He was snarling at the umpire; Asa noticed, as the ump stepped away and Coach Henderson turned his head to follow, that the coach had crooked teeth. Asa had never seen them before; he would never have expected them to be crooked. The opposing coach, a consistently jolly Greek man named Stravros who owned the Table Talk Bakery, was out of his dugout, trying to catch Coach Henderson by one of his elbows. There seemed to be four or five of them in the air, but he couldn't snag one. Then the umpire, his face full of fear, shot his arm into the air.

Still Asa did not know; he stood there not knowing, his fists of celebration still made. It was only when Coach Henderson stormed by, flushed with anger and, now, with what Asa recognized as shame, and said, "Sorry, Asa, but you were safe, my boy," that he realized. He was not safe. He was out. The umpire had called him out.

He walked back to the dugout. A couple of boys patted him and said, "We got one anyhow." On the field, as if in a hurry to reestablish the nature of things, a Cool Guy swung at a bad pitch and popped out. Asa found his glove and trotted out to center.

Out? Well, perhaps. How did he know? He hadn't been watching: he had been in there, inside the moment—tangled in legs and red shin guards and twisting arms at the end of the tunnel, not watching, not thinking, just concentrating on getting to the plate. What kind of judge was he? For once, it was up to somebody else to see the sequence of things, and somebody had done so. Out? It could be. There were only two choices, and one had been made. Asa would have preferred being safe, but preference was not knowledge. He wasn't angry. In a way, he was thrilled, simply to have been too involved to know.

The Table Talk batter swung at the first pitch and lofted a long fly to left. Asa watched without surprise as it soared, peaked, kept flying, and cleared the fence by twenty feet. The Baptist child choir woke up. He did not watch the hitter jump and dance as he ran the bases; they all did that, and he hated it. If *he* ever hit a home run, he would put his head down and scurry. He supposed he would be proud, but pride was private. Eventually the gamboling Table Talk boy touched home, and the game was tied.

Next up, the pitcher cracked a line drive that hit the shortstop in the chest. The Cool Guy collapsed, cringing and crying, while the ball spun like a planet in the dirt. He came out of the game, replaced by the kid who had been coaching third base when Asa had run around it. The runner was held at first. The next batter popped up a bunt. Pete snatched it out of the air and nearly doubled the runner off first. One away. Left-handed hitter. He swung at the first pitch and bounced it on one hop over the right-field fence. Men on second and third. One out.

The next Table Talk hitter knocked a grounder that Tim dove to his left to spear. Springing up, he drew back his arm at the runner who had taken off from third, until the boy dove back. Then Tim hummed a throw across to first and beat the runner by a stride. It was a great play. Asa hollered Tim's name. *Great* play. Two out. They could get out of this. If they did not let up, they could get out of it.

James Neal sauntered to the plate. He was a right-handed hitter but his power was to center. He was the best hitter in their league: every swing was level and true, no matter what the pitch, a disciplined slash that swept the ball through the infield in a blink. When James hit home runs—and Asa could think of half a dozen he had seen—they were line drives that just kept rising as they flew. Once he had struck one over Asa's head into the tin scoreboard, and its impact had sprung five numbers off their nails onto Asa's grass.

Asa looked around at his teammates. They were watching James Neal advance to the batter's box, and they were all slinking. *No!* Asa wanted to holler. *Stop! We can do this guy! There are two out! Just one out to get and we are back at bat and we can win it.* He wanted them to see this—it was so simple! Asa kicked at the grass. They were giving up. He did not understand giving up—that was all. Giving up did not *work.*

The first pitch whizzed in. James Neal took a cut and everybody gasped. Asa leaped a step forward, but it was a foul back up over the Quik-E-Freeze dugout into the night. The runners, cocky in their trots, touched up, and waited; with two out they would fly on any hit. Both would score on a single. James Neal waved his bat and stared at the pitcher. He was a very emotional player, but there was no feeling in his face right now, only concentration. And here came the pitch.

Asa realized as soon as James Neal started his swing that he ought to have been playing in closer. So he started his run just as the ball sprang off the bat dead on a line four feet above second base. Asa did not slow down; he sprinted from his jump start, straight at where the ball was dipping, dipping, touching the wet grass, and rising in a long, low bounce right at him. Somewhere in his awareness he registered the whirling arms of the base runners romping safely home, the yowls from the Table Talk dugout, the cheers of half the parents springing to their feet in the stands. But mostly he was aware of three things—the ball he was speeding to intercept, the moon face of his first baseman turned this way to watch the hit, and James Neal, his grin bright with the grandest pleasure, his arms held straight up, his legs scissoring as he celebrated with a couple of leaps on his way to first. Somewhere inside Asa there was a whiz of physics that added these things up, and though he hadn't time to feel it, he knew there would be happiness in a moment. For now, he gloved the ball and plucked it out with his throwing hand and planted his left foot perfectly, then with every ounce of momentum developed over fifty feet of sprint he whipped his hips and snapped his arm and spun into a follow-through. He watched the ball. It flickered through the air and smacked into the barely opened mitt of the first baseman while James Neal was coming down from his last scissor leap, six feet from first.

The first baseman stared into his mitt at the ball, then looked down at his foot on the bag. Nobody cheered. James Neal stopped, gaped, then shook his head and looked around. He walked to first and stomped on it. "It's a clean *single*," he said to no one, his voice winding up for tears.

The Cool Guy infielders still didn't get it; neither did most of the boys on the Table Talk bench. But they all began to see that Asa got it. He trotted in with his head down, and one by one the players grew still and watched him. His rubber spikes crunched on the infield dirt. No one spoke but James Neal; he ran to the umpire, who stood between first and second, watching Asa approach.

"It's a clean *single*," he pleaded. His cheeks were red as match heads. He grabbed the umpire by the left arm but the ump shook him off without looking at him. Then, slowly, the man raised his right arm until his fist poised high above his ear, as if he had a knife. He watched Asa; only James Neal did not.

As Asa crunched by, he glanced up and met the umpire's look. "Out," said the man clearly.

4

After a couple of weeks on a low twilit field not far from their house, Asa found he and Dave were communicating entirely through the baseball itself. At first there were a few blunt instructions, but it became clear that not only did Dave dislike baseball— he also did not know it very well. After telling Asa he should "watch the ball" and "not try to kill it" he hadn't much to add that Asa couldn't pick up better simply by swinging. So Dave pitched, hard, from a bag of old baseballs he had wangled from a semipro team sponsored by the company he worked for. Asa stood and swung and stood and swung and stood and swung.

It also became clear that the absence of words did not mean they had nothing to say. Between them, suddenly, the air crackled with danger; through that air passed the ball. Asa could feel shoves of anger or doubt or pure competitiveness in the spin and speed of the pitch at the moment he struck it—always as hard as he could— with his bat. He was certain his replies were just as clear: high-strung line drives, overmatched popups, meek ground balls, and spirited, sloping flies he watched with a burning in his chest that could not have been more violent and celebratory if he had strode out to Dave and socked him. Two hours might pass without a word, but at the end they would both be drained.

It was not fun, but it was practice. And it worked: pitch by pitch Asa learned things, and soon he was becoming a hitter. Occasionally he sensed some grudging satisfaction in Dave when he lashed out six or seven tough pitches in a row to all parts of the field; they both seemed to remember, if only for the moment, that Asa's progress meant they were *both* doing well.

But sometimes they forgot. If Asa hit too many pitches too hard, Dave would hum one way inside at him, and Asa would have to spin away from it into the dirt. The first time this happened, he said, "Hey!" and Dave said, "Hey what? Part of the game," and motioned for him to stand back in; the next pitch was right over the plate. After that Asa said nothing. He saved his energy to bash the next ball.

One day, Asa stroked a long fly to dead center and stood watching it contentedly, holding a hand up to Dave as a signal that he should wait until Asa finished gloating. The ball landed far out in the green; Asa sighed happily. When he lowered his hand, Dave hit him with the ball. There was no pretense about it. He did not even wind up the way he did for a pitch: he let Asa step up to the plate and then he drew his arm back and threw—hard, always hard—directly at the boy's ribs. Asa froze. The ball seemed to take forever to arrive, but then it sprang at him and burrowed into his bones. He dropped backward and landed flat, screaming and rolling over and over. He knew he was crying because he felt mud on his cheeks from tears and dust, but he did not hear a thing, nor did he notice any vision: the whole world was a hole in his side. But before he could think, the pain switched over, and the world became a fury in his heart. He stood up.

Dave was out in the outfield collecting the balls Asa had hit, putting them in the canvas bag. His back was turned, and Asa knew he would keep it turned. Asa looked around home plate. There were three balls he had fouled into the backstop. He picked up his bat and one of the balls. In left center, Dave bent, straightened, bent, and straightened. Asa tossed his ball and hit it viciously. It sailed toward Dave with good distance, but tailed away toward right; Asa watched as it whizzed over Dave's head and landed twenty feet beyond him. Dave looked up and watched it land, too, but he did not turn around. In fact, he remained upright and motionless, as if offering his back in case Asa wanted to hit another. Asa did not. He left the other two balls and took his bat home.

The family ate dinner as usual that night—or almost as usual. It was obvious that something had happened, but neither Dave nor Asa spoke of it. Asa saw his mother studying Dave, and knew she was studying him when he wasn't looking. He wondered if Dave would tell; he certainly wouldn't.

The next day he remained in his room after school, reading comics. As the hour for their daily practice approached, he reached for more comic books; there was no question about whether or not the workouts would continue. They were finished.

But about ten minutes past the time, someone knocked on his door. He said, "What?" and the door opened. His mother stepped in.

She was wearing white tennis shoes and one of Dave's golf caps and holding Asa's bat in her right hand. His glove hung over her left wrist: she wore it like a bracelet. He stared. She smiled. "Let's go," she said.

"But—"

"Come on. Your tryout is in two weeks. Let's go chuck a few."

He started to protest. But in her eyes was a look that made him rise. It was part command, part entreaty; part confidence, part loss. He went with her.

On their way to the field she did not say anything to explain why she was taking Dave's place; instead, she pointed out weeds that were coming into flower or trees that had brought forth buds. Asa nodded and commented politely, softly. In his life there had been half a dozen times when the air around him filled with an aching sweetness, a thick feeling of fragile bliss that poured into him and out of him at once, and moved with him as he moved. Always it was sad as well as happy, and always it ended suddenly. It came when someone gave him something and he took it without knowing. When the feeling was gone, sometimes the gift was too. He did not know, as he walked to the park beside his chatty mother, whether what she gave would last for him or not, but the swelling of sweetness and woe clouded around them, and he drew it in all the way to the pitcher's mound. By the time he explained why this strange little hill was here and showed her how to put on his glove, the cloud had vanished.

Her first pitch was six feet outside and ten feet high. Her second was lower, but farther away. Her third arrived near the plate on second bounce, and he gave it a tap into right field. "See," she yelled, gleefully. "Hooray for us!"

They had brought only the one ball. Asa retrieved it. When he came back, he went to the mound.

"Know what?" he said. "I've really pretty much done nothing but bat up to now, for two weeks."

She looked at him warily, unwilling to be patronized. "So?"

He tried to sound chipper and spontaneous. "What I need is the chance to field a lot."

"Field?" She looked around. "A lot?"

"Sorry—it means to catch the ball, make throws: play defense. I, um, only got the chance to do offense before. There didn't seem to be much interest in the other side. But it's just as important. At the tryouts they watch you hit, but they also make you catch and throw. It's actually more complicated than swinging the bat."

She thought, liked it, nodded. "Okay." She smiled. "I'm your defensive coach. What do I do?"

He had a feeling she could be taught to toss the ball up and hit grounders to him, certainly more easily than she could be taught to pitch. He was right. In a few minutes she had learned to toss it, grip the bat, wait for the ball to come down, and chop at it with a short stroke. He moved out to the shortstop spot, and for almost an hour she pounded it at him, slow, high-bouncing balls sprayed all over the infield. It was actually wonderful: after a dozen grounders he was breathless and sweaty and fully stretched. It was plainly wonderful for his mother, too, though she had apparently decided to play it cool. She was all business as she hit the ball, dropped the bat, crouched with her hands apart in front of her, and clapped them over the soft rollers he sent back to her after making his catch. There was no more "Hooray!" and self-celebration: she made it clear this was a natural thing now, no big deal. Nevertheless, it was just as clear they were supposed to be having fun and they were. The next day he did not wait for her to come to his room; he got the equipment and stood at her bedroom door while she tied her sneakers.

Within a few days she was able to pop little line drives at him. From there she moved easily into short fly balls. Before long, he was getting all the defensive work he could wish for. She had a good instinct for mixing up her hits, moving him around, making him go back to his left and then drawing him into a charge to his right. Her grounders got trickier; she could smash them on a lower trajectory now, or squib them with English[4] so they trickled away from him if he got lazy and waited on one knee instead of running forward. The better she got, the less serious she pretended to be; the more she yanked him around, the more she chattered and laughed. He laughed too, even, sometimes, in the middle of a lunging catch that required all his reach and concentration. Every ball she hit had wit behind it. He got the joke as he made the play.

The tryouts approached; soon they arrived at the Friday before the Sunday when he would report, alone, to the municipal park at eight in the morning. Two more days! He was excited; he leaned toward the date with confidence that his chance to show something unexpected was at hand. Two days! Still, he tried to focus on the remaining practices. His workouts with his mother had gotten longer, so the two of them took breaks in the middle and sat for ten minutes by a creek that ran along one side of the field. On this Friday the weather was hot. Before sitting, he took off his shirt.

Squinting at the water, he saw his mother stare at him, look away, then stare again. He looked at her. Her eyes were on his torso. He looked down. There, in the ribs

4. Make them spin.

beneath his left arm, was the baseball-sized bruise he had carried for two weeks. It was an old bruise by now, greenish and blotchy, with one weird feature: the raised stitches of the ball had left two perfect curved marks of a deeper bruise, exact in their replication of the tiny bird-feet pattern, purple and geometric. The mark held no horror for Asa; indeed, he had quickly come to regard it as a fascinating study in the quirkiness of skin tissue, noting each change in color and texture. He checked it coolly each morning, then forgot about it. Following his mother's eyes now, he realized it was an ugly thing. He pretended to shiver, said, "Actually, it's a little breezy," and put his shirt back on.

His mother was looking him in the eye now. He did not know what to say, so he shrugged. She did not let him off with that. He said, "No big deal, you know?"

"Oh sure," she said. "Of course not." She held his eyes for a moment longer; he had to say something, so he said, "It's, like, just something guys don't mind." He grinned, gave himself a smack right on the bruise. She winced but he didn't. "See?" he said. "Doesn't hurt." He chuckled, shook his head, smiled at the creek. In his peripheral vision he saw her continue to stare at him. It was unnerving. So, without really intending to, he began to talk. He had thought he might just say a couple of reassuring things about his relationship with Dave, but before he knew it, he had drifted into deeper waters. He found himself defending his stepfather rather cleverly, though his mother had not charged him with anything. It must be *very* difficult being a stepfather, he said; especially if you married the woman you had loved long ago and now here she was at last—but this time she had a *kid* with her! Asa joked about the terrible inconvenience of this—how the kid must get in the way, change everything; he did a cute job of imitating the frustration of the adults. He chuckled at his own wit; his mother looked at the creek.

As he listened to himself chatter, Asa knew he was not pleading a trumped-up defense of Dave just to soothe his mother's anguish. He was pleading because he knew that despite Dave's roughness, the man was mostly trying to do strong, decent, difficult things with his stepson and his wife. Especially his wife. Asa was aware that *he* was not the main challenge in Dave's life. He had witnessed this marriage for years now. His head whirled sometimes with a sense of the history of these two people, fading back into the past, beyond his conscious understanding. But he did understand a great deal, really; at certain moments he knew he was in the presence of something big. It was true that much of the time this big, sweet force couldn't be easily perceived beneath the shadows of Dave's tyranny and his mother's torment. But sometimes it did shine, even from Dave. Asa had watched Dave coax her, without a trace of impatience, out of several of the fits of despair to which she so often seemed doomed—fits that, left unchecked, took over her life in a matter of hours. Twice in the previous year she had spun so quickly into her own darkness that Dave had handed her over to the state hospital at Butner,[5] for nearly a month each time. Coaxing her out early was work that required a strength and self-assurance Asa knew he could not approach—but he could readily admire it in Dave. At other times he had watched Dave gently, teasingly build long, slow jokes from sly references to this and that old business from their life, as they drove along in the car for hours—jokes that accumulated power as they tickled deeper and deeper, drawing her up through perfectly paced stages of amusement and laughter until she reached a reckless, weeping hilarity that left her spread-eagled over the car seat shaking, sniffling, wailing. During these crescendos Dave simply watched the road and smiled.

5. The town in North Carolina where the John Umstead Psychiatric Hospital is located.

So now, filled with this urgent sympathy, Asa went on babbling to his mom about how difficult being a stepfather must be. And it wasn't just difficult being a stepfather in general. It must be *really* tough being *his* stepfather—Asa's. He was, he knew, a very weird kid. He said this lightly, with a wry shake of the head and a rueful smile, *Oh, that Asa*. It was an expression he had often inspired—with a less kindly humor to it—in his stepfather.

His mother surprised him by wheeling around in a sudden fury. "What is this?" she sputtered. "What is supposed to be so weird about *you*, Asa?"

Her flare burned off his pretense of lightheartedness. But he had started something, so he plugged on, without playacting now. "Well," he said, "you know. I'm— *different*. I mean—here we are in the South and Dave has this big family and all the kids are normal Southern kids. They go to church all the time, they take it very easy, they don't worry about much. *Great* sense of humor—tease a lot, but it's because they like you, you know. That's the way Dave was when he was a kid, I know, and that's the way he *likes* kids. That's what kids *are*, to him. But I'm different. I care too much about things they don't even notice. Stupid things I know don't really matter, really. Like, I mind that they crease my comic books. When they come over, they come in, all friendly, and I really like them, I like my cousins—I wish *I* was that friendly all the time—and they plop down and yank out a bunch of my comics. That's okay. I can put them back in order. But they *fold* them, fold the covers back, sometimes they wad them up and put them in their back pockets to go down and eat. It's dumb to care so much about it, I know, but—I try to keep them kind of neat. I take care of them, is all. But I know it doesn't matter. What matters is that we are all cousins, we are all family. You're not supposed to let junk like that—like stupid comic books—come in the way of your love of your family. But I can't help it—before the love comes on, I start worrying about my comics, and I hate doing it, and Dave is right."

"Right? What does he say that is right?"

Asa had not planned on this, but now he was nervous and upset and he couldn't seem to stop. He tried to back off. "Oh, nothing. I mean, he's *right*. He's just trying to help me."

"What does he say?"

"He lets me know I'm being sort of a nervous finicky guy. Like maybe I like *things* better than *people*, you know? And that's wrong, I know it is. So I ought to be different. It *is* better to be kind of loose and easy about stuff."

"Oh yes," she said. "Like Dave. He's very loose and easy about stuff, isn't he? That's probably how you got that bruise."

Asa shut up and plucked grass. His mother watched him for a minute, then stared back out across the creek. He snuck a look at her; she wasn't crying or anything, at least. After a few minutes he asked if they could resume their practice.

She was grave for the rest of their workout. On the way home, silence waited between them. Then she said, "I'm very sorry, Asa."

He pretended not to know what she was talking about. A few minutes later she added, "It's no good."

"No, don't," he said. He had to say *something*. "It's fine." He gave her a pretty good smile. Then he took her hand, and they held hands all the way home.

In the middle of the night he woke up to find Dave shaking him. He smelled coffee, but it was too dark for morning and he could feel he hadn't been asleep long enough.

"Wake up," said Dave. "I need your help. We have to get some coffee in her." Then he ran from the room. Asa pushed his covers away and followed him downstairs.

Dave, in pajama bottoms, was in the kitchen pouring coffee into a mug. "Too hot," he said. "Ice." He yanked open the freezer and pulled out an ice tray and smacked it very hard against the edge of the counter. Chips of ice sprayed all over. He picked a few off the counter and put them in the coffee, then said, "Come on," and walked past Asa, leaving the freezer door open.

They went into the bedroom. The light was on. His mother lay diagonally across their bed, her arms at her sides; to Asa she looked strangely heavy and still, like a slab of wet clay. His throat went cold. "Is she—"

"She's—asleep," said Dave, giving him a quick look. He was on the far side of the bed, at her head. "Come here. We've got to get some coffee in her." He was flustered; it gave him an odd gentleness. "Do you want to hold her head or pour?"

"I'll hold her head." Asa went around and lifted his mother behind the neck. Dave held the mug up to her mouth and poured some coffee in. A little ran out of the corners of her mouth onto the sheets; the rest seemed to vanish until she coughed and spewed it.

"More," said Dave. This time her throat executed a kind of swallow.

Asa's arms were trembling; he was glad, actually. He knew he was in the middle of something that ought to be making him frantic, and instead he felt all cool and easy. The trembling showed he felt *something*, he guessed. "Why is she so asleep?" he asked.

Most of the coffee was in. Dave looked down into her throat, frowning. "Okay," he said. "Lie her back down."

Asa resisted the temptation to correct Dave's *lie* to *lay*; instead he said, "Maybe we should sit her up."

Dave looked at him. "Right," he said. He jammed pillows against the headboard of the bed, and they pushed her against them. Her head fell forward, and Dave pushed it back until the pillows held it up. Her head didn't seem to care. She was out. The only thing about her that moved was her lower lip, which pulled in a bit whenever she sucked a raggedy breath.

"Why is she so asleep?" Asa asked again.

Dave ran his fingers through his hair. "You want some coffee too? I got to have some too."

Asa followed him into the kitchen. "If you don't tell me, I'm calling an ambulance," he said.

Dave was pouring coffee into the same mug. He turned as he poured. "No," he said, far more reasonably than Asa expected. "I mean, we don't need the ambulance. She's all right. Really. Just sleepy." He slurped some of the coffee and winced at the heat.

"Why is she so sleepy? Why do we have to wake her?"

Dave watched him over the edge of the mug as he took another, longer swallow. "Well, Sport," he said, with a tone almost cheery, "she kind of goofed. She had a headache, and she went into the bathroom in the middle of the night, and she took what she thought was an aspirin. But it was a sleeping pill. They look the same." He shrugged and lifted the mug.

"One sleeping pill?" Asa said.

Dave paused and considered, the mug an inch from his mouth. "Two," he said, and drank.

Asa went back into his mother's room. She had slumped sideways. The friction of the skin of her left cheek against the wooden headboard was all that held her up from lying down again; the pressure pulled her lip up above her gum on that side and opened her left eye. Asa looked at the eye. Nothing but white was showing.

He straightened her, and went into the bathroom. In the medicine cabinet there was nothing but shaving stuff and toothpaste. He looked under the sink. The wastebasket was on its side and a few wads of tissue lay near it. There was a brown prescription bottle upright on the floor there. Asa picked it up and read the name of the medicine: Seconal.[6] Inside he found a single red, oval pill. There was no aspirin or aspirin bottle anywhere.

He went back into the bedroom. Dave was there, leaning close to her, watching for some sign; from his face it was obvious he had no clue about what he was waiting for. Asa said, "I'm calling the hospital."

"No!" Dave roared, spinning on him. The gentility was gone. "You will do nothing but what I say, you hear? This isn't a time for a kid to interfere, I don't care how smart he thinks he is." He glared at Asa; the boy held his eye for a moment, then started to walk toward the kitchen. Dave said, "Wait," more gently, and came over to him.

"Listen, please," he said. *Please* was not a word Asa heard from him often; he listened.

Dave put his hands on Asa's shoulders and looked straight into his face. "Listen, son. That's my wife over there. Your mother, and my wife. We want her to wake up and be okay. Both of us. I would not let her sit there in danger, understand?"

"You lied about the pills," said Asa. "I can't trust you."

Dave groaned in exasperation, and with an offhanded force that seemed weary, almost casual, he thrust Asa straight back until the boy slammed into the side of a bureau. Asa's ears filled with a buzzing from the back of his head, but he stayed erect; Dave stepped close and squatted, sticking his face close.

"You'll pardon me for not giving a dingle," he said, "but right now I just don't feel all torn up with the need for your 'trust.' It's not something your mother's pining for over there, either. Frankly, boy, I don't think you're the kind of person who will ever trust *anybody*. It kind of takes an honest heart to do that, you understand what I mean?"

"Yes," said Asa, "I do." Then with a concentration of all his strength he snapped his arm out and punched Dave flush on the temple. The shock of it felt good; he left his arm, stiff and solid, in the air between them as Dave jerked backward and sat down hard. Dave shook his head and blinked fast for a moment, but quickly his eyes found Asa's and they stared at each other. For some time neither spoke or looked away. Then Asa lowered his fist, and Dave smiled grimly. There was a red circle near his left eye.

"Well," he said. His voice gurgled a little; he cleared his throat. "Well. Now, I guess, we're even." He started to stand up, careful to lean away from Asa as he did so.

"We'll never be even," said Asa. "We shouldn't try."

Dave hesitated, then chuckled darkly and shook his head. He stood all the way up, stepped past Asa, and went to bend over Asa's mother. Asa walked to the other side of the room and sat on the floor with his back against the wall.

Dave left after a few minutes. Asa remained, watching her. From time to time Dave checked in, bringing coffee, which he got down her without Asa's assistance. In a

---

6. The trademark of a variety of barbiturate; its uses include the treatment of sleeplessness, anxiety, and convulsions.

couple of hours her breathing got a little easier, but she showed no signs of waking up. At one point Asa went over and tried to hold her hand, but he felt stupid. So he sat on the floor and waited, and after a while he fell asleep.

He woke to the sound of heavy footsteps and Dave's voice cursing. He opened his eyes. The light was off and the room was pretty dark, but it was dawn beyond the curtained windows; a long shape was just falling forward onto the bed with a thick *WHUMP*. The bathroom light went on and Asa heard Dave curse again. He stood up and went to the door.

Dave was looking into the sink. It was full of jagged pieces of glass, some of them covered with amber goo. Thinking back, Asa realized that before the footsteps he had heard—and incorporated into his dream, something about a science class—the sound of glass breaking. It was probably what had brought him to the surface. Glass breaking, heavy footsteps, his mother collapsing onto the bed, Dave cursing—he tried to put it together.

Dave turned. "She wanted to wash her hair," he said. But he spoke with a pitiful lack of conviction, and a moment later he added, in a low, defeated voice: "Get dressed, son."

They carried her out to the car in the faint blue light, and stretched her out in the backseat on some blankets. She seemed to be as heavily asleep as ever; Asa wondered how she could have waked up and gotten to and from the bathroom and then slipped back. But he didn't need to understand: there she was. They climbed into the front seat.

Dave took turns that led them out of town, onto the road that went north. Asa had not really expected they would go only to the hospital in town; things seemed too big for town, all of a sudden. "Excuse me," he said. "Are we going to Raleigh?"

Headlights flashed over Dave's face. "Yes we are."

He offered no explanation. But then Asa and his mother never needed an explanation when they were taken to Raleigh: It was Dave's hometown, where all his family lived, and it drew them whenever they did not have a good reason to stay where they lived. He remembered suddenly that it was his mother's hometown too; this was a fact, but not one that he felt very keenly. For one thing, he had known her first in Washington; for another, they always spent all their time in Raleigh with Dave's family. She seemed as much of an outsider with them as Asa did, despite her native ability to talk the talk and mimic the behavior of the Southern wives who had never left.

"Is Mom going to Butner?" Asa said.

"Yes," Dave said. "She is."

Asa waited a long time to ask his next question. He waited while they rode between tobacco fields and past gas stations opening up for the day, while the sun rose, pink and then yellow and then white in a white sky. He listened for his mother's breathing over the rumble of the car, and every so often he heard a snaggled intake of air. Dave stopped for takeout coffee at a diner an hour up the road and bought Asa a honey bun. Asa waited until he had eaten his bun and Dave had drunk his coffee. He waited a while longer. Then, trying to sound very light, trying to sound as if it did not really matter a bit, he was just wondering, no problem at all, he asked: "Will we spend the night?"

Dave looked at him as if he must be nuts. "Of course," he said. He shook his head at the boy's strangeness, and Asa knew just what he was thinking. Imagine going to Raleigh and not spending the weekend!

Asa said nothing; he vowed he would not. But Dave surprised him. After only five minutes, he said, "Oh!" and hit the steering wheel with the palm of his right hand. He turned and looked at Asa.

"I'm sorry," he said. "You were supposed to try out for Little League tomorrow morning."

"It's all right," Asa said, looking straight ahead.

Dave hit the steering wheel another, harder lick, and cursed. And suddenly Asa could feel clearly that Dave's anger was curling toward the woman in the backseat. It was *her* fault. She had *done* this, deprived his stepson of a chance to be a regular boy. Asa had seen how Dave's shifty anger could work, and he knew that soon his missed tryout—indeed, perhaps the entirety of his strange life, all predicated upon this lost shot at normalcy—would be another black mark against her, another sin.

Well, for this Asa would not stand. If *he* could get by without anger, what right did Dave have to be mad? Whose tryout was it, anyway? So, looking over, Asa said firmly, "Oh, no. It's all right. I wasn't going to try out."

Dave frowned. "You weren't?"

"No," said Asa.

"Why not?"

Asa took a breath. Outside, a sparrow hawk fluttered in the wind over a red clay field. "Well," he said, "it's a complicated game."

Dave thought for a moment. Then he let out a long breath. "Well," he said, "I told you so."

"Yes," said Asa, "you did." And that seemed to do it. They spoke no more. Asa turned then to watch out the side window, in which he could see a reflection of his face, watching. The drive went on in silence. After a couple of hours, as he stretched, he decided the scrub shortstop, the one who had come in after the line drive popped the other boy in the chest—he decided this kid would hit a home run in the top of the eighth. Yes, he liked that. Quik-E-Freeze would win. He felt a little guilty about this, a little selfish. But what the heck, he would do it: the Cool Guys would win, and he would feel great. Somehow, he hoped, he deserved this.

1992

Timeline

CHILDREN'S LITERATURE IN CONTEXT

8th century B.C.E.–1483

8th century B.C.E.–3rd century C.E. Invention of the phonetic alphabet, with vowels, in Greece • Classical myths from Greece and Rome

ca. 700 B.C.E. The *Iliad*, dealing with the Trojan War, and (probably later) the *Odyssey*

ca. 560 B.C.E. Death of Aesop on the Greek island of Samos

ca. 300 B.C.E. Demetrius of Phalerum, librarian of the great library at Alexandria, assembles a collection, now lost, of two hundred Aesopic fables

43 B.C.E.–ca. 420 C.E. Romans conquer Britons; until ca. 420, Britannia is a province of the Roman Empire

before 50 C.E. Phaedrus, a freed Greek slave in Rome, puts Aesop's fables into Latin verse, adding topical anecdotes and stories of his own

2nd century C.E. Apuleius's *Metamorphoses*, or *The Golden Ass*, including "Cupid and Psyche," the source of many later versions of "Beauty and the Beast" • Valerius Babrius, another freed Greek slave, renders his own versions of Aesop in Greek verse

307–37 Reign of Constantine the Great leads to adoption of Christianity as the official religion of the Roman Empire

ca. 450 Withdrawal of Roman legions from Britain; Anglo-Saxon conquest of Britons begins

1066 Norman conquest by William I establishes French-speaking ruling class in England

ca. 1135–38 Geoffrey of Monmouth's *History of the Kings of Britain*, written in Latin, gives pseudohistorical status to Arthurian and other legends

1137–1453 Hundred Years' War

1326 *Gesta Romanorum* (*Deeds of the Romans*), a collection of stories in Latin, compiled by monks

ca. 1375–1400 *Sir Gawain and the Green Knight*

1376 Earliest record of drama performance at York

1455–85 Wars of the Roses

ca. 1475 *The Babees Book,* a courtesy book, or book of manners

1476–77 The Ulm Aesop, the first printed collection of all the known Aesopic fables, compiled in German by Heinrich Steinhöwell

1476 William Caxton sets up first printing press in England

ca. 1479 *Stans Puer ad Mensam*, ascribed to John Lydgate, a courtesy book, including table manners, designed as an etiquette book for boys preparing to serve at court; earliest known printing is by Caxton

1483 Caxton publishes an English translation of Jacobus de Voragine's *The Golden Legend* (*Legenda Aurea*), which was used in schools and at home to educate children about the lives of saints and ecclesiastical teachings

1484 Caxton, translating from Steinhöwell, prints *Subtyl Historyes and Fables of Esop*

1485 Sir Thomas Malory's *Morte D'Arthur,* source of many later romances

1492 Christopher Columbus sails to the Bahamas

ca. 1510–15 Earliest English translation of the *Gesta Romanorum* (*Deeds of the Romans*) printed by Wynkyn de Worde; fables are among its many stories

ca. 1553–58 *A New Interlude for Children to Play Named Jack Juggler, both Witty and Very Pleasant,* first play created in English specifically for children

1558–1603 Reign of Elizabeth I

1563 John Foxe's *Actes and Monumentes,* popularly known as the *Book of Martyrs;* used for over three centuries as a source in many books for Protestant children, including the *New-England Primer*

1570 John Hart's *A Method or Comfortable Beginning for All Unlearned,* the first known printed pictorial alphabet

1601 John Weever's *An Agnus Dei* (*A Lamb of God*), an abridged New Testament in rhymed couplets; a very early example of the miniature books known as Thumb Bibles

1607 Jamestown colony established in Virginia

1630–43 Arrival of English Puritans at the Massachusetts Bay Colony

1659 First English translation of Johann Amos Comenius's *Orbis Sensualium Pictus,* under the title *Visible World,* an educational compendium with a pictorial alphabet arranged according to sounds

1660 Thomas White's *A Little Book for Little Children,* setting out Puritan ideals for children, published as part of his *Manual for Parents*

1668 Publication in Paris of the first six books of Jean de La Fontaine's *Fables choisies, mises en vers* (*Selected Fables, Set in Verse*); first translated into English in 1734

1678 John Bunyan's *The Pilgrim's Progress*

ca. 1687–90 Publication in Boston of the *New-England Primer;* no copy printed before 1727 survives

1692 Roger L'Estrange's *Fables of Aesop, and Other Eminent Mythologists;* still a popular translation

1693 John Locke's *Some Thoughts Concerning Education,* a founding philosophical text of modern education; Locke argued against set curricula and for treating children, mainly boys, in a more humane and liberal manner; he also sought to combine instruction with amusement, believing that children could learn to discipline themselves by modeling themselves upon their parents and tutors

1697 Charles Perrault's *Histoires ou contes du temps passé* (*Stories or Tales of Past Times*), often considered the first major collection of fairy tales for children, though it was issued for adults. The book was first published in English in 1729; many of the tales were separately published as chapbooks and later as picture books for children. The collection was sometimes given the title "Tales of Mother Goose."

1715 Isaac Watts's *Divine Songs,* for two centuries an inescapable part of Protestant childhood

1717 Publication in Boston of *The Holy Bible in Verse,* an abridged rhyming version of the Bible by Benjamin Harris

1719 Daniel Defoe's *Robinson Crusoe*

1720–60 William Dicey was a prolific publisher of chapbooks from 1720 to 1760. He traded first in Northampton, then from ca. 1730 in London, where he issued chapbooks from Bow Churchyard; he was joined in 1736 by his son Cluer. In 1764 Cluer was in partnership with Richard Marshall, with premises in Aldermary Churchyard.

1722 Samuel Croxall's *Fables of Aesop and Others*, illustrated by Elisha Kirkall

1726 *A Compendious History of the Old and New Testament*, the first Bible rewritten in prose "adapted to all capacities" (as the title page claims) • Jonathan Swift's *Gulliver's Travels*

1744 John Newbery's *A Little Pretty Pocket-Book*, which contains an early play alphabet; and Mary Cooper's *Tommy Thumb's Song Book*, the earliest nursery rhyme collection • Jane Johnson's *A Very Pretty Story to Tell Children when they are about five or six years of Age*; Mrs. Johnson is important for having produced, in the spirit of Locke, inspired and playful teaching materials for her own children, including interactive card games and mobiles.

1749 Sarah Fielding's *The Governess; or, Little Female Academy*, one of the first books published specifically for girls; it contains two didactic fairy tales

1761 First publication of "Beauty and the Beast," in *The Young Misses' Magazine*, a translation of Mme Leprince de Beaumont's *Le Magasin des enfans* (1757)

1762 Jean-Jacques Rousseau's *Émile; ou, De l'éducation* (Eng. translation 1762); Rousseau developed a critique of traditional education and schools by depicting how he would raise a boy in a natural setting, and how the boy would learn from experience rather than from reading. Above all, he was to be protected from social institutions that might corrupt him. Rousseau also attacked organized religion; the work was so controversial that it was banned by the church.

1765 *The History of Little Goody Two-Shoes* published by John Newbery

1773 Boston Tea Party

1775–83 American War of Independence

1776 U.S. Declaration of Independence

1777–79 Anna Laetitia Barbauld's *Lessons for Children*, the first modern primers taking into account the idea that a child's first reading lessons are best met in a small book with lots of white space and big print

1780 Sunday School Movement initiated when Robert Raikes starts a Sunday school in Gloucester, England, to teach poor children to read

ca. 1785 First American edition of *Mother Goose's Melodies*

1786 Sarah Trimmer's *Economy of Charity*, written to promote and advise on Sunday schools

1787 U.S. Constitution adopted

1789 William Blake's *Songs of Innocence and Experience* • Fall of the Bastille (beginning of the French Revolution)

1792 Mary Wollstonecraft's *A Vindication of the Rights of Woman*

1793 Execution of Louis XVI and Marie Antoinette. France declares war against Britain (and then Britain against France). The Reign of Terror begins

1793–1815 Napoleonic Wars

1795–98 Hannah More's *Cheap Repository Tracts*, designed for the newly literate readers being taught in Sunday schools

1796 Maria Edgeworth's *The Parent's Assistant*; her *Early Lessons* follows in 1801

1799 Foundation in London of the Religious Tract Society, later publishers of much Sunday school fiction

ca. 1800 Mason Locke Weems's *The Life and Memorable Actions of George Washington*

1802–06 Sarah Trimmer's *The Guardian of Education*, the earliest critical journal of children's literature in English

1804 Napoleon crowned emperor of France, putting a virtual end to the French Revolution

1805 William Godwin's *Fables Ancient and Modern*, an adaptation for young children; Godwin opens a children's book shop with his wife, Mary Clairmont • French fleet defeated by the British at Trafalgar

1807 Abolition of the slave trade in Britain

1808 *The Cries of New-York,* probably the first American book of street cries, published by Samuel Wood

1812–15 War between Britain and the United States

1813 Catnach Press established in London by James Catnach. Its publications include street ballads, execution sheets, and cheap children's books, many of them fairy tales and nursery rhymes, ranging in price from a quarter penny to a penny.

1815 Napoleon defeated at Waterloo

1816–48 Period of restoration in Europe, also known as the Metternich Era, after the reactionary chancellor of the Austro-Hungarian Empire who brought about a restoration of archconservative governments throughout Europe

1817 Foundation of American Sunday-School Union

ca. 1818–88 The firm of Richardson in Derby, founded by Thomas Richardson; publishes many children's educational chapbooks

1818 Mary Martha Sherwood's *The History of the Fairchild Family* (part 1), familiar Sunday reading in most Victorian nurseries

1819 Washington Irving's "Rip Van Winkle" and "The Legend of Sleepy Hollow"

1820 *The History of an Apple Pie. Written by Z* published by J. Harris and Son as a picture book

ca. 1821–32 Solomon King, in New York, publishes many traditional chapbook titles

1823 Edgar Taylor's *German Popular Stories,* a translation of selected tales from Jacob and Wilhelm Grimm's *Kinder- und Hausmärchen* (1812–15, *Children's and Household Tales*) • Clement C. Moore's *A Visit from St. Nicholas*

1827 The American Tract Society (founded 1825) begins publishing for children

1837 Victoria becomes queen of England.

1843 Charles Dickens's *A Christmas Carol*

1844 Heinrich Hoffmann's *Struwwelpeter* (Germany), the most influential picture book of the nineteenth century

1846 Mary Howitt's translation of *Wonderful Stories for Children* by Hans Christian Andersen; one of the first English translations of Andersen's fairy tales, which began appearing in Danish in 1835 • Edward Lear's *A Book of Nonsense,* an early use of the children's book as adult therapy

1848 Revolutions throughout Europe

1850 North London Collegiate School for Girls established

1851 Nathaniel Hawthorne's *A Wonder-Book for Girls and Boys; Tanglewood Tales* follows in 1853

1856 Charles Kingsley's *The Heroes,* a reply to Hawthorne

1861–65 American Civil War

1863 Charles Kingsley's *The Water-Babies* • Jules Verne's *Cinq semaines en ballon, voyage de découvertes en Afrique* (*Five Weeks in a Balloon*), the first major science fiction novel

1864 George MacDonald's "The Light Princess" first published in the novel *Adela Cathcart*

1865 Lewis Carroll's *Alice's Adventures in Wonderland*

1867 Hesba Stretton's *Jessica's First Prayer* begins a fashion for waif stories • British North America Act passes in the British Parliament, making Canada an independent country

1868 Louisa May Alcott's *Little Women*

1870 The Elementary Education Act passes in Britain

1872 Christina Rossetti's *Sing-Song*

1873 Foundation of *St. Nicholas Magazine*, with Mary Mapes Dodge as the first editor. This American magazine for young people, published until 1943, included stories by such leading writers as Frances Hodgson Burnett, Mark Twain, Frank Stockton, and Louisa May Alcott.

1874 First comic paper, *Funny Folks*, debuts in England

1875 Foundation of the New York Society for the Prevention of Cruelty to Children

1878 Randolph Caldecott's first "Toy Books"

1879 Kate Greenaway's *Under the Window* sets new clothing fashions for children • Thomas Edison invents the electric lightbulb

1880 Joel Chandler Harris's *Uncle Remus, His Songs and Sayings, the Folk-lore of the Old Plantation*, the first collection of fables of black Americans

1881 Robert Louis Stevenson's *Treasure Island*

1884 Mark Twain's *The Adventures of Huckleberry Finn* • Flora Annie Steele's *Wide-Awake Stories*, a collection of retold Indian tales • National Society for the Prevention of Cruelty to Children founded in England by Angela Burdett-Coutts

1885 Robert Louis Stevenson's *A Child's Garden of Verses*

ca. 1888 First comic sold in the United States: *Impossible Adventures*, originally published by Jean-Charles Pellerin in Epinal, France

1891 Free elementary education mandated throughout the United States

1892 First U.S. comic strip, "Little Bears and Tykes," *San Francisco Examiner*

1894–95 Rudyard Kipling's *Jungle Books*

1895 First appearance of the Golliwogg in Florence and Bertha Upton's *The Adventures of Two Dutch Dolls and a Golliwogg* • H. G. Wells's *The Time Machine*

1897 W. H. D. Rouse's *The Giant Crab*, a collection and retelling of Indian Jataka—stories of the previous births of the Buddha. In 1899 Rouse published a second collection, *The Talking Thrush* • Louise Mack's *Teens: A Story of Australian Schoolgirls*

1898 Ernest Thompson Seton's *Wild Animals I Have Known*

1899 Helen Bannerman's *Little Black Sambo*

1900 L. Frank Baum's *The Wizard of Oz*

1901 Seymour Hicks's *Bluebell in Fairyland*, one of the first commercial theatrical productions for children, opens in London • Queen Victoria dies • Australia becomes an independent country

1902 Beatrix Potter's *The Tale of Peter Rabbit* • Ernest Thompson Seton sets up first Woodcraft Tribe in Wyndygoul, New York

1903 Howard Pyle's *The Story of King Arthur and His Knights*. Three more Arthurian collections followed (1905–10) • Founding of the Children's Educational Theatre at the Educational Alliance in New York City

1904 J. M. Barrie's *Peter Pan* premiers in London and is produced with great success the following year in New York

1905 Frances Hodgson Burnett's *A Little Princess*

1906 Richard F. Outcault's *Hairbreadth Harry*, first U.S. serial comic strip

1907 Robert Baden-Powell runs experimental scout camp for boys on Brownsea Island in England

1908 L. M. Montgomery's *Anne of Green Gables* • Kenneth Grahame's *The Wind in the Willows*

1910 *Tom Swift and His Motor-Cycle*, the first Tom Swift novel (by Howard R. Garis, writing as Victor Appleton), one of many novels published by Edward Stratemeyer, a pioneer in syndicated series for boys and girls • Founding of the Drama League of America, which fostered productions of plays for children

1911 J. M. Barrie's novel *Peter and Wendy* • Frances Hodgson Burnett's *The Secret Garden* • Winsor McCay's animated short, *Little Nemo*, based on his comic strip *Little Nemo in Slumberland* (1905–11)

1914–18 World War I

1914 Brownsville Children's Library, the first library devoted exclusively to children's books, founded in New York City

1915 King Features founded to syndicate cartoon strips in newspapers

1916 Bureau of Educational Experiments (later, the Bank Street College of Education) founded in New York City by Lucy Sprague Mitchell • Creation of Lincoln Logs by John Lloyd Wright (son of the architect Frank Lloyd Wright)

1918 Johnny Gruelle's *Raggedy Ann Stories*

1920–21 Publication of *The Brownies' Book*, a periodical founded by W. E. B. Du Bois and designed for African American youth

1924 *Horn Book Magazine*, the first serial publication about children's books, founded in Boston

1926 Sir William Nicholson's *Clever Bill*, an important early use of chromolithography • A. A. Milne's *Winnie-the-Pooh* • Hugo Gernsback founds *Amazing Stories* in America, the first science fiction magazine with a mass circulation

1929 *The Funnies* #1, first U.S. comic book • First definitive publication of J. M. Barrie's play *Peter Pan; or The Boy Who Would Not Grow Up* • U.S. stock market crash; the Great Depression begins

1930 First *Mickey Mouse* comic strip

1932 Laura Ingalls Wilder's *Little House in the Big Woods*

1933 Hitler comes to power in Germany

1936–39 Spanish Civil War

1936 Munro Leaf and Robert Lawson's pacifist *The Story of Ferdinand*

1937 *And to Think That I Saw It on Mulberry Street*, first book by Theodor Seuss Geisel (Dr. Seuss) • J. R. R. Tolkien's *The Hobbit* • Walt Disney's animated film *Snow White and the Seven Dwarfs*, with backgrounds by Arthur Rackham

1938 First *Superman* comic

1939–45 World War II

1939 Robert L. May's *Rudolph the Red-Nosed Reindeer*, distributed free as a Christmas promotion by Montgomery Ward department stores

1940 James Thurber's *Fables for Our Time*, variations on Aesopic themes. *Further Fables for Our Time* follows (1956)

1941 Robert McCloskey's *Make Way for Ducklings*

1945 United States drops atomic bombs on Hiroshima and Nagasaki

1947 Margaret Wise Brown's *Goodnight Moon* • Robert Heinlein's *Rocket Ship Galileo*, his first important juvenile science fiction novel

1948 Unicorn Theatre, one of the most important theaters for children, founded in London by Caryl Jenner

1950 Ray Bradbury's *The Martian Chronicles* • C. S. Lewis's *The Lion, the Witch, and the Wardrobe*, the first of the seven Narnia chronicles (1950–56) • *Eagle* #1, first of new-style U.K. comics

1951 J. D. Salinger's *The Catcher in the Rye*

1952 Anne Frank's *Diary of a Young Girl* • E. B. White's *Charlotte's Web*

1953 IBBY (International Board on Books for Young People) founded by Jella Lepman in Zurich, Switzerland. There are now more than sixty-five chapters throughout the world.

1954 Frederic Wertham's *Seduction of the Innocent*, a critique of the influence of comic books • *Brown v. Board of Education*, U.S. Supreme Court decision declaring segregated schools unconstitutional

1955–91 *Captain Kangaroo*, television program for children hosted by Robert (Bob) Keeshan

1957 Dr. Seuss's *The Cat in the Hat*

1959 Ruth Handler creates the Barbie doll, named for her daughter; the Ken doll, named for her son, would debut in 1961; Christie, an African American doll, in 1968

1961 Roald Dahl's *James and the Giant Peach*

1962 Cuban missile crisis

1963 Ezra Jack Keats's *The Snowy Day* • Madeleine L'Engle's *A Wrinkle in Time*, a blend of science, fantasy, and religious themes • Maurice Sendak's *Where the Wild Things Are* • Martin Luther King Jr. leads the March on Washington and delivers his "I Have a Dream" speech

1964 Louise Fitzhugh's *Harriet the Spy* • Lloyd Alexander's *The Book of Three*

1965–73 Vietnam War

1967–2001 *Mister Rogers' Neighborhood*, created and hosted by Fred Rogers; the longest-running program on PBS

1968–74 At high schools and universities in the United States and United Kingdom, student movements bring about major reforms in teaching and curriculums that lead to the questioning of the canon and traditional pedagogy

1968 Eric Carle's *The Very Hungry Caterpillar* • Ursula Le Guin's *A Wizard of Earthsea*, the first in the Earthsea series (1968–2001)

1969 *Sesame Street*, featuring Jim Henson's muppets, begins its telecast on PBS • First landing of humans on the moon

1970 Judy Blume's *Are You There, God? It's Me, Margaret*, a young adult novel that depicts teenage life candidly and realistically • *Signal: Approaches to Children's Books* founded by Nancy Chambers and Aidan Chambers

1971 Foundation of the International Research Society for Children's Literature (IRSCL) in Europe; Klaus Doderer elected first president

1973 Foundation of the Children's Literature Association by Anne Devereaux Jordan and Francelia Butler

1974 Robert Cormier's *The Chocolate War*, the first of his dark and compelling young adult novels

1975 Natalie Babbitt's *Tuck Everlasting* • Mitsumasa Anno's *Anno's Alphabet*

1976 Leo and Diane Dillon's *Ashanti to Zulu* • Mildred D. Taylor's *Roll of Thunder, Hear My Cry*

1977 Katherine Paterson's *Bridge to Terabithia* • Robert Crowther's *The Most Amazing Hide-and-Seek Alphabet Book*, a movable picture book

1978 Raymond Briggs's *The Snowman*, a wordless picture book in comic-strip form

1979 Leonard Clark's *Tales from the Panchatantra*, ancient Indian fables, many of which have passed into European folklore

1980 Toshi Maruki's *Hiroshima no Pika*, a depiction of the bombing of Hiroshima • Isaac Bashevis Singer's *The Power of Light: Eight Stories for Hanukkah*, stories about Jewish life and traditions • Robert Munsch's *The Paper Bag Princess*, a feminist picture book

1982 David McKee's *I Hate My Teddy Bear*, a surrealistic tale

1985 Virginia Hamilton's *The People Could Fly: American Black Folktales*

1988–2004

1988 David Macaulay's *The Way Things Work*

1989 *The Simpsons,* animated prime-time television show created by Matt Groening, begins • David Macaulay's *Black and White,* a nonlinear picture story • Successful production of *The Little Mermaid* brings about the resurgence of Disney's animated fairy-tale films such as *Beauty and the Beast, Aladdin,* and *Mulan* • Fall of the Berlin Wall • Demonstration and massacre at Beijing's Tiananmen Square

1991 Collapse of the Soviet Union

1992 Lane Smith and Jon Scieszka's *The Stinky Cheese Man,* a postmodern picture book

1993 Lois Lowry's *The Giver* • Alma Flor Ada's *My Name Is María Isabel* • Child_lit listserve founded by Michael Joseph at Rutgers, an unmoderated, international, cross-disciplinary discussion group bringing together authors (including Julius Lester, Philip Pullman, and Jane Yolen), illustrators, teachers, publishers, editors, scholars, librarians, and others interested in talking about children's literature

1994 Zlata Filipović's *Zlata's Diary: A Child's Life in Sarajevo* • Eve Bunting's *Smoky Night* (illustrated by David Diaz), a picture-book response to the Los Angeles riots of 1992

1995–2000 Philip Pullman's *His Dark Materials* trilogy

1997–2004 *Teletubbies,* children's television program broadcast in Britain; developed by Anne Wood and Andrew Davenport

1997 J. K. Rowling's *Harry Potter and the Philosopher's Stone* (U.S. title: *Harry Potter and the Sorcerer's Stone*)

1999 Jenni Overend and Julie Vivas's *Hello Baby* (Australia), an explicit depiction of natural childbirth

2001 *Shrek,* digital film adaptation of William Steig's *Shrek!* (1990), followed by *Shrek 2* in 2004, both intended to challenge the formulaic Disney fairy-tale films

2003 Mark Haddon's *The Curious Incident of the Dog in the Night-time,* winner of the Whitbread award; a crossover book originally published for children

2004 Film adaptation of Chris Van Allsburg's *The Polar Express* (1985)

General Bibliography

Histories

Children's books are intimately linked with the social, cultural, political, and pedagogical contexts of their production. Thus, the most helpful histories in the field situate themselves in the cultural fabric of the world being described. The best place to begin research into children's literature studies is in the first historical survey of the subject, *Children's Books in England: Five Centuries of Social Life*, (1932) by F. J. Harvey Darton, who was descended from one of the oldest families of publishers in Britain. Darton's original work was revised and updated by Brian Alderson in 1982, and this third edition still stands as a best first resource for information about the field—a new edition was published by the British Library in 1998. Other good general histories include *Written for Children* (1965) by John Rowe Townsend. The revised sixth edition was published in 1998. *A Critical History of Children's Literature* (1969 edition ed. Cornelia Meigs, Anne Eaton, Elizabeth Nesbitt, and Ruth H. Viguers) is still worth reading, as it offers quick access to the historical record. For research that begins in a more specific time or place or has a more explicit context, there are several options. Mary V. Jackson's *Engines of Instruction, Mischief, and Magic: Children's Literature in England from Its Beginnings to 1839* (1989) is helpful in its attention to publishing and marketing strategies. C. John Sommerville's *The Discovery of Childhood in Puritan England* (1992) remains an excellent resource for study of the Puritan ideologies underlying much of the early publishing history of children's literature. Gillian Avery's *Behold the Child: American Children and Their Books, 1621–1922* (1994) is an excellent comprehensive study. Andrew O'Malley's *The Making of the Modern Child: Children's Literature and Childhood in the Late Eighteenth Century* (2003) is a recent study of this significant period in the history of children's literature. John Goldthwaite's *The Natural History of Make-Believe: A Guide to the Principal Works of Britain, Europe and America* (1996) is original and well-researched. And Humphrey Carpenter's *Secret Gardens: A Study of the Golden Age of Children's Literature* (1985) offers literary insights into nineteenth- and early-twentieth-century children's books, a particularly important period in children's literature history.

Introductions to Children's Literature and Children's Literature Criticism: Essay Collections and Monographs

Because the academic study of children's literature is still so new, one of the best ways to get an initial sense of the theoretical scope of the field is by reading essay collections. Some volumes consist of essays composed for specific occasions; others are important scholarly essays selected from leading journals and assembled to offer a wide view of the field. The major benefit of reading such volumes is that they provide very good access, very quickly, to the work of prominent critics and scholars in the field and to the major theoretical and critical concerns that undergird children's literature scholarship. Two helpful early general collections are *The Cool Web: The Pattern of Children's Reading* (1977), ed. Griselda Barton, Aidan Warlow, and Margaret Meek, and *Only Connect: Readings in Children's Literature*, ed. Sheila Egoff, first published in 1969, but revised for a third edition and published in 1996. For a good collection of essays on illustration and publishing history, see *Children and Their Books: A Celebration of the Work of Iona and Peter Opie* (1989), ed. Gillian Avery and Julia Briggs. Three helpful collections of critical articles about children's literature are *The Signal Approach to Children's Books* (1980), ed. Nancy Chambers, and *Children's Literature: The Development of Criticism* (1990) and *Literature for Children: Contemporary Criticism* (1992), both ed. Peter Hunt. *Stories and Society* (1992), ed. Dennis Butts, offers good introductory critical essays to some of the most familiar genres in children's literature, while Margery Hourihan's *Deconstructing the Hero: Literary Theory and Children's Literature* (1997) explores the structure and meaning of the adventure story. Two recent though more specialized collections of essays edited by Sandra Beckett offer valuable insights into trends in contemporary criticism: *Reflections of Change: Children's Literature Since 1945* (1997) and *Transcending Boundaries: Writing for a Dual Audience of Children and Adults* (1999). Two important monographs about the nature of children's fiction are *The Case of Peter Pan: Or the Impossibility of Children's Fiction* (1984, rev. ed. 1994) by Jacqueline Rose and *The Narrator's Voice: The Dilemma of Children's Fiction* (1991) by Barbara Wall. Helpful discussions about the changing states of children's literature are found in Michele Landsberg's *The World of Children's Books: A Guide to Choosing the Best* (1988), Zohar Shavit's *The Poetics of Children's Literature* (1986), Maria Nikolajeva's *Children's Literature Comes of Age: Toward a New Aesthetic* (1995), Eliza Dresang's *Radical Change: Books for Youth in a Digital Age* (1999), and Jack Zipes's *Sticks and Stones: The Troublesome Success of Children's Literature from Slovenly Peter to Harry Potter* (2002).

Multiculturalism

In the last forty or so years, children's books about non-white, non-Eurocentric children began to be published in greater numbers and increasing attention has been paid to the development of a critical discourse about those books. For a good general start, see *A Multicultural Guide to Children's Books 0–16+* (1999), ed. Rosemary Stones. See also Mingshui Cai's *Multicultural Literature for Children and Young Adults: Reflections on Critical Issues* (2002). Althea K. Helbig and Agnes Regan Perkins have assembled a helpful study, *Many Peoples, One Land: A Guide to New Multicultural Literature for Children and Young Adults* (2001). There are also studies specific to particular groups: *Literature for Children about Asians and Asian-Americans: Analysis and Annotated Bibliography* (1987) by Esther C. Jenkins and Mary C. Austin; Barbara J. Kuipers's *American Indian References and Resource Book for Children and Young Adults* (2nd ed. 1995); Michelle H. Martin's *Brown Gold: Milestones of African-American Children's Picture Books, 1845–2002* (2004); Kate Capshaw Smith's *Children's Literature and the Harlem Renaissance* (2004); Frances Ann Day's *Lesbian and Gay Voices: An Annotated Bibliography and Guide to Literature for Children and Young Adults* (2000) and *Latina and Latino Voices in Literature for*

Children and Teenagers (1997); Cheryl Silberberg Grossman's *Jewish Literature for Children: A Teaching Guide* (1985); and Barbara Rollock's *Black Authors and Illustrators of Children's Books: A Biographical Dictionary* (2nd ed. 1992). Also very good is *A Guide to Canadian Children's Books* (2003) by Deirdre Baker and Ken Setterington. For a discussion of Australian children's, books, see *The Written World: Youth and Literature* (1994), ed. Agnes Nieuwenhuizen. Dan Hade's "Reading Children's Literature Multiculturally," in *Reflections of Change* (1997), ed. Sandra Beckett, is a useful introduction to finding multicultural books that are more than costumed attempts to placate current trends. And see Lissa Paul's "Boutique Inclusiveness in Literacy Education," in *Signal* 93 (Sept. 2000), for an account of the misuses to which multiculturalism is being put in some settings.

Gender

The rise of feminism in the early 1970s was co-incident with the rise of children's literature studies as a formal academic discipline. For an excellent introductory collection of essays covering the way gender studies have informed children's literature studies, see *Girls, Boys, Books, Toys: Gender in Children's Literature and Culture* (1999), ed. Beverly Lyon Clark and Margaret Higonnet. For a historical account of the lives and literatures of girls and women, see Lynne Vallone's *Disciplines of Virtue: Girls' Culture in the Eighteenth and Nineteenth Centuries* (1995). *Girls Only? Gender and Popular Fiction in Britain, 1880–1910* (1990) by Kimberley Reynolds offers an account of a subsequent wave of stories aimed at girls. See also Claudia Nelson's *Boys Will Be Girls: The Feminine Ethic and British Children's Fiction, 1857–1917* (1991). The influence of feminist theory on children's literature studies is found in *What Katy Read:Feminist Re-readings of 'Classic' Stories for Girls* (1995) by Shirley Foster and Judy Simons and in *Waking Sleeping Beauty: Feminist Voices in Children's Novels* (1997) by Roberta Seelinger Trites. See also *Reading Otherways* (1998) by Lissa Paul for an account of reading children's books in ways informed by feminist theory. For discussions on a masculine perspective, see *Ways of Being Male: Representing Masculinities in Children's Literature and Film* (2002), ed. John Stephens, and Kenneth Kidd's *Making American Boys: Boyology and the Feral Tale* (2004).

Picture Books

The combination of text and image in picture books creates unique narrative structures. For good introductions to reading picture books, see Jane Doonan's *Looking at Pictures in Picture Books* (1993), Perry Nodelman's *Words about Pictures: The Narrative Art of Children's Picture Books* (1988), and Maria Nikolajeva and Carole Scott's *How Picturebooks Work* (2001). More advanced techniques of analysis are found in David Lewis's *Reading Contemporary Picturebooks: Picturing Text* (2001) and Scott McCloud's *Understanding Comics* (1993). There are several good accounts of picture book history. Brian Alderson's *Sing a Song for Sixpence: The English Picture Book Tradition and Randolph Caldecott* (1986) is an authoritative study of the British picture book tradition. For discussions of American picture book history, see Barbara Bader's *American Picturebooks: From Noah's Ark to the Beast Within* (1976) and *Myth, Magic and Mystery: One Hundred Years of American Book Illustration* (1996) by Michael Patrick Hearn, Trinkett Clark, and H. Nichols Clark.

Reading and Understanding Children's Literature

Because reading children's books isn't quite like reading texts for adults, it is helpful to consider the different interpretive possibilities available in children's book discourse. *Tell Me: Children, Reading and Talk* (1993) by Aidan Chambers, an introduction to a form of reader-response theory particularly useful in interpreting children's books, is a good place to begin. For a solid overview of the field of children's literature and some of the major theoretical approaches, see *Understanding Children's Literature* (2005), ed. Peter Hunt, which consists of a sequence of essays originally published in Hunt's *International Companion Encyclopedia of Children's Literature*. For an individual account of contemporary theoretical approaches to children's literature, see Roderick McGillis's *The Nimble Reader: Literary Theory and Children's Literature* (1996). For in-depth discussions of ideology and children's books, see Peter Hollindale's *Ideology and the Children's Book* (1988) and John Stephens's *Language and Ideology in Children's Fiction* (1992). In *Children's Literature: Criticism and the Fictional Child* (1994), Karín Lesnik-Oberstein offers a psychological investigation of children's literature that continues the work of Jacqueline Rose. Valuable books that focus on the connections between the child reader and children's literature include *The Braid of Literature: Children's Worlds of Reading* (1992) by Shirley Brice Heath and Shelby Wolf, Nicholas Tucker's *The Child and the Book: A Psychological and Literary Exploration* (1981), Margaret Meek's *How Texts Teach What Readers Learn* (1998) and *Information and Book Learning* (1996), and Kay Vandergrift's *Children's Literature, Research and Teaching* (1990).

Reference Books, Bibliographies, and Encyclopedias

For essay-length analyses of major issues in children's literature, see the *International Companion Encyclopedia of Children's Literature* (2nd ed. 2004), ed. Peter Hunt. *The Cambridge Guide to Children's Books in English* (2001), ed. Victor Watson, and *The Continuum Encyclopedia of Children's Literature* (2001), ed. Bernice Cullinan and Diane G. Person, offer brief introductions to a large number of authors, texts, and issues. A slightly older but still dependable and well-written reference source is Humphrey Carpenter and Mari Prichard's *The Oxford Companion to Children's Literature* (1984). See also *Children's Books and Their Creators* (1995), ed. Anita Silvey. The Something about the Author series (ongoing since 1971) offers useful biographical and bibliographical information on authors and illustrators of children's books. For a quick reference source on twentieth-century children's authors, see *The St. James Guide to Children's Writers* (5th ed. 1999).

Selected Bibliographies

The Selected Bibliographies offer suggestions for further reading for each of the sections in the anthology. We have included author bibliographies, ordered alphabetically within the sections, for those whose work has influenced other writers for children and been the subject of much scholarship. For authors who have written for both children and adults or whose work has been adopted by a young reading audience, we have listed important scholarship that speaks to their influence within children's literature.

ALPHABETS

For general background the entry under "ABC Books" in Humphrey Carpenter and Mari Pritchard's *Oxford Companion to Children's Literature* (1984) gives a historical summary of the genre. Anne Rowe provides a similar survey in Victor Watson's *Cambridge Guide to Children's Books in English* (2001). Mrs. E. M. Field's *The Child and His Book* (1891) has a chapter on ABCs, as has Irene Whalley's *Cobwebs to Catch Flies: Illustrated Books for the Nursery and Schoolroom 1700–1900* (1974). Ian Michael's *The Teaching of English: From the Sixteenth Century to 1870* (1987) has an extensive bibliography of early spellers and readers.

Andrew Tuer's lavishly illustrated *History of the Horn Book* (1897, rep. 1979) describes how the alphabet was originally taught. Beulah Folmsbee's *Little History of the Horn-book* (1942, rep. 1965) is a useful shorter work. John E. Sadler's *John Amos Comenius: Orbis Pictus* (1968) reproduces in facsimile the first English translation of this seventeenth-century schoolbook, which begins with a picture alphabet. For American classroom teaching, see Clifton Johnson's *Old-Time Schools*

and School-books (1904, rep. 1963)—there is no index, but chapter 3 is devoted to the *New England Primer* and there are examples of alphabet books in chapter 8, "Other Spellers." Both P. L. Ford (1899) and Charles F. Heartman (1934) wrote studies of the *New England Primer.*

Iona and Peter Opie's *The Oxford Dictionary of Nursery Rhymes* (1951) gives five examples of early ABC rhymes, and the same authors' *A Nursery Companion* (1980) reproduces two early-nineteenth-century colored alphabet picture books. Mary F. Thwaite (1966) edited a facsimile of John Newbery's *A Little Pretty Pocket Book* (1744), which contains "A New Attempt to Teach Children the Use of the English Alphabet, by Way of Diversion." Ruari McLean's *Pictorial Alphabets* (1969) reproduces examples from the sixteenth century to 1941. Ruth M. Baldwin's *One Hundred Nineteenth-Century Rhyming Alphabets* (1972) gives both English and American examples. Peter Stockham's *Chapbooks ABC's* (1974) gives five facsimile examples published from 1830 to 1870.

CHAPBOOKS

Humphrey Carpenter and Mari Prichard give a summary of the history of chapbooks and their

printers in *The Oxford Companion to Children's Literature* (1984); there are also articles on individual titles. Louise Field (Mrs. E. M. Field) discusses chapbooks in *The Child and His Book* (1895). F. J. Harvey Darton's "The Pedlar's Pack," chapter 5 in *Children's Books in England* (3rd ed. 1982), includes illustrations and a bibliography. Harry B. Weiss's *A Book about Chapbooks* (1942) discusses chapbooks and their authors and printers in England, Scotland, and the United States. Victor E. Neuburg's *The Penny Histories* (1968) includes facsimile reproductions of seven chapbooks, an introduction describing the material and the more important British and American printers, and a valuable bibliography. Margaret Spufford's *Small Books and Pleasant Histories* (1981) describes the readership for popular literature in seventeenth-

century England. William Ashton's *Chapbooks of the Eighteenth Century* (1882) reprints with useful comments text and illustrations from 103 popular eighteenth-century titles. Robert L. Collison's *The Story of Street Literature: Forerunner of the Popular Press* (1973) widens the field to discuss religious tracts, lampoons, cartoons, and crime stories.

The Other Print Tradition: Essays on Chapbooks, Broadsides, and Related Ephemera (1995), ed. Cathy Lynn Preston and Michael Preston, and Andrew O'Malley's *The Making of a Modern Child: Children's Literature and Childhood in the Late Eighteenth Century* (2003) contain important historical discussions of the chapbook in relation to children's literature.

PRIMERS AND READERS

Although the histories of reading instruction, schooling, and education are related, no single volume offers an overview. The most useful general introduction for the three linked fields is *Opening the Nursery Door: Reading, Writing and Childhood, 1600–1900* (1997), a collection of essays edited by Mary Hilton, Morag Styles, and Victor Watson. For an introduction to children's literature, F. J. Harvey Darton's classic *Children's Books in England* (1998), revised by Brian Alderson, is always the first place to begin. Mary Jackson's *Engines of Instruction, Mischief, and Magic: Children's Literature in England from Its Beginnings to 1839* (1989) is also helpful—besides tracing the children's book industry, it tracks patterns of audience response. Also useful as general introductions are R. A. Houston's *Literacy in Early Modern Europe: Culture and Education* (2002), Alan Richardson's *Literature, Education and Romanticism: Reading as Social Practice, 1780–1832* (1994), Gillian Avery's *Behold the Child: American Children and Their Books, 1621–1922* (1994), and John C. Sommerville's *The Discovery of Childhood in Puritan England* (1992). For a general literary discussion of reading, see *A History of Reading* (1996) by Alberto Manguel. For a good collection of essays on theories of literacy education, see *New Readings: Contributions to an Understanding of Literacy* (1992), ed. Keith Kimberly, Margaret Meek, and Jane Miller. Lawrence Stone's *Schooling and Society: Studies in the History of Education* (1976) is still regarded as a standard source book. R. A. Houston's *Literacy in Early Modern Europe* (2002) is the most comprehensive historical study of lit-

eracy, education, and religion. A general account of what it means to be literate is found in Margaret Meek's *On Being Literate* (1991). A good discussion on North American literacy instruction in the second half of the twentieth century is offered in *Literacy, Textbooks and Ideology: Postwar Literacy Instruction and the Mythology of Dick and Jane* (1988) by Allan Luke.

Anna Laetitia Barbauld
For a general introduction to Barbauld's works, see *Anna Letitia Barbauld: Selected Poetry and Prose* (2002), ed. William McCarthy and Elizabeth Kraft. To read about Barbauld as a working poet in the context of her contemporaries, see *Eighteenth-Century Women Poets: An Oxford Anthology* (1989), ed. Roger Lonsdale. For the most part, Barbauld's works for children, including *Lessons for Children* (1778), are available only in collections of rare children's books, but her *Hymns in Prose for Children* (1781) appears in a modern reprint edition, published by Garland in 1977. The only easily available general book on Barbauld is *Georgian Chronicle: Mrs. Barbauld and Her Family* (1958) by Betsy Rodgers. For essays about Barbauld as an author for children, see Sarah Robbins's "Re-Making Barbauld's Primers: A Case Study in the Americanization of British Literary Pedagogy," *Children's Literature Association Quarterly* 21.4 (1996–97), and Lynne Vallone's " 'A Humble Spirit Under Correction': Tracts, Hymns, and the Ideology of Evangelical Fiction for Children, 1780–1820," *The Lion and the Unicorn* 15.2 (1991).

FAIRY TALES

The best general introductions to the history of the fairy tale for children include Roger Sale's *Fairy Tales and After: From Snow White to E. B. White* (1978), Jack Zipes's *Fairy Tales and the Art of Subversion: The Classical Genre for Children and the Process of Civilization* (1983) and *When Dreams*

Came True: Classical Fairy Tales and Their Tradition (1999), and Steven Swann Jones's *The Fairy Tale: The Magic Mirror of Imagination* (1995). Gillian Avery provides important historical background about the development of the fairy tale in America in *Behold the Child: American Children* and Their Books, 1621–1922 (1994). Maria Tatar's introductions in The Classic Fairy Tales (1990), Martin Hallett and Barbara Karasek's Folk and Fairy Tales (2nd ed. 1996), and U. C. Knoepflmacher's Ventures into Childland: Victorians, Fairy Tales, and Femininity (1998) analyze the rise of the fairy tale in England. General historical studies include Ruth Bottigheimer, ed., Fairy Tales and Society: Illusion, Allusion, and Paradigm (1986), James McGlathery, ed., The Brothers Grimm and Folktale (1988), and Nancy Canepa, ed., Out of the Woods: The Origins of the Literary Fairy Tale in Italy and France (1997). For a structural analysis, see Max Lüthi's Once Upon a Time: On the Nature of Fairy Tales (1970). The psychological approach is emphasized in Julius Heuscher's A Psychiatric Study of Fairy Tales (1963), Bruno Bettelheim's The Uses of Enchantment: The Meaning and Importance of Fairy Tales (1976), and Maria Tatar's Off with Their Heads: Fairy Tales and the Culture of Childhood (1992). The feminist perspective is developed in Marcia Lieberman's "Some Day My Prince Will Come: Female Acculturation Through the Fairy Tale," College English 34 (1972); Jennifer Waelti-Walters's Fairy Tales and the Female Imagination (1982); Jack Zipes, ed., Don't Bet on the Prince: Contemporary Feminist Fairy Tales in North America and England (1986); Marina Warner's From the Beast to the Blonde: On Fairytales and Their Tellers (1995); and Elizabeth Harries's Twice Upon a Time: Women Writers and the Fairy Tale (2001). Among the useful textbooks that discuss how to use folk and fairy tales in the classroom are Gloria T. Blatt's Once Upon a Folktale: Capturing the Folklore Process with Children (1993), Cynthia Dresser's The Rainmaker's Dog: International Folktales to Build Communicative Skills (1994), Gail de Vos and Anna E. Altmann's New Tales for Old: Folktales as Literary Fictions for Young Adults

(1999), and Eric K. Taylor's Using Folktales (2000). Jacques Barchilon and Peter Flinders offer an important study of the canonical author in Charles Perrault (1981). Individual tales are analyzed in depth in Jack Zipes's The Trials and Tribulations of Little Red Riding Hood: Versions of the Tale in Socio-cultural Context (1983), Betsy Hearne's Beauty and the Beast: Visions and Revisions of an Old Tale (1989), and Jerry Griswold's The Meanings of "Beauty and the Beast": A Handbook (2004). Among the most perceptive books dealing with the fairy tale and film are Richard Schickel's The Disney Version: The Life, Times, Art and Commerce of Walt Disney (1968), Marc Eliot's Walt Disney: Hollywood's Dark Prince (1993), and Elizabeth Bell, Lynda Haas, and Laura Sells, eds., From Mouse to Mermaid: The Politics of Film, Gender, and Culture (1995). The most thorough reference work is Jack Zipes, ed., The Oxford Companion to Fairy Tales (2000). The major Anglophone journal is Marvels & Tales: Journal of Fairy-Tale Studies.

The Brothers Grimm

Important studies of the Brothers Grimm include Maria Tatar's The Hard Facts of the Grimms' Fairy Tales (1987); Christa Kamenetsky's The Brothers Grimm and Their Critics: Folktales and the Quest for Meaning (1992); Donald Haase, ed., The Reception of the Grimms' Fairy Tales: Responses, Reactions, Revisions (1993); and Jack Zipes's The Brothers Grimm: From Enchanted Forests to the Modern World (1988).

Hans Christian Andersen

Two good biographies of Andersen are Elias Bredsdorff's Hans Christian Andersen (1975) and Jackie Wullschlager's Hans Christian Andersen: The Life of a Storyteller (2000).

ANIMAL FABLES

In The Fables of Aesop (1894), the folklorist Joseph Jacobs selected the fables he considered the "most effective and the most familiar" and traced their history. F. J. Harvey Darton's Children's Books in England (1998) opens with a chapter on fables. Anne Stevenson Hobbs's Fables (1986) offers a selection of fable illustrations from over five hundred years with accompanying text, historical introduction, and bibliography. Gerald Gottlieb's Early Children's Books and Their Illustration (1975) shows examples from the Pierpont Morgan Library, including a fragment from a third-or fourth-century papyrus with the earliest surviving Greek texts of three fables. Barbara Quinnam's Fables

from Incunabula to Modern Picture Books: A Selective Bibliography (1966) covers Indian and related fables, Aesop, La Fontaine, and Krylov. Margaret Blount includes fables in Animal Land: The Creatures of Children's Fiction (1974). With its copious illustrations, Mary V. Jackson's Engines of Instruction, Mischief, and Magic: Children's Literature in England from Its Beginnings to 1839 (1989) gives a splendid panoramic view of pre-Victorian literature. The Ancient Fable: An Introduction (2001) by Niklas Holzberg and Christine Jackson-Holzberg is a solid introduction to the historical origins of the fable.

CLASSICAL MYTHS

There are many hundreds of retellings, perhaps the most scholarly of which is Robert Graves's Greek

Myths (2 vols. 1955), which also includes some commentary. Stephen L. Harris's Classical Mythology: *Images and Insights* (1997) includes both theory and an extensive anthology. A good introductory handbook is Barry B. Powell's *Classical Myths* (3rd ed. 2000).

Major reference works include Richard Buxton's *Complete World of Greek Mythology* (2004), Michael Grant and John Hazel's *Who's Who in Classical Mythology* (2001), Henry March's *Cassell Dictionary of Classical Mythology* (2001), and Bernard Evslin's *Gods, Demigods and Demons: An Encyclopedia of Greek Mythology* (1988). Useful general reference books are the *Oxford Classical Dictionary* (1970) and the *New Larousse Encyclopedia of Mythology* (1968). Genealogies and original sources are listed in P. Grimal's *Dictionary of Classical Mythology* (1985).

Good introductions to the myths and their historical period include Fritz Graf's *Greek Mythology: an Introduction* (1993), Lowell Edmunds, ed., *Approaches to Greek Myth* (1990), and Jane F. Gardner's *Roman Myths* (1993).

Historical and archeological examinations of the period include Robert Tuscan's *The Gods of Ancient Rome* (2000) and Timothy Gantz's *Early Greek Myths: A Guide to Literary and Artistic Sources* (1993). Extensive illustrations are offered by T. H. Carpenter's *Art and Myth in Ancient Greece* (1991).

Analyses of the myths can be found in Ken Dowden's *The Uses of Greek Myth* (1992), Michael Grant's *Myths of the Greeks and Romans* (1962), G. S. Kirk's *The Nature of the Greek Myths* (1974), and Jan Bremmer, ed. *Interpretations of Greek Mythology* (1987). Two examinations of the female in the myths are Robert E. Bell's *Women of Classical Mythology: A Biographical Dictionary* (1991) and M. Lefkowitz's *Women in Greek Myth* (1986).

The standard examination of myths and legends (and fairy tales) from an educational point of view remains Elizabeth Cook's *The Ordinary and the Fabulous* (2nd ed. 1976).

LEGENDS

To date there has not been a thorough study of the legend for young readers. The most important theoretical work is Linda Dégh's *Legend and Belief: Dialectics of a Folklore Genre* (2001). Maurice Saxby's "Myth and Legend," in *International Companion Encyclopedia of Children's Literature*, ed. Peter Hunt (2nd ed. 2004), is helpful. Studies that place the legend within the history of folklore include Benjamin A. Botkin's *A Treasury of American Folklore* (1944); Walter Blair's *Tall Tale America: A Legendary History of Our Humorous Heroes* (1944); Maurice Keen's *The Outlaws of Medieval Legend* (1961); Jan Brunvand's *The Study of American Folklore* (1968), Wayland D. Hand, ed., *American Folk Legend: A Symposium* (1971); John J. Marcatante and Robert R. Potter's *American Folklore and Legends* (1971); Heda Jason's "Concerning the 'Historical' and the 'Local' Legends and Their Relatives," *Journal of American Folklore* 84 (1971); Richard Dorson's *America in Legend: Folklore from the Colonial Period to the Present* (1973); Gladys-Marie Fry's *Night Riders in Black Folk History* (1975); Tristram Potter Coffin's *The Female Hero in Folklore and Legend* (1978); Kemp B. Battle's *Great American Folklore* (1986); Bengt Klintberg's "Do the Legends of Today and Yesterday Belong to the Same Genre?" in *Storytelling in Contemporary Societies* (1990), ed. Lutz Röhrich and Sabine Weinker-Piepho; Donald Ward's "On the Genre Morphology of Legendry: Belief Story versus Belief Legend," *Western Folklore* 50 (1991); Ulf Palmenfelt, "On the Understanding of Folk Legends," in *Telling Reality: Folk Studies in Memory of Bengt Holbek* (1993), ed. Michael Chesnutt.

Some useful pedagogical books include Bette Bosma's *Fairy Tales, Fables, Legends, and Myths: Using Folk Literature in Your Classroom* (1992) and Gloria T. Blatt, ed., *Once Upon a Folktale: Capturing the Folklore Process with Children* (1993).

Important books that contain information about the legend for children and its relationship to the chapbook include Mary F. Thwaite's *From Primer to Pleasure in Reading* (1972); Mary Lystad's *From Dr. Mather to Dr. Seuss: 200 Years of American Books for Children* (1980); Eric Quayle's *Early Children's Books: A Collector's Guide* (1983); Mary V. Jackson's *Engines of Instruction, Mischief, and Magic: Children's Literature in England from Its Beginnings to 1839* (1989); Gillian Avery's *Behold the Child: American Children and Their Books, 1621–1922* (1994); Cathy Lynn Preston and Michael J. Preston, eds., *The Other Print Tradition: Essays on Chapbooks, Broadsides, and Related Ephemera* (1995); and Andrew O'Malley's *The Making of the Modern Child: Children's Literature and Childhood in the Late Eighteenth Century* (2003). Useful anthologies include John T. Flanagan and Arthur Palmer Hudson, eds., *Folklore in American Literature* (1958); Kevin Crossley-Holland, ed., *The Faber Book of Northern Legends* (1981); Robert D. San Souci, ed., *Cut from the Same Cloth: American Women of Myth, Legend, and the Tall Tale* (1993); Amy Cohn, ed., *From Sea to Shining Sea: A Treasury of American Folklore and Folk Songs* (1993); Richard Cavendish, ed., *Legends of the Word* (1994); David Leeming and Jake Page, eds., *Myths, Legends and Folktales of America* (1999); and Richard Barber, ed., *Myths and Legends of the British Isles* (1999).

Significant studies of individual legends include James Stevens's *Paul Bunyan* (1925); Guy B. Johnson's *John Henry: Tracking Down a Negro Legend* (1929); Louis W. Chappell's *John Henry: A Folk-Lore Study* (1933); Walter Blair and Franklin J. Meine's *Mike Fink, King of Mississippi Keelboatman* (1933); Constance Rourke's *Davy Crockett* (1934); Richard Dorson, ed., *Davy Crockett: American Comic Legend* (1939); Daniel Hoffman's

Paul Bunyan, Last of the Frontier Demigods (1952); Robert Price's *Johnny Appleseed, Man and Myth* (1954); Earl C. Beck's *They Knew Paul Bunyan* (1956); Roger Sherman Loomis, ed., *Arthurian Literature in the Middle Ages: A Collaborative History* (1959); Grace Steele Woodward's *Pocahontas* (1969); Valentine Harris's *The Truth about Robin Hood* (1969); A. J. Pollard's *Imagining Robin Hood* (2003); Philip Barbour's *Pocahontas and Her World* (1970); Eugene Vinaver's *The Rise of Romance* (1971); Richard Barber's *King Arthur in Legend and History* (1974); Glenys Goetinck's *Peredur: A Study of Welsh Traditions in the Grail Legends* (1975); J. C. Holt's *Robin Hood* (1982); Julian Scutts's "The Pied Piper of Hamelin as a Motif in European Poetry," *Wascana Review* (1985); Wolfgang Mieder's "The Pied Piper of Hamelin: Origin, History, and Survival of the Legend," in *Tradition and Innovation in Folk Literature* (1987); Alan Lupack and Barbara Tepa Lupack's *King Arthur in America* (1999); and Barbara Tepa Lupack's *Adapting the Arthurian Legends for Children: Essays on Arthurian Juvenilia* (2004). For a useful guide to legends, see Maria Leach, ed., *Funk and Wagnalls Standard Dictionary of Folklore, Mythology, and Legend* (1972).

RELIGION: JUDEO-CHRISTIAN STORIES

International Companion Encyclopedia of Children's Literature, ed. Peter Hunt (2nd ed. 2004), includes particularly useful chapters on "Catechistical, Devotional and Biblical Writing" by Ruth B. Bottigheimer and "Contemporary Religious Writing" by Rita Ghesquière. F. J. Harvey Darton's *Children's Books in England* (3rd ed. 1982) has a chapter on the Puritan "Good Godly Books," as well as chapters on such writers as Isaac Watts and Mrs. Sherwood. Gillian Avery's *Behold the Child: American Children and Their Books, 1621–1922* (1994) gives an account of early religious education and the later Sunday school fiction. Ruth B. Bottigheimer describes the different ways the Bible has been taught in *The Bible for Children: From the Age of Gutenberg to the Present* (1996).

Ian Green's *The Christian's ABC: Catechisms and Catechizing in England, c. 1540–1740* (1995) describes early religious education. William Sloane's *Children's Books in England and America in the Seventeenth Century* (1955) is invaluable, as is the 1977 Garland facsimile edition of five seventeenth-century books (James Janeway's *A Token for Children*; Benjamin Harris's *The Holy Bible in Verse*; *The History of the Holy Jesus*; *The School of Good Manners*; and *The Prodigal Daughter*). C. John Sommerville's *The Discovery of Childhood in Puritan England* (1992) discusses some of the books available to Puritan children. In *Isaac Watts: Divine Songs* (1971), J. H. P. Pafford provides an important introduction and extensive bibliography to accompany facsimile reproductions of the 1715 edition and an illustrated one of c. 1840. Paul Sangster's *Pity My Simplicity* (1963) discusses the evangelical revival and the religious education of children from 1738 to 1800.

Margaret Nancy Cutt's *Ministering Angels* (1979) discusses nineteenth-century evangelical fiction for children and provides useful book lists of some authors. Cutt writes at greater length about Mrs. Sherwood in *Mrs. Sherwood and Her Books for Children* (1974), which contains facsimile reproductions of two short tales and a checklist of all Sherwood's known publications. Gillian Avery's *Childhood's Pattern* (1975) has three chapters on Sunday school books and religious education from 1780 to 1880.

Modern classics in Jewish children's literature include *Letters from Rifka* (rep. ed. 1993), *The Stone Lamp* (2003), and *The Cats in Krasinski Square* (2004) by Karen Hesse; *The Gift* (1995) by Joseph Kertes; *Golem* (1997) by David Wisniewski; and *Too Young for Yiddish* (2002) by Richard Michelson. Collections of traditional, Jewish children's literature include Golda Goldreich, ed., *A Treasury of Jewish Literature* (1982) and Alfred J. Kolatch and Harry Araten, eds., *Classic Bible Stories for Jewish Children* (1994).

Critical works on Jewish children's literature include Cheryl Silberberg Grossman and Suzy Engman's *Jewish Literature for Children: A Teaching Guide* (1985); Naomi B. Sokoloff's *Imagining the Child in Modern Jewish Fiction* (1992); and Penny Schine Gold's *Making the Bible Modern: Children's Bibles and Jewish Education in Twentieth-Century America* (2003). There are many books addressing how the Holocaust is treated in children's literature, including Edward T. Sullivan's *The Holocaust in Literature for Youth* (1999); Adrienne Kertzer's *My Mother's Voice: Children, Literature, and the Holocaust* (2001); Hamida Bosmajian's *Sparing the Child: Children's Literature about Nazism and the Holocaust* (2002); and Lydia Kokkola's *Representing the Holocaust in Children's Literature* (2002). *The Lion and the Unicorn* devoted a special issue to "The Jewish Presence in Children's Literature," 27.3 (Sept. 2003).

FANTASY

A good jumping-off point for exploring the scholarship of fantasy literature is George MacDonald's "The Fantastic Imagination" (1893) and J. R. R. Tolkien's influential essay "On Fairy-Stories" (*Tree and Leaf* [1964]). Inspired by Tolkien in her own writing, Ursula K. Le Guin's defense of imagination in her essays and speeches from the 1970s, collected in *The Language of the Night: Essays on Fantasy and Science Fiction* (1979), complement Tolkien's theories. Providing critical commentary, definitions, theories, and histories of the development of fantasy literature are several solid resources: *The Fantastic: A Structural Approach to a Literary Genre* (1973) by Tzvetan Todorov, *Fantasy: The Literature of Subversion* (1981) by Rosemary Jackson, *Theorising the Fantastic* (1996) by Lucie Armitt, *The Fantastic in Literature* (1976) by Eric S. Rabkin, *The Game of the Impossible: A Rhetoric of Fantasy* (1976) by W. R. Irwin, and *Strategies of Fantasy* (1992) by Brian Attebery. A general introduction is given by Peter Hunt in *Alternative Worlds in Fantasy Fiction* (2001). Surveying the English and American fantasy traditions, respectively, are *The Fantasy Literature of England* (1999) by Colin Manlove and *The Fantasy Tradition in American Literature: From Irving to Le Guin* (1980) by Brian Attebery. An annotated bibliography for students, teachers, and librarians is *Fantasy Literature: A Core Collection and Reference Guide* (1978) by Marshall B. Tymn, Kenneth J. Zahorski, and Robert H. Boyer. A clear and concise introduction to children's fantasy literature is *Children's Fantasy* (1989) by Francis J. Molson. Two comprehensive and valuable studies on the historical development of children's fantasy are *Worlds Within: Children's Fantasy from the Middle Ages to Today* (1988) by Sheila Egoff and *The Fabulous Realm: A Literary-Historical Approach to British Fantasy, 1780–1990* (1993) by Karen Patricia Smith. Smith contextualizes fantasy literature written for children within changing concepts of the child and childhood and includes brief discussions of Australian and New Zealand fantasy for children. Several books that focus on particular fantasy writers for children from the Victorian era to the present warrant mention: *The Annotated Alice: The Definitive Edition* by Martin Gardner (1999); *Ventures in Childland: Victorians, Fairy Tales, and Femininity* (1998) by U. C. Knoepflmacher, which includes substantial chapters on writers such as Lewis Carroll, George MacDonald, John Ruskin, Jean Ingelow, Christina Rossetti and Juliana Horatia Ewing; *Classic Fantasy Writers* (1994), ed. Harold Bloom, which includes chapters on canonical fantasy writers from the Victorian era as well as Kenneth Grahame, L. Frank Baum, and Beatrix Potter; *Alternative Worlds in Fantasy Fiction* (2001) by Peter Hunt and Millicent Lenz, which focuses on Ursula K. Le Guin, Terry Pratchett, and Philip Pullman; and *Presenting Young Adult Fantasy Literature* (1998) by Cathi Dunn MacRae, which features four contemporary authors—Terry Brooks, Barbara Hambly, Jane Yolen, and Meredith Ann Pierce—and the responses of a young adult fantasy enthusiasts' club to a large variety of fantasy literature. The Twayne Author series offers short critical biographies of several writers of children's fantasy: *Natalie Babbitt* (1991) by Michael M. Levy, *Susan Cooper* (1998) by Nina Mikkelsen, *Virginia Hamilton* (1994) by Nina Mikkelsen, *Madeleine L'Engle* (1993) by Donald R. Hettinga, *Robert Lawson* (1997) by Gary D. Schmidt, *Presenting Ursula K. Le Guin* (1997) by Suzanne Elizabeth Reid, and *Laurence Yep* (1995) by Dianne Johnson-Feelings. An excellent annotated bibliography and research guide to children's fantasy literature is *Fantasy Literature for Children and Young Adults* (4th ed. 1995) by Ruth Nadelman Lynn. *A Reference Guide to Modern Fantasy for Children* (1984) by Pat Pflieger is a useful introduction to the plots and characters of thirty-six British and American fantasy authors for children.

Lloyd Alexander

Jill P. May's critical biography *Lloyd Alexander* (1991) is a useful introduction. Substantial chapters on Alexander's work can be found in Kath Filmer-Davies's *Fantasy Fiction and Welsh Myth: Tales of Belonging* (1996) and Donna R. White's *A Century of Welsh Myth in Children's Literature* (1998). See also *Welsh Celtic Myth in Modern Fantasy* (1989) by C. W. Sullivan III.

L. Frank Baum

The first biography of L. Frank Baum was *The Wizard of Oz and Who He Was* (1957) by Martin Gardner and Russel B. Nye. *To Please A Child: A Biography of L. Frank Baum, Royal Historian of Oz* (1961) was jointly written by Baum's oldest son, Frank Joslyn Baum, and Russell P. Macfall. A more recent biography is Katharine M. Rogers's *L. Frank Baum: Creator of Oz* (2002). See Michael Patrick Hearn's *The Annotated Wizard of Oz: A Centennial Edition* (rev. ed. 2000) for an excellent biographical introduction to Baum. *L. Frank Baum: Royal Historian of Oz* (1992) by Angelica Shirley Carpenter and Jean Shirley is a well-illustrated and researched short biography for young readers. *Oz and Beyond: The Fantasy World of L. Frank Baum* (1997) by Michael O'Neal Riley covers the development of Baum's complete oeuvre of other-world fantasies. Important critical works on Baum's fantasy fiction include *Wonderful Wizard, Marvelous Land* (1974) by Raylyn Moore and *L. Frank Baum's World of Oz: A Classic Series at 100* (2003), ed. Suzanne Rahn, a collection of critical essays on Baum that includes discussions of stage and screen adaptations of the Oz books. See also Jack Zipes's introduction to the Oz series in *The Wonderful World of Oz* (1998). Brian Attebery pays substantive attention to Baum's work in *The Fantasy Tradition in American Literature: From Irving to Le Guin* (1980). *The Baum Bugle* is a periodical devoted to Baum studies that has been continuously published since 1957.

E. Nesbit

E. Nesbit has been the subject of a number of biographies, including Anthea Bell's *E. Nesbit* (1964) and Doris L. Moore's *E. Nesbit: A Biography* (rev. ed. 1966). The standard biography is *A Woman of Passion: The Life of E. Nesbit* (1987) by Julia Briggs. Important critical issues in Nesbit's novels are explored in Noel Streatfeild's *Magic and the Magician: E. Nesbit and Her Children's Books* (1958) and Marcus Crouch's *The Nesbit Tradition: The Children's Novel in England, 1945–1970* (1972).

SCIENCE FICTION

The best historical studies of the development of British and American science fiction for young readers are Margaret Esmonde's "Children's Science Fiction," in *Signposts to Criticism of Children's Literature* (1983), ed. Robert Bator; Brian Stableford's *Scientific Romance in Britain, 1890–1950* (1985); Thomas J. Weber's "Children's Science Fiction," in *Masterpieces of Children's Literature*, ed. William Moynihan and Mary Shaner (1986); C. W. Sullivan III, ed., *Science Fiction for Young Readers* (1993); Suzanne Reid's *Presenting Young Adult Science Fiction* (1998); Karen Sands and Marietta Frank's *Back in the Spaceship Again: Juvenile Science Fiction Series since 1945* (1999); and C. W. Sullivan III, ed., *Young Adult Science Fiction* (1999). More general historical studies include Samuel Moskowitz's *The Immortal Storm: A History of Science Fiction Fandom* (1951); Robert M. Philmus's *Into the Unknown: The Evolution of Science Fiction from Francis Godwin to H. G. Wells* (1970); Brian Aldiss's *Billion-Year Spree: The True History of Science Fiction* (1973); H. Bruce Franklin's *Future Perfect: American Science Fiction of the Nineteenth Century* (1978); Brian Aldiss and David Wingrove's *Trillion-Year Spree: The History of Science Fiction* (1986); Thomas D. Clareson's *Understanding Contemporary American Science Fiction: The Formative Period, 1926–1970,* (1990); Paul K. Alkon's *Science Fiction before 1900: Imagination Discovers Technology* (1994); and Brooks Landon's *Science Fiction after 1900: From the Steam Man to the Stars* (1997).

For theoretical examinations, see David Ketter's *New World for Old: The Apocalyptic Imagination, Science Fiction, and American Literature* (1974); Darko Suvin's *Metamorphoses of Science Fiction* (1979); Gary K. Wolfe's *The Known and the Unknown: The Iconography of Science Fiction* (1979); Darko Suvin's *Victorian Science Fiction in the UK: Discourses of Knowledge and Power* (1983); Tom Moylan's *Demand the Impossible: Science Fiction and the Utopian Imagination* (1986); Paul K. Alkon's *Origins of Science Fiction* (1987); John Huntington's *Rationalizing Genius: Ideological Strategies in the Classic American Science Fiction Short Story* (1989); Carl D. Malmgren's *Worlds Apart: Narratology of Science Fiction* (1991); Edward James's *Science Fiction in the twentieth Century* (1994); and Carl Freedman's *Critical Theory and Science Fiction* (2000). Feminist approaches to science fiction include Marleen S. Barr's *Future Females: A Critical Anthology* (1981); Sarah Lefanu's *In the Chinks of the World Machine: Feminism and Science Fiction* (1988); Barr's *Lost in Space: Probing Feminist Science Fic-*

tion and Beyond (1993); and Jenny Wolmark's *Aliens and Others: Science Fiction, Feminism, and Postmodernism* (1994).

The Lion and the Unicorn, a scholarly journal of children's literature, dedicated Volume 28, No. 2 (April 2004), to "Children and Science Fiction"; it includes essays on virtual war, human cloning, and four generations of Tom Swift as well as theoretical articles that endeavor to redefine children's science fiction.

Important texts that analyze the impact of science fiction on film include George E. Slusser and Eric S. Rabkin's *Shadows of the Magic Lamp: Fantasy and Science Fiction in Film* (1985); Vivian Sobchack's *Screening Space: The American Science Fiction Film* (2nd ed. 1988); Brooks Landon's *The Aesthetics of Ambivalence: Rethinking Science Fiction Film in the Age of Electronic (Re)production* (1992); and Scott Bukatman's *Terminal Identity: The Virtual Subject in Postmodern Science Fiction* (1993). Guides to science fiction include Peter Nicholls, ed., *The Science Fiction Encyclopedia* (1979); Thomas D. Clareson's *Science Fiction in America, 1870s–1970s: An Annotated Bibliography of Primary Sources* (1984); Thomas B. Clarson's *Some Kind of Paradise: The Emergence of Science Fiction* (1985); Neil Barron's *Anatomy of Wonder: A Critical Guide to Science Fiction* (3rd ed. 1987); Everett F. Bleiler's *Science-Fiction: The Early Years* (1990); and John Clute and Peter Nicholls, eds., *The Encyclopedia of Science Fiction* (1993). The major Anglophone journals are *Science Fiction Studies, Extrapolation,* and *Foundation: The Review of Science Fiction.*

Robert A. Heinlein

Works that examine Heinlein and his influence on science fiction include George Edgar Slusser's *The Classic Years of Robert A. Heinlein* (1977); Joseph D. Olander and Martin Harry Greenberg, eds., *Robert A. Heinlein* (1978); H. Bruce Franklin's *Robert A. Heinlein: America as Science Fiction* (1980); Peter Nicholls's *Robert A. Heinlein* (1982); and Marietta A. Frank's "Women in Heinlein's Juveniles," in *Young Adult Science Fiction*, ed. C. W. Sullivan III (1999).

H. G. Wells

Among useful works on Wells are Darko Suvin and Robert M. Philmus, eds., *H. G. Wells and Modern Science Fiction* (1977); Frank McConnell's *The Science Fiction of H. G. Wells* (1981); John Huntington's *The Logic of Fantasy: H. G. Wells and Science Fiction* (1982); and John Huntington's *Critical Essays on H. G. Wells* (1991).

PICTURE BOOKS

The standard book on the history of British picture books is Joyce Irene Whalley and Tessa Rose Chester's *A History of Children's Book Illustration* (1988), and on the American picture book Barbara Bader's *American Picture Books from Noah's Ark to the Beast Within* (1976). Other illustrated guides and popular histories (which also deal with the illustrated book) include Brian Alderson's *Sing a Song for Sixpence: The English Picture Book Tradition and Randolph Caldecott* (1986), John Barr's *Illustrated Children's Books* (1986), William Feaver's *When We Were Young: Two Centuries of Children's Book Illustration* (1977), Marcie Muir's *A History of Australian Children's Book Illustration* (1982), and *Myth, Magic, and Mystery: One Hundred Years of American Children's Book Illustration* (1996), ed. Michael Patrick Hearne, Trinkett Clark, and H. Nichols B. Clark.

Attractive accounts of contemporary picture book artists include Quentin Blake's *Magic Pencil: Children's Book Illustration Today* (2003) and Douglas Martin's *The Telling Line: Essays on Fifteen Contemporary Book Illustrators* (1989).

Picture book and illustration theory was pioneered by Joseph H. Schwarcz in *Ways of the Illustrator: Visual Communication in Children's Literature* (1982), Perry Nodelman in *Words About Pictures: The Narrative Art of Children's Picture Books* (1988), and Jane Doonan in *Looking at Pictures in Picture Books* (1993) and has been developed extensively in David Lewis's *Reading Contemporary Picturebooks: Picturing Text* (2001),

Maria Nikolajeva and Carole Scott's *How Picture Books Work* (2001), and Michele Anstey and Geoff Bull's *Reading the Visual* (2000). Useful art theory that can be applied to picture books can be found in Gunter Kress and Theo van Leeuwen's *Reading Images: The Grammar of Visual Design* (1996).

The educational aspects of the picture book are dealt with in Evelyn Arizpe and Morag Styles's *Children Reading Pictures; Interpreting Visual Texts* (2003), Victor Watson and Morag Styles's *Talking Pictures: Pictorial Texts and Young Readers* (1996), and Pam Baddeley and Chris Eddershaw's *Not So Simple Picture Books* (1994).

There are many specialized historical works, for example, R. McLean's *Victorian Book Design and Colour Printing* (1972) and Richard Dalby's *The Golden Age of Children's Book Illustration* (1991), and books on major illustrators, such as Coy Ludwig's *Maxfield Parrish* (1973), Judy Taylor's *Beatrix Potter: Artist, Storyteller and Countrywoman* (1986), Derek Hudson's *Arthur Rackham: His Life and Work* (1973), Selma G. Lanes's *The Art of Maurice Sendak* (1981), John Cech's *Angels and Wild Things: The Archetypal Poetics of Maurice Sendak* (1995), and Brian Alderson's *Ezra Jack Keats* (2003).

Picture books figure strongly in several general histories of children's literature, among them Percy Muir's *English Children's Books 1600–1900* (1985), and a useful selective reference guide is Sylvia S. Marantz and Kenneth A. Marantz's *The Art of Children's Picture Books* (1995).

COMICS

The most comprehensive of the scholarly and entertaining reference books on comics is *The World Encyclopedia of Comics* (1999), ed. Maurice Horn. Another notable reference work is *The Encyclopedia of American Comics* (1990), ed. Ron Goulart.

There are many fully illustrated popular guides and histories, such as Denis Gifford's *Happy Days! One Hundred Years of Comics* (1975) and *The International Book of Comics* (1984), Jerry Robinson's *The Comics: An Illustrated History of Comic Strip Art* (1974), Mike Benton's *The Comic Book in America* (1990), Bill Blackbeard's *A Century of Comics* (1995), Alan and Laurel Clark's *Comics: An Illustrated History* (1991), Gerard Jones and Will Jacobs's *The Great Comic Book Heroes* (1997), and *Penny Dreadfuls and Comics: English Periodicals for Children from Victorian Times to the Present Day* (1983), ed. Kevin Carpenter. One of the best historical and theoretical studies of the rise of the comic book in America is W. Bradford Wright's *Comic Book Nation: The Transformation of Youth Culture in America* (1994).

The most extensive theorizing of the comic can

be found in Scott McCloud's *Understanding Comics: The Invisible Art* (1993), which is in all-comic form. Other analytical treatments are R. C. Harvey's *The Art of the Funnies: An Aesthetic History of the Comic Strip* (1995), Inge M. Thomas's *Comics as Culture* (1990), Will Eisner's *Comic and Sequential Art* (1992), and Roger Sabin's *Comics, Comix & Graphic Novels: A History of Comic Art* (1996). There are several serious bibliographies, notably John A. Lent's *An International Bibliography of Comic Art* (4 vols. 1994–96). The many notable collections of comics around the world are examined in, for example, *The Smithsonian Collection of Newspaper Comics* (1978), ed. Bill Blackbeard and Martin Williams, and Denis Gifford's *American Comic Strip Collections* (1990).

Specialized studies of various kinds include Trina Robbins's *A Century of Women Cartoonists* (1994); *The Comic-Book Book* (rev. 1998), ed. Don Thompson and Dick Lupoff, and Frederick Wertham's *Seduction of the Innocent* (1954). Stan Lee and George Mair's *Excelsior! The Amazing Life of Stan Lee* (2002) is a fascinating biography/autobiography of the man who has left among the most lasting imprints on comics.

Accounts of individual comic characters and writers include Bob Kane's *Batman and Me* (1989), Stan Lee's *Origins of Marvel Comics* (1974), Michael Teitelbaum's *The Story of the X-Men: How It All Began* (2000), Scott Beatty's *Superman: The Ultimate Guide to the Man of Steel* (2002), M. Farr's *Tintin: The Complete Companion* (2001), and *Mickey Mouse: The Evolution, the Legend, the Phenomenon* by Robert Heide and John Gilman

with Monique Peterson and Patrick White (2001).

Accounts of comics in other English-speaking countries include Michael Hirsh and Patrick Lambert's *The Great Canadian Comic-Books* (1971), John Bell's *Canuk Comics* (1986), and John Ryan's *Panel by Panel: An Illustrated History of Australian Comics* (1979). The highly influential Japanese comics are examined in Frederick L. Schodt's *Manga! Manga! The World of Japanese Comics* (1983).

VERSE

The category of children's poetry includes both nursery and playground verse (largely from the oral tradition) and authored poetry for children. Iona and (the late) Peter Opie, collectors and scholars of children's literature and culture, produced the most comprehensive standard reference sources for nursery and playground verse in English. The best general reference source is *The Oxford Dictionary of Nursery Rhymes*, first published in 1951, and revised in 1997. Because the Opies were such attentive scholars of children's culture, they also produced wonderful accounts of these, including *The Lore and Language of Schoolchildren* (1961), *Children's Games in the Street and Playground: Chasing, Catching, Seeking, Hunting, Racing, Duelling, Exerting, Daring, Guessing, Acting, Pretending* (1984), and *The Singing Game* (1985). Anthologies of verse for children still provide the most useful general overviews of the field. Walter de la Mare's *Come Hither*, first published in 1923, but available in modern reprints, provides a thorough sense of the range of verse considered suitable for children in the first part of the twentieth century. *The Golden Treasury of Poetry* (1959), ed. Louis Untermeyer, is the American model of its kind. *The Rattle Bag* (1982), ed. Seamus Heaney and Ted Hughes, stands as an example of the best verse considered suitable for late-twentieth-century children. As the twentieth century came to a close, anthologies tended to lose their Anglo-American tone and reflect a more diverse range. *Ranters, Ravers and Rhymers: Poems by Black and Asian Poets* (1990), ed. Farrukh Dhondy, is an excellent introduction to the newer looks and sounds of revitalized verse for children. *Shimmy, Shimmy, Shimmy Like My Sister Kate* (1996), ed. Nikki Giovanni, is an anthology that traces the history of African American poets through the Harlem Renaissance. *It's a Woman's World: A Century of Women's Voices in Poetry* (2000), ed. Neil Philip, shifts the typical male gender bias in anthologies. *Under the Moon and Over the Sea* (2003), ed. John Agard and Grace Nichols, was the first winner of the poetry award established by the Centre for Literacy in Primary Education in England. For the history of poetry for children, Morag Styles's *From the Garden to the Street: Three Hundred Years of Poetry for Children* (1998) is an excellent starting point. For discussions of poetry for children, Ted

Hughes's *Poetry in the Making* (1967) still stands as a classic text, as does *Rose, Where Did You Get That Red? Teaching Great Poetry to Children*, originally published by Kenneth Koch in 1973 but reissued in 1990. For information about children's poetry, see *A Guide to Poetry 0–13* (1996), ed. Chris Powling and Morag Styles. And the long essays published by the journal *Signal* each May between 1979 and 2001 provide the best critical accounts of the development of poetry for children during that period. Also see the *Children's Literature Association Quarterly* 27.1 (Spring 2002) special issue on poetry, ed. Richard Flynn and Anita Tarr. For general biographic and bibliographic information about poets, see the major reference sources in the field, including *The Cambridge Guide to Children's Books in English* (2001), *Something About the Author* (with a new volume published each year since 1971), and *The St. James Guide to Children's Writers* (5th ed. 1999).

For an analysis of the state of contemporary American poetry for children, see "Consolation Prize," by Richard Flynn in *Signal* 100 (January, May, September 2003). In the same volume of *Signal*, Alan Tucker offers a philosophical discussion on children's poetry in "The Mouse and the Doormat." For a discussion on nonsense, see "Edward Gorey, Children's Literature and Nonsense Verse" by Kevin Shortsleeves in the *Children's Literature Association Quarterly* 27.1 (Spring 2002). For a discussion of American traditions of playground verse, see "Child Poets and the Poetry of the Playground," by Joseph T. Thomas Jr. in *Children's Literature* 32 (2004).

Charles Causley

Because Causley was so prolific, writing for both adults and children, the best introductions to his work are in collections: *Collected Poems 1951–2000* (2000) offers a general overview, and his *Collected Poems, for Children* (1996) gives a more explicit look at his children's poetry. For glimpses of Causley thinking about poetry, his introductions to his anthologies are helpful, especially *The Puffin Book of Magic Verse* (1974) and *The Puffin Book of Salt-Sea Verse* (1978). In 1987 Harry Chambers compiled a cluster of critical responses to Causley, *Causley at 70: Poem and Prose Tribute*. In addition, a brief critical discussion of Causley's works for children is found in *From the Garden to the Street* (1998), by Morag Styles.

Lucille Clifton

Clifton has achieved success in her collections for both children and adults, though her first book of poems, *Good Times* (1969), and her next two collections, *The Black BC's* (1970) and *Some of the Days of Everett Anderson* (1970), were for children. Clifton produced nine collections centering on Everett Anderson, including *All Us Come Cross the Water* (1973), *Everett Anderson's Goodbye* (1983), and *Everett Anderson's Christmas Coming* (1991). Among Clifton's other books for children is one with a white protagonist, *Sonora Beautiful* (1981). Clifton published a complete collection of her poems in *Good Woman: Poems and a Memoir* (1987). For essays about Clifton, see "Kin and Kin: The Poetry of Lucille Clifton" in *Literary Influence and African-American Writers* (1996), ed. Tracy Mishkin. For a discussion of Clifton's Everett Anderson series, see Diane Johnson's "The Chronicling of African-American Life and Consciousness: Lucille Clifton's Everett Anderson Series," *Children's Literature Association Quarterly* 14.3 (Winter 1989).

Walter de la Mare

De la Mare was a versatile and prolific man of letters, publishing poetry and prose fiction for children and adults as well as introductions to other authors, critical essays, and anthologies. The *Collected Poems* was published in 1979. For a thoughtful selection, see *A Choice of de la Mare's Verse* (1963), ed. and with an introduction by W. H. Auden. De la Mare's *Collected Stories for Children*, originally published in 1947, was re-issued in 1967. *Songs of Childhood*, a reprint of the 1902 edition, was issued by Garland in 1976. *Rhymes and Verses: Collected Poems for Children* (1947) is also a standard collection. *Come Hither: A Collection of Rhymes and Poems for the Young of All Ages*, originally published in 1923, is the anthology of poetry for children that still sets the standard for sensitive choices. Most biographical material on de la Mare is dated. The most recent biography is *Imagination of the Heart: The Life of Walter de la Mare* (1993) by Theresa Whistler. John Bayley's "The Child in Walter de la Mare" (1989), in *Children and Their Books*, ed. Gillian Avery and Julia Briggs, is an appreciation of de la Mare as a writer for children.

Robert Graves

The White Goddess (1948, enl. ed. 1966), Graves's monumental study of myth, provides a critical key to his work and life and to the poets (including Ted Hughes) that it influenced profoundly. Early in his career, Graves recognized the link between his life and his art. In 1929, at age thirty-four, he published an autobiography, *Good-bye to All That* (rev. 1957), about his experiences in World War I. Among his other prose works is *I, Claudius* (1934), which was made into a successful BBC drama in the 1970s. Despite the other genres in which Graves wrote, he considered himself primarily a poet. Although *Robert Graves: The Complete Poems* (3 vols. 1995, 1997, 1999), edited by his wife, Beryl, and Dunstan Ward, is the full edition of his poems, the controversial *Collected Poems* (1975) represents the last edition over which Graves had editorial control. Some of Graves's earliest poems, such as "The Poet in the Nursery," tilt decidedly toward a children's audience, though he did not begin publishing explicitly for children until relatively late in life. *The Green Book* (1962), with illustrations by the young Maurice Sendak, was published in the Collier-Macmillan Modern Masters series. Graves produced three poetry collections for children. Besides *The Penny Fiddle* (1960), he published *Anne at Highwood Hall* (1964) and *The Poor Boy Who Followed His Star* (1986), a combination of prose and poetry. Graves's *Oxford Addresses on Poetry* (1968), first delivered as lectures, provide intimate access to his awareness of the importance of poetry's aural dimension. Because Graves was so much a part of the literary fabric of the twentieth century, two collections of his letters are useful: *In Broken Images: Selected Letters of Robert Graves, 1914–1947* and *Moon and Moon: Selected Letters of Robert Graves, 1946–1972*. Martin Seymour Smith's *Robert Graves: His Life and Works* (2nd ed. 1995), first published in 1982, is still the standard biographical study. Richard Percival Graves, a nephew, drawing on sources unavailable to Smith, wrote a three-volume biography, by far the most extensive study: *Robert Graves, the Assault Heroic, 1895–1926* (1987), *Robert Graves: The Years with Laura, 1926–1940* (1990), and *Robert Graves and the White Goddess, 1940–1985* (1995).

Randall Jarrell

The Complete Poems (1969) offers a good starting point for Jarrell, as the collection is shot through with poems about children and childhood. Besides *The Bat-Poet* (1964), toward the end of his life Jarrell wrote a few other books explicitly for children, *The Gingerbread Rabbit* (1964), illustrated by Gareth Williams, and *The Animal Family* (1965), illustrated by Maurice Sendak. *Fly by Night*, posthumously published in 1976, was also illustrated by Sendak. Because Jarrell was such an elegant critic, literary scholar, and observer of popular culture, his essays are worth reading, especially *Poetry and the Age* (1953), *A Sad Heart at the Supermarket: Essays and Fables* (1964), and *Kipling, Auden & Co.: Essays and Reviews, 1935–1964*. William H. Pritchard's *Randall Jarrell: A Literary Life* is the standard critical biography, though it is helpfully supplemented by *Critical Essays on Randall Jarrell* (1983), ed. Suzanne Ferguson. There are excellent critical books on Jarrell as a children's author, including *The Children's Books of Randall Jarrell* (1988) by Jerry Griswold and Richard Flynn's *Randall Jarrell and the Lost World of Childhood* (1990). For a fine recent study of Jarrell's poetry for children, see Joseph Thomas's " 'Levels and Opposites' in Randall Jarrell's *The Bat-Poet*," *Children's Literature Association Quarterly* 27.1 (Spring 2002).

Grace Nichols

As a poet still in mid-career, Nichols is best read in individual collections. *Come on Into My Tropical Garden* (1988), *Give Yourself a Hug* (1994), and *The Poet Cat* (2000) offer introductions to her children's work as does her autobiographical novel, *Whole of a Morning Sky* (1986). Nichols has also collaborated with her partner, poet John Agard, on collections, in *No Hickory, No Dickory, No Dock* (1991), for example, and as an editor, bringing the work of other Caribbean and Asian poets to British audiences. *A Caribbean Dozen* (1994) and *Under the Moon and Over the Sea* (2003) are two good examples. And Nichols has published a number of collections for adults, including *i is a long memoried woman* (1983), *The Fat Black Woman's Poems* (1984), and *Lazy Thoughts of a Lazy Woman* (1989). In "The Battle with Language," in *Caribbean Women Writers* (1990), ed. Selwyn Cudjoe, Nichols describes the way her poetic language moves between the Creole rhythms of the Caribbean and standard English. A critical essay on Nichols's poetry for children is Lissa Paul's "Coming 'To Sing Their Being': The Poetry of Grace Nichols," in *Girls, Boys, Books, Toys* (1999), ed. Beverly Lyon Clark and Margaret Higonnet.

Christina Rossetti

A relatively new edition of Rossetti's verse, *The Complete Poems*, was published in 2001, ed. Betty Flowers. There are additional notes and a new introduction, though the volume is based on an edition, published in three volumes (1980, 1986, 1990), ed. R. W. Crump. The Osborne Collection has issued a facsimile edition of Rossetti's *Sing-Song: A Nursery-Rhyme Book* (1872). A good place to begin studying Rossetti's work is Virginia Woolf's essay "I am Christina Rossetti," *The Second Common Reader* (1932). Jan Marsh's 1995 biography, *Christina Rossetti: A Writer's Life*, studies Rossetti in the context of her pre-Raphaelite brother, Dante Gabriel Rossetti. Poet Tom Paulin offers a wonderfully nuanced reading of her poetry, including her work for children, in "The Cadence in the Song," *Times Literary Supplement* (18 Jan. 2002). Also good are June Cummins's "You Should Not Loiter Longer: Beatrix Potter, Christina Rossetti, and Progressive Intertextual Revision," in *Beatrix Potter's "Peter Rabbit": A Children's Classic at 100* (2002), ed. Margaret Mackey, and Roderick McGillis's "The Simple Surfaces: Christina Rossetti's Work for Children," in *The Achievement of Christina Rossetti* (1987), ed. David A. Kent.

Robert Louis Stevenson

Although *A Child's Garden of Verses* is Stevenson's most enduring contribution to children's poetry, he did write other verse, so his *Collected Poems* (2nd ed. 1971), edited with an introduction by Janet Adam Smith, is a useful place to begin a study of his poetry. Stevenson's fiction—especially *Treasure Island* (1883), *Kidnapped* (1886), and *The Strange Case of Dr. Jekyll and Mr. Hyde* (1886)—are classics in the children's canon and hence are essential reading. The most recent biography of Stevenson is Frank McLynn's *Robert Louis Stevenson: A Biography* (1994). Although there is a vast amount of critical material on Stevenson, one of the most helpful essays about his poetry for children is Michael Rosen's "R. L. Stevenson and Children's Play," *Children's Literature in Education* 26.1 (March 1995). Recent critical approaches, including Ann Colley's "Writing Towards Home: The Landscape of *A Child's Garden of Verses*," are collected in *Robert Louis Stevenson Reconsidered: New Critical Perspectives* (2003).

PLAYS

There are no comprehensive histories of children's drama in the United States and the United Kingdom. Nellie McCaslin's work is the most reliable for understanding its development in America, and her works include *Children's Theatre in the United States: A History* (1971), *Theatre for Young Audiences* (1978), and *Historical Guide to Children's Theatre in America* (1987). Some of the founders and directors of children's theaters have written important autobiographies or accounts of their work that shed light on the historical development of children's theater. Among the most important are Alice Minnie Herts's *The Children's Educational Theatre* (1911), Charlotte B. Chorpening's *Twenty-One Years* (1952), Winifred Ward's *Creative Dramatics, for the Upper Grades and Junior High School* (1930), and Brian Way's *Development Through Drama* (1967). Theoretical studies include Winifred Ward's *Theatre for Children* (1939), Caroline Fisher and Hazel Robertson's *Children and the Theatre* (1950), Viola Spolin's *Improvisation for the Theater: A Handbook of Teaching and Directing Techniques* (1963), Moses Goldberg's *Children's Theatre: A Philosophy and a Method* (1974), Betty Jean Lifton, ed., *Contemporary Children's Theatre* (1974), John Allen's *Drama in Schools: Its Theory and Practice* (1979), Sandy Craig, ed., *Dreams and Deconstructions: Alternative Theatre in Britain* (1980), Brian Way's *Audience Participation* (1981), Jed Davis and Mary Jane Evans's *Theatre, Children and Youth* (1982), and Lin Wright, ed., *Professional Theatre for Children* (1984). Numerous scholars have studied the impact of theater in education, among them Nigel Dodd and Winifred Hickson, eds., *Drama and Theatre in Education* (1971), B. J. Wagner and Dorothy Heathcotte's *Drama as Learning Medium* (1976), John O'Toole's *Theatre in Education*

(1976), Albert Hunt's *Hopes for Great Happenings: Alternatives in Education and Theatre* (1977), Gavin Bolton's *Drama as Education* (1980), and Ken Robinson, ed., *Exploring Theatre and Education* (1980). Studies of individual children's dramatists are rare, but a great deal of attention has been paid to J. M. Barrie. In particular, see Janet Dunbar's *J. M. Barrie: The Man Behind the Image* (1970), Andrew Birkin's *J. M. Barrie and the Lost Boys* (1979), Gillian Avery's "The Cult of Peter Pan," in *Word & Image* (1986), Ronald Jack's *The Road to the Never Land: An Assessment of J. M. Barrie's Dramatic Art* (1991), and Jacqueline Rose's *The Case of Peter Pan; or, The Impossibility of Children's Fiction* (2nd ed. 1993). Other studies include Lowell Swortzel's *The Theatre of Aurand Harris* (1996), Diane Johnson-Feelings's *Presenting Laurence Yep* (1995), and Fred Guida's *A Christmas Carol and Its Adaptations: A Critical Examination of Dickens's Story and Its Productions on Screen and Television* (2000). Significant anthologies that provide background material on plays and their authors include Lowell Swortzell, ed., *All the World's a Stage* (1972); Coleman Jennings and Aurand Harris, eds., *Plays Children Love: A Treasury of Contemporary and Classic Plays for Children* (1981); Lowell Swortzell, ed., *Six Plays for Young People from the Federal Theatre Project (1936–1939): An Introductory Analysis and Six Representative Plays* (1986); Coleman Jennings, ed., *Theatre for Young Audiences* (1998), and *Eight Plays for Children: The New Generation Project* (1999); and Lowell Swortzel, ed., *The Twelve Plays of Christmas: Traditional and Modern Plays for the Holidays* (2000).

BOOKS OF INSTRUCTION

Because the category of books of instruction as a genre of children's literature is so vast, there is no single general reference work. A good beginning is "The Legacy of the Middle Ages: Romances and Manners," a chapter in Darton's *Children's Books in England* (3rd ed. 1982). For a detailed analysis of medieval courtesy books, see "Part One: The Place of Courtesy Books in Medieval Society," in *The Matter of Courtesy: Medieval Courtesy Books and the Gawain Poet* (1985), by Jonathan Nicholls. For an analysis of the kinds of courtesy books (by then often called "conduct books" in England) popular in the seventeenth and eighteenth centuries, see Penelope Fritzer's *Jane Austen and Eighteenth-Century Courtesy Books* (1997), especially the first two chapters. In the United States, at the same period, similar books of instruction on morals and manners were called "advice" books. For a book that addresses the issues of conduct and advice for girls and women during this period, see Lynne Vallone's *Disciplines of Virtue: Girls' Culture in the Eighteenth and Nineteenth Centuries* (1995). In the twentieth century, the idea of what children "need to know" shifts away from the courtesy / conduct / advice book (on morals and manners) and towards the genre of information books, which contain all kinds of facts about the world. Margaret Meek's *Information and Book Learning* (1996) offers useful analysis on what to look for in an information book—and what to avoid. Margaret Mallet has an excellent essay, "Children's Information Texts," in *International Companion Encyclopedia of Children's Literature* (2nd ed. 2004), ed. Peter Hunt.

Robert Baden-Powell
For a glimpse of Baden-Powell's vision, in his own words, see *Scouting for Boys* (1908) and *The Wolf Cub's Handbook* (1916), just two of the more than thirty books he published during his long life. A short personal biography of Baden-Powell, *The Chief: The Life Story of Robert Baden-Powell*, was first published in 1924 (rev. 1975) by Eileen Wade, who for many years was Baden-Powell's confidential secretary. For the literary, historical, and sociological contexts of Baden-Powell and the scouting movement, from the perspective of a late-twentieth-century author, see Robert H. MacDonald's *Songs of the Empire: The Frontier and the Boy Scout Movement, 1890–1918* (1993). Though there are many studies and histories of the Boy Scout movement, each one is soaked in the ideological perspectives of its own time and place. *The Scout Movement* (1950), by E. E. Reynolds, also the author of a biography of Baden-Powell (1943), is very different from Robert MacDonald's book. An account of the relationship between Baden-Powell and Kipling is contained in *Mowgli's Songs: Kipling and Baden-Powell's Scouts* (1987), by Hugh Brogan. Tim Jeal's *Baden-Powell* (1989) is a full and sympathetic reassessment of a complex character.

LIFE WRITING

For an overview of life writing (biography and autobiography) as a literary form, see Jill Ker Conway's *When Memory Speaks: Reflections on Autobiography* (1998). Leon Edel's *Writing Lives: Principia Biographica* (1959; rep. in 1984) and Paula Backscheider's *Reflections on Biography* (1999) introduce readers to the craft of biography. For a good comprehensive collection of essays on important topics within life writing—interpretation, theoretical approaches, autobiographies by women and persons of color, and autobiography as cultural expression—see *Studies in Autobiography* (1988), ed. James Olney. See also Robert Folkenflik's edited collection *The Culture of Autobiography: Constructions of Self-Representation* (1993). For studies on representative women's autobiographies, see Leigh Gilmore's *A Poetics of Women's Autobiography: Marginality and the Fictions of Self-Representation* (1987) and *Autobiographics: A Feminist Theory of Women's Self-Representation* (1994). A bibliography of biographies is *Biography: An Annotated Bibliography* (1992), ed. Carl Rollyson. See also the two-volume *Encyclopedia of Life Writing: Autobiographical and Biographical Forms* (2001), ed. Margaretta Jolly, for entries on Childhood and Life Writing, Adolescence and Life Writing, Family Relations and Life Writing, as well as entries on individual authors of life writing. A valuable resource on life writing and children's literature is *Biography and Children: A Study of Biography for Children and Children in Biography* (1993) by Stuart Hannabuss and Rita Marcella. *From Biography to History: Best Books for Children's Entertainment and Education* (1998), ed. Catherine Barr, offers a comprehensive annotated bibliography of biographies and related books published, for the most part, in the 1990s, for students in grades 3 through 9. *The Index to Collective Biographies for Young Readers* (4th ed. 1988) covers primarily twentieth-century collective biographies.

Anne Frank's diary has given rise to numerous literary and historical studies, memoirs, and cinematic and dramatic interpretations intended for both adults and youth. The first English translation of the diary, edited by Anne's father and titled *Diary of a Young Girl*, was published in 1952 (trans. B. M. Mooyaart). The "Definitive Edition" of the diary (1995, trans. by M. Pressler) includes the original manuscript version of the diary, Anne's revised draft, and the published diary edited by Otto Frank. *Anne Frank's Tales from the Secret Annex* (1994, trans. by M. Mok and R. Manheim) is a complete edition of Frank's short stories, fables, personal reminiscences, and unfinished novel. There are two recent biographies of Anne Frank: Melissa Müller's *Anne Frank, The Biography* (1998, trans. Rita and Robert Kimber) and Carol Ann Lee's *Roses from the Earth: The Biography of Anne Frank* (1999). Biographies for young readers that tell Anne's story through pictures as well as contextualize her life within the events of World War II include *Anne Frank, Beyond the Diary: A Photographic Remembrance* (1993) by Ruud van der Rol and Rian Verhoeven, *Anne Frank: Child of the Holocaust* (1991) by Gene Brown, and *A Picture Book of Anne Frank* (1993) by David D. Adler and illustrated by Karen Ritz. Jacob Boas's *We Are Witnesses: Five Diaries of Teenagers Who Died in the Holocaust* (1995) excerpts the diaries of young victims of the Holocaust (including Anne Frank) and provides biographical and contextual information about each diarist. The field of Holocaust studies is wide-ranging and growing and includes works about the experiences of children during and after the Holocaust years. Hamida Bosmajian's *Sparing the Child: Grief and the Unspeakable in Youth Literature about Nazism and the Holocaust* (2002) is an excellent book about Holocaust literature for youth and includes a discussion of Anne Frank. Also of interest is Lydia Kokkola's *Representing the Holocaust in Children's Literature* (2003). Adrienne Kertzer's *My Mother's Voice: Children, Literature, and the Holocaust* (2002) includes a chapter on Anne Frank.

ADVENTURE STORIES

Adventure stories is a sprawling category, including everything from desert island adventures to cowboy stories, from the medieval heroic adventures of Beowulf to the comic book and film versions of Spiderman. A good introduction to adventure as a category of children's literature is Dennis Butts's "The Adventure Story," in *Stories and Society* (1992), ed. Butts. Another version of this essay, "Shaping Boyhood: Empire Builders and Adventurers," appears in Peter Hunt's *International Companion Encyclopedia of Children's Literature* (2nd ed. 2004). Margery Fisher's *The Bright Face of Danger* (1986) reflects her intimate knowledge of the field.

Armed with a general sense of the field and its key players, a good next step is to read classic books by classic authors of the genre. A partial basic list might include Sir Walter Scott's historical novels, beginning with *Waverley* (1814); Mark Twain's *The Adventures of Tom Sawyer* (1876) and *The Adventures of Huckleberry Finn* (1884); Rider Haggard's *King Solomon's Mines* (1885) and *She* (1887); Rudyard Kipling's *Jungle Books* (1894, 1895); R. M. Ballantyne's *Coral Island* (1858), especially famous as the inspiration for William Golding's *Lord of the Flies* (1954); Owen Wister's *The Virginian* (1902); Jack London's *Call of the Wild* (1903); and Zane Grey's *Riders of the Purple Sage* (1912). Adventure stories for children tend to run in series, though the literary quality ranges from Enid Blyton's popular formulaic books about the "Secret Seven" and the "Famous Five," written mostly during the 1940s and 1950s, to J. R. R. Tolkien's literary, scholarly *Lord of the Rings* trilogy, first published in 1954 and 1955.

Adventures with female protagonists often edge into the domestic category and might include the *Little House* series, by American pioneer Laura Ingalls Wilder, published between 1932 and 1943, Louise Fitzhugh's *Harriet the Spy* (1964), and Margaret Mahy's *The Changeover* (1984). And finally, to gain a sense of what links these disparate stories together, mythographer Joseph Campbell's *Hero with a Thousand Faces* (1949) is indispensable. A second edition was published in 1971 and a commemorative edition in 2004.

SCHOOL STORIES

British public schools provide the setting for classic school stories for children. Useful social histories of British public schools include *Tom Brown's Universe: The Development of the Victorian Public School* (1977) by J. R. de S. Honey and Gillian Avery's *The Best Type of Girl: A History of Girls' Independent Schools* (1991). See also *Lessons for Life: The Schooling of Girls and Women, 1850–1950* (1987), ed. Felicity Hunt. A good collection of essays about boys' education in public schools and boys' literature is *The World of the Public School* (1977), ed. George MacDonald Fraser. For a comprehensive study of the development of American education, see Joel Spring's *The American School, 1642–1990* (2nd ed. 1990). See also Charles Carpenter's *History of American Schoolbooks* (1963). There are a number of excellent critical analyses of the school story as a literary subgenre. The essays in *Happiest Days: The Public Schools in English Fiction* (1988), ed. Jeffrey Richards, explore how examples of popular culture (including *Stalky & Co.* and *Tom Brown's Schooldays*) illuminate (masculine) British life. Similarly, P. W. Musgrave's *From Brown to Bunter: The Life and Death of the School Story* (1985) examines links between the boys' school story and wider society. Isabel Quigly's excellent *The Heirs of Tom Brown: The English School Story* (1982) is primarily concerned with examining the boys' school story in literary terms, although a chapter is devoted to girls' school stories. Beverly Lyon Clark's innovative *Regendering the School Story: Sassy Sissies and Tattling Tomboys* (1997) addresses gender issues in the genre for both boys and girls. See also Kimberley Reynolds's *Girls Only? Gender and Popular Children's Fiction in Britain, 1880–1910* (1990). *You're a Brick, Angela! A New Look at Girls' Fiction from 1839 to 1975* (1976) by Mary Cadogan and Patricia Craig includes substantial chapters on girls' school stories. A helpful bibliography is *Bullies, Beaks and Flannelled Fools: An Annotated Bibliography of Boys' School Fiction, 1742–1990* (1990) by R. J. Kirkpatrick. For coverage of the entire range of school stories combined with bibliographical information on British, Canadian, and Australasian examples of the genres, see *The Encyclopaedia of School Stories* (2 vols. 2000), ed. Rosemary Auchmuty and Joy Wotton. See also *The Encyclopaedia of Girls' School Stories* (2000) ed. Sue Sims and Hilary Clare, and *The Encyclopaedia of Boys' School Stories* (2000), ed. Robert J. Kirkpatrick.

Sarah Fielding
Fielding has lately been rediscovered as a significant eighteenth-century writer. Linda Bree's critical biography *Sarah Fielding* (1996) covers Fielding's entire career as a writer and includes a separate chapter on *The Governess*. The correspondence between Fielding and her brother, Henry Fielding, has been collected and edited by Martin C. Battestin and Clive T. Probyn (1993).

Thomas Hughes
The standard biography of Hughes is *Thomas Hughes* (1952) by Edward C. Mack and W. H. G. Armytage. *Muscular Christianity: Embodying the Victorian Age* (1994), ed. Donald E. Hall, is a collection of essays on "Muscular Christianity," a crucial concept in *Tom Brown's Schooldays*; Dennis W. Allen's "Young England: Muscular Christianity and the Politics of the Body in *Tom Brown's Schooldays*" explores this issue in depth. See also Claudia Nelson's *Boys Will Be Girls: The Feminine Ethic and British Children's Fiction, 1857–1917* (1991) for important discussions of manliness and androgyny in *Tom Brown's Schooldays*.

Rudyard Kipling
The official biography of Kipling is *The Life of Rudyard Kipling* (1955) by Charles Carrington. Other biographies have challenged or extended Carrington's treatment, however: Martin Seymour-Smith's *Rudyard Kipling* (1989) offers a controversial psychological profile of the author, and David Gilmour focuses on Kipling's political life in *The Long Recessional: The Imperial Life of Rudyard Kipling* (2002). Kipling wrote an autobiographical fragment, *Something of Myself* (1937), published the year after his death. *Kipling, Storyteller of East and West* (1985) by Gloria Kamen is intended for young readers. An excellent and comprehensive treatment of Kipling's work for children is found in a special issue of *Children's Literature* (vol. 20, 1992), ed. Judith A. Plotz. *Kipling Considered* (1989), a collection of essays edited by Phillip Mallett, includes Robin Gilmour's "*Stalky and Co.*: Revising the Code," on Kipling's work within the context of schoolboy literature. Useful reference works include *Kipling Dictionary* (1967) by W. Arthur Young and John H. McGivering and *Bibliography of the Works of Rudyard Kipling* (1972) by E. W. Martindell. *The Kipling Journal*, a periodical devoted to Kipling studies, has been in existence since 1927.

Social histories of childhood and family life offer context for the study of domestic fiction for children. The definition of childhood, however, has not remained static, and studies of the history of the family differ about the nature of childhood and the emotional tone of family life. Philippe Ariès's classic *Centuries of Childhood: A Social History of Family Life* (trans. Robert Baldick, 1962) examines the concept of childhood in *ancien régime* France and argues that childhood became a separate stage of life in the seventeenth century and a beloved center of the family in the eighteenth. Linda Pollock refutes Ariès in her comprehensive *Forgotten Children: Child-Parent Relations from 1500 to 1900* (1983) and argues for a greater consistency within the parent-child relationship over time and that family relationships were consistently characterized by affective bonds. Pollock's *A Lasting Relationship: Parents and Children over Three Centuries* (1987) is a useful anthology of source material relating to the home life of middle- and upper-class children from 1600 to 1900. For a good historical overview of childhood spanning the centuries, see Hugh Cunningham's *Children and Childhood in Western Society since 1500* (1995). In *Pictures of Innocence: The History and Crisis of Ideal Childhood* (1998), Anne Higonnet traces the visual history of ideal childhood and examines how photography has unsettled the notion of a perfect childhood. Patricia Holland analyzes the debate about what constitutes a child and childhood in *What Is a Child? Popular Images of Childhood* (1992). Gail S. Murray's *American Children's Literature and the Construction of Childhood* (1998) examines how American children's literature has shaped morals, information, and proper behavior. The anthology *Childhood in America* (2000), ed. Paula S. Fass and Mary Ann Mason, includes several essays on authors of domestic fiction and numerous important, interdisciplinary essays on the shifting perspectives of childhood.

Important social histories focused on specific periods, topics, and regions include Charles John Sommerville's *The Discovery of Childhood in Puritan England* (1992), *Small Worlds: Children and Adolescents in America, 1850–1950* (1992), ed. Elliott West and Paula Petrik, and H. Cunningham's *The Children of the Poor: Representations of Childhood since the Seventeenth Century* (1991). For analyses of the concept of the child as shown through literature, see Peter Coveney's *The Image of Childhood: The Individual and Society. A Study of a Theme in English Literature* (2nd ed. 1967), David Grylls's *Guardians and Angels: Parents and Children in Nineteenth-Century Literature* (1978), and T. G. A. Nelson's *Children, Parents, and the Rise of the Novel* (1995). Books that explore domesticity and its effects on female youth culture include *The Victorian Girl and the Feminine Ideal* (1982) by Deborah Gorham, *The Girls' Own: Cultural Histories of the Anglo-American Girl, 1830–*

1915 (1994), ed. Claudia Nelson and Lynne Vallone, and *Disciplines of Virtue: Girls' Culture in the Eighteenth and Nineteenth Centuries* (1995) by Lynne Vallone. For theory and criticism of domestic fiction and family stories from the seventeenth through the nineteenth centuries, see Gillian Avery's *Childhood's Pattern: A Study of the Heroes and Heroines of Children's Fiction, 1770–1950* (1975) and *Behold the Child: American Children and Their Books, 1621–1922* (1994); Samuel F. Pickering Jr.'s *Moral Instruction and Fiction for Children, 1749–1820* (1993); Anne Scott Macleod's *A Moral Tale: Children's Fiction and American Culture, 1820–1860* (1973); and J. S. Bratton's *The Impact of Victorian Children's Fiction* (1981). *Family Fictions* (2001) by Nicholas Tucker and Nikki Gamble focuses on the work of three popular contemporary authors for children who write realistic domestic fiction (British authors Anne Fine and Jacqueline Wilson and Australian Morris Gleitzman). The introduction, "Changing Families," is a valuable contribution to the dialogue on constructions of childhood and family life.

Louisa May Alcott

Alcott's life has inspired a number of biographies; Alcott's friend Ednah Dow Cheney published *Louisa May Alcott, Her Life, Letters and Journals* (1889) soon after the writer's death. Both Madeleine B. Stern's *Louisa May Alcott* (1950) and Martha Saxton's *Louisa May: A Modern Biography of Louisa May Alcott* (1977, rep. 1995) provide valuable insights into Alcott's work and character; Saxton's work was influenced by feminist theory. Madelon Bedell's *The Alcotts* (1981) is a collective biography of the Alcott family. The award-winning *The Story of the Author of "Little Women": Invincible Louisa* (1933) by Cornelia Meigs was written for juveniles and reprinted with a new introduction as *Invincible Louisa: The Story of the Author of "Little Women"* (1968). Alcott's journals and selected letters are available in editions by Joel Myerson and Daniel Shealy: *The Journals of Louisa May Alcott* (1997) and *The Selected Letters of Louisa May Alcott* (1995). Madeleine B. Stern's *L. M. Alcott: Signature of Reform* (2002) is a valuable sourcebook of primary materials on nineteenth-century domestic, educational, medical, and economic reforms and Alcott's writings on these subjects. *Louisa May Alcott on Race, Sex, and Slavery* (1997), edited and introduced by Sarah Elbert, contextualizes Alcott's participation in debates over race and gender. Since the 1970s, Madeleine B. Stern has publishing newly discovered anonymous and pseudonymous thriller tales written by Alcott. Stern's *Louisa May Alcott Unmasked: Collected Thrillers* (1995) assembles many of these works in one volume. Books that have advanced the state of Alcott studies include Madeleine B. Stern's edited collections, *Critical Essays on Louisa May Alcott* (1984) and *Louisa May Alcott: From Blood & Thun-*

der to Hearth & Home (1998); Charles Strickland's *Victorian Domesticity: Families in the Life and Art of Louisa M. Alcott* (1985); Sarah Elbert's *A Hunger for Home: Louisa May Alcott's Place in American Culture* (1987); and Elizabeth Lennox Keyser's *Whispers in the Dark: The Fiction of Louisa May Alcott* (1993). *Little Women and the Feminist Imagination: Criticism, Controversy, Personal Essays* (1999), ed. Janice M. Alberghene and Beverly Lyon Clark, focuses on Alcott's most famous work from a wide range of critical approaches and includes an excellent updated selected bibliography of biographical and critical treatments of Alcott. Useful reference works include *The Louisa May Alcott Encyclopedia* (2001), ed. Gregory Eiselein and Anne K. Phillips, and Alma J. Payne's *Louisa May Alcott: A Reference Guide* (1980).

Frances Hodgson Burnett
The first biography of Burnett was written by her son, Vivian Burnett, and published soon after her death: *The Romantick Lady (Frances Hodgson Burnett): The Life Story of an Imagination* (1927). Burnett published a memoir of her childhood: *The One I Knew the Best of All: A Memory in the Mind of a Child in New York* (1893). The standard biography is Ann Thwaite's *Waiting for the Party: The Life of Frances Hodgson Burnett, 1849–1924* (1974). A recent biography is *Frances Hodgson Burnett: The Unexpected Life of the Author of "The Secret Garden"* (2004) by Gretchen Gerzina. Angelica Shirley Carpenter and Jean Shirley's *Frances Hodgson Burnett: Beyond "The Secret Garden"* (1990) is intended for young readers. Offering in-depth analysis into and teaching strategies for Burnett's two most famous works for children—*The Secret Garden* and *A Little Princess*—are *The Secret Garden: Nature's Magic* (1996) by Phyllis Bixler and *A Little Princess: Gender and Empire* (1996) by Roderick McGillis.

Maria Edgeworth
The two-volume *Life and Letters of Maria Edgeworth* (1895) by Augustus J. C. Hare is useful for its selection of the author's letters. The standard critical biography of Edgeworth is Marilyn Butler's *Maria Edgeworth: A Literary Biography* (1972). The most important critical work on Edgeworth's tales for children is by Mitzi Myers. Myers's groundbreaking essays on Edgeworth are published in a variety of scholarly journals such as *Children's Literature*, *Children's Literature Association Quarterly*, and *The Lion and the Unicorn*, as well as collections of essays such as *Romanticism and Children's Literature in Nineteenth-Century England* (1991), ed. James Holt McGavran, *Infant Tongues: The Voice of the Child in Literature* (1994), ed. Elizabeth Goodenough, Mark A. Heberle, and Naomi Sokoloff, and *Romantic Women Writers: Voices and Countervoices* (1995), ed. Paula R. Feldman and Theresa M. Kelley. O. Elizabeth McWhorter Harden's *Maria Edgeworth's Art of Prose Fiction* (1971) covers Edgeworth's entire literary career, including her works for children, and Elizabeth Kowaleski-

Wallace's *Their Fathers' Daughters: Hannah More, Maria Edgeworth, and Patriarchal Complicity* (1991) considers the important relationship between Edgeworth and her father, Richard Lovell Edgeworth. See also Caroline Gonda, *Reading Daughters' Fictions, 1709–1834: Novels and Society from Manley to Edgeworth* (1996).

L. M. Montgomery
Interesting biographies of Montgomery include Mollie Gillen's *The Wheel of Things: A Biography of L. M. Montgomery, Author of "Anne of Green Gables"* (1975) and Mary Rubio and Elizabeth Waterston's *Writing a Life: L. M. Montgomery: A Biography of the Author of "Anne of Green Gables"* (1995). *Maud: The Life of L. M. Montgomery* (1992) by Harry Bruce is for young readers. Rubio and Waterston have been publishing the *Selected Journals of L. M. Montgomery*; to date four volumes have appeared. Montgomery collected her autobiographical essays as *The Alpine Path: The Story of My Career* (1917). Comprehensive critical analyses of Montgomery's fiction and journals can be found in *Harvesting Thistles: The Textual Garden of L. M. Montgomery; Essays on Her Novels and Journals* (1994), ed. Mary Rubio, and in John Robert Sorfleet's edited collection *L. M. Montgomery: An Assessment* (1976). Genevieve Wiggins's *L. M. Montgomery* (1992), a short, critical look at Montgomery's works, includes a chapter on her stories and poems. Mavis Reimer's edited collection *Such a Simple Little Tale: Critical Responses to L. M. Montgomery's "Anne of Green Gables"* (1992) and Elizabeth Waterston's *Kindling Spirit: L. M. Montgomery's "Anne of Green Gables"* (1993) focus on Montgomery's most famous work for children.

Mary Martha Sherwood
Paul Sangster's *Pity My Simplicity: The Evangelical Revival and the Religious Education of Children, 1739–1800* (1963) offers useful contexts for understanding Sherwood's work and milieu. M. N. Cutt's *Mrs. Sherwood and Her Books for Children* (1974) is an excellent introduction to Sherwood's life and late-eighteenth-century religious children's literature. See also T. W. Laqueur's *Religion and Respectability: Sunday Schools and Working-Class Culture, 1780–1850* (1976).

Mildred D. Taylor
For a full-length critical analysis of Taylor's fiction, see *Presenting Mildred D. Taylor* (1999) by Chris Crowe.

Charlotte Mary Yonge
One of Yonge's young friends, Christabel Coleridge, wrote the official biography: *Charlotte Mary Yonge: Her Life and Letters* (1903). Georgina Battiscombe's *Charlotte Mary Yonge: The Story of an Uneventful Life* (1943) is the standard biography. See also *Victorian Best-Seller: The World of Charlotte Yonge* (1947) by Margaret Mare and Alicia Percival. The best critical assessment of Yonge's work is *Charlotte Yonge* (1996) by Alethea Hayter.

For critical essays on Yonge's wide-ranging oeuvre, see Marghanita Laski's edited collection *A Chaplet for Charlotte Yonge* (1965). For more narrowly focused studies, see Barbara Dennis's *Charlotte Yonge (1823–1901), Novelist of the Oxford Movement: A Literature of Victorian Culture and Society* (1992) and June Sturrock's *"Heaven and Home": Charlotte M. Yonge's Domestic Fiction and the Victorian Debate over Women* (1995). Gillian Avery's entry on Yonge in *Writers for Children: Critical Studies of Major Authors since the Seventeenth Century* (1988), ed. Jane M. Bingham, supplies a helpful biographical essay and selected bibliography of critical and biographical sources.

Mary Wollstonecraft
Claire Tomalin's *Life and Death of Mary Wollstonecraft* (1974) and Janet Todd's *Mary Wollstonecraft:*
A Revolutionary Life (2000) emphasize different aspects of Wollstonecraft's life. *Mary Wollstonecraft*, by Moira Ferguson and Janet Todd, includes a chapter on Wollstonecraft's educational writings. The best work on Wollstonecraft's works for children can be found in Mitzi Myers's articles and book chapters, among them "Impeccable Governesses, Rational Dames, and Moral Mothers: Mary Wollstonecraft and the Female Tradition in Georgian Children's Books," *Children's Literature* 1986, and "Pedagogy as Self-Expression in Mary Wollstonecraft: Exorcising the Past, Finding a Voice" in *The Private Self: Theory and Practice of Women's Autobiography* (1988), ed. Shari Benstock. *Mary Wollstonecraft: Annotated Bibliography* (1976) by Janet Todd is a comprehensive reference book that covers early Wollstonecraft criticism as well as her works.

PERMISSIONS ACKNOWLEDGMENTS

Ada, Alma Flor. From *My Name Is María Isabel*, translated from the Spanish by Ana M. Cerro, illustrated by Dyble Thompson. Text copyright © 1993 Alma Flor Ada. Illustrations copyright © 1993 K. Dyble Thompson. Reprinted with the permission of Atheneum Books for Young Readers, an imprint of Simon & Schuster Children's Publishing Division. Text of the song "The Candles of Hannukah," © Suni Paz. Reprinted by permission of the author. Illustrations courtesy of de Grummond Children's Literature Collection, University of Southern Mississippi Libraries.

Adventures of Jack the Giant Killer. Illustrations from *The Adventures of Jack the Giant Killer.* London: Dean & Co. ca. 1850. Opie Collection of Children's Literature. The Lily Library, Indiana University Library.

Agard, John, and Grace Nichols. "Twinkle, Twinkle, Firefly," from *No Hickory No Dickory No Dock: A Collection of Caribbean Nursery Rhymes.* Copyright © 1991. Published by Candlewick Press. Reprinted by kind permission of John Agard c/o Caroline Sheldon Literary Agency. Illustration courtesy of de Grummond Children's Literature Collection, University of Southern Mississippi Libraries.

Ahlberg, Janet, and Allan Ahlberg. From *Each Peach Pear Plum.* Copyright © 1978 Janet and Allan Ahlberg. Reproduced by permission of Penguin Ltd. Illustration courtesy of de Grummond Children's Literature Collection, University of Southern Mississippi Libraries.

Aiken, Joan. "The Faithless Lollybird." Copyright © 1977 by Joan Aiken Enterprises Ltd. Reprinted by permission of Brandt & Hochman Literary Agents, Inc.

Alcott, Louisa May. Illustration from *Kitty's Class-day At Harvard-Aunt Kipp-Psyche's Art,* Boston; Loring Publisher, 1868.

Alexander, Lloyd. "The Truthful Harp" from *"The Foundling" and Other Tales of Prydain.* Copyright © 1967 by Lloyd Alexander. Reprinted by permission of Henry Holt and Company, LLC. *The Book of Three.* Copyright © 1964 by Lloyd Alexander. Reprinted by permission of Henry Holt and Company, LLC.

Angels hover over sleeping baby. Illustration from *Lullabies and Baby Songs: A Posy for Mother,* collected by Adelia J. Gossett, with illustrations by E. Roos, 1900.

Ardizzone, Edward. Text © Edward Ardizzone, 1955. Illustrations and text from *Little Tim and the Brave Sea Captain.* Copyright © Edward Ardizzone, 1955. Published by Scholastic UK. Illustration courtesy of de Grummond Children's Literature Collection, University of Southern Mississippi Libraries.

Baa baa black sheep. Illustration from *Nursery Rhymes* by Paula Rego.

Baden-Powell, Robert. Illustration from *Rovering to Success: A Guide to Young Manhood,* 1922.

Barrie, J. M. *Peter Pan.* Copyright © 1937 Great Ormond Street Hospital for Children, London. Reprinted by permission.

Bannerman, Helen. Illustration from *Little Black Sambo.* The only authorized American ed. HarperCollins, [1990?]. Courtesy of de Grummond Children's Literature Collection, University of Southern Mississippi Libraries.

Baum, L. Frank. Illustrations from *American Fairy Tales: Capture of Father Time,* L. Frank Baum, 1901. Courtesy of de Grummond Children's Literature Collection, University of Southern Mississippi Libraries.

Binch, Caroline. Illustration from *Come On into My Tropical Garden.* Copyright © 1988. Published by A&C Black (Publishers) Ltd.

Blake, Quentin. Illustration by Quentin Blake from *Joseph and the Amazing Technicolour Dreamcoat.* Copyright © 1982. Reprinted by permission of A. P. Watt Ltd. Illustration courtesy of de Grummond Children's Literature Collection, University of Southern Mississippi Libraries.

Block, Francesca Lia. "Wolf," from *The Rose and the Beast.* Text copyright © 2000 by Francesca Lia Block. Used by permission of HarperCollins Publishers.

Briggs, Raymond. From *Fungus the Bogeyman* by Raymond Briggs. Copyright © 1977 Raymond Briggs. Reproduced by permission of Penguin Books Ltd. From *The Snowman* by Raymond Briggs. Copyright © 1978 by Raymond Briggs. Used by permission of Random House Children's Books, a division of Random House, Inc., and by permission of Penguin Books Ltd. Illustration courtesy of de Grummond Children's Literature Collection, University of Southern Mississippi Libraries.

Brooks, Bruce. "Out," from *What Hearts.* Copyright © 1992 by Bruce Brooks. Reprinted by permission of HarperCollins Children's Books, a division of HarperCollins Publishers.

Brownies Book. Cover, New York: Du Bois and Dill: June, 1920. Manuscripts, Archives & Rare Books Division Schomburg Center for Research in Black Culture, The New York Public Library, Astor, Lenox and Tilden Foundations.

Bryan, Ashley. "Tortoise, Hare, and the Sweet Potatoes." Reprinted with the permission of Atheneum Books for Young Readers, an imprint of Simon & Schuster Children's Publishing Division from *Ashley Bryan's African Tales, Uh-Huh* by Ashley Bryan. Copyright © 1998 Atheneum Books for Young Readers. Copyright © 1971 Ashley Bryan.

Bunyan, John. Illustrations from *The Pilgrim's Progress* © Bodleian Library, 2002.

Burnett, Frances Hodgson. Illustrations from *Editha's Burglar,* 1888. de Grummond Children's Literature Collection, University of Southern Mississippi Libraries.

Burningham, John. From *Come Away from the Water, Shirley*. Published by Jonathan Cape. Used by permission of The Random House Group Limited. Illustration courtesy of de Grummond Children's Literature Collection, University of Southern Mississippi Libraries.

Bye, baby bunting. Illustration from R. Caldecott's second collection of pictures and songs, 1895. de Grummond Children's Literature Collection, University of Southern Mississippi Libraries.

Caldecott, Randolph. Illustration from *Sing a Song for Sixpence*, 1880. Courtesy of de Grummond Children's Literature Collection, University of Southern Mississippi Libraries.

Carle, Eric. From *The Very Hungry Caterpillar*. Copyright © 1969 and 1987 by Eric Carle. Used by permission of Philomel Books, a division of Penguin Young Readers Group, a member of Penguin Group (USA), Inc. All rights reserved. Illustration courtesy of de Grummond Children's Literature Collection, University of Southern Mississippi Libraries.

Carrier, Roch, translated by Sheila Fischman. "The Hockey Sweater," from *"The Hockey Sweater" and Other Stories*. Copyright © 1979 by House of Anansi Press. Reprinted by permission.

Causley, Charles, and Anthony Castro. *Early in the Morning*. Copyright © 1986. Reprinted by permission of David Higham Associates.

Chambers, Aidan. *The Present Takers*. Copyright © 1983 Aidan Chambers. Published in Great Britain by Red Fox, The Random House Group. Reprinted by permission.

Children in the Wood. Illustrations courtesy of the Bodleian Library, University of Oxford. Opie C 786.

Cleary, Beverly. *Ramona and Her Father* by Beverly Cleary. Text copyright © 1975, 1977 by Beverly Cleary. Illustrations by **Alan Tiegreen**. Used by permission of HarperCollins Publishers. Illustrations courtesy of de Grummond Children's Literature Collection, University of Southern Mississippi Libraries.

Clifford, Lucy Lane. Illustrations from *Anyhow Stories, Moral and Otherwise*. Clifford, W. K., Mrs. Published 1882 by MacMillan, London, and Wooden Tony. Scanned from the 1977 edition. New York: Garland Publishers. Courtesy Brooklyn College Library.

Clifton, Lucille. *Some of the Days of Everett Anderson*. Text copyright © 1970 by Lucille Clifton. Illustrations copyright © 1970 by **Evaline Ness**. Reprinted by permission of Henry Holt and Company, LLC. Reproduced by permission of the Osborne Collection of Early Children's Books, Toronto Public Library.

Comenius, Johann Amos. Illustrations from *Orbis sensualium pictus*. London, 1968. General Research Division, The New York Public Library, Astor, Lenox and Tilden Foundations.

Cotton, John. "Totleigh Riddles," from *The Crystal Zoo*. Copyright © 1985 John Cotton. Reprinted by permission of the estate of the author.

Crane, Walter. Illustrations from *The Baby's Own Aesop*, Walter Crane, 1887. General Research Division, The New York Public Library, Astor, Lenox and Tilden Foundations.

Daffy Down Dilly. Illustration from *The Nursery Rhyme Book*, edited by Andrew Lang, illustrated by Leslie Brooks. Frederick Warne, 1897. Courtesy of de Grummond Children's Literature Collection, University of Southern Mississippi Libraries.

Dahl, Roald. "Little Red Riding Hood and the Wolf," from *Roald Dahl's Revolting Rhymes*. Copyright © 1982 by Roald Dahl Nominee Limited. Used by permission of Alfred A. Knopf Children's Books, a division of Random House, Inc.

DC Comics. *Action Comics*, No.1. © 1938 DC Comics. All rights reserved. Used with permission.

de Brunhoff, Jean. From *The Story of Babar*. Translated by Merle Haas, copyright 1933, renewed 1961 by Random House, Inc. Text reprinted by permission of Random House Children's Books, a division of Random House, Inc. Art reprinted by permission of Hachette Livres. Illustration courtesy of de Grummond Children's Literature Collection, University of Southern Mississippi Libraries.

Defoe, Daniel. Illustrations from *Robinson Crusoe, version for children* published by Darton, 1823. de Grummond Children's Literature Collection, University of Southern Mississippi Libraries.

de la Mare, Walter. "Little Red Riding Hood," from *Tales Told Again: Old Tales Told Again by Walter de la Mare*, illustrated by A. H. Watson. Reprinted by permission of The Literary Trustees of Walter de la Mare and the Society of Authors as their representative.

de la Mare, Walter. Illustrations from *Peacock Pie* by Edward Ardizzone, Faber & Faber.

Dickery Dickery Dare. Illustration from *Mother Goose's Nursery Rhymes*, M. A. Donohue & Company, Chicago, 1892. Reproduced by permission of the Osborne Collection of Early Children's Books, Toronto Public Library.

Doctor Faustus. Illustration from *The Nursery Rhyme Book*, edited by Andrew Lang, illustrated by Leslie Brooks. Courtesy of de Grummond Children's Literature Collection, University of Southern Mississippi Libraries.

Dodd, Lynley. From *Hairy Maclary's Caterwaul Caper*. Copyright © 1987. Reprinted by permission of Gareth Steven Publishing.

Duties of a Lady's Maid. Illustration from *Duties of a Lady's Maid*, 1825. Reproduced by permission of the Osborne Collection of Early Children's Books, Toronto Public Library.

Eagle Comics. *Dan Dare*, April 14, 1950, Eagle Comics. Reprinted by permission of Colin Frewin & Associates Ltd.

Emberley, Michael. *Ruby*. Copyright © 1990 by Michael Emberley. By permission of Little, Brown and Company, Inc.

Estes, Eleanor. *The Hundred Dresses*. Illustrated by **Louis Slobodkin**. Copyright 1944 by Harcourt, Inc., and renewed 1971 by Eleanor Estes and Louis Slobodkin, reprinted by permission of Harcourt, Inc.

Fables of Aesop. Illustrations from Fables of Aesop and Others. London, 1786. The Carl H. Pforzheimer Collection of Shelley and His Circle, The New York Public Library, Astor, Lenox and Tilden Foundations.

Facts to Correct Fancies. Illustration from *Facts to Correct Fancies or, Short Narratives compiled from the Biography of Remarkable Women, written for children, by a Mother,* 1840. General Research Division, The New York Public Library, Astor, Lenox and Tilden Foundations.

Fatio, Louise. From *The Happy Lion.* Illustrated by **Roger Duvoisin.** Copyright © 1954 by Louise Fatio. Illustrations © 1954 by Roger Duivoisin, renewed © 1982 by Louise Fatio Duvoisin and Roger Duvoisin. Used by permission of Random House Children's Books, a division of Random House, Inc. Illustration courtesy of de Grummond Children's Literature Collection, University of Southern Mississippi Libraries.

Field, Barbara. *A Christmas Carol.* Permission granted by Barbara Field, playwright. This play was originally performed at the Guthrie Theater in November 1975 and directed by Stephen Kanee.

Field, Eugene. Illustration from *Wynken, Blynken, and Nod, Lullaby Land: Songs of Childhood,* 1898. de Grummond Children's Literature Collection, University of Southern Mississippi Libraries.

Flack, Marjorie. From *Angus and the Ducks.* Copyright © 1930 by Doubleday, Doran & Co. Copyright renewed 1957 by Marjorie Flack Benet. Reprinted by permission of Farrar, Straus and Giroux, LLC. Illustration courtesy of de Grummond Children's Literature Collection, University of Southern Mississippi Libraries.

Foreman, Michael. Illustrations from *Early in the Morning* by Charles Causley and Anthony Castro.

Four-and-twenty tailors. From *Mother Goose in Black: Mother Goose Rhymes with Silhouette Illustrations,* by J. F. Goodridge. Lothrop, Lee & Shepard Co., Boston, 1912. de Grummond Children's Literature Collection, University of Southern Mississippi Libraries.

Frank, Anne. From *The Diary of a Young Girl: The Definitive Edition,* Otto H. Frank and Mirjam Pressler, editors, translated by Susan Massotty, copyright © 1995 by Doubleday, a division of Random House, Inc. Used by permission of Doubleday, a division of Random House, Inc.

Fritz, Jean. From *The Double Life of Pocahontas.* Copyright © 1983 by Jean Fritz, text. Used by permission of G. P. Putnam's Sons, an imprint of Penguin Putnam Books for Young Readers, a division of Penguin Putnam, Inc. All rights reserved. *Homesick: My Own Story.* Illustrated by **Margot Tomes.** Copyright © 1982. Reprinted by permission of Penguin Putnam Books for Young Readers. Illustrations courtesy of de Grummond Children's Literature Collection, University of Southern Mississippi Libraries.

Gág, Wanda. "The Sorcerer's Apprentice," from *More Tales from Grimm.* Copyright © 1947. Permission granted by Administrator of the Wanda Gag Estate. From *Millions of Cats.* Copyright 1928 by Wanda Gag, renewed © 1956 by Robert Janssen. Used by permission of Coward-McCann, an imprint of Penguin Putnam Books for Young Readers, a division of Penguin Putnam, Inc. All rights reserved. Illustration courtesy of de Grummond Children's Literature Collection, University of Southern Mississippi Libraries.

Garfield, Leon, and Edward Blishen. From "The Seeds of Power," from *The God Beneath the Sea.* Copyright © 1970 by the estates of L. Garfield and E. Blishen. Reprinted by permission of John Johnson Ltd.

Garst, Shannon. *James Bowie and His Famous Knife.* Copyright © 1955. Reprinted by permission of the estate of the author.

Geisel, Theodor. From *Dr. Seuss's ABC* by Dr. Seuss, TM and copyright © by Dr. Seuss Enterprises, L.P., 1963, renewed 1981. Used by permission of Random House Children's Books, a division of Random House, Inc. From *Green Eggs and Ham* by Dr. Seuss, TM and copyright © by Dr. Seuss Enterprises, L.P. 1960, renewed 1988. Used by permission of Random House Children's Books, a division of Random House, Inc.

Goscinny and Uderno. From *Asterix in Britain* by Goscinny and Uderno. Copyright © 1966. Reprinted by permission of Les Editions Albert Rene. Illustration courtesy of de Grummond Children's Literature Collection, University of Southern Mississippi Libraries.

Graves, Robert. *The Penny Fiddle* by Robert Graves. Poems copyright © 1960 by Roturman S. A. Illustrations copyright © 1960 by Edward Ardizzone. Reprinted by permission of Carcanet Press Limited. Reproduced by permission of the Osborne Collection of Early Children's Books, Toronto Public Library.

Gray, William S., and May Hill Arbuthnot. From *Fun with Dick and Jane.* Illustrated by **Eleanor Campbell and Keith Ward.** Copyright 1946, renewed 1974 by Scott, Foresman and Company. Reprinted by permission of Pearson Education, Inc.

Green, Roger Lancelyn. "Sir Gawain and the Green Knight," from *King Arthur and His Knights of the Round Table.* Illustrated by **Lotte Reiniger.** Text copyright © Roger Lancelyn Green, 1953. Reprinted by permission of Penguin Books Ltd.

Greenaway, Kate. Illustrations from *A Apple Pie.* London, New York, 1886. General Research Division, The New York Public Library, Astor, Lenox and Tilden Foundations.

Greenaway, Kate. Illustration from *Under the Window,* Kate, 1878. Courtesy of de Grummond Children's Literature Collection, University of Southern Mississippi Libraries.

Grimes, Nikki. *Bronx Masquerade.* Copyright © 2001 by Nikki Grimes. Published by arrangement with Dial Books for Young Readers, a member of Penguin Group (USA), Inc.

Hall, Donald. From *The Ox-Cart Man* by Donald Hall. Illustrated by **Barbara Cooney.** Text copyright © 1979 by Donald Hall. Illustrations copyright © 1979 by Barbara Cooney Porter. Used by permission of Viking Penguin, an imprint of Penguin Putnam Books for Young Readers, a division of Penguin Putnam, Inc. All rights reserved.

Happy Hippos. Illustration courtesy of de Grummond Children's Literature Collection, University of Southern Mississippi Libraries.

Harris, John. Illustrations from *A Was an Archer*, 1830. Courtesy of de Grummond Children's Literature Collection, University of Southern Mississippi Libraries.

Harris, Robie. *It's Perfectly Normal* (TM). Text copyright © 1994 by Robie Harris; illustrations copyright © 1994 by **Michael Emberley**. Reproduced by permission of the publisher, Candlewick Press, Inc., Cambridge, MA. "It's Perfectly Normal" is a trademark of BEE Productions, Inc., and BIRD Productions, Inc. Illustrations courtesy of de Grummond Children's Literature Collection, University of Southern Mississippi Libraries.

Heide, Florence Parry. From *The Shrinking of Treehorn*. Illustrated by **Edward Gorey**. Text copyright © 1971 by Florence Parry Heide. Illustration copyright © 1971 by Edward Gorey. All rights reserved. Reprinted by permission of Holiday House, Inc. Illustration courtesy of de Grummond Children's Literature Collection, University of Southern Mississippi Libraries.

Heide, Robert. From *Mickey Mouse: The Evolution, the Legend*. Copyright © 2001 Robert Heide. Reprinted by permission of Hyperion Books for Children.

Heinlein, Robert A. *Podkayne of Mars*. Copyright © 1963 by Robert A. Heinlein, renewed 1991 by Virginia Heinlein. Used by permission of G. P. Putnam's Sons, a division of Penguin Putnam, Inc.

He'll toil for thee the whole day long. Illustration from *Lullabies and Baby Songs: A Posy for Mother*, collected by Adelia J. Gossett, with illustrations by E. Roos, 1900.

Hergé. From *Tintin in the Land of the Soviets* and *Tintin in America*. Used by permission of Moulinsart SA.

Hey Diddle Diddle. Illustration from *Hey Diddle Diddle and Baby Bunting*, Caldecott's Picture Books. Pub. by Warne, Frederick. de Grummond Children's Literature Collection, University of Southern Mississippi Libraries.

History of Goody Two-Shoes. Illustrations from *The History of Goody Two-Shoes*. London: T. Goode, ca. 1850. The Lily Library, Indiana University Library.

History of Robin Hood. Illustrations from *The History of Robin Hood*. Leeds, Webb Millington, 1860. © Bodleian Library, University of Oxford, 2004. Opie C 257.

History of Sir Whittington and His Cat. Illustrations from *The History of Sir Whittington and His Cat*, 1840. Courtesy of de Grummond Children's Literature Collection, University of Southern Mississippi Libraries.

Hoban, Russell. From *Dinner at Alberta's*. Illustrated by **James Marshall**. Copyright © 1975 by Russell Hoban. Illustrations copyright © 1975 by James Marshall. Used by permission of HarperCollins Publishers. Illustration courtesy of de Grummond Children's Literature Collection, University of Southern Mississippi Libraries. From *How Tom Beat Captain Najork and His Hired Sportsmen*. Illustrated by **Quentin Blake**. Copyright © 1974. Text reprinted by permission of David Higham Associates Ltd. Art reprinted by permission of A. P. Watt Ltd. *The Sea-Thing Child*. Copyright © 1972, 1999 by Russell Hoban. Reprinted by permission of Candlewick Press.

Hofmann, Heinrich. Illustration from *Struwwelpeter*, 1844. Courtesy of de Grummond Children's Literature Collection, University of Southern Mississippi Libraries.

Holden, Robert. "Twinkle, Twinkle, Southern Cross," from *Twinkle, Twinkle, Southern Cross*. Canberra: National Library of Australia, 1992. Reprinted by permission of the estate of the author.

How Many Miles to Babylon. Illustration from *Nursery Rhymes* by Paula Rego.

Hughes, Ted. *The Iron Giant*. Copyright © 1968 by Ted Hughes. Copyright © renewed 1996 by Ted Hughes. Illustration copyright © 1985 by Faber and Faber Ltd. Published by arrangement with Random House Children's Books, a division of Random House, Inc. New York, NY.

Hughes, Thomas. Illustrations from *Tom Brown's Schooldays*, 1857. Courtesy of de Grummond Children's Literature Collection, University of Southern Mississippi Libraries.

Hush-a-bye baby, on the treetop. Illustration from *The Golden Staircase: Poems and Verses for Children*, chosen by Louey Chisholm. London & Edinburgh: T. C. & E. C. Jack Ltd., T. Nelson & Sons Ltd. 1928. Reproduced by permission of the Osborne Collection of Early Children's Books, Toronto Public Library.

Hutchins, Pat. From *Rosie's Walk*. Copyright © 1968 by Patricia Hutchins; copyright renewed © 1996 by Patricia Hutchins. Reprinted with the permission of Simon & Schuster Books for Young Readers, an imprint of Simon & Schuster Children's Publishing Division. Illustration courtesy of de Grummond Children's Literature Collection, University of Southern Mississippi Libraries.

I'll Tell You a Story. Illustration from *Mother Goose's Nursery Rhymes*: Rackham, A., 1913.

Jack and Jill. Illustration from *Mother Goose's Nursery Rhymes*, M. A. Donohue & Company, Chicago, 1892. Reproduced by permission of the Osborne Collection of Early Children's Books, Toronto Public Library.

Jumblies. Illustration from *The Complete Verse and Other Nonsense*, Vivian Noakes.

Jarrell, Randall. Text of *The Bat-Poet*. Copyright © 1964 by the Macmillan Company, copyright renewed 1992 by Mary Jarrell. Reprinted by permission of Dunham Literary as agents for the author's estate.

Keats, Ezra Jack. From *The Snowy Day*. Copyright © 1962 by Ezra Jack Keats, renewed © 1990 by Martin Pope, Executor. Used by permission of Viking Penguin, an imprint of Penguin Putnam Books for Young Readers, a division of Penguin Putnam, Inc. All rights reserved. Illustration courtesy of de Grummond Children's Literature Collection, University of Southern Mississippi Libraries.

Keeping, Charles. From *The Highwayman*, by **Alfred Noyes**. Illustrations copyright 1981 © Charles Keeping. Reprinted by permission of Oxford University Press. Illustration courtesy of de Grummond Children's Literature Collection, University of Southern Mississippi Libraries.

Kipling, Rudyard. Illustration from *Just-So Stories: How the Camel Got His Hump*. Courtesy of de Grummond Children's Literature Collection, University of Southern Mississippi Libraries.

Scieszka, Jon. *Summer Reading Is Killing Me!* Text copyright © Jon Scieszka, 1998. Illustrations copyright © **Lane Smith**, 1998. Published by arrangement with Viking Children's Books, a member of Penguin Group (USA), Inc.

Sendak, Maurice. From *Where the Wild Things Are.* Copyright © 1963, 1991 by Maurice Sendak. Used by permission of HarperCollins Publishers. Illustration courtesy of de Grummond Children's Literature Collection, University of Southern Mississippi Libraries.

Seton, Ernest Thompson. Illustrations from *Raggylug* courtesy of de Grummond Children's Literature Collection, University of Southern Mississippi Libraries.

Singer, Isaac Bashevis. "Hanukkah in the Poorhouse," from *The Power of Light.* Copyright © 1980 by Isaac Bashevis Singer. Reprinted by permission of Farrar, Straus and Giroux, LLC.

Smith, Lane. From "The Princess and the Bowling Ball," from *"The Stinky Cheese Man" and Other Fairly Stupid Tales,* by Jon Scieszka. Copyright © 1992 by **Lane Smith**, illustrations. Used by permission of Viking Penguin, an imprint of Penguin Putnam Books for Young Readers, a division of Penguin Putnam, Inc. All rights reserved. Illustration courtesy of de Grummond Children's Literature Collection, University of Southern Mississippi Libraries.

Stevenson, Robert Louis. Illustrations from *A Child's Garden of Verses* by Charles Robinson, Green Tiger Press, 1975.

Storr, Catherine. "Little Polly Riding Hood," from *Clever Polly and the Stupid Wolf.* Published by Faber and Faber Ltd. Reprinted by permission of the publishers.

Strete, Craig. "The Bleeding Man," from *"The Bleeding Man" and Other Science Fiction Stories.* Text copyright © 1977 by Craig Strete. Used by permission of HarperCollins Publishers.

Taylor, Mildred. *Roll of Thunder, Hear My Cry.* Copyright © 1976 by Mildred D. Taylor. Published by arrangement with Dial Books for Young Readers, a member of Penguin Group (USA), Inc.

There Was an Old Woman Called . . . Illustration from *Mother Goose's Nursery Rhymes,* M. A. Donohue & Company, Chicago, 1892. Reproduced by permission of the Osborne Collection of Early Children's Books, Toronto Public Library.

There Was an Old Woman Who Lived in a Shoe. Illustration from *Mother Goose: Nursery Rhymes and Fairy Tales,* with illustrations. Sir John Gilbert, John Tenniel, Harrison Weir, Walter Crane, W. McConnll, J. B. Zwecker, and others. London: George Routledge, n.d. Reproduced by permission of the Osborne Collection of Early Children's Books, Toronto Public Library.

Tom Thumb. Illustrations courtesy of The Lily Library, Indiana University Library.

Three Blind Mice. Illustration from *Mother Goose's Nursery Rhymes*: Rackham, A., 1913.

Three Wise Men. Illustrations from *Mother Goose Rhymes, Jingles and Fairy Tales,* H. Altemus, 1896. Reproduced by permission of the Osborne Collection of Early Children's Books, Toronto Public Library.

Thurber, James. "The Fox and the Crow" and "Variations on the Theme," from *Further Fables for Our Time.* Copyright © 1956. Reprinted by permission of Barbara Hogenson Agency.

Twinkle Twinkle Little Star. Illustration from *Mother Goose's Nursery Rhymes and Nursery Songs Set to Music,* J. W. Elliott. de Grummond Children's Literature Collection, University of Southern Mississippi Libraries.

Tread Mill (copybook). Illustrations courtesy of Reproduced by permission of the Osborne Collection of Early Children's Books, Toronto Public Library.

Upton, Florence. Illustration from *The Adventures of Two Dutch Dolls and Golliwog.* Elizabeth Nesbitt Room, University Library System, University of Pittsburgh.

Ungerer, Tomi. "Little Red Riding Hood," from *A Storybook from Tomi Ungerer.* Copyright © 1974 by Tomi Ungerer. Reprinted by permission of Children's Press/Franklin Watts, a division of Scholastic, Inc. Illustrations courtesy of de Grummond Children's Literature Collection, University of Southern Mississippi Libraries.

Van Allsburg, Chris. "The House on Maple Street," from *The Mysteries of Harris Burdick,* by Chris Van Allsburg. Copyright © 1984 by Chris Van Allsburg. Reprinted by permission of Houghton Mifflin Company. All rights reserved. Illustration courtesy of de Grummond Children's Literature Collection, University of Southern Mississippi Libraries.

Vincent, Gabrielle. From *Merry Christmas, Ernest and Celestine.* Copyright © 1983. Used by permission of HarperCollins Publishers. Illustration courtesy of de Grummond Children's Literature Collection, University of Southern Mississippi Libraries.

Vivas, Julie. From *Possum Magic,* by **Mem Fox**. Illustrations copyright © 1983 by Julie Vivas. Reproduced by permission of Harcourt, Inc. Illustration courtesy of de Grummond Children's Literature Collection, University of Southern Mississippi Libraries.

Wagner, Jenny. From *John Brown, Rose, and the Midnight Cat,* published by Penguin Books Australia Ltd. Text copyright © 1977 Jenny Wagner. Illustrations copyright © 1977 **Ron Brooks**. Illustration courtesy of de Grummond Children's Literature Collection, University of Southern Mississippi Libraries.

Wee Willie Winkie. Illustration from *Mother Goose's Nursery Rhymes*: Rackham, A., 1913.

White, Edward Benson. Frontispiece to Edward Benson White's *Education at Home* courtesy of Reproduced by permission of the Osborne Collection of Early Children's Books, Toronto Public Library.

Willard, Nancy. From *A Visit to William Blake's Inn.* Illustrated by **Alice Provensen and Martin Provensen**. Text

Index of Illustrators
and Illustrations

Index